SAMUEL RICHARDSON was born in Derbyshire in 1689, the son of a London joiner. He received little formal education and in 1706 was apprenticed to a printer in the capital. Thirteen years later he set up for himself as a stationer and printer and became one of the leading figures in the London trade. As a printer his output included political writing, such as the Tory periodical *The True Briton*, the newspapers, *Daily Journal* (1736–7) and *Daily Gazetteer* (1738) together with twenty-six volumes of the *Journals* of the House of Commons and general law printing. He was twice married and had twelve children.

His literary career began when two booksellers proposed that he should compile a volume of model letters for unskilled letter writers. While preparing this, Richardson became fascinated by the project, and a small sequence of letters from a daughter in service, asking her father's advice when threatened by her master's advances, formed the germ of *Pamela, or, Virtue Rewarded* (1740–1). *Pamela* was a huge success and became something of a cult-novel. By May 1741 it reached fourth edition and it was dramatized in Italy by Goldoni, as well as in England. His masterpiece, *Clarissa, or The History of a Young Lady*, one of the greatest European novels, was published in 1747–8. Richardson's last novel, *The History of Sir Charles Grandison*, appeared in 1753–4. His writings brought him great personal acclaim and a coterie of devoted admirers who liked to discuss with him the moral aspects of the action in the novels. Samuel Richardson died in 1761 and is buried in St Bride's Church, London.

ANGUS ROSS is Emeritus Professor of English at the University of Sussex. He writes on eighteenth-century and other literature, and he has edited Daniel Defoe's *Robinson Crusoe*, Tobias Smollett's *The Expedition of Humphry Clinker* and *Selections from the Tatler and the Spectator* for Penguin, as well as a number of other texts and anthologies.

SAMUEL RICHARDSON

CLARISSA

or

The History of a Young Lady

EDITED
WITH AN INTRODUCTION
AND NOTES BY ANGUS ROSS

PENGUIN BOOKS

PENGUIN BOOKS

Published by the Penguin Group
Penguin Books Ltd, 27 Wrights Lane, London W8 5TZ, England
Penguin Putnam Inc., 375 Hudson Street, New York, New York 10014, USA
Penguin Books Australia Ltd, Ringwood, Victoria, Australia
Penguin Books Canada Ltd, 10 Alcorn Avenue, Toronto, Ontario, Canada M4V 3B2
Penguin Books (NZ) Ltd, Private Bag 102902, NSMC Auckland, New Zealand

Penguin Books Ltd, Registered Offices: Harmondsworth, Middlesex, England

First published 1747-8
This edition published 1985
Published simultaneously by Viking
16

This edition, Introduction and Notes copyright © Angus Ross, 1985
All rights reserved

Printed and bound in Great Britain by
The Bath Press, Bath

Filmset in VIP Times

To
Stephanie, Victoria, Anthea

CONTENTS

PREFACE

This volume offers a complete text of the first edition [C1] of Richardson's *Clarissa, or the History of a Young Lady*. The reasons for this choice are given on p. 17. The text of the novel has been modernized according to the principles set out in the Note on the Text on p. 31.

As the author finally left it [C3], the novel contains eight letters in addition to those in [C1]. The letters in the present edition are numbered from 1 to 537, corresponding to Richardson's numbering in [C3]; the numbers of the additional letters are omitted from the series. A few of the letters are left unnumbered by Richardson, and some of the numbered letters contain the text of letters left unnumbered by him. For ease of reference, such letters have been assigned interserial numbers, e.g. [486.1 Clarissa to John Belford]. The Table of Letter Numbers in Other Editions on p. 1512 allows the present volume to be used with two of the modern editions most commonly found.

Richardson placed a Table of Contents at the beginning of the first volume of the second edition of Clarissa [C2], to show 'the connexion of the whole'. He came to believe that this had injured the sale of the book by making 'many persons master of the story' (letter to Aaron Hill, 12 July 1749): and in [C3] he distributed the table between the ends of the volumes. As part of Richardson's tactics to control his readers' responses, the table was also meant by italicized phrases to answer criticisms which had been made of the work. Although an important document in the latter regard, its late introduction excludes it from the present text, and it could only be made to fit [C1] by clumsy omissions or bracketing. In its place, however, a Table of Letters (pp. 1500–1511) has been provided, listing the letter numbers, headings and dates.

Richardson's own notes are placed at the foot of the page, cued by his own superscript letters, e.g. 'my promise.^{a}' Editorial Notes, to be found on pp. 1513–26, are cued in the text by superscript numbers. There is a Glossary of Words and Phrases on pp. 1527–33 covering old words and phrases, words that have significantly changed their meanings, all phrases in foreign languages (e.g. *padusoy*, *gallery green-box*, *resentment(s)*, *in petto*).

ABBREVIATIONS
AND SIGNS

[ ]	Square brackets enclose matter provided by the editor.
Bysshe	Edward Bysshe, *The Art of English Poetry* (1702; nine editions to 1739): contains an anthology of passages which was used by SR for quotation.
[C1] [C2] [C3]	First (1747–8), second (1749), and third (1751) editions of *Clarissa*: see pp. 15–16.
EK	Eaves and Kimpel, *Samuel Richardson: A Biography* (1971): see p. 27.
L100	A letter with the number assigned to it in this edition: L1 to L537.
*ODEP*³	F. P. Wilson (ed.), *The Oxford Dictionary of English Proverbs*, 3rd edition (OUP, 1970).
OED	*The Oxford English Dictionary.*
SR	Samuel Richardson.
Otway¹	Superscript numbers in the text refer to the Notes on pp. 1513ff.

CHRONOLOGY

1689   Samuel Richardson baptized at Mackworth, near Derby, the son of a London joiner, who later returns with his family to the city.

1706   Apprenticed (printer) to John Wilde for seven years.

1715   Freeman of the Stationers' Company and of the City of London.

1719   Defoe, *Robinson Crusoe*.

1721   SR in business as a stationer and printer near St Bride's Church, off Fleet Street; marries Martha, daughter of his former master.

1722   Delated to the Secretary of State as an extreme Tory printer. Defoe, *Moll Flanders*.

1723   Probably printing the (Jacobite) Duke of Wharton's twice-weekly periodical, *The True Briton*.

1724   Starts printing the *Daily Journal*. Defoe, *Roxana, or, The Fortunate Mistress*.

1727   SR elected Renter Warden of the Stationers' Company.

1728   Francis Hutcheson, *Nature and Conduct of the Passions and Affections*.

1733   SR, now a widower, marries Elizabeth Leake, daughter of a former employer; writes and publishes a pamphlet, *The Apprentice's Vade Mecum; or, Young Man's Pocket Companion*.

1735   Starts to print the pro-Government *Daily Gazetteer* (to 1746).

1737   SR's revision of the fourth edition of Defoe's *Complete English Tradesman*.

1738   SR *et al.*, revision of second edition of Defoe's *Tour thro' the Whole Island of Great Britain*.

1739   SR's extensive revision of L'Estrange's *Aesop's Fables*.

1740   SR completes *Pamela*, written in a few months; 6 November: anonymous publication, 2 vols. 12°.

1741   SR's *Letters written to and for Particular Friends, on the most Important Occasions* . . ., begun before *Pamela* and prompting it, published by Rivington and Osborn. Henry Fielding, *Shamela*. February: second edition of *Pamela* with changes. March: third edition. May: fourth edition; spurious *Pamela's Conduct in High Life*. September: fifth edition of *Pamela*; French translation of *Pamela*; SR elected to Court of Assistants of Stationers' Company. 7 December: *Pamela II* published, not so successful as part I.

1742   Fielding, *Joseph Andrews*. *Pamela*, de luxe 8° published, vol. i.

1743   *Pamela*, de luxe 8°, vols. ii and iii published; second edition of *Pamela II*.

1744   Outline of *Clarissa* in being. July: SR has 'finished' some draft of the novel. November: SR sending MS. to a friend requesting suggestions for cuts.

1745   Portions of drafts of *Clarissa* seen by correspondents.

1746   SR begins a thorough revision and is perplexed by contradictory advice.

1747   1 December: *Clarissa* vols. i and ii published at 6s. bound.

1748   28 April: *Clarissa* vols. iii and iv published; indiscreet talk of impending conclusion provokes discussion and revision. 1 October: *Clarissa* vol. v printed. 7 November: vols. vi and vii printed. 8 December: *Clarissa* vols. v, vi and vii published. Smollett, *Roderick Random*.

1749   June: second edition of *Clarissa* (vols. i–iv revised, enough copies of v, vi and vii printed to make the new edition). SR [Clarissa's] *Meditations Collected from the Sacred Books* (for private circulation). Fielding, *Tom Jones*.

1750   SR begins serious consideration of *Sir Charles Grandison*.

1751   Prévost's French translation of *Clarissa* (severely cut, mostly in last two vols.; removal of 'low' scenes). April: third edition of *Clarissa*, 8 vols. 12° (adding 'Moral Sentiments' table); SR, *Letters and Passages Restored from the Original MSS of the History of Clarissa*. Smollett, *Peregrine Pickle*. December: Fielding, *Amelia*.

1752   German translation of *Clarissa*. Dutch translation starts to appear (completed 1755).

1753   SR, *Sir Charles Grandison* starts publication; vols. i–iv in 12° (first edition) and 8° (second edition). 11 December: vols. v and vi. Smollett, *Ferdinand, Count Fathom*.

1754   14 March: *Sir Charles Grandison* vol. vii, 12° and 8°. 19 March: 7 vols. 12° (third edition). Death of Fielding. SR elected Master of the Stationers' Company.

1755   SR, *Moral and Instructive Sentiments . . . contained in . . . Pamela, Clarissa and Sir Charles Grandison*.

1756   Abridgement of *Clarissa* (Dublin).

1759   *Clarissa*, fourth edition, 7 vols. 12° (omits table of Sentiments).

1760   Sterne, *Tristram Shandy* vols. i and ii.

1761   4 July: death of SR. Rousseau, *La Nouvelle Héloïse*. Diderot, *Éloge de Richardson*.

INTRODUCTION

The first impression the reader receives from Samuel Richardson's masterpiece is of its great length; and rightly so, since that is an integral part of the work's reach and meaning. When we can breach this barrier, for so it often is to us, however initially sympathetic we may be to the novelist's purposes and the concerns of his fiction, the next and lasting impression is one of power and effective complexity. To read *Clarissa* is not only to meet an indispensable document in the history of English (and indeed European) fiction in the eighteenth century, but also to become engaged with one of the greatest European novels, the haunting life of which has been acknowledged by many and diverse successors of Richardson himself and which in surprising places in the text still has the force to startle, and the spirit to enmesh, its modern audience.

Certain problems, not without their own intrinsic interest, are met at the outset in reading *Clarissa*, problems that were present at the start of the novel's career. In this respect, the circumstances of the book's publication are more important in our own dealings with Richardson's fiction than is often the case with other works of literature.

When the first two volumes of the first edition of *Clarissa* appeared on 1 December 1747, the fifty-eight-year-old Richardson was already well known and established, not only as one of the leading master-printers in London, with a substantial business in Salisbury Square off Fleet Street, but also as the author of *Pamela*. The latter indeed had quickly become a cult-novel after its first (anonymous) publication seven years before, at the end of 1740. Nevertheless, in the run-up to the appearance of his second and greatest novel, despite his apparently secure position as a citizen and as a writer, Richardson adopted a strangely deferential posture, and that in a society for which deference, received and given, was of prime importance. As early as 1744–5, he was sending out manuscript portions of some draft of the novel, asking for help and receiving contradictory advice. He turned to two kinds of correspondents. A small group of professional men of letters formed part of his circle, friends such as the Rev. Edward Young, satirist, poet and himself something of a cult-writer with his blank-verse *Night Thoughts* then in progress, and Aaron Hill, dramatist, poet, translator and projector. More important, though, was a group of ladies, several young and unmarried, others older, for whom as the fame of *Pamela* grew Richardson became something of a guru in matters of private conduct and moral feeling. The subsequent impact of *Clarissa* widened this cluster of the novelist's intimates.

Richardson was early worried about the length of his new work. Young, though asked to outline possible cuts, wisely refused. Aaron Hill more rashly sent suggestions that frightened and wounded the apparently deferential author. In this a pattern may be discerned, in which Richardson invites collaboration but ultimately demonstrates a very firm and conscious, even dictatorial, adherence to his original purposes. Professional advisers became less important, but Richardson continued to ask for comments from his other acquaintances. So at the outset, 'the author', that apparently dominant actor in the drama of reading, has a strangely shifting stance in the writing and publishing of *Clarissa*.

As well as discussing the major questions of the shape of the book and the incidents and conduct of the narrative, questions on which he never significantly gave ground to his critics or accepted the advice he was offered, Richardson and his correspondents worried over the surface and details of the text. Just as he had revised *Pamela* for the second and subsequent editions, and was still revising it, so he worked on *Clarissa*, first in the changes he made in at least two drafts, then in his adjustments to volumes i–iv of the second edition of 1749 [C2], later in the revision of the entire text for the third edition of 1751 [C3], and finally in the negligible alterations made for the fourth edition of 1759. The first four volumes of [C2] contain several thousand small, but cumulatively important, modifications of the text, and to these are added in [C3] several larger alterations, mostly additions. Forty-two of the latter are more than a page in length, and six are more than eight pages long. In all, [C3] is 200 pages longer than [C1]. Two articles by S. Van Marter (see p. 28) set out a useful summary of these changes, with examples, and with some indication of the patterns that may be discerned in them. Richardson had several ends in view in making the changes, but opinions vary not only as to his success in reaching these objectives but, more contentiously, whether the sum of the changes is a better work of art, a more pleasing creation, a more convincing story, a truer tale, a more imaginative, engaging and lively text. In short, the text too has a shifting quality, though it is easy (particularly for an editor, harmless drudge!) to exaggerate the final importance of all this in a tract of writing so long, complex and dense. It is also worth remembering that, for good or ill, Richardson's novels were printed on his own presses in his own shop.

Richardson himself was careful to suggest that the additions were restorations 'by particular desire' (letter to David Graham, 3 May 1750). He further printed 127 of these passages in a volume of *Letters and Passages Restored from the Original MSS of . . . Clarissa*, which he published in 1751 for the benefit of those who had bought copies of [C1] or [C2]: also, in [C3] he signalled by marginal marks 168 such passages, of a line or more, though Shirley Van Marter reckons there are 739 of them. Mark Kinkead-Weekes as long ago as 1959 (see p. 28) argued that much of this material was not restored at all, but new, and inserted by Richardson to answer criticism by his readers, written, oral or implied, which seemed to him to arise from inattention or misreading. It is difficult to judge in many cases whether a substantial passage has truly come from an earlier version (though on extraneous evidence one or two clearly have), or was for whatever reason newly provided by Richardson for [C2] or (in most cases) for [C3]. One addition in [C3] is a complete letter, L208: Lovelace to John Belford. In this, the former outlines his fantasy of revenging himself on Anna Howe and her mother by kidnapping them on their journey to the Isle of Wight, and arranging the rape of the maidservant as well as the mother and daughter, all this culminating in the trial of Lovelace and his 'vassals'; the men in court 'in their hearts' acquitting the accused and the women 'disclaiming prosecution, were the case to be their own'.

The final outcome is Lovelace's cynical expectation of his own acquittal as leader, 'were it but for family sake'. All this is a typically bravura performance by Lovelace, both as a letter and as a piece of impudent defiance, well over the top and a pity to lose. It is designed, as many of the new additions were, to blacken Lovelace's character, yet it is apparently truly *omitted* from the first edition. Sarah Wescomb wrote to Richardson on 14 April 1747, nominating this scheme for excision to shorten the book.

One class of additions is, however, clearly new material, though only carrying further a feature of the text already present in [C1]. This consists of twenty-two omniscient footnotes by the 'editor' added to [C2] and retained in [C3]; eighteen of these also set out to blacken Lovelace or (another reaction of Richardson to criticism) raise Clarissa. Many of the notes act against the subtle process of unfolding the story in the letters, by brusquely pointing forward into the following narrative, and the whole exercise must surely be seen as an attempt by Richardson to restore his control of the readers' interpretations of the novel (letter-texts as well as story). In turn, Richardson risks incurring some resentment by such 'distrust of his audience'. A related class of alteration is to be found in [C2] in the increased use of italics to nudge the reader's attention to significant words, phrases and longer passages, another development in directly forcing the reader's response that works to some extent against the strengths of the epistolary form.

Although there is not much surviving correspondence on the subject, it is hard not to suspect that he was following advice in the widespread if small touches he introduced to make the writing throughout more 'noble' and 'correct'. This marks a stage in the flux and reflux in the novel as a whole, between generalized meaning and significant detail, usually the 'low mimetic comedy' which the French translators, for example, did not like. Lovelace is deprived of 'puppy' and 'cunning whelp' in remonstrance, and is given instead 'awkward fellow' and 'foolish'; Clarissa's 'sooner than it agrees with my stomach' dwindles to 'sooner than I should otherwise choose'. Details of aristocratic titles and address are adjusted, a subject on which Richardson later defensively claimed to be ignorant, and Clarissa from [C2] onwards refers to her 'father' and 'mother' instead of the warmer 'papa' and 'mamma'.

All modern reprints, except Philip Stevick's abridgement of 1971, have reproduced some form of [C3]. It might be argued that the best text would be one that gave the reader a record of all the significant changes that Richardson made in the text over the years. But this would be impossible in a clear, readable version of the novel, since not only additions are involved but also omissions and revisions. It has therefore been decided that on balance it is best to reprint the text of the first edition. This may not please all readers, though it means that at last the earlier and later versions are easily available for comparison. The decision is taken, not because [C1] represents Richardson's 'real' intention later frustrated by his reactions to criticism (though there is something in this), but because the first version is appreciably shorter, often livelier and, though the additions occasionally present worthwhile improvements, to a large extent the added material seems relatively inert. Among the latter may be found the doubling in length of Joseph Leman's 'funny servant' writing in L96, and two additional letters of the pedantic Elias Brand, L468 and L469. Here also are located more than a score of substantial passages praising Clarissa, most inserted after her death. The loss of a few scenes of lively writing and some improved syntax (the best of which is incorporated in editorial brackets) is judged to be outweighed by the gains.

The latter point brings us to the *critical* significance of the publication history. Richardson's apparently deferential posture as author has in the past led to his being incautiously patronized, to the extent of prompting surprise that one, as Coleridge expressed it, of '. . . so very vile a mind, so oozy, so hypocritical, praise-mad, canting, envious, concupiscent' could command admiration, and great admiration, for a great book. The social inferior, in contemporary terms, of many of his correspondents, he was put down by later critics as a man of narrow reading, little education and apt to quote 'inaccurately'. His careful use of quotations, assembled from several handy anthologies such as Edward Bysshe's *Art of English Poetry* (1702, and many later editions) or *The Beauties of the English Stage* (1737 etc.) to establish Lovelace's background in literature and self-dramatizing fantasies, is comparable to many modern assemblages and is charted in the Notes (pp. 1513 ff). He is also preachy, and for this reason, perhaps, his use of devotional literature was not given the careful consideration such a deliberate literary gesture deserves as a potent source of imaginative power.

Despite all this, in *Clarissa* he had the luck or prescience to hit on a story that became a myth to his own age, and remains so yet. He also had the imagination and ability to give this story life in a fashion that awakens complexity within complexity, some of which it is interesting to observe becoming activated to rich effect by recent developments in economic and social thought, women's consciousness and critical theory. F. R. Leavis judged that *Clarissa* is 'a really impressive work', but went on to say: 'it's no use pretending that Richardson can ever be made a current classic again'. It has always been in print, however, and read. Terry Eagleton (see p. 28) seems pushing on an open door when he suggests that only by using his particular box of tools might it possibly 'now become a great novel for us'. His lively version of *The Rape of Clarissa* does indeed clamp a powerful reading on the struggling novel, reminiscent, it is ironic to note, of the opposing, consistent and unyielding interpretation that Richardson himself, in terms of another apocalyptic vision, also sought to bolt together. It is not only some modern interests that have made *Clarissa* into a classic; it has always been one.

Richardson's fable is dramatic, full of (perhaps irresolvable) tension, and violent. Clarissa Harlowe is a beautiful young girl of high intelligence, scrupulous moral judgement, strong resolution and warm humanity. She becomes the victim of her greedy and implacable family. They seek to force her to marry Roger Solmes, whom she detests; but she becomes attracted to Robert Lovelace, handsome, intelligent, witty and debonair, whom she allows herself to think may be rescued from a life of wickedness. He turns the full effect of his heartless and resourceful sexual encroachment on her, and in circumstances of cruel chance as well as deceit, she is inveigled out of her family house. At the centre of a web of lying harassment, she is imprisoned in a brothel, defies Lovelace, escapes, but is lured back to captivity, drugged and raped. She again escapes, and having been isolated from her family and friends turns to the consolations for the oppressed virtuous of the future life, and dies. Lovelace himself is killed in a duel with her cousin.

Some of the tensions in the fable are worth pausing over. Clarissa, 'my girl' as Richardson often calls her in his letters, is clearly intended to be a model. But she is the victim (although an unlucky and to an extent a pitiable one) of her own pride in thinking that she could 'rescue' Lovelace from his evil courses. Richardson plays down his original motivation by many small changes to the text, and by his comments on the novel as he attempts to raise her and defend her against charges of 'over-niceness' in not closing with Lovelace's ambiguous offers of marriage, i.e. accepting social necessity. Clarissa does however say in L467 as she nears death: 'Poor man . . . I once could have loved him . . .' A little earlier (L368), she is momentarily allowed something approaching despair: '. . . for I must own, my dear, that sometimes still my griefs, and my reflections, are too heavy for me; and all the aid I can draw from *religious duties* is hardly sufficient to support by staggering reason. I am a very young creature . . .' Although the modern reader might wish for more such 'flaws' in her character, Richardson, despite his hankering after a paragon, does manage the difficult task of keeping us interested and involved in the inner life of 'the lady'.

Lovelace caused Richardson the opposite difficulty. Many readers of the novel have jibbed at the idea that Lovelace is at once so attractive, amusing and so bad; a liar and a bully, spying through key-holes. The tension between the attractive side of Lovelace and his corrupt and villainous behaviour, behaviour insolently justified by his code of honour, *personal* integrity and misguided intelligence, is a very powerful one. Richardson was stung by the wish expressed by many of his contemporaries for a 'happy ending' that would show Lovelace to have been good after all, a fit subject for repentance; and he consistently tried by many changes to make Lovelace more consistently wicked. The tension is increased because Richardson has so completely imagined himself into the role of Lovelace that most of his letters are *tours-de-force*, amusing and skilful. It is the contemplation of his actions and their effect, what his friend Belford calls (L258) 'thy barbarous villainy', that condemns him unutterably: cf. L279, '. . . as to that part of [Clarissa's sufferings] which arises from extreme sensibility, I know nothing of that; and cannot therefore be answerable for it.'

Severe contradictory demands are made on the members of a propertied family of Clarissa's day, such as Richardson embodies (though to an extreme) in the Harlowes. On the one hand, the duty of a daughter is to obey and the right of a father is to require obedience; on the other, a daughter has a right to be an individual living in peace and integrity, and a father's duty is not to be an oppressor. Perhaps Richardson's choice of *James* as the Christian names of the Harlowes, father and son, is an indication of the wider reverberation of this conflict of legitimacies. The two Stuart monarchs James I ('the Royal Insignificant', as the lawless and lordly Lovelace calls him in L272) and his grandson, James II, both claimed the divine right of kings, the supreme manifestation in the state of that male *patria potestas*, the divinely given right to life and death over his dependants assigned to the head of a Roman family. But James II, like James Harlowe, Younger, carried this notion to demented lengths and destroyed his own power as king. It is rather curious that James Harlowe says (L459) of Lovelace: 'I had rather see the rebel die a hundred deaths . . . than . . . [be] a relation to my family'. Were the Harlowes imagined as having been supporters of James II during his brief reign, as a quick way of advancement, and perhaps Jacobites for a space (thus explaining the son's name) before 1714, when the Hanoverians came in? Just as politically the rights of subjects in the late seventeenth century and thereafter could successfully withstand such naked exercise of the sovereign power as James II's autocracy, so the notion of personal independence, first in young men but by Richardson's time in women too, could at least be plausibly asserted against parental power, if, as many sad instances more than prove, it was not always vindicated. In the latter argument, Richardson in his correspondence shows himself unequivocally in favour of the dependence of women, but in his story itself, the conflict is unmediated. Clarissa's defiance of her father is right, but her sense of guilt at her conduct is also apparently right in the eyes of 'the author'. In the novel there are many direct expressions of defiance by women, chiefly Clarissa's *confidante*, Anna Howe. The events of the tale, however, frustrate Anna's most active initiatives, or make them counter-productive, though this would argue that she was 'wrong' only in a simple allegory, certainly not in Richardson's complex fiction. Clarissa herself in her farewell letter to her brother (L490) effectively rebukes him with the comment that he is (however unjustly) 'an only son, more worth in the family account than several daughters'. The word *account* with its commercial overtones is an indictment of the mercantile ethos of the Harlowes, who in their calculations oppress the human spirit at their peril.

Other points of tension in the story also concern Clarissa's role. One is her categorical refusal to enter into any relationship with Lovelace except on her own scrupulous personal terms. This criticism of the story, which first surfaced at the time the novel was published as strictures on her 'over-niceness', is touched on later, and caused Richardson trouble. A related point is the part her rape plays in the story. Lovelace's fantasy of his own life is often taken from the theatre. He constantly associates himself with the *macho*, autocratic princes of Restoration heroic tragedy, seeming ironically to forget that they mostly perished by their attempts at dominance; but he also seeks to turn Clarissa's part in his sexual pursuit into a part in a Restoration comedy, a comedy in which her abduction, harassment and rape would be followed by his (at least expressed) repentance, a country-dance and marriage. Clarissa, however, turns the story into something else. A tragedy? She certainly at the end styles herself as a heroine, appearing in the heroine's white costume of the tragic stage, and apparently accepts her own death as the only outcome of her rape.

All these, and other, tensions in the story are the tensions of myth, not the discontinuities of a poorly constructed tale. They resist allegorizing, and touch on conflicts in the life of Richardson's day between social and communal norms and personal assertion, conflicts which are also as yet unresolved in our own time, and in some respects exacerbated.

Richardson inserts this powerfully contradictory story in that required constituent of the realist novel, an elaborate, well-worked-out context of economic relationships.

The Harlowe family, relatively newly established as extensive landowners, are consolidating their landed property. Hence the importance of matching Clarissa, a pawn in the chess-game of competitive asset winning, with the holder of contiguous estates, Roger Solmes. The match appears to the lady not unlike the union of Beauty and the Beast, with no magical resolution possible. Solmes is thus presented by Clarissa: 'sitting asquat . . . squatting in it with his ugly weight . . . beginning to set his splay feet' (L16); '. . . Ugly creature! What, at the close of day, quite dark, brought him hither? . . .' (L21). The amassing of property has driven James Harlowe, Senior, unnaturally to resign his power as head of the family to his rash and thrusting heir. The consequent demoralizing psychic disturbance has forced Mrs Harlowe into withdrawal, in abdicating her responsibility as wife and mother. Arabella Harlowe is bent on asserting her superiority as elder sister with all the rights and privileges in rank and property that she imagines this place may make hers. Clarissa, however, has been endowed by her grandfather with an estate: 'my estate, the enviable estate which has been the original cause of all my misfortunes' (L230). Yearning to be the obedient daughter to a loving father, she resigns the profits of the estate entirely into his hands, but the very fact that this part of the family possessions was bequeathed to her affronts her brother. In L231, Lovelace himself comments on her reproach that she 'is cast from a state of *independency* into one of *obligation*. She never was in a state of independency; nor is it fit a woman should, of any age, or in any state of life'.

It is perhaps worth noting Clarissa's position in law, had she married Solmes or Lovelace. By the common law, which governed parties in marriage until the Married Women's Property Act of 1882, the husband on marriage became entitled to the rents and profits derived from his wife's lands, and acquired a freehold estate in them during the time she was his wife. After her death, he was entitled to a life estate (*courtesy*) in the freehold lands of his wife while he survived her, if there had been or were children of the marriage capable of inheriting. The husband also acquired an absolute property in the chattels, personal or movable goods belonging to his wife. He could dispose of them during his life or by his will, and if he died intestate, his wife had no claim to them. The wife, it is true, was entitled on her husband's death to an estate for life in one third of his lands. The settlement made before marriage, a constant bait dangled by Lovelace, could by negotiation provide for more 'generous' provision for the wife. Divorce could be obtained, before 1857, only in two ways: 'from bed and board', a kind of judicial separation granted by the ecclesiastical courts; and 'from the bond of marriage' by private (and costly) Act of Parliament.

Clarissa's attempts to give her father the profits of her estate failed to ameliorate her brother's anger or her sister's jealousy, or indeed her father's displeasure at her apparent independence. Richardson never brings the angry father into a directly reported scene of action; he is left growling downstairs, raging through the claustrophobic interior of Harlowe Place in terrorizing proximity to his tormented younger daughter, a sign perhaps of the difficulty Richardson had with the representation of such a complex and contradictory situation.

Lovelace is much grander than the Harlowes, whose country house he scorns in lofty tones: 'Everybody knows Harlowe Place – for, like Versailles, it is sprung up from a dunghill within every elderly person's remembrance' (L34). He is the nephew of a peer, albeit a rather middle-class nobleman. Lovelace himself behaves aristocratically enough; he is rich, and expects to inherit more. His uncle, Lord M., would like him to go into Parliament, and on his own death can probably ensure that his nephew in turn would be *granted* a peerage, since he cannot inherit one. Lovelace is the leader of a band of young men-about-town, not quite 'Mohawks' and bully-boys. He has travelled abroad and is well read (cf. the notes to his letters, detailing references to books and plays, irrespective of where Richardson himself got the references he assembles). Lovelace may be seen as a leader who is unable to exercise to any useful purpose the dangerous, aristocratic, and perhaps outmoded, talents for fighting, stratagem and organization which have been bred in him, and which are inimical to the society in which he lives. This society seems receptive only to the rise of the Harlowes and their like, with their greed, mercenary relationships and more obsessive family cohesion. It is tempting to oppose the 'old' aristocratic family of which Lovelace is next in line as head, and the 'new', 'middle-class' Harlowe family; but we have to take into account the Harlowe-like origin of some of the aristocratic families of the time, and the fact that the Harlowes themselves are country gentlemen. Richardson does use names, though (Lovelace, recalling the Cavalier poet; or Mowbray, Tourville, Montague, Belton), to suggest the insolencies of the ancient, aristocratic 'Norman yoke'.

As well as estates, bequests and inheritances, other financial connections are important and detailed, such as the rents of lodgings and houses, the business of shopkeepers (like the Smiths, in whose house Clarissa dies), the cost of Clarissa's coffin, her will and benefactions. Patrick M'Donald, *alias* Captain Tomlinson, the out-of-work Irish actor who is available to assist Lovelace in his schemes, is also a smuggler. He perishes by that apparently glamorous, self-interested trade, dangerous entrepreneurial lawlessness legitimated by dubious political dissent; in short, he is a down-market version of Lovelace's own arrogance, forced to steal for his living. Mrs Sinclair's brothel is a superior establishment, run on business-like lines; and her strongest objection to Lovelace's obsessive conduct over Clarissa is that it is interrupting trade. The personal, moral, social, and of course economic, aspects of prostitution were constant preoccupations of eighteenth-century London, and in the second and third decades of the century it was widely canvassed, in periodical writing and elsewhere, that the problem of prostitution was out of control. Though lightly, if pervasively, touched on in *Clarissa*, where it is constantly juxtaposed with the heroine's purity, this question is a good example both of the protean shapes which any single theme is likely to assume in the hands of Richardson and of the way in which the threads of social history are woven into the moral fabric of his novel and used in the elaboration of his characters.

The presentation of the novel through letters is of course at the centre of Richardson's art, and it is in fact a phrase from a letter by Lovelace (L224) that is often used to draw attention to one of the strengths of this form of fiction: 'I love to write to the moment'. As well as thoroughly exploring all the psychological richness and the narrative force of indirection which the complex of interweaving letters creates, Richardson allows his imagination to play around the letters as constructed objects. In the letter just mentioned, Lovelace goes on to remark (editor's italics): '*these* trembling fingers, which twice have refused to direct the pen, and *thus* curvedly deform the paper . . .' A little later (L229), he physically, before our very eyes, exults in his scrupulous dishonesty: 'I am always careful to open covers cautiously, and to preserve seals entire . . .' In L232, his demonic energy is embodied in 'my shorthand writing', and he adds a little later one of the inimitable touches that made him the model-villain of the contemporary European imagination: 'Lovelaces in every corner, Jack'. Lovelace's 'language', the most intricately powerful of the 'languages' that Richardson creates in the letters, is just that, a 'language': in L256 he says 'I write it as it was spoken . . . one of my peculiars . . .', adding later (L268) '*familiar writing* is but *talking*, Jack.' The body of the novel is made up of letters written between Lovelace (just over 170, including inserts unnumbered by Richardson) and his friend Belford (almost eighty), and between Clarissa (about 190) and her *confidante*, Anna Howe (just sixty). In its sparkling surface, the impulsive Anna Howe's 'language' goes with Lovelace's, creating for her a character of amusing and likeable warmth, though her well-meant interventions are sometimes damaging to Clarissa's interests. 'The lady' has a sharp edge in her writing, a directness that underlines her own final superiority as a human being to her stylish, and at first apparently all-powerful, oppressor. The regretful shift of the self-critical Belford's allegiance, from the masterful Lovelace to the finally Christ-like Clarissa, is charted with believable sobriety in a 'language' that is a kind of norm.

The disposition of the letters from the different correspondents is an important part of Richardson's *conscious* artistry working with careful indirection, and is in contrast to the naked direction of the reader's judgement discussed above in outlining the changes he made to successive editions of the novel. Roughly, from L1 to L190 (into Clarissa's captivity), the story is seen through the eyes of Clarissa, with Anna Howe's comments and reactions, coming to rest on matching choric remarks by Belford and Lord M. Lovelace's voice does not sound, even briefly, until L26; from L191 to L293 (Clarissa's escape after the rape), Lovelace's is by far the dominant voice; thereafter to the end, Belford's becomes increasingly the reporter's voice, with dramatic insertions and finally the inclusion of Clarissa's posthumous messages. The movement of the book may be broadly outlined as follows: the invasion of Clarissa's life by Lovelace, who becomes more and more dominant up to her flight from Harlowe Place, which he instigates but does not force in outright terms; in her captivity Lovelace finally over-plays his hand with the brutal aggression of the 'fire'; from the time she escapes, even though he tricks her back, Clarissa's power increases; the rape is Lovelace's act of despair and marks his concomitant decline; thereafter she moves towards an apotheosis and he collapses; the book ends in an enigmatic coda, with Lovelace's death.

A more elaborate analysis would reveal more elaborate symmetry, with earlier passages in letters, or episodes, finding their answering voices in later parts, and effective juxtapositions of powerful and affecting writing or action with comic narrative and 'low' scenes. The variety and strength of this well-worked-out texture lie in the careful manipulation of point-of-view and self-examination, as well as comment and judgement.

The chronology of the story is only one of the more obvious instances of Richardson's extreme care and meticulous arrangement. The first letter is dated 10 January and the last (L537), reporting the death of Lovelace two days before, is dated 7 December. The year is not specified, and indeed a footnote to Clarissa's will (L507) says: 'The date of the year is left blank for particular reasons.' No day of the week is given with a date of the month until L11, 'Wednesday, March 1', so that we cannot know whether or not it is a leap year. The relevant years on which 1 March fell on a Wednesday are 1721, 1727, 1732. In L130 and L130.1, detailing Lovelace's pretence at finding a house for Clarissa to live in after their marriage, mention is made of 'some of the new streets about Grosvenor Square'. Since this square and the surrounding streets were laid out by the Grosvenor estate from 1725 onwards, perhaps 1732 is the most likely year. The precision of the dating (Clarissa's leaving Harlowe Place on the evening of Monday, 10 April; her rape on the night of 12–13 June; her death at 6.40 p.m. on the evening of Thursday, 7 September) puts the carefully arranging author, full of artifice, at the centre of one feature of the novel, namely, its sampler-like quality, the presence in it of fixed and elaborate objects for contemplation.

This static aspect of Richardson's fiction is acknowledged by his preparation and publication of *A Collection of Moral and Instructive Sentiments, Maxims, Cautions and Reflections contained . . . in the Histories of Pamela, Clarissa and Sir Charles Grandison, Digested under proper Heads, with Reference to the Volume and Page . . .* (1755). This, too, in a particular form, lies behind Dr Johnson's famous remark recorded by Boswell, 'Why, Sir, if you were to read Richardson for the story, your impatience would be so much fretted that you would hang yourself. But you must read him for the sentiment, and consider the story as giving occasion to the sentiment.' There is a contrasting, dynamic side to *Clarissa*, however, where all the sentiments, the arrangements, the objects of contemplation are qualified and further complicated by the movement of the story, the languages of the correspondents, the process of reading. It is perhaps here that Richardson's supreme genius as a novelist lies.

Many of the important constituents of Richardson's fiction discussed above, indirection, juxtaposition, movement, unfolding of psychological life, shifts of tone, the establishment of the author's solid presence, need a great deal of room in the novel and a substantial commitment of readers' time. The length of the book looks daunting, but familiarity with it turns the length into a virtue. It is easy to see why Richardson was, as he expressed it, 'a poor pruner'. As he went to cut, the novel grew under his hand. He simply saw more of the fiction locked in the text, waiting for embodiment. There are further exchanges of letters frozen in passages of indirect reporting (e.g. L157.1, L158.1), and there are whole novels implied in episodes like the involvement of James Harlowe, Junior, with a lawless ship-master, or Anna Howe's plan to rescue Clarissa by means of the higgler, Mrs Townsend, and *her* free traders.

It may easily be seen that the richness of the novel is likely to be explored to good purpose by many of the different kinds of theoretical and contextual criticism of fiction which have been developed in recent years. The way in which the characters are established by their own writing at length is open to comment in psychological terms. Two good (and related) examples of this are Clarissa's dream (L84: '. . . Mr Lovelace . . . stabbed me to the heart . . .') and Lovelace's (L417). The reading of Lovelace's dream, at least, would seem, however, to be quite complex, since Richardson himself has clearly constructed part of it, indicated by Clarissa's 'azure robe (all stuck with stars of embossed silver) . . .', as a symbolic, baroque religious painting of the Virgin Mary: in it, Lovelace is a damned soul, '. . . And then (horrid to relate!) the floor sinking under *me*, as the firmament opened for *her*, I dropped into a hole more frightful than that of Elden . . .' The psychological theory must become a complex analysi involving traditional and developed Christian symbolism. A similarly symbolic touch, one of myriads that are witness to Richardson's relation to older forms of art, is to be found in L233. Lovelace, 'slouched and muffled up' as an old man, has run Clarissa to earth at Mrs Moore's in Hampstead; as he pries around, ready to throw off his disguise and pounce on the lady like a pantomime demon (a long-running characterization of him by Richardson), he stumps 'towards the closet, over the door of which hung a picture . . . of St Cecilia . . . A common print . . . after an Italian master . . .' It is presumably a print of Raphael's painting of St Cecilia, a Roman lady of good family who wished to devote herself to Heaven by a life of celibacy, but who was compelled by her family to marry a young nobleman, Valerian, whom she converted and who joined her in martyrdom. The text invites theoretical analysis, but itself offers many (some conflicting) lines of suggestion. Richardson's conscious, and perhaps also unconscious, elaboration of text in the letters themselves, as well as his shimmering presence as 'author', create a work that is not only fruitfully tackled by structuralists and post-structuralists, but seems in certain ways to be designed by the author to be so tackled.

The myth Richardson employs is a powerful one, involving the relationship between women and men, the family, and marriage. Since Clarissa's part is so extensively and solidly imagined, feminist criticism is vital, not only of the story as Richardson's construct, but also of Clarissa's and Anna Howe's writing. This should go far beyond a critique of the novel as a report by a man, even a very empathetic man, on 'women's place in eighteenth-century society'. The novel is strong and substantial enough to search to the most fundamental truths about the relations between the sexes. Richardson has a straight, expressed, conventional opinion, stressing male dominance and the necessity for this in a well-organized family, but his fiction as a whole seems more bleakly to suggest encroachment on the one part and submission on the other, by women and men both, as the likely outcome of many, if not most, relationships. The historical and economic context of the myth, impressively imagined, has also elicited compelling readings of the novel. To all these theories must be added Richardson's own, increasingly crude, didacticism, as he worked on the successive versions.

Clarissa's death proves to be the test of all theories. In her death lies one of the most difficult problems for Richardson himself. She cannot be seen to will her death; that would be suicide and, for a paragon, impossible. She has been forced to abandon any hope for the expression of her love in this world. The only opening for her is the expectation of a future state. It is a remarkable feature of the book, and doubly so in our eyes, that Clarissa's rape is only mentioned but her death is embodied at great length, with elaborate Christian symbolism. She becomes, like Job whose words she constantly quotes, the type of Christ, and takes on herself the sins that men (and women) have committed against her. Her death confers grace on believers. This is difficult to accept for most modern readers, who are yet deeply affected by her end, even if they may feel that Richardson moved towards celebrating it too elaborately. Is her death a denial of life, a manifestation (like Lovelace's life and death) of a destructive love (or lack of it), or does she merely die 'of a galloping consumption' to complete the pattern? Is it a technical and formal problem in a great baroque composition of running figures, answering passages, symbolism and doctrine?

We may conclude by saying that Richardson's great work has up to now resisted being a mere exemplification of any theory, including his own. His book lives, however, not only by the complexity that the theories (again including his own) usefully organize and tease out, but also and perhaps primarily because he is at the same time a master of staple skills of narrative, such as suspense, indirection, even speed where necessary. His fiction also moves the reader deeply. We come to trust the text, or where we do distrust it, our distrust leads us to ask really important questions about human life and conduct. The narrative is like the snake with its tail in its mouth on Clarissa's coffin-plate, and the novel ends as it begins, with a duel. Duelling is touched on as a kind of running motif (e.g. in L346, where Hickman stands up to Lovelace's bullying, and, balancing this, in L442 and L443, where Lovelace and Colonel Morden growl at each other like two wary dogs), mostly in Lovelace's mocking but serious assent to the male, chauvinist 'Rake's Creed'. But the serious and dense use of all this comes when the reader is faced with Lovelace's last words, reported by La Tour in L537, 'LET THIS EXPIATE'. Duelling is not completely 'wrong'; the 'Rake's Creed' represents something that cannot be completely dismissed; Lovelace's death at the hands of Clarissa's cousin does not 'expiate'. It is the final act of Lovelace's fantasy, his imperious will to make all actions meet his own interpretations. At the same time, it is not without pathos, if not tragedy, since it is a distorted image of excellent qualities. Lovelace's death and last words are to be contrasted with Clarissa's, and placed in a context of death-beds, Belton's and Mrs Sinclair's. It also reflects back on Clarissa's death, and that reflection becomes less simple. This is the kind of echoing meaning that gives *Clarissa* its peculiar power.

ACKNOWLEDGEMENTS

I am grateful for the insights I have been given by members of my seminars on the English novel at the University of Sussex, who over some years have agreed to include *Clarissa* in their reading and discussion. I am indebted to Paul Boucé, Frank Gloversmith, Jocelyn Harris, Geoff Hemstedt, Rodney Hillman, Pat Hodgart, Tony Inglis, Tony Nuttall, Hermann Real, Ian Ross, Peter Sabor, Cedric Watts and others who considered queries or politely and often amiably endured questions and conversation about Richardson's work. I wish also to thank Pam Hall and Judith Wardman for assistance in preparing the volume.

SELECTED
FURTHER READING

BIBLIOGRAPHY

J. Carroll, 'Samuel Richardson' in A. E. Dyson, ed., *The English Novel: Select Bibliographical Guides* (OUP, 1974): useful annotated discussion and list.

R. G. Hannaford, *Samuel Richardson: An Annotated Bibliography of Critical Studies* (N.Y., 1980): entries up to 1978; comprehensive.

W. M. Sale, *Samuel Richardson: A Bibliographical Record of his Literary Career* (New Haven, Conn., 1936; repr. Hamden, Conn., 1968): best and fullest information on early editions.

BIOGRAPHY

J. Carroll, ed., *Selected Letters of Samuel Richardson* (OUP, 1964).

B. Downs, *Richardson* (1928; repr. N.Y., 1968).

T. C. Duncan Eaves and B. D. Kimpel, *Samuel Richardson: A Biography* (OUP, 1971).

A. D. McKillop, *Samuel Richardson: Printer and Novelist* (Chapel Hill, N.C., 1936; repr. Hamden, Conn., 1960).

W. M. Sale, *Samuel Richardson: Master Printer* (Ithaca, N.Y., 1950): now needs serious revision.

GENERAL WORKS ON RICHARDSON

D. L. Ball, *Samuel Richardson's Theory of Fiction* (The Hague, 1971).

E. B. Brophy, *Samuel Richardson: The Triumph of Craft* (Knoxville, Tenn., 1974).

J. Carroll, ed., *Samuel Richardson: A Collection of Critical Essays* in 20C Views series (Englewood Cliffs, N.J., 1967): essays on *Clarissa* are identified below by an asterisk.

M. A. Doody, *A Natural Passion: A Study of the Novels of Samuel Richardson* (OUP, 1974): chapters V, VI, VII, VIII and X deal with *Clarissa*.

M. A. Doody and P. Sabor, eds., *Samuel Richardson: Tercentenary Essays* (CUP, 1989): among the fifteen good essays are four on *Clarissa* noted below, and a relevant piece by S. Kilfeather on 'The Rise of Richardson Criticism'.

C. H. Flynn, *Samuel Richardson: A Man of Letters* (Princeton, N.J., 1982): useful background bibilography on family, sex, marriage and morals, rakes and fallen women, crime etc.

M. Golden, *Richardson's Characters* (Ann Arbor, Mich., 1963).

J. Harris, *Samuel Richardson* (CUP, 1987): an excellent brief but full discussion.

A. M. Kearney, *Samuel Richardson* (London, 1968).

M. Kinkead-Weekes, *Samuel Richardson: Dramatic Novelist* (London, 1973): Part Two, pp. 123–219, deals with *Clarissa*.

I. Konigsberg, *Samuel Richardson and the Dramatic Novel* (Lexington, Ken., 1968).

A. D. McKillop, *The Early Masters of English Fiction* (Lawrence, Kansas, 1956).

V. G. Myer, ed., *Samuel Richardson: Passion and Prudence* (London, 1986): Part II contains six short essays on aspects of *Clarissa*.

L. Brandy, 'Penetration and Impenetrability in *Clarissa*' [1974], in L. Damrosch, ed., *Modern Essays on Eighteenth-Century Literature* (OUP, 1988).

T. Castle, *Clarissa's Ciphers: Meaning and Disruption in Richardson's 'Clarissa'* (Ithaca, N.Y., 1982): political and feminist deconstruction gives some good readings.

S. W. Doederlein, 'Clarissa in the Hands of the Critics', *Eighteenth-Century Studies* 16 (1982–3).

M. A. Doody and P. Sabor, op. cit., contains J. A. Dussinger, 'Truth and Story-telling in *Clarissa*'; E. Copeland, 'Remapping London: *Clarissa* and the Woman in the Window'; J. G. Turner, 'Lovelace and the paradoxes of Libertinism'; T. Keymer, 'Richardson's *Meditations*: Clarissa's *Clarissa*'.

T. Eagleton, *The Rape of Clarissa* (London, 1982): some post-structuralist textuality; some feminist psychology; much historical materialism.

R. A. Erickson, *Mother Midnight: Birth, Sex and Fate in Eighteenth-Century Fiction (Defoe, Richardson, Sterne)* (N.Y., 1986): 'Part Four: Clarissa and the "Womb of Fate" '.

W. J. Farrell, 'The Style and Action in *Clarissa*' in *Studies in English Literature: 1500–1900*, III (Rice University, 1963).*

I. Gopnik, *A Theory of Style and Richardson's Clarissa* (The Hague, 1970): an interpretation along Russian Formalist lines.

C. Hill, 'Clarissa Harlowe and her Times', in *Essays in Criticism*, v (1955).*

F. W. Hilles, 'The Plan of Clarissa', *Philological Quarterly*, xiv (1966).*

A. M. Kearney, *Samuel Richardson: Clarissa* (Edward Arnold Studies in Literature, 1975).

M. Kinkead-Weekes, '*Clarissa* Restored?', *Review of English Studies* n.s. X (1959).

M. Price, 'Clarissa and Lovelace', in *To the Palace of Wisdom* (Carbondale, Ill., 1964).

J. Traugott, '*Clarissa's* Richardson: An Essay to Find the Reader' in M. Novak, ed., *English Literature in the Age of Disguise* (Berkeley, Cal., 1977).

D. Van Ghent, 'On *Clarissa Harlowe*', in *The English Novel: Form and Function* (N.Y., 1953).*

S. Van Marter, 'Richardson's Revisions of *Clarissa* in the second Edition', *Studies in Bibliography*, 26 (1973); '. . . in the third and fourth Editions', *ibid.*, 28 (1975).

W. B. Warner, *Reading Clarissa: The Struggles of Interpretation* (New Haven, Conn., 1979).

I. Watt, 'Richardson as Novelist: *Clarissa*', chapter VII of *The Rise of the Novel* (London, 1957).*

*Reprinted in J. Carroll, ed., *SR: Critical Essays* (1967), listed above.

BACKGROUND READING

J. G. Altman, *Epistolarity: Approaches to a Form* (Columbus, Ohio, 1984).

P. Ariès, *Western Attitudes towards Death: From the Middle Ages to the Present* (Baltimore, Md., 1974).

P.-G. Boucé, ed., *Sexuality in Eighteenth-Century Britain* (Manchester, 1982).

R. F. Brissenden, *Virtue in Distress: Studies in the Novel of Sentiment from Richardson to Sade* (London, 1974).

R. A. Day, *Told in Letters: Epistolary Fiction before Richardson* (Ann Arbor, Mich., 1960).

I. Donaldson, *The Rape of Lucretia: A Myth and its Transformations* (OUP, 1982): a line of thought that could be carried much further in relation to *Clarissa*.

F. Garber, *The Anatomy of the Self* (Boston, Mass., 1981).

R. Goldberg, *Sex and Enlightenment: Women in Richardson and Diderot* (CUP, 1984): substantial discussions of *Clarissa*; interesting treatment of Richardson's use of conduct books; useful bibliography.

J. Goody, *The Development of the Family and Marriage in Europe* (CUP, 1983): the speculative argument has been challenged but the book is instructive in drawing to the attention of historians a wider anthropological approach missing from much writing on the history of the family in Europe.

J. H. Hagstrum, *Sex and Sensibility: Ideal and Erotic Love from Milton to Mozart* (London, 1980): contains a reading of *Clarissa*.

Sir H. S. Maine, *Ancient Law: Its Connection with the Early History of Society and Its Relation to Modern Ideas* (1861; repr. in World's Classics, 1931, 1939 and 1946): although old-fashioned, still very relevant to the study of the history of marriage and the family in a wide perspective.

N. K. Miller, *The Heroine's Text: Readings in the French and English Novel: 1722–1782* (N.Y., 1980).

R. Perry, *Women, Letters and the Novel* (N.Y., 1980).

J. Preston, *The Reader's Role in Eighteenth-Century Fiction* (London, 1970): contains suggestive comments on *Clarissa*.

K. Rogers, *Feminism in Eighteenth-Century England* (Hemel Hempstead, 1982): informative.

L. Stone, *The Family, Sex, and Marriage in England: 1500–1800* (London, 1977): informative; needs qualification.

R. P. Utter and G. B. Needham, *Pamela's Daughters* (N.Y., 1937).

C. G. Wolff, *Samuel Richardson and the Eighteenth-Century Puritan Character* (Hamden, Conn., 1972).

A NOTE ON THE TEXT

The text is based on the copy of [C1] in the library of Trinity College, Cambridge (Rothschild Collection, RW 72. 8–14). There is no textual apparatus. The aim has been to give a smooth readable text without unduly distorting possible nuances in the old pages. Richardson's spelling is mostly modern; only a few old forms are altered. Capitalization in the text of the novel is very close to modern usage, but in the prefatory material and elsewhere, capitals have been reduced to conform to modern practice. Long ʃ is reduced to s; elisions are expanded (serv'd, altho': served, although). [C1] employs italics less frequently than [C2] and [C3], but some adjustment has been made silently; for example, quoted verse is turned from italic to roman, since the earlier conventions create an emphasis for the modern reader which is not usually required. Obvious errors of the press have also been silently corrected. Richardson uses both round and square brackets; but though some system may be discerned, his usage overall is inconsistent. All his brackets, therefore, are made round. All square brackets are editorial, usually marking the few occasions when [C2] and [C3] adjust minor tangles in [C1] which might interrupt reading, and the later smoothing has been adopted. The punctuation presents problems. Richardson employs both single and double marks of quotation, but apparently inconsistently; all quotation marks are made single. The eighteenth-century convention of placing a series of quotation marks down the outer margins of a long passage is abandoned. Within sentences Richardson made use of the contemporary printers' heavy and intrusive syntactic punctuation. This is made much lighter, in conformity with present taste. Very long sentences, divided by colons and semi-colons, are occasionally broken up into two or three units. At certain points, Richardson *adds* to his heavy syntactic punctuation a rhetorical punctuation of dashes. Such passages seem usually to represent agitation or emotion in the letter-writer, or in the events or speech being written about, or both. Richardson is clearly often himself writing fast in some of these passages, as well as experimenting in the presentation of 'writing to the moment'. The co-existence of the two parallel systems of punctuation sometimes leads to visual muddle. Modern readers are perhaps more receptive of authorial experimentation than audiences of the past, and less hung-up on 'correctness'. When the circumstances seem appropriate, therefore, Richardson's experiments are taken seriously; the rhetorical punctuation is given precedence and the dashes are retained; the 'correct' syntactical punctuation is omitted. The result, it is hoped, is a livelier and more direct text.

CLARISSA

OR, THE

HISTORY

OF A

YOUNG LADY:

Comprehending

THE MOST IMPORTANT CONCERNS

OF PRIVATE LIFE

And particularly showing

THE DISTRESSES THAT MAY ATTEND THE

MISCONDUCT BOTH OF PARENTS AND CHILDREN,

IN RELATION TO MARRIAGE

PUBLISHED BY THE EDITOR OF

PAMELA

PREFACE

THE following history is given in a series of letters written principally in a double yet separate correspondence: between two young ladies of virtue and honour, bearing an inviolable friendship for each other and writing upon the most interesting subjects: and between two gentlemen of free lives; one of them glorying in his talents for stratagem and invention, and communicating to the other in confidence all the secret purposes of an intriguing head, and resolute heart.

But it is not amiss to premise, for the sake of such as may apprehend hurt to the morals of youth from the more freely-written letters, that the gentlemen, though professed libertines as to the fair sex, and making it one of their wicked maxims to keep no faith with any of the individuals of it who throw themselves into their power, are not, however, either infidels or scoffers; nor yet such as think themselves freed from the observance of other moral obligations.

On the contrary, it will be found in the progress of the collection, that they very often make such reflections upon each other, and each upon himself and upon his actions, as reasonable beings who disbelieve not a future state of rewards and punishments (and who one day propose to reform) must sometimes make—one of them actually reforming, and antidoting the poison which some might otherwise apprehend would be spread by the gayer pen and lighter heart of the other.

And yet that other, although in unbosoming himself to a select friend he discover wickedness enough to entitle him to general hatred, preserves a decency, as well in his images as in his language, which is not always to be found in the works of some of the most celebrated modern writers, whose subjects and characters have less warranted the liberties they have taken.

Length will be naturally expected, not only from what has been said, but from the following considerations: that the letters on both sides are written while the hearts of the writers must be supposed to be wholly engaged in their subjects: the events at the time generally dubious—so that they abound not only with critical situations, but with what may be called instantaneous descriptions and reflections, which may be brought home to the breast of the youthful reader: as also, with affecting conversations, many of them written in the dialogue or dramatic way. To which may be added, that the collection contains not only the history of the excellent person whose name it bears, but includes the lives, characters, and catastrophes of several others, either principally or incidentally concerned in the story.

But yet the editor to whom it was referred to publish the whole in such a way as he should think would be most acceptable to the public was so diffident in relation to this article of *length*, that he thought proper to submit the letters to the perusal of several judicious friends, whose opinion he desired of what might be best spared.

One gentleman, in particular, of whose knowledge, judgement, and experience, as well as candour, the editor has the highest opinion advised him to give a narrative turn to the letters, and to publish only what concerned the principal heroine—striking off the collateral incidents and all that related to the second characters; though he allowed the parts which would have been by this means excluded to be both instructive and entertaining. But being extremely fond of the affecting story, he was desirous to have everything parted with, which he thought retarded its progress.

This advice was not relished by other gentlemen. They insisted that the story could not be reduced to a dramatic unity, nor thrown into the narrative way, without divesting it of its warmth and of a great part of its efficacy, as very few of the reflections and observations, which they looked upon as the most useful part of the collection, would then find a place.

They were of opinion that in all works of this, and of the dramatic kind, *story* or *amusement* should be considered as little more than the vehicle to the more necessary *instruction*: that many of the scenes would be rendered languid were they to be made less busy: and that the whole would be thereby deprived of that variety which is deemed the soul of a feast, whether mensal or mental.

They were also of opinion that the parts and characters which must be omitted if this advice were followed were some of the most natural in the whole collection, and no less instructive, especially to youth, which might be a consideration perhaps overlooked by a gentleman of the adviser's great knowledge and experience. For, as they observed, there is a period in human life in which, youthful activity ceasing and hope contenting itself to look from its own domestic wicket upon bounded prospects, the half-tired mind aims at little more than amusement—and with reason; for what in the instructive way can appear either new or needful to one who has happily got over those dangerous situations which call for advice and cautions, and who has filled up his measures of knowledge to the top?

Others likewise gave their opinions. But no two being of the same mind as to the parts which could be omitted, it was resolved to present the world the two first volumes by way of specimen, and to be determined with regard to the rest by the reception those should meet with.

If that be favourable, two others may soon follow, the whole collection being ready for the press: that is to say, if it be not found necessary to abstract or omit some of the letters in order to reduce the bulk of the whole.

Thus much in general. But it may not be amiss to add in particular that in the great variety of subjects which this collection contains, it is one of the principal views of the publication: to caution parents against the undue exertion of their natural authority over their children in the great article of marriage: and children against preferring a man of pleasure to a man of probity, upon that dangerous but too commonly received notion, *that a reformed rake makes the best husband.*

But as the characters will not all appear in the two first volumes, it has been thought advisable, in order to give the reader some further idea of them, and of the work, to prefix a brief account of the principal characters throughout the whole.

THE PRINCIPAL CHARACTERS

MISS CLARISSA HARLOWE, a young lady of great delicacy, mistress of all the accomplishments, natural and acquired, that adorn the sex, having the strictest notions of filial duty.

ROBERT LOVELACE, Esq., a man of birth and fortune, haughty, vindictive, humorously vain, equally intrepid and indefatigable in the pursuit of his pleasures—making his addresses to Miss Clarissa Harlowe.

JAMES HARLOWE, Esq., the father of Miss Clarissa, Miss Arabella, and Mr James Harlowe: despotic, absolute, and when offended not easily forgiving.

LADY CHARLOTTE HARLOWE, his wife, mistress of fine qualities, but greatly under the influence not only of her arbitrary husband but of her son.

JAMES HARLOWE, jun., proud, fierce, uncontrollable and ambitious, jealous of the favour his sister Clarissa stood in with the principals of the family, and a bitter and irreconcilable enemy to Mr Lovelace.

MISS ARABELLA HARLOWE, elder sister of Miss Clarissa, ill-natured, overbearing, and petulant, envying her sister, and the more as Mr Lovelace was first brought to make his address to herself.

JOHN HARLOWE, Esq., elder brother of Mr James Harlowe, sen., an unmarried gentleman, good-natured, and humane, but easily carried away by more boisterous spirits.

ANTONY HARLOWE, third brother, who had acquired a great fortune in the Indies, positive, rough, opinionated.

MR ROGER SOLMES, a man of sordid manners, disagreeable in his person and address, immensely rich, proposed with a high hand for a husband to Miss Clarissa Harlowe.

MRS HERVEY, half-sister of Lady Charlotte Harlowe, a lady of good sense and virtue, in her heart against the measures taken to drive her niece to extremities, but not having courage to oppose herself to so strong a stream, sailing with it.

MISS DOLLY HERVEY, her daughter, good-natured, gentle, sincere, and a great admirer of her cousin Clarissa.

MRS NORTON, a gentlewoman of piety and good understanding, the daughter of an unpreferred clergyman of great merit whose amanuensis she was, married unhappily and left a widow, engaged to nurse Miss Clarissa Harlowe, in whose education likewise she had a principal share.

COLONEL MORDEN, a man of fortune, generosity, and courage, nearly related to the Harlowe family, for some time past residing at Florence.

MISS HOWE, the most intimate friend, companion, and correspondent of Miss Clarissa Harlowe, of great vivacity, fire and fervency in her friendships and enmities.

MRS HOWE, mother of Miss Howe, a widow lady of high spirit, a notable manager having high notions of the parental authority.

MR HICKMAN, a man of family, fortune, sobriety and virtue, encouraged by Mrs Howe in his address to her daughter.

LORD M., uncle to Mr Lovelace, a nobleman of middle genius, and a great proverbialist.

LADY SARAH SADLEIR, LADY BETTY LAWRANCE, half-sisters of Lord M., widow ladies of honour and fortune.

Miss Charlotte and Patty Montague, maiden ladies of character, nieces of the same nobleman.

Dr Lewin, a divine of great piety and learning, to whom Miss Clarissa Harlowe owed much of her improvement.

Dr H., a physician of humanity, generosity and politeness.

Mr Elias Brand, a pedantic young clergyman, fond of Latin scraps and classical quotations.

Richard Mowbray, Thomas Doleman, James Tourville, Thomas Belton, libertine gentlemen, companions of Mr Lovelace.

John Belford, Esq., a fifth friend and companion of Mr Lovelace, and his principal intimate and confidant.

Mrs Sinclair, the pretended name of a private brothel keeper in London.

Capt. Tomlinson, the assumed name of a vile and artful pander to the debaucheries of Mr Lovelace.

Mrs Moore, a widow gentlewoman, keeping a lodging-house at Hampstead.

Miss Rawlins, a notable young gentlewoman in that neighbourhood.

Mrs Bevis, a lively widow of the same place.

Sally Martin, Polly Horton, assistants of, and partners with, the infamous Mrs Sinclair.

Joseph Leman, William Summers, Hannah Burton, Betty Barnes, Dorcas Wykes and others, servants to the principal persons.

THE HISTORY OF
MISS CLARISSA HARLOWE

Letter 1: MISS ANNA HOWE TO MISS CLARISSA HARLOWE

Jan. 10

I AM extremely concerned, my dearest friend, for the disturbances that have happened in your family. I know how it must hurt you to become the subject of the public talk; and yet upon an occasion so generally known it is impossible but that whatever relates to a young lady, whose distinguished merits have made her the public care, should engage everybody's attention. I long to have the particulars from yourself, and of the usage I am told you receive upon an accident you could not help and in which, as far as I can learn, the sufferer was the aggressor.

Mr Diggs,[a] whom I sent for at the first hearing of the rencounter to inquire for *your* sake how your brother was, told me that there was no danger from the wound, if there were none from the fever, which it seems has been increased by the perturbation of his spirits.

Mr Wyerley drank tea with us yesterday; and though he is far from being partial to Mr Lovelace, as it may be well supposed, yet both he and Mr Symmes blame your family for the treatment they gave him when he went in person to inquire after your brother's health, and to express his concern for what had happened.

They say that Mr Lovelace could not avoid drawing his sword: and that either your brother's unskilfulness or violence left him from the very first pass entirely in his power. This, I am told, was what Mr Lovelace said upon it, retreating as he spoke: 'Have a care, Mr Harlowe—Your violence puts you out of your defence. You give me too much advantage! For your sister's sake I will pass by everything—if—'

But this the more provoked his rashness to lay himself open to the advantage of his adversary, who, after a slight wound in the arm, took away his sword.

There are people who love not your brother, because of his natural imperiousness and fierce and uncontrollable temper: these say that the young gentleman's passion was abated on seeing his blood gush plentifully down his arm; and that he received the generous offices of his adversary (who helped him off with his coat and waistcoat and bound up his arm, till the surgeon could come) with such patience as was far from making a visit afterwards from that adversary to inquire after his health appear either insulting or improper.

Be this as it may, everybody pities you. So steady, so uniform in your conduct;

a Her brother's surgeon.

39

so desirous, as you always said, of sliding through life to the end of it unnoted; and, as I may add, not wishing to be observed even for your silent benevolence; sufficiently happy in the noble consciousness which rewards it: *Rather useful than glaring*, your deserved motto; though now pushed into blaze, as we see, to your regret; and yet blamed at home for the faults of others. How must such a virtue suffer on every hand!—Yet it must be allowed that your present trial is but proportioned to your prudence!

As all your friends without doors are apprehensive that some other unhappy event may result from so violent a contention, in which it seems the families on both sides are now engaged, I must desire you to enable me, on the authority of your own information, to do you occasional justice.

My mamma, and all of us, like the rest of the world, talk of nobody but you on this occasion, and of the consequences which may follow from the resentments of a man of Mr Lovelace's spirit; who, as he gives out, has been treated with high indignity by your uncles. My mamma will have it that you cannot now, with any decency, either see him or correspond with him. She is a good deal prepossessed by your uncle Antony, who occasionally calls upon us, as you know; and, on this rencounter, has represented to her the crime which it would be in a sister to encourage a man, who is to *wade* into her favour (this was his expression) through the blood of her brother.

Write to me therefore, my dear, the whole of your story from the time that Mr Lovelace was first introduced into your family; and particularly an account of all that passed between him and your sister, about which there are different reports; some people supposing that the younger sister (at least by her uncommon merit) has stolen a lover from the elder. And pray write in so full a manner as may gratify those who know not so much of your affairs as I do. If anything unhappy should fall out from the violence of such spirits as you have to deal with, your account of all things previous to it will be your justification.

You see what you draw upon yourself by excelling all your sex. Every individual of it who knows you, or has heard of you, seems to think you answerable to *her* for your conduct in points so very delicate and concerning.

Every eye, in short, is upon you with the expectation of an example. I wish to heaven you were at liberty to pursue your own methods; all would then, I dare say, be easy and honourably ended. But I dread your directors and directresses; for your mamma, admirably well qualified as she is to lead, must submit to be led. Your sister and brother will certainly put you out of your course.

But this is a point you will not permit me to expatiate upon: pardon me therefore, and I have done.—Yet, why should I say, Pardon me? When your concerns are my concerns? When your honour is my honour? When I love you, as never woman loved another? And when you have allowed of that concern and of that love, and have for years, which in persons so young may be called many, ranked in the first class of your friends.

Your ever-grateful and affectionate
ANNA HOWE?

Will you oblige me with a copy of the preamble to the clauses in your grandfather's will in your favour; and allow me to send it to my aunt Harman? She is very desirous to see it. Yet your character has so charmed her that, though a stranger to you personally, she assents to the preference given you in it, before she knows his reasons for that preference.

Letter 2: MISS CLARISSA HARLOWE TO MISS HOWE

Harlowe Place, Jan. 13

How you oppress me, my dearest friend, with your politeness! I cannot doubt your sincerity; but you should take care that you give me not reason from your kind partiality to call in question your judgement. You do not distinguish that I take many admirable hints from you, and have the art to pass them upon you for my own. For in all you do, in all you say, nay, in your very looks (so animated!) you give lessons, to one who loves you and observes you as I love and observe you, without knowing that you do. So, pray, my dear, be more sparing of your praise for the future, lest after this confession we should suspect that you secretly intend to praise yourself, while you would be thought only to commend another.

Our family has indeed been strangely discomposed—*Discomposed!*—It has been in *tumults*, ever since the unhappy transaction; and I have borne all the blame; yet should have had too much concern from myself had I been more justly spared by everyone else.

For, whether it be owing to a faulty impatience, having been too indulgently treated to be *inured* to blame, or to the regret I have to hear those censured on my account whom it is my duty to vindicate; I have sometimes wished that it had pleased God to have taken me in my last fever, when I had everybody's love and good opinion; but oftener, that I had never been distinguished by my grandpapa as I was: which has estranged me, I doubt, my brother's and sister's affections; at least, has raised a jealousy, with regard to the apprehended favour of my two uncles, that now and then overshadows their love.

My brother being happily recovered of his fever and his wound in a hopeful way, although he has not yet ventured abroad, I will be as particular as you desire in the little history you demand of me. But heaven forbid that anything should ever happen which may require it to be produced for the purpose you so kindly mention!

I will begin as you command, with Mr Lovelace's address to my sister, and be as brief as possible. I will recite facts only, and leave you to judge of the truth of the report raised that the younger sister has robbed the elder.

It was in pursuance of a conference between Lord M. and my uncle Antony, that Mr Lovelace (my papa and mamma not forbidding) paid his respects to my sister Arabella. My brother was then in Scotland, busying himself in viewing the condition of the considerable estate which was left him there by his generous godmother, together with one as considerable in Yorkshire. I was also absent at my *dairy-house*, as it is called,*a* busied in the accounts relating to the estate which my grandfather had the goodness to bequeath me, and which once a year

a Her grandfather, in order to invite her to him as often as her other friends would spare her, indulged her in erecting and fitting-up a dairy-house in her own taste. When finished, it was so much admired for its elegant simplicity and convenience that the whole seat, before of old time from its situation called *The Grove*, was generally known by the name of *The Dairy-house*. Her grandfather, particularly, was fond of having it so called.

are left to my inspection, although I have given the whole into my papa's power.

My sister made me a visit there the day after Mr Lovelace had been introduced, and seemed highly pleased with the gentleman. His birth, his fortune in possession a clear 2000 [pounds a year] as Lord M. had assured my uncle; presumptive heir to that nobleman's large estate; his great expectations from Lady Sarah Sadleir and Lady Betty Lawrance who, with his uncle, interested themselves very warmly (he being the last of his line) to see him married.

'So handsome a man!—Oh her beloved Clary!' (for then she was ready to love me dearly, from the overflowings of her good humour on his account!) 'He was but *too* handsome a man for *her!*—Were she but as amiable as *somebody*, there would be a probability of *holding* his affections!—For he was wild; she heard; *very* wild, very gay; loved intrigue. But he was young; a man of sense: would see his error, could she but have patience with his faults, if his faults were not cured by marriage.'

Thus she ran on; and then wanted me 'to see the charming man,' as she called him. Again concerned 'that she was not handsome enough for him'; with 'a sad thing, that the man should have the advantage of the woman in that particular.'— But then, stepping to the glass she complimented herself, 'That she was very *well*: that there were many women deemed passable who were inferior to herself: that she was always thought comely; and, let her tell me, that comeliness having not so much to lose as beauty had would hold, when that would evaporate and fly off— Nay, for that matter' (and again she turned to the glass), 'her features were not irregular, her eyes not at all amiss.' And I remember they were more than usually brilliant at that time.—'Nothing, in short, to be found fault with, though nothing very engaging, she doubted—was there, Clary?'

Excuse me, my dear, I never was thus particular before; no, not to you. Nor would I now have written thus freely of a sister, but that she makes a merit to my brother of disowning that she ever liked him, as I shall mention hereafter: and then you will always have me give you minute descriptions, nor suffer me to pass by the air and manner in which things are spoken that are to be taken notice of; rightly observing that air and manner often express more than the accompanying words.

I congratulated her upon her prospects. She received my compliments with a great deal of self-complacency.

She liked the gentleman still more at his next visit; and yet he made no particular address to her, although an opportunity was given him for it. This was wondered at, as my uncle had introduced him into our family declaredly as a visitor to my sister. But as we are ever ready to make excuses, when in good humour with ourselves, for the supposed slights of those whose approbation we wish to engage, so my sister found out a reason, much to Mr Lovelace's advantage, for his not improving the opportunity that was given him—It was bashfulness, truly, in him. (Bashfulness in Mr Lovelace, my dear!)—Indeed, gay and lively as he is, he has not the look of an *impudent* man. But I fancy it is many, many years ago, since he was bashful.

Thus, however, could my sister make it out—'Upon her word, she believed Mr Lovelace deserved not the bad character he had as to women. He was really, to *her* thinking, a *modest* man. He *would* have spoken out, she believed; but once or twice, as he seemed to intend to do so, he was under so *agree*-able a confusion!

Such a profound respect he seemed to show her; a perfect *reverence*, she thought. She loved dearly that a gentleman in courtship should show a reverence to his mistress.'—So indeed we all do, I believe; and with reason, since, if I may judge from what I have seen in many families, there is little enough of it shown afterwards—And she told my aunt Hervey that she would be a little less upon the reserve next time he came: 'She was not one of those *flirts*, not she, who would give pain to a person that deserved to be well treated; and the more for the greatness of his value for her.'—I wish she had not somebody whom I love in her eye. Yet is not her censure unjust, I believe. Is it, my dear?—Excepting in one undue and harsh word?

In this third visit, Bella governed herself by this kind and considerate principle; so that, according to her own account of the matter, the man *might* have spoken out—but he was still *bashful*; he was not able to overcome this *unseasonable reverence*. So this visit went off as the former.

But now she began to be dissatisfied with him. She compared his general character with this particular behaviour to her; and having never been courted before, owned herself puzzled how to deal with so odd a lover. 'What did the man mean!—Had not her uncle brought him *declaredly* as a suitor to her?—It could not be bashfulness (now she thought of it), since he might have opened his mind to her *uncle*, if he wanted courage to speak directly to *her*—Not that she cared much for the man neither; but it was right, surely, that a woman should be put out of doubt, early, as to a man's intentions in such a case as this, from his own mouth.—But, truly, she had begun to think that he was more solicitous to cultivate her *mamma's* good opinion than *hers!*—Everybody, she owned, admired her mamma's conversation—But he was mistaken if he thought that would do with *her*. And then, for his own sake, surely he should put it into her power to be complaisant to him, if he gave her cause of approbation. This distant behaviour, she must take upon her to say, was the more extraordinary, as he continued his visits and declared himself extremely desirous to cultivate a friendship with the whole family; and as he could have no doubt about her sense, if she might take upon her to join her own with the general opinion, he having taken great notice of, and admired many of her *good things* as they fell from her lips—Reserves were painful, she must needs say, to open and free spirits like hers; and yet she must tell my aunt' (to whom all this was directed) 'that she should never forget what she owed to her sex, and to herself, were Mr Lovelace as unexceptionable in his morals as in his figure, and were he to urge his suit ever so warmly.'

I was not of her council. I was still absent. And it was agreed between my aunt Hervey and her that she was to be quite solemn and shy in his next visit, if there were not a peculiarity in his address to her.

But my sister, it seems, had not considered the matter well. This was not the way, as it proved, to be taken with a man of Mr Lovelace's penetration, for matters of *mere omission*—nor with *any* man; since if love has not taken root deep enough to cause it to shoot out into declaration, if an opportunity be fairly given for it, there is little room to expect that the blighting winds of anger or resentment will bring it forward. Then my poor sister is not naturally good-humoured. This is too well-known a truth for me to endeavour to conceal it, especially from you. She must therefore, I doubt, have appeared to great disadvantage when she aimed to be worse-tempered than ordinary.

How they managed it in this conversation I know not. One would be tempted to think by the issue that Mr Lovelace was ungenerous enough to seek the occasion given,[a] and to improve it. Yet he thought fit to put the question too. But, she says, it was not till by some means or other (she knew not how) he had wrought her up to such a pitch of displeasure with him that it was impossible for her to recover herself at the instant. Nevertheless he re-urged his question, as expecting a definitive answer, without waiting for the return of her temper, or endeavouring to mollify her; so that she was under a necessity of persisting in her denial; yet gave him reason to think that she did not dislike his address, only the *manner* of it; his court being rather made to her mamma than to herself, as if he were sure of *her* consent at any time.

A good encouraging denial, I must own—as was the rest of her plea, to wit, 'a disinclination to change her state. Exceedingly happy as she was, she never could be happier!' And such-like *consenting negatives*, as I may call them, and yet not intend a reflection upon my sister; for what can any young creature in the like circumstances say, when she is not sure but a too ready consent may subject her to the slights of a sex that generally values a blessing either more or less as it is obtained with difficulty or ease? Miss Biddulph's answer to a copy of verses from a gentleman, reproaching our sex as acting in disguise, is not a bad one, although you perhaps may think it too acknowledging for the female character.

> Ungen'rous sex!—To scorn us, if we're *kind*;
>   And yet upbraid us, if we seem *severe!*
> Do *You*, t'encourage us to tell our mind,
>   Yourselves put off disguise, and be sincere.
> You talk of coquetry!—Your own false hearts
> *Compel* our sex to act dissembling parts.

Here I am obliged to lay down my pen. I will soon resume it.

Letter 3: MISS CLARISSA HARLOWE TO MISS HOWE

Jan. 13, 14

AND thus, as Mr Lovelace thought fit to *take it*, had he his answer from my sister. It was with very great regret, as he pretended (I doubt the man is a hypocrite, my dear!), that he acquiesced in it. 'So much determinedness; such a noble firmness in my sister; that there was no hope of prevailing upon her to alter sentiments she had adopted on full consideration.' He sighed, as Bella told us, when he took his leave of her: 'Profoundly sighed: grasped her hand and kissed it with *such* an ardour—withdrew with *such* an air of solemn respect—she had him then before her. She could almost find in her heart, although he had vexed her, to pity him.' A good intentional preparative [to love], this pity, since at the time, she little thought that he would not renew his offer.

He waited on my mamma after he had taken leave of Bella, and reported his ill success in so respectful a manner, both with regard to my sister and to the whole family, and with so much concern that he was not accepted as a relation to it, that

   a   See Mr Lovelace's Letter, No. 31, in which he briefly accounts for his conduct in this affair.

it left upon them all (my brother being then, as I have said, in Scotland) impressions in his favour, and a belief that this matter would certainly be brought on again. But Mr Lovelace going up directly to town, where he stayed a whole fortnight, and meeting there with my uncle Antony, to whom he regretted his niece's unhappy resolution not to change her state, it was seen that there was a total end put to the affair.

My sister was not wanting to herself on this occasion, but made a virtue of necessity; and the man was quite another man with her. 'A vain creature! Too well knowing his advantages; yet those not what she had conceived them to be!—Cool and warm by fits and starts; an ague-like lover. A steady man, a man of virtue, a man of morals was worth a thousand of such gay flutterers. Her sister Clary might think it worth her while perhaps to try to engage such a man; she had patience; she was mistress of persuasion; and indeed, to do the girl justice, had *something* of a person. But as for *her*, she would not have a man of whose heart she could not be sure for one moment; no, not for the world; and most sincerely glad was she that she had rejected him.'

But when Mr Lovelace returned into the country, he thought fit to visit my papa and mamma, hoping, as he told them, that however unhappy he had been in the rejection of the wished-for alliance, he might be allowed to keep up an acquaintance and friendship with a family which he should always respect. And then, unhappily, as I may say, was I at home, and present.

It was immediately observed that his attention was fixed on me. My sister, as soon as he was gone, in a spirit of bravery, seemed desirous to promote his address, should it be tendered.

My aunt Hervey was there, and was pleased to say we should make the finest couple in England, if my sister had no objection—No, indeed! with a haughty toss, was my sister's reply. It would be strange if she had, after the denial she had given him upon full deliberation.

My mamma declared that her only dislike of his alliance with either daughter was on account of his faulty morals.

My uncle Harlowe, that his *daughter* Clary, as he delighted to call me from childhood, would reform him if any woman in the world could.

My uncle Antony gave his approbation in high terms; but referred, as my aunt had done, to my sister.

She repeated her contempt of him, and declared that were there not another man in England she would not have him. She was ready, on the contrary, she could assure them, to resign her pretensions under hand and seal, if Miss Clary were taken with his tinsel, and if everyone else approved of his address to the girl.

My papa, indeed, after a long silence, being urged to speak his mind by my uncle Antony, said that he had a letter from his son James, on his hearing of Mr Lovelace's visits to his daughter Arabella, which he had not shown to anybody but my mamma, that treaty being at an end when he received it; that in this letter he expressed great dislikes to an alliance with Mr Lovelace on the score of his immoralities; that he knew, indeed, there was an old grudge between them; [but] that, being desirous to prevent all occasions of disunion and animosity in his family, he would suspend the declaration of his own mind, till his son arrived and till he had heard his further objections; that he was the more inclined to make his son this compliment, as Mr Lovelace's general character gave but too much ground for his son's dislike of him, adding, that he had heard (so he supposed had everyone) that he was a very extravagant man; that he had contracted debts in his travels; and, indeed, he was pleased to say, he had the air of a spendthrift.

These particulars I had partly from my aunt Hervey, and partly from my sister; for I was called out as soon as the subject was entered upon. And when I returned, my uncle Antony asked me how *I* should like Mr Lovelace? Everybody saw, he was pleased to say, that I had made a conquest.

I immediately answered, Not at all: he seemed to have too good an opinion both of his person and parts to have any great regard to his wife, let him marry whom he would.

My sister particularly was pleased with this answer, and confirmed it to be just; with a compliment to my judgement—for it was *hers.*

But the very next day Lord M. came to Harlowe Place: I was then absent: and in his nephew's name, made a proposal in form, declaring that it was the ambition of all his family to be related to ours; and he hoped his kinsman would not have such an answer on the part of the younger sister as he had had on that of the elder.

In short, Mr Lovelace's visits were admitted as those of a man who had not deserved disrespect from our family; but, as to his address to me, with a reservation as above on my papa's part, that he would determine nothing without his son. My discretion, as to the rest, was confided in; for still I had the same objections as to the man: nor would I when we were better acquainted hear anything but general talk from him, giving him no opportunity of conversing with me in private.

He bore this with a resignation little expected from his natural temper, which is generally reported to be quick and hasty, unused it seems from childhood to check or control: a case too common in considerable families where there is an only son; and *his* mother never had any other child. But, as I have heretofore told you, I could perceive notwithstanding this resignation that he had so good an opinion of himself, as not to doubt that his person and accomplishments would insensibly engage me; and could that be once done, he told my aunt Hervey, he should hope from so steady a temper that his hold in my affections would be durable. While my sister accounted for his patience in another manner, which would perhaps have had more force if it had come from a person less prejudiced: 'That the man was not fond of marrying at all; that he might perhaps have half-a-score mistresses; and that delay might be as convenient for his *roving,* as for my *well-acted* indifference.'— That was her kind expression.

Whatever were his motive for a patience so generally believed to be out of his usual character, and where the object of his address was supposed to be of fortune considerable enough to engage his warmest attention, he certainly escaped many mortifications by it. For while my papa suspended his approbation till my brother's arrival, he received from everyone those civilities which were due to his birth; and although we heard from time to time reports to his disadvantage with regard to morals, yet could we not question him upon them without giving him greater advantages than the situation he was in with us would justify to prudence, since it was much more likely that his address would *not* be allowed of than it *would.*

And thus was he admitted to converse with our family almost upon his own terms; for while my friends saw nothing in his behaviour but what was extremely respectful and observed in him no violent importunity, they seemed to have taken a great liking to his conversation; while I considered him only as a common guest when he came, and thought myself no more concerned in his visits, nor at his entrance or departure, than any other of the family.

But this indifference of my side was the means of procuring him one very great advantage; for upon it was grounded that correspondence by letters which succeeded—and which, had it been to be begun when the family animosity broke out, would never have been entered into on my part. The occasion was this:

My uncle Hervey has a young gentleman entrusted to his care, whom he has thoughts of sending abroad a year or two hence, to make the Grand Tour, as it is called; and finding Mr Lovelace could give a good account of everything necessary for a young traveller to observe upon such an occasion, he desired him to write down a description of the courts and countries he had visited, and what was most worthy of curiosity in them.

He consented, on condition that I would *direct* his subjects, as he called it: and as everyone had heard his manner of writing commended, and thought his relations might be agreeable amusements in winter evenings; and that he could have no opportunity particularly to address me in them, since they were to be read in full assembly before they were to be given to the young gentleman, I made the less scruple to write, and to make observations and put questions for our further information—Still the less, perhaps, as I love writing; and those who do are fond, you know, of occasions to use the pen: and then, having everyone's consent, and my uncle Hervey's desire that I would, I thought that if I had been the only scrupulous person, it would have shown a particularity that a vain man would construe to his advantage, and which my sister would not fail to animadvert upon.

You have seen some of these letters, and have been pleased with his account of persons, places, and things; and we have both agreed that he was no common observer upon what he had seen.

My sister herself allowed that the man had a tolerable knack of writing and describing; and my papa, who had been abroad in his youth, said that his remarks were curious and showed him to be a person of reading, judgement, and taste.

Thus was a kind of correspondence begun between him and me with general approbation; while everyone wondered at, and was pleased with, his patient veneration of me, for so they called it. However, it was not doubted that he would soon be more importunate, since his visits were more frequent and he acknowledged to my aunt Hervey a passion for me, accompanied with an awe that he had never known before; to which he attributed what he called his but *seeming* acquiescence with my papa's pleasure and the distance I kept him at. And yet, my dear, this may be his usual manner of behaviour to our sex; for had not my sister, at first, all his reverences?

Meantime, my father, expecting this importunity, kept in readiness the reports he had heard in his disfavour, to charge them upon him then, as so many objections to his address. And it was highly agreeable to me, that he did so: it would have been strange, if it were not, since the person who could reject Mr Wyerley's address for the sake of his *free opinions* must have been inexcusable had she not rejected another's for his *freer practices*.

But I should own that in the letters he sent me upon the general subject, he more than once enclosed a particular one declaring his passionate regards for me, and complaining with fervour enough of my reserves: but of these I took not the least notice; for as I had not written to him at all, but upon a subject so general, I thought it was but right to let what he wrote upon one so particular pass off as if I never had seen it; and the rather as I was not then at liberty, from the approbation his letters met with, to break off the correspondence without assigning the true reason for doing so. Besides, with all his respectful assiduities, it was easy to observe (if it had not been his general character) that his temper is naturally haughty and violent; and I had seen [too much] of that untractable spirit in my brother to like it in one who hoped to be still nearer related to me.

I had a little specimen of this temper of his upon the very occasion I have mentioned; for after he had sent me a third particular letter with the general one, he asked me the next time he came to Harlowe Place if I had not received such a one from him? I told him I should never answer one so sent, and that I had waited for such an occasion as he had now given me to tell him so. I desired him therefore not to write again on the subject, assuring him that if he did, I would return both, and never write another line to him.

You cannot imagine how saucily the man looked; as if, in short, he was disappointed that he had not made a more sensible impression upon me; and when he recollected himself (as he did immediately), what a visible struggle it cost him to change his haughty airs for more placid ones! But I took no notice of either, for I thought it best to convince him by the coolness and indifference with which I repulsed his forward hopes (at the same time intending to avoid the affection of pride or vanity) that he was not considerable enough in my eyes to make me take over-ready offence at what he said, or how he looked: in other words, that I had not value enough for him to treat him with peculiarity either by smiles or frowns. Indeed, he had cunning enough to give me, undesignedly, a piece of instruction which taught me this caution; for he had said in conversation once, 'That if a man could not make a lady in courtship own herself *pleased* with him, it was as *much* and oftentimes *more* to his purpose to make her *angry* with him.'

I must break off here. But will continue the subject the very first opportunity. Meantime, I am,

Your most affectionate friend and servant,
CL. HARLOWE

Letter 4: MISS CLARISSA HARLOWE TO MISS HOWE

Jan. 15

THIS, my dear, was the situation Mr Lovelace and I were in when my brother arrived from Scotland.

The moment Mr Lovelace's visits were mentioned to him, he, without either hesitation or apology, expressed his disapprobation of them. He found great flaws in his character, and took the liberty to say in so many words that he wondered how it came into the hearts of his uncles to encourage such a man for *either* of his sisters; at the same time returning his thanks to my father for declining his consent till *he* arrived, in such a manner, I thought, as a superior would do when he commended an inferior for having well performed his duty in his absence.

He justified his avowed inveteracy by common fame, and by what he had known of him at college; declaring that he had ever hated him; ever should hate him; and would never own him for a brother, or me for a sister, if I married him.

That college-begun antipathy I have heard accounted for in this manner:

Mr Lovelace was always noted for his vivacity and courage; and no less, it seems, for the swift and surprising progress he made in all parts of literature; for diligence in his studies, in the hours of study, he had hardly his equal. This, it seems, was his general character at the university, and it gained him many friends among the more learned youth; while those who did not love him feared him by reason of the offence his vivacity made him too ready to give, and of the courage he showed in supporting the offence when given, which procured him as many followers as he pleased among the mischievous sort. No very amiable character, you'll say, upon the whole.

But my brother's temper was not happier. His native haughtiness could not bear a superiority so visible; and whom we fear more than love, we are not far from hating: and having less command of his passions than the other, was evermore the subject of his, perhaps *indecent*, ridicule: so that they never met without quarrelling. And everybody, either from love or fear, siding with his antagonist, he had a most uneasy time of it, while both continued in the same college. It was the less wonder, therefore, that a young man who is not noted for the gentleness of his temper should resume an antipathy early begun, and so deeply-rooted.

He found my sister, who waited but for the occasion, ready to join him in his resentments against the man he hated. She utterly disclaimed all manner of regard for him: 'Never liked him at all—His estate was certainly much encumbered: it was impossible it should be otherwise, so entirely devoted as he was to his pleasures. He kept no house; had no equipage: nobody pretended that he wanted pride: the reason therefore was easy to be guessed at.' And then did she boast of, and my brother praise her for, refusing him; and both joined on all occasions to depreciate him, and not seldom *made* the occasions; their displeasure against him causing every subject to run into this, if it began not with it.

I was not solicitous to vindicate him when I was not joined in their reflections. I told them I did not value him enough to make a difference in the family on his account; and as he was supposed to have given too much cause for their ill opinion of him, I thought he ought to take the consequence of his own faults.

Now and then, indeed, when I observed that their vehemence carried them beyond all bounds of probability, I thought it but justice to put in a word for him. But this only subjected me to reproach, as having a prepossession in his favour that I would not own. So that when I could not change the subject, I used to retire either to my music or to my closet.

Their behaviour to him when they could not help seeing him was very cold and disobliging; but as yet not directly affrontive; for they were in hopes of prevailing upon my papa to forbid his visits. But as there was nothing in his behaviour that might warrant such a treatment of a man of his birth and fortune, they succeeded not; and then they were very earnest with *me* to forbid them. I asked what authority I had to take such a step in my father's house; and when my behaviour to him was so distant, that he seemed to be as much the guest of any other person of the family, themselves excepted, as mine? In revenge, they told me that it was cunning management between us; and that we both understood one another better than we pretended to do. And at last they gave such a loose to their passions all of a sudden,*ᵃ* as I may say, that instead of withdrawing as they used to do when he came, they threw themselves in his way purposely to affront him.

Mr Lovelace, you may believe, very ill brooked this; but nevertheless contented himself to complain of it to me, in high terms, however, telling me that but for my sake my brother's treatment of him was not to be borne.

I was sorry for the merit this gave him, in his own opinion, with me; and the more as some of the affronts he received were too flagrant to be excused. But I told him that I was determined not to fall out with my brother, if I could help it, whatever were his faults; and since they could not see one another with temper, should be glad that he would not throw himself in my brother's way, and I was sure my brother would not seek *him.*

He was very much nettled at this answer; but said he must bear his affronts if I would have it so. He had been accused himself of violence in his temper, but he hoped to show on this occasion that he had a command of his passions which few young men, so provoked, would be *able* to show; and doubted not but it would be attributed to a *proper motive* by a person of my generosity and penetration.

My brother had just before, with the approbation of my uncles, employed a person related to a discharged bailiff or steward of Lord M. who had had the management of some part of Mr Lovelace's affairs (from which he was also dismissed by him) to inquire into his debts, after his companions, into his amours, and the like.

My aunt Hervey, in confidence, gave me the following particulars of what the man said of him.

'That he was a generous landlord; that he spared nothing for solid and lasting improvements upon his estate; and that he looked into his own affairs and understood them; that he had, when abroad, been very expensive, and contracted a large debt (for he made no secret of his affairs); yet chose to limit himself to an annual sum and to decline equipage in order to avoid being obliged to his uncle and aunts, from whom he might have what money he pleased; but that he was very jealous of their control; had often quarrels with them and treated them so freely, that they were all afraid of him. However, that his estate was never mortgaged, as my brother had heard it was; his credit was always high; and, he believed, he was by this time near upon, if not quite, clear of the world.

He was a sad gentleman, he said, as to women. If his tenants had pretty daughters, they chose to keep them out of his sight. He believed he kept no particular mistress, for he had heard *newelty*, that was the man's word, was everything with him. But for his uncle's and aunt's teasings, fancied he would not think of marriage; was never known to be disguised with liquor; but was a great plotter and a great writer; that he lived a wild life in town, by what he had heard; had six or seven companions as bad as himself whom now and then he brought down with him; and the country was always glad when they went up again. He would have it that, although passionate, he was good humoured; loved as well to take a jest as to give one, and would rally himself, upon occasion, the freest of any man he ever knew.'

This was his character from an enemy; for, as my aunt observed, everything the man said commendably of him came grudgingly, with a *must needs say—to do him*

a The reason of this their more openly shown animosity is given in Letter 13.

justice, etc., while the contrary was delivered with a free good will. And this character, as a worse was expected, though this was bad enough, not answering the end of inquiring after it, my brother and sister were more apprehensive than before that his address would be encouraged, since the worst part of it was known, or supposed, when he was first introduced to my sister.

But with regard to myself, I must observe in his disfavour that, notwithstanding the merit he wanted to make with me for his patience upon my brother's ill-treatment of him, I owed him no compliments for trying to conciliate with *him*. Not that I believe it would have signified anything if he had made ever such court either to him or to my sister; yet one might have expected from a man of his politeness, and from his pretensions, you know, that he would have been willing to *try*. Instead of which, such a hearty contempt he showed of them both, of my brother especially, that I ever heard of it with aggravations. And for me to have hinted at an alteration in his behaviour to my brother was an advantage I knew he would have been proud of, and which therefore I had no mind to give him. But I doubted not that having so very little encouragement from *any*body, his pride would soon take fire and he would of himself discontinue his visits or go to town, where, till he came acquainted with our family, he used chiefly to reside; and in this latter case he had no reason to expect that I would *receive*, much less *answer*, his letters, the occasion which he led me to receive *any* of his being by this time over.

But my brother's antipathy would not permit him to *wait* for such an event; and after several excesses, which Mr Lovelace still returned with contempt and a haughtiness too much like that of the aggressor, my brother took upon himself to fill up the doorway once when he came, as if to oppose his entrance; and upon his asking for me, demanded what his business were with his sister?

The other, with a challenging air, as my brother says, told him he would answer a gentleman *any* question, but he wished that Mr James Harlowe, who had of late given himself high airs, would remember that he was not *now* at college.

Just then the good Dr Lewin, who frequently honours me with a *visit of conversation* as he is pleased to call it, and had parted with me in my own parlour, came to the door; and hearing the words, interposed, both having their hands upon their swords; and telling Mr Lovelace where I was, he burst by my brother, to come to me, leaving him chafing he said like a hunted boar at bay.

This alarmed us all. My father was pleased to hint to Mr Lovelace, and I by his command spoke a great deal plainer, that he wished he would discontinue his visits for the peace-sake of the family.

But Mr Lovelace is not a man to be easily brought to give up his purpose, in a point especially wherein he pretends his heart is so much engaged; and an absolute prohibition not having been given, things went on for a little while as before. For I saw plainly that to have denied myself to his visits (which, however, I declined receiving as often as I could) was to bring forward some desperate issue between the two, since the offence so readily given on one side was only brooked by the other out of consideration to me. And thus did my brother's rashness lay me under an obligation where I would least have owed it.

The intermediate proposals of Mr Symmes and Mr Mullins, both (in turn) encouraged by my brother, were inducements for him to be more patient for a while, he being in hopes, as nobody thought me over-forward in Mr Lovelace's favour, that he should engage my father and uncles to espouse the one or the other in opposition to *him*. But when he found that I had interest enough to disengage myself from their addresses, as I had (before he went to Scotland and before Mr Lovelace visited here) of Mr Wyerley's, he then kept no measures; and first set himself to upbraid me for a supposed prepossession, which he treated as if it were criminal; and then to insult Mr Lovelace in person. And it being at Mr Edward Symmes's, the brother of the other Symmes, two miles off, and no good Dr Lewin again to interpose, the unhappy rencounter followed. My brother was disarmed in it, as you have heard; and on being brought home, and giving us ground to suppose he was much worse hurt than he really was, and a fever ensuing, everyone flamed out; and all was laid at my door.

Mr Lovelace for three days together sent twice each day to inquire after my brother's health, and although he received rude and even shocking returns he thought fit, on the fourth day, to make in person the same inquiries, and received still greater incivilities from my two uncles who happened to be both there. My papa also was held by force from going to him with his sword in his hand, although he had the gout upon him.

I fainted away with terror, seeing everyone so violent; and hearing his voice swearing he would not depart without seeing me, or making my uncles ask his pardon for the indignities he had received at their hands; a door being also held fast locked between them; my mamma struggling with my papa; and my sister, after treating him with virulence, insulting me, as fast as I recovered. But when he was told how ill I was, he departed, vowing revenge.

He was ever a favourite with our domestics. His bounty to them, and having always something facetious to say to each, had made them all of his party; and on this occasion they privately blamed everybody else, and reported his patience and gentlemanly behaviour (till the provocations given him ran very high) in such favourable terms that those reports, and my apprehensions of the consequence of this treatment, induced me to *read a letter* he sent me that night; and, it being written in the most respectful terms, offering to submit the whole of my decision, and to govern himself entirely by my will, *to answer* it some days after.

To this unhappy necessity was owing our renewed correspondence, as I may call it; yet I did not write till I had informed myself from Mr Symmes's brother, that he was really insulted into the act of drawing his sword by my brother's repeatedly threatening, upon his excusing himself out of regard to me, to brand him if he did not; and, by all the inquiry I could make, that he was again the sufferer from my uncles in a more violent manner than I have related.

The same circumstances were related to my papa, and other friends, by Mr Symmes; but they had gone too far in making themselves parties to the quarrel either to retract or forgive; and I was forbid corresponding with him, or to be seen a moment in his company.

But one thing I can say, but that in confidence, because my mamma commanded me not to mention it: that, expressing her apprehension of the consequences of the indignities offered to Mr Lovelace, she told me she would leave it to my prudence to prevent, all I could, the impending mischief on *one* side.

I am obliged to break off. But I believe I have written enough to answer very fully all that you have commanded from me. It is not for a child to seek to clear her own character, or to justify her actions, at the expense of the most revered ones;

yet, as I know that the account of all those further proceedings by which I may be affected will be interesting to so dear a friend (who will communicate to others no more than what is fitting), I will continue to write as I have opportunity, as minutely as we are used to write to each other. Indeed I have no delight, as I have often told you, equal to that which I take in conversing with you—by *letter*, when I cannot in *person*.

Meantime, I can't help saying that I am exceedingly concerned to find, that I am become so much the public talk, as *you* tell me, and as *everybody* tells me, I am. Your kind, your *precautionary* regard for my fame, and the opportunity you have given me to tell my own story, previous to any new accident (which heaven avert!), is so like the warm friend I have ever found my dear Miss Howe, that with redoubled obligation you bind me to be

Your ever-grateful and affectionate
CLARISSA HARLOWE

Copy of the requested PREAMBLE *to the clauses in her grandfather's will, in her favour, enclosed in the preceding letter*

As the particular estate I have mentioned and described above is principally of my own raising; as my three sons have been uncommonly prosperous, and are very rich: the eldest by means of the unexpected benefits he reaps from his new-found mines; the second by what has as unexpectedly fallen in to him on the deaths of several relations of his present wife, the worthy daughter by both sides of very honourable families, over and above the very large portion which he received with her in marriage; my son Antony by his East India traffic and successful voyages: As furthermore my grandson James will be sufficiently provided for by his godmother Lovell's kindness to him, who having no near relations assures me that she has, as well by deed of gift as by will, left him both her Scottish and English estates: for never (blessed be God therefore!) was there a family more prosperous in all its branches: and as my second son James will very probably make it up to my grandson, and also to my grand-daughter Arabella; to whom I intend no disrespect, nor have reason, for she is a very hopeful and dutiful child: and as my sons John and Antony seem not inclined to a married life, so that my son James is the only one who has children, or is likely to have any: For all these reasons; and because my dearest and beloved grand-daughter Clarissa Harlowe has been from infancy a matchless young creature in her duty to me, and admired by all who knew her as a very extraordinary child; I must therefore take the pleasure of considering her as my own peculiar child; and this without intending offence, and I hope it will not be taken as any, since my son James can bestow his favours accordingly, and in greater proportion, upon Miss Arabella and Master James: These, I say, are the reasons which move me to dispose of the above-described estate in the precious child's favour, who is the delight of my old age; and I verily think has contributed, by her amiable duty, and kind and tender regards, to prolong my life.

Wherefore it is my express will and commandment, and I enjoin my three sons John, James and Antony, and my grandson James, and my grand-daughter Arabella, as they value my blessing, and my memory, and would wish with their own last wills and desires to be fulfilled by *their* survivors, that they will not impugn or contest the following bequests and dispositions in favour of my said grand-daughter Clarissa, although they should not be strictly conformable to law, or the forms thereof; nor suffer them to be controverted or disputed on any pretence whatsoever.

And in this confidence, etc.

Letter 5: MISS CLARISSA HARLOWE TO MISS HOWE

Jan. 20

I HAVE been hindered from prosecuting my intention. Neither nights nor mornings have been my own. My mamma has been very ill and would have no other nurse but me. I have not stirred from her bedside, for she kept her bed, and two nights I had the honour of sharing it with her.

Her disorder was a very violent colic. The contentions of these fierce, these masculine spirits, and the apprehension of mischiefs that may arise from the increasing animosity which all *here* have against Mr Lovelace, and his too-well-known resentful and intrepid character, she cannot bear. Then the foundations laid, as she dreads, for jealousy and heart-burnings in her own family, late so happy and so united, afflict exceedingly a gentle and sensible mind, which has from the beginning on all occasions sacrificed its own inward satisfaction to outward peace. My brother and sister, who used very often to jar, are now so much one and are so much together (*caballing* was the word that dropped from her, as if at unawares) that she is full of fears of consequences that may follow—to my prejudice, perhaps, is her kind concern, since she sees that they behave to me every hour with more and more shyness and reserve; yet would she but exert that authority which the superiority of her fine talents gives her, all these family-feuds might perhaps be crushed in their but yet beginnings; especially as she may be assured that all fitting concessions shall be made by me, not only as they are my elders, but for the sake of so excellent and so indulgent a mother.

For, if I may say to you my dear, what I would not to any other person living, it is my opinion that had she been of a temper that would have borne less, she would have had ten times less to bear than she has had. No commendation, you'll say, of the generosity of those spirits which can turn to its own disquiet so much condescending goodness.

Upon my word, I am sometimes tempted to think that we may make the world allow for and respect us as we please, if we can but be sturdy in our wills, and set out accordingly. It is but being the *less* beloved for it, that's all; and if we have power to oblige those we have to do with, it will not appear to *us* that we are. Our flatterers will tell us anything sooner than our faults.

Were there not truth in this observation, is it possible that my brother and sister could make their very failings, their vehemences, of such importance to all the family? 'How will my *son*, how will my *nephew*, take this or that measure? What will *he* say to it? Let us consult *him* about it,' are references always previous to every resolution taken by his superiors, whose will ought to be his. Well may he expect to be treated with this deference by every other person, when my papa himself, generally so absolute, constantly pays it to him, and the more since his godmother's bounty has given independence to a spirit that was before under too little restraint. But whither may these reflections lead me? I know you do not love any of us, but my mamma and me; and, being above all disguises, make me sensible that you do *not*, oftener than I wish you did. Ought I then to add force to your dislikes of those whom I wish you more to like?—my father, especially; for he, poor gentleman! has some excuse for his impatience of contradiction. He is not naturally an ill-tempered man; and in his person and air and in his conversation too, when not under the torture of a gouty paroxysm, everybody distinguishes the gentleman born and educated.

Our sex perhaps must expect to bear a little *uncourtliness* shall I call it?—from the *husband* whom, as the *lover*, they let know the preference their hearts gave him to all other men—Say what they will of generosity being a *manly* virtue; but, upon my word, my dear, I have ever yet observed that it is not to be met with in that sex one time in ten that it is to be found in ours. But my father was soured by the cruel distemper I have named, which seized him all at once in the very prime of life, in so violent a manner as to take from the most active of minds as *his* was all power of activity, and that, in all appearance, for life. It imprisoned, as I may say, his lively spirits in himself and turned the edge of them against his own peace, his extraordinary prosperity adding but to his impatiency; for those, I believe, who want the fewest earthly blessings most regret that they want any.

But my brother! what excuse can be made for his haughty and morose temper? He is really, my dear, I am sorry to have occasion to say it, an ill-tempered young man, and treats my mamma sometimes—indeed he is not dutiful. But possessing everything, he has the vice of age mingled with the ambition of youth, and enjoys nothing—but his own haughtiness and ill-temper, I was going to say. Yet again am I adding force to your dislikes of some of us. Once, my dear, it was perhaps in your power to have moulded him as you pleased—Could you have been my sister!— Then had I had a friend in a sister—But no wonder that he don't love you now; who could nip in the bud, and that with a disdain, let me say, too much of kin to his haughtiness, a passion that would not have wanted a fervour worthy of the object, and which possibly would have *made* him so—

But no more of this. I will prosecute my former intention in my next, which I will sit down to as soon as breakfast is over, dispatching this by the messenger whom you have so kindly sent to inquire after us, on my silence. Meantime, I am,

> Your most affectionate and obliged
> friend and servant,
> CL. HARLOWE

Letter 6: MISS CLARISSA HARLOWE TO MISS HOWE

Harlowe Place, Jan. 20

I WILL now resume my narrative of proceedings here. My brother being in a good way, although you may be sure that his resentments are rather heightened than abated by the galling disgrace he has received, my friends (my papa and uncles, however, if not my brother and sister) begin to think that I have been treated unkindly. My mamma has been so good as to tell me this since I sent away my last.

Nevertheless I believe they all think that I receive letters from Mr Lovelace. But Lord M. being inclined rather to support than to blame his nephew, they seem to be so much afraid of him that they do not put it to me whether I do or not, conniving on the contrary, as it should seem, at the only method left to allay the vehemence of a spirit which they have so much provoked, for he still insists upon satisfaction from my uncles, and this possibly (for he wants not art) as the best way to be introduced again with some advantage into our family. And indeed my aunt Hervey has put it to my mamma, whether it were not best to prevail upon my brother to take a turn to his Yorkshire estate, which he was intending to do before, and to tarry there till all is blown over.

But this is very far from being his intention, for he has already begun to hint again that he shall never be easy or satisfied till I am married, and finding neither Mr Symmes nor Mr Mullins will be accepted, has proposed Mr Wyerley once more on the score of his great passion for me. This I have again rejected, and but yesterday he mentioned one who has applied to him by letter, making high offers. This is Mr Solmes; *rich* Solmes, you know they call him. But this has not met with the attention of one single soul.

If none of his schemes of marrying me take effect, he has thoughts, I am told, of proposing to me to go to Scotland in order, as the compliment is, to put his house there in such order as our own is in. But this my mamma intends to oppose for her own sake; because, having relieved her, as she is pleased to say, of the household cares (for which my sister, you know, has no turn) they must again devolve upon her if I go. And if *she* did not oppose it, *I* should; for, believe me, I have no mind to be his housekeeper; and I am sure, were I to go with him, I should be treated rather as a servant than a sister—perhaps not the better because I *am* his sister. And if Mr Lovelace should follow me, things might be worse than they are now.

But I have besought my mamma, who is apprehensive of Mr Lovelace's visits, and for fear of whom my uncles never stir out without arms and armed servants (my brother also being near well enough to go abroad again) to procure me permission to be your guest for a fortnight, or so—Will your mamma, think you, my dear, give me leave?

I dare not ask to go to my dairy-house, as my good grandfather would call it; for I am now afraid of being thought to have a wish to enjoy that independence to which his will has entitled me: and as matters are situated, such a wish would be imputed to my favour to the man whom they have now so great an antipathy to. And, indeed, could I be as easy and happy here as I used to be, I would defy that man, and all his sex, and never repent that I have given the power of my fortune into my papa's hands.

Just now, my mamma has rejoiced me with the news that my requested permission is granted. Everyone thinks it best that I should go to you, except my brother. But he was told that he must not expect to rule in everything. I am to be sent for into the great parlour, where are my two uncles and my aunt Hervey, and to be acquainted with this concession in form.

You know, my dear, that there is a good deal of solemnity among us. But never was there a family more united in its different branches than ours. Our uncles consider us as their own children, and declare that it is for our sakes they live single. So that they are advised with upon every article relating to, or that may affect, us. It is therefore the less wonder, at a time when they understand that Mr Lovelace is determined to pay us an *amicable* visit as he calls it (but which I am sure cannot end so) that they should both be consulted upon the permission I had desired to attend you.

I will acquaint you with what passed at the general leave given me to be your guest. And yet I know that you will not love my brother the better for my communication. But I am angry with him myself, and cannot help it. And, besides, it is proper to let you know the terms I go upon, and their motives for permitting me to go.

Clary, said my mamma, as soon as I entered the great parlour, your request, to go to Miss Howe's for a few days has been taken into consideration and granted—

Much against my liking, I assure you, said my brother, rudely interrupting her.

Son James! said my father, and knit his brows.

He was not daunted. His arm is in a sling. He often has the mean art to look upon *that*, when anything is hinted that may be supposed to lead towards the least favour to, or reconciliation with, Mr Lovelace—Let the *girl* then (I am often *the girl* with him!) be prohibited seeing that vile libertine.

Nobody spoke.

Do you hear, sister Clary? taking their silence for approbation of what *he* had dictated; you are not to receive visits from Lord M.'s nephew.

Everyone still remained silent.

Do you so understand the licence you have, miss? interrogated he.

I would be glad, sir, said I, to understand that you are my *brother*—and that *you* would understand, that you are *only* my brother.

Oh the fond, fond heart! with a sneer of insult, lifting up his hands.

Sir, said I to my papa, to your justice I appeal. If I have deserved reflection, let me not be spared. But if I am to be answerable for the rashness—

No more!—No more, of either side, said my papa. You are not to receive the visits of that Lovelace, though—Nor are you, son James, to reflect upon your sister. She is a worthy child.

Sir, I have done, replied he—and yet I have *her* honour at heart, as much as the honour of the rest of the family.

And *hence*, sir, retorted I, your unbrotherly reflections upon me!

Well, but you observe, miss, said he, that it is not *I*, but your *papa*, that tells you that you are not to receive the visits of that Lovelace.

Cousin Harlowe, said my aunt Hervey, allow me to say that my cousin Clary's prudence may be confided in.

I am *convinced* it may, joined my mamma.

But aunt, but madam (put in my sister), there is no hurt, I presume, in letting my sister know the condition she goes to Miss Howe upon, since, if he gets a knack of visiting her there—

You may be sure, interrupted my uncle Harlowe, he will endeavour to see her there.

So would such an impudent man *here*, said my uncle Antony: and 'tis better *there* than *here*.

Better *nowhere*, said my papa—I command you, turning to me, on pain of my displeasure, that you see him not at all.

I will not, sir, in any way of encouragement, I do assure you; nor at all, if I can decently avoid it.

You know with what indifference, said my mamma, she has hitherto seen him—
Her prudence may be trusted to, as my sister Hervey says.

With what ap-*pa*-rent indifference, drolled my brother—

Son James! said my father, sternly—

I have done, sir, said he. But again, in a provoking manner, reminded me of the prohibition.

Thus ended this conference.

Will you engage, my dear, that the hated man shall not come near your house?—
but what an inconsistence is this, when they consent to my going, thinking his visits *here* no otherwise to be avoided! But if he does come I charge you never leave us alone together.

As I have no reason to doubt a welcome from your mamma, I will put everything in order here and be with you in two or three days.

Meantime, I am

Your most affectionate and obliged
CLARISSA HARLOWE

Letter 7: MISS CLARISSA HARLOWE TO MISS HOWE

(After her return from her)

Harlowe Place, Feb. 20

I BEG your excuse for not writing sooner. Alas, my dear, I have sad prospects before me! My brother and sister have succeeded in all their views. They have found out another lover for me; a hideous one!—yet he is encouraged by everybody. No wonder that I was ordered home so suddenly!—at an hour's warning!—No other notice, you know, than what was brought with the chariot that was to carry me back.—It was for fear, as I have been informed (an unworthy fear!), that I should have entered into any concert with Mr Lovelace had I known their motive for commanding me home; apprehending, 'tis evident, that I should dislike the man.

And well might they apprehend so—For who do you think he is?—No other than that *Solmes!*—Could you have believed it?—And they are all determined too; my mamma with the rest!—Dear, dear excellence! how could she be thus brought over!—when I am assured that, on his first being proposed, she was pleased to say that had Mr Solmes the *Indies* in possession, and would endow me with them, she should not think him deserving of her Clarissa Harlowe.

The reception I met with at my return, so different from what I used to meet with on every little absence (and now I had been from them three weeks), convinced me that I was to suffer for the happiness I had had in your company and conversation for that most agreeable period. I will give you an account of it.

My brother met me at the door, and gave me his hand when I stepped out of the chariot. He bowed very low. 'Pray, miss, favour me.'—I thought it in good humour, but found it afterwards mock-respect; and so he led me in great form, I prattling all the way, inquiring of everybody's health (although I was so soon to see them, and there was hardly time for answers), into the great parlour, where were my father, mother, my two uncles and my sister.

I was struck all of a heap as soon as I entered to see a solemnity which I had been so little used to on the like occasions in the countenance of every dear relation. They all kept their seats. I ran to my papa, and kneeled; then to my mamma; and met from both a cold salute; from my papa a blessing but half-pronounced; my mamma, indeed, called me, child, but embraced me not with her usual indulgent ardour.

After I had paid my duty to my uncles and my compliments to my sister, which she received with solemn and stiff form, I was bid to sit down. But my heart was full: and I said it became me to stand, if I *could* stand a reception so awful and unusual. I was forced to turn my face from them and pull out my handkerchief.

My unbrotherly accuser hereupon stood forth and charged me with having received no less than *five or six visits* at Miss Howe's from the man they had all so much reason to hate (that was the expression) notwithstanding the commands I had received to the contrary. And he bid me deny it if I could.

I had never been used, I said, to deny the truth; nor would I now. I owned I had, in the past three weeks, seen the person I presumed he meant *oftener* than five or six times. (Pray hear me out, brother, said I; for he was going to flame)—But he always came and asked for Mrs or Miss Howe.

I proceeded that I had reason to believe that both Mrs Howe and Miss, as matters stood, would much rather have excused his visits; but they had more than once apologized that, having not the same reason my papa had to forbid him their house, his rank and fortune entitled him to civility.

You see, my dear, I made not the pleas I might have made.

My brother seemed ready to give a loose to his passion; my papa put on the countenance which always portends a gathering storm; my uncles mutteringly whispered; and my sister aggravatingly held up her hands. While I begged to be heard out—and my mamma said, let the *child*, that was her kind word, be heard—

I hoped, I said, there was no harm done; that it became not me to prescribe to Mrs or Miss Howe who should be their visitors; that Mrs Howe was always diverted with the raillery that passed between Miss and him; that I had no reason to challenge *her* guest for *my* visitor, as I should seem to have done had I refused to go into their company when he was with them; that I had never seen him out of the presence of one or both of those ladies, and had signified to him once, on his urging for a few moments' private conversation with me, that unless a reconciliation were effected between my family and his he must not expect that I would countenance his visits, much less give him an opportunity of that sort.

I told them further that Miss Howe so well understood my mind that she never left me a moment while he was there; that when he came, if I was not below in the parlour, I would not suffer myself to be called to him; although I thought it would be an affectation which would give him advantage rather than the contrary if I had left company when he came in, or refused to enter into it when I found he would stay any time.

My brother heard me out with such a kind of impatience as showed he was resolved to be dissatisfied with me, say what I would. The rest, as the event has proved, behaved as if they *would* have been satisfied had they not further points to carry by intimidating me. All this made it evident, as I mentioned above, that they themselves expected not my voluntary compliance, and was a tacit confession of the disagreeableness of the person they had to propose.

I was no sooner silent than my *brother* swore, although in my papa's presence (swore, unchecked either by eye or countenance), that, for his part, he would *never* be reconciled to that libertine; and that he would renounce me for a sister if I encouraged the addresses of a man so obnoxious to them all.

A man who had like to have been my brother's murderer, my *sister* said, with a face even bursting with restraint of passion.

The poor Bella has, you know, a plump, high-fed face, if I may be allowed the expression—you, I know, will forgive me for this liberty of speech sooner than I can myself; yet how can one be such a reptile as not to turn when trampled upon!—

My *papa*, with vehemence both of action and voice (my father has, you know, a terrible voice, when he is angry!), told me that I had met with too much indulgence in being allowed to refuse *this* gentleman and the *other* gentleman, and it was now *his* turn to be obeyed.

Very true, my *mamma* said—and hoped his will would not now be disputed by a child so favoured.

To show they were all of a sentiment, my uncle *Harlowe* said he hoped his beloved niece only wanted to know her papa's will to obey it.

And my uncle *Antony*, in his rougher manner, that I would not give them reason to apprehend that I thought my grandfather's favour to me had made me independent of them all—If I did, he could tell me, the will *could* be set aside, and *should*.

I was astonished, you must needs think—Whose addresses now, thought I, is this treatment preparative to!—Mr Wyerley's again!—or whose?—And then, as high comparisons where *self* is concerned sooner than low come into young people's heads, be it for whom it will, this is wooing as the English did for the heiress of Scotland in the time of Edward the Sixth.[1] But that it could be for Solmes, how should it enter into my head?

I did not know, I said, that I had given occasion for this harshness; I hoped I should always have a just sense of their favour to me, superadded to the duty I owed as a daughter and a niece; but that I was so much surprised at a reception so unusual and unexpected that I hoped my papa and mamma would give me leave to retire in order to recollect myself.

No one gainsaying, I made my silent compliments and withdrew—leaving my brother and sister, as I thought, pleased, and as if they wanted to congratulate each other on having occasioned so severe a beginning to be made with me.

I went up to my chamber, and there with my faithful Hannah deplored the determined face which the new proposal it was plain they had to make me wore.

I had not recovered myself when I was sent for down to tea. I begged, by my maid, to be excused attending; but on the repeated command went down with as much cheerfulness as I could assume, and had a new fault to clear myself of; for my brother, so pregnant a thing is determined ill-will, by intimations equally rude and intelligible charged my desire of being excused coming down to sullens, because a certain person had been spoken against; upon whom as he supposed my fancy ran.

I could easily answer you, sir, said I, as such a reflection deserves, but I forbear. If I do not find a brother in *you*, you shall have a sister in *me*.

Pretty meekness! Bella whisperingly said, looking at my brother and lifting up her lip in contempt.

He, with an imperious air, bid me *deserve* his love, and I should be sure to *have* it.

As we sat, my mamma in her admirable manner expatiated upon brotherly and sisterly love, indulgently blamed my brother and sister upon having taken up displeasure too lightly against me, and politically, if I may so say, answered for my obedience to my papa's will—*Then it would be all well*, my papa was pleased to say. *Then they should dote on me*, was my brother's expression. *Love me as well as ever*, was my sister's. And my uncles', *That I should then be the pride of their hearts*—But, alas! what a forfeiture of all these must I make!

This was the reception I had on my return from you!

Mr Solmes came in before we had done tea. My uncle Antony presented him to me, as a gentleman he had a particular friendship for. My uncle Harlowe in terms equally favourable for him. My father said, Mr Solmes is my friend, Clarissa Harlowe. My mamma looked at him, and looked at me, now and then, as he sat near me, I thought with concern—I at *her*, with eyes appealing for pity—At *him*, when I could glance at him, with disgust, little short of affrightment. While my brother and sister Mr *Solmes*'d him, and *sir*'d him up with high favour. So caressed, in short, by all—yet such a wretch!—But I will at present only add my humble thanks and duty to your honoured mamma (to whom I will particularly write to express the grateful sense I have of her goodness to me) and that I am,

> Your ever obliged
> CL. HARLOWE

Letter 8: MISS CLARISSA HARLOWE TO MISS HOWE

Feb. 24

THEY drive on here at a furious rate. The man lives here, I think. He courts them and is more and more a favourite. Such terms, such settlements! That's the cry!

Oh, my dear, that I had not reason to deplore the family fault, immensely rich as they all are! But this I may the more unreservedly say to you, as we have often joined in the same concern; I for a father and uncles, you for a mother, in every other respect faultless.

Hitherto, I seem to be delivered over to my brother who pretends as great love to me as ever.

You may believe I have been very sincere with him, but he affects to rally me, and not to believe it possible that one so dutiful and so discreet as his sister Clary can resolve to disoblige all her friends.

Indeed, I tremble at the prospect before me, for it is evident that they are strangely determined.

My father and mother industriously avoid giving me opportunity of speaking to them alone. They ask not for my approbation, intending, as it should seem, to *suppose* me into their will. And with them I shall hope to prevail, or with nobody. They have not the *interest* in compelling me, as my brother and sister have. I say less therefore to them, reserving my whole force for an audience with my father, if he will permit me a patient ear. How difficult is it, my dear, to give a negative where both duty and inclination join to make one wish to oblige!—

I have already stood the shock of three of this man's particular visits, besides my share in his more general ones, and find it is impossible I should ever endure him. He has but a very ordinary share of understanding, is very illiterate, knows nothing but the value of estates and how to improve them, and what belongs to land-jobbing, and husbandry. Yet am I as one stupid, I think. They have begun so cruelly with me that I have not spirit enough to assert my own negative.

My good Mrs Norton they had endeavoured, it seems, to influence, before I came home, so intent are they to carry their point; and her opinion not being to their liking, she has been told that she would do well to decline visiting here for the present; yet she is the person of all the world, next to my mamma, the most likely to prevail upon me were the measures they are engaged in, reasonable measures, or such as she could think so.

My aunt likewise having said that she did not think her niece could ever be brought to like Mr Solmes has been obliged to learn another lesson.

I am to have a visit from her tomorrow. And since I have refused so much as to hear from my brother and sister what the noble settlements are to be, she is to acquaint me with the particulars, and to receive from me my determination; for my father, I am told, will not have patience but to *suppose* that I shall stand in opposition to his will.

Meantime it has been signified to me that it will be acceptable if I do not think of going to church next Sunday.

The same signification was made me for last Sunday, and I obeyed. They are apprehensive that Mr Lovelace will be there with design to come home with me.

Help me, dear Miss Howe, to a little of your charming spirit; I never more wanted it.

The man, you may suppose, has no reason to boast of his progress with me. He has not the sense to say anything to the purpose. His courtship, indeed, is to *them*; and my brother pretends to court me as his proxy, truly! I utterly to my brother refuse his application, but thinking a person so well received and recommended by all my family entitled to good manners, all I say against him is affectedly attributed to coyness; and he, not being sensible of his own imperfections, believes that my avoiding him when I can and the reserves I express are owing to nothing else—For, as I said, all his courtship is to *them*, and I have no opportunity of saying No, to one who asks me not the question. And so, with an air of *mannish* superiority, he seems rather to pity the bashful girl than apprehend that he shall not succeed.

February 25

I have had the expected conference with my aunt.

I have been obliged to hear the man's proposals from her, and all their motives for espousing him as they do. I am even loath to mention how equally unjust it is for him to make such offers, or for those I am bound to reverence to accept of them. I hate him more than before. One great estate is already obtained at the expense of the relations to it, though distant relations, my brother's, I mean, by his godmother; and this has given the hope, however chimerical that hope, of procuring others, and that my own at least may revert to the family. And yet, in my opinion, the world is but one great family; originally it was so; what then is this narrow selfishness that reigns in us, but relationship remembered against relationship forgot?

But here, upon my absolute refusal of him upon *any* terms, have I had a signification made me that wounds me to the heart. How can I tell it you? Yet I must. It is, my dear, that I must not for a month to come or till licence obtained correspond with *any*body out of the house.

My brother, upon my aunt's report (made, however, as I am informed, in the gentlest manner and even giving remote hopes which she had no commission from me to give), brought me in authoritative terms the prohibition.

Not to Miss Howe? said I.

No, not to Miss Howe, *madam*, tauntingly: for have you not acknowledged that Lovelace is a favourite there?

See, my dear Miss Howe!—

And do you think, brother, this is the way?—

Do *you* look to that—But your letters will be stopped, I can tell you—and away he flung.

My sister came to me soon after—Sister Clary, you are going on in a fine way, I understand. But, as there are people who are supposed to harden you against your duty, I am to tell you that it will be taken well if you avoid visits or visitings for a week or two, till further order.

Can this be from those who have authority—

Ask them, ask them, child, with a twirl of her finger—I have delivered my message. Your papa will be obeyed. He is willing to hope you to be all obedience, and would prevent all *incitements* to refractoriness.

I knew my duty, I said; and hoped I should not find impossible conditions annexed to it.

A pert young creature vain and conceited, she called me. I was the only judge, in my own wise opinion, of what was right and fit. She, for her part, had long seen through my specious ways; and now I should show everybody what I was at bottom.

Dear Bella, said I! hands and eyes lifted up—why all this?—Dear, dear Bella, why—

None of your dear, dear Bella's to me—I tell you I see through your *witchcrafts*— That was her strange word; and away she flung, adding as she went—And so will everybody else very quickly, I dare say.

Bless me, said I to myself, what a sister have I!—How have I deserved this? Then I again regretted my grandfather's too distinguishing goodness to me.

Feb. 25 in the evening

What my brother and sister have said against me I cannot tell—But I am in heavy disgrace with my papa.

I was sent for down to tea. I went with a very cheerful aspect, but had occasion soon to change it.

Such a solemnity in everybody's countenance!—My mamma's eyes were fixed upon the tea-cups; and when she looked up it was heavily, as if her eyelids had weights upon them, and then not to me. My papa sat half-aside in his elbow-chair, that his head might be turned from me; his hands folded, and waving, as it were, up and down; his fingers, poor dear gentleman! in motion, as if angry to the very ends of them. My sister sat swelling. My brother looked at me with scorn, having measured me, as I may say, with his eyes, as I entered, from head to foot. My aunt was there and looked upon me as if with kindness restrained, bending coldly to my compliment to her as she sat; and then cast an eye first on my brother, then on my sister, as if to give the reason (so I am willing to construe it) of her unusual stiffness—Bless me, my dear! that they should choose to intimidate rather than invite a mind till now not thought either unpersuadable or ungenerous!—

I took my seat. Shall I make tea; madam, to my mamma?—I always used, you know, my dear, to make tea.

No! a very short sentence in one very short word was the expressive answer; and she was pleased to take the canister in her own hand.

My sister's Betty attending, my brother bid her go—he would fill the water.

My heart was up at my mouth. I did not know what to do with myself. What is to follow? thought I.

Just after the second dish out stepped my mamma—A word with you, sister Hervey! taking her in her hand. Presently my sister dropped away. Then my brother. So I was left alone with my papa.

He looked so very sternly that my heart failed me, as twice or thrice I would have addressed myself to him; nothing but solemn silence on all hands having passed before.

At last, I asked, if it were his pleasure that I should pour him out another dish?

He answered me with the same angry monosyllable which I had received from my mamma before, and then arose and walked about the room. I arose too, with intent to throw myself at his feet, but was too much over-awed by his sternness even to make such an expression of my duty to him as my heart overflowed with.

At last, as he supported himself because of his gout on the back of a chair, I took a little more courage, and approaching him, besought him to acquaint me in what I had offended him?

He turned from me and, in a strong voice, Clarissa Harlowe, said he, know that I will be obeyed.

God forbid, sir, that you should not!—I have never yet opposed your will—

Nor I your whimsies, Clarissa Harlowe, interrupted he—Don't let me run the fate of all who show indulgence to your sex, to be the more contradicted for mine to you.

My papa, you know, my dear, has not (any more than my brother) a kind opinion of our sex, although there is not a more condescending wife in the world than my mamma.

I was going to make protestations of duty—No protestations, girl!—No words—I will not be prated to!—I will be obeyed!—I have no child—I will have no child, but an obedient one.

Sir, you never had reason, I hope—

Tell me not what I never *had*, but what I *have*, and what I *shall* have—

Good sir, be pleased to hear me—My brother and my sister, I fear—

Your brother and sister shall not be spoken against, girl!—They have a just concern for the honour of my family.

And I hope, sir,—

Hope nothing—Tell me not of *hopes*, but of *facts*. I ask nothing of you but what is in your power to comply with, and what it is your duty to comply with.

Then, sir, I will comply with it—But yet I hope from your goodness—

No expostulations!—No *but's*, girl!—No qualifyings!—I will be obeyed, I tell you!—and cheerfully too!—or you are no child of mine!—

I wept.

Let me beseech you, my dear and ever-honoured papa (and I dropped down on my knees), that I may have only your's and my mamma's will, and not my brother's, to obey—I was going on, but he was pleased to withdraw, leaving me on the floor, saying that he would not hear me thus by subtlety and cunning aiming to distinguish away my duty, repeating that he would be obeyed.

My heart is too full—so full that it may endanger my duty were I to unburden it to you on this occasion; so I will lay down my pen—But can—Yet, positively, I will lay down my pen!—

Letter 9: MISS CLARISSA HARLOWE TO MISS HOWE

Feb. 26, in the morning

MY aunt who stayed here last night made me a visit this morning as soon as it was light. She tells me that I was left alone with my papa yesterday on purpose that he might talk with me on my expected obedience, but that he owned he was put beside his purpose by reflecting on something my brother had told him in my disfavour, and by his impatience but to suppose that such a gentle spirit as mine had hitherto seemed to be should presume to dispute his will in a point where the advantage of the whole family was to be so greatly promoted by my compliance.

I find by a few words which dropped from her unawares, that they have all an absolute dependence upon what they suppose to be a meekness in my temper. But in this they may be mistaken, for I verily think upon a strict examination of myself that I have almost as much in me of my father's as of my mother's family.

My uncle Harlowe, it seems, is against driving me upon extremities; but his unbrotherly nephew has engaged that the regard I have for my reputation and my principles will bring me *round to my duty*, that's the expression. Perhaps I shall have reason to wish I had not known this.

My aunt advises me to submit for the present to the interdicts they have laid me under; and indeed to encourage Mr Solmes's address. I have absolutely refused the latter, let what will as I have told her be the consequence. The visiting prohibition I will conform to. But as to that of not corresponding with you, nothing but the menace that our letters shall be intercepted can engage my observation of it.

She believes that this order is from my father without consulting my mother upon it; and that purely, as she supposes, in consideration to me lest I should mortally offend him; and this from the incitements of *other* people (meaning you and Miss Lloyd, I make no doubt) rather than by my own will. For still, as she tells me, he speaks kind and praiseful things of me.

Here is clemency! Here is indulgence!—and so it is, to prevent a headstrong child, as a good prince would wish to do disaffected subjects, from running into rebellion and so forfeiting everything! But this is all my brother's young man's wisdom; a plotter without a head, and a brother without a heart!

How happy might I have been with any other brother in the world but Mr James

Harlowe; and with any other sister but *his* sister! Wonder not, my dear! that I, who used to chide you for these sort of liberties with my relations, now am more undutiful than you ever were unkind. I cannot bear the thought of being deprived of the principal pleasure of my life, for such is your conversation by person and by letter. And who besides can bear to be made the dupe of such low cunning, operating with such high and arrogant passions?

But can you, my dear Miss Howe, condescend to carry on a private correspondence with me? If you can, there is one way I have thought of by which it may be done.

You must remember the Green Lane, as we call it, that runs by the side of the wood-house and poultry-yard where I keep my bantams, pheasants and pea-hens, which generally engage my notice twice a day, the more my favourites because they were my grandfather's, and recommended to my care by him, and therefore brought hither from my dairy-house, since his death.

The lane is lower than the floor of the wood-house, and in the side of the wood-house the boards are rotted away down to the floor for half an ell together in several places. Hannah can step into the lane and make a mark with chalk where a letter or parcel may be pushed in under some sticks, which may be so managed as to be an unsuspected cover for the written deposits from either.

I HAVE been just now to look at the place and find it will answer. So your faithful Robert may, without coming near the house, and as only passing through the green lane which leads to two or three farmhouses (out of livery, if you please), very easily take from thence my letters and deposit yours.

This place is the more convenient because it is seldom resorted to but by myself or Hannah on the above-mentioned account, for it is the general store-house for firing, the wood for constant use being nearer the house.

One corner of this being separated off for the roosting-place of my little poultry, either she or I shall never want a pretence to go thither.

Try, my dear, the success of a letter this way, and give me your opinion and advice what to do in this disgraceful situation, as I cannot but call it, and what you think of my prospects, and what you would do in my case.

But beforehand I must tell you that your advice must not run in favour of this Solmes; and yet it is very likely they will endeavour to engage your mamma in order to induce you, who have such an influence over me, to favour him.

Yet, on second thoughts, if you incline to that side of the question I would have you write your whole mind. Determined as I think I am, and cannot help it, I would at least give a patient hearing to what may be said on the other side. For my regards are not so much engaged (upon my word they are not; I know not myself if they be) to another person, as some of my friends suppose; and as you, giving way to your lively vein, upon his last visits affected to suppose. What preferable favour I may have for him to any other person is owing more to the usage he has received, and for my sake borne, than to any personal consideration.

I write a few lines of grateful acknowledgement to your mamma for her favours to me in the late happy period. I fear I shall never know such another!—I hope she will forgive me that I did not write sooner.

The bearer if suspected and examined is to produce *that*, as the only one he carries. How do needless watchfulness and undue restraint produce artifice and contrivance! I should abhor these clandestine correspondencies, were they not forced upon me. They have so mean, so low an appearance to myself, that I think I ought not to expect that you should take part in them.

But why (as I have also expostulated with my aunt) must I be pushed into a state which, although I reverence, I have no wish to enter into?—Why should not my brother, so many years older and so earnest to see me engaged, be first engaged?—and if not so, why not my sister be first provided for?

But here I conclude these unavailing expostulations with the assurance that I am, and ever will be,

Your affectionate
CLARISSA HARLOWE

Letter 10: MISS HOWE TO MISS CLARISSA HARLOWE

Feb. 27

WHAT odd heads some people have!—Miss Clarissa Harlowe to be sacrificed in marriage to Mr Roger Solmes! Astonishing!

I must not, you say, *give my advice in favour of this man!*—You now half convince me, my dear, that you are allied to the family that could think of so preposterous a match, or you could never have had the least notion of my advising in his favour.

Ask me for his picture. You know I have a good hand at drawing an ugly likeness. But I'll see a little farther first; for who knows what may happen since matters are in such a train, and since you have not the *courage* to oppose so overwhelming a torrent?

You ask me to help you to a little of my spirit. Are you in earnest? But it will not now, I doubt, do you service—It will not sit naturally upon you. You are your mamma's girl, think what you will, and have violent spirits to contend with. Alas! my dear, you should have borrowed some of mine a little sooner—that is to say, before you had given the management of your estate into the hands of those who think they have a prior claim to it. What though a *father*'s?—Has not that father two elder children?—And do they not both bear his stamp and image more than you do?—Pray, my dear, call me not to account for this free question, lest your *application* of my meaning prove to be as severe as *that*.

Now I have launched out a little, indulge me one word more in the same strain; I will be decent, I promise you. I think you might have known, that AVARICE and ENVY are two passions that are not to be satisfied, the one by *giving*, the other by the envied person's continuing to *deserve* and *excel*—Fuel, fuel both, all the world over, to flames insatiate and devouring.

But since you ask for *my* opinion, you must tell me all you know or surmise of *their* inducements. And if you will not forbid me to make extracts from your letters for the entertainment of my cousin in the little island, who longs to hear more of your affairs, it will be very obliging.

But you are so tender of some people who have no tenderness for anybody but themselves, that I must conjure you to speak out. Remember that a friendship like ours admits of no reserves. You may trust my impartiality. It would be an affront to your own judgement if you did not; for do you not *ask* my advice? And have you not taught me that friendship should never give a bias against justice?—Justify them therefore, if you can. Let us see if there be any *sense*, whether sufficient *reason* or not, in their choice. At present I cannot (and yet I know a good deal of your family) have any conception how *all* of them, your mamma in particular and your aunt Hervey, can join with the rest against judgements given. As to some of the others, I cannot wonder at anything they do, or attempt to do, where self is concerned.

You ask why may not your brother be first engaged in wedlock?—I'll tell you why. His temper and his arrogance are too well known to induce women he would aspire to, to receive his addresses, notwithstanding his great independent acquisitions and still greater prospects. Let me tell you, my dear, those acquisitions have given him more pride than reputation. To me he is the most intolerable creature that I ever saw. The treatment you blame, he merited from one whom he would have addressed with the air of a person intending to confer, rather than hoping to receive a favour. I ever loved to mortify proud and insolent spirits. What, think you, makes me bear Hickman near me, but that the man is humble and knows his distance?

As to your question, why your elder sister may not be first provided for? I answer, because she must have no man but who has a great and clear estate, that's one thing. Another is because she has a younger sister—Pray, my dear, be so good as to tell me what man of a great and clear estate would think of that elder sister while the younger were single?

You are all too rich to be happy, child. For must not each of you by the constitutions of your family marry to be *still* richer? People who know in what their *main* excellence consists are not to be blamed (are they?) for cultivating and improving what they think most valuable? Is true happiness any part of your family-view?—So far from it, that none of your family but yourself could be happy were they not rich. So let them fret on, grumble and grudge, and accumulate; and wondering what ails them that they have not happiness when they have riches, think the cause is want of more; and so go on heaping up till Death, as greedy an accumulator as themselves, gathers them into his garner!

Well then, once more I say, do you, my dear, tell *me* what you know of their avowed and general motives, and I will tell *you* more than you will tell *me* of their failings! Your aunt Hervey, you say,[a] has told *you*—Why, as I hinted above, must I ask you to let me know them, when you condescend to ask my advice on the occasion?

That they prohibit your corresponding with *me* is a wisdom I neither wonder at, nor blame them for, since it is an evidence to me that they know their own folly; and if they do, is it strange that they should be afraid to trust another's judgement upon it?

I am glad you have found out a way to correspond with me. I approve it much. I shall *more* if this first trial of it proves successful. But should it not, and should it fall into their hands, it would not concern me but for your sake.

We had heard before you wrote that all was not right between your relations and you at your coming home; that Mr Solmes visited you and that with a prospect

a   See p. 62.

of success. But I concluded the mistake lay in the person, and that his address was to Miss Arabella; and indeed had she been as good-natured as your plump ones generally are, I should have thought her too good for him by half—Thought I, this *must* be the thing, and my beloved friend is sent for to advise and assist in her nuptial preparations. Who knows, said I to my mamma, but that when the man has thrown aside his yellow, full-buckled peruke and his broad-brimmed beaver, both of which I suppose were Sir Oliver's best of long standing, he may cut a tolerable figure dangling to church with Miss Bell!—The woman, as she observes, *should* excel the man in features; and where can she match so well for a foil?

I indulged this surmise against rumour, because I could not believe that the absurdest people in England could be so *very* absurd as to think of this man for you.

We heard moreover that you received no visitors. I could assign no reason for this, except that the preparations for your sister were to be private, and the ceremony sudden. Miss Lloyd and Miss Biddulph were with me to inquire what I knew of this, and of your not being at church either morning or afternoon, the Sunday after your return from us, to the disappointment of a little hundred of your admirers, to use their words. It was easy for me to guess the reason to be what you confirm—their apprehensions that Lovelace would be there and attempt to wait on you home.

My mamma takes very kindly your compliments in your letter to her. Her words upon reading it were: 'Miss Clarissa Harlowe is an admirable young lady. Wherever she goes, she confers a favour; whomever she leaves, she fills with regret.' And then a little comparative reflection: 'Oh my Nancy, that you had a little of her sweet obligingness!'

No matter. The praise was yours. You are me, and I enjoyed it. The more enjoyed it because—shall I tell you the truth?—because I think myself as well as I am—were it but for this reason, that had I twenty brother James's and twenty sister Bell's, not one of them, nor all of them joined together, would dare to treat me as yours presume to treat you. The person who will bear much shall have much to bear all the world through: 'tis your own sentiment, grounded upon the strongest instance that can be given in your own family, though you have so little improved by it.

The result is this: that I am fitter for *this* world than you, you for the *next* than me—that's the difference. But long, long, for my sake, and for hundreds of sakes, may it be before you quit us for company more congenial and more worthy of you!

I communicated to my mamma the account you give of your strange reception; also what a horrid wretch they have found out for you, and the compulsory treatment they give you. It only set her on magnifying her lenity to me on my *tyrannical* behaviour, as she *will* call it (mothers must have their way, you know), to the man she so warmly recommends, against whom, it seems, there can be no just exception; and expatiating upon the complaisance I owe her for her indulgence. So I believe I must communicate to her nothing farther—especially as I know she would condemn the correspondence between us, and that between you and Lovelace, as a clandestine and undutiful thing; for *duty implicit* is her cry. And moreover she lends a pretty open ear to the preachments of that starch old bachelor your uncle Antony, and for an example to *her* daughter would be more careful how she takes your part be the cause ever so just. Yet is not this right policy neither. For people who will allow nothing will be granted nothing; in other words, those who aim at carrying too many points will not be able to carry any.

But can you divine, my dear, what that old preachment-making plump-hearted soul, your uncle Antony, means by his frequent amblings hither?—There is such smirking and smiling between my mamma and him! Such mutual praises of economy, and '*That* is my way!'—and '*This* I do!'—and 'I am glad it has *your* approbation, sir!'—and '*You* look into everything, madam!'—'Nothing would be done, if I *did not!*'—Such exclamations against servants; such exaltings of self!— And *dear-heart* and *good-lack!*—and *'las-a-day!*—And now and then their conversation sinking into a whispering accent if *I* come cross them!—I'll tell you, my dear, I don't above half like it.

Only that these old bachelors usually take as many years to resolve upon matrimony as they can reasonably expect to live, or I should be ready to fire upon his visits, and recommend Mr Hickman as a much properer man to my mamma's acceptance; for what he wants in years, he makes up in gravity; and if you will not chide me, I will say, that there is a primness in *both*, especially when the man has presumed too much with me upon my mamma's favour for him and is under discipline on that account, as makes them seem near of kin; and then in contemplation of my sauciness, and what they both bear from it, they sigh away!— and seem so mightily to compassionate each other that if pity be but one remove from love, I am in no danger, while they both are in a great deal and don't know it.

Now, my dear, I know you will be upon me with your grave airs; *so in for the lamb*, as the saying is, *in for the sheep* ; and do you yourself look about you; for I'll have a pull with you by way of being aforehand. Hannibal, we read, always advised to attack the Romans upon their own territories.[1]

You are pleased to say, and *upon your word too!*—that your *regards* (a mighty quaint word for *affections) are not so much engaged, as some of your friends suppose, to another person*. What need you give one to imagine, my dear, that the last month or two has been a period extremely favourable to that *other* person!— whom it has made an obliger of the niece for his patience with the uncles.

But, to pass that by—*So much* engaged!—*How much*, my dear? Shall I infer? *Some of your friends* suppose *a great deal*—You seem to own *a little*.

Don't be angry. It is all fair, because you have not acknowledged to me that *little*. People, I have heard you say, who affect secrets always excite curiosity.

But you proceed with a kind of drawback upon your averment, as if recollection had given you a doubt—*You know not yourself, if they be* (so much engaged). Was it necessary to say this to me?—and to say it *upon your word* too?—But you know best—Yet you don't neither, I believe. For a beginning love is acted by a subtle spirit; and oftentimes discovers itself to a bystander when the person possessed (why should I not call it *possessed*?) knows not it has such a demon.

But further you say, what PREFERABLE *favour you may have for him to any other person is owing more to the usage he has received, and for your sake borne, than to any personal consideration*.

This is generously said. It is in character. But, oh my friend, depend upon it you are in danger. Depend upon it, whether you know it or not, you are a little in for't. Your native generosity and greatness of mind endanger you; all your friends by fighting *against* him with impolitic violence fight *for him*. And Lovelace, my life for yours, notwithstanding all his veneration and assiduities has seen further than that veneration and those assiduities (so well calculated to your meridian) will let him own he has seen—has seen, in short, that his work is doing for him more effectually than he could do it for himself. And have you not before now said that nothing is so penetrating as the vanity of a lover, since it makes the person who has it frequently see in his own favour what is *not*, and hardly ever fail of observing what *is*. And who says Lovelace wants vanity?

In short, my dear, it is my opinion, and that from the easiness of his heart and behaviour that he has seen more than *I* have seen; more than you think *could* be seen—more than I believe you *yourself* know, or else you would have let *me* know it.

Already, in order to restrain him from resenting the indignities he has received and which are daily offered him, he has prevailed upon you to correspond with him privately. I know he has nothing to boast of from *what* you have written. But is not his inducing you to receive his letters, and to answer them, a great point gained?— By your insisting that he should keep this correspondence private, it appears that there is *one secret* that you do not wish the world should know; and *he* is master of that secret. He is indeed *himself*, as I may say, that secret!—What an intimacy does this beget for the lover!—How is it distancing the parent!

Yet who, as things are situated, can blame you?—Your condescension has no doubt hitherto prevented great mischiefs. It must be continued for the same reasons while the cause remains. You are drawn in by a perverse fate against inclination; but custom, with such laudable purposes, will reconcile the inconveniency and *make* an inclination—And I would advise you (as you would wish to manage on an occasion so critical with that prudence which governs all your actions) not to be afraid of entering upon a close examination into the true springs and grounds of this your *generosity* to that happy man.

It is my humble opinion, I tell you frankly, that on inquiry it will come out to be LOVE—Don't start, my dear!—Has not your man himself had natural philosophy enough to observe already to your aunt Hervey that Love takes the deepest root in the steadiest minds? The deuce take his sly penetration, I was going to say; for this was six or seven weeks ago.

I have been tinctured, you know. Nor, on the coolest reflection, could I account how and when the jaundice began; but had been over head and ears, as the saying is, but for some of that advice from you which I now return you. Yet *my* man was not half so—so *what*, my dear?—To be sure Lovelace is a charming fellow—And were he only—But I will not make you *glow* as you read!—Upon *my word*, I won't—Yet, my dear, don't you find at your heart somewhat unusual make it go throb, throb, throb, as you read just here?—If you do, don't be ashamed to own it—It is your *generosity*, my love! that's all—But, as the Roman augur said, Caesar, beware of the ides of March!

Adieu, my dearest friend, and forgive; and very speedily by the new-found expedient tell me that you forgive

Your ever-affectionate
ANNA HOWE

Letter II: MISS CLARISSA HARLOWE TO MISS HOWE

Wednesday, March 1

You both nettled and alarmed me, my dearest Miss Howe, by the concluding part of your last. At first reading it I did not think it necessary, said I to myself, to guard against a critic when I was writing to so dear a friend. But then recollecting myself, is there not more in it, said I, than the result of a vein so naturally lively? Surely I must have been guilty of an inadvertence—Let me enter into the close examination of myself which my beloved friend advises.

I did so, and cannot own any of the *glow*, any of the *throbs* you mention—*Upon my word*, I will repeat, I cannot. And yet the passages in my letter upon which you are so humorously severe lay me fairly open to your agreeable raillery. I own they do. And I cannot tell what turn my mind had taken to dictate so oddly to my pen.

But pray now, is it saying so much, when one who has no very particular regard to *any* man says, there are *some* who are preferable to *others*? And is it blameable to say, *those* are the preferable who are not well used by one's relations, yet dispense with that usage out of regard to one's self, which they would otherwise resent? Mr Lovelace, for instance, I may be allowed to say, is a man to be preferred to Mr Solmes; and that I *do* prefer him to that man. But surely this may be said, without its being a necessary consequence that one must be in love with him.

Indeed I would not be *in love* with him, as it is called, for the world: first, because I have no opinion of his morals, and think it a fault in which our whole family, my brother excepted, has had a share, that he was permitted to visit us with a hope, which however being distant did not, as I have observed heretofore, entitle any of us to call him to account for such of his immoralities as came to our ears. Next, because I think him to be a vain man, capable of triumphing, secretly at least, over a person whose heart he thinks he has engaged. And, thirdly, because the assiduities and veneration which you impute to him seem to carry a haughtiness in them, as if his address had a merit in it that would be an equivalent for a lady's favour. In short, he seems to me so to behave when most unguarded as if he thought himself above the very politeness which his birth and education (perhaps therefore more than his choice) oblige him to show. In other words, his very politeness appears to me to be constrained; and, with the most remarkably easy and genteel *person*, something seems to be behind in his *manner* that is too studiously kept in. Then, good-humoured as he is thought to be in the main to *other people's* servants, and this even to familiarity (although, as you have observed, a familiarity that has dignity in it not unbecoming a man of quality), he is apt sometimes to break out into passion with *his own*; an oath or a curse follows, and such looks from those servants as plainly show terror, and that they should have fared worse, had they not been in my hearing; with a confirmation in the master's looks of a surmise too well justified.

Indeed, my dear, THIS man is not THE man. I have great objections to him. My heart *throbs* not after him; I *glow* not, but with indignation against myself for having given room for such an imputation—But you must not, my dearest friend, construe common gratitude into love. I cannot bear that you should. But if ever I should have the misfortune to think it love, I promise you, *upon my word*, which is the same as *upon my honour*, that I will acquaint you with it.

You bid me to tell you very speedily and by the new-found expedient that I am not displeased with you for your agreeable raillery. I dispatch this therefore immediately, postponing to my next the account of the inducements which my friends have to promote with so much earnestness the address of Mr Solmes.

Be satisfied, my dear, meantime, that I am *not* displeased with you; indeed I am not. On the contrary, I give you my hearty thanks for your friendly premonitions. And I charge you, as I have often done, that if you observe anything in me so very faulty, as would require from you to others in my behalf the palliation of friendly and partial love, you acquaint me with it; for, methinks, I would so conduct myself as not to give reason even for an *adversary* to censure me; and how shall so weak and so young a creature avoid the censure of such, if my *friend* will not hold a looking-glass before me to let me see my imperfections?

Judge me then, my dear, as any indifferent person (knowing what *you* know of me) would do—I may at first be a little pained; may *glow* a little, perhaps, to be found less worthy of your friendship than I wish to be; but assure yourself that your kind correction will give me reflection that shall *amend* me. If it do not, you will have a fault to accuse me of that will be utterly *in*-excusable; a fault, let me add, that should you *not* accuse me of it, if in your opinion I am guilty, you will not be so much, so *warmly* my friend, as I am yours, who have never spared you, you know, my dear, on the like occasions.

Here I break off to begin another letter to you, with the assurance, meantime, that I am, and ever will be,

Your equally affectionate
and grateful
CL. HARLOWE

Letter 12: MISS HOWE TO MISS CLARISSA HARLOWE

Thursday morn. March 2

INDEED you would not be in love with him for the world!—Your servant, my dear. Nor would I have you; for I think, with all the advantages of person, fortune and family, he is not by any means worthy of you. And this opinion I give as well from the reasons you mention, which I cannot but confirm, as from what I have heard of him but a few hours ago from Mrs Fortescue, a favourite of Lady Betty Lawrance, who knows him well—But let me congratulate you, however, on your being the first of our sex that ever I heard of who has been able to turn that lion, Love, at her own pleasure, into a lap-dog.

Well but, if you have not the throbs and the glows, you have not; and are not in love; good reason why—because you would not be in love, and there's no more to be said—Only, my dear, I shall keep a good look out upon you; and so I hope you will upon yourself, for it is no manner of argument that because you would not be in love, you are not—But before I part entirely with this subject, a word in your ear, my charming friend—'Tis only by way of caution, and in pursuance of the general observation that a stander-by is often a better judge of the game than those that play—May it not be, that you have had, and have, such cross creatures and such odd heads to deal with as have not allowed you to attend to the throbs?—Or, if you had them a little now and then, whether, having had two accounts to place them to, you have not by mistake put them to the wrong one?

But whether you have a value for this Lovelace or not, I know you'll be impatient to hear what Mrs Fortescue has said of him. Nor will I keep you longer in suspense.

A hundred wild stories she tells of him from childhood to manhood; for, as she observes, having never been subject to contradiction, he was always as mischievous as a monkey. But I shall pass over these whole hundred of his puerile rogueries, although *indicative* ones, as I may say, to take notice as well of some things you are not quite ignorant of, as of others you know not, and to make a few observations upon him and his ways.

Mrs Fortescue owns, what everybody knows, that he is notoriously, nay, avowedly, a man of pleasure; yet says that in anything he sets his heart upon, or undertakes, he is the most industrious and persevering mortal under the sun. He rests, it seems, not above six hours in the twenty-four, any more than you. He delights in writing. Whether at his uncle's, or at Lady Betty's, or Lady Sarah's, he has always, when he retires, a pen in his fingers. One of his companions, confirming his love of writing, has told her that his thoughts flow rapidly to his pen; and you and I, my dear, have observed, on more occasions than one, that though he writes even a fine hand, he is one of the readiest and quickest of writers. He must indeed have had early a very docile genius, since a person of his pleasurable turn and active spirit could never have submitted to take long or great pains in attaining the qualifications he is master of; qualifications so seldom attainable by youth of quality and fortune; by such especially of those of either, who like him have never known what it was to be controlled.

He had once the vanity upon being complimented on these talents (and on his surprising diligence for a man of pleasure) to compare himself to Julius Caesar, who performed great actions by day and wrote them down at night; and valued himself that he only wanted Caesar's out-setting, to make a figure among his cotemporaries.

He spoke this, indeed, she says, with an air of pleasantry; for she observed, and so have we, that he has the art of acknowledging his vanity with so much humour that it sets him above the contempt which is due to vanity and self-opinion, and at the same time half-persuades those who hear him that he really deserves the exaltation he gives himself.

But supposing it to be true, that all his vacant nightly hours are employed in writing, what can be his subjects? If, like Caesar, his own actions, he must undoubtedly be a very enterprising and very wicked man, since nobody suspects him to have a serious turn; and, decent as he is in his conversation with us, his writings are not probably such as will redound either to his own honour or to the benefit of others, were they to be read. He must be conscious of this, since Mrs Fortescue says that, in the great correspondence by letters which he holds, he is as secret and careful as if it were of a treasonable nature—yet troubles not his head with politics, though nobody knows the interests of princes and courts better than he.

That you and I, my dear, should love to write is no wonder. We have always from the time each could hold a pen delighted in epistolary correspondencies. Our employments are domestic and sedentary, and we can scribble upon twenty innocent subjects and take delight in them because they *are* innocent; though were they to be seen, they might not much profit or please others. But that such a gay, lively young fellow as this, who rides, hunts, travels, frequents the public entertainments, and has *means* to pursue his pleasures, should be able to set himself down to write for hours together, as you and I have heard him say he frequently does, that is the strange thing.

Mrs Fortescue says that he is a complete master of shorthand writing. By the way, what inducements could such a swift writer as he have to learn shorthand?

She says (and we know it as well as she) that he has a surprising memory, and a very lively imagination.

Whatever his other vices are, all the world as well as Mrs Fortescue say[s], he is a sober man. And among all his bad qualities, *gaming*, that great waster of time as well as fortune, is not his vice. So that he must have his head as cool, and his reason as clear, as the prime of youth and his natural gaiety will permit; and, by his early morning hours, a great portion of time upon his hands to employ in writing, or worse.

Mrs Fortescue says he has one gentleman who is more his intimate and correspondent than any of the rest. You remember what his dismissed bailiff said of him, and of his associates. I don't find but that man's character of him was in general pretty just. Mrs Fortescue confirms this part of it, that all his relations are afraid of him; and that his pride sets him above owing obligations to them. She believes he is clear of the world, and that he will continue so; no doubt from the same motive that makes him avoid being obliged to his relations.

A person willing to think favourably of him would hope that a *brave*, a *learned* and a *diligent* man cannot be *naturally* a *bad* man—But if he be better than his enemies say he is (and if worse, he is bad indeed), he is guilty of an inexcusable fault in being so careless as he is of his reputation. I think a man can be so but from one of these two reasons: either that he is conscious he deserves the evil spoken of him; or, that he takes a pride in being thought worse than he is—Both very bad and threatening indications; since the first must show him to be utterly abandoned; and it is but natural to conclude from the other, that what a man is not ashamed to have imputed to him he will not scruple to be guilty of whenever he has opportunity.

Upon the whole, and upon all that I could gather from Mrs Fortescue, Mr Lovelace is a very faulty man. You and I have thought him too gay, too inconsiderate, too rash, too little a hypocrite to be *deep*. You see he never would disguise his natural temper (haughty as it certainly is) with respect to your brother's behaviour to him. Where he thinks a contempt due, he pays it to the uttermost. Nor has he complaisance enough to spare your uncles.

But were he deep, and ever so deep, you would soon penetrate him, if they would leave you to yourself. His vanity would be your clue. Never man had more. Yet, as Mrs Fortescue observed, never did man carry it off so happily. There is a strange mixture in it of humorous vivacity—For but one half of what he says of himself, when he is in the vein, any other man would be insufferable.

TALK *of the devil* is an old saying—The lively wretch has made me a visit, and is but just gone away. He is all impatience and resentment at the treatment you meet with, and full of apprehensions too, that they will carry their point with you.

I told him my opinion, that you will never be brought to think of such a man as Solmes, but that it will probably end in a composition never to have either.

No man, he said, whose fortunes and alliances are so considerable ever had so little favour from a lady, for whose sake he had borne so much.

I told him my mind, as freely as I used to do. But who ever was in fault, self being judge? He complained of spies set upon his conduct, and to pry into his life and morals; and this by your brother and uncles.

I told him that this was very hard upon him, and the more so as neither the one nor the other, perhaps, would stand a fair inquiry.

He smiled, and called himself *my servant*—The occasion was too fair, he said, for Miss Howe, who never spared him, to let it pass—But, Lord help their shallow souls, would I believe it? they were for turning plotters upon *him*. They had best take care he did not pay them in their own coin. Their *hearts* were better turned for such works than their *heads*.

I asked him if he valued himself upon having a head better turned than theirs for *such works*, as he called them?

He drew off; and then ran into the highest professions of reverence and affection for you. The object so meritorious, who can doubt the reality of his professions?

Adieu, my dearest, my noble friend!—I love and admire you for the generous conclusion of your last more than I can express. Though I began this letter with impertinent raillery, knowing that you always loved to indulge my mad vein, yet never was there a heart that more glowed with friendly love than that of

Your own
ANNA HOWE

Letter 13: MISS CLARISSA HARLOWE TO MISS HOWE

Wed. March 1

I NOW take up my pen, to lay before you the inducements and motives which my friends have to espouse so earnestly the address of this Mr Solmes.

In order to set this matter in a clear light, it is necessary to go a little backward and even perhaps to mention some things which you already know; and so you may look upon what I am going to relate as a kind of supplement to my letters of the 15th and 20th of January last.

In those letters, of which I have kept memorandums, I gave you an account of my brother's and sister's implacableness to Mr Lovelace, and the methods they took (so far as they had then come to my knowledge) to ruin him in the opinion of my other friends; and I told you that after a very cold, yet not a directly affrontive[a] behaviour to him, they all of a *sudden*[a] became more violent and proceeded to personal insults; which brought on at last the unhappy rencounter between my brother and him.

Now you must know that from the last conversation which passed between my aunt and me, it comes out that this *sudden* vehemence on my brother's and sister's

―――――――――

a See Letter 4, p. 50.

parts was owing to stronger reasons than to the college-begun antipathy on his
side, or to slighted love on hers; to wit, to an apprehension that my uncles intended
to follow my grandfather's example in my favour; at least in a higher degree than
they wish they should; an apprehension founded, it seems, on a conversation
between my two uncles and my brother and sister, which my aunt communicated
to me in confidence as an argument to prevail upon me to accept of Mr Solmes's
noble settlements; urging that such a seasonable compliance would frustrate my
brother's and sister's views and establish me for ever in the opinion and love of my
father and uncles.

I will give you the substance of this communicated conversation after I have
made a brief introductory observation or two, which, however, I hardly need to
make to you who are so well acquainted with us all, did not the series or thread of
the story require it.

I have more than once mentioned to you the darling view some of us have long
had of *raising a family*, as it is called; a reflection as I have often thought upon our
own, which is no inconsiderable or upstart one, on either side; of my mamma's,
especially—A view too frequently, it seems, entertained by families which having
great substance, cannot be satisfied without rank and title.

My uncles had once extended this view to each of us three children, urging that
as they themselves intended not to marry, we each of us might be so portioned, and
so advantageously matched, as that our posterity if not ourselves might make a
first figure in our country—While my brother, as the only son, thought the two
girls might be very well provided for by ten or fifteen thousand pounds apiece; and
that all the real estates in the family, to wit, my grandfather's, father's, and two
uncles', and the remainder of their respective personal estates, together with what
he had an expectancy of from his godmother, would make such a noble fortune
and give him such an interest as might entitle him to hope for a peerage. Nothing
less would satisfy his ambition.

With this view, he gave himself airs very early: 'That his grandfather and uncles
were his stewards; that no man ever had better; that daughters were but
encumbrances and drawbacks upon a family.' And *this* low and familiar expression
was often in his mouth and uttered always with the self-complaisance which an
imagined happy thought can be supposed to give the speaker: to wit, 'That a man
who has sons brings up chickens for his own table' (though once I made his
comparison stagger with him by asking him, if the sons to make it hold were to
have their necks wrung off?) 'whereas daughters are chickens brought up for the
tables of other men.' This, accompanied with the equally polite reflection, 'that, to
induce people to take them off their hands, the family-stock must be impaired into
the bargain,' used to put my sister out of all patience; and although she now seems
to think a *younger* sister only can be an encumbrance, she was then often proposing
to me to make a party in our own favour against my brother's *rapacious views*, as
she used to call them; while I was for considering the liberties he took of this sort
as the effect of a temporary pleasantry, which in a young man not naturally good-
humoured, I was glad to see; or as a foible, that deserved raillery, but no other
notice.

But when my grandfather's will (of the purport of which in my particular favour,
until it was opened, I was as ignorant as they) had lopped off one branch of my
brother's expectation, he was extremely dissatisfied with me. Nobody indeed was

pleased: for although everyone loved me, yet being the youngest child, father, uncles, brother, sister, all thought themselves postponed as to matter of right and power (who loves not power?); and my father himself could not bear that I should be made sole, as I may call it, and independent, for such the will as to that estate and the powers it gave (unaccountably, as they all said), made me.

To obviate therefore everyone's jealousy, I gave up to my father's management, as you know, not only the estate, but the money bequeathed me (which was a moiety of what my grandfather had by him at his death, the other moiety being bequeathed to my sister), contenting myself to take, as from his bounty, what he was pleased to allow me, without desiring the least addition to my annual stipend. And then I hoped I had laid all envy asleep; but still my brother and sister (jealous, as now is evident, of my two uncles' favour for me, and of the pleasure I had given my father and them by this act of duty) were every now and then occasionally doing me covert ill offices; which I took the less notice of, having, as I imagined, removed the cause of their envy, and imputed everything of that sort to the petulance they are both pretty much noted for.

My brother's acquisition then took place. This made us all very happy, and he went down to take possession of it; and his absence (on so good an account too) made us still happier—Then followed Lord M.'s proposal for my sister; and this was an additional felicity for the time. I have told you how exceedingly good-humoured it made my sister.

You know how that went off; you know what came on in its place.

My brother then returned, and we were all wrong again; and Bella, as I observed in my letters above-mentioned, had an opportunity to give herself the credit of having refused Mr Lovelace on the score of his reputed faulty morals. This united my brother and sister in one cause. They set themselves on all occasions to depreciate Mr Lovelace, and his *family* too (a family which deserves nothing but respect); and this gave rise to the conversation I am leading to between my uncles and them; of which I now come to give the particulars; after I have observed that it happened before the rencounter and soon after the inquiry made into Mr Lovelace's affairs had come out better than my brother and sister·hoped or expected.[a]

They were bitterly inveighing against him in their usual way, strengthening their invectives with some new stories in his disfavour, when my uncle Antony having given them a patient hearing declared: 'That he thought the gentleman behaved like a gentleman, his niece Clary with prudence, and that a more honourable alliance for the family, *as he had often told them*, could not be wished for; since Mr Lovelace had a very good paternal estate, and that, by the evidence of an enemy, all clear. Nor did it appear that he was so bad a man as had been represented; wild indeed, but it was at a gay time of life. He was a man of sense, and he was sure that his niece would not have him if she had not good reason to think him reformed, or by her own example likely to be so.'

He then gave one instance, my aunt told me, as a proof of a generosity in his spirit, which showed him, he said, to be no very bad man in nature, and of a temper, he was pleased to say, like my own; which was that when he, my uncle, had represented to him that he might, if he pleased (as he had heard Lord M. say),

<hr>

[a]   See Letter 4, p. 50.

make three or four hundred pounds a year of his paternal estate more than he did; he answered, 'that his tenants paid their rents well; that it was a maxim with his family, from which he would by no means depart, never to rack-rent old tenants or their descendants, and that it was a pleasure to him, to see all his tenants look fat, sleek and contented.'

I indeed had once occasionally heard him say something like this, and thought he never looked so well as at the time—except once, on this occasion: an unhappy tenant came petitioning to my uncle Antony for forbearance, in Mr Lovelace's presence. When he had fruitlessly withdrawn, Mr Lovelace pleaded his cause so well, that the man was called in again and had his suit granted. And Mr Lovelace privately followed him out and gave him two guineas for present relief, the man having declared that at the time he had not five shillings in the world.

On this occasion, he told my uncle of the good action I hinted at, and that without any ostentatious airs: to wit, that he had once observed an old tenant and his wife in a very mean habit at church; and questioning them about it next day, as he knew they had no hard bargain in their farm, the man said he had done some very foolish things with a good intention which had put him behind-hand, and he could not have paid his rent and appear better. He asked him how long it would take him to retrieve the foolish step he had made. He said, perhaps two or three years. Well then, said he, I will abate you five pounds a year for seven years, provided you will lay it out upon your wife and self that you may make a Sunday appearance *like* MY *tenants*. Meantime take this (putting his hand in his pocket, and giving him five guineas) to put yourselves in present plight, and let me see you next Sunday at church, hand in hand like an honest and loving couple, and I bespeak you to dine with me afterwards.

Although this pleased me when I heard it, as giving an instance of generosity and prudence at the same time, not lessening, as my uncle took notice, the yearly value of the farm, yet, my dear, I had no *throbs*, no *glows* upon it—*upon my word* I had not. Nevertheless I own to you that I could not help saying to myself on the occasion, 'Were it ever to be my lot to have this man, he would not hinder me from pursuing the methods I so much delight to take'—with 'a pity that such a man were not *uniformly* good!'

Forgive me this digression.

My uncle went on, my aunt told me, 'That, besides his paternal estate, he was the immediate heir to very splendid fortunes; that when he was in treaty for his niece Arabella, Lord M. told him what great things he and his two half-sisters intended to do for him, in order to qualify him for the title (which would be extinct at his Lordship's death) and which they hoped to procure for him, or a still higher, that of those ladies' father, which had been for some time extinct on failure of heirs male; that this view made his relations so earnest for his marrying; that as he saw not where Mr Lovelace could better himself, so, truly, he thought there was wealth enough in their own family to build up three considerable ones; that therefore he must needs say he was the more desirous of this alliance as there was a great probability, not only from Mr Lovelace's descent, but from his fortunes, that his niece Clarissa might one day be a peeress of Great Britain—and upon that prospect (*here was the mortifying stroke*) he should, for his own part, think it not wrong to make such dispositions as should contribute to the better support of the dignity.'

My uncle Harlowe, it seems, far from disapproving of what his brother had said, declared: 'That there was but one objection to an alliance with Mr Lovelace: to wit, his morals; especially as so much could be done for Miss Bella, and for my brother too, by my father; and as my brother was actually possessed of a considerable estate by virtue of the deed of gift and will of his godmother Lovell.'

Had I known this before, I should the less have wondered at many things I have been unable to account for in my brother's and sister's behaviour to me, and been more on my guard than I imagined there was a necessity to be.

You may easily guess how much this conversation affected my brother at the time. He could not, you know, but be very uneasy to hear *two of his stewards* talk at this rate to his face.

He had from early days by his violent temper made himself both feared and courted by the whole family. My father himself, as I have lately mentioned, very often (long before his acquisitions had made him still more assuming) gave way to him, as to an only son who was to build up the name and augment the honour of it. Little inducement therefore had he to correct a temper which gave him so much consideration with everybody.

'See, sister Bella,' said he, in an indecent passion before my uncles, on the occasion I have mentioned—'See how it is!—You and I ought to look about us!—This little siren is in a fair way to *out-uncle* as well as *out-grandfather* us both!'

From this time, as I now find it plain upon recollection, did my brother and sister behave to me as to one who stood in their way (sometimes as to a creature in love with their common enemy); and to each other as having but one interest. And were resolved therefore to bend all their force to hinder an alliance from taking effect which they believed was likely to oblige them to contract their views.

And how was this to be done, after such a declaration from both my uncles?

My brother found out the way. My sister, as I have said, went hand in hand with him. Between them the family union was broken, and everyone was made uneasy. Mr Lovelace was received more and more coldly by all; but not being to be put out of his course by slights *only*, personal affronts succeeded, defiances next, then the rencounter. That, as you have heard, did the business; and now, if I do not oblige them, my grandfather's estate is to be litigated with me; and I, who never designed to take advantage of the independency bequeathed me, *am to be as dependent upon my papa's will as a daughter ought to be who knows not what is good for herself.* This is the language of the family now.

But if I will suffer myself to be prevailed upon, how happy, as *they* lay it out, shall we all be!—Such presents am I to have, such jewels, and I cannot tell what, from every one of the family! Then Mr Solmes's fortunes are so great, and his proposals so very advantageous (no relation whom he values), that there will be abundant room to raise mine upon them, were the high-intended favours of my own relations to be quite out of the question. Moreover it is now, with this view, found out that I have qualifications which, of *themselves*, will be a full equivalent to him for the settlements he is to make me, and leave *him*, as well as *them*, under an obligation to me for my compliance. He himself thinks so, I am told; so very poor a creature is he, even in *his own*, as well as in *their* eyes.

These charming views answered, how rich, how splendid, shall we all three be!

And I—— what obligations shall I lay upon them all!—And that only by doing an act of duty so suitable to my character and manner of thinking—if indeed I am the generous, as well as dutiful creature, I have hitherto made them believe I am.

This is the bright side that is turned to my father and uncles to captivate them; but I am afraid that my brother's and sister's design is to ruin me with them at any rate. Were it otherwise, would they not on my return from you have rather sought to court than frighten me into measures their hearts are so much bent to carry? A method they have followed ever since.

Meantime, orders are given to all the servants to show the highest respect to Mr Solmes; the *generous* Mr Solmes is now his character with some of our family! But are not these orders a tacit confession that they think his own merit will not procure him respect? He is accordingly, in every visit he makes, not only highly caressed by the principals of our family, but obsequiously attended and cringed to by the menials—and *the noble settlements* are echoed from every mouth.

Noble is the word used to enforce the offers of a man who is mean enough avowedly to *hate*, and wicked enough to propose to *rob* of their just expectations, his own family (every one of which at the same time stands in too much need of his favour), in order to settle all he is worth upon me; and, if I die without children, and he has none by any other marriage, upon a family which already abounds. Such are his proposals.

But were there no other motive to induce me to despise the upstart man, is not this unjust one to his family enough?—The *upstart man*, I repeat, for he was not born to the immense riches he is possessed of; riches left by one niggard to another, in injury to the next heir, because that other is a niggard. And should I not be as culpable, do you think, in my acceptance of such unjust settlements, as he in the offer of them, if I could persuade myself to be a sharer in them, or suffer a reversionary expectation of possessing them to influence my choice?

Indeed it concerns me not a little that my friends could be brought to encourage such offers on *such* motives as I think a person of conscience should not presume to begin the world with.

But this, it seems, is the only method that can be taken to disappoint Mr Lovelace, and at the same time to answer all my relations have to wish for each of us. And *sure* I will not stand against such an accession to the family as may happen from marrying Mr Solmes; since now a *possibility* is discovered (which such a grasping mind as my brother's can easily turn into a *probability*) that my grandfather's estate will revert to it, with a much more considerable one of the man's own. Instances of estates falling in, in cases far more unlikely than this, are insisted on; and my sister says, in the words of an old saw, *it is good to be related to an estate*.

While Solmes, smiling no doubt to himself at a hope so remote, by *offers* only obtains all their interests; and doubts not to join to his own the estate I am envied for, which, for the conveniency of its situation between two of his, will it seems be of twice the value to him that it would be of to any other person, and is therefore, I doubt not, a stronger motive with him than the wife.

These, my dear, seem to me the principal inducements of my relations to espouse so vehemently as they do this man's suit. And here, once more, must I deplore the family fault which gives those inducements such a force as it will be difficult to resist.

And thus far, let matters with regard to Mr Solmes and me come out as they will, my brother has succeeded in his views; that is to say, he has, in the first place, got my FATHER to make the cause his own, and to insist upon my compliance as an act of duty.

My MAMMA has never thought fit to oppose my father's will, when once he has declared himself determined.

My UNCLES, stiff, unbroken, highly-prosperous bachelors, give me leave to say, though very worthy gentlemen in the main, have as high notions of a child's duty as of a wife's obedience, in the *last* of which my mamma's meekness has confirmed them, and given them greater reason to expect the *first*.

My aunt HERVEY (not extremely happy in her own nuptials, and perhaps under some little obligation) is got over, and chooses not to open her lips in my favour against the wills of a father and uncles so determined.

This passiveness in her and in my mamma, in a point so contrary to their own first judgements, is too strong a proof that my papa is absolutely resolved.

Their treatment of my worthy Mrs NORTON is a sad confirmation of it; a woman deserving of all consideration for her wisdom, and everybody thinking so, but who, not being wealthy enough to have due weight in a point against which she has given her opinion, and which they seem bent upon carrying, is restrained from visiting here, and even from corresponding with me, as I am this very day informed.

Hatred to Lovelace, family aggrandizement, and this great motive *paternal authority!*—What a force *united!*—when, *singly*, each consideration is sufficient to carry all before it!

This is the formidable appearance which the address of this disagreeable man wears at present!

My BROTHER and my SISTER triumph—*They have got me down* is their expression, as Hannah, overhearing them, tells me. And so they have (yet I never knew that I was insolently *up*), for now my brother will either lay me under an obligation to comply, to my own unhappiness, and so make me an instrument of his revenge upon Lovelace, or, if I refuse, throw me into disgrace with my whole family.

Who will wonder at the intrigues and plots carried on by undermining courtiers against one another, when a private family, but three of which can possibly have clashing interests, and one of them, as she presumes to think, above such low motives, cannot be free from them?

What at present most concerns me is the peace of my mamma's mind! How can the husband of *such* a wife (a *good* man too!—But oh! this prerogative of manhood!) be so *posi*-tive, so unper-*suade*-able, to one who has brought into the family means, which they know so well the value of that methinks they should value *her* the more for *their* sake!

They do indeed value her; but, I am sorry to say, she has purchased that value by her compliances; yet has merit for which she ought to be venerated, prudence which ought of itself to be trusted and conformed to in everything.

But whither roves my pen? How dare a perverse girl take these liberties with relations so very respectable and whom she highly respects?—What an unhappy situation is that which obliges her, in her *own defence* as it were, to expose *their* failings?

But you, who know how much I love and reverence my mamma, will judge what a difficulty I am under to be obliged to oppose a scheme which she has engaged in.

Yet I *must* oppose it (to comply is impossible), and must declare without delay my opposition, or my difficulties will increase, since, as I am just now informed, a lawyer has been this very day consulted (would you have believed it?) in relation to settlements.

Were ours a Roman Catholic family, how much happier for me, that they thought a nunnery would answer all their views!—How happy, had not a certain person slighted somebody! All then would have been probably concluded on between them before my brother had arrived to thwart the match; then had I had a sister, which now I have not, and two brothers—both aspiring; possibly both titled. While I should only have valued that in either which is above title, that which is truly noble in both!

But what long-reaching selfishness is my brother governed by! By what remote, exceedingly remote views!—Views, which it is in the power of the slightest accident, of a fever for instance (the seeds of which are always vegetating, as I may say, and ready to burst forth, in his own impetuous temper), or of the provoked weapon of an adversary, to blow up and destroy!

I will break off here. Let me write ever so freely of my friends, I am sure of *your* kind construction; and I confide in your discretion, that you will avoid reading to or transcribing for others such passages as may have the appearance of treating too freely the parental, or even the fraternal character, or induce others to censure for a supposed failure in duty to the one, or decency to the other,

Your truly affectionate
CL. HARLOWE

Letter 14: MISS CLARISSA HARLOWE TO MISS HOWE

Thursday evening, March 2

ON Hannah's depositing my long letter, begun yesterday but by reason of several interruptions not finished till within this hour, she found and brought me yours of this day. I thank you, my dear, for this kind expedition—These few lines will perhaps be time enough deposited to be taken away by your servant with the others, yet they are only to thank you and to tell you my increasing apprehensions.

I must beg or seek the occasion to apply to my mamma for her mediation—for I am in danger of having a day fixed, and antipathy taken for bashfulness—Should not sisters be sisters to each other? Should they not make a common cause of it, as I may say, a cause of sex, on such occasions as the present? Yet mine, in support of my brother's selfishness, and no doubt in concert with him, has been urging in full assembly, as I am told, and that with an earnestness peculiar to herself when she sets upon anything, that an absolute day be given me, and if I comply not, to be told that it shall be to the forfeiture of all my fortunes, and of all their loves.

She need not be so officious; my brother's interest, without hers, is strong enough, for he has found means to confederate all the family against me. Upon some fresh provocation or new intelligence concerning Mr Lovelace (I know not what it is) they have bound themselves, or are to bind themselves, by a signed paper, to one another (the Lord bless me, my dear, what shall I do!), to carry this point of Mr Solmes, in support of my father's authority, as it is called, and against Lovelace, as a libertine and an enemy to the family; and if so, I am sure, I may say against *me*—How impolitic in them all to join two people in one interest whom they wish for ever to keep asunder!

What the discharged steward reported of him was bad enough; what Mrs Fortescue said not only confirms that bad, but gives room to think him still worse—And something my friends have come at, which, as Betty Barnes tells Hannah, is of so heinous a nature that it proves him to be the worst of men—But, hang the man, I had almost said—what is he to me? What *would* he be—were not this Mr Sol—— Oh, my dear, how I hate that man in the light he is proposed to me!—All of them at the same time afraid of Mr Lovelace—yet not afraid to provoke him!—How am I entangled!—to be obliged to go on corresponding with him for *their* sakes— Heaven forbid, that their persisted-in violence should so drive me as to make it necessary for *my own!*—But surely *they* will yield—Indeed *I* cannot—I believe the gentlest spirits when provoked (causelessly and cruelly provoked) are the most determined—The reason may be that not taking up resolutions lightly, their very deliberation makes them the more immoveable. And then when a point is clear and self-evident to everybody, one cannot without impatience think of entering into an argument or contention upon it.

An interruption obliges me to conclude myself, in some hurry as well as fright, what I must ever be,

Yours more than my own,
CLARISSA HARLOWE

Letter 15: MISS HOWE TO MISS CLARISSA HARLOWE

Friday, March 3

I HAVE both your letters at once. It is very unhappy, my dear, since your friends will have you marry, that such a merit as yours should be addressed by a succession of worthless creatures, who have nothing but their presumption for their excuse.

That these presumers appear not in this very unworthy light to some of your friends is because their defects are not so striking to them as to others—And why? Shall I venture to tell you?—Because they are nearer their own standard. *Modesty*, after all, perhaps has a concern in it; for how should they think that a *niece* or a *sister* of *theirs* (I will not go higher, for fear of incurring your displeasure) should be an angel?—But where indeed is the man to be found, who has the least share of due diffidence, that dares to look up to Miss Clarissa Harlowe with hope, or with anything but wishes? Thus the bold and forward, not being sensible of their defects, aspire, while the modesty of the really worthy fills them with too much reverence to permit them to explain themselves. Hence your Symmes's, your Byron's, your Mullins's, your Wyerley's (the best of the herd), and your Solmes's, in turn invade you—Wretches that, looking upon the rest of your family, need not despair of succeeding in an alliance with it—But, to you, what an inexcusable presumption!

Yet I am afraid all opposition will be in vain. You must, you will, I doubt, be sacrificed to this odious man!—I know your family!—There will be no resisting such baits as he has thrown out—Oh, my dear, my beloved friend! and are such charming qualities, is such exalted merit, to be sunk in such a marriage!—You must not, your uncle tells my mamma, dispute their authority. AUTHORITY! what a full word is that in the mouth of a narrow-minded person, who happened to be born thirty years before one!—Of your uncles I speak, for as to the *parental* authority, that ought to be sacred. But should not parents have *reason* for what they do?

Wonder not, however, at your Bell's unsisterly behaviour in this affair; I have a particular to add to the inducements your insolent brother is governed by, which will account for all her driving. Her *outward eye*, as *you* have owned, was from *the first* struck with the figure and address of the man whom she pretends to despise, and who 'tis certain thoroughly despises her; but you have not told us that *still* she loves him of all men. Bell has a meanness in her very pride, and no one is so proud as Bell. She has owned her love, her uneasy days, and sleepless nights, and her revenge grafted upon it, to her favourite Betty Barnes—To lay herself in the power of a servant's tongue!—Poor creature!— But LIKE little souls will find one another out, and mingle, as well as LIKE great ones. This, however, she told the wench in strict confidence; and thus, by way of the *female round-about*, as Lovelace had the sauciness on such another occasion, in ridicule of our sex, to call it, Betty (pleased to be thought worthy of a secret, and to have an opportunity of inveighing against Lovelace's perfidy, as she would have it to be) told it to one of *her* confidants; that confidant, with like injunctions of secrecy, to Miss Lloyd's Harriot—Harriot to Miss Lloyd—Miss Lloyd to *me*—I to you—with leave to make what you please of it. And now you will not wonder to find in Miss Bell an implacable rivaless rather than an affectionate sister; and will be able to account for the words *witchcraft*, *siren*, and such-like, thrown out against you; and for her driving on for a fixed day for sacrificing you to Solmes: in short, for her rudeness and violence of every kind— What a sweet revenge will she take, as well upon Lovelace as upon you, if she can procure her rival and all-excelling sister to be married to the man that sister hates, and so prevent her having the man whom she herself loves (whether *she* have hope of him or not), and whom she suspects her sister loves! Poisons and poniards have often been set to work by minds inflamed by disappointed love and revenge; will you wonder then, that the ties of relationship in such a case have no force, and that a sister forgets to be a sister?

This her secret motive (the more resistless, because her pride is concerned to make her disavow it), joined with her former envy and with the general and avowed inducements particularized by you, now it is known, fills me with apprehensions for you; joined also by a brother, who has such an ascendant over the whole family, and whose *interest*, slave to it as he always was, and whose *revenge*, his other darling passion, are engaged to ruin you with everyone: both having the ears of all your family, and continually misrepresenting all you say, all you do, to them: their subject the rencounter and Lovelace's want of morals, to expatiate upon— Oh, my dear! how will you be able to withstand all this?—I am sure (alas! I am *too* sure) that they will subdue such a fine spirit as yours, unused to opposition, and, *tell it not in Gath*, you *must* be Mrs Solmes!

Meantime, it is now easy, as you will observe, to guess from what quarter the report I mentioned to you in one of my former came, that the younger sister has robbed the elder of her lover; for Betty whispered it, at the time she whispered the rest, that neither Lovelace nor you had done honourably by *her* young mistress— How cruel, my dear, in you, to rob the poor Bella of the only lover she ever had!— At the instant too that she was priding herSelf that now, at last, she should have it in her power not only to gratify her own susceptibilities, but to give an example to the *flirts* of her sex (my worship's self the principal, I suppose, with her) how to govern their man with a silken rein and without a kerb-bridle!

Upon the whole, I have now no doubt of their persevering in favour of the despicable Solmes, and of their dependence upon the gentleness of your temper and the regard you have for their favour and for your own reputation. And now I am more than ever convinced of the propriety of the advice I formerly gave you, to keep in your own hands the estate bequeathed to you by your grandfather— Had you done so, it would have procured you at least an *outward* respect from your brother and sister, which would have made them conceal the envy and ill-will that now is bursting upon you from hearts so narrow.

I must harp a little more upon this string—Don't you observe how much your brother's influence has over-topped yours since he has got into fortunes so considerable, and since you have given some of them an appetite to *continue* in themselves the possession of your estate, unless you comply with their terms?

I know your dutiful, your laudable motives, and one would have thought that you might have trusted to a father who so dearly loved you. But had you been actually in possession of that estate, and living up to it and upon it (your youth protected from blighting tongues by the company of your prudent Norton, as you had purposed), do you think that your brother, grudging it to you at the time as he did, and looking upon it as his right as an only son, would have been practising about it and aiming at it?—I told you some time ago that I thought your trials but proportioned to your prudence—But you will be more than woman if you can extricate yourself with honour, having such violent spirits and sordid minds as in some, and such tyrannical and despotic wills as in others, to deal with—Indeed, all *may* be done, and the world be taught further to admire you, for your blind duty and will-less resignation, if you can persuade yourself to be Mrs Solmes!

I am pleased with the instances you give me of Mr Lovelace's benevolence to his own tenants, and with his little gift to your uncle's. Mrs Fortescue *allows* him to be the best of landlords; I might have told you that, had I thought it necessary to put you in some little conceit of him. He has qualities, in short, that may make him a tolerable creature on the other side of fifty; but God help the poor woman to whose lot he shall fall till then! *Women*, I should say perhaps, since he may break half a dozen hearts before that time. But to the point I was upon—Shall we not have reason to commend the tenant's grateful honesty, if we are told that with joy the poor man called out your uncle, and on the spot paid him in part of his debt those two guineas?—But what shall we say of that landlord who, though he knew the poor man to be quite destitute, could take it, and saying nothing while Mr Lovelace stayed, as soon as he was gone tell of it, praising the poor fellow's honesty?—Were this so, and were not that landlord related to my dearest friend, how should I despise such a wretch!—But perhaps the story is aggravated. Covetous people have everyone's ill word; and so indeed they ought, because they are only solicitous to keep that which they prefer to everyone's good one. Covetous indeed would they be who deserved *neither*, yet expected *both!*

I long for your next letter. Continue to be as particular as possible. I can think of no other subject but what relates to you and to your affairs; for I am, and ever will be, most affectionately,

All your own
ANNA HOWE

Letter 16: MISS CLARISSA HARLOWE TO MISS HOWE

(Her last not at the time received)

Friday, March 3

OH MY dear friend, I have had a sad conflict! trial upon trial; conference upon conference!—But what law, what ceremony, can give a man a right to a heart which abhors him more than it does any of God Almighty's creatures?

I hope my mamma will be able to prevail for me—But I will recount all, though I sit up the whole night to do it, for I have a vast deal to write and will be as minute as you wish me to be.

In my last I told you in a fright, my apprehensions, which were grounded upon a conversation that passed between my mamma and my aunt, part of which Hannah overheard. I need not give you the further particulars, since what I have to relate to you from different conversations that have passed between my mamma and me in the space of a very few hours, will include them all. I will begin then.

I went down this morning when breakfast was ready with a very uneasy heart, from what Hannah had told me yesterday afternoon; wishing for an opportunity, however, to appeal to my mamma in hopes to engage her interest in my behalf, and purposing to try to find one, when she retired to her own apartment after breakfast—But, unluckily, there was the odious Solmes sitting asquat between my mamma and sister, with *so much* assurance in his looks!—But you know, my dear, that those we love not cannot do anything to please us.

Had the wretch kept his seat, it might have been well enough, but the bent and broad-shouldered creature must needs rise and stalk towards a chair, which was just by that which was set for me.

I removed it at a distance, as if to make way to my own; and down I sat, abruptly I believe; what I had heard all in my head.

But this was not enough to daunt him. The man is a very confident, he is a very bold, staring man!—Indeed, my dear, the man is very confident.

He took the removed chair and drew it so near mine, squatting in it with his ugly weight, that he pressed upon my hoop—I was so offended (all I had heard, as I said, in my head) that I removed to another chair. I own I had too little command of myself. It gave my brother and sister too much advantage. I dare say they took it—but I did it involuntarily, I think; I could not help it—I knew not what I did.

I saw my papa was excessively displeased. When angry, no man's countenance ever showed it so much as my papa's. Clarissa Harlowe! said he with a big voice, and there he stopped—Sir! said I, and curtsied—I trembled and put my chair nearer the wretch, and sat down; my face I could feel all in a glow.

Make tea, child, said my kind mamma. Sit by me, love, and make tea.

I removed with pleasure to the seat the man had quitted, and being thus indulgently put into employment, soon recovered myself; and in the course of the breakfasting officiously asked two or three questions of Mr Solmes, which I would not have done, but to make up with my papa. *Proud spirits may be brought to*, whispering spoke my sister to me over her shoulder, with an air of triumph and scorn; but I did not mind her.

My mamma was all kindness and condescension. I asked her once if she were pleased with the tea? She said softly, and again called me *dear*, she was pleased with all I did. I was very proud of this encouraging goodness; and all blew over, as I hoped, between my papa and me, for he also spoke kindly to me two or three times.

Small incidents these, my dear, to trouble you with; only as they lead to greater, as you shall hear.

Before the usual breakfast-time was over my papa withdrew with my mamma, telling her he wanted to speak to her. My sister and my aunt, who was with us, next dropped away.

My brother gave himself some airs of insult that I understood well enough, but which Mr Solmes could make nothing of, and at last he arose from his seat—Sister, said he, I have a curiosity to show you. I will fetch it. And away he went, shutting the door close after him.

I saw what all this was for. I arose, the man hemming up for a speech, rising and beginning to set his splay feet (indeed, my dear, the man in all his ways is hateful to me) in an approaching posture—I will save my brother the trouble of bringing to me his curiosity, said I. I curtsied—Your servant, sir—The man cried, Madam, Madam, twice, and looked like a fool—But away I went—to find my brother to save my word—But my brother was gone, indifferent as the weather was, to walk in the garden with my sister. A plain case that he had left his curiosity with me and designed to show me no other.

I had but just got into my own apartment and began to think of sending Hannah to beg an audience of my mamma (the more encouraged by her condescending goodness at breakfast), when Shorey, her woman, brought me her commands to attend her in her closet.

My papa, Hannah told me, had just gone out of it with a positive, angry countenance. Then I as much dreaded the audience as I had wished for it before.

I went down, however; but, apprehending the subject, approached her trembling and my heart in visible palpitations.

She saw my concern. Holding out her kind arms as she sat, Come kiss me, my dear, said she with a smile like a sunbeam breaking through the cloud that overshadowed her naturally benign aspect. Why flutters my jewel so?

This preparative sweetness, with her goodness just before, confirmed my apprehensions. My mamma saw the bitter pill wanted gilding.

Oh my mamma! was all I could say, and I clasped my arms round her neck and my face sunk into her bosom.

My child! my child! restrain, said she, your powers of moving!—I dare not else trust myself with you. And my tears trickled down her bosom as hers bedewed my neck.

Oh the words of kindness, all to be expressed in vain, that flowed from her lips!

Lift up your sweet face, my best child, my own Clarissa Harlowe!—Oh my daughter, best-beloved of my heart, lift up a face so ever-amiable to me!—Why these sobs?—Is an apprehended duty so affecting a thing that before I can speak—But I am glad, my love, you can guess at what I have to say to you. I am spared the pains of breaking to you what was a task upon me reluctantly enough undertaken to break to you.

Then rising, she drew a chair near her own and made me sit down by her, overwhelmed as I was with tears of apprehension of what she had to say, and of gratitude for her truly maternal goodness to me, sobs still my only language.

And drawing her chair still nearer to mine, she put her arms round my neck and my glowing cheek, wet with my tears, close to her own. Let me talk to you, my child, since silence is your choice; hearken to me, and *be* silent.

You know, my dear, what I every day forgo and undergo, for the sake of peace. Your papa is a very good man and means well; but he will not be controlled, nor yet persuaded. You have seemed to pity *me* sometimes, that I am obliged to give up every point. Poor man! *his* reputation the less for it; *mine* the greater; yet would I not have this credit, if I could help it, at so dear a rate to *him* and to *myself*. You are a dutiful, a prudent and a *wise* child, she was pleased to say (in hope, no doubt, to make me so); you would not add, I am sure, to my trouble. You would not wilfully break that peace which costs your mamma so much to preserve. Obedience is better than sacrifice. Oh my Clary Harlowe, rejoice my heart by telling me I have apprehended too much!—I see your concern! I see your perplexity! I see your conflict (loosing her arm and rising, not willing I should see how much she herself was affected). I will leave you a moment—Answer me not (for I was essaying to speak and had, as soon as she took her dear cheek from mine, dropped down on my knees, my hands clasped and lifted up in a supplicating manner). I am not prepared for your irresistible expostulation, she was pleased to say—I will leave you to recollection. And I charge you, on my blessing, that all this my truly maternal tenderness be not thrown away upon you.

And then she withdrew into the next apartment, wiping her eyes as she went from me, as mine overflowed, my heart taking in the whole compass of her meaning.

She soon returned, having recovered more steadiness.

Still on my knees, I had thrown my face cross the chair she had sat in.

Look up to me, my Clary Harlowe. No sullenness, I hope!

No, indeed, my ever-to-be-revered mamma—and I arose. I bent my knee.

She raised me. No kneeling to me, but with knees of duty and compliance—Your heart, not your knees, must bend—It is absolutely determined—Prepare yourself therefore to receive your *papa* when he visits you by and by, as he would wish to receive *you*. But on this one quarter of an hour depends the peace of my future life, the satisfaction of all the family, and your own security from a man of violence. And I charge you *besides*, on my blessing, that you think of being Mrs Solmes.

There went the dagger to my heart and down I sunk; and when I recovered, found myself in the arms of my Hannah, my sister's Betty holding open my reluctantly-opened palm, my laces cut, my linen scented with hartshorn; and my mamma gone—Had I been *less* kindly treated, the hated name still forborne to be mentioned, or mentioned with a little more preparation and reserve, I had stood the horrid sound with less visible emotion—But to be bid, on the blessing of a mother so dearly beloved, so truly reverenced, to think of being Mrs SOLMES, what a denunciation was that!

Shorey came in with a message, delivered in her solemn way: Your mamma, miss, is concerned for your disorder; she expects you down again in an hour, and bid me say, that she then hopes everything from your duty.

I made no reply; for what could I say? And leaning upon my Hannah's arm, withdrew to my own apartment. There you will guess how the greatest part of the hour was employed.

Within that time, my mamma came up to *me*.

I love, she was pleased to say, to come into *this* apartment!—No emotions, child! No flutters!—Am I not your mother!—Am I not your fond, your indulgent mother! Do not discompose *me* by discomposing *yourself!*—Do not occasion *me* uneasiness, when I would give *you* nothing but pleasure. Come, my dear, we will go into your library!

She took my hand, led the way, and made me sit down by her; and after she had inquired how I did, she began in a strain as if she had supposed I had made use of the intervening space to overcome all my objections.

She was pleased to tell me that my papa and she, in order to spare my natural modesty, had taken the whole affair upon themselves—

Hear me out, and then speak (for I was going to expostulate). You are no stranger to the end of Mr Solmes's visits—

Oh madam—

Hear me out, and then speak. He is not indeed everything I wish him to be; but he is a man of probity, and has no vices—

No vices, madam!—

Hear me out, child—You have not behaved much amiss to him. We have seen with pleasure that you have not—

Oh madam, must I not now speak!—

I shall have done presently—A young creature of your virtuous and *pious* turn, she was pleased to say, cannot surely love a profligate. You love your brother too well to wish to marry one who had like to have killed him, and who threatened your uncles, and defies us all. You have had your own way six or seven times. We want to secure you against a man so vile. Tell me; I have a right to know; whether you prefer this man to all others?—Yet God forbid that I should know you do! for such a declaration would make us all miserable. Yet, tell me, are your affections engaged to this man?

I knew what the inference would be, if I had said they were not.

You hesitate; you answer me not; you cannot answer me—*Rising*—Never more will I look upon you with an eye of favour—

Oh madam, madam! Kill me not with your displeasure. I would not, I *need* not, hesitate one moment, did I not dread the inference if I answer you as you wish— Yet be that inference what it will, your threatened displeasure will make me speak. And I declare to you that I know not my own heart if it be not absolutely free. And pray, let me ask, my dearest mamma, in what has my conduct been faulty that, like a giddy creature, I must be forced to marry, to save me from—from what? Let me beseech you, madam, to be the guardian of my reputation—Let not your Clarissa be precipitated into a state she wishes not to enter into with any man! And this upon a supposition that otherwise she shall marry herself, and disgrace her whole family.

Well then, Clary (passing over the force of my plea), if your heart be free—

Oh my beloved mamma, let the usual generosity of your dear heart operate in my favour. Urge not upon me the inference that made me hesitate.

I won't be interrupted, Clary—You have seen in my behaviour to you on this occasion, a truly maternal tenderness; you have observed that I have undertaken this task, with some reluctance, because the man is not everything, and because I know you carry your notions of perfection in a man too high—

Dearest madam, this one time excuse me!—Is there *then* any danger that I should be guilty of an imprudent thing for the man's sake you hint at?

Again interrupted!—Am I to be questioned and argued with? You know this won't do somewhere else. You know it won't. What reason then, ungenerous girl, can you have for arguing with me thus, but because you think from my indulgence to you, you may?

What *can* I say? What *can* I do? What must that cause be, that will not bear being argued upon?

Again! Clary Harlowe!—

Dearest madam, forgive me. It was always my pride and my pleasure to obey you. But look upon that man—see but the disagreeableness of his person—

Now, Clary, do I see whose person you have in your eye!—Now is Mr Solmes, I see, but *comparatively* disagreeable, disagreeable only as another man has a much more specious person.

But, madam, are not his manners equally so?—Is not his person the true representative of his mind?—That other man is not, shall not, be anything to me, release me but from this one man, whom my heart, unbidden, resists.

Condition thus with your papa. Will *he* bear, do you think, to be thus dialogued with? Have I not conjured you, as you value my peace—What is it that *I* do not give up?—This very task, because I apprehended you would not be *easily* persuaded, is a task *indeed* upon me. And will *you* give up nothing? Have you not refused as many as have been offered to you? If you would not have us guess for whom, comply; for comply you must, or be looked upon as in a state of defiance with your whole family.

And saying this, she arose and went from me. But at the chamber door stopped and turned back: I will not say below in what a disposition I leave you. Consider of everything. The matter is resolved upon. As you value your father's blessing and mine, and the satisfaction of all the family, resolve to comply. I will leave you for a few moments. I will come up to you again. See that I find you as I wish to find you, and since *your heart is free*, let your duty govern it.

In about half an hour, my mamma returned. She found me in tears. She took my hand: It is my part evermore to be of the acknowledging side. I believe I have needlessly exposed myself to your opposition, by the method I have taken with you. I first began as if I expected a denial and by my indulgence brought it upon myself.

Do not, my dearest mamma! do not say so!

Were the occasion for this debate, proceeded she, to have risen from myself;

were it in my power to dispense with your compliance; you too well know what you can do with me—

Would anybody, my dear Miss Howe, wish to marry, when one sees a necessity for such a sweet temper as my mamma's either to be ruined or deprived of all power?

—When I came to you a second time, knowing that your contradiction would avail you nothing, I refused to hear your reasons. And in this I was wrong too, because a young creature who loves to reason, and *used* to love to be convinced by reason, ought to have all her objections heard. I now, therefore, this third time, see you; and am come resolved to hear all you have to say: And let me, my dear, by my patience engage your gratitude, your *generosity*, I will call it, because it is to you I speak, who used to have a mind wholly generous. Let me, if your heart *be really free*, let me see what it will induce you to do to oblige me. And so as you permit your usual discretion to govern you, I will hear all you have to say; but with this intimation, that say what you will, it will be of no avail elsewhere.

What a dreadful saying is that! But could I engage your pity, madam, it would be somewhat.

You have as much of my pity as of my love. But what is *person*, Clary, with one of your prudence, and *your heart disengaged?*—

Should the eye be disgusted, when the heart is to be engaged?—Oh madam, who can think of marrying when the heart must be shocked at the first appearance, and where the disgust must be confirmed by every conversation afterwards?

This, Clary, is owing to your prepossession. Let me not have cause to regret that noble firmness of mind in so young a creature, which I thought your glory, and which was my boast in your character. In this instance it would be obstinacy, and want of duty—Have you not made objections to several—

That was to their *minds*, their *principles*, madam—But this man—

Is an honest man, Clary Harlowe. He has a good mind—He is a virtuous man.

He an honest man! *His* a good mind, madam! *He* a virtuous man!—

Nobody denies him these qualities.

Can *he* be an honest man who offers terms that will rob all his own relations of their just expectations?—Can *his* mind be good—

You, Clary Harlowe, for whose sake he offers so much are the last person that should make this observation.

Give me leave to say, madam, that a person preferring happiness to fortune, as I do; that want not even what I *have*, and can give up the use of *that* as an instance of duty—

No more, no more of your merits!—You know you will be a gainer by that cheerful instance of your duty, not a loser. You know you have but *cast your bread upon the waters*—So no more of that!—For it is not understood as a merit by everybody, I assure you, though I think it a high one; and so did your papa and uncles at the time—

At the time, madam!—How unworthily do my brother and sister, who are afraid that the favour I was so lately in—

I hear nothing against your brother and sister—What family feuds have I in prospect, at a time when I hoped most comfort from you all!

God bless my brother and sister, in all their *worthy* views! You shall have no family feuds, if I can prevent them. You yourself, madam, shall tell me what I shall bear from them, and I will bear it. But let *my* actions, not *their* misrepresentations (as I am sure has been the case by the disgraceful prohibitions I have met with), speak for me—

Just then, up came my papa, with a sternness in his looks that made me tremble!—He took two or three turns about my chamber—And then said to my mamma, who was silent as soon as she saw him—

My dear, you are long absent—Dinner is near ready. What you had to say lay in a very little compass. Surely you have nothing to do but to declare *your* will, and *my* will!—But, perhaps, you may be talking of the preparations—Let us have you soon down—your daughter in your hand, if worthy of the name.

And down he went, casting his eye upon me with a look so stern that I was unable to say one word to him, or even for a few minutes to my mamma.

Was not this very intimidating, my dear?

My mamma, seeing my concern, seemed to pity me. She called me her good child and kissed me; told me my papa should not know that I had made such opposition. He has kindly furnished us with an excuse for being so long together. Come, my dear—Dinner will be upon table presently—Shall we go down? And took my hand.

This made me start: What, madam, go down, to let it be supposed we were talking of *preparations!*—Oh my beloved mamma, command me not down upon such a supposition.

You see, child, that to stay longer together will be owning that you are debating about an absolute duty: and that will not be borne. Did not your papa himself, some days ago tell you he would be obeyed? I will a third time leave you. I must say something by way of excuse for you; and that you desire not to go down to dinner—That your modesty on the occasion—

Oh madam! say not my modesty on *such* an occasion; for that will be to give hope—

And design you *not* to give hope?—Perverse girl!—*Rising and flinging from me*, take more time for consideration!—Since it is necessary, *take* more time—And when I see you next, let me know what blame I have to cast upon myself, or to bear from your papa, for my indulgence to you.

She made, however, a little stop at the chamber door, and seemed to expect that I would have besought her to make the gentlest construction for me; for hesitating, she was pleased to say, I suppose you would not have me make a report—

Oh madam, interrupted I, whose favour can I hope for, if I lose my mamma's?

To have desired a *favourable* report, you know, my dear, would have been qualifying upon a point that I was too much determined upon to give room for any of my friends to think I have the least hesitation about. And so my mamma went downstairs.

I will deposit thus far; and as I know you will not think me too minute in my relation of particulars so very interesting to one you honour with your love, proceed in the same way. As matters stand, I don't care to have papers so freely written about me.

Pray let Robert call every day, if you can spare him, whether I have anything ready or not.

I should be glad you would not send him empty-handed. What a generosity in you to write as frequently from friendship as I am forced to do from misfortune!

The letters being taken away will be an assurance that you have them. As I shall write and deposit as I have opportunity, the formality of *super-* and *sub-*scription will be excused. For I need not say how much I am,

Your sincere and ever-affectionate,
CL. HARLOWE

Letter 17: MISS CLARISSA HARLOWE TO MISS HOWE

MY mamma on her return, which was as soon as she had dined, was pleased to inform me that she told my papa, on his questioning her about my *cheerful* compliance (for it seems, the *cheerful* was all that was doubted), that she was willing on so material a point to give a child whom she had so *much reason to love* (as she condescended to acknowledge were her words) liberty to say all that was in her heart to say, that her compliance might be the freer; letting him know that when he came up, she was attending to my pleas, for that she found I had rather not marry at all.

She told me that to this my papa angrily said, let her take care—let her take care—that she give me not ground to suspect her of a preference somewhere else. But if it be to ease her heart, and not to dispute my will, you may hear her out.

So, Clary, said my mamma; I am returned in a temper accordingly, if you do not again by *your* peremptoriness show *me* how I ought to treat *you.*

Indeed, madam, you did me justice to say I have no inclination to marry at all. I have not, I hope, made myself so *very* unuseful in my papa's family, as—

No more of your merits, Clary! You have been a good child; you have eased me of all the family cares; but do not now add more than ever you relieved me from. You have been richly repaid in the reputation your skill and management have given you—But now there is soon to be a period to all those assistances from you. If you marry, there will be a natural and, if to please us, a desirable period; because your own family will employ all your talents in that way: if you do not, there will be a period likewise, but *not* a natural one—You understand me, child.

I wept.

I have made inquiry already after a housekeeper. I would have had your good Norton, but I suppose you will yourself wish to have the worthy woman with you. If you desire it, that shall be agreed upon for you.

But, why, dearest madam, why am I, the *youngest*, to be precipitated into a state that I am very far from wishing to enter into with anybody?

You are going to question me, I suppose, why your sister is not thought of for Mr Solmes?

I hope, madam, it will not displease you if I were?

I might refer you for an answer to your *papa*—Mr Solmes has reasons for preferring *you*—

And so have I, madam, for disliking *him.* And why am I—

This quickness upon me, interrupted my mamma, is not to be borne! I am gone, and your father comes, if *I* can do no good with you.

Madam, I would rather die, than—

She put her hand to my mouth—No peremptoriness, Clary Harlowe! Once you declare yourself inflexible, I have done.

I wept for vexation. This is all, all, my brother's doings—His grasping views—

No reflections upon your brother. He has entirely the honour of the family at heart.

I would no more dishonour my family, madam, than my brother would.

I believe it; but I hope you'll allow your papa and me and your uncles to judge what will do it honour, what dishonour!

I then offered to live single; never to marry at all; or never but with their full approbation.

If I meant to show my duty and my obedience, I must show it in *their* way, not *my own*.

I said, I hoped I had so behaved myself hitherto that there was no need of such a trial of my obedience as this.

Yes, she was pleased to say, I had behaved extremely well; but I had no trials till now. And she hoped that now I was called to one, I should not fail in it. Parents, said she, when children are young are pleased with everything they do—You have been a good child upon the whole; but we have hitherto rather complied with you than you with us. Now that you are grown up to marriageable years is the test, especially as your grandfather has made you independent, as we may say, in preference to those who had prior expectations upon that estate—

Madam, my grandfather knew, and expressly mentions in his will his desire, that my papa will more than make it up to my sister—I did nothing but what I thought my duty to procure his favour. It was rather a mark of his affection than any advantage to me. For, do I either seek or wish to be independent? Were I to be queen of the universe, that dignity should not absolve me from my duty to you and my papa. I would kneel for your blessings, were it in the presence of millions—So that—

I am loath to interrupt *you*, Clary, though you could more than once break in upon me—You are young and unbroken—But with all this ostentation of your duty, I desire you to show a little more deference to me when I am speaking.

I beg your pardon, dear madam, and your patience with me on such an occasion as this—If I did not speak with earnestness upon it, I should be supposed to have only maidenly objections against a man I never can abide—

Clary Harlowe—

Dearest, dearest madam, permit me to speak what I have to say, this once—It is hard, it is very hard, to be forbid to enter into the cause of all, because I must not speak disrespectfully of one who supposes me in the way of his ambition, and treats me like a slave—

Whither, whither, Clary—

My dearest mamma!—My duty will not permit me so far to suppose my father arbitrary, as to make a plea of that arbitrariness to you—

How now, Clary!—Oh girl!—

Your patience, my dearest mamma—You were pleased to *say* you would hear me with patience—PERSON in a man is nothing, because I am supposed to be prudent, So my eye is to be disgusted and my reason not convinced—

·Girl, girl!—

Thus are my imputed good qualities to be made my punishment, and I am to be wedded to a *monster*—

Astonishing!—Can this, Clarissa, be from you?—

The man, madam, person and mind, is a monster in my eye—And that I may be induced to bear this treatment, I am to be complimented with being indifferent to all men. Yet, at other times, and to serve other purposes, am I to be thought prepossessed in favour of a man against whose moral character lie just objections—Confined, as if, like the giddiest of creatures, I would run away with this man, and disgrace my whole family!—Oh my dearest mamma! who can be patient under such treatment?

Now, Clary, I suppose you will allow *me* to speak. I think I have had patience indeed with you. Could I have thought—But I will put all upon a short issue. Your *mamma*, Clarissa, shall show you an example of that patience you so boldly claim from *her*, without having *any yourself*.

Oh my dear, how my mamma's condescension distressed me at the time! Infinitely more distressed me than rigour could have done. But she *knew*, she was to be sure *aware*, that she was put upon a harsh service; an unreasonable service, let me say; or she would not, she could not, have had so much patience with me.

Let me tell you then, proceeded she, that all lies in a small compass, as your papa said. You have been hitherto, as you are pretty ready to plead, a dutiful child—You have indeed had no *cause* to be otherwise; no child was ever more favoured—Whether you will discredit all your past actions; whether, at a time and upon an occasion that the highest instance of duty is expected from you (an instance that is to crown all), and when you declare that *your heart is free*—you will give that instance; or whether, having a view to the independence you may claim (for so, Clary, whatever be your motive, it will be judged), and which any man you favour can assert *for you against* us all, or rather *for himself* in *spite* of us—whether, I say, you will break with us all; and stand in defiance of a jealous papa; needlessly jealous, I will venture to say, of the prerogatives of his sex as to me, and still ten times more jealous of the authority of a father—this is now the point with us. You know your papa has made it a point; and did he ever give up one he thought he had a right to carry?

Too true, thought I to myself! And now my brother has engaged my father, his fine scheme will *walk alone* without needing his leading-strings; and it is become my father's will that I oppose, not my brother's grasping views.

I was silent. To say the truth, I was just then *sullenly* silent. My heart was too big. I thought it was hard to be thus given up by my mamma, and that she should make a will so uncontrollable as my brother's, her will.

But this silence availed me still less—

I see, my dear, said she, that you are convinced. Now, my good child, now, my Clary, do I love you! It shall not be known that you have argued with me at all. All shall be imputed to that modesty which has ever so much distinguished you. You shall have the full merit of your resignation.

I wept.

She tenderly wiped the tears from my eyes and kissed my cheek—Your papa expects you down with a cheerful countenance—But I will excuse your going. All your scruples, you see, have met with an indulgence truly maternal from me. I rejoice in the hope that you are convinced. This indeed seems to be a proof of the welcome truth you have asserted, that *your heart is free*.

Did not this seem to border upon *cruelty*, my dear, in so indulgent a mamma?—It would be wicked (would it not?) to suppose my mamma capable of *art*—But she is put upon it; and obliged to take methods her heart is naturally above stooping to; and all intended for my good, because she sees that no arguing will be admitted anywhere else.

I will go down, proceeded she, and excuse your attendance at afternoon tea, as I did to dinner; for I know you will have some little reluctances to conquer. I will allow you those, and also some little natural shynesses—And so you *shan't* come down, if you choose *not* to come down—Only, my dear, don't disgrace my report when you come to supper. And be sure behave as you used to do to your brother and sister; for your behaviour to them will be one test of your cheerful obedience to us. I advise as a friend, you see, rather than command as a mother—So adieu, my love; and again she kissed me, and was going.

Oh my dear mamma, said I, forgive me!—But surely you cannot believe I can ever think of having that man!

She was very angry, and seemed to be greatly disappointed. She threatened to turn me over to my papa and my uncles—She bid me (generously bid me) consider, if I thought my brother and sister had views to serve by making my uncles dissatisfied with me, what a handle I gave them. She told me that she had early said all that she thought could be said against the present proposal, on a supposition that I, who had refused several others (whom she owned to be preferable as to person), should *not* approve of it; and could she have prevailed, I had never heard of it. And if SHE could not, how could *I* expect it?—That it was equally my good (in order to preserve to me the share I had hitherto held in everybody's affections), and her own peace, that she wished to promote by the task she had undertaken—That my papa would flame out, upon my refusal to comply—That my uncles were so much convinced of the consistence of the measure with their favourite views of aggrandizing the family, that they were as much determined as my papa—That my aunt Hervey and my uncle Hervey were of the same party—That it was hard, if a father and mother, and uncles and aunt, all conjoined, could not be allowed to direct my choice—That, surely, I was not the *more* averse, because the *family view* would be promoted by the match—That this would be the light, she could assure me, in which my refusal would be taken by everybody—That all the asseverations I could make of living single, while the man who was so obnoxious to everybody remained unmarried, and while he *buzzed* about me was the word, would have no weight with any of them—That if Mr Lovelace were an angel, and my father made it a point that I should not have him, I must be sensible he would not have his will disputed; especially, as it was not doubted that I corresponded with him; to the belief of which, and that it was by Miss Howe's means, were owing the prohibition laid upon me, so much against her liking, she was pleased to say.

I answered to every article she had spoken to as above, in such a manner as I am sure would have satisfied her, could she have been permitted to judge for herself; and then inveighed with bitterness against the disgraceful prohibitions laid upon me.

They would serve to show me, she was pleased to say, how much in earnest my papa was. They might be taken off, whenever I thought fit, and no harm done, nor disgrace received. But if I were to be contumacious, I might thank myself for all that would follow.

I sighed. I wept. I was silent.

Shall I, Clary, said she, tell your papa that these prohibitions are as unnecessary as I hoped they would be? That you know your *duty*, and will not offer to controvert his will?—What say you, my love?

Oh madam, what can I say to questions so indulgently put? I do indeed *know* my duty; no creature in the world is more willing to *practise* it. But, pardon me, dearest madam, if I say that I must bear these prohibitions, if I am to pay so dear to have them taken off.

Determined and perverse, my dear mamma called me; and after walking twice or thrice in anger about the room, she turned to me—Your heart *free!* Clarissa! How can you tell me your heart is free? Such extraordinary antipathies to a particular person must be owing to extraordinary prepossessions in another's favour!—Tell me, Clary, and tell me truly—Do you not continue to correspond with Mr Lovelace?

Dearest madam, replied I, you know my motives; to prevent mischief, I answered his letters. The reason for our apprehensions of this sort are not over.

I own to you, Clary, although now I would not have it known, that I once thought a little qualifying among such violent spirits was not amiss. I did not know but all things would come round again by Lord M.'s and his two sisters' mediation. But as they all three think proper to resent for their nephew; and as their nephew thinks fit to defy us all; and as terms are offered on another hand, that could not be asked, which will very probably prevent your grandfather's estate going out of the family and may be a means to bring a still greater into it; I see not, that the continuance of your correspondence with him either can, or ought to be permitted. I therefore now forbid it to you, as you value my favour.

Be pleased, madam, only to advise me how to break it off with safety to my brother and uncles; and it is all I wish for. Would to heaven the man so hated had not the pretence to make of having been too violently treated, when he meant peace and reconciliation! It would always have been in my own power to have broke with him—His reputed immoralities would have given me a just pretence at any time to do so—But, madam, as my uncles and my brother will keep no measures—as he has heard what the view is; and as I have reason to think that he is only restrained by his regard for me from resenting their violent treatment of him and his family; what can I do?—Would you have me, madam, make him desperate?

The law will protect us, child!—Offended magistracy will assert itself—

But, madam, may not some dreadful mischief first happen?—The law asserts not itself till it is offended.

You have made offers, Clary, if you might be obliged in the point in question— Are you really in earnest on that condition to break off all correspondence with Mr Lovelace?—Let me know this.

Indeed, I am; and I will. You, madam, shall see every letter that has passed between us. You shall see I have given him no encouragement, independent of my duty—And when you have seen them, you will be better able to direct me how, on that condition, to break entirely with him.

I take you at your word, Clarissa. Give me *his* letters; and the copies of *yours*.

I am sure, madam, you will keep the knowledge that I write, and what I write—

No conditions with your mamma—Surely my prudence may be trusted to.

I begged her pardon, and besought her to take the key of the private drawer in my escritoire where they lay, that she herself might see that I had no reserves to my mamma.

She did; and took all his letters, and the copies of mine—*un*-conditioned with; she was pleased to say, they shall be yours again, unseen by anybody else.

I thanked her; and she withdrew to read them, saying she would return them when she had.

You, my dear, have seen all the letters that have passed between him and me till my last return from you. You have acknowledged that he has nothing to boast of from them. Three others I have received since, by the private conveyance I told you of; the last I have not yet answered.

In these three, as in those you have seen, after having besought my favour and, in the most earnest manner, professed the sincerity of his passion for me and set forth the indignities done him, the defiances my brother throws out against him in all companies, the menaces and hostile appearance of my uncles, wherever they go, or come, and the methods they take to defame him; he declares, 'that neither his own honour, nor his family's (involved as that is in the undistinguishing reflections cast upon him for an unhappy affair, which he would have shunned, but could not), permit him to bear these confirmed indignities: that as my inclinations, if not favourable to *him*, cannot be, nor are, to such a man as the new-set-up Solmes, he is interested the more to resent my brother's behaviour; who to everybody avows his rancour and malice, and glories in the probability he has through this Solmes's address of mortifying *me*, and avenging himself on *him*: that it is impossible he should not think himself concerned to frustrate a measure so directly levelled at him, had he not still a higher motive for hoping to frustrate it: that I must forgive him if he enters into conference with Solmes upon it. He earnestly insists upon what he has so often proposed, that I will give him leave in company with Lord M. to wait upon my uncles, and even upon my papa or mamma, promising patience if new provocations, absolutely beneath a man to bear, are not given:' which, by the way, I am far from being able to engage for.

In my answer, I absolutely declare, as I tell him I have often done, 'that he is to expect no favour from me, against the approbation of my friends: that I am sure their consents for his visiting any of them will never be obtained: that I will not be either so undutiful, or so indiscreet, as to suffer my interests to be separated from the interests of my family, for any man on earth: that I do not think myself *obliged* to him for the forbearance I desire one flaming spirit to have with others: that in this desire I require nothing of him, but what prudence, justice and the laws of his country oblige from him: that if he has any expectations of favour from me, on that account, he deceives himself: that I have no inclination, as I have often told him, to change my condition: that I cannot allow myself to correspond with him any longer in this clandestine manner: it is mean, low, undutiful, I tell him; and has a giddy appearance, which cannot be excused: that therefore he is not to expect, that I *will* continue it.'

To this, in his last, among other things, he replies: 'That if I am actually

determined to break off all correspondence with him, he must conclude that it is
with a view to become the wife of a man, whom no woman of honour and fortune
can think tolerable. And in that case, I must excuse him for saying that he shall
neither be able to bear the thoughts of losing for ever a person in whom all his
present, and all his future hopes are centred; nor support himself with patience
under the insolent triumphs of my brother upon it: but that he will not presume to
threaten either his own life, or that of any other man. He must take his resolutions
as such a dreaded event shall impel him at the time. If he shall know that it will be
with my own consent, he must endeavour to resign to his destiny: but if it be
brought about by compulsion, he shall not be able to answer for the consequence.'

I will send you these letters for your perusal, in a few days. I would enclose
them; but that it is possible something may happen, which may make my mamma
require to see them again—You will see, my dear, by his, how he endeavours to
hold me to this correspondence.

In about an hour my mamma returned. Take your letters, Clary: I have nothing
to task your discretion with, as to the wording of yours to him. You have even kept
up a proper dignity, as well as decorum; and you have resented, as you ought to
resent, his menacing invectives. But *can* you think from the avowed hatred of one
side, and the avowed defiance of the other, that this can be a suitable match? *Can*
you think it becomes you to encourage an address from a man who has fought a
duel with your brother, let his fortune and professions be what they will?

By no means it can, madam; you will be pleased to observe that I have said as
much to him. But now, madam, the whole correspondence is before you; and I beg
your commands what to do in a situation so very disagreeable.

One thing I will tell you, Clary Harlowe: but I charge you, as you would not
have me question the generosity of your spirit, to take no advantage of it, either
mentally or *verbally* were the words: that I am so much pleased with the offer of
your keys to me, in so cheerful and unreserved a manner, and in the prudence you
have shown in your letters, that were it practicable to bring everyone, or your
father only, into my opinion, I should readily leave all the rest to your discretion,
reserving only to myself the direction or approbation of your future letters; and to
see that you broke off the correspondence as soon as possible. But as it is not, and
as I know your papa would have no patience with you, should it be acknowledged
that you correspond with Mr Lovelace, or that you *have* corresponded with him
since the time he prohibited you so to do, I forbid you continuing such a liberty.
Yet, as the case is difficult, let me ask you, what you yourself can propose? Your
heart, you *say, is free*. You own that you cannot think, as matters are circumstanced,
that a match with a man so obnoxious as he now is to us all is proper to be thought
of. What do you propose to do?—What, Clary, are your own thoughts of the
matter?

Without hesitation (for I saw I was upon a new trial) thus I answered—What I
humbly propose is this: 'That I will write to Mr Lovelace (for I have not answered
his last) that he has nothing to do between my father and me: that I neither *ask* his
advice, nor *need* it: but that since he thinks he has some pretence for interfering,
because of my brother's avowal of the interest of Mr Solmes in malice to him, I
will assure him, without giving him any reason to impute the assurance to be in the
least favourable to himself, that I never will be that man's.' And if, proceeded I,

I may be permitted to give him this assurance; and Mr Solmes, in consequence of it, be discouraged from prosecuting his address; let Mr Lovelace be satisfied or dissatisfied, I will go no farther; nor write another line to him; nor ever see him more, if I can avoid it: and shall have a good excuse for it, without bringing in any of my family.

Ah! my love!—But what shall we do about the *terms* Mr Solmes offers. Those are the inducements with everybody. He has even given hopes to your brother that he will make exchanges of estates, or at least that he will purchase the northern one; for, you know, it must be entirely consistent with the family views that we increase our interest in this county. Your brother, in short, has given in a plan that captivates us all; and a family so rich in all its branches that has its views to honour must be pleased to see a very great probability of being on a footing with the principal in the kingdom.

And for the sake of these views, for the sake of this plan of my brother's, am I, madam, to be given in marriage to a man I never can endure!—Oh my dear mamma, save me, save me, if you can, from this heavy evil!—I had rather be buried alive, indeed I had, than have that man!

She chid me for my vehemence, but was so good as to tell me that she would venture to talk with my uncle Harlowe, and, if he encouraged her (or would engage to second her), with my papa; and I should hear further in the morning.

She went down to tea and kindly undertook to excuse my attendance at supper; and I immediately had recourse to my pen, to give you these particulars.

But is it not a sad thing, I repeat, to be obliged to stand in opposition to the will of such a mamma? Why, as I often say to myself, was such a man as this Solmes fixed upon? The only man in the world, surely, that could offer so much, and deserve so little!

Little indeed does he deserve!—Why, my dear, the man has the most indifferent of characters. Every mouth is opened against him for his sordid ways—A *foolish* man to be so base-minded!—When the difference between the obtaining of a fame for generosity and incurring the censure of being a miser will not, prudently managed, cost fifty pounds a year.

What a name have you got, at a less expense? And what an opportunity had he of obtaining credit at a very small one, succeeding such a wretched creature as Sir Oliver in fortunes so vast?—Yet has he so behaved, that the common phrase is applied to him, *That Sir* Oliver *will never be dead while Mr* Solmes *lives.*

The world, as I have often thought, ill-natured as it is said to be, is generally more just in characters (speaking by what it *feels*) than is usually apprehended; and those who complain most of its censoriousness, perhaps should look *inwardly* for the occasion oftener than they do.

My heart is a little at ease, on the hopes that my mamma will be able to procure favour for me, and a deliverance from this man; and so I have leisure to moralize: but if I had *not*, I should not forbear to intermingle occasionally these sort of remarks, because you command me never to omit them when they occur to my mind. And not to be able to make them, even in a more affecting situation, when one sits down to write, would show one's self more engaged to *self* and one's *own* concerns, than attentive to the wishes of a friend. If it be said, that it is *natural* so to be, what makes that *nature*, on occasions where a friend may be obliged or reminded of a piece of instruction, which, writing down, one's self may be the better for, but a *fault*; which it would set a person above nature to subdue?

Letter 18: MISS CLARISSA HARLOWE TO MISS HOWE

Sat. Mar. 4

WOULD you not have thought that something might have been obtained in my favour, from an offer so reasonable, from an expedient so proper, as I imagine, to put a tolerable end as *from myself* to a correspondence I hardly know how otherwise, with safety to some of my family, to get rid of!—But my brother's plan (which my mamma spoke of, and of which I have in vain endeavoured to procure a copy, with a design of taking it to pieces, and exposing it, as I question not there is room to do), together with my papa's impatience of contradiction, is irresistible.

I have not been in bed all night; nor am I in the least drowsy. Expectation, and hope, and doubt (an uneasy state!) kept me sufficiently wakeful. I stepped down at my usual time, that it might not be known I had not been in bed, and gave directions in the family way.

About eight o'clock Shorey came to me from my mamma, with orders to attend her in her chamber.

My mamma had been weeping, I saw by her eyes; but her aspect seemed to be less tender and less affectionate than the day before; and this struck me with an awe as soon as I entered her presence, which gave a great damp to my spirits.

Sit down, Clary Harlowe; I shall talk to you by and by: and was looking into a drawer among laces and linen, in a way neither busy nor unbusy.

After some time, she asked me coldly, what directions I had given for the day?

I gave her the bill of fare for this day and tomorrow, if, I said, it pleased her to approve of it.

She made a small alteration in it; but with an air so cold and so solemn, as added to the emotions I entered into her presence with.

Mr Harlowe talks of dining out today, I think, at my brother Antony's—

Mr Harlowe!—not my papa!—Have I not then a papa!—thought I?

Sit down when I bid you.

I sat down.

You look very sullen, Clary.

I hope not, madam.

If children would always be children—parents—And there she stopped.

She then went to her toilette and looked in the glass, and gave half a sigh—the other half, as if she would not have sighed could she have helped it, she gently hemmed away.

I don't love to see the girl look so sullen.

Indeed, madam, I am not sullen—And I arose and, turning from her, drew out my handkerchief, for the tears ran down my cheeks. I thought, by the glass before me, I saw the *mother* in her softened eye cast towards me—But her words confirmed not the hoped-for tenderness.

One of the provokingest things in the world is to have people cry for what they can help!

I wish to heaven I could, madam!—and I sobbed again.

Tears of penitence and sobs of perverseness are mighty well suited!—You may go up to your chamber. I shall talk with you by and by.

I curtsied with reverence—

Mock me not with outward gesture of respect. The heart, Clary, is what I want.

Indeed, madam, you have it. It is not so much mine, as my mamma's!

Fine talking!—As somebody says, if words were duty, Clarissa Harlowe would be the dutifullest child breathing.

God bless that somebody!—Be it whom it will, God bless that somebody!—And I curtsied and, pursuant to her last command, was going.

She seemed struck, but *was* to be angry with me.

So turning from me, she spoke with quickness, Whither now, Clary Harlowe?

You commanded me, madam, to go to my chamber.

I see you are very ready to go out of my presence. Is your compliance the effect of sullenness, or obedience?—You are very ready to leave me.

I could hold no longer; but threw myself at her feet: Oh my dearest mamma! Let me know all I am to suffer: let me know what I am to be! I will bear it, if I *can* bear it: But your displeasure I cannot bear!

Leave me, leave me, Clary Harlowe!—No kneeling!—limbs so supple; will so stubborn!—Rise, I tell you.

I cannot rise! I will disobey my mamma, when she bids me leave her without her being reconciled to me! No sullens, my mamma: no perverseness: but, worse than either, this is direct disobedience!—Yet tear not yourself from me! (wrapping my arms about her as I kneeled, she struggling to get from me, my face lifted up to hers, with eyes running over, that spoke not my heart if they were not all humility and reverence). You must not, must not, tear yourself from me! (for still the dear lady struggled, and looked this way and that in a sweet disorder, as if she knew not what to do)—I will neither rise, nor leave you, nor let you go, till you say you are not angry with me.

Oh thou ever-moving child of my heart! (folding her dear arms about my neck, as mine embraced her knees). Why was this task!——But leave me!—You have discomposed me beyond expression!—Leave me, my dear!—I won't be angry with you—if I can help it—if you'll be good.

I arose trembling and, hardly knowing what I did, or how I stood or walked, withdrew to my chamber. My Hannah followed me, as soon as she heard me quit my mamma's presence, and with salts and spring water just kept me from fainting; and that was as much as she could do. It was near two hours before I could so far recover myself as to take up my pen to write to you how unhappily my hopes have ended.

My mamma went down to breakfast. I was not fit to appear; but if I had been better, I suppose I should not have been sent for; my papa's hint, when in my chamber, being to bring me down, if worthy of the name of daughter. That, I doubt, I never shall be in *his* opinion, if he be not brought to change his mind as to this Mr Solmes.

Letter 19: MISS CLARISSA HARLOWE TO MISS HOWE

(In answer to Letter 15)

Sat. March 4, 12 o'clock

HANNAH has just now brought me from the usual place your favour of yesterday. The contents of it have made me very thoughtful, and you will have an answer in my gravest style—*I* to have that Mr Solmes!—No indeed!—I will sooner——But I will write first to other parts of your letter that are less concerning, that I may touch upon this part with more patience.

As to what you mention of my sister's value for Mr Lovelace, I am not very much surprised at it. She takes such *officious* pains, and it is so much her subject to have it thought that she never *did*, and never *could* like him, that she gives but too much room to suspect her. Then she never tells the story of their parting, and of her refusal of him, but her colour rises, she looks with disdain upon me, and mingles anger with the airs she gives herself—both anger and airs at least demonstrating that she refused a man whom she thought worth accepting; where else is the reason either for anger or boast?—Poor Bella! She is to be pitied!—She cannot either like or dislike with temper!—Would to heaven she had been mistress of all her wishes!—Would to heaven she had!—

As to the article of giving up to my papa's control the estate bequeathed me, my motives at the time, as you acknowledge, were not blameable. Your advice to me on the subject was grounded, as I remember, on your good opinion of me; believing that I should not make a bad use of the power willed me. Neither you nor I, my dear, although you now assume the air of a diviner (pardon me), could have believed that would have happened which has happened, as to my *father's* part particularly. You were indeed jealous of my brother's views against me, or rather of his predominant love of self; but I did not think so hardly of my brother and sister as you always did. You never loved them, and ill-will has eyes always open to the faulty side; as good-will or love is blind even to real imperfections. I will briefly recollect my motives.

I found jealousies and uneasiness rising in every breast, where all before was unity and love. The honoured testator was reflected upon: a second childhood was attributed to him; and I was censured as having taken advantage of it. All young creatures, thought I, more or less covet independency, but those who wish most for it are seldom the fittest to be trusted either with the government of themselves, or with power over others. This is certainly a very high and unusual bequest to so young a creature. We should not aim at *all* we have power to do. To take all that good nature, or indulgence, or good opinion confers, shows a want of moderation and a graspingness that is unworthy of that indulgence, and are bad indications of the *use* that may be made of the power bequeathed. It is true, thought I, that I have formed agreeable schemes of making others as happy as myself by the proper discharge of the stewardship entrusted to me (are not all estates stewardships, my dear?). But let me examine myself: is not vanity or secret love of praise a principal motive with me at the bottom?—Ought I not to suspect my own heart? If I set up for myself, puffed up with everyone's good opinion, may I not be *left* to myself?—Everyone's eyes are upon the conduct, upon the visits, upon the visit-*ors* of a young creature of our sex made independent; and are not such, moreover, the subjects of the attempts of the *worst* of the other?—And then, left to myself, should I take a wrong step though with ever so good an intention, how many should I have to triumph over me, how few to pity?—the more of the one, and the fewer of the other, for having aimed at excelling.

These were some of my reflections at the time: and I have no doubt but that in the same situation I should do the very same thing; and that upon the maturest deliberation. Who can command or foresee events? To act up to our best judgements at the time is all we can do. If I have erred, 'tis to worldly wisdom only that I have erred. If we suffer by an act of duty, or even by an act of generosity, is it not pleasurable on reflection that the fault is in others, rather than in ourselves?— I had rather, a vast deal, have reason to think others unkind, than that they should have any to think me undutiful. And so, my dear, I am sure had you.

And now for the *most* concerning part of your letter.

You think I must of necessity be Mr Solmes's wife, as matters are circumstanced. I will not be very rash, my dear, in protesting to the contrary. But I think it never, never can, nor *ought* to be!—My temper, I know, is depended upon; but I have heretofore said that I have something in me of my father's family, as well as of my mother's.[a] And have I any encouragement to follow too implicitly the example which my mamma sets of meekness and resignedness to the wills of others?—Is she not for ever obliged to be, as she was pleased to hint to me, of the *forbearing* side? In my mamma's case, your observation is verified, that those who will bear much shall have much to bear—What is it, as she says, that *she* has not sacrificed to peace?—Yet, has *she* by her sacrifices always found the peace she has deserved to find? Indeed No!—I am afraid the very contrary. And often and often have I had reason on her account, to reflect that we poor mortals, by our *over*-solicitude to preserve undisturbed the qualities we are constitutionally fond of, frequently lose the benefits we propose to ourselves from them; since the designing and encroaching, finding out what we most fear to forfeit, direct their batteries against these our weaker places and, making an artillery, if I may so phrase it, of our hopes and fears, play it upon us at their pleasure.

Steadiness of mind (a quality which the ill-bred and censorious deny to any of our sex), when one is convinced of being in the right (otherwise it is not steadiness, but obstinacy), and in *material* cases, is a quality, my good Dr Lewin was wont to say, that brings great credit to the possessor of it; at the same time that it usually, when *tried* and *known*, raises *such* above the attempts of the meanly machinating. He used therefore to inculcate upon me this steadiness upon laudable convictions. And why may I not think that I am now put upon an exercise of it?—I have said that I never can be, that I never ought to be, Mrs Solmes—I repeat, that I *ought* not; for surely, my dear, I should not give up to my brother's ambition the happiness of my future life—Surely I ought not to be the instrument to deprive Mr Solmes's relations of their natural rights and reversionary prospects, for the sake of further aggrandizing a family (although *that* I am of) which already lives in great affluence and splendour; and who might be as justly dissatisfied were what some of them aim at to be obtained, that they were not princes, as now they are that they are not peers (for when ever was an ambitious mind, as you observe in the case of avarice,[b] satisfied by acquisition?). The less, surely, ought I to give into

a   See Letter 9, p. 65.
b   See Letter 10, p. 67.

these grasping views of my brother, as I myself heartily despise the end aimed at; as I wish not either to change my state, or better my fortunes; and as I am fully persuaded that happiness and riches are *two* things, and very seldom meet together.

Yet I dread, I exceedingly dread, the conflicts I know I must encounter with. It is possible that I may be more unhappy from the due observation of the good doctor's general precept, than were I to yield the point; since what I call *steadiness* is attributed to stubbornness, to obstinacy, to prepossession, by those who have a right to put what interpretation they please upon my conduct.

So, my dear, were we perfect, which no one can be, we could not be happy in this life, unless those with whom we have to deal (those, more especially, who have any control upon us) were governed by the same principles. What have we then to do but, as I have hinted above, to choose right, and pursue it steadily, and leave the issue to Providence?

This, if you approve of my motives (and if you don't, pray inform me), must be my aim in the present case.

But what then can I plead for a palliation to *myself* of my mamma's sufferings on *my* account? Perhaps this consideration will carry some force with it—that *her* difficulties cannot last long; only till this great struggle shall be one way or other determined. Whereas *my* unhappiness, if I comply, will (from an aversion not to be overcome) be for life. To which let me add that, as I have reason to think that the present measures are not entered upon with her own natural liking, she will have the less pain should they want the success which I think in my heart they ought to want.

I have run a great length in a very little time. The subject touched me to the quick. My reflections upon it will give you reason to expect from me a perhaps *too* steady behaviour in a new conference, which I find I must have with my mamma. My father and brother, as she was pleased to tell me, dine at my uncle Antony's, on purpose, as I have reason to believe, to give an opportunity for it.

Hannah informs me that she heard my papa high and angry with my mamma at taking leave of her, I suppose for being too favourable to me, for Hannah heard her say, as in tears, 'Indeed, Mr Harlowe, you greatly distress me!—The poor girl does not deserve—' Hannah heard no more, but that he said he would break somebody's heart—Mine, I suppose—Not my mother's, I hope.

As only my sister dines with my mamma, I thought I should have been commanded down; but she sent me up a plate from her table. I wrote on. I could not touch a morsel. I ordered Hannah, however, to eat of it, that I might not be thought sullen.

I will see, before I conclude this, whether anything offers from *either* of my private correspondencies, that will make it proper to add to it; and will take a turn in the wood-yard and garden for that purpose.

I am stopped. Hannah shall deposit this. She was ordered by my mamma, who asked where I was, to tell me that she would come up and talk with me in my own closet—She is coming! Adieu, my dear.

Letter 20: MISS CLARISSA HARLOWE TO MISS HOWE

Sat. p.m.

THE expected conference is over; but my difficulties are increased. This, as my mamma was pleased to tell me, being the last *persuasory* effort that will be attempted, I will be as particular in the account of it as my head and my heart will allow me to be.

I have made, said she, as she entered my room, a short as well as early dinner, on purpose to confer with you. And I do assure you, that it will be the last conference I shall either be permitted or *inclined* to hold with you on the subject, if you should prove as refractory as some, whom I hope you'll disappoint, imagine you will; and thereby demonstrate that I have not the weight with you that my indulgence to you deserves.

Your papa both dines and sups at your uncle's, on purpose to give us this opportunity; and as I shall make my report (which I have promised to do very faithfully) on his return, he will take his measures with you.

I was offering to speak—Hear, Clarissa, what I have to tell you, said she, before you speak, unless what you have to say will signify to me your compliance—Say— *will* it?—If it *will*, you may speak.

I was silent.

She looked with concern and anger upon me—No compliance, I find!—Such a dutiful young creature hitherto!—Will you not, can you not, speak as I would have you speak?—Then (rejecting me, as it were, with her hand), then, continue silent—*I*, no more than your *father*, will bear your *avowed* contradiction!—

She paused, with a look of expectation, as if she waited for my consenting answer.

I was still silent, looking down, the tears in my eyes.

Oh thou determined girl!—But say; speak out; are you resolved to stand in opposition to us all in a point our hearts are set upon?

May I, madam, be permitted to expostulate?

To what purpose expostulate with *me*, Clarissa? Your *father* is determined. Have I not told you that there is no receding; that the honour, as well as the benefit, of the family is concerned? Be ingenuous. You used to be so, even against yourself. Who at the long run *must* submit—*all* of us to *you*; or *you* to *all* of us?—If you intend to yield at *last* if you find you cannot conquer, yield *now* and with a grace— for yield you must, or be none of our child.

I wept. I knew not what to say; or rather how to express what I had to say.

Take notice that there are flaws in your grandfather's will; not a shilling of that estate will be yours, if you do not yield. Your grandfather left it to you as a reward of your duty to *him* and to *us*—You will *justly* forfeit it, if—

Permit me, good madam, to say that, if it were *unjustly* bequeathed me, I ought not to wish to have it. But I hope Mr Solmes will be apprised of these flaws.

This was very pertly said, she was pleased to tell me; but bid me reflect, that the forfeiture of that estate, through my opposition, would be attended with the total loss of my papa's favour; and then how destitute I must be; how unable to support myself; and how many benevolent designs and good actions must I give up!

I must accommodate myself, I said, in the latter case, to my circumstances.

Much only was *required* where *much* was *given*. It became me to be thankful for what I had had; and I had reason to bless her and my good Mrs Norton, for bringing me up to be satisfied with little—with much less, I would venture to say, than my papa's indulgence annually conferred upon me—And then I thought of the old Roman and his lentils.[1]

What perverseness! said my mamma—But if you depend upon the favour of either or both your uncles, vain will be that dependence. *They* will give you up, I do assure you, if your *papa* does, and absolutely renounce you.

I told her, I was sorry that I had had so little merit as to have made no deeper impressions of favour for me in their hearts; but that I would love and honour them as long as I lived.

All this, she was pleased to say, made my prepossession in a certain man's favour the more evident. Indeed my brother and sister could not go anywhither, but they heard of these prepossessions.

It was a great grief to me, I said, to be made the subject of the public talk; but I hoped she would have the goodness to excuse me for observing that the authors of my disgrace within doors, the talkers of my prepossession without, and the reporters of it from abroad, were originally the same persons.

She severely chid me for this.

I received her rebukes in silence.

You are sullen, Clarissa! I see you are sullen!—And she walked about the room in anger. Then turning to me—You can *bear* the imputation, I see!—You have no concern to clear yourself of it. I was afraid of telling you all I was enjoined to tell you in case you were to be unpersuadeable—But I find that I had a greater opinion of your delicacy and gentleness than I needed to have—It cannot discompose so steady, so inflexible a young creature, to be told that the settlements are actually drawn; and that you will be called down, in a very few days, to hear them read, and to sign them; for it is impossible, if your heart be free, that you can make the least objection to them, except that they are so much in your favour and in all our favour be one.

I was speechless, absolutely speechless; although my heart was ready to burst, yet could I neither weep nor speak.

She was sorry, she said, for my averseness to this match (*match* she was pleased to call it!), but there was no help. The honour and interest of the family, as my aunt had told me, and as *she* had told me, were concerned; and I must comply.

I was still speechless.

She folded the *warm statue*, as she was pleased to call me, in her arms; and entreated me, for God's sake, and for her sake, to comply.

Speech and tears were lent me at the same time. You have given me life, madam, said I, clasping my uplifted hands together and falling on one knee; a happy one, till now, has *your* goodness, and my *papa*'s, made it! Oh do not, do not, make all the remainder of it miserable!

Your papa, replied she, is resolved he will not see you till he sees you as obedient a child as you used to be. You have never been put to a test till now, that deserved to be called a test. This *is*, this *must* be, my last effort with you. Give me hope, my dear child; my peace is concerned. I will compound with you but for *hope*; and yet your father will not be satisfied without an implicit, and even a cheerful obedience—Give me but hope, my child!

To give you hope, my dearest, my most indulgent mamma, is to give you everything. Can I be honest if I give a hope that I cannot confirm?

She was very angry. She again called me perverse: she upbraided me with regarding only my own inclinations, and respecting not either her peace of mind, or my own duty. 'It was a grating thing, she said, for the parents of a child, who delighted in her in all the time of her helpless infancy, and throughout every stage of her childhood, and in every part of her education to womanhood, because of the promises she gave of proving the most grateful and dutiful of children; to find, that just when the time arrived which should crown all their wishes, she should stand in the way of her own happiness, and her parents comfort, and, refusing an excellent offer and noble settlements, give suspicions to her anxious friends that she would become the property of a vile rake and libertine, who (be the occasion what it *would*) defied her family, and had actually imbrued his hands in her brother's blood.'

She added, 'That she had a very hard time of it between my father and me; that seeing my dislike, she had more than once pleaded for me; but all to no purpose. She was only treated as a too fond mother, who, from motives of a blameable indulgence, would encourage a child to stand in opposition to a father's will: she was charged, she said, with dividing the family into two parts; she and her youngest daughter standing against her husband, his two brothers, her son, her eldest daughter and her sister Hervey. She had been told that she must be convinced of the fitness as well as advantage to the whole (my brother and Mr Lovelace out of the question) of carrying the contract with Mr Solmes, on which so *many* contracts depended, into execution.'

She repeated, 'That my father's heart was in it: that he had declared, he had rather have no daughter in me, than one he could not dispose of for her own good: especially as I had owned, that my *heart was free*; and as the general good of his whole family was to be promoted by my obedience: that he had pleaded, that his frequent gouty paroxysms (every fit more threatening than the former) gave him no extraordinary prospects either of worldly happiness, or of long days: that he hoped, that I, who had been supposed to have contributed to the lengthening of his *father*'s life, would not, by my disobedience, shorten *his*.'

This was a most affecting plea, my dear; I wept in silence upon it; I could not speak to it. And my mamma proceeded: 'What therefore could be *his* motives, she asked, in the earnest desire he had to see this treaty perfected, but the welfare and aggrandizement of his family; which already having fortunes to become the highest condition, could not but aspire to greater distinctions: that, however slight such views as these might appear to me, I knew that they were not slight ones to any other of the family: and my papa would be his own judge of what was, and what was not, likely to promote the good of his children: that my abstractedness (affectation of abstractedness some called it) savoured of greater particularity than what they aimed to carry: that modesty and humility would therefore oblige me rather to mistrust myself of *peculiarity*, than censure views, which all the world pursued as opportunity offered.'

I was still silent; and she proceeded—'That it was owing to the good opinion which my papa had of me, and of my prudence, duty, and gratitude, that he had engaged for my compliance, in my absence (before I returned from Miss Howe);

and had built and finished contracts upon it, that could not be made void, or cancelled.'

But why then, thought I, did they receive me, on my return from Miss Howe, with so much intimidating solemnity?—To be sure, this argument, as well as the rest, was obtruded upon my mamma.

She went on, 'That my papa had declared, that my unexpected opposition (*unexpected*, she was pleased to call it), and Mr Lovelace's continued menaces and insults, more and more convinced him that a short day was necessary in order to put an end to all that man's hopes, and to his own apprehensions resulting from the disobedience of a child so favoured: that he had therefore actually ordered patterns of the richest silks to be sent for from London—'

I started!—I was out of breath—I gasped, at this frightful precipitance. I was going to open with warmth against it. I knew whose the *happy* expedient must be. Female minds, I once heard my brother say, that could but be brought to *balance* on the change of their state, might easily be *determined* by the glare and splendour of the nuptial preparations and the pride of becoming the mistress of a family— But she was pleased to hurry on, that I might not have time to express my disgusts at such a communication—to this effect:

'That neither for my sake, nor his own, could my father labour under a suspense so affecting to his repose: that he had even thought fit to acquaint *her*, on her pleading for me, that it became her, as she valued her own peace (how harsh to such a wife!), and as she wished that he should not suspect that she secretly favoured the address of a vile rake (a character which all the sex, he was pleased to say, virtuous and vicious, were but too fond of!), to exert her authority over me; and that this she might the less scrupulously do, as I had owned (the old string!) *that my heart was free.*'

Unworthy reflection this of our sex's valuing a libertine, in my mamma's case, surely! who made choice of my papa in preference to several suitors of equal fortune, because they were of inferior reputation for morals!

She added, 'That my papa had left her at going out, with this command, that if she found that she had not the proper influence over me, she should directly separate herself from me; and leave me, singly, to take the consequence of my double disobedience.'

She therefore entreated me in the most earnest and condescending manner, 'To signify to my papa, on his return, my ready obedience; and this, she was pleased to say, as well for *her* sake, as *mine.*'

Affected by my mamma's goodness to me, and by that part of her argument which related to her own peace and to the suspicions they had of her secretly inclining to prefer the man so hated by *them*, to the man so much *my* aversion, I could not but wish it were possible for me to obey. I therefore paused, hesitated, considered, and was silent for a considerable space. I could see that my mamma hoped that the result of this hesitation would be favourable to her arguments. But then, recollecting that all was owing to the instigations of a brother and sister, wholly actuated by selfish and envious views; that I had not deserved the treatment I had of late met with; that my disgrace was *already* become the public talk; that my aversion to their man was too generally known to make my compliance either creditable to myself or to them, as it would demonstrate less of duty than of a slavish, and even of a sordid mind, seeking to preserve its wordly fortunes by the sacrifice of its future happiness; that it would give my brother and sister a triumph over me, and over Mr Lovelace, which they would not fail to glory in; and which, although it concerned me but little to matter on *his* account, yet might be attended with fatal mischiefs—And then Mr Solmes's disagreeable person, his still more disagreeable manners; his low understanding—understanding! the glory of a man! so little to be dispensed with in the head and director of a family, in order to preserve to him that respect which a good wife (and that for the justification of her own choice) should pay him herself, and wish everybody to pay him—And as Mr Solmes's *inferiority* in this respectable faculty of the human mind (I must be allowed to say this to you, and no great self-assumption neither) would proclaim to all future, as well as present observers, what must have been my mean inducement—All these reflections, which are ever present with me, crowding upon my remembrance: I would, madam, said I, folding my hands with an earnestness that my whole heart was engaged in, bear the cruellest tortures, bear loss of limb, and even of life, to give *you* peace. But this man, every moment I would at your command think of him with favour, is the more my aversion. You cannot, indeed you cannot, think, how my whole soul resists him!—And to talk of contracts concluded upon; of patterns; of a short day!—save me, save me, oh my dearest mamma, save your child, from this heavy, from this insupportable evil!—

Never was there a countenance that expressed so significantly, as my mamma's, an anguish, which she struggled to hide under an anger she was compelled to assume—till the latter overcoming the former, she turned from me with an uplifted eye, and stamping—*strange perverseness!* were the only words I heard of a sentence that she angrily pronounced; and was going. I then, half-frantically I believe, laid hold of her gown—Have patience with me, dearest madam! said I—Do not *you* renounce me totally!—If you *must* separate yourself from your child, let it not be with *absolute* reprobation on *your own* part!—My uncles may be hard-hearted— my papa may be immovable—I may suffer from my brother's ambition and from my sister's envy!—but let me not lose my mamma's love; at least, her pity.

She turned to me with benigner rays—You *have* my love! You *have* my *pity!* But, oh my dearest girl—I have not *yours*.

Indeed, indeed, madam, you have; and all my reverence, all my gratitude, you have!—But in this *one* point—cannot I be this *once* obliged?—will no *expedient* be accepted? Have I not made a very fair proposal as to the man so hated?

I wish, for both our sakes, my dear unpersuadable girl, that the decision of this point lay with me. But why, when you know it don't, should you thus perplex and urge me?—To renounce Mr Lovelace is now but *half* what is aimed at. Nor will anybody else believe you in earnest in the offer, if *I* would. While you remain single, Mr Lovelace will have hopes—and you, in the opinion of others, inclinations.

Permit me, dearest madam, to say, that *your* goodness to me, *your* patience, *your* peace, weigh more with me, than all the rest put together: for although I am to be treated by my brother and, through his instigations, by my papa, as a slave in this point, and not as a daughter, yet my mind is not that of a slave. You have not brought me up to be mean.

So, Clary, you are already at defiance with your papa! I have had too much cause before to *apprehend* as much—What will this come to?—*I*, and then my dear mamma sighed—*I* am forced to put up with many humours—

That you are, my ever-honoured mamma, is my grief. And can it be thought that this very consideration, and the apprehension of what may result from a much *worse*-tempered man (a man, who has not half the sense of my papa) has not made an impression upon me to the disadvantage of the married life? Yet 'tis something of an alleviation, if one must bear *undue* control, to bear it from a man of sense. My papa, I have heard you say, madam, was for years a very good-humoured gentleman—Unobjectible in person and manners. But the man proposed to me—

Forbear reflecting upon your papa (did I, my dear, in what I have repeated, and I think they are the very words, reflect upon my papa?). It is not possible, I must say again and again, were all men *equally* indifferent to you, that you should be thus sturdy in your will—I am tired out with your obstinacy—The most unper-suade-able girl!—You forget that I must separate myself from you, if you will not comply. You do not remember that your papa will take you up, where I leave you—Once more, however, I will put it to you—Are you determined to brave your papa's displeasure?—Are you determined to defy your uncles?—Will you choose to break with us all, rather than encourage Mr Solmes?—Rather than give me hope?

Cruel alternative!—But is not my sincerity, is not the integrity of my heart, concerned in my answer? May not my everlasting happiness be the sacrifice? Will not the least shadow of the *hope* you just now demanded from me be driven into absolute and sudden *certainty*? Is it not sought to ensnare, to entangle me in my own desire of obeying, if I could give answers that might be construed into *hope?*—Forgive me, madam: bear with your child's boldness in such a cause as this!—Settlements drawn!—patterns sent for!—an early day!—dear, dear madam, how can I give hope, and not intend to be this man's?

Ah, girl, never say your *heart is free!* You deceive yourself if you think it is.

Thus to be driven (and I wrung my hands through impatience) by the instigations of a designing, an ambitious brother, and by a sister, that—

How often, Clary, must I forbid your unsisterly reflections?—Does not your father, do not your uncles, does not everybody, patronize Mr Solmes?—And let me tell you, ungrateful girl, and unmovable as ungrateful, let me repeatedly tell you that it is evident to me, that nothing but a love unworthy of your prudence can make a creature late so dutiful, so sturdy. You may guess what your father's first question on his return will be. He must know that I can do nothing with you. I have done my part. Seek *me*, if your mind change before he comes back. You have yet a little more time, as he stays supper: I will no more seek *you*, nor *to* you—and away she flung.

What could I do but weep?

I am extremely affected on my mamma's account—more, I must needs say, than on my own—And indeed, all things considered, and especially that the measure she is engaged in is (as I dare say it is) against her own judgement, she *deserves* more compassion than myself. Excellent woman! What pity, that meekness and condescension should not be attended with the due rewards of those charming graces!—Yet had she not let violent spirits, as I have elsewhere observed with no small regret, have found their power over hers, it could not have been thus.

But here, run away with by my pen, I suffer my dear mamma to be angry with me on her own account. She hinted to me, indeed, that I must seek *her*, if my mind *changed*; which is a condition that amounts to a prohibition—But, as she left me in displeasure, will it not have a very obstinate appearance, and look like a kind of renunciation of her mediation in my favour, if I go not down to supplicate her pity and her kind report, before my papa comes back?—

I will attend her. I had rather all the world should be angry with me, than my mamma!

Meantime, to clear my hands from papers of such a nature, Hannah shall deposit this. If two or three letters reach you together, they will but express, from one period to another, the anxieties and difficulties which the mind of your unhappy, but ever affectionate friend labours under.

Cl. H.

Letter 21: MISS CLARISSA HARLOWE TO MISS HOWE

Sat. night

I HAVE been down. I *am* to be unlucky in all I do, I think, be my intention ever so good. I have made matters worse instead of better; as I shall now tell you.

I found my mamma and sister together in my sister's parlour. My mamma, I fear, by the glow in her fine face (and as the browner, sullener glow in my sister's confirmed) had been expressing herself with warmth against her *unhappier* child; perhaps giving such an account of what had passed, as should clear herself and convince Bella, and through *her*, my brother and uncles, of the sincere pains she had taken with me!—

I entered like a dejected criminal, I believe—and besought the favour of a private audience. My mamma's return, both looks and words, gave but too much reason for my surmise.

You have, said she (looking at me with a sternness that never sits well on her sweet features), rather a *requesting* than a *conceding* countenance, Clarissa Harlowe. If I am mistaken, tell me so; and I will withdraw with you wherever you will—Yet, if so or not so, you may say what you have to say before your sister.

My mamma, I thought, might have withdrawn with me, as she knows that I have not a friend in my sister.

I came down, I said, to beg of her to forgive me for anything she might have taken amiss in what had passed above respecting herself, and to use her interest to soften my papa's displeasure when she made the report she was to make to him.

Such aggravating looks, such lifting-up of hands and eyes, such a furrowed forehead in my sister!—

My mamma was angry enough without all that; and asked me, to what purpose I came down if I were still so untractable?

She had hardly spoke the words, when Shorey came in to tell her that Mr Solmes was in the hall, and desired admittance.

Ugly creature! What, at the close of day, quite dark, brought him hither? But, on second thoughts, I believe it was contrived that he should be here at supper, to know the result of the conference between my mamma and me; and that my papa on his return might find us together.

I was hurrying away; but my mamma commanded me, since I had come down only, as she said, to mock her, not to stir; and at the same time see if I could behave so to him, as might encourage her to make the report to my papa which I had so earnestly besought her to make.

My sister triumphed. I was vexed to be so caught, and to have such an angry and cutting rebuke given me, with an aspect more like the taunting sister than the indulgent mother, if I may presume to say so—for my mamma herself seemed to enjoy the surprise upon me.

The man stalked in. His usual walk is by pauses, as if (from the same vacuity of thought which made Dryden's clown whistle[1]) he was telling his steps: and first paid his clumsy respects to my mamma, then to my sister; next to me, as if I were already his wife and therefore to be last in his notice; and sitting down by me, told us in general what weather it was. Very cold he made it; but I was warm enough. Then addressing himself to me: And how do *you* find it, miss, was his question; and would have took my hand.

I withdrew it, I believe with disdain enough: my mamma frowned; my sister bit her lip.

I could not contain myself: I never was so bold in my life, for I went on with my plea, as if Mr Solmes had not been there.

My mamma coloured and looked at him, looked at my sister, and looked at me. My sister's eyes were opener and bigger than ever I saw them before.

The man understood me. He hemmed, and removed from one chair to another.

I went on, supplicating for my mamma's favourable report: nothing but invincible dislike—

What would the girl be at? Why, Clary!—Is this a subject!—is this!—is this!—is this a time—and again she looked upon Mr Solmes.

I am sorry, on reflection, that I put my mamma into so much confusion—To be sure it was very saucy in me.

I begged pardon. But my papa, I said, would return. I should have no other opportunity. I thought it was requisite, since I was not permitted to withdraw, that Mr Solmes's presence should not deprive me of an opportunity of such importance for me to embrace; and at the same time, if he still visited on my account (looking at him), to show that it could not possibly be to any purpose.

Is the girl mad? said my mamma, interrupting me.

My sister, with the affectation of a whisper to my mamma—This is—this is *spite*, madam (very *spitefully* she spoke the word), because you commanded her to stay.

I only looked at her, and turning to my mamma, Permit me, madam, said I, to repeat my request. I have no brother, no sister! If I lose my mamma's favour, I am lost for ever!

Mr Solmes removed to his first seat, and fell to gnawing the head of his hazel, a carved head, almost as ugly as his own. I did not think the man was so *sensible*.

My sister rose with a face all over scarlet, and stepping to the table where lay a fan, she took it up and, although Mr Solmes had observed that the weather was cold, fanned herself very violently.

My mamma came to me, and angrily taking my hand led me out of that parlour into my own, which, you know, is next to it—Is not this behaviour very bold, very provoking, think you, Clary?

I beg your pardon, madam, if it has that appearance to you. But indeed, my dear mamma, there seem to be snares laying for me. Too well I know my brother's drift.

With a good word he shall have my consent for all he wishes to worm me out of—
Neither he, nor my sister, shall need to take half this pains—

My mamma was about to leave me in high displeasure.

I besought her to stay. One favour, but one favour, dearest madam, said I, give
me leave to beg of you—

What would the girl?

I see how everything is working about—I never, never can think of Mr Solmes.
My papa will be in tumults, when he is told that I cannot. They will judge of the
tenderness of your heart to a poor child who seems devoted by everyone else, from
the willingness you have already shown to hearken to my prayers. There will be
endeavours used to confine me, and keep me out of your presence, and out of the
presence of everyone who used to love me—(this, my dear, is threatened)—If this
be effected; if it be put out of my power to plead my own cause, and to appeal to
you and to my uncle Harlowe, of whom only I have hope—then will every ear be
opened against me; and every tale encouraged—It is, therefore, my humble request
that, added to the disgraceful prohibitions I now suffer under, you will not, if you
can help it, give way to my being denied your ear.

Your listening Hannah has given you this intelligence, as she does many others.

My Hannah, madam, listens not!—My Hannah—

No more in her behalf—She is known to make mischief—She is known—But no
more of that busy intermeddler—'Tis true, your father threatened to confine you
to your chamber, if you complied not, in order the more assuredly to deprive you
of the opportunity of corresponding with those who harden your heart against his
will. He bid me tell you so, when he went out, if I found you refractory. But I was
loath to deliver so harsh a declaration, being still in hope that you would come
down to us in a compliant temper. Hannah has overheard this, I suppose, and has
told you of it; as also, that he declared he would break your heart rather than you
should break his. And I now assure you, that you will be confined, and prohibited
making teasing appeals to any of us: and we shall see who is to submit, you, or
everybody *to* you!

I offered to clear Hannah, and to lay the latter part of the intelligence to my
sister's echo, Betty Barnes, who had boasted of it to another servant: but I was
again bid to be silent on that head. I should soon find, she was pleased to say, that
others could be as determined as I was obstinate; and, once for all, would add that
since she saw that I built upon her indulgence, and mattered not involving her in
contentions with my father, and his brothers and her other children, she would
now assure me that she was as much determined *against* Mr Lovelace, and *for* Mr
Solmes and the family-schemes, as anybody; and would not refuse her consent to
any measures that should be thought necessary to reduce a stubborn child to her
duty.

I was ready to sink. She was so good as to lend me her arm to support me.

And this is all I have to hope for from my mamma?

It is. But, Clary, this one further opportunity I give you—Go in again to Mr
Solmes, and behave discreetly to him; and let your papa find you together, upon
civil terms at least.

My feet moved (of themselves, I think) farther from the parlour where he was,
and towards the stairs; and there I stopped and paused.

If, proceeded she, you are determined to stand in defiance of us all—then indeed may you go up to your chamber (as you are ready to do)—and God help you!

God help me indeed! for I cannot give hope of what I cannot intend—But let me have your prayers, my dear mamma!—Those shall have mine, who have brought me into all this distress!

I was moving to go up—

And *will* you go up, Clary?

I turned my face to her. My officious tears would needs plead for me; I could not just then speak; and stood still.

Good girl, distress me not thus!—Dear, good girl, do not thus distress me!—holding out her hand, but standing still likewise—

What can I do, madam?—What *can* I do?—

Go in again, my child—Go in again, my *dear* child!—repeated she; and let your papa find you together!—

What, madam, to give *him* hope?—To give hope to Mr Solmes?

Obstinate, perverse, undutiful Clarissa Harlowe! with a rejecting hand and angry aspect; then take your own way, and go up!—But stir not down again, I charge you, without leave, or till your papa's pleasure be known concerning you.

She flung from me with high indignation: and I went up with a very heavy heart, and feet as slow as my heart was heavy.

My father is come home, and my brother with him. Late as it is, they are all shut together. Not a door opens; not a soul stirs. Hannah, as she moves up and down, is shunned as a person infected.

The angry assembly is broke up. My two uncles and my aunt Hervey are sent for, it seems, to be here in the morning to breakfast. I shall then, I suppose, know my doom. 'Tis past eleven, and I am ordered not to go to bed.

Twelve o'clock

This moment the keys of everything are taken from me. It was proposed to send for me down; but my papa said he could not bear to look upon me—Strange alteration in a few weeks! Shorey was the messenger. The tears stood in her eyes when she delivered her message.

You, my dear, are happy!—May you always be so!—And then I can never be wholly miserable. Adieu, my beloved friend!

CL. HARLOWE

Letter 22: MISS CLARISSA HARLOWE TO MISS HOWE

Sunday morning, March 5

HANNAH has just brought me, from the private place in the garden-wall, a letter from Mr Lovelace, deposited last night, signed also by Lord M.

He tells me in it, 'That Mr Solmes makes it his boast that he is to be married in a few days to one of the shyest women in England; that my brother explains his meaning to be me, assuring everyone that his youngest sister is very soon to be Mr

Solmes's wife. He tells me of the patterns bespoke, which my mamma mentioned to me.'

Not one thing escapes him that is done or said in this house!

'My sister, he says, reports the same things; and that with such particular aggravations of insult upon *him*, that he cannot but be extremely piqued, as well at the manner, as from the occasion; and expresses himself with great violence upon it.

'He knows not what my relations' inducements can be, to prefer such a man as Solmes to him. If advantageous settlements be the motive, Solmes shall not offer what he will refuse to comply with.

'As to his estate or family, the first cannot be excepted against; and for the second, he will not disgrace himself by a comparison so odious. He appeals to Lord M. for the regularity of his life and manners, ever since he has made his addresses to me, or had hope of my favour.'

I suppose he would have his Lordship's signing to this letter to be taken as a voucher for him.

'He desires my leave, in company with my Lord, in a pacific manner to attend my father or uncles, in order to make proposals that must be accepted, if they will but see him and hear what they are; and tells me that he will submit to any measures that I shall prescribe, in order to bring about a reconciliation.'

He presumes to be very earnest with me 'to give him a private meeting some night in my father's garden, attended by whom I please.'

Really, my dear, were you to see his letter, you would think I had given him great encouragement and were in direct treaty with him; or that he were sure that my friends would drive me into a foreign protection; for he has the boldness to offer, in my Lord's name, an asylum to me should I be tyrannically treated in Solmes's behalf.

I suppose it is the way of this sex to endeavour to entangle the thoughtless of ours by bold supposals and offers, in hopes that we shall be too complaisant or bashful to quarrel with them; and, if not checked, to reckon upon our silence as assents voluntarily given, or concessions made in their favour.

There are other particulars in this letter which I ought to mention to you; but I will take an opportunity to send you the letter itself, or a copy of it.

For my own part, I am very uneasy to think how I have been *drawn* on one hand, and *driven* on the other, into a clandestine, in short, into a mere lover-like correspondence, which my heart condemns.

It is easy to see that if I do not break it off, Mr Lovelace's advantages by reason of my unhappy situation will every day increase, and I shall be more and more entangled; yet if I do put an end to it, without making it a condition of being freed from Mr Solmes's address——May I, my dear—is it best to continue it a little longer, in hopes, by giving him up, to extricate myself out of the other difficulty?— Whose advice can I now ask but yours?

All my relations are met. They are at breakfast together. Solmes is expected. I am excessively uneasy. I must lay down my pen.

THEY are all going to church together. Grievously disordered they appear to be, as Hannah tells me. She believes something is resolved upon.

Sunday noon

WHAT a cruel thing is suspense!—I will ask leave to go to church this afternoon.
I expect to be denied; but if I do not ask, they may allege that my not going is
owing to myself.

I desired to speak with Shorey. Shorey came: I directed her to carry my request
to my mamma, for permission to go to church this afternoon. What think you was
the return? Tell her that she must direct herself to her brother for any favour she
has to ask—So, my dear, I am to be delivered up to my brother!——

I was resolved, however, to ask of *him* this favour. Accordingly, when they sent
me up my solitary dinner, I gave the messenger a billet, in which I made it my
humble request to my papa, through him, to be permitted to go to church this
afternoon.

This was the contemptuous answer: tell her that her request will be taken into
consideration *tomorrow*—My request to go to church *today* to be taken into
consideration *tomorrow!*—

Patience will be the fittest return I can make to such an insult. But this method
will not do, indeed it will not, with your Clarissa Harlowe. And yet it is but the
beginning, I suppose, of what I am to expect from my brother, now I am delivered
up to him.

ON recollection, I thought it best to renew my request. I did. The following is
a copy of what I wrote, and what follows, that of the answer sent me.

[*Letter* 22.1: *Clarissa Harlowe to James Harlowe, Jun.*]

SIR,

I KNOW not what to make of the answer brought to my request of being permitted
to go to church this afternoon. If you designed to show your pleasantry by it, I
hope that will continue; and then my request will be granted. You know that I
never absented myself, when well, and at home, till the two last Sundays, when I
was *advised* not to go. My present situation is such that I never more wanted the
benefit of the public prayers. I will solemnly engage only to go thither and back
again. I hope it cannot be thought that I would do otherwise. My dejection of
spirits will give a too just excuse on the score of indisposition, for avoiding visits.
Nor will I, but by distant civilities, return the compliments of any of my
acquaintance. My disgraces, if they are to have an end, need not to be proclaimed
to the whole world. I ask this favour, therefore, for my reputation's sake, that I
may be able to hold up my head in the neighbourhood, if I live to see an end of the
unmerited severities which seem to be designed for

Your unhappy sister,
CL. HARLOWE

[*Letter* 22.2: *James Harlowe, Jun.*] *to Miss Clarissa Harlowe*

FOR a girl to lay so much stress upon going to church, and yet resolve to defy her parents, in an article of the greatest consequence to them, and to the whole family, is an absurdity. You are recommended, miss, to the practice of your *private* devotions. May *they* be efficacious upon the mind of one of the most pervicacious young creatures that ever was heard of! The in-*ten*-tion is, I tell you plainly, to mortify you into a sense of your duty. The neighbours you are so solicitous to appear well with, already know, that you defy *that*. So, miss, if you have a real value for your reputation, show it as you ought. It is yet in your own power to establish or impair it.

JA. HARLOWE

Thus, my dear, has my brother got me into his snares, and I, like a poor silly bird, the more I struggle, am the more entangled.

Letter 23: MISS CLARISSA HARLOWE TO MISS HOWE

Mon. morning, Mar. 6

THEY are resolved to break my heart. My poor Hannah is discharged—disgracefully discharged!—Thus it was.

Half an hour after I had sent the poor girl down for my breakfast, that bold creature Betty Barnes, my sister's confidant and servant (if a favourite maid and confidant can be deemed a *servant*), came up.

What, miss, will you please to have for breakfast?

I was surprised. What will I have for breakfast, Betty!—How!—what!—how comes it!—Then I named Hannah—I could not tell what to say.

Don't be surprised, miss—But you'll see Hannah no more in this house!—

God forbid!—Is any harm come to Hannah!—What! What is the matter with Hannah?—

Why, miss, the short and the long is this: your papa and mamma think Hannah has stayed long enough in the house to do mischief; and so she is ordered to *troop* (that was the confident creature's word); and I am directed to wait upon you.

I burst into tears—I have no service for you, Betty Barnes, none at all—But where is Hannah?—Cannot I speak with the poor girl. I owe her half a year's wages. May I not see the honest creature and pay her her wages?—I may never see her again perhaps, for they are resolved to break my heart.

And they think, you are resolved to break theirs: so tit for tat, miss.

Impertinent I called her; and asked her if it were upon such confident terms that her service was to commence.

I was so very earnest to see the poor maid that, to oblige me, as she said, she went down with my request.

The worthy creature was as earnest to see me; and the favour was granted in presence of Shorey and Betty.

I thanked her, when she came up, for her past service to me.

Her heart was ready to break. And she fell a-vindicating her fidelity and love, and disclaiming any mischief she had ever made.

I told her that those who occasioned her being turned out of my service made no question of her integrity: that it was an indignity levelled at me: that I was very sorry for it, and hoped she would meet with as good a service.

Never, never, wringing her hands, a mistress she loved so well. And the poor creature ran on in my praises, and in professions of love to me.

We are all apt, you know, my dear, to praise our benefactors, because they *are* our benefactors; as if everybody did right or wrong as they obliged or disobliged *us*. But this good creature *deserved* to be kindly treated, so I could have no merit in favouring one whom it would have been ungrateful not to distinguish.

I gave her a little linen, some laces and other odd things; and, instead of four pounds which were due to her, ten guineas: and said, if ever I were again allowed to be my own mistress, I would think of *her* in the first place.

Betty enviously whispered Shorey upon it.

Hannah told me, before their faces, having no other opportunity, that she had been examined about letters *to* me, and *from* me: and that she had given her pockets to Miss Harlowe, who looked into them and put her fingers in her stays, to satisfy herself that she had not any.

She gave me an account of the number of my pheasants and bantams; and I said they should be my own care twice or thrice a day.

We wept over each other at parting. The girl prayed for all the family.

To have so good a servant so disgracefully dismissed is a cutting thing: and I could not help saying, that these methods might break my heart, but not any other way answer the end of the authors of my disgraces.

Betty, with a very saucy fleer, said to Shorey there would be a trial of skill about that, she fancied. But I took no notice of it. If this wench thinks I have robbed her young mistress of a lover, as you say she has given out, she may think it a merit in herself to be impertinent to me.

Thus have I been forced to part with my faithful Hannah. If you can commend the good creature to a place worthy of her, pray do, for my sake.

Letter 24: MISS CLARISSA HARLOWE TO MISS HOWE

　　　　　　　　　　　　　　　　　　　　　　　Mon. near 12 o'clock

THE enclosed letter is just now delivered to me. My brother has now carried all his points.

I send you also the copy of my answer. No more at this time can I write.

[*Letter 24.1: James Harlowe, Jun. to Clarissa Harlowe*]

Miss CLARY,　　　　　　　　　　　　　　　　　　　　　Mon. March 6

BY your papa's and mamma's command, I write expressly to forbid you to come into their presence, or into the garden when they are there: nor when they are *not* there, but with Betty Barnes to attend you, except by particular licence or command.

On their blessings, you are forbidden likewise to correspond with the vile Lovelace, as it is well known you did by means of your sly Hannah, whence her sudden discharge; as was fit.

Neither are you to correspond with Miss Howe, who has given herself high airs of late, and might possibly help on your correspondence with that libertine. Nor, in short, with anybody without leave.

You are not to enter into the presence of either of your uncles, without their leave first obtained. It is in mercy to you, after such a behaviour to your mamma, that your papa refuses to see you.

You are not to be seen in any apartment of the house you so lately governed as you pleased, unless you are commanded down.

In short, are strictly to confine yourself to your chamber, except now and then in Betty Barnes's sight (as aforesaid) you take a morning and evening turn in the garden: and then you are to go directly, and without stopping at any apartment in the way, up and down the back stairs, that the sight of so perverse a young creature may not add to the pain you have given everybody.

The hourly threatenings of your Lovelace, as well as your own unheard-of obstinacy, will account to you for all this. What a hand has the best and most indulgent of mothers had with you, who so long pleaded for you and undertook for you; even when others, from the manner of your setting out, despaired of moving you!—What must your perverseness have been, that *such* a mother can give you up! She thinks it right so to do: nor will take you to favour, unless you make the first steps, by a compliance with your duty.

As for myself, whom perhaps you think hardly of (in very good company, if you do, that is my consolation), I have advised that you may be permitted to pursue your own inclinations (some people need no greater punishment than such a permission); and not to have the house encumbered by one who must give them the more pain for the necessity she has laid them under of avoiding the sight of her, although in it.

If anything I have written appear severe or harsh, it is still in your power (but perhaps will not always be so) to remedy it; and that by a single word.

Betty Barnes has orders to obey you in all points consistent with her duty to those to whom *you* owe it, as well as *she*.

JA. HARLOWE

[*Letter 24.2: Clarissa Harlowe*] *to James Harlowe, Jun.*

Sir,
I WILL only say that you may congratulate yourself on having *so far* succeeded in all your views, that you may report what you please of me, and I can no more defend myself, than if I were dead. Yet one favour, nevertheless, I will beg of you: it is this—that you will not occasion more severities, more disgraces, than are necessary for carrying into execution your further designs, whatever they be, against

Your unhappy sister,
CL. HARLOWE

Letter 25: MISS CLARISSA HARLOWE TO MISS HOWE

Tues. March 7

BY my last deposit, you'll see how I am driven, and what a poor prisoner I am; no regard had to my reputation. The whole matter is now before you. Can *such* measures be supposed to soften?—But surely they can only mean to try to frighten me into my brother's views—All my hope is to be able to weather this point till my cousin Morden comes from Florence; and he is expected soon. Yet, if they are determined upon a short day, I doubt he will not be here time enough to save me.

It is plain, by my brother's letter, that my mamma has not spared me in the report she has made of the conferences between herself and me: yet she was pleased to hint to me, that my brother had views which she would have had me try to disappoint—But she has engaged to give a *faithful* account of what was to pass between herself and me; and it was doubtless much more eligible to give up a daughter, than to disoblige a husband, and every other person of the family.

They think they have done everything by turning away my poor Hannah: but as long as the liberty of the garden, and my poultry-visits are allowed me, they will be mistaken.

I asked *Mrs Betty* if she had any orders to watch or attend me? or, whether I were to ask *her* leave, whenever I should be disposed to walk in the garden, or to go to feed my bantams?

Lord bless her! what could I mean by such a question!—Yet she owned that she had heard that I was not to walk in the garden when my papa, mamma, or uncles were there.

However, as it behoved me to be assured on this head, I went down directly, and stayed an hour, without question or impediment: and yet a good part of the time, I walked under, and in *sight* (as I may say) of my brother's study window, where both he and my sister happened to be. And I am sure they saw me, by the loud mirth they affected by way of insult, as I suppose.

So this part of my restraint was doubtless a stretch of the authority given him. The enforcing of that may perhaps come next. But I hope not.

Tuesday night

SINCE I wrote the above, I have ventured to send a letter by Shorey to my mamma. I directed her to give it into her own hand when nobody was by.

I shall enclose the copy of it. You'll see that I would have it thought, that now Hannah is gone I have no way to correspond out of the house. I am far from thinking all I do, right. I am afraid this is a little piece of art, that is *not* so. But this is an afterthought: the letter went first.

[*Letter 25.1: Clarissa to Mrs Harlowe*]

Honoured madam,

HAVING acknowledged to you that I had received letters from Mr Lovelace full of resentment, and that I answered them purely to prevent further mischief; and having showed you copies of my answers, which you did not disapprove of, although you thought fit, after you had read them, to forbid me any further correspondence with him; I think it my duty to acquaint you that another letter from him has since come to my hand, in which he is very earnest with me to permit him to wait on my papa, or you, or my two uncles, in a pacific way, accompanied by Lord M.—On which I beg your commands.

I own to you, madam, that had not the prohibition been renewed, and had not Hannah been so suddenly dismissed my service, I should have made the less scruple to have written an answer and to have commanded her to convey it to him with all speed, in order to dissuade him from these visits, lest anything should happen on the occasion that my heart aches but to think of.

And here I cannot but express my grief that I should have all the punishment and all the blame, who, as I have reason to think, have prevented great mischief and have not been the occasion of any. For, madam, could *I* be supposed to govern the passions of *either* of the gentlemen?—Over the one indeed, I have had some little influence, without giving him hitherto any reason to think he has fastened an obligation upon me for it—Over the other, who, madam, has any?

I am grieved at heart to be obliged to lay so great blame at my brother's door, although my reputation and my liberty are both to be sacrificed to his resentment and ambition. May not, however, so deep a sufferer be permitted to speak out?

This communication being as voluntarily made as dutifully intended, I humbly presume to hope that I shall not be required to produce the letter itself. I cannot either in honour or prudence do that, because of the vehemence of his style; for having heard (not, I assure you, by my means, or through Hannah's) of some part of the harsh treatment I have met with, he thinks himself entitled to place it to his own account by reason of speeches thrown out by some of my relations equally vehement.

If I do *not* answer him, he will be made desperate, and think himself justified (though I shall not think him so) in resenting the treatment he complains of. If I *do*, and if in compliment to me he forbears to resent what he thinks himself entitled to resent, be pleased, madam, to consider the obligation he will suppose he lays me under.

If I were as strongly prepossessed in his favour as is supposed, I should not have wished this to be considered by you—And permit me, as a still further proof that I am *not* prepossessed, to beg of you to consider, whether, upon the whole, the proposal I made of declaring for the single life (which I will religiously adhere to) is not the best way to get rid of his pretensions with honour. To renounce him, and not to be allowed to aver that I will never be the other man's will make him conclude (driven as I am driven) that I am determined in that other man's favour.

If this has not its due weight, my brother's strange schemes must be tried, and I will resign myself to my destiny, with all the acquiescence that shall be granted to my prayers. And so leaving the whole to your own wisdom, and whether you choose to consult my papa and uncles upon this humble application, or not; or whether I shall be allowed to write an answer to Mr Lovelace, or not (and if allowed so to do, I beg your direction by whom to send it); I remain,

Honoured madam,
Your unhappy, but ever-dutiful daughter,
CL. HARLOWE

Wednesday morning

I have just received an answer to the enclosed letter. My mamma, you'll observe, has ordered me to burn it: but as you will have it in your safe keeping and nobody else will see it, her end will be equally answered. It has neither date nor superscription.

[*Letter 25.2: Mrs Harlowe to Clarissa*]

Clarissa,

SAY not all the blame and all the punishment is yours. I am as much blamed and as much punished as you are; yet am more innocent. When your obstinacy is equal to any other person's passion, blame not your brother. We judged right that Hannah carried on your correspondencies. Now she is gone, and you cannot write (we *think* you cannot) to Miss Howe, nor she to you, without our knowledge, one cause of uneasiness and jealousy is over.

I had no dislike to Hannah. I did not tell her so, because Somebody was within hearing when she desired to pay her duty to me at going. I gave her a caution, in a raised voice, to take care wherever she went to live next, if there were any young ladies, how she made parties, and assisted in clandestine correspondencies: but I slid two guineas into her hand. Nor was I angry to hear you were *more* bountiful to her—So much for Hannah.

I don't know what to write about your answering that man of violence. What can you think of it, that such a family as ours should have such a rod held over it?—For my part, I have not owned that I know you *have* corresponded. By your last boldness to me (an astonishing one it was, to pursue before Mr Solmes the subject that I was forced to break from above stairs) you may, as far as I know, plead that you had my countenance for your correspondence with him; and so add to the uneasiness between your papa and me. You was once all my comfort: you made all my hardships tolerable—But now!—However, nothing, it is plain, can move you; and I will say no more on that head: for you are under your papa's discipline now; and he will neither be prescribed to, nor entreated.

I should have been glad to see the letter you tell me of, as I saw the rest—You say both honour and prudence forbid you to show it me!——Oh Clarissa! what think you of receiving letters that honour and prudence forbid you to show to a mother!—But it is not for me to see it, if you would *choose* to show it me. I will not be in your secret. I will not know that you did correspond. And, as to an answer, take your own methods. But let him know it will be the last you will write. And if you do write, I won't see it: so seal it up, if you do, and give it to Shorey and she— Yet do not think I give you licence to write!

We will be upon no conditions with him, nor will *you* be allowed to be upon any. Your papa and uncles would have no patience were he to come. What have *you* to do to oblige him with your refusal of Mr Solmes?—Will not that refusal be to give *him* hope? And while he has any, can *we* be easy or free from his insults? Were even your brother in *fault*, as that fault cannot be conquered, is a sister to carry on a correspondence that shall endanger her brother? But your papa has given his sanction to your brother's dislikes, and they are now your papa's dislikes, and my dislikes, your uncles and everybody's!—No matter to *whom* owing.

As to the rest, you have by your obstinacy put it out of my power to do anything for you. Your papa takes upon himself to be answerable for all consequences. You must not therefore apply to me for any favour. I shall endeavour to be only an observer; happy, if I could be an unconcerned one!—While I had power, you would not let me use it as I *would* have used it. Your aunt has been forced to engage not to interfere but by your papa's direction. You'll have severe trials. If you have any favour to hope for, it must be from the mediation of your uncles. And yet I believe they are equally determined: for they make it a principle— (Alas! they never had children!) that that child who in marriage is not governed by her parents is to be given up as a lost creature!

I charge you, let not this letter be found. Burn it. There is too much of the *mother* in it, to a daughter so unaccountably obstinate.

Write not another letter to me. I can do nothing for you. But you can do everything for yourself.

Now, my dear, to proceed with my melancholy narrative.

After this letter, you will believe that I could have very little hopes that an application directly to my father would stand me in any stead: but I thought it became me to write, were it but to acquit myself *to* myself that I have left nothing unattempted, that has the least likelihood to restore me to his favour. Accordingly I wrote to the following effect:

[*Letter 25.3: Clarissa Harlowe to James Harlowe*]

I presume not, I say, to argue with my papa, I only beg his mercy and indulgence in this *one* point, on which depends my present and perhaps my *future* happiness; and beseech him not to reprobate his child for an aversion which it is not in her power to conquer. I beg that I may not be sacrificed to projects and remote contingencies: I complain of the disgraces I suffer in this banishment from his presence, and in being confined to my chamber. In everything but this *one* point, I promise implicit duty and resignation to his will. I repeat my offers of a single life, and appeal to him, whether I have ever given him cause to doubt my word. I beg to be admitted to his, and to my mamma's presence, and that my conduct may be under their own eye: and this with the more earnestness as I have too much reason to believe that snares are laid for me; and tauntings and revilings used, on purpose to make a handle of my words against me, when I am not permitted to speak in my own defence. I conclude with hoping that my brother's instigations may not rob an unhappy child of her father.

This is the cruel answer, sent without superscription, and unsealed, although by Betty Barnes, who delivered it with an air as if she knew the contents.

[*Letter 25.4: James Harlowe to Clarissa Harlowe*]

Wednesday

I write, perverse girl, but with all the indignation that your disobedience deserves. To desire to be forgiven a fault you own, and yet resolve to persevere in, is a boldness, no more to be equalled than passed over. It is *my* authority you defy. Your reflections upon a brother that is an honour to us all deserve my utmost resentment. I see how light all relationship sits upon *you*. The *cause* I guess at, too. I cannot bear the reflections that naturally arise from this consideration. Your behaviour to your too indulgent, and too fond mother—But, I have no patience—Continue banished from my presence, undutiful as you are, till you know how to conform to my will. Ungrateful creature! Your letter but upbraids me for my past indulgence. Write no more to me till you can distinguish better; and till you are convinced of your duty to

A justly incensed Father

This angry letter was accompanied with one from my mamma, unsealed and unsuperscribed also. Those who take so much pains to confederate everyone against me, I make no doubt obliged her to bear her testimony against the poor girl.

This letter being a repetition of some of the severe things that passed between my mamma and me, of which I have given you an account, I shall not need to give you the contents—Only thus far, that *she* also praises my brother and blames me for my freedoms with him.

Letter 26: MISS CLARISSA HARLOWE TO MISS HOWE

Thursd. morn. Mar. 9

I have another letter from Mr Lovelace, although I had not answered his former.

This man, somehow or other, knows everything that passes in our family: my confinement; Hannah's dismission; and more of the resentments and resolutions of my father, uncles, and brother, than I can possibly know, and almost as soon as things happen. He cannot come at these intelligences fairly.

He is excessively uneasy upon what he hears; and his expressions both of love to me and resentment to them are very fervent. He solicits me much 'To engage my honour to him, never to have Mr Solmes.' I think I may fairly promise him that I will not.

He begs, 'That I will not think he is endeavouring to make to himself a *merit* at any man's expense, since he hopes to obtain my favour on the foot of his *own*; nor that he seeks to *intimidate* me into a consideration for him. But declares that the treatment he meets with from my family is so intolerable that he is perpetually reproached for not resenting it; and that as well by Lord M. and his two aunts, as by all his other friends: and if he must have no hope from me, he cannot answer for what his despair will make him do.'

Indeed, he says, his relations, the ladies particularly, advise him to have recourse to a *legal* remedy: 'But how, he asks, can a man of honour go to law for verbal abuses, given by people entitled to wear swords?'

You see, my dear, that my mamma seems as apprehensive of mischief as I, and has indirectly offered to let Shorey carry my answer to the letter he sent me before.

He is full of the favour of the ladies of his family to me: to whom, nevertheless, I am personally a stranger; except, that once I saw Miss Patty Montague at Mrs Knollys's.

It is natural, I believe, for a person to be the more desirous of making new friends in proportion as she loses the favour of old ones, yet had I rather appear amiable in the eyes of my own relations and in your eyes than in those of all the world besides: but these four ladies of his family have such excellent characters that one cannot but wish to be thought well of by them. Cannot there be a way to find out by Mrs Fortescue's means, or by Mr Hickman, who has some knowledge of Lord M. (covertly, however), what their opinions are of the present situation of things in our family; and of the little likelihood there is that ever the alliance once approved of by them can take effect?—I cannot, for my own part, think so well of myself as to imagine that they can wish him to persevere in his views with regard to me, through such contempts and discouragements—Not that it would concern me should they advise him to the contrary. By my lord's signing Mr Lovelace's former letter; by Mr Lovelace's assurances of the continued favour of all his relations; and by the report of others; I seem to stand still high in their favour. But, methinks, I would be glad to have this confirmed to me, as from themselves, by the lips of an indifferent person; and the rather, as they are known to put a value upon their alliance, fortunes, and family; and take it amiss, as they have reason, to be included by *ours* in the contempt thrown upon their kinsman.

Curiosity at present is all my motive: nor will there ever, I hope, be a stronger, notwithstanding your questionable *throbs*; even were Mr Lovelace to be less exceptionable than he is.

I have answered his letters. If he take me at my word, I shall need to be the less solicitous for his relations' opinions in my favour: and yet one would be glad to be well thought of by the worthy. This is the substance of my letter:

'I express my surprise at his knowing (and so early) all that passes here. I assure him, that were there not such a man in the world as himself, I would not have Mr Solmes.'

I tell him, 'That to return, as I understand he does, defiances for defiances, to my relations, is far from being a proof with me, either of his politeness or of the consideration he pretends to have for me.

'That the moment I hear he visits any of my friends without their consent, I will make a resolution never to see him more, if I can help it.'

I apprise him, 'That I am connived at in sending this letter (although no one has seen the contents), provided it shall be the last I will ever write to him: that I had more than once told him that the single life was my choice; and this before Mr Solmes was introduced as a visitor in our family: that Mr Wyerley, and other gentlemen, knew it well to be my choice, before *he* was acquainted with any of us: that I had never been induced to receive a line from him on the subject, but that I thought he had not acted ungenerously by my brother; and yet had not been so handsomely treated by my friends as he might have expected: that had he even my friends of his side, I should have very great objections to him were I to get over my choice of a single life, so really preferable to me as it is; and that I should have declared as much to him, had I regarded him as more than a common visitor. On all these accounts, I desire that the one more letter which I will allow him to deposit in the usual place may be the very *last*; and that only to acquaint me with his acquiescence that it shall be so; at least till happier times!'

This last I put in, that he may not be quite desperate. But if he take me at my word, I shall be rid of one of my tormentors.

I have promised to lay before you all his letters and my answers. I repeat that promise; and am the less solicitous for that reason to amplify upon the contents of either. But I cannot too often express my vexation to be driven to such straits and difficulties, here at home, as oblige me to answer letters (from a man I had not absolutely intended to encourage and had really great objections to) filled as *his* are with such warm protestations, and written to me with a spirit of expectation.

For, my dear, you never knew so bold a supposer. As commentators find beauties in an author which the author perhaps was a stranger to, so he sometimes compliments me in high strains of gratitude for favours, and for a consideration, which I never designed him; insomuch that I am frequently under a necessity of explaining away the attributed goodness, which if I showed him, I should have the less opinion of myself.

In short, my dear, like a restive horse he pains one's hands, and half disjoints one's arms to rein him in. And when you see his letters, you must form no judgement upon them, till you have read my answers: if you do, you will indeed think you have cause to attribute *self-deceit*, and *throbs*, and *glows* to your friend— And yet, at other times, the contradictory creature complains that I show him as little favour, and my friends as much inveteracy, as if in the rencounter betwixt my brother and him he had been the aggressor; and as if the catastrophe had been as fatal as it might have been.

If he has a design by this conduct (sometimes complaining of my shyness, at others exulting in my imaginary favours) to induce me at one time to acquiesce with his compliments, at another to be more complaisant for his complaints; and if the contradiction be not the effect of his inattention and giddiness; I shall think him as deep and as artful (too probably, as *practised*) a creature as ever lived; and were I to be sure of it, should hate him, if possible, worse than I do Solmes.

But enough for the present of a creature so very various!—

Letter 27: MISS HOWE TO MISS CLARISSA HARLOWE

Thursday night, March 9

I have no patience with any of the people you are with. I know not what to advise you to do. How do you know that you are not punishable for being the cause, though to your own loss, that the will of your grandfather is not complied with?— Wills are sacred things, child. You see that they, even *they*, think so, who imagine they suffer by a will through the distinction paid you in it.

I allow of all your noble reasonings for what you did at the time; but since such a charming, such a generous instance of filial duty is to go thus unrewarded, why should you not resume?

Your grandfather knew the family-failing: he knew what a noble spirit you had to do good—He himself, perhaps (excuse me, my dear), had done too little in his lifetime; and therefore he put it in your power to make up for the defects of the whole family. Were it to me, I would resume it. Indeed I would.

You will say, you cannot do it, while you are with them. I don't know that. Do you think they can use you worse than they do?—And is it not your *right?* And do they not make use of your own generosity to oppress you? Your uncle Harlowe is one trustee, your cousin Morden is the other. Insist upon your right to your uncle;

and write to your cousin Morden about it. This, I dare say, will make them alter their behaviour to you.

Your insolent brother, what has *he* to do to control you?—Were it me (I wish it were for one month, and no more), I'd show him the difference. I'd be in my own mansion, pursuing my charming schemes and making all around me happy. I'd set up my own chariot. I'd visit them when they deserved it. But when my brother and sister gave themselves airs, I'd let them know that I was their sister, and not their servant; and if that did not do, I would shut my gates against them; and bid them be company for each other—

It must be confessed, however, that this brother and sister of yours, judging as such narrow spirits will ever judge, have some reason for treating you as they do. It must have long been a mortifying consideration to them (set disappointed love on her side, and avarice on his, out of the question) to be so much eclipsed by a younger sister—Such a sun in a family where there are none but faint twinklers, how could they bear it!—Why, my dear, they must look upon you as a prodigy among them: and prodigies, you know, though they obtain our admiration, never attract our love. The distance between you and them is immense. Their eyes ache to look up at you. What shades does your full day of merit cast upon them!—Can you wonder then, that they should embrace the first opportunity that offered to endeavour to bring you down to their level?

Depend upon it, my dear, you will have more of it, and more still, as you bear it.

As to this odious Solmes, I wonder not at your aversion to him. It is needless to say anything to you, who have so sincere an antipathy to him, to strengthen your dislike: yet who can resist her own talents? One of mine, as I have heretofore said, is to give an ugly likeness. Shall I indulge it?—I will. And the rather as, in doing so, you will have my opinion in justification of your aversion to him, and in approbation of a steadiness that I ever admired, and must for ever approve in your temper.

I was twice in this wretch's company. At one of the times your Lovelace was there. I need not mention to you, who have such a *pretty curiosity*, though at present, *only* a curiosity, you know! the unspeakable difference!—

Lovelace entertained the company in his lively gay way, and made everybody laugh at one of his stories. It was before this creature was thought of for you. Solmes laughed too. It was, however, *his* laugh; for his first three years, at least, I imagine, must have been one continual fit of crying; and his muscles have never yet been able to recover a risible tone. His very smile (you never saw him smile, I believe; never at least gave him cause to smile) is so little natural to his features, that it appears in him as hideous as the *grin* of a man in malice.

I took great notice of him, as I do of all the noble lords of the creation in their peculiarities, and was disgusted, nay, shocked at him even then. I was glad, I remember, on that particular occasion, to see his strange features recovering their natural gloominess, though they did this but slowly, as if the muscles which contributed to his distortions had turned upon rusty springs.

What a dreadful thing must even the love of such a husband be! For my part, were I his wife! (but what have I done to myself to make but such a supposition?) I should never have comfort but in his absence, or when I was quarrelling with him. A splenetic lady, who must have somebody to find fault with, might indeed be brought to endure such a wretch. The sight of him would always furnish out the occasion, and all her servants, for that reason, and for *that* only, would have cause to bless their master. But how grievous and apprehensive a thing must it be for his wife, had she the least degree of delicacy, to catch herself in having done something to oblige him?

So much for his person: as to the other half of him, he is said to be an insinuating, creeping mortal to anybody he hopes to be a gainer by; an insolent, overbearing one where he has no such views: and is not this the genuine spirit of meanness?—He is reported to be spiteful and malicious, even to the whole family of any single person who has once disobliged him; and to his own relations most of all. I am told that they are none of them such wretches as himself. This may be one reason why he is for disinheriting them.

My Kitty, from one of his domestics, tells me that his tenants hate him: and that he never had a servant who spoke well of him. Vilely suspicious of their wronging him, probably from the badness of his own heart, he is always changing.

His pockets, they say, are continually crammed with keys, so that when he would treat a guest (a friend he has not out of your family), he is half as long puzzling *which is which* as his niggardly treat might be concluded in—And if it be wine, he always fetches it himself: nor has he much trouble in doing so, for he has very few visitors—only those whom business or necessity brings; for a gentleman who can help it would rather be benighted than put up at his house.

Yet this is the man they have found out, for the sake of considerations as sordid as those he is governed by, for a husband (that is to say, for a lord and master) for Miss Clarissa Harlowe!

But perhaps he may not be quite so miserable as he is represented. Characters extremely good, or extremely bad, are seldom justly given. Favour for a person will exalt the one, as disfavour will sink the other. But your uncle Antony has told my mamma, who objected to his covetousness, that it was intended *to tie him* up, as he called it, *to your own terms*; which would be with a hempen, rather than a matrimonial cord, I dare say! But is not this a plain indication that even his own recommenders think him a mean creature, and that he must be articled with— perhaps for *necessaries*? But enough, and too much, of such a mortal as this!—You must not have him, my dear—that I am clear in—though not so clear how you will be able to avoid it, except you assert the independence which your estate gives you.

HERE my mamma broke in upon me. She wanted to see what I had written. I was silly enough to read Solmes's character to her.

She owned that the man was not the most desirable of men; had not the happiest appearance: but what was person in a man? And I was chidden for setting you against complying with your father's will. Then followed a lecture upon the preference to be given in favour of a man who took care to discharge all his obligations to the world and to keep all together, in opposition to a spendthrift or profligate: a fruitful subject, you know, whether any particular person be meant by it, or not. Why will these wise parents, by saying too much against the persons they dislike, put one upon defending them? Lovelace is not a spendthrift; owes not obligations to the world; though, I doubt not, profligate enough. Then, putting one upon doing *such* but common justice, we must needs be prepossessed, truly!—

And so we are put, perhaps, upon *curiosities* first, how such a one or his friends may think of one—And then, but too probably, a distinguishing preference, or something that looks like it, comes in.

My mamma charged me, at last, to write that side over again. But excuse me, my good mamma! I would not have the character lost upon any consideration, since my vein ran freely into it; and I never wrote to please myself but I pleased you. A very good reason why—we have but one mind between us—only, that sometimes you are a little too grave, methinks; I, no doubt, a little too flippant in your opinion.

This difference in our tempers, however, is probably the reason that we love one another *so* well, that in the words of Norris no *third love* can come in between: since each in the other's eye having something amiss, and each loving the other well enough to bear being told of it; and the rather, perhaps, as neither wishes to mend it; this takes off a good deal from that rivalry which might encourage a little, if not a great deal, of that latent spleen which in time might rise into envy, and that into ill-will. So, my dear, if this be the case, let each keep her fault, and much good may do her with it, say I: for there is constitution in both to plead for it: and what a hero or heroine must he or she be, who can conquer a constitutional fault? Let it be *avarice*, as in some I *dare not* name: let it be *gravity*, as in my *best friend*: or let it be *flippancy*, as in—I need not say whom.

It is proper to acquaint you that I was obliged to comply with my mamma's *curiosity*—my mamma has her share, her *full* share, of *curiosity*, my dear—and to let her see here and there some passages of your letters—

I am broke in upon—but I will tell you by and by what passed between my mamma and me on this occasion—And the rather, as she had her GIRL, her favourite HICKMAN, and your LOVELACE, all at once in her eye—

Thus it was:

'I cannot but think, Nancy, said she, after all, that there is a little hardship in Miss Harlowe's case: and yet, as her mamma says, it is a grating thing to have a child who was always noted for her duty in *smaller* points to stand in opposition to her parents will in the *greater*; yea, in the *greatest of all*. And now, to middle the matter between both, it is pity that the man they insist upon her accepting has not that sort of merit, which so delicate a mind as Miss Harlowe's might reasonably expect in a husband—But then, this man is surely preferable to a libertine: to a libertine too, who has had a duel with her own brother. *Fathers* and *mothers* must think so, were it *not* for that circumstance—And it is strange if *they* do not know best.'

And so they must, thought I, from their experience, if no little, dirty views give *them* also that prepossession in one man's favour, which they are so apt to censure their daughters for having in another's—And if, as I may add in your case, they have no creeping, old, musty, uncle Antonys to strengthen their prepossessions, as he does my mamma's—poor, creeping, positive soul, what has such an old bachelor as he to do to prate about the duties of children to parents, unless he had a notion that parents owe some to their children? But your mamma, by her indolent meekness, let me call it, has spoiled all the three brothers.

'But you see, child, proceeded by mamma, what a different behaviour MINE is to YOU. I recommend to you one of the soberest, yet politest, men in England—'

I think little of my mamma's *politest*, my dear. She judges of honest Hickman for her *daughter*, as she would have done, I suppose, twenty years ago for *herself*: for Hickman appears to me to be a man of that antiquated cut, as to his mind I mean: a great deal too much upon the formal, you must needs think him to be, yourself.

'Of a good family, continued my mamma; a fine, clear, and improving estate (a prime consideration with my mamma, as well as with some other folks whom you know): and I *beg* and I *pray* you to encourage him: at least, not to use him the *worse* for his being so obsequious to you.'

Yes, indeed! To use *him* kindly, that he may treat *me* familiarly—but distance to the men-wretches is best—I say.

'Yet all will hardly prevail upon you to do as I would have you. What would you say were I to treat you as Miss Harlowe's father and mother treat her?'

'What would I *say*, madam!—That's easily answered. I would SAY nothing. Can you think such usage, and to such a young lady, is to be borne?'

'Come, come, Nancy, be not so hasty. You have heard but one side; and that there is *more* to be said is plain, by your reading to me but parts of her letters. They are her parents. *They* must know best. Miss Harlowe, as fine a child as she is, must have *done* something, must have *said* something (you know how they loved her) to make them use her thus.'

'But if *she* should be blameless, madam, how does your own supposition condemn *them*?'

Then came up Solmes's great estate; his good management of it—'A little too NEAR indeed,' was the word! (*Oh how money-lovers*, thought I, *will palliate!* Yet my mamma is a princess in spirit to this Solmes!) 'What strange effects have prepossession and love upon young ladies!'

I don't know how it is, my dear; but people take strange delight in finding out folks in love. Curiosities *beget* curiosities; I believe that's the thing!

She proceeded to praise Mr Lovelace's person, and his qualifications natural and acquired: but then she would judge as *mothers* will judge, and as *daughters* are very loath to judge—but could say nothing in answer to your offer of living single; and breaking with him—if—if—(three or four *Ifs* she made of one good one, If) *that* could be depended on, she said.

But still *obedience without reserve*, reason what I will, is the burden of my mamma's song; and this, for *my* sake, as well as *yours*.

I must needs say, that I think duty to parents is a very meritorious excellence: but I bless God I have not your trials. We can all be good when we have no temptation nor provocation to the contrary—but few young persons (who can help themselves too) would bear what you bear.

I will not mention all that is upon my mind in relation to the behaviour of your father and uncles, and the rest of them, because I would not offend you: but I have now a higher opinion of my own sagacity than ever I had, in that I could never cordially love anyone of your family but yourself. I am not *born* to like them. But it is my *duty* to be sincere to my *friend*: and this will excuse her Anna Howe to Miss Clarissa Harlowe. I ought indeed to have excepted your mamma, a lady to be reverenced, and now to be pitied. What must have been her treatment, to be thus subjugated, as I may call it? Little did the good old Viscount think, when he married his darling, his only, daughter to so well-appearing a gentleman, and to her own liking too, that she would have been so much kept down. Another would call your father a tyrant, if you will not: all the world indeed would; and if you love your mother, you should not be very angry at the world for taking that liberty. Yet, after all, I cannot help thinking that she is the less to be pitied, as she may be said (be the gout, or what will, the occasion of his moroseness) to have long behaved unworthy of her birth and fine qualities, in yielding to encroaching spirits (you may confine the reflection to your brother, if it will pain you to extend it), and this for the sake of preserving a temporary peace to herself; which is the less worth attempting to preserve, as it always produced a strength in the will of others, and a weakness in her own, that has subjected her to an arbitrariness which grew and became established upon her patience—And now to give up the most deserving of her children, against her judgement, a sacrifice to the ambition and selfishness of the least deserving—but I fly from this subject—having, I fear, said too much to be forgiven for—and yet much less than is in my heart to say upon the over-meek subject.

Mr Hickman is expected from London this evening. I have desired him to enquire after Lovelace's life and conversation in town. If he has not, I shall be very angry with him. Don't expect a very good account of either. He is certainly an intriguing wretch, and full of inventions.

Upon my word, I most heartily despise that sex! I wish they would let our fathers and mothers alone; teasing *them* to tease *us* with their golden promises, and protestations, and settlements, and the rest of their ostentatious nonsense. How charmingly might you and I live together and despite them all!—But to be cajoled, wire-drawn, and ensnared, like silly birds, into a state of bondage or vile subordination: to be courted as princesses for a few weeks, in order to be treated as slaves for the rest of our lives—Indeed, my dear, as you say of Solmes, I cannot endure them!—But for your relations (*friends* no more will I call them, unworthy as they are even of the *other* name!) to take such a wretch's price as that; and to the cutting off all reversions from his own family!—How must a mind but commonly just resist such a measure!

Mr Hickman shall sound Lord M. upon the subject you recommend. But beforehand, I can tell you what he and what his sisters will say when they *are* sounded. Who would not be proud of such a relation as Miss Clarissa Harlowe?—Mrs Fortescue told me that they are all your very great admirers.

If I have not been clear enough in my advice about what you shall do, let me say that I can give it in one word: it is only by re-urging you to RESUME. If you do, all the rest will follow.

We are told here that Mrs Norton, as well as your aunt Hervey, has given her opinion on the *implicit* side of the question. If she can think that the part she has had in your education, and your own admirable talents and acquirements, are to be thrown away upon such a worthless creature as Solmes, I could heartily quarrel with her. You may think I say this to lessen your regard for the good woman. And perhaps not wholly without cause, if you do. For, to own the truth, methinks, I don't love her so well as I should do, did you love her so apparently less, that I could be out of doubt, that you love me better.

Your mamma tells you, 'That you will have great trials: that you are under your papa's *discipline*'—The word's enough for me to despise them who give occasion for its use!—'That it is out of her power to help you!' And again: 'That if you have any favour to hope for, it must be by the mediation of your uncles!' I suppose you will write to the oddities, since you are forbid to see them!—But can it be, that such a lady, such a sister, such a wife, such a mother, has no influence in her own family? Who indeed, as you say, would marry, that can live single? My choler is again beginning to rise. RESUME, my dear—And that's all I will give myself time to say further, lest I offend you when I cannot serve you—Only this, that I am

Your truly affectionate friend and servant
ANNA HOWE

Letter 28: MISS CLARISSA HARLOWE TO MISS HOWE

Friday, Mar. 10

YOU will permit me, my dear, to touch upon a few passages in your last favour, that affect me sensibly.

In the first place, you must allow me to say, low as I am in spirits, that I am very angry with you for your reflections on my relations, particularly on my father, and on the memory of my grandfather. Nor, my dear, does your own mamma always escape the keen edge of vivacity. One cannot one's *self* forbear to write or speak freely of those we love and honour; that is to say, when grief wrings the heart. But it goes against one to hear anybody else take the same liberties. Then you have so very strong a manner of expression where you take a distaste, that when passion has subsided and I come by reflection to see by *your* severity what I have given occasion for I cannot help condemning myself. Let me then, as matters arise, make my complaints to you; but be it your part to soothe and soften my angry passions by such advice as nobody better knows how to give: and this the rather, as you know what an influence your advice has upon me.

I cannot help owning, that I am pleased to have you join with me in opinion of the contempt which Mr Solmes deserves from me. But yet, permit me to say, that he is not quite so horrible a creature as you make him; as to his *person*, I mean: for with regard to his *mind*, by all I have heard, you have done him but justice. But you have such a talent at an ugly likeness, and such a vivacity, that they sometimes carry you out of verisimilitude. In short, my dear, I have known you in more instances than one sit down resolved to write all that wit, rather than strict justice, could suggest upon the given occasion. Perhaps it may be thought that I should say the less on this particular subject, because your dislike to him arises from love to me: but should it not be our aim to judge of ourselves, and of everything that affects us, as we may reasonably imagine other people would judge of us and of our actions?

As to the advice you give, to resume my estate, I am determined not to litigate with my papa, let what will be the consequence to myself. I may give you, at another time, a more particular answer to your reasonings on this subject: but at present will only observe, that it is my opinion that Lovelace himself would hardly think me worth addressing, were he to know *this* to be my resolution. These *men*, my dear, with all their flatteries, look forward to the PERMANENT. Indeed, it is fit they should. For love must be a very foolish thing to look back upon, when it has brought persons born to affluence into indigence; and laid a generous mind under the hard necessity of obligation and dependence.

You very ingeniously account for the love we bear to one another, from the *difference* in our tempers. I own, I should not have thought of that. There may possibly be something in it: but whether there be, or not, whenever I am cool, and give myself time to reflect, I will love you the better for the correction you give me, be as severe as you will upon me. Spare me not therefore, my dear friend, whenever you think me in the least faulty. I love your agreeable raillery: you know I always did: nor, however *over*-serious you think me, did I ever think you *flippant*, as you harshly call it. One of the first conditions of our mutual friendship was that each should say or write to the other whatever was upon her mind, without any offence to be taken; a condition that is indeed an indispensable in all friendship.

I knew your mamma would be for implicit obedience in a child. I am sorry my case is so circumstanced that I *cannot* comply: as my Mrs Norton says, it would be my duty to do so, if I could. You are indeed very happy that you have nothing but your own agreeable, yet whimsical, humours to contend with in the choice she invites you to make of Mr Hickman!—How happy should I be, to be treated with so much lenity! I should blush to have *my* mamma say that she *begged* and *prayed* me, and all in vain, to encourage a man so unexceptionable as Mr Hickman.

Indeed, my beloved Miss Howe, I am ashamed to have your mamma say with ME in her view, 'What strange effects have prepossession and love upon young creatures of our sex!' This touches me the more sensibly, because you yourself, my dear, are so ready to *persuade* me into it. I should be very blameable to endeavour to hide any the least bias upon my mind from you: and I cannot but say—that this man— this Lovelace—is a person that might be liked well enough if he bore such a character as Mr Hickman bears; and even if there were hopes of reclaiming him: but LOVE, methinks, as short a word as it is, has a *broad* sound with it. Yet do I find that one may be driven by violent measures step by step, as it were, into something that may be called—I don't know what to call it—a *conditional kind of liking*, or so. But as to the word LOVE—justifiable and charming as it is in some cases (that is to say, in all the *relative*, in all the *social* and, what is still beyond both, in all our *superior* duties, in which it may be properly called *divine*), it has, methinks, in this narrow, circumscribed, selfish, peculiar sense, no very pretty sound with it. Treat me as freely as you will in all other respects, I will love you, as I have said, the better for your friendly freedom: but, methinks, I could be glad, for SEX's sake, that you would not let this imputation pass so glibly from *your* pen, or *your* lips, as attributable to one of your own sex, whether I be the person or not: since the *other* must have a *double* triumph, when a person of your delicacy (armed with such contempts of them all, as you would have one think) can give up a friend, with an exultation over her weakness, as a silly, love-sick creature!

I could make some other observations upon the contents of your last two letters, but my mind is not free enough at present. The occasions for the above stuck with me, and I could not help taking the earliest notice of them.

I will not acquaint you with all proceedings here; but these shall be the subject of another letter.

Letter 29: MISS CLARISSA HARLOWE TO MISS HOWE

Saturday, March 11

I have had such taunting messages and such repeated avowals of ill-offices brought me from my brother and sister, if I do not comply with their wills (delivered, too, with provoking sauciness by Betty Barnes), that I have thought it proper, before I entered upon my intended address to my uncles, in pursuance of the hint given me in my mamma's letter, to expostulate a little with *them*. But, I have done it in such a manner, as will give you (if you please to take it as you have done some parts of my former letters) great advantage over me. In short, you will have more cause than ever to declare me far gone in love, if my reasons for the change of my style in these letters, with regard to Mr Lovelace, do not engage your more favourable opinion—For I have thought proper to give them their own way; and, since they will have it that I have a preferable regard for Mr Lovelace, I give them a cause rather to confirm their opinion than doubt it.

These are my reasons in brief for the alteration of my style.

In the first place, they have grounded their principal argument for my compliance with their will upon my acknowledgements that my heart is free; and so supposing I give up no preferable person, my opposition has the look of downright obstinacy in their eyes; and they argue that, at worst, my aversion to Solmes is an aversion that may be easily surmounted, and *ought* to be surmounted in duty to my father, and for the promotion of family views.

Next, although they build upon this argument in order to silence me, they seem not to believe me, but treat me as violently and as disgracefully, as if I were in love with one of my father's footmen—so that my conditional willingness to give up Lovelace has procured me no favour.

In the next place, I cannot but think that my brother's antipathy to him is far from being well-grounded. His inordinate passion for the sex is his crime that is always rung in my ears, and a very great one it is: but, does my brother recriminate upon him thus, in love to me?—No—His whole behaviour shows me, that that is not his motive, and that he thinks me rather in his way, than otherwise.

It is then the call of justice, as I may say, to speak up a little for a man who, although provoked by my brother, did not do him all the mischief he could have done him, and which my brother had endeavoured to do *him*. It might not be amiss therefore, I thought, to alarm them a little with an apprehension that the methods they are taking with me are the very reverse of those they should take to answer the end they design by them. And after all, what is the compliment I make Mr Lovelace, if I *allow* it to be thought that I do really prefer him to such a man as him they terrify me with? Then, my Miss Howe (concluded I) accuses me of a tameness, which subjects me to insults from my brother: I will keep that dear friend in my eye; and for *all* these considerations, try what a little of *her* spirit will do—sit it ever so awkwardly upon me.

In this way of thinking, I wrote to my brother and sister. This is my letter to him.

[*Letter 29.1: Clarissa Harlowe to James Harlowe, Jun.*]

TREATED, as I am treated, and, in a great measure, if not *wholly*, by your instigations, brother, you must permit me to expostulate with you upon the occasion. It is not my *intention* to displease you in what I am going to write: and yet I must deal freely with you. The occasion calls for it.

And permit me, in the first place, to remind you that I am your *sister*, and not your *servant*; and that, therefore, the bitter revilings and passionate language brought me from you, upon an occasion in which you have no reason to prescribe to me, are neither worthy of my character to bear, or of yours to offer.

Put the case that I *were* to marry the man you dislike, and that he were *not* to make a polite or tender husband; is that a reason for you to be an impolite and disobliging brother?—Why must *you*, sir, anticipate my misfortunes, were such a case to happen?—Let me tell you plainly, that the husband who could treat me, as a *wife*, worse than you, of late, have treated me as a *sister*, must be a barbarous man indeed.

Ask yourself, I pray you, sir, if you would thus have treated your sister Bella, had she thought fit to receive the addresses of the man so much hated by you?— If not, let me caution you, my brother, not to take your measures by what you think *will be* borne, but rather by what *ought* to be offered.

How would *you* take it, if you had a brother who, in a like case were to act by *you*, as you do by *me*? You cannot but remember what a laconic answer you gave even to my papa, who recommended to you Miss Nelly D'Oily—*you did not like her*, were your words: and that was thought sufficient.

You must needs think that I cannot but know to *whom* to attribute my disgraces, when I recollect my papa's indulgence to me in permitting me to decline several offers; and to *whom*, that a common cause is endeavoured to be made, in favour of a man whose person and manners are more exceptionable than those of any of the gentlemen I have been permitted to refuse.

I offer not to compare the two men together: nor is there, indeed, the least comparison to be made between them. All the difference to the one's disadvantage, if I did, is but in one point—Of the greatest importance, indeed—but to whom of *most* importance?—to *myself*, surely, were I to encourage his application: of the least to *you*. Nevertheless, if you do not by your strange policies unite *that man* and *me* as joint-sufferers in one cause, you shall find me as much resolved to renounce him as I am to refuse the other. I have made an overture to this purpose: I hope you will not give me reason to confirm my apprehensions that it will be owing to *you* if it be not accepted.

It is a sad thing to have it to say, without being conscious of ever having given you cause of offence, that I have in *you* a brother, but not a *friend*.

Perhaps you will not condescend to enter into the reasons of your late conduct with a foolish sister: but, if *politeness*, if *civility*, be not due to that character, and to my sex, *justice* is.

Let me take the liberty further to observe, that the principal end of a young gentleman's education at the university is to learn him to reason justly, and to subdue the violence of his passions. I hope, brother, that you will not give room for anybody who knows us both to conclude that the toilette has learned the one more of the latter doctrine, than the university has taught the other. I am truly sorry to have cause to say, that I have heard it often remarked that your uncontrolled passions are not a credit to your liberal education.

I hope, sir, that you will excuse the freedom I have taken with you. You have given me too much reason for it, and you have taken much greater with me, *without* reason—so, if you are offended, ought to look at the cause, and not at the effect—Then examining yourself, that cause will cease, and there will not be anywhere a more accomplished gentleman than my brother.

Sisterly affection, I do assure you, sir (unkindly, as you have used *me*), and not the pertness which of late you have been so apt to impute to me, is my motive in this hint. Let me invoke your returning kindness, my *only brother!* And give me cause, I beseech you, to call you my *compassionating friend.* For I am, and ever will be,

> Your affectionate sister,
> CL. HARLOWE

This is my brother's answer.

[Letter 29.2: James Harlowe, Jun.] to Miss Clarissa Harlowe

I know there will be no end of your impertinent scribble if I don't write to you. I write therefore: but, without entering into argument with such a conceited and pert preacher and questioner, it is to forbid you to plague me with your quaint nonsense. I know not what wit in a woman is good for, but to make her over-value herself, and despise everybody else. Yours, Miss Pert, has set you above your duty, and above being taught or prescribed to either by parents or anybody else—But go on, miss, your mortification will be the greater; that's all, child. It *shall*, I assure you, if I can make it so, so long as you prefer that villainous Lovelace, who is justly hated by all your family. We see by your letter now, as well as we too justly suspected before, most evidently what hold he has got of your forward heart. But the stronger the hold, the greater must be the force (and you shall have enough of that) to tear such a miscreant from it. In me, notwithstanding your saucy lecturing and as saucy reflections before, you are sure of a friend, as well as a brother, if it be not your own fault. But if you will still think of such a husband as that Lovelace, never expect either in

> JA. HARLOWE

I will now give you a copy of my letter to my sister, with her unsisterly answer.

[Letter 29.3: Clarissa Harlowe to Arabella Harlowe]

IN what, my dear sister, have I offended you, that instead of endeavouring to soften my father's anger against me (as I am sure I should have done for you, had my unhappy case been yours) you should in so hard-hearted a manner join to aggravate not only his displeasure, but my mamma's against me. Make but my case your own, my dear Bella, and suppose you were commanded to marry Mr Lovelace (to whom you are believed to have an antipathy), would you not think it a very grievous injunction?—Yet cannot your dislike to Mr *Lovelace* be greater than mine is to Mr *Solmes*. Nor are love and hatred voluntary passions.

My brother may, perhaps, think it a proof of a *manly* spirit to be an utter stranger to the gentle passions. We have both heard him boast that he never loved with distinction; and, having predominating passions, and checked in his first attempt, perhaps he never will. It is the less wonder then, raw from the college, so lately himself the *tutored*, that he should set up for a tutor, a prescriber to our gentler sex, whose tastes and manners are differently formed; for what, according to his account, are colleges, but classes of tyrants, from the upper students over the lower, and from them to the tutor?—That *he* with such *masculine* passions should endeavour to control and bear down an unhappy sister, in a case where his antipathy and, give me leave to say, his ambition (once you would have allowed the latter to be his fault) can be gratified by so doing, may not be quite so much to be wondered at—but that a *sister* should give up the cause of a sister and join with him to set her father and mother against her, in a case relative to sex, in a case that might have been her own—indeed, my Bella, this is not pretty in you.

There was a time that Mr Lovelace was thought reclaimable, and when it was far from being deemed a censurable view to hope to bring back to the paths of virtue and honour a man of his sense and understanding. I am far from wishing to make the experiment—but nevertheless will say, that if I have *not* a regard for him, the disgraceful methods taken to compel me to receive the address of a such a man as Mr Solmes are enough to inspire it.

Do you, my sister, for one moment lay aside all prejudice, and compare the two men in their births, their educations, their persons, their understandings, their manners, their air, and their whole deportments; and in their fortunes too, taking in reversions; and then judge of both. Yet, as I have frequently offered, I will live single with all my heart, if that will do.

I cannot thus live in displeasure and disgrace!—I would, if I could, oblige all my friends—But will it be *just*, will it be *honest*, to marry a man I cannot endure?—If I have not been used to oppose the will of my father, but have always delighted to oblige and obey, judge of the strength of my antipathy by the painful opposition I am obliged to make, and cannot help it.

Pity then, my dearest Bella, my sister, my friend, my companion, my adviser, as you used to be when I was happy, and *plead for*

> Your ever-affectionate
> CL. HARLOWE

[Letter 29.4: Arabella Harlowe] to Miss Clary Harlowe

LET it be pretty, or not pretty, in your wise opinion, I shall speak my mind, I'll assure you, both of you and your conduct in relation to this detested Lovelace. You are a fond, foolish girl, with all your wisdom. Your letter shows *that* enough in twenty places. And as to your cant of living single, nobody will believe you. This is one of your fetches to avoid complying with your duty and the will of the most indulgent parents in the world, as yours have been to you, I am sure—though now they see themselves finely requited for it.

We all, indeed, once thought your temper soft and amiable: but why was it?—

You never was contradicted before: you had always your own way. But no sooner do you meet with opposition in your wishes to throw yourself away upon a vile rake, but you show what you are!—You cannot love Mr Solmes! that's the pretence; but sister, sister, let me tell you, that is because Lovelace has got into your fond heart: a wretch hated, justly hated, by us all; and who has dipped his hands in the blood of your brother—Yet *him* you would make our relation, would you?

I have no patience with you, but for putting the case of my liking such a vile wretch as him. As to the encouragement you pretend he received formerly from all our family, it was before we knew him to be so vile. And the proofs that had such force upon *us* ought to have had some upon *you*—And *would*, had you not been a foolish forward girl; as on this occasion everybody sees you are.

Oh how you run out in favour of the wretch!—His birth, his education, his person, his understanding, his manners, his air, his fortune—reversions too taken in to augment the surfeiting catalogue! What a fond string of love-sick praises is here!—And yet you would live single—Yes, I warrant!—When so many imaginary perfections dance before your dazzled eye!—But no more—I only desire that you will not, while you seem to have such an opinion of your wit, think everyone else a fool; and that you can at pleasure by your whining flourishes make us all dance after your lead.

Write as often as you will, this shall be the last answer or notice you shall have upon this subject from

ARABELLA HARLOWE

I had in readiness a letter for each of my uncles; and meeting in the garden a servant of my uncle Harlowe, I gave them to him to deliver according to their respective directions. If I am to form a judgement by the answers I have received from my brother and sister, as above, I must not, I doubt, expect any good from them. But when I have tried every expedient, I shall have the less to blame myself for if anything unhappy should fall out. I will send you copies of both when I shall see what notice they will be thought worthy of, if of any.

Letter 30: MISS CLARISSA HARLOWE TO MISS HOWE

Sunday night, March 12

THIS man, this Lovelace, gives me great uneasiness. He is extremely bold and rash. He was this afternoon at our church: in hopes to see me, I suppose: and yet, if he had such hopes, his usual intelligence must have failed him.

Shorey was at church; and a principal part of her observation was upon his haughty and proud behaviour when he turned round in the pew where he sat to our family pew—My papa and both my uncles were there; so were my mamma and sister. My brother happily was not!—They all came home in disorder. Nor did the congregation mind anybody but him; it being his first appearance there since the unhappy rencounter.

What did the man come for, if he intended to look challenge and defiance, as Shorey says he did, and as others observed it seems as well as she? Did he come for *my* sake; and, by behaving in such a manner to those present of my family, imagine he was doing me either service or pleasure?—He knows how they hate him: nor will he take pains, would pains do, to obviate their hatred.

You and I, my dear, have often taken notice of his pride, and you have rallied him upon it; and instead of exculpating himself, he has owned it; and, by owning it, has thought he has done enough.

For my own part, I thought pride, in his case, an improper subject for raillery— People of birth and fortune to be proud is so needless, so mean a vice!—If they *deserve* respect, they will have it, without requiring it. In other words, for persons to endeavour to gain respect by a haughty behaviour is to give a proof that they mistrust their own merit: to make confession that they *know* that their *actions* will not attract it. Distinction or quality may be prided in by those to whom distinction or quality is a *new* thing. And then the reflection and contempt which such bring upon themselves by it is a counter-balance.

Such added advantages too, as this man has in his person and mien; learned also, as they say he is—*Such* a man to be haughty, to be imperious!—The lines of his own face at the same time condemning him—how wholly inexcusable!—Proud of what? Not of doing well: the only *justifiable* pride. Proud of *exterior* advantages!—Must not one be led by such a *stop-short* pride, as one may call it, in him or her who has it to mistrust the *interior*. Some people may indeed be afraid that if they did not assume, they would be trampled upon. A very narrow fear, however, since they trample upon themselves who can fear *this*. But this man must be secure, that humility would be an ornament to him.

He has talents, indeed: but those talents, and his personal advantages, have been snares to him. It is plain they have. And this shows that, weighed in an equal balance, he would be found greatly wanting.

Had my friends confided, as they did at first, in that discretion which they do not accuse me of being defective in, I dare say I should have found him out: and then should have been as resolute to dismiss *him* as I was to dismiss others, and as I *am* never to have Mr Solmes. Oh that they did but know my heart!—It shall sooner burst, than voluntarily, uncompelled, undriven, dictate a measure that shall cast a slur either upon them, my sex, or myself.

Excuse me, my dear friend, for these grave *soliloquies*, as I may call them. How have I run from reflection to reflection! But the occasion is recent!—They are all in commotion below upon it!

Shorey says that he watched my mamma's eye, and bowed to her: and she returned the compliment. He always admired my mamma. She would not, I believe, have hated *him* had she not been *bid* to hate him; and had it not been for the rencounter between him and her only son.

Dr Lewin was at church; and observing as everyone else did the disorder into which Mr Lovelace's appearance had put all our family, was so good as to engage him in conversation when the service was over, till they were all gone to their coaches.

My father it seems is more and more incensed against me. And so are my uncles. They had my letters in the morning. Their answers, if they vouchsafe to answer me, will demonstrate, I doubt not, the unseasonableness of this rash man's presence at our church.

They are angry, it seems, at my mamma, for returning his compliment. What an enemy is hatred, even to the common forms of civility! which, however, more distinguish the *payer* of a compliment, than the *receiver*. But they all see, they say, that there is but one way to put an end to his insults. So I shall suffer: and in what will the rash man have benefited himself, or mended his prospects?

I am extremely apprehensive that this worse than ghost-like appearance of his bodes some still bolder step. If he come hither (and very desirous he is of my leave to come), I am afraid there will be murder. To avoid that, if there were no other way, I would most willingly be buried alive.

They are all in consultation: upon my letters, I suppose: so they were in the morning, which occasioned my uncles to be at *our* church. I will send you the copies of those letters, as I promised in my last, when I see whether I can give you their answers with them. This letter is all—I-cannot-tell-what—the effect of apprehension and displeasure at the man who has occasioned these apprehensions. Six lines would have contained all that is in it to the purpose of my story.

Cl. H.

See Letter 36 for Mr Lovelace's account of his behaviour and intentions in his appearance at their church.

Letter 31: MR LOVELACE TO JOHN BELFORD, ESQ.

Monday, March 13

In vain dost[a] thou and thy compeers press me to go to town, while I am in such an uncertainty as I am at present with this proud beauty. All the ground I have hitherto gained with her is entirely owing to her concern for the safety of people whom I have reason to hate.

Write then, thou biddest me, if I will not come. That, indeed, I can do; and as well without a subject, as with one. And what follows shall be a proof of it.

The lady's malevolent brother has now, as I told thee at M. Hall, introduced another man; the most unpromising in his person and qualities, the most formidable in his offers, that has yet appeared.

This man has, by his proposals, captivated every soul of the Harlowe's—*soul!* did I say?—there is not a soul among them but my charmer's. And she, withstanding them all, is actually confined and otherwise maltreated by a father the most gloomy and positive; at the instigation of a brother the most arrogant and selfish—but thou knowest their characters; and I will not therefore sully my paper with them.

But is it not a confounded thing to be in love with one who is the daughter, the sister, the niece, of a family I must eternally despise? And the devil of it, that love increasing, with her—what shall I call it?—'tis not scorn—'tis not pride—'tis not the insolence of an adored beauty—but 'tis to *virtue*, it seems, that my difficulties are owing. And I pay for not being a sly sinner, a hypocrite: for being regardless of my reputation; for permitting slander to open its mouth against me. But is it necessary for such a one as I, who have been used to carry all before me upon my

a   These gentlemen affected the Roman style, as they called it, in their letters: and it was an agreed rule with them to take in good part whatever freedoms they treated each other with, if the passages were written in that style.

own terms—I, who never inspired a fear that had not a discernibly-predominant mixture of love in it, to be a hypocrite?—Well says the poet:

> He who seems virtuous does but act a part,
> And shows not his own nature, but his art.[1]

Well, but it seems I must *practise* for this art, if I would succeed with this truly admirable creature! But why *practise* for it?—Cannot I *indeed* reform?—I have but *one* vice—have I, Jack?—Thou knowest my heart, if any man living does. As far as I know it myself, thou knowest it. But 'tis a cursed deceiver—For it has many and many a time imposed upon its master—*master*, did I say? That am I not now: nor have I been from the moment I beheld this angel of a woman. Prepared indeed as I was by her character, before I saw her: for what a mind must that be, which though not virtuous itself admires not virtue in another?—My visit to Arabella, owing to a mistake of the sisters, into which, as thou hast heard me say, I was led by the blundering uncle; who was to introduce me (but lately come from abroad) to the *divinity*, as I thought; but instead of her carried me to a *mere mortal*. And much difficulty had I, so fond and so forward my lady, to get off without forfeiting all with a family that I intended should give me a goddess.

I have boasted that I was once in love before: and indeed I thought I was. It was in my early manhood—with that quality-jilt, whose infidelity I have vowed to revenge upon as many of the sex as shall come into my power. I believe, in different climes, I have already sacrificed a hecatomb to my Nemesis in pursuance of this vow. But upon recollecting what I was *then*, and comparing it with what I find in myself *now*, I cannot say that I was ever in love before.

What was it then, dost thou ask me, since the disappointment had such effects upon me, when I found myself jilted, that I was hardly kept in my senses?—Why I'll tell thee what, as near as I can remember; for it was a great while ago—It was— egad, Jack, I can hardly tell what it was—but a vehement aspiration after a novelty, I think— Those confounded poets, with their celestially-terrene descriptions, did as much with me as the lady: they fired my imagination and set me upon a desire to become a goddess-maker. I must needs try my new-fledged pinions in sonnet, elogy, and madrigal. I must have a Cynthia, a Stella, a Sacharissa, as well as the best of them: darts and flames and the devil knows what must I give to my Cupid. I must create beauty and place it where nobody else could find it: and many a time have I been at a loss for a subject, when my new-created goddess has been kinder than it was proper for my plaintive sonnet she should be.

Then I had a vanity of *another* sort in my passion: I found myself well received among the women in general; and I thought it a pretty *lady-like* tyranny (I was very young then, and very vain) to single out some *one* of the sex to make *half a score* jealous. And I can tell thee, it had its effect: for many an eye have I made to sparkle with rival indignation: many a cheek glow; and even many a fan have I caused to be snapped at a sister-beauty, accompanied with a reflection, perhaps, at being seen alone with a wild young fellow who could not be in private with both at once.

In short, Jack, it was more pride than love, as I now find it, that put me upon making such a confounded rout about losing this noble varletess. I thought she loved me at least as well as I believed I loved her: nay, I had the vanity to suppose she could not help it. My friends were pleased with my choice. They wanted me to be shackled, for early did they doubt my morals as to the sex. They saw that the dancing, the singing, the musical ladies were all fond of my company: for who (I am in a humour to be vain, I think!—for who) danced, who sung, who touched the string, whatever the instrument, with a better grace than thy friend?

I have no notion of playing the hypocrite so egregiously as to pretend to be blind to qualifications which everyone sees and acknowledges. Such praise-begging hypocrisy! such affectedly-disclaimed attributes! such contemptible praise-traps!—But yet shall my vanity extend only to *personals*, such as the gracefulness of dress, my debonair and my assurance? Self-taught, self-acquired, these!—For my PARTS, I value not myself upon *them*. Thou wilt say I have no cause. Perhaps not: but if I had anything valuable as to intellectuals, those are not my own: and to be proud of what a man is answerable for the abuse of and has no merit in the right use of is to strut, like the jay, in a borrowed plumage.

But to return to my fair jilt—I could not bear that a woman, who was the first that had bound me in silken fetters (they were not iron ones, like those I now wear) should prefer a coronet to me: and when the bird was flown, I set more value upon it than when I had it safe in my cage and could visit it when I would.

But now am I in-*deed* in love. I can think of nothing, of nobody else, but the divine Clarissa Harlowe. *Harlowe!*—How that hated word sticks in my throat—but I shall give her for it, the name of Love.[a]

> CLARISSA!—Oh, there's music in the name,
> That soft'ning me to infant tenderness,
> Makes my heart spring like the first leaps of life![2]

But could'st thou have thought that I, who think it possible for me to favour as much as I can be favoured; that I, who for this charming creature thinks of forgoing the *life of honour* for the *life of shackles*; could adopt those over-tender lines of Otway?

I check myself, and leaving the three first lines of the following of Dryden's to the family of the whiners, find the workings of the passion in my stormy soul better expressed by the three last:

> Love various minds does variously inspire;
> He stirs in gentle natures gentle fire:
> Like that of incense on the altar laid.
>
> But raging flames tempestuous souls invade:
> A fire, which ev'ry windy passion blows;
> With pride it mounts, and with revenge it glows.[3]

And with REVENGE it *shall* glow!—For, dost thou think that if it were not from the hope that this stupid family are all combined to do my work for me, I would bear their insults?—Is it possible to imagine that I would be braved as I am braved, threatened as I am threatened, by those who are afraid to see me; and by this brutal brother too, to whom I gave a life (a life, indeed, not worth my taking!), had I not a greater pride in knowing that by means of his very spy upon me I am playing him off as I please; cooling, or inflaming, his violent passions, as may best suit my purposes; permitting so much to be revealed of my life and actions, and

a Lovelace.

intentions, as may give him such a confidence in his double-faced agent, as shall enable me to dance his employer upon my own wires?

This it is that makes my pride mount above my resentment. By this engine, whose springs I am continually oiling, I play them all off. The busy old tarpaulin uncle I make but my ambassador to Queen Annabella Howe, to engage her (for example sake to her princessly daughter) to join in their cause, and to assert an authority they are resolved, right or wrong (or I could do nothing), to maintain.

And what my motive, dost thou ask? No less than this, that my beloved shall find no protection out of my family; for, if I know *hers*, fly she must, or have the man she hates. This, therefore, if I take my measures right, and my familiar fail me not, will secure her mine, in spite of them all; in spite of her own inflexible heart: mine, without condition; without reformation promises; without the necessity of a siege of years, perhaps; and to be even then, after wearing the guise of a merit-doubting hypocrisy, at an uncertainty, upon a probation unapproved of—Then shall I have all the rascals, and rascalesses of the family come creeping to me: I prescribing to them; and bringing that sordidly-imperious brother to kneel at the foot-stool of my throne.

All my fear arises from the little hold I have in the heart of this charming frost-piece: such a constant glow upon her lovely features; eyes so sparkling; limbs so divinely turned; health so florid; youth so blooming; air so animated: to have a heart so impenetrable—And *I*, the hitherto successful Lovelace, the addresser—How can it be?—Yet there are people, and I have talked with some of them, who remember that she was *born*. Her nurse Norton boasts of her maternal offices in her earliest infancy; and in her education *gradatim*—So that there is full proof that she came not from above, all at once an angel! How then can she be so impenetrable?

But here's her mistake; nor will she be cured of it—she takes the man she calls her father (her mother had been faultless, had she not been her father's wife); she takes the men she calls her uncles; the fellow she calls her brother; and the poor contemptible she calls her sister; to *be* her father, to *be* her uncles, her brother, her sister; and that as such, she owes to some of them reverence, to others respect, let them treat her ever so cruelly!—sordid ties! mere cradle-prejudices!—For had they not been imposed upon her by nature, when she was in a perverse humour, or could she have chosen her relations, would any of these have been among them?

How my heart rises at her preference of them to me, when she is convinced of their injustice to me! Convinced that the alliance would do honour to them all—herself excepted; to whom everyone owes honour; and from whom the most princely family might receive it. But how much more will my heart rise with indignation against her, if I find she hesitates but one moment (however persecuted) about preferring me to the man she avowedly hates! But she cannot surely be so mean as to purchase her peace with them at so dear a rate. She cannot give a sanction to projects formed in malice and founded in a selfishness (and that at her own expense) which she has spirit enough to despise in others; and ought to disavow, that we may not think her a Harlowe.

By this incoherent ramble thou wilt gather that I am not likely to come up in haste, since I must endeavour first to obtain some assurance from the beloved of my soul that I shall not be sacrificed to such a wretch as Solmes! Woe be to the fair one, if ever she be *driven* into my power (for I despair of a voluntary impulse in my favour), and I find a difficulty in obtaining this security!

That her indifference to me is not owing to the superior liking she has for *any* other man is what rivets my chains: but take care, fair one; take care, oh thou most exalted of female minds, and loveliest of persons, how thou debasest thyself by encouraging such a competition as thy sordid relations have set on foot in mere malice to me!—Thou wilt say I rave. And so I do!

Perdition catch my soul, but I do love her.[4]

Else, could I bear the perpetual revilings of her implacable family?—*Else*, could I basely creep about—not her proud father's house—but his paddock—and garden-walls?—Yet (a quarter of a mile's distance between us) not hoping to behold the least glimpse of her shadow?—*Else*, should I think myself repaid, amply repaid, if the fourth, fifth, or sixth midnight stroll, through unfrequented paths, and over briery enclosures, afford me a few cold lines; the even *expected* purport only to let me know that she values the most worthless person of her very worthless family more than she values me; and that she would not write at all, but to induce me to bear insults which un-*man* me to bear!—My lodging in the intermediate way, at a wretched alehouse, disguised like an inmate of it: accommodations equally vile as those I met with in my Westphalian journey. 'Tis well that the necessity for all this arises not from scorn and tyranny, but is first imposed upon herself!

But was ever hero in romance (opposing giants and dragons excepted) called upon to harder trials!—Fortune and family and reversionary grandeur on my side! Such a wretched fellow my competitor!—Must I not be deplorably in love that can go through these difficulties, encounter these contempts? By my soul, I am half ashamed of myself: I, who am perjured too, by priority of obligation, if I am faithful to any woman in the world!

And yet, why say I, I am half ashamed?—Is it not a glory to love *her* whom everyone who sees her either loves, or reveres, or both? Dryden says:

The cause of love can never be assigned;
'Tis in no face;—but in the lover's mind.[5]

And Cowley thus addresses beauty as a mere imaginary:

Beauty! thou wild fantastic ape,
Who dost in ev'ry country change thy shape:
Here black; there brown; here tawny; and there white;
Thou flatterer! who comply'st with every sight!
Who hast no certain what, nor where.[6]

But both these, had they been her cotemporaries and known her, would have confessed themselves mistaken: and taking together person, mind, and behaviour, would have acknowledged the *justice* of the universal voice in her favour.

——Full many a lady
I've ey'd with best regard; and many a time
Th' harmony of their tongues hath into bondage
Brought my too diligent ear. For *several* virtues

Have I lik'd *several* women. Never any
With so full soul, but some defect in her
Did quarrel with the noblest grace she ow'd,
And put it to the *foil*. But SHE!—OH SHE!
So perfect and so peerless is created,
Of ev'ry creature's best.[7]

Thou art curious to know, if I have not started a new game?—If it be possible for so universal a lover to be confined so long to one object? Thou knowest nothing of this charming creature, that thou canst put such questions to me; or thinkest thou knowest me better than thou dost. All that's excellent in her sex is this lady!—Until by *matrimonial* or *equal* intimacies I have found her less than angel, it is impossible to think of any other. Then there are so many stimulatives to such a spirit as mine in this affair, besides love: such a field for stratagem and contrivance, which thou knowest to be the delight of my heart. Then the rewarding end of all—to carry off such a girl as this, in spite of all her watchful and implacable friends; and in spite of a prudence and reserve that I never met with in any of the sex. What a triumph!—What a triumph over the whole sex! And then such a revenge to gratify, which is only at present politically reined in, eventually to break forth with the greater fury. Is it possible, thinkest thou, that there can be room for a thought that is not *of* her, and devoted *to* her?

BY the advices I have this moment received, I have reason to think that I shall have occasion for thee here. Hold thyself in readiness to come down upon the first summons.

Let Belton, and Mowbray, and Tourville, likewise prepare themselves. I have a great mind to contrive a method to send James Harlowe to travel for improvement. Never was there booby-'squire that more wanted it. *Contrive* it, did I say? I have *already* contrived it, could I but put it in execution without being suspected to have a hand in it. This I am resolved upon; if I have not his *sister*, I will have *him*.

But be this as it may, there is a present likelihood of room for glorious mischief. A confederacy had been for *some time* formed against me; but the uncles and the nephew are *now* to be *double*-servanted (*single*-servanted they were before), and those servants are to be *double*-armed when they attend their masters abroad. This indicates their resolute enmity to me, and as resolute favour to Solmes.

The reinforced orders for this hostile apparatus are owing, it seems, to a visit I made yesterday to their church; a good place to begin a reconciliation in, were the heads of the family christians, and did they mean anything by their prayers. My hopes were to have an invitation (or, at least, to gain a pretence) to accompany home the gloomy sire; and so get an opportunity to see my goddess: for I believed they durst not but be *civil* to me, at least. But they were filled with terror, it seems, at my entrance; a terror they could not get over. I saw it indeed in their countenances; and that they all expected something extraordinary to follow. And so it *should* have done, had I been more sure than I am of their daughter's favour. Yet not a hair of any of their stupid heads do I intend to hurt.

You shall all have your directions in writing, if there be occasion. But, after all, I dare say there will be no need but to show your faces in my company.

Such faces never could four men show—Mowbray's so fierce and so fighting:

Belton's so pert and so pimply: Tourville's so fair and so foppish: thine so rough and so resolute: and *I* your leader!—What hearts, although meditating hostility, must those be which we shall not appal?—Each man occasionally attended by a servant or two, long ago chosen for qualities resembling his master's.

Thus, Jack, as thou desirest, have I written: written upon something; upon nothing; upon revenge, which I love; upon love, which I hate, *heartily* hate, because 'tis my master: and upon the devil knows what besides: for, looking back, I'm amazed at the length of it. *Thou* mayest read it: *I* would not for a king's ransom—but so as I do *but* write, thou sayest thou wilt be pleased.

Be pleased then. I *command* thee to be pleased: if not for the writer's, or written's sake, for thy word's sake. And so in the royal style (for am I not likely to be thy king and thy emperor, in the great affair before us?) I bid thee very heartily

                                                                                   Farewell

Letter 32: MISS CLARISSA HARLOWE TO MISS HOWE

                                                              Tuesday, March 14
I NOW send you copies of my letters to my uncles: with their answers. Be pleased to return the latter by the first deposit. I leave them for *you* to make remarks upon. *I* shall make none.

[*Letter 32.1: Clarissa Harlowe to*] John Harlowe, Esq.

                                                                Sat. March 11
ALLOW me, my honoured second papa, as in my happy days you taught me to call you, to implore your interest with my papa to engage him to dispense with a command which, if insisted upon, will deprive me of my free will, and make me miserable for my whole life.

For my *whole life!* let me repeat: is that a small point, my dear uncle, to give up? Am not *I* to live with the man? Is anybody else? Shall I not therefore be allowed to judge for myself whether I *can*, or *cannot* live *happily*, with him?

Should it be ever so *un*-happily, will it be prudence to complain or appeal? If it were, to whom could I appeal with effect against a husband? And would not the invincible and avowed dislike I have for him at *setting out*, justify, as it might seem, any ill usage from him *in that state*; were I to be ever so observant of him? And if I were to be *at all so*, it must be from fear, not love—

Once more, let me repeat, that this is not a *small* point to give up: and that it is *for life*. Why, I pray you, good sir, should I be made miserable for *life?* Why should I be deprived of all comfort but that which the hope that it would be a very short one would afford me?

Marriage is a very solemn engagement, enough to make a young creature's heart ache, with the *best* prospects, when she thinks seriously of it!—To be given up to a strange man; to be engrafted into a strange family; to give up her very name, as a mark of her becoming his absolute and dependent property: to be obliged to prefer this strange man to father, mother—to everybody: and his humours to all her own—Or to contend, perhaps, in breach of a vowed duty for every innocent instance of free will: to go no-whither: to make acquaintance: to give up acquaintance—to renounce even the strictest friendships perhaps; all at his pleasure, whether she think it reasonable to do so or not. Surely, sir, a young creature ought not to be obliged to make all these sacrifices but for such a man as she can approve. If she *is*, how sad must be the case!—how miserable the life, if to be called *life!*

I wish I could obey you all. What a pleasure would it be to me, if I could! *Marry first and love will come after*, was said by one of my dearest friends! But 'tis a shocking assertion! A thousand things may happen to make that state but barely tolerable, where it is entered into with mutual affection: what must it then be, where the husband can have no confidence in the love of his wife, but has reason rather to question it from the preference he *himself* believes she would have given to somebody else, had she been at her own option? What doubt, what jealousies, what want of tenderness, what unfavourable prepossessions will there be in a matrimony thus circumstanced? How will every look, every action, even the most innocent, be liable to misconstruction?—While, on the other hand, an indifference, a carelessness to oblige may take place; and fear *only* can constrain even an *appearance* of what ought to be the real effect of undisguised love?

Think seriously of these things, dear good sir, and represent them to my papa in that strong light which the subject will bear, but in which my sex, and my tender years and inexperience, will not permit me to paint it; and use your powerful interest, that your poor niece may not be consigned to a misery so durable.

I have offered to engage not to marry at all, if that condition may be accepted. What a disgrace is it to me to be thus sequestered from company, thus banished my papa's and mamma's presence, thus slighted and deserted by you, sir, and my other kind uncle! And to be hindered from attending at that public worship which, were I *out* of the way of my duty, would be most likely to reduce me into the right path again!—Is this the way, sir, can it be thought, to be taken with a free and open spirit?—May not this strange method rather harden than convince?—I cannot bear to live in disgrace thus: the very servants, so lately permitted to be under my own direction, hardly daring to speak to me; my own servant discarded with high marks of undeserved suspicion and displeasure, and my sister's maid set over me.

The matter may be too far pushed: indeed it may: and then, perhaps, everyone will be sorry for their parts in it.

May I be suffered to mention an expedient?—If I *am* to be watched, banished, and confined; suppose, sir, it were to be at your house?—Then the neighbouring gentry will the less wonder that the person of whom they used to think so favourably appeared not at church here; and that she received not their visits.

I hope, there can be no objection to this. You used to love to have me with you, sir, when all went *happily* with me: and will you not now permit me, in my *troubles*, the favour of your house, till all this displeasure be overblown?—Upon my word, sir, I will not stir out of doors, if you require the contrary of me: nor will I see anybody, but whom you'll allow me to see, provided you will not bring Mr Solmes to persecute me there.

Procure, then, this favour for me, if you cannot procure the still greater, that of a happy reconciliation; which nevertheless I presume to hope for, if *you* will be so good as to plead for me: and you will then add to those favours and to that indulgence which have bound me, and then will for ever bind me, to be

Your dutiful and obliged niece,
CL. HARLOWE

[*Letter 32.2: John Harlowe to Clarissa Harlowe*]

Sunday night

My dear niece,

IT grieves me to be forced to deny you anything you ask. Yet it *must* be so; for unless you can bring your mind to oblige us in this one point, in which our promises and honour were engaged before we believed there could be so sturdy an opposition, you must never expect to be what you have been to us all.

In short, niece, we are an *embattled phalanx*. Your reading makes you a stranger to nothing but what you should be most acquainted with—so you will see by that expression that we are not to be pierced by your persuasions and invincible persistence. We have agreed *all* to be moved, or *none*; and not to comply without one another: so you know your destiny, and have nothing to do but to yield to it.

Let me tell you, the virtue of obedience lies not in obliging when you can be obliged again: but give up an inclination, and there is some merit in that.

As to your expedient: you shall not come to my house, Miss Clary; though this is a prayer I little thought I ever should have denied you: for were you to keep your word as to *seeing* nobody but whom we please, yet can you *write* to somebody else, and receive letters from him. This we too well know you can, and have done— more is the shame and the pity!

You offer to live single, miss—*we* wish you married: but because you mayn't have the man your heart is set upon, why, truly, you'll have nobody we shall recommend: and as we know that somehow or other you correspond with him, or at least did as long as you could; and as he defies us all, and would not dare to do it if he were not sure of you in spite of us all (which is not a little vexatious to us, you must think); we are resolved to frustrate him, and triumph over him, rather than he over us: that's one word for all. So expect not any advocateship from me: I will not plead for you; and that's enough. From

Your displeased uncle,
JOHN HARLOWE

P.S. For the rest, I refer to my brother Antony.

[*Letter 32.3: Clarissa Harlowe*] *to Antony Harlowe, Esq.*

Honoured sir,   Saturday, March 11

As you have thought fit to favour Mr Solmes with your particular recommendation, and was very earnest in his behalf, ranking him (as you told me, upon introducing him to me) amongst your select friends; and expecting my regards to him accordingly; I beg your patience, while I offer a few things, out of many that I could offer, to your serious consideration, on occasion of his address to me, if I am to use that word.

I am charged with prepossession in another person's favour. You will be pleased, sir, to consider that, till my brother returned from Scotland, that other person was not discouraged, nor was I forbid to receive his visits: and is it such a crime in me, if I *should* prefer an acquaintance of twelve months to one of two?—I believe it will not be pretended that in birth, education, or personal endowments, a comparison can be made between the two. And only let me ask you, sir, if the one would have been thought of for me had he not made such offers, as, upon my word, I think *I* ought not in justice to accept, nor *he* to propose: offers which if *he* had not made, I dare say, my *papa* would not have required them of him.

But the one, it seems, has many faults—Is the other fault-*less?*—The principal thing objected to Mr Lovelace (and a very inexcusable one) is, that he is immoral in his loves—Is not the other in his hatreds?—Nay, as I may say, in his loves too (the object only differing), if *the love of money* be *the root of all evil?*

But, sir, if I am prepossessed, what has Mr Solmes to hope for?—Why should he persevere? What must I think of the man who would wish me to be *his* against my inclination?—And is it not a very harsh thing for my friends to desire to see me married to one I *cannot* love, when they will not be persuaded but that there is one I *do* love?

Treated as I am, now is the time for me to speak out, or never. Let me review what it is Mr Solmes depends upon on this occasion. Does he believe that the disgrace which I suffer on his account will give him a merit with me? Does he think to win my esteem, through my uncles' sternness to me; by my brother's contemptuous usage; by my sister's unkindness; by being denied to visit, or be visited; and to correspond with my chosen friend, although a person of unexceptionable honour and prudence, and of my own sex; my servant to be torn from me, and another servant set over me; to be confined like a prisoner to narrow and disgraceful limits, in order avowedly to mortify me, and to break my spirit; to be turned out of that family-management which I loved, and had the greater pleasure in it, because it was an ease, as I thought, to my mamma, and what my sister chose not; and yet, though time hangs heavy upon my hands, to be so put out of my course, that I have as little inclination as liberty to pursue any of the choice delights of my life—Are these steps necessary to reduce me to a standard so low as to make me a fit wife for this man?—Yet these are all he can have to trust to—And if his reliance is on these measures, I would have him to know that he mistakes *meekness* and *gentleness* of disposition for *servility* and *baseness* of heart.

I beseech you, sir, to let the natural turn and bent of *his* mind, and *my* mind, be considered. What are his qualities, by which he would hope to win my esteem?— Dear, dear sir, if I *am* to be compelled, let it be in favour of a man that can read and write—that can *teach* me something: for what a husband must that man make, who can do nothing but command; and needs himself the instruction he should be qualified to give?

I may be conceited, sir; I may be vain of my little reading; of my writing; as of late I have more than once been told I am—but, sir, the more unequal the proposed match, if so: the better opinion I have of myself, the worse I must have of him; and the more unfit are we for each other.

Indeed, sir, I must say, I thought my friends had put a higher value upon me. My brother pretended once that it was owing to such value, that Mr Lovelace's address was prohibited. Can this be; and such a man as Mr Solmes be intended for me?

As to his proposed settlements, I hope I shall not incur your greater displeasure if I say what all who know me have reason to think, and some have upbraided me for, that I despise those motives. Dear, dear sir, what are settlements to one who has as much of her own as she wishes for?—who has more in her own power, as a single person, than it is probable she would be permitted to have at her disposal as a wife!—whose expenses and ambition are moderate; and, if she had superfluities, would rather dispense them to the necessitous, than lay them by her useless? If then such narrow motives have so little weight with me for my *own* benefit, shall the remote and uncertain view of family-aggrandizement, and that in the person of my *brother* and his *descendants*, be thought sufficient to influence me?

Has the behaviour of that brother to me of late, or his consideration for the family (which had so little weight with him, that he could choose to hazard a life so justly precious as an only son's, rather than not gratify passions which he is above attempting to subdue, and, give me leave to say, has been too much indulged in, either for his own good, or the peace of anybody related to him; has his behaviour, I say) deserved of *me* in particular that I should make a sacrifice of my temporal (and, who knows? of my eternal) happiness, to promote a plan that, if I might be permitted to examine it, I will venture to engage to demonstrate it to be, if not absurd, very precarious, and what must depend upon improbable contingencies?

I am afraid you will condemn my warmth: but does not the occasion require it? To the want of a greater degree of earnestness in my opposition, it seems, it is owing that such advances have been made as have been made. Then, dear sir, allow something, I beseech you, for a spirit raised and embittered by disgraces, which (knowing my own heart) I am confident to say, are unmerited.

But why have I said so much, in answer to the supposed charge of prepossession, when I have declared to my mamma, as now, sir, I do to you, that if it be not insisted upon that I shall marry any other person, particularly this Mr Solmes, I will enter into any engagements never to have the other, nor any man else, without their consents; that is to say, without the consents of my father and mother, and of you my uncle, and my eldest uncle, and my cousin Morden, as he is one of the trustees for my grandfather's bounty to me. As to my brother indeed, I cannot say that his treatment of me has been of late so brotherly, as to entitle him to more than civility from me: and for *this*, give me leave to add, he would be very much my debtor.

If I have not been explicit enough in declaring my dislike to Mr Solmes, that the charge of *prepossession* may not be supposed to influence me against him, I do declare solemnly, that, were there no such man as Mr Lovelace in the world, I would not have *him*. It is necessary, in some *one* of my letters to my dear friends, that I should write so clearly as to put this out of all doubt: and to whom can I better address myself, with an explicitness that can admit of no mistake, than to a gentleman who professes the highest regard for plain-dealing and sincerity?

Let me then, for these reasons, be still more particular in some of my exceptions to him.

Mr Solmes appears to me (to all the world indeed) to have a very narrow mind, and no great capacity: he is coarse and indelicate; as rough in his manners as in his person: he is not only narrow, but covetous: being possessed of great wealth, he enjoys it not; nor has the spirit to communicate to a distress of any kind. Does not his own sister live unhappily for want of a little of his superfluities? And suffers he not his aged uncle, the brother of his own mother, to owe to the generosity of strangers the poor subsistence he picks up from half a dozen families?—You know, sir, my open, free, communicative temper: how unhappy must I be, circumscribed in his narrow, selfish circle! out of which, being withheld by this diabolical parsimony, he dare no more stir, than a conjurer out of his; nor would let me.

Such a man as this, *love*!—Yes, perhaps he may, my grandfather's estate, which he has told several persons (and could not resist hinting it to me, with that sort of pleasure which a low mind takes when it intimates its own interest as a sufficient motive for it to expect another's favour) lies so extremely convenient for him, that it would double the value of a considerable part of his own. That estate, and an alliance which would do credit to his obscurity and narrowness, may make him think he *can* love, and induce him to believe he *does*: but, at most, it is but a second-place love. Riches were, are, and always will be, his predominant passion. *His* were left him by a miser, on this very account: and I must be obliged to forgo all the choice delights of my life, and be as mean as he, or else be quite unhappy! Pardon, sir, this severity of expression!—One is apt to say more than one would, of a person one dislikes, when more is said in his favour than he can possibly deserve; and when he is urged to my acceptance with so much vehemence that there is no choice left me.

Whether these things be perfectly so, or not, while I *think* they are it is impossible I should ever look upon him in the light he is offered to me. Nay, were he to be proved ten times better than I have represented him, and sincerely think him; yet would he be still ten times more disagreeable to me than any other man I know in the world. Let me therefore beseech you, sir, to become an advocate for your niece, that she may not be made a victim of, to a man so highly disgustful to her.

You and my other uncle can do a great deal for me, if you please, with my papa. Be persuaded, sir, that it is not obstinacy I am governed by: it is aversion; an aversion I cannot overcome: for, if I have but *endeavoured* to reason with myself (out of regard to the duty I owe to my papa's will), my heart has recoiled, and I have been averse to myself for offering but to argue with myself, in behalf of a man who, in the light he appears to me, has no one merit; and who, knowing this aversion, could not persevere as he does, if he had the spirit of a man, and a gentleman.

If, sir, you can think the contents of this letter reasonable, I beseech you to support them with your interest: if not—I shall be most unhappy!—Nevertheless, it is but just in me so to write, as that Mr Solmes may know what he has to trust to.

Forgive, dear sir, this tedious letter; and suffer it to have weight with you; and you will for ever oblige

                              Your dutiful and affectionate niece,
                                            CL. HARLOWE

[*Letter 32.4:*] *Mr Antony Harlowe to Miss Clarissa Harlowe*

Niece CLARY,
YOU had better not write to us, or to any of us.

To me, particularly, you had better never to have set pen to paper on the subject whereupon you have written. *He that is first in his own cause*, saith the wise man, *seemeth just: but his neighbour cometh, and searcheth him.*[1] And so, in this respect, will I be your *neighbour*, for I will search your heart to the bottom; that is to say, if your letter be written from your heart. Yet do I know what a task I have undertaken, because of the knack you are noted for at writing: but in defence of a father's authority, in behalf of the good, and honour, and prosperity of a family one comes of, what a hard thing would it be if one could not beat down all the arguments a rebel child (how loath I am to write down that word of Miss Clary Harlowe!) can bring, in behalf of her obstinacy?

In the first place, don't you declare (and that contrary to your declarations to your mother) that you prefer the man we all hate, and who hates us as bad?— Then what a character have you given of a worthy gentleman! I wonder you dare write so freely of a man we all respect. But possibly it may be for that very reason.

How you begin your letter!—Because I value Mr Solmes as my friend, you treat him the worse—That's the plain Dunstable of the matter,[2] miss!—I am not such a fool but I can see that. And so a noted whoremonger is to be chosen before a man who is a money-lover! Let me tell you, niece, this little becomes so nice a one as you have been always reckoned. Who, think you, does most injustice, a prodigal man or a saving man?—The one saves his own money; the other spends other people's: but your favourite is a sinner in grain, and upon record.

The devil's in your sex! God forgive me for saying so—The nicest of them will prefer a vile rake and wh—— I suppose I must not repeat the word. The *word* will offend when the *vicious* denominated by that word will be chosen!—I had not been a bachelor to this time, if I had not seen such a mass of contradictions in you all. Such *gnat-strainers* and *camel swallowers*, as venerable holy writ has it.[3] What names will perverseness call things by—A prudent man, who intends to be just to everybody, is a covetous man!—while a vile, profligate rake is christened with the appellation of a gallant man, and a polite man, I'll warrant you!

It is my firm opinion, Lovelace would not have so much regard for you as he professes, but for two reasons. And what are these?—Why out of spite to all of us—one of them: the other, because of your independent fortune. I wish your good grandfather had not left what he did so much in your own power, as I may say. But little did he imagine his beloved granddaughter would have turned upon all her friends as she has done!

What has Mr Solmes to hope for, if you are prepossessed! Hey-day! Is this *you*, cousin Clary!—Has he then nothing to hope for from your father's, and mother's, and our recommendations?—No, nothing at all, it seems!—Oh brave!—I should think that *this*, with a dutiful child, as we took you to be, was *enough*. Depending on this your duty, we proceeded: and now there is no help for it: for we won't be balked: Neither shall our friend Mr Solmes, I can tell you that.

If your estate is convenient for him, what then? Does that, pert cousin, make it out that he does not love you? He had need to expect some good *with* you, that has so little good to hope for *from* you; mind that. But pray, is not this estate *our* estate, as we may say? Have we not *all* an interest in it, and a prior right, if right were to have taken place? And was it more than a good old man's dotage, God rest his soul! that gave it you before us all?—Well then, ought we not to have a choice who shall have it in marriage with you? And would you have the conscience to wish us to let a vile fellow who hates us all run away with it?—You bid me weigh what you write: do you weigh this, girl: and it will appear we have more to say for ourselves than you were aware of.

As to your hard treatment, as you call it, thank yourself for that. It may be over when you will: so I reckon nothing upon that: you was not banished and confined till all entreaty and fair speeches were tried with you: mind that. And Mr Solmes can't help your obstinacy—Let that be observed too.

As to being visited and visiting, you never was fond of either: so that's a grievance put into the scale to make weight—As to disgrace, that's as bad to us as to you: so fine a young creature!—So much as we used to brag of you!—And too, besides, this is all in your power, as the rest. But your heart recoils, when you would persuade yourself to obey your parents—finely described, i'n't it!—too truly described, I own, as you go on. I know that you may love him if you will. I had a good mind to bid you hate him; then, perhaps, you'd like him the better: for I have always found a most horrid romantic perverseness in your sex. To *do* and to *love* what you should not, is meat, drink, and vesture to you all.

I am absolutely of your brother's mind, that reading and writing, though not too much for the wits of you young girls, are too much for your judgements. You say, you *may be* conceited, cousin; you *may be* vain!—And so you *are*, to despise this gentleman as you do. He can read and write as well as *most* gentlemen, I can tell you *that*. Who told you Mr Solmes can't read and write? But you must have a husband who can learn you something!—I wish you knew but your *duty* as well as you do your talents—That, niece, you have of late to learn; and Mr Solmes will therefore find something to instruct you in. I won't show him this letter of yours, though you seem to desire it, lest it should provoke him to be too severe a schoolmaster, when you are his'n.

But now I think of it, suppose you *are* readier at your pen than he—you will make the more useful wife to him; won't you? For who so good an economist as you?—And you may keep all his accounts and save yourselves a steward. And, let me tell you, this is a fine advantage in a family: for those stewards are often sad dogs, and creep into a man's estate, before he knows where he is; and not seldom is he forced to pay them interest for his own money. I know not why a good wife should be above these things. 'Tis better than lying abed half the day, and junketing and card-playing all the night, and making yourselves wholly useless to every good purpose in your own families, as is now the fashion among ye—The deuce take ye all that do so, say I!—only that, thank my stars, I am a bachelor!—Then this is a province you are admirably versed in: you grieve that it is taken from you *here*, you know. So here, miss, with Mr Solmes you will have something to keep account of, for the sake of you and your children: with t'other, perhaps, you'll have an account to keep, too—But an account of what will go over the left shoulder: only of what he squanders, what he borrows, and what he owes, and never will pay. Come, come, cousin, you know nothing of the world; a man's a man, and you may have many partners in a handsome man, and costly ones too, who may lavish away all you save. Mr Solmes therefore for my money, and I hope for yours!

But Mr Solmes is a coarse man. He is not delicate enough for your niceness, because I suppose he dresses not like a fop and a coxcomb, and because he lays not himself out in complimental nonsense, the poison of female minds. He is a man of sense, I can tell you. No man talks more to the purpose to *us*. But you fly him so that he has no opportunity given him to express it to *you*: and a man who loves, if he have ever so much sense, looks like a fool, especially when he is despised and treated as you treated him the last time he was in your company.

As to his sister; she threw herself away (as you want to do) against his full warning: for he told her what she had to trust to, if she married where she did marry. And he was as good as his word; and so an honest man ought. Offences against warning ought to be smarted for. Take care this be not your case. Mind that.

His uncle deserves no favour from *him*, for he would have circumvented him, and got Sir Oliver to leave to himself the estate he had always designed for him, his nephew; and brought him up in the hope of it. *Too ready forgiveness does but encourage offences*: that's your good father's maxim: and there would not be so many headstrong daughters as there are, if this maxim were kept in mind. Punishments are of service to offenders; rewards should be only to the meriting: and I think the former are to be dealt out rigorously, in wilful cases.

As to his *love*; he shows it but too much for your deservings, as they have been of late; let me tell you that: and this is *his* misfortune; and may in time perhaps be *yours*.

As to his parsimony, which you wickedly call diabolical—a very free word in your mouth, let me tell ye—little reason have *you* of all people for this, on whom he proposes, of his own accord, to settle all he has in the world: a proof, let him love *riches* as he will, that he loves *you* better. But that you may be without excuse on this score, we will tie him up to your own terms, and oblige him, by the marriage articles, to allow you a very handsome quarterly sum, to do what you please with. And this has been told you before; and I have said it to Mrs Howe, that good and worthy lady, before her proud daughter, that you might hear of it again.

To contradict the charge of prepossession to Lovelace, you offer never to have him without our consents: and what is this saying, but that you will hope on for our consents, and to wheedle and tire us out: Then he will always be in expectation, while you are single: and we are to live on at this rate (are we?), vexed by you, and continually watchful about you; and as continually exposed to his insolence and threats. Remember last Sunday, girl!—What *might* have happened, had your brother and he met?—Moreover, you can't do with such a spirit as his, as you can with worthy Mr Solmes: the one you make tremble; the other will make you quake. Mind that: and you will not be able to help yourself. And remember that if there should be any misunderstanding between *one* of them and you, we should all interpose; and with effect, no doubt: but with the *other* it would be *self-do self-have*, and who would either care or dare to put in a word for you? Nor let the supposition of matrimonial differences frighten you: honeymoon lasts not nowadays above a fortnight; and Dunmow flitch, as I have been informed, was *never* claimed[4]; though some say *once* it was. Marriage is a queer state, child, whether paired by the parties or by their friends. Out of three brothers of us, you know there was but one had courage to marry. And why was it, do you think? We were wise by other people's experience.

Don't despise money so much; you may come to know the value of it: that is a piece of *instruction* that you *are to learn*; and which, according to your *own* notions, Mr Solmes will be *able to teach you*.

I do indeed *condemn your warmth*. I won't *allow for disgraces you bring upon yourself*. If I thought them *unmerited*, I would be your advocate. But it was always my notion, that children should not dispute their parents' authority. When your grandfather left his estate to you, though his three sons, and a grandson, and your elder sister were in being, we all acquiesced: and why? Because it was our father's doing. Do you imitate that example: if you will not, those who set it you have the more reason to hold you inexcusable. Mind that, cousin.

You mention your brother too scornfully: and in your letter to him are very disrespectful, as well as in your sister's, to her. He is your brother; a third older than yourself; and a *man*. And while you can pay so much regard to one man of a *twelve month's acquaintance only*, pray be so good as not to forget what is due to a brother, who (next to us three brothers) is the head of the family; and on whom the name depends: as upon your dutiful compliance depends the success of the noblest plan that ever was laid down for the honour of the family you are come of. And pray now, let me ask you if the honour of that will not be an honour to you?—If you don't think so, the more unworthy you. You shall see the plan, if you promise not to be prejudiced against it, right or wrong. If you are not besotted to that man, I am sure you will like it. If you are, were Mr Solmes an angel, it would signify nothing: for the devil is love, and love is the devil, when it gets into any of your heads. Many examples have I seen of that.

If there were no such man as Lovelace in the world, you would not have Mr Solmes—you *would not*, miss!—very pretty, truly!—We *see* how your spirit is *embittered* indeed. Wonder not, since it is come to your *will nots*, that those who have authority over you say *you shall have the other*. And I am one. Mind that. And if it behoves You *to speak out*, miss, it behoves US not to *speak in*. What's *sauce for the goose is sauce for the gander*: take that in your thought too.

I humbly apprehend that Mr Solmes *has the spirit of a man, and a gentleman*. I would admonish you therefore not to provoke it. He pities you as much as he loves you. He says he will convince you of his love by deeds, since he is not permitted by you to express it by words. And all his dependence is upon your generosity hereafter. We hope he *may* depend upon that: we encourage him to think he may. And this heartens him up. So that you may lay his constancy at your parents' and your uncles' doors; and this will be another mark of your duty, you know.

You must be sensible that you reflect upon your parents, and all of us, when you tell me you cannot in *justice* accept of the settlements proposed to you. This reflection we should have wondered at from you once; but now we don't.

There are many other very censurable passages in this free letter of yours; but we must place them to the account of your *embittered* spirit: I am glad you mentioned that word, because we should have been at a loss what to have called it—much rather have had reason to give it a better name.

I love you dearly still, miss. I think you, though my niece, one of the finest young gentlewomen I ever saw. But, upon my conscience, I think you ought to obey your parents, and oblige me and my brother John: for you know very well that we have nothing but your good at heart; consistently, indeed, with the good and honour of *all* of us. What must we think of any one of it, who would not promote the good of the whole? and who would set one part of it against another?—which God forbid, say I!—You see I am for the good of *all*. What shall *I* get by it, let things go as they will? Do I want anything of anybody for my own sake? Does my brother John?—Well, then, cousin Clary, what would you be at, as I may say?

Oh but, you can't love Mr Solmes!—But, I say, you know not *what* you can do. You *encourage* yourself in your dislike. You *permit* your heart (little did I think it was such a froward one) to *recoil*. Take it to task, niece; *drive it on* as fast as it *recoils* (we do so in all our sea-fights, and land-fights too, by our sailors and soldiers, or we should not conquer); and we are all sure you will overcome it. And why? Because you *ought*. So *we* think, whatever *you* think: and whose thoughts are to be preferred? You may be wittier than we; but if you are wiser, we have lived some of us, let me tell you, to very little purpose thirty or forty years longer than you.

I have written as long a letter as yours. I may not write in so lively, or so polite a style as my niece: but I think I have all the argument on my side. And you will vastly oblige me, if you will show me, by your compliance with all our desires, that you think so too. If you do not, you must not expect an advocate, or even a friend, in me, dearly as I love you. For then I shall be sorry to be called

Your uncle,

Tuesday, two in the morning   ANTONY HARLOWE

Postscript

You must send me no more letters: but a compliable one you may send. But I need not have forbid you; for I am sure, this, by fair argument, is unanswerable: I know it is. I have written day and night, I may say, ever since Sunday morning, only church-time, or the like of that. But this is the last, I can tell you, from

A. H.

Letter 33: MISS CLARISSA HARLOWE TO MISS HOWE

Thursday, March 16

HAVING met with such bad success in my application to those of my own family, I have taken a step that will surprise you. It is no other than writing a letter to Mr Solmes himself. I sent it; and have his answer. He had certainly help in it. For I have seen a letter of his, as indifferently worded as poorly spelled. Yet the superscription is of his dictating, I dare say, for he is a formal wretch. With these, I shall enclose one from my brother to me, on occasion of mine to Mr Solmes. I did think that it was possible to discourage this man from proceeding; and that would have answered all my wishes. It was worth the trial. But you'll see nothing will do. My brother has taken his measures too securely.

[*Letter 33.1: Clarissa Harlowe*] *to Roger Solmes, Esq.*

SIR,   Wednesday, Mar. 15
You will wonder to receive a letter from me, and more still at the uncommon
subject of it. But the necessity of the case will justify me, at least in my own
apprehension, and I shall therefore make no other apology for it.

When you first came acquainted with my father's family, you found the writer
of this one of the happiest creatures in the word, beloved by the best and most
indulgent of parents, and rejoicing in the kind favour of two affectionate uncles,
and in the esteem of every one.

But how is this happy scene now changed!—You was pleased to cast a favourable
eye upon me. You addressed yourself to my friends. Your proposals were approved
of by them; approved of without consulting me, as if my choice and happiness
were of the least signification. Those who had a right to all reasonable obedience
from me, insisted upon it without reserve. I had not the felicity to think as they
did, almost the first time my sentiments differed from theirs. I besought them to
indulge me in a point so important to my future happiness: but, alas, in vain! And
then (for I thought it was but honest) I told you my mind; and even that my
affections were engaged. But, to my mortification and surprise, you persisted, and
still persist.

The consequence of all is too grievous for me to repeat: you, who have such free
access to the rest of the family, know it too well; too well you know it, either for
the credit of your own generosity, or for my reputation. I am used, on your
account, as I never before was used, and never before was thought to deserve to be
used; and this was the hard, the impossible condition of their returning favour,
that I must prefer a man *to* all others, that *of* all others I cannot prefer.

Thus distressed and made unhappy, and all for your sake, and through your
cruel perseverance, I write, sir, to demand of you the peace of mind you have
robbed me of: to demand of you the love of so many dear friends, of which you
have deprived me; and, if you have the generosity that should distinguish a man,
and a gentleman, to adjure you not to continue an address that has been attended
with such cruel effects to the creature you profess to esteem.

If you really value me, as my friends would make me believe, and as you have
declared you do, must it not be a mean and selfish value? A value that can have
no merit with the unhappy object of it, because it is attended with effects so
grievous to her? It must be for *your own sake* only, not for *mine*. And, even in this
point, you *must* be mistaken; for would a prudent man wish to marry one who has
not a heart to give? Who cannot esteem him? Who therefore must prove a bad
wife?—And how cruel would it be to make a poor creature a bad wife, whose
pride it would be to make a good one?

If I am capable of judging, our tempers and inclinations are vastly different.
Any other of my sex will make you happier than I can. The treatment I meet with,
and the obstinacy, as it is called, with which I support myself under it, ought to
convince you of this; were I *not* able to give so good a reason for this my supposed
perverseness, as that I cannot consent to marry a man whom I cannot value.

But if, sir, you have not so much generosity in your value for me, as to desist for *my own* sake, let me conjure you, by the regard due to *yourself*, and to your own future happiness, to discontinue your suit, and place your affections on a worthier object: for why should you make *me* miserable, and *yourself* not happy? By this means you will do all that is now in your power to restore me to the affection of my friends; and if that can be, it will leave me in as happy a state as you found me. You need only to say that you see there are no HOPES, as you will perhaps complaisantly call it, of succeeding with me (and indeed, sir, there cannot be a greater truth than this) and that you will therefore no more think of me; but turn your thoughts another way.

Your compliance with this request will lay me under the highest obligation to your generosity, and make me ever

Your well-wisher, and humble servant,
CLARISSA HARLOWE

[Letter 33.2: Roger Solmes] to Miss Clarissa Harlowe

These most humbly present
Thursday, March 16

Dearest miss,

YOUR letter has had a very contrary effect upon me to what you seem to have expected from it. It has doubly convinced me of the excellency of your mind and the honour of your disposition. Call it *selfish*, or what you please, I must persist in my suit; and happy shall I be, if by patience and perseverance, and a steady and unalterable devoir, I may at last overcome the difficulty laid in my way.

As your good parents, your uncles, and other friends, are absolutely determined you shall never have Mr Lovelace, if they can help it; and as I presume no other person is in the way, I will contentedly wait the issue of this matter. And, forgive me, dearest miss; but a person should sooner persuade me to give up to him my estate, as an instance of my generosity, because *he* could not be happy without it, than I would a much more valuable treasure, to promote the felicity of another, and make his way easier to circumvent myself.

Pardon me, dear miss, but I must persevere, though I am sorry you suffer on my account, as you are pleased to think; for I never before saw the lady I could love: and while there is any hope, and that you remain undisposed of to some other happier man, I must and will be

Your faithful and obsequious admirer,
ROGER SOLMES

[Letter 33.3: James Harlowe, Jun.] to Miss Clarissa Harlowe

Thursday, March 16

WHAT a fine whim you took into your head, to write a letter to Mr Solmes to persuade him to give up his pretensions to you!—Of all the pretty romantic flights you have delighted in, this was certainly one of the most extraordinary. But to say nothing of what fires us all with indignation against you (your owning your prepossession in a villain's favour, and your impertinence to me and your sister, and your uncles; one of which has given it you home, child), how can you lay at Mr

Solmes's door the usage you so bitterly complain of?—You know, little fool as you are, that it is your fondness for Lovelace that has brought upon you all these things; and which would have happened whether Mr Solmes had honoured you with his addresses or not.

As you must needs know this to be true, consider, pretty, witty miss, if your fond love-sick heart can let you consider, what a fine figure all your expostulations with us, and charges upon Mr Solmes, make!—With what propriety do you demand of *him* to restore to you your former happiness, as you call it, and *merely* call it, for if you thought our favour so, you would restore it to yourself, since it is yet in your own power to do so. Therefore, Miss Pert, none of your pathetics, except in the right place. Depend upon it, whether you have Mr Solmes or not, you shall never have your heart's delight, the vile rake Lovelace, if our parents, if our uncles, if I, can hinder it. No! you fallen angel, you shall not give your father and mother such a *son*, nor me such a *brother*, in giving yourself that profligate wretch for a *husband*. And so set your heart at rest, and lay aside all thoughts of him, if ever you expect forgiveness, reconciliation, or a kind opinion, from any of your family; but especially from him, who, at present, styles himself

Your brother,
James Harlowe

P.S. I know your knack at letter-writing. If you send me an answer to this, I'll return it unopened, for I won't argue with your perverseness in so plain a case—Only once for all, I was willing to put you right as to Mr Solmes; whom I think to blame to trouble his head about you.

Letter 34: MR LOVELACE TO JOHN BELFORD, ESQ.

Friday, March 17

I RECEIVE, with great pleasure, the early and cheerful assurances of your loyalty and love. And let our principal and most trusty friends named in my last know that I do.

I would have thee, Jack, come down as soon as thou canst. I believe I shall not want the others so soon. Yet they may come down to Lord M.'s. I will be there, if not to receive them, to satisfy my Lord, that there is no new mischief in hand which will require his second intervention.

For thyself, thou must be constantly with me: not for my *security*: the family dare do nothing but bully: they bark only at distance: but for my *entertainment*: that thou mayst from the Latin and the English classics keep my love-sick soul from drooping.

Thou hadst best come to me here, in thy old corporal's coat, thy servant out of livery, and to be upon a familiar foot with thee, as a distant relation, to be provided for by thy interest above; I mean not in heaven, thou mayst be sure. Thou wilt find me at a little alehouse; they call it an inn; the White Hart; most terribly wounded (but by the weather only) the sign—in a sorry village, within five miles from Harlowe Place. Everybody knows Harlowe Place—for, like Versailles, it is sprung up from a dunghill within every elderly person's remembrance. Every poor body, particularly, knows it: but that only for a few years past, since a certain angel has appeared there among the sons and daughters of men.

The people here at the Hart are poor but honest; and have gotten it into their heads that I am a man of quality in disguise, and there is no reining in their officious respect. There is a pretty little smirking daughter, seventeen six days ago: I call her my Rosebud. Her grandmother (for there is no mother) a good neat old woman as ever filled a wicker-chair in a chimney-corner has besought me to be merciful to her.

This is the right way with me. Many and many a pretty rogue had I spared, whom I did not spare, had my power been acknowledged and my mercy been in time implored. But the *debellare superbos* should be my motto, were I to have a new one.

This simple chit (for there is a simplicity in her thou wilt be highly pleased with: all humble; all officious; all innocent—I love her for her humility, her officiousness and even for her *innocence*) will be pretty amusement to thee, while I combat with the weather, and dodge and creep about the walls and purlieus of Harlowe Place. Thou wilt see in her mind, all that her superiors have been taught to conceal in order to render themselves less natural, and more undelightful.

But I charge thee, that thou do not (what I would not permit myself to do, for the world—I charge thee, that thou do not) crop my Rosebud. She is the only flower of fragrance that has blown in this vicinage for ten years past, or will for ten years to come: for I have looked backward to the *have-been's*, and forward to the *will-be's*, having but too much leisure upon my hands in my present waiting.

I never was so honest for so long together since my matriculation. It behoves me so to be—Some way or other, my recess may be found out; and it will then be thought that my Rosebud has attracted me. A report in my favour from simplicities so amiable may establish me; for the grandmother's relation to my Rosebud may be sworn to: and the father is an honest poor man: has no joy but in his Rosebud. Oh Jack! spare thou therefore (for I shall leave thee often alone; spare thou) my Rosebud!—Let the rule I never departed from but it cost me a long regret be observed to my Rosebud! Never to ruin a poor girl whose simplicity and innocence was all she had to trust to; and whose fortunes were too low to save her from the rude contempts of worse minds than her own, and from an indigence extreme: such a one will only pine in secret; and at last, perhaps, in order to refuge herself from slanderous tongues and virulence be induced to tempt some guilty stream, or seek an end in the knee-encircling garter that, peradventure, was the first attempt of abandoned Love. No defiances will my Rosebud breathe; no *self*-dependent, *thee*-doubting watchfulness (indirectly challenging thy inventive machinations to do their worst) will she assume. Unsuspicious of her danger, the lamb's throat will hardly shun thy knife!—Oh be not thou the butcher of my lambkin!

The less be thou so, for the reason I am going to give thee—The gentle heart is touched by Love! Her soft bosom heaves with a passion she has not yet found a name for. I once caught her eye following a young carpenter, a widow neighbour's son, living (to speak in her dialect) *at the little white house over the way*. A gentle youth he also seems to be, about three years older than herself: playmates from infancy till his eighteenth and her fifteenth year furnished a reason for a greater distance in show, while their hearts gave a better for their being nearer than ever: for I soon perceived the love reciprocal: a scrape and a bow at first seeing his pretty mistress; turning often to salute her following eye; and when a winding lane was to deprive him of her sight his whole body turned round, his hat more reverently doffed, than before. This answered (for, unseen, I was behind her) by a low curtsy, and a sigh that Johnny was too far off to hear!—Happy whelp! said I to myself!—I withdrew; and in tripped my Rosebud, as if satisfied with the dumb show, and wishing nothing beyond it.

I have examined the little heart: she has made me her confidant. She owns she could love Johnny Barton very well: and Johnny Barton has told her he could love her better than any maiden he ever saw—But, alas! it must not be thought of. Why not be thought of?—She don't know!—And then she sighed: but Johnny has an aunt who will give him a hundred pounds when his time is out; and her father cannot give her but a few things, or so, to set her out with. And though Johnny's mother says she knows not where Johnny would have a prettier, or notabler wife, yet—And then she sighed again—What signifies talking?—I would not have Johnny be unhappy and poor for me!—For what good would that do *me*, you know, sir!

What would I give (by my soul, my angel will indeed reform me if her friends' implacable folly ruin us not both!—what would I give) to have so innocent and so good a heart as either my Rosebud's, or Johnny's!

I have a confounded mischievous one—by *nature* too, I think!—A good motion now and then rises from it: but it dies away presently—a love of intrigue!—an invention for mischief!—a triumph in subduing!—fortune encouraging and supporting!—and a constitution—What signifies palliating? But I believe I had been a rogue had I been a plough-boy.

But the devil's in this sex! Eternal misguiders! Who that has once trespassed ever recovered his integrity? And yet where there is not virtue, which nevertheless we free-livers are continually plotting to destroy, what is there even in the ultimate of our wishes with them?—*Preparation* and *expectation* are, in a manner, everything: *reflection*, indeed, may be something, if the mind be hardened above feeling the guilt of a past *trespass*: but the *fruition*, what is there in that? And yet, that being the end, nature will not be satisfied without it.

See what grave reflections an innocent subject will produce! It gives me some pleasure to think that it is not out of my *power* to reform: but then, Jack, I am afraid I must keep better company than I do at present—for we certainly harden one another. But be not cast down, my boy; there will be time enough to give thee, and all thy brethren, warning to choose another leader: and I fancy thou wilt be the man.

Meantime, as I make it my rule whenever I have committed a very capital enormity to do some good by way of atonement, and as I believe I am a pretty deal indebted on that score, I intend before I leave these parts (successfully shall I leave them, I hope, or I shall be tempted to do double the mischief by way of revenge, though not to my Rosebud any) to join a hundred pounds to Johnny's aunt's hundred pounds, to make one innocent couple happy. I repeat, therefore, and for half a dozen more *therefores*, spare thou my Rosebud.

An interruption—another letter anon; and both shall go together.

Letter 35: MR LOVELACE TO JOHN BELFORD, ESQ.

I HAVE found out by my watchful spy almost as many of my charmer's motions as those of the rest of her relations. It delights me to think how the rascal is caressed by the uncles and nephew; and let into *their* secrets; yet proceeds all the time by *my* line of direction. I have charged him, however, on forfeiture of his present weekly stipend, and my future favour, to take care that neither my beloved or any of the family suspect him: I have told him, that he may indeed watch her egresses and regresses; but that only to keep off other servants from her paths; yet not to be seen by her himself.

The dear creature has tempted him, he told *them*, with a bribe (*which she never offered*), to convey a letter (*which she never wrote*) to Miss Howe; *he believes*, with one enclosed (*perhaps to me*): but he declined it: and he begged they would take no notice of it to *her*. This brought him a stingy shilling; great applause; and an injunction followed it to all the servants for the strictest look-out lest she should contrive some way to send it—And, about an hour after, an order was given him to throw himself in her way; and (expressing his concern for denying her request) to tender his service to her and to bring them her letter: which it will be *proper for him to report* that she has refused to give him.

Now seest thou not, how many good ends this contrivance answers?

In the first place, the lady is secured by it against her own knowledge, in the liberty allowed her of taking her private walks in the garden: for this attempt has confirmed them in their belief that now they have turned off her maid she has no way to send a letter out of the house: if she had, she would not have run the risk of tempting a fellow who had not been in her secret so that she can prosecute unsuspectedly her correspondence with me and Miss Howe.

In the next place, it will afford me an opportunity, perhaps, of a private interview with her, which I am meditating, let her take it as she will; having found out by my spy (who can keep off everybody else), that she goes every morning and evening to a woodhouse remote from the dwelling-house, under pretence of visiting and feeding a set of bantam poultry, which were produced from a breed that was her grandfather's, and which for that reason she is very fond of; as also of some other curious fowls brought from the same place. I have an account of all her motions here. And as she has owned to me in one of her letters that she corresponds privately with Miss Howe, I presume it is by this way.

The interview I am meditating will produce her consent, I hope, to other favours of the like kind: for, should she not choose the place I am expecting to see her in, I can attend her anywhere in the rambling, Dutch-taste garden, whenever she will permit me that honour: for my implement, hight Joseph Leman, has given me the opportunity of procuring two keys (one of which I have given him, for reasons good) to the garden door, which opens to the haunted coppice, as tradition has made the servants think it; a man having been found hanging in it about twenty years ago: and Joseph, upon the least notice, will leave it unbolted.

But I was obliged to give him previously my honour, that no mischief shall happen to any of my adversaries, from this liberty: for the fellow tells me, that he loves all his masters; and, only that he knows I am a man of honour; and that my alliance will do credit to the family; and after prejudices are overcome everybody will think so; or he would not for the world act the part he does.

There never was a rogue, who had not a salvo to himself for being so. What a praise to *honesty*, that every man pretends to it even at the instant that he knows he is pursuing the methods that will perhaps prove him a knave to the whole world, as well as to his own conscience!

But what this stupid family can mean, to make all this necessary, I cannot imagine. My REVENGE and my LOVE are uppermost by turns. If the latter succeed not, the gratifying of the former will be my only consolation: and, by all that's good, they shall feel it; although, for it, I become an exile from my native country for ever.

I will throw myself into my charmer's presence: I have twice already attempted it in vain. I shall then see what I may depend upon from her favour. If I thought I had no prospect of that, I should be tempted to carry her off—That would be a rape worthy of a Jupiter!

But all gentle shall be my movements: all respectful, even to reverence, my address to her!—Her hand shall be the only witness to the pressure of my lip—my trembling lip: I *know* it will tremble, if I do not *bid* it tremble. As soft my sighs as the sighs of my gentle Rosebud. By *my* humility will I invite *her* confidence: the loneliness of the place shall give me no advantage: to dissipate her fears, and engage her reliance upon my honour for the future, shall be my whole endeavour: but little will I complain of, not at all will I threaten those who are continually threatening me: but yet with a view to act the part of Dryden's lion; to secure my love, or to let loose my vengeance upon my hunters.

> What though his mighty soul his grief contains?
> He meditates revenge, who least complains:
> And like a lion slumb'ring in his way,
> Or sleep dissembling, while he waits his prey,
> His fearless foes within his distance draws;
> Constrains his roaring, and contracts his paws:
> Till at the last, his time for fury found,
> He shoots with sudden vengeance from the ground:
> The prostrate vulgar passes o'er, and spares;
> But, with a lordly rage, his hunters tears.[1]

Letter 36: MISS CLARISSA HARLOWE TO MISS HOWE

Sat. night, Mar. 18

I HAVE been frighted out of my wits—still am in a manner out of breath—thus occasioned—I went down under the usual pretence in hopes to find something from you. Concerned at my disappointment I was returning from the woodhouse, when I heard a rustling, as of somebody behind a stack of wood. I was extremely surprised: but still more, to behold a man coming from behind the furthermost stack. Oh thought I, at that moment, the sin of a prohibited correspondence!

In the same point of time that I saw him, he besought me not to be frighted: and still nearer approaching me, threw open a horseman's coat: and who should it be but Mr Lovelace! I could not scream out (yet attempted to scream, the moment I saw a man; and again when I saw who it was) for I had no voice: and had I not caught hold of a prop, which supported the old roof, I should have sunk.

I had hitherto, as you know, kept him at distance: and now, as I recovered myself, judge of my first emotions when I recollected his character from every mouth of my family; his enterprising temper; and found myself alone with him in a place so near a by-lane and so remote from the house.

But his respectful behaviour soon dissipated these fears, and gave me others lest we should be seen together, and information of it given to my brother: the consequences of which, I could readily think, would be, if not further mischief, an imputed assignation, a stricter confinement, a forfeited correspondence with you, my beloved friend, and a pretence for the most violent compulsion: and neither the one set of reflections, nor the other, acquitted him to me for his bold intrusion.

As soon therefore as I could speak, I expressed with the greatest warmth my displeasure; and told him that he cared not how much he exposed me to the resentments of all my friends, provided he could gratify his own impetuous humour; and I commanded him to leave the place that moment: and was hurrying from him; when he threw himself in the way at my feet, beseeching my stay for one moment; declaring that he suffered himself to be guilty of this rashness, as I thought it, to avoid one much greater—for in short, he could not bear the hourly insults he received from my family with the thoughts of having so little interest in my favour, that he could not promise himself, that his patience and forbearance would be attended with any other issue than to lose me for ever, and be triumphed over and insulted upon it.

This man, you know, has very ready knees. You have said that he ought in small points frequently to offend, on purpose to show what an address he is master of.

He run on, expressing his apprehensions that a temper so gentle and obliging as he said mine was to everybody but him (and a dutifulness so exemplary inclining me to do my part to others, whether they did theirs or not by me) would be wrought upon in favour of a man set up in part to be revenged upon myself for my grandfather's envied distinction of me; and in part to be revenged upon him for having given life to one who would have taken his; and now sought to deprive him of hopes dearer to him than life.

I told him he might be assured that the severity and ill-usage I met with would be far from effecting the intended end: that although I could with great sincerity declare for a single life, which had always been my choice; and particularly, that if ever I married, if they would not insist upon the man I had an aversion to, it should not be with the man they disliked—

He interrupted me here: he hoped I would forgive him for it; but he could not help expressing his great concern that, after so many instances of his passionate and obsequious devotion—

And pray, sir, said I, let me interrupt you in my turn—Why don't you assert, in still plainer words, the obligation you have laid me under by this your boasted devotion? Why don't you let me know, in terms as high as your implication, that a perseverance I have not wished for, which has set all my relations at variance with me, is a merit that throws upon me the guilt of ingratitude for not answering it as you seem to expect?

I must forgive him, he said, if he, who pretended only to a comparative merit (and otherwise thought no man living could deserve me), had presumed to hope for a greater share in my favour than he had hitherto met with, when such men as Mr Symmes, Mr Wyerley, and now, lastly, so vile a reptile as this Solmes, however discouraged by myself, were made his competitors. As to the perseverance I mentioned, it was impossible for him *not* to persevere: but I must needs know, that were he not in being, the terms Solmes had proposed were such as would have involved me in the same difficulties with my relations that I now laboured under. He therefore took the liberty to say, that my favour to him, far from increasing those difficulties, would be the readiest way to extricate me from them. They had made it impossible (he told me, with too much truth) to oblige them any way but by sacrificing myself to Solmes. They were well apprised besides of the difference between the two; one whom they hoped to manage as they pleased; the other who could and would protect me from every insult; and who had *natural* prospects much superior to my brother's *foolish* views, of a title.

How comes this man to know so well all our foibles? But I more wonder, how he came to have a notion of meeting me in this place!

I was very uneasy to be gone; and the more as the night came on apace. But there was no getting from him, till I had heard a great deal more of what he had to say.

As he hoped that I would one day make him the happiest man in the world, he assured me that he had so much regard for my fame that he would be as far from advising any step that were likely to cast a shade upon my reputation (although that step were to be ever so much in his own favour) as I would be to follow such advice. But since I was not to be permitted to live single, he would submit it to my consideration whether I had any way but *one* to avoid the intended violence to my inclinations: my father so jealous of his authority: both my uncles in my father's way of thinking: my cousin Morden at a distance: my uncle and aunt Hervey awed into *insignificance* was his word: my brother and sister inflaming everyone; Solmes's offers captivating: Miss Howe's mother rather of party with them, for motives respecting example to her own daughter.

And then he asked me if I would receive a letter from his aunt Lawrance on this occasion: for his aunt Sadleir, he said, having lately lost her only child, hardly looked into the world or thought of it farther than to wish him married, and, preferably to all the women in the world, with me.

To be sure, my dear, there is a great deal in what the man said—I may be allowed to say this without an imputed *glow* or *throb*—But I told him nevertheless, that although I had great honour for the ladies he was related to (for his two aunts in particular) yet I should not choose to receive a letter on a subject that had a tendency to promote an end I was far from intending to promote: that it became me, ill as I was treated at present, to *hope* everything, to *bear* everything, and to *try* everything: when my father saw my steadfastness and that I would die rather than have Mr Solmes, he would perhaps recede—

Interrupting me, he represented the unlikelihood there was of that from the courses they had entered upon; which he thus enumerated: their engaging Mrs Howe against me, in the first place, as a person I might have thought to fly to, if pushed to desperation: my brother continually buzzing in my father's ears that my cousin Morden would soon arrive, and then would insist upon giving me possession of my grandfather's estate, in pursuance of the will, which would render me independent of my father: their disgraceful confinement of me: their dismissing so suddenly my servant and setting my sister's over me: their engaging my mamma, contrary to her own judgement, against me: these, he said, were all so many flagrant proofs that they would stick at nothing to carry their point; and were what made him inexpressibly uneasy.

He appealed to me whether ever I knew my papa recede from any resolution he had once fixed, especially if he thought either his prerogative, or his authority concerned in the question. His acquaintance with our family, he said, enabled him to give several instances (but they would be too grating to me) of an arbitrariness that had few examples even in the families of princes: an arbitrariness which the most excellent of women, my mamma, too severely experienced.

He was proceeding, as I thought, with reflections of this sort; and I angrily told him I would not permit my father to be reflected upon; adding, that his severity to me, however unmerited, was not a warrant for me to dispense with my duty to him.

He had no pleasure, he said, in urging anything that could be *so* construed; for, however well warranted *he* was to make such reflections, from the provocations they were continually giving him, he knew how offensive to *me* any liberties of this sort would be—And yet he must own that it was painful to him, who had youth and passions to be allowed for, as well as others, and who had always valued himself upon speaking his mind, to curb himself under such treatment. Nevertheless, his consideration for me would make him confine himself in his observations to facts that were too flagrant, and too openly avowed, to be disputed. It could not therefore *justly* displease, he would venture to say, if he made this natural inference from the premises, that if such were my father's behaviour to a *wife* who disputed not the imaginary *prerogative* he was so unprecedently fond of asserting, what room had a daughter to hope he would depart from an *authority* he was so earnest, and so much more concerned, to maintain? family-interests at the same time engaging; an aversion, however causelessly conceived, stimulating; my brother's and sister's resentments and selfish views co-operating; and my banishment from their presence depriving me of all *personal* plea or intreaty in my own favour.

How unhappy, my dear, that there is but too much reason for these observations, and for this inference; made, likewise, with more coolness and respect to my family than one would have apprehended from a man so much provoked, and of passions so high, and generally thought uncontrollable!—

Will you not question me about *throbs* and *glows*, if from such instances of a command over his fiery temper for my sake, I am ready to infer that were my friends capable of a reconciliation with him he might be affected by arguments apparently calculated for his present and future good?

He represented to me, that my present disgraceful confinement was known to all the world: that neither my sister nor brother scrupled to represent me as an obliged and favoured child, in a state of actual rebellion: that, nevertheless, everybody who knew me was ready to justify me for an aversion to a man whom everybody thought utterly unworthy of *me*, and more fit for my *sister:* that unhappy as he was, in not having been able to make any greater impression upon me in his favour, all the world gave me to him—Nor was there but one objection made to him by his very enemies (his birth, his fortunes, his prospects all unexceptionable, and the latter splendid); and *that*, he thanked God, and my example, was in a fair way of being removed for ever, since he had seen his error, and was heartily sick of the courses he had followed; which, however, were far less enormous than malice and envy had represented them to be. But of this he should say the less, as it were much better to justify himself by his actions than by the most solemn asseverations and promises: and then complimenting my *person*, he assured me (for that he always *loved* virtue, although he had not followed its rules as he ought) that he was still more captivated with the graces of my *mind*: and would frankly own that till he had the honour to know me, he had never met with an inducement sufficient to enable him to overcome an unhappy kind of prejudice to matrimony; which had made him before impenetrable to the wishes and recommendations of all his relations.

You see, my dear, he scruples not to speak of himself, as his enemies speak of him. I can't say, but his openness in these particulars gives a credit to his other professions. I should easily, I think, detect a hypocrite: and *this* man particularly, who is said to have allowed himself in great liberties, were he to pretend to instantaneous lights and convictions—at his time of life too: habits, I am sensible, are not so easily changed. You have always joined with me in remarking that he will speak his mind with freedom, even to a degree of unpoliteness sometimes; and that his very treatment of my family is a proof that he cannot make a mean court to anybody for interest-sake. What pity, where there are such laudable traces, that they should have been so mired, and choked up, as I may say!—We have heard that the man's head is better than his heart: but do you really think Mr Lovelace can have a *very* bad heart? Why should not there be something in *blood* in the human creature, as well as in the ignobler animals? None of his family are exceptionable—but himself, indeed. The ladies' characters are admirable. But I shall incur the imputation I wish to avoid. Yet what a look of censoriousness does it carry to take one to task for doing that justice, and making those charitable inferences in favour of one particular person, which one ought without scruple to do, and to make, in the behalf of any other man living?

He then again pressed that I would receive a letter from his aunt Lawrance of offered protection. He said that people of birth stood a little too much upon punctilio, as people of virtue also did (but indeed birth, worthily lived up to, was virtue; virtue, birth; the inducements to a decent punctilio the same; the origin of both, one. How came this notion from him!): else his aunt would write to *me*: but she would be willing to be first apprised that her offer would be well received—as it would have the appearance of being made against the liking of one part of my family; and which nothing would induce her to make, but the degree of unworthy persecution which I actually laboured under, and had further reason to apprehend.

I told him that, however greatly I thought myself obliged to Lady Betty Lawrance, if this offer came from herself, yet it was easy to see to what it led. It might look like vanity in me, perhaps, to say that this urgency in him on this occasion wore the face of art, in order to engage me into measures I might not easily extricate myself from. I said that I should not be affected by the splendour of even a royal title. *Goodness* I thought was *greatness:* that the excellent characters of the ladies of his family weighed more with me than the consideration that they were half-sisters to Lord M. and daughters of an Earl: that he would not have found encouragement from me had my friends been *consenting* to his address, if he had only a *mere* relative merit to those ladies: since in that case, the very reasons that made me admire *them* would have been so many objections to their *kinsman*.

I then assured him that it was with infinite concern, that I had found myself drawn into an epistolary correspondence with him; especially since that correspondence had been prohibited—And the only agreeable use I could think of making of this unexpected and undesired interview was to let him know that I should from henceforth think myself obliged to discontinue it. And I hoped that he would not have the *thought* of engaging me to carry it on, by menacing my relations.

There was light enough to distinguish that he looked very grave upon this. He so much valued my *free* choice, he said, and my *unbiased* favour (scorning to set himself upon a foot with Solmes in the compulsory methods used in that man's behalf), that he should hate himself were he capable of a view in intimidating me by so very poor a method. But nevertheless, there were two things to be considered: first, that the continual outrages he was treated with; the spies set over him, one of which he had detected; the indignities all his family were likewise treated with; as also, myself, avowedly in malice to him, or he should not presume to take upon himself to resent for me, without my leave (the artful wretch saw he would have lain open here, had he not thus guarded): all these considerations called upon him to show a proper resentment: and he would leave it to me to judge whether it would be reasonable for him, as a man of spirit, to bear such insults, if it were not for my sake. I would be pleased to consider, in the next place, whether the situation I was in (a prisoner in my father's house, and my whole family determined to compel me to marry a man unworthy of me; and that speedily, and whether I consented or not) admitted of delay in the preventive measures he was desirous to put me upon, *in the last resort only*. Nor was there a necessity, he said, if I were actually in Lady Betty's protection, that I should be his, if I should see anything objectible in his conduct, afterwards.

But what would the world conclude would be the end, I asked him, were I to throw myself into the protection of *his* friends, but that it was with such a view?

And what less did the world think *now*, he asked, than that I was confined that I *might not*? You are to consider, madam, you have not now an option; and to whom it is owing that you have not; and that you are in the power of those (parents why should I call them?) who are determined that you shall *not* have an option. All I propose is, that you will embrace such a protection—but not till you have tried every way to avoid the necessity for it.

And give me leave to say, that if a correspondence on which I have founded all my hopes is at this critical conjuncture to be broken off; and if you are resolved not to be provided against the worst; it must be plain to me that you will at last yield to that worst—worst to *me* only—It cannot be to *you*—And *then!* (and he put his hand clenched to his forehead) how shall I bear the supposition?—*Then* will you be that Solmes's!—But, by all that's sacred, neither he, nor your brother, nor your uncles, shall enjoy their triumph—perdition seize my soul, if they shall!

The man's vehemence frightened me: yet, in resentment, I would have left him; but, throwing himself at my feet again, Leave me not thus, I beseech you, dearest madam, leave me not thus, in despair. I kneel not, repenting of what I have vowed in such a case as that I have supposed. I re-vow it, at your feet!—And so he did. But think not it is by way of menace, or to intimidate you to favour me. If your heart inclines you (and then he arose) to obey your father (your *brother*, rather) and to have Solmes, although I shall avenge myself on those who have insulted me, for their insults to myself and family; yet will I tear out my heart from this bosom (if possible, with my own hands), were it to scruple to give up its ardours to a woman capable of such a preference.

I told him that he talked to me in very high language; but he might assure himself that I never would have Mr Solmes (yet that this I said not in favour to him): and I had declared as much to my relations, were there not such a man as himself in the world.

Would I declare that I would still honour him with my correspondence?—He could not bear that, hoping to obtain *greater* instances of my favour, he should forfeit the *only one* he had to boast of.

I bid him forbear rashness or resentment to any of my family, and I would, for some time at least, till I saw what issue my present trials were likely to have, proceed with a correspondence which nevertheless my heart condemned—

And his spirit him, the impatient creature said, interrupting me, for bearing what he did; when he considered that the necessity of it was imposed upon him, not by *my* will, for then he would bear it cheerfully, and a thousand times more; but by creatures—and there he stopped.

I told him plainly that he might thank himself (whose indifferent character as to morals had given such a handle against him) for all. It was but just that a man should be spoken evil of, who set no value upon his own reputation.

He offered to vindicate himself: but I told him I would judge him by his own rule—by his *actions*, not by his *professions*.

Were not his enemies, he said, so powerful and so determined; and had they not already shown their intentions in such high acts of even *cruel* compulsion; but would leave me to my choice, or to my desire of living single; he would have been content to undergo a twelvemonth's probation, or more: but he was confident that one month would either complete all their purposes, or render them abortive: and I best knew what hopes I had of my *father*'s receding: he did not know him, if I had *any*.

I said I would try every method that either my duty or my influence upon any of them should suggest, before I would put myself into any other protection. And if nothing else would do would resign the envied estate; and that I dared to say *would*.

He was contented, he said, to abide that issue. He should be far from wishing me to embrace any other protection, but, as he had frequently said, in the last necessity. But, dearest creature, said he, catching my hand with ardour, and pressing it to his lips, if the yielding up that estate will do—resign it;—and be mine—and I will corroborate, with all my soul, your resignation!—This was not ungenerously said, my dear! But what will not these men say to obtain belief, and a power over one?

I made many efforts to go; and now it was so dark that I began to have great apprehensions—I cannot say from his behaviour: indeed, he has a good deal raised himself in my opinion by the personal respect, even to reverence, which he paid me during the whole conference: for although he flamed out once upon a supposition that Solmes might succeed, it was upon a supposition that would excuse passion, if any thing could, you know, in a man pretending to love with fervour; although it was so levelled, that I could not avoid resenting it.

He recommended himself to my favour at parting, with great earnestness, yet with as great submission; not offering to condition any thing with me; although he hinted his wishes for another meeting: which I forbid him ever attempting again in the same place—And I'll own to you, from whom I should be really blameable to conceal anything, that his arguments (drawn from the disgraceful treatment I meet with) of what I *am* to expect make me begin to apprehend, that I shall be under an obligation to be either the one man's or the other's—And if so, I fancy I shall not incur your blame were I to say *which* of the two it must be. You have said, which it must *not* be. But, Oh my dear, the single life is by far the most eligible to me: *indeed* it is. And I yet hope to obtain the blessing of making that option.

I got back without observation: but the apprehension that I should not, gave me great uneasiness; and made me begin my letter in a greater flutter than he gave me cause to be in, except at the first seeing him; for then, indeed, my spirits failed me; and it was a particular felicity that, in such a place, in such a fright, and alone with him, I fainted not away.

I should add that having reproached him with his behaviour the last Sunday at church, he solemnly assured me, that it was not what had been represented to me: that he did not *expect* to see me there: but hoped to have an opportunity to address himself to my father, and to be permitted to attend him home. But that the good Dr Lewin had persuaded him not to attempt speaking to any of the family at that time; observing to him the emotions his presence had put everybody in. He intended no pride, or haughtiness of behaviour, he assured me; and that the attributing such to him was the effect of that ill-will which he had the mortification to find insuperable: adding, that when he bowed to my mamma, it was a compliment he intended generally to everyone in the pew, as well as to *her*, whom he sincerely venerated.

If he may be believed (and I should think he would not have come purposely to defy my family, yet expect favour from me), one may see, my dear, the force of hatred which misrepresents all things—Yet why should Shorey (except officiously to please her principals) make a report in his disfavour? He told me that he would appeal to Dr Lewin for his justification on this head; adding, that the whole conversation between them turned upon his desire to attempt to reconcile himself to us all, in the *face of the Church*; and upon the doctor's endeavouring to dissuade him from making such a public overture, till he knew how it would be accepted. But, alas! I am debarred from seeing that good man, or any one who would advise me what to do in my present difficult situation!—

I fancy, my dear, however, that there would hardly be a guilty person in the world, were each *suspected* or *accused* person to tell his or her own story, and be allowed any degree of credit.

I have written a very long letter. To be so particular as you require in subjects of conversation, it is impossible to be short. I will add to it only the assurance, that I am, and ever will be,

> Your affectionate and faithful
> friend and servant,
> CL. HARLOWE

You'll be so good, my dear, as to remember that the date of your last letter to me was the 9th of this instant March.

Letter 37: MISS HOWE TO MISS CLARISSA HARLOWE

Sunday, March 19

I BEG your pardon, my dearest friend, for having given you occasion to remind me of the date of my last. I was willing to have before me as much of the workings of your *wise* relations as possible; being verily persuaded that one side or the other would have yielded by this time: and then I should have had some degree of certainty to found my observations upon. And indeed what can I write, that I have not already written?—You know that I can do nothing but rave at your stupid persecutors: and that you don't like. I have advised you to resume your own estate: that you won't do. You cannot bear the thoughts of having their Solmes: and Lovelace is resolved you shall be his, let who will say to the contrary. I think you must be either the one man's or the other's. Let us see what their *next* step will be. As to Lovelace, while he tells his own story, having behaved so handsomely on his intrusion in the woodhouse, and intended so well at church, who can say that the man is in the *least* blameworthy?—*Wicked people!* to combine against so *innocent* a man!—But, as I said, let us see what their *next* step will be and what course you will take upon it; and then we may be more enlightened.

As to your change of style to your uncles and brother and sister, since they were so fond of attributing to you a regard for Lovelace and would not be persuaded to the contrary; and since you only strengthened their arguments against yourself by denying it; you did but just as I would have done, in giving way to their suspicions and trying what that would do—But if—but if—pray, my dear, indulge me a little—You *yourself* think it was necessary to apologize to *me* for that change of style to *them*—and till you will speak out like a friend to her un-*question*-able friend, I must tease you a little—Let it run, therefore; for it will run—

If, then, there be not a reason for this change of style, which you have not thought fit to give me, be so good as to watch, as I once before advised you, how the cause for it will come on: why should it be permitted to steal upon you, and you know nothing of the matter?

When a person gets a great cold, he or she puzzles and studies how it began; how he—she got it: and when that is accounted for, down he—she sits contented and lets it have its course, or takes a sweat or the like, to get rid of it, if it be very troublesome—So, my dear, before the malady you wot of, yet wot *not* of, grows so importunate as that you must be obliged to sweat it out, let me advise you to mind how it comes on. For I am persuaded, as surely as that I am now writing to you, that their indiscreet violence on one hand, and his insinuating address on the other, if the man be not a greater fool than any body thinks him, will effectually bring it to this, and do all his work for him.

But let it—if it must be Lovelace or Solmes, the choice cannot admit of debate. Yet, if all be true that is reported, I should prefer almost any of your other lovers to either; unworthy as *they* also are. But who, indeed, can be worthy of Miss Clarissa Harlowe?

I wish you don't tax me of harping too much upon one string. I should, indeed, think myself inexcusable so to do (the rather as I am so bold as to imagine it is a point out of all doubt, from fifty places in your letters, were I to labour the proof), if you would ingenuously own—

Own what? you'll say. Why, my Anna Howe, I hope, you don't think, that I am already in love!—

No, to be sure! How can your Anna Howe have such a thought?—Love, though so *short a word*, has a *broad sound* with it. What then shall we call it? You have helped me to a phrase that has a *narrower sound* with it; but a pretty *broad* meaning, nevertheless. A *conditional kind of liking!*—that's it—Oh my friend! Did I not know how much you despise prudery; and that you are too young, and too lovely to be a prude—

But, avoiding such hard names, let me tell you one thing, my dear (which nevertheless I have told you before); and that is this, that I shall think I have reason to be highly displeased with you, if, when you write to me, you endeavour to keep from me any secret of your heart.

Let me add, that if you would clearly and explicitly tell me, how far Lovelace *has*, or has *not*, a hold in your affections, I could better advise you what to do, than at present I can. You, who are so famed for prescience, as I may call it, and than whom no young lady ever had stronger pretension to a share of it, have had, no doubt, reasonings in your heart about him, supposing you were to be one day his (no doubt but you have had the same in Solmes's case—whence the ground for the hatred of the one and of the *conditional liking* of the other). Will you tell me, my dear, what you have thought of his *best* and of his *worst?*—How far eligible for the *first*; how far rejectible for the *last?*—Then weighing both parts in opposite scales we shall see which is likely to preponderate; or rather which *does* preponderate. Nothing less than the knowledge of the inmost recesses of your heart can satisfy my love and my friendship. Surely you are not afraid to trust *yourself* with a secret of this nature: if you are, then you may the *more* allowably doubt *me*. But I dare say you will not own either: nor is there, I hope, cause for either.

Be pleased to observe one thing, my dear, that whenever I have given myself any of those airs of raillery, which have seemed to make you look about you (when, likewise, your case may call for a more serious turn from a sympathizing friend), it has not been upon those passages which are written, though perhaps not *intended* with such explicitness (don't be alarmed, my dear!) as leaves one little cause of doubt: but only when you affect reserve; when you give new words for common things; when you come with your *curiosities*, with your *conditional likings*, and with your PRUDE-encies (mind how I spell the word) in a case that with every other person defies all prudence—overt-acts of treason all these, against the sovereign friendship we have vowed to each other!—

Remember, that you found *me* out in a moment. You challenged me. I owned directly that there was only my pride between the man and me; for I could not endure, I told you, to think it in the power of any fellow living to give me a moment's uneasiness. And then my man, as I have elsewhere said, was not such a one as yours: so I had reason to impute full as much to my own inconsideration, as to his *power* over me: nay, *more*. But still more to *yours*. For you reasoned me out of the *curiosity* first; and when the liking was brought to be *conditional*—why then, you know, I *throbbed* no more about him.

Oh! *pray now*, as you say, now I have mentioned that my fellow was not such a charming fellow as yours, let Miss Biddulph, Miss Lloyd, Miss Campion, and me, have your opinion, how far *figure* ought to engage us: with a view to your own case, however—*mind that*—as Mr T'Antony says—and whether *at all*, if the man be vain of it; since, as you observe in a former, that vanity is *a stop-short pride* in such a one, that would make one justly doubt the *worthiness of his interior*. You, our pattern, so lovely in feature, so graceful in person, have none of it; and have therefore with the *best* grace always held that it is not excusable even in a woman.

You must know that this subject was warmly debated among us in our last conversation, and Miss Lloyd wished me to write to you upon it for your opinion; to which, in every debated case, we always deferred. I hope you will not be so much engrossed by your more weighty cares, as not to have freedom of spirits enough to enter upon the task—You know how much we all admire your opinion on such topics, which ever produces something new and instructive, as you handle the subjects. And pray tell us, to what you think it owing, that your man seems so careful to adorn that self-adorned person of his; yet so manages, that one cannot for one's heart think him a coxcomb!—Let this question, and the above tasks, divert, and not displease you, my dear—One subject, though ever so important, could never yet ingross your capacious mind. If they should displease you, you must recollect the many instances of my impertinence, which you have forgiven, and then say, this is a mad girl—but yet I love her!—and she is my own

ANNA HOWE

Letter 38: MISS CLARISSA HARLOWE TO MISS HOWE

Monday, March 20

YOUR last so sensibly affects me, that I must postpone every other consideration, however weighty, to reply to it: and this I will do very distinctly, and with all the openness of heart which our mutual friendship demands.

But let me observe, in the first place *gratefully* observe, that if I have in *fifty passages* of my letters given you such *undoubted* proofs of my value for Mr Lovelace, that you have spared me for the sake of my *explicitness*, it is acting by me with a generosity worthy of yourself.

But lives the man, think you, who is so very bad that he does not give even a doubting mind reason at *one* time to be better pleased with him than at *another*? And when that reason offers, is it not just to express one's self accordingly? I would do the man who addresses me as much *justice*, as if he did *not* address me: it has such a look of tyranny, it appears so ungenerous, methinks, to use a man worse for his respect to one (no other cause for disrespect occurring), that I would not by any means be that person who should do so.

But, although I may intend no more than justice, it will, perhaps, be difficult to hinder those who know the man's views from construing it as a partial favour: and especially if the eager-eyed observer has been formerly touched herself, and would triumph that her friend had been no more able to escape than she!—Noble minds, emulative of perfection (and yet the passion, properly directed, I do not take to be an *im*-perfection neither), may be allowed a little generous envy, I think!

If I meant by this a reflection, by way of revenge, it is but a revenge, my dear, in the soft sense of the word!—I love, as I have told you, your pleasantry— Although at the time it may pain one a little, yet on recollection, when one feels in the reproof more of the cautioning friend than of the satirizing observer, an ingenuous mind will be all gratitude upon it. All the business will be this, I shall be sensible of the pain in the present letter perhaps; but I shall thank you in the next, and ever after.

In this way, I hope, my dear, you will account for a little of that sensibility which you will find above, and perhaps still more as I proceed. You frequently remind me, by the *best example*, that I must not spare *you!*

I am not conscious, that I have written anything of this man that has not been more in his dispraise than in his favour. Such *is* the man, that I think I must have been faulty, and ought to take myself to account, if I had not: but if you think otherwise, I will not put you upon *labouring the proof*, as you call it! My conduct must then have a faulty *appearance* at least, and I will endeavour to rectify it. But of this I assure you, that whatever interpretation my words were capable of, I *intended not* any reserve to you. I wrote my heart, at the time—If I had had thoughts of disguising it, or been conscious that there was *reason* for doing so, perhaps I had not given you the opportunity of remarking upon my *curiosity* after his relations' esteem for me; nor upon my *conditional liking*, and such-like. All I intended by the first, I believe I honestly told you at the time. To that letter I therefore refer, whether it make for me, or against me: and by the other, that I might bear in mind what it became a person of my sex and character to *be* and to *do*, in such an unhappy situation, where the imputed love is thought an undutiful, and therefore a criminal, passion; and where the supposed object of it is a man of faulty morals too. And I am sure you will excuse my desire of appearing at those times the person I ought to be, had I no other view in it but to merit the continuance of your good opinion.

But that I may acquit myself of having reserves—Oh, my dear, I must here break off!—

Letter 39: MISS CLARISSA HARLOWE TO MISS HOWE

Monday, March 20

THIS letter will account to you, my dear, for my abrupt breaking off in the answer I was writing to yours of yesterday; and which, possibly, I shall not be able to finish and send you, till tomorrow or next day, having a great deal to say to the subjects you put to me in it. What I am now to give you are the particulars of another effort made by my friends, through the good Mrs Norton.

It seems they had sent to her yesterday, to be here this day to take their instructions, and to try what *she* could do with me. It would, at least, I suppose they thought, have this effect; to render me inexcusable with *her*; or to let *her* see that there was no room for the expostulations she had often wanted to make in my favour to my mamma.

The declaration that my heart was *free* afforded them an argument to prove obstinacy and perverseness upon me, since it could be nothing else that governed me in my opposition to their wills, if I had no particular esteem for another man: and now that I have given them reason (in order to obviate this argument) to suppose that I *have* a preference to another, they are resolved to carry their schemes into execution as soon as possible. And in order to this, they sent for this good woman, for whom they know I have even a filial regard.

She found assembled my papa and mamma, my brother and sister, my two uncles, and my aunt Hervey.

My brother acquainted her with all that had passed since she was last permitted to see me; with my letters avowing my regard to Mr Lovelace, as they all interpreted them; with the substance of their answers to them; and with their resolutions.

My mamma spoke next; and delivered herself to this effect, as the good woman told me afterwards:

After reciting how many times I had been indulged in my refusals of different gentlemen, and the pains she had taken with me to induce me to oblige my whole family, in one instance out of five or six; and my obstinacy upon it: Oh my good Mrs Norton, said the dear lady, could you have thought that *my* Clarissa and *your* Clarissa was capable of so determined an opposition to the will of parents so indulgent to her? But see what *you* can do with her. The matter is gone too far to be receded from, on our parts. Her papa had concluded everything with Mr Solmes, not doubting her compliance. Such noble settlements, Mrs Norton, and such advantages to the whole family!—In short, she has it in her power to lay an obligation upon us all. Mr Solmes, knowing she has good principles, and hoping by his patience *now* and good treatment *hereafter* to engage her gratitude, and by degrees her love, is willing to overlook all!—

(*Overlook* all, my dear! Mr Solmes to *overlook* all! There's a word!)

So, Mrs Norton, if you are convinced that it is a child's duty to submit to her parents' authority, in the most important point as well as in the least, I beg you'll try *your* influence over her: *I* have none. Her *papa* has none: her *uncles* neither. Although it is her apparent interest to oblige us all; for, on that condition, her grandfather's estate is not half of what, living and dying, is purposed to be done for her. If anybody can prevail with her, it is *you*; and I hope you will *heartily* enter upon this task with her.

She asked whether she was permitted to expostulate with them upon the occasion, before she came up to me?

My arrogant brother told her she was sent for to expostulate with his *sister*, and not with *them*. And *this*, Goody Norton (She is always *Goody* with him!), you may tell her, that matters are gone so far with Mr Solmes that there is no going back!—Of consequence, no room for *your* expostulation, or *hers* either.

Be assured of this, Mrs Norton, said my papa in an angry tone; that we will not be baffled by her. We will not appear like fools in this matter, and as if we had no authority over our own daughter. We will not, in short, be bullied out of our child by a cursed rake, who had like to have killed our only son!—And so she had better make a merit of her obedience: for comply she shall, if I live; independent as she thinks my father's indiscreet bounty hath made her of me, her father. Indeed since that, she has never been what she was before. An unjust bequest!—and it is likely to prosper accordingly!—But if she marry that vile Lovelace, I will litigate every shilling with her: tell her so; and that the will *may* be set aside, and *shall*.

My uncles joined, with equal heat.

My brother was violent in his declarations.

My sister put in with vehemence on the same side.

My aunt Hervey was pleased to say, there was no article so proper for parents to govern in, as this of marriage: and it was very fit, mine should be obliged.

Thus instructed, the good woman came up to me. She told me all that had passed; and was very earnest with me to comply; and so much justice did she to the task imposed upon her, that I more than once thought that her own opinion went with theirs. But when she saw what an immoveable aversion I had to the man, she lamented with me their determined resolution: and then examined into the sincerity of my profession that I would gladly compound with them by living single: of this being satisfied, she was so convinced that this offer (which would exclude Lovelace effectually) ought to be accepted, that she would go down, although I told her it was what I had tendered over and over to no purpose, and undertake to be guarantee for me on that score.

She went accordingly; but soon returned in tears, being used harshly for urging this alternative—They had a right to my obedience upon their own terms, they said: my proposal was an artifice, only to gain time: nothing but marrying Mr Solmes *should* do: they had told me so before: they should not be at rest till it was done, for they knew what an interest Lovelace had in my heart: I had as good as owned it in my letters to my uncles and brother and sister, although I had most disingenuously declared otherwise to my mamma. I depended, they said, upon *their* indulgence, and my *own power* over them. They had not banished me their presence, if they did not know that their consideration for *me* was greater than mine for *them*. And they *would* be obeyed, or I never should be restored to their favour, let the consequence be what it would.

My brother thought fit to tell the good woman that her whining nonsense did but harden me. There was a perverseness, he said, in female minds, a tragedy-pride, that would make a romantic young creature, such a one as me, risk anything to obtain pity. I was of an age, and a turn (the insolent said), to be fond of a lover-like distress: and my grief (which she pleaded) would never break my heart; it would sooner break that of the best and most indulgent of mothers. He added that she might once more go up to me: but that, if she prevailed not, he should suspect that the man they all hated had found a way to attach *her* to his interest.

Everybody blamed him for this unworthy reflection, which greatly affected the good woman. But nevertheless he said, and nobody contradicted him, that if she could not prevail upon her *sweet child* (as it seems she had fondly called me), she had best withdraw to her own home, and there tarry till she was sent for; and so leave her *sweet child* to her father's management.

Sure nobody ever had so insolent, so hard-hearted a brother, as I have! So much resignation to be expected from me! So much arrogance, and to so good a woman, and of so fine an understanding, to be allowed in him!

She nevertheless told him that however she might be ridiculed for speaking of the sweetness of my disposition, she must take upon her to say, that there never was a sweeter in the sex: and that she had ever found that by mild methods, and gentleness, I might at any time be prevailed upon, even in points against my own judgement and opinion.

My aunt Hervey hereupon said it was worth while to reflect upon what Mrs Norton said: and that she had sometimes allowed *herself* to doubt whether I had been begun with by such methods as generous tempers are only to be influenced by, in cases where their hearts are supposed to be opposite to the will of their friends.

She had both my brother and sister upon her for this: who referred to my mamma, whether she had not treated me with an indulgence that had hardly any example?

My mamma said, she must own that no indulgence had been wanting from *her:* but she must needs say, and had *often* said it, that the reception I met with on my return from Miss Howe, and the manner in which the proposal of Mr Solmes was made to me (which was such as left nothing to my choice), and before I had had an opportunity to. converse with him, were not what she had by any means approved of.

She was silenced, you will guess by whom—with, My dear! my dear!—You have *ever* something to say, something to palliate, for this rebel of a girl!—Remember her treatment of you, of me!—Remember that the wretch, whom we so justly hate, would not dare to persist in his pupfoses, but for her encouragement of *him* and obstinacy to *us*—Mrs Norton (angrily to her), go up to her once more—and if you think gentleness will do—you have a commission to be gentle—If it won't, never make use of that plea again.

Ay, my good woman, said my mamma, try *your* force with her. My sister Hervey and I will go up to her, and bring her down in our hands, to receive her father's blessing and assurances of everybody's love, if she will be prevailed upon: and in that case, we will all love you the better for your good offices.

She came up to me, and repeated all these passages with tears—But after what had passed between us, I told her that she could not hope to prevail upon me to comply with measures so wholly my brother's; and so much to my aversion—And then folding me to her maternal bosom, I leave you, my dearest miss, said she!— I leave you because I *must!*—But let me beseech you to do nothing rashly; nothing unbecoming your character. If all be true that is said, Mr Lovelace cannot deserve you. If you *can* comply, remember it is your *duty* to comply. They take not, I own, the right method with so generous a spirit. But remember that there would not be any merit in your compliance, if it were *not* to be against your own will. Remember also what is expected from a character so extraordinary as yours: remember it is in your power to unite or disunite your whole family for ever. Although it should at *present* be disagreeable to you to be thus compelled, your prudence, I dare say, when you consider the matter seriously, will enable you to get over all prejudices against the one, and all prepossessions in favour of the other: and then the obligation you will lay all your family under will be not only meritorious in you, with regard to *them*, but in a few months very probably highly satisfactory, as well as reputable, to *yourself*.

Consider, my dear mamma Norton, said I, *only* consider, that it is not a small thing that is insisted upon; nor for a short duration: it is for my *life*—Consider too, that all this is owing to an overbearing brother, who governs everybody. Consider how desirous I am to oblige them, if a *single life*, and breaking all correspondence with the man they hate because my brother hates him, would do it.

I consider everything, my dearest miss: and, added to what I have said, do *you* only consider that if, by pursuing your *own* will, and rejecting *theirs*, you *should* be unhappy, you will be deprived of all that consolation which those have, who have been directed by their *parents*, although the event prove not answerable to their wishes.

I *must* go, repeated she—your brother will say (and she wept) that I harden you by my *whining nonsense*. 'Tis indeed hard, that so much regard should be paid to the *humours* of one child; and so little to the *inclination* of another. But let me repeat, that it is your *duty* to acquiesce, if you *can* acquiesce: your father has given your brother's schemes *his* sanction; and they are now *his*. Mr Lovelace, I doubt, is not a man that will justify *your* choice so much as he will *their* dislike. It is too easy to see that your brother has a *view* in discrediting you with all your friends, with your uncles in particular: but for that very reason, you should comply, if possible, in order to disconcert his ungenerous measures. I will pray for you; and that is all I can do for you. I must now go down, and make a report that you are resolved never to have Mr Solmes—Must I?—Consider, miss—*must* I?

Indeed you must!—but of this I do assure you, that I will do nothing to disgrace the part you have had in my education. I will bear everything that shall be short of forcing my hand into *his*, who never can have any share in my heart. I will try, by patient duty, by humility, to overcome them. But death will I choose, in any shape, rather than that man.

I dread to go down, said she, with so determined an answer: they will have no patience with me—But let me leave you with one observation, which I beg of you always to bear in mind:

'That persons of prudence, and distinguished talents like yours, seem to be sprinkled through the world, to give credit by their example to religion and virtue. When such persons *wilfully* err, how great must be the fault! How ungrateful to that God, who blessed them with such talents! What a loss likewise to the world! What a wound to virtue! But this, I hope, will never be to be said of Miss Clarissa Harlowe!'

I could give her no answer, but by my tears. And I thought, when she went away, the better half of my heart went with her.

I listened to hear what reception she would meet with below, and found it was just such a one as she apprehended.

Will she, or will she *not*, be Mrs Solmes? None of your whining circumlocutions, Mrs Norton!—(You may guess who said this)—*Will* she, or will she *not*, comply with her parents' will?

This cut short all she was going to say.

If I *must* speak so briefly, miss will sooner die, than have—

Anybody but Lovelace! interrupted my brother—This, madam, this, sir, is your meek daughter! This is Mrs Norton's *sweet child!*—Well, Goody, you may return to your own habitation. I am empowered to forbid you to have any correspondence with this perverse girl, for a month to come, as you value the favour of our whole family, or of any individual of it.

And saying this, uncontradicted by anybody, he himself showed her to the door—no doubt with all that air of cruel insult, which the haughty rich can put on to the unhappy low who have not pleased them.

So here, [my dear Miss Howe], am I deprived of the advice of one of the most prudent and conscientious women in the world, were I to have ever so much occasion for it.

I might, indeed, write, as I presume, under your cover, and receive *her* answers to what I should write, but should such a correspondence be charged upon her, I know she would not be guilty of a falsehood for the world; nor even of an equivocation: and should she own it, after this prohibition, she would forfeit my mamma's favour for ever. And in my dangerous fever, some time ago, I engaged my mamma to promise me, that, if I died before I could do anything for the good woman, she would set her above want for the rest of her life, should her eyes fail her, or sickness befall her, and she could not provide for herself as she now so prettily does by her fine needleworks, etc.

What measures will they fall upon next?—Will they not recede when they find that it must be a rooted antipathy, and nothing else, that could make a temper, not naturally inflexible, so sturdy?

Adieu, my dear. Be you happy!—To *know* that it is in your power to be so is all that seems wanting to make you so.

CL. HARLOWE

Letter 40: MISS CLARISSA HARLOWE TO MISS HOWE

(In continuation of the subject in Letter 38)

I WILL now, though midnight (for I have no sleep in my eyes), resume the subject I was forced so abruptly to quit; and will obey yours, Miss Lloyd's, Miss Campion's and Miss Biddulph's call, with as much temper as my divided thoughts will admit. The dead stillness of this solemn hour will, I hope, contribute to calm my disturbed mind.

In order to acquit myself of so heavy a charge as that of having reserves to so dear a friend, I will acknowledge (and I thought I had over and over) that it is owing to my particular situation, if Mr Lovelace appears to me in a tolerable light: and I take upon me to say, that had they opposed to him a man of sense, of virtue, of generosity; one who enjoyed his fortune with credit; who had a tenderness in his nature for the calamities of others, which would have given a moral assurance that he would have been still less wanting in grateful returns to an obliging spirit: had they opposed such a man as this to Mr Lovelace, and been as earnest to have me married, as now they are, I do not know myself if they would have had reason to tax me with that invincible obstinacy which they lay to my charge: and this, whatever had been the *figure* of the man: since the *heart* is what we women should judge by in the choice we make, as the best security for the party's good behaviour in every relation of life.

But, situated as I am, thus persecuted and driven; I own to you that I have now and then had a little more difficulty than I wished for in passing by Mr Lovelace's tolerable qualities, to keep up my dislike to him for his others.

You say I must have argued with myself in his favour, and in his disfavour, on a supposition that I might possibly be one day his. I own that I have: and thus called upon by my dearest friend, I will set before you both parts of the argument.

And first, *what occurred to me in his favour.*

At his introduction into our family, his negative virtues were insisted upon—He was no gamester; no horse-racer; no fox-hunter; no drinker: my poor aunt Hervey had, in confidence, given us to apprehend much disagreeable evil, especially to a wife of the least delicacy, from a wine-lover: and common sense instructed us, that sobriety in a man is no small point to be secured when so many mischiefs happen daily from excess. I remember that my sister made the most of this favourable circumstance in his character, while she had any hopes of him.

He was never thought to be a niggard: not even ungenerous: nor, when his conduct came to be inquired into, an extravagant, or squanderer: his pride (so far was it a laudable pride) secured him from that. Then he was ever ready to own his errors. He was no jester upon sacred things: poor Mr Wyerley's fault, who seemed to think that there was wit in saying bold things which would shock a serious mind. His conversation with us was always unexceptionable, even chastely so; which, be his actions what they would, showed him capable of being influenced by *decent* company, and that he might probably therefore be a *led* man, rather than a *leader*, in *other*. And one late instance, so late as last Saturday evening, has raised him not a little in my opinion, with regard to this point of good (and, at the same time, of manly) behaviour.

As to the advantage of birth, that is of his side, above any man who has been found out for me: if we may judge by that expression of his, which you was pleased with at the time: 'That upon *true* quality, and *hereditary* distinction, if good sense were not wanting, honour sat as easy as his glove': that, with *as* familiar an air, was his familiar expression; 'while none but the prosperous upstart, MUSHROOMED into rank (another of his peculiars), was arrogantly proud of it.' If, I say, we may judge of him by this, we shall conclude in his favour, that he knows what sort of behaviour is to be expected from persons of birth, whether he act up to it or not. Conviction is half way to amendment.

His fortunes in possession are handsome; in expectation, splendid: so nothing need be said on that subject.

But is impossible, say some, that he should make a tender or kind husband. Those who are for imposing upon me such a man as Mr Solmes, and by methods so violent, are not entitled to make this objection: but now, on this subject, let me tell you how I have argued with myself—For still you must remember, that I am upon the extenuating part of his character.

A great deal of the treatment a wife may expect from him will possibly depend upon herself. Perhaps she must *practise*, as well as *promise*, obedience to a man so little used to control; and must be careful to oblige. And what husband expects not this?—The *more*, perhaps, if he has not reason to assure himself of the preferable love of his wife, before she became such. And how much easier and pleasanter to obey the man of her choice, if he should be even unreasonable sometimes, than one she would not have had, could she have avoided it? Then, I think, as the men were the framers of the matrimonial office, and made *obedience* a part of the woman's vow, she ought not, even in *policy*, to show him that she can break through *her* part of the contract, however lightly she may think of the instance; lest *he* should take it into his head (himself is judge) to think as lightly of other points, which *she* may hold more important. But indeed no point, so solemnly vowed, can be slight.

Thus principled, and *acting* accordingly, what a wretch must that husband be, who could treat such a wife brutally!—Will Lovelace's *wife* be the only person to whom he will not pay the grateful debt of civility and good manners? He is allowed to be brave: who ever knew a brave man, if a man of *sense*, an universally base man? And how much the gentleness of sex, and the manner of our training-up and education, make us need the protection of the brave, and the countenance of the generous, let the general approbation which we are all so naturally inclined to give to men of that character, testify.

At worst, will he confine me prisoner to my chamber? Will he deny me the visits of my dearest friend, and forbid me to correspond with her? Will he take from me the mistressly management, which I had not faultily discharged? Will he set a servant over me, with licence to insult me? Will he, as he has not a *sister*, permit his cousins Montague, or would either of those ladies *accept* of a permission to insult and tyrannize over me?—It cannot be. Why then, think I often, do you tempt me, oh my cruel friends, to try the difference?

And then has the secret pleasure intruded itself, to be able to reclaim such a man to the paths of virtue and honour: to be a *secondary* means, if I were to be his, of saving him, and preventing the mischiefs so enterprising a creature might otherwise be guilty of, if he be such a one.

In these lights when I have thought of him (and that as a man of sense he will sooner see his errors than another), I own to you, that I have had some difficulty to avoid taking the path they so violently endeavour to make me shun: and all that command of my passions, which has been attributed to me as my greatest praise, and in so young a creature, as my distinction, has hardly been sufficient for me.

And let me add, that the favour of his relations (all but himself unexceptionable) has made a good deal of additional weight, thrown into the same scale.

But now, in his disfavour. When I have reflected upon the probibition of my parents: the giddy appearance, disgraceful to sex, that such a preference would have: that there is no manner of likelihood, inflamed by the rencounter, and upheld by art and ambition on my brother's side, that ever the animosity will be got over: that I must therefore be at perpetual variance with all my own family: must go to *him*, and to *his*, as an obliged, and half-fortuned person: that his aversion to them all is as strong as theirs to him; that his whole family are hated for his sake; they hating ours in return: that he has a very immoral character as to our sex: that knowing this, it is a high degree of impurity to think of joining in wedlock with such a man: that he is young, unbroken, his passions unsubdued: that he is violent in his temper, yet artful: I am afraid vindictive too: that such an husband might unsettle me in all my own principles, and hazard my future hopes: that his own relations, two excellent aunts, and an uncle, from whom he has such large expectations, have no influence upon him: that what tolerable qualities he has are founded more in pride than in virtue: that allowing, as he does, the excellency of moral precepts, and believing the doctrine of future rewards and punishments, he can live as if he despised the one, and defied the other: the probability that the taint arising from such free principles may go down into the manners of posterity: that I knowing these things, and the importance of them, should be more inexcusable than one who knows them not; since an error *against* judgement is worse, infinitely worse, than an error *in* judgement—Reflecting upon these things, I cannot help conjuring you, my dear, to pray *with* me, and to pray *for* me, that I may not be pushed upon such indiscreet measures as will render me inexcusable *to* myself: for that is the test, after all; the world's opinion ought to be but a secondary consideration.

I have said in his praise that he is extremely ready to *own his errors* but I have sometimes made a great drawback upon this article in his disfavour; having been ready to apprehend that this ingenuity may possibly be attributable to two causes, neither of them by any means creditable to him. The one, that his vices are so much his masters that he *attempts* not to conquer them; the other, that he may think it policy to give up *one half* of his character to save the *other*, when the *whole* may be blameable: by this means, silencing by acknowledgement the objections he cannot answer; which may give him the praise of ingenuousness, when he can obtain no other; and when the *challenged* proof might bring out, upon discussion, other evils. These, you'll allow, are severe constructions; but everything his enemies say of him cannot be false.

I will proceed by and by.

SOMETIMES we have both thought him one of the most undesigning *merely* witty men we ever knew; at other times one of the deepest creatures we ever conversed with. So that, when in one visit we have imagined we fathomed him, in the next he has made us ready to give him up as impenetrable. This, my dear, is to be put among the shades in his character—Yet, upon the whole, you have been so far of his party, that you have contested that his principal fault is over-frankness, and too much regardlessness of appearances, and that he is too giddy to be very artful: you would have it, that at *the time* he says anything good, he means what he speaks; that his variableness and levity are constitutional, owing to sound health, and to a soul and body, that was your observation, fitted for, and pleased with, each other. And hence you concluded, that could this *consentaneousness*, as you called it, of corporal and animal faculties be pointed by discretion; that is to say, could his vivacity be confined within the pale of *but* moral obligations; he would be far from being rejectible as a companion for life.

But I used then to say, and I still am of opinion, that he wants a *heart*: and if he does, he wants everything. A wrong *head* may be convinced, may have a right turn given it: but who is able to give a *heart*, if a heart be wanting? Divine grace, working miracle, or next to a miracle, can only change a bad heart. Should not one fly the man who is but *suspected* of such a one?—What, oh what, do parents *do*, when they precipitate a child, and make her think better than she would otherwise think of a man of an indifferent character in order to avoid another that is odious to her!

I have said that I think him vindictive. Upon my word, I have sometimes doubted whether his perseverance in his addresses to me has not been the more obstinate, since he has found himself so disagreeable to my friends. From that time, I verily think he has been more fervent in them; yet courts them not; but sets them at defiance. For this, indeed, he pleads disinterestedness (I am sure he cannot politeness) and the more plausibly, as he is apprised of the ability they have to make it worth his while to court them. 'Tis true, he has declared, and with too much reason, or there would be no enduring him, that the lowest submissions on his part would not be accepted; and to oblige me has offered to seek a reconciliation with them, if I would give him hope of success. As to his behaviour at church, the Sunday before last, I lay no stress upon that, because I doubt there was too much outward pride in his intentional humility, or Shorey, who is not his enemy, could not have mistaken it.

I do not think him so deeply learned in human nature, or in ethics, as some have thought him. Don't you remember how he stared at the following trite observations which every moralist could have furnished him with? Complaining, as he did, in a half-menacing strain, of the obloquies raised against him—'That if he were innocent, he should despise the obloquy: if not, revenge would not wipe off his guilt.' 'That nobody ever thought of turning a sword into a sponge!' 'That it was in his own power, by reformation of an error laid to his charge by an enemy, to make that enemy one of his best friends; and (which was the noblest revenge in the world) *against his will*; since an enemy would not *wish* him to be without the faults he taxed him with.'

But the *intention*, he said, was the wound.

How so, I asked him, when *that* cannot wound without the *application?* 'That the adversary only held the sword: he himself pointed it to his breast?—And why should he resent mortally that malice, which he might be the better for, as long as he lived?'—What could be the reading he has been said to be master of, to wonder, as he did, at these observations?

But, indeed, he must take pleasure in revenge; and yet holds others to be inexcusable for the same fault—He is not, however, the only one who can see how truly blameable those errors are in another, which they hardly think such in themselves.

From these considerations; from these *over-balances*; it was, that I said in a former, that I would not be in love with this man for the world: and it was going further than prudence would warrant, when I was for compounding with you by the words *conditional liking*; which you so humorously rally.

Well but, methinks you say, what is all this to the purpose? This is still but reasoning: but, if you *are* in love, you *are*: and love, like the vapours, is the deeper rooted for having no sufficient cause assignable for its hold. And so you call upon me again to have no reserves, and so forth.

Why then, my dear, if you will have it, I think that, with all his preponderating faults, I like him better than I ever thought I should like him; and, those faults considered, better perhaps than I *ought* to like him. And, I believe, it is possible for the persecution I labour under to induce me to like him still more; especially while I can recollect to his advantage our last interview, and as every day produces stronger instances of *tyranny*, I will call it, on the other side—In a word, I will frankly own (since you cannot think anything I say too explicit), that were he *now* but a moral man, I would prefer him to all the men I ever saw.

So that this is but *conditional liking* still, you'll say. Nor, I hope, is it more. I never was in *love*; and whether this be *it*, or not, I must submit to *you*—But will venture to think it, if it be, no such *mighty* monarch, no such unconquerable power, as I have heard it represented; and it must have met with greater encouragements than I think I have given it, to be so *irresistible*—Since I am persuaded, that I could yet, without a *throb*, most willingly give up the *one* man to get rid of the *other*.

But now to be a little more serious with you: if, my dear, my particularly unhappy situation *had* driven (or *led* me, if you please) into a liking of the man; and if that liking *had*, in your opinion, inclined me to the other L, should *you*, whose mind is susceptible of the most friendly impressions; who have such high notions of the delicacy of sex; and who actually *do* enter so deeply into the distresses of one you love; should *you* have pushed so far that unhappy friend on so very nice a subject?—Especially when I aimed not (as you could *prove by fifty* instances, it seems), to guard against being found out. Had you rallied me by word of mouth in the manner you do, it might have been more in character; especially if your friend's distresses had been surmounted; and if she had affected prudish airs in revolving the subject: But to sit down to *write* it, as methinks I see you, with a gladdened eye, and with all the archness of exultation—Indeed my dear (and I take notice of it, rather for the sake of your own generosity, than for my sake; for, as I have said, I love your raillery) it is not so *very* pretty; the delicacy of the subject, and the delicacy of your own mind, considered.

I lay down my pen, here, that you may consider of it a little, if you please.

I RESUME; to give you my opinion of the force which *figure* or *person* ought to have upon our sex: and this I shall do both *generally*, and *particularly*, as to this man: whence you will be able to collect how far my friends are in the right, or in the wrong, when they attribute a good deal of prejudice in favour of one man, and in disfavour of the other, on the score of figure. But, first, let me observe that they see abundant reason, on comparing Mr Lovelace and Mr Solmes together, to believe that this *may* be a consideration with me; and therefore they believe it *is*.

There is certainly something very plausible and attractive, as well as creditable to a woman's *choice*, in *figure*. It gives a favourable impression at first sight, in which one wishes to be confirmed: and if, upon further acquaintance, we find reason so to be, we are pleased with our own judgement, and like the person the better for having given us cause to compliment our own sagacity, in our first-sighted impressions. But, nevertheless, it has been generally a rule with me to suspect a fine figure, both in man and woman; and I have had a good deal of reason to approve my rule. With regard to *men* especially; who ought to value themselves rather upon their intellectual than personal qualities. For, as to our sex, if a fine woman should be led by the opinion of the world to be vain and conceited upon her form and features; and that to such a degree, as to have neglected the more material and more *durable* recommendations; the world will be ready to excuse her; since a pretty fool, in all she says, and in all she does, will please, we know not why.

But who would grudge this pretty fool her short day! Since, with her summer's sun, when her butterfly-flutters are over, and the winter of age and furrows arrives, she will feel the just effects of having neglected to cultivate her better faculties; for then, like another Helen, she will be unable to bear the reflection even of her own glass; and being sunk into the insignificance of a *mere old woman*; she will be entitled to the contempts which follow that character. While the *discreet matron*, who carries *up* (we will not, in such a one's case, say *down*) into advanced life, the ever-amiable character of virtuous prudence, and useful experience, finds solid veneration take place of airy admiration, and more than supply the want of it.

But for a *man* to be vain of his person, how effeminate? If such a one has genius, it seldom strikes deep into intellectual subjects. His outside usually runs away with him. To adorn, and perhaps, *intending* to adorn, to render ridiculous, that person, takes up all his attention. All he does is *personal*; that is to say, *for* himself; all he admires, *is* himself: and in spite of the corrections of the stage, which so often, and so justly exposes a coxcomb, he generally dwindles down, and sinks into that character; and, of consequence, becomes the scorn of one sex, and the jest of the other.

This is generally the case of your fine figures and gay dressers of men: whence it is that, I repeat, that *mere person* in a man is a despicable consideration. But if a man, *besides* figure, has learning, and such talents as *would* have distinguished him, whatever were his form; then indeed *person* is an addition: and if he has not run too egregiously into self-admiration; and if he has preserved his morals, he is truly a valuable being.

Mr Lovelace has certainly taste; and, as far as I am able to determine, he has judgement in most of the politer arts. But although he has a humorous way of carrying it off, yet one may see, that he values himself not a little, both on his person and his parts, and even upon his dress; and yet he has so happy an ease in the latter, that it seems to be the least part of his study. And as to the former, I should hold myself inexcusable, if I were to add to his vanity by showing the least regard for what is too evidently so much his.

And now, my dear, let me ask you; have I come up to your expectation? If I have not, when my mind is more at ease, I will endeavour to please you better. For, methinks, my sentences drag; my style creeps; my imagination is sunk; my spirit serves me not; only to tell you, that whether I have little or much, it is all devoted to the commands of my dear Miss Howe.

CL. HARLOWE

Postscript

The insolent Betty Barnes has just now fired me anew, by reporting to me the following expressions of the hideous creature, Solmes—'That he is *sure* of the coy girl; and that with little labour to himself.' 'That be I ever so averse to him beforehand, he can depend upon my principles; and it will be a pleasure to him to see by what pretty degrees I shall come-to.' (Horrid wretch!) 'That it was Sir Oliver's observation, who knew the world perfectly well, that *fear* was a better security than *love* for a woman's good behaviour to her husband; although, for his part, to such a fine creature, he would try what love would do; for a few weeks at least: being unwilling to believe what the old knight used to aver, that fondness spoils more wives than it makes good.'

What think you, my dear of such a wretch as this! tutored, too, by that old surly *misogynist*, as he was deemed, Sir Oliver?—

Letter 41: MISS CLARISSA HARLOWE TO MISS HOWE

Tuesday, March 21

How willingly would my dear mamma show kindness to me, were she permitted! None of this persecution should I labour under, I am sure, if that regard were paid to her prudence and fine understanding, which they so well deserve. Whether owing to her, or to my aunt, or to both, that a new trial was to be made upon me, I cannot tell; but this morning her Shorey delivered into my hand the following condescending letter.

[*Letter 41.1: Mrs Harlowe to Clarissa Harlowe*]

My dear girl,

FOR so I must still call you, since *dear* you may be to me in every sense of the word—We have taken into particular consideration some hints that fell yesterday from your good Norton, as if we had not at Mr Solmes's first application treated you with that condescension, wherewith we have in all other instances treated you. If it *had been so*, my dear, you were not excusable to be wanting in *your* part, and to set yourself to oppose your father's will in a point he had entered too far into, to recede with honour. But all yet may be well. On your single will, my child, depends all our present happiness!—

Your father permits me to tell you, that if you now at last comply with his expectations, all past disobligations shall be buried in oblivion, as if they had never been: but withal, that this is the last time that that grace will be offered you.

I hinted to you, you must remember, that patterns of the richest silks were sent for. They are come: and as they *are* come, your papa, to show how much he is determined, will have me send them up to you. I could have wished they might not have accompanied this letter—But there is no great matter in *that*. I must tell you, that your delicacy is not to be *quite* so much regarded, as I had once thought it deserved to be.

These are the newest, as well as richest, that we could procure; answerable to our station in the world; answerable to the fortune, additional to your grandfather's estate, designed you; and to the noble settlements agreed upon.

Your papa intends you six suits (three of them dressed) at his own expense. You have an entire new suit; and one besides, which I think you never wore but twice. As the new suit is rich, if you choose to make that one of the six, your papa will present you with a hundred guineas in lieu.

Mr Solmes intends to present you with a set of jewels. As you have your grandmother's and your own, if you choose to have the former new-set and to make them serve, his present will be made in money; a very round sum—which will be given in full property to yourself; besides a fine annual allowance for pin-money, as it is called. So that your objection against the spirit of a man you think worse of than he deserves, will have no weight; but you will be more independent than a wife of less discretion than we attribute to you, perhaps *ought* to be. You know full well, that I, who first and last brought a still larger fortune into the family than you will carry to Mr Solmes, had not a provision made me of near this that we have made for you—Where people marry to their liking, terms are the least things stood upon—Yet should I be sorry if you cannot, to oblige us all, overcome a dislike.

Wonder not, Clary, that I write to you thus plainly and freely upon this subject. Your behaviour hitherto has been such, that we have had no opportunity of entering minutely into the subject with you. Yet, after all that has passed between you and me in conversation, and between you and your uncles by letter, you have no room to doubt what is to be the consequence. Either, child, we must give up *our* authority, or you *your* humour. You cannot expect the one: we have all the reason in the world to expect the other. You know I have told you more than once, that you must resolve to have Mr Solmes, or never to be looked upon to be our child.

The draft of the settlements you may see when ever you will. We think there can be no room for objection to any of the articles. There is still more in them in our family's favour than was stipulated at first, when your aunt talked of them to you. More so, indeed, than we could have asked. If, upon perusal of them, you think any alteration necessary, it shall be made—Do, my dear girl, send to me within this day or two, or rather *ask* me, for the perusal of them.

As a certain person's appearance at church so lately, and what he gives out everywhere, make us extremely uneasy, and as that uneasiness will continue while you are single, you must not wonder that a short day is intended. This day fortnight we design it to be, if you have no objection to make that I shall approve of. But, if you determine as we would have you, and signify it to us, we shall not stand with you for a week or so.

Your sightliness of person may perhaps make some think this alliance disparaging. But I hope you won't put such a personal value upon yourself; if you do, it will indeed be the less wonder that *person* should weigh with you (however contemptible the consideration!)—in another man. Thus we parents, in justice, ought to judge: that our two daughters are *equally* dear and valuable to us: if so, why should *Clarissa* think that a disparagement, which *Arabella* would not (nor we for her) have thought any, had the address been made to her?—You will know what I mean by this, without my explaining myself further.

Signify to us, now, therefore, your compliance with our wishes—And then there is an end of your confinement: an act of oblivion, as I may call it, shall pass upon all your former refractoriness: and you will once more make us happy in you, and in one another. You may, in this case, directly come down to your papa and me, in his study; where we will give you our opinions of the patterns, with our hearty forgiveness and blessings.

Come, be a good child, as you used to be, my Clarissa. I have (notwithstanding your past behaviour, and the hopelesness which some have expressed of your compliance) undertaken this one time more for you. Discredit not my hopes, my dear girl. I have promised never more to interfere between your *father* and *you*, if this my most earnest application succeed not. I expect you down, love. Your papa expects you down. But be sure don't let him see any thing uncheerful in your compliance. If you come, I will clasp you to my fond heart with as much pleasure as ever I pressed you to it in my whole life. You don't know what I have suffered within these few weeks past; nor ever will be able to guess, till you come to be in my situation; which is that of a fond and indulgent mother, praying night and day, and struggling to preserve, against the attempts of more ungovernable spirits, the peace and union of her family.

But, you know the terms: come not near us if you resolve to be undutiful: but this, after what I have written, I hope you cannot be.

If you come directly, and, as I said, *cheerfully*, as if your heart were in your duty (and you told me it was *free*, you know), I shall then, as I said, give you the most tender proofs, how much I am

                                                    Your truly affectionate mother

Think for me, my dearest friend, how I must be affected by this letter; the contents of it so surprisingly terrifying, yet so sweetly urged!—Oh why, cried I to myself, am I obliged to undergo this severe conflict between a command that I cannot obey, and language so condescendingly moving!—Could I have been sure of being struck dead at the altar before the ceremony had given the man I hate a title to my vows, I think I could have submitted to have been led to it. But to think of living *with*, and living *for*, a man one cannot abide, what a sad thing is that!—

And then, how could the glare of habit and ornament be supposed any inducement to one, who has always held that the principal view of a good wife in the adorning of her person ought to be to *preserve* the affection of her husband, and to *do credit* to his choice; and that she should be even *fearful* of attracting the eyes of *others*?—In this view, must not the very richness of the patterns add to my disgusts?—Great encouragement indeed, to think of adorning one's self to be the wife of Mr *Solmes!*—

Upon the whole, it was not possible for me to go down upon the prescribed condition. Do you think it was?—And to *write*, if my letter would have been *read*, what could I write that would be admitted, and after what I had written: and said to so little effect? I walked backward and forward: I threw down with disdain the patterns: now to my closet retired I; then, quitting it, now threw I myself upon the settee; now upon this chair; now upon that; and then into one window, then into another—I knew not what to do!—And while I was in this suspense, having again taken up the letter to re-peruse it, Betty came in, reminding me, by order, that my papa and mamma waited for me in my papa's study.

Tell my mamma, said I, that I beg the favour of seeing her here for one moment; or to permit me to attend her anywhere by herself.

I listened at the stair's-head—You see, my dear, how it is, cried my father, very angrily: all your condescension (as your indulgence heretofore) is thrown away. *You blame your son's violence*, as you call it (I had some pleasure in hearing this), but nothing else will do with her. You shall *not* see her alone. Is *my* presence an exception to the bold creature?

Tell her, said my mamma to Betty, she knows upon what terms she may come down to us. Nor will I see her upon any other.

The maid brought me this answer. I had recourse to my pen and ink; but I trembled so, that I could not write, nor knew I what to say had I had steadier fingers. At last Betty brought me these lines from my papa.

[*Letter 41.2: James Harlowe to Clarissa Harlowe*]

Undutiful and perverse Clarissa,
No condescension, I see, will move you. Your mother shall *not* see you; nor will I. Prepare however to obey. You know our pleasure. Your uncle Antony, your brother, and your sister, and your favourite Mrs Norton, shall see the ceremony performed privately at your said uncle's chapel. And when Mr Solmes can introduce you to us, in the temper we wish to behold you in, we may perhaps forgive *his* wife, although we never can, in any *other* character, our perverse daughter. As it will be so privately performed, clothes and equipage may be provided afterwards. So prepare to go to your uncle's for an early day in next week. We will not see you till all is over: And we will have it over the sooner, in order to shorten the time of your deserved confinement, and our own trouble in

contending with such a rebel as you have been of late. I'll hear no pleas. Will receive no letter, nor expostulation. Nor shall you hear from me any more till you have changed your name to my liking. This from

Your incensed father

If this resolution be adhered to, then will my papa never see me more!—For I will never be that Solmes's wife—I will die first!—

Tuesday evening

HE, this Solmes, came hither soon after I had received my papa's letter. He sent up to beg leave to wait upon me. I wonder at his assurance!

I said to Betty, who brought me his message, let him restore a lost creature to her father and mother, and then I may hear what he has to say. But, if my friends will not see *me* on *his* account, I will not see him upon his *own*.

I hope, miss, said Betty, that you will not send me down with this answer. He is with your papa and mamma.

I am driven to despair, said I. I cannot be used worse. I will not see him.

Down she went with my answer. She pretended, it seems, to be loath to repeat it: so was *commanded* out of her affected reserves, and gave it in its full force.

Oh how I heard my papa storm!—

They were all together, it seems, in his study. My brother was for having me turned out of the house that moment, to Lovelace, and my evil destiny. My mamma was pleased to put in a gentle word for me: I know not what it was: but thus she was answered—My dear, this is the provokingest thing in the world in a woman of your good sense!—To love a rebel, as well as if she were dutiful. What encouragement for duty is this?—Have I not loved her as well as ever you did, and *why* am I changed? Would to the Lord, your sex knew how to distinguish! But the fond mother ever made a hardened child!—

She was pleased, however, to blame Betty, as the wench owned, for giving my answer its full force. But my father praised her for it.

The wench says, that he would have come up in his wrath, at my refusing to see Mr Solmes: but my brother and sister prevailed upon him to the contrary.

I wish he had!—and, were it not for his own sake, that he had killed me.

Mr Solmes condescended (I am mightily obliged to him, truly!) to plead for me.

They are all in tumults! How it will end, I know not!—I am quite weary of my life!—so happy, till within these few weeks!—so miserable now!

Well, indeed, might my mamma say, that I should have great trials!—

P. S. The *idiot* (such a one am I treated like!) is *begged*, as I may say, by my brother and sister. They have desired that I may be consigned over entirely to their management. If it be granted (It *is*, on my father's side, I understand, but not *yet* on my mother's) what cruelty may I not expect from their envy, jealousy and ill-will?—I shall soon see, by its effects, if I am to be so consigned—This is a written intimation privately dropped in my woodhouse-walk, by my cousin Dolly Hervey. The dear girl longs to see me, she tells me: but is forbidden till she see me as Mrs Solmes, or consenting to be his. I will take example by *their* perseverance!—Indeed I will!—

Letter 42: MISS CLARISSA HARLOWE TO MISS HOWE

A N angry dialogue, a scolding-bout rather, has passed between my sister and me. Did you think I could scold, my dear?

She was sent up to me, upon my refusal to see Mr Solmes—Let loose upon me, I think!—No intention, on their parts, to conciliate! I am to be given up to my brother and her I suppose, by general consent.

Everything she said against me, which carried force with it, I will do justice to. As I ask for your approbation or disapprobation of my conduct, upon the facts I lay before you, I should think it the sign of a very bad cause, if I endeavoured to mislead my judge.

She began with representing to me the danger I had been in had my father come up, as he would have done had he not been hindered, by Mr *Solmes*, among the rest. She reflected upon my good Mrs Norton, as if she encouraged me in my perverseness. She ridiculed me for my supposed esteem for Lovelace. Was surprised that the *witty*, the *prudent*, nay, the *dutiful* and *pi-ous* (so she sneeringly pronounced the word) Clarissa Harlowe, should be so strangely fond of a profligate man, that her parents were forced to lock her up, to keep her from running into his arms. Let me ask you, my dear, said she, how you now keep your account of the disposition of your time? How many hours in the twenty-four do you devote to your needle? How many to your prayers? How many to letter-writing? And how many to love?—I doubt, I doubt, my little dear, was her arch expression, the latter article is like Aaron's rod, and swallows up all the rest!—Tell me; is it not so?

To these I answered, that it was a double mortification to me to owe my safety from my papa's indignation to a man I could never thank for anything—I vindicated the good Mrs Norton with a warmth that her merit required from me— With equal warmth I resented her unsisterly reflections upon me on Mr Lovelace's account. As to the disposition of my time in the twenty-four hours, I told her it would better have become her to pity a sister in distress, than to exult over her— especially when I could too justly attribute to the disposition of some of her wakeful hours no small part of that distress.

She raved extremely at this last hint: but reminded me of the gentle treatment of all my friends, my mamma's particularly, before it came to this: she said that I had discovered a spirit they never had expected: that if they had *thought* me such a championess, they would hardly have ventured to engage with me: but that now, the short and long was, that the matter had gone too far to be given up: that now it was a contention between *duty* and *wilfulness*; whether a parent's authority was to yield to a daughter's obstinacy, or the contrary: that I must therefore bend or break, that was all, child.

I told her, that I wished the subject were of such a nature that I could return her pleasantry with equal lightness of heart: but that, if Mr Solmes had such merit in everybody's eye, in *hers* particularly, why might he not be a *brother* to me, rather than a *husband*?

Oh child, she thought I was as pleasant to the full as she was: she began to have some hopes of me now. But did I think she would rob her sister of her humble servant? Had he first addressed himself to me, said she, something might have been said: but to take my younger sister's refusal! No, no, child; it is not come to that neither! Besides, that would be to leave the door open in your heart for you know who, child; and we would fain bar him out, if possible. In short (and then she changed both her tone and her looks), had I been as forward as somebody, to throw myself into the arms of one of the greatest profligates in England, who had endeavoured to support his claim to me through the blood of my brother, then might all my family join together to save me from such a wretch, and to marry me as fast as they could to some worthy gentleman, who might oppor-*tune*-ly offer himself. And now, Clary, all's out, and make the most of it.

Did not this deserve a severe return? Do say it did, to justify my reply—Alas! for my poor sister! said I—The man was not *always* so great a profligate. How true is the observation, *that unrequited love turns to deepest hate!*

I thought she would have beat me—But I proceeded—I have heard often of my brother's danger, and my brother's murderer. When so little ceremony is made with me, why should I not speak out?—Did he not seek to kill the *other*, if he could have done it? Would *he* have given him *his* life, had it been in his power?—The *aggressor* should not *complain*—And as to oppor-*tune* offers, would to heaven some-one had offered oppor-*tune*-ly to somebody. It is not my fault, Bella, the oppor-*tune* gentleman don't come!

Could *you*, my dear, have shown more *spirit*? I expected to feel the weight of her hand. She did come up to me, with it held up: then, speechless with passion, ran down half way of the stairs, and then up again.

When she could speak—God give her patience with me!

Amen, said I: but you see, Bella, how ill you bear the retort you provoke. Will you forgive me; and let me find a sister in you, as *I* am sorry if you have reason to think me unsisterly in what I have said?

Then did she pour upon me, with greater violence; considering my gentleness as a triumph of temper over her. She was resolved, she said, to let everybody know how I took the wicked Lovelace's part against my brother.

I wished, I told her, I could make the plea for *my*-self, which she might for *her*-self: that my anger was more inexusable than my judgement. But I presumed she had some other view in coming to me, than she had hitherto acquainted me with. Let me, said I, but know (after all that has passed) if you have anything to propose that I *can* comply with; anything that can make my *only* sister once more my friend?

I had before, upon her ridiculing me on my supposed character of *meekness*, said, that although I wished to be thought *meek*, I would not be *abject*; although *humble*, not *mean*: and here, in a sneering way, she cautioned me on that head.

I replied that her pleasantry was much more agreeable than her anger: but I wished she would let me know the end of a visit that had hitherto (*between* us) been so unsisterly?

She desired to be informed, in the name of *everybody* was her word, what I was determined upon: and whether to comply or not?—One word for all: my friends were not to have patience with so perverse a creature, for ever.

This then I told her I would do: absolutely break with the man they were all so determined against: upon condition, however, that neither Mr Solmes, nor any other, were urged to me with the force of a command.

And what was this, more than I had offered before? What, but ringing my changes upon the same bells, and neither receding nor advancing one tittle?

If I knew what other proposals I could make, that would be acceptable to them all, and free me from the address of a man so disagreeable to me, I would make them. I had indeed before offered, never to marry without my father's consent—

She interrupted me, that was because I depended upon my whining tricks to bring my father and mother to what I pleased.

A *poor* dependence! I said—She knew those who would make that dependence vain—

And I *should* have brought them to my own beck, very probably, and my uncle Harlowe too, as also my aunt Hervey, had I not been forbidden their sight, and thereby hindered from playing my pug's tricks before them.

At least, Bella, said I, you have hinted to me to whom I am obliged that my father and mother, and everybody else, treat me thus harshly. But surely you make them all very weak. Indifferent persons, judging of us two, from what *you* say, would either think *me* a very artful creature, or *you* a very spiteful one.

You are *indeed* a very artful one, for that matter, interrupted she in a passion: one of the artfullest I ever knew! And then followed an accusation so low! so unsisterly!—That I next-to-bewitched people, by my insinuating address: that nobody could be valued or respected but must stand like cyphers wherever I came. How often, said she, have I and my brother been talking upon a subject, and had everybody's attention till *you* came in, with your bewitching *meek* pride, and *humble* significance; and then have we either been stopped by references to Miss Clarissa's opinion, forsooth; or been forced to stop ourselves, or must have talked on unattended to by everybody.

She paused. Dear Bella, proceed!—She indeed seemed only gathering breath.

And so I will, said she. Did you not bewitch my grandfather? Could anything be pleasing to him, that *you* did not say or do? How did he use to hang, till he slabbered again, poor doting old man! on your silver tongue! Yet what did *you* say, that *we* could not have said? What did *you* do, that *we* did not endeavour to do?— And what was all this for? His last will showed what effect your *smooth* obligingness had upon him!—To leave the acquired part of his estate from the next heirs, his own sons, to a grandchild; to his *youngest* grandchild! a *daughter* too!—To leave the family pictures from his sons to you, because you could *tiddle* about them, and though you now neglect their examples, could wipe and clean them with your dainty hands! The family plate too, in such quantities, of two or three generations standing, must not be changed, because his *precious child*,[a] humouring his old *fal-lal* taste, admired it, to make it all her own.

This was too low to move me: Oh my poor sister! said I: not to be able, or at least willing, to distinguish between art and nature! If I *did* oblige, I was happy in it: I looked for no further reward: my mind is above art, from the dirty motives you mention. I wish with all my heart my grandfather had not thus distinguished me: he saw my brother likely to be amply provided for *out* of the family, as well as *in* it: he desired that *you* might have the greater share of my papa's favour for it; and no doubt but you *both* will. You know, Bella, that the estate my grandfather bequeathed *me* was not half the real estate he left.

What's all that to an estate in possession, and left you with such distinctions as gave you a reputation of greater value than the estate itself?

a Alluding to his words in the preamble to the clauses in his will in her favour. See p. 53.

Hence my misfortune, Bella, in your envy, I doubt! But have I not given up that possession in the best manner I could—

Yes, interrupting me, she hated me for that *best manner*. Specious little witch! she called me: your *best manner*, so full of art and design, had never been seen through, if you with your blandishing ways had not been put out of sight, and reduced to positive declarations!—hindered from playing your little, whining tricks; curling, like a serpent, about your mamma; and making her cry to deny you anything your little obstinate heart was set upon!

Obstinate heart, Bella!

Yes, obstinate heart! For did you ever give up anything? Had you not the art to make them think all was right you asked, though my brother and I were frequently refused favours of no greater import?

I knew not, Bella, that I ever asked anything unfit to be granted. I seldom asked favours for *myself*, but for *others*.

I was a reflecting creature for this!

All you speak of, Bella, was a long time ago. I cannot go so far back into our childish follies. Little did I think of how long standing this your late-shown antipathy is.

I was a reflecter again! Such a *saucy meekness*; such a *best manner*; and such venom in words!—Oh Clary! Clary! Thou wert always a *two-faced* girl!

Nobody thought I had two faces when I gave up all into my papa's management; taking from his bounty, as before, all my little pocket-money, without a shilling addition to my stipend, or desiring it—

Yes, cunning creature!—And that was another of your *fetches!*—For did it not engage my fond papa (as no doubt you thought it would) to tell you that, since you had done so grateful and dutiful a thing, he would keep entire, for your use, all the produce of the estate left you, and be but your steward in it; and that you should be entitled to the same allowances as before: another of your *hook-in*'s, Clary!— so that all your extravagancies have been supported gratis.

My extravagancies, Bella!—but did my papa ever give me anything he did not give you?

Yes, indeed; I got more by that means, than I should have had the conscience to ask. But I have still the greater part to show! But *you*! What have *you* to show?—I dare to say, not fifty pieces in the world!

Indeed I have not!

I believe you!—Your mamma Norton, I suppose—But mum for that!

Unworthy Bella!—The good woman, although low in circumstance, is great in mind! Much greater than those who would impute meanness to a soul incapable of it.

What then have you done with the sums given you from infancy to squander?— Let me ask you (affecting archness), has, has, has, Lovelace, has your rake put it out at interest for you?

Oh that my sister would not make me blush for her! It *is*, however, out at interest!—And I hope it will bring me interest upon interest!—Better than to lie rusting in my cabinet, as yours does.

She understood me, she said. Were I a man, she should suppose I was aiming to carry the County. Popularity! A crowd to follow me with their blessings when I went to and from church, and nobody else to be regarded, were agreeable things!

House-top proclamations! I *hid not my light under a bushel*, she would say that for me. But was it not a little hard upon me to be kept from blazing on a Sunday?—And to be hindered from my charitable ostentations?

This, indeed, Bella, is cruel in *you*, who have so largely contributed to my confinement—But go on. You'll be out of breath by and by. I cannot wish to be *able* to return this usage—*Poor* Bella! And I believe I smiled a little too contemptuously for a sister.

None of my saucy contempts (rising in her voice): none of my *poor Bella's*, with that air of superiority in a younger sister!

Well then, *rich* Bella! curtsying—that will please you better—and it is due likewise to the hoards you boast of.

Look ye, Clary, holding up her hand, if you are not a little more *abject* in your *meekness*, a little more *mean* in your *humility*, and treat me with the respect due to an elder sister—you shall find—

Not that you will treat me worse than you *have done*, Bella!—That cannot be; unless you were to let fall your uplifted hand upon me—and that would less become you to *do*, than me to *bear*.

Good, meek creature!—but you were upon your overtures just now!—I shall surprise everybody by tarrying so long. They will think some good may be done with you—and supper will be ready.

A tear would stray down my cheek—How happy have I been, said I sighing, in the supper-time conversations, with all my dear friends in my eye round the hospitable board!

I met only with insult for this—Bella has not a feeling heart: the highest joy in this life she is not capable of: but then she saves herself many griefs by her impenetrableness—Yet, for ten times the pain that such a sensibility is attended with, would I not part with the pleasure it brings with it.

She asked me, upon my turning from her, if she should say anything *below* of my *compliances*?

You may say, that I will do everything they would have me do, if they will free me from Mr Solmes's address.

This is all you desire at present, *creeper-on!* (What words she has!), but will not t'other man flame out and roar most horribly, upon a prey's being snatched from his paws, that he thought himself sure of?

I must let you talk in your own way, or we shall never come to a point. I shall not matter his *roaring*, as you call it: I will promise him, that, if I ever marry any other man, it shall not be till *he* is married. And if he be not satisfied with such a condescension as this, I shall think he *ought*: and I will give any assurances that I will neither correspond with him, nor see him. Surely this will do.

But I suppose then you will have no objection to see and converse, on a civil foot, with Mr Solmes—as your papa's friend, or so?

No! I must be permitted to retire to my apartment whenever he comes: I would no more converse with the one, than correspond with the other: that would be to make Mr Lovelace guilty of some rashness, on a belief that I broke with him to have Mr Solmes.

And so that wicked wretch is to be allowed such a control over you, that you are not to be civil to your papa's friends, at his own house, for fear of incensing *him*!—

When this comes to be represented, be so good as to tell me what it is you expect from it?

Everything, I said, or *nothing*, as she was pleased to represent it—Be so good as to give it your interest, Bella: and say farther, that I will by any means I can, in the law, or otherwise, make over to my papa, to my uncles, or even to my brother, all I am intitled to by my grandfather's will, as a security for the performance of my promises. And as I shall have no reason to expect any favour from my papa, if I break them, I shall not be worth anybody's having. And further still, unkindly as my brother has used me, I will go down to Scotland privately, as his housekeeper (I now see I may be spared here), if he will promise to treat me no worse than he would do an hired one—Or I will go to Florence, to my cousin Morden, if his stay in Italy will admit of it: and, in *either* case, it may be given out that I am gone to the *other*; or to the world's end: I care not whither it is said I am gone, or do go.

Let me ask you, child, if you will give your pretty proposal in writing?

Yes, with all my heart. And I stepped to my closet, and wrote to the purpose I have mentioned; and, moreover, a few lines to my brother with it; expressing 'my concern for having offended him; beseeching him to support with his interest the accompanying proposal; disdaining subterfuge and art; referring to him to draw up a writing to bind me to the observance of my promises; declaring, that what the *law* would not establish, my *resolution* should—I told him, that he could do more than anybody to reconcile my father and mother to me: and I should be infinitely obliged to him, if he would let me owe this favour to his brotherly mediation.'

And how do you think Bella employed herself while I was writing?—Why, playing gently upon my harpsichord: and *humming* to it, to show her unconcernedness.

When I approached her with what I had written, the cruel creature arose with an air of levity—Why, love, you have not written already!—You have, I protest!—Oh what a ready penwoman!—And may I read it?

If you please, Bella.

She read it, and burst into an affected laugh: how wise ones may be taken in!—Then you did not know that I was jesting with you all this time!—and so you would have me carry down this pretty piece of nonsense?

Don't let me be surprised at your seeming unsisterliness, Bella. I hope it is *but* seeming. There can be *no* wit in such jesting as this.

The folly of the creature! How natural it is for people, when they set their hearts upon anything, to think everybody must see with their eyes!—Pray, dear child, *what* becomes of your papa's authority *here*?—Who *stoops here*, the *parent*, or the *child*?—How does *this* square with the engagements actually agreed upon between your papa and Mr Solmes? What security that your rake will not follow you to the *world's end*? Pr'ythee, pr'ythee, take it back; and put it to thy love-sick heart, and never think I will be laughed at for being *taken-in* by thy whining nonsense. I know thee better, my dear—And, with another spiteful laugh, she flung it on my toilette; and away she went—Contempts for contempts, as she passed!—That's for your *poor Bella's!*

Nevertheless, I enclosed what I had written, in a few lines directed to my brother: as modestly as I could accounting, from my sister's behaviour, for sending it down to him; lest she, having in her passion mistaken me, as I said, should set what I had written in a worse light than, as I apprehended, it deserved to appear in. The following is the answer I received to it, delivered to me just as I was going to bed. His passion would not let him stay till morning.

[*Letter 42.1: James Harlowe, Jun. to Clarissa Harlowe*]

I wonder that you have the courage to write to me, upon whom you are so continually emptying your *whole female quiver*. I have no patience with you for reflecting upon me as the aggressor in a quarrel which owed its beginning to my consideration for *you*.

You have made such confessions in a villain's favour, as ought to cause all your relations to renounce you for ever. For my part, I will not believe any woman in the world, who promises against her *avowed* inclination. To put it out of your *power* to ruin yourself is the only way left to prevent your ruin. I did not intend to write; but your too-kind sister has prevailed upon me. As to your going into Scotland, that day of grace is over!—Nor would I advise, that you should go to *grandfather-up* your cousin Morden. Besides, that worthy gentleman might be involved in some fatal dispute, upon your account; and then be called the *aggressor*.

A fine situation you have brought yourself to, to propose to hide yourself from your rake, and to have falsehoods told to conceal you!—Your confinement, at this rate, is the happiest thing that could befall you. Your bravo's behaviour at church, looking out for you, is a sufficient indication of his power over you, had you not so shamelessly acknowledged it.

One word for all—If, for the honour of the family, I cannot carry this point, I will retire to Scotland, and never see the face of any one of it more.

                                                      JA. HARLOWE

There's a brother!—There's flaming duty to a father and mother and uncles!—But he sees himself valued, and made of consequence; and he gives himself airs accordingly!—

Letter 44: MISS CLARISSA HARLOWE TO MISS HOWE

                                        Wednesday morning, 9 o'clock
MY aunt Hervey lay here last night, and is but just gone from me. She came up to me with my sister. They would not trust my aunt without this ill-natured witness. When she entered my chamber, I told her that this visit was a high favour to a poor prisoner in her hard confinement. I kissed her hand. She, kindly saluting me, said, Why this distance to your aunt, my dear, who loves you so well?

She owned that she came to expostulate with me for the peace-sake of the family: for that she could not believe it possible, if I did not conceive myself unkindly treated, that I, who had ever shown such a sweetness of temper, as well as manners, should be thus resolute in a point *so very near* to my father, and all my friends. My mamma and she were both willing to impute my resolution to the manner I had been begun with; and to my supposing that my brother had originally more of a hand in the proposals made by Mr Solmes than my father, or other friends. And fain would she have furnished me with an excuse to come off of my opposition; Bella all the while humming a tune, and opening this book and that, without meaning; but saying nothing. After having showed me, that my opposition could not be of signification, my father's honour being engaged, she concluded with enforcing upon me my duty in stronger terms than I believe she would have done, the circumstances of the case considered, had not my sister been present. It would but be repeating what I have so often mentioned, to give you the arguments that passed on both sides. So I will only recite what she was pleased to say that carried with it the face of newness.

When she found me inflexible, as she was pleased to call it, she said—For her part, she could not but say, that if I were not to have either Mr Solmes or Mr Lovelace, and yet, to make my friends easy, must marry, she should not think amiss of Mr Wyerley. What did I think of Mr Wyerley?

Ay, Clary, put in my sister, what say you to Mr Wyerley?

I saw through this immediately. It was said on purpose, I doubted not, to have an argument against me of absolute prepossession in Lovelace's favour: since Mr Wyerley everywhere proclaims his value, even to veneration, for me; and is far less exceptionable, both in person and mind, than Mr Solmes: and I was willing to turn the tables, by trying how far Solmes's terms might be dispensed with; since the same terms could not be expected from Mr Wyerley?

I therefore desired to know, whether my answer, if it should be in favour of Mr Wyerley, would release me from Mr Solmes?—for I owned that I had not the aversion to *him* that I had to the *other*.

Nay, she had no commission to propose such a thing—She only knew that my papa and mamma would not be easy till Mr Lovelace's hopes were entirely defeated.

Cunning creature! said my sister—And this, and her joining in the question before, confirmed me that it was a designed snare for me.

Don't You, dear madam, said I, put questions that can answer no end, but to support my brother's schemes against me—But are there any hopes of an end to my sufferings and disgrace, without having this hated man imposed upon me? Will not what I have offered be accepted? I am sure it ought: I will venture to say that.

Why, niece, if there be *not* any such hopes, I presume you don't think yourself absolved from the duty due from a child to her parents?

Yes, said my sister, I do not doubt but it is Miss Clary's aim, if she does not fly to her Lovelace, to get her estate into her own hands, and go to live at *The Grove*, in that independence upon which she builds all her perverseness. And, dear heart! my little love, how will you then blaze away! Your mamma Norton, your oracle, with your poor at your gates, mingling so *proudly* and so *meanly* with the ragged herd! Reflecting, by your ostentation, upon all the ladies in the county, who do not as you do. This is known to be your scheme! And the poor *without*-doors, and Lovelace *within*, with one hand building up a name, pulling it down with the other!—Oh what a charming scheme is this!—But let me tell you, my pretty little flighty one, that my papa's *living* will shall control my grandfather's *dead* one; and that estate will be disposed of as my fond grandfather would have disposed of it, had he lived to see such a change in his favourite. In a word, miss, it will be kept out of your hands, till my papa sees you discreet enough to have the management of it, or till you can *dutifully*, by law, tear it from him.

Fie, Miss Harlowe, said my aunt, this is not pretty to your sister.

Oh madam, let her go on. This is nothing to what I have borne from Miss Harlowe. She is either commissioned to treat me ill by her *envy*, or by an *higher* authority, to which I must submit—As to revoking the estate, what hinders, if I pleased? I know my power; but have not the least thought of exerting it. Be pleased to let my papa know, that, whatever be the consequences to myself, were he to turn me out of doors (which I should rather he would, than to be confined and insulted as I am), and were I to be reduced to indigence and want, I would seek no resources, that should be contrary to his will.

For that matter, child, said my aunt, were you to marry, you must do as your *husband* will have you. If that husband be Mr Lovelace, he will be glad of any opportunity of embroiling the families more. And let me tell you, niece, if he had the respect for you he pretends to have, he would not be upon such defiances as he is. He is known to be a very revengeful man; and were I *you*, Miss Clary, I should be afraid he would wreak upon me that vengeance, though I had not offended him, which he is continually threatening to pour upon the family.

Mr Lovelace's threatened vengeance is in *return* for threatened vengeance. It is not everybody will bear insult, as, of late, I have been forced to bear it.

Oh how my sister's face shone with passion!

But Mr Lovelace, proceeded I, as I have said twenty and twenty times, would be quite out of the question, were I to be generously treated!

My sister said something with great vehemence: but only raising my voice, to be heard, without minding her, Pray, madam, provokingly interrogated I, was he not known to have been as wild a man, when he was *at first* introduced into our family, as he *now* is said to be? Yet *then*, the common phrases of *wild oats*, and *black oxen*,[1] and such-like, were qualifiers; and marriage, and the wife's discretion, were to perform wonders—But (turning to my sister) I find I have said too much.

Oh thou wicked reflecter!—And what made *me* abhor him, think you, but the proof of those villainous freedoms that ought to have had the same effect upon you, were you but half so good a creature as you pretend to be?

Proof, did you say, Bella! I thought you had not *proof*?—But *you know best.* (Was not this very spiteful, my dear?)

Now, Clary, would I give a thousand pounds to know all that is in thy little rancorous and reflecting heart, at this moment.

I might let you know for a much less sum, and not be afraid of being worse treated than I have been.

Well, young ladies, I am sorry to see things run so high between you. You know, niece (to me), you had not been confined thus to your apartment, could your mamma by condescensions, or your papa by authority, have been able to have done anything with you. But how can you expect, when there must be a concession on *one* side, that it should be on theirs? If *my* Dolly, who has not the hundredth part of your understanding, were thus to set herself up in absolute contradiction to my will, in a point *so* material, I should not take it well of her—indeed I should not.

I believe not, madam: and if Miss Hervey had just such a brother, and just such a sister (you *may* look, Bella!)—and if both were to aggravate her parents, as my brother and sister do mine—then, perhaps, you might use her as I am used: and if she hated the man you proposed to her, and with as much reason as I do Mr Solmes—

And loved a rake and libertine, miss, as you do Lovelace, said my sister—

Then might she (continued I, not minding her) beg to be excused from obeying. But yet if she did, and would give you the most solemn assurances, and security besides, that she never would have the man you disliked, against your consent—I dare say, Miss Hervey's father and mother would sit down satisfied, and not endeavour to force her inclinations.

So!—said my sister, with uplifted hands, *father* and *mother* now come in for their share!

But if, child, replied my aunt, I knew she *loved a rake*, and suspected that she sought to gain time, in order to wire-draw me into a consent—

I beg pardon, madam, for interrupting you; but if Miss Hervey could *obtain* your consent, what further would be to be said?

True, child; but she never should.

Then, madam, it never would be.

That I doubt, niece.

If you do, madam, can you think confinement and ill usage is the way to prevent the apprehended rashness?

My dear, this sort of intimation would make one but too apprehensive, that there is no trusting to yourself, when one knows your inclination.

That apprehension, madam, seems to have been conceived before this intimation was made, or the least cause for it given. Why else the disgraceful confinement I have been laid under?—Let me venture to say, that my sufferings are rather owing to *designed* terror, knowing there were too good grounds for my opposition, than doubt of my conduct; for, when they were inflicted upon me first, I had given no *cause* of doubt; nor should there now be room for any, if my discretion might be trusted to.

My aunt, after a little hesitation, said, But consider, my dear, what confusion will be perpetuated in your family, if you marry this hated Lovelace?

And let it be considered, what misery to me, madam, if I marry that hated Solmes?

Many a young creature has thought she could not love a man, with whom she has afterwards been very happy. Few women, child, marry their first loves.

That may be the reason there are so few happy marriages.

But there are few first-impressions *fit* to be encouraged.

I am afraid so too, madam. I have a very indifferent opinion of light and first impressions. But, as I have often said, all I wish for is, to have leave to live single.

Indeed you must not, miss. Your father and mother will be unhappy till they see you married, and out of Lovelace's reach. I am told that you propose to condition with him (so far are matters gone between you), never to have *any* man if you have not *him*.

I know no better way to prevent mischief on all sides, I freely own it—And there is not, if *he* be out of the question, another man in the world, I can think favourably of—Nevertheless, I would give all I have in the world, that he were married to some other person—indeed I would, Bella, for all you put on that smile of incredulity.

May be so, Clary: but I will smile for all that.

If *he* be out of the question! repeated my aunt—So, Miss Clary, I see how it is— I will go down (Miss Harlowe, shall I follow you?)—And I will endeavour to persuade your papa to let my sister herself come up: and a happier event may then result.—

Depend upon it, madam, said my sister, this will be the case: my mamma and she will be both in tears; but with this different effect; my mamma will come down softened, and cut to the heart; but will leave her favourite hardened, from the advantages she will think she has over my mamma's tenderness—Why, madam, it was for this very reason the girl is not admitted into her presence.

Thus she run on, as she went down-stairs.

Letter 45: MISS CLARISSA HARLOWE TO MISS HOWE

MY heart fluttered with the hope and the fear of seeing my mamma, and with the shame and the grief of having given her so much uneasiness. But it needed not: she was not permitted to come. But my aunt was so good as to return; yet not without my sister: and, taking my hand, made me sit down by her.

She came, she must own, *officiously*, she said, this *once* more, though against the opinion of my father: but knowing and dreading the consequence of my opposition, she could not *but* come.

She then set forth to me, my friends' expectations from me; Mr Solmes's riches (three times as rich he came out to be as anybody had thought him); the settlements proposed; Mr Lovelace's bad character; their aversion to him; all in a very strong light; but not a stronger than my mamma had before placed them in. My mamma, surely, could not have given the particulars of what had passed between herself and me: if she had, my aunt would not have repeated many of the same sentiments, as you will find she did, that had been still more strongly urged without effect by her venerable sister.

She said it would break the heart of my father to have it imagined, that he had not a power over his child; and that, as *he* thought, for my own good: a child too, whom they always had doted upon!—Dearest, dearest miss, concluded she, clasping her fingers with the most condescending earnestness, let me beg of you for *my* sake, for *your own* sake, for a *hundred* sakes, to get over this averseness, and give up your prejudices, and make everyone happy and easy once more—I would kneel to you, my dearest niece—nay, I *will* kneel to you!—

And down she dropped, and I with her, kneeling to her, and beseeching her not to kneel; clasping my arms about her, and bathing her worthy bosom with my tears!

Oh rise! rise! my beloved aunt, said I: you cut me to the heart with this condescending goodness.

Say then, my dearest niece, say then, that you will oblige all your friends! If you love us, I *beseech* you do!

How can I promise what I can sooner choose to die than to perform!—

Say then, my dear, you'll *consider* of it. Say you will but *reason* with yourself. Give us but hopes. Don't let me entreat, and *thus* entreat, in vain. For still she kneeled, and I by her.

What a hard case is mine!—Could I but *doubt*; I know I could *conquer*—That which is an inducement to my friends, is none at all to me!—How often, my dearest aunt, must I repeat the same thing!—Let me but be single—Cannot I live single? Let me be sent, as I have proposed, to Scotland, to Florence; any-whither: let me be sent a slave to the Indies; any-whither: any of these I will consent to. But I cannot, *cannot* think of giving my vows to a man I cannot endure!—

Well then rising (Bella silently, with uplifted hands, reproaching my supposed perverseness); I see nothing can prevail with you to oblige us.

What *can* I do, my dearest aunt Hervey? What *can* I do? Were I capable of giving a hope I meant not to enlarge, then could I say I would *consider* of your kind advice. But I would rather be thought *perverse* than *insincere*. Is there, however, no *medium*? Can *nothing* be thought of? Will *nothing* do but to have a man who is the *more* disgustful to me because he is unjust in the very articles he offers?

Who now, Clary, said my sister, do you reflect upon? Consider that.

Make not invidious applications of what I say, Bella. It may not be looked upon in the same light by everyone. The *giver* and the *accepter* are principally answerable, in an unjust donation. While I think of it in this light, I should be inexcusable to be the latter. But why do I enter upon a *supposition* of this nature? My heart, as I have often, *often* said, recoils at the *thoughts* of the man, in every light—Whose father, but mine, agrees upon articles where there is no prospect of a liking? Where the direct contrary is avowed, all along avowed, without the least variation, or *shadow* of a change of sentiment?—But it is not my father's doing originally. Oh my cruel, cruel brother, to cause a measure to be forced upon me, which he would not behave tolerably under, were the like to be offered to him!

The girl is got into her altitudes, aunt Hervey, said my sister. You see, madam, she spares nobody. Be pleased to let her know what she has to trust to. Nothing is to be done with her. Pray, madam, pronounce her doom

My aunt retired to the window, weeping, with my sister in her hand: I cannot, indeed I cannot, Miss Harlowe, said she, softly (but yet I heard every word she said): there is great hardship in her case. She is a noble child, after all. What pity things are gone so far! But Mr Solmes ought to be told to desist.

Oh madam, said my sister, in a kind of loud whisper, are *you* caught too by the little siren?—My mamma did well not to come up!—I question whether my papa himself, after his first indignation, would not be turned round by her. Nobody but my brother can do anything with her, I am sure.

Don't think of your brother's coming up, said my aunt, still in a low voice—He is too furious by much. I see no obstinacy, no perverseness in her manner! If your brother comes, I will not be answerable for the consequences: for I thought twice or thrice she would have gone into fits.

Oh madam, she has a strong heart!—and you see there is no prevailing upon her, though you were upon your knees to her.

My sister left my aunt musing at the window with her back towards us; and took that opportunity to insult me still more barbarously: for, stepping to my closet, she took up the patterns which my mamma had sent me up, and bringing them to me, she spread them upon the chair by me; and, offering one and then another upon her sleeve and shoulder, thus she ran on, with great seeming tranquillity, but whisperingly, that my aunt might not hear her. *This*, Clary, is a pretty pattern enough: But *this* is quite *charming!* I would advise you to make your appearance in it. And *this*, were I you, should be my wedding night-gown—and *this* my second dressed suit! Won't you give orders, love, to have your grandmother's jewels new set?—Or will you think to show away in the new ones that Mr Solmes intends to present to you? He talks of laying out two or three thousand pounds in presents, child! Dear heart!—how gorgeously will you be arrayed!—What! silent, my dear, mamma Norton's *sweet dear!* What! silent still?—But, Clary, won't you have a velvet suit? It would cut a great figure in a country church, you know: and the weather may bear it for a month yet to come. Crimson velvet, suppose! Such a fine complexion as yours, how would it be set off by it! What an agreeable blush would it give you!—High-ho! (mocking me; for I sighed to be thus fooled with): and do you sigh, love?—Well then, as it will be a solemn wedding, what think you of *black* velvet, child?—Silent still, Clary!—Black velvet, so fair as you are, with those charming eyes, gleaming through a wintry cloud, like an April sun!—Does not Lovelace tell you they are charming eyes!—How lovely will you appear to everyone!—What! silent still, love!—But about your laces, Clary!—

She would have gone on still further, had not my aunt advanced towards us, wiping her eyes—What! whispering, ladies! You seem so easy and so pleased, Miss Harlowe, with your private conference, that I hope I shall carry down good news.

I am only giving her my opinion of her patterns, *here*—unasked indeed—But she seems, by her silence, to approve of my judgement.

Oh Bella! said I, that Mr Lovelace had not taken you at your word!—You had before now been exercising your judgement on your own account: and *I* had been happy, as well as *you!*—Was it my fault, I pray you, that it was not so?—Oh how she raved!

To be so ready to *give*, Bella, and so loath to *take*, is not very fair in you.

The poor Bella descended to call names.

Why, sister, said I, you are as angry as if there were more in the hint than possibly might be designed. My wish is sincere, for both our sakes!—for the whole family's sake!—And what good now is there in it?—Do not, do not, dear Bella, give me cause to suspect, that I have found a reason for your unsisterly behaviour to me; and which till now was wholly unaccountable from sister to sister—

Fie, fie, Miss Clary! said my aunt.

My sister was more and more outrageous.

Oh how much fitter, said I, to be a *jest*, than a *jester*!—But now, Bella, turn the glass to you, and see how poorly sits the robe upon your own shoulders, which you have been so unmercifully fixing upon mine!

Fie, fie, Miss Clary! repeated my aunt.

And fie, fie, likewise, good madam, to Miss Harlowe, you would say, were you to have heard her barbarous insults upon me!

Let us go, madam, said my sister, with great violence; let us leave the creature to swell till she bursts with her own poison—The last time I will ever come near her, in the mind I am in!

It is so easy a thing, returned I, were I to be mean enough to follow an example that is so censurable in the setter of it, to vanquish such a teasing spirit as yours, with its own blunt weapons, that I am amazed you will provoke me!—Yet, Bella, since you *will* go (for she had hurried to the door), forgive me: I do you. And you have a double reason to do so, both from eldership, and the offence so studiously given to one in affliction—But may *you* be happy, though *I* never shall!—May *you* never have half the trials *I* have had! Be this your comfort, that you cannot have a sister to treat *you* as you have treated *me*! And so God bless you!

Oh thou art a—And down she flung without saying what.

Permit me, madam, said I to my aunt, sinking down and clasping her knees with my arms, to detain you one moment—Not to say anything about my poor sister—she is her own punisher—only to thank you for all your condescending goodness to me. I only beg of you, not to imput to obstinacy the immoveableness I have shown to so tender a friend; and to forgive me everything I have said or done amiss in your presence: for it has not proceeded from inward rancour to the poor Bella. But I will be bold to say, that neither she, nor my brother, nor even my father himself, knows what a heart they have set a bleeding.

I saw, to my comfort, what effect my sister's absence wrought for me—Rise, my noble-minded niece!—charming creature! (those were her kind words)—kneel not to me!—Keep to yourself what I now say to you: I admire you more than I can express—and if you can forbear claiming your estate, and can resolve to avoid Lovelace, you will continue to be the greatest miracle I ever knew at your years—But I must hasten down after your sister—These are my last words to you: Conform to your father's will, if you possibly can. How meritorious will it be in you to do so! Pray to God to *enable* you to conform. You don't know what may be done.

Only, my dear aunt, one word, *one* word more (for she was going)—Speak up all you can for my dear Mrs Norton. She is but low in the world: should ill health overtake her, she may not know how to live without my mamma's favour. I shall have no means to help her; for I will want necessaries before I will assert my right: and I do assure you, she has said so many things to me in behalf of my resigning to my father's will, that her arguments have not a little contributed to make me resolve to avoid the extremities, which nevertheless I pray to God they do not at last force me upon. And yet they deprive me of her advice, and think unjustly of one of the most excellent of women.

I am glad to hear you say this: And take *this*, and *this*, and *this*, my charming niece (for so she called me at every word almost); kissing me earnestly, and clasping her arms about my neck: and God protect you, and direct you! But you *must* submit: indeed you *must*. Some *one day* in a month from *this*, is all the choice that is left you.

And this, I suppose, was the doom my sister called for; yet not worse than what had been pronounced upon me before.

She repeated these last sentences louder than the former. And remember, miss, added she, it is your *duty* to comply—And down she went, leaving me with my heart full, and my eyes runing over.

The very repetition of this fills me with almost equal concern to that which I felt at the time. I can write no more; mistinesses of all the colours in the rainbow twinkling upon my deluged eye.

Wednesday, five o'clock

I WILL add a few lines—My aunt, as she went down from me, was met at the foot of the stairs by my sister, who seemed to think she had stayed a good while after her: and hearing her last words prescribing to me implicit duty, praised her for it, and exclaimed against my obstinacy with, Did you ever hear of such a perverseness, madam? Could you have thought that your Clarissa and everybody's Clarissa was such a girl?—And who, as *you* said, is to submit, her father or she?

My aunt said something in answer to her, compassionating me, as I thought, by her accent: but I heard not the words.

Such a strange perseverance in a measure so unreasonable!—But my brother and sister are continually misrepresenting all I say and do; and I am deprived of the opportunity of defending myself!—My sister says,[a] that had they thought me such a championess, they would not have engaged with me: and now, not knowing how to reconcile my supposed obstinacy with my general character and natural temper, they seem to hope to tire me out, and resolve to vary their measures accordingly. My brother, you see,[b] is determined to carry this point, or to abandon Harlowe Place, and never to see it more—So they are to lose a son, or to conquer a daughter—the perversest and most ungrateful that ever parents had!—This is the light he places things in: and has undertaken, it seems, to subdue me, if *his* advice be followed. It will be *further* tried, *that* I am convinced of; and what will be their next measure, who can divine?

I shall dispatch, with this, my answer to yours of Sunday last, begun on Monday,[c] but which is not yet quite finished. It is too long to copy: I have not time for it. In it I have been very free with you, my dear, in more places than one. I cannot say that I am pleased with all I have written—yet will not now alter it. My mind is not at ease enough for the subject—Don't be angry with me. Yet, if you can excuse one or two passages, it will be, because they were written by

Your Clarissa Harlowe

Letter 46: MISS HOWE TO MISS CLARISSA HARLOWE

Wednesday night, March 22

Angry!—What should I be angry for?—I am mightily pleased with your freedom, as you call it. I only wonder at your patience with me; that's all. I am sorry I gave you the trouble of so long a letter upon the occasion; notwithstanding the pleasure I received in reading it.[d]

I believe you did not intend reserves to me: for two reasons, I believe you did not: first, because you *say*, you did not: next, because you have not, *as yet*, been able to convince *yourself* how it is to be with you; and persecuted as you are, how so to separate the effects that spring from the two causes (*persecution* and *love*) as to give to each its particular due. But this I believe I hinted to you once before. And so will say no more upon that subject at present.

Robin says you had but just deposited your last parcel when he took it: for he was there but half an hour before and found nothing. He had seen my impatience; and loitered about, being willing to bring me something from you, if possible.

My cousin Jenny Fynnett is here, and desires to be my bedfellow tonight. So I shall not have an opportunity to sit down with that seriousness and attention, which the subjects of yours require. For she is all prate, you know, and loves to set

a   See p. 192.
b   In his letter, p. 198.
c   See Letter 40.
d   See Letter 37 for the occasion, and Letters 38 and 40 for the freedoms Miss Harlowe apologizes for.

me a-prating: yet comes upon a very grave occasion—on purpose to procure my mamma to go with her to her grandmother Larkin, who has been long bed-ridden; and at last has taken it into her head that she is mortal, and therefore will make her will; a work she was, till now, extremely averse to; but it must be upon condition that my mamma, who is her distant relation, will go to her and advise her as to the particulars of it: for she has a high opinion, as every one else has, of my mamma's judgement in all matters relating to wills, settlements, and such-like notable affairs.

Mrs Larkin lives about seventeen miles off; and as my mamma cannot abide to lie out of her own house, she proposes to set out early in the morning, in order to get back again at night. So, tomorrow I shall be at your devotion from day-light to day-light; nor will I be at home to anybody.

As to the impertinent man, I have put him upon escorting the two ladies, in order to attend my mamma home at night: such expeditions as these, and to give our sex a little air of vanity and assuredness at public places, is all that I know these dangling fellows are good for.

I have hinted before that I could almost wish my mamma and Mr Hickman would make a match of it: and I here repeat my wishes. What signifies a difference of fifteen or twenty years, especially when the lady has spirits that will make her young a long time, and the gentleman is a *mighty* sober man?—I think verily I could like him better for a papa, than for a nearer relation: and they are strange admirers of one another.

But allow me a perhaps still better (and, as to *years*, more suitable and happier) disposal; for the *man* at least—What think you, my dear, of compromising with your friends, by rejecting *both* your men and encouraging my parader?—If your liking of one of the two go no farther than *conditional*, I believe it will do—A rich thought, if it obtain your approbation. In this light, I should have a prodigious respect for Mr Hickman; more by half than I can have in the other. The vein is opened—shall I let it flow?—how difficult to withstand constitutional foibles!—

Hickman is certainly a man more in your taste than any of those who have hitherto been brought to address you. He is mighty sober! mighty grave! and all that. Then you have told me that he is your favourite!—But that is because he is my mamma's, perhaps—The man would certainly rejoice at the transfer: or he must be a greater fool than I take him to be.

Oh but your fierce lover would knock him o' the head—I forgot that!—What makes me incapable of seriousness when I write about this Hickman?—yet the man so good a sort of man in the main?—But who is perfect? This is one of my foibles. And something for you to chide me for.

You believe me very happy in my prospects in relation to him. Because you are so very unhappy in the foolish usage you meet with, you are apt (as I suspect) to think that tolerable which otherwise would be far from being so. I dare say you would not with all your grave airs like him for yourself; except being addressed by Solmes and him, you were obliged to have one of them. I have given you a test; let me see what you'll say to it.

For my own part, I confess to you that I have great exceptions to Hickman. *He* and *wedlock* never yet once entered into my head at one time. Shall I give you my free thoughts of him?—of his *best* and his *worst*; and that as if I were writing to one who knows him not? I think I will. Yet it is impossible I should do it gravely.

The subject won't bear to be so treated, in my opinion. We are not come so far as that yet, if ever we shall? And to do it in another strain ill becomes my present real concern for you.

HERE I was interrupted on the honest man's account. He has been here these two hours—courting my mamma for her daughter, I suppose—Yet she wants no courting neither: 'tis well one of us does, else the man would have nothing but halcyon; and be remiss, and saucy of course.

He was going. His horses at the door.

My mamma sent for me down, pretending to want to say something to me.

Something she said when I came, that signified nothing—Evidently for no reason called me, but to give me an opportunity to see what a fine bow he could make; and that he might wish me a good night. She knows I am not over-ready to oblige him with my presence, if I happen to be otherwise engaged. I could not help an air a little upon the fretful, when I found she had nothing of moment to say to me, and when I saw her end.

She smiled off the visible fretfulness, that the man might go away in good humour with himself.

He bowed to the ground, and would have taken my hand, his whip in the other: I did not like to be so companioned: I withdrew my hand, but touched his elbow with a motion, as if from his low bow I had supposed him falling, and would have helped him up. A sad slip, it might have been, said I!

A mad girl, smiled it off my mamma!

He was put quite out; took his horse-bridle, stumped back, back, back, bowing, till he run against his servant: I laughed; he mounted his horse; rid away. I mounted upstairs, after a little lecture—And my head is so filled with him, that I must resume my intention; in hopes to divert you for a few moments.

Take it then—his *best* and his *worst*, as I said before.

Hickman is a sort of fiddling, busy, yet to borrow a word from you, *un*-busy man: has a great deal to do and seems to me to dispatch nothing. Irresolute and changeable in everything, but in teasing me with his nonsense; which yet, it is evident, he must continue upon my mamma's interest, more than his own hopes; for none I have given him.

Then I have a quarrel against his face, though in his person, for a well-thriven man, tolerably genteel—not to his features so much neither—for what, as you have often observed, are features in a man!—But Hickman, with strong lines, and big cheek and chin bones, has not the manliness in his aspect, which Lovelace has with the most regular and agreeable features.

Then what a set and formal mortal is he in some things!—I have not been able yet to laugh him out of his long bib and beads: indeed that is because my mamma thinks it becomes him; and I would not be so free with him, as to own I should *choose* to have him leave it off. If he did, so particular is the man, he would certainly, if left to himself, fall into a King William cravat,[1] or some such antique chin-cushion, as by the pictures of that prince one sees was then the fashion.

As to his dress, in general, he cannot, indeed, be called a sloven, but sometimes he is too gaudy, at other times too plain, to be uniformly elegant. And for his manners, he makes such a bustle with them, and about them, as would induce one to suspect that they are more strangers to him, than familiars. You, I know, lay this to his fearfulness of disobliging, or offending. Indeed your *over-does* generally give the offence they endeavour to avoid.

The man, however, is honest: is of family: has a clear and good estate; and may one day be a baronet, and please you. He is humane and benevolent, tolerably generous, as people say; and as *I* might say too, if I would accept of his bribes, which he offers in hopes of having them all back again and the *bribed* into the bargain: a method taken by all corruptors, from old Satan, to the lowest of his servants. Yet, to speak in the language of a person I am bound to honour, he is deemed a *prudent* man; that is, a *good manager*.

Then, I cannot say that now I like anybody better, whatever I did once.

He is no fox-hunter: keeps a pack indeed, but prefers not his hounds to his fellow-creatures. No bad sign for a wife, I own. Loves his horse, but dislikes racing in a gaming way, as well as all sorts of gaming. Then he is sober; modest; they *say*, virtuous; in short, has qualities that mothers would be fond of in a husband for their daughters; and for which, perhaps, their daughters would be the happier could they judge as well for themselves, as experience possibly may teach *them* to judge for their *future* daughters.

Nevertheless, to own the truth, I cannot say I love the man; nor ever shall, I believe.

Strange! that these sober fellows cannot have a decent sprightliness, a modest assurance with them! Something debonair; which need not be separated from that awe and reverence when they address a woman, which should show the ardour of their passion, rather than the sheepishness of their nature; for who knows not that love delights in taming the lion-hearted? That those of the sex, who are most conscious of their own defect in point of courage, naturally *require*, and therefore *as* naturally *prefer*, the man who has most of it, as the most able to give them the requisite protection? That the greater their own cowardice, as it would be called in a man, the greater is their delight in subjects of heroism? As may be observed in their reading; which turns upon difficulties encountered, battles fought, and enemies overcome, 4 or 500 by the prowess of one single hero, the *more* improbable the *better*. In short, that *their* man should be a hero to every one living but themselves; and to them know no bound to his humility. A woman has some glory in subduing a heart no man living can appall; and hence too often the bravo, assuming the hero, and making himself pass for one, succeeds as only a hero should.

But as for honest Hickman, the good man is so *generally* meek, as I imagine, that I know not whether I have any *preference* paid me in his obsequiousness. And then, when I rate him, he seems to be so naturally fitted for rebuke, and so much expects it, that I know not how to disappoint him, whether he just then deserve it, or not. I am sure he has puzzled me many a time when I have seen him look penitent for faults he has not committed, whether to pity or laugh at him.

You and I have often *retrospected* the faces and minds of grown people; that is to say, have formed images from their present appearances, outside and in (as far as the manners of the persons would justify us in the latter), what sort of figures they made when boys and girls. And I'll tell you the lights in which Hickman, Solmes, and Lovelace, our three heroes, have appeared to me, supposing them boys at school.

Solmes I have imagined to be a little, sordid, pilfering rogue, who would purloin from everybody, and beg every boy's bread and butter from him; while, as I have heard a reptile brag, he would in a winter morning spit upon his thumbs, and spread his own with it, that he might keep it all to himself.

Hickman, a great over-grown, lank-haired, chubby boy, who would be hunched and punched by everybody; and go home with his finger in his eye, and tell his mother.

While Lovelace I have supposed a curl-pated villain, full of fire, fancy, and mischief; an orchard-robber, a wall-climber, a horse-rider without saddle or bridle, neck or nothing: a sturdy rogue, in short, who would kick and cuff, and do no right, and take no wrong of anybody; would get his head broke, then a plaister for it, or let it heal of itself; while he went on to do more mischief, and if not to get, to deserve, broken bones. And the same dispositions have grown up with them, and distinguish the men, with no very material alteration.

Only that all men are monkeys more or less, or else that you and I should have such baboons as these to choose out of is a mortifying thing, my dear.

I am sensible, that I am not a little out of season in treating thus ludicrously the subject I am upon, while you are so unhappy; and if my manner does not divert you, as my flightiness used to do, I am inexcusable both to you, and to my own heart: which, I do assure you, notwithstanding my seeming levity, is wholly in your case.

As this letter is entirely whimsical, I will not send it until I can accompany it with something more solid and better suited to your unhappy circumstances; that is to say, to the present subject of our correspondence. Tomorrow, as I told you, will be wholly yours, and of consequence, your

                                        ANNA HOWE'S

Letter 47: MISS HOWE TO MISS CLARISSA HARLOWE

                                        Thursday morn. 7 o'clock
MY mamma and cousin are already gone off in our chariot and four, attended by their doughty squire on horseback, and he by two of his own servants and one of my mamma's. They both love parade, when they go abroad, at least in compliment to one another; which shows, that each thinks the other does. Robin is your servant and mine, and nobody's else: and the day is all my own.

I must begin with blaming you, my dear, for your resolution not to litigate for your right, if occasion were to be given you. Justice is due to one's self, as well as to everybody else. Still more must I blame you for declaring to your aunt and sister that you will *not*: since (as they will tell it to your father and brother) the declaration must needs give advantages to spirits who have so little of that generosity for which you yourself are so much distinguished.

There never was a spirit in the world that would insult where it *dared*, but it would creep and cringe where it dared *not*. Let me remind you of a sentence of your own, the occasion for which I have forgotten: 'That little spirits will always accommodate themselves to the subject they would work upon—will fawn upon a sturdy-tempered person: will insult the meek'—and another given to Miss Biddulph upon an occasion you cannot forget: 'If we assume a dignity in what we say and do; and take care not to disgrace by arrogance our own assumption, everybody will treat us with respect and deference.'

I remember that you once made an observation, which you said you was obliged to Mrs Norton for, and she to her father, upon an excellent preacher, who was but an indifferent liver: 'That to excel in theory, and to excel in practice, generally required different talents; which not always met in the same person.' Do you, my dear (to whom theory and practice are the same thing, in almost every laudable quality) apply the observation to yourself, in this particular case, where resolution is required; and where performance of the will of the defunct is the question—No more to be dispensed with by *you*, in whose favour it was made, than by anybody else, who have only themselves in view, by breaking through it.

I know how much you despise riches in the main: but yet it behoves you to remember that in one instance you yourself have judged them valuable: 'In that they put it into one's power to *lay* obligations; while the want of them puts a person under a necessity of *receiving* favours; receiving them, perhaps, from grudging and narrow spirits, who know not how to confer them with that grace, which gives the principal merit to a beneficent action.' Reflect upon this, my dear, and see how it agrees with the declaration you have made to your aunt and sister, that you would not resume your estate, were you to be turned out of doors, and reduced to indigence and want. Their very fears that you will resume, point out to you the *necessity* of resuming, upon the treatment you meet with.

I own, that I was much affected (at first reading) with your mamma's letter sent with the patterns!—A strange measure, however, from a mother; for *she* did not intend to insult you; and I cannot but lament that so sensible and so fine a lady should stoop to so much art as that letter is written with: and which also appears in some of the conversations you have given me an account of. See you not in her passiveness, what boisterous spirits can obtain from gentler, merely by teasing and ill-nature?

I know the pride they have always taken in calling you an Harlowe—*Clarissa Harlowe*, so *formal* and so *set*, at every word, when they are grave, or proudly solemn—Your mamma has learnt it of them—And as in *marriage*, so in *will*, has been taught to bury her own superior name and family in theirs. I have often thought that the same spirit governed them, in this piece of affectation and others of the like nature (as *Harlowe* Place, and so forth, though not the elder brother's or paternal seat) as governed the tyrant Tudor,[a] who marrying Elizabeth, the heiress of the House of York, made himself a title to a throne which he would not otherwise have had (being but a base descendant of the Lancaster line), and proved a gloomy and vile husband to her; for no other cause, than because she had laid him under obligations, which his pride would not permit him to own—Nor would the unprincely wretch marry her till he was in possession of the crown, that he might not be supposed to owe it to her claim.

You have chidden me, and again will, I doubt not, for the liberties I take with some of your relations. But, my dear, need I tell *you*, that pride in *ourselves* must, and forever will, provoke contempt, and bring down upon us abasement from *others?*—Have we not, in the case of a celebrated bard, observed, that those who aim at more than their due will be refused the honours that they may justly

a　Henry VII.

claim?¹—I am very loath to offend you, yet I cannot help speaking of *them*, as well as of *others*, as I think they deserve. *Praise* or *dispraise* is the reward or punishment which the world confers or inflicts on *merit* or *demerit*; and, for my part, I neither can nor will confound them in the application. I despise them all, but your mamma: indeed I do—and as for her—But I will spare the good lady for your sake—And one argument, indeed, I think may be pleaded in her favour, in the present contention—She who has for so many years, and with such absolute resignation, borne what she has borne, to the sacrifice of her own will, may think it an easier task, than another person can imagine it, for her daughter to give up *her's*—But to think to whose instigation all this is originally owing—God forgive me; but with such usage I should have been with Lovelace before now—Yet remember, my dear, that the step which would not be wondered at from such an hasty-tempered creature as me, would be inexcusable in such a considerate person as you.

After your mamma has been thus drawn in against her judgement, I am the less surprised, that your aunt Hervey should go along with her; since the two sisters never separate. I have inquired into the nature of the obligation which Mr Hervey's indifferent conduct in his affairs has laid him under. It is only, it seems, that your brother has paid off for him a mortgage upon one part of his estate, which the mortgagee was about to foreclose; and taken it upon himself: a small favour (as he has ample security in his hands) from kindred to kindred: but such a one, it is plain, as has laid the whole family of the Herveys under obligation to the ungenerous lender, who has treated him, and his aunt too (as Miss Dolly Hervey has privately complained) with the less ceremony ever since.

Must I, my dear, call such a creature your *brother*?—I believe I must—because he is your *father's son*. There is no harm, I hope, in saying that.

I am concerned that you ever wrote at all to him. It was taking too much notice of him: it was adding to his self-significance; and a call upon him to treat you with insolence: a call which you might have been assured he would not fail to answer.

But such a pretty master as this, to run riot against such a man as Lovelace; who had taught him to put his sword into his scabbard, when he had pulled it out by accident!—These indoor insolents, who, turning themselves into bugbears, frighten women, children and servants, are generally cravens among men. Were he to come fairly cross me, and say to my face some of the free things, which, I am told, he has said of me behind my back, or that (as by your account) he has said of our sex, I would take upon myself to ask him two or three questions; although he were to send me a challenge likewise.

I repeat, you know that I will speak my mind, and *write* it too. He is not *my* brother. Can you say, he is *yours*?—So, for your life, if you are just, you can't be angry with me: for would you side with a *false brother* against a *true friend*? A brother may *not* be a friend: but a friend will be *always* a brother—*Mind that*, as your uncle *Tony* says!

I cannot descend so low, as to take very particular notice of the epistles of those poor souls, whom you call *uncles*. Yet I love to divert myself with such grotesque characters too—But I know *them*, and love *you*; and so cannot make the jest of them, which their absurdities call for.

Now I have said so much on these *touching* topics (as I am but too sensible you will think them), I must add one reflection more, and so entitle myself to your correction for all at once. It is upon the conduct of those women (for you and I know more than *one* such) who can suffer themselves to be out-blustered and out-gloomed, till they have no *will* of their own; instead of being prevailed upon, by acts of tenderness and complaisance, to be *fooled out of it*—I wish that it does not demonstrate too evidently, that, with some of the sex, insolent control is a more efficacious subduer than kindness or concession—Upon my life, my dear, I have often thought that many of us are mere babies in matrimony: perverse fools when too much indulged and humoured; creeping slaves when treated harshly. But shall it be said, that *fear* makes us more gentle obligers than *love*?—Forbid it, honour! forbid it, gratitude! forbid it, justice! that any woman of sense should give occasion to have this said of her!

Did I think you would have any manner of doubt, from the style or contents of this letter, whose saucy pen it is that has run on at this rate, I would write my name at length; since it comes too much from my heart to disavow it—but at present the initials shall serve; and I will go on again directly.

A.H.

Letter 48: MISS HOWE TO MISS CLARISSA HARLOWE

Thursday morn. 10 o'clock (Mar. 23)

I WILL postpone, or perhaps pass by, several observations which I had to make on other parts of your letters, to acquaint you that Mr Hickman, when in London, found an opportunity to inquire after Mr Lovelace's town life and conversation.

At the Cocoa Tree in Pall Mall[1] he fell in with two of his intimates, the one named Belton, the other Mowbray; very free of speech, and rakish gentlemen both: but the waiter, it seems, paid them great respect, and, on his inquiry after their characters, called them men of fortune and honour.

They began to talk of Mr Lovelace of their own accord; and upon some gentlemen in the room asking when they expected him in town, answered, that very day. Mr Hickman (as they both went on praising Lovelace) said, he had indeed heard that Mr Lovelace was a very fine gentleman—and was proceeding, when one of them, interrupting him, said—Only, sir, the finest gentleman in the world; that's all.

And so he led them on to expatiate more particularly on his qualities; which they were very fond of doing: but said not one single word in behalf of his morals—*Mind that* also, in your uncle's style.

Mr Hickman said that Mr Lovelace was very happy, as he understood, in the esteem of the ladies; and, smiling, to make them believe he did not think amiss of it, that he pushed his good fortune as far as it would go.

Well put, Mr Hickman! thought I; equally grave and sage—thou seemest not to be a stranger to their dialect, as I suppose this is!—But I said nothing; for I have often tried to find out this *mighty* sober man of my mamma's: but hitherto have only to say that he is either very moral or very cunning.

No doubt of it, replied one of them; and out came an oath, with a who would not?—that he did as every young gentleman would—

Very true! said my mamma's puritan—but I hear he is in treaty with a fine lady—

So he was, Mr Belton said—the d——l fetch her! (vile brute!) for she engrossed all his time!—But that the lady's family ought to be—something—(Mr Hickman desired to be excused repeating what, though he had repeated what was worse)— and might dearly repent their usage of a man of his family and merit.

Perhaps they may think him too wild a gentleman, cried Hickman: and theirs is, I hear, a very sober family—

SOBER! said one of them: a good honest word, Dick!—where the devil has it lain all this time?—D—— me if I have heard of it in this sense, ever since I was at college! And then, said he, we bandied it about among twenty of us, as an obsolete—

There's for you, my dear!—these are Mr Lovelace's companions: you'll be pleased to take *notice of that!*

Mr Hickman said, this put him out of countenance.

I stared at him, and with such a meaning in my eyes, as he knew how to take; and so was out of countenance again.

Don't you remember, my dear, who it was that told a young gentleman designed for the gown, who owned he was apt to be too easily put out of countenance when he came among free company: 'That it was a bad sign; that it looked as if his morals were not proof; but that his good disposition seemed rather the effect of accident and education, than of such a choice as was founded upon principle?' And don't you know the lesson the very same young lady gave him: 'To endeavour to stem and discountenance vice, and to glory in being an advocate in all companies for virtue'; particularly observing, 'That it was natural for a man to shun, or give up, what he was ashamed of?' Which she should be sorry to think his case on this occasion, adding: 'That vice was a coward, and would hide its head when opposed by such a virtue as had presence of mind, and a full persuasion of its own rectitude to support it.' The lady, you may remember, modestly put her doctrine into the mouth of a worthy preacher, Dr Lewin, as she uses to do when she has a mind not to be thought to be what she is at so early an age; and that it may give more weight to anything *she hit upon, that might appear tolerable*, was her modest manner of speech.

Mr Hickman, upon the whole, professed to me, upon his *second recovery*, that he had no reason to think well of Mr Lovelace's morals, from what he heard of him in town: yet his two intimates talked of his being *more regular* than he *used to be*: that he had made a very good resolution; *that* of old Tom Wharton[2] was the expression, that he would never *give* a challenge, nor *refuse* one; which they praised in him highly: that, in short, he was a very brave fellow, and the charmingest companion in the world: and would one day make a great figure in his country, for there was nothing he was not capable of—

I am afraid that this is too true. And this, my dear, is all that Mr Hickman could pick up about him: and is it not enough to determine such a mind as yours, if not *already* determined?

Yet it must be said too, that if there be a woman in the world that can reclaim him, it is you. And, by your account of his behaviour in the interview between you, I own I have some hope of him. At least this I will say, that all his arguments with you, then, seem to be just and right: and if you *are* to be his—But no more of that: he cannot, after all, deserve you.

Letter 49: MISS HOWE TO MISS CLARISSA HARLOWE

Thursday afternoon, March 23

AN unexpected visitor has turned the course of my thoughts, and changed the subject I had intended to pursue. The only one for whom I would have dispensed with my resolution not to see anybody all the dedicated day: a visitor, whom, according to Mr Hickman's report from the expectations of his libertine friends, I supposed to be in town—Now, my dear, have I saved myself the trouble of telling you, that it was your too-agreeable rake. Our sex is said to love to trade in surprises: yet have I, by my over-promptitude, surprised myself out of mine—I had intended, you must know, to run twice the length, before I had suffered you so much as to guess who, and of which sex, my visitor was: but since you have the discovery at so cheap a rate, you are welcome to it.

The end of his coming was, to engage my interest with my *charming friend*; and as he was sure that I knew all your mind, to acquaint him what he had to trust to. He mentioned what had passed in the interview between you: but could not be satisfied with the result of it, and with the little satisfaction he had obtained from you; the malice of your family to him increasing, and their cruelty to you not abating—his heart, he told me, was in tumults, for fear you should be prevailed upon in favour of a man despised by everybody. He gave me fresh instances of indignities cast upon himself by your uncles and brother; and declared that if you suffered yourself to be forced into the arms of the man for whose sake he was loaded with undeserved abuses, you should be one of the youngest, as you would be one of the loveliest, widows in England: and that he would moreover call your brother to account for the liberties he takes with his character to everyone he meets with.

He proposed several schemes for you to choose some one of them, in order to enable you to avoid the persecutions you labour under. One I will mention; that you will resume your estate; and if you find difficulties that can be no otherwise surmounted, that you will, either avowedly or privately, as he had proposed to you, accept of his aunt Lawrance's or Lord M.'s assistance to instate you in it. He declared that, if you did, he would leave it absolutely to your own pleasure afterwards, and to the advice which your cousin Morden on his arrival should give you, whether to encourage his address or not, as you shall be convinced of the sincerity of the reformation which his enemies make him so much want.

I had now a good opportunity to sound him (as you wished Mr Hickman would Lord M.) as to the continued or diminished favour of the ladies and of his uncle towards you, upon their being acquainted with the animosity of your relations to them, as well as to their kinsman. I took the opportunity; and he satisfied me by reading some passages of a letter he had about him from Lord M., that an alliance with you, and that on the foot of your own single merit, would be the most desirable event to them that could happen: and so far to the purpose of your wished inquiry does his lordship go, in this letter, that he assures him that whatever you suffer in fortune from the violence of your relations, on *his* account, he and his sisters will join to make it up to him. And yet the reputation of a family so splendid would, no doubt, in a case of such importance to the honour of both, make them prefer a general consent.

I told him, as you yourself I knew had done, that you were extremely averse to Mr Solmes; and that might you be left to your own choice, it would be the single life. As to himself, I plainly said that you had great and just objections to him on the score of his careless morals: that it was surprising that young gentlemen, who gave themselves the liberties he was said to take, should presume to think that, whenever they took it into their heads to marry, the most virtuous and worthy of the sex were to fall to their lot: that as to the resumption, it had been very strongly urged by myself, and would be more, though you had been averse to it hitherto: that your chief reliance and hopes were upon your cousin Morden: and that to suspend or gain time till he arrived was, as I believed, your principal aim.

I told him, that with regard to the mischief he threatened, neither the act nor the menace could serve any end but theirs who persecuted you; as it would give them a pretence for carrying into effect their compulsatory projects; and that with the approbation of all the world, since he must not think the public would give its voice in favour of a violent young man, of no extraordinary character as to morals, who should seek to rob a family of eminence of a child so valuable; and who threatened, if he could not obtain her in preference to a man chosen by themselves, that he would avenge himself upon them all by acts of violence.

I added that he was very much mistaken, if he thought to intimidate *you* by such menaces: for that, though your disposition was all sweetness, yet I knew not a steadier temper in the world than yours; nor one more inflexible (as your friends had found, and would still farther find if they continued to give occasion for its exertion) whenever you thought yourself in the right; and that you were dealt ungenerously with in matters of too much moment to be indifferent about. Miss Clarissa Harlowe, Mr Lovelace, let me tell you, said I, timid as her foresight and prudence may make her in some cases, where she apprehends dangers to those she loves, is above fear in points where her honour and the true dignity of her sex are concerned—In short, sir, you must not think to frighten Miss Clarissa Harlowe into such a mean or unworthy conduct as only a weak or unsteady mind can be guilty of.

He was so very far from intending to intimidate you, he said, that he besought me not to mention one word to you of what had passed between us: that what he had hinted at, that carried the air of a menace, was owing to the fervour of his spirits, raised by his apprehensions of losing all hope of you for ever; and on a supposition that you were to be actually forced into the arms of a man you hated: that were this to be the case, he must own that he should pay very little regard to the world or its censures: especially as the menaces of some of your family now, and their triumph over him afterwards, would both provoke and warrant all the vengeance he could take.

He added that all the countries in the world were alike to him, but on your account: so that whatever he should think fit to do, were you lost to *him*, he should have nothing to apprehend from the laws of this.

I did not like the determined air he spoke this with. He is certainly, my dear, capable of great rashness—

He palliated a little this fierceness (which by the way I warmly censured) by saying, that while you remain single he will bear all the indignities that shall be cast upon him by your family. But would you throw yourself, if you were still farther driven, into any other protection, if not his uncle's or that of the ladies of

his family (into my mamma's, suppose); or would you go to London to private
lodgings, where he would never visit you unless he had your leave; and from
whence you might make your own terms with your relations; he would be entirely
satisfied; and would, as he had said before, wait the effect of your cousin's arrival,
and your free determination as to his own fate—adding, that he knew the family
so well, and how much fixed they were upon their measures, as well as the absolute
dependence they made upon your temper and principles, that he could not but
apprehend the worst, while you remained in the power of their persuasion and
menaces.

We had a great deal of other discourse: but as the reciting of the rest would be
but a repetition of many of the things that passed between you and him, in the
interview between you in the woodhouse, I refer myself to your memory on that
occasion.[a]

And now, my dear, upon the whole I think it behoves you to make yourself
independent: all then will fall right. This man is a violent man. I should wish,
methinks, that you should not have either him or Solmes. You will find, if you get
out of your brother's and sister's way, what you *can* or can-*not* do with regard to
either. If your relations persist in their foolish scheme, I think I will take his hint,
and at a proper opportunity sound my mamma. Mean time, let me have your clear
opinion of, and reasonings upon, the resumption, which I join with Lovelace in
advising. You can but see how your demand will work. To *demand* is not to *litigate*.
But be your resolution what it will, do not by any means repeat that you will not
assert your right. If they go on to give you provocation, you may have sufficient
reason to change your mind: and let them expect that you *will* change it. They
have not the generosity to treat you the better for disclaiming the power they know
you have. *That*, I think, need not now be told you.

I am, my dearest friend, and will be ever,

> Your most affectionate and faithful
> ANNA HOWE

Letter 50: MISS CLARISSA HARLOWE TO MISS HOWE

Wed. night, March 22

ON my aunt's and sister's report of my obstinacy, my assembled relations have
taken an *unanimous* resolution (as Betty tells me it is) against me. This resolution
you will find signified to me in the enclosed letter from my brother, just now
brought me. Be pleased to return it, when perused. I may have occasion for it in
the altercations between my relations and me.

[*Letter 50.1: James Harlowe, Jun. to Clarissa Harlowe*]

I AM commanded to let you know that my father and uncles having heard your
aunt Hervey's account of all that has passed between her and you; having heard
from your sister what sort of treatment she has had from you; having recollected
all that has passed between your mamma and you; having weighed all your pleas

a See Letter 36.

and proposals; having taken into consideration their engagements with Mr Solmes, that gentleman's patience and great affection for you, and the little opportunity you have given yourself to be acquainted either with his merit, or his proposals; having considered two points more; to wit, the wounded authority of a father; and Mr Solmes's continual entreaties (little as you have deserved regard from him) that you may be freed from a confinement to which he is desirous to attribute your perverseness to him (*averseness* I should have said, but let it go), he being unable to account otherwise for so strong a one, supposing you told truth to your mamma when you asserted that your heart *was free*; and which Mr Solmes is willing to believe, though nobody else does. For all these reasons, it is resolved that you shall go to your uncle Antony's: and you must accordingly prepare yourself so to do. You will have but short notice of the day for obvious reasons.

I will honestly tell you the motive for your going: it is a double one; first, that they may be sure that you shall not correspond with anybody they do not like, for they find from Mrs Howe, that by some means or other you *do* correspond with her daughter; and through her, perhaps with somebody else: and next, that you may receive the visits of Mr Solmes, which you have thought fit to refuse to do here; by which means you have deprived yourself of the opportunity of knowing *whom* and *what* you have hitherto refused.

If after one fortnight's conversation with Mr Solmes, and after you have heard what your friends shall further urge in his behalf, unhardened by clandestine correspondence, you shall convince them that Virgil's *amor omnibus idem* (for the application of which I refer you to the Georgic, as translated by Dryden) is verified in you, as well as in the rest of the animal creation; and that you cannot, or will not, forego your prepossession in favour of the moral, the virtuous, the pious Lovelace (I would please you if I could!), it will then be considered, whether to humour you, or to renounce you for ever.

It is hoped that, as you *must* go, you will go cheerfully. Your uncle Antony will make everything at his house agreeable to you. But indeed he won't promise that he will not, at *proper times*, draw up the bridge.

Your visitors, besides Mr Solmes, will be myself, if you permit me that honour; your sister; and, as you behave to Mr Solmes, your aunt Hervey and your uncle Harlowe; and yet the two latter will hardly come neither, if they think it will be to hear your *whining vocatives*. Betty Barnes will be your attendant: and, I must needs tell you, miss, that we none of us think the worse of the faithful maid for your dislike of her: which Betty, however, who would be glad to oblige you, laments as a misfortune.

Your answer is required, whether you *cheerfully* consent to go? And your indulgent mamma bids me remind you from her, that a fortnight's visits from Mr Solmes are all that is meant at present.

I am, as you shall be pleased to deserve,

Yours, etc.
JAMES HARLOWE, JUN.

So here is the master-stroke of my brother's policy! Called upon to consent to go to my uncle Antony's, *avowedly* to receive Mr Solmes's visits!—A chapel!—a moated house!—Deprived of the opportunity of corresponding with you!—or of any possibility of escape, should violence be used to compel me to be that odious man's!

Late as it was when I received this insolent letter, I wrote an answer to it directly, that it might be ready for the writer's time of rising. I enclose the rough draught of it. You will see by it how much his vile hint from the Georgic, and his rude one of my *whining vocatives*, have set me up. Besides, as the command to get ready to go to my uncle's is in the name of my father and uncles, it is but to show a piece of the art they accuse me of to resent the vile hint I have so much reason to resent, in order to palliate the refusal of obeying, what would otherwise be interpreted an act of rebellion by my brother and sister: for, it seems plain to me, that they will work but half their ends if they do not deprive me of my father's and uncles' favour, although I should even comply with terms, which it is impossible I should ever comply with.

[*Letter 50.2: Clarissa Harlowe to James Harlowe, Jun.*]

You might have told me, brother, in three lines, what the determination of my friends was; only, that then you would not have had room to display your pedantry by so detestable an allusion or reference to the Georgic. Give me leave to tell you, sir, that if *humanity* were a branch of your studies at the university, it has not found a genius in you for mastering it. Nor is either my sex or myself, though a sister, I see, entitled to the least decency from a brother who has studied, as it seems, rather to cultivate the malevolence of his natural temper, than any tendency which one would have hoped his parentage, if not his education, might have given him to a tolerable politeness.

I doubt not that you will take amiss my freedom: but as you have deserved it from me, I shall be less and less concerned on that score, as I see you are more and more intent to show your wit at the expense of justice and compassion.

The time is indeed come that I can no longer bear those contempts and reflections which a brother, least of all men, is entitled to give. And let me beg of you one favour, officious sir—it is *this*, that you will not give yourself any concern about a husband for *me*, till I shall have the forwardness to propose a wife to *you*. Pardon me, sir; but I cannot help thinking that could I have the art to *get my papa* of my side, I should have as much right to prescribe for you, as you have for me.

As to the communication you make me, I must take upon me to say, that although I will receive, as becomes me, any of my papa's commands; yet as this signification is made me by a brother, who has shown of late so much of an unbrotherly animosity to me (for no reason in the world that I know of, but that he believes he has in me *one* sister too many for his interest), I think myself entitled to conclude that such a letter as you have sent me is all your own—And of course to declare, that while I so think it, I will not willingly, nor even without violence, go to any place avowedly to receive Mr Solmes's visits.

I think myself so much entitled to resent your infamous hint, and this as well for the sake of my sex as for my own, that I ought to declare, as I do, that I will not receive any more of your letters, unless commanded to do so by an authority I never will dispute; except in a case where I think my *future*, as well as *present* happiness concerned—And were such a case to happen, I am sure my father's

harshness will be less owing to himself than to you; and to the specious absurdities
of your ambitious and selfish schemes. Very true, sir!

One word more, provoked as I am, I will add: that had I been thought as really
obstinate and perverse as of late I am said to be, I should not have been so
disgracefully treated as I have been—Lay your hand upon your heart, brother, and
say by whose instigations—And examine what I have done to deserve to be made
thus unhappy, and to be obliged to style myself,

Your injured sister,
CL. HARLOWE

When, my dear, you have read my answer to this letter, tell me what you think
of me?—It *shall go!*—

Letter 51: MISS CLARISSA HARLOWE TO MISS HOWE

Thursday morning, Mar. 23

MY letter has set them *all* in tumults: for it seems none of them went home last
night; and they all were desired to be present to give their advice if I should refuse
compliance with a command thought so reasonable as, it seems, this was.

Betty tells me, that, at first, my father, in a rage, was for coming up to me
himself, and for turning me out of his doors directly. Nor was he restrained, till it
was hinted to him that that was no doubt my wish and would answer all my
perverse views. But the result was that my brother (having really, as my mamma
and aunt insisted, taken wrong measures with me) should write again in a more
moderate manner: for nobody else was permitted or cared to write to such a *ready
scribbler*. And, I having declared that I would not receive any more of his letters
without command from a superior authority, my mamma was to give it *hers*: and
accordingly has done so in the following lines, written on the superscription of his
letter to me: which letter also follows, together with my reply.

Clary Harlowe,
RECEIVE and read this with the temper that becomes your sex, your character,
your education and your duty: and return an answer to it directed to your brother.

CHARLOTTE HARLOWE

[*Letter 51.1: James Harlowe, Jun.*] *to Miss Clarissa Harlowe*

Thursday morning

ONCE more I write, although imperiously prohibited by a younger sister. Your
mamma will have me do so, that you may be destitute of all defence if you persist
in your *pervicacy*. Shall I be a *pedant*, miss, for this word? She is willing to indulge
in you the least appearance of that delicacy for which she once, as well as
everybody else, admired you—before you knew Lovelace; I cannot, however, help
saying *that*: and she and your aunt Hervey will have it (they would fain favour you
if they could) that I may have provoked from you the answer they nevertheless

own to be so exceedingly *unbecoming*. I am now learning, you see, to take up the softer language, where you have laid it down. This then is the case:

They *entreat*, they *pray*, they *beg*, they *supplicate*—(will either of these do, Miss Clary?) that you will make no scruple to go to your uncle Antony's: and fairly I am to tell you, for the very purpose mentioned in my last—or, 'tis presumable, they need not *entreat, pray, beg, supplicate*. Thus much is promised to Mr Solmes, who is your advocate, and very uneasy that you should be under constraint, supposing that your dislike to him arises from that. And if he finds you are not to be moved in his favour when you are absolutely freed from that you call a *control*, he will forbear thinking of you, whatever it costs him. He loves you too well: and in this, I really think his understanding, which you have reflected upon, is to be questioned.

Only for one fortnight, therefore, permit his visits. Your *education* (you tell me of *mine*, you know) ought to make you incapable of rudeness to anybody. He will not, I hope, be the first man, myself excepted, whom you ever treated rudely, purely because he is esteemed by us all. I am, what you have a mind to make me, friend, brother, or servant—I wish I could be still *more* polite, to so polite, so delicate a sister.

JA. HARLOWE

You must still write to *me*, if you condescend to reply. Your mamma will not be permitted to be disturbed with your nothing-meaning vocatives!—*Vocatives*, once more, Madam Clary, repeats the *pedant* your brother!

[*Letter 51.2: Clarissa Harlowe*] to James Harlowe, Jun.

Thursday, March 23

PERMIT me, my ever dear and honoured papa and mamma, in this manner to surprise you into an *audience* (presuming this will be read to you) since I am denied the honour of writing to you directly. Let me beg of you to believe that nothing but the most unconquerable dislike could make me stand against your pleasure. What are riches, what are settlements, to happiness? Let me not thus cruelly be given up to a man my very soul is averse to. Permit me to repeat, that I cannot *honestly* be his. Had I a slighter notion of the matrimonial duty than I have, perhaps I might. But when I am to bear all the misery, and that for *life*; when my *heart* is less concerned in this matter than my *soul*; my *temporal* perhaps than my *future* good; why should I be denied the liberty of *refusing*? That liberty is all I ask.

It were easy for me to give way to hear Mr Solmes talk for the mentioned fortnight, although it is impossible for me, say what he would, to get over my dislike to him. But the moated house, the chapel there, and the little mercy my brother and sister, who are to be there, have hitherto shown me, are what I am extremely apprehensive of. And why does my brother say my restraint is to be taken off (and that too at Mr Solmes's desire), when I am to be a still closer prisoner than before; the bridge threatened to be drawn up; and no dear papa and mamma near me to appeal to in the last resort?

Transfer not, I beseech you, to a brother and sister your own authority over your child—to a brother and sister who treat me with unkindness and reproach; and as I have too much reason to apprehend misrepresent my words and behaviour; or, greatly favoured as I used to be, it is impossible I should be sunk so low in your opinions as I unhappily am!

Let but this my hard, my disgraceful confinement be put an end to. Permit me, my dear mamma, to pursue my needleworks in your presence, as one of your maidens, and you shall be witness that it is not wilfulness or prepossession that governs me. Let me not, however, be put out of your own house. Let Mr Solmes come and go, as my papa pleases: let me but tarry or retire when he comes, as I can; and leave the rest to Providence.

Forgive me, brother, that thus, with an appearance of art, I address myself to my father and mother, to whom I am forbid to approach or to write. Hard it is to be reduced to such a contrivance! Forgive likewise the plain dealing I have used in the above, with the nobleness of a gentleman and the gentleness due from a brother to a sister. Although of late you have given me but little room to hope for your favour or compassion, yet having not deserved to forfeit *either*, I presume to claim *both*: for I am confident it is at present much in your power, although but my brother (my honoured parents both, I bless God, in being), to give peace to the greatly disturbed mind of

Your unhappy sister,
CL. HARLOWE

Betty tells me my brother has taken my letter all in pieces; and has undertaken to write such an answer to it as shall confirm the *wavering*—So, it is plain, that I should have moved somebody by it, but for this hard-hearted brother; God forgive him!

Letter 52: MISS CLARISSA HARLOWE TO MISS HOWE

Thursday night, Mar. 23

I SEND you the boasted confutation letter, just now put into my hands—My brother and sister, my uncle Antony and Mr Solmes are, I understand, exulting over the copy of it below, as an unanswerable performance.

[Letter 52.1: James Harlowe, Jun.] to Miss Clarissa Harlowe

ONCE again, my inflexible sister, I write to you: it is to let you know that the pretty piece of art you found out to make me the vehicle of your whining pathetics to your father and mother has not had the expected effect.

I do assure you that your behaviour has not been misrepresented: nor need it. Your mamma, who is solicitous to take all opportunities of putting the favourable constructions upon all you do, has been forced as you well know to give you up upon full proof: no need then of the expedient of pursuing your needleworks in her sight. She cannot bear your whining pranks: and it is for *her* sake that you are not permitted to come into her presence; nor will be but upon her own terms.

You had like to have made a simpleton of your aunt Hervey yesterday: she came down from you, pleading in your favour: but when she was asked, what concession she had brought you to? she looked about her and knew not what to answer. So your mamma, when surprised into the beginning of your cunning address to her and to your papa under my name (for I had begun to read it, little suspecting such an *ingenious* subterfuge) and would then make me read it through, wrung her hands, Oh! her dear child, her dear child, must not be so compelled!—But when she was asked, whether she would be willing to have for her son-in-law, the man who bids defiance to her whole family; and who had like to have murdered her son? And what concessions she had gained from her beloved to occasion this tenderness? And that for one who had apparently deceived her in assuring her that her heart was free? then could she look about her, as her sister had done before: then was she again brought to herself, and to a resolution to assert her authority (not to *transfer* it, witty presumer!) over the rebel who of late has so ungratefully struggled to throw it off.

You seem, child, to have a high notion of the matrimonial duty; and I'll warrant, like the rest of your sex (one or two whom I have the honour to know excepted) that you will go to church to promise what you will never think of afterwards. But, *sweet* child! as your *worthy* mamma Norton calls you, think a little less of the *matrimonial* (at least till you come into that state), and a little more of the *filial*, duty.

How can you say, you are to bear *all the misery*, when you give so large a share of it to your parents, to your uncles, to your aunt, to myself and to your sister; who all, for eighteen years of your life loved you so well?

If of late I have not given you room to hope for my favour or compassion, it is because of late you have not deserved either. I know what you mean, little reflecting fool, by saying it is much in my power, although *but* your brother (a very slight degree of relation with you), to give you that peace, which you can give yourself whenever you please.

The liberty of *refusing*, pretty miss, is denied you, because we are all sensible that the liberty of *choosing* to everyone's dislike must follow. The vile wretch you have set your heart upon speaks this plainly to everybody, though you won't. He says you are *his*, and *shall* be *his*, and he will be the death of any man who robs him of his PROPERTY. So, miss, we have a mind to try this point with him. My father supposing he has the right of a father in his child is absolutely determined not to be bullied out of that right. And what must that child be who prefers the rake to a father?

This is the light in which this whole debate ought to be taken. Blush, then, delicacy! that cannot bear the poet's *Amor omnibus idem!*—Blush then, purity! Be ashamed, virgin modesty! And if capable of conviction, surrender your whole will to the will of the honoured pair to whom you owe your being: and beg of all your friends to forgive and forget the part you have of late acted.

I have written a longer letter than ever I designed to write to you after the insolent treatment and prohibition you have given me: and now I am commissioned to tell you that your friends are as weary of confining you as you are of being confined. And therefore you must prepare yourself to go in a very few days, as you have been told before, to your uncle Antony's; who, notwithstanding your apprehensions, will draw up his bridge when he pleases, will see what company he pleases in his own house; nor will he demolish his chapel to cure you of your foolish late-commenced antipathy to a place of divine worship—The more foolish as, if we intended to use force, we could have the ceremony pass in your chamber as well as anywhere else.

Prejudice against Mr Solmes has evidently blinded you, and there is a *charitable* necessity to open your eyes: since no one but you thinks the gentleman so contemptible in his *person*; nor, for a plain country gentleman who has too much solid sense to appear like a coxcomb, justly blameable in his *manners*—And as to his *temper*, it is necessary you should speak upon fuller knowledge than at present it is plain you can have of him.

Upon the whole, it will not be amiss that you prepare for your speedy removal, as well for the sake of your own conveniency as to show your readiness, in *one* point, at least, to oblige your friends; one of whom you may, if you please to deserve it, reckon, though *but* a brother,

JAMES HARLOWE

P.S. If you are disposed to see Mr Solmes and to make some excuses to him for your past conduct, in order to be able to meet him *somewhere else* with the less concern to yourself for your freedoms with him, he shall attend you where you please. If you have a mind to read the settlements before they are read to you for your signing, they shall be sent you up—Who knows, but they will help you to some fresh objections?—Your heart is *free* you know—It *must*—For, did you not tell your mother it was? And will the *pious* Clarissa Harlowe fib to her mamma?

I desire no reply. The case requires none. Yet I will ask you, have you, miss, no more proposals to make?

I was so vexed when I came to the end of this letter (the postscript to which, perhaps, might be written, after the rest had seen the letter) that I took up my pen, with an intent to write to my uncle Harlowe about resuming my own estate, in pursuance of your advice: but my heart failed me, when I recollected that I had not one friend to stand by or support me in my claim; and that it would but the more incense them, without answering any good end. Oh that my cousin were but come!

Is it not a sad thing, beloved as I thought myself so lately by everyone, that now I have not one person in the world to plead for me, to stand by me, or who would afford me refuge were I to be under the necessity of seeking for it?—I, who had the vanity to think I had as many friends as I saw faces, and flattered myself too that it was not altogether unmerited, because I saw not my Maker's image, either in man, woman, or child, high or low, rich or poor, whom, comparatively, I loved not as myself—Would to heaven, my dear, that you were married! Perhaps, then, you could have induced Mr Hickman, upon my application, to afford me protection till these storms were overblown. But then this might have involved *him* in difficulties and dangers; and that I would not have had done for the world.

I don't know what to do, not I!—God forgive me, but I am very impatient!—I wish—but I don't know what to wish, without a sin!—Yet I wish it would please God to take me to his mercy!—I can meet with none here!—What a world is this! What is there in it desirable? The good we hope for, so strangely mixed, that one knows not what to wish for: and one half of mankind tormenting the other, and being tormented themselves in tormenting!—For here in this my particular case, my relations cannot be happy, though they make me unhappy!—Except my brother and sister, indeed—and they seem to take delight in, and enjoy, the mischief they make!

But it is time to lay down my pen, since my ink runs nothing but gall.

Letter 53: MISS CLARISSA HARLOWE TO MISS HOWE

Friday morning, six o'clock

MRS Betty tells me there is now nothing talked of but of my going to my uncle Antony's. She has been ordered, she says, to get ready to attend me thither. And, upon my expressing my averseness to go, had the confidence to say that having heard me often praise the *romantic-ness* of the place, she was *astonished* (her hands and eyes lifted up) that I should set myself against going to a house so much in *my taste*.

I asked if this was her own insolence, or her young mistress's observation?

She half astonished me by her answer; that it was hard she could not say a *good* thing without being robbed of the merit of it.

As the wench looked as if she really thought she had said a good thing, without knowing the boldness of it, I let it pass. But, to say the truth, this creature has surprised me on many occasions with her smartness: for, since she has been employed in this controlling office, I have discovered a great deal of wit in her assurance, which I never suspected before. This shows that insolence is her talent; and that fortune in placing her as a servant to my sister has not done so kindly by her as nature; for that she would make a better figure as her *companion*. And indeed I can't help thinking sometimes, that I myself was better fitted by *nature* to be the servant of *both*, than the *mistress* of the *one* or the *sister* of the *other*. And within these few months past, *fortune* has acted by me as if she were of the same mind.

Friday, ten o'clock

Going down to my poultry-yard just now, I heard my brother and sister and that Solmes laughing and triumphing together. The high yew hedge between us, which divides the yard from the garden, hindered them from seeing me.

My brother, as I found, had been reading part, or the whole perhaps, of the copy of his last letter—Mighty prudent and consistent you'll say with their views, to make me the wife of a man from whom they conceal not what, were I to be such, it would be kind in them to endeavour to conceal, out of regard to my future peace: but I have no doubt that they hate me heartily.

Indeed you was up with her there, brother, said my sister! You need not have bid her not write to you. I'll engage, with all her wit, she'll never pretend to answer it.

Why, indeed, said my brother with an air of college-sufficiency, with which he abounds (for he thinks nobody writes like himself), I believe I have given her a *choke-pear*. What say you, Mr Solmes?

Why, sir, said he, I think it is unanswerable. But will it not exasperate her more against me?

Never fear, Mr Solmes, said my brother, but we'll carry our point, if she do not tire *you* out first. We have gone too far in this method to recede. Her cousin

Morden will soon be here; so all must be over before that time, or she'll be made independent of us all.

There, Miss Howe, is the reason given for their Jehu-driving!

Mr Solmes declared that he was determined to perservere while my brother gave him any hopes, and while my father stood firm.

My sister told my brother that he *hit me charmingly* on the reason why I ought to converse with Mr Solmes. But that he should not be so smart upon the *sex* for the faults of *this perverse girl*.

Some lively, and I suppose, witty answer, my brother returned; for he and Mr Solmes laughed outrageously upon it, and Bella laughing too called him a naughty gentleman: but I heard no more of what they said; they walking on into the garden.

If you think, my dear, that what I have related, did not again fire me, you will find yourself mistaken when you read at this place the enclosed copy of my letter to my brother, struck off while the iron was red hot.

No more call me meek and gentle, I beseech you.

[Letter 53.1: Clarissa Harlowe] to Mr James Harlowe, Jun.

SIR,   Friday morning
IF, notwithstanding your prohibition, I should be silent on occasion of your last, you would perhaps conclude that I was consenting to go to my uncle Antony's upon the condition you mention. My father must do as he pleases with his child. He may turn me out of his doors, if he thinks fit, or give *you* leave to do it; but (loath as I am to say it) I should think it very hard to be carried by force to anybody's house when I have one of *my own* to go to.

Far be it from me, notwithstanding yours and my sister's provocations, to think of taking my estate into my own hands without my papa's leave: but why, if I must not stay any longer here, may I not be permitted to go thither? I will engage to see nobody they would not have me see, if this favour be permitted. *Favour* I call it, and am ready to receive and acknowledge it as such, although my grandfather's will has made it matter of right.

You ask me in a very unbrotherly manner, in the postscript to your letter, if I have not some new proposals to make. I HAVE (since you put the question) three or four: *new ones* all, I think; though I will be so bold as to say, that, submitting the case to any one impartial person whom *you* have not set against me, my *old* ones ought not to have been rejected. I *think* this, why then should I not *write* it?—Nor have you any more reason to storm at your *sister* for telling it you (since you seem in your letter to make it your boast how you turned my mamma and my aunt Hervey against me), than I have to be angry with my *brother* for treating me as no brother ought to treat a sister.

These are my new proposals then:

That, as above, I may not be hindered from going to reside (under such conditions as shall be prescribed to me, which I will most religiously observe) at my grandfather's late house. I will not again in this place call it *mine*. I have reason to think it a great misfortune that ever it was so! *Indeed* I have!

If this be not permitted, I desire leave to go for a month, or for what time shall be thought fit, to Miss Howe's. I dare say her mamma will consent to it, if I have my papa's permission to go.

If this, neither, be allowed, and I *am* to be turned out of my father's house, I beg I may be suffered to go to my aunt Hervey's, where I will inviolably observe her commands, and those of my papa and mamma.

But if this, neither, is to be granted, it is my humble request, that I may be sent to my uncle Harlowe's, instead of my uncle Antony's. I mean not by this any disrespect to my uncle Antony: but his moat, with his bridge threatened to be drawn up, and perhaps his chapel, terrify me beyond expression, notwithstanding your *witty* ridicule upon me for that apprehension.

If this likewise be refused, and I must be carried to the moated house, which used to be a delightful one to me, let it be promised me that I shall not be compelled to receive Mr Solmes's visits there; and then I will as cheerfully go, as ever I did.

So here, sir, are my new proposals. And if none of them answer your end, as each of them tends to the exclusion of that ungenerous persister's visits, be pleased to know that there is no misfortune I will not submit to rather than yield to give my hand to the man to whom I can allow no share in my heart.

If I write in a style different from my usual, and different from what I wished to have occasion to write, an impartial person who knew what I have accidentally within this hour past heard from your mouth, and my sister's, and a third person's (particularly the reason you give for driving on at this violent rate; to wit, my cousin Morden's soon-expected arrival), would think I have but too much reason for it. Then be pleased to remember, sir, that when my *whining vocatives* have subjected me to so much scorn and ridicule, it is time, were it but to *imitate* examples so excellent as *you* and my *sister* set me, that I should endeavour to assert my character, in order to be thought less an *alien*, and *nearer of kin to you both*, than either of you have of late seemed to suppose me.

Give me leave, in order to *empty my female quiver* at once, to add that I know no other reason you can have for forbidding me to reply to you, after you have written what you pleased to me, than that you are conscious you cannot answer to reason and to justice the treatment you give me.

If it be otherwise, I, an unlearned, unlogical girl, younger by near a third than yourself, will venture (so assured am I of the justice of my cause) to put my fate upon an issue with *you:* with *you*, sir, who have had the advantage of an academical education; whose mind must have been strengthened by observation and learned conversation; and who, pardon my going so *low*, have been accustomed to give *choke-pears* to those you vouchsafe to write against.

Any impartial person, your late tutor for instance, or the pious and worthy Dr Lewin, may be judge between us: and if either give it against me, I will promise to resign to my destiny: provided, if it be given against you, that my father will be pleased only to allow of my negative to the person so violently sought to be imposed upon me.

I flatter myself, brother, that you will the readier come into this proposal, as you seem to have a high opinion of your talents for argumentation; and not a *low* one of the cogency of the arguments contained in your last letter. And as I can possibly have no advantage in a contention with you, if the justice of my cause affords me not any (as you have no opinion it will), it behoves you, methinks, to show to an impartial moderator that *I* am wrong, and *you* not so.

If this be accepted, there is a necessity for its being carried on by the pen; the facts to be stated and agreed upon by both; and the decision to be given according to the force of the arguments each shall produce in support of their side of the question: for, give me leave to say, I know too well the *manliness* of your temper to offer at a *personal* debate with you.

If it be not accepted, I shall conclude that you cannot defend your conduct towards me: and shall only beg of you, that for the future you will treat me with the respect due to a sister from a brother who would be thought as polite as learned.

And now, sir, if I have seemed to show some spirit not quite foreign to the relation I have the honour to bear to *you* and to my *sister*; and which may be deemed not altogether of a piece with that part of my character which once, it seems, gained me everyone's love; be pleased to consider to *whom*, and to *what* it is owing; and that this part of that character was not dispensed with till it subjected me to that scorn and those insults which a brother, who has been *so tenacious of an independence* that I *voluntarily* gave up, and who has appeared *so exalted* upon it, ought not to have shown to *anybody*, much less to a *weak* and *defenceless* sister: who is notwithstanding an affectionate and respectful one, and would be glad to show herself to be so upon all future occasions; as she has in every action of her past life, although of late she has met with such unkind returns.

CL. HARLOWE

See the force and volubility, as I may say, of passion; for the letter I send you is my first draft, struck off without a blot or erasure.

Friday, three o'clock

As soon as I had transcribed it, I sent it down to my brother by Mrs Betty.

The wench came up soon after, all aghast with her *Lord, Miss!* What *have* you done?—What *have* you written? For you have set them all in a *joyful* uproar!

MY sister is but this moment gone from me: she came up all in a flame, which obliged me abruptly to lay down my pen: she run to me—

Oh spirit! said she; tapping my neck a little *too* hard. And is it come to this at last!—

Do you beat me, Bella?

Do you call this beating you? Only tapping your shoulder *thus*, said she; tapping again more gently—This is what we expected it would come to—You want to be independent—My papa has lived too long for you!—

I was going to speak with vehemence; but she put her handkerchief before my mouth, very rudely—You have done enough with your pen, mean listener as you are! But, know, that neither your independent scheme, nor any of your visiting ones will be granted you. Take your course, perverse one; call in your rake to help you to an *in*-dependence upon your parents and a dependence upon him!—Do so!—Prepare this moment—Resolve what you will take with you!—Tomorrow you go!—Depend upon it, tomorrow you go!—No longer shall you tarry here, watching and creeping about to hearken to what people say!—'Tis determined, child!—You go tomorrow!—My brother would have come up to tell you so!—but I persuaded him to the contrary—for I know not what had become of you, if he had—Such a letter!—Such an insolent, such a *conceited* challenger!—Oh thou vain creature!—

But prepare yourself, I say—Tomorrow you go—My brother will accept your bold challenge; but it must be *personal*; and at my uncle Antony's—or perhaps at Mr Solmes's—

Thus she ran on, almost foaming with passion, till, quite out of patience, I said: No more of your violence, Bella—Had I known in what a way you would come up, you should not have found my chamber door open!—Talk to your servant in this manner: unlike *you*, as I bless God I am, I am nevertheless your sister—And let me tell you that I won't go tomorrow, nor next day, nor next day to that—except I am dragged away by violence.

What! not if your papa, or your mamma commands it—girl? said she; intending another word, by her pause and manner, before it came out.

Let it come to *that*, Bella—then I shall know what to say—But it shall be from either of their own mouths, if I do—not from yours, nor your Betty's—And say another word to me, in this manner, and be the consequence what it may, I will force myself into their presence; and demand what I have done to be used thus!

Come along, child!—come along, meekness—taking my hand and leading me towards the door—Demand it of them now—you'll find *both* your despised parents together!—What! does your heart fail you?—(for I resisted being thus insolently led and pulled my hand from her).

I want not to be led, said I; and since I can plead your invitation, I will go: and was posting to the stairs, accordingly, in my passion—But she got between me and the door and shut it—

Let me first, bold one, apprise them of your visit—for your own sake, let me—for my brother is with them. But yet opening it again, seeing me shrink back—Go if you will!—Why don't you go!—Why don't you go, miss—following me to my closet, whither I retired with my heart full, and pulled the sash-door after me; and could no longer hold in my tears.

Nor would I answer one word to her repeated aggravations and demands upon me to open my door (for the key was on the inside) nor so much as turn my head towards her, as she looked through the glass at me. And at last, which vexed her to the heart, I drew the silk curtain that she should not see me, and down she went muttering all the way.

Is not this usage enough to provoke one to a rashness one had never thought of committing?

As it is but too probable that I may be hurried away to my uncle's without being able to give you previous notice of it, I beg that as soon as you shall hear of such a violence, you will send to the usual place to take back such of your letters as may not have reached my hands, or to fetch any of mine that may be there. May you, my dear, be always happy, prays your

CL. HARLOWE

I have received your four letters. But am in such a ferment that I cannot at present write to them.

Letter 54: MISS CLARISSA HARLOWE TO MISS HOWE

Friday night, March 24

I have a most provoking letter from my sister—I might have supposed she would resent the contempt she brought upon herself in my chamber. Her conduct, surely, can only be accounted for by the rage of a supposed rivalry.

[Letter 54.1: Arabella Harlowe] to Miss Clarissa Harlowe

I AM to tell you that your mamma has begged you off for the morrow—but that you have effectually done your business with her, as well as with everybody else.

In your proposals and letter to your brother, you have showed yourself so silly and so wise, so young and so old, so gentle and so obstinate, so meek and so violent, that never was there so mixed a character.

We all know of whom you have borrowed this new spirit. And yet the seeds of it must be in your heart, or it could not all at once show itself so rampant. It would be doing Mr Solmes a spite to wish him such a *shy, un*-shy girl; another of your contradictory qualities—I leave you to make out what I mean by it.

Here, miss, your mamma will not let you remain: she cannot have any peace of mind while such a rebel of a child is so near her. Your aunt Hervey will not take a charge all the family put together cannot manage. Your uncle Harlowe will not see you at his house till you are married. So, thanks to your own stubbornness, you have nobody that will receive you but your uncle Antony: thither you must go in a very few days, and when there, your brother will settle with you, in my presence, all that relates to your modest challenge: for it is accepted, I will assure you. Dr Lewin will possibly be there, since you make choice of him; *another* gentleman likewise, were it but to convince you that he is another sort of man than you have taken him to be: your two uncles will *possibly* be there too, to see that the *poor*, *weak*, and *defenceless sister* has fair play. So, you see, miss, what company your smart challenge will draw together.

Prepare for the day. You'll soon be called upon.

Adieu, mamma Norton's sweet child!

ARAB. HARLOWE

I transcribed this letter and sent it to my mamma, with these lines.

A very few words, my ever-honoured mamma!

IF my sister wrote the enclosed by my father's direction, or yours, I must submit to the usage, with this *only* observation, that it is short of the personal treatment I have received from her. If it be of her own head—why then, madam—But I *knew*, that when I was banished from your presence—Yet, till I know if she has or has not authority for this usage, I will only write further, that I am

Your *very* unhappy child,

CL. HARLOWE

This answer I received in an open slip of paper, but it was wet in one place. I kissed the place; for I am sure it was blistered, as I may say, with a mother's tear!—The dear lady must (I *hope* she must) have [written] it reluctantly.

To apply for protection where authority is defied is bold!—Your sister who would not in *your* circumstances have been guilty of *your* perverseness may, allowably, be angry at you for it—However, we have told her to moderate her *zeal* for our insulted authority. See if you can deserve another behaviour than that which cannot be so grievous to *you*, as the *cause* of it is to

> Your *more* unhappy mother

How often must I forbid you any address to me!

GIVE me, my dearest friend, your opinion, what I *can*, what I *ought* to do. Not what you would do (pushed as I am pushed) in *resentment* or *passion*—for in *that* spirit you tell me you should have been with somebody before now. And steps made in passion hardly ever fail of leading to repentance: but acquaint me with what you think cool judgement and after-reflection, whatever be the event, will justify.

I doubt not your *sympathizing* love: but yet you cannot possibly feel indignity and persecution so very sensibly as the immediate sufferer feels them: are *fitter* therefore to advise me, than I am myself.

I will here rest my cause. Have I, or have I not, suffered or borne enough? And if they will still persevere; if that strange persister against an antipathy so strongly avowed, will *still* persist, say, what *can* I do?—what course pursue?—Shall I fly to London, and endeavour to hide myself from Lovelace as well as from all my own relations, till my cousin Morden arrives? Or shall I embark for Leghorn in my way to my cousin? Yet my sex, my youth considered, how full of danger is that!—And may not my cousin be set out for England while I am getting thither?—What *can* I do?—Tell me, tell me, my dearest Miss Howe; for I dare not trust myself!—

> Eleven o'clock at night

I HAVE been forced to try to compose my angry passions at my harpsichord; having first shut close my doors and windows, that I might not be heard below. As I was closing the shutters of the windows, the distant whooting of the bird of Minerva as from the often-visited woodhouse gave the subject in that charming ODE TO WISDOM, which does honour to our sex, as it was written by one of it. I made an essay, a week ago, to set the three last stanzas of it, as not unsuitable to my unhappy situation; and after I had re-perused the ode, those three were my lesson: and I am sure in the solemn address they contain to the all-wise and all-powerful Deity, my heart went with my fingers.

I enclose the ode and my effort with it. The subject is solemn: my circumstances are affecting; and I flatter myself that I have not been quite unhappy in the performance. If it obtain your approbation, I shall be out of doubt: and should be still more assured could I hear it tried by your voice and by your finger.

ODE TO WISDOM[1]
By a LADY

I

THE solitary bird of night
Through the thick shades now wings his flight,
And quits his time-shook tow'r;

Where sheltered from the blaze of day,
In philosophic gloom he lay,
  Beneath his ivy bow'r.

II

With joy I hear the solemn sound,
Which midnight echoes waft around,
  And sighing gales repeat.
Fav'rite of PALLAS! I attend,
And, faithful to thy summons, bend
  At WISDOM's awful seat.

III

She loves the cool, the silent eve,
Where no false shows of life deceive,
  Beneath the lunar ray.
Here folly drops each vain disguise,
Nor sport her gaily-coloured dyes,
  As in the beam of day.

IV

Oh PALLAS! Queen of ev'ry art,
That glads the sense, and mends the heart,
  Blest source of purer joys!
In ev'ry form of beauty bright,
That captivates the *mental* sight
  With pleasure and surprise;

V

To thy unspotted shrine I bow:
Attend thy modest suppliant's vow,
  That breathes no wild desires;
But taught by thy unerring rules,
To shun the fruitless wish of fools,
  To nobler views aspires.

VI

Not FORTUNE's gem, AMBITION's plume,
Nor CYTHEREA's fading bloom,
  Be objects of my pray'r:
Let *avarice*, *vanity*, and *pride*,
Those envied glitt'ring toys divide,
  The dull rewards of care.

VII

To *me* thy *better* gifts impart,
Each moral beauty of the heart,
  By studious thought refined;
For WEALTH, the smiles of glad content,
For POW'R, its amplest, best extent,
  An empire o'er my mind.

VIII

When *Fortune* drops her gay parade,
When *Pleasure*'s transient roses fade,
    And wither in the tomb,
Unchanged is *thy* immortal prize;
Thy ever-verdant laurels rise
    In undecaying bloom.

IX

By *Thee* protected, I defy
The coxcomb's sneer, the stupid lie
    Of ignorance and spite:
Alike contemn the leaden fool,
And all the pointed ridicule
    Of undiscerning *wit*.

X

From envy, hurry, noise, and strife,
The dull impertinence of life,
    In *thy* retreat I rest:
Pursue thee to the peaceful groves,
Where PLATO's sacred spirit roves,
    In all thy beauties dressed.

XI

He bade Ilyssus' tuneful stream
Convey thy philosophic theme
    Of PERFECT, FAIR, and GOOD:
Attentive Athens caught the sound,
And all her list'ning sons around
    In awful silence stood:

XII

Reclaimed her wild, licentious youth,
Confessed the potent voice of TRUTH,
    And felt its just control.
The *Passions* ceased their loud alarms,
And *Virtue*'s soft persuasive charms
    O'er all their senses stole.

XIII

Thy breath inspires the POET's song,
The PATRIOT's free, unbiased tongue,
    The HERO's gen'rous strife;
Thine are RETIREMENT's silent joys,
And all the sweet engaging ties
    Of still, domestic life.

XIV

No more to fabled names confin'd;
To thee! Supreme all-perfect mind,
    My thoughts direct their flight.

Wisdom's thy gift, and all her force
From thee deriv'd, eternal source
  Of intellect light!

XV

Oh send her sure, her steady ray,
To regulate my doubtful way,
  Through life's perplexing road:
The mists of error to control,
And through its gloom direct my soul
  To happiness and good.

XVI

Beneath her clear discerning eye
The visionary shadows fly
  Of folly's painted show.
She sees through ev'ry fair disguise,
That all, but VIRTUE's solid joys,
  Is vanity and woe.

Letter 55: MISS CLARISSA HARLOWE TO MISS LOWE

Friday midnight

I HAVE now a calmer moment. Envy, ambition, high and selfish resentment and all the violent passions are now, most probably, asleep all around me; and shall not my own angry ones give way to the silent hour, and subside likewise?—They *have* given way to it; and I have made use of the gentler space to re-peruse your last letters. I will touch upon some passages in them: and that I may the less endanger the but just-recovered calm, I will begin with what you write about Mr Hickman.

Give me leave to say, that I am sorry you cannot yet persuade yourself to think better, that is to say, *more justly*, of that gentleman than your whimsical picture of him shows you do; or at least than the humorousness of your natural vein would make one *think* you do.

I do not imagine that you yourself will say he sat for the picture you have drawn. And yet, upon the whole, it is not greatly to his disadvantage. Were I at ease in my mind, I would venture to draw a much more amiable and just likeness.

If Mr Hickman has not that assurance which some men have, he has that humanity and gentleness which many want: and which, with the infinite value he has for you, will make him one of the properest husbands in the world for a person of your vivacity and spirit.

Although you say I would not like him myself, I do assure you, if Mr Solmes were such a man as Mr Hickman, in person, mind and behaviour, my friends and I had never disagreed about him if they would not have permitted me to live single; Mr Lovelace (having such a character as he has) would have stood no chance with me. This I can the more boldly aver, because I plainly perceive that of the two passions, *love* and *fear*, this man will be able to inspire one with a much greater proportion of the *latter* than I imagine is compatible with the *former*, to make a happy marriage.

I am glad you own that you like no one better than Mr Hickman. In a little while, I make no doubt you will be able, if you challenge your heart upon it, to acknowledge that you like not any man so well: especially when you come to consider that the very faults you find in Mr Hickman admirably fit him to make *you* happy: that is to say, if it be necessary to your happiness that you should have your own will in everything.

But let me add one thing: and that is this—you have such a spritely turn that with your admirable talents you would make any man in the world, who loved you, look like a fool, except he were such a one as Lovelace.

Forgive me, my dear, for my frankness: and forgive me also for so soon returning to subjects so immediately relative to myself as those I now must touch upon.

You again insist, strengthened by Mr Lovelace's opinion, upon my assuming my own estate: and I have given you room to expect that I will consider this subject more closely than I had done before. I must however own that the reasons that I had to offer against your advice were so obvious, that I thought you would have seen them yourself, and been determined by them against your own hastier counsel—But since this has not been so; and that both you and Mr Lovelace call upon me to assume my own estate, I will enter briefly into the subject.

In the first place, let me ask you, my dear, supposing I were inclined to follow your advice, whom have I to support me in my demand?—My uncle Harlowe is one of my trustees. He is against me. My cousin Morden is the other. He is in Italy, and may be set against me too. My brother has declared that they are resolved to carry their point before he arrives: so that, as they drive on, all will probably be decided before I could have an answer from him, were I to write. And, confined as I am, if the answer were to come in time and they did not like it, they would keep it from me.

In the next place, parents have great advantages in every eye over the child if she dispute their pleasure in the disposing of her: and so they ought: since out of twenty instances perhaps two could not be produced where *they* were not in the right, the *child* in the wrong.

You would not, I am sure, have me accept of Mr Lovelace's offered assistance in such a claim. If I would embrace any *other* person's, who else would care to appear for a child against parents, ever, till of late, so affectionate? But were such a protector to be found, what a length of time would it take up in a course of litigation?—The will and the deeds have flaws in them, they say: my brother sometimes talks of going to reside at *The Grove*: I suppose with a design to make ejectments necessary, were I to offer at assuming; or should I marry Lovelace, in order to give him all the opposition and difficulty the law would help him to give.

These cares I have put to myself for argument sake: but they are all out of the question, although anybody *were* to be found who would espouse my cause: for, I do assure you, I would sooner beg my bread than litigate for my right with my papa: since I am convinced that whether or not the parent do his duty by the child, the child cannot be exempted from doing hers to him. And to go to law with my *father*, what a sound has that? You will see that I have mentioned my wish (as an alternative, and as a favour) to be permitted, if I *must* be put out of his house, to go thither: but not one step further can I go. And you see how this is resented.

Upon the whole then, what have I to hope for but a change in my father's resolution? And is there any probability of that; such an ascendency as my brother and sister have obtained over everybody; and such an interest to pursue the enmity they have now openly avowed against me?

As to Mr Lovelace's approbation of your assumption-scheme, I wonder not at it. He, very probably, penetrates the difficulties I should have to bring it to effect without his assistance. Were I to find myself as free as I would wish myself to be, perhaps that man would stand a worse chance with me than his vanity may permit him to imagine; notwithstanding the pleasure you take in rallying me on his account. How know you, but all that appears to be specious and reasonable in his offers—such as standing his chance for my favour after I became independent, as I may call it (by which, I mean no more than having the liberty to refuse a man in that Solmes, whom it hurts me but to think of as a husband); and such as his not visiting me but by my leave; and till Mr Morden came; and till I were satisfied of his reformation—how know you, I say, that he gives not himself these airs purely to stand better in *your* graces as well as *mine*, by offering of his own accord conditions which he must needs think would be insisted on, were the case to happen?

Then am I utterly displeased with him. To threaten as he threatens—yet to pretend that it is not to intimidate me; and to beg of you not to tell me, when he must know you *would*, and no doubt must *intend* that you *should*, is so meanly artful!—The man must think he has a frighted fool to deal with—I, to join hands with such a man of violence!—My own brother the man he threatens!—And Mr Solmes!— What has Mr Solmes done to him?—Is *he* to be blamed, if he thinks a person would make a wife worth having, to endeavour to obtain her?—Oh! that my friends would but leave me to my own way in this one point!—For have I given the man encouragement sufficient to ground these threats upon? Were Mr Solmes a man to whom I could be but indifferent, it might be found that to have the merit of a sufferer given him, from such a flaming spirit, would very little answer the views of that flaming spirit. It is my fortune to be treated as a fool by my brother: but Mr Lovelace shall find—Yet I will let *him* know my mind; and then it will come with a better grace to your knowledge.

Meantime, give me leave to tell you that it goes against me, in my cooler moments, wicked as my brother is to me, to have you, my dear, who are *myself*, as it were, write such very severe reflections upon him in relation to the advantage Lovelace had over him. He is not indeed *your* brother: but you write to *his* sister, remember!—Upon my word, [Miss Howe], you dip your pen in gall whenever you are offended: and I am almost ready to question, when I read some of your expressions against others of my relations as well as him (although in my favour), whether you are so thoroughly warranted by *your own* patience as you think yourself, to call *other* people to account for *their* warmth. Should we not be particularly careful to keep clear of the faults we censure?—And yet I am so angry at both my brother and sister, that I should not have taken this liberty with my dear friend, notwithstanding I know you *never* loved them, had you not made so light of so shocking a transaction, where a brother's life was at stake: where his credit in the eye of the mischievous sex has received a still deeper wound than he *personally* sustained; and when a revival of the same wicked resentments (which may end more fatally) is threatened.

His credit, I say, in the eye of the *mischievous sex*. Who is not warranted to call it so, when it is reckoned among the men, such an extraordinary piece of self-conquest, as the two libertines his companions gloried, to resolve never to *give* a challenge; and among whom duelling is so fashionable a part of brutal bravery, that the man of temper, who is, mostly, I believe, the truly brave man, is often at a great loss how to behave in some cases to avoid incurring either a mortal guilt, or a general contempt.

To enlarge a little upon this subject, may we not infer that those who would be guilty of throwing these contempts upon a man of temper, for avoiding a greater evil, know not the measure of true magnanimity: nor how much nobler it is to *forgive*, and even how much more *manly* to *despise*, than to *resent*. Were I a man, methinks, I should have too much scorn for a person who could wilfully do me a mean injury, to put a value upon his life, equal to what I put upon my own. What an absurdity, because a man had done me a *small* injury, that I should put it in his power (at least to an *equal* risk) to do me, and those who love me, an irreparable one?—Were it not a *wilful* injury, nor *avowed* to be so, there could not be *room* for resentment.

How willingly would I run away from myself, and what most concerns myself, if I could! This digression brings me back again to the occasion of it—And that to the impatience I was in, when I ended my last letter; for my situation is not altered. I renew therefore my former earnestness, as the new day approaches and will bring with it perhaps new trials, that you will (as undivestedly as possible of favour or resentment) tell me what you would have me do—For if I am obliged to go to my uncle Antony's, all I doubt will be over with me. Yet how to avoid it—That's the difficulty!

I shall deposit this the first thing: when you have it, lose no time, I pray you, to advise (lest it be too late)

Your ever-obliged,
CL. HARLOWE

Letter 56: MISS HOWE TO MISS CLARISSA HARLOWE

Sat. March 25

WHAT *can* I advise you, my noble creature? Your merit is your crime. You can no more change *your* nature, than your persecutors can *theirs*. Your distress is owing to the vast disparity between you and them. What would you have of them? Do they not act in character?—and to whom? To an alien. You are not one of them. They have two dependencies—upon their own *impenetrableness*, one (I'd give it a properer name, if I dared); the other, on the regard you have always had for your *character* (have they not heretofore owned as much?) and upon your apprehensions from *that* of Lovelace, which would discredit you, should you take any step by his means to extricate yourself. Then they know that resentment and unpersuadableness are not natural to you; and that the anger they have wrought you up to will subside, as all *extraordinaries* soon do; and that once married, you'll make the best of it.

But surely your *father*'s eldest son and eldest daughter have a view to entail unhappiness for life upon you, were you to have the man who is already more nearly related to them, than ever he can be to you should the shocking compulsion take place; by communicating to so narrow a soul all they know of your just aversion to him.

As to that wretch's perseverance, those only who know not the man will wonder at it. He has not the least delicacy. When-*ever* he shall marry, his view will not be for mind. How should it? He has *not* a mind: and does not *like seek its like?*—and if it finds something beyond itself, how shall that be valued which cannot be comprehended? Were you to be his and show a visible want of tenderness to him, it is my opinion he would not be much concerned at it; since that would leave him the more at liberty to pursue those sordid attachments which are predominant in him. I have heard you well observe, from your Mrs Norton, that a person who has any *over-ruling* passion will compound by giving up twenty *secondary* or *under-*satisfactions, though more laudable ones, in order to have *that* gratified.

I'll give you the substance of a conversation (no fear you can be made to like him worse than you do already) that passed between Sir Harry Downeton and this Solmes, but three days ago, as Sir Harry told it but yesterday to my mamma and me. It will confirm to you that what your sister's insolent Betty reported he should say, of governing by fear, was not of her own head.

Sir Harry told him he wondered he should hope to carry you so much against your inclination, as everybody knew it would be if he did.

He mattered not that, he said: coy maids made fond wives (a sorry fellow!). It would not at all grieve him to see a pretty woman make wry faces, if she gave him cause to vex her. And your estate, by the convenience of its situation, would richly pay him for all he could bear with your shyness.

He should be sure, after a while, of your complaisance, at least, if not of your love: and in that should be happier than nine parts in ten of his married acquaintance.

What a wretch is this!

For the rest, your known virtue would be as great a security to him as he could wish for.

She will look upon you, said Sir Harry (who is a reader), if she be forced to marry you, as Elizabeth of France did upon Philip II of Spain when he received her on his frontiers as her husband, who *was* to have been but her father-in-law: that is, with fear and terror rather than with complaisance and love: and you will, perhaps, be as surly to her, as that old monarch was to *his* bride.

Terror and fear, the wretch, the horrid wretch said, looked pretty in a bride, as well as in a wife: and laughing (yes, my dear, the hideous fellow laughed immoderately, as Sir Harry told us when he said it), it should be his care to perpetuate the occasion for that *fear*, if he could not think he had the *love*. And, for his part, he was of opinion that if LOVE and FEAR must be separated in matrimony, the man who made himself *feared* fared best!

If my eyes would carry with them the execution which the eyes of the basilisk are said to do, I would make it my first business to see this creature.

My mamma, however, says it would be a prodigious merit in you if you could get over your aversion to him. Where, asks she, as you have been asked before, is the praise-worthiness of obedience if it be only paid in instances where we give up nothing?

What a fatality, that you have no better an option!—Either a *Scylla* or a *Charybdis!*

Were it not YOU, I should know how (barbarously used as you are used) to advise you in a moment. But such a noble character to suffer from a (supposed) rashness and indiscretion of such a nature would be a wound to the sex, as I have heretofore observed.

While I was in hope that the asserting of your own independence would have helped you, I was pleased that you had *one* resource, as I thought: but now that you have so well proved that such a step would not avail you, I am entirely at a loss what to say. I will lay down my pen, and think.

I HAVE considered, and considered again; but, I protest, I know no more what to say, than before. Only this: that I am young, like yourself; and have a much weaker judgement and stronger passions than you have.

I have heretofore said that you have offered as much as you ought to offer in living single. If you were never to marry, the estate they are so loath should go out of their name, would in time I suppose revert to your brother: and *he* or *his* would have it, perhaps, much more certainly this way, than by the precarious reversions Solmes makes them hope for. Have you put this into their odd heads, my dear?— The tyrant word AUTHORITY, as they use it, can be the only objection against this offer.

One thing you must consider, that, if you leave your parents, your duty and love to them will not suffer you to appeal against them to justify yourself for so doing; and so you'll have the world against you. And should Lovelace continue his wild life, and behave ungratefully to you, how will that justify their conduct to *you* (which nothing *else* can), as well as their resentments against *him?*

May heaven direct you for the best! I can only say that, for my own part, I would do anything, go any-wither, rather than be compelled to marry the man I hate; and, were he such a man as *Solmes*, must always hate. Nor could I have borne what you have borne, if from father and uncles, not from brother and sister.

My mamma will have it that after they have tried their utmost efforts to bring you into their measures, and find them ineffectual, they will recede. But I cannot say I am of her mind. She does not own she has any other authority for this but her own conjecture. I should otherwise have hoped that your uncle Antony and she had been in one secret, and that favourable to you—Woe be to one of them at least (your uncle I mean), if they should be in *any other!—*

You must, if possible, avoid being carried to that uncle's. The man, the parson, the chapel, your brother and sister present!—they'll certainly there marry you to Solmes. Nor will your newly-raised spirit support you in your resistance on such an occasion. Your meekness will return; and you will have nothing for it but tears (tears despised by them all), and ineffectual appeals and lamentations—and *these*, when the ceremony is *profaned*, as I may say, you must suddenly put a stop to, and dry up: and endeavour to dispose yourself to such an humble frame of mind as may induce your new-made lord to forgive all your past declarations of aversion.

In short, my dear, you must then blandish him over with a confession that all your past behaviour was maidenly reserve only: and it will be *your* part to convince him of the truth of his impudent sarcasm, *that the coyest maids make the fondest wives.* Thus will you begin the state with a high sense of obligation to his *forgiving goodness!* And if you will not be kept to it by that *fear* he proposes to govern by, I am much mistaken.

Yet, after all, I must leave the point undetermined, and only to *be* determined as you find they recede from their avowed purpose, or resolve to remove you to your uncle Antony's. But I must repeat my wishes, that something may fall out that *neither* of these men may call you *his!* And may you live single, my dearest friend, till some man shall offer, that may be as worthy of you as man *can* be.

But yet, methinks, I would not that you, who are so admirably qualified to adorn the matrimonial state, should be always single. You know I am incapable of flattery; and that I always speak and write the sincere dictates of my heart. Nor can you, from what you must know of your own merit (taken in a comparative light with others), doubt my sincerity. For why should a person who delights to find out and admire everything that is praise-worthy in *another* be supposed ignorant of like perfections in *herself*, when she could not so much admire them *in* another if she had them *not* herself? And why may not one give *her* those praises, which *she* would give to any other who had but half of her own excellencies?—especially when she is incapable of pride and vainglory; and neither despises others for the want of her fine qualities, nor over-values herself upon them?—*Over*-values, did I say!—How can that be?—

Forgive me, my beloved friend. My admiration of you (increased as it is by every letter you write) will not always be held down in silence; although in order to avoid offending you I generally endeavour to keep it from flowing to my pen when I write to you, or to my lips whenever I have the happiness to be in your company.

I will add nothing, though I could an hundred things, on occasion of your latest communications, but that I am,

Your ever-affectionate and faithful,
ANNA HOWE

I hope I have pleased you with my dispatch. I wish I had been able to please you with my requested advice.

You have given new beauties to the charming ode which you have transmitted to me. What pity that the wretches you have to deal with put you out of your admirable course; in the pursuit of which, like the sun, you was wont to cheer and illuminate all you shone upon.

Letter 57: MISS CLARISSA HARLOWE TO MISS HOWE

Sunday morning, Mar. 26

How soothing a thing is praise from those we love!—Whether conscious or not of deserving it, it cannot but give us great delight to see one's self stand high in the opinion of those whose favour we are ambitious to cultivate. An ingenuous mind will make this farther use of it, that if it be sensible, that it does not *already* deserve the charming attributes, it will hasten, before its friend finds herself mistaken, to obtain the graces it is complimented for: and this it will do, as well in honour to itself, as to preserve its friend's opinion, and justify her judgement!— May this be always my aim!—and then you will not only give the *praise*, but the *merit*; and I shall be more worthy of that friendship which is the only pleasure I have to boast of.

Most heartily I thank you for the kind dispatch of your last favour. How much am I indebted to you! and even to your honest servant!—Under what obligations does my unhappy situation lay me!

But let me answer the kind contents of it as well as I may.

As to getting over my disgusts to Mr Solmes, it is impossible to be done, while he wants generosity, frankness of heart, benevolence, manners and every qualification that distinguishes a worthy man. Oh my dear! what a degree of patience, what a greatness of soul, is required in the wife, not to despise a husband who is more ignorant, more illiterate, more low-minded, than herself?—The wretch, vested with prerogatives, who will claim rule in virtue of them (and not to *permit* whose claim will be as disgraceful to the *prescribing* wife, as to the *governed* husband); how shall such a husband as this be borne, were he for reasons of *convenience* and *interest* even to be one's CHOICE? But, to be *compelled* to have such a one, and that compulsion to arise from motives as unworthy of the *prescribers* as of the *prescribed*, who can think of getting over an aversion so justly founded? How much easier to bear the *temporary* persecutions I labour under, *because* temporary, than to resolve to be *such* a man's for *life*? Were I to comply, must I not leave my relations and go to him? *One month* will decide the one perhaps: but what a *duration of woe* will the other be!—every day, it is likely, rising to witness to some new breach of an altar-vowed duty!

Then, my dear, the man seems already to be meditating vengeance upon me for an aversion I cannot help: for yesterday, my saucy gaoleress assured me that all my oppositions would not signify that *pinch of snuff*, holding out her genteel finger and thumb: that I *must* have Mr Solmes: that therefore, I had not best carry my jest too far; for that Mr Solmes was a man of spirit, and had told HER, that as I should surely be his, I acted very unpoliticly; since, if he had not more *mercy* (that was *her* word; I know not if it were *his*) than I had, I might have cause to repent the usage I gave him to the last day of my life.

But enough of this man; who, by what you repeat from Sir Harry Downeton, has all the insolence of his sex, without any one quality to make that insolence tolerable.

I have received two letters from Mr Lovelace, since his visit to you; which made three that I had not answered. I doubted not his being very uneasy; but in his last he complains in high terms of my silence; not in the still small voice, or rather style, of an humble lover, but in a style like that which would probably be used by a slighted protector. And his pride is again touched, that like a *thief* or *eavesdropper*, he is forced to dodge about in hopes of a letter, and return five miles, and then to an inconvenient lodging, without any.

His letters, and the copy of mine to him, shall soon attend you: till when, I will give you the substance of what I wrote to him yesterday.

I take him severely to task for his freedom in threatening me, through you, with a visit to Mr Solmes, or to my brother. I say, 'That, surely, I must be thought to be a creature fit to bear *anything:* that violence and menaces from some of my *own family* are not enough for me to bear, in order to make me avoid *him*; but that I must have them from *him* too, upon a supposition that I will oblige those whom it is both my *inclination* and *duty* to oblige in everything that is reasonable, and in my power.

'Very extraordinary, I tell him, that a violent spirit shall threaten to do a rash and unjustifiable thing, which concerns *me* but little and himself a great deal, if I do not something *as* rash, my character and sex considered, to divert him from it.

'I even hint that, however it may affect me, if any mischief shall be done on my account, yet there are persons, as far as I know, who in my case would not think there would be reason for *much* regret were such a committed rashness as he threatens Mr Solmes with, to rid her of *two* persons, whom had she never known, she had never been unhappy.'

This is plain dealing, my dear! And I suppose he will put it into still plainer English for me.

I take his pride to task, on his disdaining to watch for my letters; and for his *eavesdropping* language: and say, 'That, surely, he has the less reason to think so hardly of his situation, since his faulty morals are the original cause of all; and since faulty morals deservedly level all distinction and bring down rank and birth to the *canaille*; and to the necessity, of which he complains, of appearing, if I must descend to his language, as an *eavesdropper* and a *thief*. And then I forbid him ever to expect another letter from me, that is to subject him to such disgraceful hardships.

'That as to the solemn vows and protestations he is so ready upon all occasions to make, they have the less weight with me, as they give a kind of demonstration that he himself thinks, from his own character, there is *reason* to make them. *Deeds* are to be the only evidences of *intentions*. And I am more and more convinced of the necessity of breaking off a correspondence with a person whose addresses I see it is impossible either to expect my friends to encourage, or him to deserve that they should.

'What therefore I repeatedly desire is, that since his birth, alliances and expectations are such as will at any time, if his immoral character be not an objection, procure him at least equal advantages, in a woman whose taste and inclinations moreover might be better adapted to his own, I insist upon it as well as advise it, that he give up all thoughts of me: and the rather as he has all along, by his threatening and unpolite behaviour to my friends, and whenever he speaks of them, given me reason to conclude that there is more malice to *them* than regard to *me* in his perseverance.'

This is the substance of the letter I have written to him.

The man, to be sure, must have the penetration to observe that my correspondence with him hitherto is owing more to the severity I meet with than to a very high value for him. And so I would have him think. What a *worse* than Moloch-deity is that which expects an offering of reason, duty and discretion to be made to its shrine!

Your mamma is of opinion that *at last* my friends will relent. Heaven grant that they may!—But my brother and sister have such an influence over everybody, and are so determined; so pique themselves upon subduing me and carrying their point; that I despair that they will—And yet, if they do not, I frankly own I would not scruple to throw myself upon any not disreputable protection by which I might avoid my present persecutions on one hand, and not give Lovelace advantage over me on the other. That is to say, were there manifestly *no other* way left me: for, if there *were*, I should think the leaving my father's house, without his consent, one of the most inexcusable actions I could be guilty of, were the protection to be ever so unexceptionable; and this notwithstanding the independent fortune willed me by my grandfather. And indeed I have often reflected with a degree of indignation and disdain upon the thought of what a low, selfish creature that child must be, who is to be reined in only by what a parent can or will do for her.

But notwithstanding all this, I owe it to the sincerity of friendship to confess, that I know not what I *should* have done had your advice been conclusive any way. Had you, my dear, been witness to my different emotions as I read your letter, when in one place you advise me of my danger, if I am carried to my uncle's; in another, when you own you could not bear what I bear and would do anything rather than marry the man you hate: yet, in another, represent to me my reputation suffering in the world's eye; and the necessity I should be under to justify my conduct at the expense of my friends, were I to take a rash step: in another, insinuate the *dishonest* figure I should be forced to make in so compelled a matrimony; endeavouring to cajole, fawn upon and play the hypocrite with a man I have an aversion to; who would have reason to believe me an hypocrite, as well from my former avowals as from the sense he *must* have (if common sense he has) of his own demerits—The necessity you think there would be for me, the more averse I really was, to seem the fonder of him: a fondness, were I capable of so much dissimulation, that would be imputable to the most disgraceful motives; as it would be too visible that love, either of person or mind, could be neither of them—Then his undoubted, his even constitutional narrowness: his too probable jealousy and unforgivingness, bearing in mind my declared aversion, and the unfeigned despites I took all opportunities to do him in order to discourage his address: a preference avowed against him from the *same* motive: with the pride he professes to take in curbing and sinking the spirits of a woman he had acquired a right to tyrannize over. Had you, I say, been witness of my different emotions as I read, now leaning this way, now that; now perplexed; now apprehensive; now angry at one, then at another; now resolving; now doubting—you would have seen the power you have over me; and would have had reason to believe that, had you given your advice in any determined or positive manner, I had been ready to have been concluded by it. So, my dear, you will find from these acknowledgements, that you must justify me to those laws of friendship which require undisguised frankness of heart; although your justification of me in that particular will perhaps be at the expense of my prudence.

But, upon the whole, this I do repeat—that nothing but the *last* extremity shall make me abandon my father's house, if they will permit me to stay; and if I can by any means, by any honest pretences, but keep off my evil destiny in it, till my cousin Morden arrives. As one of my trustees, *his* is a protection that I may, without discredit, throw myself into, if my other friends should remain determined. And this (although they seem too well aware of it) is all my hope: for as to Lovelace, were one to be sure of his tenderness to one's self, and even of his reformation, must not the thoughts of embracing the offered protection of his family be the same in the world's eye, as accepting of his own?—Could I avoid receiving his visits at his own relations? Must I not be his, whatever on seeing him in a *nearer* light I should find him out to be. For you know, it has always been my observation that both sexes too generally cheat each other by the more *distant*. Oh! my dear! how *wise* have I endeavoured to be! how anxious to choose and to avoid everything, precautiously as I may say, that might make me happy or unhappy; yet all my wisdom now, by a strange fatality, likely to become foolishness.

Then you tell me, in your usual kindly-partial manner, what is expected of *me*, more than would be of some others. This should be a lesson to me. Whatever my motives, the world would not know them: to complain of a brother's unkindness, *that* one might do. It is too common a case where interests clash. But where the unkind father cannot be separated from the faulty brother, who could bear to lighten herself by loading a father?—Then, in this particular case, must not the hatred Mr Lovelace expresses to everyone of my family, although in return for *their* hatred of him, shock one extremely? Must it not show that there is something implacable, as well as highly unpolite, in his temper?—And what creature can think of marrying so as to live at continual enmity with all her own relations?

But here, having tired myself and I dare say you, I will lay down my pen.

Mr Solmes is almost continually here: so is my aunt Hervey: so are my two uncles. Something is working against me, I doubt. What an uneasy state of suspense!—when a naked sword, too, seems hanging over one's head!

I hear nothing but what this confident creature Betty throws out in the wantonness of office. Now it is, Why, miss, don't you look up your things? You'll be called upon, depend upon it, before you are aware!—Another time she intimates darkly and in broken sentences, as if on purpose to tease me, what *one* says, what *another*; with their inquiries how I dispose of my time? And my brother's insolent question comes frequently in, whether I am not writing a history of my sufferings?

But I am now used to her pertness: and as it is only through that, that I can hear of anything intended against me before it is to be put in execution; and as she pleads a commission, when she is most impertinent; I bear with her: yet now and then not without a little of the heart-burn.

I will deposit thus far.

Adieu, my dear.
CL. HARLOWE

Written on the cover, after she went down, with a pencil:

On coming down, I found your second letter of yesterday's date.[a] I have read it, and am in hopes that the *within* will in a great measure answer your mamma's expectations of me.

My most respectful acknowledgements to her for it, and for her very kind admonitions.

You'll read to her what you please of the enclosed.

Letter 58: MISS HOWE TO MISS CLARISSA HARLOWE

Sat. Mar. 25

I FOLLOW my last of this date, by command. I mentioned in my former, my mamma's opinion of the merit you would have if you could oblige your friends, against your own inclination. Our conference upon this subject was introduced by the conversation we had had with Sir Harry Downeton; and my mamma thinks it of so much importance that she injoins me to give you the particulars of it. I the

a   See the next letter.

rather comply, as I was unable in my last to tell what to advise you to; and as you will in this recital have my mamma's opinion, at least; and perhaps, in *hers*, what the *world's* would be, were it to know only what she knows; and not so much as I know.

My mamma argues upon this case in a most discouraging manner for all such of our sex as look forward for happiness in marriage with the *man of their choice*.

Only, that I know she has a side-view to her daughter; who, at the same time that she now prefers no one to another, values not the man her mamma most regards, of one farthing; or I should lay it more to heart.

What is there in it, says she, that all this bustle is about? Is it such a mighty matter for a young lady to give up her own inclinations to oblige her friends?

Very well, my mamma, thought I! Now, may you ask this—At FORTY, you may—But what would you have said at EIGHTEEN is the question!

Either, said she, the lady must be thought to have very violent inclinations (and what nice young creature would have that supposed?) which she *could* not give up; or a very stubborn will, which she *would* not; or, thirdly, have parents she was indifferent about obliging.

You know my mamma now and then argues very notably: always very warmly at least. I happen often to differ from her; and we both think so well of our own arguments that we very seldom are so happy as to convince one another. A pretty common case, I believe, in all *vehement* debatings. She says I am *too witty*; Anglicè, *too pert*: I, that she is *too wise*; that is to say, being likewise put into English, *not so young as she has been*: in short, is grown so much into *mother*, that she has forgotten she ever was a *daughter*. So, generally, we call another cause by consent—yet fall into the old one half a dozen times over, *without* consent—quitting and resuming, with half-angry faces forced into a smile, that there might be some room to piece together again: but go to bed, if bed-time, a little sullen, nevertheless; or, if we speak, her silence is broke, with an Ah! Nancy! You are so lively! so quick! I wish you were less like your papa, child!—

I pay it off with thinking, that my mamma has no reason to disclaim her share in her Nancy: and if the matter go off with greater severity on her side than I wish for, then her favourite Hickman fares the worse for it, next day.

I know I am a saucy creature: I know, if I do not *say* so, you will *think* so; so no more of this just now. What I mention it for, is to tell you that on this serious occasion I will omit, if I can, all that passed between us that had an air of flippancy on my part, or quickness on my mamma's, to let you into the *cool* and the *cogent* of the conversation.

'Look through the families, said she, which we both know, where the gentleman and lady have been said to marry for love; which at the time it is so called is perhaps no more than a passion begun in folly, or thoughtlessness, and carried on from a spirit of perverseness and opposition (Here we had a parenthetical debate, which I omit) and see if they appear to be happier than those whose principal inducement to marry has been convenience, or to oblige their friends; or even whether they are generally *so* happy: for *convenience* and *duty*, where observed, will afford a *permanent* and even an *increasing* satisfaction, as well at the time, as upon the reflection, which seldom fail to reward themselves: while *love*, if love *be* the motive, is an idle passion'— (*Idle in* ONE SENSE *my mamma cannot say; for love is as busy as a monkey, and as mischievous as a school-boy*). 'It is a *fervour*, that, like all other *fervours*, lasts but a little while; a bow over-strained, that soon returns to its natural bent.

'As it is founded generally upon mere *notional* excellencies, which were unknown to the persons themselves, till attributed to either by the other; one, two, or three months, usually sets all right on both sides; and then with opened eyes they think of each other—just as everybody else thought of them before.

'The lovers' *imaginaries* (Her own word! notable enough! i'n't it?) are by that time gone off; nature, and old habits, painfully dispensed with or concealed, return: disguises thrown aside, all the moles, freckles and defects in the minds of *each* discover themselves; and 'tis well if each do not sink in the opinion of the other as much below the common standard, as the blinded imagination of both had set them above it. And now, said she, the fond pair, who knew no felicity out of each other's company, are so far from finding the never-ending variety each had proposed in an unrestrained conversation with the other (when they seldom were together; and always parted with something *to say*; or, on recollection, when parted, wishing they *had* said); that they are continually on the wing in pursuit of amusements out of themselves; and those, concluded my sage mamma (Did you think her wisdom so *very* modern?), will perhaps be the livelier to each, in which the other has no share.'

I told my mamma, that if *you* were to take any rash step, it would be owing to the indiscreet violence of your friends: I was afraid, I said, that these reflections upon the conduct of people in the married state, who might set out with better hopes, were but too well grounded: but that this must be allowed me, that if children weighed not these matters so thoroughly as they ought, neither did parents make those allowances for youth, inclination and inexperience, which were necessary to be made for themselves at their children's time of life.

I remembered a letter, I told her hereupon, which you wrote a few months ago, personating an anonymous elderly lady (in Mr Wyerley's day of plaguing you), to Miss Drayton's mamma, who, by her severity and restraints had like to have driven the young lady into the very fault against which her mother was most solicitous to guard her. And, I dared to say, she would be pleased with it.

I fetched the copy of it, which you had favoured me with at the time. I would have read only that part of it which was most to my purpose, but she would hear it all.[a]

a   The passage most particularly recommended by Miss Howe is the following:
'Permit me, madam (says the personated grave writer), to observe, that if persons of your experience would have young people look *forward*, in order to be wiser and better by their advice, it would be kind in them to look *backward*, and allow for their children's youth and natural vivacity; in other words, for their lively hopes, unabated by time, unaccompanied by reflection, and unchecked by disappointment. Things appear to us all in a very different light at our entrance upon a favourite party, or tour; when with golden prospects and high expectations, we rise vigorous and fresh, like the sun beginning its morning course; from what they do when we sit down at the end of our views, tired, and preparing for our journey homeward: for then we take into our *reflection*, what we had left out of our *scheme*, the fatigues, the checks, the hazards, we had met with; and make a true estimate of pleasures, which, from our raised expectations, must necessarily have fallen miserably short of what we had promised ourselves at setting out——Nothing but experience can give us a strong and efficacious conviction of this difference: and when we would inculcate the fruits of *that* upon the minds of those we love, who have not lived long enough to find those fruits, and would

My mamma was pleased with the whole letter; and said it deserved to have the effect it had. But asked me, what excuse could be offered for a young lady capable of making such reflections; and who, at her time of life, could so well assume the character of one of riper years; if she should rush into any fatal mistake herself?

She then touched upon the moral character of Mr Lovelace; and how reasonable the aversion of your relations is, to a man who gives himself the liberties he is said to take; and who, indeed, himself, denies not the accusation; having been heard to declare, that he will do all the mischief he can to the sex, in revenge for the ill usage and broken vows of his first love, at a time when he was *too young* (his own expression, it seems) to be insincere.

I replied that I had heard everyone say, that that lady really used him ill; that it affected him so much at the time, that he was forced to travel upon it; and, to drive her out of his heart, ran into courses which he had ingenuity enough himself to condemn: that, however, he had denied the menaces against the sex which were attributed to him, when charged with them by me in your presence; and declared himself incapable of so unjust and ungenerous a resentment against *all*, for the perfidy of *one*.

You remember this, my dear; as I do your innocent observation upon it, that you could believe his solemn asseveration and denial: 'For, surely, said you, the man who would resent, as the highest indignity that could be offered to a gentleman, the imputation of a *wilful* falsehood would not be guilty of one.'

I insisted upon the extraordinary circumstances in your case, particularizing them; observing that Mr Lovelace's morals were, at one time, no objection with your relations for Miss Arabella; that then much was built upon his family, and more upon his parts and learning, which made it out of doubt that he might be reclaimed by a woman of virtue and prudence: and (pray forgive me for mentioning it) I ventured to add, that although your family might be good sort of folks, as the world went, yet nobody imputed to any of them, but yourself, a very punctilious concern for religion or piety—Therefore were they the less entitled to object to the defects of that kind in others. Then, what an odious man, said I, have they picked out to supplant in a lady's affections one of the finest appearances of a man in England, and one noted for his brilliant parts and other accomplishments (whatever his morals might be); as if they were determined upon an act of power and authority, without rhyme or reason!

hope, that our *advice* should have as much force upon *them*, as *experience* has upon *us*; and which, perhaps, *our* parents' advice had not upon *ourselves* at our daughters' time of life; should we not proceed by patient reasoning and gentleness, that we may not harden where we would convince? For, madam, the tenderest and most generous minds, when harshly treated, become generally the most inflexible. If the young lady knows her *heart* to be right, however defective her *head* may be for want of years and experience, she will be apt to be very tenacious. And if she believes her friends to be wrong, although perhaps they may be only so in their methods of treating her, how much will every *unkind* circumstance on the parent's part, or *heedless* one on the child's, though ever so slight in itself, widen the difference? The parent's *prejudice* in *dis*-favour will confirm the daughter's in favour, of the same person; and the best reasonings in the world on either side will be attributed to that prejudice. In short, neither of them will be convinced. A perpetual opposition ensues; the parent grows impatient; the child desperate: and, as a too natural consequence, that falls out which the mother was most afraid of, and which, possibly, had been prevented had the child's passions been only *led*, not *driven*.'

Still my mamma insisted, that there was the greater merit in your obedience on that account, and urged that there hardly ever was a very handsome and a spritely man who made a good husband: for that they were generally such Narcissuses, as to imagine every women ought to think as highly of them as they did of themselves.

There was no danger from that consideration *here*, I said, because the lady had still greater advantages, both of person and mind, than the man; graceful and elegant as he must be allowed to be, beyond any of his sex.

She cannot endure to hear me praise any man but her favourite Hickman. Upon whom, nevertheless, she generally brings a degree of contempt, which he would escape did she not lessen the little merit he has, by giving him on all occasions more than I think he can deserve, and entering him into comparisons in which it is impossible but he must be a sufferer. And now, preposterous partiality! she thought, for *her* part, that Mr Hickman, 'bating that his *face* indeed was not so smooth, nor his complexion *quite* so good, and saving that he was not so presuming and so bold (which ought to be no fault with a modest woman!), equalled Mr Lovelace *at any hour of the day*.

To avoid entering further into such an *incomparable* comparison, I said I did not believe, had they left you to your own way and treated you generously, that you would have had the thought of encouraging any man, whom they disliked.

Then, Nancy, catching me up, the excuse is less—for, if so, must there not be more of *contradiction*, than *love* in the case?

Not so, neither, madam: for I know Miss Clarissa Harlowe would prefer Mr Lovelace to all men, if morals—

If, Nancy!—That *if* is everything!—Do you really think she loves Mr Lovelace?

What would you have had me to say, my dear?—I won't tell you what I *did* say—but had I *not* said what I *did*, who would have believed me?

Besides, I *know* you love him!—Excuse me, my dear: yet, if you deny it, what do you but reflect upon yourself, as if you thought you *ought not?*

Indeed, said I, the man is worthy of any woman's love (*If*, again, I could say)—but her parents, madam—

Her parents, Nancy—(you know, my dear, how my mamma, who accuses her daughter of quickness, is evermore interrupting!)—

May take wrong measures, said I—

Cannot do wrong—They have reason, I'll warrant, said she—

By which they may provoke a young lady, said I, to do rash things which otherwise she would not do.

But if it *be* a rash thing (returned she), should she do it! A prudent daughter will not wilfully err, because her parents err, if they *were* to err: if she *do*, the world, which blames the parents, will not acquit the child. All that can be said, in extenuation of a daughter's error, arises from a kind consideration, which Miss's letter to Lady Drayton pleads for, to be paid to *her* daughter's youth and inexperience. And will such an admirable young person as Miss Clarissa Harlowe, whose prudence, as we see, qualifies her to be an adviser of persons much older than herself, take shelter under so poor a covert?

Let her know, Nancy, out of hand, what I say; and I charge you to represent farther to her, that let her dislike one man, and approve another, ever so much, it will be expected of a young lady of her unbounded generosity and greatness of mind, that she should *deny herself*, when she can *oblige all her family* by so doing:

no less than ten or a dozen, perhaps, the nearest and dearest to her of all the persons in the world, an indulgent father and mother at the head of them. It may be *fancy* only on her side; but parents look deeper: and will not Miss Clarissa Harlowe give up her *fancy* to her parents *judgement?*

I said a great deal upon this *judgement* subject: all that you could wish I should say; and all that your extraordinary case allowed me to say. And my mamma was so sensible of the force of it, that she charged me not to write to you any part of my answer to what she said; but only what she herself had advanced; lest, in so critical a case, it should induce you to take measures that might give us both reason (I for giving it, you for following it) to repent it as long as we lived.

And thus, my dear, I set my mamma's arguments before you. And the rather, as I cannot myself tell what to advise you to do!—You know best your own heart; and what that will let you do!

Robin undertakes to deposit this very early, that you may receive it by your first morning airing.

Heaven guide and direct you for the best, is the incessant prayer, of

Your ever-affectionate,
ANNA HOWE

Letter 59: MISS CLARISSA HARLOWE TO MISS HOWE

Sunday afternoon

I AM in great apprehensions. Yet cannot help repeating my humble thanks to your mamma, and you, for your last favour. I hope her kind end is answered by the contents of my last. Yet I must not think it enough to acknowledge her goodness to me, with a pencil only, on the cover of a letter sealed up. A few lines give me leave to write with regard to my anonymous letter to Lady Drayton—If I did not at that time tell you, as I believe I did, that my excellent Mrs Norton gave me her assistance in that letter; I now acknowledge that she did.

Pray let your mamma know this, for two reasons: one, that I may not be thought to arrogate to myself a discretion which does not belong to me; the other, that I may not suffer by the severe, but just inference she was pleased to draw; *doubling* my faults upon me, if I myself should act unworthy of the advice I was supposed to give.

Before I come to what most nearly affects me, I must chide you, once more, for the severe, the very severe things, you mention of our family, to the disparagement of their morals, as I may say. Indeed, my dear, I wonder at you!—A slighter occasion might have passed me, after I have written to you so often to so little purpose, on this topic. But, affecting as my own circumstances are, I cannot, without a breach of duty, let slip the reflection I need not repeat in words.

There is not a worthier person in England than my mamma. Nor is my papa that man you sometimes make him. Excepting in one point, I know not any family which lives up more to their duty, than the principals of ours. A little too *uncommunicative* for their great circumstances—that is all. Why, then, have they not reason to insist upon unexceptionable morals in a man whose relationship to them, by a marriage in their family, they have certainly a right to allow of, or disapprove?

Another line or two, before I am ingrossed by my own concerns—upon your treatment of Mr Hickman. Is it, do you think, generous, to revenge upon an innocent person, the displeasure you receive from another quarter, where I doubt you are a trespasser too?—But one thing I can tell him; and you had not best provoke me to it; that no woman uses a man ill whom she does not absolutely reject, but she has it in her heart to make him amends, when her tyranny has had its run and he has completed the measure of his services and patience. But my mind is not enough at ease to push this matter further.

I will now give you the occasion of my present apprehensions.

I had reason to fear, as I mentioned in mine of this morning, that a storm was brewing. Mr Solmes came home this afternoon from church, with my brother. Soon after, Betty brought me up a letter, without saying from whom. It was in a cover, and directed by a hand I never saw before; as if it was supposed I would not have received and opened it, had I known it came from him. These are the contents.

[*Letter 59.1: Roger Solmes*] *to Miss Clarissa Harlowe*

Sunday, Mar. 26

Dearest madam,

I THINK myself a most unhappy man, in that I have never yet been able to pay my respects to you with youre consent, for one halfe hour. I have something to communicate to you that concernes you much, if you be pleased to admit me to youre speech. Youre honour is concerned it itt, and the honour of all youre familly. Itt relates to the designes of one whom you are sed to valew more then he deserves; and to some of his reprobat actions; which I am reddie to give you convincing proofes of the truth of. I may appear to be interested in itt: but neverthelesse, I am reddy to make oathe, that every tittle is true: and you will see what a man you are sed to favour. But I hope not so, for youre owne honour.

Pray, madam, vouchsafe me a hearing, as you valew your honour and familly: which will oblidge, dearest miss,

Youre most humble and most faithfull servant,
ROGER SOLMES

I waite below for the hope of admittance.

I have no manner of doubt, that this is a poor device to get this man into my company. I would have sent down a verbal answer; but Betty refused to carry any message which should prohibit his visiting me. So I was obliged either to see him, or to write to him. I wrote, therefore, an answer, of which I shall send you the rough draft. And now my heart aches for what may follow from it; for I hear a great hurry below.

[*Letter 59.2: Clarissa Harlowe*] *to Roger Solmes, Esq.*

SIR,

WHATEVER you have to communicate to me, which concerns my honour, may as well be done by writing, as by word of mouth. If Mr Lovelace is any of *my* concern, I know not that, *therefore*, he ought to be *yours*: for the usage I receive on *your* account (I *must* think it so!) is so harsh, that were there not such a man in the world as Mr *Lovelace*, I would not wish to see Mr *Solmes*, no, not for one half hour, in the way he is pleased to be desirous to see me. I never can be in any danger from Mr Lovelace; and, of consequence, cannot be affected by any of your discoveries, if the proposal I made be accepted. You have been acquainted with it, no doubt. If not, be pleased to let my friends know, that if they will rid *me* of my apprehensions of one gentleman, I will rid them of *theirs* of another: and then, of what consequence to *them*, or to *me*, will it be, whether Mr Lovelace be a good man, or a bad? And, if to neither of *us*, I see not how it can be of any to *you*. But if *you* do, I have nothing to say to that; and it will be a Christian part, if you will expostulate with him upon the errors you have discovered, and endeavour to make him as good a man, as no doubt, you are *yourself*, or you would not be so ready to detect and expose *him*.

Excuse me, sir: but after my former letter to you, and your ungenerous perseverance; and after this attempt to avail yourself at the expense of another man's character, rather than by your own proper merit, I see not that you can blame any asperity in her, whom you have so largely contributed to make unhappy.

CL. HARLOWE

Sunday night

MY father was for coming up to me, in great wrath, it seems; but was persuaded to the contrary. My aunt Hervey was permitted to send me this that follows— Quick work, my dear!

[*Letter 59.3: Miss Dorothy Hervey*] *to Miss Clarissa Harlowe*

Niece,

EVERYBODY is now convinced, that nothing is to be done with you by way of gentleness or persuasion. Your mamma will not let you stay in the house; for your papa is so incensed by your strange letter to his friend, that she knows not what will be the consequence, if you do. So, you are commanded to get ready to go to your uncle Antony's, out of hand.

Your uncle thinks he has not deserved of you this unwillingness to go to his house.

You don't know the wickedness of the man you think it worth while to quarrel with all your friends for.

You must not answer me. There will be no end of that.

You know not the affliction you give to everybody; but to none more than to

Your affectionate aunt,
DOROTHY HERVEY

Forbid to write to my aunt, I took a bolder liberty. I wrote a few lines to my mamma; imploring her to procure me leave to throw myself at my father's feet, and hers, if I *must* go (nobody else present), to beg pardon for the trouble I had given them both, and their blessings; and to receive their commands as to my removal, and the *when*, from their own lips.

'What new boldness this!—Take it back; and bid her learn to obey,' was my mamma's angry answer, with my letter returned, unopened.

But that I might omit nothing that was in my power, or heart, to do, that had an appearance of duty, I wrote a few lines to my papa himself, to the same purpose; begging he would not turn me out of his house, without his blessing. But this, torn in two pieces, and unopened, was brought me up again by Betty, with an air, one hand held up, the other extended, the torn letter in her open palm; and a See here!—What a *sad* thing is this!—Nothing will do but duty, miss!—Your papa said, let her tell me of *deeds!*—I'll receive no *words* from her: and so he tore the letter, and flung the pieces at my head.

So desperate my case, I was resolved not to stop even at this repulse. I took my pen, and addressed myself to my uncle Harlowe, enclosing that which my mamma had returned unopened, and the torn unopened one sent to my papa; having first scratched through a transcript for you.

My uncle was going home, and it was delivered to him just as he stepped into his chariot. What may be the fate of it, therefore, I cannot know till tomorrow.

The following is a copy of it.

[Letter 59.4: Clarissa Harlowe] to John Harlowe, Esq.

My dear and ever-honoured uncle,

I HAVE nobody now but you, to whom I can apply, with hope, so much as to have my humble addresses opened and read. My aunt Hervey has given me commands which I want to have explained; but she has forbid me writing to her. Hereupon I took the liberty to write to my papa and mamma: you will see, sir, by the torn one, and by both being returned *un*-opened, what has been the result. This, sir, perhaps you know: but, as you know not the *contents* of the disgraced letters, I beseech you to read them both, that you may be a witness for me, that they are not filled with complaints, with expostulations, nor contain anything undutiful. Give me leave to say, sir, that if deaf-eared anger will neither grant *me* a hearing, nor *what I write* a perusal, some time hence the hard-heartedness may be regretted. I beseech you, dear, good sir, to let me know what is meant by sending me to my uncle Antony's rather than to your house, or to my aunt's, or elsewhere? If it be for what I apprehend it to be, life will not be supportable upon the terms: I beg also to know, WHEN I am to be turned out of doors!—My heart strongly gives me, that once I am compelled to leave this house, I never shall see it more.

It becomes me, however, to declare, that I write not this through perverseness, or in resentment; God knows my heart, I do not!—But the treatment I apprehend I shall meet with if carried to my other uncle's, will, in all probability, give the finishing stroke to the distresses, the *undeserved* distresses I will be bold to call them, of

Your once highly favoured,
but now most unhappy, kinswoman,
CL. HARLOWE

Letter 60: MISS CLARISSA HARLOWE TO MISS HOWE

Monday morning, March 27

THIS morning early my uncle Harlowe came hither. He sent me up the enclosed very tender letter. It has made me wish I *could* oblige him!—You'll see how Mr Solmes's ill qualities are glossed over in it. What blemishes does affection hide!— So, perhaps, may they say to me, what faults does antipathy bring to light! Be pleased to send me back this letter of my uncle's, by the first return. I may possibly try to account for, and wish to obviate, my being such a formidable creature to my whole family, as I am represented in it.

[Letter 60.1: John Harlowe to Clarissa Harlowe]

Sunday night, or rather Monday morning

I MUST answer you, though against my own intention. Everybody loves you; and you know they do. The very ground you walk upon is dear to most of us. But how can we resolve to see you? There is no standing against your looks and language. It is the strength of our love makes us decline to see you. How *can* we, when you are resolved not to *do* what we are resolved you *shall* do? I never, for my part, loved any creature as I loved you from your youth till now. And indeed, as I have often said, never was there a young creature so deserving of our love. But what is come to you now!—Alas! alas, my dear! How you fail in the trial!

I have read the letters you enclosed. At a proper time, I may show them to my brother and sister. But they will receive nothing from you at present.

For my part, I could not read your letter to myself, without being unmanned. How can you be so unmoved yourself, yet be so able to move everybody else? How could you send such a letter to Mr Solmes? Fie upon you!—How strangely are you altered?

Then to treat your brother and sister as you did, that they don't care to write to you, or to see you—Don't you know where it is written, that *soft answers turn away wrath?* But if you will trust to your sharp-pointed wit, you may wound: but a club will beat down a sword: and how can you expect, that they who are hurt by you will not hurt you again?—Was this the way you used to take to make us all adore you, as we did?—No, it was your gentleness of heart and manners that made everybody, even strangers, at first sight treat you as a lady, and call you a lady, though not born one, as your mamma was, any more than your sister; while she was only plain Miss Harlowe, or Miss Arabella. If you *were* envied, why should you sharpen envy, and file up its teeth to an edge?—You see I write like an impartial man, and as one that loves you still!

But since you have displayed your talents and spared nobody, and moved everybody without being moved, you have but made us stand the closer and firmer together. This is what I likened to an embattled phalanx, once before. Your aunt Hervey forbids your writing, for the same reason that I must not countenance it. We are all afraid to see you, because we know we shall be made as so many fools. Nay, your mamma is so afraid of you, that once or twice, when she thought you was coming to force yourself into her presence, she shut the door and locked herself in, because she knew she must not see you upon *your* terms, and you are resolved you will not see her upon *hers*.

Resolve but to oblige us all, my dearest Miss Clary, and you shall see how we will clasp you every one by turns, to our rejoicing hearts!—If the one man has not the wit, and the parts, and the person, of the other, no one breathing has a worse heart than that other. And is not the love of all your friends, and a sober man (if he be not so polished), to be preferred to a debauchee, though ever so fine a man to look at? You have such fine talents, that you will be adored by the one: but the other has as much advantage in those respects, as you have yourself, and will not set by them one straw: for husbands are sometimes jealous of their authority with witty wives. You will have, in one, a man of virtue. Had you not been so rudely affronting to him, he would have made your ears tingle with what he could have told you of the other.

Come, my dear niece, let me have the honour of doing with you what nobody else yet has been able to do. Your father, mother, and I will divide the pleasure, and the *honour*, I will again call it, between us; and all past offences shall be forgiven; and Mr Solmes, we will engage, shall take nothing amiss hereafter that is just.

He knows, he says, what a jewel that man will have, who can obtain your favour; and he will think light of all he has suffered, or shall suffer, in obtaining you.

Dear, sweet creature, oblige us: and oblige us with a grace. It *must* be done, whether with a grace or not. I do assure you it *must*. You must not conquer father, mother, uncles, everybody. Depend upon that.

I have sat up half the night to write this. You don't know how I am touched at reading yours, and writing this. Yet will I be at Harlowe Place early in the morning. So, upon reading this, if you will oblige us all, send me word to come up to your apartment: and I will lead you down, and present you to the embraces of everyone. And you will then see you have more of a brother and sister, than of late your prejudices will let you think you have. This from one who used to love to style himself

Your paternal uncle,
JOHN HARLOWE

In about an hour after this kind letter was given me, my uncle sent up to know if he should be a welcome visitor, upon the terms mentioned in his letter? He bid Betty bring him down a verbal answer: a written one, he said, would be a bad sign; and he bid her therefore not bring a letter. But I had just finished the enclosed transcription of one I had been writing. She made a difficulty to carry it; but was prevailed upon to oblige me, by a token which these Mrs Betty's cannot withstand.

[*Letter 60.2: Clarissa Harlowe to John Harlowe*]

Dear and honoured sir,

How you rejoice me by your condescending goodness!—So kind, so paternal a letter!—so soothing to a wounded heart; and of late what I have been so little used to!—How am I affected with it! Tell me not, dear sir, of my way of writing: your letter has more moved *me* than I ever could move *anybody!*—It has made me, with all my heart, wish I could entitle myself to be visited upon your own terms; and to be led down to my papa and mamma, by so good and so kind an uncle.

I will tell you, dearest sir, what I will do to make my peace. I have no doubt that Mr Solmes would greatly prefer my sister to such a strange, and averse creature as me. His chief, or one of his chief motives to address me, is, as I have reason to believe, the contiguity of my grandfather's estate to his own. I will resign it; for ever I will resign it: and the resignation must be good, because I will never marry at all: I will make it over to my sister, and her heirs for ever. I shall have no heirs, but my brother and her; and I will receive, as of my papa's bounty, such an annuity (not in lieu of the estate, but as *of* his bounty), as he shall be pleased to grant me, if it be ever so small; and whenever I disoblige him, he shall withdraw it at his pleasure.

Will not this be accepted?—Sure it must!—Sure it will!—I beg of you, dearest sir, to propose it; and second it with your interest. This will answer every end. My sister has a high opinion of Mr Solmes. I never can have *any* in the light he is proposed to me. But as my sister's husband, he will be always entitled to my respect; and shall have it.

If this be accepted, grant me, sir, the honour of a visit; and do me then the inexpressible pleasure of leading me down to the feet of my honoured parents, and they shall find me the most dutiful of children; and to the arms of my brother and sister, and they shall find me the most obliging and most affectionate of sisters.

I wait, sir, for your answer to this proposal, made with the whole heart of

Your dutiful and most obliged niece,
CL. HARLOWE

Monday noon

I HOPE this will be accepted: for Betty tells me that my uncle Antony and my aunt Hervey are sent for; and not Mr Solmes, which I look upon as a favourable circumstance. With what cheerfulness will I assign over this envied estate!—What a much more valuable consideration shall I part with it for!—the love and favour of all my relations!—that love and favour, which I used for eighteen years together to rejoice in, and be distinguished by!—And what a charming pretence will this afford me of breaking with Mr Lovelace! And how easy will it possibly make him, to part with *me!*

I found this morning in the usual place, a letter from him in answer, I suppose, to mine of Friday, which I deposited not till Saturday. But I have not opened it; nor will I, till I see what effect this new offer will have.

Let me but be permitted to avoid the man I hate; and I will give up, with all my heart, the man I could prefer. To renounce the one, were I really to value him as you seem to imagine, can give but a temporary concern, which time and discretion will make light: this is a sacrifice which a child owes to parents and friends, if they insist upon its being made. But the other, to marry a man one *cannot endure*, is not only a dishonest thing, as to the man; but it is enough to make a creature who wishes to be a good wife, a bad or indifferent one, as I once wrote to the man himself: and then she can hardly be either a good mistress; a good friend; or anything but a discredit to her family, and a bad example to all around her.

Methinks I am loath, in the *suspense* I am in at present, to deposit this, because I shall then leave you in as *great*: but having been prevented by Betty's officiousness twice, I will now go down to my little poultry; and if I have an opportunity, will leave it in the usual place, where I hope to find something from you.

Letter 61: MISS CLARISSA HARLOWE TO MISS HOWE

Monday afternoon, March 27

I HAVE deposited my narrative down to this day noon; but I hope soon to follow it with another letter, that I may keep you as little a while as possible in that suspense, which I am so much affected by at this moment: for my heart is disturbed at every foot I hear stir; and every door below that I hear open or shut.

They have been all assembled some time, and are in close debate, I believe: but can there be room for long debate upon a proposal, which, if accepted, will so effectually answer all their views?—Can they insist a moment longer upon my having Mr Solmes, when they see what sacrifices I am ready to make, to be freed from his addresses?—Oh but I suppose the struggle is, first, with Bella's nicety, to persuade her to accept of the estate, and of the husband; and next, with her pride, to take her *sister's refusals*, as she once phrased it!—Or, it may be, my brother is insisting upon equivalents for his reversion in the estate: and these sort of things take up but too much the attention of some of our family. To these, no doubt, one, or both, it must be owing that my proposal admits of so much consideration. I want, methinks, to see what Lovelace in his letter says. But I will deny myself *this* piece of curiosity, till that which is raised by my present suspense is answered— Excuse me, my dear, that I thus trouble you with my uncertainties. But I have no employment, nor heart, if I had, to pursue any other but what my pen affords me.

Monday evening

WOULD you believe it?—Betty, by anticipation, tells me, that I am to be refused. I am 'a vile, artful creature. Everybody is too good to me. My uncle Harlowe has been *taken in*, that's the phrase. They knew how it would be, if he either wrote to me or saw me. He has, however, been made ashamed to be so wrought upon—A pretty thing, truly, in the eye of the world, were they to take me at my word. It would look as if they had treated me thus hardly, as *I* think it, for this very purpose. My peculiars, particularly Miss Howe, would give it that turn; and I myself could mean nothing by it but to see if it would be accepted, in order to strengthen my own arguments against Mr Solmes. It was amazing, that it could admit of a moment's deliberation: that anything could be *supposed* to be done in it. It was equally against law and equity: and a fine security Miss Bella would have, or Mr Solmes, when I could resume it when I would!—My *brother* and *she* my heirs! Oh the artful creature!—*I* to resolve to live single, when Lovelace was so *sure* of me!—and everywhere declared as much!—and could, whenever he pleased, if my husband, claim under the will!—Then the insolence—the confidence—(as Betty mincingly told me, that one said; you may easily guess who) that she, who was so justly in disgrace for downright rebellion, should pretend to prescribe to the whole family!—should name a husband for her elder sister!—What a triumph would her obstinacy go away with, to delegate her commands, not as from a prison, as she called it, but as from her throne, to her elders and betters; and to her father and mother too!—Amazing, perfectly amazing! that anybody could argue upon such a plan as this! It was a master-stroke of *finesse!*—it was ME in perfection!—Surely my uncle Harlowe will never be so taken in again!'

All this was the readier told me, because it was against me, and would tease and vex me. But as some of this fine recapitulation implied that somebody spoke up for me, I was curious to know who it was: but Betty would not tell me, for fear I should have the consolation to find that *all* were not against me.

But do you not see, my dear, what a sad creature she is whom you honour with your friendship!—You could not doubt your influence over me: why did you not let me know myself a little better?—Why did you not take the friendly liberty I have always taken with you, and tell me my faults, and what a specious hypocrite I am? For if my brother and sister could make such discoveries, how is it possible, that faults so enormous (you could see *others*, you thought, of a *more secret* nature!) could escape your penetrating eye?

Well, but now, it seems they are debating how and by whom to answer me: for they know not, nor *are* they to know, that Mrs Betty has told me all these fine things. One desires to be excused, it seems: another chooses not to have anything to say to me: another has enough of me: and of writing to so ready a scribbler there will be no end.

Thus are those imputed qualifications which used so lately to gain me applause, now become my crimes; so much do disgust and anger alter the property of things.

What will be the result of their debate, I suppose will somehow or other be communicated to me by and by. But let me tell you, my dear, that I am made so desperate, that I am afraid to open Mr Lovelace's letter, lest, in the humour I am in, I should do something, if I find it not exceptionable, that may give me repentance as long as I live!

Monday night

THIS moment the following letter is brought me by Betty.

[*Letter 61.1: James Harlowe, Jun. to Clarissa Harlowe*]

Miss Cunning-ones,   Monday, 5 o'clock
YOUR fine, new proposal is thought unworthy of a particular answer. Your uncle Harlowe is ashamed to be so taken in. Have you no new fetch for your uncle Antony? Go round with us, child, now your hand's in. But I was bid to write only one line, that you might not complain, as you did of your worthy sister, for the freedoms you provoked: it is this—prepare yourself. Tomorrow you go to my uncle Antony's. That's all, child.

JAMES HARLOWE

I was vexed to the heart at this: and immediately, in the warmth of resentment, wrote the enclosed to my uncle Harlowe; who, it seems, stays here this night.

[*Letter 61.2: Clarissa Harlowe] to John Harlowe, Esq.*

Honoured sir,   Monday night
I FIND I am a very sad creature, and did not know it. I wrote not to my brother. To *you*, sir, I wrote. From *you* I hope the honour of an answer. No one reveres her uncles more than I do. Nevertheless, I will be bold to say, that the distance, great

as it is, between uncle and niece, excludes not such a hope: and I think I have not made a proposal that deserves to be treated with scorn.

Forgive me, sir—My heart is full—Perhaps one day you may think you have been *prevailed upon* (for that is plainly the case!) to join to treat me as I do not deserve to be treated. If *you* are ashamed, as my brother hints, of having expressed any returning tenderness to me, God help me! I see I have no mercy to expect from anybody! But, sir, from *your* pen let me have an answer; I humbly beseech it of you. Till my brother can recollect what belongs to a sister, I will take no answer from *him* to the letter I wrote to *you*, nor any commands whatever.

I move everybody! This, sir, is what you are pleased to mention—but whom have I moved?—One person in the family has more moving ways than I have, or he could never so undeservedly have made everybody ashamed to show any tenderness to a poor distressed child of the same family.

Return me not this with contempt, or torn, or unanswered, I beseech you. My papa has a title to do that, or anything, by this child: but from no other person in the world of your sex, ought a young creature of mine (while she preserves a supplicating spirit), to be so treated.

When what I have before written in the humblest strain has met with such strange constructions, I am afraid that this unguarded scrawl will be very ill-received. But I beg, sir, you will oblige me with one line, be it ever so harsh, in answer to my proposal. I still think it ought to be attended to. I will enter into the most solemn engagements to make it valid by a perpetual single life. In a word, anything I *can* do, I *will* do, to be restored to all your favours. More I cannot say, but that I am, very undeservedly,

                                        A most unhappy creature

Betty scrupled again to carry this letter; and said, she should have anger; and I should but have it returned in scraps and bits.

I must take that chance, I said: I only desired she would deliver it as directed.

Sad doings! very sad! she said, that young ladies should so violently set themselves against their duty!

I told her, she should have the liberty to say what she pleased, so she would but be my messenger that one time—And down she went with it.

I bid her, if she could, slide it into my uncle's hand, unseen; at least, unseen by my brother or sister, for fear it should meet, through *their* good offices, with the fate she had bespoken for it.

She would not undertake for that, she said.

I am now in expectation of the result. But having so little ground to hope for either favour or mercy, I opened Mr Lovelace's letter.

I would send it to you, my dear, as well as those I shall enclose, by this conveyance; but not being able at present to determine in what manner I shall answer it, I will give myself the trouble of abstracting it here, while I am waiting for what may offer from the letter just gone down.

'He laments, as usual, my ill opinion of him and readiness to believe everything to his disadvantage. He puts into plain English, as I supposed he would, my hint that I might be happier if, by any rashness he might be guilty of to Solmes, he should come to an untimely end himself.'

He is concerned, he says, 'that the violence he had expressed on his extreme apprehensiveness of losing me, should have made him guilty of anything I had so much reason to resent.'

He owns, 'That he is passionate: all good-natured men, he says, are so, and a sincere man cannot hide it.' But appeals to me, 'whether, if any occasion in the world could excuse the rashness of his expressions, it would not be his present dreadful situation, through my indifference and the malice of his enemies.'

He says, 'he has more reason than ever, from the contents of my last, to apprehend that I shall be prevailed upon by force, if not by fair means, to fall in with my brother's measures; and sees but too plainly that I am preparing him to expect it.

'Upon this presumption, he supplicates, with the utmost earnestness, that I will not give way to the malice of his enemies.

'Solemn vows of reformation and everlasting truth and obligingness he makes; all in the style of desponding humility; yet calls it a cruel turn upon him, to impute his protestations to a consciousness of the necessity there is for making them from his bad character.

'He despises himself, he solemnly protests, for his past follies: thanks God he has seen his error; and nothing but my more particular instructions are wanting to perfect his reformation.

'He promises that he will do everything that I shall think he can do with honour, to bring about a reconciliation with my father; and will even, if I insist upon it, make the first overture to my brother and treat him as his own brother, because he is mine, if he will not by new affronts revive the remembrance of the past.

'He begs, in the most earnest and humble manner, for one half-hour's interview; undertaking by a key, which he owns he has to the garden door, leading into the *coppice*, as we call it (if I will but unbolt the door), to come into the garden at night, and wait till I have an opportunity to come to him, that he may reassure me of the truth of all he writes, and of the affection, and, if needful, protection, of all his family.

'He presumes not, he says, to write by way of menace to me; but if I refuse him this favour, he knows not (so desperate have some strokes in my letter made him) what his despair may make him do.'

He asks me, 'determined as my friends are, and far as they have already gone and declare they will go, what I can propose to do to avoid having Mr Solmes, if I am carried to my uncle Antony's; unless I resolve to accept of the protection he has offered to procure me; or except I will escape to London, or elsewhere, while I *can* escape?'

He advises me, 'to sue to *your* mamma for her private reception of me; only till I can obtain possession of my own estate, and procure my friends to be reconciled to me; which he is sure they will be desirous to *be*, the moment I am out of their power.'

He apprises me (it is still my wonder how he comes by his intelligence!), 'that my friends have written to my cousin Morden, to represent matters to him in their own partial way; nor doubt they to influence him on their side of the question.

'That all this shows I have but *one way*, if none of my own friends or intimates will receive me.

'If I will transport him with the honour of my choice of this *one way*, settlements shall be drawn, with proper blanks, which I shall fill up as I please. Let him but have my commands from my own mouth; all my doubts and scruples from my own lips; and only a repetition that I will not, on any consideration, be Solmes's wife; and he shall be easy. But after such a letter as I have written, nothing but an interview can make him so.' He beseeches me, therefore, 'to unbolt the door, *as that very night*—If I receive not this time enough, *this night*—and he will in a disguise, that shall not give a suspicion who he is if he should be seen come to the garden door, in hopes to open it with his key; nor will he have any other lodging than in the coppice both nights: watching every wakeful hour for the propitious unbolting, unless he has a letter with my orders to the contrary, or to make some other appointment.'

This letter was dated yesterday: so he was there last night, I suppose; and will be there this night; and I have not written a line to him: and now it is too late were I determined *what* to write.

I hope he will not go to Mr Solmes!—I hope he will not come hither!—If he does, I will break with him for ever.

What have I to do with such headstrong spirits! I wish I had never—but what signifies wishing?—I am strangely perplexed—But I need not have told you this, after such a representation of my situation.

Letter 62: MISS CLARISSA HARLOWE TO MISS HOWE

Tuesday morning, 7 o'clock

MY uncle has vouchsafed to answer me. This is his letter; but just now brought me, although written last night; late, I suppose.

[*Letter 62.1: John Harlowe to Clarissa Harlowe*]

Monday night

Miss Clary,

SINCE you are grown such a bold challenger, and teach us all our duty, though you will not practise your own, I *must* answer you—Nobody wants your estate from you. Are *you*, who refuse everybody's advice, to prescribe a husband to your *sister?* Your letter to Mr Solmes is inexcusable. I blamed you for it before. Your parents *will* be obeyed. It is fit they *should.* Your mamma has nevertheless prevailed to have your going to your uncle Antony's put off till Thursday: yet owns you deserve not that, or any other favour from her. I will receive no more of your letters. You are too artful for me. You are an ungrateful and unreasonable child! You will have your will paramount to everybody's. How are you altered!

Your displeased uncle,
JOHN HARLOWE

To be carried away on Thursday—to the moated house—to the chapel—to Solmes! How can I think of this!—They will make me desperate!

Tuesday morn, eight o'clock

I HAVE another letter from Mr Lovelace. I opened it, with the expectation of its being filled with bold and free complaints, on my not writing to prevent his two nights watching, in weather not extremely agreeable. But, instead of complaints, he is 'full of tender concern lest I may have been prevented by indisposition, or by the closer confinement which he has frequently cautioned me that I may expect.'

He says, 'he had been in different disguises loitering about our garden and park wall all the day on Sunday last; and all Sunday night was wandering about the coppice, and near the back door. It rained; and he has got a great cold, attended with feverishness, and so hoarse, that he has almost lost his voice.'

Why did he not flame out in his letter?—Treated, as I am treated by my friends, it is dangerous for me to lie under the sense of an obligation to anyone's patience, when that person suffers in health for my sake.

'He had no shelter, he says, but under the great overgrown ivy, which spreads wildly round the heads of two or three oaklings; and that was soon wet through.'

You and I, my dear, once thought ourselves obliged to the natural shade they afforded us in a sultry day.

I can't help saying, I am sorry he has suffered for my sake—but 'tis his own seeking!

His letter is dated last night at eight: 'And indisposed as he is, he tells me that he will watch till ten, in hopes of my giving him the meeting he so earnestly requests. And after that, he has a mile to walk to his horse and servant; and four miles then to ride to his inn.'

He owns, 'that he has an intelligencer in our family; who has failed him for a day or two past: and not knowing how I do, or how I may be treated, his anxiety is the greater.'

This circumstance gives me to guess who this treacherous man is: one Joseph Leman: the very creature employed and confided in, more than any other, by my brother.

This is not an honourable way of proceeding in Mr Lovelace—Did he learn this infamous practice of corrupting the servants of other families at the French Court, where he resided a good while?

I have been often jealous of this Leman in my little airings and poultry-visits: I have thought him (doubly obsequious as he was always to me) my brother's spy upon me; and although he obliged me by his hastening out of the garden and poultry-yard, whenever I came into either, have wondered that from his reports my liberties of those kinds have not been abridged. So, possibly this man may take a bribe of both, and yet betray both. Worthy views want not such obliquities as these on either side. An honest mind must rise into indignation both at the traitor-maker and the traitor.

'He presses with the utmost earnestness for an interview. He would not offer, he says, to disobey my last personal commands that he should not endeavour to attend me again in the wood-house. But says he can give me such reasons for my permitting him to wait upon my father or uncles, as he hopes will be approved by me: for he cannot help observing that it is no more suitable to my own spirit than to his, that he, a man of fortune and family, should be obliged to pursue such a clandestine address, as would only became a vile fortune-hunter. But if I will give my consent for his visiting me like a man, and a gentleman, no treatment shall provoke him to forfeit his temper.

'His uncle will accompany him, if I please: or his aunt Lawrance will first make the visit to my mamma, or to my aunt Hervey, or even to my uncles, if I choose it. And such terms shall be offered, as *shall* have weight upon them.

'He begs that I will not deny him making a visit to Mr Solmes. By all that's good, he vows that it shall not be with the least intention either to hurt or affront him; but only to set before him calmly and rationally, the consequences that may possibly flow from so fruitless a perseverance; as well as the ungenerous folly of it, to a mind so noble as mine. He repeats his own resolution to attend my pleasure, and Mr Morden's arrival and advice, for the reward of his own patience.

'It is impossible, he says, but one of these methods *must* do. Presence, he observes, even of a disliked person, takes off the edge from resentments which absence whets, and makes keen.

'He therefore most earnestly repeats his importunities for the supplicated interview.' Says, 'he has business of consequence in London: but cannot stir from the inconvenient spot where he has for some time resided in disguises unworthy of himself, until he can be absolutely certain that I shall not be prevailed upon, either by force or otherwise; and until he find me delivered from the insults of my brother. Nor ought this to be an indifferent point to one, for whose sake all the world reports me to be used so unworthily as I am used—But *one* remark, he says, he cannot help making: that did my friends know the little favour I show him, and the very great distance I keep him at, they would have no reason to confine me on his account: and *another*, that they themselves seem to think him entitled to a different usage, and expect that he receives it; when, in truth, what he meets with from me is exactly what they wish him to meet with, excepting in favour of the correspondence I honour him with: upon which, he says, he puts the highest value, and for the sake of which he has cheerfully submitted to a thousand indignities.

'He renews his professions of reformation: he is convinced, he says, that he has already run a long and dangerous course; and that it is high time to think of returning. It must be from proper convictions, he says, that a person who has lived too gay a life resolves to reclaim before age or sufferings come upon him.

'All generous spirits, he observes, hate compulsion. Upon this observation he dwells; but regrets that he is likely to owe all his hopes to this compulsion; this *injudicious* compulsion, he justly calls it; and none to my esteem for him. Although he presumes upon some merit in his implicit regard to my will: in the bearing the daily indignities offered not only to him, but to his relations, by my brother: in the nightly watchings and risks which he runs, in all weathers; and which his present indisposition makes him mention, or he had not debased the nobleness of his passion for me by such a selfish instance.' I cannot but say, I am sorry the man is not well.

I am afraid to ask you, my dear, what *you* would have done, thus situated. But what I *have* done, I *have* done. In a word, I wrote, 'that I would, if possible, give him a meeting tomorrow night, between the hours of nine and twelve, by the ivy summer-house, or in it, or near the great cascade at the bottom of the garden; and would unbolt the door that he might come in by his own key. But that, if I found the meeting impracticable, or should change my mind, I would signify as much by another line; which he must wait for until it were dark.'

Tuesday, eleven o'clock

I AM just returned from depositing my billet. How diligent is this man! It is plain he was in waiting: for I had walked but a few paces after I had deposited it, when, my heart misgiving me, I returned, to have taken it back, in order to reconsider it as I walked, and whether I should, or should not, let it go: but I found it gone.

In all probability there was but a brick wall of a few inches thick between Mr Lovelace and me at the very time I put the letter under the brick.

I am come back dissatisfied with myself. But I think, my dear, there can be no harm in meeting him: if I do *not*, he may take some violent measures: what he knows of the treatment I meet with in malice to him, and with a view to frustrate all his hopes, may make him desperate. His behaviour last time I saw him, under the disadvantages of time and place, and surprised as I was, gives me no apprehension of anything but discovery. What he requires is not unreasonable, and cannot affect my future choice and determination: it is only to assure him from my own lips that I will never be the wife of a man I hate. If I have not an opportunity to meet without hazard or detection, he must once more bear the disappointment. All his trouble, and mine too, is owing to his faulty character. This, although I hate tyranny and arrogance in all shapes, makes me think less of the risks he runs and the fatigues he undergoes, than otherwise I should do; and still less, as my sufferings (derived from the same source) are greater than his.

Betty confirms the intimation that I must go to my uncle's on Thursday. She was sent on purpose to direct me to prepare myself for going, and to help me to get up everything in order to it.

Letter 63: MISS CLARISSA HARLOWE TO MISS HOWE

Tuesday, three o'clock, March 28

I HAVE mentioned several times the pertness of Mrs Betty to me; and now, having a little time upon my hands, I will give you a short dialogue that passed just now between us: it may, perhaps, be a little relief to you from the dull subjects with which I am perpetually teasing you.

As she attended me at dinner, she took notice that nature is satisfied with a very little nourishment: and thus she complimentally proved it—For, miss, said she, you eat nothing, yet never looked more charmingly in your life.

As to the former part of your speech, Betty, said I, you observe well; and I have often thought, when I have seen how healthy the children of the labouring poor *look*, and *are*, with empty stomachs and hardly a good meal in a week, that Providence is very kind to its creatures in this respect, as well as in all others, in making *much* not necessary to the support of life; when three parts in four of its creatures, if it were, would not know how to obtain it. It puts me in mind of two proverbial sentences which are full of admirable meaning.

What, pray, miss, are they? I love to hear you talk when you are so sedate as you seem now to be.

The one is to the purpose we are speaking of; *poverty is the mother of health*: and let me tell you, Betty, if I had a better appetite and were to encourage it, with so little rest, and so much distress and persecution, I don't think I should be able to preserve my reason.

There's no inconvenience but has its convenience, said Betty, giving me proverb for proverb. But what is the other, madam?

That the *pleasures of the mighty are obtained by the tears of the poor*. It is but reaonable therefore, methinks, that the plenty of the one should be followed by distempers; and that the indigence of the other should be attended with that health which makes all its other discomforts light on the comparison. And hence a third proverb, Betty, since you are an admirer of proverbs: *better a bare foot than none at all*; that is to say, than not to be able to walk.

She was mightily taken with what I said. See, said she, what a fine thing scholarship is!—I, said she, had always, from a girl, a taste for reading, though it were but in *Mother Goose*, and concerning the *Fairies* (And then she took genteelly a pinch of snuff): could but my parents *have let go as fast as I pulled*, I should have been a very happy creature.

Very likely you would have made great improvements, Betty: but as it is, I cannot say but since I have had the favour of your attendance in this *intimate* manner, I have heard smarter things from you than I have heard at table from some of my brother's fellow-collegians.

Your servant, dear miss, dropping me one of her best curtsies: so fine a judge as you are!—It is enough to make one very proud. Then, with another pinch—I cannot indeed but say, bridling upon it, that I have heard famous scholars often and often say very silly things: things I should be ashamed myself to say—but I thought they did it out of humility, and in condescension to those who had not their learning.

That she might not be too proud, I told her I would observe that the liveliness and quickness she so happily discovered in herself was not so much an honour to her, as what she owed to her *sex*; which, as I had observed in many instances, had great advantages over the other, in all the powers that related to imagination: and hence, Mrs Betty, you'll take notice, as I have of late had opportunity to do, that your own talent at repartee and smartness, when it has *something to work upon*, displays itself to more advantage than could well be expected from one whose friends, to speak in your own phrase, could not *let go so fast as you pulled*.

The wench gave me a proof of the truth of my observation, in a manner still more alert than I had expected. If, said she, our sex have so much advantage in *smartness*, it is the less to be wondered at that *you*, miss, who have had such an education, should outdo all the men and women too, that come near you.

Bless me, Betty, said I, what a proof do you give me of your wit and your courage at the same time! This is outdoing yourself. It would make young ladies less proud, and more apprehensive, were they generally attended by such smart servants, and their mouths permitted to be unlocked upon them, as yours has lately been upon me!—But, take away, Mrs Betty.

Why, miss, you have eat nothing at all—I hope you are not displeased with your dinner for anything I have said.

No, Mrs Betty, I am pretty well used to your freedoms, now, you know—I am not displeased in the main, to observe that were the succession of modern fine ladies to be extinct, it might be supplied from those whom they place in the next rank to themselves, their chambermaids and confidants. Your young mistress has contributed a great deal to this quickness of yours. She always preferred your company to mine. As *you pulled, she let go*; and so, Mrs Betty, you have gained by *her* conversation what I have lost.

Why, miss, if you come to that, nobody says better things than Miss Harlowe. I could tell you one, if *I pleased*, upon my observing to her that you lived of late upon air, and had no stomach to anything, yet looked as charmingly as ever—

I dare say it was a very good-natured one, Mrs Betty!—Do you then *please* that I shall hear it?

Only this, miss, *that your stomachfulness had swallowed up your stomach*; and *that obstinacy was meat, drink, and cloth to you.*

Ay, Mrs Betty; and *did* she say this?—I hope she laughed when she said it, as she does at all her *good things*, as she calls them. It was very smart, and very witty. I wish my mind were so much at ease as to aim at being witty too. But if you admire such sententious sayings, I'll help you to another; and that is, *encouragement and approbation make people show talents they were never suspected to have*; and this will do both for mistress and maid: and another I'll furnish you with, the contrary of the former, that will do only for me; that *persecution and discouragement depress* ingenuous *minds, and blunt the edge of lively imaginations*—And hence may my sister's brilliancy and my stupidity be both accounted for. *Ingenuous*, you must know, Mrs Betty, and *ingenious*, are two things; and I would not arrogate the latter to myself.

Lord, miss, said the foolish, you know a great deal for your years—You are a very learned young lady!—What pity—

None of your *pities*, Mrs Betty. I know what you'd say. But tell me, if you can, is it resolved that I shall be carried to my uncle Antony's on Thursday?

I was willing to reward myself for the patience she had made me exercise, by getting at what intelligence I could from her.

Why, miss, seating herself at a little distance (excuse my sitting down), with the snuff-box tapped very smartly, the lid opened and a pinch taken with a dainty finger and thumb, the other three fingers distendedly bent, and with a fine flourish—I cannot but say, that it is my opinion, you will certainly go on Thursday; and this *noless foless*, as I have heard my young lady say in FRENCH.

Whether I am *willing* or *not willing*, you mean, I suppose, Mrs Betty?

You have it, miss.

Well but, Betty, I have no mind to be turned out of doors so suddenly. Do you think I could not be permitted to tarry one week longer?

How can I tell, miss?

Oh Mrs Betty, you can tell a great deal, if *you please*. But here I am forbid writing to any one of my family; none of it now will come near *me*; nor will any of it permit me to see *them*. How shall I do to make my request known, to tarry here a week or fortnight longer!

Why, miss, I fancy, if you were to show a compliable temper, your friends would show a compliable one too. But would you expect favours, and grant none?

Smartly put, Betty! But who knows what may be the result of my being carried to my uncle Antony's?

Who knows, miss!—Why anybody will guess what may be the result.

As how, Betty?

As how! repeated the pert wench, why, miss, you will stand in your own light, as you have hitherto done: and your parents, as such good parents *ought*, will be obeyed.

If, Mrs Betty, I had not been used to your *oughts*, and to have my duty laid down to me by your oraculous wisdom, I should be apt to stare at the liberty of your speech.

You seem angry, miss. I hope I take no unbecoming liberty.

If thou really think'st thou dost not, thy ignorance is more to be pitied than thy pertness resented. I wish thou'd'st leave me to myself.

When young ladies fall out with their *own* duty, it is not much to be wondered at that they are angry at anybody who do *theirs*.

That's a very pretty saying, Mrs Betty!—I see plainly what *thy* duty is in *thy* notion, and am obliged to those who taught it thee.

Everybody takes notice, miss, that you can say very cutting words in a cool manner, and yet not call names, as I have known *some* gentlefolks, as well as others, do, when in a passion. But I wish you had permitted 'Squire Solmes to see you; he would have told you such stories of 'Squire Lovelace, as would have turned your heart against him for ever.

And know you any of the particulars of those sad stories?

Indeed, I don't; but you'll hear all at your uncle Antony's, I suppose; and a great deal more, perhaps, than you will like to hear.

Let me hear what I will, I am determined against Mr Solmes, were it to cost me my life.

If you are, miss, the Lord have mercy on you! For what with this letter of yours to 'Squire Solmes, whom they so much value, and what with their antipathy to 'Squire Lovelace, whom they hate, they will have no patience with you.

What will they do, Betty? They won't kill me? What *will* they do?

Kill you! No!—But you will not be suffered to stir from thence, till you have complied with your duty. And *no pen and ink* will be allowed you, as here; where they are of opinion you make no good use of it: Nor would it be allowed here, only as they intend so soon to send you away to your uncle's. Nobody will be permitted to see you, or to correspond with you. What farther will be done, I can't say; and, if I could, it may not be proper. But you may prevent it all, by one word: and I wish you would, miss. All then would be easy and happy. And, if I may speak my mind, I see not why one man is not as good as another: why, especially, a sober man is not as good as a rake.

Well, Betty, said I, sighing, all thy impertinence goes for nothing. But I see I am destined to be a very unhappy creature. Yet will I venture upon one request more to them.

And so, quite sick of the pert creature, and of myself, I retired to my closet, and wrote a few lines to my uncle Harlowe, notwithstanding his prohibition; in order to get a reprieve from being carried away so soon as Thursday next, if I must go. And this, that I might, if complied with, suspend the appointment I have made with Mr Lovelace; for my heart misgives me, as to meeting him; and that more and more, I know not why. Under the superscription of the letter, I wrote these words: 'Pray, dear sir, be pleased to give this a reading.'

This is the copy of what I wrote:

[*Letter 63.1: Clarissa Harlowe to John Harlowe*]

                                                    Tuesday afternoon
Honoured sir,

LET me this once be heard with patience, and have my petition granted. It is only that I may not be hurried away so soon as next Thursday.

Why should the poor girl be turned out of doors so suddenly, so disgracefully?

Procure for me, sir, one fortnight's respite. In that space of time, I hope you will all relent. My mamma shall not need to shut her door, in apprehension of seeing her disgraced child. I will not presume to think of entering her presence, or my papa's, without leave. One fortnight's respite is but a small favour for them to grant, except I am to be refused everything I ask: but it is of the highest import to my peace of mind. Procure it for me, therefore, dear sir, and you will exceedingly oblige.

Your dutiful, though greatly afflicted niece,
CL. HARLOWE

I sent this down: my uncle was not gone: and he now stays to know the result of the question put to me in the enclosed answer, which he has given to mine:

[*Letter 63.2: John Harlowe to Clarissa Harlowe*]

YOUR going to your uncle's was absolutely concluded upon for next Thursday. Nevertheless, your mamma, seconded by Mr Solmes, pleaded so strongly to indulge you, that your request for a delay will be complied with, upon one condition; and whether for a fortnight, or a shorter time, that will depend upon yourself. If you refuse this condition, your mamma declares, she will give over all further intercession for you. Nor do you deserve this favour, as you put it upon our relenting, not your own.

This condition is, that you admit of a visit from Mr Solmes, for one hour, in company of your brother, your sister, or your uncle Antony, choose which you will.

If you comply not, you go next Thursday to a house which is become so strangely odious to you of late, whether you get ready to go, or not. Answer therefore directly to the point. No evasion. Name your day and hour. Mr Solmes will neither eat you, nor drink you. Let us see whether *we* are to be complied with *in anything*, or not.

JOHN HARLOWE

After a very little deliberation, I resolved to consent to this condition. All I fear is, that Mr Lovelace's intelligencer may inform him of it; and that his apprehensions upon it may make him take some desperate resolution: especially as now (having more time given me, here) I think to write to him to suspend the interview he is possibly so sure of. I sent down the following to my uncle:

[*Letter 63.3: Clarissa Harlowe to John Harlowe*]

Honoured sir,
ALTHOUGH I see not what end the proposed condition can answer, I comply with it. I wish I could with everything expected of me. If I must name one, in whose company I am to see the gentleman, and that one *not* my mamma, whose presence I could wish to be honoured by on the occasion, let my uncle, if he pleases, be the *person*. If I must name the *day* (a long day, I doubt, will not be permitted me), let it be next Tuesday. The *hour*, four in the afternoon. The *place*, either the ivy summer-house, or in the little parlour I used to be permitted to call mine.

Be pleased, sir, nevertheless, to prevail upon my mamma to vouchsafe me her presence on the occasion. I am, sir,

> Your ever-dutiful
> CL. HARLOWE

A reply is just sent me. I thought it became my averseness to this meeting to name a distant day: but I did not expect they would have complied with it. So here is one week gained!—This is it:

[*Letter 63.4: John Harlowe to Clarissa Harlowe*]

YOU have done well to comply. We are willing to think the best of every slight instance of your duty. Yet have you seemed to consider the day as an evil day, and so put it far off. This nevertheless is granted you, as no time need to be lost, if you are as generous *after* the day, as we are condescending *before* it. Let me advise you, not to harden your mind; nor take up your resolution beforehand. Mr Solmes has more awe, and even terror, at the thoughts of seeing you, than you can have at the thoughts of seeing him. *His* motive is *love*; let not *yours* be *hatred*. My brother Antony will be present, in hopes you will deserve well of *him* by behaving well to the friend of the family. See you use him as such. Your mamma had permission to be there, if she thought fit: but says, she would not for a thousand pounds, unless you would encourage her beforehand as she wishes to be encouraged. One hint I am to give you, meantime. It is this: to make a discreet use of your pen and ink. Methinks a young creature of niceness should be less ready to write to one man, when she is designed to be another's.

This compliance, I hope, will produce greater; and then the peace of the family will be restored: which is what is heartily wished by

> Your loving uncle,
> JOHN HARLOWE

Unless it be to the purpose our hearts are set upon, you need not write again.

This man have *more terror at seeing me, than I can have at seeing him!*—How can that be? If he had half as much, he would not wish to see me!—HIS *motive love!*—Yes indeed! Love of himself!—He knows no other!—for love that deserves the name seeks the satisfaction of the beloved object more than its own!—Weighed in this scale, what a profanation is this man guilty of!

Not to take up my resolution beforehand!—That advice comes too late!

But I must *make a discreet use of my pen*. That, I doubt, as they have managed it, in the sense they mean it is as much out of my power as the other.

But *to write to one man, when I am designed for another!* What a shocking expression is that!

Repenting of my appointment with Mr Lovelace, *before* I had this favour granted me, you may believe I hesitated not a moment about revoking it *now* that I had gained such a respite. Accordingly, I wrote 'that I found it inconvenient to meet him, as I had intended: that the risk I should run of a discovery, and the mischiefs that might flow from it, could not be justified by any end that such a meeting could answer: that I found one certain servant more in my way when I took my morning and evening airings, than any other: that he knew not but that the person who might betray the secrets of a family to *him*, might be equally watchful to oblige those whom he ought to oblige, and so, if opportunity were given him, might betray me, or him, to them: that I have not been used to a conduct so faulty, as to lay myself at the mercy of servants: and was sorry he had measures to pursue that made steps necessary in his own opinion, which, in mine, were very culpable, and which no end could justify: that things drawing towards a crisis between me and my friends, an interview could avail nothing; especially as the method by which this correspondence was carried on was not suspected, and he could write all that was in his mind to write: that I expected to be at liberty to judge of what was proper and fit upon this occasion: especially as he might be assured that I would sooner choose death, than Mr Solmes.'

Tuesday night

I HAVE deposited my letter to Mr Lovelace. Threatening as things look against me, I am much better pleased with myself, than I was before. I reckon he will be a little out of humour upon it, however. But as I reserved to myself the liberty of changing my mind; and as it is easy for him to imagine there may be reasons for it *within*-doors, which he cannot judge of *without*; and I have suggested to him some of them; I should think it strange, if he acquiesces not on this occasion, with a cheerfulness, which may show me that his last letter is the genuine product of this heart: for if he be really so much concerned at his past faults as he pretends, and has for some time pretended, must he not, of course, have corrected in some degree the impetuosity of his temper? The first step to reformation, as I conceive, is to subdue sudden gusts of passion, from which frequently the greatest evils arise, and to learn to bear disappointments. If the irascible passions cannot be overcome, what opinion shall one have of the person's power over those to which bad habit, joined to *greater* temptation, gives stronger force?

Pray, my dear, be so kind as to make inquiry by some safe hand after the disguises Mr Lovelace assumes at the inn he puts up at in the poor village of Neale, [as] he calls it. If it be the same I take it to be, I never knew it was considerable enough to have a name; nor that it has an inn in it.

As he must be much there, to be so constantly near us, I would be glad to have some account of his behaviour; and what the people think of him. In such a length of time, he must give scandal, or hope of reformation. Pray, my dear, humour me in this inquiry: I have reasons for it which you shall be acquainted with another time, if the result of the inquiry discover them not.

Letter 64: MISS CLARISSA HARLOWE TO MISS HOWE

Wednesday morning, nine o'clock

I AM just returned from my morning walk, and already have received a letter from Mr Lovelace in answer to mine deposited last night. He must have had pen, ink, and paper, with him, for it was written in the coppice with this circumstance; on one knee, kneeling with the other. Not from reverence to the written-to, however, as you'll find.

Well are we instructed early to keep this sex at a distance. An undesigning open heart, where it is loath to disoblige, is easily drawn in, I see, to oblige more than ever it designed. It is too apt to govern itself by what a bold spirit is encouraged to *expect* of it. It is very difficult for a good-natured young person to give a negative where it disesteems not.

One's heart may harden and contract, as one gains experience, and when we have smarted perhaps for our easy folly: and so it *ought*, or it would be upon very unequal terms with the world.

Excuse these grave reflections. This man has vexed me heartily. I see his gentleness was *art*; fierceness, and a temper like what I have been too much used to at home, are *nature* in him. In the mind I am in, nothing shall ever make me forgive him, since there can be no good reason for his impatience on an expectation given with reserve, and absolutely revocable—*I* so much to suffer through him; yet, to be treated as if I were obliged to bear insults *from* him!—

But here you will be pleased to read his letter; which I shall enclose.

[*Letter 64.1: Robert Lovelace*] *to Miss Clarissa Harlowe*

Good God!

WHAT is now to become of me!—How shall I support this disappointment!—No new cause!—On one knee, kneeling with the other, I write!—My feet benumbed with midnight wanderings through the heaviest dews that ever fell: my wig and my linen dripping with the hoar frost dissolving on them!—Day but just breaking— sun not risen to exhale—May it never rise again!—unless it bring healing and comfort to a benighted soul!—In proportion to the joy you had inspired (ever lovely promiser!), in such proportion is my anguish!

And *are things drawing towards a crisis between your friends and you?*—Is not this a reason for me to expect, the *rather* to expect, the promised interview?

CAN *I write all that is in my mind*, say you?— Impossible!—Not the hundredth part of what is in my mind, and in my apprehension, can I write!

Oh the wavering, the changeable sex!—But can Miss Clarissa Harlowe—

Forgive me, madam!—I know not what I write!—Yet, I must, I do, insist upon your promise—or that you will condescend to find better excuses for the failure— or convince me that stronger reasons are imposed upon *you*, than those you offer— A promise *once* given; upon *deliberation* given!—the promise-*ed* only can dispense with; or some very apparent necessity imposed upon the promise-*er*, which leaves no power to perform it.

The first promise you ever made me! Life and death, perhaps, depending upon it—My heart desponding from the barbarous methods resolved to be taken with you, in malice to me!

You would sooner choose death than Solmes (How my soul spurns the competition!) Oh my beloved creature, what are these but *words!*—*Whose* words? —sweet and ever-adorable—What?—promise-breaker—must I call you?—How shall I believe the asseveration (your supposed duty in the question! persecution so flaming! hatred to me so strongly avowed!) after this instance of your so lightly dispensing with your promise!

If, my dearest life! you would prevent my distraction, or at least distracted consequences, renew the promised hope!—My *fate* is indeed upon its crisis.

Forgive me; dearest creature, forgive me!—I know I have written in too much anguish of mind!—Writing this, in the same moment that the just-dawning light has imparted to me the heavy disappointment!

I dare not re-peruse what I have written. I *must* deposit it—It may serve to show you my distracted apprehensions that this disappointment is but a prelude to the greatest of all. Nor having here any other paper, am I able to write again if I would, on this gloomy spot. Gloomy is my soul; and all nature round me partakes of my gloom!—I trust it, therefore, to your goodness! If its fervour excites your displeasure, rather than your pity, you wrong my passion; and I shall be ready to apprehend that I am intended to be the sacrifice of more miscreants than one!— Have patience with me, dearest creature!—I mean Solmes, and your brother only—But if, exerting your usual generosity, you will excuse and *re*-appoint, may that God, whom you profess to serve, and who is the God of *truth* and of *promises*, protect and bless you, for both; and for restoring to Himself, and to hope,

Ivy-Cavern in the	Your ever-adoring, yet
Coppice—day but	almost desponding
just breaking.	LOVELACE!

This is the answer I shall return.

Wednesday morning

I AM amazed, sir, at the freedom of your reproaches. Pressed and teased against convenience and inclination to give you a private meeting, am *I* to be thus challenged and upbraided, and my sex reflected upon, because I thought it prudent to change my mind?—A liberty I had reserved to myself when I made the *appointment*, as you call it. I wanted not instances of your impatient spirit to other people: yet may it be happy for me, that I have this new one; which shows that you can as little spare *me*, when I pursue the dictates of my own reason, as you do *others* for acting up to theirs. Two motives you must be governed by in this excess. The one *my easiness*; the other *your own presumption*. Since you think you have found out the *first*; and have shown so much of the *last* upon it, I am too much alarmed not to wish and desire, that your letter of this day may conclude all the trouble you have had from, or for, .

Your humble servant,
CL. HARLOWE

I BELIEVE, my dear, I may promise myself your approbation, whenever I write or speak with spirit, be it to whom it will. Indeed, I find but too much reason to exert it, since I have to deal with people who measure their conduct to me, not by what is fit or decent, right or wrong, but by what they think my temper will bear. I have, till very lately, been praised for mine; but it has always been by those who never gave me opportunity to return the compliment to themselves. Some people have acted as if they thought forbearance on *one side* absolutely necessary for them and me to be upon good terms together; and in this case have ever taken care rather to *owe* that obligation than to *lay* it. You have hinted to me that resentment is not natural to my temper, and that therefore it must soon subside. It may be so, with respect to my relations: but not to Mr Lovelace, I assure you.

Wednesday noon, March 29

WE cannot always answer for what we *can* do: but to convince you that I can keep my above resolution, with regard to this Lovelace, angry as my letter is, and three hours as it is since it was written, I assure you that I repent it not, nor will soften it, although I find it is not taken away. And yet I hardly ever before did anything in anger and that I did not repent in half an hour; and question myself in *less* than that time, whether I was right or wrong.

In this respite till Tuesday, I have a little time to look about me, as I may say, and consider of what I *have* to do, and *can* do. And Mr Lovelace's insolence will make me go very home with myself. Not that I think I can conquer my aversion to Mr Solmes. I am sure I cannot. But if I absolutely break with Mr Lovelace, and give my friends convincing proofs of it, who knows but they will restore me to their favour, and let their views in relation to the other man go off by degrees?—Or, at least, that I may be safe till my cousin Morden arrives: to whom, I think, I will write; and the rather, as Mr Lovelace has assured me that my friends have written to him to make good their side of the question.

But, with all my courage, I am exceedingly apprehensive about Tuesday next, and about what may result from my steadfastness; for steadfast I am sure I shall be. They are resolved, I am told, to try every means to induce me to comply with what they are determined upon. I am resolved to do the like, to avoid what they would force me to do. A dreadful contention between parents and child!—Each hoping to leave the other without excuse, whatever the consequence may be.

What can I do? Advise me, my dear! Something is strangely wrong somewhere! to make parents, the most indulgent till now, seem cruel in a child's eye; and a daughter, till within these few weeks thought unexceptionably dutiful, appear in their judgement a rebel!—Oh my ambitious and violent brother!—What may he have to answer for to both!—

Be pleased to remember, my dear, that your last favour was dated on Saturday. This is Wednesday: and none of mine have been taken away since. Don't let me want *your* advice. My situation is extremely difficult. But I am sure you love me still: and not the less on *that* account. Adieu, my beloved friend.

CL. HARLOWE

Letter 65: MISS HOWE TO MISS CLARISSA HARLOWE

Thursday morning, daybreak, March 30
AN accident has occasioned my remissness, as, till you know it, you may justly think my silence.

My mamma was sent for on Sunday night, with the utmost earnestness, by her cousin Larkin, whom I mentioned in one of my former.

This poor woman was always afraid of death, and was one of those weak persons who imagine that the making of their will must be an undoubted forerunner of it.

She had always said, when urged to the necessary work, that whenever she made it, she should not live long after; and, one would think, imagined she was under an obligation to prove her words: For, though she had been long bed-rid, and was in a manner worn out before, yet she thought herself better, till she was persuaded to make it: and from that moment, remembering what she used to prognosticate (her *fears helping on what she feared*, as is often the case, particularly in the small-pox), grew worse; and had it in her head once to burn her will, in hopes to grow better upon it.

She sent my mamma word, that the doctors had given her over: but that she could not die till she saw her. I told my mamma, that if she wished her a chance for recovery, she should not, for *that* reason, go. But go she would; and, what was worse, would make me go with her; and that, at an hour's warning (Had there been more time for argumentation, to be sure I had not gone!) for she said nothing of it to me till she was rising in the morning *early*, resolving to return *at night*. So that there was a kind of necessity that my preparation to obey her should, in a manner, accompany her command—a command so much out of the way on such a solemn occasion! And this I represented—but to no purpose—There never was such a contradicting girl in the world—*My* wisdom always made *her* a fool!—But she *would* be obliged *this time*, proper or improper.

I have but one way of accounting for this sudden whim of my mamma—She had a mind to accept of Mr Hickman's offer to escort her—And I verily believe (I wish I were quite sure of it) had a mind to oblige him with my company—as far as I know, to keep me out of *worse*.

For, would you believe it?—As sure as you are alive, she is afraid for her favourite Hickman, because of the long visit your Lovelace, though so much by accident, made me in her absence, last time she was at the same place. I hope, my dear, *you* are not jealous too. But, indeed, I now and then, when she teases me with praises which Hickman cannot deserve, in return fall to praising those qualities and personalities in Lovelace which the other never will have. Indeed I do love to tease a little bit, that I do—My mamma's girl!—I had like to have said.

As you know she is as passionate as I am pert, you will not wonder to be told that we generally fall out on these occasions: she flies from me at the long run. It would be undutiful in me to leave her *first*—and then I get an opportunity to pursue our *correspondence*.

For now I am rambling, let me tell you that she does not much favour *that*—for *two* reasons, I believe: one, that I don't show her all that passes between us; the other, that she thinks I harden your mind against your duty, as it is called; and with *her*, for a reason at home, as I have hinted more than once, parents cannot do wrong; children cannot oppose and be right. This obliges me now and then to *steal* an hour, as I may say, and not let her know how I am employed.

You may guess from what I have written, how averse I was to comply with this stretch of motherly authority, made so much against rhyme and reason—But it came to be a *test of duty*; so I was obliged to yield, though with a full persuasion of being in the right.

I have always your reproofs upon these occasions: in your late letters stronger than ever. A good reason why, you'll say, because more deserved than ever. I thank you kindly for your correction. I hope to make *cor*-rection of it—But let me tell you, that your stripes, whether deserved or not, have made me sensible deeper than the skin—but of this another time.

It was Monday afternoon before we reached the old gentlewoman's. That fiddling, parading fellow, you know who I mean, made us wait for him two hours (and I to go a journey I disliked!) only for the sake of having a little more tawdry upon his housings; which he had hurried his saddler to put on to make him look fine, being to escort his dear Madam Howe, and her fair daughter. I told him that

I supposed he was afraid that the double solemnity in the case, that of the visit to a dying woman and that of his own countenance, would give him the appearance of an *undertaker*; to avoid which, he ran into as bad an extreme, and I doubted would be taken for a *mountebank*.

The man was confounded. He took it as strongly as if his conscience gave assent to the justice of the remark—otherwise he would have borne it better: for he is used enough to this sort of treatment. I thought he would have cried. I have heretofore observed, that on this side of the contract he seems to be a mighty meek sort of creature. And though I should like it in him *hereafter*, perhaps, yet I can't help despising him a little in my heart for it *now*. I believe, my dear, we all love your blustering fellows best; could we but direct the bluster, and bid it roar when, and at whom, we pleased.

The poor man looked at my mamma. She was so angry (my airs upon it, and my opposition to the journey, having all helped), that for half the way she would not speak to me. And when she did, it was, I wish I had not brought you!—You know not what it is to condescend. It is *my* fault, not *Mr Hickman*'s, that you are here, so much against your will.—Have you no eyes for this side of the chariot?

And then he fared the better from *her*, as he always does for faring worse from *me*. For there was, how do you *now*, sir? And how do you *now*, Mr Hickman? as he ambled now on this side of the chariot, now on that, stealing a prim look at me; *her* head half out of the chariot, kindly smiling as if married to the man but a fortnight herself: while I always saw something to divert myself, on the side of the chariot where the honest man was not, were it but old Robin at a distance, on his roan, Keffel.

Our courtship days, they say, are our best days. Favour destroys courtship. Distance increases it. Its essence is distance. And to see how familiar these men-wretches grow upon a smile, what an awe they are struck into when one frowns! Who would not make them stand off? Who would not enjoy a power that is to be so short-lived?

Don't chide me one bit for this, my dear. It is in nature. I can't help it. Nay, for that matter, I love it, and wish not to help it. So spare your gravity, I beseech you, on this subject. I set not up for a perfect character. The man will bear it. And what need you care? My mamma over-balances all he suffers: and if he thinks himself unhappy, he ought never to be otherwise.

Then, did he not deserve a fit of sullens, think you, to make us lose our dinner for his parade, since in so short a journey one would not bait, and lose the opportunity of coming back that night, had the old gentlewoman's condition permitted it? To say nothing of being the cause that my mamma was in the glout with her poor daughter all the way.

At our alighting I gave him another dab; but it was but a little one. Yet the manner and the air made up (as I intended they should) for that defect. My mamma's hand was kindly put into his, with a simpering altogether bridal; and with another, How do you now, sir?—All his plump muscles were in motion, and double charge of care and obsequiousness fidgeted up his whole form, when he offered to me his officious palm. My mamma, when I was a girl, always bid me hold up my head. I just then remembered her commands, and was dutiful: I never held up my head so high. With an averted supercilious eye, and a rejecting hand half-flourishing—I have no need of help, sir!—You are in my way.

He ran back, as if on wheels; with a face excessively mortified: I had thoughts else to have followed the too gentle touch, with a declaration that I had as many hands and feet as himself: but this would have been telling him a piece of news, as to the latter, that I hope he had not the presumption to guess at.

WE found the poor woman, as we thought, at the last gasp. Had we come *sooner*, we could not have got away, as we intended, that night. You see I am for excusing the man all I can; and yet, I assure you, I have not so much as a *conditional liking* to him. My mamma sat up most part of the night, expecting every hour would have been her poor cousin's last. I bore her company till two.

I never saw the approaches of death in a grown person before; and was extremely shocked. Death, to one in health, is a very terrible thing. We pity the person for what *she* suffers: and we pity ourselves for what *we* must some time hence, in like sort, suffer; and so are *doubly* affected.

She held out till Tuesday morning, eleven; and having told my mamma that she had left her an executrix, and her and me rings and mourning; we were employed all that day in matters of the will (by which my cousin Jenny Fynnett is handsomely provided for); so that it was Wednesday morning early, before we set out on our return.

It is true, we got home (having no housings to stay for) by noon; but though I sent Robin away before he alit; and he brought me back a whole packet, down to the same Wednesday noon; yet was I really so fatigued (and shocked, as I must own, at the hard death of the old gentlewoman); my mamma likewise (who has no reason to dislike this world) being indisposed from the same occasion; that I could not set about writing, time enough for Robin's return that night.

But having recruited my spirits, my mamma having also had a good night, I arose with the dawn, to write this and get it dispatched time enough for your breakfast airing; that your suspense may be as short as possible.

I WILL soon follow this with another. I will employ a person directly to find out how Lovelace behaves himself at his inn. Such a busy spirit must be traceable.

But, perhaps, my dear, you are indifferent now about him, or his employments; for this request was made before he *mortally* offended you. Nevertheless, I will have inquiry made. The result, it is very probable, will be of use to confirm you in your present unforgiving temper—And yet, if the *poor* man (Shall I pity him for *you*, my dear?) should be deprived of the greatest blessing any man on earth can receive, and which he has the presumption, with so little merit, to aspire to; he will have run great risks; caught great colds; hazarded fevers; sustained the highest indignities; braved the inclemencies of skies, and all for—nothing!—Will not this move your *generosity* (if nothing else) in his favour?—Poor Mr Lovelace!—

I would occasion no throb; nor half-throb; no flash of sensibility, like lightning darting in, and as soon suppressed, by a discretion that no one of the sex ever before could give such an example of—I *would not*, I say; and yet, for a trial of *you* to *yourself*, rather than as an impertinent overflow of raillery in your friend, as money-takers try a suspected guinea by the *sound*, let me on such a supposition, sound *you* by repeating, *poor Mr Lovelace!*—

And now, my dear, how is it with you? How do you now, as my mamma says to Mr Hickman, when her pert daughter has made him look sorrowful?

Letter 68: MISS HOWE TO MISS CLARISSA HARLOWE

Thursday morning

I WILL now take some notice of your last favour. But being so far behindhand with you, must be brief.

In the first place, as to your reproofs, thus shall I discharge myself of that part of my subject: is it likely, think you, that I should avoid of deserving them now and then, occasionally, when I admire the manner in which you give me your rebukes, and love you the better for them? And when you are so well *entitled* to give them? For what faults can *you* possibly have, unless your relations are so kind as to find you a *few* to keep their *many* in countenance?—But, they are as kind to *me* in this, as to *you*; for I may venture to affirm, that anyone who should read *your* letters, and would say you were *right*, would not on reading *mine*, condemn me for being *quite wrong*.

Your resolution, not to leave your father's house, is right—if you can stay in it, and avoid being Solmes's wife.

I think you answered Solmes's letter, as *I* should have answered it—Will you not compliment me and yourself at once, by saying that *that* was right?

You have in your letters to your uncle and the rest done all that you ought to do. You are wholly guiltless of the consequence, be it what it will. To offer to give up your estate!—That would not I have done!—You see, this offer staggered them: they took time to consider of it: they made my heart ache in the time they took. I was afraid they would have taken you at your word: and so, but for shame and for fear of Lovelace, I dare say they would—You are too noble by half for them. This, I repeat, is an offer I would not have made. Let me beg of you, my dear, never to repeat the temptation to them.

I freely own to you, that their usage of you upon it, and Lovelace's different behaviour in his letter received at the same time, would have made *me* his, past redemption. The deuce take the man, I was going to say, for not having had so much regard to his character and morals as would have entirely justified such a step in a *Clarissa Harlowe*, persecuted as she is!

I wonder not at your appointment with him. I may further touch upon some part of this subject by and by.

Pray, pray, I pray you now, my dearest friend, contrive to send your Betty Barnes to me!—Does the Coventry Act[1] extend to women, know ye?—The least I would do, should be to send her home well soused in and dragged through our deepest horsepond. I'll engage, if I get her hither, that she shall keep the anniversary of her deliverance as long as she lives.

I wonder not at Lovelace's saucy answer, saucy as it really is. If he loves you as he ought, he must be vexed at so great a disappointment. The man must have been a detestable hypocrite, I think, had he not shown his vexation. Your expectations of such a Christian command of temper in him, in disappointment of this nature especially, are too early, by almost half a century, in a man of his constitution. But, nevertheless, I am very far from blaming you for your resentment.

I shall be all impatience to know how this matter ends between you and him. But a *few inches of brick wall* between you so lately; and now such *mountains!*— And you think to hold it!—Maybe so!—

You see the temper he showed in his preceding letter was not *natural* to him, you say. And did you before think it *was?* Insolent creepers and insinuators! inch-allowed, ell-taking encroachers!—This very Hickman, I make no doubt, will be as saucy as your Lovelace, if ever he dare. He has not half the arrogant bravery of the other, and can better hide his horns; that's all. But whenever he has the power, depend upon it, he will *butt* at one as valiantly as the other.

If ever I should be persuaded to have him, I shall watch how the imperative husband *comes upon him*; how the obsequious lover *goes off*; in short, how he *ascends*, and how I *descend*, in the matrimonial wheel, never to take my turn again, but by fits and starts, like the feeble struggles of a sinking state for its dying liberty.

All good-natured men are passionate, says Mr Lovelace. A pretty plea to a beloved object in the plenitude of her power! As much as to say, greatly as I value you, madam, I will not take pains to curb my passions to oblige you—Methinks, I should be glad to hear from Mr Hickman such a plea for good-nature as this!

Indeed, we are too apt to make allowances for such tempers as *early* indulgence has made uncontrollable, and therefore habitually evil. But if a boisterous temper, when under *obligation*, is to be thus allowed for, what, when the tables are turned, will it expect? You know a husband, who, I fancy, had some of these early allowances made for him: and you see that neither himself, nor anybody else, is the happier for it!

The suiting of the tempers of two persons who are to come together is a great matter: and yet there should be boundaries fixed between them, by consent as it were, beyond which neither should go: and each should hold the other to it; or there would probably be encroachments in both. If the boundaries of the three estates that constitute our political union[2] were not known, and occasionally asserted, what would become of each? The two branches of the legislature would encroach upon each other; and the executive power would swallow up both.

If two persons of discretion, you'll say, come together—

Ay, my dear, that's true: but if none but persons of discretion were to marry—And would it not surprise you if I were to advance, that the persons of discretion are generally single?—Such persons are apt to consider too much, to resolve—Are not you and I complimented as such?—And would either of us marry, if the fellows and our friends would let us alone?

But to the former point; had Lovelace made his addresses to me (unless, indeed, I had been taken with a liking for him *more* than *conditional*), I would have forbid him upon the first *passionate* instance of his *good-nature*, as he calls it, ever to see me more: 'Thou must bear with me, honest friend, might I have said (had I condescended to say any thing to him), an hundred times more than this—Begone, therefore—I bear with no passions that are predominant to that thou hast pretended for me.'

But to one of *your* mild and gentle temper, it would be all one, were you married, whether the man be a Lovelace or a Hickman in his spirit—You are so obediently principled that perhaps you would have told a mild man, that he must not *entreat*, but *command*; and that it was beneath him not to exact from you the obedience you had so solemnly vowed to him at the altar. I know of old, my dear, your meek regard to that little piddling part of the marriage vow, which some prerogative-monger foisted into the office to make that a *duty* which he knew was not a *right*.

Our way of training-up, you say, *makes us need the protection of the brave*. Very true: and how extremely brave and gallant is it that this brave man will free us from all insults but those which will go nearest to us; that is to say, his own!

How artfully has Lovelace, in the abstract you give me of one of his letters, calculated to your meridian; *generous spirits hate compulsion!*—He is certainly a deeper creature by much than once we thought him. He knows, as you intimate, that his own wild pranks cannot be concealed; and so owns just enough to palliate (because it teaches you not to be surprised at) any new one that may come to your ears; and then, truly, he is (however faulty) a mighty *ingenuous* man, and by no means an *hypocrite:* a character, when found out, the most odious of all others to *our sex*, in the *other*; were it only because it teaches us to doubt the justice of the praises such a man gives us when we are willing to believe them to be our due.

By means of this supposed *ingenuity*, Lovelace obtains a praise, instead of a merited dispraise; and like an absolved confessionaire, wipes off, as he goes along one score, to begin another: for an eye favourable to him will not magnify his faults; nor will a woman, willing to *hope the best*, forbear to impute to ill-will and prejudice all that charity can make so imputable. And if she even give credit to such of the unfavourable imputations as may be too flagrant to be doubted, she will be very apt to take in the *future hope*, which he inculcates, and which to question would be to question her own power, and perhaps *merit:* and thus may a woman be inclined to make a *slight*, or even a *fancied*, virtue atone for the most *glaring* vice.

I have a reason, a new one, for this preachment upon a text you have given me. But, till I am better informed, I will not explain myself. If it come out as I shrewdly suspect it will, the man, my dear, is a devil; and you must rather think of——I protest I had like to have said—*Solmes*, than him.

But let this be as it will, shall I tell you how, after all his offences, he may creep in with you again?

I will. Thus then: it is but to claim for himself the *good-natured character:* and this, granted, will blot out the fault of *passionate* insolence: and so he will have nothing to do, but this hour to accustom you to insult; the next, to bring you to forgive him upon his submission. The consequence will be that he will, by this see-saw teasing, break your resentment all to pieces: and then, a little *more* of the insult, and a little *less* of the submission on his part, will go down, till nothing else but the *first* will be seen, and not a bit of the *second*. You will then be afraid to provoke so offensive a spirit; and at last will be brought so *prettily*, and so *audibly*, to pronounce the little reptile word OBEY, that it will do one's heart good to hear you. The *Muscovite* wife takes place of the *managed* mistress—And, if you doubt the progression, be pleased, my dear, to take your *mamma*'s judgement upon it.

But no more of this just now. Your story is become too arduous to dwell upon these sort of topics. And yet this is but an *affected levity* with me. My heart, as I have heretofore said, is a sincere sharer in all your distresses. My sunshine darts but through a drizzly cloud. My eye, were you to see it, when it seems to you so *gladdened* as you mention in a former, is more than ready to overflow, even at the very passages, perhaps, upon which you impute to me the *archness* of *exultation*.

But now the unheard of cruelty and perverseness of some of your friends

(*relations*, I should say; I am always blundering thus!); the *as* strange determinedness of others; your present quarrel with Lovelace; and your approaching interview
with Solmes, from which you are right to apprehend a great deal; are such
considerable circumstances in your story, that it is fit they should engross all my
attention.

You ask me to advise you how to behave upon Solmes's visit. I *cannot* for my
life. I know they expect a great deal from it: you had not else had your long day
complied with. All I will say is that if Solmes cannot be prevailed for, now that
Lovelace has so much offended you, he never will. When the interview is over, I
doubt not but that I shall have reason to say, that all you did, that all you said, was
right, and could not be better: yet, if I don't think so, I won't say so; that I promise
you.

Only, let me advise you to pull up a spirit, even to your uncle, if there be
occasion. Resent the vile and foolish treatment you meet with, in which he has
taken so large a share, and make him ashamed of it, if you can.

I know not, upon recollection, but this interview may be a good thing for you,
however designed. For when Solmes sees (if that is to *be* so), that it is impossible
he should succeed with you; and your relations see it too; the one must, I think,
recede, and the other come to terms with you; upon offers, that it is my opinion,
will go hard enough with you to comply with; when the *still* harder are dispensed
with.

There are several passages in your last letters, as well as in your former, which
authorize me to say this. But it would be unseasonable to touch this subject further
just now.

But, upon the whole, I have no patience to see you thus made the sport of your
brother's and sister's cruelty: for what, after so much steadiness on your part, in
so many trials, can be their hope?

[I urge you by all means] to send out of their reach all the letters and papers you
would not have them see. Methinks, I would wish you to deposit likewise a parcel
of clothes, linen, &c. before your interview with Solmes; lest you should not have
an opportunity for it afterwards. Robin shall fetch it away on the first orders, by
day or night.

I am in hopes to procure from my mamma, if things come to extremity, leave for
you to be privately with us.

I will condition to be good-humoured, and even *kind*, to HER favourite, if she
will show me an indulgence that shall make me serviceable to MINE. It has been
a good while in my head. But I cannot promise that I shall succeed in it.

Don't absolutely despair, however, my dear. Your quarrel with Lovelace may be
a help to it. And the offers you made, in your answer to your uncle Harlowe's
letter of Sunday night last, may be another.

I depend upon your forgiveness of all the, perhaps unseasonable, flippancies of
your naturally too lively, yet most sincerely sympathizing,

ANNA HOWE

Letter 69: MISS CLARISSA HARLOWE TO MISS HOWE

Friday, March 31

You have very kindly accounted for your silence. People in misfortune are always in doubt. They are too apt to turn even unavoidable accidents into slights and neglects; especially in those whose favourable opinion they wish to preserve.

I am sure I ought evermore to exempt my Anna Howe from the supposed possibility of her becoming one of those who bask only in the sunshine of a friend: but nevertheless her friendship is too precious to me, not to doubt my own merits on the one hand, and not to be anxious for the preservation of it on the other.

You so generously give me liberty to chide you, that I am afraid of taking it, because I could sooner mistrust my own judgement, than that of a beloved friend whose ingenuity in acknowledging an *imputed* error sets her above the commission of a *wilful* one. This makes me half afraid to ask you, if you think you are not too cruel, too *ungenerous* shall I say, in your behaviour to a man who loves you so dearly, and is so worthy and so sincere a man?

Only it is by You, or I should be ashamed to be outdone in that true magnanimity which makes one thankful for the wounds given by a true friend. I believe I was guilty of a petulance, which nothing but my uneasy situation can excuse; if *that* can. I am almost *afraid* to beg of you, and yet I repeatedly *do*, to give way to that charming spirit whenever it rises to your pen, which smiles yet goes to the quick of one's fault. What patient shall be afraid of a probe in so delicate a hand?—I say I am almost afraid to pray you to give way to it, for fear you should, for that very reason, restrain it. For the edge may be taken off, if it does not make the subject of its raillery wince a little. *Permitted* or *desired* satire many be apt, in a generous satirist, mending as it rallies, to turn too soon into panegyric. Yours is intended to instruct; and though it bites, it pleases at the same time: no fear of a wound's rankling or festering by so delicate a point as you carry; not envenomed by *personality*, not intending to expose, or ridicule, or exasperate. The most admired of our moderns know nothing of this art. Why? Because it must be founded in good nature, and directed by a right heart. The *man*, not the *fault*, is the subject of *their* satire: and were it to be *just*, how should it be *useful*? How should it answer any good purpose? When every gash (for their weapon is a broadsword, not a lancet) lets in the air of public ridicule, and exasperates where it should heal. Spare me not therefore, because I am your *friend*. For *that* very reason spare me not. I may *feel* your edge, fine as it is; I may be pained: you would lose your end if I were not: but after the first sensibility (as I have said more than once before), I will love you the better, and my amended heart shall be all yours; and it will then be more worthy to be yours.

You have taught me what to say to, and what to think of, Mr Lovelace. You have, by agreeable anticipation, let me know how it is probable he will apply to me to be excused. I will lay everything before you that shall pass on the occasion, if he *does* apply, that I may take your advice when it can come in time; and when it cannot, that I may receive your correction, or approbation, as I may happen to merit either. Only one thing must be allowed for me; that whatever course I shall be *permitted* or be *forced* to steer, I must be considered as a person out of her own direction. Tossed to and fro by the high winds of passionate control, and, as I think, unreasonable severity, I behold the desired port, the *single state*, which I would fain steer into; but am kept off by the foaming billows of a brother's and sister's envy; and by the raging winds of a supposed invaded authority; while I see in Lovelace, the rocks on one hand, and in Solmes, the sands on the other; and tremble lest I should split upon the former, or strike upon the latter.

But you, my better pilot, what a charming hope do you bid me aspire to, if things come to extremity!—I will not, as you caution me, too much depend upon your success with your mamma, in my favour: for well I know her high notions of implicit duty in a child—But yet I will *hope* too—because her seasonable protection may save me perhaps from a greater rashness: and, in this case, she shall direct all my ways: I will do nothing but by her orders, and by her advice and yours: not see anybody: nor write to anybody: nor shall any living soul, but by her direction and yours, know where I am. In any cottage place me, I will never stir out, unless, disguised as your servant, I am now and then permitted an evening walk with you: and this private protection to be granted me for no longer time than till my cousin Morden comes; which, as I hope, cannot be long.

I am afraid I must not venture to take the hint you give me, to deposit some of my clothes; although I will some of my linen, as well as papers.

I will tell you why. Betty had for some time been very curious about my wardrobe, whenever I took out any of my things before her.

Observing this, I once left my keys in the locks, on taking one of my garden airings; and on my return, surprised the creature with her hand upon the keys, as if shutting the door.

She was confounded at my sudden coming back. I took no notice: but, on her retiring, I found my clothes did not lie in the usual order.

I doubted not, upon this, that her curiosity was an effect of their orders to her; and being afraid they would abridge me of my airings if their suspicions were not obviated, it has ever since been my custom (among other contrivances), not only to leave my keys in the locks; but to employ the wench now and then, in taking out my clothes, suit by suit, on pretence of preventing their being rumpled or creased, and to see that the flowered silver suit did not tarnish; sometimes declaredly as a while-away-time, having little else to do: with which employment (super-added to the delight taken by the low as well as the high of our sex in seeing fine clothes) she seemed always, I thought, as well pleased as if it answered one of the offices she had in charge.

To this, and to the confidence they have in a spy so diligent, and to their knowing that I have not one confidante in a family, where I believe, nevertheless, every servant in it loves me; nor have attempted to make one; I suppose, I owe the freedom I enjoy of my airings: and, perhaps (finding I make no movements towards going off), they are the more secure that I shall at last be prevailed upon to comply with their measures: since they must think that, otherwise, they give me provocations enough to take some rash step, in order to free myself from a treatment so disgraceful; and which (God forgive me, if I judge amiss!), I am afraid my brother and sister would not be sorry to drive me to take.

If therefore such a step should become necessary (which I yet hope will not!) I must be contented to go away with the clothes I shall have on at the time. My custom to be dressed for the day, as soon as breakfast is over, when I have had no household employments to prevent me, will make such a step, if I am forced to take it, less suspected. And the linen I shall deposit, in pursuance of your kind hint, cannot be missed.

This custom, although a prisoner, as I may too truly say, and neither visited nor visiting, I continue. One owes to *one's self*, and to one's *sex*, you know, to be always neat; and never to be surprised in a way one should be pained to be seen in.

Besides, people in adversity, which is the state of trial of every good quality, should endeavour to preserve laudable customs, that if sunshine return they may not be losers by their trial.

Does it not, moreover, manifest a firmness of mind, in an unhappy person, to keep hope alive?

To *hope* for better days is half to *deserve* them: for could we have just ground for such a hope, if we did not resolve to deserve what that hope bids us aspire to?— Then, who shall befriend a person who forsakes herself?—These are reflections by which I sometimes endeavour to support myself.

I know you don't despise my *grave airs*, although (with a view, no doubt, to irradiate my mind in my misfortunes) you rally me upon them. Everybody has not your talent of introducing serious and important lessons, in such a happy manner as at once to delight and instruct.

What a multitude of contrivances may not young people fall upon, if the mind be not engaged by acts of kindness and condescension! I am not used by my friends, of late, as I always used their servants.

When I was entrusted with the family management, I always found it both generous and just, to repose a trust in them. Not to seem to expect or depend upon justice from them, is, in a manner, to bid them take opportunities, whenever they offer, to be *un*-just.

Mr Solmes (to expatiate a little on this low, but not unuseful, subject), in his more trifling solicitudes, would have had a sorry key-keeper in me. Were I mistress of a family, I would not either take to myself, or give to servants, the pain of keeping those I had reason to suspect. People low in station have often minds not sordid—Nay, I have sometimes thought, that, even take number for number, there are more *honest low people*, than *honest high*. In the one, honesty is their *chief* pride. In the other, the love of power, of grandeur, of pleasure, mislead; and that love, and their ambition, induce a paramount pride, which too often swallows up the more laudable one.

Many of the former would scorn to deceive a confidence. But I have seen among the most ignorant of their class a susceptibility of resentment, if their honesty has been suspected: and have more than once been forced to put a servant right, whom I have heard say, that, although she valued herself upon her *honesty*, no master or mistress should suspect her for nothing.

How far has the comparison I had in my head between my friends' treatment of *me*, and my treatment of their *servants*, carried me! But we always allowed ourselves to expatiate on such subjects, whether low or high, that might tend to enlarge our minds, or mend our management, whether notional or practical, and whether they respected our present, or might respect our probable future situations.

What I was principally leading to was to tell you, how ingenious I am in my contrivances and pretences to blind my gaoleress, and to take off the jealousy of her principals, on my going down so often into the garden and poultry yard. People suspiciously treated never, I believe, want invention. Sometimes I want *air*, and am better the moment I am out of my chamber—Sometimes *spirits*; and then my bantams and pheasants, or the cascade, divert me; the former, by their inspiriting liveliness; the latter, more solemnly, by its echoing dashings and hollow murmurs—Sometimes solitude is of all things my wish, and the awful silence of the night, the spangled element, and the rising and setting sun, how promotive of contemplation!—Sometimes, when I intend nothing, and expect not letters, I am officious to take Betty with me; and at others, bespeak her attendance when I know she is otherwise employed and cannot give it me.

These more capital artifices I branch out into lesser ones without number. Yet *all* have not only the face of truth, but are real truth; although not the principal motive. How prompt a thing is *will!* What impediments does *dislike* furnish!—How swiftly, through every difficulty, do we move with the one!—How tardily with the other!—Every trifling obstruction weighing one down, as if lead were fastened to our feet!

Friday morning, eleven o'clock

I HAVE already made up my parcel of linen; my heart ached all the time I was employed about it; and still aches at the thoughts of its being a necessary precaution.

When it comes to your hands, as I hope it safely will, you will be pleased to open it. You will find in it two parcels sealed up; one of which contains the letters you have not yet seen, being those written since I left you; in the other are all the letters, and copies of letters, that have passed between you and me since I was last with you; with some other papers on subjects so much above me, that I cannot wish them to be seen by anybody whose indulgence I am not so sure of, as I am of yours. If my judgement ripen with my years, perhaps I may review them.

Mrs Norton used to say, from her reverend father, that there was one time of life for *imagination* and *fancy* to work in: then, were the writer to lay by his works till *riper years* and *experience* should direct the fire rather to *glow* than to *flame out*, something between both might, perhaps, be produced that would not displease a judicious eye.

In a third division, folded up separately, are all Mr Lovelace's letters, since he was forbidden this house, and copies of my answers to them. I expect that you will break the seals of this parcel, and when you have perused them all, give me your free opinion of my conduct.

By the way, not a line from that man!—Not one line!—Wednesday I deposited mine. It remained there on Wednesday night. What time it was taken away yesterday I cannot tell. For I did not concern myself about it, till towards night; and then it was not there. No return at ten this day. I suppose he is as much out of humour, as I. With all my heart!

He may be mean enough, perhaps, if ever I should put it into his *power*, to avenge himself for the trouble he has had with me—But that now, I dare say, I never shall.

I see what sort of a man the encroacher is—And I hope we are equally sick of one another!—My heart is *vexedly*-easy, if I may so describe it. *Vexedly*—because of the apprehended interview with Solmes, and the consequences it may have: or else I should be *quite* easy; for why? I have not *deserved* the usage I receive. And could I be rid of Solmes, as I presume I am of Lovelace, *their* influence over my father, mother, and uncles against me, could not hold.

The five guineas tied up in one corner of a handkerchief under the linen, I beg you will let pass, as an acknowledgement for the trouble I give your trusty servant. You must not chide me, my dear. You know I cannot be easy, unless I have my way in these little matters.

I was going to put up what little money I have, and some of my ornaments; but they are portable, and I cannot forget them. Besides, should they, suspecting me, desire to see any of the jewels, and were I not able to produce them, it would amount to a demonstration of an intention which would have a guilty appearance to them.

Friday, one o'clock, in the woodhouse

No letter yet from this man!—I have luckily deposited my parcel, and have your letter of last night. If Robert takes this without the parcel, pray let him return immediately for it. But he cannot miss it, I think; and must conclude that it is put there for him to take away—You may believe, from the contents of yours, that I shall immediately write again.—

CL. HARLOWE

Letter 70: MISS HOWE TO MISS CLARISSA HARLOWE

Thursday night, March 30

THE fruits of my inquiry after your abominable wretch's behaviour and baseness at the paltry alehouse, which he calls an inn; prepare to hear.

Wrens and sparrows are not too ignoble a quarry for this villainous goshawk!— His assiduities; his watchings; his nightly risks; the inclement weather he travels in; must not be all placed to *your* account. He has opportunities of making everything light to him of that sort. A sweet pretty girl, I am told—innocent till he went thither—Now!—Ah! poor girl!—who knows what?

But just turned of seventeen!—His friend and brother rake; a man of humour and intrigue, as I am told, to share the social bottle with. And sometimes another disguised rake or two. No sorrow comes near their hearts. Be not disturbed, my dear, at his *hoarsenesses*. His pretty Betsy, his Rosebud, as the vile wretch calls her, can *hear* all he says.

He is very fond of her. They say she is innocent even yet!—Her father, her grandmother, believe her to be so. He is to fortune her out to a young lover!—Ah! the poor young lover!—Ah! the poor simple girl!

Mr Hickman tells me that he heard in town, that he used to be often at plays, and at the opera, with women; and every time with a different one!—Ah! my sweet friend!—But I hope he is nothing to you, if all this were truth—But this intelligence will do his business, if you had been ever so good friends before.

A vile wretch! Cannot such purity in pursuit, in view, restrain him? But I leave him to you!—There can be no hope of him. More of a fool, than of such a one. Yet I wish I may be able to snatch the poor young creature out of his villainous paws.

I have laid a scheme to do so; if *indeed* she is hitherto innocent and heart-free.

He appears to the people as a military man, in disguise, secreting himself on account of a duel fought in town; the adversary's life in suspense. They believe he is a great man. His friend passes for an inferior officer; upon a foot of freedom with him. He, accompanied by a third man, who is a sort of subordinate companion to the second. The wretch himself but with one servant. Oh my dear! How pleasantly can these devils, as I must call them, pass their time, while our gentle bosoms heave with pity for their supposed sufferings for us!

I AM just now informed that, at my desire, I shall see this girl and her father: I will sift them thoroughly. I shall soon find out such a simple thing as this, if he has not corrupted her already—And if he has, I shall soon find that out too. If more art than nature [appears] in either her or her father, I shall give them both up—But, depend upon it, the girl's undone.

He is said to be fond of her. He places her at the upper end of his table—He sets her a-prattling—He keeps his friend at a distance from her. She prates away. He admires for nature all she says—Once was heard to call her charming little creature!—An hundred has he called so no doubt. Puts her upon singing—Praises her wild note. Oh my dear, the girl's undone!—must be undone!—The man, you know, is LOVELACE—Let 'em bring Wyerley to you, if they will have you married—Anybody but Solmes and Lovelace be yours!—So advises

Your
ANNA HOWE

My dearest friend, consider this alehouse as his garrison. Him as an enemy. His brother-rakes as his assistants and abetters: would not your brother, would not your uncles, tremble, if they knew how near them, as they pass to and fro!—I am told, he is resolved you shall not be carried to your uncle Antony's. What can you do, *with* or *without* such an enterprising—— Fill up the blank I leave—I cannot find a word bad enough.

Letter 71: MISS CLARISSA HARLOWE TO MISS HOWE

Friday, three o'clock
You incense, alarm and terrify me, at the same time! Hasten, my dearest friend, hasten to me, what further intelligence you can gather about this vilest of men!

But never talk of innocence, of simplicity, and this unhappy girl together! Must she not know, that such a man as that, dignified in his very aspect; and no disguise able to conceal his being of condition—must mean too much, when he places her at the upper end of his table, and calls her by such tender names?—Would a girl, modest as simple, above seventeen, be set a singing at the pleasure of such a man as that? A stranger, and professedly in disguise!—Would her father and grandmother, if honest people, and careful of their simple girl, permit such freedoms?

Keep his friend at distance from her!—To be sure his *designs* are villainous, if they have not been already effected.

Warn, my dear, if not too late, the unthinking father, of his child's danger—

There cannot be a father in the world, who would sell his child's virtue. No mother!—the poor thing!

I long to hear the result of your intelligence. You shall *see* the simple creature, you tell me—Let me know what sort of a girl it is—a *sweet pretty girl*, you say—a *sweet* pretty *girl*, my dear!—They are sweet, pretty words from your pen. But are they *yours*, or *his*, of her?—If she be so simple, if she have ease and nature in her manner, in her speech, and warbles prettily her *wild notes* (how affectingly you mention this simple thing, my dear!), why, such a girl as that must engage such a profligate wretch, as now, indeed, I doubt this man is; accustomed, perhaps, to town-women, and their confident ways!—must *deeply*, and for a *long season*, engage him! Since, perhaps, when her innocence is departed, she will endeavour by art to supply the natural charms that engaged him.

Fine hopes of such a wretch's reformation!—I would not, my dear, for the world, have anything to say—but I need not make resolutions. I have not opened, nor will I open, his letter—A sycophant creature!—with his hoarsenesses—got, perhaps, by a midnight revel, singing to his wild-note singer—and only increased in the coppice!

To be already on a foot!—in his esteem, I mean, my dear. For myself, I despise him. I hate myself almost for writing so much about *him*, and of such a simpleton as *this sweet pretty girl*: but nothing can be either *sweet* or *pretty*, that is not modest, that is not virtuous.

This vile Joseph Leman had given a hint to Betty, and she to me, as if Lovelace would be found out to be a very bad man, at a place where he had been lately seen in disguise. But he would see further, he said, before he told her more; and she promised secrecy, in hope to get at further intelligence. I thought it could be no harm, to get you to inform yourself, and me, of what could be gathered. And now I see his enemies are but too well warranted in their reports of him: and if the ruin of this poor young creature is his aim, and if he had not known her but for his visits to Harlowe Place, I shall have reason to be doubly concerned for her; and doubly incensed against so vile a man. I think I hate him worse than I do Solmes himself. But I will not add one other word about him; after I have wished to know, as soon as possible, what further occurs from your inquiry; because I shall not open his letter till then; and because then, if it comes out, as I dare say it will, I'll directly put the letter unopened into the place I took it from, and never trouble myself more about him. Adieu, my dearest friend.

CL. HARLOWE

Letter 72: MISS HOWE TO MISS CLARISSA HARLOWE

Friday noon, March 31

JUSTICE obliges me to forward this after my last, on the wings of the wind, as I may say—I really believe the man is innocent. Of this *one* accusation, I think, he must be acquitted; and I am sorry I was so forward in dispatching away my intelligence by halves.

I have seen the girl. She is really a very pretty, a very neat, and what is still a greater beauty, a very innocent young creature. He who could have ruined such an undesigning home-bred must have been indeed infernally wicked. Her father is an honest simple man; entirely satisfied with his child, and with her new acquaintance.

I am almost afraid for your heart, when I tell you that I find, now I have got to the bottom of this inquiry, something noble come out in this Lovelace's favour.

The girl is to be married next week; and this promoted and brought about by him. He is resolved, her father says, to make one couple happy, and wishes he could make more so. (There's for you, my dear!) And having taken a liking also to the young fellow whom she professes to love, he has given her a hundred pounds: the grandmother actually has it in her hands, to answer to the like sum given to the youth by one of his own relations: while Mr Lovelace's companion, attracted by the example, has presented twenty-five guineas to the father, who is poor, towards clothes to equip the pretty rustic.

They were desirous, the poor man says, when they first came, of appearing beneath themselves; but now he knows the one (but mentioned it in confidence) to be Colonel Barrow, the other Capt. Sloane. The Colonel he owns was at first, very *sweet upon his girl*: but upon her grandmother's begging of him to spare her innocence, he vowed, that he never would offer anything but good counsel to her; and had kept to his word: and the pretty fool acknowledged that she never could have been better instructed by the minister himself from the *Bible-book!*—The girl, I own, pleased me so well, that I made her visit to me worth her while.

But what, my dear, will become of us now?—Lovelace not only reformed, but turned preacher!—What will become of us now?—Why, my sweet friend, your *generosity* is now engaged in his favour!—Fie, upon this *generosity!*—I think in my heart that it does as much mischief to the noble-minded, as *love* to the ignobler. What before was only a *conditional liking*, I am now afraid will turn to *liking unconditional*.

I could not endure to turn my invective into panegyric all at once, and so soon. We, or such as I, at least, love to keep ourselves in countenance for a rash judgement, even when we know it to be rash. Everybody has not your generosity in confessing a mistake. It requires a greatness of soul to do it. So I made still farther inquiry after his life and manners, and behaviour there, in hopes to find something bad: but all uniform!

Upon the whole, Mr Lovelace comes out with so much advantage from this inquiry, that were there the least room for it, I should suspect the whole to be a plot set on foot to wash a blackamoor white. Adieu, my dear.

ANNA HOWE

Letter 73: MISS CLARISSA HARLOWE TO MISS HOWE

Saturday, April 1

HASTY censurers do indeed subject themselves to the charge of variableness and inconsistency in judgement: and so they ought; for, if you, even you, were really so loath to own a mistake, as, in the instance before us, you pretend to say you were, I believe I should not have loved you so well as I really do love you. Nor could you, my dear, have so frankly thrown the reflection I hint at, upon yourself, had you not had one of the most ingenuous minds that ever woman boasted.

Mr Lovelace has faults enow to deserve very severe censure, although he be not guilty of this. If I were upon such terms with him, as he would wish me to be, I should give him a hint, that this treacherous Joseph Leman cannot be so much his friend as perhaps he thinks him. If he had, he would not have been so ready to report to his disadvantage (and to Betty Barnes too) this slight affair of the pretty rustic. Joseph has engaged Betty to secrecy, promising to let her, and her young master too, know more when he knows the whole of the matter: and this hinders her from mentioning it, as she is nevertheless agog to do, to my sister or my brother. And then she does not choose to disoblige Joseph; for although she pretends to look above him, she listens, I believe, to some love-stories he tells her. Women having it not in their power to *begin* a courtship, some of them very frequently, I believe, lend an *ear* where their *hearts* incline not.

But to say no more of these low people, neither of whom I think tolerably of; I must needs own, that as I should for ever have despised this man, had he been capable of such a vile intrigue in his way to Harlowe Place; and as I believed he *was* capable of it, it has indeed engaged my *generosity*, as you call it, in proportion (I *own* it has) in his favour: perhaps more than I may have reason to wish it had. And, rally me as you will, pray tell me fairly, my dear, would it not have had such an effect upon you?

Then the real generosity of the act—I protest, my beloved friend, if he would be good for the rest of his life from this time, I would forgive him a great many of his past errors, were it only for the demonstration he has given in this, that he is *capable* of so good and bountiful a manner of thinking.

You may believe I made no scruple to open his letter, after the receipt of your second on this subject: nor shall I of answering it, as I have no reason to find fault with it. An article in his favour procured him, however, so much the easier (as I must own) by way of amends for the undue displeasure I took against him; though he knows it not.

It is lucky enough that this matter was cleared up to me by your friendly diligence so soon: for had I wrote at all before that, it would have been to reinforce my dismission of him; and perhaps the very motive mentioned; for it had affected me more than I think it ought: and then, what an advantage would that have given him, when he could have cleared up the matter so happily for himself?

When I send you this letter of his, you will see how very humble he is: what acknowledgements of natural impatience: what confession of faults, as you prognosticated. A very different appearance, I must own, all these make, now the story of the pretty rustic is cleared up, than they would have made, had it not— And, methinks too, my dear, I can allow the girl to be prettier than before I could, though I never saw her—for *virtue* is beauty in perfection.

You will see how he accounts to me, through indisposition, 'that he could not come for my letter in person; and he labours the point, as if he thought I should be uneasy that he did not.' I am sorry he should be ill on my account; and I will allow that the suspense he has been in, for some time past, must have been vexatious enough to so impatient a spirit. But all is owing originally to himself.

You will find him (in the presumption of being forgiven) 'full of contrivances and expedients for my escaping the compulsion threatened me.'

I have always said, that next to being without fault, is the acknowledgement of a fault; since no amendment can be expected where an error is defended: but you will see, in this very letter, an haughtiness even in his submissions. 'Tis true, I know not where to find fault as to the expression, yet cannot I be satisfied, that his humility *is* humility; or even an humility upon such conviction as one should be pleased with.

To be sure, he is far from being a polite man: yet is he not directly and characteristically *un*-polite. But *his* is such a sort of politeness, as has, by a carelessness founded on a very early indulgence, and perhaps on too much success in riper years, and an arrogance built upon both, grown into assuredness, and, of course, as I may say, into indelicacy.

The distance you recommend, at which to keep this sex, is certainly right in the main. Familiarity destroys reverence: but with whom?—Not with those, surely, who are prudent, grateful and generous.

But it is very difficult for persons, who would avoid running into one extreme, to keep clear of another. Hence Mr Lovelace, perhaps, thinks it the mark of a great spirit to humour his pride, though at the expense of delicacy: but can the man be a deep man, who knows not how to make such distinctions as a person of moderate parts cannot miss?

He complains heavily of my 'readiness to take mortal offence at him, and to dismiss him for ever. It is a *high* conduct, he says he must be sincere enough to tell me; and what must be very far from contributing to allay his apprehensions of the possibility that I may be persecuted into my relations' measures in behalf of Mr Solmes.'

You will see how he puts his present and his future happiness, 'with regard to both worlds, entirely upon me.' The ardour with which he vows and promises, I think the heart only can dictate. How else can any one guess at a man's heart?

You'll also see, 'that he has already heard of the interview I am to have with Mr Solmes'; and with what vehemence and anguish he expresses himself on the occasion—I intend to take proper notice of the ignoble means he stoops to, to come at his early intelligence out of our family. If persons pretending to principle bear not their testimony against unprincipled actions, who shall check them?

You'll see how passionately he presses me to oblige him with a few lines, before the interview between Mr Solmes and me take place (if it must take place), to confirm his hope that I have no view, in my displeasure to *him*, to give encouragement to *Solmes*. An apprehension, he says, that he must be excused for repeating; especially as it is a favour granted to that man, which I have refused to him; since, as he infers, were it not with such an expectation, why should my *friends* press it?

Saturday, April 1

I HAVE written; and to this effect: 'That I had never intended to write another line to a man who could take upon himself to reflect upon my sex and myself, for having thought fit to make use of my own judgement.

'That I have submitted to this interview with Mr Solmes, purely as an act of duty, to show my friends that I will comply with their commands as far as I can; and that I hope, when Mr Solmes himself shall see how determined I am, he will no longer prosecute a suit, in which it is impossible he should succeed with my consent.

'That my aversion to him is too sincere to permit me to doubt myself on this occasion. But, nevertheless, he, Mr Lovelace, must not imagine that my rejecting of Mr Solmes is in favour to him. That I value my freedom and independency too much, if my friends will but leave me to my own judgement, to give them up to a man so uncontrollable, and who shows me beforehand, what I have to expect from him were I in his power.

'I express my high disapprobation of the methods he takes to come at what passes in a private family: that the pretence of corrupting other people's servants, by way of reprisal for the spies they have set upon him, is a very poor excuse; a justification of one meanness by another.

'That there is a *right* and a *wrong* in everything, let people put what glosses they please upon their actions. To condemn a deviation, and to follow it by as great a one, what is this doing but propagating a general corruption? A stand must be made by somebody, turn round the evil as many as may, or virtue will be lost: *and shall it not be I*, a worthy mind will say, that shall make this stand?

'I leave it to him to judge, whether *his* be a worthy one, tried by this rule: and whether, knowing the impetuosity of his disposition; and the improbability there is, that my family will ever be reconciled to him, I ought to encourage his hopes?

'That these spots and blemishes give me not earnestness enough for any sake but *his own*, to wish him in a juster and nobler train of thinking and acting; for that I truly despise many of the ways he allows himself in: our minds are therefore infinitely different: and as to his professions of reformation, I must tell him that profuse acknowledgements, without amendment, are but to me as so many stopmouth concessions, which he may find much easier to make than either to defend himself, or amend his errors.

'That I have been lately made acquainted (and so I have by Betty, and she by my brother) with the foolish liberty he gives himself of declaiming against matrimony. I severely reprehend him on this occasion: and ask him, with what view he can take so witless, so despicable a liberty, worthy only of the most abandoned, and yet presume to address *me?*

'I tell him, that if I am obliged to go to my uncle Antony's, it is not to be inferred that I must therefore *necessarily* be Mr Solmes's wife: since I may not be so sure, perhaps, that the same exceptions lie so strongly against my quitting a house to which I shall be forcibly carried, as if I left my father's house: and, at the worst, I may be able to keep them in suspense till my cousin Morden comes, who will have a right to put me in possession of my grandfather's estate, if I insist upon it.'

This, I doubt, is somewhat of an artifice; being principally designed to keep him out of mischief. For I have but little hope, if carried thither, whether sensible or senseless, if I am left to my brother's and sister's mercy, but they will endeavour to force the solemn obligation upon me. Otherwise, were there but any prospect of avoiding this, by delaying (or even by taking things to make me ill, if nothing else would do) till my cousin comes, I hope I should not think of leaving even my uncle's house. For I should not know how to square it to my own principles to dispense with the duty I owe to my father, wherever it shall be his will to place me.

But while you give me the charming hope that, in order to avoid one man, I shall not be under the necessity of throwing myself upon the friends of the other; I think my case not absolutely desperate.

I see not any of my family, nor hear from them in any way of kindness. This looks as if they themselves expected no great matters from that Tuesday's conference which makes my heart flutter every time I think of it.

My uncle Antony's intended presence I do not much like: but that is preferable to my brother's or sister's. My uncle is very impetuous in his anger. I can't think Mr Lovelace can be much more so; at least, he cannot *look it*, as my uncle, with his harder features can. These sea-prospered gentlemen, as my uncle has often made me think, not used to any but elemental control, and even ready to buffet that; bluster often as violently as the winds they are accustomed to be angry at.

I believe both Mr Solmes and I shall look like a couple of fools, if it be true, as my uncle Harlowe writes, and Betty often tells me, that he is as much afraid of seeing me as I am of seeing him.

Adieu, my happy, thrice happy, Miss Howe, who have no hard terms affixed to your duty!—Who have nothing to do but to fall in with a choice your mamma has made for you, to which you have not, nor can have, a just objection: except the frowardness of [our] sex, as our free censurers would perhaps take the liberty to say, makes it one that the choice was your mamma's, at first hand. Perverse nature, we know, loves not to be prescribed to; although youth is not so well qualified, either by sedateness or experience, to choose for itself.

To *know* your own happiness; and that it is *now*, nor to leave it to *after*-reflection to look back upon the *preferable past* with a heavy and self-accusing heart, that you did not choose it when you might have chosen it, is all that is necessary to complete your felicity!—And this power is wished you by

Your

CL. HARLOWE

Letter 74: MISS HOWE TO MISS CLARISSA HARLOWE

Sunday, April 2

I OUGHT yesterday to have acknowledged the receipt of your parcel: Robin tells me that the Joseph Leman whom you mention as the traitor saw him. He was in the poultry yard and spoke to Robin over the bank which divides that from the Green Lane. What brings you hither, Mr Robert?—but I can tell. Hie away, as fast as you can.

No doubt but their dependence upon this fellow's vigilance, and upon Betty's, leaves you more at liberty in your airings than you would otherwise be: but you are the only person I ever heard of, who, in such circumstances, had not some faithful servant to trust little offices to. A poet, my dear, would not have gone to work for an Angelica, without giving her her Violetta, her Cleanthe, her Clelia, or some such pretty-named confidante—an old nurse at the least.

I read to my mamma several passages of your letters. But your last paragraph in your yesterday's charmed her quite. You have won her heart by it, she told me. And while her fit of gratitude for it lasted, I was thinking to open my proposal and to press it with all the earnestness I could give it, when Hickman came in, making his legs, and stroking his cravat and ruffles in turn.

I could most freely have ruffled him for it—As it was—Sir—saw you not some one of the servants?—Could not one of them have come in before you?

He begged pardon: looked as if he knew not whether he had best keep his ground, or withdraw—Till my mamma. Why, Nancy, we are not upon particulars—Pray, Mr Hickman, sit down.

By your le—ave, good madam, to me. You know his drawl, when his muscles give him the respectful hesitation—

Ay, ay, pray sit down, honest man, if you are weary!—But by my *mamma*, if you please. I desire my hoop may have its full circumference. All they're good for, that I know, is to clean dirty shoes and to keep ill-mannered fellows at a distance.

Strange girl! cried my mamma, displeased; but with a milder turn. Ay, ay, Mr Hickman, sit down by *me*. I have no such *forbidding folly* in my dress—I looked serious; and in my heart was glad this speech of hers was not made to your uncle Antony.

My mamma, with the true widow's freedom, would mighty prudently have led into our subject, and have had him see, I question not, that very paragraph in your letter which is so much in his favour. He was highly obliged to dear Miss Harlowe, she would assure him; that she *did* say—

But I asked him, if he had any news by his last letters from London: a question he always understands to be a *subject-changer*; for otherwise I never put it. And so if he be *but* silent, I am not angry with him that he answers it not.

I choose not to mention my proposal before him, till I know how it will be relished by my mamma. If it be not well received, perhaps I may employ *him* on the occasion. Yet I don't like to owe him an obligation, if I could help it. For men who have his views in their heads do so parade it, so strut about, if a woman condescend to employ them in her affairs, that one has no patience with them. But if I *find* not an opportunity this day, I will *make* one tomorrow.

I shall not open either of your sealed-up parcels, but in *your* presence. There is no need. Your conduct is out of all question with me: and by the extracts you have given me from his letters and your own, I know all that relates to the present situation of things between you.

I was going to give you a little flippant hint or two. But since you wish to be thought superior to all our sex in the command of yourself; and since indeed you deserve to be so thought; I will spare you—You are, however, at times, more than half inclined to speak out. That you do not is only owing to a little bashful struggle between *you* and *yourself*, as I may say. When that is quite got over, I know you will favour me undisguisedly with the result.

I cannot forgive your taking upon you (at so extravagant a rate too) to pay my mamma's servant. Indeed I *am*, and I *will be*, angry with you for it. A year's wages at once, well nigh (only as, unknown to my mamma, I make it better for the servants, according to their merits)!—How it made the man stare!—And it may be his ruin too, as far as I know. If he should buy a ring, and marry a sorry body in the neighbourhood with the money, one would be loath, a twelvemonth hence, that the poor old fellow should think he had reason to wish the bounty never conferred!

I MUST *give you your way in these things*, you say—And I know there is no contradicting you: for you were ever putting too great a value upon little offices done for *you*, and too little upon the great ones you do for *others*. The satisfaction you have in doing so, I grant it, repays you. But why should you, by the nobleness of your mind, throw reproaches upon the rest of the world?—Particularly, upon your own family, and upon ours too?

If, as I have heard you say, it is a good rule to *give* WORDS *the hearing, but to form our judgements of men and things by* DEEDS ONLY; what shall we think of one, who seeks to find palliatives in *words*, for narrowness of heart in the very persons her *deeds* so silently, yet so forcibly, reflect upon? Why blush you not, my dear friend, to be thus singular?—When you meet with another person, whose mind is like your own, then display your excellencies as you please: but till then, for pity's sake, let your heart and your spirit suffer a little contraction.

I intended to write but a few lines; chiefly to let you know your parcels are come safe. And accordingly I began in a large hand; and I am already come to the end of my second sheet. But I could write a quire without hesitation upon a subject so copious and so beloved, as is your praise—Not for *this* single instance of your generosity; since I am really angry with you for it; but for the benevolence exemplified in the whole tenor of your life and actions; of which this is but a common instance. God direct you, in your own arduous trials, is all I have room to add; and make you as happy, as you think to be

> Your own
> ANNA HOWE

Letter 75: MISS CLARISSA HARLOWE TO MISS HOWE

Sunday night, April 2

I HAVE many new particulars to acquaint you with, that show a great change in my friends' behaviour to me. I did not think we had so much art among us, as I find we have. I will give them to you as they offered.

All the family was at church in the morning. They brought good Dr Lewin with them, in pursuance of a previous invitation. And the doctor sent up to desire my permission to attend me in my own apartment.

You may believe it was easily granted.

So the doctor came up.

We had a conversation of near an hour before dinner: but, to my surprise, he waived everything that would have led to the subject I supposed he wanted to talk about. At last I asked him, if it were not thought strange I should be so long absent from church? He made me some handsome compliments upon it: but said, for his part, he had ever made it a rule to avoid interfering in the private concerns of families, unless desired to do so.

I was prodigiously disappointed: but supposing that he was thought too just a man to be made a judge of in this cause; I led no more to it: nor, when he was called to dinner, did he take the least notice of leaving me behind him there.

But this was the first time, since my confinement, that I thought it a hardship not to dine below. And when I parted with him on the stairs, a tear would burst its way; and he hurried down; his own good-natured eyes glistening; for he saw it—nor trusted he his voice, lest the accent, I suppose, should have discovered his concern; departing in silence; though with his usual graceful obligingness.

I hear that he praised me, and my part in the conversation we had held together. To show them, I suppose, that it was not upon the interesting subjects which I make no doubt he was desired not to enter upon.

He left me so dissatisfied, yet so perplexed with this new way of treatment, that I never found myself so puzzled, and so much out of my train.

But I was to be more so. This was to be a day of puzzle to me. *Pregnant* puzzle, if I may so say—for there must great meaning lie behind it.

In the afternoon, all but my brother and sister went to church with the good doctor; who left his compliments for me. I took a walk in the garden. My brother and sister walked in it too, and kept me in their eye a good while, on purpose as I thought, that I might see how gay and good-humoured they were together. At last they came down the walk that I was coming up, hand in hand, lover-like.

Your servant, miss—your servant, sir—passed between my brother and me.

Is it not cold-ish, sister Clary? in a kinder voice than usual, said my sister, and stopped—I stopped, and curtsied low to her half-curtsy. I think not, sister, said I.

She went on. I curtsied without return; and proceeded; turning to my poultry yard.

By a shorter turn, arm in arm, they were there before me.

I think, Clary, said my brother, you must present me with some of this breed, for Scotland.

If you please, brother.

I'll choose for you, said my sister.

And while I fed them, they picked out half a dozen: yet intending nothing by it, I believe, but to show a deal of love and good-humour to each other, before me.

My uncles next (after church was done, to speak in the common phrase) were to do me the honour of *their* notice. They bid Betty tell me, they would drink tea with me in my own apartment. Now, thought I, shall I have the subject of next Tuesday enforced upon me.

But they contradicted the tea orders, and only my uncle Harlowe came up to me.

Half-distant, half-affectionate, was the air he put on to his *daughter-niece*, as he used to call me; and I threw myself at his feet, and besought his favour.

None of these discomposures, child! None of these apprehensions! You'll now have everybody's favour! All is coming about, my dear!—I was impatient to see you!—I could no longer deny myself this satisfaction. And raised me, and kissed me, and called me, charming creature!

But he waived entering into any interesting subject. All will be well now! All will be right!—No more complainings! Everybody loves you!—I only came to make my earliest court to you, were his condescending words, and to sit and talk of twenty and twenty fond things, as I used to do—And let every past disagreeable thing be forgotten; as if nothing had happened.

He understood me as beginning to hint at the disgrace of my confinement. No disgrace, my dear, can fall to your lot: your reputation is too well established. I longed to see you, repeated he—I have seen nobody half so amiable, since I saw you last.

And again he kissed my cheek, my glowing cheek, for I was impatient, I was vexed to be thus, as I thought, played upon: and how could I be grateful for a visit, that it now was evident was only a too *humble* artifice to draw me in against the next Tuesday, or to leave me inexcusable to them all!

Oh my cunning brother!—This is his contrivance! And then my anger made me recollect the triumph in his and my sister's loves to each other, acted before me; and the mingled indignation flashing from their eyes, as arm in arm they spoke to me, and the forced condescension playing upon their lips, when they called me Clary, and sister.

Do you think I could with these reflections look upon my uncle Harlowe's visit as the favour he seemed desirous I should think it to be?—Indeed I could not; and seeing him so studiously avoid all recrimination, as I may call it, I gave into the affectation; and followed him in his talk of indifferent things—while he seemed to admire this thing and that, as if he had never seen them before; and now and then condescendingly kissed the hand that wrought some of the things he fixed his eyes upon; not so much to admire them, as to find subjects to divert what was most in his head, and in my own heart.

At his going away—How can I leave you here by yourself, my dear?—You, whose company used to enliven us all. You are not expected down indeed! But I protest, I had a good mind to surprise your papa and mamma!—If I thought nothing would arise that would be disagreeable—my dear, my love! (Oh the dear artful gentleman! how could my uncle Harlowe so dissemble?) What say you?— Will you give me your hand?—Will you see your father?—Can you stand his first displeasure on seeing the dear creature who has given him and all of us so much disturbance?—Can you promise future—

He saw me rising in my temper—Nay, my dear, if you cannot be all resignation, I would not have you think of it!

My heart, struggling between duty and warmth of temper, was full. You know, my dear, I never could bear to be dealt meanly with!—How,—how *can* you, sir!— You, my papa-uncle!—How *can* you, sir!—The poor girl!—For I could not speak with connexion.

Nay, my dear, if you cannot be all duty, all resignation—better stay where you are—But after the instance you have given—

Instance, I have given!—What instance, sir?

Well, well, child, better stay where you are, if your past confinement hangs so heavy upon you—But now there will be a sudden end to it—Adieu, my dear!— Three words only—Let your compliance be sincere!—And love me, as you used to love me—Your grandfather did not do so much for you, as I will do for you.

Without suffering me to reply, he hurried away, I thought, as if he had an escape, and was glad his part was over.

Don't you see, my dear, how they are all determined?—Have I not reason to dread next Tuesday?

Up presently after came my sister: to observe, I suppose, the way I was in—She found me in tears.

Have you not a Thomas à Kempis,[1] sister? with a stiff air.

I have, madam.

Madam! How long are we to be at this distance, Clary?

No longer, if you allow me to call you, sister, my dear Bella! And I took her hand.

No fawning neither, girl!

I withdrew my hand as hastily as I should do if, reaching at a parcel from under the wood, I had been bit by a [viper].

I beg pardon—Too, too ready to make advances, I am always subjecting myself to contempts!

People who know not how to keep a middle behaviour, said she, must evermore do so.

I will fetch you the Kempis—I did—Here it is—You will find excellent things, Bella, in that little book.

I wish, retorted she, you had profited by them.

I wish *you* may, said I. Example from a sister older than one's self is a fine thing.

Older! Saucy little fool!—And away she flung.

What a captious old woman will my sister make, if she lives to be one!— Demanding the reverence; yet not aiming at the merit; and ashamed of the years, that only can entitle her to the reverence.

It is plain from what I have *related*, that they think they have got me at some advantage by obtaining my consent to this interview: but if it were *not*, Betty's impertinence just now would make it more evident. She has been complimenting me upon it; and upon the visit of my uncle Harlowe. She says, the difficulty now is more than half over with me. She is sure I would not see Mr Solmes, but to have him. Now shall she be soon better employed than of late she has been. All hands will be at work. She loves dearly to have weddings go forward!—Who knows whose turn will be next?

I found in the afternoon a reply to my answer to Mr Lovelace's letter: it is full of promises, full of gratitude, of *eternal* gratitude, is his word, among others still more hyperbolic. Yet Mr Lovelace, the *least* of any man whose letters I have seen, runs into those elevated absurdities. I should be apt to despise him for it, if he did. Such language looks always to me as if the flatterer thought to *find* a woman a fool, or hoped to *make* her one.

'He regrets my indifference to him; which puts all the hope he has in my favour upon my friends' shocking usage of me.

'As to my charge upon him of unpoliteness and uncontrollableness—What (he asks) can he say? Since being unable absolutely to vindicate himself, he has too much ingenuity to attempt to do so: yet is struck dumb by my harsh construction, that his acknowledging temper is owing more to his carelessness to defend himself, than to his inclination to amend. He had never *before* met with the objections against his morals which I had raised, *justly* raised. And he was resolved to obviate them. What is it, he asks, that he had promised, but reformation by my example? And what occasion for the promise, if he had not faults, and those very great ones, to reform of? He hopes acknowledgement of an error is no bad sign; although my severe virtue has interpreted it into one.

'He believes I may be right (*severely* right, he calls it) in my judgement against making reprisals in the case of the intelligence he receives from my family. He cannot charge himself to be of a temper that leads him to be inquisitive into anybody's private affairs; but hopes, that the circumstances of the case, and the strange conduct of my friends will excuse him; especially, when so much depends upon his knowing the movements of a family so violently bent by measures right or wrong to carry their point against me, in malice to him. People, he says, who act like angels ought to have angels to deal with. For his part, he has not yet learned the difficult lesson of returning *good for evil*: and shall think himself the less encouraged to learn it, by the treatment I have met with from the very spirits which, were he to lay himself under their feet, would trample upon him, as they do upon me.

'He excuses himself for the liberties he owns he has heretofore taken in ridiculing the marriage-state. It is a subject, he says, that he has not of late treated so lightly. He owns it to be so trite, so beaten a topic with all libertines and witlings; so frothy, so empty, so nothing-meaning, so worn-out a *theme*, that he is heartily ashamed of himself, ever to have made it *his*. He condemns it as a stupid reflection upon the laws and good order of society, and upon a man's own ancestors: and in himself, who has some reason to value himself upon his descent and alliances, more censurable than in those who have not the same advantage to boast of. He promises to be more circumspect than ever, both in his words and actions, that he may be more and more worthy of my approbation; and that he may give an assurance beforehand that a foundation is laid in his mind, for my example to work upon, with equal reputation, and effect to us both—if he may be so happy as to call me his.

'He gives me up as absolutely lost, if I go to my uncle Antony's: the close confinement; the moated house; the chapel; the implacableness of my brother and sister, and their power over the rest of my family, he sets forth in strong lights, and plainly hints that he must have a struggle to prevent my being carried thither.'

Your kind, your generous interesting of yourself in your mamma's favour for me, I hope, will prevent those harsher extremities which I might otherwise be driven to. And to you I will fly, if permitted, and keep all my promises of not corresponding with anybody, not seeing anybody, but by your mamma's direction and yours—I will close, and deposit at this place. It is not necessary to say how much I am

> Your ever-affectionate and obliged
> CL. HARLOWE

Letter 76: MISS CLARISSA HARLOWE TO MISS HOWE

Monday, April 3

I AM glad my papers are safe in your hands. I will make it my endeavour to deserve your good opinion that I may not at once disgrace your judgement, and my own heart.

I have another letter from Mr Lovelace. He is extremely apprehensive of the meeting I am to have with Mr Solmes tomorrow. He says, 'That the airs that wretch gives himself on the occasion add to his concern; and it is with infinite difficulty that he prevails upon himself not to make him a visit, to let him know what he may expect if compulsion be used towards me in his favour. He assures me that Solmes has actually talked with tradesmen of new equipages, and names the people in town with whom he has treated: that he has even (was there ever such a horrid wretch!) allotted this and that apartment in his house for a nursery, and other offices.'

How shall I bear to hear such a creature talk of love to me? I shall be out of all patience with him!—Besides, I thought that he did not dare to make or talk of these impudent preparations—so inconsistent as such are with my brother's views—but I fly the shocking subject.

Upon this confidence of Solmes, you will less wonder at that of Lovelace, 'in pressing me, in the name of all his family to escape from so determined a violence as is intended to be offered to me at my uncle's: that the forward contriver should propose his uncle's chariot and six to be at the stile that leads up to the lonely coppice, adjoining to our paddock. You will see how audaciously he mentions settlements ready drawn; horsemen ready to mount; and one of his cousins Montague to be in the chariot, or at the George in the neighbouring village, waiting to accompany me to Lord M's, or to either of his aunts, or to town, as I please; and upon such orders, or conditions, and under such restrictions, as to himself, as I shall prescribe.'

You will see how he threatens 'to watch and waylay them, and rescue me, as he calls it, by an armed force of friends and servants, if they attempt to carry me against my will to my uncle's; and this, whether I give my consent to the enterprise, or not—since he shall have no hopes if I am once there.'

Oh my dear friend! Who can think of these things, and not be extremely miserable in her apprehensions!

This mischievous sex! What had I to do with any of them; or they with me!—I had deserved this, were it by my own seeking, by my own giddiness, that I had brought myself into this situation—I wish, with all my heart—But how foolishly we are apt to wish, when we find ourselves unhappy and know not how to help ourselves.

On your mamma's goodness, however, is my reliance. If I can but avoid being precipitated on either hand till my cousin Morden arrives, a reconciliation must follow; and all will be happy!

I have deposited a letter for Mr Lovelace; in which 'I charge him to avoid any rash step, any visit to Mr Solmes, which may be followed by acts of violence, as he would not disoblige me for ever.'

I re-assure him, 'that I will sooner die than be that man's wife.

'Whatever be my usage, whatever the result of this interview, I insist upon his not presuming to offer violence to any of my friends: and express myself highly displeased that he should presume upon such an interest in my favour as to think himself entitled to dispute my father's authority in my removal to my uncle's; although I tell him that I will omit neither prayers nor contrivance, even to the making of myself ill, to avoid going.'

Tomorrow is Tuesday!—How soon comes upon us the day we dread!—Oh that a deep sleep of twenty-four hours would seize my faculties—But then the next day would be Tuesday, as to all the effects and purposes for which I so much dread it. If this reach you before the event of this so much apprehended interview can be known, pray for

Your
CL. HARLOWE

Letter 77: MISS CLARISSA HARLOWE TO MISS HOWE

Tuesday morning, six o'clock

THE day is come!—I wish it were happily over. I have had a wretched night. Hardly a wink have I slept, ruminating upon the approaching interview. The very distance of time they consented to has added solemnity to the meeting, which otherwise it would not have had.

A thoughtful mind is not a blessing to be coveted, unless it had such a happy vivacity with it as yours: a vivacity which enables a person to enjoy the *present*, without being over-anxious about the *future*.

Tuesday, eleven o'clock

I HAVE had a visit from my aunt Hervey. Betty, in her alarming way, told me, I should have a lady to breakfast with me, whom I little expected; giving me to believe it was my mamma. This fluttered me so much, on hearing a lady coming upstairs, supposing it was she (not knowing how to account for her motives in such a visit, after I had been so long banished from her presence), that my aunt at her entrance took notice of my disorder, and after the first salutation: Why, miss, said she, you seem surprised!—Upon my word, you thoughtful young ladies have strange apprehensions about nothing at all. What, taking my hand, can be the matter with you?—Why, my dear, tremble, tremble, tremble at this rate? You'll be fit to be seen by nobody. Come, my love, kissing my cheek, pluck up a courage! By this needless flutter on the approaching interview, when it is over, you will judge of your other antipathies and laugh at yourself for giving way to so apprehensive an imagination.

I said that whatever we strongly imagined was, in its effects at the time, *more* than imaginary, although to others it might not appear so: that I had not rested one hour all night: that the impertinent set over me had fluttered me with giving me room to think that it was my mamma who was coming up to me: and that, at this rate, I should be very little qualified to see anybody I disliked to see.

There was no accounting for these things, she said. Mr Solmes last night supposed he should be under as much agitation as I.

Who is it, then, madam, that so reluctant an interview on both sides is to please?

Both of you, my dear, I hope, after the first flurries are over. The most apprehensive beginnings I have often known make the happiest conclusions.

There can be but one happy conclusion to the intended visit and that is, that both sides may be satisfied it will be the last.

She then represented how unhappy it would be for me if I did not suffer myself to be prevailed upon. She pressed me to receive him as became my education: and declared that his apprehensions at seeing me were owing to his love and his awe; intimating that true love was best known by fear and reverence; and that no blustering, braving lover could deserve encouragement.

To this I answered that constitution was a great deal to be considered: that a man of spirit would act like one, and could do nothing meanly: that a creeping mind would creep in everything where it had a view to obtain a benefit by it, and insult where it had power and nothing to expect—that this was not a point now to be determined with me: that I had said as much as I could possibly say on this subject: that this interview was imposed upon me: by those, indeed, who had a right to impose it; but that it was sorely against my will complied with, and for this reason, that there was *aversion*, not *wilfulness*, in the case; and so nothing could come of it, but a pretence, as I much apprehended, to use me still more severely than I had been used.

She was then pleased to charge me with prepossession and prejudice: expatiated upon the duty of a child: imputed to me abundance of fine qualities; but told me that, in this case, *that* of persuadableness was wanting to crown all. She insisted upon the *merit* of obedience, although my will were *not* in it. From a little hint I gave of my still greater dislike to see Mr Solmes, on account of the freedom I had treated him with, she talked to me of his forgiving disposition; of his infinite respect for me; and I cannot tell what of this sort—

I never found myself so fretful in my life. I told my aunt so; and begged her pardon for it. But she said it was well disguised then; for she saw nothing but little tremors usual with young ladies, when they were to see their admirers for the *first* time, as this might be called: for that it was the first time I had consented to see him in that light—But that the *next*—

How, madam, interrupted I!—Is it then imagined I give this meeting upon that foot?—

To be sure it is, child——

To be sure it is, madam!—Then do I yet desire to decline it!—I will not, I cannot, see him, if he expects me to see him upon those terms.

Niceness, punctilio—Mere punctilio, niece!—Can you think that your appointment, day, place, hour, and knowing what the intent of it was, is to be interpreted away as a mere ceremony and to mean nothing?—Let me tell you, my dear, your father, mother, uncles, everybody, respect this appointment as the first act of your compliance with their wills; and therefore recede not, I desire you; but make a merit of what cannot be helped!—

Oh the hideous wretch!—Pardon me, madam—*I* to be supposed to meet such a man as *that*, with such a view! and *he* to be armed with such an expectation!— But it cannot be that *he* expects it, whatever others may do—It is plain he cannot, by the fear he tells you all he shall have to see me: if his *hope* were so audacious, he could not *fear* so much.

Indeed, he *has* this hope; and justly founded too. But his fear arises from his reverence, as I told you before.

His reverence!—his unworthiness!—'Tis so apparent, that he himself sees it, as well as everybody else. Hence the purchase he aims at!—Hence is it, that settlements are to make up for acknowledged want of merit!—

His *unworthiness*, say you!—Not so fast, my dear. Does not this look like setting a high value upon yourself?—We all have exalted notions of your merit, niece; but nevertheless, it would not be wrong, if you were to arrogate less to *yourself*; though more were to be your due than your friends attribute to you.

I am sorry, madam, it should be thought arrogance in me to suppose I am not worthy of a better man than Mr Solmes, both as to person and mind: And as to fortune, I thank God I despise all that can be insisted upon in his favour from so poor a plea.

She told me it signified nothing to talk: I knew the expectation of everyone—

Indeed I did not—It was impossible I could think of such a strange expectation,

upon a compliance made only to show I would comply in all that was in my power
to comply with.

I might easily, she said, have supposed that everyone thought I was beginning to
oblige them all by the kind behaviour of my brother and sister to me in the garden,
last Sunday; by my sister's visit to me afterwards in my chamber; although both
more stiffly received by me than were either wished or expected; by my uncle
Harlowe's affectionate visit to me the same afternoon; not indeed so very gratefully
received, as I used to receive his favours!—But this he kindly imputed to the
displeasure I had conceived at my confinement, and to my coming-off by degrees,
that I might keep myself in countenance for my past opposition!

See, my dear, the low cunning of that Sunday-management, which then so much
surprised me! And see the reason why Dr Lewin was admitted to visit me, yet
forbore to enter upon a subject that I thought he came to talk to me about!—For,
it seems, there was no occasion to dispute with me on a point I was to be *supposed*
to have conceded to—See, also, how unfairly my brother and sister must have
represented their pretended kindness, when (though they had an end to answer by
appearing kind) their antipathy to me seems to have been so strong, that they
could not help insulting me by their arm-in-arm lover-like behaviour to each other;
as my sister afterwards likewise did, when she came to borrow my Kempis—

I lifted up my hands and eyes!—I cannot, said I, give this treatment a name!—
The *end* so unlikely to be answered by *means* so low!—I know *whose* the whole
is!—He that could get my uncle Harlowe to contribute his part and procure the
acquiescence of the rest of my friends to it must have the power to do anything
with them against me!—

Again my aunt told me that talking and invective, now I had given the
expectation, would signify nothing. She hoped I would not show them all that they
had been too forward in their constructions of my desire to oblige them. She could
assure me that it would be worse for me if *now* I receded, than if I had never
advanced—

Advanced, madam! How can you say *advanced*? Why, this is a trick upon me!—
a poor, low trick! Pardon me, madam, I don't say you have a hand in it—But, my
dearest aunt, tell me, will not my mamma be present at this dreaded interview?—
Will she not so far favour me?—were it but to qualify—

Qualify, my dear, interrupted she—Your mamma, and your uncle Harlowe
would not be present on this occasion for the world—

Oh then, madam, how can they look upon my consent to this interview as an
advance?

My aunt was displeased at this home push. Miss Clary, said she, there is no
dealing with you. It would be happy for you and for everybody else, were your
obedience as ready as your wit. I will leave you—

Not in anger, I hope, madam! interrupted I—All I meant was to observe that
let the meeting issue as it *must* issue, it cannot be a disappointment to *any-*
body.

Oh miss! you seem to be a very determined young creature—Mr Solmes will be
here at your time: and remember once more, that upon the coming afternoon
depends the peace of your whole family, and your own happiness—

And so saying, down she hurried.

Here I stop. In what way I shall resume, or when, is not left to me to conjecture;

much less to determine. I am excessively uneasy!—No good news from your mamma, I doubt!—I will deposit thus far, for fear of the worst.

Adieu, my best, my *only* friend!

Letter 78: MISS CLARISSA HARLOWE TO MISS HOWE

Tuesday evening; and continued through the night

WELL, my dear, I am alive, and here! But how long I shall be either here, or alive, I cannot say!—I have a vast deal to write; and perhaps shall have little time for it. Nevertheless, I must tell you how the saucy Betty again fluttered me when she came up with this Solmes's message; although, as you will remember from my last, I was in a way before that wanted no additional surprises.

Miss! Miss! Miss! cried she, as fast as she could speak, with her arms spread abroad and all her fingers distended and held up, will you be pleased to walk down into your own parlour?—There is everybody, I'll assure you, in full *congregation!*— And there is Mr Solmes, as fine as a lord, with a charming white peruke, fine laced shirt and ruffles, coat trimmed with silver, and a waistcoat standing an end with lace!—Quite handsome, believe me!—You never saw such an alteration!—Ah! miss, shaking her head, 'tis pity you have said so much against him!—But you know how to come off, for all that!—I hope it will not be too late!—

Impertinence! said I—wert thou bid to come up in this fluttering way?—And I took up my fan, and fanned myself.

Bless me! said she, how soon these fine young ladies will be put into *flusterations!*—I meant not either to offend or frighten you, I am sure—

Everybody there, do you say?—who do you call everybody?—

Why, miss, holding out her left palm opened, and with a flourish and a saucy leer, patting it with the forefinger of the other at every mentioned person, there is your papa!—there is your mamma!—there is your uncle Harlowe!—there is your uncle Antony!—your aunt Hervey!—*my* young lady!—and my young master!— and Mr Solmes, with the air of a great courtier, standing up because he named you. Mrs Betty, said he (then the ape of a wench bowed and scraped as awkwardly as I suppose the person she endeavoured to imitate), pray give my humble service to miss, and tell her I wait her commands.

Was not this a wicked wench?—I trembled so, I could hardly stand. I was spiteful enough to say that her young mistress, I supposed, bid her put on these airs to frighten me out of a capacity of behaving so calmly as should procure me my uncle's compassion.

What a way do you put yourself in, miss, said the insolent!—Come, dear madam, taking up my fan which I had laid down, and approaching me with it, fanning, shall I—

None of thy impertinence!—But say you, *all* my friends are below with him? And am I to *appear* before them *all?*

I can't tell if they'll stay when you come. I think they seemed to be moving when Mr Solmes gave me his orders. But what answer shall I carry to the 'squire?

Say, I can't go!—But yet, when 'tis over, 'tis over! Say, I'll wait upon—I'll attend—I'll come presently—say anything; I care not what—but give me my fan, and fetch me a glass of water.

She went, and I fanned myself all the time, for I was in a flame; and hemmed and struggled with myself, all I could; and, when she returned, drank my water; and finding no hope presently of a quieter heart, I sent her down and followed her with precipitation; trembling so, that, had I not hurried, I question if I could have gone down at all. Oh my dear, what a poor, passive machine is the body, when the mind is disordered!

There are two doors to *my* parlour, as I used to call it. As I entered at one, my friends hurried out at the other. I saw just the gown of my sister, the last who slid away. My uncle Antony went out with them; but he stayed not long, as you shall hear: and they all remained in the next parlour, a wainscot partition only parting the two. I remember them both in one: but they were separated in favour of us girls, for each to receive her visitors in at her pleasure.

Mr Solmes approached me as soon as I entered, cringing to the ground, a visible confusion in every feature of his face. After half a dozen choked-up Madams—he was very sorry—he was very much concerned—it was his misfortune—and there he stopped, being unable presently to complete a sentence.

This gave me a little more presence of mind. Cowardice in a foe begets courage in one's self: I see that plainly now. Yet perhaps, at bottom, the new-made bravo is a greater coward than the other.

I turned from him and seated myself in one of the fireside chairs, fanning myself. I have since recollected that I must have looked very saucily. Could I have had any *thoughts* of the man, I should have despised myself for it. But what can be said in the case of an aversion so perfectly sincere?

He hemmed five or six times, as I had done above; and these produced a sentence—that I could not but see his confusion. This sentence produced two or three more. I believe my aunt was his tutoress: for it was his awe, his reverence for so superlative a lady—(I assure you)—and he hoped—he hoped—three times he hoped, before he told me what—that I was too generous (generosity, he said, was my character) to despise him for such—for such—*true* tokens of his love—

I do indeed see you under some confusion, sir; and this gives me hope, that although I have been compelled, as I may call it, to this interview, it may be attended with happier effects than I had apprehended from it.

He had hemmed himself into more courage.

You could not, madam, imagine any creature so blind to your merits and so little attracted by them, as easily to forgo the interest and approbation he was honoured with by your worthy family, while he had any hope given him that one day he might, by his perseverance and zeal, expect your favour.

I am but too much aware, sir, that it is upon the interest and approbation you mention, that you build such hope. It is impossible, otherwise, that a man who has any regard for his *own* happiness would persevere against such declarations as I have made, and think myself obliged to make, in justice to you as well as to myself.

He had seen many instances, he told me, and had heard of more, where ladies had seemed as averse, and yet had been induced, some by motives of compassion; others by persuasion of friends, to change their minds; and had been very happy afterwards: and he hoped this might be the case here.

I have no notion, sir, of compliment, in an article of such importance as this: yet am I sorry to be obliged to speak my mind so plainly as I am going to do. Know then, that I have invincible objections, sir, to your address. I have declared them with an earnestness that I believe is without example: And why?—Because I believe it is without example, that any young creature, circumstanced as I am, was ever treated as I have been treated on your account.

It is hoped, madam, that your consent may, in time, be obtained: *that* is the hope; and I shall be a miserable man if it cannot.

Better, sir, give me leave to say, you were miserable by yourself, than that you should make two so.

You may have heard, madam, things to my disadvantage—No man is without enemies. Be pleased to let me know *what* you have heard, and I will either own my faults, and amend; or I will convince you that I am basely *bespattered:* and once I understand you overheard something that I should say that gave you offence— unguardedly, perhaps; but nothing but what showed my value, and that I would persist so long as I could have hope.

I have indeed heard many things to your disadvantage—and I was far from being pleased with what I overheard fall from your lips: but as you were not anything to me, and never could be, it was not for me to be concerned about the one or the other.

I am sorry, madam, to hear this: I am sure you should not tell me of any fault that I would be unwilling to correct in myself.

Then, sir, correct this fault: do not wish to have a poor young creature compelled in the most material article of her life, for the sake of motives she despises; and in behalf of a person she cannot value: one that has, in her own right, sufficient to set her above all offers, and a spirit that craves no more than what it *has* to make itself easy and happy.

I don't see, madam, how you would be happy, if I were to discontinue my address: for——

That is nothing to you, sir, interrupted I: do you but withdraw your pretensions: and if it be thought fit to start up another man for my punishment, the blame will not lie at your door. You will be entitled to my thanks; and most heartily will I thank you.

He paused, and seemed a little at a loss: and I was going to give him still stronger and more personal instances of my plain dealing, when in came my uncle Antony!

So, niece, so!—sitting in state like a queen, giving audience!—*haughty* audience!—Mr Solmes, why stand you thus humbly?—why this distance, man? I hope to see you upon a more intimate footing before we part.

I arose, as soon as he entered—and approached him with a bent knee: let me, sir, reverence my uncle, whom I have not for so long a time seen!—Let me, sir, bespeak your favour and compassion!

You'll have the favour of everybody, niece, when you know how to deserve it.

If ever I deserved it, I deserve it now. I have been hardly used—I have made proposals that ought to have been accepted; and such as would not have been *asked* of me. What have I done that I must be banished and confined thus disgracefully? That I must be allowed to have no free will in an article that concerns my present and future happiness?—

Miss Clary, replied my uncle, you have had your will in everything till now; and this makes your parents' will sit so heavy upon you.

My will, sir! Be pleased to allow me to ask, what was my will till now, but my father's will, and yours, and my uncle Harlowe's will?—Has it not been my pride to obey and oblige?—I never asked a favour, that I did not first sit down and consider if it were fit to be granted. And now, to show my obedience, have I not offered to live single? Have I not offered to divest myself of my grandfather's bounty, and to cast myself upon my papa's, to be withdrawn whenever I disoblige him? Why, dear good sir, am I to be made unhappy in a point so concerning to my happiness?

Your grandfather's estate is not wished from you. You are not desired to live a single life. You know *our* motives, and we guess at *yours*. And let me tell you, well as we love you, we would much sooner choose to follow you to the grave than that *yours* should take place.

I will engage never to marry any man, without my father's consent, and your's, sir, and everybody's. Did I ever give you cause to doubt my word?—And here I will take the solemnest oath that can be offered me——

That is the matrimonial one, interrupted he, with a big voice—and to this gentleman. It shall, it shall, cousin Clary!—And the more you oppose it, the worse it shall be for you.

This, and before the man, who seemed to assume courage upon it, highly provoked me.

Then, sir, you shall sooner follow me to the grave *indeed*—I will undergo the cruellest death: I will even consent to enter into the awful vault of my ancestors, and to have that bricked up upon me, than consent to be miserable for life—And, Mr Solmes, (turning to him) take notice of what I say; *this*, or *any* death, I will sooner undergo (that will soon be over) than be yours, and for *ever* unhappy!

My uncle was in a terrible rage upon this. He took Mr Solmes by the hand, shocked as the man seemed to be, and drew him to the window—Don't be surprised, Mr Solmes, don't be concerned at *this*. We know, and rapped out a sad oath, what women will say: the wind is not more boisterous, nor more changeable: and again he swore to that! If you think it worth your while to wait for such an ungrateful girl as this, I'll engage she'll *veer about*; I'll engage she *shall*: and a third time violently swore to it.

Then coming up to me (who had thrown myself, very much disordered by my vehemence, into the contrary window) as if he would have beat me; his face violently working, his hands clenched, and his teeth set—Yes, yes, yes, hissed the poor gentleman, you shall, you shall, you shall, cousin Clary, be Mr Solmes's; we will see that you shall; and this in one week at farthest—And then a fourth time he confirmed it. Poor gentleman, how he swore!—Strange! that people who have suffered in their time so much by storms should be so stormy!—

I am sorry, sir, said I, to see you in such a passion. All this, I am but too sensible, is owing to my brother's instigation; who would not himself give the instance of duty that is exacted from me. It is best for me to withdraw. I shall but provoke you farther, I fear: for though I would gladly obey you, if I could, yet this is a point determined with me; and I cannot so much as *wish* to get it over.

How could one help these strong declarations, the man in presence?

I was going out at the door I came in at; the gentlemen looking upon one another, as if referring to each other what to do, or whether to engage my stay, or suffer me to go: and who should I meet at the door but my brother, who had heard all that had passed.

Judge my surprise when he bolted upon me so unexpectedly, and taking my hand, which he grasped with violence, Return, pretty miss, said he; return, if you please!—You shall not yet *be bricked up!*—Your *instigating* brother shall save you from that!—Oh thou fallen angel, said he, peering up to my downcast face—such a sweetness *here!*—and such an obstinacy *there*, tapping my neck!—Oh thou true woman!—though so young—But you shall not have your rake: remember that; in a loud whisper, as if he would be decently indecent before the man!—You shall be redeemed, and this worthy gentleman, raising his voice, will be so good as to redeem you from ruin—and hereafter you will bless him, or have reason to bless him, for his *condescension*; that was the brutal brother's word!

He had led me up to meet Mr Solmes, whose hand he took, as he himself held mine. Here, sir, said he, take the rebel daughter's hand; I give it you now; she shall confirm the gift in a week's time, or will have neither father, mother, nor uncles, to boast of.

I snatched my hand away.

How now, miss!—

And how now, sir—What right have You to dispose of my hand?—If you govern everybody else, you shall not govern *me*; especially in a point so immediately relative to myself, and in which you neither have, nor ever shall have, anything to do.

I would have broke from him, but he held my hand too fast.

Let me go, sir!—Why am I thus treated?—You *design*, I doubt not, with your unmanly gripings, to hurt me, as you do: but again I say, wherefore is it that I am to be thus treated by You?

He tossed my hand from him with a whirl that pained my very shoulder. I wept, and held my other hand to the part.

Mr Solmes blamed him; so did my uncle.

He had no patience, he said, with such a perverseness; and to think of my reflections upon himself, before he entered. He had only given me back the hand I had not deserved he should touch. It was one of my arts, to pretend to be pained.

Mr Solmes said he would sooner give up all his hopes of me, than that I should be used unkindly: and he offered to plead in my behalf to them both; and applied himself with a bow, as if for my approbation of his interposition.

But I said, I am obliged to your intention, Mr Solmes, to interpose to save me from my brother's violence: but I cannot wish to owe so poor an obligation to a man whose ungenerous perseverance is the occasion, or at least the pretence, of *that* violence, and of all my disgraceful sufferings.

How generous in you, Mr Solmes, said my brother to him, to interpose in behalf of such an immoveable spirit! But I beg of you to persist!—For all our family's sake, and for *her* sake too if you love her, persist!—Let us save her, if possible, from ruining herself. Look at her person! Think of her fine qualities!—All the world confesses them, and we all gloried in her till now: she is worth saving!—and after two or three more struggles, she will be yours and, take my word for it, will reward your patience!—Talk not, therefore, of giving up your hopes, for a little whining folly. She has entered upon a parade which she knows not how to quit with a *female* grace. You have only her pride and her obstinacy to encounter: and, depend upon it, you will be as happy a man in a fortnight, as a married man *can* be.

You have heard me say, my dear, that my brother has always taken a liberty to reflect upon our sex, and upon matrimony!—he would not, if he did not think it *wit!*—Just as poor Mr Wyerley, and others we both know, prophane and ridicule Scripture; and all to evidence their pretensions to the same pernicious talent, and to have it thought that they are too wise to be good.

Mr Solmes, with a self-satisfied air, presumptuously said, he would suffer everything to *oblige* my family, and to *save* me. And doubted not to be amply rewarded, could he be so happy as to succeed at last.

Mr Solmes, said I, if you have any regard for your own happiness (*mine* is out of the question: you have not generosity enough to make *that* any part of your scheme), prosecute no further your address. It is but *just* to tell you that I could not bring my heart to think of you without the utmost disapprobation, *before* I was used as I have been: and can you think I am such a slave, such a *poor* slave, as to be brought to change my mind by the violent usage I have met with?

And you, sir, turning to my brother, if you think that *meekness* always indicates *tameness*; and that there is no *magnanimity* without *bluster*, own yourself mistaken for once: for you shall have reason to judge from henceforth that a generous mind is not to be forced; and that—

He lifted up his hands and eyes. No more, said the imperious wretch, I charge you!—Then turning to my uncle, Do you hear, sir? This is your once faultless niece! This is your favourite!

Mr Solmes looked as if he knew not what to think of the matter; and had I been left alone with him, I saw plainly, I could have got rid of him easily enough.

My uncle came up to me, looking up to my face, and down to my feet: And is it possible this can be *you?* All this violence from *you*, Miss Clary?

Yes, it is possible, sir—and I will presume to say this vehemence on my side is but the natural consequence of the usage I have met with, and the rudeness I am treated with, even in your presence, by a brother who has no more right to control me, than I have to control him.

This usage, cousin Clary, was not till all other means were tried with you.

Tried! to what end, sir—Do I contend for anything more than a mere negative? You *may*, sir (turning to Mr Solmes), *possibly* you may be induced the *rather* to persevere, thus ungenerously, as the usage I have met with for your sake, and what you have now seen offered to me by my brother, will show you what I *can* bear were my evil destiny ever to make me yours!

Lord, madam, cried Solmes, all this time distorted into twenty different attitudes, as my brother and my uncle were blessing themselves, and speaking only to each other by their eyes and by their working features; Lord, madam, what a construction is this!

A fair construction, sir, interrupted I: for he that can see a person he pretends to value, thus treated, and approve of it, must be capable of treating her thus himself. And that you *do* approve of it is evident by your declared perseverance, when you know I am confined, banished and insulted in order to make me consent to be what I never *can be*—and this, let me tell you, as I have often told others, not from motives of obstinacy, but *aversion*.

Excuse me, sir, turning to my uncle!—To you, as to my *papa's* brother, I owe duty. I beg *your* pardon that I cannot obey you: but as for my *brother*; he is *but* my brother; he shall not constrain me. And, turning to my brother: Knit your brows, sir, and frown as you will, I will ask you, Would *you*, in my case, make the sacrifices

I am willing to make to obtain everyone's favour? If *not*, what right have you to treat me thus? and to procure me to be treated as I have been, for so long past?

I had put myself by this time into great disorder. They were silent and seemed to want to talk to one another by their looks, walking about in violent disorders too, between whiles. I sat down fanning myself (as it happened, against the glass) and I could perceive my colour go and come; and being sick to the very heart, and apprehensive of fainting, I rung. Betty came in. I called for a glass of water, and drank it: but nobody minded me—I heard my brother pronounce the words, Art! d—d Art! to Solmes; which, I suppose, kept *him* back, together with the apprehension that he would not be welcome—Else I could see the man was more affected than my brother. And I, still fearing I should faint, rising, took hold of Betty's arm, staggering with extreme disorder, yet curtsying to my uncle: Let me hold by you, Betty, said I; let me withdraw.

.Whither go you, niece, said my uncle? We have not done with you yet. I charge you depart not. Mr Solmes has something to open to you that will astonish you— and you *shall* hear it.

Only, sir, by your leave, for a few minutes into the air—I will return, if you command it—I will hear all that I am to hear; that it may be over *now*, and *for-ever*. You will go with me, Betty?

And so, without any farther prohibition, I retired into the garden; and there, casting myself upon the first seat and throwing Betty's apron over my face, leaning against her side, my hands between hers, I gave way to a violent burst of grief, or passion, or both; which, as it seemed, saved my heart from breaking, for I was sensible of an immediate relief.

I have already given you specimens of Mrs Betty's impertinence. I shall not, therefore, trouble you with more: for the wench, notwithstanding this my distress, took great liberties with me after she saw me a little recovered, and as I walked further into the garden; insomuch, that I was obliged to silence her by an absolute prohibition of saying another word to me; and then she dropped behind me quite sullen and gloomy.

It was near an hour before I was sent for in again. The messenger was my cousin Dolly Hervey, who with an eye of compassion and respect (for Miss Hervey always loved me, and calls herself my scholar, as you know) told me my company was desired.

Betty left us.

Who commands my attendance, miss, said I?—Have you not been in tears, my dear?

Who can forbear tears, said she?

Why, what's the matter, cousin Dolly?—Sure, nobody is entitled to weep in this family, but I!

Yes, I am, madam, said she, because I love you.

I kissed her; and is it for me, my sweet cousin, that you shed tears?—There never was love lost between us: but tell me, what is designed to be done with me that I have this kind instance of your compassion for me?

You must take no notice of what I tell you: but my mamma has been weeping for you, too, with me; but durst not let anybody see it. Oh my Dolly, said my mamma, there never was so set a malice in man as in your cousin James Harlowe. They will ruin the flower and ornament of their family.

As how, Miss Dolly?—Did she not explain herself?—As how, my dear?

Yes, she said, Mr Solmes would have given up his claim to you; for he said you hated him, and there were no hopes; and your mamma was willing he should; and to have you taken at your word, to renounce Mr Lovelace and to live single. My mamma was for it too; for they heard all that passed between you and my uncle Antony, and my cousin James; saying it was impossible to think of prevailing upon you to have Mr Solmes. My uncle Harlowe seemed in the same way of thinking; at least, my mamma says he did not say anything to the contrary. But your papa was immoveable, and was angry at your mamma and mine upon it: and hereupon your brother, your sister, and my uncle Antony, joined in, and changed the scene entirely. In short, she says that Mr Solmes had great matters engaged to him. He owned that you were the finest young lady in England, and he would be content to be but little beloved, if he could *not* after marriage engage your heart, for the sake of having the honour to call you his but for one twelvemonth—I suppose he would break your heart in the next—for he is a cruel-hearted man, I am sure.

My friends may break my heart, cousin Dolly; but Mr Solmes will never have it in his power.

I don't know that, miss: you'll have good luck to avoid having him, by what I can find; for my mamma says they are all now of one mind, herself excepted; and she is forced to be silent, your papa and brother are both so outrageous.

I am got above minding my brother, cousin Dolly: he is *but* my brother—but to my papa I owe duty and obedience, if I could comply.

We are apt to be fond of anybody, who will side with us when oppressed or provoked: I always loved my cousin Dolly; but now she endeared herself to me ten times more by her soothing concern for me. I asked what *she* would do, were she in my case?

Without hesitation she replied: Have Mr Lovelace out of hand, and take up her own estate, if she were me; and there would be an end of it—And Mr Lovelace, she said, was a fine gentleman—Mr Solmes was not worthy to *buckle his shoes*.

Miss Hervey told me further, that her mamma was desired to come to me, to fetch me in; but she excused herself. I should have all my friends, she said she believed, sit in judgement upon me.

I wish it had been so. But, as I have been told since, neither my papa, nor my mamma, would trust themselves with me: the one for passion-sake, it seems; my mamma for tenderer considerations.

By this time we entered the house. Miss accompanied me into the parlour, and left me, as a person devoted, I just then thought.

Nobody was there. I sat down and had leisure to weep; reflecting, with a sad heart, upon what my cousin Dolly had told me.

They were all in my sister's parlour adjoining: for I heard a confused mixture of voices, some louder than others, drowning, as it seemed, the more compassionating accents.

Female accents I could distinguish the drowned ones to be. Oh my dear! what a hard-hearted sex is the other! Children of the same parents, how came they by their cruelty?—Do they get it by travel? Do they get it by conversation with one another?—Or how do they get it?—Yet my sister too is as hard-hearted as any of them. But this may be no exception neither: for she has been thought to be masculine in her air, and in her spirit. She has then, perhaps, a soul of the *other* sex in a body of *ours*. And so, for the honour of *our own*, will I judge of every woman for the future who, imitating the rougher manners of men, acts unbeseeming the gentleness of her own sex.

Forgive me, my dear friend, breaking into my story by these reflections. Were I rapidly to pursue my narration, without thinking, without reflecting, I believe I should hardly be able to keep in my right mind, since vehemence and passion would then be always uppermost; but while I *think* as I write, I cool, and my hurry of spirits is allayed.

I believe I was above a quarter of an hour enjoying my own comfortless contemplations, before anybody came in to me; for they seemed in full debate. My aunt looked in first; Oh my dear, said she, are you there? and withdrew hastily to apprise them of it.

And then (as agreed upon, I suppose) in came my uncle Antony, crediting Mr Solmes with the words, *Let me lead you in, my dear friend*; having hold of his hand; while the new-made beau awkwardly followed, but more edgingly, as I may say, setting his feet mincingly, to avoid treading upon his leader's heels. Excuse me, my dear, this seeming levity; but those we do not love, in everything are ungraceful with us.

I stood up. My uncle looked very surly—Sit down!—sit down, girl!—And drawing a chair near me, he placed his *dear* friend in it, whether he would or not, I having taken my seat. And my uncle sat on the other side of me.

Well, niece, taking my hand, we shall have very little more to say to you than we have already said, as to the subject that is so distasteful to you—Unless, indeed, you have better considered of the matter—And first, let me know if you have?

The matter wants no consideration, sir.

Very well, very well, *madam!* said my uncle, withdrawing his hands from mine: Could I ever have thought of this from you?

For God's sake, dearest madam, said Mr Solmes, folding his hands—and there he stopped.

For God's sake, *what*, sir?—How came God's sake and your sake, I pray you, to be the same?

This silenced *him*. My uncle could *only* be angry; and that he was before.

Well, well, well, Mr Solmes, said my uncle, no more of supplication. You have not confidence enough to expect a woman's favour.

He then was pleased to hint what great things he had designed to do for me; and that it was more for *my* sake, after he returned from the Indies, than for the sake of any *other* of the family, that he had resolved to live a single life. But now, concluded he, that the perverse girl despises all the great things it was once as much in my will, as in my power, to do for her, I will change my measures.

I told him, that I most sincerely thanked him for all his kind intentions to me: but that I was willing to resign all claim to any *other* of his favours than kind looks and kind words.

He looked about him this way and that.

Mr Solmes looked pitifully down.

But both being silent, I was sorry, I added, that I had too much reason to say a very harsh thing, as it might be thought; which was that if he would but be pleased to convince my brother and sister, that he was absolutely determined to alter his generous purposes towards me, it might possibly procure me better quarter from both than I was otherwise likely to have.

My uncle was very much displeased. But he had not the opportunity to express his displeasure, as he seemed prepared to do; for in came my brother in exceeding great wrath; and called me several vile names. His success hitherto had set him above keeping even decent measures.

Was this my spiteful construction, he asked?—Was this the interpretation I put upon his brotherly care of me, and concern for me, in order to prevent my ruining myself?

It *is*, indeed it *is*, said I: I know no other way to account for your late behaviour to me: and before your face, I repeat my request to my uncle, and I will make it to my other uncle whenever I am permitted to see him, that they will confer all their favours upon you and my sister; and only make me happy (It is all I wish for!) in their kind looks and kind words—

How they all gazed upon one another!—But could I be less peremptory before the man?

And, as to *your* care and concern for me, sir, turning to my brother; once more, I desire it not. You are but my brother. My papa and mamma, I bless God, are both living; and were they *not*, you have given me abundant reason to say that you are the very last person I would wish to have any concern for me.

How, niece? And is a brother, an *only* brother, of so little consideration with you, as this comes to? And ought he to have no concern for his sister's honour, and the family's honour?

My honour, sir!—I desire none of his concern for that! It never was endangered till it had his undesired concern!—Forgive me, sir—but when my brother knows how to act like a brother, or behave like a gentleman, he may deserve more consideration from me than it is possible for me to think he now does.

I thought my brother would have beat me upon this—but my uncle stood between us.

Violent girl, however, he called me!—Who, said he, would have thought it of her?

Then was Mr Solmes told that I was unworthy of his pursuit.

But Mr Solmes warmly took my part. He could not bear, he said, that I should be treated so roughly.

And so very much did he exert himself on this occasion, and so patiently was his warmth received by my brother that I began to suspect that it was a contrivance to make me think myself obliged to him; and that it might, perhaps, be one end of the pressed-for interview.

The very suspicion of this low artifice, violent as I was thought to be before, put me still more out of patience; and my uncle and my brother again praising his wonderful generosity, and his noble return of good for evil: You are a happy man, Mr Solmes, said I, that you can so *easily* confer obligations upon a whole family, except one ungrateful person of it, whom you seem to intend *most* to oblige; but who, being made unhappy by your favour, deserves not to owe to *you* any protection from the violence of a brother.

Then was I a rude, an ungrateful, an unworthy creature.

I own it all!—all, all you can call me, or think me, brother, do I own. I own my own unworthiness with regard to this gentleman. I take your word for his abundant merit, which I have neither leisure nor inclination to examine into—it may, perhaps, be as great as your own—but yet I cannot thank him for his mediation: for who sees not, looking at my uncle, that this is giving himself a merit with everybody at my expense?

Then turning to my brother, who seemed surprised into silence by my warmth, I must also acknowledge, sir, the favour of *your* superabundant care for me. But I discharge you of it; at least, while I have the happiness of nearer and dearer relations. You have given me no reason to think better of *your* prudence, than of my *own*. I am independent of *you*, sir; though I never desire to be so of my father: and although I wish for the good opinion of my uncles, it is *all* I wish for from them: and this, sir, I repeat, to make you and my sister easy.

Instantly almost came in Betty, in a great hurry, looking at me as spitefully as if she were my *sister:* Sir, said she to my brother, my master desires to speak to you this moment at the door.

He went to that which led into my sister's parlour; and this sentence I heard thundered from the mouth of one who had a right to all my reverence: Son James, let the rebel be this moment carried away to my brother's—this very moment—she shall not stay one hour more under my roof!

I trembled; I was ready to sink. Yet, not knowing what I did or said, I flew to the door, and would have opened it—but my brother pulled it to, and held it close by the key—Oh my papa!—my dear papa, said I, falling upon my knees at the door—admit your child to your presence!—Let me but plead my cause at your feet!— Oh reprobate not thus your distressed daughter!

My uncle put his handkerchief to his eyes: Mr Solmes made a still more grievous face than he had before. But my brother's marble heart was untouched.

I will not stir from my knees, continued I, without admission—at this door I beg it!—Oh let it be the door of mercy! And open it to me, honoured sir, I beseech you!—But this once, this once! although you were afterwards to shut it against me for ever!

The door was endeavoured to be opened on the inside, which made my brother let go the key on a sudden, and I pressing against it (all the time remaining on my knees) fell flat on my face into the other parlour; however, without hurting myself. But everybody was gone, except Betty, who helped to raise me up; and I looked round that apartment, and seeing nobody there, re-entered the other, leaning upon Betty; and then threw myself into the chair which I had sat in before; and my eyes overflowed to my great relief: while my uncle Antony, my brother, and Mr Solmes, left me, and went to my other relations.

What passed among them, I know not: but my brother came in by the time I had tolerably recovered myself, with a settled and haughty gloom upon his brow— Your father and mother command you instantly to prepare for your uncle Antony's. You need not be solicitous about what you shall take with you. You may give Betty your keys. Take them, Betty, if the perverse one has them about her, and carry them to her mother. She will take care to send everything after you that you shall want. But another night you will not be permitted to stay in this house.

I don't choose to give my keys to anybody, except to my mamma, and into her own hands. You see how much I am disordered. It may cost me my life to be hurried away so suddenly. I beg to be indulged, till next Monday at least.

That will not be granted you. So prepare for this very night. And give up your keys. Give them to *me*, miss. I'll carry them to your mamma.

Excuse me, brother. Indeed, I won't.

Indeed you must. In no one instance comply, Madam Clary?

Not in this, sir.

Have you anything you are afraid should be seen by your mamma?

Not if I be permitted to attend my mamma.

I'll make a report accordingly.

He went out.

In came Miss Dolly Hervey: I am sorry, madam, to be the messenger!—But your mamma insists upon your sending up all the keys of your cabinet, library, and drawers.

Tell my mamma, that I yield them up to her commands; tell her, I make no conditions with my mamma: but if she finds nothing she disapproves of, I beg that she will permit me to tarry here a few days longer—Try, my Dolly (the dear girl sobbing with grief); try if your gentleness cannot prevail for me.

She wept still more, and said, It is sad, very sad, to see matters thus carried!

She took the keys, and wrapped her arms about me; and begged me to excuse her—And would have said more; but Betty's presence awed her, as I saw.

Don't pity me, my dear, said I. It will be imputed to you as a fault. You see who is by.

The insolent wench scornfully smiled: One young lady pitying another in things of this nature looks promising in the youngest, I must needs say.

I bid her, for a saucy creature, begone from my presence.

She would most gladly, she said, were she not to stay about me by my mamma's order.

It soon appeared for what she stayed; for I offering to go upstairs to my apartment when my cousin went from me with the keys, she told me she was commanded (to her very great regret, she must own) to desire me not to go up at present.

Such a bold face as she, I told her, should not hinder me.

She instantly rang the bell, and in came my brother, meeting me at the door.

Return, return, miss—No going up yet.

I went in again, and throwing myself upon the window-seat, wept bitterly.

Shall I give you the particulars of a ridiculously spiteful conversation that passed between my brother and me, while he, with Betty, was in office to keep me in play, and my closet was searching?—But I think I will not. It can answer no good end.

I desired several times, while he stayed, to have leave to retire to my apartment; but it was not permitted me. The search, I suppose, was not over. Bella was one of those employed in it. They could not have a more diligent searcher. How happy it was they were disappointed!

But when my sister could not find the *cunning creature*'s papers, I was to stand another visit from Mr Solmes—preceded now by my aunt Hervey, sorely against her will, I could see that; accompanied by my uncle Antony, in order to keep her steady, I suppose.

But being a little heavy (for it is now past two in the morning), I will lie down in my clothes, to indulge the kind summons, if it will be indulged.

Three o'clock, Wednesday morning

I could not sleep—only dozed away one half-hour.

My aunt Hervey accosted me thus—Oh my dear child, what troubles do you give to your parents, and to everybody!—I wonder at you!

I am sorry for it, madam.

Sorry for it, child!—*Why* then so very obstinate?—Come, sit down, my dear. I will sit next you, taking my hand.

My uncle placed Mr Solmes on the other side of me: himself over against me, almost close to me. Finely beset now, my dear! Was I not?

Your brother, child, said my aunt, is too passionate—His zeal for *your* welfare pushes him on a little too vehemently.

Very true, said my uncle: but no more of this. We would now be glad to see if milder means will do with you—though, indeed, they were tried before.

I asked my aunt, if it were necessary that that gentleman should be present?

There is a reason that he should, said my aunt, as you will hear by and by. But I must tell you, first, that thinking you was a little too angrily treated by your brother, your mamma desired me to try what gentler means would do upon a spirit so generous as we used to think yours.

Nothing can be done, madam, I must presume to say, if this gentleman's address be the end.

She looked upon my uncle, who bit his lip, and looked upon Mr Solmes, who rubbed his cheek; and shaking her head: Good, dear creature, said she, be calm— Let me ask you if something would have been done, had you been gentler used than you seem to think you have been?

No, madam, I cannot say it would, in this gentleman's favour. You know, madam, you know, sir, to my uncle, I ever valued myself upon my sincerity: and once, indeed, had the happiness to be valued for it.

My uncle took Mr Solmes aside. I heard him say, whispering: She must, she shall be still yours!—We'll see who'll conquer, parents, or child, uncles, or niece!— I doubt not to be witness to all this being got over, and many a good-humoured jest made of this high frenzy.

I was heartily vexed.

Though we cannot find out, continued he, yet we *guess* who puts her upon this obstinate behaviour. It is not natural to her, man. Nor would I concern myself so much about her, but that I know what I say to be true, and intend to do great things for her.

I will hourly pray for that happy time, whispered, as audibly, Mr Solmes. I never will revive the remembrance of what is now so painful to me.

Well, but, niece, I am to tell you, said my aunt, that the sending up your keys, without making any conditions, has wrought for you what nothing else could have done—That, and the not finding anything that could give them umbrage, together with Mr Solmes's interposition—

Oh, madam, let me not owe an obligation to Mr Solmes—I cannot repay it, except by my *thanks*; and *those* only on condition that he will decline his suit. To my thanks, sir (turning to him), if you have a heart capable of humanity, if you have any esteem for me, for my *own* sake, I beseech you to entitle yourself!—I beseech you, do!—

Oh madam, cried he, believe, believe, believe me, it is impossible!—While you are single, I will hope. While that hope is encouraged by so many worthy friends, I must persevere!—I must not slight *them*, madam, because you slight *me*.

I answered him with a look of high disdain; and, turning from him—But what favour, dear madam, (to my aunt) has the instance of duty you mention procured me?

Your mamma and Mr Solmes, replied my aunt, have prevailed, that your request to stay here till Monday next, shall be granted if you will promise to go cheerfully then.

Let me but choose my own visitors, and I will go to my uncle's house with pleasure.

Well, niece, said my aunt, we must waive this subject, I find. We will now proceed to another, which will require your utmost attention. It will give you the reason why Mr Solmes's presence is requisite—

Ay, said my uncle, and show you what sort of a man somebody is. Mr Solmes, pray favour us in the first place with the letter you received from your anonymous friend.

I will, sir. And out he pulled a letter-case, and taking out a letter: It is written in answer to one sent to the person. It is superscribed, *To Roger Solmes, Esq*. It begins thus: *Honoured sir*—

I beg your pardon, sir, said I: but what, pray, is the intent of reading this letter to me?

To let you know what a vile man you are thought to have set your heart upon, said my uncle, in an audible whisper.

If, sir, it be suspected that I have set my heart upon any other, why is Mr Solmes to give himself any farther trouble about me?

Only hear, niece, said my aunt: only hear what Mr Solmes has to read, and to say to you, on this head.

If, madam, Mr Solmes will be pleased to declare, that he has no view to serve, no end to promote, for himself, I will hear anything he shall read. But if the contrary, you must allow me to say, that it will abate with me a great deal of the weight of whatever he shall produce.

Hear it but read, niece, said my aunt—

Hear it read, said my uncle—You are so ready to take part with—

With anybody, sir, that is accused anonymously; and from interested motives.

He began to read; and there seemed to be a heavy load of charges in this letter, against the poor criminal: but I stopped the reading of it, and said: It will not be *my* fault, if this vilified man be not as indifferent to me, as one whom I never saw. If he be otherwise at present, which I neither own nor deny, it proceeds from the strange methods taken to prevent it. Do not let one cause unite him and me, and we shall not be united. If my offer to live single be accepted, he shall be no more to me than *this* gentleman.

Still—Proceed, Mr Solmes—hear it out, niece, was my uncle's cry.

But, to what purpose, sir? said I—Has not Mr Solmes a *view* in this? And, besides, can anything worse be said of Mr Lovelace, than I have heard said for several months past?

But this, said my uncle, and what Mr Solmes can tell you besides, amounts to the *fullest proof*—

Was the unhappy man, then, so freely treated in his character before, *without* full proof? I beseech you, sir, give me not *too good* an opinion of Mr Lovelace; as I may have, if such pains be taken to make him guilty, by one who means not his reformation by it; nor to do good, if I may presume to say so in this case, to anybody but himself.

I see very plainly, said my uncle, your prepossession, your fond prepossession, for the person of a man without morals.

Indeed, my dear, said my aunt, you too much justify all our apprehensions. Surprising! that a young creature of virtue and honour should thus esteem a man of a quite opposite character!

Dear madam, do not conclude against me too hastily. I believe Mr Lovelace is far from being so good as he ought to be: but if every man's private life were searched into by *prejudiced people*, set on for that purpose, I know not whose reputation would be safe. I love a virtuous character, as much in man, as in woman. I think it as requisite, and as meritorious, in the one as in the other. And, if left to myself, I would prefer a person of such a character to royalty without it.

Why then, said my uncle—

Give me leave, sir—but I may venture to say, that many of those who have escaped censure, have not merited applause.

Permit me to observe further, that Mr Solmes himself may not be absolutely faultless. I never heard of his virtues. Some vices I have heard of—excuse me, Mr Solmes, I speak to your face—the text about *casting the first stone* affords an excellent lesson. He looked down; but was silent.

Mr Lovelace may have vices *you* have not. You may have others, which *he* has not. I speak not this to defend him, or to accuse you. No man is bad, no one is good, in *everything*. Mr Lovelace, for example, is said to be implacable, and to hate my friends; that does not make me value him the more. But give me leave to say, that they hate *him* as bad. Mr Solmes has his antipathies, likewise, very *strong* ones! and those to his *own relations!* which I don't find to be the other's fault; for he lives well with *his*—Yet he may have as bad—worse, pardon me, he cannot have, in my poor opinion: for what must be the man, who *hates his own flesh?*

You know not, madam;
You know not, niece;   } all in one breath.
You know not, Clary;

I may not, nor do I desire to know his reasons. It concerns me not to know them: but the world, even the impartial part of it, accuses him. If the world is unjust, or rash, in *one* man's case, why may it not be so in *another*'s? That's all I mean by it. Nor can there be a greater sign of want of merit, than where a man seeks to pull down another's character in order to build up his own.

The poor man's face was all this time overspread with confusion; it appearing as if he were ready to cry; twisted, as it were, and all awry, neither mouth nor nose standing in the middle of it. And had he been capable of pitying me, I had certainly tried to pity him.

They all three gazed upon one another in silence. My aunt, I saw (at least I thought so), looked as if she would have been glad she might have appeared to approve of what I said. She but feebly blamed me, when she spoke, for not hearing what Mr Solmes had to say. He himself seemed not now very earnest to be heard. My uncle said: There was no talking to me. And I should have absolutely silenced both gentlemen, had not my brother come in again to their assistance.

This was the strange speech he made at his entrance, his eyes flaming with anger: This prating girl has struck you all dumb, I perceive. Persevere, however, Mr Solmes. I have heard every word she has said: and I know no other method of being even with her, than, after she is yours, to make her as sensible of your power as she now makes you of her insolence.

Fie, cousin Harlowe! said my aunt—Could I have thought a *brother* would have said this to a gentleman, of a *sister?*

I must tell you, madam, said he, that *you* give the rebel courage. You yourself seem to favour too much the arrogance of her sex in her; otherwise she durst not have thus stopped her uncle's mouth by reflections upon him; as well as denied to hear a gentleman tell her the danger she is in from a libertine, whose protection, as she plainly hinted, she intends to claim against her family.

Stopped my uncle's mouth, by reflections upon him, sir! said I. How can that be! How *dare* you to make such an application as this!

My aunt wept at his reflection upon her—Cousin, said she to him, if *this* be the thanks I have for my trouble, I have done: your father would not treat me thus— and I *will* say, that the hint you gave was an unbrotherly one.

Not more unbrotherly than all the rest of his conduct to me of late, madam, said I. I see, by this specimen of his violence, how everybody has been brought into his measures. Had I any the least apprehension of ever being in Mr Solmes's power, this *might* have affected me. But you see, sir, to Mr Solmes, what a conduct is thought necessary to enable you to arrive at your ungenerous end. You see how my brother *courts* for you!

I disclaim Mr Harlowe's violence, madam, with all my soul. I will never remind you—

Silence, worthy sir! said I; I will take care you never shall have the opportunity.

Less violence, Clary, said my uncle. Cousin James, you are as much to blame as your sister.

In then came my sister. Brother, said she, you kept not your promise. You are thought to be to blame within, as well as here. Were not Mr Solmes's generosity and affection to the girl *well* known, what you have said would be inexcusable. My papa desires to speak with you; and with you, aunt; and with you, uncle; and with you, Mr Solmes, if you please.

They all four withdrew into the next apartment.

I stood silent, as not knowing till she spoke, how to take this intervention of my sister's. Oh thou perverse thing, said she (poking out her angry face at me, when they were all gone, but speaking spitefully low)—what troubles do you give to us all!

You and my brother, Bella, said I, give trouble to yourselves; for neither you nor he have any business to concern yourselves about me.

She threw out some spiteful expressions, still in a low voice, as if she chose not to be heard without; and I thought it best to oblige her to raise her tone a little, if I could. If I *could*, did I say? It is easy to make a passionate spirit answer all our views upon it.

She accordingly flamed out in a raised tone: and this brought my cousin Dolly in to us. Miss Harlowe, your company is desired.

I will come presently, cousin Dolly.

But again provoking a severity from me which she could not bear, and calling me names; in once more came Dolly, with another message, that her company was desired.

Not mine, I doubt, Miss Dolly, said I.

The sweet-tempered girl burst out into tears, and shook her head.

Go in before me, child, said Bella (vexed to see her concern for me), with thy sharp face like a new moon. What dost thou cry for? Is it to make thy keen face look still keener?

I believe Bella was blamed, too, when she went in; for I heard her say: The *creature* was so provoking, there was no keeping a resolution.

Mr Solmes, after a little while, came in again by himself, to take leave of me: full of scrapes and compliments, but too well tutored and encouraged to give me hope of his declining. He begged me not to impute to him any of the severe things to which he had been a sorrowful witness. He besought my compassion, as he called it.

He said the result was that he had still hopes given him; and, although discouraged by me, he was resolved to persevere while I remained single: and such long and such painful services he talked of, as never were heard of.

I told him, in the strongest manner, what he had to trust to.

Yet still he determined to persist—while I was no man's else, he must hope.

What! said I, will you still persist, when I declare, as I now do, that my affections are engaged?—And let my brother make the most of it—

He knew my principles, and adored me for them.

He doubted not, that it was in his power to make me happy: and he was sure I would not want the will to be so.

I assured him that, were I to be carried to my uncle's, it should answer no end; for I would never see him; nor receive a line from him; nor hear a word in his favour, whoever were the person who should mention him to me.

He was sorry for it. He must be miserable, were I to hold in that mind. But he doubted not that I might be induced by my father and uncles to change it—

Never, never, he might depend upon it.

It was richly worth his patience, and the trial.

At my *expense?*—at the price of all my *happiness*, sir?

He hoped I should be induced to think otherwise.

And then would he have run into his fortune, his settlements, his affection—vowing that never man loved a woman with so sincere a passion as he loved me.

I stopped him, as to the first part of his speech: and to the second, of the sincerity of his passion—What then, sir, said I, is your love to one who must assure you, that never young creature looked upon man with a sincerer disapprobation than I look upon you: and tell me, what argument can you urge that this *true* declaration answers not beforehand?

Dearest madam, what can I say?—On my knees I beg—

And down the ungraceful wretch dropped on his knees.

Let me not kneel in vain, madam: let me not be thus despised—and he looked most odiously sorrowful.

I have kneeled too, Mr Solmes: often have I kneeled: and I will kneel again—even to *you*, sir, will I kneel, if there be so much merit in kneeling; provided you will not be the implement of my cruel brother's undeserved persecution—

If all the services, even to worship you during my whole life—You, madam, invoke and expect mercy, yet show none—

Am I to be cruel to myself, to show mercy to you?—Take my estate, sir, with all my heart, since you are such a favourite in this house!—only leave me *myself*—The mercy you ask for, do *you* show to others.

If you mean to my relations, madam—unworthy as they are, all shall be done that you shall prescribe.

Who, I, sir, to find you bowels you naturally have not? I to purchase *their* happiness, by the forfeiture of *my own?* What I ask you for is mercy to myself: that, since you seem to have some power over my relations, you will use it in my behalf. Tell them that you see I cannot conquer my aversion to you: tell them, if you are a wise man, that you value too much your own happiness, to risk it against such a determined antipathy: tell them that I am unworthy of your offers: and that, in mercy to yourself, as well as to me, you will not prosecute a suit so impossible to be granted.

I will risk all consequences, said the fell wretch, rising, with a countenance whitened over, as if with malice, his hollow eyes flashing fire, and biting his under-lip to show he could be *manly*. Your hatred, madam, shall be no objection with me: and I doubt not in a few days to have it in my power to show you—

You have it in your power, sir—

He came well off—*to show you* more generosity, than, noble as you are said to be to others, you show to me.

The man's face became his anger: it seems formed to express the passion.

At that instant, again came in my brother—Sister, sister, sister, said he, with his teeth set, act on the termagant part you have so newly assumed—most wonderfully well does it become you. It is but a short one, however. Tyranness in your turn! accuse others of your own guilt!—but leave her, leave her, Mr Solmes; her time is short. You'll find her humble and mortified enough very quickly!—Then, how like a little tame fool will she look, with her conscience upbraiding her, and begging of you (with a whining voice, the barbarous brother spoke) to forgive and forget!—

More he said, as he flew out, with a face as red as scarlet, upon Shorey's coming in to recall him on his violence.

I removed from chair to chair, excessively frighted and disturbed at this brutal treatment.

The man attempted to excuse himself, as being sorry for my brother's passion.

Leave me, leave me, sir, fanning—or I shall faint. And indeed I thought I should.

He recommended himself to my favour with an air of assurance; augmented as I thought by a distress so visible in me; for he even snatched my trembling, my struggling hand; and ravished it to his odious mouth.

I flung from him with high disdain: and he withdrew, bowing and cringing; self-gratified, and enjoying, as I thought, the confusion he saw me in.

The creature is now, methinks, before me; and now I see him awkwardly striding backward, as he retired, till the edge of the opened door, which he run against, remembered him to turn his welcome back upon me.

Upon his withdrawing, Betty brought me word that I was permitted to go up to my own chamber: and was bid to consider of everything: for my time was short. Nevertheless, she believed I might be permitted to stay till Saturday.

She tells me, that although my brother and sister were blamed for being so *hasty* with me, yet when they made *their* report, and my uncle Antony *his*, of my provocations, they were all more determined than ever in Mr Solmes's favour.

The wretch himself, she tells me, pretends to be more in love with me than before; and to be rather delighted than discouraged with the conversation that passed between us. He run on, she says, in raptures, about the grace wherewith I should dignify his board; and the like sort of stuff, either of *his* saying or *her* making.

She closed all with a Now is my time to submit with a grace, and to make my own terms with him—else, *she* can tell me, were *she* Mr Solmes, it should be worse for me: and who, miss, of *our* sex, proceeded the saucy creature, would admire a rakish gentleman, when she might be admired by a sober one to the end of the chapter?

The creature tells me I have had *amazing* good luck to keep my writings concealed so cunningly: I must needs think that she knows I am always at my pen: and as I endeavour to hide that knowledge from her, she is not obliged to keep my secret. But that she loves not to aggravate. She had rather reconcile by much. Peacemaking is her talent, and ever was. And had she been as much my foe, as I imagined, I had not perhaps been here now—But this, however, she said not to make a merit with me: for truly, it would be better for me the sooner everything was over with me. And better for her, and everyone else; that was certain—Yet one hint she must conclude with; that my pen and ink, she would assure me (soon as I was to go away), would not be long in my power. And then, having lost *that* amusement, it would be seen how a mind so active as mine would be able to employ itself.

This hint has such an effect upon me, that I shall instantly begin to conceal in different places pens, ink, and paper; and to deposit some in the ivy summer-house, if I can find a safe place; and at the worst I have got a pencil of black, and another of red, lead, which I use in my drawings; and my patterns shall serve for paper if I have no other.

How lucky it was that I had got away my papers! They made a strict search for them; that I can see by the disorderly manner they have left all things in: for you know that I am such an observer of method, that I can go to a bit of riband, or lace, or edging, blindfold: the same in my books, which they have strangely disordered and mismatched, to look *behind* them, and *in* some of them, I suppose. My clothes, too, are rumpled not a little. No place has escaped them. To your hint, I thank you, are they indebted for their disappointment.

The pen, through heaviness and fatigue, dropped out of my fingers at the word *indebted*. I resume it to finish the sentence; and to tell you that I am,

Your forever obliged and affectionate
CL. HARLOWE

Letter 79: MISS CLARISSA HARLOWE TO MISS HOWE

Wednesday, eleven o'clock, April 5

I MUST write as I have opportunity, making use of my concealed stores: for my pens and ink (all of each that they could find) are taken from me; as I shall tell you more particularly by and by.

About an hour ago I deposited my long letter to you; as also, in the usual place, a billet to Mr Lovelace, lest his impatience should put him upon some rashness; signifying in four lines, 'That the interview was over; and that I hoped my steady refusal of Mr Solmes would discourage any further applications to me in his favour.'

Although I was unable, through the fatigue I had undergone and by reason of sitting up all night to write to you (which made me lie longer than ordinary this morning), to deposit my letter to you sooner; yet I hope you will have it in such good time as that you will be able to send me an answer to it this night, or in the morning early; which, if ever so short, will inform me whether I may depend upon your mamma's indulgence, or not. This it behoves me to know as soon as possible; for they are resolved to hurry me away on Saturday next, at farthest; perhaps tomorrow.

I will now inform you of all that happened previous to their taking away my pen and ink, as well as of the manner in which that act of violence, as I may call it, was committed; and this as briefly as I can.

My aunt, who (with Mr Solmes and my two uncles) lives here, I think, came up to me and said she would fain have me hear what Mr Solmes had to say of Mr Lovelace—only that I might be apprised of some things that would convince me what a vile man he is, and what a wretched husband he must make. I might give them what degree of credit I pleased; and take them with abatement for Mr Solmes's interestedness, if I thought fit—but it might be of use to me, were it but to question Mr Lovelace indirectly upon some of them that related to *myself*.

I was indifferent, I said, about what he could say of me, as I was sure it could not be to my disadvantage; and as *he* had no reason to impute to me the forwardness which my unkind friends had so causelessly taxed me with.

She said that he gave himself high airs on account of his family; and spoke as despicably of ours as if an alliance with *us* were beneath him.

I replied that he was a very unworthy man, if it were true, to speak slightingly of a family which was as good as his own, 'bating that it was not allied to the peerage: that the dignity itself, I thought, conveyed more shame than honour to descendants, who had not merit to adorn, as well as to be adorned by it: that my brother's absurd pride, indeed, which made him everywhere declare he would never marry but to *quality*, gave a disgraceful preference against ours: but that were I to be assured that Mr Lovelace were capable of so mean a pride as to insult us, or value himself, on such an accidental advantage, I should think as despicably of his sense, as everybody else did of his morals.

She insisted upon it, that he *had* taken such liberties; and offered to give some instances, which, she said, would surprise me.

I answered that were it ever so certain that Mr Lovelace had taken such liberties, it would be but common justice (so much hated as he was by all our family, and so much inveighed against in all companies by them), to inquire into the provocation he had to say what was imputed to him; and whether the value some of my friends put upon the riches they possess (throwing perhaps contempt upon every other advantage, and even discrediting *their own* pretensions to family in order to depreciate *his*) might not provoke him to like contempts. Upon the whole, madam, said I, can you say that the inveteracy lies not as much on *our* side as on *his*? Can *he* say anything of *us* more disrespectful than *we* say of him?—and as to the suggestion, so often repeated, that he would make a bad husband, is it possible for him to use a wife worse than I am used; particularly by my brother and sister?

Ah, niece! ah, my dear! how firmly has this wicked man attached you!

Perhaps not, madam. But really great care should be taken by fathers and mothers, when they would have their daughters of *their* minds in these particulars, not to say things that shall necessitate the child, in honour and generosity, to take part with the man her friends are averse to. But, waiving all this, as I have offered to renounce him for ever, I see not why he should be mentioned to me, nor why I should be wished to hear anything about him.

Well, but still, my dear, there can be no harm to let Mr Solmes tell you what Mr Lovelace has said of *you*. Severely as you have treated Mr Solmes, he is fond of attending you once more: he begs to be heard on this head.

If it be proper for me to hear it, madam—

It *is*, eagerly interrupted she, very proper.

Has what he has said of *me*, madam, convinced *you* of Mr Lovelace's baseness? It has, my dear: and that you ought to abhor him for it.

Then, dear madam, be pleased to let me hear it from *your* mouth. There is no need that I should see Mr *Solmes*, when it will have double the weight from *you*. What, madam, has the man dared to say of *me*?

My aunt was quite at a loss.

At last: Well, said she, I see how you are attached. I am sorry for it, miss. For I do assure you, it will signify nothing. You must be Mrs Solmes; and that in a very few days.

If consent of heart, and assent of voice, be necessary to a marriage, I am sure I never can nor ever will be married to Mr Solmes. And what will any of my relations be answerable for, if they force my hand into his and hold it there till the service be read; I perhaps insensible, and in fits, all the time?

What a romantic picture of a forced marriage have you drawn, niece! Some people would say, you have given a fine description of your own obstinacy, child.

My brother and sister would: but you, madam, distinguish, I am sure, between obstinacy and aversion.

Supposed aversion may owe its rise to *real* obstinacy, my dear.

I know my own heart, madam. I wish *you* did.

Well, but see Mr Solmes, once more, niece. It will oblige, and make for you more than you imagine.

What should I see him for, madam?—Is the man fond of hearing me declare my aversion to him?—Is he desirous of having me more and more incense my friends against myself?—Oh my cunning, my ambitious brother!

Ah, my dear!—with a look of pity, as if she understood the meaning of my exclamation—but must that necessarily be the case?

It must, madam, if they will take offence at me for declaring my steadfast detestation of Mr Solmes as a husband.

Mr Solmes is to be pitied, said she. He adores you. He longs to see you once more. He loves you the better for your cruel usage of him yesterday. He is in raptures about you.

Ugly creature, thought I! He in raptures!—

What a cruel wretch must he be, said I, who can enjoy the distress he so largely contributes to!—But I see, I see, madam, that I am considered as an animal to be baited to make sport for my brother and sister, and Mr Solmes. They are all, all of them, wanton in their cruelty—*I*, madam, see the man!—the man so incapable of pity!—Indeed I won't see him, if I can help it—Indeed I won't.

What a construction does your lively wit put upon the admiration Mr Solmes expresses of you!—Passionate as you were yesterday, and contemptuously as you treated him, he dotes upon you for the very severity he suffers by. He is not so ungenerous a man as you think him: nor has he an unfeeling heart—Let me prevail upon you, my dear (as your *father* and *mother* expect it of you), to see him once more, and hear what he has to say to you—

How can I consent to see him again, when yesterday's interview was interpreted by you, madam, as well as by every other, as an encouragement to him? When I myself declared that if I saw him a *second* time by my own consent, it might be so taken: and when I am determined never to encourage him?

You might spare your reflections upon *me*, miss. I have no thanks either from one side, or the other.

And away she flung.

Dearest madam! said I, following her to the door—

But she would not hear me further; and her sudden breaking from me occasioned a hurry to some mean listener, as the slipping of a foot from the landing-place on the stairs discovered to me.

I had scarcely recovered myself from this attack, when up came Betty with a, miss, your company is desired below-stairs in your own parlour.

By whom, Betty?

How can I tell, miss?—Perhaps by your sister; perhaps by your brother—I know they won't come upstairs to your apartment again.

Is Mr Solmes gone, Betty?

I believe he is, miss—Would you have him sent for back, said the bold creature?

Down I went: and who should I be sent for down to, but my brother and Mr Solmes? The latter standing sneaking behind the door, that I saw him not till I was mockingly led by the hand into the room by my brother. And then I started as if I had beheld a ghost.

You are to sit down, Clary.

And what then, brother?

Why, then, you are to put off that scornful look, and hear what Mr Solmes has to say to you.

Sent for down to be baited again, thought I!

Madam, said Mr Solmes, as if in haste to speak, lest he should not have opportunity given him; and he judged right; Mr Lovelace is a declared *marriage-hater*, and has a design upon your honour, if ever—

Base accuser! said I, in a passion, snatching my hand from my brother, who was insolently motioning to give it to Mr Solmes; he has not!—he dares not! But *you* have! if endeavouring to force a free mind is to dishonour it!

Oh thou violent creature! said my brother—But not gone yet—for I was rushing away.

What mean you, sir (struggling vehemently to get away), to detain me thus against my will?

You shall not go, violence, clasping his unbrotherly arms about me.

Then let not Mr Solmes stay—Why hold you me thus? He shall not, for *your own* sake, if I can help it, see how barbarously a brother can treat a sister who deserves not evil treatment.

And I struggled so vehemently to get from him, that he was forced to quit my hand; which he did with these words—Begone, then, Fury!—How strong is will!—There is no holding her.

And up I flew to my chamber again, and locked myself in, trembling, and out of breath.

In less than a quarter of an hour, up came Betty. I let her in, upon her tapping, and asking (half out of breath too) for admittance.

The Lord have mercy upon us! said she—What a *confusion of a house* is this!—hurrying up and down, fanning herself with her handkerchief—Such angry masters and mistresses! such an obstinate young lady!—such an humble lover!—such enraged uncles!—such—Oh dear! dear! what a topsy-turvy house is this?—and all for what, trow?—Only because a young lady *may* be happy and will *not?*—Only because a young lady *will* have a husband, and will *not* have a husband?—What hurly-burlies are here, where all used to be peace and quietness?

Thus she ran on, talking to herself; while I sat as patiently as I could (being assured that her errand was not designed to be a welcome one to me) to observe when her soliloquy would end.

At last, turning to me—I must do as I am bid: I can't help it—Don't be angry with me, miss. But I must carry down your pen and ink: and that, this moment.

By whose order?

By your papa's and mamma's.

How shall I know that?

She offered to go to my closet: I stepped in before her: Touch it, if you dare.

Up came my cousin Dolly—Madam!—madam! said the poor weeping good-natured creature, in broken sentences—you must—indeed you must—deliver to Betty—or to me—your pen and ink.

Must I, my sweet cousin? Then I will to you; but not to this bold body. And so I gave my standish to her.

I am sorry, very sorry, said miss, to be the messenger: but your papa will not have you in the same house with him: he is resolved you shall be carried away tomorrow, or Saturday at farthest. And therefore your pen and ink is taken away that you may give nobody notice of it.

And away went the dear girl very sorrowfully, carrying down with her my standish and all its furniture, and a little parcel of pens beside, which having been seen when the great search was made, she was bid to ask for. As it happened, I had not diminished it, having half a dozen crow-quills which I had hid in as many different places. It was lucky; for I doubt not they had told how many were in the parcel.

Betty run on, telling me that my mamma was now as much incensed against me as anybody—that my doom was fixed!—that my violent behaviour had not left one to plead for me. That Mr Solmes bit his lip and mumbled, and seemed to have more in his head than could come out at his mouth; that was her phrase.

And yet she also hinted to me that the cruel creature took pleasure in seeing me; although so much to my disgust—and so wanted to see me again. Must he not be a savage, my dear?

The wench went on—That my uncle Harlowe said that now *he* gave me up—that he pitied Mr Solmes—yet hoped he would not think of this to my detriment hereafter: that my uncle Antony was of opinion that I ought to smart for it: *and*, for *her* part—and then, as one of the family, she gave her opinion of the same side.

As I have no other way of hearing anything that is said, or intended, below, I bear sometimes more patiently than I otherwise should do with her impertinence. And, indeed, she seems to be in all my brother's and sister's counsels.

Miss Hervey came up again, and demanded an half-pint ink-bottle, which they had seen in my closet.

I gave it her without hesitation.

If they have no suspicion of my being able to write, they will perhaps let me stay longer than otherwise they would.

This, my dear, is now my situation.

All my dependence, all my hopes, is in your mamma's favour. But for that, I know not what I might do: for who can tell what will come next?

Letter 80: MISS CLARISSA HARLOWE TO MISS HOWE

Wednesday, four o'clock in the afternoon

I AM just returned from depositing the letter I so lately finished, and such of Mr Lovelace's letters as I had not sent you. My long letter I found remaining there— so you'll have both together.

I am concerned, methinks, it is not with you—but your servant cannot always be at leisure. However, I'll deposit as fast as I write: I must keep nothing by me now; and when I write, lock myself in, that I may not be surprised, now they think I have no pen and ink.

I found in the usual place another letter from this diligent man: and by its contents a confirmation that nothing passes in this house, but he knows it; and that, as soon as it passes. For this letter must have been written before he could have received my billet; and deposited, I suppose, when that was taken away; yet he compliments me in it upon asserting myself, as he calls it, on that occasion, to my uncle and to Mr Solmes.

'He assures me, however, that they are more and more determined to subdue me.

'He sends me the compliments of his family; and acquaints me with their earnest desire to see me amongst them. Most vehemently does he press for my quitting this house while it is in my power to get away: and again craves leave to order his uncle's chariot and six to attend my orders at the stile leading to the coppice adjoining to the paddock.

'Settlements to my own will, he again offers. Lord M. and both his aunts to be guaranties of his honour and justice. But, if I choose not to go to either of his aunts, nor yet to make him the happiest of men so soon as it is nevertheless his hope that I will, he urges me to withdraw to my own house; and to accept of my Lord M. for my guardian and protector till my cousin Morden arrives. He can contrive, he says, to give me easy possession of it, and will fill it with his female relations on the first invitation from me; and Mrs Norton, or Miss Howe, may be undoubtedly prevailed upon to be with me for a time. There can be no pretence for litigation, he says, when I am once in it. Nor, if I choose to have it so, will he appear to visit me; nor presume to mention marriage to me till all is quiet and easy; till every method I shall prescribe for a reconciliation with my friends is tried; till my cousin comes; till such settlements are drawn as he shall approve of for me; and that I have unexceptionable proofs of his own good behaviour.'

As to the disgrace a person of my character may be apprehensive of upon quitting my father's house, he observes, too truly I doubt, 'That the treatment I meet with is in everyone's mouth: yet, he says, that the public voice is in my favour: My friends themselves, he says, *expect* that I will do myself what he calls this justice; why else do they confine me? He urges that, thus treated, the independence I have a right to will be my sufficient excuse, going but from their house to my own, if I choose that measure; or, in order to take possession of my own, if I do not: that all the disgrace I *can* receive, they have already given me: that his concern, and his family's concern *in* my honour will be equal to my own, if he may be so happy ever to call me his: and he presumes to aver that no family can better supply the loss of my own friends to me than his, in whatever way I do them the honour to accept of his and their protection.

'But he repeats that, in all events, he will oppose my being carried to my uncle's; being well assured, that I shall be lost to him for ever if once I enter into that house.' He tells me: 'That my brother and sister, and Mr Solmes, design to be there to receive me: that my father and mother will not come near me till the ceremony is actually over: and that then they will appear in order to try to reconcile me to my odious husband by urging upon me the obligations I shall be supposed to be under, from a double duty.'

How, my dear, am I driven between both!—This last intimation is but a too probable one. All the steps they take seem to tend to this! And, indeed, they have declared almost as much.

He owns: 'That he has already taken his measures upon this intelligence—but that he is so desirous for *my sake* (I must *suppose*, he says, that he owes *them* no forbearance *for their own*) to avoid coming to extremities, that he has suffered a person whom they do not suspect, to acquaint them as if unknown to himself with his resolutions if they persist in their design to carry me by violence to my uncle's; in hopes that they may be induced, from fear of mischief, to *change* their measures: although he runs a risk, if he cannot be benefited by their fears, from their doubly guarding themselves against him on this intimation!'

What a dangerous enterpriser, however, is this man!

'He begs a few lines from me, by way of answer to this letter, either this evening, or tomorrow morning. If he be not so favoured, he shall conclude from what he knows of their fixed determination, that I shall be under a closer restraint than before: and he shall be obliged to take his measures according to that presumption.'

You will see by this abstract, as well as by his letter preceding this (for both run in the same strain), how strangely forward the difficulty of my situation has brought him in his declarations and proposals; and in his threatenings too: which, but for that, I would not take from him.

Something, however, I must speedily resolve upon, or it will be out of my power to help myself.

Now I think of it, I will enclose his letter (so might have spared the abstract of it), that you may the better judge of all his proposals and intelligence; and lest it should fall into other hands. I cannot forget the contents, although I am at a loss what answer to return.

I cannot bear the thoughts of throwing myself upon the protection of his friends: but I will not examine his proposals closely till I hear from you. Indeed, I have no *eligible* hope but in your mamma's goodness. *Hers* is a protection I could more *reputably* fly to than to that of any other person: and from hers should be ready to return to my father's (for the breach then would not be irreparable, as it would be if I fled to his family). *To return*, I repeat, on such terms as shall secure but my *negative*; not my *independence*: I do not aim at that (so shall lay your mamma under the less difficulty); although I have a right to it if I were to insist upon it— such a right, I mean, as my brother exerts in the estate left *him*; and which nobody disputes—God forbid that I should ever think myself freed from my father's *reasonable* control, whatever right my grandfather's will has given me! He, good gentleman, left me that estate as a reward of my duty, and not to set me above it, as has been justly hinted to me: and this reflection makes me more fearful of not answering the intentions of so valuable a bequest—Oh that my friends knew but my heart!—would but think of it as they used to do—for once more, I say, if it deceive me not, it is not altered, although theirs are!

Would but your mamma permit you to send her chariot, or chaise, to the by-place where Mr Lovelace proposes his uncle's shall come (provoked, intimidated and apprehensive, as I am), I would not hesitate a moment what to do!—Place me anywhere, as I have said before!—in a cot, in a garret; anywhere—disguised as a servant—or let me pass as a servant's sister—so that I may but escape Mr Solmes on one hand, and the disgrace of refuging with the family of a man at enmity with my own on the other; and I shall be in some measure happy!—Should your good mamma refuse me, what refuge, or whose, can I fly to?—Dearest creature, advise your distressed friend.

I BROKE off here—I was so excessively uneasy that I durst not trust myself with my own reflections: so went down to the garden to try to calm my mind by shifting the scene. I took but one turn up on the filbert walk, when Betty came to me. Here, miss, is your papa!—here is your uncle Antony!—here is my young master—and my young mistress coming to take a walk in the garden; and your papa sends me to see where you are for fear he should meet you.

I struck into an oblique path and got behind the yew hedge, seeing my sister appear; and there concealed myself till they were gone past me.

My mamma, it seems, is not well. My poor mamma keeps her chamber!—Should she be worse, I should have an additional unhappiness, in apprehension that my reputed undutifulness has touched her heart!

You cannot imagine what my emotions were behind the yew hedge, on seeing my papa so near me. I was glad to look at him through the hedge as he passed by: but I trembled in every joint, when I heard him utter *these* words: Son James, to you and to Bella, and to you, brother, do I wholly commit this matter—for that I was meant, I cannot doubt. And yet, why was I so affected; since I may be said to have been given up to their cruelty for many days past?

WHILE my papa remained in the garden, I sent my dutiful compliments to my mamma, with inquiry after her health, by Shorey, whom I met accidentally upon the stairs; for none of the servants, except my gaoleress, dare to throw themselves in my way. I had the mortification of such a return as made me repent my message, though not my concern for her health. Let her not inquire after the disorders she occasions, was the harsh answer. I will not receive any compliments from her!

Very, very, hard, my dear! Indeed it is very hard!

I HAVE the pleasure to hear my mamma is already better, however. A colicky disorder, to which she is too subject—and it is hoped is gone off. God send it may!—Every evil that happens in this house is owing to me!

This good news was told me, with a circumstance very unacceptable; for Betty said she had orders to let me know that my garden walks, and poultry visits were suspected; and that both will be prohibited, if I stay here till Saturday or Monday.

Possibly this is said by order, to make me go with less reluctance to my uncle's.

My mamma bid her say, if I expostulated about these orders, and about my pen and ink: 'That reading was more to the purpose, at present, than writing: that by the one, I might be taught my duty: that the other, considering whom I was believed to write to, only stiffened my will: that my needleworks had better be pursued, than my airings; which were observed to be taken in all weathers.'

So, my dear, if I do not resolve upon something soon, I shall neither be able to avoid the intended evil, nor have it in my power to correspond with you.

Wednesday night

ALL is in a hurry below-stairs. Betty is in and out like a spy. Something is working, I know not what. I am really a good deal disordered in body as well as mind. Indeed I am quite heart-sick!

I will go down, though 'tis almost dark, on pretence of getting a little air and composure. Robert has my two former, I hope, before now: and I will deposit this with Lovelace's enclosed, if I can, for fear of another search.

I know not what I shall do!—All is so strangely busy!—Doors clapped to: going out of one apartment, hurryingly as I may say, into another. Betty in her alarming way staring, as if of frighted importance; twice with me in half an hour; called down in haste by Shorey the last time, leaving me with still more meaning in her looks and gestures!—yet possibly nothing in all this worthy of my apprehensions— Here, again, comes the creature, with her deep-drawn affected sighs, and her *Oh dear's! Oh dear's!*

MORE dark hints thrown out by this saucy creature. But she will not explain herself. 'Suppose this pretty business ends in murder, she says. I may rue my opposition as long as I live, for aught she knows. Parents will not be *baffled* out of their children by impudent gentlemen; nor is it fit they should. It may come home to me, when I least expect it.'

These are the gloomy and perplexing hints this impertinent throws out. Probably they arise from the information Mr Lovelace says he has secretly permitted them to have (from his vile double-faced agent, I suppose!) of his resolution to prevent my being carried to my uncle's.

How justly, if so, may this exasperate them!—How am I driven to and fro, like a feather in the wind, at the pleasure of the rash, the selfish and the headstrong! and when I am as averse to the proceedings of the one as I am to those of the other! But being forced into a clandestine correspondence, indiscreet measures are fallen upon by the rash man before I can be consulted: and between them, I have not an option, although my ruin (for is not the loss of reputation a ruin?) may be the dreadful consequence of the steps taken. What a perverse fate is mine!

If I am prevented depositing this and the enclosed, as I intend to try to do, late as it is, I will add to it, as occasion shall offer. Meantime, believe me to be

Your ever affectionate and grateful
CL. HARLOWE

Under the superscription, written with a pencil, after she went down.

My two former not taken away!—I am surprised!—I hope you are well—I hope all is right betwixt your mamma and you.

Letter 81: MISS HOWE TO MISS CLARISSA HARLOWE

Thursday morning, April 6

I HAVE your three letters. Never was there a creature more impatient on the most interesting uncertainty than I was, to know the event of the interview between you and Solmes.

It behoves me to account to my dear friend, in her present unhappy situation, for everything that may have the least appearance of a negligence or remissness on my part. I sent Robin in the morning early, in hopes of a deposit. He loitered about the place till near ten, to no purpose; and then came away; my mamma having given him a letter to carry to Mr Hunt's, which he was to deliver before three, when only, in the daytime, that gentleman is at home; and to bring her back an answer to it. Mr Hunt's house, you know, lies wide from Harlowe Place. Robin but just saved his time; and returned not till it was too late to send him again. I could only direct him to set out before day, this morning; and, if he got any letter, to ride, as for his life, to bring it to me.

I lay by myself; a most uneasy night I had, through impatience; and being discomposed with it, lay longer than usual. Just as I was risen, in came Kitty, from Robin, with your three letters. I was not a quarter dressed; and only slipped on my morning sacque; proceeding no further till (long as they are) I had read them all through: and yet I often stopped to rave aloud (though by myself) at the devilish people you have to deal with.

How my heart rises at them all! How poorly did they design to trick you into an encouragement of Solmes, from the interview to which they had extorted your consent!—I am very, very angry at your aunt Hervey! To give up her own judgement so tamely!—and not content with that, to become such an *active* instrument in their hands. But it is so like the world!—so like my mamma too!—Next to her own child, there is not anybody living she values so much as she does you—Yet, it is—why should we embroil ourselves, Nancy, with other people's affairs?

Other people!—How I hate the poor words, where friendship is concerned, and where the protection to be given may be of so much consequence to a friend, and of so little detriment to one's self!

I am delighted with your spirit, however. I expected it not from you. Nor did they, I am sure. Nor would *you*, perhaps, have exerted it, if Lovelace's intelligence of Solmes's nursery-offices had not set you up. I wonder not that the wretch is said to love you the better for it. What an honour to have such a wife? And he can be even with you when you are so. He must indeed be a savage, as you say—yet is he less to blame for his perseverance, than those of your own family whom most you reverence.

It is well, as I have often said, that I have not such provocations and trials; I should, perhaps, long ago have taken your cousin Dolly's advice—yet dare I not to touch that key. I shall always love the good girl, for her tenderness to you.

I know not what to say to Lovelace; nor what to think of his promises, nor of his proposals to you. 'Tis certain that you are highly esteemed by all his family. The ladies are persons of unblemished honour. My Lord M. is also, as men and peers go, a man of honour. I could tell what to advise any other person in the world to do but you. So much expected from you! Such a shining light!—Your quitting your father's house, and throwing yourself into the protection of a family, however honourable, that has a man in it whose person, parts, declarations and pretensions will be thought to have engaged your warmest esteem!—Methinks I am rather for advising that you should get privately to London; and not to let either him, or anybody else but me, know where you are, till your cousin Morden comes.

As to going to your uncle's, that you must not do, if you can help it. Nor must you have Solmes, that's certain: not only because of his unworthiness in every respect, but because of the aversion you have so openly avowed to him; which everybody knows and talks of; as they do of your approbation of the other. For your reputation-sake, therefore, as well as to prevent mischief, you must either live single or have Lovelace.

If you think of going to London, let me know; and I hope you will have *time* to allow me a farther concert as to the manner of your getting away and thither, and how to procure proper lodgings for you.

To obtain this *time*, you must palliate a little, and come into some seeming compromise if you cannot do otherwise. Driven as you are driven, it will be strange if you are not obliged to part with a few of your admirable punctilios.

You will observe from what I have written that I have not succeeded with my mamma.

I am extremely mortified and disappointed. We have had very strong debates upon it. But, besides the narrow argument of *embroiling ourselves with other people's affairs*, as above-mentioned, she will have it, that it is your duty to comply. She says she was *always* of opinion that daughters *should*, and governed herself by it; for that my papa was, at first, more her father's choice than her own.

This is what she argues in behalf of her favourite Hickman, as well as for Solmes in your case.

I must not doubt but my mamma always governed herself by this principle, because she *says* she did. I have likewise another reason to believe it; which you shall have, though it may not become me to give it—that they did not live so very happily together, as one would hope people might who married preferring each other to the rest of the world.

Somebody shall fare never the better for this double-meant policy of my mamma, I will assure him. Such a retrospection in her arguments to him and to his address, it is but fit that *he* should suffer for *my* mortification in a point I had so much set my heart upon.

Think, my dear, if in any way I can serve you. If you allow of it, I protest I will go off privately with you, and we will live and die together. Think of it. Improve upon my hint, and command me.

A little interruption. What is breakfast to the subject I am upon!

LONDON, I am told, is the best hiding-place in the world. I have written nothing but what I will stand to at the word of command. Women love to engage in knight-errantry, now and then, as well as to encourage it in the men. But in your case, what I propose will have nothing in it of what can be deemed *that*. It will enable me to perform what is no more than a duty in serving and comforting a dear and worthy friend, labouring under undeserved oppression: and you will *ennoble*, as I may say, your Anna Howe, if you will allow her to be your companion in affliction.

I'll engage, my dear, we shall not be in town together one month, before we surmount all difficulties; and this without being beholden to any men-fellows for their protection.

I must repeat what I have often said, that the authors of your persecutions would not have presumed to set on foot their selfish schemes against you, had they not depended upon the gentleness of your spirit: though now, having gone so far and having engaged *Old* AUTHORITY in it (chide me if you will!), neither *he* nor *they* know how to recede.

When they find you out of their reach, and know that I am with you, you'll see how they'll pull in their odious horns.

I think, however, that you should have written to your cousin Morden, the moment they had begun to treat you disgracefully.

I shall be impatient to hear whether they will attempt to carry you to your uncle's. I remember, that Lord M.'s dismissed bailiff reported of Lovelace, that he had six or seven companions as bad as himself; and that the country was always glad when they left it. He *has* such a knot of them now, I hear, about him. And, depend upon it, he will not suffer them quietly to carry you to your uncle's: and whose must you be, if he succeeds in taking you from them?

I tremble for you but upon *supposing* what may be the consequences of a conflict upon this occasion. To be sure, he owes some of them vengeance. This gives me a double concern that my mamma should refuse her consent to the protection I had proposed and set my heart upon procuring, for you.

My mamma will not breakfast without me. A quarrel has its conveniences sometimes: yet too much love, I think, is as bad as too little.

WE have just now had another pull. Upon my word, she is *excessively*—what shall I say?—*unpersuadable*—I must let her off with that soft word.

What old Greek was it that said: *He* governed Athens; his *wife*, him; and his *son*, her?[1]

It was not my mamma's fault (I am writing to *you*, you know) that she did not govern my *papa*. But I am but a *daughter!*—yet I thought I was not quite so powerless when I was set upon carrying a point, as I find myself to be.

Adieu, my dear!—Happier times must come!—and that quickly too—The strings cannot long continue thus overstrained. They must break, or be relaxed. In either way, the certainty must be preferable to the suspense.

One word more.

I think in my conscience you must take one of these two alternatives: 1. to consent to let us go to London together privately: in which case, I will procure a vehicle and meet you at your appointment at the stile Lovelace proposes to bring his uncle's chariot to: or, secondly, to put yourself into the protection of Lord M. and the ladies of his family.

You have another, indeed; and that is, if you are absolutely resolved against Solmes, to meet and marry Lovelace directly.

Whichsoever of those you make choice of, you'll have this plea, both to yourself and to the world, that you are concluded by the same uniform principle that has governed your whole conduct ever since the contention between Lovelace and your brother has been on foot: that is to say, that you have chosen a lesser evil in hope to prevent a greater.

Adieu! and Heaven direct for the best my beloved creature, prays

Her

ANNA HOWE

Letter 82: MISS CLARISSA HARLOWE TO MISS HOWE

Thursday, April 6

I THANK you, my dearest friend, for the kind pains you have taken in accounting so affectionately for my papers not being taken away yesterday; and for the kind protection you would have procured for me, if you could.

This kind protection was what I wished for: but my wishes, raised at first by your love, were rather governed by my despair of other refuge (having before cast about, and not being able to determine what I *ought* to do, and what I *could* do, in a situation so unhappy) than by a reasonable hope: for why, indeed, should anybody embroil themselves for another, when they can avoid it?

All my consolation is, as I have frequently said, that I have not by my own inadvertence or folly brought myself into this sad situation. If I *had*, I should not have dared to look up to anybody with the expectation of protection or assistance, nor to you for excuse of the trouble I give you. But, nevertheless, we should not be angry at a person's not doing that for ourselves, or for our friend, which she thinks she ought *not* to do; and which she has it in her option to *do*, or to *let alone*. Much less have you a right to be displeased with so prudent a mother for not engaging herself so warmly in my favour as you wished she would. If my own aunt can give me up, and that against her judgement, as I may presume to say; and if my father and mother, and uncles, who once loved me so well, can join so strenuously against me; can *I* expect, or ought *you*, the protection of your mamma in *opposition* to them?

Indeed, my dearest love (permit me to be *very* serious), I am afraid I am singled out, either for my own faults or for the faults of my family, or for the faults of both, to be a very unhappy creature!—*signally* unhappy! For see you not how irresistibly the waves of affliction come tumbling down upon me?

We have been till within these few weeks, everyone of us, too happy. No crosses, no vexations, but what we gave ourselves from the *pamperedness*, as I may call it, of our own wills. Surrounded by our heaps and stores, hoarded up as fast as acquired, we have seemed to think ourselves out of the reach of the bolts of adverse fate. I was the pride of all my friends, proud *myself* of *their* pride, and glorying in my standing. Who knows what the justice of Heaven may inflict in order to convince us that we are not out of the reach of misfortune; and to reduce us to a better reliance than that we have hitherto presumptuously made?

I should have been very little the better for the *conversation-visits* which the good Dr Lewin used to honour me with, and for the principles *wrought*, as I may say, into my earliest mind by my pious Mrs Norton, founded on her reverend father's experience as well as on her own, if I could not thus retrospect and argue in such a strange situation as we are in. *Strange*, I may well call it; for don't you see, my dear, that we seem all to be *impelled*, as it were, by a perverse fate which none of us are able to resist?—and yet all arising (with a strong appearance of self-punishment) from ourselves?—Do not my parents see the hopeful children, from whom they expected a perpetuity of worldly happiness to their branching family, now grown up to answer the *till* now distant hope, setting their angry faces against each other, pulling up by the roots, as I may say, that hope which was ready to be carried into a probable certainty?

Your partial love will be ready to acquit me of capital and intentional faults—but oh, my dear! my calamities have humbled me enough to make me turn my gaudy eye inward; to make me look into myself!—And what have I discovered there?—Why, my dear friend, more *secret* pride and vanity than I could have thought had lain in my unexamined heart.

If *I* am to be singled out to be the *punisher* of myself, and family, who so lately was the *pride* of it, pray for me, my dear, that I may not be left wholly to myself; and that I may be enabled to support my character, so as to be *justly* acquitted of wilful and premeditated faults. The will of Providence be resigned to in the rest: as *that* leads, let me patiently and unrepiningly follow!—I shall not live always!—May but my *closing* scene be happy!—

But I will not oppress you, my dearest friend, with further reflections of this sort. I will take them all into myself. Surely I have a mind that has room for them. My afflictions are too sharp to last long. The crisis is at hand. Happier times you bid me hope for. I *will* hope!

BUT yet I cannot but be impatient at times to find myself thus driven, and my character so depreciated and sunk, that were all the *future* to be happy I should be ashamed to show my face in public, or to look up. And all by the instigation of a selfish brother, and envious sister!—

But let me stop: let me reflect!—Are not these suggestions the suggestions of the *secret* pride I have been censuring? Then, *already* so impatient! But this moment so resigned! so much better disposed for reflection!—Yet 'tis hard, 'tis very hard, to subdue an embittered spirit!—in the instant of its trial too!—Oh my cruel brother!—But now it rises again!—I will lay down a pen I am so little able to govern—and I will try to subdue an impatience, which (if my afflictions are sent me for corrective ends) may otherwise lead me into still more punishable errors!—

I WILL return to a subject which I cannot fly from for ten minutes together—called upon especially as I am by your three alternatives stated in the conclusion of your last.

As to the first; to wit *your advice for me to escape to London*—Let me tell you, that that other hint or proposal which accompanies it perfectly frightens me— Surely, my dear (happy as you are, and indulgently treated as your mamma treats you), you cannot mean what you propose! What a wretch must I be, if I could, for *one* moment only, lend an ear to such a proposal as this!—*I*, to be the occasion of making such a mother's (perhaps *shortened*) life unhappy to the last hour of it!— *Ennoble* you, my dear creature! How must such an enterprise (the rashness *public*, the motives were they excusable, *private*) debase you!—But I will not dwell upon the subject—for your *own* sake I will not.

As to your second alternative, *to put myself into the protection of Lord M. and of the ladies of that family*, I own to you (as I believe I have owned before) that although to do this would be the same thing in the eye of the world, as putting myself into Mr Lovelace's protection, yet I think I would do it rather than be Mr Solmes's wife, if there were evidently no other way to avoid being so.

Mr Lovelace, you have seen, proposes to contrive a way to put me into possession of my own house; and he tells me that he will soon fill it with the ladies of his family as my visitors—upon my invitation, however, to them—A very inconsiderate proposal I think it to be, and upon which I cannot explain myself to him. What an exertion of independency does it chalk out for me! How, were I to attend to *him* (and not to the natural consequences which the following of his advice would lead me to) might I be drawn by *gentle* words into the perpetration of the most *violent* acts!——For how could I gain possession, but either by legal litigation which, were I *inclined* to have recourse to it (as I never can be), must take up time; or by forcibly turning out the persons whom my papa has placed there to look after the gardens, the house, and the furniture—persons entirely attached to himself, and who, as I know, have been lately instructed by my brother?

Your third alternative, *to meet and marry Lovelace directly*: a man with whose morals I am far from being satisfied—a step that could not be taken with the least hope of ever obtaining pardon from, or reconciliation with, any of my friends— and against which a thousand objections rise in my mind—That is not to be thought of.

What appears to me, upon the fullest deliberation, the most eligible, if I *must* be thus driven, is the escaping to London. But I would forfeit all my hopes of happiness in this life, rather than you should go off with me, as you rashly propose. If I could get safely thither, and be private, methinks I might remain absolutely independent of Mr Lovelace and at liberty, either to make proposals to my friends, or, should they renounce me (and I had no other or better way) to make terms with him; supposing my cousin Morden, on his arrival, were to join with them. But they would, perhaps, *then* indulge me in my choice of a single life, on giving him up. The renewing to them this offer, when I was at my own liberty, would at least convince them that I was in earnest when I made it first: and, upon my word, I *would* stand to it, dear as you seem to think, when you are disposed to rally me, it would cost me, *to* stand to it.

If, my dear, you can procure a conveyance for us *both*, you can perhaps procure one for me *singly*; but can it be done without embroiling *yourself* with your mamma, or *her* with our family?—Be it coach, chariot, chaise, waggon, or horse, I matter not, provided you appear not in it. Only, in case it be one of the two latter, I believe I must desire you to get me an ordinary gown and coat, or habit, of some servant; having no concert with any of our own. The more ordinary the better. They may be thrust into the wood-house; where I can put them on; and then slide down from the bank that separates the wood-yard from the green lane.

But, alas! my dear, this, even *this* alternative, is not without difficulties, which seem, to a spirit so little enterprising as mine, in a manner insuperable. These are my reflections upon it:

I am afraid, in the first place, that I shall not have time for the requisite preparations to an escape.

Should I be either detected in those preparations, or pursued and overtaken in my flight, and so brought back, then would they think themselves doubly warranted to compel me to have their Solmes: and, conscious, perhaps, of an intended fault, I should be less able to contend with them.

But were I even to get safely to London, I know nobody there, but by name; and those the tradesmen to our family; who, no doubt, would be the first wrote to, and engaged, to find me out. And should Mr Lovelace discover where I was, and he and my brother meet, what mischiefs might ensue between them, whether I were willing or not to return to Harlowe Place?

But supposing I could remain there concealed, what might not my youth, my sex, an unacquaintedness with the ways of that great, wicked town, expose me to?—I should hardly dare to go to church, for fear of being discovered. People would wonder how I lived. Who knows but I might pass for a kept mistress; and that, although nobody came to me, yet that every time I went out it might be imagined to be in pursuance of some assignation?

You, my dear, who alone would know where to direct to me would be watched in all your steps, and in all your messages; and your mamma, at present not highly pleased with our correspondence, would then have reason to be *more* displeased; and might not differences follow between you, that would make me very unhappy, were I to know it? And this the more likely, as you take it so unaccountably (and give me leave to say, so ungenerously) into your head, to revenge yourself upon the innocent Mr Hickman for all the displeasure your mamma gives you?

Were Lovelace to find out where I was; that would be the same thing in the eye of the world as if I had actually gone off with him: for (among strangers, as I should be) he would not be prevailed upon to forbear visiting me: And his unhappy character (a foolish man!) is no credit to any young creature desirous of concealment. Indeed the world, let me escape whither and to whomsoever, would conclude *him* to be at the bottom, and the contriver, of it.

These are the difficulties which arise to me on revolving this scheme; which, situated as I am, might appear surmountable to a more enterprising spirit. If you, my dear, think them surmountable, in any one of the cases put (and to be sure I can take no course, but what must have *some* difficulty in it), be pleased to let me know your free and full thoughts upon it.

Had *you*, my dear friend, been married, then should I have had no doubt but you and Mr Hickman would have afforded an asylum to a poor creature, more than half lost, in her own apprehension, for want of one kind, protecting friend!

You say I should have written to my cousin Morden the moment I was treated disgracefully. But could I have believed that my friends would not have softened by degrees when they saw my antipathy to their Solmes?

I had thoughts indeed several times of writing to him. But by the time an answer could have come, I imagined all would have been over, as if it had never been—so from day to day, from week to week, I hoped on: and, after all, I might as reasonably fear (as I have heretofore said), that my cousin would be brought to side against me, as that some of those I have named would.

And then to appeal to a *cousin* (I must have written with *warmth*, to engage him) against a *father*; this was not a desirable thing to set about! Then I had not, you know, one soul of my side; my mamma herself against me. To be sure he would have suspended his judgement till he could have arrived—He might not have been in haste to come, hoping the malady would cure itself: but *had* he written, his letters probably would have run in the qualifying style; to persuade *me* to submit, or *them* only to relax. Had his letters been more on *my* side than on *theirs*, they would not have regarded them: nor perhaps *himself*, had he come, and been an advocate for me: for you see how strangely determined they are; how they have overawed, or got in, everybody; so that no one dare open their lips in my behalf: and you have heard that my brother pushes his measures with the more violence, that all may be over with me before my cousin's expected arrival.

But you tell me that in order to gain time, I must *palliate*; that I must seem to compromise with my friends—But how *palliate?* how *seem* to compromise?—You would not have me endeavour to make them believe that I will consent to what I never intend to consent to!—You would not have me try to gain time with a view to *deceive!*

To *do evil that good may come of it* is forbidden. And shall I do evil, yet know not whether good may come of it or not?

Forbid it, Heaven! that Clarissa Harlowe should have it in her thought to *serve*, or even to *save*, herself at the expense of her sincerity and by a *studied* deceit!

And is there, after all, no way to escape one great evil, but by plunging myself into another?—What an ill-fated creature am I?—Pray for me, my dearest Nancy!—My mind is at present so much disturbed that I hardly can for myself!—

Letter 83: MISS CLARISSA HARLOWE TO MISS HOWE

Thursday night

THE alarming hurry I mentioned under my date of last night, and Betty's saucy, dark hints, come out to be owing to what I guessed they were; that is to say, to the private intimation Mr Lovelace contrived our family should have of his insolent resolution (*insolent* I must call it) to prevent my being carried to my uncle's.

I saw at the time that it was as *wrong*, with respect to answering his own view, as it was *insolent*: for could he think, as Betty (I suppose from her betters) justly observed, that parents would be insulted out of their right to the disposal of their own child by a violent man whom they hate; and who could have no pretension to dispute that right with them, unless what he had from *her*, who had none over herself? And how must this insolence of his exasperate them against me, emblazoned as my brother is able to emblazon it?

The rash man has indeed so far gained his point, as to intimidate them from attempting to carry me away: but he has put them upon a surer and a more desperate measure: and this has put me also upon one *as* desperate, the consequence of which, although he could not foresee it, may perhaps too well answer his great end, little as he deserves to have it answered.

In short, I have done as far as I know the rashest thing that ever I did in my life!

But let me give you the motive, and then the action will follow of course.

About six o'clock this evening, my aunt (who stays here all night; on my account, no doubt) came up and tapped at my door; for I was writing, and had locked myself in. I opened it; and she entering, thus delivered herself:

I come once more to visit you, my dear; but sorely against my will; because it is to impart to you matters of the utmost concern to you, and to the whole family.

What, madam, is now to be done with me? said I; wholly attentive.

You will not be hurried away to your uncle's, child; let that comfort you—They see your aversion to go—You will not be obliged to go to your uncle Antony's.

How you revive me, madam! (I little thought what was to follow this supposed condescension). This is a cordial to my heart!

And then I ran over with blessings for this good news (and she permitted me so to do, by her silence); congratulating myself that I *thought* my papa could not resolve to carry things to the last extremity—

Hold, niece, said she, at last—You must not give yourself too much joy upon the occasion neither—Don't be surprised, my dear—Why look you upon me, child, with so affecting an earnestness!—But you must be Mrs Solmes, for all that.

I was dumb.

She then told me that they had had undoubted information that a certain desperate *ruffian* (I must excuse her that word, she said) had prepared armed men to waylay my brother and uncles, and seize me and carry me off. Surely, she said, I was not consenting to a violence that might be followed by murder on one side or the other; perhaps on both—

I was still silent.

That therefore my father (still more exasperated than before) had changed his resolution as to my going to my uncle's; and was determined next Tuesday to set out thither *himself* with my mamma; and that (for it was to no purpose to conceal a resolution so soon to be put in execution)—I must not dispute it any longer—on Wednesday I must give my hand—as they would have me.

She proceeded: That orders were already given for a licence: that the ceremony was to be performed in my own chamber, in presence of all my friends, except of my father and mother; who would not return, nor see me, till all was over, and till they had a good account of my behaviour.

The very intelligence, my dear!—the very intelligence this, which Lovelace gave me!

I was still dumb—only sighing as if my heart would break.

She went on comforting me, as she thought. She laid before me the merit of obedience; and told me that if it were my desire that my Mrs Norton should be present at the ceremony, it would be complied with: that the pleasure I should receive from reconciling all my friends to me, and in their congratulations upon it, must needs overbalance with such a one as me the difference of persons, however preferable I might think the one man to the other: that love was a fleeting thing, little better than a name, where morality and virtue did not distinguish the object of it: that a choice made by its dictates was seldom happy, at least not *durably* so:

nor was it to be wondered at, when it naturally exalted the object above its merits and made the lover blind to faults that were visible to everybody else: so that when a nearer intimacy stripped it of its imaginary perfections, it left frequently both sides surprised that they could be thus cheated; and that then the indifference became stronger than the love ever was. That a woman gave a man great advantages, and inspired him with great vanity, when she avowed her love for him, and preference of him, and was generally requited with insolence and contempt: whereas the confessedly obliged man, it was probable, would be all reverence and gratitude; and I cannot tell what.

You, my dear, said she, believe you shall be unhappy, if you have Mr Solmes: your parents think the contrary; and that you will be undoubtedly so, were you to have Mr Lovelace, whose morals are unquestionably bad—Suppose it were your sad lot to be unhappy with either, let me beseech you to consider, what great consolation you will have on one hand if you pursue your parents' advice, that you did so; what mortification on the other, that, by following your own, you have nobody to blame but yourself.

This, you remember, my dear, was an argument enforced upon me by Mrs Norton.

These and other observations which she made were worthy of my aunt Hervey's good sense and experience, and, applied to almost any young creature who stood in opposition to her parents' will, but one who had offered to make the sacrifices I have offered to make, ought to have had their due weight. But although it was easy to answer some of them in my own particular case; yet, having over and over, to my mamma, *before* my confinement, and to my brother and sister, and even to my aunt Hervey, *since*, said what I must now have repeated, I was so much mortified and afflicted at the cruel tidings she brought me, that, however attentive I was to what she said, I had neither power nor will to answer one word; and had she not stopped of herself, she might have gone on an hour longer without interruption from me.

Observing this, and that I only sat weeping, my handkerchief covering my face and my bosom heaving ready to burst: What! no answer, my dear?—Why so much *silent* grief? You know *I* always loved you. You know that *I* have no interest in this affair. You would not permit Mr Solmes to acquaint you with some things which would have set your heart against Mr Lovelace. Shall I tell you some of the matters charged against him? Shall I, my dear?

Still I answered only by my tears and sighs.

Well, child, you shall be told these things afterwards, when you will be in a better state of mind to hear them, and to rejoice in the escape you will have had. It will be some excuse, then, for you to plead for your behaviour to Mr Solmes before marriage, that you could not have believed Mr Lovelace had been so very vile a man.

My heart fluttered with impatience and anger at being so plainly talked to as the wife of this man; but yet I then chose to be silent. If I had spoke, it would have been with vehemence.

Strange, my dear, such silence!—Your concern is infinitely more on this side the day, than it will be on the other. But let me ask you, and do not be displeased, Will you choose to see what generous stipulations for you there are in the settlements?— You have knowledge beyond your years—Give the writings a perusal: do, my

dear. They are engrossed, and ready for signing, and have been for some time—
Excuse me, my love—I mean not to disturb you—Your papa would oblige me to
bring them up, and to leave them with you. He commands you to read them—*But
to read them, niece*—since they are engrossed, and were, before you made them
absolutely hopeless.

And then to my great terror, out she drew some parchments from her
handkerchief, which she had kept (unobserved by me) under her apron and, rising,
put them in the opposite window. Had she produced a serpent, I could not have
been more frighted.

Oh! my dearest aunt, turning away my face and holding out my hands: Hide
from my eyes those horrid parchments!—Let me conjure you to tell me! by all the
tenderness of near relationship, and upon your honour, and by your love for me,
say, are they absolutely resolved that, come what will, I must be that man's?

My dear, you must have Mr Solmes: indeed you must.

Indeed I never will! This, as I have said over and over, is not originally my
father's will—Indeed I never will!—and that is all I will say!

It is your father's will *now*, replied my aunt: and considering how all the family
is threatened by Mr Lovelace, and the resolution he has certainly taken to force
you out of their hands; I cannot but say they are in the right not to be bullied out
of their child.

Well, madam, then nothing remains for me to say. I am made desperate. I care
not what becomes of me!

Your piety, and your prudence, my dear, and Mr Lovelace's immoral character,
together with his daring insults and threatenings, which ought to incense *you* as
much as anybody, are everyone's dependence. We are sure the time will come,
when you'll think very differently of the steps your friends take to disappoint a
man who has made himself so justly obnoxious to them all.

She withdrew; leaving me full of grief and indignation—and as much out of
humour with Mr Lovelace as with anybody; who, by his conceited contrivances,
has made things worse for me than before; depriving me of the hopes I had of
gaining time to receive your advice and private assistance to get to town; and
leaving me no other choice in all appearance than either to throw myself upon his
family, or to be made miserable for ever with Mr Solmes. But I was still resolved
to avoid both these evils, if possible.

I sounded Betty in the first place (whom my aunt sent up, not thinking it proper,
as Betty told me, that I should be left by myself, and who, I found, knew their
designs), whether it were not probable that they would forbear, at my earnest
entreaty, to push matters to the threatened extremity.

But she confirmed all my aunt said; rejoicing (as she said they all did) that
the wretch had given them so good a pretence to save me from him now, and for
ever.

She run on about equipages bespoke; talked of my brother's and sister's
exultations, that now the whole family would soon be reconciled to each other: of
the servants' joy upon it: of the expected licence: of a visit to be paid me by Dr
Lewin, or another clergyman, whom they named not to *her*; which was to crown
the work: and of other preparations, so particular, as made me dread that they
designed to surprise me into a still nearer day than next Wednesday.

These things made me excessively uneasy. I knew not what to resolve upon.

At one time, thought I, what have I to do but to throw myself at once into the protection of Lady Betty Lawrance? But then, in resentment of his *fine* contrivances which had so abominably disconcerted me, I soon resolved to the contrary. And at last concluded to ask the favour of another half-hour's conversation with my aunt.

I sent Betty to her with my request.

She came.

I put it to her, in the most earnest manner, to tell me whether I might not obtain the favour of a fortnight's respite?

She assured me it would not be granted.

Would a week? Surely a week would?

She believed a week might, if I would promise two things: the first, upon my honour, not to write a line out of the house, in that week: for it was still suspected, she said, that I found means to write to *somebody*. And, secondly, to marry Mr Solmes, at the expiration of it.

Impossible! Impossible! I said with passion—What! might I not be obliged with one week, without such a horrid condition at the last?

She would go down, she said, that she might not seem of her own head to put upon me what I thought a hardship so great.

She went down. And came up again.

Did I want, was the answer, to give the vilest of men opportunity to put his murderous schemes in execution?—It was time for them to put an end to my obstinacy (they were tired out with me) and to his hopes, at once. And an end *should* be put on Tuesday or Wednesday next, at furthest; unless I would give my honour to comply with the condition upon which my aunt had been *so good* as to allow me a longer time.

I even stamped with impatience!— I called upon her to witness, that I was guiltless of the consequence of this compulsion; this barbarous compulsion, I called it; let that consequence be what it would.

My aunt chid me in an higher strain than ever she did before.

While I, in a half frenzy, insisted upon seeing my papa: such usage, I said, set me above fear. I would rejoice to owe my death to him, as I did my life.

She owned that she feared for my head.

I did go down half way of the stairs, resolved to throw myself at his feet, wherever he was. My aunt was frighted—Indeed I was quite frenzical for a few minutes—But hearing my brother's voice, as talking to somebody in my sister's apartment just by, I stopped; and heard the barbarous designer say, speaking to my sister: This works charmingly, my dear sister!

It does! It does! said she, in an exulting accent.

Let us keep it up, said my brother—The villain is caught in his own trap!—Now she must be what we'd have her be.

Do you keep my father to it; I'll take care of my mamma, said Bella.

Never fear, said he!—and a laugh of congratulation to each other, and derision of me (as I made it out) quite turned my frenzical humour into a vindictive one.

My aunt, just then coming down to me, and taking my hand, led me up; and tried to soothe me.

My raving was turned into sullenness.

She preached patience and obedience to me.

I was silent.

At last she desired me to assure her that I would offer no violence to myself.

God, I said, had given me more grace I hoped than to be guilty of so horrid a rashness. I was His creature, and not *my own*.

She then took leave of me; and I insisted upon her taking down with her the odious parchments.

Seeing me in so ill an humour, and very earnest that she should take them with her, she did; but said that my papa should not know that she did: and hoped I would better consider of the matter, and be calmer next time they were offered to my perusal.

I revolved, after she was gone, all that my brother and sister had said: I dwelt upon their triumphings over me: and found rise in my mind a rancour that I think I may say was new to me; and which I could not withstand. And putting every thing together, dreading the near day, what could I do?—Am I, in any manner excusable for what I *did* do?—If I am condemned by the world, who know not my provocations, may I be acquitted by you?—If *not*, I am unhappy indeed—for this I did.

Having shook off Betty as soon as I could, I wrote to Mr Lovelace to let him know, 'That all that was threatened at my uncle Antony's was intended to be executed *here*. That I had come to a resolution to throw myself upon the protection of either of his two aunts, who would afford it me: in short, that by endeavouring to obtain leave on Monday to dine in the ivy summer-house, I would, if possible, meet him without the garden door at two, three, four, or five o'clock on Monday afternoon, as I should be able. That in the meantime he should acquaint me, whether I might hope for either of those ladies' protection—And if so, I absolutely insisted that he should leave me with either, and go to London himself or remain at his uncle's; nor offer to visit me till I were satisfied that nothing could be done with my friends in an amicable way; and that I could not obtain possession of my own estate, and leave to live upon it: and particularly, that he should not hint marriage to me, till I consented to hear him upon that subject—I added, that if he could prevail upon one of the Misses Montague to favour me with her company on the road, it would make me abundantly easier in an enterprise which I could not think of (although so driven) without the utmost concern; and which would throw such a slur upon my reputation in the eye of the world as, perhaps, I should never be able to wipe off.'

This was the purport of what I wrote; and down into the garden I slid with it in the dark, which at another time I should not have had the courage to do, and deposited it, and came up again, unknown to anybody.

My mind so dreadfully misgave me when I returned, that to divert in some measure my increasing uneasiness, I had recourse to my private pen; and in a very short time ran this length.

And now that I am come to this part, my uneasy reflections begin again to pour in upon me. Yet what can I do?—I believe I shall take it back again the first thing I do in the morning—yet what *can* I do?

For fear they should have an earlier day in their intention than that which will too soon come, I will begin to be very ill. Nor need I feign much; for indeed I am extremely low, weak and faint.

I hope to deposit this early in the morning for you, as I shall return from resuming my letter, if I do resume it, as my *inwardest* mind bids me.

Although it is now near two o'clock, I have a good mind to slide down once more, in order to take back my letter. Our doors are always locked and barred up at eleven; but the seats of the lesser hall windows being almost even with the ground without, and the shutters not difficult to open, I could easily get out—

Yet why should I be thus uneasy?—since, should the letter go, I can but hear what Mr Lovelace says to it. His aunts live at too great a distance for him to have an immediate answer from them; so I can scruple going off till I have invitation. I can *insist* upon one of his cousins meeting me, as I have hinted, in the chariot; and he may not be able to obtain that favour from either of them. Twenty things may happen to afford me a suspension at least: why should I be so very uneasy?—when, too, I can resume it early, before it is probable he will have the thought of finding it there. Yet he owns he spends three parts of his days, and has done for this fortnight past, in loitering about in one disguise or other, besides the attendance given by his trusty servant, when he himself is not *in waiting*, as he calls it.

But these strange forebodings!—Yet I can, if you advise, cause the chariot he shall bring with him, to carry me directly for town, whither in my London scheme, if you were to approve it, I had proposed to go: and this will save you the trouble of procuring for me a vehicle; as well as the suspicion from your mamma of contributing to my escape.

But, solicitous for your advice and approbation too, if I *can* have it, I will put an end to this letter.

Adieu, my dearest friend, adieu!

Letter 84: MISS CLARISSA HARLOWE TO MISS HOWE

Friday morning, seven o'clock, April 7

MY aunt Hervey, who is a very early riser, was walking in the garden (Betty attending her, as I saw from my window this morning), when I arose; for, after such a train of fatigue and restless nights, I had unhappily overslept myself: so all I durst venture upon was to step down to my poultry yard, and deposit mine of yesterday and last night. And I am just come up; for she is still in the garden: this prevents me from going to resume my letter, as I think still to do; and hope it will not be too late.

I said I had unhappily overslept myself. I went to bed at about half an hour after two. I told the quarters till five; after which I dropped asleep and awaked not till past six, and then in great terror from a dream which has made such an impression upon me, that, slightly as I think of dreams, I cannot help taking this opportunity to relate it to you.

'Methought my brother, my uncle Antony, and Mr Solmes had formed a plot to destroy Mr Lovelace; who discovering it turned all his rage against me, believing I had a hand in it. I thought he made them all fly into foreign parts upon it; and afterwards seizing upon me, carried me into a churchyard; and there, notwithstanding all my prayers and tears, and protestations of innocence, stabbed me to the heart, and then tumbled me into a deep grave ready dug, among two or three half-dissolved carcases; throwing in the dirt and earth upon me with his hands, and trampling it down with his feet.'

I awoke with the terror, all in a cold sweat, trembling, and in agonies; and still the frightful images raised by it remain upon my memory.

But why should I, who have such *real* evils to contend with, regard *imaginary* ones? This, no doubt, was owing to my disturbed imagination; huddling together wildly all the frightful ideas which my aunt's communications and discourse, my letter to Mr Lovelace, my own uneasiness upon it, and the apprehensions of the dreaded Wednesday, furnished me with.

Eight o'clock

THE man, my dear, has got the letter!—What a strange diligence! I wish he mean me well, that he takes so much pains!—yet, must own that I should be displeased if he took less—I wish, however, he had been an hundred miles off!— What an advantage have I given him over me!

Now the letter is out of my power, I have more uneasiness and regret than I had before. For, till now, I had a doubt whether it should, or should not go: and now I think it ought *not* to have gone. And yet is there any other way than to do as I have done, if I would avoid Solmes? But what a giddy creature shall I be thought if I pursue the course to which this letter must lead me?

My dearest friend, tell me, have I done wrong!—Yet do not *say* I have, if you *think* it; for should all the world besides condemn me, I shall have some comfort, if *you* do not. The first time I ever besought you to flatter me. That, of itself, is an indication that I have done wrong, and am afraid of hearing the truth—Oh tell me (but yet do not tell me) if I have done wrong!

Friday, eleven o'clock

MY aunt has made me another visit. She began what she had to say with letting me know, that my friends are all persuaded that I still correspond with Mr Lovelace; as is plain, she said, by hints and menaces he throws out, which shows that he is apprised of several things that have passed between my relations and me, sometimes within a very little while after they have happened.

Although I approve not of the method he stoops to take to come at his intelligence, yet is it not prudent in me to clear myself by the ruin of the corrupted servant (as his vileness has neither my connivance, nor approbation), since my doing so might occasion the detection of my own correspondence; and so frustrate all the hopes I have to avoid this Solmes. Yet it is not at all unlikely that this very agent of Mr Lovelace plays booty between my brother and him: How else can *our family* know (so *soon* too) his menaces upon the passages they hint at?

I assured my aunt that I was too much ashamed of the treatment I met with, for everyone's sake as well as for my own, to acquaint Mr Lovelace with the particulars of it, were the means of corresponding with him afforded me: that I had reason to think that if he were to know of it from me, we must be upon such terms that he would not scruple making some visits, which would give me great apprehensions. They all knew, I said, that I had no communication with any of my papa's servants, except my sister's Betty Barnes: for although I had a good opinion of them all, and believed, if left to their own inclinations, they would be glad to serve me; yet, finding by their shy behaviour, that they were under particular direction, I had forborne ever since my Hannah had been so disgracefully dismissed so much as to speak to any of them, for fear I should be the occasion of their losing their places too. They must, therefore, account among *themselves* for the intelligence Mr Lovelace met with, since neither my brother, nor sister (as Betty had frequently, in praise of their sincerity, informed me), nor perhaps their favourite Mr Solmes, were at all careful who they spoke before when they had any thing to throw out against him, or even against *me*, whom they took great pride to join with them on this occasion.

It was but too natural, my aunt said, for my friends to suppose that he had his intelligence, part of it at least, from me; who, thinking myself hardly treated, might complain of it, if not to him, to Miss Howe; which, perhaps, might be the same thing; for they knew Miss Howe spoke as freely of them, as they could do of Mr Lovelace; and must have the particulars she spoke of from somebody who knew what was done here. That this determined my papa to bring the whole matter to a speedy issue, lest fatal consequences should ensue.

I perceive you are going to speak with warmth, proceeded she (and so I was)—For my own part I am sure you would not write anything, if you *do* write, to inflame so violent a spirit—But this is not the end of my present visit—

You cannot, my dear, but be convinced that your father *will* be *obeyed*. The more you contend against his will, the more he thinks himself obliged to assert his authority. Your mamma desires me to tell you that if you will give her the least hopes of a dutiful compliance, she will be willing to see you in her closet just now, while your papa is gone to take a walk in the garden.

Astonishing persistence, said I!—I am tired with making declarations and pleadings on this subject; and had hoped that my resolution being so well known, I should not have been further urged upon it.

You mistake the purport of my present visit, miss (looking gravely). Heretofore you have been *desired* and *prayed* to obey and oblige your friends: *entreaty* is at an end: they give it up. Now it is *resolved upon*, that your father's will *is to be obeyed*; as it is fit it should. Some things are laid at your door, as if you concurred with Lovelace's threatened violence to carry you off, which your mamma will not believe. She will tell you her own good opinion of you: she will tell you how much she still loves you: and what she expects of you on the approaching occasion: but yet, that she may not be exposed to an opposition, which would the more provoke her, she desires you will first assure her that you go down with a resolution to do that with a grace which must be done with or without a grace. And besides, she wants to give you some advice how to proceed in order to reconcile yourself to your papa, and to everybody else. Will you go down, miss, or will you not?

I said, I should think myself happy, could I be admitted to my mamma's presence, after so long a banishment from it; but that I could not wish it upon those terms.

And this is your answer, miss?

It must be my answer, madam. Come what may, I never will have Mr Solmes. I am very much concerned that this matter is so often pressed upon me—I never will have that man!

Down she went with displeasure. I could not help it. I was quite tired with so many attempts, all to the same purpose. I am amazed that they are not!—So little variation! And no concession on either side!

I will go down and deposit this; for Betty has seen I have been writing. The saucy creature took a napkin, and dipped it in water, and with a fleering air: Here, miss; holding the wet corner to me.

What's that for, said I?

Only, miss, one of the fingers of your right hand, if you please to look at it. It was inky.

I gave her a look: but said nothing.

But lest I should have another search, I will close here.

CL. HARLOWE

Letter 85: MISS CLARISSA HARLOWE TO MISS HOWE

Friday, one o'clock

I HAVE a letter from Mr Lovelace, full of transports, vows, and promises. I will send it to you enclosed. You'll see how he engages in it for his aunt Lawrance's protection, and for Miss Charlotte Montague's accompanying me. 'I have nothing to do, but to persevere, he says, and prepare to receive the personal congratulations of his whole family.'

But you'll see, how he presumes upon my being *his*, as the consequence of throwing myself into that lady's protection.

The chariot and six is to be ready at the place he mentions. You'll see, as to the slur upon my reputation which I am so apprehensive about, how boldly he argues. Generously enough, indeed, were I to be *his*; and had given him reason to believe that I would!—but that I have not done.

How one step brings on another with this encroaching sex! How soon may a young creature who gives a man the least encouragement be carried beyond her intentions, and out of her own power!—You would imagine, by what he writes, that I have given him reason to think that my aversion to Mr Solmes is all owing to my favour for him!

The dreadful thing is, that comparing what he writes from his intelligencer, of what is designed against me (though he seems not to know the threatened day) with what my aunt and Betty assure me of, there can be no hope for me but that I must be Solmes's wife if I stay here.

I had better have gone to my uncle Antony's, at this rate! I should have gained time, at least, by it. This is the fruit of his fine contrivances!

'What we are to do, and how good he is to be: how I am to direct all his future steps.' All this shows, as I said before, that he is sure of me.

However, I have replied to the following effect: 'That although I had given him room to expect that I would put myself into his aunt's protection; yet, as I have three days to come, between this and Monday, and as I hope that my friends will still relent or that Mr Solmes will give up a point they will both find it impossible to carry; I shall not look upon myself as absolutely bound by the appointment: and expect therefore, if I recede, that I shall not be called to account for it by him. That I think it necessary to acquaint him, that if, by putting myself into Lady Betty Lawrance's protection, he understands that I mean directly to throw myself into *his* power, he is very much mistaken: for that there are many points in which I must be satisfied; several matters to be adjusted, even, after I have left this house (if I do leave it), before I can think of giving him any particular encouragement: that, in the first place, he must expect that I will do my utmost to procure my father's reconciliation and approbation of my future steps; and that I will govern myself entirely by his commands in every reasonable point, as much as if I had not left his house: that if he imagines that I shall not reserve to myself this liberty, but that my withdrawing is to give him any advantages which he would otherwise have had; I am determined to tarry where I am, and abide the event, in hopes that my friends will still accept of my reiterated promise, never to marry him, or anybody else, without their consent.'

This I will deposit as soon as I can. And as he thinks things are near their crisis, I dare say it will not be long before I have an answer to it.

Friday, four o'clock

I AM far from being well: yet must I make myself worse than I am, preparative to the suspension I hope to obtain of the menaced evil of Wednesday next. And if I do obtain it, I will postpone my appointment to meet Mr Lovelace.

Betty has told them I am very much indisposed. But I have no pity from anybody.

I believe I am become the object of everyone's aversion; and that they would all be glad I were dead—Indeed, I believe it!—'What ails the perverse creature,' cries one?—'Is she love-sick,' another?

I was in the ivy summer-house, and came out shivering with cold, as if aguishly seized. Betty observed this, and reported it—'Oh, no matter!—Let her shiver on!—Cold cannot hurt her. Obstinacy will defend her from that. Perverseness is a bracer to a love-sick girl, and more effectual than the cold bath to make hardy, although the constitution be ever so tender.'

This said by a cruel brother, and heard said by the dearer friends of one, for whom but a few months ago everybody was apprehensive at every blast of wind to which she exposed herself!

Betty, it must be owned, has an admirable memory on these occasions. Nothing of this nature is lost by her repetition. Even the very air she repeats with renders it unnecessary to ask, who said this or that severe thing.

Friday, six o'clock

MY aunt, who again stays all night, has just left me. She came to tell me the result of my friends' deliberations about me. It is this.

Next Wednesday morning they are all to be assembled: to wit, my father, mother, my uncles, herself, and my uncle Hervey; my brother and sister of course; my good Mrs Norton is likewise to be admitted: and Dr Lewin is to be at hand, to exhort me, it seems, if there be occasion: but my aunt is not certain whether he is to be among them, or to tarry till called in.

When this awful court is set, the poor prisoner is to be brought in, supported by Mrs Norton; who is to be first tutored to instruct me in the duty of a child; which, it seems, I have quite forgotten.

Nor is the success at all doubted, my aunt says: for it is not believed I can be so hardened as to withstand so venerable a judicature, although I have withstood several of them separately. And still the less, as she hints at extraordinary condescensions from my papa. But what condescensions, from even my father, can induce me to make such a sacrifice as is expected from me?

Yet my spirits will never bear up, I doubt, at such a tribunal: my father presiding in it.

I believed indeed that my trials would not be at an end till he had admitted me once more into his awful presence!

What is hoped from me, she says, is that I will cheerfully, on Tuesday night if not before, sign the articles; and so turn the succeeding day's solemn convention of all my friends into a day of festivity. I am to have the licence sent me up, however, and once more the settlements, that I may see how much in earnest they are.

She further hinted that my papa himself would bring up the settlements for me to sign.

Oh my dear! what a trial will this be!—How shall I be able to refuse to my father (my father! from whose presence I have been so long banished; he commanding and entreating, perhaps, in a breath! how shall I be able to refuse to my father) the writing of my name?

They are sure, she says, something is working on Mr Lovelace's part, and perhaps on mine: and my papa would sooner follow me to the grave, than see me *his* wife.

I said, I was not well; that the very apprehensions of these trials were already insupportable to me; and would increase upon me as the time approached; and I was afraid I should be extremely ill.

They had prepared themselves for such an *artifice* as that, was my aunt's unkind word; and she could assure me, it would stand me in no stead.

Artifice! repeated I: and this from my aunt Hervey?

Why my dear, said she, do you think people are fools?—Can they not see how dismally you endeavour to sigh yourself down within-doors?—how you hang down your *sweet face* (those were the words she was pleased to use) upon your bosom—how you totter, as it were, and hold by this chair, and by that door-post, when you know that anybody sees you. (This, my dear Miss Howe, is an aspersion to fasten hypocrisy and contempt upon me: my brother's or sister's aspersion!—I am not capable of arts so low.) But the moment you are down with your poultry, or advancing upon your garden walk and, as you imagine, out of everybody's sight, it is seen how nimbly you trip along; and what an alertness governs all your motions.

I should hate myself, said I, were I capable of such poor *artifices* as these. I must be a fool to use them, as well as a mean creature; for have I not had experience enough that my friends are incapable of being moved in much more *affecting instances*?—But you'll see how I shall be by Tuesday.

My dear, you will not offer any violence to your health?—I hope God has given you more grace than to do that.

I hope he has, madam. But there is violence enough offered, and threatened, to affect my health; and that will be found without my needing to have recourse to any other, or to *artifice* either.

I'll only tell you one thing, my dear: and that is; ill or well, the ceremony will probably be performed before Wednesday night—but this, also, I will tell you, although beyond my present commission, that Mr Solmes will be under an engagement (if you should require it of him as a favour) after the ceremony is passed, and Lovelace's hopes thereby utterly extinguished, to leave you at your father's, and return to his own house every evening until you are brought to a full sense of your duty, and consent to acknowledge your change of name.

There was no opening of my lips to such a speech as this. I was dumb.

And these, my dear Miss Howe, are they who, *some* of them at least, have called me a romantic girl!—This is my chimerical brother, and wise sister; both joining their heads together, I dare say. And yet my aunt told me that the last part was what took in my mamma; who had, till that was started, insisted that her child should not be married if, through grief or opposition, she should be ill, or fall into fits.

This intended violence my aunt often excused by the certain information they pretended to have of some plots or machinations, that were ready to break out from Mr Lovelace:[a] the effects of which were thus cunningly to be frustrated.

Friday, nine o'clock

AND now, my dear, what shall I conclude upon? You see how determined—But how can I expect your advice will come time enough to stand me in any stead? For here I have been down and already have another letter from Mr Lovelace (The man lives upon the spot, I think): and I must write to him either that I will or will not, stand to my first resolution of escaping hence on Monday next. If I let him know that I will not (appearances so strong *against* him, and *for* Solmes even stronger than when I made the appointment), will it not be justly deemed my own fault if I am compelled to marry their odious man? And if any mischief ensue from Mr Lovelace's rage and disappointment, will it not lie at my door?—Yet, he offers so fair!—Yet, on the other hand, to incur the censure of the world, as a giddy creature!—But that, as he hints, I have already incurred!—What can I do? Oh! that my cousin Morden!—But what signifies wishing?

I will here give you the substance of Mr Lovelace's letter. The letter itself I will send when I have answered it; but that I will defer doing as long as I can, in hopes of finding reason to retract an appointment on which so much depends. And yet it is necessary you should have all before you, as I go along, that you may be the better able to advise me in this dreadful crisis of my fate.

'He begs my pardon for writing with so much assurance; attributing it to his unbounded transport; and entirely acquiesces in my will. He is full of alternatives and proposals. He offers to attend me directly to Lady Betty's; or, if I had rather, to my own estate; and that my Lord M. shall protect me there (he knows not, my dear, my reasons for rejecting this inconsiderate advice). In either case, as soon as he sees me safe, he will go up to London or whither I please; and not come near me but by my own permission; and till I am satisfied in everything I am doubtful of, as well with regard to his reformation as to settlements, etc.

'To conduct me to you, my dear, is another of his alternatives, not doubting he says, but your mamma will receive me. Or, if that be not agreeable to you, to your mamma, or to me, he will put me into Mr Hickman's protection; whom, no doubt, Miss Howe can influence; and that it may be given out that I am gone to Bath, or Bristol, or abroad; wherever I please.

'Again, if it be more agreeable, he proposes to attend me privately to London,

a It may not be amiss to observe in this place, that Mr Lovelace artfully contrived to drive them on by permitting *his* agent and *theirs* to report machinations which he had no intention, nor power, to execute.

where he will procure handsome lodgings for me, and both his cousins Montague to receive me there, and to accompany me till all shall be adjusted to my mind; and till a reconciliation shall be effected; which, he assures me, nothing shall be wanting in him to facilitate; greatly as he has been insulted by all my family.

'These several measures he proposes to my choice; it being unlikely, he says, that he can procure in the time, a letter from Lady Betty, under her own hand, inviting me in form to her house, unless he had been himself to go to that lady for it; which, at this critical conjecture while he is attending my commands, is impossible.

'He conjures me, in the solemnest manner, if I would not throw him into utter despair, to keep to my appointment.

'However, instead of threatening my relations or Solmes if I recede, he respectfully says that he doubts not but that, if I do, it will be upon such reasons as he ought to be satisfied with; upon no slighter, he hopes, than their leaving me at full liberty to pursue my own inclinations: in which (whatever they shall be) he will entirely acquiesce; only endeavouring to make his future good behaviour the sole ground for his expectation of my favour.

'In short, he solemnly vows that his *whole* view at present is to free me from my imprisonment; and to restore me to my own free will, in a point so absolutely necessary to my future happiness. He declares that neither the hopes he has in my future favour, nor the honour of himself and family, will permit him to propose anything that shall be inconsistent with my own most scrupulous notions: and, for my mind's sake, should choose to have this end obtained by my friends' declining to compel me. But that, nevertheless, as to the world's opinion, it is impossible to imagine that the behaviour of my relations to me has not already brought upon my family those free censures which they deserve, and caused the step which I am so scrupulous about taking to be no other than the natural and expected consequence of their treatment of me.'

Indeed, I am afraid all this is true: and it is owing to some little degree of politeness, that Mr Lovelace does not say all he might say on this subject: for I have no doubt that I am the talk, and perhaps the byword of half the county. If so, I am afraid I can now do nothing that will give me more disgrace than I have already so causelessly received by their indiscreet persecutions: and let me be whose I will, and do what I will, I shall never wipe off the stain my confinement and the rigorous usage I have received have fixed upon me; at least in my own opinion.

I wish, if ever I am to be considered as one of the eminent family this man is allied to, some of them do not think the worse of me for the disgrace I have received!—In that case, perhaps, I shall be obliged to him, if *he* do not. You see how much this harsh, this cruel treatment from my own family has humbled me!—But, perhaps, I was too much exalted before.

Mr Lovelace concludes 'with repeatedly begging an interview with me; and that, *this* night, if possible: an honour, he says, he is the more encouraged to solicit for, as I had twice before made him hope for it. But whether he obtain it, or not, he beseeches me to choose one of the alternatives he offers to my acceptance; and not to depart from my resolution of escaping on Monday, unless the reason ceases on which I had taken it up; and that I have a prospect of being restored to my friends' favour; at least to my own liberty and freedom of choice.'

He renews all his vows and promises on this head, in so earnest and so solemn a manner, that (his own interest, and his family's honour, and their favour for me, co-operating) I can have no room to doubt of his sincerity.

Letter 86: MISS CLARISSA HARLOWE TO MISS HOWE

Sat. morn., 8 o'clock, April 8

WHETHER you will blame me, or not, I cannot tell, but I have deposited a letter confirming my former resolution to leave this house on Monday next, within the hours, if possible, prefixed in my former. I have not kept a copy of it. But this is the substance:

I tell him, 'That I have no way to avoid the determined resolution of my friends in behalf of Mr Solmes; but by abandoning this house by his assistance.'

I have not pretended to make a merit with him on this score, for I plainly tell him 'That could I, without an unpardonable sin, die when I *would*, I would sooner make death my choice than take a step which all the world, if not my own heart, will condemn me for taking.'

I tell him, 'That I shall not try to bring any other clothes with me than those I shall have on; and those but my common wearing apparel; lest I should be suspected. That I must expect to be denied the possession of my estate: but that I am determined never to consent to a litigation with my father, were I to be reduced to ever so low a state: so that the protection I am to be obliged for, to any one, must be alone for the distress-sake: and yet, that I have too much pride to think of marrying until I have a fortune that shall make me appear upon a foot of equality with, and void of obligation to, anybody. That, therefore, he will have nothing to hope for from this step that he had not before: and that, in every light, I reserve to myself to accept or refuse his address, as his behaviour and circumspection shall appear to me to deserve.'

I tell him, 'That I think it best to go into a private lodging in the neighbourhood of his aunt Lawrance; and not to her house; that it may not appear to the world that I have refuged myself in his family; and that a reconciliation with my friends, may not, on that account, be made impracticable: that I will send for thither my faithful Hannah; and apprise only Miss Howe where I am: that he shall instantly leave me, and go to London, or to one of his uncle's seats; and (as he had promised) not come near me, but by my leave; contenting himself with a correspondence by letter only.

'That if I find myself in danger of being discovered and carried back by violence, I will then throw myself directly into the protection of either of his aunts who will receive me: but this only in case of absolute necessity; for that it will be more to my reputation, for me by the best means I can (taking advantage of my privacy) to enter by a second or third hand into a treaty of reconciliation with my friends.

'That I must, however, plainly tell him that if, in this treaty, my friends insist upon my resolving against marrying him, I will engage to comply with them; provided they will allow me to promise him that I will never be any other man's while he remains single or is living: that this is a compliment I am willing to pay to him in return for the trouble and pains he has taken, and the usage he has met with on my account: although I intimate, that he may, in a great measure, thank himself and the little regard he has paid to his reputation for the slights he has met with.'

I tell him 'That I may, in this privacy, write to my cousin Morden, and if possible interest him in my cause.'

I take some brief notice of his alternatives.

You must think, my dear, that this unhappy force upon me, and this projected flight, makes it necessary for me to account to him much sooner than it agrees with my stomach to do, for every part of my conduct.

'It is not to be expected, I tell him, that your mamma will embroil herself, or suffer you or Mr Hickman to be embroiled, on my account: and as to his proposal of my going to London, I am such an absolute stranger to everybody there, and have such a bad opinion of the place, that I cannot by any means think of going thither; except I should be induced, some time hence, by the ladies of his family to attend them.

'As to the meeting he is desirous of, I think it by no means proper; especially as it is so likely that I may soon see him. But that if anything occurs to induce me to change my mind, as to withdrawing, I may then very probably take the first opportunity to see him, and give him my reasons for that change.'

This, my dear, I the less scrupled to write, that I might qualify him for such a disappointment, should I give it; he having, besides, behaved so very unexceptionably when he surprised me some time ago in the lonely woodhouse.

Finally, 'I commend myself, as a person in distress, and merely as such, to *his* honour, and to his *aunt*'s protection. I repeat (most cordially, I am sure!) my deep concern for being forced to take a step so disagreeable, and so derogatory to my honour. And having told him that I will endeavour to obtain leave to dine in the ivy summer-house,[a] and to send Betty of some errand when there, I leave the rest to him; but imagine that about four o'clock will be a proper time for him to contrive some signal to let me know he is at hand, and for me to unbolt the garden door.'

I added, by way of postscript: 'That their suspicions seeming to increase, I advise him to contrive to send or come to the usual place, as frequently as possible, in the interval of time till Monday morning ten or eleven o'clock; as something may possibly happen to make me alter my mind.'

Oh my dear Miss Howe!—what a sad, sad thing is the necessity, forced upon me, for all this preparation and contrivance!—But it is now too late!—But how!— *Too late*, did I say?—What a word is *that!*—what a dreadful thing, *were* I to repent, to *find* it to be too late, to remedy the apprehended evil!

Saturday, ten o'clock

Mr Solmes is here. He is to dine with his new relations, as Betty tells me he already calls them.

a The *ivy summer-house*, or *ivy bower* as it was sometimes called in the family, was a place that from a girl, this young lady delighted in. She used, in the summer months, frequently to sit and work, and read and write, and draw, and (when permitted) to breakfast and dine and sometimes to sup, in it; especially when Miss Howe, who had an equal liking to it, was her visitor and guest.

She describes it in another letter as 'angularly pointing to a pretty variegated landscape of wood, water and hilly country; which had pleased her so much, that she had drawn it; the piece hanging up in her parlour, among some of her other drawings.'

He would have thrown himself in my way, once more: But I hurried up to my prison, in my return from my garden walk, to avoid him.

I had, when in the garden, the curiosity to see if my letter were gone: I cannot say with an intention to take it back again if it had not; because I see not how I could do otherwise than I have done. Yet what a caprice was this!—for when I found it gone, I began (as yesterday morning) to wish it had not: for no other reason, I believe, than because it was out of my power.

A strange diligence in this man!—He *says*, he almost lives upon the place; and I think so too.

He mentions, as you will see in his letter, four several disguises which he put on in one day. It is a wonder, nevertheless, that he has not been seen by some of our tenants: for it is impossible that any disguise can hide the gracefulness of his figure. But this is to be said, that the adjoining grounds being all in our own hands, and no common footpaths near that part of the garden, and through the park and coppice, nothing can be more bye and unfrequented.

Then they are less watchful, I believe, over my garden walks, and my poultry visits, depending as my aunt hinted upon the bad character they have taken so much pains to fasten upon Mr Lovelace. This, they think (and justly think), must fill me with doubts. And then the regard I have hitherto had for my reputation is another of their securities. Were it not for these two, they would not surely have used me as they have done; and at the same time left me the opportunities which I have several times had, to get away, had I been disposed to do so:[a] and indeed, their dependencies on both these motives would have been well founded had they kept but tolerable measures with me.

Then, perhaps, they have no notion of the back door; as it is seldom opened, and leads to a place so pathless and lonesome.[b] If not, there *can* be no other way to go off (if one would) without discovery, unless by the plashy lane, so full of springs, by which your servant reaches the solitary woodhouse; to which lane one must descend from a high bank that bounds the poultry-yard. For, as to the front way, you know, one must pass through the house, to that, and in sight of the parlours, and the servants' hall; then have the large open courtyard to go through, and, by means of the iron gate, be full in view, as one passes over the lawn, for a quarter of a mile together; the young plantations of elms and limes affording yet but little shade or covert.

The ivy summer-house is the most convenient for this affecting purpose of any spot in the garden, as it is not far from the back door, and yet in another alley, as

---

    a They might, no doubt, make a dependence upon the reasons she gives: but their chief reliance was upon the vigilance of their Joseph Leman, little imagining what an implement he was of Mr Lovelace.
    b This, in another of her letters, is thus described: 'A piece of ruins upon it, the remains of an old chapel, now standing in the midst of the coppice; here and there an overgrown oak, surrounded with ivy and mistletoe, starting up, to sanctify, as it were, the awful solemnness of the place. A spot, too, where a man having been found hanging some years ago, it was used to be thought of by us when children, and by the maidservants, with a degree of terror; as the habitation of owls, ravens and other ominous birds; and as haunted by ghosts, goblins, spectres. The genuine result of country loneliness and ignorance; notions which, early propagated, are apt to leave impressions even upon minds grown strong enough, at the same time, to despise the like credulous follies in others.'

you may remember. Then it is seldom resorted to by anybody else, except in the summer months, because it is cool. When they loved me, they would often, for this reason, object to my long continuance in it—but now it is no matter what becomes of me. Besides, *cold is a bracer*, as my brother said yesterday.

Here I will deposit what I have written. Let me have your prayers, my dear; and your approbation, or your censure, of the steps I have taken: for yet it may not be quite too late to revoke the appointment. I am

Your most affectionate and faithful
Cl. Harlowe

Why will you send your servant empty-handed?

Letter 87: MISS HOWE TO MISS CLARISSA HARLOWE

Sat. afternoon

By your last date of ten [o'clock] in your letter of this day, you could not long have deposited it before Robin took it. He rode hard, and brought it to me just as I had risen from table.

You may justly blame me for sending my messenger empty-handed, your situation considered; and yet that very situation (so critical!) is partly the reason for it: for indeed I knew not what to write, fit to send you.

I had been inquiring privately, how to procure you a conveyance from Harlowe Place, and yet not appear in it; knowing that to oblige in the *fact*, and to disoblige in the *manner*, is but obliging by halves: my mamma being, moreover, very suspicious, and very uneasy; made more so by daily visits from your uncle Antony, who tells her that now everything is upon the point of being determined, and hopes that her daughter will not so interfere as to discourage your compliance with their wills. This I came at by a way that I cannot take notice of, or *both* should hear of it in a manner *neither* would like: and, *without* that, my mamma and I have had almost hourly bickerings.

I found more difficulty than I expected, as the time was confined and secrecy required, in procuring you a vehicle; and as you so earnestly forbid me to accompany you in your enterprise. Had you not obliged me to keep measures with my mamma, I could have managed it with ease. I could even have taken our own chariot, on one pretence or other, and put two horses extraordinary to it, if I had thought fit; and I could have sent it back from London, and nobody the wiser as to the lodgings we might have taken.

I wish to the Lord, you had permitted this! Indeed I think you are too punctilious a great deal for your situation. Would you expect to enjoy yourself with your usual placidness, and not be ruffled, in an hurricane which every moment threatens to blow your house down?

Had your distress sprung from yourself, that would have been another thing. But when all the world knows where to lay the fault, this alters the case.

How can you say I am happy, when my mamma to her power is as much an abettor of their wickedness to my dearest friend, as your aunt, or anybody else?— and this through the instigation of that odd-headed and foolish uncle of yours, who (sorry creature that he is) keeps her up to resolutions which are unworthy of her, for an example to me, and please you. Is not this cause enough for me to ground a resentment upon, sufficient to justify me for accompanying you; the friendship between us so well known?

Indeed, my dear, the importance of the case considered, I must repeat, that you are too nice. Don't they already think that your standing-out is owing a good deal to my advice? Have they not prohibited our correspondence upon that very surmise? And have I, but on *your* account, reason to value *what* they think?

Besides, what discredit have I to fear by such a step? What detriment? Would Hickman, do you believe, refuse me upon it?—If he did, should I be sorry for that?—Who is it, that has a soul, who would not be affected by such an instance of female friendship?

But I should vex and disorder my mamma!—Well, that is something! But not more than she vexes and disorders me, on her being made an implement by such a sorry creature, who ambles hither every day in spite to my dearest friend. Woe be to *both*, if it be for a *double end!*—Chide me, if you will: I don't care.

I say, and I insist upon it, such a step would *ennoble* your friend: and if still you will permit it, I will take the office out of Lovelace's hands; and, tomorrow evening or on Monday, before his time of appointment takes place, will come in a chariot, or chaise: and then, my dear, if we get off as I wish, will we make terms, and what terms we please, with them all. My mamma will be glad to receive her daughter again, I warrant ye: and Hickman will cry for *joy* on my return; or he shall for *sorrow*.

But you are so very earnestly angry with me for proposing such a step, and have always so much to say for your side of any question, that I am afraid to urge it farther—only be so good as to encourage me to resume it, if, upon farther consideration, and upon weighing matters well (and in *this* light, whether best to go off with *me*, or with *Lovelace*), you can get over your punctilious regard for my reputation. A woman going off with a woman is not so discreditable a thing, surely! and with no view but to avoid the fellows!—I say, only be so good as to *consider* this point; and if you can get over your scruples on *my* account, do. And so I will have done with this argument for the present; and apply myself to some of the passages in yours.

A time, I hope, will come, that I shall be able to read your affecting narratives without that impatience and bitterness which now boils over in my heart, and would flow to my pen were I to enter into the particulars of what you write. And, indeed, I am afraid of giving you my advice at all, or of telling you what I should do in your case (supposing you will still refuse my offer); finding too, what you have been brought, or rather driven, to, without it; lest any evil should follow it: in which case, I should never forgive myself. And this consideration has added to my difficulties in writing to you, now you are upon such a crisis, and yet refuse the only method—But I said I would not for the present touch any more that string. Yet, one word more, chide me if you please: if any harm betide you, I shall for ever blame my mamma—indeed I shall—and perhaps yourself, if you do not accept of my offer.

But one thing, in your present situation and prospects, let me advise: it is this, that if you *do* go away with Mr Lovelace, you take the first opportunity to permit the ceremony to pass. Why should you *not*, when everybody will know by *whose* assistance, and in *whose* company, you leave your father's house, go whithersoever you will?—You may, indeed, keep him at distance, until settlements are drawn and such-like matters are adjusted to your mind. But even these are matters of less consideration in your particular case, than they would be in that of most others: *because*, be his other faults what they will, nobody thinks him an ungenerous man: *because* the possession of your estate must be given up to you, as soon as your cousin Morden comes; who, as your trustee, will see it done; and done upon proper terms: *because* there is no want of fortune on his side: *because* all his family value you, and are extremely desirous that you should be their relation: *because* he makes no scruple of accepting you without conditions. You see how he has always defied your relations. (I, for my own part, can forgive him for that fault: nor know I if it be not a noble one.) And I dare say, he had rather call you *his* without a shilling, than be under obligation to those whom he has full as little reason to love, as they have to love him. You have heard that his own relations cannot make his proud spirit submit to owe any favour to them.

For all these reasons, I think, you may the less stand upon previous settlements. It is therefore my absolute opinion that, if you *do* go away with him (and in that case you must let *him* be judge when he can leave you with safety, you'll observe that), you should not postpone the ceremony.

Give this matter your most serious consideration. Punctilio is out of doors the moment you are out of your father's house. I know how justly severe you have been upon those inexcusable creatures, whose giddiness and even want of decency have made them, in the same hour, as I may say, leap from a parent's window to a husband's bed—But, considering Lovelace's character, I repeat my opinion that your reputation in the eye of the world requires that no delay be made in this point, when once you are in his power.

I need not, I am sure, make a stronger plea to *you*.

You say, in excuse for my mamma (what my fervent love for my friend very ill brooks), that we ought not to blame anyone for not doing what she has an option to do, or to let alone. This, in cases of friendship, would admit of very strict discussion. If the thing requested be of *greater* consequence, or even of *equal*, to the person sought to, and it were, as the old phrase has it, *to take a thorn out of one's friend's foot, to put it into our own*, something might be said. Nay, it would be, I will venture to say, a selfish thing in us to ask a favour of a friend which would subject that friend to the *same* or *equal* inconvenience, as that from which we wanted to be relieved. The requester would, in this case, teach his friend by his *own* selfish example, with much *better* reason, to deny him and despise a friendship so *merely* nominal. But if, by a *less* inconvenience to ourselves, we could relieve our friend from a *greater*, the refusal of such a favour makes the refuser unworthy of the name of friend: nor would I admit such a one, not even into the outermost fold of my heart.

I am well aware that this is your opinion of friendship, as well as mine: for I owe the distinction to you, upon a certain occasion; and it saved me from a very great inconvenience, as you must needs remember. But you was always for making excuses for *other* people in cases wherein you would not have allowed of one for *yourself*.

I must own, that were these excuses for a friend's indifference or denial made by anybody but *you*, in a case of such *vast* importance to herself, and of so comparative a *small* one to those whose protection she would be thought to wish for; I, who am for ever, as you have often remarked, endeavouring to trace effects to their causes, should be ready to suspect that there was a latent, unowned inclination, which balancing, or *preponderating* rather, made the issue of the alternative (however important) sit more lightly upon the excuser's mind than she cared to own.

You will understand me, my dear. But if you do not, it may be as well for me; for I am afraid I shall *have it* from you, for but starting such a notion, or giving a hint, which perhaps as you did once in another case, you will reprimandingly call, 'not being able to forgo the ostentation of sagacity, though at the expence of that tenderness which is due to friendship and charity.'

What signifies owning a fault without mending it, you'll say?—Very true, my dear. But you know I ever was a saucy creature!—ever stood in need of great allowances—and I know, likewise, that I ever had them from my dear Clarissa Harlowe. Nor do I doubt them now: for you know how much I love you!—If it be possible, *more* than *myself* I love you! believe me, my dear! And, in consequence of that belief, you will be able to judge how much I am affected by your present distressful and critical situation; which will not suffer me to pass by, without a censure, even that philosophy of temper in your own cause, which you have not in another's, and which all that know you ever admired you for.

From this critical and distressful situation, it shall be my hourly prayers that you may be delivered without blemish to that fair fame, which has hitherto, like your heart, been unspotted.

With this prayer, twenty times repeated, concludes

> Your ever affectionate
> ANNA HOWE

I hurried myself in writing this; and I hurry Robin away with it, that in a situation so very critical, you may have all the time possible to consider what I have written, upon two points so very important. I will repeat them in a very few words:

'Whether you choose not rather to go off with one of *your own sex*; with your ANNA HOWE—than with one of the *other*; with Mr LOVELACE?'

And if not,

'Whether you should not marry him as soon as possible?'

Letter 88: MISS CLARISSA HARLOWE TO MISS HOWE

(The preceding letter not received)

Saturday afternoon

ALREADY have I an ecstatic answer, as I may call it, to my letter.

'He promises compliance in every article with my will: approves of all I propose; particularly of the private lodging: and thinks it a happy expedient to obviate the censures of the busy and the unreflecting: and yet he hopes, that the putting myself into the protection of either of his aunts, treated as I am treated, would be far from being looked upon by any in a disreputable light. But everything I enjoin, or resolve upon, must, he says, be right, not only with respect to my present, but future, honour; with regard to which, he hopes so to behave himself, as to be *allowed* to be next to myself, more solicitous than anybody. He will only assure me, that his whole family are extremely desirous to take advantage of the persecutions I labour under, to make their court and endear themselves to me by their best and most cheerful services: happy, if they can, in any measure, contribute to my present freedom and future happiness.

'He will this afternoon, he says, write to his uncle and to both his aunts, that he is now within view of being the happiest man in the world, if it be not his own fault; since the only woman upon earth that can make him so will be soon out of danger of being another man's; and cannot possibly prescribe any terms to him that he shall not think it his duty to comply with.

'He flatters himself now (my last letter *confirming* my resolution) that he can be in no apprehension of my changing my mind, unless my friends change their manner of acting by me; which he is too sure they will not. And now will all his relations, who take such a kind and generous share in his interests, glory and pride themselves in the prospects he has before him.'

Thus artfully does he hold me to it!—

'As to fortune, he begs of me not to be solicitous on that score: that his own estate is sufficient for us both; not a *nominal*, but a *real*, two thousand pounds *per annum*, equivalent to some estates reputed a third more: that it never was encumbered: that he is clear of the world, both as to book and bond-debts; thanks, perhaps, to his pride more than to his virtue. That his uncle moreover resolves to settle upon him a thousand pounds *per annum* on his nuptials. And this (if he writes to his lordship's honour) more from motives of *justice*, than from those of *generosity*, as he ought to consider it but as an equivalent for an estate which he had got possession of, to which *his* (Mr Lovelace's) mother had better pretensions. That his lordship also proposed to give him up either his seat in Hertfordshire, or that in Lancashire, at his own or at his wife's option, especially if I am the person. All which it will be in my power to see done, and proper settlements drawn, *before* I enter into any farther engagements with him; if I *will* have it so.'

He says, 'That I need not be under any solicitude as to *apparel*: all *immediate* occasions of that sort will be most cheerfully supplied by his aunts, or his cousins Montague: as my others shall, with the greatest pride and pleasure (if I will allow him that honour), by himself.

'That I shall govern him as I please, with regard to anything in his power towards effecting a reconciliation with my friends: a point he knows my heart is set upon.

'He is afraid that the time will hardly allow of his procuring Miss Charlotte Montague's attendance upon me at St Albans, as he had proposed she should; because, he understands, she keeps her chamber, with a violent cold and sore throat. But both she and her sister, the first moment she is able to go abroad, shall visit me at my private lodgings; and introduce me to their aunts, or their aunts to me, as I shall choose; and accompany me to town if I please; and stay as long in it with me, as I shall think fit to stay there.

'Lord M. will also, at my own time, and in my own manner, that is to say, either publicly or privately, make me a visit. And, for his own part, when he has seen me in safety, either in their protection, or in the privacy I prefer, he will leave me and not attempt to visit me but by my own permission.

'He had thoughts once, he says, on hearing of his cousin Charlotte's indisposition, to have engaged his cousin Patty's attendance upon me, either at or about the neighbouring village, or at St Albans: but, he says, she is a low-spirited, timorous girl, who would but the more perplex us.'

So, my dear, the enterprise requires courage and high spirits, you see!—And indeed it does!—What am I about to do!—

He himself, it is plain, thinks it necessary that I should be accompanied with one of my own sex!—He might, at least, have proposed the woman of one of the ladies of his family—Lord bless me!—what am I about to do!—

AFTER all, far as I have gone, I know not but I may still recede: and if I do, a mortal quarrel, I suppose, will ensue. And what if it does?—Could there be any way to escape this Solmes, a breach with Lovelace might make way for the single life (so much my preferable wish!) to take place: and then I would defy the sex. For I see nothing but trouble and vexation that they bring upon ours: and when once entered, one is obliged to go on with them, treading with tender feet upon thorns and sharper thorns, to the end of a painful journey.

What to do, I know not. The more I think, the more I am embarrassed!—and the stronger will be my doubts, as the appointed time draw nearer.

But I will go down, and take a little turn in the garden; and deposit this, and his letters, all but the two last; which I will enclose in my next, if I have opportunity to write another.

Meantime, my dear friend—But what can I desire you to pray for?—Adieu then!—let me only say—adieu!—

Letter 89: MISS CLARISSA HARLOWE TO MISS HOWE

(In answer to Letter 87)

Sunday morning, April 9

Do not think, my beloved friend, although you have given me in yours of yesterday a *severer* instance of what nevertheless I must call your *impartial* love, than ever yet I received from you, that I will be displeased with you for it. That would be to put myself into the inconvenient situation of royalty: that is to say, out of the way of ever being told of my faults; of ever mending them; and in the way of making the sincerity and warmest friendship useless to me.

And then how brightly, how nobly, burns this sacred flame in your bosom! that you are ready to impute to the unhappy sufferer a *less degree* of warmth in *her own* cause than *you* have for her, because she endeavours to divest herself of *self*, so far as to leave others to the option which they have a right to make! Ought I, my dear, to blame, ought I not rather to admire, you for this ardour?

But, nevertheless, lest you should think that there is any foundation for a surmise, which, although it owe its rise to your friendship, would, if there *were*, leave me utterly inexcusable; I must, in justice to myself, declare that I know not my own heart, if I have any of that *latent* or *unowned inclination*, which you would impute to *any other but me.* Nor does the *important alternative sit lightly on my mind.* And yet I must excuse your mamma, were it but on this single consideration, that I could not presume to reckon upon *her* favour, as I could upon her *daughter*'s, so as to make the claim of friendship upon *her*, to whom, as the mother of my dearest friend, a veneration is owing which can hardly be compatible with that sweet familiarity, which is one of the indispensables of the sacred tie by which your heart and mine are bound in one.

What therefore I might expect from my *Anna Howe*, I *ought not* from her *mamma*; for would it not be very strange, that a person of her experience should be reflected upon because she gave not up her own judgement, where the consequence of her doing so would be, to embroil herself, as she apprehends, with a family she has lived well with, and in behalf of a child against her parents?—As she has, moreover, a daughter of her own—a daughter too, give me leave to say, of whose vivacity and charming spirits she is more apprehensive than she need to be; because her truly maternal cares make her fear more from her *youth*, than she hopes from her *prudence*; which nevertheless she, and all the world, know to be *beyond* her years.

And here let me add that whatever you may generously, and as the result of an ardent affection for your unhappy friend, urge on this head in my behalf, or harshly against anyone who may refuse me protection in such extraordinary circumstances as I find myself in; I have some pleasure in being able to curb undue expectations upon my indulgent friends, whatever were to befall myself from those circumstances; for I should be extremely mortified, were I by my selfish forwardness to give occasion for such a check, as to be told that I had encouraged an unreasonable hope; or, according to the phrase you mention, wished to take a *thorn out of my own foot, and to put it into that of my friend.* Nor should I be better pleased with myself if, having been taught by my good Mrs Norton that the best of schools is *that of affliction*, I should rather learn impatience than the contrary by the lessons I am obliged to get by heart in it; and if I should judge of the *merits of others*, as they were *kind to me*; and that at the expense of their own convenience or peace of mind. For is not this to suppose myself ever in the right; and all who do not act as I would have them act, perpetually in the wrong? In short, to make *my* sake, *God*'s sake, in the sense of Mr Solmes's pitiful plea to me.

How often, my dear, have you and I endeavoured to detect and censure this partial spirit in others?

But I know you do not always content yourself with saying what you think may *justly* be said: but in order to show the extent of a penetration which can go to the bottom of any subject, delight to say or to write all that *can* be said or *written*, or even *thought*, on the particular occasion; and this partly perhaps from being desirous (pardon me, my dear!) to be thought mistress of a sagacity that is aforehand with events. But who would wish to drain off, or dry up, a refreshing current, because it now and then puts us to some little inconvenience by its overflowings? In other words, who would not allow for the liveliness of a spirit, which for one painful sensibility gives an hundred pleasurable ones: and the *one* in consequence of the *other*?

But now I come to the two points in your letter that most sensibly concern me. Thus you put them:

'Whether I choose not rather to go off with one of my *own sex*; with my ANNA HOWE—than with one of the *other*; with Mr LOVELACE?'

And if *not*,

'Whether I should not marry him as soon as possible?'

You know, my dear, my reasons for rejecting your proposal, and even for being earnest that you should not be *known* to be assisting to me in an enterprise which a cruel necessity induced *me* to think of engaging in; and which *you* have not the same plea for. At this rate, *well* might your mamma be uneasy at our correspondence, not knowing to what inconveniencies it might subject her and you!—If *I* am hardly excusable to think of flying from my *unkind* friends, what could *you* have to say for yourself, were you to abandon a mother so *indulgent?* Does she suspect that your fervent friendship may lead you to a *small* indiscretion? and does this suspicion offend you? And would you, in revenge, show her and the world that you can voluntarily rush into the *highest error* that any of our sex can be guilty of?

And is it worthy of your generosity (I ask you, my dear, is it?) to think of taking so undutiful a step, because you believe your mamma would be glad to receive you again?

I do assure you, that were I to take this step myself, I would run all risks rather than you should accompany me in it. Have I, do you think, a desire to *double* and *treble* my own fault, in the eye of the world? In the eye of that world which, cruelly as I am used (not knowing all), would not acquit *me?*

But, my dearest, kindest friend, let me tell you that we will *neither* of us take such a step. The manner of putting your questions, abundantly convinces me that I ought not, in *your* opinion, to *attempt* it. You, no doubt, intend that I shall *so* take it; and I thank you for the equally polite and forcible conviction.

It is some satisfaction to me, taking the matter in this light, that I had begun to waver before I received your last. And now I tell you, that it has absolutely determined me *not* to go away; at least, not tomorrow.

If *you*, my dear, think the *issue of the alternative*, to use your own words, *sits so lightly upon my mind*; in short, that my *inclination* is *faulty*; the *world* would treat me much less scrupulously. When, therefore, you represent *that all punctilio must be at an end the moment I am out of my father's house*; and hint that I must submit it to Lovelace to judge *when* he can leave me with safety; that is to say, give *him* the option whether he will leave me, or not; who can bear these reflections, and resolve to incur these inconveniences, that has the question still in her own power to decide upon?

While I thought only of an escape from *this house* as an escape from Mr *Solmes*; that already my reputation suffered by my confinement; and that it would be still in my own option, either to marry Mr Lovelace or wholly to renounce him; bold as the step was, I thought, treated as I am treated, something was to be said in excuse of it—if not to the world, to *myself:* and to be *self*-acquitted is a blessing to be preferred to the opinion of all the world. But, after I have censured that indiscreet forwardness in some, who (flying from their chamber to the altar) have, without the *least* ceremony, rushed upon the *greatest:* after I have stipulated with him for time, and for an ultimate option whether to accept or refuse him; and for his leaving me as soon as I am in a place of safety (which, as you observe, *he* must be the judge of): and after he has complied with these terms; so that I cannot, if I *would*, recall them, and suddenly marry—you see, my dear, that I have nothing left me but to resolve *not* to go away with him.

But, how, on this revocation, shall I be able to pacify him?

How!—Why assert the privilege of my sex!—Surely, on *this* side of the solemnity he has no *right* to be displeased. Besides, did I not reserve a power of receding, if I saw fit? To what purpose, as I asked in the case between your mamma and you, has anybody an option, if the making use of it shall give the refused a right to be disgusted?

Far, very far, would *those* be, who according to the Old Law have a *right* of *absolving* or *confirming* a child's promise, from ratifying *mine*, had it been ever *so solemn* a one.[a] But this was rather an *appointment* than a *promise:* and suppose it had been the latter; and that I had *not* reserved to myself a liberty of revoking it, was it to preclude *better* or *maturer* consideration?—If so, how unfit to be given!—how ungenerous to be insisted upon!—and how unfitter still to be kept!—Is there a man living who ought to be angry that a woman, whom he hopes one day to call his, shall refuse to keep a rash promise, when on the maturest deliberation she is convinced that it *was* a rash one?

I resolve then, upon the whole, to stand this one trial of Wednesday next—or perhaps I should rather say, of Tuesday evening, if my father hold his purpose of endeavouring in person to make me *read*, or *hear* read, and then *sign*, the settlements. *That, that* must be the greatest trial of all.

If I am compelled to sign them overnight!—then (the Lord bless me!) must all I dread follow, as of course, on Wednesday—If I can prevail upon them, by my prayers—perhaps by fits and delirium (for the very first appearance of my father, after having been so long banished his presence will greatly affect me), to lay aside their views; or to suspend, if but for one week; if *not*, but for two or three days; still Wednesday will be a lighter day of trial—They will surely give me time to *consider*; to argue with myself—This will not be *promising*—as I have made no effort to get away they have no reason to suspect me; so I may have an opportunity, in the last resort, to escape. Mrs Norton is to be with me. She, although she should be checked for it, will in my extremity plead for me. My aunt Hervey *may*, on such extremity, join her. Perhaps my mamma may be brought over. I will kneel to each, one by one, to make a friend. They have been afraid, some of them, to see me, lest they should be moved in my favour: does not this give me a reasonable hope that

    a See Numbers 30. Where it is declared, whose vows shall be binding, and whose not. The vows of a man, or of a widow, are there pronounced to be indispensable; because they are sole and subject to no other domestic authority. But the vows of a single woman, and of a wife, if the father of the one, or the husband of the other, disallow of them, as soon as they know them, are to be of no force.

    A matter highly necessary to be known, by all young ladies especially, whose designing addressers too often endeavour to engage them by vows, and then plead conscience and honour to them to hold them down to the performance.

    It cannot be amiss to recite the very words.

    Verse 3. *If a woman vow a vow unto the Lord, and bind herself by a bond, being in her father's house in her youth;*

    4. *And her father hear her vow, and her bond wherewith she hath bound her soul, and her father shall hold his peace at her; then all her vows shall stand, and every bond wherewith she hath bound her soul shall stand.*

    5. *But if her father disallow her in the day that he heareth; not any of her vows or of her bonds wherewith she hath bound her soul shall stand: and the Lord shall forgive her, because her father disallowed her.*

    The same in the case of a wife, as said above. See verses 6, 7, 8, etc.—and all is thus solemnly closed:

    Verse 16. *These are the statutes which the Lord commanded Moses between a man and his wife, between the father and his daughter, being yet in her youth in her father's house.*

I *may* move them?—My brother's counsel, heretofore given, to turn me out of doors to my evil destiny, may again be repeated, and may prevail. *Then* shall I be in no *worse* case than *now*, as to the displeasure of my friends; and thus far *better*, that it will not be my fault that I leave them and seek another protection: which even *then*, ought to be my cousin Morden's, rather than Mr Lovelace's, or any other person's.

My heart, in short, misgives me less when I resolve *this* way, than when I think of the *other:* and in so strong and involuntary a bias, the *heart* is, as I may say, *conscience.* And well cautions the wise man: 'Let the counsel of thine own heart stand; for there is no man more faithful to thee, than it: for a man's mind is sometimes wont to tell him more than seven watchmen, that sit above in a high tower.'[a]

Forgive these indigested self-reasonings. I will close here: and instantly set about a letter of revocation to Mr Lovelace; take it as he will. It will only be another trial of temper to *him*. To *me* of infinite importance. And has he not promised temper and acquiescence, on the supposition of a change in my mind?

CL. HARLOWE

Letter 90: MISS CLARISSA HARLOWE TO MISS HOWE

Sunday morning, April 9

NOBODY, it seems, will go to church this day. No blessing to be expected perhaps upon views so worldly, and in some so cruel.

They have a mistrust that I have some device in my head. Betty has been looking among my clothes. I found her, on coming up from depositing my letter to Lovelace (for I *have* written!), peering among them, the key being in the lock. She coloured, and was confounded to be caught. But I only said I should be accustomed to *any* sort of treatment in time!—If she had her orders—those were enough for her.

She owned, in her confusion, that a motion had been made to abridge me of my airings; and the report *she* should make would be no disadvantage to me. One of my friends, she told me, urged in my behalf, that there was no need of laying me under greater restraint, since Mr Lovelace's threatening to *rescue* me by violence, were I to have been carried to my uncle's, was a conviction that I had no design to go off to him voluntarily; and that if I *had*, I should have made preparations of that kind *before now*; and, most probably, been detected in them—Hence, it was also inferred, that there was no room to doubt but I would at last comply. And, added the bold creature, if you don't intend to do so, your conduct, miss, seems strange to me. Only thus she reconciled it; that I had gone so far, I knew not how to come off *genteelly:* and she fancied I should in *full congregation* on Wednesday give Mr Solmes my hand. And then, said the confident wench, as the learned Dr Brand took his text last Sunday, *There will be joy in Heaven—*[1]

This is the substance of my letter to Mr Lovelace:

'That I have reasons, of the greatest consequence to *myself*, and which when known must satisfy *him*, to suspend, for the present, my intention of leaving my

a Ecclesiasticus 37:13, 14.

father's house: that I have hopes that matters may be brought to an happy conclusion, without taking a step which nothing but the last necessity could justify: and that he may depend upon my promise, that I will die, rather than consent to marry Mr Solmes.'

And so I am preparing myself to stand the shock of his exclamatory reply. But be that what it will, it cannot affect me so much as the apprehensions of what may happen to me next Tuesday or Wednesday; for now those apprehensions engage my whole attention, and make me sick at the very heart.

Sunday, four o'clock, p.m.

MY letter is not yet taken away!—If he should not send for it, or take it, and come hither on my not meeting him tomorrow, in doubt of what may have befallen me, what shall I do? Why had I any concerns with this sex!—I, that was so happy till I knew this man!

I dined in the ivy summer-house. It was complied with at the first word. To show I meant nothing, I went again into the house with Betty, as soon as I had dined. I thought it was not amiss to ask this liberty; the weather seeming to be set in fine. One does not know what Tuesday or Wednesday may produce.

Sunday evening, seven o'clock

THERE remains my letter still!—He is busied, I suppose, in his preparations for tomorrow. But then he has servants. Does the man think he is so *secure* of me, that having appointed he need not give himself any further concern about me, till the very moment!—He knows how I am beset. He knows not what may happen. I *might* be ill, or still more closely watched or confined than before. The correspondence *might* be discovered. It *might* be necessary to vary the scheme. I *might* be forced into measures, which might entirely frustrate my purpose. I *might* have new doubts: I *might* suggest something more convenient, for anything he knew. What can the man mean, I wonder!—Yet it shall lie; for if he has it any time before the appointed hour, it will save me declaring to him personally my changed purpose, and the trouble of contending with him on that score. If he send for it at all, he will see by the date that he might have had it in time; and if he be put to any inconvenience from shortness of notice, let him take it for his pains.

Sunday night, nine o'clock

IT is determined, it seems, to send to Mrs Norton to be here on Tuesday to dinner; and she is to stay with me for a whole week.

So she is first to endeavour to persuade me to comply and, when the violence is done, she is to comfort me and try to reconcile me to my fate. They expect *fits* and *fetches*, Betty insolently tells me, and expostulations and exclamations, *without number:* but everybody will be prepared for them: and when it's over, it's over; and I shall be easy and pacified, when I find I cannot help it.

Mon. morn. April 10, seven o'clock

OH my dear! There yet lies the letter, just as I left it!

Does he think he is so sure of me!—Perhaps he imagines that I *dare not* alter my purpose. I wish I had never known him!—I begin now to see this rashness in the light everyone else would have seen it in, had I been guilty of it—But what can I do, if he come today at the appointed time!—If he receive not the letter, I must see him, or he will think something has befallen me; and certainly will come to the house. As certainly he will be insulted. And what, in that case, may be the consequence!—Then I as good as promised that I would take the first opportunity to see him, if I changed my mind, and to give him my reasons for it. I have no doubt but he will be out of humour upon it: but better *he* meet me, and go away dissatisfied with *me*, than that *I* should go away dissatisfied with *myself*.

Yet, short as the time is, he may still perhaps send, and get the letter. Something may have happened to prevent him, which, when known, will excuse him.

After I have disappointed him more than once before, on a requested *interview* only, it is impossible he should not have *curiosity*, at least, to know if something has not happened; and if my mind hold in this more *important case*. And yet, as I rashly confirmed my resolution by a second letter, I begin now to doubt it.

Nine o'clock

MY cousin Dolly Hervey slid the enclosed letter into my hand, as I passed by her, coming out of the garden.

[*Letter 90.1: Dorothy Hervey to Clarissa Harlowe*]

Dearest madam,

I HAVE got intelligence from one as says she knows that you must be married on Wednesday morning to Mr Solmes. Maybe, howsoever, only to vex me; for it is Betty Barnes: a saucy creature, I'm sure. A licence is got, as she says: and so far she went as to tell me (bidding me say nothing; but she knew as that I would) that Mr Brand the young Oxford clergyman, and fine scholar, is to marry you. For Dr Lewin, I hear, refuses, unless you consent; and they have heard that he does not like over-well their proceedings against you; and says, as that you don't deserve to be treated so cruelly as you are treated. But Mr Brand, I am told, is to have his fortune made by uncle Harlowe, and among them.

You will know better than I what to make of all these matters; for sometimes I think Betty tells me things as if I should not tell you, and yet expects as that I will. She and all the world knows how I love you: and so I would *have* them. It is an honour to me to love such a dear young lady, who is an honour to all her family, let them say what they will. But there is such whispering between this Betty and Miss Harlowe, as you can't imagine; and when that is done, Betty comes and tells me something.

This seems to be sure (and that is why I write: but pray burn it), you are to be searched once more for letters, and for pen and ink; for they know you write. Something they pretend to have betrayed out of one of Mr Lovelace's servants, as they hope to make something of; I know not what. That must be a very vilde and wicked man, who would brag of [a] lady's goodness to him, and tell secrets. Mr Lovelace is too much of a gentleman for that, I dare say. If not, who can be safe of young innocent creatures, such as we be?

Then they have a notion, from that false Betty, I beliefe, as that you intend to take something to make yourself sick, or some such thing; and so they will search for phials and powders, and such-like.

Strange searching among them! God bless us young creatures, when we come among such suspicious relations. But, thank God, my mamma is not such a one, at the present.

. If nothing be found, you are to be used kindlier for that, by your papa, at the grand judgement, as I may call it.

Yet, sick or well, alas, my dear cousin! you must be married, belike. So says this same creature; and I don't doubt it: but your husband is to go home every night, till you are reconciled to go to him. And so illness can be no pretence to save you.

They are sure you will make a good wife, when you be one. So would not I, unless I liked my husband. And Mr Solmes is always telling them how he will purchase your love and all that, by jewels and fine things—a siccofant of a man!— I wish he and Betty Barnes were to come together; and he would beat her everyday till she was good—So, in brief, secure everything you would not have seen: and burn this, I beg you. And, pray, dearest madam, do not take nothing as may hurt your health: for that will not do. I am,

Your truly loving cousin,
D.H.

When I first read my cousin's letter, I was half inclined to resume my former intention; especially as my countermanding letter is not taken away: and as my heart aches at the thoughts of the conflict I must expect to have with him on my refusal. For, see him for a few moments I doubt I must, lest he should take some rash resolutions; especially, as he has reason to expect I will. But here your words *that all punctilio is at an end the moment I am out of my father's house*, added to the still more cogent considerations of duty and reputation, determined me once more against taking the rash step. And it will be very hard (although no seasonable fainting, or wished-for fit, should stand my friend) if I cannot gain one month, or fortnight, or week. And I have still more hopes that I shall prevail for some delay, from my cousin's intimation that the good Doctor Lewin refuses to give his assistance to their projects, if they have not my consent, and thinks me cruelly used: since, without taking notice that I am apprised of this, I can plead a scruple of conscience, and insist upon having that worthy divine's opinion upon it: which, enforced as I shall enforce it, my mamma will surely second me in. My aunt Hervey and my Mrs Norton will support *her:* the suspension must follow: and I can but get away afterwards.

But, if they *will* compel me: if they *will* give me no time: if nobody *will* be moved: if it be resolved that the ceremony shall be read over my constrained hand—why then—alas! what then!—I can but—but what? Oh my dear! This Solmes shall never have my vows I am resolved! And I will say nothing but No, as long as I shall be able to speak. And who will presume to look upon such an act of violence as a marriage?—It is impossible, surely, that a father and mother can see such a dreadful compulsion offered to their child—But if mine should withdraw and leave the task to my brother and sister, they will have no mercy!

I am grieved to be driven to have recourse to the following artifices.

I have given them a clue, by the feather of a pen sticking out, where they will find such of my hidden stores as I intend they shall find.

Two or three little essays I have left easy to be seen, of my own writing.

About a dozen lines also of a letter begun to you, in which I express my hopes (although I say that appearances are against me) that my friends will relent. They know from your mamma, by my uncle Antony, that somehow or other, I now and then get a letter to you. In this piece of a letter, I declare renewedly my firm resolution to give up the man so obnoxious to my family, on their releasing me from the address of the other.

Near the essays, I have left a copy of my letter to Lady Drayton,[a] which, affording arguments suitable to my case, may chance (thus accidentally to be fallen upon) to incline them to favour me.

I have reserves of pens and ink you may believe; and one or two in the ivy summer-house; with which I shall amuse myself in order to lighten, if possible, those apprehensions which more and more affect me as Wednesday the day of trial approaches.

                                                          CL. HARLOWE

Letter 91: MISS CLARISSA HARLOWE TO MISS HOWE

                                          Ivy summer-house, eleven o'clock
HE has not yet got my letter: and while I was contriving here, how to send my officious gaoleress from me, that I might have time for the intended interview, and had hit upon an expedient which I believe would have done, came my aunt and furnished me with a much better. She saw my little table covered, preparative to my solitary dinner; and hoped, she told me, that this would be the last day that my friends would be deprived of my company at table.

You may believe, my dear, that the thoughts of meeting Mr Lovelace, the fear of being discovered, together with the contents of my cousin Dolly's letter, gave me great and visible emotions. She took notice of them—Why these sighs, why these heavings here, said she, patting my neck?—Oh my dear niece, who would have thought so much natural sweetness could be so very unpersuadable?

I could not answer her, and she proceeded. I am come, I doubt, upon a very unwelcome errand. Some things that have been told us yesterday, which came from the mouth of one of the most desperate and insolent men in the world, convince your father and all of us, that you still find means to write out of the house. Mr Lovelace knows everything that is done here; and that as soon as done; and great mischief is apprehended from him, which you are as much concerned as anybody, to prevent. Your mamma has also some apprehensions concerning yourself, which yet she hopes are groundless; but, however, cannot be easy, nor will be permitted to be easy, if she would, unless (while you remain here in the garden, or in this summer-house) you give her the opportunity once more of looking into your closet, your cabinet, and drawers. It will be the better taken, if you give me cheerfully your keys. I hope, my dear, you won't dispute it. Your desire of dining in this place was the more readily complied with, for the sake of such an opportunity.

I thought myself very lucky to be so well prepared by my cousin Dolly's means for this search: But yet I artfully made some scruples, and not a few complaints of this treatment: after which, I not only gave her the keys of all; but even officiously emptied my pockets before her, and invited her to put her fingers in my stays, that she might be sure that I had no papers there.

This highly obliged her; and she said: She would represent my cheerful

a See Letter 58, p. 246.

compliance as it deserved, *let my brother and sister say what they would*. My mamma, in particular, she was sure, would rejoice at the opportunity given her to obviate, as she doubted not would be the case, some suspicions that were raised against me.

She then hinted that there were methods taken to come at all Mr Lovelace's secrets, and even, from his careless communicativeness, at some of *mine*; it being, she said, his custom, boastingly to prate to his very servants of his intentions in particular cases. She added that, deep as he was thought to be, my brother was as deep as he; and fairly too hard for him at his own weapons—as one day it would be found.

I knew not, I said, the meaning of these dark hints. I thought the cunning she hinted at, on *both* sides, called rather for contempt than applause. I myself might have been put upon artifices which my heart disdained to practice, had I given way to the resentment which, I was bold to say, was much more justifiable than the actions that occasioned it: that it was evident to me, from what she had said, that their present suspicions of me were partly owing to this supposed superior cunning of my brother; and partly to the consciousness, that the usage I met with might naturally produce a reason for such suspicions: that it was very unhappy for me to be made the butt of my brother's wit: that it would have been more to his praise, to have aimed at showing a kind heart, than a cunning head: that, nevertheless, I wished he knew *himself* as well as I imagined *I* knew him; and he would then have less conceit of his abilities: which abilities would, in my opinion, be less thought of, if his power to do ill offices were not much greater than them.

I was vexed. I could not help making this reflection. The dupe the other, too probably, makes of him though his own spy deserved it. But I so little approve of this low art in either, that were I but tolerably used, the vileness of that man, that Joseph Leman, should be inquired into.

She was sorry, she said, to find that I thought so disparagingly of my brother. He was a young gentleman both of learning and parts.

Learning enough, I said, to make him vain of it among us women: but not of parts sufficient to make his learning valuable either to himself or to anybody else—

She wished, indeed, that he had more good nature: but she feared that I had too great an opinion of somebody else to think so well of my brother as a sister ought: since, between the two, there was a sort of rivalry as to abilities, that made them hate one another.

Rivalry, madam, said I!—If that be the case, or whether it be or not, I wish they both understood better than either of them seems to do, what it becomes gentlemen, and men of liberal education, to be and to do—Neither of them, then, would glory in what they ought to be ashamed of.

But waiving this subject, it was not impossible, I said, that they might find a little of my writing, and a pen or two and a little ink (hated art!—or rather, hateful the necessity for it!), as I was not permitted to go up to put them out of the way: but if they did, I must be contented. And I assured her that, take what time they pleased, I would not go in to disturb them, but would be either in or near the garden, in this summer-house or in the cedar one, about my poultry yard, or near the great cascade, till I was ordered to return to my prison. With like cunning I said, that I supposed the unkind search would not be made till the servants had dined; because I doubted not that the pert Betty Barnes, who knew all the corners of my apartment and closet, would be employed in it.

She hoped, she said, that nothing could be found that would give a handle against me: for, she would assure me, the motives to the search, on my mamma's part especially, were, that she hoped to find reason rather to acquit than to blame me; and that my papa might be induced to see me tomorrow night, or Wednesday morning, with temper: with *tenderness*, I should rather say, said she; for he is resolved so to do, if no new offence be given.

Ah! madam, said I!—

Why that Ah, madam, and shaking your head so significantly?

I wish, madam, that I may not have more reason to dread my papa's continued displeasure, than to hope for his returning tenderness.

You don't *know*, my dear!—Things may take a turn—things may not be so bad as you fear—

Dearest madam, have you any consolation to give me?—

Why, my dear, it is possible, that *you* may be more compliable than you have been.

Why raised you my hopes, madam!—Don't let me think my dear aunt Hervey cruel to a niece who truly honours her.

I may tell you more perhaps, said she (but in confidence, in absolute confidence), if the inquiry within come out in your favour. Do you know of anything above, that can be found to your disadvantage?

Some papers they will find, I doubt: but I must take consequences. My brother and sister will be at hand with their good-natured constructions. I am made desperate, and care not what is found.

She hoped, she *earnestly* hoped, she said, that nothing could be found that would impeach my discretion; and then—but she might say too much—

And away she went, having added to my perplexity.

But I now can think of nothing but this man!—this interview!—would to Heaven it were over!—To meet to quarrel—but I will not stay a moment with him, let him take what measures he will upon it, if he be not quite calm and resigned.

Don't you see how crooked some of my lines are? Don't you see how some of the letters stagger more than others!—That is when this interview is more in my head than my subject.

But, after all, should I, *ought* I, to meet him? How I have taken it for granted that I should!—I wish there were time to take your advice. Yet you are so loath to speak *quite* out!—But that I owe, as you own, to the difficulty of my situation.

I should have mentioned, that in the course of this conversation I besought my aunt to stand my friend, and to put in a word for me on my approaching trial; and to endeavour to procure me time for consideration, if I could obtain nothing else.

She told me that, after the ceremony was performed (odious confirmation of a hint in my cousin Dolly's letter!) I should have what time I pleased to reconcile myself to my lot, before cohabitation.

This put me out of all patience.

She requested of me in *her* turn, she said, that I would resolve to meet them all with cheerful duty, and with a spirit of absolute acquiescence. It was in my power to make them all happy. And how affectingly joyful would it be to her, she said, to see my father, my mother, my uncles, my brother, my sister, all embracing me with raptures, and folding me by turns to their fond hearts, and congratulating each other on their restored happiness. Her own joy, she said, would probably make her motionless and speechless, for a time: and for her Dolly—the poor girl, who had suffered in the esteem of some for her *grateful* attachment to me, would have everybody love her again.

Will you doubt, my dear, that my next trial will be the most affecting that I have yet had?

My aunt set forth all this in so strong a light, and I was so particularly touched on my cousin Dolly's account that, impatient as I was just before, I was greatly moved: yet could only show by my sighs and my tears how desirable such an event would be to me could it be brought about upon conditions with which it was possible for me to comply.

Here comes Betty Barnes with my dinner—

The wench is gone. The time of meeting is at hand. Oh that he may not come!— But should I, or should I not, meet him?—How I question, without possibility of a timely answer!

Betty, according to my leading hint to my aunt, boasted to me that she was to be *employed*, as she called it, after she had eat her own dinner.

She should be sorry, she told me, to have me found out. Yet 'twould be all for my good: I should have it in my power to be forgiven for all at once, before Wednesday night. The Confidence then, to stifle a laugh, put a corner of her apron in her mouth and went to the door: and on her return to take away, as I angrily bid her, she begged my excuse—but—but—and then the saucy creature laughed again, she could not help it; to think how I had drawn myself in by my summer-house dinnering; since it had given so fine an opportunity, by way of surprise, to look into all my private hoards. She thought something was in the wind when my brother came into my dining here so readily. Her young master was too hard for everybody. 'Squire Lovelace himself was nothing at all at a quick thought, to her young master.

My aunt mentioned Mr Lovelace's boasting behaviour to *his* servants: perhaps he *may* be so mean. But as to my brother, he always took a pride in making himself appear to be a man of parts and learning to our servants. *Pride* and *Meanness*, I have often thought, are as nearly allied, and as close borderers upon each other, as the poet tells us *Wit* and *Madness* are.[1]

But why do I trouble you (and myself, at such a crisis) with these impertinencies?—yet I would forget if I could the nearest evil, the interview; because, my apprehensions increasing as the hour is at hand, I should, were my attention to be engrossed by them, be unfit to see him if he does come: and then he will have too much advantage over me, as he will have seeming reason to reproach me with change of resolution.

The *upbraider*, you know, my dear, is in some sense a superior; while the *upbraided*, if with reason upbraided, must make a figure as spiritless as conscious.

I know that this wretch will, if he *can*, be his own judge, and *mine* too. But the latter he shall *not* be.

I dare say we shall be all to pieces. But I don't care for that. It would be hard if I, who have held it out so sturdily to my father and uncles, should not—But he is at the garden-door—

*

I was mistaken!—How may noises *un*-like, be made *like* what one fears!—Why flutters the fool so!——

I will hasten to deposit this. Then I will for the last time go to the usual place, in hopes to find that he has got my letter. If he *has*, I will not meet him. If he has *not*, I will take it back and show him what I have written. That will break the ice, as I may say, and save me much circumlocution and reasoning: and a steadfast adherence to that my written mind is all that will be necessary—The interview must be as short as possible; for should it be discovered, it would furnish a new and strong pretence for the intended evil of Wednesday next.

Perhaps I shall not be able to write again one while. Perhaps not till I am the miserable property of that Solmes!—But that shall never, never be, while I have my senses.

If your servant find nothing from me by Wednesday morning, you may conclude that I can then neither write to you, nor receive your favours—

In that case, pity and pray for me, my beloved friend, and continue to me that place in your affection, which is the pride of my life, and the only comfort left to

Your
CLARISSA HARLOWE

Letter 92: MISS CLARISSA HARLOWE TO MISS HOWE

St Albans, Tuesday morn., past one

Oh my dearest friend!

AFTER what I had resolved upon, as by my former, what shall I write? What *can* I? With what consciousness, even by *letter*, do I approach you!—You will soon hear (if already you have not heard from the mouth of common fame) that your Clarissa Harlowe is gone off with a man!—

I am busying myself to give you the particulars at large. The whole twenty-four hours of each day (to begin the moment I can fix) shall be employed in it till it is finished: Every one of the hours, I mean, that will be spared me by this interrupting man, to whom I have made myself so foolishly accountable for too many of them. Rest is departed from me. I have no call for that: and that has no balm for the wounds of my mind. So you'll have all those hours without interruption till the account is ended.

But will you receive, shall you be *permitted* to receive, my letters, after what I have done?

Oh, my dearest friend!—But I must make the best of it. I hope that will not be very bad! Yet am I convinced that I did a rash, an inexcusable thing, in meeting him; and all his tenderness, all his vows, cannot pacify my inward reproaches on that account.

The bearer comes to you, my dear, for the little parcel of linen which I sent you with far better and more agreeable hopes.

Send not my letters. Send the linen only: except you will favour me with one line to tell me you will love me still; and that you will suspend your censures till you have the whole before you. I am the readier to send thus early, because if you have deposited anything for me, you may cause it to be taken back, or withhold anything you had but intended to send.

Adieu, my dearest friend!—I beseech you to love me still!—But, alas! what will your mamma say?—what will mine!—what my other relations?—and what my dear Mrs Norton? and how will my brother and sister triumph?—

I cannot at present tell you how, or where, you can direct to me. For very early shall I leave this place; harassed and fatigued to death! But, when I can do nothing else, constant use has made me able to write. Long, very long, has that been all my amusement and pleasure: yet could not that have been such to me, had I not had you, my best-beloved friend, to write to. Once more adieu. Pity, and pray for,

Your
CL. HARLOWE

Letter 93: MISS HOWE TO MISS CLARISSA HARLOWE

Tuesday, nine o'clock

I WRITE, because you enjoin me to do so—Love you still!—how can I help it, if I would?—You may believe how I stand aghast, your letter communicating the first news—Good God of heaven and earth!—but what shall I say?—I shall be all impatience for particulars.

Lord have mercy upon me!—but can it be?

My mamma will, *indeed*, be astonished!—How can I tell it to her?—It was but last night that I assured her (upon some jealousies put into her head by your foolish uncle) and this upon the strength of your own assurances that neither man nor devil would be able to induce you to take a step that was in the least derogatory to the most punctilious honour.

But, once more, can it be? What woman, at this rate!—but, God preserve you!

Let nothing escape you in your letters. Direct them for me, however, to Mrs Knollys's, till further notice.

OBSERVE, my dear, that I don't blame *you* by all this—your relations only are in fault!—Yet how you came to change your mind is the surprising thing!—

How to break it to my mamma, I know not. Yet, if she hear it first from any other, and find I knew it before, she will believe it is by my connivance!——Yet, as I hope to live, I know not how to break it to her!

But this is teasing you!—I am sure without intention.

Let me now repeat my former advice—If you are *not* married by this time, be sure delay not the ceremony—Since things are as they are, I wish it were thought that you were privately married before you went away. If these men plead AUTHORITY to our pain when we are *theirs*—why should we not, in such a case as *this*, make some good out of the hated word for our reputation, when we are induced to violate a more natural one?

Your brother and sister (that vexes me almost as much as any thing!) have now their ends. Now, I suppose, will go forward alterations of wills and suchlike spiteful doings.

Miss Lloyd and Miss Biddulph this moment send up their names—They are out of breath, Kitty says, to speak to me. Easy to guess their errand!—I must see my mamma before I see them. I have no way but to show her your letter, to clear myself. I shall not be able to say a word, till she has run herself out of her first breath—Forgive me, my dear!—Surprise makes me write thus. If your messenger did not wait and were not those young ladies below, I would write it over again, for fear of afflicting you.

I send what you write for. If there be anything else you want that is in my power, command without reserve,

> Your ever affectionate
> ANNA HOWE

Letter 94: MISS CLARISSA HARLOWE TO MISS HOWE

Tuesday night

I THINK myself obliged to thank you, my dear Miss Howe, for your condescension, in taking notice of a creature who has occasioned you so much scandal.

I am grieved on this account, as much, I verily think, as for the evil itself.

Tell me—but yet I am afraid to know—what your mamma said.

I long, and yet I dread to be told, what the young ladies my companions, now never more, perhaps, to be so, say of me.

They cannot, however, say worse of me than I will of myself. Self-accusation shall flow in every line of my narrative, where I think I am justly censurable. If any thing can arise from the account I am going to give you, for extenuation of my fault (for that is all a person can hope for, who cannot excuse herself), I know I may expect it from your friendship, though not from the charity of any other: since by this time I doubt not every mouth is opened against me; and all that know Clarissa Harlowe, condemn the fugitive daughter.

AFTER I had deposited my letter to you, written down to the last hour, as I may say, I returned to the ivy summer-house; first taking back my letter from the loose bricks: and there I endeavoured, as coolly as my situation would permit, to recollect and lay together, several incidents that had passed between my aunt and me; and comparing them with some of the contents of my cousin Dolly's letter, I began to hope, that I need not be so very apprehensive as I had been of the next Wednesday. And thus I argued with myself.

'Wednesday cannot possibly be the day they intend, although to intimidate me they may wish me to think it is: for the settlements are unsigned: nor have they been offered me to sign. I can choose whether I will, or will not, put my hand to them; hard as it will be to refuse, if my father tender them to me—besides, did not my father and mother propose, if I made compulsion necessary, to go to my uncle's themselves, in order to be out of the way of my appeals? Whereas they intend to be present on Wednesday. And however affecting to me the thought of meeting them and all my friends in full assembly is, perhaps it is the very thing I ought to wish for: since my brother and sister had such an opinion of my interest in them that they got me excluded from their presence, as a measure which they thought previously necessary to carry on their designs.

'Nor have I reason to doubt but that (as I had before argued with myself) I shall be able to bring over some of my relations to my party; and being brought face to face with my brother, that I shall expose his malevolence and, of consequence, weaken his power.

'Then supposing the very worst, challenging the minister as I shall challenge him, he will not presume to proceed: nor, surely will Mr Solmes dare to accept my refusing and struggling hand. And finally, if nothing else will do, nor procure me delay, I can plead scruples of conscience, and even pretend prior obligation; for, my dear, I have given Mr Lovelace room to hope (as you will see in one of my letters in your hands), that I will be no other man's while he is single and gives me not wilful and premeditated cause of offence against him; and this in order to rein in his resentments on the declared animosity of my brother and uncles. And as I shall appeal, or refer my scruples on this head, to the good Dr Lewin, it is impossible but that my mamma and aunt (if nobody else) should be affected with this.plea.'

Revolving cursorily these things, I congratulated myself, that I had resolved against going away with Mr Lovelace.

I told you, my dear, that I would not spare myself; and I enumerate these particulars as an argument to condemn the action I have been so unhappily betrayed into. An argument that concludes against me with the greater force, as I must acknowledge that I was apprehensive that what my cousin Dolly mentions as from Betty and from my sister was told *her*, that she should tell *me* in order to make me desperate, and perhaps to push me upon some such step as I have been drawn in to take, as the most effectual means to ruin me with my father and uncles.

God forgive me, if I judge too hardly of their views!—But if I do *not*, I must say, that they laid a wicked snare for me; and that I have been caught in it—And doubly may they triumph, if they *can* triumph, in the ruin of a sister who never wished or intended hurt to them!

As the above kind of reasoning had lessened my apprehensions as to the Wednesday, it added to those I had of meeting him—now, as it seemed, not only the nearest, but the heaviest evil; principally indeed because *nearest*; for little did I dream (foolish creature that I was, and every way beset!) of the event proving what it has proved. I expected a contention with him, 'tis true, as he had not my letter: but I thought it would be very strange, as I mentioned in one of my former,[a] if I, who had so steadily held out against characters so venerable, against authorities so sacred, as I may say, when I thought them unreasonably exerted, should not find myself more equal to such a trial as this; especially as I had so much reason to be displeased with him for not having taken away my letter.

On what a crisis, on what a point of time, may one's fate depend! Had I had but two hours more to consider of the matter, and to attend to and improve upon these new lights, as I may call them—But then perhaps I might have given him a meeting—Fool that I was, what had I to do, to give him hope that I would *personally* acquaint him with the reason for my change of mind, if I did change it?

a See Letter 90.

Oh my dear! an obliging temper is a very dangerous temper!—by endeavouring to gratify others, it is evermore disobliging itself!

When the bell rang to call the servants to dinner, Betty came to me and asked if I had any commands before she went to hers; repeating her hint that she should be *employed*; adding, that she believed it was expected that I should not come up till she came down, or till I saw my aunt or Miss Hervey.

I asked her some questions about the cascade, which had been out of order, and lately mended; and expressed a curiosity to see how it played, in order to induce her (how cunning to cheat myself, as it proved!) to go thither, if she found me not where she left me; it being at a part of the garden most distant from the ivy summer-house.

She could hardly have got into the house, when I heard the first signal—Oh, how my heart fluttered!—But no time was to be lost. I stepped to the garden door; and seeing a clear coast, unbolted the ready-unlocked door—and there was he, all impatience, waiting for me!

A panic, next to fainting seized me when I saw him. My heart seemed convulsed; and I trembled so, that I should hardly have kept my feet had he not supported me.

Fear nothing, dearest creature, said he!—Let us hasten away!—The chariot is at hand!—And by this sweet condescension, you have obliged me beyond expression, or return!

Recovering my spirits a little, as he kept drawing me after him, Oh Mr Lovelace, said I, I cannot go with you!—*Indeed* I cannot!—I wrote you word so!—Let go my hand and you shall see my letter. It has lain there from yesterday morning till within this half-hour—I bid you watch to the last for a letter from me, lest I should be obliged to revoke the appointment; and had you followed the direction, you would have found it.

I have been watched, my dearest life, said he, half out of breath—I have been watched in every step I took: and my trusty servant has been watched too, ever since Saturday; and dared not to come near your wall—And here we shall be discovered in a moment!—Speed away, my charmer!—this is the moment of your deliverance!—If you neglect this opportunity, you *never* can have such another!

What is it you mean, sir!—Let go my hand: for I tell you (struggling vehemently) that I will sooner die than go with you!—

Good God, said he! with a look of wildness and surprise, what is it I hear!—but (still drawing me after him as he retreated farther from the door) it is no time to argue—By all that's good you must go!—surely you cannot doubt my honour, nor give me cause to question your own.

As you value me, Mr Lovelace, urge me no farther. I come fixed and resolved. Let me give you the letter I had written. My further reasons shall follow; and they will convince you that I ought not to go.

Nothing, madam, can convince me—By all that's sacred, I will not leave you! To leave you now is to lose you for ever!

Am I to be thus compelled? interrupted I, with equal indignation and vehemence—Let go my hands—I am resolved not to go with you—and I will convince you that I *ought* not.

All my friends expect you, madam!—all your own are determined against you!—Wednesday next is the day! the important, perhaps the fatal day! Would you stay to be Solmes's wife?—Can this be your determination at last?

No, never, never will I be that man's!—but I will not go with you!—Draw me not thus!—How dare you, sir?—I would not have seen you, but to tell you so!—I had not met you, but for fear you would have been guilty of some rashness!—and, once more, I will *not* go!—What mean you!—striving with all my force to get from him.

What can have possessed my angel, quitting my hands and with a gentler voice, that after so much ill usage from your relations; vows so solemn on my part; an affection so ardent; you stab me with a refusal to stand by your own appointment!

It signifies nothing talking, Mr Lovelace. I will give you my reasons at a better opportunity. I cannot go with you now—and, once more, urge me no farther—surely I am not to be compelled by everybody!

I see how it is, said he, with a dejected, but passionate air—what a severe fate is mine!—at length your spirit is subdued!—Your brother and sister have prevailed; and I must give up all my hopes to a wretch so *truly* despicable—

Once more I tell you, interrupted I, I never will be his—All may end on Wednesday, differently from what you expect—

And it may *not!*—and then, good heaven!—

It is to be their last effort, as I have reason to believe—

And I have reason to believe so too!—Since, if you tarry you will inevitably be Solmes's wife.

Not so, interrupted I—I have obliged them in one point—They will be in good humour with me. I shall gain time at least—I am sure I shall—I have several ways to gain time.

And what, madam, will gaining time do?—It is plain you have not a hope beyond that!—It is plain you have not, by putting all upon that precarious issue.—Oh my dearest, dearest life! let me beseech you not to run a risk of this consequence. I can convince you that it will be *more* than a risk if you go back, that you will on Wednesday next be Solmes's wife—Prevent therefore, now that it is in your power to prevent, the fatal mischiefs that will follow such a dreadful certainty.

While I have any room for hope, it concerns *your* honour, Mr Lovelace, as well as mine (if you have the proper value for me and wish me to believe you have), that my conduct in this great point shall justify my prudence.

Your prudence, madam! When has that been questionable? Yet what stead has either your prudence or your duty stood you in with people so strangely determined?

And then he pathetically enumerated the different instances of the harsh treatment I had met with; imputing all to the malice and caprice of a brother who set everybody against him: and insisting that I had no other way to effect a reconciliation with my father and uncles than by putting myself out of the power of my brother's inveterate malice.

Your brother's whole reliance, proceeded he, has been upon your easiness to bear his insults—Your whole family will seek to *you*, when you have freed yourself from his disgraceful oppression—when they know you are with those who *can*, and *will* right you, they will give up to you your own estate—Why then, putting his arm round me and again drawing me with a gentle force after him, do you hesitate a moment?—Now is the time—fly with me then, I beseech you, my dearest creature! Trust your persecuted adorer—Have we not suffered in the same cause? If any imputations are cast upon you, give me the honour, as I shall be found to deserve it, to call you mine; and, when you are so, shall I not be able to protect both your person and character?

Urge me no more, Mr Lovelace, I conjure you—You yourself have given me a hint which I will speak plainer to, than prudence perhaps on any other occasion would allow me to speak—I am convinced that Wednesday next (if I had time, I would give you my reasons) is not intended to be the day we had both so much dreaded: and if, after that day shall be over, I find my friends to be determined in Mr Solmes's favour, I will then contrive some way to meet you with Miss Howe, who is not your enemy: and when the solemnity has passed, I shall think that step a duty which, *till* then, will be criminal to take: since now my father's authority is unimpeached by any greater.

Dearest madam—

Nay, Mr Lovelace, if you now dispute!—if, after this more favourable declaration than I had the thought of making, you are not satisfied, I shall know what to think both of your gratitude and generosity.

The case, madam, admits not of this alternative. I am all gratitude upon it. I cannot express how much I should be delighted with the charming hope you have given me, were you not next Wednesday, if you stay, to be another man's. Think, dearest creature! what an heightening of my anguish the distant hope you bid me look up to, is, taken in this light!

Depend upon it, I will die sooner than be Mr Solmes's. If you would have me rely upon *your* honour, why should you doubt of *mine?*

I doubt not your *honour*, madam; your *power* is all I doubt. You never, never can have such another opportunity—Dearest creature, permit me—and he was again drawing me after him.

Whither, sir, do you draw me?—Leave me this moment—Do you seek to keep me till my return shall grow dangerous or impracticable?—I am not satisfied with you at all! indeed I am not!—This moment let me go, if you would have me think tolerably of you.

My happiness, madam, both here and hereafter, and the safety of all your implacable family, depend upon this moment.

To Providence, Mr Lovelace, and to the Law will I leave the safety of my friends—You shall not threaten me into a rashness that my heart condemns!— Shall *I*, to promote your happiness, as you call it, destroy all my future peace of mind?

You trifle with me, my dear life, just as our better prospects begin to open. The way is clear; just now it is clear!—but you may be prevented in a moment.

What is it you doubt?—May I perish eternally if your will shall not be a law to me in everything!—All my relations expect you: your own appointment calls upon you!—Next WEDNESDAY—dearest creature!—think of next WEDNESDAY!—And what is it I urge you to but to take a step that, sooner than any other, will reconcile you to all you have most reason to value in your family?

Let me judge for myself, sir. Do not you, who blame my friends for endeavouring to compel me, *yourself* seek to compel me. I won't bear it—Your earnestness gives me greater apprehensions and greater reluctance!—Let me go back, then!—let me before it is too late go back, that it may not be worse for both. What mean you by this forcible treatment?—Is it thus that I am to judge of the entire submission to my will which you have so often vowed?—Unhand me this moment or I will cry out for help.

I will obey you, my dearest creature!—and quitted my hand with a look full of tender despondency that, knowing the violence of his temper, half-concerned me for him. Yet I was hastening from him when, with a solemn air, looking upon his sword but catching as it were his hand from it, he folded both his arms as if a sudden thought had recovered him from an intended rashness.

Stay one moment!—but one moment stay, oh best beloved of my soul!—Your retreat is secure, if you *will* go: the key lies down at the door—but, oh madam, next WEDNESDAY, and you are Mr Solmes's—Fly me not so eagerly!—hear me but a few words.

When near the garden door I stopped; and was the more satisfied, as I saw the key there, by which I could let myself in again at pleasure. But, being uneasy lest I should be missed, I told him I could stay no longer: I had already stayed too long: that I would write to him all my reasons. And depend upon it, Mr Lovelace, said I, just upon the point of stooping for the key, in order to return, I will die rather than have that man. You know what I have promised if I find myself in danger.

One word, madam, however, one word more, approaching me, his arms still folded as if (as I thought) he would not be tempted to mischief. Remember only that I come at your appointment, to redeem you at the hazard of my life from your gaolers and persecutors, with a resolution, God is my witness, or may he for ever blast me! (that was his shocking imprecation), to be a father, uncle, brother, and as I humbly hoped, in your own good time, a *husband* to you, all in one. But since I find you are so ready to cry out for *help* against me, which must bring down upon me the vengeance of all your family, I am contented to run all risks—I will not ask you to retreat with *me*; I will attend you into the garden, and into the *house*, if I am not intercepted—Nay, be not surprised, madam! The help you would have called upon, I will attend you to—I will face them all: but not as a revenger, if they provoke me not too much. You shall see what I can further bear for your sake. And let us both see if expostulation, and the behaviour of a gentleman to them, will not procure me the treatment due to a gentleman from them.

Had he offered to draw his sword upon himself, I was prepared to have despised him for supposing me such a poor novice as to be intimidated by an artifice so common. But this resolution, uttered with so serious an air, of accompanying me in to my friends, made me gasp almost with terror.

What mean you, Mr Lovelace, said I?—I beseech you leave me: leave me, sir, I beseech you.

Excuse me, madam! I beg you to excuse me!—I have long enough skulked like a thief about these lonely walls!—Long, too long, have I borne the insults of your brother and others of your relations. Absence but heightens malice. I am desperate. I have but this one chance for it; for is not the day after tomorrow WEDNESDAY? I have encouraged virulence by my tameness?—Yet *tame* I will be!—You shall see, madam, what I will bear for your sake. My sword shall be put sheathed into your hands (And he offered it to me in the scabbard)—My heart, if you please, shall afford a sheath to theirs—Life is nothing if I lose you—Be pleased, madam, to show me the way into the garden. I will attend you, though to my fate! But too happy, be it what it will, if I receive it in your presence. Lead on, dear creature!—

you shall see what I can bear for you—and he stooped and took up the key; and offered it to the lock—but dropped it again without opening the door, upon my earnest expostulation to him.

What can you mean, Mr Lovelace, said I?—Would you thus expose yourself?—would you thus expose me?—Is this your generosity?—Is everybody to take advantage thus of the weakness of my temper?

And I wept. I could not help it.

He threw himself upon his knees at my feet. Who can bear, said he, with an ardour that could not be feigned, his own eyes glistening, as I thought, who can bear to behold such sweet emotion?—Oh charmer of my heart, and respectfully still kneeling, he took my hand with both his, pressing it to his lips, command me *with* you, command me *from* you; in every way I am all implicit obedience!—But I appeal to all you know of your relations' cruelty to you, and of their determined malice against me and as determined favour to the man you tell me you hate—and, oh! madam, if you did not hate him, I should hardly think there would be a merit in your approbation, place it where you would—I appeal to everything you know, to all you have suffered, whether you have not reason to be apprehensive of *that* Wednesday, which is my terror!—whether you can possibly have such another opportunity—The chariot ready: my friends with impatience expecting the result of *your own* appointment: a man whose will shall be entirely your will, imploring you, thus on his knees imploring you—to be *your own mistress*; that is all. Nor will I ask for your favour, but as upon full proof I shall appear to deserve it: fortune, alliances unobjectible!—Oh my beloved creature, pressing my hand once more to his lips, let not such an opportunity slip! You never, never, will have such another!

I bid him rise: He rose and I told him that were I not thus unaccountably hurried by his impatience, I doubted not to convince him that both he and I had looked upon next Wednesday with greater apprehension than was necessary: and was proceeding to give him my reasons; but he broke in upon me—

Had I, madam, but the shadow of a probability to hope what *you* hope, I would be all obedience and resignation. But the licence is actually got: the parson is provided: that pedant Brand is the man: Oh my dearest creature, do these preparations mean only a trial?

You know not, sir, were the worst to be intended, and weak as you think me, what a spirit I have; you know not what I can do, and how I can resist, when I think myself meanly or unreasonably dealt with: nor do you know what I have already suffered, what I have already borne, knowing to whose unbrotherly instigations all is to be ascribed.—

I may expect all things, madam, interrupted he, from the nobleness of your mind scorning unreasonable compulsion: but your spirits may fail you. From the invincible temper of a father so positive to a daughter so dutiful, what may not be apprehended? Fainting will not save you. They will not, perhaps, be sorry for such an effect of their barbarity. What will expostulations signify against a ceremony performed? Must not all, the dreadful all, follow, that is torture to my heart but to think of?—Nobody to appeal to, of what avail will your resistance be against the consequences of a rite witnessed to by the imposers of it; and those your nearest relations?

I was sure, I said, of procuring a delay at least. Many ways I had to procure delay—Nothing could be so fatal to us both, as for me now to be found with him—my apprehensions on this score, I told him, grew too strong for my heart—I should think very hardly of him if he sought to detain me longer. But his acquiescence should engage my gratitude.

And then stooping to take up the key to let myself into the garden, he started and looked as if he had heard somebody near the door, on the inside, clapping his hand on his sword.

This frighted me so, that I thought I should have sunk down at his feet. But he instantly reassured me: he thought, he said, he had heard a rustling against the door: but *had* it been so, the noise would have been stronger. It was only the effect of his apprehension for my mind's sake.

And then taking up the key, he presented it to me.—If you *will* go, madam—yet I cannot, cannot leave you!—I must enter the garden with you—forgive me, but I *must* enter the garden with you.

And will you, will you, thus ungenerously, sir, take advantage of my fears!—of my wishes to prevent mischief?—I, vain fool, to be concerned for everyone; nobody for me!

Dearest creature! interrupted he, holding my hand, as I tremblingly offered to put the key to the lock—let *me*, if you *will* go, open the door—But once more, consider, should you prevail for that delay which seems to be your only dependence, whether you may not be closer confined? I know they have already had *that* in consideration. Will you not, in this case, be prevented from corresponding either with Miss Howe, or with me?—Who then shall assist you in your escape, if escape you would?—From your chamber window only permitted to view the garden you must not enter into, how will you wish for the opportunity you now have, if your hatred to Solmes continue?—but, alas! that cannot continue!—If you go back, it must be from the impulses of a yielding (which you'll call, a dutiful) heart, tired and teased out of your own will.

I have no patience, sir, to be thus restrained!—Must I never be at liberty to follow my own judgement!—Be the consequence what it may, I will not be thus constrained—and then freeing my hand, I again offered the key to the door.

Down the ready kneeler dropped between me and that: and can you, can you, madam, once more on my knees let me ask you, look with an indifferent eye upon the evils that may follow? Provoked as I have been, and triumphed over as I shall be, if your brother succeeds my own heart shudders, at times, at the thoughts of what *must* happen: and can *yours* be unconcerned! Let me beseech you, dearest creature! to consider all these things; and lose not this only opportunity—My intelligence—

Never, Mr Lovelace, interrupted I, pin so much faith upon the sleeve of a traitor—Your base intelligencer is but a servant: he may pretend to know more than he has grounds for, in order to earn the wages of corruption. You know not what contrivances I can find out.

I was offering the key to the lock, when, starting from his knees, with a voice of affrightment loudly whispering, and as if out of breath, *They are at the door, my beloved creature!* And taking the key from me, he flew to it, and fluttered with it as if he would double-lock it. And instantly a voice from within cried out, bursting against the door, as if to break it open, and, repeating its violent pushes: *Are you there?—Come up this moment!—this moment!—Here they are—Here they are both together!*—*Your pistol this moment!*—*your gun!*—Then another push, and another—He at the same moment drew his sword, and clapping it naked under his arm, took both my trembling hands in his; and, drawing me swiftly after him: Fly, my charmer; this moment is all you have for it! said he—Your brother!—your uncles! or this Solmes!—they will instantly burst the door!—Fly, my dearest life! if you would not be more cruelly used than ever!—if you would not see two or three murders committed at your feet, fly, fly, I beseech you!

Oh Lord!—help, help, cried the fool, all amaze and confusion, frighted beyond the power of controlling.

Now behind me, now before me, now on this side, now on that, turned I my affrighted face in the same moment; expecting a furious brother here, armed servants there, an enraged sister screaming and a father armed with terror in his countenance, more dreadful than even the drawn sword which I saw or those I apprehended. I ran as fast as he, yet knew not that I ran; my fears at the same time that they took all power of thinking from me adding wings to my feet: my fears, which probably would not have suffered me to know what course to take, had I not had him to urge and draw me after him: especially as I beheld a man, who must have come out of the garden door, keeping us in his eye, running backward and forward, beckoning and calling out to others, whom I supposed *he* saw, although the turning of the wall hindered *me* from seeing them; and whom I imagined to be my brother, my father and their servants.

Thus terrified, I was got out of sight of the door in a very few minutes: and then, although quite breathless between running and apprehension, he put my arm under his, his drawn sword in the other hand, and hurried me on still faster: my voice, however, contradicting my action; crying, No, no, no, all the while, straining my neck to look back as long as the walls of the garden and park were within sight, and till he brought me to his uncle's chariot: where attending were two armed servants of his own, and two of Lord M.'s on horseback.

Here I must suspend my relation for a while: for now I am come to this sad period of it, my indiscretion stares me in the face: and my shame and my grief give me a compunction that is more poignant, methinks, than if I had a dagger in my heart—To have it to reflect, that I should so inconsiderately give in to an interview which, had I known either myself or him, or in the least considered the circumstances of the case, I might have supposed would put me into the power of his resolution and out of that of my own reason.

For, might I not have believed that *he*, who thought he had cause to apprehend that he was on the point of losing a person who had cost him so much pains and trouble, would not hinder her, if possible, from returning? That he, who knew I had promised to give him up for ever, if insisted on as a condition of reconciliation, would not endeavour to put it out of my power to do so?—In short, that he, who had artfully forborne to send for my letter (for he could not be watched, my dear) lest he should find in it a countermand to my appointment (as I myself could apprehend, although I profited not by the apprehension), would want a device to keep me with him till the danger of having our meeting discovered might throw me absolutely into his power to avoid my own worse usage, and the mischiefs which might have ensued, perhaps in my very sight, had my friends and he met?

But if it shall come out that the person within the garden was his corrupted implement, employed to frighten me away with him, do you think, my dear, that I shall not have reason to hate him and myself still more?—I hope his heart cannot be so deep and so vile a one: I hope not: but how came it to pass, that one man could get out at the garden door, and no more? How, that that man kept aloof, as it were, and pursued us not; nor run back to alarm the house?—My fright and my distance would not let me be certain; but really this single man had the air of that vile Joseph Leman, as I recollect.

Oh why, why, my dear friends!—but wherefore blame I them, when I had argued myself into a hope, not improbable, that even the dreadful trial I was to undergo so soon, might turn out better than if I had been directly carried away from the presence of my once indulgent parents, who might possibly intend that trial to be the last I should have had?

Would to heaven that I had stood it however!—Then, if I had afterwards done what now I have been prevailed upon, or perhaps foolishly frightened to do, I should not have been stung so much by inward reproach as now I am: and this would have been a great evil avoided!

You know, my dear, that your Clarissa's mind was ever above justifying her own failings by those of others. God forgive those of my friends who have acted cruelly by me! but their faults *are* their own, and not excuses for mine. And mine began early: for I ought not to have corresponded with him.

Oh the vile encroacher! how my indignation, at times, rises at him! Thus to lead a young creature (too much indeed relying upon her own strength) from evil to evil!—This last evil, although the remote, yet sure consequence of my first—my prohibited correspondence! by a father, at least, early prohibited!

How much more properly had I acted, with regard to that correspondence, had I once for all when he was forbid to visit me, and I to receive his visits, pleaded the authority I ought to have been bound by, and denied to write to him!—But I thought I could proceed or stop as I pleased. I supposed it concerned me more than any other to be the arbitress of the quarrels of unruly spirits—and now I find my presumption punished!—punished, as other sins frequently are, by *itself!*

As to this last rashness; now that it is too late, I plainly see how I ought to have conducted myself—As he knew I had but one way of transmitting to him the knowledge of what befell me; as he knew that my fate was upon a crisis with my friends; and that I had, in my letter to him, reserved the liberty of revoking; I should not have been solicitous whether he had got my letter or not. When he had come, and found I did not answer his signal, he would presently have resorted to the loose bricks, and there been satisfied by the date of my letter that it was his own fault that he had it not before. But, governed by the same pragmatical motives which induced me to correspond with him at first, I was again afraid, truly, with my foolish and busy prescience (and indeed he pretends now, that I had reason for it, as you shall hear in its place; but which then I could only fear, and not be sure of), that the disappointment would have thrown him into the way of receiving fresh insults from the same persons; which might have made him guilty of some violence to them. And so, to save him an *apprehended* rashness, I have rushed into a *real* one myself. And what vexes me more is, that it is plain to me now, by all his behaviour, that he had as great a confidence in my weakness, as I had in my own strength. And so, in a point entirely relative to my honour, he has triumphed (can

I have patience to look at him!); for he has not been mistaken in me, while I have in myself!

Tell me, my dear Miss Howe, tell me truly if your unforced heart does not despise me?—It must! for your mind and mine were ever *one*; and I despise *myself!*—and well I may: for could the giddiest and most inconsiderate girl in *England* have done worse than I shall appear to have done in the eye of the world? Since my crime will be known without the provocations, and without the artifices of the betrayer too (indeed, my dear, he is a very artful man); while it will be a high aggravation, that better things were expected from me than from many others.

You charge me to marry the first opportunity—Ah! my dear! *another* of the blessed effects of my folly!—That's as much in my power now as—as I am myself!—For can I give a sanction immediately to his deluding arts?—can I *avoid* being angry with him for tricking me thus, as I may say (and as I have called it to him), out of myself?—for compelling me to take a step so contrary to all my resolutions, and assurances given to you; so dreadfully inconvenient to myself; so disgraceful and so grievous, as it must be, to my dear mamma, were I to be less regardful of any other!—You don't know, nor can you imagine, my dear, how I am mortified!—how much I am sunk in my own opinion!—I, that was proposed for an example, truly, to others!—Oh that I were again in my father's house, stealing down with a letter to you; my heart beating with expectation of finding one from you!

THIS is the Wednesday morning I dreaded so much that I once thought of it as my doomsday: but of the Monday, it is plain, I ought to have been most apprehensive. Had I stayed, and had the worst I dreaded happened, my friends would then have been answerable, if any bad consequences had followed—but, now, I have this *one* consolation left me (a very sad one, you'll say), that I have cleared *them* of blame, and taken it all upon *myself!*

You will not wonder to see this narrative so dismally scrawled. It is owing to different pens and ink, all bad, and written by snatches of time, my hand trembling too with fatigue and grief.

I will not add to the length of it, by the particulars of his behaviour to me, and of our conversation at St Albans and since; because those will come in course, in the continuation of my story; which no doubt you will expect from me.

Only thus much I will say, that he is extremely respectful, even obsequiously so, at present, though I am so much dissatisfied with him, and myself; that he has hitherto had no great cause to praise my complaisance to him. Indeed I can hardly at times bear the seducer in my sight.

The lodgings I am in are inconvenient. I shall not stay in them: so it signifies nothing to tell you how to direct to me hither. And where my next may be, as yet I know not.

He knows that I am writing to you; and has offered to send my letter, when finished, by a servant of his. But I thought I could not be too cautious, as I am now situated, in having a letter of this importance conveyed to you. Who knows what such a man may do? So very wicked a contriver! The contrivance, if a contrivance, so insolently mean!—But I hope it is not a contrivance neither! Yet, be that as it will, I must say that the *best* of him, and of my prospects with him, are bad: and yet, having enrolled myself among the too-late repenters, who shall pity me?

Nevertheless, I will dare to hope for a continued interest in your affections (I shall be miserable indeed, if I may not!), and to be remembered in your daily prayers. I am, my dearest friend,

Your ever affectionate
CL. HARLOWE

Letter 95: MR LOVELACE TO JOSEPH LEMAN

Sat. April 8

Honest JOSEPH,

AT length your beloved young lady has consented to free herself from the cruel treatment she has so long borne. She is to meet me without the garden door, at about four o'clock on Monday afternoon; as I told you she had promised. She has confirmed her promise. Thank God, she has confirmed her promise!

I shall have a chariot and six ready in the by-road fronting the private path to Harlowe Paddock; and several of my friends and servants not far off, armed to protect her, if there be occasion: but everyone charged to avoid mischief. That, you know, has always been my principal care.

All my fear is that when she comes to the point, the over-niceness of her principles will make her waver, and want to go back: although *her* honour is *my* honour, you know, and *mine* is *hers*. If she should, and I should be unable to prevail upon her, all your past services will avail nothing and she will be lost to me for ever: the prey, then, of that cursed Solmes, whose vile stinginess will never permit him to do good to any of the servants of the family.

I have no doubt of your fidelity, honest Joseph; nor of your zeal to serve an injured gentleman and an oppressed young lady. You see by the confidence I repose in you that I have *not*; more particularly, on this very important occasion, in which your assistance may crown the work: for if she wavers, a little innocent contrivance will be necessary.

Be very mindful, therefore, of the following directions: take them into your heart. This will probably be your last trouble, until my beloved and I are joined in holy wedlock: and then we will be sure to take care of you. You know what I have promised. No man ever reproached me for breach of word.

These, then, honest Joseph, are they:

Contrive to be in the garden in disguise, if possible, and unseen by your young lady. If you find the garden door unbolted, you'll know that she and I are together although you should not see her go out at it. It will be locked, but my key shall be on the ground at the bottom of the door, without, that you may open it with yours as it may be needful.

If you hear our voices parleying, keep at the door, till I cry Hem, hem, twice: but be watchful for this signal, for I must not hem very loud, lest she should take it for a signal: perhaps in struggling to prevail upon the dear creature, I may have an opportunity to strike the door hard with my elbow, or heel, to confirm you—Then you are to make a violent burst against the door, as if you'd break it open, drawing backward and forward the bolt in a hurry: then, with another push, but with more noise than strength, lest the lock give way, cry out (as if you saw some of the family): Come up, come up, instantly!—Here they are! Here they are!

hasten!—this instant hasten! And mention swords, pistols, guns, with as terrible a voice, as you can cry out with. Then shall I prevail upon her, no doubt, if loath before, to fly: if I cannot, I will enter the garden with her, and the house too, be the consequence what it will. But so 'frighted, there is no question but she will fly.

When you think us at a sufficient distance (and I shall raise my voice, urging her swifter flight, that you may guess at *that*), then open the door with your key: but you must be sure to open it very cautiously, lest we should not be far enough off. I would not have her know you have a hand in this matter, out of my great regard to you.

When you have opened the door, take your key out of the lock, and put it in your pocket: then, stooping for mine, put it in the lock on the *inside*, that it may appear as if the door was opened by herself, with a key they'll suppose of my procuring (it being new), and left open by us.

They should conclude she is gone off by her own consent, that they may not pursue us: that they may see no hopes of tempting her back again. In either case, mischief might happen, you know.

But you must take notice that you are only to open the door with your key, in case none of the family come up to interrupt us, and before we are quite gone: for, if they do, you'll find by what follows, that you must not open the door at all. Let them, on breaking it open, or by getting over the wall, find my key on the ground, if they will.

If they do not come to interrupt us, and if you, by help of your key, come out, follow us at a distance, and with uplifted hands and wild and impatient gestures (running backward and forward, for fear you should come too near us; and as if you saw somebody coming to your assistance), cry out for Help, help, and to hasten. Then shall we be soon at the chariot.

Tell the family that you saw me enter a chariot with her: a dozen, or more, men on horseback, attending us; all armed; some with blunderbusses, as you believe; and that we took the quite contrary way to that we shall take.

You see, honest Joseph, how careful I am, as well as you, to avoid mischief.

Observe to keep at such a distance that she may not discover who you are. Take long strides, to alter your gait; and hold up your head, honest Joseph; and she'll not know it to be you. Men's airs and gaits are as various, and as peculiar, as their faces. Pluck a stake out of one of the hedges: and tug at it, though it may come easy: this, if she turn back, will look terrible, and account for your not following us faster. Then returning with it, shouldered, brag to the family what you would have done, could you have overtaken us, rather than your young lady should have been carried off by such a——And you may call me names, and curse me. And these airs will make you look valiant and in earnest. You see, honest Joseph, I am always contriving to give you reputation. No man suffers by serving me.

But if our parley should last longer than I wish; and if any of her friends miss her before I cry, Hem, hem, twice; then, in order to save yourself (which is a very great point with me, I'll assure you), make the same noise as above: but, as I directed before, open not the door with your key. On the contrary, wish for a key, with all your heart; but, for fear any of them should, by accident, have a key about them, keep in readiness half a dozen little gravel-stones, no bigger than peas, and thrust two or three slily into the keyhole; which will hinder their key from turning round. It is good, you know, Joseph, to provide against every accident in such an important case as this. And let this be your cry, instead of the other, if any of my enemies come in your sight, as you seem to be trying to burst the door open: Sir! or madam! (as it may prove) Oh Lord, hasten! Oh Lord, hasten! Mr Lovelace!—Mr Lovelace!—and very loud—And that shall quicken me more than it shall those you call to—If it be Betty, and only Betty, I shall think worse of your art of making love[a] than of your fidelity, if you can't find a way to amuse her and put her upon a false scent.

You must tell them that your young lady seemed to run as fast off with me, as I with her. This will also confirm to them that all pursuit is in vain. An end will be hereby put to Solmes's hopes: and her friends, after a while, will be more studious to be reconciled to her, than to get her back. So you will be an happy instrument of great good to all round. And this will one day be acknowledged by both families. You will then be every one's favourite: and every good servant, for the future, will be proud to be likened to honest Joseph Leman.

If she should guess at you, or find you out, I have it already in my head to write a letter for you to copy[b]; which, occasionally produced, will set you right with her.

This one time, be diligent, be careful; this will be the crown of all: and once more, depend for a recompence upon the honour of

Your assured friend,
R. LOVELACE

You need not be so much afraid of going too far with Betty. If you *should* make match with her, she is a very likely creature, though a vixen, as you say. I have an admirable receipt to cure a termagant wife—Never fear, Joseph, but thou shalt be master of thine own house. If she be very troublesome, I can teach thee how to break her heart in a twelvemonth; and *honestly* too—Or, the precept would not be mine.

I enclose a new earnest of my future favour.

Letter 96: JOSEPH LEMAN TO MR ROBERT LOVELACE
To Robert Lovelace, Esquier, His Honner

Honnered sir,   Sunday morning, April 9
I MUST confesse I am infinnitely oblidged to your honner's bounty. But, this last command!—it seems so intricket!—Lord be merciful to me, how have I been led from littel stepps to grate stepps!—and iff I should be found out!—but your honner says, you will take me into your honner's sarvise, and protect me, if as I should at any time be found out; and raise my wages besides; or set me upp in a good inne; which is my ambishion. And you will be honnerable and kind to my dearest young lady, God love her—But who can be unkind to she?

I will do the best I am able, since your honner will be apt to lose her, as your honner says, if I do not; and a man so stindgie will be apt to gain her. But mayhap my dearest younge lady will not make all this trouble needful. If she has promised, she will stand to it, I dare to say.

I love your honner for contriveing to save mischiff so well. I thought till I knowed your honner, that you was verry mischevous, and plese your honner. But find it to

  a   See Letter 73.
  b   See Letter 113.

be quite another thing. Your honner, it is plane, means mighty well by everybody, as far as I see. As I am sure I do myself; for I am, althoff a very plane man and all that, a very honnest one, I thank my God. And have good principles, and have kept my young lady's pressepts always in mind: for she goes nowhere, but saves a soul or two, more or less.

So, commending myself to your honner's furthir favour, not forgetting the inne, when your honner shall so please, and a good one offers; for plases are no inherittances nowadays.[1] And I hope your honner will not think me a dishonest man for sarvinge your honner agenst my duty, as it may look; but only as my conshence clears me.

Be pleased, howsomever, if it like your honner, not to call me, *honnest Joseph*, and *honnest Joseph*, so often. For, althoff I think myself very honnest and all that; yet I am touched a little, for fear I should not do the quite right thing: and too-besides, your honner has such a fesseshious way with you, as that I hardly know whether you are in jest or earnest, when your honner calls me honnest so often.

I am a very plane man, and seldom have writ to such honourable gentlemen; so you will be good enuff to pass by everything, as I have often said, and need not now say over again.

As to Mrs Betty; I tho'te, indede, she looked above me. But she comes on very well, nathelesse. I could like her better, iff she was better to my young lady. But she has too much wit for so plane a man. Natheless, if she was to angre me, althoff it is a shame to bete a woman; yet I colde make shift to throe my hat at her, or so,[2] your honner.

But that same reseit, iff your honour so please, to cure a shrowish wife. It would more encurrege to wed, iff so be one knowed it beforehand, as one may say. So likewise, iff one knoed one could *honestly*, as your honner says, and as of the handy work of God, in *one* twelvemonth—

But, I shall grow impartinent to such a grate man—and *hereafter* may do for that, as she turns out—for one mought be loath to part with her, mayhap, so *verry* soon too; especially if she was to make the notable lanlady your honner put into my head.

Butt wonce moer, beging your honer's parden, and promissing all dilligince and exsacknesse, I reste,

Your honner's dewtifull sarvant to cummande,

JOSEPH LEMAN

Letter 97: MR LOVELACE TO JOHN BELFORD, ESQ.

St Albans, Monday night
I SNATCH a few moments, while my beloved is retired (as I hope, to rest), to perform my promise. No pursuit!—nor have I apprehensions of any; though I must make my charmer dread that there will be one.

And now, let me tell thee that never was joy so complete as mine!—But let me inquire! is not the angel flown away?—

Oh no! she is in the next apartment!—securely mine!—mine for ever!

Oh ecstasy!—My heart will burst my breast,
To leap into her bosom!—[1]

I knew that the whole stupid family were in a combination to do my business for me. I told thee that they were all working for me, like so many underground moles; and still more blind than the moles are said to be, unknowing that they did so. I myself, the director of their principal motions; which falling in with the malice of their little hearts, they took to be all their own.

But did I say my joy was perfect?—Oh no!—It receives some abatement from my disgusted pride. For how can I endure to think that I owe more to her relation's persecutions than to her favour for me?—Or even, as far as I know, to her preference of me to another man?

But let me not indulge this thought. Were I to do so, it might cost my charmer dear—Let me rejoice that she has passed the Rubicon: that she cannot return: that, as I have ordered it, the flight will appear to the implacables to be altogether with her own consent: and that, if I doubt her love, I can put her to trials as mortifying to her niceness, as glorious to my pride—For, let me tell thee, dearly as I love her, if I thought there was but the shadow of a doubt in her mind whether she preferred me to any man living, I would show her no mercy.

                                                              Tuesday, day-dawn

BUT, on the wings of love, I fly to my charmer, who perhaps by this time is rising to encourage the tardy dawn. I have not slept a wink of the hour and half I lay down to invite sleep. It seems to me that I am not so much body as to require such vulgar renovation.

But why, as in the chariot, as in the inn, at alighting, all heart-bursting grief, my dearest creature? So persecuted, as thou wert persecuted!—so much in danger of the most abhorred compulsion!—yet grief so unsuspectably sincere for an escape so critical!—Take care!—take care, oh beloved of my soul: for jealous is the heart in which love has erected a temple to thee,

Yet it must be allowed that such a sudden transition must affect her—must ice her over—When a little more used to her new situation: when her hurries are at an end: when she sees how religiously I shall observe all her INJUNCTIONS, she will undoubtedly have the gratitude to distinguish between the confinement she has escaped from, and the liberty she has reason to rejoice in.

She comes! she comes!—And the sun is just rising to attend her!—Adieu!—Be half as happy as I am (for all diffidences, like night fogs before the sun, exhale at her approach); and, next myself, thou wilt be the happiest man in the world.

Letter 98: MISS CLARISSA HARLOWE TO MISS HOWE

                                                              Wednesday, April 12

I WILL pursue my melancholy story.

Being thus hurried to the chariot, it would have been to no purpose to have refused entering into it, had he not, in my fright, lifted me in as he did: and it instantly drove away a full gallop, and stopped not till it brought us to St Albans; which was just as the day shut in.

I thought I should have fainted several times by the way. With lifted-up hands and eyes, God protect me, said I often to myself!—Can it be I that am here!—my eyes running over and my heart ready to burst with sighs as involuntary as my flight.

How different, how inexpressibly different, the gay wretch; visibly triumphing (as I could not but construe his almost rapturous joy) in the success of his arts! But overflowing with complimental flourishes, yet respectfully distant his address, all the way we *flew*; for that, rather than *galloping*, was the motion of the horses; which took, as I believe, a roundabout way, to prevent being traced.

I have reason to think there were other horsemen at his devotion; three or four different persons above the rank of servants galloping by us now and then, on each side of the chariot: but he took no notice of them; and I had too much grief, mingled with indignation, notwithstanding all his blandishments, to ask any questions about them, or anything else.

Think, my dear, what were my thoughts on alighting from the chariot; having no attendant of my own sex; no clothes but what I had on, and those little suited for such a journey as I had *already* taken, and was still *further* to take: neither hood nor hat, nor anything but a handkerchief about my neck and shoulders: fatigued to death: my mind still more fatigued than my body: and in such a foam the horses, that everyone in the inn we put up at guessed (they could not do otherwise) that I was a young giddy creature who had run away from her friends. This it was easy to see, by their whispering and gaping; more of the people of the house also coming in to view us, as it were, by turns, than was necessary for the attendance.

The gentlewoman of the inn, whom he sent into me, showed me another apartment; and seeing me ready to faint, brought me hartshorn and water; and then, upon my desiring to be left alone for half an hour, retired: for I found my heart ready to burst, on revolving everything in my thoughts: and the moment she was gone, fastening the door, I threw myself into an old great chair, and gave way to a violent flood of tears; which a little relieved me.

Mr Lovelace, sooner than I wished, sent up the gentlewoman, who pressed me in his name to admit my brother, or to come down to him: for he had told her I was his sister; and that he had brought me, against my will and without warning, from a friend's house where I had been all the winter, in order to prevent my marrying against the consent of my friends; to whom he was now conducting me; and that, having given me no time for a travelling-dress, I was greatly offended at him.

So, my dear, your frank, your open-hearted friend was forced to countenance this tale; which, indeed, suited me the better, because I was unable for some time to talk, speak, or look up; and so my dejection, and grief, and silence, might very well pass before the gentlewoman and her niece who attended me, as a fit of sullenness.

The room I was in being a bedchamber, I chose to go down, at his repeated message, attended by the gentlewoman of the inn, to that in which he was. He approached me with great respect, yet not exceeding a brotherly politeness, where a brother *is* polite; and, calling me his dearest sister, asked after the state of my mind; and hoped I would forgive him; for never brother half so well loved a sister, as he me.

A wretch!—How naturally did he fall into the character, although I was so much out of mine!

Unthinking creatures have some comfort in the shortness of their views; in their unapprehensiveness; and that they penetrate not beyond the present moment: in short, that they *are* unthinking!—But for a person of my thoughtful disposition, who has been accustomed to look forward, as well to the *possible* as to the *probable*, what comfort can I have in my reflections?

But let me give you the particulars of our conversation, a little before and after our supper-time, joining both in one.

When we were alone, he besought me (I cannot say but with all the tokens of a passionate and respectful tenderness) to be better reconciled to myself, and to him. He repeated all the vows of honour and inviolable affection that he ever made me: he promised to be wholly governed by me in every future step: he asked me to give him leave to propose, whether I chose to set out next day to either of his aunts?

I was silent. I knew not what to say, nor what to do.

Whether I chose to have private lodgings procured me, in either of those ladies' neighbourhood, as were once my thoughts?

I was still silent.

Whether I chose to go to either of Lord M.'s seats; that of Berks[hire], or that in the county we were in?

In lodgings, I said, anywhere, where he was not to be.

He had promised this, he owned; and he would religiously keep to his word, as soon as he found all danger of pursuit over; and that I was settled to my mind— But if the place were indifferent to me, London was the safest and the most private: and his relations should all visit me there, the moment I thought fit to admit them. His cousin Charlotte, particularly, should attend me as my companion, if I would accept of her, as soon as she was able to go abroad. Meantime, would I go to his aunt Lawrance's (his aunt Sadleir was a melancholy woman)? I should be the most welcome guest she ever received.

I told him I wished not to go (immediately, however, and in the frame I was in, and likely not to be out of) to any of his relations: that my reputation was concerned to have *him* absent from me: that, if I were in some private lodging (the meaner the less to be suspected, as it would be known that I went away by his means; and he would be supposed to have provided me handsome accommodations), it would be most suitable both to my mind and my situation: that this might be best, I should think, in the country for *me*; in town for *him*—And no matter how soon he was known to be there.

If he might deliver his opinion, he said, since I declined going to any of his relations, London was the only place in the world to be private in. Every newcomer in a country town or village excited a curiosity: a person of my figure (and many compliments he made me) would excite more. Even messages and letters, where none used to be brought, would occasion inquiry. He had not provided a lodging anywhere, supposing I would choose to go either to London, where accommodations of that sort might be fixed upon in an hour's time; or to his aunt's; or to Lord M.'s Hertfordshire seat, where was housekeeper an excellent woman, Mrs Greme, such another as my Norton.

To be sure, I said, if I were pursued, it would be in their first passion; and some one of his relations' houses would be the place they would expect to find me at— I knew not what to do!

My pleasure should determine him, he said, be it what it would. Only that I were safe, was all he was solicitous about. He had lodgings in town: but he did not offer to propose them. He knew I would have more objection to go to them than I could have to go to Lord M.'s, or to his aunt's—

No doubt of it, I replied with an indignation in my manner, that made him run over with professions, that he was far from proposing them, or wishing for my acceptance of them. And again he repeated that my honour and safety were all he was solicitous about; assuring me that my will should be a law to him in every particular.

I was too peevish, and too much afflicted, and indeed too much incensed against him, to take well anything he said.

I thought myself, I said, extremely unhappy. I knew not what to determine upon: my reputation now, no doubt, utterly ruined: destitute of clothes fit to be seen by anybody: my very indigence, as I might call it, proclaiming my folly to everyone who saw me: who would suppose that I had been taken at advantage, or had given an undue one; and had no power over either my will, or my actions: that I could not but think I had been dealt artfully with: that he had seemed to have taken what he might suppose the just measure of my weakness, founded on my youth and inexperience: that I could not forgive myself for meeting him: that my heart bled for the distresses of my father and mother on this occasion: that I would give the world, and all my hopes in it, to have been still in my father's house, whatever had been my usage: that, let him protest and vow what he would, I saw something low and selfish in his love, that he could study to put a young creature upon making such a sacrifice of her duty and conscience: when a person actuated by a generous love must seek to oblige the object of it in everything essential to her honour, and to her peace of mind.

He was very attentive to all I said; never offering to interrupt me once. His answer to every article, almost methodically, showed his memory.

What I had said, he told me, had made him very grave: and he would answer accordingly.

He was grieved at his heart that he had so little share in my favour or confidence, as he had the mortification to find, by what I had said, he had.

As to my *reputation*, he must be very sincere with me: that could not suffer half so much by the step I so much regretted to have taken, as by the confinement and equally foolish and unjust treatment I had met with from my relations: that every mouth was full of blame of them, of my brother and sister particularly; and of wonder at my patience: that he must repeat, what he had written to me, he believed more than once that my friends themselves expected that I should take a proper opportunity to free myself from their persecutions; why else did they confine me? that my exalted character would still bear me out with those who knew *me*; who knew my *brother*'s and *sister*'s motives; and who knew the wretch they were for compelling me to have.

With regard to *clothes*; who, as matters were circumstanced, could expect that I should be able to bring away any others than those I had on at the time? For *present* use or wear, all the ladies of his family would take a pride to supply me:

for *future*, the product of the best looms, not only in England, but throughout the world, were at my command.

If I wanted *money*, as no doubt I must, he should be proud to supply me: would to God he might presume to hope there were but one interest between us!—

And then he would fain have had me to accept of [a] £100 bank note; which, unawares to me, he put into my hand: but which, you may be sure, I refused with warmth.

He was inexpressibly grieved and surprised, he said, to hear me say he had acted *artfully* by me. He came provided, according to my *confirmed* appointment (a wretch! to upbraid me thus!), to redeem me from my persecutors; and little expected a change of sentiment, and that he should have so much difficulty to prevail upon me as he had met with: that perhaps I might think his offer to go *into the garden with me* and to face my assembled relations was a piece of *art* only: but that if I did, I wronged him: for, to this hour, seeing my excessive uneasiness, he wished with all his soul he had been permitted to accompany me in. It was always his maxim to brave a threatened danger—Threateners, where they have an opportunity to put in force their threats, were seldom to be feared—But had he been assured of a private stab, or of as many death's wounds as there were persons in my family (made desperate as he should have been by my return), he would have attended me into the house.

So, my dear, what I have to do is to hold myself inexcusable for meeting such a determined and audacious spirit; that's all!—I have hardly any question now, that he would have contrived some way or other to have got me away, had I met him at a midnight hour, as once or twice I had thoughts to do. And that would have been more terrible still!

He concluded this part of his talk with saying: That he doubted not but that, had he attended me in, he should have come off in everyone's opinion so well, that he should have had general leave to renew his visits.

He went on: He must be so bold as to tell me, he said, that he should have paid a visit of this kind, but indeed accompanied by several of his trusty friends, had I *not* met him—and that very afternoon too—for he could not tamely let the dreadful Wednesday come without some effort to change their determinations.

What, my dear, was to be done with such a man!

That therefore, for my sake, as well as for his own, he had reason to wish a disease so desperate had been attempted to be overcome by as desperate a remedy. We all know, said he, that great ends are sometimes brought about by the very means by which they are endeavoured to be frustrated.

My present situation, I am sure, thought I, affords a sad evidence of this truth!

I was silent all this time. My blame was indeed turned inward. Sometimes, too, I was half-frighted at his audaciousness: at others, had the less inclination to interrupt him, being excessively fatigued and my spirits sunk to nothing, with the view even of the best prospects with such a creature.

This gave him opportunity to proceed; and that he did; assuming a still more serious air.

As to what further remained for him to say, in answer to what I had said, he hoped I would pardon him; but, upon his soul, he was concerned, infinitely concerned, he repeated, his colour and his voice rising, that it was *necessary* for him to observe, how much I chose rather to have run the risk of being Solmes's wife, than to have it in my power to reward a man who, I must forgive him, had been as much insulted on *my* account as *I* had been on *his*—who had watched my commands, and (pardon me, madam) every *changeable* motion of your pen, all hours, in all weathers, and with a cheerfulness and ardour, that nothing but the most faithful and obsequious passion could inspire—

I now, miss, began to revive into a little more warmth of attention—

And all, madam, for what? (how I stared!)— *Only* to prevail upon you to free yourself from ungenerous and base oppression—

Sir, sir! indignantly said I—

Hear me but out, dearest madam!—my heart is full—I *must* speak what I have to say —To be told (for your words are yet in my ears, and at my heart!) that you would give the world, *and all your hopes in it*, to have been still in your cruel and gloomy father's house—

Not a word, sir, against my papa!—I will not bear that—

Whatever had been your usage:—and you have a credulity, madam, against all probability, if you believe you should have avoided being Solmes's wife: that I have put you upon *sacrificing your duty and conscience*—Yet, dearest creature! see you not the contradiction that your warmth of temper has surprised you into, when the reluctance you showed to the last to leave your persecutors has cleared your conscience from the least reproach of this sort—

Oh sir! sir! are you so critical then? Are you so light in your anger, as to dwell upon words!—

And indeed, my dear, I have since thought that his anger was not owing to that sudden *impetus*, which cannot be easily bridled; but rather was a sort of *manageable* anger, let loose to intimidate me.

Forgive me, madam—I have just done. Have I not, in your own opinion, hazarded my life to redeem you from oppression?—Yet is not my reward, after all, precarious?—For, madam, have you not conditioned with me (and most sacredly, hard as the condition is, will I observe it) that all my hope must be remote: that you are determined to have it in your power to favour or reject me totally, as you please?—

See, my dear! In every respect my condition changed for the worse! Is it in my power to take your advice, if I should think it ever so right to take it?—

And have you not furthermore declared, proceeded he, that you will engage to renounce me for ever if your friends insist upon that cruel renunciation as the terms of being reconciled to you?

But, nevertheless, madam, all the merit of having saved you from an odious compulsion shall be mine. I glory in it, though I were to lose you for ever—as I see I am but too likely to do, from your present displeasure; and especially if your friends insist upon the terms you are ready to comply with.

That you are *your own mistress*, through *my* means, is, I repeat, my boast—As such, I humbly implore your favour—and that only upon the conditions I have yielded to hope for it—as I do now *thus humbly* (the proud wretch falling on one knee) your forgiveness, for so long detaining your ear, and for all the plain-dealing that my undesigning heart would not be denied to utter by my lips.

Oh sir, pray rise!—Let the *obliged* kneel, if one of us must kneel!—But nevertheless, proceed not in this strain, I *beseech* you. You have had a great *deal* of trouble about me: but had you let me know in time that you expected to be rewarded for it at the price of my duty, I should have spared you much of it.

Far be it from me, sir, to depreciate merit so *extraordinary*. But let me say, that had it not been for the forbidden correspondence I was teased by you into and which I had not continued (every letter for many letters, intended to be the last) but because I thought you a sufferer from my friends, I had not been either confined or maltreated: nor would my brother's low-meant violence have had a foundation to work upon.

I am far from thinking my case would have been so very desperate as you imagine, had I stayed. My father loved me at bottom: he would not see me before; and I wanted only to *see* him, and to be *heard*; and a delay of his sentence was the least thing I expected from the trial I was to stand.

You are boasting of your merits, sir; let merit *be* your boast: nothing else can attract me. If *personal* considerations had principal weight with me, either in Solmes's disfavour, or in your favour, I should despise *myself*: if you value yourself upon them, in preference to the person of the poor Solmes, I shall despise *you*!

You may glory in your fancied merits, in getting me away: but the cause of *your* glory, I tell you plainly, is *my* shame.

Make to yourself a title to my regard which I can better approve of; or else you will not have so much merit with *me* as you have with *yourself*.

But here, like the first pair, I at least driven out of my paradise, are we recriminating. No more shall you need to tell me of your *sufferings*, and your *merits*!—your *all hours*, and *all weathers*! For I will bear them in memory as long as I live; and, if it be impossible for me to *reward* them, be ever ready to *own* the obligation. All that I desire of you now is to leave it to myself to seek for some private abode: to take the chariot with you to London or elsewhere: and, if I have any further occasion for your assistance and protection, I will signify it to you, and be still *further* obliged to you.

You are warm, my dearest life!—But indeed there is no occasion for it. Had I any views unworthy of my faithful love for you I should not have been so honest in my declarations.

Then he began again to vow the sincerity of his intentions.

But I took him up short: I am willing to *believe* you, sir. It would be unsupportable but to suppose there were a *necessity* for such solemn declarations (at this he seemed to collect himself, as I may say, into a little more circumspection). If I thought there *were*, I would not sit with you here, in a public inn, I assure you, although *cheated* hither, as far as I know, by methods (you must excuse me, sir!) that, the very suspicion that it may be so gives me too much vexation for me to have patience either with you or with myself—But no more of this just now: let me but know, I beseech you, *good sir*, bowing (I was very angry!), if you intend to leave me; or if I have only escaped from one confinement to another?—

Cheated hither, as far as you know, madam! Let you *know* (and with that air too, charming though grievous to my heart!) *if you have only escaped from one confinement to another!*—Amazing! perfectly amazing!—And can there be a necessity for me to answer this?—You are absolutely your own mistress—It were very strange if you were not. The moment you are in a place of safety, I will leave you. One condition only, give me leave to beg your consent to: it is this: that you will be pleased, now you are so entirely in your own power, to renew a promise *voluntarily* made before; *voluntarily*, or I would not *now* presume to request it; for although I would not be thought capable of growing upon concession, yet I cannot bear to think of losing the ground your goodness had given me room to hope I had gained: 'That, make up how you please with your relations, you will never marry any other man while I am living and single, unless I should be so wicked as to give new cause for high displeasure.'

I hesitate not to confirm this promise, sir, upon your *own* condition. In what manner do you expect me to confirm it?—

Only, madam, by your word.

Then I never will.

He had the assurance (I was now in his power) to salute me, as a sealing of my promise, as he called it. His motion was so sudden, that I was not aware of it. It would have looked affected to be very angry; yet I could not be pleased, considering this as a leading freedom from a spirit so audacious and encroaching; and he might see that I was not.

He passed all that by with an air peculiar to himself—Enough! enough, dearest madam!—And let me beg of you but to conquer this dreadful uneasiness, which gives me to apprehend but too, too much for my jealous love to bear: and it shall be my whole endeavour to deserve your favour, and to make you the happiest woman in the world; as I shall be the happiest of men.

I broke from him to write to you my preceding letter; but refused to send it by his servant, as I told you. The gentlewoman of the inn helped me to a messenger, who was to carry what you should give him to Lord M.'s seat in Hertfordshire, directed for Mrs Greme the housekeeper there. And early in the morning, for fear of pursuit, we were to set out that way: and there he proposed to exchange the chariot and six for a chaise and pair of his own, which happened to be at that seat, as it would be a less-noticed conveyance.

I looked over my little stock of money; and found it to be no more than seven guineas and some silver. The rest of my stock was but fifty guineas, and that five more than I thought it was, when my sister challenged me as to the sum I had by me[a]: and those I left in my escritoire, little thinking to be prevailed upon to go away with him.

Indeed my case abounds with a shocking variety of indelicate circumstances. Among the rest, I was forced to account to *him*, who knew I could have no clothes but what I had on, how I came to have linen with you (for he could not but know I sent for it); lest he should imagine I had an early design to go away with him, and made that a part of the preparation.

He most heartily wished, he said, for my mind's sake, that your mamma would have afforded me her protection; and delivered himself upon this subject with equal freedom and concern.

There are, my dear Miss Howe, a multitude of punctilios and decorums which a young creature must dispense with who, in such a situation, makes a man the intimate attendant of her person. I could now, I think, give twenty reasons stronger than any I have heretofore mentioned, why women of the least delicacy should never think of incurring the danger and disgrace of taking the step. I have been

a　See Letter 43.

drawn in to take, but with horror and aversion; and why they should look upon the man who shall tempt them to it, as the vilest and most selfish of seducers.

BEFORE five o'clock (Tuesday morning) the maid-servant came up to tell me my *brother* was ready, and that breakfast also waited for me in the parlour. I went down with a heart as heavy as my eyes, and received great acknowledgements and compliments from him on being so soon dressed, and ready, as he interpreted it, to continue our journey.

He had the thought which I had not (for what had I to do with thinking, who had it not when I stood most in need of it?) to purchase for me a velvet hood, and a handsome short cloak trimmed with silver, without saying anything to me. He must reward himself, the artful encroacher said before the landlady and her maids and niece, for his forethought; and would salute his pretty sullen sister!—He took his reward; and, as he said, a tear with it. While he assured me (still before them, a vile wretch!), that I had nothing to fear from meeting with parents who so dearly loved me—How could I be complaisant, my dear, to such a man as this?—

As soon as the chariot drove on, he asked me whether I had any objection to go to Lord M.'s Hertfordshire seat? His lordship, he said, was at his Berkshire one.

I told him I chose not to go, as yet, to any of his relations; for that would indicate a plain defiance to my own—My choice was to go to a private lodging; and for him to be at a distance from me; at least till I heard how things were taken by my friends—For that although I had but little hopes of a reconciliation as it *was*, yet if they knew I was in his protection or in that of any of his friends (which would be looked upon as the same thing), there would not be room for any at all.

I should govern him as I pleased, he solemnly assured me, in everything. But he still thought London was the best place for me; and if I were once safe there, and in a lodging to my liking, he would go to M. Hall. But, as I approved not of London, he would urge it no further.

He proposed, and I consented, to put up at an inn in the neighbourhood of *The Lawn* (as he called Lord M.'s seat in this county), since I chose not to go thither. And here I got two hours to myself; which I told him I should pass in writing another letter to you (meaning my narrative, which I had begun at St Albans, fatigued as I was), and in [writing] one to my sister, to apprise the family (whether they were solicitous about it or not), that I was well; and to beg that my clothes, some particular books, and the fifty guineas I had left in my escritoire, might be sent me.

He asked if I had considered whither to have them directed?

Indeed not I, I told him: I was a stranger to—

So was he, he interrupted me; but it struck him by chance—(wicked story-teller!)——

But, added he, I will tell you, madam, how it shall be managed—If you don't choose to go to London, it is, nevertheless, best that your relations should *think* you there; for then they will absolutely despair of finding you. If you write, be pleased to direct: To be left for you, at Mr Osgood's, near Soho Square; who is a man of reputation, and they will go very safe. And this will effectually amuse them.

Amuse them, my dear!—amuse whom?—my father!—my uncles!—But it must be so!——All his expedients ready, you see!—

I had no objection to this: and I have written accordingly. But what answer I shall have, or whether any, that is what gives me no small anxiety.

This, however, is one consolation: that, if I have an answer, and although my brother should be the writer, it cannot be more severe than the treatment I have of late received from him and my sister.

Mr Lovelace stayed out about an hour and half; and then came in; impatiently sending up to me no less than four times, to express his desire of my company. But I sent him word as often, that I was busy; and, at last, that I should be so till dinner was ready. So he hastened that, as I heard him now and then, with a hearty curse upon the cook and waiters.

This is another of his perfections. I ventured afterwards to check him for his free words, as we sat at dinner.

Having heard him swear at his servant, when below, whom, nevertheless, he owns to be a good one: It is a sad life, said I, these innkeepers live, Mr Lovelace.

No; pretty well, I believe—But why, madam, think you that fellows who eat and drink at other men's cost, or they are sorry whelps of innkeepers, should be entitled to pity?

Because of the soldiers they are obliged to quarter; who are generally, I believe, wretched profligates. Bless me! said I, how I heard one of them swear and curse just now at a modest meek man, as I judge by his low voice and gentle answers!— Well do they make it a proverb—*like a trooper*!¹

He bit his lip; arose; turned upon his heel; stepped to the glass; and looked *confidently* abashed, if I may so say—Ay, madam, said he, these troopers are sad swearing fellows. I think their officers should chastise them for it.

I am sure they deserve chastisement, replied I—for swearing is a most *unmanly* vice, and cursing as *poor* and *low* a one; since it proclaims the profligate's want of power, and his wickedness at the same time: for, could such a one *punish* as he *speaks*, he would be a fiend!

Charmingly observed, by my soul, madam!—The next trooper I hear swear and curse, I'll tell him what an *unmanly*, and what a *poor* whelp he is.

Mrs Greme came to pay her duty to me, as Mr Lovelace called it; and was very urgent with me to go to her lord's house; letting me know what handsome things she had heard her lord, and his two nieces, and all the family, say of me; and what wishes, for several months past, they had put up for the honour she now hoped soon would be done them all.

This gave me some satisfaction, as it confirmed from the mouth of a very good sort of woman all that Mr Lovelace had told me.

Upon inquiry about a private lodging, she recommended me to a sister-in-law of hers, eight miles from thence—where I now am. And what pleased me the better was that Mr Lovelace (of whom I could see she was infinitely observant) obliged her, of his own motion, to accompany me in the chaise; himself riding on horseback, with his two servants and one of Lord M.'s. And here we arrived about four o'clock.

But, as I told you in my former, the lodgings are inconvenient, and Mr Lovelace found great fault with them; telling Mrs Greme, who had said they were not worthy of us, that they came not up even to her description of them; that, as the house was a mile from a town, it was not proper for him to be so far distant from me, lest anything should happen: and yet the apartments were not separate and distinct enough for me to like, he was sure.

This must be agreeable enough from him, you'll believe.

Mrs Greme and I had a good deal of talk in the chaise about him. She was very easy and free in her answers to all I asked; and has a very serious turn, I find.

I led her on to say to the following effect; some part of it not unlike what his uncle's dismissed bailiff had said before; by which I find that all the servants' opinion of him is alike.

'That Mr Lovelace was a generous man: that it was hard to say whether the servants of her lord's family loved or feared him most: that her lord had a very great affection for him: that his two noble aunts were no less fond of him: that his two cousins Montague were as good-natured young ladies as ever lived: that his uncle and aunts had proposed several ladies to him, before he made his addresses to me; and even since; despairing to move me, and my friends, in his favour—But that he had no thoughts of marrying at all, she had heard him say, if it were not to me: that as well her lord as his sisters were a good deal concerned at the contempts and ill-usage he received from my family: but admired my character, and wished to have him married to me, although I were not to have a shilling, in preference to any other person, from the opinion that they had of the influence I should have over him: that, to be sure, she said, Mr Lovelace was a wild gentleman: but that was a distemper which would cure itself: that her lord delighted in his company, whenever he could get it: but that they often fell out; and his lordship was always forced to submit: indeed, was half afraid of him, she believed—for he would do as he pleased. She mingled a thousand pities often that he acted not up to the talents lent him—Yet would have it, that he had fine qualities to found a reformation upon; and, when the happy day came, would make amends for all: and of this all his friends were so assured, that they wished for nothing so earnestly as for his marriage.'

This, indifferent as it is, is better than my brother says of him.

The people of the house here are very honest-looking industrious folks: Mrs Sorlings is the gentlewoman's name. The farm seems well-stocked and thriving. She is a widow; has two sons, men grown, who vie with each other which shall take most pains in promoting the common good; and they are both of them, I already see, more respectful to two modest young women, their sisters, than my brother was to his sister. I believe I must stay here longer than at first I thought I should.

I should have mentioned that, before I set out for this place, I received your kind letter. Everything is kind from so dear a friend. I own you might well be surprised (I *was* myself; as by this time you will have seen)—after I had determined, too, so strongly against going away.

I have not the better opinion of Mr Lovelace for his extravagant volubility. He is too full of professions: he says too many fine things *of* me, and *to* me: True respect, true value, I think, lies not in words: words *cannot* express it. The silent awe, the humble, the doubting eye, and even the hesitating voice, better show it by much, than, as Shakespeare says,

—The rattling tongue
Of saucy and audacious eloquence.[2]

The man, to be sure, is, at times, all upon the *ecstatic*, one of his phrases; but, to my shame and confusion, I know too well what to attribute it to, in a great measure—To his *triumph*, my dear, in one word; it needs no further explanation; and, to give it *that* word, perhaps, equally exposes my vanity and condemns my folly.

We have been alarmed with notions of a pursuit, founded upon a letter from his intelligencer.

How do different circumstances sanctify or condemn an action!—What care ought we to take not to confound the distinctions of right and wrong, when *self* comes into the question! I condemned in him the corrupting of a servant of my papa's; and now I am glad to give a kind of indirect approbation of it, by inquiring what he hears, by that or any other way, of the manner in which my relations took my flight. A preconcerted, forward, and artful flight, to be sure, it must appear to them—That's a sad thing!—Yet how, as I am situated, can I put them right?

Most heavily, he says, they take it; but show not so much grief as rage—and he can hardly have patience to hear of the virulence and menaces of my brother against himself—Then a merit is made to me of his forbearance.

What a satisfaction am I robbed of, my dearest friend, by this rash action? I can now, too late, judge of the difference there is in being an *offended* rather than an *offending* person!—What would I give to have it once more in my power to say I *suffered* wrong, rather than *did* wrong? That others were more wanting in their kindness to me, than I in duty (where duty is owing) to them?—

Fie upon me! for meeting the seducer!—Let all end as happily as it now may, I have laid up for myself remorse for my whole life.

What more concerns me is that every time I see this man, I am still at a greater loss than before what to make of him. I watch every turn of his countenance: and I think I see very deep lines in it. He looks with more meaning, I verily think, than he used to look; yet not more serious; not less gay—I don't know how he looks—But with more confidence a great deal than formerly; and yet he never wanted that.

But here is the thing: I behold him with fear now, as knowing the power my indiscretion has given him over me. And well may *he* look more elate, when he sees me deprived of all the self-supposed significance which adorns and exalts a person who has been accustomed to respect; and who now, by a conscious inferiority, allows herself to be overcome, and in a state of obligation, as I may say, to her new protector.

I shall send this, as my former, by a poor man who travels every day with pedlary matters, who will leave it at Mrs Knollys's, as you direct.

If you hear anything of my father and mother, and of their health, and how my friends were affected by my unhappy step, pray be so good as to write me a few lines by the messenger, if his waiting for them can be known to you.

I am afraid to ask you whether, upon reading that part of my narrative already in your hands, you think any sort of extenuation lies for

Your unhappy
CLARISSA HARLOWE

Letter 99: MR LOVELACE TO JOHN BELFORD, ESQ.

Tuesday, Wed. Apr. 11, 12

THOU claimest my promise that I will be as particular as possible in all that passes between me and my goddess. Indeed, I never had a more illustrious subject to exercise my pen upon: and, moreover, I have leisure; for by her good will my access would be as difficult to her as that of the humblest slave to an eastern monarch. Nothing, then, but inclination to write can be wanting: and since our friendship, and thy obliging attendance upon me at the White Hart, will not excuse that, I will endeavour to keep my word.

I parted with thee and thy brethren with full resolution, thou knowest, to rejoin ye, if she once again disappointed me, in order to go together, attended by our servants for show-sake, to her gloomy father; and demand audience of the tyrant upon the freedoms taken with my character. And to have tried by fair means, if fair would do, to make them change their resolutions; and treat *her* with less inhumanity, and *me* with more civility.

I told thee my reasons for not going in search of a letter of countermand. I was right; for, if I had, I should have found such a one; and had I received it, she would not have met me. Did she think that after I had been more than once disappointed, I would not keep her to her promise; that I would not hold her to it, when I had got her in so deeply?

The moment I heard the door unbolt, I was sure of her. That motion made my heart bound to my throat. But when that was followed with the presence of my charmer, flashing upon me all at once in a flood of brightness, sweetly dressed, though all unprepared for a journey, I trod air, and hardly thought myself a mortal.

Thou shalt judge of her dress as at the moment she appeared to me, and as, upon a nearer observation, she really was. I am a critic, thou knowest, in women's dresses—Many a one have I taught to dress, and helped to undress. But there is such a native elegance in this lady that she surpasses all that I could imagine surpassing. But then her person adorns what she wears, more than dress can adorn her; and that's her excellence.

Expect therefore a faint sketch of her admirable person with her dress.

Her wax-like flesh (for, after all, flesh and blood I think she is!) by its delicacy and firmness, answers for the soundness of her health. Thou hast often heard me launch out in praise of her complexion. I never in my life beheld a skin so *illustriously* fair. The lily and the driven snow it is nonsense to talk of: her lawn and her laces one might, indeed, compare to those; but what a whited wall would a woman appear to be, who had a complexion which would justify such unnatural comparisons? But this lady is all alive, all glowing, all charming flesh and blood, yet so clear, that every meandering vein is to be seen in all the lovely parts of her which custom permits to be visible.

Thou hast heard me also describe the wavy ringlets of her shining hair, needing neither art nor powder; of itself an ornament, defying all other ornaments; wantoning in and about a neck that is beautiful beyond description.

Her head-dress was a Brussels lace mob, peculiarly adapted to the charming air and turn of her features. A sky-blue riband illustrated that—But although the weather was somewhat sharp, she had not on either hat or hood; for, besides that she loves to use herself hardily (by which means, and by a temperance truly exemplary, she is allowed to have given high health and vigour to an originally tender constitution), she seems to have intended to show me that she was determined not to stand to her appointment. Oh Jack! that such a sweet girl should be a rogue!

Her morning gown was a pale primrose-coloured paduasoy: the cuffs and robings curiously embroidered by the fingers of this ever charming Arachne in a running pattern of violets and their leaves; the light in the flowers silver; gold in the leaves. A pair of diamond snaps in her ears. A white handkerchief, wrought by the same inimitable fingers, concealed—Oh Belford! what still more inimitable beauties did it not conceal!—And I saw, all the way we rode, the bounding heart; by its throbbing motions I saw it! dancing beneath the charming umbrage.

Her ruffles were the same as her mob. Her apron a flowered lawn. Her coat white satin, quilted: blue satin her shoes, braided with the same colour, without lace; for what need has the prettiest foot in the world of ornament? Neat buckles in them: and on her charming arms a pair of black velvet glove-like muffs, of her own invention; for she makes and gives fashions as she pleases. Her hands, velvet of themselves, thus uncovered, the freer to be grasped by those of her adorer.

I have told thee what were *my* transports, when the undrawn bolt presented to me my long-expected goddess—*Her* emotions were more sweetly feminine, after the first moments; for then the fire of her starry eyes began to sink into a less dazzling languor. She trembled: nor knew she how to support the agitations of a heart she had never found so ungovernable. She was even fainting, when I clasped her in my supporting arms. What a precious moment that! How near, how sweetly near, the throbbing partners!

By her dress I saw, as I observed before, how unprepared she was for a journey; and not doubting her intention once more to disappoint me, I would have drawn her after me. Then began a contention the most vehement that ever I had with lady. It would pain thy friendly heart to be told the infinite trouble I had with her. I begged, I prayed; on my knees I begged and prayed her, yet in vain, to answer her own appointment: and had I not happily provided for such a struggle, knowing whom I had to deal with, I had certainly failed in my design; and as certainly would have accompanied her in, without thee and thy brethren. And who knows what might have been the consequence?

But my honest agent answering my signal, though not quite so soon as I expected, in the manner thou knowest I had laid down to him: They are coming! They are coming!—Fly, fly, my beloved creature, cried I, drawing my sword with a flourish, as if I would have slain half an hundred of them; and seizing her trembling hands, I drew her after me so swiftly, that *my* feet, winged by love, could hardly keep pace with *her* feet, agitated by fear—And so I became her emperor!

I'll tell thee all, when I see thee: and thou shalt then judge of my difficulties, and of her perverseness. And thou wilt rejoice with me, at my conquest over such a watchful and open-eyed charmer.

But seest thou not now (as I think I do) the wind-outstripping fair one flying *from* her love *to* her love?—Is there not such a game?—Nay, flying from friends she was resolved not to abandon to the man she was determined not to go off with?—The sex! the sex, all over!—charming contradiction!—Hah, hah, hah,

hah!—I must here lay down my pen to hold my sides; for I must have my laugh out, now the fit is upon me!

I believe—I believe—Hah, hah, hah!—I believe, Jack, my dogs conclude me mad: for here has one of them popped in, as if to see what ailed me; or whom I had with me. The whoreson caught the laugh as he went out—Hah, hah, hah!—an *im*-pudent dog!—Oh Jack, knewest thou my conceit, and were but thy laugh joined to mine, I believe it would hold me for an hour longer.

But, oh my best-beloved fair one, repine not thou at the arts by which thou suspectest thy fruitless vigilance has been over-watched. Take care that thou provokest not new ones, that may be still more worthy of thee. If once thy emperor decrees thy fall, thou shalt greatly fall. Thou shalt have cause, if that comes to pass which *may* come to pass (for why wouldst thou put off marriage to so long a day as till thou hadst reason to be convinced of my reformation, dearest?); thou shalt have cause, never fear, to sit down more dissatisfied with thy stars than with thyself. And come the worst to the worst, glorious terms will I give thee. Thy garrison, with General *Prudence* at the head, and Governor *Watchfulness* bringing up the rear, shall be allowed to march out with all the honours due to so brave a resistance. And all thy sex, and all mine, that hear of my stratagems, and thy conduct, shall acknowledge the fortress as nobly won as defended.

Thou wilt not dare, methinks I hear thee say, to attempt to reduce such a goddess as this to a standard unworthy of her excellencies. It is impossible, Lovelace, that thou shouldst intend to break through oaths and protestations so solemn.

That I did *not* intend it, is certain. That I *do* intend it, I cannot (my heart, my reverence for her, will not let me) say. But knowest thou not my aversion to the state of shackles?—And is she not IN MY POWER?

And wilt thou, Lovelace, abuse that power, which—

Which what, puppy?—which I obtained not by her own consent, but against it.

But which thou hadst never obtained, had she not esteemed thee above all men.

And which I had never taken so much pains to obtain, had I not loved her above all women. So far upon a par, Jack!—And, if thou pleadest honour, ought not honour to be mutual? If mutual, does it not imply mutual trust, mutual confidence?—and what have I had of *that* from her to boast of?—Thou knowest the whole progress of our warfare: for a warfare it has truly been; and far, very far, from an amorous warfare too. Doubts, mistrusts, upbraidings, on her part: humiliations the most abject, on mine. Obliged to assume such airs of reformation, that every varlet of ye has been afraid I should reclaim in good earnest. And hast thou not thyself frequently observed to me how awkwardly I returned to my usual gaiety, after I had been within a mile of her father's garden wall, although I had not seen her?

Does she not deserve to pay for all this?—To make an honest fellow look like an hypocrite; what a vile thing is that!

Then thou knowest what a false little rogue she has been! How little conscience she has made of disappointing me!—Hast thou not been a witness of my ravings on this score?—Have I not, in height of them, vowed revenge upon the faithless charmer?—And if I *must* be forsworn whether I answer her expectations or follow my own inclinations (as Cromwell said, if it must be my head, or the king's), and the option in my own power; can I hesitate a moment which to choose?

Then, I fancy, by her circumspection, and her continual grief, that she expects some mischief from me. I don't care to disappoint anybody I have a value for.

But oh the noble, the exalted creature! Who can avoid hesitating when he thinks of an offence against her?—Who can but pity—

Yet, on the other hand, so loath at last to venture, though threatened to be forced into the nuptial fetters with a man, whom to look upon as a rival, is to disgrace myself!—So sullen, now she has ventured!—What title has *she* to pity; and to a pity which her pride would make her disclaim?

But I resolve not *any way*. I will see how *her* will works; and how *my* will leads me on. I will give the combatants fair play. And I find, every time I attend her, that she is less in *my* power—I more in *hers*.

Yet, a foolish little rogue! to forbid me to think of marriage till I am a reformed man! till the implacables of her family change their natures, and become placable!

It is true, when she was for making those conditions, she did not think that, without any, she should be cheated out of herself; for so the dear soul, as thou mayst hear in its place, phrases it.

How it swells my pride to have been able to outwit such a vigilant charmer!—I am taller by half a yard, in my imagination, than I was!—I look *down* upon everybody now!—Last night I was still more extravagant. I took off my hat, as I walked, to see if the lace were not scorched, supposing it had brushed down a star; and, before I put it on again, in mere wantonness and heart's-ease, I was for buffeting the moon. In short, my whole soul is joy. When I go to bed, I laugh myself asleep: and I awake either laughing or singing. Yet nothing *nearly* in view, neither—For why?—*I am not yet reformed enough!*

I told thee at the time, if thou remembrest, how capable this restriction was of being turned upon the over scrupulous dear creature, could I once get her out of her father's house; and were I disposed to punish her for her family's faults, and for the infinite trouble she herself had given me. Little thinks she that I have kept an account of both; and that when my heart is soft, and all her own, I can but turn to my *memoranda*, and harden myself at once.

Oh my charmer, look to it!—Abate of thy haughty airs!—Value not thyself upon thy sincerity, if thou *art* indifferent to me!—I will not bear it *now*—Art thou *not in my* POWER?—Nor, if thou lovest me, think that the female affectation of denying thy love will avail thee *now*, with a heart so proud and so jealous?— Remember, moreover, that all thy family sins are upon thy head!—

But, ah! Jack, when I see my angel, when I am admitted to the presence of this radiant beauty, what will become of all this vapouring?—

But, be my end what it may, I am obliged by thy penetration, fair one, to proceed by the sap. *Fair and softly*—a wife at any time!—that will be always in my power.

When put to the university, the same course of *initial studies* will qualify the yonker for the one line or for the other. The genius ought to point out the future lawyer, divine, or physician!—So the same cautious conduct, with such a vigilance, will do either for the *wife*, or for the *no*-wife. When I reform, I'll marry. 'Tis time enough for the *one*, the *lady* must say—for the *other*, say *I!*

But how I ramble!—This it is to be in such a situation that I know not what to resolve upon.

I'll tell thee my *inclinings*, as I proceed. The *pro*'s and the *con*'s, I'll tell thee. But being got too far from the track I set out in, I will close here. But, perhaps, may write every day something, and send it as opportunity offers.

Regardless, however, in all I write, as I shall be, of connexion, accuracy, or of anything but of my own imperial will and pleasure.

Letter 100: MISS HOWE TO MISS CLARISSA HARLOWE

Wednesday night, April 12

I HAVE your narrative, my dear. You are the same noble creature you ever were. Above disguise, above art, above extenuating a failing.

The only family in the world, yours, surely, that could have driven such a daughter into such extremities.

But you must not be so very much too good for *them*, and for the *case*.

You lay the blame so properly and so unsparingly upon your meeting him, that nothing can be added to that subject by your worst enemies, were they to see what you have written.

I am not surprised, now I have read your narrative, that so bold and so contriving a man—I am forced to break off—

YOU stood it out much better and longer—Here again comes my bustling, jealous mother!

DON'T be so angry at yourself. Did you not do for the best at the time? As to your first fault, the answering his letters; it was almost incumbent upon you to assume the guardianship of such a family, when the bravo of it had run riot, as he did, and brought himself into danger.

Except your mamma, who is kept down, have any of them common sense?—

Forgive me, my dear—Here is that stupid uncle Antony of yours. A pragmatical, conceited positive——He came yesterday, in a fearful pucker, and puffed, and blowed, and stumped about our hall and parlour, while his message was carried up.

My mamma was dressing herself. These widows are as starched as the bachelors. She would not see him in a dishabille for the world—What can she mean by it?

His errand was to set her against you, and to show their determined rage on your going away. The issue proved it to be so too evidently.

The odd creature desired to speak with her alone. I am not used to such exceptions, whenever any visits are made to my mamma.

When my mamma was primmed out, down she came to him—The door was locked upon themselves; the two positive heads were put together—close together, I suppose—for I hearkened, but could hear nothing distinctly, though they both seemed full of their subject.

I had a good mind, once or twice, to have made them open the door—Could I have been sure of keeping but tolerably my temper, I would have demanded admittance—But I was afraid, if I had obtained it, that I should have forgot it was my mamma's house, and been for turning him out of it. To come to rave against and abuse my dearest, dearest, faultless friend! and the ravings to be listened to—and this in order to justify themselves; the one for contributing to drive her out of her father's house; the other for refusing her a temporary asylum, till the reconciliation could have been effected which her dutiful heart was set upon!—and which it would have become the love my mamma had ever pretended for you, to have mediated for—Could I have had patience!

The *issue*, as I said, showed what the errand was—Its first appearance, after the old fusty fellow was marched off (you must excuse me, my dear), was in a kind of gloomy, Harlowe-like reservedness in my mamma; which, upon a few resenting flirts of mine, was followed by a rigorous prohibition of correspondence.

This put us, you may suppose, upon terms not the most agreeable. I desired to know if I were prohibited *dreaming* of you?—for, my dear, you have all my sleeping, as well as waking hours.

I can easily allow for your correspondence with your wretch at first (and yet your motives were excellent), by the effect this prohibition has upon me; since, if possible, it has made me love you better than before; and I am more desirous than ever of corresponding with you.

But I have still a more laudable motive—I should think myself the unworthiest of creatures, could I be brought to slight a dear friend, and such a meritorious one, in her distress. I would die first—and so I told my mamma. And I have desired her not to watch me in my retired hours, nor to insist upon my lying with her constantly, which she now does more earnestly than ever. 'Twere better, I told her, that the Harlowe-Betty were borrowed to be set over me.

Mr Hickman, who greatly honours you, has unknown to me interposed so warmly in your favour with my mamma, that it makes for him no small merit with me.

I cannot, at present, write to every particular, unless I would be in *set* defiance. Tease, tease, tease, for ever! The same thing, though answered fifty times over, is every hour to be repeated—Lord bless me! what a life must my poor papa—But I must remember to whom I am writing.

If this ever active, ever mischievous monkey of a man—this Lovelace—contrived as you suspect—But here comes my mamma again—Ay, stay a little longer, my mamma, if you please—I can but be suspected! I can but be chidden for making you wait; and chidden I am sure to be, whether I do or not, in the way you are *Antonyed* into.

Bless me!—how impatient!—I must break off—

A CHARMING dialogue—but I am sent for down in a very peremptory manner, I assure you—What an incoherent letter will you have, when I can get it to you! But now I know where to send it, Mr Hickman shall find me a messenger. Yet, if he be detected, poor soul, he will be *Harlowed off*, as well as his meek mistress!—

Thursday, April 13

I HAVE this moment your continuation letter, and a little absence of my Argus-eyed mamma.

Dear creature!—I can account for all your difficulties. A person of your delicacy!—and with such a man!—I must be brief——

The man's a fool, my dear, with all his pride, and with all his complaisance, and affected regards to your injunctions. Yet his ready inventions—

Sometimes I think you should go to Lady Betty's—I know not what to advise you to. I could, if you were not so intent upon reconciling yourself to your relations. But they are implacable, you can have no hopes from them—Your uncle's errand to my mamma may convince you of that; and if you have an answer to your letter to your sister, that will confirm you, I dare say.

You need not to have been afraid of asking me whether I thought upon reading your narrative, any extenuation could lie for what you have done. I have told you above my mind as to that—And I repeat that I think, your *provocations* and *inducements* considered, you are free from blame: at least, the freest, that ever young creature was who took such a step.

But you took it not—You were driven on one side, and possibly tricked on the other. If any young person on earth shall be circumstanced as you were, and shall hold out so long as you did against her persecutors on one hand, and her seducer on the other, I will forgive her for all the rest.

All your acquaintance, you may suppose, talk of nobody but you. Some, indeed, bring your admirable character against you: but nobody does, or *can*, acquit your father and uncles.

Everybody seems apprised of your brother's and sister's motives. It is, no doubt, the very thing they aimed to drive you to, by the various attacks they made upon you; unhoping (as they might do all the time) the success. They knew that if once you were restored to favour, love suspended would be love augmented, and that you must defeat and expose them, and triumph by your amiable qualities and great talents over all their arts. And now, I hear, they enjoy their successful malice.

Your father is all rage and violence. He ought, I am sure, to turn his rage inward. All your family accuse you of acting with deep art; and are put upon supposing that you are actually every hour exulting over them, with your man, in the success of it.

They all pretend now, that your trial of Wednesday was to be the last.

Advantage would indeed, my mamma owns, have been taken of your yielding, if you had yielded. But had you not been to be prevailed upon, they would have given up their scheme and taken your promise for renouncing Lovelace—Believe them who will! They own, however, that a minister was to be present. Mr Solmes was to be at hand. And your father was previously to try his authority over you, in order to make you sign the settlements—All of it a romantic contrivance of your wild-headed foolish brother, I make no doubt. Is it likely that he and Bell would have given way to your restoration to favour, on any other terms than those their hearts had been so long set upon?

How they took your flight, when they found it out, may be better supposed than described.

Your aunt Hervey, it seems, was the first that went down to the ivy summer-house, in order to acquaint you that their search was over. Betty followed her; and they not finding you there, went on toward the cascade, according to a hint of yours.

Returning by the garden door, they met a servant (they don't say it was that Joseph Leman; but it is very likely that it *was* he) running, as he said, from pursuing

Mr Lovelace (a great hedge-stake in his hand, and out of breath), to alarm the family.

If it were this fellow, and if he were employed in the double agency of cheating them and cheating you, what shall we think of the wretch you are with?—Run away from him, my dear, if so—no matter to whom—or marry him, if you cannot.

Your aunt and all your family were accordingly alarmed by this fellow (evidently when too late for pursuit). They got together and, when a posse, ran to the place of interview; and some of them as far as to the tracks of the chariot-wheels, without stopping. And having heard the man's tale upon the spot, a general lamentation, a mutual upbraiding and rage, and grief, were echoed from the different persons, according to their different tempers and conceptions. And they returned like fools as they went.

Your brother, at first, ordered horses and armed men to be got ready for a pursuit. Solmes and your uncle Tony were to be of the party. But your mamma and your aunt Hervey dissuaded them from it, for fear of adding evil to evil; not doubting but Lovelace had taken measures to support himself in what he had done; and especially when the servant declared that he saw you run with him, as fast as you could set foot to ground; and that there were several armed men on horseback at a small distance off.

My mamma's absence was owing to her suspicion that the Knollys's were to assist in our correspondence. She made them a visit upon it. She does everything at once. And they have promised that no more letters shall be left there without her knowledge.

But Mr Hickman has engaged one Filmer, a husbandman in the lane we call Finch Lane, near us, to receive them. Thither you will be pleased to direct yours, under cover, to Mr John Soberton; and Mr Hickman himself will call for them there; and there shall leave mine. It goes against me too, to make him so useful to me—He looks already so proud upon it!—I shall have him (who knows?) give himself airs. He had best consider that the favour he has been long aiming at may put him into a very dangerous, a very ticklish situation. He that can oblige, may disoblige—happy for some people not to have it in their power to offend!

I will have patience, if I can, for a while, to see if these bustlings in my mamma will subside—but upon my word, I will not long bear this usage.

Sometimes I am ready to think that my mamma carries it thus on purpose to tire me out, and to make me the sooner marry. If I find it to be so, and that Hickman, in order to make a merit with me, is in the low plot, I will never bear him in my sight.

Plotting wretch as I doubt your man is, I wish to heaven that you were married, that you might brave them all; and not be forced to hide yourself, and be hurried from one inconvenient place to another. I charge you, omit not to lay hold on any handsome opportunity that may offer for that purpose.

Here again comes my mamma.

We look mighty glum upon each other, I can tell you. She had not best *Harlowe* me at this rate!—I won't bear it!—

I have a vast deal to write. I know not what to write first. Yet my mind is full, and seems to run over.

I am got into a private corner of the garden to be out of her way—Lord help these mothers!—Do they think they can prevent a daughter's writing, or doing anything she has a mind to do, by suspicion, watchfulness and scolding?—They had better place a confidence in one by half—a generous mind scorns to abuse a generous confidence.

You have a nice, a very nice part to act with this wretch—who yet has, I think, but one plain path before him. I pity you!—but you must make the best of the lot you have been forced to draw. Yet I see your difficulties—but if he do not offer to abuse your confidence, I would have you *seem*, at least, to place some in him.

If you think not of marrying soon, I approve of your resolution to fix somewhere out of his reach: and if he know not where to find you, so much the better. Yet I verily believe they would force you back, could they but come at you, if they were not afraid of *him*.

I think, by all means, you should demand of both your trustees to be put in possession of your own estate. Meantime I have sixty guineas at your service. I beg you will command them. Before they are gone I'll take care you shall be further supplied. I don't think you'll have a shilling or a shilling's worth of your own from your relations, unless you extort it from them.

As they believe you went off by your own consent, they are surprised, it seems, and glad that you have left your jewels and money behind you, and have contrived for clothes so ill. Very little likelihood, this shows, of their answering your requests.

Indeed everybody, not knowing what I *now* know, must be at a loss to account for your flight, as they will call it. And how, my dear, can one report it with any tolerable advantage to you?—To say you did not intend it when you met him, who will believe it?—To say that a person of your known steadiness and punctilio was over-persuaded when you gave him the meeting, how will that sound?—To say you were tricked out of yourself, and people were to give credit to it, how disreputable?—And while unmarried and yet with him, he a man of such a character, what would it not lead a censuring world to think?

I want to see how you put it in your letter for your clothes.

You may depend, I repeat, upon all the little spiteful and disgraceful things they can offer, instead of what you write for. So pray accept the sum I tender. What will seven guineas do?—And I will find a way to send you also any of my clothes and linen for present supply. I beg, my dearest Miss Harlowe, that you will not put your Anna Howe upon a foot with Lovelace, in refusing to accept of my offer. If you do not oblige me, I shall be apt to think that you rather incline to be obliged to him, than to favour me. And if I find this, I shall not know how to reconcile it with your delicacy in other respects.

Pray inform me of everything that passes between you and him. My cares for you (however needless, from your own prudence) make me wish you to continue to be very minute. If anything occur that you would tell me of if [I were] present, fail not to put it down in writing, although from your natural diffidence it should not appear to you altogether so worthy of your pen, or of my knowing. A stander-by may see more of the game than one that plays. Great consequences, like great folks, are generally attended and even *made* great by small causes, and little incidents.

Upon the whole, I do not now think it is in your power to dismiss him when you please. I apprised you beforehand that it would not. I repeat, therefore, that were I you, I would at least *seem* to place some confidence in him: so long as he is decent, you may. Very visibly observable, to such delicacy as yours, must be that behaviour in him which will make him unworthy of *some* confidence.

Your relations, according to old Antony to *my mother*, and *she* to *me* (by way of threatening that you will not gain your supposed ends upon them by your flight), seem to expect that you will throw yourself into Lady Betty's protection; and that she will offer to mediate for you: and they vow that they will never hearken to any accommodation, or terms, that shall come from that quarter. They might speak out, and say from *any* quarter; for I dare aver that your brother and sister will not let them cool—at least till their uncles have made such dispositions, and your father too perhaps, as they would have them make.

As this letter will apprise you of an alteration in the place to which you must direct your next, I send it by a friend of Mr Hickman's, who may be depended upon. He has business in the neighbourhood of Mrs Sorlings, whom he knows, and will return to Mr Hickman this night; and bring back any letter you shall have ready to send or can get ready. It is moonlight. He won't mind waiting for you. I choose not to send by any of Mr Hickman's servants—at present, however. Every hour is now, or may be, important; and may make an alteration in your resolutions and situation necessary.

I hear, from where I sit, my mamma calling about her and putting everybody into motion. She will soon, I suppose, make *me* and *my* employment the subject of her inquiry.

Adieu, my dear. May heaven preserve you, and restore you with honour as unsullied as your mind, to

Your ever affectionate
ANNA HOWE

Letter 101: MISS CLARISSA HARLOWE TO MISS HOWE

Thursday, p.m. April 13

I AM infinitely concerned, my ever dear and ever kind friend, that I am the sad occasion of the displeasure between your mamma and you—How many unhappy persons have I made!—

Had I not to console myself that my error is not owing to wicked precipitation, I should be the most miserable of all creatures. As it is, I am enough punished in the loss of my character, more valuable to me than my life; and in the cruel doubts and perplexities which, conflicting with my hopes and each getting the victory by turns, harrow up my soul between them.

I think, however, that you should obey your mamma; and decline a correspondence with so unhappy a creature—Take care how you fall into my error; for that began with carrying on a prohibited correspondence; which I thought it in my power to discontinue at pleasure. My talent is scribbling, and I the readier fell into this freedom, as I found delight in writing; having motives too which I thought laudable; and, at one time, the permission of all my friends, to write to him.[a]

Yet (although I am ready sometimes to discontinue a correspondence so dear to me, in order to make your mamma easy) what hurt could a letter now and then from each do?—mine occasionally filled with self-accusation too!—so much prudence and discretion as you have; and lying under no temptation of following so bad an example, in writing to me.

I thank you most heartily for your kind offers. You may be assured, that I would sooner be beholden to you than to anybody living. To Mr Lovelace the last. So, do not think that by declining it, I have an intention to lay myself under obligations to him.

I am willing to hope, notwithstanding what you write, that I shall have my little money, together with my clothes, sent me by my friends. They are too considerate, some of them at least, to permit that I should be put to such *low* difficulties. Perhaps they will not be in haste to oblige me. But if not, I cannot yet want. I believe you think I must not dispute with him the expenses of the road and lodgings, till I can get to a fixed one. But I hope soon to put an end even to those sort of obligations.

Small hopes, indeed, of a reconciliation, from your account of my uncle's visit to your mamma; to set her against an almost friendless creature, whom once he loved! But is it not my duty to try for it? Ought I to widen my error by obstinacy and resentment, because of *their* resentment; which must appear reasonable to them, as they suppose my flight premeditated; and as they are made to believe that I am capable of triumphing in it, and over them, with the man they hate? When I have done all in my power to restore myself to their favour, I shall have the less to reproach myself with—These considerations make me waver about following your advice in relation to marriage; especially as he is so full of his complaisance with regard to my former conditions, which he calls my *injunctions*. And, at the same time that they dispose me not to go to any of the ladies of his family, whose mediation my friends, as you tell me, have so strenuously declared against; I am ready to fix all my reliance on my cousin Morden. For I think that if I can be secure in a tolerable state of independence till he comes to England, all must then be determined in a better manner, than by any other way.

Yet, if I cannot get this man to leave me, how shall terms to my friends be proposed?—If he do, and they should get me back again by force, which you think they would attempt but for fear of him; how will the severest acts of compulsion which they can have recourse to, be justified by my flight from them?—And while we are together, and unmarried, as you observe, what censures do I expose myself to!—And must I then, to save the poor remains of my reputation in the world's eye, watch the gracious motion from this man's lips?

I will acquaint you, as you desire, with all that passes between us. Hitherto I have not discovered anything in his behaviour that is very exceptionable. Yet I cannot say that I think the respect he shows me, an easy, unrestrained and natural respect; although I can hardly tell where the fault is.

But he has doubtless an arrogant and encroaching spirit. Nor is he so polite as his education and other advantages might have made one expect him to be. He

a   See p. 47.

seems, in short, to be one who has always had too much of his own will to study to accommodate himself to that of others.

As to the placing of some confidence in him, I shall be as ready to take your advice in this particular as in all others, and as he will be to deserve it. But tricked away as I was by him, not only against my judgement, but my inclination, can he, or anybody, expect that I should immediately treat him with complaisance, as if I acknowledged obligation to him for carrying me away?—If I did, must he not either think me a vile dissembler *before* he gained that point, or *afterwards*?

Indeed, indeed, my dear, I could tear my hair on reconsidering what you write (as to the probability that the dreaded Wednesday was more dreaded than it needed to be), to think that I should be thus tricked by this man; and that, in all likelihood, through his vile agent Joseph Leman. So premeditated and elaborate a wickedness as it must be!—Must I not, with such a man, be wanting to myself, if I were not jealous and vigilant?—Yet what a life to live for a spirit so open, and naturally so unsuspicious, as mine?

I am obliged to Mr Hickman for the assistance he is so kindly ready to give to our correspondence. He is so little likely to make himself an additional merit with the *daughter* upon it, that I shall be very sorry if he risk anything with the *mother* by it.

I am now in a state of obligation: so must rest satisfied with whatever I cannot help. Whom have I the power, once so precious to me, of obliging?—What I mean, my dear, is that I ought, perhaps, to expect that my influences over you are weakened by my indiscretion. Nevertheless, I will not, if I can help it, desert myself, nor give up the privilege you used to allow me, of telling you what I think of any part of your conduct which I may disapprove of.

You must permit me therefore (severe as your mamma is against an undesigning offender) to say that I think your liveliness to her inexcusable—to pass over, for this time, what nevertheless concerns me not a little, the free treatment you almost indiscriminately give my relations.

If you will not, for your *own sake*, forbear such tauntings and impatiency as you repeat to me, let me beseech you that you will for *mine*—since otherwise your mamma may apprehend that my example, like a leaven, is working itself into the mind of her beloved daughter. And may not such an apprehension give her an irreconcilable displeasure against me?

I enclose the copy of my letter to my sister, which you are desirous to see. You'll observe, that although I have not demanded my estate in form, and of my trustees, yet that I have hinted at leave to retire to it. How joyfully would I keep my word if they would accept of the offer I renew!—It was not proper, I believe you'll think, on many accounts, to own that I was carried off against my inclination.

I am, my dearest friend,

Your ever obliged and affectionate
CL. HARLOWE

Letter 102: MISS CLARISSA HARLOWE TO MISS ARABELLA HARLOWE

(Enclosed to Miss HOWE *in the preceding)*

St Albans, Tuesday, Apr. 11

My dear sister,

I HAVE, I confess, been guilty of an action which carries with it a rash and undutiful appearance. And I should have thought it an inexcusable one, had I been used with less severity than I have been of late; and had I not had too great reason to apprehend that I was to be made a sacrifice to a man I could not bear to think of. But what is done, is done—perhaps I could wish it had not—and that I had trusted to the relenting of my dear and honoured parents. Yet this from no other motives but those of duty to them—to whom I am ready to return (if I may not be permitted to retire to *The Grove*), on conditions which I before offered to comply with.

Nor shall I be in any sort of dependence upon the person by whose means I have taken this truly reluctant step, inconsistent with any reasonable engagement I shall enter into, if I am not farther precipitated.

Let me not have it to say now (at this important crisis!) that I have a sister, but not a friend in her. My reputation, dearer to me than life (whatever you may imagine from the step I have taken), is suffering. A little lenity will, even yet, in a great measure restore it; and make that pass for a temporary misunderstanding only, which otherwise will be a stain as durable as life upon a creature who has already been treated with great unkindness, to use no harsher a word.

For your own sake therefore, for my brother's sake, who have thus precipitated me (I must say it!), and for all the family's sake aggravate not my fault, if, on recollecting everything, you think it one; nor by widening the unhappy difference, expose a sister for ever—prays

Your ever affectionate
CL. HARLOWE

I shall take it for a very great favour to have my clothes directly sent me, together with fifty guineas, which you'll find in my escritoire (of which I enclose the key); as also the divinity and miscellany classes of my little library; and, if it be thought fit, my jewels—directed for *me*: To be left at Mr Osgood's near Soho Square—Till called for.

Letter 103: MR LOVELACE TO JOHN BELFORD, ESQ.

Mr Lovelace, in continuation of his last letter [99], *gives an account to his friend, pretty much to the same effect with the lady's, of what passed between them at the inns, in the journey, and till their fixing at Mrs Sorlings's. To avoid repetition, those passages in his account are only extracted which will serve to embellish hers; to open his views; or to display the humorous talent he was noted for.*

At their alighting at the inn at St Albans on Monday night, thus he writes:

The people who came about us, as we alighted, seemed, by their jaw-fallen faces and goggling eyes, to wonder at beholding a charming young lady, majesty in her air and aspect, so composedly dressed yet with features so discomposed, come off a journey which had made the cattle smoke, and the servants sweat. I read their curiosity, and my beloved's uneasiness. She cast a conscious glance as she alighted upon her habit, which was *no habit*, and repulsively, as I may say, quitting my assisting hand, hurried into the house as fast as she could . . .

Ovid was not a greater master of metamorphoses than thy friend. To the mistress of the house I instantly changed her into a sister, brought off by surprise from a near relation's (where she had wintered), to prevent her marrying a confounded rake (I love always to go as near the truth as I can), whom her father and mother, her elder sister and all her loving uncles, aunts, and cousins abhorred. This accounted for my charmer's expected sullens; for her displeasure when she was to join me again, were it to hold; for her unsuitable dress upon a road; and, at the same time, gave her a proper and seasonable assurance of my honourable views.

Upon the debate between the lady and him, and particularly upon that part where she upbraids him with putting a young creature upon making a sacrifice of her duty and conscience, he writes:

All these, and still more mortifying things, she said.

I heard her in silence. But when it came to my turn, I pleaded, I argued, I answered her, as well as I could—And when humility would not do, I raised my voice and suffered my eye to sparkle with anger; hoping to take advantage of that sweet cowardice which is so amiable in the sex (which many of them, indeed, fantastically affect), and to which my victory over this proud beauty is principally owing.

She was not intimidated, however; and was going to rise upon me in her temper; and would have broke in upon my defence. But when a man talks to a lady upon such subjects, let her be ever so much in *alt*, 'tis strange if he cannot throw out a tub to the whale[1]—if he cannot divert her from resenting one bold thing by uttering two or three full as bold; but for which more favourable interpretations will lie.

To that part where she tells him of the difficulty she made to correspond with him at first, thus he writes:

Very true, my precious!—and innumerable have been the difficulties thou hast made me struggle with. But one day thou mayest wish that thou hadst spared this boast; as well as those other pretty haughtinesses—that thou didst not reject Solmes for *my* sake: that *my* glory, if I valued myself upon carrying thee off, was *thy* shame: that I have more merit with *myself*, than with thee, or anybody else (what a coxcomb she makes me, Jack!): that thou wishest thyself in thy father's house again, *whatever were to be the consequence*. If I forgive thee, charmer, for these hints, for these reflections, for these wishes, for these contempts, I am not the Lovelace I have been reputed to be; and that thy treatment of me shows that thou thinkest I am—

In short, her whole air throughout this debate expressed a majestic kind of indignation, which implied a believed superiority of talents over the man she spoke to.

Thou hast heard me often expatiate upon the pitiful figure a man must make, whose wife *has*, or *believes* she has, more sense than himself. A thousand reasons could I give why I ought not to think of marrying Miss Clarissa Harlowe: at least till I can be sure that she loves me with the preference I must expect from a wife.

I begin to stagger in my resolutions. Ever averse as I was to the hymeneal shackles, how easily will old prejudices recur!—Heaven give me the heart to be honest to her!—There's a prayer, Jack!—If I should not be heard, what a sad thing would that be for the most admirable of women!—Yet, as I do not often trouble Heaven with my prayers, who knows but this may be granted?

But there lie before me such charming difficulties, such scenery for intrigue, for stratagem, for enterprise—What a horrible thing that my talents point all that way!—when I know what is honourable and just; and would almost wish to be honest?—*Almost*, I say; for such a varlet am I, that I cannot altogether wish it, for the soul of me!—Such triumph over the whole sex, if I can subdue this lady!—My maiden vow, as I may call it!—For did not the sex begin with me?—and does this lady spare me?—Thinkest thou, Jack, that I should have spared my Rosebud, had I been set at defiance thus?—Her grandmother besought me, at first, to spare her Rosebud; and when a girl is put, or puts herself, into a man's power, what can he wish for further? While I always considered opposition and resistance as a challenge to do my worst.[a]

Why, why, will the dear creature take such pains to appear all ice to me?—Why will she, by *her* pride, awaken *mine?*—Hast thou not seen, in the above, how contemptibly she treats me?—What have I not suffered *for* her, and even *from* her?—Is it tolerable to be told, that she will despise me, if I value myself above that odious Solmes!—

Then she cuts me short in all my ardours. To vow fidelity is, by a cursed turn upon me, to show that there is reason, in my own opinion, for doubt of it.—The very same reflection upon me once before.[b] In my power, or out of my power, all one to her—So, Belford, my poor vows are crammed down my throat before they can well rise to my lips. And what can a lover say to his mistress, if she will neither let him lie nor swear?

One little piece of artifice I had recourse to: when she pushed so hard for me to leave her, I made a request to her, upon a condition she could not refuse; and pretended as much gratitude upon her granting it, as if it were a favour of the last consequence.

And what was this? But to promise what she had before promised: never to marry any other man while I am living, and single, unless I should give her cause for high disgust against me. This, you know, was promising nothing, because she could be offended at any time; and was to be the sole judge of the offence. But it showed her how reasonable and just my expectations were; and that I was no encroacher.

She consented and asked what security I expected?

Her word only.

She gave me her word: but I besought her excuse for sealing it: and in the same moment (since to have waited for consent would have been asking for a denial) saluted her. And, believe me or not, but, as I hope to live, it was the first time I had the courage to touch her charming lips with mine. And this I tell thee, Belford, that that single pressure (as modestly put too, as if I were as much a virgin as herself, that she might not be afraid of me another time) delighted me more than ever I was delighted by the *ultimatum* with any other woman—so precious does awe, reverence, and apprehended prohibition make a favour!

a   See p. 162.
b   See p. 242.

I am only afraid that I shall be *too* cunning; for she does not at present *talk* enough for me. I hardly know what to make of the dear creature yet.

I topped the brother's part on Monday night before the landlady at St Albans; asking my sister's pardon for carrying her off so unprepared for a journey; prated of the joy my father and mother, and all our friends, would have on receiving her; and this with so many circumstances, that I perceived, by a look she gave me, that went through my very reins, that I had gone too far. I apologized for it, indeed, when alone; but I could not penetrate for the soul of me, whether I made the matter better or worse by it. But I am of too frank a nature: my success, and the joy I have because of the jewel I am half in possession of has not only unlocked my bosom, but left the door quite open.

This is a confounded sly sex. Would she but speak out, as I do—But I must learn reserves of her.

She must needs be unprovided of money: but has too much pride to accept of any from me. I would have her go to town (to town, if possible, must I get her to consent to go), in order to provide herself with the richest of silks which that can afford. But neither is this to be assented to. And yet, as my intelligencer acquaints me, her implacable relations are resolved to distress her all they can.

These wretches have been most gloriously raving, it seems, ever since her flight; and still, thank Heaven, continue to rave; and will, I hope, for a twelvemonth to come—Now, at last, it is my day!—

Bitterly do they regret that they permitted her poultry visits and garden walks, which gave her the opportunity they know she had (though they could not find out how) to concert, as they suppose, her preconcerted escape. For, as to her dining in the ivy bower, they had a cunning design to answer upon her in that permission, as Betty told Joseph her lover.[a]

They lost, they say, an excellent pretence for *more* closely confining her, on my threatening to rescue her if they offered to carry her against her will to old Antony's moated house.[b] For this, as I told thee at the Hart, and as I once hinted to the dear creature herself,[c] they had it in deliberation to do; apprehending that I might attempt to carry her off, either with or without her consent, on some one of those connived-at excursions.

But here my honest Joseph, who gave me the information, was of admirable service to me. I had taught him to make the Harlowes believe that I was as communicative to my servants, as their stupid James was to Joseph[d]: Joseph, as they supposed, by tampering with Will,[e] got at all my secrets, and was acquainted with all my motions: and having undertaken to watch all this young lady's too[f]; the wise family were secure; and so was my beloved, and so was I.

I once had it in my head (and I hinted it to thee in a former[g]), in case such a step should be necessary, to attempt to carry her off by surprise from the woodhouse; as it is remote from the dwelling house. This, had I attempted, I should certainly

a　See p. 369.
b　See pp. 326, 336.
c　See p. 326; see also p. 362.
d　See pp. 367, 369.
e　This will be further explained in Letter 123.
f　See pp. 144–5, 164.
g　See p. 165.

have effected, by the help of the confraternity: and it would have been an action worthy of us all. But Joseph's conscience, as he called it, stood in my way; for he thought it must have been known to be done by his connivance. I could, I dare say, have overcome this scruple, as easily as I did many of his others, had I not depended at one time upon her meeting me at a midnight or late hour; when, if she had, it would have cost me a fall had she gone back; at other times, upon the cunning family's doing my work for me by driving her into my arms.

And then I knew that James and Arabella were determined never to leave off their foolish trials and provocations till, by tiring her out, they had either made her Solmes's wife; or guilty of such a rashness as should throw her for ever out of the favour of both her uncles.

Letter 104: MR LOVELACE TO JOHN BELFORD, ESQ.

(In continuation)

I OBLIGED the dear creature highly, I could perceive, by bringing Mrs Greme to attend her, and to suffer that good woman's recommendation of lodgings to take place, on her refusal to go to The Lawn.

She must observe that all my views were honourable, when I had provided for her no particular lodgings, leaving it to her choice whether she'd go to M. Hall, to The Lawn, to London, or to either of my aunts.

She was visibly pleased with my motion of putting Mrs Greme into the chaise with her, and riding on horseback myself.

Some people would have been apprehensive of what might pass between her and Mrs Greme. But as all my relations know the justice of my intentions by her, I was in no pain on that account. Especially as I had been always above hypocrisy, or wanting to be thought better than I am. And indeed, what occasion has a man to be an hypocrite, who has hitherto found his views upon the sex better answered for his being known to be a rake?—Why, even my beloved here, denied not to correspond with me, though her friends had taught her to think me one. Who then would be trying a new and worse character?

And then Mrs Greme is a pious matron, who would not have been biased against the truth on any consideration. She used formerly, while there were any hopes of my reformation, to pray for me. She hardly continues the good custom, I doubt; for her worthy lord makes no scruple, occasionally, to rave against me to man, woman and child, as they come in his way. He is very undutiful, as thou knowest. Surely, I may say so; since all duties are reciprocal. But for Mrs Greme, poor woman! when my lord has the gout, and is at The Lawn and the chaplain not to be found, she prays by him, or reads a chapter to him in the Bible or some other good book.

Was it not therefore right, to introduce such a good sort of woman to my beloved; and to leave them without reserve to their own talk?—And very busy in talk I saw they were, as they rode; and *felt* it too—for most charmingly glowed my cheeks.

I hope I shall be honest, I once more say: but as we frail mortals are not our own masters at all times, I must endeavour to keep the dear creature unapprehensive, until I can get her to our acquaintance's in London, or to some other safe place there. Should I, in the interim, give her the least room for suspicion; or offer to restrain her, or refuse to leave her at her own will; she can make her appeals to strangers, and call the country in upon me; and, perhaps, throw herself upon her relations on their own terms. And were I now to lose her, how unworthy should I be to be the prince and leader of such a confraternity as ours!—how unable to look up among men! or to show my face among women!—As things at present stand, she dare not own that she went off against her own consent; and I have taken care to make all the *implacables* believe that she escaped with it.

She has received an answer from Miss Howe, to the letter written to her from St Albans.[a]

Whatever are the contents, I know not; but she was drowned in tears; and I am the sufferer.

Miss Howe is a charming creature too; but confoundedly smart, and spiritful. I am a good deal afraid of her. Her mother can hardly keep her in. I must continue to play off *old Antony*, by my *honest Joseph*, upon that mother, in order to manage that daughter and oblige my beloved to an absolute dependence upon myself.[b]

Mistress Howe is impatient of contradiction. So is Miss. A young lady who is sensible that she has all the maternal requisites herself, to be under maternal control—fine ground for a man of intrigue to build upon! A mother over-notable; a daughter over-sensible; and their Hickman, who is—over-neither, but merely a passive—

Only that I have an object still more desirable!—

Yet how unhappy that these two young ladies lived so near each other, and are so well acquainted! Else how charmingly might I have managed them both!

But *one* man cannot have every woman worth having—pity though—when the man is such a VERY clever fellow!

Letter 105: MR LOVELACE TO JOHN BELFORD, ESQ.

(In continuation)

NEVER was there such a pair of scribbling lovers as we—yet perhaps whom it so much concerns to keep from each other what each writes. She *won't* have anything else to do. I *would*, if she'd let me. I am not reformed enough for a husband— *Patience is a virtue*, Lord M. says. *Slow and sure* is another of his sentences. If I had not a great deal of that virtue, I should not have waited the Harlowes' own time of ripening into execution my plots upon themselves, and upon their goddess daughter.

My beloved has been writing to her saucy friend, I believe, all that has befallen her, and what has passed between us hitherto. She will possibly have fine subjects for her pen, if she be as minute as I am to thee.

I would not be so barbarous as to permit old Antony to set Goody Howe against her, did I not dread the consequences of the correspondence between the two young ladies. So lively the one, so vigilant, so prudent both, who would not wish to outwit such girls, and to be able to twirl them round his finger?

a See Letter 92.
b See p. 145.

My charmer has written to her sister for her clothes, for some gold and for some of her books. What books can tell her more than she knows? But I can. So she had better study me.

She *may* write. She must be obliged to me at last, with her her pride. Miss Howe will be ready enough, indeed, to supply her; but I question whether she can do it without her mother, who is as covetous as the grave. And my agent's agent, Antony, has already given the mother a hint, which will make her jealous of *pecuniaries*.

Besides, if Miss Howe has money by her, I can put her mother upon borrowing it of her—Nor blame me, Jack, for contrivances that have their foundation in generosity. Thou knowest my spirit; and that I should be proud to lay an obligation upon my charmer to the amount of half my estate. Lord M. has more for me than I can ever wish for. My predominant passion is *girl*, not *gold*; nor value I *this*, but as it helps me to *that*, and gives me independence.

I was forced to put it into the sweet novice's head, as well for *my* sake as for hers (lest we should be traceable by *her* direction), whither to direct the sending of her clothes, if they incline to do her that small piece of justice.

If they do, I shall begin to dread a reconciliation; and must be forced to muse for a contrivance or two to prevent it; and to avoid mischief. For that (as I have told honest Joseph Leman) is a great point with me.

Thou wilt think me a sad fellow, I doubt—But are not all rakes sad fellows?—and thou, to thy little power, as bad as any? If thou dost all that's in thy head and in thy heart to do, thou art worse than me; for I do not, I assure thee.

I proposed, and she consented, that her clothes, or whatever else her relations should think fit to send her, should be directed to thee, at thy cousin Osgood's—Let a special messenger, at my charge, bring me any letter or portable parcel that shall come—If not portable, give me notice of it. But thou'lt have no trouble of this sort from her relations, I dare be sworn. And, in this assurance, I will leave them, I think, to act upon their own heads. A man would have no more to answer for than needs must.

But one thing, while I think of it (it is of great importance to be attended to)—You must hereafter write to me in character, as I shall do to you. How know we into whose hands our letters may fall? It would be a confounded thing to be blown up by a train of one's own laying.

Another thing remember; I have changed my name: Changed it without an Act of Parliament. 'Robert Huntingford' it is now. Continue *Esquire*. It is a respectable addition, although every sorry fellow assumes it, almost to the banishment of the usual travelling one of *Captain*. 'To be left till called for, at the posthouse at Hertford.'

Upon naming thee, she asked thy character. I gave thee a better than thou deservest, in order to do credit to *myself*. Yet I told her that thou wert an awkward puppy; and this to do credit to *thee*, that she may not, if ever she is to see thee, expect a cleverer fellow than she'll find. Yet thy *apparent* awkwardness befriends thee not a little: for wert thou a sightly varlet, people would discover nothing extraordinary in thee when they conversed with thee: whereas seeing a bear, they are surprised to find in thee anything that is like a man. Felicitate thyself then upon thy defects; which are so evidently thy principal perfections, and which occasion thee a distinction thou wouldst otherwise never have.

The lodgings we are in at present are not convenient. I was so delicate as to find fault with them, as communicating with each other, because I knew the lady would; and told her that were I sure she was safe from pursuit, I would leave her in them, since such was her earnest desire. The devil's in't, if I don't banish even the *shadow* of mistrust from her heart. She must be an infidel against all reason and appearances, if I don't.

Here are two young likely girls, daughters of the widow Sorlings: that's the name of our landlady.

I have only, at present, admired them in their dairy works. How greedily do the whole sex swallow praise!—So pleased was I with the youngest, for the elegance of her works, that I kissed her, and she made me a curtsy for my condescension; and blushed and seemed sensible all over. Encouragingly, yet innocently, she adjusted her handkerchief and looked towards the door, as much as to say she would not tell were I to kiss her again.

Her elder sister popped upon her. The conscious girl blushed again, and looked so confounded that I made an excuse for her which gratified both. Mrs Betty, said I, I have been so much pleased with the neatness of your dairy works, that I could not help saluting your sister: you have *your* share of merit in them, I am sure—give me leave—

Good souls!—I like them both—She curtsied too!—How I love a grateful temper! Oh that my Miss Harlowe were but half so acknowledging!

I think I must get one of them to attend my charmer when she removes. The mother seems to be a notable woman. She had not best, however, be *too* notable; for were she by suspicion to give a face of difficulty to the matter, it would prepare me for a trial with one or both the daughters.

Allow me a little rhodomontade, Jack!—but really and truly, my heart is fixed. I can think of no creature breathing of the sex but my Gloriana.

Letter 106: MR LOVELACE TO JOHN BELFORD, ESQ.

(In continuation)

THIS is Wednesday; the day that I was to have lost my charmer for ever!—With what high satisfaction and heart's-ease can I now sit down and triumph over my men in straw at Harlowe Place! Yet 'tis perhaps best for them that she got off as she did. Who knows what consequences might have followed upon my attending her in; or (if she had not met me) upon my projected visit, followed by my myrmidons?

But had I even gone in with her unaccompanied, I think I had but little reason for apprehension: for well thou knowest that the tame spirits which value themselves upon reputation, and are held within the skirts of the law by political considerations only, may be compared to an infectious spider; which will run into his hole the moment one of his threads is touched by a finger that can crush him, leaving all his toils defenceless, and to be brushed down at the will of the potent invader. While a silly fly, that has neither courage nor strength to resist, no sooner gives notice by its buzz and its struggle, of its being entangled, but out steps the self-circumscribed tyrant, winds round and round the poor insect, till he covers it with his bowel spun toils; and when so fully secured, that it can neither move leg nor wing, suspends it, as if for a spectacle to be exulted over: then stalking to the door of his cell, turns about, gloats over it at a distance; and sometimes advancing, sometimes retiring, preys at leisure upon its vitals.

But now I think of it, will not this comparison do as well for the entangled girls, as for the tame spirits?—Better, o' my conscience!—'Tis but comparing the spider to us brave fellows; and it quadrates.

Whatever our hearts are in, our heads will follow. Begin with spiders, with flies, with what we will, the girl is the centre of gravity, and we all naturally tend to it.

Nevertheless, to recur; I cannot but observe that these tame spirits stand a poor chance in a fairly offensive war with such of us mad fellows as are above all law, and scorn to skulk behind the hypocritical screen of reputation.

Thou knowest that I never scrupled to throw myself among numbers of adversaries; the more the safer. One or two, no fear, will take the part of a single adventurer, if not *intentionally*, in *fact:* holding him in, while others hold in the principal antagonist, to the augmentation of their mutual prowess, till both are prevailed upon to compromise, or one to [be] absent. So that upon the whole, the law-breakers have the advantage of the law-keepers all the world over; at least for a time, till they have run to the end of their race. Add to this, in the question between me and the Harlowes, that the whole family of them must know that they have injured me—Did they not, at their own church, cluster together like bees, when they saw me enter it? Nor knew they which should venture out first, when the service was over.

James, indeed, was not there. If he had, he would perhaps have endeavoured to *look* valiant. But there is a sort of valour in the *face*, which, by its *over*-bluster, shows fear in the *heart:* Just such a face would James Harlowe's have been, had I made them a visit.

When I have had such a face and such a heart as that to deal with, I have been all calm and serene, and left it to the friends of such a one, as I have done to the Harlowes, to do my work for me.

I am about mustering up in my memory all that I have ever done that has been thought praiseworthy, or but barely tolerable. I am afraid thou canst not help me to many remembrances of this sort; because I never was so bad as since I have known thee.

Have I not had it in my heart to do *some* good that thou canst remind me of? Study for me, Jack. I have recollected several instances, which I think will *tell in*— But see if thou canst not help me to some which I may have forgot.

This I may venture to say, that the principal blot in my escutcheon is owing to these girls, these confounded girls. But for *them*, I could go to church with a good conscience: but when I do, there they are. Everywhere does Satan spread his snares for me!

But, now I think of it, what if our governors should appoint churches for the *women* only, and others for the men?—Full as proper, I think, for the promoting of *true piety* in both (much better than the synagogue lattices) as separate boarding-schools for their *education.*

There are already male and female dedications of churches.

St Swithin's, St Stephen's, St Thomas's, St George's, and so forth, might be appropriated to the men; and the Santa Katharina's, Santa Anna's, Santa Maria's, Santa Margaretta's, for the women!

Yet, were it so, and life to be the forfeiture of being found at the female churches, I believe I should, like a second Clodius, change my dress to come at my Portia or Calpurnia,[1] though one the daughter of a Cato, the other the wife of a Caesar.

But how I *excurse!*—Yet thou usedst to say, thou likest my excursions. If thou dost, thou'lt have enow of them. For I never had a subject I so much adored; and with which I shall probably be compelled to have so much patience, before I strike the blow; if the blow I do strike.

But let me call myself back to my *recordation*-subject—Thou needest not to remind me of my *Rosebud*. I have her in my head; and moreover have contrived to give my fair one a hint of that affair, by the agency of honest Joseph Leman[a]; although I have not reaped the hoped-for credit of her acknowledgement—

That's the devil; and it was always my hard fate—Everything I do that is good is but as I *ought!*—Everything of a contrary nature is brought into the most glaring light against me!—Is this fair? Ought not a balance to be struck? and the credit carried to my account?—Yet I must own too that I half grudge Johnny this blooming maiden; for, in truth, I think a fine woman too rich a jewel to hang about a poor man's neck.

Surely, Jack, if I am in a fault in my universal adorations of the sex, the *women* in general ought to love me the better for it.

And so they do, I thank them heartily; except here and there a covetous little rogue comes cross me, who, under the pretence of loving virtue for its own sake, wants to have me all to herself—

I have rambled enough—

Adieu, for the present.

Letter 107: MISS CLARISSA HARLOWE TO MISS HOWE

Thursday night, April 13

I ALWAYS loved writing, and my unhappy situation gives me now enough of it; and you, I fear, too much—I have had another very warm debate with Mr Lovelace. It brought on the subject which you advised me not to decline when it handsomely offered. And I want to have either your acquittal or blame, for having suffered it to go off without effect.

The impatient wretch sent up to me several times, while I was writing my last to you, to desire my company; yet his business nothing particular; only to hear *him* talk. The man seems pleased with his own volubility; and, whenever he has collected together abundance of smooth things, he wants me to find ears for them. Yet he need not: for I don't often gratify him either with giving him the praise, or showing the pleasure in his verboseness, that he would be fond of.

When I had dispatched the letter, and given it to Mr Hickman's friend, I was going up again: but he besought me to stop, and hear what he had to say.

Nothing, as I said, to any new purpose—but complainings, and those in a manner, and with an air, as I thought, that bordered upon insolence—He could not live, he told me, unless he had more of my company, and of my *indulgence* too, than I had yet given him.

a See pp. 269, 284–6, 286–7.

Hereupon I stepped into the parlour, not a little out of humour with him; and the more, as he has very quietly taken up his quarters here, without talking of removing.

We began presently our angry conference. He provoked me; and I repeated several of the plainest things I had said before; and particularly told him that I was every hour more and more dissatisfied with myself, and with him: that he was not a man who, in my opinion, improved upon acquaintance: and that I should not be easy till he had left me to myself.

He might be surprised at my warmth, perhaps—But really the man looked so like a simpleton; hesitating, and having nothing to say for himself, or that should excuse the peremptoriness of his demand upon me (when he knew I was writing a letter, which a gentleman waited for), that I flung from him, declaring that I would be mistress of my own time, and of my own actions, without being called to account for either.

He was very uneasy till he could again be admitted into my company. And when I was obliged to see him, which was sooner than I liked, never did man put on a more humble and respectful demeanour.

He told me that he had, upon this occasion, been entering into himself, and had found a great deal of reason to blame himself for an impatiency and inconsideration which, although he meant nothing by it, must be very disagreeable to one of my delicacy. That having always aimed at a manly sincerity and openness of heart, he had not till now discovered that both were very consistent with that true politeness, which he feared he had too much disregarded while he sought to avoid the contrary extreme; knowing that in me he had to deal with a lady who despised a hypocrite, and who was above all flattery. But from this time forth, I should find such an alteration in his whole behaviour as might be expected from a man, who knew himself to be honoured with the presence and conversation of a person who had the most delicate mind in the world—that was his flourish.

I said that he might perhaps expect congratulation upon the discovery he had just now made, that true politeness and sincerity were very compatible: But that I, who had by a perverse fate been thrown into his company, had abundant reason for regret, that he had not sooner found this out: since, I believed, very few men of birth and education were strangers to it.

He knew not, *neither*, he said, that he had so badly behaved himself as to deserve so very severe a rebuke.

Perhaps not. But he might, if so, make another discovery from what I had said; which might be to *my own* disadvantage: since, if he had so much reason to be satisfied with *himself*, he would see what an ungenerous person he spoke to, who, when he seemed to give himself airs of humility, which perhaps he thought beneath him to assume, had not the civility to make him a compliment upon them; but was ready to take him at his word.

He had long, with infinite pleasure, the pretended flattery-hater said, admired my superior talents, and a wisdom in so young a lady, perfectly surprising!

Lady he calls me, at every word, perhaps in compliment to himself. As I endeavour to repeat his words with exactness, you'll be pleased, once for all, to excuse me for repeating this. I have no title to it. And I am sure I am too much mortified at present to take any pride in that, or any other of his compliments.

Let him stand ever so low in my opinion, he said, he should believe all were just;

and that he had nothing to do, but to govern himself for the future by my example, and by the standard I should be pleased to give him.

I told him I knew better than to value myself upon this volubility of speech. As he pretended to pay so preferable a regard to sincerity, he should confine himself to the strict rules of truth, when he spoke of me, to myself: and then, although he should be so kind as to imagine he had *reason* to make me a compliment, he would have much more to pride himself in his arts, that had made so *extraordinary* a young creature so great a fool.

Really, my dear, the man deserves not politer treatment!—And then has he not made a fool, an egregious fool, of me?—I am afraid he thinks so himself—

He was surprised! He was amazed! at so strange a turn upon him!—He was very unhappy that nothing he could do or say would give me a good opinion of him. He wished I would let him know what he *could* do to obtain my confidence—

I told him I desired his absence, of all things. I saw not that my friends thought it worth their while to give me disturbance: therefore, if he would set out for London, or Berkshire, or whither he pleased, it would be most agreeable to me, and most reputable too.

He would do so, he said, he intended to do so, the moment I was in a place to my liking—in a place convenient for me.

This would be so, I told him, when he was not here, to break in upon me, and make the apartments inconvenient.

He did not think this place safe; and as I had not had thoughts of staying here, he had not been so solicitous, as otherwise he should have been, to enjoin privacy to his servants, nor to Mrs Greme, at her leaving me; and there were two or three gentlemen in the neighbourhood, he said, with whose servants his gossiping rascals had scraped acquaintance: so that he could not think of leaving me here unguarded and unattended. But fix upon any place in England where I could be out of danger, and undiscovered, and he would go to the furthermost part of the king's dominions, if, by doing so, he could make me easy.

I told him plainly that I should never be in humour with myself for meeting him; nor with him, for seducing me away: that my regrets increased, instead of diminished: that my reputation was wounded: that nothing I could do would now retrieve it: And that he must not wonder if I every hour grew more and more uneasy both with myself and him: that upon the whole, I was willing to take care of myself; and when *he* had left me, I should best know what to resolve upon, and whither to go.

He wished, he said, he were at liberty, without giving me offence, or being thought to intend to infringe upon the articles that I had stipulated and insisted upon, to make one humble proposal to me—But the sacred regard he was determined to pay to all my injunctions (reluctantly as I had on Monday last put it into his power to serve me) would not permit him to make it, unless I would promise to excuse him, if I did not approve of it.

I asked in some confusion, what he would say?

He prefaced and paraded on; and then out came, with great diffidence and many apologies, and a bashfulness which sat very awkwardly upon him, a proposal of speedy solemnization: which, he said, would put all right: would make my first three or four months which otherwise must be passed in obscurity and apprehension, a round of visits and visitings to and from all his relations; to Miss Howe; to whom I pleased: and would pave the way to the reconciliation I had so much at heart.

Your advice had great weight with me just then, as well as his reasons, and the consideration of my unhappy situation. But what could I say? I wanted somebody to speak for me: I could not, all at once, act as if I thought that *all punctilio was at an end*. I was unwilling to suppose it *was* so soon.

The man saw I was not angry at his motion. I only blushed up to the ears; that I am sure I did: looked silly, and like a fool.

He wants not courage. Would he have had me catch at his first, at his *very* first word?—I was *silent* too!—And do not the bold sex take silence for a mark of favour?—Then, *so lately* in my father's house! Having also declared to him in my letters, before I had your advice, that I would not think of marriage till he had passed through a state of probation, as I may call it—How was it possible I could encourage with very ready signs of approbation such an early proposal? especially so soon after the free treatment he had provoked from me—If I were to die, I could not.

He looked at me with great confidence; as if (notwithstanding his contradictory bashfulness) he would look me through, while my eye but now and then could glance at him. He begged my pardon with great obsequiousness: he was *afraid* I would think he deserved no other answer, but that of a contemptuous silence. True love was fearful of offending—(Take care, Lovelace, thought I, how yours is tried by that rule.) Indeed so sacred a regard (foolish man!) would he have to all my declarations made before I honoured him—

I would hear him no further; but withdrew in too visible confusion, and left him to make his nonsensical flourishes to himself.

I will only add that, if he really wishes for a speedy solemnization, he never could have had a luckier time to press for my consent to it. But he let it go off; and indignation has taken place of it; and now it shall be my point to get him at a distance from me.

I am, my dearest friend,

Your ever faithful and obliged servant,
CL. H.

Letter 108: MR LOVELACE TO JOHN BELFORD, ESQ.

WHAT can be done with a woman who is above flattery, and despises all praise but that which flows from the approbation of her own heart?

But why will this admirable creature urge her destiny? Why will she defy the power she is absolutely dependent upon?—Why will she still wish to my face that she had never left her father's house?—Why will she deny me her company, till she makes me lose my patience, and lay myself open to her resentment?—And why, when she is offended, does she carry her indignation to the utmost length that a scornful beauty in the very height of her power and pride can go?

Is it prudent, thinkst thou, in her circumstances, to tell me, *repeatedly* to tell me that she is every hour more and more dissatisfied with herself and me? That I am not one who improve upon her in my conversation and address? (Couldst thou,

Jack, bear this from a captive!) That she shall not be easy while she is with me? That she was thrown upon me by a perverse fate? That she knew better than to value herself upon my volubility? That if I thought she deserved the compliments I made her, I might pride myself in my arts, which had made a fool of so extraordinary a person? That she should never forgive herself for *meeting me*, nor me for *seducing* her away? (Her very words!) That her regrets increase instead of diminish? That she would take care of herself; and since her friends thought it not worth while to pursue her, she would be left to that care? That I should make Mrs Sorlings's house more agreeable by my absence?—and go to Berks, to town, or wherever I would (to the devil, I suppose), with all her heart?

The impolitic charmer!—To a temper so vindictive as she thinks mine! To a free-liver, as she believes me to be, who has her in his power!—I was *before*, as thou knowest, balancing; now this scale, now that, the heaviest. I only waited to see how *her* will would work, how *mine* would lead me on. Thou seest what bias hers takes—and wilt thou doubt that mine will be determined by it?—Were not her faults before this numerous enough?—Why will she put me upon looking back?—

I will sit down to argue with myself by and by, and thou shalt be acquainted with the result.

If thou knewest, if thou but beheldest, the abject slave she made me look like!—I had given myself high airs, as *she* called them: but they were airs that showed my love for her: that showed I could not live out of her company. But she took me down with a vengeance! She made me look about me. So much advantage had she over me; such severe turns upon me; by my soul, Jack, I had hardly a word to say for myself. I am ashamed to tell thee what a poor creature she made me look like!—But I could have told her something that would have humbled her pretty pride at the instant, had she been in a proper place, and proper company about her.

To such a place then—and where she cannot fly me—And *then* to see how my will works, and what can be done by the *amorous see-saw*; now humble; now proud; now expecting, or demanding; now submitting, or acquiescing—till I have tired resistance. But these hints are at present enough—I may further explain myself as I go along; and as I confirm or recede in my future motions. If she *will* revive past disobligations!—If she *will*—But no more—No more, as I said, at present, of threatenings.

Letter 109: MR LOVELACE TO JOHN BELFORD, ESQ.

(In continuation)
AND do I not see that I shall need nothing but patience, in order to have all power with me? For what shall we say, if all these complaints of a character wounded; these declarations of increasing regrets for meeting me; of resentments never to be got over for my *seducing* her away: These angry commands to leave her—what shall we say, if all were to mean nothing but MATRIMONY?—And what if my forbearing to enter upon that subject come out to be the true cause of her petulance and uneasiness?

I had once before played about the skirts of the irrevocable obligation; but thought myself obliged to speak in clouds, and to run away from the subject as soon as she took my meaning, lest she should imagine it to be ungenerously urged, now she was in some sort in my power, as she had forbid me, beforehand, to touch upon it, till I were in a state of visible reformation, and till a reconciliation with her friends were probable. But now, out-argued, out-talented, and pushed so vehemently to *leave one*, whom I had no good pretence to *hold*, if she *would* go; and who could so easily, if I had given her cause to doubt, have thrown herself into other protection, or have returned to Harlowe Place and Solmes; I spoke out upon the subject, and offered reasons, although with infinite doubt and hesitation (*lest she should be offended at me*, Belford!), why she should assent to the legal tie, and make me the happiest of men. And oh how the mantled cheek, the downcast eye, the silent, yet trembling lip, and the heaving bosom, a sweet collection of heightened beauties, gave evidence that the tender was not mortally offensive!

Charming creature, thought I (but I charge thee, that thou let not any of the sex know my exultation), is it so *soon* come to this?—Am I *already* lord of the destiny of a Clarissa Harlowe!—Am I already the reformed man thou resolvedst I *should* be, before I had the *least* encouragement given me? Is it thus, that *the more thou knowest me*, the *less thou seest reason to approve of me?*—And can art and design enter into the breast so celestial; To banish me from thee, to insist so rigorously upon my absence, in order to bring me closer to thee, and make the blessing dear?—Well do *thy* arts justify *mine*; and encourage me to let loose my plotting genius upon thee.

But let me tell thee, charming maid, if thy wishes are at all to be answered, that thou hast yet to account to me for thy reluctance to go off with me, at a crisis when thy going off was necessary to avoid being forced into the nuptial fetters with a wretch, that were he not thy aversion, thou wert no more honest to thy own merit than to me.

I am *accustomed* to be preferred, let me tell thee, by thy equals in rank too, though thy inferiors in merit; but who is not so! And shall I marry a woman who has given me reason to doubt the preference she has for me?

No, my dearest love, I have too sacred a regard for thy *injunctions*, to let them be broke through, even by thyself. Nor will I take in thy full meaning, by blushing silence only. Nor shalt thou give me room to doubt whether it be necessity or love that inspires this condescending impulse.

Upon these principles, what had I to do, but to construe her silence into contemptuous displeasure? And I begged her pardon for making a motion which I had so much *reason* to fear would offend her: For the future I would pay a sacred regard to her previous injunctions, and prove to her, by all my conduct, the truth of that observation, that true love is always fearful of offending!—

And what could the lady say to this? methinks thou askest.

Say!—Why she looked vexed, disconcerted, teased; was at a loss, as I thought, whether to be more angry with herself or me. She turned about, however, as if to hide a starting tear; and drew a sigh into two or three but just audible quavers, trying to suppress it; and withdrew, leaving me master of the field.

Tell me not of politeness: tell me not of generosity: tell me not of compassion:— Is she not a match for me? *More* than a match? Does she not outdo me at every fair weapon? Has she not made me doubt her love? Has she not taken officious pains to declare that she was not averse to Solmes for any respect she had to me? and her sorrow for putting herself out of *his* reach; that is to say, for meeting me?

Then what a triumph would it be to the *Harlowe pride*, were I now to marry this lady?—A family beneath my own!—no one in it worthy of an alliance with, but her!—my own estate not contemptible!—living within the bounds of it, to avoid dependence upon *their* betters, and obliged to no man living!—my expectations still so much *more* considerable—my person, my talents—not to be despised, surely—yet rejected by them with scorn—obliged to carry on an underhand address to their daughter when two of the most considerable families in the kingdom have made overtures, which I have declined, partly for her sake, and partly because I never will marry if *she* be not the person: to be forced to *steal* her away; not only from *them*, but from *herself*—And must I be brought to implore forgiveness and reconciliation from the Harlowes?—beg to be acknowledged as the *son* of a gloomy tyrant, whose only boast is his riches? As a *brother* to a wretch who has conceived immortal hatred to me; and to a sister who was beneath my attempts, or I would have had her *in my own way* (and that with a tenth part of the trouble and pains that her sister, whom she has so barbarously insulted, has cost me, yet not a step advanced with *her*)? And, finally, as a *nephew* to uncles who valuing themselves upon their *acquired* fortunes would insult me, as creeping to them on that account?—Forbid it the blood of the Lovelaces, that your *last*, and, let me say, not the *meanest* of your stock, should thus creep, thus fawn, thus lick the dust, for a WIFE!—

Proceed anon.

Letter 110: MR LOVELACE TO JOHN BELFORD, ESQ.

(In continuation)

BUT is it not the divine Clarissa (Harlowe let me not say; my soul spurns them all but her) whom I am thus by implication threatening?—If virtue be the true nobility, how is she ennobled, and how would an alliance with her ennoble, were there no drawbacks from the family she is sprung from, and prefers to me?

But again let me stop—Is there not something wrong; *has* there not been something wrong in this divine creature?—And will not the reflections upon that wrong (what though it may be construed in my favour?) make me unhappy, when *novelty* has lost its charms, and she is mind and person all my own?—Libertines are nicer, if *at all* nice, than other men. They seldom meet with the stand of virtue in the women whom they attempt. And by those they have met with, they judge of all the rest. *Importunity* and *opportunity* no woman is proof against, especially from a persevering lover, who knows how to suit temptations to inclinations. This, thou knowest, is a prime article of the rake's creed.

And what! (methinks thou askest with surprise): dost thou question this most admirable of women?—The virtue of a CLARISSA dost thou question?

I do not, I dare not question it. My reverence for her will not let me, *directly*, question it. But let me, in my turn, ask thee—Is not, may not her virtue be founded rather in *pride* than *principle*?—Whose daughter is she?—And is she not a *daughter*? If impeccable, how came she by her impeccability?—The pride of setting an example to her sex has run away with her hitherto, and may have made her till *now* invincible—But is not that pride abated?—What may not both men and women be brought to do in a mortified state? What mind is superior to calamity?—Pride is perhaps the principal bulwark of female virtue. Humble a woman, and may she not be *effectually* humbled?

Then who says Miss Clarissa Harlowe is the paragon of virtue? Is virtue itself?

All who know her, and have heard of her, it will be answered.

Common bruit!—Is virtue to be established by common bruit only?—Has her virtue ever been *proved?*—Who has dared to try her virtue?

I told thee I would sit down to argue with myself; and I have drawn myself into the argumentation before I was aware.

Let me enter into a strict discussion of this subject.

I know how ungenerous an appearance what I have said, and what I have farther to say, on this topic, will have from me: but am I not bringing virtue to the touchstone with a view to exalt it, if it come out to be virtue?—Avaunt then, for one moment, all consideration that may arise from a weakness, which some would miscall *gratitude*; and is oftentimes the corrupter of a heart not ignoble!

To the test then. And I will bring this charming creature to the strictest test that all the sex, who may be shown any passages in my letters (and I know thou cheerest the hearts of all thy acquaintance with such detached parts of mine as tend not to dishonour characters, or reveal names; and this gives me an appetite to oblige thee by *interlardment*), *that all the sex*, I say, may see what they ought to be; what is expected from them; and if they have to deal with a person of reflection and punctilio (*pride*, if thou wilt), how careful they ought to be, by a regular and uniform conduct, not to give him cause to think lightly of them, by favours granted, which may be interpreted into *natural weakness.* For is not a wife the keeper of a man's honour? And do not her faults bring more disgrace upon a husband than even upon herself?

It is not for nothing, Jack, that I have disliked the life of shackles!—

To the test, then, as I said, since now I have the question brought home to me, whether I am to have a wife? And whether she be to be a wife at the first or at the second hand?

I will proceed fairly; I will do the dear creature not only strict, but generous justice; for I will try her by her own judgement, as well as by our principles.

She blames herself for having corresponded with me, a man of free character; and one indeed whose *first* view it was, to draw her into this correspondence; and who succeeded in it, by means unknown to herself.

Now, what were her inducements to this correspondence?—If not what her niceness makes her *think* blameworthy, why does she blame herself!

Has she been *capable* of error?—Of persisting in that error?

Whoever was the *tempter*, that is not the thing; nor what the *temptation.* The *fact*, the *error*, is not before us.

Did she persist in it against parental prohibition?

She owns she did.

Was there ever known to be a daughter who had higher notions of the filial duty, of the parental authority?

Never.

What must be those inducements, how strong, that were too strong for duty, in a daughter so *dutiful?*—What must *my* thought have been of them, what *my* hopes built upon them, at the time, taken in this light?

Well, but it will be said that her principal view was to prevent mischief between her brother and her other friends, and the man vilely insulted by them all.

But why should she be more concerned for the safety of others than they were for their own?—And had not the *rencounter* then happened?—Was a person of virtue to be prevailed upon to break through her *apparent*, her *acknowledged* duty, upon *any* consideration?—Much less was she to be so prevailed upon to prevent an *apprehended* evil only?

Thou, Lovelace, the tempter (thou'lt again break out and say) to be the accuser!

But I am *not* the accuser. I am an arguer only, and in my heart all the time acquit and worship the divine creature. But let me, nevertheless, examine whether the acquittal be owing to her *merit*, or to my *weakness*, the true name for love.

But shall we suppose another motive?—And that is Love; a motive which all the world will excuse her for—But let me tell all the world that do, *not* because they *ought*, but because all the world is apt to be misled by it.

Let Love then be the motive—love of *whom*?

A *Lovelace* is the answer.

Is there but one Lovelace in the world?—May not more Lovelaces be attracted by so fine a figure? by such exalted qualities?—It was her character that drew me to her: and it was her beauty and good sense that rivetted my chains; and now, all together make me think her [a] subject worthy of my attempts; worthy of my ambition.

But has she had the candour, the openness, to *acknowledge* that love?

She has not.

Well then, if love it be at bottom, is there not another vice lurking beneath the shadow of that love?—Has she not *affectation?*—or is it *pride of heart?*

And what results—Is then the divine Clarissa Harlowe capable of *loving* a man whom she ought *not* to love?—And is she capable of *affectation?* And is her virtue founded in *pride?*—And if this answer be affirmative, must she not then be a *woman?*

And can she keep this lover at bay?—Can she make *him*, who has been accustomed to triumph over other women, tremble?—Can she so conduct herself as to make him, at times, question whether she loves *him* or *any* man; yet not have the requisite command over the passion itself, in steps of the highest consequence to her honour, as *she* thinks (I am trying her, Jack, by her own thoughts)—but suffer herself to be provoked to promise to abandon her father's house, and go off with him, knowing his character; and even conditioning not to marry till improbable and remote contingencies were to come to pass?—What though the provocations were such as would justify any other woman; yet was a Clarissa to be susceptible to provocations which she thinks *herself* highly censurable for being so much moved by?

But let us see the dear creature resolving to revoke her promise; yet meeting her lover; a bold and intrepid man, who was more than once before disappointed by her; and who comes, as she must think, prepared to expect the fruits of her appointment, and resolved to carry her off. And let us see him actually carrying her off; and having her at his mercy—May there not be, I repeat, other Lovelaces; other like intrepid persevering enterprisers; although they may not go to work in the same way?

And has then a Clarissa (herself her judge) failed?—In such great points failed?—And may she not *further* fail?—Fail in the *greatest* point, to which all the other points in which she has failed, have but a natural tendency?

Nor say thou that virtue, in the eye of heaven, is as much a *manly* as a *womanly* grace (by virtue in this place I mean chastity, and to be superior to temptation; my Clarissa out of the question). Nor ask thou: Shall the man be guilty, yet expect the woman to be guiltless, and even unsuspectable?—Urge thou not these arguments, I say, since the wife by a failure may do much more injury to the husband, than the husband can do to the wife, and not only to her husband, but to all his family, by obtruding another man's children into his possessions, perhaps to the exclusion of (at least to a participation with) his own; he believing them all the time to be his. In the eye of heaven, therefore, the sin *cannot* be equal. Besides, I have read in some place *that the woman was made for the man*, not *the man for the woman*.[1] Virtue then is less to be dispensed with in the woman than in the man.

Thou, Lovelace (methinks some better man than thyself will say), to expect such perfection in a woman!—

Yes, I, may I answer. Was not the great Caesar a great rake as to women?—Was he not called, by his very soldiers, on one of his triumphant entries into Rome, *the bald-pated lecher?*—and warning given of him to the *wives*, as well as to the daughters, of his fellow-citizens?—Yet did not Caesar repudiate his wife for being only in company with Clodius, or rather because Clodius, though by surprise upon her, was found in hers? And what was the reason he gave for it?—It was this (though a rake himself, as I have said) and only this—*The wife of Caesar must not be suspected!*—

Caesar was not a prouder man than Lovelace.

Go to then, Jack; nor say, nor let anybody say in thy hearing, that Lovelace, a man valuing himself upon his ancestry, is singular in his expectations of a wife's purity, though not pure himself.

As to my CLARISSA, I own that I hardly think there ever was such an angel of a woman. But has she not, as above, already taken steps which she herself condemns? Steps which the world, and her own family, did not think her *capable* of taking?—And for which her own family will not forgive her?

Nor think it strange that I refuse to hear anything pleaded in behalf of a standard virtue, from high provocations. Are not provocations and temptations the tests of virtue?—A standard virtue must not be allowed to be *provoked* to destroy or annihilate itself.

May not then the success of him who could carry her *thus far* be allowed to be an encouragement for him to try to carry her *farther?*—'Tis but to try, Jack—Who will be afraid of a trial for this divine lady?—Thou knowest that I have more than once, twice or thrice been tempted to make this trial upon young ladies of name and character: but never yet found one of them to hold me out for a month; nor so long as could puzzle my invention. I have concluded against the whole sex upon it. And now, if I have not found a virtue that cannot be corrupted, I will swear that there is not one such in the whole sex. Is not then the whole sex concerned that this trial should be made?—and who is it that knows her, that would not stake upon her head the honour of the whole?—Let her who would refuse it, come forth and desire to stand in her place.

I must assure thee that I have a prodigious high opinion of virtue; as I have of all those graces and excellencies which I have not been able to attain myself. Every free liver would not *say* this, nor *think* thus—every argument he uses, condemnatory of his own actions, as some would think—But ingenuity was ever a signal part of my character.

Satan, whom thou mayest, if thou wilt, in this case call my instigator, put the good man of old[2] upon the severest trials. To his behaviour under these trials, that good man owed his honour and his future rewards. An innocent person, if doubted, must wish to be brought to a fair and candid trial.

Rinaldo, indeed, in Ariosto, put the Mantuan knight's cup of trial from him, which was to be the proof of his wife's chastity[a]—This was his argument for forbearing the experiment: 'Why should I seek a thing I should be loath to find? My wife is a woman: the sex is frail. I cannot believe better of her than I do. It will be to my own loss, if I find reason to think worse.' But Rinaldo would not have refused the trial of the lady before she became his wife, and when he might have availed himself by detecting her.

For my part, I would not have put the cup from me, though married, had it been but in hope of finding reason to confirm my *good* opinion of my wife's honour; and that I might know whether I had a snake or a dove in my bosom.

To my point—What must that virtue be which will not stand a trial?—What that woman, who would wish to shun it?

Well then, a trial seems necessary for the further establishment of the honour of so excellent a creature.

And who shall put her to this trial?—Who but the man who has, as she thinks, already induced her in *lesser* points to swerve?—And this for her *own sake*, in a double sense—not only as he has been able to make some impression, but as she regrets the impression made; and so may be presumed to be guarded against his further attempts.

The situation she is at present in, it must be confessed, is a disadvantageous one to her: but if she overcome, that will redound to her honour.

Shun not, therefore, my dear soul, further trials, nor hate me for making them—For what woman can be said to be virtuous till she has been tried?

Nor is one effort, one trial, to be sufficient. Why? Because a woman's heart may be at one time *adamant*, at another *wax*—as I have often experienced. And so, no doubt, hast thou.

A fine time on't, methinks, thou sayest, would the women have if they were all to be tried!

But, Jack, I am not for that, neither. Though I am a rake, I am not a rake's friend; except thine and company's.

And be this one of the morals of my tedious discussion: 'Let the little rogues who would not be *put to the question*, as I may call it, choose accordingly—Let them prefer to their favour good honest, sober fellows, who have not been used to play dogs tricks: who will be willing to take them as they *offer*; and who, being tolerable themselves, are not suspicious of others.'

But what, methinks thou askest, is to become of the lady if she fail?

What?—Why will she not *if once subdued* be *always subdued?* another of our libertine maxims—And what an immense pleasure to a marriage-hater, what

---

a The story is that whoever drank of this cup, if his wife were chaste, could drink without spilling: if otherwise, the contrary. See Ariosto's *Orlando Furioso* [(1516–32); trans. Sir John Harington (1591)], Book xliii.

rapture to thought, to be able to prevail upon such a lady as Miss Clarissa Harlowe to live with him without *real* change of name!

But if she resist—if nobly she stand her trial—

Why then I will marry her, to be sure; and bless my stars for such an angel of a wife.

But will she not hate thee?—Will she not refuse—

No, no, Jack!—Circumstanced and situated as we are, I am not afraid of that—And hate me!—Why should she hate the man who loves her upon proof?—

And then for a little hint at *reprisal*—Am I not justified in my resolutions of trying *her* virtue, who is resolved, as I may say, to try *mine?*—who has declared that she will not marry me till she has hopes of my reformation?

And now, to put an end to this sober argumentation, wilt thou not thyself (whom I have supposed an advocate for the lady, because I know that Lord M. has put thee upon using the interest he thinks thou hast in me to persuade me to enter the pale; *wilt thou not thyself*) allow me to try if I cannot awaken the *woman* in her?—to try if she, with all that glowing symmetry of parts and that full bloom of vernal graces, by which she attracts every eye, be really inflexible as to the grand article?

Let me begin then, as opportunity presents—I will—and watch her every step to find one sliding one; her every moment to find the moment critical. And the rather, as she spares not me but takes every advantage that offers to puzzle and plague me; nor expects, nor thinks me to be a good man. If she be a *woman*, and *love* me, I shall surely catch her once tripping: for love was ever a traitor to its harbourer: and Love *within*, and I *without*, she'll be *more* than woman, as the poet says, or I *less* than man, if I succeed not.[3]

Now, Belford, all is out. The lady is mine; shall be *more* mine—Marriage, I see, is in my power, now she is so (else perhaps it had not). If I can have her *without*, who can blame me for trying? If *not*, great will be her glory, and my future confidence—and well will she merit the sacrifice I shall make her of my liberty; and from all her sex honours next to divine, for giving a proof that there was once a woman whose virtue no trials, no stratagems, no temptations, even from the man she hated not, could overpower.

Now wilt thou see all my circulation: as in a glass wilt thou see it. CABALA, however, is the word[a]; nor let the secret escape thee even in thy dreams.

Nobody doubts that she is to be my wife. Let her pass for such when I give the word. Meantime reformation shall be my stalking-horse; some one of the women in London, if I can get her thither, my bird—And so much for this time.

Letter III: MISS HOWE TO MISS CLARISSA HARLOWE

(In answer to Letters 101, 107)

DON'T be so much concerned, my dearest friend, at the bickerings between my mamma and me. We love one another dearly notwithstanding. If my mamma had not me to find fault with, she must find fault with somebody else. And as to me, I am a very saucy girl; and were there not this occasion, there would be some other to show it.

a This word, whenever used by any of these gentlemen, was agreed to imply an inviolable secret.

You have heard me *say* that this was always the case between us—You could not *otherwise* have known it. For when *you* was with us, you harmonized us both; and indeed I was always more afraid of you than of my mamma. But then that awe is accompanied with love. Your reproofs (as I have always found) are so charmingly mild and instructive! so evidently calculated to improve, and not to provoke, that a generous temper must be amended by them—But here now, mind my mamma, when you are not with us—*You shall, I tell you, Nancy!—I will have it so!—Don't I know best!—I won't be disobeyed!*—How can a daughter of spirit bear such language! such looks too with the language; and not have a longing mind to disobey?

Don't advise me, my dear, to obey my mamma in her prohibition of corresponding with you. She has no reason for it. Nor would she of her own judgement have prohibited me. That odd old ambling soul your uncle (whose visits are frequenter than ever), instigated by your malicious and selfish brother and sister, is the occasion. And they only have borrowed my mamma's lips, at the distance they are from you, for a sort of speaking-trumpet for them. The prohibition, once more I say, cannot come from her heart: but if it did, is so much danger to be apprehended from my continuing to write to one of my own sex, as if I wrote to one of the other? Don't let dejection and disappointment, and the course of oppression which you have run through, weaken your mind, my dearest creature; and make you see inconveniencies where there possibly cannot be any. If your talent is *scribbling*, as you call it; so is mine—And I will scribble on, at all opportunities; and to you; let 'em say what they will—Nor let your letters be filled with the self-accusations you mention: there is no cause for them. I wish that your Anna Howe, who continues in her mother's house, were but half so good as Miss Clarissa Harlowe, who has been driven out of her father's.

I will say nothing upon your letter to your sister, till I see the effect it will have. You hope, you tell me, that you shall have your money and clothes sent you, notwithstanding what I write of my opinion to the contrary. I am sorry to have it to acquaint you, that I have just now heard that they have sat in council upon your letter; and that your mamma was the only person who was for sending you your things; and was over-ruled. I charge you therefore to accept of my offer, as by my last; and give me particular directions for what you want that I can supply you with besides.

Don't set your thoughts so much upon a reconciliation as to prevent your laying hold of any handsome opportunity to give yourself a protector; such a one as the man will be who, I imagine, husband-like, will let nobody insult you but himself.

What could he mean by letting slip such a one as that you mention?—I don't know how to blame you neither. How could you go beyond silence and blushes, when the foolish fellow came with his observances of the restrictions which you laid him under when in another situation? But, as I told you above, you really strike people into awe. And, upon my word, you did not spare him.

I repeat what I said in my last, that you have a very nice part to act: and I will add that you have a mind that is much too delicate for your part. But when the lover is exalted, the lady must be humbled. He is naturally proud and saucy. I doubt you must engage his *pride*, which he calls his *honour*: and that you must throw off a little more of the veil. And I would have you restrain your wishes before him, that you had not met him; and the like—What signifies wishing, my dear?—He will not bear it. You can hardly expect that he will.

Nevertheless it vexes me to the very bottom of my pride, that any wretch of that sex should have such a triumph over such a lady.

I cannot, however, but say that I am charmed with your spirit. So much sweetness, where sweetness is requisite; so much spirit, where spirit is called for—what a *true* magnanimity!

But I doubt, in your present circumstances, you must endeavour after a little more of the reserve, and palliate a little—That humility which he puts on when you rise upon him is not natural to him.

Methinks I see the man hesitating, and looking like the fool you paint him, under your corrective superiority!—But he is not a fool. Don't put him upon mingling resentment with his love.

You are very serious, my dear, in the first of the two letters before me, in relation to Mr Hickman and me; and in relation to my mamma and me. But, as to the latter, you must not be too grave. If we are not well together at one time, we are not ill together at another. And while I am able to make my mamma smile in the midst of the most angry fit she ever fell into on the present occasion (though sometimes she would not, if she could help it), it is a very good sign—a sign that displeasure can never go deep or be lasting. And then a kind word, or kind look, to her favourite Hickman, sets the one in raptures, and the other in tolerable humour, at any time.

But your case pains me at heart; and with all my levity, they must *both* sometimes partake of that pain, which must continue as long as you are in a state of uncertainty; and especially as I was not able to prevail for that protection for you which would have prevented the unhappy step, the necessity for which we both, with so much reason, deplore.

I have only to add (and yet that is needless to tell you) that I am, and will ever be,

Your affectionate friend and servant,
ANNA HOWE

Letter 112: MISS CLARISSA HARLOWE TO MISS HOWE

You tell me, my dear, that my clothes and the little matter of money I left behind me will not be sent me—but I will still hope. It is yet early days. When their passions subside, they will better consider of it; and especially as I have my ever dear and excellent mamma for my friend in this request.—Oh the sweet indulgence! how has my heart bled, and how does it still bleed for her!

You advise me not to depend upon a reconciliation. I do not depend upon it. I cannot. But nevertheless it is the wish next my heart. And as to this man, what can I do? You see that marriage is not absolutely in my own power, if I were inclined to prefer it to the trial which I think I ought to have principally in view to make for a reconciliation.

You say he is proud and insolent. Indeed he is. But can it be your opinion that he intends to humble me down to the level of his mean pride?

And what mean you, my dear friend, when you say that I must throw off a *little more of the veil*?—Indeed I never knew that I wore one. Let me assure you that if

I see anything in Mr Lovelace that looks like a design to humble me, his insolence shall never make me discover a weakness unworthy of a person distinguished by your friendship; that is to say, unworthy either of my sex or of my former self.

But I hope, as I am out of all other protection, that he is not capable of mean or low resentments. What extraordinary trouble I have given him, may he not thank himself for?—His character, which as I have told him gave pretence to my brother's antipathy, he may lay it to if he pleases—And did I ever make him any promises? Did I ever profess a love for him?—Did I ever wish for the continuance of his address?—Had not my brother's violence precipitated matters, would not my indifference to him, in all likelihood (as I designed it should), have tired out his proud spirit,[a] and made him set out for London where he used chiefly to reside? And if he *had*, would there not have been an end of all his pretensions and hopes? For no encouragement had I given him: nor did I then correspond with him. Nor, believe me, should I have begun to do so—the fatal rencounter not having then happened; which drew me in afterwards for others' sakes (fool that I was!) and not for my own. And can you think, or can he, that even this but temporarily-intended correspondence (which, by the way, my dear mamma connived at[b] would have ended thus, had I not been driven on one hand, and teased on the other, to continue it; the occasion which had at first induced it continuing? What pretence then has he, were I to be absolutely in his power, to avenge himself on me for the faults of others; and through which I have suffered more than he? It cannot, cannot be that I should have cause to apprehend him to be so ungenerous, so bad a man.

You bid me not be concerned at the bickerings between your mamma and you. Can I avoid concern when those bickerings are on my account?—That they are raised by my uncle, and my other relations, surely must add to my concern.

But I must observe, perhaps too critically for the state my mind is in at present, that the very sentences you give from your mamma, as so many imperatives which you take amiss, are very severe reflections upon yourself—For instance—*You shall, I tell you, Nancy* implies that you had disputed her will—and so of the rest.

And further let me observe, with respect to what you say that there cannot be the same reason for a prohibition of correspondence with me, as there was of mine with Mr Lovelace; that I thought as little of bad consequences from him at the time, as you can do from me. But if obedience be a duty, the breach of it is the fault, however circumstances may differ. Surely there is no merit in setting up our own judgements against the judgements of our parents. And if it be punishable so to do, I have been severely punished; and that is what I warned you of from my own example.

Yet, God forgive me! I advise thus against myself with very great reluctance: and to say truth have not strength of mind, at present, to decline it myself. But if the occasion go not off, I will take it into farther consideration.

You give me very good advice in relation to this man; and I thank you for it— when you bid me be more upon the *reserve* with him, perhaps I may try for it: but to *palliate*, as you call it, that cannot be done by, my dearest Miss Howe,

Your own

CLARISSA HARLOWE

a See p. 51.
b See p. 52.

Letter 113: MISS CLARISSA HARLOWE TO MISS HOWE

You may believe, my dear Miss Howe, that the circumstance of the noise and outcry within the garden door on Monday last gave me no small uneasiness, to think that I was in the hands of a man who could, by such vile premeditation, lay a snare to trick me out of myself, as I have so frequently called it.

Whenever he came in my sight, the thought of this gave me an indignation that made his presence disgustful to me; and the more, as I fancied I beheld in his face a triumph which reproached my weakness on that account; although, perhaps, it was only the same vivacity and placidness that generally sit upon his features.

I was resolved to task him upon this subject, the first time I could have patience to enter upon it with him. For, besides that it piqued me excessively from the nature of the artifice, I expected shuffling and evasion, if he were guilty, that would have incensed me: and if not confessedly guilty, such unsatisfactory declarations as still would have kept my mind doubtful and uneasy; and would, upon every new offence that he might give me, sharpen my disgusts to him.

I have had the opportunity I waited for; and will lay before you the result.

He was making his court to my good opinion in very polite terms, and with great seriousness lamenting that he had lost it; declaring that he knew not how he had deserved to do so; attributing to me a prejudice, at least an indifference to him, that seemed, to his infinite concern, hourly to increase. And he besought me to let him know my whole mind, that he might have an opportunity either to confess his faults, and amend them, or to clear his conduct to my satisfaction, and thereby entitle himself to a greater share of my confidence.

I answered him with quickness—Then, Mr Lovelace, I will tell you one thing with a frankness that is, perhaps, more suitable to *my* character, than to *yours* (he hoped not, he said), which gives me a very bad opinion of you as a designing, artful man.

I am all attention, madam.

I never can think tolerably of you, while the noise and voice I heard at the garden door, which put me into the terror you took so much advantage of, remains unaccounted for. Tell me fairly, tell me candidly, the whole of that circumstance; and of your dealings with that wicked Joseph Leman; and, according to your explicitness in this particular, I shall form a judgement of your future professions.

I will, without reserve, my dearest life, said he, tell you the whole; and hope that my sincerity in the relation will atone for anything you may think wrong in the fact.

'I knew nothing, *said he*, of this man, this Leman, and should have scorned a resort to so low a method as bribing the servant of any family to let me into the secrets of that family, if I had not detected him attempting to corrupt a servant of mine, to inform him of all my motions, of all my supposed intrigues and, in short, of every action of my private life, as well as of my circumstances and engagements; and this for motives too obvious to be dwelt upon.

My servant told me of his offers, and I ordered him, unknown to the fellow, to let me hear a conversation that was to pass between them.

In the midst of it, and just as he had made an offer of money for a particular piece of intelligence, promising more when procured, I broke in upon them, and by bluster, calling for a knife to cut off his ears (one of which I took hold of), in order to make a present of it, as I said, to his employers, I obliged him to tell me who they were.

Your brother, madam, and your uncle Antony he named.

It was not difficult, when I had given him my pardon on naming them, after I had set before him the enormity of the task he had undertaken and the honourableness of my intentions to your dear self, to prevail upon him by a larger reward to serve me; since, at the same time, he might keep your uncle['s] and brother's favour; as I desired to know nothing but what related to myself and to you, in order to guard us both against the effects of an ill-will, which he acknowledged all his fellow-servants, as well as himself, thought undeserved.

By this means, I own to you, madam, I frequently turned his principals about upon a pivot of my own, unknown to themselves: and the fellow, who is always calling himself a *plain man* and boasting of his CONSCIENCE, was the easier, as I condescended frequently to assure him of my honourable views; and as he knew that the use I made of his intelligence prevented, perhaps, fatal mischiefs.

I was the more pleased with his services as, let me acknowledge to you, madam, they procured to you, unknown to yourself, a safe and uninterrupted egress (which perhaps would not otherwise have been continued to you so long as it was) to the garden and wood-house: for he undertook to them to watch all your motions: and the more cheerfully (for the fellow loves you) as it kept off the curiosity of others.'[a]

So, my dear, it comes out that I *myself* was obliged to this deep contriver.

I sat in silent astonishment; and thus he went on.

'As to the circumstance which you, madam, think so hardly of me for, I do freely confess that having a suspicion that you would revoke your intention of getting away, and in that case, as I was determined, if possible, to prevail upon you to adhere to your resolution, apprehending that we should not have the time together that was necessary for that purpose; I had ordered him to keep off everybody he *could* keep off, and to be himself within view of the garden door'—

But pray, sir, interrupting him, how came you to apprehend that I should revoke my intention? I had indeed deposited a letter to that purpose; but you had it not: and how, as I had reserved to myself the privilege of a revocation, did you know but I might have prevailed upon my friends, and so have revoked upon good grounds?

'I will be very ingenuous, madam. You had made me hope that, if you changed your mind, you would give me a meeting to apprise me of the reasons for it: I went to the loose bricks and I saw the letter there: and as I knew your friends were immovably fixed in their schemes, I doubted not but the letter was to revoke or suspend your resolution; and probably to serve instead of a meeting too. I therefore let it lie, that, if you did revoke, you might be under the necessity of meeting me for the sake of the expectation you had given me. And as I came prepared, I was resolved, pardon me, madam, whatever were your intentions, that you should not go back. Had I taken your letter, I must have been determined by the contents of it, for the present, at least. But not having received it, and you having reason to

a See p. 165.

think I wanted not resolution in a situation so desperate to make your friends a personal visit, I depended upon the interview you had bid me hope for.'

Wicked wretch! said I; it is my grief, that I gave you opportunity to take so exact a measure of my weakness!—But *would* you have presumed to visit the family, had I not met you?

Indeed I would. I had some friends in readiness, who were to have accompanied me to them. And had they refused to see me, or to give me audience, I would have taken my friends with me to Solmes.

And what did you intend to do to Mr Solmes?

Not the least hurt, had the man been passive.

But had he *not* been passive, as you call it, what would you have done to Mr Solmes?

He was loath, he said, to tell me—yet not the least hurt to his *person*.

I repeated my question.

If he must tell me, he only proposed to carry off the *poor fellow*, and to hide him for a month or two. And this he would have done, let what would have been the consequence.

Was ever such a wretch heard of!—I sighed from the bottom of my heart—but bid him proceed from the part I had interrupted him at.

'I ordered the fellow, as I told you madam, said he, to keep within view of the garden door: and if he found any parley between us, and anybody coming (before you could retreat undiscovered) whose coming might be attended with violent effects, he would cry out; and this not only in order to save himself from their suspicions of him, but to give me warning to make off, and, if possible, to induce you (I own it, madam) to go off with me, according to your own appointment. And I hope, all circumstances considered, and the danger I was in of losing you for ever, that the acknowledgement of *this* contrivance, or if you had *not* met me, *that* upon Solmes, will not procure me your hatred. For, had they come as *I* expected, as well as *you*, what a despicable wretch had I been could I have left you to the insults of a brother, and others of your family, whose mercy was cruelty when they had *not* the pretence which this detected interview would have furnished them with!'

What a wretch, said I!—But if, sir, taking your *own* account of this strange matter to be fact, anybody were coming, how happened it that I saw only that man Leman (for I *thought* it was he) out of the door, and at a distance, look after us?

Very lucky! said he, putting his hand first in one pocket, then in another—I hope I have not thrown it away—It is, perhaps, in the coat I had on yesterday—Little did I think it would be necessary to be produced—but I love to come to a demonstration whenever I can—I *may* be giddy—I *may* be heedless. I *am* indeed—but no man, as to *you*, madam, ever had a sincerer heart.

He then stepping to the parlour door called his servant to bring him the coat he had on yesterday.

The servant did. And in the pocket, rumpled up as a paper he regarded not, he pulled out a letter written by that Joseph, dated Monday night; in which 'he begs pardon for crying out so soon.' Says, 'that his fears of being discovered to act on both sides had made him take the rushing of a little dog (that always follows him) through the phyllirea hedge for Betty's being at hand, or some of his masters: and that when he found his mistake, he opened the door by his own key (which the contriving wretch confessed he had furnished him with) and inconsiderately ran out in a hurry to have apprised him that his crying-out was owing to his fright only.' And he added, 'that they were upon the hunt for me by the time he returned.'[a]

I shook my head—Deep! deep! deep! said I, at the best!—Oh Mr Lovelace! God forgive and reform you!—But you are, I see plainly, upon the whole of your own account, a very artful, a very designing man.

Love, my dearest life, is ingenious. Night and day have I racked my stupid brains (oh sir, thought I, not stupid! 'Twere well, perhaps, if they were) to contrive methods to prevent the sacrifice designed to be made of you, and the mischief that must have ensued upon it: so little hold in your affections: such undeserved antipathy from your friends: so much danger of losing you for ever from *both* causes—I have not had, for the whole fortnight before last Monday, half an hour's rest at a time. And I own to you, madam, that I should never have forgiven myself had I omitted any contrivance or forethought that would have prevented your return without me.

Again I blamed myself for meeting him: and justly; for there were many chances to one, that I had *not* met him. And if I had not, all his fortnight's contrivances, as to me, would have come to nothing; and, perhaps, I might nevertheless have escaped Solmes.

Yet, had he resolved to come to Harlowe Place with his friends, and been insulted, as he certainly would have been, what mischiefs might have followed!

But his resolution to run away with, and to hide the poor Solmes for a month or so—Oh my dear! what a wretch have I let run away with *me*, instead of *him!*

I asked him if he thought such enormities as these, such defiances of the laws of society would have passed unpunished?

He had the assurance to say, with one of his usual gay airs, that he should by this means have disappointed his enemies, and saved me from a forced marriage. He had no pleasure in such desperate pushes. Solmes he would not have *personally* hurt. He must have fled his country for a time at least: and truly, if he had been obliged to do so, as all his hopes of my favour must have been at an end, he would have had a fellow-traveller of his own sex out of our family, whom I little thought of.

Was ever such a wretch!—To be sure he meant my brother!

And such, sir, said I, in high resentment, are the uses you make of your corrupt intelligencer—

My corrupt intelligencer, madam, interrupted he! He is to this hour your brother's as well as mine. By what I have ingenuously told you, you may see who began this corruption. Let me assure you, madam, that there are many free things which I have been guilty of, as *reprisals*, which I would not have been the *aggressor* in.

All that I shall further say on this head, Mr Lovelace, is this: That as this vile double-faced wretch has probably been the cause of great mischief on both sides, and still continues, as you own, his wicked practices, it is but my duty to have my friends apprised what a creature he is, whom some of them encourage.

What you please, madam, as to that—My service and your brother's are now almost over for him. The fellow has made a good hand of it. He does not intend to

─────────

[a] See his letter to Joseph Leman, No. 95, p. 385, where he tells him he would contrive for him a letter of this nature to copy.

stay long in his place. He is now actually in treaty for an inn, which will do his business for life. I can tell you further, that he makes love to your sister's Betty: and this by my advice. They will be married when he is established. An innkeeper's wife is every man's mistress; and I have a scheme in my head, to set some engines at work to make her repent her saucy behaviour to you to the last day of her life.

What a wicked schemer are you, sir!—Who shall avenge upon you the still greater evils which *you* have been guilty of?—I forgive Betty with all my heart. She was not my servant; and but too probably, in what she did, obeyed the commands of her to whom she owed duty, better than I obeyed those to whom I owed more.

No matter for that, the wretch said (to be sure, my dear, he must design to make me afraid of him): the decree was gone out—Betty must smart—smart too by an act of her own choice. He loved, he said, to make bad people their own punishers—Nay, madam, excuse me; but if the fellow, if this Joseph, in your opinion, deserves punishment, mine is a complicated scheme; a man and his wife cannot well suffer separately, and it may come home to *him* too—

I had no patience with him. I told him so—But, sir, said I, I see what a man I am with. Your *rattle* warns me of the *snake*. And away I flung; leaving him seemingly vexed, and in confusion.

Letter 114: MISS CLARISSA HARLOWE TO MISS HOWE

MY plain dealing with him, on seeing him again, and the free dislike I expressed to his ways, his manners and his contrivances, as well as to his speeches, have obliged him to recollect himself a little. He will have it that the menaces which he threw out just now against my brother and Mr Solmes are only the effect of an unmeaning pleasantry. He has too great a stake in his country, he says, to be guilty of such enterprises as should lay him under a necessity of quitting it for ever. Twenty things, particularly, he says, he has suffered Joseph Leman to tell of him, that were not and could not be true, in order to make himself formidable in some people's eyes, and this purely with a view to prevent mischief. He is unhappy, as far as he knows, in a quick invention, in hitting readily upon expedients; and many things are reported of him which he never said, and many which he never did, and others which he has only talked of (as just now) and which he has forgot as soon as the words have passed his lips.

This may be so, in part, my dear. No one man so young could be so wicked as he has been reported to be. But such a man at the head of such wretches as he is said to have at his beck, all men of fortune and fearlessness, and capable of such enterprises as I have unhappily found him capable of, what is not to be apprehended from him!

His carelessness about his character is one of his excuses: a very bad one. What hope can a woman have of a man who values not his reputation?—These gay wretches may, in mixed conversation, divert for an hour or so—But the man of probity, the man of virtue, is the man that is to be the partner for life. What woman, who could help it, would submit it to the courtesy of a wretch who avows a disregard to all moral sanctions, whether he will perform his part of the matrimonial obligation, and treat her with tolerable politeness?

With these notions, and with these reflections, to be thrown upon such a man myself—Would to Heaven—but what avail wishes now?—To whom can I fly, if I would fly from him?

Letter 115: MR LOVELACE TO JOHN BELFORD, ESQ.

Friday, April 14

NEVER did I hear of such a parcel of foolish toads as these Harlowes!—Why, Belford, the lady must fall, if every hair of her head were a guardian angel, unless they were to make a visible appearance for her, or, snatching her from me at unawares, would draw her after them into the starry regions.

All I had to apprehend was that a daughter so reluctantly carried off would offer terms to her father, and would be accepted upon a mutual *concedence*; *they* to give up *Solmes*; *she* to give up *me*. And so I was contriving to do all I could to guard against the latter. But they seem resolved to perfect the work they have begun.

What stupid creatures there are in the world! Cunning whelp the brother! not to know that he who would be bribed to undertake a base thing by one, would be *over*-bribed to *retort* the baseness—especially when he could be put into the way to serve himself by both!—Thou, Jack, wilt never know one half of my contrivances.

He here relates the conversation between him and the lady (upon the subject of the noise and exclamations his agent made at the garden door) to the same effect as in Letter 113, and proceeds exulting:

What a capacity for glorious mischief has thy friend!—Yet how near the truth all of it! The only deviation, my asserting that the fellow made the noises by mistake and through fright, and not by previous direction. Had she known the precise truth, her pride (to be so taken in) would never have let her forgive me.

Had I been a hero, I should have made gunpowder useless; for I should have blown up all my adversaries by dint of stratagem, turning their own devices upon them.

But these fathers and mothers—Lord help 'em!—Were not the powers of nature stronger than those of discretion, and were not that busy *dea bona* to afford her genial aids, till tardy prudence qualified parents to *manage* their future offspring, how few people would have children!

James and Arabella may have *their* motives; but what can be said for a father acting as *this* father has acted? What for a mother? What for an aunt? What for uncles?—Who can have patience with such fellows and fellowesses?

Soon will the fair one hear how high their foolish resentments run against her: and then she'll have a little more confidence in me, I hope. Then will I be jealous that she loves me not with the preference my heart builds upon: then will I bring her to confessions of grateful love: and then will I kiss her when I please; and not stand trembling, as now, like an hungry hound who sees a delicious morsel within his reach (the froth hanging about his vermilion jaws), yet dare not leap at it for his life.

But I was *originally* a bashful whelp—bashful still, with regard to this lady!—bashful, yet know the sex so well!—But that indeed is the reason that I know it so well—for, Jack, I have had abundant cause, when I have looked into *myself*, by way of comparison with the *other* sex, to conclude that a bashful man has a good deal of the soul of a woman; and so, like Tiresias, can tell what they think[1] and what they drive at, as well as themselves.

The modest ones and I, particularly, are pretty much upon a par. The difference between us is only, what they *think*, I *act*. But the immodest ones outdo the worst of us by a bar's length, both in thinking and acting.

One argument let me plead in proof of my assertion: that even we rakes love modesty in a woman; while the modest women, as they are accounted, that is to say, the slyest, love and generally prefer an impudent man. Whence can this be, but from a likeness in nature? And this made the poet say, that every woman is a rake in her heart.[2] It concerns them by their *actions* to prove the contrary, if they can.

Thus have I read in some of the philosophers, *that no wickedness is comparable to the wickedness of a woman.*[a] Canst thou tell me, Jack, who says this? Was it Socrates? for he had the devil of a wife?—or who? Or is it Solomon?—*King* Solomon—thou rememberest to have read of such a king, dost thou not? SOLOMON, I learned, when an infant (my mother was a good woman) to answer, when asked, *who was the wisest man?*—But my indulgent questioner never asked me how he came by the uninspired part of his wisdom.

Come, come, Jack, you and I are not so very bad, could we but stop where we are.

He then gives the particulars of what passed between him and the lady on his menaces relating to her brother and Mr Solmes, and of his design to punish Betty Barnes and Joseph Leman.

Letter 116: MISS CLARISSA HARLOWE TO MISS HOWE

Friday, April 14

I WILL now give you the particulars of a conversation that has just passed between Mr Lovelace and me; which I must call agreeable.

It began with his telling me that he had just received intelligence, that my friends were of a sudden come to a resolution to lay aside all thoughts of pursuing me, or of getting me back: and that therefore, he attended me, to know my pleasure; and what *I* would do, or have *him* do?

I told him that I would have him leave me directly; and that, when it was known to everybody that I was absolutely independent of him, it would pass that I had left my father's house because of my brother's ill-usage of me: which was a plea that I might make with justice, and to the excuse of my father, as well as of myself.

He mildly replied that if he could be certain that my relations would *adhere* to this their new resolution, he could have no objection, since such was my pleasure: but that, as he was well assured that they had taken it only from apprehensions that a more *active* one might involve my brother (who had breathed nothing but revenge) in some fatal misfortune, there was too much reason to believe that they would resume their former purpose, the moment they should think they *safely* might.

---

a Mr Lovelace is as much out in his conjecture of Solomon as of Socrates. The passage is in Ecclesiasticus, Chap. 25.[19].

This, madam, said he, is a risk I cannot run. You would think it strange, if I could. And yet, as soon as I knew they had so given out, I thought it proper to apprise you of it, and to take your commands upon it.

Let me hear, said I, willing to try if he had any particular view, what *you* think most advisable?

'Tis very easy to say that, if I durst—if I might not offend you—if it were not to break conditions that shall be inviolable with me.

Say then, sir, what you *would* say. I can approve or disapprove, as I think fit.

To waive, madam, what I *would* say till I have more courage to speak out (more courage—Mr Lovelace more courage, my dear!)—I will only propose what I think will be most agreeable to *you*—Suppose, if you choose not to go to Lady Betty's, that you take a turn cross the country to Windsor?

Why to Windsor?

Because it is a pleasant place: because it lies in the way either to Berkshire, to Oxford, or to London—*Berkshire*, where Lord M. is at present: *Oxford*, in the neighbourhood of which lives Lady Betty: *London*, whither you may retire at your pleasure: or, if you will *have* it so, whither I may go, you staying at Windsor; and yet be within an easy distance of you, if anything should happen, or if your friends should change their pacific resolution.

This displeased me not. But I said my only objection was the distance from Miss Howe, of whom I should be glad to be always within two or three hours' reach by a messenger, if possible.

If I had thoughts of any other place than Windsor, or nearer to Miss Howe, he wanted but my commands and would seek for proper accommodations: but, fix as I pleased, farther or nearer, he had servants, and they had nothing else to do but to obey me.

A grateful thing then he named to me—to send for my Hannah as soon as I should be fixed; unless I would choose one of the young gentlewomen *here* to attend me, both of whom, as I had acknowledged, were very obliging; and he knew I had generosity enough to make it worth either of their whiles.

This of Hannah, he might see, I took very well. I said I had thoughts of sending for her as soon as I got to more convenient lodgings. As to these young gentlewomen, it were pity to break in upon that usefulness which the whole family were of to each other: each having her proper part, and performing it with an agreeable alacrity: insomuch that I liked them all so well, that I could even pass my days among them, were he to leave me; by which means the lodgings would be more convenient to me than now they were.

He need not repeat his objections to this place, he said: but as to going to Windsor, or wherever else I thought fit, or as to *his* personal attendance, or leaving me, he would assure me (he very agreeably said), that I could propose nothing in which I thought my reputation, and even my *punctilio*, concerned, that he would not cheerfully come into. And since I was so much taken up with my pen, he would instantly order his horse to be got ready, and would set out.

Not to be off of my caution: Have you any acquaintance at Windsor? said I— Know you of any convenient lodgings there?

Except with the forest, replied he, where I have often hunted, I know the least of Windsor of any place so noted and so pleasant. Indeed, I have not a single acquaintance there.

Upon the whole, I told him, that I thought his proposal of Windsor not amiss; and that I would remove thither if I could get a lodging only for myself, and an upper chamber for Hannah; for that my stock of money was but small, as was easy to be conceived; and I should be very loath to be obliged to anybody. I added that the sooner I removed the better; for that then he could have no objection to go to London or Berkshire, as he pleased: and I should let everybody know my independence.

He again proposed himself, in very polite terms, for my banker. But I, as civilly, declined his offers.

This conversation was to be, all of it, in the main, agreeable. He asked whether I would choose to lodge in the town of Windsor, or out of it.

As near the castle, I said, as possible, for the convenience of going constantly to the public worship; an opportunity I had been too long deprived of.

He should be very glad, he told me, if he could procure me accommodations in any one of the canons' houses; which he imagined would be more agreeable to me than any other, on many accounts. And as he could depend upon my promise, never to have any other man but himself, on the condition he had so cheerfully subscribed to, he should be easy; since it was now his part, *in earnest*, to set about recommending himself to my favour, by the *only* way he knew it could be done. Adding, with a very serious air—I am but a young man, madam; but I have run a long course: let not your purity of mind incline you to despise me for the acknowledgement. It is high time to be weary of it, and to reform; since, like Solomon, I can say, There is nothing new under the sun.[1] But that it is my belief, that a life of virtue can afford such pleasures, on reflection, as will be for ever blooming, for ever new!

I was agreeably surprised. I looked at him, I believe, as if I doubted my ears and my eyes!—His features and aspect, however, became his words.

I expressed my satisfaction in terms so agreeable to him, that he said he found a delight in this early dawning of a better day to him, and in *my* approbation, which he had never received from the success of the most favoured of his pursuits.

Surely, my dear, the man *must* be in earnest. He could not have said this; he could not have *thought* it, had he not. What followed made me still readier to believe him.

In the midst of my wild vagaries, said he, I have ever preserved a reverence for religion, and for religious men. I always called another cause, when any of my libertine companions, in pursuance of Lord Shaftesbury's test[2] (which is a part of the rake's creed, and what I may call *the whetstone of infidelity*), endeavoured to turn the sacred subject into ridicule. On this very account I have been called by good men of the clergy, who nevertheless would have it that I was a *practical* rake, *the decent rake*: and indeed I had too much pride in my shame to disown the name.

This, madam, I am the readier to confess, as it may give you hope that the generous task of my reformation, which I flatter myself you will have the goodness to undertake, will not be so difficult a one as you may have imagined; for it has afforded me some pleasure in my retired hours, when a temporary remorse has struck me for anything I have done amiss, that I should *one* day take delight in another course of life: for without one *can*, I dare say no durable *good* is to be expected from the endeavour—Your example, madam, must do all, must confirm all.[a]

The divine grace or favour, Mr Lovelace, must do all, and confirm all. You know not how much you please me, that I can talk to you in this dialect.

And I then thought of his generosity to his pretty rustic; and of his kindness to his tenants.

Yet, madam, be pleased to remember one thing: reformation cannot be a *sudden* work. I have infinite vivacity: it is that which runs away with me. Judge, dearest madam, by what I am going to confess, that I have a prodigious way to journey on before a good person will think me tolerable; since, though I have read in some of our *perfectionists* enough to make a *better* man than myself either run into madness or despair about the grace you mention; yet I cannot enter into the meaning of the word, nor into the modus of its operation. Let me not then be checked when I mention *your* example for my *visible* reliance; and instead of using such words, till I can better understand them, suppose all the rest included in the profession of *that* reliance.

I told him that, although I was somewhat concerned at his expression, and surprised at so much *darkness*, as, for want of another word, I would call it, in a man of his talents and learning; yet I was pleased with his ingenuity. I wished him to encourage this way of thinking: I told him that his observation that no *durable* good was to be expected from any new course where there was not a *delight* taken in it, was just: but that the delight would follow by use.

And twenty things of this sort I even *preached* to him; taking care, however, not to be tedious, nor to let my expanded heart give him a contracted or impatient brow. And, indeed, he took visible pleasure in what I said, and even hung upon the subject, when I, to try him, seemed to be ready to drop it once or twice: and proceeded to give me a most agreeable instance that he could, at times, think both deeply and seriously—Thus it was.

He was wounded dangerously, once, in a duel, he said, in the left arm, baring it to show me the scar: that this (notwithstanding a great effusion of blood, it being upon an artery) was followed by a violent fever, which at last fixed upon his spirits; and *that* so obstinately, that neither did *he* desire life, nor his *friends* expect it: that for a month together, his heart, as he thought, was so totally changed that he despised his former courses, and particularly that rashness which had brought him to the state he was in, and his antagonist (who, however, was the aggressor) into a much worse: that, in this space, he had thoughts which, at times, gives him pleasure to reflect upon: and although these promising prospects changed, as he recovered health and spirits; yet he parted with them with so much reluctance, that he could not help showing it in a copy of verses, *truly blank* ones, he said; some of which he repeated, and (advantaged by the grace which he gives to everything he repeats) I thought them very tolerable ones; the sentiments, however, much graver than I expected from him.

He has promised me a copy of the lines; and then I shall judge better of their merit; and so shall you. The tendency of them was, 'That, since sickness only gave him a proper train of thinking, and that his restored health brought with it a return

a That he proposes one day to reform, and that he has sometimes good motions, see p. 163.

of his evil habits, he was ready to renounce the gifts of nature for those of contemplation.'

He farther declared that although all these good motions went off (as he had owned) on his recovery, yet he had better hopes now, from the influence of my example, and from the reward before him, if he persevered: and that he was the more hopeful that he should, as his present resolution was made in a full tide of health and spirits; and when he had nothing to wish for but perseverance, to entitle himself to my favour.

I will not throw cold water, Mr Lovelace, said I, on a rising flame: but look to it! For I shall endeavour to keep you up to this spirit: I shall measure your value of me by this test. And I would have you bear those charming lines of Mr Rowe for ever in your mind; you, who have by your own confession so much to repent of; and as the scar, indeed, you showed me will, in one instance, remind you to your dying day.

The lines, my dear, are from that poet's *Ulysses*. You have heard me often admire them; and I repeated them to him:

> *Habitual* evils change not on a *sudden*;
> But *many* days must pass, and *many* sorrows;
> Conscious remorse and anguish *must* be felt,
> To curb desire, to break the stubborn will,
> And work a second nature in the soul,
> Ere Virtue can resume the place she lost:
> 'Tis else DISSIMULATION—[3]

He had often read these lines, he said; but never *tasted* them before—By his *soul* (the unmortified creature swore) and as *he hoped to be saved*, he was *now* in earnest, in his good resolutions. He had said, *before* I repeated these lines from Rowe, that habitual evils could not be changed on a *sudden*: but he hoped he should not be thought a *dissembler* if he were not enabled to *hold* his good purposes; since ingratitude and dissimulation were vices that of all others he abhorred.

May you ever abhor them! said I. They are the most odious of all vices.

I hope, my dear Miss Howe, I shall not have occasion in my future letters to contradict these promising appearances. Should I have *nothing* on his side to combat with, I shall be very far from being happy, from the sense of my fault and the indignation of all my relations. So shall not fail of condign punishment for it, from my inward remorse, on account of my forfeited character. But the least ray of hope could not dart in upon me without my being willing to lay hold of the very first opportunity to communicate it to *you*, who take so generous a share in all my concerns.

Nevertheless, you may depend upon it, my dear, that these agreeable assurances and hopes of his begun reformation shall not make me forget my caution. Not that I think, at worst, any more than you, that he dare to harbour a thought injurious to my honour: but he is very various, and there is an *apparent*, and even an *acknowledged* unfixedness in his temper, which at times gives me some uneasiness. I am resolved therefore to keep him at distance from my person and my thoughts as much as I can: for whether *all* men are, or are not, encroachers, I am sure Mr Lovelace is one.

Hence it is that I have always cast about, and will continue to cast about, what ends he may have in view from *this* proposal, or from *that* report. In a word, though hopeful of the *best*, I will always be fearful of the *worst*, in everything that admits of doubt. For it is better, in such a situation as mine, to apprehend without cause than to subject myself to surprise for want of forethought.

Mr Lovelace is gone to Windsor, having left two servants to attend me. He purposes to be back tomorrow.

I have written to my aunt Hervey, to supplicate her interest in my behalf, for my clothes, books and money; signifying to her, 'That, could I be restored to the favour of my family, and be allowed a negative only, as to any man who might be proposed to me, and be used like a daughter, a niece and a sister, I would still stand by my offer to live single and submit, as I ought, to a negative from my father.' Intimating nevertheless, 'That it were perhaps better, after the usage I have received from my brother and sister, that I might be allowed to be distant from them, as well for their sakes as my own' (meaning, as I suppose it will be taken, my dairy house)—offering 'to take my father's directions, as to the manner I should live in, the servants I should have and in everything that should show the dutiful subordination that I was willing to conform to.'

My aunt will know by my letter to my sister how to direct to me, if she be permitted to favour me with a line.

I am equally earnest with *her* in *this* letter, as I was with my *sister* in *that* I wrote to *her*, to obtain for me a speedy reconciliation, that I may not be further precipitated; intimating, 'That by a timely lenity, all may pass for a misunderstanding only, which otherwise will be thought equally disgraceful to them and to me; appealing to her for the necessity I was under to do what I did.'

Here I close for the present, with the assurance that I am

> Your ever obliged and affectionate
> CLARISSA HARLOWE

Letter 117: MR LOVELACE TO JOHN BELFORD, ESQ.

Friday, April 14

THOU hast often reproached me, Jack, with my vanity, without distinguishing the humorous turn that accompanies it; and for which, at the same time that thou robbest me of the merit of it, thou admirest me highly. *Envy* gives thee the *indistinction*: nature inspires the *admiration*: unknown to thyself it inspires it. But thou art too clumsy and too shortsighted a mortal to know how to account even for the impulses by which thou thyself art moved.

Well, but this acquits thee not of my charge of vanity, Lovelace, methinks thou sayest:

And true thou sayest: for I have indeed a confounded parcel of it. But, if men of parts may not be allowed to be vain, who should? And yet, upon second thoughts, men of parts have the least occasion of any to be vain; since the world (so few of *them* are there in it) are ready to find them out and extol them. If a fool can be made sensible that there is a man who has more understanding than *himself*, he is ready enough to conclude that such a man must be a very extraordinary creature.

And what, at this rate, is the general conclusion to be drawn from the premises?—Is it not, That *no* man ought to be vain? But what if a man can't help it?—This, perhaps, may be *my* case. But there is nothing on which I value myself so much as upon my *inventions*. And, for the soul of me, I cannot help letting it be seen that I *do*. Yet this vanity may be a means, perhaps, to overthrow me with this sagacious lady.

She is very apprehensive of me, I see. I have studied before her and Miss Howe, as often as I have been with them, to pass for a giddy thoughtless fellow. What a folly then to be so *expatiatingly* sincere, in my answer to her home *put*, upon the noises within the garden?—But such success having attended that contrivance (success, Jack, has blown many a man up!), my cursed vanity got uppermost, and kept down my caution. The menace to have secreted Solmes, and that other, that I had thoughts to run away with her foolish brother, and of my project to revenge her upon the two servants, so much terrified my beloved, that I was forced to sit down to muse how to retrieve myself with her.

Some favourable incidents, at the time, tumbled in from my agent in her family; at least such as I was determined to *make* favourable: and therefore I desired admittance; and this before she could resolve anything against me; that is to say, while her admiration of my intrepidity kept resolution in suspense.

Accordingly, I prepared myself to be all gentleness, all obligingness, all serenity; and as I have now and then, and always *had*, more or less good motions pop up in my mind, I encouraged and collected everything of this sort that I had ever had from novicehood to maturity (not long in recollecting, Jack!), in order to bring the dear creature into good humour with me: and who knows, thought I, if I can hold it and proceed, but I may be able to lay a foundation fit to build my grand scheme upon?—*Love*, thought I, is not *naturally* a doubter: *fear* is: I will try to banish the latter: nothing then but love will remain. *Credulity* is the God of Love's prime minister; and they never are asunder.

He then acquaints his friend with what passed between him and the lady, in relation to his advices from Harlowe Place, and to his proposal about lodgings, pretty much to the same purpose as in hers preceding.

When he comes to mention his proposal of the Windsor lodgings, thus he expresses himself:

Now, Belford, can it enter into thy leaden head what I meant by this proposal?— I know it cannot. And so I'll tell thee.

To leave her for a day or two, with a view to serve her by my absence, would, as I thought, look like confiding in her favour—I could not think of leaving her, thou knowest, while I had reason to believe her friends would pursue us; and I began to apprehend that she would suspect that I made a pretence of that intentional pursuit to keep about her and with her. But now that they had declared against it, and that they would not receive her if she came back again (a declaration she had better hear first from me, than from Miss Howe or any other); what should hinder me from giving her this mark of my obedience; especially as I could leave Will, who is a clever fellow, and can do anything but write and spell, and my uncle's Jonas (not as guards, to be sure, but as attendants only); the latter to be dispatched to me occasionally by the former, whom I could acquaint with my motions?

Then I wanted to inform myself why I had not congratulatory letters from my aunts, and from my cousins Montague, to whom I had written, glorying in my beloved's escape; which letters, as they should be worded, might possibly be made necessary to show, as matters proceed.

As to Windsor, I had no design to carry her particularly thither: but somewhere it was proper to name, as she condescended to ask my advice about it. London, I durst not; but very cautiously; and so as to make it her own option: for I must tell thee that there is such a perverseness in the sex that, when they ask your advice, they do it only to know your opinion, that they may oppose it; though, had not the thing in question been *your* choice, perhaps it had been *theirs*.

I could easily give reasons *against* Windsor, after I had pretended to be there; and this would have looked the better, as it was a place of my own nomination; and shown her that I had no fixed scheme—Never was there in woman such a sagacious, such an all-alive apprehension, as in this—Yet it is a grievous thing to an honest man to be suspected.

Then, in my going or return, I can call upon Mrs Greme. She and my beloved had a great deal of talk together. If I knew what it was about; and that *either*, upon their first acquaintance, was for benefiting herself by the *other*, I might contrive to serve them *both*, without hurting *myself*: for these are the most prudent ways of doing friendships, and what are not followed by regrets, though the *served* should prove ungrateful. Then Mrs Greme corresponds by pen and ink with her farmer sister, where we are: something may possibly arise *that* way, either of a convenient nature which I may pursue; or an inconvenient which I may avoid.

Always be careful of back doors is a maxim with me in all my exploits. Whoever knows me, knows that I am no proud man. I can talk as familiarly to servants as to principals, when I have a mind to make it worth their while to oblige me in anything—Then servants are but as the common soldiers in an army: they do all the mischief; frequently without malice, and merely, good souls! for mischief sake.

I am most apprehensive about Miss Howe. She has a confounded deal of wit, and wants only a subject, to show as much roguery: and should I be outwitted, with all my sententious, boasting conceit of my own *nostrum-mongership*—(I love to plague thee, who art a pretender to accuracy and a *surface-skimmer* in learning, with out-of-the-way words and phrases), I should certainly hang, drown, or shoot myself.

Poor Hickman!—I pity him for the prospect he has with such a virago!—But the fellow's a fool, God wot! And now I think of it, it is absolutely necessary for complete happiness in the married state, that one *should* be a fool; an argument I once held with this very Miss Howe—But then the fool should *know* that he is so, else the obstinate one will disappoint the wise one.

But my agent Joseph has helped me to secure this quarter.

Letter 118: MR LOVELACE TO JOHN BELFORD, ESQ.

(In continuation)
BUT is it not a confounded thing that I cannot fasten an obligation upon this proud beauty? I have two motives in endeavouring to prevail upon her to accept money and raiment from me: one, the real pleasure I should have in the accommodating the haughty maid; and to think there was something near her, and upon her, that I could call *mine*: the other, in order to abate her severity, and humble her a little.

Nothing sooner brings down a proud spirit, than a sense of lying under pecuniary obligations. This has always made me solicitous to avoid laying myself under any such. Yet sometimes formerly have I been put to it, and cursed the tardy revolution of the quarterly periods. And yet I ever made shift to avoid anticipations: *I never would eat the calf in the cow's belly,*[1] as Lord M.'s phrase is: for what is that but to hold our lands upon *tenant-courtesy,* the vilest of all tenures? To be denied a fox-chase, for fear of breaking down a fence upon my own grounds? To be clamoured at for repairs *studied* for, rather than *really wanted*? To be prated to by a bumkin with his hat on, and his arms folded, as if he defied your expectations of that sort; his foot firmly fixed as if upon his own ground; and you forced to take his arch leers and stupid gibes; intimating by the whole of his conduct that he has had it in his power to oblige you and, if you behave civilly, may oblige you again?—I, who think I have a right to break every man's head I pass by, if I like not his looks, to bear this!—I no more could do it than I could borrow of an insolent uncle or inquisitive aunt, who would thence think themselves entitled to have an account of all my life and actions laid before them for their review and censure.

My charmer, I see, has a pride like my own: but she has no *distinction* in her pride: nor knows the pretty fool that there is nothing nobler, nothing more delightful, than for lovers to be conferring and receiving obligations from one another. In this very farm-yard, to give thee a familiar instance, I have more than once seen this remark illustrated. A strutting rascal of a cock have I beheld chuck, chuck, chuck, chucking his mistress to him, when he has found a single barley-corn, taking it up with his bill, and letting it drop five or six times, still repeating his chucking invitation: and when two or three of his feathered ladies strive who shall be the first for't (Oh Jack! a cock is a Grand Signor of a bird!), he directs the bill of the foremost to it; and when she has got the dirty pearl, he struts over her with an erected crest, and an exulting chuck—a chuck-aw-aw-w, circling round her, with dropped wings, sweeping the dust in humble courtship: while the obliged she, half-shy, half-willing, by her cowering tail, half-stretched wings, yet seemingly affrighted eyes, and contracted neck, lets one see that she knows the barley-corn was not all he called her for.

When he comes to that part of his narrative where he mentions the proposing of the lady's maid Hannah, *or one of the young gentlewomen, to attend her, thus he writes:*
Now, Belford, canst thou imagine what I meant by proposing Hannah, or one of the girls here, for her attendant? I'll give thee a month to guess.

Thou wilt not pretend to guess, thou sayest.

Well, then, I'll tell thee.

Believing she would certainly propose to have that favourite wench about her, as soon as she was a little settled, I had caused the girl to be inquired after, with an intent to make interest, somehow or other, that a month's warning should be insisted on by her master or mistress, or by some other means which I had not determined upon, to prevent her coming to her. But fortune fights for me. The wench is luckily ill; a violent rheumatic disorder, which has obliged her to leave her place, confines her to her chamber: poor Hannah! How I pity the girl! These things are very hard upon industrious servants!—I intend to make the poor maid a small present on the occasion—I know it will oblige my charmer.

And so, Jack, pretending not to know anything of the matter, I pressed her to send for the wench. She knew I had always a regard for this servant, because of her honest love to her lady: but *now* I have a greater regard for her than ever. Calamity, though a poor servant's calamity, will rather increase than diminish good will with a truly generous master or mistress.

As to one of the young Sorlings's attendance, there was nothing at all in proposing that; for if either of them had been chosen by *her*, and permitted by the *mother* (two chances in *that*!), it would have been only till I had fixed upon another. And if afterwards they had been loath to part, I could easily have given my beloved a jealousy, which would have done the business; or to the girl, who would have quitted her country dairy, such a relish for a London one, as would have made it very convenient for her to fall in love with Will; or perhaps I could have done still better for her with Lord M.'s chaplain, who is very desirous of standing well with his lord's presumptive heir.

A blessing on thy honest heart, Lovelace! thou'lt say; for thou art for providing for everybody.

He gives an account of the serious part of their conversation, with no great variation from the lady's account of it: and when he comes to that part of it where he bids her remember that reformation cannot be a sudden thing, he asks his friend:

Is not this fair play? Is it not dealing ingenuously? Then the observation, I will be bold to say, is founded in truth and nature. But there was a little touch of policy in it besides; that the lady, if I should fly out again, should not think me too gross an hypocrite: for, as I plainly told her, I was afraid that my fits of reformation were *but* fits and sallies; but I hoped her example would fix them into habits. But it is so discouraging a thing, to have my monitress so very good!—I protest I know not how to look up at her! Now, as I am thinking, if I could pull her down a little nearer to my own level; that is to say, could prevail upon her to do something that would argue imperfection, something to repent of; we should jog on much more equally, and be better able to comprehend one another: and so the comfort would be mutual, and the remorse not all on one side.

He acknowledges, that he was greatly affected and pleased with the lady's serious arguments at the time: but even then was apprehensive that his temper would not hold. Thus he writes:

This lady says serious things in so agreeable a manner; and then her voice is all harmony, when she touches a subject she is pleased with; that I could have listened to her for half a day together. But yet I am afraid, if she *falls*, as they call it, she will lose a good deal of that *pathos*, of that noble self-confidence which gives a good person, as I now see, a visible superiority over one *not* so good.

But, after all, Belford, I would fain know why people call such free livers as you and me *hypocrites*—That's a word I hate; and should take it very ill to be called by it. For myself, I have as good motions, and perhaps have them as frequently as anybody: all the business is, they don't hold; or, to speak more in character, I don't take the care some do to conceal my lapses.

Letter 119: MISS HOWE TO MISS CLARISSA HARLOWE

Sat. April 15

THOUGH pretty much pressed in time, and oppressed by my mamma's watchfulness, I will write a few lines upon the new light that has broke in upon your gentleman; and send it by a particular hand.

I know not what to think of him upon it—He talks well; but judge him by Rowe's lines, he is certainly a *dissembler*, odious as the sin of hypocrisy and, as he says, that other of ingratitude are to him.

And pray, my dear, let me ask you, could he have triumphed, as it is said he has done, over so many of our sex, had he not been egregiously guilty of *both* sins?

His [ingenuousness] is the thing that staggers me: yet is he cunning enough to know that whoever accuses himself first blunts the edge of an adversary's accusation.

He is certainly a man of sense: there is more hope of such a one, than of a fool: and there must be a *beginning* to a reformation. These I will allow in his favour.

But this, I think, is the only way to judge of his specious confessions and self-accusations—Does he confess anything that you knew not before, or that you are not likely to find out from others?—If nothing else, what does he confess to his own disadvantage? You have heard of his duels: you have heard of his seductions: all the world has—He owns therefore what it would be to no purpose to conceal; and his [ingenuousness] is a salvo—'Why, this, madam, is no more than Mr Lovelace *himself* acknowledges.'

Well, but what is now to be done?—You must make the best of your situation: and as you say, so say I, I hope that will not be bad: for I like all that he has proposed to you of Windsor, and his canon's house. His readiness to leave you and go himself in quest of a lodging likewise looks well—And I think there is nothing can be so properly done, as (whether you get to a canon's house or not) that the canon joins you together in wedlock as soon as possible.

I much approve, however, of all your cautions, of all your vigilance, and of everything you have done, but of your meeting of him. Yet in my disapprobation of that, I judge by the event only; for who would have divined it would have concluded as it did? But he is the devil, by his own account: and had he run away with the wretched Solmes and your more wretched brother, and been himself transported for life, he should have had my free consent for all three.

What use does he make of that Joseph Leman!—His ingenuousness, I must once more say, confounds me; but if, my dear, you can forgive your brother [for the part he put that fellow upon acting, I don't know whether you ought to be angry at [Lovelace] on that account; yet I have wished fifty times, since he got you away, that you were rid of him, whether it were by a burning fever, by hanging, by drowning, or by a broken neck; provided it were before he laid you under a necessity to go into mourning for him.

I repeat my hitherto rejected offer. May I send it safely by your old man?—I have reasons for not sending it by Hickman's servant; unless I had a bank-note or notes. Inquiring for such may cause distrust. My mamma is so busy, so inquisitive!—I don't love suspicious tempers.

And here she is continually in and out—I must break off. Mr Hickman begs his most respectful compliments to you, and offer of services. I told him I would oblige him, because minds in trouble take kindly anybody's civilities: but that he must not imagine he obliged me by this: since I should think the man or woman either blind or stupid, who admired not a person of your exalted merit for her own sake, and wished not to serve her without view to other reward than the honour of serving her.

To be sure, that was his principal motive, with great daintiness he said it: but with a kiss of his hand, and a bow to my feet, he hoped that that fine lady's being my friend did not lessen the merit of the reverence he really had for her. Believe me ever, what you shall ever find me,

> Your faithful and affectionate
> ANNA HOWE

Letter 120: MISS CLARISSA HARLOWE TO MISS HOWE

Sat. afternoon

I DETAIN your messenger while I write in answer to yours; my poor old man not being very well.

You dishearten me a good deal about this man. I may be too willing from my sad circumstances to think the best of him—If his pretences to reformation are but pretences, what must be his intent? But can the heart of man be so very vile? Can he, *dare* he, mock the Almighty?—But may I not, from one very sad reflection, think better of him; that I am thrown too much in his power to make it *necessary* for him (except he were to intend the very utmost villainy by me) to be such a shocking hypocrite?—He must, at least, be in earnest, at the *time* he gives the better hopes. Surely he must. You yourself must join with me in this hope, or you could not wish me to be so dreadfully yoked.

But after all, I had rather be independent of him, and of his family, although I have an high opinion of them; *much* rather: at least till I see what my own may be brought to—Otherwise I think it were best for me, at once, to cast myself into Lady Betty's protection. All would then be conducted with decency, and perhaps many mortifications would be spared me. But then I must be *his*, at all adventures, and be thought to defy my own family. And shall I not see the issue of one application first?—And yet I cannot make this till I am settled somewhere, and at a distance from him.

Mrs Sorlings showed me a letter this morning, which she had received from her sister Greme last night; in which (hoping I will forgive her forward zeal, if her sister thinks fit to show her letter to me) she 'wishes for all the noble family's sake, and she hopes she may say for my own, that I will be pleased to yield to make his honour, as she calls him, happy.' She grounds her *officiousness*, as she calls it, upon what he was so *condescending* (her word also) to say to her yesterday, in his way to Windsor, on her *presuming* to ask if she might soon give him joy. 'That no man ever loved a woman as he loved me: that no woman ever so well deserved to be beloved: that in every conversation, he admired me still more: that he loved me with such a purity as he had never believed himself capable of, or that a mortal creature could have inspired him with; looking upon me as all *soul*; as an angel sent down to save *his*'; and a great deal more of this sort: 'but that he apprehended my consent to make him happy was at a greater distance than he wished. And complained of my too severe restrictions upon him, before I honoured him with my *confidence*: which restrictions must be as sacred to him, as if they were parts of the marriage contract' etc.

What, my dear, shall I say to this?—How shall I take it? Mrs Greme is a good woman. Mrs Sorlings is a good woman. And this letter agrees with the conversation I thought, and still think, so agreeable—Yet what means the man by forgoing the opportunities he has had to declare himself?—What mean his complaints of my restrictions to Mrs Greme? He is not a bashful man!—But you say, I inspire people with an awe of me!—An awe, my dear!—As how?—

I am quite petulant at times, to find that I am bound to see the workings of this *subtle*, or this *giddy* spirit; which shall I call it?

How am I punished, as I frequently think, for my vanity in hoping to be an *example* to young persons of my sex! Let me be but a warning, and I will now be contented. For, be my destiny what it may, I shall never be able to hold up my head again among my best friends and worthiest companions.

It is one of the cruellest circumstances that attends the faults of the inconsiderate, that she makes all who love her unhappy, and gives joy only to her own enemies, and to the enemies of her family.

What an useful lesson would this afford, were it properly inculcated at the time that the tempted mind was balancing upon a doubtful adventure?

You know not, my dear, the worth of a virtuous man; and noble-minded as you are in most particulars, you partake of the common weakness of human nature, in being apt to slight what is in your own power.

You would not think of using Mr Lovelace, were he your suitor, as you do the much worthier Mr Hickman—would you? You know who says, in my mamma's case, 'Much *will* bear, much *shall* bear, all the world through.'[a] Mr Hickman, I fancy, would be glad to know the lady's name, who made such an observation. He would think it hardly possible but such a one should benefit by her own remark; and would be apt to wish his Miss Howe acquainted with her.

Gentleness of heart, surely, is not despicable in a man. Why, if it be, is the highest distinction a man can arrive at, that of a *gentleman*?—a distinction which a prince may not deserve. For manners, more than birth, fortune or title, are requisite in this character. Manners are indeed the essence of it. And shall it be generally said, and Miss Howe not be an exception to it (as once you wrote), that our sex are best dealt with by boisterous and unruly spirits?[b]

Forgive me, my dear; and love me as you used to do. For although my fortunes are changed, my heart is not: nor ever will, while it bids my pen tell you that it must cease to beat when it is not as much yours, as

Your

CLARISSA HARLOWE

a See p. 69.
b See p. 211.

Letter 121: MISS CLARISSA HARLOWE TO MISS HOWE

Saturday evening

MR Lovelace has seen divers apartments at Windsor; but not one, he says, that he thought fit for me, or in any manner answering my description.

He had been very solicitous to keep to the letter of my instructions: which looks well: and the better I liked him, as, although he proposed that town, he came back dissuading me from it: for he said that, in his journey from thence, he had thought Windsor, although of his own proposal, a wrong choice; because I coveted privacy and that was a place generally visited and admired.

I told him that if Mrs Sorlings thought me not an emcumbrance, I would be willing to stay there a little longer; provided he would leave me, and go to Lord M.'s or to London, which ever he thought best.

He hoped, he said, that he might suppose me absolutely safe from the insults or attempts of my brother; and therefore, if it would make me easier, he would obey, for a few days at least.

He again proposed to send for Hannah—I told him I designed to do so, through you: and shall beg of you, my dear, to cause the honest creature to be sent to? Your faithful Robert, I think, knows where she is. Perhaps she will be permitted to quit her place directly, by allowing a month's wages, which I will repay her.

He took notice of the serious humour he found me in, and of the redness of my eyes: I had just been answering your letter; and, had he not approached me on his coming off his journey, in a very respectful manner, had he not made an unexceptionable report of his inquiries, and been so ready to go from me, at the very first word; I was prepared (notwithstanding the good terms we parted upon when he set out for Windsor) to have given him a very unwelcome reception: for the contents of your last letter had so affected me, that the moment I saw him, I beheld with indignation the seducer who had been the cause of all the evils I suffer, and have suffered.

He hinted to me that he had received a letter from Lady Betty, and another, as I understood him, from one of the Miss Montagues. If they take notice of *me* in them, I wonder that he did not acquaint me with the contents. I am afraid, my dear, that his relations are among those who think I have taken a rash and inexcusable step. It is not to my credit to let even them know how I have been frighted out of myself: and who knows but they may hold me unworthy of their alliance, if they may think my flight a voluntary one?—Oh my dear, how uneasy to us are our reflections upon every doubtful occurrence, when we know we have been prevailed upon to do a wrong thing!

Sunday morning

WHAT an additional concern must I have in my reflections upon Mr Lovelace's hatred of all my relations?—He calls some of them implacable; but I am afraid that he is as implacable himself as the most inveterate of them.

I could not forbear, with great earnestness, to express my wishes for a reconciliation with them; and, in order to begin a treaty for that purpose, to re-urge his departure from me. He gave himself high airs upon the occasion, not doubting, he said, that he was to be the preliminary sacrifice; and then he reflected in a very free manner upon my brother; nor spared my father himself.

So little consideration for me, my dear!—Yet it had always, as I told him, been his polite way to treat my family with contempt; wicked creature that I was, to know it, and yet to hold correspondence with him!—

But let me tell you, sir, said I, that whatever your violent temper and contempt of me may drive you to say of my brother, I will not hear my father spoken ill of. It is enough, surely, that I have tormented his worthy heart by my disobedience; and that his once beloved child has been spirited away from him—To have his character reflected upon, by the man who has been the cause of all, is what I will not bear.

He said many things in his own defence; but not one, as I told him, that could justify a daughter to *hear*, or a man to *say*, who pretended what he pretended to that daughter.

And then, seeing me very sincerely angry, he begged my pardon, though not in a very humble manner. But to change the subject, he took notice of the two letters he had received, one from Lady Betty Lawrance, the other from Miss Montague; and read me passages out of both.

Why did not the man show them to me last night? Was he afraid of giving me too much pleasure?

Lady Betty in hers, expresses herself in the most obliging manner, in relation to me. 'She wishes him so to behave, as to encourage me to make him soon happy. She desires her compliments to me; and expresses her impatience to see, as her niece, so *celebrated* a lady (those are her high words). She shall take it for an honour, she says, to be put into a way to oblige me. She hopes I will not too long delay the ceremony; because that performed, will be to her, and to Lord M. and Lady Sarah, a sure pledge of her nephew's merits and good behaviour.'

She says, 'She was always sorry to hear of the hardships I had met with on his account. That he will be the most ungrateful of men, if he make not *all up* to me: and that she thinks it incumbent upon all their family to supply to me the lost favour of my own: and, for her part, nothing of that kind, she bids him assure me, shall be wanting.'

Her ladyship observes, 'That the treatment he had received from my family would have been more unaccountable than it was, with such natural and accidental advantages as he had, had it not been owing to his own careless manners. But she hopes that he will convince the Harlowe family that they had thought worse of him than he had deserved; since now it was in his power to establish his character for ever: which she prays God to enable him to do, as well for his own honour as for the honour of their house' (was the magnificent word). She concludes, with 'desiring to be informed of our nuptials the moment they are celebrated, that she may be with the earliest in felicitating me on the happy occasion.'

But her ladyship gives me no direct invitation to attend her before marriage. Which I might have expected from what he had told me.

He then showed me part of Miss Montague's more spritely letter, 'congratulating him upon the honour he had obtained, of the *confidence of so admirable a lady.*' Those are her words. *Confidence*, my dear! Nobody, indeed, as you say, will believe otherwise, were they to be told the truth: and you see that Miss Montague (and all his family, I suppose) think the step I have taken, an *extraordinary* one. 'She also wishes for his speedy nuptials; and to see her new cousin at M. Hall: as do Lord M. she tells him, and her sister; and in general all the well-wishers of their family.

'Whenever his happy day shall be passed, she proposes, she says, to attend me and to make one in my train to M. Hall, if his lordship shall continue so ill of the gout, as at present. But that should he get better, he will himself attend me, she is sure, and conduct me thither: and afterwards quit either of his three seats to us, till we shall be settled to our mind.'

This young lady says nothing in excuse for not meeting me on the road, or at St Albans, as he had made me expect she would: yet mentions her having been indisposed. He had also told me that Lord M. was ill of the gout; which Miss Montague's letter confirms.

Letter 123: MISS CLARISSA HARLOWE TO MISS HOWE

(In continuation)

YOU may believe, my dear, that these letters put me in good humour with him. He saw it in my countenance, and congratulated himself upon it. But yet I wondered that I could not have the contents of them communicated to me last night.

He then urged me to go directly to Lady Betty's, on the strength of her letter.

But how, said I, can I do that, were I out of all hope of a reconciliation with my friends (which yet, however improbable to be brought about, is my duty to attempt), as her ladyship has given me no particular invitation.

That, he was sure, was owing to her doubt that it would be accepted: else she had done it with the greatest pleasure in the world.

That doubt itself, I said, was enough to deter me: since her ladyship, who knew so well the boundaries of the fit and the unfit, by her not expecting I would accept of an invitation, had she given it, would have reason to think me very forward if I *had* accepted it; and much more forward to go without it. Then, said I, I thank *you*, sir, I have no clothes fit to go anywhere, or to be seen by anybody.

Oh, I was fit to appear in the drawing-room, were full dress and jewels to be excused, and should make the most amiable (*extraordinary* he must mean) figure there. He was astonished at the elegance of my dress. By what art he knew not, but I appeared to such advantage, as if I had a different suit every day. Besides, his cousins Montague would supply me with all I wanted for the present; and he would write to Miss Charlotte accordingly, if I would give him leave.

Do you think me the jay in the fable?[1] said I—Would you have me visit the owners of the borrowed dresses in their own clothes?—Surely, Mr Lovelace, you think I have either a very low, or a very confident mind.

Would I choose to go to London, for a few days only, in order to furnish myself with clothes?

Not at *his* expense. I was not prepared to wear his livery yet.

I could not have appeared in earnest to him, in my displeasure at his artful contrivances to get me away, if I were not occasionally to show my real fretfulness upon the destitute condition he has reduced me to. When people set out wrong together, it is very difficult to avoid recriminations.

He wished he knew but my mind—that should direct him in his proposals, and it would be his delight to observe it, whatever it was.

My mind was, that he should leave me out of hand.—How often must I tell him so?—

If I were anywhere but here, he would obey me, he said, if I insisted upon it. But if I would assert my right, that would be infinitely preferable, in his opinion, to any other measure *but one; which he durst only hint at:* for then, admitting *his* visits, or refusing them, as I pleased (granting a correspondence by letter only), it would appear to all the world that what I had done was but in order to do myself justice.

How often must I tell you, sir, that I will not litigate with my papa?—Do you think that my unhappy circumstances will alter my notions of my own duty, so far as it is practicable for me to perform it?—How can I obtain possession without litigation, and but by my trustees? One of them will be against me; the other is abroad. This must take up time, were I *disposed* to fall upon this measure—And what I want is present independence, and your *immediate* absence.

Upon his soul, the wretch swore, he did not think it safe, for the reasons he had before given, to leave me here—He hoped I would think of some place, to which I should like to go. But he must take the liberty to say, that he hoped his behaviour had not been so exceptionable as to make me so *very* earnest for his absence in the interim: and the less, surely, as I was almost *eternally* shutting up myself from him; although he presumed, he said, to assure me that he never went from me, but with a corrected heart and with strengthened resolutions of improving by my example.

Eternally shutting myself up from you! repeated I—I hope, sir, that you will not pretend to take it *amiss*, that I expect to be uninvaded in my retirements. I hope you do not think me so weak a creature (novice as you have found me in a very capital instance) as to be fond of occasions to hear your fine speeches, especially as no differing circumstances require your over-frequent visits; nor that I am to be addressed to as if I thought hourly professions needful to assure me of your honour.

He seemed a little disconcerted.

You know, Mr Lovelace, proceeded I, why I am so earnest for your absence. It is that I may appear to the world independent of you; and in hopes, by that means, to find it less difficult to set on foot a reconciliation with my friends. And now let me add (in order to make you easier as to the terms of that hoped-for reconciliation) that since I find I have the good fortune to stand so well with your relations, I will, from time to time, acquaint you, by letter, when you are absent, with every step I shall take, and with every overture that shall be made to me. But not with an intention to render myself accountable to you, neither, as to my acceptance or non-acceptance of those overtures. They know that I have a power given me by my grandfather's will, to bequeath the estate he left me, together with my share of the effects, in a way that may affect them, though not absolutely from them: this *consideration*, I hope, will procure me *some* from them, when their passion subsides, and they know I am independent of you.

Charming reasoning!—And let him tell me, that the assurance I had given him was all he wished for. It was more than he could ask. What a happiness to have a woman of honour and generosity to depend upon!—Had he, on his first entrance into the world, met with such a one, he had never been other than a man of strict virtue—But all, he hoped, was for the best; since, in that case, he had never, perhaps, had the happiness now in his view; because his relations had been always urging him to marry; and that before he had the honour to know me. And now, as he had not been so bad as some people's malice reported him to be, he hoped he should have more merit in his repentance than if he had never erred.

I said I took it for granted that he assented to the reasoning he seemed to approve, and would leave me. And then I asked him what he really, and in his most deliberate mind, would advise me to, in my present situation? He must needs see, I said, that I was at a great loss what to resolve upon; entirely a stranger to London, having no adviser, no protector, at present—himself, he must give me leave to tell him, greatly deficient in *practice*, if not in the *knowledge*, of those decorums which, I had apprehended, were indispensable in the character of a man of birth, fortune and education.

He imagines himself, I find, to be a very polite man, and cannot bear to be thought otherwise. He put up his lip—I am sorry for it, madam—a man of breeding, a man of politeness, give me leave to say (colouring) is much more of a black swan with you, than with any lady I ever met with.

Then that is your misfortune, Mr Lovelace, as well as mine, at present. Every woman of discernment, I am confident, knowing what I know of you now, would say as I say (I had a mind to mortify a pride that I am sure deserves to be mortified), that your politeness is not regular, nor constant. It is not habit. It is too much seen by fits and starts, and sallies, and those not spontaneous. You must be *reminded* into them.

Oh Lord! Oh Lord!—Poor I!—was the light, yet the half-angry wretch's self-pitying expression!—

I proceeded—Upon my word, sir, you are not the accomplished man which your talents and opportunities would have led one to expect you to be—You are indeed in your noviciate (he had, in a former conversation, used that word) as to every laudable attainment—

Letter 124: MISS CLARISSA HARLOWE TO MISS HOWE

(In continuation)

I WAS going on to tell him more of my mind, since the subject was introduced and treated by him so lightly; but he interrupted me—Dear, dear madam, spare me. I am sorry that I have lived to this hour for nothing at all. But surely you could not have quitted a subject so much more agreeable, and so much more suitable, I will say, to our present situation, if you had not too cruel a pleasure in mortifying a man who before looked up to you with a diffidence in his own merits too great to permit him to speak half his mind to you—Be pleased but to return to the subject we were upon; and at another time I will gladly embrace correction from the only mouth in the world so qualified to give it.

You talk of reformation, sometimes, Mr Lovelace; and in so talking acknowledge errors. But I see you can very ill bear the reproof which perhaps you are not solicitous to avoid *giving* occasion for—Far be it from me to take delight in finding fault. I should be glad for both our sakes, since my situation is what it is, that I could do nothing but praise you. But failures which affect a mind that need not be very delicate to be affected by them are too grating to be passed over in silence by a person who wishes to be thought in earnest in her own duties.

I admire your delicacy, madam, again interrupted he—although I suffer by it, yet would I not have it otherwise: indeed I would not, when I consider of it. It is an angelic delicacy which sets you above all our sex, and even above your own. It is *natural* to *you*, madam; so you may not think it extraordinary—but there is nothing like it on earth, said the flatterer—(What company has he kept?)

But let us return to the former subject—You were so good as to ask me what I would advise you to do—I want but to make you easy, I want but to see you fixed to your liking—your faithful Hannah with you—your reconciliation with those with whom you wish to be reconciled set on foot, and in a train.

And now let me mention to you different proposals; in hopes that some one of them may be acceptable to you.

I will go to Mrs Howe, or to Miss Howe, or to whomsoever you would have me go, and endeavour to prevail upon them to receive you.

Do you incline to go to Florence to your cousin Morden?—I will furnish you with the opportunity of going thither, either by sea to Leghorn, or by land through France—Perhaps I may be able to procure one of the ladies of my family to attend you. Either Charlotte or Patty would rejoice in such an opportunity of seeing France and Italy. As for myself, I will only be your escort; in disguise, if you will have it so, even in your livery, that your punctilio may not receive offence by my attendance.

I told him, I would consider of all he had said. But that I hoped for a line or two from my aunt Hervey, if not from my sister, to both of whom I had written; which, if I were to be so favoured, might help to determine me. Meantime, if he would withdraw, I would particularly consider of this proposal of his, in relation to my cousin Morden. And if it held its weight with me, so far as to take your opinion upon it, he should know my mind in an hour's time.

He withdrew with great respect: and in an hour's time returned—And then I told him it was unnecessary to trouble you for your opinion about it. My cousin Morden was soon expected. I could not admit of his accompanying me in any shape, or upon any condition. It was highly improbable that I should obtain the favour of either of his cousins' company: and if that could be done, it would be the same thing in the world's eye as if he went himself.

This led us into another conversation: which shall be the subject of my next.

Letter 125: MISS CLARISSA HARLOWE TO MISS HOWE

(In continuation)
Mr Lovelace told me that on the supposition that his proposal in relation to my cousin Morden might not be accepted, he had been studying to find out, if possible, somewhat that might be agreeable, and which might convince me that he preferred my satisfaction to his own.

He then offered to go himself, and procure my Hannah to come and attend me. As I had declined the service of either of the young Mrs Sorlings, he was extremely solicitous, he said, that I should have a servant in whose integrity I might confide.

I told him that you would be so kind as to send to engage Hannah if possible.

If anything, he said, should prevent *her* from coming, suppose he himself waited upon Miss Howe, to desire her to lend me her servant till I was provided to my mind?

I said your mamma's high displeasure at the step I had taken (as *she* supposed, voluntarily) had deprived me of any open assistance of that sort from you.

He was amazed, so much as Mrs Howe herself used to admire me; and so great an influence as Miss was supposed to have over her mamma (and *deserved* to have) that that lady should take upon herself to be so much offended with me. He wished that the man who took such pains to keep up and inflame the passions of my father and uncles were not at the bottom of this mischief too.

I was afraid, I said, that my brother *was*; or else my uncle Antony, I dared to say, would not have taken such pains to set Mrs Howe against me as I understood he had done.

Since I had declined visiting his aunts, he asked me if I would admit of a visit from his cousin Montague, and accept of a servant of hers for the present?

That was not, I said, an unacceptable proposal: but I would first see if my friends would send me my clothes, that I might not make such a giddy and runaway appearance to any of his relations.

If I pleased, he would make another journey to Windsor, to make more particular inquiry among the canons, or in any worthy family.

Were not his objections as to the publicness of the place, I asked him, as strong now as before?

I remember, my dear, in one of your former letters you mentioned London as the privatest place to be in[a]: and I said that since he made such pretences against leaving me here as showed he had no intention to do so; and since he engaged to go from me, and to leave me to pursue my own measures if I were elsewhere; and since his presence made these lodgings inconvenient to me, I should not be disinclined to go to London, did I know anybody there.

As he had several times proposed London to me, I expected that he would eagerly have embraced that motion from me. But he took not ready hold of it: yet I thought his eye approved of it.

We are both great watchers of each other's eyes; and indeed seem to be more than half afraid of each other.

He then made a grateful proposal to me; that I would send for my Mrs Norton to attend me.

He saw by my eyes, he said, that he had at last been happy in an expedient which would answer both our wishes. Why, says he, did not I think of it before?—and snatching my hand: shall I write, madam? Shall I send? Shall I go and fetch the good woman myself?

After a little consideration, I told him that this was indeed a grateful motion: but that I apprehended it would put her to a difficulty which she would not be able to get over; and as it would make a woman of her known prudence appear to countenance a fugitive daughter in opposition to her parents: and as her coming to me would deprive her of my mamma's favour, without its being in my power to make it up to her.

Oh my beloved creature! said he, generously enough, let not this be an obstacle. I will do everything for the good woman you wish to have done—Let me go for her.

More coolly than perhaps his generosity deserved, I told him it was impossible but I must soon hear from my friends. I should not, meantime, embroil anybody with them. Not Mrs Norton especially, from whose interest in, and mediation with,

a   See p. 331.

my mamma, I might expect some good, were she to keep herself in a neutral state: that, besides, the good woman had a mind above her fortune; and would sooner want than be beholden to anybody improperly.

Improperly, said he!—Have not persons of merit a *right* to all the benefits conferred upon them?—Mrs Norton is so good a woman that I shall think she lays me under an obligation, if she will put it in my power to serve her; although she were not to augment it by giving me the opportunity at the same time, of contributing to your pleasure and satisfaction.

How could this man, with such powers of right thinking, be so far depraved by evil habits as to disgrace his talents by wrong acting?

Is there not room, after all, thought I at the time, for hope (as he so lately led me to hope) that the example it will behove me, for both our sakes, to endeavour to set him, may influence him to a change of manners in which both may find their account?

Give me leave, sir, said I, to tell you there is a strange mixture in your mind. You must have taken *pains* to suppress many good motions and reflections as they arose, or levity must have been surprisingly predominant in it—But as to the subject we were upon, there is no taking any resolutions till I hear from my friends.

Well, madam, I can only say I would find out some expedient, if I could, that should be agreeable to you. But since I cannot, will you be so good as to tell me what you would *wish* to have done? Nothing in the world but I will comply with, excepting leaving you here, at such a distance from the place I shall be in, if anything should happen; and in a place where my gossiping rascals have made me in a manner public, for want of proper cautions at first.

These vermin, added he, have a pride they can hardly rein in, when they serve a man of family. They boast of their master's pedigree and descent, as if they were related to him. Nor is anything they know of him, or of his affairs, a secret to one another, were it what would hang him.

If so, thought I, men of family should take care to give them subjects worth boasting of.

I am quite at a loss, said I, what to do, or whither to go. Would you, Mr Lovelace, in earnest, advise me to think of going to London?

And I looked at him with steadfastness. But nothing could I gather from his looks.

At first, madam, said he, I was for proposing London, as I was then more apprehensive of pursuit. But as your relations seem cooler on that head, I am the more indifferent about the place you go to—So as *you* are pleased—So as *you* are easy, I shall be happy.

This indifference of his to London, I cannot but say, made me like going thither the better. I asked him (to hear what he would say) if he could recommend me to any *particular place* in London?

No, he said: none that was fit for me, or that I should like. His friend Belford indeed had very handsome lodgings near Soho Square, at a relation's, a lady of virtue and honour. These, as Mr Belford was generally in the country, he could borrow till I were better accommodated.

I was resolved to refuse these at the first mention, as I should any other he had named. Nevertheless, I will see, thought I, if he has really thoughts of these for me.

If I break off the talk here, and he resume this proposal with earnestness in the morning, I shall apprehend that he is less indifferent than he seems to be about my going to London; and that he has already a lodging in his eye for me—And then I won't go at all.

But after such generous motions from him, I really think it a little barbarous to act and behave as if I thought him capable of the blackest and most ungrateful baseness. But his character, his principles, are so faulty!—He is so light, so vain, so various, that there is no certainty that he will be next hour what he is this. Then, my dear, I have no guardian now; no father, no mother! Nothing but God and my vigilance to depend upon. And I have no reason to expect a miracle in my favour.

Well, sir, said I, rising to leave him, something must be resolved upon: but I will postpone this subject till tomorrow morning.

He would fain have engaged me longer; but I said I would see him as early as he pleased in the morning. He might think of any convenient place in London, or near it, meantime.

And so I retired from him. As I do from my pen; hoping for better rest for the few hours that will remain for that desirable refreshment, than I have had of a long time.

CL. HARLOWE

Letter 126: MISS CLARISSA HARLOWE TO MISS HOWE

(In continuation)

Monday morning, April 17

LATE as I went to bed, I have had very little rest. Sleep and I have quarrelled; and although I court it, it will not be friends. I hope its fellow-irreconcilables at Harlowe Place enjoy its balmy comforts. Else that will be an aggravation of my fault. My brother and sister, I dare say, want it not.

Mr Lovelace, who is an early riser as well as I, joined me in the garden about six; and after the usual salutations, asked me to resume our last night's subject. It was upon lodgings at London, he said.

I think you mentioned one to me, sir—did you not?

Yes, madam, but (watching the turn of my countenance) rather as what you'd be welcome to, than perhaps approve of.

I believe so too. To go to town upon an *uncertainty*, I own, is not agreeable; but to be obliged to any gentleman of your acquaintance, when I want to be thought independent of you; and to a gentleman especially, to whom my friends are to direct to me, if they vouchsafe to take notice of me at all, is an absurd thing to mention.

He did not mention it as what he imagined I would accept, but only to confirm to me what he had said, that he himself knew of none fit for me.

Has not your family, madam, some one tradesman they deal with, who has conveniencies of this kind? I would make it worth such a person's while, to keep the secret of your being at his house. Traders are dealers in pins, said he; and will be more obliged by a penny customer than a pound present, because it is in their way—yet will refuse neither.

My father's tradesmen, I said, would no douht be the first employed to find me out: so that proposal was as absurd as the other.

We had a good deal of discourse upon the same topic. But, at last, the result of all was this—He wrote a letter to one Mr Doleman, a married man of fortune and character (I excepting to Mr Belford), desiring him to provide decent apartments ready furnished (for I had told him what they should be) for a single woman; consisting of a bedchamber; another for a maidservant, with the use of a dining-room or parlour. This he gave me to peruse; and then sealed it up and dispatched it away in my presence by one of his own servants, who having business in town is to bring back an answer.

I attend the issue of it; holding myself in readiness to set out for London, unless you advise the contrary. I will only add, that I am

Your ever affectionate
CL. HARLOWE

Letter 127: MR LOVELACE TO JOHN BELFORD, ESQ.

Sat., Sunday, Monday

He gives in several letters the substance of what is contained in the last of the lady's.

He tells his friend that calling at The Lawn in his way to M. Hall (for he owns that he went not to Windsor), he found the letters from Lady Betty Lawrance and his cousin Montague, which Mrs Greme was about sending to him by a special messenger.

He gives the particulars from Mrs Greme's report of what passed between the lady and her, as in pp. 396, 397, and makes such declarations to Mrs Greme of his honour and affection to the lady, as put her upon writing the letter to her sister Sorlings, the contents of which are given by the lady in pp. 452, 453.

He then accounts, as follows, for the serious humour he found her in on his return.

Upon such good terms when we parted, I was surprised to find so solemn a brow upon my return, and her charming eyes red with weeping. But when I had understood she had received letters from Miss Howe, it was easy to imagine that that little devil had put her out of humour with me.

This gives me infinite curiosity to find out the subject of their letters. But this must not be attempted yet. An invasion in an article so sacred would ruin me beyond retrieve. Yet it vexes me to the heart to think that she is hourly writing her whole mind on all that passes between her and me—I under the same roof with her—yet kept at such awful distance, that I dare not break into a correspondence that may perhaps be a means to blow me, and all my devices up together!

Would it be very wicked, Jack, to knock her messenger o'the head as he is carrying my beloved's letters or returning with Miss Howe's? To attempt to bribe him, and not succeed, would utterly ruin me. And the man seems to be one used to poverty, one who can sit down satisfied with it, and enjoy it; contented with hand-to-mouth conveniencies, and not aiming to live better tomorrow than he does today and than he did yesterday. Such a one is above temptation, unless it could come clothed in the guise of *truth* and *trust*. What likelihood of corrupting a man who has no hope, no ambition?

Yet the rascal has but *half* life, and groans under that—Should I be answerable in his case for a *whole* one?—But hang the fellow!—Let him live.—Were I a king, or a minister of state, an Antonio Perez,[a] it were another thing. And yet, on second thoughts, am not I a rake, as it is called? And who ever knew a rake to stick at anything? But thou knowest, Jack, that the greatest half of my wickedness is vapour, to show my invention and that I *could* be mischievous if I would.

He collects the lady's expressions which his pride cannot bear: such as, that he is a stranger to the decorums which she thought inseparable from a man of birth and education; and that he is not the accomplished man he imagines himself to be; *and threatens to remember them against her.*

He values himself upon his proposals and speeches, which he gives to his friend pretty much to the same purpose that the lady does in her four last letters.

When he recites his endeavouring to put her upon borrowing a servant from Miss Howe, till Hannah could come, he writes as follows:

Thou seest, Belford, that my charmer has no notion that Miss Howe herself is but a puppet danced upon my wires, at second or third hand. To outwit and impel, as one pleases, two such girls as these, who think they know everything; and by taking advantage of the pride and ill-nature of the old ones of both families, to play them off likewise at the very time that they think they are doing me spiteful displeasure; what charming revenge!—Then the sweet lady, when I wished that her *brother* was not at the bottom of Mrs Howe's resentment, to tell me that she was afraid he *was,* or her uncle would not have appeared against her to that lady— Pretty dear! how innocent!

But don't think me the *cause* neither of her family's malice and resentment. It is all in their hearts. I work but with their materials. They, if left to their own wicked direction, would perhaps express their revenge by fire and faggot; that is to say, by the private dagger, or by Lord Chief Justice's warrants, by law, and so forth: I only point the lightning and teach it where to dart, without the thunder: in other words, I only guide the effects: the cause is in their malignant hearts: and, while I am doing a little mischief, I prevent a great deal.

Thus he exults on her mentioning London:

I wanted her to propose London herself. This made me again mention Windsor. If you would have a woman do one thing, you must always propose another!—The sex! the very sex! as I hope to be saved!—Why, they lay one under a necessity to deal doubly with them: and when they find themselves outwitted, they cry out upon an honest fellow who has been too hard for them at their own weapons.

I could hardly contain myself. My heart was at my throat—Down, down, said I to myself, exuberant exultation!—A sudden cough befriended me: I again turned to her, all as *indifferenced over* as a girl at the first long-expected question who waits for two more. I heard, out the rest of her speech: and when she had done, instead of saying anything of London, I proposed to her to send for her Mrs Norton.

As I knew she would be afraid of lying under obligations had she accepted of my offer, I could have proposed to do so much for the good woman and her son as would have made her resolve that I should do nothing—This, however, not merely to avoid expense: but there was no such thing as allowing of the presence of Mrs

---

a   Antonio Perez was first minister of Philip II, king of Spain, by whose command he caused Don Juan de Escovedo to be assassinated: which brought on his own ruin, through the perfidy of his viler master (*Geddes's Tracts*).

Norton. I might as well have had her mother or aunt Hervey with her. Hannah, had she been able to come, and had she come, I could have done well enough with. What do I keep fellows idling in the country for, but to fall in love, and even to marry whom I would have them marry?

How unequal is a modest woman to the adventure when she throws herself into the power of a rake!—Punctilio will, at any time, stand for reasons with such a one. She cannot break through a well-tested modesty. None but the impudent little rogues who can name the parson and the church before you can ask them for either, and undress and go to bed before you the next hour, should think of running away with a man.

I am in the right train now. Every hour, I doubt not, will give me an increasing interest in the affections of this proud beauty!—I have just carried *un*-politeness far enough to *make her afraid of me*; and to show her that I am *no whiner*. Every instance of politeness, *now*, will give me double credit with her! My next point will be to make her acknowledge a *lambent* flame, a preference of me to all other men at least: and then my happy hour is not far off. And *acknowledged* love sanctifies every freedom: and one freedom begets another. And if she call me *ungenerous*, I can call her *cruel*. The sex love to be called cruel. Many a time have I complained of cruelty, even in the act of yielding, because I knew it gratified their pride.

Mentioning that he had only hinted at Mr Belford's lodgings as an instance to confirm what he had said, that he knew of none in London fit for her, he says:
I had a mind to alarm her with something furthest from my purpose; for (as much as she disliked my motion) I intended nothing by it: Mrs Osgood is too pious a woman; and would have been more *her* friend than *mine*.

I had a view, moreover, to give her an high opinion of her own sagacity. I love, when I dig a pit, to have my prey tumble in with secure feet and open eyes: then a man can look down upon her, with an Oh-ho, charmer! how came you there!

Monday, April 17
I have just now received a fresh piece of intelligence from my agent, honest Joseph Leman. Thou knowest the history of poor Miss Betterton of Nottingham. James Harlowe is plotting to revive the resentments of that family against me. The Harlowes took great pains, some time ago, to get to the bottom of that story. But now the foolish devils are resolved to do something in it, if they can. My head is working to make this booby 'squire a plotter, and a clever fellow, in order to turn his plots to my advantage, supposing the lady shall aim to keep me at arm's length when in town, and to send me from her—But I will, in proper time, let thee see Joseph's letter, and what I shall answer to it.[a] To know, in time, a designed mischief, is, with me, to disappoint it, and to turn it upon the contriver's head.

Joseph is plaguy squeamish again; but, I know, he only intends by his qualms to swell his merits with me. Oh Belford, Belford! what a vile corruptible rogue, whether in poor or in rich, is human nature!

---

a   See Letters 139 and 140.

Letter 128: MISS HOWE TO MISS CLARISSA HARLOWE

(In answer to Letters 120 to 126 inclusive)

Tuesday, April 18

You have a most implacable family. Another visit from your uncle Antony has not only confirmed my mamma an enemy to our correspondence, but has almost put her upon treading in their steps.

But, to other subjects:

You plead generously for Mr Hickman. Perhaps with regard to him I may have done, as I have often done in singing or music—begun a note or key too high; and yet, rather than begin again, proceed, though I strain my voice or spoil my tune—But this is evident, the man is more observant for it; and you have taught me that the spirit which is the humbler for ill-usage will be insolent upon better. So, good and grave Mr Hickman, keep your distance a little longer, I beseech you. You have erected an altar to me; and I hope you will not refuse to bow to it.

But you ask me if I would treat Mr Lovelace, were he to be in Mr Hickman's place, as I do Mr Hickman?—Why really, my dear, I believe I should not—I have been very sagely considering this point of behaviour, in general, on both sides in courtship; and I will very candidly tell you the result. I have concluded that politeness, even to excess, is necessary on the men's part, to bring us to listen to their first address, in order to induce us to bow our necks to a yoke so unequal. But upon my conscience, I very much doubt whether a little intermingled insolence is not requisite from them, to keep up that interest, when once it has got footing. Men must not let us see that we can make fools of them. And I think that *smooth* love, that is to say, a passion without rubs; in other words, a passion without passion, is like a sleepy stream that is hardly seen to give motion to a straw. So that, sometimes to make us fear, and even, for a short space, to *hate* the wretch, is productive of the *contrary* extreme.

If this be so, Lovelace, than whom no man was ever more polite and obsequious at the *beginning*, has hit the very point. For his turbulence *since*, his readiness to offend and his equal readiness to humble himself, as he is known to be a man of sense, and of courage too, must keep a woman's passion alive; and at last tire her into a non-resistance that shall make her as passive as a tyrant husband would wish her to be.

I verily think that the different behaviour of our two heroes to their heroines makes out this doctrine to demonstration. I am so much accustomed, for my own part, to Hickman's whining, creeping, submissive courtship that I now expect nothing but whine and cringe from him; and am so little moved with his nonsense that I am frequently forced to go to my harpsichord to keep me awake and to silence his humdrum—Whereas Lovelace keeps up the ball with a witness, and all his address and conversation is one continual game at racquet.

Your frequent quarrels and reconciliations verify this observation: and I really believe that could Hickman have kept my attention alive after the Lovelace manner, only that he had preserved his morals, I should have married the man by this time. But then he must have *set out* accordingly. For now, he can never, never recover himself; that's certain: but must be a dangler to the end of the courtship chapter; and what is still worse for him, a passive to the end of his life.

Poor Hickman! perhaps you'll say. I have been called your echo—Poor Hickman! say I.

You wonder, my dear, that Mr Lovelace took not notice to you of his aunt's and cousin's letters to him, overnight. I don't like his keeping such a material and *relative* circumstance, as I may call it, one moment from you. By his communicating the contents of them to you next day, when you was angry with him, it looks as if he withheld them for occasional pacifiers; and if so, must he not have had a forethought that he might give you *cause* for anger? Of all the circumstances that have happened since you have been with him, I think I like this the least. This alone, my dear, small as it might look to an indifferent eye, in mine warrants all your cautions. Yet I think that Mrs Greme's letter to her sister Sorlings; his repeated motions for Hannah's attendance; and for that of one of the widow Sorlings's daughters; and above all, for that of Mrs Norton, are agreeable counterbalances. Were it not for those circumstances, I should have said a great deal more of the other. Yet the foolish man, to let you know overnight that he *had* such letters!—I can't tell what to make of him.

I am pleased with what these ladies write. And the more as I have caused them to be again sounded, and find that the whole family are as desirous as ever of your alliance.

I think there can be no objection to your going to London. There, as in the centre, you'll be in the way of hearing from everybody and sending to anybody. And then you will put all his sincerity to the test, as to his promised absence and such-like.

But really, my dear, I think you have nothing for it but marriage. You may try (that you may say you *have* tried) what your relations can be brought to. But the moment they refuse your proposals, submit to the yoke and make the best of it. He will be a savage indeed, if he makes you speak out. Yet it is my opinion that you *must* bend a little; for he cannot bear to be thought slightly of.

This was one of his speeches once; I believe designed for me—'A woman who means one day to favour a man should show the world, for her *own* sake, that she distinguishes her adorer from the common herd.'

Shall I give you another fine sentence of his, and in the true libertine style, as he spoke it, throwing out his challenging hand?—'D—n him' if he would marry (indelicate as some persons thought him to be) the first princess on earth, if he but thought she balanced a minute in her choice of him, or of an emperor.'

All the world, in short, expect you to have this man. They think that you left your father's house for this very purpose. The longer the ceremony is delayed, the worse appearance it will have in the world's eye. And it will not be the fault of some of your relations if a slur be not thrown upon your reputation while you continue unmarried. Your uncle Antony in particular speaks rough and vile things, grounded upon the morals of his brother Orson.[1] But hitherto your admirable character has antidoted the poison; the speaker is despised, and everyone's indignation raised against him.

I have written through many interruptions: and you'll see the first sheet creased and rumpled, occasioned by putting it into my bosom on my mamma's sudden coming upon me. We have had one very pretty debate, I'll assure you; but it is not worth while to trouble you with the particulars—But upon my word—no matter though—

Your Hannah cannot attend you. The poor girl left her place about a fortnight ago on account of a rheumatic disorder which has confined her to her room ever since. She burst into tears when Kitty carried to her your desire of having her, and called herself doubly unhappy that she could not wait upon a mistress whom she so dearly loved.

Were my mamma to have answered my wishes, I should have been sorry Mr Lovelace had been the *first* proposer of my Kitty for your attendant, till Hannah could come. To be altogether among strangers, and a stranger to attend you every time you remove, is a very disagreeable thing. But your considerateness and bounty will make you faithful ones wherever you go.

You must take your own way: but if you suffer any inconvenience either as to clothes or money, that is in my power to supply, I will never forgive you. My mamma (if *that* be your objection) need not know anything of the matter.

Your next letter, I suppose, will be from London. Pray direct it, and your future letters till further notice, to Mr Hickman at his own house. He is entirely devoted to you. Don't take so heavily my mamma's partiality and prejudices. I hope I am past a baby.

Heaven preserve you, and make you as happy as I think you deserve to be, prays

Your ever affectionate
ANNA HOWE

Letter 129: MISS CLARISSA HARLOWE TO MISS HOWE

Wedn. morn. April 19

I AM glad, my dear friend, that you approve of my removal to London.

The disagreement between your mamma and you gives me inexpressible affliction. I hope I think you both more unhappy than you are. But I beseech you let me know the particulars of the debate you call *a very pretty one*. I am well acquainted with your dialect. When you acquaint me with the whole, be your mamma ever so severe upon me, I shall be easier a great deal—Faulty people should rather deplore the occasion than resent the anger that is but the consequence of their fault.

If I am to be obliged to anybody in England for money, it shall be to you. Your mother need not know of your kindness to me, you say—But she *must* know it, if it be done, and if she challenge my beloved friend upon it—for would you either falsify or prevaricate?—I wish your mamma could be made easy on this head. Forgive me, my dear—but I know—yet once she had a better opinion of me. Oh my inconsiderate rashness!—Excuse me once more, I pray you—Pride, when it is *native*, will show itself sometimes, in the midst of mortifications!—but my stomach is down already!

I AM unhappy that I cannot have my worthy Hannah!—I am as sorry for the poor creature's illness as for my own disappointment by it. Come, my dear Miss Howe, since you press me to be beholden to you; and would think me proud if I absolutely refused your favour, pray be so good as to send her two guineas in my name.

If I have nothing for it, as you say, but matrimony, it yields a little comfort that his relations do not despise the *fugitive*, as persons of their rank and quality-pride might be supposed to do, for having *been* a fugitive.

But oh my cruel, thrice cruel uncle! to suppose—but my heart checks my pen, and will not let it proceed on an intimation so extremely shocking as that which he supposes!—Yet, if thus they have been persuaded, no wonder if they are irreconcilable. This is all my hard-hearted brother's doings!—his surmisings!—God forgive him! Prays his injured sister, and

Your ever obliged and affectionate friend,
CL. H.

Letter 130: MISS CLARISSA HARLOWE TO MISS HOWE

Thursday, April 20

MR Lovelace's servant is already returned with an answer from his friend Mr Doleman, who has taken pains in his inquiries, and is very particular. Mr Lovelace brought me the letter as soon as he had read it; and as he now knows that I acquaint you with everything that offers, I desired him to let me send it to you for your perusal. Be pleased to return it by the first opportunity. You will see by it that his friends in town have a notion that we are actually married.

[*Letter 130.1: Thomas Doleman*] to *Robert Lovelace, Esq.*

Tuesday night, April 18

Dear sir,

I AM extremely rejoiced to hear that we shall so soon have you in town after so long an absence. You will be the more welcome still, if what report says be true; which is that you are actually married to the fair lady upon whom we have heard you make such encomiums. Mrs Doleman and my sister both wish you joy, if you are, and joy upon your near prospect, if you are not. I have been in town for this week past, to get help if I could, from my paralytic complaints, and am in a course for them—which nevertheless did not prevent me from making the desired inquiries. This is the result.

You may have a first floor, well-furnished, at a mercer's in Bedford Street, Covent Garden, with what conveniencies you please for servants: and these either by the quarter or month. The terms according to the conveniencies required.

Mrs Doleman has seen lodgings in Norfolk Street and others in Cecil Street; but though the prospects to the Thames and Surrey hills look inviting from both these streets, yet I suppose they are too near the city.

The owner of those in Norfolk Street would have half the house go together. It would be too much for your description therefore: and I suppose that you will hardly, when you think fit to declare your marriage, be in lodgings.

Those in Cecil Street are neat and convenient. The owner is a widow of good character; but she insists, that you take them for a twelvemonth certain.

You may have good accommodations in Dover Street, at a widow's, the relict of an officer in the guards, who dying soon after he had purchased his commission (to which he had a good title by service, and which cost him most part of what he had), she was obliged to let lodgings.

This may possibly be an objection. But she is very careful, she says, that she takes no lodgers but of figure and reputation. She rents two good houses, distant from each other, only joined by a large handsome passage. The inner house is the genteelest, and is very elegantly furnished; but you may have the use of a very handsome parlour in the outer house, if you choose to look into the street.

A little garden belongs to the inner house, in which the old gentlewoman has displayed a true female fancy, and crammed it with vases, flower-pots and figures, without number.

As these lodgings seemed to me the most likely to please you, I was more particular in my inquiries about them. The apartments she has to let are in the inner house: they are a dining-room, two neat parlours, a withdrawing-room, two or three handsome bedchambers (one with a pretty light closet in it, which looks into the little garden); all furnished in taste.

A dignified clergyman, his wife and maiden-daughter were the last who lived in them. They have but lately quitted them on his being presented to a considerable church preferment in Ireland. The gentlewoman says that he took the lodgings but for three months certain; but liked them and her usage so well, that he continued in them two years; and left them with regret, though on so good an account. She bragged that this was the way of all the lodgers she ever had, who stayed with her four times as long as they at first intended.

I had some knowledge of the colonel, who was always looked upon as a man of honour. His relict I never saw before. I think she has a masculine air, and is a little forbidding at first: but when I saw her behaviour to two agreeable maiden gentlewomen, her husband's nieces, whom for *that* reason she calls *doubly* hers, and heard their praises of *her*, I could impute her very bulk to good humour; since we seldom see your sour peevish people plump. She lives very reputably, and is, as I find, aforehand in the world.

If these, or any other of the lodgings I have mentioned, be not altogether to your lady's mind, she may continue in them the less while, and choose others for herself.

The widow consents that you should take them for a month only, and *what* of them you please. The terms, she says, she will not fall out upon when she knows what your lady expects, and what *her* servants are to do, or *yours* will undertake; for she observed that servants are generally worse to deal with than their masters or mistresses.

The lady may board or not, as she pleases.

As we suppose you married, but that you have reason from family differences to keep it private for the present, I thought it not amiss to hint as much to the widow (but as uncertainty, however), and asked her if she could in that case accommodate you and your servants, as well as the lady and hers? She said she could; and wished by all means it were to be so; since the circumstance of a person's being single, if not as well recommended as this lady, was one of her usual exceptions.

If none of these lodgings please, you need not doubt very handsome ones in or near Hanover Square, Soho Square, Golden Square, or in some of the new streets about Grosvenor Square.[1] And Mrs Doleman, her sister and myself most cordially join to offer to your good lady the best accommodations we can make for her at

Uxbridge (and also for you, if you are the happy man we wish you to be), till she fits herself more to her mind.

Let me add that the lodgings at the mercer's, those in Cecil Street, those at the widow's in Dover Street, any of them, may be entered upon at a day's warning.

I am, my dear sir,

Your sincere and affectionate friend and servant,
THO. DOLEMAN

You will easily guess, my dear, when you have read the letter, which lodgings I made choice of. But first, to try him, as in so material a point I thought I could not be too circumspect, I seemed to prefer those in Norfolk Street, for the very reason the writer gives why he thought I would *not*; that is to say, for its neighbourhood to a city so well governed as London is said to be. Nor should I have disliked a lodging in the heart of it, having heard but indifferent accounts of the liberties sometimes taken at the other end of the town—then seeming to incline to the lodgings in Cecil Street—then to the mercer's. But he made no visible preference: and when I asked his opinion of the widow gentlewoman's, he said, he thought these the most to my taste and convenience. But as he hoped that I would think lodgings necessary but for a very little while, he knew not which to give his vote for.

I then fixed upon the widow's; and he has written accordingly to Mr Doleman, making my compliments to his lady and sister for their kind offer.

I am to have the dining-room, the bedchamber with the light closet (of which, if I stay any time at the widow's, I shall make great use), and a servant's room; and we propose to set out on Saturday morning. As for a maidservant, poor Hannah's illness is a great disappointment to me: but, as he says, I can make the widow satisfaction for one of hers, till I can get one to my mind. And you know, I want not much attendance.

MR Lovelace has just now, of his own accord, given me five guineas for poor Hannah. I send them enclosed. Be so good as to cause them to be conveyed to her; and to let her know from whom they came.

He has obliged me much by this little mark of his considerateness. Indeed I have the better opinion of him ever since he proposed her return to me.

I HAVE just now *another* instance of his considerateness. He came to me and said that on second thoughts he could not bear that I should go up to town without some attendant, were it but for the look of the thing to the widow and her nieces who, according to his friend's account, lived so genteelly; and especially as I required him to leave me soon after I arrived there; and so would be left alone among strangers. He therefore thought that I might engage Mrs Sorlings to lend me one of her two maids, or to let one of her daughters go up with me, and stay till I were provided. And if the latter, the young gentlewoman no doubt would be glad of so good an opportunity to see a little of the curiosities of the town, and would be a proper attendant to me on the same occasions.

I told him as I had done before, that the servants and the two young gentlewomen were so equally useful in their way (and servants in a busy farm were so little to be spared), that I should be loath to take them off of their laudable employments.

Nor should I think much of diversions for one while; and so the less want an attendant out of doors.

And now, my dear, lest anything should happen, in so variable a situation as mine to overcloud my prospects (which at present are more promising than ever yet they have been since I quitted Harlowe Place), I will snatch the opportunity to subscribe myself.

> Your not unhoping,
> and ever obliged friend and servant,
> CL. HARLOWE

Letter 131: MR LOVELACE TO JOHN BELFORD, ESQ.

Thursday, April 20

He begins with communicating to him the letter he wrote to Mr Doleman to procure suitable lodgings in town, and which he sent away by the lady's approbation: and then gives him a copy of the answer to it (see p. 469): upon which he thus expresses himself:

Thou knowest the widow; thou knowest her nieces; thou knowest the lodgings: and didst thou ever read a letter more artfully couched than this of Tom Doleman? Every possible objection anticipated! Every accident provided against!—Every tittle of it plot-proof!

Who could forbear smiling to see my charmer, like a farcical dean and chapter, choose[1] what was before chosen for her; and sagaciously (as they go in form to prayers, that God would direct their choice) pondering upon the different proposals, as if she would make me believe she has a mind for some other? The dear sly rogue looking upon me, too, with a view to discover some emotion in me: *that* I can tell her lay deeper than her eye could reach, though it had been a sunbeam.

No confidence in me, fair one! None at all, 'tis plain. Thou wilt not, if I were inclined to change my views, encourage me by a generous reliance on my honour!—And shall it be said, that I, a master of arts in love, shall be overmatched by so unpractised a novice?

But to see the charmer so far satisfied with my contrivance as to borrow my friend's letter, in order to satisfy Miss Howe likewise!

Silly little rogues! to walk out into by-paths on the strength of their own judgements!—when nothing but *experience* can teach them how to disappoint us, and learn them grandmother-wisdom! When they have it indeed, then may they sit down, like so many Cassandras, and preach caution to others; who will as little mind *them* as they did *their* instructresses, whenever a fine handsome confident fellow, such a one as thou knowest who, comes cross them.

But, Belford, didst thou not mind that sly rogue Doleman's naming Dover Street for the widow's place of abode!—What dost think could be meant by that?—'Tis impossible thou shouldst guess. So, not to puzzle thee about it—suppose the widow Sinclair's in Dover Street should be inquired after by some officious person in order to come at characters (Miss Howe is as *sly* as the devil, and as *busy* to the full); and neither such a name, nor such a house can be found in that street, nor a house to answer the description, then will not the keenest hunter in England be at a fault?

But how wilt thou do, methinks thou askest, to hinder the lady from resenting the fallacy, and mistrusting thee the more on that account when she finds it out to be in another street?

Pho! never mind that: either I shall have a way for it, or we shall thoroughly understand one another by that time; or if we don't, she'll know enough of me not to wonder at *such* a peccadillo.

But how wilt thou hinder the lady from apprising her friend of the real name?

She must first know it herself, monkey, must she not?

Well, but, how wilt thou do to hinder her from knowing the street, and her friend from directing letters thither; which will be the same thing as if the name were known?

Let me alone for that too.

If thou further objectest that Tom Doleman is too great a dunce to write such a letter in answer to mine;—canst thou not imagine that, in order to save honest Tom all this trouble, I, who know the town so well, could send him a copy of what he should write, and leave him nothing to do but transcribe?

What now sayest thou to *me*, Belford?

And suppose I had designed this task of inquiry for thee; and suppose the lady excepted against thee, for no other reason in the world but because of my value for thee? What sayest thou to the *lady*, Jack?

This it is to have leisure upon my hands!—What a matchless plotter thy friend! Stand by and let me swell!—I am already as big as an elephant; and ten times wiser! mightier too by far! Have I not reason to snuff the moon with my proboscis?—Lord help thee for a poor, for a very poor creature!—Wonder not that I despise thee heartily—since the man who is disposed immoderately to exalt himself cannot do it but by despising everybody else in proportion.

I shall make good use of the *Dolemanic* hint of being married. But I will not tell thee all at once. Nor, indeed, have I thoroughly digested that part of my plot. When a general must regulate himself by the motions of a watchful adversary, how can he say beforehand what he will, or what he will not do?

Widow SINCLAIR!—didst thou not say, Lovelace?—

Ay, SINCLAIR, Jack!—Remember the name! SINCLAIR, I repeat. She *has* no other. And her features being broad and full-blown, I will suppose her to be of Highland extraction; as her husband the colonel (mind that too) was a Scot, as brave as honest.

I never forget the *minutiae* in my contrivances. In all *doubtable* matters the *minutiae* closely attended to and provided for are of more service than a thousand oaths, vows and protestations made to supply the neglect of them, [especially] when jealousy has actually got into the working mind.

Thou wouldst wonder if thou knewest one half of my *providences*. To give thee but one: I have already been so good as to send up a list of books to be procured for the lady's closet, mostly at *second-hand*. And thou knowest that the women there are all well read. But I will not anticipate—besides, it looks as if I were afraid of leaving anything to my old friend CHANCE; which has many a time been an excellent second to me; and ought not to be affronted or despised; especially by one who has the art of making unpromising incidents turn out in his favour.

Wednesday, April 19

I HAVE a piece of intelligence to give you which concerns you much to know.

Your brother having been assured that you are not married, has taken a resolution to find you out, way-lay you and carry you off. A friend of his, a captain of a ship, undertakes to get you on shipboard; and to sail away with you, either [to] Hull or Leith, in the way to one of your brother's houses.

They are very wicked: for in spite of all your virtues they conclude you to be *ruined*. But if they can be assured when they have you that you are not, they will secure you till they can bring you out Mrs Solmes: and meantime, in order to give Mr Lovelace full employment, they talk of a prosecution which will be set up against him for some crime or other that they have got a notion of, which they think, if it do not cost him his life, will make him fly his country.

This is very early news. Miss Bell told it in confidence, and with mighty triumph over Lovelace, to Miss Lloyd; who is at present her favourite, though as much your admirer as ever. Miss Lloyd, being very apprehensive of the mischief which might follow such an attempt, told it to me with leave to apprise you privately of it—And yet neither she nor I would be sorry, perhaps, if Lovelace were to be fairly hanged—that is to say, if you, my dear, had no objection to it. But we cannot bear that such an admirable creature should be made the tennis-ball of two violent spirits—much less that you should be seized, and exposed to the brutal treatment of wretches who have no bowels.

If you can engage Mr Lovelace to keep his temper upon it, I think you should acquaint him with it; but not to mention Miss Lloyd. Perhaps his wicked agent may come at the intelligence and reveal it to him. But I leave it to your own discretion to do as you think fit in it. All my concern is that this daring and foolish project, if carried on, will be a means of throwing you more into his power than ever. But as it will convince you that there can be no hope of a reconciliation, I wish you were actually married, let the cause for the prosecution hinted at be what it will, short of murder or a rape.

Your Hannah was very thankful for your kind present. She heaped a thousand blessings upon you for it. She has Mr Lovelace's too, by this time.

I am pleased with Mr Hickman, I can tell you—for he has sent her two guineas by the person who carries Mr Lovelace's five, as from an unknown hand: nor am I, or you, to know it. The manner, more than the value, I am pleased with him for. But he does a great many things of this sort; and is as silent as the night; for nobody knows of them till the gratitude of the benefited will not let them be concealed. He is now and then my almoner, and I believe always adds to my little benefactions.

But his time is not come to be praised for these things; nor does he seem to want *that* encouragement.

The man has certainly a good mind. Nor can we expect in one man every good quality. But he is really a silly fellow, my dear, to trouble his head about me, when he sees how much I despise his whole sex; and must of course make a common man look like a fool, were he not to make *himself* look like one by wishing to pitch his tent so oddly. Our likings and dislikings, as I have often thought, are seldom

governed by prudence or with a view to happiness. The eye, my dear, the wicked
eye—has such a strict alliance with the heart!—and both have such enmity to the
understanding!—What an unequal union, the mind and body! All the senses, like
the family at Harlowe Place, in a confederacy against that which would animate
and give honour to the whole, were it allowed its proper precedence.

Permit me, I beseech you, before you go to London, to send you forty-eight
guineas. I mention that sum to oblige you, because by accepting back the two to
Hannah I will hold you indebted to me fifty—Surely *this* will induce you!—You
know that I cannot want the money. I told you that I have near double that sum;
and that the half of it is more than my mamma knows I am mistress of. With so
little money as you have, what can you do at such a place as London!—You don't
know what occasion you may have for messengers, intelligence and such like. If
you don't oblige me, I shall not think your stomach so much down as you say it is;
and as, in this one particular, I think it ought to be.

As to the state of things between my mamma and me, you know enough of her
temper not to need to be told that she never espouses or resents with indifference.
Yet will she not remember that I am *her* daughter. No, truly, I am all my *papa's
girl.*

She was very sensible, surely, of the violence of my poor papa's temper, that she
can so long remember *that*, when acts of tenderness and affection seem quite
forgotten. Some daughters would be tempted to think that control sat very heavy
upon a mother, who can endeavour to exert the power she has over a child; and
regret for years after death, that she had not the same over a husband.

If this manner of expression becomes not me, or my mother, it will be somewhat
extenuated by the love I always bore my father, and by the reverence I shall ever
pay to his memory: for he was a fond father, and perhaps would have been as
tender a husband had not my mamma and he been too much of one temper to
agree.

The misfortune was, in short, that when *one* was out of humour, the *other* would
be so too: yet neither of their tempers *comparatively* bad. Notwithstanding all
which, I did not imagine, girl as I was, in my papa's lifetime, that my mamma's part
of the yoke sat so heavy upon her neck as she gives me room to think it did
whenever she is pleased to disclaim *her* part of me.

Both parents, as I have often thought, should be very careful if they would
secure to themselves the undivided love of their children that, of all things, they
should avoid such *durable* contentions with each other as should distress their
children in choosing their party, when they would be glad to reverence both as
they ought.

But here is the thing: there is not a better manager of her affairs in the sex than
my mamma; and I believe a *notable* wife is more impatient of control than an
indolent one. An indolent one, perhaps, thinks she has somewhat to *compound*
for; while women of the other character, I suppose, know too well their own
significance to think highly of that of anybody else. All must be their own way. In
one word, because they are *useful*, they will be *more* than useful.

I do assure you, my dear, were I a man, and a man who loved my quiet, I would
not have one of these managing wives on any consideration. I would make it a
matter of serious inquiry beforehand, whether my mistress's qualifications, if I
heard she was notable, were *masculine* or *feminine* ones. If indeed I were an

indolent supine mortal, who might be in danger of becoming the property of my steward, I would then perhaps choose to marry for the qualifications of a steward.

But setting my mamma out of the question, because she *is* my mamma, have I not seen how Lady Hartley pranks up herself above all her sex, because she knows how to manage affairs that do not *belong* to her sex to manage? Affairs that can do no credit to her as a woman to understand; *practically*, I mean; for the *theory* of them may not be amiss to be known.

Indeed, my dear, I do not think a *man-woman* a pretty character at all: and, as I said, were I a *man*, I would sooner choose for a dove, though it were fit for nothing but, as the play says, to go tame about house and breed,[1] than a wife that is setting at work (my insignificant self *present* perhaps) every busy hour my never-resting servants, those of the stud not excepted; and who, with a besom in her hand, as I may say, would be continually filling me with apprehensions that she wanted to sweep me out of my own house as useless lumber.

Were indeed the mistress of the family, like the wonderful young lady I so *much* and so *justly* admire, to know how to confine herself within her own respectable rounds of the needle, the pen, the housekeeper's bills, the dairy, for her amusement; to see the poor fed from superfluities that *would* otherwise be wasted; and exert herself in all the really useful branches of domestic management; then would she move in her proper sphere; then would she render herself *amiably* useful and *respectably* necessary; then would she become the *mistress*-wheel of the family (whatever you think of your Anna Howe, I would not have her be the *master*-wheel); and everybody would love her, as everybody did you, before your insolent brother came back, flushed with his unmerited acquirements, and turned all things topsy-turvy.

If you will be informed of the particulars of our contention, after you have known in general that your unhappy affair was the subject; why then I think I must tell you.

Yet how shall I?—I feel my cheek glow with mingled shame and indignation—Know then, my dear—that I have been—as I may say—that I have been *beaten*—Indeed 'tis true. My mamma thought fit to slap my hands to get from me a sheet of a letter she caught me writing to you; which I tore because she would not read it, and burnt it before her face.

I know this will trouble you: so spare yourself the labour to tell me it does.

Mr Hickman came in presently after. I would not see him. I am either too much a woman to be beat, or too much a child to have an humble servant—so I told my mother. What can one oppose but sullens, when it would be unpardonable so much as to *think* of lifting up a finger!

In the Harlowe style, she *will* be obeyed, she says: and even Mr Hickman shall be forbid the house, if he contributes to the carrying on of a correspondence which she will not suffer to be continued.

Poor man! He stands a whimsical chance between us. But he knows he is *sure* of my mamma; but not of me. 'Tis easy then for him to choose his party, were it not his inclination to serve you, as it surely *is*. And this makes him a merit with me, which otherwise he would not have had; notwithstanding the good qualities which I have just now acknowledged in his favour. For, my dear, let my faults in other respects be what they may, I will pretend to say that I have in my own mind those qualities which I praised him for. And if we are to come together, I could for that reason better dispense with them in him—So if a husband who has a bountiful-tempered wife is not a niggard, nor seeks to restrain her, but has an opinion of all she does, that is enough for him. As, on the contrary, if a bountiful-tempered husband has a frugal wife, it is best for both. For one to give, the t'other to give, except they have the prudence and are at so good an understanding with each other as to compare notes, they may perhaps put it out of their power to be just. Good frugal doctrine, my dear!—But this way of putting it is middling the matter between what I have learnt of my mamma's over-prudent and your enlarged notions. But from doctrine to fact—

I shut myself up all that day; and what little I did eat, eat alone. But at night she sent up Kitty with a command, upon my obedience, to attend her at supper.

I went down: but most gloriously in the sullens. YES, and NO were great words with me, to everything she asked of me, for a good while.

That behaviour, she told me, should not do for her.

Beating should not with me, I said.

My bold resistance, she told me, had provoked her to slap my hand; and she was sorry to have been so provoked. But again insisted that I would either give up my correspondence absolutely, or let her see all that passed in it.

I must not do either, I told her. It was unsuitable both to my inclination and to my honour, at the instigation of base minds to give up a friend in distress.

She rung all the maternal changes upon the words duty, obedience, filial obligation, and so forth.

I told her that a duty too rigorously and unreasonably exacted had been your ruin, if you were ruined. If I were of age to be married, I hoped she would think me capable of *making*, or at least of *keeping* my own friendships; such a one especially as this, with a young lady whose friendship she herself, till this distressful point of time, had thought the most useful and edifying that I ever had contracted.

The greater the merit, the worse the action: the finer the talents, the more dangerous the example.

There were other duties, I said, besides that of a child to a parent; and I hoped I need not give up a suffering friend, especially at the instigation of those by whom she suffered. I told her that it was very hard to annex such a condition as that to my duty; when I was persuaded that both duties might be performed without derogating from either: that an unreasonable command (she must excuse me, I must say it, though I were slapped again) was a degree of tyranny: and I could not have expected that at these years I should be allowed no will, no choice of my own; where a woman only was concerned, and the devilish sex not in the question.

What turned most in favour of her argument was that I desired to be excused from letting her read all that passes between us. She insisted much upon this: and since, she said, you were in the hands of the most intriguing man in the world, and a man who had made a jest of her favourite Hickman, as she has been told; she knows not what consequences, unthought of by you or me, may flow from such a correspondence.

So you see, my dear, that I fare the worse on Mr Hickman's account! My mamma *might* see all that passes between us, did I not know that it would cramp your spirit, and restrain the freedom of your pen, as it would also the freedom of my own: and were she not moreover so firmly attached to the contrary side, that inferences, consequences, strained deductions, censures and constructions the most partial, would for ever be hauled in to tease me, and would perpetually subject us to the necessity of debating and canvassing.

Besides, I don't choose that she should know how much this artful wretch has outwitted, as I may call it, a lady so much his superior.

The generosity of your heart, and the greatness of your mind (a mind above selfish considerations) full well I know; but do not offer to dissuade me from this correspondence.

Mr Hickman, immediately on the contention above, offered his service; and I accepted of it, as you'll see by my last. He thinks, though he has all honour for my mamma, that she is unkind to us both. He was pleased to tell me (with an air, as I thought), that he not only *approved* of our correspondence, but admires the steadiness of my friendship; and having no opinion of your man, but a great one of me, thinks that my advice or intelligence, from time to time, may be of use to you, and on this presumption, said that it would be a thousand pities that you should suffer for want of either.

Mr Hickman pleased me in the main by his speech; and it is well the general tenor of it was agreeable—otherwise, I can tell him, I should have reckoned with him for his word *approve*; for it is a style I have not yet permitted him to talk to me in—And you see, my dear, what these men are—No sooner do they find that you have favoured them with the power of doing you an agreeable service, but they take upon them to *approve*, forsooth, of your actions!—By which is implied a right to *disapprove*, if they think fit.

I have told my mamma how much you wish to be reconciled to your relations, and how independent you are on Mr Lovelace.

Mark the end of the latter assertion, she says—And as to reconciliation, she knows nothing will do, and will have it that nothing *ought* to do, but your returning back without presuming to condition with them. And this if you do, she says, will best show your independence on Lovelace.

You see, my dear, what your duty is in my mamma's opinion.

I suppose your next directed to Mr Hickman, at his own house, will be from London.

Heaven preserve you in honour and safety is my prayer.

What you do for change of clothes, I cannot imagine.

It is amazing to me what your relations can mean by distressing you as they seem resolved to do. I see they will throw you into his arms, whether you will or not.

I send this by Robert, for dispatch sake: and can only repeat the hitherto rejected offer of my best services! Adieu, my dearest friend. Believe me ever

Your affectionate and faithful
ANNA HOWE

Letter 133: MISS CLARISSA HARLOWE TO MISS HOWE

Thursday, April 20

I SHOULD think myself utterly unworthy of your friendship did my own concerns, heavy as they are, so engross me that I could not find leisure for a few lines to declare to my beloved friend my sincere disapprobation of her conduct, in an instance where she is so *generously* faulty, that the consciousness of that very generosity may hide from her the fault, which I more than any other have reason to deplore, as being the unhappy occasion of it.

You know, you say, that your account of the contentions between your mamma and you will trouble me; and so you bid me spare myself the labour to tell you that they do.

You did not use, my dear, to forbid me thus *beforehand*. You was wont to say you loved me the better for my expostulations with you on that acknowledged warmth and quickness of your temper, which your own good sense taught you to be apprehensive of. What though I have so miserably fallen and am unhappy; if ever I had any judgement worth regarding, it is now as much worth as ever, because I can give it as freely against myself as against anybody else. And shall I not, when there seems to be an infection in my fault, and that it leads you likewise to resolve to carry on a correspondence against prohibition, expostulate with you upon it; when whatever consequences flow from your disobedience but widen my error, which is as the evil root from which such bad branches spring?

The mind that can glory in being capable of so noble, so firm, so unshaken a friendship as that of my dear Miss Howe; a friendship which no casualty or distress can lessen, but which increases with the misfortunes of its friend—such a mind must be above taking amiss the well-meant admonitions of that distinguished friend. I will not therefore apologize for my freedom on this subject: and the less need I, when that freedom is the result of an affection in the very instance, so *absolutely* disinterested that it tends to deprive myself of the only comfort left me.

Your acknowledged sullens; your tearing from your mamma's hands the letter she thought she had a right to see; and burning it, as you own, before her face; your refusal to see the man who is so willing to obey you for the sake of your unhappy friend; and this purely to vex your mamma; can you think, my dear, upon this brief recapitulation of hardly one half of the faulty particulars you give, that these faults are excusable in one who so well knows her duty?

Your mamma had a good opinion of me once: is not that a reason why she should be more regarded now, when I have, as she believes, so deservedly forfeited it? A prejudice in favour is as hard to be totally overcome as a prejudice in disfavour. In what a strong light, then, must that error appear to her, that should so totally turn her heart against me, herself not a principal in the case?

There are other duties, you say, besides that of a child to a parent: but that must be a prior duty to all other duties; a duty anterior, as I may say, to your very birth: and what duty ought not to give way to that, when they come in competition?

You are persuaded that both duties may be performed without derogating from either. *She* thinks otherwise. What is the conclusion to be drawn from these premises?

When your mamma sees how much *I* suffer in my reputation from the step I have taken, from whom she and all the world expected better things, how much reason has she to be watchful over you! One evil draws another after it; and how knows she, or anybody, where it may stop?

Does not the person who will vindicate, or seek to extenuate, a faulty step in another (in this light must your mamma look upon the matter in question between you) give an indication either of a culpable will, or a weak judgement?—And may not she apprehend that the censorious will think that such a one might probably have equally failed, under the same *inducements* and *provocations*, to *use your own words* in a former letter applied to me?

Can there be a stronger instance in human life than mine has so early furnished within a few months past (not to mention the uncommon provocations to it, which I have met with), of the necessity of the continuance of a watchful parent's care over a daughter; let that daughter have obtained ever so great a reputation for her prudence?

Is not the space from sixteen to twenty-one that which requires this care, more than any time of a young woman's life? For in that period do we not generally attract the eyes of the other sex, and become the subject of their addresses, and not seldom of their attempts? And is not that the period in which our conduct or misconduct gives us a reputation or disreputation that almost inseparably accompanies us throughout our whole future lives?

Are we not then most in danger from ourselves, because of the distinction with which we are apt to behold particulars of that sex?

And when our dangers multiply, both from *within* and *without*, do not our parents know that their vigilance ought to be doubled?—And shall that necessary increase of care sit uneasy upon us because we are grown up to stature and womanhood?

Will you tell me, if so, what is the precise stature and age at which a good child shall conclude herself absolved from the duty she owes to a parent?—and at which a parent, after the example of the dams of the brute creation, is to lay aside all care and tenderness for her offspring?

Is it so hard for you, my dear, to be treated like a child? And can you not think it as hard for a good parent to imagine herself under the unhappy *necessity* of so treating her woman-grown daughter?

Do you think if your mamma had been *you*, and you your *mamma*, and *your* daughter had struggled with you, as you did with her, that you would not have been as apt as your mamma was to have slapped your daughter's hands to have made her quit her hold to you, and give up the prohibited paper?

It is a great truth that your mamma told you, that you *provoked* her to this harshness; and a great condescension in her (and not taken notice of by you as it deserved) to say that she was *sorry for it.*

At *every* age on this side matrimony (for then we come under another sort of protection, though that is far from abrogating the filial duty) it will be found that the wings of our parents are our most necessary and most effectual safeguard, to preserve us from the vultures, the hawks, the kites and the other villainous birds of prey that hover over us with a view to seize and destroy us, the first time we are caught wandering out of the eye or care of our watchful and natural guardians and protectors.

Hard as you may suppose it, to be denied the *continuance* of a correspondence once so much approved, even by the reverend denier—yet, if your mamma think that my fault is of such a nature as that a correspondence with me will cast a shade upon your reputation; all my own friends having given me up—that hardship is to be submitted to. And must it not make her the more strenuous to support her own opinion, when she sees the first fruits of this tenaciousness of your side is to be *gloriously in the sullens*, as you call it; and in a disobedient opposition?

I know, my dear, you mean an humorousness in that expression which, in most cases, gives a delightful poignancy, both to your conversation and correspondence— but indeed, my dear, *this* case will not bear it.

Will you give me leave to add to this tedious expostulation, that I by no means approve of some of the things you write in relation to the manner in which your father and mother lived?—at times—only *at times*, I dare say; though perhaps, too often—

Your mamma is answerable to *anybody*, rather than to her *child*, for whatever was wrong in her conduct, if anything *was* wrong, towards Mr Howe; a gentleman of whose memory I will only say, that it *ought* to be revered by you—But yet, should you not examine yourself whether your displeasure at your mamma had no part in your revived reverence for your papa at the time you wrote?

No one is perfect: and although your mamma may not be so right to remember disagreeablenesses against the departed, yet should you not want to be reminded on *whose* account, and on *what* occasion, she remembered them. You cannot judge, nor ought you to attempt to judge, of what might have passed between both, to keep awake and embitter disagreeable remembrances in the survivor.

Letter 134: MISS CLARISSA HARLOWE TO MISS HOWE

(In continuation)

BUT this subject must not be pursued. Another might, with more pleasure (though not with more approbation), upon one of your lively excursions. It is upon the high airs you give yourself upon the word *approve*.

How comes it about, I wonder, that a young lady so noted for a predominating generosity should not be uniformly generous?—that your generosity should fail in an instance where policy, prudence, gratitude would not permit it to fail? Mr Hickman (as you confess) has indeed a worthy mind. If I had not long ago known that, he would never have found an advocate in me for the favour of my Anna Howe. Often and often have I been concerned, when I was your happy guest, to see him, after a conversation in which he had well supported his part in your absence, sink at once into silence the moment you came into company.

I have told you of this before: and I believe I hinted to you once that the superciliousness you put on *only* to him was capable of a construction, which at the time would have very little gratified your pride to have had made; since it was as much in his favour as in your own disfavour.

Mr Hickman, my dear, is a *modest* man. I never see a modest man, but I am sure (if he has not wanted opportunities) that he has a treasure in his mind which requires nothing but the key of encouragement to unlock it, to make him shine: while a confident man who, to *be* confident, must think as meanly of his company as highly of himself, enters with magisterial airs upon any subject; and depending upon his assurance to bring himself off when found out talks of more than he is master of.

But a *modest* man!—Oh my dear, shall not a modest woman distinguish and wish to consort with a modest man?—a man *before* whom and *to* whom she may open her lips secure of his good opinion of all she says, and of his just and polite regard for her judgement? and who must therefore inspire her with an agreeable confidence.

What a lot have I drawn!—We are all apt to turn teachers—but surely I am better enabled to talk, to write upon these subjects than ever I was!—But I will banish *myself*, if possible, from an address which, when I began to write, I was determined to confine wholly to your own particular.

My dearest, dearest friend, how ready are you to tell us what others should do, and even what a mother should have done! But indeed you once, I remember, advanced that, as different attainments required different talents to master them, so, in the writing way, a person might not be a bad critic upon the works of others, although he might himself be unable to write with excellence. But will you permit me to account for all this readiness of finding fault by placing it to human nature, which being sensible of the defects of human nature (that is to say, of its *own* defects) loves to be *correcting*? but in exercising that talent chooses rather to turn its eye *outward* than *inward*?—In other words, to employ itself rather in the *out-door* search than in the *in-door* examination?

And here give me leave to add (and yet it is with tender reluctance) that although you say very pretty things of notable wives; and although I join with you in opinion that husbands may have as many inconveniencies to encounter *with*, as conveniencies to boast *of*, from women of that character; yet Lady Hartley, perhaps, would have had milder treatment from your pen had it not been dipped in gall, with a mother in your eye.

Letter 135: MISS CLARISSA HARLOWE TO MISS HOWE

(In continuation)

AND now, my dear, a few words as to the prohibition laid upon you; a subject that I have frequently touched upon, but cursorily; because I was afraid to trust myself with it, knowing that my judgement, if I did, would condemn my practice.

You command me not to attempt to dissuade you from this correspondence; and you tell me how kindly Mr Hickman approves of it; and how obliging he is to me to permit it to be carried on under cover to him—but this does not quite satisfy me.

I am a very bad casuist; and the pleasure I take in writing to you, who are the only one to whom I can disburden my mind, may make me as I have hinted very partial to my own wishes—else, if it were not an artful evasion beneath an open and frank heart to wish to be complied with, I would be glad methinks to be permitted still to write to you; and only have such occasional returns by Mr Hickman's pen, as well as cover, as might set me right when I am wrong; confirm me when right; and guide me where I doubt. This would enable me to proceed in the difficult path before me with more assuredness. For whatever I suffer from the censures of others, if I can preserve your good opinion I shall not be altogether unhappy, let what will befall me.

And indeed, my dear, I know not how to forbear writing. I have now no other employment or diversion. I must write on, although I were not to send it to anybody. You have often heard me own the advantages I have found from writing down everything of moment that befalls me; and of all I *think* and of all I *do* that may be of future use to me—for, besides that this helps to form one to a style, and opens and expands the ductile mind, everyone will find that many a good thought evaporates in thinking; many a good resolution goes off, driven out of memory, perhaps, by some other not so good. But when I set down what I *will* do, or what I *have* done on this or that occasion; the resolution or action is before me, either to be adhered to, withdrawn or amended; and I have entered into *compact* with myself, as I may say; having given it under my own hand, to *improve* rather than go *backward*, as I live longer.

I would willingly therefore write to *you*, if I *might*; the rather as it would be more inspiriting to have some end in view in what I write; some friend to please; besides merely seeking to gratify my passion for scribbling.

But why, if your mamma will permit our correspondence on communicating to her all that passes in it, and if she will condescend to one only condition, may it not be complied with?

Would she not, do you think, my dear, be prevailed upon to have the communication made to her *in confidence*?

If there were any prospect of a reconciliation with my friends, I should not have so much regard for my *pride* as to be afraid of *anybody*'s knowing how much I have been *outwitted*, as you call it. I would in *that* case (when I had left Mr Lovelace) acquaint your mamma and all my own friends with the whole of my story. It would behove me so to do for my own reputation and for their satisfaction.

But if I have no such prospect, what will the communication of my reluctance to go away with Mr Lovelace, and of his arts to frighten me away, avail me?— Your mamma has hinted that my friends would insist upon my returning to them (as a proof of the truth of my plea) to be disposed of without condition, at their pleasure. If I scrupled this, my brother would rather triumph over me than keep my secret. Mr Lovelace, whose pride already so ill brooks my regrets for meeting him (when he thinks, if I had not, I must have been Mr Solmes's wife), would perhaps treat me with indignity—And thus, deprived of all refuge and protection, I should become the scoff of men of intrigue; and be thought a greater disgrace than ever to my sex—since love, and consequential marriage will find more excuses than perhaps *ought* to be found for actions premeditatedly rash.

But if your mamma will receive the communications in confidence, pray show her all that I have written, or shall write. If my past conduct deserves not *heavy* blame, I shall then perhaps have the benefit of her advice as well as yours. And if I shall wilfully deserve blame for the time to come, I will be contented to be denied yours as well as hers for ever.

As to cramping my spirit, as you call it (were I to sit down to write what I know your mamma must see), that, my dear, is already cramped. And do not think so unhandsomely of your mamma as to fear that she would make *partial* constructions against me. Neither you nor I can doubt but that had she been left unprepossessedly to herself, she would have shown favour to me. And so, I dare say, would my uncle

Antony—Nay, my dear, I can extend my charity still further: for I am sometimes of opinion that were my brother and sister absolutely certain that they had ruined me beyond recovery in the opinion of both my uncles, so far as that they need not be apprehensive of my clashing with their interests; they would not oppose a pardon, although they might not wish a reconciliation—especially if I would make a few sacrifices to them—which, I assure you, I should be inclined to make, were I wholly free and independent of this man. You know I never valued myself upon worldly acquisitions, nor upon my grandfather's bequests, but as they enlarged my power to do things I loved to do. And if I were denied the power, I must, as I now do, curb my inclination.

Do not, however, think me guilty of an affectation in what I have said of my brother and sister. Severe enough I am sure it is, in the most favourable sense. And an indifferent person will be of opinion that *they* are much better warranted than ever, for the sake of the family honour to seek to ruin me in the favour of all my friends.

But to the former topic—Try, my dear, if your mamma will upon the condition above given permit our correspondence, on seeing all we write. But if she will not, what a selfishness would there be in my love to you were I to wish you to forgo your duty for my sake?

And now, one word as to the freedom I have treated you with in this tedious expostulatory address. I presume upon your forgiveness of it, because few friendships are founded on such a basis as ours—which is, 'freely to *give* reproof and thankfully to *receive* it, as occasions arise; that so either may have opportunity to clear up mistakes, to acknowledge and amend errors, as well in behaviour as in words and deeds; and to rectify and confirm each other in the judgement each shall form upon persons, things, and circumstances.' And all this upon the following consideration: 'That it is much more eligible, as well as honourable, to be corrected with the gentleness of an undoubted friend, than by continuing either blind or wilful, to expose ourselves to the censures of an envious, and perhaps malignant world.'

But it is as needless, I dare say, to remind you of this, as it is to repeat my request, that you will not, in your turn, spare the follies and the faults of

> Your ever affectionate
> CL. HARLOWE

(Subjoined to the above)

I said that I would avoid writing anything of my own particular affairs in the above address, if I could.

I will write one letter more to inform you how we stand. But, my dear, you must permit that one (which will require your advice) and your answer to it, and the copy of one I have written to my aunt, to be the last that shall pass between us while the prohibition continues.

I fear, I very much fear that my unhappy situation will draw me in to be guilty of evasion, of little affectations and of curvings from the plain simple truth which I was wont to value myself upon. But allow me to say, and this for your sake and in order to lessen your mother's fears of any ill consequences that she might apprehend from our correspondence, that if I am at any time guilty of a failure in these respects, I will not go on in it: but repent and seek to recover my lost ground, that I may not bring error into habit.

I have deferred going to town, at Mrs Sorlings's earnest request. But have fixed my removal to Monday, as I shall acquaint you in my next. I have already made a progress in that next; but having an unexpected opportunity, will send this by itself.

Letter 136: MISS HOWE TO MISS CLARISSA HARLOWE

Friday morn. April 21

MY mamma will not comply with your condition, my dear. I hinted it to her, as from myself—But the *Harlowes* (excuse me) have got her entirely in with them. It is a scheme of mine, she told me, to draw her into your party against your parents—which, for her own sake, she is very careful about.

Don't be so much concerned about my mamma and me, once more, I beg of you. We shall do well enough together: now a falling out, now a falling in. It used to be so when you were not in the question.

Yet do I give you my sincere thanks for every line of your reprehensive letters; which I intend to read as often as I find my temper rises.

I will freely own that I winced a little at first reading them. But I see that in every reperusal I shall love and honour you still more, if possible, than before.

Yet I think I have one advantage over you; and which I will hold through this letter, and through all my future letters; that is that I will treat you as freely as you treat me; and yet will never think an apology necessary to you for my freedom.

But this is the effect of your gentleness of temper; with a little sketch of implied reflection on the warmth of mine—Gentleness in a woman you hold to be no fault—nor do I a little due or provoked warmth—but what is this but praising on both sides what neither of us can help; nor perhaps wish to help? You can no more go out of your road than I can go out of mine. It would be a pain to either to do so—What then is it in either's approving of her own natural bias but making a virtue of necessity?

But one observation I will add, that were *your* character and *my* character to be truly drawn, mine would be allowed to be the most natural. Shades and lights are equally necessary in a fine picture. Yours would be surrounded with such a flood of brightness, with such a glory, that it would indeed dazzle; but leave one heartless to imitate it.

Oh may you not suffer from a base world for your gentleness; while my temper, by its warmth keeping all imposition at distance, though less amiable in general, affords me not reason, as I have mentioned heretofore, to wish to make an exchange with you!

I should indeed be inexcusable to open my lips by way of contradiction to my mamma, had I such a fine spirit as yours to deal with—Truth is truth, my dear!—Why should narrowness run away with the praises due to a noble expansion of heart?—If everybody would speak out as I do (that is to say, give praise where only praise is due; dispraise where due, likewise), *shame* if not *principle* would mend the world—Nay, shame would introduce principle in a generation or two—

Very true, my dear—Do you apply—I dare not—for I *fear* you almost as much as I *love* you.

I will give you an instance, nevertheless, which will anew demonstrate that none but very generous and noble-minded people ought to be implicitly obeyed. You know what I said above, that *truth* is *truth*.

Inconveniencies will sometimes arise from having to do with persons of modesty and scrupulousness. Mr Hickman, you say, is a *modest* man. He put your corrective packet into my hand with a very fine bow and a self-satisfied air. (We'll consider what you say of this honest man by and by, my dear.) His strut was not gone off, when in came my mamma as I was reading it.

When some folks find their anger has made them considerable, they will be always angry, or seeking occasions for anger.

Why, now, Mr Hickman!—why, now, Nancy, as I was putting the packet into my bosom at her entrance—You have a letter brought you this instant—while the *modest* man, with his pausing brayings, Mad-da—mad-dam, looked as if he knew not whether he had best to run and leave me and my mamma to fight it out, or to stand his ground and see fair play.

It would have been poor to tell a lie for it—She flung away. I went out at the opposite door to read it; leaving Mr Hickman to exercise his white teeth upon his thumb-nails.

When I had read your letters, I went to find out my mamma. I told her the generous contents, and that you desired that the prohibition might be adhered to—I proposed your condition as from myself; and was rejected, as above.

She supposed she was finely painted between two young creatures who had more wit than prudence. And instead of being prevailed upon by the generosity of your sentiments made use of your opinion only to confirm her own, and renewed her prohibitions, charging me to return no other answer but that she *did* renew them. Adding, that they should stand till your relations were reconciled to you; hinting as if she had *engaged for as much*; and expected my compliance.

I thought of your reprehensions, and was *meek* though not pleased. And let me tell you, my dear, that as long as I can satisfy my own mind that good is intended, and that it is hardly possible that evil should ensue from our correspondence; as long as I know that this prohibition proceeds originally from the same spiteful minds which have been the occasion of all these mischiefs; as long as I know that it is not your fault if your relations are not reconciled to you; and that upon conditions which no reasonable people would refuse—you must give me leave, with all deference to your judgement and to your excellent lessons (which would reach almost every other case of this kind but the present), to insist upon your writing to me, and that minutely, as if this prohibition had not been laid.

It is not from humour, from perverseness, that I insist upon this. I cannot express how much my heart is in your concerns. And you must, in short, allow me to think that if I can do you service by writing, I shall be better justified by *continuing* to write than my mamma is by her prohibition.

But yet, to satisfy you all I can, I will as seldom return answers while the interdict lasts as may be consistent with my notions of friendship, and the service I owe you and can do you.

As to your expedient of writing by Hickman (and now, my dear, your modest man comes in: and as you love modesty in that sex, I will do my endeavour by a proper distance to keep him in your favour), I know what you mean by it, my sweet friend. It is to make that man significant with me. As to the correspondence, THAT *shall* go on, I do assure you, be as scrupulous as you please—so that *that* will not suffer, if I do not close with your proposal as to him.

I think I must tell you that it will be honour enough for him to have his name made use of so frequently betwixt us. This, of itself, is placing a confidence in him that will make him walk bolt upright, and display his white hand and his fine diamond ring; and most mightily lay down his services, *and* his pride to oblige, *and* his diligence, *and* his fidelity, *and* his contrivances to keep our secret; *and* his excuses, *and* his evasions to my mamma when challenged by her; with fifty *and*'s beside. And will it not moreover give him pretence and excuse oftener than ever to pad-nag it hither to good Mrs Howe's fair daughter?

But to admit him into my company *tête-à-tête*, and into my closet as often as I would wish to write to you; I only to dictate to *his* pen—my mamma all the time supposing that I was going to be heartily in love with him—to make him master of my sentiments, and of my *heart*, as I may say, when I write to you—indeed, my dear, I won't. Nor, were I married to the best H E in England, would I honour him with the communication of my correspondencies.

No, my dear, it is sufficient, surely, for him to parade it in the character of our letter-conveyer, and to be honoured in a cover. And never fear but, modest as you think him, he will make enough of that.

You are always blaming me for want of generosity to this man, and for abuse of power. But I profess, my dear, I cannot tell how to help it. Do, dear, now, let me spread my plumes a little, and now and then make myself feared. This is my time, you know, since it will be no more to *my* credit, than to *his*, to give myself those airs when I am married. He has a joy when I am pleased with him that he would not know but for the pain my displeasure gives him.

This, I am satisfied, will be the consequence, if I do not make him quake now and then, he will endeavour to make me fear. All the animals in the creation are more or less in a state of hostility with each other. The wolf, that runs away from a lion, will devour a lamb the next moment. I remember that I was once so enraged at a game-chicken that was continually pecking at another (a poor humble one, as I thought him), that I had the offender caught, and without more ado, in a pet of humanity, wrung his neck off. What followed this execution?—Why that other grew insolent, as soon as *his* insulter was gone, and was continually pecking at one or two under *him*. Peck and be hanged, said I—I might as well have preserved the first; for I see it is the *nature of the beast*.

Excuse my flippancies. I wish I were with you. I would make you smile in the midst of your gravest airs, as I used to do—Oh that you had accepted of my offer to attend you!—But nothing that I offer, will you accept—Take care! you will make me very angry with you: and when I am, you know I value nobody—for, dearly as I love you, I must be, and cannot always help it,

Your saucy
ANNA HOWE

Letter 137: MISS CLARISSA HARLOWE TO MISS HOWE

Friday, April 21

MR Lovelace communicated to me this morning early, from his intelligencer, the news of my brother's scheme. I like him the better for making very light of it; and for his treating it with contempt. And indeed, had I not had the hint of it from you, I should have suspected it to be some contrivance of his, in order to hasten me to town, where he has long wished to be himself.

He read me the passage in that Leman's letter, pretty much to the effect of what you wrote to me from Miss Lloyd; with this addition, that one Singleton, a master of a Scots vessel, is the man who is to be the principal in this act of violence.

I have seen him. He has been twice entertained at Harlowe Place as my brother's friend. He has the air of a very bold and fearless man; and I fancy it must be *his* project; as my brother, I suppose, talks to everybody of the rash step I have taken; having not spared me before he had this seeming reason to censure me.

This Singleton lives at Leith; so, perhaps, I am to be carried to my brother's house not far from that port.

Putting these passages together, I am not a little apprehensive that the design, lightly as Mr Lovelace from his fearless temper treats it, may be attempted to be carried into execution; and of the consequences that may attend it, if it be.

I asked Mr Lovelace, seeing him so frank and cool, what he would advise me to do?

Shall I ask *you*, madam, what are your own thoughts?—Why I return the question, said he, is because you have been so very earnest that I should leave you as soon as you are in London, that I know not what to propose without offending you.

My opinion is, said I, that I should studiously conceal myself from the knowledge of everybody but Miss Howe; and that you should leave me out of hand; since they will certainly conclude that where *one* is, the *other* is not far off: and it is easier to trace *you* than *me*.

You would not surely wish, said he, to fall into your brother's hands by such a violent measure as this?—I propose not to throw myself officiously in their way; but should they have reason to think I avoided them, would not that whet their diligence to find you, and their courage to attempt to carry you off; and subject me to insults that no man of spirit can bear?

Lord bless me! said I, to what has this one fatal step that I have been betrayed into—

Dearest madam! Let me beseech you to forbear this harsh language, when you see by this new scheme how determined they were upon carrying their old ones, had you not been *betrayed*, as you call it! Have I offered to defy the laws of society, as this brother of yours must do, if anything be intended by this project?—I hope you will be pleased to observe that there are as violent and as wicked enterprisers as myself—but this is so very wild a project that I think there can be no room for apprehensions from it—I know your brother well. When at college he had always a romantic turn. But never had a head for anything but to puzzle and confound himself: a half invention and a whole conceit, and without any talents to do himself good or others harm, but as those others gave him the power by their own folly built upon his presumption.

This is very volubly run off, sir!—but violent spirits are but too much alike; at least in their methods of resenting. You will not presume to make yourself a less innocent man surely, who had determined to brave my whole family in person if my folly had not saved *you* the rashness, and *them* the insult—

Dear madam!—still must it be *folly, rashness!*—It is as impossible for you to think tolerably of anybody *out* of your own family, as it is for any one *in it* to deserve your love!—Forgive me, dearest creature!—If I did not love you as no man ever loved a woman, I might appear more indifferent to preferences so undeservedly made—But let me ask you, madam, what have you borne from *me*?—what cause have I given you to treat me with so much severity, and so little confidence?—and what have you not borne from *them*?—My general character may have been against me: but what of your knowledge have you against me?

I was startled. But I was resolved not to desert myself.

Is this a time, Mr Lovelace, is this a proper occasion to give yourself these high airs to me, a young creature destitute of protection?—It is a surprising question you ask me. Had I aught against you of my own knowledge—I can tell you, sir— and away I would have flung.

He snatched my hand, and besought me not to leave him in displeasure—He pleaded his passion for me, and my severity to him and partiality for those from whom I had suffered so much; and whose intended violence, he said, was now the subject of our deliberation.

I was forced to hear him.

You condescended, dearest creature, said he, to ask my advice. It is very easy, give me leave to say, to advise you what to do. I hope I may, on this *new* occasion speak without offence, notwithstanding your former injunctions—You see that there can be no hope of reconciliation with your relations. Can you, madam, consent to honour with your hand a wretch whom you have never yet obliged with one *voluntary* favour?—

What a recriminating, what a reproachful way, my dear, was this, of putting a question of this nature!—

I expected not from him, at the time, either the question or the manner—I am ashamed to recollect the confusion I was thrown into—all your advice in my head at the moment: yet his words so prohibitory. He confidently seemed to enjoy my confusion (indeed, my dear, he knows not what respectful love is!); and gazed upon me as if he would have looked me through.

He was still more declarative afterwards indeed, as I shall mention by and by: but it was half-extorted from him.

My heart struggled violently between resentment and shame to be thus teased by one who seemed to have all *his* passions at command, at a time when I had very little over *mine*; till at last I burst into tears, and was going from him in high disgust; when, throwing his arms about me, with an air, however, the most tenderly respectful, he gave a *stupid* turn to the subject.

It was far from his heart, he said, to take so much advantage of the strait which the discovery of my brother's foolish project had brought me into, as to renew without my permission a proposal which I had hitherto discountenanced; and which for that reason—

And then he came with his half-sentences, apologizing for what he had hardly half proposed.

Surely, he had not the insolence to *intend* to tease me, to see if I could be brought to speak what became me not to speak—But, whether he had or not, it *did* tease me; insomuch that my very heart was fretted and I broke out at last into fresh tears, and a declaration that I was very unhappy. And just then recollecting how like a tame fool I stood, with his arms about me, I flung from him with indignation. But he seized my hand, as I was going out of the room, and upon his knees besought my stay for one moment: and then tendered himself, in words the most clear and explicit, to my acceptance, as the most effectual means to disappoint my brother's scheme, and set all right.

But what could I say to this?—Extorted from him, as it seemed to me, rather as the effect of his compassion, than of his love? What *could* I say?—I paused, I looked silly! I am *sure* I looked very silly. He suffered me to pause and look silly; waiting for me to say something: and at last, ashamed of my confusion, and aiming to make an excuse for it, I told him that I desired he would avoid such measures as might add to an uneasiness which was so visible upon reflecting on the irreconcileableness of my friends, and what unhappy consequences might follow from this unaccountable project of my brother.

He promised to be governed by me in everything. And again the wretch asked me if I forgave him for the humble suit he had made to me? What had I to do, but to try for a palliation of my confusion, since it served me not?

I told him I had hopes it would not be long before Mr Morden arrived; and doubted not that he would be the readier to engage in my favour, when he found that I made no other use of *his*, Mr Lovelace's, assistance than to free myself from the addresses of a man so disagreeable to me as Mr Solmes: I must therefore wish that everything might remain as it was, till I could hear from my cousin.

This, although teased by him as I was, was not a denial, you see, my dear. But he must throw himself into a heat, rather than try to persuade; which any other man, in his situation, I should think, would have done: and this warmth obliged me to adhere to my seeming negative.

This was what he said, with a vehemence that must harden any woman's mind who had a spirit above being frighted into passiveness:

Good God!—and you, madam, still resolve to show me that I am to hope for no share in your favour, while any the remotest prospect remains that you will be received by my bitterest enemies at the price of my utter rejection?

This was what I returned, with warmth, and with a salving art *too*—You have seen, Mr Lovelace, how much my brother's violence can affect me: but you will be mistaken if you let loose yours upon me with a thought of terrifying me into measures, the contrary of which you have acquiesced with.

He only besought me to suffer his future actions to speak for him; and if I saw him worthy of any favour, that I would not let him be the *only* person within my knowledge who was not entitled to my consideration.

You refer to a *future time*, Mr Lovelace; so do I, for the *future proof* of a merit you seem to think for the *past time* wanting: and *justly* you think so. And I was again going from him.

One word more he begged me to hear—He was determined studiously to avoid all mischief, and every step that might lead to mischief, let my brother's proceedings, short of a violence upon my person, be what they would: but if any attempt that should extend to that were to be made, would I have him to be a quiet spectator of my being seized, or carried back, or aboard, by this Singleton; or in case of extremity, was he not permitted to stand up in my defence?

Stand up in my defence, Mr Lovelace!—I should be very miserable were there to be a call for that: but do you think I might not be *safe* and *private* in London?—By your friend's description of the widow's house, I should think I might be safe there.

The widow's house, he replied, as described by his friend, being a back house within a front one, and looking to a garden rather than a street, had the appearance of privacy: but if, when there, it was not approved, it would be easy to find another more to my liking—though, as to his part, the method he would advise should be to write to my uncle Harlowe as one of my trustees, and wait the issue of it here at Mrs Sorlings's, fearlessly directing it to be answered *hither*. To be afraid of little spirits, was but to encourage insults, he said. The substance of the letter should be: 'To demand as a right what they would refuse if requested as a courtesy: to acknowledge that I had put myself (too well, he said, did their treatment justify me) into the protection of the *ladies* of his family (by whose orders, and Lord M.'s, he himself would appear to act): but that it was upon my own terms; which laid me under no obligation to *them* for the favour, it being no more than they would have granted to any one of my sex equally distressed.' If I approved not of this method, happy should he think himself, he said, if I would honour him with the opportunity of making such a claim in his *own* name—But this was a point (with his *buts* again!) that he durst but just touch upon. He hoped, however, that I would think their violence a sufficient inducement for me to take such a wished-for resolution.

Inwardly vexed, I told him that he himself had proposed to leave me when I was in town: that I expected he would: and that, when I was known to be absolutely independent, I should consider what to write and what to do: but that, while he was hanging about me, I neither would nor could.

He would be very sincere with me, he said: this project of my brother's had changed the face of things. He must, before he left me, see how I liked the London widow and her family, if I chose to go thither: they might be people whom my brother might buy. But if he saw they were persons of integrity, he then might go for a day or two, or so. But he must needs say, he could not leave me longer.

Do you propose, sir, said I, to take up your lodgings in the same house?

He did not, he said; as he knew the use I intended to make of his absence, and my punctilio—And yet the house where he had lodgings was new-fronting: but he could go to his friend Belford's, in Soho; or perhaps, to the same gentleman's house at Edgware, and return on mornings, till he had reason to think this wild project of my brother's laid aside. But no farther till then would he venture.

The result of all was, to set out on Monday next for town. I hope it will be in a happy hour.

I cannot, my dear, say too often, how much I am

Your ever obliged
CL. HARLOWE

Letter 138: MR LOVELACE TO JOHN BELFORD, ESQ.

Friday, April 21

As it was not probable that the lady could give so particular an account of her own confusion, in the affecting scene she mentions on his offering himself to her acceptance, the following extracts are made from his of the above date.

And now, Belford, what wilt thou say, if like the fly buzzing about the bright taper, I had like to have singed the silken wings of my liberty?—Never was man in greater danger of being caught in his own snares—all his views anticipated: all his schemes untried; and not having brought the admirable creature to town nor made an effort to know if she be really angel or woman.

I offered myself to her acceptance, with a suddenness, 'tis true, that gave her no time to wrap herself in reserve; and in terms *less tender* than *fervent*, tending to upbraid her for her past indifference, and reminding her of her injunctions—for it was her brother's plot, not love of me, that had inclined her to dispense with them.

I never beheld so sweet a confusion. What a glory to the pencil, could it do justice to it, and to the mingled impatience which visibly informed every feature of the most meaning and most beautiful face in the world. She hemmed twice or thrice: her look, now so charmingly silly, then so sweetly significant; till at last, the lovely teaser, teased by my hesitating expectation of her answer out of all power of articulate speech, burst into tears, and was turning from me with precipitation when, taking the liberty of folding her in my happy arms—Oh think not, best beloved of my heart, think not that this motion which you may believe to be so contrary to your *former injunctions* proceeds from a design to avail myself of the cruelty of your relations: if I have *disobliged* you by it (and you know with what respectful tenderness I have presumed to hint it), it shall be my utmost care for the future—There I stopped—

Then she spoke; but with vexation—I am—I am—*very* unhappy—tears trickling down her crimson cheeks; and her sweet face, as my arms still encircled the finest waist in the world, sinking upon my shoulder; the dear creature so absent that she knew not the honour she permitted me.

But why, but why unhappy, my dearest life, said I?—all the gratitude that ever overflowed the heart of the most obliged of men—Justice to myself there stopped my mouth; for what *gratitude* did I owe her for obligations so involuntary?

Then recovering herself, and her usual reserves, and struggling to free herself from my clasping arms: How now, sir! said she, with a cheek more indignantly glowing and eyes of a fiercer lustre.

I gave way to her angry struggle—but, absolutely overcome by so charming a display of innocent confusion, I caught hold of her hand as she was flying from me; and kneeling at her feet, Oh my angel, said I (quite destitute of reserve, and hardly knowing the tenor of my own speech; and had a parson been there, I had certainly been a gone man), receive the vows of your faithful Lovelace—Make him yours, and only yours, for ever!—This will answer every end!—Who will dare to form plots and stratagems against my wife? That you are not so is the ground of all their foolish attempts and of their insolent hopes in Solmes's favour. Oh be mine!—I beseech you (thus on my knee I *beseech* you) to be mine—We shall then have all the world with us: and everybody will applaud an event that everybody expects.

Was the devil in me!—I no more intended all this ecstatic nonsense than I thought the same moment of flying in the air!—All power is with this charming creature!—It is I, not she, at this rate, that must fail in the arduous trial.

Didst thou ever before hear of a man uttering solemn things by an involuntary impulse, in defiance of premeditation and of all his own proud schemes? But this sweet creature is able to make a man forgo every purpose of his heart that is not favourable to her—And I verily think I should be inclined to spare her all further trial (and yet no trial has she had), were it not for the contention that her vigilance has set on foot, *which* shall overcome the *other*. Thou knowest my generosity to my uncontending Rosebud—and sometimes do I qualify my ardent aspirations after even this very fine creature by this reflection: That the charmingest woman on earth, were she an empress, can excel the meanest, in the customary visibles only. Such is the equality of the dispensation, to the prince and the peasant, in this prime gift, WOMAN.

Well, but what was the result of this involuntary impulse on my part? Wouldst thou not think I was taken at my offer?—an offer so solemnly made, and on one knee too?

No such thing!—The pretty trifler let me off as easily as I could have wished.

Her brother's project, and to find that there were no hopes of a reconciliation for her; and the apprehension she had of the mischiefs that might ensue—these, not *my offer* nor *love of me*, were the causes to which she ascribed all her sweet confusion—High treason the *ascription* against my sovereign pride—to make marriage with me but a second-place refuge!—and as good as to tell me that her confusion was owing to her concern that there were no hopes that my enemies would accept of her intended offer to renounce a man who had ventured his life for her, and was still ready to run the same risk in her behalf!

I re-urged her to make me happy—But I was to be postponed to her cousin Morden's arrival. On him are now placed all her hopes.

I raved; but to no purpose.

Another letter was to be sent, or had been sent, to her aunt Hervey; to which she hoped an answer.

Yet sometimes I think that fainter and fainter would have been her procrastinations had I been a man of courage—but so fearful was I of offending!—

A confounded thing! The man to be so bashful; the lady to want so much courting!—How shall two such come together, no kind mediatress in the way?

But I can't help it. I must be contented. 'Tis seldom, however, that a love so ardent meets with a spirit so resigned in the same person. But true love, I am now convinced, only wishes: nor has it any active will but that of the adorable object.

But, oh the charming creature! again to mention London of herself!—Had Singleton's plot been of *my own* contriving, it could not have been a happier expedient to hasten her thither, after she had deferred her journey—for what reason deferred it, I cannot divine.

I enclose the letter from Joseph Leman which I mentioned to thee in mine of Monday last,[a] with my answer to it. I cannot resist the vanity that urges me to the

a Letter 127, p. 465.

communication. Otherwise it were better, perhaps, that I suffer thee to imagine that this lady's stars fight against her, and dispense the opportunities in my favour which are only the consequences of my own superlative invention.

Letter 139: JOSEPH LEMAN TO ROBERT LOVELACE, ESQ.

HE acquaints Mr Lovelace of the prosecution intended to be set up against him by his masters, for a rape upon Miss Betterton, whom by a stratagem he had got into his hands; and who afterwards died in child-bed; the child still living but, as Joseph says, not regarded by his honour *in the least*. His masters, he says, call it a very vile affair; but God forbid that he should, without his honour's leave. He hears, he says, that his honour went abroad to avoid the prosecution which the lady's relations otherwise would have set on foot. And that his masters will not rest till they get the Bettertons to commence it.

Joseph tells him that this was one of the stories which 'squire Solmes was to tell his young lady of, would she have heard him.[a]

He desires him to let him know if his honour's life is in danger from this prosecution; and hopes if it be, 'that he will not be hanged like as a common man; but only have his head cut off or so; and that he will *natheless* think of his faithful Joseph Leman before his head shall be condemned, because afterwards he understands that all will be king's or the shreeve's.'

He then acquaints him that Captain Singleton and his young master and young mistress are often in close conference together; and that his young master said, before his face to the captain, *that his blood boiled over for revenge* upon his honour; and at the same time praised him (Joseph) to the captain, for his fidelity and for his good head, although he looked *so seelie*. And then he offers his services, in order to prevent mischief, and to deserve his bounty, and his favour as to the Blue Boar Inn, which he hears so good an account of—

'And then the *Blue Boar* is not all neither (says Joseph), since, and please your honour, the pretty sow (God forgive me for jesting in so serious a matter) runs in my head likewise. I believe I shall love her mayhap more than your honour would have me; for she begins to be kind and good-humoured, and listens, and please your honour, like as *if she was among beans*,[1] when I talk about the Blue Boar and all that.

'Pray your honour forgive the jesting of a poor plain man. We common folks have our joys, and please your honour, like as our betters have; and if we be sometimes snubbed, we can find our underlings to snub again: and if not, we can get a wife, mayhap, and snub her: so are masters somehow or other ourselves.'

He then tells him how much his conscience smites him for what he has done; since but for the stories his honour taught him it would have been impossible for his old masters, and his lady, to have been so hard-hearted as they were, notwithstanding the malice of his young master and young mistress.

'And here is the sad thing (proceeds he); they cannot come to clear up matters with my dearest young lady because, as your honour has ordered it, they have these stories as if bribed [by me] out of your honour's servant; which must not be known for fear your honour should kill him and me too, and blacken the bribers!—

a See p. 250.

Ah, your honour!—I doubt, your honour, as that I am a very vile fellow—Lord bless my soul! and did not intend it.

'But if my dearest young lady should come to harm, and please your honour, the horsepond at the Blue Boar—but Lord preserve me from all bad mischiefs, and all bad ends, I pray the Lord!—For though your honour is kind to me in worldly pelf, yet *what shall a man get to lose his soul*,[2] as holy scripture says, and please your honour?

'But *natheless* I am in hope of repentance hereafter, being but a young man, if I do wrong through ignorance; your honour being a great man and a great wit; and I a poor creature not worthy notice; and your honour able to answer for all. But howsoever I am

Your honour's faithful servant in all duty,
JOSEPH LEMAN'

April 15 and 16

Letter 140: MR LOVELACE TO JOSEPH LEMAN

April 17

HE tells him that the affair of Miss Betterton was a youthful frolic: that there was no rape in the case: that he went not abroad on her account: that she loved him and he loved her: yet that she was but a tradesman's daughter, the father grown rich and aiming at a new line of gentry: that he never pretended marriage to her: that indeed they would have had her join to prosecute him: and that she owed her death to her friends' barbarity because she would *not*. The boy, he says, is a fine boy; no father need to be ashamed of him: that he had twice, unknown to the aunt who had the care of him, been to see him; and would have provided for him had there been occasion. But that the whole family were fond of the child, though they were so wicked as to curse the father.

These, he says, were his rules in all his amours: 'to shun common women: to marry off a former mistress before he took a new one: to set the mother above want if her friends were cruel: to maintain a lady handsomely in her lying-in: to provide for the little one according to the mother's degree: and to go in mourning for her if she died in childbed.' He challenges Joseph to find out a man of more honour than himself in these respects. No wonder, he tells him, that the women love him as they do.

There is no room to fear for either his head or his neck, he tells him, from this affair: 'A lady dying in childbed eighteen months ago; no process begun in her lifetime; herself refusing to prosecute. Pretty circumstances, Joseph, to found an indictment for a rape upon!—Again, I say, I loved her: she was taken from me by her brutal friends while our joys were young—but enough of dear Miss Betterton—Dear, I say—for death endears!—Rest to her worthy soul!—There, Joseph, off went a deep sigh to the memory of Miss Betterton!'

He encourages him in his jesting. 'Jesting, says he, better becomes a poor man than qualms. All we say, all we do, all we wish for, is a jest: he that makes it not so is a sad fellow, and has the worst of it. Whoever grudges a poor man joy ought to have none himself.'

He applauds him for his love to his young lady: professes his honourable designs by her: values himself upon his word; and appeals to him on this head: 'You know, Joseph, says he, that I have gone beyond my promises to *you*. I do to everybody: and why?—because it is the best way of showing that I have not a grudging or narrow spirit. A just man will keep his promise: a generous man will go beyond it. That is my rule.'

He lays it wholly at the lady's door that they are not married; and laments the distance she keeps him at; which he attributes to Miss Howe who, he says, is for ever putting her upon contrivances; which is the reason, he tells him, that has obliged him to play off the people at Harlowe Place upon Mrs Howe by his assistance.

He then takes advantage of the hints Joseph gives him of Singleton and James Harlowe's close conferences: 'Since Singleton, says he, who has dependencies upon James Harlowe, is taught to have so good an opinion of you, Joseph, cannot you (still pretending an abhorrence of me and of my contrivances) propose to Singleton to propose to James Harlowe (who so much thirsts for revenge upon me) to assist him with his whole ship's crew, upon occasion, to carry off his sister to Leith, where both have houses, or elsewhere?

'You may tell them that if this can be effected, it will make me raving mad; and bring your young lady into all their measures. You can inform them, as from my servant, of the distance she keeps me at, in hopes of procuring her father's forgiveness by cruelly giving me up if insisted upon. That as the only secret my servant has kept from you is the place we are in, you make no doubt that a two guinea bribe will bring that out, and also an information when I shall be at distance from her that the enterprise may be safely conducted. You may tell them (still as from my servant) that we are about removing from inconvenient lodgings to others more convenient (which is true); and that I must be often absent from her.

'If they listen to your proposal, you will promote your interest with Betty by telling it to her as a secret. Betty will tell Arabella of it. Arabella will be overjoyed at anything that will help forward her revenge upon me; and will reveal it (if her brother do not) to her uncle Antony. He probably will whisper it to Mrs Howe. She can keep nothing from her daughter, though they are always jangling. Her daughter will acquaint my beloved with it. And if it will not, or if it will, come to my ears from some of those, you can write it to me, as in confidence, by way of preventing mischief, which is the study of us both. I can then show it to my beloved. Then will she be for placing a greater confidence in me. That will convince me of her love, which now I am sometimes ready to doubt. She will be for hastening to the safer lodgings. I shall have a pretence to stay about her person as a guard. She will be convinced that there is no expectation of a reconciliation. You can give James and Singleton continual false scents, as I shall direct you; so that no mischief can possibly happen.

'And what will be the happy, happy, thrice happy consequence?—The lady will be mine in an honourable way. We shall all be friends in good time. The two guineas will be an agreeable addition to the many gratuities I have helped you to, by like contrivances, from this stingy family. Your reputation, both for head and heart, will be heightened. The Blue Boar will also be yours. Nor shall you have the least difficulty about raising money to buy the stock, if it be worth your while to have it.

'Betty will likewise then be yours. You have both saved money, it seems. The whole Harlowe family, whom you have so faithfully served ('tis serving them surely, to prevent the mischief which their violent son would have brought upon them) will throw you in somewhat towards housekeeping. I will still add to your store. So nothing but happiness before you!

'Crow, Joseph, crow! A dunghill of your own in view: servants to snub at your pleasure: a wife to quarrel with, or to love, as your humour leads you: *landlord* and *landlady* at every word: to be paid instead of paying for your eating and drinking—but not thus happy only in yourself—Happy in promoting peace and reconciliation between two good families, in the long run; without hurting any Christian soul. Oh Joseph, honest Joseph! what envy will you raise!—and who would be squeamish with such prospects before him!

'This one labour crowns your work. If you can get but such a design entertained by them, whether they prosecute it or not, it will be equally to the purpose of

Your loving friend,
R. LOVELACE'

Letter 141: MISS CLARISSA HARLOWE TO MRS HERVEY

(Enclosed in her last to Miss Howe)

Thursday, April 20

Honoured madam,

HAVING not had the favour of an answer to a letter I took the liberty to write to you on the 14th, I am in some hopes that it may have miscarried; for I had much rather it should, than to have the mortification to think that my aunt Hervey deemed me unworthy of the honour of her notice.

In this hope, having kept a copy of it, and not being able to express myself in terms better suited to the unhappy circumstance of things, I transcribe and enclose what I then wrote.[a] And I humbly beseech you to favour the contents of it with your interest.

Hitherto it is in my power to perform what I undertake for in this letter; and it would be very grievous to me to be precipitated upon measures which may render the desirable reconciliation more difficult.

If, madam, I were permitted to write to you with the hopes of being answered, I could clear my intention with regard to the step I have taken, although I could not acquit myself, perhaps, to some of my severest judges, of an imprudence previous to it—You, I am sure, would pity me, if you knew all I could say and how miserable I am in the forfeiture of the good opinion of all my friends.

I flatter myself that *their* favour is yet retrievable. But whatever be the determination at Harlowe Place, do not *you*, my dearest aunt, deny me the favour of a few lines to inform me if there can be any hope of a reconciliation upon terms less shocking than those heretofore endeavoured to be imposed upon me; or if, which God forbid!, I am to be for ever reprobated.

At least, my dear aunt, procure for me the justice of my wearing apparel, and the little money and other things which I wrote to my sister for, and mention in the

a   The contents of this letter are given on p. 446.

enclosed to you; that I may not be destitute of common conveniencies, or be under a necessity to owe an obligation for such where (at present, however) I would least of all owe it.

Allow me to say that had I *designed* what happened, I might, as to the money and jewels at least, have saved myself some of the mortifications which I have suffered, and which I still farther apprehend if my request be not complied with.

If you are permitted to encourage an *éclaircissement* of what I hint, I will open my whole heart to you and inform you of everything.

If it be any pleasure to have me mortified, be pleased to let it be known that I am extremely mortified: and yet it is *entirely* from my own reflections that I am so, having nothing to find fault with in the behaviour of the person from whom every evil was apprehended.

The bearer having business your way will bring me your answer on Saturday morning, if you favour me according to my hopes. I knew not that I should have this opportunity till I had wrote the above.

I am, my dearest aunt,

> Your ever dutiful
> CL. HARLOWE

Be pleased to direct for me, if I am to be favoured with a few lines, to be left at Mr Osgood's near Soho Square; and nobody shall ever know of your goodness to me if you desire it to be kept a secret.

Letter 142: MISS HOWE TO MISS CLARISSA HARLOWE

> Sat. April 22

I CANNOT for my life account for your wretch's teasing ways. But he certainly doubts your love of him. In this *he* is a *modest* man, as well as somebody else; and tacitly confesses that he does not deserve it.

Your Israelitish hankerings after the Egyptian onions[1] (testified still more in your letter to your aunt), your often repeated regrets for meeting him, for being betrayed away by him: these he cannot bear.

I have been retrospecting the whole of his conduct, and comparing it with his general character; and find that he is more *consistently*, more *uniformly* mean, revengeful and proud, than either of us once imagined.

From his cradle, as I may say, as an *only child*, and a *boy*, humoursome, spoiled, mischievous; the governor of his governors.

A libertine in his riper years, hardly regardful of appearances; and despising the sex in general for the faults of particulars of it who made themselves too cheap to him.

What has been his behaviour in your family, a CLARISSA in view (from the time your foolish brother was obliged to take a life from him), but defiance for defiances?—Getting you into his power by terror, by artifice. What politeness can be expected from such a man?

Well, but what in such a situation is to be done?—Why, you must despise him— You must hate him—if you can—and run away from him—But whither?—

especially now that your brother is laying foolish plots to put you in a still worse condition, as it may happen?

But if you cannot despise and hate him—if you care not to break with him, you must part with some punctilios; and if the so doing bring not on the solemnity, you must put yourself into the protection of the ladies of his family.

Their respect for you is of itself a security for his honour, if there could be any room for doubt. And at least you should remind him of his offer to bring one of the Miss Montagues to attend you at your new lodgings in town, and accompany you till all is happily over.

This, you'll say, will be as good as *declaring* yourself to be his. And so let it. You ought not now to think of anything else but to be *his*. Does not your brother's project convince you more and more of this?

Give over then, my dearest friend, any thoughts of this hopeless reconciliation which has kept you balancing thus long. You own, in the letter before me, that he made very explicit offers, though you give me not the very words—And he gave his reasons, I perceive, with his wishes that you should accept them: which very few of the sorry fellows do, whose plea is generally but a compliment to our self-love— *that we must love them*, however presumptuous and unworthy, *because they love us*.

Were I in *your place*, and had *your* charming delicacies, I should, perhaps, do as you do. No doubt but I should expect that the man should urge me with respectful warmth; that he should supplicate with constancy, and that all his words and actions should tend to the one principal point—Nevertheless, if I suspected art or delay, founded upon his doubts of my love, I would either condescend to clear up his doubts or renounce him for ever.

And in this last case, I, your Anna Howe, would exert myself, and either find you a private refuge or resolve to share fortunes with you.

What a wretch to be so easily answered by your reference to the arrival of your cousin Morden? But I am afraid that you was too scrupulous—for did he not resent that reference?

Could we have *his* account of the matter, I fancy, my dear, I should think you over-nice, over-delicate. Had you laid hold of his *acknowledged* explicitness, he would have been as much in *your* power as now you seem to be in *his?*—You wanted not to be told that the person who had been tricked into such a step as you had taken must of necessity submit to many mortifications.

But were it to *me*, a girl of spirit as I am thought to be, I do assure you I would in a quarter of an hour (all the time I would allow to punctilio in such a case as yours) know what he drives at. Since either he must mean *well* or *ill*. If *ill*, the sooner you know it the better. If *well*, whose modesty is it he distresses but that of his own wife?

And methinks you should endeavour to avoid all exasperating recriminations as to what you have heard of his failure in morals; especially while you are so happy as not to have occasion to speak of them by experience.

I grant that it gives a worthy mind some satisfaction, in having borne its testimony against a bad one: but if the testimony be not seasonably borne, and when the faulty person be fitted to receive the correction, it may probably rather harden, or make an hypocrite, than reclaim him.

I am pleased, however, as well as you, with his making light of your brother's wise project—Poor creature!—And must master Jemmy Harlowe, with his half wit, pretend to plot and contrive mischief, yet rail at Lovelace for the same things?—A witty villain deserves hanging at once (and without ceremony, if you please); but a half-witted one deserves broken bones first, and hanging afterwards. I think Lovelace has given his character in few words.

Be angry at me, if you please; but as sure as you are alive, now that this poor creature, whom some call your brother, finds he has succeeded in making you fly your father's house, and that he has nothing to fear but your getting into your *own*, and into an independence of him, he thinks himself equal to anything and so has a mind to fight Lovelace with his own weapons?

Don't you remember his pragmatical triumph, as told you by your aunt, and prided in by that saucy Betty Barnes, from his own foolish mouth?[a]

I expect nothing from your letter to your aunt. I hope Lovelace will never know the contents of it. In every one of yours I see that he as warmly resents as he dares the little confidence you have in him. I should resent it too, were I him; and knew I deserved better.

Don't be scrupulous about clothes, if you think of putting yourself into the protection of the ladies of his family. They know how matters stand between you and your relations; and love you never the worse for their cruelty—As to money, why will you let me offer in vain?

I know you won't demand possession of your estate. But give *him* a right to demand it for you; and that will be still better.

Adieu, my dear!—May Heaven guide and direct you in all your steps, is the daily prayer of

Your ever affectionate and faithful
ANNA HOWE

Letter 143: MR BELFORD TO ROBERT LOVELACE, ESQ.

Friday, April 21

THOU, Lovelace, hast been long the *entertainer*; I the *entertained*. Nor have I been solicitous to animadvert, as thou wentest along, upon thy inventions and their tendency. For I believed, that with all thy airs, the unequalled perfections and fine qualities of this lady would always be her protection and security. But now that I find thou hast so far succeeded as to induce her to come to town, and to choose her lodgings in a house, the people of which will too probably damp and suppress any honourable motions which may arise in thy mind in her favour, I cannot help writing: and that professedly in her behalf.

My inducements to this are not owing to virtue—but if they *were*, what hope could I have of affecting thee by pleas arising from it?

Nor would such a man as thou art be deterred, were I to remind thee of the vengeance which thou mayest one day expect if thou insultest a woman of her character, family and fortune.

Neither are gratitude and honour motives to be mentioned in a woman's favour, to men such as we are, who consider all those of the sex as fair prize, whom we can obtain a power over. For *our honour*, and *honour* in the *general acceptation* of the word, are two things.

a See pp. 367, 369.

What then is my motive?—Why, the true friendship that I bear thee, Lovelace; which makes me plead *thy own sake* and *thy family's sake*, in the justice thou owest to this incomparable creature; who, however, so well deserves to have *her sake* to be mentioned as the principal consideration.

Last time I was at M. Hall, thy noble uncle so earnestly pressed me to use my interest to persuade thee to enter the pale, and gave me so many family reasons for it, that I could not help engaging myself heartily on his side of the question; and the rather as I knew that thy own intentions with regard to this fine woman were then worthy of *her*. And of this I assured his lordship; who was half-afraid of thee because of the ill usage thou receivedst from her family. But now that the case is altered, let me press the matter home to thee from other considerations.

By what I have heard of this lady's perfections from every mouth, as well as from thine, and from every letter thou hast written, where wilt thou find such another woman? And why shouldst thou tempt her virtue?—Why shouldst thou be for trying, where there is no reason to doubt?

Were I in thy case, and designed to marry, and if I preferred a lady as I know thou dost this to all the women in the world, I should dread to make further trial, knowing what *we* know of the sex, for *fear* of succeeding; and especially if I doubted not that if there were a woman in the world virtuous at heart, it is she.

And let me tell thee, Lovelace, that in this lady's situation, the trial is not a fair trial. Considering the depth of thy plots and contrivances: considering the opportunities which I see thou must have with her, in spite of her own heart; all her relations' follies acting in concert, though unknown to themselves, with thy wicked scheming head: considering how destitute of protection she is: considering the house she is to be in, where she will be surrounded with thy implements; *specious, well-bred* and *genteel* creatures, not easily to be detected when they are disposed to preserve appearances, especially by a young, inexperienced lady wholly unacquainted with the town: considering all these things, I say—what glory, what cause of triumph wilt thou have, if she should be overcome?—Thou, too, a man born for intrigue, full of invention, intrepid, remorseless, able patiently to watch for thy opportunity; not hurried, as most men, by gusts of violent passion which often nip a project in the bud, and make the snail that was just putting out its horns to meet the inviter withdraw into its shell—a man who has no regard to his word or oath to the sex; the lady scrupulously strict to *her* word, incapable of art or design; apt therefore to believe well of others—It would be a miracle if she stood such an attempter, such attempts and such snares, as I see will be laid for her. And after all, I see not when men are so frail *without* importunity, that so much should be expected from women, daughters of the same fathers and mothers, and made up of the same brittle compounds (education all the difference), nor where the triumph is in subduing them.

May there not be other Lovelaces, thou askest, who, attracted by her beauty, may endeavour to prevail with her?

No; there cannot, I answer, be such another man, person, mind, fortune and thy character, as above given, taken in. If thou imaginedst there could, such is thy pride, that thou wouldst think the worse of thyself.

But let me touch upon thy predominant passion, *revenge*; for *love* (what can be the love of a rake?) is but second to that, as I have often told thee, though it has set thee into raving at me—What poor pretences for revenge are the difficulties thou hadst in getting her off; allowing that she had run a risk of being Solmes's wife had she stayed; her injunctions so cruelly turned upon her; and her preference of the single life!—If these are other than pretences, why thankest thou not those who threw her into thy power?—Besides, are not the pretences thou makest for further trial most ungratefully, as well as contradictorily, founded upon the supposition of error in her, occasioned by her *favour* to thee?

And let me, for the utter confusion of thy poor pleas of this nature, ask thee: Would she, in thy opinion, had she willingly gone off with thee, have been entitled to better quarter?—For a *mistress* indeed she might: but wouldst thou for a *wife* have had cause to like her half so well as now?

That she loves thee, wicked as thou art, and cruel as a panther, there is no reason to doubt. Yet what a command has she over herself, that such a penetrating self-flatterer as thyself art sometimes ready to doubt it? Though persecuted on the one hand as she was by her own family, and attracted on the other by the splendour of thine; every one of whom wishes for, and courts her to rank herself among them?

Thou wilt perhaps think that I have departed from my proposition, and pleaded the *lady's sake* more than *thine* in the above—but no such thing. All that I have written is more in thy behalf than in hers—since she may make *thee* happy—But it is next to impossible, I should think, if she preserves her delicacy that thou canst make *her* so. I need not give my reasons. Thou'lt have ingenuity enough, I dare say, were there occasion for it, to subscribe to my opinion.

I plead not for the state from any great liking to it myself. Nor have I, at present, thoughts of entering into it. But as thou art the last of thy name; as thy family is of note and figure in thy country; and as thou thyself thinkest that thou shalt one day marry; is it possible, let me ask thee, that thou canst have such another opportunity as thou now hast, if thou lettest this slip? A lady in her family and fortune not unworthy of thine own (though thou art so apt from pride of ancestry and pride of heart to speak slightly of the families thou dislikest); so celebrated for beauty; and so noted at the same time for prudence, for *soul* (I will say, instead of *sense*), and for virtue?

If thou art not so narrow-minded an elf as to prefer thy own *single* satisfaction to *posterity*, thou, who shouldst wish to beget children for duration, wilt not postpone till the rake's usual time; that is to say, till diseases or years, or both, lay hold of thee; since in that case thou wouldst entitle thyself to the curses of thy legitimate progeny for giving them a being altogether miserable: a being which they will be obliged to hold upon a worse tenure than that *tenant-courtesy*, which thou callest the *worst*[a]; to wit, upon the *doctor's courtesy*; thy descendants also propagating (if they shall live and be able to propagate) a wretched race that shall entail the curse, or the *reason* for it, upon remote generations.

Wicked as the sober world accounts us, we have not yet, it is to be hoped, got over all compunction. Although we find religion against us, we have not yet presumed to make a religion to suit our practices. We despise those who do. And we know better than to be even *doubters*. In short, we believe a future state of rewards and punishments. But as we have so much youth and health in hand, we hope to have time for repentance. That is to say, in plain English (nor think thou me too grave, Lovelace: thou art grave sometimes, though not often), we hope to

---

a See p. 449.

live to sense, as long as sense can relish, and purpose to reform when we can sin no longer.

And shall this admirable woman suffer for her generous endeavours to set on foot thy reformation; and for insisting upon proofs of the sincerity of thy professions before she will be thine?

Upon the whole matter let me wish thee to consider well what thou art about, before thou goest a step farther in the path which thou hast chalked out for thyself to tread, and art just going to enter into. Hitherto all is so far right, that if the lady *mistrusts* thy honour, she has no *proofs*. Be honest to her, then, in *her* sense of the word. None of thy companions, thou knowest, will offer to laugh at what *thou* dost. And if they *should* (on thy entering into a state which has been so much ridiculed by thee, and by all of us), thou hast one advantage: it is this; that thou canst not be ashamed.

Deferring to the post-day to close my letter, I find one left for my cousin Osgood, to be forwarded to the lady. It was brought within these two hours by a *particular* hand, and has a Harlowe seal upon it. As it may therefore be of importance, I dispatch it with my own, by my servant, post-haste.[a]

I suppose you will soon be in town. Without the lady, I hope. Farewell.

Be honest, and be happy.

Sat. Apr. 22 J. BELFORD

Letter 144: MRS HERVEY TO MISS CLARISSA HARLOWE

(In answer to Letter 141)
Dear niece,
IT would be hard not to write a few lines, so much pressed to write, to one I ever loved. Your former letter I received, yet was not at liberty to answer it. I break my word to answer you now.

· Strange informations are every day received about you. The wretch you are with, we are told, is every hour triumphing and defying—must not these informations aggravate? You know the uncontrollableness of the man. He loves his own humour better than he loves you—though so fine a creature as you are! I warned you over and over: no young lady was ever more warned!—Miss Clarissa Harlowe to do such a thing!

You might have given your friends the meeting. If you had *held* your aversion, it would have been complied with. As soon as I was entrusted myself with their *intention* to give up the point, I gave you a hint—a dark one perhaps![b]—but who would have thought—oh miss!—such an *artful* flight!—such *cunning* preparation!

But you want to clear up things—*What* can you clear up? Are you not gone off?—with a Lovelace too?—*What*, my dear, would you clear up?

You did not *design* to go, you say. Why did you meet him then, chariot and six, horsemen, all prepared by him? Oh, my dear, how art produces art!—Will it be believed?—If it *would*, what power will he be thought to have had over you!—

a This letter was from her sister Arabella. See Letter 147.
b See p. 368.

He!—Who?—_Lovelace!_—the vilest of libertines!—Over whom?—A _Clarissa Harlowe!_—Was your love for such a man above your reason?—above your resolution?—What credit would a belief of this, _if_ believed, bring you?—How mend the matter?—Oh! that you had stood the next meeting!—

I'll tell you all that was intended, if you had.

It was indeed imagined that you would not have been able to resist your father's entreaties and commands. He was resolved to be all condescension, if anew you had not provoked him. _I love my Clary Harlowe,_ said he, but an hour before the killing tidings were brought him; _I love her as my life; I will kneel to her, if nothing else will do, to prevail upon her to oblige me!_

Your father and mother (reverse to what should have been!) would have humbled themselves to _you:_ and if you _could_ have denied them, and refused to sign the settlements previous to the meeting, they would have yielded, although with regret.

But it was presumed, so naturally sweet your temper, so self-denying, as they thought you, that you could _not_ have withstood them, notwithstanding all your dislike of the _one_ man, without a greater degree of headstrong passion for the _other_ than you had given any of us reason to expect from you.

If you _had_, the meeting on Wednesday would have been a lighter trial to you. You would have been presented to all your assembled friends, with a short speech only. 'That this was the young creature, till very lately faultless, condescending and obliging, now having cause to glory in a triumph over the wills of father, mother, uncles, the most indulgent; over family interests, family views, and preferring her own will to everybody's; and this for a transitory preference to _person_ only; the morals of the men not to be compared with each other's.'

Thus complied with, and perhaps blessed, by your father and mother, and the consequences of your disobedience deprecated in the solemnest manner by your inimitable mother, your _generosity_ would have been appealed to, since your duty would have been found too weak an inducement, and you would have been bid to withdraw for one half-hour's consideration: then would the settlements have been again tendered for your signing by the person least disobliging to you; by your good Norton perhaps; she perhaps seconded by your father again: and if again refused, you would again have been led in to declare such your refusal. Some restrictions, which you yourself had proposed, would have been insisted upon. You would have been permitted to go home with me, or with your uncle Antony (_which_, not agreed upon, because they hoped you might be prevailed with), there to tarry till the arrival of your cousin Morden; or till your father could have borne to see you; or till assured that the views of Lovelace were at an end.

This the intention, your father so set upon your compliance, so much in hopes that you would have yielded, that you would have been prevailed upon by methods so condescending and so gentle; no wonder that _he_, in particular, was like a distracted man when he heard of your flight—of your flight, so _premeditated_— with your ivy summer-house dinings, your arts to blind me, and all of us!— naughty, naughty young creature!

I, for my part, would not believe it when told of it. Your uncle Hervey would not believe it. We rather expected, we rather feared, a still more desperate adventure. There could be but one more desperate; and I was readier to have the cascade first resorted to, than the garden back door—Your mamma fainted away, while her heart was torn between the two apprehensions. Your father, poor man! your father was beside himself for near an hour. To this day he can hardly bear your name: yet can think of nobody else. Your merits, my dear, but aggravate your fault—something of fresh aggravation almost every hour—How can any favour be expected?

I am sorry for it; but am afraid, nothing you ask will be complied with.

Why mention you, my dear, the saving you from mortifications, who have gone off with a man? What a poor pride is it to stand upon anything else?

I dare not open my lips in your favour. Nobody dare. Your letter must stand by itself. This has caused me to send it to Harlowe Place. Expect therefore great severity. May you be enabled to support the lot you have chosen! Oh my dear! How unhappy have you made everybody! Can *you* expect to be happy? Your father wishes you had never been born. Your poor mother—but why should I afflict you? There is now no help!—You must be changed indeed, if you are not very unhappy yourself in the reflections your thoughtful mind must suggest to you.

You must now make the best of your lot. Yet *not* married, it seems!

It is in your power, you say, to perform whatever you shall undertake to do: you may deceive yourself. You hope that your reputation, and your friends' favour, may be retrieved. Never, never, both, I doubt; if either. Every offended person (and that is all who loved you, and are related to you) must *join* to restore you: when can these be of *one* mind in a case so notoriously wrong?

It would be very grievous, you say, to be precipitated upon measures that may make the desirable reconciliation more difficult. Is it *now*, my dear, a time for you to be afraid of being *precipitated*? At *present*, if *ever*, there can be no thought of reconciliation. The *upshot* of your precipitation must first be seen. There may be murder yet, as far as we know. Will the man you are with part willingly with you? If *not*, what may be the consequence? If he *will*, Lord bless me! what shall we think of his reasons for it?—I will fly this thought. I know your purity—but, my dear, are you not out of all protection?—Are you not unmarried?—Have you not (making your daily prayers useless) thrown yourself into temptation? And is not the man the most wicked of plotters?

You have hitherto, you say (and I think, my dear, with an air unbecoming your declared penitence), no fault to find with the behaviour of a man from whom every evil was apprehended: like Caesar to the Roman augur, which I heard you tell of, who had bid him *beware of the ides of March*. The ides of March, said Caesar, seeing the augur among the crowd, as he marched in state to the senate house which he never was to return from alive, *the ides of March are come. But they are not past*, the augur replied. Make the application, my dear: may you be able to make this reflection upon his good behaviour to the last of your knowledge of him! May he behave himself better to you, than he ever did to anybody else whom he had power over! Amen!

No answer, I beseech you. I hope your messenger will not tell anybody that I have written to you. And I dare say you will not show what I have written to Mr Lovelace—for I have written with the less reserve, depending upon your prudence.

You have my prayers.

My Dolly knows not that I write. Nobody does: not even Mr Hervey.

Dolly would have several times written: but, having defended your fault with heat, and with a partiality that alarmed us (such a fall as yours, my dear, must be alarming to all parents), she has been forbidden on pain of losing our favour for ever: and this at your family's request, as well as by her father's commands.

You have the poor girl's hourly prayers, however, I will tell you, though she knows not that I do, as well as those of

Your truly afflicted aunt,
D. HERVEY

Friday, April 21

Letter 145: MISS CLARISSA HARLOWE TO MISS HOWE

(With the preceding)

Sat morn. April 22

I HAVE just now received the enclosed from my aunt Hervey. Be pleased, my dear, to keep her secret of having written to the unhappy wretch, her niece.

I may go to London, I see, or where I will. No matter what becomes of me.

I was the willinger to suspend my journey thither, till I heard from Harlowe Place. I thought if I could be encouraged to hope for a reconciliation, I would let this man see that he should not have me in his power but upon my own terms, if at all.

But I find I must be *his*, whether I will or not; and perhaps through still greater mortifications than those great ones which I have already met with—And must I be so absolutely thrown upon a man with whom I am not at all satisfied!

My letter is sent, you see, to Harlowe Place. My heart aches for the reception it may meet with there. One comfort only arises to me from its being sent; that my aunt will clear herself by the communication from the supposition of having corresponded with the poor creature whom they have all determined to reprobate. It is no small part of my misfortune that I have weakened the confidence one dear friend has in another, and made one look cool upon another. My poor cousin Dolly, you see, has reason to regret this, as well as my aunt. Miss Howe, my dear Miss Howe, is but too sensible of the effects of my fault, having had more words with her mother on my account than ever she had on any other. Yet the man who has drawn me into all this evil, I must be thrown upon!—Much did I consider, much did I apprehend, *before* my fault, supposing I *were* to be guilty of it: but I saw it not in all its shocking lights.

And now to know that my father, an hour before he received the tidings of my supposed flight, owned that he loved me as his life: that he would have been all condescension: that he would—Oh! my dear, how tender, how mortifyingly tender, now in him! My aunt need not have been afraid that it should be known that she has sent me such a letter as this!—A father to KNEEL to a daughter!—There would not indeed have been any bearing of that!—What I should have done in such a case, I know not. Death would have been much more welcome to me than such a sight, on such an occasion, in behalf of a man so very, very disgustful to me! But I had deserved annihilation had I suffered my father to kneel in vain.

Yet, had but the sacrifice of *inclination* and *personal preference* been *all*, less than KNEELING should have done. My *duty* should have been the conqueror of my *inclination*. But an aversion—an aversion so *very* sincere!—The triumph of a cruel and ambitious brother, ever so uncontrollable, joined with the insults of an envious sister, bringing wills to *theirs* which otherwise would have been favourable to *me*: the marriage duties so very strong, so solemnly to be engaged for: the marriage-intimacies (permit me to say to you, my friend, what the purest, although with apprehension, must think of) so *very* intimate: myself one who never looked upon any duty, much less a voluntarily-vowed one, with indifference; could it have been honest in me to have given my hand to an odious hand, and to have consented to such a more than reluctant, such an *immiscible* union, if I may so call it?—for life too!—Did I not *think* more and deeper than most young creatures think; did I not *weigh*, did I not *reflect*; I might perhaps have been less obstinate—*Delicacy* (may I presume to call it?), *thinking, weighing, reflection*, are not blessings (I have not found them such) in the degree I have them. I wish I had been able in some very nice cases to have known what *indifference* was; yet not to have my *ignorance* imputable to me as a fault. Oh! my dear! the finer sensibilities, if I may suppose mine to be such, make not happy!

What a method had my friends intended to take with me!—This, I dare say, was a method chalked out by my brother. *He*, I suppose, was to have presented me to all my assembled friends as the daughter capable of preferring her own will to the wills of them all. It would have been a sore trial, no doubt. Would to heaven, however, I had stood it—let the issue have been what it would, would to heaven I had stood it!

There may be murder, my aunt says. This looks as if she knew of Singleton's rash plot. Such an *upshot*, as she calls it, of this unhappy affair, Heaven avert!

She flies a thought that I can *less* dwell upon—a *cruel* thought!—but she has a poor opinion of the purity she compliments me with, if she thinks that I am not, by God's grace, above temptation from this sex. Although I never saw a man, whose *person* I could like, before this man; yet his faulty character allowed me but little merit from the indifference I pretended to on his account. But now I see him in nearer lights, I like him less than ever—Indeed, I never liked him so little as now. Upon my word, I think I could hate him (if I do not already hate him) sooner than any man I ever thought tolerably of—a good reason why: because I have been more disappointed in my expectations of him; although they never were so high as to have made him my choice in preference to the single life, had that been permitted me. Still, if the giving him up for ever will make my path to reconciliation easy, and if they will signify as much to me, they shall see that I never will be *his:* for I have the vanity to think my soul his soul's superior.

You will say I rave. Forbid to write to my aunt, and taught to despair of reconciliation, you, my dear, must be troubled with my passionate resentments. What a wretch was I to meet him, and thereby to leave it not in my power to stand the general meeting with my friends!—All would now have been over!—And who can tell, when my present distresses will?—Rid of both men, I had been now perhaps at my aunt Hervey's, or at my uncle Antony's; wishing for my cousin Morden's arrival; who might have accommodated all.

I *intended*, indeed, to have stood it—and if I had, how know I by whose name I might now have been called? For how should I have resisted a condescending, a *kneeling* father, had he been able to have kept his temper with me!

Yet my aunt says *he* would have relented if *I* had not. Perhaps he would have been moved by my humility before he could have shown such *undue* condescension. Such temper as he would have received me with might have been improved upon in my favour. And that he had designed *ultimately* to relent, how it clears my friends, at least to themselves, and condemns me! Oh why were my aunt's hints (I remember them now) so *very* dark?—Yet I intended to have returned after the interview; and then perhaps she would have explained herself—Oh this artful, this designing Lovelace!—Yet I must repeat that most ought I to blame myself for meeting him.

But far, far be banished from me fruitless recrimination! Far banished, *because* fruitless! Let me wrap myself about in the mantle of my own integrity, and take comfort in my unfaulty intention! Since it is now too late to look back, let me collect all my fortitude and endeavour to stand those shafts of angry providence which it will not permit me to shun! That whatever the trials may be which I am destined to undergo, I may not behave unworthily in them; but come out amended by them.

Join with me in this prayer, my beloved friend; for your own honour's sake, as well as for love's sake, join with me in it: lest a deviation on my side should, with the censorious, cast a shade upon a friendship which has no *body*, no levity in it, and whose basis is improvement as well in the greater as lesser duties.

CL. HARLOWE

Letter 146: MISS CLARISSA HARLOWE TO MISS HOWE

Saturday, p.m. April 23

OH MY best, my only friend! Now indeed is my heart broken!—It has received a blow it never will recover! Think not of corresponding with a wretch who now seems absolutely devoted! How can it be otherwise, if a parent's curses have the weight I always attributed to them and have heard so many instances of their being followed by!—Yes, my dear Miss Howe, superadded to all my afflictions, I have the consequences of a father's curse to struggle with! How shall I support this reflection!—my past and my present situation so much authorizing my apprehensions!

I have at last a letter from my unrelenting sister. Would to heaven I had not provoked it by my second letter to my aunt Hervey. It lay ready for me, it seems. The thunder slept till I awakened it. I enclose the letter itself. Transcribe it I cannot. There is no bearing the thoughts of it: for (shocking reflection!) the curse extends to the life beyond this.

I am in the depth of vapourish despondency. I can only repeat: shun, fly, correspond not with a wretch so devoted as

Your CLARISSA HARLOWE

Letter 147: MISS ARABELLA HARLOWE TO MISS CLARISSA HARLOWE

To be left at Mr Osgood's, near Soho Square

Friday, April 21

IT was expected you would send again to me or to my aunt Hervey. The enclosed has lain ready for you therefore by direction. You will have no answer from anybody, write to *whom* you will, and as *often* as you will, and *what* you *will*.

It was designed to bring you back by proper authority, or to send you whither the disgraces you have brought upon us all should be in the likeliest way, after a while, to be forgotten. But I believe that design is over: so you may *range* securely: nobody will think it worth while to give themselves any trouble about you. Yet my mamma has obtained leave to send you your clothes, of all sorts: but your clothes only. This is a favour you'll see by the within letter not *designed* you: and *now* not granted for *your* sake, but because my poor mother cannot bear in her sight anything you used to wear. Read the enclosed and tremble.

ARABELLA HARLOWE

To the most ungrateful and undutiful of daughters

Harlowe Place, Sat. April 15

Sister that was,

FOR I know not what name you are *permitted* or *choose* to go by.

You have filled us all with distraction. My father, in the first agitations of his mind on discovering your wicked, your shameful elopement, imprecated on his knees a fearful curse upon you. Tremble at the recital of it!—No less, than 'that you may meet your punishment, both *here* and *hereafter*, by means of the very wretch in whom you have chosen to place your wicked confidence.'

Your clothes will not be sent you. You seem, by leaving them behind you, to have been secure of them whenever you demanded them. But perhaps you could think of nothing but meeting your fellow—nothing but how to get off your forward self!—for everything seems to have been forgot but what was to contribute to your wicked flight. Yet you judged right, perhaps, that you would have been detected, had you endeavoured to get off your clothes!—Cunning creature! not to make *one* step that we could guess at you by!—Cunning to effect your own ruin and the disgrace of all the family!

But does the wretch put you upon writing for your things for fear you should be too expensive to him?—That's it, I suppose.

Was there ever a giddīer creature?—Yet this is the celebrated, the blazing Clarissa—Clarissa, *what?—Harlowe*, no doubt!—and Harlowe it will be to the disgrace of us all!—

Your drawings and your pieces are all taken down; as is also your own whole-length picture in the Vandyke taste, from your late parlour: they are taken down and thrown into your closet, which will be nailed up as if it were not a part of the house; there to perish together: for who can bear to see them? Yet, how did they use to be shown to everybody: the former for the magnifying of your dainty fingerworks; the latter for the imputed dignity (dignity now in the dust!) of your boasted figure[a]; and this by those fond parents whom you have run away from with so *much*, yet with *so little* contrivance!

My brother vows revenge upon your libertine—for the *family*'s sake he vows it—not for *yours!*—For he will treat you, he declares, like a common creature, if ever he sees you: and doubts not that this will be your fate.

My uncle Harlowe renounces you for ever.

So does my uncle Antony.

a   This picture is drawn as big as the life by Mr Highmore[1] and is in his possession.

So does my aunt Hervey.

So do *I*, base unworthy creature!—the disgrace of a good family and the property of an infamous rake, as questionless you will soon find yourself, if you are not already!

Your books, since they have not taught you what belongs to your family, to your sex and to your education, will not be sent you. Your money neither. Nor yet the jewels so undeservedly made yours! For it is wished you may be seen a beggar along London streets!

If all this is heavy, lay your hand to your heart and ask yourself why you have deserved it?

Every gentleman whom your pride taught you to reject with scorn (Mr Solmes excepted, who, however, has reason to rejoice that he missed you) triumphs in your shameful elopement; and now knows how to account for his being refused.

Your worthy Norton is ashamed of you, and mingles her tears with your mamma's; both reproaching themselves for their shares in you and in so fruitless an education.

Everybody, in short, is ashamed of you: but none more than

ARABELLA HARLOWE

Letter 148: MISS HOWE TO MISS CLARISSA HARLOWE

Tuesday, April 25

BE comforted; be not dejected; do not despond, my dearest and best-beloved friend. God Almighty is just and gracious, and gives not his assent to rash and inhuman curses. If he did, malice, envy and the blackest passions in the blackest hearts would triumph, and the best (blasted by the malignity of the worst) would be miserable in both worlds.

This malediction shows only what manner of spirit they are of, and how much their sordid views exceed their parental love. 'Tis all rage and disappointment, my dear; disappointment in designs proper to be frustrated; and all you have to grieve for is that their own rashness will turn upon their own hearts. God Almighty cannot succeed a curse so presumptuous as to be carried into *his* futurity!

Fie upon them!—Fie upon them will all the world say, who shall come to the knowledge of such overflowing venom!—And the more, when all shall know that what they resent so outrageously is owing to themselves!

My mother blames them for this wicked letter; and she pities you; and of her own accord wished me to write to comfort you, for this once. For she says, it is pity your heart which was so noble (and when the sense of your fault and the weight of a parent's curse are so strong upon you) should be quite broken.

Lord bless me, how your aunt writes!—Can there be two rights and two wrongs in palpable cases!—But, my dear, she *must* be wrong: so they all have been, justify themselves now as they will. They can only justify themselves *to* themselves from selfish principles, resolving to *acquit*, not fairly to *try* themselves. Did your unkind aunt in all the tedious progress of your contentions with them give you the least hope of their relenting?—Her dark hints I now recollect, as well as you. But why was anything good or hopeful to you to be *darkly* hinted?—How easy was it for *her*, who pretended always to love you so well; for *her*, who can give such flowing licence to her pen for your hurt; to have given you one word, one line (in confidence) of their pretended change of measures!

But don't mind their after-pretences, my dear—All of them serve but for tacit confessions of their vile usage of you. I will keep your aunt's secret, never fear. I would not, on any consideration, that my mother should see it.

You will now see that you have nothing left but to overcome all scrupulousness, and marry as soon as you have opportunity. Determine upon this, my dear.

I will give you a motive for it, regarding myself. For this I have resolved, and this I have vowed (Oh friend, the best beloved of my heart, be not angry with me for it!): 'That so long as your happiness is in suspense, I will never think of marrying.' In justice to the man I shall have, I have vowed this: for, my dear, must I not be miserable if you are so? And what an unworthy wife must I be to any man, who cannot have interest enough in my heart to make his obligingness a balance for an affliction he has not caused?

I would show Lovelace your sister's abominable letter, were it to me. I enclose it. It shall not have a place in this house. This will enter him of course into the subject which now you ought to have most in view. Let him see what you suffer for him. He cannot prove base to such an excellence. I should never enjoy my head or my senses, should this man prove a villain to you! With a merit so exalted, you may have punishment more than enough for your involuntary fault in that husband.

I would not have you be too sure that their project to seize you is over. The words intimating that it is over in the letter of that abominable Arabella seem calculated to give you security—She only says she *believes* that design is over— And I do not yet find from Miss Lloyd that it is disavowed. So it will be best, when you are at London, to be private and to let every direction be to a third place, for fear of the worst; for I would not for the world have you fall into the hands of such flaming and malevolent spirits by surprise.

I will myself be content to direct to you at some *third* place; and that I may have it to aver to my mother, or to any other if occasion be, that I know not where you are.

Besides, this measure will make you less apprehensive of the consequences of their violence should they resolve to attempt to carry you off in spite of Lovelace.

I would have you direct to Mr Hickman even your answer to this. I have a reason for it. Besides, my mamma, notwithstanding this particular indulgence, is very positive.

I would not have you dwell on the shocking occasion. I know how it must affect you. But don't let it. Try to make light of it (forget it you can't): and pursue other subjects—the subjects before you. And let me know your progress, and what he says (so far may you enter into this hateful subject) to this abominable letter, and diabolical curse. I expect that this will aptly introduce the grand topic between you without needing a mediator.

Come, my dear, when things are at worst they must mend. Good often comes when evil is expected. Happily improved upon, this very curse may turn to a blessing. But if you despond, there can be no hopes of cure. Don't let them break your heart; for that, it is plain to me, is now what some people have in view to do.

How poor, to withhold from you your books, your jewels and your money!—

The latter is all you can at present want, since they will vouchsafe to send your clothes—I send fifty guineas by the bearer, enclosed in single papers in my *Norris's Miscellanies*. I charge you, as you love me, return them not.

I have more at your service. So if you like not your lodgings, or his behaviour, when you get to town, leave both out of hand.

I would advise you to write to Mr Morden without delay. If he intends for England, it may hasten him. And you'll do very well till he can come. But surely Lovelace is bewitched if he takes not his happiness from *your consent*, before that of Mr Morden's is made needful by his arrival.

Come, my dear, be comforted. All is hastening to be well. This very violence shows that it is. Suppose yourself to be *me*, and me to be *you* (you *may*—for your distress is mine); and then give to yourself those consolations which, in that case, you would give me. Nothing but words has passed, vehement and horrid as those are. The divine goodness will not let them be more. Can you think that Heaven will seal to the black passions of its depraved creatures? Manage with your usual prudence the stake before you, and all will be still happy.

I have as great apprehensions as you of the weight of a parent's curse; but not of the curse of those parents who have more to answer for than the child, in the very errors they so much resent. To entitle those horrid words to efficacy, the parents' views should be pure, should be altogether justifiable; and the child's ingratitude and undutifulness without excuse; and her *choice* too, as totally inexcusable.

This is the true light, as I humbly conceive, that this matter should appear to you in, and to everybody. If you let not despondency seize you, you will strengthen, you will add more day to this but glimmering light, from

Your ever affectionate and faithful

ANNA HOWE

I hurry this away by Robert. I will inquire into the truth of your aunt's pretences about their change of measures had you not gone away.

Letter 149: MISS CLARISSA HARLOWE TO MISS HOWE

Wednesday morning, April 26

YOUR letter, my beloved Miss Howe, gives me great comfort. How sweetly do I experience the truth of the wise man's observation, *That a faithful friend is the medicine of life!*[1]

Your messenger finds me just setting out for London: the chaise at the door. Already I have taken leave of the good widow, who has obliged me with the company of her eldest daughter, at Mr Lovelace's request, while he rides by us. The young gentlewoman is to return in two or three days with the chaise, in its way to my Lord M.'s Hertfordshire seat.

I received this dreadful letter on Sunday when Mr Lovelace was out. He saw, on his return, my extreme anguish and dejection; and he was told how much worse I had been: for I had fainted away twice.

I think it has touched my head as well as my heart.

He would fain have seen it. But I would not permit that because of the threatenings he would have found in it against himself. As it *was*, the effect it had upon me made him break out into execrations and menaces. I was so ill, that he himself advised me to delay going to town on Monday, as I proposed to do.

He is extremely regardful and tender of me. All that you supposed *would* follow this violent letter, from him, *has* followed it. He has offered himself to my acceptance in so unreserved a manner that I am concerned I have written so freely and so diffidently of him. Pray, my dearest friend, keep to yourself everything that may appear disreputable of him from me.

I must own to you that this kind behaviour and my low-spiritedness, co-operating with your former advice and my unhappy situation, made me that very Sunday evening receive unreservedly his declarations: And now, indeed, I am more in his power than ever.

He presses me every hour for fresh tokens of my esteem *for* him, and confidence *in* him. He owns that he doubted the one, and was ready to despair of the other. And as I have been brought to some verbal concessions, if he should prove unworthy, I am sure I shall have great reason to blame this violent letter: for I have no resolution at all. Abandoned thus of all my natural friends, and only you to pity me; and *you* restrained as I may say; I have been forced to turn my desolate heart to such protection as I could find.

All my comfort is that your advice repeatedly given to the same purpose, in your kind letter before me, warrants me. Upon the strength of that, I now set out the more cheerfully to London: for, before, a heavy weight hung upon my heart, and although I thought it best and safest to go, yet my spirit sunk, I know not why, at every motion I made towards a preparation for it.

I hope no mischief will happen on the road—I hope these violent spirits will not meet.

Everyone is waiting for me—Pardon me, my best, my kindest friend, that I return your Norris. In these more promising prospects, I cannot have occasion for your favour. Besides, I have some hope that with my clothes they will send me what I wrote for, although it is denied me in the letter. If they do not, and if I should have occasion, I can but signify my wants to so ready a friend. But I had rather methinks you should have it still to say, if challenged, that nothing of this nature has been either requested or done. I say this, with a view entirely to my future hopes of recovering your mamma's favour which, next to that of my own father and mother, I am most solicitous to recover.

I must add one thing more, notwithstanding my hurry; and that is: Mr Lovelace offered to attend me to Lord M.'s, or to send for his chaplain, yesterday: he pressed me to consent to this proposal most earnestly; and even seemed more desirous to have the ceremony pass here than at London: for when there, I had told him, it was time enough to consider of so weighty and important a matter. Now, upon the receipt of your kind, your consolatory letter, methinks I could almost wish it *had been* in my power to comply with his earnest solicitations. But this dreadful letter has unhinged my whole frame. Then some little punctilio surely is necessary. No preparation made. No articles drawn. No licence ready. Grief so extreme: no pleasure in prospect, nor so much as in wish—Oh my dear, who could think of entering into so solemn an engagement! Who, *so* unprepared, could seem to be *so* ready!

If I could flatter myself that my indifference to all the joys of this life proceeded from *proper* motives, and not rather from the disappointments and mortifications my pride has met with, how much rather, I think, should I choose to be wedded to my shroud than to any man on earth!

Indeed I have at present no pleasure but in *your* friendship. Continue that to me, I beseech you. If my heart rises hereafter to more, it must be built on that foundation.

My spirits sink again on setting out. Excuse this depth of vapourish dejection which forbids me even *hope*, the cordial that keeps life from stagnating, and which never was denied me till within these eight-and-forty hours.

But 'tis time to relieve you.

Adieu, my best beloved and kindest friend! Pray for your

CL. HARLOWE

Letter 150: MISS HOWE TO MISS CLARISSA HARLOWE

Thursday, April 27

I AM sorry you returned my Norris. But you must be allowed to do as you please. So must I, in return. We must neither of us, perhaps, expect absolutely of the other what is the rightest to be done: and yet few folks, so young, better know *what that rightest is*. I cannot separate myself from you, my dear; although I give a double instance of my vanity in this particular compliment to myself.

I am most heartily rejoiced that your prospects are so much mended; and that, as I hoped, good has been produced out of evil. What must the man have been, what must have been his views, had he not taken such a turn upon a letter so vile, and treatment so unnatural, himself principally the occasion of it?

You *know best* your motives for suspending: but I wish you had taken him at offers so earnest. Why should you not have permitted him to send for Lord M.'s chaplain? If punctilio only was in the way, and want of a licence and of proper preparations and such-like, my service to you, my dear: and there is ceremony tantamount to your ceremony.

Don't, don't my dear friend, *again* be so very melancholy a decliner as to prefer a shroud, when the matter you wish for is in your power; and when, as you have said justly heretofore, persons cannot die when they will.

But it is a strange perverseness in human nature that we covet at a distance what when near we slight.

You have now but one point to pursue: that is marriage. Let that be compassed. Leave the rest to Providence; and follow as that leads. You'll have a handsome man, a genteel man; he would be a *wise* man if he were not vain of his endowments, and wild and intriguing. But while the eyes of many of our sex, taken by so specious a form and so brilliant a spirit, encourage that vanity, you must be contented to stay till grey hairs and prudence enter upon the stage together. You would not have everything in the same man.

I believe Mr Hickman treads no crooked paths; but he hobbles most ungracefully in a straight one. Yet Hickman, though he *pleases* not my eye, nor *diverts* my ear, will not, as I believe, *disgust* the one, nor *shock* the other. Your man, as I have lately said, will always keep up attention; you will always be alive with him, though perhaps more from fears than hopes: while Hickman will neither say anything to keep one awake, nor yet by shocking adventures make one's slumbers uneasy.

I believe I now know which of the two men so prudent a person as *you* would, at first, have chosen; nor doubt I that you can guess which *I* would have made choice of, if I might. But proud as we are, the proudest of us all can *only* refuse, and many of us accept the but half-worthy for fear a still worse should offer.

If the men had chosen for spirits like their own, although Mr Lovelace, at the long run, might have been too many for me, I don't doubt but I should have given heartache for heartache, for one half-year at least; while you, with my dull-swift, would have glided on *as* serenely, *as* calmly, *as* accountably, as the succeeding seasons; and varying no otherwise than as they, to bring on new beauties and conveniencies to all about you.

I WAS going on in this style—but my mamma broke in upon me, with a prohibitory aspect. 'She gave me leave but for one letter only.' She has seen your odious uncle; and they have been in close conference again.

She has vexed me; I must lay this by till I hear from you again; not knowing where to send it.

Direct me to a *third place*, as I desired in my former.

I told my mother (on her challenging me), that I was writing indeed, and to you: but it was only to amuse myself; for I protested that I knew not where to send to you.

I hope that your next may inform me of your nuptials, although the next to that were to acquaint me that he was the ungratefullest monster on earth; as he must be, if not the kindest husband in it.

My mamma has vexed me. But so, on revising, I wrote before—But she has *unhinged* me, as you call it—Pretended to catechize Hickman, I assure you, for contributing to our supposed correspondence. Catechize him *severely* too, upon my word!—I believe I have a sneaking kindness for the sneaking fellow; for I can't endure that anybody should treat him like a fool but myself.

I believe, between you and me, the good lady forgot herself. I heard her loud. She possibly imagined, that my papa was come to life again!—Yet the man's meekness might have sooner convinced her, I should have thought; for my papa, it seems, would talk as loud as she—I suppose, though within a few yards of each other, as if both were out of their way and were hollowing at half a mile's distance to get in again.

I know you'll blame me for this sauciness. But I told you I was vexed: and if I had not a spirit, my parentage on both sides might be doubted.

You must not chide me too severely, however, because I have learned of you not to defend myself in an error—And I own I am wrong—And that's enough. You won't be so generous in this case as you are in every other, if you don't think it is.

Adieu, my dear!—I must, I will love you; and love you for ever! So subscribes your

ANNA HOWE

Letter 151: MISS HOWE TO MISS CLARISSA HARLOWE

(Enclosed in the above)

Thursday, April 27

I HAVE been making inquiry, as I told you I would, whether your relations had really (before you left them) resolved upon that change of measures which your aunt mentions in her letter—And by laying together several pieces of intelligence, some drawn from my mamma, by your uncle Antony's communications; some from Miss Lloyd, by your sister's; and some by a third way that I shall not tell you of; I have reason to think the following a true state of the case.

That there was no intention of a change of measures, till within two or three days of your going away. On the contrary, your brother and sister, though they had no hope of prevailing with you in Solmes's favour, were resolved never to give over their persecutions till they had pushed you upon taking some step which, by help of their good offices, should be deemed inexcusable by the half-witted souls they had to play upon.

But that at last your mamma (tired with and perhaps ashamed of the passive part she had acted) thought fit to declare to Miss Bell, that she was determined to try to put an end to the family feuds; and to get your uncle Harlowe to second her endeavours.

This alarmed your brother and sister; and then a change of measures was resolved upon. Solmes's offers were however too advantageous to be given up; and your father's condescension was now to be their sole dependence, and (as they give out) your last trial.

And, indeed, my dear, this must have succeeded, I verily think, with such a daughter as they had to deal with, could that father, who never, I dare say, kneeled in his life but to God, have so far condescended, as your aunt writes he would.

But then, my dear, what would this have done?—Perhaps you would have given Lovelace the meeting in hopes to pacify him and prevent mischief; supposing that they had given you time, and not hurried you directly into the state. But if you had not met him, you see that he was resolved to visit them, and well attended too: and what must have been the consequence?

So that, upon the whole, we know not but matters may be best as they *are*, however undesirable that *best* is.

I hope your considerate and thoughtful mind will make a good use of this hint. Who would not with patience sustain even a great evil, if she could persuade herself that it was kindly dispensed, in order to prevent a *still* greater?—Especially if she could sit down, as you can, and acquit her own heart?

Permit me one further observation—Do we not see, from the above state of the matter, what might have been done before by *the worthy person* of your family, had she exerted the *mother* in behalf of a child so meritorious, yet so much oppressed?

Adieu, my dear. I will be ever yours.

ANNA HOWE

Miss Harlowe, *in her answer to the first of the two last letters, chides her friend for giving so little weight to her advice in relation to her behaviour to her mother. It may be proper to insert here the following extracts from that answer, though a little before their time.*

'I will not repeat, says she, what I have before written in Mr Hickman's behalf. I will only remind you of an observation I have made to you more than once, that you have outlived your first passion; and had the second man been an angel, he would not have been more than indifferent to you.

'My motives for suspending, *proceeds she*, were not merely ceremonious ones. I was really very ill. I could not hold up my head. The contents of my sister's letters had pierced my heart. And was I, my dear, to be as ready to accept his offer as if I were afraid he never would repeat it?'

To the second letter, among other things, she says:
'So, my dear, you seem to think that there was a fate in my error. The cordial, the considering friend is seen in the observation you make on this occasion. Yet since things have happened as they have, would to heaven I could hear that all the world acquitted my father, or, at least, my mother; for her character, before these family feuds broke out, was everyone's admiration. Don't let anybody say from you, so that it may come to *her* ear, that she might by a timely exertion of her fine talents have saved her unhappy child. You'll observe, my dear, that in her own good time, when she saw that there was not likely to be an end to my brother's persecutions, she was resolved to exert herself. But the pragmatical daughter by the fatal meeting precipitated all and frustrated her indulgent designs. Oh my dear, I am now convinced, by dear experience, that while children are so happy as to have parents or guardians whom they *may* consult, they should not presume (no, not with the best and purest intentions) to follow their own conceits in material cases.

'A ray of hope of future reconciliation, *adds she*, darts in upon my mind from the intention you tell me my mother had to exert herself in my favour, had I not gone away. And my hope is the stronger, as this communication points out to me that my uncle Harlowe's interest is likely, in my mother's opinion, to be of weight, if it could be engaged. It will behove me, perhaps, to apply to that dear uncle, if a proper occasion offer.'

Letter 152: MR LOVELACE TO JOHN BELFORD, ESQ.

Monday, April 24
FATE is weaving a whimsical web for thy friend; and I see not but I shall be inevitably manacled.

Here have I been at work, dig, dig, dig, like a cunning miner at one time, and spreading my snares like an artful fowler at another, and exulting in my contrivances to get this inimitable creature absolutely into my power. Everything made for me—Her brother and uncle were but my pioneers: her father stormed as I directed him to storm. Mrs Howe was acted by the springs I set at work: her daughter was moving for me, and yet imagined herself plumb against me: and the dear creature herself had already run her stubborn neck into my gin, and knew not that she was caught; for I had not drawn my sprindges close about her—and just as all this was completed, wouldst thou believe that I should be my own enemy, and her friend?—that I should be so totally diverted from all my favourite purposes, as to propose to marry her before I went to town, in order to put it out of my own power to resume them?

When thou knowest this, wilt thou not think that my black angel plays me booty, and has taken it into his head to urge me on to the indissoluble tie that he might be more sure of me (from the complex transgressions to which he will certainly stimulate me, when wedded) than perhaps he thought he could be from the simple sins in which I have so long allowed myself, that they seem to have the plea of habit?

Thou wilt be still the more surprised, when I tell thee that there seems to be a coalition going forward between the black angels and the white ones; for here has hers induced her in one hour, and by one retrograde accident, to *acknowledge* what the charming creature never before acknowledged, a preferable favour for me. She even owns an intention to be mine:—mine, without reformation conditions—She permits me to talk of love to her: of the irrevocable ceremony: yet, another extraordinary! postpones that ceremony; chooses to set out for London; and even to go to the widow's in town.

Well, but how comes all this about, methinks thou askest?—Thou, Lovelace, dealest in wonders, yet aimest not at the *marvellous*.—How did all this come about?

I'll tell thee—I was in danger of losing my charmer for ever—She was soaring upward to her native skies. She was got above earth, by means, too, of the *earth-born*: and something extraordinary was to be done to keep her with us sublunaries. And what so effectually as the soothing voice of love, and the attracting offer of matrimony from a man not hated, can fix the attention of the maiden heart aching with uncertainty; and before impatient of the questionable question?

This, in short, was the case—While she was refusing all manner of obligation to me, keeping me at haughty distance; in hopes that her cousin Morden's arrival would soon fix her in a full and absolute independence of me: disgusted likewise at her adorer, for holding himself the reins of his own passions, instead of giving them up to her control—she writes a letter urging an answer to a letter before written, for her apparel, her jewels and some gold which she had left behind her; all which was to save her pride from obligation and to promote the independence her heart was set upon. And what followed but a shocking answer, made still more shocking by the communication of a paternal curse upon a daughter deserving only blessings?—A curse upon the curser's heart, and a double one upon the transmitter's, the spiteful, the envious Arabella!

Absent when it came, on my return I found her recovering from fits, again to fall into stronger fits; and nobody expecting her life; half a dozen messengers dispatched to find me out. Nor wonder at her being so affected; she, whose filial piety gave her dreadful faith in a father's curses; and the curse of this gloomy tyrant extending, to use her own words when she could speak, *to both worlds*—Oh that it had turned in the moment of its utterance to a mortal quinsy, and sticking in his gullet had choked the old execrator, as a warning to all such unnatural fathers.

What a miscreant had I been, not to have endeavoured to bring her back by all the endearments, by all the vows, by all the offers that I could make her?

I did bring her back. More than a father to her; for I have given her a life her unnatural father had well-nigh taken away; shall I not cherish the fruits of my own benefaction?—I have been in earnest in my vows to marry, and my ardour to urge the present time was a *real* ardour. But extreme dejection, with a mingled delicacy that in her dying moments I doubt not she will preserve have caused her to refuse me the *time*, though not the solemnity; for she has told me that now she must be wholly in my protection, *being destitute of every other!*—More indebted still, thou seest, to her cruel friends, than to herself for her favour!

She has written to Miss Howe an account of their barbarity; but has not acquainted her how very ill she was.

Low, very low, she remains; yet dreading her stupid brother's enterprise, she wants to be in London: where, but for *this* accident and (wouldst thou have believed it?) my persuasions, seeing her so very ill, she would have been this night; and we shall actually set out on Wednesday morning if she be not worse.

And now for a few words with thee, on thy heavy preachment of Saturday last.

Thou art apprehensive that the lady is now in danger indeed; and it is a miracle thou tellest me, if she stand such an attempter: 'Knowing what we know of the sex, thou sayest, thou shouldst dread, wert thou me, to make farther trial, lest thou should succeed.' And, in another place, tellest me: 'That thou pleadest not for the state, for any favour thou hast for it.'

What an advocate art thou for matrimony!—Thou wert ever an unhappy fellow at argument. Does the trite stuff with which the rest of thy letter abounds, in *favour* of wedlock, strike with the force that this does *against* it?

Thou takest great pains to convince me, and that from the distresses the lady is reduced to (chiefly by her friends' persecutions and implacableness, I hope thou wilt own, and not from me as yet), that the proposed trial will not be a fair trial. But let me ask thee, is not calamity the test of virtue? And wouldst thou not have me value this charming creature upon proof of her merits?—Do I not intend to reward her by marriage if she stand that proof?

But why repeat I what I have said before?—Turn back, thou egregious arguer, turn back to my long letter of the 13th[a]; and thou wilt there find every syllable of what thou hast written either answered or invalidated.

But I am not angry with thee, Jack. I love opposition. As gold is tried by fire and virtue by temptation; so is sterling wit by opposition. Have I not, before thou settedst out as an advocate for my fair one, often brought thee in, as making objections to my proceedings, for no other reason than to exalt myself by proving thee a man of straw? As Homer raises up many of his champions and gives them terrible names, only to have them knocked on the head by his heroes.

However, take to thee this one piece of advice—Evermore be sure of being in the right when thou presumest to sit down to correct thy master.

Well, but to return to my principal subject; let me observe that be my future resolutions what they will as to this lady, the contents of the violent letter she has received have set me at least a month forward with her. I can now, as I hinted, talk of love and marriage without control or restriction; her injunctions no more my terror.

In this sweetly familiar way shall we set out together for London. Mrs Sorlings's eldest daughter, at my motion, is to attend her in the chaise; while I ride by way of escort: for she is extremely apprehensive of the Singleton plot; and has engaged me to be all patience if anything should happen on the road. But nothing I am sure

a See Letter 110, pp. 426–31.

will happen: for, by a letter received just now from Joseph, I understand that James Harlowe has already laid aside his stupid project: and this by the earnest desire of all his friends to whom he had communicated it; who were afraid of the consequences that might attend it. But it is not over with *me*, however; although I am not determined at present as to the uses I may make of it.

My beloved tells me she shall have her clothes sent her: she hopes also her jewels and some gold which she left behind her. But Joseph says clothes *only* will be sent. I will not, however, tell her that. On the contrary, I say there is no doubt but they will send *all* she wrote for, of personals. The greater her disappointment from them, the greater must be her dependence on me.

But after all, I hope I shall be enabled to be honest to a merit so transcendent. The devil take thee though, for thy opinion given so *mal-à-propos*, that she may be overcome.

If thou designest to be honest, methinks thou sayest, why should not Singleton's plot be over with *thee*, as it is with her *brother?*

Because, if I must answer thee, where people are so modestly doubtful of what they are able to do, it is good to leave a loop-hole. And let me add that when a man's heart is set upon a point, and anything occurs to beat him off, he will find it is very difficult, when the suspending reason ceases, to forbear resuming it.

Letter 153: MR LOVELACE TO JOHN BELFORD, ESQ.

Tuesday, April 25

ALL hands at work in preparation for London. What makes my heart beat so strong? Why rises it to my throat in such half-choking flutters, when I think of what this removal may do for me?—I am hitherto resolved to be honest: and that increases my wonder at these involuntary commotions. 'Tis a plotting villain of a heart: it ever was; and ever will be, I doubt. Such a joy when any roguery is going forward!—I so little its master!—A head likewise so well turned to answer the triangular varlet's impulses. No matter. I will have one struggle with thee, old friend; and if I cannot overcome thee now, I never will again attempt to conquer thee.

The dear creature continues extremely low and dejected. Tender blossom! How unfit to contend with the rude and ruffling winds of passion, and haughty and insolent control!—Never till now from under the wing (it is not enough to say of indulging, but) of *admiring* parents; the mother's bosom only fit to receive this charming flower!

This was the reflection that, with mingled compassion and augmented love, arose to my mind when I beheld the charmer reposing her lovely face upon the bosom of the widow Sorlings, from a recovered fit, as I entered soon after she had received her execrable sister's letter. How lovely in her tears!—and as I entered, her lifted-up face significantly bespeaking my protection, as I thought. And can I be a villain to such an angel!—I hope not. But why once more, thou varlet, puttest thou me in mind that she *may be* overcome? And why is her own reliance on my honour so late and so reluctantly shown?

But after all, so low, so dejected continues she to be that I am terribly afraid I shall have a vapourish wife, if I *do* marry. I should then be doubly undone. Not that I shall be much at home with her, perhaps, after the first fortnight or so. But when a man has been ranging like the painful bee from flower to flower, perhaps for a month together, and the thoughts of home and a wife begin to have their charms with him, to be received by a Niobe who, like a wounded vine, weeps its vitals away while it but involuntarily curls about you; how shall I be able to bear that?

May heaven restore my charmer to health and spirits, I hourly pray, that a man may see whether she can love anybody but her father and mother! In *their* power, I am confident, it will be at any time, to make her husband joyless; and that, as I hate them so heartily, is a shocking thing to reflect upon. Something *more* than woman, an *angel*, in some things, but a *baby* in others: so father-sick! so family-fond! what a poor chance stands a husband with such a wife, unless, forsooth, they vouchsafe to be reconciled to her and *continue* reconciled?

It is infinitely better for her and for me that we should not marry!—What a delightful manner of life (Oh that I could persuade her to it!) would that be with such a lady! The fears, the inquietudes, the uneasy days, the restless nights; all arising from doubts of having disobliged me! Every absence dreaded to be an absence for ever! And then, how amply rewarded, and rewarding, by the rapture-causing return! Such a passion as this keeps love in a continual fervour; makes it all alive. The happy pair, instead of sitting dozing and nodding at each other in two opposite chimney-corners in a winter-evening, and over a wintry love, always new to each other, and having always something to say.

Thou knowest, in my verses to my Stella, my mind on this occasion. I will lay those verses in her way, as if undesignedly, when we are together at the widow's; that is to say, if we do not soon go to church by consent. She will thence see what my notions are of wedlock. If she receives them with any sort of temper, that will be a foundation; and let *me* alone to build upon it.

Many a girl has been *carried*, who never would have been *attempted* had she showed a proper resentment when her ears or her eyes were first invaded. I have tried a young creature by a bad book, a light quotation, or an indecent picture; and if she has borne that, or only blushed, and not been angry, and more especially if she has leered and smiled, that girl have I, and old Mulciber, put down for our own. Oh how I could warn these little rogues if I would! Perhaps envy, more than virtue, will put me upon setting up beacons for them when I grow old and joyless.

Tuesday afternoon

IF you are in London when I get thither, you will see me soon—My charmer is a little better than she was. Her eyes show it, and her harmonious voice, hardly audible last time I saw her, now begins to cheer my heart once more. But yet she has no love, no sensibility!—There is no addressing her with those *meaning* yet *innocent* freedoms (innocent at first setting out they may be called) which soften others of her sex. The more strange this, as she now acknowledges preferable favour for me; and is highly susceptible of grief. Grief mollifies and enervates. The grieved mind looks round it, silently implores consolation, and loves the soother. Grief is ever an inmate with joy. Though they won't show themselves at the same window at *one* time; yet have they the whole house in common between them.

Letter 154: MR LOVELACE TO JOHN BELFORD, ESQ.

Wed. Apr. 26

AT last my lucky star has directed us into the desired port, and we are safely landed. Well says Rowe:

> The wise and active conquer difficulties
> By daring to attempt them. Sloth and folly
> Shiver and shrink at sight of toil and hazard,
> And *make* th' impossibility they *fear*.[1]

But in the midst of my exultation, something, I know not what to call it, checks my joys, and glooms over my brighter prospects. If it be not conscience, it is wondrously like what I thought so, many, many years ago.

Surely, Lovelace, methinks thou sayest: Thy good motions are not gone off already! Surely thou wilt not now at last be a villain to this lady.

I can't tell what to say to it—Why would not the dear creature accept of me, when I so sincerely offered myself to her acceptance? Things already appear with a very different face now I have got her here. Already have our mother and her daughters been about me. 'Charming lady! What a complexion! What eyes! What majesty in her person!—Oh Mr Lovelace, you are a happy man!—You owe us such a lady!'—Then they remind me of my revenge, and of my hatred to her whole family. Sally was so struck with her, at first sight, that she broke out to me in those lines of Dryden:

> —Fairer to be seen
> Than the fair lily on the flow'ry green!
> More fresh than May herself in blossoms new!—[2]

I sent to thy lodgings within half an hour after our arrival, to receive thy congratulations upon it: but thou wert at Edgware, it seems.

My beloved, who is charmingly amended, is retired to her constant employment, writing. I must content myself with the same amusement till she shall be pleased to admit me to her presence: having already given to every one her cue.

But here comes the widow, with Dorcas Wykes in her hand. Dorcas Wykes, Jack, is to be the maid-servant to my fair one; and I am to introduce them both to her. In so many ways will it be in my power to have the dear creature now, that I shall not know which of them to choose!

So! The honest girl is accepted!—of good parentage: but, through a neglected education, plaguy illiterate—she can neither write, nor read writing. A kinswoman of Mrs Sinclair's: so could not well be refused, the widow in person recommending her; and the wench only taken till her Hannah can come. What an advantage has an imposing or forward nature over a courteous one!—So here may something arise to lead into correspondencies, and so forth!—To be sure, a person need not be so wary, so cautious of what she writes, or what she leaves upon her table or toilet, when her attendant cannot read.

Dorcas is a neat girl both in person and dress; a countenance not vulgar. And I am in hopes that [the lady will] accept of her for her bedfellow in a strange house for a week or so. But I saw she had a dislike to her at her very first appearance—yet I thought the girl behaved very modestly—overdid it a little perhaps!—[Her lady] shrunk back and looked shy upon her. The doctrine of sympathies and antipathies is a surprising doctrine. But Dorcas will be excessively obliging, and win her lady's favour soon, I doubt not—I am secure in her *incorruptibility*. A great point that!—For a lady and her maid of one party will be too hard for half a score devils.

The dear creature was no less shy when the widow first accosted her, at her alighting. Yet I thought that honest Doleman's letter had prepared her for her masculine appearance.

And now I mention that letter, why dost thou not wish me joy, Jack?

Joy of what?

Why, joy of my nuptials—Know then, that *said* is *done* with me, when I have a mind to have it so; and that we are actually man and wife. Only that consummation has not passed: bound down to the contrary of that by a solemn vow till a reconciliation with her family take place. The women here are told so. They know it before my beloved knows it; and that's odd, thou'lt say.

But how shall I do to make my fair one [keep her temper] on the intimation? Why, is she not here?—at Mrs Sinclair's?—But if she will hear reason, I doubt not to convince her that she ought to acquiesce.

She will insist, I suppose, upon my leaving her, and that I shall not take up my lodgings under the same roof. But circumstances are changed since I first made her that promise. I have taken all the vacant apartments; and must carry this point also.

I hope in a while to get her with me to the public entertainments. She knows nothing of the town, and has seen less of its diversions than ever woman of her taste, her fortune, her endowments, did see. She has indeed a natural politeness which transcends all acquirement. The most capable of anyone I ever knew of judging what a *hundred* things are, by seeing *one* of a like nature. Indeed she took so much pleasure in her own chosen amusements till persecuted out of them, that she had neither leisure nor inclination for the town diversions.

These diversions will amuse. And the deuce is in it, if a little susceptibility will not put forth, now she receives my address, and if I can manage it so as to be allowed to live under *one* roof with her. What though the appearance be at first no more than that of an early spring flower in frosty weather, that seems afraid of being nipped by an easterly blast; that will be enough for me.

I hinted to thee in a former, that I had provided for the lady's indoor amusement.[a] Sally and Polly are readers. My beloved's light closet was their library. And several pieces of devotion have been put in, bought on purpose at second-hand.

I was always for forming a judgement of the reading part of the sex by their books. The observations I have made on this occasion have been of great use to me, as well in England as out of it. This sagacious lady may possibly be as curious in this point as her Lovelace.

So much for the present. Thou seest that I have a great deal of business before me. Yet I will write again soon.

    a Letter 131, p. 473.

Mr Lovelace sends another letter with this; in which he takes notice of young Mrs Sorlings's setting out with them, and leaving them at Barnet: but as its contents are nearly the same with those in the lady's next, it is omitted.

Letter 155: MISS CLARISSA HARLOWE TO MISS HOWE

Wed. p.m. Apr. 26

AT length, my dearest Miss Howe, I am in London, and in my new lodgings. They are neatly furnished, and the situation, for the town, is pleasant. But I think you must not ask me how I like the old gentlewoman. Yet she seems courteous and obliging. Her kinswomen just appeared to welcome me at my alighting. They seem to be genteel young women. But more of their aunt and of them, as I shall see more.

Miss Sorlings has an uncle at Barnet whom she found so very ill that her uneasiness to stay to attend him (having large expectations from him) made me comply with her desire. Yet I wished, as her uncle did not expect her, that she would first see me settled in London; and Mr Lovelace was still more earnest that she would, offering to send her back again in a day or two, and urging that her uncle's malady intimated not a sudden change. But leaving the matter to her choice, after she knew what would have been mine, she made me not the expected compliment upon it. Mr Lovelace, however, made her a handsome present at parting.

His genteel spirit on all occasions makes me often wish him more consistent.

As soon as I arrived, I took possession of my apartment. [I] shall make good use of the light closet in it, if I stay here any time.

One of his attendants returns in the morning to The Lawn; and I made writing to you by him an excuse for my retiring.

And now give me leave to chide you, my dearest friend, for your rash, and I hope revocable resolution, not to make Mr Hickman the happiest man in the world while my happiness is in suspense. Suppose I were to be unhappy, what, my dear, would your resolution avail me? Marriage is the highest state of friendship: if happy, it lessens our cares by dividing them, at the same time that it doubles our pleasures by a mutual participation. Why, my dear, if you love me, will you not rather give another friend to one who has not two that she is sure of?—Had you married on your mother's last birthday, as she would have had you, I should not, I dare say, have wanted a refuge that would have saved me so many mortifications, and so much disgrace.

HERE I was broken in upon by Mr Lovelace; introducing the widow leading in a kinswoman of hers to attend me, if I approved of her, till my Hannah should come, or till I had provided myself with some other servant. The widow gave her many good qualities; but said that she had one great defect; which was that she could not write, nor read writing; that part of her education having been neglected when she was young. But for discretion, fidelity, obligingness, she was not to be outdone by anybody. She commended her likewise for her skill in the needle.

As for her defect, I can easily forgive that. She is very likely and genteel; too genteel indeed, I think, for a servant. But what I like least of all in her, she has a strange sly eye. I never saw such an eye—half-confident, I think. But indeed Mrs Sinclair herself (for that is the widow's name) has an odd winking eye; and her respectfulness seems too much studied, methinks, for the London ease and freedom. But people can't help their looks, you know; and after all, she is extremely civil and obliging: and as for the young woman (Dorcas her name), she will not be long with me.

I accepted her: how could I do otherwise (if I had a mind to make objections, which in my present situation I had not), her aunt present and the young woman also present; and Mr Lovelace officious in his introducing of them for my sake?— But upon their leaving me, I told him, who seemed inclinable to begin a conversation with me that I desired that this apartment might be considered as my retirement: that when I saw him, it might be in the dining-room; and that I might be as little broke in upon as possible, when I am here. He withdrew very respectfully to the door; but there stopped; and asked for my company then in the dining-room. If he was about setting out for other lodgings, I would go with him now, I told him: but if he did not just then go, I would first finish my letter to Miss Howe.

I see he has no mind to leave me if he can help it. My brother's scheme may give him a pretence to try to engage me to dispense with his promise. But if I now do, I must acquit him of it entirely.

My approbation of his tender behaviour in the midst of my grief has given him a right, as he seems to think, of addressing me with all the freedom of an approved lover. I see by this man that when once a woman embarks with this sex, there is no receding. One concession is but the prelude to another with them. He has been ever since Sunday last continually complaining of the distance I keep him at; and thinks himself entitled now, to call in question my value for him; strengthening his doubts by my declared readiness to give him up to a reconciliation with my friends—and yet has himself fallen off from that *obsequious tenderness*, if I may couple the words, which drew from me the concessions he builds upon.

While we were talking at the door, my new servant came up with an invitation to us both to tea. I said *he* might accept of it, if he pleased; but I must pursue my writing; and not choosing either tea or supper, I desired him to make my excuses below, as to both; and inform them of my choice to be retired as much as possible; yet to promise for me my attendance on the widow and her nieces at breakfast in the morning.

He objected particularity in the eye of strangers as to avoiding supper.

You know, said I, and can tell them that I seldom eat suppers. My spirits are low. You must never urge me against a declared choice. Pray, Mr Lovelace, inform them of all my particularities. If they are obliging, they will allow for them. I come not here to make new acquaintance.

I have turned over the books I have found in my closet; and am not a little pleased with them; and think the better of the people of the house for their sakes.

Stanhope's *Gospels*; Sharp's, Tillotson's and South's *Sermons*; Nelson's *Feasts and Fasts*; a sacramental piece of the Bishop of Man, and another of Dr Gauden, Bishop of Exeter; and Inett's *Devotions*; are among the devout books: and among those of a lighter turn, these not ill-chosen ones; a *Telemachus* in French, another in English; Steele's, Rowe's, and Shakespeare's plays; that genteel comedy of Mr Cibber, *The Careless Husband*, and others of the same author; Dryden's *Miscel-*

lanies; the *Tatlers*, *Spectators*, and *Guardians*; Pope's, and Swift's, and Addison's works.[1]

In the blank leaves of the Nelson and Bishop Gauden is Mrs Sinclair's name; in those of most of the others, either Sarah Martin or Mary Horton, the names of the two nieces.

I AM exceedingly out of humour with Mr Lovelace: and have great reason to be so: as you will allow when you have read the conversation I am going to give you an account of; for he would not let me rest till I gave him my company in the dining-room.

He began with letting me know that he had been out to inquire after the character of the widow; which was the more necessary, he said, as he supposed that I would *expect* his frequent absence.

I did, I said; and that he would not think of taking up his lodging in the same house with me. But what was the issue of his inquiry?

Why, indeed, it was in the main what he liked well enough. But as it was Miss Howe's opinion, as I had told him, that my brother had not given over his scheme; as the widow lived by letting lodgings; and had others to let in the same part of the house which might be taken by an enemy; he knew no better way than for him to take them all, as it could not be for a long time; unless I would think of removing to others.

So far was well enough: but as it was easy for me to see that he spoke the slighter of the widow, in order to have a pretence to lodge here himself, I asked him his intention in that respect. And he frankly owned that if I chose to stay here, he could not, as matters stood, think of leaving me for six hours together; and he had prepared the widow to expect that we should be here but for a few days—only till we could fix ourselves in a house suitable to our condition; and this, that I might be under the less embarrass, if I pleased to remove.

Fix *our*selves in a house, and *we* and *our*, Mr Lovelace—pray, in what light—

He interrupted me—Why, my dearest life, if you will hear me with patience—yet I am half afraid that I have been too forward, as I have not consulted you upon it. But as my friends in town, according to what Mr Doleman has written in the letter you have seen conclude us to be married—

Surely, sir, you have not presumed—

Hear me out, dearest creature—You have received with favour my addresses—you have made me hope for the honour of your consenting hand: yet, by declining my most fervent tender of myself to you at Mrs Sorlings's have given me apprehensions of delay: I would not for the world be thought so ungenerous a wretch, now you have honoured me with your confidence, as to wish to precipitate you: yet your brother's schemes are not given up. Singleton, I am afraid, is actually in town; his vessel lies at Rotherhithe—Your brother is absent from Harlowe Place (indeed not with Singleton yet, as I can hear). If you are *known* to be mine, or if you are but *thought* to be so, there will probably be an end of your brother's contrivances. The widow's character may be as worthy as it is said to be. But the worthier she is, the more danger if your brother's agent should find us out; since she may be persuaded that she ought in conscience to take a parent's part against a child who stands in opposition to them. But if she believes us married, her good character will stand us in stead, and she will be of our party—Then I have taken care to give her a reason why two apartments are requisite for us, at the hour of retirement.

I perfectly raved at him. I would have flung from him in resentment; but he would not let me. And what could I do? Whither go, the evening advanced?

I am astonished at you! said I—If you are a man of honour, what need of all this strange obliquity? You delight in crooked ways—Let me know, since I must stay in your company (for he held my hand), let me know all you have said. Indeed, indeed, Mr Lovelace, you are a very unaccountable man.

My dearest creature, need I to have mentioned anything of this; and could I not have taken up my lodgings in this house unknown to you, if I had not intended to make you the judge of all my proceedings?—But this is what I have told the widow before her kinswomen, and before your new servant—That indeed we were privately married at Hertford; but that you had preliminarily bound me under a solemn vow, which I am most religiously resolved to keep, to be contented with separate apartments, and even not to lodge under the same roof, till a certain reconciliation shall take place which is of high consequence to both. And further, that I might convince you of the purity of my intentions, and that my whole view in this was to prevent mischief, I have acquainted them that I have solemnly promised to behave to you before everybody, as if we were only betrothed and not married; not even offering to take any of those innocent freedoms which are not refused in the most punctilious loves.

And then he solemnly vowed to me the strictest observance of the same respectful behaviour to me.

I told him that I was not by any means satisfied with the tale he had told, nor with the necessity he wanted to lay me under of appearing what I was not: that every step he took was a wry one, a needless wry one: and since he thought it necessary to tell the people below anything about me, I insisted that he should unsay all he had said, and tell them the truth.

What he had told them, he said, was with so many circumstances that he could sooner die than contradict it. And still he insisted upon the propriety of appearing to be married, for the reasons he had given before—And, dearest creature, said he, why this high displeasure with me upon so well-intended an expedient? You know that I cannot wish to shun your brother, or his Singleton, but upon your account. The first step I would take, if left to myself, would be to find them out. I have always acted in this manner when anybody has presumed to give out threatenings against me.

'Tis true I should have consulted you first, and had your leave. But since you dislike what I have said, let me implore you, dearest madam, to give the only proper sanction to it, by naming an early day. Would to heaven that were to be tomorrow!—For God's sake, let it be tomorrow! But if not (was it his business, my dear, before I spoke (yet he seemed to be afraid of me), to say, *if not*?), let me beseech you, madam, if my behaviour shall not be to your dislike, that you will not tomorrow at breakfast-time discredit what I have told them. The moment I give you cause to think that I take any advantage of your concession, that moment revoke it and expose me as I shall deserve—And once more let me remind you that I have no view either to serve or save myself by this expedient. It is only to prevent a probable mischief, for your own mind's sake; and for the sake of those who deserve not the least consideration from me.

What could I say? What could I do?—I verily think that had he urged me again, in a proper manner, I should have consented (little satisfied as I am with him) to give him a meeting tomorrow morning at a more solemn place than in the parlour below.

But this I resolve, that he shall not have my consent to stay a night under this roof. He has now given me a stronger reason for this determination than I had before.

ALAS! my dear, how vain a thing to say what we will or what we will not do, when we have put ourselves into the power of this sex!—He went down to the people below, on my desiring to be left to myself; and stayed till their supper was just ready; and then, desiring a moment's *audience*, as he called it, he besought my leave to stay that one night, promising to set out either for Lord M.'s, or for Edgware to his friend Belford's, in the morning after breakfast. But if I were against it, he said, he would not stay supper; and would attend me about eight next day—yet he added, that my denial would have a very particular appearance to the people below, from what he had told them; and the more as he had actually agreed for all the vacant apartments (indeed only for a month), for the reason he had before hinted at. But I need not stay here two days if, upon conversing with the widow and her nieces in the morning, I should have any dislike to them.

I thought, notwithstanding my resolution above-mentioned, that it would seem too punctilious to deny him; under the circumstances he had mentioned—having, besides, no reason to think he would obey me; for he looked as if he were determined to debate the matter with me. And, as now I see no likelihood of a reconciliation with my friends, and had actually received his addresses with less reserve than ever; I thought I would not quarrel with him if I could help it, especially as he asked to stay but for one night, and could have done so without my knowing it; and you being of opinion that the proud wretch, distrusting his own merits with me, or at least my regard for him, will probably bring me to some concessions in his favour. For all these reasons, I thought proper to yield *this* point; yet I was so vexed with him on the *other*, that it was impossible for me to comply with that grace which a concession should be made with, or not made at all.

This was what I said: What you *will* do, you *must* do, I think. You are very ready to promise; very ready to depart from your promise. You say, however, that you will set out tomorrow for the country. You know how ill I have been. I am not well enough now to debate with you upon your encroaching ways. I am utterly dissatisfied with the tale you have told below. Nor will I promise to appear to the people of the house tomorrow what I am not.

He withdrew in the most respectful manner, beseeching me only to favour him with such a meeting in the morning as might not make the widow and her nieces think he had given me reason to be offended with him.

I retired to my own apartment, and Dorcas came to me soon after to take my commands. I told her that I required very little attendance, and always dressed and undressed myself.

She seemed concerned, as if she thought I had repulsed her, and said it should be her whole study to oblige me.

I told her that I was not difficult to please. And should let her know from time to time what assistances I should expect from her. But for that night I had no occasion for her further attendance.

She is not only genteel, but is well-bred, and well-spoken. She must have had what is generally thought to be the polite part of education: but it is strange that fathers and mothers should make so light, as they generally do, of that preferable part in girls, which would improve their minds and give a grace to all the rest.

As soon as she was gone, I inspected the doors, the windows, the wainscot, the dark closet as well as the light one; and finding very good fastenings to the door and to all the windows, I again had recourse to my pen.

MRS SINCLAIR is just now gone from me. Dorcas, she told me, had acquainted her that I had dismissed her for the night. She came to ask me how I liked my apartment, and to wish me good rest. She expressed her concern that they could not have my company at supper. Mr Lovelace, she said, had informed them of my love of retirement. She assured me that I should not be broken in upon. She highly extolled him, and gave me a share in the praise, as to person. But was sorry, she said, that she was likely to lose us so soon as Mr Lovelace talked of.

I answered her with suitable civility; and she withdrew with great tokens of respect. With greater, I think, than should be from distance of years, as she was the wife of a gentleman; and as the appearance of everything about her, as well house as dress, carries the marks of such good circumstances as require not abasement.

If, my dear, you *will* write against prohibition, be pleased to direct, *To Miss Laetitia Beaumont*; *to be left till called for, at Mr Wilson's in Pall Mall.*

Mr Lovelace proposed this direction to me, not knowing of your desire that our letters should pass by a third hand. As his motive for it was that my brother might not trace out where we are, I am glad, as well from this instance as from others, that he seems to think he has done mischief enough already.

Do you know how my poor Hannah does?

Mr Lovelace is so full of his contrivances and expedients that I think it may not be amiss to desire you to look carefully to the seals of my letters, as I shall to those of yours. If I find him base in this particular, I shall think him capable of any evil; and will fly him as my worst enemy.

Letter 156: MISS HOWE TO MISS CLARISSA HARLOWE

(With her two last letters, 150 and 151, enclosed)

Thursday night, April 27

I HAVE yours, just brought me. Mr Hickman has helped me to a lucky expedient which, with the assistance of the post, will enable me to correspond with you every day. An honest higgler (Simon Collins his name), by whom I shall send this and the two enclosed (now I have your direction where), goes to town constantly on Mondays, Wednesdays and Fridays, and can bring back to me from Wilson's what you shall have caused to be left for me.

I congratulate you on your arrival in town so much amended in spirits. I must be brief. I hope you'll have no cause to repent returning my Norris. It is forthcoming on demand.

I am sorry your Hannah can't be with you. She is very ill still; but not in danger.

I long for your account of the women you are with. If they are not right people, you'll find them out in one breakfasting.

I know not what to write upon his reporting to them that you are actually married. His reasons for it are plausible. But he delights in odd expedients and inventions.

Whether you like the people or not, don't by your noble sincerity and plain dealing make yourself enemies. You are in the world now, you know.

I am glad you had thoughts of taking him at his offer, if he had re-urged it. I wonder he did not. But if he don't soon, and in such a way as you can accept of it, don't think of staying with him.

Depend upon it, my dear, he will not leave you either night or day if he can help it, now he has got footing.

I should have abhorred him for his report of your marriage, had he not made it with such circumstances as leave it still in your power to keep him at distance. If once he offer at the least familiarity—but this is needless to say to you. He can have, I think, no other design but what he professes; because he must needs think that his report must increase your vigilance.

You may depend upon my looking narrowly into the sealings of your letters. If, as you say, he be base in that point, he will be so in everything. But to one of your merit, of your fortune, of your virtue, he cannot be base. The man is no fool. It is his interest, as well with regard to his expectations from his own friends as from you, to be honest. Would to heaven, however, that you were really married! This is the predominant wish of

Your ANNA HOWE

Letter 157: MISS CLARISSA HARLOWE TO MISS HOWE

Thursday morning, eight o'clock

I AM more and more displeased with Mr Lovelace, on reflection, for his boldness in hoping to make me, though but *passively*, as I may say, testify to his great untruth. And I shall like him still less for it, if his view in it does not come out to be the hope of accelerating my resolution in his favour, by the difficulty it will lay me under as to my behaviour to him. He has sent me his compliments by Dorcas, with a request that I will permit him to attend me in the dining-room; perhaps that he may guess from thence whether I will meet him in good-humour, or not: but I have answered that as I shall see him at breakfast-time, I desire to be excused.

Ten o'clock

I TRIED to adjust my countenance before I went down, to an easier air than I had a heart, and was received with the highest tokens of respect by the widow and her two nieces: agreeable young women enough in their persons; but they seemed to put on an air of reserve; while Mr Lovelace was easy and free to all, as if he were of long acquaintance with them: gracefully enough, I cannot but say; an advantage which travelled gentlemen have over other people.

The widow, in the conversation we had after breakfast, gave us an account of the military merit of the colonel her husband; and upon this occasion put her handkerchief to her eye twice or thrice. I hope for the sake of her sincerity she wetted it, because she would be thought to have done so; but I saw not that she did. She wished that I might never know the loss of a husband so dear to me, as her dear colonel was to her: and again she put her handkerchief to her eyes.

It must, no doubt, be a most affecting thing to be separated from a good husband, and to be left in difficult circumstances besides, and that not by *his* fault, and exposed to the insults of the base and ungrateful; as she represented her case to be at his death. This moved me a good deal in her favour.

You know, my dear, that I have an open and free heart, and naturally have as open and free a countenance; at least my complimenters have told me so. At once, where I like, I mingle minds without reserve, encouraging reciprocal freedoms, and am forward to dissipate diffidences. But with these two young gentlewomen, I never can be intimate—I don't know why.

Only that circumstances, and what passed in conversation, encouraged not the notion, or I should have been apt to think that the young gentlewomen and Mr Lovelace were of longer acquaintance than yesterday. For he, by stealth as it were, cast glances sometimes at them, which they returned; and, on my ocular notice, their eyes fell, as I may say, under my eye, as if they could not stand its examination.

The widow directed all her talk to me as to Mrs Lovelace; and I, with a very ill grace, bore it. And once she expressed, more forwardly than I thanked her for, her wonder that any vow, any consideration however weighty, could have force enough with so charming a couple, as she called him and me, to make us keep separate beds.

Their eyes, upon this hint had the advantage of mine. Yet was I not conscious of guilt. How know I then, upon recollection, that my censures upon theirs are not too rash? There are, no doubt, many truly modest persons (putting myself out of the question) who, by blushes at an injurious charge, have been suspected by those who cannot distinguish between the confusion which guilt will be attended with, and the noble consciousness that overspreads the face of a fine spirit, to be thought but capable of an imputed evil.

The great Roman, as we read, who took his surname from one part in three (the fourth not then discovered) of the world he had triumphed over, being charged with a mean crime to his soldiery, chose rather to suffer exile (the punishment due to it, had he been found guilty) than to have it said that Scipio[1] was questioned in public on so scandalous a charge. And think you, my dear, that Scipio did not blush with indignation when the charge was first communicated to him?

Mr Lovelace, when the widow expressed her forward wonder, looked sly and leering, as if to observe how I took it; and said they might observe that his regard for my will and pleasure, calling me his dear creature, had greater force upon him than the oath by which he had bound himself.

Rebuking both him and the widow, I said it was strange to me to hear an oath or vow so lightly treated as to have it thought but of *second* consideration, whatever were the first.

The observation was just, Miss Martin said; for that nothing could excuse the breaking of a solemn vow, be the occasion of making it what it would.

I asked after the nearest church; for I have been too long a stranger to the sacred worship. They named St James's, St Anne's and another in Bloomsbury; and the two nieces said they oftenest went to St James's Church, because of the good company, as well as for the excellent preaching.

Mr Lovelace said the Royal Chapel was the place he oftenest went to, when in town. Poor man! little did I expect to hear he went to any place of devotion. I asked if the presence of the visible king of, comparatively, but a small territory, did not take off, too generally, the requisite attention to the service of the invisible King and Maker of a thousand worlds?

He believed this might be so with such as came for curiosity, when the royal family were present. But, otherwise, he had seen as many contrite faces at the Royal Chapel as anywhere else: and why not? Since the people about courts have as deep scores to wipe off as any people whatsoever.

He spoke this with so much levity, that I could not help saying that nobody questioned but he knew how to choose his company.

Your servant, my dear, bowing, were his words; and turning to them: You will observe upon numberless occasions, ladies, as we are further acquainted, that my beloved never spares me upon these topics. But I admire her as much in her reproofs, as I am fond of her approbation.

Miss Horton said there was a time for everything. She could not but say that she thought innocent mirth was mighty becoming in young people.

Very true, joined in Miss Martin. And Shakespeare says well, *That youth is the spring of life, The bloom of gaudy years*[2]; with a theatrical air she spoke it: and for her part, she could not but admire in my spouse, that charming vivacity which so well suited his time of life.

Mr Lovelace bowed. The man is fond of praise. More fond of it, I doubt, than of deserving it. Yet this sort of praise he does deserve. He has, you know, an easy free manner, and no bad voice: And this praise so expanded his gay heart that he sung the following lines, from Congreve as he told us:

> Youth does a thousand pleasures bring,
>   Which from decrepit age will fly;
> Sweets that wanton in the bosom of the spring,
>   In winter's cold embraces die.[3]

And this for a compliment, as he said, to the two nieces. Nor was it thrown away upon them. They encored it; and his compliance fixed them in my memory.

We had some talk about meals; and the widow very civilly offered to conform to any rules I would set her. I told her how easily I was pleased, and how much I chose to dine by myself, and that from a plate sent me from any single dish. But I will not trouble you with such particulars.

They thought me very singular; and with reason: but as I liked them not so very well as to forgo my own choice in compliment to them, I was the less concerned for what they thought. And still the less as Mr Lovelace had put me very much out of humour with him.

They, however, cautioned me against melancholy. I said I should be a very unhappy creature if I could not bear my own company.

Mr Lovelace said that he must let the ladies into my story; and then they would know how to allow for my ways. But, *my dear, as you love me*, said the confident wretch, give as little way to melancholy as possible. Nothing but the sweetness of your temper, and your high notions of a duty that can never be deserved where you place it, can make you so uneasy as you are—Be not angry, *my dear love*, for saying so (seeing me frown, I suppose): and snatched my hand and kissed it.

I left him with them; and retired to my closet and my pen.

Just as I have wrote thus far, I am interrupted by a message from him that he is setting out on a journey, and desires to take my commands—so here I will leave off, to give him a meeting in the dining-room.

I WAS not displeased to see him in his riding-dress.

He seemed desirous to know how I liked the gentlewomen below. I told him that although I did not think them very exceptionable, yet as I wanted not, in my present situation, new acquaintance, I should not be fond of cultivating theirs; and he must second me, particularly in my desire of breakfasting and supping (when I *did* sup) by myself.

If I would have it so, to be sure it should be so. The people of the house were not of consequence enough to be apologized to, in any point where my pleasure was concerned. And if I should dislike them still more on further knowledge of them, he hoped I would think of some other lodgings.

He expressed a good deal of regret at leaving me, declaring that it was absolutely in obedience to my commands: but that he could not have consented to go while my brother's schemes were on foot, if I had not done him the credit of my countenance in the report he had made that we were married; which, he said, had bound all the family to his interest, so that he could leave me with the greater security and satisfaction.

He hoped, he said, that on his return I would name his happy day; and the rather as I might be convinced by my brother's projects that no reconciliation was to be expected.

I told him that perhaps I might write one letter to my uncle Harlowe. He once loved me. I should be easier when I had made one direct application. I might possibly propose such terms, in relation to my grandfather's estate, as might procure me their attention; and I hoped he would be long enough absent to give me time to write to him and receive an answer from him.

That, he must beg my pardon, he could not promise. He would inform himself of Singleton's and my brother's motions; and if on his return he found no reason for apprehensions, he would go directly to Berks, and endeavour to bring up with him his cousin Charlotte, who, he hoped, would induce me to give him an earlier day than at present I seemed to think.

I told him, that I would take that young lady's company for a great favour.

I was the more pleased with this motion, as it came from himself.

He earnestly pressed me to accept of a bank note: but I declined it. And then he offered me his servant William for my attendant in his absence; who, he said, might be dispatched to him if anything extraordinary fell out. I consented to that.

He took his leave of me in the most respectful manner, only kissing my hand. He left the note unobserved by me upon the table. You may be sure I shall give it him back at his return.

I am now in a much better humour with him than I was. Where doubts of any person are removed, a mind not ungenerous is willing, by way of amends for having conceived those doubts, to construe everything that happens *capable* of a good construction, in that person's favour. Particularly, I cannot but be pleased to observe, that although he speaks of the ladies of his family with the freedom of relationship, yet it is always with tenderness. And from a man's kindness to his relations of the sex, a woman has some reasons to expect his good behaviour to herself, when married, if she be willing to deserve it from him. And thus, my dear, am I brought to such a pass as to sit myself down satisfied with this man, where I find room to infer that he is not naturally a savage.

May you, my dear friend, be always happy in your reflections, prays

Your ever affectionate
CL. HARLOWE

[*Letter 157.1: Mr Lovelace to John Belford, Esq.*]

Mr Lovelace in his next letter triumphs on his having carried his two great points of making the lady yield to pass for his wife to the people of the house, and to his taking up his lodging in it, though but for one night. He is now sure, *he says*, that he shall soon prevail, if not by persuasion, by surprise. *Yet he pretends to have some little remorse, and* censures himself as acting the part of the grand tempter. But having succeeded thus far, he cannot, *he says*, forbear trying, according to the resolution he had before made, whether he cannot go farther.

He gives the particulars of their debates on the above-mentioned subjects, to the same effect as in the lady's last letters.

It will by this time be seen that his whole merit with regard to this lady lies in doing justice to her excellencies both of mind and person by acknowledgement, though to his own condemnation. Thus he begins his succeeding letter:

And now, Belford, will I give thee an account of our first breakfast conversation.

All sweetly serene and easy was the lovely brow and charming aspect of my goddess, on her descending to us; commanding reverence from every eye; a curtsy from every knee; and silence, awful silence, from every quivering lip. While she, armed with conscious worthiness and superiority, looked and behaved as an empress would among her vassals; yet with a freedom from pride and haughtiness, as if born to dignity and to a behaviour habitually gracious.

He takes notice of the jealousy, pride and vanity of Sally Martin and Polly Horton, on his respectful behaviour to her. Creatures who, brought up too high for their fortunes, and to a taste of pleasure and the public diversions, had fallen an easy prey to his seducing arts; and for some time past been associates with Mrs Sinclair: and who, as he observes, had not yet got over that distinction in their love which makes a woman prefer one man to another.

How difficult is it, *says he*, to make a woman subscribe to a preference against herself, though ever so visible; especially where love is concerned? This violent, this partial little devil, Sally, has the insolence to compare herself with an angel— yet owns her to be an angel. I charge you, Mr Lovelace, said she, show none of your extravagant acts of kindness before me, to this sullen, this gloomy beauty!— I cannot bear it—Then her first sacrifices were remembered—What a rout do these women make about nothing at all! Were it not for what the learned bishop, in his letter from Italy, calls the delicacy of intrigue,[1] what is there, Belford, in all they can do for us?—

How do these creatures endeavour to stimulate me! A fallen woman, Jack, is a worse devil than even a profligate man. The former is above all remorse: that am not I—nor ever shall they prevail upon me, though aided by all the powers of darkness, to treat this admirable creature with indignity—So far, I mean, as indignity can be separated from the trials which will prove her to be either woman or angel.

Yet with them I am a craven. I might have had her before now, if I would. If I would treat her as flesh and blood, I should find her such. They thought that I knew, if any man living did, that to make a goddess of a woman, she would assume the goddess; to give her power, she would act up to it to the giver, if to nobody else—And D—r's wife is thrown into my dish who, thou knowest, kept her over-ceremonious husband at haughty distance, and whined in private to her insulting footman. Oh how I cursed the blaspheming wretches!—They will make me, as I tell them, hate their house; and never rest till I remove her. And by my soul, Jack, I begin to repent already that I have brought her hither—and yet, without knowing their hearts, she resolves against having any more conversation with them than she can avoid. This I am not sorry for; since jealousy in woman is not to be concealed from woman. And Sally has no command of herself.

Letter 158: MISS CLARISSA HARLOWE TO MISS HOWE

Friday, April 28

MR Lovelace is returned already. My brother's projects were his pretence. I could not but look upon this short absence as an evasion of his promise; especially as he had taken such precautions with the people below; and as he knew that I proposed to keep close within doors. I cannot bear to be dealt meanly with, and angrily insisted that he should directly set out for Berkshire, in order to engage his cousin, as he had promised.

Oh my dearest life, said he, why will you banish me.from your presence?—I cannot leave you for so long a time as you seem to expect I should. I have been hovering about town ever since I left you. Edgware was the furthest place I went to; and there I was not able to stay two hours for fear, at this crisis, anything should happen. Who can account for the workings of an apprehensive mind, when all that is dear and valuable to it is at stake?—You may spare yourself the trouble of writing to any of your friends till the happy ceremony has passed, that shall entitle me to give weight to your application. When they know we are married, your brother's plots will be at an end; and your father and mother and uncles must be reconciled to you. Why then should you hesitate a moment to confirm my happiness?—Why, once more, would you banish me from you? Why will you not give the man who has brought you into difficulties, and who so honourably wishes to extricate you from them, the happiness of doing so?

He was silent. My voice failed to second the inclination I had to say something not wholly discouraging to a point so ardently pressed.

I'll tell you, my angel, resumed he, what I propose to do, if you approve of it. I will instantly go out to view some of the handsome new squares or fine streets round them, and make a report to you of any suitable house I find to be let. I will take such a one as you shall choose, furnish it, and set up an equipage befitting our condition. You shall direct the whole. And on some early day, either before or after we fix (it must be at your own choice), be pleased to make me the happiest of men. And then will everything be in a desirable train. You shall receive in your own house (if it can be so soon furnished as I wish) the congratulations of all my relations. Charlotte shall visit you in the interim: and if it take up time, you shall choose whom you'll honour with your company, first, second or third, in the summer months; and on your return, you shall find all that was wanting in your new habitation supplied; and pleasures in a constant round shall attend us. Oh my angel, take me to you, instead of banishing me from you, and make me yours for ever.

You see, my dear, that here was no day pressed for. I was not uneasy about that; and the sooner recovered myself, as there was not. But, however, I gave him no reason to upbraid me for refusing his offer of going in search of a house.

He is accordingly gone out for this purpose. But I find that he intends to take up his lodging here tonight; and if tonight, no doubt on other nights, when he is in town. As the doors and windows of my apartment have good fastenings; as he has not, in all this time, given me cause for apprehension; as he has the pretence of my brother's schemes to plead; as the people below are very courteous and obliging, Miss Horton especially, who seems to have taken a great liking to me, and to be of a gentler temper and manners than Miss Martin; and as we are now in a tolerable way; I imagine it would look particular to them all, and bring me into a debate with a man who, let him be set upon what he will, has always a great deal to say for himself, if I insisted upon his promise. On all these accounts, I think I will take no notice of his lodging here, if he don't.

Let me know, my dear, your thoughts of everything. You may believe I gave him back his note the moment I saw him.

Friday evening

MR Lovelace has seen two or three houses; but none to his mind. But he has heard of one which looks promising, he says, and which he is to inquire about in the morning.

Saturday morning

HE has made his inquiries, and actually seen the house he was told of last night. The owner of it is a young widow lady, who is inconsolable for the death of her husband, Fretchville her name. It is furnished quite in taste, everything being new within these six months. He believes, if I like not the furniture, the use of it may be agreed for, with the house, for a time certain: but if I like it, he will endeavour to take the one and purchase the other, directly.

The lady sees nobody; nor are the best apartments above stairs to be viewed till she is either absent, or gone into the country, where she proposes to live retired; and which she talks of doing in a fortnight or three weeks, at farthest.

What Mr Lovelace saw of the house (which were the salon and two parlours) was perfectly elegant; and he was assured, all is of a piece. The offices are also very convenient; coach-house and stables at hand.

He shall be very impatient, he says, till I see the whole; nor will he, if he finds he can have it, look farther till I have seen it, except anything else offer to my liking. The price he values not.

He has just now received a letter from Lady Betty Lawrance, by a particular hand; the contents principally relating to an affair she has in Chancery. But in the postscript she is pleased to say very respectful things of me. They are all impatient, she says, for the happy day being over; which, they flatter themselves, will *ensure his reformation*.

He hoped, he told me, that I would soon enable him to answer *their* wishes, and *his own*. But although the opportunity was so inviting, he urged not for the day. Which is the more extraordinary, as he was so pressing for marriage before we came to town.

He was very earnest with me to give him, and four of his friends, my company on Monday evening, at a little collation. Miss Martin and Miss Horton cannot, he says, be there, being engaged in a party of their own, with two daughters of Colonel Solcombe, and two nieces of Sir Anthony Holmes, upon an annual occasion. But Mrs Sinclair will be present, and she gave him hope also of the company of a young maiden lady of very great fortune and merit (Miss Partington), to whom Colonel Sinclair, it seems, in his lifetime, was guardian, and who therefore calls Mrs Sinclair mamma.

I desired to be excused. He had laid me, I said, under a most disagreeable necessity of appearing as a married person; and I would see as few people as possible who were to think me so.

He would not urge it, he said, if I were *much* averse: but they were his select friends, men of birth and fortune; who longed to see me. It was true that they, as well as his friend Doleman, believed we were married: but they thought him under the restrictions that he had mentioned to the people below. I might be assured, he told me, that his politeness before them should be carried into the highest degree of reverence.

When he is set upon anything, there is no knowing, as I have said heretofore, what one *can* do. But I will not, if I can help it, be made a show of; especially to men of whose characters and principles I have no good opinion. I am, my dearest friend,

Your ever affectionate
CL. HARLOWE

[*Letter 158.1: Mr Lovelace to John Belford, Esq.*]

Mr Lovelace in his next letter to his friend Mr Belford recites the most material passages in hers preceding. He invites him to his collation on Monday evening.

Mowbray, Belton, and Tourville, *says he*, long to see my angel, and will be there. She has refused me; but must be present notwithstanding. And then will I show thee the pride and glory of the Harlowe family, my implacable enemies; and thou shalt join with me in my triumph over them all.

If I can procure you this honour, you'll be ready to laugh out, as I have often much ado to forbear, at the puritanical behaviour of the mother before this lady. Not an oath, not a curse, nor the least free word escapes her lips. She minces in her gait. She prims up her horse-mouth. Her voice, which when she pleases, is the voice of thunder, is sunk into an humble whine. Her stiff hams, that have not been bent to a civility for ten years past, are now limbered into curtsies three deep at every word. Her fat arms are crossed before her; and she can hardly be prevailed upon to sit in the presence of my goddess.

I am drawing up instructions for ye all to observe on Monday night. It will be thy care, who art a parading fellow, and pretendest to wisdom, to keep the rest from blundering.

Saturday night

MOST confoundedly alarmed—Lord, sir, what do you think? cried Dorcas—My lady is resolved to go to church tomorrow! I was at quadrille with the women below—To church! said I, and down I laid my cards. *To church!* repeated they, each looking upon the other. We had done playing for that night. Who could have dreamt of such a whim as this?—Without notice, without questions! Her clothes not come! No leave asked!—Impossible she should think to be my wife!—Why, this lady don't consider, if she go to church, I must go too!—Yet not to ask for my company!—Her brother and Singleton ready to snap her up, as far as she knows!—Known by her clothes! Her person, her features, so distinguished!—Not such another woman in England! To church of all places!—Is the devil in the girl, said I? as soon as I could speak.

Well, but to leave this subject till tomorrow morning, I will now give you the instructions I have drawn up for yours and your companions' behaviour on Monday night.

Instructions to be observed by John Belford, Richard Mowbray, Thomas Belton and James Tourville, esquires of the body to General Robert Lovelace, on their admission to the presence of his goddess.

Then follow his humorous instructions: in which he cautions them to avoid all obscene hints and even the double entendre.

You know, says he, that I never permitted any of you to talk obscenely. Time enough for that when ye grow old and can *only* talk. What! as I have often said, cannot you touch a woman's heart without wounding her ear?

I need not bid you respect me mightily. Your allegiance obliges you to that. And who that sees me respects me not?

He gives them their cue as to Miss Partington, and her history and assumed character.

So noted, *says he*, for innocent looks, yet deep discretion!—And be sure to remember that my beloved has no name but mine; and that the mother has no other than her maiden name, *Sinclair*; her husband a lieutenant-colonel.

Many other whimsical particulars he gives; and then says:

This dear lady is prodigiously learned in *theories*: but as to *practices*, as to *experimentals*, must be, as you know, from her tender years, a mere novice. Till she knew me, I dare say, she did not believe, whatever she had read, that there were such fellows in the world as she'll see in you four. I shall have much pleasure in observing how she'll stare at her company, when she finds me the politest man of the five.

And so much for instructions general and particular for your behaviour on Monday night.

And now, methinks, thou art curious to know, what can be my view in risking the displeasure of my fair one, and alarming her fears after four or five halcyon days have gone over our heads?—I'll satisfy thee.

The visitors of the two nieces will crowd the house. Beds will be scarce. Miss Partington, a sweet modest genteel girl, will be prodigiously taken with my charmer; will want to begin a friendship with her. A share in her bed for one night only, will be requested. Who knows, but on that very Monday night I may be so unhappy as to give mortal offence to my beloved? The shyest birds may be caught napping. Should she attempt to fly me upon it, cannot I detain her? Should she actually fly, cannot I bring her back by authority, civil or uncivil, if I have evidence upon evidence that she acknowledged, though but tacitly, her marriage?—And should I, or should I not succeed, and she forgive me, or if she but descend to expostulate, or if she bear me in her sight; then will she be all my own. All delicacy is my charmer. I long to see how such a delicacy, on either occasion, will behave. And in my situation it behoves me to provide against every accident.

I must take care, knowing what an eel I have to do with, that the little wriggling rogue does not slip through my fingers. How silly should I look, staring after her, when she had shot from me into the muddy river, her family, from which, with so much difficulty, I have taken her!

Well then; here are—let me see—how many persons are there who, after Monday night, will be able to swear, that she has gone by my name, answered to my name, had no other view in leaving her friends, but to go by my name? Her own relations not able nor willing to deny it. First, here are my servants; her servant Dorcas, Mrs Sinclair, her two nieces, and Miss Partington.

But for fear these evidences should be suspected, here comes the jet of the business. No less than four worthy gentlemen of fortune and family, who were all in company such a night particularly, at a collation to which they were invited by Robert Lovelace of Sandoun Hall, in the county of Lancaster, Esquire, in company with Magdalen Sinclair widow, and Priscilla Partington spinster, and the lady complainant; when the said Robert Lovelace addressed himself to the said lady, on a multitude of occasions, as *his* lady; as they and others did, as Mrs Lovelace; everyone complimenting and congratulating her upon her nuptials; and that she received such their compliments and congratulations with no other visible displeasure or repugnance than such as a young bride, full of blushes and pretty confusion, might be supposed to express upon such contemplative revolvings as those compliments would naturally inspire. Nor do thou rave at me, Jack, nor rebel—Dost think I brought the dear creature here for nothing?

And there's a faint sketch of my plot.—Stand by, varlets—Tanta-ra-ra-ra!— Veil your bonnets, and confess your master!

Letter 159: MR LOVELACE TO JOHN BELFORD, ESQ.

Sunday

HAVE been at church, Jack—behaved admirably well too!—My charmer is pleased with me now: for I was exceedingly attentive to the discourse, and very ready in the auditor's part of the service—Eyes did not much wander. How could they? when the loveliest object, infinitely the loveliest, in the whole church, was in my view.

Dear creature! how fervent, how amiable, in her devotions!—I have got her to own that she prayed for me!—I hope a prayer from so excellent a mind will not be made in vain.

There is, after all, something beautifully solemn in devotion!—The Sabbath is a charming institution to *keep* the heart right, when it *is* right. One day in seven, how reasonable!—I think I'll go to church once a day often. I fancy it will go a great way towards making me a reformed man. To see multitudes of well-appearing people, all joining in one reverent act: an exercise worthy of a sentient being! Yet it adds a sting or two to my former stings, when I think of my projects with regard to this charming creature. In my conscience, I believe if I were to go constantly to church, I could not pursue them.

I had a scheme come into my head while there: but I will renounce it, because it obtruded itself upon me in so good a place. Excellent creature! How many *ruins* has she prevented by attaching me to herself!—by engrossing my whole attention!

But let me tell thee what passed between us in my first visit of this morning; and then I will acquaint thee more largely with my good behaviour at church.

I could not be admitted till after eight. I found her ready prepared to go out. I pretended to be ignorant of her intention, having charged Dorcas not to own that she had told me of it.

Going abroad, madam?—with an air of indifference.

Yes, sir; I intend to go to church.

I hope, madam, I shall have the honour to attend you.

No: she designed to take a chair, and go to the next church.

This startled me: a chair to carry her to the next church from Mrs Sinclair's, her right name not Sinclair, and to bring her back thither, in the face of people who might not think well of the house! There was no permitting that—yet I was to appear indifferent. But said, I should take it for a favour, if she would permit me to attend her in a coach, as there was time for it, to St Paul's.

She made objections to the gaiety of my dress; and told me that, if she went to St Paul's, she could go in a coach without *me*.

I objected Singleton and her brother, and offered to dress in the plainest suit I had.

I beg the favour of attending you, dear madam, said I. I have not been at church a great while: we shall sit in different stalls: and the next time I go, I hope it will be to give myself a title to the greatest blessing I can receive.

She made some further objections: but at last permitted me the honour of attending her.

I got myself placed in her eye, that the time might not seem tedious to me; for we were there early. And I gained her good opinion, as I mentioned above, by my behaviour.

The subject of the discourse was particular enough: it was about a prophet's story or parable of an ewe lamb taken by a rich man from a poor one, who dearly loved it, and whose only comfort it was: designed to strike remorse into David, on his adultery with Uriah's wife Bathsheba, and his murder of the husband. (These women, Jack, have been the occasion of all manner of mischief from the beginning!) Now, when David, full of indignation, swore (King David would swear, Jack: but how shouldst thou know who King David was? The story is in the Bible) that the rich man should surely die; Nathan, which was the prophet's name, and a good ingenious fellow, cried out (which were the words of the text[1]), *Thou art the man!*—By my soul I thought the parson looked directly at me: and at that moment

I cast my eye full at my ewe lamb. But I must tell thee too, that I thought a good deal of my Rosebud—a better man than King David, in that point, however, thought I!

When we came home, we talked upon the subject; and I showed my charmer my attention to the discourse, by letting her know where the doctor made the most of his subject, and where it might have been touched to greater advantage (for it is really a very affecting story, and has as pretty a contrivance in it as ever I read). And this I did in such a grave way, that she seemed more and more pleased with me; and I have no doubt that I shall get her to favour me tomorrow night with her company at my collation.

                                                             Sunday evening

WE all dined together in Mrs Sinclair's parlour! All ex-*cessive*-ly right! The two nieces have topped their parts: Mrs Sinclair hers. Never so easy yet as now!—'She really thought a little oddly of these people at first, she said: Mrs Sinclair seemed very forbidding! Her nieces were persons with whom she could not wish to be acquainted. But really we should not be too hasty in our censures. Some people improve upon us. The widow seems *tolerable*.' (She went no farther than *tolerable*.) 'Miss Martin and Miss Horton are young people of good sense, and have read a good deal. What Miss Martin particularly said of marriage, and of her humble servant, was very solid. She believes, with such notions, she cannot make a bad wife.'—By the way, Sally's humble servant is a woollen-draper of great reputation; and she is soon to be married.

I have been letting her into thy character, and into the characters of my other three esquires, in hopes to excite her curiosity to see you tomorrow night. I have told her some of the *worst*, as well as *best* parts of your characters, in order to exalt myself, and to obviate any sudden surprises, as well as to teach her what sort of men she may expect to see, if she will oblige me.

By her observations upon each of you, I shall judge what I may or may not do to *obtain* or *keep* her good opinion: what she will *like*, what *not*; and so pursue the one, or avoid the other, as I see proper. So, while she is penetrating into your shallow heads, I shall enter her heart and know what to bid my own hope for.

The house is to be taken in three weeks. All will be over in three weeks, or bad will be my luck!—Who knows but in three days!—Have I not carried that great point of making her pass for my wife to the people below? And that other great one of fixing myself here night and day?—What lady ever escaped me, that lodged under one roof with me?—The house too, THE house; the people, people after my own heart: her servants Will and Dorcas both my servants. *Three days* did I say! Pho! pho!—*Three hours!*

I HAVE carried my third point, Jack; but extremely to the dislike of my charmer. Miss Partington was introduced to her; and being engaged on condition that my beloved would honour me at my collation, there was no denying her; so fine a young lady! seconded by my earnest entreaties.

I long to have your opinions of my fair prize!—If you love to see features that glow, though the heart is frozen and never yet was thawed; if you love fine sense and adages flowing through teeth of ivory, and lips of coral; an eye that penetrates all things; a voice that is harmony itself; an air of grandeur, mingled with a sweetness that cannot be described; a politeness that, if ever equalled, was never excelled—you'll see all these excellencies, and ten times more, in this my GLORIANA.[2]

> Mark her majestic fabric!—She's a temple
> Sacred by birth, and built by hands divine;
> Her soul the deity that lodges there:
> Nor is the pile unworthy of the god.[3]

Or, to describe her in a softer style, with Rowe,

> The bloom of op'ning flow'rs, unsully'd beauty,
> Softness, and sweetest innocence, she wears,
> And looks like nature in the world's first spring.[4]

Adieu, varlets four!—At six on Monday evening, I expect ye all.

Letter 160: MISS CLARISSA HARLOWE TO MISS HOWE

In the lady's next letter, dated on Monday morning, she praises his behaviour at church, his observations afterwards. Likes the people of the house better than she did. The more likes them by reason of the people of condition that visit them.

She dates again, and declares herself displeased at Miss Partington's being introduced to her: and still more for being obliged to promise to be present at Mr Lovelace's collation. She foresees, she says, a murdered evening.

Letter 161: MISS CLARISSA HARLOWE TO MISS HOWE

Monday night, May 1

I HAVE just escaped from the very disagreeable company I was obliged, so much against my will, to be in. As a very particular relation of this evening's conversation would be painful to me, you must content yourself with what you shall be able to collect from the outlines, as I may call them, of the characters of the persons, assisted by the little histories Mr Lovelace gave me of each yesterday.

The names of the gentlemen are Belton, Mowbray, Tourville, and Belford. These four, with Mrs Sinclair, Miss Partington, the great heiress mentioned in my last, Mr Lovelace, and myself, made up the company.

I gave you before the favourable side of Miss Partington's character, such as it was given me by Mrs Sinclair and her nieces. I will now add a few words from my own observations upon her behaviour in *this* company.

In *better* company, perhaps, she would have appeared to less disadvantage: but notwithstanding her innocent looks, which Mr Lovelace also highly praised, he is the last person whose judgement I would take upon real modesty. For I observed that, upon some talk from the gentlemen, not free enough to be openly censured yet too indecent in its implication to come from well-bred persons in the company of virtuous people, this young lady was very ready to apprehend; and yet, by smiles and simperings, to encourage rather than discourage the culpable freedoms of persons who, in what they went out of their way to say, must either be guilty of absurdity, meaning *nothing*; or, meaning *something*, of rudeness.

But indeed I have seen ladies, of whom I have had a better opinion than I can say I have of Mrs Sinclair, who have allowed *gentlemen* and *themselves* too, in greater liberties of this sort, than I have thought consistent with that purity of manners which ought to be the distinguishing characteristic of our sex: for what are *words* but the *body* and *dress* of *thought?* And is not the mind indicated strongly by its outward dress?

But to the gentlemen, as they must be called in right of their ancestors, it seems; for no other do they appear to have.

Mr BELTON has had university education, and was designed for the gown; but that not suiting with the gaiety of his temper, and an uncle dying who bequeathed to him a good estate, he quitted the college, came up to town and commenced fine gentleman. He is said to be a man of sense. He dresses gaily, but not quite foppishly; drinks hard; keeps all hours, and glories in doing so; games, and has been hurt by that pernicious diversion: he is about thirty years of age: his face is of a fiery red, somewhat bloated and pimply; and his irregularities threaten a brief duration to the sensual dream he is in; for he has a short consumptive cough, which seems to indicate bad lungs; yet makes himself and his friends merry by his stupid and inconsiderate jests upon very threatening symptoms, which ought to make him more serious.

Mr MOWBRAY has been a great traveller; speaks as many languages as Mr Lovelace himself, but not so fluently: is of a good family: seems to be about thirty-three or thirty-four: tall and comely in his person: bold and daring in his look: is a large-boned, strong man: has a great scar in his forehead, with a dent, as if his skull had been beaten in there; and a seamed scar in his right cheek. He dresses likewise very gaily: has his servants always about him, whom he is continually calling upon and sending on the most trifling messages; half a dozen instances of which we had in the little time I was among them; while they seem to watch the turn of his fierce eye, to be ready to run before they have half his message, and serve him with fear and trembling. Yet to his equals the man seems tolerable: talks not amiss upon public entertainments and diversions, especially upon those abroad: yet has a romancing air; and avers things strongly, which seem quite improbable. Indeed, he *doubts* nothing but what he ought to *believe:* for he jests upon sacred things; and professes to hate the clergy of all religions: has high notions of *honour*, a word hardly ever out of his mouth; but seems to have no great regard to *morals*.

Mr TOURVILLE occasionally told his age; just turned of thirty-one. He also is of an ancient family; but in his person and manners, more of what I call the coxcomb, than any of his companions: he dresses richly; would be thought elegant in the choice and fashion of what he wears; yet, after all, appears rather tawdry than fine. One sees by the care he takes of his outside, and the notice he bespeaks from *everyone*, by his *own* notice of himself, that the inside takes up the least of his attention. He dances finely, Mr Lovelace says: is a master of music; and singing is one of his principal excellencies. They prevailed upon him to sing; and he obliged them both in Italian and French; and, to do him justice, his songs in both were decent. They were all highly delighted with his performance; but his greatest admirers were Mrs Sinclair, Miss Partington, and *himself*. To me he appeared to have a great deal of affectation.

Mr Tourville's conversation and address are insufferably full of those really gross affronts upon the understandings of our sex, which the moderns call *compliments*, and are intended to pass for so many instances of good breeding, though the most hyperbolical, unnatural stuff that can be conceived, and which can only serve to show the insincerity of the *complimenter*; and the ridiculous light in which the *complimented* appears in his eyes, if he supposes a woman capable of relishing the romantic absurdities of his speeches.

He affects to introduce into his common talk Italian and French words; and often answers an English question in French, which language he greatly prefers to the barbarously hissing English. But then he never fails to translate into this his odious native tongue, the words and the sentences he speaks in the other two—lest, perhaps, it should be questioned whether he understands what he says.

He loves to tell stories: always calls them *merry*, *facetious*, *good*, or *excellent*, before he begins, in order to bespeak the attention of the hearers; but never gives himself concern, in the *progress* or *conclusion* of them, to make good what he promises in his *preface*. Indeed, he seldom brings any of them to a conclusion; for, if his company have patience to hear him out, he breaks in upon himself by so many parenthetical intrusions, as one may call them, and has so many incidents springing in upon him, that he frequently drops his own thread, and sometimes sits down satisfied half-way; or, if at other times he would resume it, he applies to his company to help him in again, with a *Devil fetch him* if he remembers what he was driving at. But enough, and too much, of Mr Tourville.

Mr BELFORD is the fourth gentleman, and one of whom Mr Lovelace seems more fond than any of the rest—being a man of tried bravery, it seems; for this pair of friends came acquainted upon occasion of a quarrel (possibly about a lady), which a rencounter at Kensington gravelpits ended, by the mediation of three gentlemen strangers.

Mr Belford is about seven- or eight-and-twenty, it seems; the youngest of the five, except Mr Lovelace: and these are, perhaps, the wickedest; for they seem capable of leading the other three as they please. Mr Belford, as the others, dresses gaily: but has not those advantages of person, nor from his dress, which Mr Lovelace is too proud of. He has, however, the appearance of a gentleman. He is well read in classical authors, and in the best English poets and writers: and by his means, the conversation took now and then a more agreeable turn: and I, who endeavoured to put the best face I could upon my situation, as I passed for Mrs Lovelace with them, made shift to join in it, at such times; and received abundance of compliments from all the company, on the observations I made.

Mr Belford seems good-natured and obliging; and although very complaisant, not so fulsomely so as Mr Tourville; and has a polite and easy manner of expressing his sentiments on all occasions. He seems to delight in a logical way of argumentation; as also does Mr Belton; these two attacking each other in this way; and both looking at us women, as if to observe whether we did not admire their learning, or their wit, when they had said a smart thing. But Mr Belford had visibly the advantage of the other, having quicker parts and, by taking the worst side of the argument, seemed to *think* he had. All together, he put me in mind of that character in Milton:

—His tongue
Dropt manna, and could make the worse appear
The better reason, to perplex and dash
Maturest counsels; for his thoughts were low;
To vice industrious: but to nobler deeds
Tim'rous and slothful: yet he pleas'd the ear.[1]

How little soever matters in general may be to our liking, we are apt to endeavour, when hope is strong enough to permit it, to make the best we can of the lot we have drawn; and I could not but observe often, how much Mr Lovelace excelled all his four friends in everything they seemed desirous to excel in. But, as to wit and vivacity, he had no equal present. All the others gave up to him, when his lips began to open. The haughty Mowbray would call upon the prating Tourville for silence, and with his elbow would punch the supercilious Belton into attention, when Lovelace was going to speak. And when he had spoken, the words, Charming fellow! with a free word of admiration or envy, fell from every mouth. He has indeed so many advantages in his person and manner, that what would be inexcusable in another, if one took not great care to watch over one's self and to distinguish what is the essence of right and wrong, would look becoming in him.

'See him among twenty men,' said Mr Belford; who, to my no small vexation and confusion, with the forwardness of a favoured and entrusted friend singled me out, on Mr Lovelace's being sent for down, to make me congratulatory compliments on my supposed nuptials; which he did with a caution, not to insist too long on the rigorous vow I had imposed upon a man so universally admired—

'See him among twenty men,' said he, 'all of distinction, and nobody is regarded but Mr Lovelace.'

It must, indeed, be confessed, that there is in his whole deportment a natural dignity, which renders all insolent or imperative demeanour as unnecessary as inexcusable. Then that deceiving sweetness which appears in his smiles, in his accent, in his whole aspect and address, when he thinks it worth his while to oblige, or endeavour to attract, how does this show that he was *born* innocent, as I may say; that he was not *naturally* the cruel, the boisterous, the impetuous creature which the wicked company he may have fallen into have made him! For he has, besides, an open and I think, an honest countenance. Don't you think so too?—On all these specious appearances, have I founded my hopes of seeing him a reformed man.

But 'tis amazing to me, I own, that with so much of the gentleman, such a general knowledge of books and men, such a skill in the learned as well as modern languages, he can take so much delight as he does in the company of such persons as I have described, and in subjects of frothy impertinence, unworthy of his talents and natural and acquired advantages. I can think of but one reason for it, and that must argue a very low mind; his VANITY; which makes him desirous of being considered as the head of the people he consorts with. A man to love praise; yet to be content to draw it from such contaminated springs!

One compliment passed from Mr Belford to Mr Lovelace, which hastened my quitting the shocking company—'You are a happy man, Mr Lovelace,' said he, upon some fine speeches made him by Mrs Sinclair, and assented to by Miss Partington: 'You have so much courage, and so much wit, that neither man nor woman can stand before you.'

Mr Belford looked at me, when he spoke: yes, my dear, he smilingly looked at me: and he looked upon his complimented friend: and all their *assenting*, and therefore *affronting* eyes, both men's and women's, were turned upon your Clarissa: at least my self-reproaching heart made me think so; for that would hardly permit my eye to look up.

Oh! my dear, were but a woman who is thought to be in love with a man (and this must be believed to be my case; or to what can my *supposed* voluntary going off with Mr Lovelace be imputed to?) to reflect one moment on the exaltation she gives *him*, and the disgrace she brings upon *herself*, the low pity, the silent contempt, the insolent sneers and whispers, to which she makes herself obnoxious from a censuring world of both sexes, how would she despise herself! And how much more eligible would she think death itself to such a discovered debasement!

What I have thus in general touched upon will account to you why I could not more particularly relate what passed in the evening's conversation: which, as may be gathered from what I have written, abounded with *approbatory* accusations, and *supposed* witty retorts.

Letter 162: MISS CLARISSA HARLOWE TO MISS HOWE

Monday midnight

I AM very much vexed and disturbed at an odd incident.

Mrs Sinclair has just now left me, I believe in displeasure, on my declining to comply with a request she made me: which was to admit Miss Partington to a share in my bed; her house being crowded by her nieces' guests and their attendants, as well as by those of Miss Partington.

There might be nothing in it; and my denial carried a stiff and ill-natured appearance. But instantly, all at once, upon her making the request, it came into my thought that I was, in a manner, a stranger to everybody in the house. Not so much as a servant I could call my own, or of whom I had any great opinion: that there were four gentlemen of free manners in the house, avowed supporters of Mr Lovelace in matters of offence; himself a man of enterprise; all, as far as I knew (and had reason to think by their noisy mirth after I had left them), drinking deeply: that Miss Partington herself is not so bashful a lady as she was represented to me to be: that officious pains were taken to give me a good opinion of her: and that Mrs Sinclair made a greater parade in prefacing the request, than such a request needed. To deny, thought I, can carry only an appearance of singularity, to people who *already* think me singular. To consent may possibly, if not probably, be attended with inconveniences. The consequences of the alternative so very disproportionate, I thought it more prudent to incur the censure, than risk the inconvenience.

I told her that I was writing a long letter: that I should choose to write till I were sleepy: and that Miss would be a restraint upon me, and I upon her.

She was loath, she said, that so delicate a young creature and so great a fortune as Miss Partington was, should be put to lie with Dorcas in a press-bed. She should be very sorry, if she had asked an improper thing: she had never been so put to it before: and Miss would stay up with *her*, till I had done writing.

Alarmed at this urgency, and it being easier to persist in a denial *given*, than to give it at *first*, I offered Miss my whole bed, and to retire into the dining-room, and there, locking myself in, write all the night.

The poor thing, she said, was afraid to lie alone. To be sure Miss Partington would not put me to such an inconvenience.

She then withdrew: but returned; begged my pardon for returning: but the poor child, she said, was in tears. Miss Partington had never seen a young lady she so much admired, and so much wished to imitate, as me. The dear girl hoped that nothing had passed in her behaviour to give me dislike to her. Should she bring her to me?

I was very busy, I said. The letter I was writing was upon a very important subject. I hoped to see Miss in the morning; when I would apologize to her for my particularity. And then Mrs Sinclair hesitating, and moving towards the door (though she turned round to me again), I desired her (lighting her) to take care how she went down.

Pray, madam, said she, on the stairs' head, don't give yourself all this trouble. God knows my heart, I meant no affront: but, since you seem to take my freedom amiss, I beg you will not acquaint Mr Lovelace with it; for he, perhaps, will think me bold and impertinent.

Now, my dear, is not this a particular incident; either as I have made it, or as it was designed? I don't love to do an uncivil thing. And if nothing were meant by the request, my refusal deserves to be called so. Then I have shown a suspicion of foul usage by it, which surely dare not be meant. If just, I ought to apprehend everything, and fly the house and the man, as I would an infection. If not just, and if I cannot contrive to clear myself of having entertained suspicions, by assigning some other plausible reason for my denial, the very staying here will have an appearance not at all reputable to myself.

I am now out of humour with him, with myself, with all the world but you. His companions are shocking creatures. Why, again I repeat, should he have been desirous to bring me into such company? Once more, I like him not. I am, my dear,

> Your affectionate
> CL. HARLOWE

Letter 163: MISS CLARISSA HARLOWE TO MISS HOWE

Tuesday, May 2

WITH infinite regret I am obliged to tell you that I can no longer write to you, or receive letters from you. Your mother has sent me a letter enclosed in a cover to Mr Lovelace, directed for him at Lord M.'s (and which was brought him just now), reproaching me on this subject in very angry terms, and forbidding me, as I would not be thought to intend to make her and you unhappy, to write to you, without her leave.

This, therefore, is the last you must receive from me, till happier times: and as my prospects are not very bad, I presume we shall soon have leave to write again; and even to see each other: since an alliance with a family so honourable as Mr Lovelace's is, will not be a disgrace.

She is pleased to write that if I would wish to *inflame* you, I should let you know her written prohibition: but otherwise find some way of my own accord (without bringing *her* into the question) to decline a correspondence, which I must know she has for some time past forbidden. But all I can say is, to beg of you *not* to be inflamed—to beg of you, not to let her *know*, or even by your behaviour to her, on this occasion, *guess*, that I have acquainted you with my reason for declining to write to you. For how else, after the scruples I have heretofore made on this very subject, yet proceeding to correspond, can I honestly satisfy you about my motives for this sudden stop? So my dear, I choose, you see, rather to rely upon your discretion, than to feign reasons you would not be satisfied with, but with your usual active penetration sift to the bottom, and at last find me to be a mean and low qualifier; and that, with an implication injurious to you, that I supposed you had not prudence enough to be trusted with the naked truth.

I repeat, that my prospects are not bad. The house, I presume, will soon be taken. The people here are very respectful, notwithstanding my nicety about Miss Partington. Miss Martin, who is near marriage with an eminent tradesman in the Strand, just now in a very respectful manner asked my opinion of some patterns of rich silks for the occasion. The widow has a less forbidding appearance than at first. Mr Lovelace, on my declared dislike of his four friends, has assured me that neither they nor anybody else shall be introduced to me, without my leave.

These circumstances I mention, as you will suppose, that your kind heart may be at ease about me; that you may be induced by them to acquiesce with your mother's commands, *cheerfully* acquiesce, and that for *my* sake, lest I should be thought an *inflamer*; who am, with very contrary intentions, my dearest, and best-beloved friend,

Your ever obliged and affectionate
CLARISSA HARLOWE

Letter 164: MISS HOWE TO MISS CLARISSA HARLOWE

Wed. May 3
I AM astonished that my mother should take such a step—purely to exercise an unreasonable act of authority; and to oblige the most remorseless hearts in the world. If I find that I can be of use to you either by advice or information, do you think I will not give it?—Were it to any other person, *less* dear to me than you are, do you think, in such a case, I would forbear giving it?—

Mr Hickman, who pretends to a little casuistry in such nice matters, is of opinion that I ought not to decline a correspondence thus circumstanced. And 'tis well he is; for my mother having set me up, I must have somebody to quarrel with.

This I will come into, if it will make you easy: I will forbear to write to you for a few days, if nothing extraordinary happen—and till the rigour of her prohibition is abated. But be assured that I will not dispense with your writing to me. My heart, my conscience, my honour, will not permit it.

But how will I help myself?—How!—Easy enough. For I do assure you that I want but very little further provocation to fly privately to London: and if I do, I will not leave you till I see you either honourably married, or absolutely quit of the wretch: and in this last case, I will take you down with me in defiance of the whole world: or, if you refuse to go with me, stay with you, and accompany you as your shadow whithersoever you go.

Don't be frighted at this declaration. There is but one consideration, and but one hope, that withhold me; watched as I am in all my retirements; obliged to read to her without a voice; to work in her presence without fingers; and to lie with her every night against my will. The *consideration* is, lest you should apprehend that a step of this nature would look like a doubling of your fault, in the eyes of such as think your going away a fault. The *hope* is, that things will still end happily, and that some people will have reason to take shame to themselves for the sorry parts they have acted— Nevertheless I am often balancing. But your resolving to give up the correspondence at this crisis will turn the scale. Write therefore, or take the consequence.

A few words upon the subject of your last letters. I know not whether your brother's wise project be given up or not. A dead silence reigns in your family. Your brother was absent three days; then at home one; and is now absent: but whether with Singleton or not, I cannot find out.

By your account of your wretch's companions, I see not but they are a set of infernals, and he the Beelzebub. What could he mean, as you say, by his earnestness to bring you into such company, and to give you such an opportunity to make him and them reflecting-glasses to one another? The man's a fool, to be sure, my dear—a silly fellow, at least. They must put on their *best* before you, no doubt—Lords of the creation!—Noble fellows these!—Yet who knows how many poor despicable souls of our sex the worst of them has had to whine after him!

You have brought an inconvenience upon yourself, as you observe, by your refusal of Miss Partington for your bedfellow. Pity you had not admitted her. Watchful as *you* are, what *could* have happened? If violence were intended, he would not stay for the night. You might have sat up after her, or not gone to bed. Mrs Sinclair pressed it too far. You was over-scrupulous.

If anything happens to delay your nuptials, I would advise you to remove: but if you marry, you may, perhaps, think it no great matter to stay where you are, till you take possession of your own estate. The knot once tied, and with so resolute a man, it is my opinion your relations will soon resign what they cannot legally hold: and were even a litigation to follow, you will not be *able*, nor ought you to be *willing*, to help it: for your estate will then be his right; and it will be unjust to wish it to be withheld from him.

One thing I would advise you to think of; and that is, of proper settlements. It will be to the credit of your prudence, and of his justice (and the more as matters stand), that something of this should be done before you marry. Bad as he is, nobody accounts him a sordid man. And I wonder he has been hitherto silent on that subject.

I am not displeased with his proposal about the widow lady's house. I think it will do very well. But if it must be three weeks before you can be certain about it; surely you need not put off his day for that space: and he may bespeak his equipages. Surprising to me that he could be so acquiescent!

I repeat—continue to write to me—I insist upon it; and that as minutely as possible: or, take the consequence. I send this by a particular hand. I am, and ever will be,

Your most affectionate
ANNA HOWE

Letter 165: MISS CLARISSA HARLOWE TO MISS HOWE

Thursday, May 4

I FORGO every other engagement, I suspend every wish, I banish every other fear, to take up my pen to beg of you that you will not think of being *guilty* of such an act of love as I can never thank you for; but must for ever regret. If I *must* continue to write to you, I must. I know full well your impatience of control when you have the least imagination that your generosity or friendship is likely to be wounded by it.

My dearest, dearest creature, would you incur a maternal, as I have a paternal, malediction? Would not the world think there was an infection in my fault, if it were to be followed by Miss Howe? There are some points so flagrantly wrong that they will not bear to be argued upon. This is one of them. I need not give reasons against such a rashness. Heaven forbid that it should be known that you had it but once in your *thought*, be your motives ever so noble and generous, to follow so bad an example! The rather as that you would, in such a case, want the extenuations that might be pleaded in my favour; and particularly that one of being *surprised* into the unhappy step.

The restraint your mamma lays you under would not have appeared heavy but on my account. Would you have once thought it a hardship to be admitted to a part of her bed?—How did I use to be delighted with such a favour from my mother!—How did I love to work in her presence!—So did you in the presence of yours once. And to read to her on winter evenings I know was one of your joys. Do not give me cause to reproach myself on the reason that may be assigned for the change.

Learn, my dear, I beseech you learn, to subdue your own passions. Be the motives what they will, excess is excess. Those passions in our sex, which we take no pains to subdue, may have one and the same source with those infinitely blacker passions which we used so often to condemn in the violent and headstrong of the other sex; and which may be heightened in them only by custom, and their freer education. Let us both, my dear, ponder well this thought; look into ourselves, and fear.

If I write, as I find I must, I insist upon *your* forbearance—Your silence to *this* shall be the sign to me that you will not think of the rashness you threaten me with; and that you will obey your mamma as to your *own* part of the correspondence, however: especially as you can inform or advise me in every weighty case, by Mr Hickman's pen.

My trembling writing will show you what a trembling heart you, my dear impetuous creature, have given to

Your ever obliged,
Or, if you take so rash a step,
Your forever disobliged,
CLARISSA HARLOWE

My clothes were brought to me just now. But you have so much discomposed me, that I have no heart to look into the trunks.

A servant of Mr Lovelace carries this to Mr Hickman for dispatch sake: Let that worthy man's pen relieve my heart from this new uneasiness.

Letter 166: MR HICKMAN TO MISS CLARISSA HARLOWE

(Sent to Wilson's by a particular hand)

Madam,   Friday, May 5

I HAVE the honour of dear Miss Howe's commands to acquaint you, without knowing the occasion, 'That she is excessively concerned for the concern she has given you in her last letter: and that, if you will but write to her, under cover as before, she will have no thoughts of what you are so very apprehensive about.'— Yet she bid me write, 'That if she has but the *least* imagination that she can *serve* you, and *save* you,' those are her words, 'all the censures of the world will be but of second consideration with her.' I have great temptations on this occasion to express my own resentments upon your present state; but not being fully apprised of what that is—only conjecturing from the disturbance upon the mind of the dearest lady in the world to me, and the most sincere of friends to you, that *that* is not altogether so happy as were to be wished; and being, moreover, forbid to enter into the cruel subject, I can only offer, *as I do*, my best and faithfullest services; and to wish you a happy deliverance from all your troubles. For I am,

> Most excellent young lady,
> Your faithful and most obedient servant,
> CH. HICKMAN

Letter 167: MR LOVELACE TO JOHN BELFORD, ESQ.

Tuesday May 2

MERCURY, as the fabulist tells us,[1] having the curiosity to know the estimation he stood in among mortals, descended in disguise, and in a statuary's shop cheapens a Jupiter, then a Juno, then one, then another, of the *Dii majores*; and at last asks, What price that same statue of *Mercury* bore? Oh, says the artist, buy one of the others, sir, and I'll throw ye in that for nothing. How sheepish must the god of thieves look upon this rebuff to his vanity!

So thou!—A thousand pounds wouldst thou give for the good opinion of this single lady: to be only thought tolerably of, and not quite unworthy of her conversation, would make thee happy. And at parting last night, or rather this morning, thou madest me promise a few lines to Edgware to let thee know what she thinks of thee, and thy brother varlets.

Thy thousand pounds, Jack, is all thy own: for most heartily does she dislike ye all: thee as much as any.

I am sorry for it too, as to thy part; for two reasons. *One*, that I think thy motive for thy curiosity was fear and consciousness: whereas that of the arch thief was vanity, intolerable vanity: and he was therefore justly sent away with a blush upon his cheeks to heaven, and could not brag. The *other*, that I am afraid if she dislikes *thee*, she dislikes *me*: for are we not birds of a feather?

I must never talk of reformation, she told me, having such companions and taking such delight as I seemed to take in their frothy conversation.

I, no more than you, imagined she could possibly like ye: but then, as *my* friends, I thought a person of her education would have been more sparing of her censures.

I don't know how it is, Belford; but women think themselves entitled to take any freedoms with *us*; while we are unpolite, forsooth, and I can't tell what, if we don't tell a pack of cursed lies, and make black white, in *their* favour—teaching us to be hypocrites, yet stigmatizing us at other times for deceivers.

I defended ye all, as well as I could: but you know there was no attempting ought but a palliative defence, to one of her principles. I will summarily give thee a few of my pleas.

To the *pure*, every little deviation seemed offensive: yet I saw not that there was anything amiss the whole evening, either in your words or behaviour. Some people could talk but upon *one* or *two* subjects: she upon every one: no wonder, therefore, *they* talked to what they understood best; and to mere objects of sense. Had she honoured us with more of *her* conversation, she would have been less disgusted with *ours*; for she saw how everyone was prepared to admire her, whenever she opened her lips. You, in particular, had said, when she retired, that virtue itself spoke when she spoke: but that you had such an awe upon you, after she had favoured us with an observation or two on a subject started, that you should ever be afraid in her company, to be found *most* exceptionable, when you intended to be *least* so.

Plainly, she said, she neither liked my companions, nor the house she was in.

I liked not the house any more than she: though the people were very obliging, and she had owned they were less exceptionable to herself than at first: and were we not about another of our own?

She did not like Miss Partington: let her fortune be what it would, she should not choose an intimacy with her. She thought it was a hardship to be put upon such a difficulty as she was put upon the preceding night, when there were lodgers in the front-house whom they had reason to be freer with, than, upon so short an acquaintance, with her.

I pretended to be an utter stranger as to this particular; and when she explained herself upon it, condemned the request, and called it a confident one.

She, *artfully*, made lighter of her denial of Miss for a bedfellow than she *thought* of it, I could see that; for it was plain she supposed there was room for me to think she had been either over-*nice*, or over-*cautious*.

I offered to resent Mrs Sinclair's freedom.

No; there was no great matter in it: it was best to let it pass. It might be thought more particular in her to *deny*, than in Mrs Sinclair to *ask*, or Miss to *expect*: but as the people below had a large acquaintance, she did not know how much she might have her retirements invaded, if she gave way. And indeed there were levities in Miss's behaviour, which she could not so far pass over, as to wish an intimacy with her. But if she were such a vast fortune, she could not but say that Miss seemed a much more suitable person for me to make my addresses to, than—

Interrupting her, with gravity, I said I liked Miss Partington as little as *she could* like her. She was a silly young creature, who seemed too likely to justify her guardians' watchfulness over her. But nevertheless, as to her general conversation and behaviour last night, I must own that I thought the girl (for *girl* she was, as to discretion) not exceptionable; only carrying herself as a free good-natured creature, who thought herself secure in the honour of her company.

It was very well said of me, she replied: but, if Miss were so *well* satisfied with her company, she left it to me, whether I was not very kind to suppose her such an *innocent*—For her own part, she had seen nothing of the London world: but thought she must tell me plainly, that she never was in such company in her life; nor ever again wished to be in it.

There, Belford!—worse off than Mercury!—art thou not?

I was nettled. Hard would be the lot of *more* discreet ladies, as far as I knew, than Miss Partington, were they to be judged by so rigid a virtue as hers.

Not so, she said: but if I really saw nothing exceptionable to a virtuous mind in that young lady's behaviour, *my* ignorance of *better* behaviour was, she must needs tell me, as pitiable as *hers:* and it were to be wished, that minds *so* paired, for their *own* sakes, should never be separated.

See, Jack, what I get by my charity!

I thanked her heartily. But I must take the liberty to say that good folks were generally so uncharitable that, devil take me, if I would choose to be good, were the consequence to be that I must think hardly of the whole world besides.

She congratulated me upon my charity: but told me that, to enlarge her *own*, she hoped it would not be expected of her to approve of the low company I had brought her into last night.

No exception for thee, Belford! Safe is thy thousand pounds.

I saw not, I said, begging her pardon, that she liked *anybody* (Plain dealing for plain dealing!—Why then did she abuse my friends?—*Love me, and love my dogs*, as Lord M. would say)—However, let me but know whom and what she did or did not like; and, if possible, I would like and dislike the very same persons and things.

She bid me then, in a pet, *dislike myself*.

Cursed severe!—Does she think she must not pay for it one day, or one night?—And if *one, many*; that's my comfort!

I was in a train of being so happy, I said, before my earnestness to procure her to favour my friends with her company, that I wished the devil had had as well my friends as Miss Partington—And yet I must say, that I saw not how good people could answer half their end, which was by their example to amend the world, were they to accompany *only* with the good.

I had like to have been blasted by two or three flashes of lightning from her indignant eyes; and she turned scornfully from me, and retired to her own apartment. Once more, Jack, safe, as thou seest, is thy thousand pounds. She says I am not a polite man—But is she, in the instance before us, more polite for a lady?

And now, dost thou not think that I owe my charmer some revenge for her cruelty in obliging such a fine young creature, and so vast a fortune, as Miss Partington, to crowd into a press-bed with her maid-servant Dorcas!—Miss Partington too (with tears) declaring by Mrs Sinclair that, would Mrs Lovelace honour her at Barnet, the best bed and best room in her guardian's house should be at her service. Thinkest thou that I could not guess at her dishonourable fears of me!—that she apprehended that the supposed *husband* would endeavour to take possession of *his own?*—and that Miss Partington would be willing to contribute to such a piece of justice?

Thus, then, thou both remindest and defiest me, charmer!—And since thou reliest more on thy own precaution than upon my honour; be it unto thee as thou apprehendest, fair one!

And now, Jack, let me know what thy opinion and the opinions of thy brother varlets are of my Gloriana.

I have just now heard that her Hannah hopes to be soon well enough to attend her young lady, when in London. It seems the girl has had no physician. I must send her one, out of pure love and respect to her mistress. Who knows but medicine may weaken nature, and strengthen the disease?—As her malady is not a fever, very likely it may do so—But perhaps her hopes are too forward. Blustering weather in this month yet—And that is bad for rheumatic complaints.

Letter 168: MR LOVELACE TO JOHN BELFORD, ESQ.

Tuesday, May 2

JUST as I had sealed up the enclosed, comes a letter to my beloved, in a cover to me directed to Lord M.'s. From whom, thinkest thou?—From Mrs Howe!—
And what the contents!

How should I know, unless the dear creature had communicated them to me? But a very cruel letter I believe it is, by the effect it had upon her. The tears ran down her cheeks as she read it; and her colour changed several times. No end of her persecutions, I think.

'What a cruelty in her fate!' said the sweet lamenter—'Now the only comfort of her life must be given up!'

Miss Howe's correspondence, no doubt.

But *should* she be so much grieved at this? This correspondence was prohibited before, and that, to the daughter, in the strongest terms: but yet carried on by *both:* although a brace of impeccables, and please ye. Could they expect that a mother would not vindicate her authority?—And finding her prohibition ineffectual with her perverse *daughter*, was it not reasonable to suppose she would try what effect it would have upon her *daughter's friend?*—And now I believe the end will be effectually answered: for my beloved, I dare say, will make a point of conscience of it.

I hate cruelty, especially in *women*; and should have been more concerned for this instance of it in Mrs Howe, had I not had a stronger instance of the same in my beloved to Miss Partington; for how did she know, since she was so much afraid for herself, whom Dorcas might let in to that innocent and less watchful young lady? But nevertheless I must needs own, that I am not very sorry for this prohibition, let it originally come from the Harlowes, or from whom it will; because I make no doubt that it is owing to Miss Howe, in a great measure, that my beloved is so much upon her guard, and thinks so hardly of me. And who can tell, as characters here are so tender, and some disguises so flimsy, what consequences might follow this undutiful correspondence?—I say, therefore, I am not sorry for it: now will she have nobody to compare notes with: nobody to alarm her: and I may be saved the guilt and disobligation of inspecting into a correspondence that has long made me uneasy.

How everything works for me!—Why will this charming creature make such contrivances necessary as will increase my trouble, and my guilt too, as some would account it? But why, rather I would ask, will she fight against her stars?—

Edgware, Tuesday night, May 2

WITHOUT staying for the promised letter from you to inform us what the lady says of *us*, I write to tell you that we are all of *one* opinion with regard to *her*; which is, that there is not of her age a finer lady in the world, as to her understanding. As for her person, she is at the age of bloom, and an admirable creature; a perfect beauty: but this *poorer* praise a man can hardly descend to give, who has been honoured with her conversation; and yet she was brought amongst us against her will.

Permit me, dear Lovelace, to be a means of saving this excellent creature from the dangers she hourly runs from the most plotting heart in the world. In a former, I pleaded your own family, Lord M.'s wishes particularly; and then I had not seen her. But now, I join her sake, honour's sake, motives of justice, generosity, gratitude and humanity, which are all concerned in the preservation of so fine a creature—Thou knowest not the anguish I should have had (whence arising, I cannot devise), had I not known before I set out this morning, that the incomparable creature had disappointed thee in thy cursed view of getting her to admit the specious Partington for a bedfellow!

There is something so awful, and yet so sweet, in this lady's aspect (I have done nothing but talk of her ever since I saw her), that were I to have the virtues and the graces all drawn in one piece, they should be taken, every one of them, from different airs and attitudes in her. She was born to adorn the age she was given to, and would be an ornament to the first dignity. What a piercing, yet gentle eye, every glance I thought mingled with love and fear of you: what a sweet smile darting through the cloud that overspread her fair face; demonstrating that she had more apprehensions and grief at her heart than she cared to express!

You may think what I am going to write too flighty; but, by my faith, I have conceived such a profound reverence for her sense and judgement that, far from thinking the man excusable who should treat her basely, I am ready to regret that such an angel of a lady should even marry. She is, in my eye, all mind: and were she to meet with a man all mind likewise, why should the charming qualities she is mistress of, be endangered? Why should such an angel be plunged so low as into the vulgar offices of domestic life? Were she mine, I should hardly wish to see her a mother unless there were a kind of moral certainty that minds like hers could be propagated. For why, in short, should not the work of bodies be left to *mere* bodies? I know that you yourself have an opinion of this lady little less exalted than mine. Belton, Mowbray, Tourville, are all of my mind; are full of her praises; and swear it would be a million of pities to ruin a lady in whose fall none but devils can rejoice.

What must that merit and excellence be that can extort this from *us*, free livers like yourself, and all of us your partial friends who have joined with you in your just resentments against the rest of her family, and offered our assistance to execute your vengeance on them? But we cannot think it reasonable that you should punish an innocent lady who loves you so well; and who is in your protection, and has suffered so much for you, for the faults of her relations.

And here let me put a serious question or two. Thinkest thou, truly admirable as this lady is, that the end thou proposest to thyself, if obtained, is answerable to the means, to the trouble thou givest thyself, and the perfidies, tricks, stratagems and contrivances thou hast already been guilty of, and still meditatest? In every real excellence she surpasses all her sex. But in the article thou seekest to subdue her for, a mere sensualist of her sex, a Partington, a Horton, a Martin, would make a sensualist a thousand times happier than she either will or can.

Sweet are the joys that come with willingness.[1]

And wouldst thou make her unhappy for her whole life, and thyself not happy for a single moment?

Hitherto, it is not too late; and that, perhaps, is as much as can be said, if thou meanest to preserve her esteem and good opinion, as well as person; for I think it is impossible she can get out of thy hands, now she is in this cursed house. Oh that damned hypocritical *Sinclair*, as thou callest her! How was it possible she should behave so speciously as she did, all the time the lady stayed with us! Be honest, and marry; and be thankful that she will condescend to have thee. If thou dost not, thou'lt be the worst of men; and will be condemned in this world and the next: as I am sure thou oughtest, and shouldst too, wert thou to be judged by one who never before was so much touched in a woman's favour, and whom thou knowest to be

Thy partial friend,
J. BELFORD

Our companions consented that I should withdraw to write to the above effect. They can make nothing of the characters we write in; so I read this to them; and they approve of it; and of their own motion each man would set his name to it. I would not delay sending it, for fear of some detestable scheme taking place.

THOMAS BELTON
RICHARD MOWBRAY
JAMES TOURVILLE

Just now are brought me both thine. I vary not my opinion, nor forbear my earnest prayers to thee in her behalf, notwithstanding her dislike of me.

Letter 170: MR LOVELACE TO JOHN BELFORD, ESQ.

Wednesday, May 3
WHEN I have already taken pains to acquaint thee in full with my views, designs and resolutions, with regard to this admirable creature, it is very extraordinary that thou shouldst vapour as thou dost in her behalf, when I have made no trial, no attempt: and yet givest it as thy opinion in a former letter, that advantage may be taken of the situation she is in; and that she may be overcome.

Most of thy reflections, particularly that which respects the difference as to the joys to be given by the virtuous and the libertine of the sex, are fitter to come in as after-reflections, than as *antecedencies*.

I own with thee, and with the poet, *that sweet are the joys that come with willingness*—but is it to be expected that a woman of education, and a lover of

forms, will yield before she is attacked?—And have I so much as summoned this
to surrender?—I doubt not but I shall meet with difficulty. I must therefore make
my first effort by surprise. There may possibly be some cruelty necessary. But
there may be consent in struggle; there may be yielding in resistance. But the first
conflict over, whether the following may not be weaker and weaker, till *willingness*
follow, is the point to be tried. I will illustrate what I have said by the simile of a
bird new caught. We begin with birds as boys, and as men go on to ladies; and both
perhaps, in turns, experience our sportive cruelty.

Hast thou not observed the charming gradations by which the ensnared volatile
has been brought to bear with its new condition? How at first, refusing all
sustenance, it beats and bruises itself against its wires, till it makes its gay plumage
fly about, and overspread its well-secured cage. Now it gets out its head; sticking
only at its beautiful shoulders: then, with difficulty, drawing back its head, it gasps
for breath, and erectedly perched, with meditating eyes, first surveys, and then
attempts, its wired canopy. As it gets breath, with renewed rage it beats and bruises
again its pretty head and sides, bites the wires, and pecks at the fingers of its
delighted tamer. Till at last, finding its efforts ineffectual, quite tired and breathless,
it lays itself down and pants at the bottom of the cage, seeming to bemoan its cruel
fate and forfeited liberty. And after a few days, its struggles to escape still
diminishing, as it finds it to no purpose to attempt it, its new habitation becomes
familiar; and it hops about from perch to perch, resumes its wonted cheerfulness,
and every day sings a song to amuse itself, and reward its keeper.

Now let me tell thee that I have known a bird actually starve itself, and die with
grief, at its being caught and caged—But never did I meet with a lady who was so
silly. Yet have I heard the dear souls most vehemently threaten their own lives on
such an occasion. But it is saying nothing in a woman's favour, if we do not allow
her to have more sense than a bird. And yet we must all own that it is more
difficult to catch a bird than a lady.

And now, Belford, were I to go no further, how shall I know whether this sweet
bird may not be brought to sing me a fine song, and in time to be as well contented
with her condition as I have brought other birds to be; some of them very shy ones?

But I guess at thy principal motive in this thy earnestness in behalf of this
charming creature. I know that thou correspondest with Lord M. who is impatient,
and long has been desirous, to see me shackled. And thou wantest to build up a
merit with that noble podagra-man, with a view to one of his nieces. But knowest
thou not that my consent will be wanting to complete it?—And what a
commendation will it be of thee to such a girl as Charlotte, when I shall acquaint
her with the affront thou puttest upon the whole sex, by asking whether I think my
reward, when I have subdued the most charming woman in the world, will be equal
to my trouble?—Which, thinkest thou, a woman of spirit will soonest forgive, the
undervaluing varlet who can put such a question; or him who prefers the pursuit
and conquest of a fine woman to all the joys of life?—Have I not known even a
virtuous woman, as she would be thought, vow everlasting antipathy to a man who
gave out that she was too old for him to attempt?

But another word or two, as to thy objection relating to my trouble and my
reward.

Does not the keen foxhunter endanger his neck and his bones in pursuit of a
vermin which, when killed, is neither fit food for men nor dogs?

Do not the hunters of the nobler game value the venison less than the sport?

· Why then should I be reflected upon, and the sex affronted, for my patience and perseverance in the most noble of all chases; and for not being a poacher in love, as thy question may be made to imply?

Learn of thy master, for the future, to treat more respectfully a sex that yields us our principal diversions and delights.

Proceed anon.

Letter 171: MR LOVELACE TO JOHN BELFORD, ESQ.

(In continuation)

WELL sayest thou, that mine is the *most plotting heart in the world*. Thou dost me honour; and I thank thee heartily. Thou art no bad judge. How like Boileau's parson I strut behind my double chin![1] Am I not obliged to deserve thy compliment?—And wouldst thou have me repent of a murder before I have committed it?

The virtues and graces are this lady's handmaids. 'She was certainly born to adorn the age she was given to.'—Well said, Jack—'And would be an ornament to the first dignity.'—But what praise is that unless the first dignity were adorned with the first merit?—Dignity! gewgaw!—First dignity! thou idiot!—Art thou, who knowest *me*, so taken with ermine and tinsel?—I, who have won the gold, am only fit to wear it. For the future therefore correct thy style, and proclaim her the ornament of the happiest man, and (respecting herself and sex) the greatest conqueror in the world.

Then, that she loves me, as thou imaginest, by no means appears clear to me— Her conditional offers to renounce me; the little confidence she places in me; entitle me to ask, What merit can she have with a man who won her in spite of herself; and who fairly, in set and obstinate battle, took her prisoner?

As to what thou inferrest from her eye when with us, thou knowest nothing of her heart from that, if thou imaginest there was one glance of love shot from it. Well did I note her eye, and plainly did I see that it was all but just civil disgust to me and to the company I had brought her into. Her early retiring that night against all entreaty might have convinced thee that there was very little of the gentle in her heart for me. And her eye never knew what it was to contradict her heart.

She is thou sayest, *all mind*. So say I. But why shouldst thou imagine that such a mind as hers, meeting with such a one as mine; and, to dwell upon the word, meeting with an inclination in hers to *meet*, should not propagate minds like her own?

No doubt of it, as thou sayest, the devils would rejoice in the fall of such a lady. But this is my confidence, that I shall have it in my power to marry when I will. And if I do her this justice, shall I not have a claim to her gratitude? And will she not think herself the obliged, rather than the obliger? Then let me tell thee, Belford, it is impossible so far to hurt the morals of this lady, as thou and thy brother-varlets have hurt others of the sex, who now are casting about the town, firebrands and double death—Take ye that thistle to mumble upon.

You will, perhaps, tell me that among all the objects of your respective attempts there was not one of the rank and merit of my charming Miss Harlowe.

But let me ask, Has it not been a constant maxim with us that the greater the *merit* on the woman's side, the nobler the victory on the man's?—And as to *rank*, sense of honour, sense of shame, pride of family, may make rifled rank get up, and shake itself to rights: and if anything come of it, such a one may suffer only in her pride, by being obliged to take up with a second-rate match instead of a first; and, as it may fall out, be the happier, as well as the more useful, for the misadventure; since (taken off of her public gaddings, and *domesticated* by her disgrace) she will have reason to think herself obliged to the man who has saved her from further reproach; while *her* fortune and alliance will lay an obligation upon *him*; and her past fall, if she have prudence and consciousness, will be his present and future security.

But a *poor* girl; such a one as my *Rosebud* for instance; having no recalls from education—being driven out of every family that pretends to reputation; persecuted most perhaps by such as have only kept their secret better; and having no refuge to fly to—the common, the stews, the street, is the fate of such a poor wretch; penury, want, and disease, her sure attendants; and an untimely end perhaps closes the miserable scene.

And will ye not now all join to say that it is more manly to attack a lion than a sheep?—Thou knowest that I always illustrated my eagleship by aiming at the noblest quarries; and by disdaining to make a stoop at wrens, *phil*-tits, and wagtails.

The worst respecting myself in the case before me, is that my triumph, when completed, will be so glorious a one, that I shall never be able to keep up to it. All my future attempts must be poor to this. I shall be as unhappy after a while, from my reflections upon this conquest, as Don John of Austria was, in his, on the renowned victory of Lepanto, when he found that none of his future achievements could keep pace with his early glory.

I am sensible that my pleas and my reasonings may be easily answered, and perhaps justly censured; but by whom censured? Not by any of the confraternity, whose constant course of life, even long before I became your general, to this hour, has justified what ye now, in a fit of squeamishness, and through envy, condemn. Having therefore vindicated myself and my intentions to You, that is all I am at present concerned for.

Be convinced then, that I (according to *our* principles) am right, *thou* wrong; or, at least, be silent. But I command thee to be convinced. And in thy next, be sure to tell me that thou art.

Letter 172: MR BELFORD TO ROBERT LOVELACE, ESQ.

Edgware, Thursday, May 4

I KNOW that thou art so abandoned a man, that to give thee the best reasons in the world against what thou hast once resolved upon, will be but acting the madman, whom once we saw trying to buffet down a hurricane with his hat. I hope, however, that the lady's merit will still avail her with thee. But if thou persistest; if thou wilt avenge thyself on this sweet lamb, which thou hast singled out from a flock thou hatest, for the faults of the dogs who kept it: if thou art not to be moved by beauty, by learning, by prudence, by innocence, all shining out in one charming object;

but she must fall; fall by the man whom she has chosen for her protector; I would not for a thousand worlds have thy crime to answer for.

Upon my faith, Lovelace, the subject sticks with me, notwithstanding I find I have not the honour of the lady's good opinion. And the more, when I reflect upon her father's brutal curse, the villainous hard-heartedness of all her family. But nevertheless, I should be desirous to know (if thou wilt proceed) by what gradations, arts, and contrivances, thou effectest thy ungrateful purpose—And, oh Lovelace, I conjure thee, if thou art a *man*, let not the specious devils thou hast brought her among, be suffered to triumph over her; nor make her the victim of unmanly artifices. If she yield to *fair seduction*, if I may so express myself; if thou canst raise a weakness in her by love, or by arts not inhuman; I shall the less pity her. And shall then conclude that there is not a woman in the world who can resist a bold and resolute lover.

A messenger is just now arrived from my uncle. The mortification, it seems, is got up to his knee; and the surgeons declare that he cannot live many days. He therefore sends for me directly, with these shocking words, that I will come and close his eyes. My servant, or his, must of necessity be in town every day on his case, or on other affairs, and one of them shall regularly attend you for any letter or commands: and it will be charity to write to me as often as you can. For although I am likely to be a considerable gainer by the poor man's death, yet I can't say that I at all love these scenes of Death and the Doctor so near me. The *Doctor* and *Death* I should have said; for that's that natural order; and, generally speaking, the one is but the harbinger to the other.

If therefore you decline to oblige me, I shall think you are displeased with my freedom. But let me tell you at the same time, that no man has a right to be displeased at freedoms taken with him for faults he is not ashamed to be guilty of.

J. BELFORD

Letter 173: MISS CLARISSA HARLOWE TO MISS HOWE

I THANK you and Mr Hickman for his letter sent me with such kind expedition; and proceed to obey my dear menacing tyranness.

She then gives the particulars of what passed between herself and Mr Lovelace on Tuesday morning, in relation to his four friends, and to Miss Partington, pretty much to the same effect as in Mr Lovelace's letter 167. And then proceeds:

He is constantly accusing me of over-scrupulousness. He says I am always out of humour with him. That I could not have behaved more reservedly to Mr Solmes: and that it is contrary to all his hopes and notions, that he should not, in so long a time, find himself able to inspire the person whom he hoped so soon to have the honour to call his, with the least distinguishing tenderness for him beforehand.

Silly and partial encroacher! not to know to what to attribute the reserve I am forced to treat him with. But his pride has eaten up his prudence. It is indeed a dirty low pride that has swallowed up the *true* pride which should have set him above the vanity that has overrun him. Have you not beheld the man, when I was your happy guest, as he walked to his chariot, looking about him, as if to observe what eyes his specious person and air had attracted? But indeed we have seen homely coxcombs as proud as if they had persons to be proud of; at the same time that it was apparent, that the pains they took about themselves but the more exposed their defects.

The man who is fond of being thought *more* or *better* than he *is*, as I have often [observed], but provokes a scrutiny into his pretensions; and that generally produces contempt. For pride, as I believe I have heretofore observed, is an infallible sign of weakness; of something wrong in the head or heart. He that exalts himself, insults his neighbour; who is provoked to question in him even that merit which, were he modest, would perhaps be allowed to be his due.

You will say, that I am very grave: and so I am. Mr Lovelace is extremely sunk in my opinion since Monday night: nor see I before me anything that can afford me a pleasing hope. For what, with a mind so unequal as his, can be my best hope?

I think I mentioned to you, in my former, that my clothes were brought me. You fluttered me so, that I am not sure I did. But I know I designed it. They were brought me on Thursday; but neither my few guineas with them, nor any of my books, except a *Drexelius on Eternity*, the good old *Practice of Piety*, and a *Francis Spira*. My brother's wit, I suppose. He thinks he does well to point out death and despair to me. I wish for the one, and every now and then, am on the brink of the other.

You will the less wonder at my being so very solemn when, added to the above, and to my uncertain situation, I tell you that they have sent me with these books a letter from my cousin Morden. It has set my heart against Mr Lovelace. Against myself too. I send it enclosed. If you please, my dear, you may read it here.

Letter [173.1: Colonel Morden] to Miss Clarissa Harlowe

Florence, April 13
I AM extremely concerned to hear of a difference betwixt the rest of a family, so near and dear to me, and *you* still dearer to me than any of the rest.

My cousin James has acquainted me with the offers you have had, and your refusals. I wonder not at either. Such charming promises at so early an age as when I left England; and those promises, as I have often heard, so greatly exceeded, as well in your person as mind, how much must you be admired! How few must there be worthy of you!

Your parents, the most indulgent in the world, to a child the most deserving, have given way, it seems, to your refusals of several gentlemen. They have contented themselves at last to name one with *earnestness* to you, because of the address of another they cannot approve of.

They had not reason, it seems, from your behaviour, to think you greatly averse; so they proceeded: perhaps too hastily for a delicacy like yours. But when all was fixed on their parts, and most extraordinary terms concluded in your favour; terms, which abundantly show the gentleman's just value for you; you fly off with a warmth and vehemence little suited to that sweetness which gave grace to all your actions.

I know very little of either of the gentlemen: but of Mr Lovelace I know more than of Mr Solmes. I wish I could say more to his advantage than I can. As to every qualification but *one*, your brother owns there is no comparison: but that *one* outweighs all the rest together—It cannot be thought, that Miss Clarissa Harlowe will dispense with MORALS in a husband.

What, my dearest cousin, shall I first plead to you on this occasion? Your duty, your interest, your temporal, and your eternal welfare, do, and may all depend upon this single point, *the morality of a husband.* A wife cannot always have it in her power to *be* good, or to *do* good, if she has a wicked husband, as a good husband may if he has a bad wife. You preserve all your religious regards, I understand. I wonder not that you do: I should have wondered had you not: but what can you promise yourself as to perseverance in them, with an immoral husband?

If your parents and you differ in sentiment on this important occasion, let me ask you, my dear cousin, who ought to give way?—I own to you that I should have thought there could not anywhere have been a more suitable match for you, than with Mr Lovelace, had he been a moral man. I should have very little to say against a man, of whose actions I am not to set up myself as a judge, did he not address my cousin. But, on this occasion, let me tell you, my dear Clarissa, that Mr Lovelace cannot possibly deserve you. He *may* reform, you'll say; but he may *not.* Habit is not soon shook off. Libertines who are libertines in defiance of talents, of superior lights, of conviction, hardly ever reform but by miracle, or by incapacity. Well do I know my own sex. Well am I able to judge of the probability of the reformation of a licentious young man, who has not been fastened upon by sickness, by affliction, by calamity: who has a prosperous run of fortune before him: his spirits high: his will uncontrollable: the company he keeps, perhaps such as himself, confirming him in all his courses, assisting him in all his enterprises.

As to the other gentleman, suppose, my dear cousin, you don't like him at *present*, it is far from being unlikely that you will *hereafter:* perhaps the more for not liking him *now.* He can hardly sink *lower* in your opinion: he may *rise.* Very seldom is it, that *high* expectations are so much as *tolerably* answered. How indeed *can* they, when a fine and extensive imagination carries its expectation infinitely beyond reality, in the highest of our sublunary enjoyments? A lady adorned with such an imagination sees no defect in a favoured object, because she is not conscious of any in herself, till it is too late to rectify the mistakes occasioned by her generous credulity.

But suppose a person of your talents were to marry a man of inferior talents; who, in this case, can be so happy in *herself*, as Miss Clarissa Harlowe? What delight do you take in doing good? How happily do you devote the several portions of the natural day to your own improvement, and to the advantage of all that move within your sphere?—And then such is your taste, such are your acquirements in the politer studies, and in the politer amusements; such your excellence in all the different parts of economy fit for a young lady's inspection and practice, that your friends would wish you to be taken off as little as possible by regards that might be called merely *personal?*

But as to what may be the consequence respecting yourself, respecting a young lady of your exalted talents, from the preference you are suspected to give to a libertine, I would have you, my dear cousin, consider what that may be—A mind so pure, to mingle with a mind more impure than most of his species! Such a man as this will engross all your solicitudes. He will perpetually fill you with anxieties for him and for yourself. The divine and civil powers defied, and their sanctions broke through by him, on every not merely *accidental*, but *meditated* occasion. To be agreeable to him, and to hope to preserve an interest in his affections, you must probably be obliged to abandon all your own laudable pursuits. You must enter into his pleasures and distastes: you must give up your own virtuous companions for his profligate ones: perhaps be forsaken by yours, because of the scandal he daily gives. Can you hope, cousin, with such a man as this, to be *long* so good as you *now* are?—If not, consider which of your present laudable delights you would choose to give up?—which of his culpable ones to follow him in? How could you brook to go backward instead of forward, in those duties which you now so exemplarily perform? And how do you know, if you once give way, where you shall be suffered, where you shall be *able*, to stop?

Your brother acknowledges that Mr Solmes is not near so agreeable in person as Mr Lovelace. But what is *person* with such a lady as I have the honour to be now writing to?—He owns likewise, that he has not the address of Mr Lovelace: but what a *mere* personal advantage is *address*, without *morals?*—A lady had better take a husband whose manners she were to fashion, than to find them ready-fashioned to her hand, at the price of his morality; a price that is often paid for travelling accomplishments. Oh my dear cousin, were you but with us here at Florence, or at Rome, or at Paris (where also I resided for many months), to see the gentlemen whose supposed *rough* English manners at setting out are to be polished, and what their improvements are in their return through the same places, you would infinitely prefer the man in his *first* stage, to the same man in his *last*. You *find* the difference on their return: foreign fashions, foreign vices, and foreign diseases too, often complete the man, and to despise his own country and countrymen, himself still more despicable than the *most* despicable of those he despises: these too generally make up, with a mixture of an unblushing effrontery, the travelled gentleman!

Mr Lovelace, I know, deserves to have an exception made in his favour; for he is really a man of parts and learning. He was esteemed so both here and at Rome; and a fine person, and a generous turn of mind, gave him great advantages. But you need not be told that a libertine man of sense does infinitely more mischief than a libertine of weak parts is able to do. And this I will tell you farther, that it was Mr Lovelace's own fault that he was not still more respected than he was among the *literati* here. There were, in short, some liberties in which he indulged himself, that endangered his person and his liberty; and made the best and most worthy of those who honoured him with their notice give him up; and his stay both at Florence and at Rome shorter than he designed.

This is all I choose to say of Mr Lovelace. I had much rather have had reason to give him a quite contrary character. But as to rakes or libertines in general, I, who know them well, must be allowed, because of the mischiefs they have always in their hearts, and too often in their power, to do your sex, to add still a few more words upon this topic.

A libertine, my dear cousin, a plotting, an intriguing libertine, must be generally remorseless—*unjust* he must always be. The noble rule of doing to others what he would have done to himself is the first rule he breaks; and every day he breaks it; the oftener, the greater his triumph. He has great contempt for your sex: he believes no woman chaste, because he is a profligate: every woman who favours him confirms him in his wicked incredulity. He is always plotting to extend the mischiefs he delights in. If a woman loves such a man, how can she bear the thought of dividing her interest in his affections with half the town, and that, perhaps, the dregs of it?—Then so sensual!—How will a young lady of your delicacy bear with so sensual a man? a man who makes a jest of his vows; and who, perhaps, will break your spirit by the most unmanly insults. To *be* a libertine, at setting out, all compunction, all humanity, must be overcome. To *continue* to be a libertine is to continue to be everything vile and inhuman. Prayers, tears and the most abject submission are but fuel to his pride: wagering perhaps with lewd companions and, not improbably, with lewder women, upon instances which he boasts of to them of your patient sufferings and broken spirit, and bringing them home to witness to both. I write what I know *has* been.

I mention not fortunes squandered, estates mortgaged or sold, and posterity robbed: nor yet a multitude of other evils, too gross, too shocking, to be mentioned to a delicacy like yours.

All these, my dear cousin, to be shunned, all the evils I have named to be avoided; the power of doing all the good you have been accustomed to do, preserved, nay, increased, by the separate provision that will be made for you: your charming diversions and exemplary employments all maintained; and every good habit perpetuated: and all by *one* sacrifice, the fading pleasure of the eye. Who would not (since everything is not to be met with in one man; who would not) to preserve so many essentials give up so light, so unpermanent a pleasure?

Weigh all these things, which I might insist upon to more advantage, did I think it needful to one of your prudence: weigh them well, my beloved cousin; and if it be not the will of your parents that you should continue single, resolve to oblige them; and let it not be said that the powers of fancy shall (as in many others of your sex) be too hard for your duty and your prudence. The less agreeable the man, the more obliging the compliance. Remember that he is a sober man: a man who has reputation to lose, and whose reputation therefore is a security for his good behaviour to you.

You have an opportunity offered you to give the highest instance that can be given of filial duty—Embrace it; it is worthy *of* you; it is expected *from* you; however, for your inclination sake, one may be sorry that you are called upon to give it. Let it be said that you have been able to lay an obligation upon your parents (a proud word, my cousin!) which you could not do, were it not laid *against* your inclination!—upon parents who have laid a thousand upon you: who are set upon this point: who will not give it up: who have given up many points to you, even of this very nature: and in *their* turn, for the sake of their own authority as well as judgement, expect to be obliged.

I hope I shall soon, in person, congratulate you upon this your meritorious compliance. To settle and give up my trusteeship is one of the principal motives of my leaving these parts. I shall be glad to settle it to everyone's satisfaction; to yours particularly. If on my arrival I find a happy union, as formerly, reign in a family so dear to me, it will be an unspeakable pleasure to me; and I shall perhaps so dispose my affairs, as to be near you for ever.

I have written a very long letter, and will add no more, than that I am, with the greatest respect, my dearest cousin,

Your most affectionate and faithful servant,
WM. MORDEN

I will suppose, my dear Miss Howe, that you have read my cousin's letter. It is now in vain to wish it had come sooner. But if it had, I might perhaps have been so rash as to give Mr Lovelace the fatal meeting, as I little thought of going off with him.

But I should hardly have given him the *expectation* of so doing, *previous* to the meeting, which made him come prepared; and the revocation of which he so artfully made ineffectual.

Persecuted as I was, and little expecting so much condescension, as my aunt, to my great mortification, has told me (and you confirm) that I should have met with, it is, however, hard to say what I should or should not have done, as to meeting him, had it come in time: but this effect I verily believe it would have had—to have made me insist with all my might on going over, out of all their ways, to the kind writer of the instructive letter, and made a father, a protector, as well as a friend, of a cousin who is one of my trustees. This, circumstanced as I was, would have been a natural, at least an unexceptionable protection. But I was to be unhappy! And how it cuts me to the heart to think that I can already subscribe to my cousin's character of a libertine, so well drawn in the letter which I suppose you now to have read!

That such a vile character, which ever was my abhorrence, should fall to my lot!—But depending on my own strength; having no reason to apprehend danger from headstrong and disgraceful impulses, I too little, perhaps, cast up my eyes to the Supreme Director: in whom, mistrusting myself, I ought to have placed my whole confidence!—and the more, when I saw myself so persistingly addressed by a man of this character.

Inexperience and presumption, with the help of a brother and sister who have low ends to answer in my disgrace, have been my *ruin!*—a hard word my dear! But I repeat it upon deliberation: since, let the best happen which *now* can happen, my reputation is destroyed; a rake is my portion: and what that portion is, my cousin Morden's letter has acquainted you.

Pray keep it by you, till called for. I saw it not myself (having not the heart to inspect my trunks) till this morning. I would not for the world this man should see it; because it might occasion mischief between the most violent spirit, and the most settled brave one, in the world, as my cousin's is said to be.

This letter was enclosed (opened) in a blank cover. Scorn and detest me as they will, I wonder that one line was not sent with it—were it but to have more particularly pointed the design of it, in the same generous spirit that sent me the Spira—The sealing of the cover was with black wax. I hope there is no new occasion in the family to give reason for black wax. But if there were, it would, to be sure, have been mentioned and laid at my door—perhaps too justly!

I had begun a letter to my cousin; but laid it by, because of the uncertainty of my situation and expecting every day, for several days past, to be at a greater certainty. You bid me write to him some time ago, you know. Then it was I began it: for I have great pleasure in obeying you in all I may. So I ought to have; for you are the only friend left me: and moreover, you generally honour me with your own observance of the advice I take the liberty to offer you: for I pretend to say, I give better advice than I have taken. And so I had need. For, I know not how it comes about, but I am, in my own opinion, a poor lost creature: and yet cannot charge myself with one criminal or faulty inclination. Do you know, my dear, how this can be?

Yet I can tell you *how*, I believe—One devious step at setting out!—That must be it: which pursued, has led me so far out of my path that I am in a wilderness of doubt and error; and never, never shall find my way out of it: for, although but one pace awry at first, it has led me hundreds and hundreds of miles out of my path: and the poor estray has not one kind friend, nor has met with one directing passenger, to help her to recover it.

But I, presumptuous creature! must rely so much upon my own knowledge of the right path!—little apprehending that an *ignis fatuus* with its false fires (and yet I had heard enough of such) would arise to mislead me!—And now, in the midst of fens and quagmires, it plays around me and around me, throwing me back again, whenever I think myself in the right track—But there is one common point in which all shall meet, err widely as they may. In that I shall be laid quietly down at last: and then will all my calamities be at an end.

But how I stray again; stray from my intention! I would only have said that I had begun a letter to my cousin Morden some time ago: but that, now, I can never end it. You will believe I cannot: for how shall I tell him that all his compliments are misbestowed: that all his advice is thrown away: all his warnings vain: and that even my highest expectation is to be the wife of that free liver whom he so pathetically warns me to shun?

Let me, however, have your prayers joined with my own (my fate depending, as it seems, upon the lips of such a man), 'That, whatever shall be my destiny, that dreadful part of my father's malediction that I may be punished by the man in whom he supposes I put my confidence may not take place! That this for *Mr Lovelace's* own sake, and for the sake of *human nature*, may not be!—Or, if it be necessary in support of the parental authority that I should be punished by *him*, that it may not be by his *premeditated* or *wilful* baseness; but that I may be able to acquit his *intention*, if not his *action!*' Otherwise, my fault will appear to be doubled in the eye of the event-judging world. And yet, methinks, I would be glad that the unkindness of my father and uncles, whose hearts have already been too much wounded by my error, may be justified in every article, excepting in this heavy curse: and that my father will be pleased to withdraw that, before it be generally known, at least that most dreadful part of it which regards futurity!

I must lay down my pen: I must brood over these reflections. Once more, before I enclose my cousin's letter, I will peruse it: and then I shall have it by heart.

Letter 174: MISS CLARISSA HARLOWE TO MISS HOWE

                                                                    Sunday night, May 7

WHEN you reflect upon my unhappy situation, which is attended with so many indelicate and even shocking circumstances, some of which my pride will not let me think of with patience; all aggravated by the contents of my cousin's affecting letter; you will not wonder that the vapourishness which has laid hold of my heart should rise to my pen. And yet it would be more kind, more friendly in me, to conceal from *you*, who take such a generous interest in my concerns, that worst part of my griefs which communication and complaint cannot relieve.

But to whom can I unbosom myself but to you?—When the man who ought to be my protector, as he has brought upon me all my distresses, adds to my apprehensions; when I have not even a servant on whose fidelity I can rely, or to whom I can break my griefs as they arise; and when his bountiful temper and gay heart attach everyone to him; and I am but a cipher, to give him significance and myself pain?—These griefs, therefore, do what I can, will sometimes burst into tears; and these mingling with my ink, will blot my paper—And I know you will not grudge me the temporary relief.

But I shall go on in the strain I left off with in my last; when I intended rather to apologize for my melancholy. But let what I have above written, once for all, be my apology. My misfortunes have given you a call to discharge the noblest offices of the friendship we have vowed to each other, in advice and consolation, and it would be an injury to it, and to you, to suppose it needed even that call.

She then tells Miss Howe that now her clothes are come, Mr Lovelace is continually teasing her to go abroad with him in a coach, attended by whom she pleases of her own sex; either for the air, or to the public diversions.

She gives the particulars of a conversation that has passed between them on that subject, and his several proposals. But takes notice that he says not the least word of the solemnity which he so much pressed upon her before they came to town; and which, as she observes, was necessary to give propriety to his proposals.

Now, my dear, *says she*, I cannot bear the life I live. I would be glad at my heart to be out of his reach. If I were, he should soon see the difference. If I must be humbled, it had better be by those to whom I owe duty, than by him. My aunt writes in her letter,[a] that SHE dare not propose anything in my favour. You tell me that, upon inquiry, you find[b] that, had I not been unhappily seduced away, a change of measures was actually resolved upon; and that my mamma, particularly, was determined to exert herself for the restoration of the family peace; and in order to succeed the better had thoughts of trying to engage my uncle Harlowe in her party.

Let me build on these foundations—I can but try, my dear—It is my duty to try all *probable* methods to restore the poor outcast to favour—And who knows but that once indulgent uncle, who has very great weight in the family, may be induced to interpose in my behalf?—I will give up all right and title to my grandfather's bequests, with all my heart and soul, to whom they shall think fit, in order to make my proposal palatable to my brother. And that my surrender may be effectual, I will engage never to marry.

What think you, my dear, of this expedient? Surely they cannot resolve to renounce me for ever. If they look with impartial eyes upon what has happened, they *will* have something to blame *themselves* for, as well as *me*.

I presume that you will be of opinion that this expedient is worth trying. But here is my difficulty: if I should write, my hard-hearted brother has so strongly confederated everybody against me that my letter would be handed about from one to another till he had hardened everyone to refuse my request; whereas, could my uncle be engaged to espouse my cause, as from *himself*, I should have some hope; as I presume to think he would soon have my mother and my aunt of his party.

a See p. 505.
b See p. 516.

What therefore I am thinking of, is this—Suppose Mr Hickman, whose good character has gained him everybody's respect, should put himself in my uncle Harlowe's way? And (as if from your knowledge of the state of things between Mr Lovelace and me) assure him not only of the above particulars, but that I am under no obligations that shall hinder me from taking his directions?

I submit the whole to your discretion, whether to pursue it at all, or in what manner. But if it be pursued, and if my uncle refuses to interest himself in my favour upon Mr Hickman's application as from you (for so, for obvious reasons, it must be put), I can then have no hope; and my next step, in the mind I am in, shall be to throw myself into the protection of the ladies of his family.

It were an impiety to adopt the following lines, because it would be throwing upon the decrees of Providence a fault too much my own. But often do I revolve them, for the sake of the general similitude which they bear to my unhappy yet undesigned error.

> To you, great gods! I make my last appeal:
> Or clear my virtues, or my crimes reveal.
> If wand'ring in the maze of life I run,
> And backward tread the steps I sought to shun,
> Impute my errors to your own decree;
> My FEET are guilty; but my HEART is free.[1]

[Letter 174.1]

Miss Harlowe dates again on Monday, to let Miss Howe know that Mr Lovelace, on observing her uneasiness, had introduced to her Mr Mennell, Mrs Fretchville's kinsman, who managed all her affairs (a young officer of sense and politeness, she calls him); and who gave her an account of the house and furniture to the same effect that Mr Lovelace had done before; as also of the melancholy way Mrs Fretchville is in.

She tells Miss Howe how extremely urgent Mr Lovelace was with the gentleman to get his spouse (as he now always calls her before company) a sight of the house: and that Mr Mennell undertook that very afternoon to show her all of it, except the apartment Mrs Fretchville should be in when she went. But that she chose not to take another step till she knew how she approved of her scheme to have her uncle sounded; and what success, if tried, it would be attended with.

[Letter 174.2]

Mr Lovelace, in his humorous way, gives his friend an account of the lady's peevishness and dejection on receiving a letter with her clothes. He regrets that he has lost her confidence; which he attributes to bringing her into the company of his four companions. Yet he thinks he must excuse them, and censure her for over-niceness; for that he never saw men behave better, at least not them.

Mentioning his introducing Mr Mennell to her, 'Now, Jack, *says he,* was it not very kind of Mr Mennell, *Captain* Mennell I sometimes called him (for among the military men there is no such officer, thou knowest, as a *Lieutenant* or an *Ensign*):

was it not very kind in him to come along with me so readily as he did, to satisfy my beloved about the vapourish lady and the house?

'But who is Captain Mennell, methinks thou askest? I never heard of such a man as Captain Mennell.'

'Very likely. But knowest thou not young Newcomb, honest Doleman's nephew?'

'Oh-ho! Is it he?'

'It is. And I have changed his name by virtue of my own single authority. Knowest thou not that I am a great name-father? Preferments I bestow, both military and civil. I give estates, and take them away at my pleasure. Quality too I create. And by a still more valuable prerogative, I *degrade* by virtue of my own imperial will, without any other act of forfeiture than my own convenience. What a poor thing is a monarch to me!

'But Mennell, now he has seen this angel of a woman, has qualms; that's the devil!—I shall have enough to do to keep him right. But it is the less wonder, that he should stagger, when a few hours' conversation with the same lady could make four much more hardened varlets find *hearts*—Only, that I am confident, that I shall at last reward her virtue, if her virtue overcome me, or I should find it impossible to persevere.—For at times, I have confounded qualms myself. But say not a word of them to the Confraternity: nor laugh at me for them thyself.'

[*Letter 174.3*]

In another letter, dated Monday night, he tells his friend: that the lady keeps him at such distance that he is sure something is going on between her and Miss Howe, notwithstanding the prohibition from Mrs Howe to both; and as he has thought it some degree of merit in himself to punish others for their transgressions, he thinks both these girls punishable for the breach of parental injunctions. And as to their letter-carrier, he has been inquiring into his way of living; and finding him to be a common poacher, a deer-stealer and warren-robber who, under pretence of higgling, deals with a set of customers who constantly take all he brings, whether fish, fowl or venison, he holds himself justified (since Wilson's conveyance must at present be sacred) to have him stripped and robbed, and what money he has about him given to the poor; since, if he take not money as well as letters, he shall be suspected.

'To serve one's self, says he, and punish a villain at the same time, is serving public and private. The law was not made for such a man as me. And I *must* come at correspondencies so disobediently carried on.

'But, on second thoughts, if I could find out that the dear creature carried any of her letters in her pockets, I can get her to a play or to a concert, and she may have the misfortune to lose her pockets.

'But how shall I find this out; since her Dorcas knows no more of her dressing or undressing than her Lovelace? For she is dressed for the day before she appears even to her servant—Vilely suspicious!—Upon my soul, Jack, a suspicious temper is a punishable temper. If a lady suspects a rogue in an honest man, is it not enough to make the honest man who knows it, a rogue?

'But as to her pockets, I think my mind hankers after them, as the less mischievous attempt—But they cannot hold all the letters that I should wish to see. And yet a woman's pockets are half as deep as she is high. Tied round them as ballast-bags, I presume, lest the wind, as they move with full sail from whale-ribbed canvas, should blow away the gypsies.'

He then, in apprehension that something is meditating between the two ladies, or that something may be set on foot to get Miss Harlowe out of his hands, relates several of his contrivances, and boasts of his instructions given in writing to Dorcas and to his servant Will Summers; and says that he has provided against every possible accident, even to bring her back if she should escape, or in case she should go abroad and then refuse to return; and hopes so to manage, as that should he make an attempt, whether he succeed in it or not, he may have a pretence to detain her.

He orders Dorcas to cultivate by all means her lady's favour; to lament her incapacity as to writing and reading; to show her lady letters from pretended country relations, and beg her advice how to answer them and to get them answered; to be always aiming at scrawling with a pen, lest inky fingers should give suspicions. And says that he has given her an ivory-leaved pocket-book with a silver pencil, that she may make memoranda on occasion.

The lady has already, he says, at Mrs Sinclair's motion removed her clothes out of the trunks they came in, into an ample mahogany repository, where they will lie at full length, and which has drawers in it for linen. A repository, *says he*, that used to hold the richest suits which some of the nymphs put on when they are to be dressed out to captivate or to ape quality. For many a countess, thou knowest, has our mother equipped; nay, two or three duchesses who live upon *quality-terms* with their lords. But this to such as will come up to her price, and can make an appearance like quality themselves on the occasion: for the reputation of persons of birth must not lie at the mercy of every under-degreed sinner.

A master key which will open every lock in this chest is put into Dorcas's hands; and she is to take care when she searches for papers, before she removes anything to observe how it lies, that she may replace all to a hair. Sally and Polly can occasionally help to transcribe. Slow and sure with such a lady must be all my movements.

It is impossible that one so young and so inexperienced can have all her caution from herself; the behaviour of the women so unexceptionable; no revellings, no company ever admitted into this inner-house; all genteel, quiet, and easy in it; the nymphs well-bred and well-read; her first disgusts to the old one got over—It must be Miss Howe, therefore, who once was in danger of being taken in by one of our class, by honest Sir George Colmar, as thou hast heard, that makes my progress difficult.

Thou seest, Belford, by the above *precautionaries*, that I forget nothing. As the song says, it is not to be imagined

> On what slight strings
> Depend those things,
> On which men build their glory![1]

So far, so good. I shall never let my goddess rest till I have first discovered where she puts her letters, and next till I have got her to a play, to a concert, or to take an airing with me of a day or so.

I GAVE thee just now some of *my* contrivances. Dorcas, who is ever attentive to all her lady's motions, has given me some instances of her *mistress's* precautions. She wafers her letters, it seems, in two places; pricks the wafers; and then seals upon them. No doubt but those brought hither are taken the same care of. And she always examines the seals of the letter before she opens them. I must, I must, come at them. This difficulty augments my curiosity. Strange, so much as she writes, and at all hours, that not one sleepy or forgetful moment has offered in our favour!

A fair contention, thou seest. Do not thou therefore reproach me for endeavouring to take advantage of her *tender years*. *Credulity* she has none. Am not I a *young fellow*, myself? As to her *fortune*, that's out of the question; fortune never had any other attractions for me than to stimulate me on; and this, as I have elsewhere said, for motives not ignoble. As to *beauty*: prithee, Jack, do thou to spare my modesty make a comparison between my Clarissa for a *woman*, and thy Lovelace for a *man!*—The only point that can admit of debate, as I conceive, is who has most *wit*, most *circumspection*: and that is what remains to be tried.

A sad life, however, for the poor lady to live, as well as for me; that is to say, if she be not *naturally* jealous. If she be, her uneasiness is constitutional, and she cannot help it; nor will it in that case hurt her. For a suspicious temper will *make* occasions for doubt, if none were to offer to her hand; and so my fair one is obliged to me for saving her the trouble of studying for these occasions—But after all, the plain way in every affair of the human life is the best, I believe. But it is not given me to choose it. Nor am I singular in the pursuit of the more intricate paths; since there are thousands and ten thousands, besides me, who had rather fish in troubled waters than in smooth.

Letter 175: MR LOVELACE TO JOHN BELFORD, ESQ.

Tuesday, May 9

I AM a very unhappy fellow. This lady is said to be one of the sweetest-tempered creatures in the world: and so I thought her. But to me, she is one of the most perverse. I never was supposed to be an ill-natured puppy neither. How can it be? I imagined for a long while that we were born to make each other happy: but, quite the contrary; we really seem to be sent to plague one another.

I will write a comedy, I think. I have a title ready; and that's half the work. *The Quarrelsome Lovers*. 'Twill do. There's something new and striking in it. Yet, more or less, all lovers quarrel. Old Terence has taken notice of that; and observes upon it, that lovers falling out occasions lovers falling in[1]; and a better understanding of course. 'Tis natural that it should be so. But with us, we fall out so often, without falling in once; and a second quarrel so generally happens before a first is made up; that it is hard to guess what event our loves will be attended with. But Shakespeare says:

> —Come what come may,
> Patience and time run through the roughest day.[2]

And that shall be my comfort. No man living bears crosses better than myself: but then they must be of *my own* making: and even this is a great merit, and a great excellence, think what thou wilt: since most of the troubles which fall to the lot of mortals are brought upon themselves, either by their *too large* desires, or *too little* deserts. But I shall make myself a common man by-and-by: which is what no one yet ever thought me. I will now lead to the occasion of this preamble.

I had been out. On my return, meeting Dorcas on the stairs—Your lady in her chamber, Dorcas? In the dining-room, sir: and if ever you hope for an opportunity to come at a letter, it must be now. For at her feet I saw one lie which, by its opened folds, she has been reading, with a little parcel of others she is now busied with. All pulled out of her pocket, as I believe: so, sir, you'll know where to find them another time.

I was ready to leap for joy, and instantly resolved to bring forward an expedient which I had held *in petto*; and entering into the dining-room with an air of transport, I boldly clasped my arms about her as she sat (she huddling up her papers in her handkerchief all the time, the dropped paper unseen): Oh my dearest life, a lucky expedient have Mr Mennell and I hit upon just now. In order to hasten Mrs Fretchville to quit the house, I have agreed, if you approve of it, to entertain her cook, her housemaid and two men-servants (about whom she was very solicitous) till you are provided to your mind. And that no accommodations may be wanted, I have consented to take the household linen at an appraisement.

I am to pay down five hundred pounds and the remainder as soon as the bills can be looked up and the amount of them adjusted. Thus will you have a charming house entirely ready to receive you, and any of my friends. They will soon be with you: they will not permit you long to suspend my happy day—And that nothing may be wanting to gratify your utmost punctilio, I will till then consent to stay here at Mrs Sinclair's, while you reside at your new house; and leave the rest to your own generosity.

Oh my beloved creature, will not this be agreeable to you? I am sure it will—It must—And clasping her closer to me, I gave her a more fervent kiss than ever I had dared to give her before: but still let not my ardour overcome my discretion; for I took care to set my foot upon the letter and scraped it farther from her, as it were behind her chair.

She was in a passion at the liberty I took. Bowing low, I begged her pardon; and stooping still lower, in the same motion took it up and whipped it in my bosom.

Pox on me for a puppy, a fool, a blockhead, a clumsy varlet, and a mere Jack Belford!—I thought myself a much cleverer fellow than I am!—Why could I not have been followed in by Dorcas; who might have taken it up while I addressed her lady?

For here, the letter being unfolded, I could not put it into my bosom without alarming her ears, as my sudden motion did her eyes—Up she flew in a moment: Traitor! Judas! her eyes flashing lightning, and a perturbation in her eager countenance, so charming!—What have you taken up?—And then, what for both my ears I durst not to have done to her, she made no scruple to seize the stolen letter, though in my bosom.

Beg-pardon apologies were all that now remained for me on so palpable a detection. I clasped her hand, which had hold of the ravished paper, between mine: Oh my beloved creature! can you think I have not *some* curiosity? Is it possible you can be thus for ever employed; and I, loving narrative letter-writing above every other species of writing, and admiring your talent that way, should not (thus upon the dawn of my happiness, as I presume to hope) burn with a desire to be admitted into so sweet a correspondence?

Let go my hand!—stamping with her pretty foot. How dare you, sir!—At this rate, I see—too plainly I see—and more she could not say: but, gasping, was ready to faint with passion and affright; the devil a bit of her accustomed gentleness to be seen in her charming face, or to be heard in her musical voice.

Having gone thus far, loath, very loath was I to lose my prize—Once more I got hold of the rumpled-up letter!—Impudent man! were her words: stamping again: for God's sake, then it was!—I let go my prize, lest she should faint away: but had the pleasure first to find my hand within both hers, she trying to open my reluctant fingers. How near was my heart, at that moment, to my hand, throbbing to my fingers' ends, to be thus familiarly, although angrily, treated by the charmer of my soul!

When she had got it in her possession, she flew to the door. I threw myself in her way, shut it, and in the humblest manner besought her to forgive me: and yet do you think the Harlowe-hearted charmer would; notwithstanding the agreeable annunciation I came in with?—No, truly! but pushing me rudely from the door, as if I had been nothing (yet do I love to try, so innocently to try, her strength too!); she gaining that force through passion, which I had lost through fear; and out she shot to her own apartment (thank my stars she could fly no further!); and as soon as she entered it, in a passion still, she double-locked and double-bolted herself in—This my comfort, on reflection, that upon a greater offence it cannot be worse!

I retreated to my own apartment with my heart full. And my man Will not being near me, gave myself a plaguy knock on the forehead with my double fist.

And now is my charmer shut up from me: refusing to see me; refusing her meals. Resolves *not* to see me, that's more—Never again, if she can help it.

In the mind she is in—I hope she has said. The dear creatures, whenever they quarrel with their humble servants, should always remember this saving clause, *that they may not be forsworn.*

But thinkest thou that I will not make it the subject of one of my first plots to inform myself of the reason why all this commotion was necessary on so slight an occasion as this would have been, were not the letters that pass between these ladies of a treasonable nature?

Wednesday morning

No admission to breakfast, any more than to supper. I wish this lady is not a simpleton, after all—I have sent up in Capt. Mennell's name. A message from Capt. Mennell, madam.

It won't do!—She is of a baby age: she cannot be—a Solomon, I was going to say, in everything. Solomon, Jack, was the wisest man—But didst ever hear who was the wisest woman?—I want a comparison for this lady. Cunning women and witches, we read of without number. But I fancy wisdom never entered into the character of a woman. It is not a requisite of the sex. Women, indeed, make better sovereigns than men: but why is that?—Because the women sovereigns are governed by men; the men sovereigns by women—Charming by my soul! For hence we guess at the rudder by which both are governed. Yet, sorry puppy as thou art, thou makest light of me for my attachment to this sex; and even of my ardours to the most excellent one of it!—

But to put wisdom out of the question, and to take *cunning* in: that is to say, to consider woman *as* a woman; what shall we do if this lady has something extraordinary in her head?—Repeated charges has she given for Wilson, by a particular messenger, to send any letter directed for her the moment it comes.

I must keep a good look-out. She is not now afraid of her brother's plot. I shan't be at all surprised if Singleton calls upon Miss Howe, as the only person who knows, or is likely to know, where Miss Harlowe is; pretending to have affairs of importance and of particular service to her, if he can but be admitted to her speech. Of compromise, who knows, from her brother?

Then will Miss Howe warn her to keep close; then will my protection be again necessary. This will do, I believe. Anything from Miss Howe must.

Joseph Leman is a vile fellow with her, and my implement. Joseph, honest Joseph as I call him, may hang himself. I have played him off enough, and have very little further use for him. No need to wear one plot to the stumps when I can find new ones every hour.

Nor blame me for the use I make of my talents. Who, that had such, would let 'em be idle?

Well then, I will find a Singleton; that's all I have to do.

Instantly find one!—Will—

Sir—

This moment call me hither thy cousin Paul Wheatly, just come from sea, whom thou wert recommending to my service if I were to marry and keep a pleasure-boat.

Presto—Will's gone!—Paul will be here presently!—Presently will he be gone to Mrs Howe's—If Paul be Singleton's mate, coming from his captain, it will do as well as if it were Singleton himself.

Sally, a little devil, often reproaches me with the slowness of my proceedings. But in a play, does not the principal entertainment lie in the first four acts? Is not all in a manner over when you come to the fifth? And what a vulture of a man must he be who souses upon his prey, and in the same moment trusses and devours?

But to own the truth, I have overplotted myself. To make my work secure, as I thought, I have frighted the dear creature with my four Hottentots, and I shall be a long time, I doubt, before I can recover my lost ground. And then these cursed folks at Harlowe Place have made her out of humour with me, with herself, and with all the world but Miss Howe, who no doubt is continually adding difficulties to my other difficulties. And then I am very unwilling to have recourse to measures which these demons below are continually urging me to take. And the rather, as I am sure that, at last, she must be legally mine. One complete trial over, and I think I will do her noble justice.

WELL, Paul's gone!—gone already!—has all his lessons!—A notable fellow!— Lord W.'s necessary man was Paul before he went to sea. A more sensible rogue Paul than Joseph!—Not such a pretender to piety neither, as the other. At what a price have I bought that Joseph!—I had two to buy, in him—his conscience as well as the man. I believe I must punish the rascal at last: but must let him marry first: then (though that may be punishment enough), as I bribed two at once in one man, I shall punish two at once in the man and his wife—And how richly does Betty deserve it for her behaviour to my goddess!

But now I hear the rusty hinges of my beloved's door give me creaking invitation. My heart creaks and throbs with respondent trepidations. Whimsical enough though! For what relation has a lover's heart to a rusty pair of hinges?—But they are the hinges that open and shut the door of my beloved's bed chamber!—Relation enough in that!

I hear not the door shut again. I shall have her commands I hope anon—What signifies her keeping me thus at a distance?—She must be mine, let me do or offer what I will. Courage whenever I assume, all is over: for should she think of escaping from hence, whither can she fly to avoid me? Her parents will not receive her. Her uncles will not entertain her. Her beloved Norton is in their direction, and cannot. Miss Howe dare not. She has not one friend in town but me: is entirely a stranger to the town. And what then is the matter with me, that I should be thus unaccountably overawed and tyrannized over by a dear creature, who wants only to know how impossible it is that she should escape me, in order to be as humble to me as she is to her persecuting relations?

Should I even make the grand attempt, and fail, and should she hate me for it, her hatred can be but temporary. She has already incurred the censure of the world. She must therefore choose to be mine for the sake of soldering up her reputation in the eye of that impudent world. For who that knows me and knows that she has been in my power, though but for twenty-four hours, will think her spotless as to fact, let her inclination be what it will?—And then human nature is such a well-known rogue, that every man and woman judges by what each knows of themselves, that inclination is no more to be trusted, where an opportunity is given, than I am; especially where a woman young and blooming loves a man well enough to go off with him; for such will be the world's construction in the present case.

She calls her maid Dorcas. No doubt that I may hear her harmonious voice, and to give me an opportunity to pour out my soul at her feet; to renew all my vows; and to receive her pardon for the past offence: and then, with what pleasure shall I begin upon a new score; and afterwards wipe out that; and begin another, and another; till the *last* offence passes; and there can be no other. And once, after that, to be forgiven, will be to be forgiven for ever.

THE door is again shut. Dorcas tells me that she denies to admit me to dine with her, as I had ordered her to request for me next time she saw her. Not uncivilly, however, denies. Coming to by degrees! Nothing but the last offence, the honest wench tells me in the language of her principals below, will do with her. The last offence is meditating. Yet this vile recreant heart of mine plays me booty—But here I conclude; though the tyranness leaves me nothing to do but read, write and fret.

Subscription is formal between us. Besides, I am so totally hers, that I cannot say how much I am thine, or any other person's.

Letter 176: MISS CLARISSA HARLOWE TO MISS HOWE

Tuesday, May 9

IF, my dear, you approve of the application to my uncle Harlowe, I wish it may be made as soon as possible. We are quite out again. I have shut myself up from him. The offence indeed not *very* great—and yet it is too. He had like to have got a letter. One of yours. But never will I write again, or re-peruse my papers, in an apartment where he thinks himself entitled to come. He did not read a line of it. Indeed he did not. So don't be uneasy: and depend upon future caution.

Thus it was. The sun being upon my closet, and Mr Lovelace abroad—

She then gives Miss Howe an account of his coming in by surprise upon her: of his fluttering speech: of his bold address: of her struggle with him for the letter, &c.

And now, my dear, *proceeds she*, I am more and more convinced that I am too much in his power to make it prudent to stay with him. And if my friends *will* but give me hope—Till I can know whether they will or not, I must do what I never studied to do before in any case—that is, try to keep this difference open: and yet it will make me look little in my own eyes; because I shall mean by it more than I can own. But this is one of the consequences of a step which will be ever deplored by

Your CLARISSA HARLOWE

Letter 177: MISS HOWE TO MISS CLARISSA HARLOWE

Wednesday, May 10

I MUCH approve of your resolution to leave this man, if you can have any encouragement from your uncle. And the rather, as I have heard but within these two hours some well-attested stories of him that show him to be one of the worst of men as to our Sex. I do assure you, my dear friend, that had he a dozen lives, if all I have heard be true, he might have forfeited them all, and been dead *twenty crimes* ago.

If ever you condescend to talk familiarly with him again, ask him after Miss Betterton, and what became of her: and if he shuffle and prevaricate, question him about Miss Lockyer—Oh my dear, the man's a villain!

I will have your uncle sounded, as you desire, and that out of hand. But yet I am afraid of the success; and this for several reasons. 'Tis hard to say what the sacrifice of your estate would do with some people: and yet I must not, when it comes to the test, permit you to make it.

As your Hannah continues ill, I would advise you to try to attach Dorcas to your interest. Have you not been impoliticly shy of her?

I wish you could come at some of his letters. Surely a man of his negligent character cannot be always guarded. If he were, and if you cannot engage your servant, I should suspect them both. Let him be called upon at a short warning when he is writing, or when he has papers lying about, and so surprise him into negligence.

Such inquiries, I know, are of the same nature with those we make at an inn in travelling, when we look into every corner and closet for fear of a villain; yet should be frighted out of our wits were we to find one. But 'tis better to detect such a one when awake and up, than to be attacked by him when in bed and asleep.

I am glad you have your clothes. But no money; no books but a *Spira*, a *Drexelius*, and a *Practice of Piety*. Those who sent the latter ought to have kept it for themselves—But I must hurry myself from this subject.

You have exceedingly alarmed me by what you hint of his attempt to get one of my letters. I am assured by my new informant that he is the head of a gang of wretches (those he brought you among, no doubt, were some of them), who join together to betray innocent creatures, and to support one another, when they have done, by violence. And were he to come at the knowledge of the freedoms I take with him, I should be afraid to stir out without a guard.

I am sorry to tell you that I have reason to think that your brother has not laid aside his foolish plot. A sun-burnt, sailor-looking fellow was with me just now, pretending great service to you from Captain Singleton, could he be admitted to your speech. I pleaded ignorance. The fellow was too well instructed for me to get anything out of him.

I wept for two hours incessantly on reading yours which enclosed that from your cousin Morden.[a] My dearest creature, do not desert yourself. Let your Anna Howe obey the call of that friendship which has united us as one soul and endeavour to give you consolation.

I wonder not at the melancholy reflections you so often cast upon yourself in your letters, for the step you have been forced upon on one hand, and tricked into on the other. A strange fatality! As if it were designed to show the vanity of all human prudence. I wish, my dear, as you hint, that both you and I have not too much prided ourselves in a perhaps too conscious superiority over others—But I will stop—How apt are weak minds to look out for judgements in any extraordinary event! 'Tis so far right that it is better, and safer and juster, to arraign ourselves, or our dearest friends, than Providence; which must always have wise ends to answer in its dispensations.

But do not talk, as in one of your former, of being a warning only[b]—You will be as excellent an example as ever you hoped to be, as well as a warning. And that will make your story, to all that shall come to know it, of double efficacy: for were it that such a merit as yours could not ensure to herself noble and generous usage from a libertine heart, who will expect any tolerable behaviour from men of his character?

If YOU think yourself inexcusable for taking a step that put you into the way of delusion, without any intention to go off with him, what must those giddy creatures think of themselves, who, without half your provocations and inducements, and without any regard to decorum, leap walls, drop from windows, and steal away from their parents' house to the seducer's bed, in the same day?

Again, if YOU are so ready to accuse yourself for dispensing with the prohibitions of the most unreasonable parents, which yet were but half-prohibitions at first, what ought those to do who wilfully shut their ears to the advice of the most

a See Letters 173 and 174.
b See p. 453.

reasonable; and that, perhaps, where apparent ruin, or undoubted inconvenience, is the consequence of the predetermined rashness?

And lastly, to all who will know your story, you will be an excellent *example* of watchfulness, and of that caution and reserve by which a prudent person who has been supposed to be a little misled endeavours to mend her error; and, never once losing sight of her duty, does all in her power to recover the path she has been rather driven out of than chosen to swerve from.

Come, come, my dearest friend, consider but these things; and steadily, without desponding, pursue your earnest purposes to amend what you think has been amiss; and it may not be a misfortune in the end that you have erred; especially as so little of your will was in your error.

And, indeed, I must say, that I use the words *misled* and *error* and such-like only in compliment to your own too ready self-accusations, and to the opinion of one to whom I owe duty: for I think in my conscience that every part of your conduct is defensible; and that those only are blameable who have no other way to clear themselves than by condemning you.

I expect, however, that such melancholy reflections as drop from your pen but too often will mingle with all your future pleasures, were you to marry Lovelace, and were he to make the best of husbands.

You was immensely happy, above the happiness of a mortal creature, before you knew him. Everybody almost worshipped you. Envy itself, which has of late reared up its venomous head against you, was awed by your superior worthiness into silence and admiration. You was the soul of every company where you visited: your elders have I seen declining to offer their opinions upon a subject till you had delivered yours; often to save themselves the mortification of retracting *theirs* when they heard *yours*. Yet, in all this, your sweetness of manners, your humility and affability caused the subscription everyone made to your sentiments, and to your superiority, to be equally unfeigned and unhesitating; for they saw that their applause and the preference they gave you to themselves subjected not themselves to insults, nor exalted you into any visible triumph over them; for you had always something to say, on every point you carried, that raised the yielding heart, and left everyone pleased and satisfied with themselves, though they carried not off the palm.

Your works were shown or referred to wherever fine works were talked of. Nobody had any but an inferior and second-hand praise for diligence, for economy, for reading, for writing, for memory, for facility in learning everything laudable, and even for the more envied graces of person and dress and an all-surpassing elegance in both, where you were known and those subjects talked of.

The poor blessed you every step you trod. The rich thought you their honour, and took a pride that they were not obliged to descend from their own class for an example that did credit to it.

Though all men wished for you and sought you, young as you was, yet, had not those who were brought to address you been encouraged out of sordid and spiteful views to attempt your presence, not one of them would have dared to lift up his eyes to you.

Thus happy in all about you, thus making happy all within your circle, could you think that nothing would happen to you to convince you that you were not to be exempted from the common lot?—to convince you that you were not *absolutely* perfect; and that you must not expect to pass through life without trial, temptation and misfortune?

Indeed, it must be owned that no trial, no temptation worthy of you, could have well attacked you sooner, or more effectually, than those heavy ones have done: for every common case you were superior to. It must be some man, or some worse spirit in the shape of one, that, formed on purpose, was to be sent to invade you; while as many other such spirits as there are persons in your family were permitted to take possession, severally, in one dark hour, of the heart of everyone of it, there to sit perching, perhaps, and directing every motion to the motions of the seducer without, in order to irritate, to provoke, to push you forward to meet him.

So, upon the whole, there seems as I have often said a kind of fate in your error, if an error; and this, perhaps, admitted for the sake of a better example to be collected from your *sufferings* than could have been given had you *never erred*: for, my dear, ADVERSITY is your SHINING-TIME: I see evidently that it must call forth graces and beauties that could not have been seen in a run of that prosperous fortune which attended you from your cradle till now; admirably as you became, and as we all thought greatly as you deserved, that prosperity.

All the matter is, the trial must be grievous to you. It is to *me*: it is to all who love you, and looked upon you as one set aloft to be admired and imitated, and not as a mark, as you have lately found, for envy to shoot its shafts at.

Let what I have written above have its due weight with you, my dear; and then, as warm imaginations are not without a mixture of enthusiasm, your Anna Howe, who on reperusal of it imagines it to be in a style superior to her usual style, will be ready to flatter herself that she has been in a manner inspired with the hints that have comforted and raised the dejected heart of her suffering friend; who, from such hard trials, in a bloom so tender, may find at times her spirits sunk too low to enable her to pervade the surrounding darkness which conceals from her the hopeful dawning of the better day which awaits her.

I will add no more at present, than that I am

Your ever-faithful and affectionate
ANNA HOWE

Letter 178: MISS CLARISSA HARLOWE TO MISS HOWE

Friday, May 12

I MUST be silent, my exalted friend, under praises that oppress my heart with a consciousness of not deserving them, at the same time that the generous design of those praises raises and comforts it: for it is a charming thing to stand high in the opinion of those we love; and to find that there are souls that can carry their friendships beyond accidents, beyond body and ties of blood. Whatever, my dearest creature, is *my* shining-time, the adversity of a friend is *yours*. And it would be almost a fault in me to regret those afflictions which give you an opportunity so gloriously to exert those qualities, which not only ennoble our sex, but dignify human nature.

But let me proceed to subjects less agreeable.

I am sorry you have reason to think Singleton's projects are not at an end. But who knows what the sailor had to propose?—Yet had any good been intended me, this method would hardly have been fallen upon.

Depend upon it, my dear, your letters shall be safe.

I have made a handle of Mr Lovelace's bold attempt and freedom, as I told you I would, to keep him ever since at distance, that I may have an opportunity to see the success of the application to my uncle, and to be at liberty to embrace any favourable overtures that may arise from it. Yet he has been very importunate, and twice brought Mr Mennell from Mrs Fretchville to talk about the house. If I should be obliged to make up with him again, I shall think I am always doing myself a spite.

As to what you mention of his newly-detected crimes, and your advice to attach Dorcas, and to come at some of his letters; these things will require more or less of my attention, as I may hope favour or not from my uncle Harlowe.

I am sorry for poor Hannah's continued illness. Pray, my dear, inform yourself, for me, whether she wants anything that befits her case.

I will not close this letter till tomorrow is over; for I am resolved to go to church; and this as well for the sake of my duty, as to see if I am at liberty to go out when I please without being attended or accompanied.

Sunday, May 14

I HAVE not been able to avoid a short debate with Mr Lovelace. I had ordered a coach to the door. When I had notice that it was come, I went out of my chamber to go to it; but met him dressed on the stairs head, with a book in his hand, but without his hat and sword—He asked with an air very solemn, yet respectful, if I were going abroad. I told him I was. He desired leave to attend me, if I were going to church. I refused him. And then he complained heavily of my treatment of him, and declared that he would not live such another week as the past, for the world.

I owned to him very frankly, that I had made an application to my friends; and that I was resolved to keep myself to myself till I knew the issue of it.

He coloured, and seemed surprised. But checking himself in something he was going to say, he pleaded my danger from Singleton, and again desired to attend me.

And then he told me that Mrs Fretchville had desired to continue a fortnight longer in the house. She found, said he, that I was unable to determine about entering upon it; and now who knows when such a vapourish creature will come to a resolution? This, madam, has been an unhappy week; for had I not stood upon such bad terms with you, you might have been now mistress of that house; and probably had my cousin Montague, if not my aunt Lawrance, actually with you.

And so, sir, taking all you say for granted, your cousin Montague cannot come to Mrs Sinclair's? What, pray, is her objection to Mrs Sinclair's? Is this house fit for me to live in a month or two, and not fit for any of your relations for a few days?—And Mrs Fretchville has taken more time too—And so, pushing by him, I hurried downstairs.

He called to Dorcas to bring him his sword and hat; and following me down into the passage, placed himself between me and the door; and again besought me to permit him to attend me.

Mrs Sinclair came out at that instant, and asked me if I did not choose a dish of chocolate?

I wish, Mrs Sinclair, said I, you would take this man in with you to your chocolate. I don't know whether I am at liberty to stir out without his leave or not—Then turning to him, I asked, if he kept me there his prisoner?

Dorcas just then bringing him his sword and hat, he opened the street door, and taking my resisting hand led me, in a very obsequious manner, to the coach. People passing by, stopped, stared, and whispered—But he is so graceful in his person and dress, that he generally takes every eye.

I was uneasy to be so gazed at; and he stepped in after me, and the coachman drove to St Paul's.

He was very full of assiduities all the way, while I was as reserved as possible: and when I returned, dined, as I had done the greatest part of the week, by myself.

He told me, upon my resolving to do so, that although he would continue his passive observance till I knew the issue of my application, yet I must expect that then I should never rest one moment till I had fixed his happy day: for that his very soul was fretted with my slights, resentments, and delays.

A wretch! when I can say, to my infinite regret, on a *double* account, that all he complains of is owing to himself!

Oh that I may have good tidings from my uncle!

Adieu, my dearest friend!—This shall lie ready for an exchange, as I hope for one tomorrow from you that will decide, as I may say, the destiny of

Your CLARISSA HARLOWE

Letter 179: MISS HOWE TO MRS JUDITH NORTON

Thursday, May 11

Good Mrs Norton,

CANNOT you, without naming *me* as an adviser who am hated by the family, contrive a way to let Mrs Harlowe know that in an accidental conversation with me you had been assured, that my beloved friend pines after a reconciliation with her relations: that she has hitherto, in hopes of it, refused to enter into any obligations that shall be in the least a hindrance to it: that she would fain avoid giving Mr Lovelace a right to make her family uneasy in relation to her grandfather's estate: that all she wishes for still is to be indulged in her choice of a single life, and, on that condition, would make her father's pleasure hers with regard to that estate: that Mr Lovelace is continually pressing her to marry him; and all his friends likewise. But that I am sure she has so little liking to the man, because of his faulty morals, and of her relations' antipathy to him, that if she had any hope given her of a reconciliation, she would forgo all thoughts of him and put herself into her father's protection. But that their resolution must be speedy; for otherwise she would find herself obliged to give way to his pressing entreaties; and it might then be out of her power to prevent disagreeable litigations.

I do assure you, Mrs Norton, upon my honour, that our dearest friend knows nothing of this procedure of mine. And therefore it is proper to acquaint you, in confidence, with my grounds for it—These are they:

She had desired me to let Mr Hickman drop hints to the above effect to her uncle Harlowe; but indirectly as from *himself*, lest, if the application should not be attended with success, and Mr Lovelace (who already takes it ill that he has so little of her favour) come to know it, she may be deprived of every protection, and be perhaps subjected to great inconveniences from so haughty a spirit.

Having this authority from her, and being very solicitous about the success of the application, I thought that if the weight of so good a wife, mother, and sister, as Mrs Harlowe is known to be, were thrown into the same scale with that of Mr John Harlowe (supposing he *could* be engaged), it could hardly fail of making a due impression.

Mr Hickman will see Mr Harlowe tomorrow: by that time you may see Mrs Harlowe. If Mr Hickman finds the old gentleman favourable, he will tell him that you will have seen Mrs Harlowe upon the same account; and will advise him to join in consultation with her how best to proceed to melt the most obdurate hearts in the world.

This is the fair state of the matter, and my true motive for writing to you. I leave all therefore to your discretion: and most heartily wish success to it; being of opinion that Mr Lovelace cannot possibly deserve our admirable friend. Nor, indeed, know I the man who can.

Pray acquaint me, by a line, of the result of your kind interposition. If it prove not such as may be reasonably hoped for, our dear friend shall know nothing of this step from me; and pray let her not from you. For, in that case, it would only give deeper grief to a heart already too much afflicted. I am, dear and worthy Mrs Norton,

Your true friend,
ANNA HOWE

Letter 180: MRS NORTON TO MISS HOWE

Saturday, May 13

Dear Madam,

MY heart is almost broken to be obliged to let you know, that such is the situation of things in the family of my ever dear Miss Harlowe, that there can be at present no success expected from any application in her favour. Her poor mother is to be pitied. I have a most affecting letter from her; but must not communicate it to you; and she forbids me to let it be known that she writes upon the subject, although she is compelled, as it were, to do it for the ease of her own heart. I mention it therefore in confidence.

I hope in God that my beloved Miss has preserved her honour inviolate. I hope there is not a man breathing who could attempt a sacrilege so detestable. I have no apprehension of a failure in a virtue so established. God for ever keep so pure a heart out of the reach of surprises and violence! Ease, dear madam, I beseech you, my over-anxious heart, by one line by the bearer, although but by one line, to acquaint me as surely you can that her honour is unsullied! If it be not, adieu to all the comforts this life can give: since none will it be able to afford

To the poor JUDITH NORTON

Letter 181: MISS HOWE TO MRS JUDITH NORTON

Saturday evening, May 13

Dear good Woman,

YOUR beloved's honour is inviolate!—*Must* be inviolate! And *will* be so, in spite of men and devils. Could I have had hope of a reconciliation, all my view was, that she should not have had this man!—All that can be said now is, she must run the risk of a bad husband: she of whom no man living is worthy.

You pity her mother!—so don't *I!*—I pity nobody that puts it out of their power to show maternal love and humanity, in order to patch up for themselves a precarious and sorry quiet, which every blast of wind shall disturb!

I hate tyrants in every form and shape. But paternal and maternal tyrants are the worst of all: for they can have no bowels.

I repeat, that I pity *none* of them!—My beloved and your beloved *only* deserves pity. She had never been in the hands of this man, but for them. She is quite blameless. You don't know all her story. Were I to tell you she had no intention to go off with this man, it would avail her nothing. It would only condemn those who drove her to extremities; and him, who now must be her refuge. I am

Your sincere friend and servant,
ANNA HOWE

Letter 182: MRS HARLOWE TO MRS JUDITH NORTON

(Not communicated till the history came to be compiled)

Saturday, May 13

I RETURN an answer in writing, as I promised, to your communication. But take no notice that I do write, either to my Bella's Betty, who I understand sometimes visits you, or to the poor wretch herself; nor to anybody. I charge you don't. My heart is full. Writing may give some vent to my griefs, and perhaps I may write what lies most upon my heart, without confining myself strictly to the present subject.

You know how dear this ungrateful creature ever was to us all. You know how sincerely we joined with every one of those who ever had seen her, or conversed with her, to praise and admire her; and exceeded in our praise even the bounds of that modesty which, because she was our own, should have restrained us; being of opinion, that to have been silent in the praise of so apparent a merit must rather have argued blindness or affectation in us, than that we should incur the censure of vain partiality to our own.

When therefore anybody congratulated us on such a daughter, we received their congratulations without any diminution. If it was said, You are happy in this child, we owned that no parents ever were happier *in* a child. If more particularly, they praised her dutiful behaviour to us, we said, She knew not how to offend. If it was said, Miss Clarissa Harlowe has a wit and penetration beyond her years; we, instead of disallowing it, would add—And a judgement no less extraordinary than her wit. If her prudence was praised, and a forethought which everyone saw supplied what only years and experience gave to others—Nobody need to scruple taking lessons from Miss Clarissa Harlowe, was our proud answer.

Forgive me, oh forgive me, my dear Norton—but I know you will—for yours, when good, was this child, and your glory as well as mine!

But have you not heard strangers, as she passed to and from church, stop to praise the angel of a creature, as they called her; when it was enough for those who knew who she was, to cry, *Why, it is Miss Clarissa Harlowe!*—As if everybody were obliged to know, or to have heard of Miss Clarissa Harlowe, and of her excellencies. While, accustomed to praise, it was too familiar to her to cause her to alter either her look or her pace.

For my own part, I could not stifle a pleasure that had perhaps a faulty vanity for its foundation, whenever I was spoken of, or addressed to, as the mother of so sweet a child: Mr Harlowe and I, all the time, loving each other the better for the share each had in such a daughter.

Still, still indulge the fond, the overflowing heart of a mother! I could dwell for ever upon the remembrance of what she *was*, would but that remembrance banish from my mind what she *is!*

In her bosom, young as she was, could I repose all my griefs—sure of receiving from *her* prudence, advice as well as comfort: and both insinuated in so humble, in so dutiful a manner, that it was impossible to take those exceptions which the distance of years and character between a mother and a daughter would, from any other daughter, have made one apprehensive of. She was our glory when abroad, our delight when at home. Everybody was even covetous of her company; and we grudged her to our brothers Harlowe, and to our sister and brother Hervey—No other contention among us, then, but who should be favoured by her next—No chiding ever knew she from us, but the chiding of lovers, when she was for shutting herself up too long together from us, in pursuit of those charming amusements and useful employments which, however, the whole family was the better for.

Our other children had reason, good children as they always were, to think themselves neglected. But they likewise were so sensible of their sister's superiority, and of the honour she reflected upon the whole family, that they confessed themselves eclipsed without envying the eclipser. Indeed there was not anybody so equal with her, in their own opinions, as to envy what all aspired but to emulate— The dear creature, you know, my Norton, gave an eminence to us all. And now that she has left us, so disgracefully left us! we are stripped of our ornament, and are but a common family!

Then her acquirements. Her skill in music, her fine needleworks, her elegance in dress; for which she was so much admired, that the neighbouring ladies used to say that they need not fetch fashions from London; since whatever Miss Clarissa Harlowe wore was the *best* fashion, because her choice of *natural* beauties set those of *art* far behind them. Her genteel ease, and fine turn of person; her deep reading; and these, joined to her open manners, and her cheerful modesty—Oh my good Norton, what a sweet child was *once* my Clary Harlowe!

This, and more, *you* knew her to be: for many of her excellencies were owing to yourself; and with the milk you gave her, you gave her what no other nurse in the world could give her.

And do you think, my worthy woman, do you think that the wilful lapse of such a child is to be forgiven? Can she herself think that she deserves not the severest punishment for the abuse of such talents as were entrusted to her?

Her fault was a fault of premeditation, of cunning, of contrivance. She has deceived everybody's expectations. Her whole sex, as well as the family she sprung from, is disgraced by it.

Would anybody ever have believed that such a young creature as this, who had by her advice saved even her over-lively friend from marrying a fop and a libertine, would herself have gone off with one of the vilest and most notorious of libertines? A man whose character she knew; and knew to be worse than his she saved her friend from; whose vices she was warned of: one who had had her brother's life in his hands; and who constantly set our whole family at defiance.

Think for me, my good Norton; think what my unhappiness must be, both as a wife and a mother. What restless days, what sleepless nights; yet my own rankling anguish endeavoured to be smoothed over to soften the anguish of fiercer spirits, and to keep them from blazing out to further mischief. Oh this naughty, naughty girl! who *knew* so well what she did; and who could look so far into consequences, that we thought she would have died, rather than have done as she has done!

Her known character for prudence leaves no plea for excuse. How then can I offer to plead for her, if through motherly indulgence I would forgive her myself?—And have we not, moreover, suffered all the disgrace that can befall us? Has not she?

If *now* she has so little liking to his morals, had she not reason *before* to have *as* little? Or has she suffered by them in her own person?—Oh my good woman, I doubt—I doubt—Will not the character of the man make one doubt an angel, if once in his power? The world will think the worst. I am told it *does*. So likewise her father fears; her brother hears; and what can I do?

Our *antipathy* to him she knew before, as well as his character. These therefore cannot be new motives without a new reason—Oh my dear Mrs Norton, how shall *I*, how can *you*, support ourselves under the apprehensions that these thoughts lead to, of my Clary Harlowe, and your Clary Harlowe!

He continually pressing her, you say, *to marry him. His friends likewise.* She has reason, no doubt she has reason, for this application to us: and her crime is glossed over to bring her to us with new disgrace!—Whither, whither, does one guilty step lead the misguided heart!—And now truly, to save a stubborn spirit, we are only to be *sounded*, that the application may be retracted or denied!

Upon the whole: were I inclined to plead for her, it is *now* the most improper of all times. *Now* that my brother Harlowe has discouraged (as he last night came hither on purpose to tell us) Mr Hickman's insinuated application; and been applauded for it. *Now*, that my brother Antony is intending to carry his great fortune, through her fault, into another family—she expecting, no doubt, herself to be put into her grandfather's estate, in consequence of a reconciliation and as a reward for her fault: and insisting still upon terms that she offered before, and were rejected—not through my fault, I am sure, rejected.

From all these things, you will return such an answer as the case requires—It might cost me the peace of my whole life, at this time to move for her. God forgive her!—If I do, nobody else will. And let it be for your own sake, as well as mine, a secret that you and I have entered upon this subject. And I desire you not to touch upon it again but by particular permission: for, Oh my dear good woman, it sets my heart a-bleeding in as many streams as there are veins in it!

Yet think me not impenetrable by a proper contrition and remorse! But what a torment is it to have a will without a power!

Adieu! adieu! God give us both comfort; and to the once dear—the ever-dear creature (for can a mother forget her child?), repentance, deep repentance! And as little suffering as may befit his blessed will, and her grievous fault, prays

Your real friend,
CHARLOTTE HARLOWE

Letter 183: MISS HOWE TO MISS CLARISSA HARLOWE

Sunday, May 14

How it is now, my dear, between you and Mr Lovelace, I cannot tell. But wicked as the man is, I am afraid he must be your lord and master.

I called him by several very hard names in my last. I had but just heard some of his vilenesses when I sat down to write, so my indignation was raised. But on inquiry and recollection, I find that the facts laid to his charge were all of them committed some time ago; not since he has had *strong* hopes of your favour. This is saying something for him. His generous behaviour to the innkeeper's daughter is a more recent instance to his credit; to say nothing of the universal good character he has as a kind landlord. And then I approve much of the motion he made to put you in possession of Mrs Fretchville's house, while he continues at the other widow's, till you agree that one house shall hold you. I wish this was done. Be sure you embrace this offer, if you do not soon meet at the altar, and get one of his cousins with you.

Were you once married, I should think you cannot be *very* unhappy, though you may not be so happy with him as you deserve to be. The stake he has in his country, and his reversions[1]: the care he takes of his affairs; his freedom from obligation; nay, his pride, with your merit, must be a tolerable security for you, I should think. Though particulars of his wickedness, as they come to my knowledge, hurt and incense me; yet, after all, when I give myself time to reflect, all that I have heard of him to his disadvantage was comprehended in the general character given of him long ago by his uncle's and his own dismissed bailiff,[a] and which was confirmed to you by Mrs Greme.[b]

You can have nothing therefore, I think, to be deeply concerned about, but his future good, and the bad example he may hereafter set to his own family. These indeed are very just concerns: but were you to *leave* him now, either *with* or *without* his consent, his fortune and alliances so considerable, his person and address so engaging (everyone excusing you now on those accounts, and because of your relations' follies), it would have a very ill appearance for your reputation. I cannot therefore, on the most deliberate consideration, advise you to think of that while you have no reason to doubt his honour. May eternal vengeance pursue the villain if he gives room for an apprehension of this nature!

a   p. 50.
b   p. 397.

Yet his teasing ways are intolerable: his acquiescence with your slight delays, and his resignedness to the distance you now keep him at (for a fault so much slighter, as he must think, than the punishment), are unaccountable. He doubts your love of *him*, that is very probable; but you have reason to be surprised at *his* want of ardour; a blessing so great within his *reach*, as I may say.

By the time you have read to this place, you will have no doubt of what has been the issue of the conference between the *two gentlemen*. I am equally shocked, and enraged against them all: against them *all*, I say; for I have tried your good Norton's weight with your mother, to the same purpose as the gentleman sounded your uncle—Never were there such determined brutes in the world! Why should I mince the matter? Yet would I fain, methinks, make an exception for your mother.

Your uncle will have it that you are ruined. 'He can believe everything bad of a creature who could run away with a man—with such a one especially as Lovelace. They all *expected* applications from you, when some heavy distress had fallen upon you—But they were all resolved not to stir an inch in your favour; no, not to save your life!'

My dearest soul! resolve to assert your right. Claim your own, and go and live upon it as you ought. Then, if you marry not, how will the wretches creep to you for your reversionary dispositions!

You were accused (as in your aunt's letter) 'of premeditation and contrivance in your escape'. Instead of pitying *you*, the mediating person was called upon 'to pity *them*; who once, [your uncle] said, doted upon you: who took no joy but in your presence: who devoured your words as you spoke them: who trod over again your footsteps as you walked before them'—And I know not what of this sort.

Upon the whole, it is now evident to me, and so it must be to you when you read this letter, that you have but one choice. And the sooner you make it the better—Shall we suppose that it is not in your power to make it?—I cannot have patience to suppose that.

I am concerned, methinks, to know how you will do to condescend, now you see you must be his, after you have kept him at such a distance; and for the revenge his pride may put him upon taking for it. But let me tell you, that if my going up and sharing fortunes with you will prevent such a noble creature from stooping too low, much more were it likely to prevent your ruin, I would not hesitate a moment about it. What's the whole world to me, weighed against such a friendship as ours—Think you that any of the enjoyments of this life could be enjoyments to me, were such a friend as you to be involved in calamities which I could either relieve her from, or alleviate, by giving them up? And what in saying this, and acting up to it, do I offer you, but the fruits of a friendship your worth has created?

Excuse my warmth of expression. The warmth of my heart wants none. I am enraged at your relations; for, bad as what I have mentioned is, I have not told you all; nor now, perhaps, ever will—I am angry at my own mother's narrowness of mind and adherence to old notions indiscriminately—And I am exasperated against your foolish, your low-vanitied Lovelace!—But let us stoop to take the wretch as he is, and make the best of him, since you are destined to stoop to keep grovellers and worldlings in countenance. He has not been guilty of direct indecency to you. Nor *dare* he. Not so much of a devil as that comes to neither!—Had he such villainous intentions, so much in his power as you are, they would have shown themselves before now to such a penetrating and vigilant eye, and to such a pure heart as yours. Let us save the wretch then, if we can, though we soil our fingers in lifting him up from his dirt.

There is yet, to a person of your fortune and independence, a good deal to do, if you enter upon those terms which *ought* to be entered upon. I don't find that he has once talked of settlements; much less of the licence. It is hard! But as your evil destiny has thrown you out of all other protection and mediation, you must be father, mother, uncle to yourself; and enter upon the requisite points for yourself. Indeed you must. Your situation requires it. What room for delicacy now? Or would you have *me* write to the wretch? Yet that would be the same thing as if you were to write yourself. Yet write you should, I think, if you cannot speak. But speaking is certainly best: for words leave no traces; they pass as breath; and mingle with air, and may be explained with latitude. But the pen is a witness on record.

I know the gentleness of your spirit; I know the laudable pride of your heart; and the just notion you have of the dignity of our sex in these delicate points. But once more, all this is nothing now. Your honour is concerned that the dignity I speak of should not be stood upon.

'Mr Lovelace,' would I say; yet hate the foolish fellow for his low, his stupid pride, in wishing to triumph over the dignity of his own wife—'I am deprived, by your means, of every friend I have in the world. In what light am I to look upon *you*? I have well considered of everything. You have made some people, much against my liking, think me a *wife*: others know I am *not* married; nor do I desire anybody should believe I am. Do you think your being here in the same house with me can be to my reputation? You talk to me of Mrs Fretchville's house— (This will bring him to renew his last discourse on that subject, if he does not revive it of himself.) [—] If Mrs Fretchville knows not her own mind, what is her house to me? You talked of bringing up your cousin Montague to bear me company: if my brother's schemes be your pretence for not going yourself to *fetch her*, you can *write* to her—I insist upon bringing these two points to an issue: off or on ought to be indifferent to *me*, if so to *them*.'

Such a declaration must bring all forward. There are twenty ways, my dear, that you would find out to advise another how to act in your circumstances. He will disdain, from his native insolence, to have it thought he has *anybody* to consult. Well then, will he not be obliged to declare himself? And if he *does*, no delays on your side, I beseech you. Give him the day. Let it be a short one. It would be derogating from your own merit, and *honour* too let me tell you, even although he should *not* be so explicit as he ought to be, to seem but to doubt his meaning; and to wait for that explanation which I should for ever despise him for if he makes necessary. Twice already have you, my dear, if not oftener, *modestied* away such opportunities as you ought not to have slipped—As to settlements, if they come not in naturally, e'en leave them to his own justice, and to the justice of his family. And there's an end of the matter.

This is *my* advice. Mend it as circumstances offer, and follow *your own*. But indeed, my dear, this, or something like it, would I do. As witness

Your ANNA HOWE

(Enclosed in the above)

I MUST trouble you with my concerns, though your own are so heavy upon you—A piece of news I have to tell you. Your uncle Antony is disposed to marry—With whom, think you?—With my mamma. True indeed. Your family know it. All is laid with redoubled malice at your door. And there the *old soul* himself lays it.

Take no notice of this intelligence, not so much as in your letters to me, for fear of accidents.

I think it can't do. But were I to provoke my mother, that might afford a pretence. Else I should have been with you before now, I fancy.

The first likelihood that appears to me of encouragement, I dismiss Hickman, that's certain. If my mother disoblige me in so important an article, I shan't think of obliging her in such another. It is impossible, surely, that the desire of popping me off to that honest man can be with such a view.

I repeat, that it cannot come to anything. But these *widows*—Then such a love in us all, both old and young, of being courted and admired!—And so irresistible to their *elderships* to be flattered, that all power is not over with them; but that they may still class and prank it with their daughters. It vexed me heartily to have her tell me of this proposal with self-complaisant simperings; and yet she affected to speak of it as if she had no intention to encourage it.

These antiquated bachelors, old before they think themselves so, imagine that when they have once persuaded *themselves*, they have nothing else to do but to make their minds known to the lady. His overgrown fortune is indeed a bait—a tempting one. A saucy daughter to be got rid of! The memory of the father of that daughter not precious enough to weigh!—But let him advance if he dare—Let her encourage—But I hope she won't.

Excuse me, my dear. I am nettled. They have fearfully rumpled my gorget. You'll think me faulty. So I won't put my name to this separate paper. Other hands may resemble mine. You did not see me write it.

Letter 184: MISS CLARISSA HARLOWE TO MISS HOWE

Monday, p.m. May 15

Now indeed is it evident, my best, my only friend, that I have but one choice to make. And now do I find that I have carried my resentment against this man too far; since now I am to appear as if under an obligation to his patience with me for conduct that perhaps he will think, if not humoursome and childish, plainly demonstrative of my little esteem of him; of but a secondary esteem at least, where before his pride rather than his merit had made him expect a *first*. Oh my dear!—to be under obligation to, and to be cast upon a man, that is not a *generous* man!—that is, indeed, a *cruel* man!—that is capable of creating a distress to a young creature, who by her evil destiny is thrown into his power; and then of *enjoying* it, as I may say! (I verily think I may say so, of this savage!)—What a fate is mine!

You give me, my dear, good advice as to the peremptory manner in which I ought to treat him: but do you consider to whom it is that you give that advice?

The occasion for it should never have been given by *me*, of all creatures; for I am unequal, utterly unequal to it!—What, *I*, to challenge a man for a husband!—*I*, to exert myself to quicken the delayer in his resolutions! And, having lost an opportunity, to begin to try to recall it, as *from myself*, and *for myself!*—to *threaten* him, as I may say, into the marriage-state!—Oh my dear! if this be right to be done, how difficult is it, where modesty and self (or where pride, if you please) is concerned to do that right? Or, to express myself in your words, to be father, mother, uncle, to myself!—Especially where one thinks a triumph over one is intended. Do, my dear, advise me, persuade me, to renounce the man for ever: and then I will for ever renounce him!

You say you have tried Mrs Norton's weight with my mamma—Bad as the returns are which my application by Mr Hickman has met with, you tell me you have not acquainted me with all the bad; nor now, perhaps, ever will. But why so, my dear? What *is* the bad, what *can* be the bad, which now you will never tell me of?—What worse, than renounce me! and for ever! 'My uncle, you say, believes me ruined: he declares that he can believe everything bad of a creature who could run away with a man: and they have all made a resolution not to stir an inch in my favour; no, not to save my life.'

Have you worse than this, my dear, behind?—Surely my father has not renewed his dreadful malediction!—Surely, if so, my mamma has not joined in it! Have my uncles given it their sanction, and made it a family act! What, my dear, is the worst, that you will leave for ever unrevealed?

Oh Lovelace! why comest thou not just now, while these black prospects are before me? For now, couldst thou look into my heart, wouldst thou see a distress worthy of thy barbarous triumph!

I WAS forced to quit my pen.

And you say you have tried Mrs Norton's weight with my mamma?

What *is* done, cannot be helped: but I wish you had not taken any step, in a matter so very concerning to me, without first consulting me—Forgive me, my dear—but that high-souled and noble friendship which you avow with so obliging, and so uncommon a warmth, at the same time that it is the subject of my grateful admiration, is no less, because of its fervour, the ground of my apprehension!

Well, but now to look forward: you are of opinion that I must be his; and that I cannot leave him with reputation to myself, whether with or without his consent. I must, if so, make the best of the bad matter.

He went out in the morning; intending not to return to dinner, unless (as he sent me word) I would admit him to dine with me.

I excused myself. The man whose anger is now to be of such high importance to me was, it seems, displeased.

As he, as well as I, expected that I should receive a letter from you this day by Collins, I suppose he will not be long before he returns; and then, possibly, he is to be mighty stately, mighty *mannish*, mighty *coy*, if you please! And then must I be very humble, very submissive, and try to whine myself into his good graces: with downcast eye, if not by speech, beg his forgiveness for the distance I have so perversely kept him at!—Yes, I warrant you!—But I'll see how this behaviour will sit upon me!—You have always rallied me upon my meekness, I think! Well then, I'll try if I can be still meeker, shall I!—Oh my dear!—

But let me sit with my hands before me, all patience, all resignation; for I think I hear him coming up—Or shall I roundly accost him, in the words, in the form, you, my dear, have prescribed?

He is come in—He has sent to me, all impatience in his aspect, Dorcas says—
But I cannot, cannot see him!

Monday night

THE contents of your letter, and my own heavy reflections, rendered me
incapable of seeing this expecting man!—The first word he asked Dorcas was, If
I had received a letter since he had been out?—She told me this; and her answer,
That I had; and was fasting, and had been in tears ever since.

He sent to desire an interview with me.

I answered by her, That I was not very well. In the morning, if better, I would
see him as soon as he pleased.

Very humble! was it not, my dear?—Yet he was too royal to take it for humility;
for Dorcas told me he rubbed one side of his face impatiently; and said a rash
word, and was out of humour; stalking about the room.

Half an hour after, he sent again; desiring very earnestly that I would admit him
to supper with me. He would enter upon no subjects of conversation but what I
should lead to.

So I should have been at *liberty*, you see, to *court him!*

I again desired to be excused.

Indeed, my dear, my eyes were swelled: I was very low-spirited; and could not
think of entering all at once, after several days' distance, into the freedom of
conversation which my friends' utter rejection of me, as well as your opinion, have
made necessary.

He sent up to tell me, that as he heard I was fasting, if I would promise to eat
some chicken which Mrs Sinclair had ordered for supper, he would acquiesce—
Very kind in his anger!—Is he not?

I promised him. Can I be more *preparatively* condescending?—How happy, I'll
warrant you, if I may meet him in a kind and forgiving humour!

I hate myself!—But I won't be insulted. Indeed I won't! for all this.

Letter 185: MISS CLARISSA HARLOWE TO MISS HOWE

Tuesday, May 16

I THINK once more we seem to be in a kind of train; but through a storm. I will
give you the particulars.

I heard him in the dining-room at five in the morning. I had rested very ill, and
was up too: but opened not my door till six: when Dorcas brought me his request
for my company.

He approached me, and taking my hand as I entered the dining-room, I went
not to bed, madam, till two, yet slept not a wink. For God's sake, torment me not,
as you have done for a week past.

He paused. I was silent.

At first, proceeded he, I thought your resentment of a mere unavailing curiosity
could not be deep; and that it would go off of itself. But when I found it was to be
kept up till you knew the success of some new overtures which you had made, and
which complied with, might have deprived me of you for ever; how, madam, could

I support myself under the thoughts of having, with such an union of interests, made so little impression upon your mind in my favour?

He paused again. I was still silent. He went on.

I acknowledge that I have a proud heart, madam. I cannot but hope for some instances of previous and preferable favour from the lady I am ambitious to call mine; and that her choice of me should not appear, not *flagrantly* appear, directed by the perverseness of her selfish persecutors, and my irreconcilable enemies.

More to the same purpose he said. You know, my dear, the room he had given me to recriminate upon him in twenty instances. I did not spare him: but I need not repeat those instances to you. Every one of these instances, I told him, convinced me of his *pride*, indeed, but not of his *merit*. I confessed that I had as much pride as himself; although I hoped it was of another kind than that he so readily avowed. But that if he had the least mixture in *his* of the laudable pride (a pride worthy of his birth, of his family, and of his fortune), he should rather wish, I would presume to say, to promote *mine*, than either to suppress, or to regret that I had it: that *hence* it was that I thought it beneath me to disown what had been my motives for declining, for some days past, any conversation with him, or visit from Mr Mennell, that might lead to points out of my power to determine upon, until I heard from my uncle Harlowe; whom, I confessed, I had caused to be sounded whether I might be favoured with his interest to obtain for me a reconciliation with my friends, upon terms which I had caused to be proposed to him.

He knew not, he said, and supposed must not presume to ask, what these terms were. But he could but too well guess at them; and that he was to have been the preliminary sacrifice. But I must allow him to say, that as much as he admired the nobleness of my sentiments in general, and in particular that *laudable* pride in me which I had spoken of; he wished that he could compliment me with such an uniformity in it, as should have set me as much above all submission to minds implacable and unreasonable (he hoped he might, without offence, say that my brother's and sister's were such), as it had above all favour and condescension to him.

Duty and *nature*, sir, call upon me to make the submissions you speak of: there is a father, there is a mother, there are uncles, in the one case, to justify and demand those submissions—What, pray, sir, can be pleaded for the *condescension*, as you call it?—Will you say your merits, either with regard to *them*, or to *myself*, may?

This to be said, after the persecutions of those relations! After what you have suffered! After what you have made me hope! Let me ask you, madam (we talked of *pride* just now), what sort of pride must *his* be, which could dispense with inclination and preference in his lady's part of it?—What must be that love—

Love, sir! who talks of *love?*—Was not *merit* the thing we were talking of?— Have *I* ever professed, have *I* ever required of *you* professions of a passion of that nature? But there is no end of these debatings, sir; each *so* faultless, each *so* full of self—

I do not think myself *faultless*, madam—But—

But what, sir!—Would you evermore argue with me, as if you were a child?— Seeking palliations, and making promises?—Promises of what, sir? Of being in future the man it is a shame a gentleman is not?—Of being the man—

Good God! interrupted he, with eyes lifted up, if *thou* wert to be thus severe—

Well, well, sir (impatiently)—I need only to observe that all this vast difference in sentiments shows how unpaired our minds are—So let us—

Let us *what*, madam!—My soul is rising into tumults! And he looked so wildly, that it startled me a good deal—Let us *what*, madam—

Why, sir, let us resolve to quit every regard for each other—Nay, flame not out—I am a poor weak-minded creature in some things: but where what I *should be*, or not deserve to live if I *am not*, is in the question, I have [a] great and invincible spirit, or my own conceit betrays me—Let us resolve to quit every regard for each other that is more than civil. *This* you may depend upon; you may, if it will fuel your pride, gratify it with this assurance; that I will never marry any other man. I have seen enough of your sex; at least of *you*. A single life shall ever be *my* choice—while I will leave you at liberty to pursue *your own*.

Indifference, worse than indifference! said he, in a passion—

Interrupting him—Indifference let it be—You have not, in *my* opinion at least, deserved it should be other: if you have in *your own*, you have cause, at least your *pride* has, to hate me for misjudging you—

Dearest, dearest creature! (snatching my hand with wildness), let me beseech you to be *uniformly* noble! *Civil regards*, madam!—*Civil regards!*—Can you so expect to narrow and confine such a passion as mine!—

Such a passion as yours, Mr Lovelace, *deserves* to be narrowed and confined—It is either the passion *you* do not think it; or *I* do not—I question whether your mind is capable of being *so* narrowed and *so* widened, as is necessary to make it be what I wish it to be. Lift up your hands and your eyes, sir, in that emphatical silent wonder, as you please: But what does it express, what does it convince me of, but that we are not born for one another?

By his soul, he said, and grasped my hand with an eagerness that hurt it, we *were* born for one another. I *must* be his—I *should* be his (and put his other arm round me), although his damnation were to be the purchase!—

I was terrified!—Let me leave you—or begone from me, sir—Is the passion you boast to be thus shockingly declared!

You must not go, madam!—You must *not* leave me in anger—

I will return—I will return—When you can be less violent—less shocking.

And he let me go.

The man quite frighted me; insomuch that when I got into my chamber, I found a sudden flow of tears a great relief to me.

In half an hour, he sent a little billet expressing his concern for the vehemence of his behaviour, and praying to see me.

I went—Because I could not help myself, I went.

He was full of his excuses—Oh my dear, what would you, even *you*, do with such a man as this; and in my situation?

It was very possible for him now, he said, to account for the workings of a frenzical disorder. For his part, he was near distraction. All last week to suffer as he had suffered; and now to talk of *civil regards* only, when he had hoped from the nobleness of my mind—

Hope what you will, interrupted I; I must insist upon it that our minds are by no means suited to each other. You have brought me into difficulties. I am deserted of every friend but Miss Howe. My true sentiments I will not conceal. It is against my will that I must submit to owe protection from a brother's projects, which Miss Howe thinks are not given over, to you, who have brought me into these straits; *not* with my own concurrence brought me into them; remember that—

I do remember that, madam! So often reminded, how can I forget it?

Yet I *will* owe to you this protection, if it be necessary, in the earnest hope that you will *shun* rather than *seek* mischief, if any further inquiry after me be made. But what hinders you from leaving me?—Cannot I send to you? The Widow Fretchville, it is plain, knows not her own mind: the people here indeed are civiller every day than other: but I had rather have lodgings more agreeable to my circumstances. I best know what will suit them; and am resolved not to be obliged to anybody. If you leave me, I will take a civil leave of these people, and retire to some one of the neighbouring villages, and there, secreting myself, wait my cousin Morden's arrival with patience.

He presumed, he told me, from what I said, that my application to my relations was unsuccessful: that therefore he hoped I would give him leave now to mention the terms in the nature of settlements, which he had long intended to propose to me; and which having till now delayed to do, through accidents not proceeding from himself, he had thoughts of urging to me the moment I entered upon my new house; and upon finding myself as independent in *appearance* as I was in *fact*. Permit me, madam, to propose these matters to you—not with an expectation of your immediate answer; but for your consideration.

Were not hesitation, a self-felt glow, a downcast eye, more than enough? Your advice was too much in my head: I hesitated.

He urged on upon my silence: he would call God to witness to the justice, nay to the *generosity* of his intentions to me, if I would be so good as to hear what he had to propose to me, as to settlements.

Could not the man have fallen into the subject without this *parade*? Many a point, you know, *is* refused, and *ought to be* refused, if leave be asked to introduce it; and when once refused, the refusal must in honour be adhered to—whereas, had it been *slid* in upon one, as I may say, it might have merited further consideration. If such a man as he knows not this, who should?

I thought myself obliged, though not to depart from this subject entirely, yet to give it a more diffuse turn; in order, on the one hand, to save myself the mortification of appearing too ready in my compliance, after such a distance as had been between us; and on the other, to avoid (in pursuance of your advice) the necessity of giving him such a repulse as might again throw us out of the course.

A cruel alternative to be reduced to!

You talk of *generosity*, Mr Lovelace, said I; and you talk of *justice*; perhaps without having considered the force of the words, in the sense you use them on this occasion. Let me tell you what *generosity* is, in my sense of the word—TRUE GENEROSITY is not confined to pecuniary instances: it is *more* than politeness: it is *more* than good faith: it is *more* than honour: it is *more* than *justice:* since all these are but duties, and what a worthy mind cannot dispense with. But TRUE GENEROSITY is greatness of soul: it incites us to do more by a fellow-creature, than can be strictly required of us: it obliges us to hasten to the relief of an object that wants relief, anticipating even hope or expectation. Generosity, sir, will not surely permit a worthy mind to doubt of its honourable and beneficent intentions: much less will it allow itself to shock, to offend anyone; and, least of all, a person thrown by adversity, mishap, or accident, into its protection.

What an opportunity had he to clear his intentions, had he been so disposed, from the *latter part* of this home observation!—But he run away with the *first*, and kept to that.

Admirably defined! he said—But who at this rate, madam, can be said to be *generous* to you?—Your *generosity* I implore, while *justice*, as it must be my sole merit, shall be my aim. Never was there a woman of such nice and delicate sentiments!

It is a reflection upon yourself, sir, and upon the company you have kept, if you think these notions either nice or delicate. Thousands of my sex are more nice than I; for they would have avoided the devious path I have been surprised into: the consequences of which surprise have laid me under the sad necessity of telling a man, who has not delicacy enough to enter into those parts of the female character which are its glory and distinction, what true generosity is.

His divine monitress, he called me!—He would endeavour to form his manners, as he had often promised, by my example. But he hoped I would now permit him to mention briefly the *justice* he proposed to do me, in the terms of the settlement; a subject so proper, before now, to have been entered upon; and which would have been entered upon long ago, had not my frequent displeasure taken from him the opportunity he had often wished for: but now having ventured to lay hold of this, nothing should divert him from improving it.

I have no spirits just now, sir, to attend to such weighty points. What you have a mind to propose, write to me: and I shall know what answer to return. Only one thing let me remind you of, that if you touch upon any subject, in which my papa has a concern, I shall judge by your treatment of the father, what value you have for the daughter.

He *looked* as if he would choose rather to speak than write: but had he *said so*, I had a severe return to have made upon him; as possibly he might see by *my* looks.

In this way are we now: a sort of calm, as I said, succeeding a storm—What may happen next, whether a storm or a calm, with such a spirit as I have to deal with, who can tell?

But be that as it will, I think, my dear, I am not *meanly* off: and that is a great point with me; and which I know you'll be glad to hear: if it were only that I can see this man without losing any of that dignity (what other word can I use, speaking of *myself*, that betokens *decency* and not *arrogance*?) which is so necessary to enable me to look *up*, or rather, with the *mind*'s eye, I may say, to look *down* upon a man of this man's cast.

Although circumstances have so offered that I could not take your advice as to the *manner* of dealing with him; yet you gave me so much courage by it, as has enabled me to conduct things to this issue; as well as determined me against leaving him: which *before*, I was thinking to do, at all adventures. Whether, when it came to the point, I *should* have done so, or not, I cannot say, because it would have depended upon his behaviour at the time.

But let his behaviour be what it will, I am afraid, with you, that should anything offer at last to oblige me to leave him, I shall not mend my situation in the world's eye; but the contrary. And yet I will not be treated by him with indignity while I have any power to help myself.

You, my dear, have accused me of having *modestied away*, as you phrase it, several opportunities of being—Being what, my dear?—Why, the wife of a libertine: and what a libertine and his wife are, my cousin Morden's letter tells us—Let me here, once for all, endeavour to account for the motives of my behaviour to this man, and for the principles I have proceeded upon, as they appear to me upon a close self-examination.

Be pleased then to allow me to think that my motives on this occasion arise not *altogether* from maidenly niceness; nor yet from the apprehension of what my present tormentor, and future husband, may think of a precipitate compliance, on such a disagreeable behaviour as his. But they arise principally from what offers to my own heart, respecting, as I may say, its own rectitude, its own judgement of the *fit* and the *unfit*; as I would without study answer *for* myself *to* myself, in the *first* place; to *him* and to the *world*, in the *second* only. Principles, that *are* in my mind; that I *found* there; implanted, no doubt, by the first gracious Planter: which therefore *impel* me, as I may say, to act up to them, that thereby I may to the best of my judgement be enabled to comport myself worthily in both states (the single and the married), let others act as they will by *me*.

I hope, my dear, I do not deceive myself, and instead of setting about rectifying what is amiss in my heart, endeavour to find excuses for habits and peculiarities which I am unwilling to cast off or overcome. The heart is very deceitful: do you, my dear friend, lay mine open (but surely it is always open before you!) and spare me not, if you find or think it culpable.

This observation, once for all, as I said, I thought proper to make, to convince you that to the best of my judgement my errors in matters as well of the lesser moment, as the greater, shall rather be the fault of my understanding than of my will.

I am, my dearest friend,

Your ever-obliged
CLARISSA HARLOWE

Letter 186: MISS CLARISSA HARLOWE TO MISS HOWE

Tuesday night, May 16

MR Lovelace has sent me, by Dorcas, his proposals, as follow:

'To spare a delicacy so extreme, and to obey you, I write: and the rather that you may communicate this paper to Miss Howe, who may consult any of her friends you shall think proper to have entrusted on this occasion. I say *entrusted* because, as you know, I have given it out to several persons that we are actually married.

'In the first place, madam, I offer to settle upon you, by way of jointure, your whole estate. And moreover to vest in trustees such a part of mine in Lancashire as shall produce a clear four hundred pounds a year, to be paid to your sole and separate use, quarterly.

'My own estate is a clear £2000 *per annum*. Lord M. proposes to give me possession either of that which he has in Lancashire (to which, by the way, I think

I have a better title than he has himself), or that we call *The Lawn* in Hertfordshire, upon my nuptials with a lady whom he so greatly admires; and to make [the one] I shall choose a clear £1000 *per annum*.

'My too great contempt of censure has subjected me to much traduction. It may not therefore be improper to assure you, on the word of a gentleman, that no part of my estate was ever mortgaged: and that although I lived very expensively abroad, and made large draughts, yet that Midsummer-Day next will discharge all that I owe in the world. My notions are not all bad ones. I have been thought, in pecuniary cases, *generous*. It would have deserved *another* name, had I not first been *just*.

'If, as your own estate is at present in your father's hands, you rather choose that I should make a jointure out of mine, tantamount to yours, be it what it will, it shall be done. I will engage Lord M. to write to *you*, what he proposes to do on the happy occasion: not as your desire or expectation, but to demonstrate that no advantage is intended to be taken of the situation you are in with your own family.

'To show the beloved daughter the consideration I have for her, I will consent that she shall prescribe the terms of agreement in relation to the large sums, which must be in her father's hands, arising from her grandfather's estate. I have no doubt but he will be put upon making large demands upon you. All those it shall be in your power to comply with, for the sake of your own peace. And the remainder shall be paid into your hands, and be entirely at your disposal, as a fund to support those charitable donations, which I have heard you so famed for *out* of your family; and for which you have been so greatly reflected upon *in* it.

'As to clothes, jewels, and the like, against the time you shall choose to make your appearance, it will be my pride that you shall not be beholden for such of these as shall be answerable to the rank of both, to those who have had the stupid folly to renounce a daughter they deserved not. You must excuse me, madam: you would mistrust my sincerity in the rest, could I speak of these people with less asperity, though so nearly related to you.

'These, madam, are my proposals. They are such as I always designed to make, whenever you would permit me to enter into the delightful subject. But you have been so determined to try every method for reconciling yourself to your relations, even by giving me absolutely up for ever, that you have seemed to think it but justice to keep me at a distance, till the event of that your *predominant* hope could be seen. It is *now* seen!—And although I *have been*, and perhaps still *am*, ready to regret the want of that preference I wished for from you as Miss Clarissa Harlowe; yet I am sure, as the husband of Mrs Lovelace, I shall be more ready to adore than to blame you for the pangs you have given to a heart, the generosity, or rather *justice* of which, my implacable enemies have taught you to doubt: and this still the readier, as I am persuaded that those pangs never would have been given by a mind so noble, had not the doubt been entertained perhaps with too great an appearance of reason; and as I hope I shall have it to reflect that the moment the doubts shall be overcome, the indifference will cease.

'I will only add, that if I have omitted anything that would have given you further satisfaction; or if the above terms be short of what you would wish; you will be pleased to supply them as you think fit. And when I know your pleasure, I will instantly order articles to be drawn up conformably; that nothing in my power may be wanting to make you happy.

'You will now, dearest madam, judge how far all the rest depends upon yourself.'

You see, my dear, what he offers. You see it is all my fault that he has not made these offers before—I am a strange creature! To be to blame in everything, and to everybody! Yet neither intend the ill at the time, nor know it to *be* the ill till too late, or so nearly too late that I must give up all the delicacy he talks of to compound for my fault!

I shall now judge how far all the rest depends upon myself! So coldly concludes he such warm, and, in the main, unobjectible proposals! Would you not, as you read, have supposed that the paper would conclude with the most earnest demand of a day?—I own I had that expectation so strong, resulting *naturally*, as I may say, from the premises, that without studying for dissatisfaction, I could not help being dissatisfied when I came to the conclusion—But you say, there is no help. I must perhaps make *further* sacrifices. All delicacy it seems is to be at an end with me! But if so, this man knows not what every *wise* man knows, that prudence, and virtue, and delicacy of mind in a *wife*, do the husband more *real* honour in the eye of the world, than the same qualities (were *she* destitute of them) in *himself*: as the *want* of them in her does him more *dis*-honour: for are not the wife's errors the husband's reproach? How *justly* his reproach, is another thing.

I will consider this paper; and write to it, if I am able: for it seems *now, all the rest depends upon myself.*

Letter 187: MISS CLARISSA HARLOWE TO MISS HOWE

Wednesday morning, May 17

MR Lovelace would fain have engaged me last night. But as I was not prepared to enter upon the subject of his proposals, intending to consider them maturely, and was not highly pleased with his conclusion (and then there is hardly any getting from him in tolerable time over-night), I desired to be excused seeing him till morning.

About seven o'clock we met in the dining-room. I find he was full of expectation that I should meet him with a very favourable, who knows but with *thankful* aspect?—And I immediately found by his sullen countenance, that he was under no small disappointment that I did not.

My dearest love, are you well?—Why look you so solemn upon me?—Will your indifference never be over?—If I have proposed terms in any respect *short* of your expectation—

I told him that he had very considerately mentioned my showing his proposals to Miss Howe, and consulting any of her friends upon them by her means; and I should have an opportunity to send them to her by Collins by-and-by, and so insisted to suspend any talk upon that subject till I had her opinion upon them.

Good God!—If there were but the least loop-hole, the least room for delay!— But he was writing a letter to his uncle, to give him an account of his situation with me, and could not finish it so satisfactorily, either to my lord or to himself, as if I would condescend to say whether the terms he had proposed were acceptable or not.

Thus far, I told him, I could say, that my principal point was peace and reconciliation with my family. As to other matters, the genteelness of his own spirit would put him upon doing more for me than I should ask or expect. Wherefore, if all he had to write about was to know what Lord M. would do on my account, he might spare himself the trouble; for that my utmost wishes as to myself were much more easily gratified than he perhaps imagined.

He asked me then, if I would so far permit him to touch upon the happy day, as to request his uncle's presence on the occasion, and to be my father?

Father had a sweet and venerable sound with it, I said. I should be glad to have a father who would own me!

Was not this plain speaking, think you, my dear? Yet it rather, I must own, appears so to me on reflection, than was *designed* freely at the time. For I then, with a sigh from the bottom of my heart, thought of my *own father*; bitterly regretting that I am an outcast from him and from my mother.

Mr Lovelace, I thought, seemed a little affected at the *manner* of my speaking, as well as at the sad reflection, I suppose.

I am but a very young creature, Mr Lovelace, said I, and wiped my averted eye, although you have *kindly*, and in *love to me*, introduced so much sorrow to me already: so you must not wonder that the word *father* strikes so sensibly upon the heart of a child ever dutiful till she knew you, and whose tender years still require the paternal wing.

He turned towards the window (rejoice with me, my dear, since I seem devoted to him, that the man is not absolutely impenetrable!)—His emotion was visible; yet he endeavoured to suppress it—Approaching me again, again he was obliged to turn from me; Angelic something, he said: but then, obtaining a heart more *suitable* to his wish, he once more approached me—For his own part, he said, as Lord M. was so subject to the gout, he was afraid that the compliment he had just proposed to make him might, if made, occasion a longer suspension than he could bear to think of: and if it did, it would vex him to the heart that he had made it.

I could not say a single word to this, you know, my dear. But you will guess at my thoughts of what he said—So much passionate love, *lip-deep!* So prudent, and so dutifully patient *at heart* to a relation he had, till now, so undutifully despised!— Why, why, am I thrown upon such a man! thought I—

He hesitated, as if contending with himself, and after taking a turn or two about the room—He was at a great loss what to determine upon, he said, because he had not the honour of knowing when he was to be made the happiest of men—Would to God it might that very instant be resolved upon!

He stopped a moment or two, staring in my downcast face (Did I not, oh my beloved friend, think you, want a father or a mother just then?): but if he could not so *soon* as he wished procure my consent to a day; in *that* case he thought the compliment might *as well* be made to Lord M. as *not*—since the settlements might be drawn and ingrossed in the intervenient time, which would pacify his impatience as no time would be lost.

You will suppose how *I* was affected by this speech, by repeating the substance of what *he* said upon it; as follows.

—But by his soul, he knew not, so much was I upon the reserve, and so much latent meaning did my eye import, whether, when he most hoped to please me, he was not farthest from doing so. Would I vouchsafe to say, whether I approved of his compliment to Lord M. or not?

'Miss Howe, thought I at that moment, says I must *not* run away from this man!

To be sure, Mr Lovelace, if this matter is *ever to be*, it must be agreeable to me to have the full approbation of *one* side, since I cannot have that of the *other*.

If this matter be ever to be! Good God! what words were those at this time of day! And full *approbation* of one side! Why that word *approbation?* when the greatest pride of all his family was that of having the honour of so dear a creature for their relation? Would to Heaven, my dearest life, added he, that, without complimenting *any*body, tomorrow might be the happiest day of my life!—What say you, my angel? with a trembling impatience that *seemed* not affected—What say you for *tomorrow?*

It was likely, my dear, I could say much to it, or name another day had I been disposed to the latter, with such an hinted delay from him.

Next day, madam, if not *tomorrow!*—Or the *day after that!*—and taking my two hands, stared me into a half-confusion.

No, no! [said I] you cannot think all of a sudden there should be reason for such a hurry. It will be most agreeable, to be sure, for my lord to be present.

I am all obedience and resignation, returned the wretch, with a self-pluming air, as if he had acquiesced to a proposal made by me, and had complimented me with a great piece of self-denial.

Modesty, I think, required it of me that it should pass so. Did it not?—I think it did. Would to Heaven—but what signifies wishing?

But when he would have *rewarded himself*, as he had heretofore called it, for this self-supposed concession, with a kiss, I repulsed him with a just and very sincere disdain.

He seemed both vexed and surprised, as one who had made proposals that he had expected everything from. He plainly said that he thought our situation would entitle him to such an innocent freedom: and he was both amazed and grieved to be thus scornfully repulsed.

No reply could be made by me. I abruptly broke from him. I recollect, as I passed by one of the pier-glasses, that I saw in it his clenched hand offered in wrath to his forehead: the words, *indifference, by his soul, next to hatred*, I heard him speak: and something of *ice* he mentioned: I heard not what.

Whether he intends to write to my lord, or to Miss Montague, I cannot tell. But as all delicacy ought to be over with me *now*, perhaps I am to blame to expect it from a man who may not know *what it is*. If he does *not*, and yet thinks himself very delicate, and intends not to be otherwise, I am rather to be pitied, than he to be censured. And after all, since I *must* take him as I find him, I *must:* that is to say, as a man so vain, and so accustomed to be admired, that not being conscious of internal defect he has taken no pains to polish more than his outside. And as his proposals are higher than my expectations; and as in his own opinion he has a great deal to bear from *me*, I *will* (no new offence preventing) sit down to answer them—And, if possible, in terms as unobjectible to him, as his are to me.

But after all, see you not, my dear, more and more, the mismatch that there is in our minds?

However, I am willing to compound for my fault, by giving up (if that may be all my punishment) the expectation of what is deemed happiness in this life, with such a husband as I fear he will make. In short, I will content myself to be a suffering person through the state to the end of my life. A long one it cannot be!—

This may qualify him (as it may prove) from stings of conscience from misbehaviour to a *first* wife, to be a more tolerable one to a *second*, though not perhaps better deserving. While my story, to all who shall know it, will afford these instructions: that the eye is a traitor, and ought ever to be mistrusted: that form is deceitful. In other words; that a fine person is seldom paired by a fine mind: and that sound principles and a good heart are the only bases on which the hopes of a *happy future*, either with respect to the *here* or to the *hereafter*, can be built.

And so much at present for Mr Lovelace's proposals: of which I desire your opinion.

I am, my dearest friend,

Your ever-obliged
CL. HARLOWE

[*Letters 187.1–4: Mr Lovelace to John Belford, Esq.*]

Four letters are written by Mr Lovelace from the date of his last, giving the state of affairs between him and the lady, pretty much the same as in hers in the same period, allowing for the humour in his; and for his resentments expressed with vehemence on her resolution to leave him, if her friends could be prevailed upon. A few extracts from them will be only given.

What, says he, might have become of me and my projects, had not her father, and the rest of the implacables, stood my friends?

(*After violent threatenings and vows of revenge, he says*—) 'Tis plain she would have given me up for ever; nor should I have been able to prevent her abandoning of me, unless I had torn up the tree by the roots to come at the fruit; which I hope still to bring down by a gentle shake or two, if I can but have patience to stay the ripening season.

(*Thus triumphing in his unpolite cruelty, he says*—) After her haughty treatment of me, I am resolved she shall speak out. There are a thousand beauties to be discovered in the face, in the accent, in the bush-beating hesitations of a woman that is earnest about a subject which she wants to introduce, yet knows not how. Silly rogues, calling themselves generous ones, would value themselves for sparing a lady's confusion: but they are silly rogues indeed; and rob themselves of prodigious pleasure by their forwardness; and at the same time deprive her of displaying a world of charms, which only can be manifested on these occasions. Hard-heartedness, as it is called, is an essential of the libertine's character. Familiarized to the distresses he occasions, he is seldom betrayed by tenderness into a complaisant weakness unworthy of himself. How have I enjoyed a charming creature's confusion, as I have sat over-against her; her eyes lost in admiration of my shoebuckles, or meditating some uncouth figure in the carpet!

(*Mentioning the settlements, he says*—) I am in earnest as to the terms. If I marry her (and I have no doubt but that I shall, after my pride, my ambition, my *revenge* if thou wilt, is gratified), I will do her noble justice. The more I do for such a prudent, such an excellent economist, the more shall I do for myself—But, by my soul, Belford, her haughtiness shall be brought down to own both love and obligation to me—Nor will this sketch of settlements bring us forwarder than I would have it. Modesty of sex will stand my friend at any time. At the very altar, our hands joined, I'd engage to make this proud beauty leave the parson and me, and all my friends present, though there were twenty of them, to look like fools upon one another, while she took wing and flew out of the church door, or window if that were open and the door shut; and this only by a very word.

He mentions his rash expression, that she should be his although damnation were to be the purchase; and owns that, at that instant, he was upon the point of making a violent attempt; but that he was checked in the very moment, and but just in time, by the awe he was struck with on again casting his eye upon her terrified but lovely face, and seeing as he thought her spotless heart in every line of it.

Oh virtue, virtue! *says he,* what is there in thee that can thus affect the heart of such a man as me, against my will!—Whence these involuntary tremors, and fear of giving mortal offence?—What art thou, that acting in the breast of a feeble woman, canst strike so much awe into a spirit so intrepid! which never before, no, not in my first attempt, young as I then was, and frighted at my own boldness (till I found myself *forgiven*), had such an effect upon me!

He paints in lively colours that part of the scene between him and the lady, where she says, 'The word father *has a sweet and venerable sound with it.'*

I was exceedingly affected, *says he,* upon the occasion. But was ashamed to be surprised by her into such a fit of unmanly weakness—so ashamed that I was resolved to subdue it at the instant, and guard against the like for the future. Yet, at that moment, I more than half regretted that I could not permit her to enjoy a triumph which she so well deserved to glory in—her youth, her beauty, her artless innocence, and her manner, equally beyond comparison or description. But her *indifference,* Belford!—That she could resolve to sacrifice me to the malice of my enemies; and carry on the design in so clandestine a manner—yet love her, as I do, to frenzy!—revere her, as I do, to adoration!—These were the recollections with which I fortified my recreant heart against her—Yet, after all, if she persevere, she must conquer!—Coward, as she has made me, that never was a coward before!

He concludes his fourth letter in a vehement rage, upon her repulsing him when he offered to salute her; having supposed, as he owns, that she would have been all condescension on his proposals to her.

This, *says he,* I will for ever remember against her, in order to steel my own heart, that I may cut through a rock of ice to hers; and repay her for the disdain, the scorn, which glowed in her countenance and was apparent in her air at her abrupt departure from me, after such obliging behaviour on my side, and after I had so earnestly pressed her for an early day—The women below say, She hates me, she despises me!—And 'tis true: she does; she must—And why cannot I take their advice?—I will not long, my fair one, be despised by thee and laughed at by them!

Let me acquaint thee, Jack, *adds he by way of postscript,* that this effort of hers to leave me, if she could have been received; her sending for a coach on Sunday; no doubt, resolving not to return, if she had gone out without me (for did she not declare that she had thoughts to retire to some of the villages about town, where she could be safe and private?); have all together so much alarmed me that I have been adding to the written instructions for my servant, and the people below, how to act in case she should elope in my absence: particularly letting my fellow know what he shall report to strangers, in case she shall throw herself upon any such with a resolution to abandon me. These instructions I shall further add to, as circumstances offer.

Letter 188: MISS HOWE TO MISS CLARISSA HARLOWE

Thursday, May 18

I HAVE neither time nor patience, my dear friend, to answer to every material article in your last letters just now received. Mr Lovelace's proposals are all I like of him. And yet (as you do) I think that he concludes them not with that warmth and earnestness which we might naturally have expected from him. Never in my life did I hear or read of so patient a man, with such a blessing in his reach. But wretches of his cast, between you and me, my dear, have not, I fancy, the ardours that honest men have. Who knows, as your Bell once spitefully said, but he may have half a dozen creatures to quit his hands of, before he engages for life?—Yet I believe you must not expect him to be honest on this side of his grand climacteric.

He, to suggest delay from a compliment to be made to Lord M. and to give time for settlements!— *He,* a part of whose character it is, not to know what complaisance to his relations is!—I have no patience with him!—You did indeed want an interposing friend on the affecting occasion which you mention in yours of yesterday morning. But, upon my word, were I to have been that moment in your situation, and been so treated, I would have torn his eyes out, and left it to his own heart, when I had done, to furnish the reason for it.

Would to Heaven tomorrow, without complimenting anybody, might be his happy day!—Villain! After he had himself suggested the compliment!—And I think he accuses YOU of delaying!—Fellow, that he is!—How my heart is wrung—

But, as matters now stand betwixt you, I am very unseasonable in expressing my resentments against him—Yet I don't know whether I am or not, neither; since it is the cruellest of states for a woman to be forced to have a man whom her heart despises. You must, at *least,* despise him; at times, however. His clenched fist offered to his forehead on your leaving him in just displeasure; I wish it had been a poleaxe, and in the hand of his worst enemy.

I will endeavour to think of some method, of some scheme, to get you from him, and to fix you safely somewhere till your cousin Morden arrives: a scheme to lie by you, and to be pursued as occasion may be given. You are sure that you can go abroad when you please; and that our correspondence is safe. I cannot, however, for the reasons heretofore mentioned respecting your own reputation, wish you to leave him while he gives you not cause to suspect his honour. But your heart, I know, would be the easier if you were sure of some asylum, in case of necessity.

Yet once more, I say, I can have no notion that he can or dare to mean you dishonour—But then the man is a fool, my dear—that's all.

However, since you are thrown upon a fool, marry the fool at the first opportunity; and though I doubt that this man will be the most ungovernable of fools, as all witty and vain fools are, take him as a punishment, since you cannot as a reward. In short, as one given to convince you that there is nothing but imperfection in this life.

I shall be impatient till I have your next. I am, my dearest friend,

Your ever-affectionate and faithful
ANNA HOWE

Letter 189: MR BELFORD TO ROBERT LOVELACE, ESQ.

Wednesday, May 17

I WOULD conceal nothing from you that relates to yourself so much as the enclosed. You will see what the noble writer apprehends from you, and wishes of you, with regard to Miss Harlowe, and how much at heart all your relations have it that you do honourably by her. They compliment me with an influence over you which I wish with all my soul you would let me have in this article.

Let me once more entreat thee, Lovelace, to reflect before it be too late, before the mortal offence be given, upon the graces and merits of this lady. Let thy frequent remorses at last end in one effectual one. Let not pride and wantonness of heart ruin thy fairer prospects. By my faith, Lovelace, there is nothing but vanity, conceit, and nonsense, in our wild schemes. As we grow older, we shall be wiser, and looking back upon our foolish notions of the present hour, shall certainly despise ourselves (our youth dissipated), when we think of the honourable engagements we might have made. Thou, more especially, if thou lettest such a matchless creature slide through thy fingers. A creature pure from her cradle. In all her actions and sentiments uniformly noble. Strict in the performance of all her even *unrewarded* duties to the most unreasonable of fathers, what a wife will she make the man who shall have the honour to call her his!

Reflect likewise upon her sufferings for thee. Actually at the time thou art forming schemes to ruin her (at least in *her* sense of the word) is she not labouring under a father's curse laid upon her by thy means, and for thy sake? And wouldst thou give operation and completion to this curse?

And what, Lovelace, all the time is thy pride? Thou that vainly imaginest that the whole family of the Harlowes, and that of the Howes too, are but thy machines, unknown to themselves, to bring about thy purposes and thy revenge: what art thou more or better than the instrument even of her implacable brother and envious sister, to perpetuate the disgrace of the most excellent of sisters, which they are moved to by vilely low and sordid motives?—Canst thou bear, Lovelace, to be thought the machine of thy inveterate enemy James Harlowe?—Nay, art thou not the cully of that still viler Joseph Leman, who serves himself as much by thy money, as he does thee by the double part he acts by thy direction?—And the devil's agent besides, who only can, and who certainly will, suitably reward thee, if thou proceedest, and if thou effectest thy wicked purpose?

Could any man but you put together upon paper the following questions with so much unconcern as you seem to have written them?—Give them a reperusal, oh heart of adamant! 'Whither can she fly to avoid me? Her parents will not receive her; her uncles will not entertain her: her beloved Norton is in their direction, and cannot. Miss Howe dare not. She has not one friend in town but ME: is entirely a stranger to the town.'[a] What must that heart be that can triumph in a distress so deep, into which she has been plunged by thy elaborate arts and contrivances? And what a sweet, yet sad reflection was that, which had almost had its due effect upon thee, arising from thy naming Lord M. for her nuptial father! Her tender years inclining her to *wish* a father, and to *hope* a friend—Oh my dear Lovelace, canst thou resolve to be, instead of the father thou has robbed her of, a devil?

Thou knowest that I have no interest, that I can have no view, in wishing thee to do justice to this admirable creature. For thy own sake, once more I conjure thee, for thy family's sake, and for the sake of our common humanity, let me beseech thee to be just to Miss Clarissa Harlowe.

No matter whether these expostulations are in character from me, or not. I *have* been, and *am*, bad enough. If thou takest my advice, which is as the enclosed will show thee the advice of all thy family, thou wilt perhaps have it to reproach me (and but perhaps neither), that thou art not a worse man than myself. But if thou dost *not*, and if thou ruinest such a virtue, all the complicated wickedness of ten devils let loose among the innocent with full power over them will not do so much vile and base mischief as thou wilt be guilty of.

It is said that the prince on his throne is not safe if a mind so desperate can be found as values not its *own* life. So may it be said that the most immaculate virtue is not safe, if a man can be met with who has no regard to his own honour, and makes a jest of the most solemn vows and protestations.

Thou mayest by trick, chicane, and false colours, thou who art worse than a pickeroon in love, overcome a poor lady so entangled as thou hast entangled her; so unprotected as thou hast made her. But consider how much more generous and just to her, and noble to thyself, it is to overcome *thyself*.

Once more, it is no matter whether my past or future actions countenance my preachment, as perhaps thou'lt call what I have written: but this I promise thee, that whenever I meet with a woman of but one half of Miss Harlowe's perfections who will favour me with her acceptance, I will take the advice I give, and marry. Nor will I attempt to try her honour at the hazard of my own. In other words, I will not degrade an excellent creature in her own eyes by trials when I have no cause for suspicion. And let me add, with respect to thy *eagleship*'s manifestation of which thou boastest, in thy attempts upon the innocent and uncorrupted, rather than upon those whom thou humorously comparest to wrens, *phil-tits*, and wagtails,[b] that I hope I have it not once to reproach myself that I ruined the morals of any one creature, who otherwise would have been uncorrupted. Guilt enough in contributing to the *continued* guilt of other poor wretches, if I am one of those who take care she shall never rise again, when she has once fallen.

Whatever the capital devil, under whose banner thou hast listed, will let thee do with regard to this incomparable woman, I hope thou wilt act with honour in

a See p. 575.
b See p. 559.

relation to the enclosed between Lord M. and me; who, as thou wilt see, desires that thou mayest not know he wrote on the subject; for reasons I think very far from being creditable to thyself: and that thou wilt take as meant, the honest zeal for thy service of

Thy real friend,
J. BELFORD

Letter 190: LORD M. TO JOHN BELFORD, ESQ.

M. Hall, Monday, May 15

Sir,

IF any man in the world has power over my nephew, it is you. I therefore write this to beg you to interfere in the affair depending between him and the most accomplished of women, as every one says; and *what everyone says, must be true.*

I don't know that he has any bad designs upon her; but I know his temper too well, not to be apprehensive upon such long delays: and the ladies here have been for some time in fear for her; my sister Sadlier, in particular, who (you know) is a wise woman, says that these delays in the present case must be from him, rather than from the lady. He had always indeed a strong antipathy to marriage; and may think of playing his dog's tricks by her, as he has by so many others. If there's any danger of this, 'tis best to prevent it in time: for, *when a thing is done advice comes too late.*

He has always had the folly and impertinence to make a jest of me for using proverbs: but as they are the wisdom of whole nations and ages collected into a small compass, I am not to be shamed out of sentences that often contain more wisdom in them, than the tedious harangues of most of our parsons and moralists. Let him laugh at them, if he pleases: you and I know better things, Mr Belford— *Though you have kept company with a wolf, you have not learnt to howl of him.*

But nevertheless, you must not let him know that I have written to you on this subject. I am ashamed to say it; but he has ever treated me as if I were a man of very common understanding. And would perhaps think never the better of the best advice in the world for coming from me.

I am sure he has no reason to slight me as he does. He may and will be the better for me, if he outlives me; though he once told me to my face that I might do as I would with my estate; for that he, for his part, loved his liberty as much as he despised money. He thought, I suppose, that *I could not cover him with my wings without pecking at him with my bill*; though I never used to be pecking at him without very great occasion: and, God knows, he might have my very heart, if he would but endeavour to oblige me by studying his own good; for that is all I desire of him. Indeed, it was his poor mother that first spoiled him; and I have been but too indulgent to him since—A fine grateful disposition, you'll say, to *return evil for good!*[1] But that was always his way.

This match, however, as the lady has such an extraordinary share of wisdom and goodness, might set all to rights: and if you can forward it, I would enable him to make whatever settlements he could wish; and should not be unwilling to put him in possession of another pretty estate besides. For what do I live for (as I have often said), but to see him and my two nieces well married and settled? May heaven settle him down to a better mind, and turn his heart to more of goodness and consideration!

If the delays are on his side, I tremble for the lady; and if on hers (as he tells my niece Charlotte), I could wish the young lady were apprised that *delays are dangerous*. Excellent as she is, I can tell her she ought not to depend on her merits with such a changeable fellow, and such a professed marriage-hater as he has been. I know you are very good at giving kind hints. *A word to the wise is enough.*

I wish you would try what you can do with him; for I have warned him so often of his wicked practices, that I begin to despair of my words having any effect upon him. But let him remember that *Vengeance, though it comes with leaden feet, strikes with iron hands*. If he behaves ill in this case, he may find it so. What a pity it is that a man of his talents and learning should be so vile a rake! Alas! alas! *Une poignée de bonne vie vaut mieux que plein muy de clergé*; a handful of good life is better than a whole bushel of learning.

You may throw in, too, as his friend, that should he provoke me, it may not be too late for me to marry. My old friend Wycherl[e]y[2] did so, when he was older than I am, on purpose to plague *his* nephew: and in spite of this gout, I might have a child or two still. And have not been without some thoughts that way, when he has angered me more than ordinary: but these thoughts have gone off again hitherto, upon my considering that *the children of very young and very old men* (though I am not so very old neither) *last not long*; and that *old men when they marry young women* are said to *make much of death*: yet who knows but that matrimony might be good against the gouty humours I am troubled with?

The sentences that I have purposely wove into my discourse may be of some service to you in talking to him; but use them sparingly, that he may not discover that you borrow your *darts* from my *quiver*.

May your good counsels, Mr Belford, founded upon the hints I have given, pierce his heart and incite him to do what will be so happy for himself, and so necessary for the honour of that admirable lady whom I long to see his wife; and, if I may, I will not think of one for myself.

Should he abuse the confidence she has placed in him, I myself shall pray that vengeance may fall upon his head—*Raro*—*Raro*—(I quite forget all my Latin! but I think it is)—*Raro antecedentem scelestum deseruit pede poena claudo*: where vice goes before, vengeance (sooner or later) will follow.

I shall make no apologies to you for this trouble. I know how well you love him and me; and there is nothing in which you could serve us both more importantly than in forwarding this match to the utmost of your power. When it is done, how shall I rejoice to see you at M. Hall! Meantime, I shall long to hear that you are likely to be successful; and am,

Dear sir,
Your most faithful friend and servant,
M.

[*Letter 190.1: Mr Belford to Robert Lovelace, Esq.*]

(*Mr Lovelace having not returned an answer to Mr Belford's expostulatory letter, so soon as Mr Belford expected, he wrote to him, expressing his apprehension, that he had disobliged him by his honest freedom. Among other things, he says*—) I pass my time here at Watford, attending my dying uncle, very heavily. I cannot therefore, by any means, dispense with thy correspondence. And why shouldst thou punish me for having more conscience and remorse than thyself? Thou, who never thoughtest either conscience or remorse an honour to thee. And I have, besides, a melancholy story to tell thee, in relation to Belton and his Thomasine; and which may afford a lesson to all the keeping class.

I have a letter from each of our three companions in the time. They have all the wickedness that thou hast, but not the wit. Some new rogueries do two of them boast of, which I think if completed deserve the gallows.

I am far from hating intrigue upon principle. But to have awkward fellows plot, and commit their plots to paper, destitute of the seasonings, of the *acumen*, which is thy talent, how extremely shocking must their letters be!—But do thou, Lovelace, whether thou art, or art not, determined upon thy measures with regard to the fine lady in thy power, enliven my heavy heart by thy communications; and thou wilt oblige

> Thy melancholy friend,
> J. BELFORD

Letter 191: MR LOVELACE TO JOHN BELFORD, ESQ.

Friday night, May 19

WHEN I have opened my views to thee so amply as I have done in my former letters, and have told thee that my principal design is but to bring virtue to a trial, that, *if* virtue, it need not be afraid of; and that the reward of it will be marriage (that is to say, if, after I have carried my point, I cannot prevail upon her to live with me the Life of Honour[a]; for that thou knowest is the wish of my heart); I am amazed at the repetition of thy wambling nonsense.

I am of opinion with thee that some time hence, when I am *grown wiser*, I shall conclude that *there is nothing but vanity, conceit, and nonsense, in my present wild schemes*. But what is this saying but that I must be *first* wiser?

I do not intend *to let this matchless creature slide through my fingers*.

Art thou able to say half the things in her praise that I have said, and am continually saying or writing?

Her gloomy father cursed the sweet creature, because she put it out of his wicked power to compel her to have the man she hated. Thou knowest how little merit she has with me on this score—and shall I not try the virtue I intend, upon full proof, to reward, because her father is a tyrant?—Why art thou thus eternally reflecting upon so excellent a woman, as if thou wert assured she would fail in the trial?—Nay, thou declarest, every time thou writest on the subject, that she *will*,

a   See pp. 430–31.

that she *must* yield, *entangled as she is:* and yet makest her virtue the pretence of thy solicitude for her.

An instrument of the vile James Harlowe, dost thou call me?—Oh Jack! how I could curse thee!—*I* an *instrument* of that brother! of that sister!—But mark the end—and thou shalt see what will become of that brother, and of that sister!

Play not against me my own acknowledged sensibilities, I desire thee. Sensibilities which, at the same time that they contradict thy charge of an *adamantine heart* in thy friend, thou hadst known nothing of, had I not communicated them to thee.

If I ruin such a virtue, sayest thou?—Eternal monotonist!—Again; *the most immaculate virtue may be ruined by men who have no regard to their honour, and who make a jest of the most solemn oaths,* &c. What must be the virtue that will be ruined without oaths? Is not the world full of these deceptions? And are not *lovers' oaths* a jest of hundreds of years' standing? And are not cautions against the perfidy of our sex a necessary part of the female education?

I do intend to endeavour to overcome *myself*; but I must first try if I cannot overcome *this lady.* Have I not said that the honour of her sex is concerned that I should *try*?

Whenever thou meetest with a woman of but half her perfections, thou wilt marry—Do, Jack.

Can a girl be *degraded by trials,* who is not *overcome*?

I am glad that thou takest crime to thyself for not endeavouring to convert the poor wretches whom *others* have ruined. I will not recriminate upon thee, Belford, as I might, when thou flatterest thyself that thou never ruinedst the morals of any young creature who otherwise would not have been corrupted—the palliating consolation of an Hottentot heart, determined rather to gluttonize on the garbage of other foul feeders, than to reform. But tell me, Jack, wouldst thou have spared such a girl as my Rosebud, had I not by my example engaged thy generosity? Nor was my Rosebud the only girl I spared—When my power was acknowledged, who more merciful than thy friend?

> It is *resistance* that inflames desire,
> Sharpens the darts of love, and blows its fire.
> Love is disarm'd that meets with too much ease;
> He languishes, and does not care to please.

The women know this as well as the men. They love to be addressed with spirit:

> And therefore 'tis their golden fruit they guard
> With so much care, to make possession hard.[1]

Whence, for a by-reflection, the ardent, the complaisant gallant is so often preferred to the cold husband. And yet the sex do not consider that variety or novelty gives the ardour and the obsequiousness, and that were the rake as much used to them as the husband is, he would be (and is to his own wife, if married) *as* indifferent to their favours; and the husband, in his turn, would to another woman be the rake. Let the women, upon the whole, take this lesson from a Lovelace— Always to endeavour to make themselves as new to a husband, and to appear as elegant and as obliging to him, as they are desirous to appear to a lover, and actually were to him as *such*; and then the rake, which all women love, will last longer in the husband than it generally does.

But to return—If I have not sufficiently cleared my conduct to thee in the above, I refer thee once more to mine of the 13th of last month.[a] And prithee, Jack, lay me not under a necessity to repeat the same things so often. I hope thou readest what I write more than once.

I am not displeased that thou art so apprehensive of my resentment, that I cannot miss a day without making thee uneasy. Thy conscience, 'tis plain, tells thee that thou hast deserved my displeasure: and if it has convinced thee of *that*, it will make thee afraid of repeating thy fault. See that this be the consequence. Else, now that thou hast told me how I can punish thee, it is very likely that I do punish thee by my silence, although I have as much pleasure in writing on this charming subject, as thou canst have in reading what I write.

When a boy, if a dog ran away from me through fear, I generally looked about for a stone, a stick, or a brickbat; and if neither offered to my hand, I skimmed my hat after him to make him afraid for something. What signifies power, if we do not exert it?

Let my lord know thou hast scribbled to me. But give him not the contents of thy epistle. Though a parcel of crude stuff, *he* would think there was something in it. Poor arguments will do in favour of what we like. But the stupid peer little thinks that this lady is a rebel to love. On the contrary, not only he, but all the world believe her to be a volunteer in his service—So I shall incur blame, and she will be pitied, if anything happen amiss.

Since my lord's heart is so set upon this match, I have written already to let him know, 'That my unhappy character has given my beloved an ungenerous diffidence of me. That she is so mother-sick and father-fond, that she had rather return to Harlowe Place than marry. That she is even apprehensive that the step she has taken of going off with me will make the ladies of a family of such name and rank as ours think slightly of her. That therefore I desire his lordship (though this hint, I tell him, must be very delicately touched) to write me such a letter as I can show her. Let him treat me in it ever so freely, I shall not take it amiss, because I know his lordship takes pleasure in writing to me in a corrective style. That he may make what offers he pleases on the marriage. That I desire his presence at the ceremony; that I may take from his hand the greatest blessing that mortal man can give me.'

I have not absolutely told the lady that I would write to his lordship to this effect; yet have given her reason to think I will. So that without the last necessity I shall not produce the answer I expect from him: for I am very loath, I own, to make use of any of my family's names for the furthering of my designs. And yet I must make all secure before I pull off the mask. This was my motive for bringing her hither.

Thus thou seest that the old peer's letter came very seasonably. I thank thee for it. But as to his sentences, they cannot possibly do me good. I was early suffocated with his *wisdom of nations*. When a boy, I never asked anything of him, but out flew a *proverb*; and if the tendency of that was to deny me, I never could obtain the least favour. This gave me so great an aversion to the very word, that when a child,

a   See pp. 424f.

I made it a condition with my tutor, who was an honest parson, that I would not read my Bible at all, if he would not excuse me one of the wisest books in it: to which, however, I had no other objection than that it was called *The Proverbs*. And as for Solomon, he was then a hated character with me, not because of his polygamy, but because I had conceived him to be such another musty old fellow as my uncle.

Well, but let us leave old saws to old men—What signifies thy tedious whining over thy departing relation? Is it not generally agreed that he cannot recover? Will it not be kind in thee to put him out of his misery? I hear that he is pestered still with visits from doctors, and apothecaries, and surgeons; that they cannot cut so deep as the mortification has gone; and that in every visit, in every scarification, inevitable death is pronounced upon him. Why then do they keep tormenting him? Is it not to take away more of his living fleece than of his dead flesh?—When a man is given over, the fee should surely be refused. Are they not now robbing his heirs?—What hast thou to do, if the will be as thou'dst have it?— He sent for thee (did he not?) to close his eyes. He is but an *uncle*, is he?

Let me see, if I mistake not it is in the Bible, or some other good book: can it be in Herodotus?—Oh, I believe it is in Josephus; a half-sacred and half-profane author. He tells us of a king of Syria, put out of his pain by his prime minister, or one who deserved to be so for his contrivance. The story says, if I am right, that he spread a wet cloth over his face, which killing him, he reigned in his place.[2] A notable fellow! Perhaps this wet cloth in the original is what we now call *laudanum*; a potion that overspreads the faculties, as the wet cloth did the face of the royal patient, and the translator knew not how to render it.

But how like a forlorn varlet thou subscribest, *Thy melancholy friend*, J. BELFORD!—Melancholy for what? To stand by and see fair play between an old man and death? I thought thou hadst been more of a man; thou that are not afraid of an acute death, a sword's point, to be so plaguily hypped at the consequences of a chronical one!—What though the scarificators work upon him day by day? it is only upon a *caput mortuum:* and prithee *Go to*, to use the *stylum veterum*, and learn of the *royal butchers*; who, for sport (a hundred times worse men than thy Lovelace) widow ten thousand at a brush, and make twice as many fatherless; and are dubbed *Magnus* or *Le Grand* for it. Learn of *them*, I say, how to support a *single* death.

I wish *my* uncle had given *me* the opportunity of setting thee a better example: thou shouldst have seen what a brave fellow I had been. And had I had occasion to write, my conclusion would have been this: 'I hope the old Trojan's happy. In that hope, I am so; and

> Thy rejoicing friend,
> R. LOVELACE'

Dwell not always, Jack, upon one subject. Let me have poor Belton's story; the sooner the better. If I can be of service to him, tell him he may command me, either in purse or person. Yet the former with a freer will than the latter; for how can I leave my goddess? But I'll issue my commands to my other vassals to attend thy summons. If ye want *head*, let me know. If not, my quota on this occasion is *money*.

Letter 192: MR BELFORD TO ROBERT LOVELACE, ESQ.

Saturday, May 20

NOT one word will I reply to such an abandoned wretch as thou hast shown thyself to be in thine of last night. I will leave the lady to the protection of that Power who only can work miracles; and to her own merits. Still I have hopes that these will save her.

I will proceed, as thou desirest, to poor Belton's case; and the rather as it has thrown me into such a train of thinking upon our past lives, our present courses, and our future views, as may be of service to both, if I can give due weight to the reflections that arise from it.

The poor man made me a visit on Thursday, in this my melancholy attendance. He began with complaints of his ill health and spirits, his hectic cough, and his increased malady of spitting of blood; and then led to his story.

A confounded one it is; and which highly aggravates his other maladies: for it has come out that his Thomasine (who truly would be new-christened, you know, that her name might be nearer in sound to the christian name of the man whom she pretended to dote upon) has for many years carried on an intrigue with a fellow who had been hostler to her father (an innkeeper at Dorking); of whom, at the expense of poor Tom, she has made a gentleman; and managed it so, that having the art to make herself his cashier, she has been unable to account for large sums which poor Belton thought forthcoming at his demand, and had trusted to her custody, in order to pay off a mortgage upon his paternal estate in Kent, which his heart had run upon leaving clear; but which cannot now be done, and will soon be foreclosed. And yet she has so long passed for his wife, that he knows not what to resolve upon about her; nor about the two boys he was so fond of, supposing them to be his; whereas now he begins to doubt his share in them.

So KEEPING don't do, Lovelace. 'Tis not the eligible life. 'A man may *keep a woman*, said the poor fellow to me, but *not his estate!*—Two interests!—Then, my tottering fabric!' pointing to his emaciated carcase.

We do well to value ourselves upon our *liberty* or, to speak more properly, upon the liberties we take! We had need to run down matrimony as we do, and to make that state the subject of our frothy jests, when we frequently render ourselves (for this of Tom's is not a *singular* case) the dupes and fools of women, who generally govern us (by arts our wise heads penetrate not) more absolutely than a wife would attempt to do!

Let us consider this point a little; and that upon our own *principles* as *libertines*, setting aside what the *laws of our country*, and its *customs*, oblige from us; which, nevertheless, we cannot get over till we have got over almost all moral obligations as members of society.

In the first place, let us consider (we, who are in possession of estates by *legal descent*) how we should have liked to have been such naked destitute varlets, as we must have been had our fathers been as wise as ourselves; and despised matrimony as we do—and then let us ask ourselves if we ought not to have the same regard for *our* posterity as we are glad our fathers had for *theirs?*

But this, perhaps, is too *moral* a consideration—To proceed therefore to those which will be more striking to *us*: how can we reasonably expect economy or frugality (or anything indeed but riot and waste) from creatures who have an *interest*, and must therefore have *views*, different from our own?

They know the uncertain tenure (our fickle humours) by which they hold: and is it to be wondered at, supposing them to be provident harlots, that they should endeavour, if they have the *power, to lay up against a rainy day*; or, if they have *not* the power, that they should squander all they can come at, when they are sure of *nothing but the present hour*; and when the life they live, and the sacrifices they have made, put conscience and honour out of the question?

Whereas a *wife*, having the same family interest with her husband, lies not under either the same *apprehensions* or *temptations*; and has not broken through (of *necessity*, at least, has not) *those* restraints which education has fastened upon her: and if she made a private purse, which we are told by anti-matrimonialists, all wives love to do, and has children, it goes all into the same family at the long run.

Then, as to the great article of fidelity to your bed, are not women of family, who are well-educated, under greater restraints than creatures who, if they ever *had* reputation, sacrifice it to sordid interest, or to more sordid appetite, the moment they give up to you? Does not the example you furnish, of having succeeded with her, give encouragement for *others* to attempt her likewise? For, with all her blandishments, can any man be so credulous, or so vain, as to believe that the woman *he* could persuade, *another* may not prevail upon?

Adultery is so capital a guilt, that even rakes and libertines, if not wholly abandoned, and as I may say *invited* by a woman's levity, disavow and condemn it: but here, in a state of KEEPING, a woman is in no danger of incurring, *legally* at least, that guilt; and you yourself have broken through, and overthrown in her, all the fences and boundaries of moral honesty, and the modesty and reserves of her sex. And what tie shall hold her against inclination or interest? And what shall deter an attempter?

While a husband has this security from *legal* sanctions, that if his wife be detected in a criminal conversation with a man of fortune (the *most* likely by bribes to seduce her) he may recover very great damages and procure a divorce besides: which, to say nothing of the ignominy, is a consideration that must have some force upon *both* parties. And a wife must be vicious indeed, and a reflection upon a man's own choice, who, for the sake of change, and where there are no qualities to seduce nor affluence to corrupt, will run so many hazards to injure her husband in the tenderest of all points.

But there are difficulties in procuring a divorce—(and so there ought)—And none, says the rake, in parting with a mistress whenever you suspect her; or whenever, weary of her, you have a mind to change her for another.

But must not the man be a brute indeed, who can cast off a woman whom he has seduced (if he take her from the town, that's another thing), without some flagrant reason; something that will better justify him to *himself*, as well as to *her* and to the *world*, than mere *power* and *novelty*?

But I don't see, if we judge by *fact* and by the *practice* of all we have been acquainted with of the *keeping class*, that we know how to part with them when we have them.

That we know we *can* if we *will*, is all we have for it: and this leads us to bear many things from a *mistress*, which we would not from a *wife*. But if we are good-natured and humane; if the woman has *art* (and what woman *wants* it, who has fallen by *art?* and to whose precarious situation *art* is so necessary?); if you have given her the credit of being called by your name; if you have a settled place of abode, and have received and paid visits in her company, as your wife; if she has brought you children: you will allow that these are strong obligations upon you in the world's eye, as well as to your own heart, against tearing yourself from such close connexions. She will stick to you as your skin: and it will be next to flaying yourself to cast her off.

Even if there be *cause* for it, by infidelity, she will have managed ill, if she have not her defenders—Nor did I ever know a cause, or a person, so *bad*, as to want advocates, either from ill-will to the one, or pity to the other; and you will then be thought a hard-hearted miscreant. And even were she to go off without credit to *herself,* she will leave *you* as little; especially with all those whose good opinion a man would wish to cultivate.

Well, then, shall this poor privilege, that we may part with a woman if we *will*, be deemed a balance for the other inconveniencies? Shall it be thought by *us*, who are men of family and fortune, an equivalent for giving up equality of degree; and taking for the partner of our bed, and very probably more than the partner in our estates (to the breach of all family rule and order), a low-born, a low-educated creature, who has not brought anything into the common stock; and can possibly make no returns for the solid benefits she receives, but those libidinous ones which a man cannot boast of but to *his* disgrace, nor think of but to the shame of *both?*

Moreover, as the man advances in years, the fury of his libertinism will go off. He will have different aims and pursuits which will diminish his appetite to ranging, and make such a regular life as the matrimonial and family life palatable to him, and every day more palatable.

If he has children, and has reason to think them *his*, and if his lewd courses have left him any estate, he will have cause to regret the *restraint* his boasted *liberty* has laid him under, and the valuable *privilege* it has deprived him of; when he finds that it must descend to some relation, for whom, whether near or distant, he cares not one farthing; and who perhaps [for] his dissolute life, if a man of virtue, has held him in the utmost contempt.

And were we to suppose his estate in his power to bequeath as he pleases; why should a man resolve, for the gratifying of his wicked humour only, to bastardize his race? Why should he wish to expose them to the scorn and insults of the rest of the world?—Why should he, whether they are men or women, lay them under the necessity of complying with proposals of marriage, either inferior as to fortune, or unequal as to age?—Why should he deprive the children he loves, and who are themselves guilty of no fault (if they have regard to morals, and to legal and social sanctions), of the respect they would wish to have, and to deserve?—and of the opportunity of associating themselves with proper, that is to say with *reputable*, company?—And why should he make them think themselves under obligation to every person of character, who should vouchsafe to visit them? What little reason, in a word, would such children have to bless their father's obstinate defiance of the laws and customs of his country; and for giving them a mother whom they could not think of with honour; to whose *crime* it was, that they owed their very beings, and whose example it was their duty to shun?

If the education and morals of these children are left to chance, as too generally they are (for the man who has humanity and a feeling heart, and who is capable of fondness for his offspring, I take it for granted will marry); the case is still worse; his crime is perpetuated, as I may say, by his children: and the sea, the army, perhaps the highway, for the boys; the common for the girls; too often point out the way to a worse catastrophe.

What therefore, upon the whole, do we get by treading in these crooked paths, but danger, disgrace, and a too late repentance?

And after all, do we not frequently become the cullies of our own libertinism; sliding into the very state with those half-worn-out doxies; which perhaps we might have entered into with their ladies; at least with their superiors, both in degree and fortune? And all the time lived handsomely like ourselves; not sneaking into holes and corners; and, when we crept abroad with our women, looking about us at every opening into the street or day, as if we were confessedly accountable to the censures of all honest people.

My cousin Tony Jenyns, thou knewest. He had not the actively mischievous spirit that thou, Belton, Mowbray, myself, and Tourville, have: but he imbibed the same notions we do, and carried them into practice.

How did he prate against wedlock! How did he strut about as a *wit* and a *smart!* And what a *wit* and a *smart* did all the boys and girls of our family, myself among the rest, then an urchin, think him, for the airs he gave himself?—Marry! No, not for the world; what man of sense would bear the insolences, the petulances, the expensiveness of a wife! He could not for the heart of him think it tolerable that a woman of *equal* rank and fortune, and as it might happen *superior* talents to his own, should look upon herself to have a right to share the benefit of that fortune which she brought him.

So, after he had fluttered about the town for two or three years, in all which time he had a better opinion of himself than anybody else had, what does he do, but enter upon an affair with his fencing-master's daughter?

He succeeds; takes private lodgings for her at Hackney; visits her by stealth, both of them tender of reputations that were *extremely* tender, but which neither had quite given over; for rakes of either sex are always the last to condemn or cry down themselves: visited by nobody, nor visiting: the life of a thief, or of a man beset by creditors, afraid to look out of his own house or to be seen abroad with her. And thus went he on for twelve years and, though he had a good estate, hardly making both ends meet; for, though no glare, there was no economy; and besides, he had every year a child, and very fond of them was he. But none of them lived above three years. And being now, on the death of the dozenth, grown as dully sober as if he had been a real husband, his good Mrs Thomas (for he had not permitted her to take his own name) prevailed upon him to think the loss of their children a judgement upon the parents for their wicked way of life (there is a time when calamities will beget reflection! The royal cully of France, thou knowest, was *Maintenon*ed into it by his ill successes in the field[1]): and so, when more than half worn-out *both* of them, the sorry fellow took it into his head to marry her. And then had leisure to sit down, and contemplate the many offers of persons of family and fortune which he had declined in the prime of his life: his expenses *equal* at least: his reputation not only *less*, but *lost:* his enjoyments *stolen:* his partnership *unequal*, and such as he had always been ashamed of. But the women said, that after twelve years' cohabitation, Tony did an honest thing by her. And that was all my poor cousin got by making his old mistress his new wife—Not a drum, not a trumpet, not a fife, not a tabret, nor the expectation of a new joy, to animate him on!

What Belton will do with his Thomasine, I know not; nor care I to advise him: for I see the poor fellow does not like that anybody should curse her but himself: and that he does very heartily. And so low is he reduced that he blubbers over the reflection upon his past fondness for her cubs, and upon his present doubts of their being his: 'What a damned thing is it, Belford, if Tom and Hal should be the hostler dog's puppies, and not mine!' Very true! and I think the strong health of the chubby-faced, muscular whelps confirms the too great probability. But I say not so to him.

You, he says, are such a gay, lively mortal, that this sad tale would make no impression upon you: especially now that your whole heart is engaged as it is. Mowbray would be too violent upon it; he has not, he says, a feeling heart: Tourville has no discretion: and, a pretty jest! although he and his Thomasine lived without reputation in the world (people guessing that they were not married, notwithstanding she went by his name); yet 'he would not *too much* discredit the *cursed ingrate* neither!'—Could a man act a weaker part, had he been really married; and were he sure he was going to separate from the mother of his own children?

I leave this as a lesson upon thy heart, without making any application: only with this remark, that after we libertines have indulged our licentious appetites, reflecting in the conceit of our vain hearts, both with our lips and by our lives, upon our ancestors and the good old ways, we find out, when we come to years of discretion, if we live till then (what all who knew us found out before, that is to say, we find out) our own despicable folly; that those good old ways would have been best for *us*, as well as for the rest of the world; and that in every step we have deviated from them, we have only exposed our vanity and our ignorance at the same time.

J. BELFORD

Letter 193: MR LOVELACE TO JOHN BELFORD, ESQ.

Saturday, May 20

I AM pleased with the sober reflection thou concludest thy last with; and I thank thee for it. Poor Belton!—I did not think his Thomasine would have proved so very a devil. But this must everlastingly be the risk of a keeper who takes up with a low-bred girl. This I never did. Nor had I occasion to do. Such a one as *I*, Jack, needed only, till now, to shake the stateliest tree, and the mellowed fruit dropped into my mouth: always of Montaigne's taste, thou knowest—thought it a glory to subdue a girl of family[1]—More truly delightful to me the seduction progress than the crowning act—for that's a vapour, a bubble!—And most cordially do I thank thee for thy indirect hint that I am right in my present pursuit.

From such a lady as Miss Harlowe, a man is secured from all the inconveniencies thou expatiatest upon.

Once more, therefore, do I thank thee, Belford, for thy approbation!—One need not, as thou sayest, sneak into holes and corners and shun the day, in the company of such a lady as this. How friendly in thee, thus to abet the favourite purpose of my heart!—Nor can it be a disgrace to me to permit such a lady to be called by my name!—Nor shall I be at all concerned about the world's censure, if I live to the *years of discretion* which thou mentionest, should I be taken in, and prevailed upon to tread with her the good old path of my ancestors.

A blessing on thy heart, thou honest fellow! I *thought* thou wert but in jest, or acting but by my uncle's desire, when thou wert pleading for matrimony in behalf of this lady!—It could not be principle, I knew, in thee: it could not be compassion—A little *envy* indeed I suspected!—But now I see thee once more thyself. And once more, say I, a blessing on thy heart, thou true friend, and very honest fellow!

Now will I proceed with courage in all my schemes, and oblige thee with the continued narrative of my progressions towards bringing them to effect!—But I could not forbear to interrupt my story, to show my gratitude!

Letter 194: MR LOVELACE TO JOHN BELFORD, ESQ.

Saturday, May 20

AND now will I favour thee with a brief account of our present situation.

From the highest to the lowest we are all extremely happy—*Dorcas* stands well in her lady's graces. *Polly* has asked her advice in relation to a courtship affair of her own. No oracle ever gave better. *Sally* has had a quarrel with her woollen draper; and made my beloved lady chancellor in it. She blamed Sally for behaving tyrannically to a man who loves her. Dear creature! to stand against a glass, and to shut her eyes because she will not see her face in it!—Mrs Sinclair has paid *her* court to so unerring a judge by requesting her advice with regard to both nieces.

This the way we have been in for several days with the people below. Yet *sola* generally at her meals, and seldom at other times in their company. They now, used to her ways (perseverance must conquer), never press her; so when they meet, all is civility on both sides. Even married people, I believe, Jack, prevent abundance of quarrels by seeing one another but seldom.

But how stands it between thyself and the lady, methinks thou askest, since her abrupt departure from thee, and undutiful repulse of Wednesday morning? Why, pretty well in the main. Nay, very well. For why? The dear saucy-face knows not how to help herself. Can fly to no other protection. And has, besides, overheard a conversation (who would have thought she had been so near?) which passed between Mrs Sinclair, Miss Martin, and myself, that very Wednesday afternoon; which has set her heart at ease with respect to several doubtful points.

Such as, particularly, Mrs Fretchville's unhappy state of mind—most humanely pitied by Miss Martin, who knows her very well; the husband she has lost and herself, lovers from their cradles. Pity from one begets pity from another; and so many circumstances were given to poor Mrs Fretchville's distress, that it was impossible but my beloved must *extremely* pity her, whom the less tender-hearted Miss Martin *greatly* pitied.

My Lord M.'s gout his only hindrance from visiting my spouse.

Lady Betty and Miss Montague soon expected in town.

My earnest desire signified to have my spouse receive them in her own house, if Mrs Fretchville would but know her own mind.

My intention to stay at their house notwithstanding, *as I said I had told them before*, in order to gratify her utmost punctilio.

My passion for my beloved, which I told them in a high and fervent accent was the truest that man could have for woman, I boasted of. It was, in short, I said, of the *true platonic kind*; or I had no notion of what platonic love was.

So it is, Jack; and must end as platonic love generally does end.

Sally and Mrs Sinclair praised, *but not grossly*, my beloved. Sally particularly admired her purity, called it exemplary; yet, to avoid suspicion, expressed her thoughts that she was *rather over-nice*, if she might presume to say so before me. But applauded me for the strict observation I made of my vow.

I more freely blamed her reserves to me; called her cruel; inveighed against her relations; doubted her love. Every favour I asked of her denied me. Yet my behaviour to her as pure and delicate when alone, as when before them. Hinted at something that had passed between us that very day, that showed her indifference to me in so strong a light that I could not bear it. But that I would ask her for her company to the play of *Venice Preserved*, given out for Saturday night, as a benefit play[1]; the prime actors to be in it; and this to see if I were to be denied every favour—Yet, for my own part, I loved not tragedies; though she did, for the sake of the instruction, the warning, and the example generally given in them.

I had too much *feeling*, I said. There was enough in the world to make our hearts sad, without carrying grief into our diversions, and making the distresses of others our own.

True enough, Belford; and I believe, generally speaking, that all the men of our cast are of my mind—They love not any tragedies but those in which they themselves act the parts of tyrants and executioners; and, afraid to trust themselves with serious and solemn reflections, run to comedies, to laugh away the distresses they have occasioned, and to find examples of as immoral men as themselves. For very few of our comic performances, as thou knowest, give us good ones—I answer, however, for myself—Yet thou, I think, on recollection, lovest to deal in the *lamentable*.

Sally answered for Polly, who was absent, Mrs Sinclair for herself, and for all her acquaintance, even for Miss Partington, in preferring the comic to the tragic scenes—And I believe they are right; for the devil's in it, if a confided-in rake does not give a girl enough of tragedy in his comedy.

I asked Sally to oblige my fair one with her company.

She was engaged (that was right, thou'lt suppose). I asked Mrs Sinclair's leave for Polly. To be sure, she answered, Polly would think it an honour to attend Mrs Lovelace: but the poor thing was tender-hearted; and as the tragedy was deep, would weep herself blind.

Sally, mean time, objected Singleton, that *I* might answer the objection, and save my beloved the trouble of making it, or debating the point with me.

I then, from a letter just before received from one in her father's family, warned them of a person who had undertaken to find us out, and whom I thus in writing (calling for pen and ink) described, that they might arm all the family against him—'A sun-burnt, pock-fretten sailor, ill-looking, big-boned; his stature about six foot; an heavy eye, an overhanging brow, a deck-treading stride in his walk; a couteau generally by his side; lips parched from his gums, as if by staring at the sun in hot climates; a brown coat; a coloured handkerchief about his neck; an oaken plant in his hand, near as long as himself, and proportionably thick.'

No questions must be answered, that he should ask. They should call me to him. But not let my beloved know a tittle of this, so long as it could be helped. And I added, that if her brother or Singleton came, and if they behaved civilly, I would for her sake be civil to *them:* and in this case, she had nothing to do but to own her marriage, and there could be no pretence for violence on either side. But most fervently I swore, that if she was conveyed away, either by persuasion or force, I would directly, on missing her but one day, go to demand her at her father's whether she were there or not; and if I recovered not a sister, I would have a brother; and should find out a captain of a ship as well as he. And now, Jack, dost thou think she'll attempt to get from me, do what I will?

Mrs Sinclair began to be afraid of mischief in her house—I was apprehensive that she would overdo the matter, and be out of character. I therefore winked at her. She primmed; nodded, to show she took me, twanged out a High-ho, lapped one horse-lip over the other, and was silent.

Here's preparation, Belford!—Dost think I will throw it all away, for anything thou canst say, or Lord M. write?—*No indeed!*—as my charmer says, when she bridles.

AND what must necessarily be the consequence of all this, with regard to my beloved's behaviour to me?—Canst thou doubt that it was all complaisance next time she admitted me into her presence?

Thursday we were very happy. All the morning *extremely* happy. I kissed her charming hand—I need not describe to thee her hand and arm. When thou sawest her, I took notice that thy eyes dwelt upon them, whenever thou couldst spare them from that beauty-spot of wonders, her face. *Fifty* times kissed her hand, I believe—Once her cheek, intending her lip, but so rapturously, that she could not help seeming angry.

Had she not thus kept me at arms-length; had she not denied me those innocent liberties which our sex, from degree to degree, aspire to; could I but have gained access to her in her hours of heedlessness and dishabille (for full dress creates dignity, augments consciousness, and compels distance), we had been familiarized to each other long ago. But keep her up ever so late; meet her ever so early; by breakfast-time dressed for the day; and at her earliest hour, as nice as others dressed—All her forms thus kept up, wonder not that I have made so little progress in the proposed trial—But how must all this distance stimulate!

Thursday morning, [as] I said, we were extremely happy—About *noon,* she numbered the hours she had been with me; all of them to me but as one minute; and desired to be left to herself. I was loth to comply: but observing the sunshine begin to shut in, I yielded.

I dined out. Returned; talked of the house, and of Mrs Fretchville: had seen Mennell—Had pressed him to get the widow to quit—She pitied Mrs Fretchville—another good effect of the overheard conversation—Had written to my uncle; expected an answer soon from him. I was admitted to sup with her. Urged for her approbation or correction of my written terms. She promised an answer as soon as she had heard from Miss Howe.

Then I pressed for her company to the play on Saturday night. She made objections, as I had foreseen: her brother's projects, warmth of the weather, etc. But in such a manner as if half-afraid to disoblige me (another happy effect of the overheard conversation). Got over these therefore; and she consented to favour me.

Friday passed as the day before.

Here were two happy days to both!—Why cannot I make every day equally happy? It looks as if it were in my power to do so.—Strange I should thus delight in teasing a woman I so dearly love!—I must, I doubt, have something in my temper like Miss Howe, who loves to plague the man who puts himself in her power—But I could not do thus by such an angel as this, did I not believe that after her probation-time is expired, and if there is no bringing her to *cohabitation* (my darling view), I shall reward her as she wishes.

Saturday is half-over, equally happy—preparing for the play—Polly has offered, and is accepted. I have directed her where to weep—and this not only to show her humanity (a weeping eye indicates a gentle heart), but to have a pretence to hide her face with her fan or handkerchief; yet Polly is far from being every man's girl— And we shall sit in the gallery green-box.

The woes of others so well represented, as those of Belvidera particularly will be, must I hope unlock and open my charmer's heart. Whenever I have been able to prevail upon a girl to permit me to attend her to a play, I have thought myself sure of her. The female heart, all gentleness and harmony when obliged, expands and forgets its forms when attention is carried out of itself at an agreeable or affecting entertainment: music, and perhaps a collation afterwards, co-operating. I have no hope of such an effect here; but I have more than one end to answer by my earnestness in getting her to a play. To name but one: Dorcas has a master-key, as I have told thee—And it were worth carrying her to *Venice Preserved*, were it but to show her that there have been, and may be, much deeper distresses than she can possibly know.

Thus exceedingly happy are we at present. I hope we shall not find any of Nat. Lee's left-handed gods at work, to dash our bowl of joy with wormwood.

Letter 195: MISS CLARISSA HARLOWE TO MISS HOWE

The lady, in her next letter, dated Friday, May 19, acquaints her friend that her prospects are once more mended; and that she has known four and twenty hours together, since her last, not unhappy ones, her situation considered. 'How willing am I, *says she*, to compound for tolerable appearances! how desirous to turn the sunny side of things towards me, and to hope, where reason for hope offers! and this, not only for my own sake, but for yours, who take such generous concern in all that befalls me.'

She then gives the particulars of the conversation which she had overheard between Mr Lovelace, Mrs Sinclair, and Miss Martin; but accounts more minutely than he had done, for the opportunity she had of overhearing it, unknown to them.

She gives the reason she has to be pleased with what she heard from each: but is shocked at the measure he is resolved to take, if he misses her but for one day. Yet is pleased that he proposes to avoid *aggressive* violence, if her brother and he meet in town.

She thought herself obliged, she says, from what passed between them on Wednesday, and from what she overheard him say, to consent to go with him to the play; especially as he had the discretion to propose one of the nieces to accompany her.

She expresses herself pleased that he has actually written to Lord M.

She tells her that she has promised to give him an answer to his proposals, as soon as she has heard from *her* on the subject: and hopes that in her future letter she shall have reason to confirm these favourable appearances. 'Favourable, *says she*, I must think them in the wreck I have suffered.'

She thinks it not amiss, however, that she should perfect her scheme [whatever it be[1]]. He is certainly, she says, a deep and dangerous man; and it is therefore but prudence to be watchful, and to provide against the worst.

She is certain, she tells her, that her letters are safe.

He would never be out of her company by his good-will; otherwise she has no doubt that she is mistress of her goings-out and comings-in; and did she think it needful, and were she not afraid of her brother and Capt. Singleton, would oftener put it to trial.

Letter 196: MISS HOWE TO MISS CLARISSA HARLOWE

Saturday, May 20

I DID not know, my dear, that you deferred giving an answer to Mr Lovelace's proposals till you had my opinion of them. A particular hand occasionally going to town will leave this at Wilson's, that no delay may be made on that account.

I never had any doubt of the man's justice and generosity in matters of settlement; and all his relations are as noble in their spirits as in their descent: but *now*, it may not be amiss for you to wait to see what returns my lord makes to his letter of invitation.

The scheme I think of is this.

There is a person (I believe you have seen her with me), one Mrs Townsend, who is a great dealer in Indian silks, Brussels and French laces, cambrics, linen, and other valuable goods; which she has a way of coming at, duty-free; and has a great vend for them, and for other curiosities which she imports, in the private families of the gentry round us.

She has her days of being in town, and then is at a chamber she rents in an inn in Southwark, where she has patterns of all her silks and much of her portable goods, for the conveniency of her London customers. But her place of residence, and where she has her principal warehouse, is at Deptford, for the opportunity of getting her goods on shore.

She was first brought to me by my mother, to whom she was recommended, on the supposal of my speedy marriage; that I might have an opportunity to be as fine as a princess, was my mamma's expression, at a moderate expense.

Now, my dear, I must own that I do not love to encourage these contraband traders. What is it, but bidding defiance to the laws of our country when we do; and hurting fair traders; and at the same time robbing our prince of his legal due, to the diminution of those duties which possibly must be made good by new levies upon the whole public?

But, however, Mrs Townsend and I, though we have not yet dealt, are upon a very good foot of understanding. She is a sensible woman; she has been abroad, and often goes abroad, in the way of her business; and gives very entertaining accounts of all she has seen. And having applied to me, to recommend her to you (as it is her view to be known to young ladies who are likely to change their condition), I am sure I can engage her to give you protection at her house at Deptford; which she says is a populous village; and one of the last, I should think, that you would be sought for in. She is not much there, you will believe, by the course of her dealings; but no doubt must have somebody on the spot in whom she can confide: and there perhaps you might be safe, till your cousin comes. And I should not think it amiss, that you write to him out of hand. I cannot suggest to you what you should write. That must be left to your own discretion. For you will be afraid, no doubt, of the consequence of a variance between the two men.

I will think further of this scheme of mine in relation to Mrs Townsend, if you find it necessary that I should. But I hope there will be no occasion to do so, since your prospects seem to be changed, and that you have had *twenty-four not unhappy hours together*. How my indignation rises for this poor consolation in the courtship (*courtship* must I call it?) of such a lady!

Mrs Townsend, as I have recollected, has two brothers, each a master of a vessel; and who knows, as she and they have great concerns together, but that, in case of need, you may have a whole ship's crew at your devotion? If he give you cause to leave him, take no thought for the people at Harlowe Place. Let them take care of one another. It is a care they are *used* to. The law will help to secure them. The wretch is no assassin, no night-murderer. He is an *open*, because a *fearless* enemy; and should he attempt anything that should make him obnoxious to the laws of society, you might have a fair riddance of him either by flight or the gallows; no matter which.

Had you not been so minute in your account of the circumstances that attended the opportunity you had of overhearing the dialogue between Mr Lovelace and two of the women, I should have thought the conference contrived on purpose for your ears.

I showed Mr Lovelace's proposals to Mr Hickman, who had chambers once at Lincoln's Inn, being designed for the law had his elder brother lived. He looked so wise, so proud, and so important, upon the occasion; and wanted to take so much consideration about them—would take them home if I pleased—and weigh them well—and so forth—and the like—and all that—that I had no patience with him, and snatched them back with anger.

Oh dear!—to be so angry, and please me, for his zeal—

Yes, zeal without knowledge, I said—like most other zeals—if there were no objections that struck him at once, there were none.

So *hasty*, dearest madam!—

And so *slow*, un-dearest sir, I could have said—But, SURELY, said I, with a look which implied, *Would you rebel, sir!*—

He begged my pardon—*Saw* no objection, indeed!—But might he be allowed once more—

No matter—no matter—I would have shown them to my mother, I said, who, though of no Inn of Court, knew more of these things than half the lounging lubbers of them; and that at first sight—only that she would have been provoking upon the confession of our continued correspondence.

But, my dear, let the articles be drawn up, and ingrossed; and solemnize upon them; and there's no more to be said.

Let me add, that the sailor fellow has been tampering with my Kitty, and offered a bribe to find where to direct to you. Next time he comes, I will have him drawn through one of our deepest fish-ponds, if I can get nothing out of him. His attempt to corrupt a servant of mine will justify my orders.

I send this away directly. But will follow it by another; which shall have for its subject only my mother, myself, and your uncle Antony. And as your prospects are more promising than they have been, I will endeavour to make you smile upon this occasion. For you will be pleased to know that my mamma has had a formal tender from that grey goose; which may make her skill useful to herself, were she to encourage it.

May your prospects be still more and more happy, prays

Your own
Anna Howe

Letter 197: MISS HOWE TO MISS CLARISSA HARLOWE

Sat., Sunday, May 20, 21

Now, my dear, for the promised subject. You must not ask me how I came by the *originals* (such they really are) that I am going to present you with: for my mamma would not read to me those parts of your uncle's letter which bore hard upon myself, and which leave him without any title to mercy from me: nor would she let me hear but what she pleased of hers in answer; for she has condescended to answer him; with a denial, however—but such a denial as no one but an *old bachelor* would take from a widow.

Anybody, except myself, who could have been acquainted with such a fal-lal courtship as this must have been had it proceeded, would have been glad it had gone on; and I dare say, but for the saucy daughter, it had. My mamma, in that case, would have been ten years the younger for it, perhaps: and could I but have approved of it, I should have been considered as if ten years older than I am: since very likely it would then have been: 'We widows, my dear, know not how to keep men at a distance—so as to give them pain, in order to try their love. You must advise me, child: you must teach me to be cruel—yet not *too* cruel neither—so as to make a man heartless, who has no time, God wot, to throw away.' Then would my behaviour to Mr Hickman have been better liked; and my mother would have bridled like her daughter!

Oh my dear, how we might have been diverted by the practisings for recovery of the *long-forgottens!* could I have been sure that it would have been in my power to have put them asunder, in the Irish style, *before they had come together*. But there's no trusting to a widow whose goods and chattels are in her own hands, addressed by an old bachelor who has fine things, and offers to leave her ten thousand pounds better than he found her, and sole mistress besides, of all her *notables!* for these, as you'll see by and by, are his proposals.

The old Triton's address carries the writer's marks upon the very superscription—*To the equally amiable, and worthily admired* (There's for you) *Mrs* ANNABELLA HOWE, *Widow*; the last word added, I suppose, as *Esquire* to a man; or for fear the *bella* to *Anna* should not enough distinguish the person meant from the spinster (vain hussy you'll call me, I know): and then follows—*These humbly present*—Put down as a memorandum, I presume, to make a leg, and behave handsomely at presenting it; he intending very probably to deliver it himself.

And now stand by—to see

Enter OLD NEPTUNE

His head adorned with seaweed, and a crown of cockle-shells, as we see him decked out in Mrs Robinson's ridiculous grotto.

[*Letter 197.1: Antony Harlowe to Mrs Annabella Howe*]

Monday, May 15

Madam,

I DID make a sort of resolution ten years ago never to marry. I saw in other families, where they lived *best*, you'll be pleased to mark that, *queernesses* I could not away with. Then, liked well enough to live single for sake of my brother's family; and for one child in it, more than the rest. But that girl has turned us all off of the hinges: and why I should deny myself any comforts for them as will not thank me for so doing, I don't know.

So much for my motives, as from self and family: but the dear Mrs Howe makes me go further.

I have a very great fortune, I bless God for it, all of my own getting, or *most* of it; you'll be pleased to mark that; for I was the younger brother of three. You have also, God be thanked, a great estate which you have improved by your own frugality and wise management. Frugality, let me stop to say, is one of the greatest virtues in this mortal life, because it enables us to do justice to *all*, and puts it in our power to benefit *some* by it, as we see they *deserve*.

You have but one child; and I am a bachelor, and have never a one—All bachelors cannot say so. Wherefore your daughter may be the better for me if she will keep up with my humour; which was never thought bad: especially to my equals. Servants, indeed, I don't matter being angry with, when I please: they are paid for bearing it, and too, too often deserve it; as we have very frequently taken notice of to one another. But this won't hurt neither you nor Miss.

I will make very advantageous settlements; such as any common friend shall judge to be so. But must have all in my own power, while I live: because, you know, madam, it is as creditable to the wife as the husband, that it should be so.

I aim not at fine words. We are not children; though it is hoped we may have some; for I am a very healthy sound man, I bless God for it: and never brought home from my voyages and travels a worser constitution than I took out with me. I was none of those, I will assure you. But this I will undertake, that if you are the survivress, you shall be at *the least* ten thousand pounds the better for me. What in the contrary case I shall be the better for you, I leave to you, as you shall think my kindness to you shall deserve.

But one thing, madam, I should be glad of, that Miss Howe might not live with us then (she need not know I write thus)—But go home to Mr Hickman, as she is upon the point of marriage, I hear. And if she behaves dutifully, as she should do, to us both, she shall be the better; for so I said before.

You shall manage all things, both mine and your own; for I know little of land matters. All my opposition to you shall be out of love, when I think you take too much upon you for your health.

It will be very pretty for you, I should think, to have a man of experience, in a long winter's evening, to sit down and tell you stories of foreign parts, and the customs of the nations he has consorted with. And I have fine curiosities of the Indian growth, such as ladies love, and some that even my niece Clary, when she was good, never saw. These, one by one, as you are kind to me (which I make no question of, because I shall be kind to you) shall all be yours—Prettier entertainment by much, than sitting with a too smartish daughter, sometimes out of humour, and thwarting and vexing, as daughters will, when women grown especially (as I have heard you often observe); and thinking their parents old, without paying them the reverence due to years; when, as in your case, I make no sort of doubt they are young enough to wipe their noses. You understand me, madam.

As for me myself, it will be very happy, and I am delighted with the thinking of it, to have after a pleasant ride or so, a lady of like experience with myself to come home to, and but one interest betwixt us: to reckon up our comings-in together; and what this day and this week has produced—Oh how this will increase love!—Most mightily will it increase it!—And I believe I should never love you enough, or be able to show you all my love.

I hope, madam, there need not be *such* maiden niceties and hangings-off, as I may call them, between us, for hanging-off sake, as that you will deny me a line or two to this proposal, written down, although you would not answer me so readily when I spoke to you: your daughter being, I suppose, hard by; for you looked round you, as if not willing to be overheard. So I resolved to write: that my writing may stand, as upon record, for my upright meaning; being none of your Lovelaces; you'll mark that, madam; but a downright, true, honest, faithful Englishman. So hope you will not disdain to write a line or two to this my proposal: and I shall look upon it as a great honour, I will assure you, and be proud thereof—What can I say more?—For you are your own mistress, as I am my own master: and you shall *always* be your own mistress: be pleased to mark that; for so a lady of your prudence and experience ought to be.

This is a long letter. But the subject requires it; because I would not write twice where once would do: so would explain my sense and meaning at one time.

I have had writing in my head *two whole months very near*; but hardly knew how, being unpractised in these matters, to begin to write. And now, good lady, be favourable to

Your most humble lover,
and obedient servant,
ANT. HARLOWE

Here's a letter of courtship, my dear!—And let me subjoin to it, that if now, or hereafter, I should treat this hideous lover who is so free with me to my mother with asperity, and you should be disgusted at it; I shall think you don't give me that preference in your love which you have in mine.

And now, which shall I first give you; the answer of my mamma; or the dialogue that passed between the widow mother and the pert daughter, upon her letting the latter know that she had a letter?

I *think* you shall have the *dialogue*. But let me premise one thing; that if you *think* me too free, you must not let it run in your head that I am writing of *your* uncle, or of *my* mother: but of a couple of old lovers, no matter whom. Reverence is too apt to be forgotten by second persons, where the *reverends* forget *first*.

Well then, suppose my mamma, after twice coming into my closet to me, and as often going out, with very meaning features and lips ready to burst open, but still closed as it were by compulsion, a speech going off in a slight cough that never went near the lungs; grown more resolute, the third time of entrance, and sitting down by me, thus begin:

Mother. I have a very serious matter to talk with you upon, Nancy, when you are disposed to attend to matters *within* ourselves, and not let matters *without* ourselves wholly engross you.

A good *selves*-ish speech!—But I thought that friendship, and gratitude, and humanity, were matters that ought to be deemed of the most *intimate* concern to us. But not to dwell upon her words:

Daughter. I am *now* disposed to attend to everything my mamma is *disposed* to say to me.

M. Why then, child—why then, my dear—(and the good lady's face looked *so* plump! *so* smooth! and *so* shining!)—I see you are all attention, Nancy!—but don't be surprised!—don't be uneasy!—but I have—I have—where is it?—(And yet it lay next her heart, never another near it—so no difficulty to have found it)— I have a *letter*, my dear!—(and out from her bosom it came: but she still held it in her hand)—I have a *letter*, child—It is—it is—it is from—from a gentleman, I assure you!—lifting up her head, and smiling.

There is no delight to a daughter, thought I, in such surprises as seem to be *collecting*: I will deprive my mamma of the satisfaction of making a *gradual* discovery.

D. From Mr Antony Harlowe, I suppose, madam?

M. (Lips drawn closer: eye raised) Why, my dear!—but how, I wonder, could you think of Mr Antony Harlowe?

D. How, madam, could I think of anybody *else*?

M. How could you think of anybody *else!*—(angrily, and drawing back her face). But do you know the subject, Nancy?

D. You have told it, madam, by your manner of breaking it to me. But, indeed, I questioned not that he had *two* motives in his visits here—*both* equally agreeable to me; for all that family love me dearly.

M. No love lost, if so, between you and them. But this (*rising*) is what I get—so like your papa!—I never could open my heart to *him!*

D. Dear madam, excuse me. Be so good as to open your heart to *me*—I don't love the Harlowes. But pray excuse me.

M. You have put me quite out with your forward temper!—(angrily sitting down again).

D. I will be all patience and attention. May I be allowed to read his letter?

M. I wanted to *advise* with you upon it—But you are such a strange creature!— You are always for answering one before one speaks!

D. You'll be so good as to forgive me, madam—But I thought everybody (he among the rest) knew that you had always declared against a second marriage.

M. And so I have. But then it was in the mind I was in. Things may offer—
I stared.

M. Nay, don't be surprised!—I don't intend—I don't intend—

D. Not, perhaps, in *the mind you are in*, madam.

M. Pert creature!—(*rising again!*)—We shall quarrel, I see!—There's no—

D. Once more, dear madam, I beg your excuse. I will attend in silence—Pray, madam, sit down again—Pray do—(she sat down)—May I see the letter?

No; there are some things in it, you won't like—Your temper is known, I find, to be unhappy—But nothing *bad* against you; intimations, on the contrary, that you shall be the better for him, if you oblige him.

Not a living soul but the Harlowes, I said, thought me ill-tempered: and I was contented that *they* should, who could do as they had done by the most universally acknowledged sweetness in the world.

Here we broke out a little; but, at last, she read me some of the passages in it— But not the *most mightily* ridiculous; yet I could hardly keep my countenance neither. And when she had done:

M. Well now, Nancy, tell me what you think of it?

D. Nay, pray, madam, tell me what *you* think of it?

M. I expect to be answered by an answer; not by a question!—You don't *use* to be shy to speak your mind.

D. Not when my mamma commands me to do so.

M. Then speak it now.

D. Without hearing it all?

M. Speak to what you *have* heard.

D. Why then, madam—you won't be my mamma Howe, if you give way to it.

M. I am surprised at your assurance, Nancy!

D. I mean, madam, you will then be my mamma Harlowe.

M. Oh dear heart!—But I am not a fool.

And her colour went and came.

D. Dear, madam!—(but, indeed, I don't love a Harlowe—that's what I meant). I *am* your child, and *must* be your child, do what you will.

M. A very pert one, I am sure, as ever mother bore! And you *must* be my child, do what I *will!*— As much as to say, you would not, if you could help it, if I—

D. How could I have such a thought!—It would be *forward*, indeed, if I had— when I don't know what your *mind* is as to the proposal—when the proposal is so very advantageous a one too.

M. (Looking a little less discomposed) Why, indeed, ten thousand pounds—

D. And to be sure of outliving him, madam!

This staggered her a little—

M. Sure! Nobody can be sure!—but it is very likely that—

D. Not at all, madam; you was going to read something (but stopped) about his constitution: his sobriety is well known—Why, madam, these gentlemen who have been at sea, and in different climates, and come home to relax from cares in a temperate one, and are sober—are the likeliest to live long of any men in the world—Don't you see that his very skin is a fortification of buff?

M. Strange creature!

D. God forbid that anybody I love and honour should *marry a man* in hopes to *bury him*. But suppose, madam, at your time of life—

M. My time of life!—Dear heart!—What is my time of life, pray?

D. Not old, madam; and that may be your danger!

As I hope to live (my dear) my mamma smiled, and looked not displeased with me.

M. Why, indeed, child—why, indeed, I must needs say—and then I should choose to do nothing (froward as you are sometimes) to hurt *you*.

D. Why, as to that, madam—I can't expect you should deprive yourself of any satisfaction—

M. Satisfaction, my dear!—I don't say it would be a *satisfaction*—But could I do anything that would benefit *you*, it would perhaps be an inducement to hold *one* conference upon the subject.

D. My fortune already will be more considerable than my match, if I am to have Mr Hickman.

M. Why so?—Mr Hickman's fortune is enough to entitle him to yours.

D. If *you* think so, that's enough.

M. Not but I should think the worse of myself, if I desired anybody's death; but I think, as you say, Mr Antony Harlowe is a healthy man, and bids fair for a long life.

Bless me, thought I, how shall I do to know whether this be an objection or a recommendation!

D. Will you forgive me, madam?

M. What would the girl say—(looking as if she was half afraid to hear what).

D. Only, that if you marry a man of *his* time of life, you stand two chances instead of one, to be a nurse at *your* time of life.

M. Saucebox!

D. Dear madam!—What I mean is only that these healthy old men sometimes fall into lingering disorders all at once. And I humbly conceive that the infirmities of age are too uneasily borne with, where the remembrance of the pleasanter season comes not in to relieve the healthier of the two.

M. A strange girl!—I always told you that you know either too much to be argued with, or too little for me to have patience with you.

D. I can't but say I would be glad of your commands, madam, how to behave myself to Mr Harlowe next time he comes.

M. How to behave yourself!—Why, if you retire with contempt of him when he next comes, it will be but as you have been used to do of late.

D. Then he *is* to come again, madam?

M. And suppose he be?

D. I can't help it, if it be your pleasure, madam—He desires a line in answer to his fine letter. If he comes, it will be in pursuance of that line, I presume?

M. None of your arch and pert leers, girl!—You know I won't bear them. I had a mind to hear what you would say to this matter. I have not wrote; but I shall presently.

D. It is mighty good of you, madam; I hope the man will think so; to answer his first application by letter—Pity *he should write twice, if once will do*.

M. That fetch won't let you into my intention as to what I shall write: it is too saucily put.

D. Perhaps I can guess at your intention, madam, were it to become me so to do.

M. Perhaps I would not make a *Mr Hickman* of any gentleman; using him the worse for respecting me.

D. Nor, perhaps, would I, madam, if I *liked* his respects.

M. I understand you. But perhaps it is in *your* power to make me hearken, or not, to Mr Harlowe.

D. Young gentlemen, who have probably a great deal of time before them, need not be in haste for a wife. Mr Hickman, poor man! must stay his time, or take his remedy.

M. He bears more from you than a man *ought*.

D. Then, I doubt, he gives a *reason* for the treatment he meets with.

M. Provoking creature!

D. I have but one request to make you, madam.

M. A *dutiful* one, I suppose. What is it, pray?

D. That if *you* marry, *I* may be permitted to live single.

M. Perverse creature!—I am sure.

D. How can I expect, madam, that you should refuse such terms? *Ten thousand pounds!*—At the *least* ten thousand pounds!—A very handsome proposal!—So many fine things too, to give you one by one! Dearest madam, forgive me!—I hope it is not yet so far gone, that rallying *this man* will be thought want of duty to *you*.

M. Your rallying of *him*, and your reverence to *me*, it is plain, have *one* source.

D. I hope not, madam. But ten thousand pounds—

M. Is no unhandsome proposal.

D. Indeed I think so. I hope, madam, you will not be behindhand with him in generosity.

M. He won't be ten thousand pounds the better for me, if he survive me.

D. No, madam, he can't expect that, as you have a daughter, and as he is a *bachelor and has not a child*—poor old soul!

M. Old soul, Nancy!—And thus to call him for being a bachelor and not having a child?—Does this become you?

D. Not old soul for that, madam—but half the sum; five thousand pounds; you can't engage for less, madam.

M. That sum has your approbation then?—(looking as if she'd be even with me).

D. As he leaves it to your generosity, madam, and as the reward of his kindness to you, it can't be less—Do, dear madam, permit me without incurring your displeasure to call him poor old soul again.

M. Never was such a whimsical creature!—(turning away, for I believe I looked very archly, at least I intended to do so, to hide her involuntary smiling)—I hate that wicked sly look. You give yourself very free airs—don't you?

D. I snatched her hand, and kissed it—My dear mamma, be not angry with your girl!—You have told me that *you* was very lively formerly.

M. Formerly! Good lack!—But were I to encourage his proposals, you may be sure that for Mr Hickman's sake, as well as yours, I should make a wise agreement.

D. You have both lived to years of prudence, madam.

M. Yes, I suppose I am an *old soul* too.

D. He also is for making a wise agreement, or hinting at one at least.

M. Well, the short and the long I suppose is this: I have not your consent to marry?

D. Indeed, madam, you have not my *wishes* to marry.

M. Let me tell you, that if prudence consists in wishing well to *one's self*, I see not but the *young flirts* are as prudent as the *old souls*.

D. Dear madam, would you blame me, if to wish you not to marry Mr Antony Harlowe is wishing well *to myself*?

M. You are mighty witty. I wish you were as dutiful.

D. I am more dutiful, I hope, than witty; or I should be a fool, as well as a saucebox.

M. Let *me* judge of both—Parents are only to live for their children, let them deserve it or not. That's *their* dutiful notion!

D. Heaven forbid that I should wish, if there be two interests between my mamma and me, that my mamma postpone her own for mine! or give up anything that would add to the real comforts of her life, to oblige me!—Tell me, my dear mamma, if you think this proposal will?

M. I say that ten thousand pounds is such an acquisition to one's family, that the offer of it deserves a civil return.

D. Not the *offer*, madam: the *chance* only!—If you have a view to an increase of family, the money may provide—

M. You cannot keep within tolerable bounds!—That saucy fleer I cannot away with—

D. Dearest, dearest madam, forgive me, but *old soul* ran in my head again!— Nay, indeed and upon my word, I won't be robbed of that charming smile; and again I kissed her hand.

M. Away, bold creature! Nothing can be so provoking as to be made to smile when one would *choose*, and *ought*, to be angry.

D. But, dear madam, if it be to *be*, I presume you won't think of it before next winter.

M. What now would the pert one be at?

D. Because he only proposes to entertain you with pretty stories of foreign nations in a winter's evening. Dearest, dearest madam, let me have the reading of his letter through. I will forgive him all he says about *me*.

M. It may be a very difficult thing perhaps for a man of the best sense to write a love-letter that may not be cavilled at.

D. That's because lovers, in their letters, hit not the medium—They either write too much nonsense, or too little. But do you call this *odd* soul's letter (no more will I call him *old* soul, if I can help it) a love-letter?

M. Well, well, I see you are averse to this matter. I am not to be your *mamma*; you will live single if I marry. I had a mind to see if generosity governed you in your views. I shall pursue my own inclinations; and if they should happen to be suitable to yours, pray let me for the future be better rewarded by you, than hitherto I have been.

And away she flung, without staying for a reply—vexed, I dare say, that I did not better approve of the proposal—were it only that the merit of denying might have been all her own, and to lay the stronger obligation upon her saucy daughter.

She wrote such a widow-like refusal when she went from me, as might not exclude hope in any other wooer; whatever it may do in Mr Tony Harlowe.

It will be my part to take care to beat her off of the visit she half-promises to make him upon condition of withdrawing his suit, as you will observe in [her answer]: for who knows what effect the old bachelor's exotics (*far fetched and dear-bought*, you know, is a proverb[1]) might otherwise have upon a woman's mind, wanting nothing but unnecessaries, gewgaw[s], and fineries, and offered such as are not easily to be met with or purchased?

Well, but now I give you leave to read here, in this place, the copy of my mother's answer to your uncle's letter. Not one comment will I make upon it. I know my duty better. And here therefore, taking the liberty to hope that I may in your present less disagreeable, if not wholly agreeable, situation, provoke a smile from you, I conclude myself,

> Your ever-affectionate and faithful
> ANNA HOWE

[*Letter 197.2:*] *Mrs Annabella Howe to Antony Harlowe, Esq.*

Mr Antony Harlowe,
Sir,   Friday, May 19
IT is not usual, I believe, for our sex to answer by pen and ink the first letter on these occasions. The *first* letter!—How odd is that!—As if I expected another; which I do not. But then, I think, as I do not judge proper to encourage your proposal, there is no reason why I should not answer in civility, where so great a civility is intended. Indeed I was always of opinion, that a person was entitled to that, and not to ill-usage, because he had a respect for me. And so I have often and often told my daughter.

A woman, I think, makes but a poor figure in a man's eye afterwards, and does no reputation to her sex neither, when she behaves like a tyrant to him before-hand.

To be sure, sir, if I were to change my condition, I know not a gentleman whose proposal could be more agreeable. Your nephew and nieces have enough without you: my daughter is a fine fortune without me, and I should take care to double it, living or dying, were I to do such a thing: so nobody need to be the worse for it. But Nancy would not think so.

All the comfort I know of in children is that when young they do with us what they will, and all is pretty in them to their very faults; and when they are grown up, they think their parents must live for them only; and deny themselves everything for their sakes. I know Nancy could not bear a father-in-law. She would fly at the very thought of my being in earnest to give her one. Not that I stand in fear of my daughter neither: it is not fit I should. But she has her poor papa's spirit: a very violent one that was—And one would not choose, you know, sir, to enter into any affair that one knows one must renounce a daughter for, or she a mother—Except indeed one's heart were much in it—which, I bless God, mine is not.

I have now been a widow these ten years; nobody to control me—And I am said not to bear control: so, sir, you and I are best as we are, I believe—nay, I am sure of it—for we want not what either has—having both more than we know what to do with. And I know I could not be in the least accountable for any of my ways.

My daughter indeed, though she is a fine girl, as girls go (she has too much sense indeed for her sex; and knows she has it), is more a check to me than one would wish a daughter to be—for one would not be always snapping at each other. But she will soon be married; and then, not living together, we shall only come together when we are pleased, and stay away when we are not; and so, like other lovers, never see anything but the best sides of each other.

I own, for all this, that I love her dearly; and she me, I dare say. So would not wish to provoke her to do otherwise. Besides, the girl is so much regarded everywhere, that having lived so much of my prime a widow, I would not lay myself open to her censures, or even to her indifference, you know.

Your generous proposal requires all this explicitness. I thank you for your good opinion of me. When I know you acquiesce with this my civil refusal; and indeed, sir, I am as much in earnest in it, as if I had spoke broader; I don't know but Nancy and I may, with your permission, come to see your fine things; for I am a great admirer of rarities that come from abroad.

So, sir, let us only converse occasionally as we meet, as we used to do, without any other view to each other than good wishes: which I hope may not be lessened for this declining. And then I shall always think myself

> Your obliged servant,
> ANNABELLA HOWE

I sent word by Mrs Lorimer, that I would write an answer: but would take time for consideration. So hope, sir, you won't think it a slight I did not write sooner.

Letter 198: MR LOVELACE TO JOHN BELFORD, ESQ.

Sunday, May 21

I AM too much disturbed in my mind to think of any think but revenge; or I had intended to give thee an account of Miss Harlowe's curious observations on the play. *Miss Harlowe's*, I say. Thou knowest that I hate the name of *Harlowe*; and I am exceedingly out of humour with her, and with her saucy friend.

What's the matter *now*, thou'lt ask?—Matter enough; for while we were at the play, Dorcas, who had her orders and a key to her lady's chamber, as well as a master-key to her drawers and mahogany chest, closet-key and all, found means to come at some of Miss Howe's last-written letters. The vigilant wench was directed to them by seeing her lady take a letter out of her stays, and put it to the others, before she went out with me—afraid, as the women upbraidingly tell me, that I should find it there.

Dorcas no sooner found them, than she assembled three ready writers of the *non-apparents*, and Sally, and she and they employed themselves with the utmost diligence, in making extracts according to former directions, from these cursed letters, for my use. *Cursed*, I may well call them—Such abuses, such virulence! Oh this little fury Miss Howe!—Well might her saucy friend (who has been equally free with me, or the occasion could not have been given) be so violent as she lately was at my endeavouring to come at one of these letters.

I was sure that this fair one, at so early an age, with a constitution so firm, health so blooming, eyes so sparkling, could not be absolutely, and from her own vigilance, so guarded and so apprehensive as I have found her to be—Sparkling eyes, Jack, when the poetical tribe have said all they can for them, are an infallible sign of a rogue, or room for a rogue, in the heart.

Thou may'st go on with thy preachments, and Lord M. with his wisdom of nations, I am now more assured of her than ever. And now my revenge is up, and joined with my love, all resistance must fall before it. And most solemnly do I swear, that Miss Howe shall come in for her snack.[1]

And here, just now, is another letter brought from the same little virulent devil—I hope to procure transcripts from that too, very speedily, if it be put to the rest; for the saucy lady is resolved to go to church this morning; not so much from a spirit of devotion, I have reason to think, as to try whether she can go out without check or control, or my attendance.

I HAVE been denied breakfasting with her. Indeed she was a little displeased with me last night; because, on our return from the play, I obliged her to pass the rest of the night with the women and me, in their parlour, and to stay till near one. She told me at parting that she expected to have the whole next day to herself—I had not read the extracts then; so was all affectionate respect, awe, and distance; for I had resolved to begin a new course, and, if possible, to banish all jealousy and suspicion from her heart: and yet I had no reason to be much troubled at her past suspicions; since, if a woman will continue with a man whom she suspects, when she can get from him, or *thinks* she can, I am sure it is a very hopeful sign.

SHE is gone. Slipped down before I was aware. She had ordered a chair, on purpose to exclude my personal attendance. But I had taken proper precautions. Will attended her by consent; Peter, the house-servant, was within Will's call.

I had, by Dorcas, represented her danger from Singleton, in order to dissuade her from going at all, unless she allowed me to attend her; but I was answered, that if there was no cause of fear at the playhouse, when there were but *two* playhouses, surely there was less at church, when there were so *many* churches. The chairmen were ordered to carry her to St James's Church.[2]

But she would not be so careless of obliging me, if she knew what I have already come at, and how the women urge me on; for they are continually complaining of the restraint they lie under in their behaviour, in their attendance; neglecting all their concerns in the front house and keeping this elegant back one entirely free from company, that she may have no suspicion of them. They doubt not my generosity, they say: but *why* for my own sake, in Lord M.'s style, *should I make so long a harvest of so little corn?*—Women, ye reason well. I think I will begin my operations the moment she comes in.

I HAVE come at the letter brought her from Miss Howe today—Plot, conjuration, sorcery, witchcraft, all going forward!—I shall not be able to see this *Miss Harlowe* with patience. As the nymphs below say, why is *night* necessary?—And Sally and Polly upbraidingly remind me of my first attempts upon themselves—Yet force answers not my end—And yet it may, if there be truth in that part of the libertine's creed, *that once subdued, is always subdued!* And what woman answers *affirmatively* to the question?

SHE is returned—But refuses to admit me. Desires to have the day to herself. Dorcas tells me that she believes her denial is from motives of piety—Oons, Jack, is there impiety in seeing me!—Would it not be the highest act of piety to reclaim me? And is this to be done by her refusing to see me when she is in a devouter frame than usual? But I hate her, hate her heartily!—She is old, ugly, and deformed—But Oh, the blasphemy!—Yet she is an Harlowe—and I hate her for that.

But since I must not see her (she will be mistress of her *own will*, and of her *time* truly!), let me fill up mine by telling thee what I have come at.

The first letter the women met with is dated April 27.[a] Where can she have put the preceding ones? It mentions Mr Hickman as a busy fellow between them. Hickman had best take care of himself. She says in it, *I hope you have no cause to repent returning my Norris—It is forthcoming on demand.* Now, what the devil can this mean!—Her Norris forthcoming on demand!—The devil take me, if I am *out-Norrised!*—If such innocents can allow themselves to plot, to *Norris,* well may I.

She is sorry that *her Hannah can't be with her*—And what if she could?—What could Hannah do for her in such a house as this?

The women in the house are to be found out in one breakfasting. The women are enraged at both the correspondents for this; and more than ever make a point of conquering her. I had a good mind to give them Miss Howe in full property. Say but the word, Jack, and it shall be done.

She is glad that Miss Harlowe had thoughts of taking me at my word. She wondered I did not offer again. Advises her, if I don't soon *not to stay with me.* Cautions her *to keep me at distance; not to permit the least familiarity*—See, Jack—see Belford—exactly as I thought!—Her vigilance all owing to a cool friend; who can sit down quietly, and give that advice which, in her own case, she could not take—She tells her, *it is my interest to be honest*—INTEREST, fools!—I thought these girls knew that my *interest* was ever subservient to my *pleasure.*

What would I give to come at the copies of the letters to which those of Miss Howe are answers!

The next letter is dated May 3.[b] In this the little termagant expresses her astonishment that her mother should write to Miss Harlowe to forbid her to correspond with her daughter. Mr Hickman, she says, is of opinion *that she ought not to obey her mother.* How the creeping fellow trims between both! I am afraid that I must punish him as well as this virago; and I have a scheme rumbling in my head that wants but half an hour's musing to bring into form, that will do my business upon both. I cannot bear that the parental authority should be thus despised, thus trampled under foot—But observe the vixen, *'Tis well he is of her opinion; for her mother having set her up, she must have somebody to quarrel with*—Could a Lovelace have allowed himself a greater licence? This girl's a devilish rake in her heart. Had she been a man, and one of us, she'd have outdone us all in enterprise and spirit.

She wants but very little farther provocation, she says, *to fly privately to London. And if she does, she will not leave her till she sees her either honourably married, or*

a See p. 529.
b See p. 548.

quit of the wretch. Here, Jack, the transcriber Sally has added a prayer—'For the Lord's sake, dear Mr Lovelace, get this fury to London!'—Her fate, I can tell thee, Jack, if we had her among us, should not be so long deciding as her friend's. What a gantlope would she run, when I had done with her, among a dozen of her own pitiless sex, whom my charmer shall never see!—But more of this anon.

I find by this letter that my saucy captive had been drawing the characters of every varlet of ye. Nor am I spared in it more than you. *The man's a fool, to be sure, my dear.* Let me die, if they either of them find me one. *A silly fellow, at least.* Cursed contemptible!—*I see not but they are a set of infernals*—There's for thee, Belford—*and he the Beelzebub.* There's for thee, Lovelace!—And yet she would have her friend marry a Beelzebub—And what have any of us done, to the knowledge of Miss Harlowe, that she should give such an account of us, as should warrant so much abuse from Miss Howe?—But that's to come!

She blames her for *not admitting Miss Partington to her bed*—*Watchful as you are, what could have happened?*—*If violence were intended, he would not stay for the night.* Sally writes upon this hint—'See, sir, what is expected from you. An hundred and an hundred times have we told you of this'—And so they have. But, to be sure, the advice from them was not of half the efficacy as it will be from Miss Howe—*You might have sat up after her, or not gone to bed.* But can there be such apprehensions between them, yet the one advise her to stay, and the other resolve to wait my imperial motion for marriage? I am glad I know that.

She approves of my proposal about Mrs Fretchville's house. She puts her upon expecting settlements; upon naming a day. And concludes with insisting upon her writing, notwithstanding her mother's prohibition; or bids her *take the consequence.* Undutiful wretches!

Thou wilt say to thyself by this time: And can this proud and insolent girl be the same Miss Howe who sighed for honest Sir George Colmar; and who, but for this her beloved friend, would have followed him in all his broken fortunes, when he was obliged to quit the kingdom?

Yes, she is the very same. And I always found in others, as well as in myself, that a first passion thoroughly subdued, made the conqueror of it a rover; the conqueress a tyrant.

Well, but now comes mincing in a letter from one who has *the honour of dear Miss Howe's commands,* [a] to acquaint Miss Harlowe that Miss Howe is *excessively concerned for the concern she has given her.*

I have great temptations, on this occasion, says the prim Gothamite, *to express my own resentments upon your present state.*

My own resentments!—And why did he not fall into this *temptation?*—Why, truly, because he knew not what that state was, which gave him so *tempting* a subject—*only by conjecture,* and so forth.

He then dances in his style, as he does in his gait! To be sure, to be sure, he must have made the grand tour, and come home by the way of Tipperary.

And being moreover forbid, says the prancer, *to enter into the cruel subject*—This prohibition was a mercy to thee, friend Hickman!—But why *cruel subject,* if thou knowest not what it is, but *conjecturest* only from the disturbance it gives to a girl that is her mother's disturbance, will be thy disturbance, and the disturbance, in

a See p. 551.

turn, of everybody with whom she is intimately acquainted, unless I have the humbling of her?

In another letter,[a] *She approves of her design to leave me, if she can be received by her friends.*

Has heard some strange stories of me, that show me to be the worst of men. Had I a dozen lives, I might have forfeited them all twenty crimes ago—An odd way of reckoning, Jack!

Miss Betterton, Miss Lockyer, are named—*The man* (so she irreverently calls me!), she says, *is a villain.* Let me perish if I am called a villain for nothing!—She *will have her uncle* (as Miss Harlowe desires) *sounded about receiving her. Dorcas is to be attached to her interest: my letters are to be come at by surprise or trick*—See, Jack!

She is alarmed at my attempt to come at a letter of hers.

Were I to come at the knowledge of her freedoms with my character, she says, *she should be afraid to stir out without a guard*—I would advise the vixen to get her guard ready.

I am at the head of a gang of wretches (thee, Jack, and thy brother varlets, she owns she means), *who join together to betray innocent creatures, and to support one another in their villainies*—What sayest thou to this, Belford?

She wonders not at her melancholy reflections for meeting me, for being forced upon me, and tricked by me—I hope, Jack, thou'lt have done preaching after this!

But she comforts her, *that she will be both a warning and example to all her sex*—I hope the sex will thank me for this.

The nymphs had not time, they say, to transcribe all that was worthy of my resentment in this letter—so I must find an opportunity to come at it myself. Noble rant, they say it contains—But I am a *seducer*, and a hundred vile fellows, in it—*And the devil*, it seems, *took possession of my heart, and of the hearts of all her friends, in the same dark hour, in order to provoke her to meet me.* Again, *there is a fate in her error*, she says—why then should she grieve?—*Adversity is her shining-time*, and I cannot tell what—Yet never to thank the man to whom she owes the *shine!*

In the next,[b] wicked as I am, *she fears I must be her lord and master*—I hope so.

She retracts what she said against me in her last—My behaviour to my Rosebud; Miss Harlowe to take possession of Mrs Fretchville's house; I to stay at Mrs Sinclair's; the stake I have in my country; my reversions; my economy; my person; my address; all are brought in my favour, to induce her now *not* to leave me. How do I love to puzzle these *long*-sighted girls!

Yet *my teasing ways*, it seems, *are intolerable*—Are women only to tease, I trow?—The sex may thank themselves for learning me to out-tease them. So the headstrong Charles XII of Sweden learned the Czar Peter to beat him, by continuing a war with the Muscovites against the ancient maxims of his kingdom.

May eternal vengeance PURSUE *the villain* (thank Heaven, she does not say *overtake*), *if he give room to doubt his honour!*—Women can't swear, Jack—Sweet souls! they can only curse.

I am said *to doubt her love*—Have I not reason? And she *to doubt my ardour?*—Ardour, Jack!—Why, 'tis very right—Women, as Miss Howe says, and as every rake knows, love ardours!

She apprises her of the *ill success of the application made to her uncle*—by

a   p. 576.
b   p. 586.

Hickman, no doubt!—I must have this fellow's ears in my pocket, very quickly, believe.

She says, *she is equally shocked and enraged against all her family: Mrs Norton's weight has been tried upon Mrs Harlowe, as well as Mr Hickman's upon the uncle: but never were there*, says the vixen, *such determined brutes in the world. Her uncle concludes her ruined already*—Is not that a call upon me, as well as a reproach?— *They all expected applications from her when in distress—but were resolved not to stir an inch to save her life.* She was *accused of premeditation and contrivance.* Miss Howe is *concerned*, she tells her, *for the revenge my pride may put me upon taking for the distance she has kept me at*—And well she may—*She has now but one choice* (for her cousin Morden, is seems, is set against her too), *and that's to be mine*—An act of necessity, of convenience—Thy friend, Jack, to be already made a woman's convenience!—Is this to be borne by a Lovelace?

I shall make great use of this letter. From Miss Howe's hints of what passed between her uncle Harlowe and Hickman (it must be Hickman), I can give room for my *invention* to play, for she tells her that *she will not reveal all.* I must endeavour to come at this letter myself; I must have the very words; extracts will not do. This letter, when I have it, must be my compass to steer by.

The fire of friendship then blazes out and crackles. I never before imagined that so fervent a friendship could subsist between two sister-beauties, both toasts. But even here it may be inflamed by opposition, and by that contradiction which gives spirit to female spirits of a warm and romantic turn.

She raves about *coming up, if by so doing she could prevent so noble a creature from stooping too low, or save her from ruin*—One reed to support another! These girls are frenzical in their friendship. They know not what a steady fire is.

How comes it to pass, that I cannot help being pleased with this virago's spirit, though I suffer by it? Had I her but here, I'd engage in a week's time to teach her submission without reserve. What pleasure should I have in breaking such a spirit! I should wish for her but for one month, in all, I think. She would be too tame and spiritless for me after that. How sweetly pretty to see the two lovely friends, when humbled and tame, both sitting in the darkest corner of a room, arm in arm, weeping and sobbing for each other!—And I their emperor, their then *acknowledged* emperor, reclined on a sophee, in the same room, Grand Signor-like, uncertain to which I should first throw out my handkerchief?[3]

Mind the girl: *she is enraged at the Harlowes:* she *is angry at her own mother; she is exasperated against her foolish and low-vanitied Lovelace*—FOOLISH, a little toad! (God forgive me for calling a virtuous girl a toad!) *Let us stoop to lift the wretch out of his dirt, though we soil our fingers in doing it! He has not been guilty of direct indecency to you*—It seems *extraordinary* to Miss Howe that I have not— *Nor dare he*—She should be sure of that. If women have such things in their heads, why should not I in my heart?—*Not so much of a devil as that comes to, neither. Such villainous intentions would have shown themselves before now, if I had them*— Lord help them!—

She then puts her friend upon urging for *settlements, licence*, and so forth—*No room for delicacy now*, she says—And tells her what she shall say, to *bring all forward from me*—Dost think, Jack, that I should not have carried my point long ago, but for this vixen?—She *reproaches her for having* MODESTY'D *away*, as she calls it, *more than one opportunity that she ought not to have slipped*—Thus thou seest that the noblest of the sex mean nothing in the world by their shyness and distance, but to pound a poor fellow whom they dislike not, when he comes into their purlieus.

Annexed to this letter is a paper the most saucy that ever was wrote of a mother by a daughter. There are in it such free reflections upon widows and bachelors, that I cannot but wonder how Miss Howe came by her learning. Sir George Colmar, I can tell thee, was a greater fool than thy friend, if she had it all for nothing.

The contents of this paper acquaint Miss Harlowe that her uncle Antony has been making proposals of marriage to her mother. The old fellow's heart ought to be a tough one, if he succeed, or she who broke that of a much worthier man, the late Mr Howe, will soon get rid of him. But be this as it may, the stupid family is more irreconcilable than ever to their goddess-daughter for old Antony's thoughts of marrying: so I am more secure of her than ever; since, as Miss Howe says, *she can have but one choice now.* Though this disgusts my pride, yet I believe at last my tender heart will be moved in her favour. For I did not wish that she should have nothing but persecution and distress—But why loves she the *brutes*, as Miss Howe justly calls them, so much; me so little?—But I have still more unpardonable transcripts from other letters.

Letter 199: MR LOVELACE TO JOHN BELFORD, ESQ.

THE next letter is of such a nature, that I dare say these proud varletesses would not have had it fall into my hands for the world.[a]

I see by it to what her displeasure with me, in relation to my proposals, was owing. They were not summed up, it seems, with the warmth, with the *ardour*, which she had expected. This whole letter was transcribed by Dorcas, to whose lot it fell. Thou shalt have copies of them all at full length shortly.

Men of our cast, this little devil says, *she fancies, cannot have the ardours that honest men have.* Miss Howe has very pretty fancies, Jack. Charming girl! Would to heaven I knew whether my fair one answers her as freely as she writes! 'Twould vex a man's heart, that this virago should have come honestly by her *fancies.*

Who knows but I may have half a dozen creatures to get off my hands, before I engage for life?—Yet, lest this should mean me a compliment, as if I would reform, she adds her belief, *that she must not expect me to be honest on this side my grand climacteric.* She has an high opinion of her sex, to think they can charm so long, with a man so well acquainted with their *identicalness.*

He to suggest delays, she says, *from a compliment to be made to Lord M.!*—Yes, *I*, my dear—Because a man has not been accustomed to be dutiful, must he never be dutiful? In so important a case as this too; the hearts of his whole family engaged in it? *You did indeed*, says she, *want an interposing friend—But were I to have been in your situation, I would have tore his eyes out, and left it to his own heart to furnish the reason for it.* See! See! What sayest thou to this, Jack?

Villain—fellow that he is! follow. And for what? Only for wishing that the next day were to be my happy one; and for being dutiful to my nearest relation.

It is the cruellest of fates, she says, *for a woman to be forced to have a man whom*

a   p. 603.

her heart despises—That is what I wanted to be sure of—I was afraid that my beloved was too conscious of her talents; of her superiority!—I was afraid that she *indeed* despised me; and I cannot bear it. But, Belford, I do not intend that this lady shall be bound down by so cruel a fate. Let me perish, if I marry a woman who has given her most intimate friend reason to say she despises me!—A Lovelace to be despised, Jack!

His clenched fist to his forehead on your leaving him in just displeasure—that is, when she was not satisfied with my ardours, and please ye!—I remember the motion: but her back was toward me at the time. Are these watchful ladies all eye?—But observe her wish, *I wish it had been a pole-axe, and in the hands of his worst enemy*—I *will* have patience, Jack; I *will* have patience! My day is at hand—Then will I steel my heart with these remembrances.

But here is a scheme to be thought of, in order to *get my fair prize out of my hands in case I give her reason to suspect me.*

This indeed alarms me. Now the contention becomes arduous. Now wilt thou not wonder, if I let loose my plotting genius upon them both. I will not be *out-Norrised*, Belford.

But once more, *she has no notion*, she says, *that I can or dare to mean her dishonour.* But *then the man is a fool—that's all*—I should indeed be a fool to proceed as I do and mean matrimony! *However, since you are thrown upon a fool*, says she, *marry the fool at the first opportunity; and though I doubt that this man will be the most unmanageable of fools, as all witty and vain fools are, take him as a punishment, since you cannot as a reward*—Is there any bearing this, Belford?

But in the letter I came at today, while she was at church, her scheme is further opened, and a cursed one it is.

Mr Lovelace then transcribes from his shorthand notes that part of Miss Howe's letter, which relates to the design of engaging Mrs Townsend (in case of necessity) to give her protection till Colonel Morden comes[a]: and repeats his vows of revenge; especially for those words: *that should he attempt anything that would make him obnoxious to the laws of society, she might have a fair riddance of him, either by flight or the gallows; no matter which.*

He then adds: 'Tis my pride to subdue girls who know *too much* to *doubt* their knowledge; and to convince them that they know *too little* to defend themselves from the inconveniencies of knowing *too much.*

How passion drives a man on! I have written, as thou'lt see, a prodigious quantity in a very few hours! Now my resentments are warm, I will see, and perhaps will punish, this proud, this *double*-armed beauty. I have sent to tell her that I must be admitted to sup with her. We have neither of us dined: she refused to drink tea in the afternoon—and I believe neither of us will have much stomach to our supper.

a pp. 621–2.

Letter 200: MISS CLARISSA HARLOWE TO MISS HOWE

Sunday morning, 7 [a.m.], May 21

I WAS at the play last night with Mr Lovelace and Miss Horton. It is, you know, a deep and most affecting tragedy in the reading. You have my remarks upon it, in the little book you made me write upon the principal acting plays. You will not wonder that Miss Horton, as well as I, was greatly moved at the representation, when I tell you, and have some pleasure in telling you, that Mr Lovelace himself was very sensibly touched with some of the most affecting scenes. I mention this in praise of the author's performance; for I take Mr Lovelace to be one of the most hard-hearted men in the world. Upon my word, my dear, I do.

His behaviour, however, on this occasion, and on our return, was unexceptionable, only that he would oblige me to stay to supper with the women below when we came back, and to sit up with him and them till near one o'clock this morning. I was resolved to be even with him; and indeed I am not very sorry to have the pretence; for I love to pass the Sundays by myself.

To have the better excuse to avoid his teasing, I am ready dressed to go to church this morning. I will go only to St James's church, and in a *chair*; that I may be sure I can go out and come in when I please, without being obtruded upon by him, as I was twice before.

Near nine o'clock

I HAVE your kind letter of yesterday. He knows I have. And I shall expect that he will be inquisitive next time I see him after your opinion of his proposals. I doubted not your approbation of them, and had written an answer on that presumption; which is ready for him. He must study for occasions of procrastination, and to disoblige me, if now anything happens to set us at variance again.

He is very importunate to see me; he has desired to attend me to church. He is angry that I have declined to breakfast with him. I was sure that I should not be at my own liberty if I had—I bid Dorcas tell him that I desired to have this day to myself; I would see him in the morning, as early as he pleased. She says she knows not what ails him, but that he is out of humour with everybody.

He has sent again, in a peremptory manner. He warns me of Singleton. But surely, I sent him word, if he was not afraid of Singleton at the playhouse last night, I need not at church today: so many churches to one playhouse—I have accepted of his servant's proposed attendance—But he is quite displeased, it seems. I don't care. I will not be perpetually at his insolent beck—Adieu, my dear, till I return. The chair waits. He won't stop me, sure, as I go down to it.

I DID not see him as I went down. He is, it seems, excessively out of humour. Dorcas says, not with me neither, she believes: but something has vexed him. This is put on, perhaps, to make me dine with him. But I won't, if I can help it. I shan't get rid of him for the rest of the day if I do.

HE was very earnest to dine with me. But I was resolved to carry this one small point; and so denied to dine myself. And indeed I was endeavouring to write to my cousin Morden; and had begun three different letters, without being able to please myself; so uncertain and so unpleasing is my situation.

He was very busy in writing, Dorcas says, and pursued it without dining, because I denied him my company.

He afterwards *demanded*, as I may say, to be admitted to afternoon tea with me: and appealed by Dorcas to his behaviour to me last night; as if, as I sent him word by her, he thought he had a merit in being unexceptionable. However, I repeated my promise to meet him as early as he pleased in the morning, or to breakfast with him.

Dorcas says he raved. I heard him loud, and I heard his servant fly from him, as I thought. You, my dearest friend, say, in one of yours,[a] that you must have somebody to be angry at when your mother sets you up—I should be very loath to draw comparisons—But the workings of passion, when indulged, are but too much alike, whether in man or woman.

HE has just sent me word that he insists upon supping with me. As we had been in a good train for several days past, I thought it not prudent to break with him for little matters. Yet, to be in a manner threatened into his will, I know not how to bear that.

WHILE I was considering, he came up and, tapping at my door, told me, in a very angry tone, he must see me this night. He could not rest, till he had been told what he had done to deserve this treatment.

I must go to him. Yet perhaps he has nothing new to say to me—I shall be very angry with him.

As the lady could not know what Mr Lovelace's designs were, nor the cause of his ill humour, it will not be improper to pursue the subject from his letter.

[*Letter 199 as before: Mr Lovelace to John Belford, Esq.*]

(*Having described his angry manner of demanding in person her company at supper; he proceeds as follows:*)
'Tis hard, answered the fair perverse, that I am to be so little my own mistress. I will meet you in the dining-room half an hour hence.

I went down to wait that half-hour. All the women set me hard to give her cause for this tyranny. They demonstrated, as well from the nature of the *sex*, as of the *case*, that I had nothing to hope for from my tameness, and could meet with no worse treatment were I to be guilty of the last offence. They urged me vehemently to *try* at least what effect some greater familiarities than I had ever used with her would have: and their arguments being strengthened by my just resentments on the discoveries I had made, I was resolved to take some liberties and, as they were received, to take still greater, and lay all the fault upon her tyranny. In this humour I went up, and never had paralytic so little command of his joints as I had as I walked about the dining-room, attending her motions.

With an erect mien she entered, her face averted, her lovely bosom swelling, and the more charmingly protuberant for the erectness of her mien. Oh Jack! that sullenness and reserve should give this haughty maid new charms! But in every attitude, in every humour, in every gesture, is beauty beautiful—By her averted

a   p. 548.

face and indignant aspect, I saw the dear insolent was disposed to be angry—But by the fierceness of mine, as my trembling hands seized hers, I soon made fear her predominant passion. And yet the moment I beheld her, my heart was dastardized, damped, and reverenced-over. Surely this is an angel, Jack!—And yet, had she not been known to be female, they would not from *babyhood* have dressed her as such, nor would she, but upon that conviction, have continued the dress.

Let me ask you, madam, I beseech you tell me, what I have done to deserve this distant treatment?

And let me ask you, Mr Lovelace, why are my retirements to be thus invaded?— What can you have to say to me since last night, that I went with you so much against my will to the play? And after sitting up with you, equally against my will, till a very late hour!—

This I have to say, madam, that I cannot bear to be kept at this distance from you under the same roof. I have a thousand things to say, to talk of, relating to our present and future prospects; but when I want to open my whole soul to you, you are always contriving to keep me at a distance; you make me inconsistent with myself; your heart is set upon delays; you must have views that you will not own. Tell me, madam, I conjure you to tell me, this moment, without subterfuge or reserve, in what light am I to appear to you in future? I cannot bear this distance; the suspense you hold me in I cannot bear.

In what light, Mr Lovelace? In no bad light, I hope—Pray, Mr Lovelace, do not grasp my hands so hard (endeavouring to withdraw her hands). Pray let me go—

You hate me, madam—

I hate nobody, sir—

You *hate* me, madam, repeated I.

Instigated and resolved, as I came up, I wanted some new provocation. The devil indeed, as soon as my angel made her appearance, crept out of my heart; but he had left the door open and was no farther off than my elbow.

You come up in no good temper, I see, Mr Lovelace—But pray be not violent— I have done you no hurt—Pray be not violent—

Sweet creature! And I clasped one arm about her, holding one hand in my other—*You have done me no hurt!*—You have done me the greatest hurt!—In what have I deserved the distance you keep me at?—I knew not what to say.

She struggled to disengage herself—Pray, Mr Lovelace, let me withdraw. I know not why this is—I know not what I have done to offend you. I see you are come with a design to quarrel with me. If you would not terrify me by the ill-humour you are in, permit me to withdraw. I will hear all you have to say another time— Tomorrow morning, as I sent you word; but indeed you frighten me—I beseech you, if you have any value for me, permit me to withdraw.

Night, *mid*-night, *is* necessary, Belford. Surprise, terror, *must* be necessary to the ultimate trial of this charming creature, say the women below what they will— I could not hold my purposes—This was not the first time that I had *intended* to try if she could forgive.

I kissed her hand with a fervour, as if I would have left my lips upon it— Withdraw then, dearest and ever dear creature—Indeed I entered in a very ill humour: I cannot bear the distance you so causelessly keep me at—Withdraw, however, madam, since it is your will to withdraw; and judge me generously; judge me but as I deserve to be judged; and let me hope to meet you tomorrow morning early, in such a temper as becomes our present situation, and my future hopes. And so saying, I conducted her to the door, and left her there. But instead of going down to the women, went into my own chamber, and locked myself in; ashamed of being awed by her majestic loveliness and apprehensive virtue into so great a change of purpose, notwithstanding I had such just provocations from the letters of her saucy friend, founded on her own representations of facts and situations between herself and me.

[*Letter 200 as before: Miss Clarissa Harlowe to Miss Howe, Sunday night*]

(The lady thus describes her terrors, and Mr Lovelace's behaviour, on this occasion:)

On my entering the dining-room, he took my hands in his, in such a humour as I saw plainly he was resolved to quarrel with me—*And for what?*—I never in my life beheld in anybody such a wild, such an angry, such an impatient spirit. I was terrified; and instead of being as angry as I intended to be, I was forced to be all mildness. I can hardly remember what were his first words, I was so frighted. But, *You hate me,—madam! You hate me,—madam!* were some of them—with such a fierceness—I wished myself a thousand miles distant from him. I hate nobody, said I; I thank God I hate nobody—You terrify me, Mr Lovelace—Let me leave you— The man, my dear, looked quite ugly—I never saw a man look so ugly, as passion made him look—*And for what?*—And he so grasped my hands—fierce creature! He so grasped my hands! In short, he seemed by his looks, and by his words (once putting his arms about me), to wish me to provoke him—So that I had nothing to do but to beg of him, which I did repeatedly, to permit me to withdraw; and to promise to meet him at his own time in the morning.

It was with a very ill grace that he complied, on that condition; and at parting he kissed my hand with such a savageness, that a redness remains upon it still.

Perfect for me, my dearest Miss Howe, perfect for me, I beseech you, your kind scheme with Mrs Townsend—and I will then leave this man. See you not how from step to step, he grows upon me?—I tremble to look back upon his encroachments. And now to give me cause to apprehend more evil from him than indignation will permit me to express!—Oh my dear, perfect your scheme, and let me fly from so strange a wretch! He must certainly have views in quarrelling with me thus, which he dare not own! Yet what can they be?

I WAS so disgusted with him, as well as frighted by him, that on my return to my chamber, in a fit of passionate despair, I tore almost in two, the answer I had written to his proposals.

I will see him in the morning, because I promised I would. But I will go out, and that without him, or any attendant. If he account not tolerably for his sudden change of behaviour, and a proper opportunity offer of a private lodging in some creditable house, I will not any more return to this—At present I think so. And there will I either attend the perfecting of your scheme; or, by your epistolary mediation, make my own terms with the wretch; since it is your opinion that I must be his, and cannot help myself. Or perhaps take a resolution to throw myself at once into Lady Betty's protection; and this will hinder him from making his insolently threatened visit to Harlowe Place.

The lady writes again on Monday evening; and gives her friend an account of all that has passed between herself and Mr Lovelace that day; and of her being terrified out of her purpose of going abroad: but Mr Lovelace's next letters giving a more ample account of all, hers are omitted.

It is proper, however, to mention that she re-urges Miss Howe (from the dissatisfaction she has reason for from what passed between Mr Lovelace and herself) to perfect her scheme in relation to Mrs Townsend.

She concludes this letter in these words:

I should say something of your last favour (but a few hours ago received), and of your dialogue with your mother—Are you not very whimsical, my dear?—I have but two things to wish for on this occasion. The one, that your charming pleasantry had a better subject than that you find for it in this dialogue. The other, that my situation were not such as must too often damp that pleasantry, and will not permit me to enjoy it as I used to do. Be, however, happy in yourself, though you cannot in

Your CLARISSA HARLOWE

Letter 201: MR LOVELACE TO JOHN BELFORD, ESQ.

Monday morn. May 22

No generosity in this lady. None at all. Wouldst thou not have thought that after I had permitted her to withdraw, primed for mischief as I was, that she would meet me next morning early; and that with a smile; making me one of her best curtsies?

I was in the dining-room before six, expecting her. She opened not her door. I went upstairs and down, and hemmed, and called Will, called Dorcas: threw the doors hard to; but still she opened not her door. Thus till half an hour after eight, fooled I away my time; and then, breakfast ready, I sent Dorcas to request her company.

But I was astonished, when, following the wench at the first invitation, I saw her enter dressed, all but her gloves, and those and her fan in her hand; in the same moment, bidding Dorcas direct Will to get her a chair to the door.

Cruel creature, thought I, to expose me thus to the derision of the women below!

Going abroad, madam?

I am, sir.

I looked cursed silly, I am sure—You will breakfast first, I hope, madam, in a very humble strain: yet with an hundred tenter-hooks in my heart.

Had she given me more notice of her intention, I had perhaps wrought myself up to the frame I was in the day before, and begun my vengeance. And immediately came into my head all the virulence that had been transcribed for me from Miss Howe's letters, and in that I had transcribed myself.

Yes, she would drink one dish; and then laid her gloves and fan in the window just by.

I was perfectly disconcerted. I hemmed and hawed, and was going to speak several times; but knew not in what key. Who's modest now, thought I! Who's insolent now!—How a tyrant of a woman confounds a bashful man!—She was my Miss Howe, I thought; and I the spiritless Hickman.

At last, I *will* begin, thought I.

She a dish—I a dish.

Sip, her eyes her own, she; like an haughty and imperious sovereign, conscious of dignity, every look a favour.

Sip, like her vassal, I; lips and hands trembling, and not knowing that I sipped or tasted.

I was—I was—I sipped—drawing in my breath and the liquor together, though I scalded my mouth with it—I was in hopes, madam—

Dorcas came in just then—Dorcas, said she, is a chair gone for?

Damned impertinence, thought I, putting me out of my speech! And I was forced to wait for the servant's answer to the insolent mistress's question.

William is gone for one, madam.

This cost me a minute's silence before I could begin again—And then it was with my hopes, and my hopes, and my hopes, that I should have been early admitted to—

What weather is it, Dorcas? said she, as regardless of me, as if I had not been present.

A little lowering, madam—The sun is gone in—It was very fine half an hour ago.

I had no patience—Up I rose. Down went the tea-cup, saucer and all—Confound the weather, the sunshine, and the wench!—Begone for a devil, when I am speaking to your lady, and have so little opportunity given me.

Up rose the lady, half frighted; and snatched from the window her gloves and fan.

You must not go, madam!—by my soul, you must not—taking her hand.

Must not, sir!—But I must—You can curse your maid in my absence, as well as if I were present—Except—except—you intend for *me*, what you direct to *her*.

Dearest creature, you must not go!—You must not leave me!—Such determined scorn! Such contempts!—Questions asked your servant of no meaning but to break in upon me; who could bear it?

Detain me not (struggling)—I will not be withheld—I like you not, nor your ways—You sought to quarrel with me yesterday for no reason in the world that I can think of, but because I was too obliging. You are an ungrateful man; and I hate you with my whole heart, Mr Lovelace!

Do not make me desperate, madam—Permit me to say that you shall not leave me in this humour. Wherever you go, I will attend you—Had Miss Howe been my friend, I had not been thus treated—It is but too plain to whom my difficulties are owing. I have long observed that every letter you receive from her makes an alteration in your behaviour to me. She would have *you* treat *me*, as *she* treats Mr Hickman, I suppose: but neither does that treatment become your admirable temper to offer, nor me to receive.

This startled her. She did not care to have me think hardly of Miss Howe.

But recollecting herself, Miss Howe, said she, is a friend to virtue, and to good men—If she like not you, it is because you are not one of those.

Yes, madam; and therefore, to speak of Mr Hickman and myself, as you both, I suppose, think of each, she treats *him* as she would not treat a *Lovelace*—I challenge you, madam, to show me but one of the many letters you have received from her, where I am mentioned.

Whither will this lead us? replied she. Miss Howe is just; Miss Howe is good— She writes, she speaks, of everybody as they deserve. If you point me out but any one occasion upon which you have reason to build a merit to yourself, as either just or good, or even generous, I will look out for her letter on that occasion (if it be one I have acquainted her with); and will engage it shall be in your favour.

Devilish severe! And as indelicate as severe, to put a modest man upon hunting backward after his own merits.

She would have flung from me: I *will* go out, Mr Lovelace. I will *not* be detained.

Indeed you must not, madam, in this humour. And I placed myself between her and the door—And then she threw herself into a chair, fanning herself, her sweet face all crimsoned over with passion.

I cast myself at her feet—Begone, Mr Lovelace, said she, with a rejecting motion, her fan in her hand; for your own sake leave me!—My soul is above thee, man! With both her hands pushing me from her!—Urge me not to tell thee how sincerely I think my soul above thee!—Thou hast a proud, a too proud heart, to contend with!—Leave me, and leave me for ever!—Thou hast a proud heart to contend with!

Her air, her manner, her voice, were bewitchingly noble, though her words were so severe.

Let me worship an angel, said I, no woman. Forgive me, dearest creature!— Creature if you be, forgive me!—Forgive my inadvertencies! Forgive my inequalities!—Pity my infirmity!—Who is equal to my Clarissa?

I trembled between admiration and love; and wrapped my arms about her knees as she sat. She tried to rise at the moment; but my clasping round her thus ardently drew her down again; and never was woman more affrighted. But free as my clasping emotion might appear to her apprehensive heart, I had not, at the instant, any thought but what reverence inspired. And till she had actually withdrawn (which I permitted under promise of a speedy return, and on her consent to dismiss the chair), all the motions of my heart were as pure as her own.

She kept not her word. An hour I waited, before I sent to claim her promise. She could not possibly see me yet, was the answer. As soon as she could, she would.

Dorcas says she still excessively trembled; and ordered her to give her water and hartshorn.

A strange apprehensive creature!—Her terror is too great for the occasion— Evils in apprehension are often greater than evils in reality. Hast thou never observed that the terrors of a bird caught, and actually in the hand, bear no comparison to what we might have supposed those terrors would be, were we to have formed a judgement of the same bird by its shyness before taken?

Dear creature!—Did she never romp? Did she never from girlhood to now, hoyden? The *innocent* kinds of freedom taken and allowed on these occasions would have familiarized her to greater. Sacrilege but to touch the hem of her garment!—Excess of delicacy!—Oh, the consecrated beauty!—How can she think to be a wife!

But how do I know till I try, whether she may not by a less alarming treatment be prevailed upon, or whether (day, I have done with thee!) she may not yield to nightly surprises? This is still the burden of my song, I can marry her when I will.

And if I do, after prevailing (whether by surprise or reluctant consent), whom but myself shall I have injured?

IT is now eleven o'clock. She will see me as soon as she can, she tells Polly Horton, who made her a tender visit, and to whom she is less reserved than to anybody else. Her emotion, she assures her, was not owing to perverseness, to nicety, to ill-humour; but to *weakness of heart*. She has not *strength of mind* sufficient, she says, to enable her to support her condition, and her apprehensions under the weight of a father's curse; which she fears is more than beginning to operate.

Yet what a contradiction!—*Weakness of heart*, says she, with such a *strength of will!*—Oh Belford! she is a lion-hearted lady in every case where her honour, her punctilio rather, calls for spirit. But I have had reason more than once in her case, to conclude that the passions of the gentlest, slower to be moved than those of the quick, are the most flaming, the most irresistible, when raised—Yet her charming body is not equally organized. The unequal partners pull two ways; and the divinity within her tears her silken frame. But had the same soul informed a masculine body, never would there have been a truer hero.

Monday, two o'clock

MY beloved not yet visible. She is not well. What *expectations* had she from my ardent admiration of her!—More rudeness than revenge apprehended. Yet, how my soul thirsts for revenge upon both these ladies!—I must have recourse to my master-strokes. This cursed project of Miss Howe and her Mrs Townsend, if I cannot contrive to render it abortive, will be always a sword hanging over my head. Upon every little disobligation my beloved will be for taking wing; and the pains I have taken to deprive her of every other refuge or protection, in order to make her absolutely dependent upon me, will be all thrown away. But perhaps I shall find out a smuggler to counteract Miss Howe.

Thou rememberest the contention between the sun and the north wind, in the fable; which should first make an honest traveller throw off his cloak.

Boreas began first. He puffed away most vehemently; and often made the poor fellow curve and stagger: but with no other effect than to cause him to wrap his surtout the closer about him.

But when it came to Phoebus's turn, he so played upon the traveller with his beams, that he made him first unbutton, and then throw it quite off—nor left he, till he obliged him to take to the friendly shade of a spreading beech; where prostrating himself on the thrown-off cloak, he took a comfortable nap.

The victor-god then laughed outright, both at Boreas and the traveller, and pursued his radiant course, shining upon, and warming and cherishing a thousand new objects, as he danced along: and at night, when he put up his fiery coursers, he diverted his Thetis with the relation of his pranks in the passed day.

I, in like manner, will discard all my boisterous inventions; and if I can oblige my sweet traveller to throw aside, but for one moment, the cloak of her rigid virtue, I shall have nothing to do but, like the sun, to bless new objects with my rays—But my chosen hours of conversation and repose, after all my peregrinations, will be devoted to my goddess.

AND now, Belford, according to my new system, I think this house of Mrs Fretchville an embarrass upon me. I will get rid of it; for some time at least. Mennell, when I am out, shall come to her, inquiring for me. What for? thou'lt ask. What for!—Hast thou not heard what has befallen poor Mrs Fretchville!—Then I'll tell thee.

One of her maids, about a week ago, was taken with the small-pox. The rest kept their mistress ignorant of it till Friday; and *then* she came to know it by accident—The greater half of the plagues poor mortals of condition are tormented with proceed from the servants they take, partly for show, partly for use and with a view to lessen their cares.

This has so terrified the widow, that she is taken with all the symptoms which threaten an attack from that dreadful enemy of fair faces—so must not think of removing: yet cannot expect that we should be further delayed on her account.

She now wishes, with all her heart, that she had known her own mind, and gone into the country at first when I treated about the house: this evil then had not happened!—A cursed cross accident for *us*, too!—Heigh-ho! Nothing else, I think, in this mortal life!—People need not study to bring crosses upon themselves by their petulancies.

So this affair of the house will be over; at least, for one while. But then I can fall upon an expedient which will make amends for this disappointment. Since I must move *slow*, in order to be *sure*, I have a charming contrivance or two in my head—even supposing she should get away, to bring her back again.

But what is become of Lord M. I trow, that he writes not to me, in answer to my invitation? If he would send me such a letter as I could show, it might go a great way towards a perfect reconciliation. I have written to Charlotte about it. He shall soon hear from me, and that in a way he won't like, if he writes not quickly. He has sometimes threatened to disinherit *me:* but if I should renounce *him*, it would be but justice, and would vex him ten times more than anything he can do will vex me. Then, the settlements unavoidably delayed, by his neglect!—How shall I bear such a life of procrastination! I, who, as to my will and impatience and so forth, am of the true *lady-make!* and can as little bear control and disappointment as the best of them!

ANOTHER letter from Miss Howe. I suppose it is *that* which she promises in her last to send her, relating to the courtship between old Tony the uncle and Annabella the mother. I should be extremely rejoiced to see it. No more of the smuggler plot in it, I hope. This, it seems, she has put in her pocket. But I hope I shall soon find it deposited with the rest.

Monday evening

AT my repeated request she condescended to meet me in the dining-room to afternoon tea, and not before.

She entered with bashfulness, as I thought; in a pretty confusion for having carried her apprehensions too far. Sullen and slow moved she towards the tea-table—Dorcas present, busy in tea-cup preparations. I took her reluctant hand, and pressed it to my lips—Dearest, loveliest of creatures, why this distance? Why this displeasure?—How can you thus torture the faithfullest heart in the world?—She disengaged her hand. Again I would have snatched it.

Be quiet, peevishly withdrawing it; and down she sat; a gentle palpitation in the beauty of beauties indicating mingled sullenness and resentment; her snowy handkerchief rising and falling, and a sweet flush overspreading her charming cheeks.

For God's sake, madam!—And a third time I would have taken her repulsing hand.

And for the same sake, sir; no more teasing.

Dorcas retired; I drew my chair nearer hers, and with the most respectful tenderness took her hand; and told her that I could not, without the utmost concern, forbear to express my apprehensions (from the distance she was so desirous to keep me at) that if any man in the world was more *indifferent* to her, to use no harsher a word, than another, it was the unhappy wretch before her.

She looked steadily upon me for a moment, and with her other hand, not withdrawing that I held, pulled her handkerchief out of her pocket; and by a twinkling motion, tried to dissipate a tear or two, which stood ready in each eye to meander themselves a passage down her glowing cheeks; but answered me only with a sigh and an averted face.

I urged her to speak; to look up at me; to bless me with an eye more favourable.

I had reason, she told me, for my complaint of her indifference. She saw nothing in my mind that was generous. I was not a man to be obliged or favoured. My strange behaviour to her since Saturday night, for no cause at all that she knew of, convinced her of this. Whatever hopes she had conceived of me were utterly dissipated: all my ways were disgustful to her.

This cut me to the heart. The guilty, I believe, in every case less patiently bear the detecting truth than the innocent do the degrading falsehood.

I bespoke her patience, while I took the liberty to account for this change on my part—I re-acknowledged the pride of my heart, which could not bear the thought of that want of preference in the heart of a lady whom I hoped to call mine, which she had always manifested. Marriage, I said, was a state that was not to be entered upon with indifference on either side.

It is insolence, interrupted she, it is presumption, sir, to expect tokens of value without resolving to *deserve* them. You have no whining creature before you, Mr Lovelace, overcome by weak motives, to love where there is no merit. Miss Howe can tell you, sir, that I never loved the *faults* of my friend; nor ever wished her to love me for mine. It was a rule with us not to spare each other. And would a man who has nothing but faults (for pray, sir, what are your virtues?) expect that I should show a value for him? Indeed, if I did, I should not deserve even *his* value, but ought to be despised by him.

Well have you, madam, kept up to this noble manner of thinking. You are in no danger of being despised for any marks of tenderness or favour shown to the man before you. You have been perhaps, *you'll* think, *laudably* studious of making and taking occasions to declare that it was far from being owing to your choice, that you had any thoughts of me. My whole soul, madam, in all its errors, in all its wishes, in all its views, had been laid open and naked before you, had I been encouraged by such a share in your confidence and esteem, as would have secured me against your apprehended worst constructions of what I should from time to time have revealed to you, and consulted you upon. For never was there a franker heart; nor a man so ready to accuse himself. (This, Belford, is true.) But you know, madam, how much otherwise it has been between us—Doubt, distance, reserve, on your part, begat doubt, fear, awe, on mine—How little confidence! as if we apprehended each other to be a plotter rather than a lover. How have I dreaded every letter that has been brought you from Wilson's!—And with reason; since the last, from which I expected so much, on account of the proposals I had made you in writing, has, if I may judge by the effects, and by your denial of seeing me yesterday (though you could go abroad, and in a *chair* too, to avoid my attendance on you), set you against me more than ever.

I was guilty, it seems, of going to church, said the indignant charmer; and without the company of a man whose choice it would not have been to go, had I not gone. I was guilty of desiring to have the whole Sunday to myself, after I had obliged you against my will at a play; and after you had detained me, equally to my dislike, to a very late hour over night—These were my faults: for these I was to be punished; I was to be compelled to see you, and to be terrified when I did see you, by the most shocking ill-humour that was ever shown to a creature in my circumstances, and not bound to bear it. You have pretended to find free fault with my father's temper, Mr Lovelace: but the worst that he ever showed *after* marriage, was not in the least to be compared to what you have shown twenty times *beforehand*—And what are my prospects with you, at the very best?—My indignation rises against you, Mr Lovelace, while I speak to you, when I recollect the many instances, equally ungenerous and unpolite, of your behaviour to one whom you have brought into distress—and I can hardly bear you in my sight.

She turned from me, standing up; and lifting up her folded hands and charming eyes, swimming in tears—Oh my dear papa, said the inimitable creature, you might have spared your heavy curse, had you known how I have been punished, ever since my swerving feet led me out of your garden doors to meet this man! Then, sinking into her chair, a burst of passionate tears forced their way down her glowing cheeks.

My dearest life, taking her still folded hands in mine, who can bear an invocation so affecting, though so passionate?

And, as I hope to live, my nose tingled as I once when a boy remember it did (and indeed once more very lately), just before some tears came into my eyes; and I durst hardly trust my face in view of hers.

What have I done to deserve this impatient exclamation?—Have I, at any time, by word, by deeds, by looks, given you cause to doubt my honour, my reverence, my *adoration*, I may call it, of your virtues?—All is owing to misapprehension, I hope, on both sides—Condescend to clear up but your part, as I will mine, and all must speedily be happy—Would to Heaven I loved that Heaven as I love you! And yet, if I doubted a return in love, let me perish if I should know how to wish you mine!—Give me hope, dearest creature, give me but hope, that I am your preferable choice!—Give me but hope, that you hate me not; that you do not despise me.

Oh Mr Lovelace, we have been long enough together to be tired of each other's humours and ways; ways and humours so different, that perhaps you ought to dislike *me*, as much as I do *you*—I think, I think, that I cannot make an answerable return to the value you profess for me. My temper is utterly ruined. You have given me an ill opinion of all mankind; of yourself in particular: and withal so bad a one of myself that I shall never be able to look up, having utterly and for ever lost all that self-complacency and conscious pride, which are so necessary to carry a woman through this life with tolerable satisfaction to herself.

She paused. I was silent. By my soul, thought I, this sweet creature will at last undo me!

She proceeded—What now remains, but that you pronounce me free of all obligation to you? And that you will not hinder me from pursuing the destiny that shall be allotted me?

Again she paused. I was still silent; meditating whether to renounce all further designs upon her; whether I had not received sufficient evidence of a virtue, and of a greatness of soul, that could not be questioned or impeached.

She went on: Propitious to me be your silence, Mr Lovelace!—Tell me that I am free of all obligation to you. You know I never made *you* promises—You know that you are not under any to *me*—My broken fortunes I matter not—

She was proceeding—My dearest life, said I, I have been all this time, though you fill me with doubts of your favour, busy in the nuptial preparations—I am actually in treaty for equipage.

Equipage, sir!—Trappings, tinsel!—What is equipage; what is life; what is anything, to a creature sunk so low as I am in my own opinion!—Labouring under a father's curse!—Unable to look backward without reproach, or forward without terror!—These reflections strengthened by every cross accident!—And what but cross accidents befall me!—All my darling schemes dashed in pieces; all my hopes at an end; deny me not the liberty to refuge myself in some obscure corner, where neither the enemies you have made me, nor the few friends you have left me, may ever hear of the supposed rash one, till those happy moments are at hand, which shall expiate for all!

I had not a word to say for myself. Such a war in my mind had I never known. Gratitude, and admiration of the excellent creature before me, combating with villainous habit, with resolutions so premeditate[d]ly made, and with views so much gloried in!—An hundred new contrivances in my head, and in my heart, that, to be honest, as it is called, must all be given up by a heart delighting in intrigue and difficulty—Miss Howe's virulences endeavoured to be recollected— yet recollection refusing to bring them forward with the requisite efficacy—I had certainly been a lost man, had not Dorcas come seasonably in with a letter—On the superscription written—*Be pleased, sir, to open it now*.

I returned to the window—opened it—It was from herself—These the contents— 'Be pleased to detain my lady; a paper of importance to transcribe. I will cough when I have done.'

I put the paper in my pocket, and turned to my charmer, less disconcerted, as she, by that time, had also a little recovered herself—One favour, dearest creature—Let me but know whether Miss Howe approves or disapproves of my proposals?—I know her to be my enemy. I was intending to account to you for the change of behaviour you accused me of at the beginning of this conversation; but was diverted from it by your vehemence—Indeed, my beloved creature, you was *very* vehement—Do you think it must not be matter of high regret to me to find my wishes so often delayed and postponed, in favour of your predominant view to a reconciliation with relations who will not be reconciled to you?—To this was owing your declining to celebrate before we came to town, though you were so atrociously treated by your sister, and your whole family; and though so ardently pressed to celebrate by me? To this was owing the ready offence you took at my four friends; and at the unavailing attempt I made to see a dropped letter, little imagining that there could be room for mortal displeasure on that account, from what two such ladies could write to each other—To this was owing the week's distance you held me at, till you knew the issue of another application—But when they had rejected that; when you had sent my coldly-received proposals to Miss Howe for her approbation or advice, as indeed I advised, and had honoured me with your company at the play on Saturday night (my whole behaviour unobjectible to the last hour); must not, madam, the sudden change in your conduct, the very next morning, astonish and distress me?—And this persisted in with still stronger declarations, after you had received the impatiently-expected letter from Miss Howe; must I not conclude, that all was owing to her influence; and that some other application or project was meditating, that made it necessary to keep me again at distance till the result were known, and which was to deprive me of you for ever? for was not that your constantly proposed preliminary?—Well, madam, might I be wrought up to a half-frenzy by this apprehension; and well might I charge you with hating me—And now, dearest creature, let me know, I once more ask you, what is Miss Howe's opinion of my proposals?

Were I disposed to debate with you, Mr Lovelace, I could very easily answer your fine harangue. But at present, I shall only say that your ways have been very unaccountable. You seem to me, if your meanings were always just, to have taken great pains to embarrass them. Whether owing in you to the want of a clear head, or a sound heart, I cannot determine; but it is to the want of one of them, I verily think, that I am to ascribe the greatest part of your strange conduct.

Curse upon the heart of the little devil, said I, who instigates you to think so hardly of the faithfullest heart in the world!

How dare you, sir?—And there she stopped; having almost overshot herself; as I designed she should.

How dare I *what*, madam? And I looked with meaning. How dare I *what*?

Vile man!—And do you—and there again she stopped.

Do I *what*, madam?—And why *vile man*?

How dare you to curse *anybody* in my presence?

Oh the sweet receder!—But that was not to go off so with a Lovelace.

Why then, dearest creature, is there *anybody* that instigates you?—If there be, again I curse them, be they who they will.

She was in a charming pretty passion—And this was the first time that I had the odds in my favour.

Well, madam, it is just as I thought. And now I know how to account for a temper, that I hope is not *natural* to you.

Artful wretch! And is it thus you would entrap me?—But know, sir, that I receive letters from nobody but Miss Howe. Miss Howe likes some of your ways as little as I do; for I have set everything before her—Yet she is thus far *your* enemy, as she is *mine*—she thinks I should not refuse your offers; but endeavour to make the best of my lot. And now you have the truth. Would to Heaven you were capable of dealing with equal sincerity!

I *am*, madam. And here, on my knee, I renew my vows, and my supplication, that you will make me yours—yours for ever—And let me have cause to bless you and Miss Howe in the same breath.

To say the truth, Belford, I had before begun to think that that vixen of a girl, who certainly likes not Hickman, was in love with *me*.

Rise, sir, from your too-ready knees; and mock me not.

Too-ready knees, thought I!—Though this humble posture so little affects this proud beauty, she knows not how much I have obtained of others of her sex, nor how often I have been forgiven the last attempts, by kneeling.

Mock you, madam!—and I arose, and re-urged her for the day. I blamed myself at the same time, for my invitation to Lord M., as it might subject me to delay from his infirmities: but told her that I would write to him to excuse me, if she had no objection; or to give him the day she would give me, and not wait for him, if he could not come in time.

My day, sir, said she, is never. Be not surprised. A person of politeness judging between us would not be surprised that I say so. But indeed, Mr Lovelace (and wept through impatience), you either know not how to treat with a mind of the least degree of delicacy, notwithstanding your birth and education, or you are an ungrateful man; and (after a pause) a worse than ungrateful one. But I will retire. I will see you again tomorrow. I cannot before. I think I hate you—You may look—Indeed I think I hate you. And if, upon a re-examination of my own heart, I find I do, I would not for the world that matters should go on farther between us.

I was too much vexed, disconcerted, mortified, to hinder her retiring—and yet she had not gone, if Dorcas had not coughed.

The wench came in, as soon as her lady had retired, and gave me the copy she had taken. And what should it be of, but the answer the truly admirable creature had intended to give to my written proposals in relation to settlements?

I have but just dipped into this affecting paper. Were I to read it attentively, not a wink should I sleep this night. Tomorrow it shall obtain my serious consideration.

Letter 202: MR LOVELACE TO JOHN BELFORD, ESQ.

Tuesday morning, May 23

THE dear creature desires to be excused seeing me till evening. She is not very well, Dorcas tells me.

Read here, if thou wilt, the paper transcribed by Dorcas. It is impossible that I should proceed with my projects against this admirable woman, were it not that I am resolved, after a few trials more, as nobly sustained as those she has already passed through, to make her (if she really hate me not) legally mine.

To Mr LOVELACE.

'WHEN a woman is married, that supreme earthly obligation requires her, in all instances of natural justice, and where her husband's honour may be concerned, to yield her own will to his—But, beforehand, I could be glad, conformably to what I have always signified, to have the most explicit assurances, that every possible way should be tried to avoid litigation with my father. Time and patience will subdue all things. My prospects of happiness are extremely contracted. A husband's right will be always the same. In my life-time I could wish nothing to be done of this sort. Your circumstances, sir, will not oblige you to extort violently from him what is in his hands. All that depends upon *me*, either with regard to my person, to my diversions, or to the economy that no married woman, of whatever rank or quality, should be above inspecting, shall be done, to prevent a necessity for such measures being taken. And, if there will be no *necessity* for them, it is to be hoped that motives *less* excusable will not have force—motives which must be founded in a littleness of mind, which a woman, who has *not* that littleness of mind, will be under such temptations as her duty will hardly be able at all times to check, to despise her husband for having; especially in cases where her own family, so much a part of herself, and which will have obligations upon her (though then but *secondary* ones) from which she never can be freed, are intimately concerned.

'This article, then, I urge to your most serious consideration, as what lies next my heart. I enter not here minutely into the fatal misunderstanding between them and you: the fault may be in both. But, sir, *yours* was the foundation-fault: at least, you gave a too plausible pretence for my brother's antipathy to work upon. Condescension was no part of your study. You chose to bear the imputations laid to your charge, rather than to make it your endeavour to obviate them.

'But this may lead into hateful recrimination—Let it be remembered, I will only say in this place, that, in *their* eye, you have robbed them of a daughter they doted upon; and that their resentments on this occasion rise but in proportion to their love, and their disappointment. If they were faulty in some of the measures they took, while they themselves did not think so, who shall judge for *them?* You, sir, who will judge everybody as you please, and will let nobody judge you, in *your own* particular, must not be their judge—It may therefore be expected that they will stand out.

'As for *myself*, sir, I must leave it (so seems it to be destined) to your justice, to treat me as you shall think I deserve: but if your future behaviour to *them* is not governed by that harsh-sounding implacableness, which you charge upon some of their tempers, the splendour of your family, and the excellent character of *some* of them (of *all* indeed, except your own conscience furnishes you with one *only* exception) will, on better consideration, do everything with them: for they *may* be overcome; perhaps, however, with the more difficulty, as the greatly prosperous less bear control and disappointment than others: for I will own to you, that I have often in secret lamented that their great acquirements have been a snare to them; perhaps as great a snare as some *other* accidentals have been to you; which being less immediately your own gifts, you have still less reason than they to value yourself upon them.

'Let me only, on this subject, further observe that condescension is not meanness. There is a glory in yielding, that hardly any violent spirit can judge of. My brother perhaps is no more sensible of *this* than you. But as you have talents he has not (who, however, has, as I hope, that regard for morals, the want of which makes one of his objections to you), I could wish it may not be owing to *you* that your mutual dislikes to each other do not subside; for it is my earnest hope that in time you may see each other, without exciting the fears of a wife and a sister for the consequence. Not that I should wish you to yield in points that truly concerned your honour: no, sir, I would be as delicate in such, as you yourself: *more* delicate, I will venture to say, because more *uniformly* so. How vain, how contemptible, is that pride, which shows itself in standing upon diminutive observances; and gives up, and makes a jest of, the most important!

'This article being considered as I wish, all the rest will be easy. Were I to accept of the handsome separate provision you seem to intend me; added to the considerable sums arisen from my grandfather's estate since his death (more considerable than perhaps you may suppose from your offer); I should think it my duty to lay up for the family good, and for unforeseen events out of it: for, as to my donations, I would generally confine myself, in them, to the tenth of my income, be it what it would. I aim at no glare in what I do of that sort: all I wish for is the power of relieving the lame, the blind, the sick, and the industrious poor, whom accident has made so, or sudden distress reduced. The common or bred beggars I leave to others, and to the public provision. They cannot be lower: perhaps they wish not to be higher: and, not able to do for everyone, I aim not at works of supererogation. Two hundred pounds a year would do all I wish to do of the separate sort: for all above, I would content myself to ask you; except, mistrusting your own economy, you would give up to my management and keeping, in order to provide for future contingencies, a larger portion; for which, as your steward, I would regularly account.

'As to clothes, I have particularly two suits, which, having been only, in a manner, tried on, would answer for any present occasion. Jewels I have of my grandmother's, which want only new setting: another set I have, which on particular days I used to wear. Although these are not sent me, I have no doubt, being merely personals, that they will, when I send for them in another name: till when I should not choose to wear any.

'As to your complaints of my diffidences, and the like, I appeal to your own heart, if it be possible for you to make my case your own for one moment, and to retrospect some parts of your behaviour, words, and actions, whether I am not rather to be justified than censured—and whether, of all men in the world, avowing what you avow, you ought not to think so. If you do not, let me admonish you, sir, that there must be too great a mismatch, as I may call it, in our minds, ever to make you wish to bring about a more intimate union of interests between yourself and

May 20   CLARISSA HARLOWE.'

THE original of this charming paper, as Dorcas tells me, was torn almost in two—in one of her pets, I suppose!—What business have the sex, whose principal glory is meekness, and patience, and resignation, to be in a passion, I trow?—Will not she, who allows herself such liberties as a maiden lady, take greater when a married one?

And a *wife*, to be in a passion!—Let me tell the ladies, it is a d——ned impudent thing, begging their pardon, and as *imprudent* as impudent, for a *wife* to be in a passion, if she mean not eternal separation, or wicked defiance, by it: for is it not rejecting at once all that expostulatory meekness and gentle reasoning, mingled with sighs as gentle, and graced with bent knees, supplicating hands, and eyes lifted up to your imperial countenance, just running over, that should make a reconciliation speedy, and as lasting as speedy? Even suppose the husband is wrong, will not his being so give the greater force to her expostulation?

Now I think of it, a man *should* be wrong now and then, to make his wife shine. Miss Howe tells my charmer that adversity is *her* shining time. 'Tis a generous thing in a man to make his wife shine at his own expense: to give her leave to triumph over him by patient reasoning: for were he to be too *imperial* to acknowledge his fault on the spot, she will find the benefit of her duty and submission *in future*, and in the high opinion he will conceive of her prudence and obligingness—and so, by degrees, she will be her master's master.

But for a wife to come up with a kemboed arm, the other hand thrown out, perhaps, with a pointing finger—Look ye here, sir!—Take notice!—If *you* are wrong, *I'll* be wrong!—If *you* are in a passion, *I'll* be in a passion!—Rebuff for rebuff, sir!—If *you* fly, *I'll* tear!—If *you* swear, *I'll* curse!—And the same room, and the same bed, shall not hold us, sir!—For, remember, I am married, sir!—I'm a wife, sir!—You can't help yourself, sir!—Your honour, as well as your peace, is in my keeping!—And, if you like not this treatment, you may have worse, sir!

Ah! Jack, Jack! What man who has observed these things, either *implied*, or *expressed*, in *other* families, would wish to be an husband!

Dorcas found this paper in one of the drawers of her lady's dressing-table: she was re-perusing it, as she supposes, when the honest wench carried my message to desire her to favour me at the tea-table; for she saw her pop a paper into the drawer, as she came in; and there, on her mistress's going to meet me in the dining-room, she found it: and to be this.

But I had better not to have had a copy of it, as far as I know: for, determined as I was before upon my operations, it instantly turned all my resolutions in her favour. Yet I would give something to be convinced that she did not pop it into her drawer before the wench, in order for me to see it; and perhaps (if I were to take notice of it) to discover whether Dorcas, according to Miss Howe's advice, were most *my* friend, or *hers*.

The very suspicion of this will do her no good: for I cannot bear to be artfully treated. People love to enjoy their own peculiar talents in *monopoly*, as I may say. I am aware that it will strengthen thy arguments against me in her behalf. But I know every tittle thou canst say upon it: so spare thy wambling nonsense, I desire thee; and leave this sweet excellence and me to our fate: that will determine for us, as it shall please itself: for, as Cowley says,

> An unseen hand makes all our moves:
> And some are great, and some are small;
> Some climb to good, some from good fortune fall:
> Some wise men, and some fools we call:
> Figures, alas! of speech!—For destiny plays us all.[1]

But, after all, I am sorry, *almost* sorry (for how shall I do to be *quite* sorry, when it is not *given* to me to be so?), that I cannot, without making any further trials, resolve upon wedlock.

I have just read over again this intended answer to my proposals: and how I adore her for it!

But yet; another *yet!*—She has not given it or sent it to me—So it is not *her* answer. It is not written *for* me, though *to* me.

Nay, she has not *intended* to send it to me: she has even torn it, perhaps with indignation, as thinking it too *good* for me. By this action she absolutely retracts it. Why then does my foolish fondness seek to establish for her the same merit in my heart, as if she avowed it? Prithee, dear Belford, once more leave us to our fate; and do not thou interpose with thy nonsense, to weaken a spirit already too squeamish, and strengthen a conscience that has declared itself of her party.

Then again, remember thy recent discoveries, Lovelace!—Remember her indifference, attended with all the appearance of contempt and hatred. View her, even *now*, wrapt up in reserve and mystery; meditating plots, as far as thou knowest, against the sovereignty thou hast, by right of conquest, obtained over her: remember, in short, all thou hast *threatened* to remember against this insolent beauty, who is a rebel to the power she has listed under!

But yet, how dost thou propose to subdue thy sweet enemy?—Abhorred be *force*, be the *necessity* of force, if that can be avoided! There is no triumph in *force!* No conquest over the will!—No prevailing, by gentle degrees, over the gentle passions! *Force* is the devil!

My cursed character, as I have often said, was against me at setting out!—yet is she not a *woman?* Cannot I find one but half-yielding moment, if she do not absolutely hate me?

But with what can I tempt her?—RICHES she was born to, and despises, knowing what they are. JEWELS and ornaments, to a mind so much a jewel, and so richly set, her worthy consciousness will not let her value. LOVE, if she be susceptible of love, it seems to be so much under the direction of prudence, that one unguarded moment, I fear, cannot be reasonably hoped for: and so much VIGILANCE, so much apprehensiveness, that her fears are ever aforehand with her dangers. Then her LOVE OF VIRTUE seems to be *principle*, native, or if *not* native, so deeply rooted that its fibres have struck into her heart, and, as she grew up, so blended and twisted themselves with the strings of life that I doubt there is no separating of the one, without cutting the others asunder.

What then can be done to make such a matchless creature as this get over the first tests, in order to put her to the grand proof, whether once overcome, she will not be always overcome?

By my faith, Jack, as I sit gazing upon her, my whole soul in my eyes, contemplating her perfections, and thinking, when I have seen her easy and serene, what would be her thoughts, did *she* know my heart as well as *I* know it; when I behold her disturbed and jealous, how *just* her apprehensions, and that she cannot fear so much as there is *room* for her to fear; my heart often misgives me.

And must, think I, oh creature so divinely excellent, and so beloved of my soul, those arms, those encircling arms, that would make a monarch happy, be used to repel brutal force; all their strength, unavailingly perhaps, exerted to repel it, and to defend a person so delicately framed? Can violence enter into the heart of a wretch, who might entitle himself to all [her] willing yet virtuous love, and make the blessings [he aspires] after, her *duty* to confer?—Begone, villain-purposes!—Sink ye all to the hell that could only inspire ye!—And I am ready to throw myself at her feet, confess my villainous designs, avow my repentance, and put it out of my power to act unworthily by such a peerless excellence.

How then comes it, that all these compassionate, and, as some would call them, *honest* sensibilities go off?—Why, Miss Howe will tell thee: she says I am the *devil*—By my conscience, I think he has at present a great share in me.

There's ingenuity!—How I lay myself open to thee!—But seest thou not that the more I say against myself, the less room there is for thee to take me to task?—Oh Belford, Belford! I cannot, cannot (at least at present I cannot) marry.

Then her family, my bitter enemies!—To supple to them, or, if I do not, to make her *as* unhappy as she can be from my *attempts*——

Then must she love them too much, me too little.

She now seems to despise me: Miss Howe declares, that she really does despise me. To be *despised by a* WIFE!—What a thought is that!—To be *excelled by a* WIFE too, in every part of praiseworthy knowledge!—To *take lessons*, to *take instructions*, from a WIFE!—*More* than despise me, she herself has taken time to consider whether she does not *hate* me—*I hate you*, Lovelace, *with my whole heart*, said she to me but yesterday!—*My soul is above thee, man!*—*Urge me not to tell thee, how sincerely I think my soul above thee!*—How poor indeed was I then, even in my own heart!—So *visible* a superiority, to so proud a spirit as mine!—And *here* from below, from BELOW indeed! I am so goaded on—

Yet 'tis poor too, to think myself a machine—I am *no* machine—Lovelace, thou art base to thyself, but to *suppose* thyself a machine.

But having gone thus far, I should be unhappy, if, after marriage, in the petulance of ill humour, I had it to reproach myself that I did not try her to the utmost. And yet I don't know how it is, but this lady, the moment I come into her presence, half assimilates me to her own virtue—Once or twice (to say nothing of her triumph over me on Sunday night) I was prevailed upon to fluster myself, with an intention to make some advances, which, if obliged to recede, I might lay upon raised spirits: but the instant I beheld her, I was soberized into awe and reverence: and the majesty of her even *visible* purity first damped, and then extinguished, my *double* flame.

What a surprisingly powerful effect, so much and so long in my power, *she!* so instigated by some of her own sex, and so stimulated by passion, *I!*—How can this be accounted for, in a Lovelace!

But what a heap of stuff have I written!—How have I been run away with!—By what?—Canst thou say by what?—Oh thou lurking varletess CONSCIENCE!—Is it thou that has thus made me of party against myself?—How camest thou in?—In what disguise, thou egregious haunter of my more agreeable hours?—Stand *thou*, with *fate*, but neuter in this controversy; and, if I cannot do credit to human nature, and to the female sex, by bringing down such an angel as this to class with and adorn it (for adorn it she does in her very foibles), then I am all yours, and never will resist you more.

Here I arose. I shook myself. The window was open. Away the troublesome bosom-visiter, the intruder, is flown—I see it yet!—I see it yet!—And now it lessens to my aching eye!—And now the cleft air has closed after it, and it is out of sight!—And once more I am

ROBERT LOVELACE

· Letter 203: MR LOVELACE TO JOHN BELFORD, ESQ.

Tuesday, May 23

WELL did I, and but just in time, conclude to have done with Mrs Fretchville and the house: for here Mennell has declared that he cannot in conscience and honour go any farther—He would not for the world be accessory to the deceiving of such a lady!—I was a fool to let either you or him see her; for ever *since*, ye have both had scruples, which neither would have had, were a *woman* to have been in the question.

Well, I can't help it!

He has, however, though with some reluctance, consented to write me a letter, provided I will allow it to be the last step he shall take in this affair.

I presumed, I told him, that if I could make Mrs Fretchville's *woman* supply his place, he would have no objection to that.

None, he says—*But is it not pity—*

A pitiful fellow! Such a ridiculous kind of pity *his*, as those silly souls have, who would not kill an innocent chicken for the world; but when killed to their hands, are always the most greedy devourers of it.

Now this letter gives the servant the small-pox: and she has given it to her unhappy vapourish lady. Vapourish people are perpetual subjects for diseases to work upon. *Name* but the malady, and it is *theirs* in a moment. *Ever* fitted for inoculation.—The physical tribe's milch-cows—A vapourish or splenetic patient is a fiddle for the doctors; and they are eternally playing upon it. Sweet music does it make them. All their difficulty, except a case extraordinary happens (as poor Mrs Fretchville's, who has *realized* her apprehensions), is but to hold their countenance, while their patient is drawing up a bill of indictment against himself—and when they have heard it, proceed to *punish*—The right word for *prescribe*. Why should they not, when the criminal has confessed his guilt?—And *punish* they generally do with a vengeance.

Yet, silly toads too, now I think of it! For why, when they know they cannot do good, may they not as well endeavour to gratify, as to nauseate, the patient's palate?

Were I a physician, I'd get all the trade to myself: for Malmsey, and Cyprus, and the generous products of the Cape,[1] a little disguised, should be my principal doses: as these would create new spirits, how would the revived patient covet the physic, and adore the doctor!

Give all the paraders of the faculty whom thou knowest, this hint—There could but one inconvenience arise from it. The APOTHECARIES would find their medicines cost them *something:* but the demand for quantities would answer that: since the honest NURSE would be the patient's taster; perpetually requiring repetitions of the last cordial julap.

Well, but to the letter—Yet what need of further explanation after the hints in my former? The widow cannot be removed; and that's enough: and Mennell's work is over; and his conscience left to plague him for his own sins, and not another man's: and very possibly plague enough will it give him for those.

This letter is directed, *To Robert Lovelace, Esq; or, in his absence, to his lady.* She had refused dining with me, or seeing me; and I was out when it came. She opened it: so is my lady by her own consent, proud and saucy as she is.

I am glad at my heart that it came before we entirely make up. She would else, perhaps, have concluded it to be contrived for a delay: and now, moreover, we can accommodate our old and new quarrels together; and that's contrivance, you know. But how is her dear haughty heart humbled to what it was when I knew her first, that she can apprehend *any* delays from me; and have nothing to do but to vex at them!

I came in to dinner. She sent me down the letter, desiring my excuse for opening it. Did it before she was aware. Lady pride, Belford!—Recollection, then retrogradation!

I requested to see her upon it that moment. But she desires to suspend our interview till morning. I will bring her to own, before I have done with her, that she can't see me too often.

My impatience was so great, on an occasion so *unexpected*, that I could not help writing, to tell her, 'how much vexed I was at the accident: But that it need not delay my happy day, as that did not depend upon the house (she knew that before, she'll think, and so did I): and as Mrs Fretchville, by Mr Mennell, so handsomely expressed her concern upon it, and her wishes that it could suit us to bear with the unavoidable delay, I hoped that going down to The Lawn for two or three of the summer months, when I was made the happiest of men, would be favourable to all round.'

The dear creature takes this incident to heart, I believe: and sends word to my repeated request to see her, notwithstanding her denial, that she cannot till the morning. It shall be then at six o'clock, if I please!

To be sure I *do* please!

Can see her but once a day now, Jack!

Did I tell thee, that I wrote a letter to my cousin Montague, wondering that I heard not from Lord M. as the subject was so very interesting? In it I acquainted her with the house I was about taking; and with Mrs Fretchville's vapourish delays.

I was very loth to engage my own family, either man or woman, in this affair; but I must take my measures securely: and already they all think as bad of me as they well can. You observe by my Lord M.'s to yourself, that the well-mannered peer is afraid I should play this admirable creature one of my *usual dog's tricks*.

I have received just now an answer from Charlotte.

Charlotte i'n't well. A stomach disorder.

No wonder a girl's stomach should plague her. A single lady; that's it. When she has a man to plague, it will have something besides itself to prey upon. Knowest thou not moreover, that man is the woman's sun; woman is the man's earth?— How dreary, how desolate, the earth, that is deprived of the all-salubriating sunshine!

Poor Charlotte! But I *heard* she was not well; that encouraged me to write to her; and to express myself a little concerned that she had not of her own accord thought of a visit in town to my charmer.

Here follows a copy of her letter: Thou wilt see by it, that every little monkey is to catechize me. They all depend upon my good-nature.

[*Letter 203.1: Lady Charlotte Montague to Robert Lovelace, Esq.*]

M. Hall, May 22

Dear cousin,

WE have been in daily hope for a long time, I must call it, of hearing that the happy knot was tied. My lord has been very much out of order: and yet nothing would serve him, but he would himself write an answer to your letter. It was the only opportunity he should ever have, perhaps, to throw in a little good advice to you, with the hope of its being of any signification; and he has been several hours in a day, as his gout would let him, busied in it: it wants now only his last revisal.

He hopes it will have the greater weight with you, if it appear all in his own handwriting.

Indeed, Mr Lovelace, his worthy heart is wrapped up in you. I wish you loved yourself but half as well. But I believe too, that if all the family loved you less, you would love yourself more.

His lordship has been very busy, at the times he could not write, in consulting Pritchard about those estates which he proposes to transfer to you on the happy occasion, that he may answer your letter in the most acceptable manner; and show by effects, how kindly he takes your invitation. I assure you, he is mighty proud of it.

As for myself, I am not at all well, and have not been for some weeks past, with my old stomach disorder. I had certainly else before now have done myself the honour you wonder I have *not* done myself. My aunt Lawrance, who would have accompanied me (for we had laid it all out), has been exceedingly busy in her law affair; her antagonist, who is actually on the spot, having been making proposals for an accommodation. But you may assure yourself, that when our dear relation-elect shall be entered upon the new habitation you tell me of, we will do ourselves the honour of visiting her; and if any delay arises from the dear lady's want of courage, which, considering her man, let me tell you, may very well be, we will endeavour to inspire her with it, and be sponsors for you: for, cousin, I believe you have need to be christened over again before you are entitled to so great a blessing. What think you?

Just now, my lord tells me he will dispatch a man on purpose with his letter tomorrow: so I need not have written. But now I have, let it go; and by Empson, who sets out directly on his return to town.

My best compliments, and sister's, to the most deserving lady in the world (you will need no other direction to the person meant) conclude me

Your affectionate cousin and servant,
Charl. Montague

Thou seest how seasonably this letter comes. I hope my lord will write nothing but what I may show my beloved. I have actually sent her up this letter of Charlotte's; and hope for happy effects from it.

[*Letter 203.2: Miss Clarissa Harlowe to Miss Howe*]

The lady, in her next letter, gives Miss Howe an account of what has passed between Mr Lovelace and herself. She resents his behaviour with her usual dignity: but when she comes to mention Mr Mennell's letter, she re-urges Miss Howe to perfect her scheme for her deliverance; being resolved to leave him. But, dating again on his sending up to her Miss Montague's letter, she alters her mind, and desires her to suspend, for the present, her application to Mrs Townsend.

I had begun, *says she*, to suspect all he had said of Mrs Fretchville and her house; and even Mr Mennell himself, though so well appearing a man. But now that I find Mr Lovelace had apprised his relations of his intention to take it; and had engaged some of the ladies to visit me there; I could hardly forbear blaming myself for censuring him as capable of so vile an imposture. But may he not thank himself for acting so very unaccountably, and taking such needlessly wry steps, as he has done; embarrassing, as I told him, his own meanings, if they were good?

Letter 204: MR LOVELACE TO JOHN BELFORD, ESQ.

Wed. May 24

(He gives his friend an account of their interview that morning; and of the happy effects of his cousin Montague's letter in his favour. Her reserves, however, he tells him, are not absolutely banished. But this he imputes to form.)

IT is *not* in the power of woman, *says he*, to be altogether sincere on these occasions. But why?—Do they think it so great a disgrace to be found out to be really what they *are?*

I regretted the illness of Mrs Fretchville; as the intention I had to fix her dear self in the house before the happy knot was tied would have set her in that independence in *appearance*, as well as *fact*, which was necessary to show to all the world that her choice was free; and *as* the ladies of my family would have been proud to make their court to her there; while the settlements and our equipages were preparing. But on any other account, there was no great matter in it; since when my happy day was over, we could, with so much convenience, go down to The Lawn, or to my Lord M.'s, or to either of my aunts in town; which would give full time to provide ourselves with servants, and other accommodations.

How sweetly the charmer listened!

I asked her if she had had the small-pox?

'Twas always a doubtful point with her mother and Mrs Norton, she owned. But although she was not afraid of it, she chose not unnecessarily to rush into places where it was.

Right, thought I—Else, I said, it would not have been amiss for her to see the house before she went into the country; for, if *she* liked it not, I was not obliged to have it.

She asked if she might take a copy of Miss Montague's letter?

I said she might keep the letter itself, and send it to Miss Howe if she pleased; for that, I supposed, was her intention. She bowed her head to me. There, Jack!—I shall have her curtsy to me, by and by, I question not. What a-devil had I to do, to terrify the sweet creature by my termagant projects!—Yet it was not amiss, I believe, to make her afraid of me. She *says*, I am an unpolite man—and every polite instance from such a one is deemed a favour.

Talking of the settlements, I told her that I had rather Pritchard (mentioned by my cousin Charlotte), had not been consulted on this occasion. Pritchard, indeed, was a very honest man; and had been for a generation in the family; and knew the estates, and the condition of them, better than either my lord or myself: but Pritchard, like other old men, was diffident and slow; and valued himself upon his skill as a draughtsman; and for the sake of that paltry reputation, must have all his forms preserved, were an imperial crown to depend upon his dispatch.

I kissed her unrepulsing hand no less than five times during this conversation. Lord, Jack, how my generous heart run over!—She was quite obliging at parting— She in a manner asked me *leave* to retire, to reperuse Charlotte's letter—I think she bent her knees to me; but I won't be sure—How happy might we have both been long ago, had the dear creature been always as complaisant to me! For I do love respect, and, whether I deserved it or not, always had it, till I knew this proud beauty.

And now, Belford, are we in a train, or the deuce is in it. Every fortified town has its strong and its weak place. I had carried on my attacks against the impregnable parts. I have no doubt but I shall either *shine* or *smuggle* her out of her cloak, since she and Miss Howe have intended to employ a smuggler against *me*—All we wait for now is my lord's letter.

But I had like to have *forgot* to tell thee, that we have been not a little alarmed, by some inquiries that have been made after me and my beloved, by a man of good appearance; who yesterday procured a tradesman in the neighbourhood to send for Dorcas; of whom he asked several questions relating to us; and particularly (as we boarded and lodged in one house), whether we were married?

This has given my beloved great uneasiness. And I could not help observing upon it to her, how right a thing it was that we had given out below that we were married. The inquiry, most probably, I said, was from her brother's quarter; and now, perhaps, that our marriage was owned, we should hear no more of his machinations. The person, it seems, was curious to know the day that the ceremony was performed. But Dorcas refused to give him any other particulars, than that we *were* married; and was the more reserved, as he declined to tell her the motives of his enquiry.

Letter 205: MR LOVELACE TO JOHN BELFORD, ESQ.

May 24

THE devil take this uncle of mine! He has at last sent me a letter, which I cannot show without exposing the head of our family for a fool. A confounded parcel of pop-guns has he let off upon me. I was in hopes he had exhausted his whole stock of this sort, in his letter to you—To keep it back, to delay sending it till he had recollected all this *farrago* of nonsense—Confound his *wisdom of nations*, if so much of it is to be scraped together, in disgrace of itself, to make one egregious simpleton!—But I am glad I am fortified with this piece of flagrant folly, however; since, in all human affairs, the *convenient* and *inconvenient*, the *good* and the *bad*, are so mingled, that there is no having the one without the other.

I have already offered the bill enclosed in it to my beloved; and read to her part of the letter. But she refused the bill: and I, being in cash, shall return it. She seemed very desirous to peruse the whole letter. And when I told her that were it not for exposing the writer I would oblige her, she said, it would not be exposing his lordship to show it to her; and that she always preferred the heart to the head. I knew her meaning—but did not thank her for it.

All that makes for me in it, I will transcribe for her—Yet, hang it, she shall have the letter, and my soul with it, for one consenting kiss.

SHE has got the letter from me, without the reward. Deuce take me if I had the courage to propose the condition! A new character this of bashfulness in thy friend—I see that a truly modest woman may make even a confident man keep his distance. By my soul, Belford, I believe that the nine women in ten who fall, fall either from their own vanity, or levity, or for want of circumspection, and proper reserves.

I DID intend to take my reward on her returning a letter so favourable to us both. But she sent it to me, sealed up, by Dorcas—I might have thought that there were two or three hints in it that she would be too nice immediately to appear to. I send it to thee; and here will stop, to give thee time to read it. Return it as soon as thou hast perused it.

Letter 206: LORD M. TO ROBERT LOVELACE, ESQ.

Tuesday, May 23

It is a long lane that has no turning—Do not despise me for my proverbs—You know I was always fond of them; and if you had been so too, it would have been the better for you, let me tell you. I dare swear the fine lady you are so likely to be soon happy with will be far from despising them; for I am told that she writes well, and that all her letters are full of sentences. God convert you! for nobody but He and this lady, can.

I have no manner of doubt now but that you will marry, as your father, and all your ancestors, did before you: else you would have had no title to be my heir; nor can your descendants have any title to be yours, unless they are legitimate; that's worth your remembrance, sir!—*No man is always a fool, every man sometimes*— But your follies, I hope, are now at an end.

I know you have vowed revenge against this fine lady's family: but no more of that, now. You must look upon them all as your relations; and forgive and forget. And when they see you make a good husband, and a good father (which God send, for all our sakes!), they will wonder at their nonsensical antipathy, and beg your pardon: but while they think you a vile fellow, and rake, how can they either love you, or excuse their daughter?

And methinks I could wish to give a word of comfort to the lady, who, doubtless, must be under great fears how she shall be able to hold-in such a wild creature as you have hitherto been. I would hint to her, that by strong arguments and gentle words, she may do anything with you; for though you are too apt to be hot, gentle words will cool you and bring you into the temper that is necessary for your cure.

Would to God, *my* poor lady, your aunt, who is dead and gone, had been a proper patient for the same remedy! God rest her soul! No reflections upon her memory! *Worth is best known by want!* I know *hers* now; and if I had went first, she would by this time have known *mine.*

There is great wisdom in that saying, *God send me a friend that may tell me of my faults: if not, an enemy, and he will.* Not that I am your enemy; and that you know well. *The more noble anyone is, the more humble:* so bear with me, if you would be thought noble—Am I not your uncle? And do I not design to be better to you than your father could be? Nay, I will be your father too, when the happy day comes; since you desire it: and pray make my compliments to my dear niece; and tell her I wonder much that she has so long deferred your happiness.

Pray let her know, I will present HER (not *you*) either my Lancashire seat or *The*

Lawn in Hertfordshire; and settle upon her a thousand pounds a year, penny-rents; to show her that we are not a family to take base advantages: and you may have writings drawn, and settle as you will—Honest Pritchard has the rent-roll of both these estates at his fingers end; and has been a good old servant. I recommend him to your lady's favour. I have already consulted him: he will tell you what is best for you, and most pleasing to me.

I am still very bad with my gout; but will come in a litter, as soon as the day is fixed: it would be the joy of my heart to join your hands. And let me tell you, if you do not make the best of husbands to so good a young lady, and one who has had so much courage for your sake, I will renounce you; and settle all I can upon her and hers by you, and leave you out of the question.

If anything be wanting for your further security, I am ready to give it (though you know that my word has always been looked upon as my bond): and when the Harlowes know all this, let us see whether they are able to blush, and take shame upon themselves.

Your two aunts want only to know the day, to make all the country round them blaze, and all their tenants mad. And, if any one of mine be sober upon the occasion, Pritchard shall eject him. And, on the birth of the first child, if a son, I will do something more for you, and repeat all our rejoicings.

I ought indeed to have written sooner. But I knew that if you thought me long, and were in haste as to your nuptials, you would write and tell me so. But my gout was very troublesome: and I am but a slow writer, you know, at best: for composing is a thing that, though formerly I was very ready at it (as my Lord Lexington used to say), yet having left it off a great while, I am not so now. And I chose, on this occasion, to write all out of my own head and memory; and to give you my best advice; for I may never have such an opportunity again. You have had (God mend you!) a strange way of turning your back upon all I have said; this once, I hope, you will be more attentive to the advice I give you for your own good.

I had still another end; nay, two other ends.

The one was: That now you are upon the borders of wedlock, as I may say, and *all your wild oats will be sown*, I would give you some instructions as to your public as well as private behaviour in life; which, intending you so much good as I do, you ought to hear; and perhaps would never have listened to, on any less extraordinary occasion.

The second is: That your dear lady-elect (who is, it seems, herself so fine and so sententious a writer) will see by this, that it is not our faults, nor for want of the best advice, that you was not a better man than you have hitherto been.

And now, in few words, for the conduct I would wish you to follow in public, as well as in private, if you would think me worthy of advising. It shall be short; so be not uneasy.

As to the *private* life: Love your lady as she deserves. *Let your actions praise you.* Be a good husband; and so give the lie to all your enemies; and make them ashamed of their scandals: and let us have pride in saying that Miss Harlowe has not done either herself, or family, any discredit by coming among us. Do this; and I, and your aunts, will love you for ever.

As to your *public* conduct—this is what I could wish: but I reckon your lady's wisdom will put us both right—No disparagement, sir; since, with all your wit, you have not hitherto shown much wisdom, you know.

Get into Parliament as soon as you can: for you have talents to make a great figure there. Who so proper to assist in making new holding laws, as those whom no law in being could hold?

Then, for so long as you will give attendance in St Stephen's Chapel[1]—its being called a chapel, I hope, will not *disgust* you: I am sure I have known many a riot there—a Speaker has a hard time of it! But we *peers* have more decorum—but what was I going to say?—I must go back.

For so long as you will give your attendance in Parliament, for so long will you be out of mischief; out of *private* mischief, at least: and may St Stephen's fate be yours, if you wilfully do *public* mischief!

When a new election comes, you will have two or three boroughs, you know, to choose out of—but if you stay till then, I had rather you were for the shire.[2]

You'll have interest enough, I am sure; and being so handsome a man, the women will make their husbands vote for you.

I shall long to read your speeches. I expect you will speak, if occasion offers, the very first day. You want no courage; and think highly enough of yourself, and lowly enough of everybody else, to speak on all occasions.

As to the methods of the House, you have spirit enough, I fear, to be too much above them: take care of that—I don't so much fear your want of good-manners. To *men*, you want no decency, if they don't provoke you: as to that, I wish you'd only learn to be as patient of contradiction from others as you would have other people be to *you*.

Although I would not have you to be a courtier; neither would I have you be a malcontent.[3] I remember (for I have it down) what my old friend Archibald Hutcheson said, and it was a very good saying—to Mr Secretary Craggs, I think it was—'I look upon an administration as entitled to every vote I can with good conscience give it; for a House of Commons should not needlessly put drags upon the wheels of Government: and, when I have not given it my vote, it was with regret: and for my country's sake, I wished with all my heart the measure had been such as I could have approved.'[4]

And another saying he had, which was this: 'Neither can an Opposition, neither can a Ministry, be always wrong. To be a plumb man therefore with either, is an infallible mark that that man must mean more and worse than he will own he does mean.'

Are these sayings bad, sir? Are they to be despised?—Well then, why should I be despised for remembering them, and quoting them, as I love to do? Let me tell you, if you loved my company more than you do, you would not be the worse for it: I may say so without any vanity; since it is other men's wisdom, and not my own, that I am so fond of. But to add a word or two more, on this occasion; and I may never have such another; for you *must* read this through—*Love honest men, and herd with them, in the House and out of the House*; by whatever names they be dignified or distinguished: *Keep good men company, and you shall be of the number*. But did I, or did I not, write this before!—Writing, at so many different times, and such a quantity, one may forget.

You may come in for the title when I am dead and gone—God help me!—So I would have you keep an equilibrium. If once you get the name of being a fine speaker, you may have anything: and, to be sure, you have naturally a great deal of elocution; a tongue that would delude an angel, as the women say: to their sorrow, some of them, poor creatures!—A leading man in the House of Commons is a very important character; because that House has the giving of money: and *Money makes the mare to go*; ay, and queens and kings too, sometimes, to go in a manner very different from what they might otherwise choose to go, let me tell you.

However, methinks I would not have you take a place neither—It will double your value, and your interest, if it be believed that you will not: for, as you will then stand in no man's way, you will have no envy; but pure sterling respect; and both sides will court you.

For your part, you will not want a place, as some others do, to piece up their broken fortunes. If you can now live reputably upon two thousand pounds a year, it will be hard if you cannot hereafter upon seven or eight—Less you will not have, if you oblige me; as now by marrying so fine a lady, very much you will—and all this, beside Lady Betty's and Lady Sarah's favours!—What, in the name of wonder, could possibly possess the proud Harlowes! That son, that son of theirs!—But, for his dear sister's sake, I will say no more of him.

I never was offered a place myself: and the only one I would have taken, had I been offered it, was *Master of the Buckhounds*; for I loved hunting when I was young; and it carries a good sound with it, for us who live in the country. Often have I thought of that excellent old adage: *He that eats the king's goose shall be choked with his feathers.* I wish to the Lord this was thoroughly considered by place-hunters! It would be better for them, and for their poor families—I could say a great deal more, and all equally to the purpose. But really I am tired; and so I doubt are you. And besides, I would reserve something for conversation.

My cousins Montague, and my two sisters, join in compliments to my niece that is to be. If she would choose to have the knot tied among us, pray tell her that we shall see it *securely done:* and we will make all the country ring, and blaze, for a week together. But so, I believe, I said before.

If anything farther may be needful toward promoting your reciprocal felicity, let me know it; and how you order about the day; and all that. The enclosed bill is very much at your service: 'tis payable at sight, as whatever else you may have occasion for shall be.

So God bless you both; and make things as convenient to my gout as you can; though be it whenever it will, I will hobble to you; for I long to see you; and my niece full as much as you; and am, in expectation of that happy time,

Your most affectionate uncle,
M.

Letter 207: MR LOVELACE TO JOHN BELFORD, ESQ.

Thursday, May 25

THOU seest, Belford, how we now drive before the wind—The dear creature now comes almost at the first word, whenever I desire the honour of her company. I told her last night that, apprehending delay from Pritchard's slowness, I was determined to leave it to my lord to make his compliments in his own way; and had actually that afternoon put my writings into the hands of a very eminent lawyer,

Counsellor Williams, with directions for him to draw up settlements from my own estate, and conformable to those of my own mother; which I put into his hands at the same time. It had been, I said, no small part of my concern, that her frequent displeasure, and our mutual misapprehensions, had hindered me from advising with her before on this subject. Indeed, indeed, my dearest life, said I, you have hitherto afforded me but a very thorny courtship.

She was silent. *Kindly* silent. For well know I, that she could have recriminated upon me with a vengeance—But I was willing to see if she were not loth to disoblige me now—I comforted myself, I said, with the hopes that all my difficulties were over; and that every past disobligation would now be buried in oblivion.

Now, Belford, I have actually deposited these writings with Counsellor Williams; and I expect the drafts in a week at furthest. So shall be doubly armed. For if I attempt, and fail, these will be ready to throw in to make her have patience with me till I can try again.

I have more contrivances still in embryo. I could tell thee of an hundred, and still hold another hundred *in petto*, to pop in as I go along, to excite thy surprise, and to keep up thy attention. Nor rave thou at me; but, if thou art my friend, think of Miss Howe's letters, and of her smuggling scheme. All owing to my fair captive's informations and incitements—Am I not a *villain*, a *fool*, a *Beelzebub*, with them already?—Yet no harm done by me, nor so much as attempted?

Everything of this nature, the dear creature answered (with a downcast eye, and a blushing cheek), she left to me.

I proposed my lord's chapel for the celebration, where we might have the presence of Lady Betty, Lady Sarah, and my two cousins Montague.

She seemed not to favour a public celebration; and waived this subject for the present. I did suppose that she would not choose to be married in public, any more than me: so I pressed not this matter further just then.

But patterns I actually produced; and a jeweller was to bring as this day several sets of jewels, for her choice. But the patterns she would not open. She sighed at the mention of them; the second patterns, she said, that had been offered to her[a]: and very peremptorily forbid the jeweller's coming; as well as declined my offer of getting my own mother's to be new-set; at least for the present.

I do assure thee, Belford, I was in earnest in all this. My whole estate is nothing to me, put in competition with her hoped-for favour.

She then told me that she had written her opinion of my general proposals; and there had expressed her mind as to clothes and jewels—But on my behaviour to her, for no cause that she knew of, on Sunday night she had torn the paper in two. I earnestly pressed her to let me be favoured with a sight of this paper, torn as it was. And after some hesitation, she withdrew, and sent it to me by Dorcas.

I perused it again. It was in a manner new to me, though I had read it so lately; and by my soul I could hardly stand it. An hundred admirable creatures I called her to herself—But I charge thee, write not a word to me in her favour, if thou meanest her well; for if I spare her, it must be all *ex mero motu*.

You may easily suppose, when I was re-admitted to her presence, that I ran over in her praises, and in vows of gratitude and everlasting love. But here's the devil; she still receives all I say with reserve; or if it be not with reserve, she receives it

a   See p. 188.

so much as her due, that she is not at all raised by it. Some women are undone by praise, by flattery. I myself am proud of praise—Perhaps thou wilt say that those are most proud of it, who least deserve it—as those are of riches and grandeur who are not born to either. I own that it requires a soul to be superior to these foibles. Have I not then a soul?—Surely, I have—Let me then be considered as an exception to the rule.

Now have I a foundation to go upon in my terms. My lord, in the exuberance of his generosity, mentions a thousand pounds a year penny-rents. *This* I know, that were I to marry this lady, he would rather settle upon her all he has a mind to settle, than upon me: and has even threatened that if I prove not a good husband to her, he will leave all he can at his death, from me, to her—Yet considers not that a woman so perfect can never be displeased with her husband but to *his* disgrace; for who will blame *her?* Another reason why a Lovelace should not wish to marry a CLARISSA.

But what a pretty fellow of an uncle mine, to think of making a wife independent of her emperor, and a rebel of course—yet smarted himself for an error of this kind!

My beloved, in her torn paper, mentions but two hundred pounds a year for her separate use. I insisted upon her naming a larger sum. She said it might then be three; and I, for fear she should suspect very large offers, named five, and the entire disposal of all arrears in her father's hands, for the benefit of Mrs Norton, or whom she pleased.

She said that the good woman would be uneasy, if anything more than a competency were done for her. She was for suiting all her dispositions of this kind, she said, to the usual way of life of the person. To go beyond it was but to put the benefited upon projects, or to make them awkward in a new state, when they might shine in that they were accustomed to. And to put it into so good a mother's power to give her son a beginning in his business at a proper time; yet to leave her something for herself, to set her above want, or the necessity of taking back from her child what she had been enabled to bestow upon him, would be the height of such a worthy parent's ambition.

Here is prudence! Here is judgement in so young a creature! How do I hate the Harlowes for producing such an angel!—Oh why, why, did she refuse my sincere address to tie the knot before we came to this house!

But yet, what mortifies my pride is, that this exalted creature, if I were to marry her, would not be governed in her behaviour to me by love, but by generosity merely, or by blind duty; and had rather live single, than be mine.

I cannot bear this. I would have the woman whom I honour with my name, if ever I confer this honour upon any, forgo even her superior duties for me. I would have her look after me when I go out, as far as she can see me, as my Rosebud after her Johnny; and meet me at my return with rapture. I would be the subject of her dreams, as well as of her waking thoughts. I would have her look upon every moment lost, that is not passed with me: sing to me, read to me, play to me when I pleased; no joy so great as in obeying me. When I should be inclined to love, overwhelm me with it; when to be serious or solitary, if intrusive, awfully so; retiring at a nod; approaching me only if I smiled encouragement: steal into my presence with silence; out of it, if not noticed, on tiptoe. Be a *Lady Easy* to all my pleasures, and valuing those most, who most contributed to them; only sighing in private, that it was not *herself* at the time—Thus of old did the contending wives of the honest patriarchs; each recommending her handmaid to her lord, as she thought it would oblige him, and looking upon the genial product as her own.

The gentle Waller says, *Women are born to be controlled.*[1] Gentle as he was, he knew that. A tyrant-husband makes a dutiful wife. And why do the sex love rakes, but because they know how to direct their uncertain wills, and manage them?

ANOTHER agreeable conversation. The day of days the subject. As to fixing a particular one, that need not be done till the settlements are completed. As to marrying at my lord's chapel, the ladies of my family present, that would be making a public affair of it; and my charmer observed with regret, that it seemed to be my lord's intention to make it so.

It could not be imagined, I said, but that his lordship's setting out in a litter, and coming to town, as well as his taste for glare, and the joy he would take to see me married at last, would give it as much the air of a public marriage, as if the ceremony were performed at his own chapel, all the ladies present.

She could not bear the thoughts of a public day. It would carry with it an air of insult upon her whole family. And, for her part, if my lord would not take it amiss (and perhaps he would not, as the motion came not from himself, but from me), she would very willingly dispense with his lordship's presence; the rather, as dress and appearance would then be unnecessary. For she could not bear to think of decking her person, while her parents were in tears.

How excellent this, did not her parents richly deserve to be in tears!

See, Belford, with so charming a niceness, we might have been a long time ago upon the verge of the state, and yet found a great deal to do, before we entered into it.

All obedience, all resignation—no will but hers. I withdrew, and wrote directly to my lord; and she not disapproving of it, sent it away. The purport as follows; for I took no copy.

'That I was much obliged to his lordship for his intended goodness to me, on an occasion that was the most solemn and awful of my life. That the admirable lady, whom he so justly praised, thought his lordship's proposals in her favour too high. That she chose not to make a public appearance, if, without disobliging my friends, she could avoid it, till a reconciliation with her own could be effected. That although she expressed a grateful sense of his lordship's consent to give her to me with his own hand; yet presuming that the motive to his kind intention was rather to do her honour, than that it otherwise would have been his own choice (especially as travelling would be at this time so inconvenient to him), she thought it advisable to save his lordship trouble on this occasion; and hoped he would take, as meant, her declining the favour.

'The Lawn, I tell him, will be most acceptable to retire to; and still the more, as it is so to his Lordship.

'But, if he pleases, the jointure may be made from my own estate; leaving to his lordship's goodness the alternative.

'That I had offered to present to the lady his lordship's bill; but on her declining to accept of it (having myself no present occasion for it), I returned it enclosed, with my thanks, etc.'

And is not this going a plaguy length? What a figure should I make in rakish annals, if at last I should be caught in my own gin?

The sex may say what they will, but a poor innocent fellow had need to take great care of himself, when he dances upon the edge of the matrimonial precipice. Many a faint-hearted man, when he began in jest, or only designed to ape gallantry, has been forced into earnest, by being over-prompt, and taken at his word, not knowing how to own that he meant less than the lady supposed he meant. I am the better enabled to judge that this must have been the case of many a sneaking varlet; because I, who know the female world as well as any man in it of my standing, am so frequently in doubt of myself, and know not what to make of the matter.

Then these little sly rogues, how they lie couchant, ready to spring upon us harmless fellows the moment we are in their reach!—When the ice is once broken for them, how swiftly can they make to port!—Meantime, the subject they can least *speak* to, they most *think* of. Nor can you talk of the ceremony before they have laid out in their minds how it is all to be—Little saucy-face designers! how first they draw themselves in, then us!

But be all these things as they will, Lord M. never in his life received so handsome a letter as this from his nephew

LOVELACE

[*Letter 207.1: Miss Clarissa Harlowe to Miss Howe*]

(*The lady, after having given to Miss Howe the particulars which are contained in Mr Lovelace's last letter, thus expresses herself:*)

A principal consolation arising from these favourable appearances is that I, who have now but one only friend, shall most probably, and if it be not my own fault, have as many new ones as there are persons in Mr Lovelace's family; and this whether Mr Lovelace treat me kindly, or not. And who knows, but that by degrees, those new friends, by their rank and merit, may have weight enough to get me restored to the favour of my relations? Till which can be effected, I shall not be tolerably easy. Happy I never expect to be. Mr Lovelace's mind and mind are vastly different; different in *essentials*.

But as matters are at present circumstanced, I pray you, my dear friend, to keep to yourself everything that, revealed, might bring discredit to him—Better anybody expose a husband than a wife, if I am to be so; and what is said by you will be thought to come from me.

It shall be my constant prayer, that all the felicities which this world can afford, may be yours. And that the Almighty will never suffer you nor yours to the remotest posterity, to want such a friend as my Anna Howe has been to

Her CLARISSA HARLOWE

Mr Lovelace, to show the wantonness of his invention, in his next gives his friend an account of a scheme he had framed to be revenged on Miss Howe, when she set out for the Isle of Wight; which he heard she was to do, accompanied by her mother and Mr Hickman, in order to visit a rich aunt there, who desired to see her, and her future consort, before she changed her name. But as he does not intend to carry it into execution, it is omitted [see p. 16].

Letter 209: MR LOVELACE TO JOHN BELFORD, ESQ.

IF, Belford, thou likest not my plot upon Miss Howe, I have three or four more as good in my own opinion; better, perhaps, they will be in thine: and so 'tis but getting loose from thy present engagement, and thou shalt pick and choose. But as for thy three brethren, they must do as I'd have them: and so, indeed, must thou—else why am I your general?—But I will refer this subject to its proper season. Thou knowest that I never absolutely conclude upon a project, till 'tis time for execution: and then lightning strikes not quicker than I.

And now to the subject next my heart.

Wilt thou believe me, when I tell thee that I have so many contrivances rising up and crowding upon me for preference, with regard to my Gloriana, that I hardly know which to choose?—I could tell thee of no less than six princely ones, any of which *must* do. But as the dear creature has not grudged giving me trouble, I think I ought not, in gratitude, to spare combustibles for her; but, on the contrary, to make her stare and stand aghast, by springing three or four mines at once.

Thou rememberest what Shakespeare, in his *Troilus and Cressida*, makes Hector, who however is not used to boast, say to Achilles in an interview between them; and which, applied to this watchful lady, and to the vexation she has given me, and to the certainty I now think I have of subduing her; will run thus—supposing the charmer before me; and I meditating her sweet person from head to foot:

> Henceforth, *oh watchful* fair one, guard thee well:
> For I'll not kill thee There! nor There! nor There!
> But, by the *zone that circles Venus' waist*,
> I'll kill thee Ev'ry-where; yea, o'er and o'er.
> Thou, wisest *Belford*, pardon me this brag:
> Her watchfulness draws folly from my lips;
> But I'll endeavour *deeds* to match the *words*,
> Or may I never——

Then, I imagine thee interposing to qualify my impatience, as Ajax did to Achilles:

> —Do not chafe thee, cousin:
> —And let these threats alone,
> Till *accident* or *purpose* bring thee to it.[1]

And now, Jack, what dost think?

That thou art a cursed fellow, if—

If! No if's—But I shall be very sick tomorrow. I shall, 'faith.

Sick!—Why sick?—What a devil shouldst thou be sick for?

For more good reasons than one, Belford.

I should be glad to hear but one—Sick, quotha! Of all thy roguish inventions, I should not have thought of this.

Perhaps thou thinkest my view to be, to draw the lady to my bedside: that's a trick of three or four thousand years old; and I should find it much more to my purpose, if I could get to hers. However, I'll condescend to make thee as wise as myself.

I am excessively disturbed about this smuggling scheme of Miss Howe. I have no doubt that my fair one will fly from me, if she can, were I to make an attempt, and miscarry. I once believed she loved me: but now I doubt whether she does or not: at least, that it is with such an *ardour*, as Miss Howe calls it, as will make her overlook a premeditated fault, should I be guilty of one.

And what will being sick do for thee?

Have patience. I don't intend to be so very bad as Dorcas shall represent me to be. But yet I know I shall retch confoundedly, and bring up some clotted blood. To be sure, I shall break a vessel: there's no doubt of that; and a bottle of Eaton's styptic shall be sent for; but no doctor. If she has *humanity*, she will be concerned. But if she has *love*, let it have been pushed ever so far back, it will, on this occasion, come forward, and show itself; not only in her eye, but in every line of her sweet face.

I will be very intrepid. I will not fear death, or anything else. I will be sure of being well in an hour or two, having formerly found great benefit by this balsamic medicine, on occasion of an inward bruise by a fall from my horse in hunting, of which, perhaps, this malady may be the remains. And this will show her, that though those about me may make the most of it, I don't; and so can have no design in it.

Well, methinks thou sayest, I begin to think tolerably of this device.

I knew thou wouldst, when I explained myself. Another time prepare to wonder; and banish doubt.

Now, Belford, if she be not much concerned at the broken vessel, which, in one so fiery in his temper as I have the reputation to be thought, may be very dangerous; a malady that I shall calmly attribute to the harasses and doubts that I have laboured under for some time past; which will be a further proof of my love, and will demand a grateful return—

What then, thou egregious contriver?

Why then I shall have the less remorse, if I am to use a little violence: for can she deserve compassion, who shows none?

And what if she show a great deal of concern?

Then shall I be in hope of building on a good foundation. Love hides a multitude of faults, and diminishes those it cannot hide. Love, when found out or acknowledged, authorizes freedom; and freedom begets freedom; and I shall then see how far I can go.

Well but, Lovelace, how the deuce wilt thou, with that full health and vigour of constitution, and with that bloom in thy face, make anybody believe thou art sick?

How!—Why take a few grains of ipecacuanha; enough to make me retch like a fury.

Good!—But how wilt thou manage to bring up blood, and not hurt thyself?

Foolish fellow! Are there not pigeons and chickens in every poulterer's shop?

Cry thy mercy.

But then I will be persuaded by Mrs Sinclair, that I have of late confined myself too much; and so will have a chair called, and be carried to the Park; where I will try to walk half the length of the Mall, or so; and in my return, amuse myself at White's or the Cocoa.

And what will this do?

Questioning again?—I am afraid thou'rt an infidel, Belford—Why then shall I not know if my beloved offers to go out in my absence?—And shall I not see whether she receives me with tenderness at my return? But this is not all: I have a foreboding that something affecting will happen while I am out. But of this more in its place.

And now, Belford, wilt thou, or wilt thou not, allow that it is a right thing to be sick?—Lord, Jack, so much delight do I take in my contrivances, that I shall be half sorry when the occasion for them is over; for never, never shall I again have such charming exercise for my invention.

Meantime these plaguy women are so impertinent, so full of reproaches, that I know not how to do anything but curse them. And then, truly, they are for helping me out with some of their trite and vulgar artifices—Sally particularly, who pretends to be a mighty contriver, has just now in an insolent manner told me, on my rejecting her proffered aids, that I had no mind to conquer; and that I was so *wicked* as to intend to marry, though I would not own it to her.

Because this little devil made her first sacrifice at my altar, she thinks she may take any liberty with me: and what makes her outrageous at times, is, that I have for a long time *studiously*, as she says, slighted her too readily offered favours: but is it not very impudent in her to think that I will be any man's successor? It is not come to that, neither. This, thou knowest, was always my rule—*Once any other man's*, and *I* know it, and *never more mine*. It is for such as thou, and thy brethren, to take up with *harlots*. I have been always aiming at the merit of a first discoverer.

The more devil I, perhaps thou'lt say, to endeavour to corrupt the uncorrupted. But I say, *not*; since, hence, I have but very few adulteries to answer for.

One affair, indeed, at Paris, with a married lady (I believe I never told thee of it) touched my conscience a little: yet brought on by the spirit of intrigue, more than by sheer wickedness. I'll give it thee in brief:

'A French marquis, somewhat in years, employed by his court in a public function at that of Madrid, had put his charming, young, new-married wife under the control and *wardship*, as I may say, of his insolent sister, an old prude.

'I saw the lady at the opera. I liked her at first sight, and better at second, when I knew the situation she was in. So, pretending to make my addresses to the prude, got admittance to both.

'The first thing I had to do, was to compliment my prude into shyness, by complaints of shyness: next to take advantage of the marquise's situation, between her husband's jealousy and his sister's arrogance, to inspire her with resentment; and, as I hoped, with a regard to my person. The French ladies have no dislike to intrigue.

'The sister began to suspect me: the lady had no mind to part with the company of the only man who had been permitted to visit there; and told me of her sister's suspicions—I put her upon concealing the prude, as if unknown to me, in a closet in one of her own apartments, locking her in, and putting the key in her own pocket: and she was to question me on the sincerity of my professions to her sister, in her sister's hearing.

'She complied. My mistress was locked up. The lady and I took our seats. I owned fervent love, and made high professions: for the marquise put it home to me. The prude was delighted with what she heard.

'And how dost think it ended?—I took my advantage of the lady herself, who durst not for her life cry out: drew her after me to the next apartment, on pretence of going to seek her sister, who all the time was locked up in the closet.

'No woman ever gave me a private meeting for nothing; my dearest Miss Harlowe excepted.

'My ingenuity obtained my pardon: the lady being unable to forbear laughing through the whole affair, to find both so uncommonly tricked; her gaoleress her prisoner, safe locked up, and as much pleased as either of us.

'The English, Jack, do not often outwit the French.

'We had contrivances afterwards equally ingenious, in which the lady, the ice once broken (*once subdued, always subdued*), co-operated—But a more tender tell-tale revealed the secret—revealed it, before the marquis could come to cover the disgrace. The sister was inveterate; the husband irreconcilable; in every respect unfit for a husband, even for a *French* one—made, perhaps, more delicate to these particulars by the customs of a people among whom he was then resident, so contrary to those of his own countrymen. She was obliged to throw herself into my protection—nor thought herself unhappy in it, till childbed pangs seized her: then penitence, and death, overtook her in the same hour!'

Excuse a tear, Belford!—She deserved a better fate! What has such a vile inexorable husband to answer for!—The sister was punished effectually! That pleases me on reflection! The sister was punished effectually!—But perhaps I have told thee this story before.

Letter 210: MR LOVELACE TO JOHN BELFORD, ESQ.

Friday evening

JUST returned from an airing with my charmer; complied with after great importunity. She was attended by the two nymphs. They both topped their parts; kept their eyes within bounds; made moral reflections now and then. Oh Jack! what devils are women, when all tests are got over, and we have completely ruined them!

The coach carried us to Hampstead, to Highgate, to Muswell Hill; back to Hampstead to the Upper Flask[1]: there, in compliment to the nymphs, my beloved consented to alight, and take a little refection. Then home early by Kentish Town.

Delightfully easy she: and so respectful and obliging I, all the way, and as we walked out upon the Heath, to view the variegated prospects which that agreeable elevation affords, that she promised to take now and then a little excursion with me. I think, Miss Howe—I *think*, said I to myself, every now and then as we walked, that thy wicked devices are superseded.

We have both been writing ever since we came home. I am to be favoured with her company for an hour before she retires to rest.

All that obsequious love can suggest, in order to engage her tenderest sentiments for me against tomorrow's sickness, will I aim at when we meet. But at parting will complain of a disorder in my stomach.

WE have met. All was love and unexceptionable respect on my part. Ease and complaisance on hers. She was concerned for my disorder. So sudden!—Just as we parted. But it was nothing. I should be quite well by morning.

Faith, Jack, I think I am sick already!—Is it possible for such a giddy fellow as me to persuade myself to be ill? I am a better mimic at this rate than I wish to be. But every nerve and fibre of me is always ready to contribute its aid, whether by health or by ailment, to carry a resolved-on roguery into execution.

Dorcas has transcribed for me the whole letter of Miss Howe, dated Sunday May 14,[a] of which before I had only extracts. But she found no other letter added to that parcel. But this, and that which I copied myself in character last Sunday while she was at church, relating to the smuggling scheme,[b] are enough for me.

DORCAS tells me that her lady has been removing her papers from the mahogany chest into a wainscot box, which held her linen, and which she put into her dark closet. We have no key of that at present. No doubt but all her letters, previous to those I have come at, are in that box. Dorcas is uneasy upon it: yet hopes that her lady does not suspect her; for she is sure that she laid in everything as she found it.

Letter 211: MR LOVELACE TO JOHN BELFORD, ESQ.

Cocoa Tree,[1] Saturday, May 27

THIS ipecacuanha is a most disagreeable medicine! That these cursed physical folks can find out nothing to do us good, but what would poison the devil! In the other world, were they only to take physic, it would be punishment enough of itself for a mis-spent life. A doctor at one elbow, and an apothecary at the other, and the poor soul labouring under their prescribed operations, he need no worse tormentors.

But now this was to take down my countenance. It has done it: for, with violent retchings, having taken enough to make me sick, and not enough water to carry it off, I presently looked as if I had kept my bed a fortnight. *Ill-jesting*, as I thought in the midst of the exercise, *with edge-tools*, and worse with *physical ones*.

Two hours it held me. I had forbid Dorcas to let my beloved know anything of the matter; out of tenderness to her; being willing, when she knew my prohibition, to let her see that I *expected* her to be concerned for me—What a worthless fellow must *he* be, whose own heart gives him up as deserving of no one's regard!

Well, but Dorcas nevertheless is a *woman*, and she can *whisper* to her lady the secret she is enjoined to keep!

Come hither, you toad (sick as a devil at the instant); let me see what a mixture of grief and surprise may be beat up together in thy pudden-face.

That won't do. That dropped jaw, and mouth distended into the long oval, is more upon the horrible, than the grievous.

Nor that pinking and winking with thy *odious eyes*, as my charmer once called them.

A little better *that*; yet not quite right: but keep your mouth closer. You have a muscle or two which you have no command of, between your cheek-bone and your

a   Letter 184.
b   Letter 196.

lips, that should carry one corner of your mouth up towards your crow's-foot, and that down to meet it.

There! Begone! Be in a plaguy hurry running up stairs and down, to fetch from the dining-room what you carry up on purpose to fetch, till motion extraordinary put you out of breath, and give you the sigh natural.

What's the matter, Dorcas?

Nothing, madam.

My beloved wonders she has not seen me this morning, no doubt; but is too shy to say she wonders. Repeated What's the matter's, however, as Dorcas runs up and down stairs by her door, bring on. Oh! madam! my master!—my master!

What! How! When!—and all the monosyllables of surprise.

(Within parenthesis let me tell thee that I have often thought, that the little words in the republic of letters, like the little folks in a nation, are the most significant. The *trisyllables*, and the *rumblers* of syllables more than *three*, are but the good for little *magnates*.)

I must not tell you, madam—My master ordered me not to tell you—But he is in a worse way than he thinks for!—But he would not have *you* frighted.

High concern took possession of every sweet feature. She pitied me!—By my soul, she pitied me!

Where is he?

Too much in a hurry for good manners (another parenthesis, Jack! Good manners are so little natural, that we ought to be *composed* to observe them: politeness will not live in a storm), I cannot stay to answer questions, cries the wench—though desirous to answer (a third parenthesis—like the people crying proclamations, running away from the customers they want to sell to). This hurry puts the lady in a hurry to ask (a fourth, by way of embellishing the third! as the other does the people in a hurry to buy). And I have in my eye now a whole street raised, and running after a proclamation or express crier, as if the first was a thief, the other his pursuers.

At last: Oh Lord! let Mrs Lovelace know!—There is danger, to be sure! whispered from one nymph to another, in her hearing; but at the door, and so loud, that my listening fair one might hear.

Out she darts—As how! as how, Dorcas!

Oh madam—a vomiting of blood! a vessel broke, to be sure!

Down she hastens; finds everyone as busy over my blood in the entry, as if it were that of the Neapolitan saint.

In steps my charmer! with a face of sweet concern.

How do you, Mr Lovelace!

Oh my best love!—Very well!—Very well!—Nothing at all! Nothing of consequence!—I shall be well in an instant!—straining again; for I was indeed plaguy sick, though no more blood came.

In short, Belford, I have gained my end. I see the dear soul loves me. I see she forgives me all that's past. I see I have credit for a new score.

Miss Howe, I defy thee, my dear—Mrs Townsend!—who the devil are you?—Troop away with your contrabands. No smuggling! nor smuggler, but myself! Nor will the choicest of my fair one's favours be long prohibited goods to me!

EVERYONE now is sure that she loves me. Tears were in her eyes more than once for me. She suffered me to take her hand, and kiss it as often as I pleased. On Mrs Sinclair's mentioning that I too much confined myself, she pressed me to take an airing, but obligingly desired me to be careful of myself. Wished I would advise with a physician. *God made physicians*, she said.

I did not think that, Jack. God indeed made us all. But I fancy she meant *physic* instead of *physicians*; and then the phrase might mean what the vulgar phrase means—*God sends meat, the devil cooks*.

I was well already, on taking the styptic from *her* dear hands.

On her requiring me to take the air, I asked if I might have the honour of her company in a coach; and this, that I might observe if she had an intention of going out in my absence.

If she thought a chair were not a more proper vehicle for my case, she would with all her heart!

There's a precious!

I kissed her hand again! She was all goodness!—Would to Heaven I better deserved it, I said!—But all were golden days before us!—Her presence and generous concern had done everything. I was well! Nothing ailed me. But since my beloved will have it so, I'll take a little airing!—Let a chair be called!—Oh my charmer!—were I to have owed this indisposition to my late harasses, and to the uneasiness I have had for disobliging you; all is infinitely compensated by your goodness!—All the art of healing is in your smiles!—Your late displeasure was the only malady!

While Mrs Sinclair, and Dorcas, and Polly, and even poor silly Mabel (for Sally went out, as my angel came in), with uplifted hands and eyes, stood thanking Heaven that I was better, in audible whispers: See the power of love, cried one!—What a charming husband, another!—Happy couple, all!

Oh how the dear creature's cheek mantled!—How her eyes sparkled!—How sweetly acceptable is praise to conscious merit, while it but reproaches when applied to the undeserving!—What a new, what a gay creation it makes at once in a diffident or dispirited heart!—

And now, Belford, was it not worth while to be sick? And yet I must tell thee, that too many pleasanter expedients offer themselves, to make trial any more of this confounded ipecacuanha.

Letter 212: MISS CLARISSA HARLOWE TO MISS HOWE

Saturday, May 27

MR Lovelace, my dear, has been very ill. Suddenly taken. With a vomiting of blood in great quantities. Some vessel broken. He complained of a disorder in his stomach over-night. I was the more affected with it, as I am afraid it was occasioned by the violent contentions between us—But was I in fault?

How lately did I think I hated him!—But hatred and anger, I see, are but temporary passions with me. One cannot, my dear, hate people in danger of death, or who are in distress or affliction. My heart, I find, is not proof against kindness and acknowledgement of errors committed.

He took great care to have his illness concealed from me as long as it could. So tender in the violence of his disorder!—So desirous to make the best of it!—I wish he had not been ill in my sight. I was too much affected—Everybody alarming me with his danger—The poor man, from such high health so *suddenly* taken!—And so unprepared!—

He is gone out in a chair. I advised him to do so. I fear that my advice was wrong; since quiet in such a disorder must needs be best. We are apt to be so ready, in cases of emergency, to give our advice without judgement, or waiting for it!—I proposed a physician indeed; but he would not hear of one. I have great honour for the faculty; and the greater, as I have always observed that those who treat the professors of the art of healing contemptuously, too generally treat higher institutions in the same manner.

I am really very uneasy. For I have, I doubt, exposed myself to him, and to the women below. *They* indeed will excuse me, as they think us married. But if he be not generous, I shall have cause to regret this surprise; which has taught me more than I knew of myself; as I had reason to think myself unaccountably treated by him.

Nevertheless let me tell you (what I hope I may justly tell you), that if again he give me cause to resume distance and reserve, I hope my reason will gather strength enough from his imperfections (for Mr Lovelace, my dear, is not a wise man in all his ways) to enable me to keep my passions under—What can we do more than govern ourselves by the temporary lights lent us?

You will not wonder that I am grave on this detection—*Detection*, must I call it? What can I call it?—I have not had heart's ease enough to inspect that heart as I ought.

Dissatisfied with myself, I am afraid to look back upon what I have written. And yet know not how to have done writing. I never was in such an odd frame of mind—I know not how to describe it—Was *you* ever *so?*—Afraid of the censure of her I love—Yet not conscious that I deserve it.

Of this, however, I am convinced, that I should *indeed* deserve censure if I kept any secret of my heart from you.

But I will not add another word, after I have assured you that I will look still more narrowly into myself: and that I am

> Your equally sincere and affectionate
> CLARISSA HARLOWE

Letter 213: MR LOVELACE TO JOHN BELFORD, ESQ.

Sat. evening

I HAD a charming airing. No return of my malady. My heart perfectly easy, how could my stomach be otherwise?

But when I came home, I found that my sweet soul had been alarmed by a new incident. The inquiry after us both, in a very suspicious manner, and that by description of our persons, and not by names, by a servant in a blue livery turned up and trimmed with yellow.

Dorcas was called to him, as the upper servant, and she refusing to answer any of his questions, unless he told his business and from whom he came, the fellow, as short as she, said that if she would not answer *him*, perhaps she might answer somebody *else*; and went away out of humour.

Dorcas hurried up to her lady, and alarmed her not only with the fact, but with her own conjectures; adding, that he was an ill-looking fellow, and she was sure could come for no good.

The livery and the features of the servant were particularly inquired after, and as particularly described—*Lord bless her! no end of her alarms, she thought!* And then was she aforehand with every evil that could happen.

She wished Mr Lovelace would come in.

Mr Lovelace came in soon after; all lively, grateful, full of hopes, of duty, of love, to thank his charmer, and to congratulate with her upon the cure she had performed. And then she told the story, with all its circumstances; and Dorcas, to point her lady's fears, told us that the servant was a sun-burnt fellow, and looked as if he had been at sea.

He was then, no doubt, Captain Singleton's servant, and the next news she should hear was that the house was surrounded by a whole ship's crew; the vessel lying no farther off, as she understood, than Rotherhithe.

Impossible, I said. Such an attempt would not be ushered in by such a manner of inquiry. And why may it not rather be a servant of your cousin Morden's, with notice of his arrival, and of his design to attend you?

This surmise delighted her. Her apprehensions went off, and she was at leisure to congratulate me upon my sudden recovery; which she did in the most obliging manner.

But we had not sat long together, when Dorcas again came fluttering up to tell us that the footman, the *very* footman, was again at the door, and inquired, whether Mr Lovelace and his lady, by name, had not lodgings in this house? He asked, he told Dorcas, for no harm: but this was a demonstration with my apprehensive fair one that harm was intended. And as the fellow had not been answered by Dorcas, I proposed to go down to the street parlour, and hear what he had to say.

I see your causeless terror, my dearest life, said I, and your impatience—Will you be pleased to walk down—And without being observed, as he shall come no farther than the parlour door, you may hear all that passes?

She consented. We went down. Dorcas bid the man come forward—Well, friend, what is your business with Mr or Mrs Lovelace?

Bowing, scraping, I am sure you are the gentleman, sir. Why, sir, my business is only to know if your honour be here, and to be spoke with; or if you shall be here for any time?

Who came you from?

From a gentleman who ordered me to say, if I was *made* to tell, but not else, it was from a friend of Mr John Harlowe's, Mrs Lovelace's eldest uncle.

The dear creature was ready to sink upon this. It was but of late that she had provided herself with salts. She pulled them out.

Do you know anything of Colonel Morden, friend? said I.

No; I never heard of his name.

Of Captain Singleton?

No, sir. But the gentleman, my master, is a captain too.

What is his name?

I don't know if I should tell.

There can be no harm in telling the gentleman's name, if you come upon a good account.

That I do; for my master told me so; and there is not an honester gentleman on the face of *God's yearth*—His name is Captain Tomlinson, sir.

I don't know such a one.

I believe not, sir. He was pleased to say he don't know your honour, sir; but I heard him say, as how he should not be an unwelcome visitor to you, for all that.

Do you know such a man as Captain Tomlinson, my dearest life (*aside*), your uncle's friend?

No; but my uncle may have acquaintance, no doubt, that I don't know—But I hope (*trembling*), this is not a trick.

Well, friend, if your master has anything to say to Mr Lovelace, you may tell him that Mr Lovelace is here; and will give him a meeting whenever he pleases.

The dear creature looked as if afraid that my engagement was too prompt for my own safety; and away went the fellow—*I* wondering, that *she* might not wonder, that this Captain Tomlinson, whoever he was, came not himself, or sent not a letter the second time, when he had reason to suppose that I might be here.

Meantime, for fear that this should be a contrivance of James Harlowe's who, I said, loved plotting, though he had not a head turned for it, I gave some precautionary directions to the servants, and the women, whom, for the greater parade, I assembled before us: and my beloved was resolved not to stir abroad till she saw the issue of this odd affair.

And here must I close, though in so great a puzzle.

Only let me add, that poor Belton wants thee; for I dare not stir for my life.

Mowbray and Tourville skulk about like vagabonds, without heads, without hands, without souls; having neither thee nor me to conduct them. They tell me, they shall rust beyond the power of oil or action to brighten them up, or give them motion.

How goes it with thy uncle?

Letter 214: MR LOVELACE TO JOHN BELFORD, ESQ.

Sunday, May 28

THIS story of Captain Tomlinson employed us not only for the time we were together last night, but all the while we sat at breakfast this morning. She would still have it that it was the prelude to some mischief from Singleton. I insisted that it might much more probably be a method taken by Colonel Morden to alarm her, previous to a personal visit. Travelled gentlemen affected to surprise in this manner. And why, dearest creature, said I, must everything that happens, which we cannot immediately account for, be what we least wish?

She had had so many disagreeable things befall her of late, that her fears were too often stronger than her hopes.

And this, madam, makes me apprehensive that you will get into so low-spirited a way, that you will not be able to enjoy the happiness that seems to await us.

Her duty and her gratitude, she gravely said, to the Dispenser of all good, would secure her she hoped against unthankfulness. And a thankful spirit was the same as a joyful one.

So, Belford, for all her future joys she depends entirely upon the Invisible Good. She is certainly right; since those who fix least upon second causes are the least likely to be disappointed—And is not this gravity for her gravity.

She had hardly done speaking, when Dorcas came running up in a hurry—She set even *my* heart into a palpitation—Thump, thump, thump, like a precipitated pendulum in a clock-case—Flutter, flutter, flutter my charmer's, as by her sweet bosom rising to her chin I saw.

This lower class of people, my beloved herself observed, were for ever aiming at the stupid wonderful, and for making even common incidents matter of surprise.

Why the devil, said I to the wench, this alarming hurry?—and with your spread fingers, and your Oh madams, and Oh sirs!—and be cursed to you: would there have been a second of time difference, had you come up slowly?

Captain Tomlinson, sir!

Captain Devilson, what care I!—Do you see how you have disordered your lady?

Good Mr Lovelace, said my charmer, trembling (see, Jack, when she has an end to serve, I am *good* Mr Lovelace), if—if my brother—if Captain Singleton should appear—Pray now—I beseech you—Let me beg of you—to govern your temper—My brother is my brother—Captain Singleton is but an *agent*.

My dearest life, folding my arms about her (when she asks favours, thought I, the devil's in it if she will not allow of such innocent freedoms as this from *good* Mr Lovelace too), you shall be witness of all that passes between us. Dorcas, desire the gentleman to walk up.

Let me retire to my chamber first! Let me not be known to be in the house!

Charming dear!—Thou seest, Belford, she is afraid of leaving me!—Oh the little witchcrafts! Were it not for surprise now and then, how would an honest man know where to have them?

She withdrew to listen—and though this incident has not turned out to answer all I wished from it, yet is it necessary, if I would acquaint thee with my whole circulation, to be very particular in what passed between Captain Tomlinson and me.

Enter Captain Tomlinson in a riding dress, whip in hand.

Your servant, sir—Mr Lovelace, I presume?

My name is Lovelace, sir.

Excuse the day, sir—Be pleased to excuse my garb. I am obliged to go out of town directly, that I may return at night.

The day is a good day. Your garb needs no apology.

When I sent my servant, I did not know that I should *find time to do myself this honour*. All that I thought I could do to oblige my friend this journey, was *only* to assure myself of your abode; and whether there was a probability of being admitted to your speech, or to your lady's.

Sir, you know best your own motives. What your time will permit you to do, you also best know. And here I am, attending your pleasure.

My charmer owned afterwards her concern on my being so short. Whatever I shall mingle of her emotions, thou wilt easily guess I had afterwards.

Sir, I hope no offence. I intend none.

None—none at all, sir.

Sir, I have no interest in the affair I come about. I may appear officious; and if I thought I should, I would decline any concern in it, after I have just hinted what it is.

And what, pray, sir, is it?

May I ask you, sir, without offence, whether you wish to be reconciled, and to co-operate upon honourable terms with *one* gentleman of the name of Harlowe; preparative, as it may be hoped, to a general reconciliation?

Oh how my heart fluttered, cried my charmer!

I can't tell, sir (*and then it fluttered still more, no doubt*): the whole family have used me extremely ill. They have taken greater liberties with my character than are justifiable, and with my family *too*; which I can less forgive.

Sir, sir, I have done. I beg pardon for this intrusion.

My beloved then was ready to sink, and thought very hardly of me.

But pray, sir, to the immediate purpose of your present commission; since a commission it seems to be?

It *is* a commission, sir; and such a one, as I thought would be agreeable to all parties, or I should not have given myself concern about it.

Perhaps it *may*, sir, when known. But let me ask you one previous question? Do you know Colonel Morden, sir?

No, sir. If you mean *personally*, I do not. But I have heard my good friend Mr John Harlowe talk of him with great respect; and as a co-trustee with him in a certain trust.

I thought it probable, sir, said I, that the colonel might be arrived; that you might be a gentleman of his acquaintance; and that something of an agreeable surprise might be intended.

Had Colonel Morden been in England, Mr John Harlowe would have known it; and then I should not have been a stranger to it.

Well but, sir, have you then any commission to me from Mr John Harlowe?

Sir, I will tell you, as briefly as I can, the whole of what I have to say; but you'll excuse *me* also a previous question, for which curiosity is not my motive; but it is necessary to be answered before I can proceed; as you will judge when you hear it.

What, pray, sir, is your question?

Briefly, Whether you are actually, and *bona fide*, married to Miss Clarissa Harlowe?

I started, and, in a haughty tone, Is this, sir, a question that *must* be answered before you can proceed in the business you have undertaken?

I mean no offence, Mr Lovelace. Mr Harlowe sought to me to undertake this office. I have daughters and nieces of my own. I thought it a good office, or I, who have many considerable affairs upon my hands, had not accepted of it. I know the world; and will take the liberty to say, that if that young lady—

Captain Tomlinson, I think you are called?

My name is Tomlinson.

Why then, Captain Tomlinson, no *liberty*, as you call it, will be taken well, that is not extremely delicate, when that lady is mentioned.

When you had heard me out, Mr Lovelace, and had found I had so behaved as to make the caution necessary, it would have been just to have given it—Allow me

CLARISSA [L214

to say, I know what is due to the character of a woman of virtue, as well as any man alive.

Why, sir! Why, Captain Tomlinson, you seem warm. If you intend anything by this (*Oh how I trembled!* said the lady, *when she took notice of this part of our conversation afterwards*), I will only say that this is a privileged place. It is at present my home, and an asylum for any gentleman who thinks it worth his while to inquire after me, be the manner or end of his inquiry what it will.

I know not, sir, that I have given occasion for this. I make no scruple to attend you *elsewhere*, if I am troublesome here. I was told, I had a warm young gentleman to deal with: but as I knew my intention, and that my commission was an amicable one, I was the less concerned about that. I am twice your age, Mr Lovelace, I dare say: but I do assure you, that if either my message, or my manner, give you offence, I can suspend the one or the other for a day, or for ever, as you like. And so, sir, any time before eight tomorrow morning, you will let me know your further commands—And was going to tell me where he might be found.

Captain Tomlinson, said I, you answer well. I love a man of spirit. Have you not been in the army?

I have, sir; but have *turned my sword into a ploughshare*, as the Scripture has it (*There was a clever fellow, Jack!—He was a good man with somebody, I warrant!*)— And all my delight, added he, for some years past, has been in cultivating my paternal estate. I love a brave man, Mr Lovelace, as well as ever I did in my life. But, let me tell you, sir, that when you come to my time of life, you will be of opinion that there is not so much true bravery in youthful choler as you may now think there is.

A clever fellow again, Belford—Ear and heart, both at once, he took in my charmer—'*Tis well, she says, there are some men who have wisdom in their anger*.

Well, captain, that is reproof for reproof. So we are upon a foot. And now give me the pleasure of hearing your commission.

Sir, you must first allow me to repeat my question: Are you really, and *bona fide*, married to Miss Clarissa Harlowe? Or are you not yet married?

Bluntly put, captain. But if I answer that I *am*, what then?

Why then, sir, I shall say that you are a man of honour.

That I hope I am, whether you *say* it or not, Captain Tomlinson.

Sir, I will be very frank in all I have to say on this subject—Mr John Harlowe has lately found out that you and his niece are both in the same lodgings; that you have been long so; and that the lady was at the play with you yesterday was se'ennight; and he hopes, that you are actually married. He has indeed heard that you are; but, as he knows your enterprising temper, and that you have declared that you disdain a relation to their family, he is willing by me to have your marriage confirmed from your own mouth, before he takes the steps he is inclined to take in his niece's favour. You will allow me to say, Mr Lovelace, that he will not be satisfied with an answer that admits of the least doubt.

Let me tell you, Captain Tomlinson, that it is a damned degree of vileness for any man to suppose—

Sir—Mr Lovelace—don't put yourself into a passion. The lady's relations are jealous of the honour of their family. They have prejudices to overcome as well as you—Advantage may have been taken—and the lady, at the *time*, not to blame.

This lady, sir, could give no such advantages: and if she *had*, what must the *man* be, Captain Tomlinson, who could have taken them?—Do you know the lady, sir?

I never had the honour to see her but once; and that was at church; and should not know her again.

Not know her again, sir!—I thought that there was not a man living who had once seen her, and would not know her among a thousand.

I remember, sir, that I thought I never saw a finer woman in my life. But, Mr Lovelace, I believe you will allow that it is better that her relations should have wronged *you*, than you the *lady*. I hope, sir, you will permit me to repeat my question.

Enter Dorcas, in a hurry.

A *gentleman*, this minute, sir, desires to speak with your honour—*My lady, sir!* (*aside*)

Could the dear creature put *Dorcas* upon telling this fib, yet want to save *me* one?—

Desire the gentleman to walk into one of the parlours. I will wait on him presently.

(Exit Dorcas.

The dear creature, I doubted not, wanted to instruct me how to answer the captain's home-put. I knew how I intended to answer it—plumb, thou may'st be sure—But Dorcas's message staggered me. And yet I was upon one of my master-strokes—which was, to take advantage of the captain's inquiries, and to make her own her marriage before him, as she had done to the people below; and if she had been brought to that, to induce her, for her uncle's satisfaction, to write him a letter of gratitude; which of course must have been signed *Clarissa Lovelace*. I was loath, therefore, thou may'st believe, to attend her sudden commands: and yet, afraid of pushing matters beyond recovery with her, I thought proper to lead him from the question, to account for himself, for Mr Harlowe's coming at the knowledge of where we are, and for other particulars which I knew would engage her attention; and which might possibly convince her of the necessity there was for her to acquiesce in the affirmative I was disposed to give. And this for her own sake; for what, as I asked her afterwards, is it to me, whether I am ever reconciled to a family I must for ever despise?

You think, captain, that I have answered doubtfully to the question you have put. You *may* think so. And you must know that I have a good deal of pride: and only that you are a gentleman, and seem in this affair to be governed by generous principles, or I should ill brook being interrogated as to my honour to a lady so dear to me—But before I answer more directly to the point, pray satisfy me in a question or two that I shall put to *you*.

With all my heart, sir. Ask me what questions you please, I will answer them with sincerity and candour.

You say that Mr Harlowe has found out that we were at a play together: and that we are both in the same lodgings—How, pray, came he at his knowledge?—For, let me tell you, that I have, for certain considerations not respecting myself, condescended that our abode should be kept secret. And this has been so strictly observed, that even Miss Howe, though she and my beloved correspond, knows not directly whither to send to us.

Why, sir, the person who saw you at the play was a tenant of Mr John Harlowe. He watched all your motions. When the play was done, he followed your coach to your lodgings. And early the next day, Sunday, he took horse, and acquainted his landlord with what he had observed.

How oddly things come about, Captain Tomlinson!—But does any other of the Harlowes know where we are?

It is an absolute secret to every other person of the family; and so it is intended to be kept: as also that Mr John Harlowe is willing to enter into treaty with you, by me, if his niece be actually married; for perhaps he is aware that he shall have difficulty enough with some people to bring about the desirable reconciliation, although he could give them this assurance.

I doubt it not, captain—To James Harlowe is all the family folly owing—Fine fools! (*heroically stalking about*) to be governed by one to whom malice, and not genius, gives the busy liveliness that distinguishes him from a natural!—But how long, pray, sir, has Mr John Harlowe been in this pacific disposition?

I will tell you, Mr Lovelace, and the occasion; and be very explicit upon it, and upon all that concerns you to know of me, and of the commission I have undertaken; and this the rather, as when you have heard me out, you will be satisfied that I am not an officious man in this my present address to you.

I am all attention, Captain Tomlinson.

And so I doubt not was my beloved.

'You must know, sir, said the captain, that I have not been many months in Mr John Harlowe's neighbourhood. I removed from Northamptonshire, partly for the sake of better managing one of two executorships, which I could not avoid engaging in (the affairs of which frequently call me to town, and are part of my present business), and partly for the sake of occupying a neglected farm which has lately fallen into my hands. But though an acquaintance of no longer standing, and that commencing on the bowling-green (uncle John is a great bowler, Belford), upon my decision of a point to everyone's satisfaction, which was appealed to me by all the gentlemen, and which might have been attended with bad consequences, no two brothers have a more cordial esteem for each other. You know, Mr Lovelace, that there is a *consent*, as I may call it, in some minds, which will unite them stronger in a few hours, than years will do with others, whom yet we see not with disgust.'

Very true, captain.

'It was on the foot of this avowed friendship on both sides, that on Monday the 15th, as I very well remember, Mr Harlowe invited himself home with me. And when there, he acquainted me with the whole of the unhappy affair that had made them all so uneasy. Till then I knew it only by report; for, intimate as we were, I forbore to speak of what was so near his heart, till he began first. And then he told me that he had had an application made to him two or three days before by a gentleman whom he named,[a] to induce him not only to be reconciled to his niece himself, but to forward for her a general reconciliation.

'A like application, he told me, had been made to his sister Harlowe, by a good woman whom everybody respected; who had intimated that his niece, if encour-

a   See Miss Howe's letters, 177 and 183.

aged, would again put herself into the protection of her friends, and leave you: but if not, that she must unavoidably be yours.'

I hope, Mr Lovelace, I make no mischief—You look concerned—you sigh, sir. Proceed, Captain Tomlinson. Pray proceed. *And I sighed still more profoundly.*

'They all thought it extremely particular that a lady should decline marriage with a man she had so lately gone away with.'

Pray, captain—pray, Mr Tomlinson—no more of this subject. My beloved is an angel. In every thing unblamable. Whatever faults there have been, have been theirs and mine. What you would further say, is, that the *unforgiving* family rejected her application. They did. She and I had had a misunderstanding. *The falling out of lovers*'—you know, captain—We have been happier ever since.

'Well, sir; Mr John Harlowe could not but better consider the matter afterwards. And he desired my advice how to act in it. He told me that no father ever loved a daughter as he loved this niece of his; whom, indeed, he used to call his *daughter-niece*. He said she had really been unkindly treated by her brother and sister: and as your alliance, sir, was far from being a discredit to their family, he would do his endeavour to reconcile all parties, if he could be sure that ye were actually man and wife.'

And what, pray, captain, was your advice?

'I gave it as my opinion, that if his niece were unworthily treated, and in distress, as he apprehended from the application to him, he would soon hear of her again. But that it was likely that this application was made without expecting it would succeed; and as a salvo only, to herself, for marrying without their consent. And the rather, as he had told me, that it came from a young lady her friend, and not in a direct way from herself; which young lady was no favourite of the family, and therefore would hardly have been employed had success been expected.'

Very well, Captain Tomlinson—Pray proceed.

'Here the matter rested till last Sunday evening, when Mr John Harlowe came to me with the man who had seen you and your lady (as I hope she is) at the play; and who had assured him that you both lodged in the same house—And then the application having been so lately made, which implied that you were not then married, he was so uneasy for his niece's honour, that I advised him to dispatch to town some one in whom he could confide, to make proper inquiries.'

Very well, captain.—And was such a person employed on such an errand by her uncle?

'A trusty and discreet person was accordingly sent; and last Tuesday, I think it was (for he returned to us on the Wednesday), he made the inquiries among the neighbours first (*The very inquiry, Jack, that gave us all so much uneasiness*[a]); but finding that none of them could give any satisfactory account, the lady's woman was come at, who declared that you were actually married. But the inquirist keeping himself on the reserve as to his employers, the girl refused to tell the day, or to give him other particulars.'

You give a very clear account of everything, Captain Tomlinson. Pray go on.

'The gentleman returned; and on his report, Mr Harlowe having still doubts, and being willing to proceed on some grounds in so important a point, besought me, as my affairs called me frequently to town, to undertake this matter. You, Mr

a See p. 663.

Tomlinson, he was pleased to say, have children of your own: you know the world: you know what I drive at: you will proceed, I know, with understanding and spirit: and whatever you are satisfied with shall satisfy me.'

Enter Dorcas again, in a hurry.

Sir, the gentleman is impatient.

I will attend him presently.

The captain then accounted for his not calling in person, when he had reason to think us here.

He said he had business of consequence a few miles out of town, whither he thought he must have gone yesterday; and having been obliged to put off his little journey till this day, and understanding that we were within, not knowing whether he should have such another opportunity, he was willing to try his good fortune before he set out; and this made him come booted and spurred, as I saw him.

He dropped a hint in commendation of the people of the house; but it was in such a way, as to give no room for suspicion that he thought it necessary to make any inquiries after the character of persons who make so genteel an appearance as he observed they do.

And here let me remark, to the same purpose, that my beloved might collect another circumstance in their favour, had she doubted them, from the silence of her uncle's inquirist on Tuesday among the neighbours.

And now, sir, said he, that I believe I have satisfied you in everything relating to my commission, I hope you will permit me to repeat my question—which is—

Enter Dorcas again, out of breath.

Sir, the gentleman will step up to *you*—*My lady is impatient. She wonders at your honour's delay* (*aside*).

Excuse me, captain, for one moment.

I have stayed my full time, Mr Lovelace—What may result from my question and your answer, whatever it shall be, may take us up time—and you are engaged—Will you permit me to attend you in the morning before I set out on my return?

You will then breakfast with me, captain?

It must be early if I do. I must reach my own house tomorrow night, or I shall make the best of wives unhappy. And I have two or three places to call at in my way.

It shall be by seven o'clock, if you please, captain. We are early folks. And this I will tell you, that if ever I am reconciled to a family so implacable as I have always found the Harlowes to be, it must be by the mediation of so cool and so moderate a gentleman as yourself.

And so, with the highest civilities on both sides, we parted. But for the private satisfaction of so good a man, I left him out of doubt that we were man and wife, though I did not directly aver it.

Letter 215: MR LOVELACE TO JOHN BELFORD, ESQ.

Sunday night

THIS Captain Tomlinson is one of the happiest, as well as one of the best men in the world. What would I give to stand as high in my beloved's opinion as he does! But yet, I am as good a man as he, were I to tell my own story, and have equal credit given to it. But the devil should have had him before I had seen him on the account he came upon, had I thought I should not have answered my principal end in it—I hinted to thee in my last what that was.

But to the particulars of the conference between my fair one, and me, on her hasty messages; which I was loath to come to, because she has had a half triumph over me in it.

After I had attended the captain down to the very passage, I returned to the dining-room, and put on a joyful air, on my beloved's entrance into it—Oh my dearest creature, let me congratulate you on a prospect so agreeable to your wishes!—And I snatched her hand, and smothered it with my kisses.

I was going on; when, interrupting me—You see, Mr Lovelace, said she, how you have embarrassed yourself by your own obliquities!—You see that you have not been able to return a direct answer to a plain and honest question, though upon it depends all the happiness you congratulate me upon the prospect of.

You know, my best love, what my prudent, and I will say, my *kind* motives were, for giving out that we were married. You see that I have taken no advantage of it; and that no inconvenience has followed it—You see that your uncle wants only to be assured from ourselves that it is so—

Not another word to this purpose, Mr Lovelace. I will not only risk, but I will forfeit, the reconciliation so near my heart, rather than I will go on to countenance a story so untrue!

My dearest soul—would you have me appear—

I would have you appear, sir, as *you are*! I am resolved that I will appear to my uncle's friend, and to my uncle, as *I am*.

For one week, my dearest life, cannot you for one week, only till the settlements—

Not for one hour, with my own consent—You don't know, sir, how much I have been afflicted that I have appeared to the people below what I am not. But my uncle, sir, shall never have it to upbraid me, nor will I to upbraid myself, that I have wilfully passed myself upon him in false lights.

What, my dear, would you have me to say to the captain tomorrow morning?— I have given him room to think—

Then put him right, Mr Lovelace. Tell the truth. Tell him what you please of your relations' favour to me: tell him what you will about the settlements: and if when drawn, you will submit them to his perusal and approbation, it will show him how much you are in earnest.

My dearest life—do you think that he would disapprove of the terms I have offered?—

No.

Then may I be accursed, if I willingly submit to be trampled under foot by my enemies!

And may I, Mr Lovelace, never be happy in this life, if I submit to the passing upon my uncle Harlowe a wilful and premeditated falsehood for truth!—I have too long laboured under the affliction which the rejection of all my friends has given me, to purchase their reconciliation now at so dear a price as at that of my veracity.

The women below, my dear—

What are they to me?—I want not to establish myself with them. Need they know all that passes between my relations and you and me?

Neither are they anything to me, madam. Only, that when, for the sake of preventing the fatal mischiefs which might have attended your brother's projects, I have made them think us married, I would not appear to them in a light which you yourself think so shocking. By my soul, madam, I had rather die, than contradict myself so flagrantly, after I have related to them so many circumstances of our marriage.

Well, sir, the women may believe what they please. That I have given countenance to what you told them, is my error. The many circumstances which you own *one* untruth has drawn you in to relate, is a justification of my refusal in the present case.

Don't you see, madam, that your uncle wishes to find us married? May not the ceremony be privately over before his mediation can take place?

Urge this point no farther, Mr Lovelace. If *you* will not tell the truth, *I* will tomorrow morning, if I see Captain Tomlinson, tell it myself. Indeed I will.

Will you, madam, consent that things pass as before with the people below? This mediation of Tomlinson *may* come to nothing. Your brother's schemes *may* be pursued; the rather, that now he will know (perhaps from your uncle), that you are not under a legal protection—You will, at least, consent that things pass *here* as before?

To permit this, is to go on in an error, Mr Lovelace. But as the occasion for so doing (if there *can* be an occasion in your opinion, that will warrant an untruth), will, as I presume, soon be over, I shall the less dispute that point with you. But a new error I will not be guilty of, if I can avoid it.

Can I, do you think, madam, have any dishonourable view in the step I supposed you would not scruple to take towards a reconciliation with your own family?— Not for *my own* sake, you know, did I hope you to take it—for what is it to me, if I am never reconciled to your family? I want no favours from them.

I hope, Mr Lovelace, there is no occasion in our present *not* disagreeable situation to answer such a question. And let me say, that I shall think my prospects still more agreeable if, tomorrow morning, you will not only own the very truth, but give my uncle's friend such an account of the steps you have taken, and are taking, as may keep up my uncle's favourable intentions towards me. This you may do under what restrictions of secrecy you please. Captain Tomlinson is a prudent man; a promoter of family peace, you find; and, I dare say, may be made a friend.

I saw there was no help. I saw that the inflexible Harlowe spirit was all up in her—A little witch!—a little—Forgive me, Love, for calling her names: and so I said, with an air, We have had too many misunderstandings, madam, for me to wish for new ones; I will obey you without reserve. Had I not thought I should have obliged you by the other method (especially as the ceremony might have been over before anything could have operated from your uncle's intentions, and of consequence no untruth persisted in), I would not have proposed it—But think not, my beloved creature, that you shall enjoy, without condition, this triumph over my judgement.

And then, clasping my arms about her, I gave her struggled-away cheek (her charming lip designed) a fervent kiss—And your forgiveness of this sweet freedom (bowing) is that condition.

She was not mortally offended—And now must I make out the rest as well as I can. But this I will tell thee, that although her triumph has not diminished my love for her; yet has it stimulated me more than ever to *revenge*, as thou wilt be apt to call it. But *victory* or *conquest* is the more proper name.

There is a pleasure, 'tis true, in subduing one of these watchful beauties. But, by my soul, Belford, men of our cast take twenty times the pains to be rogues, that it would cost them to be honest; and dearly, with the sweat of our brows, and to the puzzling of our brains (to say nothing of the hazards we run), do we earn our purchase: and ought not therefore to be grudged our success, when we meet with it—especially as, when we have obtained our end, satiety soon follows; and leaves us little or nothing to show for it. But this, indeed, may be said of all worldly delights—and is not that a grave reflection from me?

I was willing to write up to the time. Although I have not carried my principal point, I shall make something turn out in my favour from Captain Tomlinson's errand—But let me give thee this caution; that thou do not pretend to judge of my devices by *parts*; but have patience till thou seest the *whole*. But once more I swear, that I will not be *out-Norrised* by a pair of novices. And yet I am very apprehensive, at times, of the consequences of Miss Howe's smuggling scheme.

'Tis late, or rather early; for the day begins to dawn upon me. I am plaguy heavy. Perhaps I need not to have told thee that. But will only indulge a doze in my chair, for an hour; then shake myself, wash, and refresh. At my time of life, with my constitution, that's all that's wanted.

Good night to me!—It cannot be broad day till I am awake—Aw-w-w-w-haugh—Pox of this yawning!

Is not thy uncle dead yet?

· What's come to mine, that he writes not to my last!—Hunting after more *wisdom of nations*, I suppose!—Yaw-Yaw-Yawning again!—Pen, begone!

Letter 216: MR LOVELACE TO JOHN BELFORD, ESQ.

Monday, May 29

Now have I established myself for ever in my charmer's heart.

The captain came at seven, as promised, and ready equipped for his journey. My beloved chose not to give us her company till our first conversation was over—Ashamed, I suppose (but to my shame, if she was), to be present at that part of it which was to restore her to her virgin state by my confession, after her *wifehood* had been reported to her uncle. But she took her cue nevertheless, and listened to all that passed.

The modestest women, Jack, must *think*, and think deeply sometimes—I wonder whether they ever blush at those things by themselves, at which they have so charming a knack of blushing in company—If not; and if blushing be a sign of grace or modesty, have not the sex as great a command over their blushes, as they are said to have over their tears? This reflection would lead me a great way into female minds, were I disposed to pursue it.

I told the captain that I would prevent his question; and accordingly, after I had enjoined the strictest secrecy that no advantage might be given to James Harlowe; and which he answered for as well on Mr Harlowe's part as his own; I acknowledged nakedly and fairly the whole truth—To wit, 'That we were not yet married—I gave him hints of the causes of procrastination—Some of them owing to unhappy misunderstanding: but chiefly to the lady's desire of previous reconciliation with her friends; and to a delicacy that had no example.'

Less nice ladies than this, Jack, love to have delays, wilful and *studied* delays, imputed to them in these cases—yet are indelicate in their affected delicacy; for do they not thereby tacitly confess that they expect to be the greatest gainers in wedlock; and that there is *self-denial* in the pride they take in delaying?

'I told him the reason of our passing to the people below as married—yet as under a vow of restriction as to consummation, which had kept us both to the height, one of *forbearing*, the other of *vigilant* punctilio; even to the denial of those innocent freedoms which betrothed lovers never scruple to allow and to take.

'I then communicated to him a copy of my proposals of settlement; the substance of her written answer; the contents of my letter of invitation to Lord M. to be her nuptial father; and of my Lord's generous reply. But said that having apprehensions of delay from his infirmities, and my beloved choosing by all means (and that from principles of *unrequited* duty) a private solemnization, I had written to excuse his lordship's presence; and expected an answer every hour.

'The settlements, I told him, were actually drawing by counsellor Williams, of whose eminence he must have heard (he had); and of the truth of this he might satisfy himself before he went out of town.

'When these were drawn, approved, and engrossed, nothing, I said, but signing, and the nomination of my happy day, would be wanting. I had a pride, I declared, in doing the highest justice to so beloved a creature, of my own voluntary motion, and without the intervention of a family from whom I had received the greatest insults. And this being our present situation, I was contented that Mr John Harlowe should suspend his reconciliatory purposes till our marriage were actually solemnized.'

The captain was highly delighted with all I had said: yet owned, that as his dear friend Mr Harlowe had expressed himself greatly pleased to hear that we were actually married, he could have wished it *had* been so. But, nevertheless, he doubted not that all would be well.

He saw my reasons, he said, and approved of them, for making the gentlewomen below (whom again he *understood to be good sort of people*) believe, that the ceremony had passed; which so well accounted for what the lady's maid had told Mr Harlowe's friend. Mr James Harlowe, he said, had certainly ends to answer in keeping open the breach; and *as* certainly had formed a design to get his sister out of my hands. Wherefore it as much imported his worthy friend to keep this treaty a secret, as it did me; at least till he had formed his party, and taken his measures. Ill-will and passion were dreadful misrepresenters. It was amazing to him that animosity could be carried so high against a man capable of views so pacific and so honourable, and who had shown such a command of his temper, in this whole transaction. Generosity, indeed, in every case, where love of stratagem and intrigue (I would excuse him) were not concerned, was a part of my character—

He was proceeding, when breakfast being ready, in came the empress of my heart, irradiating all around her as with a glory—A benignity and graciousness in her aspect, that, though natural to it, had been long banished from it.

Next to prostration lowly bowed the captain. Oh how the sweet creature smiled her approbation of him! Reverence from one, begets reverence from another. Men are more of monkeys in imitation, than they think themselves—Involuntarily, in a manner, I bent my knee—My dearest life—and made a very fine speech on presenting the captain to her. No title, myself, to her lip or cheek, 'tis well he attempted not either—He was indeed ready to worship her—could only touch her charming hand—

I have told the captain, my dear creature—And then I briefly repeated, as if I had supposed she had not heard it, all I had told him.

He was astonished, that anybody could be displeased one moment with such an angel. He undertook her cause as the highest degree of merit to himself.

Never, I must needs say, did the angel so much *look* the angel. All placid, serene, smiling, self-assured: a more lovely flush than usual heightening her natural graces, and adding charms, even to radiance, to her charming complexion.

After we had seated ourselves, the agreeable subject was renewed, as we took our chocolate. How happy should she be in her uncle's restored favour!

The captain engaged for it—No more delays, he hoped, of her part! Let the happy day be but *once* over, all would then be right!—But was it improper to ask for copies of my proposals, and of her answer, in order to show them to his dear friend her uncle?

As Mr Lovelace pleased—Oh that the dear creature would always say so!

It must be in strict confidence then, I said—But would it not be better to show her uncle the draught of the settlements, when drawn?

And will you *be so good* as to allow of this, Mr Lovelace?

There, Belford! We were once *The Quarrelsome*, but now we are *The Polite, Lovers*—

Indeed, my dearest creature, I will, *if you desire it*; and if Captain Tomlinson will engage that Mr Harlowe shall keep them absolutely a secret; that I may not be subjected to the cavil and control of any other of a family that have used me so very ill.

Now indeed, sir, you are very obliging.

Dost think, Jack, that my face did not now also shine?

I held out my hand (first consecrating it with a kiss) for hers. She condescended to give it me. I pressed it to my lips: You know not, Captain Tomlinson (with an air), all storms overblown, what a happy man—

Charming couple! (his hands lifted up)—How will my good friend rejoice!—Oh that he were present!—You know not, madam, how dear you still are to your uncle Harlowe!—

I am unhappy ever to have disobliged him!

Not too much of that, however, fairest, thought I!

He repeated his resolutions of service, and that in so acceptable a manner, that the dear creature wished that neither he, nor any of his, might ever want a friend of equal benevolence.

None of his, she said; for the captain brought it in that he had five children living by one of the best of wives and mothers, whose excellent management made him as happy as if his eight hundred pounds a year (which was all he had to boast of) were two thousand.

Without economy, the oraculous lady said, no estate was large enough. *With* it, the least was not too small.

Lie still, teasing villain! lie still!—I was only speaking to my conscience, Jack.

And let me ask you, Mr Lovelace, said the captain; yet not so much from doubt, as that I may proceed upon sure grounds—You are *willing* to co-operate with my dear friend in a general reconciliation?

Let me tell you, Mr Tomlinson, that if it can be distinguished that my readiness to make up with a family, of whose generosity I have not had reason to think highly, is entirely owing to the value I have for this angel of a woman, I will not only co-operate with Mr John Harlowe, as you ask; but I will meet Mr James Harlowe senior, and his lady, all the way. And furthermore, to make the son James and Arabella quite easy, I will absolutely disclaim any further interest, whether living or dying, in any of the three brothers' estates; contenting myself with what my beloved's grandfather has bequeathed to her: for I have reason to be abundantly satisfied with my own circumstances and prospects—enough rewarded, were she not to bring a shilling in dowry, in a lady who has a merit superior to all the goods of fortune. True as the Gospel, Belford! Why had not this scene a real foundation?

The dear creature, by her eyes, expressed her gratitude before her lips could utter it. Oh Mr Lovelace, said she—you have infinitely—and there she stopped—

The captain run over in my praise. He was really affected.

Oh that I had not such a mixture of revenge and pride in my love, thought I!— But (my old plea) cannot I make her amends at any time?—and is not her virtue now in the height of its probation?—Would she lay aside, like the friends of my uncontending Rosebud, all thought of defiance—Would she throw herself upon my mercy, and try me but one fortnight in the life of honour—What then?—I cannot say, what then.

Do not despise me, Jack, for my inconsistency—in no two letters perhaps agreeing with myself—Who expects consistency in men of our character?—But I am mad with love—fired by revenge—puzzled with my own devices—My inventions are my curse—my pride my punishment—drawn five or six ways at once—Can *she* possibly be so unhappy as *I*? Oh why, why was this woman so divinely excellent!— yet how know I that she is?—What have been her trials? Have I had the courage to make a single one upon her *person*, though fifty upon her *temper*?—Enough, I hope, to make her afraid of ever disobliging me more!—

I MUST banish reflection, or I am a lost man. For these two hours past have I hated myself for my own contrivances. And this not only from what I *have* related to thee; but from what I have *further* to relate. But I have now once more steeled my heart. My vengeance is uppermost; for I have been re-perusing some of Miss Howe's virulence. The contempt they have both held me in, I cannot bear—

The happiest breakfast-time, my beloved owned, that she had ever known since she had left her father's house. *She might have let this alone.* The captain renewed all his protestations of service. He would write me word how his dear friend received the account he should give him of the happy situation of our affairs, and what he thought of the settlements, as soon as I should send him the kindly-promised drafts. And we parted with great professions of mutual esteem; my beloved putting up vows for the success of his generous mediation.

When I returned from attending the captain downstairs, which I did to the outward door, my beloved met me as I entered the dining-room; complacency reigning in every lovely feature.

You see me already, said she, another creature. You know not, Mr Lovelace, how near my heart this hoped-for reconciliation is. I am now willing to banish every disagreeable remembrance. You know not, sir, how much you have obliged me. And Oh, Mr Lovelace, how happy shall I be, when my heart is lightened from the all-sinking weight of a father's curse! When my dear mamma (you don't know, sir, half the excellencies of my dear mamma! and what a kind heart she has, when it is left to follow its own impulses—when this blessed mamma) shall once more fold me to her indulgent bosom! When I shall again have uncles and aunts, and a brother and sister, all striving who shall show most kindness and favour to the poor outcast, then *no more* an outcast!—and you, Mr Lovelace, to behold all this, and to be received into a family so dear to me, with welcome—What though a little cold at first? when they come to know you better, and to see you oftener, no fresh causes of disgust occurring, and you, as I hope, having entered upon a new course, all will be warmer and warmer love on both sides, till everyone perhaps will wonder how they came to set themselves against you.

Then drying her eyes with her handkerchief, after a few moments pausing, on a sudden, as if recollecting that she had been led by her joy to an expression of it, which she had not intended I should see, she retired to her chamber with precipitation—leaving me almost as unable to stand it as herself.

In short, I was—I want words to say how I was—My nose had been made to tingle before; my eyes have before been made to glisten by this soul-moving beauty; but so *very* much affected, I never was—for, trying to check my sensibility, it was too strong for me, and I even sobbed—Yes, by my soul, I *audibly* sobbed, and was forced to turn from her before she had well finished her affecting speech.

I want, methinks, now I have owned the odd sensation, to describe it to thee— The thing was so strange to me—something choking, as it were, in my throat—I know not how—yet, I must needs say, though I am out of countenance upon the recollection, that there was something very pretty in it; and I wish I could know it again, that I might have a more perfect idea of it, and be better able to describe it to thee.

But this effect of her joy on such an occasion gives me a high notion of what that virtue must be (what other name can I call it?) which in a mind so capable of delicate transport, should be able to make so charming a creature in her very bloom, all frost and snow to every advance of love from the man she hates not. This must be all from education too—must it not, Belford? Can *education* have stronger force in a woman's heart than *nature*?—Sure it cannot. But if it can, how entirely right are parents to cultivate their daughters' minds, and to inspire them with notions of reserve and distance to our sex; and indeed to make them think highly of their own? For pride is an excellent substitute, let me tell thee, where virtue shines not out, as the sun, in its own unborrowed lustre.

AND now it is time to confess (and yet I know that thy conjectures are aforehand with my exposition), that this Captain Tomlinson, who is so great a favourite with my charmer, and who takes so much delight in healing breaches, and reconciling differences, is neither a great man nor a less, than honest Patrick McDonald, attended by a discarded footman of his own finding out.

Thou knowest what a various-lifed rascal he is; and to what better hopes born and educated. But that ingenious knack of forgery, for which he was expelled the Dublin University, and a detection since in evidenceship, have been his ruin. For these have thrown him from one country to another; and at last, into the way of life which would make him a fit husband for Miss Howe's Townsend with her contrabands. He is, thou knowest, admirably qualified for any enterprise that requires adroitness and solemnity. And can there, after all, be a higher piece of justice aimed at, than to keep one smuggler in readiness to play against another?

'Well but, Lovelace (methinks thou questionest), how camest thou to venture upon such a contrivance as this, when, as thou hast told me, the lady used to be a month at a time at this uncle's; and must therefore, in all probability, know that there was not a Captain Tomlinson in all his neighbourhood; at least no one of the name so intimate with him, as this man pretends to be?—'

This objection, Jack, is so natural a one, that I could not help observing to my charmer that she must surely have heard her uncle speak of this gentleman. No, she said, she never had. Besides, she had not been at her uncle Harlowe's for near ten months (*This I had heard her say before*): and there were several gentlemen who used the same green, whom she knew not.

We are all very ready, thou knowest, to believe what we like.

And what was the reason, thinkest thou, that she had not been of so long time at this uncle's?—Why, this old sinner, who imagines himself entitled to call me to account for my freedoms with the sex, has lately fallen into familiarities, as it is suspected, with his housekeeper, who assumes airs upon it—A cursed deluding sex!—In youth, middle age, or dotage, they take us all in.

Dost thou not see, however, that this housekeeper knows nothing, nor is to know anything, of the treaty of reconciliation designed to be set on foot; and therefore the uncle always comes to the captain, the captain goes not to the uncle: and this I surmised to the lady. And then it was a natural suggestion that the captain was the rather applied to, as he is a stranger to the rest of the family. Need I tell thee the meaning of all this?

But this intrigue of the *ancient* is a piece of private history, the truth of which my beloved cares not to own, and indeed, affects to disbelieve. As she does also some puisne gallantries of her foolish brother; which, by way of recrimination, I have hinted at, without naming my informant in their family.

Well but, methinks, thou questionest again, Is it not probable that Miss Howe will make inquiry after such a man as Tomlinson?—And when she cannot—

I know what thou wouldst say—but I have no doubt that Wilson will be so good, if I desire it, as to give into my own hands any letter that may be brought by Collins to his house, for a week to come. And now I hope thou'rt satisfied.

I will conclude with a short story.

'Two neighbouring sovereigns were at war together, about some pitiful chuck-farthing thing or other; no matter what; for the least trifles will set princes and children at loggerheads. Their armies had been drawn up in battalia some days, and the news of a decisive action expected every hour to arrive at each court. At last, issue was joined; a bloody battle was fought; and a fellow, who had been a spectator of it, arriving with the news of a complete victory, at the capital of one of the princes, some time before the appointed couriers, the bells were set a-ringing, bonfires and illuminations were made, and the people went to bed intoxicated with joy and good liquor. But the next day all was reversed. The victorious enemy, pursuing his advantage, was expected every hour at the gates of the almost defenceless capital. The first reporter was hereupon sought for, and found; and being questioned, pleaded a great deal of merit, in that he had in so dismal a situation taken such a space of time from the distress of his fellow-citizens, and given it to festivity, as were the hours between the false good news and the real bad.'

Do thou, Belford, make the application. This I know, that I have given greater joy to my beloved, than she had thought would so soon fall to her share. And as the human life is properly said to be chequerwork, no doubt but a person of her prudence will make the best of it, and set off so much good against so much bad, in order to strike as just a balance as possible.

The lady in three several letters acquaints her friend with the most material passages and conversations contained in those of Mr Lovelace's preceding.

[Letter 217.1: Miss Clarissa Harlowe to Miss Howe]

These are her words, on relating what the commission of the pretended Tomlinson was, after the apprehensions that his distant inquiry had given her.

'At last, my dear, all these doubts and fears were cleared up, and banished; and in their place a delightful prospect was opened to me. For it comes happily out (but at present it must be an absolute secret, for reasons which I shall mention in the sequel), that the gentleman was sent by my uncle Harlowe (I thought he could not be angry with me for ever); all owing to the conversation that passed between your good Mr Hickman and him. For although Mr Hickman's application was too harshly rejected at the time, my uncle could not but think better of it afterwards, and of the arguments that worthy gentleman used in my favour.

'Who, upon a passionate repulse, would despair of having a reasonable request granted?—Who would not, by gentleness and condescension, endeavour to leave favourable impressions upon an angry mind; which, when it comes coolly to reflect, may induce it to work itself into a condescending temper? To request a favour, as I have often said, is one thing; to challenge it as our due, is another. And what right has a petitioner to be angry at a *repulse*, if he has not a right to *demand* what he sues for as a *debt*?'

She describes Captain Tomlinson, on his breakfast visit, to be 'a grave good sort of man.' And in another place, 'a genteel man, of great gravity, and a good aspect; she believes upwards of fifty years of age. I liked him; says she as soon as I saw him.'

[*Letter 217.2: Miss Clarissa Harlowe to Miss Howe*]

As her prospects are now more favourable than heretofore, she wishes that her hopes of Mr Lovelace's so often promised reformation were better grounded than she is afraid they can be.

'We have both been extremely puzzled, my dear, says she, to reconcile some parts of Mr Lovelace's character with other parts of it: his good with his bad; such of the former in particular, as his generosity to his tenants; his bounty to the innkeeper's daughter; his readiness to put me upon doing kind things by my good Norton, and others.

'A strange mixture in his mind, as I have told him! For he is certainly (as I have reason to say, looking back upon his past behaviour to me in twenty instances) a hard-hearted man—Indeed, my dear, I have thought more than once that he had rather see me in tears, than give me reason to be pleased with him.

'My cousin Morden says that free livers are remorseless.[a] And so they must be in the very nature of things.

'Mr Lovelace is a proud man. That we have long observed. And I am truly afraid that his very generosity is more owing to his *pride* and his *vanity*, than to that *philanthropy* which distinguishes a beneficent mind.

'Money he values not, but as a means to support his pride and his independence. And it is easy, as I have often thought, for a person to part with a *secondary* appetite, when, by so doing, he can promote or gratify a *first*.

'I am afraid, my dear, that there must have been some fault in his education. His natural bias was not, I fancy, sufficiently attended to. He was instructed, perhaps (as his power was likely to be large), to do good and beneficent actions; but not from *proper motives*, I doubt.

'If he *had*, his generosity would not have stopped at *pride*, but would have struck into *humanity*; and then would he not have contented himself with doing praiseworthy things by fits and starts, or, as if relying on the doctrine of merits, he hoped by a good action to atone for a bad one[b]; but he would have been uniformly noble and done the good for its *own* sake.

'Oh my dear! what a lot have I drawn! *Pride* his *virtue*; and *revenge* his other predominating quality!—This one consolation, however, remains: he is not an infidel, an unbeliever. Had he been an *infidel*, there would have been no room at

a p. 563. See also Mr Lovelace's own confession of the delight he takes in a lady's tears, in different parts of his letters; particularly in p. 601.

b That the lady judges rightly of him in this place, see p. 163, where, giving the motive for his generosity to his Rosebud, he says: 'As I make it my rule, whenever I have committed a very capital enormity, to do some good by way of atonement; and as I believe I am a pretty deal indebted on that score; I intend to join a hundred pounds to Johnny's aunt's hundred pounds, to make one innocent couple happy'—Besides which motive, he had a further view to answer in that instance of his generosity; as may be seen [in] Letters 70, 71, 72, 73.

To show the consistence of his actions, as they *now* appear, with his views and principles as he lays them down in his *first letters*, it may not be amiss to refer the reader to his Letters, 34 and 35.

See also pp. 140, 141 and 181–4 for Clarissa's early opinion of Mr Lovelace—Whence the coldness and indifference to him, which he so repeatedly accuses her of, will be accounted for, more to her glory than to his honour.

all for hope of him; but (priding himself, as he does, in his fertile invention) he would have been utterly abandoned, irreclaimable, and a savage.'

[*Letter 217.3: Miss Clarissa Harlowe to Miss Howe*]

(*When she comes to relate those occasions, which Mr Lovelace in his narrative acknowledges himself to be affected by, she thus expresses herself:*)

'He endeavoured, as once before, to conceal his emotion. But why, my dear, should these men (for Mr Lovelace is not singular in this) think themselves above giving these beautiful proofs of a feeling heart? Were it in my power again to choose, or refuse, I would reject the man with contempt who sought to suppress, or offered to deny, the power of being affected upon *proper* occasions, as either a savage-hearted creature, or as one who was so ignorant of the principal glory of the human nature as to place his pride in a barbarous insensibility.

These lines translated from Juvenal by Mr Tate I have been often pleased with.

> Compassion *proper* to *mankind* appears,
> Which nature witness'd when she lent us tears.
> Of tender sentiments *We* only give
> These proofs: to weep is *Our* prerogative;
> To show by pitying looks, and melting eyes,
> How with a suff'ring friend we sympathize.
> Who can all sense of others' ills escape,
> Is but a brute at best, in human shape.
> *This natural piety* did first refine
> Our wit, and rais'd our thoughts to things divine.
> *This* proves our spirit of the gods descent,
> While that of beasts is prone and downward bent.
> To *them*, but earth-born life they did dispense;
> To *us*, for *mutual aid*, celestial sense.[1]

(*She takes notice, to the advantage of the people of the house, that such a good man as Captain Tomlinson had spoken well of them, upon inquiry.*)

Letter 218: MR LOVELACE TO JOHN BELFORD, ESQ.

Tuesday, May 30

I HAVE a letter from Lord M. Such a one as I would wish for if I intended matrimony. But as matters are circumstanced, I cannot think of showing it to my beloved.

My Lord regrets, 'that he is not to be the Lady's nuptial father. He seems apprehensive that I have still, specious as my reasons are, some mischief in my head.'

He graciously consents, 'that I may marry when I please; and offers one or both of my cousins to assist my bride, and to support her spirits on the occasion; since, as he understands, she is so much afraid to venture with me.

'Pritchard, he tells me, has his final orders to draw up deeds, to assign over to me in perpetuity £1000 *per annum*; which he will execute the same hour that the lady in person owns her marriage.'

He consents, 'that the jointure be made from my own estate.'

He wishes, 'that the lady would have accepted of his draft; and commends me for tendering it to her. But reproaches me for pride in not keeping it myself. *What the right side gives up, the left*, he says, *may be the better for.*'

The girls, he means.

With all my heart. If I can have Miss Clarissa Harlowe, the devil take everything else.

A good deal of other stuff writes this stupid peer; scribbling in several places half a dozen lines, apparently for no other reason but to bring in as many musty words in an old saw.

If thou askest, How I can manage, since my beloved will wonder that I have not an answer from my lord to such a letter as I wrote to him; and if I own I have one, will expect that I should show it to her, as I did my letter?—This I answer—That I can be informed by Pritchard that my lord has the gout in his right hand; and has ordered him to attend me in form, for my particular orders about the transfer: and I can see Pritchard, thou knowest, at the King's Arms, or where I please in town; and he, by word of mouth, can acquaint me with everything in my lord's letter that is necessary for her to know.

Whenever it suits me, I can restore the old peer to his right hand, and then can make him write a much more sensible letter than this he has now sent me.

Thou knowest that an adroitness in the art of *manual imitation* was one of my earliest attainments. It has been said on this occasion, that had I been a *bad* man in *meum* and *tuum* matters, I should not have been fit to live. As to the girls, we hold it no sin to cheat them. And are we not told that in being *well* deceived consists the whole of human happiness?[1]

Wednesday, May 31

ALL still happier and happier. A very high honour done me: a chariot, instead of a coach, permitted, purposely to indulge me in the subject of subjects.

Our discourse in this sweet airing turned upon our future manner of life. The day is bashfully promised me. *Soon*, was the answer to my repeated urgency. Our equipage, our servants, our liveries, were parts of the delightful subject. A desire that the wretch who had given me intelligence out of the family (honest Joseph Leman) might not be one of our menials; and her resolution to have her faithful Hannah, whether recovered or not; were signified; and both as readily assented to.

The reconciliation prospect was enlarged upon. If her uncle Harlowe will but pave the way to it, and if it can be brought about, she shall be happy—Happy, with a sigh, *as it is now possible she can be!*—She won't forbear, Jack!

I told her that I had heard from Pritchard, just before we set out, and expected him in town tomorrow from Lord M. to take my directions. I spoke with gratitude of my lord's kindness to me; and with pleasure of my aunt's and cousin's veneration for her: as also of his lordship's concern that his gout hindered him from writing a reply with his own hand to my last.

She pitied my lord. She pitied poor Mrs Fretchville too; for she had the goodness to inquire after her. The dear creature pitied everybody that seemed to want pity.

Happy in her own prospects, she has leisure to look abroad, and wishes everybody equally happy.

It is likely to go very hard with Mrs Fretchville. Her face, which she had valued herself upon, will be utterly ruined. This good, however, she may reap from so great an evil—As the greater malady generally swallows up the less, she may have a grief on this occasion, that may diminish the other grief and make it tolerable.

I had a gentle reprimand for this light turn on so heavy an evil—For what was the loss of beauty to the loss of a good husband?—Excellent creature!

Her hopes, and her pleasure upon those hopes, that Miss Howe's mother would be reconciled to her, were also mentioned. *Good* Mrs Howe was her word, for a woman so covetous, and so remorseless in her covetousness, that no one else would call her *good*. But this dear creature has such an extension in her love, as to be capable of valuing the most insignificant animal related to those whom she respects. *Love me, and love my dog*, I have heard Lord M. say—Who knows but that I may in time, in compliment to myself, bring her to think well of thee, Jack?

But what am I about?—Am I not all this time arraigning my own heart?—I know I am, by the remorse I feel in it, while my pen bears testimony to her excellence. But yet I must add (for no selfish consideration shall hinder me from doing justice to this admirable creature), that in this conversation she demonstrated so much prudent knowledge in everything that relates to that part of the domestic management, which falls under the care of a mistress of a family, that I believe she has no equal of her years in the world.

I break off, to re-peruse some of Miss Howe's virulence.

Cursed letters, these of Miss Howe, Jack!—Do thou turn back to those of mine, where I take notice of them—I proceed—

Upon the whole, my charmer was all gentleness, all ease, all serenity, throughout this sweet excursion. Nor had she reason to be otherwise: for it being the first time that I had the honour of her company *sola*, I was resolved to encourage her by my respectfulness, to repeat the favour.

On our return, I found the counsellor's clerk waiting for me, with a draft of the marriage settlements.

They are drawn, with only the necessary variations, from those made for my mother. The original of which (now returned by the counsellor), as well as the new drafts, I have put into my beloved's hands.

This made the lawyer's work easy; nor can she have a better precedent; the great Lord S. having settled them, at the request of my mother's relations; all the difference, my charmer's are £100 *per annum* more than my mother's.

I offered to read to her the old deed, while she looked over the draft; for she had refused her presence at the examination with the clerk: but this she also declined.

I suppose she did not care to hear of so many children, first, second, third, fourth, fifth, sixth, and seventh sons, and as many daughters, *to be begotten upon the body of the said Clarissa Harlowe.*

Charming matrimonial recitativoes!—Though it is always said *lawfully begotten* too—as if a man could beget children *unlawfully* upon the body of his own wife— But thinkest thou not that these arch rogues the lawyers hereby intimate, that a man may have children by his wife *before* marriage?—This must be what they mean. Why will these sly fellows put an honest man in mind of such rogueries?—

But hence, as in numberless other instances, we see that *Law* and *Gospel* are two very different things.

Dorcas, in our absence, tried to get at the wainscot box in the dark closet. But it cannot be done without violence. And to run a risk of consequence now, for mere curiosity sake, would be inexcusable.

Mrs Sinclair and the nymphs are all of opinion that I am now so much of a favourite, and have such a visible share in her confidence, and even in her affections, that I may do what I will, and plead violence of *passion*; which, they will have it, makes violence of *action* pardonable with their sex; as well as an allowed extenuation with the unconcerned of both sexes; and they all offer their helping hands. Why not? they say: has she not passed for my wife before them all?—and is she not in a fine way of being reconciled to her friends; which was the pretence for postponing consummation?

They again urge me, since it is so difficult to make *night* my friend, to an attempt in the *day*. They remind me that the situation of their house is such, that no noises can be heard out of it; and ridicule me for making it necessary for a lady to be undressed. *It was not always so with me*, poor old man! Sally told me; saucily slinging her handkerchief in my face.

Letter 219: MR LOVELACE TO JOHN BELFORD, ESQ.

Friday, June 2

NOTWITHSTANDING my studied-for politeness and complaisance for some days past; and though I have wanted courage to throw the mask quite aside; yet I have made the dear creature more than once look about her by the warm though decent expressions of my passion. I have brought her to own that I am *more* than indifferent [with] her: but as to LOVE, which I pressed her to acknowledge, *What need of acknowledgements of that sort, when a woman consents to marry?*—And once repulsing me with displeasure, *The proof of the true love I was vowing for her, was* respect, *not* freedom. And offering to defend myself, she told me that all the conception she had been able to form of a faulty passion was that it must demonstrate itself as mine sought to do.

I endeavoured to justify my passion, by laying over-delicacy at her door. That was *not*, she said, *my* fault, if it were *hers*. She must plainly tell me that I appeared to her incapable of distinguishing what were the requisites of a pure mind. Perhaps had the *libertine* presumption to imagine that there was no difference in *heart*, nor any but what proceeded from *education* and *custom*, between the pure and the impure—And yet custom *alone*, as she observed, would make a second nature, as well in good as in bad habits.

I HAVE just now been called to account for some innocent liberties which I thought myself entitled to take before the women; as they suppose us married, and now within view of consummation.

I took the lecture very hardly; and with impatience wished for the happy day and hour when I might call her all my own, and meet with no check from a niceness that had no example.

She looked at me with a bashful kind of contempt. I thought it *contempt*, and required the reason for it; not being conscious of offence, as I told her.

This is not the first time, Mr Lovelace, said she, that I have had cause to be displeased with you, when *you*, perhaps, have not thought yourself exceptionable—But, sir, let me tell you that the married state, in my eye, is a state of purity, and (I think she told me) not of *licentiousness*; so at least, I understood her.

Marriage purity, Jack!—Very comical, 'faith—Yet, sweet dears, half the female world ready to run away with a rake, *because* he is a rake; and for no *other* reason; nay, every other reason *against* their choice.

But have not you and I, Belford, seen young wives, who would be thought modest; and when maids, were fantastically shy; permit freedoms in public from their *lambent* husbands which have shown that they have forgot what belongs either to prudence or decency? While every modest eye has sunk under the shameless effrontery, and every modest face been covered with blushes for those who could not blush.

I once, upon such an occasion, proposed to a circle of a dozen, thus scandalized, to withdraw; since they must needs see that as well the *lady*, as the gentleman, wanted to be in private. This motion had its effect upon the amorous pair; and I was applauded for the check given to their licentiousness.

But, upon another occasion of this sort, I acted a little more in character—for I ventured to make an attempt upon a bride, which I should not have had the courage to make, had not the unblushing passiveness with which she received her fond husband's public toyings (looking round her with triumph rather than with shame, upon every lady present), incited my curiosity to know if the same complacency might not be shown to a private friend. 'Tis true, I was in honour obliged to keep the secret. But I never saw the turtles bill afterwards, but I thought of number two to the same female; and in my heart thanked the fond husband for the lesson he had taught his wife.

From what I have said, thou wilt see that I approve of my beloved's exception to *public* loves. That, I hope, is all the charming icicle means by *marriage purity*.

From the whole of the above, thou wilt gather that I have not been a mere dangler, a Hickman, in the past days, though not absolutely active and a Lovelace.

The dear creature now considers herself as my wife-elect. The *unsaddened* heart, no longer prudish, will not now, I hope, give the sable turn to every action of the man she dislikes not. And yet she must keep up so much reserve as will justify past inflexibilities. Many and many a pretty soul would yield, were she not afraid that the man she favoured would think the worse of her for it. This is also a part of the rake's creed. But should she resent ever so strongly, she cannot now break with me; since, if she does, there will be an end of the family reconciliation; and that in a way highly discreditable to herself.

Sat. June 3

JUST returned from Doctors' Commons. I have been endeavouring to get a licence.[1] Very true, Jack. I have the mortification to find a difficulty in obtaining this all-fettering instrument, as the lady is of rank and fortune, and as there is no consent of father or *next friend*.

I made report of this difficulty. It is very right, she says, that such difficulties should be made. But not to a man of my known fortune, surely, Jack, though the woman were the daughter of a duke.

I asked if she approved of the settlements? She said she had compared them with my mother's, and had no objection. She had written to Miss Howe upon the subject, she owned; and to inform her of our present situation.[a]

JUST now, in high good humour, my beloved returned me the drafts of the settlements; a copy of which I had sent to Captain Tomlinson. She complimented me that she never had any doubt of my honour in cases of this nature—In matters between man and man nobody ever had, thou knowest. I had need, thou'lt say, to have some good qualities.

Great faults and great virtues are often found in the same person. In nothing *very* bad, but as to women: and did not one of them begin with me?[b]

We have held that women have no souls: I am a very Jew in this point, and willing to believe they have not.[2] And if so, to whom shall I be accountable for what I do to them? Nay, if souls they have, as there is no sex in ethereals,[3] nor need of any, what plea can a lady hold of injuries done her in her lady-*state*, when there is an end of her lady-*ship*?

Letter 220: MR LOVELACE TO JOHN BELFORD, ESQ.

Monday, June 5

I AM now almost in despair of succeeding with this charming frost-piece by love or gentleness—A copy of the drafts, as I told thee, has been sent to Captain Tomlinson; and that by a special messenger. Ingrossments are proceeding with. I have been again at the Commons. Should in all probability have procured a licence by Malory's means, had not Malory's friend the proctor been suddenly sent for to Cheshunt, to make an old lady's will. Pritchard has told me by word of mouth, *though my charmer saw him not*, all that was necessary for her to know in the letter my lord wrote, which I could not show her; and taken my directions about the estates to be made over to me on my nuptials—Yet with all these favourable appearances no conceding moment to be found, no improvable tenderness to be raised.

Twice indeed with rapture, which once she called rude, did I salute her; and each time, resenting the freedom, did I retire; though, to do her justice, she favoured me again with her presence at my first entreaty, and took no notice of the cause of her withdrawing.

Is it policy to show so open a resentment for innocent liberties which, in her situation, she must so soon forgive?

Yet the woman who resents not initiatory freedoms must be lost. For love is an encroacher. Love never goes backward. Love is always aspiring. Always must aspire. Nothing but the highest act of love can satisfy an indulged love. And what advantages has a lover who values not breaking the peace, over his mistress who is solicitous to keep it!

I have now at this instant wrought myself up, for the dozenth time, to a half-resolution. A thousand agreeable things I have to say to her. She is in the dining-room. Just gone up. She always expects me when there.

---

a As this letter of the lady contains no new matter, but what may be collected from those of Mr Lovelace, it is omitted.

b See Letter 31, p. 143.

HIGH displeasure!—followed by an abrupt departure.

I sat down by her. I took both her hands in mine. I would *have* it so. All gentle my voice—Her father mentioned with respect. Her mother with reverence. Even her brother amicably spoken of. I never thought I could have wished so ardently, as I told her I did wish, for a reconciliation with her family.

A sweet and grateful flush then overspread her fair face; a gentle sigh now and then heaved her handkerchief.

I perfectly longed to hear from Captain Tomlinson. It was impossible for her uncle to find fault with the draft of the settlements: I would not, however, be understood by sending them down, that I intended to put it in her uncle's power to delay my happy day. When, when, was it to be?

I would hasten again to the Commons; and would not return without the licence.

The Lawn I proposed to retire to, as soon as the happy ceremony was over. This day and that day I proposed.

It was time enough to name the day when the settlements were completed, and the licence obtained. Happy should she be, could the kind Captain Tomlinson obtain her uncle's presence privately!

A good hint!—It may perhaps be improved upon—either for a *delay*, or a *pacifier*.

No new delays, for heaven's sake, I besought her; reproaching her gently for the past. Name but the day—an early day, I hoped in the following week—that I might hail its approach and number the tardy hours.

My cheek reclined on her shoulder—kissing her hands by turns. Rather bashfully than angrily reluctant, her hands sought to be withdrawn; her shoulder avoiding my reclined cheek—apparently loath and more loath to quarrel with me; her downcast eye confessing more than her lips could utter—Now surely, thought I, it is my time to try if she can forgive a still bolder freedom than I had ever yet taken.

I then gave her struggling hands liberty. I put one arm round her waist: I imprinted a kiss on her sweet lips, with a *Be quiet* only, and an averted face, as if she feared another.

Encouraged by so gentle a repulse, the tenderest things I said; and then, with my other hand, drew aside the handkerchief that concealed the beauty of beauties, and pressed with my burning lips the charmingest breast that ever my ravished eyes beheld.

A very contrary passion to that which gave her bosom so delightful a swell immediately took place. She struggled out of my encircling arms with indignation. I detained her reluctant hand. Let me go, said she. I see there is no keeping terms with you. Base encroacher! Is this the design of your flattering speeches?—Far as matters have gone, I will for ever renounce you. You have an odious heart. Let me go, I tell you—

I was forced to obey, and she flung from me, repeating *base*, and adding *flattering*, encroacher.

IN vain have I urged by Dorcas for the promised favour of dining with her. She would not dine *at all*. She *could not*.

But why makes she every inch of her person thus sacred?—so near the time too, that she must suppose, that all will be my own by deed of purchase and settlement? She has read, no doubt, of the art of the Eastern monarchs, who sequester themselves from the eyes of their subjects, in order to excite their adoration when, upon some solemn occasions, they think fit to appear in public.

But let me ask thee, Belford, whether (on these solemn occasions) the preceding cavalcade; here a great officer, and there a great minister, with their satellites and glaring equipages; do not prepare the eyes of the wondering beholders, by degrees, to bear the blaze of canopied majesty (what though but an ugly old man perhaps himself? yet) glittering in the collected riches of his vast empire?

And should not my beloved, for her own sake, descend by *degrees* from *goddesshood* into *humanity*? If it be *pride* that restrains her, ought not that pride to be punished? If, as in the Eastern emperors, it be *art* as well as *pride*, *art* is what she of all women need not use. If *shame*, what a shame to be ashamed to communicate to her adorer's sight the most admirable of her personal graces?

Let me perish, Belford, if I would not forgo the brightest diadem in the world for the pleasure of seeing a twin Lovelace at each charming breast, drawing from it his first sustenance; the pious task continued for one month, and no more!¹

I now, methinks, behold this most charming of women in this sweet office, pressing with her fine fingers the generous flood into the purple mouths of each eager hunter by turns: her conscious eye now dropped on one, now on the other, with a sigh of maternal tenderness; and then raised up to my delighted eye, full of wishes, for the sake of the pretty varlets, and for her own sake, that I would deign to legitimate; that I would condescend to put on the nuptial fetters.

Letter 221: MR LOVELACE TO JOHN BELFORD, ESQ.

Monday, p.m.

A LETTER received from the worthy Captain Tomlinson, has introduced me into the presence of my charmer sooner than perhaps I should otherwise have been admitted.

Sullen her brow at her first entrance into the dining-room. But I took no notice of what had passed, and her anger slid away upon its own ice.

'The captain, after letting me know that he chose not to write till he had the promised draft of the settlements, acquaints me that his friend Mr John Harlowe, in their first conference (which was held as soon as he got down), was extremely surprised and even grieved (as he feared he would be) to hear that we were not married. The world, he said, who knew my character, would be very censorious, were it owned that we had lived so long together unmarried in the same lodgings; although our marriage were now to be ever so publicly celebrated.

'His nephew James, he was sure, would make a great handle of it against any motion that might be made towards a reconciliation; and with the greater success, as there was not a family in the kingdom more jealous of their honour than theirs.'

This is true of the Harlowes, Jack: they have been called *the proud Harlowes*: and I have ever found that all young honour is supercilious and touchy.

But seest thou not how right I was in my endeavour to persuade my fair one to allow her uncle's friend to think us married; especially as he came *prepared* to believe it; and as her uncle *hoped* it was so?—But nothing on earth is so perverse as a woman when she is set upon carrying a point, and has a *meek* man, or one who loves his *peace*, to deal with.

My beloved was vexed. She pulled out her handkerchief: but was more inclined to blame me, than herself.

Had you kept your word, Mr Lovelace, and left me when we came to town—and there she stopped; for she knew that it was her own fault that we were not married before we left the country; and how could I leave her afterwards while her brother was plotting to carry her off by violence?

Nor has he yet given over his machinations.

For, as the Captain proceeds, 'Mr John Harlowe owned to him (but in confidence) that his nephew is at this time busied in endeavouring to find out where we are; being assured, as I am not to be heard of at any of my relations, or at my usual lodgings, that we are together. And that we are not married is plain, as he will have it, from Mr Hickman's application so lately made to her uncle, and which was seconded by Mrs Norton to her mother. And he cannot bear that I should enjoy such a triumph unmolested.'

A profound sigh, and the handkerchief again lifted to the eye. But did not the sweet soul deserve this turn upon her, for her felonious intention to rob me of herself?

I read on to the following effect:

'Why (Mr Harlowe asked) was it said to his other inquiring friend that we *were* married—and that by his niece's woman, who ought to know? Who could give *convincing* reasons, no doubt—'

Here again she wept, took a turn cross the room; then returned—Read on, said she—

Will you, my dearest life, read it yourself?

I will take the letter with me by and by—I cannot *see* to read it just now, wiping her eyes—Read on—Let me hear it all—that I may know your sentiments upon this letter, as well as give my own.

'The captain then told uncle John the reasons that induced me to give out that we were married; and the conditions on which my beloved was brought to countenance it; which had kept us at the most punctilious distance.

'But still my character was insisted upon. And Mr Harlowe went away dissatisfied. And the captain was also so much concerned, that he cared not to write what the result of this first conference was.

'But in the next, which was held on receipt of the drafts, at his the captain's house (as the former was, for the greater secrecy), when the old gentleman had read them and had the captain's opinion, he was much better pleased. And yet he declared that it would not be easy to persuade any other person of his family to believe so favourably of the matter as he was *now* willing to believe, were they to know that we had lived so long together unmarried.

'And then the captain says his dear friend made a proposal: it was this—*That we should marry out of hand, but as privately as possible, as indeed he found we intended* (for he could have no objection to the drafts)—*But yet he expected to have present one trusty friend of his own, for his better satisfaction—*'

Here I stopped, with a design to be angry—but she desiring me to read on, I obeyed—

'*—but that it should pass to every one living, except to that trusty person, to himself, and to the captain, that we were married from the time that we had lived*

together in one house; and that this time should be made to agree with that of Mr
Hickman's application to him from Miss Howe.'

This, my dearest life, said I, is a very considerate proposal. We have nothing to
do but to caution the people below properly on this head. I did not think your
uncle Harlowe capable of such an expedient. But you see how much his heart is in
the reconciliation.

This was the return I met with—You have always, as a mark of your politeness,
let me know how *meanly* you think of every one of my family.

Yet thou wilt think, Belford, that I could forgive her for the reproach.

'The captain does not know, he says, how this proposal will be relished by us.
But, for his part, he thinks it an expedient that will obviate many difficulties, and
may possibly put an end to Mr James Harlowe's further designs: and on this
account he has, by the uncle's advice, already declared to two several persons, by
whose means it may come to that young gentleman's ears, that he (Captain
Tomlinson) has very great reason to believe that we were married soon after Mr
Hickman's application was rejected.

'And this, Mr Lovelace (says the captain), will enable you to pay a compliment
to the family that will not be unsuitable to the generosity of some of the
declarations you was pleased to make to the lady before me (and which Mr John
Harlowe may make some advantage of in favour of a reconciliation); in that you
have not demanded your lady's estate so soon as you were entitled to make the
demand.' An excellent contriver surely she must think this worthy Mr Tomlinson
to be!

'But the captain adds that if either the lady or I disapprove of his report of our
marriage, he will retract it. Nevertheless he must tell me, that Mr John Harlowe
is very much set upon this way of proceeding; as the only one, in his opinion,
capable of being improved into a general reconciliation. But if we do acquiesce in
it, he beseeches my fair one not to suspend my day, that he may be authorised in
what he says, as to the truth of the main fact (*how conscientious this good man!*):
nor must it be expected, he says, that her uncle will take one step towards the
wished-for reconciliation till the *solemnity is actually over.'*

He adds, 'that he shall be very soon in town on other affairs; and then proposes
to attend us, and give us a more particular account of all that passed, or shall
further pass, between Mr Harlowe and him.'

Well, my dearest life, what say you to your uncle's expedient? Shall I write to
the captain and acquaint him that we have no objection to it?

She was silent for a few minutes. At last, with a sigh—See, Mr Lovelace, said
she, what you have brought me to, by treading after you in such crooked paths!—
See what disgrace I have incurred!—Indeed you have not acted like a wise man.

My beloved creature, do you not remember how earnestly I besought the honour
of your hand before we came to town?—Had I been *then* favoured—

Well, well, sir—there has been much amiss somewhere; that's all I will say at
present. And since what's past cannot be recalled, my uncle must be obeyed, I
think.

Charmingly dutiful!—I had nothing then to do, that I might not be behindhand
with the worthy captain and her uncle, but to press for the day. This I fervently
did. But (as I might have expected) her former answer was repeated, That when
the settlements were completed; when the licence was actually obtained; it would

be time enough to name the day: and, Oh Mr Lovelace, said she, turning from me with a grace inimitably tender, her handkerchief at her eyes, what a happiness, if my dear uncle could be prevailed upon to be personally a father on this occasion, to *the poor fatherless girl!*—

What's the matter with me!—Whence this dew-drop!—a tear!—as I hope to be saved, it is a tear, Jack!—Very ready methinks!—only on reciting!—But her lively image was before me, in the very attitude she spoke the words—and indeed at the *time* she spoke them, these lines of Shakespeare came into my head:

> Thy heart is big. Get thee apart, and weep!
> Passion, I see, is catching:—For my eyes,
> Seeing those beads of sorrow stand in thine,
> Begin to water—¹

I withdrew, and wrote to the captain to the following effect—'That he would be so good as to acquaint his dear friend that we entirely acquiesced with what he had proposed; and had already *properly* cautioned the gentlewomen of the house, and their servants, as well as our own: that if he would in person give me the blessing of his dear niece's hand, it would crown the wishes of both: that his own day, in this case, as I presumed it would be a short one, should be ours: that by this means the secret would be in fewer hands: that I myself thought the ceremony could not be too privately performed; and this not only for the sake of the wise end he had intended to be answered by it, but because I would not have Lord M. think himself slighted; as he had once intended (as I had told him) to be our nuptial father, had we not declined his offer in order to avoid a public wedding; which his beloved niece would not come into while she was in disgrace with her friends—But that, if he chose not to do us this honour, I wished that Captain Tomlinson might be the trusty person whom he would have to be present on the happy occasion.'

I showed this letter to my fair one. She was not displeased with it. So, Jack, we cannot now move too fast, as to settlements and licence: the day is her *uncle's day*, or *Captain Tomlinson's* perhaps, as shall best suit the occasion. Miss Howe's smuggling scheme is now surely provided against in all events.

But I will not by anticipation make thee a judge of all the benefits that may flow from this my elaborate contrivance. Why will these girls put me upon my *master-strokes*?

And now for a little mine which I am getting ready to spring. The *first*, and at the rate I go on (now a *resolution*, and now a *remorse*), perhaps the *last*.

A *little* mine, I call it. But it may be attended with great effects. I shall not, however, absolutely depend upon the success of it, having much more effectual ones in reserve. And yet great engines are often moved by little springs. A small spark falling by accident into a powder magazine has sometimes done more execution than an hundred cannon.

Come the worst to the worst, the *hymeneal torch*, and a *white sheet*,² must be my *amende honorable*, as the French have it.

Letter 222: MR BELFORD TO ROBERT LOVELACE, ESQ.

Tuesday, June 6

UNSUCCESSFUL as hitherto my application to thee has been, I cannot for the heart
of me forbear writing once more in behalf of this admirable woman: and yet am
unable to account for the zeal which impels me to take her part with an earnestness
so sincere.

But all her merit thou acknowledgest; all thy own vileness thou confessest, and
even gloriest in it; what hope then of moving so hardened a man?—Yet, as it is not
too late, and thou art nevertheless upon the crisis, I am resolved to try what
another letter will do. It is but my writing in vain, if it do no good; and if thou wilt
let me prevail, I know thou wilt hereafter think me richly entitled to thy thanks.

To *argue* with thee would be folly. The case cannot require it. I will only *entreat*
thee, therefore, that thou wilt not let such an excellence lose the reward of her
vigilant virtue.

I believe there never were libertines so vile but purposed, at some future period
of their lives, to set about reforming; and let me beg of thee, that thou wilt in this
great article make thy future repentance as easy as some time hence thou wilt wish
thou *hadst* made it. If thou proceedest, I have no doubt that this affair will end
tragically, one way or other. It must. Such a woman must interest both gods and
men in her cause. But what I most apprehend is, that with her own hand, in
resentment of the perpetrated outrage, she (like another Lucretia) will assert the
purity of her heart: or, if her piety preserve her from this violence, that wasting
grief will soon put a period to her days. And in either case, will not the
remembrance of thy *ever-during* guilt, and *transitory* triumph, be a torment of
torments to thee?

'Tis a seriously sad thing, after all, that so fine a creature should have fallen into
such vile and remorseless hands: for, from thy cradle, as I have heard thee own,
thou ever delightedst to sport with and torment the animal, whether bird or beast,
that thou lovedst, and hadst a power over.

How different is the case of this fine woman from that of any other whom thou
hast seduced! I need not mention to thee, nor insist upon the striking difference;
justice, gratitude, thy interest, thy vows, all engaging thee; and thou certainly
loving her, as far as thou art capable of love, above all her sex. She not to be drawn
aside by art, or to be made to suffer from credulity, nor for want of wit and
discernment (that will be another cutting reflection to so fine a mind as hers): the
contention between you only unequal, as it is between naked innocence and armed
guilt. In everything else, as thou ownest, her talents greatly superior to thine!—
What a fate will hers be, if thou art not at last overcome by thy reiterated remorses!

At first, indeed, when I was admitted into her presence[a](and till I observed her
meaning air, and heard her speak), I supposed that she had no very uncommon
judgement to boast of: for I made, as I thought, but *just* allowances for her
blossoming youth, and for that loveliness of person, and easiness of dress, which I
imagined must have taken up half her time and study to cultivate; and yet I had
been prepared by thee to entertain a very high opinion of her sense and her
reading. Her choice of this gay fellow, upon such hazardous terms (thought I), is

a See p. 544.

a confirmation that her *wit* wants that maturity which only *years* and *experience* can give it. Her *knowledge* (argued I to myself) must be all *theory*; and the complaisance ever consorting with an age so green and so gay will make so inexperienced a lady at least forbear to show herself *disgusted* at freedoms of discourse, in which those present of her own sex, and some of ours (so learned, so well read, and so travelled), allow themselves.

In this presumption, I [ran] on; and having the advantage, as I conceited, of all the company but thee, and being desirous to appear in her eyes a mighty clever fellow, I thought I *showed away*, when I said any foolish things that had more sound than sense in them; and when I made silly jests, which attracted the smiles of thy Sinclair, and the specious Partington; and that Miss Harlowe did not smile too, I thought was owing to her youth or affectation, or to a mixture of both, perhaps to a greater command of her features—Little dreamt I that I was incurring her contempt all the time.

But when, as I said, I heard her speak; which she did not till she had fathomed us all; when I heard her sentiments on two or three subjects, and took notice of that searching eye, darting into the very inmost cells of our frothy brains, by my faith, it made me look about me; and I began to recollect, and be ashamed of all I had said before; in short, was resolved to sit silent, till every one had talked round, to keep my folly in countenance. And then I raised the subjects that she *could* join in, and which she *did* join in, so much to the confusion and surprise of every one of us!—For even thou, Lovelace, so noted for smart wit, repartee, and a vein of raillery that delighteth all who come near thee, sattest in palpable darkness, and looked about thee, as well as we.

One instance only, of this, shall I remind thee of?

We talked of *wit*, and of *wit*, and aimed at it, bandying it like a ball from one to another of us, and resting it chiefly with thee, who wert always proud enough and vain enough of the attribute; and then more especially, as thou hadst assembled us, as far as I know, principally to show the lady thy superiority over us; and us thy triumph over her. And then Tourville (who is always satisfied with wit at second-hand; wit upon memory; other men's wit) repeated some verses, as applicable to the subject; which two of us applauded, though full of double entendre. Thou, seeing the lady's serious air on one of those repetitions, appliedst thyself to her, desiring her notions of wit: a quality, thou saidst, which everyone prized, whether flowing from himself, or found in another.

Then it was she took all our attention—It was a quality much talked of, she said, but, she believed, very little understood—At least, if she might be so free as to give her judgement of it, from what had passed in the present conversation, she must say that wit with gentlemen was one thing; with ladies, another.

This startled us all—How the women looked!—How they pursed in their mouths, a broad smile the moment before upon each, from the verses they had heard repeated, so well understood, as we saw, by their looks—While I besought her to let us know, for our instruction, what wit was with *ladies:* for such I was sure it *ought* to be, with *gentlemen*.

Cowley, she said, had defined it prettily by negatives.

Thou desiredst her to repeat his definition.

She did; and with so much graceful ease, and beauty, and propriety of accent, as would have made bad poetry delightful.

> A thousand diff'rent shapes it bears,
> Comely, in thousand shapes appears.
> 'Tis not a *tale*: 'Tis not a *jest*,
> Admir'd, *with laughter*, at a *feast*,
> Nor *florid talk*, which must this title gain:
> The proofs of wit for ever must remain.
> Much less can that have any place
> At which a virgin hides her face.
> Such dross the fire must purge away:—'Tis just
> The author blush there, where the reader must.[1]

Here she stopped, looking round her upon us all with conscious superiority, as I thought. Lord! how we stared! Thou attemptedst to give us thy definition of wit, that thou mightest have something to say, and not seem to be surprised into silent modesty.

But, as if she cared not to trust thee with the subject, referring to the same author as for his more positive decision, she thus, with the same harmony of voice and accent, emphatically decided upon it.

> *Wit*, like a luxuriant vine,
> Unless to *Virtue's* prop it join,
> Firm and erect, tow'rd heaven bound,
> Tho' it with beauteous leaves and pleasant fruit be crown'd; }
> It lies deform'd, and rotting on the ground.[2]

If thou recollectest this part of the conversation, and how like fools we looked at one another: how much it put us out of conceit with ourselves, and made us *fear* her; when we found our conversation thus excluded from the very character which our vanity had made us think unquestionably ours: and if thou profitest properly by the recollection, thou wilt be of my mind that there is not so much wit in wickedness, as we had flattered ourselves there was.

And after all, I have been of opinion ever since *that* conversation, that the wit of all the rakes and libertines I ever conversed with, from the brilliant Bob Lovelace down to little Johnny Hartop the punster, consists mostly in saying bold and shocking things with such courage as shall make modest people blush, the impudent laugh, and the ignorant stare.

And why dost thou think I mention these things, so mal-à-propos, as it may seem?—Only, let me tell thee, as an instance, among many that might be given from the same evening's conversation, of this fine lady's superiority in those talents which ennoble nature, and dignify her sex: evidenced not only to each of us, as we offended, but to the flippant Partington, and the grosser, but egregiously hypocritical Sinclair, in the correcting eye, the discouraging blush, in which was mixed as much displeasure as modesty, and sometimes, as the occasion called for it (for we were some of us hardened above the sense of feeling *delicate* reproof), by the sovereign contempt, mingled with a disdainful kind of pity, that showed at once her own conscious worth, and our despicable worthlessness.

Oh Lovelace! what then was the triumph, even in my eye, and what is it still upon reflection, of *true* modesty, of *true* wit, and *true* politeness, over frothy jest, laughing impertinence, and an obscenity so shameful even to the guilty, that they cannot hint at it but under a double meaning!

Then, as thou hast somewhere observed, all her correctives *avowed* by her eye. Not poorly, like the generality of her sex, affecting ignorance of meanings too obvious to be concealed; but so resenting, as to show each impudent laugher the offence given to, and taken by, a purity that had mistaken its way when it fell into such company.

Such is the woman, such is the angel, whom thou hast betrayed into thy power, and wouldst deceive and ruin—Sweet creature! did she but know how she is surrounded (as I then thought as well as now think), and what is *intended*, how much sooner would death be her choice than so dreadful a situation!—And how effectually would her story, were it generally known, warn all the sex against throwing themselves into the power of ours, let our vows, oaths, and protestations, be what they will!

But let me beg of thee, once more, my dear Lovelace, if thou hast any regard for thy honour, for the honour of thy family, for thy future peace, or for my opinion of thee (who yet pretend not to be so much moved by principle, as by that dazzling merit which ought still more to attract *thee*), to be prevailed upon— to be—to be *humane*, that's all—Only, that thou wouldst not disgrace our common humanity!

Hardened as thou art, I know that they are the abandoned people in the house who keep thee up to a resolution against her. Oh that the sagacious fair one, with so much innocent charity in her own heart, had not so resolutely held those women at distance!—That, as she boarded there, she had oftener tabled with them. Specious as they are, in a week's time she would have seen through them; they could not have been always so guarded as they were when they saw her but seldom, and when they prepared themselves to see her; and she would have fled their house as a place infected. And yet, perhaps, with so determined an enterpriser, this discovery might have accelerated her ruin.

I know that thou art nice in thy loves. But are there not hundreds of women, who, though not utterly abandoned, would be taken with thee for mere *personal* regards? Make a toy, if thou wilt, of principle, with regard to such of the sex as regard it as a toy; but rob not an angel of those purities which, in her own opinion, constitute the difference between angelic and brutal qualities.

With regard to the passion itself, the less of soul in either man or woman, the more sensual are they. Thou, Lovelace, hast a soul, though a corrupted one; and art more intent (as thou even gloriest) upon the preparative stratagem, than upon the end of conquering.

See we not the natural bent of idiots and the crazed?—The very appetite is *body*; and when we ourselves are most fools, and crazed, then are we most eager in these pursuits. See what fools this passion makes the wisest men! What snivellers, what dotards, when they suffer themselves to be run away with by it!—An *unpermanent passion!*—since, if (ashamed of its *more proper* name) we must call it *love, love gratified, is love satisfied—and love satisfied, is indifference begun*. And this is the case where *consent* on one side adds to the obligation on the other. What then but remorse can follow a forcible attempt?

Do not even chaste lovers choose to be alone in their courtship preparations, ashamed to have even a child to witness to their foolish actions, and more foolish expressions?—Is this deified passion, in its greatest altitudes, fitted to stand the day?—Do not the lovers, when mutual consent awaits their wills, retire to coverts and to darkness, to complete their wishes? And shall such a sneaking passion as this, which can be so easily gratified by viler objects, be permitted to debase the noblest?

Were not the delays of thy vile purposes owing more to the awe which her majestic virtue has inspired thee with, than to thy want of adroitness in villainy (I *must* write my free sentiments in this case; for have I not *seen* the angel?); I should be ready to censure some of thy contrivances and pretences to suspend the expected day as *trite*, *stale*, and (to me, who know thy intention) *poor*; and too often resorted to, as nothing comes of them, to be gloried in; particularly that of Mennell, the vapourish lady, and the ready-furnished house.

She must have thought so too, at times, and in her heart despised thee for them, or love thee (ungrateful as thou art) to her misfortune; as well as entertain hope against probability. But this would afford another warning to the sex, were they to know her story; as it would show them what poor pretences they must *seem* to be satisfied with, if once they put themselves into the power of a designing man.

If *trial* only was thy end, as once was thy pretence,^a enough surely hast thou tried this paragon of virtue and vigilance. But I knew thee too well to expect, at the *time*, that thou wouldst stop there. Men of our cast, whenever they form a design upon any of the sex, put no other bound to the views than what want of power gives them. I knew that from one advantage gained, thou wouldst proceed to attempt another. Thy habitual aversion to wedlock too well I knew; and indeed thou avowest thy hope to bring her to *cohabitation*, in that very letter in which thou pretendest *trial* to be thy principal view.^b

But do not even thy own frequent and involuntary remorses, when thou hast time, place, company, and every other circumstance to favour thee in thy wicked design, convince thee that there can be no room for a hope so presumptuous?— Why then, since thou wouldst choose to marry her rather than lose her, wilt thou make her hate thee for ever?

But if thou darest to meditate *personal* trial, and art sincere in thy resolution to reward her as she behaves in it, let me beseech thee to remove her from this vile house: that will be to give her and thy conscience fair play. So entirely now does the sweet deluded excellence depend upon her supposed happier prospects, that thou needest not to fear that she will fly from thee, or that she will wish to have recourse to that scheme of Miss Howe, which has put thee upon what thou callest thy *master-strokes*.

But whatever be thy determination on this head; and if I write not in time, but that thou hast actually pulled off the mask; let it not be one of thy devices, if thou wouldst avoid the curses of every heart, and hereafter of thy own, to give her, no not for one hour (be her resentment ever so great), into the power of that villainous woman, who has, if possible, less remorse than thyself; and whose *trade* it is to break the resisting spirit, and utterly to ruin the heart unpractised in evil.—Oh Lovelace, Lovelace, how many dreadful stories could this horrid woman tell the sex! And shall that of Miss Clarissa Harlowe swell the guilty list?

But this I might have spared. Of this, devil as thou art, thou canst not be capable.

a   See p. 430, Letter 110.
b   pp. 431, 436.

Thou couldst not enjoy a triumph so disgraceful to thy wicked pride, as well as to humanity.

Shouldst thou think that the melancholy spectacle hourly before me has made me more serious than usual, perhaps thou wilt not be mistaken. But nothing more is to be inferred from hence (were I even to return to my former courses), but that whenever the time of cool reflection comes, whether brought on by our own disasters, or by those of others, we shall undoubtedly, if capable of thought, and if we have time for it, think in the same manner.

We neither of us are such fools as to disbelieve a futurity, or to think, whatever be our practice, that we came hither by chance, and for no end but to do all the mischief that we have in our power to do—Nor am I ashamed to own that in the prayers which my poor uncle makes me read to him, in the absence of a very good clergyman who regularly attends him, I do not forget to put in a word or two for myself.

If, Lovelace, thou laughest at me, thy ridicule will be more conformable to thy *actions*, than to thy *belief—Devils believe and tremble*.[3] Canst thou be more abandoned than they?

And here let me add, with regard to my poor old man, that I often wish thee present but for one half hour in a day, to see the dregs of a gay life running off in the most excruciating tortures that the colic, the stone, and the gangrene, can unitedly inflict; and to hear him bewail the dissoluteness of his past life in the bitterest anguish of a spirit every hour expecting to be called to its last account— Yet, by all his confessions, he has not to accuse himself in sixty-seven years of life, of half the *very* vile enormities which you and I have committed in the last seven only.

I conclude with recommending to thy serious consideration all I have written, as proceeding from the heart and soul of

Thy assured friend,
JOHN BELFORD

Letter 223: MR LOVELACE TO JOHN BELFORD, ESQ.

Tuesday, p.m., June 6

DIFFICULTIES still to be got over in procuring this plaguy licence. I ever hated, and ever shall hate, these spiritual lawyers, and their court.

And now, Jack, if I have not secured *victory*, I have a *retreat*.

But hold—Thy servant with a letter—

A confounded long one! though not a narrative one—Once more in behalf of the lady.—Lie thee down oddity! What canst thou write that can have force upon me at this crisis?—And have I not, as I went along, made thee to say all that was necessary for thee to say?

Yet once more, I'll take thee up.

Trite, stale, poor (sayest thou) are some of my contrivances? That of the widow's particularly!—I have no patience with thee—Had not that contrivance its effect at the time, for a procrastination?—And had I not then reason to fear that she would find enough to make her dislike this house? And was it not right (intending what I intended) to lead her on from time to time, with a notion that a house of her own would be ready for her soon, in order to induce her to continue here till it was?

Trite, stale, and *poor!*—Thou art a silly fellow, and no judge, when thou sayest this. Had I not, like a blockhead, revealed to thee, as I *went along*, the secret purposes of my heart, but had kept all in, till the event had explained my mysteries, I would have defied thee to have been able, any more than the lady, to have guessed at what was to befall her, till it had actually come to pass. Nor doubt I in this case that, instead of presuming to reflect upon her for credulity, as *loving me to her misfortune*, and for *hoping against probability*, thou wouldst have been readier by far to censure her for nicety and overscrupulousness. And let me tell thee, that had she loved me, as I wished her to love me, she could not possibly have been so very apprehensive of my designs; nor so ready to be influenced by Miss Howe's precautions, as she has always been, although my general character made not for me with her.

But in thy opinion, I suffer for that simplicity in my contrivances which is their principal excellence. No machinery make I necessary. No unnatural flights aim I at. All pure nature, taking advantage of nature, as nature tends; and so simple my devices, that when they are known, thou, even thou, imaginest thou couldst have thought of the same. And indeed thou seemest to *own* that the slight thou puttest upon them is owing to my letting thee into them beforehand; undistinguishing, as well as ungrateful as thou art!

Yet, after all, I would not have thee think that I do not know my weak places. I have formerly told thee that it is difficult for the ablest general to say what he *will* do, or what he *can* do, when he is obliged to regulate his motions by those of a watchful enemy.[a] If thou givest due weight to this consideration, thou wilt not wonder that I should make many marches and countermarches, some of which may appear to a slight observer unnecessary.

But let me cursorily enter into this debate with thee on this subject, now I am within sight of my journey's end.

Abundance of impertinent things thou tellest me in this letter; some of which thou hadst from myself; others that I knew before.

All that thou sayest in this charming creature's praise is short of what I have said and written on this inexhaustible subject.

Her virtue, her resistance, which are her merits, are my *stimulatives*. Have I not told thee so twenty times over?

Devil, as these girls between them call me, what of devil am I, but in my *contrivances?* I am not more a devil than others, in the *end* I aim at; for when I have carried my point, it is still but *one* seduction. And I have perhaps been spared the guilt of many seductions in the time.

What of uncommon would there be in this case, but for her watchfulness?—As well as I love intrigue and stratagem, dost think that I had not rather have gained my end with less trouble and less guilt?

The man, let me tell thee, who is as wicked as he *can* be, is a worse man than I

a p. 473.

am. Let me ask any rake in England, if, resolving to carry his point, he would have been so long about it? or have had so much compunction as I have had?

Were every rake, nay, were every man, to sit down, as I do, and write all that enters into his head or into his heart, and to accuse himself with equal freedom and truth, what an army of miscreants should I have to keep me in countenance!

It is a maxim with some that if they are left alone with a woman, and make not an attempt upon her, she will think herself affronted—Are not such men as these worse than I am?—What an opinion must they have of the whole sex?

Let me defend the sex I so dearly love—If these elder brethren of ours think they have general reason for their assertion, they must have kept very bad company, or must judge of women's hearts by their own. She must be an abandoned woman, who will not shrink as a snail into its shell, at a gross and sudden attempt. A modest woman must be naturally cold, reserved, and shy. She cannot be so much and so soon affected as libertines are apt to imagine; and must, at least, have some confidence in the honour and silence of a man, before desire can possibly put forth in her, to encourage and meet his flame. For my own part, I have been always decent in the company of women, till I was sure of them. Nor have I ever offered a *great* offence, till I have found *little* ones passed over; and that they shunned me not, when they knew my character.

My divine Clarissa has puzzled me, and beat me out of my play. At one time I hoped to overcome by *intimidating* her, at another by *love*; by the amorous *see-saw*, as I have called it.[a] And I have only now to join *surprise* to the other two, and see what can be done by all three.

And whose property, I pray thee, shall I invade, if I pursue my schemes of love and vengeance?—Have not those who have a right in her, renounced that right?—Have they not wilfully exposed her to dangers?—yet must know that such a woman would be considered as lawful prize by as many as could have the opportunity to attempt her?—And had they not thus cruelly exposed her, is she not a *single woman?*—And need I tell thee, Jack, that men of our cast, the *best* of them (the *worst* stick at nothing) think it a great grace and favour done to the married men if they leave them their wives to themselves, and compound for their sisters, daughters, wards, and nieces?—Shocking as these principles must be to a reflecting mind; yet such thou knowest are the principles of thousands (who would not act by the sex as I have acted by them, when in my power); and as often carried into practice as their opportunities or courage will permit—Such therefore have no right to blame me.

Thou repeatedly pleadest her sufferings from her family. But I have too often answered this plea to need to say any more now, than that she has not suffered for *my sake*. For has she not been made the victim of the malice of her rapacious brother and envious sister, who only waited for an occasion to ruin her with her other relations; and took this as the first, to drive her out of the house, and, as it happened, into my arms?—Thou knowest how much *against her inclination*.

As for her *own* sins, how many has the dear creature to answer for to *love* and to *me!*—Twenty [times], and twenty times twenty, has she not told me that she refused not the odious Solmes in favour to me? And as often has she not offered to renounce me for the single life, if the implacables would have received her on that condition?—What repetitions does thy weak pity make me guilty of?

a p. 424.

To look a little farther back: canst thou forget what my sufferings were from this haughty beauty, in the whole time of my attendance upon her proud motions, in the purlieus of Harlowe Place, and at the little White Hart at Neale, as we called it?—Did I not threaten vengeance upon her then (and had I not reason?) for disappointing me (I will give but this one instance) of a promised interview?

Oh Jack! what a night had I of it in the bleak coppice adjoining to her father's paddock!—My linen and wig frozen; my limbs absolutely numbed; my fingers only sensible of so much warmth as enabled me to hold a pen; and that obtained by rubbing the skin off, and beating with my hands my shivering sides—Kneeling on the hoar moss on one knee, writing on the other, if the stiff scrawl could be called writing—My feet, by the time I had done, seeming to have taken root, and actually unable to support me for some minutes!—Love and rage kept then my heart in motion (and only love and rage could do it), or how much more than I *did* suffer, must I have suffered?

I told thee, at my melancholy return, what were the contents of the letter I wrote.[a] And I showed thee afterwards her tyrannical answer to it.[b] Thou then, Jack, lovedst thy friend; and pitiedst thy poor suffering Lovelace. Even the affronted god of love approved then of my threatened vengeance against the fair promiser; though now with thee in the day of my power, forgetful of the night of my sufferings, he is become an advocate for her.

Nay, was it not he himself that brought to me my adorable *Nemesis*; and both together put me upon this very vow, 'That I would never rest till I had drawn in this goddess-daughter of the Harlowes to cohabit with me; and that in the face of all their proud family?'—Nor canst thou forget this vow—At this instant I have thee before me, as then thou sorrowfully lookedst.

Thy strong features glowing with compassion for me; thy lips twisted; thy forehead furrowed; thy whole face drawn out from the stupid round into the ghastly oval; every muscle contributing its power to complete the aspect grievous; and not one word couldst thou utter, but *amen* to my vow.

And what of distinguishing love, or favour, or confidence, have I had from her since, to make me forego this vow?

I *renewed* it not, indeed, afterwards; and actually for a long season, was willing to forget it; till repetitions of the same faults revived the remembrance of the former—And now adding to those the contents of some of Miss Howe's virulent letters, so lately come at, what canst thou say for the rebel, consistent with thy loyalty to thy friend?

Every man to his genius and constitution. Hannibal was called *The father of warlike stratagems*. Had Hannibal been a private man, and turned his plotting head against the *other sex*; or had I been a general, and turned mine against such of my fellow-creatures of *my own*, as I thought myself entitled to consider as my enemies because they were born and lived in a different climate—Hannibal would have done less mischief—Lovelace more—That would have been the difference.

Not a sovereign on earth, if he be not a *good man*, and if he be of a warlike temper, but must do a thousand times more mischief than me. And why? Because he has it in his *power* to do more.

An honest man, perhaps thou'lt say, will not wish to have it in his power to do

a   p. 270.
b   p. 271.

hurt. He *ought not*, let me tell him: for, if he have it, a thousand to one but it makes him both wanton and wicked.

In what, then, am I so *singularly* vile?

In my *contrivances*, thou'lt say (for thou art my echo), if not in my proposed *end* of them.

How difficult does every man find it, as well as me, to forgo a predominant passion? I have three passions that sway me by turns; all imperial ones. Love, revenge, ambition, or a desire of conquest.

As to this particular contrivance of Tomlinson and the uncle, which thou'lt think a black one perhaps; that had been spared, had not these *innocent* ladies put me upon finding a husband for their Mrs Townsend. That device, therefore, is but a *preventive* one. Thinkest thou that I could bear to be outwitted? And may not this very contrivance save a world of mischief; for, dost thou think I would have tamely given up the lady to Townsend's tars?

What meanest thou, except to overthrow thy own plea, when thou sayest, *that men of our cast know no other bound to their wickedness, but want of power*; yet knowest this lady to be in mine?

Enough, sayest thou, *have I tried this paragon of virtue*. Not so; for I have not tried her at all—All I have been doing is but preparation to a trial.

But thou art concerned for the *means* that I may have recourse to in the *trial*, and for my *veracity*.

Silly fellow!—Did ever any man, thinkest thou, deceive a girl but at the expense of his veracity? How otherwise can he be said to *deceive*?

As to the *means*, thou dost not imagine that I expect a *direct* consent—My main hope is but in a yielding reluctance, without which I will be sworn, whatever rapes have been attempted, none ever were committed, one person to one person. And good Queen Bess of England, had she been living, and appealed to, would have declared herself of my mind.

It would not be amiss for the sex to know what our opinions are upon this subject—I love to warn them. I wish no man to succeed with them but myself. I told thee once, that *though a rake, I am not a rake's friend*.[a]

Thou sayest that I ever hated wedlock. And true thou sayest. And yet *as* true, when thou tellest me that I *would rather marry than lose this lady*. And *will she detest me for ever*, thinkest thou, if I try her, and succeed not?—Take care—Take care, Jack!—Seest thou not that thou warnest me, that I do not try, without resolving to conquer?

I must add, that I have for some time been convinced that I have done wrong to scribble to thee so freely as I have done (and the more so, if I make the lady legally mine); for has not every letter I have written to thee been a bill of indictment against myself? I may partly curse my vanity for it; and I think I will refrain for the future; for thou art really very impertinent.

A good man, I own, might urge many of the things thou urgest; but, by my soul, they come very awkwardly from thee. And thou must be sensible, that I can answer every tittle of what thou writest, upon the foot of the *maxims we have long held and pursued*—By the specimen above, thou wilt see that I can.

And prithee tell me, Jack, what but this that follows would have been the

a   p. 430.

epitome of mine and my beloved's story, *after ten years cohabitation*; had I never written to thee upon the subject, and had I not been my own accuser?

'Robert Lovelace, a notorious woman-eater, makes his addresses in an honourable way to Miss Clarissa Harlowe; a young lady of the highest merit—fortunes on both sides out of the question.

'After encouragement given, he is insulted by her violent brother; who thinks it his interest to discountenance the match; and who at last challenging him, is obliged to take his worthless life at his hands.

'The family, as much enraged as if he had *taken* the life he *gave*, insult him personally, and find out an odious lover for the young lady.

'To avoid a forced marriage, she is prevailed upon to throw herself into Mr Lovelace's protection.

'Yet, disclaiming any passion for him, she repeatedly offers to renounce him for ever if, on that condition, her relations will receive her, and free her from the address of the hated lover.

'Mr Lovelace, a man of strong passions and, as some say, of great pride, thinks himself under very little obligation to her on this account; and not being naturally fond of marriage, and having so much reason to hate her relations, endeavours to prevail upon her to live with him what he calls *the life of honour*. And at last, by stratagem, art, and contrivance, prevails.

'He resolves never to marry any other woman: takes a pride to have her called by his name: church-rite all the difference between them: treats her with deserved tenderness. Nobody questions their marriage but these proud relations of hers whom he wishes to question it. Every year a charming boy. Fortunes to support the increasing family with splendour—a tender father. Always a warm friend; a generous landlord, and a punctual paymaster—Now and then, however, perhaps, indulging with a new object, in order to bring him back with greater delight to his charming Clarissa—His only fault love of the sex—which nevertheless the women say will cure itself—Defensible thus far, that he breaks no contracts by his rovings—'

And what is there so very greatly amiss, as the world goes, in all this?—

Let me aver that there are thousands and ten thousands, who have worse stories to tell than this would appear to be, had I not interested thee in the progress to my great end. And besides, thou knowest that the character I gave myself to Joseph Leman, as to my treatment of my mistresses, is pretty near the truth.[a]

Were I to be as much in earnest in my defence as thou art warm in my arraignment, I could convince thee, by other arguments, observations, and comparisons (*Is not all human good and evil comparative?*) that though from my ingenuous temper (writing only to thee, who art master of every secret of my heart) I am so ready to accuse myself in my narrations; yet I have something to say *for* myself *to* myself, as I go along; though no one else, perhaps, that was not a rake would allow any weight to it—And this caution might I give to thousands, who would stoop for a stone to throw at me: 'See that your own *predominant passions*, whatever they be, hurry you not into as much wickedness, as *mine* do *me*—See, if ye happen to be better than me in some things, that ye are not worse in others; and in points too that may be of more extensive bad consequence, than that of seducing

a   p. 495.

a girl (and taking care of her afterwards), who from her cradle is armed with cautions against the delusions of men.' And yet I am not so partial to my own faults as to think lightly of *that*, when I allow myself to think.

Another grave thing will I add, now my hand's in: 'So dearly do I love the sex, that had I found that a character for virtue had been generally necessary to recommend me to them, I should have had a much greater regard to my morals, as to the sex, than I have had.'

To sum up all—I am sufficiently apprised that men of worthy and honest hearts, who never allowed themselves in *premeditated* evil, and who take into the account the excellencies of this fine creature, will, and must, not only condemn, but *abhor* me, were they to know as much of me as thou dost—But, methinks, I would be glad to escape the censure of those men, and of those women too, who have never known what capital trials and temptations are; who have no genius for enterprise; and most particularly of those who have only kept their secret better than I have kept, or wished to keep, mine.

I THREATENED above to refrain writing to thee. But take it not to heart, Jack— I must write on, and cannot help it.

Letter 224: MR LOVELACE TO JOHN BELFORD, ESQ.

Wednesday night, 11 o'clock

FAITH, Jack, thou hadst half undone me with thy nonsense, though I would not own it in my yesterday's letter; my conscience of thy party before. But I think I am my own man again.

So near to execution my plot! So near springing my mine! All agreed upon between the women and me, or I believe thou hadst overthrown me.

I have time for a few lines preparative to what is to happen in an hour or two; and I love to write to the moment—

We have been extremely happy. How many agreeable days have we known together! What may the next two hours produce!—

When I parted with my charmer (which I did with infinite reluctance, half an hour ago), it was upon her promise that she would not sit up to write or read. For so engaging was the conversation to me (and indeed my behaviour throughout the whole of it was confessedly agreeable to her), that I insisted, if she did not directly retire to rest, that she should add another happy hour to the former.

To have sat up writing or reading half the night, as she sometimes does, would have frustrated my view, as thou wilt observe when my little plot unravels.

WHAT—what—what now!—bounding villain! wouldst thou choke me!— I was speaking to my heart, Jack!—It was then at my throat—And what is all this for?—These shy ladies, how, when a man thinks himself near the mark, do they tempest him!—

Is all ready, Dorcas? Has my beloved kept her word with me?—Whether are these billowy heavings owing more to love or to fear? I cannot tell for the soul of me which I have most of. If I can but take her before her apprehension, before her eloquence, is awake—

Limbs, why thus convulsed!—Knees, till now so firmly knit, why thus relaxed? Why beat ye thus together? Will not these trembling fingers, which twice have refused to direct the pen, and thus curvedly deform the paper, fail me in the arduous moment?

Once again, Why and for what all these convulsions? This project is not to end in matrimony surely!

But the consequences must be greater than I had thought of till this moment— My beloved's destiny or my own may depend upon the issue of the two next hours!—

I will recede, I think!—

SOFT, oh virgin saint, and safe as soft, be thy slumbers!—

I will now once more turn to my friend Belford's letter. Thou shalt have fair play, my charmer. I'll re-peruse what thy advocate has to say for thee. Weak arguments will do, in the frame I am in!—

BUT, what's the matter!—What's the matter!—What a *double*—But the uproar abates!—What a *double coward* am I?—Or is it that I am taken in a cowardly minute? for heroes have their fits of *fear*; cowards their *brave* moments: and virtuous ladies, all but my Clarissa, their moment *critical*—

But thus coolly enjoying thy reflections in a hurricane!—Again the confusion's renewed!—

What! Where!—How came it!—

Is my beloved safe!—

Oh wake not too roughly my beloved!—

Letter 225: MR LOVELACE TO JOHN BELFORD, ESQ.

Thursday morning, five o'clock (June 8)
Now is my reformation secured; for I never shall love any other woman!—Oh she is all variety! She must be ever new to me!—*Imagination* cannot form; much less can the pencil paint; nor can the soul of painting, *poetry*, describe an angel so exquisitely, so elegantly lovely!—But I will not by anticipation pacify thy impatience. Although the subject is too hallowed for profane contemplation, yet shalt thou have the whole before thee as it passed: and this not from a spirit wantoning in description upon so rich a subject; but with a design to put a bound to thy roving thoughts—It will be iniquity greater than a Lovelace ever was guilty of, to carry them farther than I shall acknowledge.

Thus then, connecting my last with the present, I lead to it.

Didst thou not, by the conclusion of my former, perceive the consternation I was in, just as I was about to re-peruse thy letter, in order to prevail upon myself to recede from my purpose of awaking in terrors my slumbering charmer? And what dost thou think was the matter?

I'll tell thee—

At a little after two, when the whole house was still, or seemed to be so, and, as it proved, my Clarissa abed and fast asleep; I also in a manner undressed for an hour before, and in my gown and slippers though, to oblige thee, writing on—I was alarmed by a trampling noise overhead, and a confused buzz of mixed voices, some louder than others, like scolding, and little short of screaming, all raised to vocatives, as in a fright: and while I was wondering what could be the matter, downstairs ran Dorcas, and at my door, in an accent rather frightedly and hoarsely inward than shrilly clamorous, cried out Fire! Fire! And this the more alarmed me, as she seemed to endeavour to cry out louder, but could not.

My pen (its last scrawl a benediction on my beloved) dropped from my fingers; and up started I; and making but three steps to the door, opened it, and cried Where! Where! almost as much terrified as the wench. While she, more than half-undressed, her petticoats in her hand, unable to speak distinctly, pointed up-stairs.

I was there in a moment, and found all owing to the carelessness of Mrs Sinclair's cook-maid, who, having sat up to read the simple history of Dorastus and Faunia[1] when she should have been in bed, had set fire to an old pair of calico window-curtains.

She had had the presence of mind in her fright, to tear down the half-burnt valance as well as curtains, and had got them, though blazing, into the chimney, by the time I came up; so that I had the satisfaction to find the danger happily over.

Meantime Dorcas, after she had directed me upstairs, not knowing the worst was over, and expecting every minute the house would be in a blaze, out of tender regard for her lady (I shall for ever love the wench for it) ran to her door, and rapping loudly at it, in a recovered voice, cried out with a shrillness equal to her love, Fire! Fire!—The house is on fire!—Rise, madam!—This instant rise—if you would not be burnt in your bed!

No sooner had she made this dreadful outcry, but I heard her lady's door with hasty violence unbar, unbolt, unlock, and open, and my charmer's voice sounding like that of one going into a fit.

You may believe how much I was affected. I trembled with concern for her, and hastened down faster than the alarm of fire had made me run up, in order to satisfy her that all the danger was over.

When I had *flown down* to her chamber door, there I beheld the charmingest creature in the world, supporting herself on the arm of the gasping Dorcas, sighing, trembling, and ready to faint, with nothing on but an under-petticoat, her lovely bosom half-open, and her feet just slipped into her shoes. As soon as she saw me, she panted, and struggled to speak; but could only say, oh, Mr Lovelace! and down was ready to sink.

I clasped her in my arms with an ardour she never felt before: My dearest life! fear nothing: I have been up—the danger is over—the fire is got under—And how (foolish devil! to Dorcas) could you thus, by your hideous yell, alarm and frighten my angel!

Oh Jack! how her sweet bosom, as I clasped her to mine, heaved and panted! I could even distinguish her dear heart flutter, flutter, flutter, against mine; and for a few minutes, I feared she would go into fits.

Lest the half-lifeless charmer should catch cold in this undress, I lifted her to her bed, and sat down by her upon the side of it, endeavouring with the utmost tenderness, as well of action as expression, to dissipate her terrors.

But what did I get by this my generous care of her, and by my *successful* endeavour to bring her to herself?—Nothing, ungrateful as she was! but the most passionate exclamations: for we had both already forgot the occasion, dreadful as it was, which had thrown her into my arms; I, from the joy of encircling the almost disrobed body of the loveliest of her sex; she, from the greater terrors that arose from finding herself in my arms, and both seated on the bed from which she had been so lately frighted.

And now, Belford, reflect upon the distance the watchful charmer had hitherto kept me at. Reflect upon my love, and upon my sufferings for her: reflect upon her vigilance, and how long I had lain in wait to elude it; the awe I had stood in, because of her frozen virtue and over-niceness; and that I never before was so happy with her; and then think how ungovernable must be my transports in those happy moments!—And yet, in my own account, I was both decent and generous. The following lines, altered to the first person, come nearest of any I can recollect, to the rapturous occasion:

> Bowing, I kneel'd, and her forc'd hand I press'd,
> With sweet compulsion, to my beating breast;
> O'er it, in ecstasy, my lips bent low,
> And tides of sighs 'twixt her grasp'd fingers flow.
> High beat my hurry'd pulse, at each fierce kiss,
> And ev'ry burning sinew ach'd with bliss.[2]

But, far from being affected by an address so fervent (although from a man she had so lately owned a regard for, and with whom, but an hour or two before, she had parted with so much satisfaction), that I never saw a bitterer, or more moving grief, when she came fully to herself.

She appealed to Heaven against my *treachery*, as she called it; while I, by the most solemn vows, pleaded my own equal fright, and the reality of the danger that had alarmed us both.

She conjured me, in the most solemn and affecting manner, by turns threatening and soothing, to quit her apartment, and permit her to hide herself from the light, and from every human eye.

I besought her pardon, yet could not avoid offending; and repeatedly vowed that the next morning's sun should witness our espousals. But taking, I suppose, all my protestations of this kind, as an indication that I intended to proceed to the last extremity, she would hear nothing that I said; but, redoubling her struggles to get from me, in broken accents, and exclamations the most vehement, she protested that she would not survive what she called a treatment so disgraceful and villainous; and, looking all wildly round her as if for some instrument of mischief, she espied a pair of sharp-pointed scissors on a chair by the bedside, and endeavoured to catch them up, with design to make her words good on the spot.

Seeing her desperation, I begged her to be pacified; that she would hear me speak but one word, declaring that I intended no dishonour to her: and having seized the scissors, I threw them into the chimney; and she still insisting vehemently upon my distance, I permitted her to take the chair.

But, oh the sweet discomposure!—Her bared shoulders and arms, so inimitably fair and lovely: her spread hands crossed over her charming neck; yet not half concealing its glossy beauties: the scanty coat, as she rose from me, giving the whole of her admirable shape and fine-turned limbs: her eyes running over, yet seeming to threaten future vengeance: and at last her lips uttering what every indignant look and glowing feature portended; exclaiming as if I had done the worst I could do, and vowing never to forgive me; wilt thou wonder that I could avoid resuming the incensed, the already too-much-provoked fair one?

I did; and clasped her once more to my bosom: but, considering the delicacy of her frame, her force was amazing, and showed how much in earnest she was in her resentment; for it was with the utmost difficulty that I was able to hold her: nor could I prevent her sliding through my arms, to fall upon her knees: which she did at my feet. And there, in the anguish of her soul, her streaming eyes lifted up to my face with supplicating softness, hands folded, dishevelled hair; for her night head-dress having fallen off in her struggling, her charming tresses fell down in naturally shining ringlets, as if officious to conceal the dazzling beauties of her neck and shoulders; her lovely bosom too heaving with sighs, and broken sobs, as if to aid her quivering lips in pleading for her—in this manner, but when her grief gave way to her speech, in words pronounced with that emphatical propriety which distinguishes this admirable creature in her elocution from all the women I ever heard speak; did she implore my compassion, and my honour.

'Consider me, *dear* Lovelace,' were her charming words! 'on my knees I beg you to consider me, as a poor creature who has no protector but you; who has no defence but your honour: by that honour! by your humanity! by all you have vowed! I conjure you not to make me abhor myself! Not to make me vile in my own eyes!'

I mentioned the morrow as the happiest day of my life.

Tell me not of tomorrow; if indeed you mean me honourably, *now*, this very instant NOW! you must show it, and begone! You can never in a whole long life repair the evils you may NOW make me suffer!

Wicked wretch!—insolent villain!—Yes, she called me insolent villain, although so much in my power! And for what?—only for kissing (with passion indeed) her inimitable neck, her lips, her cheeks, her forehead, and her streaming eyes, as this assemblage of beauties offered itself at once to my ravished sight; she continuing kneeling at my feet, as I sat.

If I *am* a villain, madam—And then my grasping but trembling hand—I hope I did not hurt the tenderest and loveliest of all her beauties—If I am a villain, madam—

She tore my ruffle, shrunk from my happy hand, with amazing force and agility, as with my other arm I would have encircled her waist.

Indeed you are!—The worst of villains!—Help! dear blessed people! and screamed—No help for a poor creature!—

Am I then a villain, madam?—*Am* I then a villain, say you?—and clasped both my arms about her, offering to raise her to my bounding heart—

Oh no!—and yet you are!—And again I was her *dear* Lovelace!—Her hands again clasped over her charming bosom—Kill me! kill me!—if I am odious enough in your eyes, to deserve this treatment; and I will thank you!—Too long, much too long, has my life been a burden to me!—or, wildly looking all around her, give me but the means, and I will instantly convince you that my honour is dearer to me than my life!

Then, with still folded hands, and fresh-streaming eyes, I was her *blessed* Lovelace; and she would thank me with her latest breath if I would permit her to make that preference, or free her from farther indignities.

I sat suspended for a moment. By my soul, thought I, thou art upon full proof an angel and no woman! Still, however, close clasping her to my bosom, as I had raised her from her knees, she again slid through my arms, and dropped upon them:—'See, Mr Lovelace!—Good God! that I should live to see this hour, and to bear this treatment!—see, at your feet a poor creature, imploring your pity, who for your sake is abandoned of all the world! Let not my father's curse thus dreadfully operate! Be not *you* the inflicter, who have been the *cause* of it! But spare me! I beseech you spare me!—for how have I deserved this treatment from you?—For your own sake, if not for my sake, and as you would that God Almighty, in your last hour, should have mercy upon you, spare me!'—

What heart but must have been penetrated?

I would again have raised the dear suppliant from her knees; but she would not be raised, till my softened mind, she said, had yielded to her prayer, and bid her rise to be innocent.

Rise then, my angel, rise, and be what you are, and all you wish to be! Only pronounce me pardoned for what has passed, and tell me you will continue to look upon me with that eye of favour and serenity, which I have been blessed with for some days past, and I will submit to my beloved conqueress, whose power never was at so great an height with me, as now; and retire to my apartment.

God Almighty, said she, hear your prayers in your most arduous moments, as you have heard mine! And now leave me, this moment leave me, to my own recollection: in *that* you will leave me to misery enough, and more than you ought to wish to your bitterest enemy.

Impute not everything, my best beloved, to design; for design it was not—

Oh Mr Lovelace!—

Upon my soul, madam, the fire was real—(and so it was, Jack!)—The house might have been consumed by it, as you will be convinced in the morning by ocular demonstration.

Oh Mr Lovelace!—

Let my passion for you, madam, and the unexpected meeting of you at your chamber door, in an attitude so charming—

Leave me, leave me, this moment!—I beseech you, leave me; looking wildly and in confusion, now about her, and now upon herself.

Excuse me, dearest creature, for those liberties which, innocent as they were, your too great delicacy may make you take amiss.

No more! no more!—Leave me, I beseech you! Again looking upon herself, and around her, in a sweet confusion.— Begone! Begone!—Then weeping, she struggled vehemently to withdraw her hands, which all the while I held between mine—Her struggles! Oh what additional charms, as I now reflect, did her struggles give to every feature, every limb, of a person so sweetly elegant and lovely!

Impossible! my dearest life, till you pronounce my pardon!—Say but you forgive me!—Say you do!

I beseech you, begone! Leave me to myself, that I may think what I *can* do, and what I *ought* to do.

That, my dearest creature, is not enough. You must tell me that I am forgiven; that you will see me tomorrow, as if nothing had happened.

And then, clasping her again in my arms, hoping she would not forgive me—

I will—I do forgive you—wretch that you are!

Nay, my Clarissa! And is it such a reluctant pardon, mingled with a word so upbraiding, that I am to be put off with, when you are thus (clasping her close to me) in my power?

I do, I *do* forgive you!

Heartily?

Yes, heartily!

And freely?

Freely!

And will you look upon me tomorrow, as if nothing had passed?

Yes, yes!

I cannot take these peevish affirmatives, so much like intentional negatives!— Say you will, upon your honour!

Upon my honour, then—Oh now, begone! begone! and never—

What, never, my angel!—Is this forgiveness?

Never, said she, let what has passed be remembered more!

I insisted upon one kiss to seal my pardon—and retired like a fool, a woman's fool, as I was!—I sneakingly retired!—Couldst thou have believed it?

But I had no sooner entered my own apartment, than, reflecting upon the opportunity I had lost, and that all I had gained was but an increase of my own difficulties; and upon the ridicule I should meet with below, upon a weakness so much out of my usual character; I repented, and hastened back, in hope that through the distress of mind which I left her in, she had not so soon fastened her door; and I was fully resolved to execute all my purposes, be the consequence what it would; for, thought I, I have already sinned beyond *cordial* forgiveness, I doubt; and if fits and desperation ensue, I can but marry at last, and then I shall make her amends.

But I was justly punished—for her door was fast: and hearing her sigh and sob, as if her heart would burst, My beloved creature, said I, rapping gently, and her sobbings ceasing, I want but to say three words to you, which must be the most acceptable you ever heard from me. Let me see you but for one moment.

I thought I heard her coming to open the door, and my heart leaped in that hope; but it was only to draw another bolt to make it still the faster, and she either could not, or would not, answer me, but retired to the further end of her apartment, to her closet, probably: and more like a fool than before, again I sneaked away.

This was my mine, my plot!—And this was all I made of it!

I love her more than ever!—And well I may!—Never saw I such polished ivory as her arms and shoulders seemed to be; never touched I velvet so soft as her skin. Then such an elegance! Oh Belford, she is all perfection! Her pretty foot, in her struggling, losing her shoe but just slipped on, as I told thee, equally white and delicate as the hand of any other lady, or even as her own hand!

But seest thou not, that I have a claim of merit for a grace that everybody hitherto had denied me? And that is, for a capacity of being moved by prayers and tears: Where, where, on this occasion, was the *callus*, where the flint, that my heart was said to be surrounded by?

This, indeed, is the first instance, in the like case, that ever I was wrought upon. But why? Because I never before encountered a resistance so much in earnest: a resistance, in short, so irresistible.

What a triumph has her sex obtained in my thoughts by this trial, and this resistance!

But if she can *now* forgive me—*Can!*—She *must*. Has she not upon her honour already done it?—But how will the dear creature keep that part of her promise, which engages her to see me in the morning as if nothing had happened?

She would give the world, I fancy, to have the first interview over!—She had not best reproach me—yet *not* to reproach me!—What a charming puzzle! Let her break her word with me at her peril. Fly me she cannot: no appeals lie from my tribunal—What friend has she in the world, if my compassion exert not itself in her favour?—And then the worthy Captain Tomlinson, and her Uncle Harlowe, will be able to make all up for me, be my next offence what it will.

As to thy apprehensions of her committing any rashness upon herself, whatever she might have done in her passion, if she could have seized upon her scissors, or found any other weapon, I dare say there is no fear of that from her *deliberate* mind. A man has trouble enough with these truly pious, and truly virtuous girls (now I believe there are such); he had need to have some benefit *from*, some security *in*, the rectitude of their minds.

In short, I fear nothing in this lady but grief; yet that's a slow worker, you know; and gives time to pop in a little joy between its sullen fits.

Letter 226: MR LOVELACE TO JOHN BELFORD, ESQ.

Thursday morning, eight o'clock

HER chamber door has not yet been opened. I must not expect she will breakfast with me: nor dine with me, I doubt. A little silly soul, what troubles does she make to herself by her over-niceness!—All I have done to her would have been looked upon as a frolic only, a romping-bout, and laughed off by nine parts in ten of the sex accordingly. The more she makes of it, the more painful to herself, as well as to me.

Why now, Jack, were it not better, upon *her own* notions, that she seemed not so sensible, as she will make herself to be if she is very angry?

But perhaps I am more afraid than I need. I believe I am. From her *over* niceness arises my fear, more than from any extraordinary reason for resentment. Next time, she may count herself very happy if she come off no worse.

The dear creature was so frightened, and so fatigued last night, no wonder she lies it out this morning.

I hope she has had more rest than I have had: soft and balmy, I hope, have been her slumbers, that she may meet me in tolerable temper. All sweetly blushing and confounded—I *know* how she will look!—But why should she, the *sufferer*, be ashamed, when I, the *trespasser*, am not?

But custom is a prodigious thing. The ladies are told how much their blushes heighten their graces: they practise for them therefore: blushes come as readily when they call them, as their tears: aye, that's it! While we men, taking blushes for a sign of guilt or sheepishness, are equally studious to suppress them.

BY my troth, Jack, I am half as much ashamed to see the women below, as my fair one can be to see me. I have not yet opened my door, that I may not be obtruded upon by them.

After all, what devils may one make of the sex! To what a height of—what shall I call it?—must those of it be arrived, who once loved a man with so much distinction as both Polly and Sally loved me, and yet can have got so much above the pangs of jealousy, so much above the mortifying reflections that arise from dividing and sharing with new objects, the affections of him they prefer to all others, as to wish for, and promote a competitorship in his love, and make their supreme delight consist in reducing others to their level!—For thou canst not imagine how even Sally Martin rejoiced last night in the thought that the lady's hour was approaching.

Past ten o'clock

I NEVER longed in my life for anything with so much impatience, as to see my charmer. She has been stirring, it seems, these two hours.

Dorcas just now tapped at her door, to take her morning commands.

She had none for her, was the answer.

She desired to know if she would not breakfast?

A sullen and low-voiced *negative* she received.

I will go myself.

THREE different times tapped I at the door, but had no answer.

Permit me, dearest creature, to inquire after your health. As you have not been seen today, I am impatient to know how you do.

Not a word of answer; but a deep sigh, even to sobbing.

Let me beg of you, madam, to accompany me up another pair of stairs—you'll rejoice to see what a happy escape we have all had.

A happy escape indeed, Jack!—for the fire had scorched the window-board, singed the hangings, and burned through the slit-deal lining of the window-jambs.

No answer, madam!—Am I not worthy of one word?—Is it thus you keep your promise with me?—Shall I not have the favour of your company for two minutes, only for two minutes, in the dining-room?

Hem!—and a deep sigh!—was all the answer.

Answer me, but how you do! Answer me but that you are well!—Is this the forgiveness that was the condition of my obedience?

Then, in a faintish but angry voice, Begone from my door!—wretch, inhuman, barbarous, and all that's base and treacherous!—Begone from my door! Nor tease thus a poor creature, entitled to protection, not outrage.

Well, madam, I see how you keep your word with me!—*If* a sudden impulse, the effects of an unthought-of accident, cannot be forgiven—

Oh the dreadful weight of a father's curse, thus in the letter of it so likely to be fulfilled!

And then her voice dying away into inarticulate murmurs, I looked through the keyhole, and saw her on her knees, her face, though not towards me, lifted up, as well as hands, and these folded, deprecating I suppose that gloomy tyrant's curse.

I could not help being moved.

My dearest life! admit me to your presence, but for two minutes, and confirm your promised pardon; and may lightning blast me on the spot if I offer anything but my penitence at a shrine so sacred!—I will afterwards leave you for the whole day; and till tomorrow morning; then to attend, with writings, all ready to sign, a licence obtained, or, if it cannot, a minister without one. This once, believe me. When you see the reality of the danger that gave occasion for this your unhappy resentment, you will think less hardly of me. And let me beseech you to perform a promise, on which I made a reliance not altogether ungenerous.

I cannot see you! Would to Heaven I never had! If I write, that's all I can do.

Let your writing then, my dearest life, confirm your promise. And I will withdraw in expectation of it.

Past eleven o'clock

JUST now she rung her bell for Dorcas; and, with her door in her hand, only half-opened, gave her a billet for me.

How did the dear creature look, Dorcas?

She was dressed. Turned her face quite from me. Sighed as if her heart would break.

Sweet creature!—I kissed the wet wafer, and drew it from the paper with my breath.

These are the contents—No inscriptive Sir! No Mr Lovelace!

I CANNOT see you: nor will I, if I can help it. Words cannot express the anguish of my soul on your baseness and ingratitude.

If the circumstances of things are such that I can have no way for reconciliation with those who would have been my natural protectors from such outrages, but through *you* (the only inducement I can have to stay a moment longer in your knowledge), pen and ink must be, at present, the only means of communication between us.

Vilest of men! and most detestable of plotters! how have I deserved from you the shocking indignities—But no more—only for your own sake, wish not, at least for a week to come, to see

The undeservedly injured and insulted,
CLARISSA HARLOWE

So thou seest, nothing could have stood me in stead but this plot of Tomlinson and her uncle: to what a pretty pass, nevertheless, have I brought myself!—Had Caesar been such a fool, he had never passed the Rubicon. But, after he *had* passed it, had he retreated, *re infecta*, intimidated by a senatorial edict, what a pretty figure would he have made in history!—I might have known that to attempt a robbery and put a person in bodily fear is as punishable as if the robbery had been actually committed.

But not to see her for a week!—Dear pretty soul! how she anticipates me in everything! The counsellor will have finished the writings, ready to sign, today or tomorrow at furthest: the licence with the parson, or the parson without the licence, must be also procured within the next four-and-twenty hours: Pritchard is as good as ready with his indentures tripartite: Tomlinson is at hand with a favourable answer from her uncle—*Yet not to see her for a week!*—Dear sweet soul!—Her good angel is gone a journey: is truanting at least. But nevertheless, in thy week's time, and much less, my charmer, I doubt not to have completed my triumph!

But what vexes me of all things is that such an excellent creature should break her word—Fie, fie, upon her!—but nobody is absolutely perfect! *'Tis human to err*, but *not to persevere*—I hope my charmer cannot be inhuman!

Letter 227: MR LOVELACE TO JOHN BELFORD, ESQ.

King's Arms, Pall Mall, Thursday, two o'clock
SEVERAL billets passed between us before I went out, by the internuncioship of Dorcas: for which reason mine are superscribed by her married name—She would not open her door to receive them; lest I should be near it, I suppose: so Dorcas was forced to put them under the door (after copying them for thee); and thence to take the answer. Read them, if thou wilt, at this place.

[Letter 227.1: Lovelace] to Mrs Lovelace

INDEED, my dearest life, you carry this matter too far. What will the people below, who suppose us one as to the ceremony, think of so great a niceness? Liberties so innocent; the occasion so accidental!—You will expose *yourself* as well as *me*—Hitherto they know nothing of what has passed. And what, indeed, *has* passed, to occasion all this resentment?—I am sure you will not by a breach of your word of honour give me reason to conclude that, had I *not* obeyed you, I could have fared no worse.

Most sincerely do I repent the offence given to your delicacy—But must I, for so accidental an occurrence, be branded by such shocking names? *Vilest of men*, and *most detestable of plotters*, are hard words!—from such a lady's pen too.

If you step up another pair of stairs, you'll be convinced that, however *detestable* to you, I am no *plotter* in this affair.

I must insist upon seeing you, in order to take your directions upon some of the subjects that we talked of yesterday in the evening.

All that's more than necessary is too much. I claim your promised pardon, and wish to plead it on my knees.

I beg your presence in the dining-room for one quarter of an hour, and I will then leave you for the day. I am, my dearest life,

Your ever-adoring and truly penitent,
LOVELACE

[Letter 227.2: Clarissa Harlowe] to Mr Lovelace

I WILL not see you. I cannot see you. I have no directions to give you. Let Providence decide for me as it pleases.

The more I reflect upon your vileness, your ungrateful, your barbarous vileness, the more I am exasperated against you.

You are the *last* person whose judgement I would take upon what is or is not carried too far, in matters of decency.

'Tis grievous to me to write, or even to think of you at present. Urge me no more then. Once more, I will *not* see you. Nor care I, now you have made me vile to myself, what other people think of me.

[Letter 227.3: Lovelace] to Mrs Lovelace

AGAIN, madam, I remind you of your promise: and beg leave to say I insist upon the performance of it.

Remember, dearest creature, that the fault of a blameable person cannot warrant a fault in one more perfect. Over-niceness may be under-niceness!

I cannot reproach myself with anything that deserves this high resentment.

I own that the violence of my passion for you might have carried me beyond fit bounds—but that your commands and adjurations had such a power over me at such a moment, I humbly presume to say deserves some consideration.

You enjoin me not to see you for a week. If I have not your pardon before Captain Tomlinson comes to town, what shall I say to *him*?

I beg once more your presence in the dining-room. By my soul, madam, I *must* see you.

I want to consult you about the licence, and other particulars of great importance. The people below think us married; and I cannot talk to you, the door between us, upon such subjects.

For Heaven's sake, favour me with your presence for a few minutes: and I will leave you for the day.

If I am to be forgiven, according to your promise, the earliest forgiveness must be the least painful to yourself, as well as to

Your truly contrite and afflicted,
LOVELACE

[Letter 227.4: Clarissa Harlowe] to Mr Lovelace

THE more you tease me, the worse will it be for you.

Time is wanted to consider whether I ever should think of you at all. At present, it is my sincere wish that I may never more see your face.

All that can afford you the least shadow of favour from me arises from the hoped-for reconciliation with my *real*, not my *Judas* protector.

I am careless at present of consequences. I hate myself: and who is it I have reason to value?—Not the man who could form a plot to disgrace his own hopes, as well as a poor friendless creature (made friendless by himself), by outrages not to be thought of with patience.

[Letter 227.5: Lovelace] to Mrs Lovelace

Madam,

I WILL go to the Commons, and proceed in every particular as if I had not the misfortune to be under your displeasure.

I must insist upon it, that however faulty my passion on so unexpected an incident made me appear to a lady of your delicacy, yet my compliance with your entreaties at such a moment, as it gave you an instance of your power over me which few men could have shown, ought, duly considered, to entitle me to the effects of that solemn promise which was the condition of my obedience.

I hope to find you in a kinder and, I will say, *juster* disposition on my return. Whether I get the licence, or not, let me beg of you to make the *soon* you have been pleased to bid me hope for, tomorrow morning. This will reconcile everything, and make me the happiest of men.

The settlements are ready to sign, or will be by night.

For Heaven's sake, madam, do not carry your resentment into a displeasure so disproportionate to the offence. For that would be to expose us both to the people below; and, what is of infinite more consequence to us, to Captain Tomlinson. Let us be able, I beseech you, madam, to assure him, on his next visit, that we are one.

As I have no hope to be permitted to dine with you, I shall not return till evening: and then, I presume to say, I *expect* (your *promise* authorizes me to use the word) to find you disposed to bless, by your consent for tomorrow,

Your adoring
LOVELACE

WHAT pleasure did I propose to take, how to *enjoy* the sweet confusion I expected to find her in, while all was so recent!—But she *must*, she *shall* see me on my return. It were better for *herself*, as well as for *me*, that she had not made *so much ado about nothing*. I must keep my anger alive, lest it sink into compassion. *Love* and *compassion*, be the provocation ever so great, are hard to be separated: while *anger* converts what would be *pity* without it, into *resentment*. Nothing can be lovely in a man's eye, with which he is thoroughly displeased.

I ordered Dorcas, on putting the last billet under the door and finding it taken up, to tell her that I hoped an answer to it before I went out.

Her reply was verbal, *Tell him that I care not whither he goes, nor what he does—And this*, re-urged by Dorcas, *was all she had to say to me*.

I looked through her keyhole at my going by her door, and saw her on her knees at her bed's feet, her head and bosom on the bed, her arms extended (sweet creature!), and in an agony she seemed to be, sobbing, as I heard at that distance, as if her heart would break—By my soul, Jack, I am a *pity*-ful fellow. Recollection is my enemy!—Divine excellence!—Happy for so many days together!—Now so unhappy!—and for what?—But she is purity itself—And why, after all, should I thus torment—But I must not trust myself with myself, in the humour I am in.

WAITING here for Mowbray and Mallory, by whose aid I am to get the licence, I took papers out of my pocket to divert myself; and thy last popped itself officiously the first into my hand. I gave it the honour of a re-perusal; and this revived the subject with me, which I had resolved not to trust myself with.

I remember that the dear creature, in her torn answer to my proposals, says *that condescension is not meanness*. She better knows how to make this out than any mortal breathing. Condescension, indeed, *implies* dignity: and dignity ever *was* there in *her* condescension. Yet such a dignity as gave grace to the condescension; for there was no pride, no insult, no apparent superiority, indicated by it—This Miss Howe confirms to be a part of her general character.[a]

a See p. 578.

I can tell her how she might behave to make me her own for ever. She knows she cannot fly me. She knows she must see me sooner or later; the sooner the more gracious—I would allow her to resent (not because the liberties I took with her require resentment, were she not a CLARISSA; but as it becomes her particular niceness to resent): but would she show more *love* than *abhorrence* of me in her resentment; would she *seem*, if it were *but* to *seem*, to believe the fire no device, and all that followed merely accidental; and descend, upon it, to tender expostulation and upbraiding for the advantage I would have taken of her surprise; and would she, at last, be satisfied (as *well* she may) that it was attended with no further consequence; and place some generous confidence in my honour (power loves to be trusted, Jack); I think I would put an end to all her trials and pay her my vows at the altar.

Yet, to have taken such bold steps, as with Tomlinson and her uncle—to have made such a progress—Oh Belford, Belford, how have I puzzled myself as well as her!—This cursed aversion to wedlock how has it entangled me!—What contradictions has it not made me guilty of!

How pleasing to myself, to look back upon the happy days I gave her; though mine would doubtless have been more unmixedly so, could I have determined to lay aside my contrivances, and to be as sincere all the time as she deserved that I should be!

If I find this humour hold but till tomorrow morning (and it has now lasted two full hours, and I seem, methinks, to have *pleasure* in encouraging it), I will make thee a visit, I think, or get thee to come to me; and then will I consult thee upon it.

But she will not trust me. She will not confide in my honour. Doubt, in this case, is defiance. She loves me not well enought to forgive me generously. She is so greatly above me! How can I forgive her for a merit so mortifying to my pride! She *thinks*, she *knows*, she has *told* me, that she is above me. These words are still in my ears, 'Begone, Lovelace!—My soul is above thee, man!—Thou hast a proud heart to contend with!—My soul is above thee, man!' [a] Miss Howe thinks her above me too. Thou, even thou, my friend, my *intimate* friend and companion, art of the same opinion. I fear her as much as I love her—How shall my pride bear these reflections?—My wife (as I have so often said, because it so often recurs to my thoughts) to be so *much* my superior!—Myself to be considered but as the second person in my own family!—Canst thou teach me to bear such a reflection as this!—To tell me of my acquisition in her, and that she, with all her excellencies, will be *mine* in full property, is a mistake—It cannot be so—For shall I not be *hers*; and not *my own*?—Will not every act of her duty (as I cannot deserve it) be a condescension, and a triumph over me?—And must I owe it merely to her *goodness*, that she does not despise me?—To have her condescend to bear with my follies!—to wound me with an eye of pity!—a daughter of the Harlowes thus to excel the last and, as I have heretofore said, not the meanest of the Lovelaces—forbid it!—

Yet forbid it not—for do I not now—do I not every moment—see her before me all over charms, and elegance, and purity, as in the struggles of the past midnight? And in these struggles, heart, voice, eyes, hands, and sentiments, so greatly, so

a See p. 646.

gloriously consistent with the character she has sustained from her cradle to the present hour?

But what advantages do I give thee?

Yet have I not always done her justice? Why then thy teasing impertinence?

However, I forgive thee, Jack—since (so much generous love am I capable of!) I had rather all the world should condemn *me*, than that *her* character should suffer the least impeachment.

The dear creature herself once told me that there was a strange mixture in my mind.[a]

I have been called *Devil*, and *Beelzebub*, between the two proud beauties: I must indeed be a Beelzebub, if I had not some tolerable qualities.

But as Miss Howe says, her *suffering-time* is her *shining-time*.[b] Hitherto she has done nothing but shine.

She called me *villain*, Belford, within these few hours. And what is the sum of the present argument; but that had I *not* been a villain in her sense of the word, she had not been so much an *angel*?

Oh Jack, Jack! This midnight attempt has made me mad; has utterly undone me! How can the dear creature say I have made her vile in her *own* eyes, when her behaviour under such a surprise, and her resentment under such circumstances, have so greatly exalted her in *mine*?

Whence, however, this strange rhapsody?—Is it owing to my being *here*? That I am not at *Sinclair*'s? But if there be infection in that house, how has my beloved escaped it?

But no more in this strain!—I will see what her behaviour will be on my return—Yet already do I begin to apprehend some little sinkings, some little retrogradations; for I have just now a doubt arisen, whether, for *her own* sake, I should wish her to forgive me *lightly*, or with *difficulty*—

I AM in a way to come at the wished-for licence.

I have now given everything between my beloved and me a full consideration; and my puzzle is over. What has brought me to a speedier determination is that I think I have found out what she means by the *week*'s distance she intends to hold me at. It is that she may have time to write to Miss Howe, to put in motion that cursed scheme of hers, and to take measures upon it, which shall enable her to abandon and renounce me for ever—Now, Jack, if I obtain not admission to her presence on my return; but am refused with haughtiness, if her *week* be insisted upon (such prospects before her); I shall be confirmed in my conjecture; and it will be plain to me that weak at best was that love which could give place to punctilio, at a time that the all-reconciling ceremony (so she must think) waits her command—Then will I recollect all her perversenesses; then will I re-peruse Miss Howe's letters, and the transcripts from others of them; and give way to my aversion to the life of shackles: and then shall she be mine in my own way.

But, after all, I am in hopes that she will have better considered of everything by the evening. That her threat of a *week's* distance was thrown out in the heat of passion; and that she will allow that I have as much cause to quarrel with her for breach of her word, as she has with me for breach of the peace.

  a   See p. 461.
  b   See p. 579.

These lines of Rowe have got into my head; and I shall repeat them very devoutly all the way the chairmen shall poppet me towards her by and by.

> Teach me, some power, the happy art of speech,
> To dress my purpose up in gracious words;
> Such as may softly steal upon her soul,
> And never waken the tempestuous passions.

Letter 228: MR LOVELACE TO JOHN BELFORD, ESQ.

Thursday evening, June 8

OH for a curse to kill with!—Ruined! Undone! Outwitted, tricked!—Zounds, man, the lady is gone off!—Absolutely gone off!—Escaped!—

Thou knowest not, nor canst conceive, the pangs that wring my heart!—What can I do!—Oh Lord, oh Lord, oh Lord!

And thou, too, who hast endeavoured to weaken my hands, wilt but clap thy dragon's wings at the tidings!—

Yet I must write, or I shall go distracted. Little less have I been these two hours; dispatching messengers to every stage; to every inn; to every waggon or coach, whether flying or creeping, and to every house with a bill up, for five miles round.

The little hypocrite, who knows not a soul in this town (*I thought I was sure of her at any time*) such an inexperienced traitress; giving me hope too, in her first billet, that her expectation of the family reconciliation would withhold her from taking such a step as this—Curse upon her contrivances!—I thought that it was owing to her bashfulness; to her modesty, that after a few innocent freedoms she could not look me in the face; when, all the while, she was impudently (yes, I say *impudently*, though she be Clarissa Harlowe) contriving to rob me of the dearest property I had ever purchased—Purchased by a painful servitude of many months; fighting through the wild beasts of her family for her, and combating with a windmill virtue, that hath cost me millions of perjuries only to attempt; and which now, with its damned air-fans, has tossed me a mile and a half beyond hope!—And this, just as I had arrived within view of the consummation of all my wishes!

Oh devil of love! god of love no more!—How have I deserved this of thee!— Never before the friend of frozen virtue!—*Powerless* demon, for powerless thou must be if thou meanedst not to play me booty; who shall henceforth kneel at thy altars!—May every enterprising heart abhor, despise, execrate, renounce thee, as I do—But what signifies cursing now!

How she could effect this her wicked escape is my astonishment; the whole sisterhood having charge of her—for, as yet, I have not had patience enough to inquire into the particulars, nor to let a soul of them approach me.

Of this I am sure, *or I had not brought her hither*, there is not a creature belonging to this house that could be corrupted either by virtue or remorse: the highest joy every infernal nymph of this worse than infernal habitation *could* have known, would have been to reduce this proud beauty to her own level—And as to my villain, who also had charge of her, he is such a seasoned varlet that he delights in mischief, for the sake of it: no bribe could seduce him to betray his trust, were there but wickedness in it!—'Tis well, however, he was out of my way when the cursed news was imparted to me!—Gone, the villain! in quest of her: not to return, nor to see my face (so it seems he declared), till he has heard some tidings of her; and all the out-of-place varlets of his numerous acquaintance are summoned and employed in the same business.

To what purpose brought I this angel (angel I must yet call her!) to this hellish house!—And was I not meditating to do her deserved honour? By my soul, Belford, I was resolved—But thou knowest what I had *conditionally* resolved—And now, though I was determined so much in her favour, who can tell what hands she may have fallen into?

I am mad, stark mad, by Jupiter, at the thoughts of this!—Unprovided, destitute, unacquainted—some villain, worse than myself, who adores her not as I adore her, may have seized her, and taken advantage of her distress!—Let me perish, Belford, if a whole hecatomb of *innocents*, as the little plagues are called, shall atone for the broken promise and wicked artifices of this cruel creature.

COMING home with resolutions so favourable to her, judge thou of my distraction when her escape was first hinted to me, although but in broken sentences. I knew not what I said, nor what I did; I wanted to kill somebody. I flew out of one room into another, while all avoided me but the veteran Betty Carberry, who broke the matter to me: I charged bribery and corruption, in my first fury, upon all; and threatened destruction to old and young, as they should come in my way.

Dorcas continues *locked* up from me: Sally and Polly have not yet dared to appear: the vile Sinclair—

But here comes the odious devil: she taps at the door, though that's only ajar, whining and snuffling, to try, I suppose, to coax me into temper.

WHAT a helpless state, where a man can only execrate himself and others; the occasion of his rage remaining; the evil increasing upon reflection; time itself conspiring to deepen it!—Oh how I cursed her!

I have her now, methinks, before me, blubbering—How odious does sorrow make an ugly face!—Thine, Jack, and this old beldam's, in penitentials, instead of moving compassion, must evermore confirm hatred; while beauty in tears is beauty heightened, and what my heart has ever delighted to see—

What excuse!—Confound you, and your cursed daughters, what excuse can you make! Is she not gone!—Has she not escaped!—But before I am quite distracted! before I commit half a hundred murders, let me hear how it was.

I HAVE heard her story!—Art, damned, confounded, wicked, unpardonable art, in a woman of her character—But show me a woman, and I'll show thee a plotter!—This plaguy sex is *art* itself: every individual of it is a plotter by nature.

This is the substance of the old wretch's account.

She told me, 'That I had no sooner left the vile house, than Dorcas acquainted the siren' (do, Jack, let me call her names!—I beseech thee, Jack, let me call her names!) 'than Dorcas acquainted her lady with it; and that I had left word that I was gone to Doctors' Commons, and should be heard of for some hours at the Horn there, if inquired after by the counsellor, or anybody else: that afterwards I should be either at the Cocoa Tree, or King's Arms; and should not return till late. She then urged her to take some refreshment.

'She was in tears, when Dorcas approached her; her saucy eyes swelled with weeping: she refused either to eat or drink; sighed as if her heart would break.' False, devilish grief! not the humble, silent grief that only deserves pity!— Contriving to ruin me, to despoil me of all that I held valuable, in the very midst of it!

'Nevertheless, being resolved not to see me for a week at least, she ordered her to bring her up three or four French rolls, with a little butter, and a decanter of water; telling her she would dispense with her attendance; and that should be all she would live upon in the interim. So, artful creature! pretending to lay up for a week's siege'—For, as to substantial food, she, no more than other angels'— Angels, said I!—The devil take me if she shall be any more an angel!—for she is odious in my eyes; I hate her mortally!—

But oh! Lovelace, thou liest!—She is all that is lovely! All that is excellent!—

But *is* she, *can* she, be gone!—Oh how Miss Howe will triumph!—But if that little fury receive her, fate shall make me rich amends; for then will I contrive to have them both.

I was looking back for connexion—but the devil take connexion; I have no business with it: the contrary best befits distraction, and that will soon be my lot! 'Dorcas consulted the old wretch about obeying her: Oh yes, by all means, for Mr Lovelace knew how to come at her at any time; and directed a bottle of sherry to be added.

'This cheerful compliance so obliged her, that she was prevailed upon to go up and look at the damage done by the fire; and seemed not only shocked at it, but satisfied it was no trick, as she owned she had at first apprehended it to be. All this made them secure; and they laughed in their sleeves, to think what a childish way of showing her resentment she had found out; Sally throwing out her witticisms, that Mrs Lovelace was right, however, *not to quarrel with her bread and butter.*'

Now this very childishness, as *they* thought it, in such a genius, would have made *me* suspect either her head, after what had happened the night before; or her intention, when the marriage was, so far as she knew, to be completed within the week she was resolved to secrete herself from me in the same house. 'She sent Will with a letter to Wilson's, directed to Miss Howe, ordering him to inquire if there were not one for her there.

'He only pretended to go, and brought word there was none; and put her letter in his pocket for me.

'She then ordered him to carry another (which she gave him) to the Horn Tavern to me—All this done without any seeming hurry; yet she appeared to be very solemn; and put her handkerchief frequently to her eyes.

'Will pretended to come to me with this letter, but though the dog had the sagacity to mistrust something, on her sending him out a second time (and to *me,* whom she had refused to see); which he thought extraordinary; and mentioned his mistrusts to Sally, Polly, and Dorcas; yet they made light of his suspicions; Dorcas assuring them all that her lady seemed more stupid with her grief than active; and that she really believed she was a little turned in her head, and knew not what she did—But all of them depended upon her inexperience, her open temper, and upon her not making the least motion towards going out, or to have a coach or chair called, as sometimes she had done; and still more upon the preparations she had made for a week's siege, as I may call it.

'Will went out, pretending to bring the letter to me; but quickly returned; his heart still misgiving him; on recollecting my frequent cautions that he was not to judge for himself, when he had *positive* orders; but if any doubt occurred, from circumstances I could not foresee, literally to follow them, as the only way to avoid blame.

'But it must have been in this little interval, that she escaped; for soon after his return, they made fast the street door and hatch, the mother and the two nymphs taking a little turn into the garden; Dorcas going upstairs, and Will (to avoid being seen by his lady, or his voice heard) down into the kitchen.

'About half an hour after, Dorcas, who had planted herself where she could see her lady's door open, had the curiosity to go to look through the keyhole, having a misgiving, as she said, that her lady might offer some violence to herself, in the mood she had been in all day; and finding the key in the door, which was not very usual, she tapped at it three or four times, and having no answer, opened it, with madam, madam, did you call?—supposing her in her closet.

'Having no answer, she stepped forward, and was astonished to find her not there: she hastily ran into the dining-room, then into my apartments, searched every closet; dreading all the time to behold some sad catastrophe.

'Not finding her anywhere, she ran down to the old creature, and her nymphs, with a Have you seen my lady?—Then she's gone!—She's nowhere above!

'They were sure she could not be gone out.

'The whole house was in an uproar in an instant; some running upstairs, some down, from the upper rooms to the lower; and all screaming, How should they look me in the face!

'Will cried out, he was a dead man! *He* blamed *them*; *they*, *him*; and everyone was an *accuser* and an *excuser* at the same time.

'When they had searched the whole house, and every closet in it, ten times over to no purpose: they took it into their heads to send to all the porters, chairmen, and hackney-coachmen that had been near the house for two hours past, to inquire if any of them saw such a young lady; describing her.

'This brought them some light: the only dawning for hope that I can have, and which keeps me from absolute despair. One of the chairmen gave them this account: That he saw such a one come out of the house a little before four (in a great hurry, and as if frighted), with a little parcel tied up in a handkerchief, in her hand: that he took notice to his fellow, who plied her, without her answering, that she was a fine young lady: that he'd warrant she had either a bad husband, or very cross parents, for that her eyes seemed swelled with crying. Upon which, a third fellow replied, That it might be a Doe escaped from Mother *Damnable*'s park. This Mrs Sinclair told me with a curse, and a wish that she knew the saucy villain—She thought, truly, that she had a better reputation; so handsomely as she lived, and so justly as she paid everybody for what she bought; her house visited by the best and civillest of gentlemen; and no noise or brawls ever heard or known in it!

'From these appearances, the fellow who gave this information had the curiosity to follow her, unperceived. She often looked back. Everybody who passed her, turned to look after her; passing their verdicts upon her tears, her hurry, and her charming person; till coming to a stand of coaches, a coachman plied her; was accepted; alighted, opened the coach door in a hurry, seeing *her* hurry; and in it she stumbled for haste; and the fellow believed, hurt her shins with the stumble.'

The devil take me, Belford, if my generous heart is not moved for her, notwithstanding her wicked deceit, to think what must be her reflections and apprehensions at the time!—A mind so delicate, heeding no censures; yet, probably, afraid of being laid hold of by a Lovelace in everyone she saw! At the same time, not knowing to what dangers she was going to expose herself; nor of whom she could obtain shelter; a stranger to the town, and to all its ways; the afternoon far gone; but little money; and no clothes but those she had on.

It is impossible, in this little interval since last night, that Miss Howe's Townsend could be co-operating.

But how she must abhor me, to run all these risks; how heartily must she detest me for my freedoms of last night! Oh that she had had greater reason for a resentment so violent!—As to her *virtue*, I am too much enraged to give her the merit due to that: to virtue it cannot be owing that she should fly from the charming prospects that were before her: but to malice, hatred, contempt, Harlowe-pride, the worst of pride, and to all the deadly passions that ever reigned in a female breast—And if I can but recover her—But be still, be calm, be hushed, my stormy passions; for is it not Clarissa (*Harlowe* must I say?), that thus I rave against!

'The fellow heard her say, Drive fast! Very fast!

'Where, madam?—To Holborn Bars, answered she; repeating, Drive very fast!—And up she pulled both the windows: and he lost sight of the coach in a minute.

'Will, as soon as he had this intelligence, speeded away in hopes to trace her out; declaring, that he would never think of seeing me, till he had heard some tidings of his lady.'

And now, Belford, all my hope is that this fellow (who attended us in our airing to Hampstead, to Highgate, to Muswell Hill, to Kentish Town) will hear of her at some one or other of those places—And on this I the rather build, as I remember she was once, after our return, very inquisitive about the stages, and their prices; praising the conveniency to passengers in their going off every hour; and this in Will's hearing, who was then in attendance. Woe be to the villain, if he recollect not this!

I HAVE been traversing her room, meditating, or taking up everything she but touched or used: the glass she dressed at I was ready to break, for not giving me the personal image it was wont to reflect, of *her*, whose idea is for ever present with me. I call for her, now in the tenderest, now in the most reproachful terms, as if within hearing: wanting *her*, I want my own soul, at least everything dear to it. What a void in my heart! what a chillness in my blood, as if its circulation were arrested! From her room to my own; in the dining-room, and in and out of every place where I have seen the beloved of my heart, do I hurry; in none can I tarry; her lovely image in every one, in some lively attitude, rushing cruelly upon me, in differently remembered conversations.

But when in my first fury, at my return, I went up two pair of stairs, resolved to find the locked-up Dorcas, and beheld the vainly-burnt window-board, and recollected my baffled contrivances, baffled by my own weak folly, I thought my distraction completed, and down I ran as one frighted at a spectre, ready to howl for vexation; my head and my temples shooting with a violence I had never felt before; and my back aching as if the vertebrae were disjointed, and falling in pieces.

But now that I have heard the mother's story, and contemplated the dawning hopes given by the chairman's information, I am a good deal easier, and can make cooler reflections. Most heartily pray I for Will's success, every four or five minutes. If I lose her, all my rage will return with redoubled fury. The disgrace to be thus outwitted by a novice, an infant, in stratagem and contrivance, added to the violence of my passion for her, will either break my heart or (what saves many a heart in evils insupportable) turn my brain. What had I to do to go out a licence-hunting, at least till I had seen her, and made up matters with her? And indeed, were it not the privilege of a principal to lay all his own faults upon his underlings, and never be to blame himself, I should be apt to reflect that I am more in fault than anybody. And as the sting of this reflection will sharpen upon me if I recover her not, how shall I be able to bear it?

If ever—

Here Mr Lovelace lays himself under a curse, too shocking to be repeated, if he revenge not himself upon the lady, should he once more get her into his hands.

I HAVE just now dismissed the snivelling toad Dorcas, who was introduced to me for my pardon by the whining mother. I gave her a kind of negative and ungracious forgiveness—Yet I shall as violently curse the two nymphs, by and by, for the consequences of my own folly: and this will be a good way too, to prevent their ridicule upon me for losing so glorious an opportunity as I had last night, or rather this morning.

I have collected, from the result of the inquiries made of the chairman, and from Dorcas's observations before the cruel creature escaped, a description of her dress; and am resolved, if I cannot otherwise hear of her, to advertise her in the Gazette as an eloped wife, both by her maiden and acknowledged name; for her elopement will soon be known by every *enemy*, why then should not my *friends* be made acquainted with it, from whose inquiries and informations I may expect some tidings of her?

She had on a brown lustring nightgown, fresh, and looking like new, as everything she wears does, whether new or not, from an elegance natural to her. A beaver hat, a black riband about her neck, and blue knots on her breast. A quilted petticoat, of carnation-coloured satin; a rose-diamond ring supposed on her finger; and in her whole person and appearance, as I shall express it, a dignity, as well as beauty, that commands the repeated attention of everyone who sees her.

The description of her person I shall take a little more pains about. My mind must be more at ease before I can undertake that. And I shall threaten that if, after a certain period given for her voluntary return, she be not heard of, I will prosecute any person who presumes to entertain, harbour, abet, or encourage her, with all the vengeance that an injured gentleman and husband may be warranted to take by law, or otherwise.

FRESH cause of aggravation!—But for this scribbling vein, or I should still run mad!

Again going into her chamber, because it was hers, and sighing over the bed and every piece of furniture in it, I cast my eye towards the drawers of the dressing-glass, and saw peep out, as it were, in one of the half-drawn drawers, the corner of a letter. I snatched it out, and found it superscribed by her, *To Mr Lovelace*. The sight of it made my heart leap, and I trembled so, that I could hardly open the seal.

How does this damned love unman me!—But nobody ever loved as I love!—It is even increased by her unworthy flight, and my disappointment. Ungrateful creature, to fly from a passion thus ardently flaming! which, like the palm, rises the more for being depressed and slighted!

I will not give thee a copy of this letter. I owe her not so much service.

But wouldst thou think that this haughty promise-breaker could resolve, as she does, absolutely and for ever to renounce me for what passed last night? That she could resolve to forgo all her opening prospects of reconciliation; *that* reconciliation with a worthless family, on which she had set her whole heart?—Yet she does!—She acquits me of all obligation to her, and herself of all expectations from me!—And for what?—Oh that indeed I had given her real cause! Damned confounded niceness, prudery, affectation, or pretty ignorance, if not affectation!—By my soul, Belford, I told thee all—I was more indebted to her struggles, than to my own forwardness. I cannot support my own reflections upon a decency so ill-requited. She could not, she would not have been so much a Harlowe in her resentment had I deserved, as I *ought* to have done, her resentment. All she feared had then been over, and her own good sense, and even modesty, would have taught her to make the best of it.

But if ever again I get her into my hands, *art* and more *art*, and *compulsion* too, if she make it necessary (*and 'tis plain that nothing else will do*), shall she experience from the man whose fear *of* her has been above even his passion *for* her; and whose gentleness and forbearance she has thus *perfidiously* triumphed over. Well says the poet:

> 'Tis nobler like a lion to invade
> When appetite directs, and seize my prey,
> Than to wait tamely, like a begging dog,
> Till dull consent throws out the scraps of love.[2]

Thou knowest what I have so lately vowed—And yet, at times (cruel creature, and ungrateful as cruel!), I can subscribe with too much truth to those lines of another poet:

> She reigns more fully in my soul than ever;
> She garrisons my breast, and mans against me
> Ev'n my own rebel thoughts, with thousand graces,
> Ten thousand charms, and new-discover'd beauties![3]

Letter 229: MR LOVELACE TO JOHN BELFORD, ESQ.

A LETTER is put into my hands by Wilson himself—
Such a letter!—
A letter from Miss Howe to her cruel friend!—
I made no scruple to open it.

It is a miracle that I fell not into fits at the reading of it; and at the thought of what might have been the consequence had it come to the hands of *this Clarissa Harlowe*. Let my justly excited rage excuse my irreverence.

Collins, though not his day, brought it this afternoon to Wilson's with a particular desire that it might be sent with all speed to Miss Beaumont's lodgings, and given, if possible, into her own hands. He had before been here (at Mrs Sinclair's), with intent to deliver it to her himself, but was told (*too truly told!*), that she was abroad; but that they would give her anything he should leave for her, the moment she returned—But he cared not to trust them with his business, and went away to Wilson's (as I find by the description of him at both places), and there left the letter; but not till he had a second time called here, and found her not come in.

The letter (which I shall enclose; for it is too long to transcribe) will account to thee for his coming hither.

Oh this devilish Miss Howe!—Something must be resolved upon, and done with that little fury!

THOU wilt see the margin of this cursed letter crowded with indices (☞). I put them to mark the places devoted for vengeance, or requiring animadversion. Return thou it to me the moment thou hast read it.

Read it here; and avoid trembling for me, if thou canst.

[*Letter 229.1: Anna Howe*] to Miss Laetitia Beaumont

Wednesday, June 7

My dearest friend,

You will perhaps think that I have been too long silent. But I had begun two letters at different times since my last, and written a great deal each time; and
☞ with spirit enough, I assure you; incensed as I was against the abominable wretch you are with; particularly on reading yours of the 21st of the past month.[a]

☞   The *first* I intended to keep open till I could give you some account of my proceedings with Mrs Townsend. It was some days before I saw her: and this intervenient space giving me time to re-peruse what I had written, I thought
☞ it proper to lay that aside, and to write in a style a little less fervent; for you would have blamed me, I know, for the freedom of some of my expressions
☞ (*execrations*, if you please). And when I had gone a good way in the *second*, the change in your prospects, on his communicating to you Miss Montague's letter, and his better behaviour, occasioning a change in your mind, I laid that aside also. And in this uncertainty, thought I would wait to see the issue of affairs between you, before I wrote again; believing that all would soon be decided one way or other.

I had still, perhaps, held this resolution (as every appearance, according to your letters, was more and more promising), had not the two past days furnished me with intelligence which it highly imports you to know.

☞   But I must stop here, and take a little walk, to try to keep down that just

a   See Letter 200, pp. 640–41, 643–4.

indignation which rises to my pen, when I am about to relate to you what I must communicate.

    I AM not my own mistress enough—then my mother—always up and
☞ down—and watching as if I were writing to a fellow—but I will try if I can contain myself in tolerable bounds—
    The women of the house where you are—oh my dear—the women of the house—but you never thought highly of them—so it cannot be so very
☞ surprising—nor would you have stayed so long with them, had not the notion of removing to one of your own made you less uneasy, and less curious about
☞ their characters, and behaviour. Yet I could *now* wish that you had been less
☞ reserved among them—but I tease you—In short, my dear, you are certainly in a devilish house!—Be assured that the woman is one of the vilest of women!—nor does she go to you by her right name—Very true—her name is *not* Sinclair—nor is the street she lives in, Dover Street—Did you never go out by yourself, and discharge the coach or chair, and return by another coach
☞ or chair? If you did (yet I don't remember that you ever wrote to me, that you did), you would never have found your way to the vile house, either by the woman's name, *Sinclair*, or by the street's name, mentioned by that Doleman in his letter about the lodgings.[a]
☞   The wretch might indeed have held out these false lights a little more excusably had the house been an honest house; and had his end only been to prevent mischief from your brother—But this contrivance was antecedent, as I think, to your brother's project: so that no excuse can be made for his intentions at the *time*—The man, whatever he may *now* intend, was certainly
☞ then, even *then,* a villain in his heart!

☞   I AM excessively concerned that I should be prevailed upon, between *your* over-niceness on one hand, and my *mother*'s positiveness on the other, to be satisfied without knowing how to direct to you at your lodgings. I think too, that the proposal that I should be put off to a *third-hand* knowledge, or rather veiled in a *first-hand* ignorance, came from him—and that it was only acquiesced in by you, as it was by me,[b] upon needless and weak considerations—because, truly, I might have it to say, if challenged, that I knew not where to send to you!—I am ashamed of myself!—Had this been at *first* excusable, it could not be a good reason for going on in the folly, when you
☞ had no liking to the house, and when he began to play tricks and delay with you—What! I was to mistrust myself, was I?—I was to allow it to be thought
☞ that I could not keep my own secret?—But the house to be taken at this time,
☞ and at that time, led us both on—like fools, like tame fools in a string—Upon
☞ my life, my dear, this man is a vile, a contemptible villain—I must speak

    a See p. 472.
    b See pp. 511 and 515, where the reader will observe that the proposal came from herself; which, as it was also mentioned by Mr Lovelace (as will be seen in Miss Harlowe's letter, p. 529), she may be presumed to have forgot. So that Clarissa had a double inducement for acquiescing with the proposed method of carrying on the correspondence between Miss Howe and herself by Wilson's conveyance, and by the name of Laetitia Beaumont.

out!—How has he laughed in his sleeve at us both, I warrant, for I can't tell
how long!

And yet who could have thought that a man of fortune, and some *reputation*
☞ (This Doleman, I mean; not your wretch, to be sure!)—formerly a rake
indeed—(I have inquired after him—long ago; and so was the easier satisfied)—
but married to a woman of family—having had a palsy-blow—and one would
☞ think a penitent—should recommend such a house—(Why, my dear, he could
not *inquire* of it, but must find it to be bad)—to such a man as Lovelace, to
bring his future, nay, his *then* supposed bride, to?

☞   I WRITE, perhaps, with too much violence to be clear. But I cannot help it.
Yet I lay down my pen, and take it up every ten minutes, in order to write with
some temper—My mother too in and out—What need I (she asks me) lock
myself in, if I am only reading past correspondencies?—for that is my
☞ pretence, when she comes poking in with her face sharpened to an edge, as I
☞ may say, by a curiosity that gives her more pain than pleasure—The Lord
forgive me; but I believe I shall huff her next time she comes in.

Do *you* forgive me too, my dear. My mother *ought*; because she says I am
☞ my father's girl; and because I am sure I am *hers*. I don't know what to do—
I don't know what to write next—I have so much to write, yet have so little
patience, and so little opportunity.

But I will tell you how I came by my intelligence.
☞   *That* being a *fact*, and requiring the less attention, I will try to account to
you for *that*.

Thus then it came about—'Miss Lardner (whom you have seen at her cousin
Biddulph's) saw you at St James's church on Sunday was fortnight. She kept
you in her eye during the whole time; but could not once obtain the notice of
yours, though she curtsied to you twice. She thought to pay her compliments
to you when the service was over; for she doubted not but you were married—
☞ and for an odd reason—*because you came to church by yourself*—Every eye
as usual, she said, was upon you; and this seeming to give you hurry, and you
being nearer the door than she, you slid out before she could get to you. But
she ordered her servant to follow you till you were housed. This servant saw
you step into a chair, which waited for you; and you ordered the men to carry
you to the place where they took you up.

'The next day, Miss Lardner sent the same servant, out of mere curiosity,
to make private inquiry whether Mr Lovelace were, or were not, with you
☞ there. And this inquiry brought out, from *different* people, that the house was
suspected to be one of those genteel wicked houses, which receive and
accommodate fashionable people of both sexes.

'Miss Lardner, confounded at this strange intelligence, made further
inquiry; enjoining secrecy to the servant she had sent, as well as to the
☞ gentleman whom she employed: who had it confirmed from a rakish friend,
who knew the house; and told him that there were two houses; the one, in
which all decent appearances were preserved, and guests rarely admitted; the
other, the receptacle of those who were absolutely engaged, and broken to the
vile yoke—'

🖙   Say–my dear creature—say—shall I not execrate the wretch?—But words are weak—What can I say that will suitably express my abhorrence of such a villain as he must have been, when he meditated to bring a Clarissa Harlowe to such a place!

'Miss Lardner kept this to herself some days, not knowing what to do; for she loves you, and admires you of all women. At last, she revealed it, but in confidence, to Miss Biddulph, by letter. Miss Biddulph, in like confidence, being afraid it would distract *me*, were I to know it, communicated it to Miss Lloyd; and so, like a whispered scandal, it passed through several canals; and then it came to me. Which was not till last Monday.'

I thought I should have fainted upon the surprising communication. But 🖙 rage taking place, it blew away the sudden illness. I besought Miss Lloyd to re-enjoin secrecy to everyone. I told her that I would not for the world, that 🖙 my mother, or any of your family, should know it. And I instantly caused a trusty friend to make what inquiries he could about Tomlinson.

🖙   I had thoughts to have done it before: but not imagining it to be needful, and little thinking that you could be in such a house, and as you were pleased 🖙 with your changed prospects, I forbore. And the rather forbore, as the matter is so laid, that Mrs Hodges is supposed to know nothing of the projected treaty of accommodation; but, on the contrary, that it was designed to be a secret to her, and to everybody but immediate parties; and it was Mrs Hodges that I had proposed to sound by a *second* hand.

🖙   Now, my dear, it is certain, without applying to that too-much-favoured housekeeper, that there is not such a man within ten miles of your uncle. Very true! One *Tomkins* there is, about four miles off; but he is a day-labourer: and one *Thompson*, about five miles distant the other way; but he is a parish schoolmaster, poor, and about seventy.

🖙   A man, though but of £800 a year, cannot come from one county to settle in another but everybody in both must know it, and talk of it.

🖙   Mrs Hodges may yet be sounded at a distance, if you will. Your uncle is an old man. Old men imagine themselves under obligation to their paramours, if younger than themselves, and seldom keep anything from their knowledge. 🖙 But if we suppose him to make a secret of the designed treaty, it is impossible, *before* that treaty was thought of, but she must have seen him, at least have *heard* your uncle speak praisefully of a man he is said to be so intimate with, let him have been ever so little a while in those parts.

🖙   Yet, methinks, the story is so plausible, Tomlinson, as you describe him, is so good a man, and so much of a gentleman; the end to be answered by his 🖙 being an impostor, so much *more than necessary* if Lovelace has villainy in his head; and as you are in such a house—your wretch's behaviour to him was so 🖙 petulant and lordly; and Tomlinson's answer so full of spirit and circumstance; 🖙 and then what he communicated to you of Mr Hickman's application to your uncle, and of Mrs Norton's to your mother (some of which particulars, I am 🖙 satisfied, his vile agent Joseph Leman could not reveal to his viler employer); his pressing on the marriage-day, in the name of your uncle, which it could not answer any *wicked* purpose for him to do; and what he writes of your 🖙 uncle's proposal to have it thought that you were married from the time that you had lived in one house together; and that to be made to agree with the

☞ time of Mr Hickman's visit to your uncle: the insisting on a trusty person's being present at the ceremony, at that uncle's nomination—These things make me willing to try for a tolerable construction to be made of all; though I am so much puzzled by what occurs on both sides of the question, that I
☞ cannot but abhor the devilish wretch, whose inventions and contrivances are
☞ for ever employing an inquisitive head, without affording the means of absolute detection.

But this is what I am ready to conjecture: that Tomlinson, specious as he is, is a machine of Lovelace; and that he is employed for some end, which has
☞ not yet been answered—This is certain, that not only Tomlinson, but Mennell, who I think attended you more than once at this vile house, must know it to *be* a vile house.

What can you then think of Tomlinson's declaring himself in *favour* of it, upon inquiry?

Lovelace too must know it to be so; if not before he brought you to it, soon after.

☞ Perhaps the *company he found there* may be the most probable way of accounting for his bearing with the house, and for his strange suspensions of marriage, when it was in his power to call such an angel of a woman his—

☞ Oh my dear, the man is a villain! the greatest of villains in every light!—I am convinced that he is—and this Doleman must be another of his implements!

☞ There are so many wretches who think *that* to be no sin, which is one of the greatest and the most ungrateful of all sins; to ruin young creatures of our sex who place their confidence in them; that the wonder is less than the shame, that people of figure, of *appearance* at least, are found to promote the horrid purposes of profligates of fortune and interest!—

☞ But can I think (you will ask with indignant astonishment), that Lovelace can have designs upon your honour?

☞ That such designs he *has had*, if he *still* hold them not, I can have no doubt, now that I know the house he has brought you to, to be a vile one. This is a clue that has led me to account for all his behaviour to you ever since you have been in his hands.

Allow me a brief retrospection of it all.

☞ We both know, that pride, revenge, and a delight to tread in unbeaten paths, are principal ingredients in the character of this finished libertine.

☞ He hates all your family, yourself excepted; and I have several times thought that I have seen him stung and mortified that love has obliged him to
☞ kneel at your footstool, because you are a *Harlowe*—Yet is this wretch a savage in love—Love that humanizes the fiercest spirits has not been able to
☞ subdue his. His *pride*, and the credit which a few *plausible qualities* sprinkled
☞ among his *odious ones* have given him, have secured him too good a reception from our eye-judging, our undistinguishing, our self-flattering, our too-confiding sex, to make assiduity and obsequiousness, and a conquest of his unruly passions, any part of his study.

☞ He has some reason for his animosity to *all* the men, and to *one* woman of your family. He has always shown you, and all his own family too, that he
☞ prefers his pride to his interest. He is a declared marriage-hater: a notorious intriguer: full of his inventions; and glorying in them—He never could draw

you in to declarations of love: nor, till your *wise* relations persecuted you as they did, to receive his addresses as a lover—He knew that you professedly disliked him for his immoralities; he could not therefore justly blame you for the coldness and indifference of your behaviour to him.

☞   The prevention of mischief was your first main view in the correspondence he drew you into. He ought not, then, to have wondered that you declared your preference of the *single life* to *any* matrimonial engagement. He knew

☞ that this was *always* your preference; and that before he tricked you away so artfully. What was his conduct to you afterwards, that you should of a sudden change it?

Thus was your whole behaviour regular, consistent, and dutiful to those to whom by birth you owed duty; and neither prudish, coquettish, nor tyrannical to him.

☞   He had agreed to go on with you upon those your own terms, and to rely only on his own merits and future reformation for your favour.

☞   It was plain to me, indeed, to whom you communicated all that *you knew* of your own heart, though not all of it that *I found out*, that love had pretty early gained footing in it. And this you yourself would have discovered sooner

☞ than you did, had not his alarming, his unpolite, his rough conduct, kept it under.

☞   I knew by experience that love is a fire that is not to be played with without burning one's fingers; I knew it to be a dangerous thing for two single persons of different sexes to enter into familiarity and correspondence with each other; since, as to the latter, must not a person be capable of premeditated art who can sit down to write, and not write from the heart?—and a woman to write her heart to a man practised in deceit, or even to a man of some character, what advantage does it give him over her?

☞   As this man's vanity had made him imagine that no woman could be proof against love, when his address was honourable; no wonder that he struggled, like a lion held in toils, against a passion that he thought not returned—and how could you, *at first*, show a return in love to so fierce a spirit, and who had seduced you away by vile artifices, but to the approval of those artifices?

☞   Hence, perhaps, it is not difficult to believe that it became possible for such a wretch as this to give way to his old prejudices against marriage; and to that revenge which had always been a first passion with him.

This is the only way, I think, to account for his horrid views in bringing you to a vile house.

☞   And now may not all the rest be naturally accounted for?—His delays—his teasing ways—his bringing you to bear with his lodging in the same house— his making you pass to the people of it as his wife; though restrictively so,

☞ yet with hope, no doubt (vilest of villains as he is!), to take you at advantage—

☞   His bringing you into the company of his libertine companions; the attempt of imposing upon you that Miss Partington for a bedfellow, very probably his own invention, for the worst of purposes; his terrifying you at many different times; his obtruding himself upon you when you went out to church; no doubt to prevent your finding out what the people were: the advantages he made of your brother's foolish project with Singleton.

See, my dear, how naturally all this follows from the discovery made by
☞ Miss Lardner—See how the monster, whom I thought, and so often called a
☞ *fool*, comes out to have been all the time one of the greatest villains in the
world!

But if this be so, what (it would be asked by an indifferent person) has
hitherto saved you? Glorious creature!—What (morally speaking) but your
watchfulness! What but that, and the majesty of your virtue; *the native dignity*
which, in a situation so very difficult (friendless, destitute, passing for a wife,
cast into the company of creatures accustomed to betray and ruin innocent
hearts), has hitherto enabled you to baffle, over-awe, and confound, such a
dangerous libertine as this; so habitually remorseless as you have observed
him to be; so very various in his temper; so inventive; so seconded, so
supported, so instigated, too probably, as he has been!—That *native dignity*,
that *heroism* I will call it, which has, on all proper occasions, exerted itself in
☞ its *full* lustre, unmingled with that charming obligingness and condescending
sweetness, which is evermore the *softener* of that dignity when your mind is free
and unapprehensive!

☞   Let me stop to admire and to bless my beloved friend who, unhappily for
herself, at an age so tender, unacquainted as she was with the world and with
the vile arts of libertines, having been called upon to sustain the hardest and
most shocking trials from persecuting relations on one hand, and from a
villainous lover on the other, has been enabled to give such an illustrious
example of fortitude and prudence, as never woman gave before her; and
who, as I have heretofore observed,[a] has made a far greater figure in adversity,
than she possibly could have made had all her shining qualities been exerted
☞ in their full force and power by the continuance of that prosperous run of
fortune, which attended her for eighteen years of life out of nineteen.

☞   BUT now, my dear, do I apprehend that you are in greater danger than ever
yet you have been in; if you are not married in a week; and yet stay in this
abominable house. For were you out of it, I own, I should not be much afraid
for you.

☞   These are my thoughts on the most deliberate consideration: 'That he is
now convinced that he has not been able to draw you off your guard: that
therefore, if he can obtain no new advantage over you as he goes along, he is
resolved to do you all the *poor justice* that it is in the power of such a wretch
as he to do you. He is the rather induced to this, as he sees that all his own
family have warmly engaged themselves in your cause; and that it is his *highest*
☞ *interest* to be just to you. Then the horrid wretch loves you, as well he may,
above all women. I have no doubt of this—with *such* a love as such a wretch
is capable of: with *such* a love as Herod loved his Mariamne[1]—He is now
therefore very probably at last, in earnest.'

I took time for inquiries of different natures, as I knew by the train you are
in, that whatever his designs are, they cannot ripen either for good or evil till
☞ something shall result from this new device of his about Tomlinson and your
uncle.

a See p. 579.

Device I have no doubt that it is, whatever this dark, this impenetrable spirit, intends by it.

☞   And yet I find it to be true, that Counsellor Williams (whom Mr Hickman knows to be a man of eminence in his profession) has actually as good as finished the settlements: that two drafts of them have been made; one
☞ avowedly to be sent to one Captain Tomlinson, as the clerk says: and I find that a licence has actually been more than once endeavoured to be obtained;
☞ and that difficulties have hitherto been made, equally to Lovelace's vexation and disappointment. My mother's proctor, who is very intimate with the proctor applied to by the wretch, has come at this information in confidence; and hints that, as Mr Lovelace is a man of high fortunes, these difficulties will probably be got over.

But here follow the causes of my apprehension of your danger; which I should
☞ not have had a thought of (since nothing *very* vile has yet been attempted) but on finding what a house you are in and, on that discovery, laying together and ruminating on past occurrences.

'You are obliged, from the present favourable appearances, to give him
☞ your company whenever he requests it—You are under a necessity of forgetting, or seeming to forget, past disobligations; and to receive his addresses as those of a betrothed lover—You will incur the censure of prudery and affectation, even perhaps in your own apprehension, if you keep him at
☞ that distance which has hitherto been your security—His sudden (and as suddenly recovered) illness has given him an opportunity to find out that you love him. (*Alas, my dear, I knew you loved him!*) He is, as you relate, every
☞ hour more and more an encroacher upon it. He has seemed to change his nature, and is all love and gentleness. The wolf has put on the sheep's clothing;
☞ yet more than once has shown his teeth, and his hardly sheathed claws. The instance you have given of his freedom with your person, which you could not but resent; and yet, as matters are circumstanced between you, could not but pass over, when Tomlinson's letter called you into his company,[a] show the
☞ advantage he has now over you; and also that if he can obtain greater he will—And for this very reason (as I apprehend) it is, that Tomlinson is
☞ introduced; that is to say, to give you the greater security, and to be a mediator if mortal offence be given you by any villainous attempt—The day seems not now to be so much in your power as it ought to be, since that now partly depends on your uncle, whose presence, at your own motion, he has wished on the occasion—a wish, were all real, very unlikely, I think, to be granted.'

☞   And thus situated, should he offer greater freedoms, must you not forgive him?

I fear nothing (as I know who has said), that devil carnate or incarnate can
☞ fairly do against a virtue so established[b]—But surprises, my dear, in such a house as that you are in, and in such circumstances as I have mentioned, I greatly fear!—The man, one who has already triumphed over persons worthy of his alliance.

a   See pp. 704, 705, 706.
b   See Letter 180 from Mrs Norton, p. 582.

☞   What then have you to do, but to fly this house, this infernal house!—Oh that your heart would let you fly *him!*

☞   If you should be disposed so to do, Mrs Townsend shall be ready at your command—But if you meet with no impediments, no new causes of doubt, I think your reputation in the eye of the world, though not your happiness, is

☞   concerned that you should be his—And yet I cannot bear that these libertines should be rewarded for their villainy with the best of the sex, when the worst of it are too good for them.

But if you meet with the least ground for suspicion; if he would detain you at the odious house, or wish you to stay, now you know what the people are,

☞   fly *him*, whatever your prospects are, as well as *them*.

☞   In one of your next airings, if you have no other way, refuse to return with him. Name *me* for your intelligencer, that you are in a bad house; and if you think you cannot now break with him, seem rather to believe that he may not

☞   know it to be so; and that I do not believe he does: and yet this belief in us both must appear to be very gross.

☞   But suppose you desire, and insist upon it, to go out of town for the air, this sultry weather?—You may plead your health for so doing. He dare not resist such a plea. Your brother's foolish scheme, I am told, is certainly given up; so you need not be afraid on that account.

If you do not fly the house upon reading of this, or some way or other get out of it, I shall judge of his power over you by the little you will have over either him or yourself.

☞   One of my informants has made slight inquiries concerning Mrs Fretchville. Did he ever name to you the street or square she lived in?—I don't remember

☞   that you in any of yours mentioned either to me. Strange, very strange, this, I think! No such person or house can be found, near any of the new streets or squares, where the lights I had from your letters led me to imagine her house

☞   might be—Ask him what street the house is in, if he has not told you. And let me

☞   know. If he make a difficulty of that circumstance, it will amount to a detection—And yet, I think, you have enough without this.

I shall send this long letter by Collins, who changes his day to oblige me; and that he may try (now I know where you are), to get it into your own hands. If he cannot, he will leave it at Wilson's. As none of our letters by that conveyance have miscarried when you have been in more *apparently* disagreeable situations than you are in at present, I hope that this will go safe, if Collins should be obliged to leave it there.

☞   I wrote a short letter to you in my first agitations. It contained not above twenty lines, all full of fright, alarm, and execration. But being afraid that my vehemence would too much affect you, I thought it better to wait a little, as well for the reasons already hinted at, as to be able to give you as many particulars as I could; and my thoughts upon all. And now, I think, taking to your aid other circumstances as they *have* offered, or *may* offer, you will be sufficiently armed to resist all his machinations, be they what they will.

☞   One word more. Command me up, if I can be of the least service or pleasure to you. I value not fame: I value not censure; nor even life itself, I verily think, as I do your honour, and your friendship—for, is not your honour my honour? And is not your friendship the pride of my life?

May heaven preserve you, my dearest creature, in honour and safety, is the prayer, the hourly prayer, of

Your ever-faithful and affectionate
ANNA HOWE

Thursday morn. 5. I have
  written all night.

[Letter 229.2: 'Clarissa Harlowe'] to Miss Howe

My dearest creature,
How you have shocked, confounded, surprised, astonished me, by your dreadful communication!—My *heart is too weak* to bear up against such a stroke as this!—When all hope was with me! When my prospects were so much mended!—But can there be such villainy in men, as in this vile principal, and equally vile agent!

I am really ill—very ill—Grief and surprise, and now I will say, despair, have overcome me!—All, all, you have laid down as conjecture, appears to me now to be *more* than conjecture!

Oh that your mother would have the goodness to permit me the presence of the only comforter that my afflicted, my half-broken heart, could be raised by! But I charge you, think not of coming up without her indulgent permission—I am too ill at present, my dear, to think of combating with this dreadful man; and of flying from this horrid house!—My bad writing will show you this—But my illness will be my present security, should he indeed have meditated villainy—Forgive, oh forgive me, my dearest friend, the trouble I have given you!—All must soon—But why add I grief to grief, and trouble to trouble?—But I charge you, my beloved creature, not to think of coming up without your mother's leave, to the truly desolate and broken-spirited

CLARISSA HARLOWE

WELL, Jack!—And what thinkest thou of this last letter?—Miss Howe values not either *fame* or censure; and thinkest thou that this letter will not bring the little fury up, though she could procure no other conveyance than her higgler's panniers, one for herself, the other for her maid?—She knows where to come now!—Many a little villain have I punished for knowing more than I would have her know; and that by adding to her knowledge and experience—What thinkest thou, Belford, if by getting hither this virago, and giving *cause* for a lamentable letter from her to the fair fugitive, I should be able to recover *her?*—Would she not visit that friend in *her* distress, thinkest thou, whose intended visit to her in *hers* brought her into the condition she herself had so perfidiously escaped from?

Let me enjoy the thought!

Shall I send this letter?—Thou seest I have left room, if I fail in the exact imitation of so charming a hand, to avoid too strict a scrutiny—Do they not both deserve it of me?—Seest thou not how the raving girl threatens her mother?—Ought she not to be punished?—And can I be a worse devil, or villain, or monster, than she calls me in this letter; and has called me in her former letters; were I to punish them both, as my vengeance urges me to punish them. And when I have executed that my vengeance, how charmingly satisfied may they both go down into the country, and keep house together, and have a much better reason than their pride could give them for living the single life they have both seemed so fond of?

I will set about transcribing it this moment, I think. I can resolve afterwards. Yet what has poor Hickman done to deserve this of me?—But gloriously would it punish the mother (as well as daughter) for all her sordid avarice; and for her undutifulness to honest Mr Howe, whose heart she actually broke. I am on tiptoe, Jack, to enter upon this project—Is not one country as good to me as another, if I should be obliged to take another tour upon it?

BUT I will not venture. Mr Hickman is a good man, they tell me. I love a good man. I hope one of these days to be a good man myself. Besides, I have heard within this week, something of this honest fellow that shows he has a soul; when I thought, if he had one, that it lay a little of the deepest to emerge to notice, except on very extraordinary occasions; and that then it presently sunk again into its *cellula adiposa*—The man is a *plump man*—Didst ever see him, Jack?

But the principal reason that withholds me (for 'tis a tempting project!) is, for fear of being utterly blown up if I should not be quick enough with my letter, or if Miss Howe should deliberate on setting out, or try her mother's consent first; in which time, a letter from my frighted beauty might reach her; for I have do doubt, wherever she has refuged, but her first work was to write to her vixen friend. I will therefore go on patiently; and take my revenge upon the little fury at my leisure.

But, in spite of my compassion for Hickman, whose better character is sometimes my envy, and who is one of those mortals that bring clumsiness into credit with the *mothers*, to the disgrace of us clever fellows, and often to our disappointment with the *daughters*; and who has been very busy in assisting these double-armed beauties against me; I swear by all the *dii majores*, as well as *minores*, that I will have Miss Howe, if I cannot have her more exalted friend!—And then, if there be so much flaming love between these girls as they pretend, what will my charmer profit by her escape?

And now that I shall permit Miss Howe to reign a little longer, let me ask thee if thou hast not, in the enclosed letter, a *fresh* instance that a great many of my difficulties with her sister-toast are owing to this flighty girl?—'Tis true that here was naturally a confounded sharp wintry air; and, if a little cold water was thrown into the path, no wonder that it was instantly frozen; and that a poor honest traveller found it next to impossible to keep his way; one foot sliding back as fast as the other advanced; to the endangering of his limbs or neck. But yet I think it impossible that she should have baffled me as she has done (novice as she is, and never before from under her parents' wing), had she not been armed by a virago, who was formerly very near showing that she could better advise than practise. But this, I believe, I have said more than once before.

I am loath to *reproach myself*, now the cruel creature has escaped me; for what would that do but add to my torment? Since evils self-caused and avoidable admit not of palliation or comfort. And yet, if *thou* tellest me that all *her* strength was owing to *my* weakness, and that I have been a cursed coward in this whole affair; why then, Jack, I may blush, and be vexed; but, by my soul, I cannot contradict thee.

But this, Belford, I hope—that if I can turn the poison of this letter into wholesome aliment; that is to say, if I can make use of it to my advantage; I shall have *thy* free consent to do it.

I am always careful to open covers cautiously, and to preserve seals entire. I will draw out from this cursed letter an alphabet. Nor was Nick Rowe ever half so diligent to learn Spanish, at the Quixote recommendation of a certain peer,[2] as I will be to gain a mastery of this vixen's hand.

Letter 230: MISS CLARISSA HARLOWE TO MISS HOWE

Thursday evening, June 8

AFTER my last, so full of other hopes, the contents of this will surprise you. Oh my dearest friend, the man has at last proved himself to be a villain! It was with the utmost difficulty last night, that I preserved myself from the vilest dishonour. He extorted from me a promise of forgiveness; and that I would see him next day, as if nothing had happened: but if it were possible to escape from a wretch who, as I have too much reason to believe, formed a plot to fire the house, to frighten me almost naked into his arms, how could I see him next day?

I have escaped, Heaven be praised, I have! And have now no other concern than that I fly from the only hope that could have made such an husband tolerable to me; the reconciliation with my friends, so agreeably undertaken by my uncle.

All my present hope is to find some reputable family, or person of my own sex, who is obliged to go beyond sea, or who lives abroad; I care not whither; but if I might choose, in some one of our American colonies—never to be heard of more by my relations, whom I have so grievously offended.

Nor let your generous heart be moved at what I write: if I can escape the dreadfullest part of my father's malediction (for the temporary part is already in a manner fulfilled, which makes me tremble in apprehension of the other), I shall think the wreck of my worldly fortunes a happy composition.

Neither is there need of the renewal of your so often tendered goodness to me: for I have with me rings and other valuables that were sent me with my clothes, which will turn into money, to answer all I can want till Providence shall be pleased to put me into some way to help myself, if, for my further punishment, my life is to be lengthened beyond my wishes.

Impute not this scheme, my beloved friend, either to dejection on one hand, or to that romantic turn on the other, which we have supposed generally to obtain with our sex from fifteen to twenty-two: for, be pleased to consider my unhappy situation in the light in which it really must appear to every considerate person who knows it. In the first place, the man who has had the assurance to think me, and to endeavour to make me, his *property*, will hunt me from place to place, and search after me as an estray: and he knows he may do so with impunity; for whom have I to protect me from him?

Then as to my estate, the enviable estate which has been the original cause of all my misfortunes, it shall never be mine upon litigated terms. What is there in being enabled to boast that I am worth more than *I can use*, or *wish to use?*—And if my power is circumscribed, I shall not have that to answer for, which I should have if I did not use it as I ought: which very few do. I shall have no husband, of whose interest I ought to be so regardful as to prevent me doing *more* than justice to others, that I may not do *less* to him—If therefore my father will be pleased (as I shall presume, in proper time, to propose to him) to pay two annuities out of it, one to my dear Mrs Norton, which may make her easy for the remainder of her life, as she is now growing into years; the other of £50 *per annum*, to the same good woman, for the use of—*my poor*, as I have had the vanity to call a certain set of people, concerning whom she knows all my mind; that so as few as possible may suffer by the consequences of my error; God bless them, and give them heart's-ease and content with the rest.

Other reasons for my taking the step I have hinted at, are these:

This wicked man knows I have no friend in the world but you: your neighbourhood therefore would be the first he would seek for me in, were you to think it possible for me to be concealed in it: and in this case you might be subjected to inconveniences greater even than those which you have already sustained on my account.

From my cousin Morden, were he to come, I could not hope protection; since, by his letter to me, it is evident that my brother has engaged him in his party: nor would I, by any means, subject so worthy a man to danger; as might be the case, from the violence of this ungovernable spirit.

These things considered, what better method can I take than to go abroad to some one of the English colonies; where nobody but yourself shall know anything of me; nor you, let me tell you, presently, nor till I am fixed and, if it please God, in a course of living tolerably to my mind. For it is no small part of my concern that my indiscretions have laid so heavy a tax upon you, my dear friend, to whom once I hoped to give more pleasure than pain.

I am at present at one Mrs Moore's at Hampstead. My heart misgave me at coming to this village, because I had been here with him more than once: but the coach hither was so ready a conveniency, that I knew not what to do better. Then I shall stay here no longer than till I can receive your answer to this: in which you will be pleased to let me know if I cannot be hid, according to your former contrivance (happy, had I given into it at the time!) by Mrs Townsend's assistance, till the heat of his search be over. The Deptford road, I imagine, will be the right direction to hear of a passage, and to get safely aboard.

Oh why was the great fiend of all unchained, and permitted to assume so specious a form, and yet allowed to conceal his feet and his talons, till with the one he was ready to trample upon my honour, and to strike the other into my heart!— And what had I done that he should be let loose particularly upon me!

Forgive me this murmuring question, the effect of my impatience, my *guilty* impatience, I doubt: for, as I have escaped with my honour, and nothing but my worldly prospects, and my pride, my ambition, and my vanity, have suffered in this wreck of my hopefuller fortunes, may I not still be more happy than I deserve to be? And is it not in my own power still, by the divine favour, to secure the great stake of all? And who knows, that this very path into which my inconsideration has thrown me, strewed as it is with briars and thorns, which tear in pieces my gaudier trappings, may not be the right path to lead me into the great road to my future happiness; which might have been endangered by evil communication?

And after all, are there not still more deserving persons than I, who never failed in any capital point of duty, that have been more humbled than myself; and some too, by the errors of parents and relations, by the tricks and baseness of guardians and trustees, and in which their own rashness or folly had no part?

I will then endeavour to make the best of my present lot. And join with me, my best, my only friend, in praying that my punishment may end here; and that my present afflictions may be sanctified to me.

This letter will enable you to account for a line or two, which I sent to Wilson's, to be carried to you, only for a feint, to get his servant out of the way. He seemed to be left, as I thought, for a spy upon me. But returning too soon, I was forced to write a few lines for him to carry to his master, to a tavern near Doctors Commons, with the same view: and this happily answered my end.

I wrote early in the morning a bitter letter to the wretch, which I left for him obvious enough; and I suppose he has it by this time. I kept no copy of it. I shall recollect the contents, and give you the particulars of all, at more leisure.

I am sure you will approve of my escape—the rather, as the people of the house must be very vile: for they, and that Dorcas too, did hear me (I know they did) cry out for help. If the fire had been other than a villainous plot (although in the morning, to blind them, I pretended to think it otherwise), they would have been alarmed as much as I; and have run in, hearing me scream, to *comfort me*, supposing my terror was the fire; to *relieve me*, supposing it were anything else. But the vile Dorcas went away, as soon as she saw the wretch throw his arms about me!—Bless me, my dear, I had only my slippers and an under-petticoat on. I was frighted out of my bed by her cries of Fire; and that I should be burnt to ashes in a moment!—And she to go away, and never to return, nor anybody else: and yet I heard women's voices in the next room; indeed I did—An evident contrivance of them all—God be praised, I am out of their house!

My terror is not yet over: I can hardly think myself safe: every well-dressed man I see from my windows, whether on horseback or on foot, I think to be him.

I know you will expedite an answer. A man and horse will be procured me tomorrow early, to carry this. To be sure, you cannot return an answer by the same man, because you must see Mrs Townsend first: nevertheless, I shall wait with impatience till you *can*; having no friend but you to apply to; and being such a stranger to this part of the world, that I know not which way to turn myself; whither to go; nor what to do!—What a dreadful hand have I made of it!

Mrs Moore, at whose house I am, is a widow, and of a good character: and of this, one of her neighbours, of whom I bought a handkerchief purposely to make inquiry before I would venture, informed me.

I will not set my foot out of doors till I have your direction: and I am the more secure, having dropped words to the people of the house where the coach set me down, as if I expected a chariot to meet me in my way to Hendon, a village a little distance from this—And when I left their house, I walked backward and forward upon the hill, at first not knowing what to do, and afterwards, to be certain that I was not watched, before I ventured to inquire after a lodging.

You will direct for me, my dear, by the name of Mrs Harriot Lucas.

Had I not made escape when I did, I was resolved to attempt it again and again. He was gone to the Commons for a licence, as he wrote me word; for I refused to see him, notwithstanding the promise he extorted from me.

How hard, how next to impossible, my dear, to avoid many lesser deviations when we are betrayed into a capital one!

For fear I should not get away at my first effort, I had apprised him that I would not set eye upon him under a week, in order to gain myself time for it in different ways—And were I so to have been watched as to have made it necessary, I would, after such an instance of the connivance of the women of the house, have run out into the street, and thrown myself into the next house I could have entered, or claimed protection from the first person I had met—Women to desert the cause of a poor creature of their own sex in such a situation, what must they be!—Then, such poor guilty sort of figures did they make in the morning after he was gone out—so earnest to get me upstairs, and to convince me, by the scorched window-boards, and burnt curtains and valance, that the fire was real—that (although I seemed to believe all they would have me believe) I was more and more resolved to get out of their house at all adventures.

When I began, I thought to write but a few lines. But, be my subject what it will, I know not how to conclude when I write to you. It was *always* so: it is not therefore owing peculiarly to that most interesting and unhappy situation, which you will allow, however, to engross at present the whole mind of

Your unhappy, but ever-affectionate,
CLARISSA HARLOWE

Letter 231: MR LOVELACE TO JOHN BELFORD, ESQ.

Friday morning, past two o'clock

Io Triumphe! Io Clarissa, sing!—Once more, what a happy man thy friend!—A silly dear novice, to be heard to tell the coachman whither to carry her!—And to go to *Hampstead*, of all the villages about London!—The place where we had been together more than once!

Methinks I am sorry she managed no better!—I shall find the recovery of her too easy a task, I fear! Had she but known how much difficulty enhances the value of anything with me, and had she had the least notion of obliging me, she would never have stopped short at *Hampstead*, surely.

Well, but after all this exultation, thou wilt ask, If I have already got back my charmer?—I have not—But knowing where she is, is almost the same thing as having her in my power: and it delights me to think how she will start and tremble, when I first pop upon her! How she will look with conscious guilt, that will more than wipe off my guilt of Wednesday night, when she sees her injured lover, and acknowledged husband, from whom, the greatest of felonies, she would have stolen herself.

But thou wilt be impatient to know how this came about. Read the enclosed here, and remember the instructions which, from time to time, I have given my fellow, in apprehension of such an elopement; and that will tell thee all, and what I may reasonably expect from the rascal's diligence and management, if he wishes ever to see my face again.

I received it about half an hour ago, just as I was going to lie down in my clothes: and it has made me so much alive, that, midnight as it is, I have sent for a Blunt's chariot,[1] to attend me here by day-peep, with *my usual coachman*, if possible; and knowing not else what to do with myself, I sat down, and, in the joy

of my heart, have not only wrote thus far, but have concluded upon the measures
I shall take when admitted to her presence: for well am I aware of the difficulties
I shall have to contend with from her perverseness.

[*Letter 231.1: Will Summers to Mr Lovelace*]

Honnored Sur,

THIS is to sertifie your honner, as how I am heer at Hamestet, wher I have found
out my lady to be in logins at one Mrs Moore's near upon Hamestet hethe. And
I have so ordered matters, that her ladiship cannot stur but I must have notice of
her goins and comins. As I knowed I dursted not look into your Honner's fase, if
I had not found out my lady, thoff she was gone off the prems's in a quartir off an
hour, as a man may say; so I knowed you would be glad at heart to know I had
found her out: and so I send thiss Petur Partrick, who is to haf 5 shillins, it being
now nere 12 of the clock at nite; for he would not stur without a hartie drinck too
besides: and I was willing all shulde be snug likewayes at the logins befoer I sent.

I have munny of youre Honner's, but I thout as how if the man was payed by me
beforend, he mought play trix; so left that to youre Honner.

My lady knows nothing of my being hereaway. But I thoute it best not to leve
the plase, because she has tacken the logins but for a fue nites.

If your Honner cum to the Upper Flax, I will be in site all the day about the
tapp-house or the Hethe; I have borroued an othir cote, instead off your Honner's
liferie, and a blacke wigge; soe cannot be knoen by my lady, iff as howe she shuld
see me: and have made as if I had the toothe-ake; so with my hancriffe at my
mothe, the tethe which your Honner was plesed to bett out with your Honner's
fyste, and my dam'd wide mothe, as youre Honner notifys it to be, cannot be
knoen to be mine.

The tow inner letters I had from my lady, before she went off the prems's. One
was to be left at Mr Wilson's for Miss Howe. The next was to be for your Honner.
But I knew you was not at the plase directed; and being afeared of what fell out,
so I kept them for your Honner, and so could not give um to you, until I seed you.
Miss How's I only made belief to her ladiship as I carried it, and sed as how there
was nothing left for hur, as shee wished to knoe: so here they be bothe.

I am, may it pless your Honner,

> Your Honner's most dutiful,
> and, wonce more, happy servant,
> WM. SUMMERS

THE two *inner* letters, as Will calls them, 'tis plain, were wrote for no other
purpose, but to send him out of the way with them, and one of them to amuse me.
That directed to Miss Howe is only this:

[*Letter 231.2: Miss Clarissa Harlowe to Miss Howe*]

Thursday, June 8
I WRITE this, my dear Miss Howe, only for a feint, and to see if it will go current.
I shall write at large very soon, if not miserably prevented!!!

                                                                    CL. H.

Now, Jack, will not her *feints* justify mine? Does she not invade my province,
thinkest thou? And is it not now fairly come to *Who shall most deceive and cheat
the other?* So, I thank my stars, we are upon a par, at last, as to this point—which
is a great ease to my conscience, thou must believe. And if what Hudibras tells us
is true, the dear fugitive has also abundance of pleasure to come.

> Doubtless the pleasure is as great
> In being cheated, as to cheat.
> As lookers-on find most delight,
> Who least perceive the juggler's sleight;
> And still the less they understand,
> The more admire the sleight of hand.[2]

THIS is my dear juggler's letter to me; the other *inner* letter sent by Will.

[*Letter 231.3: Miss Clarissa Harlowe to Mr Lovelace*]

                                                            Thursday, June 8
Mr Lovelace,
Do not give me cause to dread your return. If you would not that I should hate
you for ever, send me half a line by the bearer, to assure me that you will not
attempt to see me for a week to come. I cannot look you in the face without equal
confusion and indignation. The obliging me in this is but a poor atonement for
your last night's vile behaviour.
    You may pass this time in a journey to your uncle's; and I cannot doubt, if the
ladies of your family are as favourable to me as you have assured me they are, but
that you will have interest enough to prevail with one of them, to oblige me with
her company. After your baseness of last night, you will not wonder that I insist
upon this proof of your future honour.
    If Captain Tomlinson comes meantime, I can hear what he has to say, and send
you an account of it. But in less than a week, if you see me, it must be owing to a
fresh act of violence, of which you know not the consequence.
    Send me the requested line, if ever you expect to have the forgiveness confirmed;
the promise of which you extorted from
                                                              The unhappy
                                                                  CL. H.
    NOW, Belford, what canst thou say in behalf of this sweet rogue of a lady? What
canst thou say for her? 'Tis apparent that she was fully determined upon an
elopement when she wrote it: and thus would she make me of party against myself,
by drawing me in to give her a week's time to complete it in: and, wickeder still,
send me upon a fool's errand to bring up one of my cousins—When we came, to

have the satisfaction of finding her gone off, and me exposed for ever!—What punishment can be bad enough for such a little villain of a lady!

But mind, moreover, how plausibly she accounts by this billet (supposing she had no opportunity of eloping before I returned) for the resolution of not seeing me for a week; and for the bread and butter expedient!—So childish as we thought it!

The chariot is not come; and if it were, it is yet too soon for everything but my impatience. And as I have already taken all my measures, and can think of nothing but my triumph, I will resume her violent letter, in order to strengthen my resolutions against her. I was *before* in too gloomy a way to proceed with it: but now the subject is all alive to me, and my gayer fancy, like the sunbeams, will irradiate it, and turn the solemn deep green into a brighter verdure.

When I have called upon my charmer to explain some parts of her letter, and to atone for others, I will send it, or a copy of it, to thee.

Suffice it at present to tell thee, in the first place, that *she is determined never to be my wife*—To be sure, there ought to be no compulsion in so material a case. Compulsion was her parents' fault, which I have censured so severely that I shall hardly be guilty of the same. And I am glad I know her mind as to this essential point.

I have *ruined* her, she says!—Now that's a fib, take it in her own way—If I had, she would not perhaps have run away from me.

She is *thrown upon the wide world:* Now I own that Hampstead Heath affords very pretty, and very *extensive* prospects; but 'tis not the *wide world* neither: and suppose *that* to be her grievance, I hope soon to restore her to a *narrower.*

I am the *enemy of her soul, as well as of her honour!*—Confoundedly severe! Nevertheless, another fib!—For I love her soul very well; but think no more of it in this case than of my own.

She is to be *thrown upon strangers!*—And is not that her own fault?—Much against my will, I am sure!

She is cast from a state of *independency into one of obligation.* She never was in a state of *independency*; nor is it fit a woman should, of any age, or in any state of life. And as to the state of obligation, there is no such thing as living without being beholden to somebody. Mutual obligation is the very essence and soul of the social and commercial life—Why should *she* be exempt from it?—I am sure the person she raves at, desires not such an exemption—has been long *dependent* upon her, and would rejoice to owe *further obligations* to her than he can boast of hitherto.

She talks of her *father's curse*—But have I not repaid him for it an hundred-fold in the same coin? But why must the faults of other people be laid at my door? Have I not enow of my own?

But the grey-eyed dawn begins to peep—Let me sum up all.

In short, then, the dear creature's letter is a collection of invectives not very new to *me*; though the occasion for them, no doubt, is new to *her*. A little sprinkling of the romantic and contradictory runs through it. She loves, and she hates: she encourages me to pursue her by telling me I safely may; and yet she begs I will not: she apprehends poverty and want, yet resolves to give away her estate: to gratify whom?—Why, in short, those who have been the cause of her misfortunes. And finally, though she resolves never to be mine, yet she has some regrets at leaving me because of the opening prospects of a reconciliation with her friends.

But never did morning dawn so tardily as this!—The chariot not yet come neither.

A GENTLEMAN to speak with me, Dorcas?—Who can want me thus early?

Captain Tomlinson, sayest thou! Surely he must have travelled all night!—Early riser as I am, how could he think to find me up *thus* early?

Let but the chariot come, and he shall accompany me in it to the bottom of the hill (though he return to town on foot; for the captain is all obliging goodness), that I may hear all he has to say, and tell him all my mind, and lose no time.

Well, now am I satisfied that this rebellious flight will turn to my advantage, as all crushed rebellions do to the advantage of a sovereign in possession.

DEAR captain, I rejoice to see you: just in the nick of time—See! see!

> The rosy-finger'd morn appears,
> And from her mantle shakes her tears;
> The sun arising, mortals cheers,
> And drives the rising mists away,
> In promise of a glorious day.[3]

Excuse me, sir, that I salute you from my favourite bard. He that rises with the lark, will sing with the lark. Strange news since I saw you, captain! Poor mistaken lady!—But you have too much goodness, I know, to reveal to her uncle Harlowe the errors of this capricious beauty. It will all turn out for the best. You must accompany me part of the way. I know the delight you take in composing differences. But 'tis the task of the prudent to heal the breaches made by the rashness and folly of the imprudent.

AND now (all around me so still, and so silent) the rattling of the chariot-wheels at a street's distance do I hear!—And to this angel of a lady I fly!

Reward, oh God of Love (the cause is thy own); reward thou, as it deserves, my suffering perseverance!—Succeed my endeavours to bring back to thy obedience, this charming fugitive!—Make her acknowledge her rashness; repent her insults; implore my forgiveness; beg to be reinstated in my favour, and that I will bury in oblivion the remembrance of her heinous offence against thee, and against me, thy faithful votary.

THE chariot at the door!—I come! I come!—

I attend you, good captain—

Indeed, sir—

Pray, sir—civility is not ceremony.

And now, dressed like a bridegroom, my heart elated beyond that of the most desiring one (attended by a footman whom my beloved never saw), I am already at Hampstead!

Letter 232: MR LOVELACE TO JOHN BELFORD, ESQ.

Upper Flask, Hampstead, Friday (June 9) morn. 7 o'clock
I AM now here, and here have been this hour and half. What an industrious spirit
have I! Nobody can say that I eat the bread of idleness. I take true pains for all the
pleasure I enjoy. I cannot choose but to admire myself strangely; for, certainly,
with this active soul, I should have made a very great figure in whatever station I
had filled. But had I been a prince!—To be sure I should have made a most *noble*
prince! I should have led up a military dance equal to that of the great
Macedonian.[1] I should have added kingdom to kingdom, and robbed all my
neighbour sovereigns in order to have obtained the name of *Robert the Great*. And
I would have gone to war with the Great Turk, and the Persian, and the Mogul, for
their seraglios; for not one of those Eastern monarchs should have had a pretty
woman to bless himself with, till I had done with her.

And now I have so much leisure upon my hands, that, after having informed
myself of all necessary particulars, I am set to my shorthand writing, in order to
keep up with time as well as I can: for the subject is now become worthy of me;
and it is yet too soon, I doubt, to pay my compliments to my charmer, after all her
fatigues for two or three days past. And, moreover, I have abundance of matters
preparative to my future proceedings to recount, in order to connect and render
all intelligible.

I parted with the captain at the foot of the hill, trebly instructed; that is to say,
as to the *fact*, to the *probable*, and to the *possible*. If my beloved and I can meet
and make up, without the mediation of this worthy gentleman, it will be so much
the better. As little foreign aid as possible, in my amorous conflicts, has always
been a rule with me; though here I have been obliged to call in so much. And who
knows but it may be the better for her, the less she makes necessary? I cannot bear
that she should sit so indifferent to me as to be in earnest to part with me for ever,
upon so *slight*, or even upon *any* occasion. *If I find she is*—But no more threatenings
till she is in my power—thou knowest what I have vowed.

All Will's account, from the lady's flight to his finding her again, all the accounts
of the people of the house, the coachman's information to Will, and so forth,
collected together, stand thus.

'The Hampstead coach, when the lady came to it, had but two passengers in it.
But she made the fellow go off directly, paying for the vacant places.

'The two passengers directing the coachman to set them down at the Upper
Flask, she bid him set her down there also.

'They took leave of her (very respectfully no doubt), and she went into the
house, and asked if she could not have a dish of tea, and a room to herself for half
an hour?

'They showed her up to the very room where I now am. She sat at the very table
I now write upon; and I believe the chair I sit in was hers.' Oh Belford, if thou
knowest what love is, thou wilt be able to account for these *minutiae*.

'She seemed spiritless and fatigued. The gentlewoman herself chose to attend so
genteel and lovely a guest. She asked her if she would have bread and butter to her
tea? No. She could not eat. They had very good biscakes. As she pleased. The
gentlewoman stepped out for some; and returning on a sudden, she observed the

sweet fugitive endeavouring to restrain a violent burst of grief which she had given way to in that little interval.

'However, when the tea came, she made her sit down with her, and asked her abundance of questions about the villages and roads in that neighbourhood.

'The gentlewoman took notice to her, *that she seemed to be troubled in mind*.

'Tender spirits, she replied, could not part with *dear* friends without concern.' She meant *me*, no doubt.

'She made no inquiry about a lodging, though by the sequel, thou'lt observe that she seemed to intend to go no farther that night than Hampstead. But after she had drank two dishes, and put a biscake in her pocket—(sweet soul, to serve for her supper perhaps—) she laid down half a crown; and refusing change, sighing, took leave, saying she would proceed towards Hendon; the distance to which had been one of her questions.

'They offered to send to know if a Hampstead coach were not to go to Hendon that evening. No matter, she said—perhaps she might meet the chariot.' Another of her *feints*, I suppose; for how, or with whom, could anything of this sort have been concerted since yesterday morning?

'She had, as the people took notice to one another, something so uncommonly noble in her air, and in her person and behaviour, that they were sure she was of quality. And having no servant with her of either sex, her eyes (her fine eyes, the gentlewoman called them, stranger as she was, and a woman!) being swelled and red, they were sure there was an elopement in the case, either from parents or guardians; for they supposed her too young and too maidenly to be a married lady: and were she married, no husband would let such a fine young creature be unattended and alone; nor give her cause for so much grief as seemed to be settled in her countenance. Then, at times, she seemed to be so bewildered, they said, that they were afraid she had it in her head to make away with herself.

'All these things put together excited their curiosity; and they engaged a *peery* servant, as they called a footman who was drinking with Kit the hostler at the tap-house, to watch all her motions. This fellow reported the following particulars, as they were re-reported to me.

'She indeed went towards Hendon, passing by the sign of the Castle on the Heath; then, stopping, looked about her, and down into the valley before her. Then, turning her face towards London, she seemed, by the motion of her handkerchief to her eyes, to weep; repenting (who knows?) the rash step she had taken, and wishing herself back again'—

Better for her if she do, Jack, once more I say!—Woe be to the girl who could think of marrying me, yet be able to run away from me, and renounce me for ever!

'Then, continuing on a few paces, she stopped again; and, as if disliking her road, again seeming to weep, directed her course back towards Hampstead.'

I am glad she wept so much, because no heart bursts (be the occasion for the sorrow what it will) which has that kindly relief. Hence I hardly ever am moved at the sight of these pellucid fugitives in a fine woman. How often, in the past twelve hours, have I wished that I could cry most confoundedly!

'She then saw a coach and four driving towards her empty. She crossed the path she was in, as if to meet it; and seemed to intend to speak to the coachman, had he stopped, or spoke first. He, as earnestly, looked at *her*. Everyone did so, who passed her (so the man who dogged her was the less suspected)'—Happy rogue of a coachman, hadst thou known whose notice thou didst engage, and whom thou mightest have obliged!—It was the divine Clarissa Harlowe at whom thou gazedst!—My own Clarissa Harlowe!—But it was well for me that thou wert as undistinguishing as the beasts thou drovest; otherwise, what a wild-goose chase had I been led?

'The lady, as well as the coachman, in short, seemed to want resolution; the horses kept on; the fellow's head and eyes, no doubt, turned behind him; and the distance soon lengthened beyond recall. With a wistful eye she looked after him; sighed and wept again; as the servant, who then slyly passed her, observed.

'By this time she had reached the houses. She looked up at every one, as she passed; now and then breathing upon her bared hand, and applying it to her swelled eyes, to abate the redness, and dry the tears. At last, seeing a bill up for letting lodgings, she walked backwards and forwards half a dozen times, as if unable to determine what to do. And then went farther into the town; and there the fellow being spoken to by one of his familiars, he lost her for a few minutes: but soon saw her come out of a linen-drapery shop, attended with a servant-maid, having, as he believed, bought some little matters, and, as it proved, got that maid-servant to go with her to the house she is now at.[a]

'The fellow, after waiting about an hour and not seeing her come out, returned, concluding that she had taken lodgings there.'

And here, supposing my narrative of the dramatic kind, ends Act the First. And now begins

ACT II. Scene, Hampstead Heath continued
Enter my Rascal

WILL, having got at all these particulars by exchanging others as frankly against them, which I had formerly prepared him with, both verbally and in writing; I found the people already of my party, and full of good wishes for my success, repeating to me all they told him.

But he had first acquainted me with the accounts he had given them of his lady and me. It is necessary that I give thee the particulars of his tale—and I have a little time upon my hands; for the maid of the house, who had been out of an errand, tells us that she saw Mrs Moore (with whom must be my first business) go into the house of a young gentleman, within a few doors of her, who has a maiden sister, Miss Rawlins by name, *so notified* for prudence, that none of her acquaintance undertake anything of consequence without consulting her.

Meanwhile my honest coachman is walking about Miss Rawlins's door, in order to bring me notice of Mrs Moore's return to her own house. I hope her gossip's tale will be as soon told as mine. Which take as follows.

Will told them, before I came, 'That his lady was but lately married to one of the finest gentlemen in the world. But that, he being very gay and lively, she was *mortal* jealous of him; and in a fit of that sort, had eloped from him. For although she loved him dearly, and he doted upon her (as well he might, since, as they had seen, she was the finest creature *that ever the sun shone upon*), yet she was apt to be very wilful and sullen, if he might take the liberty to say so—but truth was truth—and if she could not have her own way in everything, would be for leaving him. That she had three or four times played his master such tricks; but with all

a See p. 756.

the virtue and innocence in the world; running away to an intimate friend of hers, who, though a young lady of honour, was but too indulgent to her in this her *only* failing: for which reason his master had brought her to London lodgings; their usual residence being in the country: and that, on his refusing to satisfy her about a lady he had been seen with in the park, she had, for the first time since she came to town, served his master thus: whom he had left half-distracted on that account.'

And truly well he might, poor gentleman! cried the honest folks, pitying me before they saw me.

'He told them how he came by his intelligence of her; and made himself such an interest with them, that they helped him to a change of clothes for himself; and the landlord, at his request, privately inquired if the lady actually remained at Mrs Moore's; and for how long she had taken the lodgings: which he found only to be for a week certain: but she had said that she believed she should hardly stay so long. And then it was that he wrote his letter, and sent it by honest Peter Partrick, as thou hast heard.'

When I came, my person and dress having answered Will's description, the people were ready to worship me. I now and then sighed, now and then put on a lighter air; which, however, I designed should show more of vexation ill-disguised, than of real cheerfulness. And they told Will it was a thousand pities so fine a lady should have such *skittish tricks*; adding, that she might expose herself to great dangers by them; for that there were rakes everywhere (*Lovelaces in every corner, Jack!*), and many about that town who would leave nothing unattempted to get into her company: and although they might not prevail upon her, yet might they nevertheless hurt her reputation; and, in time, estrange the affections of so fine a gentleman from her.

Good sensible people, these!—Hey, Jack!

Here, landlord; one word with you. My servant, I find, has acquainted you with the reason of my coming this way. An unhappy affair, landlord! A very unhappy affair! But never was there a more virtuous woman.

So, sir, she seems to be. A thousand pities her ladyship has such ways—And to so good-humoured a gentleman as you seem to be, sir.

Mother-spoilt, landlord!—Mother-spoilt! that's the thing!—But, sighing, I must make the best of it. What I want *you* to do for me, is to lend me a great-coat. I care not what it is. If my spouse should see me at a distance, she would make it very difficult for me to get at her speech. A great-coat with a cape, if you have one. I must come upon her before she is aware.

I am afraid, sir, I have none fit for such a gentleman as you.

Oh, anything will do!—The worse the better.

Exit landlord. Re-enter with two great-coats

Ay, landlord, this will be best; for I can button the cape over the lower part of my face. Don't I look devilishly down and concerned, landlord?

I never saw a gentleman with a better-natured look. 'Tis pity you should have such trials, sir.

I must be very unhappy, no doubt of it, landlord. And yet I am a little pleased, you must needs think, that I have found her out before any great inconvenience has arisen to her. However, if I cannot break her of these freaks, she'll break my heart; for I do love her with all her failings.

The good woman, who was within hearing of all this, pitied me much.

Pray, your honour, said she, if I may be so bold, was madam ever a mamma?

No!—and I sighed—We have been but a little while married; and, as I may say to *you*, it is her own fault that she is not in that way. (Not a word of a lie in this, Jack.) But to tell you truth, madam, she may be compared to the dog in the manger—

I understand you, sir (simpering)—She is but young, sir. I have heard of one or two such skittish young ladies in my time, sir—But when madam is in that way, I dare say, as she loves you (and it would be strange if she did not!), all this will be over, and she may make the best of wives.

That's all my hope.

She is as fine a lady as I ever beheld. I hope, sir, you won't be too severe. She'll get over all these freaks if once she be a mamma, I warrant.

I can't be severe to her; she knows that. The moment I see her, all resentment is over with me if she give me but one kind look.

All this time, I was adjusting my horseman's coat, and Will was putting in the ties of my wig, and buttoning the cape over my chin.

I asked the gentlewoman for a little powder. She brought me a powder-box, and I lightly shook the puff over my hat, and flapped one side of it, though the lace looked a little too gay for my covering; and slouching it over my eyes, Shall I be known, think you, madam?

Your honour is so expert, sir!—I wish, if I may be so bold, your lady has not some *cause* to be jealous. But it will be impossible, if you keep your laced clothes covered, that anybody should know you in that dress to be the same gentleman—except they find you out by your clocked stockings.

Well observed—Can't you, landlord, lend or sell me a pair of stockings that will draw over these? I can cut off the feet, if they won't go into my shoes.

He could let me have a pair of coarse, but clean, stirrup-stockings, if I pleased.

The best in the world for the purpose.

He fetched them. Will drew them on; and my legs then made a good gouty appearance.

The good woman, smiling, wished me success; and so did the landlord. And as thou knowest that I am not a bad mimic, I took a cane which I borrowed of the landlord, and stooped in the shoulders to a quarter of a foot of less height, and stumped away cross to the bowling-green, to practise a little the hobbling gait of a gouty man. The landlady whispered her husband, as Will tells me, He's a good one, I warrant him!—I dare say the fault lies not all of one side. While mine host replied that I was so lively and so good-natured a gentleman, that he did not know who could be angry with me, do what I would. A sensible fellow!—I wish my charmer were of the same opinion.

And now I am going to try if I can't agree with goody Moore for lodgings and other conveniences for my sick wife.

Wife, Lovelace! methinks thou interrogatest.

Yes, *wife*; for who knows what cautions the dear fugitive may have given in apprehension of me?

But has goody Moore any other lodgings to let?

Yes, yes; I have taken care of that; and find that she has just such conveniencies as I want. And I know that my wife will like them. For, although married, I can do everything I please; and that's a bold word, you know. But had she only a garret to let, I would have liked it; and been a poor author afraid of arrests, and made that my place of refuge; yet would have made shift to pay beforehand for what I had. I can suit myself to any condition, that's my comfort.

THE widow Moore returned! say you—Down, down, flutterer!—This impertinent heart is more troublesome to me than my conscience, I think—I shall be obliged to hoarsen my voice, and roughen my character, to keep up with its puppily dancings.

But let me see—Shall I be angry or pleased when I am admitted to my beloved's presence?

Angry, to be sure—Has she not broken her word with me?—at a time, too, when I was meditating to do her grateful justice?—And is not breach of word a dreadful crime in good folks? I have ever been for forming my judgement of the nature of things and actions, not so much from what they are in themselves, as from the character of the actors. Thus it would be as odd a thing in such as we to *keep* our words with a lady, as it would be wicked in her to *break* hers to us.

Seest thou not, that this unseasonable gravity is admitted to quell the palpitations of this unmanageable heart? But still it will go on with its boundings. I'll try, as I ride in my chariot, to *tranquillize*.

Ride, Bob! so little a way?

Yes, ride, Jack; for am I not lame? And will it not look well to have a lodger who keeps his chariot? What widow, what servant, asks questions of a man with an equipage?

My coachman, as well as my other servant, is under Will's tuition.

Never was there such a hideous rascal as he has made himself. The devil only, and his other master, can know him. They both have set their marks upon him. As to my honour's mark, it will never be out of *his damned wide mothe*, as he calls it. For the dog will be hanged before he can lose the rest of his teeth by age.

I am gone.

Letter 233: MR LOVELACE TO JOHN BELFORD, ESQ.

Hampstead, Friday night, June 9

Now, Belford, for the narrative of narratives. I will continue it as I have opportunity; and that so dextrously, that if I break off twenty times, thou shalt not discern where I piece my thread.

Although grievously afflicted with the gout, I alighted out of my chariot (leaning very hard on my cane with one hand, and on my new servant's shoulder with the other) the same instant almost that he had knocked at the door, that I might be sure of admission into the house.

I took care to button my greatcoat about me, and to cover with it even the pommel of my sword; it being a little too gay for my years. I knew not what occasion I might have for my sword. I stooped forward; blinked with my eyes to conceal their lustre (no vanity in saying that, Jack!); my chin wrapped up for the

CLARISSA
[L233]

toothache; my slouched laced hat, and so much of my wig as was visible, giving me all together the appearance of an antiquated beau.

My wife, I resolved beforehand, should have a complication of disorders.

The maid came to the door. I asked for her mistress. She showed me into one of the parlours; and I sat down, with a gouty Oh!—

Enter goody Moore

Your servant, madam—but you must excuse me; I cannot well stand—I find by the bill at the door that you have lodgings to let (mumbling my words as if, like my man Will, I had lost some of my fore-teeth): be pleased to inform me what they are; for I like your situation—and I will tell you my family—I have a wife, a good old woman—older than myself, by the way, a pretty deal. She is in a bad state of health, and is advised into the Hampstead air. She will have two maidservants and a footman. The coach or chariot (I shall not have them up both together) we can put up anywhere, and the coachman will be with his horses.

When, sir, shall you want to come in?

I will take them from this very day; and, if convenient, will bring my wife in the afternoon.

Perhaps, sir, you would board, as well as lodge?

That as you please. It will save me the trouble of bringing my cook, if we do. And I suppose you have servants who know how to dress a couple of dishes. My wife must eat plain food, and I don't love kickshaws.

We have a single lady, who will be gone in two or three days. She has one of the best apartments: that will then be at liberty.

You have one or two good ones meantime, I presume, madam, just to receive my wife; for we have lost time—These damned physicians—Excuse me, madam, I am not used to curse; but it is owing to the love I have for my wife—They have kept her in hand, till they are ashamed to take more fees, and now advise her to the air. I wish we had sent her hither at first. But we must now make the best of it.

Excuse me, madam (for she looked hard at me), that I am muffled up thus in this warm weather. I am but too sensible that I have left my chamber sooner than I ought, and perhaps shall have a return of my gout for it. I came out thus muffled up, with a dreadful pain in my jaws; an ague in them, I believe. But my poor dear will not be satisfied with anybody's care but mine. And, as I told you, we have lost time.

You shall see what accommodations I have, if you please, sir. But I doubt you are too lame to walk upstairs.

I can make shift to hobble up, now I have rested a little. I'll just look upon the apartment my wife is to have. Anything may do for the servants: and as you seem to be a good sort of gentlewoman, I shan't stand for a price, and will pay well besides, for the trouble I shall give.

She led the way; and I, leaning upon the banisters, made shift to get up with less fatigue than I expected from ankles so weak. But oh! Jack, What was Sixtus the Vth's artful depression of his natural powers to mine, when, as the half-dead Montalto, he gaped for the pretendedly unsought Pontificate, and, the moment he was chosen, leapt upon the prancing beast, which it was thought by the amazed conclave he was not able to mount without help of chairs and men? Never was there a more joyous heart and lighter heels than mine joined together, yet both denied their functions; the one fluttering in secret, ready to burst its bars for reliefful expression, the others obliged to a hobbling motion; when, unrestrained, they would, in their master's imagination, have mounted him to the lunar world without the help of a ladder.

There were three rooms on a floor; two of them handsome; and the third, she said, still handsomer; but the lady was in it.

I saw!—I saw, she was! for as I hobbled up, crying out upon my weak ankles in the hoarse mumbling voice I had assumed, I beheld a little piece of her, just casting an eye, with the door ajar, as they call it, to observe who was coming up; and, seeing such an old clumsy fellow great-coated in weather so warm, slouched and muffled up, she withdrew, shutting the door without any emotion. But it was not so with me; for thou canst not imagine how my heart danced to my mouth at the very glimpse of her; so that I was afraid the thump, thump, thumping villain, which had so lately thumped as much to no purpose, would have choked me.

I liked the lodgings well; and the more, as she said the third room was still handsomer. I must sit down, madam (and chose the darkest part of the room). Won't you take a seat yourself? No price shall part us. But I will leave the terms to you and my wife, if you please: and also whether for board or not. Only please to take this for earnest, putting a guinea into her hand—And one thing I will say; my poor wife loves money; but is not an ill-natured woman. She was a great fortune to me: but, as the real estate goes away at her death, I would fain preserve her for that reason, as well as for the love I bear her as an honest man. But if she makes too close a bargain with you, tell *me*; and, unknown to *her*, I will make it up. This is my constant way: she loves to have her pen'worths; and I would not have her vexed or made uneasy on any account.

She said I was a very considerate gentleman; and, upon the condition I had mentioned, she was content to leave the terms to my lady.

But, madam, cannot a body just peep into the other apartment, that I may be more particular to my wife in the furniture of it?

The lady desires to be private, sir—but—and was going to ask her leave.

I caught hold of her hand—However, stay, stay, madam: it mayn't be proper, if the lady loves to be private. Don't let me intrude upon the lady—

No intrusion, sir, I dare say: the lady is good-humoured. She will be so kind as to step down into the parlour, I dare say. As she stays so little a while, I am sure she will not wish to stand in my way.

No, madam, that's true, if she be good-humoured, as you say—Has she been with you long, madam?

But yesterday, sir—

I believe I just now saw the glimpse of her. She seems to be an elderly lady.

No, sir; you're mistaken. She's a young lady; and one of the handsomest I ever saw.

Cot so, I beg her pardon! Not but that I should have liked her the better, were she to stay longer, if she had been elderly. I have a strange taste, madam, you'll say, but I really, for my wife's sake, love every elderly woman. Indeed I ever thought age was to be reverenced, which made me (taking the fortune into the scale too, *that* I own) make my addresses to my present dear.

Very good of you, sir, to respect age: we all hope to live to be old.

Right, madam. But you say the lady is beautiful. Now you must know, that though I choose to converse with the elderly, yet I love to see a beautiful young woman, just as I love to see fine flowers in a garden. There's no casting an eye upon her, is there, without her notice? For in this dress, and thus muffled up about my jaws, I should not care to be seen, any more than she, let her love privacy as much as she will.

I will go ask, if I may show a gentleman the apartment, sir; and, as you are a married gentleman, and not *over*-young, she'll perhaps make the less scruple.

Then, like me, she loves elderly folks best, perhaps. But it may be she has suffered by young ones?

I fancy she has, sir, or is afraid she shall. She desired to be very private, and if by description inquired after, to be denied.

Thou art true woman, goody Moore, thought I!

Good lack!—Good lack!—What may be her story then, I pray?

She is pretty reserved in her story; but, to tell you my thoughts, I believe *love* is in the case: she is always in tears, and does not much care for company.

Nay, madam, it becomes not me to dive into ladies' secrets; I want not to pry into other people's affairs. But, pray, how does she employ herself?—Yet she came but yesterday; so you can't tell.

Writing continually, sir.

These women, Jack, when you ask them questions by way of information, don't care to be ignorant of anything.

Nay, excuse me, madam, I am very far from being an inquisitive man. But if her case be difficult, and not merely *love*, as she is a friend of yours, I would give her my advice.

Then you are a lawyer, sir—

Why, indeed, madam, I was sometime at the Bar; but I have long left practice; yet am much consulted by my friends in difficult points. In a pauper case I frequently *give* money; but never *take* any from the richest.

You are a very good gentleman, then, sir.

Ay, madam, we cannot live always here; and we ought to do what good we can—But I hate to appear officious. If the lady stays any time, and thinks fit, upon better acquaintance, to let me in to her case, it may be a happy day for her if I find it a just one; for, you must know, that when I was at the Bar, I never was such a sad fellow as to undertake, for the sake of a paltry fee, to make white black and black white; for what would that have been, but to endeavour to establish iniquity by quirks while I robbed the innocent?

You are an excellent gentleman, sir: I wish (and then she sighed) I had had the happiness to know there was such a lawyer in the world; and to have been acquainted with him.

Come, come, Mrs Moore, I think your name is, it may not be too late—when you and I are better acquainted, I may help *you* perhaps.—But mention nothing of this to the lady; for, as I said, I hate to appear officious.

This prohibition, I knew, if goody Moore answered the specimen she had given of her womanhood, would make her take the first opportunity to tell, were it to be necessary to my purpose that she should.

I appeared, upon the whole, so indifferent about seeing the room, or the lady, that the good woman was the more eager I should see both. And the rather, as I, to stimulate her, declared that there was more required in my eye to merit the character of a handsome woman, than most people thought necessary; and that I had never seen six truly lovely ladies in my life.

To be brief, she went in; and after a little while came out again. The lady, sir, is retired to her closet, so you may go in and look at the room.

Then how my heart began again to play its pug's tricks!

I hobbled in, and stumped about, and liked it very much; and was sure my wife would. I begged excuse for sitting down, and asked who was the minister of the place? If he were a good preacher? Who preached at the chapel? And if *he* were a good preacher, and good *liver* too, madam—I must inquire after *that*: for I love, I must needs say, that the clergy should practise what they preach.

Very right, sir; but that is not so often the case as were to be wished.

More's the pity, madam. But I have a great veneration for the clergy in general. It is more a satire upon human nature than upon the cloth, if we suppose those who have the *best* opportunities to be good, less perfect than other people. For my part, I don't love *professional* any more than *national* reflections—But I keep the lady in her closet. My gout makes me rude.

Then up from my seat stumped I—What do you call these window-curtains, madam?

Stuff-damask, Sir.

It looks mighty well, truly. I like it better than silk. It is warmer to be sure, and much fitter for lodgings in the country; especially for people in years. The bed is in a pretty taste.

It is neat and clean, sir: that's all we pretend to.

Ay, mighty well—very well—a silk camlet, I think—very well, truly!—I am sure my wife will like it. But we would not turn the lady out of her lodging for the world. The other two apartments will do for us at the present.

Then stumping towards the closet, over the door of which hung a picture—What picture is that?—Oh! I see: A St Cecilia!

A common print, sir—

Pretty well, pretty well! It is after an Italian master—I would not for the world turn the lady out of her apartment. We can make shift with the other two, repeated I, louder still: but yet mumblingly hoarse; for I had as great regard to uniformity in accent, as to my words.

Oh Belford! to be so near my angel, think what a painful constraint I was under!—

I was resolved to fetch her out, if possible: and pretending to be going—You can't agree as to any *time*, Mrs Moore, when we can have this third room, can you?—Not that (whispered I, loud enough to be heard in the next room); not that I would incommode the lady: but I would tell my wife *when*abouts—and women, you know, Mrs Moore, love to have everything before them of this nature.

Mrs Moore, says my charmer (and never did her voice sound so harmonious to me. Oh how my heart bounded again! It even talked to me, in a manner; for I thought I *heard*, as well as *felt*, its unruly flutters; and every vein about me seemed a pulse): Mrs Moore, you may acquaint the gentleman that I shall stay here only for two or three days, at most, till I receive an answer to a letter I have written into the country; and rather than be your hindrance, I will take up with any apartment a pair of stairs higher.

Not for the world! Not for the world, young lady, cried I!—My wife, well as I love her, should lie in a garret, rather than put such a considerate lady as you seem to be, to the least inconveniency.

She opened not the door yet; and I said, But since you have so much goodness, madam, if I could but just look into the closet, as I stand, I could tell my wife whether it is large enough to hold a cabinet she much values, and will have with her wherever she goes.

Then my charmer opened the door, and blazed upon me, as it were in a flood of light, like what one might imagine would strike a man who, born blind, had by some propitious power been blessed with his sight, all at once, in a meridian sun.

Upon my soul, I never was so strangely affected before. I had much ado to forbear discovering myself that instant: but, hesitatingly, and in great disorder, I said, looking into the closet, and around it, There is room, I see, for my wife's cabinet; and it has many jewels in it of high price; but, upon my soul (for I could not forbear swearing, like a puppy:—habit is a cursed thing, Jack)—nothing so valuable as the lady I see, can be brought into it!—

She started, and looked at me with terror. The truth of the compliment, as far as I know, had taken dissimulation from my accent.

I saw it was impossible to conceal myself longer from her, any more than (from the violent impulses of my passion) to forbear manifesting myself. I unbuttoned therefore my cape, I pulled off my flapped, slouched hat; I threw open my great-coat and, like the devil in Milton (an odd comparison though!),

> I started up in my own form divine,
> Touched by the beam of her celestial eye,
> More potent than Ithuriel's spear!—[1]

Now, Belford, for a similitude—now for a likeness to illustrate the surprising scene, and the effect it had upon my charmer and the gentlewoman!—But nothing *was* like it, or equal to it. The plain fact can only describe it, and set it off. Thus then take it.

She no sooner saw who it was, than she gave three violent screams; and, before I could catch her in my arms (as I was about to do the moment I discovered myself), down she sunk at my feet in a fit; which made me curse my indiscretion for so suddenly, and with so much emotion, revealing myself.

The gentlewoman, seeing so strange an alteration in my person, and features, and voice, and dress, cried out, Murder, help! Murder, help! by turns, for half a dozen times running. This alarmed the house, and up ran two servant-maids, and *my* servant after them. I cried out for water and hartshorn, and everyone flew a different way, one of the maids as fast down as she came up; while the gentlewoman ran out of one room into another, and by turns up and down the apartment we were in, without meaning or end, wringing her foolish hands, and not knowing what she did.

Up then came running a gentleman and his sister, fetched and brought in by the maid who had run down; and who having let in a cursed crabbed old wretch, hobbling with his gout and mumbling with his hoarse broken-toothed voice, was metamorphosed all at once into a lively gay young fellow, with a clear accent, and all his teeth; and she would have it that I was neither more nor less than the devil, and could not keep her eye from my foot; expecting, no doubt, every minute to see it discover itself to be cloven.

For my part, I was so intent upon restoring my angel that I regarded nobody else. And at last, she slowly recovering motion, with bitter sighs and sobs (only the whites of her eyes however appearing for some moments), I called upon her in the tenderest accent, as I kneeled by her, my arm supporting her head; My angel! My charmer! My Clarissa! look upon me, my dearest life!—I am not angry with you!— I will forgive you, my best beloved!—

The gentleman and his sister knew not what to make of all this: and the less, when my fair one, recovering her sight, snatched another look at me; and then again groaned, and fainted away.

I threw up the closet-sash for air, and then left her to the care of the young gentlewoman, the same notable Miss Rawlins, whom I had heard of at the Flask; and to that of Mrs Moore; who by this time had recovered herself; and then retiring to one corner of the room, I made my servant pull off my gouty stockings, brush my hat, and loop it up into the usual smart cock.

I then stepped to the closet to Mr Rawlins, whom, in the general confusion, I had not much minded before.—Sir, said I, you have an uncommon scene before you. The lady is my wife, and no gentleman's presence is necessary here but my own.

I beg pardon, sir: *If* the lady is your wife, I have no business here. *But*, sir, by her concern at seeing you—

Pray, sir, none of your *if*'s, and *but*'s, I beseech you: nor *your* concern about the *lady*'s concern. You are a very qualified judge in this cause; and I beg of you, sir, to oblige me with your absence. The ladies only are proper to be present on this occasion, added I; and I think myself obliged to them for their care and kind assistance.

'Tis well he made not another word: for I found my choler begin to rise. I could not bear that the finest neck, and arms, and foot, in the world, should be exposed to the eyes of any man living but mine.

I withdrew once more from the closet, finding her beginning to recover, lest the sight of me too soon should throw her back again.

The first words she said, looking round her with great emotion, were, Oh hide me! hide me! Is he gone!—Oh hide me! Is he gone!

Sir, said Miss Rawlins, coming to me with an air somewhat peremptory and assured, this is some surprising case. The lady cannot bear the sight of you. What you have done is best known to yourself. But another such fit will probably be her last. It would be but kind, therefore, for you to retire.

It behoved me to have so notable a person of my party; and the rather, as I had disobliged her impertinent brother.

The dear creature, said I, may *well* be concerned to see me. If *you*, madam, had a husband who loved you, as I love her, you would not, I am confident, fly from him and expose yourself to hazards, as she does whenever she has not all her way—and yet with a mind not capable of intentional evil—But, mother-spoilt! This is her fault, and all her fault: and the more inexcusable it is, as I am the man of her choice, and have reason to think she loves me above all the men in the world.

Here, Jack, was a story to support to the lady; face to face too![a]

You *speak* like a gentleman; you *look* like a gentleman, said Miss Rawlins—But, sir, this is a strange case; the lady seems to dread the sight of you.

No wonder, madam; taking her a little on one side, nearer to Mrs Moore. I have three times already forgiven the dear creature—But this *jealousy*—there is a spice of *that* in it—and of *frenzy* too (whispered I, that it might have the face of a secret, and of consequence the more engage their attention)—but our story is too long—

I then made a motion to go to the lady. But they desired that I would walk into the next room; and they would endeavour to prevail upon her to lie down.

I begged that they would not suffer her to talk; for that she was accustomed to fits and would, when in this way, talk of anything that came uppermost; and the more she was suffered to run on, the worse she was; and if not kept quiet would fall into ravings; which might possibly hold her a week.

They promised to keep her quiet; and I withdrew into the next room; ordering everyone down but Mrs Moore and Miss Rawlins.

She was full of exclamations. Unhappy creature! miserable! ruined! and undone! she called herself; wrung her hands, and begged they would assist her to escape from the terrible evils she should otherwise be made to suffer.

They preached patience and quietness to her; and would have had her to lie down; but she refused; sinking, however, into an easy chair; for she trembled so, she could not stand.

[a] And here, Belford, lest thou through inattention shouldst be surprised at my assurance, let me remind thee (and that, thus by way of marginal observation, that I may not break in upon my narrative), that this my intrepidity was but a consequence of the measures I had previously concerted (as I have from time to time acquainted thee) in apprehension of such an event as has fallen out. For had not the dear creature already passed for my wife before no less than four worthy gentlemen of family and fortune*? And before Mrs Sinclair and her household, and Miss Partington?—And had she not agreed to her uncle's expedient that she *should* pass for such, from the time of Mr Hickman's application to that uncle †; and that the worthy Captain Tomlinson should be allowed to propagate that belief; as he had actually reported it to two families (*they possibly to more*); purposely that it might come to the ears of James Harlowe; and serve for a foundation for uncle John to build his reconciliation scheme upon ‡? And canst thou think that nothing was meant by all this contrivance? And that I am not still *further* prepared to support my story?

Indeed, I little thought at the time that I formed these precautionary schemes, that she would ever have been able, *if willing*, to get out of my hands. All that I hoped I should have occasion to have recourse to them for, was only that in case I should have the courage to make the grand attempt, and should succeed in it, to bring the dear creature (and this out of tenderness to her; for what attention did I ever yet pay to the grief, the execrations, the tears of a woman I had triumphed over?) to bear me in her sight; to expostulate with me; to be pacified by my pleas, and by her own future hopes, founded upon the reconciliatory project, upon my reiterated vows, and upon the captain's assurances—Since, in that case, to forgive me, to have gone on with me for a week, would have been to forgive me, to have gone on with me for ever. And then had my eligible life of honour taken place; her trials would all have been then over; and she would have known nothing but gratitude, love, and joy, to the end of one of our lives. For never would I, never could I, have abandoned such an admirable creature as this. Thou knowest I never was a sordid villain to any of her inferiors—*her inferiors*, I may say,—for who is not her inferior?

*See p. 539.   †See p. 707.   ‡See p. 708.

By this time, I hoped that she was enough recovered to bear a presence, that it behoved me to make her bear; and fearing she would throw out something in her exclamations that would still more disconcert me, I went into the room again.

Oh! there he is! said she, and threw her apron over her face—I cannot see him!—I cannot look upon him!—Begone! begone! touch me not!—

For I took her struggling hand, beseeching her to be pacified; and assuring her that I would make all up with her, upon her own terms and wishes.

Base man! said the violent lady, I have no wishes, but never to behold you more! Why must I be thus pursued and haunted? Have you not made me miserable enough already? Despoiled of all succour and help, and of every friend, I am contented to be poor, low, and miserable, so I may be free from your persecutions!—

Miss Rawlins stared at me (a confident slut this Miss Rawlins, thought I!): so did Mrs Moore—I told you so! whisperingly said I, turning to the women; shaking my head with a face of great concern and pity; and then to my charmer, My dear creature, how you rave!—You will not easily recover from the effects of this violence! Have patience, my love! Be pacified! and we will coolly talk this matter over: for you expose yourself, as well as me. These ladies will certainly think you have fallen among robbers; and that I am the chief of them.

So you are! so you are! stamping, her face still covered (she thought of Wednesday night, no doubt); and, sighing as if her heart were breaking, she put her hand to her forehead—I shall be quite distracted!

I will not, my dearest love, uncover your face. You shall *not* look upon me, since I am so odious to you. But this is a violence I never thought you capable of—

And I would have pressed her hand, as I held it, with my lips; but she drew it from me with indignation.

Unhand me, sir, said she. I will not be touched by you. Leave me to my fate. What right, what title, have you to persecute me thus?

What right, what title, my dear!—But this is not a time—I have a letter from Captain Tomlinson—Here it is—offering it to her—

I will receive nothing from your hands—Tell me not of Captain Tomlinson—Tell me not of anybody—You have no right to invade me thus—Once more, leave me to my fate—Have you not made me miserable enough?—

I touched a delicate string, on purpose to set her in such a passion before the women as might confirm the intimation I had given of a frenzical disorder. What a turn is here!—Lately so happy!—Nothing wanting but a reconciliation between you and your friends!—that reconciliation in such a happy train!—shall so *slight*, so *accidental* an occasion be suffered to overturn all our happiness?

She started up with a trembling impatience, her apron falling from her indignant face—Now, said she, that thou darest to call the occasion *slight* and *accidental*, and that I am happily out of thy vile hands, and out of a house I have reason to believe *as* vile, traitor and wretch that thou art, I will venture to cast an eye upon thee—and Oh that it were in my power, in mercy to my sex, to look thee first into shame and remorse, and then into death!

This violent tragedy speech, and the high manner in which she uttered it, had its desired effect. I looked upon the women, and upon her, by turns, with a pitying eye; and they shook their wise heads, and besought *me* to retire, and *her* to lie down to compose herself.

This hurricane, like other hurricanes, was presently allayed by a shower. She threw herself once more into her armed chair—and begged pardon of the women for her passionate excess; but not of me: yet I was in hopes that when compliments were stirring, I should have come in for a share.

Indeed, ladies, said I (with assurance enough, thou'lt say), this violence is not natural to my beloved's temper—misapprehension—

Misapprehension, wretch!—and want I excuses from thee!

What a scorn was every lovely feature agitated by!

Then turning her face from me, I have not patience, Oh thou guileful betrayer, to look upon thee!—Begone! Begone! With a face so unblushing, how darest thou my presence?

I thought then that the character of a husband obliged me to be angry.

You may one day, madam, repent this treatment—by my soul you may—You know I have not deserved it of you—you *know* I have not.

Do I know you have not?—wretch! Do I know—

You do, madam!—and never did man of my figure and consideration (I thought it was proper to throw that in) meet with such treatment. (She lifted up her hands: indignation kept her silent)—But all is of a piece with the charge you bring against me of *despoiling you of all succour and help*, of making you *poor* and *low*, and with other unprecedented language. I will only say, before these two gentlewomen, that since it *must* be so, and since your former esteem for me is turned into so riveted an aversion, I will soon, *very* soon, make you entirely easy. I *will* be gone:—I *will* leave you to *your own fate*, as you call it; and may that be happy!—Only, that I may not appear to be a spoiler, a robber indeed, let me know whither I shall send your apparel, and everything that belongs to you, and I *will* send it.

Send it to this place; and assure me that you will never molest me more; never more come near me; and that is all I ask of you.

I *will* do so, madam, said I, with a dejected air. But did I ever think I should be so indifferent to you?—However, you must permit me to insist on your reading this letter; and on your seeing Captain Tomlinson, and hearing what he has to say from your uncle. He will be here by and by.

Don't trifle with me, said she, in an imperious tone—Do as you offer. I will not receive any letter from your hands. If I see Captain Tomlinson, it shall be on his *own* account; not on *yours*. You tell me you will send me my apparel: if you would have me believe anything you say, let this be the test of your sincerity—Leave me *now*, and send my things.

The women stared. They did nothing but stare; and appeared to be more and more at a loss what to make of the matter between us.

I pretended to be going from her in a pet: but when I had got to the door, I turned back; and, as if I had recollected myself, One word more, my dearest creature!—charming even in your anger!—Oh my fond soul! said I, turning half round, and pulling out my handkerchief.

I believe, Jack, my eyes did glisten a little—I have no doubt but they did—The women pitied me. Honest souls!—they showed that they had each of them a handkerchief as well as I. So, hast thou not observed (to give a familiar illustration) every man in a company of a dozen or more, obligingly pull out his watch, when some one has asked what's o'clock?

One word only, madam, repeated I as soon as my voice had recovered its tone—

I have represented to Captain Tomlinson in the most favourable light the cause of our present misunderstanding. You know what your uncle insists upon; and which you have acquiesced with. The letter in my hand (and again I offered it to her) will acquaint you with what you have to apprehend from your brother's active malice.

She was going to speak in a high accent, putting the letter from her, with an open palm—Nay, hear me out, madam—The captain, you know, has reported our *marriage* to two different persons. It is come to your brother's ears. My own relations have also heard of it. Letters were brought me from town this morning, from Lady Betty Lawrance and Miss Montague. Here they are (I pulled them out of my pocket, and offered them to her, with that of the captain; but she held back her still open palm, that she might not receive them). Reflect, madam, I beseech you reflect, upon the fatal consequences which this your high resentment may be attended with.

Ever since I knew you, said she, I have been in a wilderness of doubt and error. I bless God that I am out of your hands. I will transact for myself what relates to myself. I dismiss all your solicitude for me. Am I not my own mistress!—Am I not—

The women stared. (The devil stare ye, thought I, can ye do nothing but stare?) It was high time to stop her here. I raised my voice to drown hers—You used, my dearest creature, to have a tender and apprehensive heart—You never had so much reason for such a one as now.

Let me judge for myself upon what I shall *see*, not upon what I shall *hear*—Do you think I shall ever—

I dreaded her going on—I *must* be heard, madam, raising my voice still higher. You must let me read one paragraph or two of this letter to you, if you will not read it yourself—

Begone from me, man!—Begone from me with thy letters! What pretence hast thou for tormenting me thus—

Dearest creature, what questions you ask! Questions that you can as well answer yourself—

I *can*, I *will*—And *thus* I answer them—

Still louder raised I my voice. She was overborne. Sweet soul! It would be hard, thought I (and yet I was very angry with her), if such a spirit as thine cannot be brought to yield to such a one as mine!

I lowered my voice on her silence. All gentle, all *intreative*, my accent: my head bowed; one hand held out; the other on my honest heart—For Heaven's sake, my dearest creature, resolve to see Captain Tomlinson with temper. He would have come along with me: but I was willing to try to soften your mind first, on this fatal misapprehension; and this for the sake of your own wishes: for what is it otherwise to me, whether your friends are, or are not, reconciled to us? *Do I want any favour from them?*—For your own mind's sake therefore, frustrate not Captain Tomlinson's negotiation. That worthy gentleman will be here in the afternoon—Lady Betty will be in town with my cousin Montague in a day or two. They will be your visitors. I beseech you do not carry this misunderstanding so far, as that Lord M. and Lady Betty, and Lady Sarah, may know it. (*How considerable this made me look to the women!*) Lady Betty will not let you rest till you consent to accompany her to her own seat—and to that lady may you safely entrust your cause.

Again, upon my pausing a moment, she was going to break out. I liked not the turn of her countenance, nor the tone of her voice— 'And thinkest thou, base wretch,' were the words she *did* utter. I again raised my voice, and drowned hers— *Base wretch*, madam!—You know that I have not deserved the violent names you have called me. Words so opprobrious from a mind so gentle—but this treatment is from *you*, madam!—from *you*, whom I love more than my own soul—By that soul, I swear that I do—(The women looked upon each other. They seemed pleased with my ardour. Women, whether wives, maids, or widows, love ardours. Even Miss Howe, thou knowest, speaks up for ardours[a])—Nevertheless, I must say that you have carried matters too far for the occasion. I see you hate me—

She was just going to speak—If we are to *separate for ever*, in a strong and solemn voice, proceeded I, this island shall not long be troubled with me— Meantime, only be pleased to give these letters a perusal, and consider what is to be said to your uncle's friend; and what he is to say to your uncle—Anything will I come into (renounce me if you will), that shall make for *your* peace, and for the reconciliation your heart was so lately set upon. But I humbly conceive that it is necessary that you should come into better temper with me, were it but to give a favourable appearance to what *has passed*, and weight to any *future application* to your friends, in whatever way you shall think proper to make it.

I then put the letters into her lap, and retired into the next apartment with a low bow, and a very solemn air.

I was soon followed by the two women. Mrs Moore withdrew to give the fair perverse time to read them: Miss Rawlins for the same reason; and because she was sent for home.

The widow besought her speedy return. I joined in the same request; and she was ready enough to promise to oblige us.

I excused myself to Mrs Moore for the disguise I had appeared in at first, and for the story I had invented. I told her that I held myself obliged to satisfy her for the whole floor we were upon; and for an upper room for my servant; and that for a month certain.

She made many scruples, and begged she might not be urged on this head till she had consulted Miss Rawlins.

I consented; but told her that she had taken my earnest; and I hoped there was no room for dispute.

Just then Miss Rawlins returned with an air of eager curiosity; and having been told what had passed between Mrs Moore and me, she gave herself airs of office immediately: which I humoured, plainly perceiving that if I had *her* with me, I had the other.

She wished, if there were time for it, and if it were not quite impertinent in her to desire it, that I would give Mrs Moore and her a brief history of an affair which, as she said, bore the face of novelty, mystery, and surprise: for sometimes it looked to her as if we were married; at other times that point appeared doubtful; and yet the lady did not absolutely deny it; but, upon the whole, thought herself highly injured.

I said that ours was a very particular case: that were I to acquaint them with it, some part of it would hardly appear credible. But, however, I would give them, as they seemed to be persons of discretion, a brief account of the whole; and this in

a pp. 587, 603.

so plain and sincere a manner that it should clear up to their satisfaction everything that had passed, or might hereafter pass between us.

They sat down by me, and threw every feature of their faces into attention. I was resolved to go as near the truth as possible, lest anything should drop from my spouse to impreach my veracity; and yet keep in view what passed at the Flask.

It is necessary, although thou knowest my whole story, and a good deal of my views, that thou shouldst be apprised of the substance of what I told them.

'I gave them in as concise a manner as I was able the history of our families, fortunes, alliances, antipathies (her brother's, and mine, particularly). I averred the truth of our private marriage.' The captain's letter, which I will enclose, will give thee my reasons for that: and besides, the women might also, perhaps, have proposed a parson to me by way of compromise. 'I told them the condition my spouse had made me swear to; and which she held me to, in order, I said, to induce me the sooner to be reconciled to her relations.

'I owned that this restraint made me sometimes ready to fly out.' And Mrs Moore was so good as to declare that she did not much wonder at it.

Thou art a very good sort of woman, Mrs Moore, thought I.

As Miss Howe has actually detected our mother; and might possibly find some way still to acquaint her friend with her discoveries; I thought it proper to prepossess them in Mrs Sinclair's favour; and in that of her two nieces.

I said, 'They were gentlewomen born; had not bad hearts; that indeed my spouse did not love them; they having once jointly taken the liberty to blame her for her over-niceness with regard to me. People, I said, even *good* people, who knew themselves to be guilty of a fault they had no inclination to mend, were too often least patient when told of it; as they could less bear than others to be thought indifferently of.'

Too often the case, they owned.

'Mrs Sinclair's house was a very handsome house, and fit to receive the first quality. (True enough, Jack!) Mrs Sinclair was a woman very easy in her circumstances: a widow-gentlewoman—as *you*, Mrs Moore, are. Lets lodgings—as *you*, Mrs Moore, do. Once had better prospects—as *you*, Mrs Moore, may have had: the relict of Colonel Sinclair: you, Mrs Moore, might know Colonel Sinclair—he had lodgings at Hampstead.'

She had heard of the name.

'Oh, he was related to the best families in Scotland: and his widow is not to be reflected upon because she lets lodgings, you know Mrs Moore;—you know, Miss Rawlins.'

Very true, and, very true: and they must needs say, it did not look quite so pretty in such a lady as my spouse, to be so censorious.

A foundation here, thought I, to procure these women's help to get back the fugitive, or their connivance at least at my doing so; as well as for anticipating any future information from Miss Howe.

I gave them a character of that virago: and intimated, 'that for a head to contrive mischief, and a heart to execute it, she had hardly her equal in her sex.'

To *this* Miss Howe it was, Mrs Moore said she supposed, that my spouse was so desirous to dispatch a man and horse, by day-dawn, with a letter she wrote before she went to bed last night; proposing to stay no longer than till she had received an answer to it.

The very same, said I. I *knew* she would have immediate recourse to her. I should have been but too happy, could I have prevented such a letter from passing, or so to have managed as to have it given into Mrs Howe's hands instead of her daughter's. Women who had lived some time in the world, knew *better* than to encourage such skittish pranks in young wives.

Let me just stop to tell thee, while it is in my head, that I have since given Will his cue to find out where the man lives who is gone with the fair fugitive's letter; and, if possible, to see him on his return before he sees her.

I told the women, 'That I despaired it would ever be better with us while Miss Howe had so strange a predominance over my spouse, and remained herself *unmarried*; and until the reconciliation with her friends could be effected; or a *still* happier event—as I should think it, who am the last male of my family; and which my foolish vow, and her rigour, had hitherto'—

Here I stopped, and looked modest, turning my diamond ring round my finger: while goody Moore looked mighty significant, calling it a very particular case; and the maiden lady fanned away, and primmed and pursed, to show that what I said needed no farther explanation.

'I told them the occasion of our present difference: avowed the reality of the fire: but owned that I would have made no scruple of breaking the unnatural oath she had bound me in (having a husband's right of my side), when she was so accidentally frighted into my arms: and I blamed myself excessively that I did not; since she thought fit to carry her resentment so high, and had the injustice to suppose the fire to be a contrivance of mine.'

Nay, for that matter, Mrs Moore said—as we were married, and *madam* was so odd—every gentleman would not—and there stopped Mrs Moore.

'To suppose I should have recourse to such a *poor* contrivance, said I, when I saw the dear creature *every hour*—' Was not this a bold put, Jack?

A most extraordinary case, truly! the maiden lady: fanning, yet coming in with her *Well buts*, and her sifting *Pray, sir's!*—And her restraining *Enough, sir's!*—flying *from* the question *to* the question; her seat now and then uneasy, for fear my want of delicacy should hurt her abundant modesty; and yet it was difficult to satisfy her *super*-abundant curiosity.

'My beloved's jealousy; which of itself, to female minds, accounts for a thousand unaccountablenesses; and the imputation of her half-frenzy brought upon her by her father's wicked curse, and by the previous persecutions she had undergone from all her family; were what I dwelt upon in order to provide against what might happen.'

In short, 'I owned against myself most of the offences which I did not doubt but she would charge me with in their hearing: and as every cause has a black and white side, I gave the worst parts of our story the gentlest turn. And when I had done, gave them some *partial* hints of the contents of Captain Tomlinson's letter, which I had left with her: with a caution to be guarded against the inquiries of James Harlowe and of Captain Singleton, or of sailor-looking men.' This thou wilt see from the letter itself was necessary to be done. Here therefore thou mayest read it. And a charming letter to my purpose, if thou givest the least attention to its contents, wilt thou find it to be.

[*Letter 233.1*: '*Captain Tomlinson*'] *to Robert Lovelace, Esq.*

Wed. June 7

Dear sir,

ALTHOUGH I am obliged to be in town tomorrow, or next day at farthest, yet I would not dispense with writing to you by one of my servants (whom I send up before me upon a particular occasion), in order to advertise you *that it is probable you will hear from some of your own relations on your (supposed[a]) nuptials.* One of the persons (Mr Lilburne by name) to whom I hinted my belief of your marriage, happens to be acquainted with Mr Spurrier, Lady Betty Lawrance's steward; and (not being under any restriction) mentioned it *to* Mr Spurrier, and he to Lady Betty, as a thing certain: and this (though I have not the honour *to be personally known to her ladyship*) brought on an inquiry from her ladyship to me by her gentleman; who coming to me in company with Mr Lilburne, I had no way but to confirm the report. And I understand that Lady Betty takes it amiss, that she was not acquainted with so desirable a piece of news from yourself.

Her ladyship, it seems, has *business that calls her to town*; (and you will possibly choose to put her right. If you do, it will, I presume, *be in confidence*; that nothing may perspire from your *own* family to contradict what I have given out.)

(I have ever been of opinion, *that truth ought to be strictly adhered to on all occasions:* and am concerned that I have departed (though with so good a view), from my old maxim. But my dear friend Mr John Harlowe would have it so. Yet I never knew a departure of this kind a *single* departure. But, to make the best of it now, allow me, sir, once more to beg the lady as soon as possible to authenticate the report given out.) When you both join in the acknowledgement [of your marriage], it will be impertinent in anyone to be inquisitive as to the *day or week:* (and, if as privately celebrated as you intend, while the gentlewomen with whom you lodge are properly instructed as you say they are, and who actually believe you are married long ago, who shall be able to give a contradiction to my report?)

And yet it is very probable that minute inquiries will be made; and this is what renders precaution necessary. For Mr James Harlowe will not believe that you are married; and is sure, he says, that you both lived together when Mr Hickman's application was made to Mr John Harlowe: and if you lived together *any* time unmarried, he infers from *your* character, Mr Lovelace, that it is not probable that you would ever marry. And he leaves it to his two uncles to decide, if you even *should be* married, whether there be not room to believe that his sister was first dishonoured; and if so, to judge of the title she will have to their favour, or to the forgiveness of any of her family. I believe, sir, this part of my letter had best to be kept from the lady.

What makes young Mr Harlowe the more earnest to find this out—and find it out he is resolved, and to come at his sister's speech too; and for that purpose sets out tomorrow, as I am well-informed, with a large attendance, armed, and Mr Solmes is to be of the party—is this: Mr John Harlowe has told the whole family that he will alter and new-settle his will. Mr Antony Harlowe is resolved to do the same by his; for, it seems, he has now given over all thoughts of changing his

---

a What is between hooks ( ) thou mayest suppose, Jack, I sunk upon the women in the account I gave them of the contents of this letter.

condition; *having lately been disappointed in a view he had of that sort with Mrs Howe.* These two brothers generally act in concert; and Mr James Harlowe dreads, and let me tell you that he has reason for it, on *my* Mr Harlowe's account, that his younger sister will be at last more benefited than he wishes for, by the alteration intended. He has already been endeavouring to sound his uncle Harlowe on this subject; and wanted to know whether any new application had been made to him on his sister's part. Mr Harlowe avoided a direct answer, and expressed his wishes for a general reconciliation, and his hopes that his niece was married. This offended the furious young man, and he reminded his uncle of engagements they had all entered into at his sister's going away, *not to be reconciled but by general consent.*

Mr John Harlowe complains to me often of the uncontrollableness of his nephew; and says that now that the young man has not anybody of whose superior sense he stands in awe, he observes not decency in his behaviour to any of them. And this makes *my* Mr Harlowe still more desirous than ever of bringing his younger niece into favour again. I will not say all I might of this young man's extraordinary rapaciousness—but one would think *that these grasping men expect to live for ever!*

'I took the liberty but within these two hours to propose to set on foot, and offered my cover, to a correspondence between *my friend, and his daughter-niece,* as he still sometimes fondly calls her. She was mistress of so much prudence, I said, that I was sure she could better direct everything to its desirable end than anybody else could. But he said, he did not think himself entirely at liberty to take such a step *at present*; and that it was best that he should have it in his power to say, occasionally, that he had not any correspondence *with* her, or letter *from* her.

'You will see, sir, from all this, the necessity of keeping our treaty an *absolute secret*; and if the lady has mentioned it to her *worthy* friend Miss Howe, I hope it is in confidence.'

(And now, sir, a few lines in answer to yours of Monday last.)

(Mr Harlowe was very well pleased with your readiness to come into his proposal. But as to what you *both* desire, that he will be present at the ceremony, he said that his nephew watched all his steps so narrowly, that he thought it was not practicable, if he were inclinable, to oblige you: but that he consented with all his heart that I should be the person privately present at the ceremony, on his part.)

(However, I think I have an *expedient* for this, if your lady *continues* to be very desirous of her uncle's presence, except he should be more determined than his answer seemed to import; of which I shall acquaint you, and perhaps of what he says to it, when I have the pleasure to see you in town. But, indeed, I think you have no time to lose. Mr Harlowe is impatient to hear that you are actually one; and I hope I may carry him down word, when I leave you next, that I saw the ceremony performed.)

(If any obstacle arises from the lady, from *you* it cannot, I shall be tempted to think a little hardly of her punctilio.)

Mr Harlowe hopes, sir, that you will rather take pains to *avoid,* than to *meet,* this violent young man. He has the better opinion of you, let me tell you, sir, from the account I gave him of your moderation and politeness; neither of which are qualities with his nephew. *But we have all of us something to amend.*

You cannot imagine how dearly my friend still loves this excellent niece of his—

I will give you an instance of it, which affected me a good deal—'If once more, said he, the last time but one we were together, I can but see this sweet child gracing the upper end of my table, as mistress of my house, in my *allotted month*; all the rest of the family present but as her guests; for so I *would* have it; and had her *mother's consent for it*'—There he stopped; for he was forced to turn his reverend face from me. Tears ran down his cheeks. Fain would he have hid them: but he could not—'Yet—yet,' said he—'How—how'—poor gentleman, he perfectly sobbed—'how shall I be able to bear the first meeting!'

I bless God I am *no hard-hearted man*, Mr Lovelace: my eyes showed to my worthy friend that he had no reason to be ashamed of his humanity before me.

I will put an end to this long epistle. Be pleased to make my compliments acceptable to the most excellent of women; as well as believe me to be, dear sir,

Your faithful friend, and humble servant,
ANTONY TOMLINSON

During the above conversation [between me and the women], I had planted myself at the further end of the apartment we were in, over against the door, which was open; and opposite to the lady's chamber-door, which was shut. I spoke so low, that it was impossible, at that distance, that she should hear what we said; and in this situation I could see if her door opened.

I told the women that what I had mentioned of Lady Betty's and her niece's coming to town, and of their intention to visit my spouse, whom they had never seen, nor she them, was real; and that I expected news of their arrival every hour. I then showed them copies of the other two letters which I had left with her; the one from lady Betty, the other from my cousin Montague—And here thou mayest read them if thou wilt.

Eternally reproaching, eternally upbraiding me, are my impertinent relations. But they are fond of occasions to find fault with me. Their love, their love, Jack, and their dependence on my known good humour, their inducement!

[*Letter 233.2: Lady Elizabeth Lawrance*] *to Robert Lovelace, Esq.*

Wed. morn. June 7

Dear Nephew,

I UNDERSTAND that at length all our wishes are answered in your happy marriage. But I think we might as well have heard of it directly from you, as from the roundabout way by which we have been made acquainted with it. Methinks, sir, the *power* and the *will* we have to oblige you should not expose us the more to your slights and negligence. My brother had set his heart upon giving to you the wife we have all so long wished you to have. But if you were actually married at the time you made him that request (supposing, perhaps, that his gout would not let him attend you), it is but like *you*ᵃ—If your lady had *her* reasons to wish it to be private while the differences between her family and self continue, you might nevertheless have communicated it to us, with *that* restriction; and we should have forborne the public manifestations of our joy upon an event we have so long desired.

a I gave [Mrs Moore and Miss Rawlins] room to think this reproach *just*, Jack.

The distant way we have come to know it is by my steward; who is acquainted with a friend of Captain Tomlinson, to whom that gentleman revealed it: and he, it seems, had it from yourself and lady, with such circumstances as leave it not to be doubted.

I am, indeed, very much disobliged with you: so is my sister Sadleir. But I shall have a very speedy opportunity to tell you so in person; being obliged to go to town on my old Chancery affair. My cousin Leeson, who is, it seems, removed to Albermarle Street, has notice of it. I shall be at *her* house, where I bespeak your attendance on Sunday night. I have written to my cousin Charlotte for either her, or her sister, to meet me at Reading, and accompany me to town. I shall stay but a few days; my business being matter of form only. On my return I shall pop upon my brother at M. Hall, to see in what way his last fit has left him.

Meantime, having told you my mind on your negligence, I cannot help congratulating you both upon the occasion: your fair lady particularly, upon her entrance into a family which is prepared to admire and love her.

My principal intention of writing to you (dispensing with the necessary punctilio) is, that you may acquaint my dear new niece that I will not be denied the honour of her company down with me into Oxfordshire. I understand that your proposed house and equipages cannot be soon ready. She shall be with me till they are. I insist upon it. This shall make all up. My house shall be her own: my servants and equipages hers.

Lady Sarah, who has not been out of her own house for months, will oblige me with her company for a week, in honour of a niece so dearly beloved as I am sure she will be of us all.

Being but in lodgings in town, neither you nor your lady can require much preparation.

Some time on Monday I hope to attend the dear young lady, to make her my compliments; and to receive *her* apology for *your* negligence: which, and her going down with me, as I said before, shall be full satisfaction. Meantime, God bless *her* for her courage (tell her I say so): and bless you *both* in each other; and that will be happiness to us all—particularly to

Your truly affectionate aunt,
ELIZ. LAWRANCE

[*Letter 233.3: Miss Charlotte Montague*] *to Robert Lovelace, Esq.*

Dear Cousin,

AT last, as we understand, there is some hope of you. Now does my good lord run over his bead-roll of proverbs; of *black oxen, wild oats, long lanes*, and so forth.

Now, cousin, say I, is your time come; and you will be no longer, I hope, an infidel either to the power or excellence of the sex you have pretended hitherto so much to undervalue; nor a ridiculer or scoffer at an institution which all sober people reverence and all rakes sooner or later are brought to reverence, or to wish they had.

I want to see how you become your silken fetters: whether the charming yoke sits light upon your shoulders. If, with such a sweet yoke-fellow it does not, my lord, and my sister as well as I, think that you will deserve a closer tie about your neck.

His lordship frets like taffaty, that you have not written him word of the day, the hour, the manner, and everything. But I ask him how he can *already* expect any mark of deference or politeness from you? He must stay, I tell him, till that sign of reformation, among others, must appear from the influence and example of your lady: but that, if ever you will be good for anything, it will be quickly seen. And oh cousin, what a vast, vast, journey have you to take from the dreary land of libertinism, through the bright province of reformation, into the serene kingdom of happiness!—You had need to lose no time. You have many a weary step to tread, before you can overtake those travellers who set out for it from a less remote quarter. But you have a charming pole-star to guide you, that's your advantage. I wish you joy of it: and as I have never yet expected any highly complaisant thing from you, I make no scruple to begin first; but it is purely, I must tell you, in respect to my new cousin; whose accession into our family we most heartily congratulate and rejoice in.

I have a letter from Lady Betty. She commands my attendance, or my sister's, at Reading, to proceed with her to the great beastly town, to cousin Leeson's. She puts Lord M. in hopes that she shall certainly bring down with her our lovely new relation; for she says she will not be denied. His lordship is the willinger to let *me* be the person, as I am in a manner wild to see her; my sister having two years ago had that honour at Sir Robert Biddulph's. So get ready to accompany us in our return; except your lady has objections strong enough to satisfy us all. Lady Sarah longs to see her; and says this accession to the family will supply to it the loss of her beloved daughter.

I shall soon, I hope, pay my compliments to the dear lady in person: so have nothing to add, but that, I am

Your old mad playfellow and cousin,
CHARLOTTE MONTAGUE

The women having read the copies of these two letters, I thought that I might then threaten and swagger—'But very little heart have I, said I, to encourage such a visit from Lady Betty and Miss Montague to my spouse. For after all, I am tired out with her strange ways. She is not what she was, and (as I told her in your hearing, ladies) I will leave this plaguy island, though the place of my birth, and though the stake I have in it is very considerable; and go and reside in France or Italy, and never think of myself as a married man, *nor live like one*.'

Oh dear! said one.

That would be a sad thing! said the other.

Nay, madam, turning to Mrs Moore—Indeed, madam, to Miss Rawlins—I am quite desperate. I can no longer bear such usage. I have had the good fortune to be favoured by the smiles of very fine ladies, though I say it (and I looked modest), both abroad and at home—(Thou knowest this to be true, Jack). With regard to my spouse here, I had but one hope left (for as to the reconciliation with her friends, I scorn them all too much to value that, but for her sake); and that was, that if it pleased God to bless us with children, she might entirely recover her usual serenity; and we might then be happy. But the reconciliation her heart was so much set upon is now, as I hinted before, entirely hopeless—made so by this rash step of hers, and by the rasher temper she is in; since (as you will believe) her brother and sister, when they come to know it, will make a fine handle of it against us both;—

affecting as they do at present to disbelieve our marriage—and the dear creature herself too ready to countenance such a disbelief—as nothing *more than the ceremony*—

Here I was bashful; for Miss Rawlins by her preparatory primness, put me in mind that it was *proper to be so*—

I turned half round; then facing the fan-player, and the matron—You *yourselves*, ladies, knew not what to believe till *now*, that I have told you our story: and I do assure you that I shall not give myself the same trouble to convince people I hate: people from whom I neither expect nor desire any favour; and who are determined *not* to be convinced. And what, pray, must be the issue when her uncle's friend comes, although he seems to be a *truly worthy man*? Is it not natural for him to say, 'To what purpose, Mr Lovelace, should I endeavour to bring about a reconciliation between Mrs Lovelace and her friends, by means of her elder uncle, when a good understanding is wanting between yourselves?'—A fair inference, Mrs Moore!—A fair inference, Miss Rawlins!—And here is the unhappiness—till she is reconciled to them, this cursed oath, in her notion, is binding!

The women seemed moved; for I spoke with great earnestness, though low—and besides, they love to have their sex and its favours appear of importance to us. They shook their deep heads at each other, and looked sorrowful: and this moved my tender heart too.

'Tis an unheard-of case, ladies—Had she not preferred me to all mankind— There I stopped—and that, resumed I feeling for my handkerchief, is what staggered Captain Tomlinson when he heard of her flight; who, the last time he saw us together, saw the most affectionate couple on earth!—the most affectionate couple on earth!—in the accent grievous, repeated I.

Out then I pulled my handkerchief and, putting it to my eyes, arose and walked to the window—It makes me weaker than a woman!—Did I not love her as never man loved *his wife* (I have no doubt but I do, Jack)—

There again I stopped; and resuming—Charming creature, as you see she is, I wish I had never beheld her face!—Excuse me, ladies; traversing the room. And having rubbed my eyes till I supposed them red, I turned to the women; and pulling out my letter-case, I will show you one letter—here it is—read it, Miss Rawlins, if you please—It will confirm to you how much all my family are prepared to admire her. I am freely treated in it—so I am in the two others: but after what I have told you, nothing need be a secret to you two.

She took it with an air of eager curiosity, and looked at the seal, ostentatiously coronetted; and at the superscription, reading out, *To Robert Lovelace, Esq*;—Ay, madam—Ay, miss—that's my name (giving myself an air, though I had told it to them before). I am not ashamed of it. My wife's maiden name—*unmarried* name, I should rather say—fool that I am!—and I rubbed my cheek for vexation (fool enough in conscience, Jack!) was Harlowe—Clarissa Harlowe—you heard me call her *my Clarissa*.—

I did—but thought it to be a feigned or love-name said Miss Rawlins.

I wonder what is Miss Rawlins's love-name, Jack. Most of the fair romancers have in their early womanhood chosen love-names. No parson ever gave more *real* names, than I have given *fictitious* ones. And to very good purpose: many a sweet dear has answered me a letter for the sake of owning a name which her godmother never gave her.

No—it was her real name, I said.

I bid her read out the whole letter. If the spelling be not exact, Miss Rawlins, said I, you will excuse it; the writer is a lord. But, perhaps I may not show it to my spouse; for if those I have left with her have no effect upon her, neither will this: and I shall not care to expose my Lord M. to her scorn. Indeed I begin to be quite careless of consequences.

Miss Rawlins, who could not but be pleased with this mark of my confidence, looked as if she pitied me.

And here thou mayest read the letter, No. [4].

[*Letter 233.4: Lord M.*] *to Robert Lovelace, Esq.*

M. Hall, Wed. June 7

Cousin Lovelace,

I THINK you might have found time to let us know of your nuptials being actually solemnized. I might have expected this piece of civility from you. But perhaps the ceremony was performed at the very time that you asked me to be your lady's father—but I shall be angry if I proceed in my guesses—and *little said is soon amended.*

But I can tell you that Lady Betty Lawrance, whatever Lady Sarah does, will not so soon forgive you as I have done. *Women resent slights longer than men.* You that know so much of the sex (I speak it not however to your praise) might have known *that.* But never was you before acquainted with a lady of such an amiable character. I hope there will be but one soul between you. I have before now said that I will disinherit you, and settle all I can upon her, if you prove not a good husband to her.

May this marriage be crowned with a great many fine boys (I desire no girls) to build up again a family so antient! The first boy shall take my surname by Act of Parliament. That is in my will.

Lady Betty and niece Charlotte will be in town about business *before you know where you are.* They long to pay their compliments to your fair bride. I suppose you will hardly be at The Lawn when they get to town; because Greme informs me you have sent no orders there for your lady's accommodation.

Pritchard has all things in readiness for signing. I will take no advantage of your slights. Indeed I am too much used to them—more praise to my patience than to your complaisance, however.

One reason for Lady Betty's going up, as I may tell you *under the rose,* is, to buy some suitable presents for Lady Sarah and all of us to make on this agreeable occasion.

We would have blazed it away, could we have had timely notice, and thought it would have been agreeable to all round. The *like occasions don't happen every day.*

My most affectionate compliments and congratulations to my new niece; conclude me, for the present, in violent pains that with all your heroicalness would make you mad,

Your truly affectionate uncle,
M.

This letter clenched the nail. Not but that, Miss Rawlins said, she saw I had been a wild gentleman; and, truly, she thought so the moment she beheld me.

They began to intercede for my spouse (so nicely had I turned the tables), and that I would not go abroad and disappoint a reconciliation so much wished for on one side, and such desirable prospects on the other in my own family.

Who knows, thought I to myself, but more may come of this plot than I had even promised myself? What a happy man shall I be if these women can be brought to join to carry my marriage into consummation?

Ladies, you are exceeding good to us both. I should have some hopes, if my unhappily-nice spouse could be brought to dispense with the unnatural oath she has laid me under. You see what my case is. Do you think I may not insist upon her absolving me from this abominable oath? Will you be so good as to give your advice, that one apartment may serve for a man and his wife at the hour of retirement?—Modestly put, Belford!—And let me here observe that few rakes, besides me, would find a language so decent as to engage modest women to talk with him in, upon such subjects.

They both simpered, and looked upon one another.

These subjects always make women simper at least. No *need* but of the most delicate hints to *them*. A man who is gross in a woman's company ought to be knocked down with a club: for, like so many musical instruments, touch but a single wire, and the dear souls are sensible all over.

To be sure, Miss Rawlins learnedly said, playing with her fan, a casuist would give it that the matrimonial vow ought to supersede any other obligation.

Mrs Moore, for her part, was of opinion that, if the lady owned herself to be a wife, she ought to behave *like* one.

Whatever be my luck, thought I, with this *all-eyed* fair one, any other woman in the world, from fifteen to five-and-twenty, would be mine upon my own terms before the morning.

And now, that I may be at hand to take all advantages, I will endeavour, said I to myself, to make sure of good quarters.

I am your lodger, Mrs Moore, in virtue of the earnest I have given you for these apartments, and for any one you can spare above for my servants; indeed for *all* you have to spare—for who knows what my spouse's brother may attempt? I will pay you your own demand: and that for a month or two certain (board included), as I shall or shall not be your hindrance. Take *that* as a pledge; or in part of payment—offering her a thirty pound bank note.

She declined taking it; desiring she might consult the lady first; adding that she doubted not my honour; and that she would not let her apartments to any other person, whom she knew not something of, while I and the lady were here.

The lady, The lady! from both the women's mouths continually (which still implied a doubt in their hearts): and not *Your spouse*, and *Your lady*, sir.

I never met with such women, thought I—so thoroughly convinced but this moment, yet already doubting! I am afraid I have a couple of sceptics to deal with.

I knew no reason, I said, for my wife to object to my lodging in the same house with her here, any more than in town at Mrs Sinclair's. But were she to make such objection, I would not quit possession; since it was not unlikely that the same freakish disorder which brought her to Hampstead might carry her absolutely out of my knowledge.

They both seemed embarrassed; and looked upon one another; yet with such an air as if they thought there was reason in what I said. And I declared myself her boarder, as well as lodger; and, dinner-time approaching, was not denied to be the former.

Letter 234: MR LOVELACE TO JOHN BELFORD, ESQ.

I THOUGHT it was now high time to turn my whole mind to my beloved; who had had full leisure to weigh the contents of the letters I had left with her.

I therefore requested Mrs Moore to step in, and desire to know whether she would be pleased to admit me to attend her in her apartment, on occasion of the letters I had left with her; or whether she would favour me with her company in the dining-room?

Mrs Moore desired Miss Rawlins to accompany her in to the lady. They tapped at her door, and were both admitted.

I cannot but stop here for one minute to remark, though against myself, upon that security which innocence gives, that nevertheless had better have in it a greater mixture of the serpent with the dove. For here, heedless of all I could say behind her back, because she was satisfied with her own worthiness, she permitted me to go on with my own story without interruption, to persons as great strangers to her as to me; and who, as strangers to *both*, might be supposed to lean to the side most injured: and that, as I managed it, was to mine. A dear silly soul! thought I, at the time, to depend upon the goodness of her own heart, when the heart cannot be seen into but by its actions; and she, to appearance, a runaway, an eloper, from a tender, a most indulgent husband!—to neglect to cultivate the opinion of individuals, when the whole world is governed by appearance!

Yet, what can be expected of an angel under twenty?—She has a world of knowledge; knowledge *speculative*, as I may say; but no *experience*! How should she?—Knowledge by theory only is a vague uncertain light: a will o' the wisp, which as often misleads the doubting mind as puts it right.

There are many things in the world, could a moraliser say, that would afford inexpressible pleasure to a reflecting mind, were it not for the mixture they come to us with. To be graver still; I have seen parents (perhaps my own did so) who delighted in those very qualities in their children, while young, the natural consequences of which (too much indulged and encouraged) made them, as they grew up, the plague of their hearts—To bring this home to my present purpose, I must tell thee, that I adore this charming creature for her vigilant prudence; but yet I would not, methinks, wish her, by virtue of that prudence, which is, however, necessary to carry her above the *devices* of all the rest of the world, to be too wise for *mine*.

My revenge, my *sworn* revenge, is nevertheless (adore her as I will) uppermost in my heart!—Miss Howe says that my love is a *Herodian* love[a]: by my soul, that girl's a witch!—I am half sorry to say that I find a pleasure in playing the tyrant over what I love. Call it an ungenerous pleasure, if thou wilt: softer hearts than

a See p. 749.

mine know it. The women to a woman know it, and *show* it too, whenever they are trusted with power. And why should it be thought strange that I, who love them so dearly, and study them so much, should catch the infection of them?

Letter 235: MR LOVELACE TO JOHN BELFORD, ESQ.

I WILL now give thee the substance of the dialogue that passed between the two women and the lady.

Wonder not that a perverse wife makes a listening husband. The event, however, as thou wilt find, justified the old observation, *that listeners seldom hear good of themselves.* Conscious of their own demerits (if I may guess by myself: There's ingenuity, Jack!), and fearful of censure, they seldom find themselves disappointed. There is something of sense, after all, in these proverbs, in these phrases, in this *wisdom of nations.*

Mrs Moore was to be the messenger; but Miss Rawlins began the dialogue.

Your SPOUSE, madam—(Devil!—Only to fish for a negative or affirmative declaration.)

Cl. My *spouse*, madam—

Miss R. Mr Lovelace, madam, avers, that you are married to him; and begs admittance, or your company in the dining-room, to talk upon the subject of the letters he left with you.

Cl. He is a poor wicked wretch. Let me beg of you, madam, to favour me with your company as often as possible while he is hereabouts, and I remain here.

Miss R. I shall with pleasure attend you, madam. But, methinks, I could wish you would *see* the gentleman, and hear what he has to say on the subject of the letters.

Cl. My case is a hard, a very hard one—I am quite bewildered!—I know not what to do!—I have not a friend in the world that can or will help me!—yet had none but friends till I knew *that man*!

Miss R. The gentleman neither looks nor talks like a bad man—Not a *very* bad man; as men go.

As men go!—Poor Miss Rawlins, thought I!—And dost thou know, *how men go*?

Cl. Oh madam, you know him not!—He can put on the appearance of an angel of light; but has a black, a very black heart!—

Poor I!—

Miss R. I could not have thought it, truly!—But men are very deceitful nowadays!

Nowadays!—a fool!—Have not her history books told her that they were always so?

Mrs Moore, sighing. I have found it so, I am sure, to my cost!—

Who knows but in her time, poor goody Moore may have met with a Lovelace, or a Belford, or some such vile fellow?—My little harum-scarum beauty knows not what strange histories every woman living, who has had the least independence of will, could tell her, were such to be as communicative as she is—But here's the thing—I have given her cause enough of offence; but not enough to make her hold her tongue.

Cl. As to the letters he has left with me, I know not what to say to *them*—but am resolved never to have anything to say to *him*.

Miss R. If, madam, I may be allowed to say so, I think you carry matters very far.

Cl. Has he been making a bad cause a good one with you, madam?—*That* he can do, with those who know him not. Indeed I heard him talking, though not what he said, and am indifferent about it. But what account does he give of himself?

I was pleased to hear this. To arrest, to stop her passion, thought I, in the height of its career, is a charming presage.

Then the busy Miss Rawlins fished on, to find out from her either a *confirmation* or *disavowal* of my story. Was Lord M. my uncle?—Did I court her at first with the allowance of her friends, her brother excepted? Had I a rencounter with that brother? Was she so persecuted in favour of a very disagreeable man, one Solmes, as to induce her to throw herself into my protection?

None of these were denied. All the objections she *could* have made were stifled, or kept in, by the consideration (as she mentioned) that she should stay there but a little while; and that her story was too long. But Miss Rawlins would not be thus easily answered.

Miss R. He says, madam, that he could not prevail for marriage, till he had consented under a solemn oath to separate beds, while your family remained unreconciled.

Cl. Oh the wretch!—What can be still in his head, to endeavour to pass these stories upon strangers!

So no direct denial, thought I!—Admirable!—All will do by and by!

Miss R. He has owned that an accidental fire had frightened you very much on Wednesday night—and that—and that—and that—an accidental fire had frightened you—very much frightened you—last Wednesday night!—

Then, after a short pause—In short, he owned that he had taken some innocent liberties, which might have led to a breach of the oath you had imposed upon him: and that this was the cause of your displeasure.

I would have been glad to see how my charmer then looked—To be sure she was at a loss in her own mind, to justify herself for resenting so highly an offence so trifling. She hesitated—did not presently speak—When she did, she wished that she, Miss Rawlins, might never meet with any man who would take such innocent liberties with *her*.

Miss Rawlins pushed further.

Your case, to be sure, madam, is very particular. But if the hope of a reconciliation with your own friends is made more distant by your leaving him, give me leave to say that 'tis pity—'tis pity—(I suppose the maiden then primmed, fanned, and blushed)—'tis pity the oath cannot be dispensed with; especially as he owns he has not been so strict a liver—

I could have gone in, and kissed the girl.

Cl. You have heard *his* story. Mine, as I told you before, is too long, and too melancholy; my disorder on seeing the wretch is too great; and my time here is too short, for me to enter upon it. And if he has any end to serve by his own vindication, in which I shall not be a *personal* sufferer, let him make himself appear as white as an angel; with all my heart.

My love for her, and the excellent character I gave her, were then pleaded.

Cl. Specious seducer!—Only tell me if I cannot get away from him by some back way?

How my heart then went *pit-a-pat*!

Cl. Let me look out—(I heard the sash lifted up). Whither does that path lead to? Is there no possibility of getting to a coach?—Surely he must deal with some fiend, or how could he have found me out?—Cannot I steal to some neighbouring house, where I may be concealed till I can get quite away?—You are good people!—I have not been always among such!—Oh help me, help me, ladies (with a voice of impatience), or I am ruined!

Then pausing, Is that the way to Hendon? (pointing, I suppose)—Is Hendon a private place?—The Hampstead coach, I am told, will carry passengers thither.

Mrs Moore. I have an honest friend at Mill Hill (Devil fetch her, thought I); where, if such be your determination, madam, and if you think yourself in danger, you may be safe, I believe.

Cl. Anywhither, if I can but escape from *this man*!—Whither does that path lead to, out yonder?—What is that town on the right hand called?

Mrs M. Highgate, madam.

Miss R. On the side of the heath is a little village called North End. A kinswoman of mine lives there. But her house is small. I am not sure she could accommodate such a lady.

Devil take her too, thought I!—I imagined that I had made myself a better interest in these women. But the whole sex love plotting; and plot-*ters*, too, Jack.

Cl. A barn, an outhouse, a garret, will be a palace to me, if it will but afford me a refuge from *this man*!—

Her senses, thought I, are much livelier than *mine*. What a devil have I done, that she should be so *very* implacable!—I told thee, Belford, all I did: was there anything in it so *very* much amiss!—Such prospects of family reconciliation before her too!—To be sure she is a very *sensible* lady!—

She then espied my new servant walking under the window, and asked if he were not one of mine?—

Will was on the look-out for old Grimes (so is the fellow called whom my beloved has dispatched to Miss Howe). And being told that the man she saw *was* my servant; I see, said she, that there is no escaping, unless you, madam (to Miss Rawlins, I suppose), can befriend me till I can get farther. I have no doubt that that fellow is planted about the house to watch my steps. But the wicked wretch his master has no right to control me. He shall not hinder me from going whither I please. I will raise the town upon him if he molests me. Dear ladies, is there no back door for me to get out at while you hold him in talk?

Miss R. Give me leave to ask you, madam, is there no room to hope for accommodation? Had you not better see him? He certainly loves you dearly: he is a fine gentleman: you may exasperate him and make matters more unhappy for yourself.

Cl. Oh Mrs Moore, Oh Miss Rawlins! you know not the man!—I wish not to see his face, nor to exchange another word with him as long as I live.

Mrs Moore. I don't find, Miss Rawlins, that the gentleman has misrepresented anything. You see, madam (to my Clarissa), how respectful he is; not to come in till permitted. He certainly loves you dearly. Pray, madam, let him talk to you, as he wishes to do, on the subject of the letters.

Very kind of Mrs Moore. Mrs Moore, thought I, is a very good woman—I did not curse her then.

Miss Rawlins said something; but so low, that I could not hear what it was. Thus it was answered.

Cl. I am greatly distressed! I know not what to do!—But, Mrs Moore, be so good as to give his letters to him—Here they are—Be pleased to tell him that I wish him and his aunt and cousin a happy meeting. He never can want excuses to them for what has happened, any more than pretences to those he would delude. Tell him that he has ruined me in the opinion of my own friends. I am for that reason the less solicitous how I appear to his.

Mrs Moore then came to me; and being afraid that something would pass meantime between the other two, which I should not like, I took the letters and entered the room, and found them retired into the closet; my beloved whispering with an air of earnestness to Miss Rawlins, who was all attention.

Her back was towards me; and Miss Rawlins, by pulling her sleeve, giving intimation of my being there, Can I have no retirement uninvaded, sir, said she with indignation, as if she was interrupted in some talk her heart was in?—What business have you here, or with me?—You have your letters, han't you?

Lovel. I have, my dear; and let me beg of you to consider what you are about. I every moment expect Captain Tomlinson here. Upon my soul, I do. He has promised to keep from your uncle what has happened—But what will he think, if he finds you hold in this strange humour?

Cl. I will endeavour, sir, to have patience with you for a moment or two, while I ask you a few questions before this lady and Mrs Moore (who just then came in), both whom you have prejudiced in your favour by your specious stories—Will you say, sir, that we are married together? Lay your hand upon your heart, and answer me, Am I your wedded wife?

I am gone too far, thought I, to give up for such a push as this—home one as it is.

My dearest soul! how can you put such a question?—Is it either for *your* honour or *my own*, that it should be doubted?—Surely, surely, madam, you cannot have attended to the contents of Captain Tomlinson's letter.

She complained often of want of spirits throughout our whole contention, and of weakness of person and mind, from the fits she had been thrown into: but little reason had *she* for this complaint, as I thought, who was able to hold me to it, as she did. I own that I was excessively concerned for her several times.

You and I! *Vilest of men—*

My name is Lovelace, madam—

Therefore it is, that I call you the *vilest of men.* (Was this pardonable, Jack?) *You* and *I* know the truth, the *whole* truth—I want not to clear up my reputation with these gentlewomen—that is already lost with every one I had most reason to value: but let me have this *new* specimen of what you are capable of—Say, wretch (say, Lovelace, if thou hadst rather), art thou really and truly my wedded husband?—Say! answer without hesitation!—

She trembled with impatient indignation; but had a wildness in her manner, which I took some advantage of, in order to parry this cursed thrust—and a cursed

CLARISSA

[L235

thrust it was; since, had I positively averred it, she never would have believed
anything I had said: and had I owned that I was not married, I had destroyed my
own plot, as well with the women as with her; and could have had no pretence for
pursuing her, or hindering her from going whithersoever she pleased. Not that I
was ashamed to aver it, had it been consistent with policy. I would not have thee
think me such a milksop neither.

Lovel. My dearest love, how wildly you talk! What would you *have* me answer?
Is it necessary that I *should* answer? May I not re-appeal this to your own breast,
as well as to Captain Tomlinson's treaty and letter? You know yourself how matters
stand between us—and Captain Tomlinson—

Cl. Oh wretch! Is this an answer to my question? Say, are we married, or are we
not?

Lovel. What *makes a marriage*, we all know. If it be the union of two hearts,
(there was a turn, Jack!) to my utmost grief I must say we are *not*; since now I see
you hate me. If it be the completion of marriage, to my confusion and regret I
must own we are *not*. But, my dear, will you be pleased to consider what answer
half a dozen people whence you came could give to your question? And do not
now, in *the disorder of your mind*, and in the height of passion, bring into question
before these gentlewomen a point you have acknowledged before those who know
us better.

I would have whispered her about the treaty with her uncle, and the contents of
the Captain's letter; but, retreating, and with a rejecting hand, Keep thy distance,
man, cried the dear insolent—To thy own heart I appeal, since thou evadest me
thus pitifully!—I own no marriage with thee! Bear witness, ladies, I do not. And
cease to torment me, cease to follow me. Surely, surely, faulty as I have been, I
have not deserved to be *thus* persecuted!—I resume, therefore, my former
language: you have no right to pursue me: you *know* you have not: begone, then;
and leave me to make the best of my hard lot. Oh my dear cruel papa! said she, in
a violent fit of grief (falling upon her knees, and clasping her uplifted hands
together), thy heavy curse is completed upon thy devoted daughter! I am *punished*,
dreadfully punished, *by the very wretch in whom I had placed my wicked
confidence*!

By my soul, Belford, the little witch with her words, but more by her manner,
moved *me*! Wonder not then, that her action, her grief, her tears, set the women
into the like compassionate manifestations.

Had not I a cursed task of it?

The two women withdrew to the further end of the room, and whispered: A
strange case! There is no frenzy here—I just heard said.

The charming creature threw her handkerchief over her head and neck,
continuing kneeling, her back towards me, and her face hid upon a chair, and
repeatedly sobbed with grief and passion.

I took this opportunity to step to the women to keep them steady.

You see, ladies (whispering), what an unhappy man I am! You see what a spirit
this dear creature has!—all, all owing to her implacable relations, and to her
father's curse—A curse upon them all; they have turned the head of the most
charming woman in the world.

Ah! sir, sir, replied Miss Rawlins, whatever be the fault of her relations, all is not as it should be between you and her. 'Tis plain she does not think herself married: 'Tis *plain* she does not: and if you have any value for the poor lady, and would not totally deprive her of her senses, you had better withdraw, and leave to time and cooler consideration the event in your favour.

She will compel me to this at last, I fear, Miss Rawlins; I *fear* she will; and then we are both undone: for I cannot live without her; she knows it too well—And she has not a friend will look upon her: this also she knows. Our marriage, when her uncle's friend comes, will be proved incontestably. But I am ashamed to think I have given her room to believe it no marriage: that's what she harps upon!

Well, 'tis a strange case, a very strange one, said Miss Rawlins; and was going to say further, when the angry beauty, coming towards the door, said, Mrs Moore, I beg a word with you. And they both stepped into the dining-room.

I saw her, just before, put a parcel into her pocket, and followed them out, for fear she should slip away; and stepping to the stairs that she *might not go by me*, Will cried I, aloud (though I knew he was not near)—Pray, child, to a maid who answered, call either of my servants to me.

She then came up to me, with a wrathful countenance: Do you call your servant, sir, to hinder me, between you, from going whither I please?

Don't, my dearest life, misinterpret everything I do. Can you think me so mean and so unworthy as to employ a servant to constrain you?—I call him to send to the public houses, or inns in this town, to inquire after Captain Tomlinson, who may have alighted at some one of them, and be now, perhaps, needlessly adjusting his dress; and I would have him come, were he to be without clothes, God forgive me! for I am stabbed to the heart by your cruelty.

Answer was returned, that neither of my servants was in the way.

Not in the way, said I!—Whither can the dogs be gone?

Oh sir! with a scornful air; not far, I'll warrant. One of them was under the window just now; according to order, I suppose, to watch my steps—But I will do what I please, and go whither I please; and that to your face.

God forbid that I should hinder you in anything that you may do with safety to yourself!

Now I verily believe that her design was to slip out in pursuance of the closet-whispering between her and Miss Rawlins; perhaps to Miss Rawlins's house.

She then stepped back to Mrs Moore, and gave her something, which proved to be a diamond ring, and desired her, not whisperingly, but with an air of defiance to me, that that might be a pledge for her till she defrayed her demands; which she should soon find means to do; having no more money about her than she might have occasion for before she came to an acquaintance's.

Mrs Moore would have declined taking it; but she would not be denied; and then, wiping her eyes, she put on her gloves—Nobody has a right to stop me, said she!—I *will* go!—Who should I be afraid of?—Her very question, charming creature! testifying her fear.

I beg pardon, madam (turning to Mrs Moore, and curtsying), for the trouble I have given you—I beg pardon, madam, to Miss Rawlins (curtsying likewise to her)—You may both hear of me in a happier hour, if such a one falls to my lot—and God bless you both!—struggling with her tears till she sobbed—and away was tripping.

I stepped to the door: I put it to; and setting my back against it, took her struggling hand—My dearest life! my angel! said I, why will you thus distress me?—Is this the forgiveness which you so solemnly promised?—

Unhand me, sir!—You have no business with me! You have no right over me! You *know* you have not.

But whither, whither, my dearest love, would you go?—Think you not that I will follow you, were it to the world's end?—Whither would you go?

Well do you ask me whither I would go, who have been the occasion that I have not a friend left!—But God, who knows my innocence, and my upright intentions, will not wholly abandon me when I am out of your power—But while in it, I cannot expect a gleam of the divine grace or favour to reach me.

How severe is this!—how shockingly severe!—Out of *your* presence, my angry fair one! I can neither hope for the one nor the other. As my cousin Montague in the letter you have read, observes, you are my pole-star and my guide; and if ever I am to be happy either here or hereafter, it must be in and by you.

She would then have urged me from the door. But respectfully opposing her, Begone, man! Begone, Mr Lovelace, said she—Stop not my way—if you would not that I should attempt the window, give me passage by the door; for, once more, you have no right to detain me!

Your resentments, my dearest life, I will own to be well grounded—I will acknowledge that I have been all in fault. On my knee (and down I dropped) I ask your pardon. And can you refuse to ratify your own *promise*?—Look forward to the happy prospect before us. See you not my Lord M. and Lady Sarah longing to bless *you*, for blessing me and their whole family? Can you take no pleasure in the promised visit of Lady Betty and my cousin Montague? And in the protection *they* offer you if you are dissatisfied with *mine*?—Have you no wish to see your uncle's friend?—Stay only till Captain Tomlinson comes—Receive from him the news of your uncle's compliance with the wishes of both.

She seemed altogether distressed; was ready to sink; and forced to lean against the wainscot, as I kneeled at her feet. A stream of tears at last burst from her less indignant eyes—Good heaven, said she, lifting up her lovely face and clasped hands, what is at last to be my destiny!—Deliver me from this dangerous man; and direct me!—I know not what I do; what I can do; nor what I ought to do!—

The women, as I had owned our marriage to be but half completed, heard nothing in this whole scene to contradict (not flagrantly to contradict) what I had asserted: they believed they saw in her returning temper and staggered resolution, a love for me, which her indignation had before suppressed; and they joined to persuade her to tarry till the captain came, and to hear his proposals; representing the dangers to which she would be exposed; the fatigues she might endure; a lady of her appearance, unguarded, unprotected. On the other hand, they dwelt upon my declared contrition, and on my promises: for the performance of which they offered to be bound—So much had my kneeling humility affected them.

Women, Jack, tacitly acknowledge the inferiority of their own sex in the pride they take to behold a kneeling lover at their feet.

She turned from me, and threw herself into a chair.

I arose, and approached her with reverence—My dearest creature, said I—and was proceeding—But with a face glowing with conscious dignity, she interrupted me—Ungenerous, ungrateful Lovelace!—You know not the value of the heart you have insulted! Nor can you conceive how much my soul despises your meanness. But meanness must ever be the portion of the man who can act vilely!—

The women believing we were likely to be on better terms, retired. The dear perverse opposed their going; but they saw I was desirous of their absence. And when they had withdrawn, I once more threw myself at her feet, and acknowledged my offences; implored her forgiveness for this one time, and promised the exactest circumspection for the future.

It was impossible for her, she said, to keep her *memory*, and *forgive* me. What hadst thou *seen* in the conduct of Clarissa Harlowe, that should encourage such an insult upon her as thou didst dare to make? How meanly must thou think of *her*, that *thou* couldst presume to be so guilty, and expect *her* to be so weak as to forgive thee?—

I besought her to let me go over with her Captain Tomlinson's letter. I was sure it was impossible she could have given it the requisite attention.

I *have* given it the requisite attention, said she; and the other letters too. So that what I say is upon deliberation. And what have I to fear from my brother and sister!—They can but *complete* the ruin of my fortunes with my father and uncles. Let them, and welcome. You, sir, I thank you, have lowered my fortunes: but, I bless God, that my mind is not sunk with my fortunes. It is, on the contrary, raised above fortune, and above you; and for half a word, they shall have the estate they have envied me for, and an acquittal of all expectations from my family that may make them uneasy.

I lifted up my hands and eyes in silent admiration of her!

My brother, sir, may think me ruined. To the praise of *your* character, by whom I have been seduced from them, he may think it is impossible to be with *you* and be innocent. You have but too well justified their harshest censures in every part of your conduct. But I will, now that I have escaped from you, and that I am out of the reach of your mysterious devices, wrap myself up in my own innocence (and then she passionately folded her arms about herself), and leave to time, and to my future circumspection, the re-establishment of my character—Leave me then, sir—pursue me not!—

Good God! interrupting her—And all this, for what?—Had I *not* yielded to your entreaties (forgive me, madam), you could not have carried farther your resentments—

Wretch!—Was it not crime enough to give *occasion* for those *entreaties*? Wouldst thou make a merit to me that thou didst not utterly ruin *her* whom thou oughtest to have protected?—Begone, man! Turning from me, her face crimsoned over with passion—See me no more!—I cannot bear thee in my sight!—

Dearest, dearest creature!—

If I forgive thee, Lovelace—and there she stopped. To endeavour, proceeded she, to endeavour, to terrify a poor creature by *premeditation*, by *low contrivance*, by *cries of fire*—a poor creature who had consented to take a wretched chance with thee for life!

For Heaven's sake—offering to take her repulsing hand, as she was flying from me towards the closet—

What hast thou to do, to plead the sake of Heaven in thy favour, oh darkest of human minds!

Then turning from me, wiping her eyes, and again turning towards me, but her

sweet face half-aside, What difficulties hast thou involved me in!—Thou that hadst
a plain path before thee, after thou hadst betrayed me into thy power—At once
my mind takes in the whole of thy crooked behaviour; and if thou thinkest of
Clarissa Harlowe as her proud heart tells her thou oughtest to think of her, thou
wilt seek thy fortunes elsewhere. How often hast thou provoked me to tell thee,
that my soul is above thee?

For God's sake, madam, for a soul's sake, which it is in your power to save from
perdition, forgive me the past offence. I am the greatest villain on earth, if it was
a premeditated one. Yet I presume not to excuse myself. On your mercy I throw
myself. I will not offer at any plea but that of penitence. See but Captain
Tomlinson. See but my aunt and cousin; let *them* plead for me; let *them* be
guaranties for my honour.

If Captain Tomlinson come while I stay here, I may see *him*. But as for *you*,
sir—

Dearest creature! let me beg of you not to aggravate my offence to the captain
when he comes. Let me beg of you—

What askest thou?—Is it not that I shall be of party against myself?—that I shall
palliate—

Do not charge me, madam, interrupted I, with villainous premeditation!—Do
not give such a construction to my offence as may weaken your uncle's opinion—
as may strengthen your brother's—

She flung from me to the further end of the room; *she could go no further*—and
just then Mrs Moore came up and told her that dinner was ready; and that she had
prevailed upon Miss Rawlins to give her her company.

You must excuse me, Mrs Moore, said she. Miss Rawlins I hope also will—but
I cannot eat. I cannot go down. As for *you*, sir, I suppose you will think it right to
depart hence; at least till the gentleman comes whom you expect.

I respectfully withdrew into the next room, that Mrs Moore might acquaint her
(I durst not myself) that I was her lodger and boarder, as (whisperingly) I desired
she would: and meeting Miss Rawlins in the passage, Dearest Miss Rawlins, said
I, stand my friend: join with Mrs Moore to pacify my spouse if she has any new
flights upon my having taken lodgings, and intending to board here. I hope she will
have more generosity than to think of hindering a gentlewoman from letting her
lodgings.

I suppose Mrs Moore (whom I left with my fair one) had appraised her of this
before Miss Rawlins went in; for I heard her say, while I withheld Miss Rawlins—
'No, indeed: he is much mistaken—Surely he does not think I will.'

They both expostulated with her, as I could gather from bits and scraps of what
they said; for they spoke so low, that I could not hear any distinct sentence but
from the fair perverse, whose anger made her louder. And to this purpose I heard
her deliver herself in answer to different parts of their talk to her: 'Good Mrs
Moore, dear Miss Rawlins, press me no further—I cannot sit down at table with
him!'

They said something, as I suppose in my behalf—'Oh the insinuating wretch!—
what defence have I against a man who, go where I will, can turn everyone, even
of the virtuous of my sex, in his favour?'

After something else said, which I heard not distinctly—'This is execrable
cunning!—Were you to know his wicked heart, he is not without hope of engaging

you two good persons to second him in the vilest of his machinations.'

How came she (thought I at the instant) by all this penetration? My devil surely does not play me booty. If I thought he did, I would marry and live honest, to be even with him.

I suppose then, they urged the plea which I hinted to Miss Rawlins at going in, that she would not be Mrs Moore's hindrance; for thus she expressed herself—'He will no doubt pay you your own price. You need not question his liberality. But one house cannot hold us. Why, if it would, did I fly from him to seek refuge among strangers?'

Then, in answer to somewhat else they pleaded—' 'Tis a mistake, madam; I am *not* reconciled to him. I will believe nothing he says. Has he not given you a flagrant specimen of what a man he is, and of what he is capable, by the disguises you saw him in? My story is too long, and my stay here will be but short; or I could convince you that my resentments against him are but too well founded.'

I suppose then, that they pleaded for *her* leave for *my* dining with them: for she said: 'I have nothing to say to that—It is your own house, Mrs Moore—It is your own table—You may admit whom you please to it—Only leave me at my liberty to choose my company.'

Then in answer, as I suppose to their offer of sending her up a plate—'A bit of bread, if you please, and a glass of water: that's all I can swallow at present. I am really very much discomposed. Saw you not how bad I was?—Indignation only could have supported my spirits!—

'I have no objection to his dining with you, madam,' added she in reply, I suppose, to a farther question of the same nature—'But I will not stay a night in the house where he lodges, if I can help it.'

I presume Miss Rawlins had told her that she would not stay dinner—for she said, 'Let me not deprive Mrs Moore of your company, Miss Rawlins. You will not be displeased with his talk. He can have no design upon you.'

Then I suppose they pleaded what I might say behind her back to make my own story good—'I care not what he says, or what he thinks of me. Repentance and amendment are all the harm I wish him, whatever becomes of me!'

By her accent, she wept when she spoke these last words.

They came out both of them wiping their eyes; and would have persuaded me to relinquish the lodgings, and to depart till her uncle's friend came. But I knew better. I did not care to trust the devil, well as she and Miss Howe suppose me to be acquainted with him, for finding her out again if once more she escaped me.

What I am most afraid of, is, that she will throw herself among her own relations; and if she does, I am confident they will not be able to withstand her affecting eloquence. But yet, as thou'lt see, the captain's letter to me is admirably calculated to obviate my apprehensions on this score; particularly in that passage where it is said that her uncle thinks not himself at liberty to correspond directly with her, or to receive applications from her—*but through Captain Tomlinson*, as is strongly implied.[a]

I must own (notwithstanding the revenge I have so solemnly vowed) that I would very fain have made for her a merit with myself *in her returning favour*, and

a See p. 782.

owed as little as possible to the mediation of Captain Tomlinson. My pride was concerned in this. And this was one of my reasons for not bringing him with me. Another was; that, if I were obliged to have recourse to his assistance, I should be better able (by visiting her without him) to direct him what to say or to do, as I should find out the turn of her humour.

I was, however, glad at my heart that Mrs Moore came up so seasonably with notice that dinner was ready. The fair fugitive was all in all. She had the game in her own hands; and by giving me so good an excuse for withdrawing, I had time to strengthen myself; the captain had time to come; and the lady to cool. Shakespeare advises well:

> Oppose not rage, while rage is in its force;
> But give it way awhile, and let it waste.
> The rising deluge is not stopt with dams;
> Those it o'erbears, and drowns the hope of harvest.
> But, wisely manag'd, its divided strength
> Is sluic'd in channels, and securely drain'd:
> And when its force is spent, and unsupply'd,
> The residue with mounds may be restrain'd,
> And dry-shod we may pass the naked ford.[1]

I went down with the women to dinner. Mrs Moore sent her fair boarder up a plate; but she only ate a little bit of bread, and drank a glass of water. I doubted not but she would keep her word, when it was once gone out. Is not she an Harlowe?—She seems to be inuring herself to hardships, which, at the worst, she can never know; since, though she should ultimately refuse to be obliged to me, or, to express myself more suitably to my own heart, to *oblige me*, everyone who sees her must befriend her.

But let me ask thee, Belford, art thou not solicitous for me, in relation to the contents of the letter which the angry beauty has written and dispatched away by man and horse; and for what may be Miss Howe's answer to it? Art thou not ready to inquire, whether it be not likely that Miss Howe, when she knows of her saucy friend's flight, will be concerned about her letter, which she must know could not be at Wilson's till after that flight; and so, probably, would fall into my hands?—

All these things, as thou'lt see in the sequel, are provided for with as much contrivance as human foresight can admit.

I have already told thee that Will is upon the look-out for old Grimes—Old Grimes is, it seems, a gossiping, sottish rascal; and if Will can but light of him, I'll answer for the consequence: for has not Will been my servant upwards of seven years?

Letter 236: MR LOVELACE TO JOHN BELFORD, ESQ.

(In continuation)

WE had at dinner, besides Miss Rawlins, a young widow-niece of Mrs Moore, who is come to stay a month with her aunt—*Bevis* her name; very forward, very lively, and a great admirer of *me*, I assure you—hanging smirkingly upon all I said; and prepared to approve of every word before I spoke: and who, by the time we had half-dined (by the help of what she had collected before), was as much acquainted with our story as either of the other two.

As it behoved me to prepare them in my favour against whatever might come from Miss Howe, I improved upon the hint I had thrown out above-stairs against that mischief-making lady. I represented her to be an arrogant creature, revengeful, artful, enterprising, and one who, had she been a man, would have sworn and cursed, and committed rapes, and played the devil, as far as I knew (and I have no doubt of it, Jack): but who, nevertheless, by advantage of a female education, and pride, and insolence, I believed was *personally* virtuous.

Mrs Bevis allowed that there was a *vast deal* in education—and in *pride* too, she said. While Miss Rawlins came with a prudish God forbid that virtue should be owing to education only! However, I declared that Miss Howe was a subtle contriver of mischief; one who had always been *my* enemy: her motives I knew not: but despising the man whom her mother was desirous she should have, one Hickman; although I did not directly aver, that she would rather have had me; yet they all immediately imagined that *that* was the ground of her animosity to me, and of her envy to my beloved; and it was pity, they said, that so fine a young lady did not see through such a pretended friend.

And yet nobody (added I) has more reason than she to know by *experience* the force of a hatred founded in envy; as I hinted to *you* above, Mrs Moore, and to *you*, Miss Rawlins, in the case of her sister Arabella.

I had compliments made to my person and talents on this occasion; which gave me a singular opportunity of displaying my modesty, by disclaiming the merit of them, with a *No, indeed!—I should be very vain, ladies, if I thought so*. While thus abasing myself, and exalting Miss Howe, I got their opinion both for modesty and generosity; and had all the graces which I disclaimed thrown in upon me besides.

In short, they even oppressed that modesty, which (to speak modestly of myself) their praises *created*, by disbelieving all I said against myself.

And, truly, I must needs say they have almost persuaded even me myself, that Miss Howe is actually in love with me. I have often been willing to hope this. And who knows but she may? The captain and I have agreed that it shall be so insinuated *occasionally*—And what's thy opinion, Jack? She certainly hates Hickman: and girls who are *disengaged* seldom *hate*, though they may not *love:* and if she had rather have *another*, why not that *other* ME? For am I not a smart fellow, and a rake? And do not your sprightly ladies love your smart fellows, and your rakes? And where is the wonder that the man who could engage the affections of Miss Harlowe should engage those of a lady (with her[a] *Alas's*) who would be honoured in being deemed her second?

Nor accuse thou me of SINGULAR vanity in this presumption, Belford. Wert thou to know the secret vanity that lurks in the hearts of those who *disguise* or *cloak it best*, thou wouldst find great reason to acquit, at least to allow for, *me:* since it is generally the *conscious over-fulness of conceit* that makes the hypocrite most upon his guard to conceal it—Yet with these fellows, proudly-humble as they are, it will break out sometimes in spite of their cloaks, though but in self-denying, compliment-begging self-degradation.

But now I have appealed this matter to thee, let me use another argument in

a   See p. 750, where Miss Howe says: *Alas, my dear, I knew you loved him!*

favour of my observation that the ladies generally prefer a rake to a sober man; and of my presumption upon it that Miss Howe is in love with me: It is this— Common fame says that Hickman is a very virtuous, a very innocent fellow—a *male-virgin*, I warrant!—An odd dog I always thought him—Now women, Jack, like not novices. They are pleased with a love of the sex that is founded in the knowledge of it. Reason good. Novices expect more than they can possibly find in the commerce with them. The man who knows them yet has *ardours* for them, to borrow a word from Miss Howe,^a though those ardours are generally owing more to the devil *within* him than to the witch *without* him, is the man who makes them the highest and most grateful compliment. He knows what to expect, and with what to be satisfied.

Then the merit of a woman, in some cases, must be *ignorance*, whether *real* or *pretended*. The man, in *these* cases, must be an *adept*. Will it then be wondered at that a woman prefers a libertine to a novice?—While she expects in the one the confidence *she* wants; she considers the other and herself as two parallel lines; which, though they run side by side, can never meet.

Yet in this the sex is generally mistaken too; for these sheepish fellows are sly— I myself was modest once: and this, as I have elsewhere hinted to thee,^b has better enabled me to judge of both—But to proceed with my narrative:

Having thus prepared everyone against any letter should come from Miss Howe, and against my beloved's messenger returns, I thought it proper to conclude that subject with a hint that my spouse could not bear to have anything said *that reflected upon Miss Howe*; and, with a deep sigh, added that I had been made very unhappy more than once by the ill-will of ladies whom I had never offended.

The widow Bevis believed that might very easily be.

These hints within-doors, joined with others to Will both without and within (for I intend he shall fall in love with widow Moore's maid, and have saved one hundred pounds in my service, at least), will be great helps, as things may happen.

Letter 237: MR LOVELACE TO JOHN BELFORD, ESQ.

(In continuation)

WE had hardly dined, when my coachman, who kept a look-out for Captain Tomlinson, as Will did for old Grimes, conducted hither that worthy gentleman attended by one servant, *both* on horseback. He alighted. I went out to meet him at the door.

Thou knowst his solemn appearance, and unblushing freedom; and yet canst not imagine what a dignity the rascal assumed, nor how respectful to him I was.

I led him into the parlour, and presented him to the women, and them to him— I thought it highly imported me (as they might still have some diffidences about our marriage, from my fair-one's home-pushed questions on that head) to convince them entirely of the truth of all I had asserted. And how could I do this better than by dialoguing with him before them a little?

Dear captain, I thought you long; for I have had a terrible conflict with my spouse.

a pp. 587 and 603.
b p. 440.

Capt. I am sorry that I am later than my intention—My account with my banker—(there's a dog, Jack!) took me up longer time to adjust than I had foreseen (all the time pulling down and stroking his ruffles): for there was a small difference between us—only twenty pounds, indeed, which I had taken no account of. The rascal has not seen twenty pounds of his own these ten years.

Then had we between us the characters of the Harlowe family: I railing against them all; the captain taking his dear friend Mr John Harlowe's part; with a *Not so fast!—not so fast, young gentleman!*—and the like free assumptions.

He accounted for *their* animosity by *my* defiances: no good family, having such a charming daughter, would care to be *defied* instead of *courted:* he *must* speak his mind: never was a double-tongued man—He appealed to the ladies, if he were not right.

He got them of his side.

The correction I had given the brother, he told me, must have aggravated matters.

How valiant this made me look to the women!—The sex love us mettled fellows at their hearts.

Be that as it would, I should never love any of the family but my spouse; and, wanting nothing from them, would not, but for *her* sake, have gone so far as I *had* gone towards a reconciliation.

This was very good of me, Mrs Moore said.

Very good indeed; Miss Rawlins.

Good!—It is *more* than good; it is very generous, said the widow.

Capt. Why, so it is, I must needs say: for I am sensible that Mr Lovelace has been rudely treated by them all—More rudely than it could have been imagined a man of his *quality* and *spirit* would have put up with. But then, sir (turning to me), I think you are amply rewarded in such a lady; and that you ought to forgive the father for the daughter's sake.

Mrs M. Indeed so I think.

Miss R. So must everyone think who has seen the lady.

Widow B. A fine lady! to be sure! But she has a violent spirit; and some very odd humours too, by what I have heard. The value of good husbands is not known till they are lost!

Her conscience then drew a sigh from her.

Lovel. Nobody must reflect upon my angel—An angel she is—Some little blemishes, indeed, as to her over-hasty spirit, and as to her unforgiving temper. But this she has from the Harlowes; instigated too by *that* Miss Howe—But her innumerable excellencies are all her own.

Capt. Ay, talk of spirit, there's a spirit, now you have named Miss Howe! (And so I led him to confirm all I had said of that vixen.) Yet she was to be pitied too, looking with meaning at me.

As I have already hinted, I had before agreed with him to impute secret love *occasionally* to Miss Howe, as the best means to invalidate all that might come from her in my disfavour.

Capt. Mr Lovelace, but that I know your modesty, or *you* could give a reason—

Lovel. Looking down, and very modest—I can't think so, captain—but let us call another cause.

Every woman present could look me in the face, so bashful was I.

Capt. Well, but, as to our *present* situation—Only it mayn't be proper—looking upon me, and round upon the women.

Lovel. Oh captain, you may say anything before this company—only, Andrew, to my new servant who attended us at table, do you withdraw: This good girl (looking at the maid-servant) will help us to all we want.

Away went Andrew: he wanted not his cue; and the maid seemed highly pleased at my honour's preference of her.

Capt. As to our *present* situation, I say, Mr Lovelace—why, sir, we shall be all *untwisted*, let me tell you, if my friend Mr John Harlowe were to know what *that* is. He would as much question the truth of your being married, as the rest of the family do.

Here the women perked up their ears; and were all silent attention.

Capt. I asked you before for particulars, Mr Lovelace: but you *declined giving them*—Indeed it may not be *proper* for me to be acquainted with them—But I must own that it is past my comprehension that a wife can resent anything a husband can do (that is not a breach of the peace), so far as to think herself justified for *eloping* from him.

Lovel. Captain Tomlinson—sir—I do assure you, that I shall be offended—I shall be extremely concerned—if I hear that word mentioned again—

Capt. Your nicety, and your love, sir, may make you take offence—but it is my way to call everything by its proper name, let who will be offended—

Thou canst not imagine, Belford, how brave, and how independent, the rascal looked.

Capt. When, *young gentleman*, you shall think proper to give us particulars, we will find a word that shall please you better, for this rash act in so admirable a lady—You see, sir, that being the representative of my dear friend Mr John Harlowe, I speak as freely as I suppose *he* would do, if present. But you blush, sir—I beg your pardon, Mr Lovelace: it becomes not a modest man to pry into those secrets which a modest man cannot reveal.

I did not blush, Jack; but denied not the compliment, and looked down: the women seemed delighted with my modesty: but the widow Bevis was more inclined to laugh at me, than praise me for it.

Capt. Whatever be the cause of this step (I will not again, sir, call it *elopement*, since that harsh word wounds your tenderness), I cannot but express my surprise upon it, when I recollect the affectionate behaviour, which I was witness to between you, when I attended you last. *Over-love*, sir, I think you once mentioned—but *over-love* (smiling), give me leave to say, sir, is an odd cause of quarrel—Few ladies—

Lovel. Dear captain! And I tried to blush.

The women also tried; and, being more used to it, succeeded better—Mrs Bevis, indeed, has a red-hot countenance, and always blushes.

Miss R. It signifies nothing to mince the matter: but the lady above as good as denies her marriage. You *know*, sir, that she does; turning to me.

Capt. Denies her marriage! Heavens! how then have I imposed upon my dear friend Mr John Harlowe!

Lovel. Poor dear!—but let not her *veracity* be called in question. She would not be guilty of a wilful untruth for the world.

Then I had all their praises again.

Lovel. Dear creature!—she thinks she has reason for her denial. You know, Mrs Moore; you know, Miss Rawlins; what I owned to you above, as to my vow——

I looked down, and, as once before, turned round my diamond ring.

Mrs Moore looked awry; and with a leer at Miss Rawlins, as to her partner in the hinted-at reference.

Miss Rawlins looked down as well as I; her eye-lids half-closed, as if mumbling a paternoster, meditating her snuff-box, the distance between her nose and chin lengthened by a close-shut mouth.

She put me in mind of the pious Mrs Fetherstone at Oxford, whom I pointed out to thee once among other grotesque figures at St Mary's church, where we went to take a view of her two sisters: her eyes shut, not daring to trust her heart with them open; and but just half-rearing the lids to see who the next comer was; and falling them again when her curiosity was satisfied.

The widow Bevis gazed as if on the hunt for a secret.

The captain looked archly, as if half in possession of one.

Mrs Moore at last broke the bashful silence. Mrs Lovelace's behaviour, she said, could be no otherwise so well accounted for as by the ill-offices of *that* Miss Howe; and by the severity of her relations; which might but too probably have affected her head a little at times; adding that it was very generous in me to give way to the storm when it was up, rather than to exasperate at such a time.

But let me tell you, sirs, said the widow Bevis, that is not what one husband in a thousand would have done.

I desired that *no part of this conversation might be hinted to my spouse*; and looked still more bashfully. Her great fault, I must own, was over-delicacy.

The captain leered round him; and said he believed he could guess from the hints I had given him in town (of my *over-love*), and from what had now passed, that we had not consummated our marriage.

Oh Jack! how sheepishly then looked, or endeavoured to look, thy friend! how primly goody Moore! how affectedly Miss Rawlins!—while the honest widow Bevis gazed around her fearless; and though only simpering with her mouth, her eyes laughed outright, and seemed to challenge a laugh from every eye in the company.

He observed, that I was a phoenix of a man, if so; and he could not but hope that all matters would be happily accommodated in a day or two; and that then he should have the pleasure to aver to her uncle that he was present, as he might say, on our wedding-day.

The women seemed all to join in the same hope.

Ah, captain! ah, ladies!—how happy should I be if I could bring my dear spouse to be of the same mind!

It would be a very happy conclusion of a very knotty affair, said widow Bevis; and I see not why we may not make this very night a merry one.

The captain superciliously smiled at me. He saw plainly enough, he said, that we had been at *children's play* hitherto. A man of my character must have a prodigious value for his lady, who could give way to such a caprice as this. But one thing he would venture to tell me; and that was this—that however desirous young skittish ladies might be to have their way in this particular, it was a very bad setting-out for the man; as it gave his bride a very high proof of the power she had over him: and he would engage that no woman, *thus* humoured, ever valued the man the more for it; but very much the contrary—and there were *reasons to be given why she should not*.

Well, well, captain, no more of this subject before the ladies—*One* feels (in a bashful *try-to-blush* manner, shrugging my shoulders), that *one* is *so* ridiculous—I have been punished enough for my tender folly.

Miss Rawlins had taken her fan, and would needs hide her face behind it: I suppose because her blush was not quite ready.

Mrs Moore hemmed, and looked down, and by that, gave hers over.

While the jolly widow, laughing out, praised the captain as one of Hudibras's metaphysicians, repeating,

> He knew what's what, and that's as high
> As metaphysic wit can fly.[1]

This made Miss Rawlins blush indeed—Fie, fie, Mrs Bevis! cried she, unwilling I suppose to be thought absolutely ignorant.

Upon the whole, I began to think that I had not made a bad exchange of our professing mother, for the un-professing Mrs Moore. And indeed the women and I, and my beloved too, all mean the same thing: we only differ about the manner of coming at the proposed end.

Letter 238: MR LOVELACE TO JOHN BELFORD, ESQ.

(In continuation)

IT was now high time to acquaint my spouse that Captain Tomlinson was come. And the rather, as the maid told us that the lady had asked her if such a gentleman (describing him) was not in the parlour?

Mrs Moore went up, and requested in my name that she would give us audience.

But she returned with a desire that Captain Tomlinson would excuse her for the present. She was very ill. Her spirits were too weak to enter into conversation with him; and she must lie down.

I was vexed, and at first extremely disconcerted. The captain was vexed too. And my concern, thou mayst believe, was the greater on his account.

She had been very much fatigued, I own. Her fits in the morning must have weakened her: and she had carried her resentment so high, that it was the less wonder she should find herself low when her raised spirits had subsided. *Very* low, I may say, if sinkings are proportioned to risings; for she had been lifted up above the standard of a common mortal.

The captain, however, sent up in his own name, that if he could be admitted to drink one dish of tea with her, he should take it for a favour; and would go to town and dispatch some necessary business, if possible, to leave his morning free to attend her.

But she pleaded a violent headache; and Mrs Moore confirmed the plea to be just.

I would have had the captain lodge there that night, as well in compliment to him, as introductory to my intention of entering myself upon my new-taken apartment. But his hours were of too much importance to him to stay the evening.

It was indeed very inconvenient for him, he said, to return in the morning; but he was willing to do all in his power to heal this breach, and that as well for the sakes of me and my lady, as for that of his dear friend Mr John Harlowe; who must not know how far this misunderstanding had gone. He would therefore only drink one dish of tea with the ladies and me.

And accordingly, after he had done so, and I had had a little private conversation with him, he hurried away.

His fellow had given him, in the interim, a high character to Mrs Moore's servants: and this reported by the Widow Bevis (who, being no proud woman, is *hail fellow well met*, as the saying is, with all her aunt's servants), he was a *fine* gentleman, a *discreet* gentleman, a man of *sense* and *breeding*, with them all: and it was pity that, with such great business upon his hands, he should be obliged to come again.

My life for yours, audibly whispered the Widow Bevis, there is *humour* as well as *head-ache* in somebody's declining to see this worthy gentleman—Ah, Lord! how happy might some people be if they would!—

No perfect happiness in this world, said I, very gravely, and with a sigh; for the widow must know that I heard her. If we have not *real* unhappiness, we can make it, even from the overflowings of our own good fortune.

Very true, and, very true, the two widows: a charming observation, Mrs Bevis. Miss Rawlins smiled *her* assent to it; and I thought she called me in her heart, charming man! for she professes to be a great admirer of moral observations.

I had hardly taken leave of the captain, and sat down again with the women, when Will came; and calling me out, 'Sir, sir,' said he, grinning with a familiarity in his looks, as if what he had to say entitled him to take liberties: 'I have got the fellow down!—I have got old Grimes—Hah, hah, hah, hah—He is at the Lower Flask—almost in the condition of *David's sow*,[1] and please your honour—(The dog himself not much better) Here is his letter—from—from Miss Howe—Ha, ha, ha, ha,' laughed the varlet; holding it fast, as if to make conditions with me, and to excite my praises, as well as my impatience.

I could have knocked him down; but he would have his *say* out—'Old Grimes knows not that I have the letter—I must get back to him before he misses it—I only made a pretence to go out for a few minutes—But—but'—and then the dog laughed again—'He *must* stay—old Grimes *must* stay—till I go back to pay the reckoning.'

D—n the prater!—grinning rascal!—The letter—the letter!—

He gathered in his *wide mothe*, as he calls it, and gave me the letter; but with a *strut*, rather than a *bow*; and then sidled off like one of Widow Sorlings's dunghill cocks, exulting after a great feat performed. And all the time that I was holding up the billet to the light, to try to get at its contents without breaking the seal (for, dispatched in a hurry, it had no cover), there stood he laughing, shrugging, playing off his legs; now stroking his shining chin; now turning his hat upon his thumb; then leering in my face, flourishing with his head—Oh Christ! now and then cried the rascal—

What joy has this dog in mischief!—More than I can have in the completion of my most favourite purposes!—These fellows are ever happier than their masters.

I was once thinking to rumple up this billet till I had broken the seal. *Young* families (Miss Howe's is not an ancient one) love ostentatious sealings: and it might have been supposed to have been squeezed in pieces, in old Grimes's breeches pocket. But I was glad to be *saved* the guilt as well as suspicion of having a hand in so dirty a trick; for thus much of the contents (enough for my purpose) I was enabled to scratch out in character without it; the folds depriving me only of a few connecting words; which I have supply'd between hooks.

My Miss Harlowe, thou knowest, had *before* changed her name to Miss Laetitia Beaumont. Another *alias* now, Jack: I have learned her to be half a rogue in this instance; for this billet was directed to her by the name of *Mrs* Harriot Lucas.

[*Letter 238.1: Anna Howe to 'Mrs Harriot Lucas'*]

I CONGRATULATE you, my dear, with all my heart and soul upon (your escape) from the villain. (I long) for the particulars of all. (My mamma) is out: but expecting her return every minute, I dispatched (your) messenger instantly. (I will endeavour to come at) Mrs Townsend without loss of time; and will write at large in a day or two, if in that time I can see her. (Meantime I) am excessively uneasy for a letter I sent you yesterday by Collins, (who must have left it at) Wilson's after you got away. (It is of very) great importance. (I hope the) villain has it not. I would not for the world (that he should.) Immediately send for it, if by so doing the place you are at (will not be) discovered. If he has it, let me know it by some way (out of) hand. If not, you need not send.

June 9   Ever, ever yours,
                                                                                          A. H.

Oh Jack, what heart's ease does this *interception* give me!—I sent the rascal back with the letter to old Grimes, and charged him to drink no deeper. He owned that he was *half seas over*, as he phrased it.

Dog! said I, are you not to court one of Mrs Moore's maids tonight?—

Cry your mercy, sir!—I will be sober—I had forgot that—but old Grimes is plaguy tough—I thought I should never have got him down.

Away, villain!—Let old Grimes come; and on horseback, too, to the door—

He shall, and please your honour, if I can get him on the saddle, and if he can sit—

And charge him not to have alighted, nor to have seen *any*body—

Enough, sir! familiarly nodding his head, to show he took me. And away went the villain: into the parlour, among the women, I.

In a quarter of an hour old Grimes on horseback, waving to his saddle-bow, now on this side, now on that; his head, at others, joining to that of his more sober beast.

It looked very well to the women that I made no effort to speak to old Grimes (though I wished *before them*, that I knew the contents of what he brought); but, on the contrary, desired that they could instantly let my spouse know that her messenger was returned. Down she flew, violently as she had the head-ache!

Oh how I prayed for an opportunity to be revenged of her, for the ungrateful trouble she had given to her uncle's friend!

She took the letter from old Grimes with her own hands, and retired to an inner parlour to read it.

She presently came out again to the fellow, who had much ado to sit his horse—
Here is your money, friend. I thought you long. But what shall I do to get
somebody to go to town immediately for me? I see *you* cannot.

Old Grimes took his money; let fall his hat in doffing it; had it given him; and
rode away; his eyes isinglass, and set in his head, as I saw through the window; and
in a manner speechless; all his language hiccoughs. My dog need not have gone so
deep with this *tough* old Grimes—But the rascal was in his kingdom with him.

The lady applied to Mrs Moore: she mattered not the price. Could a man and
horse be engaged for her?—Only to go for a letter left for her at one Mr Wilson's
in Pall Mall.

A poor neighbour was hired. A horse procured for him. He had his directions.

In vain did I endeavour to engage my beloved when she was below. Her head-
ache, I suppose, returned. She, like the rest of her sex, can be ill or well when she
pleases.—

I see her drift, thought I: it is to have all her lights from Miss Howe before she
resolves; and to take her measures accordingly.

Up she went, expressing great impatience about the letter she had sent for; and
desired Mrs Moore to let her know if I offered to send any of my servants to
town—to get at the letter, I suppose, was her fear. But she might have been quite
easy on that head; and yet perhaps would not, had she known that the worthy
Captain Tomlinson (who will be in town before her messenger) will leave there the
important letter: which I hope will help to pacify her, and to reconcile her to
me.

Oh Jack! Jack! thinkest thou that I will take all this roguish pains, and be so
often called villain, for nothing?

But yet, is it not taking pains to come at the finest creature in the world, not for
a *transitory moment* only, but for one of our lives?—The struggle, whether I am to
have her in *my own way*, or in *hers?*

But now I know thou wilt be frightened out of thy wits for me—What, Lovelace!
wouldst thou let her have a letter that will inevitably blow thee up; and blow up
the mother, and all her nymphs!—yet not intend to reform, to marry?

Patience, puppy! Canst thou not trust thy master?

Letter 239: MR LOVELACE TO JOHN BELFORD, ESQ.

(In continuation)

I WENT up to my new-taken apartment, and fell to writing in character, as usual.
I thought I had made good my quarters. But the cruel creature, understanding that
I intended to take up my lodgings there, declared with so much violence against
it, that I was obliged to submit, and to accept of another lodging about twelve
doors off, which Mrs Moore recommended. And all the advantage I could obtain
was that Will, unknown to my spouse and for fear of a freak, should lie in the
house.

Mrs Moore, indeed, was unwilling to disoblige *either* of us. But Miss Rawlins
was of opinion, that nothing more ought to be allowed me: and yet Mrs Moore
owned that the refusal was a strange piece of tyranny to an husband, if I *were* an
husband.

I had a good mind to make Miss Rawlins smart for it. Come and see Miss Rawlins, Jack—If thou likest her, I'll get her for thee with a *wet finger*, as the saying is!

The Widow Bevis indeed stickled hard for me (an innocent or injured man will have friends everywhere). She said that to *bear much* with some wives, was to be obliged to bear more: and I reflected, with a sigh, *that tame spirits must always be imposed upon*. And then, in my heart, I renewed my vows of revenge upon this haughty and perverse beauty.

The second fellow came back from town about nine o'clock, with Miss Howe's letter of Wednesday last. 'Collins, *it seems*, when he left it, had desired that it might be safely and speedily delivered into Miss Laetitia Beaumont's own hands. But Wilson, understanding that neither she nor I were in town (*He could not know of our difference, thou must think*), resolved to take care of it till our return, in order to give it into one of our own hands; and now delivered it to her messenger.' This was told *her*. Wilson, I doubt not, is in her favour upon it.

She took the letter with great eagerness, opened it in a hurry (I am glad she did: yet, I believe, all was right) before Mrs Moore and Mrs Bevis (Miss Rawlins was gone home); and said, she would not for the world that I should have had that letter; for the sake of her dear friend the writer; who had written to her very uneasily about it.

Her *dear friend!* repeated Mrs Bevis, when she told me this—such mischief-makers are always deemed *dear friends* till they are found out!

The widow says that I am the finest gentleman she ever beheld.

I have found a warm kiss now and then very kindly taken.

I might be a very wicked fellow, Jack, if I were to do all the mischief in my power. But I am evermore for quitting a too-easy prey to *reptile-rakes*. What but difficulty (though the lady is an angel), engages me to so much perseverance here? And *here, conquer or die* is now the determination!

I HAVE just now parted with this honest widow. She called upon me at my new lodgings. I told her that I saw I must be further obliged to her in the course of this difficult affair. She must allow me to make her a handsome present when all was happily over. But I desired that she would take no notice of what should pass between us, *not even to her aunt*; for that she, as I saw, was in the power of Miss Rawlins: who, being a maiden gentlewoman, knew not the *right* and the *fit* in matrimonial matters, as she, my dear widow, did.

Very true: how *should* she? said Mrs Bevis, proud of knowing—nothing! But, for her part, she desired no present. It was enough if she could contribute to reconcile man and wife, and disappoint mischief-makers. She doubted not that such an envious creature as Miss Howe was glad that Mrs Lovelace had eloped—jealousy and love *was* old Nick!

See, Belford, how charmingly things work between me and my new acquaintance, the widow!—Who knows but that she may, after a little farther intimacy (though I am banished the house on nights), contrive a midnight visit for me to my spouse, when all is still and fast asleep?

Where can a woman be safe, who has once entered the lists with a contriving and intrepid lover?

But as to this *letter*, methinks thou sayest, of Miss Howe?

I knew thou would be uneasy for me: but did not I tell thee that I had provided for everything? That I always took care to keep seals entire, and to preserve covers?[a] Was it not easy then, thinkest thou, to contrive a shorter letter out of a longer; and to copy the very words?

I can tell thee it was so well ordered that, not being suspected to have been in my hands, it was not easy to find me out. Had it been my beloved's hand, there would have been no imitating it for such a length. Her delicate and even mind is seen in the very cut of her letters. Miss Howe's hand is no bad one; but is not so equal and regular. That little devil's natural impatience hurrying on her fingers gave, I suppose, from the beginning, her handwriting, as well as the rest of her, its fits and starts, and those peculiarities which, like strong muscular lines in a face, neither the pen nor the pencil can miss.

Hast thou a mind to see what it was I *permitted* Miss Howe to write to her lovely friend? Why then read it here, as if by way of marginal observation, as extracted from hers of Wednesday last[b]; with a few additions of my own—the additions underscored.[c]

[*Letter 239.1: 'Anna Howe' to Clarissa*]

My dearest Friend,
You will perhaps think that I have been too long silent. But I had begun two letters at different times since my last, and written a great deal each time; and with spirit enough, I assure you; incensed as I was against the abominable wretch you are with, particularly on reading yours of the 21st of the past month.

The FIRST I intended to keep open till I could give you some accounts of my proceedings with Mrs Townsend. It was some days before I saw her: and this intervenient space giving me time to reperuse what I had written, I thought it proper to lay that aside, and to write in a style a little less fervent; for you would have blamed me, I knew, for the freedom of some of my expressions (execrations, if you please). And when I had gone a good way in the SECOND, the change in your prospects on his communicating to you Miss Montague's letter, and his better behaviour occasioning a change in your mind, I laid that aside also: and in this uncertainty thought I would wait to see the issue of affairs between you, before I wrote again; believing that all would soon be decided one way or other—

Here I was forced to break off. I am *too little* my own mistress—My mother[d] always up and down; and watching as if I were writing to a fellow. What need I (she asks me) lock myself in,[e] if I am only reading past correspondencies? For that is my pretence, when she comes poking in with her face sharpened to an edge, as I may say, by a curiosity that gives her more pain than pleasure—The Lord forgive me; but I believe I shall huff her, next time she comes in.

Do you forgive me too, my dear. My mother ought; because she says I am my father's girl; and because I am sure I am hers.

a   p. 754.   b   See p. 743.
c   Mr Lovelace's additions and connexions in this letter are printed in the italic character.
d   See p. 744   e   p. 745.

Upon my life, my dear, I am sometimes of opinion that this vile man was capable of meaning you dishonour. When I look back upon his past conduct, I cannot help thinking so: what a villain, if so!—But now I hope, and verily believe, that he has laid aside such thoughts. My reasons for both opinions I will give you.

For the first, to wit, that he had it once in his head to take you at advantage if he could; I consider[a] that pride, revenge, and a delight to tread in unbeaten paths, are principal ingredients in the character of this finished libertine. He hates all your family, yourself excepted—yet is a savage in love. His pride, and the credit which a few plausible qualities sprinkled among his odious ones, have given him, have secured him too good a reception from our eye-judging, our undistinguishing, our self-flattering, our too-confiding sex, to make assiduity and obsequiousness, and a conquest of his unruly passions, any part of his study.

He has some reason for his animosity to all the men, and to one woman, of your family. He has always shown you and his own family too, that he prefers his pride to his interest. He is a declared marriage-hater; a notorious intriguer; full of his inventions, and glorying in them. As his vanity had made him imagine that no woman could be proof against his love, no wonder that he struggled like a lion held in toils,[b] against a passion that he thought not returned.[c] Hence, perhaps, it is not difficult to believe that it became possible for such a wretch as this to give way to his old prejudices against marriage; and to that revenge which had always been a first passion with him.[d]

And hence may we account for his delays; his teasing ways; his bringing you to bear with his lodging in the same house; his making you pass to the people of it as his wife; his bringing you into the company of his libertine companions; the attempt of imposing upon you that Miss Partington for a bedfellow, etc.

My reasons for the contrary opinion; to wit, that he is now resolved to do you all the justice in his power to do you; are these: that he sees that all his own family[e] have warmly engaged themselves in your cause; that the horrid wretch loves you— with such a love, *however,* as Herod loved his Mariamne: that, on inquiry, I find it to be true that counsellor Williams (whom Mr Hickman knows to be a man of eminence in his profession) has actually as good as finished the settlements: that two drafts of them have been made; one avowedly to be sent to this very Captain Tomlinson: and I find that a licence has actually been more than once endeavoured to be obtained, and that difficulties have hitherto been made equally to Lovelace's vexation and disappointment. My mother's proctor, who is very intimate with the proctor applied to by the wretch, has come at this information in confidence; and hints that as Mr Lovelace is a man of high fortunes, these difficulties will probably be got over.

I had once resolved to make strict inquiry about Tomlinson; and still, if you will, your uncle's favourite housekeeper may be sounded, at distance.

I know that the matter is so laid[f] that Mrs Hodges is supposed to know nothing of the treaty set on foot by means of Captain Tomlinson. But your uncle is an old man,[g] and old men imagine themselves to be under obligation to their paramours, if younger than themselves, and seldom keep anything from their knowledge—Yet,

a   p. 747.   b   p. 748.
c   ibid.   d   ibid.
e   p. 749.   f   p. 746.   g   ibid.

methinks, there can be no need; since Tomlinson, as you describe him, is so good a man, and so much of a gentleman; the end to be answered by his being an impostor so much more than necessary, if Lovelace has villainy in his head—And thus what he communicated to you of Mr Hickman's application to your uncle, and of Mrs Norton's to your mother (some of which particulars I am satisfied his vile agent Joseph Leman could not reveal to his viler employer); his pushing on the marriage-day in the name of your uncle; which it could not answer any wicked purpose for him to do; and what he writes of your uncle's proposal, to have it thought that you were married from the time that you had lived in one house together; and that to be made to agree with the time of Mr Hickman's visit to your uncle; the insisting on a trusty person's being present at the ceremony, at that uncle's nomination—these things made me *assured that he now at last means honourably.*

But if any unexpected delays should happen on his side, acquaint me, my dear, of the very street where Mrs Sinclair lives; and where Mrs Fretchville's house is situated (which I cannot find that you have ever mentioned in your former letters—which is a little odd); and I will make strict inquiries of them, and of Tomlin: on too; and I will (if your heart will let you take my advice) soon procure you a refuge from him with Mrs Townsend.

But why do I now, when you seem to be in so good a train, puzzle and perplex you with my retrospections? And yet they may be of use to you, if any delay happen on his part.

But that I think cannot well be. What you have therefore now to do, is, so to behave to this proud-spirited wretch, as may banish from his mind all remembrance of past disobligations,[a] *and to receive his addresses as those of a betrothed lover. You will incur the censure of prudery and affectation, if you keep him at that distance which you have hitherto* kept him at. *His sudden (and as suddenly recovered) illness has given him an opportunity to find out that you love him (Alas, my dear, I knew you loved him!): he has seemed to change his nature, and is all love and gentleness: and no more quarrels now, I beseech you.*

I am very angry with him, nevertheless, for the freedoms which he took with your person[b]; *and I think some guard is necessary, as he is certainly an encroacher. But indeed all men are so; and you are such a charming creature, and have kept him at such a distance!—But no more of this subject. Only, my dear, be not over-nice, now you are so near the state. You see what difficulties you laid yourself under when* Tomlinson's letter called you again into the wretch's company.

If you meet with no impediments, no new causes of doubt,[c] your reputation in the eye of the world is concerned that you should be his, *and, as your uncle rightly judges, be thought to have been his before now.* And yet, *let me tell you,* I can *hardly* bear *to think* that these libertines should be rewarded for their villainy with the best of the sex, when the worst of it are too good for them.

I shall send this long letter by Collins,[d] who changes his day to oblige me. As none of our letters by Wilson's conveyance have miscarried, when you have been in more apparently disagreeable situations than you are in at present, I *have no doubt* that this will go safe.

a   p. 750.   b   See pp. 704, 705.
c   p. 751.   d   ibid.

Miss Lardner[a] (whom you have seen at her cousin Biddulph's) saw you at St James's Church on Sunday was fortnight. She kept you in her eye during the whole time; but could not once obtain the notice of yours, though she curtsied to you twice. She thought to pay her compliments to you when the service was over; for she doubted not but you were married—and for an odd reason—because you came to church by yourself—Every eye, as usual, she said was upon you; and this seeming to give you hurry, and you being nearer the door than she, you slid out before she could go to you. But she ordered her servant to follow you till you were housed. This servant saw you step into a chair which waited for you; and you ordered the men to carry you to the place where they took you up. She *describes the house* as a very genteel house, and fit to receive people of fashion: *and what makes me mention this is, that perhaps you will have a visit from her; or message, at least.*

So that you have Mr Doleman's testimony to the credit of the house and people you are with[b]; *and he is* a man of fortune and some reputation; formerly a rake indeed; but married to a woman of family; and, having had a palsy blow, one would think, a penitent. You have *also Mr Mennell's at least passive testimony; Mr* Tomlinson's; *and now, lastly, Miss Lardner's; so that there will be the less need for inquiry: but you know my busy and inquisitive temper, as well as my affection for you, and my concern for your honour. But all doubt will soon be lost in certainty.*

Nevertheless I must add, that I would have you command me up, if I can be of the least service or pleasure to you.[c] I value not fame; I value not censure; nor even life itself, I verily think, as I do your honour, and your friendship—For is not your honour my honour? And is not your friendship the pride of my life?

May heaven preserve you, my dearest creature, in honour and safety, is the prayer, the hourly prayer, of

Your ever faithful and affectionate

Thursday morn. 5th   ANNA HOWE

I have written all night. *Excuse indifferent writing. My crow-quills are worn to the stumps, and I must get a new supply.*

These ladies always write with crow-quills, Jack.

If thou art capable of taking in all my *precautionaries* in this letter, thou wilt admire my sagacity and contrivance almost as much as I do myself. Thou seest that Miss Lardner, Mrs Sinclair, Tomlinson, Mrs Fretchville, Mennell, are all mentioned in it. My first liberties with her person also. (Modesty, modesty, Belford, I doubt, is more confined to time, place, and occasion, even by the most delicate minds, than those minds would have it believed to be.) And why all these taken notice of by me from the genuine letter, but for fear some future letter from the vixen should escape my hands, in which she might refer to these names? And if none of them were to have been found in this that is to pass for hers, I might be routed *horse and foot*, as Lord M. would phrase it, in a like case.

Devilish hard (and yet I may thank myself) to be put to all this plague and trouble!—And for *what*, dost thou ask? Oh Jack, for a triumph of more value to

a   pp. 745, 749.
b   p. 745.
c   p. 751.

me *beforehand* than an imperial crown!—Don't ask me the value of it a *month hence*. But what indeed is an imperial crown itself, when a man is used to it?

Miss Howe might well be anxious about the letter she wrote. Her sweet friend, from what I have let pass of hers, has reason to rejoice in the thought that it fell not into my hands.

And now must all my contrivances be set at work to intercept the expected letter from Miss Howe; which is, as I suppose, to direct her to a place of safety, and out of my knowledge. Mrs Townsend is, no doubt, in this case to smuggle her off. I hope the *villain*, as I am so frequently called between these two girls, will be able to manage this point.

But what, perhaps thou askest, if the lady should take it into her head, by the connivance of Miss Rawlins, to quit this house privately in the night?

I have thought of this, Jack. Does not Will lie in the house? And is not the Widow Bevis my fast friend?

Letter 240: MR LOVELACE TO JOHN BELFORD, ESQ.

Saturday, 6 o'clock, June 10

THE lady gave Will's sweetheart a letter last night to be carried to the post-house as this morning, directed for Miss Howe, under cover to Hickman. I dare say neither cover nor letter will be seen to have been opened. The contents but eight lines—to own—'The receipt of her double-dated letter in safety: and referring to a longer letter which she intends to write, when she shall have a quieter heart, and less trembling fingers. But mentions something to have happened (My detecting her, she means), which has given her very great flutters, confusions, and apprehensions: but which she will await the issue of (some hopes for me hence, Jack!) before she gives her fresh perturbation or concern on her account—She tells her how impatient she shall be for her next, etc.'

Now, Belford, I thought it would be but kind in me to save Miss Howe's concern on these alarming hints; since the curiosity of such a spirit must have been prodigiously excited by them. Having therefore so good a copy to imitate, I wrote; and, taking out that of my beloved, put under the same cover the following short billet; inscriptive and conclusive parts of it in her own words.

[*Letter 240.1: 'Clarissa Harlowe' to Anna Howe*]

Hampstead, Tuesday evening

My ever-dear Miss Howe,

A FEW lines only, till calmer spirits and quieter fingers be granted me, and till I can get over the shock which your intelligence has give me—to acquaint you—that your kind long letter of Wednesday, and, as I may say, of Thursday morning, is come safe to my hands. On receipt of yours by my messenger to you, I sent for it from Wilson's. There, thank heaven! it lay. May that heaven reward you for all your past, and for all your *intended* goodness to

Your for-ever obliged,
CL. HARLOWE

I took great pains in writing this. It cannot, I hope, be suspected. Her hand is so *very* delicate. Yet hers is written less beautifully than she usually writes: and I hope Miss Howe will allow somewhat for *hurry of spirits*, and *unsteady fingers*.

My consideration for Miss Howe's *ease of mind* extended still farther than to the instance I have mentioned.

That this billet might be with her as soon as possible (and before it could have reached Hickman by the post), I dispatched it away by a servant of Mowbray's. Miss Howe, had there been any failure or delay, might, as thou wilt think, have communicated her anxieties to her fugitive friend; and she *to me*, perhaps, in a way I should not have been pleased with.

Once more wilt thou wonderingly question—All this pains for a single girl?

Yes, Jack!—but is not this girl a CLARISSA?—And who knows, but kind fortune, as a reward for my perseverance, may toss me in her charming friend? Less likely things have come to pass, Belford!—and to be sure I shall have her, if I resolve upon it.

Letter 241: MR LOVELACE TO JOHN BELFORD, ESQ.

Eight o'clock, Sat. morn. June 10

I AM come back from Mrs Moore's, whither I went in order to attend my charmer's commands. But no admittance. A very bad night.

Doubtless she must be as much concerned, that she has carried her resentments so very far, as I have reason to be that I made such a poor use of the opportunity I had on Wednesday night.

But now, Jack, for a brief review of my present situation; and a slight hint or two of my precautions.

I have seen the women this morning, and find them half right, half doubting.

Miss Rawlins's brother tells her that she *lives* at Mrs Moore's.

Mrs Moore can do nothing without Miss Rawlins.

People who keep lodgings at public places expect to get by everyone who comes into their purlieus. Though not permitted to lodge there myself, I have engaged all the rooms she has to spare, to the very garrets; and *that* as I have told thee before, for a month certain, and at her own price, board included; my spouse's and all: but she must not, at present, know it. So I hope I have Mrs Moore fast *by the interest*.

This, devil-like, is suiting temptations to inclinations.

I have always observed, and I believe I have hinted as much formerly,[a] that all dealers, though but for pins, may be taken in by customers for pins, sooner than by a direct bribe of ten times the value; especially if pretenders to conscience: for the offer of a bribe would not only give room for suspicion; but would startle and alarm their scrupulousness; while a high price paid for what you buy, is but submitting to be cheated in the method the person makes a profession to get by. Have I not said that human nature is a rogue?[b]—And do not I know it?

To give a higher instance, how many proud senators, in the year 1720 were induced by presents or subscriptions of South Sea stock to contribute to a scheme big with national ruin; who yet would have spurned the man who. should have

a   See p. 462.
b   See pp. 465 and 575.

presumed to offer them even twice the sum certain, that they had a chance to gain by the stock?—But to return to my *review*, and my *precautions*.

Miss Rawlins fluctuates as she hears the lady's story, or as she hears mine. Somewhat of an infidel, I doubt, is this Miss Rawlins. I have not yet considered *her* foible. The next time I see her, I will take particular notice of all the moles and freckles in her mind; and then *infer* and *apply*.

The Widow Bevis, as I have told thee, is all my own.

My man Will lies in the house. My other new fellow attends upon *me*; and cannot therefore be quite stupid.

Already is Will over head and ears in love with one of Mrs Moore's maids. He was struck with her the moment he set his eyes upon her. A raw country wench too. But all women, from the countess to the cookmaid, are put into high good humour with themselves, when a man is taken with them at first sight. Be they ever so *plain* (no woman can be *ugly*, Jack!), they'll find twenty good reasons besides the great one, for *sake's sake*, by the help of the glass without (and perhaps in spite of it) and conceit within, to justify the honest fellow's *caption*.

'The rogue has saved £150 in my service'—more by 50 than I bid him save. No doubt he thinks he *might* have done so; though I believe not worth a groat. 'The best of masters I—passionate, indeed: but soon appeased.'

The wench is extremely kind to him already. The other maid is also very civil to him. He has a husband for *her* in his eye. She cannot but say that Mr Andrew, my *other* servant (the girl is for fixing the *person*), is a very well-spoken civil young man.

'We common folks have our joys, and please your honour, says honest Joseph Leman, like as our betters have.'[a] And true says honest Joseph—Did I prefer ease to difficulty, I should envy these low-degree sinners some of their joys.

But if Will had *not* made amorous pretensions to the wenches, we all know that servants, united in one common *compare-note* cause, are intimate the moment they see one another—great genealogists too; they know immediately the whole kin and kin's kin of each other, though dispersed over the three kingdoms, as well as the genealogies and kin's kin of those they serve.

But my precautions end not here.

Oh Jack, with such an invention, what occasion had I to carry my beloved to Mrs Sinclair's?

My spouse may have *further* occasion for the messengers whom she dispatched, one to Miss Howe, the other to Wilson's. With one of these Will is already well acquainted, as thou hast heard—to mingle liquor is to mingle souls with these fellows: with the other he will soon be acquainted, if he be not *already*.

The captain's servant has *his* uses and instructions assigned him. I have hinted at some of them already.[b] *He* also serves a most humane and considerate master. I love to make everybody respected to my power.

The post, general and penny,[1] will be strictly watched likewise.

Miss Howe's Collins is remembered to be described. Miss Howe's and Hickman's liveries also.

James Harlowe and Singleton are warned against. I am to be acquainted with any inquiry that shall happen to be made after my spouse, whether by her married

a See p. 494.
b See p. 807.

or maiden name, before *she* shall be told of it—and this that I may have it in my power to *prevent mischief.*

I have ordered Mowbray and Tourville (and Belton, if his health permit) to take their quarters at Hampstead for a week, with their fellows to attend them. I spare thee for the present, because of thy private concerns. But hold thyself in cheerful readiness however, as a mark of thy *allegiance.*

As to my spouse herself, has she not reason to be pleased with me for having permitted her to receive Miss Howe's letter from Wilson's? A plain case, either that I am no deep plotter, or that I have no further views but to make my peace with her for an offence so slight, and so *accidental.*

Miss Howe says, though prefaced with an *alas!* that her charming friend loves me: she must therefore yearn after this reconciliation—prospects so fair—if she used me with less rigour, and more politeness; if she showed me any *compassion*; seemed inclinable to spare me, and to make the most favourable constructions; I cannot but say that it would be impossible not to show *her* some. But to be insulted and defied by a rebel in one's power, what prince can bear that?

But I return to the scene of action. I must keep the women steady. I had no opportunity to talk to my worthy Mrs Bevis in private.

Tomlinson, a dog, not come yet!

Letter 242: MR LOVELACE TO JOHN BELFORD, ESQ.

From my apartments at Mrs Moore's Miss Rawlins at her brother's; Mrs Moore engaged in household matters; Widow Bevis dressing; I have nothing to do but write. This cursed Tomlinson not yet arrived! Nothing to be done without him.

I think he shall complain in pretty high language of the treatment he met with yesterday. 'What are our affairs to him? He can have no view but to serve us. Cruel, to send back to town, *unaudienced*, unseen, a man of his business and importance. He never stirs a foot, but something of consequence depends upon his movements. A confounded thing to trifle thus humoursomely with such a gentleman's moments!—These women think that all the business of the world must stand still for their *figaries* (a good female word, Jack!): the greatest triflers in the creation, to fancy themselves the most important beings in it—*Marry come up!* as I have heard goody Sorlings say to her servants when she has rated at them, with mingled anger and disdain.'

After all, methinks I want these *tostications* (thou seest how women, and women's words, fill my mind) to be over, *happily* over, that I may sit down quietly, and reflect upon the dangers I have passed through, and the troubles I have undergone. I have a *reflecting* mind, as thou knowest; but the very word [*reflecting*] implies, *all got over.*

What briers and thorns does the wretch rush into (a scratched face and tattered garments the unavoidable consequence), who will needs be for striking out a new path through overgrown underwood; quitting *that* beaten out for him by those who have travelled the same road before him!

A VISIT from the Widow Bevis in my own apartment. She tells me that my spouse had thoughts last night, after I was gone to my lodgings, of removing from Mrs Moore's. I almost wish she had attempted to do so.

Miss Rawlins, it seems, who was applied to upon it, dissuaded her from it.

Mrs Moore also, though she did not own that Will lay in the house (or rather sat up in it, courting), set before her the difficulties which, in her opinion, she would have to get clear off without my knowledge; assuring her that she could be nowhere safer than with her, till she had fixed whither to go. And the lady herself recollected that if she went, she might miss the expected letter from her dear friend Miss Howe; which, as she owned, was to direct her future steps.

She must also surely have some curiosity to know what her uncle's friend had to say to her from her uncle, contemptuously as she yesterday treated a man of his importance. Nor could she, I should think, be absolutely determined to put herself out of the way of receiving the visits of two of the principal ladies of my family, and to break entirely with me in the face of them all—Besides, whither could she have gone?—Moreover, Miss Howe's letter coming, after her elopement, so safely to her hands, must surely put her into a more confiding temper with me, and with everyone else, though she would not immediately own it.

But these good folks have so *little* charity!— are such *severe* censurers!—yet who is *absolutely perfect?*—It were to be wished, however, that *they* would be so modest as to doubt themselves sometimes: then would they allow for others, as others (excellent as they imagine themselves to be) must for them.

Saturday, one o'clock

TOMLINSON at last is come. Forced to ride five miles about (though I shall impute his delay to great and important business) to avoid the sight of two or three impertinent rascals, who, little thinking whose affairs he was employed in, wanted to obtrude themselves upon him. I think I will make this fellow easy, if he behave to my liking in this affair.

I sent up the moment he came.

She desired to be excused receiving his visit till four this afternoon.

Intolerable!—No consideration!—None at all in this sex, when their cursed humours are in the way!—Pay-day, pay-*hour*, rather, will come!—Oh that it were to be the next!

The captain is in a pet. Who can blame him? Even the women think a man of his consequence, and generously coming to serve us, hardly used. Would to heaven she had attempted to get off last night: the women not my enemies, who knows but the husband's exerted authority might have met with such connivance as might have concluded either in carrying her back to her former lodgings, or in consummation at Mrs Moore's, in spite of exclamations, fits, and the rest of the female obsecrations?

My beloved has not appeared to anybody this day, except to Mrs Moore. Is, it seems, extremely low: unfit for the interesting conversation that is to be held in the afternoon. Longs to hear from her dear friend Miss Howe—yet cannot expect a letter for a day or two. Has a bad opinion of all mankind—No wonder!—Excellent creature as she is! with such a *father*, such *uncles*, such a *brother*, as she has!

How does she look?

Better than could be expected from yesterday's fatigue, and last night's ill rest.

These tender doves know not, till put to it, what they can bear; especially when engaged in love-affairs; and their attention wholly engrossed. But the sex love busy scenes. Still-life is their aversion. A woman will *create* a storm, rather than be without one. So as they can preside in the whirlwind, and direct it, they are happy—But my beloved's misfortune is, that she must live in tumults; yet neither raise them herself, nor be able to control them.

Letter 243: MR LOVELACE TO JOHN BELFORD, ESQ.

Sat. night, June 10

WHAT will be the issue of all my plots and contrivances, devil take me if I am able to divine! But I will not, as Lord M. would say *forestall my own market.*

At four, the appointed hour, I sent up to desire admittance in the captain's name and my own.

She would wait upon the *captain* presently (not upon *me!*); and in the parlour, if it were not engaged.

The dining-room being *mine*, perhaps that was the reason of her naming the parlour—mighty nice again, if so!—no good sign for me, thought I, this stiffness.

In the parlour, with me and the captain, were Mrs Moore, Miss Rawlins, and Mrs Bevis.

The women said they would withdraw when the lady came down.

Lovel. Not except she chooses you should, ladies—People who are so much above-board as I am, need not make secrets of any of their affairs. Besides, you three ladies are now acquainted with all our concerns.

Capt. I have some things to say to your lady, that perhaps she would not herself choose that anybody should hear; not even *you*, Mr Lovelace, as you and her family are not upon such a good foot of understanding as were to be wished.

Lovel. Well, well, captain, I must submit. Give us a sign to withdraw; and we will withdraw.

It was better that the exclusion of the women should come from him, than from me.

Capt. I will bow, and wave my hand, thus——when I wish to be alone with the lady. Her uncle dotes upon her: I hope, Mr Lovelace, you will not make a reconciliation more difficult, for the earnestness which my dear friend shows to bring it to bear: but indeed I must tell you, *as I told you more than once before*, that I am afraid you have made lighter of the occasion of this misunderstanding to me, than it ought to have been made.

Lovel. I hope, Captain Tomlinson, you do not question my veracity!

Capt. I beg your pardon, Mr Lovelace—but those things which we men may think lightly of, may not be so to a lady of delicacy—and then, if you *have* bound yourself by a vow, you ought——

Miss Rawlins bridling, her lips closed (but her mouth stretched to a smile of approbation, the longer for not buttoning), tacitly showed herself pleased with the captain for his delicacy.

Mrs Moore *could* speak—*Very true*, however, was all she said, with a motion of her head that expressed the bow-approbatory.

For my part, said the jolly widow, staring with eyes as big as eggs, I know what

I know—but man and wife *are* man and wife; or they are *not* man and wife—I have no notion of standing upon such niceties.

But here she comes! cried one—hearing her chamber door open—here she comes! another—hearing it shut after her—and down dropped the angel among us.

We all stood up, bowing and curtsying; and could not help it. For she entered with such an air as commanded all our reverence. Yet the captain looked plaguy grave.

Cl. Pray keep your seats, ladies—Pray do not go (for they made offers to withdraw; yet Miss Rawlins would have burst, had she been suffered to retire). Before this time you have heard all my story, I make no doubt—Pray keep your seats—at least all Mr Lovelace's.

A very saucy and whimsical beginning, thought I.

Captain Tomlinson, your servant, addressing herself to him with inimitable dignity. I hope you did not take amiss my declining your visit yesterday. I was really incapable of talking upon any subject that required attention.

Capt. I am glad I see you better now, madam. I hope I do.

Cl. Indeed I am not well. I would not have excused myself from attending you some hours ago, but in hopes I should have been better. I beg your pardon, sir, for the trouble I have given you; and shall the rather expect it, as *this day will*, I hope, *conclude it all*.

Thus set! thus determined! thought I—yet to have *slept* upon it!—But, as what she said was capable of a good, as well as a bad construction, I would not put an unfavourable one upon it.

Lovel. The captain was sorry, my dear, he did not offer his attendance the moment he arrived yesterday. He was afraid that you took it amiss that he did not.

Cl. Perhaps I thought that my *uncle*'s friend might have wished to see me as soon as he came (how we stared!)—but, sir (to me), it might be *convenient to you* to detain him.

The devil, thought I!—so there really was resentment as well as head-ache, as my good friend Mrs Bevis observed, in her refusing to see the honest gentleman.

Capt. You *would* detain me, Mr Lovelace—I was for paying my respects to the lady the moment I came—

Cl. Well, sir (interrupting him), to waive this; for I would not be thought captious—If you have not suffered inconveniency in being obliged to come again, I shall be easy.

Capt. (half-disconcerted) A *little*, I can't say but I have. I have, indeed, too many affairs upon my hands. But the desire I have to serve you and Mr Lovelace, as well as to oblige my dear friend your uncle Harlowe, make great inconveniencies but small ones.

Cl. You are very obliging, sir.——Here is a great alteration since you parted with us last.

Capt. A great one indeed, madam! I was very much surprised at it on Thursday evening, when Mr Lovelace conducted me to your lodgings, where we hoped to find you.

Cl. Have you anything to say to me, sir, from my uncle himself, that requires my *private* ear? Don't go, ladies (for the women stood up, and offered to withdraw)—If Mr Lovelace stays, I am sure *you* may.

I frowned. I bit my lip. I looked at the women; and shook my head.

Capt. I have nothing to offer, but what Mr Lovelace is a party to and may hear, except one private word or two which may be postponed to the last.

Cl. Pray, ladies, keep your seats—Things are altered, sir, since I saw you. You can mention nothing that relates to *me* now, to which *that gentleman* can be a party.

Capt. You surprise me, madam! I am sorry to hear this!—sorry for your *uncle*'s sake!—sorry for *your* sake!—sorry for Mr *Lovelace*'s sake—and yet I am sure he must have given greater occasion than he has mentioned to me, or——

Lovel. Indeed, captain, indeed, ladies, I have told you great part of my story!— and what I told you of my offence was the truth—What I concealed of my story was only what I apprehended would, if known, cause this dear creature to be thought more censorious than charitable.

Cl. Well, well, sir, say what you please. Make me as black as you please. Make yourself as white as you can. I am not now in your power: that will comfort me for all.

Capt. God forbid that I should offer to plead in behalf of a crime that a lady of virtue and honour cannot forgive. But surely, surely, madam, this is going too far.

Cl. Do not blame me, Captain Tomlinson. I have a good opinion of you, as my *uncle*'s friend. But if you are Mr *Lovelace*'s friend, that is another thing; for my interests and Mr Lovelace's must now be for ever separated.

Capt. One word with you, madam, if you please—offering to retire.

Cl. You may say all that you please to say before these gentlewomen. Mr Lovelace may have secrets. I have none. You seem to think me faulty: I should be glad that all the world knew my heart. Let my enemies sit in judgement upon my actions: fairly scanned, I fear not the result. Let them even ask me my most secret thoughts, and, whether they make for me or against me, I will reveal them.

Capt. Noble lady! who can say as you say?

The women held up their hands and eyes; each, as if she had said, Not I.

No disorder here, said Miss Rawlins! But (judging by her own heart) a confounded deal of improbability, I believe she thought.

Finely *said*, to be sure, said the Widow Bevis, shrugging her shoulders.

Mrs Moore sighed.

Jack Belford, thought I, knows all mine: and in this I am more ingenuous than any of the three, and a fit match for this paragon.

Cl. How Mr Lovelace has found me out here, I cannot tell. But such mean devices, such artful, such worse than Waltham disguises put on, to obtrude himself into my company; such bold, such shocking untruths——

Capt. The favour of but one word, madam, in private——

Cl. In order to support a right which he has not over me!—Oh sir, oh captain Tomlinson!—I think I have reason to say that the man is capable of any vileness!——

The women looked upon one another, and upon me, by turns, to see how I bore it. I had such dartings in my head at the instant, that I thought I should have gone distracted. My brain seemed on fire. What would I have given to have had her alone with me!—I traversed the room; my clenched fist to my forehead. Oh that I had anybody here, thought I, that, Hercules-like, when flaming in the tortures of Deianira's poisoned shirt, I could tear in pieces?[1]

Capt. Dear lady! see you not how the poor gentleman—Lord, how have I imposed upon your uncle, at this rate! How happy, did I tell him, I saw you! How happy I was sure you would be in each other!

Cl. Oh, sir, you don't know how many premeditated offences I had forgiven when I saw you last, before I could appear to you what I hoped then I might for the future be!—But now you may tell my uncle, if you please, that I cannot hope for his mediation. Tell him that my guilt in giving this man an opportunity to spirit me away from my *tried*, my *experienced*, my *natural* friends, harshly as they treated me, stares me every day more and more in the face; and still the more, as my fate seems to be drawing to a crisis, according to the malediction of my offended father!

And then she burst into tears, which even affected that dog, who, brought to abet me, was himself all *Belforded* over.

The women, so used to cry without grief, as they are to laugh without reason, by mere force of example (confound their promptitudes!) must needs pull out *their* handkerchiefs. The less wonder, however, as I myself, between confusion, surprise, and concern, could hardly stand it.

What's a tender heart good for!—Who can be happy that has a *feeling* heart?—And yet thou'lt say that he who has it not, must be a tiger, and no man.

Capt. Let me beg the favour of one word with you, madam, in private; and that on my *own* account.

The women hereupon offered to retire. She insisted, that if *they* went, *I* should not stay.

Capt. Sir, bowing to me, shall I beg——

I hope, thought I, that I may trust this solemn dog, instructed as he is. She does not doubt him. I'll stay out no longer than to give her time to spend her first fire.

I then passively withdrew, with the women—but with such a bow to my goddess, that it won for me every heart but that I wanted *most* to win; for the haughty maid bent not her knee in return.

The conversation between the captain and the lady, when we were retired, was to the following effect: They both talked loud enough for me to hear them. The lady from anger, the captain with design; and thou mayst be sure there was no listener but myself. What I was imperfect in was supplied afterwards; for I had my vellum-leaved book to note all down—If she had known this, perhaps she would have been more sparing of her invectives—and but *perhaps* neither.

He told her, that as her brother was absolutely resolved to see her; and as he himself, in compliance with her uncle's expedient, had reported her marriage; and as that report had reached the ears of Lord M., Lady Betty, and the rest of my relations; and as he had been obliged, in consequence of his first report, to vouch it; and as her brother might find out where she was, and apply to the women here, for a confirmation or refutation of the marriage; he had thought himself obliged to countenance the report before the women: that this had embarrassed him not a little, as he would not for the world that she should have cause to think him capable of prevarication, contrivance, or double-dealing: and that this made him desirous of a private conversation with her.

It was true, she said, she *had* given her consent to such an expedient, believing it was her *uncle*'s; and little thinking that it would lead to so many errors. Yet she might have known that one error is frequently the parent of many. Mr Lovelace had made her sensible of the truth of that observation on more occasions than one; and it was an observation that he the captain had made, in one of the letters that was shown her yesterday.[a]

He hoped that she had no mistrust of *him*. That she had no doubts of *his honour*. If, madam, you suspect me—if you think me capable—What a man—the Lord be merciful to me!—what a man must you think me!

I hope, sir, there cannot be a man in the world who could deserve to be suspected in such a case as this. I do *not* suspect you. If it were possible there could be *one* such man, I am sure Captain Tomlinson, a father of children, a man in years, of sense and experience, cannot be that man.

He told me that just then, he thought he felt a sudden flash from her eye, an *eye-beam* as he called it, dart through his shivering reins; and he could not help trembling.

The dog's conscience, Jack! Nothing else!—I have felt half a dozen such flashes, such eye-beams, in as many different conversations with this soul-piercing beauty.

Her uncle, she must own, was not accustomed to think of such expedients: but she had reconciled this to herself, as the case was unhappily uncommon; and by the regard he had for her honour.

This set the puppy's heart at ease, and gave him more courage.

She asked him if he thought Lady Betty and Miss Montague intended her a visit?

He had no doubt but they did.

And does he imagine, said she, that I could be brought to countenance to them the report you have given out?

(*I had hoped to bring her to this, Jack, or she had not seen their letters*. But I had told the captain that I believe I must give up this expectation.)

No. He believed that I had no such a thought. He was pretty sure that I intended, when I saw *them*, to tell them (as in confidence) the naked truth.

He then told her that her uncle had already made some steps towards a general reconciliation. The moment, madam, that he knows you are really married, he will enter into conference with your *father* upon it; having actually expressed his desire to be reconciled to you, to your *mother*.

And what, sir, said my mother? What said my *dear* mother? (with great emotion; holding out her sweet face, as the captain described her, with the most earnest attention, as if she would shorten the way which his words were to have to her heart).

Your mother, madam, burst into tears upon it: and your uncle was so penetrated by *her* tenderness, that he could not proceed with the subject. But he intends to enter upon it with her in form, as soon as he hears that the ceremony is over.

By the tone of her voice she wept. The dear creature, thought I, begins to relent!—and I grudged the dog his eloquence. I could hardly bear the thought that any man breathing should have the power, which I had lost, of persuading this high-souled lady, though in my own favour. And, wouldst thou think it? this reflection gave me more uneasiness at the moment than I felt from her reproaches, violent as they were; or than I had pleasure in her supposed relenting. For there is beauty in everything she says and does: beauty in her passion: beauty in her

a See p. 781.

tears!—Had the captain been a young fellow, and of rank and fortune, his throat would have been in danger; and I should have thought very hardly of her!

Oh Captain Tomlinson, said she, you know not what I have suffered by this man's strange ways. He had, as I was not ashamed to tell him yesterday, a *plain path before him*. He at first betrayed me into his power: but when I *was* in it—There she stopped. Then resuming—Oh, sir, you know not what a strange man he has been!—an unpolite, a rough-mannered man!—in disgrace of his birth and education, and knowledge, an unpolite man!—and so acting, as if his worldly and personal advantages set him above those graces which distinguish a gentleman.

The first woman that ever said or that ever thought so of me, that's my comfort, thought I!—But this (spoken to her *uncle's friend* behind my back) helps to heap up thy already too-full measure, dearest!—It is down in my vellum-book.

Cl. When I look back on his whole behaviour to a poor young creature (for I am but a *very* young creature), I cannot acquit him either of great folly, or of deep design—And, last Wednesday—(There she stopped; and I suppose turned away her face. I wonder she was not ashamed to hint at what she thought so shameful; and that to a *man*, and *alone* with him.)

Capt. Far be it from me, madam, to offer to enter too closely into so tender a subject. He owns that you have reason to be displeased with him. But he so solemnly clears himself to me, of *premeditated* offence——

Cl. He cannot clear himself, Mr Tomlinson. The people of the house must be very vile, as well as he. I am convinced that there was a wicked confederacy—but no more upon such a subject.

Capt. Only one word more, madam: he tells me that he gave you such an instance of your power over him, as never man gave: and that you promised to pardon him.

Cl. He knew that he deserved not pardon, or he had not extorted that promise from me. Nor had I given it to him, but to shield myself from the vilest outrage——

Capt. I could wish, madam, inexcusable as his behaviour has been, since he has *something* to plead in the reliance he made upon your *promise*; that, for the sake of appearances to the world, and to avoid the mischiefs that may follow if you absolutely break with him, you could prevail upon your naturally generous mind, to lay an obligation upon him by your forgiveness.

She was silent.

Capt. Your father and mother, madam, deplore a daughter lost to them, whom your generosity to Mr Lovelace may restore. Do not put it to the possible chance that they may have cause to deplore a double loss; the losing of a *son*, as well as a *daughter*, who, by his own violence, which you may perhaps prevent, may be for ever lost to them, and to the whole family.

She paused. She wept. She owned that she felt the force of this argument.

I will be the making of this fellow, thought I!

Capt. Permit me, madam, to tell you that I do not think it would be difficult to prevail upon your uncle, if you insist upon it, to come up privately to town, and to give you with his own hand to Mr Lovelace—except, indeed, your present misunderstanding were to come to his ears.

Cl. But why, sir, should I be so much afraid of my *brother*? My brother has injured *me*, not I *him*. Shall I seek protection from my brother of Mr Lovelace?

And who shall protect me from Mr Lovelace?—Will the one offer to me, what the other has offered!—Wicked, ungrateful man! to insult a friendless, unprotected creature, made friendless by himself—I cannot, cannot think of him in the light I once thought of him. He has no business with me. Let him leave me. Let my brother find me. I am not such a poor creature as to be afraid to face the brother who has injured me.

Capt. Were you and your brother to meet only to confer together, to expostulate, to clear up difficulties, it were another thing. But what, madam, can you think will be the issue of an interview (Mr Solmes with him), when he find you *unmarried*, and resolved never to have Mr Lovelace; supposing Mr Lovelace were *not* to interfere; which cannot be supposed?

Cl. Well, sir, I can only say I am a very unhappy creature!—I must resign to the will of Providence, and be patient under evils which *that* will not permit me to shun. But I have taken my measures. Mr Lovelace can never make *me* happy, nor I *him*. I wait here only for a letter from Miss Howe. That must determine me——

Determine you as to Mr Lovelace, madam? interrupted the captain.

Cl. I am already determined as to him.

Capt. If it be not in his favour, I have done. I cannot use stronger arguments than I have used, and it would be impertinent to repeat them—If you cannot forgive his offence, I am sure it must have been much greater than he has owned to me—If you are absolutely determined, be pleased to let me know what I shall say to your uncle? You was pleased to tell me that this day would put an end to what you called my trouble: I should not have thought it any, could I have been an humble means of reconciling persons of worth and honour to each other.

Here I entered with a solemn air.

Lovel. Mr Tomlinson, I have heard a great part of what has passed between you and this unforgiving, however otherwise excellent lady. I am cut to the heart to find the dear creature so determined. I could not have believed it possible, with such prospects, that I had so little a share in her esteem. Nevertheless I must do myself justice with regard to the offence I was so unhappy as to give, since I find you are ready to think it much greater than it really was.

Cl. I hear not, sir, your recapitulations. I am, and ought to be, the sole judge of insults offered to my person. I enter not into discussion with you, nor hear you on the shocking subject. And was going.

I put myself between her and the door—You *may* hear all I have to say, madam. My *fault* is not of such a nature, but that you *may*. I will be a just accuser of myself; and will not wound your ears.

I then protested that the fire was a real fire (so it was). I disclaimed (less truly indeed) premeditation. I owned that I was hurried on by the violence of a youthful passion, and by a sudden impulse, which few other persons in the like situation would have been able to check: that I withdrew at her command and entreaty, on the promise of *pardon*, without having offered the least indecency, or any freedom that would not have been forgiven by persons of delicacy, surprised in an attitude so charming—her terror, on the alarm of fire, calling for a soothing behaviour, and personal tenderness, she being ready to fall into fits: my hoped-for happy day so near, that I might be presumed to be looked upon as a betrothed lover—and that this excuse might be pleaded even for the women of the house, that they, thinking us actually married, might suppose themselves to be the less concerned to interfere on so tender an occasion—There, Jack, was a bold insinuation in behalf of the women!

High indignation filled her disdainful eye, eye-beam after eye-beam flashing at me. Every feature of her sweet face had soul in it. Yet she spoke not. Perhaps, Jack, she had a thought that this *plea for the women* accounted for my contrivance to have her pass to them as married, when I *first carried her thither*.

Capt. Indeed, sir, I must say that you did not well to add to the apprehensions of a lady so much terrified before.

She offered to go by me. I set my back against the door, and besought her to stay a few moments. I had not said thus much, my dearest creature, but for your sake, as well as for my own, that Captain Tomlinson should not think I had been viler than I was. Nor will I say one word more on the subject, after I have appealed to your own heart whether it was not necessary that I should say so much; and to the captain, whether otherwise he would not have gone away with a much worse opinion of me if he had judged of my offence by the violence of your resentment.

Capt. Indeed I *should*. I *own* I should. And I am very glad, Mr Lovelace, that you are able to defend yourself thus far.

Cl. That cause must be well tried, where the offender takes his seat upon the same bench with the judge—I submit not mine to men—nor, give me leave to say, to you, Captain Tomlinson, though I am willing to have a good opinion of you. Had not the man been assured that he had influenced you in his favour, he would not have brought you up to Hampstead.

Capt. That I am *influenced*, as you call it, madam, is for the sake of your uncle, and for your own sake, more (I will say to Mr Lovelace's face) than for his. What can I have in view, but peace and reconciliation? I have from the *first* blamed, and I now *again* blame, Mr Lovelace, for adding distress to distress, and terror to terror; the lady, as you acknowledge, sir (*looking valiantly*), ready *before* to fall into fits.

Lovel. Let me own to you, Captain Tomlinson, that I have been a very faulty, a very foolish man; and, if this dear creature *ever* honoured me with her love, an *ungrateful* one. But I have had too much reason to doubt it. And this is now a flagrant proof that she never had the value for me which my proud heart wished for, that, with such prospects before us; a day so near; settlements approved and drawn; her uncle mediating a reconciliation, which for *her* sake not *my own*, I was desirous to give into; she can, for an offence so *really* slight, on an occasion so *truly* accidental, renounce me for ever; and, with me, all hopes of that reconciliation in the way her uncle had put it in, and she had acquiesced with; and risk all consequences, fatal ones as they may too possibly be—By my soul, Captain Tomlinson, the dear creature must have hated me all the time she was intending to honour me with her hand. And now she must resolve to abandon me, as far as I know, with a preference in her heart of the most odious of men—in favour of *that Solmes*, who, as you tell me, accompanies her brother: and with what hopes, with what view, accompanies him?—How can I bear to think of this?—

Cl. It is fit, sir, that you should judge of my regard for you by your own conscious demerits. Yet you know, or you would not have dared to behave to me as sometimes you did, that you had more of it than you deserved.

She walked from us; and then returning, Captain Tomlinson, said she, I will own to you that I was not capable of resolving to give my *hand*, and—*nothing but my hand*—Have I not given a flagrant proof of this to the once most indulgent of parents? which has brought me into a distress, which this man has heightened, when he ought in gratitude and honour to have endeavoured to render it supportable. I had even a *bias*, sir, in his favour, I scruple not to own it. Long, too long! bore I with his unaccountable ways, attributing his errors to unmeaning gaiety, and to a want of knowing what true delicacy, and true generosity, required from a heart susceptible of grateful impressions to one involved by his means in unhappy circumstances. It is now *wickedness* in him (a wickedness which discredits all his *professions*) to say that his last cruel and ungrateful insult was not a *premeditated* one—But what need I say more of this insult, when it was of such a nature that it has changed that bias in his favour, and made me choose to forgo all the inviting prospects he talks of, and to run all hazards, to free myself from his power?

Oh my dearest creature! how happy for us both, had I been able to *discover that bias*, as you condescend to call it, through such reserves as man never encountered with!—

He did *discover* it, Captain Tomlinson. He brought me, *more than once to own it*; the more needlessly brought me to own it, as I dare say his own *vanity* gave him *no cause to doubt it*; and as I had no other motive in not being *forward* to own it, than my too just apprehensions of his want of generosity. In a word, Captain Tomlinson (and now that I am determined upon my measures, I the less scruple to say it), I should have despised myself, had I found myself capable of affectation or tyranny to the man I intended to marry. I have always blamed the dearest friend I have in the world for a fault of this nature. In a word——

Lovel. And had my angel really and indeed the favour for me she is pleased to own?—Dearest creature, forgive me. Restore me to your good opinion. Surely I have not sinned beyond forgiveness. You say that I extorted from you the promise you made me. But I could not have presumed to make that promise the condition of my obedience, had I not thought there was room to expect forgiveness. Permit, I beseech you, the prospects to take place, that were opening so agreeably before us. I will go to town, and bring the licence. All difficulties to the obtaining of it are surmounted. Captain Tomlinson shall be witness to the deeds. He will be present at the ceremony on the part of your uncle. Indeed he gave me hope, that your uncle himself——

Capt. I *did*, Mr Lovelace: and I will tell you my grounds for the hope I gave. I proposed to my dear friend (your uncle, madam), that he should give out that he would take a turn with me to my little farm-house, as I call it, near Northampton, for a week or so—Poor gentleman! he has of late been very little abroad! Too visibly indeed declining!—Change of air, it might be given out, was good for him—But I see, madam, that this is too *tender* a subject——

The dear creature wept. She knew how to apply, as meant, the captain's hint to the *occasion* of her uncle's declining state of health.

Capt. We might indeed, I told him, set out in that road, but turn short to town *in my chariot*; and he might see the ceremony performed with his own eyes, and be the desired father, as well as the beloved uncle.

She turned from us, and wiped her eyes.

Capt. And, really, there seem now to be but two objections to this; as Mr

Harlowe discouraged not the proposal—The one, the unhappy misunderstanding between you; which I would not by any means he should know; since then he might be apt to give weight to Mr James Harlowe's unjust surmises—The other, that it would necessarily occasion some delay to the ceremony; which I cannot see but may be performed in a day or two—if——

And then he reverently bowed to my goddess—Charming fellow!—But often did I curse my stars, for making me so much obliged to his adroitness.

She was going to speak; but, not liking the turn of her countenance (although, as I thought, its severity and indignation seemed a little abated), I said, and had like to have blown myself up by it—One expedient I have just thought of——

Cl. None of your expedients, Mr Lovelace! I abhor your expedients, your inventions—I have had too many of them.

Lovel. See, Captain Tomlinson!—See, sir—Oh how we expose ourselves to you!—Little did you think, I dare say, that we have lived in such a continued misunderstanding together! But you will make the best of it all. We may yet be happy. Oh that I could have been assured that this dear lady loved me with the hundredth part of the love I have for her!—Our diffidences have been mutual. This dear creature has too much punctilio: I am afraid that I have too little. Hence our difficulties. But I have a heart, Captain Tomlinson, a heart that bids me hope for her love, because it is resolved to deserve it, as much as man *can* deserve it.

Capt. I am indeed surprised at what I have seen and heard. I defend not Mr Lovelace, madam, in the offence he has given you—As a father of daughters myself, I *cannot* defend him, though his fault seems to be lighter than I had apprehended—but in my conscience I think that you, madam, carry your resentment too high.

Cl. Too high, sir!—too high, to the man that might have been happy if he would!—too high to the man that has held *my soul in suspense* an hundred times since (by artifice and deceit) he obtained a power over me!—Say, Lovelace, thyself say, art thou not the *very* Lovelace that, by insulting *me*, hast wronged thy *own hopes*?—The wretch that appeared in vile disguises, personating an old lame creature seeking for lodgings for thy sick wife?—Telling the gentlewomen here stories all of thy own invention; and asserting to them an husband's right over me, which thou hadst not?—And is it (turning to the captain) to be expected that I should give credit to the protestations of such a man?

Lovel. Treat me, dearest creature, as you please, I will bear it: and yet your scorn and your violence have fixed daggers in my heart—But was it possible, without those disguises, to come at your speech?—And could I lose you, if study, if invention, would put it in my power to arrest your anger, and give me hope to engage you to confirm to me the *promised pardon*?—The address I made to you before the women, as if the marriage-ceremony had passed, was in consequence of what your uncle *had advised*, and what *you had acquiesced with*; and the rather made, as your brother, and Singleton, and Solmes, were resolved to find out whether what was reported of your marriage were true or not, that they might take their measures accordingly; and in hopes to prevent that mischief, which I have been but too studious to prevent, since this tameness has but invited insolence from your brother and his confederates.

Cl. Oh thou strange wretch, how thou talkest!—But, Captain Tomlinson, give me leave to say that, were I inclined to talk any farther upon this subject, I would appeal to Miss Rawlins's judgement (who else have I to appeal to?); she seems to be a person of prudence and honour; but not to any *man*'s judgement, whether I carry my resentment beyond fit bounds, when I resolve——

Capt. Forgive, madam, the interruption—but I think there can be no reason for this. You ought, as you said, to be the *sole judge* of indignities offered you. The gentlewomen here are strangers to you. You will perhaps stay but a little while among them. If you lay the state of your case before any of them, and your brother come to inquire of them, your uncle's intended mediation will be discovered and rendered abortive—*I* shall appear in a light that I never appeared in, in my life— for these women may not think themselves obliged to keep the secret.

Cl. Oh what difficulties has one fatal step involved me in!—but there is no necessity for such an appeal. I am resolved on my measures.

Capt. Absolutely resolved, madam?

Cl. I am.

Capt. What shall I say to your uncle Harlowe, madam?—Poor gentleman! how will he be surprised!—You see, Mr Lovelace—you see, sir—turning to me with a flourishing hand—but you may thank yourself—and admirably stalked he from us.

True, by my soul, thought I. I traversed the room, and bit my unpersuasive lips, now upper, now under, for vexation.

He made a profound reverence to her—and went to the window, where lay his hat and whip; and, taking them up, opened the door. Child, said he, to somebody he saw, pray, order my servant to bring my horse to the door——

Lovel. You won't go, sir—I hope you won't!—I am the unhappiest man in the world!—You won't go—yet, alas!—But you won't go, sir!—There may be yet hopes that Lady Betty may have some weight——

Capt. Dear Mr Lovelace; and may not my worthy friend, an affectionate uncle, hope for some influence upon his *daughter-niece*?—but I beg pardon—A letter will always find me disposed to serve the lady, and that as well for her sake as for the sake of my dear friend.

She had thrown herself into a chair; her eyes cast down: she was motionless, as in a profound study.

The captain bowed to her again: but met with no return to his bow. *Mr Lovelace*, said he (with an air of equality and independence), *I am yours*.

Still the dear unaccountable sat as immovable as a statue; stirring neither hand, foot, head, nor eye—I never before saw anyone in so profound a reverie, in so waking a dream.

He passed by her to go out at the door she sat near, though the other door was his direct way; and bowed again. She moved not. I will not disturb the lady in her meditations, sir—Adieu, Mr Lovelace——*No farther, I beseech you*.

She started, sighing—Are you going, sir?

Capt. I am, madam. I could have been glad to do you service: but I see it is not in my power.

She stood up, holding out one hand, with inimitable dignity and sweetness—I am sorry you are going, sir—I can't help it—I have no friend to advise with—Mr Lovelace has the art (or good-fortune, perhaps, I should call it) to make himself many—Well, sir—if you will go, I can't help it.

Capt. I will *not* go, madam, his eyes twinkling (again seized with a fit of humanity!). I will *not* go if my longer stay can do you either service or pleasure.

What, sir (turning to me), what, Mr Lovelace, was your expedient?—Perhaps something may be offered, madam——

She sighed, and was silent.

REVENGE, *invoked I to myself, keep thy throne in my heart—If the usurper* LOVE *once more drive thee from it, thou wilt never regain possession!*

Lovel. What I had thought of, what I had intended to propose, and I sighed—was this, That the dear creature, if she will not forgive me as she promised, would suspend the displeasure she has conceived against me, till Lady Betty arrives—That lady may be the mediatrix between us. This dear creature may put herself into *her* protection, and accompany her down to her seat in Oxfordshire. It is one of her ladyship's purposes to prevail on her supposed new niece to go down with her. It may pass to everyone but to Lady Betty, and to you, Captain Tomlinson, and to your friend Mr Harlowe (as he desires), that we have been some time married: and her being with my relations will amount to a proof to James Harlowe that we *are*; and our nuptials may be privately, and at this beloved creature's pleasure, solemnized; and your report, captain, authenticated.

Capt. Upon my honour, madam, clapping his hand upon his breast, a charming expedient! This will answer every end.

She mused—she was greatly perplexed—at last, God direct me, said she! I know not what to do—a young unfriended creature, whom have I to advise with?—Let me retire, if I *can* retire.

She withdrew with slow and trembling feet, and went up to her chamber.

For Heaven's sake, said the penetrated varlet, his hands lifted up, for Heaven's sake, take compassion upon this admirable lady!—I cannot proceed—I cannot proceed—She deserves all things—

Softly!—damn the fellow!—the women are coming in.

He sobbed up his grief—turned about—hemmed up a more *manly* accent—Wipe thy cursed eyes—He did. The sunshine took place on one cheek, and spread slowly to the other, and the fellow had his whole face again.

The women all three came in, led by that ever-curious Miss Rawlins. I told them that the lady was gone up to consider of everything: that we had hopes of her. And such a representation we made of all that had passed, as brought either tacit or declared blame upon the fair perverse, for hardness of heart, and over-delicacy.

The Widow Bevis, in particular, put out one lip, tossed up her head, wrinkled her forehead, and made such motions with her now lifted-up, now cast-down eyes, as showed that she thought there was a great deal of perverseness and affectation in the lady. Now and then she changed her censuring looks to looks of pity of me—But (as she said) she loved not to aggravate!—a poor business, *God help*'s! shrugging up her shoulders, to make such a rout about! and then her eyes laughed heartily—Indulgence was a good thing! Love was a good thing!—But too much was too much!

Miss Rawlins, however, declared, after she had called the Widow Bevis, with a prudish simper, a *comical gentlewoman!* That there must be something in our story which she could not fathom; and went from us into a corner, and sat down, seemingly vexed that she could not.

(In continuation)

THE lady staying longer above than we wished; and [I] hoping that (lady-like) she only waited for an invitation to return to us; I desired the Widow Bevis, in the captain's name (who wanted to go to town), to request the favour of her company.

I cared not to send up either Miss Rawlins or Mrs Moore on the errand, lest my beloved should be in a *communicative disposition*; especially as she had hinted at an appeal to Miss Rawlins; who, besides, has such an unbounded curiosity.

Mrs Bevis presently returned with an answer (winking and pinking at me), that the lady would follow her down. Miss Rawlins could not but offer to retire, as the others did. Her eyes, however, intimated that she had rather stay. But they not being answered as she seemed to wish, she went with the rest, but with slower feet; and had hardly left the parlour, when the lady entered it by the other door; a melancholy dignity in her person and air.

She sat down. Pray, Mr Tomlinson, be seated. He took his chair over against her. I stood behind hers, that I might give him *agreed-upon* signals, should there be occasion for them.

As thus—A wink of the left eye was to signify, *Push that point, captain.*

A wink of the right, and a nod, was to indicate *approbation* of what he had said.

My forefinger held up, and biting my lip, *Get off of that as fast as possible.*

A right forward nod, and a frown—*Swear to it, captain.*

My whole spread hand, *To take care not to say too much on that particular subject.*

And these motions I could make, even those with my hand, without holding up my arm or moving my wrist, had the women been there; as, when they were agreed upon, I knew not but they would.

A scowling brow, and a positive nod, was to bid him *rise in his temper.*

She hemmed—I was going to speak, to spare her supposed confusion: but this lady never wants presence of mind, when presence of mind is necessary either to her honour, or to that conscious dignity which distinguishes her from all the women I ever knew.

I have been considering, said she, as well as I was able, of everything that has passed; and of all that has been said; and of my unhappy situation. I mean no ill; I wish no ill to any creature living, Mr Tomlinson. I have always delighted to draw favourable rather than unfavourable conclusions, sometimes, as it has proved, for very bad hearts. Censoriousness, whatever faults I have, is not *naturally* my fault—But, circumstanced as I am; treated as I have been, unworthily treated by a man who is full of contrivances, and glories in them——

Lovel. My dearest life!—but I will not interrupt you.

Cl. Thus treated, it becomes me to doubt—It concerns my honour to doubt, to fear, to apprehend—*Your* intervention, sir, is so seasonable, so kind, for *this man*—My uncle's expedient, the first of the kind he ever, I believe, thought of; a plain, honest, good-minded man, as he is, not affecting such expedients—Your report in conformity to it—The consequences of that report; the alarm taken by my brother; his rash resolution upon it—the alarm taken by Lady Betty, and the rest of Mr Lovelace's relations—the *sudden* letters written to him upon it, which, with yours, he showed me—all ceremony, among persons *born observers of ceremony* and entitled to value themselves upon *their distinction*, dispensed with— all these things have happened *so* quick, and some of them *so* seasonable——

Lovel. Lady Betty, you see, madam, in her letter, dispenses with punctilio, avowedly in compliment to you. Charlotte, in hers, professes to do the same for the same reason. Good Heaven, that the respect intended you by my relations, who, in every other case, are really punctilious, should be thus construed! They were glad, madam, to have an opportunity to compliment you at my expense. Every one of my family takes delight in rallying me. But their joy on the supposed occasion——

Cl. Do I doubt, sir, that you have not something to say for anything you think fit to do?—I am speaking to Captain Tomlinson, sir—I wish you would be pleased to withdraw—at least to come from behind my chair.

And she looked at the captain, observing, no doubt, that his eyes seemed to take lessons from mine.

A fair match, by Jupiter!

The captain was disconcerted. The dog had not such a blush upon his face for ten years before. I bit my lip for vexation: walked about the room; but nevertheless took my post again; and blinked with my eyes to the captain, as a caution for him to take more care of *his:* and then scowling with my brows, and giving the nod positive, I as good as said, *Resent that, captain.*

Capt. I hope, madam, you have no suspicion that I am capable——

Cl. Be not displeased with me, Captain Tomlinson. I have told you that I am not of a suspicious temper. Excuse me for the sake of my sincerity. There is not, I will be bold to say, a sincerer heart in the world than hers before you.

She took out her handkerchief, and put it to her eyes.

I was going at the instant, after her example, to vouch for the honesty of *my* heart; but my conscience *Mennelled* upon me; and would not suffer the meditated vow to pass my lips—A devilish thing, thought I, for a man to be so little himself, when he has most occasion for himself!

The villain Tomlinson looked at me with a rueful face, as if he begged leave to cry for company. It might have been as well, if he *had* cried. A feeling heart, or the tokens of it, given by a sensible eye, are very reputable things when kept in countenance by the occasion.

And here let me fairly own to thee, that twenty times in this trying conversation I said to myself, that could I have thought that I should have all this trouble, and incurred all this guilt, I would have been honest at first. But why, questioned I, is this dear creature so lovely?—yet so invincible?—Ever heardst thou before, that the sweets of May blossomed in December?

Capt. Be pleased—be pleased, madam—if you have doubts of my honour—

A whining varlet! He should have been quite angry—for what gave I him the nod positive? He should have stalked to the window, as for his whip and hat.

Cl. I am only making such observations as my youth, my inexperience, and my present unhappy circumstances, suggest to me—A worthy heart (such, I hope, is Captain Tomlinson's) need not fear an examination—need not fear being looked into—Whatever doubt *that* man, who has been the cause of my errors, and, as my severe father imprecated, the punisher of the errors he has caused, might have had of me, or of my honour, I would have forgiven him for them, if he had fairly proposed them to me: for he might, perhaps, have had some doubt of the future conduct of a creature, whom he could induce to correspond with him against parental prohibition, and against the lights which her own judgement threw in upon her: and if he had propounded them to me like a man and a gentleman, I would have been glad of the opportunity given me to clear my intentions,·and to have shown myself entitled to his good opinion—And I hope *you*, sir——

Capt. I am ready to hear all your doubts, madam, and to clear them up——

Cl. I can only put it, sir, to your conscience and honour——

The dog sat uneasy: he shifted his feet: her eye was upon him; he was therefore, after the rebuff he had met with, afraid to look at me for my motions; and now turned his eyes towards me, then from me, as if he would *unlook* his own looks; his head turning about like a weathercock in a hurricane.

Cl.—that all is true that you have written, and that you have told me.

I gave him a right-forward nod, and a frown—as much as to say, *Swear to it, captain.* But the varlet did not round it off as I would have had him. However, he averred that it was.

He had hoped, he said, that the circumstances with which his commission was attended, and what he had communicated to her, which he could not know but from his dear friend her uncle, might have shielded him even from the *shadow* of suspicion—But I am contented, said he, stammering, to be thought—to be thought—what—what you please to think me—till, till, you are satisfied——

A whore's-bird!

Cl. The circumstances you refer to, I must own, ought to shield you, sir, from suspicion—but the man before you is a man that would make an angel suspected, should that angel plead for him.

I came forward. Traversed the room—was indeed in a bloody passion—I have no patience, madam!—and again I bit my unpersuasive lip——

Cl. No man ought to be impatient at imputations he is not ashamed to deserve. An innocent man *will not* be outrageous upon such imputations. A guilty man *ought not.* (Most excellently would this charming creature cap sentences with Lord M.!) But I am not now trying you, sir, on the foot of your *merits.* I am only sorry that I am constrained to put questions to this *worthier* gentleman, which perhaps I ought not to put, so far as they regard *himself*—And I hope, Captain Tomlinson, that you, who know not Mr Lovelace so well as, to my unhappiness, I do, and who have children of your own, will excuse a poor young creature who is deprived of all worthy protection, and who has been insulted and endangered by the most *designing man in the world*, and perhaps *by a confederacy of his creatures.*

There she stopped; and stood up, and looked at me; fear, nevertheless, apparently mingled with her anger. And so it ought. I was glad, however, of this poor sign of love—No one fears whom they value not.

Women's tongues were licensed, I was going to say—but my conscience would not let me call her a *woman*; nor use to her so vulgar a phrase. I could only rave by my motions; lift up my eyes, spread my hands, rub my face, pull my wig, and look like a fool. Indeed, I had a great mind to run mad. Had I been alone with her, I would; and she should have taken consequences.

The captain interposed in my behalf; gently, however, and as a man not quite sure that he was himself acquitted. Some of the pleas we had both insisted on, he again enforced—and, speaking low—Poor gentleman! said he, who can but pity him!—Indeed, madam, it is easy to see, with all his failings, the power you have over him!

Cl. I have no pleasure, sir, in distressing anyone—Not even *him*, who has so much distressed me—But, sir, when I THINK, and when I see him before me, I cannot command my temper!—Indeed, indeed, Captain Tomlinson, Mr Lovelace has not acted by me either as a grateful, a generous, or a prudent man!—He knows not, as I told him yesterday, the value of the heart he has insulted!

There the angel stopped; her handkerchief at her eyes!

Oh Belford, Belford! that she should so greatly excel, as to make me, at times, a villain in my own eyes!

I besought her pardon. I promised that it should be the study of my whole life to deserve it. My faults, I said, *whatever* they had been, were rather faults in her *apprehension*, than in *fact*. I besought her to give way to the expedient I had hit upon—I repeated it. The captain enforced it, for her uncle's sake. I, once more, for the sake of the general reconciliation; for the sake of all my family; for the sake of preventing future mischief——

She wept—she seemed staggered in her resolution—she turned from me. I mentioned the letter of Lord M. I besought her to resign to Lady Betty's mediation all our differences, if she would not forgive me before she saw her.

She turned towards me—she was going to speak; but her heart was full—and again she turned away her face—Then, half turning it to me, her handkerchief at her eyes—And do you *really* and *indeed* expect Lady Betty and Miss Montague?— And do you—again she stopped——

I answered in a solemn manner.

She turned from me her whole face, and paused, and seemed to consider. But, in a passionate accent, again turning towards me (Oh how difficult, Jack, for a Harlowe spirit to forgive!)—Let her ladyship come if she pleases, said she—I cannot, cannot wish to *see* her—and if she plead for you, I cannot wish to *hear* her!—The more I *think*, the less can I forgive an attempt that I am convinced was intended to *destroy* me. (A plaguy strong word for the occasion, supposing she was right!) What has my conduct been, that an insult of *such* a nature should be offered to me, as it would be a *weakness* to forgive? I am sunk in my own eyes!— and how can I receive a visit that must depress me more?

The captain urged her in my favour with greater earnestness than before. We both even clamoured, as I may say, for mercy and forgiveness. (Didst thou never hear the good folks talk of taking heaven by storm?)—Contrition repeatedly avowed—a total reformation promised—the happy expedient again pleaded——

Cl. I have taken my measures. I have gone too far to recede, or to *wish* to recede. My mind is prepared for adversity. That I have not *deserved* the evils I have met with is my consolation!—I have written to Miss Howe what my intentions are. My heart is not *with* you—it is *against* you, Mr Lovelace. I had not written to you, as I did, in the letter I left behind me, had I not resolved, whatever became of me, to renounce you for ever.

I was full of hope now. Severe as her expressions were, I saw she was afraid that I should think of what she had written. And indeed her letter is violence itself. *Angry people, Jack, should never write while their passion holds.*

Lovel. The severity you have shown me, madam, whether by pen or by speech, shall never have place in my remembrance, but for your *honour*. In the light you

CLARISSA [L244

have taken things, all is deserved, and but the natural result of virtuous resentment; and I adore you, even for the pangs you have given me.

She was silent. She had employment enough with her handkerchief at her eyes.

Lovel. You lament sometimes that you have no friends of your own sex to consult with. Miss Rawlins, I must confess, is too inquisitive to be confided in. (I liked not, thou mayest think, her appeal to Miss Rawlins.) She *may* mean well. But I never in my life knew a person who was fond of prying into the secrets of others, that was fit to be trusted. The curiosity of such is governed by pride, which is not gratified but by whispering about a secret till it becomes public, in order to show either their consequence, or their sagacity. It is so in every case. What man or woman, who is *covetous* of *power* or of *wealth*, is covetous of either for the sake of making a right use of it?—But in the ladies of my family you *may* confide. It is their ambition to think of you as one of themselves. Renew but your consent to pass *to the world*, for the sake of your uncle's expedient, and for the prevention of mischief, as a lady some time married. Lady Betty may be acquainted with the naked truth; and you may (as she hopes you will) accompany her to her seat; and, if it *must* be so, consider me as in a state of penitence or probation, to be accepted or rejected as I may appear to deserve.

The captain again clapped his hand on his breast, and declared upon his honour that this was a proposal that, were the case that of his own daughter, and she were not resolved upon *immediate* marriage (which yet he thought by far the more elegible choice), he should be very much concerned were she to refuse it.

Cl. Were I with Mr Lovelace's relations, and to pass as his wife to the world, I could not have any choice. And how could he be then in a state of probation? Oh Mr Tomlinson, you are too much his *friend* to see into his drift.

Capt. His friend, madam, as I said before, as I am *yours* and your *uncle's*, for the sake of a general reconciliation, which must begin with a better understanding between yourselves.

Lovel. Only, my dearest life, resolve to attend the arrival and visit of Lady Betty: and permit her to arbitrate between us.

Capt. There can be no harm in *that*, madam—You can suffer no inconvenience from *that*. If Mr Lovelace's offence be such that a lady of that lady's character judges it to be unpardonable, why then—

Cl. (interrupting; and to me) If am not invaded by you, sir—if I am (as I ought to be) my own mistress, I think to stay here, in this *honest house* (and then had I an *eye-beam*, as the captain calls it, flashed at me), till I receive a letter from Miss Howe. That, I hope, will be in a day or two. If in that time the ladies come whom you expect, and if they are desirous to see the creature whom you have made unhappy, I shall know whether I can, or cannot, receive their visit.

She turned short to the door, and retiring, went upstairs to her chamber.

Oh, sir, said the captain, as soon as she was gone, what an angel of a woman is this!—I *have been*, and I *am*, a very wicked man—but if anything should happen amiss to this admirable lady, through my means, I shall have more cause for self-reproach than for all the bad actions of my life put together.

And his eyes glistened.

Nothing can happen amiss, thou sorrowful dog!—What *can* happen amiss?—Are we to form our opinion of things by the romantic notions of a girl who supposes *that* to be the greatest which is the slightest of evils? Have I not told thee our whole story? Has she not broken her promise? Did I not generously spare her, when in my power? I was decent, though I had her at such advantage. Greater liberties have I taken with girls of character at a common romping bout, and all has been laughed off, and handkerchief and headcloths adjusted, and petticoats shaken to rights, in my presence. Never man, in the like circumstances, and resolved as I was resolved, goaded on as I was goaded on, as well by her own sex, as by the impulses of a violent passion, was ever so decent. Yet what mercy does she show me?

Now, Jack, this pitiful dog was such another unfortunate one as thyself—his arguments serving to confirm me in the very purpose he brought them to prevail upon me to give up. Had he left me to myself, to the tenderness of my own nature, moved as I was when the lady withdrew, and had sat down and made odious faces, and said nothing; it is very possible that I should have taken the chair over-against him, which she had quitted; and have cried and blubbered with him for half an hour together. But the varlet to *argue* with me! To pretend to *convince* a man, who knows in his heart that he is doing a wrong thing!—He must needs think that this would put me upon trying what I could say for myself; and when the excited compunction can be carried from the heart to the lips, it must evaporate in words.

Thou perhaps, in this place, wouldst have urged the same pleas that he urged. What I answered to him therefore may do for thee, and spare thee the trouble of writing, and me of reading, a good deal of nonsense.

Capt. You was pleased to tell me, sir, that you only proposed to try her virtue; and that you believed you should actually marry her.

Lovel. So I shall, and cannot help it. I have no doubt but I shall. And as to *trying* her, is she not now in the height of her trial? Have I not reason to think that she is coming about? Is she not now yielding up her resentment for an attempt which she thinks she ought *not* to forgive?—and if she do, may she not forgive the *last attempt?*—Can she, in a word, resent *that* more than she does *this?*—Women often, for their own sakes, will keep the *last secret*; but will ostentatiously din the ears of gods and men with their clamours upon a successless offer. It was my folly, my weakness, that I gave her not more cause for this her unsparing violence!

Capt. Oh sir, you never will be able to subdue this lady without force.

Lovel. Well, then, puppy, must I not endeavour to find a proper time and place——

Capt. Forgive me, sir! but can you think of force to such a fine creature?

Lovel. Force, indeed, I abhor the thought of; and for what, thinkest thou, have I taken all the pains I have taken, and engaged so many persons in my cause, but to avoid the necessity of *violent* compulsion? But yet, imaginest thou that I expect *direct consent* from such a lover of forms as this lady is known to be? Let me tell thee, McDonald, that thy master Belford has urged on thy side of the question, all that thou canst urge. Must I have every puppy's conscience to pacify, as well as my own?—By my soul, Patrick, she has a friend *here* (clapping my hand on my breast) that pleads for her with greater and more irresistible eloquence, than all the men in the world can plead for her. And had she not escaped me?—And yet how have I answered my first design of trying her,[a] and in *her* the virtue of the most virtuous

a   See Letter 110, pp. 427 ff.

of the sex?—Thou puppy! wouldst thou have me decline a trial that may make for the honour of a sex we all so dearly love?

Then, sir, you have no thoughts—no thoughts—(looking still more sorrowfully) of marrying this wonderful lady?

Yes, puppy, but I have. But let me, first, to gratify *my* pride, bring down *hers*. Let me see that she loves me well enough to forgive me for my *own* sake. Has she not heretofore lamented that she stayed not in her father's house, though the consequence must have been, if she *had*, that she would have been the wife of the odious Solmes? If now she be brought to consent to be mine, seest thou not that the *reconciliation* with her *detested relations* is the *inducement*, as it *always* was, and not *love* of *me?*—Neither her virtue nor her love can be established but upon full trial; the *last* trial—But if her resistance and resentment be such as hitherto I have reason to expect they will be, and if I find in that resentment less of hatred of *me*, than of the fact, then shall she be mine in her own way. Then, hateful as is the *life of shackles* to me, will I *marry her*.

Well, sir, I can only say that I am dough in your hands, to be moulded into what shape you please. But if, as I said before—

None of your *saids-before*. I remember all thou saidst—and I know all thou canst *further* say—Thou art only, Pontius Pilate like, washing thine own hands (don't I know thee?), that thou mayst have something to silence thy conscience with by loading me. But we have gone too far to recede. Are not all our engines in readiness?—Dry up thy sorrowful eyes. Let unconcern and heart's-ease once more take possession of thy solemn features. Thou hast hitherto performed extremely well. Shame not thy past by thy future behaviour; and a rich reward awaits thee. If thou *art* dough, *be* dough; and I slapped him on the shoulder— Resume but thy former shape—and I'll be answerable for the event.

He bowed assent and compliance: went to the glass; and began to untwist and unsadden his features: pulled his wig right, as if that, as well as his head and heart, had been discomposed by his compunction; and once more became old Mulciber's and mine.

But didst thou think, Jack, that there was so much—what-shall-I-call it?—in this Tomlinson? Didst thou imagine that such a fellow as that had bowels? That nature, so long dead and buried in him, as to all humane effects, should thus revive and exert itself?—Yet why do I ask this question of thee, who, to my equal surprise, hast shown, on the same occasion, the like compassionate sensibilities?

As to Tomlinson, it looks as if poverty had made him the wicked fellow he is; as plenty and wantonness have made us what we are. Necessity, after all, is the test of principle. But what is there in this dull word or thing called HONESTY, that even I, who cannot in my present views be served by it, cannot help thinking even the accidental emanations of it amiable in Tomlinson, though demonstrated in a *female case*; and judging better of him for being capable of such?

Letter 245: MR LOVELACE TO JOHN BELFORD, ESQ.

This debate between the captain and me was hardly over, when the three women led by Miss Rawlins, entered, hoping, No intrusion—but very desirous the maiden said, to know if we were likely to accommodate.

Oh yes, I hope so. You know, ladies, that your sex must in these cases preserve their forms. They must be courted to comply with their own happiness. A lucky expedient we have hit upon. The uncle has his doubts of our marriage. He cannot believe, nor will anybody, that it is possible that a man so much in love, the lady so desirable——

They all took the hint—It was a very extraordinary case, the two widows allowed. Women, Jack, as I believe I have observed elsewhere, have a high opinion of what they can do for us—Miss Rawlins desired, if I pleased, to let them know the expedient; and looked as if there was no need to proceed in the rest of my speech.

I begged that they would not let the lady know that I had told them what this expedient was.

They promised.

It was this: That to oblige and satisfy Mr Harlowe, the ceremony was to be again performed. He was to be privately present, and to give his niece to me with his own hands—And she was retired to consider of it.

Thou seest, Jack, that I have provided an excuse to save my veracity to the women here, in case I should incline to marriage, and she should choose to have Miss Rawlins's assistance at the ceremony. Nor doubted I to bring my fair one to save my credit on this occasion, if I could get her to consent to be mine.

A charming expedient! cried the widow. They were all three ready to clap their hands for joy upon it. Women love to be married twice at least, Jack; though not indeed to the *same man*; and all blessed the reconciliatory scheme, and the proposer of it; and, supposing it came from the captain, they looked at him with pleasure, while his face shined with the applause implied. He should think himself very happy if he could bring about a general reconciliation; and he flourished with his head like my man Will on his victory over old Grimes; bridling by turns, like Miss Rawlins in the height of a prudish fit.

But now it was time for the captain to think of returning to town, having a great deal of business to dispatch before morning: nor was he certain that he should again be able to attend us at Hampstead before he went home.

And yet I did not intend that he should leave Hampstead this night: everything drawing on to a crisis.

A message to the above effect was carried up, at my desire, by Mrs Moore; with the captain's compliments, and to know if she had any commands for him to her uncle?

But I hinted to the women, that it would be proper for them to withdraw if the lady did come down; lest she should not care to be so free before *them* on a proposal so particular, as she would be to *us* who had offered it to her consideration.

Mrs Moore brought down word that the lady was following her. They all three withdrew; and she entered at one door, as they went out at the other.

The captain accosted her, repeating the contents of the message sent up; and desired that she would give him her commands in relation to the report he was to make to her uncle Harlowe.

I know not what to say, sir, nor what I would have *you* to say to my uncle. Perhaps you may have business in town—perhaps you need not see my uncle till I have heard from Miss Howe; till after Lady Betty—I don't know what to say.

I implored the return of that value which she had so generously acknowledged once to have had for me. I presumed, I said, to flatter myself that Lady Betty, in her own person, and in the name of all my family, would be able, on my promised reformation and contrition, to prevail in my favour; especially as our prospects in other respects, with regard to the general reconciliation wished for, were so happy. But let me owe to your own generosity, my dearest creature, said I, rather than to the mediation of any person on earth, the forgiveness I am an humble suitor for. How much more agreeable to yourself, oh best beloved of my soul, must it be, as well as obliging to me, that your first personal knowledge of my relations, and theirs of you (for they will not be denied attending you), should not be begun in recriminations and appeals! As Lady Betty will be here so soon, it will not perhaps be possible for you to receive her visit with a brow absolutely serene. But, dearest, dearest creature, I beseech you, let the misunderstanding pass as a slight one—as a misunderstanding cleared up. Appeals give pride and superiority to the persons appealed to, and are apt to lessen the appellant, not only in their eye, but in her own. Exalt not into judges those who are prepared to take lessons and instructions from you. The individuals of my family are as proud as I am said to be. But they will cheerfully resign to your superiority—You will be the first woman of the family in everyone's eyes.

This might have done with any other woman in the world but *this*; and yet she is the only woman in the world of whom it may with truth be said—But thus, angrily, did she disclaim the compliment.

Yes, indeed!—(and there she stopped a moment, her sweet bosom heaving with a noble disdain)—Tricked out of myself from the very first—a fugitive from my own family! renounced by my relations! insulted by you!—laying humble claim to the protection of yours!—is not this the light in which I must appear not only to the ladies of your family, but to all the world?—Think you, sir, that in these circumstances, or even had I been in the *happiest*, that I could be affected by this plea of undeserved superiority?—You are a stranger to the mind of Clarissa Harlowe, if you think her capable of so poor and so *undue* a pride!

She went from us to the farther end of the room.

The captain was again affected—Excellent creature! I called her; and, reverently approaching her, urged further the plea I had last made.

It is but lately, said I, that the opinions of my relations have been more than indifferent to me, whether good or bad; and it is for *your* sake, more than for *my own*, that I now wish to stand well with my whole family. The principal motive of Lady Betty's coming up is to purchase presents for the whole family to make on the happy occasion.

This consideration, turning to the captain, with so noble-minded a dear creature, I know, can have no weight; only as it will show their value and respect. But what a damp would their worthy hearts receive, were they to find their admired new niece, as they now think her, not only *not* their niece, but capable of renouncing me for ever! They love me. They *all* love me. I have been guilty of carelessness and levity to them, indeed; but of carelessness and levity only; and *that* owing to a pride that has set me above meanness, though it has not done everything for me.

My whole family will be guaranties for my good behaviour to this dear creature, their niece, their daughter, their cousin, their friend, their chosen companion and directress, all in one—Upon my soul, captain, we *may*, we *must* be happy.

But, dearest, dearest creature, let me on my knees (and down I dropped, her face all the time turned half from me, as she stood at the window, her handkerchief often at her eyes) plead your *promised* forgiveness; and let us not appear to them on their visit thus unhappy with each other. Lady Betty, the next hour that she sees you, will write her opinion of you, and of the likelihood of our future happiness, to Lady Sarah, her sister, a weak-spirited woman who now hopes to supply to herself, in my bride, the lost daughter she still mourns for!

The captain then joined in, re-urging her uncle's hopes and expectations; and his resolution effectually to set about the general reconciliation: the mischief that might be prevented: the certainty he was in that her uncle might be prevailed upon to give her to me with his own hand, if she made it her choice to wait for his coming up. But, for his own part, he humbly advised, and fervently pressed her, to make the very next day, or Monday at farthest, my happy day.

Permit me, dearest lady, said he, and I could kneel to you myself (bending his knee); though I have no interest in my earnestness but the pleasure I should have to be able to serve you all; to beseech you to give me an opportunity to assure your uncle that I myself saw with my own eyes the happy knot tied!—All misunderstandings, all doubts, all diffidences, will then be at an end.

And what, madam, rejoined I, still kneeling, can there be in your new measures, be they what they will, that can so happily, so reputably I will presume to say for all round, obviate the present difficulties?

Miss Howe herself, if she loves you, and loves your fame, madam, urged the captain, his knee still bent, must congratulate you on such a happy conclusion.

Then turning her face, she saw the captain half-kneeling—Oh sir! Oh Captain Tomlinson!—why this *undue* condescension? extending her hand to his elbow to raise him—I cannot bear this!—Then casting her eye to me, Rise, Mr Lovelace. Kneel not to the poor creature whom you have insulted!—How cruel the occasion for it!—and how mean the submission!

Not mean to such an angel!—nor can I rise, but to be forgiven!——

The captain then re-urged once more the day—He was amazed, he said, if she ever valued me—

Oh Captain Tomlinson, interrupted she, how much are you the friend of this man!—*If I had never valued him, he never would have had it in his power to insult me*; nor could I have *taken to heart as I do*, the insult (execrable as it was) so undeservedly, so ungratefully given—But let him retire—for a moment let him retire.

I was more than half afraid to trust the captain by himself with her—He gave me a sign that I might depend upon him—And then I took out of my pocket his letter to me, and Lady Betty's, and Miss Montague's, and Lord M.'s (which last she had not then seen), and giving them to him: Procure for me in the first place, Mr Tomlinson, a re-perusal of these three letters; and of *this* from Lord M. And I beseech you, my dearest life, give them due consideration: and let me on my return find the happy effects of it.

I then withdrew; with slow feet, however, and a misgiving heart.

The captain insisted upon this re-perusal previously to what she had to say to him, as he tells me. She complied, but with some difficulty; as if she was *afraid* of being *softened in my favour!*

She lamented her unhappy situation; destitute of friends, and not knowing whither to go, or what to do—She asked questions, *sifting* questions, about her uncle, about her family, and after what he knew of Mr Hickman's fruitless application in her favour.

He was well prepared in this particular; for I had shown him the letters, and extracts of letters, of Miss Howe, which I had so happily come at.[a] Might she be assured, she asked him, that her brother, with Singleton, and Solmes, were actually in quest of her?

He averred that they were.

She asked, If he thought I had hopes of prevailing on her to go back to town?

He was sure I had not.

Was he really of opinion that Lady Betty would pay her a visit?

He had no doubt of it.

But, sir; but, Captain Tomlinson—(then impatiently turning from him, and again to him) I know not what to do—but were I *your* daughter, sir—were *you* my own father—Alas, sir, I have neither father nor mother!

He turned from her, and wiped his eyes.

Oh sir! you have humanity! (She wept too.) There are some men in the world, thank Heaven, that *can* be moved. Oh sir, I have met with hard-hearted men; and in my own family too—or I could not have been so unhappy as I am—but I make everybody unhappy!

I suppose his eyes run over.

Dearest madam! Heavenly lady!—Who can—who can—hesitated and blubbered the dog, as he owned. And indeed I heard some part of what passed, though *they both* talked lower than I wished; for, from the nature of *their* conversation, there was no room for altitudes.

THEM, and BOTH, and THEY!—How it goes against me to include this angel of a creature, and any man on earth but myself, in *one* word!

Capt. Who can forbear being affected?—But, madam, you *can* be no other man's.

Cl. Nor would I be. But he is so sunk with me!—To fire the house!—an artifice so vile!—contrived for the worst of purposes!—Would you have a daughter of yours—but what would I say?—Yet you see that I have nobody in whom I can confide!—Mr Lovelace is a vindictive man!—He could not love the creature whom he could insult as he has insulted me! Then pausing—In short, I never, never can forgive *him*, nor he *me*—Do you think, sir, I would have gone so far as I have gone, if I had intended ever to draw with him in one yoke?—I left behind me *such* a letter——

You know, madam, he has acknowledged the justice of your resentment——

Oh sir, he can acknowledge, and he can retract, fifty times a day—But do you think I am trifling with myself and you, and want to be *persuaded* to forgive him, and to be *his*—There is not a creature of my sex, who would have been *more*

a   See pp. 632 ff.

explicit, and *more frank*, than I would have been, from the moment I *intended* to be his, had I had a heart like *my own* to deal with. I was always *above reserve*, sir, I will presume to say, where I had no cause of doubt. Mr Lovelace's conduct has made me appear, perhaps, *over-nice*, when my heart wanted to be *encouraged* and *assured*; and when, if it had been so, my whole behaviour would have been governed by it.

She stopped, her handkerchief at her eyes. I inquired after the minutest part of her behaviour, as well as after her words. I love, thou knowest, to trace human nature, and more particularly female nature, through its most secret recesses.

The pitiful fellow was lost in silent admiration of her—And thus the noble creature proceeded.

It is the fate of unequal unions, that tolerable creatures through them frequently incur censure, when, more happily yoked, they might be entitled to praise. And shall I not shun an union with a man that might lead into errors a creature who flatters herself that she is blest with an inclination to be good; and who wishes to make everyone happy with whom she has any connexion, even to her very servants?

She paused, taking a turn about the room—the fellow, devil fetch him, a mummy all the time: then proceeded.

Formerly, indeed, I hoped to be an humble means of reforming him. But, when I have *no such hope*, is it right (you are a serious man, sir) to make a venture that shall endanger *my own morals!*

Still silent was the varlet. If my advocate had nothing to say for me, what hope of carrying my cause?

And now, sir, what is the result of all?—It is this—that you will endeavour, if you have that influence over him which a man of your sense and experience ought to have, to prevail upon him, and that for *his own* sake as well as *mine*, to leave me free to pursue my own destiny. And of this you may assure him that I never will be any other man's.

Impossible, madam!—I know that Mr Lovelace would not hear me with patience on such a topic. And I do assure you that I have some spirit, and should not care to take an indignity from him, or from any man living.

She paused—then resuming—And think you, sir, that my uncle will refuse to receive a letter from me?—*How averse, Jack, to concede a tittle in my favour!*

I know, madam, as matters are circumstanced, that he would not *answer* it. If you please I will carry one down from you.

And will he not pursue his intentions in *my* favour, nor be himself reconciled to me, except I am married?

From what your brother gives out, and affects to believe, on Mr Lovelace's living with you in the same——

No more, sir—I am an unhappy creature!

He then re-urged that it would be in her power instantly, or on the morrow, to put an end to all her difficulties.

How can that *be*, said she? The licence *still* to be obtained? The settlements *still* to be signed? Miss Howe's answer to my last *unreceived?*—And shall I, sir, be in such a HURRY as if I thought my *honour in danger if I delayed?* Yet *marry* the man from whom only it *can* be endangered?—Unhappy, thrice unhappy, Clarissa Harlowe!—in how many difficulties has one rash step involved thee?—and she turned from him, and wept.

The varlet, by way of comfort, wept too: yet her tears, as he might have observed, were tears that indicated rather a *yielding* than a *perverse* temper.

There is a sort of stone, thou knowest, so soft in the quarry that it may, in a manner, be cut with a knife; but if the opportunity be not taken, and it is exposed to the air for any time, it will become as hard as marble, and then with difficulty it yields to the chisel.[a] So this lady, not taken at the moment, after a turn or two cross the room, gained more resolution; and then she declared, as she had done once before, that she would wait the issue of Miss Howe's answer to the letter she had sent her from hence, and take her measures accordingly; leaving it to him, meantime, to make what report he thought fit to her uncle; the kindest that *truth* could bear, she doubted not from Captain Tomlinson: and she should be glad of a few lines from him, to hear what *that* was.

She wished him a good journey. She complained of her head; and was about to withdraw: but I stepped round to the door next the stairs, as if I had but just come in from the garden; which, as I entered, I called a very pretty one; and took her reluctant hand, as she was going out: My dearest life, you are not going?—What hopes, captain?—Have you not some hopes to give me of pardon and reconciliation?

She said, she would not be detained. But I would not let her go till she had promised to return, when the captain had reported to me what her resolution was.

And when he had, I claimed her promise; and she came down again, and repeated it, as what she was determined upon.

I expostulated with her upon it, in the most submissive and earnest manner. She made it necessary for me to repeat many of the pleas I had before urged. The captain seconded me with equal earnestness. At last, each fell down on his knees before her.

She was distressed. I was afraid at one time she would have fainted. Yet neither of us would rise without some concessions. I pleaded my own sake; the captain his dear friend her uncle's; and *both* the prevention of future mischief; and the peace and happiness of the two families.

She owned herself unequal to the conflict. She sighed, she sobbed, she wept, she wrung her hands.

I was perfectly eloquent in my vows and protestations. Her tearful eyes were cast down upon me; a glow upon each charming cheek; a visible anguish in every lovely feature—At last, her trembling knees seeming to fail her, she dropped into the next chair; her charming face, as if seeking for a hiding-place (which a mother's bosom would have best supplied), sinking upon her own shoulder.

I forgot at the instant all my vows of revenge. I threw myself at her feet as she sat; and, snatching her hand, pressed it with my lips. I besought Heaven to forgive my past offences, and prosper my future hopes, as I designed honourably and justly by the charmer of my heart, if once more she would restore me to her favour. And I thought I felt drops of scalding water (could they be tears?) trickle down upon my cheeks; while my cheeks, glowing like fire, seemed to scorch up the unwelcome strangers.

I then arose, not doubting of an implied pardon in this silent distress. I raised

---

a   The nature of the Bath stone, in particular.

the captain. I whispered him—By my soul, man, I am in earnest—Now talk of reconciliation, of her uncle, of the licence, of settlements—And raising my voice, If now at last, Captain Tomlinson, my angel will give me leave to call so great a blessing mine, it will be impossible that you should say too much to her uncle in praise of my gratitude, my affection, and fidelity to his charming niece; and he may begin as soon as he pleases, his kind schemes for effecting the desirable reconciliation!—Nor shall he prescribe any terms to me that I will not comply with.

The captain blessed me with his eyes and hands—Thank God, whispered he. We approached the lady together.

What hinders, dearest madam, said he, what now hinders, but that Lady Betty Lawrance, when she comes, may be acquainted with the truth of everything? And assist privately at your nuptials?—I will stay till they are celebrated; and then shall I go down with the happy tidings to my dear Mr Harlowe—and all will, all must, soon be happy.

I must have an answer from Miss Howe, replied the still trembling fair one. I cannot change my new measures, but with her advice. I will forfeit all my hopes of happiness in this world, rather than her good opinion, and that she should think me giddy, unsteady, or precipitate. All I will further say on the present subject is this, that, when I have her answer to what I *have* written, I will write to her the whole state of the matter, as I shall then be enabled to do.

Lovel. Then must I despair for ever—Oh Captain Tomlinson, Miss Howe hates me!—Miss Howe—

Capt. Not so, perhaps—When Miss Howe knows your concern for having offended, she will never advise that, with such prospects of general reconciliation, the hopes of so many considerable persons in both families should be frustrated. Some little time, as that excellent lady has foreseen and hinted, will necessarily be taken up in actually procuring the licence, and in perusing and signing the settlements. In that time Miss Howe's answer may be received; and Lady Betty may arrive; and she, no doubt, will have weight to dissipate the lady's doubts, and to accelerate the day. It shall be my part, meantime, to make Mr Harlowe easy. All I fear from delay is from Mr James Harlowe's quarter; and therefore all must be conducted with prudence and privacy—as your uncle, madam, has proposed.

She was silent: I rejoiced in her silence: the dear creature, thought I, has actually forgiven me in her heart!—But why will she not lay me under obligation to her by the generosity of an explicit declaration?—And yet, as that would not accelerate anything while the licence is not in my hands, she is the less to be blamed (if I do her justice), that she took more time to *descend*.

I proposed, as on the morrow night, to go to town; and doubted not to bring the licence up with me on Monday morning. Would she be pleased to assure me that she would not depart from Mrs Moore's?

She should stay at Mrs Moore's till she had an answer from Miss Howe.

I told her that I hoped I might have her *tacit* consent, at least, to the obtaining of the licence.

I saw by the turn of her countenance, that I should not have asked this question. She was so far from *tacitly* consenting, that she declared to the contrary.

As I never intended, I said, to ask her to enter again into a house, with the people of which she was so much offended, would she be pleased to give orders for her clothes to be brought up hither? Or should Dorcas attend her for any of her commands on that head?

She desired not ever more to see anybody belonging to that house. She might perhaps get Mrs Moore or Mrs Bevis to go thither for her, and take her keys with them.

I doubted not, I said, that Lady Betty would arrive by that time. I hoped she had no objection to my bringing that lady and my cousin Montague up with me?

She was silent.

To be sure, Mr Lovelace, said the captain, the lady can have no objection to this.

She was still silent. So silence in this case was assent.

Would she be pleased to write to Miss Howe?—

Sir! Sir! peevishly interrupting—No more questions: no prescribing to me—You will do as you think fit. So will I, as I please. I own no obligation to you. Captain Tomlinson, your servant. Recommend me to my uncle Harlowe's favour: and was going.

I took her reluctant hand, and besought her only to promise to meet me early in the morning.

To what purpose meet you? Have you more to say than has been said?—I have had enough of vows and protestations, Mr Lovelace. To what purpose should I meet you tomorrow morning?

I repeated my request, and that in the most fervent manner, naming six in the morning.

'You know that I am always stirring before that hour at this season of the year,' was the half-expressed consent.

She then again recommended herself to her uncle's favour; and withdrew.

And thus, Belford, has she *mended her markets*, as Lord M. would say, and I worsted mine. Miss Howe's next letter is now the hinge on which the fate of both must turn. I shall be absolutely ruined and undone if I cannot intercept it.

Letter 246: MR LOVELACE TO JOHN BELFORD, ESQ.

Sat. midnight

No rest, says a text that I once heard preached upon, *to the wicked*—and I cannot close my eyes; yet wanted only to compound for half an hour in an elbow-chair. So must scribble on.

I parted with the captain after another strong debate with him in relation to what is to be the fate of this lady. As the fellow has an excellent head, and would have made an eminent figure in any station of life, had not his early days been tainted with a deep crime, and he detected in it; and as he had the right side of the argument; I had a good deal of difficulty with him; and at last brought myself to promise that if I could prevail upon her generously to forgive me, and to reinstate me in her favour, I would make it my whole endeavour to get off of my contrivances as happily as I could (only that Lady Betty and Charlotte must come); and then, substituting him for her uncle's proxy, take shame to myself, and marry.

But if I should, Jack (with the strongest antipathy to the state that ever man had), what a figure shall I make in rakish annals? And can I have taken all this pains for nothing? Or for a wife only, that, however excellent (and *any* woman, do I think, I could make good, because I could make any woman *fear* as well as *love* me), might have been obtained without the plague I have been at, and much more reputably than with it? And hast thou not seen that this haughty lady knows not how to forgive with graciousness? Indeed has not at all forgiven me? But holds my soul in a *suspense*, which has been so grievous to her own.

At this silent moment I think that if I were to pursue my former scheme, and resolve to try whether I cannot make a greater fault serve as a sponge to wipe out a less; and then be forgiven for that; I can justify myself to *myself*; and that, as the fair implacable would say, is all in all.

It is my intention in all my reflections to avoid repeating, at least dwelling upon, what I have before written to thee, though the state of the case may not have varied; so I would have thee reconsider the *old* reasonings (particularly those contained in my answer to thy last expostulatory nonsense[a]); and add the *new* as they fall from my pen; and then I shall think myself invincible—at least, as arguing rake to rake.

I take the gaining of this lady to be essential to my happiness: and is it not natural for *all men* to aim at obtaining whatever they think will make them happy, be the object more or less considerable in the eyes of others?

As to the manner of endeavouring to obtain her, by falsification of oaths, vows, and the like—do not the poets of two thousand years and upwards tell us that Jupiter laughs at the perjuries of lovers? And let me add to what I have heretofore mentioned on that head a question or two.

Do not the mothers, the aunts, the grandmothers, the governesses of the pretty innocents, always, from their very cradles to riper years, preach to them the deceitfulness of men?—That they are not to regard their oaths, vows, promises?— What a parcel of fibbers would all these reverend matrons be, if there were not now and then a pretty credulous rogue taken in for a justification of their preachments, and to serve as a beacon lighted up for the benefit of the rest?

Do we not then see that an honest prowling fellow is a necessary evil on many accounts? Do we not see that it is highly requisite that a sweet girl should be now and then drawn aside by him?—And the more eminent the lady, in the graces of person, mind, and fortune, is not the example likely to be the more efficacious?

If these *postulata* be granted me, who I pray, can equal my charmer in all these? Who therefore so fit for an example to the rest of the sex?—At worst, I am entirely within my worthy friend Mandeville's rule, *That private vices are public benefits.*[1]

Well then, if this sweet creature must *fall*, as it is called, for the benefit of all the pretty fools of the sex, she *must*; and there's an end of the matter. And what would there have been in it of uncommon or rare, had I not been so long about it?—And so I dismiss all further argumentation and debate upon the question: and I impose upon thee, when thou writest to me, an eternal silence on this head.

(Wafered on, as an after-written introduction to the paragraphs which follow.)
LORD, Jack, what shall I do now!—How one evil brings on another!—Dreadful news to tell thee!—While I was meditating a simple robbery, here have I (in my own defence indeed) been guilty of murder! A bloody murder!—So I believe it will

---

a See pp. 715 ff.

prove—At her last gasp!—Poor impertinent opposer! Eternally resisting!—Eternally contradicting! There she lies, weltering in her blood! Her death's wound have I given her!—But she was a thief, an impostor, as well as a tormentor. She had stolen my pen. While I was sullenly meditating, doubting as to my future measures, she stole it; and thus she wrote with it, in a hand exactly like my own; and would have faced me down, that it was really my own handwriting.

'But let me reflect, before it be too late. On the manifold perfections of this ever-admirable creature, let me reflect. The hand yet is only held up. The blow is not struck. Miss Howe's next letter may blow thee up. In policy thou shouldest be now at least honest. Thou canst not live without her. Thou wouldst rather marry her than lose her absolutely. Thou mayest undoubtedly prevail upon her, inflexible as she seems to be, for marriage. But if now she find thee a villain, thou mayest never more engage her attention, and she perhaps will refuse and abhor thee.

'Yet already have I not gone too far? Like a repentant thief, afraid of his gang and obliged to go on in fear of hanging till he comes to be hanged, I am afraid of the gang of my cursed contrivances.

'As I hope to live, I am sorry at the present writing, that I have been such a foolish plotter as to put it, as I fear I have done, out of my *own power* to be honest. I hate compulsion in all forms; and cannot bear, even to be *compelled* to be the wretch my choice has made me!—So now, Belford, as thou hast said, I am a machine at last, and no free agent.

'Upon my soul, Jack, it is a very foolish thing for a man of spirit to have brought himself to such a height of iniquity, that he must proceed, and cannot help himself; and yet to be next to certain that his very victory will undo him.

'Why was such a woman as this thrown in my way, whose very fall will be her glory, and perhaps not only my shame, but my destruction?

'What a happiness must that man know, who moves regularly to some laudable end, and has nothing to reproach himself with in his progress to it! When by honest means he attains this end, how great and unmixed must be his enjoyments! What a happy man, in this particular case had I been, had it been given me to *be* only what I wished to *appear* to be!'

Thus far had my *conscience* written with my pen; and see what a recreant she had made me!—I seized her by the throat—*There!*—*There*, said I, thou vile impertinent!—Take *that*, and *that!*—How often have I given thee warning!—And now, I hope, thou intruding varletess, have I done thy business!

Puling, and *in-voiced*, rearing up thy detested head, in vain implorest thou *my* mercy, who, in *thy* day, hast showed me so little!—Take *that*, for a rising blow!—And now will *thy* pain, and *my* pain from *thee*, soon be over!—Lie there!—Welter on!—Had I not given thee thy death's wound, thou wouldst have robbed me of all my joys. Thou couldst not have mended me, 'tis plain. Thou couldst only have thrown me into despair. Didst thou not see that I had gone too far to recede?—Welter on, once more I bid thee!—Gasp on!—*That* thy last gasp, surely!—How hard diest thou!—ADIEU!—'Tis kind in thee, however, to bid me *Adieu!*—Adieu, Adieu, Adieu, to thee, Oh thou inflexible and, till now, unconquerable bosom-intruder—Adieu to thee for ever!

Letter 247: MR LOVELACE TO JOHN BELFORD, ESQ.

Sunday morn. (June 11) 4 o'clock

A FEW words to the information thou sentest me last night concerning thy poor old man; and then I rise from my seat, shake myself, refresh, new-dress, and so to my charmer, whom, notwithstanding her reserves, I hope to prevail upon to walk out with me on the heath, this warm and fine morning.

The birds must have awakened her before now. They are in full song. She always gloried in accustoming herself to behold the sun-rise; one of God's natural wonders, as once she called it.

Her window salutes the east. The valleys must be gilded by his rays, by the time I am with her; for already have they made the up-lands smile, and the face of nature cheerful.

How unsuitable wilt thou find this gay preface to a subject so gloomy, as that I am now turning to!

I am glad to hear thy tedious expectations are at last answered.

Thy servant tells me that thou art plaguily grieved at the old fellow's departure.

I can't say but thou mayst look as if thou wert; harassed as thou hast been for a number of days and nights with a close attendance upon a dying man, beholding his drawing-on hour—pretending, for decency's sake, to whine over his excruciating pangs—to be in the way to answer a thousand impertinent inquiries after the health of a man thou wished to die—to pray by him—for so once thou wrotest to me!—to read by him—to be forced to join in consultations with a parcel of solemn would-seem-wise doctors, and their officious zanies the apothecaries, joined with the butcherly tribe of scarificators; all combined to carry on the physical farce, and to cut out thongs both from his flesh and his estate—to have the superadded apprehension of dividing thy interest in what he shall leave with a crew of eager-hoping, never-to-be-satisfied relations, legatees, and the devil knows who, of private gratificators of passions laudable and illaudable—in these circumstances, I wonder not that thou lookest to servants (as little grieved at heart as thyself, and who are gaping after legacies as thou after *heirship*) as if thou indeed wert grieved; and as if the most wry-facing woe had befallen thee.

Then, as I have often thought, the reflection that must naturally arise from such mortifying objects as the death of one with whom we have been familiar must afford, when we are obliged to attend it in its slow approaches, and in its face-twisting pangs, that it will one day be our own case, goes a great way to credit the appearance of grief.

And this it is that, seriously reflected upon, may temporarily give a fine air of sincerity to the wailings of lively widows, heart-exulting heirs, and residuary legatees of all denominations; since, by keeping down the inward joy, those interesting reflections must sadden the aspect, and add an appearance of real concern to the assumed sables.

Well, but now thou art come to the reward of all thy watchings, anxieties, and close attendances, tell me what it is; tell me if it compensate thy trouble, and answer thy hope?

As to myself, thou seest by the gravity of my style how the subject has helped to mortify me. But the necessity I am under of committing either speedy matrimony, or a rape, has saddened over my gayer prospects, and, more than the case itself, contributed to make me sympathize with thy present joyful sorrow.

Adieu, Jack. I must be soon out of my pain; and my Clarissa shall be soon out of hers—for so does the arduousness of the case require.

Letter 248: MR LOVELACE TO JOHN BELFORD, ESQ.

Sunday morning

I HAVE had the honour of my charmer's company for two complete hours. We met before six in Mrs Moore's garden: a walk on the heath refused me.

The sedateness of her aspect, and her kind compliance in this meeting, gave me hopes. And all that either the captain or I had urged yesterday to obtain a full and free pardon, that re-urged I; and I told her besides, that Captain Tomlinson was gone down with hopes to prevail upon her uncle Harlowe to come up in person, in order to present me with the greatest blessing that man ever received.

But the utmost I could obtain was, that she would take no resolution in my favour till she received Miss Howe's next letter.

I will not repeat the arguments used by me: but I will give thee the substance of what she said in answer to them.

She had considered of everything, she told me. My whole conduct was before her. The house I carried her to must be a vile house. The people early showed what they were capable of, in the earnest attempt made to fasten Miss Partington upon her; as she doubted not, with my approbation—(Surely, thought I, she has not received a duplicate of Miss Howe's letter of detection!) They heard her cries. My insult was undoubtedly premeditated. By my whole recollected behaviour to her, previous to it, it must be so. I had the vilest of views, no question. And my treatment of her put it out of all doubt.

Soul all over, Belford! She seems sensible of liberties that my passion made me insensible of having taken.

She besought me to give over all thoughts of her. Sometimes, she said, she thought herself cruelly treated by her nearest and dearest relations: at *such* times, a spirit of repining, and even of resentment, took place, and the reconciliation, at other times so desirable, was not then so much the favourite wish of her heart, as was the scheme she had formerly planned—of taking her good Norton for her directress and guide, and living upon her own estate in the manner her grandfather had intended she should live.

This scheme she doubted not that her cousin Morden, who was one of her trustees for that estate, would enable her (and that as she hoped, without litigation) to pursue. And if he can, and does, what, sir, let me ask you, said she, have I seen in your conduct that should make me prefer to it an union of interests, where there is such a disunion in minds?

So thou seest, Jack, there is *reason*, as well as *resentment*, in the preference she makes against me!—Thou seest that she presumes to think that she can be happy *without* me; and that she must be unhappy *with* me!

I had besought her, in the conclusion of my re-urged arguments, to write to Miss Howe before Miss Howe's answer could come, in order to lay before her the present state of things; and if she *would* defer to her judgement, to let her have an opportunity to give it on the full knowledge of the case—

So I would, Mr Lovelace, was the answer, if I were in doubt myself which I would prefer; marriage, or the scheme I have mentioned. You cannot think, sir, but the latter must be my choice. I wish to part with you with temper—don't put me upon repeating—

Part with me, madam, interrupted I!—I cannot bear those words!—But let me beseech you, however, to write to Miss Howe. I hope, if Miss Howe is not my enemy—

She is not the enemy of your *person*, sir—as you would be convinced if you *saw her last letter to me.*[a] But were she not an enemy to your *actions*, she would not be *my* friend, nor the friend of *virtue*. Why will you provoke from me, Mr Lovelace, the harshness of expression, which, however deserved by you, I am unwilling just now to use; having suffered enough in the two past days from my own vehemence?

I bit my lip for vexation. I was silent.

Miss Howe, proceeded she, knows the full state of matters already, sir. The answer I expect from her respects *myself*, not *you*. Her heart is too warm in the cause of friendship, to leave me in suspense one moment longer than is necessary as to what I want to know. Nor does her answer depend absolutely upon herself. She must see a person first; and that person perhaps must see others.

The cursed smuggler-woman, Jack!—Miss Howe's Townsend, I doubt not!— Plot, contrivance, intrigue, stratagem!—Underground moles these ladies—But let the earth cover me! let me be a mole too, thought I, if they carry their point!—and if this lady escape me now.

She frankly owned that she had once thought of embarking *out of all our ways* for some one of our American colonies. But now that she had been *compelled* to see me (which had been her greatest dread, and which she would have given her life to avoid), she thought she might be happiest in the resumption of her former favourite scheme, if Miss Howe could find her a reputable and private asylum till her cousin Morden could come. But if he came not soon, and if she had a difficulty to get to a place of refuge, whether from her brother or from *anybody else* (meaning me, I suppose), she might yet perhaps go abroad: for, to say the truth, she could not think of returning to her father's house; since her brother's rage, her sister's upbraidings, her father's anger, her mother's still more affecting sorrowings, and her own consciousness under them all, would be insupportable to her.

Oh Jack! I am sick to death, I pine, I die, for Miss Howe's next letter! I would bind, gag, strip, rob, and do anything but murder, to intercept it.

But, determined as she seems to be, it was evident to me, nevertheless, that she had still some tenderness for me.

She often wept as she talked, and much oftener sighed. She looked at me twice with an eye of *undoubted* gentleness, and three times with an eye *tending* to compassion and softness: but its benign rays were as often *snatched* back, as I may say, and her face averted, as if her sweet eye were not to be trusted, and could not stand against my eager eyes; seeking, as they did, for a lost heart in hers, and endeavouring to penetrate to her very soul.

More than once I took her hand. She struggled not *much* against the freedom.

---

a   The lady innocently means Mr Lovelace's forged one, p. 811.

I pressed it once with my lips. She was not *very* angry. A frown indeed; but a frown that had more distress in it than indignation.

How came the dear soul (clothed as it is with such a silken vesture) by all its steadiness?[a]—Was it necessary that the active gloom of such a tyrant of a *father* should commix with such a passive sweetness of a will-less *mother*, to produce a constancy, an equanimity, a steadiness, in the *daughter*, which never woman before could boast of?—If so, she is more obliged to that despotic father than I could have imagined a creature to be, who gave distinction to everyone related to her, beyond what the crown itself can confer.

I hoped, I said, that she would admit of the intended visit of the two ladies, which I had so often mentioned.

She was *here*. She *had* seen me. She could not help herself at present. She ever had the highest regard for the ladies of my family, because of their worthy characters. There she turned away her sweet face, and vanquished a half-risen sigh.

I kneeled to her then. It was upon a verdant cushion; for we were upon the grass-walk. I caught her hand. I besought her with an earnestness that called up, as I could feel, my heart to my eyes, to make me by her forgiveness and example more worthy of them, and of her own kind and generous wishes. By my soul, madam, said I, you stab me with your goodness, your undeserved goodness! and I cannot bear it!

Why, why, thought I, as I did several times in this conversation, will she not *generously* forgive me? Why will she make it necessary for me to bring my aunt and my cousin to my assistance? Can the fortress expect the same advantageous capitulation, which yields not to the summons of a resistless conqueror, as if it gave not the trouble of bringing up, and raising its heavy artillery against it?

What *sensibilities*, said the divine creature, withdrawing her hand, must thou have suppressed!—What a dreadful, what a judicial hardness of heart must thine be; who canst be capable of such emotions as sometimes thou hast shown; and of such sentiments as sometimes have flowed from thy lips; yet canst have so far overcome them all as to be able to act as thou hast acted, and that from settled purpose and premeditation; and this, as it is *said*, throughout the whole of thy life, from infancy to this time!

I told her that I had hoped from the generous concern she had expressed for me, when I was so suddenly and dangerously taken ill—(the ipecacuanha experiment, Jack!).

She interrupted me—Well have you rewarded me for the concern you speak of!—However, I will frankly own, that I am determined to think no more of you, that you might (unsatisfied as I nevertheless was with you) have made an interest——

She paused. I besought her to proceed.

Do you suppose, sir, and turned away her sweet face as we walked; do you suppose that I had not thought of laying down a plan to govern myself by, when I found myself so unhappily over-reached, and cheated, as I may say, out of myself?—When I found that I could not *be*, and *do*, what I wished *to be*, and *to do*, do you imagine that I had not cast about, what was the next proper course to

---

[a] See pp. 65, 84, 105 for what she herself says on that steadiness which Mr Lovelace, though a deserved sufferer by it, cannot help admiring.

take?—And do you believe that this next course has not cost me some pain, to be obliged to—

There again she stopped.

But let us break off discourse, resumed she. The subject grows too—she sighed—Let us break off discourse—I will go in—I will prepare for church—(The devil! thought I.) Well as I *can* appear in these everyday worn clothes—looking upon herself—I will go to church.

She then turned from me to go into the house.

Bless me, my beloved creature, bless me with the continuance of this affecting conversation—Remorse has seized my heart!—I have been excessively wrong—Give me further cause to curse my heedless folly, by the continuance of this calm, but soul-penetrating conversation.

No, no, Mr Lovelace. I have said too much. Impatience begins to break in upon me. If you can excuse me to the ladies, it will be better for my mind's sake and for your credit's sake, that I do not see them. Call me to *them* over-nice, petulant, prudish; what you please, call me to them. Nobody but Miss Howe, to whom, next to the Almighty, and my own mother, I wish to stand acquitted of wilful error, shall know the whole of what has passed. Be happy, as you may!—*Deserve* to be happy, and happy you will be, in your own reflection at least, were you to be ever so unhappy in other respects. For myself, if I shall be enabled, on due reflection, to look back upon my own conduct without the great reproach of having wilfully, and against the light of my own judgement, erred, I shall be more happy than if I had all that the world accounts desirable.

The noble creature proceeded; for I could not speak.

This self-acquittal, when spirits are lent me to dispel the darkness which at present too often overclouds my mind, will, I hope, make me superior to all the calamities that can befall me.

Her whole person was informed by her sentiments. She seemed to be taller than before. How the God within her exalted her, not only above me, but above herself.

Divine creature! (as I *thought* her) I *called* her. I acknowledged the superiority of her mind; and was proceeding—But she interrupted me—All human excellence, said she, is comparative only. My mind, I believe, is indeed superior to yours, debased as yours is by evil habits. But I had not known it to be so, if you had not *taken pains* to convince me of the inferiority of yours.

How great, how sublimely great, this creature!—By my soul, I cannot forgive her for her virtues!—There is no bearing the consciousness of the infinite inferiority she charged me with—But why will she break from me, when good resolutions are taking place?—The red-hot iron she refuses to strike—Oh why will she suffer the yielding wax to harden?

We had gone but a few paces towards the house, when we were met by the impertinent women, with notice that breakfast was ready. I could only, with uplifted hands, beseech her to give me hope of a renewed conversation after breakfast.

No; she would go to church.

And into the house she went, and upstairs directly. Nor would she oblige me with her company at the tea-table.

I offered by Mrs Moore to quit both the table and the parlour, rather than she should exclude herself, or deprive the two widows of the favour of her company.

That was not all the matter, she told Mrs Moore. She had been struggling to keep down her temper. It had cost her some pains to do it. She was desirous to compose herself, in hopes to receive benefit by the divine worship she was going to join in.

Mrs Moore hoped for her presence at dinner.

She had rather be excused. Yet, if she could obtain the frame of mind she hoped for, she might not be averse to show that she had got above those sensibilities, which gave consideration to a man who deserved not to be to her what he had been.

This said, no doubt, to let Mrs Moore know that the garden conversation had not been a reconciling one.

Mrs Moore seemed to wonder that we were not upon a better foot of understanding, after so long a conference; and the more, as she believed that the lady had given in to the proposal for the repetition of the ceremony, which I had told them was insisted upon by her uncle Harlowe. But I accounted for this, by telling both widows that she was resolved to keep on the reserve till she heard from Captain Tomlinson, whether her uncle would be present in person at the solemnity, or would name that worthy gentleman for his proxy.

Again I enjoined strict secrecy as to this particular; which was promised by the widows, as well for themselves as for Miss Rawlins; of whose taciturnity they gave me such an account as showed me that she was *secret-keeper-general* to all the women of fashion at Hampstead.

The Lord, Jack! What a world of mischief, at this rate, must Miss Rawlins know!—What a Pandora's box must her bosom be!—Yet, had I nothing that was more worthy of my attention to regard, I would engage to open it, and make my uses of the discovery.

And now, Belford, thou perceivest, that all my reliance is upon the mediation of Lady Betty and Miss Montague; and upon the hope of intercepting Miss Howe's next letter.

THE fair inexorable is actually gone to church, with Mrs Moore and Mrs Bevis. But Will closely attends her motions; and I am in the way to receive any occasional intelligence from him.

She did not *choose* (a mighty word with the sex! as if they were always to have their own wills!) that I should wait upon her. I did not much press it, that she might not apprehend that I thought I had reason to doubt her voluntary return.

I once had it in my head to have found the widow Bevis other employment. And I believe she would have been as well pleased with my company as to go to church; for she seemed irresolute when I told her that two out of a family were enough to go to church for one day. But having her things on, as the women call everything, and her aunt Moore expecting her company, she thought it best to go—*Lest it should look oddly, you know*, whispered she, to one who was above regarding how it looked.

Letter 250: MR LOVELACE TO JOHN BELFORD, ESQ.

Sunday afternoon

OH Belford! what a hair's-breadth escape have I had!—Such a one, that I tremble between terror and joy at the thoughts of what *might* have happened and did not.

What a perverse girl is this, to contend with her fate, yet has reason to think that her very stars fight against her! I am the luckiest of men!—But my breath almost fails me when I reflect upon what a slender thread my destiny hung.

But not to keep thee in suspense; I have, within this half-hour, obtained possession of the expected letter from Miss Howe—and by *such* an accident! But here, with the former, I dispatch this; thy messenger waiting.

Letter 251: MR LOVELACE TO JOHN BELFORD, ESQ.

(In continuation)

THUS it was—My charmer accompanied Mrs Moore again to church this afternoon. I had been very earnest, in the *first* place, to obtain her company at dinner: but in vain. According to what she had said to Mrs Moore,[a] I was *too considerable* to her to be allowed that favour. In the *next* place, I besought her to favour me after dinner with another garden walk. But she *would* again go to church. And what reason have I to rejoice that she did!

My worthy friend Mrs Bevis thought one sermon a day, *well*-observed, enough; so stayed at home to bear me company.

The lady and Mrs Moore had not been gone a quarter of an hour, when a young country fellow on horseback came to the door, and inquired for Mrs *Harriot Lucas*. The widow and I (undetermined how we were to entertain each other) were in the parlour next the door; and hearing the fellow's inquiry, Oh my dear Mrs Bevis, said I, I am undone, undone for ever, if you don't help me out!—Since here, in all probability, is a messenger from that implacable Miss Howe with a letter; which, if delivered to Mrs Lovelace, may undo all we have been doing.

What, said she, would you have me do?

Call the maid in this moment, that I may give her her lesson; and if it be as I imagine, I'll tell you what you shall do.

Widow. Margaret!—Margaret! come in this minute.

Lovel. What answer, Mrs Margaret, did you give the man, upon his asking for Mrs *Harriot Lucas*?

Peggy. I only asked, What was his business, and who he came from? (for, sir, your honour's servant had told me how things stood): and I came at your call, madam, before he answered me.

Lovel. Well, child, if ever you wish to be happy in wedlock yourself, and would have people disappointed who want to make mischief between you and your husband, get out of him his message, or letter, if he has one, and bring it to me, and say nothing to Mrs Lovelace when she comes in; and here is a guinea for you.

Peggy. I will do all I can to serve your honour's worship for nothing (nevertheless,

a p. 854.

with a ready hand taking the guinea). For Mr William tells me what a good gentleman you be.

Away went Peggy to the fellow at the door.

Peggy. What is your business, friend, with Mrs *Harry Lucas?*

Fellow. I must speak to her, her own self.

Lovel. My dearest widow, do you personate Mrs Lovelace—for Heaven's sake do you personate Mrs Lovelace!

Wid. I personate Mrs Lovelace, sir! How can I do that?—She is fair: I am a brown woman. She is slender: I am plump—

Lovel. No matter, no matter—The fellow may be a new come servant: he is not in livery, I see. He may not know her person. You can but be bloated, and in a dropsy.

Wid. Dropsical people look not so fresh and ruddy as I do—

Lovel. True—but the clown may not know that—'Tis but for a present deception.

Peggy, Peggy, called I, in a female tone, softly at the door. Madam, answered Peggy; and came up to me to the parlour door.

Lovel. Tell him the lady is ill, and has lain down upon the couch. And get his business from him, whatever you do.

Away went Peggy.

Lovel. Now, my dear widow, lie along on the settee, and put your handkerchief over your face, that, if he *will* speak to you himself, he may not see your eyes and your hair—so—that's right. I'll step into the closet by you.

I did so.

Peggy. (returning) He won't deliver his business to me. He will speak to Mrs Harry Lucas her own self.

Lovel. (holding the door in my hand) Tell him that this is Mrs Harriot Lucas; and let him come in. Whisper him, if he doubts, that she is bloated, dropsical, and not the woman she was.

Away went Margery.

Lovel. And now, my dear widow, let me see what a charming Mrs Lovelace you'll make!—Ask if he comes from Miss Howe. Ask if he live with her. Ask how she does. Call her, at every word, your dear Miss Howe. Offer him money—take this half-guinea—complain of your head, to have a pretence to hold it down; and cover your forehead and eyes with your hand, where your handkerchief hides not your face—that's right—and dismiss the rascal—(here he comes)—as soon as you can.

In came the fellow, bowing and scraping, his hat poked out before him with both his hands.

Fellow. I am sorry, madam, and please you, to find you be'n't well.

Widow. What is your business with me, friend?

Fellow. You are Mrs Harriot Lucas, I suppose, Madam?

Widow. Yes. Do you come from Miss Howe?

Fellow. I do, madam.

Widow. Dost thou know my right name, friend?

Fellow. I can give a shrewd guess. But that is none of my business.

Widow. What *is* thy business? I hope Miss Howe is well.

Fellow. Yes, madam; pure well, I thank God. I wish you were so too.

Widow. I am too full of grief to be well.

Fellow. So belike I have *hard* say.

Widow. My head aches so dreadfully, I cannot hold it up. I must beg of you to let me know your business?

Fellow. Nay, and that be all, my business is soon known. It is but to give this letter into your own *partiklar* hands—Here it is.

Widow. [*Taking it.*] From my dear friend Miss Howe?—Ah, my head!

Fellow. Yes, madam: but I am sorry you are so bad.

Widow. Do you live with Miss Howe?

Fellow. No, madam: I am one of her tenant's sons. Her lady mother must not know as how I came of this errand. But the letter, I suppose, will tell you all.

Widow. How shall I satisfy you for this kind trouble?

Fellow. Nahow at all. What I do is for love of Miss Howe. She will satisfy me more than enough. But mayhap you can send no answer, you are so ill.

Widow. Was you ordered to wait for an answer?

Fellow. No. I can't say I was. But I was bidden to observe how you looked, and how you was; and if you did write a line or so, to take care of it, and give it only to our young landlady, in secret.

Widow. You see I look strangely. Not so well as I used to do.

Fellow. Nay, I don't know that I ever saw you but once before; and that was at a stile, where I met you and my young landlady; but knew better than to stare a gentlewoman in the face; especially at a stile.

Widow. Will you eat, or drink, friend?

Fellow. A cup of small ale, I don't care if I do.

Widow. Margaret, take the young man down, and treat him with what the house affords.

Fellow. Your servant, madam. But I stayed to eat as I came along, just upon the Heath yonder, or else, to say the truth, I had been here sooner. (*Thank my stars, thought I, thou didst.*) A piece of powdered beef was upon the table, at the sign of the Castle,[1] where I stopped to inquire for this house: and so, thoff I only intended to whet my whistle, I could not help eating. So shall only taste of your ale; for the beef was woundily corned.

He withdrew, bowing and scraping.

Pox on thee, thought I. Get thee gone for a prating dog!

Margaret, whispered I, in a female voice, whipping out of the closet, and holding the parlour door in my hand, get him out of the house as fast as you can, lest they come from church and catch him here.

Peggy. Never fear, sir.

The fellow went down and, it seems, drank a large draught of ale; and Margaret finding him very talkative, told him she begged his pardon; but she had a sweetheart just come from sea, whom she was forced to hide in the pantry; so was sure he would excuse her from staying with him.

Ay, ay, to be sure, the clown said: *For if he could not make sport, he would spoil none.* But he whispered her, that one 'Squire Lovelace was a *damnation rogue*, if the truth might be told.

For what, said Margaret? And could have given him, she said, a good dowse of the chaps.

For kissing all the women he came near.

At the same time, the dog wrapped himself round Margery, and gave her a smack that, she told Mrs Bevis afterwards, she might have heard into the parlour.

Such, Jack, is human nature: thus does it operate in all degrees; and so does the clown, as well as his betters, practise what he censures; and censure what he practises! Yet this sly dog knew not but the wench had a sweetheart locked up in the pantry. If the truth were known, some of the ruddy-faced dairy wenches might perhaps call him a *damnation rogue*, as justly as their betters of the same sex, might 'Squire Lovelace.

The fellow told the maid that, by what he discerned of the young lady's face, it looked very *rosy* to what he took it to be; and he thought her a good deal fatter, as she lay, and not so tall.

All women are born to intrigue, Jack; and practise it more or less, as fathers, guardians, governesses, from dear experience can tell; and in love affairs are naturally expert, and quicker in their wits by half than men. This ready, though raw, wench gave an instance of this, and improved on the dropsical hint I had given her. The lady's seeming plumpness was owing to a dropsical disorder, and to the round posture she lay in—Very likely, truly. Her appearing to him to be shorter, he might have observed was owing to her drawing her feet up, from pain, and because the couch was too short, she supposed—Ad-so, he did not think of that. Her rosy colour was owing to her grief and head-ache—Ay, that might very well be—But he was highly pleased he had given the letter into Mrs Harriot's own hand, as he should tell Miss Howe.

He desired once more to see the lady, at his going away, and would not be denied. The widow therefore sat up, with her handkerchief over her face, leaning her head against the wainscot.

He asked if she had any *partiklar* message.

No: she was so ill she could not write, which was a great grief to her.

Should he call next day? for he was going to London, now he was so near; and should stay at a cousin's that night, who lived in a street called Fetter Lane.

No: she would write as soon as able, and send by the post.

Well then, if she had nothing to send by him, mayhap he might stay in town a day or two; for he had never seen the Lions in the Tower, nor Bedlam, nor the Tombs[2]; and he would make a holiday or two, as he had leave to do, if she had no business or message that required his posting down next day.

She had not.

She offered him the half-guinea I had given her for him; but he refused it, with great professions of disinterestedness, and love, as he called it, to Miss Howe; to serve whom, he would ride to the world's end, or *even* to Jericho.

And so the shocking rascal went away: and glad at my heart was I when he was gone; for I feared nothing so much as that he would have stayed till they came from church.

Thus, Jack, got I my *heart's-ease*, the letter of Miss Howe; and through such a train of accidents, as make me say that the lady's stars fight against her. But yet I must attribute a good deal to my own precaution in having taken right measures: for had I not secured the widow by my stories, and the maid by my servant, all would have signified nothing. And so heartily were they secured, the one by a single guinea, the other by half a dozen warm kisses, and the aversion they both had to such wicked creatures as delighted in making mischief between man and wife, that they promised that neither Mrs Moore, Miss Rawlins, Mrs Lovelace, nor anybody living, till a week at least were past, and till I gave leave, should know anything of the matter.

The widow rejoiced that I had got the mischief-maker's letter. I excused myself to her, and instantly withdrew with it; and, after I had read it, fell to my shorthand, to acquaint thee with my good luck: and they not returning so soon as church was done (stepping, as it proved, in to Miss Rawlins's, and tarrying there a while, to bring that busy girl with them to drink tea); I wrote thus far to thee, that thou mightest, when thou camest to this place, rejoice with me upon the occasion.

They are all three just come in—I hasten to them.

Letter 252: MR LOVELACE TO JOHN BELFORD, ESQ.

I HAVE begun another letter to thee, in continuation of my narrative: but I believe I shall send thee this before I shall finish that. By the enclosed thou wilt see that neither of the correspondents deserve mercy from me: and I am resolved to make the ending with one, the beginning with the other.

If thou sayest that the provocations I have given to *one* of them will justify *her* freedoms; I answer, so they *will* to any other person but myself. But he that is capable of giving those provocations, and has the power to punish those who abuse him *for* giving them, *will* show his resentment; and the more vindictively, perhaps, as he has *deserved* the freedoms?

If thou sayest it is, however, wrong to do so; I reply that it is nevertheless human nature—and wouldst not have me be a man, Jack?

Here read the letter, if thou wilt. But thou art not my friend if thou offerest to plead for either of the saucy creatures, after thou *hast* read it.

[*Letter 252.1: Anna Howe*] *to Mrs Harriot Lucas, at Mrs Moore's at Hampstead*

AFTER the discoveries I had made of the villainous machinations of the *most abandoned of men*, particularized in my long letter of Wednesday last,[a] you will believe, my dearest friend, that my surprise upon perusing yours of Thursday evening from Hampstead[b] was not so great as my indignation. Had the *villain* attempted to fire a city instead of a house, I should not have wondered at it. All that I am amazed at, is, that he (whose boast, as I am told it is, that no woman shall keep him out of her bedchamber, when he has made a resolution to be in it) did not discover *his foot* before.[1] And it is as strange to me that, having got you at such a shocking advantage, and in such an horrid house, you could, at the time, *escape dishonour*, and afterwards get from such a set of *infernals*.

I gave you, in my long letter of Wednesday and Thursday last, reasons why you

a See p. 743.
b See p. 754.

ought to mistrust that specious Tomlinson. That man, my dear, must be a solemn villain. *May lightning from Heaven blast the wretch, who has set him, and the rest of his* REMORSELESS GANG, *at work, to endeavour to destroy the most consummate virtue!* Heaven be praised! you have escaped from all their snares, and *now are out of danger*—So I will not trouble you at present with the particulars that I have further collected relating to this abominable imposture.

For the same reason, I forbear to communicate to you some *new stories* of the *abhorred wretch himself,* which have come to my ears. One in particular, of so *shocking* a nature!—Indeed, my dear, the man is a devil.

The whole story of Mrs Fretchville and her house, I have no doubt to pronounce, likewise, an absolute fiction—*Fellow!—How my soul spurns the villain!*

Your thought of going abroad, and your reasons for so doing, most sensibly affect me. But, be comforted my dear; I hope you will not be under a necessity of quitting your native country. Were I sure that that must be the cruel case, I would abandon all my own better prospects, and soon be with you. And I would accompany you whithersoever you went, and share fortunes with you: for it is impossible that I should be happy if I knew that you were exposed not only to the perils of the sea, but to the attempts of other vile men; your personal graces attracting every eye, and exposing you to those hourly dangers which others, less distinguished by the gifts of nature, might avoid—All that I know, that beauty (so greatly coveted, and so greatly admired) is good for!

Oh, my dear, were I ever to marry, and to be the mother of a CLARISSA (*Clarissa* must be the name, if promisingly lovely!), how often would my heart ache for the dear creature as she grew up, when I reflected that a prudence and discretion unexampled in woman had not, in *you,* been a sufficient protection to that beauty, which had drawn after it as many admirers as beholders!—How little should I regret the attacks of that *cruel* distemper, as it is called, which frequently makes the greatest ravages in the finest faces!

Sat. afternoon

I HAVE just parted with Mrs Townsend.[a] I thought you had once seen her with me: but she says she never had the honour to be personally known to you. She has a *manlike spirit.* She knows the world. And her two brothers being in town, she is sure she can engage them, in so good a cause and (if there should be occasion) *both their ships' crews,* in your service.

Give your consent, my dear; and the *horrid villain* shall be repaid with *broken bones, at least,* for all his vileness!

The misfortune is, Mrs Townsend cannot be with you till *Thursday next,* or *Wednesday at soonest.* Are you sure you can be safe where you are till then? I think you are too near London; and perhaps you had better be *in it.* If you remove, let me know *whither,* the very moment.

How my heart is torn to think of the necessity so dear a creature is driven to, of hiding herself! *Devilish fellow!* He must have been sportive and wanton in his inventions—Yet that cruel, that savage sportiveness has saved you from sudden violence which he has had recourse to in the violation of others, of names and families not contemptible. For such the *villain* always gloried to spread his snares.

The *vileness* of this *specious monster* has done more than any other consideration

---

a   For the account of Mrs Townsend etc., see pp. 621–2.

could do, to bring Mr Hickman into credit with me. Mr Hickman alone knows, for me, of your flight, and the reason of it. Had I not given him the reason, he might have thought *still worse* of the vile attempt. I communicated it to him by showing him your letter from Hampstead. When he had read it (*and he trembled* and *reddened*, as he read), he threw himself at my feet, and besought me to permit him to attend you, and to give you the protection of his house. The good-natured man had tears in his eyes, and was repeatedly earnest on this subject; proposing to take his chariot-and-four, or a set, and in person, in the face of all the world, give himself the glory of protecting such an oppressed innocent.

I could not but be pleased with him. And I let him know that I was. I hardly expected so much spirit from him. But a man's passiveness to a beloved object of our sex may not, perhaps, argue want of courage on proper occasions.

I thought I ought, in return, to have some consideration for his safety, as such an open step would draw upon him the vengeance of the most *villainous enterpriser* in the world, who has always a *gang of fellows*, such as himself, at his call, ready to support one another in the vilest outrages. But yet, as Mr Hickman might have strengthened his hands by legal recourses, I should not have stood upon it, had I not known your delicacies (since such a step must have made a great noise, and given occasion for scandal, as if some advantage had been gained over you), and were there not the greatest probability that all might be more silently, and more effectually, managed by Mrs Townsend's means.

Mrs Townsend will in person attend you—she *hopes* on Wednesday—Her brothers, and some of their people, will scatteringly, and as if they knew nothing of you (so we have contrived), see you safe not only to London, but to her house at Deptford.

She has a kinswoman who will take your commands there, if she herself be obliged to leave you. And there you may stay till the wretch's fury on losing you, and his search, are over.

He will very soon, 'tis likely, enter upon some *new villainy*, which may engross him: and it may be given out that you are gone to lay claim to the protection of your cousin Morden at Florence.

Possibly, if he can be made to believe it, he will go over in hopes to find you there.

After a while, I can procure you a lodging in one of the neighbouring villages; where I may have the happiness to be your daily visitor. And if this Hickman be not silly and apish, and if my mother do not do unaccountable things, I may the sooner think of marrying, that I may without control receive and entertain the darling of my heart.

Many, very many, happy days, do I hope we shall yet see together: and as this is *my* hope, I expect that it will be *your* consolation.

As to your estate, since you are resolved not to litigate for it, we will be patient, either till Col. Morden arrives, or till shame compels some people to be just.

Upon the whole, I cannot but think your prospects *now* much happier than they could have been, had you been actually married to such a man as this. I must therefore congratulate you upon your escape, not only from a *horrid libertine*, but from *so vile a husband* as he *must* have made to any woman; but more especially to a person of your virtue and delicacy.

You hate him, heartily hate him, I hope, my dear—I am sure you do. It would be strange if so much purity of life and manners were not to abhor what is so repugnant to itself.

In your letter before me, you mention one written to me for a *feint*.[a]—I have not received any such. Depend upon it therefore, that he must have it. And if he has, it is a wonder that he did not likewise get my long one of the 7th. Heaven be praised that he did not; *and that it came safe to your hands!*

I send this by a young fellow whose father is one of our tenants, with command to deliver it to no other hands but yours. He is to return directly, if you give him any letter. If not, he will proceed to London upon his own pleasures. He is a simple fellow; but very honest. So you may say anything to him. If you write not by him, I desire a line or two as soon as possible.

My mother knows nothing of his going to you. Nor yet of your abandoning *the fellow!* Forgive me!—but he's not entitled to good manners.

I shall long to hear how you and Mrs Townsend order matters. I wish she could have been with you sooner. But I have lost no time in engaging her, as you will suppose. I refer to *her*, what I have further to say and advise. So shall conclude with my prayers that Heaven will direct, and protect, my dearest creature, and make your future days happy!

ANNA HOWE

AND now, Jack, I will suppose that thou hast read this cursed letter. Allow me to make a few observations upon some of its contents, which I will do in my crow-quill short-hand, that they may have the appearance of notes upon the vixen's text.

It is strange to Miss Howe, that having got her friend at such a shocking advantage, etc.) And it is strange to me, too. If ever I have such another opportunity given me, the cause of both our wonder, I believe, will cease.

So thou seest Tomlinson is further detected. No such person as Mrs Fretchville. *May lightning from heaven*——Oh Lord, oh Lord, oh Lord!——What a horrid vixen is this!——My *gang*, my *remorseless gang*, too, is brought in——and thou wilt plead for these girls again; wilt thou?——*Heaven be praised*, she says, that her friend is out of danger——Miss Howe should be sure of *that*: and that she herself is safe. But for this termagant (as I have often said), I must surely have made a better hand of it——

New stories of me, Jack!——What can they be?—I have not found that my generosity to my Rosebud ever did me *due* credit with this pair of friends. Very hard, Belford, that credits cannot be set against debits, and a balance struck in a rake's favour, as well as in that of every *common* man!—But he, from whom no good is expected, is not allowed the merit of the good he does.

I ought to have been a little more attentive to *character* than I have been. For, notwithstanding that the measures of right and wrong are said to be so manifest, let me tell thee that *character* biases and runs away with all mankind. Let a man or woman once establish themselves in the world's opinion, and all that either of them do will be sanctified. Nay, in the very courts of justice, does not *character* acquit or condemn as often as facts, and sometimes even in spite of facts?—Yet (impolitic that I have been, and am!) to be so careless of mine!—And now, I doubt, it is irretrievable—But to leave moralizing.

  a See pp. 756–9.

Thou, Jack, knowest almost all my enterprises worth remembering. Can this particular story, which this girl hints at, be that of Lucy Villars?—Or can she have heard of my intrigue with the pretty gipsy, who met me in Norwood, and of the trap I caught her cruel husband in (a fellow as gloomy and tyrannical as old Harlowe), when he pursued a wife who would not have deserved ill of *him*, if he had deserved well of *her*?—But he was not quite drowned. The man is alive at this day: and Miss Howe mentions the story as a *very* shocking one. Besides, both these are a twelvemonth old, or more.

But evil fame and scandal are always *new*. When the offender has forgot a vile fact, it is often told to one and to another, who, having never heard of it before, trumpet it about as a novelty to others. But well said the honest corregidor at Madrid, a saying with which I enriched Lord M.'s collection—*Good actions are remembered but for a day: bad ones for many years after the life of the guilty*—— Such is the relish that the world has for scandal. In other words, such is the desire which everyone has to exculpate himself by blackening his neighbour. You and I, Belford, have been very kind to the world in furnishing it with many opportunities to gratify its devil.

Miss Howe will abandon her own better prospects, and share fortunes with her were she to go abroad.) Charming romancer!—I must set about this girl, Jack. I have always had hopes of a woman whose passions carry her into such altitudes!— Had I attacked Miss Howe first, her passions (inflamed and guided as I could have managed them) would have brought her to my lure in a fortnight.

But thinkest thou (and yet I think thou dost), that there is anything in these high flights among the sex? Verily, Jack, these vehement friendships are nothing but chaff and stubble, liable to be blown away by the very wind that raises them. Apes! mere apes of *us!* they think the word *friendship* has a pretty sound with it; and it is much talked of; a fashionable word: and so, truly, a single woman who thinks she has a soul, and knows that she wants something, would be thought to have found a fellow-soul for it in her own sex. But I repeat that the word is a *mere* word, the thing a mere name with them; a cork-bottomed shuttlecock, which they are fond of striking to and fro, to make one another glow in the frosty weather of a single state; but which, when a *man* comes in between the pretended *inseparables*, is given up like their music and other maidenly amusements; which, nevertheless, may be necessary to keep the pretty rogues out of more active mischief. They then, in short, having caught the *fish*, lay aside the net.[a]

Thou hast a mind, perhaps, to make an exception for these two ladies. With all my heart. My Clarissa has, if *woman* has, a soul capable of friendship. Her flame is bright and steady. But Miss Howe's, were it not kept up by her mother's opposition, is too vehement to endure. How often have I known opposition not only cement friendship, but create love? I doubt not but poor Hickman would fare the better with this vixen, if her mother were as heartily against him as she is for him.

Thus much indeed, as to these two ladies, I will grant thee; that the active spirit of the one, and the meek disposition of the other, may make their friendship more

a He alludes here to the story of a pope, who (once a poor fisherman), through every preferment he rose to, even to that of the cardinalate, hung up in view of all his guests, his net, as a token of humility. But, when he arrived at the pontificate, he took it down, saying that there was no need of the net, when he had caught the fish.

durable than it would otherwise be; for this is certain, that in every friendship, whether male or female, there must be a man and a woman spirit (that is to say, one of them a *forbearing* one) to make it permanent.

But this I pronounce as a truth, which all experience confirms; that friendship between women never holds to the sacrifice of capital gratifications, or to the endangering of life, limb or estate, as it often does in our nobler sex.

Well, but next comes an indictment against poor *beauty!*—What has beauty done that *Miss Howe* should be offended at it?—Miss Howe, Jack, is a charming girl. *She* has no reason to quarrel with beauty!—Didst ever see her?—Too much fire and spirit in her eye indeed, for a girl!—But that's no fault with a man that can lower that fire and spirit at pleasure; and I know I am the man that can.

A sweet auburn beauty is Miss Howe. A first beauty among beauties, when her sweeter friend (with such a commixture of serene gracefulness, of natural elegance, of native sweetness, yet conscious, though not arrogant, dignity, every feature glowing with intelligence) is not in company.

The difference between the two, when together, I have sometimes delighted to *read* in the addresses of a stranger entering into the presence of both, when standing side by side. There never was an instance, on such an occasion, where the stranger paid not his first devoirs to my Clarissa.

A respectful solemn awe sat upon every feature of the addresser's face. His eye seemed to ask leave to approach her; and lower than common, whether man or woman, was the bow or curtsy. And although this awe was immediately diminished by her condescending sweetness, yet went it not so entirely off, but that you might see the reverence remain, as if the person saw more of the goddess than the woman in her.

But the moment the same stranger turns to Miss Howe (though proud and saucy, and erect and bridling, she) you will observe by the turn of his countenance, and the air of his address, a kind of equality assumed. He appears to have discovered the woman in her, charming as that woman is. He smiles. He seems to expect repartee and smartness, and is never disappointed. But then visibly he prepares himself to *give* as well as *take*. He dares, after he has been a while in her company, to dispute a point with her——Every point yielded up to the other, though no assuming or dogmatical air compels it.

In short, with Miss Howe a bold man sees (no doubt but Sir George Colmar did), that he and she may either very soon be familiar together (I mean with innocence), or he may so far incur her displeasure, as to be forbid her presence for ever.

For my own part, when I was first introduced to this lady, which was by my goddess, when she herself was a visitor at Mrs Howe's; I had not been half an hour with her, but I even hungered and thirsted after a romping bout with the lively rogue; and in the second or third visit was more deterred by the delicacy of her friend, than by what I apprehended from her own. This charming creature's presence, thought I, awes us both. And I wished her absence, though any other lady were present, that I might try the difference in Miss Howe's behaviour before her friend's face, or behind her back.

Delicate ladies make delicate ladies, as well as decent men. With all Miss Howe's fire and spirit, it was easy to see, by her very eye, that she watched for lessons, and feared reproof from the penetrating eye of her milder-dispositioned friend*: and yet it was as easy to observe, in the candour and sweet manners of the other, that the fear which Miss Howe stood in of her was more owing to her own generous apprehension, that she fell short of her excellencies, than to Miss Harlowe's consciousness of excellence over *her*. I have often, since I came at Miss Howe's letters, revolved this just and fine praise contained in one of them.* 'Everyone saw that the preference each gave *you* to *herself* exalted you not into any visible triumph over her; for you had always something to say, on every point you carried, that raised the yielding heart, and left every one pleased and satisfied with herself, though she carried not off the palm.'

As I propose in my more advanced life, to endeavour to atone for my youthful freedoms with individuals of the sex by giving caution and instructions to the whole, I have made a memorandum to enlarge upon this doctrine; to wit, that it is full as necessary to direct daughters in the choice of their female companions, as it is to guard them against the designs of men.

I say not this, however, to the disparagement of Miss Howe. She has from *pride*, what her friend has from *principle*. (The Lord help the sex, if they had not pride!)—But yet I am confident that Miss Howe is indebted to the conversation and correspondence of Miss Harlowe for her highest improvements. But, both these ladies out of the question, I make no scruple to aver (and I, Jack, should know something of the matter), that there have been more girls ruined, at least *prepared* for ruin, by their own sex (taking in servants, as well as companions), than *directly* by the attempts and delusions of men.

But it is time enough when I am old and joyless to enlarge upon this topic.

As to the comparison between the two ladies, I will expatiate more on that subject (for I like it) when I have *had them both*—which this letter of the vixen girl's I hope thou wilt allow warrants me to try for.

I return to the consideration of a few more of its contents, to justify my vengeance, so nearly now in view.

As to Mrs Townsend; her manlike spirit; her two brothers; and their ships' crews—I say nothing but this to the insolent threatening—Let 'em come!—

But as to her sordid menace—To *repay the horrid villain*, as she calls me, *for all my vileness*, by BROKEN BONES!—Broken bones, Belford!—Who can bear this porterly threatening!—Broken bones, Jack!—Damn the little vulgar—Give me a name for her—But I banish all furious resentment. If I get these two girls into my power, Heaven forbid that I should be a second Phalaris, and turn his bull upon the artist!² No bones of theirs will I break!—They shall come off with me upon much lighter terms!—

But these fellows are smugglers, it seems. And am not I a smuggler too?—I have not the least doubt that I shall have secured my goods before Thursday or Wednesday either.

But did I want a plot, what a charming new one does this letter of Miss Howe strike me out? I am almost sorry that I have fixed upon one—for here, how easy would it be for me to assemble a crew of swabbers, and to create Mrs Townsend

---

a Miss Howe on p. 432 says that she was always more afraid of her than of her mother; and on p. 486 that she fears her as much as she loves her; and in many other places in her letters to Miss Harlowe, verifies this observation of Mr Lovelace.

b See p. 578.

(whose person, thou seest, my beloved knows not) to come on Tuesday, at Miss Howe's *renewed* urgency, in order to carry my beloved to a warehouse of my own providing?

This, however, is my triumphant hope, that at the very time, that these ragamuffins will be at Hampstead (looking for us), my dear Miss Harlowe and I (so the fates, I imagine, have ordained) shall be fast asleep in each other's arms in town—Lie still, villain, till the time comes—My heart, Jack; my heart!—It is always thumping away on the remotest prospects of this nature.

But it seems that *the vileness of this specious monster* (meaning me Jack!) has brought Hickman into credit with her. So I have done *some* good!—But to whom, I cannot tell: for this poor fellow, should I permit him to have this termagant, will be punished, as many times we all are, by the enjoyment of his own wishes—Nor can she be happy, as I take it, with him, were he to govern himself by her will, and have none of his own; since never was there a directing wife who knew where to stop. Power makes such a one wanton—she despises the man she can govern. Like Alexander, who wept that he had no more worlds to conquer, she will be looking out for new exercises for her power, till she grow uneasy to herself, a discredit to her husband, and a plague to all about her.

But this honest fellow, it seems, with *tears in his eyes*, and with *humble prostration*, besought the vixen to *permit* him to set out in his *chariot and four*, in order to *give himself the glory of protecting such an oppressed innocent, in the face of the whole world*—Nay, he *reddened*, it seems; and *trembled* too! as he read the fair complainant's letter—How *valiant* is all this!—Women love *brave* men; and no wonder that his *tears*, his *trembling*, and his *prostration*, gave him high reputation with the *meek* Miss Howe.

But dost think, Jack, that I, in the like case (and equally affected with the desires) should have acted thus?—Dost think that I should not first have rescued the lady, and then, if needful, have asked excuse for it, the lady in my hand?— Wouldst not *thou* have done thus, as well as I?

But 'tis best as it is. Honest Hickman may now sleep in a whole skin. And yet that is more perhaps than he would have done (the lady's deliverance *unattempted*), had I come at this *requested permission* of his any other way than by a letter that it must not be known I have intercepted.

She thinks I may be diverted from pursuing my charmer by some new-started *villainy*. *Villainy* is a word that she is extremely fond of. But I can tell her that it is impossible I should, till the end of this *villainy* be obtained. Difficulty is a *stimulus* with such a spirit as mine. I thought Miss Howe knew me better. Were she to offer herself, person for person, in the romancing zeal of her friendship, to save her friend, it should not do while the dear creature is on this side the moon.

She thanks Heaven that her friend has received her letter of the 7th. We are all glad of it. She ought to thank me too. But I will not at present claim her thanks.

But when she rejoices that that letter went safe, does she not, in effect, call out for vengeance, and *expect* it?—All in good time, Miss Howe. *When settest thou out for the Isle of Wight, love?*

I will close at this time with desiring thee to make a *list* of the virulent terms with which the enclosed letter abounds: and then, if thou supposest that I have made such another, and have added to it all the flowers of the same blow in the former letters of the same saucy creature, and those in that of Miss Harlowe, left for me on her elopement, thou wilt certainly think that I have provocations sufficient to justify me in all I shall do to either.

Return the enclosed the moment thou hast perused it.

Letter 253: MR LOVELACE TO JOHN BELFORD, ESQ.

Sunday night—Monday morning

I WENT down with revenge in my *heart*; the contents of Miss Howe's letter almost engrossing me, the moment that Miss Harlowe and Mrs Moore, accompanied by Miss Rawlins, came in: but in my countenance all the gentle, the placid, the serene, that the glass could teach; and in my behaviour all the polite that such an unpolite creature, as she has often told me I am, could put on.

Miss Rawlins was sent for home almost as soon as she came in, to entertain an unexpected visitor; to her great regret, as well as to the disappointment of my fair one, as I could perceive from the looks of both: for they had agreed, it seems, if I went to town as I said I intended to do, to take a walk upon the heath; at least in Mrs Moore's garden; and who knows what might have been the issue had the spirit of curiosity in the one met with the spirit of communication in the other?

Miss Rawlins promised to return, if possible: but sent to excuse herself; her visitor intending to stay with her all night.

I rejoiced in my heart at her message; and after much supplication obtained the favour of my beloved's company for another walk in the garden, having, as I told her, abundance of things to say, to propose, and to be informed of, in order ultimately to govern myself in my future steps.

She had vouchsafed, I should tell thee, with eyes turned from me, and in an *half aside* attitude, to sip two dishes of tea in my company—Dear soul!—How anger *unpolishes* the most polite! for I never saw Miss Harlowe behave so awkwardly. I imagined she knew not how to be awkward.

When we were in the garden, I poured my whole soul into her attentive ear; and besought her returning favour.

She told me that she had formed her scheme for her future life: that, vile as the treatment was which she had received from me, that was not all the reason she had for rejecting my suit: but that, on the maturest deliberation, she was convinced that she could neither be happy with me, nor make me happy; and she enjoined me, for both our sakes, to think no more of her.

The captain, I told her, was rid down post in a manner, to forward my wishes with her uncle.

Lady Betty and Miss Montague were undoubtedly arrived in town by this time. I would set out early in the morning to attend them.

They adored her. They longed to see her. They *would* see her—They would not be denied her company into Oxfordshire.

Where could she better go, to be free from her brother's insults?—Where, to be absolutely made unapprehensive of anybody else?—Might I have any hopes of her returning favour, if Miss Howe could be prevailed upon to intercede for me?

Miss Howe prevailed upon to intercede for you! repeated she, with a scornful bridle, but a very pretty one—And there she stopped.

I *repeated* the concern it would be to me, to be under a necessity of mentioning the misunderstanding to Lady Betty and my cousin as a misunderstanding still to be made up; and as if I were of very *little* consequence to a dear creature, who was of so *much* to me; urging, that it would extremely lower me, not only in my own opinion, but in that of my relations.

But still she referred to Miss Howe's next letter; and all the concession I could bring her to in this whole conference, was, that she would wait the arrival and visit of the two ladies, if they came in a day or two, or before she received the expected letter from Miss Howe.

Thank Heaven for this! thought I. And now may I go to town with hopes at my return to find thee, dearest, where I shall leave thee.

But yet I shall not entirely trust to this, as she may find reasons to change her mind in my absence. My fellow, therefore, who is in the house, and who by Mrs Bevis's kind intelligence will know every step she can take, shall have Andrew and a horse ready, to give me immediate notice of her motions; and moreover, go where she will, he shall be one of her retinue, though unknown to herself, if possible.

This was all I could make of the fair inexorable. Should I be glad of it, or sorry for it?—

Glad, I believe: and yet my pride is confoundedly abated to think that I had so little hold in the affections of this daughter of the Harlowes.

Don't tell me that virtue and principle are her guides on this occasion!—'Tis *pride*, a greater pride than my own, that governs her. Love she has none, thou seest; nor ever had; at least not in a superior degree—Love never was under the dominion of *prudence*, or of any *reasoning* power—She cannot bear to be thought a *woman*, I warrant!—and if, in the last attempt, I find her *not* one, what will she be the worse for the trial?—No one is to blame for suffering an evil he cannot shun or avoid.

Were a general to be overpowered and robbed by a highwayman, would he be less fit for the command of an army on that account?—If indeed the general, pretending great valour, and having boasted that he never would be robbed, were to make but faint resistance when he was brought to the test, and to yield his purse when he was master of his own sword, then indeed will the highwayman, who robs him, be thought the braver man.

But from these last conferences am I furnished with an argument in defence of my favourite purpose, which I never yet pleaded.

Oh Jack! what a difficulty must a man be allowed to have, to conquer a predominant passion, be it what it will, when the gratifying of it is in his *power*, however wrong he knows it to be to resolve to gratify it! Reflect upon this; and then wilt thou be able to account for, if not to excuse, a projected crime, which has *habit* to plead for it in a breast as stormy, as uncontrollable!—

This my new argument——

Should she fail in the trial; should I succeed; and should she refuse to go on with me; and even to marry me; which I can have no notion of—and should she disdain to be obliged to me for the handsome provision I should be proud to make for her, even to the *half of my estate*; yet cannot she be altogether unhappy—Is she not entitled to an independent fortune? Will not Colonel Morden, as her trustee, put her in possession of it? And did she not, in our former conference, point out the *way of life* that she always preferred to the *married life?*—To take her good Norton for her directress and guide, and to live upon her own estate in the manner her grandfather desired she should live?[a]

It is moreover to be considered that she cannot, according to her own notions, recover above *one half* of her fame, were we now to intermarry; so much does she think she has suffered by her going off with me. And will she not be always repining and mourning for the loss of the *other half?*—And if she must live a life of such uneasiness and regret for *half*, may she not as well repine and mourn for the *whole*?

Nor, let me tell thee, will her own scheme of penitence in this case be half so perfect if she do *not* fall, as if she *does*: for what a foolish penitent will she make, who has nothing to repent of?—She piques herself, thou knowest, and makes it matter of reproach to me, that she went not off with me by her own consent; but was tricked out of herself.

Nor upbraid thou me upon the meditated breach of vows so repeatedly made. She will not, thou seest, *permit* me to fulfil them. And if she *would*, this I have to say, that at the time I made the most solemn of them, I was fully determined to keep them. But what prince thinks himself obliged any longer to observe the articles of the most sacredly sworn-to treaties, than suits with his interest or inclination; although the consequence of the infraction must be, as he knows, the destruction of thousands?

Is not this then the result of all, that Miss Clarissa Harlowe, if it be not her own fault, may be as virtuous *after* she has lost her honour, as it is called, as she was *before*? She may be a more eminent example to her sex; and if she yield (a *little* yield) in the trial, may be a *completer penitent*. Nor can she, but by her own wilfulness, be reduced to *low fortunes*.

And thus may her *old* nurse and she; an *old* coachman; and a pair of *old* coach-horses; and two or three *old* maid-servants, and perhaps a *very old* footman or two (for everything will be old and penitential about her), live very comfortably together; reading *old* sermons, and *old* prayer-books; and relieving *old* men, and *old* women; and giving *old* lessons, and *old* warnings upon new subjects, as well as *old* ones, to the young ladies of her neighbourhood; and so pass on to a good *old* age, doing a great deal of good, both by precept and example, in her generation.

And is a lady who can live thus prettily without *control*; who ever did prefer, and who *still* prefers, the *single* to the *married life*; and who will be enabled to do everything that the plan she had formed will direct her to do; be said to be ruined, undone, and such sort of stuff?—I have no patience with the pretty fools who use those strong words to describe the most transitory evil; and which a mere church-form makes none?

At this rate of romancing, how many *flourishing ruins* dost thou, as well as I, know? Let us but look about us, and we shall see some of the haughtiest and most *censorious* spirits among our acquaintance of that sex, now passing for chaste

a   See p. 850.

wives, of whom strange stories might be told; and others, whose husbands' hearts have been made to ache for their gaieties, both before and after marriage; and yet know not half so much of them as some of us honest fellows could tell them.

But, having thus satisfied myself in relation to the worst that can happen to this *charming creature*; and that it will be her own fault if she be unhappy; I have not at all reflected upon what is likely to be *my own lot*.

This has always been my notion, though Miss Howe grudges us the best of the sex, and says that the worst is too good for us[a]; that the wife of a libertine ought to be pure, spotless, uncontaminated. To what purpose has such a one lived a free life, but to know the world, and to make his advantages of it?—And, to be *very* serious, it would be a misfortune to the public for two persons, heads of a family, to be both bad; since, between two such, a race of varlets might be propagated, Lovelaces and Belfords if thou wilt, who might do great mischief in the world.

Thou seest at bottom that I am not an abandoned fellow; and that there is a mixture of gravity in me. This, as I grow older, may increase; and when my active capacity begins to abate, I may sit down with the preacher, and resolve all my past life into vanity and vexation of spirit.

This is certain, that I shall never find a woman so well suited to my taste as Miss Clarissa Harlowe. I only wish (if I live to see that day), that I may have such a lady as her to comfort and adorn my setting sun. I have often thought it very unhappy for us both, that so excellent a creature sprung up a little too late for my *setting out*, and a little too early in my *progress*, before I can think of *returning*. And yet, as I have picked up the sweet traveller in my way, I cannot help wishing that she would bear me company in the *rest* of my journey, although she were to step out of her own path to oblige me. And then, perhaps, we could put up in the *evening* at the same *inn*; and be very happy in each other's conversation; recounting the difficulties and dangers we had passed in our way to it.

I imagine that thou wilt be apt to suspect that some passages in this letter were written in town. Why, Jack, I cannot but say that the Westminster air is a little grosser than that at Hampstead; and the conversation of Mrs Sinclair and the Nymphs less innocent than Mrs Moore's and Miss Rawlins's. And I think in my heart, that I can say and write those things at one place, which I cannot at the other; nor indeed anywhere else.

I came to town about seven this morning—All necessary directions and precautions remembered to be given.

I besought the favour of an audience before I set out. I was desirous to see which of her lovely faces she was pleased to put on after another night had passed. But she was resolved, I found, to leave our quarrel open. She would not give me an opportunity so much as to entreat her again to close it, before the arrival of Lady Betty and my cousin.

I had notice from my proctor, by a few lines brought by man and horse, just before I set out, that all difficulties had been for two days past surmounted; and that I might have the licence for fetching.

I sent up the letter to my beloved by Mrs Bevis. It procured me not admittance, though my request for *that* was sent with it.

And now, Belford, I set out upon business.

a See p. 751.

Letter 254: MR LOVELACE TO JOHN BELFORD, ESQ.

Monday, June 12

DIDST ever see a licence, Jack?

N.N. by divine permission, Lord Bishop of London, to our well beloved in Christ, Robert Lovelace (Your servant, my good lord! What have I done to merit so much goodness, who never saw your lordship in my life?), *of the parish of St Martin's in the Fields, bachelor, and Clarissa Harlowe of the same parish, spinster, sendeth greeting. WHEREAS ye are, as is alleged, determined to enter into the holy state of matrimony* (This is only alleged, thou observest), *by and with the consent of, etc. etc. etc., and are very desirous of obtaining your marriage to be solemnized in the face of the church: We are willing that such your honest desires* (honest desires, Jack!) *may more speedily have their due effect: and therefore that ye may be able to procure such marriage to be freely and lawfully solemnized in the parish church of St Martin in the Fields, or St Giles's in the Fields, in the county of Middlesex, by the rector, vicar, or curate thereof, at any time of the year* (at ANY time of the year, Jack!), *without publication of banns: Provided, that by reason of any precontract* (I verily think, that I have had three or four precontracts in my time, but the good girls have not claimed upon them of a long time), *consanguinity, affinity, or any other lawful cause whatsoever, there be no lawful impediment in this behalf; and that there be not at this time any action, suit, plaint, quarrel, or demand, moved or depending before any judge ecclesiastical or temporal, for or concerning any marriage contracted by or with either of you; and that the said marriage be openly solemnized in the church above-mentioned, between the hours of eight and twelve in the forenoon; and without prejudice to the minister of the place where the said woman is a parishioner: We do hereby, for good causes* (It cost me—let me see, Jack— what did it cost me?), *give and grant our licence, or faculty, as well to you the parties contracting, as to the rector, vicar, or curate of the said church, where the said marriage is intended to be solemnized, to solemnize the same in manner and form above-specified, according to the rites and ceremonies prescribed in the Book of Common Prayer in that behalf published by authority of Parliament. Provided always, that if hereafter any fraud shall appear to have been committed, at the time of granting this licence, either by false suggestions, or concealment of the truth* (Now this, Belford, is a little hard upon us: for I cannot say that every one of our suggestions is literally true—So, in good conscience, I ought not to marry under this licence), *the licence shall be void to all intents and purposes, as if the same had not been granted. And in that case, we do inhibit all ministers whatsoever, if anything of the premises shall come to their knowledge, from proceeding to the celebration of the said marriage, without first consulting Us, or our Vicar-general. Given, etc.*

Then follow the registrar's name, and a large pendent seal, with these words round it: SEAL OF THE VICAR-GENERAL AND OFFICIAL-PRINCIPAL OF THE DIOCESE OF LONDON.

A good whimsical instrument, take it all together!—But what, thinkest thou, are the arms to this matrimonial harbinger?—Why, in the first place, *two crossed swords*; to show that marriage is a state of offence as well as defence: *three lions*; to denote that those who enter into the state ought to have a triple proportion of courage. And (couldst thou have imagined that these priestly fellows, in so solemn a case, would cut their jokes upon poor souls who come to have their *honest desires* put in a way to be gratified?) there are *three crooked horns*, smartly top-knotted with ribands; which being the ladies' wear seem to indicate that they may very probably adorn, as well as bestow, the bull's feather.

To describe it according to heraldry art, if I am not mistaken: Gules, two swords, saltire-wise, Or; second coat, a chevron sable between three buglehorns, Or (*so it ought to be*): on a chief of the second, three lions rampant of the first—But the devil take them for their hieroglyphics, should I say, if I were determined in good earnest to marry!

And determined to marry I would be, were it not for this consideration: that once married, and I am married for life.

That's the plague of it!—Could a man do as the birds do, change every Valentine's day (a *natural* appointment! for birds have not the *sense*, forsooth, to fetter themselves, as we wiseacre men take great and solemn pains to do); there would be nothing at all in it. And what a glorious time would the *lawyers* have, on the one hand, with their *noverint universi*'s, and suits commenceable on restitution of goods and chattels; and the *parsons*, on the other, with their indulgences (renewable annually, as *other* licences) to the *honest desires* of their clients?

Then, were a stated mulct, according to rank or fortune, to be paid on every change, towards the exigencies of the State (but none on *renewals* with the *old loves*, for the sake of encouraging constancy, especially among the *minores*), the change would be made sufficiently difficult, and the whole public would be the better for it; while those children which the parents could not agree about maintaining might be considered as the *children of the public*, and provided for like the children of the ancient Spartans; who were (as ours would in this case be) a nation of heroes. How, Jack, could I have improved upon Lycurgus's institutions,[1] had I been a lawgiver?

Did I never show thee a scheme, which I drew up on such a notion as this? In which I demonstrated the *conveniences*, and obviated the *inconveniencies*, of changing the present mode to this? I believe I never did.

I remember I proved, to a demonstration, that such a change would be a means of annihilating, absolutely annihilating, four or five very atrocious and capital sins—*rapes*, vulgarly so called; adultery, and fornication; nor would *polygamy* be panted after. Frequently would it prevent *murders* and *duelling*: hardly any such thing as *jealousy* (the cause of shocking violences) would be heard of: and hypocrisy between man and wife be banished the bosoms of each. Nor, probably, would the reproach of *barrenness* rest, as now it too often does, where it is least deserved—Nor would there possibly be such a person as a barren woman.

Moreover, what a multitude of domestic quarrels would be avoided, were such a scheme carried into execution? Since both sexes would bear with each other, in the view that they could help themselves in a few months.

And then what a charming subject for conversation would be the gallant and generous last partings between man and wife! Each, perhaps, a new mate in eye, and rejoicing secretly in the manumission, could *afford* to be complaisantly sorrowful in appearance. 'He presented *her* with this jewel, it will be said by the reporter, for *example* sake: she *him* with that. How *he* wept! How *she* sobbed! How they looked after one another!' Yet, that's the jest of it, neither of them wishing to stand another twelvemonth's trial.

And if giddy fellows, or giddy girls, misbehave in a first marriage, whether from *noviceship*, having expected to find more in the matter than can be found; or from perverseness on *her* part, or *positiveness* on *his*, each being mistaken in the other (a mighty difference, Jack, in the same person, an *inmate*, or a *visitor*); what a fine opportunity will each have, by this scheme, of recovering a lost character, and of setting all right in the next adventure?

And Oh Jack, with what joy, with what rapture, would the *changelings* (or *changeables*, if thou like that word better) number the weeks, the days, the hours, as the annual obligation approached to its desirable period!

As for the spleen or vapours, no such malady would be known or heard of. The physical tribe would, indeed, be the sufferers, and the only sufferers; since fresh health and fresh spirits, the consequences of sweet blood and sweet humours (the mind and body continually pleased with each other), would perpetually flow in; and the joys of *expectation*, the highest of all our joys, would salubriate and keep all alive.

But, that no body of men might suffer, the *physicians*, I thought, might turn *parsons*, as there would be a great demand for parsons. Besides, as they would be partakers in the general benefit, they must be sorry fellows indeed if they preferred themselves to the public.

Everyone would be married a dozen times, at least. Both men and women would be careful of their characters, and polite in their behaviour, as well as delicate in their *persons*, and elegant in their *dress* (a great matter each of these, let me tell thee, to keep passion alive), either to induce a *renewal* with the *old love*, or to recommend themselves to a *new*. While the newspapers would be crowded with paragraphs, all the world their readers, as all the world would be concerned to see *who and who's together*——

'Yesterday, for instance, entered into the holy state of matrimony (We should all speak reverently of matrimony then) the Right Honourable Robert, Earl Lovelace (I shall be an Earl by that time), with her Grace the Duchess Dowager of Fifty-manors; his lordship's one-and-thirtieth wife'—I shall then be contented, perhaps, to take up, as it is called, with a widow. But she must not have had more than one husband neither. Thou knowest that I am nice in these particulars.

I know, Jack, that thou, for thy part, wilt approve of my scheme.

As Lord M. and I, between us, have three or four boroughs at command, I think I will get into Parliament, in order to bring in a Bill for this good purpose.

Neither will the Houses of Parliament, nor the Houses of Convocation, have reason to object to it. And all the courts, whether *spiritual* or *sensual, civil* or *uncivil*, will find their account in it, when passed into a law.

By my soul, Jack, I should be apprehensive of a general insurrection, and that incited by the women, were such a Bill to be thrown out—For here is the excellency of the scheme: the women will have equal reason with the men to be pleased with it.

Dost think that *old prerogative Harlowe*, for example, must not, if such a law were in being, have pulled in his horns?—So excellent a lady as he has would never else have *renewed* with such a gloomy tyrant: who, as well as all other tyrants, must have been upon good behaviour from year to year.

A termagant wife, if such a law were to pass, would be a phoenix.

The *churches* would be the only *market-places* for the fair sex; and *domestic excellence* the capital recommendation.

Nor would there be an *old maid* in Great Britain and all its territories. For what an odd soul must she be, who could not have her *twelvemonth's trial*?

In short, a total alteration for the better in the *morals* and *way of life* in both sexes must, in a very few years, be the consequence of such a salutary law.

Who would have expected such a one from me? I wish the devil owe me not a spite for it.

Then would not the distinction be very pretty, Jack; as in flowers—such a gentleman, or such a lady, is an ANNUAL—such a one a PERENNIAL.

One difficulty, however, as I remember, occurred to me, upon the probability that a wife might be *enciente*, as the lawyers call it. But thus I obviated it.

That no man should be allowed to marry another woman without his *then* wife's consent, till she were brought to bed, and he had defrayed all incident charges; and till it was agreed upon between them, whether the child should be *his*, *hers*, or the *public*'s. The women, in this case, to have what I call the *coercive option*: for I would not have it in the man's power to be a dog neither.

And indeed, I gave the turn of the scale, in every part of my scheme, in the women's favour: for dearly do I love the sweet rogues.

How infinitely more preferable this my scheme, than the polygamy one of the old patriarchs; who had wives and concubines without number! I believe David and Solomon had their hundreds *at a time*. Had they not, Jack?

Let me add, that *annual Parliaments*,[2] and *annual marriages*, are the projects next my heart. How could I expatiate upon the benefits that would arise from both!

Letter 255: MR LOVELACE TO JOHN BELFORD, ESQ.

WELL, but now my plots thicken; and my employment of writing to thee on this subject will soon come to a conclusion. For now, having got the licence; and Mrs Townsend, with her tars, being to come to Hampstead next Wednesday or Thursday; and another letter possibly, or message from Miss Howe, to inquire how Miss Harlowe does, upon the rustic's report of her ill health, and to express her wonder that she has not heard from her in answer to hers on her escape—I must soon blow up the lady, or be blown up myself. And so I am preparing, with Lady Betty and my cousin Montague, to wait upon my beloved with a coach and four, or a set; for Lady Betty will not stir out with a pair for the world; though but for two or three miles. And this is a well-known part of her character.

But as to her arms and crest upon the coach and trappings?

Dost thou not know that a Blunt's must supply her, while her own is new lining and repairing? An opportunity she is willing to take now she is in town. Nothing of this kind can be done to her mind in the country. Liveries nearly Lady Betty's.

Thou hast seen Lady Betty Lawrance several times—hast thou not, Belford?

No, never in my life.

But thou hast; and lain with her too; or fame does thee more credit than thou deservest—Why, Jack, knowest thou not Lady Betty's other name?

Other name!—Has she two?

She has. And what thinkest thou of Lady Bab Wallis?

Oh the devil!

Now thou hast it. Lady Barbara, thou knowest, lifted up in circumstances and by pride, never appears or produces herself, but on occasions special—to pass to men of quality or price for a duchess, or countess at least. She has always been admired for a grandeur in her air that few women of quality can come up to: and never was supposed to be other than what she passed for; though often and often a paramour for lords.

And who, thinkest thou, is my cousin Montague?

Nay, how should I know?

How indeed! Why, my little Johanetta Golding, a lively, yet modest-looking girl, is my cousin Montague.

There, Belford, is an aunt!—There's a cousin! Both have wit at will. Both are accustomed to ape quality. Both are genteelly descended. Mistresses of themselves; and well educated—yet past pity. True *Spartan* dames; ashamed of nothing but *detection*—always, therefore, upon their guard against that. And in their own conceit, when assuming top parts, the very quality they ape.

And how dost think I dress them out?—I'll tell thee.

Lady Betty in a rich gold tissue, adorned with jewels of high price.

My cousin Montague in a pale pink, standing [on] end with silver flowers of her own working. Charlotte, as well as my beloved, is admirable at her needle. Not quite so richly jewelled out as Lady Betty; but ear-rings and solitaire very valuable, and infinitely becoming.

Johanetta, thou knowest, has a good complexion, a fine neck, and ears remarkably fine—So has Charlotte. She is nearly of Charlotte's stature too.

Laces both, the richest that could be procured.

Thou canst not imagine what a sum the loan of the jewels cost me; though but for three days.

This sweet girl will half ruin me. But seest thou not by this time, that her reign is short?—It must be so. And Mrs Sinclair has already prepared everything for her reception once more.

HERE come the ladies—attended by Susan Morrison, a tenant-farmer's daughter, as Lady Betty's woman; with her hands before her, and thoroughly instructed.

How dress advantages women!—especially those, who have naturally a genteel air and turn, and have had education!

Hadst thou seen how they paraded it—cousin, and cousin, and nephew, at every word; Lady Betty bridling and looking haughtily-condescending: Charlotte galanting her fan, and swimming over the floor without touching it.

How I long to see my niece-elect! cries one—for they are told that we are not married; and are pleased that I have not put the slight upon them that they had apprehended from me.

How I long to see my dear cousin that is to be, the other!

Your la'ship, and your la'ship, and an awkward curtsy at every address, prim Susan Morrison.

Top your parts, ye villains!—You know how nicely I distinguish. There will be no passion in *this case* to blind the judgement, and to help on meditated delusion, as when you engage with titled sinners. My charmer is as cool and as distinguishing, though not quite so learned in her own sex, as I am. Your commonly assumed dignity won't do for me now. Airs of superiority, as if *born* to rank—but no over-do!—doubting nothing. Let not your faces arraign your hearts.

Easy and unaffected!—Your very dresses will give you pride enough.

A little *graver*, Lady Betty. More significance, less bridling,.in your dignity. That's the air! Charmingly hit—Again—You have it.

Devil take you!—Less arrogance. You are got into airs of *young quality*. Be less sensible of your new condition. People born to dignity command respect without needing to require it.

Now for *your* part, cousin Charlotte!—

Pretty well. But a little too frolicky that air—Yet have I prepared my beloved to expect in you both, great vivacity and quality-freedom.

Curse those eyes!—Those glancings will never do. A down-cast bashful turn, if you can command it—Look upon me. Suppose me now to be my beloved.

Devil take that leer. Too *significantly* arch!—Once I knew you the girl I would now have you to be.

Sprightly, but not confident, cousin Charlotte!—Be sure forget not to look down, or aside, when looked at. When eyes meet eyes, be yours the retreating ones. Your face will bear examination.

Oh Lord! Oh Lord! that so young a creature can so soon forget the innocent appearance she first charmed by; and which I thought born with you all!—Five years to ruin what twenty had been building up! How natural the latter lesson! How difficult to regain the former!

A stranger, as I hope to be saved, to the principal arts of your sex!—Once more, what a devil has your heart to do in your eyes?

Have I not told you that my beloved is a great observer of the eyes? She once quoted upon me a text,[a] which showed me how she came by her knowledge—Dorcas's were found guilty of treason the first moment she saw her.

Once more, suppose me to be my charmer—Now you are to encounter my *examining* eye, and my *doubting* heart—

That's my dear!

Study that air in the pier-glass!—

Charming!—Perfectly right!

Your honours, now, devils!—

Pretty well, cousin Charlotte, for a young country lady!—Till form yields to familiarity, you *may* curtsy low. You must not be supposed to have forgot your boarding-school airs.

But too low, too low, Lady Betty, for your years and your quality. The common fault of your sex will be your danger: aiming to be young too long!—The devil's in you all, when you judge of yourselves by your wishes, and by your vanity! Fifty will then never be more than fifteen.

Graceful ease, conscious dignity, like that of my charmer, oh how hard to hit!

Both together now—

---

a Eccl[esiastic]us 26:[9 and 11]. The whoredom of a woman may be known in her haughty looks and eye-lids. Watch over an impudent eye, and marvel not if it trespass against thee.

Charming!—That's the air, Lady Betty!—That's the cue, cousin Charlotte, suited to the character of each!—But, once more, be sure to have a guard upon your eyes.

Never fear, nephew!—

Never fear, cousin.

A dram of Barbados each—

And now we are gone—

Letter 256: MR LOVELACE TO JOHN BELFORD, ESQ.

At Mrs Sinclair's, Monday afternoon

ALL's right as heart can wish!—In spite of all objection—in spite of a reluctance next to fainting—in spite of all her foresight, vigilance, suspicion, once more is the charmer of my soul in her new lodgings!

Now throbs away every pulse! Now thump, thump, thumps my bounding heart for something!

But I have not time for the particulars of our management.

My beloved is now directing some of her clothes to be packed up—never more to enter this house! Nor ever more will she, I dare say, when once again out of it!

Yet not so much as a condition of forgiveness!—The Harlowe-spirited fair one will not *deserve* my mercy!—She will wait for Miss Howe's next letter; and then, if she find a *difficulty in her new schemes* (thank her for nothing)—will—Will what?——Why even *then* will take time to consider whether I am to be forgiven, or for ever rejected. An indifference that revives in my heart the remembrance of a thousand of the like nature—And yet Lady Betty and Miss Montague (one would be tempted to think, Jack, that they wish her to provoke my vengeance) declare that I ought to be satisfied with such a proud suspension!

They are entirely attached to her. Whatever she says *is, must be*, gospel!—They are guarantees for her return to Hampstead this night. They are to go back with her. A supper bespoke by Lady Betty at Mrs Moore's. All the vacant apartments there, by my permission (for I had engaged them for a month certain), to be filled with them and their attendants, for a week at least, or till they can prevail upon the dear perverse, as they hope they shall, to restore me to her favour, and to accompany Lady Betty to Oxfordshire.

The dear creature has thus far condescended—that she will write to Miss Howe, and acquaint her with the present situation of things.

If she write, I shall see what she writes. But I believe she will have other employment soon.

Lady Betty is sure, she tells her, that she shall prevail upon her to forgive me; though she dares say, that I deserve not forgiveness. Lady Betty is too delicate to inquire strictly into the nature of my offence. But it must be an offence against herself, against Miss Montague, against the virtuous of the whole sex, or it could not be so highly resented. Yet she will not leave her till she forgive me, and till she see our nuptials privately celebrated. Meantime, as she approves of her *uncle's expedient*, she will address her as *already my wife, before strangers*.

Stedman her solicitor may attend her for orders, in relation to her Chancery affair, at Hampstead. Not one hour they *can* be favoured with, will they lose from the company and conversation of so dear, so charming a new relation.

Hard then if she had not obliged them with her company, in their coach and four, to and from their cousin Leeson's, who longed (as they themselves had done) to see a lady so justly celebrated!

'How will Lord M. be raptured when he sees her, and can salute her as his niece!

'How will Lady Sarah bless herself!—She will now think her loss of the dear daughter she mourns for, happily supplied!'

Miss Montague dwells upon every word that falls from her lips. She perfectly adores her new cousin:

'For her cousin she *must* be. And her cousin will she call her! She answers for equal admiration in her sister Patty.'

'Ay, cry I (whispering loud enough for her to hear), how will my cousin Patty's dove's eyes glisten, and run over, on the very first interview!—So gracious, so noble, so unaffected a dear creature!'

'What a happy family,' chorus we all, 'will ours be!'

These, and such-like congratulatory admirations, every hour repeated: her modesty hurt by the ecstatic praises—'Her graces are too natural to herself for her to be proud of them—but she must be content to be punished for excellencies that cast a shade upon the *most* excellent!'

In short, we are here, as at Hampstead, all joy and rapture: all of us, except my beloved, in whose sweet face (her almost fainting reluctance to re-enter these doors not overcome) reigns a kind of anxious serenity!—But how will even *that* be changed in a few hours!

Methinks I begin to pity the half-apprehensive beauty!—But avaunt, thou unseasonably-intruding pity! Thou hast more than once already well nigh undone me!—And, adieu, reflection! Begone, consideration! and commiseration! I dismiss ye all, for at least a week to come!—Be remembered her broken word! Her flight, when my fond soul was meditating mercy to her!—Be remembered her treatment of me in her letter on her escape to Hampstead!—her Hampstead virulence!— What is it she ought not to expect from an unchained Beelzebub, and a plotting villain?

Be her preference of the single life to *me* also remembered!—that she despises me!—that she even refuses to be my WIFE!—A proud Lovelace to be denied a *wife*!—to be more proudly rejected by a daughter of the *Harlowes*!—The ladies of my own family (she thinks them the ladies of my family) supplicating in vain for her returning favour to their despised kinsman, and taking laws from her still prouder punctilio!

Be the execrations of her vixen friend likewise remembered, poured out upon me from *her* representations, and thereby made her *own* execrations!

Be remembered still more particularly, the Townsend plot, set on foot between them, and now, in a day or two, ready to break out; and the *sordid threatenings* thrown out against me by that little fury.

Is not *this* the crisis for which I have been long waiting? Shall Tomlinson, shall these women, be engaged; shall so many engines be set at work, at an immense expense, with infinite contrivance; and all to no purpose?

Is not *this* the hour of her trial—and in *her*, of the trial of the virtue of her whole sex, so long premeditated, so long threatened?—Whether her frost is frost indeed?

Whether her virtue is principle? Whether, if *once subdued, she will not be always subdued*? And will she not want the very crown of her glory, the proof of her till now all-surpassing excellence, if I stop short of the ultimate trial?

Now is the end of purposes long over-awed, often suspended, at hand. And need I to throw the sins of her cursed family into the too weighty scale?

Abhorred be force!—be the thoughts of force! There's no triumph over the will in force! This I know I have said.[a] But would I not have avoided it if I could?—Have I not tried every other method? And have I any other recourse left me? Can she resent the *last outrage* more than she has resented a *fainter effort*?—And if her resentments run ever so high, cannot I repair by matrimony?—She will not refuse me, I know, Jack; the haughty beauty will not refuse me, when her pride of being corporally inviolate is brought down; when she can tell no tales, but when (be her resistance what it will) even her own sex will suspect a yielding in resistance; and when that modesty, which may fill her bosom with resentment, will lock up her speech.

But how know I that I have not made my own difficulties?—Is she not a woman?—What redress lies for a perpetrated evil?—Must she not *live*?—Her piety will secure her life. And will not *time* be my friend?—What, in a word, will be her behaviour afterwards?—She cannot fly me!—She must forgive me—And, as I have often said, *once forgiven, will be for ever forgiven.*

Why then should this enervating pity unsteel my foolish heart?—

It shall not. All these things will I remember; and think of nothing else, in order to keep up a resolution which the women about me will have it I shall be still unable to hold.

I'll teach the dear charming creature to emulate me in contrivance!—I'll teach her to weave webs and plots against her conqueror!—I'll show her that in her smuggling schemes she is but a spider compared to me, and that she has all this time been spinning only a cobweb!

WHAT shall we do now!—We are immersed in the depth of grief and apprehension!—How ill do women bear disappointment!—Set upon going to Hampstead, and upon quitting for ever a house she re-entered with infinite reluctance; what things she intended to take with her ready packed up; herself on tip-toe to be gone; and I prepared to attend her thither; she begins to be afraid that she shall not go this night; and, in grief and despair, has flung herself into her old apartment; locked herself in; and, through the key-hole, Dorcas sees her on her knees—praying, I suppose, for a safe deliverance.

And from what?—And wherefore these agonizing apprehensions?

Why, here, this unkind Lady Betty, *with* the dear creature's knowledge, though to her concern, and this mad-headed cousin Montague *without* it, while she was employed in directing her package, have hurried away in the coach to their own lodgings—Only, indeed, to put up some night-clothes, and so forth, in order to attend their sweet cousin to Hampstead; and, no less to my surprise than hers, are not yet returned.

I have sent to know the meaning of it.

In a great hurry of spirits, she would have had me gone myself. Hardly any

a See p. 657.

pacifying her!—The girl, God bless her! is wild with her own idle apprehensions!—
What is she afraid of?

I curse them both for their delay—My tardy villain, how he stays!—Devil fetch
them! Let them send their coach, and we'll go without them. In her hearing, I bid
the fellow tell them so—Perhaps he stays to bring the coach, if anything happens
to hinder the ladies from attending my beloved this night.

DEVIL take them, again say I!—They *promised* too, they would not stay, because
it was but two nights ago that a chariot was robbed at the foot of Hampstead hill;
which alarmed my fair one, when told of it!

Oh! here's my aunt's servant, with a billet.

[*Letter 256.1: 'Lady Elizabeth Lawrance'*] *to Robert Lovelace, Esq.*

Monday night

EXCUSE us, dear nephew, I beseech you, to my dearest kinswoman. One night
cannot break squares. For here Miss Montague has been taken violently ill with
three fainting fits, one after another. The hurry of her joy, I believe, to find your
dear lady so much surpass all expectation (never did family-love, you know, reign
so strong as among us), and the too eager desire she had to attend her, have
occasioned it: for she has but weak spirits, poor girl! well as she looks.

If she be better, we will certainly go with you tomorrow morning, after we have
breakfasted with her at your lodgings. But, whether she be, or not, I will do
myself the pleasure to attend your lady to Hampstead; and will be with you, for
that purpose, about nine in the morning. With due compliments to your most
worthily beloved, I am

Yours affectionately,
ELIZAB. LAWRANCE

Faith and troth, Jack, I know not what to do with myself: for here, just now,
having sent in the above note by Dorcas, out came my beloved with it in her hand:
in a fit of frenzy!—True, by my soul!

She had indeed complained of her head all the evening.

Dorcas ran to me, out of breath, to tell me that her lady was coming in some
strange way: but she followed her so quick, that the frighted wench had not time
to say in what way.

It seems, when she read the billet—Now indeed, said she, am I a lost creature!
Oh the poor Clarissa Harlowe!

She tore off her head-clothes; inquired where I was: and in she came, her shining
tresses flowing about her neck; her ruffles torn, and hanging in tatters about her
snowy hands; with her arms spread out; her eyes wildly turned as if starting from
their orbits—Down sunk she at my feet, as soon as she approached me; her
charming bosom heaving to her uplifted face; and, clasping her arms about my
knees, Dear Lovelace, said she, if ever—if ever—if ever—And, unable to speak
another word, quitting her clasping hold, down prostrate on the floor sunk she,
neither in a fit nor out of one.

I was quite astonished—All my purposes suspended for a few moments, I knew
neither what to say, nor what to do. But, recollecting myself, am I *again*, thought

I, in a way to be overcome and made a fool of!—If I now recede, I am gone for ever.

I raised her: but down she sunk, as if quite disjointed; her limbs failing her—yet not in a fit neither. I never heard of, or saw, such a dear unaccountable: almost lifeless, and speechless too for a few moments!—What must her apprehensions be at that moment! And for what?—A high-notioned dear soul!—Pretty ignorance! thought I.

Never having met with a repugnance so *greatly* repugnant, I was staggered—I was confounded—Yet how should I know that it would be so till I tried?—And how, having proceeded thus far, could I stop, were I *not* to have had the women to goad me on, and to make light of circumstances which they pretended to be better judges of than me.

I lifted her, however, into a chair; and, in words of disordered passion, told her all her fears were needless: wondered at them: begged of her to be pacified: besought her reliance on my faith and honour: and re-vowed all my old vows, and poured forth new ones.

At last, with an heart-breaking sob, I see, I see, Mr Lovelace, in broken sentences she spoke—I see, I see—that at last—at last—I am ruined!—ruined—if *your* pity—Let me implore your pity!—And down on her bosom, like a half-broken-stalked lily, top-heavy with the overcharging dews of the morning, sunk her head with a sigh that went to my heart.

All I could think of to reassure her, when a little recovered, I said.

Why did I not send for their coach, as I had intimated? It might return in the morning for the ladies.

I had actually done so, I told her, on seeing her strange uneasiness. But it was then gone to fetch a doctor for Miss Montague, lest his chariot should not be so ready.

Ah! Lovelace! said she, with a doubting face; anguish in her imploring eye.

Lady Betty would think it very strange, I told her, if she were to know it was so disagreeable to her to stay one night, for *her* company, in a house where she had passed *so many*!

She called me names upon this.—She had called me names before—I was patient.

Let her go to Lady Betty's lodgings, then; *directly* go; if the person I called Lady Betty was really Lady Betty.

If! my dear! Good Heaven! What a villain does that IF show you believe me to be!

I cannot help it—I beseech you once more, let me go to Mrs Leeson's, if *that* IF ought not to be said.

Then assuming a more resolute spirit—I will go! I will inquire my way!—I will go by myself!—And would have rushed by me.

I folded my arms about her to detain her; pleading the bad way I heard poor Charlotte was in; and what a farther concern her impatience, if she went, would give her.

She would believe nothing I said, unless I would instantly order a coach (since she was not to have Lady Betty's, nor was permitted to go to Mrs Leeson's), and let her go in it to Hampstead, late as it was; and all alone; so much the better: for in the house of *people*, of whom Lady Betty upon inquiry had heard a bad character (*dropped foolishly this, by my prating new relation, in order to do credit to herself by depreciating others*); everything, and every face, looking with so much meaning vileness, as well as *my own* (*thou art still too sensible, thought I, my charmer!*), she was resolved not to stay another night.

Dreading what might happen as to her intellects, and being very apprehensive that she might possibly go through a great deal before morning (though more violent she could not well be with the worst she dreaded), I humoured her, and ordered Will to go and endeavour to get a coach directly, to carry us to Hampstead; I cared not at what price.

Robbers, whom I would have terrified her with, she feared not—*I* was all her fear, I found; and this house her terror: for I saw plainly that she now believed that Lady Betty and Miss Montague were both impostors.

But her mistrust is a little of the latest to do her service.

And, oh Jack, the rage of love, the rage of revenge is upon me! By turns they tear me!—The progress already made!—the women's instigations!—the power I shall have to try her to the utmost, and still to marry her if she be not to be brought to cohabitation!—Let me perish, Belford, if she escape me now!

Will is not yet come back—Near eleven.—

Will is this moment returned—No coach to be got, *for love or money*.

Once more she urges—To Mrs Leeson's let me go!—Lovelace! Good Lovelace! Let me go to Mrs Leeson's!—What is Miss Montague's illness to my terror?—For the Almighty's sake, Mr Lovelace!—her hands clasped—

Oh my angel! What a wildness is this!—Do you know, do you see, my dearest life, what an appearance your causeless apprehensions have given you?—Do you know it is past eleven o'clock?

Twelve, one, two, three, four—any hour——I care not—If you mean me honourably, let me go out of this hated house!

Thou'lt observe, Belford, that though this was written afterwards, yet (as in other places) I write it as it was spoken, and happened; as if I had retired to put down every sentence as spoken. I know thou likest this lively *present-tense* manner, as it is one of my peculiars.

Just as she had repeated the last words, *If you mean me honourably, let me go out of this hated house*, in came Mrs Sinclair, in a great ferment—And what, pray, madam, has *this house* done to you?—Mr Lovelace, you have known me some time; and, if I have not the niceness of this lady, I hope I do not deserve to be treated thus!

She set her huge arms a-kembo: *Hoh!* madam, let me tell you, I am amazed at your freedoms with my character! And, Mr Lovelace (holding up and violently shaking her head), if you are a gentleman, and a man of honour——

Having never before seen anything but obsequiousness in this woman, little as she liked her, she was frighted at her masculine air, and fierce look—God help me! cried she. What will become of me now! Then, turning her head hither and thither, in a wild kind of amaze, Whom have I for a protector! What will become of me now!

I will be your protector, my dearest love!—But indeed you are uncharitably severe upon poor Mrs Sinclair! Indeed you are!—She is a gentlewoman born, and the relic of a man of honour; and though left in such circumstances as oblige her to let lodgings, yet would she scorn to be guilty of a wilful baseness.

I hope so—it may be so—I may be mistaken——But—but there is no crime, I presume, no treason, to say I don't like her house.

The old dragon straddled up to her, with her arms kemboed again—her eyebrows erect, like the bristles upon a hog's back and, scowling over her shortened nose, more than half-hid her ferret eyes. Her mouth was distorted. She pouted out her blubber-lips, as if to bellows up wind and sputter into her horse-nostrils; and her chin was curdled, and more than usually prominent with passion.

With two *Hoh-madams* she accosted the frighted fair one; who, terrified, caught hold of my sleeve.

I feared she would fall into fits; and, with a look of indignation, told Mrs Sinclair that these apartments were mine; and I could not imagine what she meant, either by listening to what passed between me and my spouse, or to come in, uninvited; much less to give herself these violent airs.

I may be to blame, Jack, for suffering this wretch to give herself these airs: but her coming in was without my orders.

The old beldam, throwing herself into a chair, fell a blubbering and exclaiming. And the pacifying of her, and endeavouring to reconcile the lady to her, took up till near one o'clock.

And thus, between terror, and the late hour, and what followed, she was diverted from the thoughts of getting out of the house to Mrs Leeson's, or anywhere else.

Letter 257: MR LOVELACE TO JOHN BELFORD, ESQ.

Tuesday morn. June 13

AND now, Belford, I can go no farther. The affair is over. Clarissa lives. And I am

Your humble servant,
R. LOVELACE

The whole of this black transaction is given by the injured lady to Miss Howe, in her subsequent letters, dated Thursday July 6. To which the reader is referred. [See Letters 312, 313, 314.]

Letter 258: MR BELFORD TO ROBERT LOVELACE, ESQ.

Watford, Wed. June 14

O THOU savage-hearted monster! What work hast thou made in *one guilty hour*, for a *whole age* of repentance!

I am inexpressibly concerned at the fate of this matchless lady! She could not have fallen into the hands of any other man breathing, and suffered as she has done with thee.

I had written a great part of another long letter, to try to soften thy flinty heart in her favour; for I thought it but too likely that thou shouldst succeed in getting her back again to the accursed woman's. But I find it would have been too late, had I finished it and sent it away. Yet cannot I forbear writing, to urge thee to make the *only* amends thou now canst make her, by a proper use of the licence thou hast obtained.

Poor, poor lady! It is a pain to me that I ever saw her. Such an adorer of virtue to be sacrificed to the vilest of her sex; and thou their implement in the devil's hands for a purpose so base, so ungenerous, so inhuman!—Pride thyself, oh cruellest of men, in this reflection; and that thy triumph over a lady, who for thy sake was abandoned of every friend she had in the world, was effected, not by advantages taken of her weakness and credulity; but by the blackest artifice; after a long course of studied deceits had been tried to no purpose.

I can tell thee, it is well either for thee or for me, that I am not the brother of the lady. Had I been her brother, her violation must have been followed by the blood of one of us.

Excuse me, Lovelace; and let not the lady fare the worse for my concern for her. And yet I have but one *other* motive to ask thy excuse; and that is, because I owe to thy own communicative pen the knowledge I have of thy barbarous villainy; since thou mightest, if thou wouldst, have passed it upon me for a common seduction.

CLARISSA LIVES, thou sayest. That she does is my wonder; and these words show that thou thyself (though thou couldst, nevertheless, proceed) hardly expectedst she would have survived the outrage. What must have been the poor lady's distress (watchful as she had been over her honour), when dreadful certainty took place of cruel apprehension!—And yet a man may guess what it must have been, by that which thou paintest, when she suspected herself tricked, deserted, and betrayed, by thy pretended aunt and cousin.

That thou couldst behold her frenzy on this occasion, and her half-speechless, half-fainting prostration at thy feet, and yet retain thy evil purposes, will hardly be thought credible, even by those who know *thee*, if they have seen *her*.

Poor, poor lady! With such noble qualities as would have adorned the most exalted married life, to fall into the hands of the *only* man in the world who could have treated her as thou hast treated her!—And to let loose the old dragon, as thou properly callest her, upon the before-affrighted innocent, what a barbarity was *that!* What a *poor* piece of barbarity! in order to obtain by terror, what thou despairedst to do by love, though supported by stratagems the most insidious!

Oh LOVELACE! LOVELACE! *had I doubted it before, I should now be convinced that there must be a* WORLD AFTER THIS, *to do justice to injured merit, and to punish such a barbarous perfidy!* Could the divine SOCRATES, and the divine CLARISSA, otherwise have suffered?

But let me, if possible, for one moment try to forget this villainous outrage on the most excellent of women.

I have business here, which will hold me yet a few days; and then perhaps I shall quit this house for ever.

I have had a solemn and tedious time of it. I should never have known that I had half the respect I really find I had for the old gentleman, had I not so closely, at his earnest desire, attended him, and been a witness of the tortures he underwent.

This melancholy occasion may possibly have contributed to humanize me: but surely I never could have been so remorseless a caitiff as *thou* hast been, to a woman of *half* this lady's excellence.

But prithee, dear Lovelace, if thou'rt a man and not a devil, resolve out of hand to repair thy sin of ingratitude, by conferring upon thyself the highest honour thou *canst* receive, in making her lawfully thine.

But if thou canst not prevail upon thyself to do her this justice, I think I should not scruple a tilt with thee (an everlasting rupture at least must follow), if thou sacrificest her to the accursed women.

Thou art desirous to know what advantage I reap by my uncle's demise. I do not certainly know; for I have not been so greedily solicitous on this subject, as some of the kindred have been, who ought to have shown more decency, as I have told them, and suffered the corpse to have been cold before they had begun their hungry inquiries. But, by what I gathered from the poor man's talk to me, who oftener than I wished touched upon the subject, I deem it will be upwards of £5000 in cash, and in the funds, after all legacies paid, besides the real estate, which is a clear £500 a year.

I wish from my heart thou wert a money lover! Were the estate to be of double the value, thou shouldst have it every shilling; only upon one condition (for my circumstances before were as easy as I wish them to be while I am single)—that thou wouldst permit me the honour of being this fatherless lady's *father*, as it is called, at the altar.

Think of this, my dear Lovelace: be honest: and let me present thee with the brightest jewel that man ever possessed; and then, body and soul, wilt thou bind to thee for ever, thy

BELFORD

Letter 259: MR LOVELACE TO JOHN BELFORD, ESQ.

Thursday, June 15

LET me alone, you great dog, you!—Let me alone!—have I heard a lesser boy, his coward arms held over his head and face, say to a bigger, who was pummelling him for having run away with his apple, his orange, or his gingerbread.

So say I to thee, on occasion of thy severity to thy poor friend, who, as thou ownest, has furnished thee (ungenerous as thou art!) with the weapons thou brandishest so fearfully against him—And to what purpose, when the mischief is done; when, of consequence, the affair is irretrievable? and when a CLARISSA could not move me?

Well, but after all, I must own that there is something very singular in this lady's case: and at times I cannot help regretting that I ever attempted her; since not one power either of body or soul could be moved in my favour; and since, to use the expression of the philosopher, on a much graver occasion, There is no difference to be found between the skull of king Philip and that of another man.[1]

But people's extravagant notions of things alter not facts, Belford: and, when all's done, Miss Clarissa Harlowe has but run the fate of a thousand others of her sex—only that they did not set such a romantic value upon what they call their *honour*; that's all.

And yet I will allow thee this—That if a person sets a high value upon anything, be it ever such a trifle in itself, or in the eye of others, the robbing of that person of it is *not* a trifle to *him*. Take the matter in this light, I own I have done wrong, great wrong, to this admirable creature.

But have I not known twenty and twenty of the sex, who have seemed to carry their notions of virtue high; yet, when brought to the test, have abated of their severity? And how should we be convinced that *any* of them are proof, till they are tried?

A thousand times have I said that I never yet met with such a woman as this. If I *had*, I hardly ever should have attempted Miss Clarissa Harlowe. Hitherto she is all angel: and was not that the point which at setting out I proposed to try?[a] And was not *cohabitation* ever my darling view? And am I not now, at last, in the high road to it?—It is true, that I have nothing to boast of as to her will. The very contrary. But now are we come to the test, whether she cannot be brought to make the best of an irreparable evil?—If she exclaim (she has reason to exclaim, and I will sit down with patience by the hour together to hear her exclamations, till she is tired of them), she will then descend to expostulation perhaps. Expostulation will give me hope: expostulation will show that she hates me not. And if she hate me not, she will forgive: and if she *now* forgive; then will all be over; and she will be mine upon my own terms: and it shall then be the whole study of my future life to make her happy.

So, Belford, thou seest that I have journeyed on to this stage (indeed, through infinite mazes and as infinite remorses), with one determined point in view from the first. To thy urgent supplication then, that I will do her grateful justice by marriage, let me answer in Matt Prior's two lines on his hoped-for auditorship; as put into the mouths of his St John and Harley:

> —Let that be done, which Matt doth say.
> YEA, quoth the Earl—BUT NOT TODAY.[2]

Thou seest, Jack, that I make no resolutions, however, against doing her, one time or other, the wished-for justice, even were I to succeed in my principal view, *cohabitation*. And of this I do assure thee, that, if I ever marry, it must, it shall, be Miss Clarissa Harlowe—Nor is her honour at all impaired with *me*, by what she has *so far* suffered: but the contrary. She must only take care that, if she be at last brought to forgive me, she show me that her Lovelace is the only man on earth whom she could have forgiven on the like occasion.

But, ah, Jack! what, in the meantime, shall I do with this admirable creature? At present—I am loath to say it—but, at present she is quite stupefied.

I had rather, methinks, she should have retained all her active powers, though I had suffered by her nails and her teeth, than that she should be sunk into such a state of absolute—insensibility (shall I call it?) as she has been in ever since Tuesday morning. Yet, as she begins a little to revive, and now and then to call names and to exclaim, I dread almost to engage with the anguish of a spirit that owes its extraordinary agitations to a niceness that has no example either in ancient or modern story. For, after all, what is there in her case that should *stupefy* such a glowing, such a *blooming* charmer?—Excess of grief, excess of terror, has made

a   See pp. 429–30.

a person's hair stand on end, and even (as we have read) changed the colour of it. But that it should so stupefy, as to make a person at times insensible to those imaginary wrongs, which would raise others *from* stupefaction, is very surprising!

But I will leave this subject, lest it should make me too grave.

I was yesterday at Hampstead, and discharged all obligations there, with no small applause. I told them that the lady was now as happy as myself: and that is no great untruth; for I am not altogether so when I allow myself to *think*.

Mrs Townsend, with her tars, had not been then there. I told them what I would have them say to her, if she come.

Well, but, after all (how many *after-all's* have I?), I could be very grave, were I to give way to it—The devil take me for a fool! What's the matter with me, I wonder!—I must breathe a fresher air for a few days.

But what shall I do with this admirable creature the while?—Hang me, if I know!—For, if I stir, the venomous spider of this habitation will want to set upon the charming fly, whose silken wings are already so entangled in my enormous web that she cannot move hand or foot: for so much has grief stupefied her, that she is at present as destitute of will, as she always seemed of desire. I must not therefore think of leaving her yet for two days together.

Letter 260: MR LOVELACE TO JOHN BELFORD, ESQ.

I HAVE just now had a specimen of what this dear creature's resentment will be when quite recovered: an affecting one!—For, entering her apartment after Dorcas; and endeavouring to soothe and pacify her disordered mind; in the midst of my blandishments, she held up to Heaven, in a speechless agony, the innocent licence (which she has in her own power); as the poor distressed Catalans held up their English treaty,[1] on an occasion that keeps the worst of my actions in countenance.

She seemed about to call down vengeance upon me; when, happily, the leaden god in pity to her trembling Lovelace waved over her half-drowned eyes his somniferous wand, and laid asleep the fair exclaimer before she could go half through with her intended imprecation.

Thou wilt guess, by what I have written, that some *little* art has been made use of; but it was with a *generous* design (if thou'lt allow me the word on such an occasion) in order to lessen the too quick sense she was likely to have of what she was to suffer. A contrivance I never had occasion for before, and had not thought of now if Mrs Sinclair had not proposed it to me: to whom I left the management of it: and I have done nothing but curse her ever since, lest the quantity should have for ever damped her charming intellects.

Hence my concern—for I think the poor lady ought not to have been so treated. *Poor lady*, did I say?—What have I to do with thy creeping style?—But have not I the worst of it; since her insensibility has made me but a thief to my own joys?

I did not intend to tell thee of this little *innocent* trick; for such I designed it to be; but that I hate disingenuity: to thee especially: and as I cannot help writing in a more serious vein than usual, thou wouldst, perhaps, had I not hinted the true cause, have imagined that I was sorry for the fact itself: and this would have given *thee* a good deal of trouble in scribbling dull persuasives to repair by matrimony; and *me*, in reading thy crude nonsense. Besides, one day or other, thou mightest, had I not confessed it, have heard of it in an aggravated manner; and I know thou hast such an high opinion of this lady's virtue, that thou wouldst be disappointed if thou hadst reason to think that she was subdued by *her own* consent, or any the *least* yielding in her will. And so is she beholden to me in some measure, that at the expense of *my* honour she may so justly form a plea, which will entirely salve *hers?*

And now is the whole secret out.

Thou wilt say I am a horrid fellow!—as the lady does that I am the *unchained Beelzebub*, and a *plotting villain:* and as this is what you both said beforehand, and nothing worse *can* be said, I desire, if thou wouldst not have me quite serious with thee, and that I should think thou meanest more by thy tilting-hint than I am willing to believe thou dost, that thou wilt forbear thy invectives: for is not the thing done?—Can it be helped?—And must I not now try to make the best of it?—And the rather do I enjoin thee this, and inviolable secrecy; because I begin to think that my punishment will be greater than the fault, were it to be only from my own reflection.

Letter 261: MR LOVELACE TO JOHN BELFORD, ESQ.

Friday, June 16

I AM sorry to hear of thy misfortune; but hope thou wilt not long lie by it. Thy servant tells me what a narrow escape thou hadst with thy neck. I wish it may not be ominous: but I think thou seemest not to be in so enterprising a way as formerly; and yet, merry or sad, thou seest a rake's neck is always in danger, if not from the hangman, from his own horse. But 'tis a vicious toad, it seems; and I think thou shouldst never venture upon his back again; for 'tis a plaguy thing for rider and horse both to be vicious.

Thy fellow tells me thou desirest me to continue to write to thee, to *divert* thy chagrin on thy forced confinement: but how can I think it in my *power* to divert, when my subject is not pleasing to myself?

Caesar never knew what it was to be *hypped*, I will call it, till he came to be what Pompey was; that is to say, till he arrived at the height of his ambition: nor did thy Lovelace know what it was to be gloomy, till he had completed his wishes upon the charmingest creature in the world, as the other did his upon the most potent republic that ever existed.

And yet why say I, *completed?* when the *will*, the *consent*, is wanting—and I have still views before me of obtaining that?

Yet I could almost join with thee in the wish, which thou sendest me up by thy servant, unfriendly as it is, that I had had thy misfortune before Monday night last: for here the poor lady has run into a contrary extreme to that I told thee of in my last: for now is she as much too lively, as before she was too stupid; and, 'bating that she has pretty frequent lucid intervals, would be deemed raving mad, and I should be obliged to confine her.

I am most confoundedly disturbed about it: for I begin to fear that her intellects are irreparably hurt.

Who the devil could have expected such strange effects from a cause so common, and so slight?

But these high-souled and high-sensed girls, who had set up for shining lights and examples to the rest of the sex (I now see that such there are!) are with such difficulty brought down to the common standard, that a wise man, who prefers his peace of mind to his glory in subduing one of that exalted class, would have nothing to say to them.

I do all in my power to quiet her spirits, when I force myself into her presence.

I go on, begging pardon one minute; and vowing truth and honour another.

I would at first have persuaded her, and offered to call witnesses to the truth of it, that we were actually married. Though the licence was in her hands, I thought the assertion might go down in her disorder; and charming consequences I hoped would follow. But this would not do—

I therefore gave up that hope: and now I declare to her that it is my resolution to marry her the moment her uncle Harlowe informs me that he will grace the ceremony with his presence.

But she believes nothing I say; nor (whether in her senses or not) bears me with patience in her sight.

I pity her with all my soul; and I curse myself, when she is in her wailing fits, and when I apprehend that intellects so charming as hers are for ever damped—But more I curse these women who put me upon such an expedient!—Lord! Lord! what a hand have I made of it!—And all for what?

Last night, for the first time since Monday last, she got to her pen and ink: but she pursues her writing with such eagerness and hurry, as show too evidently her discomposure.

I hope, however, that this employment will help to calm her spirits.

JUST now Dorcas tells me that what she writes she tears, and throws the paper in fragments under the table, either as not knowing what she does, or disliking it: then gets up, wrings her hands, weeps, and shifts her seat all round the room: then returns to her table, sits down, and writes again.

ONE odd letter, as I may call it, Dorcas has this moment given me from her— *Carry this*, said she, *to the vilest of men.* Dorcas, a toad! brought it, without any further direction, to *me*—I sat down, intending (though 'tis pretty long) to give thee a copy of it: but, for my life, I cannot; 'tis so extravagant. And the original is too much an original to let it go out of my hands.

But some of the scraps and fragments, as either torn through, or flung aside, I will copy for the novelty of the thing, and to show thee how her mind works now she is in this whimsical way. Yet I know I am still furnishing thee with new weapons against myself. But spare thy comments. My own reflections render them needless. Dorcas thinks her lady will ask for them: so wishes to have them to lay again under her table.

By the first thou'lt guess that I have told her that Miss Howe is very ill, and can't write; that she may account the better for not having received the letter designed for her.

PAPER I
(Torn in two pieces)

My dearest Miss Howe!

OH! What dreadful, dreadful things have I to tell you!

But yet I cannot tell you neither. But say, are you really ill, as a vile, vile creature informs me you are?

But he never yet told me truth, and I hope has not in this: and yet, if it were not true, surely I should have heard from you before now!—But what have I to do, to upbraid?—You may well be tired of me!—And if you are, I can forgive you; for I am tired of myself: and all my own relations were tired of me long before you were.

How good you have always been to me, mine own dear Anna Howe!—But how I ramble!

I sat down to say a great deal—my heart was full—I did not know what to say first—and thought, and grief, and confusion, and (Oh my poor head!) I cannot tell what—And thought, and grief, and confusion came crowding so thick upon me; *one* would be first, *another* would be first, *all* would be first; so I can write nothing at all—only that, whatever they have done to me, I cannot tell; but I am no longer what I was in any one thing.—In any one thing did I say? Yes, but I am; for I am still, and I ever will be,

Your true—

Plague on it! I can write no more of this eloquent nonsense myself; which rather shows a raised, than a quenched, imagination: but Dorcas shall transcribe the others in separate papers, as written by the whimsical charmer: and some time hence, when all is over, and I can better bear to read them, I may ask thee for a sight of them. Preserve them therefore; for we often look back with pleasure even upon the heaviest griefs, when the cause of them is removed.

PAPER II
(Scratched through, and thrown under the table)

—AND can you, my dear honoured papa, resolve for ever to reprobate your poor child?—But I am sure you would not, if you knew what she has suffered since her unhappy—And will nobody plead for your poor suffering girl?—No one good body?—Why, then, dearest sir, let it be an act of your own innate goodness, which I have so much experienced, and so much abused—I don't presume to think you should receive me—no, indeed—my name is—I don't know what my name is!—I never dare to wish to come into your family again!—But your heavy curse, my papa—Yes, I *will* call you papa, and help yourself as you can—for you are my own dear papa, whether you will or not—And though I am an unworthy child—yet I *am* your child—

PAPER III

A LADY took a great fancy to a young lion, or a bear, I forget which—but a bear, or a tiger, I believe, it was. It was made her a present of when a whelp. She fed it with her own hand: she nursed up the wicked cub with great tenderness; and would play with it, without fear or apprehension of danger: and it was obedient to all her commands: and its tameness, as she used to boast, increased with its growth; so that, like a lap-dog, it would follow her all over the house. But mind what followed. At last, somehow, neglecting to satisfy its hungry maw, or having otherwise disobliged it on some occasion, it resumed its nature; and on a sudden fell upon her, and tore her in pieces—And who was most to blame, I pray? The brute, or the lady? The lady, surely!—For what *she* did, was *out* of nature, *out* of character at least: what *it* did, was *in* its own nature.

PAPER IV

How art thou now humbled in the dust, thou proud Clarissa Harlowe! Thou that never steppedst out of thy father's house, but to be admired! Who wert wont to turn thine eye, sparkling with healthful life, and self-assurance, to different objects at once, as thou passedst, as if (for so thy penetrating sister used to say) to plume thyself upon the expected applauses of all that beheld thee! Thou that usedst to go to rest satisfied with the adulations paid thee in the past day, and couldst put off everything but thy vanity!—

PAPER V

REJOICE not now, my Bella, my sister, my friend; but pity the humbled creature, whose foolish heart you used to say you beheld through the thin veil of humility, which covered it.

It must have been so! My fall had not else been permitted—

You penetrated my proud heart with the jealousy of an elder sister's searching eye.

You knew me better than I knew myself.

Hence your upbraidings, and your chidings, when I began to totter.

But forgive now those vain triumphs of my heart.

I thought, poor proud wretch that I was, that what you said was owing to your envy.

I thought I could acquit my intention of any such vanity.

I was too secure in the knowledge I thought I had of my own heart.

My supposed advantages became a snare to me.

And what now is the end of all?—

PAPER VI

WHAT now is become of the prospects of a happy life, which once I thought opening before me?—Who now shall assist in the solemn preparations? Who now shall provide the nuptial ornaments, which soften and divert the apprehensions of the fearful virgin? No court now to be paid to my smiles! No encouraging compliments to inspire thee with hope of laying a mind not unworthy of thee under obligation! No elevation now for conscious merit, and applauded purity, to look down from on a prostrate adorer, and an admiring world, and up to pleased and rejoicing parents and relations!

PAPER VII

THOU pernicious caterpillar, that preyest upon the fair leaf of virgin fame, and poisonest those leaves which thou canst not devour!

Thou fell blight, thou eastern blast, thou overspreading mildew, that destroyest the early promises of the shining year! that mockest the laborious toil, and blastest the joyful hopes, of the painful husbandman!

Thou fretting moth that corruptest the fairest garment!

Thou eating canker-worm that preyest upon the opening bud, and turnest the damask rose into livid yellowness!

If, as religion teaches us, God will judge us in a great measure by our benevolent or evil actions to one another—Oh wretch! bethink thee, in time bethink thee, how great must be thy condemnation!

PAPER VIII

AT first I saw something in your air and person that displeased me not. Your birth and fortunes were no small advantages to you—You acted not ignobly by my passionate brother. Everybody said you were brave: everybody said you were generous. A *brave* man, I thought, could not be a *base* man: a *generous* man could not, I believed, be *ungenerous* where he acknowledged *obligation*. Thus prepossessed, all the rest that my soul loved and wished for in your reformation, I hoped!—I knew not, but by report, any flagrant instances of your vileness. You seemed frank, as well as generous: frankness and generosity ever attracted me: whoever kept up those appearances, I judged of their hearts by my own; and whatever qualities *I wished* to find in them, I was *ready* to find; and, *when* found, I believed them to be natives of the soil.

My fortunes, my rank, my character, I thought a further security. I was in none of those respects unworthy of being the niece of Lord M. and of his two noble sisters—Your vows, your imprecations—But, oh! you have barbarously and basely conspired against that honour, which you ought to have protected: and now you have made me—what is it of vile that you have *not* made me?—

Yet, God knows my heart, I had no culpable inclinations!—I honoured virtue!—I hated vice!—But I knew not that you were vice itself!

PAPER IX

HAD the happiness of any the poorest outcast in the world, whom I had never seen, never known, never before heard of, lain as much in *my* power as my happiness did in *yours*, my benevolent heart would have made me fly to the succour of such a poor distressed—With what pleasure would I have raised the dejected head, and comforted the desponding heart!—But who now shall pity the poor wretch who has increased, instead of diminished, the number of the miserable!

PAPER X[1]

LEAD me, where my own thoughts themselves may lose me;
Where I may doze out what I've left of life,
Forget myself; and that day's guilt!—
Cruel remembrance!—how shall I appease thee?

  —Oh! you have done an act
That blots the face and blush of modesty;
    Takes off the rose
From the fair forehead of an innocent love,
And makes a blister there!—

    Then down I laid my head,
Down on cold earth, and for a while was dead;
And my freed soul to a strange somewhere fled!
    Ah! sottish soul! said I,
When back to its cage again I saw it fly,
    Fool! to resume her broken chain,
    And row the galley here again!
    Fool! to that body to return,
Where it condemn'd and destin'd is to *mourn*.

Oh my Miss Howe! if thou hast friendship, help me,
And speak the words of peace to my divided soul,
    That wars within me,
And raises ev'ry sense to my confusion.
    I'm tott'ring on the brink
Of peace; and thou art all the hold I've left!
Assist me in the pangs of my affliction!

When honour's lost, 'tis a relief to die:
Death's but a sure retreat from infamy.

    Then farewel, youth,
      And all the joys that dwell
    With youth and life!
      And life itself, farewel!

For life can never be sincerely blest.
Heaven punishes the *Bad*, and proves the *Best*.

Death only can be dreadful to the bad:
To innocence 'tis like a bugbear dress'd
To frighten children. Pull but off the mask
And he'll appear a friend.

I could a tale unfold—
Would harrow up thy soul!—

By swift misfortunes
How am I pursu'd!
Which on each other are,
Like waves, renew'd!

AFTER all, Belford, I have just skimmed over these transcriptions of Dorcas; and I see there is method and good sense in some of them, wild as others of them are; and that her memory, which serves her so well for these poetical flights, is far from being impaired. And this gives me hope that she will soon recover her charming intellects—though I shall be the sufferer by their restoration, I make no doubt.

But, in the letter she wrote to me, there are yet greater extravagancies; and though I said it was too affecting to give thee a copy of it, yet, after I have let thee see the loose papers enclosed, I think I may throw in a transcription of that. Dorcas, therefore, shall here transcribe it: *I* cannot. The reading of it affected me ten times more than the severest reproaches of a regular mind.

[*Letter 261.1: Clarissa Harlowe*] *to Mr Lovelace*

I NEVER intended to write another line to you. I would not see you, if I could help it. Oh that I never had!

But tell me of a truth, is Miss Howe really and truly ill?—very ill?—and is not her illness poison? And don't *you* know who gave it her?—

What you, or Mrs Sinclair, or somebody I cannot tell who, have done to my poor head, you best know: but I shall never be what I was. My head is gone. I have wept away all my brain, I believe; for I can weep no more. Indeed I have had my full share; so it is no matter.

But, good now, Lovelace, don't set Mrs Sinclair upon me again! I never did her any harm. She *so* affrights me when I see her!—Ever since—when was it? I cannot tell. *You* can, I suppose. She may be a good woman, as far as I know. She was the wife of a man of honour—very likely!—though forced to let lodgings for her livelihood. Poor gentlewoman! Let her know I pity her: but don't let her come near me again—pray don't!

Yet she may be a very good woman—

What would I say!—I forget what I was going to say.

Oh Lovelace, you are Satan himself; or he helps you out in everything; and that's as bad!

But have you really and truly sold yourself to him? And for how long? What duration is your reign to have?

Poor man! The contract *will* be out; and then what will be your fate!

Oh! Lovelace! if you could be sorry for yourself, I would be sorry too—but when all my doors are fast, and nothing but the key-hole open, and the key of late put into that, to be where you are, in a manner without opening any of them—Oh wretched, wretched Clarissa Harlowe!

For I never will be Lovelace—let my uncle take it as he pleases.

Well, but now I remember what I was going to say—It is for *your* good—not *mine*—for nothing can do me good now!—Oh thou villainous man! thou hated Lovelace!

But Mrs Sinclair may be a good woman—If you love me—but that you don't—but don't let her bluster up with her worse than mannish airs to me again! Oh she is a frightful woman! If she *be* a woman!—She needed not to put on that *fearful mask* to scare me out of my poor wits. But don't tell her what I say—I have no hatred to her—It is only fright, and foolish fear, that's all—She may not *be* a bad woman—but neither are all *men*, any more than all *women*, alike—God forbid they should be like you!

Alas! you have killed my head among you—I don't say who did it—God forgive you all!—But had it not been better to have put me out of all your ways at once? You might safely have done it! For nobody would require me at your hands—no, not a soul—except, indeed, Miss Howe would have said, when she should see you, what, Lovelace, have you done with Clarissa Harlowe?—And then you could have given any slight gay answer—Sent her beyond sea; or, she has run away from me as she did from her parents. And this would have been easily credited; for you know, Lovelace, she that could run away from *them*, might very well run away from *you*.

But this is nothing to what I wanted to say. Now I have it!

I have lost it again—This foolish wench comes teasing me—For what purpose should I eat? For what end should I wish to live?—I tell thee, Dorcas, I will neither eat nor drink. I cannot be worse than I am.

I will do as you'd have me—Good Dorcas, look not upon me so fiercely—But thou canst not look so bad as I have seen somebody look.

Mr Lovelace, now that I remember what I took pen in hand to say, let me hurry off my thoughts, lest I lose them again—Here I am sensible—And yet I am hardly sensible neither—But I know my head is not as it should be, for all that—Therefore let me propose one thing to you: it is for *your* good—not *mine:* and this is it:

I must needs be both a trouble and an expense to you. And here my uncle Harlowe, when he knows how I am, will never wish any man to have me: no, not even *you*, who have been the occasion of it—Barbarous and ungrateful!—A less complicated villainy cost a Tarquin[2]—but I forget what I would say again—

Then this is it: I never shall be myself again: I have been a very wicked creature—a vain, proud, poor creature—full of secret pride—which I carried off under an humble guise, and deceived everybody—My sister says so—and now I am punished—so let me be carried out of this house, and out of your sight; and let me be put into that Bedlam privately, which once I saw: but it was a sad sight to me then! Little as I thought what I should come to *myself!*—That is all I would say: this is all I have to wish for—then I shall be out of all your ways; and I shall be taken care of; and bread and water, without your tormentings, will be dainties; and my straw bed the easiest I have lain in—for—I cannot tell how long!—

My clothes will sell for what will keep me there, perhaps, as long as I shall live. But, Lovelace, *dear* Lovelace I will call you; for you have cost me enough, I'm sure!—don't let me be made a show of, for my *family*'s sake; nay, for your *own sake*, don't do that—For when I know all I have suffered, which yet I do not, and no matter if I never do—I may be apt to rave against you by name, and tell of all your baseness to a poor humbled creature, that once was as proud as anybody—but of what I can't tell—except of my own folly and vanity—but let that pass—since I am punished enough for it—

So, suppose, instead of Bedlam, it were a private madhouse where nobody comes!—That will be better a great deal.

But, another thing, Lovelace: don't let them use me cruelly when I am there—*You* have used me cruelly enough, you know! Don't let them use me cruelly; for I will be very tractable; and do as anybody would have me do—except what you would have me do—for that I never will.—Another thing, Lovelace: don't let this *good* woman; I was going to say *vile* woman; but don't tell her that—because she won't let you send me to this happy refuge perhaps, if she were to know it—

Another thing, Lovelace: and let me have pen, and ink, and paper, allowed me—It will be all my amusement—But they need not send to anybody I shall write to, what I write, because it will but trouble them: and somebody may do you a mischief, maybe—I wish not that anybody do anybody a mischief upon my account.

You tell me that Lady Betty Lawrance and your cousin Montague were here to take leave of me; but that I was asleep, and could not be waked. So you told me at first, I was married, you know; and that you were my husband—Ah! Lovelace! look to what you say—But let not them (for they will sport with my misery), let not *that* Lady Betty, let not *that* Miss Montague, whatever the *real* ones may do; nor Mrs Sinclair neither, nor any of her lodgers, nor her nieces, come to see me in my place—*Real* ones, I say; for, Lovelace, I shall find out all your villainies in time—indeed I shall—so put me there as soon as you can—It is for *your* good—Then all will pass for ravings that I can say, as, I doubt not, many poor creatures' exclamations do pass, though there may be too much truth in them for all that—and you know *I began to be mad at Hampstead*—so you said—Ah! villainous man! what have you not to answer for!

A little interval seems to be lent me. I had begun to look over what I have written. It is not fit for anyone to see, so far as I have been able to re-peruse it: but my head will not hold, I doubt, to go through it all. If therefore I have not already mentioned my earnest desire, let me tell you, it is this: that I be sent out of this abominable house without delay, and locked up in some private madhouse about this town; for such, it seems, there are; never more to be seen, or to be produced to anybody, except in your own vindication, if you should be charged with the murder of my person; a much lighter crime than that of my honour, which the greatest villain on earth has robbed me of. And deny me not this my last request, I beseech you; and one other, and that is, never to let me see you more! This surely may be granted to

> The miserably abused
> CLARISSA HARLOWE

I WILL not hear thy heavy preachments upon this plaguy letter. So, not a word of that sort! The paper, thou'lt see, is blistered with the tears even of the hardened transcriber; which has made her ink run here and there.

Mrs Sinclair is a true heroine and, I think, shames us all. And she is a *woman* too! Thou'lt say the best things corrupted become the worst. But this is certain, that whatever the sex set their hearts upon, they make thorough work of it. And hence it is, that a mischief which would end in simple robbery among men-rogues, becomes murder if a woman be in it.

I know thou wilt blame me for having had recourse to *art*. But do not physicians prescribe opiates in acute cases, where the violence of the disorder would be apt to throw the patient into a fever or delirium? I aver that my motive for this expedient was *mercy*; nor could it be anything else. For a rape, thou knowest, to us rakes is far from being an undesirable thing. Nothing but the law stands in our way, upon that account; and the opinion of what a modest woman will suffer, rather than become a *viva voce* accuser, lessens much an honest fellow's apprehensions on that score. Then, if these *somnivolences* (I hate the word *opiates* on this occasion) have turned her head, that is an effect they frequently have upon some constitutions; and in this case was rather the fault of the dose, than the design of the giver.

But is not wine itself an opiate in degree?—How many women have been taken advantage of by wine, and other still more intoxicating viands?—Let me tell thee, Jack, that the *experience* of many of the *passive* sex, and the *consciences* of many more of the *active*, appealed to, will testify that thy Lovelace is not the worst of villains. Nor would I have *thee* put me upon clearing myself, by comparisons.

If she escape a settled delirium when my plots unravel, I think it is all I ought to be concerned about. What therefore I desire of thee is, that if two constructions may be made of my actions, thou wilt afford me the most favourable. For this, not only friendship, but my own ingenuity, which has furnished thee with the knowledge of the facts against which thou art so ready to inveigh, require of thee.

WILL is just returned from an errand to Hampstead; and acquaints me that Mrs Townsend was yesterday at Mrs Moore's, accompanied by three or four rough fellows. She was strangely surprised at the news that my spouse and I are entirely reconciled; and that two fine ladies, my relations, came to visit her, and went to town with her: where she is very happy with me. *She* was sure we were not married, she said, unless it was while we were at Hampstead: and *they* were sure the ceremony was not performed there. But that the lady *is* happy and easy is unquestionable: and a fling was thrown out by Mrs Moore and Mrs Bevis at *mischief-makers*, as they knew Mrs Townsend to be acquainted with Miss Howe.

Now, since my fair one can neither receive nor send away letters, I am pretty easy as to this Mrs Townsend and her employer. And I fancy Miss Howe will be puzzled to know what to think of the matter, and afraid of sending by Wilson's conveyance; and perhaps suppose that her friend slights her; or has changed her mind in my favour, and is ashamed to own it; as she has not had an answer to what she wrote; and will believe that the rustic delivered her last letter into her own hand.

Meantime, I have a little project come into my head, of a *new* kind; just for amusement sake, that's all: variety has irresistible charms. I cannot live without intrigue. My charmer has no passions; that is to say, none of the passions that I want her to have. She engages all my reverence. I am at present more inclined to regret what I have done, than to proceed to new offences: and shall regret it till I see how she takes it, when recovered.

Shall I tell thee my project? 'Tis not a high one—'Tis this—to get hither Mrs Moore, Miss Rawlins, and my Widow Bevis; for they are desirous to make a visit to my spouse, now we are so happy together. And, if I can order it right, Belton, Mowbray, Tourville, and I, will show them a little more of the ways of this wicked town than they at present know. Why should they be *acquainted* with a man of my character, and not be the *better* and *wiser* for it?—I would have everybody rail against rakes with *judgement* and *knowledge*, if they *will* rail. Two of these women gave me a great deal of trouble: and the third, I am confident, will forgive a merry evening.

I am really sick at heart for a frolic, and have no doubt but this will be an agreeable one. These women already think me a wild fellow; *nor do they like me the less for it*, as I can perceive; and I shall take care that they shall be treated with so much freedom before one another's faces, that in policy they shall keep each other's counsel. And won't this be doing a kind thing by them? since it will knit an indissoluble band of union and friendship between three women who are neighbours, and at present have only *common* obligations to one another: for thou wantest not to be told that secrets of love, and secrets of this nature, are generally the strongest cement of female friendships.

But, after all, if my beloved should be happily restored to her intellects, we may have scenes arise between us, that will be sufficiently busy to employ all the faculties of thy friend, without looking out for new occasions. Already, as I have often observed, has she been the means of saving scores; yet without her own knowledge.

Sat. night

BY Dorcas's account of her lady's behaviour, the dear creature seems to be recovering. I shall give the earliest notice of this to the worthy Captain Tomlinson, that he may apprise uncle John of it. I must be properly enabled from that quarter, to pacify her, or, at least, to rebate her first violence.

Letter 262: MR LOVELACE TO JOHN BELFORD, ESQ.

Sunday afternoon, 6 o'clock (June 18)

I WENT out early this morning, and returned not till just now; when I was informed that my beloved, in my absence, had taken it into her head to attempt to get away.

She tripped down with a parcel tied up in a handkerchief, her hood on; and was actually in the entry, when Mrs Sinclair saw her.

Pray, madam, whipping between her and the street door, be pleased to let me know whither you are going?

Who has a right to control me? was the word.

I have, madam, by order of your spouse: And, kemboing her arms, as she owned, I desire you will be pleased to walk up again.

She would have spoken; but could not: and bursting into tears, turned back and went up to her chamber: and Dorcas was taken to task for suffering her to be in the passage before she was seen.

This shows, as we hoped last night, that she is recovering her charming intellects.

Dorcas says she was visible to her, but once before, the whole day; and then seemed very solemn and sedate.

I will endeavour to see her. It must be in her own chamber, I suppose; for she will hardly meet me in the dining-room. What advantage will the confidence of our sex give me over the modesty of hers, if she be recovered!—*I*, the most confident of men: *she*, the most delicate of women. Sweet soul! methinks I have her before me: her face averted: speech lost in sighs—abashed—conscious—What a triumphant aspect will this give me, when I gaze in her downcast countenance!

THIS moment Dorcas tells me she believes she is coming to find me out. She asked her after me: and Dorcas left her drying her red-swollen eyes at her glass (no design of moving me by her tears!); sighing too sensibly for my courage. But to what purpose have I gone thus far, if I pursue not my principal end?—Niceness must be a little abated. She knows the worst. That she cannot fly me; that she must see me; and that I can look her into a sweet confusion; are circumstances greatly in my favour. What can she do, but rave and exclaim? I am used to raving and exclaiming—but, if recovered, I shall see how she behaves upon this our first sensible interview after what she has suffered.

Here she comes!—

Letter 263: MR LOVELACE TO JOHN BELFORD, ESQ.

Sunday night

NEVER blame me for giving way to have art used with this admirable creature. All the princes of the air, or beneath it, joining with me, could never have subdued her while she had her senses.

I will not anticipate—only to tell thee that I am too much awakened by her to think of sleep, were I to go to bed; and so shall have nothing to do, but to write an account of our odd conversation, while it is so strong upon my mind that I can think of nothing else.

She was dressed in a white damask night-gown, with less negligence than for some days past. I was sitting, with my pen in my fingers; and stood up when I first saw her, with great complaisance, as if the day were still her own. And so indeed it is.

She entered with such dignity in her manner, as struck me with great awe, and prepared me for the poor figure I made in the subsequent conversation. A poor figure indeed!—but I will do her justice.

She came up with quick steps, pretty close to me; a white handkerchief in her hand; her eyes neither fierce nor mild, but very earnest; and a fixed sedateness in her whole aspect, which seemed to be the effect of deep contemplation: and thus she accosted me, with an air and action that I never saw equalled.

You see before you, sir, the wretch whose preference of you to all your sex you have rewarded—as it indeed deserved to be rewarded. My father's dreadful curse has already operated upon me in the very letter of it as to this life; and it seems to me too evident that it will not be your fault that it is not entirely completed in the loss of my soul, as well as of my honour—which you, villainous man! have robbed me of, with a baseness so unnatural, so inhuman, that it seems, you, even *you*, had not the heart to attempt it, till my senses were made the previous sacrifice.

Here I made an hesitating effort to speak, laying down my pen—but she proceeded. Hear me out, guilty wretch!—abandoned man!—*Man* did I say?—Yet what name else can I? since the mortal worryings of the fiercest beast would have been more natural, and infinitely more welcome, than what you have acted by me; and that with a premeditation and contrivance worthy only of that single heart, which now, *base* as well as ungrateful as thou art, seems to quake within thee— And well mayest thou quake; well mayest thou tremble and falter; and hesitate as thou dost, when thou reflectest upon what I have suffered for thy sake, and the returns thou hast made me!

By my soul, Belford, my whole frame was shaken: for not only her looks, and her action, but her voice, so solemn, was inexpressibly affecting: and then my cursed guilt, and her innocence and merit, and rank, and superiority of talents, all stared me at that instant in the face so formidably, that my present account, to which she unexpectedly called me, seemed, as I then thought, to resemble that general one to which we are told we shall be summoned, when our conscience shall be our accuser.

But she had had time to collect all the powers of her eloquence. The whole day probably in her intellects. And then I was the more disappointed, as I had thought I could have gazed the dear creature into confusion—but it is plain that the sense she has of her wrongs sets this matchless woman *above all lesser, all weaker* considerations.

My dear—my love—I—I—I never—no never—lips trembling, limbs quaking, voice inward, hesitating, broken—Never surely did miscreant look so *like* a miscreant! While thus she proceeded, waving her snowy hand, with all the graces of moving oratory.

I have no pride in the confusion visible in thy whole person. I have been all the day praying for a composure, if I could not escape from this vile house, that should once more enable me to look up to my destroyer with the consciousness of an innocent sufferer—Thou seest me, since my wrongs are beyond the power of *words to express*, thou seest me *calm enough* to wish that thou mayest continue harassed by the workings of thy own conscience, till effectual repentance take hold of thee, that so thou mayest not forfeit all title to *that* mercy which thou hast not shown to the poor creature now before thee, who had so well deserved to meet with a faithful friend, where she met with the worst of enemies.

But tell me (for no doubt thou hast *some* scheme to pursue), tell me, since I am a prisoner as I find, in the vilest of houses, and have not a friend to protect or save me, what thou intendest shall become of the remnant of a life not worth the keeping? Tell me if yet there are more evils reserved for me; and whether thou hast entered into a compact with the grand deceiver, in the person of his horrid agent in this house; and if the ruin of my soul, that my father's curse may be fulfilled, is to complete the triumphs of so vile a confederacy?—Answer me!—Say, if thou hast courage to speak out to her whom thou hast ruined, tell me what *further* I am to suffer from thy barbarity?

She stopped here; and, sighing, turned her sweet face from me, drying up with her handkerchief those tears which she endeavoured to restrain; and, when she could not, to conceal from my sight.

As I told thee, I had prepared myself for high passions, raving, flying, tearing, execration: these transient violences, the workings of sudden grief and shame, and vengeance, would have set us upon a par with each other, and quitted scores. These have I been accustomed to; and, as nothing violent is lasting, with these I could have wished to encounter. But such a majestic composure—seeking me— whom yet, it is plain by her attempt to get away, she would have avoided seeing— No Lucretia-like vengeance[1] upon herself in her thought—yet swallowed up, her whole mind swallowed up, as I may say, by a grief so heavy, as, in her own words, to be beyond the power of speech to express—and to be able, discomposed as she was to the very morning, to put such a home question to me, as if she had penetrated my future view—How could I avoid looking like a fool, and answering as before, in broken sentences, and confusion?

What—what-a—what—has been done—I, I, I—cannot but say—must own—must confess—hem—hem—is not right—is not what should have been—But-a—but—but—I am truly—truly—sorry for it—Upon my soul I am—And —and—will do all—do everything—do what—whatever is incumbent upon me—all that you—that you—that you shall require, to make you amends!——

Oh Belford! Belford! whose the triumph now!—HERS, or MINE?

Amends! Oh thou truly despicable wretch!—Then, lifting up her eyes—Good Heaven! who shall pity the creature who could fall by so base a mind!—Yet—and then she looked indignantly upon me—yet, I hate thee not, base and low-souled as thou art! half so much as I hate myself, that I saw thee not sooner in thy proper colours!—that I hoped either morality, gratitude, or humanity from a libertine, who, to *be* a libertine, must have got over and defied all moral sanctions.[a]

She then called upon her cousin Morden's name, as if he had warned her against a man of free principles; and walked towards the window; her handkerchief at her eyes: but, turning short towards me, with an air of mingled scorn and majesty (*What, at the moment, would I have given never to have injured her!*)—What amends hast *thou* to propose!—What amends can such a one as thou make to a person of spirit or common sense, for the evils thou hast so inhumanly made me suffer?

As soon, madam—as soon—as—as soon as your uncle—or—not waiting——

Thou wouldst tell me, I suppose—I know what thou wouldst tell me—but thinkest thou that marriage will satisfy for a guilt like thine? Destitute as thou hast made me both of friends and fortune, I too much despise the wretch *who could rob himself of his wife's virtue*, to endure the thoughts of thee in the light thou seemest to hope I will accept thee in!—

I hesitated an interruption: but my meaning died away upon my trembling lips. I could only pronounce the word *marriage*—and thus she proceeded:

Let me therefore know whether I am to be controlled in the future disposal of myself? Whether, in a country of liberty as *this*, where the sovereign of it must not be guilty of *your* wickedness; and where *you* neither durst have attempted it, had I one friend or relation to look upon me, I am to be kept here a prisoner, to sustain fresh injuries? Whether, in a word, you intend to hinder me from going whither my destiny shall lead me?

After a pause; for I was still silent:

Can you not answer me this plain question?—I quit all claim, all expectation upon you—what right have you to detain me here?

I could not speak. What could I say to such a question?

Oh wretch! wringing her uplifted hands, had I not been robbed of my senses, and that in the *basest* manner—you best know how—had I been able to account for myself, and your proceedings, or to have known but how the days passed; a whole week should not have gone over my head, as I find it has done, before I had told you what I now tell you—*That the man who has been the villain to me you have been, shall never make me his wife.* I will write to my uncle to lay aside his kind intentions in my favour—All my prospects are shut in—I give myself up for a lost creature as to this world—Hinder me not from entering upon a life of severe penitence, for corresponding, after prohibition, with a wretch who has too well justified all their warnings and inveteracy; and for throwing myself into the power

---

a   Her cousin Morden's words to her in his letter from Florence. See p. 564.

of your vile artifices—Let me try to secure the only hope I have left—This is all the amends I ask of you. I repeat, therefore, Am I *now* at liberty to dispose of myself as I please?

Now comes the fool, the miscreant again, hesitating his broken answer: My dearest love, I am confounded, quite confounded, at the thought of what—of what has been done; and at the thought of—to whom. I see, I see, there is no withstanding your eloquence!—Such irresistible proofs of the love of virtue for its own sake—did I never hear of, nor meet with in all my reading. And if you can forgive a repentant villain, that thus on his knees implores your forgiveness (then down I dropped, absolutely in earnest in all I said), I vow by all that's sacred and just (and may a thunderbolt strike me dead at your feet, if I am not sincere!), that I will by marriage, before tomorrow noon, without waiting for your uncle, or anybody, do you all the justice I now *can* do you. And you shall ever after control and direct me as you please; till you have made me more worthy of your angelic purity than now I am: nor will I presume so much as to touch your garment till I have the honour to call so great a blessing lawfully mine.

Oh thou guileful betrayer! There is a just God, whom thou invokest: yet the thunderbolt descends not; and thou livest to imprecate and deceive!

My dearest life! rising; for I hoped she was relenting——

Hadst thou not sinned beyond the *possibility* of forgiveness, interrupted she; and had this been the first time that thus thou solemnly promisest and invokest the vengeance thou hast as often defied; the desperateness of my condition might have induced me to think of taking a wretched chance with a man so profligate. But, *after what I have suffered by thee*, it would be *criminal* in me to wish to bind my soul in covenant to a man so nearly allied to perdition.

Good God!—how uncharitable!—I offer not to defend—Would to Heaven that I could recall—*so nearly allied to perdition*, madam!—so *profligate* a man, madam!——

Oh how short is expression of *thy* crimes, and *my* sufferings!—Such premeditation in thy baseness!—to prostitute the characters of persons of honour of thy own family!—and all to delude a poor creature, whom thou oughtest—But why talk I to thee?—Be thy crimes upon thy head!—Once more I ask thee, Am I, or am I not, at my own liberty *now?*

I offered to speak in defence of the women, declaring that they really were the very persons——

Presume not, interrupted she, base as thou art, to say one word in thine own vindication on this head. I have been contemplating their behaviour, their conversation, their over-ready acquiescencies to my declarations in thy disfavour; their free, yet affectedly reserved light manners: and now that the sad event has opened my eyes, and I have compared facts and passages together in the little interval that has been lent me, I wonder I could not distinguish the behaviour of the unmatron-like jilt whom thou broughtest to betray me, from the worthy lady whom thou hast the honour to call thy aunt: and that I could not detect the superficial creature whom thou passedst upon me for the virtuous Miss Montague.

Amazing uncharitableness in a lady so good herself!—That the high spirits those ladies were in to see *you*, should subject them to such censures!—I do most solemnly vow, madam——

That they were, interrupting me, *verily* and *indeed* Lady Betty Lawrance, and thy cousin Montague!—Oh wretch! I see by thy solemn averment (*I had not yet averred it*) what credit ought to be given to all the rest. Had I no other proof——

Interrupting her, I besought her patient ear. 'I had found myself,' I told her, 'almost *avowedly* despised and hated. I had no hope of gaining her love, or her confidence. The letter she had left behind her, on her removal to Hampstead, sufficiently convinced me that she was entirely under Miss Howe's influence, and waited but the return of a letter from her to enter upon measures that would deprive me of her for ever: Miss Howe had *ever* been my enemy: more so *then*, no doubt, from the contents of the letter she had written to her on her first coming to Hampstead: that I dared not to stand the event of such a letter; and was glad of an opportunity, by Lady Betty's and my cousin's means (though they knew not my motive), to get her back to town; far, at the *time*, from *intending* the outrage which my despair, and her want of confidence in me, put me so vilely upon'——

I would have proceeded; and particularly would have said something of Captain Tomlinson and her uncle; but she would not hear me further. And indeed it was with visible indignation, and not without several angry interruptions that she heard me say so much.

Would I dare, she asked me, to offer at a palliation of my baseness?—The two women, she was convinced, were impostors—She knew not but Captain Tomlinson and Mr Mennell were so too. But, whether *they* were so or not, *I* was. And she insisted upon being at her own disposal for the remainder of her short life—for indeed she abhorred me in every light; and more particularly in that in which I offered myself to her acceptance.

And saying this, she flung from me; leaving me absolutely shocked and confounded at her part of a conversation, which she began with such uncommon, however severe composure, and concluded with so much sincere and unaffected indignation.

And now, Jack, I must address one serious paragraph *particularly* to thee.

I have not yet touched upon cohabitation—her uncle's mediation she does not absolutely discredit, as I had the pleasure to find by one hint in this conversation—yet she suspects my future views, and has doubts about Mennell and Tomlinson.

I *do* say, if she come *fairly* at her *lights*, at her *clues*, or what shall I call them? her penetration is *wonderful*.

But if she do *not* come at them fairly, *then* is her incredulity, *then* is her antipathy to me, evidently accounted for.

I will speak out—Thou couldst not, surely, play me booty, Jack?—Surely thou couldst not let thy weak pity for *her* lead thee to an unpardonable breach of trust to thy *friend*, who has been so unreserved in his communications to thee?

I cannot believe thee capable of such a baseness. Satisfy me, however, upon this head. I must make a cursed figure in her eye, vowing and protesting, as I shall not scruple occasionally to vow and protest, if all the time she has had unquestionable informations of my perfidy!—I know thou as little fearest me, as I do thee, in any point of manhood; and wilt scorn to deny it, if thou *hast* done it, when thus home pressed.

And here I have a good mind to stop, and write no farther, till I have thy answer. And so I will.

Monday morn. past three

Letter 264: MR LOVELACE TO JOHN BELFORD, ESQ.

Monday morn. 5 o'clock (June 19)

I *must* write on. Nothing else can divert me: and I think thou canst not have been a dog to me.

I would fain have closed my eyes: but sleep flies me. Well says *Horace*, as translated by *Cowley*:

> The halcyon *Sleep* will never build his nest
> In any stormy breast.
> 'Tis not enough, that he does find
> *Clouds* and *Darkness* in the mind:
> *Darkness* but half his work will do.
> 'Tis not enough: he must find *Quiet* too.[1]

Now indeed do I from my heart wish that I had never known this lady. But who would have thought there had been such a woman in the world? Of all the sex I have hitherto known, or heard, or read of, it was *once subdued, and always subdued*. The *first* struggle was generally the *last*; or at least the subsequent struggles were so much fainter and fainter, that a man would rather have them than be without them. But how know I yet——

IT is now near six—The sun has been illuminating, for several hours, everything about me: for that impartial orb shines upon mother Sinclair's house, as well as upon any other: but nothing within me can it illuminate.

At day-dawn I looked through the keyhole of my beloved's door. She had declared she would not put off her clothes any more in this house. There I beheld her in a sweet slumber, which I hope will prove refreshing to her disturbed senses; sitting in her elbow-chair, her apron over her head, and that supported by one sweet hand, the other hanging down upon her side, in a sleepy lifelessness; half of one pretty foot only visible.

See the difference in our cases, thought I! She, the charming injured, can sweetly sleep, while the varlet injurer cannot close his eyes; and has been trying to no purpose, the whole night, to divert his melancholy, and to fly from himself!

As every vice generally brings on its own punishment, even in *this* life, if anything were to tempt me to doubt of *future* punishment, it would be that there can hardly be a greater than that which I at this instant experience in my own remorse.

I hope it will go off—If not, well will the dear creature be avenged; for I shall be the most miserable of men.

Six o'clock

JUST now Dorcas tells me that her lady is preparing openly, and without disguise, to be gone. Very probable. The humour she flew away from me in last night, has given me expectation of such an enterprise.

Now, Jack, to be thus hated and despised!—And if I *have* sinned beyond forgiveness——

But she has sent me a message by Dorcas that she will meet me in the dining-room; and desires (odd enough!) that the wench may be present at the conversation that shall pass between us. This message gives me hope.

Nine o'clock

Confounded art, cunning, villainy!—By my soul, she had like to have slipped through my fingers. She meant nothing by her message, but to get Dorcas out of the way, and a clear coast. Is a fancied distress sufficient to justify this lady for dispensing with her principles? Does she not show me that she can wilfully deceive, as well as I?

Had she been in the fore-house, and no passage to go through to get at the street door, she had certainly been gone. But her haste betrayed her: for Sally Martin happening to be in the fore-parlour, and hearing a swifter motion than usual, and a rustling of silks, as if from somebody in a hurry, looked out; and seeing who it was, stepped between her and the door, and set her back against it.

You must not go, madam. Indeed you must not.

By what right?—and how dare you?—and such-like imperious airs the dear creature gave herself—while Sally called out for her aunt; and half a dozen voices joined instantly in the cry for me to hasten down, to hasten down, in a moment.

I was gravely instructing Dorcas abovestairs, and wondering what would be the subject of the conversation which she was to be a witness to, when these outcries reached my ears. And down I flew—and there was the charming creature, the sweet deceiver, panting for breath, her back against the partition, a parcel in her hand (women make no excursions without their parcels), Sally, Polly (but Polly obligingly pleading for her), the Mother, Mabel, and Peter (the footman of the house), about her; all, however, keeping their distance; the Mother and Sally between her and the door—In her soft rage the dear soul repeating, I *will* go!—Nobody has a right—I *will* go!—If you kill me, women, I won't go up again!

As soon as she saw me, she stepped a pace or two towards me; Mr Lovelace, I *will* go! said she—Do you authorize these women—What right have they, or *you* either, to stop me?

Is this, my dear, preparative to the conversation you led me to expect in the dining-room? And do you think I can part with you thus?—Do you think I will?

And am I, sir, to be thus beset?—Surrounded thus?—What have these women to do with me?

I desired them to leave us, all but Dorcas, who was down as soon as I. I then thought it right to assume an air of resolution, having found my tameness so greatly triumphed over. And now, my dear, said I (urging her reluctant feet), be pleased to walk into the fore-parlour. Here, since you will not go upstairs—here we may *hold our parley:* and Dorcas *be witness to it*—And now, madam, seating her, and sticking my hands in my sides, your pleasure!

Insolent villain! said the furious lady. And rising, ran to the window, and threw up the sash. (She knew not, I suppose, that there were iron rails before the windows.) And when she found she could not get out into the street, clasping her uplifted hands together—having dropped her parcel—For the love of God, good honest man!—For the love of God, mistress—to two passers-by—a poor, poor creature, said she, ruined!——

I clasped her in my arms, people beginning to gather about the window: and then she cried out, Murder! Help! Help!—and carried her up to the dining-room, in spite of her little plotting heart (as I may now call it), although she violently struggled, catching hold of the banisters here and there, as she could. I would have seated her there, but she sunk down half-motionless, pale as ashes. And a violent burst of tears happily relieved her.

Dorcas wept over her. The wench was actually moved for her!

Violent hysterics succeeded. I left her to Mabel, Dorcas, and Polly; the latter the most supportable to her of the sisterhood.

This attempt, so resolutely made, alarmed me not a little.

Mrs Sinclair and her nymphs are much more concerned; because of the reputation of their house, as they call it, having received some insults (broken windows threatened) to make them produce the young creature who cried out.

While the mobbish inquisitors were in the height of their office, the women came running up to me, to know what they should do; a constable being actually fetched.

Get the constable into the parlour, said I, with three or four of the forwardest of the mob, and produce one of the nymphs, onion-eyed, in a moment, with disordered head-dress and neck-kerchief, and let her own herself the person: the occasion, a female skirmish; but satisfied with the justice done her. Then give a dram or two to each fellow, and all will be well.

Eleven o'clock

ALL done, as I advised; and all *is* well.

Mrs Sinclair wishes she never had seen the face of so skittish a lady; and she and Sally are extremely pressing with me, to leave the perverse beauty to their *breaking*, as they call it, for four or five days. But I cursed them into silence; only ordering double precaution for the future.

Polly, though she consoled the dear perverse one all she could, when *with her*, insists upon it *to me* that nothing but terror will procure me tolerable usage.

Dorcas was challenged by the women upon her tears. She owned them real. Said she was ashamed of herself; but could not help it. So sincere, so *unyielding* a grief, in so *sweet* a lady!—

The women laughed at her: but I bid her make no apologies for her tears, nor mind their laughing. I was glad to see them *so ready*. Good use might be made of such strangers. In short, I would have her indulge them often, and try if it were not possible to gain her lady's confidence by her concern for her.

She said that her lady *did* take kind notice of them to her; and was glad to see such tokens of humanity in her.

Well then, said I, your *part*, whether anything come of it or not, is to be *tender-hearted*. It can do no harm, if no good. But take care you are not *too suddenly*, or *too officiously* compassionate.

So Dorcas will be a humane good sort of creature, I believe, very quickly with her lady. And as it becomes women to be so, and as my beloved is willing to think highly of her own sex; it will the more readily pass with her.

I thought to have had one trial (having gone so far) for *cohabitation*. But what hope can there be of succeeding?—She is invincible!—Against all my notions, against all my conceptions (thinking of her as a woman, and in the very bloom of her charms), she is absolutely invincible!—My whole view at the present is to do her legal justice! if I can but once more get her out of her altitudes!

The *consent* of such a lady must make her ever new, ever charming. But, astonishing! Can the want of a church ceremony make such a difference!

She *owes* me her consent; for hitherto I have had nothing to boast of. All, of my side, has been deep remorse, anguish of mind, and love increased rather than abated.

How her proud rejection stings me!—And yet I hope still to get her to listen to my stories of the family reconciliation, and of her uncle and Captain Tomlinson—And as she has given me a pretence to detain her against her will, she *must* see me, whether in temper, or not—she cannot help it. And if love will not do, terror, as the women advise, must be tried.

A nice part, after all, has my beloved to act. If she forgive me easily, I resume, perhaps, my projects—If she carry her rejection into violence, that violence may make me desperate, and occasion fresh violence—She ought, since she thinks she has found the women out, to consider *where she is*.

I am confoundedly out of conceit with myself. If I give up my contrivances, my joy in stratagem, and plot, and invention, I shall be but a common man: such another dull heavy creature as thyself. Yet what does even my success in my machinations bring me, but disgrace, repentance, regret? But I am overmatched, egregiously overmatched, by this lady. What to do with her, or without her, I know not.

Letter 265: MR LOVELACE TO JOHN BELFORD, ESQ.

I HAVE this moment intelligence from Simon Parsons, one of Lord M.'s stewards, that his lordship is very ill. Simon, who is my obsequious servant in virtue of my presumptive heirship, gives me a hint in his letter that my presence at M. Hall will not be amiss. So I must accelerate whatever be the course I shall be allowed or compelled to take.

No bad prospects for this charming creature, if the old peer would be so kind as to surrender; and many a summons has his gout given him. A good £8000 a year and perhaps the title reversionary would help me up with her.

Proudly as this lady pretends to be above all pride, grandeur will have its charms with her; for grandeur always makes a man's face shine in a woman's eye. I have a pretty good, because a clear, estate, as it is: but what a noble variety of mischief will £8000 a year enable a man to do?

Perhaps thou'lt say I do *already* all that comes into my head: but that's a mistake—not one half, I will assure thee. And even *good folks*, as I have heard, love to have the *power* of doing mischief, whether they make *use of it*, or *not*. The late Queen Anne, who was a very good woman, was always fond of *prerogative*. And her ministers, in her name, in more instances than one, made a *ministerial* use of this her foible.

BUT now, at last, am I to be admitted to the presence of my angry fair one: after three denials, nevertheless; and a *peremptory* from me, by Dorcas, that I must see her in her chamber, if I cannot see her in the dining-room.

Dorcas, however, tells me that she says if she were at her own liberty, she would never see me more; and that she has been asking after the characters and conditions of the neighbours. I suppose, now she has found her voice to call out for help from them, if there were any to hear her.

She will have it now, it seems, that I had the wickedness, from the very beginning, to contrive for her ruin, a house so convenient for dreadful mischief.

Dorcas begs of her to be pacified—entreats her to see me with patience—tells her that I am one of the most determined of men, as she has heard say—that gentleness may do with me; but that nothing else will, she believes. And what, as her ladyship (as she always styles her) is *married*, if I *had* broke my oath, or *intended* to break it!—

She hinted plain enough to the honest wench that she was *not* married—but Dorcas would not understand her.

This shows that she is resolved to keep no measures. And now is to be a trial of skill, whether she shall or not.

Dorcas has hinted to her my lord's illness, as a piece of intelligence that dropped in conversation from me.

But here I stop. My beloved, pursuant to my peremptory message, is just gone up into the dining-room.

Letter 266: MR LOVELACE TO JOHN BELFORD, ESQ.

Monday afternoon, June 19

PITY me, Jack, for pity's sake; since, if thou dost not, nobody else will: and yet never was there a man of my genius and lively temper that wanted it more. We are apt to attribute to the devil everything that happens to us which we would not *have* happen: but here, being (as perhaps thou'lt say) the devil myself, my plagues arise from an angel. I suppose all mankind is to be plagued by its *contrary*.

She began with me like a true woman (*she* in the fault, *I* to be blamed) the moment I entered the dining-room—Not the least apology, not the least excuse, for the uproar she had made, and the trouble she had given me.

I come, said she, into thy detested presence, because I cannot help it. But why am I to be imprisoned here?—Although to no purpose, I cannot help—

Dearest madam, interrupted I, give not way to so much violence. You must know that your detention is entirely owing to the desire I have to make you all the amends that is in my power to make you. And this, as well for *your* sake as *my own*—Surely there is still *one* way left to repair the wrongs you have suffered——

Canst thou blot out the past week? *Several* weeks past, I should say; ever since I have been with thee? Canst thou call back time?—If thou canst——

Surely, madam, again interrupting her, if I may be permitted to call you *legally* mine, I might have but anticip——

Wretch, that thou art! Say not another word upon this subject. When thou vowedst, when thou promisedst at Hampstead, I had begun to think that I must be thine. If I had consented at the request of those I thought thy relations, this would have been a principal inducement, that I could then have brought thee what was *most* wanted, an unsullied honour in dowry to a wretch destitute of all honour; and could have met the gratulations of a family, to which thy life has been one continued disgrace, with a consciousness of *deserving* their gratulations. But thinkest thou that I will give a harlot-niece to thy honourable uncle, and to thy *real* aunts; and a cousin to thy cousins from a brothel? For such, in my opinion, is this detested house!—Then, lifting up her clasped hands, 'Great and good God of Heaven, said she, give me patience to support myself under the weight of those afflictions, which thou for wise and good ends, though at present impenetrable by me, hast permitted!'

Then, turning towards me, who knew neither what to say *to* her, nor *for* myself: I renounce thee for ever, Lovelace!—Abhorred of my soul! for ever I renounce thee!—Seek thy fortunes wheresoever thou wilt!—only now, that thou hast already ruined me——

Ruined you, madam—The world need not—I knew not what to say——

Ruined me in my *own* eyes, and that is the same to me, as if *all the world* knew it—Hinder me not from going whither my mysterious destiny shall lead me——

Why hesitate you, sir? What right have you to stop me, as you lately did; and to bring me up by force, my hands and arms bruised with your violence? What right have you to detain me here?

I am cut to the heart, madam, with invectives so violent. I am but too sensible of the wrong I have done you, or I could not *bear* your reproaches. The man who perpetrates a villainy, and resolves to go on with it, shows not the compunction I show. Yet, if you think yourself in my power, I would caution you, madam, not to make me desperate. For you *shall* be mine, or my life shall be the forfeit! Nor is life worth having without you!——

Be *thine!*—I be *thine!*—said the passionate beauty. Oh how lovely in her violence!—

Yes, madam, be *mine!*—I repeat, you *shall* be mine!—My very crime is your glory. My love, my admiration of you is increased by what has passed: *and so it ought.* I am willing, madam, to court your returning favour: but let me tell you, were the house beset by a thousand armed men resolved to take you from me, they should not effect their purpose while I had life.

I never, never will be yours, said she, clasping her hands together, and lifting up her eyes!—I never will be yours!

We may yet see many happy years, madam. All your friends may be reconciled to you. The treaty for that purpose is in greater forwardness than you imagine. You know *better* than to think the *worse* of yourself for suffering what you *could not help.* Enjoin but the terms I can make my peace with you upon, and I will instantly comply.

Never, never, repeated she, will I be yours!—

Only forgive me, my dearest life, this *one* time!—A virtue so invincible! what further view *can* I have against you?—Have I attempted any further outrage?—If you will be mine, your injuries will be injuries done to myself. You have too well guessed at the unnatural arts that have been used?—But can a greater testimony be given of your virtue?—And now I have only to hope that although I cannot make you *complete* amends, yet that you will permit me to make you *all* the amends that can possibly be made.

Hear me out, I beseech you, madam; for she was going to speak with an aspect unpacifiedly angry: the God whom you serve requires but repentance and amendment. Imitate *Him*, my dearest love, and bless me with the *means* of reforming a course of life that begins to be hateful to me. *That* was *once* your favourite point. Resume it, dearest creature: in charity to a soul as well as body which once, as I flattered myself, was *more* than indifferent to you, resume it. And let tomorrow's sun witness to our espousals.

I cannot judge thee, said she; but the GOD to whom thou so boldly referrest, can; and assure thyself *He* will. But, if compunction has *really* taken hold of thee; if *indeed* thou art touched for thy ungrateful baseness, and meanest anything by pleading the holy example thou recommendest to my imitation; in this thy pretended repentant moment, let me sift thee thoroughly; and by thy answer I shall judge of the sincerity of thy pretended declarations.

Tell me then, is there any reality in the treaty thou hast pretended to be on foot between my uncle and Captain Tomlinson, and thyself?—Say, and hesitate not, is there any truth in that story?—But remember, if there be *not*, and thou avowest that there *is*, what further condemnation attends thy averment, if it be as solemn as I require it to be!

This was a cursed thrust. What could I say?—Surely this merciless lady is resolved to damn me, thought I, and yet accuses me of a design against her soul!—But was I not obliged to proceed as I had begun?

In short, I solemnly averred that there was!—How one crime, as the good folks say, brings on another?

I added that the captain had been in town, and would have waited on her, had she not been indisposed: that he went down much afflicted, as well on her account as on that of her uncle; though I had not acquainted him either with the nature of her disorder, or the ever-to-be-regretted occasion of it; having told him that it was a violent fever: that he had twice since, by her uncle's desire, sent up to inquire after her health: and that I had already dispatched a man and horse with a letter to acquaint him (and her uncle through him) with her recovery; making it my earnest request that he would renew his application to her uncle for the favour of his presence at the private celebration of our nuptials; and that I expected an answer, if not this night, as tomorrow.

Let me ask thee next, said she (Thou knowest the opinion I have of the women thou broughtest to me at Hampstead; and who have seduced me hither to my ruin); let me ask thee, if *really* and *truly* they were Lady Betty Lawrance and thy cousin Montague?—What sayest thou—hesitate not—what sayest thou to this question?

Astonishing, my dear, that you should suspect them!—but, knowing your strange opinion of them, what can I say to be believed?

And is *this* the answer thou returnest me? Dost thou *thus* evade my question? But let me know, for I am trying thy sincerity now, and shall judge of thy new professions by thy answer to this question; let me know, I repeat, whether those women be *really* Lady Betty Lawrance and thy cousin Montague?

Let me, my dearest love, be enabled tomorrow to call you lawfully mine, and we will set out the next day, if you please, to Berkshire, to my Lord M.'s, where they both are at this time, and you shall convince yourself by your own eyes, and by your own ears; which you will believe sooner than all I can say or swear.

Now, Belford, I had really some apprehension of treachery from thee; which made me so miserably evade; for else I could *as* safely have sworn to the truth of this, as to that of the former: but she pressing me still for a categorical answer, I ventured plumb; and swore to it (*lovers' oaths, Jack*) that they were really and truly Lady Betty Lawrance and my cousin Montague.

She lifted up her hands, and eyes—What can I think!—What *can* I think!—

You *think* me a devil, madam; a very devil! or you could not, after you have put these questions to me, seem to doubt the truth of answers so solemnly sworn to.

And if I do think thee so, have I not cause? Is there another man in the world (I hope, for the sake of human nature, there is not) who could act by any poor friendless creature as thou hast acted by *me*, whom thou hast *made* friendless—and who, before I knew thee, had for a friend everyone who knew me?

I told you, madam, *before*, that my aunt and cousin were actually here, in order to take leave of you before they set out for Berkshire. But the effects of my ungrateful crime (such, with shame and remorse, I own it to be!) were the reason you could not see them. Nor could I be fond that they should see *you:* since they never would have forgiven me, had they known what had passed—and what reason had I to expect your silence on the subject, had you been recovered?

It signifies nothing, now that the cause of their appearance has been answered in my ruin, *who* or *what* they are: but, if thou hast averred thus solemnly to two falsehoods, what a wretch do I see before me!—

I thought she had now reason to be satisfied; and I begged her to allow me to talk to her of tomorrow, as of the happiest day of my life. We have the licence, madam—and you *must* excuse me that I cannot let you go hence till I have tried every way I *can* try, to obtain your forgiveness.

And am I then (with a kind of frantic wildness) to be detained a prisoner in this horrid house?—Am I, sir?—Take care!—Take care! holding up her hand, menacing, how you make me desperate!—If I fall, though by my own hand, inquisition will be made for my blood: and be not out in thy plot, Lovelace, if it *should* be so—Make *sure* work, I charge thee: dig a hole deep enough to cram in and conceal this unhappy body: for, depend upon it, that some of those who will not stir to protect me living, will move heaven and earth to avenge me dead!

A horrid dear creature!—By my soul, she made me shudder! She had need, indeed, to talk of *her* unhappiness, in falling into the hands of the only *man* in the world who could have used her as I have used her! She is the only *woman* in the world who could have shocked and disturbed me as she has done—So we are upon a foot in that respect. And I think I have the *worst* of it by much. Since very little has been my joy; very much my trouble: and *her* punishment, as she calls it, is *over:* but when *mine* will, or what it *may be*, who can tell?

Here, only recapitulating (think, then, how I must be affected at the time), I was forced to leave off, and sing a song to myself. I aimed at a lively air; but I croaked rather than sung: and fell into the old dismal thirtieth of January strain.[1] I hemmed up for a sprightlier note; but it would not do: and at last I ended, like a malefactor, in a dead psalm melody.[2]

High-ho!—I gape like an unfledged kite in its nest, wanting to swallow a chicken, bobbed at its mouth by its marauding dam!—

What a devil ails me!—I can neither think nor write!—

Lie down, pen, for a moment!—

Letter 267: MR LOVELACE TO JOHN BELFORD, ESQ.

THERE is certainly a good deal in the observation, *that it costs a man ten times more pains to be wicked, than it would cost him to be good*. What a confounded number of contrivances have I had recourse to, in order to carry my point with this charming creature; and, after all, how have I puzzled myself by it; and yet am near tumbling into the pit, which it was the end of all my plots to shun! What a happy man had I been with such an excellence, could I have brought my mind to marry when I first prevailed upon her to quit her father's house! But *then*, as I have often reflected, how had I *known* that a but blossoming beauty, who could carry on a private correspondence and run such risks with a notorious wild fellow, was not prompted by inclination, which one day might give such a free liver as myself as much pain to reflect upon, as at the time it gave me pleasure? Thou rememberest the host's tale in Ariosto. And *thy* experience, as well as *mine*, can furnish out twenty *Fiamettas* in proof of the imbecility of the sex.[1]

But to proceed with my narrative.

The dear creature resumed the topic her heart was so firmly fixed upon; and insisted upon quitting the *odious house*, and that in very high terms.

I urged her to meet me the next day at the altar, in either of the two churches mentioned in the licence. And I besought her, whatever were her resolution, to let me debate this matter calmly with her.

If, she said, I would have her give what I desired the least moment's consideration, I must not hinder her from being her own mistress. To what purpose did I ask her *consent*, if she had not a power over either her own person or actions?

Will you give me your honour, madam, if I consent to your quitting a house so disagreeable to you?—

My honour, sir! said the dear creature—alas!—And turned weeping from me with inimitable grace—as if she had said—Alas!—You have robbed me of my honour!

I hoped then that her angry passions were subsiding!—But I was mistaken!— For, urging her warmly for the day; and that for the sake of our mutual honour and the honour of both our families, in this high-flown, and high-souled strain she answered me:

And canst thou, Lovelace, be so *mean*—as to wish to make a wife of the creature thou hast insulted, dishonoured, and abused, as thou hast me? Was it necessary to humble Clarissa Harlowe down to the low level of thy baseness, before she could be a wife meet for thee? Thou hadst a father who was a man of honour: a mother who deserved a better son—Thou hast an uncle who is no dishonour to the peerage of a kingdom, whose peers are more respectable than the nobility of any other country. Thou hast other relations also, who may be *thy* boast, though thou canst not be *theirs*. And canst thou not imagine that thou hearest them calling upon thee; the dead from their monuments; the living from their laudable pride; not to dishonour thy ancient and splendid house by entering into wedlock with a creature whom thou hast levelled with the dirt of the street, and classed with the vilest of her sex?

I extolled her greatness of soul, and her virtue. I execrated myself for my guilt:

and told her how grateful to the *manes* of my ancestors, as well as to the wishes of the living, the honour I supplicated for would be.

But still she insisted upon being a free agent; of seeing herself in other lodgings before she would give what I urged the *least* consideration. Nor would she promise me favour even then, or to permit my visits. How then, as I asked her, could I comply, without resolving to lose her for ever?

She put her hand to her forehead often as she talked; and at last, pleading disorder in her head, retired; neither of us satisfied with the other. But *she* ten times more dissatisfied with me, than I with her.

Dorcas seems to be coming into favour with her—

What now!—What now!—

Monday night

How determined is this lady!—Again had she like to have escaped us!—What a fixed resentment!—She only, I find, assumed a little calm in order to quiet suspicion. She was got down, and actually had unbolted the street door before I could get to her; alarmed as I was by Mrs Sinclair's cookmaid, who was the only one that saw her fly through the passage: yet lightning was not quicker than I.

Again I brought her back to the dining-room, with infinite reluctance on her part. And before her face, ordered a servant to be placed constantly at the bottom of the stairs for the future.

She seemed even choked with grief and disappointment.

Dorcas was exceedingly assiduous about her; and confidently gave it as her own opinion that her dear lady should be permitted to go to another lodging, since *this* was so disagreeable to her: were she to be killed for saying so, she would say it. And was *good* Dorcas for this afterwards.

But for some time the dear creature was all passion and violence—

I see, I see, said she, when I had brought her up, what I am to expect from your new professions, oh vilest of men!—

Have I offered to you, my beloved creature, anything that can justify this impatience, after a more hopeful calm?

She wrung her hands. She disordered her headdress. She tore her ruffles. She was in a perfect frenzy.

I dreaded her returning malady: but entreaty rather exasperating, I affected an angry air—I bid her expect the worst she had to fear—and was menacing on, in hopes to intimidate her, when, dropping down at my feet:

'Twill be a mercy, said she, the highest act of mercy you can do, to kill me outright upon this spot—This happy spot, as I will in my last moments call it!— Then, baring with a still more frantic violence, part of her enchanting neck—here, here, said the soul-harrowing beauty, let thy pointed mercy enter! And I will thank thee, and forgive thee for all the dreadful past!—With my latest gasp will I forgive and thank thee!—Or help *me* to the means, and I will myself put out of thy way so miserable a wretch! And bless thee for those means!

Why all this extravagant passion, why all these exclamations? Have I offered any new injury to you, my dearest life! What a frenzy is this! Am I not ready to make you all the reparation that I *can* make you? Had I not reason to hope—

No, no, no, no—half a dozen times, as fast as she could speak.

Had I not reason to hope that you were meditating upon the means of making

me happy, and yourself not miserable, rather than upon a flight so causeless and
so precipitate?—

No, no, no, no, as before, shaking her head with wild impatience, as resolved not
to attend to what I said.

My resolutions are so honourable, if you will permit them to take effect, that I
need not be solicitous whither you go, if you will but permit my visits, and receive
my vows. And, God is my witness, that I bring you not back from the door with
any view to your dishonour, but the contrary: and this moment I will send for a
minister to put an end to all your doubts and fears.

Say this, and say a thousand times more, and bind every word with a solemn
appeal to that God whom thou art accustomed to invoke to the truth of the vilest
falsehoods, and all will still be short of what thou *hast* vowed and promised to me.
And, were *not* my heart to abhor thee and to rise against thee for thy *perjuries*, as
it *does*, I would not, I tell thee once more, I would not bind my soul in covenant
with such a man for a thousand worlds!

Compose yourself, however, madam; for *your own sake*, compose yourself.
Permit me to raise you up; *abhorred* as I am of your soul!—

Nay, if I must not touch you; for she wildly slapped my hands; but with such a
sweet passionate air, her bosom heaving and throbbing as she looked up to me,
that although I was most sincerely enraged, I could with transport have pressed her
to mine—

If I must not touch you, I will not—But depend upon it (and I assumed the
sternest air I could assume, to try what *that* would do), depend upon it, madam,
that this is not the way to avoid the evils you dread. Let me do what I will, I cannot
be used worse!—Dorcas, be gone!

She arose, Dorcas being about to withdraw, and wildly caught hold of her arm:
Oh Dorcas! If thou art of mine own sex, leave me not, I charge thee!—Then
quitting Dorcas, down she threw herself upon her knees in the furthermost corner
of the room, clasping a chair with her face laid upon the bottom of it!—Oh where
can I be safe?—Where, where can I be safe, from this man of violence?—

This gave Dorcas an opportunity to confirm herself in her lady's confidence: the
wench threw herself at my feet, while I seemed in violent wrath; and, embracing
my knees, Kill me, sir, kill me, sir, if you please!—I must throw myself in your way
to save my lady. I beg your pardon, sir—but you must be set on!—God forgive the
mischief-makers!—But your own heart, if left to itself, would not permit these
things!—Spare, however, sir! spare my lady, I beseech you! bustling on her knees
about me, as if I were intending to approach her lady had I not been restrained by
her.

This, humoured by me, Begone, devil!—Officious devil, begone!—startled the
dear creature; who, snatching up hastily her head from the chair, and as hastily
popping it down again in terror, hit her nose, I suppose, against the edge of the
chair; and it gushed out with blood, running in a stream down her bosom; she
herself too much affrighted to heed it!—

Never was mortal man in such terror and agitation as I; for I instantly concluded
that she had stabbed herself with some concealed instrument.

I ran to her in a wild agony—for Dorcas was frighted out of all her mock
interposition—

What have you done!—Oh what have you done!—Look up to me, my dearest life!—Sweet injured innocence, look up to me! What have you done!—Long will I not survive you!—And I was upon the point of drawing my sword to dispatch myself, when I discovered—(what an unmanly blockhead does this charming creature make me at her pleasure!) that all I apprehended was but a bloody nose, which, as far as I know (for it could not be stopped in a quarter of an hour), may have saved her head and her intellects.

But I see by this scene that the sweet creature is but a pretty coward at bottom; and that I can terrify her out of her virulence against me, whenever I put on sternness and anger: but then, as a qualifier to the advantage this gives me over her, I find myself to be a coward too, which I had not before suspected, since I was capable of being so easily terrified by the apprehensions of her offering violence to herself.

Letter 268: MR LOVELACE TO JOHN BELFORD, ESQ.

BUT, with all this dear creature's resentment against me, I cannot for my heart think but she will get all over, and consent to enter the pale with me. Were she even to die tomorrow, and to know she should, would not a woman of her sense, of her punctilio, and in her situation, and of so proud a family, rather die married, than otherwise?—No doubt but she would; although she were to hate the man ever so heartily. If so, there is now but one man in the world whom she can have— and that is *me*.

Now I talk (*familiar writing* is but *talking*, Jack) thus glibly of entering the pale, thou wilt be ready to question me, I know, as to my intentions on this head.

As much of my heart as I know of it myself will I tell thee—When I am *from* her, I cannot still help hesitating about marriage, and I even frequently resolve against it; and am resolved to press my favourite scheme for cohabitation. But when I am *with* her, I am ready to say, to swear, and to do, whatever I think will be most acceptable to her: and were a parson at hand, I should plunge at once, no doubt of it, into the state.

I have frequently thought, in *common* cases, that it is happy for many giddy fellows (there are giddy fellows, as well as giddy girls, Jack; and perhaps *those* are as often drawn in, as *these*), that ceremony and parade are necessary to the irrevocable solemnity; and that there is generally time for a man to recollect himself in the space between the heated overnight, and the cooler next morning; or I know not who could escape the sweet gipsies, whose fascinating powers are so much aided by our own raised imaginations.

A wife at any time, I used to say. I had ever confidence and vanity enough to think that no woman breathing could deny her hand, when I held out mine. I am confoundedly mortified to find that this lady is able to hold me at bay, and to refuse all my *honest* vows.

What force (allow me a serious reflection, Jack: it *will* be put down!), what force have evil habits upon the human mind! When we enter upon a devious course, we think we shall have it in our power, when we will, to return to the right path. But it is not so, I plainly see: for, who can acknowledge with more justice this dear creature's merits, and his own errors, than I? Whose regret, at times, can

be deeper than mine, for the injuries I have done her? Whose resolutions to repair
those injuries stronger?—Yet how transitory is my penitence!—How am I hurried
away—Canst thou tell by what?—Oh devil of youth, and devil of intrigue, how do
ye mislead me!—How often do we end in occasions for the deepest remorse, what
we begin in wantonness!—

At the present writing, however, the turn of the scale is in favour of matrimony—
for I despair of carrying with her my favourite point.

The lady tells Dorcas that her heart is broken; and that she shall live but a little
while. I think nothing of that, if we marry. In the first place, she knows not what
a mind unapprehensive will do for her, in a state to which all the sex look forward
with high satisfaction. How often have the whole sacred conclave been thus
deceived in their choice of a pope; not considering that the new dignity is of itself
sufficient to give new life!—A few months' heart's ease will give my charmer a
quite different notion of things: and I dare say, as I have heretofore said,[a] once
married, and I am married for life.

I will allow that her pride, in *one* sense, has suffered abasement: but her triumph
is the greater in every other. And while I can think that all her trials are but
additions to her honour, and that I have laid the foundations of her glory in my
own shame, can I be called cruel if I am *not* affected with her grief as some men
would be?—

And for what should her heart be broken? Her will is unviolated—at *present*,
however, her will is unviolated. The destroying of good habits, and the introducing
of bad, to the corrupting of the whole heart, is the violation. That her will is not
to be corrupted, that her mind is not to be debased, she has hitherto unquestionably
proved. And if she give cause for further trials, and hold fast her integrity; what
ideas will she have to dwell upon, that will be able to corrupt her morals?—What
vestigia, what *remembrances*, but such as will inspire abhorrence of the attempter?

What nonsense then to suppose that such a mere notional violation as she has
suffered should be able to cut asunder the strings of life?

Her religion, married or not married, will set her above making such a trifling
accident, such an *involuntary* suffering, fatal to her.

Such considerations as these, they are, that support me against all apprehension
of bugbear consequences: and I would have them have weight with thee; who art
such a doughty advocate for her. And yet I allow thee this; that she really makes
too much of it: takes it too much to heart. To be sure she ought to have forgot it
by this time, except the charming, charming consequence happen, that still I am
in hopes will happen, were I to proceed no further. And if she apprehend this
herself, then has the dear over-nice soul some reason for taking it so much to
heart: and yet would not, I think, refuse to legitimate.

Oh Jack! had I an imperial diadem, I swear to thee that I would give it up, even
to my *enemy*, to have one charming boy by this lady. And should she *escape me*,
and no such effect follow, my revenge on her family, and in *such* a case on herself,
would be incomplete, and I should reproach myself as long as I lived.

Were I to be sure that this foundation is laid (and why may I not hope it is?), I
should not doubt to have her still (should she withstand her day of grace) on my
own conditions: nor should I, if it were so, question that *revived* affection in *her*

a See p. 872.

which a woman seldom fails to have for the father of her first child, whether born in wedlock or out of it.

And prithee, Jack, see in this *aspiration*, let me call it, a distinction in my favour from other rakes; who almost to a man follow their inclinations without troubling themselves about consequences. In imitation, as one would think, of the strutting villain of a bird, which from feathered lady to feathered lady pursues his imperial pleasures, leaving it to his sleek paramours to hatch the genial product, in holes and corners of their own finding out.

Letter 269: MR LOVELACE TO JOHN BELFORD, ESQ.

Tuesday morn. June 20

WELL, Jack, now are we upon another foot together. This dear creature will not *let me be good*. She is now authorizing all my plots by her own example.

Thou must be partial in the highest degree, if now thou blamest me for resuming my former schemes, since in that case I shall but follow her clue. No forced construction of her actions do I make on this occasion in order to justify a bad cause, or a worse intention. A little pretence, indeed, served the wolf, when he had a mind to quarrel with the lamb; but this is not now my case.

For here (wouldst thou have thought it?), taking advantage of Dorcas's compassionate temper, and of some warm expressions which the tender-hearted wench let fall against the cruelty of men; and wishing to have it in her power to serve her; has she given her the following note, signed by her maiden name: for she has thought fit, in positive and plain words, to own to the pitying Dorcas that she is not married.

Monday, June 19

I the underwritten do hereby promise that, on my coming into possession of my own estate, I will provide for Dorcas Martindale in a gentlewoman-like manner, in my own house: or, if I do not soon obtain that possession, or should first die, I do hereby bind myself, my executors, and administrators, to pay to her, or her order, during the term of her natural life, the sum of five pounds on each of the four usual quarterly days in the year; that is to say, twenty pounds by the year; on condition that she faithfully assist me in my escape from an illegal confinement, which I now labour under. The first quarterly payment to commence, and be payable, at the end of three months immediately following the day of my deliverance. And I do also promise to give her, as a testimony of my honour in the rest, a diamond ring, which I have showed her. Witness my hand, this nineteenth day of June, in the year above-written.

CLARISSA HARLOWE

Now, Jack, what terms wouldst thou have me to keep with such a sweet corruptress?—Seest thou not how she hates me?—Seest thou not that she is resolved never to forgive me?—Seest thou not, however, that she must disgrace herself in the eye of the world, if she actually should escape?—that she must be subjected to infinite distress and hazard?—for whom has she to receive and protect her?—Yet to determine to risk all these evils!—And furthermore to stoop to artifice, to be guilty of the reigning vice of the times, of bribery and corruption! Oh Jack, Jack! say not, *write* not, another word in her favour!—

Thou hast blamed me for bringing her to this house: but had I carried her to any other in England, where there would have been one servant or inmate capable either of *compassion* or *corruption*, what must have been the consequence?

But seest thou not, however, that in this flimsy contrivance the dear implacable, like a drowning man, catches at a straw to save herself!—A straw shall she find to be the refuge she has resorted to.

Letter 270: MR LOVELACE TO JOHN BELFORD, ESQ.

Tuesday morn. 10 o'clock

VERY ill!—exceeding ill!—as Dorcas tells me, in order to avoid seeing me—and yet the dear soul may be so in her *mind*—But is not that equivocation?—Some one passion predominating in every human breast breaks through principle, and controls us all. Mine is *love* and *revenge* taking turns. Hers is *hatred*—But this is my consolation, that *hatred appeased is love begun*; or *love renewed*, I may rather say, if love ever had footing here.

But *reflectioning* apart, thou seest, Jack, that her plot is beginning to work. Tomorrow it is to break out.

I have been abroad, to set on foot a plot of circumvention. All fair now, Belford!—

I insisted upon visiting my indisposed fair one. Dorcas made officious excuses for her. I cursed the wench in her hearing for her impertinence; and stamped and made a clutter—which was improved into an apprehension to the lady, that I would have flung her faithful confidante from the top of the stairs to the bottom.

He is a violent wretch!—But, Dorcas (*dear* Dorcas now it is), thou shalt have a friend in me to the last day of my life.

And what now dost think the name of her *good angel* is?—Why *Dorcas Martindale*, christian and super (no more Wykes) as in the promissory note in my former—and the dear creature has bound her to her by the *most solemn* obligations, *besides* the tie of interest.

Whither, madam, do you design to go when you get out of this house?

I will throw myself into the first open house I can find; and beg protection till I can get a coach, or a lodging in some honest family.

What will you do for clothes, madam?—I doubt you'll not be able to take any away with you, but what you'll have on.

Oh no matter for clothes, if I can but get out of this house.

What will you do for money, madam? I have heard his honour express his concern that he could not prevail upon you to be obliged to him, though he apprehended that you must be short of money.

Oh, I have rings, and other valuables. Indeed I have but four guineas, and two of them I found lately wrapped up in a bit of lace, designed for a charitable use: but now, alas! charity begins at home! But I have one dear friend left, if she be living, as I hope in God she is! to whom I can be obliged, if I want. Oh Dorcas! I must ere now have heard from her, if I had had fair play.

Well, madam, yours is a hard lot. I pity you at my heart!

Thank you, Dorcas!—I am unhappy that I did not think *before*, that I might have confided in thy pity, and in thy sex!

I pitied you, madam, often and often: but you were always, as I thought, diffident of me. And then I doubted not but you were married; and I thought his honour was unkindly used by you. So that I thought it my duty to wish well to his honour, rather than to what I thought to be your humours, madam. Would to heaven that I had known before that you were not married!—Such a lady!—Such a fortune!—To be so sadly betrayed!—

Ah, Dorcas! I was basely drawn in! My youth! My ignorance of the world!— And I have some things to reproach myself with, when I look back!

Lord, madam, what deceitful creatures are these men!—Neither oaths, nor vows!—I am sure! I am sure!—and then with her apron she gave her eyes half a dozen hearty rubs—I may curse the time that I came into this house!—

Here was accounting for her bold eyes! And was it not better to give up a house which her lady could not think worse of than she did, in order to gain the reputation of sincerity, than by offering to vindicate it to make her proffered services suspected?

Poor Dorcas!—Bless me! how little do we, who have lived all our time in the country, know of this wicked town!—

Had I *been able to write*, cried the veteran wench, I should certainly have given some other near relations I have in Wales a little *inkling* of matters; and they would have saved me from—from—from—

Her sobs were enough. The apprehensions of women on such subjects are ever aforehand with speech.

And then, sobbing on, she lifted her apron to her face again. She showed me how.

Poor Dorcas!—Again wiping her own charming eyes.

All love, all compassion, is this dear creature to every one in affliction, but me.

And would not an aunt protect her kinswoman?—Abominable wretch!

I can't—I can't—I can't—say my aunt was privy to it. She gave me good advice. She knew not for a great while, that I was—that I was—that I was—ugh!—ugh!— ugh!—

No more, no more, good Dorcas!—What a world we live in!—What a house am I in! But come, don't weep (though she herself could not forbear): my being betrayed into it, though to my own ruin, may be a happy event for thee: and, if I live, it shall.

I thank you, my good lady, blubbering. I am sorry, very sorry, you have had so hard a lot. But it may be the saving of my soul if I can get to your ladyship's house—Had I but known that your ladyship was not married, I would have eat my own flesh, before, before, before—

Dorcas sobbed and wept. The lady sighed and wept also.

But now, Jack, for a serious reflection upon the premises.

How will the good folks account for it that Satan has such faithful instruments, and that the bond of wickedness is a stronger bond than the ties of virtue?—As if it were the nature of the human mind to be villainous. For here, had Dorcas been *good*, and tempted, as she was tempted, to anything *evil*, I make no doubt but she would have yielded to the temptation.

And cannot our fraternity, in an hundred instances, give proof of the like predominance of vice over virtue? And that we have risked more to serve and promote the interests of the former, than ever a good man did to serve a good man, or a good cause? For have we not been prodigal of life and fortune? Have we not defied the civil magistrate upon occasion; and have we not attempted rescues, and dared all things, only to extricate a pounded profligate?—

Whence, Jack, can this be?

Oh I have it, I believe. The vicious are as bad as they can be; and do the devil's work without looking after; while he is continually spreading snares for the others; and like a skilful angler, suiting his baits to the fish he angles for.

Nor let even *honest* people, *so called*, blame poor Dorcas for her fidelity in a bad cause. For does not the *general*, who implicitly serves an ambitious prince in his unjust designs upon his neighbours, or upon his own oppressed subjects; and even the *lawyer*, who for the sake of a paltry fee undertakes to whiten a black cause, and to defend it against one he knows to be good, do the very same thing as Dorcas? And are they not both every whit as culpable? Yet the one shall be dubbed a hero, the other a charming fellow and be contended for by every client; and his double-paced abilities shall carry him through all the high preferments of the law with reputation and applause.

Well but, what shall be done, since the lady is so much determined on removing?—Is there no way to oblige her, and yet to make the very act subservient to my own views?—I fancy such a way may be found out.

I will study for it——

Suppose I suffer her to make an escape? Her heart is in it. If she effect it, the triumph she will have over me upon it will be a counterbalance for all she has suffered.

I will oblige her if I can.

Letter 271: MR LOVELACE TO JOHN BELFORD, ESQ.

TIRED with a succession of fatiguing days and sleepless nights, and with contemplating the precarious situation I stand in with my beloved, I fell into a profound reverie; which brought on sleep; and that produced a dream; a fortunate dream; which, as I imagine, will afford my working mind the means to effect the obliging double purpose my heart is now once more set upon.

What, as I have often contemplated, is the enjoyment of the finest woman in the world, to the contrivance, the bustle, the surprises, and at last the happy conclusion of a well-laid plot?—The charming *roundabouts*, to come the *nearest way home*— the doubts; the apprehensions; the heartachings, the meditated triumphs—These are the joys that make the blessing dear—For all the rest, what is it?—What but to find an angel in imagination dwindled down to a woman in fact?—But to my dream——

Methought it was about nine on Wednesday morning, that a chariot with a dowager's arms upon the doors, and in it a grave matronly lady (not unlike Mother H. in the face; but in her heart oh how unlike!), stopped at a grocer's shop about ten doors on the other side of the way, in order to buy some groceries: and methought Dorcas, having been out to see if the coast were clear for her lady's flight, and if a coach were to be got near the place, espied this chariot with the dowager's arms, and this matronly lady: and what, methought, did Dorcas, that subtle traitress, do, but whip up to the old matronly lady, and lifting up her voice say, Good my lady, permit me one word with your ladyship.

What thou hast to say to me, say on, quoth the old lady; the grocer retiring and standing aloof, to give Dorcas leave to speak; who, methought, in words like these, accosted the lady:

'You seem, madam, to be a very good lady; and here in this neighbourhood, at a house of no high repute, is an innocent lady of rank and fortune, beautiful as a May morning, and youthful as a rosebud, and full as sweet and lovely; who has been tricked thither by a wicked gentleman practised in the ways of the town; and this very night will she be ruined if she get not out of his hands. Now, oh lady! if you will extend your compassionate goodness to this fair young lady, in whom, the moment you behold her, you will see cause to believe all I say; and let her but have a place in your chariot, and remain in your protection for one day only, till she can send a man and a horse to her rich and powerful friends; you may save from ruin a lady who has no equal for virtue as well as beauty.'

Methought the old lady, moved with Dorcas's story, answered and said: 'Hasten, oh damsel, who in a happy moment art come to put it in my power to serve the innocent and the virtuous, which it has always been my delight to do: hasten to this young lady, and bid her hie hither to me with all speed; and tell her that my chariot shall be her asylum: and if I find all that thou sayest true, my house shall be her sanctuary, and I will protect her from all her oppressors.'

Hereupon, methought, this traitress Dorcas hied back to the lady, and made report of what she had done. And, methought, the lady highly approved of Dorcas's proceeding, and blessed her for her good thought.

And I lifted up mine eyes, and behold the lady issued out of the house, and without looking back, ran to the chariot with the dowager's coat upon it, and was received by the matronly lady with open arms, and 'Welcome, welcome, welcome, fair young lady, who so well answer the description of the faithful damsel: and I will carry you instantly to my house, where you shall meet with all the good usage your heart can wish for, till you can apprise your rich and powerful friends of your past dangers, and present escape.'

'Thank you, thank you, thank you, thank you, worthy, thrice worthy lady, who afford so kindly your protection to a most unhappy young creature who has been basely seduced and betrayed, and brought to the very brink of destruction.'

Methought then, the matronly lady, who had by the time the young lady came to her bought and paid for the goods she wanted, ordered her coachman to drive home with all speed; who stopped not till he had arrived in a certain street, not far from Lincoln's Inn Fields, where the matronly lady lived in a sumptuous dwelling, replete with damsels who wrought curiously in muslins, cambricks, and fine linen, and in every good work that industrious damsels love to be employed about, except the loom and the spinning-wheel.

And methought, all the way the young lady and the old lady rode, and after they came in, till dinner was ready, the young lady filled up the time with the dismal account of her wrongs and her sufferings, the like of which was never heard by mortal ear; and this in so moving a manner, that the good old lady did nothing but weep, and sigh, and sob, and inveigh against the arts of wicked men, and against that abominable 'Squire Lovelace, who was a *plotting villain*, methought she said; and, more than that, an *unchained Beelzebub*.

Methought I was in a dreadful agony when I found the lady had escaped; and in my wrath had like to have slain Dorcas, and our mother, and everyone I met. But, by some quick transition, and strange metamorphosis which dreams do not usually account for, methought all of a sudden, this matronly lady was turned into the famous Mother H. herself; and, being an old acquaintance of Mother Sinclair, was prevailed upon to assist in my plot upon the young lady.

Then, methought, followed a strange scene; for Mother H. longing to hear more of the young lady's story, and night being come, besought her to accept of a place in her own bed in order to have all the talk to themselves. For methought, two young nieces of hers had broken in upon them in the middle of the dismal tale.

Accordingly going early to bed, and the sad story being resumed, with as great earnestness on one side as attention on the other, before the young lady had gone far in it, Mother H. methought was taken with a fit of the colic; and her tortures increasing, was obliged to rise, to get a cordial she used to find specific in this disorder, to which she was unhappily subject.

Having thus risen, and stepped to her closet, methought she let fall the wax taper in her return; and then (Oh metamorphosis still stranger than the former! What unaccountable things are dreams!), coming to bed, again in the dark, the young lady, to her infinite astonishment, grief, and surprise, found Mother H. turned into a young person of the other sex: and although Lovelace was the *abhorred of her soul*, yet fearing it was some *other* person, it was matter of some consolation to her, when she found it was no other than himself, and that she had been still the bedfellow of but one and the same man.

A strange promiscuous huddle of adventures followed; scenes perpetually, shifting; now nothing heard from the lady, but sighs, groans, exclamations, faintings, dyings—from the gentleman, but vows, promises, protestations, disclaimers of purposes pursued; and all the gentle and ungentle pressures of the lover's warfare.

Then, as quick as thought (for dreams, thou knowest, confine not themselves to the rules of the drama), ensued recoveries, lyings-in, christenings, the smiling boy amply, even in *her own* opinion, rewarding the suffering mother.

Then the grandfather's estate yielded up, possession taken of it—living very happily upon it—her beloved Norton her companion; Miss Howe her visitor; and (admirable! thrice admirable!) enabled to *compare notes* with her; a charming girl, by the same father, to her friend's charming boy; who, as they grow up, in order to consolidate their mammas' friendships (for neither have dreams regard to *consanguinity*), intermarry; change names by Act of Parliament, to enjoy my estate—and I know not what of the like incongruous stuff.

I awoke, as thou mayest believe, in great disorder, and rejoiced to find my charmer in the next room, and Dorcas honest.

Now thou wilt say this was a very odd dream. And yet (for I am a strange dreamer) it is not altogether improbable that something like it may happen; as the pretty simpleton has the weakness to confide in Dorcas, whom till now she disliked.

But I forgot to tell thee one part of my dream; and that was, that the next morning the lady gave way to such transports of grief and resentment, that she was with difficulty diverted from making an attempt upon her own life. But, however, at last, was prevailed upon to resolve to live, and to make the best of the matter. A letter, methought, from Captain Tomlinson helping to pacify her, written to apprise me that her uncle Harlowe would certainly be at Kentish Town on Wednesday night June 28, the following day, the 29th, being his anniversary birthday; and he doubly desirous, on that account, that our nuptials should be then privately solemnized in his presence.

But *is* Thursday the 29th her uncle's anniversary, methinks thou askest?—It is; or else the day of celebration should have been earlier still. Three weeks ago I heard her say it was; and I have down the birthday of every one of her family, and the wedding-day of her father and mother. The minutest circumstances are often of great service in matters of the last importance.

And what sayest thou now to my dream?

Who says that, sleeping and waking, I have not fine helps from some *body*, some *spirit* rather, as thou'lt be apt to say?—But no wonder that a Beelzebub has his devilkins to attend his call.

I can have no manner of doubt of succeeding in Mother H.'s part of the scheme; for will the lady (who resolves to throw herself into the *first house she can enter*, or to bespeak the protection of the *first person she meets*; and who thinks there can be no danger *out* of this house equal to what she apprehends from me *in* it) scruple to accept of the chariot of a dowager accidentally offering? And the lady's protection engaged by her faithful Dorcas, so highly bribed to promote her escape?—And then Mrs H. has the air and appearance of a venerable matron, and is not such a forbidding devil as Mrs Sinclair.

The pretty simpleton knows nothing of the world; nor that people who have money never want assistants in their views, be they what they will. How else could the princes of the earth be so implicitly served as they are, change they hands ever so often, and be their purposes ever so wicked?

If I can but get her to *go on* with me till Wednesday next week, we shall be settled together pretty quietly by that time. And indeed if she has any gratitude, and has in her the least of her sex's foibles, she must think I deserve her favour, by the pains she has cost me. For dearly do they all love that men should take pains about them, and for them.

And here, for the present, I will lay down my pen, and congratulate myself upon my happy invention (since her obstinacy puts me once more upon exercising it)—but with this resolution, I think that, if the present contrivance fail me, I will exert all the faculties of my mind, all my talents, to procure for myself a legal right to her favour, and that in defiance of all my antipathies to the married state; and of the suggestions of the great devil out of the house, and of his secret agents in it—since, if *now* she is not to be prevailed upon, or drawn in, it will be in vain to attempt her further.

Letter 272: MR LOVELACE TO JOHN BELFORD, ESQ.

Tuesday night, June 20

No admittance yet to my charmer! She is very ill—in a violent fever, Dorcas thinks. Yet will have no advice.

Dorcas tells her how much I am concerned at it.

But again let me ask, Does this lady do right to make herself ill, when she is *not* ill? For my own part, libertine as people think me, when I had *occasion* to be sick, I took a dose of ipecacuanha, that I might not be guilty of a falsehood; and most heartily sick was I; as she, who then pitied me, full well knew. But here to pretend to be very ill, only to get an opportunity to run away in order to avoid forgiving a man who has offended her, how unchristian!—If good folks allow themselves in these breaches of a known duty, and in these presumptuous contrivances to deceive, who, Belford, shall blame us?

I have a strange notion that the matronly lady will be certainly at the grocer's shop at the hour of nine tomorrow morning: for Dorcas heard me tell Mrs Sinclair that I shall go out at eight precisely; and then she is to try for a coach: and if the dowager's chariot should happen to be there, how lucky will it be for my charmer! How strangely will my dream be made out!

I HAVE just received a letter from Captain Tomlinson. Is it not wonderful! For that was part of my dream!

I shall always have a prodigious regard to dreams henceforward. I know not but I may write a book upon that subject; for my own experience will furnish out a great part of it. *Glanville of Witches*, and *Baxter's History of Spirits and Apparitions*, and the Royal Insignificant's *Demonology*,[1] will be nothing at all to *Lovelace's Reveries*.

The letter is just what I dreamed it to be. I am only concerned that uncle John's anniversary did not happen three or four days sooner; for should any *new* misfortune befall my charmer, she may not be able to support her spirits so long as till Thursday in the next week. Yet it will give me the more time for new expedients, should my present contrivance fail; which I cannot, however, suppose.

[*Letter 272.1:* '*Captain Tomlinson*'] *to Robert Lovelace, Esq.*

Monday, June 19

Dear sir,

I CAN now return you joy, for the joy you have given me, as well as my dear friend Mr Harlowe, in the news of his beloved niece's happy recovery; for he is determined to comply with *her* wishes, and *yours*, and to give her to you with his own hand.

As the ceremony has been necessarily delayed by reason of her illness, and as Mr Harlowe's birthday is on Thursday the 29th of this instant June, when he enters into the seventy-fourth year of his age; and as time may be wanted to complete the dear lady's recovery; he is very desirous that the marriage shall be solemnized upon it; that he may afterwards have double joy on that day, to the end of his life.

For this purpose he intends to set out privately so as to be at Kentish Town on Wednesday se'nnight in the evening.

All the family used, he says, to meet to celebrate it with him; but as they are at present in too unhappy a situation for that, he will give out that, not being able to bear the day at home, he has resolved to be absent for two or three days.

He will set out on horseback, attended only with one trusty servant, for the greater privacy. He will be at the most creditable-looking public house there, expecting you both next morning, if he hear nothing from me to prevent him. And he will go to town with you after the ceremony is performed, in the coach he supposes you will come in.

He is very desirous that I should be present on the occasion. But this I have promised him, at his request, that I will be up before the day, in order to see the settlements executed, and everything properly prepared.

He is very glad that you have the licence ready.

He speaks very kindly of you, Mr Lovelace; and says that, if any of the family stand out after he has seen the ceremony performed, he will separate from them, and unite himself to his dear niece and her interests.

I owned to you, when in town, that I took slight notice to my dear friend of the misunderstanding between you and his niece; and that I did this for fear the lady should have shown any little discontent in his presence, were I to have been able to prevail upon him to go up in person, as then was doubtful. But I hope nothing of that discontent remains now.

My absence, when your messenger came, must excuse me for not writing by him.

Be pleased to make my most respectful compliments acceptable to the admirable lady, and believe me to be

> Your most faithful and obedient servant,
> ANTONY TOMLINSON

This letter I sealed, and broke open. It was brought, thou mayest suppose, by a particular messenger; the seal such a one as the writer need not be ashamed of. I took care to inquire after the Captain's health, in my beloved's hearing; and it is now ready to be produced as a pacifier, according as she shall *take on*, or *resent*, if the two metamorphoses happen pursuant to my wonderful dream; as, having great faith in dreams, I dare say they will—I think it will not be amiss in changing my clothes, to have this letter of the worthy Captain lie in my beloved's way.

Letter 273: MR LOVELACE TO JOHN BELFORD, ESQ.

Wed. noon, June 21

WHAT shall I say now!—I who but a few hours ago had such faith in dreams, and had proposed out of hand to begin my treatise of *Dreams sleeping* and *Dreams waking*, and was pleasing myself with the dialoguings between the old matronly lady and the young lady; and with the two metamorphoses (absolutely assured that everything would happen as my dream chalked it out); shall never more depend upon those flying follies, those illusions of a fancy depraved, and run mad.

Thus confoundedly have matters happened.

I went out at eight o'clock in high good humour with myself, in order to give the sought-for opportunity to the plotting mistress and corrupted maid; only ordering Will to keep a good look-out for fear his lady should mistrust my plot, or mistake a hackney-coach for the dowager-lady's chariot. But first I sent to know how she did; and received for an answer, Very ill—had a very bad night: which latter was but too probable: since this *I* know, that people who have plots in their heads as seldom *have* as *deserve* good ones.

I desired a physician might be called in; but was refused.

I took a walk in St James's park, congratulating myself all the way on my rare inventions: then, impatient, I took coach, with one of the windows *quite* up, the other *almost* up, playing at bo-peep at every chariot I saw pass in my way to Lincoln's Inn Fields: and when arrived there, I sent the coachman to desire any one of Mother H.'s family to come to me to the coach-side, not doubting but I should have intelligence of my fair fugitive there; it being then half an hour after ten.

A servant came to me, who gave me to understand that the matronly lady was just returned by herself in the chariot.

Frighted out of my wits, I alighted, and heard from the Mother's own mouth, that Dorcas had engaged her to protect the lady; but came to tell her afterwards that she had changed her mind, and would not quit the house.

Quite astonished, not knowing what might have happened, I ordered the coachman to lash away to our mother's.

Arriving here in an instant, the first word I asked, was, if the lady were safe?

Mr Lovelace gives here a very circumstantial relation of all that passed between the lady and Dorcas. But as he could only guess at her motives for refusing to go off, when Dorcas told her that she had engaged for her the protection of the dowager lady, it is thought proper to omit his relation, and to supply it by some *memoranda* of the lady's. But it is first necessary to account for the occasion on which those *memoranda* were made.

The reader may remember that in the letter wrote to Miss Howe on her escape to Hampstead,[a] she promises to give her the particulars of her flight at leisure.

She had indeed thoughts of continuing her account of everything that had passed between her and Mr Lovelace since her last narrative letter. But the uncertainty she was in from that time, with the execrable treatment she met with on her being deluded back again; followed by a week's delirium; had hitherto hindered her from prosecuting her intention. But, nevertheless, having it still in her view to perform her promise, as soon as she had opportunity, she made minutes of everything as it passed, in order to help her memory—which, as she observes, in one place, she could less trust to since her late disorders than before.

In these minutes, or book of *memoranda*, she observes: 'That having apprehensions that Dorcas might be a traitress, she would have got away while she was gone out to see for a coach; and actually slid downstairs with that intent. But that, seeing Mrs Sinclair in the entry' (whom Dorcas had planted there while she went out) 'she speeded up again, unseen.'

She then went up to the dining-room, and saw the letter of Captain Tomlinson: on which she observes in her memorandum-book, as follows:

a　See p. 756.

'How am I puzzled now!—He might leave this letter on purpose: none of the other papers left with it being of any consequence—What's the alternative?—To stay and be the wife of the vilest of men—How my heart resists that!—To attempt to get off and fail, ruin inevitable!—Dorcas *may* betray me!—I doubt she is *still* his implement!—At his going out, he whispered her, as I saw, unobserved—in a very familiar manner too—Never fear, sir, with a curtsy.

'In her agreeing to connive at my escape, she provided not for her own safety if I got away! Yet had reason, in that case, to expect his vengeance; and wants not forethought—To have taken her *with me*, was to be in the power of her intelligence, if a faithless creature—Let me, however, though I part not with my caution, keep my charity!—Can there be any woman so vile to woman?—Oh yes!—Mrs Sinclair: her aunt—The Lord deliver me!—But, alas! I have put myself out of the course of his protection by the *natural* means—and am already ruined!—A father's curse likewise against me!—Having made vain all my friends' cautions and solicitudes, I must not hope for miracles in my favour!

'If I do escape, what may become of me, a poor, helpless, deserted creature!—Helpless from sex!—from circumstances!—Exposed to every danger!—Lord protect me!

'His vile man not gone with him!—lurking hereabouts, no doubt, to watch my steps!—I *will* not go away by the chariot, however.

'That this chariot should come so opportunely!—So like his many *opportunelies!*—That Dorcas should have the sudden thought!—should have the *courage* with the thought, to address a lady in behalf of an absolute stranger to that lady!—That the lady should so readily consent!—yet the transaction between them to take up so much time; their distance in degree considered: for, arduous as the case was, and precious as the time, Dorcas was gone above half an hour! Yet the chariot was said to be ready at a grocer's not many doors off!

'Indeed some elderly ladies are talkative: and there are, no doubt, *some* good people in the world——

'But that it should chance to be a widow lady, who could do what she pleased: that Dorcas should know her to be so, by the lozenge! Persons in her station not usually so knowing, I believe, in heraldry.

'Yet some may!—for servants are fond of deriving *collateral* honours and distinctions, as I may call them, from the quality, or people of rank, whom they serve.

'But his sly servant not gone with him!—Then this letter of Tomlinson's!——

'Although I am resolved never to have this wretch, yet, may I not *throw myself into my uncle's protection at Kentish Town or Highgate, if I cannot escape before*; *and so get clear of him?*—May not the evil I know be less than what I may fall into, if I can avoid further villainy?—Further villainy he has not yet threatened—freely and justly as I have treated him!—I will not go, I think. At least, unless I can send this fellow out of the way.[a]

---

a She tried to do this; but was prevented by the fellow's pretending to put his ankle out, by a slip downstairs—'A trick,' says his contriving master, in his omitted relation, 'I had learned him, on a like occasion, at Amiens'.

'The fellow a villain! The wench, I doubt, a vile wench. At last concerned for her own safety. Plays off and on about a coach.

'All my hopes of getting off, at present, over!— Unhappy creature!— to what further evils art thou reserved!— Oh how my heart rises, at the necessity I must still be under to see and converse with so very vile a man!'

Letter 274: MR LOVELACE TO JOHN BELFORD, ESQ.

Wednesday afternoon

DISAPPOINTED in her meditated escape—obliged, against her will, to meet me in the dining-room—and perhaps apprehensive of being upbraided for her art in feigning herself ill; I *expected* that the dear perverse would *begin* with me with spirit and indignation. But I was in hopes, from the gentleness of her natural disposition, from the consideration which I expected from her, on her situation on the letter of Captain Tomlinson, which Dorcas told me she had seen, and from the time she had had to cool and reflect, since she last admitted me to her presence, that she would not have carried it so strongly through as she did.

As I entered the dining-room, I congratulated her and myself upon her *sudden* recovery. And would have taken her hand, with an air of respectful tenderness. But she was resolved to begin where she left off.

She turned from me, drawing in her hand with a repulsing and indignant aspect—I meet you once more, said she, because I cannot help it. What have you to say to me? Why am I to be thus detained against my will?

With the utmost solemnity of speech and behaviour, I urged the ceremony. I saw I had nothing else for it—I had a letter in my pocket, I said (feeling for it, although I had not taken it from the table where I left it, and which we were then near), the contents of which, if attended to, would make us both happy. I had been loath to show it to her before, because I hoped to prevail upon her to be mine sooner than the day mentioned in it.

I felt for it in all my pockets, watching her eye meantime, which I saw glance towards the table where it lay.

I was uneasy that I could not find it—At last, directed again by her sly eye, I spied it on the table at the further end of the room.

With joy I fetched it. Be pleased to read that letter, madam, with an air of satisfied assurance.

She took it, and cast her eye over it in such a careless way, as made it evident that she had read it before: and then unthankfully tossed it into the window-seat before her.

I urged her to bless me tomorrow, or Friday morning: at least, that she would not render vain her uncle's journey, and kind endeavours to bring about a reconciliation among us all.

Among us all, repeated she, with an air equally disdainful and incredulous. Oh Lovelace, thou art surely nearly allied to the grand deceiver in thy endeavour to suit temptations to inclinations!—But what honour, what faith, what veracity, were it possible that I could enter into parley with thee on this subject, which it is not, may I expect from such a man as thou hast shown thyself to be?

I was touched to the quick. A lady of your perfect character, madam, who has feigned herself sick, on purpose to avoid seeing the man who adored her, should——

I know what thou wouldst say, interrupted she!—Twenty and twenty low things, that my soul would have been above being guilty of, and which I have despised myself for, have I been brought into by the infection of thy company, and by the necessity thou hast laid me under of appearing mean. But I thank God, destitute as I am, that I am not, however, sunk so low as to wish to be thine.   ···

I, madam, as the injurer, *ought* to have patience. It is for the injured to reproach. But your uncle is not in a plot against you, it is to be hoped. There are circumstances in the letter you have cast your eyes over——

Again she interrupted me, Why, once more I ask thee, am I detained in this house?—Do I not see myself surrounded by wretches, who, though they wear the habit of my sex, may yet, as far as I know, lie in wait for my perdition?

She would be very loath, I said, that Mrs Sinclair and her nieces should be called up to vindicate themselves and their house.

Would but they kill me, let them come, and welcome. I will bless the hand that will strike the blow; indeed I will.

'Tis idle, very idle, to talk of dying. Mere young-lady talk, when controlled by those they hate—But let me beseech you, dearest creature——

Beseech me nothing. Let me not be detained thus against my will!—Unhappy creature, that I am, said she, in a kind of frenzy, wringing her hands at the same time, and turning from me, her eyes lifted up! Thy curse, oh my cruel father, seems to be now in the height of its operation!—I am in the way of being a lost creature as to both worlds! Blessed, blessed God, said she, falling on her knees, save me, Oh save me from myself, and from this man!

I sunk down on my knees by her, excessively affected—Oh that I could recall yesterday!—Forgive me! my dearest creature, forgive what is past, as it cannot now but by one way be retrieved. Forgive me only on this condition—that my future faith and honour——

She interrupted me, rising—If you mean to beg of me, never to seek to avenge myself by law, or by an appeal to my relations, to my cousin Morden in particular, when he comes to England——

D—n the law, rising also (she started), and all those to whom you talk of appealing!—I defy both the one and the other—All I beg, is YOUR forgiveness; and that you will, on my unfeigned contrition, re-establish me in your favour——

Oh no, no, no! lifting up her clasped hands, I never, never *will*, never, never *can* forgive you!—And it is a punishment worse than death to me, that I am obliged to meet you, or to see you!

This is the last time, my dearest life, that you will ever see me in this posture, on this occasion: and again I kneeled to her—Let me hope that you will be mine next Thursday, your uncle's birthday, if not before. Would to Heaven I had never been a villain! Your indignation is not, cannot be, greater than my remorse—and I took hold of her gown; for she was going from me.

Be remorse thy portion!—For thy own sake, be remorse thy portion!—I never, never will forgive thee!—I never, never will be thine!—Let me retire!—Why kneelest thou to the wretch whom thou hast so vilely humbled?

Say but, dearest creature, you will *consider*—Say but you will take time to reflect upon what the honour of both our families require of you. I will not rise. I will not permit you to withdraw (still holding her gown), till you tell me you will *consider*—Take this letter. Weigh well *your* situation, and *mine*. Say you will withdraw to *consider*; and then I will not presume to withhold you.

Compulsion shall do nothing with me. Though a slave, a prisoner, in circumstance, I am no slave in my will!—Nothing will I promise thee—Withheld, compelled—nothing will I promise thee—

Noble creature!—but not implacable, I hope!—Promise me but to return in an hour!—

Nothing will I promise thee!—

Say but you will see me again this evening!

Oh that I could say—that it were in my *power* to say—I never will see thee more!—Would to Heaven I never were to see thee more!

Passionate beauty—still holding her——

I speak, though with vehemence, the deliberate wish of my heart—Oh that I could avoid *looking down* upon thee, mean groveller, and abject as insulting—Let me withdraw! My soul is in tumults! Let me withdraw!

I quitted my hold to clasp my hands together—Withdraw, oh sovereigness of my fate!—Withdraw, if you *will* withdraw!—My destiny is in your power!—It depends upon your breath!—Your scorn but augments my love!—Your resentment is but too well founded!—But, dearest creature, return, return, with a resolution to bless with pardon and peace your faithful adorer!

She flew from me. As soon as she found her wings, the angel flew from me. I, the reptile kneeler, the despicable slave, no more the proud victor, arose; and, retiring, tried to comfort myself that, circumstanced as she is, destitute of friends and fortune; her uncle moreover, who is to reconcile all so soon (as, I thank my stars, she still believes), expected.

Oh that she would forgive me!—Would she but generously forgive me, and receive my vows at the altar, at the *instant* of her forgiving me, that I might not have time to relapse into my old prejudices!—By my soul, Belford, this dear girl gives the lie to all our rakish maxims. There must be something more than a *name* in virtue!—I now see that there is!—*Once subdued, always subdued*—'Tis an egregious falsehood!—But oh, Jack, she never *was subdued*. What have I obtained but an increase of shame and confusion!—While her glory has been established by her sufferings!

This one merit is, however, left me, that I have laid all her sex under obligations to me, by putting this noble creature to trials which, so gloriously supported, have done honour to them all.

But yet—but no more will I add—What a force have evil habits—I will take an airing, and try to fly from myself—Do not thou upbraid me on my weak fits—on my contradictory purposes—on my irresolution—and all will be well.

Letter 275: MR LOVELACE TO JOHN BELFORD, ESQ.

Wednesday night

A MAN is just now arrived from M. Hall, who tells me that my lord is in a very dangerous way. The gout in his stomach to an extreme degree, occasioned by drinking a great quantity of lemonade.

A man of £8000 a year to prefer his appetite to his health!—He deserves to die!—But we have all of us our inordinate passions to gratify!—and they generally bring their punishment along with them. So witnesses the nephew, as well as the uncle.

The fellow was sent up on other business; but stretched his orders a little to make his court to a successor.

I am glad I was not at M. Hall at the time my lord took the grateful dose (It was certainly grateful to *him* at the time): there are people in the world who would have had the wickedness to say that I had persuaded him to drink it.

The man says that his lordship was so bad when he came away, that the family began to talk of sending for me in post-haste. As I know the old peer has a good deal of cash by him, of which he seldom keeps account, it behoves me to go down as soon as I can. But what shall I do with this dear creature the while?—Tomorrow over, I shall, perhaps, be able to answer my own question—I am afraid she will make me desperate.

For here have I sent to implore her company, and am denied with scorn.

I HAVE been so happy as to receive, this moment, a third letter from my dear correspondent Miss Howe. A little severe devil!—It would have broke the heart of my beloved had it fallen into her hands. I will enclose a copy of it. Read it here.

[*Letter 275.1: Miss Howe to Miss Clarissa Harlowe*]

Tuesday, June 20

My dearest Miss Harlowe,

AGAIN I venture to write to you (almost against inclination); and that by your former conveyance, little as I like it.

I know not how it is with you. It may be bad; and then it would be hard to upbraid you for a silence you may not be able to help. But if not, what shall I say severe enough, that you have not answered either of my last letters? The first[a] of which (and I think it imported you too much to be silent upon it) you owned the receipt of. The other, which was delivered into your own hands,[b] was so pressing for the favour of a line from you, that I am amazed I could not be obliged—and still *more*, that I have not heard from you since.

The fellow made so strange a story of the condition he saw you in, and of your speech to him, that I know not what to conclude from it: only, that he is a simple, blundering, and yet conceited fellow, who aiming at description, and the rustic wonderful, gives an air of bumkinly romance to all he tells. That this is his character, you will believe, when you are informed that he described you in grief excessive,[c] yet so improved in your person and features, and so *rosy*, that was his word, in your face, and so flush-coloured, and so plump in your arms, that one would conclude you were labouring under the operation of some malignant poison; and so much the rather, as he was introduced to you when you were upon a couch, from which you offered not to rise, or sit up.

Upon my word, Miss Harlowe, I am greatly distressed upon your account; for

a   See p. 743.
b   See p. 859.
c   See pp. 856–8.

I must be so free as to say that, in your ready return with your deceiver, you have not at all answered my expectations, nor acted up to your own character: for Mrs Townsend tells me, from the women at Hampstead, how cheerfully you put yourself into his hands again: yet, at the time, it was impossible you should be married!

Lord, my dear, what pity it is that you took so much pains to get from the man! But you know best!—Sometimes I think it could not be *you* to whom the rustic delivered my letter. But it must too: yet it is strange I could not have one line by him: not one—and you so soon well enough to go with him back again!

I am not sure that the letter I am now writing will come to your hands: so shall not say half that I have upon my mind to say. But if you think it *worth your while* to write to me, pray let me know what fine ladies, his relations, those were, who visited you at Hampstead, and carried you back again so joyfully to a place that I had so fully warned you—But I will say no more: at least till I *know* more: for I can do nothing but wonder, and stand amazed!

Notwithstanding all the man's baseness, 'tis plain there was more than a lurking love—Good God!—But I have done!—Yet I know not how to have done, neither!—Yet I must—I *will*.

Only account to me, my dear, for what I cannot at all account for: and inform me whether you are really married, or not—And then I shall know whether there *must*, or must *not*, be a period shorter than that of one of our lives, to a friendship which has hitherto been the pride and boast of

Your ANNA HOWE

DORCAS tells me that she has just now had a *searching* conversation, as she calls it, with her lady. She is willing, she tells the wench, still to place a confidence in her. Dorcas hopes she has reassured her; but wishes me not to depend upon it. Yet Captain Tomlinson's letter must assuredly weigh with her. I sent it in just now by Dorcas, desiring her to re-peruse it. And it was not returned me, as I feared it would be. And that's a good sign, I think.

I say, *I think*, and *I think*; for this charming creature, entangled as I am in my own inventions, puzzles *me* ten thousand times more than I *her*.

Letter 276: MR LOVELACE TO JOHN BELFORD, ESQ.

Thursday noon, June 22

LET me perish, if I know what to make either of myself, or of this surprising creature—now calm, now tempestuous—but I know thou lovest not anticipation any more than me.

At my repeated requests, she met me at six this morning. She was ready dressed; for she has not had her clothes off ever since she declared that they never more should be off in this house. And charmingly she looked, with all the disadvantages of a three hours' violent stomach-ache (for Dorcas told me that she had been really ill), no rest, and eyes red and swelled with weeping. Strange to me that those charming fountains have not been long ago exhausted. But she is a woman. And I believe anatomists allow *that women have more watery heads than men*.

Well, my dearest creature, I hope you have now thoroughly considered of the contents of Captain Tomlinson's letter. But as we are thus early met, let me beseech you to make this my happy day.

She looked not favourably upon me. A cloud hung upon her brow at her entrance: but as she was going to answer me, a still greater solemnity took possession of her charming features.

Your air, and your countenance, my beloved creature, are not propitious to me. Let me beg of you, before you speak, to forbear all further recriminations. For already I have such a sense of my vileness to you, that I know not how to bear the reproaches of my own mind.

I have been endeavouring, said she, since I am not permitted to avoid you, after a composure which I never more expected to see you in. How long I may enjoy it, I cannot tell. But I hope I shall be enabled to speak to you without that vehemence which I expressed yesterday, and could not help it.[a]

After a pause (for I was all attention) thus she proceeded.

It is easy for me, Mr Lovelace, to see that further violences are intended me if I comply not with your purposes, whatever they are. I will suppose them to be what you so solemnly profess they are. But I have told you as solemnly my mind, that I never *will*, that I never *can*, be yours; nor, if so, any man's upon earth. All vengeance, nevertheless, for the wrongs you have done me, I disclaim. I want but to slide into some obscure corner, to hide myself from you, and from everyone who once loved me. The desire lately so near my heart, of a reconciliation with my friends, is much abated. They shall not receive me *now*, if they *would*. Sunk in my own eyes, I now think myself unworthy of their favour. In the anguish of my soul, therefore, I conjure you, Lovelace (tears in her eyes), to leave me to my fate. In doing so, you will give me a pleasure, the highest I now can know.

Whither, my dearest life——

No matter whither. I will leave to Providence, when I am out of this house, the direction of my future steps. I am sensible enough of my destitute condition. I know that I have not now a friend in the world. Even Miss Howe has given me up—or you are—but I would fain keep my temper!—By your means I have lost them all—and you have been a barbarous enemy to me. You know you have.

She paused.

I could not speak.

The evils I have suffered, proceeded she (turning from me), however irreparable, are but *temporary* evils—Leave me to my hopes of being enabled to obtain the Divine forgiveness for the offence I have been drawn in to give to my parents, and to virtue; that so I may avoid the evils that are *more than temporary*. This is now all I have to wish for. And what is it that I demand, that I have not a right to, and from which it is an illegal violence to withhold me?

It was impossible for me, I told her plainly, to comply. I besought her to give me her hand as this very day. I could not live without her. I communicated to her my lord's illness, as a reason why I wished not to stay for her uncle's anniversary. I

---

a The lady, in her minutes, says, 'I fear Dorcas is a false one. May I not be able to prevail upon him to leave me at my liberty? Better to try than to trust to her. If I cannot prevail, but must meet him and my uncle, I hope I shall have fortitude enough to renounce him then. But I would fain avoid qualifying with the wretch, or to give him an expectation which I intend not to answer. If I am mistress of my own resolutions, my uncle himself shall not prevail with me to bind my soul in covenant with so vile a man.'

besought her to bless me with her consent; and, after the ceremony was passed, to accompany me down to Berkshire. And thus, my dearest life, said I, will you be freed from a house to which you have conceived so great an antipathy.

This, thou wilt own, was a princely offer. And I was resolved to be as good as my word. I thought I had killed my conscience, as I told thee, Belford, some time ago. But conscience, I find, though it may be temporarily stifled, cannot die; and when it dare not speak aloud, will whisper. And at this instant, I thought I felt the revived varletess (on but a slight retrograde motion) writhing round my pericardium like a serpent; and, in the action of a dying one (collecting all its force into its head), fix its plaguy fangs into my heart.

She hesitated and looked down, as if irresolute. And this set my heart up at my mouth. And believe me, I had instantly popped in upon me in imagination, an old spectacled parson with a white surplice thrown over a black habit (a fit emblem of the halcyon office which, under a benign appearance, often introduces a life of storms and tempests), whining and snuffling through his nose the irrevocable ceremony.

I hope now, my dear life, said I, snatching her hand, and pressing it to my lips, that your silence bodes me good. Let me, my beloved creature, have but your tacit consent this moment, to step out and engage a minister—and then I promised how much my whole future life should be devoted to her commands, and that I would make her the best and tenderest of husbands.

At last, turning to me, I have told you my mind, Mr Lovelace, said she. Think you that I could thus solemnly—There she stopped—I am too much in your power, proceeded she; your prisoner, rather than a person free to choose for myself, or to say what I will *do* or *be*. But, as a testimony that you mean me well, let me instantly quit this house; and I will then give you such an answer in writing as best befits my unhappy circumstances.

And imaginest thou, fairest, thought I, that this will go down with a Lovelace? Thou oughtest to have known that free-livers, like ministers of state, never part with a power put into their hands, without an equivalent of twice the value.

I pleaded that if we joined hands *this morning* (if not, *tomorrow*; if not, on *Thursday*, her uncle's birthday, and in his presence); and afterwards, as I had proposed, set out for Berkshire; we should, of course, quit this house; and, on our return to town, should have in readiness the house I was in treaty for.

She answered me not, but with tears and sighs: *fond of believing what I hoped*, I imputed her silence to the modesty of her sex. The dear creature, thought I, solemnly as she began with me, is ruminating, in a sweet suspense, how to put into fit words the gentle purposes of her condescending heart. But, looking in her averted face with a soothing gentleness, I plainly perceived that it was resentment, and not bashfulness, that was struggling in her bosom.[a]

At last, she broke silence—I have no patience, said she, to find myself a slave, a prisoner in a vile house—Tell me, sir, in so many words tell me, whether it be, or be not, your intention to permit me to quit it?—To permit me the freedom which is my birthright as an English subject?

---

a The lady, in her minutes, owns the difficulty she lay under to keep her temper in this conference. 'But when I found, says she, that all my entreaties were ineffectual, and that he was resolved to detain me, I could no longer withhold my impatience.'

Will not the consequence of your departure hence be, that I shall lose you for ever, madam?—and can I bear the thoughts of that?

She flung from me—My soul disdains to hold parley with thee, were her violent words—But I threw myself at her feet, and took hold of her reluctant hand, and began to imprecate, to vow, to promise—But thus the passionate beauty, interrupting me, went on:

I am sick of thee, MAN!—One continued string of vows, oaths, and protestations, varied only by time and place, fill thy mouth!—Why detainest thou me? My heart rises against thee, Oh thou *cruel implement of my brother's causeless vengeance*— All I beg of thee is that thou wilt remit me the future part of my father's dreadful curse! The temporary part, base and ungrateful as thou art! thou hast completed!

I was speechless!—Well I might!—Her *brother's* implement!—*James Harlowe's* implement!—Zounds, Jack! what words were these!

I let go her struggling hand. She took two or three turns cross the room, her whole haughty soul in her air—Then approaching me, but in silence, turning from me, and again to me, in a milder voice—I see thy confusion, Lovelace. Or is it thy remorse?—I have but one request to make thee—the request so often repeated— that thou wilt this moment permit me to quit this house. Adieu then, let me say, for *ever* adieu! And mayst thou enjoy that happiness in this world which thou hast robbed me of; as thou hast of every friend I have in it!

And saying this, away she flung, leaving me in a confusion so great that I knew not what to think, say, or do.

But Dorcas soon roused me—Do you know, sir, running in hastily, that my lady is gone downstairs!

No, sure!—And down I flew, and found her once more at the street door, contending with Polly Horton to get out.

She rushed by me into the fore parlour, and flew to the window, and attempted once more to throw up the sash—Good people! Good people! cried she.

I caught her in my arms, and lifted her from the window. But being afraid of hurting the charming creature (charming in her very rage), she slid through my arms on the floor—Let me die here! Let me die here! were her words; remaining jointless and immoveable till Sally and Mrs Sinclair hurried in.

She was visibly terrified at the sight of the old wretch; while I, sincerely affected, appealed, Bear witness, Mrs Sinclair!—Bear witness, Miss Martin!—Miss Horton!—Everyone bear witness, that I offer not violence to this beloved creature!

She then found her feet—Oh house (looking towards the windows, and all round her, Oh house) contrived on purpose for my ruin! said she—But let not that woman come into my presence—nor that Miss Horton neither, who would not have dared to control me, had she not been a base one!

Hoh, sir! Hoh, madam! vociferated the old creature, her arms kemboed, and flourishing with one foot to the extent of her petticoats—What ado's here about nothing!—I never knew such work in my life, between a chicken of a gentleman, and a tiger of a lady!——

She was visibly affrighted: and upstairs she hastened. A bad woman is certainly, Jack, more terrible to her own sex, than even a bad man.

I followed her up. She rushed by her own apartment into the dining-room: no terror can make her forget her punctilio.

To recite what passed there of invective, exclamations, threatenings, even of her own life, on one side; of expostulations, supplications, and sometimes menaces, on the other, would be too affecting; and, after my particularity in like scenes, these things may as well be imagined as expressed.

I will therefore only mention that, at length, I extorted a concession from her. She had reason[a] to think it would have been worse for her on the spot, if she had not made it. It was, *that she would endeavour to make herself easy, till she saw what next Thursday, her uncle's birthday, would produce.* But Oh that it were not a sin, she passionately exclaimed, on making this poor concession, to put an end to her own life, rather than yield to give me but *that* assurance!

This, however, shows me, that she is aware that the reluctantly given assurance may be fairly construed into a matrimonial expectation on my side. And if she will *now*, even *now*, look forward, I think from my heart that I will put on her livery, and wear it for life.

What a situation am I in, with all my cursed inventions? I am puzzled, confounded, and ashamed of myself, upon the whole. To take such pains to be a villain!—But (for the *fiftieth* time) let me ask thee, who would have thought that there had been such a woman in the world?—Nevertheless, she had best take care that she carries not her obstinacy much further. She knows not what revenge for slighted love will make me do.

The busy scenes I have just passed through have given emotions to my heart which will not be quieted one while. My heart, I see (on reperusing what I have written), has communicated its tremors to my fingers; and in some places the characters are so indistinct and unformed that thou'lt hardly be able to make them out. But if one *half* of them only are intelligible, that will be enough to expose me to thy contempt, for the wretched hand I have made of my plots and contrivances. But surely, Jack, I have gained some ground by this promise.

And now, one word to the assurances thou sendest me that thou hast not betrayed my secrets in relation to this charming creature. Thou mightest have spared them, Belford. My suspicions held no longer than while I wrote about them.[b] For well I knew, when I allowed myself time to think, that thou hadst no *principles*, no *virtue*, to be misled by. A great deal of strong envy, and a little of weak pity, I knew to be thy motives. Thou couldst not provoke my anger, and my compassion thou ever hadst; and art now more especially entitled to it; because thou art a *pitiful* fellow.

All thy new expostulations in my beloved's behalf I will answer when I see thee.

---

a The lady mentions, in her memorandum-book, that she had no other way, as she apprehended, to save herself from instant dishonour but by making this concession. Her only hope, now, she says, if she cannot escape by Dorcas's connivance (whom, nevertheless, she suspects) is to find a way to engage the protection of her uncle, and even of the civil magistrate, on Thursday next, if necessary. 'He shall see, she says, tame and timid as he has thought her, what she dare to do to avoid so hated a compulsion; and a man capable of a baseness so premeditatedly vile and inhuman.'

b See p. 903.

Letter 277: MR LOVELACE TO JOHN BELFORD, ESQ.

Thursday night

CONFOUNDEDLY out of humour with this perverse lady. Nor wilt thou blame me, if thou art my friend. She regards the concession she made, as a concession extorted from her: and we are but just where we were before she made it.

With great difficulty I prevailed upon her to favour me with her company for one half-hour this evening. The necessity I was under to go down to M. Hall was the subject I wanted to talk to her upon.

I told her, that as she had been so good as to promise that she would endeavour to make herself easy till she saw the Thursday in next week over, I hoped that she would not scruple to oblige me with her word that I should find her here at my return from M. Hall.

Indeed she would make me no such promise. Nothing of *this house* was mentioned to me, said she: you know it was not. And do you think that I would have given *my consent to my imprisonment in it?*

I was plaguily nettled, and disappointed too. If I go not down to M. Hall, madam, you'll have no scruple to stay here, I suppose, till Thursday is over?

If I cannot help myself, I must. But I insist upon being permitted to go out of this house, whether you leave it, or not.

Well, madam, then I will comply with your commands. And I will go out this very evening, in quest of lodgings that you shall have no objection to.

I will have no lodgings of your providing, sir—I will go to Mrs Moore's at Hampstead.

Mrs Moore's, madam?—I have no objection to Mrs Moore's. But will you give me your promise to admit me there to your presence?

As I do here—when I cannot help it.

Very well, madam—Will you be so good as to let me know what you intended by your promise to *make yourself easy*——

To *endeavour*, sir, to make myself easy—were the words——

—*Till you saw what next Thursday would produce?*

Ask me no questions that may ensnare me. I am too sincere for the company I am in.

Let me ask you, madam, what meant you, when you said, 'that, were it not a sin, you would die before you gave me that assurance'?

She was indignantly silent.

You thought, madam, you had given me room to hope your pardon by it?

When I think I ought to answer you with patience, I will speak.

Do you think yourself in my power, madam?

If I were not—And there she stopped——

Dearest creature, speak out—I beseech you, dearest creature, speak out.

She was silent; her charming face all in a glow.

Have you, madam, any reliance upon my honour?

Still silent.

You hate me, madam. You despise me more than you do the most odious of God's creatures.

You ought to despise me if I did not.

You say, madam, you are in a *bad* house. You have *no reliance* upon my honour—you believe you *cannot avoid me*——

She arose. I beseech you, let me withdraw.

I snatched her hand, rising, and pressed it first to my lips, and then to my heart, in wild disorder. She might have felt the bounding mischief ready to burst its bars—You *shall* go—to your own apartment, if you please—but, by the great God of Heaven, I will accompany you thither.

She trembled—Pray, pray, Mr Lovelace, don't terrify me so!

Be seated, madam! I beseech you be seated!—

I will sit down——

Do then, madam—do then—all my soul in my eyes, and my heart's blood throbbing at my fingers' ends.

I will—I will—you hurt me—pray, Mr Lovelace, don't—don't frighten me so— and down she sat, trembling; my hand still grasping hers.

I hung over her throbbing bosom, and putting my other arm round her waist— And you say you hate me, madam—and you say you despise me!—and you say you promised me nothing——

Yes, yes, I did promise you—let me not be held down thus—you see I sat down when you bid me—Why (struggling) need you hold me down thus?—I did promise *to endeavour to be easy till Thursday was over!* But you won't let me!—How can I be easy?—Pray, let me not be thus terrified.

And what, madam, meant you by your promise? Did you mean anything in my favour?—You designed that I should, at the time, *think* you did. Did you mean anything in my favour, madam?—Did you intend that I should *think* you did?

Let go my hand, sir—take away your arm from about me, struggling, yet trembling—*Why do you gaze upon me so?*

Answer me, madam—Did you mean anything in my favour by your promise?

Let me not be thus constrained to answer.

Then pausing, and gaining more spirit, Let me go, said she: I am but a woman— but a weak woman—but my life is in my own power, though my person is not—I will not be thus constrained.

You shall not, madam, quitting her hand, bowing, but my heart at my mouth, and hoping farther provocation.

She arose, and was hurrying away.

I pursue you not, madam—I will try your generosity—Stop—return—This moment stop, return, if, madam, you would not make me desperate.

She stopped at the door; burst into tears—Oh Lovelace!—How, how, have I deserved——

Be *pleased*, dearest angel, to return.

She came back—but with declared reluctance; and imputing her compliance to terror.

Terror, Jack, as I have heretofore found out, though I have so little benefited by the discovery, must be my resort if she make it necessary—Nothing else will do with the inflexible charmer.

She seated herself over against me; extremely discomposed—but indignation had a visible predominance in her features.

I was going towards her with a countenance intendedly changed to love and softness: Sweetest, dearest angel, were my words, in the tenderest accent—but, rising up, she insisted upon my being seated at distance from her.

I obeyed—and begged her hand over the table, to my extended hand; to see, as I said, if in anything she would oblige me—But nothing gentle, soft, or affectionate would do. She refused me her hand!—Was she wise, Jack, to confirm to me that nothing but terror would do?

Let me only know, madam, if your promise to *endeavour* to wait with patience the event of next Thursday meant me favour?

Do you expect any voluntary favour from one to whom you give not a free choice?

Do you intend, madam, to honour me with your hand, in your uncle's presence, or do you not?

My heart and my hand shall never be separated. Why, think you, did I stand in opposition to the will of my best, my natural friends?

I know what you mean, madam—Am I then as hateful to you as the vile Solmes?

Ask me not such a question, Mr Lovelace.

I *must* be answered. Am I as hateful to you as the vile Solmes?

Why do you call Mr Solmes vile?

Don't *you* think him so, madam?

Why should I? Did Mr Solmes ever do vilely by me?

Dearest creature! don't distract me by hateful comparisons! And perhaps by a more hateful preference.

Don't you, sir, put questions to me that you know I will answer truly, though my answer were ever so much to enrage you.

My heart, madam, my soul is all yours at present. But you *must* give me hope that your promise, in your own construction, binds you, no *new cause* to the contrary, to be mine on Thursday. How else can I leave you?

Let me go to Hampstead; and trust to my favour.

May I trust to it?—Say, only, *may* I trust to it?

How will you trust to it, if you extort an answer to this question?

Say only, dearest creature, say only, *may* I trust to your favour if you go to Hampstead?

How *dare* you, sir, if I must speak out, expect a promise of favour from me?—What a mean creature must you think me, after your ungrateful baseness to me, were I to give you such a promise?

Then standing up, Thou hast made me, Oh vilest of men! (her hands clasped, and a face crimsoned over with indignation) an inmate of the vilest of houses—nevertheless, while I am in it, I shall have a heart incapable of anything but abhorrence of *that* and of *thee!*

And round her looked the angel, and upon me, with fear in her sweet aspect of the consequence of her free declaration. But what a devil must I have been, I, who love bravery in a man, had I not been more struck with admiration of her fortitude at the instant, than stimulated by revenge?

Noblest of creatures!—And do you think I can leave you, and my interest in such an excellence, precarious? No promise!—No hope!—If you make me not desperate, may lightning blast me if I do you not all the justice 'tis in my power to do you!

If you have any intention to oblige me, leave me at my own liberty, and let me not be detained in this abominable house. To be constrained as I have been constrained! To be stopped by your vile agents! To be brought up by force, and to be bruised in my own defence against such illegal violence!—I dare to die, Lovelace—and the person that fears not death is not to be intimidated into a meanness unworthy of her heart and principles!

Wonderful creature! But why, madam, did you lead me to hope for something favourable for next Thursday?—Once more, make me not desperate—With all your magnanimity, glorious creature! (I was more than half frantic, Belford) you *may*, you *may*—but do not, do not make me brutally threaten you!—do not, do not make me desperate!

My aspect, I believe, threatened still more than my words. I was rising—she arose—Mr Lovelace, be pacified—You are even more dreadful than the Lovelace I have long dreaded—let me retire—I ask your *leave* to retire—you really frighten me—yet I give you no hope—from my heart I ab——

Say not, madam, you *abhor* me—You must, for your own sake, conceal your hatred—at least not avow it. I seized her hand.

Let me retire—let me retire, said she—in a manner out of breath.

I will only say, madam, that I refer myself to your generosity. My heart is not to be trusted at this instant. As a mark of my submission to your will, you shall, *if you please*, withdraw—but I will not go to M. Hall—Live or die my uncle, I will not go to M. Hall—but will attend the effect of your promise. Remember, madam, you have promised *to endeavour to make yourself easy, till you see the event of next Thursday*—Next Thursday, remember, your uncle comes up to see us married—*that's the event*—You think ill of your Lovelace—Do not, madam, suffer your own morals to be degraded by the *infection*, as you called it, of his example.

Away flew the charmer, with this half-permission—and no doubt thought that she had an escape—nor without reason.

I knew not for half an hour what to do with myself. Vexed at the heart, nevertheless (now she was from me, when I reflected upon her hatred of me, and her defiances), that I suffered myself to be so over-awed, checked, restrained——

And now I have written thus far (having of course recollected the whole of our conversation), I am more and more incensed against myself.

But I will go down to these women—and perhaps suffer myself to be laughed at by them.

Devil fetch them, they pretend to know their own sex. Sally was a woman well educated—Polly also—Both have read—both have sense—of parentage not contemptible—once modest both—still they say had been modest, but for me—not entirely indelicate *now*; though too little nice for my *personal* intimacy, loath as they both are to have me think so. The old one, too, a woman of family, though thus (from bad inclination, as well as at first from low circumstances) miserably sunk—And hence they all pretend to remember what *once* they were; and vouch for the inclinations and hypocrisy of the whole sex; and wish for nothing so ardently as that I will leave the perverse lady to their management while I am gone to Berkshire; undertaking absolutely for her humility and passiveness on my return; and continually boasting of the many perverse creatures whom they have obliged to draw in their traces.

They often upbraidingly tell me that they are sure I shall marry at last: and

Sally, the last time I was with her, had the confidence to hint that, when a wife, some other person would not find half the difficulty that I had found—Confidence, indeed! But yet I must say, that this dear creature is the only woman in the world of whom I should not be jealous. And yet, if a man gives himself up to the company of these devils, they never let him rest till he either suspect or hate his wife.

But a word or two of other matters, if possible.

Methinks I long to know how causes go at M. Hall. I have another private intimation that the old peer is in the greatest danger.

I must go down. Yet what to do with this lady the meanwhile!—These cursed women are full of cruelty and enterprise. She will never be easy with them in my absence. They will have provocation and pretence therefore. But woe be to them, if—

Yet what will vengeance do, after an insult committed? The two nymphs will have jealous rage to goad them on—and what will withhold a jealous and already ruined woman?

To let her go elsewhere; that cannot be done. I am still resolved to be honest, if she'll give me hope: if yet she'll *let me* be honest—But I'll see how she'll be after the contention she will certainly have between her resentment, and the terror she had reason for from our last conversation. So let this subject rest till the morning. And to the old peer once more.

I shall have a good deal of trouble, I reckon, though no sordid man, to be decent on the expected occasion. Then how to act (I who am no hypocrite) in the days of condolement! What farces have I to go through; and to be a principal actor in them—I'll try to think of my own latter end; a grey beard, and a graceless heir; in order to make me serious.

Thou, Belford, knowest a good deal of this sort of grimace; and canst help a gay heart to a little of the dismal. But then every feature of thy face is cut out for it. My heart may be touched, perhaps, sooner than thine; for, believe me or not, I have a very tender one—but then, no man looking in my face, be the occasion for grief ever so great, will believe *that* heart to be deeply distressed.

All is placid, easy, serene, in my countenance. Sorrow cannot sit half an hour together upon it. Nay, I believe that Lord M.'s recovery, should it happen, would not affect me above a quarter of an hour. Only the new scenery (and the pleasure of aping an Heraclitus to the family, while I am a Democritus among my private friends[1]), or I want nothing that the old peer can leave me. Wherefore then should grief sadden and distort such blithe, such jocund features as mine?

But as for thine, were there murder committed in the street, and thou wert but passing by, the murderer even in sight, the pursuers would quit *him*, and lay hold of *thee*: and thy very looks would hang, as well as apprehend, thee.

But one word to business, Jack. Whom dealtest thou with for thy blacks?—Wert thou well used?—I shall want a plaguy parcel of them. For I intend to make every soul of the family mourn—*outside*, if not *in*——

Letter 278: MR LOVELACE TO JOHN BELFORD, ESQ.

June 23. Friday morning

I WENT out early this morning, on a design that I know not yet whether I shall or shall not pursue; and on my return found Simon Parsons, my lord's Berkshire bailiff (just before arrived), waiting for me with a message in form, sent by all the family, to press me to go down, and that at my lord's particular desire; who wants to see me before he dies.

Simon has brought my lord's chariot and six (perhaps *my own* by this time), to carry me down. I have ordered it to be in readiness by four tomorrow morning. The cattle shall smoke for the delay; and by the rest they'll have in the interim, will be better able to bear it.

I am still resolved upon matrimony, if my fair perverse will accept of me. But, if she will not—why then I must give an uninterrupted hearing, not to my conscience, but to these women below.

Dorcas had acquainted her lady with Simon's arrival and errand. My beloved had desired to see him. But my coming in prevented his attendance on her, just as Dorcas was instructing him what questions he should not answer to, that might be asked of him.

I am to be admitted to her presence immediately, at my repeated request— Surely the acquisition in view will help me to make all up with her—She is just gone up to the dining-room.

NOTHING will do, Jack!—I can procure no favour from her, though she has obtained from me the point which she had set her heart upon.

I will give thee a brief account of what passed between us.

I first proposed instant marriage; and this in the most fervent manner: but was denied as fervently.

Would she be pleased to assure me that she would stay here only till Tuesday morning? I would but just go down and see how my lord was—to know whether he had anything particular to say, or enjoin me, while yet he was sensible, as he was very earnest to see me—perhaps I might be up on Sunday—Concede in something!—I beseech you, madam, show me some little consideration.

Why, Mr Lovelace, must I be determined by your motions?—Think you that I will voluntarily give a sanction to the imprisonment of my person? Of what importance to me ought to be your stay or your return?

Give a sanction to the imprisonment of your person! Do you think, madam, that I fear the law?——

I might have spared this foolish question of defiance—but my pride would not let me. I thought she threatened me, Jack.

I *don't* think so, sir—You are too *brave* to have any regard either to moral or divine sanctions.

'Tis well, madam!—But ask me anything I can do to oblige *you*; and I *will* oblige you, though in nothing will you oblige *me*.

Then I ask you, then I request of you, to let me go to Hampstead.

I paused—and at last—By my soul you shall——This very moment I will wait upon you, and see you fixed there, if you'll promise me your hand on Thursday, in presence of your uncle.

I want not *you* to see me fixed—I will promise nothing.

Take care, madam, that you don't let me see that I can have no reliance upon your future favour.

I have been used to be threatened by you, sir—but I will accept of your company to Hampstead—I will be ready to go in a quarter of an hour—My clothes may be sent after me.

You know the condition, madam—next Thursday.

You dare not trust—

My infinite demerits tell me that I *ought* not—Nevertheless I *will* confide in your generosity—Tomorrow morning (no *new cause* arising to give reason to the contrary), as early as you please, you may go to Hampstead.

This seemed to oblige her. But yet she looked with a face of doubt.

I will go down to the women. And having no better judges at hand, will hear what they say upon my critical situation with this proud beauty, who has so insolently rejected a Lovelace kneeling at her feet, though making an earnest tender of himself for a husband, in spite of all his prejudices to the state of shackles.

Letter 279: MR LOVELACE TO JOHN BELFORD, ESQ.

JUST come from the women.

'Have I gone so far, and am I afraid to go farther?—Have I not already, as it is evident by her behaviour, sinned beyond forgiveness?—A woman's tears used to be to me but as water sprinkled on a glowing fire, which gives it a fiercer and brighter blaze: what defence has this lady, but her tears and her eloquence? She was before taken at *no weak* advantage. She was *insensible* in her moments of trial. *Had* she been sensible, she *must* have been sensible. So they say. The methods taken with her have augmented her glory and her pride. She has now a tale to tell, that she *may* tell with honour to herself. No accomplice-inclination. She can look me into confusion, without being conscious of so much as a *thought* which she need to be ashamed of.'

This, Jack, the substance of my conference with the women.

To which let me add, that the dear creature now sees the necessity I am in to leave her. Detecting me is in her head. My contrivances are of such a nature, that I must appear to be the most odious of men if I am detected on this side matrimony. And yet I have promised as thou seest, that she shall set out to Hampstead as soon as she pleases in the morning, and that without condition on her side.

Dost thou ask, what I meant by this promise?

No *new cause* arising, was the proviso on my side, thou'lt remember. But there *will be* a new cause.

Suppose Dorcas should drop the promissory-note given her by her lady? Servants, especially those who cannot read or write, are the most careless people in the world of written papers. Suppose I take it up?—at a time, too, that I was determined that the dear creature should be her own mistress?—Will not this detection be a *new cause*?—a cause that will carry against her the appearance of ingratitude with it?

That she designed it a *secret from me* argues a *fear of detection*, and indirectly a *sense of guilt*. I wanted a pretence. Can I have a better? If I am in a violent passion upon the detection, is not passion an universally allowed extenuator of violence?— Is not every man and woman obliged to excuse that fault in another, which at times they find attended with such ungovernable effects in themselves?

The mother and sisterhood, suppose, brought to sit in judgement upon the vile corrupted?—The least benefit that must accrue from the accidental discovery, if not a pretence for *perpetration* (which, however, may be the case), an excuse for renewing my orders for her detention till my return from M. Hall (the fault her own); and for keeping a stricter watch over her than before; with direction to send me any letters that may be written *by* her or *to* her. And when I return, the devil's in it if I find not a way to make her choose lodgings for herself (since these are so hateful to her), that shall answer all my purposes; and yet no more appear to direct her choice than I did before in these.

Thou wilt curse me when thou comest to this place. I know thou wilt. But thinkest thou that, after such a series of contrivance, I will lose this inimitable woman for want of a little more? A rake's a rake, Jack!—And what rake is withheld by *principle* from the perpetration of any evil his heart is set upon, and in which he thinks he can succeed?—Besides, am I not in earnest as to marriage?— Will not the generality of the world acquit me, if I *do* marry? And what is that injury which a *church rite* will at any time repair? Is not *the catastrophe of every story that ends in wedlock accounted happy*, be the difficulties in the progress to it ever so great?

But here, how am I engrossed by this lady, while poor Lord M. as Simon tells me lies groaning in the dreadfullest agonies?—What must he suffer!—Heaven relieve him!—I have a too compassionate heart. And so would the dear creature have found, could I have thought the worst of *her* sufferings equal to the lightest of *his*. I mean as to fact; for, as to that part of hers which arises from extreme sensibility, I know nothing of that; and cannot therefore be answerable for it.

Letter 280: MR LOVELACE TO JOHN BELFORD, ESQ.

JUST come from my charmer. She will not suffer me to say half the obliging, the tender things, which my honest heart is ready to overflow with. A confounded situation that, when a man finds himself in humour to be eloquent and pathetic at the same time, yet cannot engage the mistress of his fate to lend an ear to his fine speeches.

I can account now, how it comes about that lovers, when their mistresses are cruel, run into solitude, and disburthen their minds to *stocks* and *stones*: for am I not forced to make my complaints to *thee*?

She claimed the performance of my promise, the moment she saw me, of *permitting* her (haughtily she spoke the word) to go to Hampstead as soon as I were gone to Berkshire.

Most cheerfully I renewed it.

She desired me to give orders in her hearing.

I sent for Dorcas and Will. They came—Do you both take notice (but, perhaps, sir, I may take *you* with me), that your lady is to be obeyed in all her commands. She purposes to return to Hampstead as soon as I am gone—My dear, will you not have a servant to attend you?

I shall want no servant there.

Will you take Dorcas?

If I should want Dorcas, I can send for her.

Dorcas could not but say, she should be very proud——

Well, well, that may be at my return, if your lady permit—Shall I, my dear, call up Mrs Sinclair, and give her orders to the same effect, in your hearing?

I desire not to see Mrs Sinclair; nor any that belong to her.

As you please, madam.

And then (the servants being withdrawn) I urged her again for the assurance that she would meet me at the altar on Thursday next. But to no purpose. May she not thank herself for all that may follow?

One favour, however, I would not be denied; to be admitted to pass the evening with her.

All sweetness and obsequiousness will I be on this occasion. My whole soul shall be poured out to move her to forgive me. If she will not, and if the promissory-note should fall in my way, my revenge will doubtless take total possession of me.

All the house in my interest, and everyone in it not only engaging to intimidate, and assist, as occasion shall offer; but staking all their experience upon my success if it be not my own fault, what must be the consequence?

This, Jack, however, shall be her last trial; and if she behave as nobly *in* and *after* this *second* attempt (*all her senses about her*), as she has done after the *first*, she will come out an angel upon full proof, in spite of man, woman, and devil: then shall there be an end of all her sufferings. I will then renounce that vanquished devil, and reform. And if any vile machination start up, presuming to mislead me, I will sooner stab it in my heart as it rises, than give way to it.

A few hours will now decide all. But whatever be the event, I shall be too busy to write again, till I get to M. Hall.

Meantime I am in strange agitations. I must suppress them, if possible before I venture into her presence—My heart bounces my bosom from the table. I will lay down my pen, and wholly resign to its impulses.

Letter 281: MR LOVELACE TO JOHN BELFORD, ESQ.

Fri. night, or rather Sat. morn. 1 o'clock

I THOUGHT I should not have had either time or inclination to write another line before I got to M. Hall. But have the first; must find the last; since I can neither sleep, nor do anything but write, if I can do that. I am most *confoundedly* out of humour. The reason let it follow; if it will follow—no preparation for it, from me.

I tried by gentleness and love to soften—What?—Marble. A heart incapable either of love or gentleness. Her past injuries for ever in her head. Ready to receive a favour; the permission to go to Hampstead; but neither to deserve it, nor return any. So my scheme of the gentle kind was soon given over.

I then wanted her to provoke me: like a coward boy who waits for the first blow before he can persuade himself to fight, I half challenged her to challenge or defy me: she seemed aware of her danger; and would not directly brave my resentment: but kept such a middle course that I neither could find a pretence to offend, nor reason to hope; yet she believed my tale that her uncle would come to Kentish Town; and seemed not to apprehend that Tomlinson was an impostor.

She was very uneasy, upon the whole, in my company: wanted often to break from me: yet so held me to my promise of permitting her to go to Hampstead, that I knew not how to get off of it; although it was impossible, in my precarious situation with her, to think of performing it.

In this situation; the women ready to assist; and, if I proceeded not, as ready to ridicule me; what had I left me but to pursue the concerted scheme, and seek a pretence to quarrel with her in order to revoke my promised permission; and to convince her that I would not be upbraided as the most brutal of ravishers for nothing?

I had agreed with the women, that if I could not find a pretence in her presence to begin my operations, the note should lie in my way, and I was to pick it up soon after her retiring from me. But I began to doubt at near ten o'clock (so earnest was she to leave me, suspecting my over-warm behaviour to her, and eager grasping of her hand two or three times, with eye-strings, as I felt, on the strain, while her eyes showed uneasiness and apprehension), that if she actually retired for the night, it might be a chance, whether it would be easy to come at her again. Loath therefore to run such a risk, I stepped out at a little after ten, with intent to alter the pre-concerted disposition a little; saying I would attend her again instantly. But as I returned, I met her at the door, intending to withdraw for the night. I could not persuade her to go back: nor had I presence of mind (so full of complaisancy as I was to her just before) to stay her by force: so she slid through my hands into her own apartment. I had nothing to do, therefore, but to let my former concert take place.

I should have premised (but care not for order of time, connexion, or anything else) that, between eight and nine o'clock in the evening, another servant of Lord M.'s, on horseback, came to desire me to carry down with me Dr S., my uncle having been once (*in extremis*, as they judge he is now) relieved and reprieved by him. I sent, and engaged the doctor to accompany me down; and am to call upon him by four this morning: or the devil should have uncle and doctor, if I'd stir till I got all made up.

Poke thy damned nose forward into the event, if thou wilt—curse me, if thou shalt have it till its proper time and place—and too soon then.

She had hardly got into her chamber, but I found a little paper, as I was going into mine; which I took up; and, opening it (for it was carefully pinned in another paper), what should it be but a promissory note, given as a bribe, with a further promise of a diamond ring, to induce Dorcas to favour her mistress's escape?

How my temper changed in a moment!—Ring, ring, ring, ring, my bell, with a violence enough to break the string, and as if the house were on fire.

Every devil frighted into active life: the whole house in an uproar: up runs Will—Sir—sir—sir!—eyes goggling, mouth distended—Bid the damned toad Dorcas come hither (as I stood at the stair head), in a horrible rage, and out of breath, cried I.

In sight came the trembling devil—but standing aloof, from the report made her by Will of the passion I was in, as well as from what she heard.

Flash came out my sword immediately; for I had it ready on—Cursed, confounded, villainous, bribery and corruption!—

Up runs she to her lady's door, screaming out for safety and protection.

Good your honour, interposed Will, for God's sake—Oh Lord, Oh Lord!—receiving a good cuff—

Take that, varlet, for saving the ungrateful *wretch* from my vengeance!—

Wretch! I *intended* to say; but if it were some other word of like ending, passion must be my excuse.

Up ran two or three of the sisterhood: What's the matter! What's the matter!

The matter! (for still my beloved opened not her door; on the contrary, drew another bolt). This *abominable* Dorcas!—(Call her aunt up!—Let her see what a traitress she has placed about me!—And let her bring the toad to answer for herself)—has taken a bribe, a provision for life, to betray her trust; by that means to perpetuate a quarrel between a man and his wife, and frustrate for ever all hopes of reconciliation between us!

Let me perish, Belford, if I have patience to proceed with the farce!

Up came the aunt puffing and blowing!—As she hoped for mercy, she was not privy to it!—She never knew such a plotting perverse lady in her life!—Well might servants be at the pass they were, when such ladies as Mrs Lovelace made no conscience of corrupting them. For *her* part, she desired no mercy for the wretch: no niece of hers, if she were not faithful to her trust!—But what was the proof?—

She was shown the paper—

But too evident!—Cursed, cursed toad, devil, jade, passed from each mouth—and the vileness of the *corrupted* and the unworthiness of the *corruptress* were inveighed against.

Up we all went, passing the lady's door into the dining-room, to proceed to trial—

Stamp, stamp, stamp up, each on her heels; rave, rave, rave, every tongue!—

Bring up the creature before us all, this instant!—

And would she have got out of the house, say you!—

These the noises and the speeches, as we clattered by the door of the fair briberess—

Up was brought Dorcas (whimpering) between two, both bawling out—You must go! You shall go!—'Tis fit you should answer for yourself!—You are a discredit to all worthy servants!—as they pulled and pushed her upstairs—she whining, I cannot see his honour!—I cannot look so good and so generous a gentleman in the face!—Oh how shall I bear my aunt's ravings!—

Come up, and be damned—Bring her forward, her imperial judge!—What a plague, it is the *detection*, not the *crime*, that confounds you. You could be quiet enough for days together, as I see by the date, under the villainy. Tell me, ungrateful devil, tell me, who made the first advances.

Ay, disgrace to my family and blood, cried the old one!—Tell his honour! Tell the truth—Who made the first advances!—

Ay, cursed creature, cried Sally, Who made the first advances?

I have betrayed one trust already!—Oh let me not betray another!—My lady is a good lady!—Oh let not *her* suffer!—

Tell all you know. Tell the whole truth, Dorcas, cried Polly Horton—His honour loves his lady too well to make her suffer *much*; little as she requites his love!—

Everybody sees that, cried Sally—Too well indeed, *for* his honour, I was going to say.

Till now, I thought she deserved my love! But to bribe a servant thus, whom she supposed had orders to watch her steps for fear of another elopement; and to impute that precaution to me as a crime!—Yet I must love her!—Ladies, forgive my weakness!—

Curse upon my grimaces!—if I have patience to repeat them!—but thou shalt have them all—Thou canst not despise me more than I despise myself!—

BUT suppose, sir, said Sally, you have my lady and the wench face to face? You see she cares not to confess.

Oh my *carelessness*! cried Dorcas—Don't let my poor lady suffer!—Indeed if you all knew what I know, you would say her ladyship has been cruelly treated—

See!—see!—see!—see!—repeatedly, everyone at once—Only sorry for the *detection*, as your honour said—not the *fault*—

Cursed creature, and devilish creature, from every mouth.

Your lady *won't*, she *dare* not come out to save you, cried Sally, though it is more his honour's mercy than your desert, if he does not cut your vile throat this instant.

Say, repeated Polly, was it your lady that made the first advances, or was it you, you creature?—

If the lady has so much honour, bawled the mother, excuse me, *so*—excuse me, sir—(confound the old wretch! she had like to have said *son!*)—If the lady has so much honour, as we have supposed, she will appear to vindicate a poor servant, misled as she has been by such large promises!——But I hope, sir, you will do them *both* justice; I *hope* you will!—Good lack! Good lack! clapping her hands together, to grant her everything she could ask: to indulge her in her unworthy hatred to my poor innocent house!—to let her go to Hampstead, though your honour told us you could get no condescension from her: no, not the least!——Oh sir——Oh sir——I hope——I hope——if your lady will not come out—I hope you will find a way to hear this cause in her presence. I value not my doors on such an occasion as this. Justice I ever loved. I desire you will come at the bottom of it, in *clearance* to me!—I'll be sworn I had no privity in this black corruption.

Just then, we heard the lady's door unbar, unlock, unbolt——

Now, sir!

Now, Mr Lovelace.

Now, sir! from every encouraging mouth!—

But, oh Jack! Jack! Jack! I can write no more!

IF you must have it all, you must!

Now, Belford, see us all sitting in judgement, resolved to punish the fair briberess—I, and the mother, the hitherto *dreaded* mother, the nieces Sally, Polly, the traitress Dorcas, and Mabel, a guard as it were over [Dorcas] that she might not run away and hide herself: all pre-determined, and of *necessity* pre-determined, from the journey I was going to take, and my precarious situation with her: and hear her *unbolt*, *unlock*, *unbar*, the door; then, as it proved afterwards, put the key into the lock on the outside, lock the door, and put it in her pocket; Will I knew below, who would give me notice if, while we were all above, she should mistake her way and go downstairs, instead of coming into the dining-room; the street doors also doubly secured, and every shutter to the windows round the house fastened, that no noise or screaming should be heard (such was the brutal preparation)—and then *hear* her step towards us, and instantly *see* her enter among us, confiding in her own innocence; and with a majesty in her person and manner that is *natural* to her; but which then shone out in all its glory!—Every tongue silent, every eye awed, every heart quaking, mine, in a particular manner, sunk, throbless, and twice below its usual region, to once at my throat—a shameful recreant!—She silent too, looking round her, first on me; then on the mother, as no longer fearing her; then on Sally, Polly; and the culprit Dorcas!—Such the glorious power of innocence exerted at that awful moment!

She would have spoken, but could not, looking down my guilt into confusion: a mouse might have been heard passing over the floor, her own light feet and rustling silks could not have prevented it; for she seemed to tread air, and to be all soul—She passed to the door, and back towards me, two or three times, before speech could get the better of indignation, and at last, after twice or thrice hemming, to recover her articulate voice—Oh thou contemptible and abandoned Lovelace, thinkest thou that I see not through this poor villainous plot of thine, and of these thy wicked accomplices?

Thou woman, looking at the mother, once my terror! always my dislike! but now my detestation! shouldst once more (for thine perhaps was the preparation) have provided for me intoxicating potions, to rob me of my senses—

And then, *turning to me*, Thou, wretch, mightest more securely have depended upon such a low contrivance as this!—

And ye, vile women, who perhaps have been the ruin, body and soul, of hundreds of innocents (you show me *how*, in full assembly), know that I am not married—ruined as I am by your helps, I bless God, I am *not* married to this miscreant—And I have friends that will demand my honour at your hands!—And to whose authority I will apply; for none has this man over me. Look to it then, what further insults you offer me, or incite him to offer me. I am a person, though thus vilely betrayed, of rank and fortune. I never will be his; and to your utter ruin will find friends to pursue you: and now I have this full proof of your detestable wickedness, and have heard your base incitements, will have no mercy upon you!—

They could not laugh at the poor figure I made.—Lord! how every devil, conscience-shaken, trembled!—

What a dejection must ever fall to the lot of guilt, were it given to innocence always thus to exert itself!—

And as for thee, thou vile Dorcas!—thou *double* deceiver!—whining out thy pretended love for me!—begone, wretch!—Nobody will hurt thee!—Begone, I say!—Thou hast too well acted thy part to be blamed by *any* here but myself—Thou art safe: thy guilt is thy security in such a house as this!—Thy shameful, thy poor part thou hast as well acted as the low farce could give thee to act!—as well as they each of them (thy superiors, though not thy betters), thou seest, can act

, theirs. Steal away into darkness! No inquiry after this will be made, whose the first advances, thine or mine.

And, as I hope to live, the wench, confoundedly frightened, slunk away; so did her sentinel, Mabel; though I, endeavouring to rally, cried out for Dorcas to stay: but I believe the devil could not have stopped her, when an angel bid her begone.

Madam, said I, let me tell you; and was advancing towards her with a fierce aspect, most cursedly vexed and ashamed too—

But she turned to me: Stop where thou art, Oh vilest and most abandoned of men!—Stop where thou art!—Nor, with that determined face, offer to touch me, if thou wouldst not that I should be a corpse at thy feet!

To my astonishment, she held forth a penknife in her hand, the point to her own bosom, grasping resolutely the whole handle, so that there was no offering to take it from her.

I offer not mischief to anybody but myself. You, sir, and ye women, are safe from every violence of mine. The LAW shall be all my resource: the LAW, and she spoke the word with emphasis, that to such people carries natural terror with it, and now struck a panic into them.

No wonder, since those who will damn themselves to procure ease and plenty in this world will tremble at everything that seems to threaten their methods of obtaining that ease and plenty—

The LAW only shall be my refuge!—

The infamous mother whispered me that it were better to *make terms* with this *strange* lady, and let her go.

Sally, notwithstanding all her impudent bravery at other times, said: *If* Mr Lovelace had told *them* what was *not true* of her being his wife—

And Polly Horton: That she must *needs* say, the lady, if she were *not* my wife, had been very much injured; that was all.

That is not now a matter to be disputed, cried I: you and I know, madam—

We do so, said she; and I thank God, I am *not* thine—*Once more*, I thank God for it! I have no doubt of the further baseness that thou hadst intended me by this vile and low trick: but I have my SENSES, Lovelace: and from my heart I despise thee, thou very poor Lovelace! How canst thou stand in my presence!—Thou, that—

Madam, madam, madam——these are insults not to be borne—and was approaching her. She withdrew to the door, and set her back against it, holding the pointed knife to her heaving bosom; while the women held me, beseeching me not to provoke the violent lady——For their *house* sake, and be cursed to them, they besought me—and all three hung upon me—while the truly heroic lady braved me at that distance:

Approach me, Lovelace, with resentment, if thou wilt. I dare die. It is in defence of my honour. God will be merciful to my poor soul!—I expect no mercy from thee! I have gained this distance, and two steps nearer me and thou shalt see what I dare do!—

Leave me, women, to myself, and to my angel!—They retired at a distance—Oh my beloved creature, how you terrify me!—Holding out my arms, and kneeling on one knee—Not a step, not a step further, except to receive the death myself at that injured hand that threatens its own. I am a villain! the blackest of villains!—Say you will sheathe your knife in the injurer's, not the injured's, heart; and then will I indeed approach you, but not else.

The mother twanged her damned nose; and Sally and Polly pulled out their handkerchiefs, and turned from us. They never in their lives, they told me afterwards, beheld such a scene—

Innocence so triumphant: villainy so debased, they must mean!

Unawares to myself, I had moved onward to my angel—And dost thou, dost thou, *still* disclaiming, *still* advancing—Dost thou, dost thou, *still* insidiously move towards me? (and her hand was extended)—I dare—I dare—not rashly neither—My heart from *principle* abhors the act which *thou* makest *necessary*!—God, in thy mercy!—lifting up her eyes, and hands—God, in thy mercy!—

I threw myself to the further end of the room. An ejaculation, a silent ejaculation, employing her thoughts that moment; Polly says the whites of her lovely eyes were only visible: and, in the instant that she extended her hand, *assuredly* to strike the fatal blow (how the very recital tumults me!), she cast her eye towards me, and saw me at the utmost distance the room would allow, and heard my broken voice (my voice was utterly broken; nor knew I what I said, or whether to the purpose or not): and her charming cheeks that were all in a glow before turned pale, as if terrified at her own purpose; and lifting up her eyes—Thank God!—Thank God! said the angel—Delivered *for the present*; for the *present* delivered from myself. Keep, sir, keep that distance (looking down towards me, who was prostrate on the floor, my heart pierced as with an hundred daggers!): that distance has saved a life; to what reserved, the Almighty only knows!—

To *be* happy, madam; and to *make* happy!—And Oh let me but hope for your favour for tomorrow—I will put off my journey till then—And may God—

Swear not, sir!—with an awful and piercing aspect—You have too, too often sworn!——God's eye is upon us!—His more *immediate* eye; and looked wildly. But the women looked up to the ceiling, and trembled, as if *afraid* of God's eye. And well they might; and *I* too, who so very lately had each of us the devil in our hearts.

If not tomorrow, madam, say but next Thursday, your uncle's birthday; say but next Thursday!—

This I say, of this you may assure yourself, I never, never *will* be yours—And let me hope that I may be entitled to the performance of your promise, to permit me to leave this *innocent* house, as one called it (but long have my ears been accustomed to such inversions of words), as soon as the day breaks.

Did my perdition depend upon it, that you cannot, madam, but upon terms. And I hope you will not terrify me—still dreading the accursed knife.

Nothing less than an attempt upon my honour shall make me desperate—I have no view but to defend my honour: with such a view only I entered into treaty with your infamous agent below. The resolution you have seen, I trust God will give me again upon the same occasion. But for a *less*, I wish not for it. Only take notice, women, that I am no wife of *this man*: basely as he has used me, I am not his wife. He has no authority over me. If he go away by and by, and you act by his authority to detain me, look to it.

Then, taking one of the lights, she turned from us; and away she went, unmolested. Not a soul was *able* to molest her.

Mabel saw her, tremblingly and in a hurry, take the key of her chamber door out of her pocket and unlock it; and, as soon as she entered, heard her double-lock, bar, and bolt it.

By her taking out her key, when she came out of her chamber to us, she no doubt suspected my design: which was to have carried her in my arms thither, if she made such force necessary, after I had intimidated her, and to have been her companion for that night.

She was to have had several bedchamber women to assist to undress her upon occasion: but, from the moment she entered the dining-room with so much intrepidity, it was absolutely impossible to think of prosecuting my villainous designs against her.

THIS, this, Belford, was the hand I made of a contrivance I expected so much from!—And now am I ten times worse off than before!

Thou never sawest people in thy life look so like fools upon one another, as the mother, her partners, and I did for a few minutes. And at last, the two devilish nymphs broke out into insulting ridicule upon me; while the old wretch was concerned for her house, the reputation of her house. I cursed them all together; and, retiring to my chamber, locked myself in.

And now it is time to set out: all I have gained, detection, disgrace, fresh guilt by repeated perjuries, and to be despised by her I *doat upon*; and, what is still worse to a proud heart, by *myself.*

Success, success in projects, is everything. What an admirable fellow did I think myself till now! Even for this scheme among the rest! But how pitifully foolish does it appear to me now!—Scratch out, erase, never to be read, every part of my preceding letters, where I have boastingly mentioned it—And never presume to rally me upon the cursed subject: for I cannot bear it.

But for the lady, by my soul I love her, I admire her, more than ever!—I *must* have her. I *will* have her still—*With* honour, or *without*, as I have often vowed. My cursed fright at her accidental bloody nose, so lately, put her upon improving upon me thus: had she threatened ME, I should soon have been mistress of *one* arm, and *in both*!—but for so sincere a virtue to threaten *herself*, and not offer to intimidate *any other*, and with so much presence of mind as to distinguish, in the very passionate intention, the necessity of the act in defence of her *honour*, and so *fairly* to disavow *lesser* occasions; showed such a deliberation, such a choice, such a principle; and then keeping me so watchfully at a distance that I could not seize her hand, so soon as she could have given the fatal blow, how impossible not to be subdued by so *true* and so *discreet* a magnanimity!

But she is not *gone*; shall not go. I will press her with letters for the Thursday— She shall yet be mine, legally mine. For, as to cohabitation, there is now no such thing to be thought of.

The captain shall give her away, as proxy for her uncle. My lord will die. My fortune will help my *will*, and set me above everything and everybody.

But here is the curse—She despises me, Jack!—What man, as I have heretofore said, can bear to be despised—especially by his wife?—Oh Lord! Oh Lord! What a hand, what a cursed hand have I made of this plot!—and here ends

The history of the Lady and the Penknife!!!—The devil take the penknife!—It goes against me to say, God bless the lady.

Near 5, Sat. morn.

Letter 282: MR LOVELACE TO MISS CLARISSA HARLOWE

(Superscribed, To Mrs Lovelace)

M. Hall, Sat. night, June 24

My dearest life,

IF you do not impute to love, and to terror raised by love, the poor figure I made before you last night, you will not do me justice. I thought I would try to the very last moment if, by complying with you in *everything*, I could prevail upon you to promise to be mine on Thursday next, since you refused me an earlier day. Could I have been so happy, you had not been hindered going to Hampstead, or wherever else you pleased. But when I could not prevail upon you to give me this assurance, what room had I (my demerit so great) to suppose that your going thither would not be to lose you for ever?

I will own to you, madam, that yesterday afternoon I picked up the paper dropped by Dorcas; who has confessed that she would have assisted you in getting away, if she had had an opportunity so to do; and undoubtedly dropped it by *accident*. And could I have prevailed upon you as to the Thursday next, I would have made no use of it; secure as I should then have been in your word given to be mine. But when I found you inflexible, I was resolved to try if, by resenting Dorcas's treachery, I could not make *your* pardon of *me* the condition of *mine* to *her*: and if not, to make a handle of it to revoke my consent to your going away from Mrs Sinclair's; since the consequence of that must have been so fatal to me.

So far, indeed, was my proceeding *low* and *artful*: and when I was challenged with it as such, in so high and noble a manner, I could not avoid taking shame to myself upon it.

But you must permit me, madam, to hope that you will not punish me too heavily for so poor a contrivance, since no dishonour was meant you; and since, in the moment of its execution, you had as great an instance of my incapacity to defend a wrong, a low measure, and at the same time of your power over me, as mortal man could give: in a word, since you must have seen that I was absolutely under the control both of conscience, and of love.

I will not offer to defend myself for *wishing you to remain where you are*, till either you give me your word to meet me at the altar, on Thursday; or till I have the honour of attending you, preparative to the solemnity which will make that day the happiest of my life.

I am but too sensible that this kind of treatment may appear to you with the face of an arbitrary and illegal imposition: but as the consequences, not only to ourselves but to both our families, may be fatal if you cannot be moved in my favour; let me beseech you to forgive this act of compulsion on the score of the necessity you your dear self have laid me under to be guilty of it; and to permit the solemnity of next Thursday to include an act of oblivion of all past offences.

The orders I have given to the people of the house are: 'That you shall be obeyed in every particular that is consistent with my expectations of finding you there on my return to town on Wednesday next: that Mrs Sinclair and her nieces, having incurred your just displeasure, shall not without your orders come into your presence: that neither shall Dorcas, till she has fully cleared her conduct to your satisfaction, be permitted to attend you: but Mabel, in her place; of whom, you seemed some time ago to express some liking. Will I have left behind me to attend your commands. If he be either negligent or impertinent, *your* dismission shall be a dismission of him from my service for ever. But, as to letters which may be sent you, or any which you may have to send, I must humbly entreat that none such pass *from* or *to* you, for the few days that I shall be absent.' But I do assure you, madam, that the seals of both sorts shall be sacred: and the letters, if such be sent, shall be given into your own hands the moment the ceremony is performed, or before, if you require it.

Meantime I will inquire, and send you word, how Miss Howe does; and to what, if I can be informed, her long silence is owing.

Dr Perkins I found here attending my lord, when I arrived with Dr S. He acquaints me that your father, mother, uncles, and the still *less* worthy persons of your family, are well; and intend to be all at your uncle Harlowe's next week; I presume to keep his anniversary. This can make no alteration but a happy one, as to *persons*, on Thursday; because Mr Tomlinson assured me that, if anything fell out to hinder your uncle's coming up in person (which, however, he did not then expect), he would be satisfied if his friend the captain were proxy for him. I shall send a man and horse tomorrow to the captain, to be at greater certainty.

I send this by a special messenger, who will wait your pleasure: which I humbly hope will be signified in a line, in relation to the impatiently-wished-for Thursday.

My lord, though hardly sensible, and unmindful of everything but of our felicity, desires his most affectionate compliments to you. He has in readiness to present you several valuables; which he hopes will be acceptable, whether he lives to see you adorn them or not.

Lady Sarah and Lady Betty have also their tokens of respect ready to court your acceptance: but may Heaven incline you to give the opportunity of receiving their personal compliments, and those of my cousins Montague, before the next week be out!

His lordship is exceeding ill. Dr S. has no hopes of him: the only consolation I can have for the death of a relation who loves me so well, if he *do* die, must arise from the additional power it will put into my hands of showing how much I am,

> My dearest life,
> Your ever-affectionate and faithful
> LOVELACE

Letter 283: MR LOVELACE TO MISS CLARISSA HARLOWE

(Superscribed, To Mrs Lovelace)

M. Hall, Sunday night, June 25

My dearest love,

I CANNOT find words to express how much I am mortified at the return of my messenger without a line from you.

Thursday is so near, that I will send messenger after messenger every four hours, till I have a favourable answer; the one to meet the other till its eve arrives, to know if I may venture to appear in your presence with the hope of having my wishes answered on that day.

Your love, madam, I neither expect, nor ask for; nor will, till my future behaviour gives you cause to think I deserve it. All I at present presume to wish is to have it in my power to do you all the justice I can now do you: and to your generosity will I leave it, to reward me as I shall merit, with your affection.

At present, revolving my poor behaviour of Friday night before you, I think I should sooner choose to go to my last audit, unprepared for it as I am, than to appear in your presence, unless you give me some hope that I shall be received as your elected husband, rather than (however deserved) as a detested criminal.

Let me therefore propose an expedient, in order to spare my own confusion; and to spare you the necessity for that soul-harrowing recrimination, which I cannot stand, and which must be disagreeable to yourself—to name the church; and I will have everything in readiness; so that our next interview will be, in a manner, at the very altar; and then you will have the kind husband to forgive for the faults of the ungrateful lover. If your resentment be still too high to write more, let it only be in your own dear hand these words, St Martin's church, Thursday—or these, St Giles's church, Thursday; nor will I insist upon any inscription, or subscription, or so much as the initials of your name. This shall be all the favour I will expect, till the dear hand itself is given to mine in presence of that Being whom I invoke as a witness of the inviolable faith and honour of

Your adoring
LOVELACE

Letter 284: MR LOVELACE TO MISS CLARISSA HARLOWE

(Superscribed, To Mrs Lovelace)

M. Hall, Monday, June 26

ONCE more, my dearest love, do I conjure you to send me the four requested words. There is no time to be lost. And I would not have next Thursday go over without being entitled to call you mine, for the world; and that as well for your sake as my own. Hitherto all that has passed is between you and me only; but, after Thursday, if my wishes are unanswered, the whole will be before the world.

My lord is extremely ill, and endures not to have me out of his sight for one half-hour. But this shall not weigh with me one iota, if you be pleased to hold out the olive-branch to me in the four requested words.

I have the following intelligence from Captain Tomlinson.

All your family are at your uncle Harlowe's. Your uncle finds he cannot go up; and names Captain Tomlinson for his proxy. He proposes to keep all your family with him till the captain assures him that the ceremony is over.

Already he has begun, with hope of success, to try to reconcile your mother to you.

My Lord M. but just now has told me how happy he should think himself to have an opportunity, before he dies, to salute you as his niece. I have put him in hopes that he shall see you; and have told him that I will go to town on Wednesday, in order to prevail upon you to accompany me down on Thursday or Friday. I have ordered a set to be in readiness to carry me up; and, were not my lord so very ill, my cousin Montague tells me she would offer *her* attendance on you. If you please, therefore, we can set out for this place the moment the solemnity is performed.

Do not, dearest creature, dissipate all these promising appearances, and, by refusing to save your own and your family's reputation in the eye of the world, use yourself worse than the ungratefullest wretch on earth has used you. For, if we are married, all the disgrace you imagine you have suffered while a single lady will be my own; and only known to ourselves.

Once more then, consider well the situation we are both in; and remember, my dearest life, that Thursday will be soon here; and that you have no time to lose.

In a letter sent by the messenger whom I dispatch with this, I have desired that my friend Mr Belford, who is your very great admirer and who knows all the secrets of my heart, will wait upon you to know what I am to depend upon, as to the chosen day.

Surely, my dear, you never could, at any time, suffer half so much from cruel suspense as I do.

If I have not an answer to this, either from your own goodness, or through Mr Belford's intercession, it will be too late for me to set out: and Captain Tomlinson will be disappointed, who goes to town on purpose to attend your pleasure.

One motive for the gentle restraint I have presumed to lay you under is to prevent the mischiefs that might ensue (as probably to the *more* innocent, as to the *less*) were you to write to anybody, while your passions were so much raised and inflamed against me. Having apprised you of my direction on this head, I wonder you should have endeavoured to send a letter to Miss Howe, although in a cover directed to that young lady's [a] servant; as you must think it would be likely to fall into my hands.

The just sense of what I have deserved the contents *should be* leaves me no room to doubt what they *are*. Nevertheless, I return it you enclosed with the seal, as you will see, unbroken.

Relieve, I beseech you, dearest madam, by the four requested words, or by Mr Belford, the anxiety of

> Your ever-affectionate and obliged
> LOVELACE

Remember, there will not, there *cannot* be time for further writing, and for my coming up by Thursday, *your uncle's birthday*.

Letter 285: MR LOVELACE TO JOHN BELFORD, ESQ.

Monday, June 26

THOU wilt see the situation I am in with Miss Harlowe by the enclosed copies of three letters; to two of which I am too much scorned to have one word given me in answer; and of the third (now sent by the messenger who brings thee this) I am afraid as little notice will be taken—and if so, her day of grace is absolutely over.

One would imagine (so long used to constraint too as she has been), that she might have been satisfied with the triumph she had over us all on Friday night: a triumph that to this hour has sunk my pride and my vanity so much, that I almost

---

a The lady had made an attempt to send away a letter.

hate the words *plot*, *contrivance*, *scheme*, and shall mistrust myself in future for every one that rises to my inventive head.

But seest thou not that I am under a necessity to continue her at Sinclair's, and to prohibit all her correspondences?

Now, Belford, as I really in my present mood think of nothing less than marrying her if she let not Thursday slip; I would have thee, in pursuance of the intimation I have given her in my letter of this date, to attend her; and vow for me, swear for me, bind thy soul to her for my honour, and use what arguments thy friendly heart can suggest, in order to procure me an answer from her; which, as thou wilt see, she may give in four words only. And then I purpose to leave Lord M. (dangerously ill as he is) and meet her at her appointed church, in order to solemnize. If she will sign but *Cl. H.* to *thy* writing the four words, that shall do; for I would not come up to be made a fool of in the face of all my family and friends.

If she should let the day go off—I shall be desperate!—I am entangled in my own devices, and cannot bear that she should detect me.

Oh that I had been honest!—What a devil are all my plots come to! What do they end in, but one grand plot upon myself, and a title to eternal infamy and disgrace! But, depending on thy friendly offices, I will say no more of this. Let her send me but one line!—but one line!—not treat me as *unworthy* of her notice; yet be altogether in my power—I cannot—I will not bear that.

My lord, as I said, is extremely ill: the doctors give him over. He gives himself over. Those who would not have him die, are afraid he will. But as to myself, I am doubtful: for these long and violent struggles between the constitution and the disease, though the latter has three physicians and an apothecary to help it forward (and all three, as to their prescriptions, of different opinions too), indicate a plaguy tough habit, and favour more of recovery than death: and the more so, as he has no sharp or acute animal organs to whet out his bodily ones, and to raise his fever above the symptomatic helpful one.

Thou wilt see in the enclosed what pains I am at to dispatch messengers; who are constantly on the road to meet each other, and one of them to link in the chain with a fourth, whose station is in London and five miles onward, or till met. But, in truth, I have some other matters for them to perform at the same time, with my lord's banker and his lawyer; which will enable me, if his lordship is so good as to die this bout, to be an over-match for some of my other relations. I don't mean Charlotte and Patty; for they are noble girls; but others, who have been scratching and clawing under-ground like so many moles in my absence; and whose workings I have discovered since I have been down, by the little heaps of dirt they have thrown up.

A speedy account of thy commission, dear Jack! The letter travels all night.

Letter 286: MR BELFORD TO ROBERT LOVELACE, ESQ.

London, June 27. Tuesday

You must excuse me, Lovelace, from engaging in the office you would have me undertake, till I can be better assured you really intend honourably at last by this much-injured lady.

I believe you know your friend Belford too well to think he would be easy with you, or with any man alive, who should seek to make him promise for him what he never intended to perform. And let me tell thee that I have not much confidence in the honour of a man, who by *imitation of hands* (I will only call it) has shown so little regard to the honour of his own relations.

Only that thou hast such jesuitical qualifyings, or I should think thee at last touched with remorse, and brought within view of being ashamed of thy cursed inventions by the ill success of thy last: which I heartily congratulate thee upon.

Oh the divine lady!—But I will not aggravate!

Yet when thou writest that in thy *present mood* thou thinkest of marrying; and yet canst so *easily* change thy *mood*: when I know thy heart is against the state—that the four words thou courtest from the lady are as much to thy purpose as if she wrote forty; since it will show she can forgive the highest injury that can be offered to woman: and when I recollect how easily thou canst find excuses to postpone; thou must be more explicit a good deal as to thy real intentions, and future honour, than thou art: for I cannot trust to a temporary remorse; which is brought on by disappointment too, and not by principle; and the like of which thou hast so often got over!

If thou canst convince me time enough for the day, that thou meanest to do honourably by her, in *her own* sense of the word; or, if not time enough, wilt fix some other day (which thou oughtest to leave to her option, and not bind her down for the Thursday; and the rather, as thy pretence for so doing is founded on an absolute fiction); I will then most cheerfully undertake thy cause; by *person*, if she will admit me to her presence; if not, by *pen*. But, in this case, thou must allow me to be guarantee for thy faith. And, if so, as much as I value thee and respect thy skill in all the qualifications of a gentleman, thou mayst depend upon it that I will act up to the character of a guarantee, with more honour than the princes of our day usually do—to their shame be it spoken.

Meantime, let me tell thee that my heart bleeds for the wrongs this angelic lady has received: and if thou dost *not* marry her, if she will *have* thee; and, when married, make her the best and tenderest of husbands; I would rather be a dog, a monkey, a bear, a viper, or a toad, than thee.

Command me with honour, and thou shalt find none readier to oblige thee than

Thy sincere friend,
JOHN BELFORD

Letter 287: MR LOVELACE TO JOHN BELFORD, ESQ.

M. Hall, June 27. Tuesday night, near 12

YOURS reached me this moment, by an extraordinary push in the messengers.

What a man of honour, thou, of a sudden!

And so, in the imaginary shape of a guarantee, thou threatenest me!

Had I *not* been in earnest as to the lady, I should not have offered to employ thee in the affair. But, let me tell thee, that *hadst* thou undertaken the task, and I had afterwards thought fit to change my mind, I should have contented myself to tell thee that that *was* my mind when thou engagedst for me; and to have given thee the reasons for the change; and then left thee to thy own direction. For never knew I what fear of man was—nor fear of woman neither, till I became acquainted with Miss Clarissa Harlowe; nay, what is *most* surprising, till I came to have her in my power.

And so thou wilt not wait upon the charmer of my heart, but upon terms and conditions!—Let it alone, and be cursed; I care not—But so much credit did I give to the value thou expressedst for *her*, that I thought the office would have been as acceptable to *thee* as serviceable to me; for what was it but to endeavour to persuade her to consent to the reparation of her own honour? For what have I done but disgraced myself, and been a thief to my own joys?—And if there be an union of hearts, and an intention to solemnize, what is there wanting but the foolish ceremony?—And that I still offer. But if she will keep back her hand; if she will make me hold out mine in vain—how can I help it?

I write her one more letter, and if after she has received that she keep sullen silence, she must thank herself for what is to follow.

But, after all, my heart is wholly hers. I love her beyond expression; and cannot help it. I hope therefore she will receive this last tender as I wish. I hope she intends not, like a true woman, to plague, and vex, and tease me, now she has found her power. If she will take me to mercy now these remorses are upon me; though I scorn to condition with *thee* for my sincerity; all her trials, as I have heretofore declared, shall be over; and she shall be as happy as I can make her: for, ruminating upon all that has passed between us, from the first hour of our acquaintance till the present, I must pronounce that she is virtue itself, and, once more I say, has no equal.

As to what you hint of leaving to her choice another day, do you consider that it will be impossible that my contrivances and stratagems should be much longer concealed?—This makes me press *that* day, though so near; and the more, as I have made so much ado about her uncle's anniversary. If she send me the *four words*, I will spare no fatigue to be in time, if not for the canonical hour at church,[1] for some other hour of the day in her own apartment, or any other; for money will do everything: and *that* I have never spared in this affair.

To show thee that I am not at enmity with thee, I enclose the copies of two letters: one to her: it is the *fourth*, and *must* be the *last* on the subject: the other to Captain Tomlinson; calculated, as thou wilt see, for him to show her.

And now, Jack, interfere in this case or not, thou knowest the mind of

R. LOVELACE

Letter 288: MR LOVELACE TO MISS CLARISSA HARLOWE

(Superscribed, To Mrs Lovelace)

M. Hall, Wed. morn. one o'clock, June 28

NOT one line, my dearest life, not one word, in answer to three letters I have written! The time is now so short that this *must* be the last letter that can reach you on this side of the important hour that might make us legally one.

My friend Mr Belford is apprehensive that he cannot wait upon you in time, by reason of some urgent affairs of his own.

I the less regret the disappointment, because I have procured a *more* acceptable person, as I hope, to attend you; Captain Tomlinson I mean: to whom I had applied for this purpose, before I had Mr Belford's answer.

I was the more solicitous to obtain this favour from him because of the office he is to take upon him, as I humbly presume to hope, tomorrow. That office obliged him to be in town as this day: and I acquainted him with my unhappy situation with you; and desired that he would show me, on this occasion, that I had as much of his favour and friendship as your uncle had; since the whole treaty must be broken off, if he could not prevail upon you in my behalf.

He will dispatch the messenger directly; whom I propose to meet in person at Slough; either to proceed onward to London with a joyful heart, or to return back to M. Hall with a broken one.

I ought not (but cannot help it) to anticipate the pleasure Mr Tomlinson proposes to himself, in acquainting you with the likelihood there is of your mother's seconding your uncle's views. For, it seems, he has privately communicated to her his laudable intentions: and *her* resolution depends, as well as *his*, upon what tomorrow will produce.

Disappoint not then, I beseech you, for an hundred persons' sakes, as well as for mine, *that* uncle and *that* mother, whose displeasure I have heard you so often deplore.

You may think it impossible for me to reach London by the canonical hour. If it should, the ceremony may be performed in your own apartment at any time in the day, or at night: so Captain Tomlinson may have it to aver to your uncle, that it was performed on his anniversary.

Tell but the captain that you *forbid me not* to attend you: and that shall be sufficient for bringing to you, on the wings of love,

> Your ever grateful and affectionate
> LOVELACE

Letter 289: [MR LOVELACE] TO MR PATRICK M'DONALD, AT HIS LODGINGS AT MR BROWN'S, PERUKEMAKER, IN ST MARTIN'S LANE, WESTMINSTER

> M. Hall, Wed. morning, two o'clock, June 28

Dear M'DONALD,

THE bearer of this has a letter to carry to the lady.[a] I have been at the trouble of writing a copy of it; which I enclose, that you may not mistake your cue.

You will judge of my reasons for antedating the enclosed sealed one,[b] directed to you by the name of Tomlinson, which you are to show the lady, as in confidence. You will open it of course.

I doubt not your dexterity and management, dear M'Donald; nor your zeal, especially as the hope of cohabitation must now be given up. Impossible to be carried is that scheme. I might break her heart, but not incline her will. Am in earnest therefore to marry her, if she let not the day slip.

Improve upon the hint of her mother: that must touch her. But John Harlowe, *remember*, has *privately* engaged that lady—*privately*, I say; else (not to mention

a   See the preceding letter.
b   See the next letter.

the reason for her uncle Harlowe's former expedient) you know she might find means to get a letter away to the one or the other, to know the truth; or to Miss Howe, to engage *her* to inquire into it: and if she should, the word *privately* will account for the uncle's and mother's denying it.

However, fail not as from me to charge our mother and her nymphs to redouble their vigilance both as to her person and letters. All's upon a crisis now. But she must not be treated ill neither.

Thursday over, I shall know what to resolve upon.

If necessary, you must assume authority. The devil's in't, if such a girl as this shall awe a man of your years and experience. Fly out if she doubt your honour. Spirits *naturally* soft may be beat out of their play and borne down (though ever so much raised) by higher anger. All women are cowards at bottom: only violent when they *may*. I have often stormed a girl out of her mistrusts, and made her yield (before she knew where she was) to the point indignantly *mistrusted*; and that to make up with me, though I was the aggressor.

If this matter succeed as I'd have it (or if *not*, and do not fail by your fault), I will take you off of the necessity of pursuing your cursed smuggling; which otherwise may one day end fatally for you.

We are none of us perfect, M'Donald. This sweet lady makes me serious sometimes in spite of my heart. But as private vices are less blameable than public; and as I think *smuggling* (as it is called) a national evil; I have no doubt to pronounce you a much worse man than myself, and as such shall take pleasure in reforming you.

I send you enclosed ten guineas, as a small earnest of further favours. Hitherto you have been a very clever fellow.

As to clothes for Thursday, Monmouth Street[1] will afford a ready supply. Clothes quite new would make your condition suspected. But you may defer that care till you see if she can be prevailed upon. Your riding-dress will do for the first visit. Nor let your boots be over clean: I have always told you the consequence of attending to the *minute*, where art (or *imposture*, as the ill-mannered would call it) is designed—your linen rumpled and soily when you wait upon her—easy terms these!—just come to town—remember (as formerly) to loll, to throw out your legs, to stroke and grasp down your ruffles, as if of significance enough to be careless. What though the presence of a fine lady would require a different behaviour, are you not of years to dispense with politeness? You have no design upon her, you know. Are a father yourself of daughters as old as she. Evermore is *parade* and *obsequiousness* suspectable: it must show either a foolish head, or a knavish heart. Make yourself of *consequence* therefore; and you will be treated as a *man* of consequence. I have often more than half ruined myself by my complaisance and, being afraid of control, have brought control upon myself.

I think I have no more to say at present. I intend to be at Slough, or on the way to it, as by mine to the lady. Adieu, honest M'Donald.

R. L.

Letter 290: [MR LOVELACE] TO CAPTAIN ANTONY TOMLINSON

(Enclosed in the preceding; to be shown to the lady as in confidence)

M. Hall, Tuesday morn. June 27

Dear Captain Tomlinson,

AN unhappy misunderstanding having arisen between the dearest lady in the world and me (the particulars of which she perhaps may give you, but I will not, because I might be thought partial to myself); and she refusing to answer my most pressing and respectful letters; I am at a most perplexing uncertainty whether she will meet us or not next Thursday to solemnize.

My lord is so extremely ill that if I thought she would not oblige me, I would defer going up to town for two or three days. He cares not to have me out of his sight: yet is impatient to salute my beloved as his niece before he dies. This I have promised to give him an opportunity to do; intending, if the dear creature will make me happy, to set out with her for this place directly from church.

With regret I speak it of the charmer of my soul; but irreconcileableness is her family fault: the less excusable indeed in *her*, as she herself suffers by it in so high a degree from her own relations.

Now, sir, as you *intended* to be in town some time before Thursday, if it be not too great an inconvenience to you I could be glad you would go up as soon as possible, for my sake: and this I the more boldly request, as I presume that a man who has so many great affairs of his own in hand as you have would be glad to be at a certainty himself as to the day.

You, sir, can so pathetically and justly set before her the unhappy consequences that will follow if the day be postponed, as well with regard to her uncle's disappointment as to the part *you have assured me* her mother is willing to take in the wished-for reconciliation, that I have great hopes she will suffer herself to be prevailed upon. And a man and horse shall be in waiting to take your dispatches, and bring them to me.

But if you cannot prevail in my favour, you will be pleased to satisfy your friend Mr John Harlowe, that it is not my fault that he is not obliged. I am, dear sir,

Your extremely obliged and faithful servant,

R. LOVELACE

Letter 291: [PATRICK M'DONALD] TO ROBERT LOVELACE, ESQ.

Wed. June 28, near 12 o'clock

Honoured sir,

I RECEIVED yours, as your servant desired me to acquaint you, *by ten this morning*. Horse and man were in a foam.

I instantly equipped myself, as if come off from a journey, and posted away to the lady, intending to plead great affairs that I came not before, in order to favour your *ante-date*; and likewise to be in a *hurry*, to have a pretence to *hurry her ladyship*, and to take no denial for her giving a *satisfactory* return to your messenger: but, upon my entering Mrs Sinclair's house, I found all in the greatest consternation.

You must not, sir, be surprised. It is a trouble to me to be the relater of the bad news: but so it is, the lady is gone off. She was missed but half an hour before I came.

Her waiting-maid is run away, or hitherto is not to be found: so that they conclude it was by her connivance.

They had sent before I came to my honoured masters Mr Belton, Mr Mowbray, and Mr Belford. Mr Tourville is out of town.

High words are passing between Madam Sinclair, and Madam Horton, and Madam Martin; as also with Dorcas. And your servant William threatens to hang or drown himself.

They have sent to know if they can hear of Mabel the waiting-maid at her mother's, who it seems lives in Chick Lane, West Smithfield; and to an uncle of hers also, who keeps an alehouse at Cowcross, hard by, and with whom she lived last.

Your messenger, having just changed his horse, is come back: so I will not detain him longer than to add, that I am, with great concern for this misfortune, and thanks for your seasonable favour and kind intentions towards me (I am sure this was not my fault), honoured sir,

Your most obliged humble servant,
PATRICK M'DONALD

Letter 292: MR MOWBRAY TO ROBERT LOVELACE, ESQ.

Wednesday, 12 o'clock

Dear Lovelace,

I HAVE plaguy news to acquaint thee with. Miss Harlowe is gon off!—Quite gon, by my soul!—I have not time for particulars, your servant being going off. But iff I had, we are not yet come to the bottom of the matter. The ladies here are all blubbering like devils, accusing one another most confoundedly: whilst Belton and I damn them all together in thy name.

If thou shouldst hear that thy fellow Will is taken dead out of some horse-pond, and Dorcas cutt down from her bed's tester, from dangling in her own garters, be not surprised. Here's the devill to pay. Nobody serene but Jack Belford, who is taking minnutes of examminations, accusations, and confessions, with the significant air of a Middlesex Justice, and intends to write at large all particulars, I suppose.

I heartily condole with thee: so does Belton. But it may turn out for the best: for she is gone away with thy marks, I understand. A foolish little devill! Where will she mend herself? For nobody will look upon her. And they tell me that thou wouldst certainly have married her had she stayed—but I know thee better.

Dear Bobby, adieu. If thy uncle will die now, to comfort thee for this loss, what a *seasonable* exit would he make! Let's have a letter from thee: prithee do. Thou canst write devil-like to Belford, who shows us nothing at all.

Thine heartily,
RD. MOWBRAY

Letter 293: MR BELFORD TO ROBERT LOVELACE, ESQ.

Thursday, June 29

THOU hast heard from M'Donald and Mowbray the news. Bad or good, I know not which thou'lt deem it. I only wish I could have given thee joy upon the same account, before the unhappy lady was seduced from Hampstead: for then of what an ungrateful villainy hadst thou been spared the perpetration, which now thou hast to answer for!

I came to town purely to serve thee with her, expecting that thy next would satisfy me that I might endeavour it without dishonour: and at first when I found her gone, I half pitied thee; for now wilt thou be inevitably blown up: and in what an execrable light wilt thou appear to all the world! Poor Lovelace! Caught in thy own snares! Thy punishment is but beginning!

But to my narrative; for I suppose thou expectest all particulars from me, since Mowbray has informed thee that I have been collecting them.

'The noble exertion of spirit she had made on Friday night had, it seems, greatly disordered her; insomuch that she was not visible till Saturday evening; when Mabel saw her, and she seemed to be very ill: but on Sunday morning, having dressed herself as if designing to go to church, she ordered Mabel to get her a coach to the door.

'The wench told her she was to obey her in everything but the calling of a coach or chair.

'She sent for Will and gave him the same command.

'He pleaded his master's orders to the contrary, and desired to be excused.

'Upon this, down she went herself, and would have gone out without observation: but finding the street door double locked, and the key not in the lock, she stepped into the street parlour, and would have thrown up the sash to call out to the people passing by, as they doubted not: but that, since her last attempt of the same nature, had been fastened down.

'Hereupon she resolutely stepped into Mrs Sinclair's parlour in the back-house; where were the old devil and her two partners; and demanded the key of the street door, or to have it opened for her.

'They were all surprised; but desired to be excused, pleading your orders.

'She asserted that you had no authority over her; and never should have any: that their present refusal was their own act and deed: she saw the intent of their back-house, and the reason of putting her there: she pleaded her condition and fortune; and said they had no way to avoid utter ruin but by opening their doors to her, or by murdering her and burying her in her garden or cellar too deep for detection: that already what had been done to her was punishable by death: and bid them at their peril detain her.'

What a noble, what a right spirit has this charming creature, in cases that will justify an exertion of spirit!——

'They answered that Mr Lovelace could prove his marriage, and would indemnify them. And they all would have vindicated their behaviour on Friday night, and the reputation of their house: but refusing to hear them on that topic, she flung from them, threatening.

'She then went up half a dozen stairs in her way to her own apartment: but, as if she had bethought herself, down she stepped again, and proceeded towards the street parlour; saying, as she passed by the infamous Dorcas, I'll make myself protectors, though the windows suffer: but that wench, of her own head, on the lady's going out of that parlour to Mrs Sinclair's, had locked the door, and taken out the key: so that finding herself disappointed, she burst into tears, and went menacing and sobbing upstairs again.

'She made no other attempt till the effectual one. Your letters and messages, they supposed, coming so fast upon one another (though she would not answer one of them), gave *her* some amusement, and an assurance to *them* that she would at last forgive you; and that then all would end as you wished.

'The women, in pursuance of your orders, offered not to obtrude themselves upon her; and Dorcas also kept out of her sight all the rest of Sunday; also on Monday and Tuesday. But by the lady's condescension (even to familiarity) to Mabel, they imagined that she must be working in her mind all that time to get away. They therefore redoubled their cautions to the wench: who told them so faithfully all that passed between her lady and her, that they had no doubt of her fidelity to her wicked trust.

' 'Tis probable she might have been contriving something all this time; but saw no room for perfecting any scheme. The contrivance by which she effected her escape seems to me not to have been fallen upon till the very day; since it depended partly upon the *weather*, as it proved. But it is evident she hoped something from Mabel's simplicity, or gratitude, or compassion, by cultivating all the time her civility to her.

'Polly waited on her early on Wednesday morning; and met with a better reception than she had *reason* to expect. She complained however with warmth of her confinement. Polly said, there would be an happy end to it (if it *were* a confinement) next day, she presumed. She absolutely declared to the contrary, in the way Polly meant it; and said that Mr Lovelace, on his *return* (*which looked as if she intended to wait for it*), should have reason to repent the orders he had given, as *they all should* their observance of them: let him send twenty letters, she would not answer one, be the consequence what it would; nor give him hope of the least favour while she was in that house. She had given Mrs Sinclair and themselves fair warning, she said: no orders of another ought to make them detain a free person: but having made an open attempt to *go*, and been detained by them, she was the calmer, she told Polly; let *them* look to the consequence.

'But yet she spoke this with temper; and Polly gave it as her opinion (with apprehension for their own safety) that, having so good a handle to punish them all, she would not go away if she might. And what, inferred Polly, is the indemnity of a man who has committed the vilest of rapes on a person of condition; and must himself, if prosecuted for it, either fly, or be hanged?

'Sinclair, so I will still call her, upon this representation of Polly, foresaw, she said, *the ruin of her poor house* in the issue of this *strange* business, as she called it; and Sally and Dorcas bore their parts in the apprehension: and this put them upon thinking it advisable for the future, that the street door should generally in the daytime be only left upon a bolt-latch, as they called it, which anybody might open on the inside; and that the key should be kept in the door; that their numerous *comers* and *goers*, as they called their guests, should be able to give evidence that she might have gone out if she would: not forgetting, however, to renew their orders to Will, to Dorcas, to Mabel, and the rest, to redouble their vigilance on this occasion to prevent her escape—none of them doubting, at the same time, that her love of a man so considerable in *their* eyes, and the prospect of what was to happen as she had reason to believe on Thursday, her uncle's birthday, would (though perhaps not till the last hour, for her *pride-sake* was their word) engage her to change her temper.

'They believe that she discovered the key to be left in the door; for she was down more than once to walk in the little garden, and seemed to cast her eye each time to the street door.

'About eight yesterday morning, an hour after Polly had left her, she told Mabel she was sure she should not live long; and having a good many suits of apparel, which after her death would be of no use to anybody she valued, she would give her a brown lustring gown, which with some alterations to make it more suitable to her degree would a great while serve her for a Sunday wear; for that she (Mabel) was the only person in that house of whom she could think without terror or antipathy.

'Mabel expressing her gratitude upon the occasion, the lady said she had nothing to employ herself about; and if she could get a workwoman directly, she would look over her things then, and give her what she intended for her.

'Her mistress's mantua-maker, the maid replied, lived but a little way off; and she doubted not that she could procure *her*, or one of her journey-women, to alter the gown out of hand.

'I will give you also, said she, a quilted coat, which will require but little alteration, if any; for you are much about my stature: but the gown I will give directions about, because the sleeves and the robings and facings must be altered for your wear, being I believe above your station: and try, said she, if you can get the workwoman, and we'll advise about it. If she cannot come now, let her come in the afternoon; but I had rather now, because it will amuse me to give you a lift.

'Then stepping to the window, It rains, said she (and so it had done all the morning): slip on the hood and short cloak I have seen you wear, and come to me when you are ready to go out, because you shall bring me in something that I want.

'Mabel equipped herself accordingly, and received her commands to buy her some trifles, and then left her; but, in her way out, stepped into the back parlour, where Dorcas was with Mrs Sinclair, telling her where she was going, and on what account, bidding Dorcas look out till she came back. So faithful was the wench to the trust reposed in her, and so little had the lady's generosity wrought upon her.

'Mrs Sinclair commended her; Dorcas envied her, and took her cue: and Mabel soon returned with the mantua-maker's journeywoman (she was resolved, she said, she would not come without her); and then Dorcas went off guard.

'The lady looked out the gown and petticoat and, before the workwoman, caused Mabel to try it on; and, that it might fit the better, made the willing wench pull off her upper petticoat, and put on that she gave her. Then she bid them go into Mr Lovelace's apartment, and contrive about it before the pier-glass there, and stay till she came to them, to give them her opinion.

'Mabel would have taken her own clothes, and hood, and short cloak with her:

but her lady said, No matter; you may put them on again here when we have considered about the alterations: there's no occasion to litter the other room.

'They went; and instantly, as it is supposed, she slipped on Mabel's gown and petticoat over her own, which was white damask, and put on the wench's hood, short cloak, and ordinary apron, and down she went.

'Hearing somebody tripping along the passage, both Will and Dorcas whipped to the inner hall door, and saw her; but taking her for Mabel, Are you going far, Mabel, cried Will?

'Without turning her face, or answering, she held out her hand, pointing to the stairs; which they construed as a caution for them to look out in her absence; and supposing she would not be long gone, as she had not formally repeated her caution to them, up went Will tarrying at the stairs-head in expectation of the supposed Mabel's return.

'Mabel and the workwoman waited a good while, amusing themselves not disagreeably, the one with contriving in the way of her business, the other delighting herself with her fine gown and coat: but at last, wondering the lady did not come in to them, Mabel tiptoed it to her door, and tapping and not being answered, stepped into the chamber.

'Will at that instant, from his station at the stairs-head, seeing Mabel in her *lady*'s clothes; for he had been told of the present (gifts to servants fly from servant to servant in a minute) was very much surprised, having, as he thought, just seen her go out in *her own*; and stepping up, met her at the door. How the devil can this be, said he? Just now you went out in your own dress! How came you here in this? And how could you pass me unseen? But nevertheless, kissing her, said he would now brag he had kissed his lady, or one in her clothes.

'I am glad, Mr William, cried Mabel, to see you here so diligently. But know you where my lady is?

'In my master's apartment, i'n't she? interrogated Will. Was she not talking with you this moment?

'No, that's Mrs Dolins's journeywoman.

'They both stood aghast, as they said; Will again recollecting he had seen Mabel, as he thought, go out in her own clothes. And while they were debating and wondering, up comes Dorcas with your fourth letter, just then brought for her lady; and seeing Mabel dressed out (whom she had likewise beheld a little before, as she supposed, in her common clothes), she joined in the wonder; till Mabel, re-entering the lady's apartment, missed her own clothes; and then suspecting what had happened, and letting the others into the ground of her suspicion, they all agreed that she had certainly escaped. And then followed such an uproar of mutual accusation, and *You should have done this*, and *You should have done that*, as alarmed the whole house; every apartment in both houses giving up its devil, to the number of fourteen or fifteen, including the mother and her partners.

'Will told them *his* story; and then ran out, as on the like occasion formerly, to make inquiry whether the lady was seen by any of the coachmen, chairmen, or porters, plying in that neighbourhood: while Dorcas cleared herself immediately, and that at the poor Mabel's expense, who made a figure as guilty as awkward, having on the suspected price of her treachery; which Dorcas, out of envy, was ready to tear from her back.

'Hereupon all the pack opened at the poor wench, while the mother, foaming at the mouth, bellowed out her orders for seizing the suspected offender; who could neither be heard in her own defence, nor, *had* she been heard, would have been believed.

'That such a perfidious wretch should ever disgrace *her* house! was the mother's cry! *Good* people *might* be corrupted; but it was a fine thing if such a house as *hers* could not be faithfully served by cursed creatures, who hired themselves upon *character*, and had no pretence to *principle!*—Damn her, the wretch proceeded!— she had no patience with her! Call the cook, and call the scullion!

'They were at hand.

'See that guilty *pieball* devil was her word (her lady's gown upon her back)—But I'll punish her for a warning to all betrayers of their trust. Put on the great gridiron this moment (an oath or a curse at every word): make up a roaring fire—the cleaver bring me this instant—I'll cut her into quarters with my own hands; and carbonade and broil the traitress for a feast to all the dogs and cats in the neighbourhood; and eat the first slice of the toad myself, without salt or pepper.

'The poor Mabel, frightened out of her wits, expected every moment to be torn in pieces, having half a score open-clawed paws upon her all at once. She promised to confess all: but that all, when she had obtained a hearing, was nothing; for *nothing* had she to confess.

'Sally hereupon, with a *curse of mercy*, ordered her to retire; undertaking that she and Polly would examine her themselves, that they might be able to write all particulars to *his honour*; and then, if she could not clear herself, or if guilty, give some account of the lady (who had been so *wicked* as to give them all this trouble) so as they might get her again, then the cleaver and gridiron might go to work with all their hearts.

'The wench, glad of this reprieve, went upstairs; and while Sally was laying out the law and prating away in her usual dictatorial manner, whipped on another gown, and sliding downstairs escaped to her relations. And this flight, which was certainly more owing to *terror* than *guilt*, was in the true Old Bailey construction made a confirmation of the latter.'

These are the particulars of Miss Harlowe's flight. Thou'lt hardly think me too minute—How I long to triumph over thy impatience and fury on the occasion!

Let me beseech thee, my dear Lovelace, in thy next letter to rave most gloriously!—I shall be grievously disappointed if thou dost not.

Where, Lovelace, can the poor lady be gone? And who can describe the distress she must be in?

By your former letters, it may be supposed that she can have very little money: nor, by the suddenness of her flight, more clothes than those she has on. And thou knowest who once said,[a] 'Her parents will not receive her: her uncles will not entertain her: her Norton is in their direction, and cannot: Miss Howe dare not: she has not one friend or intimate in town; entirely a stranger to it.' And, let me add, has been despoiled of her honour by the man for whom she made all these sacrifices; and who stood bound to her by a thousand oaths and vows, to be her husband, her protector, and friend!

How strong must be her resentment of the barbarous treatment she has received! How worthy of herself that it has made her *hate* the man she once *loved!* And,

a   See p. 575.

rather than marry him, choose to expose her disgrace to the whole world; to forgo the reconciliation with her friends which her heart was so set upon; and to hazard a thousand evils to which her youth and her sex may too probably expose an indigent and friendless beauty.

Rememberest thou not that home push upon thee, in one of the papers written in her delirium; of which however it savours not?—

I will assure thee that I have very often since most seriously reflected upon it: and as thy intended second outrage convinces me that it made no impression upon thee then, and perhaps thou hast never thought of it since, I will transcribe the sentence.

'If, as religion teaches us, God will judge us in a great measure by our benevolent or evil actions to one another—oh wretch, bethink thee, in time bethink thee, how great must be thy condemnation!'[a]

And is this amiable doctrine the sum of religion? Upon my faith I believe it is. For, to indulge a serious thought, since we are not atheists, except in *practice*, does God, the BEING of beings, want anything of us for HIMSELF? And does he not enjoin us works of mercy to one another as the means to obtain *His* mercy? A sublime principle, and worthy of the SUPREME SUPERINTENDENT and FATHER of all things!—But, if we *are* to be judged by this noble principle, what *indeed* must be *thy* condemnation on the score of this lady only! And what *mine*, and what all our *confraternity*'s, on the score of other women; though we are none of us half so bad as thou art, as well for want of inclination, I hope, as of opportunity!

I must add that, as well for thy *own* sake as for the *lady*'s, I wish ye were yet to be married to each other. It is the only medium that can be hit upon to salve the honour of both. All that's past may yet be concealed from the world, and from her relations; and thou mayst make amends for all her sufferings if thou resolvest to be a tender and kind husband to her.

And if this really be thy intention, I will accept with pleasure of a commission from thee, that shall tend to promote so good an end, whenever she can be found; that is to say, if she will admit to her presence a man who professes friendship to thee. Nor can I give a greater demonstration, that I am

Thy sincere friend,
J. BELFORD

P.S. *Mabel's clothes were thrown into the passage this morning: nobody knows by whom.*

Letter 294: MR LOVELACE TO JOHN BELFORD, ESQ.

Friday, June 30

I AM ruined, undone, blown-up, destroyed, and worse than annihilated, that's certain!—But was not the news shocking enough, dost thou think, without thy throwing into the too weighty scale reproaches which thou couldst have had no opportunity to make, but for my own voluntary communications? At a time too, when, as it falls out, I have another very sensible disappointment to struggle with?

I imagine, if there be such a thing as future punishment, it must be none of the

a See p. 892.

smallest mortifications that a *new* devil shall be punished by a worse *old one*. And, *take that!* And, *take that!* to have the old satyr cry to the screaming sufferer, laying on with a cat-o'-nine-tails, with a star of burning brass at the end of each: and, *for what! for what!*—Why, if the truth might be fairly told, for not being so bad a devil as myself!

Thou art, surely, casuist good enough to know (what I have insisted upon[a] heretofore), that the sin of seducing a credulous and easy girl is as great as that of bringing to your lure an incredulous and watchful one.

However ungenerous an appearance what I am going to say may have from *my* pen, let me tell thee that if such a lady as Miss Harlowe chose to enter into the matrimonial state (*I am resolved to disappoint thee in thy meditated triumph over my rage and despair!*) and, according to the old patriarchal system, to go on contributing to get sons and daughters with no other view than to bring them up piously, and to be good and useful members of the commonwealth, what a devil had she to do to let her fancy run a gadding after a rake? One whom she *knew* to be a rake?

Oh but truly, she hoped to have the merit of reclaiming him. She had formed pretty notions how charmingly it would look to have a penitent of her own making dangling at her side to church, through an applauding neighbourhood: and, as their family increased, marching with her thither at the head of their boys and girls, processionally, as it were, boasting of the fruits of their *honest desires*, as my good lord bishop has it in his licence. And then, what a comely sight, all kneeling down together in one pew, according to eldership, as we have seen in effigy, a whole family upon some old monument, where the honest chevalier, in armour, is presented kneeling with uplift hands, and half a dozen jolter-headed crop-eared boys behind him, ranged *gradatim*, or step-fashion, according to age and size, all in the same posture—facing his pious dame, with a ruff about her neck, and as many whey-faced girls, all kneeling behind *her*: an altar between them, and an opened book upon it: over their heads semilunary rays darting from gilded clouds, surrounding an achievement-motto, IN COELO SALUS—or QUIES—perhaps, if they have happened to live the usual married life of brawl and contradiction.

It is certainly as much my misfortune to have fallen in with Miss Clarissa Harlowe, were I to have valued my reputation or ease, as it is that of Miss Harlowe to have been acquainted with me. And, after all, what have I done more than prosecute the maxims by which thou and I and every rake are governed, and which, before I knew this lady, we have pursued from pretty girl to pretty girl, as fast as we had set one down, taking another up—just as the fellows do with their flying-coaches and flying-horses at a country fair—with a *Who rides next! Who rides next!*

But here, in the present case, to carry on the volant metaphor (for I must either be merry, or mad), is a pretty little miss just come out of her hanging-sleeve coat, brought to buy a pretty little fairing; for the world, Jack, is but a great fair, thou knowest; and, to give thee serious reflection for serious, all its toys but tinselled hobby-horses, gilt gingerbread, squeaking trumpets, painted drums, and so forth——

Now behold this pretty little miss skimming from booth to booth in a very pretty manner. One pretty little fellow called Wyerly, perhaps; another jiggeting rascal

a   See p. 559.

called Biron, a third simpering varlet of the name of Symmes, and a more hideous villain than any of the rest with a long bag under his arm, and parchment settlements tagged to his heels, ycleped Solmes; pursue her from raree-show to raree-show, shouldering upon one another at every turning, stopping when she stops, and set a spinning again when she moves—And thus dangled after, but still in the eye of her watchful guardians, traverses the pretty little miss through the whole fair, equally delighted and delighting: till at last, taken with the invitation of the *laced-hat orator*, and seeing several pretty little bib-wearers stuck together in the flying-coaches, cutting safely the yielding air in the one-go-up, the other-go-down picture-of-the-world vehicle, and all with as little fear as wit, is tempted to ride next.

In then suppose she slily pops, when *none of her friends are near her*: and if, after two or three ups and downs, her pretty head turns giddy, and she throws herself out of the coach when at its elevation, and so dashes out her pretty little brains, who can help it!—And would you hang the poor fellow, whose *professed trade* it was to set the pretty little creatures a-flying?

'Tis true, this pretty little miss, being a *very* pretty little miss, being a *very much admired* little miss, being a very *good* little miss, who always minded her book and had passed through her sampler-doctrine with high applause; had even stitched out in gaudy propriety of colours an Abraham offering up Isaac, a Samson and the Philistines, and flowers, and knots, and trees, and the sun and the moon, and the seven stars, all hung up in frames with glasses before them for the admiration of her future grandchildren: who likewise was entitled to a very pretty little estate: who was descended from a pretty little family upwards of one hundred years' gentility; which lived in a very pretty little manner, respected a very little on their own accounts, a great deal on hers—

For such a pretty little miss as this to come to so very great a misfortune must be a very sad thing: but tell me, would not the losing of any ordinary child, of any other less considerable family, of less shining or amiable qualities, have been as great and as heavy a loss to that family as the losing this pretty little miss to hers?

To descend to a very low instance, and that only as to *personality*; hast thou any doubt that thy strong-muscled bony face was as much admired by thy mother as if it had been the face of a Lovelace, or any other handsome fellow; and had thy picture been drawn, would she have forgiven the painter, had he not expressed so exactly thy lineaments as that everyone should have discerned the likeness? The *handsome* likeness is all that is wished for. Ugliness made familiar to us, with the partiality natural to fond parents, will be beauty all the world over—Do thou apply.

BUT, alas, Jack, all this is but a copy of my countenance, drawn to evade thy malice!—Though it answer thy unfriendly purpose to own it, I cannot forbear to own it, that I am stung to the very soul with this unhappy—*accident*, must I call it?—Have I nobody, whose throat, either for carelessness or treachery, I ought to cut in order to pacify my vengeance!——

When I reflect upon my *last* iniquitous intention, the *first* outrage so nobly resented, as well as so far as she was able so nobly *resisted*, I cannot but conclude that I was under the power of fascination from these accursed Circes; who, pretending to know their own sex, would have it that there is in every woman a yielding, or a weak-resisting moment to be met with: and that *yet*, and *yet*, and *yet*, I had not tried enough—but that, if neither love nor terror should enable me to hit that lucky moment, when by help of their cursed arts she was *once overcome*, she would be for *ever overcome*—appealing to all my experience, to all my knowledge of the sex, for a justification of their assertion.

My appealed-to experience, I own, was but too favourable to their argument: for dost thou think I could have held my purpose against such an angel as this, had I ever before met with one so much in earnest to defend her honour against the unwearied artifices and perseverance of the man she loved? Why then were there not more examples of a virtue so immovable? Or, why was this singular one to fall to my lot? Except indeed to *double my guilt*; and at the same time to convince all that should hear of her story *that there are angels as well as devils in the flesh?*

So much for confession; and for the sake of humouring my conscience; with a view likewise to disarm thy malice by acknowledgement: since no one shall say worse of me than I will of myself on this occasion.

One thing I will nevertheless add, to show the sincerity of my contrition: 'Tis this, that if thou canst by any means find her out within these three days, or any time before she has discovered the stories relating to Captain Tomlinson and her uncle to be what they are; and if thou canst prevail upon her to consent; I will actually, in thy presence, and his (he to represent her uncle), marry her.

I am still in hopes it may be so—She cannot be long concealed—I have already set all engines at work to find her out; and if I do, what *indifferent* persons (and no one of her *friends*, as thou observest, will look upon her) will care to embroil themselves with a man of my figure, fortune and resolution?—Show her this part then, or any other part of this letter, at thy own discretion, if thou *canst* find her: for, after all, methinks, I would be glad that this affair, which is bad enough in itself, should go off without worse personal consequences to anybody else; and yet it runs in my mind, I know not why, that sooner or later it will draw a few drops of blood after it; except she and I can make it up between ourselves. And this may be another reason why she should not carry her resentment too far—not that such an affair would give me much concern neither, were I to choose my man or men; for I heartily hate all her family but herself; and ever shall.

LET me add that the lady's plot to escape appears to me no extraordinary one. There was much more luck than probability that it should do: since, to make it succeed, it was necessary that Dorcas and Will and Sinclair and her nymphs should be all deceived, or off their guard. It belongs to me, when I see them, to give them my hearty thanks that they were; and that their selfish care to provide for their own future security should induce them to leave their outward door upon their bolt-latch, and be cursed to them!——

Mabel deserves a pitch-suit and a bonfire, rather than the lustring; and as her clothes are returned, let the lady's be put to her others, to be sent to her when it can be told whither—But not till I give the word, neither; for we must get the dear fugitive back again, if possible.

I suppose that my stupid villain, who knew not such a goddess-shaped lady with a mien so noble from the awkward and bent-shouldered Mabel, has been at Hampstead to see after her: and yet I hardly think she would go thither. He ought to go through every street where bills for lodgings are up, to inquire after a newcomer. The houses of such as deal in women's matters, and tea, coffee, and suchlike, are those to be inquired at for her. If some tidings be not quickly heard of her, I would not have either Dorcas, Will or Mabel, appear in my sight, whatever their superiors think fit to do.

This, though written in character, is a very long letter, considering it is not a narrative one or a journal of proceedings, like some of my former; for such will unavoidably and naturally, as I may say, run into length. But I have so used myself to write a great deal of late, that I know not how to help it. Yet I must add to its length, in order to explain myself on a hint I gave at the beginning of it, which was that I have another disappointment besides this of Miss Harlowe's escape, to bemoan.

And what dost think it is? Why, the old peer, *pox* of his tough constitution! (for that would have helped him on), has made shift by fire and brimstone, and the devil knows what, to force the gout to quit the counterscarp of his stomach, just as it had collected all its strength in order to storm the citadel of his heart. In short they have, by the mere force of stink-pots, hand-grenades, and pop-guns, drove the slow-working pioneer quite out of the trunk into the extremities; and there it lies nibbling and gnawing upon his great toe; when I had hoped a fair end both of the distemper, and the distempered.

But I, who could write to *thee* of laudanum and the wet cloth[1] formerly, yet let £8,000 a year slip through my fingers, when I had entered upon it more than in imagination (for I had begun to ask the stewards questions, and to hear them talk of fines and renewals, and such sort of stuff), *deserve* to be mortified.

Thou canst not imagine how differently the servants, and even my cousins, look upon me since yesterday, to what they did before. Neither the one nor the other bow and curtsy half so low—Nor am I a quarter so often *his honour*, and *your honour*, as I was within these few hours with the former: and as to the latter—it is *cousin Bobby* again, with the usual familiarity, instead of *sir*, and *sir*, and, *If you please, Mr Lovelace.* And now they have the insolence to congratulate me on the recovery of the *best of uncles*, while I am forced to seem as much delighted as they, when, would it do me good, I could sit down and cry my eyes out.

I had bespoken my mourning in imagination, after the example of a certain foreign minister, who, before the death, or even last illness of Charles II, as honest White Kennet tells us,[2] had half exhausted Blackwell Hall of its sables: an indication, as the historian would insinuate, that the monarch was to be poisoned, and the ambassador in the secret—and yet, fool that I was, I could not take the hint!—What a devil does a man read history for, if he cannot but profit by the examples he finds in it?

But thus, Jack, is an observation of the old peer's verified, *that one misfortune seldom comes alone:* and so concludes

Thy doubly-mortified
LOVELACE

Letter 295: MISS CLARISSA HARLOWE TO MISS HOWE

Wednesday night, June 28

Oh, my dearest Miss HOWE!

ONCE more have I escaped—but, alas! *I*, my *best self*, have not escaped!—Oh! your poor Clarissa Harlowe! *You* also will hate me, I fear!—Yet you won't, when you know all!——

But no more of myself! my *lost* self. You that can rise in a morning to be blessed and to bless; and go to rest delighted with your own reflections, and in your unbroken, unstarting slumbers, conversing with saints and angels, the former only more pure than yourself, as they have shaken off the encumbrance of body; you shall be my subject, as you have long, long, been my only pleasure. And let me, at awful distance, revere my beloved Anna Howe, and in *her* reflect upon what her Clarissa Harlowe once was!——

FORGIVE, oh! forgive my rambling. My peace is destroyed. My intellects are touched. And what flighty nonsense must you read, if now you will vouchsafe to correspond with me, as formerly!——

Oh! my best, my dearest, my *only* friend! What a tale have I to unfold!—But still upon *self*, this vile, this hated *self!*—I will shake it off, if possible; and why should I not, since I think, except one wretch, I hate nothing so much!—Self, then, be banished from *self* one moment (for I doubt it *will* for no longer) to inquire after a *dearer* object, my beloved Anna Howe!—whose mind, all robed in spotless white, charms and irradiates—but what would I say?——

AND how, my dearest friend, after this rhapsody, which, on re-perusal, I would not let go but to show you what a distracted mind dictates to my trembling pen; *how do you?* You have been very ill, it seems. That you are *recovered*, my dear, let me hear!—That your mamma is well, pray let me hear, and hear quickly!—This comfort, surely, is owing to me; for if life is no *worse* than chequer-work, I must now have a little white to come, having seen nothing but black, all unchequered dismal black, for a great, great while!

AND what is all this wild incoherence for?—It is only to beg to know how you have been, and how you now do, by a line directed for Mrs Rachel Clark, at Mr Smith's, a glove shop, in King Street, Covent Garden; which (although my abode is a secret to everybody else) will reach the hands of—*your unhappy*—but that's not enough——

Your miserable
CLARISSA HARLOWE

Letter 296: MRS HOWE TO MISS CLARISSA HARLOWE

(Superscribed as directed in the preceding)

Friday, June 30

Miss CLARISSA HARLOWE,

YOU will wonder to receive a letter from me. I am sorry for the great distress you seem to be in. Such a hopeful young lady as you were!—But see what comes of disobedience to parents!

For my part; although I pity you; yet I much more pity your poor father and mother. Such education as they gave you! such improvements as you made! and such delight as they took in you!—and all come to this!——

But pray, miss, don't make my Nancy guilty of your fault; which is that of disobedience. I have charged her over and over not to correspond with one who has made such a giddy step. It is not to her reputation, I am sure. You *knew* that I so charged her; yet you go on corresponding together, to my very great vexation; for she has been very perverse upon it, more than once. *Evil communication*[1] miss—You know the rest.

Here, people cannot be unhappy by themselves, but they must involve their friends and acquaintance, whose discretion has kept them clear of their errors, into near as much unhappiness as if they had run into the like of their own heads. Thus my poor daughter is always in tears and grief. And she has postponed her own felicity truly, because *you* are unhappy!

If people who seek their own ruin could be the only sufferers by their headstrong doings, it were something: but, oh miss, miss, what have *you* to answer for, who have made as many grieved hearts as have known you? The whole sex is indeed wounded by you: for who but Miss Clarissa Harlowe was proposed by every father and mother for a pattern for their daughters?

I write a long letter where I proposed to say but a few words; and those to forbid you writing to my Nancy: and this as well because of the false step you have made, as because it will grieve her poor heart and do you no good. If you love her, therefore, write not to her. Your sad letter came into my hands, Nancy being abroad, and I shall not show it her: for there would be no comfort for her if she saw it, nor for me whose delight she is—as you once was to your parents——

But you seem to be sensible enough of your errors now! So are all giddy girls, when it is too late—and what a crest-fallen figure then does their self-willed obstinacy and headstrongness compel them to make!

I may say too much: only as I think it proper to bear that testimony against your rashness, which it behoves every careful parent to bear. And none more than

Your compassionating well-wisher,
ANNABELLA HOWE

I send this by a special messenger who has business only so far as Barnet, because you shall have no need to write again; knowing how you love writing: and knowing likewise, *that misfortune makes people plaintive.*

Letter 297: MISS CLARISSA HARLOWE TO MRS HOWE

Saturday, July 1

PERMIT me, madam, to trouble you with a few lines, were it only to thank you for your reproofs; which have nevertheless drawn fresh streams of blood from a bleeding heart.

My story is a dismal story. It has circumstances in it that would engage pity, and possibly a judgement not altogether unfavourable, were those circumstances known. But it is my business, and shall be *all* my business, to repent of my failings and not endeavour to extenuate them.

But I will not seek to distress your worthy mind. If *I cannot suffer alone*, I will make as few parties as I can in my sufferings. And, indeed, I took up my pen with this resolution, when I wrote the letter which has fallen into your hands: it was only to know, that for a very particular reason, as well as for affection unbounded, if my dear Miss Howe, from whom I had not heard of a long time, were ill; as I had been told she was; and if so, how she now does. But my injuries being recent, and my distresses having been exceeding great, *self* would crowd into my letter. When distressed, the human mind is apt to turn itself to everyone in whom it imagined or wished an interest, for pity and consolation—or, to express myself better and more concisely, in your own words, *misfortune makes people plaintive*: and to whom, if not to a friend, can the afflicted complain?

Miss Howe being abroad when my letter came, I flatter myself that she is recovered. But it would be some satisfaction to me to be informed if she *has been ill*. Another line from *your* hand would be too great a favour. But, if you will be pleased to direct any servant to answer *yes* or *no* to that question, I will not be farther troublesome.

Nevertheless, I must declare that my Miss Howe's friendship was all the comfort I had, or expected to have, in this world; and a line from her would have been a cordial to my fainting heart. Judge then, dearest madam, how reluctantly I must obey your prohibition—but yet I will endeavour to obey it; although I should have hoped, as well from the tenor of all that has passed between Miss Howe and me, as from *her* established virtue, that she could not be tainted by *evil communication*, had one or two letters been permitted. This, however, I ask not for, since I think I have nothing to do, but to beg of God (who, I hope, has not yet withdrawn his grace from me, although he is pleased to let loose his justice upon my faults) to give me a truly broken spirit, if it be not already broken enough, and then to take to his mercy

The unhappy
CLARISSA HARLOWE

Two favours, good madam, I have to beg of you—The first—that you will not let any of my relations know that you have heard from me. The other—that no living creature be apprised where I am to be heard of, or directed to. This is a point that concerns me more than I can express—In short, my preservation from further evils may depend upon it.

Letter 298: MISS CLARISSA HARLOWE TO HANNAH BURTON

Thursday, June 29

My good HANNAH,

STRANGE things have happened to me since you were dismissed my service (so sorely against my will), and your pert fellow-servant set over me. But that must be all forgotten now——

How do you, my Hannah? Are you recovered of your illness? If you are, do you choose to come and be with me? Or *can* you conveniently?

I am a very unhappy creature and, being among all strangers, should be glad to have *you* with me, of whose fidelity and love I have had so many acceptable instances.

Living or dying, I will endeavour to make it worth your while, my Hannah.

If you are recovered, as I hope, and if you have a good place, it may be they would bear with your absence, and suffer somebody in your room, *for a month or so*: and, by that time, I hope to be provided for, and you may then return to your place.

Don't let any of my friends know of this my desire, whether you can come or not.

I am at Mr Smith's, a hosier's and glove shop, in King Street, Covent Garden.

You must direct to me by the name of Rachel Clark.

Do, my good Hannah, come if you can to your poor young mistress, who always valued you, and always will, whether you come or not.

I send this to your mother at St Albans, not knowing where to direct to you. Return me a line that I may know what to depend upon: and I shall see you have not forgotten the pretty hand you were taught, in happy days, by

Your true friend,
CLARISSA HARLOWE

Letter 299: HANNAH BURTON [TO MISS CLARISSA HARLOWE]

(In answer)

Monday, July 3

Honored Maddam,

I HAVE not forgot to write, and never will forget anything you, my dear young lady, was so good as to larn me. I am very sorrowfull for your misfortens, my dearest young lady; so sorrowfull, I do not know what to do. Gladd at harte would I be to be able to come to you. But indeed I have not been able to stir out of my rome here at my mother's, ever since I was forsed to leave my plase with a roomatise, which has made me quite and clene helpless. I will pray for you night and day, my dearest, my kindest, my goodest young lady, who have been so badly used; and I am very sorry I cannot come to do you love and sarvice; which will ever be in the harte of mee to do, if it was in my power: who am

Your most dewtifull sarvant to command,
HANNAH BURTON

Letter 300: MISS CLARISSA HARLOWE TO MRS JUDITH NORTON

Thursday, June 29

My dear Mrs NORTON,

I ADDRESS myself to you after a very long silence (which, however, was not owing either to want of love or duty) principally to desire you to satisfy me in two or three points, which it behoves me to know.

My father, and all the family, I am informed, are to be at my uncle Harlowe's this day, as usual. Pray acquaint me if they have been there? And if they were cheerful on the anniversary occasion? And also, if you have heard of any journey, or intended journey, of my brother, in company with Captain Singleton and Mr Solmes.

Strange things have happened to me, my dear worthy and maternal friend!— very strange things!—Mr Lovelace has proved a very barbarous and ungrateful man to me. But, God be praised, I have escaped from him!—Being among absolute strangers (though I think worthy folks), I have written to Hannah Burton to come and be with me. If the good creature fall in your way, pray encourage her to come to me. I always intended to have her, she knows—but hoped to be in happier circumstances.

Say nothing to any of my friends that you have heard from me.

Pray, do you think my father would be prevailed upon, if I were to supplicate him by letter, to take off the heavy curse he laid upon me at my going from Harlowe Place?—I can expect no other favour from him: but that being literally fulfilled, as to my prospects in this life, I hope it will be thought to have operated far enough.

I am afraid *my poor*, as I used to call the good creatures to whose necessities I was wont to administer, by your faithful hands, have missed me of late. But now, alas! I am poor myself. It is not the least aggravation of my fault, nor of my regrets, that with such inclinations as God had given me, I have put it out of my power to do the good I once pleased myself to think I was born to do. It is a sad thing, my dearest Mrs Norton, to render ourselves unworthy of the talents Providence has entrusted to us!

But these reflections are not too late; and perhaps I ought to have kept them to myself. Let me, however, hope that you love me still. Pray let me hope that you do: and then, notwithstanding my misfortunes, which have made me seem ungrateful to the kind and truly maternal pains you have taken with me from my cradle, I shall have the happiness to think that there is *one* worthy person, who hates not

The unfortunate
CLARISSA HARLOWE

Pray remember me to my foster-brother. I hope he continues dutiful and good to you.

Be pleased to direct for Rachel Clark, at Mr Smith's in King Street, Covent Garden. But keep the direction an absolute secret.

Letter 301: MRS NORTON [TO MISS CLARISSA HARLOWE]

(*In answer*)   Saturday, July 1

YOUR letter, my dearest young lady, cuts me to the heart! Why will you not let me know all your distresses!—Yet you have said enough!

My son is very good to me. A few hours ago he was taken with a feverish disorder. But I hope it will go off happily, if his ardour for business will give him the recess from it, which his good master is willing to allow him. He presents his duty to you, and shed tears at hearing your sad letter read.

You have been misinformed as to your family's being at your uncle Harlowe's. They did not intend to be there. Nor was the day kept at all. Indeed, they have not stirred out, but to church (and that but three times), ever since the day you went away—Unhappy day for them, and for all who know you!—to me, I am sure, most particularly so!—My heart now bleeds more and more for you.

I have not heard a syllable of such a journey as you mention, of your brother, Captain Singleton, and Mr Solmes. There has been some talk, indeed, of your brother's setting out for his northern estates: but I have not heard of it lately.

I am afraid no letter will be received from you. It grieves me to tell you so, my dearest young lady. No evil can have happened to you, which they do not *expect* to hear of; so great is their antipathy to the wicked man, and so bad is his character.

I cannot but think hardly of their unforgivingness: but there is no judging for others by one's self. Nevertheless I will add, that if you had had as gentle spirits to deal with as your own, or, I will be bold to say, as mine, these evils had never happened either to them, or to you. I knew your virtue, and your love of virtue, from your very cradle; and I doubted not but *that*, with God's grace, would always be your guard—But you could never be driven; nor was there occasion to drive you—so generous, so noble, so discreet—But how does my love of your amiable qualities increase my affliction; as these recollections must do yours!

You are escaped, my dearest miss—happily, I hope—that is to say, with your honour—else, how great must be your distress!—Yet from your letter I dread the worst.

I am very seldom at Harlowe Place. The house is not the house it used to be since you went from it. Then they are *so* relentless! And, as I cannot say harsh things of the beloved child of my *heart*, as well as *bosom*, they do not take it *amiss* that I stay away.

Your Hannah left her place ill some time ago; and, as she is still at her mother's at St Albans, I am afraid she continues ill. If so, as you are among strangers, and I cannot encourage you at present to come into *these* parts, I shall think it my duty to attend you (let it be taken as it will) as soon as my Tommy's indisposition will permit; which I hope will be soon.

I have a little money by me. You say you *are poor yourself*—How grievous are those words from one entitled and accustomed to affluence!—Will you be so good to command it, my beloved young lady?—It is most of it your own bounty to me. And I should take a pride to restore it to its original owner.

Your poor bless you, and pray for you continually. I have so managed your last benevolence, and they have been so healthy, and have had such constant employ, that it has held out; and will still hold out, till happier times, I hope, betide their excellent benefactress.

Let me beg of you, my dearest young lady, to take to yourself all those aids, which good persons like you draw from RELIGION in support of their calamities. Let your sufferings be what they will, I am sure you have been innocent in your intention. So do not despond. None are made to suffer above what they *can*, and therefore *ought* to bear.

We know not the methods of Providence, and what wise ends it may have to serve in its dispensations to its poor creatures.

Few persons have greater reason to say this than myself. And since we are apt in calamities to draw more comfort from example than precept, you will permit me to remind you of my own lot: for who has had a greater share of afflictions than myself?

To say nothing of the loss of an excellent mother, at a time of life when motherly care is most wanted; the death of a dear father, who was an ornament to his cloth (and who had qualified me to be his scribe and amanuensis), just as he came within view of a preferment which would have made his family easy, threw me friendless into the wide world; threw me upon a very careless and, which was much worse, a very unkind husband. Poor man!—But he was spared long enough, thank God, in a tedious illness, to repent of his neglected opportunities and his light principles; which I have always thought of with pleasure, although I was left the more destitute for his chargeable illness, and ready to be brought to bed, when he died, of my Tommy.

But this very circumstance, which I thought the unhappiest that I could have been left in (so short-sighted is human prudence), became the happy means of recommending me to your mother, who, in regard to my character and in compassion to my very destitute circumstances, permitted me, as I made a conscience of not parting with my poor boy, to nurse both you and him, born within a few days of each other. And I have never since wanted any of the humble blessings which God has made me contented with.

Nor have I known what a very great grief was, from the day of my poor husband's death, till the day that your parents told me how much they were determined that you should have Mr Solmes; when I was apprised not only of your aversion to him, but how unworthy he was of you: for then I began to dread the consequences of forcing so generous a spirit; and, till then, I never feared Mr Lovelace, attracting as was his person and specious his manners and address. For I was sure you would never have him, if he gave you not good reason to be convinced of his reformation; nor till your friends were as well satisfied in it as yourself. But that unhappy misunderstanding between your brother and Mr Lovelace, and their joining so violently to force you upon Mr Solmes, did all that mischief which has cost you and them so dear, and poor me all my peace! Oh what has not this ungrateful, this doubly-guilty man to answer for!

Nevertheless, you know not what God has in store for you yet!—But if you are to be punished all your days here, for example-sake, in a case of such importance, for your one false step, be pleased to consider that this life is but a state of probation; and if you have your purification in it, you will have your reward hereafter in a greater degree for submitting to the dispensation with patience and resignation.

You see, my dearest Miss Clary, that I make no scruple to call the step you took a false one. In *you* it was less excusable than it would have been in any other young lady; not only because of your superior talents, but because of the opposition between *your* character and *his*: so that if you had been provoked to quit your father's house, it needed not to have been with him. Nor needed I, indeed, but as an instance of my *impartial* love, to have written this to you.[a]

After this, it will have an unkind, and perhaps at this time, an unseasonable appearance, to express my concern that you have not before favoured me with a line—Yet, if you can account to yourself for your silence, I dare say I ought to be satisfied; for I am sure you love me: as I both love and honour you, and ever will, and the more for your misfortunes.

One consolation, methinks, I have, even when I am sorrowing for your calamities; and that is that I know not any young person so qualified to shine the brighter for the trials she may be exercised with: and yet it is a consolation that ends in adding to my regrets for your afflictions, because you are blessed with a mind so well able to bear prosperity, and to make everybody round you the better for it. *Woe unto him!*—Oh this wretched, wretched man!—But I will forbear till I know more.

Ruminating on everything your melancholy letter suggests, and apprehending from the gentleness of your mind, the amiableness of your person, and your youth, the further misfortunes and inconveniencies to which you may possibly be subjected, I cannot conclude without asking for your leave to attend you, and that in a very earnest manner—and I beg of you not to deny me, on any consideration relating to *myself*, or even to the indisposition of my *other* beloved child; if I can be either of use or comfort to you. Were it, my dearest young lady, but for two or three days, permit me to attend you, although my son's illness should increase, and compel me to come down again at the end of those two or three days—I repeat my request likewise, that you will command from me the little sum remaining in my hands of your bounty to your poor, as well as that dispensed to

> Your ever-affectionate and faithful servant,
> JUDITH NORTON

Letter 302: MISS CLARISSA HARLOWE TO LADY BETTY LAWRANCE

Thursday, June 29

Madam,

I HOPE you'll excuse the freedom of this address from one who has not the honour to be personally known to you, although you must have heard much of Clarissa Harlowe. It is only to beg the favour of a line from your ladyship's hand (by the next post, if convenient) in answer to the following questions:

1. Whether you wrote a letter dated, as I have a memorandum, Wed. June 7, congratulating your nephew Lovelace on his supposed nuptials, as reported to you by Mr Spurrier, your ladyship's steward, as from one Captain Tomlinson—and in

a Mrs Norton having only the family representation and invectives to form her judgement upon, knew not that Clarissa had determined against going off with Mr Lovelace; nor how solicitous she had been to procure for herself *any other* protection than his; when she apprehended that if she stayed, she had no way to avoid being married to Mr Solmes.

it reproaching Mr Lovelace, as guilty of slight, etc., in not having acquainted your ladyship and the family with his marriage?

2. Whether your ladyship wrote to Miss Montague to meet you at Reading, in order to attend you to your cousin Leeson's in Albemarle Street; on your being obliged to be in town on your *old Chancery affair*, I remember are the words? And whether you bespoke your nephew's attendance there on Sunday night the 11th?

3. Whether your ladyship and Miss Montague *did* come to town at that time? And whether you went to Hampstead on Monday, in a hired coach and four, your own being repairing; and took from thence to town the young creature whom you visited there?

Your ladyship will probably guess that these questions are not asked for reasons favourable to your nephew Lovelace. But be the answer what it will, it can do *him* no hurt, nor *me* any good; only that I think I owe it to my former hopes (however deceived in them), and even to charity, that a person of whom I was once willing to think better should not prove so egregiously abandoned as to be wanting in *every* instance to that veracity, which is an indispensable in the character of a gentleman.

Be pleased, madam, to direct to me (keeping the direction a secret for the present) to be left at the Belle Savage on Ludgate Hill till called for. I am,

Your ladyship's most humble servant,
CLARISSA HARLOWE

Letter 303: LADY BETTY LAWRANCE TO MISS CLARISSA HARLOWE

Saturday, July 1

Dear madam,

I FIND that all is not as it should be between you and my nephew Lovelace. It will very much afflict me, and all his friends, if he has been guilty of any designed baseness to a lady of your character and merit.

We have been long in expectation of an opportunity to congratulate you and ourselves, upon an event most earnestly wished for by us all; since all our hopes of *him* are built upon the power *you* have over him: for if ever man adored a woman, he is that man, and you, madam, are that woman.

Miss Montague in her last letter to me, in answer to one of mine inquiring if she knew from him, whether he could call you his, or was likely soon to have that honour; has these words: 'I know not what to make of my cousin Lovelace, as to the point your ladyship is so earnest about. He sometimes says he is actually married to Miss Cl. Harlowe: at other times, that it is her own fault if he be not— He speaks of her not only with love, but with reverence: yet owns that there is a misunderstanding between them; but confesses that she is wholly faultless. An angel, and not a woman, he says she is: and that no man living can be worthy of her'—This is what my niece Montague writes.

God grant, my dearest young lady, that he may not have so heinously offended you that you *cannot* forgive him! If you are not already married, and refuse to be his, I shall lose all hopes that he ever will marry, or be the man I wish him to be. So will Lord M. So will Lady Sarah Sadleir.

I will now answer your questions: but indeed I hardly know what to write, for fear of widening still more the unhappy difference between you. But yet such a young lady must command everything from me. This then is my answer:

I wrote not any letter to him on or about the 7th of June.

Neither I nor my steward know such a man as Captain Tomlinson.

I wrote not to my niece to meet me at Reading, nor to accompany me to my cousin Leeson's in town.

My Chancery affair, though like most Chancery affairs it be of long standing, is nevertheless now in so good a way, that it cannot give me occasion to go to town.

Nor have I been in town these six months: nor at Hampstead for several years.

Neither shall I have any temptation to go to town, except to pay my congratulatory compliments to Mrs Lovelace. On which occasion I should go with the greatest pleasure; and should hope for the favour of your accompanying me to Glenham Hall for a month at least.

Be what will the reason of your inquiry, let me entreat you, my dear young lady, for Lord M.'s sake; for my sake; for this giddy man's sake, soul as well as body; and for all our family's sakes; not to suffer this answer to widen differences so far as to make you refuse him, if already he has not the honour of calling you his; as I am apprehensive he has not, by your signing by your family name.

And here let me offer to you my mediation to compose the difference between you, be it what it will. Your cause, my dear young lady, cannot be put into the hands of anybody living more devoted to your service, than into those of

> Your sincere admirer, and humble servant,
> ELIZ. LAWRANCE

Letter 304: MISS CLARISSA HARLOWE TO MRS HODGES

Enfield, June 29

Mrs HODGES,

I AM under a kind of necessity to write to you, having no one among my relations to whom I dare write, or hope a line from, if I did. It is but to answer a question. It is this:

Whether you know such a man as Captain Tomlinson? And, if you do, whether he be very intimate with my uncle Harlowe?

I will describe his person, lest possibly he should go by another name among you; although I know not why he should.

'He is a thin, tallish man, a little pock-fretten; of a sallowish complexion. Fifty years of age, or more. Of a good aspect, when he looks up. He seems to be a serious man, and one who knows the world. He stoops a little in the shoulders. Is of Berkshire. His wife of Oxfordshire; and has several children. He removed lately into your parts from Northamptonshire.'

I must desire you, Mrs Hodges, that you will not let my uncle, nor any of my relations, know that I write to you.

You used to say that you would be glad to have it in your power to serve me. That, indeed, was in my prosperity. But, I dare say, you will not refuse me in a particular that will oblige me, without hurting yourself.

I understand that my father, mother, and sister, and, I presume, my brother, and my uncle Antony, are to be at my uncle Harlowe's this day. God preserve them all, and may they rejoice in many happy birthdays! You will write six words to me concerning their healths.

Direct, for a particular reason, to Mrs Dorothy Salcomb; to be left, till called for, at the Four Swans Inn, Bishopsgate Street.

You know my handwriting well enough, were not the contents of the letter sufficient to excuse my name, or any other subscription, than that of

Your friend.

Letter 305: MRS HODGES [TO MISS CLARISSA HARLOWE]

(In answer)

Sat. July 1

Maddam,

I RETURN you an anser, as you wish me to doe. Master is acquented with no sitch man. I am shure no sitch ever came to our house. And master sturs very little out. He has no harte to stur out. For why? Your obstincy makes um not care to see one another. Master's birthday never was keept soe before: for not a sole heere; and nothing but sikeing and sorrowin from master, to think how it yused to bee.

I axsed master if soe bee he knoed sitch a man as one Captain Tomlinson? But sayed not whirfor I axsed. He sed, No, not he.

Shure this is no trix nor forgary bruing agenst master by won Tomlinson—Won knoes not what cumpany you may have bin forsed to keep, sen you went away, you knoe, maddam. Ecscuse me, maddam; but Lundon is a pestilent plase; and that Squire Luveless is a devil (for all he is sitch a like gentleman to look to), as I hev herd everyboddy say; and thinke as how you have found by thiss.

I truste, maddam, you wulde not let master cum to harme, if you knoed it, by anyboddy, whoe may pretend too be acquented with him: but, for fere, I querid with myself iff I shulde not tell him. Butt I was willin to show you that I wulde pleasure you in advarsity, if advarsity bee youre lott, as wel as prosprity; for I am none of those as woulde doe otherwis. Soe noe more frum

Your humbell sarvant, to wish you well,
SARAH HODGES

Letter 306: MISS CLARISSA HARLOWE TO LADY BETTY LAWRANCE

Monday, July 3

Maddam,

I CANNOT excuse myself from giving your ladyship this one trouble more; to thank you, as I most heartily do, for your kind letter.

I must own to you, madam, that the honour of being related to ladies as eminent for their virtue as for their descent was at first no small inducement with me, to lend an ear to Mr Lovelace's address. And the rather, as I was determined had it come to effect, to do everything in my power to deserve your favourable opinion.

I had another motive, which I knew would of itself give me merit with your whole family; a presumptuous one (a punishably presumptuous one, as it has proved), in the hope that I might be an humble means, in the hand of Providence, to reclaim a man who had, as I thought, good sense enough at bottom to be reclaimed; or, at least, gratitude enough to acknowledge the intended obligation, whether the generous hope were to succeed, or not.

But I have been most egregiously mistaken in Mr Lovelace; the only man, I persuade myself, pretending to be a gentleman, in whom I could have been so *much* mistaken: for while I was endeavouring to save a drowning wretch, I have been, not accidentally but premeditatedly, and of set purpose, drawn in after him. And he has had the glory to add to the list of those he has ruined, a name that, I will be bold to say, would not have disparaged his own. And this, madam, by means that would shock humanity to be made acquainted with.

My whole end is served by your ladyship's answer to the questions I took the liberty to put to you in writing. Nor have I a wish to make the unhappy man more odious to you than is necessary to excuse myself for absolutely declining your offered mediation.

When your ladyship shall be informed of the following particulars:

That after he had compulsatorily, as I may say, tricked me into the act of going off with him, he could carry me to one of the vilest houses, as it proved, in London:

That he could be guilty of a wicked attempt, in resentment of which I found means to escape from him to Hampstead:

That, after he had found me out there (I know not how), he could procure two women dressed out richly, to personate your ladyship and Miss Montague; who, under pretence of engaging me to make a visit in town to your cousin Leeson (promising to return with me that evening to Hampstead), betrayed me back again to the vile house: where, again made a prisoner, I was first robbed of my senses; and then (why should I seek to conceal that disgrace from others, which I cannot hide from myself?) of my honour:

When your ladyship shall know that, in the shocking progress to this ruin, wilful falsehoods, repeated forgeries (particularly of one letter from your ladyship, another from Miss Montague, and a third from Lord M.), and numberless perjuries, were not the least of his crimes:

You will judge that I can have no principles that will make me worthy of an alliance with ladies of yours and your noble sister's character, if I could not from my soul declare that such an alliance can never *now* take place.

I will not offer to clear myself entirely of blame: but, as to *him*, I have no fault to accuse myself of. My crime was the corresponding with him at first, when prohibited so to do by those who had a right to my obedience; made still more inexcusable by giving him a clandestine meeting, which put me into the power of his arts. And for this, I am content to be punished: thankful that at last I have escaped from him; and have it in my power to reject so wicked a man for my husband: and glad if I may be a warning, since I cannot be an example: which once (very vain, and very conceited as I was!) I proposed to myself to be!

All the ill I wish him is that he may reform; and that I may be the last victim of his baseness. Perhaps this desirable wish may be obtained when he shall see how his wickedness, his unmerited wickedness to a poor creature made friendless by his cruel arts, will end.

I conclude with my humble thanks to your ladyship, for your favourable opinion of me; and with the assurance that I will be, while life is lent me,

Your ladyship's grateful and obliged servant,
CL. HARLOWE

Letter 307: MISS CLARISSA HARLOWE TO MRS NORTON

Sunday evening, July 2

How kindly, my beloved Mrs Norton, do you soothe the anguish of a bleeding heart! Surely you are my own mamma; and by some unaccountable mistake, I must have been laid to a family that, having newly found out or at least suspected the imposture, cast me from their hearts with the indignation that such a discovery will warrant.

Oh that I had indeed been your own child, born to partake of your humble fortunes, an heiress only to that content in which you are so happy! Then should I have had a *truly* gentle spirit to have guided my ductile heart, which force and ungenerous usage sit so ill upon; and nothing of what has happened would have been.

But let me take heed that I enlarge not by impatience, the breach already made in my duty by my rashness; since, had I not erred, my *mother* at least could never have been thought hard-hearted and unforgiving—Am I not then answerable, not only for my own faults, but for the consequences of them; which tend to depreciate and bring disgrace upon a maternal character never before called in question?

It is kind however in you to endeavour to extenuate the fault of one so greatly sensible of it—and could it be wiped off entirely, it would render me more worthy of the pains you have taken in my education: for it must add to your grief, as it does to my confusion, that after such promising beginnings I should have so behaved as to be a disgrace instead of a credit to you, and my other friends.

But that I may not make you think me more guilty than I am, give me leave briefly to assure you, that when my story is known, I shall be entitled to more compassion than blame, even on the score of going away with Mr Lovelace.

As to all that happened afterwards, let me only say that, although I must call myself a lost creature as to this world, yet have I this consolation left me, that I have not suffered either for want of circumspection, or through credulity, or weakness. Not one moment was I off my guard, or unmindful of your early precepts. But (having been enabled to baffle many base contrivances) I was at last ruined by arts the most inhuman. But had I not been rejected by every friend, this low-hearted man had not dared, nor would have had opportunity, to treat me as he has treated me.

More I cannot at this time, nor need I, say: and this I desire you to keep to yourself, lest resentments should be taken up when I am gone, that may spread the evil which I hope will end with me.

I have been misinformed, you say, as to my principal relations being at my uncle Harlowe's. The day, you say, was not kept. Nor have my brother and Mr Solmes—Astonishing—What complicated wickedness has this wretched man to answer for!—Were I to tell you, you would hardly believe there could have been such a heart in man—

But one day you may know my whole story!—At present I have neither inclination nor words—Oh my bursting heart!—Yet a happy, a wished relief!—Were you present, my tears would supply the rest!

I RESUME my pen!

And so you fear no letter will be received from me. But DON'T *grieve to tell me so!* I expect everything bad!—And such is my distress that had you not bid me hope for mercy from the Throne of Mercy, I should have been afraid that my father's dreadful curse would be completed with regard to both worlds.

For, here, an additional misfortune!—In a fit of frenzical heedlessness, I sent a letter to my beloved Miss Howe, without recollecting her private address; and it is fallen into her angry mother's hands: and so that dear friend perhaps has anew incurred displeasure on my account. And here too, your worthy son is ill; and my poor Hannah, you think, cannot come to me—Oh my dear Mrs Norton, *will* you, *can* you, censure *those* whose resentments against me Heaven seems to approve of? and will you acquit *her* whom *that* condemns?

Yet you bid me not despond—I will not, if I can help it—And, indeed, most seasonable consolation has your kind letter afforded me—Yet to God Almighty do I appeal, to avenge my wrongs, and vindicate my inno—

But hushed be my stormy passions!—Have I not but this moment said that your letter gave me consolation?—May *those* be forgiven who hinder my father from forgiving *me!*—And this, as to *them*, shall be the harshest thing that shall drop from my pen.

But although your son should recover, I charge you, my dear Mrs Norton, that you do not think of coming to me. I don't know still but your mediation with my mother (although at present your interposition would be so little attended to) may be of use to procure me the revocation of that most dreadful part of my father's curse, which only remains to be fulfilled. The voice of nature must at last be heard in my favour, surely. It will only plead at first to my friends in the still, conscious plaintiveness of a young and unhardened beggar!—But it will grow more clamorous when *I* have the courage to be so, and shall demand, perhaps, the paternal protection from further ruin; and that forgiveness, which those will be little entitled to expect for their own faults, who shall interpose to have it refused to me for an *accidental*, not a *premeditated*, error: and which, but for them, I had never fallen into.

But again impatiency, founded perhaps on self-partiality, that strange misleader! prevails.

Let me briefly say, that it is necessary to my present and future hopes that you keep well with my family. And, moreover, should you come, I may be traced out by your means by the most abandoned of men. Say not then that you think you ought to come up to me, *let it be taken as it will*—For *my sake*, let me repeat (were my foster-brother recovered, as I hope he is), you must *not* come. Nor can I want your advice while *I* can write, and *you* can answer me. And write I will, as often as I stand in need of your counsel.

Then the people I am now with seem to be both honest and humane: and there is in the same house a widow-lodger of low fortunes, but of great merit—almost such another serious and good woman as the dear one to whom I am now writing; who has, as she says, given over all other thoughts of the world but such as shall assist her to leave it happily—How suitable to my own views!—There seems to be a comfortable providence in *this* at least!—So that at present there is nothing of exigence; nothing that can *require*, or even *excuse*, your coming, when so many better ends may be answered by your staying where you are. A time *may* come, when I shall want your last and best assistance: and *then*, my dear Mrs Norton— and *then*, I will bespeak it, and embrace it with my whole heart—and *then*, will it not be denied me by anybody.

You are very obliging in your offer of money. But although I was forced to leave my clothes behind me, yet I took several things of value with me, which will keep me from present want. You'll say I have made a miserable hand of it—So indeed I have!—and, to look backwards, in a very little while too.

But what shall I do if my father cannot be prevailed upon to recall his grievous malediction?—Of all the very heavy evils wherewith I have been afflicted, this is *now* the heaviest; for I can neither live nor die under it.

Oh my dear Mrs Norton, what a weight must a father's curse have upon a mind so apprehensive of it as mine is!—Did I think I should ever have *this* to deprecate?

But you must not be angry with me that I wrote not to you before. You are very right, and very kind, to say you are sure I love you. Indeed I do. And what a generosity is there (so like yourself) in your praise, to attribute to me more than I merit, in order to raise an emulation in me to *deserve* your praises!—You tell me what you expect from me in the calamities I am called upon to bear. May I but behave answerably!

I *can* a little account *to myself* for my silence to you, my kind, my dear maternal friend (how equally sweetly and politely do you express yourself on this occasion!)— I was very desirous, for your sake as well as for my own, that you should have it to say that we did not correspond. Had they thought we did, every word you could have dropped in my favour would have been rejected; and my mother would have been forbid to see you, or to pay any regard to what you should say.

Then I had sometimes better and sometimes worse prospects before me. My worst would only have troubled you to know: my better made me frequently hope that, by the next post, or the next, and so on for weeks, I should have the best news to impart to you, that *then* could happen; cold as the wretch had made my heart to *that best*—For how could I think to write to you, with a confession that I was not married, yet lived in the house (nor could I help it) with such a man?—who likewise had given it out to several, that we were actually married, although with restrictions that depended on the reconciliation with my friends? And to disguise the truth, or be guilty of a falsehood either direct or equivocal, that was what you had never learnt me.

But I might have written to you for advice, in my precarious situation, perhaps you will think. But, indeed, my dear Mrs Norton, I was not lost for want of advice. And this will appear clear to you from what I have already hinted, were I to explain myself no further—For what need had the cruel spoiler to have had recourse to unprecedented arts—I will speak out plainer still (but you must not at present report it); to stupefying potions, and to the most brutal and outrageous force; had I been wanting in my duty?

A few words more upon this grievous subject—

When I reflect upon all that has happened to me, it is apparent that this generally supposed *thoughtless* seducer has acted by me upon a regular and preconcerted plan of villainy.

In order to set all his vile plots in motion, nothing was wanting from the first, but to prevail upon me either by force or fraud, to throw myself into his power: and when this was effected, nothing less than the intervention of the paternal authority (which I had not deserved to be exerted in my behalf) could have saved me from the effect of his deep machinations. Opposition from any other quarter would but too probably have precipitated his barbarous and ungrateful violence: and had *you yourself* been with me, I have reason *now* to think, that somehow or other you would have suffered in endeavouring to save me: for never was there, as now I see, a plan of wickedness more steadily and uniformly pursued, than *his* has been, against an unhappy creature who merited better of *him*. But the Almighty has thought fit, according to the general course of his providence, to make the fault bring on its own punishment: and that, perhaps, in consequence of my father's dreadful imprecation, 'That I might be punished *here*' (Oh my mamma Norton, pray with me that *here* it stop!) 'by the very wretch in whom I had placed my wicked confidence!'

I am sorry for your sake to leave off so heavily. Yet the rest must be brief.

Let me desire you to be secret in what I have communicated to you; at least till you have my consent to divulge it.

God preserve to you your more faultless child!

I will hope for His mercy, although I should not obtain that of any other person.

And I repeat my prohibition—You must not think of coming up to

Your ever-dutiful
CL. HARLOWE

The obliging person who left yours for me this day promised to call tomorrow to see if I should have anything to return. I would not lose so good an opportunity.

Letter 308: MRS NORTON TO MISS CLARISSA HARLOWE

Monday night, July 3

OH THE barbarous villainy of this detestable man!

And is there a man in the world who could offer violence to so sweet a creature! And are you sure you are now out of his reach?

You command me to keep secret the particulars of the vile treatment you have met with; or else, upon an unexpected visit which Miss Harlowe favoured me with, soon after I had received your melancholy letter, I should have been tempted to own I had heard from you, and to have communicated to her such parts of your two letters as would have demonstrated your penitence, and your earnestness to obtain the revocation of your father's malediction, as well as his protection from outrages that may still be offered to you. But then your sister would probably have expected a sight of the letters, and even to have been permitted to take them with her to the family.

Yet they *must* one day be acquainted with the sad story—and it is impossible but they must pity you, and forgive you, when they know your early penitence, and your unprecedented sufferings; and that you have fallen by the brutal force of a barbarous ravisher, and not by the vile arts of a seducing lover.

The wicked man gives it out at Lord M.'s, as Miss Harlowe tells me, that he is actually married to you—yet she believes it not; nor had I the heart to let her know the truth.

She put it close to me, whether I had not corresponded with you from the time of your going away? I could safely tell her (as I did), that I had not: but I said that I was well informed that you took extremely to heart your father's imprecation; and that, if she would excuse me, I would say it would be a kind and sisterly part, if she would use her interest to get you discharged from it.

Among other severe things, she told me that my partial fondness for you made me very little consider the honour of the rest of the family: but, if I had not heard this from you, she supposed I was set on by Miss Howe.

She expressed herself with a good deal of bitterness against that young lady: who, it seems, everywhere, and to everybody (for you must think that your story is the subject of all conversations), rails against your family; treating them, as your sister says, with contempt and even with ridicule.

I am sorry such angry freedoms are taken, for two reasons; first, because such liberties never do any good. I have heard you own that Miss Howe has a satirical vein; but I should hope that a young lady of her sense and right cast of mind must know, that the end of satire is not to exasperate, but amend; and should never be personal. If it be, as my good father used to say, it may make an impartial person suspect that the satirist has a natural spleen to gratify; which may be as great a fault in *him*, as any of those which he pretends to censure and expose in *others*.

Perhaps a hint of this from you will not be thrown away.

My second reason is, that these freedoms from so warm a friend to you as Miss Howe is known to be are most likely to be charged to your account.

My resentments are so strong against this vilest of men, that I dare not touch upon the shocking particulars which you mention of his baseness. What defence, indeed, could there be against so determined a wretch, after you were in his power? I will only repeat my earnest supplication to you that, black as appearances are, you will not despair. Your calamities are exceeding great, but then you have talents proportioned to your trials. This everybody allows.

Suppose the worst, and that your family will not be moved in your favour, your cousin Morden will soon arrive, as Miss Harlowe told me. If he should even be got over to their side, he will however see justice done you; and then may you live an exemplary life, making hundreds happy, and teaching young ladies to shun the snares in which you have been so dreadfully entangled.

As to the man you have lost, is an union with such a perjured heart as his with such an admirable one as yours, to be wished for? A base, *low-hearted* wretch, as you justly call him, with all his pride of ancestry; and more an enemy to himself with regard to his present and future happiness, than to you in the barbarous and ungrateful wrongs he has done you; I need not, I am sure, exhort you to despise such a man as this; since not to be able to do so would be a reflection upon a sex to which you have always been an honour.

Your moral character is untainted: the very nature of your sufferings, as you well observe, demonstrates *that*. Cheer up, therefore, your dear heart, and do not despair: for is it not GOD who governs the world, and permits some things, and directs others, as He pleases? And will he not reward *temporary sufferings*, innocently incurred and piously supported, with *eternal felicity?*—And what, my dear, is this poor needle's point of NOW to a *boundless* ETERNITY?

My heart, however, labours under a double affliction: for my poor boy is very, very bad!—A violent fever!—Nor can it be brought to intermit!—Pray for *him*, my dearest miss—for his recovery if God sees fit—I hope God *will* see fit!—If not (how can I bear to suppose that!)—pray for *me*, that he will give me that patience and resignation which I have been wishing to you. I am, my dearest young lady,

> Your ever-affectionate
> JUDITH NORTON

Letter 309: MISS CLARISSA HARLOWE TO MRS JUDITH NORTON

Thursday, July 6

I OUGHT not, especially at this time, to add to your afflictions—But yet I cannot help communicating to you (who are now my *only* soothing friend) a new trouble that has befallen me.

I had but one friend in the world, besides you; and she is utterly displeased with me.*a* It is grievous, but for one moment, to lie under a beloved person's censure; and this through imputations that affect one's honour and prudence. There are points so delicate, you know, my dear Mrs Norton, that it is a degree of dishonour to have a vindication of one's self from them appear to be *necessary*. In the present case, my misfortune is that I know not how to account, but by guess (so subtle have been the workings of the dark spirit I have been unhappily entangled by), for some of the facts that I am called upon to explain.

Miss Howe, in short, supposes she has found a flaw in my character. I have just now received her severe letter: but I shall answer it, perhaps, in better temper if I first consider yours. For indeed my patience is almost at an end. And yet I ought to consider *that faithful are the wounds of a friend.*[1] But so *many* things at once!— Oh, my dear Mrs Norton, how shall so young a scholar in the school of affliction be able to bear such heavy and such various evils!

But to leave this subject for a while, and turn to your letter.

I am very sorry Miss Howe is so lively in her resentments on my account. I have always blamed her very freely for her liberties of this sort with my friends. I once had a good deal of influence over her kind heart, and she made all I said a law to her. But people in calamity have but little weight in anything, or with anybody. Prosperity and independence are charming things on this account, that they give force to the counsels of a friendly heart; while it is thought insolence in the miserable to advise, or so much as remonstrate.

Yet is Miss Howe an invaluable person: and is it to be expected that she should preserve the same regard for my judgement that she had before I forfeited all title to discretion? With what face can I take upon me to reproach a want of prudence in *her?* But if I can be so happy as to re-establish myself in her ever-valued opinion, I shall endeavour to enforce upon her your just observations on this head.

You need not, you say, exhort me to despise such a man as him by whom I have

a See the next letter.

suffered—Indeed you need not: for I would choose the cruellest death rather than to be his. And yet, my dear Mrs Norton, I will own to you that once I could have loved him—ungrateful man!—had he permitted me, I *once* could have loved him. Yet he never deserved my love. And was not this a fault? But now, if I can but keep out of his hands, and procure the revocation of my father's malediction, it is all I wish for.

Reconciliation with my friends I do not expect; nor pardon from them; at least, till in extremity, and as a *viaticum*.

Oh, my beloved Mrs Norton, you cannot imagine what I have suffered!—But indeed my heart is broken! I am sure I shall not live to take possession of that independence which you think would enable me to atone in some measure for my past conduct.

While this is my opinion, you may believe I shall not be easy till I can procure the revocation of that dreadful curse; and, if possible, a last forgiveness.

I wish to be left to take my own course in endeavouring to procure this grace. Yet know I not at present what that course shall be.

I will write. But to *whom* is my doubt. Calamity has not yet given me the assurance to address myself to my FATHER. My UNCLES (well as they once loved me) are hard-hearted. They never had their masculine passions humanized by the tender name of FATHER. Of my BROTHER I have no hope. I have then but my MOTHER and my SISTER to whom I can apply—'And may I not, my dearest mamma, be permitted to lift up my trembling eye to your all-cheering, and your once *more* than indulgent, your *fond* eye, in hopes of seasonable mercy to the poor sick heart that yet beats with life drawn from your own dearer heart?—Especially when pardon only, and not restoration, is implored?'

Yet were I able to engage my mother's pity, would it not be a means to make *her* still more unhappy than I have already made her, by the opposition she would meet with were she to try to give force to that pity?

To my SISTER, then, I think I will apply—Yet how hard-hearted has my sister been!—But I will not ask for protection; and yet I am in hourly dread that I shall want protection—All I will ask for shall be only to be freed from the heavy curse that has operated as far as it *can* operate as to *this* life.—And surely it was passion and not intention, that carried it so very far as to the *other!*

But why do I thus add to your distresses?—It is not, my dear Mrs Norton, that I have so *much* feeling for my *own* calamity that I have *none* for *yours*: since yours is indeed an addition to my own. But you have one consolation (a very great one) which I have not—that *your* afflictions, whether respecting your *more* or your *less* deserving child, rise not from any fault of your own.

But what can I do for you more than pray?—Assure yourself that in every supplication I put up for myself, I will with equal fervour remember both you and your son. For I am, and ever will be,

> Your truly sympathizing and dutiful
> CLARISSA HARLOWE

Letter 310: MISS HOWE TO MISS CLARISSA HARLOWE

(Superscribed, For Mrs Rachel Clark, etc.)

Wednesday, July 5

My dear Clarissa,

I HAVE at last heard from you from a quarter I little expected.

From my mamma.

She had for some time seen me uneasy and grieving; and justly supposed it was about you. And this morning dropped a hint, which made me conjecture that she must have heard something of you more than I knew. And when she found that this added to my uneasiness, she owned she had a letter in her hands of yours, dated the 29th of June, directed for me.

You may guess that this occasioned a little warmth that could not be wished for by either.

(It is surprising, my dear, *mighty* surprising! that, knowing the prohibition I lay under of corresponding with you, you could send a letter for me to our own house: since it must be fifty to one that it would fall into my mother's hands, as you find it did.)

In short, *she* resented that I should disobey her: *I* was as much concerned that she should open and withhold from me *my* letters: and at last she was pleased to compromise the matter with me; by giving up the letter and permitting me to write to you *once* or *twice*; she to see the contents of what I wrote. For, besides the value she has for you, she could not but have a great curiosity to know the occasion of so sad a situation as your melancholy letter shows you to be in.

(But I shall get her to be satisfied with hearing me read what I write; putting in between hooks, thus ( ), what I intend not to read to her.)

Need I to remind you, Miss [Clarissa] Harlowe, of *three* letters I wrote to you, to none of which I had any answer; except to the *first*, and that a few lines only, promising a letter at large; though you were well enough the day after you received my *second* to go joyfully back again with him to the vile house? But more of these by and by. I must hasten to take notice of your letter of Wednesday last week; which you could *contrive* should fall into my mother's hands.

Let me tell you that that letter has almost broken my heart. Good God! what have you brought yourself to, Miss Clarissa Harlowe?—Could I have believed that after you had escaped from the miscreant (with such mighty pains and earnestness escaped), and after such an attempt as he had made, you would have been prevailed upon, not only to forgive him, but (without being married too) to return with him to that horrid house!—A house I had given you such an account of!—Surprising!—What an intoxicating thing is *this love?*—I *always* feared, that you, even you, were not proof against it.

You your *best self* have not escaped!—Indeed I see not how you could expect to escape.

What a tale have you to unfold!—You need not unfold it, my dear: I would have engaged to prognosticate all that has happened, had you but told me that you would once more have put yourself into his power after you had taken such pains to get out of it.

Your peace is destroyed!—I wonder not at it: since now you must reproach yourself for a credulity so ill-placed.

Your intellect is touched!—I am sure my heart bleeds for you: but, excuse me, my dear, I doubt your intellect was touched before you left Hampstead; or you would never have let him find you out there; or, when he did, suffer him to prevail upon you to return to the horrid brothel.

I tell you I sent you *three letters*: the *first* of which, dated the 7th and 8th of June[a] (for it was wrote at twice), came safe to your hands, as you sent me word by a few lines dated the ninth: had it not, I should have doubted my own safety; since in it I gave you such an account of the abominable house, and threw such cautions in your way as to that Tomlinson, as the more surprised me that you could think of going back to it again after you had escaped from it, and from Lovelace—Oh my dear!—But nothing now will I ever wonder at!

The *second*, dated June 10,[b] was given into your own hand at Hampstead on Sunday the 11th, as you was lying upon a couch in a strange way, according to my messenger's account of you, bloated, and flush-coloured; I don't know how.

The *third* was dated the 20th of June.[c] Having not heard one word from you since the promising billet of the 9th, I own I did not spare you in it. I ventured it by the usual conveyance, by that Wilson's, having no other: so cannot be sure you received it. Indeed I rather think you might not; because in yours, which fell into my mamma's hands, you make no mention of it: and if you had had it, I believe it would have touched you too much to have been passed by unnoticed.

You have heard that I have been ill, you say. I had a cold indeed; but it was so slight a one that it confined me not an hour. But I doubt not that strange things you have *heard*, and *been told*, to induce you to take the step you took. And, till you did take that step (the going back with this villain, I mean), I knew not a more pitiable case than yours—for everybody must have excused you before who knew how you was used at home, and was acquainted with your prudence and vigilance. But, alas! my dear, we see that the *wisest people* are not to be depended upon when *love*, like an *ignis fatuus*, holds up its misleading lights before their eyes.

My mother tells me she sent you an answer desiring you not to write to me, because it would grieve me. To be sure I *am* grieved; *exceedingly* grieved; and *disappointed* too, you must permit me to say. For I had always thought that there never was such a woman, at your years, in the world.

But I remember once an argument you held on occasion of a censure passed in company upon an excellent preacher, who was not a very excellent liver: *preaching* and *practising*, you said, required quite different talents: which, when united in the same person, made the man a saint; as *wit* and *judgement* going together constituted a genius.

You made it out, I remember, very prettily: but you never made it out, excuse me my dear, more convincingly than by that part of your late conduct which I complain of.

My love for you, and my concern for your honour, may possibly have made me a little of the severest: if you think so, place it to its proper account; to *that* love, and to *that* concern: which will but do justice, to

Your afflicted and faithful,
A.H.

a See p. 743.
b See p. 855.
c See pp. 931, 932.

POSTSCRIPT

My mother would not be satisfied without reading my letter herself; and that before I had fixed my proposed hooks. She knows, by this means, and has excused, our former correspondence.

She indeed suspected it before: and so she very well might; knowing me, and knowing my love of you.

She has so much real concern for your misfortunes that, thinking it will be a consolation to *you*, and that it will oblige *me*, she consents that you shall write to me the *particulars at large of your sad story*: but it is on condition that I show her all that has passed between us relating to yourself and the vilest of men. I have the more cheerfully complied, as the communication cannot be to your disadvantage.

You may therefore write freely, and direct to our own house.

My mother promises to show me the copy of her letter to you, and your reply to it; which latter she has but just told me of. She already apologizes for the severity of hers: and thinks the sight of your reply will affect me too much. But having her promise, I will not dispense with it.

I doubt hers is severe enough. So I fear you will think mine: but you have taught me never to spare the *fault* for the *friend's* sake; and that a great error ought rather to be more inexcusable in the person we value, than in one we are indifferent to; because it is a reflection upon our choice of that person, and tends to a breach of the love of mind; and to expose us to the world for our partiality. To the *love of mind*, I repeat; since it is impossible but the errors of the dearest friend must weaken our inward opinion of that friend; and thereby lay a foundation for future distance, and perhaps disgust.

God grant that you may be able to clear your conduct *after* you had escaped from Hampstead; as all *before* that time was noble, generous, and prudent: the man a devil, and you a saint!—Yet I hope you can; and therefore expect it from you.

I send by a particular hand. He will call for your answer at your own appointment.

I am afraid this horrid wretch will trace out by the post offices where you are, if not careful.

To have *money*, and *will*, and *head*, to be a villain, is too much for the rest of the world when they meet in one man.

Letter 311: MISS CLARISSA HARLOWE TO MISS HOWE

Thursday, July 6

FEW young persons have been able to give more convincing proofs than myself, how little true happiness lies in the enjoyment of our own wishes.

To produce one instance only of the truth of this observation; what would I have given for weeks past for the favour of a letter from my dear Miss Howe, in whose friendship I placed all my remaining comfort? Little did I think that the next letter she would honour me with should be in such a style as should make me look more than once at the subscription, that I might be sure (the name not being written at length) that it was not signed by another A.H. For surely, thought I, this

is my sister Arabella's style: surely Miss Howe (blame me as she pleases in other
points) could never repeat so *sharply* upon her friend, words written in the
bitterness of spirit, and in the disorder of head; nor remind her, with asperity and
with mingled strokes of wit, of an argument held in the gaiety of an heart elated
with prosperous fortunes (as mine then was), and very little apprehensive of the
severe turn that argument would one day take against herself.

But what have *I*, sunk in my fortunes; my character forfeited; my honour lost
(while *I* know it, I care not *who* knows it); destitute of friends, and even of hope;
what have *I* to do to show a spirit of repining and expostulation to a dear friend,
because she is not *more* kind than a sister?——

I find, by the rising bitterness which will mingle with the gall in my ink, that I am
not yet subdued enough to my condition: and so, begging your pardon that I
should rather have formed my expectations of favour from the indulgence you
used to show me, than from what I *now deserve* to have shown me, I will endeavour
to give a particular answer to your letter; although it will take me up too much
time to think of sending it by your messenger tomorrow. He can put off his journey,
he says, till Saturday. I will endeavour to have the whole narrative ready for you
by Saturday.

But how to defend myself in everything that has happened, I cannot tell: since
in some part of the time in which my conduct appears to have been censurable, I
was not myself; and to this hour know not all the methods taken to deceive and
ruin me.

You tell me that in your first letter you gave me such an account of the vile
house I was in, and such cautions about that Tomlinson, as make you wonder how
I could think of going back.

Alas, my dear! I was tricked, most vilely tricked back, as you shall hear in its
place.

Without *knowing* the house was so very *vile* a house from your *intended*
information, I disliked the people too much, ever *voluntarily* to have returned to
it. But had you really written such cautions about Tomlinson, and the house, as
you seem to have *purposed* to do, they must, had they come in time, have been of
infinite service to me. But not one word of either, whatever was your *intention*, did
you mention to me in that *first* of the *three* letters you so warmly TELL ME you *did*
send me. *I will enclose it to convince you.*[a]

But your account of your messenger's delivering to me your second letter, and
the description he gives of me as *lying upon a couch, in a strange way, bloated and
flush-coloured, you don't know how*, absolutely puzzles and confounds me.

Lord have mercy upon the poor Clarissa Harlowe! What can this mean!—*Who*
was the messenger you sent? Was *he* one of Lovelace's creatures too!—Could
nobody come near me but that man's confederates, either *setting out so*, or *made
so?*—I know not what to make of any one syllable of this!—Indeed I don't!

Let me see. You say this was *before* I went from Hampstead!—My intellects had
not then been touched!—Nor had I ever been surprised by wine (strange if I had!):
how then could I be found in such a *strange way, bloated, and flush-coloured; you
don't know how!*—Yet what a vile, what a hateful figure has your messenger
represented me to have made!

a The letter she encloses was Mr Lovelace's forged one. See pp. 811 ff.

But indeed, I know nothing of ANY messenger from you.

Believing myself secure at Hampstead, I stayed longer there than I would have done, in hopes of the letter promised me in your short one of the 9th, brought me by my own messenger, in which you undertake to send for and engage Mrs Townsend in my favour.[a]

I wondered I heard not from you: and was told you were sick; and, at another time, that your mother and you had had words on my account, and that you had refused to admit Mr Hickman's visits upon it: so that I supposed at one time that you was not *able* to write; at another that your mother's prohibition had its *due* force with you. But now I have no doubt that the wicked man must have intercepted your letter; and I wish he found not means to *corrupt your messenger* to tell you so strange a story.

It was on Sunday June 11 you say, that the man gave it me. I was at church twice that day with Mrs Moore. Mr Lovelace was at her house the while, where he boarded, and wanted to have lodged; but I would not permit that, though I could not help the other. In one of these spaces *it must be* that he had time to work upon the man. You'll easily, my dear, find that out by inquiring the time of his arrival at Mrs Moore's, and other circumstances of the *strange way* he pretended to see me in, *on a couch*, and the rest.

Had anybody seen me afterwards, when I was betrayed back to the vile house, struggling under the operation of wicked potions, and robbed *indeed* of my intellects (for this, as you shall hear, was my dreadful case!), I might then perhaps have appeared *bloated*, and *flush-coloured*, and *I know not how myself*. But were you to see your poor Clarissa *now* (or ever to have seen her at Hampstead, *before* she suffered the vilest of all outrages), you would not think her *bloated*, or *flush-coloured:* indeed you would not.

In a word, it could not be *me* your messenger saw; nor (if anybody) who it was can I divine.

I will now, as *briefly* as the subject will permit, enter into the darker part of my sad story: and yet I must be somewhat circumstantial, that you may not think me capable of *reserve* or *palliation*. The *latter* I am not conscious that I need. I should be utterly inexcusable, were I guilty of the *former* to you. And yet, if you knew how my heart sinks under the thoughts of a recollection so painful, you would pity me.

As I shall not be able, perhaps, to conclude what I have to write in even two or three letters, I will begin a new one with my story; and send the whole of it together, although written at different periods, as I am able.

Allow me a little pause, my dear, at this place; and to subscribe myself

Your ever-affectionate and obliged
CLARISSA HARLOWE

a   See p. 808.

Letter 312: MISS CLARISSA HARLOWE TO MISS HOWE

(Referred to on p. 883)

Thursday night

HE had found me out at Hampstead: strangely found me out; for I am still at a loss to know by what means.

I was loath, in my billet of the 9th,[a] to tell you so, for fear of giving you apprehensions for me; and besides I hoped then to have a shorter and happier issue account to you for, through your assistance, than I met with.

(She then gives a narrative of all that passed at Hampstead between herself, Mr Lovelace, Captain Tomlinson and the women there, to the same effect with that so amply given by Mr Lovelace.)

Mr Lovelace, finding all he could say, and all Captain Tomlinson could urge, ineffectual to prevail upon me to forgive an outrage so flagrantly premeditated; rested all his hopes on a visit which was to be paid me by Lady Betty Lawrance and Miss Montague.

In my uncertain situation, my prospects all so dark, I knew not to whom I might be obliged to have recourse in the last resort: and as those ladies had the best of characters, insomuch that I had reason to regret that I had not from the first thrown myself upon their protection (when I had forfeited *that* of my own friends), I thought I would not *shun* an interview with them, though I was too indifferent to their kinsman to *seek* it, as I doubted not that one end of their visit would be to reconcile me to him.

On Monday the 12th of June, these pretended ladies came to Hampstead, and I was presented to them, and they to me, by their kinsman.

They were richly dressed and stuck out with jewels; the pretended Lady Betty's were particularly very fine.

They came in a coach and four, hired, as was confessed, while their own was repairing in town: a pretence made, I now perceive, that I should not guess at the imposture by the want of the real lady's arms upon it. Lady Betty was attended by her woman, whom she called Morrison; a modest country-looking person.

I had heard that Lady Betty was a fine woman, and that Miss Montague was a beautiful young lady, genteel and graceful, and full of vivacity: such were these impostors; and having never seen either of them, I had not the least suspicion that they were not the ladies they personated; and being put a little out of countenance by the richness of their dresses, I could not help, fool that I was! to apologize for my own.

The pretended Lady Betty then told me that her nephew had acquainted them with the situation of affairs between us. And although she could not but say that she was very glad that he had not put such a slight upon his lordship and them, as report had given them cause to apprehend (the reasons for which report, however, she much approved of); yet it had been matter of great concern to her, and to her niece Montague, and would to the whole family, to find so great a misunderstanding subsisting between us as, if not made up, might distance all their hopes.

She could easily tell who was in fault, she said—and gave him a look both of anger and disdain; asking him how it was possible for him to give an offence of

a See p. 815.

such a nature to so charming a lady (so she called me) as should occasion a resentment so strong?

He pretended to be awed into shame and silence.

My dearest niece, said she, and took my hand (I *must* call you niece, as well from love, as to humour your uncle's laudable expedient), permit me to be, not an advocate, but a mediatrix for him; and not for his sake so much as for my own, my Charlotte's, and all our family's. The indignity he has offered to you may be of too tender a nature to be inquired into. But as he declares that it was not a premeditated offence; whether, my dear (for I was going to rise upon it in my temper), it were or not; and as he declares his sorrow for it (and never did creature express a deeper sorrow for any offence than he!); and as it is a reparable one; let *us*, for this one time, forgive him; and thereby lay an obligation upon this man of errors—Let US, I say, my dear: for, sir (turning to him), an offence against such a peerless lady as this must be an offence against *me*, against your *cousin*, here; and against *all the virtuous* of our sex.

See, my dear, what a creature he had picked out! Could you have thought there was a woman in the world who could thus express herself, and yet be vile? But she had her principal instructions from him, and those written down too, as I have reason to think: for I have recollected since, that I once saw this Lady Betty (who often rose from her seat and took a turn to the other end of the room with such emotion as if the joy of her heart would not let her sit still) take out a paper from her stays and look into it, and put it there again. She might oftener, and I not observe it; for I little thought that there could be such impostors in the world.

I could not forbear paying great attention to what she said. I found tears ready to start; I drew out my handkerchief and was silent. I had not been so indulgently treated a great while by a person of character and distinction (such I thought her), and durst not trust to the accent of my voice.

The pretended Miss Montague joined in on this occasion; and drawing her chair close to me, took my other hand and besought me to forgive her cousin; and consent to rank myself as one of the principals of a family that had long, very long, coveted the honour of my alliance.

I am ashamed to repeat to you, my dear, now I know what wretches they are, the tender, the obliging, and the respectful things I said to them.

The wretch himself then came forward. He threw himself at my feet. How was I beset!—The women grasping one my right hand, the other my left: the pretended Miss Montague pressing to her lips more than once the hand she held: the wicked man on his knees, imploring my forgiveness; and setting before me my happy and my unhappy prospects, as I should forgive or not forgive him. All that he thought would affect me in his former pleas and those of Captain Tomlinson, he repeated. He vowed, he promised, he bespoke the pretended ladies to answer for him; and they engaged their honours in his behalf.

Indeed, my dear, I was distressed, perfectly distressed. I was sorry that I had given way to this visit. For I knew not how, in tenderness to relations (as I thought them) so worthy, to treat so freely as he deserved, a man nearly allied to them—so that my arguments and my resolutions were deprived of their greatest force.

I pleaded, however, my application to you. I expected every hour, I told them, an answer from you to a letter I had written, which would decide my future destiny.

They offered to apply to you themselves in person, in *their own behalf* as they politely termed it. They besought me to write to you to hasten your answer.

I said I was sure that you would write the moment that the event of an application to be made to a third person enabled you to write—But as to the success of their requests in behalf of their kinsman, that depended not upon the expected answer; for *that*, I begged their pardon, was out of the question. I wished him well. I wished him happy. But I was convinced that I neither could make *him* so, nor he *me*.

Then, again, how the wretch promised!—How he vowed!—How he entreated!— And how the women pleaded! And they engaged themselves, and the honour of their whole family, for his just, his kind, his tender behaviour to me.

In short, my dear, I was so hard set that I was obliged to come to a more favourable compromise with them than I had intended. I would wait for your answer to my letter, I said: and if it made doubtful or difficult the change of measures I had resolved upon, and the scheme of life I had formed, I would then consider of the matter; and, if they would permit me, lay all before them, and take their advice upon it, in conjunction with yours, as if the one were my own aunt, and the other were my own cousin.

They shed tears upon this—of joy they called them—but since, I believe, to their credit, bad as they are, that they were tears of temporary remorse; for the pretended Miss Montague turned about and, as I remember, said there was no standing it.

But Mr Lovelace was not so easily satisfied. He was fixed upon his villainous measures perhaps; and so might not be sorry to have a pretence against me. He bit his lip—He had been but too much used, he said, to such indifference, such coldness, in the very midst of his happiest prospects—I had on twenty occasions shown him, to his infinite regret, that any favour I was to confer upon him was to be the result of—there he stopped—and not of my choice.

This had like to have set all back again. I was exceedingly offended. But the pretended ladies interposed. The elder severely took him to task. He ought, she told him, to be satisfied with what I had said. She *desired* no other condition. And what, sir, said she with an air of authority, would you commit errors, and expect to be *rewarded* for them?

They then engaged me in more agreeable conversation—The pretended lady declared that she, Lord M., and Lady Sarah would directly and personally interest themselves to bring about a general reconciliation between the two families, and this either in open or private concert with my uncle Harlowe, as should be thought fit. Animosities on one side had been carried a great way, she said; and too little care had been shown on the other to mollify or heal. My father should see that they could treat him as a brother and a friend; and my brother and sister should be convinced that there was no room either for the jealousy or envy they had conceived from motives too unworthy to be avowed.

Could I help, my dear, being pleased with them?—

Permit me here to break off. The task grows too heavy, at present, for the heart of

                                        Your CLARISSA HARLOWE

Letter 313: MISS CLARISSA HARLOWE TO MISS HOWE

(In continuation)

I was very ill, and obliged to lay down my pen. I thought I should have fainted. But am better now—so will proceed.

The pretended ladies, the more we talked, seemed to be the fonder of me. And *the* Lady Betty had Mrs Moore called up; and asked her, if she had accommodations for her niece and self, her woman, and two menservants, for three or four days?

Mr Lovelace answered for her that she had.

She would not ask her dear niece Lovelace (*Permit me, my dear*, whispered she, *this charming style before strangers!—I will keep your uncle's secret*) whether she should be welcome or not to be so near her. But for the time she should stay in these parts, she would come up every night—What say *you*, niece Charlotte?

The pretended Charlotte answered she should like to do so, of all things.

The Lady Betty called her an obliging girl. She liked the place, she said. Her cousin Leeson would excuse her. The air and my company would do her good. She never chose to lie in the smoky town if she could help it. In short, my dear, said she to me, I will stay till you hear from Miss Howe; and till I have your consent to go with me to Glenham Hall. Not one moment will I be out of your company, when I can have it. Stedman my solicitor, as the distance from town is so small, may attend me here for instructions. Niece Charlotte, one word with you, child.

They retired to the farther end of the room, and talked about their nightdresses. *The* Miss Charlotte said Morrison might be dispatched for them.

True, the other said—But she had some letters in her private box, which she must have up. And you know, Charlotte, that I trust nobody with the keys of that.

Could not Morrison bring up that box?

No. She thought it safest where it was. She had heard of a robbery committed but two days ago at the foot of Hampstead Hill; and she should be ruined if she lost her box.

Well then, it was but going to town to undress, and she would leave her jewels behind her, and return; and should be the easier a great deal on all accounts.

For my part, I wondered they came up with them. But that was to be taken as a respect paid to me. And then they hinted at another visit of ceremony which they had thought to make, had they not found me so inexpressibly engaging.

They talked loud enough for me to hear them; on purpose, no doubt, though in affected whispers; and concluded with high praises of me.

I was not fool enough to believe, or to be puffed up with their encomiums; yet not suspecting them, I was not displeased at so favourable a beginning of acquaintance with ladies (whether I were to be related to them or not) of whom I had always heard honourable mention. And yet at the time, I thought, highly as they exalted *me*, that in some respects (though I hardly knew in what) they fell short of what I expected *them* to be.

The grand deluder was at the farther end of the room, another way; probably to give me an opportunity to hear these preconcerted praises—looking into a book which, had there not been a preconcert, would not have taken his attention for one moment. It was *Taylor's Holy Living and Dying*.[1]

When the pretended ladies joined me, he approached me with it in his hand—

A smart book, this, my dear!—This old divine affects, I see, a mighty flowery style upon a very solemn subject. But it puts me in mind of an ordinary country funeral, where the young women, in honour of a defunct companion, especially if she were a virgin, or *passed for such*, make a flower-bed of her coffin.

And then, laying down the book, turning upon his heel, with one of his usual airs of gaiety, And are you determined, ladies, to take up your lodgings with my charming creature?

Indeed they were.

Never were there more cunning, more artful impostors, than these women. Practised creatures, to be sure: yet genteel; and they must have been well educated—Once, perhaps, as much the delight of their parents, as I was of mine: and who knows by what arts ruined, body and mind!—Oh my dear! how pregnant is this reflection!

But the *man!*—Never was there a man so deep! Never so consummate a deceiver! except that detested Tomlinson; whose years, and seriousness, joined with a solidity of sense and judgement, that seemed uncommon, gave him, one would have thought, advantages in villainy the other had not time for. Hard, very hard, that I should fall into the knowledge of two such wretches; when two more such I hope are not to be met with in the world—both so determined to carry on the most barbarous and perfidious projects against a poor young creature who never did or wished harm to either!

Take the following slight account of these women's and of this man's behaviour to each other before me.

Mr Lovelace carried himself to his pretended aunt with high respect, and paid a great deference to all she said. He permitted her to have all the advantage over him in the repartees and retorts that passed between them. I could, indeed, easily see that it *was* permitted; and that he forbore that *acumen*, that quickness, which he never spared showing to the pretended Miss Montague; and which a man of wit seldom knows how to spare showing, when an opportunity offers to display his wit.

The pretended Miss Montague was still more reverent in her behaviour to her aunt. While the aunt kept up the dignity of the character she had assumed, rallying both of them with the air of a person who depends upon the superiority which years and fortune give over younger persons; who might have a view to be obliged to her, either in her life, or at her death.

The severity of her raillery, however, was turned upon Mr Lovelace, on occasion of the character of the people who kept the lodgings, which, she said, I had thought myself so well warranted to leave privately.

This startled me. For having then no suspicion of the vile Tomlinson, I concluded (and your letter of the 7th[a] favoured my conclusion), that if the house were notorious, either he, or Mr Mennell, would have given me or him some hints of it—nor, although I liked not the people, did I observe anything in them very culpable till the Wednesday night before, that they offered not to come to my assistance, although within hearing of my distress (as I am sure they were), and having as much reason to be frighted as I, at the fire, had it been real.

I looked with indignation upon Mr Lovelace, at this hint.

a　His forged letter. See p. 811.

He seemed abashed. I have not patience but to recollect the specious looks of this vile deceiver. But how was it possible that even this florid countenance of his should enable him to command a blush at his pleasure? For blush he did, more than once: and the blush, on this occasion, was a deep-died crimson, unstrained-for, and natural, as I thought—But he is so much of the actor that he seems able to enter into any character; and his muscles and features appear entirely under obedience to his wicked will.[a]

The pretended lady went on, saying she had taken upon herself to inquire after the people, on hearing that I had left the house in disgust; and though she heard not anything much amiss, yet she heard enough to make her wonder that he would carry his spouse, a person of so much delicacy, to a house that, if it had not a *bad* fame, had not a *good* one.

You must think, my dear, that I liked the pretended Lady Betty the better for this. I suppose it was designed I should.

He was surprised, he said, that her ladyship should hear a bad character of the people. It was what he had never before heard that they deserved. It was easy, indeed, to see that they had not very great delicacy, though they were not indelicate. The nature of their livelihood, letting lodgings and taking people to board (and yet he had understood that they were nice in these particulars), led them to aim at being free and obliging: and it was difficult, he said, for persons of cheerful dispositions so to behave as to avoid censure: openness of heart and countenance in the sex (more was the pity!) too often subjected good people, whose fortunes did not set them above the world, to uncharitable censure.

He wished, however, that her ladyship would tell *what* she had heard: although now it signified but little, because he would never ask me to set foot within their doors again: and he begged she would not mince the matter.

Nay, no great matter, she said. But she had been informed that there were more women lodgers in the house than men: yet that their visitors were more men than women. And this had been hinted to her (perhaps by ill-willers, she could not answer for that) in such a way as if somewhat further were meant by it than was spoken.

This, he said, was the true innuendo way of characterizing used by detractors. Everybody and everything had a black and a white side, as ill-willers and well-willers were pleased to report. He had observed that the front house was well let, and he believed more to the one sex, than to the other; for he had seen, occasionally passing to and fro, several genteel modest-looking women; and who, it was very probable, were not so ill-beloved but they might have visitors and relations of both sexes: but they were none of them anything to us, or we to them: we were not once in any of their companies: but in the genteelest and most retired house of the two, which we had in a manner to ourselves, with the use of a parlour to the street, to

---

a It is proper to observe that there was a more natural reason than this that the lady gives for Mr Lovelace's blushing. It was a blush of indignation, as he owned afterwards to his friend Belford, in conversation; for his pretended aunt had mistaken her cue in condemning the house; and he had much ado to recover the blunder; being obliged to follow her lead, and vary from his first design; which was to have the people of the house spoken well of, in order to induce her to return to it, were it but on pretence to direct her clothes to be carried to Hampstead.

serve us for a servants' hall, or to receive common visitors, or our traders only, whom we admitted not upstairs.

He always loved to speak as he found. No man in the world had suffered more from calumny than he himself had done.

Women, he owned, ought to be more scrupulous than men needed to be where they lodged. Nevertheless, he wished that fact rather than surmise were to be the foundation of their judgements, especially when they spoke of one another.

He meant no reflection upon her ladyship's informants, or rather *surmisants* (as he might call them), be they who they would: nor did he think himself obliged to defend characters impeached, or not thought well of, by women of virtue and honour. Neither were these people of importance enough to have so much said about them.

The pretended Lady Betty said, all who knew her would clear her of censoriousness: that it gave her some opinion, she must needs say, of the people, that he had continued there so long with me; that I had rather *negative* than *positive* reasons of dislike to them; and that so shrewd a man, as she heard Captain Tomlinson was, had not objected to them.

I think, niece Charlotte, proceeded she, as my nephew has not parted with these lodgings, you and I (for, as my dear Miss Harlowe *dislikes* the people, I would not ask *her* for her company) will take a dish of tea with my nephew there before we go out of town, and then we shall see what sort of people they are. I have heard that Mrs Sinclair is a mighty forbidding creature.

With all my heart, madam. In your *ladyship*'s company I shall make no scruple of going any whither.

It was *ladyship* at every word; and as she seemed proud of her title, and of her dress too, I might have guessed that she was not used to *either*.

What say *you*, cousin Lovelace? Lady Sarah, though a melancholy woman, is very inquisitive about all your affairs. I must acquaint her with every particular circumstance when I go down.

With all his heart. He would attend her whenever she pleased. She would see very handsome apartments, and very civil people.

The deuce is in them, said *the* Miss Montague, if they appear other to us.

They then fell into family talk: family happiness on my hoped-for accession into it. They mentioned Lord M.'s and Lady Sarah's great desire to see me. How many friends and admirers, with up-lift hands, I should have! (*Oh my dear, what a triumph must these creatures, and he, have over the poor devoted all the time!*)— What a happy man he would be—They would not, *the* Lady Betty said, give themselves the mortification but to suppose, that I should not be one of them!

Presents were hinted at. She resolved that I should go with her to Glenham Hall. She would not be refused, although she were to stay a week beyond her time for me.

She longed for the expected letter from you. I must write to hasten it, and to let Miss Howe know how everything stood since I wrote last. That might dispose me absolutely in *their* favour, and in her nephew's; and then she hoped there would be no occasion for me to think of entering upon any new measures.

Indeed, my dear, I did at the time intend if I heard not from you by morning, to dispatch a man and horse to you with the particulars of *all*, that you might (if you thought proper) at least put off Mrs Townsend's coming up to another day—But I was miserably prevented.

She made me promise that I would write to you upon this subject, whether I heard from you or not. One of her servants should ride post with my letter, and wait for Miss Howe's answer.

She then launched out in deserved praises of you, my dear. How fond should she be of the honour of your acquaintance!

The pretended Miss Montague joined in with her, as well for herself as for her sister.

Abominably well-instructed were they both.

Oh my dear! What risks may poor giddy girls run when they throw themselves out of the protection of their natural friends, and into the wide world?

They then talked again of reconciliation and intimacy with every one of my friends; with my mother particularly; and gave the dear good lady the praises that everyone gives her, who has the happiness to know her.

Ah, my dear Miss Howe! I had almost forgot my resentments against the pretended nephew!—So many agreeable things said, made me think that, if you should advise it, and if I could bring my mind to forgive the wretch for an outrage so *premeditatedly* vile, and could forbear despising him for that and his other ungrateful and wicked ways, I might not be unhappy in an alliance with such a family. Yet, thought I at the time, with what intermixtures does everything come to me that has the appearance of good!—However, as my lucid hopes made me see fewer faults in the behaviour of these pretended ladies than recollection and abhorrence have helped me since to see, I began to reproach myself that I had not at first thrown myself into their protection.

But amidst all these delightful prospects, I must not, said *the* Lady Betty, forget that I am to go to town.

She then ordered her coach to be got to the door—We will all go to town together, said she, and return together. Morrison shall stay here, and see everything as I [am] used to have it in relation to my apartment and my bed; for I am very particular in some respects. My cousin Leeson's servants can do all I want to be done with regard to my nightdresses, and the like. And it will be a little airing for you, my dear, and a good opportunity for Mr Lovelace to order what you want of your apparel to be sent from your former lodgings to Mrs Leeson's; and we can bring it up with us from thence.

I had no intention to comply. But as I did not imagine that she would insist upon my going to town with them, I made no answer to that part of her speech.

I must here lay down my tired pen!

Recollection! Heart-affecting recollection! How it pains me!

Letter 314: MISS CLARISSA HARLOWE TO MISS HOWE

IN the midst of these agreeablenesses, the coach came to the door. The pretended Lady Betty besought me to give them my company to their cousin Leeson's. I desired to be excused: yet suspected nothing. She would not be denied. How happy would a visit so condescending make her cousin Leeson!—Her cousin

Leeson was not unworthy of my acquaintance: and would take it for the greatest favour in the world.

I objected my dress. But the objection was not admitted. She bespoke a supper of Mrs Moore to be ready at nine.

Mr Lovelace, vile hypocrite and wicked deceiver, seeing as he said my dislike to go, desired her ladyship not to insist upon it.

Fondness for my company was pleaded. She begged me to oblige her: made a motion to help me to my fan herself: and, in short, was so very urgent that my feet complied against my speech, and my mind: and being in a manner led to the coach by her, and made to step in first, she followed me; and her pretended niece, and the wretch, followed her: and away it drove.

Nothing but the height of affectionate complaisance passed all the way: over and over, what a joy would this unexpected visit give her cousin Leeson! What a pleasure must it be to such a mind as mine to be able to give so much joy to everybody I came near!

The cruel, the savage seducer (as I have since recollected) was in rapture all the way; but yet such a sort of rapture as he took visible pains to check.

Hateful villain!—How I abhor him!—What mischief must be then in his plotting heart!—What a devoted victim must I be in all their eyes!

Though not pleased, I was nevertheless just then thoughtless of danger; they endeavouring thus to lift me up above all apprehension of that, and above myself too.

But think, my dear, what a dreadful turn all had upon me, when, through several streets and ways I knew nothing of, the coach slackening its pace came within sight of the dreadful house of the dreadfullest woman in the world; as she proved to me.

Lord be good unto me! cried the poor fool, looking out of the coach—Mr Lovelace!—Madam! turning to the pretended aunt—Madam! turning to the niece, my eyes and hands lifted up—Lord be good unto me!

What! What! What, my dear!

He pulled the string—What need to have come this way? said he—But since we are, I will but ask a question—My dearest life! why this apprehension?

The coachman stopped: his servant, who with one of hers was behind, alighted—ask, said he, if I have any letters?—Who knows, my dearest creature, turning to me, but we may already have one from the captain?—We will not go out of the coach!—Fear nothing—Why so apprehensive?—Oh! these fine spirits!—cried the execrable insulter.

Dreadfully did my heart then misgive me: I was ready to faint. Why this terror, my life? You shall not stir out of the coach!—But one question, now the fellow has drove us this way!

Your lady will faint! cried the execrable Lady Betty, turning to him. My dearest niece! I *will* call you, taking my hand, we must alight if you are so ill—Let us alight—only for a glass of water and hartshorn—Indeed we must alight.

No, no, no—I am well—quite well—Won't the man drive on?—I am well—quite well—indeed I am—*Man*, drive on, putting my head out of the coach—*Man*, drive on!—though my voice was too low to be heard.

The coach stopped at the door. How I trembled!

Dorcas came to the door on its stopping.

My dearest creature! said the vile man, gasping as it were for breath, you shall *not* alight—Any letters for me, Dorcas?

There are two, sir. And here is a gentleman, Mr Belton, sir, waits for your honour; and has done so above an hour.

I'll just speak to him. Open the door—You sha'n't step out, my dear—A letter, perhaps, from the captain already!—You sha'n't step out, my dear.

I sighed as if my heart would burst.

But we *must* step out, nephew: your lady will faint—Maid, a glass of hartshorn and water!—My dear, you *must* step out—You will faint, child—We must cut your laces—(I believe my complexion was all manner of colours by turns)—Indeed, you must step out, my dear.

He knew, he said, I should be well, the moment the coach drove from the door. I should *not* alight. By his soul, I should not.

Lord, Lord, nephew, Lord, Lord, cousin, both women in a breath, What ado you make about nothing!—You *persuade* your lady to be afraid of alighting!—See you not that she is just fainting?

Indeed, madam, said the vile seducer, my dearest love must not be moved in this point against her will!—I beg it may not be insisted upon.

Fiddle-faddle, foolish man!—what a pother is here!—I guess how it is: you are ashamed to let us see what sort of people you carried your lady among!—But do you go out and speak to your friend, and take your letters.

He stepped out; but shut the coach door after him, to oblige me.

The coach may go on, madam! said I.

The coach *shall* go on, my dear life, said he—but he gave not, nor intended to give, orders that it should.

Let the coach go on! said I—Mr Lovelace may come after us.

Indeed, my dear, you are ill!—Indeed you must alight!—Alight but for one quarter of an hour!—Alight but to give order yourself about your things. Whom can you be afraid of, in my company and my niece's?—These people must have behaved shockingly to you!—Please the Lord, I'll inquire into it!—I'll see what sort of people they are!

Immediately came the old creature to the door. A thousand pardons, dear madam, stepping to the coachside, if we have any way offended you!—Be pleased ladies (to the other two), to alight.

Well, my dear, whispered *the* Lady Betty, I now find that an hideous description of a person we never saw is an advantage to them. I thought the woman was a monster! But, really, she seems tolerable.

I was afraid I should have fallen into fits: but still refused to go out!—Man!—Man!—Man! cried I, gaspingly, my head out of the coach and in, by turns, half a dozen times running, drive on!—Let us go!

My heart misgave me beyond the power of my own accounting for it; for still I did not suspect these women. But the antipathy I had taken to the vile house, and to find myself so near it when I expected no such matter, with the sight of the old creature, all together made me behave like a distracted person.

The hartshorn and water was brought. The pretended Lady Betty made me drink it. Heaven knows if there were anything else in it!

Besides, said she, whisperingly, I must see what sort of creatures the *nieces* are. Want of delicacy cannot be hid from me. You could not surely, my dear, have this aversion to re-enter a house for a few minutes in our company, in which you lodged and boarded several weeks, unless these women could be so presumptuously vile as my nephew ought not to know.

Out stepped the pretended lady; the servant, at her command, having opened the door.

Dearest madam, said the other, let me follow you (for I was next the door). Fear nothing: I will not stir from your presence.

Come, my dear, said the pretended lady: Give me your hand; holding out hers. Oblige me this once!

I will bless your footsteps, said the old creature, if once more you honour my house with your presence.

A crowd by this time was gathered about us; but I was too much affected to mind that.

Again the pretended Miss Montague urged me (standing up as ready to go out if I would give her room). Lord, my dear, said she, who can bear this crowd?— What will people think?

The pretended lady again pressed me, with both her hands held out—Only, my dear, to give orders about your things.

And thus pressed, and gazed at (for then I looked about me), the women so richly dressed, people whispering; in an evil moment, out stepped I, trembling, forced to lean with both hands (frighted too much for ceremony) on the pretended Lady Betty's arm—Oh that I had dropped down dead upon the guilty threshold!

We shall stay but a few minutes, my dear!—but a few minutes! said the same specious jilt—out of breath with her joy, as I have since thought, that they had thus triumphed over the unhappy victim!

Come, Mrs Sinclair, I think your name is, show us the way—following her, and leading me. I am very thirsty. You have frighted me, my dear, with your strange fears. I must have tea made, if it can be done in a moment. We have further to go, Mrs Sinclair, and must return to Hampstead this night.

It shall be ready in a moment, cried the wretch. We have water boiling.

Hasten, then—Come, my dear, to me, as she led me through the passage to the fatal inner house—Lean upon me—How you tremble!—how you falter in your steps!—Dearest niece Lovelace (the old wretch being in hearing), why these hurries upon your spirits?—We'll begone in a minute.

And thus she led the poor sacrifice into the old wretch's too well-known parlour.

Never was anybody so gentle, so meek, so low-voiced, as the odious woman; drawling out, in a puling accent, all the obliging things she could say: awed, I then thought, by the conscious dignity of a woman of quality; glittering with jewels.

The called-for tea was ready presently.

There was no Mr Belton, I believe: for the wretch went not to anybody, unless it were while we were parleying in the coach. No such person, however, appeared at the tea-table.

I was made to drink two dishes, with milk, complaisantly urged by the pretended ladies helping me each to one. I was stupid to their hands; and when I took the tea almost choked with vapours; and could hardly swallow.

I thought, *transiently*, that the tea, the last dish particularly, had an odd taste. They, on my palating it, observed that the milk was *London milk*; far short in goodness of what they were accustomed to from their own dairies.

I have no doubt that my two dishes, and perhaps my hartshorn, were prepared for me; in which case it was more proper for their purpose that *they* should help me than that I should help *myself*. Ill before, I found myself still more and more disordered in my head; a heavy torpid pain increasing fast upon me. But I imputed it to my terror.

Nevertheless, at the pretended ladies' motion, I went upstairs, attended by Dorcas; who affected to weep for joy that once more she saw my *blessed* face, that was the vile creature's word; and immediately I set about taking out some of my clothes, ordering what should be put up, and what sent after me.

While I was thus employed, up came the pretended Lady Betty in a hurrying way—My dear, you won't be long before you are ready. My nephew is very busy in writing answers to his letters: so I'll just whip away and change my dress, and call upon you in an instant.

Oh madam!—I *am* ready! I am *now* ready!—You must not leave me here: and down I sunk, affrighted, into a chair.

This instant, this instant, I will return—before you can be ready—before you can have packed up your things—We would not be late—the robbers we have heard of may be out—don't let us be late.

And away she hurried before I could say another word. Her pretended niece went with her, without taking notice to me of her going.

I had no suspicion yet that these women were not indeed the ladies they personated; and I blamed myself for my weak fears—It cannot *be*, thought I, that *such* ladies will abet treachery against a poor creature they are so fond of. They must undoubtedly *be* the persons they *appear* to be—what folly to doubt it! The air, the dress, the dignity, of women of quality—How unworthy of them, and of my charity, concluded I, is this ungenerous shadow of suspicion!

So, recovering my stupefied spirits as well as they could be recovered (for I was heavier and heavier; and wondered to Dorcas what ailed me; rubbing my eyes, and taking some of her snuff, pinch after pinch, to very little purpose), I pursued my employment: but when that was over, all packed up that I designed to be packed up; and I had nothing to do but to *think*; and found them tarry so long; I thought I should have gone distracted. I shut myself into the chamber that had been mine; I kneeled, I prayed; yet knew not what I prayed for: then ran out again. It was almost dark night, I said: where, where, was Mr Lovelace?

He came to me, taking no notice at first of my consternation and wildness (what they had given me made me incoherent and wild): All goes well, said he, my dear!—A line from Captain Tomlinson!

All indeed did go well for the villainous project of the most cruel and most villainous of men!

I *demanded* his aunt!—I *demanded* his cousin!—The evening, I said, was closing!—My head was very, *very* bad, I remember, I said—And it grew worse and worse.

Terror, however, as yet kept up my spirits; and I insisted upon his going himself to hasten them.

He called his servant. He raved at the *sex* for *their* delay: 'twas well that business of consequence seldom depended upon such parading, unpunctual triflers!

His servant came.

He ordered him to fly to his cousin Leeson's; and to let his aunt and cousins know how uneasy we both were at their delay: adding, of his own accord, Desire them, if they don't come instantly, to send their coach and we will go without them. Tell them I wonder they'll serve me so!

I thought this was considerately and fairly put. But now, indifferent as my head was, I had a little time to consider the man and his behaviour. He terrified me with his looks, and with his violent emotions as he gazed upon me. Evident *joy-suppressed* emotions, as I have since recollected. His sentences short, and pronounced as if his breath were touched. Never saw I his abominable eyes look, as then they looked—triumph in them!—fierce and wild; and more disagreeable than the women's at the vile house appeared to me when I first saw them: and at times, such a leering, mischief-boding cast!—I would have given the world to have been an hundred miles from him. Yet his behaviour was decent—a decency, however, that I might have seen to be struggled for—for he snatched my hand two or three times with a vehemence in his grasp that hurt me; speaking words of tenderness through his shut teeth, as it seemed; and let it go with a beggar-voiced humble accent, like the vile woman's just before; half-inward; yet his words and manner carrying the appearance of strong and almost convulsed passion!—Oh my dear! What mischiefs was he not then meditating!

I complained once or twice of thirst. My mouth seemed parched. At the time, I supposed that it was my terror (gasping often as I did for breath) that parched up the roof of my mouth. I called for water: some table-beer was brought me. Beer, I suppose, was a better vehicle (if I were not dosed enough before) for their potions. I told the maid that she knew I seldom tasted malt-liquor: yet, suspecting nothing of this nature, being extremely thirsty I drank it, as what came next: and instantly, as it were, found myself much worse than before; as if inebriated, I should fancy: I know not how.

His servant was gone twice as long as he needed: and, just before his return, came one of the pretended Lady Betty's, with a letter for Mr Lovelace.

He sent it up to me. I read it: and then it was that I thought myself a lost creature; it being to put off her going to Hampstead that night, on account of violent fits which Miss Montague was pretended to be seized with: for then immediately came into my head his vile attempt upon me in this house; the revenge that my flight might too probably inspire him with on that occasion, and because of the difficulty I made to forgive him and to be reconciled to him; his very looks wild and dreadful to me; and the women of the house such as I had more reason than ever, even from the pretended Lady Betty's hints, to be afraid of: all these crowding together in my apprehensive mind, I fell into a kind of frenzy.

I have not remembrance how I was for the time it lasted: but I know that in my first agitations I pulled off my head-dress, and tore my ruffles in twenty tatters; and ran to find him out.

When a little recovered, I insisted upon the hint he had given of their coach. But the messenger, he said, had told him that it was sent to fetch a physician, lest his chariot should be put up, or not ready.

I then insisted upon going directly to Lady Betty's lodgings.

Mrs Leeson's was now a crowded house, he said: and as my earnestness could be owing to nothing but groundless apprehension (and oh what vows, what protestations of his honour did he then make!), he hoped I would not add to their present concern. Charlotte, indeed, was used to fits, he said, upon any great surprises, whether of joy or grief; and they would hold her for a week together if not got off in a few hours.

You are an *observer of eyes*, my dear, said the villain; perhaps in secret insult: saw you not in Miss Montague's now and then, at Hampstead, something wildish?—I was afraid for her then—Silence and quiet only do her good: your concern for *her*, and her love for *you*, will but augment the poor girl's disorder, if you should go.

All impatient with grief and apprehension, I still declared myself resolved not to stay in that house till morning. All I had in the world, my rings, my watch, my little money, for a coach! or, if one were not to be got, I would go on foot to Hampstead that night, though I walked it by myself.

A coach was hereupon sent for, or pretended to be sent for. Any price, he said, he would give to oblige me, late as it was; and he would attend me with all his soul—But no coach was to be got.

Let me cut short the rest. I grew worse and worse in my head; now stupid, now raving, now senseless. The vilest of vile women was brought to frighten me. Never was there so horrible a creature as she appeared to me at the time.

I remember, I pleaded for mercy—I remember that I said *I would be his*— *indeed I would be his*—to obtain his mercy—But no mercy found I!—My strength, my intellects, failed me!—And then such scenes followed—Oh my dear, such dreadful scenes!—fits upon fits (faintly indeed, and imperfectly remembered) procuring me no compassion—but death was withheld from me. That would have been too great a mercy!

Thus was I tricked and deluded back by blacker hearts of my own sex, than I thought there were in the world; who appeared to me to be persons of honour: and, when in his power, thus barbarously was I treated by this villainous man!

I was so senseless that I dare not aver that the horrid creatures of the house were personally aiding and abetting: but some visionary remembrances I have of female figures flitting, as I may say, before my sight; the wretched woman's particularly. But as these confused ideas might be owing to the terror I had conceived of the worse than masculine violence she had been permitted to assume to me, for expressing my abhorrence of her house; and as what I suffered from his barbarity wants not that aggravation; I will say no more on a subject so shocking as this must ever be to my remembrance.

I never saw the personating wretches afterwards. He persisted to the last (dreadfully invoking Heaven as a witness to the truth of his assertion), that they were really and truly the ladies they pretended to be; declaring, that they could not take leave of me when they left the town, because of the state of senselessness and frenzy I was in. For their intoxicating, or rather stupefying, potions had almost deleterious effects upon my intellects, as I have hinted; insomuch that, for several days together, I was under a strange delirium; now moping, now dozing, now weeping, now raving, now scribbling, tearing what I scribbled as fast as I wrote it: *most* miserable when now and then a ray of reason brought confusedly to my remembrance what I had suffered.

Letter 315: MISS CLARISSA HARLOWE [TO MISS HOWE]

(In continuation)

The lady next gives an account

Of her recovery from her frenzical and sleepy disorders:

Of her attempt to get away in his absence:

Of the conversations that followed, at his return, between them:

Of the guilty figure he made:

Of her resolution not to have him:

Of her several efforts to escape:

Of her treaty with Dorcas to assist her in it:

Of Dorcas's dropping the promissory note, undoubtedly, as she says, on purpose to betray her:

Of her triumph over all the creatures of the house assembled to terrify her; and perhaps to commit fresh outrages upon her:

Of his setting out for M. Hall:

Of his repeated letters to induce her to meet him at the altar on her uncle's anniversary:

Of her determined silence to them all:

Of her second escape, effected, *as she says*, contrary to her own expectation: that attempt being at first but the intended prelude to a more promising one, which she had formed in her mind:

And of other particulars; which being to be found in Mr Lovelace's preceding letters, and that of his friend Belford, are omitted. She then proceeds:

The very hour that I found myself in a place of safety, I took pen to write to you. When I began, I designed only to write six or eight lines, to inquire after your health: for, having heard nothing from you, I feared *indeed* that you *had been*, and *still were*, too ill to write. But no sooner did my pen begin to blot the paper, but my sad heart hurried it into length. The apprehensions I had lain under that I should not be able to get away; the fatigue I had in effecting my escape; the difficulty of procuring a lodging for myself; having disliked the people of two houses, and those of a third disliking me; for you must think I made a frighted appearance—these, together with the recollection of what I had suffered from him, and my farther apprehensions of my insecurity, and my desolate circumstances, had so disordered me that I remember I rambled strangely in that letter.

In short, I thought it on re-perusal a half-distracted one: but I then despaired (were I to begin again) of writing better: so I let it go: and can have no excuse for directing it as I did, if the cause of the incoherence in it will not furnish me with a very pitiable one.

The letter I received from your mother was a dreadful blow to me. But nevertheless, it had the good effect upon me (labouring as I was just then under a violent fit of vapourish despondency, and almost yielding to it) which profuse bleeding and blisterings have in paralytical or apoplectical strokes; reviving my attention, and restoring me to spirits to combat the evils I was surrounded by—sluicing off, and diverting into a new channel (if I may be allowed another metaphor), the overcharging woes which threatened once more to overwhelm my intellects.

But yet I most sincerely lamented (and still lament), in your mamma's words, *that I cannot be unhappy by myself*: and was grieved, not only for the trouble I had given you before; but for the new one I had brought upon you by my inattention.

She then gives the contents of the letters she wrote to Mrs Norton, to Lady Betty Lawrance, and to Mrs Hodges; as also of their answers; whereby she detected all Mr Lovelace's impostures.

I cannot, however, says she, forbear to wonder how the vile Tomlinson could come at the knowledge of several of the things he told me of, and which contributed to give me confidence in him.[a]

I doubt not, continues she, that the stories of Mrs Fretchville and her house would be found as vile impostures as any of the rest, were I to inquire; and had I not enough, and too much, already against the perjured man.

How have I been led on! says she—What will be the end of such a false and perjured creature; Heaven not less profaned and defied by him than myself deceived and abused! This, however, against myself I must say, that if what I have suffered is the natural consequence of my first error, I never can forgive *myself*, although you are so partial in my favour, as to say that I was not censurable for what passed before my first escape.

And now, honoured madam, and my dearest Miss Howe, who are to sit in judgement upon my case, permit me to lay down my pen with one request which, with the greatest earnestness I make to you both: and that is that you will neither of you open your lips in relation to the potions and the violences I have hinted at— Not that I am solicitous that my disgrace should be hidden from the world, or that it should not be generally known that the man has proved a villain to me: for this, it seems, everybody but myself expected from his character. But suppose, as his actions by me are really of a *capital nature*, it were insisted upon that I should appear to prosecute him and his accomplices in a Court of Justice, how do you think I could bear that?

But since my character *before* the capital enormity was lost in the eye of the world; and that from the very hour I left my father's house; and since all my own hopes of worldly happiness are entirely over; let me slide quietly into my grave; and let it not be remembered, except by one friendly tear, and no more, dropped from your gentle eye, my own dear Anna Howe, on the happy day that shall shut up all my sorrows, that there was such a creature as

Saturday, July 8   CLARISSA HARLOWE

---

a The attentive reader need not be referred back for what the lady nevertheless could not account for, as she knew not that Mr Lovelace had come at Miss Howe's letters; particularly that on p. 586, which he comments upon on p. 636.

Letter 316: MISS HOWE TO MISS CLARISSA HARLOWE

Sunday, July 9

MAY heaven signalize its vengeance in the face of all the world upon the most abandoned and profligate of men!—And in its own time, I doubt not but it will— And we must look to a WORLD BEYOND THIS for the reward of your sufferings!—

Another shocking detection, my dear!—How have you been deluded!—Very watchful I have thought you; very sagacious—but, alas! not watchful, not sagacious enough, for the horrid villain you have had to deal with!—

The letter you sent me enclosed as mine, of the 7th of June, is a villainous forgery.[a] The hand, indeed, is astonishingly like mine; and the cover, I see, is actually my cover: but yet the letter is not so exactly imitated but that (had you had any suspicions about his vileness at the time) you, who so well know my hand, might have detected it.

In short, this vile forged letter, though a long one, contains but a few extracts from mine. Mine was a *very* long one. He has omitted everything, I see, in it that could have shown you what a detestable house the house is; and given you suspicions of the vile Tomlinson—You will see this, and how he has turned Miss Lardner's information and my advices to you (execrable villain!) to his own horrid ends, by the rough draught of the genuine letter which I shall enclose.[b]

Apprehensive for *both* our safeties, from such a daring and profligate contriver, I must call upon you, my dear, to resolve upon taking legal vengeance of the infernal wretch. And this not only for our own sakes, but for the sakes of innocents who otherwise may yet be deluded and outraged by him.

She then gives the particulars of the report made by the young fellow whom she sent to Hampstead with her letter; and who supposed he had delivered it into her own hand[c]; and then proceeds:

I am astonished that the vile wretch, who could know nothing of the time my messenger (whose honesty I can vouch for) would come, could have a creature ready to personate you! Strange that the man should happen to arrive just as you were gone to church, as I find was the fact, on comparing what he says with your hint that you were at church twice that day; when he might have got to Mrs Moore's two hours before!—But had you told me, my dear, that the villain had found you out, and was about you!—You should have done that—yet I blame you upon a judgement founded on the *event* only!

I never had any faith in the stories that go current among country girls, of spectres, familiars, and demons; yet I see not any other way to account for this wretch's successful villainy, and for his means of working up his specious delusions, but by supposing (if he be not the devil himself), that he has a familiar constantly at his elbow. Sometimes it seems to me that this familiar assumes the shape of that solemn villain Tomlinson: sometimes that of the execrable Sinclair, as he calls her: sometimes it is permitted to take that of Lady Betty Lawrance—but, when it

a See pp. 811 ff.
b See p. 743.
c See p. 856.

would assume the angelic shape and mien of my beloved friend, see what a bloated figure it made!

'Tis my opinion, my dear, that you will be no longer safe where you are, than while the V. is in the country. Words are poor!—or how could I execrate him! I have hardly any doubt that he has sold himself for a time. Oh may the time be short!—or may his infernal prompter no more keep covenant with him than he does with others!

I enclose not only the rough draught of my long letter mentioned above; but the heads of that which the young fellow thought he delivered into your own hands at Hampstead. And when you have perused them, I will leave you to judge how much reason I had to be surprised that you wrote me not an answer to either of those letters; one of which you owned you had received (though it proved to be his forged one); the other delivered into your own hands, as I was assured; and both of them of so much concern to your honour; and still how much more surprised I must be when I received a letter from Mrs Townsend, dated June 15 from Hampstead, importing 'That Mr Lovelace, who had been with you several days, had, on the Monday before, brought his aunt and cousin, richly dressed, and in a coach and four, to visit you: who, with your own consent, had carried you to town with them—to your former lodgings; where you still were: that the Hampstead women believed you to be married; and reflected upon me as a fomenter of differences between man and wife: that he himself was at Hampstead the day before; viz. [Wednesday] the 14th; and boasted of his happiness with you; inviting Mrs Moore, Mrs Bevis, and Miss Rawlins to go to town to visit his spouse; which they promised to do: that he declared that you were entirely reconciled to your former lodgings—and that, finally, the women at Hampstead told Mrs Townsend that he had very handsomely discharged theirs.'

I own to you, my dear, that I was so much surprised and disgusted at these appearances, against a conduct till then unexceptionable, that I was resolved to make myself as easy as I could, and wait till you should think fit to write to me. But I could rein in my impatience but for a few days; and on the 20th of June I wrote a sharp letter to you; which I find you did not receive.

What a fatality, my dear, has appeared in your case, from the very beginning till this hour! Had my mother permitted—

But can I blame *her*; when you have a *father* and *mother* living, who have so much to answer for?—so much!—as no father and mother, considering the child they have driven, persecuted, exposed, renounced—ever had to answer for!—

But again I must execrate the abandoned villain—yet, as I said before, *all* words are poor, and beneath the occasion!

But see we not, in the horrid perjuries and treachery of this man, what rakes and libertines will do when they get a young creature into their power? It is probable that he might have the intolerable presumption to hope an easier conquest: but, when your unexampled vigilance and exalted virtue made potions, and rapes, and the utmost violences, necessary to the attainment of his detestable end, we see that he never boggled at them. I have no doubt that the same or equal wickedness would be *oftener* committed by men of his villainous cast, if the folly and credulity of the poor inconsiderates who throw themselves into their hands did not give them an easier triumph.

With what comfort must those parents reflect upon these things, who have happily disposed of their daughters in marriage to a virtuous man! And how happy the young women who find themselves safe in a worthy protection!—If such a person as Miss Clarissa Harlowe could not escape, who can be secure?—since, though every rake is not a LOVELACE, neither is every woman a CLARISSA: and his attempts were but proportioned to your resistance and vigilance.

My mother has commanded me to let you know her thoughts upon the whole of your sad story. I will do it in another letter; and send it to you with this by a special messenger.

But, for the future, if you approve of it, I will send my letters by the usual hand (Collins's), to be left at the Saracen's Head on Snow Hill: whither you may send yours (as we both used to do, to Wilson's), except such as we shall think fit to transmit by the post: which I am afraid, after my next, must be directed to Mr Hickman as before: since my mother is for fixing a condition to our correspondence which, I doubt, you will not comply with, though I wish you would. This condition I shall acquaint you with by and by.

Meantime, begging excuse for all the harsh things in my last, I beseech you, my dearest creature, to believe me to be,

> Your truly sympathizing,
> and unalterable friend,
> ANNA HOWE

Letter 317: MISS HOWE TO MISS CLARISSA HARLOWE

> Monday, July 10

I NOW, my dearest friend, resume my pen to obey my mother in giving you her opinion upon your unhappy story.

She still harps upon the old string; and will have it that all your calamities are owing to your first fatal step; for she believes (what I cannot) that your relations had intended, after one general trial more, to comply with your aversion, if they had found it as riveted a one as, let me say, it was a folly to suppose it would not be found to be, after so many *ridiculously* repeated experiments.

As to your latter sufferings from that vilest of miscreants, she is unalterably of opinion that if all be as you have related (which she doubts not), with regard to the potions, and to the violences you have sustained, you ought by all means to set on foot a prosecution against him, and his devilish accomplices.

She asks what murderers, what ravishers, would be brought to justice if *modesty* were to be a general plea, and allowable, against appearing in a court to prosecute?

She says that the good of society requires that such a beast of prey should be hunted out of it: and if you do not prosecute him, she thinks you will be answerable for all the mischiefs he may do in the course of his future villainous life.

Will it be thought, Nancy, said she, that Miss Harlowe can be in earnest when she says she is not solicitous to have her disgraces concealed from the world, if she is afraid or ashamed to appear in court to do justice to herself and her sex against him? Will it not be rather surmised that she may be apprehensive that some weakness, or lurking love, will appear upon the trial of the strange cause? If, inferred she, such complicated villainy as this (where perjury, potions, forgery, subornation, are all combined to effect the ruin of an innocent creature, and to dishonour a family of eminence, and where those very crimes, as may be supposed, are proofs of her innocence) is to go off impunely, what case will deserve to be brought into judgement; or what malefactor ought to be hanged?

Then she thinks, and so do I, that the vile creatures, his accomplices, ought by all means to be brought to condign punishment, as they must and will be, upon bringing him to his trial: and this may be a means to blow up and root out a whole nest of vipers, and save many innocent creatures.

She added that, if Miss Clarissa Harlowe could be so indifferent about having this public justice done upon such a wretch, for her *own* sake, she ought to overcome her scruples out of regard to her family, her acquaintance, and her sex, which are all highly injured and scandalized by his villainy to her.

For her own part, she declares that were *she* your mother, she would forgive you upon no other terms: and upon your compliance with these, she herself will undertake to reconcile all your family to you.

These, my dear, are my mother's sentiments upon your sad story.

I cannot say but there are reason and justice in them: and it is my opinion that it would be very right for the law to *oblige* an injured woman to prosecute, and to make seduction on the man's part capital, where his studied baseness, and no fault in her will, appeared.

To this purpose, the custom in the Isle of Man is a very good one—

'If a single woman there prosecutes a single man for a rape, the ecclesiastical judges impanel a jury; and, if this jury finds him guilty, he is returned *guilty* to the temporal courts: where, if he be convicted, the deemster, or judge, delivers to the woman a rope, a sword, and a ring; and she has it in her choice to have him hanged, beheaded, or to marry him.'

One of the two former, I think, should always be her option.

I long for the full particulars of your story. You must have but too much time upon your hands for a mind so active as yours, if tolerable health and spirits be afforded you.

The villainy of the worst of men, and the virtue of the most excellent of women, I expect will be exemplified in it, were it to be written in the same connected and particular manner that you used to write to me in.

Try for it, my dearest friend; and since you cannot give the *example* without the *warning*, give *both*, for the sakes of all those who shall hear of your unhappy fate; beginning from yours of June 5, your prospects then not disagreeable. I pity you for the task; though I cannot willingly exempt you from it.

My mother will have me add that she must *insist* upon your prosecuting. She repeats that she makes that a condition on which she permits our future correspondence—so let me know your thoughts upon it. I asked her if she would be willing that I should appear to support you in court if you complied?—By all means, she said, if that would induce you to begin with him, and with the horrid women. I think I could attend you; I am sure I could, were there but a probability of bringing the monster to his deserved end.

Once more your thoughts of it, supposing it were to meet with the approbation of your relations.

But whatever be your determination on this head, it shall be my constant prayer that God will give you patience to bear your heavy afflictions as a person ought to do, whose faulty will has not brought them upon herself; that He will speak peace and comfort to your wounded mind; and give you many happy years.

I am, and ever will be,

Your affectionate and faithful
ANNA HOWE

The two preceding letters were sent by a special messenger: In the cover were written the following lines:

Monday, July 10

I CANNOT, my dearest friend, suffer the enclosed to go unaccompanied by a few lines to signify to you that they are both less tender in some places than I would have written had they not been to pass my mamma's inspection. The principal reason, however, of my writing thus separately is to beg of you to permit me to send you money and necessaries; which you must needs want: and that you will let me know if either I, or *anybody I can influence*, can be of service to you. I am excessively apprehensive that you are not enough out of his reach where you are. Yet London, I am persuaded, is the place of all others, to be private in.

I could tear my hair for vexation that I have it not in my power to afford you *personal* protection!—I am,

Your ever-devoted
ANNA HOWE

Letter 318: MISS CLARISSA HARLOWE TO MISS HOWE

Tuesday, July 11

I APPROVE, my dearest friend, of the method you prescribe for the conveyance of our letters; and have already caused the porter of the inn to be engaged to bring to me yours, the moment that Collins arrives with them: as the servant of the house where I am will be permitted to carry mine to Collins for you.

As you are so earnest to have all the particulars of my sad story before you, I will, if life and spirits be lent me, give you an ample account of all that has befallen me from the time you mention. But this, it is very probable, you will not see till after the close of my last scene: and as I shall write with a view to that, I hope no other voucher will be wanted for the veracity of the writer.

I am far from thinking myself out of the reach of this man's further violence. But what can I do? Whither can I fly?—Perhaps my bad state of health (which must grow worse, as recollection of the past evils, and reflections upon them, grow heavier and heavier upon me) may be my protection. Once, indeed, I thought of going abroad; and had I the prospect of many years before me, I would go—But, my dear, the blow is given—Nor have you reason, now, circumstanced as I am, to be concerned that it is. What a heart must I have if it be not broken!—And, indeed, my *dear*, my *best*, I had almost said my *only* friend, I do so earnestly wish for the last closing scene, and with so much comfort find myself in a declining way, that I even sometimes ungratefully regret that naturally healthy constitution which used to double upon me all my enjoyments.

As to the earnestly recommended prosecution, I may possibly touch upon it more largely hereafter, if ever I shall have better spirits; for they are at present extremely sunk and low—But, just now, will only say that I would sooner suffer every evil (the repetition of the capital one excepted), than appear publicly in a court to do myself justice.[a] And I am heartily grieved that your mother prescribes such a measure as the condition of our future correspondence—for the continuance of your friendship, my dear, and the desire I had to correspond with you to my life's end, were all my remaining hopes and consolation. Nevertheless, as that friendship is in the power of the *heart*, not of the *hand* only, I hope I shall not forfeit that.

Oh my dear! what weight has a parent's curse—You cannot imagine—But I will not touch this string to you, who never loved them!—A reconciliation with them is not to be hoped for!

I have written a letter to Miss Rawlins of Hampstead; the answer to which, just now received, has helped me to the knowledge of the vile contrivance by which this wicked man got your letter of June the 10th. I will give you the contents of both.

In mine to her, I briefly acquaint her 'with what had befallen me, through the vileness of the women who had been passed upon me as the aunt and cousin of the wickedest of men; and own that I never was married to him. I desire her to make particular inquiry, and to let me know, who it was at Mrs Moore's, that on Sunday afternoon, June 11, while I was at church, received a letter from Miss Howe, pretending to be me, and lying on a couch—which letter, had it come to my hands, would have saved me from ruin. I excuse myself (from the delirium which the barbarous usage I had received threw me into, and from a confinement as barbarous and illegal), that I had not before applied to Mrs Moore for an account of what I was indebted to her: which I now desired. And, for fear of being traced by Mr Lovelace, I directed her to superscribe her answer, To Mrs Mary Atkins; to be left till called for, at the Bell Savage Inn, on Ludgate Hill.'

In her answer she tells me, 'that the vile wretch prevailed upon Mrs Bevis to personate me. A sudden motion of his, it seems, on the appearance of your messenger—persuaded to lie along on a couch: a handkerchief over her neck and face; pretending to be ill; drawn in, by false notions of your ill offices to keep up a variance between a man and his wife—and so taking the letter from your messenger as me.

'Miss Rawlins takes pains to excuse Mrs Bevis's intention. She expresses their astonishment and concern at what I communicate: but is glad, however, and so they are all, that they know in time the vileness of the base man; the two widows and herself having, at his earnest invitation, designed me a visit at Mrs Sinclair's; supposing all to be happy between him and me; as he assured them was the case. Mr Lovelace, she informs me, had handsomely satisfied Mrs Moore. And Miss Rawlins concludes with wishing to be favoured with the particulars of so extraordinary a story, as they may be of use to let her see what wicked creatures (women as well as men) there are in the world.'

I thank you for the drafts of your two letters which were intercepted by this horrid man. I see the great advantage they were of to him, in the prosecution of

[a] Dr Lewin, as will be seen hereafter, presses her to this public prosecution by arguments worthy of his character: which she answers in a manner worthy of hers.

his villainous designs against the poor wretch whom he has so long made the sport of his abhorred inventions.

Let me repeat that I am quite sick of life; and of an earth in which *innocent* and *benevolent* spirits are sure to be considered as *aliens*, and to be made sufferers by the *genuine sons* and *daughters* of *that earth*.

How unhappy that those letters only which could have acquainted me with his horrid views, and armed me against them, and against the vileness of the base women, should fall into his hands!—Unhappier still, in that my very escape to Hampstead gave him the opportunity of receiving them!

Nevertheless, I cannot but still wonder how it was possible for that Tomlinson to know what passed between Mr Hickman and my uncle Harlowe*a*: a circumstance which gave that vile impostor most of his credit with me.

How the wicked wretch himself could find me out at Hampstead must also remain wholly a mystery to me. He *may* glory in his contrivances—he, who has more wickedness than wit, *may* glory in his contrivances!—but, after all, I shall, I humbly presume to hope, be happy, when he, poor wretch, will be—alas!—who can say what!—

Adieu, my dearest friend!—May *you* be happy!—And then your Clarissa Harlowe cannot be wholly miserable!

Letter 319: MISS HOWE TO MISS CLARISSA HARLOWE

Wedn. night, July 12

I WRITE, my dearest creature, I cannot *but* write, to express my concern on your dejection. Let me beseech you, my charming excellence, let me beseech you, not to give way to it.

Comfort yourself, on the contrary, in the triumphs of a virtue unsullied; a will wholly faultless. Who could have withstood the trials that you have surmounted?— Your cousin Morden will soon come. He will see justice done you, I make no doubt, as well with regard to what concerns your person as your estate. And many happy days may you yet see; and much good may you still do, if you will not heighten unavoidable accidents into guilty despondency.

But why, my dear, this pining solicitude continued after a reconciliation with relations as unworthy as implacable; whose wills are governed by an all-grasping brother, who finds his account in keeping the breach open? On this over-solicitude, it is now plain to me that the vilest of men built all his schemes. He saw you had a thirst after it, beyond all reason for hope. The view, the hope, I own extremely desirable, had your family been Christians; or even had they been pagans, who had bowels.

I shall send this short letter (I am obliged to make it a short one) by young Rogers, as we call him; the fellow I sent to you to Hampstead; an innocent, though pragmatical rustic. Admit him, I pray you, into your presence, that he may report to me how you look, and how you are.

Mr Hickman should attend you; but I apprehend that all his motions, and my own too, are watched by the execrable wretch: as indeed his are by an agent of mine; for I own that I am so apprehensive of his plots and revenge, now I know

a See the note at the bottom of p. 1013.

that he has intercepted my vehement letters against him, that he is the subject of my dreams, as well as of my waking fears.

My mother, at my earnest importunity, has just given me leave to write, and to receive your letters—but fastened this condition upon the concession, that yours must be under cover to Mr Hickman (this with a view, I suppose, to give him consideration with me); and upon this further condition, that she is to see all we write—'When girls are set upon a point,' she told one, who told me again, 'it is better for a mother, if possible, to make herself of their party, rather than to oppose them; since there will be then hopes that she will still hold the reins in her own hands.'

Pray let me know what the people are with whom you lodge?—Shall I send Mrs Townsend to direct you to lodgings, either more safe, or more convenient for you?

Be pleased to write to me by Rogers; who will wait on you for your answer, at your own time.

Adieu, my dearest creature. Comfort *yourself*, as you would in the like unhappy circumstances comfort

Your own
ANNA HOWE

Letter 320: MISS CLARISSA HARLOWE TO MISS HOWE

Thursday, July 13

I AM extremely concerned, my dear Miss Howe, for being primarily the occasion of the apprehensions you have of this wicked man's vindictive attempts. What a wide-spreading error is mine!—

If I find that he sets on foot any machination against you, or Mr Hickman, I do assure you I will consent to prosecute him, although I were sure I should not survive my first appearance at the bar he should be arraigned at.

I own the justice of your mother's arguments on that subject; but must say that I think there are circumstances in my particular case which will excuse me, although (on a slighter occasion than *that* above apprehended) I should decline to appear against him. I have said that I may one day enter more particularly into this subject.

Your messenger has now indeed seen me. I talked with him on the imposture put upon him at Hampstead: and am sorry to have reason to say that had not the poor young man been very *simple*, and very *self-sufficient*, he had not been so grossly deluded. Mrs Bevis has the same plea to make for herself. A good-natured, thoughtless woman; not used to converse with so vile and so specious a deceiver as him who made his advantage of both these shallow creatures.

I think I cannot be more private than where I am. I hope I am safe. All the risk I run is in going out and returning from morning prayers; which I have two or three times ventured to do; once at Lincoln's Inn chapel, at eleven; once at St Dunstan's, Fleet Street, at seven in the morning, in a chair both times; and twice at six in the morning, at the neighbouring church in Covent Garden. The wicked wretches I have escaped from will not, I hope, come to church to look for me;

especially at so early prayers; and I have fixed upon the privatest pew in the latter church to hide myself in; and perhaps I may lay out a little matter in an ordinary gown, by way of disguise; my face half hid by my mob—I am very careless, my dear, of my appearance now. Neat and clean takes up the whole of my attention.

The man's name, at whose house I lodge, is Smith—a glove-*maker*, as well as *seller*. His wife is the shopkeeper. A dealer also in stockings, ribands, snuff and perfumes. A matron-like woman, plain-hearted, and prudent. The husband an honest, industrious man. And they live in good understanding with each other. A proof with me that their hearts are right; for where a married couple live together upon ill terms, it is a sign, I think, that each knows something amiss of the other, either with regard to temper or morals, which if the world knew as well as themselves, it would as little like them as such people like each other. Happy the marriage where neither man nor wife has any wilful or premeditated evil in their general conduct to reproach the other with!—for even persons who have bad hearts will have a veneration for those who have good ones.

Two neat rooms, with plain, but clean furniture, on the first floor, are mine; one they call the dining-room.

There is, up another pair of stairs, a very worthy widow lodger, Mrs Lovick by name; who, although of low fortunes, is much respected, as Mrs Smith assures me, by people of condition of her acquaintance, for her piety, prudence, and understanding. With her I propose to be well acquainted.

I thank you, my dear, for your kind, your seasonable advice and consolation. I hope I shall have more grace given me than to despond, in the *religious* sense of the word—especially as I can apply to myself the comfort you give me that neither my will nor my inconsiderateness has contributed to my calamity. But, nevertheless, the irreconcileableness of my relations, whom I love with an unabated reverence; my apprehensions of fresh violences (this wicked man, I doubt, will not yet let me rest); my destituteness of protection; my youth, my sex, my unacquaintedness with the world, subjecting me to insults; my reflections on the scandal I have given, added to the sense of the indignities I have received from a man of whom I deserved not ill; all together will undoubtedly bring on the effect that cannot be undesirable to me—the slower, however, perhaps from my natural good constitution; and as I presume to imagine, from principles which I hope will, in due time, and by due reflection, set me *above the sense of all worldly disappointments*.

At present my head is much disordered. I have not indeed enjoyed it with any degree of clearness since the violence done to that, and to my heart too, by the wicked arts of the abandoned creatures I was cast among.

I must have more conflicts. At times I find myself not subdued enough to my condition. I will welcome those conflicts as they come, as *probationary* ones—But yet my father's malediction—yet I hope even *that* may be made of so much use to me as to cause me to *double my attention to render it ineffectual*.

All I will at present add are my thanks to your mother for her indulgence to us. Due compliments to Mr Hickman; and my request that you will believe me to be, to my last hour, and beyond it, if possible, my beloved friend, and my *dearer* self (for what is now my self?),

Your obliged and affectionate
CLARISSA HARLOWE

Letter 321: MR LOVELACE TO JOHN BELFORD, ESQ.

Friday, July 7

I HAVE three of thy letters at once before me to answer; in each of which thou complainest of my silence; and in one of them tellest me that thou canst not live without I scribble to thee every day, or every other day at least.

Why then, die, Jack, if thou wilt—What heart, thinkest thou, can I have to write, when I have lost the only subject worth writing upon?

Help me again to my angel, to my CLARISSA; and thou shalt have a letter from me, or writing at least, part of a letter, every hour. All that the charmer of my heart shall say, that will I put down: every motion, every air of her beloved person, every look, will I try to describe; and when she is silent, I will endeavour to tell thee her thoughts, either what they are, or what I'd have them to be—so that, having *her*, I shall never want a subject. Having lost her, my whole soul is a blank: the whole creation round me, the elements above, beneath, and everything I *behold* (for nothing can *I enjoy*) is a blank without her!

Oh return, return, my soul's *fondledom*, return to thy adoring Lovelace! What is the light, what the air, what the town, what the country, what's anything, without thee? Light, air, joy, harmony, in my notion are but parts of thee; and could they be all expressed in one word, that word would be CLARISSA.

Oh my beloved CLARISSA, return thou then; once more return to bless thy LOVELACE, who now by the loss of thee knows the value of the jewel he has slighted; and rises every morning but to curse the sun that shines upon everybody but him!

WELL but, Jack, 'tis a surprising thing to me that the dear fugitive cannot be met with; cannot be heard of. She is so poor a plotter (for plotting is not her talent), that I am confident, had I been at liberty, I should have found her out before now; although the different emissaries I have employed about town, round the adjacent villages, and in Miss Howe's vicinage, have hitherto failed of success. But my lord continues so weak and low-spirited, that there is no getting from him. I would not disoblige a man whom I think in danger still: for would his gout, now it has got him down, but give him, like a fair boxer, the rising blow, all would be over with him. And here (Pox of his fondness for me! it happens at a very bad time) he makes me sit hours together entertaining him with my rogueries (a pretty amusement for a sick man!): and yet, whenever he has the gout, he prays night and morning with his chaplain. But what must *his* notions of religion be, who, after he has nosed and mumbled over his responses, can give a sigh or groan of satisfaction, as if he thought he had made up with heaven; and return with a new appetite to my stories?—Encouraging them by shaking his sides with laughing at them, and calling me a sad fellow in such an accent as shows he takes no small delight in his kinsman.

The old peer has been a sinner in his day, and suffers for it now: a sneaking sinner, *sliding* rather than *rushing* into vices, for fear of his reputation: or, rather, for fear of detection and positive proof; for these sort of fellows, Jack, have no real regard for reputation—Paying for what he never had, and never daring to rise to the joy of an enterprise at first hand, which could bring him within view of a tilting, or of the honour of being considered as the principal man in a court of justice.

To see such an old Trojan as this, just dropping into the grave which I hoped ere this would have been dug, and filled up with him; crying out with pain, and grunting with weakness; yet in the same moment crack his leathern face into an horrible laugh, and call a young sinner charming varlet, encoring him, as formerly he used to do the Italian eunuchs[1]; what a preposterous, what an unnatural adherence to old habits!

My two cousins are generally present when I *entertain*, as the old peer calls it. Those stories must drag horribly that have not more hearers and applauders, than relaters.

Applauders!—

Ay, Belford, *applauders*, repeat I; for although these girls pretend to blame me sometimes for the facts, they praise my manner, my invention, my intrepidity— Besides, what other people call *blame*, that call I *praise*: I ever did; and so I very early discharged *shame*, that cold-water damper to an enterprising spirit.

These are smart girls; they have life and wit; and yesterday, upon Charlotte's raving against me upon a related enterprise, I told her that I had had it in debate several times, whether she were or were not too near of kin to me: and that it was once a moot point with me whether I could not love her dearly for a month or so: and perhaps it was well for her that another pretty little puss started up and diverted me, just as I was entering upon the course.

They all three held up their hands and eyes at once. But I observed that though the girls exclaimed against me, they were not so angry at this plain speaking as I have found my beloved upon hints so dark, that I have wondered at her quick apprehension.

I told Charlotte that, grave as she pretended to be in her *smiling* resentments on this declaration, I was sure I should not have been put to the expense of above two or three stratagems (for nobody admired a good invention more than she), could I but have disentangled her conscience from the embarrasses of consanguinity.

She pretended to be highly displeased: so did her sister for her: I told her that she seemed as much in earnest, as if she had thought *me* so; and *dared* the trial. Plain words, I said, in these cases were more shocking to their sex than gradatim actions. And I bid Patty not be displeased at my distinguishing her sister; since I had a great respect for *her* likewise.

An Italian air, in my usual careless way, a half-struggled-for kiss from me, and a shrug of the shoulder by way of admiration from each pretty cousin, and Sad, sad fellow, from the old peer, attended with a side-shaking laugh, made us all friends.

There, Jack!—wilt thou, or wilt thou not, take this for a letter? There's quantity, I am sure—How have I filled a sheet (not a shorthand one indeed) without a subject! My fellow shall take this; for he is going to town. And if thou canst think tolerably of such execrable stuff, I will soon send thee another.

Letter 322: MR LOVELACE TO JOHN BELFORD, ESQ.

Six Sat. morning, July 8

HAVE I nothing new, nothing diverting, in my whimsical way, thou askest, in one of thy three letters before me, to entertain thee with?—And thou tellest me that, when I have least to *narrate*, to speak in the Scottish phrase,[1] I am most diverting. A pretty compliment, either to thyself, or to me. To both indeed!—A sign that thou hast as frothy a heart as I a head. But canst thou suppose that this admirable woman is not all, is not everything, with me? Yet I dread to think of her too; for detection of all my contrivances, I doubt, must come next.

The old peer is also full of Miss Harlowe; and so are my cousins. He hopes I will not be such a dog (there's a specimen of his peer-like dialect), as to think of doing dishonourably by a woman of so much merit, beauty, and fortune; and, he says, of so good a family. But I tell him that this is a string he must not touch: that it is a very tender point: in short, is my sore place; and that I am afraid he would handle it too roughly, were I to put myself into the power of so ungentle an operator.

He shakes his crazy head. He thinks all is not as it should be between us; longs to have me present her to him, as my wife; and often tells me what great things he will do, additional to his former proposals; and what presents he will make on the birth of the first child. But I hope the whole will be in my hands before such an event take place. No harm in *hoping*, Jack! My uncle says, *Were it not for hope, the heart would break.*

EIGHT o'clock at midsummer, and these lazy varletesses (in full health) not come down yet to breakfast!—What a confounded indecency in young ladies, to let a rake know that they love their beds so dearly, and, at the same time, *where to have them!* But I'll punish them: they shall breakfast with their old uncle, and yawn at one another, as if for a wager: while I drive my phaeton to Colonel Ambrose's, who yesterday gave me invitation both to breakfast and dine, on account of two Yorkshire nieces, celebrated toasts, who have been with him this fortnight past; and who, he says, want to see *me*. So, Jack, all women do not run away from me, thank Heaven!—I wish I could have leave of my heart, since the dear fugitive is so ungrateful, to drive her out of it with another beauty. But who can supplant her? Who can be admitted to a place in it, after Miss Clarissa Harlowe?

At my return, if I can find a subject, I will scribble on, to oblige thee.

My phaeton's ready: my cousins send me word they are just coming down: so in spite I'll be gone—

Saturday afternoon

I DID stay to dine with the colonel, and his lady and nieces: but I could not pass the afternoon with them, for the heart of me. There was enough in the persons and faces of the two young ladies to set me upon comparisons. Particular features held my attention for a few moments: but those served but to whet my impatience to find the charmer of my soul; who, for person, for air, for mind, had never any equal. My heart recoiled and sickened upon comparing minds and conversation. Pert wit, a too studied-for desire to please; each in high good humour with herself; an open-mouth affectation in both to show white teeth, as if the principal excellence; and to invite amorous familiarity by the promise of a sweet breath; at the same time reflecting tacitly upon breaths arrogantly implied to be less pure.

Once I could have borne them.

They seemed to be disappointed that I was so soon able to leave them. Yet have I not at present so much vanity (my Clarissa has cured me of my vanity!) as to attribute their disappointment so much to particular liking of me, as to their own self-admiration. They looked upon me as a connoisseur in beauty. They would have been proud of engaging my attention, as such: but so affected, so flimsy-witted, mere skin-deep beauties!—They had looked no further into themselves than what their glasses had enabled them to see: and their glasses were flattering-glasses too; for I thought them passive-faced, and spiritless; with eyes, however, upon the hunt for conquests, and bespeaking the attention of others in order to countenance their own—I believe I could, with a little pains, have given them life and soul, and to every feature of their faces sparkling information—But my Clarissa!—Oh Belford, my Clarissa has made me eyeless and senseless to every other beauty!—Do thou find her for me, as a subject worthy of my pen, or this shall be the last from

Thy LOVELACE

Letter 323: MR LOVELACE TO JOHN BELFORD, ESQ.

Sunday night, July 9

NOW, Jack, have I a subject with a vengeance. I am in the very height of my trial for all my sins to my beloved fugitive. For here, yesterday, at about five o'clock, arrived Lady Sarah Sadleir and Lady Betty Lawrance, each in her chariot and six. Dowagers love equipage; and these cannot travel ten miles without a set, and half a dozen horsemen.

My time had hung heavy upon my hands; and so I went to church after dinner. Why may not handsome fellows, thought I, like to be looked at as well as handsome wenches?—I fell in, when service was over, with Major Warneton; and so came not home till after six; and was surprised, at entering the courtyard here, to find it littered with equipages and servants. I was sure the owners of them came for no good to me.

Lady Sarah, I soon found, was raised to this visit by Lady Betty; who has health enough to allow her to look out of herself, and out of her own affairs, for business. Yet congratulation to my uncle on his amendment (spiteful devils on both accounts!) was the avowed errand. But coming in my absence, I was their principal subject: and they had opportunity to set each other's heart against me.

Simon Parsons hinted this to me, as I passed by the steward's office; for it seems they talked loud; and he was making up some accounts with old Pritchard.

However, I hastened to pay my duty to them. Other people not performing theirs is no excuse for the neglect of our own, you know.

And now I enter upon my TRIAL

WITH horrible grave faces was I received. The two antiques only bowed their tabby heads; making longer faces than ordinary; and all the old lines appearing strong in their furrowed foreheads and fallen cheeks. How do you, cousin? and, How do you, Mr Lovelace? looking all round at one another, as who should say, Do you speak first; and, Do you: for they seemed resolved to lose no time.

I had nothing for it but an air as manly as theirs was womanly. Your servant, madam, to Lady Betty; and, Your servant, madam—I am glad to see you abroad, to Lady Sarah.

I took my seat. Lord M. looked horribly glum; his fingers clasped, and turning round and round, under and over, his but just disgouted thumbs; his sallow face, and goggling eyes, cast upon the floor, on the fireplace, on his two sisters, on his two kinswomen, by turns; but not once deigning to look upon me.

Then I began to think of the laudanum and wet cloth I had told thee of long ago¹; and to call myself in question for a tenderness of heart that will never do me good.

At last, Mr Lovelace—Cousin Lovelace!—Hem!—Hem!—I am sorry, very sorry, hesitated Lady Sarah, that there is no hope of your ever taking up—

What's the matter *now*, madam?

The matter now!—Why, Lady Betty has two letters from Miss Harlowe, which have *told* us what's the matter—Are all women alike with you?

Yes; I could have answered; 'bating the difference which pride makes.

Then they all chorused upon me—Such a character as Miss Harlowe's! cried one—A lady of so much generosity and good sense! another—How charmingly she writes! the two maiden monkies, looking at her fine handwriting: her perfections my crimes. What can you expect will be the end of these things? cried Lady Sarah—Damned, damned doings! vociferated the peer, shaking his loose-fleshed wabbling chaps, which hung on his shoulders like an old cow's dew-lap.

For my part I hardly knew whether to sing or say what I had to reply to these all-at-once attacks upon me!—Fair and softly, ladies—One at a time, I beseech you. I am not to be hunted down without being heard, I hope. Pray let me see these letters. I beg you will let me see them.

There they are—that's the first—Read it out, if you can.

I opened a letter from my charmer, dated *Thursday, June 29*, our wedding-day that was to be, and written to Lady Betty Lawrance—By the contents, to my great joy, I find the dear creature is alive and well, and in charming spirits. But the direction where to send an answer was so scratched out, that I could not read it; which afflicted me much.

She put three questions in it to Lady Betty.

1st, About a letter of hers, dated *June 7*, congratulating our nuptials, and which I was so good as to save my aunt the trouble of writing: a very civil thing of me, I think.

Again, 'Whether she and one of her nieces Montague were to go to town on an old Chancery suit?' And, 'Whether they actually did go to town accordingly, and to Hampstead afterwards?' and 'Whether they brought to town from thence the young creature whom they visited?' was the subject of the second and third questions.

A little inquisitive dear rogue! And what did she expect to be the better for these questions?—But curiosity, damned curiosity, is the itch of the sex—yet when didst thou know it turned to their benefit?—for they seldom inquire but when they fear—and the proverb, as my lord has it, says *It comes with a fear*. That is, I suppose, what they fear generally happens because there is generally occasion for the fear.

Curiosity indeed she avows to be her only motive for these interrogatories: for though she says her ladyship may suppose the questions are not asked for good to *me*, yet the answer can do me no harm, nor her good, only to give her to understand whether I have told her—a parcel of damned lies; that's the plain English of her inquiry.

Well, madam, said I, with as much philosophy as I could assume; and may I ask, pray, What was your ladyship's answer?

There's a copy of it, tossing it to me, very disrespectfully.

This answer was dated *July 1*. A very kind and complaisant one to the lady, but very so-so to her poor kinsman—That people can give up their own flesh and blood with so much ease!—She tells her 'how proud all our family would be of an alliance with such an excellence.' She does me justice in saying how much I adore her, as an angel of a lady; and begs of her for I know not how many sakes, besides my soul's sake, 'that she will be so good as to have me for an husband:' and answers—thou wilt guess how—to the lady's questions.

Well, madam; and, pray, may I be favoured with the lady's other letter? I presume it is in reply to yours.

It is, said the peer: but, sir, let me ask you a few questions, before you read it— Give *me* the letter, Lady Betty.

There it is, my lord.

Then on went the spectacles, and his head moved to the lines—A charming pretty hand!—I have often heard, that this lady is a *genus*.

And so, Jack, repeating my lord's wise comments and questions will let thee into the contents of this merciless letter.

'*Monday, July 3*' (reads my lord)—Let me see!—That was last *Monday*; no longer ago! '*Monday July the third*—Madam—I cannot excuse myself—um, um, um, um, um, um (humming inarticulately, and skipping)—I must own to you, madam, that the honour of being related'—

Off went the spectacles—Now, tell me, sir, has not this lady lost all the friends she had in the world, for your sake?

She has very implacable friends, my lord: we all know that.

But has she not lost all for your sake?—Tell me that.

I believe so, my lord.

Well then!—I am glad thou art not so graceless as to deny that.

On went the spectacles again—'I must own to you, madam, that the honour of being related to ladies as eminent for their virtue, as for their descent'—*Very pretty, truly!* said my lord, repeating, '*as eminent for their virtue as for their descent*, was, at first, no small inducement with me to lend an ear to Mr Lovelace's address.'

—There is dignity, born dignity, in this lady, cried my lord.

Lady Sarah. She would have been a grace to our family.

Lady Betty. Indeed she would.

Lovel. To a royal family, I will venture to say.

Ld M. Then what a devil—

Lovel. Please to read on, my lord. It cannot be *her* letter, if it does not make you admire her more and more as you read. Cousin Charlotte, Cousin Patty, pray attend—Read on, my lord.

Miss Charlotte. Amazing fortitude!

Miss Patty only lifted up her dove's eyes.

Lord M. (reading) 'And the rather, as I was determined, had it come to effect, to do everything in my power to deserve your favourable opinion.'

Then again they chorused upon me!

A blessed time of it, poor I!—I had nothing for it but impudence!

Lovel. Pray read on, my lord—I told you how you would all admire her—or shall I read?

Lord M. Damned assurance! (reading) 'I had another motive, which I knew would of itself give me merit with your whole family—*They were all ear*—a presumptuous one; a punishably presumptuous one, as it has proved; in the hope that I might be an humble means in the hand of Providence, to reclaim a man, who had, as I thought, good sense enough at bottom to be reclaimed; or at least gratitude enough to acknowledge the intended obligation, whether the generous hope were to succeed or not'—Excellent young creature!—Excellent young creature! echoed the ladies, with their handkerchiefs at their eyes, attended with nose-music.

Lovel. By my soul, Miss Patty, you weep in the wrong place: you shall never go with me to a tragedy.

Lady Betty. Hardened wretch!—

His lordship had pulled off his spectacles to wipe them. His eyes were misty; and he thought the fault in his spectacles.

I saw they were all cocked and primed—To be sure that is a very pretty sentence, said I—that is the excellency of this lady, that in every line as she writes on, she improves upon herself. Pray, my lord, proceed—I know her style; the next sentence will still rise upon us.

Lord M. Damned fellow! (again saddling and reading). 'But I have been most egregiously mistaken in Mr Lovelace!'—(Then they all clamoured again.) 'The *only* man, I persuade myself—'

Lovel. Ladies may persuade themselves to anything—But how can she answer for what *other* men would or would not have done in the same circumstances?

I was forced to say anything to stifle their outcries. Pox take ye all together, thought I, as if I had not vexation enough in losing her!

Lord M. (reading) 'The only man, I persuade myself, pretending to be a gentleman, in whom I could have been so much mistaken.'

They were all beginning again—Pray, my lord, proceed!—Hear, hear—Pray, ladies, hear!—Now, my lord, be pleased to proceed. The ladies are silent.

So they were; lost in admiration of me, hands and eyes uplifted.

Lord M. I will, to thy confusion; for he had looked over the next sentence.

What wretches, Belford, what spiteful wretches, are poor mortals!—So rejoiced to sting one another! to see each other stung!

Lord M. (reading) 'For while I was endeavouring to save a drowning wretch, I have been, not accidentally, but premeditatedly and of set purpose, drawn in after him'—What say you to this, sir-r?

Lady S. ⎱
Lady B. ⎰ Ay, sir, what say you to this?

Lovel. Say! Why I say it is a very pretty metaphor, if it would but hold—But if you please, my lord, read on. Let me hear what is further said, and I will speak to it all together.

Lord M. I will—'And he has had the glory to add to the list of those he has ruined, a name that I will be bold to say, would not have disparaged his own.'

They all looked at me, as expecting me to speak.

Lovel. Be pleased to proceed, my lord: I will speak to this by and by. How came she to know, I *kept a list?*—I will speak to this by and by.

Lord M. (reading on) 'And this, madam, by means that would shock humanity to be made acquainted with.'

Then again, in a hurry, off went the spectacles.

This was a plaguy stroke upon me. I thought myself an oak in impudence; but, by my troth, this had almost felled me.

Lord M. What say you to this, SIR-R!—

Remember, Jack, to read all their *sirs* in this dialogue with a double *rr, sirr!*—denoting indignation rather than respect.

They all looked at me, as if to see if I could blush.

Lovel. Eyes off, my lord!—Eyes off, ladies! (looking bashfully, I believe)—What say I to this, my lord!—Why, I say that this lady has a strong manner of expressing herself!—That's all—There are many things that pass among lovers, which a man cannot explain himself upon before grave people.

Lady Betty. Among lovers, sir-r!—But, Mr Lovelace, can you say that this lady behaved either like a weak, or a credulous person?—Can you say—

Lovel. I am ready to do the lady all manner of justice—But, pray now, ladies, if I am to be thus interrogated, let me know the contents of the rest of the letter, that I may be prepared for my defence, as you are all for my arraignment. For, to be required to answer piecemeal thus, without knowing what is to follow, is a cursed ensnaring way of proceeding.

They gave me the letter: I read it through to myself—and by the repetition of what I said, thou wilt guess at the remaining contents.

You shall find, ladies; you shall find, my lord, that I will not spare myself. Then holding the letter in my hand, and looking upon it, as a lawyer upon his breviate:

Miss Harlowe says, 'That when your ladyship' (turning to Lady Betty) 'shall know that in the progress to her ruin, wilful falsehoods, repeated forgeries, and numberless perjuries were not the least of my crimes, you will judge that she can have no principles that will make her worthy of an alliance with ladies of yours, and your noble sister's character, if she could not, from her soul, declare that such an alliance can never now take place.'

Surely, ladies, this is passion! This is not reason. If our family would not think themselves dishonoured by my marrying a person whom I had so treated; but, on the contrary, would rejoice that I did her this justice; and if she has come out pure gold from the assay; and has nothing to reproach herself with; why should it be an impeachment of her principles to consent that such an alliance should take place?

She cannot think herself the worse, *justly* she cannot, for what was done against her will.

Their countenances menaced a general uproar—But I proceeded.

Your lordship read to us that she had an *hope*, a *presumptuous* one; nay, a *punishably presumptuous* one, she calls it; 'that she might be a means in the hands of Providence to reclaim me; and that this, she knew, if effected, would give her a merit with you all.' But from *what* would she reclaim me?—She had *heard*, you'll say (but she had *only* heard, at the time she held *that hope*), that, to express myself in the women's dialect, I was *a very wicked fellow*—Well, and what then?— Why, truly, the very moment she was *convinced* by her own experience that the charge against me was *more* than *hearsay*; and that, of consequence, I was a fit subject for her *generous endeavours* to work upon; she would needs give me up. Accordingly, she flies out, and declares that the ceremony which would repair all shall never take place!—Can this be from any other motive than *female resentment?*

This brought them all upon me, as I intended it should: it was as a tub to the whale; and after I had let them play with it awhile, I claimed their attention, and knowing that they always loved to hear me prate, went on.

The lady, it is plain, thought that the reclaiming of a man from bad habits was a much *easier task* than, in the *nature of things*, it *can* be.

She writes, as your lordship has read, 'That in endeavouring to save a drowning wretch, she had been, not accidentally, but premeditatedly and of set purpose, drawn in after him.' But how is this, ladies?—You see by her own words that I am still far from being out of danger myself. Had she found me, in a quagmire suppose, and I had got out of it by her means, and left her to perish in it; that would have been a crime indeed—But is not the fact quite otherwise? Has she not, if her allegory proves what she would have it prove, got out herself and left me floundering still deeper and deeper in?—What she should have done, had she been in earnest to save me, was to join her hand with mine, that so we might by our united strength help one another out—I held out my hand to her, and besought her to give me hers—but no, truly! she was determined to get out herself as fast as she could, let me *sink or swim:* refusing her assistance (against her own principles), because she saw I wanted it. You see, ladies, you see, my lord, how pretty tinkling words run away with ears inclined to be musical!—

They were all ready to exclaim again: but I went on, *proleptically*, as a rhetorician would say, before their voices could break out into words.

But my fair accuser says that, 'I have added to the list of those I have ruined, a name that would not have disparaged my own.' It is true I have been gay and enterprising. It is in my constitution to be so. I know not how I came by such a constitution: but I was never accustomed to check or control; that you all know. When a man finds himself hurried by passion into a slight offence, which, however slight, will not be forgiven, he may be made desperate: as a thief, who only intends a robbery, is often by resistance, and for self-preservation, drawn in to commit a murder.

I was a strange, a horrid wretch, with everyone. But he must be a silly fellow who has not something to say for himself, when every cause has its black and its white side—Westminster Hall, Jack, affords every day as confident defences as mine.

But what right, proceeded I, has this lady to complain of me, when she as good as says—Here, Lovelace, you have acted the part of a villain by me—You would *repair your fault:* but I won't let you, that I may have the satisfaction of exposing you; and the pride of refusing you?

But, was that the case? Was that the case? Would I pretend to say I would *now* marry the lady, if she would have me?

Lovel. You find she renounces Lady Betty's mediation—

Lord M. (interrupting me) *Words are wind; but deeds are mind:* what signifies your cursed quibbling, Bob?—Say plainly, if she will have you, will you have her? Answer me, Yes or No; and lead us not *a wild goose-chase* after your meaning.

Lovel. She knows I would. But here, my lord, if she thus goes on to expose herself and me, she will make it a dishonour to us both to marry.

Charl. But how must she have been treated—

Lovel. (interrupting her) Why now, cousin Charlotte, chucking her under the chin, would you have me tell you all that has passed between the lady and me? Would YOU care, had you a bold and enterprising lover, that proclamation should be made of every little piece of amorous roguery that he offered to you?

Charlotte reddened. They all began to exclaim. But I proceeded.

The lady says, 'She has been dishonoured' (Devil take me, if I spare myself!) 'by means that would shock humanity to be made acquainted with them.' She is a very innocent lady, and may not be a *judge* of the means she hints at. *Over-niceness may be under-niceness:* have you not such a proverb, my lord?—tantamount to, *One extreme produces another!*—Such a lady as this may possibly think her case more extraordinary than it is. This I will take upon me to say, that if she has met with the only man in the world who would have treated her as she says I have treated her, I have met in her, with the *only woman in the world* who would have made such a rout about a case that is uncommon only from the circumstances that attend it.

This brought them all upon me, hands, eyes, voices, all lifted up at once. But my Lord M., who has in his *head* (the last seat of retreating lewdness) as much wickedness as I have in my *heart*, was forced (upon the air I spoke this with, and Charlotte's and all the rest reddening) to make a mouth that was big enough to swallow up the other half of his face; crying out, to avoid laughing, Oh! Oh!—as if under the power of a gouty twinge.

Hadst thou seen how the two tabbies, and the young grimalkins, looked at one another, at my lord, and at me, by turns, thou too wouldst have been ready to split thy ugly face just in the middle. Thy mouth has already done half the work. And, after all, I found not seldom in this conversation, that my humorous undaunted way forced a smile into my service from the prim mouths of the *younger* ladies especially: for the case not being likely to be theirs, they could not be so much affected by it as the elders; who, having had roses, that is to say, daughters, of their own, would have been very loath to have had them nipped in the bud, without saying By your leave, Mrs Rose-bush, to the mother of it.

The next article of my indictment was for forgery; and for personating of Lady Betty and my cousin Charlotte. Two shocking charges! thou'lt say: and so they were!—The peer was outrageous upon the *forgery*-charge. The ladies vowed never to forgive the *personating* part. Not a peace-maker among them. So we all turned women, and scolded.

My lord told me that he believed in his conscience there was not a viler fellow upon *God's earth* than me—What signifies mincing the matter, said he?—And that it was not the first time I had forged his hand.

To this I answered, that I supposed when the statute of *scandalum magnatum* was framed, there were a good many in the peerage who knew they deserved hard names; and that that law therefore was rather made to privilege their qualities than to whiten their characters.

He called upon me to explain myself, with a *sir-r*, so pronounced as to show that one of the most ignominious words in our language was in his head.

People, I said, that were fenced in by their quality and by their years, should not take freedoms that a man of spirit could not put up with, unless he were able heartily to despise the insulter.

This set him in a violent passion. He would send for Pritchard instantly. Let Pritchard be called. He would alter his will; and all he *could* leave from me, he *would*.

Do, do, my lord, said I: I always valued my own pleasure above your estate. But I'll let Pritchard know that if he draws, he shall sign and seal.

Why, what would I do to Pritchard?—shaking his crazy head at me.

Only, what he, or any man else, writes with his pen, to despoil me of what I think my right, he shall seal with his ears; that's all, my lord.

Then the two ladies interposed.

Lady Sarah told me that I carried things a great way; and that neither Lord M. nor any of them deserved the treatment I gave them.

I said I could not bear to be used ill by my lord, for two reasons; first, because I respected his lordship above any man living; and next, because it looked as if I were induced by selfish considerations to take that from him, which nobody else would offer to me.

And what, returned he, shall be my inducement to take what I do at your hands?—Hey, sir?

Indeed, cousin Lovelace, said Lady Betty with great gravity, we do not any of us, as Lady Sarah says, deserve at your hands the treatment you give us: and let me tell you that I don't think my character, and your cousin Charlotte's, ought to be prostituted in order to ruin an innocent lady. She must have known early the good opinion we all have of her, and how much we wished her to be your wife. This good opinion of ours has been an inducement to her (You see she says so) to listen to your address. And this, with her friends' folly, has helped to throw her into your power. How you have requited her is too apparent. It becomes the character we all bear to disclaim your actions by her. And, let me tell you, that to have her abused by wicked people raised up to personate us, or any of us, makes a double call upon us to disclaim them.

Lovel. Why this is talking somewhat like. I would have you all disclaim my actions. I own I have done very vilely by this lady. One step led to another. I am cursed with an enterprising spirit. I hate to be foiled.

Foiled! interrupted Lady Sarah. What a shame to talk at this rate!—Did the lady set up a contention with you? All nobly sincere, and plain-hearted, have I heard Miss Clarissa Harlowe is: above art, above disguise; neither the coquette, nor the prude!—Poor lady! She deserved a better fate from the man for whom she took the step which she so freely blames!

This above half affected me—Had this dispute been so handled by everyone, I had been ashamed to look up. I began to be bashful—

Charlotte asked if I did not still seem inclinable to do the lady justice, if she would have *me?* It would be, she dared to say, the greatest felicity the family could know (She would answer for one), that this fine lady were of it.

They all declared to the same effect; and Lady Sarah put the matter home to me.

But my Lord *Marplot* would have it that I could not be serious for six minutes together.

I told his lordship that he was mistaken; light as he thought I made of this subject, I never knew any that went so near my heart.

Miss Patty said she was glad to hear *that:* indeed she was glad to hear *that:* and her soft eyes glistened with pleasure.

Lord M. called her sweet soul, and was ready to cry.

Not from humanity neither, Jack. This peer has no bowels; as thou mayst observe by his treatment of *me.* But when people's minds are weakened by a sense of their own infirmities, and when they are drawing on to their latter ends, they will be moved on the slightest occasions, whether those offer from *within,* or *without* them. And this, frequently, the unpenetrating world calls *humanity,* when all the time, in compassionating the miseries of human nature, they are but pitying themselves; and were they in strong health and spirits would care as little for anybody else as thou or I do.

Here broke they off my trial for this sitting. Lady Sarah was much fatigued. It was agreed to pursue the subject in the morning. They all, however, retired together, and went into private conference.

Letter 324: MR LOVELACE [TO JOHN BELFORD, ESQ.]

(In continuation)

THE ladies, instead of taking up the subject where we had laid it down, must needs touch upon passages in my fair accuser's letter, which I was in hopes they would have let rest, as we were in a tolerable way. But, truly, they must hear all they could hear of our story, and what I had to say to those passages that they might be better enabled to mediate between us if I were really and indeed inclined to do her the hoped-for justice.

These passages were: 1st, 'That after I had tricked her against her will into the act of going off with me, I carried her to one of the worst houses in London.'

2. 'That I had made a wicked attempt upon her; in resentment of which, she fled to Hampstead, privately.'

3dly, Came the forgery, and personating charges again; and we were upon the point of renewing our quarrel, before we could get to the next charge: which was still worse.

For that, 4thly, was, 'That having tricked her back to the vile house, I had first robbed her of her senses, and then of her honour; detaining her afterwards a prisoner there.'

Were I to tell thee the glosses I put upon these heavy charges, what would it be but to repeat many of the extenuating arguments I have used in my letters to thee?—Suffice it, therefore, to say that I insisted much, by way of palliation, on the lady's extreme niceness: on her diffidence in my honour: on Miss Howe's contriving spirit; plots on their parts, begetting plots on mine: on the high passions of the sex: I asserted that my whole view in gently restraining her was to oblige her to forgive me, and to marry me; and this, for the honour of both families. I boasted of my own good qualities; some of which, none that know me deny; and which few libertines can lay claim to.

They then fell into warm admirations and praises of the lady; all of them preparatory, as I knew, to the grand question: and thus it was introduced by Lady Sarah.

We have said as much as I think we can say upon these letters of the poor lady. To dwell upon the mischiefs that may ensue from the abuse of a person of her rank, if all the reparation be not made that now can be made, would perhaps be to little purpose. But you seem, sir, still to have a just opinion of her, as well as affection for her. Her virtue is not in the least questionable. She could not resent as she does, had she anything to reproach herself with. She is, by everybody's account, a fine woman; has a good estate in her own right; is of no contemptible family; though I think with regard to her they have acted as imprudently as unworthily. For the excellency of her mind, for good economy, the common speech of her, as the worthy Dr Lewen once told me, is *that her prudence would enrich a poor man, and her piety reclaim a licentious one*. I, who have not been abroad twice this twelvemonth, came hither purposely, so did Lady Betty, to see if justice may not be done her; and also whether we, and my Lord M. (your nearest relations, sir) have, or have not, any influence over you. And, for my own part, as your determination shall be in this article, such shall be mine, with regard to the disposition of all that is within my power.

Lady Betty. And mine.

And mine, said my lord: and valiantly he swore to it.

Lovel. Far be it from me to think slightly of favours you may, any of you, be glad I would deserve. But as far be it from me to enter into conditions against my own liking, with sordid views—As to future mischiefs, let them come. I have not done with the Harlowes yet. They were the aggressors; and I should be glad they would let me hear from them, in the way they should hear from me in the like case. Perhaps I should not be sorry to be *found*, rather than be obliged to *seek*, on this occasion.

Miss Charlotte (reddening). Spoke like a man of violence, rather than a man of reason! I hope you'll allow that, cousin.

Lady Sarah. Well, but since what is done, *is* done, and cannot be undone, let us think of the next best. Have you any objection against marrying Miss Harlowe, if she will have you?

Lovel. There can possibly be but one: that she is everywhere, no doubt, as well as to Lady Betty, pursuing that maxim, peculiar to herself (*and let me tell you, so it ought to be*), that what she cannot conceal from herself, she will publish to all the world.

Miss Patty. The lady, to be sure, writes this in the bitterness of her grief, and in despair.

And this from *you*, cousin Patty!—*Sweet girl!* And would *you*, my dear, in the like case (whispering her), have meant no more by the like exclamations?

I had a rap with her fan, and a blush; and from Lord M. a reflection that I turned into jest everything they said.

I asked if they thought the Harlowes deserved any consideration from me; and whether that family would not exult over me, were I to marry their daughter as if I *dared* not to do otherwise?

Lady Sarah. Once I was angry with that family, as we all were. But now I pity them; and think that you have but too well justified the worst treatment they gave you.

Lord M. Their family is of standing. All gentlemen of it, and rich, and reputable. Let me tell you that many of our coronets would be glad they could derive their descents from no worse a stem than theirs.

Lovel. They are a narrow-souled and implacable family. I hate them: and though I revere the lady, scorn all relation to them.

Lady Betty. I wish no worse could be said of *him*, who is such a scorner of common failings in *others*.

Lord M. How would my sister Lovelace have reproached herself for all her indulgent folly to this favourite boy of hers, had she lived till now, and been present on this occasion!

Lady Sarah. Well but, begging your lordship's pardon, let us see if anything can be done for this poor lady.

Miss Ch. If Mr Lovelace has nothing to object against the lady's character (and I presume to think he is not *ashamed* to do her justice, though it may make against himself), I cannot see but honour and generosity will compel from him all that we expect. If there be any levities, any weaknesses, to be charged upon the lady, I should not open my lips in her favour; though in private I would pity her, and deplore her hard hap. And yet, even then, there might not want arguments from honour and gratitude, in so particular a case, to engage you, sir, to make good the vows it is plain you have broken.

Lady Betty. My niece Charlotte has called upon you so justly, and has put the question to you so properly, that I cannot but wish you would speak to it directly, and without evasion.

All in a breath then bespoke my seriousness, and my justice: and in this manner I delivered myself, assuming an air sincerely solemn.

'I am very sensible that the performance of the task you have put me upon will leave me without excuse: but I will not have recourse either to evasion, or palliation.

'As my cousin Charlotte has severely observed, I am not *ashamed* to do justice to Miss Harlowe's merit in words, although I will confess that I ought to blush that I have done it so little in deeds.

'I own to *you* all, and what is more, with high regret (if not with *shame*, cousin Charlotte), that I have a great deal to answer for in my usage of this lady. The sex has not a nobler mind, nor a lovelier person of it. And, for *virtue*, I could not have believed (excuse me, ladies) that there ever was a woman who *gave*, or *could* have given, such illustrious, such uniform proofs of it: for, in her whole conduct, she has shown herself to be equally above temptation and art; and, I had almost said, human frailty.

'The step she so freely blames herself for taking was truly what she calls *compulsatory*: for though she was provoked to *think* of going off with me, she intended it not, nor was provided to do so: neither would she ever have had the *thought* of it, had her relations left her free, upon her offered composition, to renounce the man she did *not* hate, in order to avoid the man she *did*.

'It piqued my pride, I own, that I could so little depend upon the force of those impressions which I had the vanity to hope I had made in a heart so delicate; and in my worst devices against her, I encouraged myself that I abused no confidence; for none had she in my honour.

'The evils she has suffered, it would have been more than a miracle had she avoided. Her watchfulness rendered more plots abortive than those which contributed to her fall; and they were many and various. And all her greater trials and hardships were owing to her noble resistance and just resentment.

'I know, proceeded I, how much I condemn myself in the justice I am doing to this excellent creature. But yet I *will* do her justice, and cannot help it if I would. And I hope this shows, that I am not so totally abandoned as I have been thought to be.

'Indeed with me, she has done more honour to the sex in her fall, if it be to be called a fall (in truth it ought not), than ever any other could do in her standing.

'When, at length, I had given her watchful virtue cause of suspicion, I was then indeed obliged to make use of power and art to hinder her from escaping from me. She then formed contrivances to elude mine; but all *hers* were such as strict truth and punctilious honour would justify. She could not stoop to deceit and falsehood, no, not to save herself. More than once, justly did she tell me, fired by conscious worthiness, that her soul was my soul's superior!—Forgive me, ladies, for saying that till I knew *her*, I questioned a soul in a sex, created, as I was willing to suppose, only for temporary purposes—It is not to be imagined into what absurdities men of free principles run, in order to justify to themselves their free practices; and to make a religion to their minds. And yet, in this respect, I have not been so faulty as some others.

'No wonder that such a noble creature as this looked upon every studied artifice as a degree of baseness, not to be forgiven: no wonder that she could so easily become averse to the man (though once she beheld him with an eye not wholly indifferent) whom she thought capable of premeditated guilt—nor, give me leave on the other hand to say, is it to be wondered at that the man who found it so difficult to be forgiven for the *slighter* offences, and who had not the grace to recede or repent (made desperate), should be hurried on to the commission of the *greater*.

'In short, ladies, in a word, my lord, Miss Clarissa Harlowe is an angel; if ever there was or could be one in human nature: and is, and ever was, as pure as an angel in her will: and this justice I must do her, although the question, I see by every glistening eye, is ready to be asked, What, then, Lovelace, are you?—'

Lord M. A devil!—A damned devil! I must answer. And may the curse of God follow you in all you undertake, if you do not make her the best amends now in your power to make her!

Lovel. From you, my lord, I could expect no other: but from the ladies I hope for less violence from the ingenuity of my confession.

The ladies, elder and younger, had their handkerchiefs to their eyes, at the just testimony which I bore to the merits of this exalted creature; and which I would make no scruple to bear at the bar of a court of justice, were I to be called to it.

Lady Betty. Well, sir, this is a noble character. If you think as you speak, surely you cannot refuse to do the lady all the justice now in your power to do her.

They all joined in this demand.

I pleaded that I was sure she would not have me: that, when she had taken a resolution, she was not to be moved: unpersuadableness was an Harlowe sin: that, and her name, I told them, were all she had of theirs.

All were of opinion that she might, in her present desolate circumstances, be brought to forgive me. Lady Sarah said that her sister and she would endeavour to find out the *noble sufferer*, as they justly called her; and would take her into their protection, and be guaranties to her of the justice that I would do her; as well after marriage, as before.

It was some pleasure to me, to observe the placability of these ladies of my own family, had they, any or either of them, met with a LOVELACE. But 'twould be hard upon us honest fellows, Jack, if all women were CLARISSAS.

Here I am obliged to break off.

Letter 325: MR LOVELACE [TO JOHN BELFORD, ESQ.]

(In continuation)
IT is much better, Jack, to tell your own story when it *must* be known, than to have an adversary tell it for you. Conscious of this, I gave them a particular account, how urgent I had been with her to fix upon the Thursday after I left her (it being her uncle Harlowe's anniversary birthday, and named to oblige her) for the private celebration; having some days before actually procured a licence, which still remained with her.

That, not being able to prevail upon her to promise anything, while under a supposed restraint; I offered to leave her at full liberty, if she would give me the least hope for that day. But neither did this offer avail me.

That this inflexibleness making me desperate, I resolved to add to my former fault, by giving directions that she should not either go, or correspond, out of the house, till I returned from M. Hall; well knowing that, if she were at full liberty, I must for ever lose her.

That this constraint had so much incensed her, that although I wrote no less than four different letters, I could not procure a single word in answer; though I pressed her but for four words to signify the day and the church.

I referred to my two cousins to vouch for me the extraordinary methods I took to send messengers to town, though they knew not the occasion: which now I told them, was *this*.

I acquainted them that I even had wrote to you, Jack, and to another gentleman, of whom I thought she had a good opinion, to attend her, in order to press for her compliance; holding myself in readiness the last day, at Salt Hill, to meet the messenger they should send, and proceed to London if his message were favourable: but that, before they could attend her, she had found means to fly away once more: and is now, said I, perched perhaps, somewhere under Lady Betty's window at Glenham Hall; and there, like the sweet Philomela, a thorn in her breast, warbles forth her melancholy complaints against her barbarous Tereus.[1]

Lady Betty declared that she was not with *her*; nor did she know where she was. She should be, she added, the most welcome guest to her, that she ever received.

In truth, I had a suspicion that she was already in their knowledge, and taken into their protection; for Lady Sarah I imagined incapable of being roused to this spirit by a letter only from Miss Harlowe, and that not directed to herself; she being a very indolent and melancholy woman. But her sister, I find, had wrought her up to it: for Lady Betty is as officious and managing a woman as Mrs Howe; but of a much more generous and noble disposition—She is *my aunt*, Jack.

I supposed, I said, that her ladyship might have a private direction where to send to her. I spoke, as I wished: I would have given the world to have heard that she was inclined to cultivate the interest of any of my family.

Lady Betty answered that she had no direction but what was in the letter; which she had scratched out, and which it was probable was only a temporary one, in order to avoid me: Otherwise she would hardly have directed an answer to be left at an inn. And she was of opinion, that to apply to Miss Howe would be the only certain way to succeed in any application for forgiveness, would I enable that young lady to interest herself in procuring it.

Miss Charlotte. Permit me to make a proposal—Since we are all of one mind in relation to the justice due to Miss Harlowe, if Mr Lovelace will oblige himself to marry her, I will make Miss Howe a visit, little as I am acquainted with her; and endeavour to engage her interest to forward the desired reconciliation. And if this can be done, I make no question but all may be happily accommodated; for everybody knows the love there is between Miss Harlowe and Miss Howe.

MARRIAGE, *with these women, thou seest, Jack, is an atonement for all we can do to them. A true dramatic recompense!*

This motion was highly approved of; and I gave my honour, as desired, in the fullest manner they could wish.

Lady Sarah. Well then, cousin Charlotte, begin your treaty with Miss Howe, out of hand.

Lady Betty. Pray do. And let Miss Harlowe be told that I am ready to receive her as the welcomest of guests: and I will not have her out of my sight till the knot is tied.

Lady Sarah. Tell her from me that she shall be my daughter!—instead of my poor Betsey!—and shed a tear in remembrance of her lost daughter.

Lord M. What say you, sir, to this?

Lovel. CONTENT, my lord. I speak in the language of your House.

Lord M. We are not to be fooled, nephew. No quibbling. We will have no slur put upon us.

Lovel. You shall not. And yet I did not intend to marry if she exceeded the appointed Thursday. But I think, according to her own notions, that I have injured her beyond reparation, although I were to make her the best of husbands; as I am resolved to be if she will *condescend*, as I will call it, to have me. And be this, cousin Charlotte, *my* part of your commission to say.

This pleased them all.

Lord M. Give thy hand, Bob!—Thou talkest like a man of honour at last. I hope we may depend upon what thou sayest?

The ladies' eyes put the same question to me.

Lovel. You may, my lord. You may, ladies. Absolutely you may.

Then was the personal character of the lady, as well as her extraordinary talents and endowments, again expatiated upon: and Miss Patty, who had once seen her, launched out more than all the rest in her praise. These were followed by *family-cogencies*; what never are forgotten to be inquired after in marriage-treaties, the *principal inducements* to the *sages* of a family, and the *least to be mentioned* by the *parties* themselves, although even by *them*, perhaps, the *first* thought of: That is to say, inquisition into the lady's fortune; into the particulars of the grandfather's estate; and what her father, and her single-souled uncles, will probably do for her if a reconciliation be effected; as, by *their* means, they make no doubt but it will, between both families, if it be not my fault. The two venerables (no longer tabbies with me now) hinted at rich presents on their own parts; and my lord declared that he would make such overtures in my behalf as should render my marriage with Miss Harlowe the best day's work I ever made; and what, he doubted not, but would be as agreeable to that family as to myself.

Thus, at present, by a single hair, hangs over my head the matrimonial sword. And thus ended my trial. And thus are we all friends; and cousin and cousin, and nephew and nephew, at every word.

Did ever comedy end more happily than this long trial?

Letter 326: MR LOVELACE TO JOHN BELFORD, ESQ.

Wed. July 12

So, Jack, they think they have gained a mighty point. But, *were* I to change my mind, were I to repent, I fancy I am safe—And yet this very moment it rises to my mind that 'tis hard trusting too; for surely there must be some embers where there was fire so lately, that may be stirred up to give a blaze to combustibles strewed lightly upon them. Love (like some self-propagating plants or roots which have taken strong hold in the earth), when once got deep into the heart, is hardly ever *totally* extirpated, except by matrimony indeed, which is the grave of love, because it allows of the end of love. Then these ladies all advocates *for* herself, *with* herself, Miss Howe at their head, perhaps—not in favour to me—I don't expect that from Miss Howe—but perhaps in favour to *herself:* for Miss Howe has reason to apprehend vengeance from me, I ween. Her Hickman will be safe too, as she may think, if I marry her beloved friend: for he has been a busy fellow, and I have long wished to have a slap at him!—The lady's case desperate with her friends too; and likely to be so, while single, and her character exposed to censure.

A husband is a charming cloak; a fig-leafed apron for a wife: and for a lady to be protected in liberties, in diversions which her heart pants after—and all her faults, even the most criminal, were she to be detected, to be thrown upon the husband, and the ridicule too; a charming eligible for a wife!

But I shall have one comfort, if I marry, which pleases me not a little. If a man's wife has a dear friend of her sex, a hundred liberties may be taken with that friend, which could *not* be taken if the *single lady* (knowing what a title to freedoms marriage has given him with her *friend*) was not less scrupulous with him than she ought to be, as to *herself.* Then there are *broad* freedoms (shall I call them?) that may be taken by the husband with his wife, that may not be *quite* shocking, which if the wife *bears before her friend* will serve for a lesson to *that friend*; and if that friend *bears* to be present at them without check or bashfulness, will show a sagacious fellow that she can bear as much herself, at *proper time* and *place*. *Chastity*, Jack, like *piety*, is an uniform thing. If in *look*, if in *speech*, a girl gives way to undue levity, depend upon it the devil has got one of his cloven feet in her heart already—So, Hickman, take care of thyself, I advise thee, whether I marry or not.

Thus, Jack, have I at once reconciled myself to all my relations—and, if the lady refuses me, thrown the fault upon her. This, I knew, would be in my power to do at any time: and I was the more arrogant to them, in order to heighten the merit of my compliance.

But after all, it would be very whimsical, would it not, if all my plots and contrivances should end in wedlock? What a punishment would this come out to be, upon myself too, that all this while I have been plundering my own treasury?

But, Jack, two things I must insist upon with thee, if this is to be the case— Having put secrets of so high a nature between me and my spouse into thy power, I must, for my own honour and the honour of my wife and my illustrious progeny, first oblige thee to give up the letters I have so profusely scribbled to thee; and, in the next place, do by thee as I have heard whispered in France was done by the *true* father of a certain monarque[1]; that is to say, cut thy throat to prevent thy telling of tales.

I have found means to heighten the kind opinion my friends here have begun to have of me, by communicating to them the contents of the four last letters which I wrote to press my elected spouse to solemnize. My lord has repeated one of his phrases in my favour, that he hopes it will come out, *That the devil is not quite so black as he is painted.*

Now prithee, dear Jack, since so many good consequences are to flow from these our nuptials (one of which to *thyself*; since the sooner thou diest, the less thou wilt have to answer for); and that I now and then am apt to believe there may be something in the old fellow's notion, who once told us that he who kills a man has all that man's sins to answer for, as well as his own, because he gave him not the time to repent of them that Heaven designed to allow him (A fine thing for thee, if thou consentest to be knocked of the head; but a cursed one for the manslayer!); and since there may be room to fear that Miss Howe will not give us her help; I prithee now exert thyself to find out my Clarissa Harlowe, that I may make a LOVELACE of her. Set all the city bellmen, and the country criers for ten miles round the metropolis, at work, with their 'Oh yes's! and if any man, woman or child can give tale or tidings'—Advertise her in all the newspapers; and let her know, 'That if she will repair to Lady Betty Lawrance, or to Miss Charlotte Montague, she may hear of something greatly to her advantage.'

MY two cousins Montague are actually to set out tomorrow to Mrs Howe's, to engage her vixen daughter's interest with her friend: to flaunt it away in a chariot and six for the greater state and significance.

Confounded mortification to be reduced thus low!—My pride hardly knows how to brook it.

Lord M. has engaged the two venerables to stay here, to attend the issue: and I, standing very high at present in their good graces, am to gallant them to Oxford, to Blenheim, and several other places.

Letter 327: MISS HOWE TO MISS CLARISSA HARLOWE

Thursday night, July 13

COLLINS sets not out tomorrow. Some domestic occasion hinders him. Rogers is but now returned from you, and cannot well be spared. Mr Hickman is gone upon an affair of my mother's, and has taken both his servants with him to do credit to his employer: so I am forced to venture this by the post, directed by your assumed name.

I am to acquaint you that I have been favoured with a visit from Miss Montague and her sister, in Lord M.'s chariot and six. My lord's gentleman rode here yesterday with a request that I would receive a visit from the two young ladies, on a *very particular occasion*; the greater favour if it might be the next day.

As I had so little personal knowledge of either, I doubted not but it must be in relation to the interests of my dear friend; and so consulting with my mother, I sent them an invitation to favour me (because of the distance) with their company at dinner; which they kindly accepted.

I hope, my dear, since things have been so *very* bad, that their errand to me will be as agreeable to you as anything that can now happen. They came in the name of Lord M. and his two sisters, to desire my interest to engage you to put yourself into the protection of Lady Betty Lawrance; who will not part with you till she sees all the justice done you that now can be done.

Lady Sarah Sadleir had not stirred out for a twelve-month before, never since she lost her agreeable daughter, whom you and I saw at Mrs Benson's: but was induced to take this journey by her sister, purely to procure you reparation, if possible. And their joint strength, united with Lord M.'s, has so far succeeded, that the wretch has bound himself to them, and to these young ladies, in the solemnest manner, to wed you in their presence if they can prevail upon you to give him your hand.

This consolation you may take to yourself, that all this honourable family have a *due*, that is the *highest*, sense of your merit, and greatly admire you. The horrid creature has not spared himself in doing justice to your virtue; and the young ladies gave us such an account of his confessions, and self-condemnation, that my mother was quite charmed with you; and we all four shed tears of joy that there is one of our sex (I, that that one is my dearest friend), who has done so much honour to it as to deserve the self-convicted praises he gave you; though pity for the excellent creature mixed with the sensibility.

He promises by them to make the best of husbands; and my lord and his two sisters are both to be guarantees that he will be so. Noble settlements, noble presents, they talked of: they say they left Lord M. and his two sisters talking of nothing else but of those presents and settlements, how most to do you honour, the greater in proportion for the indignities you have suffered; and of changing of names by Act of Parliament, preparative to the interest they will all join to make to get the titles to go where the bulk of the estate must go at my lord's death, which they apprehend to be nearer than they wish. Nor doubt they of a thorough reformation in his morals from your example and influence over him.

I made a great many objections for you—all, I believe, that you could have made yourself, had you been present. But I have no doubt to advise you, my dear (and so does my mother), instantly to put yourself into Lady Betty's protection, with a resolution to take the wretch for your husband: all his future grandeur (he wants not pride) depends upon his sincerity to you; and the young ladies vouch for the depth of his concern for the wrongs he has done you.

All his apprehension is in your readiness to communicate to everyone, as he fears, the evils you have suffered; which he thinks will expose you both. But had you not revealed them to Lady Betty, you had not had so warm a friend; since it is owing to two letters you wrote to her, that all this good, as I hope it will prove, was brought about. But I advise you to be more sparing in exposing what is past, whether you have thoughts of accepting him or not: for what, my dear, can that avail now but to give a handle to vile wretches to triumph over your friends; since everyone will not know how much to your honour your very sufferings have been?

Your melancholy letter brought by Rogers,*a* with his account of your indifferent health, confirmed to Rogers by the woman of the house, as well as by your looks and by your faintness while you talked with him, would have given me inexpressible affliction, had I not been cheered by this agreeable visit from the young ladies. I hope you will be equally so, on my imparting the subject of it to you.

Indeed, my dear, you must not hesitate: you *must* oblige them: the alliance is splendid and honourable. Very few will know anything of his brutal baseness to you. All must end in a little while in a genteel reconciliation; and you will be able to resume your course of doing the good to every deserving object, which procured you blessings wherever you set your foot.

I am concerned to find that your father's rash wish affects you so much as it does. Upon my word, my dear, your mind is weakened grievously. You must not, indeed you must not, desert yourself. The penitence you talk of—It is for *them* to be penitent who hurried you into evils you could not well avoid. You judge by the unhappy event rather than upon the true merits of your case. Upon my honour, I think you faultless in almost every step you have taken. What has not that vilely insolent and ambitious, yet stupid, brother of yours to answer for?—that spiteful thing your sister too!—

· But come, since what is past cannot be helped, let us look forward. You have now happy prospects opening to you: a family, *already noble*, ready to receive and embrace you with open arms and joyful hearts; and who, by their love to you, will teach another family (who know not what an excellence they have confederated to persecute) how to value you. Your prudence, your piety, will crown all: it will reclaim a wretch that for an hundred sakes more than for his own one would wish to be reclaimed.

Like a traveller who has been put out of his way by the overflowing of some rapid stream, you have only had the fore-right path you were in overwhelmed. A few miles about, a day or two only lost, as I may say, and you are in a way to recover it; and, by quickening your speed, will get up the lost time. The hurry upon your spirits, meantime, will be all your inconvenience; for it was not your fault you were stopped in your progress.

Think of this, my dear; and improve upon the allegory, as you know how. If you can, without impeding your progress, be the means of assuaging the inundation,

a See Letter 320, p. 1021, preceding.

of bounding the waters within their natural channel, and thereby of recovering the overwhelmed path for the sake of future passengers who travel the same way, what a merit will yours be!—

I shall impatiently expect your next letter. The young ladies proposed that you should put yourself, if in town, or near it, into the Reading stage-coach, which inns somewhere in Fleet Street: and if you give notice of the day, you will be met on the road, and that pretty early in your journey, by some of both sexes; one of whom you won't be sorry to see.

Mr Hickman shall attend you at Slough; and Lady Betty herself, and one of the Misses Montague, with proper equipages, will be at Reading to receive you; and carry you directly to the seat of the former: for I have expressly stipulated that the wretch himself shall not come into your presence till your nuptials are to be solemnized, unless you give leave.

Adieu, my dearest friend: be happy: and hundreds will then be happy of consequence. Inexpressibly so, I am sure, will then be

Your ever-affectionate
ANNA HOWE

Letter 328: MISS HOWE TO MISS CLARISSA HARLOWE

Sunday night, July 16

My dearest friend,

WHY would you permit a mind so much devoted to your service to labour under such an impatience as you must know it *would* labour under, for want of an answer to a letter of such consequence to *you*, and therefore to *me?*—Rogers told me last Thursday, you were *so* ill: your letter sent by him was *so* melancholy!—Yet you must be ill indeed, if you could not write something to such a letter; were it but a line to say you would write as soon as you could. Sure you have received it. The master of our nearest post office will pawn his reputation that it went safe: I gave him particular charge of it.

God send me good news of your health, of your ability to write; and then I will chide you—indeed I will—as I never yet did chide you.

I suppose your excuse will be that the subject required consideration—Lord! my dear, so it might: but you have so right a mind, and the matter in question is so obvious, that you could not want half an hour to determine—Then you intended, probably, to wait Collins's call for your letter as on tomorrow!—Suppose—Miss!— (indeed I am angry with you! suppose) something were to happen, as it did on Friday, that he should not be able to go to town tomorrow?—How, child, could you serve me so?—I know not how to leave off scolding you!

Dear, honest Collins, make haste. He will: he will. He sets out, and travels all night: for I have told him that the dearest friend I have in the world has it in her own choice to be happy, and to make me so; and that the letter he will bring from her will assure it to me.

I have ordered him to go directly (without stopping at the Saracen's Head inn) to you at your lodgings. Matters are now in so good a way, that he safely may.

Your expected letter is ready written, I hope: if it be not, he will call for it at your hour.

You can't be so happy as you deserve to be: but I doubt not that you will be as happy as you *can*; that is, that you will choose to put yourself instantly into Lady Betty's protection. If you would not have him for *your own* sake; have him you must, for *mine*, for your *family*'s for your *honour*'s sake!—Dear, honest Collins, make haste! make haste! and relieve the impatient heart of my beloved's

Ever-faithful, ever-affectionate,
ANNA HOWE

Letter 329: MISS HOWE TO MISS CHARLOTTE MONTAGUE

Tuesday morning, July 18

Madam,

I TAKE the liberty to write to you, by this special messenger: in the frenzy of my soul I write to you, to demand of you, and of any of your family who can tell, news of my beloved friend; who, I doubt, has been spirited away by the base arts of one of the blackest—Oh help me to a name bad enough to call him by!—Her piety is proof against self-attempts: it must, it must be him, the only him who could injure such an innocent; and now—who knows what he has done with her!

If I have patience, I will give you the occasion of this distracted vehemence.

I wrote to her the very moment you and your sister left me. But being unable to procure a special messenger, as I intended, was forced to send by the post. I urged her (you know, I promised, that I would), I urged her with earnestness, to comply with the desires of all your family. Having no answer, I wrote again on Sunday night; and sent it by a particular hand, who travelled all night; chiding her for keeping a heart so impatient as mine in such cruel suspense upon a matter of so much importance to her; and therefore to me. And very angry I was with her in my mind.

But, judge my astonishment, my distraction, when last night, the messenger, returning post-haste, brought me word that she had not been heard of since Friday morning! And that a letter lay for her at her lodgings, which came by the post; and must be mine.

She went out about six that morning; only intending, as they believe, to go to morning prayers at Covent Garden church, just by her lodgings, as she had done divers times before. Went on foot!—Left word she should be back in an hour—Very poorly in health!

Lord, have mercy upon me! What shall I do!—I was a distracted creature all last night!

Oh madam! You know not how I love her!—She was my earthly saviour, as I may say!—My own soul is not dearer to me than my Clarissa Harlowe!—Nay, she *is* my soul!—for I now have none!—only a miserable one, however!—for she was the joy, the stay, the prop of my life! Never woman loved woman as we love one another! It is impossible to tell you half her excellencies. It was my glory and my pride that I was capable of so fervent a love of so pure and matchless a creature!— But now!—Who knows whether the dear injured has not all her woes, her undeserved woes! completed in death; or is not reserved for a worse fate!—This I leave to your inquiry—for—your—(shall I call the man—your) relation, I understand, is still with you.

Surely, my good ladies, you were well authorized in the proposals you made me in presence of my mother! Surely he dare not abuse your confidence, and the confidence of your noble relations. I make no apology for giving you this trouble, nor for desiring you to favour with a line by this messenger

> Your almost distracted
> ANNA HOWE

Letter 330: MR LOVELACE TO JOHN BELFORD, ESQ.

> M. Hall, Sat. night, July 15

ALL undone, undone, by Jupiter!—Zounds, Jack, what shall I do now! A curse upon all my plots and contrivances!—But I have it!—in the very heart and soul of me, I have it!

Thou toldest me that my punishments were but beginning!—Canst thou, oh fatal prognosticator! canst thou tell me where they will end?

Thy assistance I bespeak: the moment thou receivest this, I bespeak thy assistance. This messenger rides for life and death!—and I hope he'll find you at your town lodgings; if he meet not with you at Edgware; where, being Sunday, he will call first.

This cursed, cursed woman, on Friday dispatched man and horse with the joyful news, as she thought it would be to me, in an exulting letter from Sally Martin, that she had found out my angel as on Wednesday last; and on Friday morning, after she had been at prayers at Covent Garden church—praying for my reformation, perhaps!—got her arrested by two sheriff's officers as she was returning to her lodgings, who put her into a chair they had in readiness, and carried her to one of the cursed fellows' houses.

She has arrested her for £150 pretendedly due for board and lodgings: a sum, besides the low villainy of the proceeding, which the dear soul could not possibly raise; all her clothes and effects, except what she had on and with her when she went away, being at the old devil's!

And here, for an aggravation, has the dear creature lain already two days; for I must be gallanting my two aunts and my two cousins, and giving Lord M. an airing after his lying-in: pox upon the whole family of us!—and returned not till within this hour: and now returned to my distraction, on receiving the cursed tidings, and the exulting letter.

Hasten, hasten, dear Jack; for the love of God, hasten to the injured charmer! My heart bleeds for her!—She deserved not this!—I dare not stir!—It will be thought done by my contrivance—and if I am absent from this place, that will confirm the suspicion.

Damnation seize quick this accursed woman!—Yet she thinks she has made no small merit with me!—Unhappy, thrice unhappy circumstance!—At a time too, when better prospects were opening for the sweet creature!

Hasten to her!—Clear me of this cursed job. Most sincerely, by all that's sacred,

I swear you may!—Yet have I been such a villainous plotter that the charming sufferer will hardly believe it; although the proceeding be so dirtily low!

Set her free the moment you see her: without conditioning, free!—On your knees, for me, beg her pardon: and assure her that, wherever she goes, I will not molest her: no, nor come near her without her leave: and be sure allow not any of the damned crew to go near her—Only, let her permit *you* to receive her commands from time to time: you have always been her friend and advocate. What would I now give, had I permitted you to have been a successful one!

Let her have all her clothes and effects sent her instantly, as a small proof of my sincerity. And force upon the dear creature, who must be moneyless, what sums you can get her to take. Let me know how she has been treated: if roughly, woe be to the guilty!

Take thy watch in thy hand, after thou hast freed her, and damn the whole brood, dragon and serpents, by the hour, till thou'rt tired: and tell them I bid thee do so for their cursed officiousness.

They had nothing to do, when they had found her, but to wait my orders how to proceed.

The great devil fly away with them all, one by one, through the roof of their own cursed house, and dash them to pieces against the tops of chimneys, as he flies; and let the lesser devils collect their scattered scraps, and bag them up, in order to put them together again in their allotted place, in the element of fire, with cements of molten lead.

A line! a line! a kingdom for a line! with tolerable news, the first moment thou canst write!—This fellow waits to bring it.

Letter 331: MISS CHARLOTTE MONTAGUE TO MISS HOWE

M. Hall, Tuesday afternoon

Dear Miss HOWE,

YOUR letter has infinitely disturbed us all.

This wretched man has been half distracted ever since Saturday night.

We knew not what ailed him, till your letter was brought.

Vile wretch as he is, he is however innocent of this new evil.

Indeed he is, he *must* be; as I shall more at large acquaint you.

But will not now detain your messenger.

Only to satisfy your just impatience, by telling you that the dear young lady is safe, and, we hope, well.

A horrid mistake of his general orders has subjected her to the terror and disgrace of an arrest.

Poor dear Miss Harlowe! her sufferings have endeared her to us, almost as much as her excellencies can have done to you.

But she must be now quite at liberty.

He has been a distracted man ever since the news was brought him; and we knew not what ailed him.

But that I said before.

My Lord M., my Lady Sarah Sadleir, and my Lady Betty Lawrance, will all write to you this very afternoon.

And so will the wretch himself.

And send it by a servant of their own, not to detain yours.

I know not what I write.

But you shall have all the particulars, just, and true, and fair, from,

Dear madam,
Your most faithful and obedient servant,
CH. MONTAGUE

Letter 332: MISS MONTAGUE TO MISS HOWE

M. Hall, July 18

Dear madam,

IN pursuance of my promise, I will minutely inform you of everything we know, relating to this shocking transaction.

When we returned from you on Thursday night, and made our report of the kind reception both we and our message met with, in that you had been so good as to promise to use your interest with your dear friend; it put us all into such good humour with one another, and with my cousin Lovelace, that we resolved upon a little tour of two days, the Friday and Saturday, in order to give an airing to my lord, and Lady Sarah; both having been long confined, one by illness, the other by melancholy. My lord, his two sisters, and myself, were in the coach; and all our talk was of dear Miss Harlowe, and of our future happiness with her. Mr Lovelace, and my sister who is his favourite, as he is hers, were in his phaeton: and whenever we joined company, that was still the subject.

As to him, never man praised a lady as he did her: never man gave greater hopes, and made better resolutions. He is none of those that are governed by interest. He is too proud for that. But most sincerely delighted was he in talking of her; and of his hopes of her returning favour. He said, however, more than once, that he feared she would not forgive him; for, from his heart, he must say he deserved not her forgiveness: and often, and often, that there was not such a woman in the world.

This I mention to show you, madam, that he could not at this very time be privy to such a barbarous and disgraceful treatment.

We returned not till Saturday night, all in as good humour with one another as we went out. We never had such pleasure in his company before: if he would be good, and as he ought to be, no man would be better beloved by relations than he. But never was there a greater alteration in man when he came home, and received a letter from a messenger, who, it seems, had been flattering himself in hopes of a reward, and had been waiting for his return from the night before. In *such* a fury!—The man fared but badly. He instantly shut himself up to write, and ordered man and horse to be ready to set out before day-light the next morning, to carry the letter to a friend in London.

He would not see us all that night; neither breakfast nor dine with us next day. He ought, he said, never to see the light; and bid my sister, whom he called an *innocent* (and she being very desirous to know the occasion of all this), shun him;

saying he was a wretch, and made so by his own inventions, and the consequences of them.

None of us could get out of him what so disturbed him. We should too soon hear, he said, to the utter dissipation of all *his* hopes, and all *ours*.

We could easily suppose that all was not right with regard to the worthy young lady.

He was out each day; and said he wanted to run away from himself.

Late on Monday night he received a letter from Mr Belford, his most favoured friend, by his own messenger; who came back in a foam, man and horse. Whatever were the contents, he was not easier, but like a madman rather: but still would not let us know the occasion. But to my sister, he said, Nobody, my dear Patsey, who can think but of half the plagues that pursue an intriguing spirit, would ever quit the right path.

He was out when your messenger came: but soon came in; and bad enough was his reception from us all. And he said that his own torments were greater than ours, than Miss Harlowe's, or yours, madam, all put together. He would see your letter. He always carries everything before him: and said when he had read it that he thanked God he was not such a villain as you, with too much reason, thought him.

Thus then he owned the matter to be:

He had left general directions to the people of the lodgings the dear lady went from, to find out where she was gone to, if possible, that he might have an opportunity to importune her to be his, before their difference was public. The wicked people, *officious* at least, if not wicked, discovered where she was on Wednesday; and, for fear she should remove before they could have his orders, they put her under a *gentle restraint*, as they call it; and dispatched away a messenger to acquaint him with it; and to take his orders.

This messenger arrived here on Friday afternoon; and tarried till we returned on Saturday night—And when he read the letter he brought—I have told you, madam, what a fury he was in.

The letter he retired to write, and which he dispatched away so early on Sunday morning, was to conjure his friend Mr Belford, on receipt of it, to fly to the lady, and set her free; and to order all her things to be sent her; and to clear him of so black and villainous a fact, as he justly called it.

And by this time, he doubts not that all is happily over; and the beloved of his soul (as he calls her at every word) in an easier and happier way than she was before the horrid fact. And now he owns that the reason why Mr Belford's letter set him into stronger ravings was because of his keeping him wilfully, and on purpose to torment him, in suspense; and reflecting very heavily upon him (for Mr Belford, he says, was ever the lady's friend and advocate), and only mentioning that he had waited upon her; referring to his next for further particulars; which he could have told him at the time.

He declares, and we can vouch for him, that he has been ever since last Saturday night the miserablest of men.

He forbore going up himself, that it might not be imagined he was guilty of so black a contrivance; and went up to complete any base views in consequence of it.

Believe us all, dear Miss Howe, under the deepest concern at this unhappy accident; which will, we fear, exasperate the charming sufferer; not too much for the occasion, but too much for our hopes.

Oh what wretches are these free-living men who love to tread in intricate paths; and, when once they err, know not how far out of the way their headstrong course may lead them!

My sister joins her thanks with mine to your good mother and self, for the favours you heaped upon us last Thursday. We beseech your continued interest as to the subject of our visit. It shall be all our studies to oblige and recompense the dear lady to the utmost of our power, for what she has suffered from the unhappy man.

We are, dear madam,

Your obliged and faithful servants,
CHARLOTTE ⎱
MARTHA   ⎰ MONTAGUE

[*Letter 332.1: Lady Sarah Sadleir and Lady Elizabeth Lawrance to Anna Howe*]

Dear Miss HOWE,
WE join in the above request of Miss Charlotte and Miss Patty Montague for your favour and interest; being convinced that the accident was an accident; and no plot or contrivance of a wretch too full of them. We are, madam,

Your most obedient humble servants,
M.
SARAH SADLEIR
ELIZ. LAWRANCE

[*Letter 332.2: Lovelace to Anna Howe*]

Dear Miss HOWE,
AFTER what is written above, by names and characters of such unquestionable honour, I might have been excused signing a name almost as hateful to myself, as I KNOW it is to you. But the above will have it so. Since therefore I *must* write, it shall be the truth; which is, that if I may be once more admitted to pay my duty to the most deserving and most injured of her sex, I will be content to do it with a halter about my neck; and attended by a parson on my right hand, and the hangman on my left, be doomed, at her will, either to the church or the gallows.

Your most humble servant,
Tuesday, July 18   ROBT. LOVELACE

Letter 333: MR BELFORD TO ROBERT LOVELACE, ESQ.

Sunday night, July 16
WHAT a cursed piece of work hast thou made of it, with the most excellent of women! Thou mayest be in earnest, or in jest, as thou wilt; but the poor lady will not be long either thy sport, or the sport of fortune!

I will give thee an account of a scene that wants but her affecting pen to represent it justly; and it would wring all the black blood out of thy callous heart.

Thou only, who art the author of her calamities, shouldst have attended her in her prison. I am unequal to such a task: nor know I any other man but would.

This last act, however unintended by thee, yet a consequence of thy general orders, and too likely to be thought agreeable to thee by those who know thy other villainies by her, has finished thy barbarous work. And I advise thee to trumpet forth everywhere, how much in earnest thou art to marry her, whether thou art or not.

Thou mayest *safely* do it. She will not live to put thee to the trial; and it will a little palliate for thy enormous usage of her, and be a means to make mankind, who know not what I know of the matter, herd a little longer with thee, and forbear to hunt thee to thy fellow-savages in the Libyan wilds and deserts.

Your messenger found me at Edgware, expecting to dinner with me several friends, whom I had invited three days before. I sent apologies to them, as in a case of life and death; and speeded to town to the wicked woman's: for how knew I but shocking attempts might be made upon her by the cursed wretches; perhaps by thy contrivance, in order to mortify her into thy measures?

Little knows the public what villainies are committed in these abominable houses, upon innocent creatures drawn into their snares!

Finding the lady not there, I posted away to the officer's, although Sally told me that she had been but just come from thence; and that she had refused to see her, or, as she sent down word, anybody else; being resolved to have the remainder of that Sunday to herself, as it might, perhaps, be the last she should ever see.

I had the same thing told me when I got thither.

I sent up to let her know that I came with a commission to set her at liberty. I was afraid of sending up the name of a man known to be thy friend. She absolutely refused to see *any man*, however, for that day, or to answer further to anything said from me.

Having therefore informed myself of all that the officer, and his wife and servant, could acquaint me with, as well in relation to the horrid arrest, as to her behaviour, and the women's to her; and her ill state of health; I went back to Sinclair's, as I will still call her, and heard the three women's story: from all which I am enabled to give thee the following shocking particulars: which may serve till I can see the unhappy lady herself tomorrow, if then I can gain admittance to her. Thou wilt find that I have been very minute in my inquiries.

Thy villain it was, that set the poor lady, and had the impudence to appear and abet the sheriff's officers in the cursed transaction. He thought, no doubt, that he was doing the most acceptable service to his blessed master. They had got a chair; the head ready up, as soon as service was over. And as she came out of the church, at the door fronting Bedford Street, the officers stepping to her, whispered that they had an action against her.

She was terrified, trembled, and turned pale.

Action! said she. What is that?—I have committed *no bad action!*—Lord bless me! Men, what mean you?

That you are our prisoner, madam.

Prisoner, sirs!—What—How—Why—What have I done?

You must go with us. Be pleased, madam, to step into this chair.

With *you!*—With *men!*—Must go with *men!*—I am not used to go with *strange men!*—Indeed you must excuse me!

We can't excuse you: we are sheriff's officers—We have a writ against you. You *must* go with us, and you shall know at whose suit.

Suit! said the charming innocent; I don't know what you mean. Pray, men, don't lay hands upon me!—They offering to put her into the chair. I am not used to be thus treated!—I have done nothing to deserve it.

She then spied thy villain—Oh thou wretch, said she, where is thy vile master?—Am I again to be *his* prisoner? Help, good people!

A crowd had before begun to gather.

My master is in the country, madam, many miles off: if you please to go with these men, they will treat you civilly.

The people were most of them struck with compassion. A fine young creature!—A thousand pities! some—while some few threw out vile and shocking reflections: but a gentleman interposed, and demanded to see the fellows' authority.

They showed it. Is your name Clarissa Harlowe, madam? said he.

Yes, yes, indeed, ready to sink, my name *was* Clarissa Harlowe—but it is now *Wretchedness!*—Lord, be merciful to me! what is to come next?

You *must* go with these men, madam, said the gentleman: they have authority for what they do. He pitied her, and retired.

Indeed you must, said one chairman.

Indeed you must, said the other.

Can nobody, joined in another gentleman, be applied to, who will see that so fine a creature is not ill used?

Thy villain answered, Orders were given particularly for that. She had rich relations. She need but ask and have. She would only be carried to the officer's house, till matters could be made up. The people she had lodged with, loved her: but she had left her lodgings privately.

Oh! had she those tricks already? cried one or two.

She heard not this—but said, Well, if I must go, I must!—I cannot resist—But I will not be carried to the woman's!—I will rather die at your feet, than be carried to the woman's!

You won't be carried there, madam, cried thy fellow.

Only to *my* house, madam, said one of the officers.

Where is that?

In High Holborn, madam.

I know not where High Holborn is: but anywhere, except to the woman's—But am I to go with *men* only?

Looking about her, and seeing the three passages, to wit, that leading to Henrietta Street, that to King Street, and the fore-right one, to Bedford Street, crowded, she started—Anywhere—anywhere, said she, but to the woman's! And stepping into the chair, threw herself on the seat, in the utmost distress and confusion—Carry me, carry me out of sight—Cover me—Cover me up—for ever!—were her words.

Thy villain drew the curtains: she had not power; and they went away with her, through a vast crowd of people.

Here I must rest. I can write no more at present. Only, Lovelace, remember, *all this was to a Clarissa!!!*

THE unhappy lady fainted away when she was taken out of the chair at the officer's house.

Several people followed the chair to the very house, which is in a wretched court. Sally was there; and satisfied some of the inquirers that the young gentlewoman would be exceedingly well used: and they soon dispersed.

Dorcas was also there; but came not in her sight. Sally, as a favour, offered to carry her to her former lodgings: but she declared they should carry her thither a corpse, if they did.

Very gentle usage the women boast of: so would a vulture, could it speak, with the entrails of its prey upon its rapacious talons. Of this thou'lt judge, from what I have to recite.

She asked, What was meant by this usage of her?—People told me, said she, that I *must* go with the men!—that they had authority to take me: so I submitted. But now, what is to be the end of this disgraceful violence?

The end, said the vile Sally Martin, is for honest people to come at their own.

Bless me! Have I taken away anything that belongs to those who have obtained this power over me?—I have left very valuable things behind me; but have taken nothing away that is not my own.

And who do you think, *Miss Harlowe*, for I understand, said the cursed creature, you are not married; who do you think is to pay for your board and your lodgings; such handsome lodgings! for so long a time as you were at Mrs Sinclair's?

Lord have mercy upon me! Miss Martin (I think you are Miss Martin)!—and is this the cause of such a disgraceful insult upon me in the open streets?

And cause enough, *Miss Harlowe* (fond of gratifying her jealous revenge by calling her *Miss*)—One hundred and fifty guineas, or pounds, is no small sum to lose—and by a young creature, who would have bilked her lodgings!

You amaze me, Miss Martin!—What language do you talk in?—*Bilk my lodgings!*—What is that?

She stood astonished and silent for a few moments.

But recovering herself, and turning from her to the window, she wrung her hands (the cursed Sally showed me how!); and lifting them up—*Now*, Lovelace! Now indeed do I think I *ought* to forgive thee!—But who shall forgive Clarissa Harlowe!—Oh my sister! Oh my brother! Tender mercies were your cruelties to *this!*

After a pause, her handkerchief drying up her falling tears, she turned to Sally! *Now*, have I nothing to do but acquiesce—only let me say that if this aunt of yours, this Mrs Sinclair; or this man, this Mr Lovelace; come near me; or if I am carried to the horrid house (for that I suppose is to be the end of this new outrage); God be merciful to the poor Clarissa Harlowe!—look to the consequence!—look, I charge you, to the consequence!

The vile wretch told her it was not designed to carry her anywhither against her will: but, if it were, they should take care not to be frighted again by a *penknife*.

She cast up her eyes to heaven, and was silent—and went to the farthest corner of the room and, sitting down, threw her handkerchief over her face.

Sally asked her several questions: but not answering her, she told her she would wait upon her by and by, when she had found her speech.

She ordered the people to press her to eat and drink. She must be fasting:

nothing but her prayers and tears, poor thing! were the merciless devil's words, as she owned to me—Dost think I did not curse her?

She went away; and, after her own dinner, returned.

The unhappy lady, by this devil's account of her, then seemed either mortified into meekness, or to have made a resolution not to be provoked by the insults of this cursed creature.

Sally inquired, in her presence, whether she had eat or drank anything; and being told by the woman that she could not prevail upon her to taste a morsel, or drink a drop, she said, This is wrong, *Miss Harlowe!* Very wrong!—Your religion, I think, should teach you that starving yourself is self-murder.

She answered not.

The wretch owned she was resolved to make her speak.

She asked if Mabel should attend her till it were seen what her friends would do for her, in discharge of the debt? Mabel, said she, has not *yet* earned the clothes you were so good as to give her.

Am I not worth an answer, *Miss Harlowe?*

I would answer you (said the sweet sufferer, without any emotion), if I knew how.

I have ordered pen, ink and paper, to be brought you, *Miss Harlowe*. There they are. I know you love writing. You may write to whom you please. Your friend Miss Howe will expect to hear from you.

I have no friend, said she. I deserve none.

Rowland, for that is the officer's name, told her, she had friends enow to pay the debt, if she would write.

She would trouble nobody; she had no friends; was all they could get from her, while Sally stayed: but yet spoken with a patience of spirit as if she enjoyed her griefs.

The insolent creature went away, ordering them in her hearing to be very civil to her, and to let her want for nothing. Now had she, she owned, the triumph of her heart over this haughty beauty, who kept them all at such a distance in their own house!

What thinkest thou, Lovelace, of this!—This wretch's triumph was over a Clarissa!

About six in the evening, Rowland's wife pressed her to drink tea. She said she had rather have a glass of water; for her tongue was ready to cleave to the roof of her mouth.[1]

The woman brought her a glass, and some bread and butter. She tried to taste the latter; but could not swallow it: but eagerly drank the water; lifting up her eyes in thankfulness for that!!!

The divine Clarissa, Lovelace—reduced to rejoice for a cup of cold water!—By whom *reduced!*

About nine o'clock she asked if anybody were to be her bedfellow?

Their maid, if she pleased; or, as she was so weak and ill, the girl should sit up with her, if she chose she should.

She chose to be alone, both night and day, she said. But might she not be trusted with the keys of the room where she was to lie down; for she should not put off her clothes?

That, they told her, could not be.

She was afraid not, she said—But indeed she would not get away, if she could.

They told me that they had but one bed, besides that they lay in themselves (which they would fain have had her accept of), and besides *that* their maid lay in, in a garret, which they called a hole of a garret: and that *that* one bed was the prisoner's bed; which they made several apologies to me about. I suppose it is shocking enough.

But the lady would not lie in theirs. Was she not a prisoner, she said?—Let her have the prisoner's room.

Yet they owned that she started when she was conducted thither. But recovering herself, Very well, said she—Why should not all be of a piece?—Why should not my wretchedness be complete?

She found fault that all the fastenings were on the outside, and none within; and said she could not trust herself in a room where others could come in at their pleasure, and she not go out. She had not *been used* to it!!!

Dear, dear soul!—My tears flow as I write—Indeed, Lovelace, she had not been used to such treatment!

They assured her that it was as much their duty to protect her from other persons' insults, as from escaping herself.

Then they were people of more honour, she said, than she had of late been used to!

She asked if they knew Mr Lovelace?

No, was their answer.

Have you heard of him?

No.

Well then, you may be good sort of folks in your way.

Pause here a moment, Lovelace!—and reflect—I must.

AGAIN they asked her if they should send any word to her lodgings?

These are my lodgings now, are they not?—was all her answer.

She sat up in a chair all night, the back against the door; having, it seems, thrust a broken piece of a poker through the staples where a bolt had been on the inside.

NEXT morning Sally and Polly both went to visit her.

She had begged of Sally the day before, that she might not see Mrs Sinclair, nor Dorcas, nor the broken-toothed servant, called William.

Polly would have ingratiated herself with her; and pretended to be concerned for her misfortunes. But she took no more notice of her than of the other.

They asked if she had any commands?—If she *had*, she only need to mention what they were, and she should be obeyed.

None at all, she said.

How did she like the people of the house? Were they civil to her?

Pretty well, considering she had no money to give them.

Would she accept of any money? They could put it to her account.

She would contract no debts.

Had she any money about her?

She meekly put her hand in her pocket, and pulled out half a guinea, and a little silver. Yes, I have a little—But here should be fees paid, I believe. Should there not? I have heard of entrance money to compound for not being stripped. But these people are very civil people, I fancy; for they have not offered to take away my clothes.

They have *orders* to be civil to you.

It is very kind.

But we two will bail you, *miss*, if you will go back with us to Mrs Sinclair's.

Not for the world!

Hers are very handsome apartments.

The fitter for those who own them!

These are very sad ones.

The fitter for *me!*

You may be very happy yet, *miss*, if you will.

I hope I shall.

If you refuse to eat or drink, we will give bail, and take you with us.

Then I will *try* to eat and drink. Anything but go with you.

Will you not send to your new lodgings? The people will be frighted.

So they will, if I send. So they will, if they know where I am.

But have you no things to send for from thence?

There is what will pay for their lodgings and trouble: I shall not lessen their security.

But perhaps letters or messages may be left for you there.

I have very few friends; and to those I *have*, I will spare the mortification of knowing what has befallen me.

We are surprised at your indifference, *Miss* Harlowe. Will you not write to any of your friends?

No.

Why, you don't think of tarrying *here* always?

I shall not *live* always.

Do you think you are to stay here, as long as you live?

That's as it shall please God, and those who have brought me hither.

Should you like to be at liberty?

I am miserable!—What is liberty to the miserable, but to be *more* miserable!

How, miserable, *miss*?—You may make yourself as happy as you please.

I hope *you* are both happy.

We are.

May you be more and more happy!

But we wish *you* to be so too.

I never shall be of your opinion, I believe, as to what happiness is.

What do you take our opinion of happiness to be?

To live at Mrs Sinclair's.

Perhaps, said Sally, we were once as squeamish and narrow-minded as you.

How came it over with you?

Because we saw the ridiculousness of prudery.

Do you come hither to persuade me to hate prudery, as you call it, as much as you do?

We came to offer our service to you.

It is out of your power to serve me.

Perhaps not.

It is not in my inclination to trouble you.

You may be worse offered.

Perhaps I may.

You are mighty short, *miss*.

As I wish your visit to be, ladies.

They owned to me, that they cracked their fans and laughed.

Adieu, perverse beauty!

Your servant, ladies.

Adieu, Haughty-airs!

You see me humbled—

As you deserve, *Miss* Harlowe. Pride will have a fall.

Better fall with what *you* call pride, than stand with meanness.

Who does?

I had once a *better* opinion of *you*, Miss Horton!—Indeed you should not insult the miserable.

Neither should the *miserable*, said Sally, insult people for their civility.

I should be sorry if I did.

Mrs Sinclair shall attend you by and by, to know if you have any commands for *her*.

I have no wish for any liberty but that of refusing to see her, and *one* more person.

What we came for, was to know if you had any proposals to make for your enlargement?

Then, it seems, the officer put in. You have very good friends, madam, I understand. Is it not better that you make it up? Charges will run high. A hundred and fifty guineas are easier paid than two hundred. Let these ladies bail you, and go along with them; or write to your friends to make it up.

Sally said, There is a gentleman who saw you taken, and was so much moved for you, *Miss Harlowe*, that he would gladly advance the money for you, and leave you to pay it when you can.

See, Lovelace, what cursed devils these are! This is the way, we know, that many an innocent heart is thrown upon keeping, and then upon the town. But for these wretches thus to go to work with such an angel as this!—How glad would have been the devilish Sally to have had the least handle to report to thee a listening ear, or patient spirit, upon this hint!

Sir, said she, with high indignation to the officer, did not you say last night that it was as much your business to protect me from the insults of others, as from escaping?—Cannot I be permitted to see whom I please; and to refuse admittance to those I like not?

Your creditors, madam, will expect to see you.

Not if I declare I will not treat with them.

Then, madam, you will be sent to prison.

Prison, friend!—What dost thou call thy house?

Not a prison, madam.

Why these iron-barred windows then? Why these double locks, and bolts all on the outside, none on the in?

And down she dropped into her chair, and they could not get another word from her. She threw her handkerchief over her face, as once before, which was soon wet with tears; and grievously, they own, she sobbed.

Gentle treatment, Lovelace!—Perhaps thou, as well as these wretches, wilt think it so!

Sally then ordered a dinner, and said they would soon be back again, and see that she eat and drink as a good Christian should, comporting herself to her condition, and making the best of it.

What has not this charming creature suffered; what has she not come through in these last three months, that I know of!—Who would think such a delicately-framed person could have sustained what she has sustained? We sometimes talk of bravery, of courage, of fortitude!—Here they are in perfection!—Such bravoes as thou and I should never have been able to support ourselves under half the persecutions, the disappointments, and contumelies, that *she* has met with; but, like cowards, should have slid out of the world, basely, by some back door; that is to say, by a sword, by a pistol, by a halter, or knife!—But here is a fine-principled lady who, by dint of this noble consideration, as I imagine (what else can support her?)—that she has *not deserved the evils she contends with*; and that *this world is designed but as a transitory state of probation*; and that she is *travelling to another, and better*; puts up with all the hardships of the *journey*; and is not to be diverted from her course by the attacks of *thieves* and *robbers*, or any other terrors and difficulties; *being assured of an ample reward at the end of it!*

If thou thinkest this reflection uncharacteristic, from a companion and friend of thine, imaginest thou that I profited nothing by my attendance on my uncle for so long a time, in his dying state; and from the pious reflections of the good clergyman who, day by day, at the poor man's own request, visited and prayed by him?—And could I have another such instance *as this*, to bring all these reflections home to me?

Then who can write of good persons, and of good subjects, and be capable of *admiring them*, and not be made serious for the *time*, if he write in character?—And hence may we gather what a benefit to the morals of men the keeping of *good* company must be; while those who keep only *bad* must necessarily more and more harden, and be hardened.

'TIS twelve of the clock, Sunday night—I can think of nothing but of this excellent creature. Her distresses fill my head and my heart. I was drowsy for a quarter of an hour; but the fit is gone off. And I will continue the melancholy subject from the information of these wretches. Enough, I dare say, will arise in the visit I shall make, if admitted tomorrow, to send by thy servant, as to the way I am likely to find her in.

After the women had left her, she complained of her head and her heart; and seemed terrified with apprehensions of being carried once more to Sinclair's.

Refusing anything for breakfast, Mrs Rowland came up to her, and told her (as these wretches owned they had ordered her, for fear she should starve herself), that she *must* and *should* have tea, and bread and butter; and that, as she had friends who could support her if she wrote to them, it was a wrong thing both for herself and *them* to starve herself thus.

If it be for *your own sakes*, said she, that is another thing: let coffee, or tea, or chocolate, or what you will, be got: and put down a chicken to my account every day, if you please, and eat it yourselves. I will taste it, if I can. I would do nothing to hinder you: I have friends will pay you liberally, when they know I am gone.

They wondered at her strange composure, in such distresses.

They were nothing, she said, to what she had suffered already from the vilest of all men. The disgrace of seizing her in the street; multitudes of people about her; shocking imputations wounding her ears; had indeed been very affecting to her. But that was over—Everything soon would!—And she should be still *more* composed, were it not for the apprehensions of seeing one man, and one woman; and being tricked or forced back to the vilest house in the world.

Then were it not better to give way to the two gentlewomen's offer to bail her?— They could tell her, it was a very kind proffer; and what was not to be met with every day.

She believed so.

The ladies might, possibly, dispense with her going back to the house she had such an antipathy to. Then the compassionate gentleman, who was inclined to make it up with her creditors on her own bond, it was strange to them she hearkened not to so generous a proposal.

Did the two ladies tell you who the gentleman was?—or did they say any more on that subject?

Yes, they did; and hinted to me, said the woman, that you had nothing to do but to receive a visit from the gentleman, and the money they believed would be laid down on your own bond or note.

She was startled.

I charge you, said she, as you will answer it one day to my friends, that you bring no gentleman into my company. I charge you don't. If you do, you know not what may be the consequence.

They apprehended no bad consequence, they said, in doing their duty: and if she knew not her own good her friends would thank them for taking any innocent steps to serve her, though against her will.

Don't push me upon extremities, man!—Don't make me desperate, woman!— I have no small difficulty, notwithstanding the seeming composure you just now took notice of, to bear, as I ought to bear, the evils I suffer. But if you bring a man or men to me, be the pretence *what* it will—

She stopped there, and looked so earnestly, and so wildly, they said, that they did not know but she would do some harm to herself if they disobeyed her; and that would be a sad thing in *their* house, and might be their ruin. So they promised that no man should be brought to her, but by her own consent.

Mrs Rowland prevailed on her to drink a dish of tea, and taste some bread and butter, about eleven on Saturday morning: which she probably did to have an excuse not to dine with the women when they returned.

But she would not quit her *prison-room*, as she called it, to go into their parlour. 'Unbarred windows, and a lightsomer apartment, she said, had too cheerful an appearance for her mind.'

At another time, 'The light of the sun was irksome to her. The sun seemed to shine in to mock her woes.'

And when, soon after, a shower fell, she looked at it through the bars: 'How kindly, said she, do the elements weep, to keep me company!'

'Methought, added she, the sun darting in a while ago, and gilding those iron bars, played upon me like the two women who came to insult my haggard looks by the word *Beauty*; and my dejected heart, with the word *Haughty-airs!*'

Sally came again at dinner-time, *to see how she fared,* as she told her; and that she did not starve herself: and as she wanted to have some talk with her, if she gave her leave she would dine with her.

I cannot eat.

You must try, *Miss Harlowe.*

And, dinner being ready just then, she offered her hand, and desired her to walk down.

No; she would not stir out of her *prison-room.*

These sullen airs won't do, *Miss Harlowe:* indeed they won't.

She was silent.

You will have harder usage than any you have ever yet known, I can tell you, if you come not into some humour to make matters up.

She was still silent.

Come, *miss,* walk down to dinner. Let me entreat you, do. Miss Horton is below: she was once your favourite.

She waited for an answer: but received none.

We came to make some proposals to you, for your good; though you affronted us so lately. And we would not let Mrs Sinclair come in person, because we thought to oblige you.

That is indeed obliging.

Come, give me your hand, *Miss Harlowe.* You *are* obliged to me, I can tell you that: and let us go down to Miss Horton.

Excuse me: I will not stir out of this room.

Would you have me and Miss Horton dine in this filthy bedroom?

It is not a bedroom to me. I have not been in bed; nor will, while I am here.

And yet you care not, as I see, to leave the house—And so you won't go down, *Miss Harlowe?*

I won't, except I am forced to it.

Well, well, let it alone. I sha'nt ask Miss Horton to dine in this room, I assure you. I will send up a plate.

And away the little saucy toad fluttered down.

And when they had dined, up they came together.

Well, miss, you would not eat anything, it seems!—Very pretty sullen airs these!—No wonder *the honest gentleman had such a hand with you.*

She only held up her hands and eyes; the tears trickling down her cheeks.

Insolent devils!—How much more cruel and insulting are bad women, even than bad men!

Methinks, miss, said Sally, you are a little *soily,* to what we have seen you. Pity such a nice lady should not have changes of apparel. Why won't you send to your lodgings for linen, at least?

I am not nice now.

Miss looks well and clean in anything, said Polly. But, dear madam, why won't you send to your lodgings? It is but kind to the *people.* They must have a concern about you. And your Miss Howe will wonder what's become of you; for no doubt, you correspond.

She turned from them, and, to herself said, *Too much! Too much!*—She tossed her handkerchief, wet before with her tears, from her, and held her apron to her eyes.

Don't weep, miss! said the vile Polly.

Yet *do*, cried the viler Sally, if it be a relief. Nothing, as Mr Lovelace once told *me*, dries sooner than tears. For once I too wept mightily.

I could not bear the recital of this with patience. Yet I cursed them not so much as I should have done, had I not had a mind to get from them all the particulars of their *gentle* treatment; and this for two reasons; the one, that I might stab thee to the heart with the repetition; the other, that I might know upon what terms I am likely to see the unhappy lady tomorrow.

Well, but, *Miss Harlowe*, cried Sally, do you think these *forlorn airs* pretty? You are a good Christian, child. Mrs Rowland tells me she has got you a Bible book— Oh there it lies!—I make no doubt but you have doubled down the *useful places*, as honest Matt Prior says.[2]

Then rising, and taking it up—Ay, so you have—The *Book of Job!* One opens naturally here, I see—*My* mamma made me a fine Bible scholar.—*Ecclesiasticus* too!—That's Apocrypha, as they call it—You see, Miss Horton, I know something of the book.

They proposed once more to bail her, and to go home with them. A motion which she received with the same indignation as before.

Sally told her that she had written in a very favourable manner, in her behalf, to you; and that she every hour expected an answer; and made no doubt that you would come up with the messenger, and generously pay the whole debt, and ask her pardon for neglecting it.

This disturbed her so much, that they feared she would have fallen into fits. She could not bear your name, she said. She hoped she should never see you more: and were you to intrude yourself, dreadful consequences might follow.

Surely, they said, she would be glad to be released from her confinement.

Indeed she *should*, now they had begun to alarm her with *his* name, who was the author of all her woes: and who, she now saw plainly, gave way to this new outrage in order to bring her to his own infamous terms.

Why then, they asked, would she not write to her friends to pay Mrs Sinclair's demand?

Because she hoped she should not long trouble anybody: and because she knew that the payment of the money, if she were able to pay it, was not what was aimed at.

Sally owned that she told her that, truly, she had thought herself as well descended and as well educated as herself, though not entitled to such considerable fortunes. And had the impudence to insist upon it to me to be truth.

She had the insolence to add to the lady, that she had as much reason as *she*, to expect Mr Lovelace would marry her; he having contracted to do so *before* he knew Miss Clarissa Harlowe: and that she had it under his hand and seal too—or else he had not obtained his end: therefore, it was not likely she should be so officious as to do his work against herself, if she thought Mr Lovelace had designs upon her, like what she *presumed* to hint at: that, for her part, her only view was to procure liberty to a young gentlewoman who made those things grievous to her, which would not be made such a rout about by anybody else—and to procure the payment of a just debt to her friend Mrs Sinclair.

She besought them to leave her. She wanted not these instances, she said, to convince her of the company she was in: and told them that, to get rid of such visitors, and of still worse that she apprehended, she would write to one friend to raise the money for her; though it would be death for her to do so; because that friend could not do it without her mother, in whose eye it would give a selfish appearance to a friendship that was above all sordid alloys.

They advised her to write out of hand.

But how much must I write for? What is the sum? Should I not have had a bill delivered me?—God knows, I took not your lodgings. But he that could treat me, as he has done, could do this!

Don't speak against Mr Lovelace, *Miss Harlowe*. He is a man I greatly esteem (cursed toad!). And, 'bating that he will take his advantage where he can of *us* silly credulous girls, he is a man of honour.

She lifted up her hands and eyes, instead of speaking: and well she might! For any words she could have used could not have expressed the anguish she must feel on being comprehended in the U S.

She must write for one hundred and fifty guineas, at least: two hundred, if she were short of money, might as well be written for.

Mrs Sinclair, she said, had all her clothes. Let them be sold, *fairly* sold, and the money go as far as it would go. She had also a few other valuables; but no money (none at all), but the poor half-guinea, and the little silver they had seen. She would give bond to pay all that her apparel, and the other matters she had, would fall short of. She had great effects belonging to her of right. Her bond would, and must, be paid, were it for a thousand pounds. But her clothes she should never want. She believed, if not too much undervalued, those, and her few valuables, would answer everything. She wished for no surplus, but to discharge the last expenses; and forty shillings would do as well for those, as forty pounds. Let my ruin, said she, lifting up her eyes, be LARGE, be COMPLETE, *in this life!*—for a *composition*, let it be COMPLETE—and there she stopped. No doubt alluding to her father's futurely-extended curse!

The wretches could not help wishing to me for the opportunity of making such a purchase for their own wear. How I cursed *them!* and, in my heart, *thee!*—But too probable, thought I, that this vile Sally Martin may hope (though thou art incapable of it), that *her* Lovelace, as she has the assurance, behind thy back, to call thee, may present her with some of the poor lady's spoils!

Will not Mrs Sinclair, proceeded she, think my clothes a security, till they can be sold? They are very good clothes. A suit or two but just put on, as it were; never worn. They cost much more than is demanded of me. *My father loved to see me fine*—All shall go. But let me have the particulars of her demand. I suppose I must pay for my *destroyer* (that was her well-adapted word!), and his servants, as well as for myself—I am content to do so—indeed I am content to do so—I am above wishing that anybody, who could *thus* act, should be so much as expostulated with as to the justice and equity of it. If I have but enough to pay the demand, I shall be satisfied; and will leave the baseness of such an action as this, as an aggravation of a guilt which I thought could *not* be aggravated.

I own, Lovelace, I have malice in this particularity, in order to sting thee to the heart. And, let me ask thee, What now thou canst think of thy barbarity, thy unprecedented barbarity, in having reduced a person of her rank, fortune, talents, and virtue, so low?

The wretched women, it must be owned, act but in their profession; a profession thou hast been the principal means of reducing these two to act in. And they know what thy designs have been, and how far prosecuted. It is, in their opinions, using her *gently*, that they have forborne to bring to her the woman so justly odious to her; and that they have not threatened her with the introducing to her strange men: nor yet brought into her company their *spirit-breakers*, and *bumbling-drones* (fellows not allowed to carry stings), to trace and force her back to their detested house; and, when there, into all their measures.

Till I came, they thought thou wouldst not be displeased at anything she suffered, that could help to mortify her into a state of shame and disgrace; and bring her to comply with thy views when thou shouldst come to release her from these wretches, as from a greater evil than cohabiting with thee.

When thou considerest these things, thou wilt make no difficulty of believing that this their own account of their behaviour to this admirable lady, has been far short of their insults: and the less, when I tell thee that all together their usage had such effects upon her, that they left her in violent hysterics; ordering an apothecary to be sent for if she should continue in them and be worse; and particularly (as they had done from the first) that they kept out of her way any edged or pointed instrument; especially a penknife; which, pretending to mend a pen, they said she might ask for.

At twelve Saturday night, Rowland sent to tell them that she was so ill that he knew not what might be the issue; and wished her out of his house.

And this made them as heartily wish to hear from you. For their messenger, to their great surprise, was not then returned from M. Hall. And they were sure he must have reached that place by Friday night.

Early on Sunday morning, both devils went to see how she did. They had such an account of her weakness, lowness, and anguish, that they forbore, out of compassion, they said, finding their visits so disagreeable to her, to see her. But their apprehension of what might be the issue was, no doubt, their principal consideration: nothing else could have softened such flinty bosoms.

They sent for the apothecary Rowland had had to her, and gave him, and Rowland, and his wife, and maid, paradeful injunctions for the utmost care to be taken of her: no doubt with an Old Bailey forecast.[3] And they sent up to let her know what orders they had given: but that, understanding she had taken something to compose herself, they would not disturb her.

She had scrupled, it seems, to admit the apothecary's visit overnight, because he was a MAN—and could not be prevailed upon, till they pleaded *their own safety* to her.

They went again, from church—Lord, Bob, these creatures go to church!—But she sent them down word that she must have all the remainder of the day to herself.

When I first came, and told them of thy execrations for what they had done, and joined my own to them, they were astonished. The mother said she had thought she had known Mr Lovelace better; and expected thanks, and not curses.

While I was with them, came back halting and cursing most horribly their messenger; by reason of the ill-usage he had received from you, instead of the reward he had been taught to expect, for the supposed good news that he carried down, of the lady's being found out, and secured. A pretty fellow! art thou not, to abuse people for the consequences of thy own faults?

Under what shocking disadvantages, and with this addition to them, that I am thy friend and intimate, am I to make a visit to this unhappy lady tomorrow morning. In thy *name* too!—Enough to be refused, that I am of a *sex* to which, for *thy* sake, she has so justifiable an aversion: nor, having such a tyrant of a father, and such an implacable brother, has she reason to make an exception in favour of *any* of it on *their* accounts.

It is three o'clock. I will close here; and take a little rest: what I have written will be a proper preparative for what shall offer by and by.

Thy servant is not to return without a letter, he tells me; and that thou expectest him back in the morning. Thou hast fellows enough where thou art, at thy command. If I find any difficulty in seeing the lady, thy messenger shall post away with this—Let him look to broken bones, and other consequences, if what he carries answer not thy expectation. But, if I am admitted, thou shalt have *this* and the result of my audience both together. In the former case, thou mayest send another servant to wait the next advices, from

J. BELFORD

Letter 334: MR BELFORD TO ROBERT LOVELACE, ESQ.

Monday, July 17

ABOUT six this morning I went to Rowland's. Mrs Sinclair was to follow me, in order to dismiss the action; but not to come in sight.

Rowland, upon inquiry, told me that the lady was extremely ill; and that she had desired not to let anybody but his wife or maid come near her.

I said I *must* see her. I had told him my business overnight; and I *must* see her.

His wife went up: but returned presently, saying she could not get her to speak to her; yet that her eyelids moved; though she either would not, or could not, open them, to look up at her.

Oons, woman, said I, the lady may be in a fit: the lady may be dying—Let me go up. Show me the way.

A horrid hole of a house, in an alley they call a court; stairs wretchedly narrow, even to the first-floor rooms: and into a den they led me, with broken walls which had been papered, as I saw by a multitude of tacks, and some torn bits held on by the rusty heads.

The floor indeed was clean, but the ceiling was smoked with variety of figures, and initials of names, that had been the woeful employment of wretches who had no other way to amuse themselves.

A bed at one corner, with coarse curtains tacked up at the feet to the ceiling; because the curtain rings were broken off; but a coverlid upon it with a cleanish look, though plaguily in tatters, and the corners tied up in tassels, that the rents in it might go no farther.

The windows dark and double-barred, the tops boarded up to save mending; and only a little four-paned eylet-hole of a casement to let in air; more, however, coming in at broken panes than could come in at that.

Four old turkey-worked chairs, bursten-bottomed, the stuffing staring out.

An old, tottering, worm-eaten table, that had more nails bestowed in mending it to make it stand, than the table cost fifty years ago when new.

On the mantelpiece was an iron shove-up candlestick, with a lighted candle in it, twinkle, twinkle, twinkle, four of them, I suppose, for a penny.

Near that, on the same shelf, was an old looking-glass, cracked through the middle, breaking out into a thousand points; the crack given it, perhaps, in a rage, by some poor creature to whom it gave the representation of his heart's woes in his face.

The chimney had two half-tiles in it on one side, and one whole one on the other; which showed it had been in better plight; but now the very mortar had followed the rest of the tiles in every other place, and left the bricks bare.

An old half-barred stove-grate was in the chimney; and in that a large stone-bottle without a neck, filled with baleful yew as an evergreen, withered southern-wood, and sweet-briar, and sprigs of rue in flower.

To finish the shocking description, in a dark nook stood an old, broken-bottomed cane couch, without a squab or coverlid, sunk at one corner, and unmortised, by the failing of one of its worm-eaten legs, which lay in two pieces under the wretched piece of furniture it could no longer support

And this, thou horrid Lovelace, was the bedchamber of the divine Clarissa!!!

I had leisure to cast my eye on these things: for, going up softly, the poor lady turned not about at our entrance nor, till I spoke, moved her head.

She was kneeling in a corner of the room, near the dismal window, against the table, on an old bolster (as it seemed to be) of the cane couch, half-covered with her handkerchief; her back to the door; which was only shut to (no need of fastenings!); her arms crossed upon the table, the fore-finger of her right hand in her Bible. She had perhaps been reading in it, and could read no longer. Paper, pens, ink, lay by her book on the table. Her dress was white damask, exceeding neat; but her stays seemed not tight-laced. I was told afterwards, that her laces had been cut when she fainted away at her entrance into this cursed place; and she had not been solicitous enough about her dress to send for others. Her headdress was a little discomposed; her charming hair, in natural ringlets, as you have heretofore described it, but a little tangled, as if not lately kembed, irregularly shading one side of the loveliest neck in the world; as her disordered, rumpled handkerchief did the other. Her face (Oh how altered from what I had seen it! yet lovely in spite of all her griefs and sufferings!) was reclined, when we entered, upon her crossed arms; but so as not more than one side of it to be hid.

When I surveyed the room around, and the kneeling lady, sunk with majesty too in her white, flowing robes (for she had not on a hoop), spreading the dark, though not dirty, floor, and illuminating that horrid corner; her linen beyond imagination white, considering that she had not been undressed ever since she had been here; I thought my concern would have choked me. Something rose in my throat, I know not what, which made me for a moment guggle, as it were, for speech: which, at last, forcing its way, Con–Con–Confound you both, said I to the man and woman, is this an apartment for such a lady? And could the cursed devils of her own sex, who visited this suffering angel, see her, and leave her, in so damned a nook?

Sir, we would have had the lady to accept of our own bedchamber; but she refused it. We are poor people—and we expect nobody will stay with us longer than they can help it.

You are people chosen purposely, I doubt not, by the damned woman who has employed you: and if your usage of this lady has been but half as bad as your house, you had better never to have seen the light.

Up then raised the charming sufferer her lovely face; but with such a significance of woe overspreading it that I could not, for the soul of me, help being visibly affected.

She waved her hand two or three times towards the door, as if commanding me to withdraw; and displeased at my intrusion; but did not speak.

Permit me, madam—I will not approach one step farther without your leave—permit me, for one moment, the favour of your ear!

No—No—go, go; MAN, with an emphasis—and would have said more; but, as if struggling in vain for words, she seemed to give up speech for lost, and dropped her head down once more, with a deep sigh, upon her left arm; her right, as if she had not the use of it (numbed, I suppose), self-moved, dropping down on her side.

Oh that thou hadst been there! and in my place!—But by what I then felt in myself, I am convinced that a capacity of being moved by the distresses of our fellow-creatures is far from being disgraceful to a manly heart. With what pleasure, at that moment, could I have given up my own life, could I but first have avenged this charming creature, and cut the throat of her *destroyer*, as she emphatically calls thee, though the friend that I best love! And yet, at the same time, my heart and my eyes gave way to a softness, of which (though not so hardened a wretch as thou) it was never before so susceptible.

I dare not approach you, dearest lady, without your leave: but on my knees I beseech you to permit me to release you from this damned house, and out of the power of the accursed woman who was the occasion of your being here!

She lifted up her sweet face once more, and beheld me on my knees. Never knew I before what it was to pray so heartily.

Are you not—are you not Mr Belford, sir? I think your name is Belford?

It is, madam, and I ever was a worshipper of your virtues, and an advocate for you; and I come to release you from the hands you are in.

And in whose to place me? Oh leave me, leave me! Let me never rise from this spot! Let me never, never more believe in man!

This moment, dearest lady, this very moment, if you please, you may depart whithersoever you think fit. You are absolutely free, and your own mistress.

I had now as lieve die here in this place, as anywhere. I will owe no obligation to any friend of *him* in whose company you have seen me. So, pray, sir, withdraw.

Then turning to the officer, Mr Rowland I think your name is? I am better reconciled to your house than I was at first. If you can but engage that I shall have nobody come near me but your wife; no *man!* and neither of those women who have sported with my calamities; I will die with you, and in this very corner. And you shall be well satisfied for the trouble you have had with me—I have value enough for that—for, see, I have a diamond ring; taking it out of her bosom; and I have friends will redeem it at a high price, when I am gone.

But for *you*, sir, looking at me, I beg you to withdraw. If you mean me well, God, I hope, will reward you for your good meaning; but to the friend of my *destroyer* will I not owe an obligation.

You will owe no obligation to me, nor to anybody. You have been detained for a debt you do not owe. The action is dismissed; and you will only be so good as to give me your hand into the coach which stands as near to this house as it could draw up. And I will either leave you at the coach-door, or attend you whithersoever you please, till I see you safe where you would wish to be.

Will you then, sir, *compel* me to be beholden to you?

You will inexpressibly oblige me, madam, to command me to do you either service or pleasure.

Why then, sir—looking at me—but why do you mock me in that humble posture! Rise, sir! I cannot speak to you else.

I arose.

Only, sir, take this ring. I have a sister who will be glad to have it, at the price it shall be valued at, for the *former* owner's sake!—Out of the money she gives, let this man be paid; handsomely paid: and I have a few valuables more at my lodgings (Dorcas, or the MAN William, can tell where that is); let them, and my clothes at the wicked woman's where you have seen me, be sold for the payment of my lodging first, and next of your *friend*'s debts, that I have been arrested for; as far as they will go; only reserving enough to put me into the ground, anywhere, or anyhow, no matter—Tell your friend I wish it may be enough to satisfy the whole demand; but if it be not, he must make it up himself; or, if he think fit to draw for it on Miss Howe, she will repay it, and with interest, if he insist upon it—And this, sir, if you promise to perform, you will do me, as you offer, both pleasure and service: and say you *will*, and take the ring, and withdraw. If I want to say anything more to you (you seem to be an humane man), I will let you know—and so, sir, God bless you.

I approached her, and was going to speak——

Don't speak, sir: Here's the ring.

I stood off.

And won't you take it? Won't you do this last office for me?—I have no other person to ask it of; else, believe me, I would not request it of *you*. But take it or not, laying it upon the table—you must withdraw, sir: I am very ill. I would fain get a little rest, if I could. I find I am going to be bad again.

And offering to rise, she sunk down through excess of weakness and grief, in a fainting fit.

Why, Lovelace, wast thou not present thyself?—Why dost thou commit such villainies as even thou thyself art afraid to appear in; and yet puttest a weaker heart and head upon encountering with?

The maid coming in just then, the woman and she lifted her up on the decrepit couch; and I withdrew with this Rowland; who wept like a child, and said he never in his life was so moved.

Yet so hardened a wretch art thou, that I question whether thou wilt shed a tear at my relation.

They recovered her by hartshorn and water: I went down mean while; for the detestable woman had been below some time. Oh how did I curse her! I never before was so fluent in curses.

She tried to wheedle me; but I renounced her; and, after she had dismissed the action, sent her away crying, or pretending to cry, because of my behaviour to her.

You will observe that I did not mention one word to the lady about *you*. I was afraid to do it. For 'twas plain that she could not bear your name: your *friend*, and the *company* you have seen me in were the words nearest to naming you she could speak: and yet I wanted to clear your intention of this brutal, this sordid-looking, villainy.

I sent up again, by Rowland's wife, when I heard that the lady was recovered, beseeching her to quit that devilish place; and the woman assured her that she was at full liberty to do so; for that the action was dismissed.

But she cared not to answer her: and was so weak and low that it was almost as much out of her power as inclination, the woman told me, to speak.

I would have hastened away for my friend Doctor H., but the house is such a den, and the room she was in such a hole, that I was ashamed to be seen in it by a man of his reputation, especially with a woman of such an appearance, and in such uncommon distress; and I found there was no prevailing on her to quit it for the people's bedroom, which was neat and lightsome.

The strong room she was in, the wretches told me, should have been in better order, but that it was but the very morning that she was brought in, that an unhappy man had quitted it; for a more eligible prison, no doubt; since there could hardly be a worse.

Being told that she desired not to be disturbed, and seemed inclined to doze, I took this opportunity to go to her lodgings in Covent Garden; to which Dorcas (who first discovered her there, as Will was the setter from church) had before given me a direction.

The man's name is Smith, a dealer in gloves, snuff, and such petty merchandise: his wife the shopkeeper: he a maker of the gloves they sell. Honest people, it seems.

I thought to have got the woman with me to the lady; but she was not within.

I talked with the man, and told him what had befallen the lady; owing, as I said, to a mistake of orders; and gave her the character she deserved; and desired him to send his wife, the moment she came in, to the lady; directing him whither; not doubting that her attendance would be very welcome to her: which he promised.

He told me that a letter was left for her there on Saturday; and, about half an hour before I came, another, superscribed by the same hand; the first by the post; the other by a countryman; who, having been informed of her absence, and of all the circumstances they could tell him of it, posted away full of concern, saying that the lady he was sent from would be ready to break her heart at the tidings.

I thought it right to take the two letters back with me; and, dismissing my coach, took a chair, as a more proper vehicle for the lady, if I (the friend of her *destroyer*) could prevail upon her to leave Rowland's.

And here being obliged to give way to an indispensable avocation, I will make thee taste a little in thy turn of the plague of suspense; and break off, without giving thee the least hint of the issue of my further proceedings. I know that those least bear disappointment who love most to give it. In twenty instances hast thou afforded me proof of the truth of this observation. And I matter not thy raving.

Another letter, however, shall be ready, send for it as soon as thou wilt. But, were it not, have I not written enough to convince thee, that I am

Thy ready and obliging friend,
J. BELFORD?

Letter 335: MR LOVELACE TO JOHN BELFORD, ESQ.

Monday, July 17, eleven at night

CURSE upon thy hard heart, thou vile caitiff! How hast thou tortured me by thy designed *abruption!* 'Tis impossible that Miss Harlowe should have ever suffered as thou hast made me suffer, and as I now suffer!

That sex is made to bear pain. It is a curse that the first of it entailed upon all her succeeding daughters, when she brought the curse upon us all. And they love those best, whether man or child, who give them most—But to stretch upon thy damned tenterhooks such a spirit as mine—No rack, no torture, can equal my torture!

And must I still wait the return of another messenger? Confound thee for a malicious devil! I wish thou wert a post-horse, and I upon the back of thee! How would I whip and spur, and harrow up thy clumsy sides, till I made thee a ready-roasted, ready-flayed mess of dog's meat; all the hounds in the county howling after thee as I drove thee, to wait my dismounting, in order to devour thee piecemeal; life still throbbing in each churned mouthful!

Give this fellow the sequel of thy tormenting scribble. Dispatch him away with it. Thou hast promised it shall be ready. Every cushion or chair I shall sit upon, the bed I shall lie down upon (if I go to bed), till he return, will be stuffed with bolt-upright awls, bodkins, corking-pins, and packing-needles: already I can fancy that to pink my body like my mind, I need only to be put into a hogshead stuck full of steel-pointed spikes, and rolled down a hill three times as high as the Monument.

But I lose time, yet know not how to employ it, till this fellow returns with the sequel of thy soul-harrowing intelligence!

Letter 336: MR BELFORD TO ROBERT LOVELACE, ESQ.

Monday night, July 17

ON my return to Rowland's, I found that the apothecary was just gone up. Mrs Rowland being above with him, I made the less scruple to go up too, as it was probable that to ask for leave would be to ask to be denied; hoping also that the letters I had with me would be a good excuse.

She was sitting on the side of the broken couch, extremely weak and low; and, I observed, cared not to speak to the man; and no wonder; for I never saw a more shocking fellow, of a profession tolerably genteel, nor heard a more illiterate one prate—physician in ordinary to this house, and others like it, I suppose! He put me in mind of Otway's apothecary in his Caius Marius:

> Meagre and very rueful were his looks:
> Sharp misery had worn him to the bones.
> — Famine in his cheeks:
> Need and oppression staring in his eyes:
> Contempt and beggary hanging on his back:
> The world no friend of his, nor the world's law.[1]

As I am in black, he took me at my entrance, I believe, to be a doctor, and slunk behind me with his hat upon his two thumbs, and looked as if he expected the oracle to open, and give him orders.

The lady looked displeased, as well at me as at Rowland, who followed me, and at the apothecary. It was not, she said, the least of her present misfortunes, that she could not be left to her own sex; and to her option to see whom she pleased.

I besought her excuse; and, winking for the apothecary to withdraw (which he did), told her that I had been at her new lodgings, to order everything to be got ready for her reception; presuming she would choose to go thither: that I had a chair at the door: that Mr Smith, and his wife (I named their names, that she should not have room for the least fear of Sinclair's), had been full of apprehensions for her safety: that I had brought two letters which were left there for her; one by the post, the other that very morning.

This took her attention. She held out her charming hand for them; took them, and, pressing them to her lips—From the only friend I have in the world! said she, kissing them again; and looking at the seals, as if to see whether they had been opened. I can't read them, said she, my eyes are too dim; and put them in her bosom.

I besought her to think of quitting that wretched hole.

Where could she go, she asked, to be safe and uinterrupted for the short remainder of her life; and to avoid being again visited by the creatures who had insulted her before?

I gave her the solemnest assurances that she should not be invaded in her new lodgings by anybody; and said that I would particularly engage my honour that *the person who had most offended her should not come near her, without her own consent.*

Your honour, sir! Are you not that man's friend?

I am not a friend, madam, to his vile actions to the *most excellent of women*.

Do you flatter me, sir? Then are you a MAN—But Oh, sir, your friend, holding her face forward with great earnestness, your *barbarous* friend, what has he not to answer for!

There she stopped: her heart full; and putting her hand over her eyes and forehead, the tears trickled through her fingers: resenting thy barbarity, it seemed, as Caesar did the stab from his distinguished Brutus!

Though she was so very much disordered, I thought I would not lose this opportunity to assert your innocence of this villainous arrest.

There is no defending the unhappy man, in any of his vile actions by you, madam; but of this last outrage, by all that's good and sacred, he is innocent!

Oh wretches! what a sex is yours!—Have you all one dialect? *Good and sacred!*—If, sir, you can find an oath, or a vow, or an adjuration, that my ears have not been twenty times a day wounded with, then speak it, and I may again believe a MAN.

I was excessively touched at these words, knowing thy baseness, and the reason she had for them.

But say you, sir; for I would not, methinks, have the wretch capable of this sordid baseness!—Say you, that he is innocent of this *last* wickedness? Can you *truly* say that he is?

By the great God of Heaven!——

Nay, sir, if you swear, I must doubt you!—If you yourself think your WORD insufficient, what reliance can I have on your OATH!—Oh that this my experience had not cost me so dear! But, were I to live a *thousand* years, I would always suspect the veracity of a swearer. Excuse me, sir; but is it likely, that *he* who makes so free with his GOD, will scruple anything that may serve his turn with his *fellow-creature*?

This was a most affecting reprimand!

Madam, said I, I have a regard, a regard a gentleman *ought* to have, to my word; and whenever I forfeit it to you——

Nay, sir, don't be angry with me. It is grievous to me to question a gentleman's veracity. But your friend calls himself a *gentleman*—You know not what I have suffered by a *gentleman!*—And then again she wept.

I would give you, madam, demonstration, if your griefs and your weakness would permit it, that he has no hand in this barbarous baseness: and that he resents it as it ought to be resented.

Well, well, sir (with quickness), he will have his account to make up somewhere else; not to me. I should not be sorry to find him able to acquit his intention on this occasion. Let him know, sir, only one thing, that, when you heard me in the bitterness of my spirit most vehemently exclaim against the undeserved usage I have met with from him, that even *then*, in *that* passionate moment, I was able to say (and never did I see such an earnest and affecting exaltation of hands and eyes), Give him, good God! repentance and amendment; that I may be the last poor creature who shall be ruined by him!—and, in thy own good time, receive to *thy* mercy, the poor wretch who had *none* on me!

By my soul, I could not speak—She had not her Bible before her for nothing.

I was forced to turn my head away, and to take out my handkerchief.

What an angel is this!—Even the gaoler, and his wife and maid, wept.

Again I wish thou hadst been there, that thou mightest have sunk down at her feet, and begun that moment to reap the effect of her generous wishes for thee; undeserving, as thou art, of anything but perdition!

I represented to her that she would be less free where she was, from visits she liked not, than at her own lodging. I told her that it would probably bring her, in particular, *one visitor*, who otherwise I would engage (but I durst not swear again, after the severe reprimand she had just given me) should not come near her without her consent. And I expressed my surprise, that she should be unwilling to quit such a place as this; when it was more than probable that some of her friends, when it was known how bad she was, would visit her.

She said the place, when she was first brought into it, was indeed very shocking to her: but that she had found herself so weak and ill, and her griefs had so sunk her, that she did not expect to have lived till now: that therefore all places had been alike to her; for to die in a prison *was* to die; and equally eligible as to die in a palace (Palaces, she said, could have no attractions for a dying person): but that, since she feared she was not so soon to be released as she had hoped; since she was so little mistress of herself *here*; and since she might, by removal, be in the way of her dear friend's letters; she would hope that she might depend upon the assurances I gave her of being at liberty to return to her last lodgings (otherwise she would provide herself with new ones, out of my knowledge, as well as out of yours); and that I was too much of a gentleman to be concerned in carrying her back to the house she had so much reason to abhor; and to which she had been once before most vilely betrayed, to her ruin.

I assured her in the strongest terms (*but swore not*) that you were resolved not to molest her: and, as a proof of the sincerity of my professions, besought her to give me directions (in pursuance of my friend's express desire) about sending all her apparel, and whatever belonged to her, to her new lodgings.

She seemed pleased; and gave me instantly out of her pocket her keys; asking me if Mrs Smith, whom I had named, might not attend me; and she would give *her* further directions? To which I cheerfully assented; and then she told me that she would accept of the chair I had offered her.

I withdrew; and took the opportunity to be civil to Rowland and his maid; for she found no fault with their behaviour, for what they *were*; and the fellow seems to be miserably poor. I sent also for the apothecary, who is as poor as the gaoler (and still poorer, I dare say, as to the skill required in his business), and satisfied him beyond his hopes.

The lady, after I had withdrawn, attempted to read the letters I brought her. But she could read but a little way in one of them, and had great emotions upon it.

She told the woman she would take a speedy opportunity to acknowledge their civilities, and to satisfy the apothecary; who might send her his bill to her lodgings.

She gave the maid something; probably the only half-guinea she had: and then, with difficulty, her limbs trembling under her, and supported by Mrs Rowland, got downstairs.

I offered my arm: she was pleased to lean upon it. I doubt, sir, said she as she moved, I have behaved rudely to you: but, if you knew all, you would forgive me.

I know enough, madam, to convince me that there is not such purity and honour in any woman upon earth; nor anyone that has been so barbarously treated.

She looked at me very earnestly. What she thought I cannot say; but, in general, I never saw so much soul in a lady's eyes, as in hers.

I ordered my servant (whose mourning made him less observable as such, and who had not been in the lady's eye) to keep the chair in view; and to bring me word, how she did, when set down. The fellow had the thought to step into the shop just before the chair entered it, under pretence of buying snuff; and so enabled himself to give me an account that she was received with great joy by the good woman of the house; who told her she was but just come in; and was preparing to attend her in High Holborn—Oh Mrs Smith, said she, as soon as she saw her, did you not think I was run away?—You don't know what I have suffered since I saw you. I have been in prison!—Arrested for debts I owe not!—But, thank God, I am here!—Will you permit your maid—I have forgot her name already—

Katharine, madam—

Will you let Katharine assist me to bed?—I have not had my clothes off since Thursday night.

What she further said the fellow heard not, she leaning upon the maid, and going upstairs.

But dost thou not observe what a strange, what an uncommon, openness of heart reigns in this lady: *she had been in a prison*, she said before a stranger in the shop, and before the maid-servant: and so, probably, she would have said, had there been twenty people in the shop.

The disgrace she cannot hide from *herself*, as she says in her letter to Lady Betty, she is not solicitous to conceal from the *world!*

But this makes it evident to me that she is resolved to keep no terms with thee. And yet to be able to put up such a prayer for thee, as she did in her prison (I will often mention the *prison-room*, to tease thee!); does not this show that revenge has very little sway in her mind; though she can retain so much proper resentment?

And this is another excellence in this admirable woman's character: for whom, before her, have we met with in the whole sex, or in ours either, that know how, in *practice*, to distinguish between REVENGE and RESENTMENT for base and ungrateful treatment?

'Tis a cursed thing, after all, that such a woman as this should be treated as she has been treated. Hadst thou been a king, and done as thou *hast* done by such a meritorious innocent, I believe in my heart it would have been adjudged to be a national sin, and the sword, the pestilence, or famine, must have atoned for it!— But, as thou art a private man, thou wilt certainly meet with thy punishment (besides what thou mayest expect from the justice of thy country, and the vengeance of her friends), as she will her reward, HEREAFTER.

It *must* be so, if there be really such a thing as *future remuneration*; as now I am more and more convinced there must—else, what a hard fate is hers, whose punishment, to all appearance, has so much exceeded her fault? And, as to thine, how can *temporary* burnings, wert thou by some accident to be consumed in thy bed, expiate for thy abominable vileness to her, in breach of all obligations moral and divine?

I was resolved to lose no time in having everything which belonged to the lady at the cursed woman's sent her. Accordingly, I took coach to Smith's, and procured the lady (to whom I sent up my compliments, and inquiries how she bore her removal), ill as she sent me down word she was, to give proper directions to Mrs Smith: whom I took with me to Sinclair's; and who saw everything looked out and put into the trunks and boxes they were first brought in, and carried away in two coaches.

Had I not been there, Sally and Polly would each of them have taken to herself something of the poor lady's spoils. This they declared: and I had something to do to get from Sally a fine Brussels lace head, which she had the confidence to say she would wear for *Miss Harlowe*'s sake. Nor should either I or Mrs Smith have known she had got it, had she not been in search after the ruffles belonging to it.

My resentment on this occasion, and the conversation which Mrs Smith and I had (in which I not only expatiated upon the merits of the lady, but expressed my concern for her sufferings; though I left her room to suppose her married, yet without averring it), gave me high credit with the good woman: so that we are perfectly well-acquainted already: by which means I shall be enabled to give you accounts, from time to time, of all that passes: and which I will be very industrious to do, provided I may depend upon the solemn promises I have given the lady, in your name as well as my own, that she shall be free from all personal molestation from you. And thus shall I have it in my power to return *in kind* your writing favours; and preserve my shorthand besides: which, till this correspondence was opened, I had pretty much neglected.

I ordered the abandoned women to make out your account. They answered *that* they would do with a *vengeance*. Indeed they breathe nothing but revenge. For now they say you will assuredly marry; and your example will be followed by all your friends and companions—as the old one says, to the utter ruin of her poor house.

Letter 337: MR BELFORD TO ROBERT LOVELACE, ESQ.

Tuesday morn. (July 18) 6 o'clock

HAVING sat up late to finish and seal up in readiness my letter to the above period, I am disturbed before I wished to have risen by the arrival of thy second fellow; man and horse in a foam.

While he baits, I will write a few lines, most heartily to congratulate thee on thy *expected* rage and impatience; and on thy recovery of mental feeling.

How much does the idea thou givest me of thy deserved torments, by thy upright awls, bodkins, pins, and packing-needles, by thy rolling hoghead with iron spikes, and by thy macerated sides, delight me!

I will, upon every occasion that offers, drive more spikes into thy hogshead, and roll thee downhill and up, as thou recoverest to sense, or rather returnest back to *senselessness*. Thou knowest therefore the terms on which thou art to enjoy my correspondence. Am not I, who have all along, and *in time*, protested against thy barbarous and ungrateful perfidies to a lady so noble, entitled to drive remorse, if possible, into thy hitherto callous heart?

Only let me reinforce one thing, which perhaps I mentioned too slightly before, that the lady was prevailed upon by my solemn assurances *only*, that she might depend upon being free from *your* visits, not to remove to new lodgings where neither you nor I should be able to find her.

These assurances I thought I might give her, not only because of your promise, but because it is necessary for you to know where she is, in order to address yourself to her by your friends.

Enable me therefore to make good to her this my solemn engagement; or adieu to all friendship, at least to all correspondence, with thee for ever.

J. BELFORD

Letter 338: MR BELFORD TO ROBERT LOVELACE, ESQ.

Tuesday, July 18, afternoon

I RENEWED my inquiries after the lady's health, in the morning, by my servant: and, as soon as I had dined, I went myself.

I had but a poor account of it: yet sent up my compliments. She returned me thanks for all my good offices; and her excuses that they could not be *personal* just then, being very low and faint: but if I gave myself the trouble of coming about six this evening, she should be able, she hoped, to drink a dish of tea with me, and would then thank me herself.

I am very proud of this condescension; and think it looks not amiss for you, as I am your *avowed* friend. Methinks I want fully to remove from her mind all doubts of you in this last villainous action: and who knows then, what your noble relations may be able to do for you with her, if you hold your mind? For your servant acquainted me with their having actually engaged Miss Howe in their and your favour, before this cursed affair happened. And I desire the particulars of all from yourself, that I may the better know how to serve you.

She has two handsome apartments, a bedchamber and dining-room, with light closets in each. She has already a nurse (the people of the house having but one maid); a woman whose care, diligence, and honesty, Mrs Smith highly commends. She has likewise the benefit of the voluntary attendance, and *love*, as it seems, of a widow gentlewoman, Mrs Lovick her name, who lodges over her apartment, and of whom she seems very fond, having found something in her, she thinks, resembling the qualities of her worthy Mrs Norton.

About seven o'clock this morning, it seems, the lady was so ill that she yielded to their desires to have an apothecary sent for—Not the fellow, thou mayest believe, she had had before at Rowland's; but one Mr Goddard, a man of skill and eminence; and of conscience too; demonstrated as well by general character, as by his prescriptions to this lady: for, pronouncing her case to be grief, he ordered for the present only innocent juleps by way of cordial; and as soon as her stomach should be able to bear it, light kitchen-diet; telling Mrs Lovick that that, with air, moderate exercise, and cheerful company, would do her more good than all the medicines in his shop.

This has given me, as it seems it has the lady (who also praises his modest behaviour, paternal looks, and genteel address), a very good opinion of the man; and I design to make myself acquainted with him; and if he advises to call in a doctor, to wish him, for the fair patient's sake more than the physician's (who wants not practice), my worthy friend Dr H.—whose character is above all exception, as his humanity I am sure will distinguish him to the lady.

Mrs Lovick gratified me with an account of a letter she had written from the lady's mouth to Miss Howe; she being unable to write herself with steadiness. It was to this effect; in answer, it seems, to her two letters, whatever were the contents of them:

'That she had been involved in a dreadful calamity, which she was sure, when known, would exempt her from the effects of her friendly displeasure for not answering her first; having been put under an arrest—Could she have believed it?—That she was released but the day before: and was now so weak, and so low, that she was obliged to get a widow gentlewoman in the same house to account thus for her silence to her two letters of the 13th and 16th: that she would, as soon as able, answer them. Begged of her, meantime, not to be uneasy for her; since (only that this was a calamity which came upon her when she was far from being well; a load laid upon the shoulders of a poor wretch, ready before to sink under too heavy a burden) it was nothing to the evil she had before suffered: and one felicity seemed likely to issue from it; which was, that she should be at rest in an honest house, with considerate and kind-hearted people; having assurance given her that she should not be molested by the wretch whom it would be death for her to see. So that now she (Miss Howe) needed not to send to her by private and expensive conveyances: nor need Collins to take precautions for fear of being dogged to her lodgings; nor she to write by a fictitious name to her, but by her own.'

You see I am in a way to oblige you: you see how much she depends upon my engaging for your forbearing to intrude yourself into her company. Let not your flaming impatience destroy all; and make me look like a villain to a lady who has reason to suspect *every man she sees* to be so—Upon this condition, you may expect all the services that can flow from true friendship, and from

Your sincere well-wisher,
JOHN BELFORD

Letter 339: MR BELFORD TO ROBERT LOVELACE, ESQ.

Tuesday night, July 18

I AM just come from the lady. I was admitted into the dining-room, where she was sitting in an elbow-chair, in a very weak and low way. She made an effort to stand up when I entered; but was forced to keep her seat. You'll excuse me, Mr Belford: I ought to rise to thank you for all your kindness to me. I was to blame to be so loath to leave that sad place; for I am in Heaven here, to what I was there: and good people about me too!—I have not had good people about me for a long, long time before; so that (with a half-smile) I had begun to wonder whither they were all gone.

Her nurse and Mrs Smith, who were present, took occasion to retire: and, when we were alone, You seem to be a person of humanity, sir, said she: You hinted, as I was leaving *my prison*, that you were not a stranger to my sad story. If you know it *truly*, you must know that I have been most barbarously treated; and have not deserved it at the man's hands by whom I have suffered.

I told her I knew enough to be convinced that she had the merit of a saint, and the purity of an angel: and was proceeding, when she said, No flighty compliments! No undue attributes, sir! I offered to plead for my sincerity; and mentioned the word *politeness*, and would have distinguished between that and *flattery*. Nothing can be polite, said she, that is not just: Whatever I *may* have had, I have *now* no vanity to gratify.

I disclaimed all intention of compliment: All I *had* said, and what I *should* say, was, and should be, the effect of sincere veneration. My unhappy friend's account of her had entitled her to that.

I then mentioned your grief, your penitence, your resolutions of making her all the amends that were possible now to be made her: and, in the most earnest manner, I asserted your innocence as to the last villainous outrage.

Her answer was to this effect: It is painful to me to think of him. The amends you talk of cannot be made. This last violence you speak of is nothing to what preceded it. That cannot be atoned for; nor palliated: this may: and I shall not be sorry to be convinced that he cannot be guilty of so very low a wickedness—Yet, after his vile forgeries of hands—after his personating basenesses—what are the iniquities he is not capable of?

I would then have given her an account of the trial you stood with your friends: your own previous resolutions of marriage, had she honoured you with the requested *four words*: all your family's earnestness to have the honour of her alliance: and the application of your two cousins to Miss Howe, by general consent, for that young lady's interest with her. But, having just touched upon these topics, she cut me short, saying that was a cause before another tribunal: Miss Howe's letters to her were upon that subject; and she should write her thoughts to *her*, as soon as she was able.

I then attempted more particularly to clear you of having any hand in the vile Sinclair's officious arrest; a point she had the generosity to *wish* you cleared of: and having mentioned the outrageous letter you had written to me on this occasion, she asked if I had that letter about me?

I owned I had.

She wished to see it.

This puzzled me horribly: for you must needs think that most of the free things which among us rakes pass for wit and spirit, must be shocking stuff to the ears or eyes of persons of delicacy of that sex: and then such an air of levity runs through thy most serious letters; such a false bravery, endeavouring to carry off ludicrously the subjects that most affect thee; that those letters are generally the least fit to be seen which ought to be most to thy credit.

Something like this I observed to her; and would fain have excused myself from showing it: but she was so earnest, that I undertook to read some parts of it, resolving to omit the most exceptionable.

I know thou'lt curse me for that; but I thought it better to oblige her, than to be suspected myself; and so not have it in my power to serve thee with her when so good a foundation was laid for it; and when she knows as bad of thee as I can tell her.

Thou rememberest the contents, I suppose, of thy furious letter.[a] Her remarks upon the different parts of it which I read to her were to the following effect:

Upon thy two first lines, *All undone! undone, by Jupiter!—Zounds, Jack, what shall I do now! A curse upon all my plots and contrivances!* thus she expressed herself:

'Oh how light, how unaffected with the sense of its own crimes is the heart that could dictate to the pen this libertine froth!'

The paragraph which mentions the vile arrest affected her a good deal.

In the next I omitted thy curse upon thy relations, whom thou wert gallanting: and read on the seven subsequent paragraphs, down to thy execrable wish; which was too shocking to read to her. What I read produced the following reflections from her:

'The plots and contrivances which he curses, and the exultings of the wicked wretches on finding me out, show me that all his guilt was premeditated: nor doubt I, that his dreadful perjuries, and inhuman arts, as he went along, were to pass for fine stratagems; for witty sport; and to demonstrate a superiority of inventive talents!—Oh my cruel, cruel brother! had it not been for thee, I had not been thrown upon so pernicious and so despicable a plotter!—But proceed, sir; pray proceed.'

At that part, *Canst thou, oh fatal prognosticator! tell me where my punishments will end?*—she sighed: and when I came to that sentence, *Praying for my reformation, perhaps*—Is that there? said she, sighing again—Wretched man!—and shed a tear for thee. By my faith, Lovelace, I believe she hates thee not!—She

---

a See pp. 1046–7.

has at least a concern, a generous concern, for thy future happiness!—What a noble creature hast thou injured!

She made a very severe reflection upon me, on reading these words—*On your knees, for me, beg her pardon*. 'You had all your lessons, sir, said she, when you came to redeem me—You was so condescending as to kneel: I thought it was the effect of your own humanity, and good-natured earnestness to serve me. Excuse me, sir, I knew not that it was in consequence of a prescribed lesson.'

This concerned me not a little: I could not bear to be thought such a wretched puppet, such a Joseph Leman, such a Tomlinson—I endeavoured therefore, with some warmth to clear myself of this reflection; and she again asked my excuse. 'I was avowedly, she said, the friend of a man whose friendship, she had reason to be sorry to say, was no credit to anybody.' And desired me to proceed—I did; but fared not much better afterwards: for,

On that passage where you say, *I had always been her friend and advocate*, this was her unanswerable remark: 'I find, sir, by this expression, that he had always designs against me; and that you all along knew that he had: would to Heaven you had had the goodness to have contrived some way that might not have endangered your own safety, to give me notice of his baseness, since you approved not of it! But you gentlemen, I suppose, had rather see an innocent fellow-creature ruined, than be thought capable of an action which, however generous, might be likely to loosen the bands of a wicked friendship!'

After this severe but just reflection I would have avoided reading the following, although I had unawares begun the sentence (but she held me to it): *What would I now give, had I permitted you to have been a successful advocate!* And this was her remark upon it—'So, sir, you see, if you had been the happy means of preventing the evils designed me, you would have had your friend's thanks for it when he came to his consideration. This satisfaction, I am persuaded, everyone in the long run will enjoy who has the virtue to withstand, or prevent, a wicked purpose. I was obliged, *I see*, to your kind wishes—but it was a point of honour with you to keep his secret; the greater honour, perhaps, the viler the secret. Yet permit me to wish, Mr Belford, that you were capable of relishing the pleasures that arise to a benevolent mind from VIRTUOUS friendship!—None *other* is worthy of the sacred name. You seem an humane man: I hope, for your own sake, you will one day experience the difference: and when you do, think of Miss Howe and Clarissa Harlowe (I find you know much of my sad story), who were the happiest creatures on earth in each other's friendship, till this friend of yours—' And there she stopped and turned from me.

Where thou callest thyself *A villainous plotter*; 'To take crime to himself, said she, without shame, oh what a hardened wretch is this man!'

On that passage where thou sayest, *Let me know how she has been treated: if roughly, woe be to the guilty!* this was her remark, with an air of indignation: 'What a man is your friend, sir!—Is such a one as *he* to set himself up to punish the guilty?—All the *rough* usage I could receive from them was infinitely *less*'—And there she stopped a moment or two: then proceeding—'And who shall punish *him*? What an assuming wretch!—Nobody but *himself* is entitled to injure the innocent?—He is, I suppose, on earth to act the part which the malignant fiend is supposed to act below, dealing out punishments at his pleasure to every inferior instrument of mischief!'

What, thought I, have I been doing! I shall have this savage fellow think I have been playing him booty in reading part of his letter to this sagacious lady!—Yet, if thou art angry, it can only, in reason, be at thyself; for who would think I might not communicate to her some of the least exceptionable parts of a letter (as a proof of thy sincerity in exculpating thyself from a criminal charge), which thou wrotest to thy friend to convince *him* of thy innocence? But a bad heart, and a bad cause, are confounding things: and so let us put it to its proper account.

I passed over thy charge to me to curse them by the hour; and thy names of *dragon* and *serpents*, though so applicable; since, had I read them, thou must have been supposed to know from the first what creatures they were; vile fellow as thou wert, for bringing so much purity among them! And I closed with thy own concluding paragraph, *A line! A line! A kingdom for a line!* etc. However telling her, since she saw that I omitted some sentences, that there were further vehemences in it; but as they were better fitted to show to me the sincerity of the writer than for so delicate an ear as hers to hear, I chose to pass them over.

You have read enough, said she—He is a wicked, wicked man!—I see he intended to have me in his power at any rate; and I have no doubt of what his purposes were, by what his actions have been. You know his vile Tomlinson, I suppose—you know—But what signifies talking?—Never was there such a premeditately false heart in man (*nothing can be truer, thought I!*). What has he not vowed! What has he not invented! And all for what?—Only to ruin a poor young creature whom he ought to have protected; and whom he had first deprived of all other protection?

She arose and turned from me, her handkerchief at her eyes: and after a pause, came towards me again—'I hope, said she, I talk to a man, who has a better heart: and I thank you, sir, for all your kind, though ineffectual, pleas in my favour formerly, whether the motives for them were compassion, or principle, or both. That they *were* ineffectual, might very probably be owing to your want of earnestness; and *that* as *you* might think, to my want of merit. I might not, in your eye, *deserve* to be saved!—I might appear to you a giddy creature who had run away from her true and natural friends; and who therefore ought to take the consequence of the lot she had drawn.'

I was afraid, for thy sake, to let her know how *very* earnest I had been: but assured her that I had been her zealous friend; and that my motives were founded upon a merit that, I believed, was never equalled: that, however indefensible Mr Lovelace was, he had always done justice to her virtue: that to a full conviction of her untainted honour it was owing, that he so earnestly desired to call so inestimable a jewel his—and was proceeding, when she again cut me short—

Enough, and too much, of this subject, sir!—If he will never more let me behold his face, that is all I have now to ask of him—Indeed, indeed, clasping her hands, *I never will*, if I can by any means not criminally desperate avoid it.

What could I say for thee?—There was no room, however, *at that time* to touch this string again, for fear of bringing upon myself a prohibition, not only of the subject, but of ever attending her again.

I gave some distant intimations of money matters. I should have told thee that, when I read to her that passage where thou biddest me force what sums upon her I can get her to take—she repeated, No, no, no, no! several times with great quickness; and I durst no more than just intimate it again—and that so darkly, as left her room to seem not to understand me.

Indeed I know not the person, man or woman, I should be so much afraid of disobliging, or incurring a censure from, as from her. She has so much true dignity in her manner, without pride or arrogance; which, in those who have either, one is tempted to mortify; such a piercing eye, yet softened so sweetly with rays of benignity, that she commands all one's reverence.

Methinks I have a kind of holy love for this angel of a woman; and it is matter of astonishment to me that thou couldst converse with her a quarter of an hour together, and hold thy devilish purposes.

Guarded as she was by piety, prudence, virtue, dignity, family, fortune, and a purity of heart, that never woman before her boasted, what a true devil must he be (yet I doubt I shall make thee proud!), who could resolve to break through so many fences!

For my own part, I am more and more sensible that I ought not to have contented myself with *representing against*, and *expostulating with thee upon*, thy base intentions: and indeed I had it in my head, more than once, to try to do something for her. But, wretch that I was! I was withheld by notions of false honour, as she justly reproached me, because of thy own *voluntary* communications to me of thy purposes. And then, as she was brought into such a cursed house, and was so watched by thyself, as well as by thy infernal agents, I thought (knowing my man!) that I should only accelerate the intended mischiefs—Moreover, finding thee so much overawed by her virtue that thou hadst not, at thy *first* carrying her thither, the courage to attempt her; and that she had, more than once, without knowing thy base views, obliged thee to abandon them, and to resolve to do her justice, and thyself honour; I hardly doubted that her merit would be triumphant at last.

It is my opinion (if thou holdest thy purposes to marry), that thou canst not do better than to procure thy real aunts, and thy real cousins, to pay her a visit, and to be thy advocates. But, if they decline personal visits, letters from them, and from my Lord M., supported by Miss Howe's interest, may perhaps effect something in thy favour.

But these are only my hopes, founded on what I *wish* for thy sake. The lady, I really think, would choose death rather than thee: and the two women are of opinion, though they know not half of what she has suffered, that her heart is actually broken.

At taking my leave, I tendered my best services to her, and besought her to permit me frequently in inquire after her health.

She made me no answer, but by bowing her head.

Letter 340: MR BELFORD TO ROBERT LOVELACE, ESQ.

Wednesday, July 19

THIS morning I took chair to Smith's; and, being told that the lady had a very bad night, but was up, I sent for her worthy apothecary; who, on his coming to me, approving of my proposal of calling in Dr H. I bid the women acquaint her with the designed visit.

It seems she was at first displeased; yet withdrew her objection: but, after a pause, asked them what she should do? She had effects of value, some of which she intended as soon as she *could* to turn into money; but, till then, had not a single guinea to give the doctor for his fee.

Mrs Lovick said she had five guineas by her: they were at her service.

She would accept of three, she said, if she would take *that* (pulling a diamond ring from her finger), till she repaid her; but on no other terms.

Having been told I was below with Mr Goddard, she desired to speak one word with me, before she saw the doctor.

She was sitting in an elbow-chair, leaning her head on a pillow; Mrs Smith and the widow on each side her chair; her nurse with a phial of hartshorn behind her; in her own hand, her salts.

Raising her head at my entrance, she inquired if the doctor knew Mr Lovelace?

I told her no; and that I believed you never saw him in your life.

Was the doctor my friend?

He was; and a very worthy and skilful man. I named him for his eminence in his profession: and Mr Goddard said he knew not a better physician.

I have but one condition to make before I see the gentleman; that he refuse not his fees from me. If I am poor, sir, I am proud. I will not be under obligation. You may *believe*, sir, I will not. I suffer this visit, because I would not appear ungrateful to the few friends I have left, nor obstinate to such of my relations as may some time hence, for their private satisfaction, inquire after my behaviour in my sick hours. So, sir, you know the condition. And don't let me be vexed: I am very ill; and cannot debate the matter.

Seeing her so determined, I told her if it must be so, it should.

Then, sir, the gentleman may come. But I shall not be able to answer many questions. Nurse, you can tell him at the window there, what a night I have had, and how I have been for two days past. And Mr Goddard, if he be here, can let him know what I have taken. Pray let me be as little questioned as possible.

The doctor paid his respects to her, with the gentlemanly address for which he is noted: and she cast up her sweet eyes to him, with that benignity which accompanies her every graceful look.

I would have retired; but she forbid it.

He took her hand, the lily not of so beautiful a white; Indeed, madam, you are very low, said he: But, give me leave to say, that you can do more for yourself than all the faculty can do for you.

He then withdrew to the window. And, after a short conference with the women, he turned to me and to Mr Goddard, at the other window: We can do nothing here, speaking low, but by cordials and nourishment. What friends has the lady? She seems to be a person of condition; and, ill as she is, a very fine woman——a single lady, I presume?

I whisperingly told him she was. That there were extraordinary circumstances in her case; as I would have apprised him, had I met with him yesterday. That her friends were very cruel to her; but that she could not hear them named, without reproaching herself; though they were much more to blame than she.

I knew I was right, said the doctor. A love case, Mr Goddard! A love case, Mr Belford! There is one person in the world who can do her more service than all the faculty.

Mr Goddard said he had apprehended her disorder was in her mind; and had treated her accordingly: and then told the doctor what he had done: which he approving of, again taking her charming hand, said, My good young lady, you will require very little of our assistance. You must, in a great measure, be your own doctress. Come, *dear* madam (forgive me the familiar tenderness; your aspect commands love, as well as reverence; and a father of children, some of them older than yourself, may be excused for them), cheer up your spirits. Resolve to do all in your power to be well; and you'll soon grow better.

You are very kind, sir, said she. I will take whatever you direct. My spirits have been hurried. I shall be better, I believe, before I am worse. The care of my good friends here, looking at the women, shall not meet with an ungrateful return.

The doctor wrote. He would fain have declined his fee. As her malady, he said, was rather to be relieved by the soothings of a friend, than by the prescriptions of a physician, he should think himself greatly honoured to be admitted rather to *advise* her in the *one* character, than to *prescribe* to her in the *other*.

She answered that she should be always glad to see so humane a gentleman: that his visits would *keep her in charity with his sex*: but that, were she to *forget* that he was her *physician*, she might be apt to abate of the confidence in his skill which might be necessary to effect the amendment that was the end of his visits.

And when he urged her still further, which he did in a very polite manner, and as passing by the door two or three times a day, she said she should always have pleasure in considering him in the kind light he *offered himself to her*: that *that* might be very generous in one person to offer, which would be as ungenerous in another to accept: that indeed she was not at present high in circumstance; and he saw by the tender (which he *must* accept of), that she had greater respect to *her own convenience*, than to *his merit*, or than to the *pleasure* she should take in his visits.

We all withdrew together; and the doctor and Mr Goddard having a great curiosity to know something more of her story, at the motion of the latter we went into a neighbouring coffee-house, and I gave them in confidence a brief relation of it; making all as light for you as I could; and yet you'll suppose that, in order to do but common justice to the lady's character, heavy must be that light.

Three o'clock, afternoon
I JUST now called again at Smith's; and am told she is somewhat better; which she attributed to the soothings of her doctor. She expressed herself highly pleased with both gentlemen; and said that their behaviour to her was perfectly *paternal*—

Paternal, poor lady!—Never having been, till very lately, from under her parents' wings, and now abandoned by all her friends, she is for finding out something *paternal* and *maternal* in everyone (the latter qualities in Mrs Lovick and Mrs Smith), to supply to herself the father and mother her dutiful heart pants after!

Mrs Smith told me that after we were gone she gave the keys of her trunks and drawers to her and the widow Lovick, and desired them to take an inventory of them; which they did, in her presence.

They also informed me that she had requested them to find her a purchaser for two rich dressed suits; one never worn, the other not above once or twice.

This shocked me exceedingly: *perhaps it may thee a little!!!*—Her reason for so doing, she told them, was that she should never live to wear them: that her sister, and other relations were above wearing them: that her mother would not endure in her sight anything that was hers: that she wanted the money: that she would not be obliged to anybody when she had effects by her, which she had no occasion for. And yet, said she, I expect not that they will fetch a price answerable to their value.

They were both very much concerned, as they owned; and asked my advice upon it: and the richness of her apparel having given them a still higher notion of her rank than they had before, they supposed she must be of quality; and again wanted to know her story.

I told them that she was indeed a lady of family and fortune: I still gave them room to suppose her married: but left it to her to tell them all in her own time and manner. All I would say was, that she had been very vilely treated; deserved it not; and was all innocence and purity.

You may suppose that they both expressed their astonishment that there could be a man in the world who could ill-treat so fine a creature.

As to disposing of the two suits of apparel, I told Mrs Smith that she should pretend that upon inquiry she had found a friend who would purchase the richest of them; but (*that she might not mistrust*) would stand upon a good bargain. And having twenty guineas about me, I left them with her in part of payment; and bid her *pretend* to get her to part with it for as little more as she could induce her to take.

I am setting out for Edgware with poor Belton—more of whom in my next. I shall return tomorrow; and leave this in readiness for your messenger, if he shall call in my absence. Adieu!

Letter 341: MR LOVELACE TO JOHN BELFORD, ESQ.

(In answer to Letter 339)

M. Hall, Wed. night, July 19

THOU mightest well apprehend that I should think thou wert playing me booty, in communicating my letter to the lady.

Thou askest who would think thou mightest not read to her the least exceptionable parts of a letter written in my own defence to thee?—*I'll tell thee who*—the man who in the same letter that he asks this question tells the friend whom he exposes to her resentment, 'That there is such an air of levity runs through his most serious letters that those of his are *least fit to be seen*, which ought to be *most to his credit*.' And now, what thinkest thou of thy self-condemned folly? Be, however, I charge thee, more circumspect for the future, that so this clumsy error may stand singly by itself.

'It is painful to her to think of me!' 'Libertine froth!' 'So pernicious and so despicable a plotter!' 'A man whose friendship is no credit to anybody!' 'Hardened wretch!' 'The devil's counterpart!' 'A wicked, wicked man!'—But *did* she, *could* she, *dared* she, to say or *imply* all this?—And say it to a man whom she praises for humanity, and prefers to myself for that virtue; when all the humanity *he* shows, and *she knows it too*, is by *my* direction—so robs me of the credit of my own works? Admirably entitled, all this shows her, to thy refinement upon the words *resentment* and *revenge*. But thou wert always aiming and blundering at something thou never couldst make out.

The praise thou givest to her *ingenuousness* is another of thy peculiars. I think not as *thou* dost of her tell-tale recapitulations and exclamations—What end can they answer?—Only that thou hast an *holy* love (The devil fetch thee for thy oddity!), or it is extremely provoking to suppose one sees such a charming creature stand upright before a libertine, and talk of the sin against her that cannot be forgiven!—I wish at my heart that these chaste ladies would have a little modesty in their anger!—It would sound very strange if I, Robert Lovelace, should pretend to have more true delicacy in a point that requires the utmost, than Miss Clarissa Harlowe.

I think I will put it into the head of her Nurse Norton, and her Miss Howe, by some one of my agents, to chide the dear novice for her proclamations.

But to be serious; let me tell thee that severe as she is, and saucy, in asking so contemptuously, 'What a man is your friend, sir, to set himself to punish guilty people!' I will never forgive the cursed woman who could commit this last horrid violence on so excellent a creature.

The barbarous insults of the two nymphs in their visits to her; the choice of the most execrable den that could be found out, in order no doubt to induce her to go back to theirs; and the still more execrable attempt to propose to her a man who would pay the debt; a snare, I make no question, laid for her despairing and resenting heart by that devilish Sally (thinking her, no doubt, a *woman*), in order to ruin her with me; and to provoke me, in a fury, to give her up to their remorseless cruelty; are outrages that, to express myself in her style, I never *can*, never *will*, forgive.

But as to thy opinion, and the two women's at Smith's, that her heart is broken; that is the true women's language: I wonder how *thou* camest into it: thou who hast seen and heard of so many *female deaths* and *revivals*.

I'll tell thee what makes *against* this notion of theirs.

Her time of life and charming constitution: the good she ever delighted to do, and fancied she was born to do: and which she may still continue to do, to as high a degree as ever; nay, higher; since I am no sordid varlet, thou knowest: her religious turn; a turn that will always teach her to bear *inevitable* evils with patience: the contemplation upon her last noble triumph over me, and over the whole crew; and upon her succeeding escape from us all: her will unviolated: and the inward pride of having not deserved the treatment she has met with.

How is it possible to imagine that a woman who has all these *consolatories* to reflect upon will die of a broken heart?

On the contrary, I make no doubt but that, as she recovers from the dejection into which this last scurvy villainy (which none but wretches of her own sex *could* have been guilty of) has thrown her, returning love will re-enter her time-pacified mind: her thoughts will then turn once more on the conjugal pivot: of course she will have livelier notions in her head; and these will make her perform all her circumvolutions with ease and pleasure; though not with so high a degree of either, as if the dear proud rogue could have exalted herself above the rest of her sex as she turned round.

Thou askest, on reciting the bitter invectives that the lady made against thy poor friend (standing before her, I suppose, with thy fingers in thy mouth), *What couldst thou say* FOR *me?*

Have I not, in my former letters, suggested an hundred things, which a friend *in earnest* to vindicate or excuse a friend might say on such an occasion?

But now to current topics, and the present state of matters here—It is true, as my servant told thee, that Miss Howe had engaged, before this cursed woman's officiousness, to use her interest with her friend in my behalf: and yet she told my cousins, in the visit they made her, that it was her opinion that she would never forgive me.

I long to know what Miss Howe wrote to her friend, in order to induce her to marry the *despicable plotter*; the *man whose friendship is no credit to anybody*; the *wicked, wicked man*. Thou hadst the two letters in thy hand. Had they been in mine, the seal would have yielded to the touch of my warm finger (perhaps without the help of the post-office bullet[1]), and the folds, as other plications have done, opened of themselves to oblige my curiosity. A wicked omission, Jack, not to contrive to send them down to me, by man and horse! It might have passed that the messenger who brought the second letter took them both back. I could have returned them by another, when copied, as from Miss Howe, and nobody but myself and thee the wiser.

My two aunts, finding the treaty, upon the success of which they have set their foolish hearts, likely to run into length, are about departing to their own seats; having taken from me the best security the nature of the case will admit of, that is to say, *my word*, to marry the lady if she will have me.

All I have to do in my present uncertainty is to brighten up my faculties, by filing off the rust they have contracted by the town smoke, a long imprisonment in my close attendance to so little purpose on my fair perverse; and to brace up, if I can, the relaxed fibres of my mind, which have been twitched and convulsed like the nerves of some tottering paralytic, by means of the tumults she has excited in it; that so I may be able to present to her a husband as worthy as I can be of her acceptance; or, if she reject me, be in a capacity to resume my usual gaiety of heart, and show others of the misleading sex that I am not discouraged by the difficulties I have met with from this sweet individual of it, from endeavouring to make myself as acceptable to them as before.

In this latter case, one tour to France and Italy, I dare say, will do the business. Miss Harlowe will by that time have forgotten all she has suffered from the ungrateful Lovelace: though it will be impossible that her Lovelace should ever forget a woman whose equal he despairs to meet with, were he to travel from one end of the world to the other.

If thou continuest paying off the heavy debts my long letters for so many weeks together have made thee groan under, I will endeavour to restrain myself in the desires I have (importunate as they are) of going to town, to throw myself at the feet of my soul's beloved. *Policy* and *honesty* both join to strengthen the restraint my *own promise* and *thy engagement* have laid me under on this head. I would not afresh provoke: on the contrary, would give time for her resentments to subside, that so all that follows may be her own act and deed.

HICKMAN (I have a mortal aversion to that fellow!) has by a line which I have just now received requested an interview with me on Friday at Mr Dormer's, as at a *common friend*'s. Does the business he wants to meet me upon require that it should be at a *common friend*'s?—A challenge implied; i'n't it, Belford?—I shall not be civil to him, I doubt. He has been an intermeddler!—Then I envy him on Miss Howe's account: for if I have a right notion of this Hickman, it is impossible that that virago can ever love him.

A charming encouragement for a man of intrigue, when he has reason to believe that the woman he has a view upon has no love for her husband! What good principles must that wife have, who is kept in against temptation by a sense of her duty and plighted faith, where affection has no hold of her!

Prithee let's know, very particularly how it fares with poor Belton—'Tis an honest fellow—Something more than his Thomasine seems to stick with him.

Tourville, Mowbray, and myself, pass away our time as pleasantly as possibly we can without thee. I wish we don't add to Lord M.'s gouty days by the joy we give him.

This is one advantage, as I believe I have elsewhere observed, that we male-delinquents in love matters have of the other sex—for while they, poor things! sit sighing in holes and corners, or run to woods and groves to bemoan themselves for their baffled hopes, we can rant and roar, hunt and hawk; and by new loves banish from our hearts all remembrance of the old ones.

Merrily, however, as we pass our time, my reflections upon the injuries done to this noble creature bring a qualm upon my heart very often. But I know she will permit me to make her amends, after she has plagued me heartily; and that's my consolation.

An honest fellow still!—Clap thy wings, and crow, Jack!—

Letter 342: MISS HOWE TO MISS CLARISSA HARLOWE

Thursday morn. July 20

WHAT, my dearest creature, have been your sufferings!—What must have been your anguish on so disgraceful an insult, committed in the open streets, and in the open day!

No end, I think, of the undeserved calamities of a dear soul who has been so unhappily driven and betrayed into the hands of a vile libertine!—How was I shocked at the receiving of your letter written by another hand, and only dictated by you!—You must be very ill. Nor is it to be wondered at. But I hope it is rather from hurry and surprise, and lowness, which *may* be overcome, than from a grief given way to, which may be attended with effects I cannot bear to think of.

But whatever you do, my dear, you must not despond! Indeed you must not despond! Hitherto you have been in no fault: but despair would be all your own; and the worst fault you can be guilty of.

I cannot bear to look upon another hand instead of yours. My dear creature, send me a few lines, though *ever so few*, in your own hand, if possible—for they will revive my heart; especially if they can acquaint me of your amended health.

I expect your answer to my letter of the 13th. We *all* expect it with impatience.

His relations are persons of *so much* honour—They are so *very* earnest to rank you among them—The wretch is so *very* penitent: *every one* of *his* family says he is—*Your own* are so implacable—Your last distress, though the consequence of his former villainy, yet neither brought on by his direction, nor with his knowledge; and so much resented by him—that my mamma is absolutely of opinion that *you should be his*—especially if, yielding to my wishes as in my letter and those of all his friends, you *would* have complied had it not been for this horrid arrest.

I will enclose the copy of the letter I wrote to Miss Montague last Tuesday, on hearing that nobody knew what was become of you; and the answer to it, underwritten and signed by Lord M. and Lady Sarah Sadleir, and Lady Betty Lawrance, as well as by the young ladies—and also by the wretch himself.

I own that I like not the turn of what he has written to me; and before I will further interest myself in his favour, I have determined to inform myself by a friend, from his own mouth, of his sincerity, and whether his *whole inclination* be in his request to me, exclusive of the *wishes of his relations*. Yet my heart rises against him, on the supposition that there is the shadow of a reason for such a question, the lady Miss Clarissa Harlowe. But, I think with my mother, that marriage is now the only means left to make your future life tolerably easy—*happy* there is no saying—In the eye of the world itself, his disgraces, in *that* case, will be more than yours—and to those who know you, glorious will be your triumph.

I am obliged to accompany my mother soon to the Isle of Wight. My aunt Harman is in a declining way, and insists upon seeing us both; and Mr Hickman too, I think.

His sister, of whom we had heard so much, with her lord, were brought t'other day to visit us. She strangely likes me, or says she does.

I can't say but that I think she answers the excellent character we have heard of her.

It would be death to me to set out for the little island, and not see you first: and yet my mother (fond of exerting an authority that she herself, by that exertion, often brings into question) insists that my next visit to you *must* be a congratulatory one, as Mrs Lovelace.

When I know what will be the result of the questions to be put in my name to that wretch, and what is your mind on my letter of the 13th, I shall tell you more of mine.

The bearer promises to make so much dispatch, as to attend you this very afternoon. May he return with good tidings to

Your ever affectionate
ANNA HOWE

Letter 343: MISS CLARISSA HARLOWE TO MISS HOWE

Thursday afternoon

YOU oppress me, my dearest Miss Howe, by your flaming, yet steady love. I will be very brief, because I am not well; yet a good deal better than I was; and because I am preparing an answer to yours of the 13th. But, beforehand, I must tell you, my dear, I will *not* have that man—Don't be angry with me—But indeed I won't. So let him be asked no questions about me, I beseech you.

I do *not* despond, my dear. I hope I may say, *I will* not despond. Is not my condition greatly mended? I thank Heaven it is!

I am no prisoner now in a vile house. I am not now in the power of that man's devices. I am not now obliged to hide myself in corners for fear of him. One of his intimate companions is become my warm friend, and engages to keep him from me, and that by his own consent. I am among honest people. I have all my clothes and effects restored me. The wretch himself bears testimony to my honour.

Indeed I am very weak and ill: but I have an excellent physician, Dr H., and as worthy an apothecary, Mr Goddard—Their treatment of me, my dear, is perfectly *paternal!* My mind too, I can find, begins to strengthen: and methinks at times I find myself superior to my calamities.

I shall have sinkings sometimes. I must expect such. And my father's maledict— But you will chide me for introducing that, now I am enumerating my comforts.

But I charge you, my dear, that you do not suffer my calamities to sit too heavy upon your own mind: if you do, that will be to new-point some of those arrows that have been blunted and lost their sharpness.

If you would contribute to *my* happiness, give way, my dear, to *your own*; and to the cheerful prospects before you!

You will think very meanly of your Clarissa Harlowe, if you do not believe that the greatest pleasure she can receive in this life is in your prosperity and welfare. Think not of me, my only friend, but as we were in times past: and suppose me gone a great, great way off!—a long journey!—How often are the dearest of friends, at their country's call, thus parted—with a *certainty* for years—with a *probability* for ever!

Love me still, however. But let it be with a weaning love. I am not what I was when we were *inseparable* lovers, as I may say—Our *views* must now be different— Resolve, my dear, to make a worthy man happy, because a worthy man must make *you* so—And so, my dearest love, for the present adieu!—Adieu, my dearest love!—But I shall soon write again, I hope!

Letter 344: MR BELFORD TO ROBERT LOVELACE, ESQ.

(In answer to Letter 341)

Thursday, July 20

I READ that part of your conclusion to poor Belton, where you inquire after him, and mention how merrily you and the rest pass your time at M. Hall. He fetched a deep sigh; *You are all very happy!* were his words—I am sorry they *were* his words; for, poor fellow, he is going very fast. Change of air, *he* hopes, will mend him, joined to the cheerful company I have left him in. But nothing, I dare say, will.

A consuming malady and a consuming mistress, to an indulgent keeper are dreadful things to struggle with both together. Violence must be used to get rid of the latter: and yet he has not spirit left him to exert himself. His house is Thomasine's house; not his. He has not been within his doors for a fortnight past. Vagabonding about from inn to inn; entering each for a bait only; and staying two or three days without power to remove; and hardly knowing which to go to next. His malady is within him; and he cannot run away from it.

Her boys (once he thought them his) are sturdy enough to shoulder him in his own house as they pass by him. Siding with the mother, they in a manner expel him; and in his absence riot away on the remnant of his broken fortunes. As to their mother, who was once so tender, so submissive, so studious to oblige, that we all pronounced him happy, and his course of life the eligible, she is now so termagant, so insolent, that he cannot contend with her, without doing infinite prejudice to his health. A broken-spirited defensive, *hardly a defensive* therefore reduced to: and this to a heart for so many years waging *offensive* war (nor valuing whom the opponent), what a reduction!—Now comparing himself to the super-annuated lion in the fable, kicked in the jaws and laid sprawling by the spurning heel of an ignoble ass!

I have undertaken his cause. He has given me leave, yet not without reluctance, to put him into possession of his own house; and to place in it for him his unhappy sister, whom he has hitherto slighted, *because* unhappy. It is hard, he told me (and wept, poor fellow, when he said it), that he cannot be permitted to die quietly in his own house!—The fruits of blessed keeping these!—

Though but lately apprised of her infidelity, it now comes out to have been of so long continuance, that he has no room to believe the boys to be his: yet how fond did he use to be of them!

If I have occasion for your assistance, and that of our compeers, in reinstating the poor fellow, I will give you notice. Meantime, I have just now been told that Thomasine declares she will not stir: for it seems she suspects that measures will be fallen upon to make her quit. She is Mrs Belton, she says, and will prove her marriage.

If she give herself these airs in his lifetime, what would she attempt to do after his death?

Her boys threaten anybody who shall presume to insult their *mother*. Their *father* (as they *call* poor Belton) they speak of as an unnatural one. And their probably *true father* is for ever there, *hostilely* there, passing for her cousin, as usual: now her *protecting cousin*.

Hardly ever, I dare say, was there a keeper that did not make a keeperess; who lavished away on her kept-fellow what she obtained from the extravagant folly of him who kept her.

I will do without you, if I can. The case will be only, as I conceive, like that of the ancient Sarmatians, returning after many years absence to their homes, their wives then in possession of their slaves: so that they had to contend not only with those *wives*, conscious of their infidelity, and with their *slaves*, but with the *children* of those slaves, grown up to manhood, resolute to defend their mothers and their long manumitted fathers. But the noble Sarmatians, scorning to attack their slaves with equal weapons, only provided themselves with the same sort of whips with which they used formerly to chastise them. And, attacking them with them, the miscreants fled before them. In memory of which, to this day the device on the coin in Novogrod in Russia, a city of the ancient Sarmatia, is a man on horseback with a whip in his hand.[1]

The poor fellow takes it ill that you did not press him more than you did to be of your party at M. Hall. It is owing to Mowbray, he is sure, that he had so very slight an invitation from one whose invitations used to be so warm.

Mowbray's speech to him, he says, he never will forgive: 'Why, Tom,' said the brutal fellow with a curse, 'thou droopest like a pip or roup-cloaking chicken.

Thou shouldst grow perter, or submit to a solitary quarantine, if thou wouldst not infect the whole brood.'

For my own part, only that this poor fellow is in distress, as well in his affairs as in his mind, or I should be sick of you all. Such is the relish I have of the conversation, and such my admiration of the deportment and sentiments of this divine lady, that I would forgo a month, even of thy company, to be admitted into hers but for one hour: and I am highly in conceit with myself, greatly as I used to value *thine*, for being able, spontaneously as I may say, to make this preference.

It is, after all, a devilish life we have lived. And to consider how it all ends in a very few years: to see what a state of ill health this poor fellow is so soon reduced to: and then to observe how every one of ye run away from the unhappy being, as rats from a falling house, is fine comfort to help a man to look back upon companions ill-chosen, and a life misspent!

For my own part, if I can get some good family to credit me with a sister or a daughter, as I have now an increased fortune which will enable me to propose handsome settlements, I will desert ye all; marry, and live a life of reason, rather than a life of brute, for the time to come.

Letter 345: MR BELFORD TO ROBERT LOVELACE, ESQ.

Thursday night
I WAS forced to take back my twenty guineas. How the women managed it, I can't tell (I suppose too readily found a purchaser for the rich suit); but she mistrusted that I was the advancer of the money; and would not let the clothes go. But Mrs Lovick has actually sold, for fifteen guineas some rich lace, worth three times the sum: out of which she repaid her the money she borrowed for fees to the doctor, in an illness occasioned by the barbarity of the most savage of men. *Thou knowest his name!*

The doctor called on her in the morning, it seems, and had a short debate with her about fees. She insisted that he should take one every time he came, write or not write; mistrusting that he only gave verbal directions to Mrs Lovick, or the nurse, to avoid taking any.

He said that it would have been impossible for him, had he *not* been a physician, to forbear inquiries after the health and welfare of so excellent a person. He had not the thought of paying her a compliment in declining the offered fee: but he knew her case could not so suddenly vary as to demand his daily visits. She must permit him, therefore, to inquire after her health of the women below; and he must not think of coming up, if he were to be *pecuniarily* rewarded for the satisfaction he was so desirous to give himself.

It ended in a compromise for a fee each other time: which she unwillingly submitted to; telling him that though she was at present desolate and in disgrace, yet her circumstances were, of right, high; and no expenses could rise so as to be scrupled, whether she lived or died. But she submitted, she added, to the compromise, in hopes to see him as often as he had opportunity; for she really looked upon him and Mr Goddard, from their kind and tender treatment of her, with a regard next to filial.

I hope thou wilt make thyself acquainted with this worthy doctor, when thou comest to town; and give him thy thanks for putting her into conceit with the sex that thou hast given her so much reason to execrate.

Farewell.

Letter 346: MR LOVELACE TO JOHN BELFORD, ESQ.

M. Hall, Friday, July 21

JUST returned from an interview with this Hickman: a precise fop of a fellow, as starched as his ruffles.

Thou knowest I love him not, Jack; and whom we love not, we cannot allow a merit to; perhaps not the merit they should be granted—However, I am in earnest when I say that he seems to me to be so set, so prim, so affected, so mincing, yet so clouterly in his person, that I dare engage for thy opinion if thou dost justice to him, and to thyself, that thou never beheldest such another, except in a pier-glass.

I'll tell thee how I played him off.

He came in his own chariot to Dormer's; and we took a turn in the garden, at his request. He was devilish ceremonious, and made a bushel of apologies for the freedom he was going to take; and, after half a hundred hums and haws, told me that he came—that he came—to wait on me—at the request of *dear Miss Howe*, on the account—on the account—of Miss Harlowe.

Well, sir, speak on, said I: but give me leave to say, that if your book be as long as your preface, it will take up a week to read it.

This was pretty rough, thou'lt say: but there's nothing like balking these formalists at first. When they're put out of their road, they are filled with doubts of themselves, and can never get into it again: so that an honest fellow, impertinently attacked as I was, has all the game in his own hand quite through the conference.

He stroked his chin, and hardly knew what to say. At last, after parenthesis within parenthesis, apologizing for apologies, in imitation I suppose of Swift's Digressions in Praise of Digressions[1]—I presume, I presume, sir, you were privy to the visit made to Miss Howe by the young ladies your cousins, in the name of Lord M. and Lady Sarah Sadleir, and Lady Betty Lawrance?

I *was*, sir: and Miss Howe had a letter afterwards, signed by his lordship and those ladies, and underwritten by myself. Have you seen it, sir?

I can't say but I have. It is the principal cause of this visit: for Miss Howe thinks your part of it is written with such an air of levity—pardon me, sir—that she knows not whether you are in earnest or not, in your address to *her* for her interest to her friend.[a]

Will Miss Howe permit me to explain myself in person to her, Mr Hickman?

Oh sir, by no means: Miss Howe, I am sure, would not give you that trouble.

I should not think it a trouble. I will most readily attend you, sir, to Miss Howe, and satisfy her in all her scruples. Come, sir, I will wait upon you now. You have a chariot. Are alone. We can talk as we ride.

He hesitated, wriggled, winced, stroked his ruffles, set his wig, and pulled his

---

a See p. 1050.

neckcloth which was long enough for a bib—I am not going directly back to Miss Howe, sir. It will be as well, if you will be so good as to satisfy Miss Howe by me.

What is it she scruples, Mr Hickman?

Why, sir, Miss Howe observes that in your part of the letter, you say—but let me see, sir: I have a copy of what you wrote (pulling it out). Will you give me leave, sir?—Thus you begin—*Dear Miss Howe*—

No offence, I hope, Mr Hickman?

None in the least, sir!—None at all, sir!—Taking aim as it were to read.

Do you use spectacles, Mr Hickman?

Spectacles, sir! His whole broad face lifted up at me. Spectacles!—What makes you ask me such a question? Such a young man as I use spectacles, sir!—

They do in Spain, Mr Hickman; young as well as old; to save their eyes. Have you ever read Prior's *Alma*, Mr Hickman?

I have, sir—*Custom* is everything in nations, as well as with individuals: I know the meaning of your question—But 'tis not the *English* custom—[2]

Was you ever in Spain, Mr Hickman?

No, sir: I have been in Holland.

In Holland, sir!—Never in France or Italy?—I was resolved to travel with him into the land of *Puzzledom*.

No, sir, I cannot say I have, as yet.

That's a wonder, sir, when on the continent!

I went on a particular affair: I was obliged to return soon.

Well, sir; you was going to read—Pray be pleased to proceed.

Again he took aim, as if his eyes were older than the rest of him; and read, *After what is written above, and signed by names and characters of such unquestionable honour*—To be sure, taking off his eye, nobody questions the honour of Lord M., nor that of the good ladies, who signed the letter.

I hope, Mr Hickman, nobody questions mine neither?

If you please, sir, I will read on—*I might have been excused signing a name, almost as hateful to myself* (you are pleased to say), *as I KNOW it is to* YOU—

Well, Mr Hickman, I must interrupt you at this place. In what I wrote to Miss Howe, I distinguished the word KNOW. I had a reason for it. Miss Howe has been very free with my character. I have never done her any harm. I take it very ill of her. And I hope, sir, you come in her name to make excuses for it.

Miss Howe, sir, is a very polite young lady. She is not accustomed to treat any gentleman's character unbecomingly.

Then *I* have the more reason to take it amiss, Mr Hickman.

Why, sir, you know the friendship—

No friendship should warrant such freedoms as Miss Howe has taken with my character.

I believe he began to wish he had not come near me. He seemed quite disconcerted.

Have you not heard Miss Howe treat my name with great—

Sir, I come not to offend or affront you: but you know what a love there is between Miss Howe and Miss Harlowe—I doubt, sir, you have not treated Miss Harlowe as so fine a young lady deserved to be treated: and if love for her friend has made Miss Howe take freedoms, as you call them, a generous mind on such an occasion will rather be sorry for having given the *cause*, than—

I know your consequence, sir!—But I'd rather have this reproof from a lady than from a gentleman. I have a great desire to wait upon Miss Howe. I am persuaded we should soon come to a good understanding. Generous minds are always of kin. I know we should agree in everything. Pray, Mr Hickman, be so kind as to introduce me to Miss Howe.

Sir—I can signify your desire, if you please, to Miss Howe.

Do so. Be pleased to read on, Mr Hickman.

He did very formally, as if I remembered not what I had written; and when he came to the passage about the halter, the parson, and the hangman, reading it, Why, sir, says he, does not this look like a jest?—Miss Howe thinks it does. It is not in the lady's *power*, you know, sir, to doom you to the gallows.

Then, if it were, Mr Hickman, you think she would?

You say here to Miss Howe, proceeded he, that Miss Harlowe is the *most injured of her sex*. I know from Miss Howe that she highly resents the injuries you own: insomuch that Miss Howe doubts that she shall ever prevail upon her to overlook them: and as your family are all desirous you should repair her wrongs, and likewise desire Miss Howe's interposition with her friend; Miss Howe fears from this part of your letter that you are too much in jest; and that your offer to do her justice is rather in compliment to your friends' entreaties, than proceeding from your own inclinations: and she desires to know your true sentiments on this occasion before she interposes further.

Do you think, Mr Hickman, that if I am capable of deceiving my own relations, I have so much obligation to Miss Howe, who has always treated me with great freedom, as to acknowledge to *her* what I don't to *them*?

Sir, I beg pardon—but Miss Howe thinks that, as you have written to her, she may ask you by me for an explanation of what you have written.

You see, Mr Hickman, something of me—Do *you* think I am in jest or in earnest?

I see, sir, you are a gay gentleman, of fine spirits, and all that—All I beg in Miss Howe's name is to know if you really, and *bona fide*, join with your friends in desiring her to use her interest to reconcile you to Miss Harlowe?

I should be extremely glad to be reconciled to Miss Harlowe; and should owe great obligations to Miss Howe if she could bring about so happy an event.

Well, sir, and you have no objections to marriage, I presume, as the terms of that reconciliation?

I never liked matrimony in my life. I must be plain with you, Mr Hickman.

I am sorry for it: I think it a very happy state.

I hope you will find it so, Mr Hickman.

I doubt not but I shall, sir. And I dare say, so would you, if you were to have Miss Harlowe.

If I could be happy in it with anybody, it would be with Miss Harlowe.

I am surprised, sir!—Then, after all, you don't think of marrying Miss Harlowe!—after the hard usage—

What hard usage, Mr Hickman? I don't doubt but a lady of her niceness has represented what would appear trifles to any other, in a very strong light.

If what I have had hinted to me, sir—excuse me—has been offered to the lady, she has more than trifles to complain of.

Let me know what you have heard, Mr Hickman? I will very truly answer to the accusations.

Sir, you know best what you have done: you own the lady is the *most injured, as well as the most deserving, of her sex.*

I do, sir; and yet, I would be glad to know what you have *heard*; for on that, perhaps, depends my answer to the questions Miss Howe puts to me by you.

Why then, sir, since you ask it, you cannot be displeased if I answer you. In the first place, sir, you will acknowledge, I suppose, that you promised Miss Harlowe marriage, and all that?

Well, sir, and I suppose what you have to charge me with is that I was desirous to have *all that* without marriage.

Cot-so, sir, I know you are deemed to be a man of wit: but may I not ask if these things sit not too light upon you?

When a thing is done, and cannot be helped, 'tis right to make the best of it. I wish the lady would think so too.

I think, sir, ladies should not be deceived. I think a promise to a lady should be as binding as to any other person, at the least.

I *believe* you think so, Mr Hickman: and I believe you are a very honest good sort of a man.

I would always keep my word, sir, whether to man or woman.

You say well. And far be it from me to persuade you to do otherwise. But what have you farther heard?

Thou wilt think, Jack, I must be very desirous to know in what light my elected spouse had represented things to Miss Howe; and how far Miss Howe had communicated them to Mr Hickman.

Sir, this is no part of my present business.

But, Mr Hickman, 'tis part of mine. I hope you would not expect that I should answer *your* questions, at the same time that you refuse to answer *mine*. What, pray, have you farther heard?

Why then, sir, if I must say, I am told that Miss Harlowe was carried to a very bad house.

Why, indeed, the people did not prove so good as they should be—What farther have you heard?

I have heard, sir, that the lady had strange advantages taken of her, very *unfair* ones; but what I cannot say.

And *cannot* you say? Cannot you *guess*? Then I'll tell you, sir. Perhaps some liberty was taken with her, when she was asleep. Do you think no lady ever was taken at such an advantage?—You know, Mr Hickman, that ladies are very shy of trusting themselves with the modestest of our sex, when they are disposed to sleep; and why so, if they did not *expect* that advantages would be taken of them at such times?

But, sir, had not the lady something given her to make her sleep?

Ay, Mr Hickman, that's the question: I want to know if the lady says she had?

I have not seen all she has written; but by what I have heard, it is a very black affair—excuse me, sir.

I do excuse you, Mr Hickman: but, supposing it were so, do you think a lady was never imposed upon by wine, or so?—Do you think the most cautious woman in the world might not be cheated by a stronger liquor for a smaller, when she was thirsty, after a fatigue in this very warm weather? And do you think if she was thus thrown into a profound sleep, that she is the only lady that was ever taken at such advantage?

Even as you make it, Mr Lovelace, this matter is not a light one. But I fear it is a great deal heavier than as you put it.

What reasons have you to fear this, sir? What has the lady said? Pray, let me know. I have *reason* to be so earnest.

Why, sir, Miss Howe herself knows not the whole. The lady promises to give her all the particulars at a proper time, if she lives; but has said enough to make it out to be a very bad affair.

I am glad Miss Harlowe has not yet given all the particulars. And, since she has not, you may tell Miss Howe from me that neither she, nor any lady in the world, can be more virtuous than Miss Harlowe is to this hour, as to her own mind. Tell her that I hope she never *will* know the particulars; but that she has been unworthily used: tell her, that though I know not what she has said, yet I have such an opinion of her veracity that I would blindly subscribe to the truth of every tittle of it, though it make me ever so black. Tell her that I have but *three* things to blame her for: *one*, that she won't give me an opportunity of repairing her wrongs: the *second*, that she is so ready to acquaint everybody with what she has suffered, that it will put it out of my power to redress those wrongs with any tolerable reputation to either of us. Will this, Mr Hickman, answer any part of the intention of this visit?

Why, sir, this is talking like a man of honour, I own. But you say there is a *third* thing you blame the lady for; may I ask what that is?

I don't know, sir, whether I ought to tell it you or not. Perhaps you won't believe it if I do. But though the lady will tell the *truth*, and nothing *but* the truth, yet perhaps she will not tell the *whole* truth.

Pray, sir—but it mayn't be proper—Yet you give me great curiosity: sure there is no misconduct in the lady. I hope there is not. I am sure, if Miss Howe did not believe her to be faultless in every particular, she would not interest herself so much in her favour as she does, dearly as she loves her.

I love the lady too well, Mr Hickman, to wish to lessen her in Miss Howe's opinion; especially as she is abandoned of every other friend. But, perhaps, it would hardly be credited, if I should tell you.

I should be very sorry, sir, and so would Miss Howe, if this poor lady's conduct had laid her under obligation to you for this reserve—You have so much the appearance of a gentleman, as well as are so much distinguished in your family and fortunes, that I hope you are incapable of loading such a young lady as this, in order to lighten yourself—excuse me, sir.

I do, I do, Mr Hickman. You say you came not with any intention to affront me. I take freedom, and I give it—I should be very loath, I repeat, to say anything that may weaken Miss Harlowe in the good opinion of the only friend she thinks she has left.

It may not be proper, said he, for me to know your *third* article against this unhappy lady: but I never heard of anybody, out of her own implacable family, that had the least doubt of her honour. Mrs Howe, indeed, once said after a conference with one of her uncles, that she feared all was not right of her side— But else, I never heard——

Oons, sir, in a fierce tone, and with an erect mien, stopping short upon him, which made him start back—'Tis next to blasphemy to question the lady's honour. She is more pure than a vestal; for vestals have been often warmed by their own fires. No age, from the first to the present, ever produced, nor will the future to the end of the world, I dare aver, ever produce, a young blooming lady, tried as she has been tried, who has stood all trials as she has done—Let me tell you, sir, that you never saw, never knew, never heard of, such another lady as Miss Harlowe.

Sir, sir, I beg your pardon. Far be it from me to question the lady. You have not heard me say a word, that could be so construed. I have the utmost honour for her. Miss Howe loves her, as she loves her own soul; and that she would not do if she were not sure she were as virtuous as herself.

As herself, sir!—I have a high opinion of Miss Howe, sir—but, I dare say—

What, sir, dare you say of Miss Howe?—I hope, sir, you will not presume to say anything to the disparagement of Miss Howe!

Presume, Mr Hickman!—That is *presuming* language, let me tell you, Mr Hickman!

The *occasion* for it, Mr Lovelace, if designed, is *presuming*, if you please—I am not a man ready to take offence, sir—especially where I am employed as a mediator. But no man breathing shall say disparaging things of Miss Howe, in my hearing, without observation.

Well said, Mr Hickman. I dislike not your spirit, on such a *supposed* occasion. But what I was going to say is this, that there is not, in my opinion, a woman in the world who ought to compare herself with Miss Clarissa Harlowe, till she has stood *her* trials, and has behaved *under* them, and *after* them, as she has done. You see, sir, I speak against myself. You see I do. For, libertine as I am thought to be, I never will attempt to bring down the measures of right and wrong to the standard of my actions.

Why, sir, this is very right. It is very *noble*, I will say. But 'tis pity—excuse me, sir—'tis pity that the man who can pronounce so fine a sentence, will not square his actions accordingly.

That, Mr Hickman, is another point. We all err in some things. I wish not that Miss Howe should have Miss Harlowe's trials: and I rejoice that she is in no danger of any such from so good a man.

Poor Hickman!—He looked as if he knew not whether I meant a compliment or a reflection!

But, proceeded I, since I find that I have excited your curiosity, that you may not go away with a doubt that may be injurious to the most admirable of women, I am inclined to hint to you, what I have in the *third* place to blame her for.

Sir, as you please—It may not be proper—

It cannot be very *improper*, Mr Hickman—So let me ask you, what would Miss Howe think if her friend is the *more* determined against me, because she thinks (in revenge to me, I verily believe that!) of encouraging another lover?

How, sir!—Sure this cannot be the case!—I can tell you, sir, if Miss Howe thought this, she would not approve of it at all: for, little as you think Miss Howe likes you, sir, and little as she approves of your actions by her friend, I know she is of opinion that she ought to have nobody living, but you: and should continue single all her life, if she be not yours.

Revenge and obstinacy, Mr Hickman, will make women, the best of them, do very unaccountable things—Rather than not put out both eyes of the man they are offended with, they will give up one of their own.

I don't know what to say to this, sir: but, sure, she cannot encourage any other person's address!—So soon too—Why, sir, she is, as we are told, so ill, and so *weak*—

Not in resentment weak, I'll assure you. I am well acquainted with all her movements—and I tell you, believe it, or not, that she refuses *me* in view of *another* lover.

Can it be?

'Tis true, by my soul!—Has she not hinted this to Miss Howe, do you think?

No indeed, sir. If she had, I should not have troubled you at this time from Miss Howe.

Well then, you see I am right: that though she cannot be guilty of a falsehood, yet she has not told her friend the whole truth.

What shall a man say to these things! looking most stupidly perplexed.

Say! say! Mr Hickman!—Who can account for the workings and ways of a passionate and offended lady? Endless would be the histories I could give, within my own knowledge, of the dreadful effects of women's passionate resentments, and what that sex will do when disappointed. But can there be a stronger instance than this, of such a person as Miss Harlowe, who, at this very instant, and ill as she is, not only encourages, but in a manner makes court to, one of the most odious dogs that ever was seen? I think Miss Howe should not be told this. And yet she ought too, in order to dissuade her from such a preposterous rashness.

Oh fie! Oh strange! Miss Howe knows nothing of this! To be sure she won't look upon her, if this be true!

'Tis true, very true, Mr Hickman! True as I am here to tell you so!—And he is an ugly fellow too; uglier to look at than me.

Than *you*, sir! Why, to be sure, you are one of the handsomest men in England.

Well, but the wretch she so spitefully prefers to me is a misshapen, meagre varlet; more like a skeleton than a man! Then he dresses—you never saw a devil so bedizened! Hardly a coat to his back, nor a shoe to his foot: a bald-pated villain, yet grudges to buy a peruke to hide his baldness: for he is as covetous as hell, never satisfied, yet plaguy rich.

Why, sir, there is some joke in this, surely. A man of common parts knows not how to take such gentlemen as you. But, sir, if there be any truth in the story, what is he? Some Jew, or miserly citizen, I suppose, that may have presumed on the lady's distressful circumstances; and your lively wit points him out as it pleases.

Why the rascal has estates in every county *in* England, and *out of* England too.

Some East-India governor, I suppose, if there be anything in it. The lady once had thoughts of going abroad. But, I fancy, all this time you are in jest, sir. If not, we must surely have heard of him——

Heard of him! Ay, sir, we have all heard of him—but none of us care to be intimate with him—except this lady—and that, as I told you, in spite to me—His name, in short, is DEATH!—DEATH, sir, stamping, and speaking loud, and full in his ear; which made him jump half a yard high.

Thou never beheldest any man so disconcerted. He looked as if the frightful skeleton was before him, and he had not his accounts ready. When a little recovered, he fribbled with his waistcoat buttons, as if he had been telling his beads.

This, sir, proceeded I, is her wooer!—Nay, she is so forward a girl, that she *woos him*: but I hope it never will be a match.

He had before behaved, and now looked, with more spirit than I expected from him.

I came, sir, said he, as a mediator of differences. It behoves me to keep my temper. But, sir, and turned short upon me, as much as I love peace and to promote it, I will not be ill-used.

As I had played so much upon him, it would have been wrong to take him at his *more* than half-menace: yet, I think, I owe him a grudge for his presuming to address Miss Howe.

You mean no defiance, I presume, Mr Hickman, any more than I do offence. On that presumption, I ask your excuse. But this is my way. I mean no harm. I cannot let sorrow touch my heart. I cannot be grave six minutes together, for the blood of me. I am a descendant of old Chancellor More, I believe[3]; and should not forbear to cut a joke, were I upon the scaffold. But you may gather from what I have *said*, that I prefer Miss Harlowe, and that upon the justest grounds, to all the women in the world. And I wonder that there should be any difficulty to believe, from what I have signed, and from what I have promised to my relations, and enabled them to promise for me, that I should be glad to marry that excellent lady upon her own terms. I acknowledge to you, Mr Hickman, that I have basely injured her. If she will honour me with her hand, I declare that it is my intention to make her the best of husbands. But nevertheless, I must say that, if she goes on appealing her case, and exposing us both, as she does, it is impossible to think the knot can be knit with reputation to either. And although, Mr Hickman, I have delivered my apprehensions under so ludicrous a figure, I am afraid that she will ruin her constitution; and by seeking death when she may shun him, will not be able to avoid him when she would be glad to do so.

This cool and honest speech let down his stiffened muscles into complacency. He was my very obedient and faithful humble servant several times over, as I waited on him to his chariot: and I was his almost as often.

And so *exit* Hickman.

Letter 347: MR LOVELACE TO JOHN BELFORD, ESQ.

(In answer to Letters 340, 344, 345)

Friday night, July 21

I WILL throw away a few paragraphs upon the contents of thy last shocking letters, just brought me; and send what I shall write by the fellow who carries mine on the interview with Hickman.

Reformation, I see, is coming fast upon thee. Thy uncle's slow death, and thy attendance upon him through every stage towards it, prepared thee for it. But go thou on in thy own way, as I will in mine. Happiness consists in being pleased with what we do: and if thou canst find delight in being *sad*, it will be as well for thee as if thou wert *merry*, though no other person should join to keep thee in countenance.

I am, nevertheless, exceedingly disturbed at the lady's ill health. It is entirely owing to the cursed arrest. She was absolutely triumphant over me and the whole crew, before. Thou believest me guiltless of that: so, I hope, does she—The rest, as I have often said, is a common case; only a little uncommonly circumstanced; that's all: why then, all these severe things from her and thee?

As to selling her clothes, and her laces, and so forth, it has, I own, a shocking sound with it. What an implacable, as well as unjust set of wretches are those of her unkindredly kin; who have money of hers in their hands, as well as large arrears of her own estate; yet withhold both, *avowedly* to distress her! But may she not have money of that proud and saucy friend of hers, Miss Howe, more than she wants?—And should I not be overjoyed, thinkest thou, to serve her?—What then is there in the parting with her apparel but female perverseness?—And I am not sure, whether I ought not to be glad if she does this out of *spite to me*—Some disappointed fair ones would have hanged, some drowned, themselves. My beloved only revenges herself upon her clothes. Different ways of working has passion in different bosoms, as humour and complexion induce—Besides, dost think I shall grudge to replace, to three times the value, what she disposes of? So, Jack, there is no great matter in this.

Thou seest how sensible she is of the soothings of the polite doctor. This will enable thee to judge how dreadfully the horrid arrest, and her gloomy father's curse, must have hurt her. I have great hope, if she will but see me, that my behaviour, my contrition, my soothings, may have some happy effects upon her.

But thou art too ready to give me up. Let me seriously tell thee that, all excellence as she is, I think the earnest interposition of my relations; the implored mediation of that little fury Miss Howe; and the commissions thou actest under from myself; are such instances of condescension and high value in *them*, and such contrition in *me*, that nothing farther can be done—So here let the matter rest for the present, till she considers better of it.

But now a few words upon poor Belton's case. I own I was, at first, a little startled at the infidelity of his Thomasine: her hypocrisy to be for so many years undetected!—I have very lately had some intimations given me of her vileness; and had intended to mention it to thee when I saw thee. To say the truth, I always suspected her *eye*: the *eye*, thou knowest, is the *casement* at which the *heart* generally looks out. Many a woman who will not show herself at the *door*, has tipped the sly, the intelligible *wink* from the *windows*.

But Tom had no management at all. A very careless fellow. Would never look into his affairs. The estate his uncle left him was his ruin: wife, or mistress, whoever was, must have had his fortune to sport with.

I have often hinted his weaknesses of this sort to him; and the danger he was in of becoming the property of designing people. But he hated to take pains. He would ever run away from his accounts; as now, poor fellow! he would be glad to do from himself. Had he not had a *woman* to fleece him, his *coachman* or *valet* would have been his *prime minister*, and done it as effectually.

But yet, for many years I thought she was true to his bed. At least, I thought the boys were his own. For though they are muscular and big-boned, yet I supposed the healthy mother might have furnished them with legs and shoulders: for she is not of a delicate frame; and then Tom, some years ago, looked up, and spoke more like a man than he has done of late; squeaking inwardly, poor fellow! for some time past, from contracted quail-pipes, and wheezing from lungs half spit away.

He complains, thou sayest, that we all run away from him. Why, after all, Belford, it is no pleasant thing to see a poor fellow one loves dying by inches, yet unable to do him good. There are friendships which are only *bottle-deep:* I should be loath to have it thought that mine for any of my vassals is such a one. Yet, to gay hearts, which *became intimate because they were gay*, the reason for their first intimacy ceasing, the friendship will fade; that sort of friendship, I mean, which may be distinguished more properly by the word *companionship*.

But mine, as I said, is deeper than this: I would still be as ready as ever I was in my life, to the utmost of my power, to do him service.

As one instance of this my readiness to extricate him from all his difficulties as to Thomasine, dost thou care to propose to him an expedient that is just come into my head?

It is this: I would engage Thomasine, and her cubs if Belton be convinced they are neither of them his, in a party of pleasure: she was always complaisant to me. It should be in a boat hired for the purpose, to sail to Tilbury, to the Isle of Sheppey, or a pleasuring up the Medway; and 'tis but contriving to turn the boat bottom-upward. I can swim like a fish. Another boat should be ready to take up whom I should direct, for fear of the worst: and then, if Tom has a mind to be decent, one suit of mourning will serve for all three. Nay, the ostler cousin may take his plunge from the steerage: and who knows but they may be thrown up on the beach, Thomasine and he, hand in hand?

This, thou'lt say, is no *common* instance of friendship.

Meantime, do thou prevail upon him to come down to us: he never was more welcome in his life than he shall be now. If he will not, let him find me some other service; and I will clap a pair of wings to my shoulders and he shall see me come flying in at his windows at the word of command.

As for thy resolution of repenting and marrying; I would have thee consider which thou wilt set about first. If thou wilt follow my advice, thou shalt make short work of it. Let matrimony take place of the other; for then thou wilt, very possibly, have repentance come tumbling in fast upon thee as a consequence, and so have both in one.

Letter 348: MR BELFORD TO ROBERT LOVELACE, ESQ.

Friday noon, July 21

THIS morning I was admitted as soon as I sent up my name, into the presence of the divine lady. Such I may call her; as what I have to relate will fully prove.

She had had a tolerable night, and was much better in spirits; though weak in person; and visibly declining in looks.

Mrs Lovick and Mrs Smith were with her; and accused her, in a gentle manner, of having applied herself too assiduously to her pen for her strength, having been up ever since five. She said she had rested better than she had done for many nights: she had found her spirits free, and her mind tolerably easy: and having, as she had reason to think, but a short time, and much to do in it; she must be a good housewife of her hours.

She had been writing, she said, a letter to her sister; but had not pleased herself in it; though she had made two or three essays: but that the last must go.

By hints I had dropped, from time to time, she had reason, she said, to think that I knew everything that concerned her and her family; and, if so, must be acquainted with the heavy curse her father had laid upon her; which had been dreadfully fulfilled in one part, as to her temporary prospects, and that in a very short time; which gave her great apprehensions for the other. She had been applying herself to her sister to obtain a revocation of it. I hope my father will revoke it, said she, or I shall be very miserable—Yet (and she gasped as she spoke, with apprehension)—I am ready to tremble at what the answer may be; for my sister is hard-hearted.

I said something reflecting upon her friends; as to what they would deserve to be thought of, if the unmerited imprecation were not withdrawn—Upon which she took me up, and talked in such a dutiful manner of her parents, as must doubly condemn them (if they remain implacable) for their inhuman treatment of such a daughter.

She said I must not blame her parents: it was her dear Miss Howe's fault [to do so]. But what an enormity was there in her crime, which could set the best of parents (as they had been to her till she disobliged them) in a bad light for resenting the rashness of a child, from whose education they had reason to expect better fruits! There were some hard circumstances in her case, it was true: but my *friend* could tell me that no *one* body, throughout the whole fatal transaction, had acted out of character, but *herself.* She submitted therefore to the penalty she had incurred. If they had any fault, it was only that they would not inform themselves of some circumstances, which would alleviate a little her misdeed; and that, supposing her a guiltier creature than she was, they punished her without a hearing.

Lord!—*I was going to curse thee, Lovelace! How every instance of excellence, in this all-excelling creature, condemns thee!—Thou wilt have reason to think thyself of all men most accursed, if she die!*

I then besought her, while she was capable of such glorious instances of generosity and forgiveness, to extend her goodness to a man whose heart bled in every vein of it for the injuries he had done her; and who would make it the study of his whole life to repair them.

The women would have withdrawn when the subject became so particular. But she would not permit them to go. She told me that if, after this time, I was for entering with so much earnestness into a subject so very disagreeable to *her,* my visits must not be repeated. Nor was there occasion, she said, for my friendly offices in your favour; since she had begun to write her whole mind upon that subject to Miss Howe, in answer to letters from her, in which Miss Howe urged the same arguments, in compliment to the wishes of your noble and worthy relations.

Meantime, you may let him know, said she, that I reject him with my whole heart—yet that, although I say this with such a determination as shall leave no room for doubt, however I say it not with passion. On the contrary, tell him that I am trying to bring my mind into such a frame as to be able to *pity* him (poor perjured wretch! what has he not to answer for!); and that I shall not think myself qualified for the state I am aspiring to, if, after a few struggles more, I cannot *forgive* him too: and I hope, clasping her hands together, uplifted, as were her eyes, my dear *earthly* father will set me the example my *heavenly* one has already set us all; and by forgiving his fallen daughter teach her to forgive the man who then, I hope, will not have destroyed my eternal prospects, as he has my temporal!

Stop here, thou wretch!—But I need not bid thee—for I can go no farther!

Letter 349: MR BELFORD [TO ROBERT LOVELACE, ESQ.]

(In continuation)

YOU will imagine how affecting her noble speech and behaviour was to me, at the time, when the bare recollection and transcription obliged me to drop my pen. The women had tears in their eyes. I was silent for a few moments—At last, Matchless excellence! Inimitable goodness! I called her, with a voice so accented that I was half-ashamed of myself, as it was before the women—But who could stand such sublime generosity of soul in so young a creature, her loveliness giving grace to all she said?—Methinks, said I (and I really, in a manner involuntarily, bent my knee), I have before me an angel indeed. I can hardly forbear prostration, and to beg your influence to draw me after you to the world you are aspiring to!— Yet—but what shall I say?—Only, dearest excellence, make me, in some small instances, serviceable to you, that I may (if I survive you) have the glory to think I was able to contribute to your satisfaction, while among us.

Here I stopped. She was silent. I proceeded—Have you no commission to employ me in; deserted as you are by all your friends; among strangers, though I doubt not worthy people? Cannot I be serviceable by message, by letter-writing, by attending personally, with either message or letter, your father, your uncles, your brother, your sister, Miss Howe, Lord M., or the ladies his sisters? Any office to be employed in to serve you, absolutely *independent* of my *friend*'s wishes, or of my own wishes to oblige him. Think, madam, if I cannot?

I thank you, sir; very heartily I thank you: but in nothing that I can at present think of, or at least resolve upon, can you do me service. I will see what return the letter I have written will bring me—Till then—

My life and my fortune, interrupted I, are devoted to your service. Permit me to observe that here you are without one natural friend; and (so much do I know of your unhappy case) that you must be in a manner destitute of the means to *make* friends—

She was going to interrupt me with a prohibitory kind of earnestness in her manner—

I beg leave to proceed, madam: I have cast about twenty ways how to mention this before, but never dared till now. Suffer me, now that I have broke the ice, to tender myself—as your *banker* only—I know you will not be obliged: you *need* not. You have sufficient of your own, if it were in your hands; and from *that*, whether you live or die, will I consent to be reimbursed. I do assure you that the unhappy man shall never know either *my* offer, or *your* acceptance—Only permit me this small—

And down behind her chair I dropped a bank note of £100 which I had brought with me, intending somehow or other to leave it behind me: nor shouldst thou ever have known it, had she favoured me with the acceptance of it; and so I told her.

You give me great pain, Mr Belford, said she, by these instances of your humanity. And yet, considering the company I have seen you in, I am not sorry to find you capable of such. Methinks I am glad, for the sake of human nature, that there could be but *one* such man in the world as him you and I know—But as to your kind offer, whatever it be, if you take it not up, you will greatly disturb me. I have no need of your kindness. I have effects enough, which I never can want, to supply my present occasions; and, if needful, can have recourse to Miss Howe. I have promised that I would—So, pray, sir, urge not upon me this favour—Take it up yourself—If you mean me peace and ease of mind, urge not this favour—and she spoke with impatience.

I beg, madam, but one word—

Not one, sir, till you have taken back what you have let fall. I doubt not either the *honour*, or the *kindness*, of your offer; but you must not say one word more on this subject. I cannot bear it.

She was stooping, but with pain. I therefore prevented her; and besought her to forgive me for a tender which I saw had been more discomposing to her than I had hoped (from the purity of my intentions) it would be. But I could not bear to think that such a mind as hers should be distressed: since the want of the conveniencies she was used to abound in might affect and disturb her in the divine course she was in.

You are very kind to me, sir, said she, and very favourable in your opinion of me. But I hope that I cannot now be easily put out of my present course. My declining health will more and more confirm me in it. Those who arrested and confined me, no doubt thought they had fallen upon the ready method to distress me so as to bring me into all their measures. But I presume to hope that I have a mind that cannot be debased, in *essential instances*, by *temporary calamities*: little do those poor wretches know of the force of innate principles, forgive my own *implied* vanity was her word, who imagine that a prison, or penury, or want, can bring a right turned mind to be guilty of a wilful baseness, in order to avoid such *short-lived evils*.

She then turned from me towards the window, with a dignity suitable to her words; and such as showed her to be more of soul than of body at that instant.

What magnanimity!—No wonder a virtue so solidly based could baffle all thy arts—and that it forced thee (in order to carry thy accursed point) to have recourse to those unnatural ones, which robbed her of her charming senses.

The women were extremely affected, Mrs Lovick especially—who said whisperingly to Mrs Smith, We have an angel, not a woman, with us, Mrs Smith!

I repeated my offers to write to any of her friends; and told her that, having taken the liberty to acquaint Dr H. with the cruel displeasure of her relations, as what I presumed lay nearest her heart, he had proposed to write himself, to acquaint her friends how ill she was, if she would not take it amiss.

It was kind in the *doctor*, she said: but begged that no step of that sort might be taken without her knowledge and consent. She would wait to see what effects her letter to her sister would have. All she had to hope for was that her father would revoke his malediction: for the rest, her friends would think she could not suffer too much; and she was content to suffer: for now nothing could happen, that could make her wish to live.

Mrs Smith went down; and soon returning, asked if the lady and I would not dine with her that day: for it was her wedding-day. She had engaged Mrs Lovick, she said; and should have nobody else, if we would do her that favour.

The charming creature sighed and shook her head—*Wedding-day*, repeated she!—I wish you, Mrs Smith, many happy wedding-days!—But you will excuse *me*.

Mr Smith came up with the same request. They both applied to me.

On condition the *lady* would, I should make no scruple; and would suspend an engagement: which I actually had.

She then desired they would all sit down. You have several times, Mrs Lovick and Mrs Smith, hinted your wishes that I would give you some little history of myself. Now, if you are at leisure, that this gentleman who I have reason to believe knows it all is present, and can tell you if I give it justly or not; I will oblige your curiosity.

They all eagerly, the man Smith too, sat down; and she began an account of herself which I will endeavour to repeat as nearly in her own words as I possibly can: for I know you will think it of importance to be apprised of her manner of relating your barbarity to her, as well as what her sentiments are of it; and what room there is for the hopes your friends have in your favour, from her.

'At first when I took these lodgings, said she, I thought of staying but a short time in them; and so, Mrs Smith, I told you: I therefore avoided giving any other account of myself than that I was a very unhappy young creature, seduced from good friends, and escaped from very vile wretches.

'This account I thought myself obliged to give, that you might the less wonder at seeing a young body rushing through your shop into your back apartment, all trembling and out of breath; an ordinary garb over my own; craving lodging and protection; only giving my bare word that you should be handsomely paid: all my effects contained in a pocket-handkerchief.

'My sudden absence for three days and nights together when arrested must still further surprise you: and although this gentleman, who perhaps knows more of the darker part of my story than I do myself, has informed you (as you, Mrs Lovick, tell me) that I am only an *unhappy*, not a *guilty* creature; yet I think it incumbent upon me not to suffer honest minds to be in doubt about my character.

'You must know, then, that I have been, in one instance (I had like to have said *but* in one instance; but that was a capital one), an undutiful child to the most indulgent of parents: for what some people call cruelty in them is owing but to the excess of their love, and to their disappointment; having had reason to expect better from me.

'I was visited (at first with my friends' connivance) by a man of birth and fortune, but of worse principles, as it proved, than I believed any man could have. My brother, a very headstrong young man, was absent at that time; and when he returned (from an old grudge, and knowing the gentleman, it is plain, better than I knew him), entirely disapproved of his visits: and having a great sway in our family, brought other gentlemen to address me. And at last (several having been rejected) he introduced one extremely disagreeable: in every *indifferent* body's eyes disagreeable. I could not love him. They all joined to compel me to have him;

a rencounter between the gentleman my friends were set against and my brother, having confirmed them all his enemies.

'To be short: I was confined and treated so very hardly, that in a rash fit I appointed to go off with the man they hated. A wicked intention, you'll say: but I was greatly provoked. Nevertheless, I repented; and resolved not to go off with him; yet I did not mistrust his honour to me neither; nor his love; because nobody thought me unworthy of the latter, and my fortune was not to be despised. But foolishly (wickedly, as my friends still think, and contrivingly, with a design as they imagine to abandon them) giving him a private meeting, I was tricked away; poorly enough tricked away, I must needs say; though others who had been first guilty of so rash a step as the meeting of him was, might have been so deceived and surprised as well as I.

'After remaining some time at a farm-house in the country, behaving to me all the time with honour, he brought me to handsome lodgings in town till still better provision could be made for me. But they proved to be, as he indeed knew and designed, at a vile, a very vile creature's; though it was long before I found her out to be so; for I knew nothing of the town or its ways.

'There is no repeating what followed: such unprecedented vile arts!—for I gave him no opportunity to take me at any disreputable advantage—'

And here (half covering her sweet face with her handkerchief put to her tearful eyes) she stopped.

Hastily, as if she would fly from the hateful remembrance, she resumed: 'I made my escape afterwards from the abominable house in his absence, and came to yours: and this gentleman has almost prevailed on me to think that the ungrateful man did not connive at the vile arrest: which was made no doubt in order to get me once more to those wicked lodgings: for nothing do I owe them, except I were to pay them—' (She sighed, and again wiped her charming eyes—adding in a softer, lower voice)—'*for being ruined!*—'

Indeed, madam, said I, guilty, abominably guilty as he is in all the rest, he is innocent of this last wicked outrage.

'Well, and so I wish him to be. That evil, heavy as it was, is one of the slightest evils I have suffered. But hence you'll observe, Mrs Lovick (for you seemed this morning curious to know if I were not a wife), that I *never was married*. You, Mr Belford, no doubt, knew before that I am no wife: and now I never will be one. Yet I bless God that I am not a guilty creature!

'As to my parentage, I am of no mean family: I have in my own right, by the intended favour of my grandfather, a fortune not contemptible: independent of my *father*, if I had pleased; but I never will please.

'My father is very rich. I went by another name when I came to you first: but that was to avoid being discovered to the perfidious man; who now engages, by this gentleman, not to molest me.

'My real name you now know to be Harlowe: *Clarissa* Harlowe. I am not yet twenty years of age.

'I have an excellent mother, as well as father; a woman of family, and fine sense—worthy of a better child!—They both doted upon me.

'I have two good uncles: men of great fortune; jealous of the honour of their family; which I have wounded.

'I was the joy of their hearts; and, with theirs and my father's, I had three houses to call my own; for they used to have me with them by turns, and almost kindly to quarrel for me: so that I was two months in the year at one's house; two months at the other's: six months at my father's; and two at the houses of others of my dear friends, who thought themselves happy in me: and whenever I was at any one's, I was crowded upon with letters by all the rest, who longed for my return to them.

'In short, I was beloved by everybody. The poor—I used to make glad *their* hearts: I never shut my hand to any distress, wherever I was—but now I am poor myself!

'So, Mrs Smith, so, Mrs Lovick, I am *not* married. It is but just to tell you so. And I am now, as I ought to be, in a state of humiliation and penitence for the rash step which has been followed by so much evil. God, I hope, will forgive me, as I am endeavouring to bring my mind to forgive all the world, even the man who has ungratefully, and by dreadful perjuries (poor wretch! he thought all his wickedness to be *wit!*) reduced to this, a young creature who had *his* happiness in her *view*, and in her *wish*, even beyond this life; and who was believed to be of rank, and fortune, and expectations, considerable enough to make it the *interest* of any gentleman in England to be faithful to his vows to her. But I cannot expect that my parents will forgive me: my refuge must be death; the most painful kind of which I would suffer, rather than be the wife of one who could act by me as the man has acted, upon whose birth, education, and honour, I had so much reason to found better expectations.

'I see, continued she, that I, who once was everyone's delight, am now the cause of grief to everyone—You that are strangers to me are moved for me! 'Tis kind!—But 'tis time to stop. Your compassionate hearts, Mrs Smith and Mrs Lovick, are too much touched' (for the women sobbed again, and the man was also affected). 'It is barbarous in me, with my woes, thus to sadden your wedding-day.' Then turning to Mr and Mrs Smith—'May you see many happy ones, honest, good couple!—How agreeable is it to see you both join so kindly to celebrate it after many years are gone over you!—I once—But no more!—All my prospects of felicity as to this life are at an end. My hopes, like opening buds or blossoms in an over-forward spring, have been nipped by a severe frost!—blighted by an eastern wind!—But I can but *once die*; and if life be spared me but till I am discharged from a heavy malediction which my father in his wrath laid upon me, and which is fulfilled literally in every article relating to this world, it is all I have to wish for; and death will be welcomer to me than rest to the most wearied traveller that ever reached his journey's end.'

And then she sunk her head against the back of her chair, and, hiding her face with her handkerchief, endeavoured to conceal her tears from us.

Not a soul of us could speak a word. Thy presence, perhaps, thou hardened wretch, might have made us ashamed of a weakness, which perhaps thou wilt deride *me* in particular for, when thou readest this!—

She retired to her chamber soon after, and was forced, it seems, to lie down. We all went down together; and, for an hour and half, dwelt upon her praises; Mrs Smith and Mrs Lovick repeatedly expressing their astonishment that there could be a man in the world capable of offending, much more of wilfully injuring, such a lady; and repeating that they had an angel in their house—I thought they had; and that as assuredly as there was a devil under the roof of good Lord M.

I hate thee heartily!—By my faith I do!—Every hour I hate thee more than the former!—

J. BELFORD

Letter 350: MR LOVELACE TO JOHN BELFORD, ESQ.

Sat. July 22

WHAT dost hate me for, Belford?—And why more and more?—Have I been guilty of any offence thou knewest not before?—If *pathos* can move such a heart as thine, can it alter facts?—Did I not always do this incomparable creature as much justice as thou canst do her for the heart of thee, or as she can do herself?—What nonsense then thy hatred, thy *augmented* hatred, when I still persist to marry her, pursuant to word given to thee, and to faith plighted to all my relations? But hate if thou wilt, so thou dost but write: thou canst not hate me so much as I do myself: and yet I know, if thou really hatedst me, thou wouldst not venture to tell me so.

Well, but after all, what need of her history to these women? She will certainly repent, some time hence, that she has thus needlessly exposed us both.

Sickness palls every appetite, and makes us hate what we loved: but renewed health changes the scene; disposes us to be pleased with ourselves; and then we are in a way to be pleased with everyone else. Every hope, then, rises upon us: every hour presents itself to us on dancing feet: and what Mr Addison says of liberty, may with still greater propriety be said of *health* (*for what is liberty itself without health?*):

> It makes the gloomy face of nature gay;
> Gives beauty to the sun, and pleasure to the day.[1]

And I rejoice that she is already so much better as to hold, with strangers, such a long and interesting conversation.

Strange, confoundedly strange, and as perverse (that is to say, as *womanly*) as strange, that she should refuse, and sooner choose to die—(Oh the obscene word! and yet how free does thy pen make with it to me!) than be mine, who offended her by acting *in* character, while her parents acted shamefully *out of theirs*, and when I am now willing to act *out of my own* to oblige her: Yet I not to be forgiven! they to be faultless with her!—And marriage the only medium to repair all breaches, and to salve her own honour!—Surely thou must see the inconsistence of her *forgiving* unforgivingness, as I may call it!—Yet, heavy varlet as thou art, thou wantest to be drawn up after her! And what a figure dost thou make with thy speeches, stiff as Hickman's ruffles, with thy aspirations and prostrations!—unused thy weak head to bear the sublimities that fall, even in common conversation, from the lips of this ever-charming creature!

But the prettiest whim of all was to drop the bank note behind her chair, instead of presenting it on thy knees to her hand!—To make such a lady as this *doubly* stoop—by the acceptance, and to take it from the ground!—What an ungraceful *benefit-conferrer* art thou! How awkward to take it into thy head that the best way of making a present to a lady was to throw the present behind her chair!

I am very desirous to see what she has written to her sister; what she is about to write to Miss Howe; and what return she will have from the Harlowe Arabella. Canst thou not form some scheme to come at the copies of these letters, or at the substance of them at least, and of that of her other correspondencies? Mrs Lovick, thou seemest to say, is a pious woman: the lady, having given such a particular history of herself, will acquaint her with everything. And art thou not about to reform?—Won't this consent of minds between thee and the widow (what age is she, Jack? the devil never trumped up a friendship between a man and a woman, of anything like years, which did not end in matrimony, or the dissipation of both their morals! Won't it) strike out an intimacy between ye, that may enable thee to gratify me in this particular? A proselyte, I can tell thee, has great influence upon your good people: Such a one is a saint of their own creation; and they will water, and cultivate, and cherish him as a plant of their own raising; and this from a pride truly spiritual!

But one consolation arises to me from the pretty regrets this admirable creature seems to have in indulging reflections on the people's wedding-day—*I* ONCE!—thou makest her break off with saying.

She once! What?—Oh Belford! why didst thou not urge her to explain what she *once* hoped?

What once a lady hopes, in love matters, she always hopes while there is room for hope: and are we not both single? Can she be any man's but mine? Will I be any woman's but hers?

I never will! I never can!—And I tell thee that I am every day, every hour, more and more in love with her: and at this instant have a more vehement passion for her than ever I had in my life!—And that with views absolutely honourable, in *her own sense* of the word: nor have I varied, so much as in *wish*, for this week past: firmly fixed and wrought into my very nature as the *life of honour*, or of generous confidence in me, was, in preference to the life of *doubt* and *distrust*. That must be a *life of doubt* and *distrust*, surely, where the woman confides nothing, and ties up a man for his good behaviour for life, taking church and state sanctions in aid of the obligation she imposes upon him.

I shall go on Monday morning to a kind of ball, to which Colonel Ambrose has invited me. It is given on a family account. I care not on what: for all that delights me in the thing is that Mrs and Miss Howe are to be there; Hickman, of course; for the old lady will not stir abroad without him. The colonel is in hopes that Miss Arabella Harlowe will be there likewise; for all the fellows and women of fashion round him are invited.

I fell in by accident with the colonel who, I believe, hardly thought I would accept of the invitation. But he knows me not if he thinks I am ashamed to appear at any place where ladies dare show their faces. Yet he hinted to me that my name *was up*, on Miss Harlowe's account. But, to allude to one of my uncle's phrases, if it be, I will not *lie abed* when anything joyous is going forward.

As I shall go in my lord's chariot, I would have had one of my cousins Montague to go with me: but they both refused: and I sha'n't choose to take either of thy brethren. It would look as if I thought I wanted a bodyguard: besides, one of them is too rough, the other too smooth and too great a fop for some of the staid company that will be there; and for *me* in particular. Men are known by their companions; and a fop (as Tourville, for example) takes great pains to hang out a sign, by his dress, of what he has in his shop. Thou, indeed, art an exception; dressing like a coxcomb, yet a very clever fellow. Nevertheless so clumsy a beau, that thou seemest to me to owe thyself a double spite, making thy ungracefulness appear the *more* ungraceful by thy remarkable tawdriness when thou art out of mourning.

I remember when I first saw thee, my mind laboured with a strong puzzle whether I should put thee down for a great fool, or a smatterer in wit: something I saw was wrong in thee, by thy *dress*. If this fellow, thought I, delights not so much in *ridicule* that he will not spare *himself*, he must be plaguy silly to take so much pains to make his ugliness more conspicuous than it would otherwise be.

Plain dress, for an ordinary man or woman, implies at least *modesty*, and always procures kind quarter from the censorious. Who will ridicule a personal imperfection in one that seems conscious that it *is* an imperfection? *Who ever said, an anchoret was poor?* But to such as appear proud of their deformity, or bestow tinsel upon it in hopes to set it off, who would spare so very absurd a wronghead?

But, although I put on these lively airs, I am sick at my soul!—My whole heart is with my charmer! With what indifference shall I look upon all the assembly at the colonel's, my beloved in my ideal eye, and engrossing my whole heart?

Letter 351: MISS HOWE TO MISS ARABELLA HARLOWE

Thursday, July 20

Miss HARLOWE,

I CANNOT help acquainting you, however it may be received as coming from *me*, that your poor sister is dangerously ill at the house of one Smith, who keeps a glover's and perfume shop, in King Street, Covent Garden. She knows not that I write. Some violent words, in the nature of an imprecation, from her father, afflict her greatly in her weak state. I presume not to direct to you what to do in this case. You are her sister. I therefore could not help writing to you, not only for her sake, but for your own.

I am, madam, Your humble servant,
ANNA HOWE

Letter 352: MISS ARABELLA HARLOWE TO MISS ANNA HOWE

Thursday, July 20

Miss HOWE,

I HAVE yours of this morning. All that has happened to the unhappy body you mention is what we foretold and expected. Let *him* for whose sake she abandoned us be her comfort. We are told he has remorse, and would marry her. We don't believe it, indeed. She *may* be very ill. Her disappointment may make her so, or ought. Yet is she the only one I know, who is disappointed.

I cannot say, miss, that the notification from you is the *more* welcome for the liberties you have been pleased to take with our whole family, for resenting a conduct that it is a shame any young lady should justify. Excuse this freedom, occasioned by greater.

I am, miss, Your humble servant,
ARABELLA HARLOWE

Letter 353: MISS HOWE [TO MISS ARABELLA HARLOWE]

(In reply)

Friday, July 21

Miss ARABELLA HARLOWE,

IF you had half as much sense as you have ill-nature, you would (notwithstanding the exuberance of the latter) have been able to distinguish between a kind intention to you all (that you might have the less to reproach yourselves with if a deplorable case should happen), and an officiousness I owed you not, by reason of freedoms at least reciprocal. I will not for the *unhappy body*'s sake, as you call a sister you have helped to make so, say all that I *could* say. If what I fear happen, you shall hear (whether desired or not) all the mind of

ANNA HOWE

Letter 354: MISS ARABELLA HARLOWE TO MISS HOWE

Friday July 21

Miss ANN HOWE,

YOUR pert letter I have received. You that spare nobody, I cannot expect should spare me. You are very happy in a prudent and watchful mother—but else—mine cannot be exceeded in prudence: but we had all too good an opinion of somebody, to think watchfulness needful. There may possibly be some reason why *you* are so much attached to her, in an error of this flagrant nature.

I help to make a sister unhappy!—It is false, miss!—It is all her own doings!—Except, indeed, what she may owe to somebody's advice—You know who can best answer for that.

Let us *know your mind* as soon as you please: as we shall know it to be *your* mind, we shall judge what attention to give it. That's all, from, etc.

AR. H.

Letter 355: MISS HOWE TO MISS ARABELLA HARLOWE

Sat. July 22

IT may be the *misfortune* of some people to engage *every*body's notice: others may be the *happier*, though they may be the more *envious*, for nobody's thinking them worthy of any. But one would be glad people had the sense to be thankful for that want of consequence, which subjected them not to hazards they would hardly have been able to manage under.

I own to you, that had it not been for the prudent advice of that admirable somebody (whose principal fault is the superiority of her talents, and whose misfortune to be brothered and sistered by a couple of creatures who are not able to comprehend her excellencies), I might at one time have been plunged into difficulties. But, pert as the superlatively pert may think me, I thought not myself *wiser* because I was *older*; nor for that *poor* reason qualified to prescribe to, much less to maltreat, a genius so outsoaring.

I repeat it with gratitude, that the dear creature's advice was of very great service to me—and this before my mother's *watchfulness* became necessary. But how it would have fared with me, I cannot say, had I had a brother or sister, who had deemed it their *interest*, as well as a gratification of their *sordid envy*, to misrepresent me.

Your admirable sister, in effect, saved *you*, miss, as well as *me*—with this difference—you, *against* your will—me, *with* mine: and but for *your* own brother, and *his* own sister, would not have been lost herself.

Would to God both sisters had been obliged with their own wills!—The most admirable of her sex would never then have been out of her father's house!—*You*, miss—I don't know what had become of *you*—But, let what would have happened, you would have met with the humanity you have not shown, whether you had deserved it or not—nor, at worst, lost either a kind sister, or a pitying friend, in the most excellent of sisters.

But why run I into length to such a poor thing?—Why push I so weak an adversary? whose first letter is all low malice, and whose next is made up of falsehood and inconsistence, as well as spite and ill-manners. Yet I was willing to give you a *part* of my mind—call for more of it; it shall be at your service: from one who, though she thanks God she is not your *sister*, is not your *enemy*: but that she is *not* the latter is withheld but by two considerations; one, that you bear, though unworthily, a relation to a sister so excellent; the other, that you are not of consequence enough to engage anything but the pity and contempt of

A. H.

Letter 356: MRS HARLOWE TO MRS HOWE

Sat. July 22

Dear madam,

I SEND you enclosed copies of five letters that have passed between Miss Howe and my Arabella. You are a person of so much prudence and good sense, and (being a mother yourself) can so well enter into the distresses of all our family, upon the rashness and ingratitude of a child we once doted upon, that I dare say you will not countenance the strange freedoms your daughter has taken with us all. These are not the only ones we have to complain of; but we were silent on the others, as they did not, as these have done, spread themselves out upon paper. We only beg that we may not be reflected upon by a young lady, who knows not what we have suffered, and do suffer, by the rashness of a naughty creature who has brought ruin upon herself, and disgrace upon a family which she has robbed of all comfort. I offer not to prescribe to your known wisdom in this case; but leave it to you to do as you think most proper.

I am, madam, Your most humble servant,
CHARL. HARLOWE

Letter 357: MRS HOWE [TO MRS HARLOWE]

(In answer)

Sat. July 22

Dear madam,

I AM highly offended with my daughter's letters to Miss Harlowe. I knew nothing at all of her having taken such a liberty. These young creatures have such romantic notions, some of *love*, some of *friendship*, that there is no governing them in either. Nothing but time, and dear experience, will convince them of their absurdities in both. I have chidden Miss Howe very severely. I had before so just a notion of what your whole family's distress must be, that, as I told your brother Mr Antony Harlowe, I had often forbid her corresponding with the poor fallen angel—for surely never did young lady more resemble what we imagine of angels, both in person and mind. But, tired out with her headstrong ways (I am sorry to say this of my own child), I was forced to give way to it again: and, indeed, so sturdy was she in her will, that I was afraid it would end in a fit of sickness, as too often it did in fits of sullens.

None but parents know the trouble that children give: they are happiest, I have often thought, who have none. And these women-grown girls, bless my heart! how ungovernable!—

I believe, however, you will have no more such letters from my Nancy. I have been forced to use compulsion with her, upon Miss Clary's illness (and it seems she is very bad); or she would have run away to London, to attend upon her: and this she calls doing the duty of a friend; forgetting that she sacrifices to her romantic friendship her duty to a fond indulgent mother.

There are a thousand excellencies in the poor sufferer, notwithstanding her fault: and, if the hints she has given to my daughter be true, she has been most grievously abused. But I think your forgiveness and her father's forgiveness of her ought to be all at your own choice; and nobody should intermeddle in that, for the sake of due authority in parents: and besides, as Miss Harlowe writes, it was what everybody expected, though Miss Clary would not believe it till she smarted for her credulity. And, for these reasons, I offer not to plead anything in alleviation of her fault, which is aggravated by her admirable sense, and a judgement above her years.

I am, madam, with compliments to good Mr Harlowe, and all your afflicted family,

Your most humble servant,
ANNABELLA HOWE

I shall set out for the Isle of Wight in a few days with my daughter. I will hasten our setting-out, on purpose to break her mind from her friend's distresses; which afflict us as much, nearly, as Miss Clary's rashness has done you.

Letter 358: MISS HOWE TO MISS CLARISSA HARLOWE

Sat. July 22

My dearest friend,

WE are busy in preparing for our little journey and voyage: but I will be ill, I will be very ill, if I cannot hear you are better before I go.

Rogers greatly afflicted me by telling me the bad way you are in. But now you have been able to hold a pen, and as your sense is strong and clear, I hope that the amusement you will receive from writing will make you better.

I dispatch this by an extraordinary way, that it may reach you time enough to move you to *consider well* before you absolutely decide upon the contents of mine of the 13th, on the subject of the two Misses Montague's visit to me; since, according to what you write, must I answer them.

In your last, you conclude very positively that you will not be his. To be sure, he rather deserves an infamous death than such a wife. But, as I really believe him innocent of the arrest, and as all his family are such earnest pleaders, and will be guarantees for him, I think the compliance with *their* entreaties, and *his own*, will be now the best step you can take; your own family remaining implacable, as I *can assure you they do*. He is a man of sense; and it is not impossible but he may make you a good husband, and in time may become no bad man.

My mother is entirely of my opinion: and on Friday, pursuant to a hint I gave you in my last, Mr Hickman had a conference with the strange wretch. And though he liked not, by any means, his behaviour to himself; nor, indeed, had reason to do so; yet he is of opinion that he is sincerely determined to marry you, if you will condescend to have him.

Perhaps Mr Hickman may make you a private visit before we set out. If I may not attend you myself, I shall not be easy except he does. And he will then give you an account of the admirable character the surprising wretch gave of you, and of the justice he does to your virtue.

He was as acknowledging to his relations, though to his own condemnation, as his two cousins told me. All that he apprehends, as he said to Mr Hickman, is that if you go on appealing your case, and exposing *him*, wedlock itself will not wipe off the dishonour to both: and moreover, 'that you would ruin your constitution by your immoderate sorrow; and by seeking death when you might avoid it, would not be able to escape it when you would wish to do so.'

So, my dearest friend, I charge you, if you *can*, to get over your aversion to this vile man. You may yet live to see many happy days, and be once more the delight of all your friends, neighbours, and acquaintance, as well as a stay, a comfort, and a blessing, to your Anna Howe.

I long to have your answer to mine of the 13th. Pray keep the messenger till it be ready. If he return on Monday night, it will be time enough for his affairs, and to find me come back from Colonel Ambrose's; who gives a ball on the anniversary of Mrs Ambrose's birth and marriage, both in one. The gentry all round the neighbourhood are invited this time, on some good news they have received from Mrs Ambrose's brother the Governor.

My mother promised the colonel for me and herself, in my absence. I would fain have excused myself to her; and the rather, as I had exceptions on account of the day[a] : but she is almost as young as her daughter; and thinking it not so well to go without me, she told me she could propose *nothing* that was agreeable to me. And having had a *few sparring blows* with each other very lately, I think I must comply. For I don't love jangling when I can help it; though I seldom make it my study to avoid the occasion when it offers of itself. I don't know, if either were not a little afraid of the other, whether it would be possible that we could live together—I, *all my father!*—my mamma—what?—*all my mother*—What else should I say?

Oh my dear, how many things happen in this life to give us displeasure! how few to give us joy!—I am sure I shall have none on this occasion; since the true partner of my heart, the principal half of the *one soul* that, it used to be said, animated *the pair of friends*, as we were called; YOU, my dear (who used to irradiate every circle you set your foot into, and to give me *real* significance, in a *second* place to yourself), cannot be there!—One hour of your company, my ever-instructive friend (I thirst for it!), how infinitely preferable to me, to all the diversions and amusements with which our sex are generally most delighted!—Adieu, my dear!—

A. HOWE

Letter 359: MISS CLARISSA HARLOWE TO MISS HOWE

Sunday, July 23

WHAT pain, my dearest friend, does your kind solicitude for my welfare give me! How much more binding and tender are the ties of pure friendship, and the union of like minds, than the ties of nature! Well might the sweet singer of Israel, when he was carrying to the utmost extent the praises of the friendship between him and his beloved friend, say that the love of Jonathan to him was wonderful; that it surpassed the *love of women!* What an exalted idea does it give of the soul of Jonathan, sweetly attempered for this sacred band, if we may suppose it but equal to that of my Anna Howe for her fallen Clarissa! But although I can glory in your kind love for me, think, my dear, what concern must fill a mind, not ungenerous, when the obligation lies all on one side: and when, at the same time that your light is the brighter for my darkness, I must give pain to a dear friend to whom I delighted to give pleasure; and, at the same time, discredit, for supporting my blighted fame against the busy tongues of uncharitable censurers!—

This it is that makes me, in the words of my admired exclaimer very little altered, often repeat: 'O! that I were as in months past, as in the days when God preserved me! When his candle shined upon my head, and when by his light I walked through darkness! As I was in the days of my *childhood*—when the Almighty was yet with me; when *I was in my father's house:* when I washed my steps with butter, and the rock poured me out rivers of oil!'[1]

You set before me your reasons, enforced by the opinion of your honoured mother, why I should think of Mr Lovelace for a husband.[b]

And I have before me your letter of the 13th,[c] containing the account of the visit and proposals, and kind interposition, of the two Misses Montague, in the names of the good Ladies Sarah Sadleir and Betty Lawrance, and that of Lord M.

a The 24th of July, Miss Clarissa Harlowe's anniversary birthday.
b See the preceding letter.
c See p. 1042.

Also yours of the 18th,[a] *demanding* me, as I may say, of those ladies, and of that family, when I was so infamously and cruelly arrested, and you knew not what was become of me:

The answer likewise of those ladies, signed in so full and so generous a manner by themselves,[b] and by that nobleman, and those two venerable ladies; and, in his light way, by the wretch himself:

These, my dearest Miss Howe, and your letter of the 16th,[c] which came when I was under arrest, and which I received not till some days after:

Are all before me.

And I have as well weighed the whole matter, and your arguments in support of your advice, as at present my head and my heart will let me weigh them.

I am, moreover, willing to believe, not only from your own opinion, but from the assurances of one of Mr Lovelace's friends, Mr Belford, a good-natured and humane man, who spares not to censure the author of my calamities (*I think*, with undissembled and undesigning sincerity), that that man is innocent of the disgraceful arrest:

And even, if you please, in sincere compliment to your opinion, and to that of Mr Hickman, that (over-persuaded by his friends, and ashamed of his unmerited baseness to me) he, in earnest, would marry *me* if I would have *him*.

'Well, [d] and now, what is the result of all?—It is this—that I must abide by what I have already declared—and that is (don't be angry at me, my best friend) that I have much more pleasure in thinking of death, than of such a husband. In short, as I declared in my last, that I cannot—forgive me, if I say I *will* not—ever be his.

'But you will expect my reasons: I know you will: and if I give them not, will conclude me either obstinate, or implacable, or both: and those would be sad imputations, if just, to be laid to the charge of a person who thinks and talks of *dying*. And yet, to say that resentment and disappointment have no part in my determination would be saying a thing hardly to be credited. For I own I *have* resentments, strong resentments, but not unreasonable ones, as you will be convinced if already you are not so, when you know all my story—if ever you do know it—For I begin to fear (so many things more necessary to be thought of, than either this man, or my own vindication, have I to do) that I shall not have time to compass what I have intended, and, in a manner, promised you.[e]

'I have one reason to give in support of my resolution that, I believe, yourself will allow of: but having owned that I have resentments, I will begin with those considerations, in which anger and disappointment have too great a share; in hopes that having once disburdened my mind upon paper, and to my Anna Howe, of those corroding uneasy passions, I shall prevent them for ever from returning to my heart, and to have their place supplied by better, milder, and more agreeable ones.

a   See p. 1045.
b   See p. 1048.
c   See p. 1044.
d   Those parts of this letter which are marked with inverted commas (thus ') were transcribed afterwards by Miss Howe, in a letter to the ladies of Mr Lovelace's family, dated July 29, and are thus distinguished to avoid the necessity of repeating them when that letter comes to be inserted.
e   See Letter 318.

'My pride, then, my dearest friend, although a great deal mortified, is not *sufficiently* mortified if it be necessary for me to submit to make that man my choice, whose actions are, and ought to be, my abhorrence!—What!—shall I, who have been treated with such premeditated and perfidious barbarity as is painful to be thought of, and cannot with modesty be described, think of taking the violator to my heart? Can I vow duty to one so wicked, and hazard my salvation by joining myself to so great a profligate, now I *know* him to be so? Do you think your Clarissa Harlowe so lost, so *sunk* at least, as that she could for the sake of patching up in the world's eye a broken reputation, meanly appear indebted to the generosity, or *compassion* perhaps, of a man who has, by means so inhuman, robbed her of it? Indeed, my dear, I should not think my penitence for the rash step I took anything better than a specious delusion, if I had not got above the least wish to have Mr Lovelace for my husband.

'Yes, I warrant, I must *creep* to the violator, and be thankful to him for doing me poor justice!

'Do you not already see me (pursuing the advice you give), with a downcast eye, appear before his friends, and before *my own* (supposing the latter would at last condescend to own me), divested of that *noble confidence* which arises from a mind unconscious of having deserved reproach?

'Do you not see me creep about my own house, preferring all my honest maidens to myself—as if afraid, too, to open my lips, either by way of reproof or admonition, lest their bolder eyes should bid me look inward, and not expect perfection from *them?*

'And shall I entitle the wretch to upbraid me with his generosity, and his pity; and perhaps to reproach me for having been *capable* of forgiving crimes of *such* a nature?

'I once indeed hoped, little thinking him so *premeditatedly* vile a man, that I might have the happiness to reclaim him: I vainly believed that he loved me well enough to suffer my advice for his good, and the example I humbly presumed I should be enabled to set him to have weight with him; and the rather, as he had no mean opinion of my morals and understanding: but now, what hope is there left for this my *prime* hope?—*Were* I to marry him, what a figure should I make, preaching virtue and morality to a man whom I had trusted with opportunities to seduce me from all my own duties?—And then, supposing I were to have children by such a husband, must it not, think you, cut a thoughtful person to the heart, to look round upon her little family and think she had given them a father destined, without a miracle, to perdition; and whose immoralities, propagated among them by his vile example, might too probably bring down a curse upon them? And, after all, who knows but that my own sinful compliances with a man who would think himself entitled to my obedience might taint my own morals, and make me, instead of a reformer, an imitator of him?—for who *can touch pitch, and not be defiled?*

'Let me then repeat that I truly despise this man! If I know my own heart, indeed I do!—I pity him!—*Beneath* my very pity as he is, I nevertheless pity him!—But this I could not do if I still loved him: for, my dear, one must be greatly sensible of the baseness and ingratitude of those we love. I love him not, therefore! My soul disdains communion with him.

'But although thus much is due to resentment, yet have I not been so far carried away by its angry effects, as to be rendered incapable of casting about what I *ought* to do, and what *could be done*, if the Almighty, in order to lengthen the time of my penitence, were to bid me to live.

'The single life, at such times, has offered to me as the life, the *only* life, to be chosen. But in *that*, must I not *now* sit brooding over my past afflictions, and mourning my faults till the hour of my release? And would not everyone be able to assign the reason why Clarissa Harlowe chose solitude, and to sequester herself from the world? Would not the look of every creature who beheld me appear as a reproach to me? And would not my conscious eye confess my fault, whether the eyes of others accused me or not? One of my delights was to enter the cots of my poor neighbours, to leave lessons to the boys, and cautions to the elder girls: and how should I be able, unconscious and without pain, to say to the latter, Fly the delusions of men, who had been supposed to have run away with one?

'What then, my dear and only friend, can I wish for but death?—And what, after all, *is* death? 'Tis but a cessation from mortal life: 'tis but the finishing of an appointed course: the refreshing inn after a fatiguing journey: the end of a life of cares and troubles; and, if happy, the beginning of a life of immortal happiness.

'If I die not now, it may possibly happen that I may be taken when I am less prepared. Had I escaped the evils I labour under, it might have been in the midst of some gay promising hope; when my heart had beat high with the desire of life; and when the vanity of this earth had taken hold of me.

'But now, my dear, for *your* satisfaction let me say, that although I wish not for life, yet would I not like a poor coward desert my post, when I *can* maintain it, and when it is my *duty* to maintain it.

'More than once, indeed, was I urged by thoughts so sinful: but then it was in the height of my distress: and once, particularly, I have reason to believe I saved myself by my desperation from the most shocking personal insults: from a repetition, as far as I know, of his vileness; the base women (with so much reason dreaded by me) present to intimidate *me*, if not to assist *him!*—Oh my dear, you know not what I suffered on that occasion!—Nor do I what I *escaped* at the time, if the wicked man had approached me to execute the horrid purposes of his vile heart. High resolution, a courage I never knew before; a settled, not a rash courage; and such a command of my passions—I can only say I know not how I came by such an uncommon elevation of mind, if it were not given me in answer to my earnest prayers to Heaven for such a command of myself, before I entered into the horrid company.'

As I am of opinion, that it would have manifested more of revenge and despair, than of principle, had I committed a violence upon myself when the villainy was *perpetrated*; so I should think it equally criminal, were I now *wilfully* to neglect myself; were I *purposely* to run into the arms of death (as that man supposes I shall do) when I might avoid it.

Nor, my dear, whatever are the suppositions of such a short-sighted, such a low-souled man, must you impute to gloom, to melancholy, to despondency, nor yet to a spirit of faulty pride, or still *more* faulty revenge, the resolution I have taken never to marry *this*; and if not *this*, *any* man. So far from deserving this imputation, I do assure you (my dear and *only* love) that I will do everything I can to prolong my life, till God in mercy to me shall be pleased to call for it. I have reason to think my punishment is but the due consequence of my fault, and I will not run away from it; but beg of Heaven to sanctify it to me. When appetite serves, I will eat and drink what is sufficient to support nature. A very little, you know, will do for that. And whatever my physicians shall think fit to prescribe, I will take, though ever so disagreeable. In short, I will do everything I can do, to convince all my friends, who hereafter may think it worth their while to inquire after my last behaviour, that I possessed my soul with tolerable patience; and endeavoured to bear with a lot of my own drawing: for thus, in humble imitation of the sublimest exemplar, I often say: Lord, it is thy will; and it shall be mine. Thou art just in all thy dealings with the children of men; and I know thou wilt not afflict me beyond what I can bear: and, if I *can* bear it, I *ought* to bear it; and (thy grace assisting me) I *will* bear it.

'But here, my dear, is another reason; a reason that will convince you yourself that I ought not to think of wedlock; but of a quite different preparation: I am persuaded, as much as that I am now alive, that I shall not long live. The strong sense I have ever had of my fault, the loss of my reputation, my disappointments, the determined resentment of my friends, *aiding* the barbarous usage I have met with where I least deserved it, have seized upon my heart: seized upon it before it was so well fortified by *religious considerations*, as I hope it now is. Don't be concerned, my dear—But I am sure, if I may say it with as little presumption as grief, in the words of Job, That God will soon *dissolve my substance*; and *bring me to death, and to the house appointed for all living.*'[2]

And now, my dearest friend, you know all my mind. And you will be pleased to write to the ladies of Mr Lovelace's family, that I think myself infinitely obliged to them for their good opinion of me; and that it has given me greater pleasure than I thought I had to come in this life, that upon the little knowledge they have of me, and that not personal, I was thought worthy (after the ill usage I have received) of an alliance with their honourable family: but that I can by no means think of their kinsman for a husband: and do you, my dear, extract from the above, such reasons as you think have any weight in them.

I would write myself to acknowledge their favour, had I not more employment for my head, my heart, and my fingers, than I doubt they will be able to go through.

I should be glad to know when you set out on your journey; as also your little stages; and your time of stay at your aunt Harman's; that my prayers may locally attend you, whithersoever you go, and wherever you are.

CLARISSA HARLOWE

Letter 360: MISS CLARISSA HARLOWE TO MISS HOWE

Sunday, July 23

THE letter accompanying this being upon a very peculiar subject, I would not embarrass it, as I may say, with any other. And yet having some further matters upon my mind, which will want your excuse for directing them to you, I hope the following lines will *have* that excuse.

My good Mrs Norton, so long ago as in a letter dated the 3rd of this month,[a] hinted to me that my relations took amiss some severe things you was pleased, in

<hr>

a See p. 990.

love to me, to say of them. Mrs Norton mentioned it with that respectful love which she bears to my dearest friend: but wished, for *my* sake, that you would rein in a vivacity which, on most other occasions, so charmingly becomes you. This was her sense. You know that *I* am warranted to speak and write freer to my Anna Howe, than Mrs Norton would do.

I durst not mention it to you at that time, because appearances were *so* strong against me on Mr Lovelace's getting me again into his power (after my escape to Hampstead), as made you very angry with me when you answered mine on my second escape. And soon afterwards I was put under that barbarous arrest; so that I could not well touch upon that subject till now.

Now, therefore, my dearest Miss Howe, let me *repeat* my earnest request (for this is not the first time by several that I have been obliged to chide you on this occasion), that you will spare my parents, and other relations, in all your conversations about me—Indeed, I wish they had thought fit to take other measures with me: but who shall judge for them?—The event has justified them, and condemned me. They expected nothing good of this vile man; *he* has not, therefore, deceived *them:* but they expected other things from *me*; and *I* have. And they have the more reason to be set against me, if (as my aunt Hervey wrote formerly*a*) they intended not to force my inclinations, in favour of Mr Solmes; and if they believe, that my going off was the effect of choice and premeditation.

I have no desire to be received to favour by them: for why should I sit down to wish for what I have no reason to expect?—Besides, I could not look them in the face if they *would* receive me. Indeed I could not. All I have to hope for is, first, that my father will absolve me from his heavy malediction: and next, for a last blessing. The obtaining of these favours are needful to my peace of mind.

I have written to my sister; but have only mentioned the absolution.

I am afraid, I shall receive a very harsh answer from her. My fault in the eyes of my family is of so enormous a nature, that my *first* application will hardly be encouraged. Then they know not (nor perhaps will believe), that I am so very ill as I am. So that, were I actually to die before they could have time to take the necessary informations, you must not blame them too severely. You must call it a fatality. I know not what you must call it: for, alas! I have made them as miserable as I am myself. And yet sometimes I think that, were they cheerfully to pronounce me forgiven, I know not whether my concern for having offended them would not be augmented: since I imagine that nothing can be more wounding to a spirit not ungenerous, than a *generous forgiveness*.

I hope your mamma will permit our correspondence for *one* month more, although I do not take her advice as to having this man. Only for *one* month, I will not desire it longer. When catastrophes are consummating, what changes (changes that make one's heart shudder to think of) may *one* short month produce!—But if she will not—why then, my dear, it becomes us both to acquiesce.

You can't think what my apprehensions would have been, had I known Mr Hickman was to have had a meeting (on such a questioning occasion as must have been his errand from you) with that haughty and uncontrollable man.

You give me hope of a visit from him: let him *expect* to see me greatly altered. I know he loves me: for he loves everyone whom you love. A painful interview, I

---

a See Letter 144.

doubt! But I shall be glad to see a man, whom *you* will one day, and an *early* day, I hope, make happy; and whose gentle manners, and unbounded love for you, will make *you* so, if it be not your own fault.

I am, my dearest, kindest friend, the sweet companion of my happy hours, the friend ever dearest and nearest to my fond heart,

Your equally obliged and faithful,
CLARISSA HARLOWE

Letter 361: MRS NORTON TO MISS CLARISSA HARLOWE

Monday, July 24

EXCUSE, my dearest young lady, my long silence. I have been extremely ill. My poor boy has also been at death's door; and, when I hoped that he was better, he has relapsed. Alas! my dear, he is very dangerously ill. Let us both have your prayers!

Very angry letters have passed between your sister and Miss Howe. Everyone of your family is incensed against that young lady. I wish you would remonstrate against her warmth; since it can do no good; for they will not believe but that her interposition has your connivance; nor that you are so ill as Miss Howe assures them you are.

Before she wrote, they were going to send up young Mr Brand the clergyman, to make private inquiries of your health, and way of life—But now they are so exasperated, that they have laid aside their intention.

We have flying reports here, and at Harlowe Place, of some fresh insults which you have undergone: and that you are about to put yourself into Lady Betty Lawrance's protection. I believe they would now be glad (as I should be) that you would do so; and this perhaps will make them suspend for the present any determination in your favour.

How unhappy am I that the dangerous way my son is in prevents my attendance on you! Let me beg of you to write me word how you are, both as to person and mind. A servant of Sir Robert Beachcroft, who rides post on his master's business to town, will present you with this; and perhaps will bring me the favour of a few lines in return. He will be obliged to stay in town several hours for an answer to his dispatches.

This is the anniversary that used to give joy to as many as had the pleasure and honour of knowing you. May the Almighty bless you, and grant that it may be the only unhappy one that may be ever known by you, my dearest young lady; and by

Your ever-affectionate
JUDITH NORTON

Letter 362: MISS CLARISSA HARLOWE TO MRS NORTON

Monday night, July 24

My dear Mrs NORTON,

HAD I not fallen into fresh troubles, which disabled me for several days from holding a pen, I should not have forborne inquiring after your health and that of your son; for I should have been but too ready to impute your own silence to the cause, to which to my very great concern I find it was owing. I pray to Heaven, my dear good friend, to give you comfort in the way most desirable to yourself.

I am exceedingly concerned at Miss Howe's writing about me to my friends. I do assure you that I was as ignorant of her intention so to do, as of the contents of her letter. Nor has she yet let me know (discouraged I suppose by her ill success), that she *did* write. Impossible to share the delight which such charming spirits give, without the inconvenience that will attend their volatility—So mixed are our best enjoyments!

It was but yesterday that I wrote to chide the dear creature for freedoms of that nature, which her unseasonable love for me had made her take as you wrote me word in your former. I was afraid that all such freedoms would be attributed to *me*. And I am sure that nothing but my own application to my friends, and a full conviction of my contrition, will procure me favour. Least of all can I expect that either your mediation or hers (both of whose fond and partial love of me is so well known) will avail me.

She then gives a brief account of the arrest: of her dejection under it: of her apprehensions of being carried to her former lodgings: of Mr Lovelace's avowed innocence as to that insult: of her release by Mr Belford: of Mr Lovelace's promise not to molest her: of her clothes being sent her: of the earnest desire of all his friends, and of himself, to marry her: of Miss Howe's advice to comply with their requests: and of her declared resolution rather to die than be his, sent to Miss Howe to be given to his relations, but as yesterday. After which, she thus proceeds:

Now, my dear Mrs Norton, you will be surprised perhaps that I should have returned such an answer: but when you have everything before you, you, who know me so well, will not think me wrong. And, besides, I am upon a better preparation than for an earthly husband.

Nor let it be imagined, my dear and ever-venerable friend, that my present turn of mind proceeds from gloominess or melancholy; for although it was *brought on* by disappointment (the world showing me early, even at my first *rushing* into it, its true and ugly face); yet I hope that it has obtained a better root, and will every day more and more by its fruits demonstrate to me, and to all my friends, that it has.

I have written to my sister. Last Friday I wrote. So the die is thrown. I hope for a gentle answer. But perhaps they will not vouchsafe me *any*. It is my *first* direct application, you know. I wish Miss Howe had left me to my own workings in this tender point.

It will be a great satisfaction to me to hear of your perfect recovery; and that my foster-brother is out of danger. But why said I, *out of danger?*—When can *this* be justly said of creatures who hold by so uncertain a tenure? This is one of those forms of common speech that proves the *frailty* and the *presumption* of poor mortals at the same time.

Don't be uneasy you cannot answer your wishes to be with me. I am happier than I could have expected to be among mere strangers. It was grievous at first; but use reconciles everything to us. The people of the house where I am are courteous and honest. There is a widow who lodges in it (have I not said so formerly?), a good woman; who is the better for having been a proficient in the school of affliction.

An excellent school! my dear Mrs Norton, in which we are taught to know ourselves, to be able to compassionate and bear with one another, and to look up to a better hope.

I have as humane a physician (whose fees are his least regard), and as worthy an apothecary, as ever patient was visited by. My nurse is diligent, obliging, silent, and sober. So I am not unhappy *without:* and *within*—I hope, my dear Mrs Norton, that I shall be every day more and more happy *within*.

No doubt, it would be one of the greatest comforts I could know to have you with me: you who love me so dearly: who have been the watchful sustainer of my helpless infancy: you, by whose precepts I have been so much benefited!—In your dear bosom could I repose all my griefs: and by your piety, and experience in the ways of Heaven, should I be strengthened in what I am still to go through.

But, as it must not be, I will acquiesce; and so I hope will you: for you see in what respects I am *not* unhappy; and in those that I *am*, they lie not in your power to remedy.

Then, as I have told you, I have all my clothes in my own possession. So I am rich enough, as to this world, and in common conveniencies.

So you see, my venerable and dear friend, that I am not always turning the dark side of my prospects, in order to move compassion; a trick imputed to me, too often, by my hard-hearted sister; when, if I know my own heart, it is above all trick or artifice. Yet I hope at last I shall be so happy as to receive *benefit* rather than *reproach* from this talent, if it *be* my talent. At *last*, I say; for whose heart have I *hitherto* moved?—Not one, I am sure, that was not *predetermined* in my favour!

As to the day—I have passed it, as I ought to pass it—It has been a very heavy day to me!—More for my friends' sake, too, than for my own!—How did *they* use to pass it!—What a gala!—How have they now passed it!—To *imagine* it, how grievous!—Say not that those are cruel who suffer so much for my fault; and who, for eighteen years together, rejoiced in me, and rejoiced me, by their indulgent goodness!—But I will *think* the rest!—Adieu, my dearest Mrs Norton!—Adieu!

Letter 363: MISS CLARISSA HARLOWE TO MISS ARABELLA HARLOWE

Friday, July 21

IF, my dearest sister, I did not think the state of my health very precarious, and that it was my duty to take this step, I should hardly have dared to approach you, although but with my pen, after having found your censures so dreadfully justified as they have been.

I have not the courage to write to my father himself; nor yet to my mother. And it is with trembling that I address myself to you, to beg of you to intercede for me, that my father will have the goodness to revoke that heaviest part of the very heavy curse he laid upon me, which relates to HEREAFTER: for, as to the HERE, *I have*, indeed, *met with my punishment from the very wretch in whom I was supposed to place my confidence.*

As I hope not for restoration to favour, I may be allowed to be very earnest on this head: yet will I not use any arguments in support of my request, because I am sure my father cannot wish to have his poor child miserable for ever!

I have the most grateful sense of my mother's goodness in sending me up my clothes. I would have acknowledged the favour the moment I received them, with the most thankful duty, but that I feared any line from me would be unacceptable.

I would not give fresh offence: so will decline all other commendations of duty and love; appealing to my heart for both, where *both* are flaming with an ardour that nothing but death can extinguish: therefore only subscribe myself, without so much as a name,

My dear and happy sister, Your afflicted servant.

A letter directed for me, at Mr Smith's, a glover, in King Street, Covent Garden, will come to hand.

Letter 364: MR BELFORD TO ROBERT LOVELACE, ESQ.

(In answer to Letters 347 and 350)

Edgware, Monday, July 24

WHAT pains thou takest to persuade thyself that the lady's ill health is owing to the vile arrest, and to her friends' implacableness! Both, primarily (if they were), to be laid at thy door. What poor excuses will good heads make for the evils they are put upon by bad hearts!—But 'tis no wonder, that he who can sit down premeditatedly to do a bad action will content himself with a bad excuse: and yet, what fools must he suppose the rest of the world to be, if he imagines them as easily to be imposed upon as he can impose upon himself?

In vain dost thou impute to pride or wilfulness the necessity to which thou hast reduced this lady of parting with her clothes: for can she do otherwise, and be the noble-minded creature she is?

Her implacable friends have refused her the current cash she left behind her; and wished, as her sister wrote to her, to see her reduced to want. Probably therefore they will not be sorry that she is reduced to such straits; and will take it for a justification from Heaven of their wicked hard-heartedness. Thou canst not suppose she would take supplies from thee: to take them from me would, in her opinion, be taking them from thee. Miss Howe's mother is an avaricious woman; and perhaps the daughter could do nothing of that sort unknown to her; and, if she *could*, is too noble a girl to deny it, if charged. And then Miss Harlowe is firmly of opinion that she shall never want nor wear the things she disposes of.

Having heard nothing from town that obliges me to go thither, I shall gratify poor Belton with my company till tomorrow, or perhaps till Wednesday: for the unhappy man is more and more loath to part with me. I shall soon set out for Epsom, to endeavour to serve him there, and reinstate him in his own house. Poor fellow! he is most horribly low-spirited; mopes about; and nothing diverts him. I pity him at my heart; but can do him no good. What consolation can I give him, either from his past life, or from his future prospects?

Our friendships and intimacies, Lovelace, are only calculated for strong life and health. When sickness comes, we look round us, and upon one another, like frighted birds at the sight of a kite ready to souse upon them. Then, with all our bravery, what miserable wretches are we!

Thou tellest me that thou seest reformation is coming swiftly upon me. I hope it is. I see so much difference in the behaviour of this admirable woman in *her* illness, and that of poor Belton in *his*, that it is plain to me the sinner is the real coward, and the saint the true hero; and sooner or later we shall all find it to be so, if we are not cut off suddenly.

The lady shut herself up at six o'clock yesterday afternoon; and intends not to see company till seven or eight this; not even her nurse; imposing upon herself a severe fast. And why? It is her birthday!—Blooming, yet declining in her blossom!—Every birthday till this, no doubt, happy!—What must be her reflections!—What ought to be thine!

What sport dost thou make with my aspirations and my prostrations, as thou callest them; and with my dropping of the bank note behind her chair. I had too much awe of her at the time, and too much apprehended her displeasure at the offer, to make it with the grace that would better have become my intention. But the action, if awkward, was modest. Indeed, the fitter subject for ridicule with thee; who canst no more taste the beauty and delicacy of modest obligingness than of modest love. For the same may be said of inviolable respect, that the poet says of unfeigned affection:

> I *speak*, I know not what!—
> Speak ever so; and if I *answer* you
> I know not what, it shows the more of love.
> Love is a child that talks in broken language;
> Yet then it speaks most plain.[1]

The like may be pleaded in behalf of that modest respect which made the humble offerer afraid to invade the awful eye, or the revered hand; but awkwardly to drop its incense beside the altar it should have been laid upon. But how should that soul, which could treat delicacy itself brutally, know anything of this?

But I am still more amazed at thy courage, to think of throwing thyself in the way of Miss Howe, and Miss Arabella Harlowe!—Thou wilt not dare, surely, to carry this thought into execution!

As to *my* dress, and *thy* dress, I have only to say that the sum total of thy observation is this: that *my* outside is the *worst* of me; and *thine* the *best* of thee: and what gettest thou by the comparison? Do thou reform the one, and I'll try to mend the other. I challenge thee to begin.

Mrs Lovick gave me, at my request, the copy of a meditation she showed me, which was extracted by the lady from the Scriptures,[2] while under arrest at Rowland's, as appears by the date. She is not to know that she has taken such a liberty.

You and I always admired the noble simplicity, and natural ease and dignity of style, which are the distinguishing characteristics of these books, whenever any passages from them by way of quotation in the works of other authors, popped upon us. And once I remember you, even *you*, observed that those passages always appeared to you like a rich vein of golden ore, which runs through baser metals; embellishing the work they were brought to authenticate.

Try, Lovelace, if thou canst relish a divine beauty. I think it must strike transient (if not permanent) remorse into thy heart. Thou boastest of thy [ingenuousness]; let this be the test of it; and whether thou canst be serious on a subject so deep, the occasion of it resulting from thyself.

MEDITATION

Saturday, July 15

Oh that my grief were thoroughly weighed, and my calamity laid in the balance together!

For now it would be heavier than the sand of the sea: therefore my words are swallowed up.

For the arrows of the Almighty are within me; the poison whereof drinketh up my spirit. The terrors of God do set themselves in array against me.

When I lie down, I say, When shall I arise? When will the night be gone? And I am full of tossings to and fro, unto the dawning of the day.

My days are swifter than a weaver's shuttle, and are spent without hope—mine eye shall no more see good.

Wherefore is light given to *her* that is in misery; and life unto the bitter in soul?

Who longeth for death; but it cometh not; and diggeth for it more than for hid treasures?

Why is light given to *one* whose way is hid; and whom God hath hedged in?

For the thing which I greatly feared is come upon me!

I was not in safety; neither had I rest; neither was I quiet: yet trouble came.

Oh that my words were now written! Oh that they were printed in a book! that they were graven with an iron pen and lead in the book for ever!

I have a little leisure, and am in a scribbling vein: indulge me, Lovelace, a few reflections on these sacred books.

We are taught to read the Bible when children, and as a rudiment only; and, as far as I know, this may be the reason why we think ourselves above it when at a maturer age. For you know that our parents, as well as we, wisely rate our proficiency by the books we are advanced to, and not by our understanding what we have passed through. But, in my uncle's illness, I had the curiosity in some of my dull hours (lighting upon one in his closet), to dip into it: and then I found, wherever I turned, that there were *admirable things in it*. I have borrowed one, on receiving from Mrs Lovick the above meditations; for I had a mind to compare them by the book, hardly believing they could be so exceedingly apposite as I find they are. And one time or other, it is very likely that I shall make a resolution to give it a thorough perusal, by way of *course*, as I may say.

This, meantime, I will venture to repeat, is certain, that the style is that truly easy, simple, and natural one, which we should admire in other authors excessively. Then all the world join in an opinion of its antiquity, and authenticity too; and the learned are fond of strengthening their different arguments by its sanctions. Indeed, I was so much taken with it at my uncle's, that I was half ashamed that it appeared so *new* to me. And yet, I cannot but say that I have some of the Old Testament history, as it is called, in my head: but perhaps am more obliged for it to Josephus, than to the Bible itself.

Odd enough, with all our pride of learning, that we choose to derive the little we know from the undercurrents, perhaps muddy ones too, when the clear, the pellucid fountain-head is much nearer at hand, and easier to be come at—Slighted the more, possibly, for that very reason!

But man is a pragmatical foolish creature; and the more we look into him, the more we must despise him—Lords of the creation!—Who can forbear indignant laughter! When we see not one of the individuals of that creation, except his perpetually eccentric self, but acts within its own natural and original appointments: and all the time, proud and vain as the conceited wretch is of fancied and self-dependent excellence, he is obliged not only for the ornaments, but for the necessaries of life (that is to say, for food as well as raiment) to all the other creatures; strutting with their blood and spirits in his veins, and with their plumage on his back: for what has he of his own, but a very mischievous, monkey-like, bad nature? Yet thinks himself at liberty to kick, and cuff, and elbow out every worthier creature: and when he has none of the animal creation to hunt down and abuse, will make use of his power, his strength, or his wealth, to oppress the less powerful and weaker of his own species!

When you and I meet next, let us enter more largely into this subject: and I dare say we shall take it by turns, in imitation of the two sages of antiquity, to laugh and to weep[3] at the thoughts of what miserable yet conceited beings men in general, but we libertines in particular, are.

I fell upon a piece at Dorrell's this very evening, entitled, *The Sacred Classics*, written by one Blackwall.[4]

I took it home with me; and had not read a dozen pages, when I was convinced that I ought to be ashamed of myself to think how greatly I have admired less noble and less natural beauties in pagan authors; while I have known nothing of this all-excelling collection of beauties, the Bible! By my faith, Lovelace, I shall for the future have a better opinion of the good sense and taste of half a score parsons, whom I have fallen in with in my time, and despised for *magnifying*, as I thought they did, the language and the sentiments to be found in it, in preference to all the ancient poets and philosophers. And this is now a convincing proof to me, and shames as much an infidel's presumption as his ignorance, that those who know least are the greatest scoffers. A pretty pack of would-be wits of us, who censure without knowledge, laugh without reason, and are most noisy and loud against things we know least of!

Letter 365: MR BELFORD TO ROBERT LOVELACE, ESQ.

Wednesday, July 26

I CAME not to town till this morning early; poor Belton clinging to me, as a man destitute of all other hold.

I hastened to Smith's; and had but a very indifferent account of the lady's health. I sent up my compliments; and she desired to see me in the afternoon.

Mrs Lovick told me that, after I went away on Saturday, she actually parted with one of her best suits of clothes to a gentlewoman who is her (Mrs Lovick's) benefactress, and who bought them for a niece who is very speedily to be married, and whom she fits out and portions as her intended heiress. The lady was so jealous that the money might come from you or me, that she would see the purchaser: who owned to Mrs Lovick, that she bought them for half their worth: but yet, though her conscience permitted her to take them at such an under-rate, the widow says her friend admired the lady as one of the loveliest of her sex: and having been let into a little of her story, could not help tears at taking away her purchase.

She may be a good sort of woman: Mrs Lovick says she *is*: but SELF is an odious devil, that reconciles to some people the most cruel and dishonest actions. But, nevertheless, it is my opinion that those who can suffer themselves to take advantage of the necessities of their fellow-creatures, in order to buy anything at a less rate than would allow them the legal interest of their purchase-money (supposing they purchase *before they want*), are no better than robbers for the difference—To plunder a wreck, and to rob at a fire, are indeed higher degrees of wickedness: but do not these as well as the others heighten the distresses of the distressed, and heap more misery on the miserable, whom it is the duty of every-one to relieve?

About three o'clock I went again to Smith's. The lady was writing when I sent up my name; but admitted of my visit. I saw a visible alteration in her countenance for the worse; and Mrs Lovick respectfully accusing her of too great assiduity to her pen, early and late, and of her abstinence the day before. I took notice of the alteration; and told her that her physician had greater hopes of her than she had of herself; and I would take the liberty to say that despair of recovery allowed not room for cure.

She said she neither despaired nor hoped. Then stepping to the glass, with great composure, My countenance, says she, is indeed an honest picture of my heart. But the mind will run away with the body at any time.

Writing is all my diversion, continued she; and I have subjects that cannot be dispensed with. As to my hours, I have always been an early riser: but now rest is less in my power than ever: sleep has a long time ago quarrelled with me, and will not be friends, although I have made the first advances. What *will* be, *must*.

She then stepped to her closet, and brought to me a parcel sealed up with three seals. Be so kind, said she, as to give this to your friend. A very grateful present it ought to be to him: for, sir, this packet contains all his letters to me. Such letters they are, as, compared with his actions, would reflect dishonour upon all his sex, were they to fall into other hands.

As to my letters to him, they are not many. He may either keep or destroy them as he pleases.

I thought I ought not to forgo this opportunity to plead for you: I therefore, with the packet in my hand, urged all the arguments I could think of in your favour.

She heard me out with more attention than I could have promised myself, considering her determined resolution.

I would not interrupt you, Mr Belford, said she, though I am far from being pleased with the subject of your discourse. The motives for your pleas in his favour are generous. I love to see instances of generous friendship in either sex. But I have written my full mind on this subject to Miss Howe, who will communicate it to the ladies of his family. No more, therefore, I pray you, upon a topic that may lead to disagreeable recriminations.

Her apothecary came in. He advised her to the air, and blamed her for so great an application as he was told she made to her pen; and he gave it as the doctor's opinion, as well as his own, that she would recover if she herself desired to recover, and would use the means.

The lady may indeed write too much for her health, perhaps; but I have observed on several occasions, that when the physical men are at a loss what to prescribe, they forbid their patients what they best like, and are most diverted with.

But, noble-minded as they see this lady is, they know not half her nobleness of mind, nor how deeply she is wounded; and depend too much upon her *youth*, which I doubt will not do in this case, and upon *time*, which will not alleviate the woes of such a mind: For, having been bent upon doing good, and upon reclaiming a libertine whom she loved, she is disappointed in all her darling views, and will never be able, I fear, to look up with satisfaction enough in herself to make life desirable to her. For this lady had *other* views in living, than the common ones of eating, sleeping, dressing, visiting, and those other fashionable amusements which fill up the time of most of her sex, especially of those of it who think themselves fitted to shine in and adorn polite assemblies. Her grief, in short, seems to me to be of such a nature that *time*, which alleviates most other persons' afflictions, will, as the poet says, *give increase to hers*.[1]

Thou, Lovelace, mightest have seen all this superior excellence, as thou wentest along. In every word, in every sentiment, in every action, is it visible—But thy cursed inventions and intriguing spirit ran away with thee. 'Tis fit that the subject of thy wicked boast, and of talents so egregiously misapplied, should be *thy* punishment and thy curse.

Mr Goddard took his leave; and I was going to do so too, when the maid came up and told her a gentleman was below, who very earnestly inquired after her health, and desired to see her: his name Hickman.

She was overjoyed; and bid the maid desire the gentleman to walk up.

I would have withdrawn; but I suppose she thought it was likely I should have met him upon the stairs, and so she forbid it.

She shot to the stairs-head to receive him, and, taking his hand, asked half a dozen questions (without waiting for any answer) in relation to Miss Howe's health; acknowledging, in high terms, her goodness in sending him to see her before she set out upon her little journey.

He gave her a letter from that young lady; which she put into her bosom, saying she would read it by and by.

He was visibly shocked to see how ill she looked.

You look at me with concern, Mr Hickman, said she—Oh! sir, times are strangely altered with me since I saw you last at my dear Miss Howe's!—What a cheerful creature was I then!—My heart at rest! My prospects charming! And beloved by everybody!—But I will not pain you!

Indeed, madam, said he, I am grieved for you at my soul.

He turned away his face with visible grief in it.

Her own eyes glistened: but she turned to each of us, presenting one to the other: him to me, as a gentleman *truly* deserving to be *called so*; me to him, as *your* friend, indeed (how was I, at that instant, ashamed of myself!); but, nevertheless, as a man of humanity; detesting my friend's baseness; and desirous of doing her all manner of good offices.

Mr Hickman received my civilities with a coldness, which, however, was rather to be expected on your account, than that it deserved exception on mine. And the lady invited us both to breakfast with her in the morning; he being obliged to return next day.

I left them together, and called upon Mr Dorrell, my attorney, to consult him upon poor Belton's affairs; and then went home, and wrote thus far, preparative to what may occur in my breakfasting visit in the morning.

Letter 366: MR BELFORD TO ROBERT LOVELACE, ESQ.

Thursday, July 27

I WENT this morning, according to the lady's invitation, to breakfast, and found Mr Hickman with her. A good deal of heaviness and concern hung upon his countenance; but he received me with more respect than he did yesterday: which, I presume, was owing to the lady's favourable character of me.

He spoke very little; for I suppose they had all their talk out yesterday and before I came this morning.

By the hints that dropped, I perceived that Miss Howe's letter gave an account of your interview with her at Colonel Ambrose's—of your professions to Miss Howe; and Miss Howe's opinion that marrying you was the only way now left to repair her wrongs.

Mr Hickman, as I also gathered, had pressed her, in Miss Howe's name, to let her find her, on her return from the Isle of Wight, at a neighbouring farmhouse, where neat apartments would be made ready to receive her. She asked how long it would be before they returned? And he told her it was proposed to be no more than a fortnight out and in. Upon which she said, she should then perhaps have time to consider of that kind proposal.

He had tendered her money from Miss Howe; but could not induce her to take any. No wonder I was refused! She only said that if she had occasion, she would be obliged to nobody but Miss Howe.

Mr Goddard, her apothecary, came in before breakfast was over. At her desire he sat down with us. Mr Hickman asked him if he could give him any consolation in relation to Miss Harlowe's recovery, to carry down to a lady who loved her as she loved her own life?

The lady, said he, will do very well if she will resolve upon it herself. Indeed you *will*, madam. The doctor is entirely of this opinion; and has ordered nothing for you but weak jellies, and innocent cordials, lest you should starve yourself. And, let me tell you, madam, that so much watching, so little nourishment, and so much grief as you seem to indulge, is enough to impair the most vigorous health, and to wear out the strongest constitution.

What, sir, said she, can I do? I have no appetite. Nothing you call nourishing will stay on my stomach. I do what I can: and have such kind directors in Dr H. and you, that I should be inexcusable if I did not.

I'll give you a regimen, madam, replied he; which I am sure the doctor will approve of, and will make physic unnecessary in your case. And that is, 'Go to rest at ten at night. Rise not till seven in the morning. Let your breakfast be water-gruel, or milk-pottage, or weak broths: your dinner anything you like, so you will *but* eat: a dish of tea with milk in the afternoon; and sago for your supper: and, my life for yours, this diet and a month's country air will set you up.'

We were much pleased with the worthy gentleman's disinterested regimen: and she said, referring to her nurse (who vouched for her), Pray, Mr Hickman, let Miss Howe know the good hands I am in: and as to the kind charge of the gentleman, assure her that all I promised to her, in the longest of my two last letters, on the subject of my health, I do and will, to the utmost of my power, observe. I have engaged, sir (to Mr Goddard), I have engaged, sir (to me) to Miss Howe, to avoid all wilful neglects. It would be an unpardonable fault, and very ill become the character I would be glad to deserve, or the temper of mind I wish my friends hereafter to think me mistress of, if I did not.

Mr Hickman and I went afterwards to a neighbouring coffee-house; and he gave me some account of your behaviour at the ball on Monday night, and of your treatment of him in the conference he had with you before that; which he represented in a more favourable light than you had done yourself: and yet he gave his sentiments of you with great freedom, but with the politeness of a gentleman.

He told me how very determined the lady was against marrying you; that she had, early this morning, set herself to write a letter to Miss Howe, in answer to one he brought her, which he was to call for at twelve, it being almost finished before he saw her at breakfast; and that at three he proposed to set out on his return.

He told me that Miss Howe, and her mother, and himself, were to begin their little journey for the Isle of Wight on Monday next: but that he must make the most favourable representation of Miss Harlowe's bad health, or they should have a very uneasy absence. He expressed the pleasure he had in finding the lady in such good hands: proposed to call on Dr H. to take his opinion whether it was likely she would recover; and hoped he should find it favourable.

As he was resolved to make the best of the matter, and as the lady had refused to accept of money offered by Mr Hickman, I said nothing of her parting with her clothes. I thought it would serve no other end to mention it but to shock Miss Howe: for it has such a sound with it, that a lady of her rank and fortune should be so reduced, that I cannot myself think of it with patience; nor know I but *one* man in the world who can.

This gentleman is a little finical and formal; but I think him an agreeable sensible man, and not at all deserving of the treatment, or the character, you give him.

But you are really a strange mortal. Because you have advantages in your person, in your air, and intellect, above all the men I know, and a face that would deceive the devil, you can't think any man else tolerable.

It is upon this modest principle that thou deridest some of us who, not having thy confidence in their outside appearance, seek to hide their defects by the tailor's and peruke-maker's assistance (mistakenly enough, if it be really done so absurdly as to expose them more); and sayest that we do but hang out a sign in our dress, of what we have in the shop of our minds. This no doubt thou thinkest is smartly observed: but prithee, Lovelace, tell me, if thou canst, what sort of a sign must thou hang out, wert thou obliged to give us a clear idea by it of the furniture of *thy* mind?

Mr Hickman tells me he should have been happy with Miss Howe some weeks ago (for all the settlements have been some time engrossed); but that she will not marry, she declares, while her dear friend is so unhappy.

This is truly a charming instance of the force of *female friendship*; which you and I, and our brother rakes, have constantly ridiculed as a chimerical and impossible thing in ladies of equal age, rank, and perfections.

But really, Lovelace, I see more and more that there are not in the world, with all our conceited pride, narrower-souled wretches than we rakes and libertines are. And I'll tell thee how it comes about.

Our early love of roguery makes us generally run away from instruction; and so we become mere smatterers in the sciences we are put to learn; and because we *will* know no more, think there is no more to be *known*.

With an infinite deal of vanity, unreined imaginations, and no judgements at all, we next commence *half-wits*; and then think we have the whole field of knowledge in possession, and despise everyone who takes more pains and is more serious than ourselves, as phlegmatic stupid fellows, who have no taste for the most poignant pleasures of life.

This makes us insufferable to men of modesty and merit, and obliges us to herd with those of our own cast; and by this means we have no *opportunities* of seeing or conversing with anybody who could or would show us what we are; and so we conclude that we are the cleverest fellows in the world, and the only men of spirit in it; and, looking down with supercilious eyes on all who give not themselves the liberties we take, imagine the world made for us, and for us only.

Thus, as to useful knowledge, while others go to the bottom, we only skim the surface; are despised by people of solid sense, of true honour, and superior talents; and, shutting our eyes, move round and round (like so many blind mill-horses) in one narrow circle, while we imagine we have all the world to range in.

I THREW myself in Mr Hickman's way, on his return from the lady; and we took a small repast at the Lebeck's Head in Chandos Street.[1]

He was excessively moved at taking leave of her; being afraid, as he said to me (though he would not tell her so), that he should never see her again. She charged him to represent everything to Miss Howe in the most favourable light that the truth would bear.

He told me of a tender passage at parting; which was, that having saluted her at her closet door, he could not help once more taking the same liberty, in a more fervent manner, at the stairs-head, whither she accompanied him; and this in the thought that it was the last time he should ever have that honour; and offering to apologize for his freedom (for he had pressed her to his heart with a vehemence that he could neither account for or resist)—Excuse you, Mr Hickman! that I will: you are my brother, and my friend: and to show you that the good man who is to be happy with my beloved Miss Howe is very dear to me, you shall carry to her this token of my love (offering her sweet face to his salute, and pressing his hand between hers); and perhaps her love of *me* will make it more agreeable to her, than her punctilio would otherwise allow it to be. And tell her, said she, dropping on one knee, with clasped hands and uplifted eyes, that in this posture you see me, in the last moment of our parting, begging a blessing upon you both, and that you may be the delight and comfort of each other for many, very many, happy years!

Tears, said he, fell from my eyes: I even sobbed with mingled joy and sorrow; and she retreating as soon as I raised her, I went downstairs, highly dissatisfied with myself for going; yet unable to stay, my eyes fixed the contrary way to my feet, as long as I could behold the skirts of her raiment.

I went into the back shop, continued the worthy man, and recommended the angelic lady to the best care of Mrs Smith; and, when I was in the street, cast my eye up at her window: there, for the last time I doubt, said he, that I shall ever behold her, I saw her; and she waved her charming hand to me, and with such a look of smiling goodness and mingled concern, as I cannot describe.

Prithee tell me, thou vile Lovelace, if thou hast not a notion, even from these jejune descriptions of mine (as I have from reflecting upon the occasion), that there must be a more exalted pleasure in intellectual friendship than ever thou couldst taste in the grosser fumes of sensuality? And whether it may not be possible for thee, in time, to give that preference to the *infinitely* preferable, which I hope now that I shall always give?

I will leave thee to make the most of this reflection, from

Thy true friend,
J. BELFORD

Letter 367: MISS HOWE TO MISS CLARISSA HARLOWE

Tuesday, July 25

YOUR two affecting letters were brought to me (as I had directed any letter from you should be), to the colonel's, about an hour before we broke up. I could not forbear dipping into them there; and shedding more tears over them than I will tell you of; although I dried my eyes, as well as I could, that the company I was obliged to return to, and my mamma, should see as little of my concern as possible.

I am yet (and was then still more) excessively fluttered. The occasion I will communicate to you by and by: for nothing but the flutters given by the stroke of death could divert my *first* attention from the sad and solemn contents of your last favour. These therefore I must begin with.

How can I bear the thoughts of losing so dear a friend! I will not so much as suppose it. Indeed I *cannot!* Such a mind as yours was not vested in humanity to be snatched away from us so soon. There must be still a great deal for you to do, for the good of all who have the happiness to know you.

You enumerate, in your letter of Thursday last,[a] the particulars in which your situation is already mended: let me see, by effects, that you are in earnest in that enumeration; and that you really have the courage to resolve to get above the sense of injuries you could not avoid; and then will I trust to Providence, and my humble prayers, for your perfect recovery; and glad at my heart shall I be, on my return from the little island, to find you well enough to be near us, according to the proposal Mr Hickman has to make you.

You chide me, in yours of Sunday, on the freedom I take with your friends.[b]

I *may* be warm. I know I *am*—too warm—Yet warmth in friendship, surely, cannot be a crime; especially when our friend has great merit, labours under oppression, and is struggling with undeserved calamity.

I have no notion of coldness in friendship, be it dignified or distinguished by the name of *prudence*; or what it will.

You may excuse your relations. It was ever your way to do so. But, my dear, other people must be allowed to judge as they please. I am not their daughter, nor the sister of your brother and sister—I thank Heaven, I am not.

But if you are displeased with me, for the freedoms I took so long ago, as you mention, I am afraid if you knew what passed upon an application I made to your sister very lately, to procure you the absolution your heart is so much set upon,

a   Letter 343.
b   See pp. 1118–19.

that you would be still *more* concerned. But they have been even with me. But I must not tell you all. I hope however that these *unforgivers* (my mother is among them) were always good, dutiful, passive children to *their* parents.

Once more, forgive me. I owned I was too warm. But I have no example to the contrary, but from you: and the treatment you meet with is very little encouragement to me to endeavour to imitate you in your dutiful meekness.

You leave it to me to give a negative to the hopes of the noble family, whose only disgrace is that so very vile a man is so nearly related to them. But yet—alas! my dear, I am so fearful of consequences, so *selfishly* fearful if this negative *must* be given—I don't know what I should say—But give me leave to suspend, however, this negative, till I hear from you again.

Their earnest courtship of you into their splendid family is so *very* honourable to you—they *so justly* admire you—you must have had such a *noble triumph* over the base man—he is so *much* in earnest—the world knows so *much* of the unhappy affair—you may do *still* so *much* good—your will is *so* inviolate—your relations are *so* implacable—Think, my dear, and *re*-think.

And let me leave you to do so, while I give you the occasion of the flutter I mentioned at the beginning of this letter; in the conclusion of which, you will find the obligation I have consented to lay myself under, to refer this important point once more to your discussion, before I give, in your name, the negative that cannot, when given, be with honour to yourself repented of or recalled.

KNOW then, my dear, that I accompanied my mother to Colonel Ambrose's, on the occasion I mentioned to you in my former. Many ladies and gentlemen were there, whom you know; particularly Miss Kitty D'Oily, Miss Lloyd, Miss Biddy D'Ollyffe, Miss Biddulph, and their respective admirers, with the colonel's two nieces, fine women both; besides many whom you know not; for they were strangers to me, but by name. A splendid company, and all pleased with one another, till Colonel Ambrose introduced one, who the moment he was brought into the great hall set the whole assembly into a kind of agitation.

It was your villain.

I thought I should have sunk as soon as I set my eyes upon him. My mother was also affected; and coming to me, Nancy, whispered she, can you bear the sight of that wretch without too much emotion?—If not, withdraw into the next apartment.

I could not remove. Everybody's eyes were glanced from him to me. I sat down, and fanned myself, and was forced to order a glass of water. Oh that I had the eye the basilisk is reported to have, thought I, and that his life were within the power of it—directly would I kill him!

He entered with an air so hateful to me, but so agreeable to every other eye, that I could have looked him dead for that too.

After the general salutations, he singled out Mr Hickman, and told him he had recollected some parts of his behaviour to him when he saw him last, which had made him think himself under obligation to his patience and politeness.

And so, indeed, he was.

Miss D'Oily, upon his complimenting her among a knot of ladies, asked him, in their hearing, how Miss Clarissa Harlowe did?

He heard, he said, you were not so well as he wished you to be, and as you deserved to be.

Oh Mr Lovelace, said she, what have you to answer for on that young lady's account, if all be true that I have heard?

I have a great deal to answer for, said the unblushing villain: but that dear lady has so many excellencies, and so much delicacy, that little sins are great ones in her eye.

Little sins! replied the lady: Mr Lovelace's character is so well known that nobody believes he can commit *little* sins.

You are very good to me, Miss D'Oily.

Indeed I am not.

Then I am the only person to whom you are *not* very good: and so I am the less obliged to you.

He turned with an unconcerned air to Miss Playford, and made her some genteel compliments. I believe you know her not. She visits his cousins Montague. Indeed, he had something in his specious manner to say to everybody: and this too soon quieted the disgust each person had at his entrance.

I still kept my seat, and he either saw me not, or would not yet see me; and addressing himself to my mother, taking her unwilling hand with an air of high assurance, I am glad to see you here, madam: I hope Miss Howe is well. I have reason to complain greatly of her: but hope to owe to her the highest obligations that can be laid on man.

My daughter, sir, is accustomed to be too warm and too zealous in her friendships for either my tranquillity or her own.

There had indeed been some late occasion given for mutual displeasure between my mother and me: but I think she might have spared this to *him*; though nobody heard it, I believe, but the person to whom it was spoken and the lady who told it to me; for my mother spoke it low.

We are not wholly, madam, to live for ourselves, said the vile hypocrite. It is not everyone who has a soul capable of friendship: and what a heart must that be, which can be insensible to the interests of a suffering friend?

This sentiment from Mr Lovelace's mouth, said my mother!—Forgive me, sir; but you can have no end, surely, in endeavouring to make *me* think as well of you, as some innocent creatures have thought of you, to their cost.

She would have flung from him. But, detaining her hand—Less severe, dear madam, said he, be less severe in *this* place, I beseech you. You will allow that a very faulty person may see his errors; and when he does, and owns them, and repents, should he not be treated mercifully?

Your air, sir, seems not to be that of a penitent. But the place may as properly excuse this subject, as what you call my severity.

But, dearest madam, permit me to say that I hope for your interest with your *charming* daughter (was his sycophant word) to have it put into my power to convince all the world that there never was a truer penitent. And why, why this anger, dear madam (for she struggled to get her hand out of his); these violent airs, so *maidenly!*—Impudent fellow!—May I not ask if Miss Howe be here?

She would not have been here, replied my mother, had she known whom she had been to see.

And is she here, then?—Thank Heaven!—He disengaged her hand, and stepped forward into company.

Dear Miss Lloyd, said he, with an air (taking her hand, as he quitted my mother's), tell me, tell me, is Miss Arabella Harlowe here? Or will she be here? I was informed she would: and this, and the opportunity of paying my compliments to your friend Miss Howe, were great inducements with me to attend the colonel.

Superlative assurance! Was it not, my dear?

Miss Arabella Harlowe, excuse me, sir, said Miss Lloyd, would be very little inclined to meet you here, or anywhere else.

Perhaps so; my dear Miss Lloyd: but perhaps for that very reason, I am more desirous to see *her*.

Miss Harlowe, sir, said Miss Biddulph with a threatening air, will hardly be here without her *brother*. I imagine, if one come, both will come.

Heaven grant they both may! said the wretch. Nothing, Miss Biddulph, shall *begin* from me to disturb this assembly, I assure you, if they do. One calm half-hour's conversation with that brother and sister would be a most fortunate opportunity to me, in presence of the colonel and his lady, or whom else they should choose.

Then turning round, as if desirous to find out the one or the other, or both, he 'spied me, and, with a very low bow, approached me.

I was all in a flutter, you may suppose. He would have taken my hand. I refused it, all glowing with indignation: everybody's eyes upon us.

I went from him to the other end of the room and sat down, as I thought out of his hated sight: but presently I heard his odious voice, whispering, behind my chair (he leaning upon the back of it with impudent unconcern): *Charming Miss Howe!* looking over my shoulder: *One request*—I started up from my seat, but could hardly stand neither, for very indignation—Oh this sweet, but becoming, disdain, whispered on the insufferable creature!—I am sorry to give you all this emotion: but either here, or at your own house, let me entreat from you one quarter of an hour's audience—I beseech you, madam, but one quarter of an hour, in any of the adjoining apartments.

Not for a kingdom, fluttering my fan—I knew not what I did—But I could have killed him.

We are so much observed—else on my knees, my dear Miss Howe, would I beg your interest with your charming friend.

She'll have nothing to say to you.

I had not then your letters, my dear.

Killing words!—But indeed I have deserved them, and a dagger in my heart besides—I am so conscious of my demerits, that I have no hope but in *your* interposition—Could I owe that favour to Miss Howe's mediation, which I cannot hope for on any other account——

My mediation, vilest of men!—my mediation!—I abhor you!—from my soul, I abhor you, vilest of men!—Three or four times I repeated these words, stammering too. I was excessively fluttered.

You can call me nothing, madam, so bad as I will call myself—I *have* been, indeed, the vilest of men—but now I am not so—Permit me (everybody's eyes upon us) but one moment's audience—to exchange but ten words with you, dearest Miss Howe—in whose presence you please—for your dear friend's sake—but ten words with you in the next apartment.

It is an insult upon me to presume that I would exchange *one* with you, if I could help it!—Out of my way, and my sight, fellow!

And away I would have flung: but he took my hand. I was excessively disordered—everybody's eyes more and more intent upon us.

Mr Hickman, whom my mother had drawn on one side to enjoin him a patience which perhaps need not to have been enforced, came up just then with my mother, who had him by his leading-strings—by his sleeve, I should say.

Mr Hickman, said the bold wretch, be my advocate but for ten words in the next apartment with Miss Howe, in your presence, and in yours, madam, to my mother.

Hear, Nancy, what he has to say to you. To get rid of him, hear his *ten words*.

Excuse me, madam. His very breath—Unhand me, sir!

He sighed, and looked—Oh how the practised villain sighed and looked! He then let go my hand, with such a reverence in his manner as brought blame upon me from some, that I would not hear him—And this incensed me the more. Oh my dear, this man is a devil!—This man is indeed a devil!—So much patience, when he pleases! so much gentleness!—yet so resolute, so persisting, so audacious!

I was going out of the assembly in great disorder. He was at the door as soon as I.

How kind this is! said the wretch; and, ready to follow me, opened the door for me.

I turned back upon this, and, not knowing what I did, snapped my fan just in his face as he turned short upon me; and the powder flew from his wig.

Everybody seemed as much pleased as I was vexed.

He turned to Mr Hickman, nettled at the powder flying and at the smiles of the company upon him; Mr Hickman, you will be one of the happiest men in the world; because you are a *good* man, and will do nothing to provoke this passionate lady; and because she has too much good sense to be provoked without reason: but else, the Lord have mercy upon you!

This man, this Mr Hickman, my dear, is too meek for a man. Indeed he is—But my patient mother twits me that her passionate daughter ought to like him *the better* for that. But meek men abroad are not always meek men at home. I have observed that, in more instances than one: And if they *were*, I should not, I verily think, like them the better for being so.

He then turned to my mother, resolved to be even with *her* too: Where, good madam, could miss get all this spirit?

The company round smiled; for I need not tell you that my mother's high-spiritedness is pretty well known; and she, sadly vexed, said, Sir, you treat me, as you do the rest of the world—but——

I beg pardon, madam, interrupted he: I might have spared my question—And instantly (I retiring to the other end of the hall) he turned to Miss Playford: What would I give, miss, to hear you sing that song you obliged us with at Lord M.'s?

He then, as if nothing had happened, fell into a conversation with her and Miss D'Ollyffe, upon music; and whisperingly sung to Miss Playford, holding her two hands, with such airs of genteel unconcern, that it vexed me not a little to look round and see how pleased half the giddy fools of our sex were with him, notwithstanding his notorious wicked character. To this it is, that such vile fellows owe much of their vileness; whereas, if they found themselves shunned and despised, and treated as beasts of prey, as they are, they would run to their caverns, there howl by themselves; and none but such as sad accident, or unpitiable presumption threw in their way, would suffer by them.

He afterwards talked very seriously, at times, to Mr Hickman: at *times*, I say; for it was with such breaks and starts of gaiety, turning to this lady and to that, and then to Mr Hickman again, resuming a serious or a gay air at pleasure, that he took everybody's eye, the women's especially; who were full of their whispering admirations of him, qualified with *if*'s, and *but*'s, and *what pity*'s, and such sort of stuff, that showed, in their very dispraises, too much liking.

Well may our sex be the sport and ridicule of such libertines! Unthinking eye-governed creatures!—Would not a little reflection teach us that a man of merit must be a man of modesty, because a diffident one? And that such a wretch as this must have taken his degrees in wickedness, and gone through a course of vileness before he could arrive at this impenetrable effrontery? An effrontery which can proceed only from the light opinion he has of us, and the high one of himself.

But our sex are generally modest and bashful themselves, and are too apt to consider that, which in the main is their principal grace, as a defect: and *finely* do they judge, when they think of supplying that defect by choosing a man who cannot be ashamed.

His discourse to Mr Hickman turned upon you, and his acknowledged injuries of you, though he could so lightly start from the subject and return to it.

I have no patience with such a devil—*man* he cannot be called. To be sure he would behave in the same manner anywhere, or in any presence, even at the altar itself, if a lady were with him there.

It shall ever be a rule with me, that he who does not regard a woman with some degree of reverence will look upon her, and occasionally *treat* her, with contempt.

He had the confidence to offer to take me out; but I absolutely refused him, and shunned him all I could, putting on the most contemptuous airs: but nothing could mortify him.

I wished twenty times I had not been there.

The gentlemen were as ready as I to wish he had broken his neck rather than been present, I believe: for nobody was regarded but him. So little of the fop, yet so elegant and rich in his dress: his person so specious: his manner so intrepid: so much meaning and penetration in his face: so much gaiety, yet so little of the monkey: though a travelled gentleman, yet no affectation; no mere toupet-man; but all manly; and his courage and wit, the one so known, the other so dreaded, you must think the *petits-maîtres* (of which there were four or five present) were most deplorably off in his company: and one grave gentleman observed to me (pleased to see me shun him as I did) that the poet's observation was too true, that the generality of ladies were *rakes in their hearts*,[1] or they could not be so much taken with a man who had so notorious a character.

I told him the reflection both of the poet and applier was much too general, and made with more ill-nature than good manners.

When the wretch saw how industriously I avoided him (shifting from one part of the hall to another), he at last boldly stepped up to me, as my mother and Mr Hickman were talking to me; and thus, before them, accosted me:

I beg your pardon, madam; but, by your mother's leave, I must have a few moments' conversation with you, either here or at your own house; and I beg you will give me the opportunity.

Nancy, said my mother, hear what he has to say to you. In my presence you may: and better in the adjoining apartment, if it must be, than to come to you at our own house.

I retired to one corner of the hall, my mother following me, and he, taking Mr Hickman under the arm, following her—Well, sir, said I, what have you to say?— Tell me *here*.

I have been telling Mr Hickman, said he, how much I am concerned for the injuries I have done to the most excellent woman in the world: and yet, that she obtained such a glorious triumph over me the last time I had the honour to see her, as, with my penitence, ought to have qualified her former resentments: but that I will, with all my soul, enter into any measures to obtain her forgiveness of me. My cousins Montague have told you this. Lady Betty, and Lady Sarah, and my Lord M. are engaged for my honour. I know your power with the dear creature. My cousins told me you gave them hopes you would use it in my behalf. My Lord M. and his two sisters are impatiently expecting the fruits of it. You must have heard from her before now: I hope you have. And will you be so good as to tell me, if I may have any hopes?

If I must speak on this subject, let me tell you that you have broken her heart. You know not the value of the lady you have injured. You deserve her not. And she despises you as she ought.

Dear Miss Howe, mingle not passion with denunciations so severe. I must know my fate. I will go abroad once more, if I find her absolutely irreconcilable. But I hope she will give me leave to attend upon her, to know my doom from her own mouth.

It would be death immediate for her to see you. And what must *you* be, to be able to look her in the face?

I then reproached him (with vehemence enough, you may believe) on his baseness, and the evils he had made you suffer: the distress he had reduced you to: all your friends made your enemies: the vile house he had carried you to: hinted at his villainous arts; the dreadful arrest: and told him of your present deplorable illness, and resolution to die rather than have him.

He vindicated not any part of his conduct, but that of the arrest; and so solemnly protested his sorrow for his usage of you, accusing himself in the freest manner, and by *deserved* appellations, that I promised to lay before you this part of our conversation. And now you have it.

My mother, as well as Mr Hickman, believes, from what passed on this occasion, that he is touched in conscience for the wrongs he has done you: but, by his whole behaviour, I must own it seems to me that nothing can touch him for half an hour together. Yet I have no doubt that he would willingly marry you; and it piques his pride, I could see, that he should be denied: as it did mine, that such a wretch had dared to think it in his power to have such a woman whenever he pleased; and that it must be accounted a condescension, and matter of obligation (by all his own family at least), that he would vouchsafe to think of marriage.

Now, my dear, you have the reason before you why I suspend the decisive negative to the ladies of his family. My mother, Miss Lloyd, and Miss Biddulph, who were inquisitive after the subject of our retired conversation, and whose curiosity I thought it was right, in some degree, to gratify (especially as those young ladies are of our select acquaintance), are all of opinion that you should be his.

You will let Mr Hickman know your whole mind; and when he acquaints me with it, I will tell you all my own.

Meantime, may the news he will bring me of the state of your health be favourable! prays, with the utmost fervency,

Your ever-faithful and affectionate
ANNA HOWE

Letter 368: MISS CLARISSA HARLOWE TO MISS HOWE

Thursday, July 27

My dearest Miss HOWE,

AFTER I have thankfully acknowledged your favour in sending Mr Hickman to visit me before you set out upon your intended journey, I must chide you (in the sincerity of that faithful love, which could not be the love it is if it would not admit of that *cementing* freedom) for suspending the decisive negative, which, upon such full deliberation, I had entreated you to give to Mr Lovelace's relations.

I am sorry that I am obliged to *repeat* to you, my dear, who know me so well, that were I sure I should live *many years* I would not have Mr Lovelace: much less can I think of him, as it is probable I may not live *one*.

As to the *world*, and its *censures*, you know, my dear, that, however desirous I always was of a fair fame, yet I never thought it right to give more than a *second place* to the world's opinion. The challenges made to Mr Lovelace by Miss D'Oily in public company are a fresh proof that I have lost my reputation: and what advantage would it be to me, were it retrievable, and were I to live long, if I could not acquit myself to *myself*?

Having in my former said so much on the freedoms you have taken with my friends, I shall say the less now: but *your* hint that something else has newly passed between some of them and you gives me great concern, and that as well for *my own* sake, as for *theirs*; since it must necessarily incense them against me. I wish, my dear, that I had been left to my own course on an occasion so *very* interesting to myself. But since what is done cannot be helped, I must abide the consequences: yet I dread, *more than before*, what may be my sister's answer, if an answer be at all vouchsafed.

Will you give me leave, my dear, to close this subject with one remark?—It is this: that my beloved friend, in points where her own laudable *zeal* is concerned, has ever seemed more ready to fly from the *rebuke*, than the *fault*. If you will excuse this freedom, I will acknowledge thus far in favour of your way of thinking as to the conduct of some parents in these nice cases, that *indiscreet* opposition does frequently as much mischief as *giddy* love.

As to the invitation you are so kind as to give me, to remove privately into your neighbourhood, I have told Mr Hickman that I will consider of it: but believe, if you will be so good as to excuse me, that I shall not accept of it, even should I be *able* to remove. I will give you my reasons for declining it; and so I ought, when both my love, and my gratitude, would make a visit now and then from my dear Miss Howe, the most consolatory thing in the world to me.

You must know then, that this great town, wicked as it is, wants not opportunities of being better; having daily prayers at several churches in it; and I am desirous, as my strength will admit, to embrace those opportunities. The method I have proposed to myself (and was beginning to practise, when that cruel arrest deprived me both of freedom and strength), is this: when I was disposed to gentle exercise, I took a chair to St Dunstan's Church in Fleet Street, where are prayers at seven in the morning: I proposed, if the weather favoured, to walk (if not, to take chair) to Lincoln's Inn Chapel; where, at eleven in the morning, and at five in the afternoon, are the same desirable opportunities; and at other times to go no farther than Covent Garden Church, where are early morning prayers likewise.

This method pursued, I doubt not will greatly help, as it has already done, to calm my disturbed thoughts, and to bring me to that perfect resignation which I aspire after: for I must own, my dear, that sometimes still my griefs, and my reflections, are too heavy for me; and all the aid I can draw from *religious duties* is hardly sufficient to support my staggering reason. I am a very young creature, you know, my dear, to be left to my own conduct in such circumstances as I am in.

Another reason why I choose not to go down into your neighbourhood is the displeasure that might arise on my account between your mother and you.

If, indeed, you were actually married, and the worthy man (who would then have a title to all your regard) were earnestly desirous of my near neighbourhood, I know not what I might do: for although I might not perhaps intend to give up my other important reasons at the *time* I should make you a congratulatory visit, yet I might not know how to deny myself the pleasure of continuing near you, when there.

I send you enclosed the copy of my letter to my sister. I hope it will be thought to be written with a true penitent spirit; for indeed it is. I desire that you will not think I stoop too low in it; since there can be no such thing as that, in a child, to parents whom she has unhappily offended.

But if still (perhaps more disgusted than before at your freedom with them) they should pass it by with the contempt of silence (for I have not yet been favoured with an answer), I must learn to think it right in them so to do; especially as it is my first direct application: for I have often censured the boldness of those, who, applying for a favour which it is in a person's option to grant or to refuse, take the liberty of being offended if they are not gratified; as if the *petitioned-to* had not as good a right to reject, as the *petitioner* to ask.

But if my letter should be answered, and that in such terms as will make me loath to communicate it to so warm a friend—you must not, my dear, take upon you to censure my relations; but allow for them, as they know not what I have suffered; as being filled with *just* resentments against me (*just* to them, if they *think* them just); and as not being able to judge of the reality of my penitence.

And after all, what can they do for me?—They can only pity me: and what will that do but augment their own *grief*; to which, at present, their *resentment* is an alleviation? For can they by their pity restore to me my lost reputation? Can they by it purchase a sponge that will wipe out from the year the past fatal five months of my life?[a]

Your account of the gay, unconcerned behaviour of Mr Lovelace at the colonel's does not surprise me at all, after I am told that he had the intrepidity to go thither,

---

a She takes in the time that she appointed to meet Mr Lovelace.

knowing who were *invited* and *expected*—Only this, my dear, I really wonder at, that Miss Howe could imagine that I could have a thought of such a man for a husband.

Poor wretch! I pity him, to see him fluttering about; abusing talents that were given him for excellent purposes; taking courage for wit; and dancing, fearless of danger, on the edge of a precipice!

But, indeed, his threatening to see me most sensibly alarms and shocks me. I cannot but hope that I never, never more shall see him in this world.

Since you are so loath, my dear, to send the desired negative to the ladies of his family, I will only trouble you to transmit the letter I shall enclose for that purpose; directed indeed to yourself, because it was to you that those ladies applied themselves on this occasion; but to be sent by you to any one of the ladies, at your own choice.

I commend myself, my dearest Miss Howe, to your prayers; and conclude with repeated thanks for sending Mr Hickman to me; and with wishes for your health and happiness, and for the speedy celebration of your nuptials,

Your ever-affectionate and obliged
CLARISSA HARLOWE

Letter 369: MISS CLARISSA HARLOWE TO MISS HOWE

(Enclosed in the preceding)

Thursday, July 27

My dearest MISS HOWE,
SINCE you seem loath to acquiesce in my determined resolution, signified to you as soon as I was able to hold a pen, I beg the favour of you, by this or by any other way you think most proper, to acquaint the worthy ladies who have applied to you in behalf of their relation, that, although I am infinitely obliged to their generous opinion of me, yet I cannot consent to *sanctify*, as I may say, Mr Lovelace's repeated breaches of all moral sanctions, and hazard my *future* happiness by a union with a man, through whose premeditated injuries, in a long train of the basest contrivances, I have forfeited my *temporal* hopes.

He himself, when he reflects upon his own actions, must surely bear testimony to the justice, as well as fitness, of my determination. The ladies I dare say would, were they to know the whole of my unhappy story.

Be pleased to acquaint them that I deceive myself, if my resolution on this head (however ungratefully, and even inhumanly, he has treated me) be not owing more to *principle* than *passion*. Nor can I give a stronger proof of the truth of this assurance, than by declaring that I *can* and *will* forgive him on this one easy condition, *that he will never molest me more*.

In whatever way you choose to make this declaration, be pleased to let my most respectful compliments to the ladies of the noble family, and to my Lord M., accompany it. And do you, my dear, believe, that I shall be to the last moment of my life,

Your ever-obliged and affectionate
CLARISSA HARLOWE

Letter 370: MR LOVELACE TO JOHN BELFORD, ESQ.

Friday, July 28

I HAVE three letters of thine to take notice of[a]: but am divided in my mind whether to quarrel with thee on thy unmerciful reflections, or to thank thee for thy acceptable particularity and diligence. But several of my sweet dears have I, indeed, in my time made to cry and laugh in a breath; nay, one side of their pretty faces laugh, before the cry could go off of the other: why may I not therefore curse and applaud thee in the same moment? So take both in one: and what follows, as it shall rise from my pen.

How often have I ingenuously confessed my sins against this excellent creature?—Yet thou never sparest me, although as bad a man as myself. Since then I get so little by my confessions, I had a good mind to try to defend myself; and that not only from ancient and modern story, but from common practice; and yet avoid repeating anything I have suggested before in my own behalf.

I am in a humour to play the fool with my pen: briefly then, from ancient story first—Dost thou not think that I am as much entitled to forgiveness on Miss Harlowe's account, as Virgil's hero was on Queen Dido's? For what an ungrateful varlet was that vagabond to the *hospitable* princess, who had *willingly* conferred upon him the last favour?—Stealing away (whence, I suppose, the ironical phrase of *trusty Trojan*[1] to this day) like a thief; pretendedly indeed at the command of the gods; but could that be, when the errand he went upon was to rob other princes, not only of their dominions, but of their lives?—Yet this fellow is at every word the *pius* Aeneas with the immortal bard who celebrates him.

Should Miss Harlowe even break her heart (which Heaven forbid!) for the usage she has received (to say nothing of her disappointed pride, to which her death would be attributable more than to reason), what comparison will *her* fate hold to Queen Dido's? And have I half the obligation to her that Aeneas had to the Queen of Carthage? The latter placing a confidence, the former none, in her man?—Then, whom *else* have I robbed? Whom *else* have I injured? Her brother's worthless life I gave him, instead of taking any man's, as the Trojan vagabond did the lives of thousands. Why then should it not be the *pius* Lovelace, as well as the *pius* Aeneas? For, dost thou think had a conflagration happened, and had it been in my power, that I would not have saved my old Anchises (as he did his from the Ilion bonfire) even at the expense of my Creüsa,[2] had I had a wife of that name?

But for a more modern instance in my favour—Have I used Miss Harlowe as our famous maiden queen, as she was called, used one of her own blood, a sister-queen; who threw herself into her protection from her rebel subjects; and whom she detained prisoner eighteen years, and at last cut off her head? Yet (credited by worse and weaker reigns, a succession four deep[3]) do not honest Protestants pronounce *her* pious too?—And call her particularly *their* queen?

As to *common practice*—Who, let me ask, that has it in his power to gratify a predominant passion, be it what it will, denies himself the gratification?—Leaving it to cooler deliberation; and, if he be a great man, to his flatterers; to find a reason for it afterwards?

[a] Letters 364, 365, 366.

Then, as to the worst part of my treatment of this lady—How many men are there, who as well as I have sought, by intoxicating liquors, first to inebriate, then to subdue? What signifies what the *potations* were, when the same end was in view?

Let me tell thee upon the whole, that neither the Queen of Carthage, nor the Queen of Scots, would have thought they had any reason to complain of cruelty, had they been used no worse than I have used the queen of my heart: and then do I not aspire with my whole soul to repair by marriage? Would the *pius* Aeneas, thinkest thou, have done such a piece of justice by Dido had she lived?

Come, come, Belford, let people run away with notions as they will, I am *comparatively* a very innocent man. And if by these, and other like reasonings, I have quieted my own conscience, a great end is answered. What have I to do with the world?

And now I sit me peaceably down to consider thy letters.

I hope thy pleas in my favour,[a] when she gave thee (so generously gave thee) for me, my letters, were urged with an honest energy. But I suspect thee much for being too ready to give up thy client. Then thou hast such a misgiving aspect; an aspect rather inviting rejection than carrying persuasion with it; and art such an hesitating, such an humming and hawing caitiff; that I shall attribute my failure, if I do fail, rather to the inability and ill looks of my advocate, than to my cause. Again, thou art deprived of the force men of our cast give to arguments; for she won't let thee *swear!*—Art moreover a very heavy, thoughtless fellow; tolerable only at a second rebound; a horrid dunce at the *impromptu*. These, encountering with such a lady, are great disadvantages—And still a greater is thy balancing (as thou dost at present) between old rakery and new reformation: since this puts thee into the same situation with her, as they told me at Leipzig Martin Luther was in, at the first public dispute which he held in defence of his supposed *new* doctrines, with Eckius. For Martin was then but a linsey-wolsey reformer. He retained some dogma[s], which, by natural consequence, made others that he held untenable. So that Eckius in some points had the better of him. But, from that time, he made clear work, renouncing all that stood in his way: and then his doctrines ran upon all fours. He was never puzzled afterwards; and could boldly declare that he would defend them in the face of angels and men; and to his friends, who would have dissuaded him from venturing to appear before the emperor Charles the Fifth at Spires, *That, were there as many devils at Spires, as tiles upon the houses, he would go.* An answer that is admired by every Protestant Saxon to this day.

Since then thy unhappy awkwardness destroys the force of thy arguments, I think thou hadst better (for the present, however) forbear to urge her on the subject of accepting the reparation I offer; lest the continual teasing of her to forgive me should but strengthen her in her denials of forgiveness; till, for *consistency* sake, she'll be forced to adhere to a resolution so often avowed. Whereas, if left to herself, a little time and better health, which will bring on better spirits, will give her quicker resentments; those quicker resentments will lead her into vehemence; that vehemence will subside, and turn into expostulation and parley: my friends will then interpose, and guarantee for me: and all our trouble on both sides will be over—Such is the natural course of things.

a See p. 1127.

I cannot endure thee for thy hopelessness in the lady's recovery[a]; and that in contradiction to the doctor and apothecary.

Time, in the words of Congreve, thou sayest *will give increase to her afflictions*.[4] But why so? Knowest thou not that those words (so contrary to common experience) were applied to the case of a person while passion was in its full vigour?—At such a time, everyone in a heavy grief thinks the same: but as enthusiasts do by Scripture, so dost thou by the poets thou hast read: anything that carries the most distant allusion from *either* to the case in hand, is put down by both for gospel, however incongruous to the general scope of either, and to *that case*. So once, in a pulpit, I heard one of the former very vehemently declare himself to be a *dead dog*[5]; when every man, woman, and child were convinced to the contrary by his howling.

I can tell thee that if nothing else will do I am determined, in spite of thy buskin-airs and of thy engagements for me to the contrary, to see her myself.

Face to face have I known many a quarrel made up, which distance would have kept alive and widened. Thou wilt be a madder Jack than him in the *Tale of a Tub*, if thou givest an active opposition to this interview.

In short, I cannot bear the thought that a lady whom once I had bound to me in the silken cords of love, should slip through my fingers, and be able, while *my* heart flames out with a violent passion for her, to despise me, and to set both love and me at defiance. Thou canst not imagine how much I envy *thee*, and her *doctor*, and her *apothecary*, and everyone whom I hear of being admitted to her presence and conversation; and wish to be the *one* or the *other* in turn.

Wherefore, if nothing else will do, I *will* see her. I'll tell thee of an admirable expedient just come cross me, to save *thy* promise and *my own*.

Mrs Lovick, you say, is a good woman: if the lady be worse, she shall advise her to send for a parson to pray by her: unknown to her, unknown to the lady, unknown to *thee* (for so it may pass), I will contrive to be the man, petticoated out, and vested in a gown and cassock. I once, for a certain purpose, did assume the canonicals; and I was thought to make a fine sleek appearance, my broad rose-bound beaver[6] became me *mightily*, and I was much admired upon the whole by all who saw me.

Methinks it must be charmingly apropos to see me kneeling down by her bedside (I am sure I shall pray heartily), beginning out of the Common Prayer Book the Sick Office for the restoration of the languishing lady, and concluding with an exhortation to charity and forgiveness for myself.

I will consider of this matter. But, in whatever shape I shall choose to appear, of this thou mayest assure thyself, I will apprise thee beforehand of my determined-upon visit, that thou mayest contrive to be out of the way, and to know nothing of the matter. This will save *thy* word; and, as to *mine*, can she think worse of me than she does at present?

An indispensable of true love and profound respect, in thy wise opinion,[b] is absurdity or awkwardness—'Tis surprising that *thou* shouldst be one of those partial mortals, who take their measures of right and wrong from what they find *themselves to be*, and cannot *help being!*—So awkwardness is a perfection in the awkward!—At this rate, no man ever can be in the wrong. But I insist upon it that

a See p. 1127.
b See p. 1124.

an awkward fellow will do everything awkwardly: and if he be like thee, will rack his unmeaning brain for excuses as awkward as his first fault. Respectful love is an inspirer of actions worthy of itself; and he who cannot show it where he most means it manifests that he is an unpolite rough creature, a perfect Belford, and has it not in him.

But here thou'lt throw out that notable witticism, that my outside is the best of *me*, thine the worst of *thee*; and that, if I set about mending my mind, thou wilt mend thy appearance.

But, prithee, Jack, don't stay for *that*; but set about thy amendment in dress when thou leavest off thy mourning; for why shouldst thou prepossess in thy disfavour all those who never saw thee before?—It is hard to remove early-taken prejudices, whether of liking or distaste: people will *hunt*, as I may say, for reasons to confirm first impressions, in compliment to their own sagacity: nor is it every mind that has the ingenuity to confess itself mistaken when it finds itself to be wrong. Thou thyself art an adept in the pretended science of reading of men; and, whenever thou art out, wilt study to find some reasons why it was more probable that thou shouldst have been right; and wilt watch every motion and action, and every word and sentiment, in the person thou hast once censured, for proofs, in order to help thee to revive and maintain thy first opinion. And, indeed, as thou seldom errest on the *favourable side*, human nature is so vile a thing that thou art likely to be right five times in six on the *other:* and perhaps it is but guessing of others, by what thou findest in thy own heart, to have reason to compliment thyself on thy penetration.

Here is preachment for thy preachment: and I hope, if thou likest thy own, thou wilt thank me for mine; the rather as thou mayest be the better for it, if thou wilt: since it is calculated for thy own meridian.

Well, but the lady refers my destiny to the letter she has written, actually written, to Miss Howe; to whom it seems she has given her reasons why she will not have me. I long to know the contents of this letter: but am in great hopes that she has so expressed her denials, as shall give room to think she only wants to be persuaded to the contrary, in order to reconcile herself to herself.

I could make some pretty observations upon one or two places of the lady's meditation: but, wicked as I am thought to be, I never was so abandoned as to turn into ridicule, or even to treat with levity, things sacred. I think it the highest degree of ill manners to jest upon those subjects, which the world in general look upon with veneration and call divine. I would not even treat the mythology of the heathen, to a heathen, with the ridicule that perhaps would fairly lie from some of the absurdities that strike every common observer. Nor, when at Rome and in other popish countries, did I ever behave shockingly at those ceremonies which I thought very extraordinary: for I saw some people affected and seemingly edified by them; and I contented myself to think, though they were beyond my comprehension, that, if they answered any good end to the *many*, there was religion enough in them, or civil policy at least, to exempt them from the ridicule of even a *bad* man who had common sense, and good manners.

For the like reason, I have never given noisy or tumultuous instances of dislike to a new play, if I thought it ever so indifferent: for, I concluded first, that every-one was entitled to see quietly what he paid for: and, next, as the theatre (the epitome of the world) consisted of pit, boxes, and gallery, it was hard, I thought, if there could be such a performance exhibited as would not please somebody in that mixed multitude: and, if it did, those somebodies had as much right to enjoy their own judgements undisturbedly, as I had to enjoy mine.

This was *my* way of showing my disapprobation; I never went again. And as a man is at his option whether he will go to a play, or not, he has not the same excuse for expressing his dislike clamorously, as if he were *compelled* to see it.

I have ever, thou knowest, declared against those shallow libertines who could not make out their pretensions to wit, but on two subjects, to which every man of *true* wit will scorn to be beholden: PROFANENESS and OBSCENITY, I mean; which must shock the ears of every man or woman of sense, without answering any end but of showing a very low and abandoned nature. And, till I came acquainted with the brutal Mowbray (no great praise to myself from such a tutor), I was far from making so free, as I now do, with oaths and curses; for then I was forced to outswear him sometimes, to keep him in his allegiance to me his general: nay, I often check myself to myself for this empty, unprofitable liberty of speech; in which we are outdone by the sons of the common sewer.

All my vice is women, and the love of plots and intrigues; and I cannot but wonder how I fell into those shocking freedoms of speech; since, generally speaking, they are far from helping forward my main end: only now and then, indeed, a little novice rises to one's notice, who seems to think dress, and oaths and curses, the diagnostics of the rakish spirit she is inclined to favour: and, indeed, they are the only qualifications that some, who are called rakes, and pretty fellows, have to boast of. But what must the women be, who can be attracted by such *empty-souled* profligates?—since wickeness *with* wit is hardly excusable; but, *without* it, is equally shocking and contemptible.

There again is preachment for thy preachment; and thou wilt be apt to think that I am reforming too: but no such matter. If this were *new light* darting in upon me, as thy morality seems to be to thee, something of this kind might be apprehended: but this was *always* my way of thinking; and I defy thee, or any of thy brethren, to name a time when I have either ridiculed religion, or talked obscenely. On the contrary, thou knowest how often I have checked that bear in love-matters, Mowbray, and the finical Tourville, and thyself too, for what ye have called the double entendre. In *love*, as in points that required a *manly resentment*, it has always been my maxim, to *act* rather than *talk*; and I do assure thee, as to the first, the ladies themselves will excuse the one sooner than the other.

As to the admiration thou expressest for the books of Scripture, thou art certainly right in it. But 'tis strange to me that thou wert ignorant of their beauty and noble simplicity, till now. Their antiquity always made me reverence them: and how was it possible that thou couldst not for that reason, if for no other, give them a perusal?

I'll tell thee a short story which I had from my tutor, admonishing me against exposing myself by *ignorant wonder* when I should quit college, go to town, or travel.

'The first time Dryden's *Alexander's Feast*' fell into his hands, he told me, he was prodigiously charmed with it: and, having never heard anybody speak of it before, thought, as thou dost of the Bible, that he had made a new discovery.

'He hastened to an appointment which he had with several wits (for he was then in town), one of whom was a noted critic, who according to him had more merit than good fortune; for all the little nibblers in wit, whose writings would not stand the test of criticism, made it, he said, a common cause to run him down, as men would a mad dog.

'The young gentleman (for young he then was) set forth magnificently in the praises of that inimitable performance; and gave himself airs of second-hand merit, for finding out its beauties.

'The old bard heard him out with a smile, which the collegian took for approbation, till he spoke; and then it was in these mortifying words: " 'Sdeath, sir, where have you lived till now, or with what sort of company have you conversed, young as you are, that you have never before heard of the finest piece in the English language!" '

This story had such an effect upon *me*, who had ever a proud heart, and wanted to be thought a clever fellow, that in order to avoid the like disgrace I laid down two rules to myself. The first, whenever I went into company where there were strangers, to hear every one of them speak, before I gave myself liberty to prate: the other, if I found any of them above my match, to give up all title to new discoveries, contenting myself to praise what they praised, as beauties familiar to me, though I had never heard of them before. And so, by degrees, I got the reputation of a wit myself: and when I threw off all restraint, and books, and learned conversation, and fell in with some of our brethren who are now wandering in Erebus, and with such others as Belton, Mowbray, Tourville, and thyself, I set up on my own stock; and, like what we have been told of Sir Richard, in his latter days, valued myself on being the emperor of the company; for, having fathomed the depth of them all, and afraid of no rival but thee, whom also I had got a little under (by my gaiety and promptitude at least), I proudly, like Addison's Cato, delighted to give laws to my little senate.[8]

Proceed with thee by and by.

Letter 371: MR LOVELACE TO JOHN BELFORD, ESQ.

BUT now I have cleared myself of any intentional levity on occasion of my beloved's meditation; which, as thou observest, is finely suited to her case (that is to say, as she and you have drawn her case); I cannot help expressing my pleasure, that by one or two verses of it (the *arrow*, Jack, and *what she feared being come upon her!*) I am encouraged to hope, what it will be very surprising to me if it do not happen: that is, in plain English, that the dear creature is in the way to be a mamma.

This cursed arrest, because of the ill effects the terror might have had upon her in that hoped-for circumstance, has concerned me more than on any other account. It would be the pride of my life to prove, in this charming frost-piece, the triumph of nature over principle, and to have a young Lovelace by such an angel: and then, for its sake, I am confident she will live, and will legitimate it. And what a meritorious little cherub would it be, that should lay an obligation upon both parents before it was born, which neither of them would be able to repay!—Could I be sure it is so, I should be out of all pain for her recovery: *pain*, I say; since, were she to *die*—(*die!* abominable word! how I hate it!) I verily think I should be the most miserable man in the world.

As for the earnestness she expresses for death, she has found the words ready to her hand in honest Job; else she would not have delivered herself with such strength and vehemence.

Her innate piety (as I have more than once observed) will not permit her to shorten her own life, either by violence or neglect. She has a mind too noble for that; and would have done it before now, had she designed any such thing: for, to do it like the Roman matron, when the mischief is over, and it can serve no end; and when the man, however a Tarquin, as some may think him in this action, is not a Tarquin in power, so that no national point can be made of it; is what she has too much good sense to think of.

Then, as I observed in a like case a little while ago, the distress, when this was written, was strong upon her; and she saw no end of it: but all was darkness and apprehension before her. Moreover, has she it not in her power to *disappoint*, as much as she has been *disappointed?* Revenge, Jack, has induced many a woman to cherish a life, which grief and despair would otherwise have put an end to.

And, after all, death is no such eligible thing as Job in his *calamities* makes it. And a death desired merely from worldly disappointment shows not a right mind, let me tell this lady, whatever she may think of it.*ᵃ* You and I, Jack, although not afraid in the height of passion or resentment to rush into those dangers which might be followed by a sudden and violent death, whenever a point of honour calls upon us, would shudder at his cool and deliberate approach in a lingering sickness which had debilitated the spirits.

So we read of a French general, in the reign of Harry the IVth (I forget his name, if it were not Mareschal Biron) who, having faced with intrepidity the ghastly varlet on an hundred occasions in the field, was the most dejected of wretches when, having forfeited his life for treason, he was led with all the cruel parade of preparation, and surrounding guards, to the scaffold.

The poet says well:

> 'Tis not the Stoic lesson, got by rote,
> The pomp of words, and pedant dissertation,
> That can support us in the hour of terror.
> Books have taught cowards to talk nobly of it:
> But when the *trial* comes, they start, and stand aghast.[1]

Very true: for then it is the old man in the fable with his bundle of sticks.[2]

The lady is well read in Shakespeare, our English pride and glory; and must sometimes reason with herself in his words, so greatly expressed that the subject, affecting as it is, cannot produce anything more so.

> Ay, but to die, and go we know not where;
> To lie in cold obstruction, and to rot;
> *This* sensible, warm motion to become

---

a Mr Lovelace could not know that the lady was *so* thoroughly sensible of the solidity of this doctrine, as she really was: for in Letter 362 to Mrs Norton (p. 1121) she says: 'Nor let it be imagined that my present turn of mind proceeds from gloominess or melancholy; for, although it was brought on by disappointment (the world showing me early, even at my first *rushing* into it, its true and ugly face); yet, I hope that it has obtained a better root, and will every day more and more, by its fruits demonstrate to me, and to all my friends, that it has.'

> A kneaded clod; and the delighted spirit
> To bathe in fiery floods, or to reside
> In thrilling regions of thick-ribbed ice:
> To be imprisoned in the viewless winds,
> Or blown, with restless violence, about
> The pendent worlds; or to be worse than worst
> Of those that lawless and uncertain thought
> Imagines howling: 'tis too horrible!
> The weariest and most loaded worldly life,
> That pain, age, penury, and *imprisonment*,
> Can lay on nature, is a paradise
> To what we fear of death.[3]

I find, by one of thy three letters, that my beloved had some account from Hickman of my interview with Miss Howe, at Colonel Ambrose's. I had a very agreeable time of it there; although severely rallied by several of the assembly. It concerns me, however, not a little, to find our affair so generally known among the *flippanti* of both sexes. It is all her own fault. There never, surely, was such an odd little soul as this—Not to keep her own secret, when the revealing of it could answer no possible good end; and when she wants not (one would think) to raise to herself either pity or friends, or to me enemies, by the proclamation!—Why, Jack, must not all her own sex laugh in their sleeves at her weakness! What would become of the peace of the world, if all women should take it into their heads to follow her example? What a fine time of it would the heads of families have? Their wives always filling their ears with their confessions; their daughters with theirs: sisters would be every day setting their brothers about cutting of throats, if they had at heart *the honour of their families*, as it is called; and the whole world would either be a scene of confusion, or cuckoldom must be as much the fashion as it is in Lithuania.[a]

I am glad, however, that Miss Howe, as much as she hates me, kept her word with my cousins on their visit to her, and with me at the colonel's, to endeavour to persuade her friend to make up all matters by matrimony; which, no doubt, is the best, nay, the *only* method she can take for her own honour, and that of her family.

I had once thoughts of revenging myself on that little vixen, and particularly as thou mayst[b] remember, had planned something to this purpose on the journey she is going to take, which had been talked of some time. But, I think—let me see— yes, I *think*, I will let this Hickman have her safe and entire, as thou believest the fellow to be a tolerable sort of a mortal, and that I had made the worst of him: and I am glad, for his own sake, he has not launched out too virulently against me to thee.

And thus, if I pay thee not in quality, I do in quantity (and yet leave a multitude of things unobserved upon): for I begin not to know what to do with myself here— Tired with Lord M., who in his recovery has played upon me the fable of the nurse, the crying child, and the wolf—tired with my cousins Montague, though

---

a   In Lithuania, the women are said to have *so allowedly* their gallants, called *adjutores*, that the husbands hardly ever enter upon any party of pleasure without them.

b   This plot of his is mentioned on p. 671.

charming girls, were they not so near of kin—tired with Mowbray and Tourville, and their everlasting identity—tired with the country—tired of myself: longing for what I have not; I must go to town; and there have an interview with the charmer of my soul: for desperate diseases must have desperate remedies; and I only wait to know my doom from Miss Howe; and then, if it be rejection, I will try my fate, and receive my sentence at her feet—But I will apprise thee of it beforehand, as I told thee, that thou mayest keep thy parole with the lady in the best manner thou canst.

Letter 372: MISS HOWE TO MISS CLARISSA HARLOWE

(In answer to hers of July 27, Letter 368)

Friday night, July 28

I WILL now, my dearest friend, write to you all my mind without reserve, on your resolution not to have this vilest of men. You gave me, in yours of Sunday the 23rd, reasons so worthy of the pure mind of my Clarissa Harlowe in support of this your resolution, that nothing but self-love, lest I should lose my ever-amiable friend, could have prevailed upon me to wish you to alter it.

Indeed, I thought it was impossible there could be (however desirable) so noble an instance given by any of our sex, of a passion conquered, when there were so many inducements to give way to it. And, therefore, I was willing to urge you once more to overcome your just indignation, and to be prevailed upon by the solicitations of *his* friends, before you carried your resentments to so great a height that it would be more difficult for you, and less to your honour, to comply, than if you had complied at first.

But now, my dear, that I see you fixed in your noble resolution; and that it is impossible for your pure mind to join itself with that of so perjured a miscreant; I congratulate you most heartily upon it; and beg your pardon for but seeming to doubt that *theory* and *practice* were not the same thing with my beloved Clarissa Harlowe.

I have only one thing that saddens my heart on this occasion; and that is the bad state of health Mr Hickman (unwillingly) owns you are in: for, although you so well observe the doctrine you always laid down to me, that a censured person should first seek to be justified to herself, and give but a second place to the world's opinion of her; and, in all cases where the two could not be reconciled, to prefer the first to the last; and though you *are* so well justified to your Anna Howe, and to your own heart; yet, my dear, let me beseech you to endeavour to recover your health and spirits by all possible means: and this, as what, if it *can* be effected, will crown the work, and show the world that you were *indeed* got above the base wretch; and, though put out of your course for a little while, could resume it again and go on blessing all within your knowledge, as well by your example as by your precepts.

For Heaven's sake, then, for the world's sake, for the honour of our sex, and for *my* sake, once more I beseech you, try to overcome this shock: and, if you *can* overcome it, I shall then be as happy as I wish to be; for I cannot, indeed I cannot, think of parting with you, for many, many years to come.

The reasons you give for discouraging my wishes to have you near us, are so convincing, that I ought at present to acquiesce in them: but, my dear, when your mind is fully settled, as (now you are so absolutely determined in it, with regard to this wretch) I hope it will soon be, I shall expect you with us, or near us: and then you shall chalk out every path that I will set my foot in; nor will I turn aside either to the right hand or to the left.

You wish I had not mediated for you to your friends. I wish so too; because it was ineffectual; because it may give new ground for the malice of some of them to work upon; and because you are angry with me for doing so. But how, as I said in my former, could I sit down quietly, knowing how uneasy their implacableness must make you? But I will tear myself from the subject—for I see I shall be warm again—and displease you—And there is not one thing in the world that I would do, however agreeable to myself, if I thought it would disoblige you; nor any one that I would omit to do, if I knew it would give you pleasure. And, indeed, my dear, half-severe friend, I will try if I cannot avoid the *fault*, as willingly as I would the *rebuke*.

For this reason, I forbear saying anything on so nice a subject as your letter to your sister. It *must* be right, because you think it so—and, if it be taken as it ought, that will show you that it *is*. But if it beget insults and revilings as it is but too likely—I find you don't intend to let me know it.

You were always so ready to accuse yourself for other people's faults, and to suspect your own conduct, rather than the judgement of your relations, that I have often told you I cannot imitate you in this. It is not a necessary point of belief with me that all people in *years* are *therefore* wise; or that all *young people* are *therefore* rash and headstrong: it may be *generally* the case, as far as I know: and possibly it may be so in the case of *my* mother and *her* girl: but I will venture to say that it has not yet appeared to be so between the principals of Harlowe Place, and their second daughter.

You are for excusing them beforehand for their expected cruelty, as not knowing what you have suffered, nor how ill you are. They have *heard* of the former, and are not sorry for it: of the latter, they have been *told*, and *I* have most reason to know how they have taken it—But I shall be far from avoiding the *fault*, and as surely shall incur the *rebuke*, if I say any more upon this subject. I will therefore only add at present, that your reasonings in their behalf show *you* to be all excellence; their returns to you, that *they* are all—Do, my dear, let me end with a little bit of spiteful justice—but you won't, I know—so I have done, quite done, however reluctantly: yet, if you think of the word I would have said, don't doubt the justice of it, and fill up the blank with it.

You put me in hope that, were I actually married and Mr Hickman to *desire* it, you would think of obliging me with a visit on the occasion; and that, perhaps, when with me, it would be difficult for you to remove far from me.

Lord, my dear, what a stress do you seem to lay upon Mr Hickman's *desiring* it! To be sure he does, and would of all things desire to have you *near* us, and *with* us. if we might be so favoured. Policy, as well as veneration for *you*, would undoubtedly make the man, if not a fool, *desire* this. But let me tell you that if Mr Hickman, after marriage, should pretend to dispute with me my friendships, as I hope I am not quite a fool, I should let him know how far his own quiet was concerned in such an impertinence; especially if they were such friendships as were contracted before I knew him.

I know I always differed from you on this subject; for you think more highly of a *husband*'s prerogative, than most people do of the *royal* one—These notions, my dear, from a person of your sense and judgement are no-way advantageous to us; inasmuch as they justify that insolent sex in their assumptions; when hardly one out of ten of them, their opportunities considered, deserve any prerogative at all. Look through all the families we know; and we shall not find one third of them have half the sense of their wives—And yet these are to be vested with prerogatives!—And a woman of twice their sense has nothing to do but hear, tremble, and obey—and for *conscience*-sake too, I warrant!

But Mr Hickman and I may perhaps have a little discourse upon these sort of subjects before I suffer him to talk of the day: and then I shall let him know what he has to trust to; as he will me, if he be a sincere man, what he pretends to expect from me. But let me tell you, my dear, that it is more in *your* power than perhaps you think it, to hasten the day so much pressed-for by my mother, as well as wished-for by you—for the very day that you can assure me that you are in a tolerable state of health, and have discharged your doctor and apothecary at their own motions on that account—some day in a month from that desirable news shall be it—So, my dear, make haste and be well; and then this matter will be brought to effect in a manner more agreeable to your Anna Howe than it otherwise ever can.

I send this day by a particular hand to the Misses Montague, your letter of just reprobation of the greatest profligate in the kingdom; and hope I shall not have done amiss that I transcribe some of the paragraphs of your letter of the 23rd, and send them with it, as you at first intended should be done.

You are, it seems (and that too much for your health), employed in writing. I hope it is in penning down the particulars of your tragical story. And my mother has put me in mind to press you to it, with a view that one day, if it might be published under feigned names, it would be of as much use as honour to the sex. My mother says she cannot help admiring you for the propriety of your resentment in your refusal of the wretch; and she would be extremely glad to have her advice of penning your sad story complied with. And then, she says, your noble conduct throughout your trials and calamities will afford not only a shining example to your sex; but, at the same time (those calamities befalling SUCH a person), a fearful warning to the inconsiderate young creatures of it.

On Monday we shall set out on our journey; and I hope to be back in a fortnight, and on my return will have one pull more with my mother for a London journey: and, if the *pretence must* be the buying of clothes, the *principal motive* will be that of seeing once more my dear friend, *while* I can say I have not finally given consent to the change of a visitor into a relation; and so can call myself MY OWN, as well as

                                                    Your
                                            ANNA HOWE

Letter 373: MISS HOWE TO THE TWO MISSES MONTAGUE

Sat. July 29

Dear ladies,

I HAVE not been wanting to use all my interest with my beloved friend to induce her to forgive and be reconciled to your kinsman (though he has so ill deserved it); and have even *repeated* my earnest advice to her on this head. This repetition, and the waiting for her answer, having taken up time, have been the cause that I could not sooner do myself the honour of writing to you on this subject.

You will see, by the enclosed, her immovable resolution, grounded on noble and high-souled motives, which I cannot but *regret* and *applaud* at the same time: *applaud*, for the justice of her determination, which will confirm all your worthy house in the opinion you had conceived of her unequalled merit; and *regret*, because I have but too much reason to apprehend, as well by that as by the report of a gentleman just come from her, that she is in such a declining way as to her health, that her thoughts are very differently employed than on a continuance here.

The enclosed letter she thought fit to send to me unsealed, that, after I had perused it, I might forward it to you; and this is the reason it is superscribed by myself, and sealed with my seal. It is very full and peremptory; but as she had been pleased in a letter to me, dated the 23rd instant (as soon as she could hold a pen), to give me ampler reasons why she could not comply with your pressing requests, as well as mine, I will transcribe some of the passages in that letter, which will give one of the wickedest men in the world (if he sees them) reason to think himself one of the unhappiest, in the loss of so incomparable a wife as he might have gloried in, had he not been so *superlatively* wicked. These are the passages:

(See, for these passages, Miss Harlowe's Letter 359, dated July 23, marked with turned commas, thus: ')

And now, ladies, you have before you my beloved friend's reasons for her refusal of a man unworthy of the relation he bears to so many excellent persons: and I will add (for I cannot help it) that, the merit and rank of the person considered, and the vile manner of his proceedings, there never was a greater villainy committed: and since she thinks her first and *only* fault cannot be expiated but by death, I pray to God *daily*, and will *hourly* from the moment I shall hear of that sad catastrophe, that He will be pleased to make him the subject of his vengeance, in some such way as that all who know of his perfidious crime may see the hand of Heaven in the punishment of it.

You will forgive me, ladies; I love not my own soul better than I do Miss Clarissa Harlowe: and the distresses she has gone through; and the persecutions she suffers from all her friends; the curse she lies under for his sake, from her implacable father; her reduced health and circumstances, from high health and affluence; and that execrable arrest and confinement, which have deepened all her other calamities (and which must be laid at his door, as the action of his vile agents, that, whether from his immediate orders or not, naturally flowed from his preceding baseness); the sex dishonoured in the eye of the world, in the person of one of the greatest ornaments of it; his unmanly methods, whatever they were (for I know not all as yet), of compassing her ruin; all join to justify my warmth and my execrations against a man, whom I think excluded by his crimes from the benefit even of Christian forgiveness—and were you to see all she writes, and the admirable talents she is mistress of, you yourselves would join to admire her and execrate him as I do.

Believe me to be, with a high sense of your merits,

Dear ladies,
Your most obedient humble servant,
ANNA HOWE

Letter 374: MRS NORTON TO MISS CLARISSA HARLOWE

Friday, July 28

My dearest young lady,

I HAVE the consolation to tell you that my son is once again in an hopeful way, as to his health. He desires his duty to you. He is very low and weak. And so am I. But this is the first time that I have been able for several days past to sit up to write, or I would not have been so long silent.

Your letter to your sister is received and answered. You have the answer by this time, I suppose. I wish it may be to your satisfaction: but am afraid it will not: for, by Betty Barnes, I find they were in a great ferment on receiving yours, and much divided whether it should be answered or not. They will not yet believe that you are so ill as to my infinite concern I find you are. What passed between Miss Harlowe and Miss Howe, as I feared, has been an aggravation.

I showed Betty two or three passages in your letter to me; and she seemed moved, and said she would report them favourably, and would procure me a visit from Miss Harlowe, if I would promise to show the same to *her*. But I have heard no more of that.

Methinks I am sorry you refuse the wicked man: but doubt not, nevertheless, that your motives for doing so are righter than my wishes that you would not. But as you would be resolved as I may say on life, if you gave way to such a thought; and as I have so much interest in it; I cannot forbear showing this regard to myself, as to ask you, Cannot you, my dear young lady, get over your just resentments?— But I dare say no more on this subject.

What a dreadful thing indeed was it for my dearest tender young lady to be arrested in the streets of London!—How does my heart go over again for you, what yours must have suffered at that time!—Yet this, to such a mind as yours, must be light compared to what you had suffered before.

Oh my dearest Miss Clary, how shall we know what to pray for, when we pray for anything but that *God's will may be done*, and that we may be *resigned to it!*— When at nine years old, and afterwards at eleven, you had a dangerous fever, how incessantly did we all grieve, and pray, and put up our vows to the throne of grace, for your recovery! For all our lives were bound up in your life—Yet *now*, my dear, as it has proved (especially if we are *soon* to lose you) what a much more desirable event, both for you and for us, had we *then* lost you!

A sad thing to say! But as it is in pure love to you that I say it, and in full conviction that we are not always fit to be our own choosers, I hope it may be excusable; and the rather, as the same reflection will naturally lead both you and me to acquiesce under the present dispensation; since we are assured that nothing happens by chance; and that the greatest good may, for aught we know, be produced from the heaviest evils.

I am glad you are with such honest people; and that you have all your effects restored—How dreadfully have you been used, that one should be glad of such a poor piece of justice as that?

Your talent at moving the passions is always hinted at; and this Betty of your sister's never comes near me, that she is not full of it. But, as you say, whom has it moved that you *wished* to move? Yet, were it not for this unhappy notion, I am sure your mamma would relent. Forgive me, my dear Miss Clary; for I must try one way to be convinced if my opinion be not just. But I will not tell you what that is, unless it succeeds. I will try, in pure duty and love to *them*, as well as to *you*.

May Heaven be your support in all your trials, is the constant prayer, my dearest young lady of

> Your ever-affectionate friend and servant,
> JUDITH NORTON

Letter 375: MRS NORTON TO MRS HARLOWE

Friday, July 28

Honoured madam,

BEING forbidden, without leave, to send you anything I might happen to receive from my beloved Miss Clary, and so ill that I cannot attend to *ask* your leave, I give you this trouble to let you know that I have received a letter from her; which, I think, I should hereafter be held inexcusable, as things may happen, if I did not desire permission to communicate it to you, and that as soon as possible.

Applications have been made to the dear young lady from Lord M., from the two ladies his sisters, and from both his nieces, and from the wicked man himself, to forgive and marry him. This, in noble indignation for the usage she has received from him, she has absolutely refused. And perhaps, madam, if you and the honoured family should be of opinion that to comply with their wishes is *now* the properest measure that *can* be taken, the circumstances of things may require your authority or advice, either to induce her to change her mind or to confirm her in it.

I have reason to believe that one motive for her refusal, is her full conviction that she shall not long be a trouble to anybody; and so she would not give a husband a right to interfere with her family, in relation to the estate her grandfather bequeathed to her. But of this, however, I have not the least intimation from her. Nor would she, I dare say, mention it *as* a reason, having still stronger to refuse him, from his vile treatment of her.

The letter I have received will show how truly penitent the dear creature is; and if I have your permission, I will send it sealed up with a copy of mine to which it is an answer. But as I resolve upon this step without her knowledge (and indeed I do), I will not acquaint her with it unless it be attended with desirable effects: because, otherwise, besides making me incur her displeasure, it might quite break her already half-broken heart.

I am, honoured madam,

Your dutiful and ever-obliged servant,
JUDITH NORTON

Letter 376: MRS HARLOWE TO MRS JUDITH NORTON

Sunday, July 30

WE all know your virtuous prudence, worthy woman; we all do. But your partiality to this your rash favourite is likewise known. And we are no less acquainted with the unhappy body's power of painting her distresses so as to pierce a stone.

Everyone is of opinion that the dear naughty creature is working about to be forgiven and received; and for this reason it is that Betty has been forbidden (not by me, you may be sure!) to mention any more of her letters; for she did speak to my Bella of some moving passages you read to her.

This will convince you that nothing will be heard in her favour: to what purpose then, should I mention anything about her?—But you may be sure that I *will*, if I can have but one second. However, that is not at all likely, until we see what the *consequences* of her crime will be: and who can tell that?—She may—How can I speak it, and my once darling daughter unmarried!—She may be with child!—This would perpetuate her stain. Her brother may come to some harm; which God forbid!—One child's ruin, I hope, will not be followed by another's murder!

As to her grief, and her present misery, whatever it be, she must bear with it; and it must be short of what I hourly bear for her! Indeed I am afraid nothing but her being at the last extremity of all will make her father, and her uncles, and her other friends, forgive her.

The easy pardon perverse children meet with, when they have done the rashest and most rebellious thing they can do, is the reason (*as is pleaded to us every day*) that so *many* follow their example. They depend upon the indulgent weakness of their parents' tempers, and in *that* dependence harden their own hearts: and a little humiliation, when they have brought themselves into the foretold misery, is to be a sufficient atonement for the greatest perverseness.

But for such a child as this (*I mention what others hourly say, but what I must sorrowfully subscribe to*) to lay plots and stratagems to deceive her parents, as well as herself; and to run away with a libertine; can there be any atonement for her crime? And is she not answerable to God, to us, to you, and to all the world who knew her, for the abuse of such talents as *she* has abused?

You say her heart is half-broken: is it to be wondered at? Was not her sin committed equally against warning, and the light of her own knowledge?

That *he* would now marry her, or that *she* would refuse him if she believed him in earnest, as she has circumstanced herself is not at all probable; and were *I* inclined to believe it, *nobody else* here would. He values not his relations; and would deceive them as soon as any others: his aversion to marriage he has always openly declared; and still occasionally declares it. But if he be now in earnest, which everyone who knows him must doubt; which do you think (hating us too, as he professes to hate and despise us all) would be soonest to be chosen here, to hear of her death, or of her marriage with such a vile man?

To all of us, yet, I cannot say! For Oh! my good Mrs Norton, you know what a mother's tenderness for the child of her heart would make her choose, notwithstanding all that child's faults, rather than lose her for ever!

But I must sail with the tide; my own judgement also joining with it, or I should make the unhappiness of the more worthy still greater (my dear Mr Harlowe's particularly); which is already more than enough to make them unhappy for the remainder of their days. This I know; if I were to oppose the rest, our son would fly out to find this libertine; and who could tell what would be the issue of that, with such a man of violence and blood as that Lovelace is known to be?

All I can expect to prevail for her is that in a week or so, Mr Brand may be sent up to inquire privately about her present state and way of life, and to see she is not altogether destitute: for nothing she writes herself will be regarded.

Her father indeed has at her earnest request withdrawn the curse which, in a passion, he laid upon her at her first wicked flight from us. But Miss Howe (it is a sad thing, Mrs Norton, to suffer so many ways at once!) had made matters so difficult by her undue liberties with us all, as well by speech in all companies as by letters written to my Bella, that we could hardly prevail upon him to hear her letter read.

These liberties of Miss Howe with us; the general cry against us abroad, wherever we are spoken of; and the *visible* and not seldom *audible* disrespectfulness which high and low treat us with to our faces, as we go to and from church, and even *at* church (for nowhere else have we the heart to go), as if none of us had been regarded but upon her account; and as if she were innocent, we all in fault; are constant aggravations, you must needs think, to the whole family.

She has made my lot heavy, I am sure, that was far from being light before!—I am enjoined (to tell you truth) not to receive anything of hers, from any hand, without leave. Should I therefore gratify my yearnings after her so far as to receive privately the letter you mention, what would the case be but to torment myself, without being able to do her good?—And were it to be known—Mr Harlowe is *so* passionate—And should it throw his gout into his stomach, as her rash flight did—Indeed, indeed, I am very unhappy!—For Oh, my good woman, she is my child still!—But unless it were more in my power—Yet do I long to see the letter—you say it tells of her present way and circumstances—The poor child, who ought to be in possession of thousands!—and *will!*—for her father will be a faithful steward for her—But it must be in his own way, and at his own time.

And is she *really* ill?—so *very* ill?—But she *ought* to sorrow.—She has given a double measure of it.

But does she *really* believe she shall not *long* trouble us?—But Oh, my Norton!—she must, she *will* long trouble us—for can she think her death, if we should be deprived of her, will put an end to our afflictions?—Can it be thought that the fall of such a child will not be regretted by us to the last hour of our lives?

But in the letter you have, does she without *reserve* express her contrition? Has she in it no reflecting hints? Does she not aim at extenuations?—If I *were* to see it, will it not shock me so much that my *apparent* grief may expose me to harshnesses?—Can it be contrived——

But to what purpose?—Don't send it—I charge you don't—I dare not see it——

Yet——

But, alas!——

Oh forgive the distracted-thoughted mother! You *can*—you know how to allow for all this—so I will let it go—I will not write over again this part of my letter.

But I choose not to know more of her than is communicated to us all—no more than I dare *own* I have seen—and what some of them may rather communicate *to* me than receive *from* me: and this for the sake of my outward quiet: although my inward peace suffers more and more by the compelled reserve.

I was forced to break off. But I will now try to conclude my long letter.

I am sorry you are ill. But if you were well, I could not for your own sake wish you to go up, as Betty tells us you long to do. If you *went*, nothing would be minded that came from you. As they already think you too partial in her favour, your going up would confirm it, and do yourself prejudice and her no good. And as everybody values you here, I advise you not to interest yourself too warmly in her favour, especially before my Bella's Betty, till I can let you know a *proper* time. Yet to forbid you to love the dear naughty creature, who can? Oh my Norton! you *must* love her!—and so must I!

I send you five guineas to help you in your present illness, and your son's; for it must have lain heavy upon you. What a sad, sad thing, my dear good woman, that all *your* pains, and all *my* pains, for eighteen or nineteen years together, have in so few months been rendered thus deplorably vain! Yet I must be always your friend, and pity you, for the very reason that I myself deserve everyone's pity.

Perhaps I may find an opportunity to pay you a visit, as in your illness, and then may weep over the letter you mention, with you. But, for the future, write nothing to me about the poor girl, that you think may not be communicated to us all.

And I charge you, as you value my friendship, as you wish my peace, not to say anything of a letter you have from me, either to the naughty one, or to anybody else. It was some little relief (the occasion given) to write to you, who must in so particular a manner share my affliction. A mother, Mrs Norton, cannot forget her child, though that child could abandon her mother; and in so doing run away with all her mother's comforts!—As I can truly say is the case of

Your unhappy friend,
CHARLOTTE HARLOWE

Letter 377: MISS CLARISSA HARLOWE TO MRS JUDITH NORTON

Sat. July 29

I congratulate you, my dear Mrs Norton, with all my heart on your son's recovery; which I pray to God, with your own health, to perfect.

I write in some hurry, being apprehensive of the consequence of the hints you give of some method you propose to try in my favour (with my relations, I presume you mean): but you will not tell me what, you say, if it prove unsuccessful.

Now I must beg of you that you will not take any step in my favour, with which you do not first acquaint me.

I have but one request to make to them, besides what is contained in my letter to my sister; and I would not, methinks, for their own future peace of mind's sake, that they should be teased so by your well-meant kindness, and Miss Howe's, as to be put upon denying me that. And why should more be asked for me than I can partake of? More than is absolutely necessary for my own peace?

You suppose I should have my sister's answer to my letter by the time yours reached my hand. I have it; and a severe one, a very severe one, it is. Yet, considering my fault in their eyes, and the provocations I am to suppose they so newly had from my dear Miss Howe, I am to look upon it as a favour that it was answered at all. I will send you a copy of it soon; as also of mine, to which it is an answer.

I have reason to be very thankful that my father has withdrawn that heavy malediction, which affected me so much—A parent's curse, my dear Mrs Norton, what child could die in peace under a parent's curse; so literally fulfilled too as this has been in what relates to this life!

My heart is too full to touch upon the particulars of my sister's letter. I can make but *one* atonement for my fault. May *that* be accepted! And may it soon be forgotten, by *every* dear relation, that there was such an unhappy daughter, sister or niece, as Clarissa Harlowe!

My cousin Morden was one of those who was so earnest in prayers for my recovery, at nine and eleven years of age, as you mention. My sister thinks he will be one of those who will wish I never had a being. But pray, when he does come, let me hear of it with the first.

You think that were it not for that unhappy notion of my moving talent, my mamma would relent. What would I give to see her once more, and although unknown to her to kiss but the hem of her garment!

Could I have thought that the last time I saw her would *have been the last*, with what difficulty should I have been torn from her embraced feet!—And when, screened behind the yew hedge on the 5th of April last,[a] I saw my father, and my uncle Antony, and my brother and sister, how little did I think that that would be the last time I should ever see them; and in so short a space that so many dreadful evils would befall me!

But I can write nothing but what must give you trouble. I will therefore, after repeating my desire that you will not intercede for me but with my previous consent, conclude with the assurance that I am, and ever will be,

Your most affectionate and dutiful
CLARISSA HARLOWE

a   See p. 327.

Letter 378: MISS ARABELLA HARLOWE TO MISS CLARISSA HARLOWE

(In answer to hers of Friday, July 21, p. 1122)

Thursday, July 27

Oh my unhappy lost sister!

WHAT a miserable hand have you made of your romantic and giddy expedition! I pity you at my heart!

You may *well* grieve and repent!—Lovelace has left you!—In what way or circumstances you know best.

I wish your conduct had made your case more pitiable. But 'tis your own seeking!

God help you!—for you have not a friend will look upon you!—Poor, wicked, undone creature!—Fallen as you are, against warning, against expostulation, against duty!

But it signifies nothing to reproach you. I weep over you!

My poor mamma!—Your rashness and folly have made *her* more miserable than *you* can be! Yet she has besought my papa to grant your request.

My uncles joined with her; for they thought there was a little more modesty in your letter than in those of your pert advocate: and he is pleased to give me leave to write; but only these words for *him*, and no more: 'That he withdraws the curse he laid upon you at the first hearing of your wicked flight, so far as it is in his power to do it; and hopes that your present punishment may be all you will meet with. For the rest, he will never own you, nor forgive you; and grieves he has such a daughter in the world.'

All this, and more, you have deserved from him, and from all of *us*: but what have you done to this abandoned libertine, to deserve what you have met with at *his* hands?—I fear, I fear, sister!—But no more!—A blessed four months' work have you made of it!

My brother is now at Edinburgh, sent thither by my father (though he knows not this to be the motive), that he may not meet this triumphant deluder.

We are told he would be glad to marry you: but why, then, did he abandon you? He had kept you till he was tired of you, no question; and it is not likely he would wish to have you but upon the terms you have already without all doubt been *his*.

You ought to advise your friend Miss Howe to concern herself less in your matters than she does, except she could do it with more decency. She has written three letters to me: very insolent ones. Your favourer, poor Mrs Norton, thinks you know nothing of the pert creature's writing. I hope you don't. But then the more impertinent the writer. But, believing the fond woman, I sat down the more readily to answer your letter, and write with less severity than otherwise I should have done, if I had answered it at all.

Monday last was your birthday. Think, poor ungrateful wretch as you are! how we all used to keep it; and you will not wonder to be told that we ran away from one another that day. But God give you true penitence, if you have it not already! And it *will* be true, if it be equal to the shame and the sorrow you have given us all.

Your afflicted sister,
ARABELLA HARLOWE

Your cousin Morden is every day expected in England. He, as well as others of the family, when he comes to hear what a blessed piece of work you have made of it, will wish you never had a being.

Letter 379: MISS CLARISSA HARLOWE TO MISS HOWE

Sunday, July 30

You have given me great pleasure, my dearest friend, by your approbation of my reasonings, and of my resolution founded upon them, never to have Mr Lovelace. This approbation is so *right* a thing, give me leave to say, from the nature of the case, and from the strict honour and true dignity of mind which I always admired in my Anna Howe, that I could hardly tell to what but to my evil destiny, that of late would not let me please anybody, to attribute the advice you gave me to the contrary.

But let not the ill state of my health, and what that may naturally tend to, sadden you. I have told you that I will not run away from life, nor avoid the means that may continue it, if God see fit: and if he do *not*, who shall repine at his will?

If it shall be found that I have not acted unworthy of your love and of my own character in my greater trials, that will be a happiness to both on reflection.

The shock which you so earnestly advise me to try to get over, was a shock, the greatest that I could receive. But, my dear, as it was not incurred by my *fault*, I hope I am already got above it. I hope I am!

I am more grieved (at times however) for *others*, than for *myself*. And so I *ought*. For as to *myself*, I cannot but reflect that I have had an escape, rather than a loss, in missing Mr Lovelace for a husband: even had he *not* committed the vilest of all outrages.

Let anyone who knows my story collect his character from his behaviour to *me*, *before* that outrage; and then judge whether it was in the least probable for such a man to make me happy. But to collect his character from his principles with regard to the *sex in general*, and from his enterprises upon many of them, and to consider the cruelty of his nature and the sportiveness of his invention, together with the high opinion he has of himself, it will not be doubted that a wife of his must have been miserable; and more miserable if she loved him, than if she could have been indifferent to him.

A *twelvemonth* might, very probably, have put a period to my life; situated as I was with my friends; persecuted and harassed as I had been by my brother and sister; and my very heart torn in pieces by the *wilful*, and (as it is now apparent) *premeditated* suspenses of the man whose gratitude I wished to engage, and whose protection I was the more entitled to expect, as he had robbed me of every other, and hating my own family had reduced me to an absolute dependence upon himself. This once, as I thought, all his view; and uncomfortable enough for me, if it had been all.

Can it be thought, my dear, that my heart was not affected (happy as I was before I knew Mr Lovelace) by such an unhappy change in my circumstances?— Nor, perhaps, was the wicked violence *wanting* to have cut short, though not so *very* short perhaps, a life that he has sported with.

Had I been his but a *month*, he must have possessed the estate on which my relations had set their hearts; the more to their regret, as they hated *him* as much as he hated *them*.

Have I not reason, these things considered, to think myself happier without Mr Lovelace than with him?—My will too unviolated; and very little, nay, not anything as to him, to reproach myself with?

But with my *relations* it is *otherwise*. They indeed deserve to be pitied. They are, and no doubt will long be, unhappy.

To judge of their resentments, and of their conduct, we must put ourselves in their situation: and while *they* think me more in fault than themselves (whether my favourers are of their opinion, or not) and have a right to judge for themselves, they ought to have great allowances made for them; my parents especially. They stand at least *self*-acquitted (that cannot I); and the rather as they can recollect to their pain their past indulgencies to me, and their unquestionable love.

Your partiality for the friend you so much value will not easily let you come into this way of thinking. But only, my dear, be pleased to consider the matter in the following light.

Here was my MOTHER, one of the most prudent persons of her sex, married into a family not perhaps so happily tempered as herself; but every one of which she had the address, for a great while, absolutely to govern as she pleased by her directing wisdom, at the same time that they knew not but her prescriptions were the dictates of their own hearts; such a sweet art had she of conquering by seeming to yield. Think, my dear, what must be the pride and the pleasure of such a mother, that in my brother she could give a *son* to the family she distinguished with her preferable love, not unworthy of their wishes; a *daughter*, in my *sister*, of whom she had no reason to be ashamed; and in *me*, a *second* daughter whom everybody complimented (such was their partial favour to me) as being the still more immediate likeness of herself? How, self-pleased, could she smile round upon a family she had so blessed! What compliments were paid her upon the example she had given us, which were followed with such hopeful effects! With what a noble confidence could she look upon her dear Mr Harlowe, as a person made happy by her; and be delighted to think that nothing but purity streamed from a fountain so pure!

Now, my dear, reverse, as I daily do, this charming prospect. See my dear *mamma* sorrowing in her closet; endeavouring to suppress her sorrow at her table, and in those retirements where sorrow was before a stranger: hanging down her pensive head: smiles no more beaming over her benign aspect: her virtue made to suffer for faults she could not be guilty of: her patience continually tried (because she has more of it than any other) with repetitions of faults she is as much wounded by, as those can be from whom she so often hears of them: taking to herself, as the fountain-head, a taint which only had infected one of the undercurrents: afraid to open her lips (were she willing) in my favour, lest it should be thought she has any bias in her own mind to failings that never otherwise could have been suspected in her: robbed of that conscious merit which the mother of hopeful children may glory in: everyone who visits her, or is visited by her, by dumb-show, and looks that mean more than words can express, condoling where they used to congratulate: the affected silence wounding: the compassionating look reminding: the half-suppressed sigh in *them* calling up deeper sighs from *her*; and their averted eyes endeavouring to restrain the rising tear, provoking tears from *her* that will not be restrained.

When I consider these things, and added to these the pangs that tear in pieces my FATHER's stronger heart, because it cannot relieve itself by those tears which carry the torturing grief to the eyes of softer spirits: the overboiling tumults of my impatient and uncontrollable BROTHER, piqued to the heart of his honour in the fall of a sister in whom he once gloried: the pride of an ELDER SISTER, who had given unwilling way to the honours paid over her head to one born after her: and lastly the dishonour I have brought upon TWO UNCLES who each contended which should most favour their then happy niece. When, I say, I reflect upon my fault in these strong, yet just lights, what room can there be to censure anybody but my unhappy self? And how much reason have I to say: *If I justify myself, mine own heart shall condemn me: If I say, I am perfect, it shall also prove me perverse?*[1]

Here permit me to lay down my pen for a few moments.

You are very obliging to me, *intentionally* I know, when you tell me it is in my power to hasten the day of Mr Hickman's happiness. But yet, give me leave to say, that I admire this kind assurance less than any other paragraph of your letter.

In the first place, you know it is *not* in my power to say *when* I can dismiss my physician; and you should not put the celebration of a marriage *intended* by *yourself*, and so *desirable* to your *mother*, upon so precarious an issue. Nor will I accept of a compliment which must mean a slight to *her*.

If anything could give me a relish for life, after what I have suffered, it would be the hopes of the continuance of the more than sisterly love which has for years uninterruptedly bound us together as one mind—And why, my dear, should you defer giving (by a tie still stronger) another friend to one who has so few?

I am glad you have sent my letter to Miss Montague. I hope I shall hear no more of this unhappy man.

I had begun the particulars of my tragical story: but it is so painful a task, and I have so many more important things to do and as I apprehend so little time to do them in, that could I avoid it, I would go no farther in it.

Then, to this hour, I know not by what means several of his machinations to ruin me were brought about; so that some material parts of my sad story must be defective if I were to sit down to write it. But I have been thinking of a way that will answer the end wished for by your mother and you full as well; perhaps better.

Mr Lovelace, it seems, has communicated to his friend Mr Belford all that has passed between himself and me, as he went on. Mr Belford has not been able to deny it. So that (as we may observe by the way) a poor young creature whose indiscretion has given a libertine power over her, has a reason *she little thinks of* to regret her folly; since these wretches, who have no more honour in one point than in another, scruple not to make her weakness a part of their triumph to their brother libertines.

I have nothing to apprehend of this sort, if I have the justice done me in his letters which Mr Belford assures me that I have: and therefore the particulars of my story, and the base arts of this vile man will, I think, be best collected from those very letters of his (if Mr Belford can be prevailed upon to communicate them); to which I dare appeal with the same truth and fervour as he did, who

says:—*Oh that one would hear me! and that mine adversary had written a book!—
Surely, I would take it upon my shoulders, and bind it to me as a crown! For I
covered not my transgressions as Adam, by hiding mine iniquity in my bosom.*[2]

There is one way which may be fallen upon to induce Mr Belford to communicate
these letters; since he seems to have (and declares he always had) a sincere
abhorrence of his friend's baseness to me: but that, you'll say when you hear it, is
a strange one. Nevertheless, I am very earnest upon it, at present.

It is no other than this:

I think to make Mr Belford the executor of my last will (don't be surprised!):
and with this view I permit his visits with the less scruple: and every time I see him,
from his concern for me am more and more inclined to do so. If I hold in the same
mind, and if he accept the trust and will communicate the materials in his power,
those, joined with what you can furnish, will answer the whole end.

I know you will start at my notion of such an executor: but pray, my dear,
consider in my present circumstances what I can do better, as I am empowered to
make a will, and have considerable matters in my own disposal.

Your mother, I am sure, would not consent that *you* should take this office upon
you. It might subject *Mr Hickman* to the insults of that violent man. *Mrs Norton*
cannot, for several reasons respecting herself. My *brother* looks upon what I ought
to have as his right: My *uncle Harlowe* is already my trustee, with my cousin
Morden, for the estate my grandfather left me: but you see I could not get from my
own family the few pieces I left behind me at Harlowe Place; and my *uncle Antony*
once threatened to have my grandfather's will controverted. My *father!*—To be
sure, my dear, I could not expect that my *father* would do all I wish should be
done: and a *will* to be executed by a father for a daughter (parts of it, perhaps,
absolutely against his own judgement) carries somewhat daring and prescriptive
in the very *word*.

If indeed my *cousin Morden* were to come in time and would undertake this
trust—but even *him* it might subject to hazards; and the more as he is a man of
great spirit; and as the other man (of *as* great) looks upon me (unprotected as I
have long been) as his property.

Now Mr Belford knows, as I have already mentioned, everything that has passed.
He is a man of spirit, and it seems as fearless as the other, with more humane
qualities. You don't know, my dear, what instances of sincere humanity this Mr
Belford has shown, not only on occasion of the cruel arrest, but on several
occasions since. And Mrs Lovick has taken pains to inquire after his general
character; and hears a very good one of him, for justice and generosity in all his
concerns of *meum* and *tuum*, as they are called: he has a knowledge of law matters;
and has two executorships upon him at this time, in the discharge of which his
honour is unquestioned.

All these reasons have already in a manner determined me to ask this favour of
him; although it will have an odd sound with it, to make an intimate friend of Mr
Lovelace my executor.

This is certain: my brother will be more acquiescent a great deal in such a case
with the articles of my will, as he will see that it will be to no purpose to controvert
some of them, which else I dare say he would controvert, or persuade my other
friends to do so. And who would involve an executor in a lawsuit, if they could
help it? Which would be the case, if anybody were left whom my brother could

hope to awe or control; since my father (who is governed by him) has possession of all: nor would I wish, you may believe, to have effects torn out of my father's hands: while Mr Belford, who is a man of fortune (and a good economist in his own affairs), would have no interest but to do justice.

Then he exceedingly presses for some occasion to show his readiness to serve me: and he would be able to manage his violent friend, over whom he has more influence than any other person.

But, after all, I know not if it were not more eligible by far, that my story should be forgotten as soon as possible; and myself too. And of this I shall have the less doubt, if the character of my parents cannot be guarded (you will forgive me, my dear) from the unqualified bitterness which, from your affectionate zeal for me, has sometimes mingled with your ink. A point that ought and (I insist upon it) must be well considered of, if anything be done which your mother and you are desirous should be done.

My father has been so good as to take off from me the heavy malediction he laid me under. I must be now solicitous for a last blessing; and that is all I shall presume to ask. My sister's letter, communicating this grace, is a severe one. But as she writes to me as *from everybody*, how could I expect it to be otherwise?

If you set out tomorrow, this letter cannot reach you till you get to your aunt Harman's. I shall therefore direct it thither, as Mr Hickman instructed me.

I hope you will have met with no inconveniencies in your little journey and voyage; and that you will have found in good health all whom you wish to see well.

Let me recommend to you, my dear, that if your friends and relations in the little island join their solicitations with your mother's commands to have your nuptials celebrated before you leave them, you do not refuse to oblige them. How grateful will the notification that you have done so, be to

Your ever-faithful and affectionate
CL. HARLOWE!

Letter 380: MISS CLARISSA HARLOWE TO MISS HARLOWE

Saturday, July 29

I REPINE not, my dear sister, at the severity you have been pleased to express in the letter you favoured me with; because that severity was accompanied with the grace I had petitioned for: and because the reproaches of my own heart are stronger than any other person's reproaches can be; although I am not half so culpable as I am imagined to be; as would be allowed if all the circumstances of my unhappy story were known; and which I shall be ready to communicate to Mrs Norton, if she be commissioned to inquire into them; or to you, my sister, if you can have patience to hear them.

I remembered with a bleeding heart what day the 24th of July was. I began with the eve of it; and I passed the day itself—as it was fit I should pass it. Nor have I any comfort to give to my dear and ever-honoured father and mother, and to you, my Bella, but this—that, as it was the first *unhappy* anniversary of my birth, in all probability it will be the *last*.

Believe me, my dear sister, I say not this merely to move compassion; but from the *best* grounds: and as I think it of the highest importance to my peace of mind to obtain one further favour, I would choose to owe to your intercession, as my sister, the leave I beg to address half a dozen lines with the hope of having them answered as I wish, to either or to both my honoured parents, to beg their *last blessing*.

This blessing is all the favour I have now to ask: it is all I *dare* to ask: yet am afraid to rush at once, though by *letter*, into the presence of either. And if I did not ask it, it might seem to be owing to stubbornness and want of duty, when my heart is all humility and penitence. Only, be so good as to embolden me to attempt this task: write but this one line, 'Clary Harlowe, you are at liberty to write as you desire.' This will be enough—and shall to my last hour be acknowledged as the greatest favour by

Your truly penitent sister,
CLARISSA HARLOWE

Letter 381: MRS NORTON TO MISS CLARISSA HARLOWE

Monday, July 31

My dearest young lady,
I MUST indeed own that I took the liberty to write to your mamma offering to enclose to her, if she gave me leave, yours of the 24th: by which I thought she would see what was the state of your mind; what the nature of your last troubles was, from the wicked arrest; what the people are where you lodge; what proposals were made you from Lord M.'s family; also your sincere penitence; and how much Miss Howe's writing to them, in the terms she wrote in, disturbed you—But, as you have taken the matter into your own hands, and forbid me in your last to act in this nice affair unknown to you, I am glad the letter was *not required of me:* and indeed it may be better that the matter lie wholly between you and them; since my affection for you is thought to proceed from partiality.

They would choose, no doubt, that you should owe to themselves, and not to my humble mediation, the favour you so earnestly sue for, and which I would not have you despair of: for I will venture to assure you that your mother is ready to take the first opportunity to show her maternal tenderness for you: and this I gather from several hints I am not at liberty to explain myself upon.

I long to be with you, now I am better, and now my son is in a fine way of recovery. But is it not hard to have it signified to me that at present it will not be taken well if I go?—I suppose while the reconciliation, which I hope will take place, is negotiating by means of the correspondence so newly opened between you and your sister. But if you would have me come, I will rely on my good intentions and risk everyone's displeasure.

Mr Brand has business in town, to solicit for a benefice which it is expected the incumbent will be obliged to quit for a better preferment: and when there, he is to inquire privately after your way of life, and of your health.

He is a very officious young man; and, but that your uncle Harlowe (who has chosen him for this errand) regards him as an oracle; your mother had rather anybody else had been sent.

He is one of those puzzling, over-doing gentlemen, who think they see farther into matters than anybody else, and are fond of discovering mysteries where there are none, in order to be thought a shrewd man.

I can't say I like him, either in the pulpit or out of it: I who had a father one of the soundest divines and finest scholars in the kingdom; who never made an ostentation of what he knew; but loved and venerated the gospel he taught, preferring it to all other learning; to be obliged to hear a young man depart from his text as soon as he has named it (so contrary, too, to the example set him by his learned and worthy principal,*a* when his health permits him to preach), and throwing about to a Christian and country audience scraps of Latin and Greek from the pagan classics; and not always brought in with great propriety neither (if I am to judge by the only way given me to judge of them, by the English he puts them into); is an indication of something wrong, either in his head or his heart, or both; for, otherwise, his education at the university must have taught him better. You know, my dear Miss Clary, the honour I have for the cloth: it is owing to *that*, that I say what I do.

I know not the day he is to set out; and as his inquiries are to be private, be pleased to take no notice of this intelligence. I have no doubt that your life and conversation are such as may defy the scrutinies of the most officious inquirer.

I am just now told that you have written a second letter to your sister: but am afraid they will wait for Mr Brand's report, before further favour will be obtained from them; for they will not yet believe you are so ill as I fear you are.

But you would soon find that you have an indulgent mother, were she at liberty to act according to her own inclination. And this gives me great hopes that all will end well at last: for I verily think you are in the right way to reconciliation. God give a blessing to it, and restore your health, and you to all your friends, prays

Your ever-affectionate servant,
JUDITH NORTON

Your good mamma has privately sent me five guineas: she is pleased to say, to help us in the illness we have been afflicted with; but, more likely, that I might send them to you as from myself. I hope, therefore, I may send them up, with ten more I have still left.

I will send you word of Mr Morden's arrival, the moment I know it.

If agreeable, I should be glad to know all that passes between your relations and you.

Letter 382: MISS CLARISSA HARLOWE TO MRS NORTON

Wednesday, Aug. 2

You give me, my dear Mrs Norton, great pleasure in hearing of yours and your son's recovery. May you continue, for many, many years, a blessing to each other!

You tell me that you did actually write to my mamma, *offering* to enclose mine of the 24th past: and you say it was not *required* of you. That is to say, although you cover it over as gently as you could, that your offer was rejected; which makes it evident that no plea will be heard for me. Yet, you bid me hope that the grace I sued for would, *in time*, be granted.

a Dr Lewin.

The grace I then sued for was indeed granted: but you are afraid, you say, that they will wait for Mr Brand's report before favour will be obtained in return to the second letter which I wrote to my sister: and you add, that I have an indulgent mamma, were she at liberty to act according to her own inclination; and that all will end well at last.

But what, my dear Mrs Norton, what is the grace I sue for in my second letter?—It is not that they will receive me into favour—if they think it is, they are mistaken. I do not, I cannot expect that: nor, as I have often said, should I, if they *would* receive me, bear to live in the eye of those dear friends whom I have so grievously offended. 'Tis only, simply, a blessing I ask: a blessing to *die* with; not to *live* with—Do they know that? And do they know that their unkindness will perhaps shorten my date? So that their favour, if ever they intend to grant it, may come too late?

Once more I desire you not to think of coming to me. I have no uneasiness now, but what proceeds from the apprehension of seeing a man I would not see for the world, if I could help it; and from the severity of my nearest and dearest relations: a severity entirely their own, I doubt; for you tell me that my brother is at Edinburgh! You would therefore heighten their severity, and make yourself enemies besides, if you were to come to me—Don't you see that you would?

Mr Brand may come if he will. He is a clergyman, and must mean well; or I must think so, let him say of me what he will. All my fear is that, as he knows I am in disgrace with a family whose esteem he is desirous to cultivate; and as he has obligations to my uncle Harlowe and to my father; he will be but a languid acquitter. Not that I am afraid of what he, or anybody in the world, can hear as to my conduct. You may, my beloved and dear friend, indeed you may, rest satisfied, that that is such as may warrant me to challenge the inquiries of the most officious.

I will send you copies of what passes, as you desire, when I have an answer to my second letter. I now begin to wish that I had taken the heart to write to my father himself; or to my mother at least; instead of to my sister; and yet I doubt my poor mother can do nothing for me of *herself*. A strong confederacy, my dear Mrs Norton (a strong confederacy indeed!), against a poor girl, their daughter, sister, niece!—My brother, perhaps, got it renewed before he left them. He needed not—his work is done; and more than done.

Don't afflict yourself about money matters on my account. I have no occasion for money. I am glad my mother was so considerate to you. I was in pain for you on the same subject. But Heaven will not permit so good a woman to want the humble blessings she was always satisfied with. I wish every individual of our family were but as rich as you!—Oh my mamma Norton, you are rich; you are rich indeed!—The true riches are such content as you are blessed with—And I hope in God that I am in the way to be rich too.

Adieu, my ever-indulgent friend. You say all will be at last happy—and I *know* it will—I confide that it will, with as much security as you may that I will be to my last hour,

Your ever-grateful and affectionate
CL. HARLOWE

Letter 383: MR LOVELACE TO JOHN BELFORD, ESQ.

Tuesday, Aug. 1

I AM most confoundedly chagrined and disappointed: for here, on Saturday, arrived a messenger from Miss Howe, with a letter to my cousins[a]; which I knew nothing of till yesterday; when my two aunts were procured to be here to sit in judgement upon it with the old peer, and my two kinswomen. And never was bear so miserably baited as thy poor friend!—And for what?—Why, for the cruelty of Miss Harlowe: for have I committed any *new* offence? And would I not have succeeded in her favour upon her own terms, if I could? And is it fair to punish me for what is my misfortune, and not my fault? Such event-judging fools as I have for my relations! I am ashamed of them all.

In that of Miss Howe was enclosed one to *her* from Miss Harlowe,[b] to be sent to my cousins, containing a final rejection of me; and that in very vehement and positive terms; yet pretends that in this rejection she is governed more by *principle* than *passion*—(damned lie as ever was told!). And as a proof that she is says that she *can* forgive me, and *does*, on this one condition, that I will never molest her more: the whole letter so written as to make *herself* more admired, *me* more detested.

What we have been told of the agitations and workings, and sighings and sobbings of the French prophets among us formerly, were nothing at all to the scene exhibited by these maudlin souls at the reading of these letters; and of some affecting passages extracted from another of my fair implacable's to Miss Howe— Such lamentations for the loss of so charming a relation! Such applaudings of her virtue, of her exaltedness of soul and sentiment! Such menaces of disinherisons! I, not needing *their* reproaches to be stung to the heart with my own reflections, and with the rage of disappointment; and as sincerely as any of them admiring her—What the devil, cried I, is all this for?—Is it not enough to be despised and rejected? Can I help her implacable spirit?—Would I not repair the evils I have made her suffer?—Then was I ready to curse them all, herself and Miss Howe for company—and heartily I swore that she should yet be mine.

I now swear it over again to thee—Were her death to follow in a week after the knot is tied, by the Lord of Heaven, it *shall* be tied, and she shall die a Lovelace. Tell her so, if thou wilt: but, at the same time, tell her that I have no *view to her fortune*; and that I will solemnly resign that, and all pretensions to it, in whose favour she pleases, if she resign life issueless. I am not so low-minded a wretch as to be *guilty* of any sordid views to her fortune: let her judge for herself then, whether it be not for her honour rather to leave this world a Lovelace than a Harlowe.

But do not think I will entirely rest a cause so near my heart, upon an advocate who so much more admires his client's adversary than his client. I will go to town in a few days, in order to throw myself at her feet: bringing with me, or having at hand, a *resolute, well-prepared* parson; and the ceremony shall be performed, let what will be the consequence.

But if she will permit me to attend her for this purpose at either of the churches

a   See Letter 373.
b   See Letter 379.

mentioned in the licence (which she has by her, and, thank Heaven! has not returned me with my letters); then will I not disturb her; but meet her at the altar in either church, and will engage to bring my two cousins to attend her, and even Lady Sarah and Lady Betty, and my Lord M. in person, to give her to me.

Or, if it will be still more agreeable to her; I will undertake that either or both my aunts shall go to town and attend her down; and the marriage shall be celebrated in theirs and Lord M.'s presence, here, or elsewhere, at her own choice.

Do not play me booty, Belford; but sincerely and warmly use all the eloquence thou art master of to prevail upon her to choose one of these three methods. One of them she *must* choose—by my soul, she must.

Here is Charlotte tapping at my closet door for admittance. What a devil wants Charlotte?—I will bear no more reproaches!—Come in, girl!

My cousin Charlotte, finding me writing on with too much earnestness to have any regard for politeness to her, and guessing at my subject, besought me to let her see what I had written.

I obliged her. And she was so highly pleased on seeing me so much in earnest, that *she* offered and I accepted her offer, to write herself to Miss Harlowe; with permission to treat me in it as she thought fit.

I shall enclose a copy of her letter.

When she *had* written it, she brought it to me with apologies for the freedom taken with me in it: but I excused it; and she was ready to give me a kiss for joy of my approbation: and I gave her two for writing it; telling her I had hopes of success from it; and that I thought she had luckily hit it off.

Everyone approves of it, as well as I, and is pleased with me for so patiently submitting to be abused and undertaken for. If it do not succeed, all the blame will be thrown upon the dear creature's perverseness: her charitable or forgiving disposition, about which she makes such a parade, will be justly questioned; and the pity of which she is now in full possession will be transferred to me.

Putting therefore my whole confidence in this letter, I postpone all my other alternatives, as also my going to town, till my empress send an answer to my cousin Montague.

But if she persist, and will not promise to take time to *consider* of the matter, thou mayest communicate to her what I had written, as above, before my cousin entered; and if she be still perverse, assure her that I *must* and *will* see her—but this with all honour, all humility. And if I cannot move her in my favour, I will then go abroad and perhaps never more return to England.

I am sorry thou art, at *this critical time*, so busily employed as thou informest me thou art, in thy Watford affairs, and in preparing to do Belton justice. If thou wantest my assistance in the latter, command me. Though engrossed and plagued as I am with this perverse beauty, I will obey thy first summons.

I have great dependence upon thy zeal and thy friendship: hasten back to her, therefore, and resume a task *so* interesting to me that it is equally the subject of my dreams as of my waking hours.

Letter 384: MISS MONTAGUE TO MISS CLARISSA HARLOWE

Tuesday, Aug. 1

Dearest madam,

ALL our family is deeply sensible of the injuries you have received at the hands of one of it, whom YOU only can render in any manner worthy of the relation he stands in to us all: and if, as an act of mercy and charity, the greatest your pious heart can show, you will be pleased to look over his past wickedness and ingratitude, and suffer yourself to be our kinswoman, you will make us the happiest family in the world: and I can engage that Lord M. and Lady Sarah Sadleir, and Lady Betty Lawrance, and my sister, who are all admirers of your virtues, and of your nobleness of mind, will for ever love and reverence you, and do everything in all our powers to make you amends for what you have suffered from Mr Lovelace. This, madam, we should not, however, dare to petition for, were we not assured that he is most sincerely sorry for his past vileness to you; and that he will, on his knees, beg your pardon and vow eternal love and honour to you.

Wherefore, *my dearest cousin* (how you will charm us all, if this agreeable style may be permitted!), for *all* our sakes, for his *soul*'s sake (you must, I am sure, be so good a lady as to wish to save a soul!), and allow me to say for *your own fame*'s sake, condescend to our joint requests: and if, by way of encouragement, you will but say you will be glad to see, and to be as much known personally as you are by fame to Charlotte Montague, I will in two days' time from the receipt of your permission wait upon you, *with* or *without* my sister, and receive your further commands.

Let me, *our dearest cousin* (we cannot deny ourselves the pleasure of calling you so), let me entreat you to give me your permission for my journey to London; and put it in the power of Lord M. and of the ladies of the family to make you what reparation they can make you, for the injuries which a person of the greatest merit in the world has received from one of the most audacious men in it; and you will infinitely oblige us all; and particularly her, who repeatedly presumes to style herself,

Your affectionate *cousin*, and obliged servant,
CHARLOTTE MONTAGUE

Letter 385: MR BELFORD TO ROBERT LOVELACE, ESQ.

Thursday morning, Aug. 3, six o'clock

I HAVE been so much employed in my own and Belton's affairs that I could not come to town till last night; having contented myself with sending to Mrs Lovick, to know from time to time the state of the lady's health; of which I received but very indifferent accounts, owing in a great measure to letters or advices brought her from her implacable family.

I have now completed my own affairs; and next week shall go to Epsom to endeavour to put Belton's sister into possession of his own house for him: after which I shall devote myself wholly to your service, and to that of the lady.

I was admitted to her presence last night; and found her visibly altered for the worse. When I went home, I had your letter of Tuesday last put into my hands. Let me tell thee, Lovelace, that I insist upon the performance of thy engagement to me that thou wilt not personally molest her.

Mr Belford dates again on Thursday morning ten o'clock; and gives an account of a conversation which he had just held with the lady, upon the subject of Miss Montague's letter to her, preceding, and upon Mr Lovelace's alternatives as mentioned in Letter 383, which Mr Belford supported with the utmost earnestness. But, as the result of this conversation will be found in the subsequent letters, Mr Belford's pleas and arguments and the lady's answers are omitted.

Letter 386: MISS CLARISSA HARLOWE TO MISS MONTAGUE

Thursday, Aug. 3

Dear madam,

I AM infinitely obliged to you for your kind and condescending letter. A letter, however, which heightens my regrets, as it gives me a new instance of what a happy creature I might have been in an alliance so much approved of by such worthy ladies; and which, on their accounts, and on that of Lord M., would have been so reputable to myself and [was] once so desirable.

But indeed, indeed, madam, my heart sincerely repulses the man who, descended from such a family, could be guilty, *first*, of such premeditated violence as he has been guilty of; and as *he* knows *further* intended me on the night previous to the day he set out for Berkshire; and, *next*, pretending to spirit, be so mean as to wish to list into that family a person he was capable of abasing into a companionship with the most abandoned of her sex.

Allow me then, dear madam, to declare with fervour, that I think I never could deserve to be ranked with the ladies of a family so splendid and so noble, if, by vowing love and honour at the altar to such a violator, I could *sanctify* as I may say his unprecedented and elaborate wickedness.

Permit me, however, to make one request to my good Lord M. and to the two ladies his lordship's sisters, and to your kind self and your sister—It is, that you will all be pleased to join your authority and interests to prevail upon Mr Lovelace not to molest me further.

Be pleased to tell him that if I am designed for *life*, it will be very cruel in him to attempt to hunt me out of it; for I am determined never to see him more if I can help it. The more cruel, because he knows that I have nobody to protect me from him: nor do I wish to engage anybody to *his* hurt, or to their own.

If I am, on the other hand, destined for *death*, it will be no less cruel if he will not permit me to die in peace—since a peaceable and happy end I wish him. Indeed I do.

Every worldly good attend you, dear madam, and every branch of the honourable family, is the wish of one whose misfortune it is that she is obliged to disclaim any other title than that of,

Dear madam, your and their obliged and faithful servant,
CLARISSA HARLOWE

Letter 387: MR BELFORD TO ROBERT LOVELACE, ESQ.

Thursday afternoon, Aug. 3

I AM just now agreeably surprised by the following letter, delivered into my hands by a messenger from the lady. The letter she mentions as enclosed,[a] I have returned, without taking a copy of it. The contents of it will soon be communicated to you, I presume, by another way. They contain an absolute rejection of thee— *Poor Lovelace:*——

[*Letter 387.1: Miss Clarissa Harlowe*] *to John Belford, Esq.*

Aug. 3

Sir,

You have frequently offered to oblige me in anything that shall be within your power: and I have such an opinion of you as to be willing to hope you meant me at the times more than mere compliment.

I have therefore two requests to make to you; the first I will now mention; the other, if this shall be complied with, otherwise not.

It behoves me to leave behind me such an account as may clear up my conduct to several of my friends who will not at present concern themselves about me: and Miss Howe and her mother are very solicitous that I will do so.

I am apprehensive that I shall not have time to do this; and you will not wonder that I have less and less inclination to set about such a painful task; especially as I find myself unable to look back with patience on what I have suffered; and shall be too much discomposed by it to proceed with the requisite temper in a task of *still greater* importance which I have before me.

It is very evident to me that your wicked friend has given you, from time to time, a circumstantial account of all his behaviour *to* me and devices *against* me; and you have more than once assured me that, both by writing and speech, he has done my character all the justice I could wish for.

Now, sir, if I may have a fair, a faithful specimen from his letters or accounts to you, upon some of the most interesting occasions, I shall be able to judge whether there will or will not be a necessity for me, for my honour's sake, to enter upon the solicited task.

You may be assured from my enclosed answer to the letter which Miss Montague has honoured me with (and which you'll be pleased to return me as soon as read), that it is impossible for me ever to think of your friend in the way I am importuned to think of him. He cannot therefore receive any detriment from the requested specimen: and I give you my honour that no use shall be made of it to his prejudice, in law, or otherwise. And that it may *not* after I am no more, I assure you that it is a *main part of my view* that the passages you shall oblige me with shall be always in your own power, and not in that of any other person.

If, sir, you think fit to comply with my request, the passages I would wish to be transcribed (making neither better nor worse of the matter) are those which he has written to you, on or about the 7th and 8th of June, when I was alarmed by the

a   See Miss Montague's letter [384].

wicked pretence of a fire; and what he has written from Sunday June 11 to the 19th. And in doing this you will much oblige

> Your humble servant,
> CL. HARLOWE

Now, Lovelace, since there are no hopes for thee of her returning favour; since some praise may lie for thy ingenuity, having never offered (as more diminutive-minded libertines would have done) to palliate thy crimes by aspersing the lady or her sex; since she may be made easier by it; since thou must fare better from thy own pen than from hers; and finally since thy actions have manifested that thy letters are not the most guilty part of what she *knows* of thee; I see not why I may not oblige her, upon her honour and under the restrictions, and for the reasons she has given; and this without breach of the confidence due to friendly communications; especially as I might have added, *Since thou gloriest in thy pen, and in thy wickedness, and canst not be ashamed.*

But, be this as it may, she *will* be obliged before thy remonstrances or clamours against it can come; so, prithee now, make the best of it, and rave not; except for the sake of a pretence against me, and to exercise thy talent of execration!—And, if thou likest to do so for these reasons, rave and welcome.

I long to know what the second request is: but this I know, that if it be anything less than cutting *thy* throat or endangering *my own* neck, I will certainly comply; and be proud of having it in my power to oblige her.

And now I am actually going to be busy in the extracts.

Letter 388: MR BELFORD TO MISS CLARISSA HARLOWE

Aug. 3, 4

Madam,

YOU have engaged me to communicate to you, upon honour (making neither better nor worse of the matter), what Mr Lovelace has written to me in relation to yourself, in the period preceding your going to Hampstead, and in that between the 11th and 19th of June: and you assure me you have no view in this request, but to see if it be necessary for you, from the account he gives, to touch the painful subjects yourself, for the sake of your own character.

Your commands, madam, are of a very delicate nature, as they may seem to affect the secrets of private friendship: but as I know you are not capable of a view, the motives to which you will not own; and as I think the communication may do some credit to my unhappy friend's character as an *ingenuous* man; though his actions by the most excellent woman in the world have lost him all title to that of an *honourable* one; I obey you with the greater cheerfulness.

He then proceeds with his extracts, and concludes them with an address to her in his friend's behalf in the following words:

'And now, madam, I have fulfilled your commands; and, I hope, not disserved my friend with you; since you will hereby see the justice he does to your virtue in every line he writes. He does the same in all his letters, though to his own condemnation: and give me leave to add that if this ever-amiable sufferer could but think it in any manner consistent with her honour to receive his vows at the altar, on his truly penitent turn of mind, I have not the least doubt but that he would make her the best and tenderest of husbands. What obligation would not the admirable lady hereby lay upon all *his* noble family, who so greatly admire her! and, I will presume to say, upon *her own*, when the unhappy family aversion (which certainly has been carried to an unreasonable height against him) is got over, and a general reconciliation take place! For who is it that would not give these two admirable persons to each other, were not his morals an objection?'

However this be, I would humbly refer to you, madam, whether, as you will be mistress of very delicate particulars from *me* his friend, you should not in honour think yourself concerned to pass them by as if you had never seen them; and not to take any advantage of the communication, not even in argument, as some perhaps might lie, with respect to the *premeditated* design he seems to have had, not against you *as* you; but as against the *sex*; over whom (I am sorry I can bear witness myself) it is the villainous aim of all libertines to triumph: and I would not, if any misunderstanding should arise between him and me, give him room to reproach me that his losing of you, or (through his usage of you) his losing of his own friends, were owing to what perhaps he would call breach of trust, were he to judge rather by the events, if such should happen, than by my intention.

I am, madam, with the most profound veneration,

Your most faithful humble servant,
J. Belford

Letter 389: MISS CLARISSA HARLOWE TO JOHN BELFORD, ESQ.

Friday, Aug. 4

Sir,

I HOLD myself extremely obliged to you for your communications. I will make no use of them that you shall have reason to reproach either yourself or me with. I wanted no new lights to make the unhappy man's premeditated baseness to me unquestionable, as my answer to Miss Montague's letter might convince you.[a]

I must own in his favour, that he has observed some decency in his accounts to you of the most indecent and shocking actions. And if all his strangely-communicative narrations are equally decent, nothing will be rendered criminally odious by them but the vile heart that could meditate such contrivances as were much stronger evidences of his inhumanity, than of his wit: since men of very contemptible parts and understanding may succeed in the vilest attempts, if they can get above regarding the moral sanctions which bind man to man; and sooner upon an innocent heart, than upon any other; because, knowing its own integrity, it is the less apt to suspect that of others.

I find I have had great reason to think myself obliged to your intention in the whole progress of my sufferings. It is however impossible, sir, to miss the natural inference on this occasion that lies against his predetermined baseness. But I say

---

a See Letter 386.

the less, because you shall not think I borrow from your communications aggravations that are needed.

And now, sir, that I may spare you the trouble of offering any future arguments in his favour, let me tell you that I have weighed everything thoroughly: all that human vanity could suggest; all that a desirable reconciliation with my friends and the kind respects of his own could bid me hope for: the enjoyment of Miss Howe's friendship, the dearest consideration to me now of all worldly ones: all these I have weighed: and the result is, and *was* before you favoured me with these communications, that I have more satisfaction in the hope that in one month there will be an end of all with me, than in the most agreeable things that could happen from an alliance with Mr Lovelace, although I were to be assured he would make the best and tenderest of husbands. But as to the rest; if, satisfied with the evils he has brought upon me, he will forbear all further persecutions of me, I will to my last hour wish him good: although *he hath overwhelmed the fatherless, and digged a pit for his friend*[1]: fatherless may *she* well be called, and motherless too, who has been denied all paternal protection and motherly forgiveness.

AND now, sir, acknowledging gratefully your favour in the extracts, I come to the second part of my request: which requires a great deal of courage to mention to you: and which courage nothing but a great deal of distress, and a very destitute condition, can give. But, if improper, I can but be denied; and dare to say I shall be at least excused. Thus, then, I preface it:

You see, sir, that I am thrown absolutely into the hands of strangers, who, although as kind and compassionate as strangers can be wished to be, are nevertheless persons from whom I cannot expect anything more than pity and good wishes; nor can my memory receive from them any more protection than my person, if either should need it.

If then I request it of the *only* gentleman possessed of materials that will enable him to do my character justice;

And who has courage, independence, and ability to oblige me;

To be the protector of my memory, as I may say;

And to be my *executor*; and to see some of my dying requests performed;

(And if I leave it to him to do the whole in his own way, manner, and time; consulting, however, in requisite cases, my dear Miss Howe);

I presume to hope that this part of my request may be granted.

And if it may, these satisfactions will accrue to me from the favour done me, and the office undertaken:

It will be an honour to my memory, with all those who shall know that I was so well satisfied of my innocence, that having not time to write my own story I could entrust it to the relation which the destroyer of my fame and fortunes has given of it.

I shall not be apprehensive of involving anyone in troubles or hazards by this task, either with my own relations, or with your friend; having dispositions to make which perhaps my own friends will not be so well pleased with as it were to be wished they would be; for I intend not unreasonable ones: but you know, sir, where *self* is judge, matters, even with *good people*, will not always be rightly judged of.

I shall also be freed from the pain of recollecting things that my soul is vexed at;

and this at a time when its tumults should be allayed in order to make way for the most important preparation.

And who knows but that the man who already, from a principle of humanity, is touched at my misfortunes, when he comes to revolve the whole story placed before him in one strong light, and when he shall have the catastrophe likewise before him; and shall become in a manner interested in it: who knows but that from a still higher principle, he may so regulate his future actions as to find his own reward in the everlasting welfare which is wished him by his

Obliged servant,
CLARISSA HARLOWE?

Letter 390: MR BELFORD TO MISS CLARISSA HARLOWE

Friday, Aug. 4

Madam,

I AM so sensible of the honour done me in yours of this day, that I would not delay for one moment the answering of it. I hope you will live to see many happy years; and to be your own executrix in those points which your heart is most set upon. But in case of survivorship, I most cheerfully accept of the sacred office you are pleased to offer me; and you may absolutely rely upon my fidelity, and if possible upon the literal performance of every article you shall enjoin me.

The effect of the kind wish you conclude with has been my concern ever since I have been admitted to the honour of your conversation. It shall be my whole endeavour that it be not vain. The happiness of approaching you, which this trust, as I presume, will give me frequent opportunities of doing, must necessarily promote the desirable end; since it will be impossible to be a witness of your piety, equanimity, and other virtues, and not aspire to emulate you. All I beg is, that you will not suffer any future candidate, or event, to displace me; unless some new instances of unworthiness appear, either in the morals or behaviour of,

Madam, your most obliged and faithful servant,
J. BELFORD

Letter 391: MR BELFORD TO ROBERT LOVELACE, ESQ.

Friday night, Aug. 4

I HAVE actually delivered to the lady the extracts she requested me to give her from thy letters. I do assure thee that I have made the very best of the matter for thee, *not* that conscience, but that friendship could oblige me to make. I have changed or omitted some free words. The warm description of her person in the *fire scene*, as I may call it, I have omitted. I have told her that I have done justice to you, in the justice you have done to her unexampled virtue. But take the very words which I wrote to her immediately following the extracts:

'And now, madam,'—*see the paragraph marked with inverted commas* (' *thus*), *pp. 1174–5.*

The lady is extremely uneasy at the thoughts of your attempting to visit her. For Heaven's sake (your word being given), and for pity's sake (for she is really in a very weak and languishing way), let me beg of you not to think of it.

Yesterday afternoon she received a cruel letter, as Mrs Lovick supposes it to be by the effect it had upon her, from her sister, in answer to one written last Saturday entreating a blessing and forgiveness from her parents.

She acknowledges that, if all thy letters are written with equal decency and justice, as I have assured her they are, she shall think herself freed from the necessity of writing her own story: and this is an advantage to thee accruing from the extracts I have obliged her with; though thou perhaps wilt not thank me for so doing.

But what thinkest thou is the second request she had to make to me? No other than that I would be her *executor!*—Her motives will appear before thee in proper time; and then, I dare answer for them, will be satisfactory.

You cannot imagine how proud I am of this trust. I am afraid I shall too soon come into the execution of it. As she is always writing, what a melancholy pleasure will the perusal and disposition of her papers afford me! Such a sweetness of temper, so much patience and resignation, as she seems to be mistress of; yet writing of and in the midst of *present* distresses! How much more lively and affecting, for that reason, must her style be, than all that can be read in the dry, narrative, unanimated style of persons relating difficulties and dangers surmounted! The minds of such not labouring in suspense, not tortured by the pangs of uncertainty about events still hidden in the womb of fate; but on the contrary perfectly at ease; the relater unmoved by his own story, how then able to move the hearer or reader?

Saturday morning, Aug. 5

I AM just returned from visiting the lady and thanking her in person for the honour she has done me; and assuring her, if called to the sacred trust, of the utmost fidelity and exactness. I found her very ill. I took notice of it. She said she had received a second hard-hearted letter from her sister; and she had been writing a letter (and that on her knees) directly to her mother; which before she had not the courage to do. It was for a last blessing and forgiveness. No wonder, she said, that I saw her affected. Now that I had accepted of the last charitable office for her (for which, as well as for complying with her other request, she thanked me), I should one day have all these letters before me: and could she have a kind one in return to that she had been now writing, to counterbalance the unkind one she had from her sister, she might be induced to show me both together.

I knew she would be displeased if I had censured the cruelty of her relations; I therefore only said that surely she must have enemies, who hoped to find their account in keeping up the resentments of her friends against her.

It may be so, Mr Belford, said she: the unhappy never want enemies. One fault wilfully committed authorizes the imputation of many more. Where the ear is opened to accusations, accusers will not be wanting; and everyone will officiously come with stories against a disgraced child, where nothing dare be said in her favour. I should have been wise in time, and not have needed to be convinced by my own misfortunes of the truth of what common experience daily demonstrates. Mr Lovelace's baseness, my father's inflexibility, my sister's reproaches, are the natural consequences of my own rashness; so I must make the best of my hard lot. Only, as these consequences follow one another so closely, while they are *new* how can I help being anew affected?

I asked if a letter written by myself, by her doctor or apothecary, to any of her friends, representing her low state of health, and great humility, would be acceptable? Or if a journey to any of them would be of service, I would gladly undertake it in person, and strictly conform to her orders, to whomsoever she would direct me to apply.

She earnestly desired that nothing of this sort might be attempted, especially without her knowledge and consent. Miss Howe, she said, had done harm by her kindly-intended zeal; and if there were room to expect favour by mediation, she had ready at hand a kind friend, Mrs Norton, who for piety and prudence had few equals; and who would let slip no opportunity to do her service.

I let her know that I was going out of town till Monday: she wished me pleasure; and said she should be glad to see me on my return.

Adieu!

Letter 392: MISS ARABELLA HARLOWE TO MISS CLARISSA HARLOWE

(In answer to hers of Saturday, July 29, Letter 380)

Thursday morn. Aug. 3

Sister CLARY,

I WISH you would not trouble me with any more of your letters. You had always a knack at writing; and depended upon making everyone do what you would when you wrote. But your wit and your folly have undone you. And now, as all naughty creatures do when they can't help themselves, you come begging and praying, and make others as uneasy as yourself.

When I wrote last to you, I *expected* that I should not be at rest.

And so you'd creep on, by little and little, till you'll want to be received again.

But you only hope for *forgiveness*, and a *blessing*, you say. A blessing for what, sister Clary? Think for what?—However, I read your letter to my father and mother.

I won't tell you what my papa said—One who has the true sense you boast to have of your misdeeds may guess, without my telling you, what a justly incensed father would say on such an occasion.

My poor mamma—Oh wretch! What has not your ungrateful folly cost my poor mamma!—Had you been less a darling, you would not perhaps have been so graceless: but I never in my life saw a cockered favourite come to good.

My heart is full, and I can't help writing my mind; for your crimes have disgraced us all; and I am afraid and ashamed to go to any public or private assembly or diversion: and why?—I *need* not say why, when your actions are the subjects either of the open talk, or of the affronting whispers, of both sexes at all such places.

Upon the whole, I am sorry I have no more comfort to send you: but I find nobody willing to forgive you. I don't know what *time* may do for you; and when it is seen that your penitence is not owing more to disappointment than true conviction: for it is too probable, Miss Clary, that had you gone on as swimmingly as you expected, and had not your feather-headed villain abandoned you, we should have heard nothing of these moving supplications: nor of anything but defiances from *him*, and a guilt gloried in from *you*. And this is everyone's opinion, as well as that of

Your grieved sister,
ARABELLA HARLOWE

I send this by a particular hand, who undertakes to give it you or leave it for you by tomorrow night.

Letter 393: MISS CLARISSA HARLOWE TO HER MOTHER

Sat. Aug. 5

Honoured madam,

No self-convicted criminal ever approached her angry and just judge with greater awe, nor with a truer contrition than I do you by these lines.

Indeed I must say that if the matter of my humble prayer had not respected my future welfare, I had not dared to take this liberty. But my heart is set upon it, as upon a thing next to God Almighty's forgiveness necessary for me.

Had my happy sister known my distresses, she would not have wrung my heart as she has done, by a severity which I must needs think unkind and unsisterly.

But complaint of any unkindness from her belongs not to me: yet, as she is pleased to write that it must be seen that my penitence is less owing to disappointment than to true conviction, permit me, madam, to insist upon it that I am actually *entitled* to the blessing I sue for; since my humble prayer is founded upon a true and unfeigned repentance: and this you will the readier believe, if the creature who never to the best of her remembrance told her mamma a wilful falsehood may be credited, when she declares, as she does, in the most solemn manner, that she met the seducer with a determination not to go off with him: that the rash step was owing more to compulsion than infatuation: and that her heart was so little in it that she repented and grieved from the moment she found herself in his power; and for every moment after, for several weeks *before* she had any cause from him to apprehend the usage she met with.

Wherefore, on my knees, my ever-honoured mamma (for on my knees I write this letter), I do most humbly beg your blessing: say but in so many words (I ask you not to call me your daughter)—*Lost, unhappy wretch, I forgive you! and may God bless you!*—This is all! Let me, on a blessed scrap of paper but see one sentence to this effect, under your dear hand, that I may hold it to my heart in my most trying struggles, and I shall think it a passport to Heaven. And if I do not too much presume, and it were WE instead of I, and *both* your honoured names subjoined to it, I should then have nothing more to wish. Then would I say, 'Great and merciful God! thou seest here in this paper thy poor unworthy creature absolved by her justly-offended parents: Oh join, for my Redeemer's sake, thy all-gracious *fiat*, and receive a repentant sinner to the arms of thy mercy!'

I can conjure you, madam, by no subject of motherly tenderness, that will not in the opinion of my severe censurers, before whom this humble address must appear, add to my reproach: let me therefore, for God's sake, prevail upon you to pronounce me blessed and forgiven, since you will thereby sprinkle comfort through the last hours of

Your
CLARISSA HARLOWE

Letter 394: MISS MONTAGUE TO MISS CLARISSA HARLOWE

(In answer to hers of Thursday, August 3, Letter 386)

Monday, Aug. 7

Dear madam,

WE were all of opinion, *before* your letter came, that Mr Lovelace was utterly unworthy of you and deserved condign punishment rather than the blessing of such a wife: and hoped far *more* from your kind consideration for *us*, than any we supposed you could have for so base an *injurer*. For we were all determined to love you and admire you, let *his* behaviour to you be what it would.

But, after your letter, what can be said?

I am, however, commanded to write in all the subscribing names, to let you know how greatly your sufferings have affected us: to tell you that my Lord M. has forbid him ever more to darken the doors of the apartments where he shall be: and as you labour under the unhappy effects of your friends' displeasure, which may subject you to inconveniencies, his lordship and Lady Sarah and Lady Betty beg of you to accept for your life, or at least till you are admitted to enjoy your own estate, of one hundred guineas *per* quarter, which will be regularly brought you by an especial hand, and of the enclosed bank bill for a beginning. And do not, dearest madam, we all beseech you, do not think you are beholden for this token of Lord M.'s and Lady Sarah's and Lady Betty's love to you, to the *friends of this vile man*; for he has not one friend left among us.

We each of us desire to be forward with a place in your esteem; and to be considered upon the same foot of relationship, as if what once was so much our pleasure to hope *would* be, *had* been. And it shall be our united prayer that you may recover health and spirits, and live to see many happy years: and since this wretch can no more be pleaded for, that, when he is gone abroad, as he now is preparing to do, we may be permitted the honour of a personal acquaintance with a lady who has no equal. These are the earnest requests, dearest young lady, of

Your affectionate friends, and most faithful servants,
M.
SARAH SADLEIR.
ELIZ. LAWRANCE.
CHARL. MONTAGUE.
MARTH. MONTAGUE.

YOU will break the hearts of the three first-named more particularly, if you refuse them your acceptance. Dearest Miss Harlowe, punish not *them* for *his* crimes. We send by a particular hand, which will bring us, we hope, your accepting favour.

Mr Lovelace writes by the same hand; but he knows nothing of ours, nor we of his: for we shun each other; and one part of the house holds *us*, another *him*, the remotest from each other.

Letter 395: MR LOVELACE TO JOHN BELFORD, ESQ.

Sat. Aug. 5

I AM so excessively disturbed at the contents of Miss Harlowe's answer to my cousin Charlotte's letter of Tuesday last (which was given her by the same fellow that gave me yours), that I have hardly patience or consideration enough to weigh what you write.

She had need, indeed, to cry out for mercy herself from *her* friends, who knows not how to show any! She is a true daughter of the Harlowes—by my soul, Jack, she is a true daughter of the Harlowes! Yet has she so many excellencies, that I must love her; and, fool that I am, love her the more for her despising me.

Thou runnest on with thy cursed nonsensical *reformado* rote, of dying, dying, dying! and, having once got the word by the end, canst not help foisting it in at every period! The devil take me, if I don't think thou wouldst give her poison with thy own hands, rather than she should recover and rob thee of the merit of being a conjurer!

But no more of thy cursed knell; thy changes upon death's candlestick turned botton-upwards: she'll live to bury me; I see that: for, by my soul, I can neither eat, drink, nor sleep; nor, what's still worse, love any woman in the world but her. Nor care I to look upon a woman now; on the contrary, I turn my head from every one I meet; except by chance an eye, an air, a feature, strikes me resembling hers in some glancing-by face; and then I cannot forbear looking again; though the second look recovers me; for there can be nobody like her.

But surely, Belford, the devil's in this lady! The more I think of her nonsense and obstinacy, the less patience I have with her. Is it possible she can do herself, her family, her friends, so much justice any *other* way, as by marrying me! Were she sure she should live but a day, she ought to die a wife. If her *Christian revenge* will not let her wish to do so for her *own* sake, ought she not for the sake of her family, and of her sex, which she pretends sometimes to have so much concern for? And if no *sake* is dear enough to move her Harlowe spirit in my favour, has she any title to the pity thou so pitifully art always bespeaking for her?

As to the difference which her letter has made between me and the stupid family here (and I must tell thee we are all broke in pieces), I value not that of a button. They are fools to anathematize and curse me, who can give them ten curses for one, were they to hold it for a day together.

I have one half of the house to myself; and that the best; for the great enjoy that least, which costs them most: *grandeur* and *use* are two things: the common part is theirs; the state part is mine: and here I lord it, and *will* lord it, as long as I please; while the two pursy sisters, the old gouty brother, and the two musty nieces, are stived up in the other half, and dare not stir for fear of meeting me: whom (that's the jest of it) they have forbidden coming into their apartments, as I have them into mine. And so I have them all prisoners while I range about as I please. Pretty dogs and doggesses, to quarrel and bark at me, and yet, whenever I appear, afraid to pop out of their kennels; or if out before they see me, at the sight of me run growling in again, with their flapped ears, their sweeping dewlaps, and their quivering tails curling inwards.

And here, while I am thus worthily waging war with beetles, drones, wasps, and hornets, and am all on fire with the rage of slighted love, thou art regaling thyself with phlegm and rock-water, and art going on with thy reformation scheme, and thy exultations in my misfortunes!

The devil take thee for an insensible dough-baked varlet: I have no more patience with thee than with the lady; for thou knowest nothing either of love or friendship, but art as incapable of the one as unworthy of the other; else wouldst thou not rejoice as thou dost under the *grimace of pity* in my disappointments.

And thou art a pretty fellow, art thou not? to engage to transcribe for her some parts of my letters written to thee in confidence? Letters that thou shouldst sooner have parted with thy cursed tongue than have owned thou ever hadst received such: yet these are now to be communicated to *her*! But I charge thee, and woe be to thee if it be too late! that thou do not oblige her with a line of mine.

If thou *hast* done it, the least vengeance I will take is to break through *my* honour given to thee not to visit her, as thou wilt have broken through *thine* to me in communicating letters written under the seal of friendship.

I am now convinced, too sadly for my hopes, by her letter to my cousin Charlotte, that she is determined never to have me.

Unprecedented wickedness, she calls mine to her. But how does *she* know what the ardour of flaming love will stimulate? How does *she* know the requisite distinctions of the words she uses in this case?—To think the *worst*, and to be able to *make comparisons* in these *very* delicate situations, must she not be less delicate than I had imagined her to be?—But she has heard that the devil is black; and having a mind to make one of me, brays together in the mortar of her wild fancy twenty chimney-sweepers, in order to make one sootier than ordinary rise out of the dirty mass.

But what a whirlwind does she raise in my soul by her proud contempts of me! Never, never, was mortal man's pride so mortified. How does she sink me, even in my own eyes!—Her heart sincerely repulses me, she says, for my MEANNESS—Yet she intends to reap the benefit of what she calls so!—Curse upon her *haughtiness* and her *meanness* at the same time!—Her haughtiness to *me*, and her meanness to *her own relations*; more unworthy of kindred with her, than I can be, or I am *mean* indeed.

Yet who but must admire, who but must adore her?—Oh that cursed, cursed house! But for the women of that!—Then their damned potions! But for *those*, had her *unimpaired* intellects and the *majesty of her virtue* saved her, as once it did by her humble eloquence,[a] another time by her terrifying menaces against her own life.[b]

Yet in both these to find her power over me, and my love for her, and to hate, to despise, and to refuse me!—She might have done this with some show of justice had the last intended violation been perpetrated—but to go away conqueress and triumphant in every light!—Well may she despise me for suffering her to do so.

She left me *low* and *mean* indeed!—and the impression holds with her—I could

a   In the fire scene, pp. 725 ff.
b   In the penknife scene, pp. 949 ff.

tear my flesh that I gave her not cause—that I humbled her not *indeed*—or that I stayed not in town till I could have exalted myself by giving myself a wife superior to all trial, to all temptation.

I will venture one more letter to her, however; and if that don't do, or procure me an answer, then will I endeavour to see her, let what *will* be the consequence. If she get out of my way, I will do some noble mischief to the vixen girl whom she most loves, and then quit the kingdom for ever.

And now, Jack, since thy hand is in at communicating the contents of private letters, tell her this if thou wilt. And add to it, that if SHE abandon me, GOD will; and it is no matter *then* what becomes of

Her LOVELACE!

Letter 396: MR LOVELACE TO JOHN BELFORD, ESQ.

(In answer to his of Friday night, August 4, Letter 391)

Monday, Aug. 7

AND so you have actually delivered to the fair implacable extracts of letters written in the confidence of friendship! Take care—take care, Belford—I do indeed love you better than I love any man in the world: but this is a very delicate point. The matter is grown very serious to me. My heart is bent upon having her. And have her I will, though I marry her in the agonies of death.

She is very earnest, you say, that I will not offer to molest her. *That*, let me tell her, will absolutely depend upon herself and the answer she returns, whether by pen and ink, or the contemptuous one of silence which she bestowed upon my last four to her: and I will write it in such humble and in such reasonable terms, that if she is not a true Harlowe she *shall* forgive me. But as to the *executorship* she is for conferring upon thee—thou shalt not be her *executor*. Let me perish if thou shalt—Nor shall she die. Nobody shall be anything, nobody shall *dare* to be anything to her, but me—Thy happiness is already too great, to be admitted daily to her presence; to look upon her, to talk to her, to hear her talk, while I am forbid to come within view of her window—What a reprobation is this, of the man who was once more dear to her than all the men in the world!—And now to be able to look down upon me, while her exalted head is hid from me among the stars, sometimes with low scorn, at other times with abject pity, I cannot bear it.

This I tell thee, that if I have not success in my effort by letter, I will overcome the creeping folly that has found its way to my heart, or I will tear it out in her presence and throw it at hers, that she may see how much more tender than her own that organ is, which she and you and everyone else have taken the liberty to call callous.

Give notice to the people who live back and edge, and on either hand of the cursed mother, to remove their best effects if I am rejected: for the first vengeance I shall take will be to set fire to that den of serpents. Nor will there be any fear of taking them when they are in any act that has *the relish of salvation in it*, as Shakespeare says[1]—so that my revenge, if they perish in the flames I shall light up, will be complete as to them.

Letter 397: MR LOVELACE TO MISS CLARISSA HARLOWE

Monday, Aug. 7

LITTLE as I have reason to expect either your patient ear or forgiving heart, yet cannot I forbear to write to you once more (as a more pardonable intrusion perhaps than a visit would be), to beg of you to put it in my power to atone, as far as it is possible to atone for the injuries I have done you.

Your angelic purity, and my awakened conscience, are standing records of your exalted merit and of my detestable baseness: but your forgiveness will lay me under an eternal obligation to you—Forgive me then, my dearest life, my earthly good, the visible anchor of my future hope! As you (who believe you have something to be forgiven for) hope for pardon yourself, forgive me and consent to meet me upon your own conditions, and in whose company you please, at the holy altar, and to give yourself a title to the most repentant and affectionate heart that ever beat in a human bosom.

But perhaps a time of probation may be required. It may be impossible for you, as well from indisposition as doubt, so soon to receive me to absolute favour as my heart wishes to be received. In this case, I will submit to your pleasure; and there shall be no penance which you can impose that I will not cheerfully undergo, if you will be pleased to give me hope that after an expiation, suppose of months wherein the regularity of my future life and actions shall convince you of my reformation, you will at last be mine.

Let me beg the favour then of a few lines encouraging me in this *conditional* hope, if it must not be a still *nearer* hope, and a more generous encouragement.

If you refuse me this, you will make me desperate. But even then I must, at all events, throw myself at your feet that I may not charge myself with the omission of any earnest, any humble effort, to move you in my favour: for in YOU, madam, in YOUR *forgiveness*, are centred my hopes as to *both worlds:* since to be reprobated finally by *you* will leave me without expectation of mercy from *above!*—For I am now awakened enough to think that to be forgiven by injured innocents is *necessary* to the Divine pardon; the Almighty putting into the power of such (as is reasonable to believe) the wretch who causelessly and capitally offends them. And *who* can be entitled to this power if YOU are not?

Your cause, madam, in a word, I look upon to be the *cause of virtue*, and, as such, the *cause of God*. And may I not expect that He will assert it in the perdition of a man who has acted by a person of the most spotless purity, as I have done, if *you*, by rejecting me, show that I have offended beyond the possibility of forgiveness?

I do most solemnly assure you that no temporal or worldly views induce me to this earnest address. I deserve not forgiveness from *you*. Nor do my Lord M. and his sisters from *me*. I despise them from my heart for presuming to imagine that I will be controlled by the prospect of any benefits in their power to confer. There is not a person breathing but yourself, who shall prescribe to me. Your whole conduct, madam, has been so nobly principled and your resentments are so admirably just, that you appear to me even in a divine light; and in an infinitely more amiable one at the same time than you could have appeared in had you not suffered the barbarous wrongs that now fill my mind with anguish and horror at my own recollected villainy to the most excellent of women.

I *repeat* that all I beg for the present is a few lines to guide my doubtful steps; and (if possible for you so far to condescend) to encourage me to hope that, if I can justify my present vows by my future conduct, I may be permitted the honour to style myself

Eternally yours,
R. Lovelace

Letter 398: MISS CLARISSA HARLOWE TO LORD M. AND TO THE LADIES OF HIS HOUSE

(In reply to Miss Montague's of Monday, August 7, Letter 394)

Tuesday, Aug. 8

EXCUSE me, my good lord, and my ever-honoured ladies, from accepting of your noble quarterly bounty; and allow me to return with all grateful acknowledgement and true humility, the enclosed earnest of your goodness to me. Indeed I have no need of the one, and cannot possibly want the other: but, nevertheless, have such a sense of your generous favour that, to my last hour, I shall have pleasure in contemplating upon it, and be proud of the place I hold in the esteem of such venerable personages, to whom I once had the ambition to hope to be related.

But give me leave to express my concern that you have banished your kinsman from your presence and favour: since now, perhaps, he will be under less restraint than ever; and since I in particular, who had hoped by your influences to remain unmolested for the remainder of my days, may be again subjected to his persecutions.

He has not, my good lord and my dear ladies, offended against *you*, as he has against *me*; and yet you could all very generously intercede for him with *me*: and shall I be *very* improper, if I desire for my own peace-sake; for the sake of other poor creatures who may be still injured by him if he be made quite desperate; and for the sake of all your worthy family; that you will extend to *him* that forgiveness which you hoped for from *me*? and this the rather as I presume to think that his daring and impetuous spirit will not be subdued by violent methods; since I have no doubt that the gratifying of a present passion will be always more prevalent with him than any future prospects, however unwarrantable the one, or beneficial the other.

Your resentments on my account are extremely generous, as your goodness to me is truly noble: but I am not without hope that he will be properly affected by the evils he has made me suffer; and that when I am laid low and forgotten, your whole honourable family will be enabled to rejoice in his reformation; and see many of those happy years together which, my good lord and my dear ladies, you so kindly wish to

Your ever-grateful and obliged
CLARISSA HARLOWE

Letter 399: MR BELFORD TO ROBERT LOVELACE, ESQ.

Thursday night, Aug. 10

You have been informed by Tourville how much Belton's illness and affairs have engaged *me*, as well as Mowbray and him, since my former. I called at Smith's on Monday, in my way to Epsom.

The lady was gone to chapel: but I had the satisfaction to hear she was not worse; and left my compliments, and an intimation that I should be out of town for three or four days.

I refer myself to Tourville, who will let you know the difficulty we had to drive out this *meek* mistress and *frugal* manager, with her cubs, and to give the poor fellow's sister possession for him of his own house; he skulking meanwhile at an inn at Croydon, too dispirited to appear in his own cause.

But I must observe that we were probably but just in time to save the shattered remains of his fortune from this rapacious woman and her accomplices: for, as he cannot live long, and she thinks so, we found she had certainly taken measures to set up a marriage, and keep possession of all for herself and her sons.

Tourville will tell you how I was forced to chastise the quondam hostler in her sight, before I could drive him out of the house. He had the insolence to lay hands on me: and I made him take but one step from the top to the bottom of a pair of stairs. I thought his neck and all his bones had been broken. And then, he being carried out neck-and-heels, Thomasine thought fit to walk out after him.

Charming consequences of *keeping*; the state we have been so fond of extolling!— Whatever it may be in strong health, *sickness* and *declining spirits* in the keeper will let him see the difference.

She should soon have him, she told a confident, in the space of six foot by five; meaning his bed: and then she would let nobody come near him but whom she pleased. The hostler fellow, I suppose, would then have been his physician; his will ready made for him—and widow's weeds probably ready provided; who knows but [she] to appear in them in his own sight; as once I knew an instance in a wicked wife insulting a husband she hated, when she thought him past recovery: though it gave the man such spirits, and such a turn, that he got over it and lived to see her in her coffin, dressed out in the very weeds she had insulted him in.

So much, for the present, for Belton and his Thomasine.

I BEGIN to pity thee heartily, now I see thee in earnest in the fruitless love thou expressest to this angel of a lady; and the rather as, say what thou wilt, it is impossible she should get over her illness, and her friends implacableness, of which she has had fresh instances.

I hope thou art not indeed displeased with the extracts I have made from thy letters for her. The letting her know the justice thou hast done to her virtue in them is so much in favour of thy [ingenuousness], that I think in my heart I was right; though to any other woman, and to one who had not known the worst of thee that she could know, it might have been wrong.

If the end will justify the means, it is plain that I have done well with regard to you both; since I have made *her* easier, and *you* appear in a better light to her than otherwise you would have done.

But if, nevertheless, you are dissatisfied with my having obliged her in a point which I acknowledge to be delicate, let us canvass this matter at our first meeting: and then I will show you what the extracts *were*, and what connexions I gave them in your favour.

But surely thou dost not pretend to say what I shall, or shall not do, as to the executorship.

I am my own man, I hope. I think thou shouldst be glad to have the justification of her memory left to one who at the same time, thou mayest be assured, will treat thee and thy actions with all the lenity the case will admit.

I cannot help expressing my surprise at one instance of thy self-partiality; and that is where thou sayest she had need, indeed, to cry out for mercy herself from *her* friends, who knows not how to show any!

Surely thou canst not think the cases alike!—For she, as I understand, desires but a last blessing and a last forgiveness, for a fault in a manner *involuntary* if a fault at all; and *hopes* not to be *received:* thou, to be forgiven *premeditated* wrongs (which, nevertheless, she forgives, on condition to be no more molested by thee); and hopest to be *received into favour*, and to make the finest jewel in the world thy absolute property in consequence of that forgiveness.

I will now briefly proceed to relate what has passed since my last, as to the poor lady; by which thou wilt see she has troubles enough upon her, all springing originally from thee, without thy needing to add more to them by new vexations. And as long as thou canst exert thyself so very cavalierly at M. Hall, where everyone is thy prisoner, I see not but the bravery of thy spirit may be as well gratified in domineering there over half a dozen persons of rank and distinction, as it could be over a helpless orphan, as I may call this lady, since she has not a single friend to stand by her, if I do not; and who will think herself happy if she can refuge herself from thee, and from all the world, in the arms of death.

My last was dated on Saturday.

On Sunday, in compliance with her doctor's advice, she took a little airing. Mrs Lovick, and Mr Smith and his wife, were with her. After being at Highgate Chapel at divine service, she treated them with a little repast; and in the afternoon was at Islington Church, in her way home; returning tolerably cheerful.

She had received several letters in my absence, as Mrs Lovick acquainted me, besides yours. Yours, it seems, much distressed her; but she ordered the messenger, who pressed for an answer, to be told that it did not require an immediate one.

On Wednesday she received a letter from her uncle Harlowe,[a] in answer to one she had written to her mother on Saturday on her knees. It must be a very cruel one, Mrs Lovick says, by the effects it had upon her: for, when she received it, she was intending to take an afternoon airing in a coach; but was thrown into so violent a fit of hysterics upon it, that she was forced to lie down; and (being not recovered thereby) to go to bed about eight o'clock.

On Thursday morning she was up very early; and had recourse to the Scriptures to calm her mind, as she told Mrs Lovick: and, weak as she was, would go in a chair to Lincoln's Inn Chapel about eleven. She was brought home a little better; and then sat down to write to her uncle. But was obliged to leave off several times—to struggle, as she told Mrs Lovick, for a humble temper. 'My heart, said

a See Letter 402.

she to the good woman, is a proud heart, and not yet I find enough mortified to my condition; but, do what I can, will be for prescribing resenting things to my pen.'

I arrived in town from Belton's this Thursday evening; and went directly to Smith's. She was too ill to receive my visit. But on sending up my compliments, she sent me down word that she should be glad to see me in the morning.

Mrs Lovick obliged me with the copy of a meditation collected by the lady from the Scriptures. She has entitled it, *Poor mortals the cause of their own misery*; so entitled, I presume, with intention to take off the edge of her repinings at hardships so disproportioned to her fault, were her fault even as great as she is inclined to think it. We may see by this, the method she takes to fortify her mind, and to which she owes in a great measure the magnanimity with which she bears her undeserved persecutions.

MEDITATION
Poor mortals the cause of their own misery.

SAY not thou, It is through the Lord that I fell away; for thou oughtest not to do the thing that He hateth.

Say not thou, He hath caused me to err; for He hath no need of the sinful man.

He Himself made man from the beginning, and left him in the hand of his own counsel;

If thou wilt, to keep the Commandments, and to perform acceptable faithfulness.

He hath set fire and water before thee: stretch forth thine hand to whether thou wilt.

He hath commanded no man to do wickedly; neither hath He given any man licence to sin.

And now, Lord, what is my hope? Truly my hope is *only* in Thee.

Deliver me from all my offences; and make me not a rebuke unto the foolish.

When Thou with rebuke dost chasten man for sin, Thou makest his beauty to consume away, like as it were a moth fretting a garment: every man therefore is vanity.

Turn Thee unto me, and have mercy upon me; for I am desolate and afflicted.

The troubles of my heart are enlarged. Oh bring thou me out of my distresses!

MRs Smith gave me the following particulars of a conversation that passed between herself and a young clergyman on Tuesday afternoon, who, as it appears, was employed to make inquiries about the lady by her friends.

He came into the shop in a riding-habit, and asked for some Spanish snuff; and finding only herself there, he desired to have a little talk with her in the back shop.

He beat about the bush in several distant questions, and at last began to talk more directly about Miss Harlowe.

He said he knew her before her *fall* (that was his impudent word); and gave the substance of the following account of her, as I collected it from Mrs Smith.

'She was then, he said, the admiration and delight of everybody: he lamented with great solemnity her *backsliding*; another of his phrases. Mrs Smith said he was a fine scholar; for he spoke several things she understood not; and either in Latin or Greek, she could not tell which; but was so good as to give her the English of them without asking. A fine thing, she said, for a scholar to be so condescending!'

He said, 'Her going off with so vile a rake had given great scandal and offence to all the neighbouring ladies, as well as to her friends.'

He told Mrs Smith 'how much she used to be followed by everyone's eye whenever she went abroad or to church, and praised and blessed by every tongue as she passed; especially by the poor: that she gave the fashion to the fashionable, without seeming herself to intend it, or to know she did: that, however, it was pleasant to see ladies imitate her in dress and behaviour who, being unable to come up to her in grace and ease, exposed but their own affectation and awkwardness, at the time that they thought themselves secure of a general approbation because they wore the same things, and put them on in the same manner that *she* did, who had everybody's admiration; little considering, that were *her* person like *theirs*, or if she had had *their* defects, she would have brought up a very different fashion; for that *nature* was her guide in everything, and *ease* her study; which, joined with a mingled dignity and condescension in her air and manner, whether she received or paid a compliment, distinguished her above all her sex.

'He spoke not, he said, his own sentiments only on this occasion, but those of everybody: for that the praises of Miss Clarissa Harlowe were such a favourite topic, that a person who could not speak well upon any other subject was sure to speak well upon that; because he could say nothing but what he had heard repeated and applauded twenty times over.'

Hence it was, perhaps, that this gentleman accounted for the best things that he said himself; though I must own that the personal knowledge of the lady which I am favoured with, made it easy to me to lick into shape what the good woman reported to me, as the character given her by the young Levite: for who even now, in her decline of health, sees not that all these attributes belong to her?

I suppose he has not been long come from college, and now thinks he has nothing to do but to blaze away for a scholar among the *ignorant*; as such young fellows are apt to think those who cannot cap verses with them, and tell us how an ancient author expressed himself in Latin on a point which, however, they may know how as well as that author, to express in English.

Mrs Smith was so taken with him that she would fain have introduced him to the lady, not questioning but it would be very acceptable to her to see one who knew her and her friends so well. But this he declined for several reasons, which he gave. One was that persons of his cloth should be very cautious of the *company they were in*, especially where *sex* was concerned, and where a lady had *slurred her reputation*—(I wish I had been there when he gave himself these airs.) Another, that he was desired to inform himself of her present way of life and who her visitors were; for, as to the praises Mrs Smith gave the lady, he hinted that *she* seemed to be a good-natured woman, and might (though for the lady's sake he hoped not) be too partial and short-sighted to be trusted to absolutely, in a concern of so high a nature as he intimated the task was which he had undertaken; nodding out words of doubtful import, and assuming airs of great significance (as I could gather), throughout the whole conversation. And when Mrs Smith told him that the lady was in a very bad state of health, he gave a careless shrug—She may be very ill, says he: her disappointments must have touched her to the quick: but she is not bad enough, I dare say, yet, to atone for her very great lapse, and to expect to be forgiven by those whom she has so much disgraced.

A starched conceited novice! What would I give he had fallen in my way?

He went away highly satisfied with himself, no doubt, and assured of Mrs Smith's great opinion of his sagacity and learning: but bid her not say anything to the lady about him, or his inquiries. And I, for very different reasons, enjoined the same thing.

I am glad, however, for her peace of mind's sake, that they begin to think it behoves them to inquire about her.

Letter 400: MR BELFORD TO ROBERT LOVELACE, ESQ.

Friday, Aug. 11

Mr Belford acquaints his friend with the generosity of Lord M. and the ladies of his family; and with the lady's grateful sentiments upon the occasion.

He says that in hopes to avoid the pain of seeing him, she intends to answer his letter of the 7th, though much against her inclination. 'She took great notice, *says Mr Belford,* of that passage in yours which makes necessary to the *Divine* pardon, the forgiveness of a person causelessly injured.

'Her grandfather, I find, has enabled her at eighteen years of age to make her will, and to devise great part of his estate to whom she pleases of the family, and the rest out of it (if she die single) at her own discretion; and this to create respect to her; as he apprehended that she would be envied: and she now resolves to set about making her will out of hand.'

Mr Belford insists upon the promise he had made him, not to molest the lady: and gives him the contents of her answer to Lord M. and the ladies, declining their generous offers. See Letter 398.

Letter 401: MISS CLARISSA HARLOWE TO ROBERT LOVELACE, ESQ.

Friday, Aug. 11

'Tis a cruel alternative to be either forced to see you or to write to you. But a will of my own has been long denied me; and to avoid a greater evil, nay, now I may say the greatest, I write.

Were I capable of disguising or concealing my real sentiments, I might safely I dare say give you the remote hope you request, and yet keep all my resolutions. But I must tell you, sir; it becomes my character to tell you; that were I to live more years than perhaps I may weeks, and there were not another man in the world, I could not, I would not, be yours.

There is no *merit* in performing a *duty*.

Religion enjoins me not only to forgive injuries, but to return good for evil. It is all my consolation, and I bless God for giving me that, that I am now in such a state of mind with regard to you, that I can cheerfully obey its dictates. And accordingly I tell you that wherever you go, I wish you happy. And in this I mean to include every good wish.

And now having, with great reluctance I own, complied with one of your compulsatory alternatives, I expect the fruits of it.

CLARISSA HARLOWE

Letter 402: MR JOHN HARLOWE TO MISS CLARISSA HARLOWE

Monday, Aug. 7

Poor ungrateful, naughty kinswoman,

YOUR mother neither caring, nor being *permitted* to write, I am desired to set pen to paper though I had resolved against it.

And so I am to tell you that your letters, joined to the occasion of them, almost break the hearts of us all.

Were we sure you had seen your folly, and were *truly* penitent, and at the same time that you were so very ill as you intimate, I know not what might be done for you. But we are all acquainted with your moving ways when you want to carry a point.

Unhappy girl! how miserable have you made us all! We, who used to visit with so much pleasure, now cannot endure to look upon one another.

If you had not known upon an hundred occasions how dear you once was to us, you might judge of it now, were you to know how much your folly has unhinged us all.

Naughty, naughty girl! You see the fruits of preferring a rake and libertine to a man of sobriety and morals. Against full warning, against better knowledge. And such a modest creature too, as you was! How could you think of such an unworthy preference?

Your mother *can't* ask, and your sister knows not in modesty *how* to ask; and so *I* ask you, if you have any reason to think yourself with child by this villain?— You *must* answer this, and answer it truly, before any thing can be resolved upon about you.

You may well be touched with a deep remorse for your misdeeds. Could I ever have thought that my doting-piece, as everyone called you, would have done thus? To be sure I loved you too well. But that is over now. Yet, though I will not pretend to answer for anybody but myself, for my own part I say, God forgive you! And this is all from

Your afflicted uncle,
JOHN HARLOWE

The following MEDITATION *was stitched to the bottom of this letter with black silk.*

MEDITATION

Oh that Thou wouldst hide me in the grave! That Thou wouldst keep me secret, till Thy wrath be past!

My face is foul with weeping: and on my eyelid is the shadow of death.

My friends scorn me; but mine eye poureth out tears unto God.

A dreadful sound is in my ears; in prosperity the destroyer came upon me!

I have sinned! What shall I do unto Thee, O thou Preserver of men! Why hast Thou set me as a mark against Thee; so that I am a burden to myself!

When I say, My bed shall comfort me; My couch shall ease my complaint;

Then Thou scarest me with dreams, and terrifiest me through visions.

So that my soul chooseth strangling, and death rather than life.

I loathe it! I would not live alway!—Let me alone; for my days are vanity!

He hath made me a byword of the people; and aforetime I was as a tabret.

My days are past, my purposes are broken off, even the thoughts of my heart.

When I looked for good, then evil came unto me; and when I waited for light, then came darkness.

And where now is my hope?—

Yet all the days of my appointed time will I wait, till my change come.

Letter 403: MISS CLARISSA HARLOWE TO JOHN HARLOWE, ESQ.

Thursday, Aug. 10

Honoured sir,

IT was an act of charity I begged: only for a last blessing, that I might die in peace. I ask not to be received again, as my severe sister (Oh! that I had not written to her!) is pleased to say is my view. Let that grace be denied me when I do!

I could not look forward to my last scene with comfort, without seeking, at least, to obtain the blessing I petitioned for; and that with a contrition so deep, that I deserved not, were it known, to be turned over from the tender nature of a mother to the upbraiding pen of an uncle; and to be wounded by a cruel question, put by him in a shocking manner; and which a little, a very little time, will better answer than I can: for I am not either a hardened or shameless creature: if I were, I should not have been so solicitous to obtain the favour I sued for.

And permit me to say that I asked it as well for my father and mother's sake, as for my own; for I am sure *they* at least will be uneasy, after I am gone, that they refused it to me.

I should still be glad to have theirs, and yours sir, and all your blessings and your prayers: but, denied in such a manner, I will not presume again to ask it: relying entirely on the Almighty's; which is never denied when supplicated for with such true penitence as I hope mine is.

God preserve my dear uncle, and all my honoured friends! prays

Your unhappy
CLARISSA HARLOWE

Letter 404: MISS ANNA HOWE TO MISS CLARISSA HARLOWE

Yarmouth, Isle of Wight, Monday, Aug. 7

My dearest creature,

I CAN write just now but a few lines. I cannot tell how to bear the *sound* of that Mr Belford for your executor, cogent as your reasons for that measure are: and yet I am firmly of opinion that none of your relations should be named for the trust. But I dwell the less upon this subject, as I hope (and cannot bear to apprehend the contrary) that you will still live many, many years.

Mr Hickman, indeed, speaks very handsomely of Mr Belford. But he, poor man! has not much penetration. If he had, he would hardly think so well of *me* as he does.

I have a particular opportunity of sending this by a friend of my aunt Harman's; who is ready to set out for London (and this occasions my hurry), and is to return out of hand. I expect therefore by him a large packet from you; and hope and long for news of your amended health: which Heaven grant to the prayers of

Your ever-affectionate
ANNA HOWE

Letter 405: MISS CLARISSA HARLOWE TO MISS HOWE

Friday, Aug. 11

I WILL send you a large packet, as you desire and expect; since I can do it by so safe a conveyance: but not all that is come to my hand—for I must own that my friends are very severe; too severe for anybody who loves them not, to see their letters. You, my dear, would not call them my *friends*, you said long ago; but my *relations:* indeed I cannot call them my *relations*, I think!—But I am ill; and therefore perhaps more peevish than I should be. It is difficult to go out of ourselves to give a judgement against ourselves; and yet oftentimes to pass a *just* judgement, we ought.

I thought I should alarm you in the choice of my executor. But the sad necessity I am reduced to must excuse me.

I shall not repeat anything I have said before on that subject: but if your objections will not be answered to your satisfaction by the papers and letters I shall enclose, marked 1, 2, 3, 4, to 9, I must think myself in another instance unhappy; since I am engaged too far (and with my own judgement too) to recede.

As I have the accompanying transcripts from Mr Belford in confidence from his friend's letters to him, I must insist that you suffer no soul but yourself to peruse them; and that you return them by the very first opportunity; that so no use may be made of them that may do hurt either to the original writer, or to the communicator. You'll observe I am bound by promise to this care. If through *my* means any mischief should arise between this *humane* and that *inhuman* libertine, I should think myself utterly inexcusable.

I subjoin a list of the papers or letters I shall enclose. You must return them all when perused.*

I am very much tired and fatigued—with—I don't know what—with writing, I think—but most with myself, and with a situation I cannot help aspiring to get out of, and above!

Oh, my dear, 'tis a sad, a very sad world!—While under our parents' protecting wings, we know nothing at all of it. Book-learned and a scribbler, and looking at people as I saw them as visitors or visiting, I thought I knew a great deal of it. Pitiable ignorance!—Alas! I knew nothing at all!

With zealous wishes for your happiness, and the happiness of every one dear to you, I am, and will ever be,

Your gratefully affectionate
CL. HARLOWE

* 1. A letter from Miss Montague, dated Aug. 1
2. A copy of my answer. Aug. 3
3. Mr Belford's letter to me, which will show you what my request was to

him; and his compliance with it; and the desired extracts from his friend's
letters. Aug. 3, 4

4. A copy of my answer, with thanks; and requesting him to undertake the
executorship. Aug. 4
5. Mr Belford's acceptance of the trust. Aug. 4
6. Miss Montague's letter, with a generous offer from Lord M. and the ladies
of that family. Aug. 7
7. Mr Lovelace's to me. Aug. 7
8. Copy of mine to Miss Montague, in answer to hers of the day before.
Aug. 8
9. Copy of my answer to Mr Lovelace. Aug. 11

You will see by these several letters, written and received in so little a space of
time (to say nothing of what I have received and written, which I *cannot*
show you), how little opportunity or leisure I can have for writing my own
story.

Letter 406: MR ANTONY HARLOWE TO MISS CLARISSA HARLOWE

(In reply to hers to her uncle [John] Harlowe of Thursday, August 10, Letter 403)

Aug. 12

Unhappy girl!

As your uncle Harlowe chooses not to answer your pert letter to him; and as mine
written to you before[a] was written as if it were in the spirit of prophecy, as you
have found to your sorrow; and as you are now making yourself worse than you
are in your health, and better than you are in your penitence, *as we are very well
assured*, in order to move compassion; which you do not deserve, having had so
much warning: for all these reasons, I take up my pen once more; though I had
told your *brother, at his going to Edinburgh*, that I would not write to you, even
were you to write to me, without letting him know. So indeed *had we all*; for he
prognosticated what would happen, as to your applying to us when you knew not
how to help it.

Brother John has hurt your niceness, it seems, by asking you a plain question,
which your mother's heart is too full of grief to let her ask; and modesty will not
let your sister ask, though but the consequence of your actions—And yet it *must*
be answered before you'll obtain from your father and mother, and us, the notice
you hope for, I can tell you that.

You lived several guilty weeks with one of the vilest fellows that ever drew
breath, at bed as well as board no doubt (for is not his character known?); and
pray don't be ashamed to be asked after what may naturally come of such free
living. This modesty, indeed, would have become you for eighteen years of your
life—you'll be pleased to mark that—but makes no good figure compared with
your behaviour since the beginning of April last. So pray don't take it up, and
wipe your mouth upon it, as if nothing had happened.

But maybe I likewise am too shocking to your niceness!—Oh, girl, girl! your
modesty had better been shown at the right time and place!—Everybody but you

a   See Letter 32.4.

believed what the rake was: but you would believe nothing bad of him—What think you now?

Your folly has ruined all our peace. And who knows where it may yet end?— Your poor father but yesterday showed me this text: with bitter grief he showed it me, poor man! And do you lay it to your heart:

'A father waketh for his daughter when no man knoweth; and the care for her taketh away his sleep—When she is young, lest she pass away the flower of her age (*and you know what proposals were made to you at different times*): and, being married, lest she should be hated: in her virginity, lest she should be defiled, and gotten with child in her father's house (*I don't make the words, mind that*): and having an husband, lest she should misbehave herself.' *And what follows?* 'Keep a sure watch over a shameless daughter (*yet no watch could hold you!*), lest she make thee a laughing-stock to thine enemies (*as you have made us all to this cursed Lovelace*), and a byword in the city, and a reproach among the people, and make thee ashamed before the multitude.' *Eccl[esiastic]us* xlii. 9, 10, etc.

Now will you wish you had not written pertly. Your sister's severities!—Never, girl, say that is *severe* that is *deserved*. You know the meaning of words. Nobody better. Would to the Lord you had acted up but to one half of what you know. Then had we not been disappointed and grieved, as we all have been: and nobody more than him who was

Your loving uncle,
ANTONY HARLOWE

This will be with you tomorrow. Perhaps you may be suffered to have some part of your estate, after you have smarted a little more. Your pertly answered uncle John, who is your trustee, will not have you be destitute. But we hope all is not true *that we hear of you*—Only take care, I advise you, that bad as you have acted you act not still worse, if it be possible to act worse. *Improve upon the hint.*

Letter 407: MISS CLARISSA HARLOWE TO ANTONY HARLOWE, ESQ.

Sunday, Aug. 13

Honoured sir,

I AM very sorry for my pert letter to my uncle Harlowe. Yet I did not intend it to be pert. People *new* to misfortune may be too easily moved to impatience.

The fall of a regular person no doubt is dreadful and inexcusable. It is like the sin of apostasy. Would to Heaven, however, that I had had the circumstances of mine inquired into!

If, sir, I make myself worse than I am in my health, and better than I am in my penitence, it is fit I should be punished for my double dissimulation: and *you* have the pleasure of being one of my punishers. My sincerity in both respects will, however, be best justified by the event. To *that* I refer—May Heaven give you always as much comfort in reflecting upon the reprobation I have met with, as you seem to have pleasure in mortifying a poor creature, *extremely* mortified; and that from a *right* sense as she presumes to hope of her own fault!

What you have *heard of me* I cannot tell. When the nearest and dearest relations give up an unhappy wretch, it is not to be wondered at that those who are *not* related to her are ready to take up and propagate slanders against her. Yet I think I may defy calumny itself, and (excepting the fatal, though involuntary step of April 10) wrap myself in my own innocence and be easy. I thank you, sir, nevertheless, for your *caution*, mean it what it will.

As to the question required of me to answer, and which is allowed to be too shocking either for a mother to put to a daughter, or a sister to a sister; and which, however, *you* say, I *must* answer—Oh sir!—and *must* I answer?—This then be my answer: 'A *little* time, a much *less* time than is imagined, will afford a more satisfactory answer to my whole family, and even to my *brother* and *sister*, than I can give in words.'

Nevertheless, be pleased to let it be remembered that I did not petition for a restoration to favour. I could not hope for that. Nor yet to be put in possession of any part of my own estate. Nor even for means of necessary subsistence from the produce of that estate—But only for a blessing; for a *last* blessing!

And this I will further add, because it is *true*, that I have no wilful crime to charge against myself: no free living at bed and at board, as you phrase it!

Why, why, sir, were not other inquiries made of me, as well as this shocking one?—inquiries that modesty *would* have permitted a mother or a sister to make; and which, if I may be excused to say so, would have been still *less* improper and *more* charitable to have been made by *uncles* (were the mother *forbid*, or the sister *not inclined* to make them), than those they have made.

Although my humble application has brought upon me so much severe reproach, I repent not that I have written to my mamma (although I cannot but wish that I had not written to my sister); because I have satisfied a dutiful consciousness by it, however unanswered by the wished-for success. Nevertheless, I cannot help saying that mine is indeed a hard fate, that I cannot beg pardon for my capital error without doing it in such terms as shall be an aggravation of the offence.

But I had best leave off, lest, as my full mind I find is rising to my pen, I have other pardons to beg as I multiply lines, where none at all will be given.

God Almighty bless, preserve, and comfort my dear sorrowing and grievously offended father and mother!—And continue in honour, favour, and merit, my happy sister!—May God forgive my brother, and protect him from the violence of his own temper, as well as from the destroyer of his sister's honour!—And may you, my dear uncle, and your no less now than ever dear brother, my second papa, as he used to bid me call him, be blessed and happy in them all, and in each other!—And, in order to this, may you all speedily banish from your remembrance for ever

The unhappy
CLARISSA HARLOWE

Letter 408: MRS NORTON TO MISS CLARISSA HARLOWE

Monday, Aug. 14

ALL your friends here, my dear young lady, now seem set upon proposing to you to go to one of the plantations. This, I believe, is owing to some misrepresentations of Mr Brand; from whom they have received a letter.

I wish with all my heart that you could, consistently with your own notions of honour, yield to the pressing requests of all Mr Lovelace's family in his behalf. This, I think, would stop every mouth; and in time reconcile everybody to you. For your own friends will not believe that he is in earnest to marry you; and the hatred between the families is such, that they will not condescend to inform themselves better; nor would believe *him*, if he were ever so solemnly to avow that he is.

I should be very glad to have in readiness, upon occasion, some brief particulars of your sad story under your own hand. But let me tell you at the same time, that no misrepresentations, nor even your own confession, shall lessen my opinion, either of your piety or of your prudence in essential points; because I know it was always your humble way to make light faults heavy against yourself: and well might you, my dearest young lady, aggravate your own failings, who have ever had so few; and those few so slight that your ingenuity has turned most of them into excellencies.

Nevertheless, let me advise you, my dear Miss Clary, to discountenance any visits that may with the censorious affect your character. As *that* has not hitherto suffered by your *wilful* default, I hope you will not in a desponding negligence (satisfying yourself with a consciousness of your own innocence) permit it to suffer. Difficult situations, you know, my dear young lady, are the tests not only of prudence, but of virtue.

I think I must own to you that, since Mr Brand's letter has been received, I have a renewed prohibition to attend you. However, if you will give me leave, that shall not detain me from you. Nor would I stay for that leave, if I were not in hopes that, in this critical situation, I may be able to do you service here.

I have often had messages and inquiries after your health from the truly reverend Dr Lewen, who has always expressed, and still expresses, infinite concern for you. He entirely disapproves of the measures of the family with regard to you. He is too much indisposed to go abroad. But were he in good health, he would not, as I understand, visit at Harlowe Place; having been unhandsomely treated some time ago by your brother, on his offering to mediate between your family and you.

I AM just now informed that your cousin Morden is arrived in England. He is at Canterbury, it seems, looking after some concerns he has there; and is soon expected in these parts. Who knows what may arise from his arrival?—God be with you, my dearest Miss Clary, and be your comforter and sustainer. And never fear but He will; for I am sure, I am very sure, that you put your whole trust in Him.

And what, after all, is this world on which we so much depend for durable good, poor creatures that we are!—When all the joys of it, and (what is a balancing comfort) all the *troubles* of it, are but momentary, and vanish like a morning dream?

And be this remembered, my dearest young lady, that worldly joy claims no kindred with the joys we are bid to aspire after. These latter we must be fitted for by affliction and disappointment. You are therefore in the direct road to glory, however thorny the path you are in. And I had almost said that it depends upon yourself, by your patience and by your resignedness to the dispensation (God enabling you, who never fails the true penitent and sincere invoker), to be an heir of a blessed immortality.

But this glory I humbly pray that you may not be permitted to enter into, ripe as you are so soon likely to be for it, till with your gentle hand (a pleasure I have so often, as you know, promised to myself) you have closed the eyes of

Your maternally affectionate
JUDITH NORTON

Letter 409: MISS CLARISSA HARLOWE TO MRS NORTON

Thursday, Aug. 17

WHAT Mr Brand, or anybody, can have written or said to my prejudice, I cannot imagine; and yet some evil reports have gone out against me; as I find by some hints in a very severe letter written to me by my uncle Antony. Such a letter as I believe was never written to any poor creature, who by ill health of body as well as of mind was before tottering on the brink of the grave. But my friends may possibly be better justified than the reporters—for who knows what they may have heard?

You give me a kind caution, which seems to imply *more* than you express, when you advise me against countenancing of visitors that may discredit me. You should, in so tender a point, my dear Mrs Norton, have spoken quite out. Surely, I have had afflictions enow to make my mind fitted to bear anything. But I will not puzzle myself by *conjectural evils*. I *might*, if I had not enow that were *certain*. And I shall hear all when it is thought proper that I should. Meantime, let me say for *your* satisfaction, that I know not that I have anything criminal or disreputable to answer for either in word or deed, since the fatal 10th of April last.

You desire an account of what passes between me and my friends; and also particulars or brief heads of my sad story, in order to serve me as occasions shall offer. My dear good Mrs Norton, you shall have a whole packet of papers which I have sent to my Miss Howe, when she returns them; and you shall have, besides, another packet (and that with this letter), which I cannot at present think of sending to that dear friend, for the sake of my *own relations*; whom she is already but too eager to censure heavily. From these you will be able to collect a great deal of my story. But for what is previous to these papers, and which more particularly relates to what I have suffered from Mr Lovelace, you must have patience; for at present I have neither head nor heart for such subjects. The papers I send you with this will be those mentioned in the margin.* You must restore them to me, as soon as perused; and, upon your honour, make no use of any intelligence you have from me, but by my consent.

These communications you must not, my good Mrs Norton, look upon as appeals against my relations. On the contrary, I am heartily sorry that they have

*   1. A copy of mine to my sister, begging off my father's malediction, dated July 21.
    2. My sister's answer, dated July 27.
    3. Copy of my second letter to my sister, dated July 29.
    4. My sister's answer, dated Aug. 3.
    5. Copy of my letter to my mother, dated Aug. 5.
    6. My uncle Harlowe's letter, dated Aug. 7.
    7. Copy of my answer to it, dated the 10th.
    8. Letter from my uncle Antony, dated the 12th.
    9. And lastly, the copy of my answer to it, dated the 13th.

incurred the displeasure of so excellent a divine as Dr Lewen. But you desire to have everything before you; and I think you *ought*; for who knows, as you say, but you may be applied to at last, to administer comfort from their conceding hearts to one that wants it; and who sometimes, judging by what she knows of her own heart, thinks herself entitled to it?

I know that I have a most indulgent and sweet-tempered mother; but having to deal with violent spirits, she has too often forfeited that peace of mind which she so much prefers, by her over-concern to preserve it.

I am sure she would not have turned me over for an answer to a letter written with so contrite and fervent a spirit, as was mine to her, to a *manly* spirit, had she been left to herself.

But, my dear Mrs Norton, might not, think you, the revered lady have favoured me with one *private* line?—If not, might not she have permitted *you* to have written by her order, or connivance, one softening, one *motherly* line, when she saw her poor girl borne so hard upon?

Oh no, she might not!—because her heart, to be sure, is in their measures!—and if *she* think them right, perhaps they *must be right!*—at least knowing only what *they* know!—and yet they *might* know all, if they would!—and possibly in their own good time, they think to make proper inquiry—My application was made to them but *lately*—yet how grievous will it be to their hearts, if *their* time should be *out of time!*

By the letters I have sent to Miss Howe, you will see when you have them before you, that Lord M. and the ladies of his family, jealous as they are of the honour of *their house* (to express myself in their language), think better of me than my own relations do. You will see an instance of their generosity to me, which has extremely affected me.

Some of the letters in the same packet will also let you into the knowledge of a strange step which I have taken (strange you will think it); and, at the same time, give you my reasons for it.[a]

It must be expected that situations uncommonly difficult will make necessary some extraordinary steps, which but for those situations would be hardly excusable. It will be very happy indeed, and somewhat wonderful, if all the measures I have been driven to take should be right. A pure intention, void of all undutiful resentment, is what must be my consolation, whatever others may think of those measures when they come to know them: which, however, will hardly be till it is out of my power to justify them or to answer for myself.

I am glad to hear of my cousin Morden's safe arrival. I should wish to see him methinks: but I am afraid that he will sail with the stream; as it must be expected that he will hear what they have to say first—But what I most fear is that he will take upon himself to avenge me—Rather than this should happen, I would have him look upon me as a creature utterly unworthy of his concern; at least of his *vindictive* concern.

How soothing to the wounded heart of your Clarissa, how balmy, are the assurances of your continued love and favour!—Love me, my dear mamma Norton, continue to love me to the end!—I now think that I may, without presumption, promise to *deserve* your love to the end. And when I am gone, cherish my memory

a　She means that of making Mr Belford her executor.

in your worthy heart; for in so doing you will cherish the memory of one who loves and honours you more than she can express.

But when I am no more, get over, I charge you, as soon as you can, the smarting pangs of grief that will attend a recent loss; and let all be early turned into that sweetly melancholy regard to MEMORY, which, engaging us to forget all faults and to remember nothing but what was thought amiable, gives more pleasure than pain to survivors—especially if they can comfort themselves with the humble hope that the Divine mercy has taken the dear departed to itself.

And what is the space of time to look backward upon, between an early departure and the longest survivance?—And what the consolation attending the sweet hope of meeting again, never more to be separated, never more to be pained, grieved, or aspersed!—But mutually blessing, and being blessed, to all eternity!

In the contemplation of this happy state, in which I hope in God's good time to rejoice with you, my beloved Mrs Norton, and also with my dear relations, all reconciled to, and blessing, the child against whom they are now so much incensed, I conclude myself

Your ever dutiful and affectionate
CLARISSA HARLOWE

Letter 410: MR LOVELACE TO JOHN BELFORD, ESQ.

Sunday, Aug. 13

I DON'T know what a devil ails me; but I never was so much indisposed in my life. At first I thought some of my blessed relations here had got a dose administered to me, in order to get the whole house to themselves. But as I am the hopes of the family, I believe they would not be so wicked.

I must lay down my pen. I cannot write with any spirit at all. What a plague can be the matter with me!

LORD M. paid me just now a cursed gloomy visit, to ask how I do after bleeding. His sisters both drove away yesterday, God be thanked. But they asked not my leave; had hardly bid me good-bye. My lord was more tender and more dutiful than I expected. Men are less unforgiving than women. I have reason to say so, I am sure. For, besides implacable Miss Harlowe and the old ladies, the two Montague apes han't been near me yet.

NEITHER eat, drink, nor sleep!—A piteous case, Jack! If I should die like a fool now, people would say Miss Harlowe had broke my heart—That she *vexes* me to the heart is certain.

Confounded squeamish! I would fain write it off. But must lay down my pen again. It won't do. Poor Lovelace!—What a devil ails thee?

WELL, but now let's try for't—Hoy—hoy—hoy! Confound me for a gaping puppy, how I yawn!—Where shall I begin? At thy executorship?—Thou shalt have a double office of it: for I really think thou mayest send me a coffin and a shroud. I shall be ready for them by the time they can come down.

What a little fool is this Miss Harlowe! I warrant she'll now repent that she refused me. Such a lovely young widow—what a charming widow would she have made! How would she have adorned the weeds! To be a widow in the first twelvemonth is one of the greatest felicities that can befall a fine lady. Such pretty employment in *new dismals* when she had hardly worn round her *blazing joyfuls!* Such lights and such shades! how would they set off one another and be adorned by the wearer!—

Go to the devil!—I *will* write!—Can I do anything else?

They would not have me write, Belford—I must be ill indeed when I can't write—

BUT thou seemest nettled, Jack! Is it because I was stung? It is not for two friends, any more than for man and wife, to be out of patience at one time—What must be the consequence, if they are?—I am in no fighting mood just now: but as patient and passive as the chickens that are brought me in broth—for I am come to that already.

But I can tell thee, for all this, be *thy own man*, if thou wilt, as to the executorship, I will never suffer thee to expose my letters. They are too ingenuous by half to be seen. And I absolutely insist upon it that, on receipt of this, thou burn them all.

I will never forgive thee that impudent and unfriendly reflection of my *cavaliering* it here over half a dozen persons of distinction: remember, too, thy poor *helpless orphan*—these reflections are too serious; and thou art also too serious for me to let these things go off as jesting; notwithstanding the Roman style is preserved; and, indeed, but just preserved. By my soul, Jack, if I had not been taken thus egregiously cropsick, I would have been up with thee, and the lady too, before now.

But write on, however: and send me copies, if thou canst, of all that passes between our Charlotte and Miss Harlowe. I'll take no notice of what thou communicatest of that sort. I like not the people here the worse for their generous offer to the lady. But you see she is as proud as implacable. There's no obliging her. She'd rather sell her clothes than be beholden to anybody, although she would oblige by permitting the obligation.

Oh Lord! Oh Lord!—Mortal ill—Adieu, Jack!

I WAS forced to leave off, I was so ill, at this place. And what dost think? My uncle brought the parson of the parish to pray by me; for his chaplain is at Oxford. I was lain down in my night-gown over my waistcoat, and in a doze: and when I opened my eyes, who should I see, but the parson kneeling on one side the bed; Lord M. on the other; Mrs Greme, who had been sent for to *tend me*, as they call it, at the feet: God be thanked, my lord, said I in an ecstasy!—Where's miss?—For I thought they were going to marry me.

They thought me delirious at first, and prayed louder and louder.

This roused me: off the bed I started; slid my feet into my slippers; put my hand in my waistcoat pocket, and pulled out thy letter with my beloved's meditations in it: my lord, Dr Wright, Mrs Greme, you have thought me a very wicked fellow: but, see! I can read you as good as you can read me.

They stared at one another. I gaped, and read, Poor mo-or-tals the cau-o-ause of their own—their own mis-ser-ry.

It is as suitable to my case as to the lady's, as thou'lt observe if thou readest it again.[a] At the passage where it is said That when a man is chastened for sin, his beauty consumes away, I stepped to the glass: A poor figure, by Jupiter, cried I!— And they all praised and admired me; lifted up their hands and their eyes; and the doctor said he always thought it impossible that a man of my sense could be so wild as the world said I was. My lord chuckled for joy; congratulated me; and, thank my dear Miss Harlowe, I got high reputation among good, bad, and indifferent. In short, I have established myself for ever with all here—But oh Belford, even this will not do!—I must leave off again.

A VISIT from the Montague sisters, led in by my hobbling uncle, to congratulate my amendment and reformation both in one. What a lucky event this illness, with this meditation in my pocket; for we were all to pieces before! Thus, when a boy, have I joined with a crowd coming out of church, and have been thought to have been there myself.

I am incensed at the insolence of the young Levite. Thou wilt highly oblige me, if thou'lt find him out and send me his ears in the next letter.

My charmer mistakes me if she thinks I proposed her writing to me as an alternative that should dispense with my attendance upon her. That it shall *not* do, nor did I intend it should, unless she had pleased me better in the contents of it than she has done. Bid her read again. I gave no such hopes. I would have been with her in spite of you both, by tomorrow at farthest, had I not been laid by the heels thus, like a helpless miscreant.

But I grow better and better every hour, *I* say: the *doctor* says not: but I am sure I know best: and I will soon be in London, depend on't. But say nothing of this to my dear, cruel, and implacable Miss Harlowe.

A–dieu–u, Ja–aack—What a gaping puppy (yaw–n! yaw–n! yaw–n!).

                                                                    Thy LOVELACE

Letter 411: MR BELFORD TO ROBERT LOVELACE, ESQ.

                                                                    Monday, Aug. 14

I AM extremely concerned for thy illness. I should be very sorry to lose thee. Yet if thou diest so soon, I could wish from my soul it had been before the beginning of last April: and this as well for thy sake as for the sake of the most excellent woman in the world: for then thou wouldst not have had the most crying sin of thy life to answer for.

I was told on Saturday that thou wert very much out of order; and this made me forbear writing till I heard further. Harry, on his return from thee, confirmed the bad way thou art in. But I hope Lord M. in his unmerited tenderness for thee thinks the worst of thee. What can it be, Bob? A violent fever, they say; but attended with odd and severe symptoms.

I will not trouble thee, in the way thou art in, with what passes here with Miss Harlowe. I wish thy repentance as swift as thy illness; and as efficacious if thou diest; for it is else to be feared that she and you will never meet in one place.

    a See p. 1189.

I told her how ill you are. Poor man! said she. *Dangerously* ill, say you? Dangerously *indeed*, madam!—So Lord M. sends me word!

God be merciful to him if he die! said the admirable creature—Then, after a pause, Poor wretch!—May he meet with the mercy he has not shown!

I send this by a special messenger: for I am impatient to hear how it goes with thee—If I have received thy *last* letter, what melancholy reflections will that *last*, so full of shocking levity, give to

Thy true friend,
JOHN BELFORD

Letter 412: MR LOVELACE TO JOHN BELFORD, ESQ.

Tuesday Aug. 15

THANK thee, Jack, most heartily I thank thee, for the sober conclusion of thy last!—I have a good mind for the sake of it to forgive thy till now absolutely unpardonable extracts.

But dost think I will lose such an angel, such a *forgiving* angel, as this?—By my soul, I will not!—To pray for mercy for such an ungrateful miscreant!—How she wounds, how she cuts me to the soul by her exalted generosity!—But SHE must have mercy upon me first!—Then will she teach me a reliance for the sake of which her prayer for me will be answered.

But hasten, hasten to me, particulars of her health, of her employments, of her conversation.

I am sick only of love!—Oh that I could have called her mine!—It would then have been worth while to be sick!—To have sent for her down to me from town; and to have had her with healing in her dove-like wings flying to my comfort; her duty and her choice to pray for me, and to bid me live for her sake!—Oh Jack! what an angel have I—

But I *have not* lost her!—I *will not* lose her! I am almost well; should be quite well but for these prescribing rascals, who to do credit to their skill will make the disease of importance—And I will make her mine!—And be sick again, to entitle myself to her *dutiful* tenderness, and *pious* as well as *personal* concern!

God for ever bless her!—Hasten, hasten particulars of her!—I am sick of love!—Such generous goodness!—By all that's great and good, I will not lose her! So tell her!—She says that she could not pity me, if she thought of being mine! This, according to Miss Howe's transcriptions to Charlotte—But bid her hate me, and have me: and my behaviour to her shall soon turn that hate to love!—For, body and mind, I will be wholly hers.

Letter 413: MR BELFORD TO ROBERT LOVELACE, ESQ.

Thursday, Aug. 17

I AM sincerely rejoiced to hear that thou art already so much amended as thy servant tells me thou art. Thy letter looks as if thy morals were mending with thy health. This was a letter I *could* show, as I *did*, to the lady.

She is very ill (cursed letters received from her implacable family!): so I could not have much conversation with her in thy favour upon it—But what passed will make thee more and more adore her.

She was very attentive to me, as I read it; and, when I had done, Poor man! said she; what a letter is this! He had timely instances that my temper was not ungenerous, if generosity could have obliged him! But his remorse, and that for *his own* sake, is all the punishment I wish him. Yet I must be more reserved if you write to him everything I say!

I extolled her unbounded goodness—How could I help it, though to her face!

No goodness in it! she said—It was a frame of mind she had endeavoured after for her own sake. She suffered too much in want of mercy, not to wish it to a penitent heart. He *seems* to be penitent, said she; and it is not for me to judge beyond appearances—If he be not, he deceives himself more than anybody else.

She was so ill that this was all that passed on the occasion.

What a fine subject for tragedy would the injuries of this lady, and her behaviour under them, both with regard to her implacable friends and to her persecutor, make! With a grand objection as to the moral, nevertheless[a]; for here virtue is punished! Except indeed we look forward to the rewards of HEREAFTER, which, morally, *she* must be sure of, or who can? Yet, after all, I know not, so sad a fellow art thou and so vile an husband mightest thou have made, whether her virtue is not rewarded in missing thee: for things the most grievous to human nature, when they happen, as this charming creature once observed, are often the happiest for us in the event.

I have frequently thought in my attendance on this lady, that if Belton's admired author, Nick Rowe, had such a character before him, he would have drawn another sort of a penitent than he *has* done, or given his play which he calls *The Fair Penitent*, a fitter title.[1] Miss Harlowe is a penitent indeed! I think, if I am not guilty of a contradiction in terms, a penitent without a fault; her parents conduct towards her from the first considered.

The whole story of the other is a pack of damned stuff. Lothario, 'tis true, seems such another wicked ungenerous varlet as thou knowest who: the author knew how to draw a rake; but not to paint a penitent. Calista is a desiring luscious wench, and her penitence is nothing else but rage, insolence, and scorn. Her passions are all storm and tumult; nothing of the finer passions of the sex, which if naturally drawn will distinguish themselves from the masculine passions by a softness that will even shine through rage and despair. Her character is made up of deceit and disguise. She has no virtue; is all pride; and her devil is as much *within* her as *without* her.

How then can the fall of such a one create a proper distress, when all the circumstances of it are considered? For does she not brazen out her crime even

---

a Mr Belford's objection that virtue ought not to suffer in a tragedy is not well considered: Monimia in *The Orphan*, Belvidera in *Venice Preserved*, Athenais in *Theodosius*,[2] Cordelia in Shakespeare's *King Lear*, Desdemona in *Othello*, Hamlet, to name no more, are instances that a tragedy could hardly be justly called a tragedy, if virtue did not temporarily suffer, and vice for a while triumph. But he recovers himself in the same paragraph; and leads us to look up to the FUTURE for the reward of virtue, and for the punishment of guilt: and observes not amiss, when he says he knows not but that the virtue of such a woman as Clarissa is rewarded in missing such a man as Lovelace.

after detection? Knowing her own guilt, she calls for Altamont's vengeance on his best friend, as if he had traduced her; yields to marry Altamont, though criminal with another; and actually beds that whining puppy, when she had given up herself body and soul to Lothario; who, nevertheless, refused to marry her.

Her penitence, when begun, she justly styles *the frenzy of her soul*; and as I said, after having as long as she could most audaciously brazened out her crime, and done all the mischief she could do (occasioning the death of Lothario, of her father, and others), she stabs herself.

And can this be an act of penitence?

But, indeed, our poets hardly know how to create a distress without horror and murder; and must shock your soul to bring tears from your eyes.

Altamont indeed, who is an amorous blockhead, a credulous cuckold, and (though painted as a brave fellow and a soldier)—a whining Tom Essence,[3] and a quarreller with his best friend, dies like a fool without sword or pop-gun, of mere grief and nonsense, for one of the vilest of her sex: But the *Fair Penitent*, as she is called, dies by her own hand; and having no title by her past crimes to *laudable* pity, forfeits all claim to *true* penitence and in all probability to future mercy.

But here is MISS [CLARISSA] HARLOWE, virtuous, noble, wise, pious, unhappily ensnared by the vows and oaths of a vile rake, whom she believes to be a man of honour: and being ill used by her friends for *his sake* is in a manner *forced* to throw herself upon his protection; who, in order to obtain her confidence, never scruples the deepest and most solemn protestation of honour. After a series of plots and contrivances, all baffled by her virtue and vigilance, he basely has recourse to the vilest of arts, and to rob her of her honour is forced first to rob her of her senses. Unable to bring her notwithstanding to his ungenerous views of cohabitation, she awes him in the very entrance of a fresh act of premeditated guilt, in presence of the most abandoned of women assembled to assist his cursed purpose; triumphs over them all by virtue only of her innocence; and escapes from the vile hands he had put her into: nobly, not franticly, resents: refuses to see, or to marry the wretch; who, repenting his usage of so divine a creature, would fain move her to forgive his baseness and make him her husband: and, though persecuted by all her friends and abandoned to the deepest distress, obliged from ample fortunes to make away with her apparel for subsistence, surrounded by strangers, and forced (in want of others) to make a friend of the friend of her seducer. Though longing for death, and making all the proper preparatives for it, convinced that grief and ill usage have broken her noble heart, she abhors the impious thought of shortening her allotted period; and, as much a stranger to revenge as despair, is able to forgive the author of her ruin; wishes his repentance, and that she may be the last victim to his barbarous perfidy: and is solicitous for nothing so much in this life as to prevent vindictive mischief *to* and *from* the man who has used her so basely.

This is penitence! This is piety! And hence a distress naturally arises that must *worthily* affect every heart.

Whatever the ill-usage of this excellent lady is from her relations, [she] breaks not out into excesses: she strives on the contrary to find reason to justify them at her own expense; and seems more concerned for their cruelty to her for their sakes hereafter, when she shall be no more, than for her own: for, as to herself, she is sure, she says, God will forgive her, though nobody else will.

On every extraordinary provocation she has recourse to the Scriptures, and endeavours to regulate her vehemence by sacred precedents. Better people, she says, have been more afflicted than she, grievous as she sometimes thinks her afflictions: and shall she not bear what less faulty persons have borne? On the very occasion I have mentioned (some new instances of implacableness from her friends), the enclosed meditation will show how mildly she complains, and yet how forcibly. See if thou, in the wicked levity of thy heart, canst apply it as thou didst the other, to thy case: if thou canst not, give way to thy conscience, and that will make the properest application.

MEDITATION⁴

How long will ye vex my soul, and break me in pieces with words!

Be it indeed that I have erred, mine error remaineth with myself.

To *her* that is afflicted, pity should be shown from her friend.

But she that is ready to slip with *her* feet, is as a lamp despised in the thought of *them* that *are* at ease.

There is a shame which bringeth sin, and there is a shame which bringeth glory and grace.

Have pity upon me, have pity upon me, oh ye, my friends! for the hand of God hath touched me.

If your soul were in my soul's stead, I also could speak as ye do: I could heap up words against you—

But I would strengthen you with my mouth, and the moving of my lips should assuage your grief.

Why will ye break a leaf driven to and fro? *Why will ye* pursue the dry stubble? *Why will ye* write bitter words against me, and make me possess the iniquities of my youth?

Mercy is seasonable in the time of affliction, as clouds of rain in the time of drought.

Are not my days few? Cease then, and let me alone, that I may take comfort a little—before I go whence I shall not return; even to the land of darkness, and shadow of death!

POSTSCRIPT

This excellent lady is informed, by a letter from Mrs Norton, that Colonel Morden is just arrived in England. He is now the only person she wishes to see.

I expressed some jealousy upon it, lest he should have place given over me in the executorship. She said that she had no thoughts to do so now; for that such a trust, were he to accept of it (which she doubted) might, from the nature of some of the papers which in that case would necessarily pass through his hands, occasion mischiefs between my friend and him, that would be worse than death for her to think of.

Poor Belton, I hear, is at death's door. A messenger is just come from him, who tells me he cannot die till he sees me. I hope the poor fellow will not go off yet; since neither his affairs in this world, nor for the other, are in tolerable order. I cannot avoid going to the poor man. Yet am unwilling to stir, till I have an assurance from thee that thou wilt not disturb the lady: for I know he will be very loath to part with me, when he gets me to him.

Tourville tells me how fast thou mendest: let me conjure thee not to think of molesting this incomparable woman. For thy own sake I request this, as well as for hers, and for the sake of thy given promise: for, should she die within a few weeks, as I fear she will, it will be said, and perhaps too justly, that thy visit has hastened her end.

In hopes thou wilt not, I wish thy perfect recovery: else, that thou mayest relapse, and be confined to thy bed.

Letter 414: MR BELFORD TO MISS CLARISSA HARLOWE

Sat. morn. Aug. 19

Madam,

I THINK myself obliged in honour to acquaint you that I am afraid Mr Lovelace will try his fate by an interview with you.

I wish to Heaven you could prevail upon yourself to receive his visit. All that is respectful, even to veneration, and all that is penitent, will you see in his behaviour, if you can admit of it. But as I am obliged to set out directly for Epsom (to perform, as I apprehend, the last friendly offices for poor Mr Belton, whom once you saw), and as I think it more likely that Mr Lovelace will *not* be prevailed upon, than that he *will*, I thought fit to give you this intimation, lest otherwise, if he should come, you should be too much surprised.

He flatters himself that you are not so ill as I represent you to be. When he sees you, he will be convinced that the most obliging things he can do will be as proper to be done for the sake of his own future peace of mind, as for your health-sake; and I dare say in fear of hurting the latter, he will forbear the thoughts of any further intrusion; at least while you are so much indisposed: so that *one half-hour's shock*, if it *will* be a shock to see the unhappy man (but just got up himself from a dangerous fever), will be all you will have occasion to stand.

I beg you will not too much hurry and discompose yourself. It is impossible he can be in town till Monday at soonest. And if he resolve to come, I hope to be at Mr Smith's before him.

I am, madam, with the profoundest veneration,

Your most faithful and most obedient servant,
J. BELFORD

Letter 415: MR LOVELACE TO JOHN BELFORD, ESQ.

(In answer to his of Aug. 17, Letter 413)

Sunday, Aug. 20

WHAT an unmerciful fellow art thou! A man has no need of a conscience who has such an impertinent monitor. But if Nick Rowe wrote a play that answers not his title, am I to be reflected upon for that?—I have sinned! I repent! I would repair!—She forgives my sin! She accepts my repentance! But she won't let me repair!—What wouldst have me do?

But get thee gone to Belton as soon as thou canst. Yet whether thou goest or not, up I *must* go, and see what I can do with the sweet oddity myself. The moment these *prescribing* varlets will let me, depend upon it, I go. Nay, Lord M. thinks she ought to permit me one interview. His opinion has great authority with me—when it squares with my own: and I have assured him, and my two cousins, that I will behave with all the decency and respect that man can behave with to the person whom he *most* respects. And so I will. Of this, if thou choosest not to go to Belton meantime, thou shalt be witness.

Colonel Morden, thou hast heard me say, is a man of honour and bravery—but Colonel Morden has had his girls as well as you and I. And indeed, either openly or secretly, who has not? The devil always baits with a pretty wench when he angles for a man, be his age, rank, or degree, what it will.

I have often heard my beloved speak of the colonel with great distinction and esteem. I wish he could make matters a little easier, for her mind's sake, between the rest of the implacables and herself.

Methinks I am sorry for honest Belton. But a man cannot be ill or vapourish, but thou liftest up thy shriek-owl note and killest him immediately. None but a fellow who is fit for a drummer in death's forlorn-hope could take so much delight, as thou dost, in beating a dead-march with thy goose-quills.

I shall call thee seriously to account, when I see thee, for the extracts thou hast given the lady from my letters, notwithstanding what I said in my last; especially if she continue to refuse me. An hundred times have I known a woman deny, yet comply at last: but by these extracts, thou hast I doubt made her bar up the door of her heart, as she used to do her chamber-door, against me—This therefore is a disloyalty that friendship cannot bear, nor honour allow me to forgive.

Letter 416: MR LOVELACE TO JOHN BELFORD, ESQ.

London, Aug. 21. Monday

I BELIEVE I am bound to curse thee, Jack. Nevertheless I won't anticipate, but proceed to write thee a longer letter than thou hast had from me for some time past. So here goes.

That thou mightest have as little notice as possible of the time I was resolved to be in town, I set out in my lord's chariot and six yesterday as soon as I had dispatched my letter to thee, and arrived in town last night: for I knew I could have no dependence on thy friendship where Miss Harlowe's humour was concerned.

I had no other place so ready, and so was forced to go to my old lodgings, where also my wardrobe is; and there I poured out millions of curses upon the whole crew, and refused to see either Sally or Polly; and this not only for suffering the lady to escape; but for the villainous arrest, and for their insolence to her at the officer's house.

I dressed myself in a never worn suit, which I had intended for one of my wedding suits—and like myself so well, that I began to think with thee that my outside was the best of me.

I took a chair to Smith's, my heart bounding in almost audible thumps to my throat, with the assured expectation of seeing my beloved. I clasped my fingers as I was danced along: I charged my eyes to languish and sparkle by turns: I talked to my knees, telling them how they must bend; and in the language of a charming describer acted my part in fancy, as well as spoke it to myself:

Tenderly kneeling, *thus* will I complain:
Thus court her pity; and *thus* plead my pain:
Thus sigh for fancied frowns, if frowns should rise;
And *thus* meet favour in her soft'ning eyes.[1]

In this manner entertained I myself till I arrived at Smith's; and there the fellows set down their gay burden. Off went their hats; Will ready at hand in a new livery; up went the head; out rushed my honour; the woman behind the counter all in flutters—respect and fear giving due solemnity to her features; and her knees, I doubt not, knocking against the inside of her wainscot fence.

Your servant, madam—Will, let the fellows move to some distance and wait.

You have a young lady lodges here; Miss Harlowe, madam: is she above?

Sir, sir, and please your honour (the woman is struck with my figure, thinks I): Miss Harlowe, sir! There is, indeed, such a young lady lodges here—but, but—

But what, madam?—I must see her—One pair of stairs; is it not?—Don't trouble yourself—I shall find her apartment. And was making towards the stairs.

Sir, sir, the lady, the lady is not at home—she is abroad—she is in the country—

In the country! Not at home!—Impossible! You will not pass this story upon me, good woman. I *must* see her. I have business of life and death with her.

Indeed, sir, the lady is not at home! Indeed, sir, she is abroad—

She then rung a bell: John, cried she, pray step down!—Indeed, sir, the lady is not at home.

Down came John, the good man of the house, when I expected one of his journeymen, by her saucy familiarity.

My dear, said she, the gentleman will not believe Miss Harlowe is abroad.

John bowed to my fine clothes. Your servant, sir—Indeed the lady is abroad. She went out of town this morning by six o'clock—into the country—by the doctor's advice.

Still I would not believe either John or his wife. I am sure, said I, she cannot be abroad. I heard she was very ill—she is not able to go out in a coach. Do you know Mr Belford, friend?

Yes, sir; I have the honour to know 'Squire Belford. He is gone into the country to visit a sick friend. He went on Saturday, sir.

This had also been told from thy lodgings to Will, whom I sent to desire to see thee on my first coming to town.

Well, and Mr Belford wrote me word that she was exceeding ill. How then can she be gone out?

Oh sir, she is very ill; very ill, indeed—could hardly walk to the coach.

Belford, thought I, *himself* knew nothing of the time of my coming; neither can he have received my letter of yesterday: and so ill, 'tis impossible she would go out.

Where is her servant? Call her servant to me.

Her servant, sir, is her nurse: she has no other. And *she* is gone with her.

Well, friend, I must not believe you. You'll excuse me; but I must go upstairs myself. And was stepping up.

John hereupon put on a serious and a less respectful face—Sir, this house is mine; and——

And what, friend? not doubting then but she was above—I must and will see her. I have authority for it. I am a Justice of Peace. I have a search-warrant.

And up I went; they following me muttering, and in a plaguy flutter.

The first door I came to was locked. I tapped at it.

The lady, sir, has the key of her own apartment.

On the inside, I question not, my honest friend; tapping again. And being assured if she heard my voice that her timorous and soft temper would make her betray herself by some flutters to my listening ear. I said aloud, I am confident Miss Harlowe is here: dearest madam, open the door: admit me but for one moment to your presence.

But neither answer nor fluttering saluted my ear; and the people being very quiet, I led on to the next apartment; and the key being on the outside, I opened it and looked all round it, and into the closet.

The man said he never saw so uncivil a gentleman in his life.

Hark thee, friend, said I: Let me advise thee to be a little decent; or I shall teach thee a lesson thou never learnedst in all thy life.

Sir, said he, 'tis not like a gentleman, to affront a man in his own house.

Then prithee, man, replied I, don't crow upon thine own dunghill.

I stepped back to the locked door: My dear Miss Harlowe, I beg of you to open the door or I'll break it open—pushing hard against it, that it cracked again.

The man looked pale; and, trembling with his fright, made a plaguy long face; and called to one of his bodice-makers above, *Joseph, come down quickly*.

Joseph came down: a lion's-face grinning fellow; thick and short, and bushy-headed, like an old oak pollard. Then did master John put on a sturdier look. But I only hummed a tune, traversed all the other apartments, sounded the passages with my knuckles to find whether there were private doors, and walked up the next pair of stairs, singing all the way; John, and Joseph, and Mrs Smith, following me trembling.

I looked round me there, and went into two open-door bedchambers; searched the closets, the passages, and peeped through the keyhole of another: No Miss Harlowe, by Jupiter! What shall I do!—What shall I do!—Now will she be grieved that she is out of the way.

I said this on purpose to find out whether these people knew the lady's story; and had the answer I expected from Mrs Smith—I believe not, sir, said she.

Why so, Mrs Smith? Do you know who I am?

I can guess, sir.

Whom do you guess me to be?

Your name is Mr Lovelace, sir, I make no doubt.

The very same. But how came you to guess so well, Dame Smith? You never saw me before—did you?

Here, Jack, I laid out for a compliment, and missed it.

'Tis easy to guess, sir; for there cannot be two such gentlemen as you.

Well said, Dame Smith—but mean you *good* or *bad*?—*Handsome* was the least I thought she would have said.

I leave you to guess, sir.

Condemned, thinks I, by myself, on this appeal.

Why, Father Smith, thy wife is a wit, man!—Didst thou ever find that out before?—But where is widow Lovick, Dame Smith? My cousin John Belford says she is a very good woman. Is she within? Or is *she* gone with Miss Harlowe too?

She will be within by and by, sir. She is not with the lady.

Well, but my good dear Mrs Smith, where is the lady gone? And when will she return?

I can't tell, sir.

Don't tell fibs, Dame Smith; don't tell fibs; chucking her under the chin: which made John's upper lip, with chin shortened, rise to his nose—I am sure you know!—But here's another pair of stairs: let us see; who lives up there?—But hold, here's another room locked up, tapping at the door—Who's at home, cried I?

That's Mrs Lovick's apartment. She is gone out and has the key with her.

Widow Lovick! rapping again, I believe you are at home: pray open the door.

John and Joseph muttered and whispered together.

No whispering, honest friends: 'tis not manners to whisper. Joseph, what said John to thee?

JOHN, sir! disdainfully repeated the good woman.

I beg pardon, Mrs Smith: but you see the force of example. Had *you* showed your honest man more respect, *I* should. Let me give you a piece of advice—Women who treat their husbands irreverently teach strangers to use them with contempt. There, honest Master John; why dost not pull off thy hat to me—Oh, so thou wouldst, if thou hadst it on: but thou never wearest thy hat in thy wife's presence, I believe; dost thou?

None of your fleers and your jeers, sir, cried John. I wish every married pair lived as happily as we do.

I wish so too, honest friend. But I'll be hanged if thou hast any children.

Why so, sir?

Hast thou?—Answer me, man: hast thou, or not?

Perhaps not, sir. But what of that?

What of that?—Why I'll tell thee. The man who has no children by his wife must put up with plain John. Hadst thou a child or two, thou'dst be called Mr Smith, with a curtsy, or a smile at least, at every word.

You are very pleasant, sir, replied my dame. I fancy if either my husband or I had as much to answer for as I know whom, we should not be so merry.

Why then, Dame Smith, so much the worse for those who were obliged to keep you company. But I am not merry—I am sad!—Hey-ho!—Where shall I find my dear Miss Harlowe?

My beloved Miss Harlowe! (calling at the foot of the third pair of stairs) if you are above, for God's sake answer me. I am coming up.

Sir, said the good man, I wish you'd walk down. The servants' rooms and the working rooms are up those stairs, and another pair; and nobody's there that you want.

Shall I go up, and see if Miss Harlowe be there, Mrs Smith?

You may, sir, if you please.

Then I won't; for if she was, you would not be so obliging.

I am ashamed to give you all this attendance: you are the politest traders I ever knew. Honest Joseph, slapping him upon the shoulders on a sudden, which made him jump, didst ever grin for a wager, man?—For the rascal seemed not displeased with me; and cracking his flat face from ear to ear, with a distended mouth, showed his teeth, as broad and as black as his thumb-nails. But don't I hinder thee? What canst earn a day, man?

Half a crown I can earn a day; with an air of pride and petulance at being startled.

There then is a day's wages for thee. But thou needest not attend me further.

Come, Mrs Smith, come, John, Master Smith I should say; let's walk down, and give me an account where the lady is gone and when she will return.

So downstairs led I. John and Joseph (though I had discharged the latter), and my dame, following me, to show their complaisance to a stranger.

I re-entered one of the first-floor rooms. I have a great mind to be your lodger: for I never saw such obliging folks in my life. What rooms have you to let?

None at all, sir.

I am sorry for that. But whose is this?

Mine, sir, chuffily said John.

Thine, man! Why then I will take it of thee. This, and a bed-chamber, and garret for my servant, will content me. I will give thee thy own price, and half a guinea a day over, for those conveniences.

For ten guineas a day, sir——

Hold, John! Master Smith, I should say—before thou speakest, consider—I won't be affronted, man.

Sir, I wish you'd walk down, said the good woman. Really, sir, you take—

Great liberties, I hope you would not say, Mrs Smith?

Indeed, sir, I was going to say something like it.

Well, then, I am glad I prevented you; for the words better become my mouth than yours. But I must lodge with you till the lady returns. I *believe* I must. However, you may be wanted in the shop; so we'll talk that over there.

Down I went, they paying diligent attendance on my steps.

When I came into the shop, seeing no chair or stool, I went behind the counter and sat down under an arched kind of canopy of carved work, which these proud traders, emulating the royal niche-fillers, often give themselves, while a joint-stool perhaps serves those by whom they get their bread: such is the dignity of trade in this mercantile nation!

I looked about me, and above me, and told them I was very proud of my seat; asking if John were ever permitted to fill this superb niche?

Perhaps he was, he said, very surlily.

That is it, cried I, that makes thee look so like a statue, man.

John looked plaguy glum upon me. But his man Joseph and my man Will turned round with their backs to us, to hide their grinning, with each his fist in his mouth.

I asked, What it was they sold?

Powder, and wash-balls, and snuff, they said; and gloves and stockings.

Oh come, I'll be your customer. Will, do I want wash-balls?

Yes, and please your honour, you can dispense with one or two.

Give him half a dozen, Dame Smith.

She told me she must come where I was to serve them. Pray, sir, walk from behind the counter.

Indeed but I won't. The shop shall be mine. Where are they if a customer should come in?

She pointed over my head, with a purse-mouth, as if she would not have simpered could she have helped it. I reached down the glass, and gave Will six. There—put 'em up, sirrah.

He did, grinning with his teeth out before; which touching my conscience, as the loss of them was owing to me, Joseph, said I, come hither. Come hither, man, when I bid thee.

He stalked towards me, his hands behind him, half willing, and half unwilling.

I suddenly wrapped my arm round his neck. Will, thy penknife this moment. D—n the fellow, where's thy penknife?

Oh Lord! said the pollard-headed dog, struggling to get his head loose from under my arm, while my other hand was muzzling about his cursed chaps, as if I would take his teeth out.

I will pay thee a good price, man: don't struggle thus! The penknife, Will!

Oh Lord! cried Joseph, struggling still more and more: and out comes Will's pruning-knife; for the rascal is a gardener in the country. I have only this, sir.

The best in the world to lance a gum. D—n the fellow, why dost struggle thus?

Master and Mistress Smith being afraid, I suppose, that I had a design upon Joseph's throat, because he was their champion (and this, indeed, made me take the more notice of him), coming towards me with countenances tragi-comical, I let him go.

I only wanted, said I, to take out two or three of this rascal's broad teeth, to put them into my servant's jaws—And I would have paid him his price for them—I would, by my soul, Joseph.

Joseph shook his ears; and with both hands stroked down, smooth as it would lie, his bushy hair; and looked at me as if he knew not whether he should laugh or be angry: but, after a stupid stare or two, stalked off to the other end of the shop, nodding his head at me as he went, still stroking down his hair, and took his stand by his master, facing about and muttering that I was plaguy strong in the arms, and he thought would have throttled him. Then folding his arms, and shaking his bristled head, added, 'Twas well I was a gentleman, or he would not have taken such an affront.

I demanded where their rappee was? The good woman pointed to the place; and I took up a scollop-shell of it, refusing to let her weigh it, and filled my box. And now, Mrs Smith, said I, where are your gloves?

She showed me; and I chose four pair of them, and set Joseph, who looked as if he wanted to be taken notice of again, to open the fingers.

A female customer, who had been gaping at the door, came in for some Scots snuff; and I would serve her. The wench was plaguy homely; and I told her so; or else, I said, I would have treated her. She in anger (no woman is homely in her own opinion) threw down her penny; and I put it in my pocket.

Just then, turning my eye to the door, I saw a pretty genteel lady with a footman after her peeping in with a What's the matter, good folks? to the starers; and I ran to her from behind the counter, and, as she was making off, took her hand and drew her into the shop, begging that she would be my customer; for that I had but just begun trade.

What do you sell, sir, said she, smiling; but a little surprised.

Tapes, ribands, silk-laces, pins, and needles; for I am a pedlar: powder, patches, wash-balls, stockings, garters, snuffs, and pin-cushions—don't we, Goody Smith?

So in I gently drew her to the counter, running behind it myself, with an air of great diligence and obligingness. I have excellent gloves and wash-balls, madam, rappee, Scots, Portugal, and all sorts of snuff.

Well, said she, in very good humour, I'll encourage a young beginner for once. Here, Andrew (to her footman) you want a pair of gloves, don't you?

I took down a parcel of gloves, which Mrs Smith pointed to, and came round to the fellow to fit them on myself.

No matter for opening them, said I: thy fingers, friend, are as stiff as drumsticks. Push—thou'rt an awkward dog! I wonder such a pretty lady will be followed by such a clumsy varlet.

The fellow had no strength for laughing: and Joseph was mightily pleased, in hopes I suppose I would borrow a few of Andrew's teeth to keep him in countenance: and, like all the world, as the jest was turned from themselves, Father and Mother Smith seemed diverted with the humour.

The fellow said the gloves were too little.

Thrust, and be d—ned to thee, said I: why, fellow, thou hast not the strength of a cat.

Sir, sir, said he, laughing, I shall hurt your honour's side.

D—n thee, thrust, I say.

He did; and burst out the sides of the glove.

Will, said I, where's thy pruning-knife? By my soul, friend, I had a good mind to pare thy cursed paws. But come, here's a larger pair: try them when thou gettest home; and let thy sweetheart, if thou hast one, mend the other; and so take both.

The lady laughed at the humour; as did my fellow, and Mrs Smith, and Joseph: even John laughed, though he seemed by the force put upon his countenance to be but half pleased with me neither.

Madam, said I, and steppped behind the counter, bowing over it, now I hope you will buy something for yourself. Nobody shall use you better, nor sell you cheaper.

Come, said she, give me sixpennyworth of Portugal snuff.

They showed me where it was, and I served her; and said, when she would have paid me, I took nothing at my opening.

If I treated her footman, she told me, I should not treat her.

Well, with all my heart, said I: 'tis not for us tradesmen to be saucy—is it, Mrs Smith?

I put her sixpence in my pocket; and seizing her hand, took notice to her of the crowd that had gathered about the door, and besought her to walk into the back shop with me.

She struggled her hand out of mine, and would stay no longer.

So I bowed, and bid her kindly welcome, and thanked her, and hoped I should have her custom another time.

She went away smiling; and Andrew after her; who made me a fine bow.

I began to be out of countenance at the crowd, which thickened apace; and bid Will order the chair to the door.

Well, Mrs Smith, with a grave air, I am heartily sorry Miss Harlowe is abroad. You don't tell me where she is?

Indeed, sir, I cannot.

You *will* not, you mean—She could have no notion of my coming. I came to town but last night—Have been very ill. She has almost broke my heart by her cruelty. You know my story, I doubt not. Tell her I must go out of town tomorrow morning. But I will send my servant to know if she will favour me with one half-hour's conversation; for, as soon as I get down, I shall set out for Dover, in my way to France, if I have not a countermand from her who has the sole disposal of my fate.

And so, flinging down a Portugal six-and-thirty, I took Mr Smith by the hand, telling him I was sorry we had not more time to be better acquainted; and bidding honest Joseph farewell; who pursed up his mouth as I passed by him, as if he thought his teeth still in jeopardy; and bidding Mrs Smith adieu, and to recommend me to her fair lodger, hummed an air, and the chair being come whipped into it; the people about the door seeming to be in good humour with me; one crying, A pleasant gentleman, I warrant him! And away I was carried to White's,[2] according to direction.

As soon as I came thither, I ordered Will to go and change his clothes, and to disguise himself by putting on his black wig and keeping his mouth shut; and then to dodge about Smith's to inform himself of the lady's motions.

I GIVE thee this impudent account of myself, that thou mayest rave at me, and call me hardened and what thou wilt. For in the first place, I who had been so lately ill was glad I was alive; and then I was so balked by my charmer's unexpected absence, and so ruffled by that and by the bluff treatment of Father John, that I had no other way to avoid being out of humour with all I met with. Moreover I was rejoiced to find by the lady's absence, and by her going out at six in the morning, that it was impossible she should be so ill as thou representedest her to be; and this gave me still higher spirits. Then I know the sex always love cheerful and humorous fellows. The dear creature herself used to be pleased with my gay temper and lively manner; and had she been told that I was blubbering for her in the back shop, she would have despised me still more than she does.

Furthermore, I was sensible that the people of the house must needs have a terrible notion of me, as a savage, bloody-minded, obdurate fellow; a perfect woman-eater; and no doubt expected to see me with the claws of a lion, and the fangs of a tiger; and it was but policy to show them what a harmless, pleasant fellow I am, in order to familiarize the John's and the Joseph's to me. For it was evident to me by the good woman's calling them down, that she thought me a dangerous man. Whereas now, John and I having shaken hands together, and Dame Smith having seen that I have the face and hands and looks of a man, and walk upright, and prate and laugh and joke like other people; and Joseph, that I can talk of taking his teeth out of his head without doing him the least hurt; they will all at my next visit be much more easy and pleasant with me than Andrew's gloves were to him; and we shall be *hail, fellow, well met*, as the saying is, and as thoroughly acquainted as if we had known one another a twelvemonth.

When I returned to our mother's, I again cursed her and all her nymphs together; and still refused to see either Sally or Polly. I raved at the horrid arrest; and told the old dragon, that it was owing to her and hers that the fairest virtue in the world was ruined; my reputation for ever blasted; and that I was not married and happy in the love of the most excellent of her sex.

She, to pacify me, said she would show me a new face that would please me; since I would not see my Sally, who was dying for grief.

Where is this new face, cried I? Let me see her, though I shall never see any face with pleasure but Miss Harlowe's.

She won't come down, replied she. She will not be at the word of command yet—is but just in the trammels; and must be waited upon, I'll assure you; and courted much besides.

Ay! said I, that looks well. Lead me to her this instant.

I followed her up: and who should she be but that little toad, Sally.

Oh curse you, said I, for a devil, is it you? Is yours the new face?

Oh my dear, dear Mr Lovelace? cried she, I am glad anything will bring you to me! And so the little beast threw herself about my neck, and there clung like a cat. Come, said she, what will you give me, and I'll be virtuous for a quarter of an hour and mimic your Clarissa to the life.

I was *Belforded* all over. I could not bear such an insult upon the dear creature (for I have a soft and generous nature in the main, whatever you think); and cursed her most devoutly for taking her name in her mouth in such a way. But the little devil was not to be balked; but fell a crying, sobbing, praying, begging, exclaiming, fainting, so that I never saw my lovely girl so well aped; and I was almost taken in; for I could have fancied I had her before me once more.

Oh this sex! this artful sex! There's no minding them. At first, indeed, their grief and their concern may be real: but give way to the hurricane, and it will soon die away in soft murmurs, trilling upon your ears like the notes of a well-tuned viol. And, by Sally, one sees that art will generally so well supply the place of nature, that you shall not easily know the difference. Miss Harlowe, indeed, is the only woman in the world, I believe, that can say, in the words of her favourite Job (for I can quote a text as well as she), *But it is not so with me.*

They were very inquisitive about my fair one. They told me that you seldom came near them; that when you did, you put on plaguy grave airs; would hardly stay five minutes; and did nothing but praise Miss Harlowe and lament her hard fate. In short, that you despised them; was full of sentences; and they doubted not in a little while would be a lost man, and marry.

A pretty character for thee, is it not? Thou art in a blessed way, yet hast nothing to do but to *go on in it*; and then what a work hast thou to go through! If thou turnest back, these sorceresses will be like the Czar's Cossacks (at Pultowa,[3] I think it was), who were planted with ready primed and cocked pieces behind the regulars, in order to shoot them dead if they did not push on and conquer; and then wilt thou be most lamentably despised by every harlot thou hast made—and, Oh Jack! how formidable in that case will be the number of thy enemies!

I intend to regulate my motions by Will's intelligence; for see this dear creature I must and will. Yet I have promised Lord M. to be down in two or three days at farthest; for he is grown plaguy fond of me since I was ill.

I am in hopes that the word I left that I am to go out of town tomorrow morning will soon bring the lady back again.

Meantime, I thought I would write to divert thee, while thou art of such importance about the dying; and as thy servant it seems comes backward and forward every day, perhaps I may send thee another tomorrow, with the particulars of the interview between the dear lady and me; after which my soul thirsteth.

Letter 417: MR LOVELACE TO JOHN BELFORD, ESQ.

Thursday, Aug. 22

I MUST write on to divert myself: for I can get no rest; no refreshing rest. I awaked just now in a cursed fright. How a man may be affected by dreams!

'Methought I had an interview with my beloved. I found her all goodness, condescension, and forgiveness. She suffered herself to be overcome in my favour by the joint intercessions of Lord M., Lady Sarah, Lady Betty, and my two cousins Montague, who waited upon her in deep mourning; the ladies in long trains sweeping after them; Lord M. in a long black mantle trailing after *him*. They told her they came in these robes to express their sorrow for my sins against her, and to implore her to forgive me.

'I myself, I thought, was upon my knees and with a sword in my hand, offering either to put it up in the scabbard, or to thrust it into my heart, as she should command the one or the other.

'At that moment her cousin Morden, I thought, all of a sudden flashed in through a window, with his drawn sword—Die, Lovelace, said he! this instant die, and be damned, if in earnest thou repairest not by marriage my cousin's wrongs!

'I was rising to resent this insult, I thought, when Lord M. run between us with his great black mantle, and threw it over my face: and instantly, my charmer, with that sweet voice which has so often played upon my ravished ears, wrapped her arms round me, muffled as I was in my Lord M.'s mantle: Oh spare, spare my Lovelace! And spare, Oh Lovelace, my beloved cousin Morden! Let me not have my distresses augmented by the fall of either or both of those who are so dear to me.

'At this, charmed with her sweet mediation, I thought I would have clasped her in my arms: when immediately the most angelic form I had ever beheld, vested all in transparent white, descended from a ceiling, which, opening, discovered a ceiling above that, stuck round with golden cherubs and glittering seraphs, all exulting: Welcome, welcome, welcome! and, encircling my charmer, ascended with her to the region of seraphims; and instantly, the opening ceiling closing, I lost sight of *her*, and of the *bright form* together, and found wrapped in my arms her azure robe (all stuck thick with stars of embossed silver), which I had caught hold of in hopes of detaining her; but was all that was left me of my beloved Miss Harlowe. And then (horrid to relate!) the floor sinking under *me*, as the ceiling had opened for *her*, I dropped into a hole more frightful than that of Elden[1] and tumbling over and over down it, without view of a bottom, I awaked in a panic; and was as effectually disordered for half an hour, as if my dream had been a reality.'

Wilt thou forgive me troubling thee with such visionary stuff? Thou wilt see by it only that, sleeping or waking, my Clarissa is always present with me.

But here this moment is Will come running hither to tell me that his lady actually returned to her lodgings last night between eleven and twelve, and is now there, though very ill.

I hasten to her. But that I may not add to her indisposition by any rough or boisterous behaviour, I will be as soft and gentle as the dove herself in my addresses to her.

> That I do love her, oh all ye host of heaven,
> Be witness!—That she is dear to me!
> Dearer than day to one whom sight must leave;
> Dearer than life, to one who fears to die.[2]

The chair is come. I fly to my beloved.

Letter 418: MR LOVELACE TO JOHN BELFORD, ESQ.

CURSE upon my stars!—Disappointed again!

It was about eight when I arrived at Smith's—The woman was in the shop.

So, old acquaintance, how do you now? I know my love is above—Let her be acquainted that I am here, waiting for admission to her presence and can take no denial. Tell her that I will approach her with the most respectful duty and in whose company she pleases; and I will not touch the hem of her garment without her leave.

Indeed, sir, you're mistaken. The lady is not in this house, nor near it.

I'll see that—Will! beckoning him to me, and whispering, see if thou canst any way find out (without losing sight of the door, lest she should be below stairs) if she be in the neighbourhood, if not within.

Will bowed and went off. Up went I, without further ceremony; attended now only by the good woman.

I went into each apartment, except that which was locked before, and was now also locked: and I called to Miss Harlowe in the voice of love; but by the still silence was convinced she was not there. Yet, on the strength of my intelligence, I doubted not but she was in the house.

I then went up two pair of stairs, and looked round the first room: but no Miss Harlowe.

And who, pray, is in this room? stopping at the door of another.

A widow gentlewoman, sir—Mrs Lovick.

Oh my dear Mrs Lovick! said I, I am intimately acquainted with her character from my cousin John Belford. I must see Mrs Lovick by all means. Good Mrs Lovick, open the door.

She did.

Your servant, madam. Be so good as to excuse me—You have heard my story. You are an admirer of the most excellent woman in the world. Dear Mrs Lovick, tell me what is become of her?

The poor lady, sir, went out yesterday on purpose to avoid you.

How so? She knew not that I would be here.

She was afraid you would come when she heard you were recovered from your illness—Ah! sir, what pity it is that so fine a gentleman should make such ill returns for God's goodness to him!

You are an excellent woman, Mrs Lovick: I know that, by my cousin John Belford's account of you; and Miss Harlowe is an angel.

Miss Harlowe is indeed an angel, replied she; and soon will be company for angels.

No jesting with such a woman as this, Jack.

Tell me of a truth, good Mrs Lovick, where I may see this dear lady. Upon my soul, I will neither fright nor offend her. I will only beg of her to hear me speak for one half-quarter of an hour; and if she will have it so, I will never trouble her more.

Sir, said the widow, it would be death for her to see you. She was at home last night; I'll tell you truth: but fitter to be in bed all day. She came home, she said, to die; and if she could not avoid your visit, she was unable to fly from you; and believed she should die in your presence.

And yet go out again this morning early? How can that be, widow?

Why, sir, she rested not two hours, for fear of you. Her fear gave her strength, which she'll suffer for when that fear is over. And finding herself, the more she thought of it, the less able to stay to receive your visit, she took chair and is gone nobody knows whither. But I believe she intended to be carried to the water-side, in order to take boat; for she cannot bear a coach. It extremely incommoded her yesterday.

But before we talk any further, said I, if she be gone abroad, you can have no objection to my looking into every apartment above and below; because I am told she is actually in the house.

Indeed, sir, she is *not*. You may satisfy yourself, if you please: but Mrs Smith and I waited on her to her chair. We were forced to support her, she was so weak. She said, Where *can* I go, Mrs Lovick? Whither *can* I go, Mrs Smith?—Cruel, cruel man! Tell him I called him so, if he come again!—God give him that peace which he denies me!

Sweet creature! cried I, and looked down and took out my handkerchief.

The widow wept. I wish, said she, I had never known so excellent a lady, and so great a sufferer! I love her as my own child!

Mrs Smith wept.

I then gave over the hope of seeing her for this time. I was extremely chagrined at my disappointment, and at the account they gave of her ill health.

Would to Heaven, said I, she would put it in my power to repair her wrongs! I have been an ungrateful wretch to her. I need not tell you, Mrs Lovick, how much I have injured her, nor how much she suffers by her relations' implacableness. 'Tis the latter, Mrs Lovick, 'tis that, Mrs Smith, that cuts her to the heart. Her family is the most implacable family on earth; and the dear creature, in refusing to see me and to be reconciled to me, shows her relation to them a little too plainly.

Oh sir, said the widow, not one syllable of what you say belongs to this lady. I never saw so sweet a creature! so edifying a piety! and one of so forgiving a temper! She is always accusing herself and excusing her relations. And, as to you, sir, she forgives you: she wishes you well; and happier than you will let her be. Why will you not, sir, why will you not let her die in peace? 'Tis all she wishes for. You don't look like a hard-hearted gentleman!—How can you thus hunt and persecute a poor lady whom none of her relations will look upon? It makes my heart bleed for her.

And then she wept again. Mrs Smith wept also. My seat grew uneasy to me. I shifted to another several times; and what Mrs Lovick farther said and showed me made me still more uneasy.

Bad as the poor lady was last night, said she, she transcribed into her book a meditation on your persecuting her thus. I have a copy of it. If I thought it would have any effect, I would read it to you.

Let me read it myself, Mrs Lovick.

She gave it to me. It has a Harlowe spirited title. And from a forgiving spirit, intolerable. I desired to take it with me. She consented, on condition that I showed it to 'Squire Belford. So here, Mr 'Squire Belford, thou may'st read it, if thou wilt.

On being hunted after by the enemy of my soul[1]
Monday, Aug. 21

DELIVER me, oh Lord, from the evil man. Preserve me from the violent man.
Who imagines mischief in his heart.
He hath sharpened *his* tongue like a serpent. Adder's poison is under *his* lips.
Keep me, oh Lord, from the hands of the wicked. Preserve me from the violent man; *who hath* purposed to overthrow my goings.
He hath hid a snare for me. *He hath* spread a net by the wayside. *He hath* set gins for me in the way wherein I walked.
Keep me from the snares which *he hath* laid for me, and the gins of *this* worker of iniquity.
The enemy hath persecuted my soul. He hath smitten my life down to the ground. He hath made me dwell in darkness, as those that have been long dead.
Therefore is my spirit overwhelmed within me. My heart within me is desolate.
Hide not thy face from me in the day when I am in trouble.
For my days are consumed like smoke: and my bones are burnt as the hearth.
My heart is smitten and withered like grass: so that I forget to eat my bread.
By reason of the voice of my groaning, my bones cleave to my skin.
I am like a pelican of the wilderness. I am like an owl of the desert.
I watch; and am as a sparrow alone upon the house-top.
I have eaten ashes like bread; and mingled my drink with weeping:
Because of thine indignation and thy wrath: for thou hast lifted me up, and cast me down.
My days are like a shadow that declineth, and I am withered like grass.
Grant not, oh Lord, the desires of the wicked: further not his devices, lest he exalt himself.

Why now, Mrs Lovick, said I, when I had read this meditation, as she called it, I think I am very severely treated by the lady, if she mean *me* in all this. For how is it that I am the *enemy of her soul*, when I love her both soul and body?

She says that I am a *violent* man, and a *wicked* man—That I have been so, I own: but I repent, and only wish to have it in my power to repair the injuries I have done her.

The *gin*, the *snare*, the *net*, mean matrimony, I suppose—but is it a crime in me to wish to marry her? Would any other woman think it so? and choose to become a *pelican in the wilderness* or a *lonely sparrow on the house-top*, rather than to have a mate that would chirp about her all day and all night?

She says she has *eaten ashes like bread*—a sad mistake to be sure!—and *mingled her drink with weeping*— sweet maudlin soul! should I say of anybody confessing this but Miss Harlowe.

She concludes with praying that *the desires of the wicked* (meaning poor me, I doubt) *may not be granted*; that *my devices may not be furthered, lest I exalt myself*—I should undoubtedly exalt myself, and with reason, could I have the honour and the blessing of such a wife. And if my *desires* have so honourable an end, I know not why I should be called *wicked*, and why I should not be allowed to hope that my honest *devices* may be *furthered*, that I MAY exalt myself.

But here, Mrs Lovick, let me ask, as something is undoubtedly meant by the *lonely sparrow on the house-top*, is not the dear creature at this very instant (tell me truly) concealed in Mrs Smith's cockloft?—What say you, Mrs Lovick; what say you, Mrs Smith, to this?

They assured me to the contrary; and that she was actually abroad, and they knew not where.

Thou seest, Jack, that I would fain have diverted the chagrin given me by the women's talk, and by this collection of Scripture-texts drawn up in array against me. And several other whimsical and light things I said (all I had for it!) for this purpose. But the widow would not let me come off so. She stuck to me; and gave me, as I told thee, a good deal of uneasiness, by her sensible and serious expostulations. Mrs Smith put in now and then; and the two Jack-pudding fellows, John and Joseph, not being present, I had no provocation to turn the conversation into a farce; and at last they both joined warmly to endeavour to prevail upon me to give up all thoughts of seeing the lady. But I could not hear of that. On the contrary, I besought Mrs Smith to let me have one of her rooms but till I could see her; and were it but for one, two, or three days, I would pay a year's rent for it; and quit it the moment the interview was over. But they desired to be excused; and were sure the lady would not come to the house till I was gone, were it for a *month*.

This pleased me; for I found they did not think her so very ill as they would have me believe her to be; but I took no notice of the slip, because I would not guard them against more of the like.

In short, I told them I *must* and *would* see her: but that it should be with all the respect and veneration that heart could pay to excellence like hers. And that I would go round to all the churches in London and Westminster, where there were prayers or service, from sunrise to sunset, and haunt their house like a ghost till I had the opportunity my soul panted after.

This I bid them tell her. And thus ended our serious conversation.

I took leave of them, and went down; and stepping into my chair, caused myself to be carried to Lincoln's Inn; and walked in the gardens till Chapel was opened; and then I went in, and stayed prayers, in hopes of seeing the dear creature enter: but to no purpose; and yet I prayed most devoutly that she might be conducted thither, either by my good angel, or her own. And indeed I burn more than ever with impatience to be once more permitted to kneel at the feet of this adorable woman. And had I met her, or spied her in the Chapel, it is my firm belief that I should not have been able (though it had been in the midst of the sacred office, and in the presence of thousands) to have forborne prostration to her, and even clamorous supplication for her forgiveness: a Christian act; the exercise of it therefore worthy of the place.

After service was over, I stepped into my chair again, and once more was carried to Smith's in hopes I might have surprised her there: but no such happiness for thy friend. I stayed in the back shop an hour and half by my watch; and again underwent a good deal of preachment from the women. John was mainly civil to me now; won over a little by my serious talk, and the honour I professed for the lady; and they all three wished matters could be made up between us: but still insisted that she could never get over her illness; and that her heart was broken. A cue, I suppose, they had from you.

While I was there, a letter was brought for her by a particular hand. They seemed very solicitous to hide it from me; which made me suspect it was for her. I desired to be suffered to cast an eye upon the seal and the superscription; promising to give it back to them unopened.

Looking upon it, I told them I knew the hand and seal. It was from her sister.[a] And I hoped it would bring her news that she would be pleased with.

They joined most heartily in the same hope: and giving the letter to them again, I civilly took my leave and went away.

But I will be there again presently; for I fancy my courteous behaviour to these women will, on their report of it, procure me the favour I so earnestly covet. And so I will leave my letter unsealed, to tell thee the event of my next visit at Smith's.

THY servant just calling, I send thee this. And will soon follow it by another. Meantime, I long to hear how poor Belton is. To whom my best wishes.

Letter 419: MR BELFORD TO ROBERT LOVELACE, ESQ.

Tuesday, Aug. 22

I HAVE been under such concern for the poor man whose exit I almost hourly expect, and at the shocking scenes his illness and his agonies exhibit, that I have been only able to make memoranda of the melancholy passages, from which to draw up a more perfect account for the instruction of us all, when the writing appetite shall return.

IT is returned! Indignation has revived it, on receipt of thy letters of Sunday and yesterday; by which I have reason to reproach thee in very serious terms that thou hast not kept thy honour with me: and if thy breach of it be attended with such effects as I fear it will be, I shall let thee know more of my mind on this head.

If thou would'st be thought in earnest in thy wishes to move the poor lady in thy favour, thy ludicrous behaviour at Smith's, when it comes to be represented to her, will have a very *consistent* appearance; will it not?—It will, indeed, confirm her in her opinion that the *grave* is more to be wished-for, by one of her serious and pious turn, than a *husband* incapable either of reflection or remorse; just recovered, as thou art, from a dangerous, at least a sharp illness.

I am extremely concerned for the poor unprotected lady; she was so excessively low and weak on Saturday, that I could not be admitted to her speech: and to be driven out of her lodgings, when it was fitter for her to be in bed, is such a piece of cruelty as he only could be guilty of, who could act as thou hast done by such an angel.

Canst thou thyself say, on reflection, that it has not the look of a wicked and hardened sportiveness in thee, for the sake of a wanton humour only (since it can answer no end that thou proposest to thyself, but the direct contrary), to hunt from

  a See Letter 429.

place to place a poor lady who, like a harmless deer that has already a barbed shaft in her breast, seeks only a refuge from thee in the shades of death?

But I will leave this matter upon thy own conscience, to paint thee such a scene from my memoranda, as thou perhaps wilt be moved by more effectually than by any other: because it is such a one as thou thyself must one day be a principal actor in; and, as I thought, hadst very lately in apprehension: and is the last scene of one of thy most intimate friends, who has been for the four past days labouring in the agonies of death. For, Lovelace, let this truth, this undoubted truth, be engraven on thy memory in all thy gaieties, that the life we are so fond of, is hardly life; a mere breathing-space only; and that at the end of its longest date,

Thou must die, as well as BELTON.

Thou knowest by Tourville what we had done as to the poor man's worldly affairs; and that we had got his unhappy sister to come and live with him (little did we think him so very near his end); and so I will proceed to tell thee that when I arrived at his house on Saturday night, I found him excessively ill: but just raised, and in his elbow-chair, held up by his nurse and Mowbray (the roughest and most untouched creature that ever entered a sick man's chamber), while the maid-servants were trying to make that bed easier for him which he was to return to; his mind ten times uneasier than that could be, and the true cause that the down was no softer to him.

He had so much longed to see me, his sister told me (whom I sent for down to inquire how he was), that they all rejoiced when I entered: Here, said Mowbray, here, Tommy, is honest Jack Belford!

Where, where? said the poor man.

I hear his voice, cried Mowbray, coming upstairs.

In a transport of joy, he would have raised himself at my entrance, but had like to have pitched out of the chair: and when recovered, called me his best friend! his *kindest* friend! but burst out into a flood of tears, Oh Jack! Oh Belford! said he, see the way I am in! See how weak! So *much*, and so soon reduced! Do you know me? Do you know your poor friend Belton?

You are not so much altered, my dear Belton, as you think you are. But I see you are weak; very weak—and I am sorry for it.

Weak! weak, indeed, my dearest Belford, said he, and weaker in my mind, if possible, than in my body; and wept bitterly—or I should not thus unman myself. I, who never feared *anything*, to be forced to show myself such a *nursling*!—I am quite ashamed of myself!—But don't despise me, dear Belford, don't despise me, I beseech thee.

I ever honoured a man that could weep for the distresses of *others*; and ever shall, said I; and such a one cannot be insensible to *his own*.

However, I could not help being *visibly* moved at the poor fellow's emotion.

Now, said the brutal Mowbray, do I think thee insufferable, Jack. Our poor friend is already a peg too low; and here thou art letting him down lower and lower still. This soothing of him in his dejected moments, and joining thy womanish tears with his, is not the way; I am sure it is not. If our Lovelace were here, he'd tell thee so.

Thou art an impenetrable creature, replied I; unfit to be present at a scene thou wilt not be able to feel the terrors of, till thou feelest them in thyself; and then, if thou has *time for feeling*, my life for thine, thou behavest as pitifully as those thou thinkest *most* pitiful.

Then turning to the poor sick man, Tears, my dear Belton, are no signs of an *unmanly*, but contrarily of a humane nature; they ease the over-charged heart, which would burst but for that kindly and natural relief.

> Give sorrow *words* (says Shakespeare);
> — The grief that does not speak,
> Whispers the o'er-fraught heart, and bids it break.[1]

I know, my dear Belton, thou usedest to take pleasure in repetitions from the poets; but thou must be tasteless of their beauties now: yet be not discountenanced by this uncouth and unreflecting Mowbray, for as Juvenal says, *Tears are the prerogative of manhood.*[2]

'Tis at least seasonably said, my dear Belford; it is kind to keep me in countenance for this *womanish weakness*, as Mowbray has been upbraidingly calling it ever since he has been with me. And in so doing (whatever I might have thought in such high health as he enjoys) has convinced me that bottle-friends feel nothing but what moves in that little circle.

Well, well proceed in your own way, Jack. I love my friend Belton as well as you can do; yet for the blood of me, I cannot but think that soothing a man's weakness is increasing it.

If it be a weakness to be touched at great and concerning events in which our humanity is concerned, said I, thou mayest be right.

I have seen many a man, said the rough creature, going up Holborn Hill,[3] that has behaved more like a man than either of you.

Ay, but Mowbray, replied the poor man, those wretches have not had such infirmities of body as I have long laboured under, to enervate their minds. Thou art a shocking fellow, and ever wert. But to be able to remember nothing in these moments but what reproaches me, and to know that I cannot hold it long, and what may *then* be my lot, if—But interrupting himself and turning to me, Give me thy pity, Jack, 'tis balm to my wounded soul; and let Mowbray sit indifferent enough to the pangs of a dying friend to laugh at us both.

The hardened fellow then retired, with the air of a Lovelace; only more stupid; yawning and stretching, instead of humming a tune as thou didst at Smith's.

I assisted to get the poor man into bed. He was so weak and low that he could not bear the fatigue, and fainted away; and I verily thought was quite gone. But recovering, and his doctor coming and advising to keep him quiet, I retired, and joined Mowbray in the garden; who took more delight to talk of the living Lovelace and his levities, than of the dying Belton and his repentance.

I just saw him again on Saturday night before I went to bed: which I did early; for I was surfeited with Mowbray's frothy insensibility, and could not bear him. It is such a horrid thing to think of, that a man who had lived in such strict terms of *amity* with another (the proof does not come out so as to say *friendship*); who had pretended so much love for him; could not bear to be out of his company; would ride a hundred miles an end to enjoy it, and would fight for him be the cause right or wrong: yet now could be so little moved to see him in such misery of body and mind as to be able to rebuke him, and rather ridicule than pity him, because he was more affected by what he felt than he had seen a malefactor (hardened perhaps by liquor and not softened by previous sickness) on his going to execution.

This put me strongly in mind of what the divine Miss HARLOWE once said to me, talking of friendship, and what my friendship to *you* required of me: 'Depend upon it, Mr Belford,' said she, 'that one day you will be convinced that what *you* call friendship is chaff and stubble; and that nothing is worthy of that sacred name,

'THAT HAS NOT VIRTUE FOR ITS BASE.'

Sunday morning I was called up at six o'clock at his earnest request, and found him in a terrible agony. Oh Jack! Jack! said he, looking wildly, as if he had seen a spectre—Come nearer me! reaching out both arms—Come nearer me!—Dear, dear Belford, save me! Then clasping my arm with both his hands and rearing up his head towards me, his eyes strangely rolling, Save me! dear Belford, save me! repeated he.

I put my other arm about him—Save you from what, my dear Belton! Save you from what!—Nothing shall hurt you!—What must I save you from?

Recovering from his terror, he sunk down again, Oh save me from myself! said he; save me from my own reflections. Oh dear Jack! what a thing it is to die; and not to have one comfortable reflection to revolve!—What would I give for one year of my passed life?—only *one* year—and to have the same sense of things that I now have?

I tried to comfort him as well as I could: but free-livers to free-livers are sorry death-bed comforters. And he broke in upon me: Oh my dear Belford, said he, I am told (and I have heard you ridiculed for it) that the excellent Miss Harlowe has wrought a conversion in you. May it be so! You are a man of sense; Oh may it be so! Now is your time! Now, that you are in full vigour of mind and body! But your poor Belton, alas! kept his vices till they left him. And see the miserable effects in debility of mind and despondency! Were Mowbray here, and were he to *laugh* at me, I would own that this is the cause of my despair: that God's *justice* cannot let his *mercy* operate for my comfort: for oh! I have been very, *very* wicked; and have despised the offers of his grace, till he has withdrawn it from me for ever.

I used all the arguments I could think of to give him consolation; and what I said had such an effect upon him, as to quiet his mind for the greatest part of the day; and in a lucid hour his memory served him to repeat those lines of Dryden, grasping my hand and looking wistfully upon me:

> Oh that I less could fear to lose this being,
> Which, like a snow-ball, in my coward-hand,
> The more 'tis grasp'd, the faster melts away!

In the afternoon of Sunday he was inquisitive after you and your present behaviour to Miss Harlowe. I told him how you had been, and how light you made of it. Mowbray was pleased with your impenetrable hardness of heart, and said, Bob Lovelace was a good edge-tool, and steel to the back: and such coarse but hearty praises he gave thee, as an abandoned man might *give*, and only an abandoned man could wish to *deserve*.

But hadst thou heard what the poor, dying, wise-too-late Belton said on this occasion, perhaps it would have made thee serious an *hour or two* at least.

When poor Lovelace is brought, said he, to a sick-bed, as I am now, and his mind forebodes that it is impossible he should recover, which *his* could not do in his late illness: if it had, he could not have behaved so lightly in it—when he revolves his past mis-spent life; his actions of offence to helpless innocents; in Miss Harlowe's case particularly: what then will he think of himself, or of his past actions? His mind debilitated; his strength turned into weakness; unable to stir or to move without help; not one ray of hope darting in upon his benighted soul; his conscience standing in the place of a thousand witnesses; his pains excruciating; weary of the poor remnant of life he drags, yet dreading that in a few short hours his bad will be changed to worse, nay, to worst of all; and that worst of all to last beyond time and to all eternity; Oh Jack! what will he then think of the poor transitory gratifications of sense which now engage all his attention? Tell him, dear Belford, tell him, how happy he is if he knows his own happiness; how happy compared to his poor dying friend, that he has recovered from his illness, and has still an opportunity lent him, for which I would give a thousand worlds, had I them to give!

I approved exceedingly of what he said, as reflections suited to his present circumstances; and inferred consolations to him from a mind so properly touched.

He proceeded in the like penitent strain. I have lived a very wicked life; so have we all. We have never made a conscience of doing all the mischief that either force or fraud put it in our power to do. We have laid snares for the innocent heart; and have not scrupled by the too-ready sword to extend, as occasions offered, the wrongs we did to the persons whom we had before injured in their dearest relations. But yet I think in my heart that I have less to answer for than either Lovelace or Mowbray; for I, by taking to myself that accursed deceiver from whom thou hast freed me (and who for years, unknown to me, was retaliating upon my own head some of the evils I had brought upon others), and retiring and living with her as a wife, was not party to half the mischiefs that I doubt they, and Tourville, and even you, Belford, committed. As to the ungrateful Thomasine, I hope I have met with my punishment in her. But notwithstanding this, dost thou not think that *such* an action—and *such* an action—and *such* an action (and then he recapitulated several enormities in which, led on by false bravery and the heat of youth and wine, we have all been concerned); dost thou not think that these villainies (let me call them *now* by their proper name), joined to the wilful and gloried-in neglect of every duty that our better sense and education gave us to know were required of us as men and Christians, are not enough to weigh down my soul into despondency?—Indeed, indeed, they are! And now to hope for *mercy!* And to depend upon the efficacy of that gracious attribute when that no less shining one of *justice* forbids me to hope; how can I!—I, who have despised all warnings, and taken no advantage of the benefit I might have reaped from the lingering consumptive illness I have laboured under, but left all to the last stake; hoping for recovery, against hope, and driving off repentance till that grace is denied me; for oh! my dear Belford! I can now neither repent nor pray as I ought; my heart is hardened, and I can do nothing but despair!—

More he would have said; but overwhelmed with grief and infirmity, he bowed his head upon his pangful bosom, endeavouring to hide from the sight of the hardened Mowbray, who just then entered the room, those tears which he would not restrain.

Prefaced by a phlegmatic Hem; Sad, very sad, truly! cried Mowbray; who sat himself down on one side of the bed, as I on the other: his eyes half closed, and his lips pouting out to his turned-up nose, his chin curdled (to use one of thy descriptions), leaving one at a loss to know whether stupid drowsiness or intense contemplation had got most hold of him.

An excellent, however uneasy lesson, Mowbray, said I! by my faith it is!—It may one day, who knows how soon? be our own case!

I thought of thy yawning fit, as described in thy letter of Aug. 13. For up started Mowbray, writhing and shaking himself as in an ague-fit; his hands stretched over his head—with thy hoy! hoy! hoy! yawning—And then recovering himself with another stretch and a shake, What's a clock, cried he? pulling out his watch—and stalking by long tip-toe strides through the room, downstairs he went; and meeting the maid in the passage, I heard him say—Betty, bring me a bumper of claret; thy poor master and this damned Belford are enough to throw a Hercules into the vapours.

Mowbray, after this, amusing himself in our friend's library, which is as thou knowest chiefly classical and dramatical, found out a passage in Lee's *Oedipus*, which he would needs have to be extremely apt, and in he came full fraught with the notion of the courage it would give the dying man, and read it to him. 'Tis poetical and pretty. This is it.

> When the *sun sets*, shadows that show'd at *noon*
> But small, appear most long and terrible:
> So when we think fate hovers o'er our heads,
> Our apprehensions shoot beyond all bounds:
>   Owls, ravens, crickets seem the watch of death:
> Nature's worst vermin scare her god-like sons.
> Echoes, the very leavings of a voice,
> Grow babbling ghosts, and call us to our graves.
> Each mole-hill thought swells to a huge Olympus;
> While we, fantastic dreamers, heave and puff,
> And sweat with our imagination's weight.[5]

He expected praises for finding this out. But Belton turning his head from him, Ah, Dick! (said he) these are not the reflections of a dying man! What thou wilt one day feel, if it be what I now feel, will convince thee that the evils *before* thee, and *with* thee, are more than the effects of imagination.

I was called twice on Sunday night to him; for the poor fellow, when his reflections on his past life annoy him most, is afraid of being left with the women; and his eyes, they tell me, hunt and roll about for me. Where's Mr Belford?—But I shall tire him out, cries he—yet beg of him to step to me—yet don't—yet do; were once the doubting and changeful orders he gave: and they called me accordingly.

But, alas! What could Belford do for him? Belford, who had been but too often the companion of his guilty hours, who wants mercy as much as he does; and is unable to promise it to himself, though 'tis all he can bid his poor friend *rely* upon!

What miscreants are we! What figures shall we make in these terrible hours!

If Miss HARLOWE's glorious *example*, on one hand, and the *terrors of this* poor man's on the other, affect me not, I must be abandoned to perdition; as I fear thou wilt be if thou benefittest not thyself from both.

He then readily took it; but said he could have sworn that Tom Metcalfe had been in the room, and had drawn him out of bed by the throat, upbraiding him with the injuries he had first done his sister, and then him in the duel to which he owed that fever which cost him his life.

Thou knowest the story, Lovelace, too well to need my repeating it: but mercy on us if in these terrible moments all the evils we do rise to our affrighted imaginations! If so, what shocking scenes have I, but still more hast thou, to go through if, as the noble poet says:

> If any sense at that sad time remains.

The doctor ordered him an opiate this morning early, which operated so well that he dozed and slept several hours more quietly than he had done for the two past days and nights, though he had sleeping draughts given him before. But it is more and more evident every hour that nature is almost worn out in him.

Mowbray, quite tired with this house of mourning, intends to set out in the morning to find you. He was not a little rejoiced to hear you were in town; I believe to have a pretence to leave us.

He has just taken leave of his poor friend, intending to go away early: an everlasting leave, I may venture to say; for I think he will hardly live till tomorrow night.

I believe the poor man would not have been sorry had he left him when I arrived; for 'tis a shocking creature, and enjoys too strong health to know how to pity the sick. Then (to borrow an observation from thee), he has by nature strong bodily organs, which those of his soul are not likely to whet out; and he, as well as the wicked friend he is going to, may last a great while from the strength of their constitutions, though so greatly different in their talents; if neither the sword nor the halter interpose.

I must repeat that I cannot but be very uneasy for the poor lady whom thou so cruelly persecutest; and that I do not think thou hast kept thy honour with me. I was apprehensive, indeed, that thou wouldst attempt to see her as soon as thou gottest well enough to come up; and I told her as much, making use of it as an argument to prepare her for thy visit, and to induce her to stand it. But she could not, it is plain, bear the shock of it; and, indeed, she told me that she would not see thee, though but for one half hour, for the world.

Could she have prevailed upon herself, I know that the sight of her would have been as affecting to thee as thy visit could have been to her; when thou hadst seen to what a lovely skeleton (for she is really lovely still, nor can she with such a form and features be otherwise) thou hast, in a few weeks, reduced one of the most charming women in the world; and that in the full bloom of her youth and beauty.

Mowbray undertakes to carry this, that he may be more welcome to you, he says. Were it to be sent unsealed, the characters we write in would be Hebrew to the dunce. I desire you to return it; and I'll give you a copy of it upon demand; for I intend to keep it by me as a guard against the infection of thy company which might otherwise perhaps, some time hence, be apt to weaken the impressions I always desire to have of the awful scene before me. God convert us both!

Letter 420: MR BELFORD TO ROBERT LOVELACE, ESQ.

Wednesday morn. 11 o'clock

I BELIEVE no man has two such servants as I have. Because I treat them with kindness, and do not lord it over my inferiors and damn and curse them by looks and words like Mowbray; or beat their teeth out like Lovelace; but cry, Prithee, Harry, do this, and Prithee, Jonathan, do that, the fellows pursue their own devices, and regard nothing I say but what falls in with thee. Here, this vile Harry, who might have brought your letter of yesterday in good time, came not in with it till past eleven last night (drunk, I suppose); and concluding that I was in bed, as he pretends (because he was told I sat up the preceding night), brought it not to me; and having over-slept himself, just as I had sealed up my letter, in comes the villain with the forgotten one, shaking his ears, and looking as if he himself did not believe the excuses he was going to make. I questioned him about it, and heard his pitiful pleas, and though I never think it becomes a gentleman to treat people insolently who by their stations are humbled beneath his feet, yet could I not forbear to *Lovelace* and *Mowbray* him, most cordially.

And this detaining Mowbray (who was ready to set out to thee before) while I write a few lines upon it, the fierce fellow, who is impatient to exchange the company of a dying Belton for that of a too lively Lovelace, affixed a *supplement* of curses upon the staring fellow that was larger than my *book*—nor did I offer to take off the bear from such a mongrel, since he deserved not of me on this occasion the protection which every master owes to a good servant.

He has not done cursing him yet; for stalking about the courtyard with his boots on (the poor fellow dressing his horse, and unable to get from him), he is at him without mercy; and I will heighten his impatience (since being just under the window where I am writing, he will not let me attend to my pen) by telling thee how he fills my ears as well as the fellow's, with his—Hey, sir! and G—d d—n ye, sir! and were you my servant, ye dog ye! and must I stay here till the mid-day sun scorches me to a parchment, for such a mangy dog's drunken neglect?—Ye lie, sirrah! ye lie, I tell you—(I hear the fellow's voice in an humble excusatory tone, though not articulately). Ye lie, ye dog!—I'd a good mind to thrust my whip down your drunken throat. Damn me if I would not flay the skin from the back of such a rascal, if thou wert mine, and have dogskin gloves made of it for thy brother scoundrels to wear in remembrance of thy abuses of such a master.

The poor horse suffers for this, I doubt not; for, What now! and, Stand still, and be damned to ye, cries the fellow, with a kick, I suppose, which he better deserves himself. For these varlets, where they can, are Mowbrays and Lovelaces to man or beast; and not daring to answer *him*, is flaying the poor *horse*.

I hear the fellow is just escaped, the horse (better curried than ordinary, I suppose, in half the usual time) by his clanking shoes, and Mowbray's silence, letting me know that I may now write on: and so I will tell thee that, in the first place (little as I, as well as you, regard dreams), I would have thee lay thine to heart; for I could give thee such an interpretation of it as would shock thee, perhaps: if thou asketh me for it, I will.

Mowbray calls to me from the courtyard, that 'tis a cursed hot day, and he shall be fried by riding in the noon of it: and that poor Belton longs to see me. So I will only add my earnest desire that thou wilt give over all thoughts of seeing the lady if, when this comes to thy hand, thou hast not seen her: and that it would be kind if thoud'st come, and for the last time thou wilt ever see thy poor friend, share my concern *for* him; and *in* him, see what, in a little time, will be thy fate and mine, and that of Mowbray, Tourville and the rest of us—for what are ten, fifteen, twenty, or thirty years, to look back to: in which period forward we shall all, perhaps, be mingled with the dust we sprung from?

Letter 421: MR LOVELACE TO JOHN BELFORD, ESQ.

Wednesday morn. Aug. 23

ALL alive, dear Jack! and in ecstasy! Likely to be once more a happy man! For I have received a letter from my beloved Miss HARLOWE; in consequence I suppose of advices that I mentioned in my last, from her sister. And I am setting out for Berkshire directly, to show the contents to my Lord M. and to receive the congratulations of all my kindred upon it.

I went last night, as I intended, to Smith's: but the dear creature was not returned at near ten o'clock. And lighting upon Tourville, I took him home with me, and made him sing me out of my megrims. I went to bed tolerably easy at two; had bright and pleasant dreams, not such a frightful one as that I gave thee an account of: and at eight this morning, as I was dressing to be in readiness against Will came back, whom I had sent to inquire after his lady's return, I had this letter brought me by a chairman.

[Letter 421.1: Clarissa Harlowe] to Robert Lovelace, Esq.

Tuesday night, 11 o'clock (Aug 22)

Sir,

I HAVE good news to tell you. I am setting out with all diligence for my father's house. I am bid to hope that he will receive his poor penitent with a goodness peculiar to himself; for I am overjoyed with the assurance of a thorough reconciliation through the interposition of a dear blessed friend, whom I always loved and honoured. I am so taken up with my preparation for this joyful and long-wished-for journey, that I cannot spare one moment for any other business, having several matters of the last importance to settle first. So, pray, sir, don't disturb or interrupt me—I beseech you don't—You may in time, possibly, see me at my father's, at least, if it be not your own fault.

I will write a letter which shall be sent you when I am got thither and received: till when, I am, etc.

CLARISSA HARLOWE

I dispatched instantly a letter to the dear creature, assuring her with the most thankful joy, 'That I would directly set out for Berkshire, and wait the issue of the happy reconciliation, and the charming hopes she had filled me with. I poured out upon her a thousand blessings. I declared that it should be the study of my whole life to merit such transcendent goodness. And that there was nothing which her father or friends should require at my hands, that I would not for *her* sake comply with, in order to promote and complete so desirable a reconciliation.'

I hurried it away without taking a copy of it; and I have ordered the chariot and six to be got ready; and hey for M. Hall!—Let me but know how Belton does. I hope a letter from thee is on the road. And if the poor fellow can spare thee, make haste, I advise thee, to attend this truly divine lady, or else thou mayest not see her of months perhaps; at least, not while she is Miss HARLOWE. And favour me with one letter before she sets out, if possible, confirming to me, and accounting for, this generous change.

But what accounting for it is necessary? The dear creature cannot receive consolation herself, but she must communicate it to others. How noble!—She would not see me in her adversity: but no sooner does the sun of prosperity begin to shine upon her, than she forgives me.

I know to whose mediation all this is owing. It is to Colonel Morden's. She always, as she says, loved and honoured him: and he loved her above all his relations.

I shall now be convinced that there is something in dreams. The ceiling opening is the reconciliation in view. The bright form, lifting her up through it to another ceiling stuck round with golden Cherubims and Seraphims, indicates the charming little boys and girls that will be the fruits of this happy reconciliation. The welcomes, thrice repeated, are those of her family, now no more to be deemed implacable. Yet are they a family too, that my soul cannot mingle with.

But then what is my tumbling over and over, through the floor, into a frightful hole (*descending* as she *ascends*)? Ho! only this; it alludes to my disrelish to matrimony: which is a bottomless pit, a gulf, and I know not what. And I suppose, had I not awoke (in such a plaguy fright) I had been soused into some river at the bottom of the hole, and then been carried (mundified or purified from my past iniquities) by the same bright form (waiting for me upon the mossy banks) to my beloved girl; and we should have gone on, cherubiming of it, and carolling, to the end of the chapter.

But what are the black sweeping mantles and robes of my Lord M. thrown over my face, and what are those of the ladies? Oh, Jack! I have these too: they indicate nothing in the world but that my lord will be so good as to die, and leave me all he has. So, rest to thy good natured soul, honest Lord M.

Lady Sarah Sadleir and Lady Betty Lawrance will also die, and leave me swingeing legacies.

Miss Charlotte and her sister—what will become of them?—Oh! they will be in mourning of course for their uncle and aunts—That's right!

As to Morden's flashing through the window, and crying, Die, Lovelace, and be damned, if thou wilt not repair my cousin's wrongs! That is only that he would have sent me a challenge had I not been disposed to do the lady justice.

All I dislike is this part of the dream: for, even in a dream, I would not be thought to be threatened into any measure, though I liked it ever so well.

And so much for my prophetic dream.

Dear charming creature! What a meeting will there be between her and her father and mother and uncles! What transports, what pleasure, will this happy, long-wished-for reconciliation give her dutiful heart! And indeed, now, methinks I am glad she *is* so dutiful to them; for her duty to parents is a conviction to me that she will be *as* dutiful to her husband: since duty upon principle is an uniform thing.

Why prithee, now, Jack, I have not been so much to blame as thou thinkest: for had it not been for me, who have led her into so much distress, she could neither have *received* nor *given* the joy that will now overwhelm them all. So here rises great and durable good out of temporary evil!

I knew they loved her (the pride and glory of their family) too well to hold out long!

I wish I could have seen Arabella's letter. She has always been so much eclipsed by her sister, that I dare say she has signified this reconciliation to her with intermingled phlegm and wormwood; and her invitation most certainly runs all in the rock-water style.

I shall long to see the promised letter too, when she is got thither, which I hope will give an account of the reception she will meet with.

There is a solemnity, however, I think, in the style of her letter, which pleases and affects me at the same time. But as it is evident she loves me still, and hopes soon to see me at her father's; she could not help being a little solemn and half-ashamed (dear blushing pretty rogue!) to own her love, after my usage of her.

And then her subscription: *Till when, I am,* CLARISSA HARLOWE: as much as to say, *after that* I shall be, if not *your own fault,* CLARISSA LOVELACE!

Oh my best love! My ever generous and adorable creature! How much does this thy forgiving goodness exalt us both!—[Me] for the occasion given thee! [Thee] for turning it so gloriously to thy advantage, and to the honour of both!

And if, my beloved creature, you will but connive at the imperfections of your adorer, and not play the *wife* upon me: if, while the charms of novelty have their force with me, I should happen to be drawn aside by the intricacies of intrigue, and of plots that my soul loves to form and pursue; and if thou wilt not be open-eyed to the follies of my youth (a transitory state!), every excursion shall serve but the more to endear thee to me, till in time, and in a very little time too, I shall get above sense; and then, charmed by thy soul-attracting converse, and brought to despise my former courses, what I now at distance consider as a painful duty will be my joyful choice, and all my delight will centre in thee!

MOWBRAY is just arrived with thy letters. I therefore close my agreeable subject, to attend to one which I doubt will be very shocking. I have engaged the rough varlet to bear me company in the morning to Berkshire; where I shall file off the rust he has contracted in his attendance upon the poor fellow.

He tells me that between the dying Belton and the preaching Belford, he shan't be his own man these three days. And says that thou addest to the unhappy fellow's weakness, instead of giving him courage to help him to bear his destiny.

I am sorry he takes the unavoidable lot so heavily. But he has been long ill; and sickness enervates the mind as well as the body; as he himself very significantly observed to thee.

Letter 422: MR LOVELACE TO JOHN BELFORD, ESQ.

Wed. evening

I HAVE been reading thy shocking letter—Poor Belton! what a multitude of lively hours have we passed together! 'Twas a fearless, cheerful fellow!—Who'd ha' thought all should end in such dejected whimpering and terror?

But why didst thou not comfort the poor man about the rencounter between him and that poltroon Metcalfe? He acted in that affair like a man of true honour, and as I should have acted in the same circumstances. Tell him I say so, and what happened he could neither help nor foresee.

Some people are as sensible of a scratch from a pin's point, as others from a push of a sword: and who can say anything for the sensibility of such fellows? Metcalfe would resent for his sister, when his sister resented not for herself. Had she demanded her brother's protection and resentment, that would have been *another man's matter*, as Lord M. phrases it: but she herself thought her brother a coxcomb to busy himself, undesired, in her affairs, and wished for nothing but to be provided for decently and privately in her lying-in; and was willing to take the chance of *Maintenon-ing* his conscience in her favour,ᵃ and getting him to marry when the little stranger came; for she knew what an easy, good-natured fellow he was. And, indeed, if she *had* prevailed upon him, it might have been happy for both; as then he would not have fallen in with his cursed Thomasine. But truly this officious brother of hers must interpose. This made a trifling affair important: and what was the issue? Metcalfe challenged; Belton met him; disarmed him; gave him his life: but the fellow, more sensible in his *skin* than in his *head*, having received a scratch, he was frighted; it gave him first a puke, then a fever, and then he died. That was all. And how could Belton help that?—But sickness, a long tedious sickness, will make a bugbear of anything to a languishing heart, I see that. And so far was Mowbray *apropos* in the verses from *Nat Lee* which thou hast transcribed.

Merely to die, no man of reason fears is a mistake, say thou, or say thy author, what ye will. And thy solemn parading about the natural repugnance between life and death is a proof that it is.

Let me tell thee, Jack, that so much am I pleased with this world, in the main; though in some points, too, the world (to make a *person* of it) has been a rascal to me; so delighted am I with the joys of youth; with my worldly prospects as to fortune; and now, newly, with the charming hopes given me by dear, thrice dear, and forever dear Miss HARLOWE; that were I even sure that nothing bad would come hereafter, I should be very loath (very much *afraid* if thou wilt have it so) to lay down my life and them together; and yet upon a call of honour, no man fears death less than myself.

But I have not either inclination or leisure to weigh thy *leaden* arguments, except in the *pig*, or as thou wouldst say in the *lump*.

If I return thy letters, let me have them again some time hence, that is to say when I am married, or when poor Belton is half-forgotten; or when *time* has

---

ᵃ Madam Maintenon was reported to have prevailed upon Lewis XIV of France, in his old age (sunk, as he was, by ill success in the field) to marry her, by way of compounding with his conscience for the freedoms of his past life, to which she attributed his public losses.[1]

enrolled the honest fellow among those whom we have *so long* lost, that we may remember them with more pleasure than pain; and then I may give them a serious perusal, and enter with thee as deeply as thou wilt into the subject.

When I am married, said I?—What a sound has that!

I must wait with patience for a sight of this charming creature, till she is at her father's: and yet, as the but blossoming beauty as thou tellest me is reduced to a shadow, I should have been exceedingly delighted to see her now, and every day till the happy one; that I might have the pleasure of beholding how sweetly, hour by hour, she will rise to her pristine glories, by means of that state of ease and contentment which will take place of the stormy *past*, upon her reconciliation with her friends, and our happy nuptials.

Letter 423: MR LOVELACE TO JOHN BELFORD, ESQ.

WELL, but now my heart is a little at ease, I will condescend to take some brief notice of some other passages in thy letters.

I find I am to thank *thee* that the dear creature has avoided my visit. Things are now in so good a train, that I must forgive thee; else shouldest thou have heard more of this new instance of disloyalty to thy general.

Thou art continually giving thyself high praise by way of *opposition*, as I may say, to others; gently and artfully blaming thyself for qualities thou wouldst at the same time have to be thought, and which generally are thought, praiseworthy.

Thus, in the airs thou assumest about thy servants, thou wouldst pass for a mighty humane mortal, and that at the expense of Mowbray and me; whom thou representest as kings and emperors to our menials. Yet art thou always unhappy in thy attempts of this kind, and never canst make us, who know thee, believe that to be a virtue in thee which is but the effect of constitutional phlegm and absurdity.

Knowest thou not that some men have a native dignity in their manner that makes them more regarded by a look, than either thou canst be in thy low style, or Mowbray in his high?

I am fit to be a prince, I can tell thee; for I reward well, and I punish seasonably and properly; and I am generally as well served as any man.

The art of governing these under-bred varlets lies more in the dignity of looks than in words, and thou art a sorry fellow to think humanity consists in acting by thy servants as men must act who are not able to pay them their wages; or had made them masters of secrets, which if divulged, would lay them at the mercy of such wretches.

Now to me, who never did anything I was ashamed to own, and who have more [ingenuousness] than ever man had; who can call a villainy by its right name, though practised by myself, and (by my own readiness to reproach myself) anticipate all reproach from others; who am not such a hypocrite as to wish the world to think me other or better than I am: it is my part to *look* a servant into his duty, if I can. Nor will I keep one who knows not how to take me by a nod, or a wink; and who, when I smile, shall not be all transport; when I frown, all terror. If, indeed, I am out of the way a little, I always take care to reward the varlets for bearing patiently my displeasure. But this I hardly ever am, but when a fellow is egregiously stupid in any plain points of duty, or will be wiser than his master; and when he shall tell me that he thought acting contrary to my orders was the way to serve me best.

One time or other, I will enter the lists with thee upon thy conduct and mine to servants; and I will convince thee that what thou wouldst have pass for humanity, if it be indiscriminately practised to all tempers, will perpetually subject thee to the evils thou complainest of; and *justly* too; and that *he* only is fit to be a master of servants, who can command their attention as much by a *nod*, as if he were to *prithee* a fellow to do his duty on one hand, or to talk of *flaying* and *horsewhipping*, like Mowbray, on the other: for the servant who being *used* to *expect* thy creeping style will always be master of his master; and he who deserves to be treated as the other is not fit to be any man's servant; nor would I keep such a fellow to rub my horse's heels.

I shall be the readier to enter the lists with thee upon this argument, because I have presumption enough to think that we have not in any of our dramatic poets, that I can at present call to mind, one character of a servant of either sex that is justly hit off. So absurdly wise *some*, and so sottishly foolish *others*; and *both* sometimes in the *same* person. *Foils* drawn from the lees or dregs of the people to set off the characters of their masters and mistresses; nay, sometimes, which is still more absurd, introduced with more wit than the poet has to bestow upon their principals—Mere *flints* and *steels* to strike fire with—or to vary the metaphor, to serve for whetstones to wit, which *otherwise* could not be made apparent—or for engines to be made use of like the *machinery* of the ancient poets (or the still *more* unnatural soliloquy) to help on a sorry plot, or to bring about a necessary *éclaircissement*, to save the poet the trouble of thinking deeply for a better way to wind up his bottoms.

Of this I am persuaded (whatever my *practice* be to my own servants), that thou wilt be benefited by my *theory* when we come to controvert the point. For then I shall convince thee that the *dramatic* as well as *natural* characteristics of a good servant ought to be fidelity, common sense, cheerful obedience, and silent respect: that wit in his station, except to his companions, would be sauciness: that he should never presume to give his advice: that if he ventured to expostulate upon any unreasonable command, or such a one as appeared to him to be so, he should do it with humility and respect, and take a proper season for it. But such lessons do most of the dramatic performances I have seen give, where servants are introduced as characters essential to the play, or to act very significant or long parts in it (which, of itself, I think a fault); such lessons, I say, do they give to the footmen's gallery, that I have not wondered we have so few modest or good menservants among those who often attend their masters or mistresses to plays. Then how miserably evident must that poet's conscious want of genius be, who can stoop to raise or give force to a clap by the indiscriminative roar of the party-coloured gallery!

But this subject I will suspend to a better opportunity; that is to say, to the happy one when my nuptials with my Clarissa will oblige me to increase the number of my servants, and of consequence to enter more nicely into their qualifications.

ALTHOUGH I have the highest opinion that man can have of the generosity of my dear Miss Harlowe, yet I cannot for the heart of me account for this agreeable change in her temper but one way. Faith and troth, Belford, I verily believe, laying all circumstances together, that the dear creature unexpectedly finds herself in the way I have so ardently wished her to be in; and that this makes her at last incline to favour me, that she may set the better face upon her gestation when at her father's.

If this be the case, all her falling away and her fainting fits are charmingly accounted for. Nor is it surprising that such a sweet novice in these matters should not know to what to attribute her frequent indispositions. If this should be the case, how shall I laugh at *thee!* and (when I am sure of her) at the dear novice *herself*, that all her grievous distresses shall end in a man-child: which I shall love better than all the Cherubims and Seraphims that may come after; though there were to be as many of them as I beheld in my dream; in which a vast expanse of ceiling was stuck as full of them as it could hold.

I shall be afraid to open thy next, lest it bring me the account of poor Belton's death. Yet, as there are no hopes of his recovery—But what should I say, unless the poor man were better fitted—But thy heavy sermon shall not affect me too much neither.

I enclose thy papers: and do thou transcribe them for me or return them; for there are some things in them which, at a proper season, a *mortal* man should not avoid attending to: and thou seemest to have entered deeply into the shocking subject—But here I will end, lest I grow too serious.

THY servant called here about an hour ago, to know if I had any commands: I therefore hope that thou wilt have this early in the morning. And if thou *canst* let me hear from thee, do. I'll stretch an hour or two in expectation of it. Yet I must be at Lord M.'s tomorrow night, if possible, though ever so late.

Thy fellow tells me the poor man is much as he was when Mowbray left him.

Wouldst thou think that this varlet Mowbray is sorry that I am so near being happy with Miss Harlowe. And, 'egad, Jack, I know not what to say to it, now the fruit seems to be within my reach. But, let what will come, I'll stand to't: for I find I can't live without her.

Letter 424: MR BELFORD TO ROBERT LOVELACE, ESQ.

Wed. three o'clock

I WILL proceed where I left off in my last.

As soon as I had seen Mowbray mounted, I went to attend upon poor Belton, whom I found in dreadful agonies, in which he awoke, as he generally does.

The doctor came in presently after; and I was concerned at the scene that passed between them.

It opened with the dying man's asking him, with melancholy earnestness, if nothing, if nothing at all, could be done for him?

The doctor shook his head, and told him he doubted not.

I *cannot* die, said the poor man; I cannot *think* of dying. I am very desirous of living a little longer, if I could but be free from these horrible pains in my stomach and head. Can you give me nothing to make me pass one week, but *one* week, in tolerable ease, that I may die like a man?—if I *must* die!

But, doctor, I am *yet* a young man: in the prime of my years—Youth is a good subject for a physician to work upon: can you do nothing, nothing *at all* for me, doctor?

Alas, sir, replied his physician, you have been long in a bad way. I fear, I fear, nothing in physic can help you.

He was then out of all patience: What, then, is your art, sir?—I have been a passive machine for a whole twelvemonth, to be wrought upon at the pleasure of you people of the faculty. I verily believe, had I not taken such doses of nasty stuff, I had been now a well man—But who the plague would regard physicians, whose art is to cheat us with hopes while they help to destroy us? And who, not one of you, know anything but by guess?

Sir, continued he fiercely (and with more strength of voice and coherence than he had shown for several hours before), if you give *me* over, I give *you* over—The only honest and certain part of the art of healing is surgery. A good surgeon is worth a thousand of you. I have been in surgeons' hands often, and have always found reason to depend upon their skill: but *your* art, sir, what is it?—but to daub, daub, daub; load, load, load; plaster, plaster, plaster; till ye utterly destroy the appetite first, and the constitution afterwards, which you are called in to help. I had a companion once—my dear Belford, thou knewest honest Blomer—as pretty a physician he would have made as any in England, had he kept himself from excess in wine and women; and he always used to say there was nothing at all but pick-pocket parade in the physician's art; and that the best guesser was the best physician; and I used to believe him too: and yet, fond of life, and fearful of death, what do we do when we are taken ill, but call ye *in*? And what do *ye* do when called in, but nurse our distempers, till from pigmies you make giants of them?— And then ye come creeping with solemn faces when ye are ashamed to prescribe, or when the stomach won't bear its natural food by reason of your poisonous potions, *Alas! I am afraid physic can do no more for him!*—Nor need it, when it has brought to the brink of the grave the poor wretch who placed all his reliance in your cursed slops and the flattering hopes you gave him.

The doctor was out of countenance; but said, If we could make mortal men *immortal*, and *would not*, all this might be just.

I blamed the poor man; yet excused him to the physician. To die, dear doctor, when like my poor friend, we are so desirous of life, is a melancholy thing. We are apt to hope too much, not considering that the seeds of death are sown in us when we begin to live, and grow up, till, like rampant weeds, they choke the tender flower of life; which declines in us as those weeds flourish. We ought therefore to begin early to study what our constitutions will bear, in order to root out by temperance, the weeds which the soil is most apt to produce; or at least to keep them down as they rise; and not, when the flower or plant is withered at the root, and the weed in its full vigour, expect that the medical art will restore the one or destroy the other; when that other, as I hinted, has been rooting itself in the habit from the time of our birth.

This speech, Bob, thou wilt call a *prettiness*; or a WHITE BEAR—but the allegory is just; and thou hast not quite cured me of the metaphorical.

Very true, said the doctor, you have brought a good metaphor to illustrate the thing. I am sorry I can do nothing for the gentleman; and can only recommend patience, and a better frame of mind.

Well, sir, said the poor angry man, vexed at the doctor, but more at death; you will perhaps recommend the next in succession to the physician, when he can do no more; and I suppose will send your brother to pray by me for those virtues which you wish me.

It seems the physician's brother is a clergyman in the neighbourhood.

I was greatly concerned to see the gentleman thus treated; and so I told poor Belton when he was gone: but he continued impatient, and would not be denied, he said, the liberty of talking to a man who had taken so many guineas of him for doing nothing, or worse than nothing, and never declined one, though he knew all the time he could do him no good.

It seems the gentleman, though rich, is noted for being greedy after fees; and poor Belton went on raving at the extravagant fees of English physicians, compared with those of the most eminent foreign ones. But, poor man! he, like the Turks who judge of a general by his success (out of patience to think he must die), would have worshipped the doctor, and not grudged three times the sum; could he have given him hopes of recovery.

But nevertheless I must needs say that gentlemen of the faculty should be more moderate in their fees, or take more pains to deserve them: for generally they only come into a room, feel the sick man's pulse, ask the nurse a few questions, inspect the patient's tongue and perhaps his water; then sit down, look plaguy wise; and *write*. The golden fee finds the ready hand, and they hurry away as if the sick man's room were infectious. So to the next they troll, and to the next, if men of great practice; valuing themselves upon the number of visits they make in a morning, and the little time they make them in. They go to dinner, and unload their pockets; and sally out again to refill them. And thus, in a little time, they raise vast estates; for, as Ratcliffe said[1] when first told of a great loss which befell him, it was only going up and down a hundred pair of stairs to fetch it up.

Mrs Sambre (Belton's sister) had several times proposed to him a minister to pray by him; but the poor man could not, he said, bear the thoughts of one; for that he should certainly die in an hour or two after: and he was willing to hope still, against all probability, that he might recover; and was often asking his sister if she had not seen people as bad as he was who, almost to a miracle, when everybody gave them over, had got up again?

She, shaking her head, told him she had: But, once saying that *their* disorders were of an acute kind, and such as had a crisis in them, he called her *small-hopes*, and *Job's comforter*; and bid her say *nothing* if she could not say more to the purpose, and what was fitter for a sick man to hear. And yet, poor fellow! he has no hopes himself, as is plain by his desponding terrors; one of which he fell into, and a very dreadful one, soon after the doctor went.

Wednesday, 9 o'clock at night

THE poor man has been in convulsions, terrible convulsions! for an hour past. Oh Lord! Lovelace, death is a shocking thing! By my faith, it is!—I wish thou wert present on this occasion. It is not merely the concern a man has for his friend; but, as death is the common lot, we see, in *his* agonies how it will be one day with ourselves. I am all over as if cold water were poured down my back, or as if I had a strong ague fit upon me. I was obliged to come away. And I write, hardly knowing what—I wish *thou* wert here.

THOUGH I left him because I could stay no longer, I can't be easy by myself, but must go to him again.

Eleven o'clock

POOR Belton!—Drawing on apace! Yet was he sensible when I went in: too sensible, poor man! He has something upon his mind to reveal, he tells me, that is the worst action of his life; worse than ever you or I knew of him, he says. It *must* be then very bad!

He ordered everybody out; but was seized with another convulsion fit, before he could reveal it: and in it he lies struggling between life and death. But I'll go in again.

One o'clock in the morning

ALL now must soon be over with him: poor! poor fellow! He has given me some hints of what he wanted to say; but all incoherent, interrupted by dying hiccoughs and convulsions.

Bad enough it must be, heaven knows! by what I can gather. Alas! Lovelace, I fear, I fear, he came *too soon* into his uncle's estate.

If a man were to live always, he might have some temptation to do base things, in order to procure to himself, as it would then be, *everlasting* ease, plenty or affluence: but, for the sake of ten, twenty, thirty years of poor life, to be a villain— can that be worth while? with a conscience stinging him all the time too! And when he comes to wind up all such agonizing reflections upon his past guilt! All then appearing as nothing! What he most valued, most disgustful! and not one thing to think of, as the poor fellow says twenty and twenty times over, but what is attended with anguish and reproach!

To hear the poor man wish he had never been born! To hear him pray to be nothing after death! Good God! how shocking!

By his incoherent hints, I am afraid, 'tis very bad with him. No pardon, no mercy, he repeats, can lie for him!

I hope I shall make a proper use of this lesson. Laugh at me if thou wilt, but never, never more will I take the liberties I have taken; but whenever I am tempted, will think of Belton's dying agonies, and what my own may be.

Thursday, three in the morning

HE is now at the last gasp—rattles in the throat: has a new convulsion every minute almost. What horror is he in! His eyes look like breath-stained glass! They roll ghastly no more; are quite set: his face distorted and drawn out by his sinking jaws and erected staring eyebrows, with his lengthened furrowed forehead, to double its usual length as it seems. It is not, it cannot be, the face of Belton, thy Belton, and my Belton, whom we have beheld with so much delight over the social bottle, comparing notes that one day may be brought against us, and make *us* groan, as they very lately did *him*—that is to say, while he had strength to groan; for now his voice is not to be heard; all inward, lost; not so much as speaking by his eyes: yet, strange! how can it be? the bed rocking under him like a cradle!

Four o'clock

> Alas! he's gone! That groan, that *dreadful* groan,
> Was the last farewell of the parting mind!
> The struggling soul has bid a long adieu
> To its late mansion—Fled!—Ah! whither fled?[2]

Now is all indeed over!—Poor, poor Belton! By this time thou knowest if thy crimes were above the size of God's mercies! Now are everyone's cares and attendance at an end! Now do we, thy friends, poor Belton! know the worst of thee, as to this life! Thou art released from insufferable tortures, both of body and mind! May those tortures, and thy repentance, expiate for thy offences, and mayest thou be happy to all eternity!

We are told that God desires not the death, the *spiritual* death of a sinner: and 'tis certain that thou didst deeply repent! I hope therefore as thou wert not cut off in the midst of thy sins by the sword of injured friendship, which more than once thou hadst braved (the dreadfullest of all deaths, next to suicide, because it gives no opportunity for repentance), that this is a merciful earnest that thy penitence is accepted; and that thy long illness, and dreadful agonies in the last stages of it, will be thy only punishment.

I wish indeed, I *heartily* wish, we could have seen one ray of comfort darting in upon his benighted mind before he departed. But all, alas! to the very last gasp was horror and confusion. And my only fear arises from this, that till within the four last days of his life, he could not be brought to think he should die, though in a visible decline for months; and in that presumption was too little inclined to set about a serious preparation for a journey which he hoped he should not be obliged to take; and when he began to apprehend that he could not put it off, his impatience, and terror, and apprehension, showed too little of that reliance and resignation which afford the most comfortable reflections to the *friends* of the dying, as well as to the *dying* themselves.

But we must leave poor Belton to that mercy which we have all so much need of; and, for my own part (do you, Lovelace, and the rest of the fraternity, as ye will), I am resolved I will endeavour to begin to repent of my follies while my health is sound, my intellects untouched, and while it is in my power to make some atonement, as near to restitution as is possible, to those I have wronged or misled. And do ye *outwardly*, and from a point of *false bravery*, make as light as ye will of my resolution, as ye are none of ye of the class of abandoned and stupid sots who endeavour to disbelieve the future existence which ye are afraid of, I am sure you will justify me in your *hearts*, if not by your *practices*; and one day you will wish you had joined with me in the same resolution, and will confess there is more good sense in it than now perhaps you will own.

Seven o'clock, Thursday morning

You are very earnest, by your last letter (just given me), to hear again from me before you set out for Berkshire. I will therefore close with a few words upon the *only* subject in your letter which I can at present touch upon, and this is the letter you give me a copy of from the lady.

Want of rest, and the sad scene I have before my eyes, have rendered me altogether incapable of accounting for it in any shape. You are in ecstasies upon it. You have reason to be so, if it be as you think. Nor would I rob you of your joy: but I must say that I am amazed at it.

Surely Lovelace this surprising letter cannot be a forgery of thy own, in order to carry on some view, and to impose upon me. Yet by the style of it, it cannot; though thou art a perfect Proteus too.

I will not, however, add another word, after I have desired the return of this, and have told you, that I am,

Your true friend and well-wisher,
J. BELFORD

Letter 425: MR LOVELACE TO JOHN BELFORD, ESQ.

Aug. 24. Thursday morn

I RECEIVED thy letter in such good time, by thy fellow's dispatch, that it gives me an opportunity of throwing in a few paragraphs upon it. I read a passage or two of it to Mowbray; and we both agree that thou art an absolute master of the lamentable.

Poor Belton! what terrible conflicts were thy last conflicts!—I hope, however, that he is happy: and I have the more hope, because the hardness of his death is likely to be such a warning to *thee*. If it have the effect thou declarest it shall have, what a world of mischief will it prevent! How much good will it do! How many poor wretches will rejoice at the occasion (if they know it), however melancholy in itself, which shall bring them in a compensation for injuries they had been forced to sit down contented with? But, Jack, though thy uncle's death has made thee a rich fellow, art thou sure that the making good of such a vow will not totally bankrupt thee?

Thou sayest I may laugh at thee if I will. Not I, Jack: I do not take it to be a laughing subject: and I am heartily concerned at the loss we all have in poor Belton: and when I get a little settled, and have leisure to contemplate the vanity of all sublunary things (a subject that will now and then, in my gayest hours, obtrude itself upon me), it is very likely that I may talk seriously with thee upon these topics; and, if thou hast not got too much the start of me in the repentance thou art entering upon, will go hand-in-hand with thee in it. If thou hast, thou wilt let me just keep thee in my eye; for it is an uphill work, and I shall see thee, at setting out, at a great distance; but as thou art a much heavier and clumsier fellow than myself, I hope that without much puffing and sweating, only keeping on a good round dogtrot, I shall be able to overtake thee.

Meantime take back thy letter as thou desirest; I would not have it in my pocket upon any account at present; nor read it once more.

I am going down without seeing my beloved. I was a hasty fool to write her a letter promising that I would not come near her till I saw her at her father's. For as she is now actually at Smith's, and I so near her, one short visit could have done no harm.

I sent Will two hours ago with my grateful compliments, and to know how she does. How must I adore this charming creature! For I am ready to think my servant a happier fellow than myself for having been within a pair of stairs and an apartment of her!

Mowbray and I will drop a tear apiece, as we ride along, to the memory of poor Belton—*as we ride along*, I say: for we shall have so much joy when we arrive at Lord M.'s, and when I communicate to him and my cousins the dear creature's letter, that we shall forget everything grievous: since now their family-hopes in my reformation (the point which lies so near their hearts) will all revive; it being an article of their faith, that if I marry, repentance and mortification will follow of course.

Neither Mowbray nor I shall accept of thy *verbal* invitation to the funeral. We like not these dismal formalities. And as to the respect that is supposed to be shown to the memory of a deceased friend in such an attendance, why should we do anything to reflect upon those who have made it a fashion to leave this parade to people whom they *hire for that purpose?*

Adieu, and be cheerful. Thou canst now do no more for poor Belton, wert thou to howl for him to the end of thy life.

Letter 426: MR BELFORD TO ROBERT LOVELACE, ESQ.

Sat. Aug. 26

ON Thursday afternoon I assisted at the opening of poor Belton's will, in which he has left me his sole executor, and bequeathed me a legacy of 100 guineas: which I shall present to his unfortunate sister, to whom he has not been so kind as I think he ought to have been. He has also left £20 apiece to Mowbray, Tourville, thyself, and me, for a ring to be worn in remembrance of him.

After I had given some particular orders about the preparations to be made for his funeral, I went to town; but having made it late before I got in on Thursday night, and being fatigued for want of rest several nights before, and low in my spirits (I could not help it, Lovelace!), I contented myself to send my compliments to the innocent sufferer, to inquire after her health.

My servant saw Mrs Smith, who told him she was very glad I was come to town; for that the lady was worse than she had yet been.

It is impossible to account for the contents of her letter to you; or to reconcile those contents to the facts I have to communicate.

I was at Smith's by seven yesterday (Friday) morning; and found that the lady was just gone in a chair to St Dunstan's to prayers; she was too ill to get out by six to Covent Garden Church; and was forced to be supported to her chair by Mrs Lovick. They would have persuaded her against going; but she said she knew not but it would be her last opportunity. Mrs Lovick, dreading that she would be taken worse at church, walked thither before her.

Mrs Smith told me she was so ill on Wednesday night, that she had desired to receive the Sacrament; and accordingly it was administered to her by the parson of the parish: whom she besought to take all opportunities of assisting her in her solemn preparation.

This the gentleman promised: and called in the morning to inquire after her health; and was admitted at the first word. He stayed with her about half an hour; and when he came down, with his face turned aside and a faltering accent, 'Mrs Smith, said he, you have an angel in your house—I will attend her again in the evening, as she desires, and as often as I think it will be agreeable to her.'

Her increased weakness she attributed to the fatigues she had undergone by your means; and to a letter she had received from her sister, which she answered the same day.

Mrs Smith told me that two different persons had called there, one on Thursday morning, one in the evening, to inquire after her state of health; and seemed as if commissioned from her relations for that purpose; but asked not to see her, only were very inquisitive after her visitors (particularly, it seems, after *me*: what could they mean by that?), after her way of life, and expenses; and one of them inquired after her manner of supporting them; to the latter of which, Mrs Smith said, she had answered, as the truth was, that she had been obliged to sell some of her clothes, and was actually about parting with more; at which the inquirist (a grave old farmer-looking man) held up his hands, and said, Good God!—this will be sad, sad news to somebody! I believe I must not mention it. But Mrs Smith says she desired he *would*, let him come from whom he would. He shook his head, and said if she died, the flower of the world would be gone, and the family she belonged to would be no more than a common family.[a] I was pleased with the man's expression.

You may be curious to know how she passed her time when she was obliged to leave her lodging to avoid you.

Mrs Smith tells me 'that she was very ill when she went out on Monday morning, and sighed as if her heart would break as she came downstairs, and as she went through the shop into the coach, her nurse with her, as you had informed me before: that she ordered the coachman (whom she hired for the day) to drive anywhither, so it was into the air: he accordingly drove her to Hampstead and thence to Highgate. There she alighted at the Bowling Green House, extremely ill, and having breakfasted, ordered the coachman to drive very slowly, anywhere. He crept along to Muswell Hill, and put up at a public house there; where she employed herself two hours in writing, though exceedingly weak and low; till the dinner she had ordered was brought in: she endeavoured to eat; but could not; her appetite was gone, quite gone, she said. And then she wrote on for three hours more: after which, being heavy, she dozed a little in an elbow-chair. When she awoke, she ordered the coachman to drive her very slowly to town, to the house of a friend of Mrs Loviok, whom, as agreed upon, she met there: but, being extremely ill, she would venture home at a late hour, although she heard from the widow that you had been there, and had reason to be shocked at your behaviour. She said, she found there was no avoiding you: she was apprehensive she should not live many hours, and it was not impossible but the shock the sight of you must give her would determine her fate in your presence.

'She accordingly went home. She heard the relation of your astonishing vagaries, with hands and eyes often lifted up; and with the words, Shocking creature! Incorrigible wretch! and, Will nothing make him serious! intermingled. And not being able to bear an interview with a man so hardened, she took to her usual chair early in the morning, and was carried to the Temple stairs, whither she had ordered her nurse before her, to get a pair of oars in readiness (for her fatigues the day before made her unable to bear a coach); and then she was rowed to Chelsea, where she breakfasted; and after rowing about, put in at the Swan at Brentford Ait, where she dined; and would have written, but had no conveniency either of tolerable pens, or ink, or private room; and then proceeding to Richmond, they rowed her back to Mortlake; where she put in and drank tea at a house her waterman recommended to her. She wrote there for an hour; and returned to the Temple; and, when she landed, made one of the watermen get her a chair, and so

---

a This man came from her cousin Morden; as will be seen hereafter.

was carried to the widow's friend, as the night before; where she again met the widow, who informed her that you had been after her twice that day.

'Mrs Lovick gave her there her sister's letter[a]; and she was so much affected with the contents of it, that she was twice very near fainting away; and wept bitterly, as Mrs Lovick told Mrs Smith; dropping some warmer expressions than ever they had heard proceed from her lips in relation to her friends; calling them cruel, and complaining of ill offices done her, and of vile reports raised against her.

'While she was thus disturbed, Mrs Smith came to her, and told her that you had been there a third time, and was just gone (at half an hour after nine), having left word how civil and respectful you would be; but that you was determined to see her at all events.

'She said it was hard she could not be permitted to die in peace: that her lot was a severe one: that she began to be afraid she should not forbear repining, and to think her punishment greater than her fault; but recalling herself immediately, she comforted herself that her life would be short, and with the assurance of a better.'

By what I have mentioned, you will conclude with me that the letter brought her by Mrs Lovick (the superscription of which you saw to be written in her sister's hand) could not be the letter on the contents of which she grounded *that* she wrote to you on her return home: and yet neither Mrs Lovick, nor Mrs Smith, nor the servant of the latter, know of any other brought her. But as the women assured me that she actually *did* write to you, I was eased of a suspicion which I had begun to entertain, that you (for some purpose I could not guess at) had forged the letter from her of which you sent me a copy.

On Wednesday morning, when she received your letter in answer to hers, she said, Necessity may well be called the mother of invention—But calamity is the test of integrity. I hope I have not taken an inexcusable step—and there she stopped a minute or two, and then said, I shall now perhaps be allowed to die in peace.

I stayed till she came in. She was glad to see me; but, being very weak, said, she must sit down before she could go upstairs; and so went into the back shop; leaning upon Mrs Lovick: and when she had sat down, 'I am glad to see you, Mr Belford, said she; I *must* say so—let misreporters say what they will.'

I wondered at this expression[b]; but would not interrupt her.

Oh! sir, said she, I have been grievously harassed. Your friend, who would not let me live with reputation, will not permit me to die in peace—You see how I am—Is there not a great alteration in me within this week?—But 'tis all for the better. Yet were I to wish for life, I must say that your friend, your barbarous friend, has *hurt* me greatly.

She was so very weak, so short-breathed, and her words and action so very moving, that I was forced to walk from her; the two women and her nurse, turning away their faces also, weeping.

I have had, madam, said I, since I saw you, a most shocking scene before my eyes for days together. My poor friend Belton is no more. He quitted the world yesterday morning in such dreadful agonies that the impression it has left upon me has *so weakened* my mind—I was loath to have her think that my grief was owing to the weak state I saw her in, for fear of dispiriting her.

a   See Letter 429.
b   Explained hereafter.

That is only, Mr Belford, interrupted she, in order to *strengthen* it, if a proper use be made of the impression—But I should be glad, since you are so humanely affected with the solemn circumstance, that you could have written an account of it in the style and manner you are master of, to your gay friend. Who knows, as it would have come *from* an associate and *of* an associate, how it might have affected him?

That I *had* done, I told her, in such a manner as had, I believed, some effect upon you.

His behaviour in this honest family so lately, said she, and his cruel pursuit of me, give but little hopes that anything serious or solemn will affect him.

We had some talk about Belton's dying behaviour, and I gave her several particulars of the poor man's impatience and despair; to which she was very attentive; and made fine observations upon the subject of procrastination.

A letter and packet were brought her by a man on horseback from Miss Howe, while we were talking. She retired upstairs to read it; and while I was in discourse with Mrs Smith and Mrs Lovick, the doctor and apothecary both came in together. They confirmed to me my fears as to the dangerous way she is in. They had both been apprised of the new instances of implacableness in her friends, and of your persecutions: and the doctor said, he would not for the world be either the unforgiving father of that lady, or the man who had brought her to this distress. Her heart's broke; she'll die, said he: there is no saving her. But how, were I either the one or the other of the people I have named, I should support myself afterwards, I cannot tell.

When she was told we were all three together, she desired us to walk up. She arose to receive us, and after answering two or three general questions relating to her health, she addressed herself to us to the following effect.

As I may not, said she, see you three gentlemen together again, let me take this opportunity to acknowledge my obligations to you all. I am inexpressibly obliged to you, sir, and to you, sir (curtsying to the doctor and to Mr Goddard) for your *more* than friendly, your *paternal* care and concern for me. Humanity in your profession, I dare say, is far from being a rare qualification, because you are gentlemen *by* your profession: but so much kindness, so much humanity, did never desolate creature meet with, as I have met with from you both. But indeed I have always observed that where a person relies upon Providence, it never fails to raise up a new friend for every old one that falls off.

This gentleman (bowing to me) who, some people think, should have been one of the last I should have thought of as my executor—is nevertheless (such is the strange chance of things!) the only one I can choose; and therefore I have chosen him for that charitable office, and he has been so good as to accept of it: for rich as I may boast myself to be, I am rather so in *right* than in *fact*, at this present. I repeat therefore my humble thanks to you all three, and beg of God to return to you and yours (looking to each) an hundredfold, the kindness and favour you have shown me; and that it may be in the power of you and of yours to the end of time, to confer benefits, rather than to be obliged to receive them. This is a god-like power, gentlemen: I once rejoiced in it, in some little degree; and much more in the prospect I had of its being enlarged to me; though I have had the mortification to experience the reverse, and to be obliged almost to everybody I have seen or met with: but all, originally, through my own fault; so I ought to bear the punishment without repining: and I hope I do—Forgive these impertinencies: a grateful heart, that wants the power it wishes for, to express itself suitably to its own impulses, will be at a loss what properly to dictate to the tongue; and yet, unable to restrain its overflowings, will force it to say weak and silly things, rather than appear ungratefully silent. Once more then, I thank ye all three for your kindness to me: and God Almighty make you that amends which at present I cannot!

She retired from us to her closet with her eyes full; and left us looking upon one another.

We had hardly recovered ourselves, when she, quite easy, cheerful, and smiling, returned to us. Doctor, said she (seeing we had been moved), you will excuse me for the concern I give you; and so will you, Mr Goddard, and you, Mr Belford; for 'tis a concern that only generous natures can show; and to such natures *sweet* is the pain, if I may so say, that attends such a concern. But as I have some few preparations still to make, and would not (though in ease of Mr Belford's future cares, which is, and ought to be, part of my study) undertake more than it is likely I shall have time lent me to perform, I would beg of you to give me your opinions (you see my way of living; and you may be assured that I will do nothing wilfully to shorten my life) how long it may possibly be before I may hope to be released from all my troubles.

They both hesitated, and looked upon each other. Don't be afraid to answer me, said she, each sweet hand pressing upon the arm of each gentleman, with that mingled freedom and reserve which virgin modesty, mixed with conscious dignity, can only express, and with a look serenely earnest: Tell me how long you think I may hold it? And believe me, gentlemen, the shorter you tell me my time is likely to be, the more comfort you will give me.

With what pleasing woe, said the doctor, do you fill the minds of those who have the happiness to converse with you, and see the happy frame you are in! What you have undergone within a few days past has much hurt you: and should you have fresh troubles of those kinds, I could not be answerable for your holding it—and there he paused.

How long, doctor?—I believe I *shall* have a little more ruffling—I am afraid I shall—but there can happen only one thing that I shall not be tolerably easy under—How long then, sir?—

He was silent.

A fortnight, sir?

He was still silent.

Ten days?—a week?—how long, sir? with smiling earnestness.

If I *must* speak, madam; if you have not better treatment than you have lately met with, I am afraid—There again he stopped.

Afraid of what, doctor? Don't be afraid—How long, sir?

That a fortnight or three weeks may deprive the world of the finest flower in it.

A fortnight or three weeks yet, doctor!—But, God's will be done! I shall, however, by this means have full time, if I have but strength and intellect, to do all that is now upon my mind to do. And so, sirs, I can but once more thank you, turning to each of us, for all your goodness to me; and, having letters to write, will take up no more of your time—only, doctor, be pleased to order me some more of those drops: they cheer me a little when I am low; and, putting a fee into his unwilling hand—You know the terms, sir!—Then, turning to Mr Goddard, You'll be so good, sir, as to look in upon me tonight, or tomorrow, as you have the opportunity: and you, Mr Belford, I know will be desirous to set out to prepare for the last office for your late friend: so I wish you a good journey, and hope to see you when that is performed.

She then retired with a cheerful and serene air. The two gentlemen went away together. I went down to the women, and inquiring, found that Mrs Lovick was this day to bring her twenty guineas more for some other of her apparel.

The widow told me that she had taken the liberty to expostulate with her upon the *occasion* she had for raising this money, to such great disadvantage; and it produced the following short, and affecting conversation between them.

None of my friends will wear anything of mine, said she. I shall leave a great many good things behind me—And as to what I want the money for—don't be surprised—but suppose I want it to purchase a house?

You are all mystery, madam, I don't comprehend you.

Why, then, Mrs Lovick, I will explain myself: I have a man, not a woman, for my executor: and think you that I will leave to his care anything that concerns my own person?—Now, Mrs Lovick, smiling, do you comprehend me?

Mrs Lovick wept.

Oh fie! proceeded the lady, drying up her tears with her own handkerchief, and giving her a kiss—Why this kind weakness for one whom you have been so little a while acquainted with? Dear, good Mrs Lovick, don't be concerned for me on a prospect which I have occasion to be pleased with; but go tomorrow to your friends, and bring me the money they have agreed to give you.

Thus, Lovelace, is it plain, that she means to bespeak her *last* house! Here's presence of mind; here's tranquillity of heart on the most affecting occasion!—This is magnanimity indeed!—Couldst thou, or could I, with all our boisterous bravery and offensive false courage, act thus?—Poor Belton! how unlike was thy behaviour?

Mrs Lovick tells me that the lady spoke of a letter she had received from her favourite divine Dr Lewen, in the time of my absence. And of an answer she had returned to it. But Mrs Lovick knows not the contents of either.

When thou receivest this letter, thou wilt see what will soon be the end of all thy injuries to this divine lady. I say, *when thou receivest* it; for I will delay it for some little time, lest thou shouldst take it into thy head (under pretence of resenting the disappointment her letter must give thee) to molest her again.

This letter having detained me by its length, I shall not now set out for Epsom till tomorrow.

I should have mentioned, that the lady explained to me what the *one thing* was that she was afraid might happen to ruffle her. It was the apprehension of what may result from a visit which Colonel Morden, as she is informed, designs to make *you*.

Letter 427: THE REV. DR LEWEN TO MISS CLARISSA HARLOWE

Friday, Aug. 18

PRESUMING, dearest and ever-respectable young lady, upon your former favour, and upon your opinion of my judgement and sincerity, I cannot help addressing you by a few lines, on your present unhappy situation.

I will not look back upon the measures which you have either been *led* or *driven* into: but will only say as to *those*, that I think you are the least to blame of any young lady that was ever reduced from happy to unhappy circumstances; and I have not been wanting to say as much, where I hoped my freedom would have been better received than I have had the mortification to find it to be.

What I principally write for now is to put you upon doing a piece of justice to yourself, and to your sex, in the prosecuting for his life (I am assured his life is in your power) the most profligate and abandoned of men, as *he* must be, who could act so basely as I understand Mr Lovelace has acted by you.

I am very ill; and am now forced to write upon my pillow; my thoughts confused; and incapable of method. I shall not therefore aim at method: but to give you in general my opinion; and that is that your religion, your duty to your family, the duty you owe to your honour, and even charity to your sex, oblige you to give public evidence against this very wicked man.

And let me add another consideration; the prevention by this means of the mischiefs that may otherwise happen between your brother and Mr Lovelace, or between the latter and your cousin Morden, who is now I hear arrived, and resolves to have justice done you.

A consideration which ought to affect your conscience (forgive me, dearest young lady, I think I am now in the way of my duty); and to be of more concern to you than that hard pressure upon your modesty, which I know the appearance against him in an open court must be of to such a lady as you: and which, I conceive, will be your great difficulty. But I know, madam, that you have dignity enough to *become* the blushes of the most naked truth, when necessity, justice and honour, exact it from you. Rakes and ravishers would meet with encouragement *indeed*, and most from those who had the greatest abhorrence of their actions, if violated modesty were never to complain of the injury it received from the villainous attempters of it.

In a word, the reparation of your family dishonour now rests in your own bosom: and which only one of these two alternatives *can* repair; to wit, either to marry, or to prosecute him at law. Bitter expedients for a soul so delicate as yours.

He and all his friends, I understand, solicit you to the first: and it is certainly, now, all the amends within his power to make. But I am assured that you have rejected *their* solicitations, and *his*, with the indignation and contempt that his foul actions have deserved: but yet, that you refuse not to extend to him the Christian forgiveness he has so little reason to expect, provided he will not disturb you further.

But, madam, the prosecution I advise will not let your present and future exemption from fresh disturbance from so vile a molester depend upon his *courtesy:* I should think so noble and so rightly-guided a spirit as yours would not permit that it should, if you could help it.

And can indignities of any kind be *properly pardoned* till we have it in *our power to punish them?* To pretend to pardon, while we are labouring under the pain or dishonour of them, will be thought by some to be but the vaunted mercy of a pusillanimous heart trembling to resent them. The remedy I propose is a severe one; but what pain can be more severe than the injury? or how will injuries be believed to grieve us, that are never honourably complained of?

I am sure Miss Clarissa Harlowe, however injured and oppressed, remains unshaken in her sentiments of honour, and virtue: and although she would sooner die than *deserve* that her modesty should be drawn into question; yet she will think no truth immodest that is to be uttered in the vindicated cause of innocence and chastity. Little, very little difference is there, my dear young lady, between a *suppressed* evidence, and a *false* one.

It is a terrible circumstance, I once more own, for a young lady of your delicacy to be under the obligation of telling so shocking a story in public court: but it is still a worse imputation that she should pass over so mortal an injury unresented.

Conscience, honour, justice, and the cares of Heaven are on your side: and modesty would, by some, be thought but an empty name should you refuse to obey their dictates.

I have been consulted, I own, on this subject. I have given it as my opinion, that you ought to prosecute the abandoned man. But without my reasons. These I reserved, with a resolution to lay them before you, unknown to anybody; that the result (if what I wish) might be *your own*.

I will only add that the misfortunes which have befallen you, had they been the lot of a child of my own, could not have affected me more than yours have done. My own child I love: but I both love and honour you: since to love you is to love virtue, good sense, prudence, and everything that is good and noble in woman.

Wounded as I think all these are by the injuries you have received, you will believe that the knowledge of your distresses must have afflicted, beyond what I am able to express,

Your sincere admirer, and humble servant,
ARTHUR LEWEN

I just now understand that your sister will, by proper authority, propose this prosecution to you. I humbly presume that the reason why you resolved not upon this step from the first was that you did not know that it would have the *countenance and support of your relations.*

Letter 428: MISS CLARISSA HARLOWE TO THE REV. DR LEWEN

Sat. Aug. 19

Reverend and dear sir,

I THOUGHT, till I received your affectionate and welcome letter, that I had neither father, uncle, brother left; nor hardly a friend among my former favourers of your sex. Yet, knowing *you* so well, and having no reason to upbraid myself with a faulty will, I was to blame (even although I had doubted the continuance of your good opinion) to decline the trial whether I had forfeited it or not; and if I had, whether I could not, *honourably*, reinstate myself in it.

But, sir, it was owing to different causes that I did not; partly to *shame,* to think how high in my happier days I stood in your esteem, and how much I must be sunk in it, since those so much nearer in relation to me gave me up; partly to *deep distress*, which makes the humbled heart diffident; and made mine afraid to claim the kindred mind in yours, which would have supplied to me, in some measure, all the dear and lost relations I have named.

Then, so loath as I sometimes was to be thought to want to make a *party* against those whom both duty and inclination bid me reverence: so long *trailed* on between *hope and doubt:* so *little mine own mistress* at one time; so fearful of *making or causing mischief* at another; and not being encouraged to hope, by *your kind notice*, that my application to you would be acceptable—apprehending that my relations had engaged your *silence* at least.[a]

THESE——But why these unavailing retrospections now? I *was* to be unhappy—in order to *be* happy; that is my hope. Resigning therefore to that hope, I will without any further preamble write a few lines (if writing to *you*, I can write *but* a few) in answer to the subject of your kind letter.

Permit me then to say, that I believe your arguments would have been unanswerable in almost every *other* case of this nature but in that of the unhappy *Clarissa Harlowe*.

It is certain that creatures who cannot stand the shock of *public shame* should be doubly careful how they expose themselves to the danger of incurring *private guilt*, which may possibly bring them to it: But as to *myself,* suppose there were no objections from the declining way I am in as to my health; and supposing I could have prevailed upon myself to appear against this man, was there not room to apprehend that the end so much wished for by my friends (to wit, his condign punishment) would not have been obtained, when it came to be seen that I had consented to give him a clandestine meeting; and in consequence of that, had been weakly tricked out of myself; and further still, had not been able to avoid living under one roof with him for several weeks; which I did, not only without complaint, but without *cause* of complaint.

Little advantage *in a court* (perhaps bandied about, and jested profligately with) would some of those pleas in my favour have been, which *out of court*, and to a *private* and *serious* audience, would have carried the greatest weight against him—Such, particularly, as the infamous methods to which he had recourse.

It would no doubt have been a ready retort from *every* mouth, that I ought not to have thrown myself into the power of such a man, and that I ought to take for my pains what had befallen me.

But had the prosecution been carried on to *effect*, and had he even been *sentenced to death*, can it be thought that his family would not have had interest enough to obtain his pardon for a crime thought too lightly of, though one of the greatest that can be committed against a creature valuing her honour above her life?—While I had been censured as pursuing with sanguinary views a man who offered me early all the reparation in his power to make?

And had he been *pardoned*, would he not then have been at liberty to do as much mischief as ever?

a   The stiff visit this good divine was prevailed upon to make her, as mentioned on p. 293 (of which, however, she was too generous to remind him) might warrant the lady to think that he had rather inclined to their party, as the *parental side*, than to hers.

I dare say, sir, such is the assurance of the man upon whom my unhappy destiny threw me; and such his inveteracy to my family (which would then have appeared to be justified by their known inveteracy to *him*, and by their earnest endeavours to take away his life), that he would not have been sorry to have an opportunity to confront me and my father, uncles, and brother, at the bar of a court of justice, on such an occasion. In which case, would not, on his acquittal or pardon, resentments have been reciprocally heightened? And then would my brother, or my cousin Morden, have been more secure than now?

How do these considerations aggravate my fault? My motives, at first, were not indeed blamable: but I had forgotten the excellent caution, which yet I was not ignorant of, *that we ought not to do evil that good may come of it.*

In full conviction of the purity of my heart, and of the firmness of my principles (why may I not, thus called upon, say what I am conscious of, and yet without faulty pride; since all is but a *duty*, and I should be utterly inexcusable, could I not justly say what I do?—In this full conviction) he has offered me marriage. He has avowed his penitence: a *sincere* penitence I have reason to think it, though perhaps not a *Christian* one. And his noble relations (kinder to the poor sufferer than her own), on the same conviction, and his own not ungenerous acknowledgements, have joined to intercede with me to *forgive* and *accept* of him. Although I cannot comply with the latter part of their intercession, have not you, sir, from the *best* rules, and from the *divinest* example, taught me to forgive injuries?

The injury I have received from him is indeed of the highest nature, and it was attended with circumstances of unmanly baseness and premeditation; yet, I bless God, it has not tainted my mind; it has not hurt my morals. No thanks, indeed, to the wicked man, that it has not. No vile courses have followed it. My will is unviolated. The evil (respecting *myself*, and not my *friends*) is merely personal. No credulity, no weakness, no want of vigilance, have I to reproach myself with. I have, through grace, triumphed over the deepest machinations. I have escaped from him. I have renounced him. The man whom once I could have loved, I have been enabled to despise: and shall not *charity* complete my triumph? And shall I not *enjoy* it?—And where would be my triumph if he *deserved* my forgiveness?— Poor man! He has had a loss in losing me! I have the pride to think so, because I think I know my own heart. I have had none in losing him!

But I have *another* plea to make, which alone would have been enough (as I presume) to answer the contents of your very kind and friendly letter.

I know, my dear and reverend friend, the spiritual guide and director of my happier days! I know that you will allow of my endeavour to bring myself to this charitable disposition, when I tell you how near I think myself to that great and awful moment *in* which, and even in the ardent preparation *to* which, every sense of indignity or injury that concerns not the immortal soul ought to be absorbed in higher and more important contemplations.

Thus much for *myself.*

And for the satisfaction of my *friends* and *favourers*, Miss Howe is solicitous to have all those letters and materials preserved, which will set my whole story in a true light. The good Dr Lewen is one of the principal of those friends and favourers.

The warning that may be given from those papers to all such young creatures as may have known or heard of me, may be more efficacious, as I humbly presume to think, to the end wished for, than my appearance could have been in a court of justice, pursuing a doubtful event, under the disadvantages I have mentioned. And if, my dear and good sir, you are now on considering everything, of *this* opinion, and I could *know* it, I should consider it as a particular felicity; being as solicitous as ever to be justified in what I may in your eyes.

I am sorry, sir, that your indisposition has reduced you to the necessity of writing upon your pillow. But how much am I obliged to that kind and generous concern for me, which has *impelled* you, as I may say, to write a letter containing so many paternal lines, with such inconvenience to yourself!

May the Almighty bless you, dear and reverend sir, for all your goodness to me, both of now and of long standing! Continue to esteem me to the last, as I do and will venerate you! And let me bespeak your prayers; the *continuance*, I should say, of your prayers; for I doubt not that I have always had them: and to them, perhaps, has in part been owing (as well as to your pious precepts through my earlier youth) that I have been able to make the stand I have made; although everything that you prayed for has not been granted to me by that Divine Wisdom, which knows what is best for its poor creatures.

My prayers for *you* are that it will please God to restore you to your affectionate flock; and after as many years of life as shall be for *His* service, and to *your own* comfort, give us a happy meeting in those regions of blessedness which you have taught me, as well by *example* as by *precept*, to aspire to!

                                                                    CLARISSA HARLOWE

Letter 429: MISS ARABELLA HARLOWE TO MISS CLARISSA HARLOWE

(In answer to hers to her uncle Antony of Aug. 13, Letter 407)

                                                                    Monday, Aug. 21
Sister CLARY,

I FIND by your letters to my uncles, that they, as well as I, are in great disgrace with you for writing our minds to you.

We can't help it, sister Clary.

You don't think it worth your while, I find, to press for the blessing you pretend to be so earnest about, a second time: you think, no doubt, that you have done your duty in asking for it: so you'll sit down satisfied with that, I suppose, and leave it to your wounded parents to repent hereafter that they have not done *theirs* in giving it to you at the *first* word; and in making such inquiries about you, as you think ought to have been made. Fine encouragement to inquire after a runaway daughter! living with her fellow, as long as he would live with her! You repent also (with your *full mind*, as you modestly call it) that you wrote to me.

So we are not likely to be applied to any more, I find, in this way.

Well then, since this is the case, sister Clary, let me, *with all humility*, address myself with a proposal or two to you; to which you will be *graciously* pleased to give an answer.

Now you must know that we have had hints given us from several quarters that you have been used in such a manner by the villain you ran away with, that his life would be answerable for his crime if it were fairly to be proved. And, by your own hints, something like it appears to us.

If, Clary, there be anything but jingle and affecting period in what proceeds from your *full mind*, and your *dutiful consciousness*; and if there be truth in what Mrs Norton and Mrs Howe have acquainted us with; you may yet justify your character to us, and to the world, in everything but your scandalous elopement; and the law may reach the villain: and, could we but bring him to the gallows, what a meritorious revenge would that be to our whole injured family, and to the innocents he has deluded, as well as the saving from ruin many others?

Let me, therefore, know (if you please) whether you are willing to appear to do *yourself*, and *us*, and your *sex*, this justice? If *not*, sister Clary, we shall know what to think of you; for neither *you* nor *we* can suffer more than we have done from the scandal of your fall: and, if *you will*, Mr Ackland and Counsellor Derham will both attend you to make *proper inquiries*, and to take minutes of your story to found a process upon, if it will bear one with as great a probability of success as we are told it may be prosecuted with.

But, by what Mrs Howe intimates, this is not likely to be complied with; for it is what she hinted to you, it seems, by her lively daughter, but without effect[a]; and then again, possibly you may not at present behave so prudently in some certain points as to entitle yourself to public justice; which if true, the Lord have mercy upon you!

One word only more as to the above proposal—your admirer, Dr Lewen, is clear in his opinion that you should prosecute the villain.

But if you will not agree to this, I have another proposal to make to you, and that in the name of everyone in the family; which is, that you will think of going to Pennsylvania, to reside there for some few years till all is blown over; and if it please God to spare you, and your unhappy parents, till they can be satisfied that you behave like a true and uniform penitent; at least till you are one-and-twenty; you may then come back to your own estate, or have the produce of it sent you thither, as you shall choose. A period which my papa fixes because it is the *custom*; and because he thinks your *grandfather* should have fixed it; and because, let *me* add, you have fully proved by your fine conduct that you were not at years of discretion at *eighteen*. Poor doting, though good old man!—your grandfather, he thought—But I would not be too severe.

Mr Hartley has a widow sister at Pennsylvania, with whom he will undertake you may board, and who is a sober, sensible, and well-read woman. And if you were once well there, it would rid your father and mother of a world of cares, and fears, and scandal; and I think is what you should wish for of all things.

Mr Hartley will engage for all accommodations in your passage suitable to your rank and fortune; and he has a concern in a ship which will sail in a month; and you may take your secret-keeping Hannah with you, or whom you will of your newer acquaintance. 'Tis presumed it will be of your own sex.

These are what I had to communicate to you; and if you'll oblige me with an answer (which the hand that conveys this will call for on Wednesday morning) it will be very condescending.

ARABELLA HARLOWE

a See Letter 317.

Letter 430: MISS CLARISSA HARLOWE TO MISS ARABELLA HARLOWE

Tuesday, Aug. 22

WRITE to me, my hard-hearted sister, in what manner you please, I shall always be thankful to you for your notice. But (think what you will of me) I cannot see Mr Ackland and the counsellor on such a business as you mention.

The Lord have mercy upon me indeed! For none else will.

Surely I am believed to be a creature past all shame, or it could not be thought of sending two *gentlemen* to me on such an errand.

Had my mother required of me (or would *modesty* have permitted you to inquire into) the particulars of my sad story, or had Mrs Norton been directed to receive them from me, methinks it had been more fit; and, I presume to think, more in everyone's character too, had they been required of me before such heavy judgement had passed upon me as has been passed.

I know that this is Dr Lewen's opinion. He has been so good as to enforce it in a kind letter to me. I have answered his letter; and given such reasons as I hope will satisfy *him:* I could wish it were thought worth while to ask to see them.[a]

To your other proposal, of going to Pennsylvania; this is my answer: If nothing happen within a month which may full as effectually rid my parents and friends of that world of cares, and fears, and scandals, which you mention, and if I am *then* able to be carried on board of ship, I will cheerfully obey my father and mother, although I were sure to die in the passage. And, if I may be forgiven for saying so, you shall set over me, instead of my poor obliging but really unculpable Hannah, your Betty Barnes: to whom I will be answerable for all my conduct. And I will make it worth her while to accompany me.

I am equally surprised and concerned at the hints which both you and my uncle Antony give of *new* points of misbehaviour in me!—What can be meant by them?

I will not tell you, Miss Harlowe, how much I am afflicted at your severity, and how much I suffer by it, and by your hard-hearted levity of style, because what I shall say may be construed into *jingle* and *period*, and because I know it is *intended* (very possibly for *kind* ends) to mortify me. All I will therefore say is that it does not lose its end, if that be it.

But nevertheless (divesting myself as much as possible of all resentment) I will only pray that heaven will give you, for *your own* sake, a kinder heart than at present you seem to have; since a kind heart, I am convinced, is a greater blessing to its possessor than it can be to any other person. Under this conviction I subscribe myself, my dear Bella,

Your ever-affectionate sister,
CL. HARLOWE

a   This letter was not asked for; and the reverend gentleman's death, which fell out soon after he had received it, was the reason that it was not communicated to the family till it was too late to do the service that might have been hoped for from it.

Letter 431: MRS JUDITH NORTON TO MISS CLARISSA HARLOWE

(In answer to hers of Thursday, Aug. 17, Letter 409)

Tuesday, Aug. 22

My dearest young lady,

THE Letters you sent me I now return by the hand that brings you this.

It is impossible for me to express how much I have been affected by them, and your last of the 17th. Indeed, my dear Miss Clary, you are very harshly used; indeed you are! And if you should be taken from us, what grief, and what punishment, are they not treasuring up against themselves, in the heavy reflections which their rash censures and unforgiveness will occasion them!

But I find what your uncle Antony's cruel letter is owing to, as well as one you will be still more afflicted by, (God help you, my poor dear child!) when it comes to your hand, written by your sister, with proposals to you.

It was finished to send you yesterday, I know; and I apprise you of it, that you should fortify your heart against the contents of it.

The motives which incline them all to this severity, if well-grounded, would authorize any severity they could express, and which, while they believe them to be so, both they and you are to be equally pitied.

They are owing to the information of that officious Mr Brand, who has acquainted them from some enemy of yours in the neighbourhood about you, that visits are made you, highly censurable, from a man of a free character and an intimate of Mr Lovelace; who is often in private with you; sometimes twice or thrice a day.

Betty gives herself great liberties of speech upon this occasion, and all your friends are too ready to believe that things are not as they should be: which makes me wish, that, let the gentleman's views be ever so honourable, you could entirely drop acquaintance with him.

Something of this nature was hinted at by Betty to me before, but so darkly, that I could not tell what to make of it; and this made me mention it to you so *generally* as I did in my last.

Your cousin Morden has been among them: he is exceedingly concerned for your misfortunes; and as they will not believe Mr Lovelace would marry you, he is determined to go to Lord M.'s, in order to inform himself from Mr Lovelace's own mouth whether he intends to do you that justice or not.

He was extremely caressed by everyone at his first arrival; but I am told there is some little coldness between them and him at present.

I was in hopes of getting a sight of this letter of Mr Brand's (a rash, officious man!). But, it seems, Mr Morden had it given him yesterday to read, and he took it away with him.

God be your comfort, my dear miss! But indeed I am exceedingly disturbed at the thoughts of what may still be the issue of all these things. I am,

My beloved young lady,
Your most affectionate and faithful
JUDITH NORTON

Letter 432: MRS NORTON TO MISS CLARISSA HARLOWE

Tuesday, Aug. 22

AFTER I had sealed up the enclosed, I had the honour of a private visit from your aunt Hervey, who has been in a very low-spirited way, and kept her chamber for several weeks past; and is but just got abroad.

She longed, she said, to see me, and to weep with me on the hard fate that had befallen her beloved niece.

I will give you a faithful account of what passed between us; as I expect that it will, upon the whole, administer hope and comfort to you.

'She pitied very much your good mamma who, she assured me, is obliged to act a part entirely contrary to her inclinations; as she herself, she owns, had been in a great measure.

'She said that the poor lady was with great difficulty withheld from answering your letter to her; which had (as was your aunt's expression) almost broken the heart of everyone: that she had reason to think that she was neither consenting to your two uncles writing; nor approving of what they wrote.

'She is sure they all love you dearly; but have gone so far that they know not how to recede.

'That, but for the *abominable league* which your brother had got everybody into (he refusing to set out for Scotland till it was renewed and till they had all promised to take no step towards a reconciliation in his absence but by his consent; and to which your sister's resentments kept them up), all would before now have happily subsided.

'That nobody knew the pangs which their inflexible behaviour gave them, ever since you had begun to write to them in so affecting and humble a style.

'That, however, they were not inclined to believe that you were either so ill or so penitent as you really are; and still less that Mr Lovelace is in earnest in his offers of marriage.

'She is sure, she says, that all will soon be well: and the sooner for Mr Morden's arrival: who is very zealous in your behalf.

'She wished to heaven that you would accept of Mr Lovelace, wicked as he has been, if he were now in earnest.

'It had always, she said, been matter of astonishment to her, that so weak a pride in her cousin James, of making himself the *whole family* should induce them all to refuse an alliance with such a family as Mr Lovelace's was.

'She would have it that your going off with Mr Lovelace was the unhappiest step for your honour and your interest that could have been taken; for that although you would have had a severe trial the next day; yet it would probably have been the *last*; and your pathetic powers must have drawn you off some friends—hinting at your mamma, at your uncle Harlowe, at your uncle Hervey, and herself.'

But here I must observe (that the regret that you did not trust to the event of that meeting may not in your present low way too much afflict you) that it seems a little too evident from this opinion of your aunt's, that it was not so absolutely determined that all compulsion was designed to be avoided, since your freedom from it must have been owing to the party to be made among them by your persuasive eloquence, and dutiful expostulation.

'She owned that some of them were as much afraid of meeting you, as you could be of meeting them'—But why so if they designed in the last instance, to give you your way?

She told me, 'that Mrs Williams, your mamma's former housekeeper, had been with *her*, to ask her opinion if it would be taken amiss, if she desired leave to go up to attend her *dearest young lady in her calamity*. She referred her to your mamma; but had heard no more of it.

'Her daughter, Miss Dolly, she said, had been frequently earnest with her on the same subject; and renewed her request with the greatest fervour when your first letter came to hand.

'Your aunt says that being then very ill, she wrote to your mother upon it, hoping it would not be taken amiss if she permitted Miss Dolly to go; but that your sister, as from your mamma, answered her that now you seemed to be coming to, and to have a due sense of your faults, you must be left entirely to their own management.

'Miss Dolly, she said, had pined ever since she had heard of Mr Lovelace's baseness; being doubly mortified by it: first, on account of your sufferings; next, because she was one who rejoiced in your getting off; and vindicated you for it: and had incurred censure and ill-will on that account; especially from your brother and sister; so that she seldom went to Harlowe Place.'

Make the best use of these intelligences, my dearest young lady, for your consolation.

I will only add that I am, with the most fervent prayers for your recovery and restoration,

> Your ever-faithful
> JUDITH NORTON

Letter 433: MISS CLARISSA HARLOWE TO MRS JUDITH NORTON

> Thursday, Aug. 24

THE relation of such a conversation as passed between my aunt and you would have given me pleasure had it come some time ago; because it would have met with a spirit more industrious than mine *now* is, to pick out remote comfort in the hope of a favourable turn that might one day have rewarded my patient duty.

I did not doubt my aunt's good-will to me. Her affection I did not doubt. But shall we wonder that kings and princes meet with so little control in their passions, be they ever so violent, when in a private family, an aunt, nay, even a mother in that family, shall choose to give up a once favoured child against their own inclinations, rather than oppose an aspiring young man who had armed himself with the authority of a father, who, when once determined, never would be expostulated with?

And will you not *blame* me, if I say that good sense, that relationly indulgence, must be a little offended at the treatment I have met with, and if I own that I think that great rigour has been exercised towards me? And yet I am now authorized to call it *rigour* by the judgement of two excellent sisters, my mother and my aunt, who acknowledge (as you tell me from my aunt) that they have been obliged to join against me, contrary to their inclinations; and that even in a point which concerns my eternal welfare.

But I must not go on at this rate. For may not the inclination my mother has given up be the effect of a too fond indulgence, rather than that I merit the indulgence? And yet, so petulantly perverse am I, that I must tear myself from the subject.

All then that I will say further to it, at this time, is that were the intended goodness to be granted to me but a week hence; it would possibly be too late— Too late, I mean, to be of the consolation to me that I would wish from it: for what an inefficacious preparation must I have been making, if it has not by this time carried me above—But above what?—Poor mistaken creature!—Unhappy self-deluder!—that finds herself above nothing! Nor able to subdue her own faulty impatience!

But in*deed* to have done with a subject that I dare not trust myself with; if it come in your way, let my aunt Hervey, let my dear cousin Dolly, let the worthy Mrs Williams, know, how exceedingly grateful to me their kind intentions and concern for me are: and as the best warrant or justification of their good opinions (since I know that their favour for me is founded on the belief that I loved virtue) tell them that I *continued* to love virtue to my last hour, as I presume to hope it may be said; and assure them that I never made the least *wilful* deviation, however unhappy I became for one faulty step; which nevertheless was not owing to unworthy or perverse motives.

I am very sorry that my cousin Morden has taken a resolution to see Mr Lovelace.

My apprehensions on this intelligence are a great abatement to the pleasure I have in knowing that he still loves me.

My sister's letter to me is a most afflicting one—So *needlessly*, so *ludicrously* taunting. But for that part of it that is so, I ought rather to pity her than to be so much concerned at it as I am.

I wonder what I have done to Mr Brand—I pray God to forgive both him and his informants, whoever they be. But if the scandal arise solely from Mr Belford's visits, a very little time will confute it—Meanwhile, the packet I shall send you, which I sent to Miss Howe, will I hope satisfy *you*, my dear Mrs Norton, as to my reasons for admitting his visits.

My sister's taunting letter, and the inflexibleness of my dearer friends—But how do remoter-begun subjects tend to the point which lies nearest the heart!—as new-caught bodily disorders all crowd to a fractured or distempered part.

I will break off, with requesting your prayers that I may be blessed with patience and due resignation; and with assuring you that I am, and will be to the last hour of my life,

> Your equally grateful and affectionate
> CL. HARLOWE

Letter 434: MISS HOWE TO MISS CLARISSA HARLOWE

(In reply to hers of Friday, Aug. 11, Letter 405)

Yarmouth, Isle of Wight, Aug. 23

My dearest friend,

I HAVE read the letters and copies of letters you favoured me with: and I return them by a particular hand.

I am extremely concerned at your indifferent state of health: but I approve all your proceedings and precautions in relation to the naming of a man for an office that, I hope, will not require to be filled up for many, many years.

I admire, and so we do all, that greatness of mind which can make you so steadfastly despise (through such inducements as no other woman could resist, and in such desolate circumstances as you are in) the wretch that ought to be so heartily despised and detested.

What must the contents of those letters from your relations be, which you will not communicate to me! Fie upon them! How my heart rises—But I dare say no more—though you yourself now begin to think they use you with great severity.

Everybody here is so taken with Mr Hickman (and the more from the horror they conceive at the character of such a wretch as Lovelace), that I have been teased to death almost to name a day. This has given him airs; and, did I not keep him to it, he would behave himself as carelessly and as insolently as if he were sure of me. I have been forced to mortify him no less than four times since we have been here.

I made him lately undergo a severe penance for some negligences that were not to be passed over: not *designed* ones, he said: but that was a poor excuse, as I told him: for, had they been *designed*, he should never have come into my presence more: that they were *not*, showed his want of thought and attention; and those were inexcusable in a man only in his probatory state.

He hoped he had been more than in a *probatory* state, he said.

And therefore, sir, might be more *careless?*—So you add *ingratitude* to *negligence*, and make what you plead as *accident* that *itself* wants an excuse, *design* which deserves none.

I would not see him for two days, and he was so penitent and so humble, that I had like to have lost myself, to make him amends: for, as you have said, a resentment carried too high often ends in an amends too humble.

I long to be nearer to you: but that must not yet be, it seems. Pray, my dear, let me hear from you as often as you can.

May heaven increase your comforts, and restore your health, are the prayers of

Your ever faithful and affectionate
ANNA HOWE

P.S. Excuse me that I did not write before; it was owing to a little coasting voyage I was obliged to give into.

Letter 435: MISS CLARISSA HARLOWE TO MISS HOWE

Friday, Aug. 25

You are very obliging, my dear Miss Howe, to account to me for your silence. I was easy in it, as I doubted not that among such near and dear friends as you are with, you was diverted from writing by some such agreeable excursion as that you mention.

I was in hopes that you had given over, at this time of day, those very spritely airs which I have taken the liberty to blame you for as often as you have given me occasion for it; and that has been *very* often.

I was always very grave with you upon this subject: and while your own and a worthy man's future happiness are in the question, I must enter into it whenever you forget yourself, although I had not a day to live: and indeed I am very ill.

I am sure it was not your intention to take your future husband with you to the little island to make him look weak and silly among those of your relations who never before had seen him. Yet do you think it possible for them (however prepared and resolved they may be to like him) to forbear smiling at him when they see him suffering under your whimsical penances? A modest man should no more be made little in *his own eyes* than in the eyes of *others*. If he be, he will have a diffidence which will give an awkwardness to everything he says or does: and this will be no more to the credit of your choice, than to that of the approbation he meets with from your friends, or to his own credit.

I love an obliging, and even an *humble* deportment in a man to the woman he addresses. It is a mark of his politeness, and tends to give her that opinion of herself which it may be supposed bashful merit wants to be inspired with. But if the lady exacts it with a high hand, she shows not either her own politeness or gratitude; although I must confess she does her courage. I gave you expectation that I would be very serious with you.

Oh my dear, that had it been my lot (as I was not permitted to live single) to have met with a man by whom I could have acted generously and unreservedly!

Mr Lovelace, it is now plain, in order to have a pretence against me, taxed my behaviour to him with stiffness and distance. You, at one time, thought me guilty of some degree of prudery. Difficult situations should be allowed for; which often make occasions for censure unavoidable. I deserved not blame from *him* who made mine difficult. And you, my dear, if I had had any other man to deal with, or had he had but half the merit which Mr Hickman has, should have found that my doctrine on this subject should have governed my practice!

But to put myself out of the question—I'll tell you what I should think were I an indifferent bystander, of these high airs of yours in return for Mr Hickman's humble demeanour. 'The lady thinks of having the gentleman, I see plainly, would I say. But I see, as plainly, that she has a very great indifference to him. And to what may this indifference be owing? To one or all of these considerations, no doubt: that she receives his addresses rather from motives of convenience than choice: that she thinks meanly of *his* endowments and intellects; at least more highly of *her own:* or she has not the generosity to use that power with moderation, which his great affection for her puts into her hands.'

How would you like, my dear, to have any of these things said?

Then, to give but the shadow of a reason for free-livers and free-speakers to say, or to imagine, that Miss Howe gives her hand to a man who has no reason to expect any share in her heart, I am sure you would not wish that such a thing should be so much as supposed. Then, all the regard from you to come *afterwards*; none to be shown *before*; must, I should think, be capable of being construed as a compliment to the *husband* made at the expense of the *wife's delicacy*.

There is no fear that attempts could be formed by the most audacious (two Lovelaces there cannot be!) upon a character so revered for virtue, and so charmingly spirited as Miss Howe's: yet, to have any man encouraged to despise a husband by the example of one who is most concerned to do him honour; what, my dear, think you of that?—It is but too natural for envious men (and who that knows Miss Howe will not envy Mr Hickman?) to scoff at, and to jest upon, those who are treated with or will bear indignity from a woman. If a man so treated have a true and ardent love for the woman he addresses, he will be easily over-awed by her displeasure: and this will put him upon acts of submission which will be called *meanness*. And what woman of true spirit would like to have it said that she would impose anything upon the man from whom she one day expected protection and defence, that should be capable of being construed as a meanness, or unmanly abjectness in his behaviour, even to herself?—Nay, I am not sure, and I ask it of you, my dear, to resolve me, whether in your own opinion it is not likely that a woman of spirit will *despise* rather than *value* more the man who will take patiently an insult at her hands; especially *before company?*

I have always observed that prejudices in *disfavour* of a person, at his first appearance, fix deeper and are much more difficult to be removed *when* fixed, than prejudices in *favour*: whether owing to envy, or to that malignant principle so eminently visible in little minds, which makes them wish to bring down the more worthy characters to their own level, I pretend not to determine. When once, therefore, a woman of your good sense gives room to the world to think she has not an high opinion of the *lover* whom, nevertheless, she *entertains*, it will be very difficult for her afterwards to make that world think so well as she would have it of the *husband* she has chosen.

Give me leave to observe that to condescend with *dignity*, and to command with such *kindness*, and *sweetness of manners*, as should let the condescension, while single, be seen and acknowledged, are points which a wise woman, *knowing her man*, should aim at: and a wise woman, I should think, would choose to live single all her life, rather than give herself to a man whom she thinks unworthy of a treatment so noble.

But when a woman lets her lover see that she has the generosity to approve of and reward a well-meant service; that she has a mind that lifts her above the little captious follies which some (too licentiously, I hope) attribute to the sex in general: that she resents not (if ever she thinks she has reason to be displeased) with petulance, or through pride: nor thinks it necessary to insist upon little points, to come at or secure great ones perhaps not proper to be aimed at: nor leaves room to suppose she has so much cause to doubt her own merit, as to put the love of the man she intends to favour upon disagreeable or arrogant trials: but lets reason be the principal guide of her actions—she will then never fail of that true respect, of that sincere veneration, which she wishes to meet with; and which will make her judgement, after marriage, consulted, sometimes with a *preference* to a man's own, at other times, as a delightful *confirmation* of it.

And so much, my beloved Miss Howe, for this subject *now*, and I dare say, *for ever!*

I will begin another letter by and by, and send both together—Meantime, I am, etc.

Letter 436: MISS CLARISSA HARLOWE TO MISS HOWE

In the promised next letter the lady acquaints Miss Howe with Mr Brand's report; with her sister's proposals, either that she will go abroad, or prosecute Mr Lovelace; she complains of the severe letter of her uncle Antony and her sister; but in milder terms than they deserved.

She sends her Dr Lewen's letter, and the copy of her answer to it.

She tells her of the difficulties she had been under to avoid seeing Mr Lovelace. Gives her the contents of the letter she wrote to him: is afraid, she says, that it is a step that is not strictly right, if allegory and metaphor be not allowable to one in her circumstances.

She informs her of her cousin Morden's arrival and readiness to take her part with her relations; of his designed interview with Mr Lovelace; and tells her what her apprehensions are upon it.

She gives her the purport of the conversation between her aunt Hervey and Mrs Norton. And then adds:

But were they ever so favourably inclined to me now, what can they do for me? I wish, and that for their sakes more than for my own, that they would yet relent— But I am very ill—I must drop my pen—a sudden faintness overspreads my heart— Excuse my crooked writing!—Adieu, my dear!—Adieu!

Three o'clock, Friday

ONCE more, I resume my pen. I thought I had taken my last farewell of you. I never was so very oddly affected: something that seemed totally to overwhelm my faculties—I don't know how to describe it!—I believe I do amiss in writing so much, and taking too much upon me: but an active mind, though clouded by bodily illness, cannot be idle.

I'll see if the air, and a discontinued attention will help me—But if it will not, don't be concerned for me, my dear!—I shall be happy. Nay, I am more so already, than of late I thought I could ever be in this life—Yet how this *body* clings!—How it encumbers!

Seven o'clock

I could not send this letter away with so melancholy an ending as *you* would have thought it. So I deferred closing it, till I saw how I should be on my return from my airing: and now I must say, I am quite another thing: so alert!—that I could proceed with as much spirit as I begun, and add more preachment to your lively subject, if I had not written more than enough upon it already.

I wish you would let me give you and Mr Hickman joy. Do, my dear!—I should take some to *myself*, if you would.

My respectful compliments to all your friends, as well to those I have the honour to know, as to those I do not know.

I HAVE just now been surprised with a letter from one whom I long ago gave up all thoughts of hearing from. From Mr Wyerley. I will enclose it. You'll be surprised at it as much as I was. This seems to be a man whom I *might* have reclaimed. But I could not love him. Yet I hope I never treated him with arrogance. Indeed, my dear, if I am not too partial to myself, I think I refused him with more gentleness than you retain somebody else. And this recollection gives me less pain than I should have had in the other case, on receiving this instance of a generosity that affects me. I will also enclose the rough draught of my answer as soon as I have transcribed it.

If I begin another sheet, I shall write to the end of it: wherefore I will only add my prayers for your honour and prosperity, and for a long, long, happy life; and that, when it comes to be wound up, you may be as calm and as easy at quitting it, as I hope in God I shall be. Who am, and will be, to the latest moment,

Your truly affectionate and obliged servant,
·CL. HARLOWE

Letter 437: MR WYERLEY TO MISS CLARISSA HARLOWE

Wednesday, Aug. 23

Dearest madam,

YOU will be surprised to find renewed, at this distance of time, an address so positively though so politely discouraged: but, however it be received, I *must* renew it. Everybody has heard that you have been vilely treated by a man who, to treat *you* ill, must be the vilest of men. Everybody knows your just resentment of his base treatment: that you are determined never to be reconciled to him: and that you persist in these sentiments against all the entreaties of his noble relations, against all the prayers and repentance of his ignoble self. And all the world that have the honour to know *you*, or have heard of *him*, applaud your resolution as worthy of yourself; worthy of your virtue, and of that strict honour which was always attributed to you by every one who spoke of you.

But, madam, were all the world to have been of a different opinion, it could never have altered mine. I ever loved you; I ever *must* love you. Yet have I endeavoured to resign to my hard fate. When I had so many ways, in vain, sought to move you in my favour, I sat down seemingly contented. I even wrote to you that I *would* sit down contented. And I endeavoured to make all my friends and companions think I was. But nobody knows what pangs this self-denial cost me! In vain did the chase, in vain did travel, in vain did lively company, offer themselves: though embraced each in its turn, yet with redoubled force did my passion for you bring on my unhappiness, when I looked into myself, into my own heart; for there did your charming image sit enthroned; and you engrossed me all.

I truly deplore those misfortunes, and those sufferings, for your *own* sake; which, nevertheless, encourage *me* to renew my bold hope. I know not particulars. I dare not inquire after them; because *my* sufferings would be increased with the knowledge of what *yours* have been. I therefore desire not to know more than what common report wounds my ears with; and what is given me to know, by your absence from your cruel family, and from the sacred place where I, among numbers of your rejected admirers, used to be twice a week sure to behold you, doing credit to that service of which your example gave me the highest notions. But whatever be those misfortunes, of whatsoever nature those sufferings, I shall bless the occasion for *my own* sake (though for *yours* curse the author of them) if they may give me the happiness to know that this my renewed address may not be absolutely rejected. Only give me hope that it may one day meet with encouragement, if in the interim nothing happen either in my morals or behaviour to give you fresh offence. Give me but hope of this—Not absolutely to *reject* me is all the hope I ask for; and I will love you, if possible, still more than I ever loved you—and that for your sufferings; for well you deserve to be loved, even to adoration, who can for honour and for virtue's sake subdue a passion which common spirits (I speak by cruel experience) find invincible; and this at a time when the black offender kneels and supplicates, as I am well assured he does (all his friends likewise supplicating for him), to be forgiven.

That you cannot forgive him; not forgive him so as to receive him again to favour, is no wonder. His offence is against virtue: that is a part of your essence— What magnanimity is this! How just to yourself, and to your spotless character! Is it any merit to admire more than ever so exalted a distinguisher? It is not. I cannot plead it.

What hope have I left, may it be said, when my address was *before* rejected, now that your sufferings, so *nobly borne*, have with all *good judges* exalted your character? Yet, madam, I have to pride myself in this, that while your friends (not looking upon you in the just light I do) persecute and banish you; while your fortune and estate is withheld from you, and threatened (as I *know*) to *be* withheld, as long as the chicaning law, or rather the chicaneries of its practisers, can keep it from you: while you are destitute of protection; everybody standing aloof, either through fear of the injurer of one family, or of the hard-hearted of the other; I pride myself, I say, to stand forth and offer my fortune, and my life, at your devotion: with a *selfish* hope indeed: I should be too great an hypocrite not to own this: and I know how much you abhor insincerity.

But, whether you encourage that hope or not, accept my best services, I beseech you, madam: and be pleased to excuse me for a piece of honest art, which the nature of the case (doubting the honour of your notice otherwise) makes me choose to conclude with—It is this:

If I am to be still the most unhappy of men, let your pen, by *one line*, tell me so. If I am permitted to indulge a hope, however distant, your *silence* shall be deemed by me the happiest indication of it that you can give—except that *still* happier— (the happiest that *can* befall me) a signification that you will accept the tender of that life and fortune, which it would be my pride and my glory to sacrifice in your service, leaving the reward to *yourself*.

Be your determination as it may, I must for ever admire and love you: nor will I ever change my condition while you live, whether you change yours or not: for, having once had the presumption to address *you*, I cannot stoop to think of any other woman: and this I solemnly declare in the presence of that God, whom I daily pray to bless and protect you, be your determination what it will with regard to, dearest madam,

> Your most devoted and ever-affectionate and faithful servant,
> ALEXANDER WYERLEY

Letter 438: MISS CLARISSA HARLOWE TO ALEXANDER WYERLEY, ESQ.

Sat. Aug. 26

Sir,

THE generosity of your purpose would have commanded not only my notice, but my thanks, although you had *not* given me the alternative you are pleased to call *artful*. And I do therefore give you my thanks for your kind letter.

At the time you distinguished me by your favourable opinion, I told you, sir, that my choice was the single life. And most *truly* did I tell you so.

When that was not permitted me, and I looked round upon the several gentlemen who had been proposed to me, and had reason to believe that there was not one of them against whose morals or principles there lay not some exception, it would not have been *much* to be wondered at if FANCY *had* been allowed to give a preference, where JUDGEMENT was at a loss to determine.

Far be it from me to say this with a design to upbraid you, sir, or to reflect upon you. I always wished you well. You had reason to think I did. You had the generosity to be pleased with the frankness of my behaviour to you; as I had with that of yours to me: and I am sorry to be now told that the acquiescence you obliged me with gave you so much pain.

Had the option I have mentioned been allowed me *afterwards* (as I not only wished but proposed), things had not happened that did happen. But there was a kind of fatality, by which our whole family was impelled, as I may say; and which none of us were permitted to avoid. But this is a subject that cannot be dwelt upon.

As matters are, I have only to wish, for your own sake, that you will encourage and cultivate those good motions in your mind, to which many passages in your kind and generous letter now before me must be owing. Depend upon it, sir, that such motions wrought into habit will yield you pleasure at a *time* when nothing else can. And at *present*, shining out in your actions and conversation, will commend you to the worthiest of our sex. For, sir, the man who is good upon *choice*, as well as by *education*, has that quality in himself which ennobles the human race, and without which the most dignified by birth or rank are ignoble.

As to the resolution you so solemnly make not to marry while I live, I should be concerned at it, were I not morally sure that you may keep it and yet not be detrimented by it. Since a few, a very few days, will convince you that I am got above all human dependence—and that there is no need of that protection and favour, which you so generously offer to, sir,

> Your obliged well-wisher, and humble servant,
> CL. HARLOWE

Letter 439: MR LOVELACE TO JOHN BELFORD, ESQ.

Monday noon, Aug. 28

ABOUT the time of poor Belton's interment last night, as near as we could guess, Lord M., Mowbray and myself toasted once, *To the memory of honest Tom Belton*; and by a quick transition to the living, *Health to Miss Harlowe*; which Lord M. obligingly began, and, *To the happy reconciliation*; and then we stuck in a remembrance *To honest Jack Belford*, who of late we all agreed was become a useful and humane man; preferring his friend's service to his own.

But what is the meaning I hear nothing from thee[a]? And why dost thou not let me into the grounds of the sudden reconciliation between my beloved and her friends, and the cause of the generous invitation which she gives me of attending her at her father's some time hence?

Thou must certainly have been let into the secret by this time; and I can tell thee I shall be plaguy jealous if there be any one thing pass between my angel and thee that is to be concealed from me. For either I am a principal in this cause, or I am nothing. I have dispatched Will to know the reason of thy neglect.

But let me whisper a word or two in thy ear. I begin to be afraid, after all, that this letter was a stratagem to get me out of town, and for nothing else: for, in the first place, Tourville, in a letter I received this morning, tells me that the lady is actually very ill—(I am sorry for it with all my soul!). This, thou'lt say, I may think a reason why she cannot *set out as yet*: but then I have heard on the other hand, but last night, that the family is as implacable as ever; and my lord and I expect this very afternoon a visit from Colonel Morden; who undertakes, it seems, to question me as to my intention with regard to his cousin.

This convinces me that if she *has* apprised them of my offers to her, they will not believe me to be in earnest till they are assured that I am so from my own mouth. And then I understand that the intended visit is an officiousness of Morden's own, without the desire of any of her friends.

Now, Jack, what can a man make of all this? My intelligence as to the continuance of her family's implacableness is not to be doubted; and yet when I read her letter, what can one say? Surely the dear little rogue will not lie!

I never knew her dispense with her word, but once: and that was when she promised to forgive me, after the dreadful fire that had like to have happened at our mother's, and yet would not see me next day, and afterwards made her escape to Hampstead in order to avoid forgiving me: and as she severely smarted for this departure from her honour given (for it is a sad thing for good people to break their word when it is in their power to keep it), one would not expect that she should set about deceiving again; more especially by the *premeditation of writing*. You perhaps will ask: What honest man is obliged to keep his promise with a highwayman? for well I know your unmannerly way of making comparisons: but I say, *every* honest man is—and I will give you an illustration.

Here is a marauding varlet who demands your money with his pistol at your breast. You have neither money nor valuable effects about you; and promise solemnly, if he will spare your life, that you will send him an agreed-upon sum, by

a   Mr Belford had not yet sent him his last-written letter. His reason for which see p. 1250.

such a day, to such a place. The question is, If your life is not in the fellow's power?

How he came by the power is another question; for which he must answer with *his* life, when caught—so he runs risk for risk.

Now if he gives you *your life*, does he not give, think you, a valuable consideration for the money you engage your honour to send him? If not, the sum must be exorbitant, or your life is a very paltry one, even in your own opinion.

I need not make the application; and I am sure that even thou thyself, who never sparest me, and thinkest thou knowest *my* heart by *thy own*, canst not possibly put the case in a stronger light against me.

Then, why do good people take upon themselves to censure, as they do, persons *less* scrupulous than themselves? Is it not because the latter allow themselves in *any* liberty, in order to carry a point? And can my not doing *my* duty, warrant another for not doing *his*? Thou wilt not say it can.

And how would it sound, to put the case as strongly once more as my greatest enemy would put it, both as to *fact* and in *words*: Here has that profligate wretch Lovelace broken his vow with and deceived Miss Clarissa Harlowe—A vile fellow! would an enemy say: but it is *like* him. But when it comes to be said that the pious Miss Clarissa Harlowe has broken her word with and deceived Lovelace; Good Lord! would everyone say! Sure it cannot be!

Upon my soul, Jack, such is the veneration I have for this admirable woman that I am shocked barely at putting the case; and so wilt thou, if thou respectest her as thou oughtest: for thou knowest that men and women all the world over form their opinions of one another by each person's professions and known practices. In this lady therefore it would be as unpardonable to tell a wilful untruth, as it would be strange if I kept my word—In love-cases, I mean; for as to the rest, I am an honest moral man, as all who know me can testify.

And what, after all, would this lady deserve if she has deceived me in this case? For did she not set me prancing away upon Lord M.'s best nag to Lady Sarah's, and to Lady Betty's, with an erect and triumphing countenance, to show them her letter to me? And I have received their congratulations upon it: Well, and now, cousin Lovelace, cries one; Well and now, cousin Lovelace, cries t'other; I hope you'll make the best of husbands to so excellent and so forgiving a lady! And now we shall soon have the pleasure of looking upon you as a reformed man, added one! And now we shall see you in the way we have so long wished you to be in, exulted the other!

My cousins Montague also have been ever since rejoicing in the new relationship. Their charming cousin, and their lovely cousin, at every word!—And how dearly they will love her!—What lessons will they take from her!—And yet Charlotte, who pretends to have the eye of an eagle, was for finding out some mystery in the style and manner, till I overbore her, and laughed her out of it.

As for Lord M., he has been in hourly expectation of being sent to with proposals of one sort or other from the Harlowes: and still will have it that such proposals will be made by Colonel Morden when he comes; and that the Harlowes only put on a face of irreconcileableness, till they know the issue of Morden's visit, in order to make the better terms with us.

Indeed, if I had not undoubted reason, as I said, to believe the continuance of their antipathy to *me*, and implacableness to *her*, I should be apt to think there might be some foundation to my lord's conjecture; for there is a cursed deal of low cunning in all that family, except in the angel of it, who has so much generosity of soul that she despises cunning, both name and thing.

What I mean by all this is to let thee see what a stupid figure I should make to all my own family, if my Clarissa has been capable, as Gulliver in his abominable Yahoo story phrases it, of saying the *thing that is not*. By my soul, Jack, if it were only that I should be *outwitted* by such a novice at plotting, and that it would make me look silly to my kinswomen here who know I value myself upon my contrivances, it would vex me to the heart; and I would instantly clap a feather-bed into a coach and six, and fetch her away, sick or well, and marry her at my leisure.

But Colonel Morden is come and I must break off.

Letter 440: MR BELFORD TO ROBERT LOVELACE, ESQ.

Monday night, Aug. 28

I DOUBT you will be all impatience that you have not heard from me since mine of Thursday last. You would be still more so, if you knew that I had by me a letter ready-written.

I went early yesterday morning to Epsom; and found everything disposed according to the directions I had left on Friday; and at night the solemn office was performed. Tourville was there; and behaved very decently, and with greater concern than I thought he would ever have expressed for anybody.

Thomasine, they told me, in a kind of disguise was in an obscure pew out of curiosity (for it seems she was far from showing any tokens of grief) to see the last office performed for the man whose heart she had so largely contributed to break.

I was obliged to stay till this afternoon, to settle several necessary matters, and to direct inventories to be taken in order for appraisement; for everything is to be turned into money, by his will. I presented his sister with the 100 guineas the poor man left me as his executor, and desired her to continue in the house, and take the direction of everything, till I could hear from his nephew at Antigua, who is *heir at law*. He had left her but £50, although he knew her indigence; and that it was owing to a vile husband, and not to herself, that she *was* indigent.

The poor man left about £200 in money, and £200 in two East India bonds; and I will contrive, if I can, to make up the poor woman's £50 and my 100 guineas, £200 to her; and then she will have some little matter coming in certain, which I will oblige her to keep out of the hands of a son who has completed that ruin which his father had very near effected.

I gave Tourville his £20 and will send you and Mowbray yours by the first order. And so much for poor Belton's affairs till I see you.

I got to town in the evening, and went directly to Smith's. I found Mrs Lovick and Mrs Smith in the back shop, and I saw they had been both in tears. They rejoiced to see me, however, and told me that the doctor and Mr Goddard were but just gone; as was also the worthy clergyman who often comes to pray by her; and all three were of opinion that she would hardly live to see the entrance of another week. I was not so much surprised as grieved; for I had feared as much when I left her on Saturday.

I sent up my compliments; and she returned that she would take it for a favour if I would call upon her in the morning, by eight o'clock. Mrs Lovick told me that she had fainted away on Saturday, while she was writing, as she had done likewise the day before; and having received benefit then by a little turn in a chair, she was carried abroad again. She returned somewhat better; and wrote till late; yet had a pretty good night; and went to Covent Garden Church in the morning: but came home so ill, that she was obliged to lie down.

When she arose, seeing how much grieved Mrs Lovick and Mrs Smith were for her, she made apologies for the trouble she gave them—You were happy, said she, before I came hither. It was a cruel thing in me to come among honest strangers, and to be sick, and die with you.

When they touched upon the irreconcileableness of her friends, she said, she had ill offices done her to them, and they did not know how ill she was, nor would they believe anything she should write. But yet she could not but sometimes think it a little hard that she should have so many near and dear friends living, and not one to look upon her—No old servant, no old friend, she said, to be permitted to come near her, without being sure of incurring displeasure; and to have such a great work to go through by herself, a young creature as she was, and to have everything to think of as to her temporal matters, and to order, to her very interment! No dear mother, said she, to pray by me and bless me!—No kind sister to soothe and comfort me!—But come, said she, how do I know but all is for the best—if I can but make a right use of the dispensation?—Pray for me, Mrs Lovick—Pray for me, Mrs Smith, that I may—I have great need of your prayers. This cruel man has discomposed me. His persecutions have given me a pain just here—putting her hand to her heart. What a step has he made me take to avoid him!—Who can *touch pitch, and not be defiled?* He has made a bad spirit take possession of me, I think—broken in upon all my duties. And will not yet, I doubt, let me be at rest. Indeed he is very cruel—But this is one of my trials, I believe. By God's grace I shall be easier tomorrow, and especially if I have no more of his tormentings, and if I can get a tolerable night. And I will sit up till eleven, that I may.

She said, that though this was so heavy a day with her, she was at other times within those few days past especially blessed with bright hours; and particularly, that she had now and then such joyful assurances (which she hoped were not presumptuous ones) that God would receive her to His mercy, that she could hardly contain herself and was ready to think herself above this earth while she was in it: and what, inferred she to Mrs Lovick, must be the state itself, the very aspirations after which have often cast a beamy light through the thickest darkness, and when I have been at the lowest ebb have dispelled the black clouds of despondency?—as I hope they soon will this spirit of repining.

She had a pretty good night, it seems, and this morning went in a chair to St Dunstan's church.

The chairmen told Mrs Smith that after prayers (for she did not return till between nine and ten) they carried her to a house in Fleet Street, where they never waited on her before. And where dost think this was?—Why, to an undertaker's! Good God! what a woman is this! She went into the back shop and talked with the master of it about half an hour, and came from him with great serenity; he waiting upon her to her chair with a respectful countenance, but full of curiosity and seriousness.

'Tis evident that she then went to bespeak her *house* that she talked of[a].—*As soon as you can, sir*, were her words to him as she got into the chair. Mrs Smith told me this with the same surprise and grief, that I heard it.

She was so ill in the afternoon, having got cold either at St Dunstan's or at chapel, that she sent for the clergyman to pray by her; and the women, unknown to her, sent both for Dr H. and Mr Goddard: who were just gone, as I told you, when I came to pay my respects to her this evening.

And thus I have recounted from the good women what passed to this night since my absence.

I long for tomorrow that I may see her: and yet 'tis such a melancholy longing as I never experienced, and know not how to describe.

Tuesday, Aug. 29

I was at Smith's at half an hour after seven. They told me that the lady was gone in a chair to St Dunstan's; but was better than she had been in either of the two preceding days; and said to Mrs Lovick and Mrs Smith, as she went into the chair, I have a good deal to answer for to you, my good friends, for my vapourish conversation of last night.

If, Mrs Lovick, said she smiling, I have no new matters to discompose me, I believe my spirits will hold out purely.

She returned immediately after prayers.

Mr Belford, said she, as she entered the back shop where I was, and upon my approaching her, I am very glad to see you. You have been performing for your poor friend a kind last office. 'Tis not long ago, since you did the same for a near relation. Is it not a little hard upon you that these troubles should fall so thick to your lot? But they are charitable offices: and it is a praise to your humanity that poor dying people know not where to choose so well.

I told her I was sorry to hear she had been so ill since I had the honour to attend her; but rejoiced to find that now she seemed a good deal better.

It will be sometimes better and sometimes worse, replied she, with poor creatures when they are balancing between life and death. But no more of these matters just now. I hope, sir, you'll breakfast with me. I was quite vapourish yesterday. I had a very bad spirit upon me. Had I not, Mrs Smith? But I hope I shall be no more so. And today I am perfectly serene. This day rises upon me as if it would be a bright one.

She desired me to walk up, and invited Mr Smith and his wife, and Mrs Lovick also, to breakfast with her. I was better pleased with her liveliness than with her looks.

The good people retiring after breakfast, the following conversation passed between us.

Pray, sir, let me ask you, said she, if you think I may promise myself that I shall be no more molested by your friend?

I hesitated: for how could I answer for such a man?

What shall I do if he comes again?—You see how I am—I cannot fly from him

a See p. 1250.

now—If he has any pity left for the poor creature whom he has thus reduced, let him not come—But have you heard from him lately? And will he come?

I hope not, madam; I have not heard from him since Thursday last, that he went out of town rejoicing in the hopes your letter gave him of a reconciliation between your friends and you, and that he might in good times see you at your father's; and he is gone down to give all his friends joy of the news, and is in high spirits upon it.

Alas for me! I shall then surely have him come up to persecute me again! As soon as he discovers that that was only a stratagem to keep him away, he will come up; and who knows but even *now* he is upon the road? I thought I was so bad that I should have been out of his and everybody's way before now; for I expected not that this contrivance would serve me above two or three days; and by this time he must have found out that I am not so happy as to have any hope of a reconciliation with my family; and then he will come, if it be only in revenge for what he will think a deceit.

I believe I looked surprised to hear her confess that her letter was a stratagem only; for she said, You wonder, Mr Belford, I observe, that I could be guilty of such an artifice. I doubt it is not right. But how could I see a man who had so mortally injured me; yet, pretending sorrow for his crimes, and wanting to see me, could behave with so much shocking levity as he did to the honest people of the house? Yet, 'tis strange too, that neither you nor he found out my meaning on perusal of my letter. You have seen what I wrote, no doubt?

I have, madam. And then I began to account for it as an *innocent* artifice.

Thus far indeed, sir, it is *innocent*, that I meant him no hurt, and had a right to the effect I hoped for from it; and he had none to invade me. But have you, sir, that letter of his, in which he gives you (as I suppose he does) the copy of mine?

I have, madam. And pulled it out of my letter-case: but hesitating—Nay, sir, said she, be pleased to read my letter to yourself—I desire not to see *his*—and see if you can be longer a stranger to a meaning so obvious.

I read it to myself—Indeed, madam, I can find nothing but that you are going down to Harlowe Place to be reconciled to your father and other friends: and Mr Lovelace presumed that a letter from your sister, which he saw brought when he was at Mr Smith's, gave you the welcome news of it.

She then explained all to me, and that, as I may say, in six words—A *religious* meaning is couched under it, and that's the reason that neither you nor I could find it out.

Read but for my *father's house, Heaven*, said she; and for the interposition of my dear blessed friend, suppose the *mediation* of my *Saviour*; which I humbly rely upon; and all the rest of the letter will be accounted for.

I read it so, and stood astonished for a minute at her invention, her piety, her charity, and at thine and my own stupidity, to be thus taken in.

And now, thou vile Lovelace, what hast thou to do (the lady all consistent with herself, and no hopes left for thee) but to hang, drown, or shoot thyself, for an outwitted triumpher?

My surprise being a little over, she proceeded: As to the letter that came from my sister while your friend was here, you will *soon* see, sir, that it is the cruellest letter she ever wrote me.

And then she expressed a deep concern for what might be the consequence of Colonel Morden's intended visit to you; and besought me that if now, or at any time hereafter, I had opportunity to prevent any further mischief, without detriment or danger to myself, I would do it.

I assured her of the most particular attention to this and to all her commands; and that in a manner so agreeable to her that she invoked a blessing upon me for my goodness, as she called it, to a desolate creature who suffered under the worst of orphanage; those were her words.

She then went back to her first subject, her uneasiness for fear of your molesting her again; and said, If you have any influence over him, Mr Belford, prevail upon him that he will give me the assurance that the short remainder of my time shall be all my own. I have need of it. Indeed I have. Why will he wish to interrupt me in my duty? Has he not punished me enough for my preference of him to all his sex? Has he not destroyed my fame and my fortune? And will not his causeless vengeance upon me be complete, unless he ruins my soul too?—Excuse me, sir, this vehemence! But indeed it greatly imports me to know that I shall be no more disturbed by him. And yet, with all this aversion, I would sooner give way to his visit, though I were to expire the moment I saw him, than to be the cause of any fatal misunderstanding between you and him.

I assured her that I would make such a representation of the matter to you, and of the state of her health, that I would undertake to *answer for you* that you would not attempt to come near her.

And for this reason, Lovelace, do I lay the whole matter before you, and desire you will authorize me, as soon as this and mine of Saturday last come to your hands, to dissipate her fears.

This gave her a little satisfaction; and then she said that had I not told her I *could* promise for you, she was determined, ill as she is, to remove somewhere out of my knowledge as well as out of yours. And yet, to have been obliged to leave people I am but just got acquainted with, said the poor lady, and to have died among perfect strangers, would have completed my hardships.

This conversation, I found, as well from the length as the nature of it, had fatigued her; and seeing her change colour once or twice, I made that my excuse, and took leave of her: desiring her permission to attend her in the evening; and as often as possible; for I could not help telling her that every time I saw her, I more and more considered her as a beatified spirit; and as one sent from heaven to draw me after her out of the miry gulf in which I had been so long immersed.

And laugh at me if thou wilt; but it is true that every time I approach her, I cannot but look upon her as one just entering into a companionship with saints and angels. This thought so wholly possessed me, that I could not help begging as I went away, her prayers and her blessing; and that with the reverence due to an angel, and with an earnestness like that which expecting intimates manifest, when they seek to make an interest with a person who is just exalted into a prime degree of power, by the favour of his prince.

In the evening she was so low and weak, that I took my leave of her, in less than a quarter of an hour. I went directly home. Where, to the pleasure and wonder of my cousin and her family, I now pass many honest evenings: which they impute to your being out of town.

I shall dispatch my packet tomorrow morning early by my own servant, to make you amends for the suspense I must have kept you in: you'll thank me for that, I hope; but will not, I am sure, for sending your servant back without a letter.

I long for the particulars of the conversation between you and Mr Morden: the lady, as I have hinted, is full of apprehensions about it. Send me back this packet when perused, for I have not had either time or patience to take a copy of it—And I beseech you enable me to make good my engagements to the poor lady that you will not invade her again.

Letter 441: MR BELFORD TO ROBERT LOVELACE, ESQ.

Wednesday, Aug. 30

I HAVE a conversation to give you that passed between this admirable lady and Dr H. which will furnish a new instance of the calmness and serenity with which she can talk of death, and prepare for it, as if it were an occurrence as familiar to her as dressing and undressing.

As soon as I had dispatched my servant to you with my letters of the 26th, 28th, and yesterday the 29th, I went to pay my duty to her, and had the pleasure to find her, after a tolerable night, pretty lively and cheerful. She was but just returned from her usual devotions. And Doctor H. alighted as she entered the door.

After inquiring how she did, and hearing her complaints of shortness of breath (which she attributed to inward decay, precipitated by her late harasses, as well from her friends as from you) he was for advising her to go into the air.

What will that do for me, said she? Tell me truly, good sir, with a cheerful aspect (you know you cannot disturb me by it), whether now you do not put on the *true* physician; and despairing that anything in medicine will help me, advise me to the air, as the last resource?—Can you think the air will avail in such a malady as mine?

He was silent.

I ask, said she, because my friends (who will possibly some time hence inquire after the means I used for my recovery) may be satisfied that I omitted nothing which so worthy and so skilful a physician prescribed?

The air, madam, may possibly help the difficulty of breathing, which has so lately attacked you.

But, sir, you see how weak I am. You must see that I have been consuming from day to day; and now, if I can judge by what I feel in myself, putting her hand to her heart, I cannot continue long. If the air would *very* probably add to my days, though I am far from being *desirous* to have them lengthened, I would go into it; and the rather as I know Mrs Lovick would kindly accompany me. But if I were to be at the trouble of removing into new lodgings (a trouble which I think now would be too much for me) and this only to *die* in the country, I had rather the scene were to be shut up here. For here have I meditated the spot, and the manner, and everything, as well of the minutest as of the highest consequence, that can attend the solemn moments. So, doctor, tell me truly, may I stay here and be clear of any imputations of curtailing, through wilfulness or impatiency, or through resentments which I hope I am got above, a life that might otherwise be prolonged?—Tell me, sir, you are not talking to a coward in this respect; indeed you are not!—unaffectedly smiling.

The doctor turning to me was at a loss what to say, lifting up his eyes only in admiration of her.

Never had any patient, said she, a more indulgent and more humane physician—But since you are loath to answer my question directly, I will put it in other words. You don't *enjoin* me to go into the air, doctor, do you?

I do *not*, madam. Nor do I now visit you as a physician; but as a person whose conversation I admire, and whose sufferings I condole. And to explain myself more directly as to the occasion of this day's visit in particular, I must tell you, madam, that understanding how much you suffer by the displeasure of your friends; and having no doubt but that if they knew the way you are in, they would alter their conduct to you; and believing it must cut them to the heart when too late they shall be informed of everything; I have resolved to apprise them by letter (stranger as I am to their persons) how necessary it is for some of them to attend you very speedily. For *their* sakes, madam, let me press for your approbation of this measure.

She paused, and at last said, This is kind, very kind in you, sir. But I hope that you do not think me so perverse and so obstinate as to have left till now any means unessayed, which I thought likely to move my friends in my favour. But now, doctor, said she, I should be too much disturbed at their grief, if they were any of them to come or to send to me: and perhaps if I found they still loved me, wish to live; and so should quit unwillingly that life which I am now really fond of quitting, and hope to quit, as becomes a person who has had such a weaning-time as I have been favoured with.

I hope, madam, said I, we are not so near as you apprehend to that deplorable deprivation you hint at with such an amazing presence of mind. And therefore I presume to second the doctor's motion, if it were only for the sake of your father and mother, that they may have the satisfaction, if they *must* lose you, to think they were first reconciled to you.

It is very kindly, very humanely considered, said she. But if you think me not so *very* near my last hour; let me desire this may be postponed till I see what effect my cousin Morden's mediation may have. Perhaps he may vouchsafe to make me a visit yet, after his intended interview with Mr Lovelace is over; of which, who knows Mr Belford, but your next letters may give an account? I hope it will not be a fatal one to *any*body!—Will you promise me, doctor, to forbear writing for two days only, and I will communicate to you anything that occurs in that time; and then you shall take your own way? Meantime, I repeat my thanks for your goodness to me—Nay, dear doctor, hurry not away from me so precipitately (for he was going for fear of an offered fee): I will no more affront you with tenders that have pained you for some time past: and since I must now, from this kindly offered favour, look upon you only as a friend, I will assure you henceforth that I will give you no more uneasiness on that head: and now, sir, I know I shall have the pleasure of seeing you oftener than heretofore.

The worthy gentleman was pleased with this assurance, telling her that he had always come to see her with great pleasure, but parted with her on the account she hinted at, with as much pain; and that he should not have forborn to double his visits, could he have had this kind assurance as early as he wished for it.

There are few instances of like disinterestedness, I doubt, in this tribe. Till now I always held it for gospel, that *friendship* and *physician* were incompatible things;

and little imagined that a man of medicine, when he had given over his patient to death, would think of any visits but those of ceremony, that he might stand well with the family against it came to their turns to go through his turnpike.

After the doctor was gone, she fell into a very serious discourse of the vanity of life, and the wisdom of preparing for death while health and strength remained, and before the infirmities of body impaired the faculties of the mind, and disabled them from acting with the necessary efficacy and clearness: the whole calculated for everyone's meridian, but particularly, as it was easy to observe, for thine and mine.

She was very curious to know further particulars of the behaviour of poor Belton in his last moments. You must not wonder at my inquiries, Mr Belford, said she; for who is it that is to undertake a journey into a country they never travelled to before, that inquires not into the difficulties of the road, and what accommodations are to be expected in the way?

I gave her a brief account of the poor man's terrors, and unwillingness to die: and when I had done: Thus, Mr Belford, said she, must it always be with poor souls who have never thought of their long voyage till the moment they are to embark for it.

She made such other observations upon this subject, as coming from the mouth of a person who will so soon be a companion for angels, I shall never forget. And indeed, when I went home, that I might engraft them the better on my memory, I entered them down in writing: but I will not let you see them until you are in a frame more proper to benefit by them, than you are likely to be in one while.

Thus far I had written, when the unexpected early return of my servant with your packet (yours and he meeting at Slough, and exchanging letters) obliged me to leave off to give its contents a reading—Here, therefore, I close this letter.

Letter 442: MR LOVELACE TO JOHN BELFORD, ESQ.

Tuesday morn. Aug. 29

Now, Jack, will I give thee an account of what passed on occasion of the visit made us by Colonel Morden.

He came on horseback, attended by one servant; and Lord M. received him as a relation of Miss Harlowe's, with the highest marks of civility and respect.

After some general talk of the times and of the weather, and such nonsense as Englishmen generally make their introductory topics to conversation, the colonel addressed himself to Lord M. and to me, as follows:

I need not, my lord, and Mr Lovelace, as you know the relation I bear to the Harlowe family, make any apology for entering upon a subject which, on account of that relation, you must think is the principal reason of the honour I have done myself in this visit.

Miss Harlowe, Miss Clarissa Harlowe's affair, said Lord M. with his usual forward bluntness. That, sir, is what you mean. She is, by all accounts, the most excellent woman in the world.

I am glad to hear that is your lordship's opinion of her. It is everyone's.

It is not only my opinion, Colonel Morden (proceeded the prating peer) but it is the opinion of all my family. Of my sisters, of my nieces, and of Mr Lovelace himself.

Col. Would to heaven it had been always Mr Lovelace's opinion of her!

Lovel. You have been out of England, colonel, a good many years. Perhaps you are not yet fully apprised of all the particulars of this case.

Col. I have been out of England, sir, about seven years. My cousin Clary Harlowe was then about *twelve* years of age: but never was there at *twenty* so discreet, so prudent, and so excellent a creature. All that knew her, or saw her, admired her. Mind and person, never did I see such promises of perfection in any young lady: and I am told, nor is it to be wondered at, that as she advanced to maturity, she more than justified and made good those promises. Then, as to fortune—what her father, what her uncles, and what I myself intended to do for her, besides what her grandfather had done—There is not a finer fortune in the county.

Lovel. All this, colonel, and more than this, is Miss Clarissa Harlowe; and had it not been for the implacableness and violence of her family (all resolved to push her upon a match as unworthy *of* her, as hateful *to* her) she had still been happy.

Col. I own, Mr Lovelace, the truth of what you observed just now, that I am not thoroughly acquainted with all that has passed between you and my cousin. But permit me to say, that when I first heard that you made your addresses to her, I knew but of one objection against you. That, indeed, a very great one: and upon a letter sent me, I gave her my free opinion upon the subject.[a] But had it not been for that, I own, that in my private mind there could not have been a more suitable match: for you are a gallant gentleman, graceful in your person, easy and genteel in your deportment, and in your family, fortunes, and expectations happy as a man can wish to be. Then the knowledge I had of you in Italy (although give me leave to say, your conduct there was not wholly unexceptionable) convinces me that you are brave: and few gentlemen come up to you in wit and vivacity. Your education has given you great advantages; your manners are engaging, and you have travelled; and I know, if you'll excuse me, you make better observations than you are governed by. All these qualifications make it not at all surprising that a young lady should love you: and that this love, joined to that indiscreet warmth wherewith my cousin's friends would have forced her inclinations in favour of men who are far your inferiors in the qualities I have named, should throw her upon your protection: but then, if there were these two strong motives, the one to *induce*, the other to *impel* her, let me ask you, sir, if she were not doubly entitled to generous usage from a man whom she chose for her protector; and whom, let me take the liberty to say, she could so amply reward for the protection he was to afford her?

Lovel. Miss Clarissa Harlowe was entitled, sir, to the best usage that man could give her. I have no scruple to own it. I will always do her the justice she so well deserves. I know what will be your inference; and have only to say, that time past cannot be recalled. Perhaps I wish it could.

The colonel then in a very manly strain set forth the wickedness of attempting a woman of virtue and character. He said that men had generally too many advantages over the weakness, credulity, and inexperience of the fair sex, who were too apt to be hurried into acts of precipitation by their reading inflaming

a See Letter 173.1.

novels, and idle romances; that his cousin, however, he was sure, was above the reach of common seduction, or to be influenced to the rashness her parents accused her of, by weaker motives than *their* violence, and the most solemn promises on *my part*: but, nevertheless, *having* those motives, and her prudence (eminent as it was) being rather the effect of *constitution* than *experience* (a fine advantage, however, he said, to ground an unblamable future life upon), she might not be apprehensive of bad designs in a man she loved: it was, therefore, a very heinous thing to abuse the confidence of such a lady.

He was going on in this trite manner: but, interrupting him, I said: These general observations, colonel, perhaps, suit not this particular case. But you yourself are a man of gallantry; and possibly were you to be put to the question, might not be able to vindicate every action of your life, any more than I.

Col. You are welcome, sir, to put what questions you please to me. And, I thank God, I can both *own* and be *ashamed* of my errors.

Lord M. looked at *me*; but as the colonel did not by his manner seem to intend a reflection, I had no occasion to take it for one; especially as I can as readily *own* my errors as he, or any man can his, whether *ashamed* of them or not.

He proceeded. As you seem to call upon me, Mr Lovelace, I will tell you (without boasting of it) what has been my general practice, till lately, that I hope I have reformed it a good deal.

I have taken liberties, which the laws of morality will by no means justify; and once I should have thought myself warranted to cut the throat of any young fellow who should make as free with a sister of mine, as I have made with the sisters and daughters of others. But then I took care never to promise anything I intended not to perform. A modest ear should as soon have heard downright obscenity from my lips as matrimony, if I had not intended it. Young ladies are generally ready enough to believe we mean honourably if they love us; and it would look like a strange affront to their virtue and charms that it should be supposed *needful* to put the question whether in your address you mean a wife. But when once a man makes a promise, I think it ought to be performed; and a woman is well warranted to appeal to every one against the perfidy of a deceiver; and is always sure to have the world of her side.

Now, sir, continued he, I believe you have so much honour as to own that you could not have made way to so eminent a virtue, without promising marriage; and that very explicitly and solemnly—

I know very well, colonel, interrupted I, all you would say—You will excuse me, I am sure, that I break in upon you, when you find it is to answer the end you drive at.

I own to you then that I have acted very unworthily by Miss Clarissa Harlowe; and I'll tell you further, that I heartily repent of my ingratitude and baseness to her. Nay, I will say *still* further, that I am so grossly culpable *as to her*, that even to plead that the abuses and affronts I daily received from her implacable relations were in any manner a provocation to me to act vilely by her would be a mean and low attempt to excuse myself—so low and so mean, that it would doubly condemn me. And if you can say worse, speak it.

He looked upon Lord M. and then upon me, two or three times. And my lord said: My kinsman speaks what he thinks, I'll answer for him.

Lovel. I do, sir; and what can I say more? And what further, in your opinion, can be done?

Col. Done! sir? Why, sir (in a haughty tone he spoke), I need not tell you that reparation follows repentance. And I hope you make no scruple of justifying your sincerity as to the one by the other.

I hesitated (for I relished not the manner of his speech, and his haughty accent), as undetermined whether to take proper notice of it, or not.

Col. Let me put this question to you, Mr Lovelace—Is it true, as I have heard it is, that you would marry my cousin, if she would have you?—What say you, sir?—

This wound me up a peg higher[.]

Lovel. Some questions, as they may be put, imply *commands*, colonel. I would be glad to know how I am to take yours? And what is to be the end of your interrogatories?

Col. My questions are not meant by me as commands, Mr Lovelace. The *end* is to prevail upon a gentleman to act *like* a gentleman, and a man of honour.

Lovel. (*briskly*) And by what arguments, sir, do you propose to prevail upon me?

Col. By what arguments, sir, prevail upon a gentleman to act like a gentleman!— I am surprised at that question from Mr Lovelace.

Lovel. Why so, sir?

Col. Why so, sir (*angrily*)—Let me—

Lovel. (*interrupting*) I don't choose, colonel, to be repeated upon in that accent.

Lord M. Come, come, gentlemen, I beg of you to be willing to understand one another. You young gentlemen are so warm—

Col. Not I, my lord—I am neither very young, nor unduly warm. Your nephew, my lord, can make me be everything he would have me to be.

Lovel. And that shall be, whatever you please to be, colonel.

Col. (*fiercely*) The choice be yours, Mr Lovelace. Friend or foe! as you do or are willing to do justice to one of the finest women in the world.

Lord M. I guessed from both your characters what would be the case when you met. Let me interpose, gentlemen, and beg you but to understand one another. You *both shoot at one mark*; and if you are patient, will both *hit it*. Let me beg of you, colonel, to give no challenges—

Col. Challenges, my lord—They are things I ever was readier to accept than to offer. But does your lordship think that a man so nearly related as I have the honour to be to the most accomplished woman on earth—

Lord M. (*interrupting*) We all allow the excellencies of the lady—and we shall all take it as the greatest honour to be allied to her that can be conferred upon us.

Col. So you ought, my lord!—

A perfect *Chamont!* thought I.[a]

Lord M. So we *ought*, colonel! And so we *do!*—And pray let *every one* do as he ought!—and no *more* than he *ought*; and you, colonel, let me tell you, will not be so hasty.

Lovel. (*coolly*) Come, come, Colonel Morden, don't let this dispute, whatever you intend to make of it, go farther than with you and me. You deliver yourself in

a See Otway's *Orphan*.[1]

very high terms. Higher than ever I was talked to in my life. But here, beneath this roof, 'twould be inexcusable for me to take that notice of it, which perhaps it would become me to take elsewhere.

Col. This is spoken as I wish the man to speak, whom I should be pleased to call my friend, if all his actions were of a piece; and as I would have the man speak, whom I would think it worth my while to call my foe. I love a man of spirit, as I love my soul. But, Mr Lovelace, as my lord thinks we aim at *one mark*, let me say that were we permitted to be alone for six minutes, I dare say we should soon understand one another perfectly well—And he moved to the door.

Lovel. I am entirely of your opinion, sir, and will attend you.

My lord rung, and stepped between us: Colonel, return, I beseech you, said he; for he had stepped out of the room while my lord held me—Nephew, you shall not go out.

The bell and my lord's raised voice brought in Mowbray, and Clements, my lord's gentleman; the former in his careless way, with his hands behind him; What's the matter, Bobby? What's the matter, my lord?

Only, only, only, stammered the agitated peer, these young gentlemen are, are, are—*young* gentlemen, that's all.—Pray, Colonel Morden (who again entered the room, with a sedater aspect) let this cause have a fair trial, I beseech you.

Col. With all my heart, my lord.

Mowbray whispered me: What is the cause, Bobby?—Shall I take the gentleman to task, for thee, my boy?

Not for the world, whispered I. The colonel is a gentleman, and I desire you'll not say one word.

Well, well, well, Bobby, I have done. I can turn thee loose to the best man upon God's earth, that's all, Bobby; strutting off to the other end of the room.

Col. I am sorry, my lord, I should give your lordship the least uneasiness. I came not with such a design.

Lord M. Indeed, colonel, I thought you did, by your taking fire so quickly. I am glad to hear you say you did not. How soon a little *spark kindles into a flame*; especially when it meets with such combustible spirits!

Col. If I had had the least thought of proceeding to extremities, I am sure Mr Lovelace would have given me the honour of a meeting where I should have been less an intruder; but I came with an amicable intention—to reconcile differences rather than to widen them.

Lovel. Well then, Colonel Morden, let us enter upon the subject in your own way. I don't know the man I should sooner choose to be upon terms with than one whom Miss Clarissa Harlowe so much respects. But I cannot bear to be treated either in word or accent in a menacing way.

Lord M. Well, well, well, well, gentlemen, this is somewhat like. *Angry men make to themselves beds of nettles*, and when they lie down in them, are uneasy with everybody. But I hope you are friends. Let me hear you say you are—I am persuaded, colonel, that you don't know all this unhappy story. You don't know how desirous my kinsman is, as well as all of us, to have this matter end happily. You don't know, do you, colonel, that Mr Lovelace at all our requests is disposed to marry the lady?

Col. At all your requests, my lord?—I should have hoped that Mr Lovelace was disposed to do justice for the *sake* of justice; and when at the same time the doing of justice was doing himself the highest honour.

Mowbray lifted up his before half-closed eyes to the colonel, and glanced them upon me.

Lovel. This is in very high language, colonel.

Mowbr. By my soul, I thought so.

Col. High language, Mr Lovelace? Is it not *just* language?

Lovel. It is, colonel. And I think the man that does honour to Miss Clarissa Harlowe does me honour. But, nevertheless, there is a manner in speaking that may be liable to exception, where the words without that manner can bear none.

Col. Your observation in the general is undoubtedly just; but *if* you have the value for my cousin that you say you have, you must needs think—

Lovel. You must allow me, sir, to interrupt you—IF I have the value *I say* I have—I hope, sir, when *I say* I *have* that value, there is no room for that *if*, pronounced as you pronounced it with an emphasis.

Col. You have broken in upon me twice, Mr Lovelace. I am as little accustomed to be broken in upon, as you are to be *repeated* upon.

Lord M. Two barrels of gunpowder, by my conscience! What a devil will it signify talking, if thus you are to blow one another up at every wry word?

Lovel. No man of honour, my lord, will be easy to have his veracity called in question, though but by implication.

Col. Had you heard me out, Mr Lovelace, you would have found that my *if* was rather an *if* of *inference*, than of *doubt*. But 'tis, really, a strange liberty gentlemen of free principles take; who at the same time that they would resent unto death the imputation of being capable of telling an untruth to a man, will not scruple to break through the most solemn oaths and promises to a woman. I must assure you, Mr Lovelace, that I always made a conscience of my vows and promises.

Lovel. You did right, colonel. But let me tell you, sir, that you know not the man you talk to, if you imagine he is not able to rise to a proper resentment when he sees his generous confessions taken for a mark of base-spiritness.

Col. (*warmly, and with a sneer*) Far be it from me, Mr Lovelace, to impute to you the baseness of spirit you speak of; for what would that be, but to imagine that a man who has done a very flagrant injury is not ready to show his *bravery* in defending it—

Mowbr. This is damned severe, colonel. It is, by Jove. I could not take so much at the hands of any man breathing as Mr Lovelace before this took at yours.

Col. Who are you, sir? What pretence have you to interpose in a cause where there is an acknowledged guilt on one side, and the honour of a considerable family wounded in the tenderest part by that guilt on the other?

Mowbr. (*whispering to the colonel*) My dear child, you will oblige me highly if you will give me the opportunity of answering your question. And was going out.

The colonel was held in by my lord. And I brought in Mowbray.

Col. Pray, my good lord, let me attend this officious gentleman. I beseech you, do. I will wait upon your lordship in three minutes, depend upon it.

Lovel. Mowbray, is this acting like a friend by me, to suppose me incapable of answering for myself? And shall a man of honour and bravery, as I know Colonel Morden to be (rash as perhaps in this visit he has shown himself), have it to say that he comes to my Lord M.'s house, in a manner naked as to attendants and friends, and shall not for that reason be rather borne with than insulted! This moment, my dear Mowbray, leave us. You have really no concern in this business; and if you are my friend, I desire you'll ask the colonel pardon for interfering in it in the manner you have done.

Mowbr. Well, well, Bob; thou shalt be arbiter in this matter. I know I have no business in it—And, colonel, (*holding out his hand*), I leave you to one who knows how to defend his own cause as well as any man in England.

Col. (*taking Mowbray's hand, at Lord M.'s request*) You need not tell me *that*, Mr Mowbray. I have no doubt of Mr Lovelace's ability to defend his own cause, were it a cause to be defended. And let me tell you, Mr Lovelace, that I am astonished to think that a brave man, and a generous man, as you have appeared to be in two or three instances that you have given in the little knowledge I have of you, should be capable of acting as you have done by the most excellent of her sex.

Lord M. Well, but gentlemen, now Mr Mowbray is gone; and you have both shown instances of courage and generosity to boot, let me desire you to lay your heads together amicably, and think whether there be anything to be done to make all end happily for the lady?

Lovel. But hold, my lord, let me say one thing, now Mowbray *is* gone; and that is, that I think a gentleman ought not to put up tamely one or two severe things that the colonel has said.

Lord M. What the devil canst thou mean? I thought all had been over. Why, thou hast nothing to do but to confirm to the colonel that thou art willing to marry Miss Harlowe, if she will have thee.

Col. Mr Lovelace will not scruple to say *that*, I suppose, notwithstanding all that has passed. But if you think, Mr Lovelace, I have said anything I should *not* have said, I suppose it is this: that the man who has shown so little of the *thing* honour to a defenceless unprotected woman, ought not to stand so nicely upon the *empty name* of it with a man who is expostulating with him upon it. I am sorry to have cause to say this, Mr Lovelace; but I would on the same occasion repeat it to a king in all his glory, and surrounded by all his guards.

Lord M. But what is all this, but more *sacks upon the mill?* more *coals upon the fire?* You have a mind to quarrel both of you, I see that. Are you not willing, nephew, are you not *most* willing to marry this lady if she can be prevailed upon to have you?

Lovel. Damn me, my lord, if I'd marry an empress upon such treatment as this.

Lord M. Why now, Bob, thou art more choleric than the colonel. It was *his* turn just now. And now you see he is cool, you are all gunpowder.

Lovel. I own the colonel has many advantages over me; but perhaps there is one advantage he has not, if it were put to the trial.

Col. I came not hither, as I said before, to seek the occasion: but if it be offered me, I won't refuse it—And since we find we disturb my good Lord M., I'll take my leave, and will go home by the way of St Alban's.

Lovel. I'll see you part of the way, with all my heart, colonel.

Col. I accept your civility very cheerfully, Mr Lovelace.

Lord M. (*interposing again, as we were both for going out*) And what will this do, gentlemen? Suppose you kill one another, will the matter be bettered or worsted by that? Will the lady be made happier or unhappier do you think, by either or both of your deaths? Your characters are too well known to make fresh instances of the courage of either needful. And I think, if the honour of the lady is your view, colonel, it can be no other way so effectually promoted as by marriage. And, sir, if *you* would use your interest with her, it is very probable that *you* may succeed, though nobody else can.

Lovel. I think, my lord, I have said all that a man can say (since what is passed cannot be recalled) and you see Colonel Morden rises in proportion to my coolness, till it is necessary for me to assert myself, or even *he* would despise me.

Lord M. Let me ask you, colonel: Have you any way, any method, that you think reasonable and honourable to propose, to bring about a reconciliation with the lady. That is what we all wish for. And I can tell you, sir, it is not a little owing to her family, and to their implacable usage of her, that her resentments are heightened against my kinsman; who, however, has used her vilely; but is willing to repair her wrongs—

Lovel. Not, my lord, for the sake of her family; nor for this gentleman's haughty behaviour; but for *her own sake*, and in full sense of the wrongs I have done her.

Col. As to my haughty behaviour, as you call it, sir, I am mistaken if you would not have gone beyond it in the like case of a relation so meritorious and so unworthily injured. And, sir, let me tell you, that if your motives are not love, honour, and justice, and if they have the least tincture of mean compassion for *her*, or of an uncheerful assent on *your part*, I am sure it will neither be desired or accepted by a person of my cousin's merit and sense; nor shall I wish that it should.

Lovel. Don't think, colonel, that I am meanly compounding off a debate, that I should as willingly go through with you as to eat or drink if I have the occasion given me for it: but thus much I will tell you, that my lord, that Lady Sarah Sadleir, Lady Betty Lawrance, my two cousins Montague, and myself, have written to her in the most solemn and sincere manner, to offer her such terms as no one but herself would refuse, and this long enough before Colonel Morden's arrival was dreamt of.

Col. What reason, sir, may I ask, does she give against listening to so powerful a mediation, and to such offers?

Lovel. It looks like capitulating, or else—

Col. It looks not like any such thing to *me*, Mr Lovelace, who have as good an opinion of your spirit as man can have. And what, pray, is the part I act, and my motives for it? Are they not, in desiring that justice may be done to my cousin Clarissa Harlowe, that I seek to establish the honour of *Mrs Lovelace* if matters can once be brought to bear?

Lovel. Were she to honour me with her acceptance of that name, Mr Morden, I should not want you or any man to assert the honour of Mrs Lovelace.

Col. I believe it. But till she *has* honoured you with that acceptance, she is nearer to me than to you, Mr Lovelace. And I speak this only to show you, that in the part I take, I mean rather to deserve your thanks than your displeasure, though against *yourself*, were there occasion. Nor ought you to take it amiss if you rightly weigh the matter: for, sir, whom does a lady want protection against, but her injurers? And who has been her *greatest* injurer?—Till, therefore, she becomes entitled to your protection, as *your wife*, you yourself cannot refuse me some merit in wishing to have justice done *my cousin*. But, sir, you was going to say that if it were not to look like capitulating, you would hint the reasons my cousin gives against accepting such an honourable mediation?

I then told him of my sincere offers of marriage; 'I made no difficulty, I said, to own my apprehensions that my unhappy behaviour to her had greatly affected her: but that it was the implacableness of her friends that had thrown her into despair, and given her a contempt for life.' I told him, 'That she had been so good as to send me a letter to divert me from a visit my heart was set upon making her: a letter on which I built great hopes, because she assured me in it, that she was *going to her father's*; and that *I might see her there, when she was received, if it were not my own fault.*'

Col. Is it possible? And were you, sir, thus earnest? And did she send you such a letter?

Lord M. confirmed both; and also that, in obedience to her desires and that intimation, I had come down without the satisfaction I had proposed to myself in seeing her.

It is very true, colonel, said I: and I should have told you this before: but your heat made me decline it; for, as I said, it had an appearance of meanly capitulating with you. An abjectness of heart, of which had I been capable, I should have despised *myself* as much as I might have expected *you* would despise me.

Lord M. proposed to enter into the proof of all this: he said in his phraseological way *that one story was good, till another was heard:* that the Harlowe family and I, 'twas true, had behaved like so many *Orsons* to one another; and that they had been very free with all our family besides: that nevertheless, for the lady's sake more than for theirs, or even for *mine* (he could tell me), he would do greater things for me than they could ask, if she could be brought to have me: and that this he *wanted* to declare, and would *sooner* have declared if he could have brought us sooner to patience and a good understanding.

The colonel made excuses for his warmth on the score of his affection to his cousin.

My regard for her made me readily admit them: and so a fresh bottle of Burgundy and another of Champagne being put upon the table, we sat down in good humour after all this blustering, in order to enter closer into the particulars of the case: which I undertook at both their desires to do.

But these things must be the subject of another letter which shall immediately follow this, if it do not accompany it.

Meantime you will observe that a bad cause gives a man great disadvantages: for I myself think that the interrogatories put to me with so much spirit by the colonel made me look cursedly mean; at the same time that it gave him a superiority which I know not how to allow to the best man in Europe. So that, literally speaking, as a *good man* would infer, guilt is its own punisher; in that it makes the most lofty spirit look like the miscreant he is—*good man*, I say: so, Jack, *proleptically* I add, *thou* hast no right to make the observation.

Letter 443: MR LOVELACE [TO JOHN BELFORD, ESQ.]

(In continuation)

Tuesday afternoon, Aug. 29

I WENT back in this part of our conversation to the day that I was obliged to come down to attend my lord, in the dangerous illness which some feared would have been his last.

I told the colonel 'what earnest letters I had written to a particular friend, to engage him to prevail upon the lady not to slip a day that had been proposed for the private celebration of our nuptials; and of my letters*a* written to herself on that subject'; for I had stepped to my closet and fetched down all the letters and drafts and copies of letters relating to this affair.

I read to him 'several passages in the copies of those letters which, thou wilt remember, make not a little to my honour.' And I told him 'that I wished I had kept copies of those to my friend on the same occasion; by which he would have seen how much in earnest I was in my professions to her, although she would not answer one of them.' And thou mayest remember that one of those four letters accounted to herself why I was desirous she should remain where I had left her.*b*

I then proceeded to give him an account 'of the visit made by Lady Sarah and Lady Betty to Lord M. and me, in order to induce me to do her justice: of my readiness to comply with their desires; and of their high opinion of her merit. Of the visit made to Miss Howe by my cousins Montague in the name of us all, to engage her interest with her friend in my behalf. Of my conversation with Miss Howe at a private assembly, to whom I gave the same assurances, and besought her interest with her friend.'

I then read the copy of the letter (though so much to my disadvantage) which was written to her by Miss Charlotte Montague, Aug. 1,*c* entreating her alliance in the names of all our family.

This made him ready to think that his fair cousin carried her resentment against me too far. He did not imagine, he said, that either myself or our family had been so much in earnest.

So thou seest, Belford, that it is but glossing over *one* part of a story, and omitting *another*, that will make a bad cause a good one at any time. What an admirable lawyer should I have made! And what a poor hand would this charming creature, with all her innocence, have made of it in a court of justice against a man who had so much to *say*, and to *show* for himself.

I then hinted at the generous annual tender which Lord M. and his sisters made to his fair cousin, in apprehension that she might suffer by her friends' implacableness.

And this also the colonel highly applauded, and was pleased to lament the unhappy misunderstanding between the two families, which had made the Harlowes less fond of an alliance with a family of so much honour as this instance showed ours to be.

I then told him, 'that having, by my friend (meaning thee), who was admitted

a See pp. 953–60.
b See p. 953.
c See p. 1171.

into her presence (and who had always been an admirer of her virtues and had given me such advice from time to time in relation to her as I wished I had followed), been assured that a visit from me would be very disagreeable to her, I once more resolved to try what a letter would do; and that accordingly, on the 7th of August I wrote her one.

'This, colonel, is the copy of it. I was then out of humour with my Lord M. and the ladies of my family. You will therefore read it to yourself.'[a]

This letter gave him high satisfaction. You write here, Mr Lovelace, from your heart. 'Tis a letter full of penitence and acknowledgement. Your request is reasonable—to be forgiven only as you shall appear to deserve it after a time of probation, which you leave to her to fix. Pray, sir, did she return an answer to this letter?

She did, but with *reluctance*, I own, and not till I had declared by my friend that if I could not procure one, I would go up to town and throw myself at her feet.

I wish I might be permitted to see it, sir, or to hear such parts of it read as you shall think proper.

Turning over my papers. Here it is, sir.[b] I will make no scruple to put it into your hands.

This is very obliging, Mr Lovelace.

He read it. My charming cousin!—How strong her resentments!—Yet how charitable her wishes! Good God! that such an excellent creature!—But, Mr Lovelace, it is to your regret, as much as to mine, I doubt not—

Interrupting him, I swore that it was.

So it ought, said he. Nor do I wonder that it should be so. I shall tell you by and by, proceeded he, how much she suffers with her friends by false and villainous reports. But, sir, will you permit me to take with me these two letters? I shall make use of them to the advantage of you both.

I told him I would oblige him with all my heart. And this he took very kindly, as he had reason, and put them in his pocket-book, promising to return them in a few days.

I then told him 'that upon this refusal, I took upon myself to go to town, in hopes to move her in my favour; and that though I went without giving her notice of my intention, yet had she got some notion of my coming, and so contrived to be out of the way: and at last, when she found I was fully determined at all events to see her before I went abroad (which I shall do, said I, if I cannot prevail upon her), she sent me the letter I have already mentioned to you, desiring me to suspend my purposed visit: and that for a reason which amazes and confounds me, because I don't find there is any thing in it: and yet I never knew her once dispense with her word; for she always made it a maxim, that *it was not lawful to do evil that good might come of it:* and yet in this letter, for no reason in the world but to avoid seeing me (to gratify a humour only), has she sent me out of town, depending upon the assurance she had given me.'

Col. This is indeed surprising. But I cannot believe that my cousin, for such an end *only* or indeed for *any* end, according to the character I hear of her, should stoop to make use of such an artifice.

a See p. 1185.
b See p. 1191.

Lovel. This, colonel, is the thing that astonishes me; and yet, see here!—This is the letter she wrote me—nay, sir, 'tis her own hand.

Col. I see it is; and a charming hand it is.

Lovel. You observe, colonel, that all her hopes of reconciliation with her parents are from you. You are her *dear blessed friend!* She always talked of you with delight.

Col. Would to heaven I had come to England before she left Harlowe Place. Nothing of this had then happened. Not a man of those whom I have heard that her friends proposed for her should have had her. Nor you, Mr Lovelace, unless I had found you to be the man everyone who sees you must wish you to be: and if you *had* been that man, no one living should I have preferred to you for such an excellence.

My lord and I both joined in the wish: and 'faith, I wished it most cordially.

The colonel read the letter twice over, and then returned it to me. 'Tis all a mystery, said he: I can make nothing of it. For, alas! her friends are as averse to a reconciliation as ever.

Lord M. I could not have thought it. But don't you think there is something very favourable to my nephew in this letter?—something that looks as if the lady would comply at last?

Col. Let me die if I know what to make of it. This letter is very different from her preceding one!—You returned an answer to it, Mr Lovelace?

Lovel. An answer, colonel! No doubt of it. And an answer full of transport. I told her 'I would directly set out for Lord M.'s in obedience to her will. I told her that I would consent to anything she should command, in order to promote this happy reconciliation. I told her that it should be my hourly study, to the end of my life, to deserve a goodness so transcendent.' But I cannot forbear saying that I am not a little shocked and surprised, if nothing more be meant by it than to get me into the country without seeing her.

Col. That can't be the thing, depend upon it, sir. There must be more in it than that. For were that all, she must think you would soon be undeceived, and that you would then most probably resume your intention—unless, indeed, she depended upon seeing *me* in the interim, as she knew I was arrived. But I own I know not what to make of it. Only that she does me a great deal of honour, if it be me that she calls her *blessed friend, whom she always loved and honoured.* Indeed, I ever loved her: and if I die unmarried and without children, shall be as kind to her as her grandfather was: and the rather, as I fear that there is too much of envy and self-love in the resentments her brother and sister endeavour to keep up in her father and mother against her. But I shall know better how to judge of this, when my cousin James comes from Edinburgh; and he is every hour expected.

But let me ask you, Mr Lovelace, What is the name of your friend who is admitted so easily into my cousin's presence? Is it not Belford, pray?

Lovel. It is, sir; a man of honour, and a great admirer of your fair cousin.

Was I right as to the *first*, Jack? The *last* I have such strong proof of, that it makes me question the *first*; since she would not have been out of the way of my intended visit but for thee.

Col. Are you sure, sir, that Mr Belford is a man of honour?

Lovel. I can swear for him, colonel. What makes you put this question?

Col. Only this: that an officious pragmatical novice has been sent up to inquire into my cousin's life and conversation: and, would you believe it! the frequent visits of this gentleman have been interpreted basely to her disreputation?—Read that letter, Mr Lovelace, and you will be shocked at every part of it.

This cursed letter, no doubt, is from the young Levite whom thou, Jack, describedst as making inquiry of Mrs Smith about Miss Harlowe's character and visitors.[a]

I believe I was a quarter of an hour in reading it: for I made it, though not a short one, six times as long as it is by the additions of oaths and curses to every pedantic line. Lord M. too helped to lengthen it, by the like execrations. And thou, Jack, wilt have as much reason to curse it as we.

You cannot but see, said the colonel, when I had done reading it, that this fellow has been *officious* in his malevolence; for what he says is mere hearsay, and that hearsay conjectural scandal without fact or the appearance of fact to support it; so that an unprejudiced eye, upon the face of the letter, would condemn the writer of it as I did, and acquit my cousin. But yet, such is the spirit by which the rest of my relations are governed, that they run away with the belief of the worst it insinuates, and the dear creature has had shocking letters upon it; the pedant's hints are taken; and a voyage to one of the colonies has been proposed to her, as the only way to avoid Mr Belford and you. I have not seen these letters indeed; but they took a pride in repeating some of their contents, which must have cut the poor soul to the heart; and these, joined to her former sufferings—What have you not, Mr Lovelace, to answer for?

Lovel. Who the devil could have expected such consequences as these? Who could have believed there could be parents so implacable? Brother and sister so envious? And give me leave to say, a lady so immovably fixed against the only means that could be taken to put all right with everybody?—And what now can be done?

Lord M. I have great hopes that Colonel Morden may yet prevail upon his cousin. And by her last letter, it runs in my mind that she has some thoughts of forgiving all that's past. Do you think, colonel, if there should *not* be such a thing as a reconciliation going forward at present, that her letter may not imply that if we *could* bring such a thing to bear with her friends, she would be reconciled to Mr Lovelace?

Col. Such an artifice would better become the Italian subtlety than the English simplicity. Your lordship has been in Italy, I presume?

Lovel. My lord has read Boccacio, perhaps, and that's as well, as to the hint he gives, which may be borrowed from one of that author's stories. But Miss Clarissa Harl~ ~e is above all artifice. She must have some meaning I cannot fathom.

Col. Well, my lord, I can only say that I will make some use of the letters Mr Lovelace has obliged me with: and after I have had some talk with my cousin James, who is hourly expected; and when I have dispatched two or three affairs that press upon me; I will pay my respects to my dear cousin; and shall then be able to form a better judgement of things. Meantime I will write to her; for I have sent to inquire about her, and find she wants consolation.

Lovel. If you favour me, colonel, with the damned letter of that fellow Brand for a day or two, you will oblige me.

Col. I will. But remember, the man is a parson, Mr Lovelace; an innocent one

a   See pp. 1189 f.

too, they say. Else I had been at him before now. And these college novices who think they know everything in their cloisters, and that all learning lies in *books*, make dismal figures when they come into the world among *men* and *women*.

Lord M. Brand! Brand! It should have been *Fire-Brand*, I think in my conscience!

Thus ended this doughty conference.

I cannot say, Jack, but I am greatly taken with Colonel Morden. He is brave and generous, and knows the world; and then his contempt of the parsons is a certain sign that he is one of *us*.

We parted with great civility; Lord M. (not a little pleased that we did, and as greatly taken with the colonel) repeated his wish, after the colonel was gone, that he had arrived in time to save the lady; if that would have done it.

I wish so too. For by my soul, Jack, I am every day more and more uneasy about her. But I hope she is not so ill as I am told she is.

I enclose this *Fire-Brand*'s letter, as my Lord calls him. I reckon it will rouse all thy phlegm into vengeance.

I know not what to advise as to showing it to the lady. Yet perhaps she will be able to reap more satisfaction than concern from it, knowing her own innocence; in that it will give her to hope that her friends' treatment of her is owing as much to misrepresentation, as to their own natural implacableness. Such a mind as hers, I know, would be glad to find out the shadow of a reason for the shocking letters the colonel says they have sent her, and for their proposal to her of going to some one of the colonies. (Confound them all—but if I begin to curse, I shall never have done.)—Then it may put her upon such a defence as she might be glad of an opportunity to make, and to shame them for their monstrous credulity—But this I leave to thy own fat-headed prudence—only it vexes me to the heart that even scandal and calumny should dare to surmise the bare possibility of any man's sharing the favours of a lady, whom now methinks I could worship with a veneration due only to a divinity.

Charlotte and her sister could not help weeping at the base aspersion: When, when, said Patty, lifting up her hands, will this sweet lady's sufferings be at an end?—Oh cousin Lovelace!—

And thus am I blamed for everyone's faults!—When her brutal father curses her, it is I. I upbraid her with her severe mother. Her stupid uncles' implacableness is all mine. Her brother's virulence, and her sister's spite and envy, are entirely owing to me. This rascal Brand's letter is of my writing—Oh Jack, what a wretch is thy Lovelace!

RETURNED without a letter!—This damned fellow Will is returned without a letter! Yet the rascal tells me that he hears you have been writing to me these two days!

Plague confound thee, who must know my impatience, and the reason for it!

To send a man and horse on purpose; as I did! My imagination chained to the belly of the beast, in order to keep pace with him! Now he is got to this place; now to that; now to London; now to thee.

Now (a letter given him) whip and spur upon the return. This town just entered, not staying to bait: that village passed by: leaves the wind behind him; in a foaming sweat, man and horse.

And in this way did he actually enter Lord M.'s courtyard.

The reverberating pavement brought me down—The letter, Will! The letter, dog!—The letter sirrah!

No letter, sir!—Then wildly staring round me, fists clenched, and grinning like a maniac, Confound thee for a dog, and him that sent thee without one!—This moment out of my sight, or I'll scatter thy stupid brains through the air, snatching from his holsters a pistol, while the rascal threw himself from the foaming beast and run to avoid the fate which I wished with all my soul thou hadst been within the reach of me to have met with.

But, to be as meek as a lamb to one who has me at his mercy, and can wring and torture my soul as he pleases, *What canst thou mean* to send back my varlet without a letter?—I will send away by day-dawn another fellow upon another beast for what thou hast written; and I charge thee on thy allegiance, that thou dispatch him not back empty-handed.

Letter 444: MR BRAND TO JOHN HARLOWE, ESQ.

(Enclosed in the preceding)

Worthy sir, my very good friend and patron,

I ARRIVED in town yesterday, after a tolerable pleasant journey (considering the hot weather and dusty roads). I put up at the Bull and Gate in Holborn, and hastened to Covent Garden. I soon found the house where the unhappy lady lodges. And in the back shop had a good deal of discourse[a] with Mrs Smith (her landlady), whom I found to be so *highly prepossessed* in her *favour*, that I saw it would not answer your desires to take my informations *altogether* from her, and being obliged to attend my patron; who, to my sorrow,

(Miserum est aliena vivere quadra)

I find wants much waiting upon, and is *another* sort of man than he was at college: for sir (*inter nos*), *honours change manners*. For the *aforesaid causes* I thought it would best answer all the ends of the commission you honoured me with, to engage in the desired scrutiny the wife of a *particular friend*, who lives almost over against the house where she lodges, and who is a gentlewoman of *character* and *sobriety*, a *mother of children*, and one who *knows* the *world* well.

To her I applied myself, therefore, and gave her a short history of the case, and desired she would very particularly inquire into the *conduct* of the unhappy young lady; her *present way of life* and *substance*; her *visitors*, her *employments*, and such-like; for these, sir, you know, are the things whereof you wished to be informed.

Accordingly, sir, I waited upon the gentlewoman aforesaid this day; and, to *my* very great trouble (because I know it will be to *yours*, and likewise to all your worthy family's) I must say that I do find things look a little more *darkly* than I hoped they would. For, alas! sir, the gentlewoman's report turns not out so *favourable* for miss's reputation as *I* wished, as *you* wished, and as *every one* of her friends wished. But so it is throughout the world, that *one false step* generally brings on *another*; and peradventure *a worse*, and *a still worse*; till the poor *limed*

a   See pp. 1189 f.

soul (a very fit epithet of the divine Quarles's![1]) is quite *entangled* and (without infinite *mercy*) lost for ever.

It seems, sir, she is notwithstanding in a very *ill state of health*. In this, both gentlewomen (that is to say, Mrs Smith her landlady, and my friend's wife) agree. Yet she goes often out in a chair to *prayers* (as it is said). But my friend's wife tells me that nothing is more common in London than that the frequenting of the church at morning prayers is made the *pretence* and *cover* for *private assignations*. What a sad thing is this! that what was designed for *wholesome nourishment* to the *poor soul* should be turned into *rank poison*! But as Mr Daniel de Foe, an ingenious man, though a *dissenter*, observes (but indeed it is an old proverb; only I think he was the first that put it into verse):

> God never had a house of pray'r,
> But Satan had a chapel there.[2]

Yet, to do the lady *justice*, nobody comes home with her: nor, indeed *can* they, because she goes forward and backward in a *sedan* or *chair* (as they call it). But then there is a gentleman of *no good character* (an *intimado* of Mr Lovelace's) who is a *constant* visitor of her, and of the people of the house, whom he *regales* and *treats*, and has (of consequence) their *high good words*.

I have hereupon taken the trouble (for I love to be *exact* in any *commission* I undertake) to inquire *particularly* about this *gentleman*, as he is called (albeit I hold no man so but by his actions: for, as Juvenal says:

—Nobilitas sola est, atque unica virtus).[3]

And this I did *before* I would sit down to write to you.

His name is Belford. He has a paternal estate of upwards of £1000 by the year; and is now in mourning for an uncle who left him very considerably besides. He bears a very profligate character as to *women* (for I inquired *particularly* about *that*), and is Mr Lovelace's more especial *privado*, with whom he holds a *regular correspondence*; and has been often seen with miss (*tête à tête*) at the *window*: in no *bad way*, indeed: but my friend's wife is of opinion that all is not *as it should be*. And, indeed, it is mighty strange to me, if miss be so *notable a penitent* (as is represented) and if she have such an *aversion* to Mr Lovelace, that she will admit his *privado* into *her retirements*, and see *no other company*.

I understand from Mrs Smith that Mr Hickman was to see her some time ago, from Miss Howe; and I am told by *another* hand (you see, sir, how diligent I have been to excute the *commissions* you had given me) that he had no *extraordinary opinion* of this Belford at first; though they were seen together one morning by the opposite neighbour, at *breakfast with miss:* and another time this Belford was observed to *watch* Mr Hickman's coming from her; so that, as it should seem, he was mighty zealous to *ingratiate* himself with Mr Hickman; no doubt to engage him to make a *favourable report to Miss Howe* of the *intimacy* he was admitted into by her unhappy friend; who (*as she is very ill*) may *mean no harm* in allowing his visits (for he, it seems, brought to her, or recommended at least, the doctor and apothecary that attend her): but I think upon the whole it *looketh not well*.

I am sorry, sir, I cannot give you a better account of the young lady's *prudence*. But what shall we say?

Uvaque conspecta livorem ducit ab uva,

as Juvenal observes.⁴

One thing I am afraid of; which is, that miss may be under *necessities*; and that this Belford (who, as Mrs Smith owns, has *offered her money* which she, *at the time*, refused) may find an opportunity to *take advantage* of those *necessities:* and it is well observed by the poet, that

> Aegre formosam poteris servare puellam:
> Nunc prece, nunc [pretio] forma petita ruit.⁵

And this Belford (who is a *bold man*, and has, as they say, the *look* of one) may make good that of Horace (with whose writings you are so well acquainted; nobody better):

> Audax omnia perpeti,
> Gens humana ruit per vetitum nefas.⁶

Forgive me, sir, for what I am going to write: but if you could prevail upon the rest of your family to join in the scheme which *you* and her *virtuous sister*, Miss Arabella, and the archdeacon and I, once talked of (which is, to persuade the unhappy young lady to go in some *creditable* manner to some one of the foreign colonies), it might save not only her *own credit* and *reputation*, but the *reputation* and *credit* of all her *family*, and a great deal of *vexation* moreover. For it is my humble opinion that you will hardly, any of you, enjoy yourselves while this (*once innocent*) young lady is in the way of being so frequently heard of by you: and this would put her *out of the way* both of *this Belford* and of *that Lovelace*, and it might peradventure prevent as much *evil* as *scandal*.

You will forgive me, sir, for this my *plainness*. Ovid pleads for me,

> —Adulator nullus amicus erit.⁷

And I have no view but that of approving myself a *zealous well-wisher* to *all* your worthy family (whereto I owe a great number of obligations) and very particularly, sir,

Your obliged and humble servant,
Wedn. Aug. 9.   ELIAS BRAND

P.S. I shall give you *further hints* when I come down (which will be in a few days), and who my *informants* were; but by *these* you will see that I have been very assiduous (for the time) in the task you set me upon.

The *length* of my letter you will excuse; for I need not tell you, sir, what *narrative, complex*, and *conversation* letters (such a one as *mine*) require. Everyone to his *talent. Letter writing* is mine, I will be bold to say; and that my *correspondence* was much coveted at the university, on that account. But this I should not have taken upon me to mention; only in defence of the *length* of my letter; for nobody writes *shorter*, or *pithier*, when the subject is upon *common forms* only—But in apologizing for my *prolixity* I am *adding* to the *fault* (if it were one, which however I cannot think it to be, the *subject* considered: but this I have said before in other words): so, sir, if you will excuse my *postscript*, I am sure you will not find fault with my *letter*.

I think I have nothing to add until I have the honour of attending you in *person*; but that I am, as above, etc. etc. etc. E.B.

Letter 445: MR BELFORD TO ROBERT LOVELACE, ESQ.

Wednesday night, Aug. 30

It was lucky enough that our two servants met at Hannah's,[a] which gave them so good an opportunity of exchanging their letters time enough for each to return to his master early in the day.

Thou dost well to brag of thy capacity for managing servants, and to set up for correcting our poets in their characters of this class of people,[b] when like a madman thou canst beat their teeth out, and attempt to shoot them through the head for not bringing to thee what they had no power to obtain.

You well observe[c] that you would have made a thorough-paced lawyer. The whole of the conversation-piece between you and the colonel affords a convincing proof that there is a black and a white side to every cause: but what must the conscience of a partial whitener of his *own* cause, or blackener or *another*'s, tell him while he is throwing dust in the eyes of his judges, and all the time he knows his own guilt?

The colonel, I see, is far from being a faultless man: but while he sought not to carry his point by breach of faith, he has an excuse which thou hast not. But with respect to him, and to us all, I can now with a detestation of some of my own actions see that the taking advantage of another person's good opinion of us to injure (perhaps to ruin) that other, is the most ungenerous wickedness that can be committed.

Man acting thus by *man*, we should not be at a loss to give such actions a name: but is it not doubly and trebly aggravated when such advantage is taken of an inexperienced and innocent young creature whom we pretend to love above all the women in the world; and when we seal our pretences by the most solemn vows and protestations of inviolable honour that we can invent?

I see that this gentleman is the best match thou ever couldst have had, upon all accounts: his spirit such another impetuous one as thy own; soon taking fire: vindictive; and only differing in this, that the cause he engages in is a just one. But commend me to honest brutal Mowbray, who before he knew the cause offers his sword in thy behalf against a man who had taken the injured side, and whom he had never seen before.

As soon as I had run through your letters and that incendiary Brand's (by the latter of which I saw to what cause a great deal of this last implacableness of the Harlowe family is owing), I took coach to Smith's, although I had been come from thence but about an hour, and had taken leave of the lady for the night.

I sent down for Mrs Lovick, and desired her in the first place to acquaint the lady (who was busied in her closet) that I had letters from Berkshire: in which I was informed that the interview between Colonel Morden and Mr Lovelace had ended without ill consequences; that the colonel intended to write to her very

a The windmill near Slough.
b See p. 1237.
c See p. 1287.

soon, and was interesting himself meanwhile in her favour with her relations; that I hoped that this agreeable news would be a means of giving her good rest; and I would wait upon her in the morning, by the time she should return from prayers, with all the particulars.

She sent me word that she should be glad to see me in the morning; and was highly obliged to me for the good news I had sent her up.

I then in the back shop read to Mrs Lovick and to Mrs Smith Brand's letter, and asked them if they could guess at the man's informant? They were not at a loss, Mrs Smith having seen the same fellow Brand who had talked with her, as I mentioned in a former,*a* come out of a milliner's shop over-against them; which milliner, she said, had also been lately very inquisitive about the lady.

I wanted no further hint; but, bidding them take no notice to the lady of what I had read, I shot over the way, and asking for the mistress of the house, she came to me.

Retiring with her, at her invitation, into her parlour, I desired to know if she was acquainted with a young country clergyman of the name of Brand. She hesitatingly, seeing me in some emotion, owned that she had some small knowledge of the gentleman. Just then came in her husband, who is it seems a petty officer in the excise, and not an ill-behaved man, who owned fuller knowledge of him.

I have the copy of a letter, said I, from this Brand, in which he has taken great liberties with my character, and with that of the most unblamable lady in the world, which he grounds upon informations that you, madam, have given him. And then I read to them several passages in his letter; and asked what foundation she had for giving that fellow such impressions of either of us?

They knew not what to answer: but at last said that he had told them how wickedly the young lady had run away from her parents: what worthy and rich people they were: in what favour *he* stood with them; and that they had employed him to inquire after her behaviour, visitors, etc.

They said that indeed they knew very little of the young lady; but that (curse upon their censoriousness!) it was but too natural to think that where a lady had given way to a delusion, and taken so wrong a step, she would not stop there: that the most sacred places and things were but too often made a cloak for bad actions. That Mr Brand had been informed (perhaps by some enemy of mine) that I was a man of very free principles, and an *intimado*, as he calls it, of the man who had ruined her. And that their cousin Barker, a mantua-maker who lodged up one pair of stairs (and who, at their desire, came down and confirmed what they said), had often from her window seen me with the lady in her chamber talking very earnestly together: and that Mr Brand being unable to account for her admitting my visits, and knowing I was but a new acquaintance of hers and an old one of Mr Lovelace's, thought himself obliged to lay these matters before her friends.

This was the sum and substance of their tale. Oh how I cursed the censoriousness of this plaguy triumvirate! A parson, a milliner, and a mantua-maker! The two latter not more by *business* led to adorn the person than generally by *scandal* to destroy the *reputations* of those they have a mind to exercise their talents upon!

The two women took great pains to persuade me that they were people of conscience—of consequence, I told them, too much addicted I doubted to censure

a   See pp. 1189 f.

other people who pretended not to their strictness; for that I had ever found censoriousness, narrowness, and uncharitableness to prevail too much with those who affected to be thought more pious than their neighbours.

That was not them, they said; and that they had since inquired into the lady's character and manner of life, and were very much concerned to think anything they had said should be made use of against her: and as they heard from Mrs Smith that she was not likely to live long, they should be sorry she should go out of the world a sufferer by their means, or with an ill opinion of them, though strangers to her. The husband offered to write, if I pleased, to Mr Brand, in vindication of the lady; and the two women said they should be glad to wait upon her in person, to beg her pardon for anything she had reason to take amiss from them; because they were now convinced that there was not such another young lady in the world.

I told them that the least said of the affair to the lady in her present circumstances was best. That she was fond of taking all occasions to find excuses for her relations on their implacableness to her; that therefore I should take some notice to her of the uncharitable and weak surmises which gave birth to so vile a scandal. But that I would have him, Mr Walton (for that is the husband's name), write to his acquaintance Brand, as soon as possible, as he had offered—And so I left them.

Letter 446: MR BELFORD TO ROBERT LOVELACE, ESQ.

Thursday, 11 o'clock, Aug. 31

I AM just come from the lady, whom I left cheerful and serene.

She thanked me for my communication of the preceding night. I read to her such parts of your letters as I *could* read to her; and I thought it was a good test to distinguish the froth and whipped-syllabub in them from the cream, in what one *could* and could *not* read to a woman of so fine a mind; since four parts out of six of thy letters, which I thought entertaining as I read them to myself, appeared to me when I would have read them to her, most abominable stuff, and gave me a very contemptible idea of thy talents, and of my own judgement.

She was far from rejoicing, as I had done, at the disappointment her letter gave you when explained.

She said she meant only an innocent allegory that might carry instruction and warning to you when the meaning was taken, as well as answer her own hopes for the time. It was run off in a hurry. She was afraid it was not quite right in *her*. But hoped the end would excuse, if it could not justify, the means. And then she again expressed a good deal of apprehension lest you should still take it into your head to molest her, when her time, she says, is so short that she wants every moment of it; repeating what she had once said before, that when she wrote she was so ill, that she believed she should not have lived till now: if she had thought she should, she must have thought of an expedient that would have better answered her intentions; hinting at a removal out of the knowledge of us both.

But she was much pleased that the conference between you and Colonel Morden ended so amicably, after two or three such violent sallies as I acquainted her you had had between you; and said she must absolutely depend upon the promise I had given her to use my utmost endeavours to prevent further mischief on her account.

She was pleased with the justice you did her character to her cousin.

She was glad to hear that he had so kind an opinion of her, and that he would write to her.

I was under an unnecessary concern how to break to her that I had the copy of Brand's vile letter: *unnecessary*, I say; for she took it just as you thought she would, as an excuse she wished to have for the implacableness of her friends; and begged I would let her read it herself; for, said she, the contents cannot disturb me, be they what they will.

I gave it her, and she read it to herself, a tear now and then ready to start, and a sigh sometimes interposing.

She gave me back the letter with great and surprising calmness, considering the subject.

There was a time, said she, and that not long since, when such a letter as this would have greatly pained me. But I hope I have now got above all these things; for I can refer to your kind offices and Miss Howe's, the justice that will be done to my memory among my friends. There is a good and a bad light in which everything that befalls us may be taken. If the human mind will busy itself to make the worst of every disagreeable occurrence, it will never want woe. This letter, affecting as the subject of it is to my reputation, gives me more pleasure than pain, because I can gather from it that had not my friends been prepossessed by misinformed, or rash and officious persons, who are always at hand to flatter or soothe the passions of the affluent, they could not have been so immovably determined against me. But now they are sufficiently cleared from every imputation of unforgiveness; for while I appeared to them in the character of a vile hypocrite, pretending to true penitence, yet giving up myself to profligate courses, how could I expect either their pardon or blessing?

But, madam, said I, you'll see by the date of this letter, August 9, that their severity *previous* to that cannot be excused by it.

It imports me much, replied she, on account of my present wishes as to the office you are so kind to undertake, that you should not think harshly of my friends. I must own to you that I have been apt sometimes myself to think them not only severe, but cruel. Suffering minds will be partial to their own cause and merits. Knowing their own hearts, if sincere, they are apt to murmur when harshly treated: but if they are not *believed* to be innocent by persons who have a right to decide upon their conduct according to their own judgements, how can it be helped? Besides, sir, how do you know that there are not about my friends as well-meaning misrepresenters as Mr Brand really seems to be? But be this as it will, there is no doubt that there are and have been multitudes of persons as innocent as myself, who have suffered upon surmises as little probable as those on which Mr Brand founds his judgement. Your intimacy, sir, with Mr Lovelace, and (may I say?) a character which it seems you have been less solicitous formerly about justifying than perhaps you will be for the future; and your frequent visits to me, may well be thought to be questionable circumstances in my conduct.

I could only admire her in silence.

But you see, sir, proceeded she, how necessary it is for young people of our sex to be careful of our company: and how much at the same time it behoves young gentlemen to be chary of their own reputation, were it only for the sake of such of ours as they may mean honourably by; and who otherwise may suffer in their good names for being seen in their company.

As to Mr Brand, continued she, he is to be pitied; and let me enjoin you, Mr Belford, not to take up any resentments against him which may be detrimental either to his person or his fortunes. Let his function and his good meaning plead for him. He will have concern enough, when he finds everybody whose displeasure I now labour under acquitting my memory of perverse guilt, and joining in a general pity for me.

This, Lovelace, is the lady whose life thou hast curtailed in the blossom of it!— How many opportunities must thou have had of admiring her inestimable worth, yet couldst have thy senses so much absorbed in the WOMAN in her charming person as to be blind to the ANGEL that shines out in such full glory in her mind? Indeed, I have ever thought myself when blessed with her conversation, in the company of a real angel: and I am sure it would be impossible for me, were she to be as beautiful and as crimsoned over with health as I have seen her, to have the least thought of sex when I heard her talk.

Thursday, three o'clock, Aug. 31

ON my revisit to the lady, I found her almost as much a sufferer from joy as she had sometimes been from grief: for she had just received a very kind letter from her cousin Morden; which she was so good as to communicate to me. As she had already begun to answer it, I begged leave to attend her in the evening, that I might not interrupt her in it.

The letter is a very tender one . . .

Here Mr Belford gives the substance of it upon his memory [but that is omitted]; see the next letter. And then adds:

But, alas! all will be now too late. For the decree is certainly gone out. The world is unworthy of her!

Letter 447: COLONEL MORDEN TO MISS CLARISSA HARLOWE

Tuesday, Aug. 29

My dear cousin,

PERMIT me to condole those misfortunes which have occasioned so unhappy a difference between you and the rest of your family: and to offer my assistance to enable you to make the best of what has happened.

You have fallen into most unworthy hands. The letter I wrote to you from Florence[a] I find came too late to have its hoped-for effect. I am very sorry it did: as I am that I did not come sooner to England in person.

But forgetting past things, let us look forward. I have been with Mr Lovelace, and Lord M. I need not tell *you*, it seems, how desirous all the family are of the honour of an alliance with you; nor how exceedingly earnest the former is to make you all the reparation in his power.

I think, my dear cousin, that you cannot now do better than to give him the honour of your hand. He says such just and great things of your virtue, and so

a See p. 561.

heartily condemns himself, that I think there is great and honourable room for your forgiving him: and the more as it seems you are determined against a legal prosecution.

Your effectual forgiveness of him, it is evident to me, will accelerate a general reconciliation: for at present my other cousins cannot persuade themselves that he is in earnest to do you justice; or that you would refuse him if you believed he was.

But, my dear cousin, there may possibly be something in this affair to which I may be a stranger. If there be, and you will acquaint me with it, all that a *naturally* warm heart can do in your behalf shall be done.

Nothing but my endeavour to serve you here has hitherto prevented me from assuring you of this by word of mouth: for I long to see you after so many years' absence. I hope I shall be able in my next visits to my several cousins, to set all right. Proud spirits when convinced that they have carried resentments too high want but a good excuse to condescend: and parents must *always* love the child they *once* loved.

Meanwhile, I beg the favour of a few lines, to know if you have reason to doubt Mr Lovelace's sincerity. For my part, I can have none if I am to judge from the conversation that passed yesterday between him and me, in presence of Lord M.

You will be pleased to direct for me at your uncle Antony's.

Permit me, my dearest cousin, till I can procure a happy reconciliation between you and your father, and brother and uncles, to supply the place to you of all those near relations, as well as that of

> Your affectionate kinsman, and humble servant,
> WM. MORDEN

Letter 448: MISS CLARISSA HARLOWE TO WM. MORDEN, ESQ.

Thursday, Aug. 31

I MOST heartily congratulate you, dear sir, on your return to your native country.

I heard with much pleasure that you were come; but I was both afraid and ashamed, till you encouraged me by a first notice, to address myself to you.

How consoling is it to my wounded heart to find that you have not been carried away by that tide of resentment and displeasure with which I have been so unhappily overwhelmed—But that, while my still nearer relations have not thought fit to examine into the truth of vile reports raised against me, you have informed yourself (and generously *credited* the information) that my error was owing more to my misfortune than my fault.

I have not the least reason to doubt Mr Lovelace's sincerity in his offers of marriage: nor that all his relations are heartily desirous of ranking me among them. I have had noble instances of their esteem for me, on their apprehending that my father's displeasure must have subjected me to difficulties: and this after I had absolutely refused *their* pressing solicitations in their kinsman's favour, as well as *his own*.

Nor think me, my dear cousin, blamable for refusing him. I had given Mr Lovelace no reason to think me a weak creature. If I *had*, a man of his character might have thought himself warranted to endeavour to make ungenerous advantage of the weakness he had been able to inspire. The consciousness of *my own* weakness (in that case) might have brought me to a composition with *his* wickedness.

I can indeed forgive him. But that is because I think his crimes have set me above him. Can I be above the man, sir, to whom I shall give my hand and my vows; and with them a sanction to the most premeditated baseness? No, sir, let me say that your cousin Clarissa, were she likely to live many years and *that* (if she married not this man) in penury and want, despised and forsaken by all her friends, puts not so high a value upon the conveniencies of life, nor upon life itself, as to seek to re-obtain the one, or to preserve the other, by giving *such* a sanction: a sanction which (*were she to perform her duty*) would reward the violater.

Nor is it so much from pride, as from principle, that I say this. What, sir, when virtue, when chastity is the crown of a woman, and particularly of a wife, shall your cousin stoop to marry the man who could not form an attempt upon *hers* but upon a presumption that she was capable of receiving his offered hand, when he had found himself mistaken in the vile opinion he had conceived of her? Hitherto he has not had reason to think me weak. Nor will I give him an instance so flagrant, that weak I am in a point in which it would be criminal to be *found* weak.

One day, sir, you will perhaps know all my story. But, whenever it is known, I beg that the author of my calamities may not be vindictively sought after. He could not have been the author of them but for a strange concurrence of unhappy causes. As the law will not be able to reach him when I am gone, any other sort of vengeance terrifies me but to think of it: for, in such a case, should my friends be *safe*, what honour would his death bring to my memory? If any of them should come to misfortune, how would my fault be aggravated!

God long preserve you, my dearest cousin, and bless you but in *proportion* to the consolation you have given me in letting me know that you still love me; and that I have one near and dear relation who can pity and forgive me (and then will you be *greatly* blessed); is the prayer of

> Your ever-grateful and affectionate
> CLARISSA HARLOWE

Letter 449: MR LOVELACE TO JOHN BELFORD, ESQ.

(In answer to his letters of August 26, 28–9, Letters 426, 440)

Thursday, Aug. 31

I CANNOT but own that I am cut to the heart by *this* Miss Harlowe's interpretation of her letter. She ought never to be forgiven. *She*, a meek person, and a penitent, and innocent, and pious, and I know not what, who can deceive with a foot in the grave!—

'Tis evident that she sat down to write this letter with a design to mislead and deceive. And if she be capable of that at such a crisis, she has much need of *God*'s forgiveness, as I have of *hers*: and, with all her cant of *charity* and *charity*, if she be not more sure of it than I am of her *real pardon*; and if she take the thing in the light she ought to take it in; she will have a few darker moments yet to come than she seems to expect.

Lord M. himself, who is not one of those (to speak in his own phrase) *who can penetrate a millstone*, sees the deceit and thinks it unworthy of her; though my cousins Montague vindicate her. And no wonder: this cursed partial sex (I hate 'em all—by my soul, I hate 'em all!) will never allow anything against an individual of it, where ours is concerned. And why? Because if they censure deceit in another, they must condemn their own hearts.

She is to send me a letter after she is in heaven, is she? The devil take such *allegories*; and the devil take thee for calling this absurdity an *innocent* artifice!

I insist upon it that if a woman of her character at such a critical time is to be justified in such a deception, a man in full health and vigour of body and mind, as I am, may be excused for all his stratagems and attempts against her. And, thank my stars, I can now sit me down with a quiet conscience on that score. By my soul, I can, Jack. Nor has anybody who can acquit *her*, a right to blame *me*. But with some, indeed, everything *she* does must be good, everything *I* do must be bad— And why? Because she has always taken care to coax the stupid misjudging world like a *woman*: while I have constantly defied and despised its censures, like a *man*.

But notwithstanding all, you may let her know from me that I will *not* molest her, since my visits would be so shocking to her: and I hope she will take this into her consideration as a piece of generosity that she could hardly expect, after the deception she has put upon me. And let her further know that if there be anything in my power that will contribute either to her ease or honour, I will obey her at the very first intimation, however disgraceful or detrimental to myself. All this to make her unapprehensive, and that she may have nothing to pull her back.

If her cursed relations could be brought as cheerfully to perform *their* parts, I'd answer life for life for her recovery.

But who that has so many ludicrous images raised in his mind by thy awkward penitence, can forbear laughing at thee? Spare, I beseech thee, dear Belford, for the future, all thy own aspirations, if thou wouldst not dishonour those of an angel indeed.

When I came to that passage where thou sayest that thou considerest her[a] as one sent from heaven to draw thee after her—for the heart of me, I could not for an hour put thee out of my head in the attitude of Dame Elizabeth Carteret on her monument in Westminster Abbey.[1] If thou never observedst it, go thither on purpose; and there wilt thou see this dame in effigy, with uplifted head and hand, the latter taken hold of by a cupid every inch of stone, one clumsy foot lifted up also, aiming, as the sculptor designed it, to ascend; but so executed as would rather make one imagine that the figure (without shoe or stocking as it is, though the rest of the body is robed) was looking up to its corn-cutter: the other riveted to its native earth, bemired like thee (*immersed* thou callest it), beyond the possibility of unsticking itself. Both figures thou wilt find, seem to be in a contention, the bigger, whether it should pull down the lesser about its ears—the lesser (a chubby fat little varlet, of a fourth part of the other's bigness, with wings not much larger than those of a butterfly), whether it should raise the larger to a heaven it points to, hardly big enough to contain the great toes of either.

Thou wilt say perhaps that the dame's figure in *stone* may do credit in the comparison to thine, both in grain and shape, *wooden* as thou art all over. But that

a   See p. 1275.

the lady, who in everything but in the trick she has played me so lately is truly an angel, is but sorrily represented by the fat flanked cupid. This I allow thee. But yet there is enough in thy aspirations to strike my mind with a resemblance of thee and the lady to the figures on the wretched monument; for thou oughtest to remember that, prepared as she may be to mount to her native skies, it is impossible for her to draw after her a heavy fellow who has so much to repent of and amend.

But now, to be serious once more, let me tell you, Belford, that if the lady be really so ill as you write she is, it will become you (*no Roman style here!*) in a case so very affecting, to be a little less pointed and sarcastic in your reflections. For, upon my soul, the matter begins to grate me most confoundedly.

I am now so impatient to hear oftener of her, that I take the hint accidentally given me by our two fellows meeting at Slough, and resolve to go to our friend Doleman's at Uxbridge; whose wife and sister, as well as he, have so frequently pressed me to give them my company for a week or two: there shall I be within two hours' ride, if anything should happen to induce her to see me: for it will well become her piety and avowed charity, should the worst happen (the Lord of heaven and earth, however, avert that worst!), to give me that pardon from her *lips*, which she has not denied me by *pen and ink*. And as she wishes my reformation, she knows not what good effects such an interview may have upon me.

I shall accordingly be at Doleman's tomorrow morning, by eleven at furthest. My fellow will find me there at his return from you (with a letter, I hope). I shall have Joel with me likewise, that I may send the oftener, as matters fall out. Were I to be *still nearer*, or in town, it would be impossible to withhold myself from seeing her.

But if the worst happen!—as by your continual knelling I know not what to think of it!—(Yet, once more, Heaven avert that worst!—How natural is it to pray, when one cannot help one's self!)—THEN say not in so many dreadful words what the event is—only that you advise me to take a trip to Paris: and that will stab me to the heart.

I so well approve of your generosity to poor Belton's sister, that I have made Mowbray give up his legacy, as I do mine, towards her India Bonds. When I come to town, Tourville shall do the like; and we will buy each a ring to wear in memory of the honest fellow, with our own money, that we may perform *his* will as well as our *own*.

My fellow rides the rest of the night. I charge you, Jack, if you would save his life, that you send him not back empty-handed.

Letter 450: MR BELFORD TO ROBERT LOVELACE, ESQ.

Thursday night, Aug. 31

WHEN I concluded my last, I hoped that my next attendance upon this surprising lady would furnish me with some particulars as agreeable as now could be hoped for from the declining way she is in, by reason of the welcome letter she had received from her cousin Morden. But it proved quite otherwise to *me*, though not to *herself*; for I think I never was more shocked in my life than on the occasion I shall mention presently.

When I attended her about seven in the evening, she told me that she had found herself since I went, in a very petulant way. Strange, she said, that the pleasure she had received from her cousin's letter should have had such an effect upon her. But she had given way to a *comparative* humour, as she might call it, and thought it very hard that her nearer relations had not taken the methods with her, which her cousin Morden had begun with; by inquiring into her merit or demerit, and giving her cause a fair audit before condemnation.

She had hardly said this, when she started, and a blush overspread her face, on hearing, as I also did, a sort of lumbering noise upon the stairs, as if a large trunk were bringing up between two people: and looking upon me with an eye of concern, Blunderers! said she, they have brought in something two hours before the time—Don't be surprised, sir: it is all to save *you* trouble.

Before I could speak, in came Mrs Smith: Oh madam, said she, what have you done?—Mrs Lovick, entering, made the same exclamation. Lord have mercy upon me, madam, cried I, what have you done!—For, she stepping at the instant to the door, the women told me it was a coffin. Oh Lovelace! that thou hadst been there at the moment!—Thou, the causer of all these shocking scenes! Surely thou couldst not have been less affected than I, who have no guilt as to *her*, to answer for.

With an intrepidity of a piece with the preparation, having directed them to carry it into her bedchamber, she returned to us: They were not to have brought it in till after dark, said she—Pray, excuse me, Mr Belford: and don't you, Mrs Lovick, be concerned: nor you, Mrs Smith. Why should you? There is nothing more in it than the unusualness of the thing. Why may we not be as reasonably shocked at going to the church where are the monuments of our ancestors, with whose dust we even *hope* our dust shall be one day mingled, as to be moved at such a sight as this?

We all remaining silent, the women having their aprons at their eyes—Why this concern for nothing at all, said she?—If I am to be blamed for anything, it is for showing too much solicitude, as it may be thought, for this earthly part. I love to do everything for myself that I can do. I ever did. Every other material point is so far done and taken care of, that I have had *leisure* for things of lesser moment. Minutenesses may be observed, where greater articles are not neglected for them. I might have had this to order, perhaps, when less fit to order it. I have no mother, no sister, no Mrs Norton, no Miss Howe, near me. Some of you must have seen *this* in a few days, if not now; perhaps have had the friendly trouble of directing it. And what is the difference of a few days to *you*, when *I* am gratified rather than discomposed by it?—I shall not die the sooner for such a preparation—Should not everybody make their will, that has anything to bequeath? And who that makes a will, should be afraid of a coffin?—My dear friends (to the women), I have considered these things; do not give me reason to think *you* have not, with such an object before you as you have had in *me*, for weeks.

How reasonable was all this!—It showed, indeed, that she herself had well considered of it. But yet we could not help being shocked at the thoughts of the coffin thus brought in: the lovely person before our eyes, who is in all likelihood so soon to fill it.

We were all silent still, the women in grief, I in a manner stunned. She would not ask *me*, she said; but would be glad, since it had thus earlier than she had intended been brought in, that her two good friends would walk in and look upon it. They would be less shocked when it was made more familiar to their eye, than while their thoughts ran large upon it. Don't you lead back, said she, a starting steed to the object he is apt to start at, in order to familiarize him to it and cure his starting? The same reason will hold in this case. Come, my good friends, I will lead you in.

I took my leave; telling her she had done wrong, very wrong; and ought not, by any means, to have such an object before her.

The women followed her in—'Tis a strange sex! Nothing is too shocking for them to look upon, or see acted, that has but novelty and curiosity in it.

Down I posted; got a chair; and was carried home, extremely shocked and discomposed: yet, weighing the lady's arguments, I know not why I was so affected—except as she said, at the unusualness of the thing.

While I waited for a chair, Mrs Smith came down, and told me that there were devices and inscriptions upon the lid. Lord bless me! Is a coffin a proper subject to display fancy upon?—But these great minds cannot avoid doing extraordinary things!

Letter 451: MR BELFORD TO ROBERT LOVELACE, ESQ.

Friday morn. Sept 1

IT is surprising that I, a *man*, should be so much affected as I was at such an object as is the subject of my former letter; who also, in my late uncle's case, and poor Belton's, had the like before me, and the directing of it: when she, a *woman*, of so weak and tender a frame, who was to fill it (so soon, perhaps, to fill it!) could give orders about it, and draw out the devices upon it, and explain them with so little concern as the women tell me she did to them last night, after I was gone.

I really was ill and restless all night. Thou wert the subject of my execration, as she of my admiration, all the time I was quite awake: and when I dozed, I dreamt of nothing but of flying hour-glasses, death's-heads, spades, mattocks, and eternity; the hint of her devices (as given me by Mrs Smith) running in my head.

However, not being able to keep away from Smith's, I went thither about seven. The lady was just gone out: she had slept better, I found, than I, though her solemn repository was under her window not far from her bedside.

I was prevailed upon by Mrs Smith and her nurse Shelburne (Mrs Lovick being abroad with her) to go up and look at the devices. Mrs Lovick has since shown me a copy of the draft by which all was ordered. And I will give thee a sketch of the symbols.

The principal device, neatly etched on a plate of white metal, is a crowned serpent, with its tail in its mouth, forming a ring, the emblem of eternity, and in the circle made by it is this inscription:

CLARISSA HARLOWE.
APRIL X.
[Then the year]
AETAT. XIX.

For ornaments: at top, an hour-glass winged. At bottom, an urn.

Under the hour-glass, on another plate, this inscription:

HERE the wicked cease from troubling: and HERE the weary be at rest. Job iii. 17.

Over the urn, near the bottom:

Turn again unto thy rest, Oh my soul! For the Lord hath rewarded thee. And why? Thou hast delivered my soul from death; mine eyes from tears; and my feet from falling. Ps[alm] cxvi. 7, 8.

Over this text is the head of a white lily snapped short off, and just falling from the stalk; and this inscription over that, between the principal plate and the lily:

The days of man are but as grass. For he flourisheth as a flower of the field: for, as soon as the wind goeth over it, it is gone; and the place thereof shall know it no more. Ps[alm] ciii. 15, 16.

She excused herself to the women, on the score of her youth, and being used to draw for her needleworks, for having shown more fancy than would perhaps be thought suitable on so solemn an occasion.

The date April 10 she accounted for, as not being able to tell what her closing-day would be; and as that was the fatal day of her leaving her father's house.

She discharged the undertaker's bill after I was gone, with as much cheerfulness as she could ever have paid for the clothes she sold to purchase this her *palace*: for such she called it; reflecting upon herself for the expensiveness of it, saying that they might observe in *her*, that pride left not poor mortals to the last: but indeed she did not know but her father would permit it, when furnished, to be carried down to be deposited with her ancestors; and in that case she ought not to discredit them in her *last appearance*.

It is covered with fine black cloth, and lined with white satin; soon she said to be tarnished by viler earth than any it could be covered by.

The burial-dress was brought home with it. The women had curiosity enough, I suppose, to see her open that, if she did open it—And, perhaps, thou wouldst have been glad to have been present to have admired it too!

Mrs Lovick said she took the liberty to blame her; and wished the removal of such an object—from her *bed-chamber* at least: and was so affected with the noble answer she made upon it, that she entered it down the moment she left her.

To persons in health, said she, this sight may be shocking; and the preparation, and my unconcernedness in it, may appear affected: but to me, who have had so gradual a weaning-time from the world, and so much reason not to love it, I must say I dwell on, I indulge (and, strictly speaking, I enjoy) the thoughts of death. For believe me (looking steadfastly at the awful receptacle): believe what at this instant I feel to be most true, that there is such a vast superiority of weight and importance in the thought of death, and its hoped-for happy consequences, that it in a manner annihilates all other considerations and concerns. Believe me, my good friends, it does what nothing else can do; it teaches me, by strengthening in me the force of the divinest example, to forgive the injuries I have received; and shuts out the remembrance of past evils from my soul.

And now let me ask thee, Lovelace, Dost thou think, that when the time shall come that thou shalt be obliged to launch into the boundless ocean of eternity, thou wilt be able (any more than poor Belton was) to act thy part with such true heroism as this sweet and tender blossom of a woman has manifested, and continues to manifest!

Oh no! it cannot be!—And why cannot it be?—The reason is evident: she has no wilful errors to look back upon with self-reproach—and her mind is strengthened by the consolations which flow from that religious rectitude which has been the guide of all her actions; and which has taught her rather to choose to be a sufferer than an aggressor!

This was the support of the divine Socrates, as thou hast read. When led to execution, his wife lamenting that he should suffer being innocent, Thou fool, said he, wouldst thou wish me to be guilty?

Letter 452: MR BELFORD TO ROBERT LOVELACE, ESQ.

Friday, Sept. 1

How astonishing in the midst of such affecting scenes is thy mirth on what thou callest my *own aspirations*! Never, surely, was there such another man in this world, thy talents and thy levity taken together!—Surely, what I shall send thee with this will affect thee. If not, nothing can, till *thy own hour* come—and heavy will then thy reflections be!

I am glad however that thou enablest me to assure the lady that thou wilt no more molest her; that is to say, in other words, that after having ruined her fortunes and all her worldly prospects, thou wilt be so gracious as to let her lie down and die in peace.

Thy giving up to poor Belton's sister the little legacy, and thy undertaking to make Mowbray and Tourville follow thy example is, I must say to thy honour, of a piece with thy generosity to thy Rosebud and her Johnny; and to a number of other good actions in pecuniary matters; although thy Rosebud's is, I believe, the only instance where a pretty woman was concerned, of such a disinterested bounty.

Upon my faith, Lovelace, I love to praise thee; and often and often, as thou knowest, have I *studied* for occasions to do it: insomuch that when for the life of me I could not think of anything done by thee that deserved it, I have taken pains to applaud the not ungraceful manner in which thou hast performed actions that merited the gallows.

Now thou art so near, I will dispatch my servant to thee if occasion requires. But I fear I shall soon give thee the news thou apprehendest. For I am just now sent for by Mrs Smith; who has ordered the messenger to tell me that she knew not if the lady will be alive when I come.

Friday, Sept. 1, two o'clock, at Smith's

I COULD not close my letter in such an uncertainty as must have added to your impatience. For you have on several occasions convinced me, that the suspense you love to *give* would be the greatest torment to you that you could *receive*. A common case with all aggressive and violent spirits, I believe. I will just mention then (your servant waiting here till I have written), that the lady has had two very severe fits: in the last of which, whilst she lay, they sent to the doctor and Mr Goddard, who both advised that a messenger should be dispatched for me, as her executor; being doubtful whether, if she had a third, it would not carry her off.

She was tolerably recovered by the time I came; and the doctor made her promise before me, that she would not attempt any more, while so weak, to go abroad; for by Mrs Lovick's description, who attended her, the shortness of her breath, her extreme weakness, and the fervour of her devotions when at church, were contraries, which pulling different ways (the soul aspiring, the body sinking) tore her tender frame in pieces.

So much for the present. I shall detain Will no longer than just to beg that you will send me back this packet, and the last. Your memory is so good, that once reading is all you ever give, or need to give, to anything. And who but ourselves can make out our characters, were you inclined to let anybody see what passes between us? If I cannot be obliged, I shall be tempted to withhold what I write, till I have time to take a copy of it.*a*

A letter from Miss Howe is just now brought by a particular messenger, who says he must carry back a few lines in return. But, as the lady is just retired to lie down, the man is to call again by and by.

Letter 453: MR LOVELACE TO JOHN BELFORD, ESQ.

Uxbridge, Sept. 1, twelve o'clock at night

I SEND you the papers with this. You must account to me honestly and fairly when I see you for the earnestness with which you write for them. And then also will we talk about the contents of your last dispatch, and about some of your severe and unfriendly reflections.

Meantime, whatever thou dost, don't let the wonderful creature leave us! Set before her the sin of her preparation, as if she thought she could depart when she pleased. She'll persuade herself at this rate, that she has nothing to do when all is ready, but to lie down and go to sleep: and such a lively fancy as hers will make a reality of a jest at any time.

A *jest* I call all that has passed between her and me; a mere jest to die for!—for has she not, from first to last, infinitely more triumphed over me than suffered from me?

Would the sacred regard I have for her purity, even for her *personal* as well as *intellectual* purity, permit, I could prove this as clear as the sun. Therefore tell the dear creature she must not be wicked in her piety. There is a *too much*, as well as a *too little*, even in righteousness. Perhaps she does not think of that—Oh that she would have permitted my attendance as obligingly as she does of thine!—The dear soul used to love humour. I remember the time that she knew how to smile at a piece of apropos humour. And let me tell thee, a smile upon the lips must have had its correspondent cheerfulnesses in a heart so sincere as hers.

Tell the doctor I will make over all my possessions and all my reversions to him, if he will but prolong her life for one twelvemonth to come. But for one twelvemonth, Jack!—He will lose all his reputation with me, and I shall treat him as Belton did his doctor, if he cannot do this for me, on so young a subject. But *nineteen*, Belford!—*nineteen* cannot so soon die of grief, if the doctor deserve that name; and so blooming and so fine a constitution as she had but three or four months ago!

a It may not be amiss to observe that Mr Belford's solicitude to get back his letters was owing to his desire of fulfilling the lady's wishes that he would furnish Miss Howe with materials to vindicate her memory.

But what need the doctor have asked her leave to write to her friends? Could he not have done it without letting her know anything of the matter? That was one of the likeliest means that could be thought of to bring some of them about her, since she is so desirous to see them. At least it would have induced them to send up her favourite Norton. But these plaguy solemn fellows are great traders in parade: and for the hearts of them, cannot get out of it, be the occasion what it will. They'll cram down your throat their poisonous drugs by wholesale without asking you a question; and have the assurance to *own* it to be *prescribing*: but when they are to do good, they are to ask your consent.

How the dear creature's character rises in every line of thy letters!—But it is owing to the uncommon occasions she has met with that she blazes out upon us with such a meridian lustre!—How, but for those occasions, could her noble sentiments, her prudent consideration, her forgiving spirit, her exalted benevolence, and her equanimity in view of the most shocking prospects (which set her in a light so superior to all her sex, and even to the philosophers of antiquity) have been manifested?

I know thou wilt think I am going to claim some merit to myself for having given her such opportunities of signalizing her virtue. But I am not; for if I did, I must share that merit with her implacable relations, who would justly be entitled to *two thirds* of it at least: and my soul disdains a partnership in anything with such a family.

But this I mention as an answer to thy reproaches that I could be so little edified by perfections, to which thou supposest I was for so long together daily and hourly a personal witness—when, admirable as she was in all she said, and in all she did, occasion had not at that time ripened and called forth those amazing perfections which now astonish and confound me.

Hence it is that I admire her more than ever I did; and that my love for her is less *personal*, as I may say, more *intellectual* than ever I thought it could be to woman.

Hence also it is, that I am confident (would it please the Fates to spare her and make her mine) I could love her with a purity that would draw on *my own* FUTURE, as well as ensure *her* TEMPORAL, happiness—And hence, by necessary consequence, shall I be the most miserable of all men if I am deprived of her.

Thou severely reflectest upon me for my levity in the Abbey instance. And I will be ingenuous enough to own, that as thou seest not my heart, there may be passages in every one of my letters which (the melancholy occasion considered) deserve thy most pointed rebukes. But, faith, Jack, thou art such a tragi-comical mortal, with thy leaden aspirations at one time, and thy flying hour-glasses and dreaming terrors at another, that as Prior says, *What serious is, thou turn'st to farce*[1]; and it is impossible to keep within the bounds of decorum or gravity when one reads what thou writest.

But to restrain myself (for my constitutional gaiety was ready to run away with me again), I will repeat, I must ever repeat, that I am most egregiously affected with the circumstances of the case: and were this paragon actually to quit the world, should never enjoy myself one hour together, though I were to live to the age of Methusalem.

Indeed it is to this *deep concern* that my very *levity* is owing: for I struggle and struggle, and try to buffet down these reflections as they rise; and when I cannot do it, I am forced as I have often said to try to make myself laugh that I may not cry; for one or other I must do: and is it not philosophy carried to the highest pitch, for a man to conquer such tumults of soul as I am sometimes agitated by, and in the very height of the storm to be able to quaver out an horse-laugh?

Your Seneca's, your Epictetuses, and the rest of your stoical tribe, with all their apathy nonsense, could not come up to this. They could *forbear* wry faces: bodily pains they could well enough *seem* to support; and that was all: but the pangs of their own smitten-down souls they could not *laugh* over, though they could at the follies of others. They read grave lectures; but they *were* grave. This high point of philosophy, to laugh and be merry in the midst of the most soul-harrowing woes, when the heart-strings are just bursting asunder, was reserved for thy Lovelace.

There is something owing to constitution, I own; and that this is the laughing-time of my life. For what a woe must that be which for an hour together can mortify a man of six or seven and twenty, in high blood and spirits, of a naturally gay disposition, who can sing, dance, and scribble, and take and give delight in them all?—But then my grief, as my joy, is sharper-pointed than most other men's; and, like what Dolly Welby once told me, describing the parturient throes, if there were not lucid intervals—if they did not come and go—there would be no bearing them.

AFTER all, as I am so little distant from the dear creature, and as she is so very ill, I think I cannot excuse myself from making her *one* visit. Nevertheless, if I thought her so near——(what word shall I use that my soul is not shocked at!) and that she would be *too much discomposed* by a visit; I would not think of it—Yet how can I bear the recollection that, when she last went from me (her innocence so triumphant over my premeditated guilt as was enough to reconcile her to life, and to set her above the sense of injuries so nobly sustained), that she should then depart with an incurable fracture in her heart; and that *that* should be the last time I should ever see her!—How, how can I bear this reflection!

Oh Jack! how my conscience, that gives edge even to thy blunt reflections, tears me!—Even this moment would I give the world to push the cruel reproacher from me by one gay intervention!—Sick of myself!—Sick of the remembrance of my vile plots; and of my *light*, my *momentary* ecstasy (villainous burglar, felon, thief that I was!) which has brought upon me such *durable* and such *heavy* remorse! what would I give that I had not been guilty of such barbarous and ungrateful perfidy to the most excellent of God's creatures!

I would end, methinks, with one spritelier line!—but it will not be—Let me tell thee then, and rejoice at it if thou wilt, that I am

Inexpressibly miserable.

Letter 454: MR BELFORD TO ROBERT LOVELACE, ESQ.

Sat. morning, Sept. 2

I HAVE some little pleasure given me by thine, just now brought me. I see now that thou hast a little humanity left. Would to heaven, for the dear lady's sake as well as for thy own, that thou hadst rummaged it up from all the dark forgotten corners of thy soul a little sooner!

The lady is alive and serene, and calm, and has all her noble intellects clear and strong: but nineteen will not however save her. She says she will now content herself with her closet duties and the visits of the parish minister; and will not attempt to go out. Nor indeed will she, I am afraid, ever walk up or down a pair of stairs again.

I am sorry at my soul to have this to say: but it would be a folly to flatter thee.

As to thy seeing her, I believe the least hint of that sort now, would cut off some hours of her life.

What has contributed to her serenity, it seems, is that taking the alarm her fits gave her, she has entirely finished, and signed and sealed her last will: which she had deferred doing till this time, in hopes, as she said, of some good news from Harlowe Place; which would have occasioned the alterations of some passages in it.

Miss Howe's letter was not given her till four in the afternoon, yesterday; at what time the messenger returned for an answer. She admitted him to her presence in the dining-room, ill as she then was; and would have written a few lines, as desired by Miss Howe; but not being able to hold a pen, she bid the messenger tell her that she hoped to be well enough to write a long letter by the next day's post; and would not now detain him.

Saturday, six in the afternoon

I CALLED just now, and found the lady writing to Miss Howe. She made me a melancholy compliment, that she showed me not Miss Howe's letter because I should soon have that and all her papers before me. But she told me that Miss Howe had very considerately obviated to Colonel Morden several things which might have occasioned misapprehensions between him and me; and had likewise put a lighter construction, for the sake of peace, on some of your actions than they deserved.

She added that her cousin Morden was warmly engaged in her favour with her friends: and one good piece of news Miss Howe's letter contained; that her father would give up some matters, which (appertaining to her of right) would make my executorship the easier in some particulars that had given her a little pain.

She owned she had been obliged to leave off (in the letter she was writing) through weakness.

Will says he shall reach you tonight. I shall send in the morning; and if I find her not worse, will ride to Edgware, and return in the afternoon.

Letter 455: MISS HOWE TO MISS CLARISSA HARLOWE

Tuesday, Aug. 29

My dearest friend,

I AM at length returned to this place; and had intended to wait on you in London: but my mamma is very ill—Alas! my dear, she is very ill indeed—And you are likewise very ill—I see *that* by yours of the 25th—What shall I do if I lose two such near, and dear, and tender friends? She was taken ill yesterday at our last stage in our return home—and has a violent surfeit and fever, and the doctors are doubtful about her.

If she should die, how will all my pertnesses to her fly in my face!—Why, why, did I ever vex her?—She says I have been all duty and obedience!—She kindly forgets all my faults, and remembers everything I have been so happy as to oblige her in. And this cuts me to the heart.

I see, I see, my dear, you are very bad—and I cannot bear it. Do, my beloved Miss Harlowe, if you *can* be better, do, for *my* sake, *be* better; and send me word of it. Let the bearer bring me a line. Be sure you send me a line. If I lose you, my more than sister, and lose my mamma, I shall distrust my own conduct, and will not marry. And why should I?—Creeping, cringing in courtship:—Oh my dear, these men are a vile race of *reptiles* in *our day*, and mere *bears* in *their own*. See in Lovelace all that was desirable in figure, in birth, and in fortune: but in his heart a devil!—See in Hickman—Indeed, my dear, I cannot tell what anybody can see in Hickman, to be always preaching in his favour. And is it to be expected that I, who could hardly bear control from a mother, should take it from a husband?—from one too, who has neither more wit, nor more understanding, than myself? Yet he to be my instructor!—So he will, I suppose; but more by the insolence of his will than by the merit of his counsel. It is in vain to think of it—I cannot be a wife to any man breathing whom I at present know—This I the rather mention now, because on my mother's danger I know you will be for pressing me the sooner to throw myself into another sort of protection, should I be deprived of her. But no more of this subject, or indeed of any other; for I am obliged to attend my mamma, who cannot bear me out of her sight.

Wednesday, Aug. 30

My mother, Heaven be praised! has had a fine night and is much better. Her fever has yielded to medicine! And now I can write once more with freedom and ease to you, in hopes that *you* also are better. If this be granted to my prayers, I shall again be happy. I write with still the more alacrity, as I have an opportunity given me to touch upon a subject in which you are nearly concerned.

You must know then, my dear, that your cousin Morden has been here with me. He told me of an interview he had on Monday at Lord M.'s with Lovelace; and asked me abundance of questions about you, and about that villainous man.

I could have raised a fine flame between them if I would: but, observing that he is a man of very lively passions, and believing you would be miserable if anything should happen to him from a quarrel with a man who is known to have so many advantages at his sword, I made not the worst of the subjects we talked of. But, as I could not tell untruths in his favour, you must think I said enough to make him curse the wretch.

I don't find, well as they all used to respect Colonel Morden, that he has influence enough upon them to bring them to any terms of reconciliation.

'What can they mean by it!—But your brother is come home, it seems: so, the honour of the house—the reputation of the family, is all the cry!

The colonel is exceedingly out of humour with them all. Yet has he not hitherto, it seems, seen your brutal brother—I told him how ill you were, and communicated to him some of the contents of your letter. He admired *you*, cursed *Lovelace*, and raved against all your *family*—He declared that they were all unworthy of you.

At his earnest request, I permitted him to take some brief notes of such of the contents of your letter to me as I thought I *could* read to him; and particularly of your melancholy conclusion.[a]

a   See p. 1265.

He says that none of your friends think you so ill as you are; nor will believe it— He is sure they all love you, and that dearly too.

If they do, their present hardness of heart will be the subject of everlasting remorse to them should you be taken from us—But now it seems (barbarous wretches!) you are to *suffer within an inch of your life.*

He asked me questions about Mr Belford: and when he had heard what I had to say of that gentleman and his disinterested services to you, he raved at some villainous surmises thrown out against you by that officious pedant, Brand: who, but for his gown, I find would come off poorly enough between your cousin and Lovelace.

He was so uneasy about you himself, that on Thursday the 24th he sent up an honest serious man,[a] one Alston, a gentleman farmer, to inquire of your condition, your visitors etc., who brought him word that you was very ill, and was put to great straits to support yourself: but as this was told him by the gentlewoman of the house where you lodge, who it seems mingled with it some tart though deserved reflections upon your relations' cruelty, it was not credited by them: and I myself hope it cannot be true; for surely you could not be so *unjust,* I will say, to my friendship, as to suffer any inconveniencies for want of money. I think I could not forgive you if it were so.

The colonel (as one of your trustees) is resolved to see you put into possession of your estate: and in the meantime he has actually engaged them to remit to him, for you, the produce of it accrued since your grandfather's death (a very considerable sum); and proposes himself to attend you with it. But by a hint he dropped, I find you had disappointed some people's littleness by not writing to them for money and supplies; since they were determined to distress you, and to put you at defiance.

Like all the rest!—I hope I may say that without offence.

Your cousin imagines that before a reconciliation takes place, they will insist that you shall make such a will as to that estate as they shall approve of: but he declares he will not go out of England till he has seen justice done you by *everybody*; and that you shall not be imposed on either by friend or foe—

By *relation* or foe, should he not have said?—For a friend will not impose upon a friend.

So, my dear, you are to *buy your peace,* if some people were to have their wills!

Your cousin (not *I,* my dear, though it was always my opinion[b]) says that the whole family is *too rich* to be either *humble, considerate,* or *contented.* And as for himself, he has an ample fortune he says, and thinks of leaving it wholly to you.

Had this villain Lovelace consulted his worldly interest only, what a fortune would he have had in you, even although your marrying him had deprived you of your paternal share?

I am obliged to leave off here. But having a good deal still to write, and my mother better, I will pursue the subject in another letter, although I send both together. I need not say how much I am, and will ever be,

Your affectionate, etc.

ANNA HOWE

a .See p. 1246.
b   See p. 68.

Letter 456: MISS HOWE TO MISS CLARISSA HARLOWE

Thursday, Aug. 31

THE colonel thought fit once to speak it to the praise of Lovelace's *generosity*, that (*as a man of honour ought*) he took to himself all the blame and acquitted you of the consequences of the precipitate step you had taken; since, he said, as you loved him, and was in his power, he *must* have had advantages which he would *not* have had if you had continued at your father's, or at any friend's.

Mighty generous, I said (were it as he supposed) in such insolent reflectors, the best of them; who pretend to *clear* reputations which never had been *sullied*, but by falling into their dirty acquaintance! But in this case, I added, that there was no need of anything but the strictest truth, to demonstrate Lovelace to be the blackest of villains, you the brightest of innocents.

This he catched at; and swore that could he find that there were anything uncommon or barbarous in the seduction, as one of your letters had indeed seemed to imply (that is to say, my dear, anything *worse* than perjury, breach of faith, and abuse of a generous confidence!—sorry fellows!), he would avenge his cousin to the utmost,

I urged your apprehensions on this head from your last letter to me: but he seemed capable of taking what I know to be real greatness of soul in an unworthy sense: for he mentioned directly upon it, the expectation your friends had that you should (previous to any reconciliation with them) appear in a court of justice against the villain—IF you could do it with the advantage to yourself that I hinted might be done.

And truly, if I would have heard him, he had indelicacy enough to have gone into the nature of the proof of the crime upon which they wanted to have Lovelace arraigned: yet this is a gentleman improved by travel and learning!—Upon my word, my dear, I who have been accustomed to the most delicate conversation ever since I had the honour to know you, despise this sex from the gentleman to the peasant.

Upon the whole I find that Mr Morden has a very slender notion of women's virtue in particular cases: for which reason I put him down, though your favourite, as one who is not entitled *to cast the first stone*.

I never knew a man who deserved to be well thought of himself for his morals, who had a slight opinion of the virtue of our sex in general. For if from the *difference* of *temperament* and *education*, modesty, chastity, and piety too (and these from *principle*) are not to be found in our sex preferably to the other, I should think it a sign of a much worse nature in *ours*.

He even hinted (as from your relations indeed) that it is impossible but there must be some *will* where there is much *love*. These sort of reflections are enough to make a woman who has at heart her own honour and the honour of her sex, to look about her and consider what she is doing when she enters into an intimacy with these wretches; since it is plain that whenever she throws herself into the power of a man, and leaves for him her parents or guardians, everybody will believe it to be owing more to her good luck than to her discretion if there be not an end of her virtue: and let the man be ever such a villain to her, she must take into her own bosom a share of his guilty baseness.

I am writing to general cases. You, my dear, are out of the question. Your story, as I have heretofore said, will afford a warning as well as an example[a]: for who is it that will not infer that if a person of your fortune, character, and merit could not escape ruin after she had put herself into the power of her *hyaena*, what can a thoughtless, fond, giddy creature expect?

Every man, they will say, is not a LOVELACE—true: but then, neither is every woman a CLARISSA—and allow for the one and the other, the example must be of general use.

I prepared this gentleman to expect your appointment of Mr Belford for an office that we both hope he will have no occasion to act in (nor anybody else) for many, very many years to come. He was at first startled at it: but upon hearing your reasons, which had satisfied me, he only said that such an appointment, were it to take place, would exceedingly affect his other cousins.

He told me he had a copy of Lovelace's letter to you imploring your pardon, and offering to undergo any penance to procure it[b]; and also of your answer to it.[c]

I find he is willing to hope that a marriage between you may still take place; which he says will heal up all breaches.

I would have written much more—on the following particulars especially; to wit, of the wretched man's hunting you out of your lodgings: of your relations' strange *implacableness* (I am in haste, and cannot think of a word you would like better, *just now*): of your last letter to Lovelace, to divert him from pursuing you: of your aunt Hervey's penitential conversation with Mrs Norton: of Mr Wyerley's renewed address: of your lessons in Hickman's behalf, so approvable were the man more so than he is: but indeed I am offended with him at this instant, and have been these two days—of your sister's transportation project—and of twenty and twenty other things—But am obliged to leave off to attend my two cousins Spilsworth, and my cousin Herbert, who are come to visit us on account of my mother's illness. I will therefore dispatch these by Rogers; and if my mother gets well soon (as I hope she will) I am resolved to see you in town, and tell you everything that now is upon my mind: and particularly, mingling my soul with yours, how much I am, and will ever be, my dearest dear friend,

Your affectionate
ANNA HOWE

Let Rogers bring one line, I pray you. I thought to have sent him this afternoon; but he cannot set out till tomorrow morning early.

I cannot express how much your staggering lines, and your conclusion, affect me!

a   See p. 577.
b   See p. 1185.
c   See p. 1191.

Letter 457: MR BELFORD TO ROBERT LOVELACE, ESQ.

Sunday evening, Sept. 3

I WONDER not at the impatience your servant tells me you express to hear from me. I was designing to write you a long letter, and was just returned from Smith's for that purpose; but since you are so urgent, you must be contented with a short one.

I attended the lady this morning, just before I set out for Edgware. She was so ill overnight, that she was obliged to leave her letter to Miss Howe unfinished: but early this morning she made an end of it, and had just sealed it up as I came. She was so fatigued with writing, that she told me she would lie down after I was gone, and endeavour to recruit her spirits.

They had sent for Mr Goddard when she was so ill last night; and not being able to see him out of her own chamber, he for the first time saw her *house*, as she calls it. He was extremely shocked and concerned at it; and chid Mrs Smith and Mrs Lovick for not persuading her to have such an object removed from her bedchamber: and when they excused themselves on the *little authority* it was reasonable to suppose they must have with a lady so much their superior, he reflected warmly on those who had *more* authority, and who left her to proceed in such a shocking and solemn whimsy, as he called it.

It is placed near the window like a harpsichord, though covered over to the ground: and when she is so ill that she cannot well go to her closet, she writes and reads upon it, as others would upon a desk or table. But (only as she was so ill last night) she chooses not to see anybody in that apartment.

I went to Edgware; and returning in the evening, attended her again. She had a letter brought her from Mrs Norton (a long one, as it seems by its bulk) just before I came. But she had not opened it; and said that as she was pretty calm and composed, she was afraid to look into the contents lest she should be ruffled; expecting now to hear of nothing that could do her good or give her pleasure from that good woman's *dear hard-hearted neighbours*, as she called her own relations.

Seeing her so weak and ill, I withdrew; nor did she desire me to tarry, as sometimes she does when I make a motion to depart.

By Mrs Smith I had some hints as I went away, that she had appropriated that evening to some offices that were to save trouble, as she called it, after her departure; and had been giving her nurse and Mrs Lovick and Mrs Smith orders about what she would have done when she *was gone*; and I believe they were of a very delicate and affecting nature; but Mrs Smith descended not to particulars.

The doctor had been with her, as well as Mr Goddard; and they both joined with great earnestness to persuade her to have her *house* removed out of her sight: but she assured them that it gave her pleasure and spirits; and, being a necessary preparation, she wondered they should be surprised at it, when she had not any of her family about her, or any old acquaintance, on whose care and exactness in these punctilios, as she called them, she could rely.

The doctor told Mrs Smith that he believed she would hold out long enough for any of her friends to have notice of her state, and to see her, and hardly longer; and since he could not find that she had any certainty of hearing from or seeing her cousin Morden (which made it plain that her relations continued inflexible) he would go home and write a letter to her father, take it as she would.

She had spent great part of the day in intense devotions; and tomorrow morning she is to have with her the same clergyman who has often attended her; from whose hands she will again receive the Sacrament.

Thou seest, Lovelace, that all is preparing, that all will be ready; and I am to attend her tomorrow afternoon to take some instructions from her in relation to my part in the office to be performed for her. And thus, omitting the particulars of a fine conversation between her and Mrs Lovick, which the latter acquainted me with, as well as another between her and the doctor and apothecary, which I had a design this evening to give you, they being of a very affecting nature, I have yielded to your impatience.

I shall dispatch Harry tomorrow morning early with her letter to Miss Howe: an offer she took very kindly; as she is extremely solicitous to lessen that young lady's apprehensions for her on not hearing from her by Saturday's post: and yet, to write the truth, how can her apprehensions be lessened?

Letter 458: MISS CLARISSA HARLOWE TO MISS HOWE

Saturday, Sept. 2

I WRITE, my beloved Miss Howe, though very ill still: but I could not by the return of your messenger; for I was then unable to hold a pen.

Your mother's illness (as by the first part of your letter) gave me great distress for you, till I read further: you bewail it as it becomes a daughter so sensible. May you be blessed in each other for many, very many, happy years to come! I doubt not that even this sudden and grievous indisposition, by the frame it has put you in and the apprehension it has given you of losing so dear a mother, will contribute to the happiness I wish you: for, alas! my dear, we never know how to value the blessings we enjoy, till we are in danger of losing them, or have actually lost them: and then what would we give to have them restored to us?

What, I wonder, has again happened between you and Mr Hickman? Although I know it not, I dare say it is owing to some pretty petulance, to some half-ungenerous advantage taken of his obligingness and assiduity. Will you never, my dear, give the weight you and all our sex ought to give to the qualities of sobriety and regularity of life and manners in that sex? Must bold creatures and forward spirits, for ever, and by the best and wisest of us, as well as by the indiscreetest, be the most kindly used?

My dear friends know not that I *have* actually suffered within *less* than *an inch of my life*.

Poor Mr Brand! He meant well, I believe—I am afraid all will turn heavily upon him when he probably thought that he was taking the best method to oblige: but were he *not* to have been so light of belief, and so weakly officious; but had given a more favourable and, it would be strange if I could not say, a *juster* report; things would have been nevertheless exactly as they are.

I must lay down my pen. I am very ill. I believe I shall be better by and by. The bad writing would betray me, although I had a mind to keep from you what the event must soon——

Now I resume my trembling pen. Excuse the unsteady writing. It *will* be so—

I have wanted no money: so don't be angry about such a trifle as money. Yet am I glad of what you incline me to hope, that my friends will give up the produce of my grandfather's estate since it has been in their hands: because, knowing it to be my right and that *they* could not want it, I had already disposed of a good part of it: and could only hope they would be willing to give it up at my last request. And now how rich shall I think myself in this my last stage!—And yet I did not want before—indeed I did not—for who, that has many *superfluities*, can be said to want?

Do not, my dear friend, be concerned that I call it my *last stage*; for what is even the long life which in high health we wish for? What; but as we go along, a life of apprehension, sometimes for our friends, oftener for ourselves? And at last, when arrived at the old age we covet, one heavy loss or deprivation having succeeded another, we see ourselves stripped, as I may say, of everyone we loved; and find ourselves exposed as uncompanionable poor creatures, to the slights, to the contempts, of jostling youth, who want to push us off the stage, in hopes to possess what we have—and, superadded to all, our own infirmities every day increasing: of themselves enough to make the life we wished for the greatest disease of all! Don't you remember the lines of Howard, which once you read to me in my ivy-bower[a]?

In the disposition of what belongs to me, I have endeavoured to do everything in the justest and best manner I could think of; putting myself in my relations' places, and in the greater points ordering my matters as if no misunderstanding had happened.

I hope they will not think much of some bequests where wanted, and where due from my gratitude: but if they should, what is done, is done; and I cannot now help it. Yet I must repeat that I hope, I hope, I have pleased every one of them. For I would not, on any account, have it thought that, in my last disposition, anything undaughterly, unsisterly, or unlike a kinswoman, should have had place in a mind that is *so* truly free (as I will presume to say) from all resentment that it now overflows with gratitude and blessings for the good I *have* received, although it be not all that my heart wished to receive. Were it even an *hardship* that I was not favoured with more, what is it but an hardship of half a year, against the *most* indulgent goodness of eighteen years and an half that ever was shown to a daughter?

a   These are the lines the lady refers to:

From death we rose to life: 'Tis but the same,
Through life to pass again from whence we came.
With shame we see our PASSIONS can prevail,
Where *Reason, Certainty*, and *Virtue* fail.
HONOUR, that empty name! can death despise:
SCORN'D LOVE, to death, as to a *refuge*, flies;
And SORROW waits for death with longing eyes.
HOPE triumphs o'er the thoughts of death; and FATE
Cheats fools, and flatters the unfortunate.
We fear to lose, what a *small time* must waste,
Till life itself grows the *disease* at last.
Begging for life, we beg for *more decay*,
And to be *long a dying* only pray.[1]

My cousin, you tell me, thinks I was off my guard, and that I was taken at some advantage. Indeed, my dear, I was not. Indeed I gave no room for advantage to be taken of me. I hope, one day, that will be seen, if I have the justice done me which Mr Belford assures me of.

I should hope that my cousin has not taken the liberties which you, by an observation (not unjust), seem to charge him with. For it is sad to think that the generality of that sex should make so light of crimes which they justly hold so unpardonable in their own most intimate relations of ours—Yet cannot commit them without doing such injuries to other families and individuals as they think themselves obliged to resent unto death, when offered to their own families.

But we women are too often to blame on this head; since the most virtuous among us seldom make *virtue* the test of their approbation of the other: insomuch that a man may glory in his wickedness of this sort without being rejected on that account, even to the faces of women of unquestionable virtue. Hence it is, that a libertine seldom thinks himself concerned so much as to save appearances: and what is it not that our sex suffers in their opinions on this very score? And what have I, more than many others, to answer for on this very account in the world's eye?

May my story be a warning to all, how they prefer a libertine to a man of true honour; and how they permit themselves to be misled (where they mean the *best*) by the specious yet foolish hope of subduing riveted habits, and as I may say of altering natures!—The *more* foolish, as experience might convince us, that there is hardly one in ten of even tolerably happy marriages, in which the wife keeps the hold in the *husband*'s affections which she had in the *lover*'s. What influence then can she hope to have over the morals of an avowed libertine, who marries perhaps for conveniency, who despises the tie, and whom, it is too probable, nothing but old age, or sickness, or disease (the consequence of ruinous riot) can reclaim?

I am very glad you gave my cous—

Sunday morning (Sept. 3) six o'clock

HITHER I had written, and was forced to quit my pen. And so much weaker and worse I grew, that had I resumed it to have closed here, it must have been with such trembling unsteadiness that it would have given you more concern for me, than the delay of sending it away by last night's post can do: so I deferred it, to see how it would please God to deal with me. And I find myself after a better night than I expected, lively and clear; and hope to give you a proof that I do, in the continuation of my letter, which I will pursue as currently as if I had not left off.

I am glad you so considerately gave my cousin Morden favourable impressions of Mr Belford; since, otherwise, some misunderstanding might have happened between *them*: for although I hope this gentleman is an altered man, and in time will be a reformed one, yet is he one of those high spirits that has been accustomed to resent *imaginary indignities* to *himself*, when I believe he has not been studious to avoid giving *real offences* to *others*; men of this cast acting as if they thought all the world was made to bear with them, and they with nobody in it.

Mr Lovelace, you tell me, thought fit to entrust my cousin with the copy of his letter of penitence to me, and with my answer to it rejecting him and his suit: and Mr Belford moreover acquaints me how much concerned Mr Lovelace is for his baseness, and how freely he accused himself to my cousin. This shows that the true bravery of spirit is to be above doing a vile action; and that nothing subjects the human mind to such meannesses as to be guilty of wilful wrongs to our fellow-creatures. How low, how sordid, are the submissions which elaborate baseness compels! That that wretch could treat me as he did, and then could so poorly creep to me to be forgiven, and to be allowed to endeavour to repair crimes so wilful, so black, and so premeditated! How my soul despised him for his meanness on a certain occasion, of which you will one day be informed![a] And him whom one's heart despises, it is far from being difficult to reject had one ever so partially favoured him once.

Yet am I glad this violent spirit *can* thus creep; that, like a poisonous serpent, he *can* thus coil himself and hide his head in his own narrow circlets; because this stooping, this abasement, gives me hope that no further mischief will ensue.

All my apprehension is what may happen when I am gone; lest then my cousin, or any other of my family, should endeavour to avenge me and risk their own more precious lives on that account.

If that part of Cain's curse were Mr Lovelace's, *to be a fugitive and vagabond in the earth*[2]; that is to say, if it meant no more harm to him than that he should be obliged to travel, as it seems he intends (though I wish him no ill in his travels), and I could know it; then should I be easy in the hoped-for safety of my friends from his skilful violence. Oh that I could hear he was a thousand miles off!

When I began this letter, I did not think I could have run to such a length. But 'tis to YOU, my dearest friend, and *you* have a title to the spirits you raise and support; for they are no longer mine, and will subside the moment I cease writing to you.

But what do you bid me hope for when you tell me that if your mother's health will permit, you will see me in town? I *hope* your mother's health will be perfected as you wish; but I dare not promise myself so great a favour; so great a *blessing*, I will call it—And, indeed, I know not if I should be able to bear it now!—

Yet one comfort it is in your power to give me; and that is, let me know, and very speedily it must be if you wish to oblige me, that all matters are made up between you and Mr Hickman; to whom, I see, you are resolved with all your bravery of spirit to owe a multitude of obligations for his patience with your flightiness. Think of this, my dear proud friend! and think, likewise, of what I have often told you, that PRIDE in man or woman is an extreme that hardly ever fails, sooner or later, to bring forth its mortifying CONTRARY.

May you, my dear Miss Howe, have no discomforts but what you make to yourself! Those, as it will be in your own power to lessen them, ought to be your own punishment if you do not. As there is no such thing as *perfect happiness* here, since the busy mind will *make* to itself evils were it to *find* none, you will pardon this limited wish, strange as it may appear till you consider it: for to wish you no infelicities, either within or without you, were to wish you what can never happen in this world; and what perhaps ought not to be wished for, if by a wish one *could* give one's friend such an exemption; since we are not to live here always.

We must not, in short, expect that our roses will grow without thorns: but then they are useful and instructive thorns; which by pricking the fingers of the too

_____

[a] Meaning his meditated second violence (see Letter 281) and his succeeding letters to her supplicating her pardon.

hasty plucker teach future caution, at the same time that they add sweets, and poignancy too, to enjoyments which are not over-easily attained.

I *must* conclude—

God for ever bless you, and all you love and honour, and reward you here and hereafter for your kindness to

Your ever obliged and affectionate
CLARISSA HARLOWE!

Letter 459: MRS NORTON TO MISS CLARISSA HARLOWE

(In answer to hers of Thursday, August 24, Letter 433)

Thursday, Aug. 31

I HAD written sooner, my dearest young lady, but that I have been endeavouring ever since the receipt of your last letter to obtain a private audience of your mother, in hopes of leave to communicate it to her. But last night I was surprised by an invitation to breakfast at Harlowe Place this morning: and the chariot came early to fetch me: an honour I did not expect.

When I came, I found there was to be a meeting of all your family with Colonel Morden at Harlowe Place; and it was proposed by your mother, and consented to, that I should be present. Your cousin, I understand, had with difficulty brought this meeting to bear; for your brother had before industriously avoided all conversation with him on the affecting subject; urging, that it was not necessary to talk to Mr Morden upon it, who being a remoter relation than themselves had no business to make himself a judge of their conduct to their daughter, their niece, and their sister; especially as he had declared himself in her favour; adding, that he should hardly have patience to be questioned by him on that head.

I was in hopes that your mamma would have given me an opportunity of talking with her alone before the company met; but she seemed studiously to avoid it: I dare say, however, not with her inclination.

I was ordered in just before Mr Morden came; and was bid to sit down—which I did in the window.

The colonel, when he came, began the discourse by *renewing* as he called it his solicitations in your favour. He set before them your penitence; your ill health; your virtue, though once betrayed and basely used. He then read to them Mr Lovelace's letter, a most contrite one indeed[a]; and your *high-souled* answer[b]; for that was what he justly called it; and he treated as it deserved Mr Brand's officious information (of which I had before heard he had made them ashamed) by representations founded upon inquiries made by Mr Alston,[c] whom he procured to go up on purpose to acquaint himself with your manner of life, and what was meant by the visits of that Mr Belford.

He then told them that he had the day before waited upon Miss Howe, and had been shown a letter from you to her,[d] and permitted to take some memorandums

a See p. 1185.
b See p. 1191.
c See p. 1246.
d See p. 1265.

from it, in which you appeared both by hand-writing and the contents to be so very ill, that it seemed doubtful to him if it were possible for you to get over it. And when he read to them that passage where you ask Miss Howe, 'What can be done for you now, were your friends to be ever so favourable? and wish, for *their* sakes more than for your *own*, that they would still relent'; and then say, 'You are very ill—You must drop your pen—and ask excuse for your crooked writing; and take, as it were, a last farewell of Miss Howe; *Adieu, my dear, adieu,*' are your words—

Oh my child! my child! said your mamma, weeping, and clasping her hands.

Dear madam, said your brother, be so good as to think you have more children than this ungrateful one.

Yet your sister seemed affected.

Your uncle Harlowe wiping his eyes, Oh cousin, said he, if one thought the poor girl was *really* so ill—

She *must*, said your uncle Antony. This is written to her private friend. God forbid she should be quite lost!

Your uncle Harlowe wished they did not carry their resentments too far.

I begged for God's sake, wringing my hands, and with a bended knee, that they would permit me to go up to you; engaging to give them a faithful account of the way you were in. But I was chidden by your brother; and this occasioned some angry words between him and Mr Morden.

I believe, sir, I believe, madam, said your sister to her father and mother, we need not trouble my cousin to read any more. It does but grieve and disturb you. My sister Clary seems to be ill: I think if Mrs Norton were permitted to go up to her it would be right. Wickedly as she has acted, if she be truly penitent—

Here she stopped; and everyone being silent, I stood up once more, and besought them to let me go: and then I offered to read a passage or two in your letter to me of the 24th. But I was taken up again by your brother; and this occasioned still higher words between the colonel and him.

Your mamma, hoping to gain upon your inflexible brother, and to divert the anger of the two gentlemen from each other, proposed that the colonel should proceed in reading the minutes he had taken from your letter.

He accordingly read 'of your resuming your pen: that you thought you had taken your last farewell; and the rest of that very affecting passage in which you are obliged to break off more than once, and afterwards to take an airing in a chair.' Your brother and sister were affected at this; and he had recourse to his snuff-box. And where you comfort Miss Howe, and say, 'You shall be happy': It is more, said he, than she will let anybody else be.

Your sister called you sweet soul; but with a low voice: then grew hard-hearted again; yet said, nobody could help being affected by your pathetic grief—but that it was your talent.

The colonel then went on to the good effect your airing had upon you; to your good wishes to Miss Howe and Mr Hickman; and to your concluding sentence, that when the happy life you wish *her* comes to be wound up, she may be as calm and as easy at quitting it as you hope in God you shall be. Your mamma could not stand this, but retired to a corner of the room and sobbed and wept. Your father for a few minutes could not speak, though he seemed inclined to say something.

Your uncles were also both affected—but your brother went round to each; and again reminded your mamma that she had other children: what was there, he said, in what was read, but the result of the talent you had of moving the passions? And he blamed them for choosing to hear read what they knew their abused indulgence could not be proof against.

This set Mr Morden up again: Fie upon you, cousin Harlowe! said he—I see plainly to whom it is owing that all relationship and ties of blood with regard to this sweet sufferer are laid aside. Such rigours as these make it difficult for a sliding virtue ever to recover itself.

Your brother pretended the honour of the family; and declared that no child ought to be forgiven who abandoned the most indulgent of parents, against warning, against the light of knowledge, as you had done.

But, sir and ladies, said I, rising from my seat in the window, and humbly turning round to each, if I may be permitted to speak, my dear miss asks only for a blessing: she begs not to be received to favour: she is very ill, and asks only for a last blessing.

Come, come, goody Norton (I need not tell you who said this), you are up again with your lamentables!—A good woman, as you are, to forgive so readily a crime that has been as disgraceful to your part in her education as to her family, is a weakness that would induce one to suspect your virtue, if you were to be encountered by a temptation *properly adapted.*

By some such charitable logic as this, said Mr Morden, is my cousin Arabella captivated, I doubt not. If to be uncharitable and unforgiving is to give a proof of virtue, you, Mr James Harlowe, are the most virtuous young man in the world.

I knew how it would be, replied your brother in a passion, if I met Mr Morden upon this business. I would have declined it: but you, sir, to his father, would not permit me so to do. But, sir, turning to the colonel, in no other presence—

Then, Cousin James, interrupted the other gentleman, that which is *your* protection, it seems is *mine.* I am not used to bear defiances thus—You are my cousin, sir—and the son and nephew of persons as dear as near to me—There he paused—

Are we, said your father, to be made still more unhappy among ourselves, when the villain lives that ought to be the object of everyone's resentment who has either a value for the family, or for this ungrateful girl?

That's the man, said your cousin, whom last Monday, as you know, I went purposely to make the object of mine. But what could I say when I found him so willing to repair his crime?—and I give it as my opinion, and have written accordingly to my poor cousin, that it is best for all round that his offer should be accepted: and let me tell you—

Tell me nothing, said your father, quite enraged, of that very vile fellow! I have a riveted hatred to him. I would rather see the rebel die a hundred deaths, were it possible, than that she should give such a villain as him a relation to my family.

Well, but there is no room to think, said your mamma, that she will give us such a relation, my dear. The poor girl will lessen, I fear, the number of our relations; not increase it. If she be so ill as we are told she is, let us send Mrs Norton up to her—That's the *least* we can do—Let us take her, however, out of the hands of that Belford.

Both your uncles supported this motion; the latter part of it especially.

Your brother observed, in his ill-natured way, what a fine piece of consistency it was in you to refuse the vile injurer, and the amends he offered; yet to throw yourself upon the protection of his fast friend.

Miss Harlowe was apprehensive, she said, that you would leave all you *could* leave to that pert creature Miss Howe (so she called her) if you should die.

Oh do not, do not suppose *that*, my Bella, said your poor mother: I cannot think of parting with my Clary—With all her faults, she is my child—Her reasons for her conduct are not heard. It would break my heart to lose her. I think, my dear, to your papa, none so fit as I, if you will give me leave, to go up. And Mrs Norton shall accompany me.

This was a sweet motion; and your father paused upon it. Mr Morden offered his service to escort her. Your uncles seemed to approve of it. But your brother dashed all. I hope, sir, said he to his father; I hope, madam, to his mother, that you will not endeavour to recover a faulty daughter by losing an unculpable son. I do declare that if ever my sister Clary darkens these doors again, I never will. I will set out, madam, the same hour you go to London (on such an errand), to Edinburgh; and there I will reside; and try to forget that I have relations in England so near and so dear as you are now all to me.

Good God, said the colonel! What a declaration is this!—And suppose, sir, and suppose, madam (turning to your father and mother) this *should* be the case, whether is it better, think you, that you should lose for ever such a daughter as my cousin Clary, or that your son should go to Edinburgh and reside there upon an estate which will be the better for his residence upon it?—

Your brother's passionate behaviour hereupon is hardly to be described. He resented it as promoting an alienation of the affection of the family to him. And to such a height were resentments carried, everyone siding with him, that the colonel, with hands and eyes lifted up, cried out, What hearts of flint am I related to!—Oh cousin Harlowe, to your father, are you resolved to have but one daughter? Are you, madam, to be taught by a son who has no bowels, to forget that you are a mother?

The colonel turned from them to draw out his handkerchief, and could not for a minute speak. The eyes of everyone, but the hard-hearted brother, caught tears from his.

But then turning to them (with the more indignation, as it seemed, as he had been obliged to show a humanity which, however, no brave heart should be ashamed of), I leave ye all, said he, fit company for one another. I will never open my lips to any of you more upon this subject. I will instantly make my will, and in me shall the dear creature have the father, uncle, brother, she has lost. I will prevail upon her to take the tour of France and Italy with me; nor shall she return till ye know the value of *such* a daughter.

And saying this, he hurried out of the room, went into the courtyard, and ordered his horse.

Mr Antony Harlowe went to him there, just as he was mounting; and said he hoped he should find him cooler in the evening (for he till then had lodged at his house) and that then they would converse calmly; and everyone meantime would weigh all matters well—But the angry gentleman said, Cousin Harlowe, I shall endeavour to discharge the obligations I owe to your civility since I have been in England; but I have been so treated by that hot-headed young man (who, as far as I know, has done more to ruin his sister than Lovelace himself, and *this* with the approbation of you all) that I will not again enter into *your* doors or *theirs*. My servant shall have orders whither to bring what belongs to me from your house. I will see my dear cousin Clary as soon as I can. And so God bless you all together! Only this one word to your nephew, if you please: That he wants to be taught the difference between courage and bluster; and it is happy for him, perhaps, that I am *his* kinsman; though I am sorry he is *mine*.

I wondered to hear your uncle, on his return to them all, repeat this; because of the consequences it may be attended with, though I hope it will not have bad ones: yet it was considered as a sort of challenge, and so it confirmed everybody in your brother's favour; and Miss Harlowe forgot not to inveigh against that error which had brought on all these evils.

I took the liberty again, but with fear and trembling, to desire leave to attend you.

Before any other person could answer, your brother said, He supposed I looked upon myself to be my own mistress. Did I want their consents, and *courtship*, to go up? If he might speak his mind, we were *fittest* to be together—yet he wished I would not trouble my head about their family matters till I was desired so to do.

But don't you know, brother, said Miss Harlowe, that the error of any branch of a family splits that family all in pieces, and makes not only every common friend and acquaintance, but even *servants*, judges over both?—This is one of the blessed effects of my sister Clary's fault!

There never was a creature so criminal, said your father, looking with displeasure at me, who had not some weak heads to pity and side with her.

I wept. Your mamma was so good as to take me by the hand: Come, good woman, said she, come along with me. You have too much reason to be afflicted at what afflicts us, to want additions to your grief.

But, my dearest young lady, I was more touched for your sake than for my own: for I have been low in the world for a great number of years; and of consequence must have been accustomed to snubs and rebuffs from the affluent. But I hope that patience is written as legibly on my forehead, as haughtiness on that of any of my obligers.

Your mamma led me to her chamber; and there we sat and wept together for several minutes, without being able to speak either of us one word to the other. At last she broke silence; asking me, If you were really and indeed so ill as it was said you were?

I answered in the affirmative; and would have shown her your last letter; but she declined seeing it.

I would fain have procured from her the favour of a line to you, with her blessing. I asked what was *intended* by your brother and sister? Would nothing satisfy them but your final reprobation?—I insinuated how easy it would be, did not your duty and humility govern you, to make yourself independent as to circumstances; but that nothing but a blessing, a *last* blessing, was requested by you. And many other things I urged in your behalf. The following brief repetition of what she was pleased to say, in answer to my pleas, will give you a notion of it all; and of the present situation of things.

She said: 'She was very unhappy! She had lost the little authority she once had over her other children, through one child's failing; and all influence over Mr Harlowe and his brothers. Your father, she said, had besought her to leave it to him to take his own methods with you; and (as she valued him) to take no step in your favour unknown to him and your uncles: yet she owned that they were too much governed by your brother. They would, however, give way in time, she knew, to a reconciliation: they designed no other; for they all still loved you.

'Your brother and sister, she owned, were very jealous of your coming into favour again: yet, could but Mr Morden have kept his temper, and stood her son's first sallies, who had carried his resentment so high (having always had the family grandeur in view) that he knew not how to descend, the conferences, so abruptly broken off just now, would have ended more happily; for that she had reason to think that a few concessions on your part, with regard to your grandfather's estate, and your cousin's engaging for your submission, as from *proper* motives, would have softened them all.

'Mr Brand's account of your intimacy with the friend of the obnoxious man, she said, had for the time very unhappy effects; for she had (before that) gained some ground: but afterwards dared not, nor indeed had inclination, to open her lips in your behalf. Your continued intimacy with that Mr Belford was wholly unaccountable, and as wholly inexcusable.

'What made the wished-for reconciliation, she said, more difficult was, first, that you yourself acknowledged yourself dishonoured; and it was too well known that it was your own fault that you ever were in the power of so great a profligate; of consequence, that their and your disgrace could not be greater than it was: yet, that you refused to prosecute the wretch. Next, that the pardon and blessing hoped for must probably be attended with your marriage to the man they hate, and who hates them as much: very disagreeable circumstances, she said, I must allow, to found a reconciliation upon.

'As to her own part, she must needs say that if there were any hope that Mr Lovelace would become a reformed man, the letter her cousin Morden had read to them from him to you, and the justice (as she hoped it was) he did your character, though to his own condemnation (his family and fortunes being unexceptionable), and all his relations earnest to be related to you, were arguments that would have weight with her, could they have any with your father and uncles.'

To my plea of your illness, 'She could not but flatter herself, she answered, that it was from lowness of spirits and temporary dejection. A young creature, she said, so very considerate as you naturally were, and fallen so low, must have enough of that. Should they lose you, which God forbid! the scene would then indeed be sadly changed; for then those who now most resented, would be most grieved; all your fine qualities would rise to their remembrance, and your unhappy error would be quite forgotten.

'She wished you would put yourself into your cousin's protection entirely, and have nothing more to say to Mr Belford.'

And I would recommend it to your most serious consideration, my dear Miss Clary, whether now, as your cousin (who is your trustee for your grandfather's estate) is come, you should not give over all thoughts of Mr Lovelace's intimate friend for your executor; more especially as that gentleman's interfering in the concerns of your family, should the sad event take place (which my heart aches but to think of), might be attended with those consequences which you are so desirous, in other cases, to obviate and prevent. And suppose, my dear young lady, you were to write one letter more to each of your uncles, to let them know how ill you are?—and to ask their advice, and offer to be governed by it in relation to the disposition of your estate and effects?

I find they will send you up a large part of what has been received from that estate, since it was yours; together with your current cash which you left behind you. And this by your cousin Morden, for fear you should have contracted debts which may make you uneasy.

They seem to expect that you will wish to live at your grandfather's house, in a private manner, if your cousin prevail not upon you to go abroad for a year or two.

Friday morning

BETTY was with me just now. She tells me that your cousin Morden is so much displeased with them all, that he has refused to lodge any more at your uncle Antony's; and has even taken up with inconvenient lodgings till he is provided with others to his mind. This very much concerns them; and they repent their violent treatment of him: and the more, as he is resolved, he says, to make you his heir general, and his full and whole executrix.

What noble fortunes still, my dearest young lady, await you! I am thoroughly convinced, if it please God to preserve your life and your health, that everybody will soon be reconciled to you, and that you will see many happy days.

Your mamma wished me not to attend you as yet, because she hopes that I may give myself that pleasure soon with everybody's good liking, and even at their desire. Your cousin Morden's reconciliation with them, which they are very desirous of, I am ready to hope will include theirs with you.

But if that should happen which I so much dread, and I not with you, I should never forgive myself. Let me, therefore, my dearest young lady, desire you to command my attendance, if you find any danger, and if you wish me peace of mind; and no consideration shall withhold me.

I hear that Miss Howe has obtained leave from her mother to see you; and intends next week to go to town for that purpose; and (as it is believed) to buy clothes for her approaching nuptials.

Mr Hickman's mother-in-law is lately dead. Her jointure of £600 a year is fallen in to him; and she has moreover, as an acknowledgement of his good behaviour to her, left him all she was worth, which was very considerable, a few legacies excepted to her own relations.

These good men are uniformly good: indeed could not else *be* good; and never fare the worse for being so. All the world agrees he will make that fine young lady an excellent husband. And I am sorry they are not as much agreed in her making him an excellent wife. But I hope a lady of her principles would not encourage his address if, whether she at present loves him or not, she thought she could *not* love him; or if she preferred any other man to him.

Mr Pocock undertakes to deliver this; but fears it will be Saturday night first, if not Sunday morning.

May the Almighty protect and bless you! I long to see you—my dearest young lady, I long to see you; and to fold you once more to my fond heart. I dare to say happy days are coming. Be but cheerful. Give way to hope.

Whether for this world, or the other, you *must* be happy. Wish to live, however, were it only because you are so well fitted in mind to make everyone happy who has the honour to know you. What signifies this transitory eclipse? You are as near perfection, by all I have heard, as any creature in this world can be: for here is your glory: you are brightened and purified, as I may say, by your sufferings!— How I long to hear your whole sad yet instructive story from your own lips!

For Miss Howe's sake, who in her new engagements will so much want you; for your cousin Morden's sake; for your mother's sake, if I must go no further in your family; and yet I can say, for all their sakes; and for my sake, my dearest young lady; let your resumed and accustomed magnanimity bear you up. You have many things to do, which I know not the person who will do, if you leave us.

Join your prayers then to mine, that God will spare you to a world that wants you and your example; and, although your days may seem to have been numbered, who knows but that, with the good King Hezekiah, you may have them prolonged?[1] which God grant, if it be his blessed will, to the prayers of

Your JUDITH NORTON

Letter 460: MR BELFORD TO ROBERT LOVELACE, ESQ.

Monday, Sept. 4

THE LADY would not read the letter she had from Mrs Norton till she had received the Communion, for fear it should contain anything that might disturb that happy calm which she had been endeavouring to obtain for it. And when that solemn office was over, she was so composed, she said, that she thought she could receive any news, however affecting, with tranquillity.

Nevertheless, in reading it, she was forced to leave off several times through weakness and a dimness in her sight, of which she complained; if I may say *complained*; for so easy and soft were her complaints, that they could hardly be called such.

She was very much affected at divers parts of this letter. She wept several times, and sighed often. Mrs Lovick told me that these were the gentle exclamations she broke out into, as she read: *Her unkind, her cruel brother!—How* unsisterly!— *Poor dear woman!* seeming to speak of Mrs Norton. *Her kind cousin!—Oh these flaming spirits!*—and then reflecting upon herself more than once—*What a deep error is mine!—What evils have I been the occasion of!*—

When I was admitted to her presence, I have received, said she, a long and not very pleasing letter from my dear Mrs Norton: it will soon be in your hands. I am advised against appointing you to the office you have so kindly accepted: but you must resent nothing of these things. My choice will have an odd appearance to them: but it is now too late to alter it, if I would.

I would fain write an answer to it, continued she: but I have no distinct sight, Mr Belford, no steadiness of fingers—This mistiness, however, will perhaps be gone by and by—Then turning to Mrs Lovick: I don't think I am dying yet—not *actually* dying, Mrs Lovick—for I have no bodily pain—no numbnesses; no signs of immediate death, I think—and my breath, which used of late to be so short, is now tolerable—my head clear, my intellects free—I think I cannot be dying yet—I shall have agonies, I doubt—Life will not give up so blessedly easy, I fear—Yet how merciful is the Almighty to give his poor creature such a sweet serenity!—'Tis what I have prayed for!—What encouragement, Mrs Lovick, so near one's dissolution to have it to hope that one's prayers are answered!

Mrs Smith, as well as Mrs Lovick, was with her. They were both in tears; nor had I, any more than they, power to say a word in answer: yet she spoke all this, as well as what follows, with a surprising composure of mind and countenance.

But, Mr Belford, said she, assuming a still spritelier air and accent, let me talk a little to you while I am thus able to say what I have to say.

Mrs Lovick, don't leave us; for the women were rising to go—Pray sit down; and do you, Mrs Smith, sit down too—Dame Shelburne, take this key and open that upper drawer. I will move to it.

She did, with trembling knees. Here, Mr Belford, is my will. It is witnessed by three persons of Mr Smith's acquaintance.

I dare to hope that my cousin Morden will give you assistance, if you request it of him. My cousin Morden continues his affection for me: but as I have not seen *him*, I leave all the trouble upon *you*, Mr Belford. This deed may want forms; and it does, no doubt: but the less as I have my grandfather's will almost by heart, and have often enough heard that canvassed. I will lay it by itself in this corner; putting it at the further end of the drawer.

She then took up a parcel of letters enclosed in one cover, sealed with three seals of black wax: this, said she, I sealed up last night. The cover, sir, will let you know what is to be done with what it encloses. This is the superscription (holding it close to her eyes, and rubbing them): *As soon as I am certainly dead, this to be broke open by Mr Belford*—Here, sir, I put it (placing it by the will)—These folded papers are letters and copies of letters, disposed according to their dates. Miss Howe will do with those as you and she shall think fit. If I receive any more, or more come when I cannot receive them, they may be put into this drawer (pulling out and pushing in the looking-glass drawer), you'll be so kind as to observe that, Mrs Lovick and Dame Shelburne, to be given to Mr Belford be they from whom they will.

Here, sir, proceeded she, I put the keys of my apparel (putting them into the drawers with her papers). All is in order, and the inventory upon them, and an account of what I have disposed of: so that nobody need to ask Mrs Smith any questions.

There will be no immediate need to open or inspect the trunks which contain my wearing apparel. Mrs Norton will open them, or order somebody to do it for her, in your presence, Mrs Lovick; for so I have directed in my will. They may be sealed up now: I shall never more have occasion to open them.

She then, though I expostulated to the contrary, caused me to seal them up with my seal.

After this, she locked the drawer where were her papers; first taking out her book of *Meditations*, as she called it; saying she should perhaps have use for that; and then desired me to take the key of that drawer; for she should have no further occasion for that neither.

All this in so composed and cheerful a manner, that we were equally surprised and affected with it.

You can witness for me, Mrs Smith, and so can you, Mrs Lovick, proceeded she, if anyone ask after my life and conversation since you have known me, that I have been very orderly; have kept good hours, and never have lain out of your house, but when I was in prison; and then, you know, I could not help it.

Oh Lovelace! that thou hadst heard her, or seen her, unknown to herself, on this occasion!—Not one of us could speak a word.

I shall leave the world in perfect charity, proceeded she. And turning towards the women, Don't be so much concerned for me, my good friends. This is all but needful preparation; and I shall be very happy.

Then again rubbing her eyes, which she said were misty, and looking more intently round upon each, particularly on me—God bless you all, said she! how kindly are you concerned for me!—Who says I am friendless? Who says I am abandoned and among strangers?—Good Mr Belford, don't be so *generously* humane—Indeed (putting her handkerchief to her charming eyes) you will make me less happy than I am sure you wish me to be.

While we were thus solemnly engaged, a servant came with a letter from her cousin Morden—Then, said she, he is not come *himself!*

She broke it open; but every line, she said, appeared two to her: so that, being unable to read it herself, she desired I would read it to her. I did so; and wished it were more consolatory to her: but she was all patient attention; tears, however, often trickling down her cheeks. By the date, it was written yesterday; and this is the substance of it.

He tells her 'that the Thursday before, he had procured a general meeting of her principal relations at her father's; though not without difficulty, her haughty brother opposing it, and, when met, rendering all his endeavours to reconcile them to her ineffectual. He censures him as the most ungovernable young man he ever knew: some great sickness, he says, some heavy misfortune is wanted to bring him to a knowledge of himself and of what is due from him to others; and he wishes that he were not *her* brother, and *his* cousin. Nor does he spare her father and uncles for being so implicitly led by him.'

He tells her, 'That he parted with them all in high displeasure, and thought never more to darken any of their doors: that he declared as much to her two uncles, who came to him on Saturday, to try to accommodate with him; and who found him preparing to go to London to attend her; and that, notwithstanding their pressing entreaties, he determined so to do, and not to go with them to Harlowe Place, or to either of their own houses; and accordingly dismissed them with such an answer.

'But that her noble letter, as he calls it, of Aug. 31[a] being brought him about an hour after their departure, he thought it might affect them as much as it did him; and give them the exalted opinion of her virtue and honour which was so well deserved; and at the same time convince them of what they made such difficulty to believe; to wit, that you and all your relations were solicitous to obtain the honour of her alliance, on her own terms: and that this induced him to turn his horse's head back to her uncle Antony's, instead of forward towards London.

'That accordingly arriving there, and finding her two uncles together, he read to them the affecting letter; which left neither of the three a dry eye: that the absent, as is usual in such cases, bearing all the load, they accused her brother and sister; and besought him to put off his journey to town, till he could carry with him the

---

a See Letter 448.

blessings which she had formerly in vain solicited for; and (as they hoped) the happy tidings of a general reconciliation.

'That not doubting but his visit would be the more welcome to her, if these good ends could be obtained, he the more readily complied with their desires. But not being willing to subject himself to the possibility of receiving fresh insults from her brother, he had given her uncles a copy of her letter for the family to assemble upon; and desired to know, as soon as possible, the result of their deliberations.

'He tells her that he shall bring her up the accounts relating to the produce of her grandfather's estate, and adjust them with her; having actually in his hands the arrears due to her from it.

'He highly applauds the noble manner in which she resents your usage of her. It is impossible, he owns, that you can either deserve her, or to be forgiven. But as you do justice to her virtue, and offer to make her all the reparation now in your power; and as she is so very earnest with him not to resent that usage; and declares that you could not have been the author of her calamities but through a strange concurrence of unhappy causes; and as he is not at a loss to know how to place to a *proper account* that strange concurrence; he desires her not to be apprehensive of any vindictive measures from him.'

Nevertheless (as may be expected) 'he inveighs against you; as he finds that she gave you no advantage over her. But he forbears to enter further into this subject, he says, till he has the honour to see her; and the rather as she seems so much determined against you. However, he cannot but say that he thinks you a gallant man, and a man of sense; and that you have the reputation of being thought a generous man in every instance but where the sex is concerned. In *such*, he owns that you have taken inexcusable liberties. And he is sorry to say that there are very few young men of fortune but who allow themselves in the same. Both sexes, he observes, too much love to have each other in their power: yet he hardly ever knew man or woman who was very fond of power make a right use of it.

'If she be so absolutely determined against marrying you, as she declares she is, he hopes, he says, to prevail upon her to take (as soon as her health will permit) a little tour abroad with him, as what will probably establish it; since travelling is certainly the best physic for all those disorders which owe their rise to grief and disappointment. An absence of two or three years will endear her to everyone on her return, and everyone to her.

'He expresses his impatience to see her. He will set out, he says, the moment he knows the result of her family's determination; which he doubts not will be favourable. Nor will he wait long for that.'

When I had read the letter through to the languishing lady, And so, my friends, said she, have I heard of a patient who actually died while five or six principal physicians were in a consultation, and not agreed upon what name to give to his distemper. The patient was an emperor: the Emperor Joseph, I think.

I asked if I should write to her cousin, as he knew not how ill she was, to hasten up.

By no means, she said; since, if he were not already set out, she was persuaded that she should be so low by the time he could receive my letter and come, that his presence would but discompose and hurry *her*, and afflict *him*.

I hope, however, she is not so very near her end. And without saying any more to her, when I retired I wrote to Colonel Morden that if he expects to see his beloved cousin alive, he must lose no time in setting out. I sent this letter by his own servant.

Dr H. sent away *his* letter to her father by a particular hand this morning.

Mrs Walton the milliner has also just now acquainted Mrs Smith, that her husband had a letter brought by a special messenger from Parson Brand within this half-hour, enclosing the copy of one he had written to Mr John Harlowe, recanting his officious one.

And as all these, and the copy of the lady's letter to Colonel Morden, will be with them pretty much at a time, the devil's in the family if they are not struck with a remorse that shall burst open the double-barred doors of their hearts.

Will engages to reach you with this (late as it will be) before you go to rest. He begs that I will testify for him the hour and the minute I shall give it him. It is just half an hour after ten.

I pretend to be (now by use) the swiftest shorthand writer in England, next to yourself. But were matter to arise every hour to write upon, and I had nothing else to do, I cannot write so fast as you expect. And let it be remembered, that your servants cannot bring letters or messages before they are written or sent.

J. BELFORD

Letter 461: DR H. TO JAMES HARLOWE, SENIOR, ESQ.

London, Sept. 4

Sir,

IF I may judge of the hearts of other parents by my own, I cannot doubt but you will take it well to be informed that you have yet an opportunity to save yourself and family great future regret, by dispatching hither someone of it with your last blessing, and your lady's, to the most excellent of her sex.

I have some reason to believe, sir, that she has been represented to you in a very different light from the true one. And this it is that induces me to acquaint you that I think her, on the best grounds, absolutely irreproachable in all her conduct which has passed under my eye or come to my ear; and that her very misfortunes are made glorious to her, and honourable to all that are related to her, by the use she has made of them; and by the patience and resignation with which she supports herself in a painful, lingering, and dispiriting decay; and by the greatness of mind with which she views her approaching dissolution. And all this from proper motives; from motives in which a dying saint might glory.

She knows not that I write. I must indeed acknowledge that I offered to do so some days ago, and that very pressingly: nor did she refuse me from obstinacy— she seems not to know what that is—but desired me to forbear for two days only, in hopes that her newly arrived cousin, who, as she heard, was soliciting for her, would be able to succeed in her favour.

I hope I shall not be thought an officious man on this occasion: but if I am, I cannot help it; being driven to write by a kind of *parental* and irresistible impulse.

But, sir, whatever you do, or permit to be done, must be speedily done; for she cannot, I verily think, live a week: and how long of that short space she may enjoy her admirable intellects, to take comfort in the favours you may think proper to confer upon her, cannot be said. I am, sir,

> Your most humble servant,
> R.H.

Letter 462: MR BELFORD TO WILLIAM MORDEN, ESQ.

> London, Sept 4

Sir,

THE urgency of the case and the opportunity by your servant, will sufficiently apologize for this trouble from a stranger to your person; who, however, is not a stranger to your merit.

I understand you are employing your good offices with Miss Clarissa Harlowe's parents and other relations, to reconcile them to the most meritorious daughter and kinswoman that ever family had to boast of.

Generously as this is intended by you, we *here* have too much reason to think all your solicitudes on this head will be unnecessary: for, it is the opinion of everyone who has the honour of being admitted to her presence, that she cannot live over three days: so that if you wish to see her alive you must lose no time to come up.

She knows not that I write. I had done it sooner if I had had the least doubt that before now she would not have received from you some news of the happy effects of your kind mediation in her behalf. I am, sir,

> Your most humble servant,
> J. BELFORD

Letter 463: MR LOVELACE TO JOHN BELFORD, ESQ.

(In answer to Letter 460)

> Uxbridge, Tuesday morn. between 4 and 5

AND can it be that this admirable creature will so soon leave this cursed world? For cursed I shall think it, and more cursed myself, when she is gone. Oh Jack! thou, who canst sit so cool, and like Addison's Angel, *direct*, and even *enjoy*, the storm[1] that tears up my happiness by the roots, blame me not for my impatience, however unreasonable! If thou knewest that already I feel the torments of the damned, in the remorse that wrings my heart on looking back upon my past actions by her, thou wouldst not be the devil thou art to halloo on a worrying conscience which, without thy merciless aggravations, is altogether intolerable.

I know not what I write, nor what I would write. When the company that used to delight me is as uneasy to me as my reflections are painful, and I can neither help nor divert myself, must not every servant about me partake in a perturbation so sincere?

Shall I give thee a faint picture of the horrible uneasiness with which my mind struggles? And faint indeed it must be; for nothing but outrageous madness can exceed it; and *that* only in the apprehension of others; since as to the sufferer, it is certain that actual distraction (take it out of its lucid intervals) must be an infinitely more happy state than the suspense and anxieties that bring it on.

Forbidden to attend the dear creature, yet longing to see her, I would give the world to be admitted once more to her beloved presence. I ride towards London three or four times a day, resolving *pro* and *con* twenty times in two or three miles; and at last ride back; and in view of Uxbridge, loathing even the kind friend and hospitable house, turn my horse's head again towards the town and resolve to gratify my humour, let her take it as she will; but, at the very entrance of it, after infinite canvassings, once more alter my mind, dreading to offend and shock her, lest by that means I should curtail a life so precious.

Yesterday, in particular, to give you an idea of the strength of that impatience which I cannot avoid suffering to break out upon my servants, I had no sooner dispatched Will, than I took horse to meet him on his return.

In order to give him time, I loitered about on the road, riding up *this* lane to the one highway, down *that* to the other, just as my horse pointed; all the way cursing my very being; and though so lately looking *down* upon all the world, wishing to change conditions with the poorest beggar that cried to me for charity as I rode by him—and throwing him money, in hopes to obtain by his prayers the blessing my heart pants after.

After I had sauntered about an hour or two (which seemed three or four tedious ones), fearing I had slipped the fellow, I inquired at every turnpike whether a servant in such a livery had not passed through in his return from London on a full gallop (for woe had been to the dog had I met him on a sluggish trot!). And lest I should miss him at one end of Kensington, as he might take either the Acton or Hammersmith road; or at the other, as he might come through the Park, or not; how many score times did I ride backwards and forwards from the Palace to the Gore, making myself the subject of observation to all passengers, whether on horseback or on foot; who, no doubt, wondered to see a well-dressed and well-mounted man, sometimes ambling, sometimes prancing (as the beast had more fire than his master) backwards and forwards in so short a compass!

Yet all this time, though longing to espy the fellow, did I dread to meet him, lest he should be charged with fatal tidings.

When at distance I saw any man galloping towards me, my resemblance-forming fancy immediately made it to be him; and then my heart bounded to my mouth, as if it would have choked me. But when the person's nearer approach undeceived me, how did I curse the varlet's delay and thee by turns; and how ready was I to draw my pistol at the stranger for having the impudence to gallop; which none but my messenger, I thought, had either right or reason to do! For all the business of the world, I am ready to imagine, should stand still on an occasion so melancholy and so interesting to myself. Nay, for this week past, I could cut the throat of any man or woman I see laugh while I am in such dejection of mind.

I am now convinced that the wretches who fly from a heavy scene labour under ten times more distress in the intermediate suspense and apprehension, than *they* can do who are present at it, and see and know the worst; so much greater are the evils we dread than those we see!—and so able is fancy or imagination, the more immediate offspring of the soul, to outdo fact, let the subject be either joyous or grievous.

And hence, as I conceive, it is that all pleasures are greater in the *expectation*, or in the *reflection*, than in *fruition*; as all pains, which press heavy upon both parts of that unequal union by which frail mortality holds its precarious tenure, generally are most acute in the *present tense:* for how easy sit upon the *reflection* the heaviest misfortunes, especially when surmounted!—But *most* easy, I confess, those in which body has more concern than soul. This, however, is a point of philosophy I have neither time nor head just now to weigh. So take it as it falls from a madman's pen.

Woe be to either of the wretches who shall bring me the fatal news that she is no more! For it is but too likely that a shriek-owl so hated will never whoot or scream again; unless the shock that will probably disorder my whole frame on so sad an occasion (by *unsteadying* my hand) shall divert my aim from his head, heart, or bowels, if it turn not against my own.

But, surely, she will not, she cannot yet die! Such a matchless excellence,

> —whose mind
> Contains a world, and seems for all things fram'd,[2]

could not be lent to be so soon demanded back again!

But may it not be that thou, Belford, art in a plot with the dear creature (who will not let me attend her to convince myself) in order to work up my soul to the deepest remorse and penitence; and that, when she is convinced of the sincerity of both, and when my mind is made such wax as to be fit to take what impression she pleases to give it, she will then raise me up with the joyful tidings of her returning health and acceptance of me?

What would I give to have it so! And when the happiness of *hundreds*, as well as the peace and reconciliation of several eminent families, depend upon *her* restoration and happiness, why should it not be so?

But let me presume it will. Let me indulge my former hope, however improbable—*I will*; and *enjoy* it too. And let me tell thee how ecstatic my delight would be on the unravelling of such a plot as this!

Do, *dear* Belford, let it be so!—And, Oh my dearest, and ever-dear Clarissa, keep me no longer in this cruel suspense; in which I suffer a thousand times more than ever I made thee suffer. Nor fear thou that I will resent, or recede, on an *éclaircissement* so desirable: for I will adore thee for ever and, without reproaching thee for the pangs thou hast tortured me with, confess thee as much my superior in noble and generous contrivances, as thou art in virtue and honour!

But, once more—should the worst happen—say not what that worst is—and I am gone from this hated island—gone for ever—and may eternal—But I am crazed already—and will therefore conclude myself,

> Thine more than my own
> (And no great compliment neither),
> R.L.

Letter 464: MR BELFORD TO ROBERT LOVELACE, ESQ.

Tuesday, 5 Sept. 9 in the morn. at Mr Smith's

WHEN I read yours of this morning, I could not help pitying you for the account you give of the dreadful anxiety and suspense you labour under. I wish from my heart all were to end as you are so willing to hope: but it will not be; and your suspense, if the worst part of your torment as you say it is, will soon be over; but, alas! in a way you wish not.

I attended the lady just now. She is extremely ill: yet is she aiming at an answer to her Mrs Norton's letter, which she began yesterday in her own chamber, and has written a good deal; but in a hand not like her own fine one, as Mrs Lovick tells me, but much larger, and the lines crooked.

I have accepted of the offer of a room adjoining to the widow Lovick's till I see how matters go; but unknown to the lady; and I shall go home every night for a few hours—I would not lose a sentence that I could gain from lips so instructive nor the opportunity of receiving any command from her, for an estate.

In this my new apartment, I now write, and shall continue to write as occasions offer, that I may be the more circumstantial: but I depend upon the return of my letters, or copies of them, on demand, that I may have together all that relates to this affecting story; which I shall reperuse with melancholy pleasure to the end of my life.

I think I will send thee Brand's letter to Mr John Harlowe, recanting his base surmises. It is a matchless piece of pedantry; and may perhaps a little divert thy deep chagrin: some time hence at least it may, if not now.

What wretched creatures are there in the world! What strangely mixed characters!—So sensible and so foolish at the same time! What a *various*, what a *foolish* creature is man!—

Three o'clock

THE lady has just finished her letter, and has entertained Mrs Lovick, Mrs Smith, and me, with a noble discourse on the vanity and brevity of life, which I cannot do justice to in the repetition: and indeed I am so grieved for her that, ill as she is, my intellects are not half so clear as hers.

A few things which made the strongest impression upon me, as well from the sentiments themselves, as from her manner of uttering them, I remember. She introduced them thus:

I am thinking, said she, what a gradual and happy death God Almighty (blessed be His Name!) affords me! Who would have thought that, suffering what I have suffered, and abandoned as I have been, with such a tender education as I have had, I should be so long a dying!—But see how by little and little it has come to this. I was first taken off from the power of *walking*: then I took a *coach*—a coach grew too violent an exercise: then I took a *chair*—The prison was a large DEATH-STRIDE upon me—I should have *suffered longer else!*—Next, I was unable to go to *church*; then to go *up* or *down stairs*; now hardly can move from one *room* to *another*; and a *less room* will soon hold me—My *eyes* begin to fail me, so that at times I cannot see to read distinctly; and now I can hardly *write* or hold a pen—Next, I presume, I shall know nobody, nor be able to thank any of you: I therefore now once more thank you, Mrs Lovick, and you, Mrs Smith, and you, Mr Belford, while I *can* thank you, for all your kindness to me. And thus by little and little, in such a gradual sensible death as I am blessed with, God dies away in us, as I may say, all human satisfactions, in order to subdue his poor creatures to Himself.

Thou mayest guess how affected we all were at this moving account of her progressive weakness. We heard it with wet eyes; for what with the women's example, and what with her moving eloquence, I could no more help it than they. But we were silent nevertheless; and she went on, applying herself to me.

Oh Mr Belford! This is a poor transitory life in its best enjoyments. We flutter about here and there, with all our vanities about us, like painted butterflies, for a gay but a very short season, till at last we lay ourselves down in a quiescent state, and turn into vile worms: and who knows in what form, or to what condition, we shall rise again?

I wish you would permit me, a young creature just turned of nineteen years of age, blooming and healthy as I was a few months ago, now nipped by the cold hand of death, to influence you in *these my last hours* to a life of regularity and repentance for any past evils you may have been guilty of. For, believe me, sir, that now in this last stage very few things will bear the test, or be passed as laudable, if *pardonable*, at our own bar, much less at a more tremendous one, in all we have done or delighted in, even in a life not very offensive neither, as *we* may think!— Ought we not then to study in our *full day*, before the dark hours approach, so to live as may afford reflections that will soften the agony of the last moments when they come, and let in upon the departing soul a ray of Divine Mercy to illuminate its passage into an awful eternity?

She was ready to faint, and choosing to lie down, I withdrew, I need not say with a melancholy heart: and when I was got to my new-taken apartment, my heart was still more affected by the sight of the solemn letter the admirable lady had so lately finished. It was communicated to me by Mrs Lovick; who had it to copy for me; but it was not to be *delivered to me* till after her departure. However, I trespassed so far as to prevail upon the widow to let me take a copy of it; which I did directly in character.

I send it enclosed. If thou canst read it, and thy heart not bleed at thy eyes, thy remorse can hardly be so deep as thou hast inclined me to think it is.

Letter 465: MISS CLARISSA HARLOWE TO MRS NORTON

(In answer to Letter 459ᵃ)
My dearest Mrs Norton,
I AM afraid I shall not be able to write all that is upon my mind to say to you upon the subject of your last. Yet I will try.

As to my friends, and as to the sad breakfasting, I cannot help being afflicted for *them*. What, alas! has not my mother, in particular, suffered by my rashness!—Yet to allow so much for a son!—so little for a daughter!—But all now will soon be over, as to me. I hope they will bury all their resentments in my grave.

As to your advice in relation to Mr Belford, let me only say that the unhappy reprobation I have met with, and my short time, must be my apology now—I wish

---

ᵃ Begun on Monday Sept. 4 and by piecemeal finished on Tuesday; but not sent till the Thursday following.

I *could* have written to my mother and my uncles, as you advise. And yet, favours come *so* slowly from them!—

The granting of one request only now remains as a desirable from them. Which nevertheless, when granted, I shall not be sensible of. It is, that they will be pleased to permit my remains to be laid with those of my ancestors—placed at the feet of my dear grandfather, as I have mentioned in my will. This, however, as they please. For, after all, this vile body ought not so much to engage my cares. It is a weakness—but let it be called a *natural* weakness, and I shall be excused; especially when a reverential gratitude shall be known to be the foundation of it. You know, my dear woman, how my grandfather loved me. And you know how much I honoured him, and that from my very infancy to the hour of his death. How often since have I wished that he had not loved me so well!

I wish not now, at the writing of this, to see even my cousin Morden. Oh my blessed woman! My dear maternal friend! I am entering upon a better tour than to France or Italy either!—or even than to settle at my once beloved dairy-house!—All these prospects and pleasures, which used to be so agreeable to me in health, how poor seem they to me now!—

Indeed, indeed, my dear mamma Norton, I shall be happy! I *know* I shall!—I have charming forebodings of happiness already!—Tell all my dear friends, for their comfort, that I shall!—Who would not bear the punishments I have borne, to have the prospects and assurances I rejoice in!—Assurances I might *not have had*, were all my own wishes to have been granted me!

Neither do I want to see even *you*, my dear Mrs Norton. Nevertheless, I must, in justice to my own gratitude, declare that there *was* a time that your presence and comfortings would have been balm to my wounded mind, could you have been permitted to come without incurring displeasure from those whose esteem it is necessary for you to cultivate and preserve. But were you now, even by consent and with reconciliatory tidings, to come, it would but add to your grief: and the sight of one I so dearly love, so happily fraught with good news, might but draw me back to wishes I have had great struggles to get above. And let me tell you for your comfort, that I have not left undone anything that ought to be done, either respecting *mind* or *person*; no, not to the minutest preparation: so that nothing is left for *you* to do for me. Everyone has her direction as to the last offices—And my desk, that I now write upon—Oh my dearest Mrs Norton, all is provided!—All is ready! And all will be as decent as it should be!

And pray let my Miss Howe know that by the time you will receive this, and she *your* signification of the contents of it, it will in all probability be too late for *her* to do me the inestimable favour, as I should once have thought it, to see me. *God will have no rivals in the hearts of those he sanctifies.* By various methods he deadens all other sensations, or rather absorbs them all in the love of Him.

I shall nevertheless love *you*, my mamma Norton, and my Miss Howe, whose love to me *has passed the love of women*, to my latest hour!—But yet I am now above the quick sense of those pleasures which once most delighted me: and once more I say, that I do not wish to see objects so dear to me, which might bring me back again into sense, and rival my *supreme love*.

TWICE have I been forced to leave off. I *wished* that my last writing might be to YOU, or to Miss Howe, if it might not be to my dearest ma—

Mamma, I would have wrote—is the word distinct?—My eyes are *so* misty!—If when I apply to you, I break off in half-words, do you supply them—The kindest are your due—Be sure take the kindest, to fill up chasms with, if any chasms there be—

ANOTHER breaking off!—But the new day seems to rise upon me with healing in its wings. I have gotten, I think, a recruit of strength: spirits, I bless God, I have not of late wanted.

Let my dearest Miss Howe purchase her wedding garments—and may all temporal blessings attend the charming preparation!—Blessings *will*, I make no question, notwithstanding the little cloudinesses that Mr Hickman encounters with now and then, which are but prognostics of a future golden day to him: for her heart is good and her head not wrong—But great merit is coy, and that coyness has not always its foundation in pride: but, if it should *seem* to be pride, take off the skin-deep covering, and in her it is noble diffidence, and a love that wants but to be assured!

Tell Mr Hickman I write this, and write it as I believe with my last pen; and bid him *bear* a little at first, and *forbear*; and all the future will be crowning gratitude and rewarding love: for Miss Howe has great sense, fine judgement, and exalted generosity; and can such a one be ungrateful or easy under those obligations which his assiduity and obligingness (when he shall be so happy as to call her his) will lay her under to him!

As for me, never bride was so ready as I am. My wedding garments are bought—and though not fine or gaudy to the sight, though not adorned with jewels and set off with gold and silver (for I have no beholders' eyes to wish to glitter in), yet will they be the easiest, the *happiest* suit, that ever bridal maiden wore—for they are such as carry with them a security against all those anxieties, pains, and perturbations, which sometimes succeed to the most promising outsettings.

And now, my dear Mrs Norton, do I wish for no other.

Oh hasten, good God, if it be thy blessed will, the happy moment that I am to be decked out in this all-quieting garb! And sustain, comfort, bless, and protect with the all-shadowing wing of thy mercy, my dear parents, my uncles, my brother, my sister, my cousin Morden, my ever-dear and ever-kind Miss Howe, my good Mrs Norton, and every deserving person to whom *they* wish well! is the ardent prayer, first and last, of every beginning hour, as the clock tells it me (hours now are days, nay years), of

> Your now not sorrowing or afflicted, but happy
> CLARISSA HARLOWE

Letter 466: MR LOVELACE TO JOHN BELFORD, ESQ.

Wed. morn. Sept 6, half an hour after three

I AM *not* the savage which you and my worst enemies think me. My soul is *too much* penetrated by the contents of the letter which you enclosed in your last, to say one word more to it than that my heart has bled over it from every vein!—I will fly from the subject—But what other can I choose that will not be as grievous, and lead into the same?

I could quarrel with all the world; with thee as well as the rest; obliging as thou supposest thyself for writing to me hourly. How daredst thou (though unknown to her) to presume to take an apartment under the same roof with her?—I cannot bear to think that thou shouldst be seen at all hours passing to and repassing from her apartments, while *I*, who have so much reason to call her mine, and once was preferred by her to all the world, am forced to keep aloof and hardly dare to enter the *city* where she is!

If there be anything in Brand's letter that will divert me, hasten it to me. But nothing now will ever divert me, will ever again give me joy or pleasure! I can neither eat, drink, nor sleep. I am sick of all the world.

Surely it will be better when *all is over*—when I know the *worst* the Fates can do against me—Yet how shall I bear that *worst?*—Oh Belford, Belford! write it not to me; but if it *must* happen, get somebody else to write; for I shall curse the pen, the hand, the head, and the heart, employed in communicating to me the fatal tidings. But what is this saying, when already I curse the whole world except her—myself most?

In fine, I am a most miserable being. Life is a burden to me. I would not bear it upon these terms for one week more, let what would be my lot; for already is there a hell begun in my own mind. Never more mention to me, let *her* or who will say it, the *prison*—I cannot bear it—May damnation seize quick the accursed woman who could set death upon taking that *large stride*, as the dear creature calls it!—I had no hand in it! But her relations, her implacable relations, have done the business. All else would have been got over. Never persuade me but it would. The fire of youth, and the violence of passion would have pleaded for me to good purpose with an individual of a sex which loves to be addressed with passionate ardour, even to tumult, had it not been for that cruelty and unforgivingness, which (the object and the penitence considered) have no example, and have aggravated the heinousness of my faults.

Unable to rest, though I went not to bed till two, I dispatch this ere the day dawn—Who knows what this night, this dismal night, may have produced!

I must after my messenger. I have told the varlet I will meet him, perhaps at Knightsbridge, perhaps in Piccadilly; and I trust not myself with pistols, not only on his account, but my own: for pistols are *too ready* a mischief.

I hope thou hast a letter ready for him. He goes to thy lodgings first: for surely thou wilt not presume to take thy rest in an apartment near hers. If he miss thee there, he flies to Smith's, and brings me word whether in being, or not.

I shall look for him through the air as I ride, as well as on horseback; for if the prince of it serve *me* as well as I have served *him*, he will bring the dog by his ears, like another Habakkuk[1] to my saddle-bow, with the tidings that my heart pants after.

Nothing but the excruciating pangs the condemned soul feels at its entrance into the eternity of the torments we are taught to fear, can exceed what I now feel, and have felt for almost this week past; and mayest thou have a spice of those, if thou hast not a letter ready written for

                                        Thy LOVELACE

Letter 467: MR BELFORD [TO ROBERT LOVELACE, ESQ.]

(In continuation)

Tuesday, Sept. 5, six o'clock

THE lady remains exceedingly weak and ill. Her intellects nevertheless continue clear and strong, and her piety and patience are without example. Everyone thinks this night will be her last. What a shocking thing is that to say of such an excellence! She will not however send away her letter to her Norton, as yet. She endeavoured in vain to superscribe it: so desired me to do it. Her fingers will not hold her pen with the requisite steadiness. She has, I fear, written and read her last!

Eight o'clock

SHE is somewhat better than she was. The doctor has been here, and thinks she will hold out yet a day or two. He has ordered her, as for some time past, only some little cordials to take when ready to faint. She seemed disappointed when he told her she might yet live two or three days; and said she longed for dismission!—Life was not so easily extinguished, she saw, as some imagine—*Death from grief* was, she believed, *the slowest of deaths*. But God's will must be done!—Her only prayer was now for submission to it: for she doubted not but by the Divine goodness she should be an happy creature as soon as she could be divested of these *rags of mortality*.

Of her own accord she mentioned you; which, till then, she had avoided to do. She asked with great serenity where you were?

I told her where; and your motives of being so near; and read to her a few lines of yours of this morning, in which you mention your wishes to see her, your sincere affliction, and your resolution not to approach her without her consent.

I would have read more; but she said: Enough, Mr Belford, enough!—Poor man! Does his conscience begin to find him!—Then need not anybody to wish him a greater punishment!—May it work upon him to a happy purpose!

I took the liberty to say that as she was in such a frame that nothing now seemed capable of discomposing her, I could wish that you might have the benefit of her exhortations, which I dared to say, while you were so seriously affected, would have a greater force upon you than a thousand sermons; and how happy you would think yourself if you could but receive her forgiveness on your knees.

How can you think of such a thing, Mr Belford, said she with some emotion? My composure is owing, next to the Divine goodness blessing my earnest supplications for it, to the *not* seeing him. Yet let him know that I now again repeat that I forgive him—and may God Almighty, clasping her fingers and lifting up her eyes, forgive him too; and perfect his repentance, and sanctify it to him!—Tell him I say so! And tell him that if I could not say so with my whole heart, I should be very uneasy, and think that my hopes of mercy to myself were but weakly founded; and that I had still, in any harboured resentments, some hankerings after a life which he has been the cause of shortening.

The divine creature then turning aside her head—Poor man, said she! I once could have loved him. This is saying more than ever I could say of any other man out of my own family! Would he have permitted me to have been a humble instrument to have made him good, I think I could have made him happy!—But tell him not this, if he be *really* penitent—It may too much affect him!—There she paused.

Admirable creature!—Heavenly forgiver!—Then resuming: But pray tell him that if I could know that my death might be a means to reclaim and save him, it would be an inexpressible satisfaction to me!

But let me not, however, be made uneasy with the apprehension of seeing him. I cannot *bear* to see him!

Just as she had done speaking, the minister, who had so often attended her, sent up his name; and was admitted.

Being apprehensive that it would be with difficulty that you could prevail upon that impetuous spirit of yours not to invade her dying hours, and of the agonies into which a surprise of this nature would throw her, I thought this gentleman's visit afforded a proper opportunity to renew the subject; and (having asked her leave) acquainted him with the topic we had been upon.

The good man urged that some condescensions were usually expected on these solemn occasions, from pious souls like hers, however satisfied with *themselves*, for the sake of showing the *world*, and for *example's sake*, that all resentments against those who had most injured them were subdued: and if she would vouchsafe to a heart so truly penitent, as I had represented Mr Lovelace's to be, that *personal* pardon which I had been pleading for, there would be no room to suppose the least lurking resentment remained; and it might have very happy effects upon the gentleman.

I have no lurking resentment, sir, said she—This is not a time for resentment: and you will be the readier to believe me when I can assure you (looking at me) that even what I have most rejoiced in, the truly friendly love that has so long subsisted between my Miss Howe and her Clarissa, although to my last gasp it will be the dearest to me of all that is dear in this life, has already abated of its fervour; has already given place to supremer fervours: and shall the remembrance of Mr Lovelace's *personal* insults which, I bless God, never corrupted that *mind* which her friendship so much delighted, be stronger in these hours with me than the remembrance of love as pure as the human heart ever boasted? Tell, therefore, the *world*, if you please, and (if you think what I said to you before, Mr Belford, not strong enough) tell the poor man that I not only forgive him, but have *such* earnest wishes for the good of his soul, and that from considerations of its immortality, that could my penitence avail for more sins than my own, my last tear should fall for him by whom I die!

Our eyes and hands expressed for us both what our lips could not utter.

Say not then, proceeded she, nor let it be said, that my resentments are unsubdued!—And yet these eyes, lifted up to Heaven as witness to the truth of what I have said, shall never if I can help it behold him more!—For do ye not consider, sirs, how short my time is; what much more important subjects I have to employ it upon; and how unable I should be (so weak as I am) to contend even with the avowed penitence of a person in strong health, governed by passions unabated, and always violent?—And now I hope you will never urge me more on this subject.

The minister said it were pity ever to urge this plea again.

You see, Lovelace, that I did not forget the office of a friend, in endeavouring to prevail upon her to give you her last forgiveness personally. And I hope, as she is so near her end, you will not invade her in her last hours; since she must be extremely discomposed at such an interview; and it might make her leave the world the sooner for it.

This reminds me of an expression which she used on your barbarous hunting her at Smith's on her return to her lodgings; and that with a serenity unexampled (as Mrs Lovick told me, considering the occasion, and the trouble given her by it, and her indisposition at the time): He will not let me die decently, said the angelic sufferer!—He will not let me enter into my Maker's presence with the composure that is required in entering into the drawing room of an earthly prince!

I cannot, however, forbear to wish that the heavenly creature could have prevailed upon herself, in these her last hours, to see you; and that for my sake, as well as yours: for although I am determined never to be guilty of the crimes which have, till within these few past weeks, blackened my former life; and for which at present I most heartily hate myself; yet should I be less apprehensive of a relapse, if (wrought upon by the solemnity which such an interview must have been attended with) you had become a reformed man: for no devil do I fear, but one in your shape.

IT is now eleven o'clock at night. The lady, who retired to rest an hour ago, is in a sweet slumber, as Mrs Lovick tells me.

I will close here. I hope I shall find her the better for it in the morning. Yet, alas! how frail is hope! How frail is life; when we are apt to build so much on every shadowy relief; although in such a desperate case as this, sitting down to reflect, we *must* know that it is *but* shadowy!

I will enclose Brand's horrid pedantry. And for once am aforehand with thy ravenous impatience.

Mr Brand's recantation letters (one directed to his friend Mr [John Walton], the other to his patron Mr John Harlowe) are thought to be originals in their way: but as they are long, and as the reader has already been let into his singular character (see p. 1167 and p. 1189, and his Letter 444) and as this collection is run into an undesirable length, they are omitted.

Letter 470: MR LOVELACE TO JOHN BELFORD, ESQ.

Wed. morn. Sept. 6

AND is she somewhat better!—Blessings upon thee without number or measure! Let her still be better and better! *Tell* me so at least, if it be *not* so: for thou knowest not what a joy that poor temporary reprieve, that she will hold out yet a day or two, gave me.

But who told this hard-hearted and death-pronouncing doctor that she will hold it no longer? By what warrant says he this? What presumption in these parading solemn fellows of a college, which will be my contempt to the latest hour of my life, if this brother of it (eminent as he is deemed to be) cannot work an ordinary miracle in *her* favour, or rather in *mine*.

Let me tell thee, Belford, that already he deserves the *utmost* contempt for suffering this charming clock to run down so low. What must be his art, if it could not wind it up in a quarter of the time he has attended her, when at his first visits the springs and wheels of life and motion were so good that they seemed only to want common care and oiling!

I am obliged to you for endeavouring to engage her to see me. 'Twas like a friend. If she had vouchsafed me that favour, she should have seen at her feet the most abject adorer that ever kneeled to justly offended beauty.

What she bid you, and what she *forbid* you, to tell me (the latter for *tender* considerations); that she forgives me; and that, could she have made me a *good* man, she could have made me a *happy* one! That she even loved me! At such a moment to own that she once loved me! Never before loved any man! That she prays for me! That her last tear should be shed for me, could she by it save a soul, without *her*, doomed to perdition!—Oh Belford, Belford! I cannot bear it!—What a dog, what a devil, have I been to so superlative a goodness!—Why does she not inveigh against me?—Why does she not execrate me?—Oh the triumphant subduer! Ever above me!—And now to leave me so infinitely below her!

Marry and repair, at any time; this (wretch that I was!) was my plea to myself. To give her a lowering sensibility; to bring her down from among the stars which her beamy head was surrounded by, that my wife, so greatly above me, might not too much despise me—this was part of my reptile envy, owing to my *more* reptile apprehension of inferiority—Yet [she], from step to step, from distress to distress, to maintain her superiority; and, like the sun, to break out upon me with the greater refulgence for the clouds that I had contrived to cast about her—And now to escape me thus!—No power left me to repair her wrongs!—No alleviation to my self-reproach!—No dividing of blame with her!—

Tell her, Oh tell her, Belford, that her prayers and wishes, her superlatively generous prayers and wishes, shall *not* be vain: that I *can*, and *do*, repent—and *long* have repented—Tell her of my frequent deep remorses—It was impossible that such remorse should not at last produce *effectual* remorses—Yet she must not leave me—she must live, if she would wish to have my contrition perfect—for what can despair produce?—

I WILL do everything you would have me do in the return of your letters. You have infinitely obliged me by this last, and by pressing for an admission for me, though it succeeded not.

Once more, how could I be such a villain to so divine a creature! Yet love her all the time, as never man loved woman!—Curse upon my contriving genius! Curse upon my intriguing head, and upon my seconding heart!—To sport with the fame, with the honour, with the life, of such an angel of a woman!—Oh my damned incredulity!—that, believing her to *be* a woman, I must hope to *find* her a woman!—On my incredulity that there could be such virtue (virtue for *virtue*'s sake) in the sex, founded I my hope of succeeding with her.

But say not, Jack, that she must leave us yet—If she recover—and if I can but re-obtain her favour, then indeed will life be life to me—The world never *saw* such an husband as I will make. I will have no will but hers: she shall conduct me in all my steps: she shall open and direct my prospects, and turn every motion of my heart, as she pleases.

You tell me in your letter that at eleven o'clock she had sweet rest; and my servant acquaints me from Mrs Smith that she has had a good night. What hopes does this fill me with! I have given the fellow five guineas for his good news, to be divided between him and his fellow-servant.

Dear, dear Jack! confirm this to me in thy next—for Heaven's sake do!—Tell the doctor I will make him a present of a thousand guineas if he recover her—Ask if a consultation be necessary.

Adieu, dear Belford!—Confirm, I beseech thee, the hopes that now with sovereign gladness have taken possession of a heart that, next to hers, is

Thine.

Letter 471: MR BELFORD TO ROBERT LOVELACE, ESQ.

Wed. morn, eight o'clock (6 Sept.)

YOUR servant arrived here before I was stirring. I sent him to Smith's to inquire how the lady was; and ordered him to call upon me when he came back. I was pleased to hear she had had tolerable rest; and as soon as I had dispatched him with the letter I had written overnight, I went to attend her.

I found her up and dressed; in a white satin nightgown. Ever elegant; but now more so than I had seen her for a week past; her aspect serenely cheerful.

She mentioned the increased dimness of her eyes, and the tremor which had invaded her limbs. If this be dying, said she, there is nothing at all shocking in it. My body hardly sensible of pain, my mind at ease, my intellects clear and perfect as ever. What a good and gracious God have I!—For this is what I always prayed for.

I told her it was not so serene with you.

There is not the same reason for it, replied she. 'Tis a choice comfort, Mr Belford, at the winding-up of our short story, to be able to say I have rather *suffered* injuries *myself*, than *offered* them to *others*. I bless God, though I have been unhappy as the *world* deems it, and once I thought more so than at present I do; yet have I not wilfully made any one creature so. I have no reason to grieve for anything but for the sorrow I have given my friends.

But pray, Mr Belford, remember me in the best manner to my cousin Morden; and desire him to comfort them and to tell them that all would have been the same, had they accepted of my true penitence, as I wish and as I trust the Almighty has done.

I was called down; it was to Harry, who was just returned from Miss Howe's to whom he carried the lady's letter. The stupid fellow, being bid to make haste with it and return as soon as possible, stayed not till Miss Howe had it, she being at the distance of five miles, although Mrs Howe would have had him stay, and sent a man and horse purposely with it to her daughter.

Wednesday morning, 10 o'clock

THE poor lady is just recovered from a fainting fit, which has left her at death's door. Her late tranquillity and freedom from pain seemed but a *lightening*, as Mrs Lovick and Mrs Smith call it.

By my faith, Lovelace, I had rather part with all the friends I have in the world, than with this lady: I never knew what a virtuous, a holy friendship, as I may call mine to her, was before. But to be so *new* to it, and to be obliged to forgo it so soon, what an affliction! Yet, thank Heaven, I lose her not by *my own* fault!—But 'twould be barbarous not to spare thee now.

She has sent for the divine who visited her before, in order to pray with her.

Letter 472: MR LOVELACE TO JOHN BELFORD, ESQ.

Kensington, Wednesday noon

LIKE Aesop's traveller, thou blowest hot and cold, life and death, in the same breath, with a view no doubt to distract me. How familiarly dost thou use the words, *dying, dimness, tremor?* Never did any mortal ring so many changes on so few bells. Thy true father, I dare swear, was a butcher, or an undertaker, by the delight thou seemest to take in scenes of horror and death. Thy barbarous reflection that thou losest her not by thy own fault is never to be forgiven. Thou hast but one way to atone for the torments thou givest me, and that is by sending me word that she is better, and will recover. Whether it be true or not, let me be told so, and I will go abroad rejoicing and believing it, and my wishes and imagination shall make out all the rest.

If she live but one year, that I may acquit myself *to* myself (no matter for the world!) that her death is not owing to me, I will compound for the rest.

Will neither vows nor prayers save her? I never prayed in my life, put all the years of it together, as I have done for this fortnight past: and I have most sincerely repented of all my baseness to her—And will nothing do?

But after all, if she recover not, this reflection must be my comfort; and it is *truth*; that her departure will be owing rather to wilfulness, to downright female wilfulness, than to any other cause.

It is difficult for people who pursue the dictates of a violent resentment to stop where first they designed to stop.

I have the charity to believe that even James and Arabella Harlowe at first intended no more by the confederacy they formed against this their angel sister, than to disgrace and keep her down, lest (sordid wretches!) their uncles should follow the example her grandfather had set, to *their* detriment.

Many a man who at first intended only to try if a girl would resent a petty freedom, finding himself unchecked, or only lightly and laughingly put by, has been encouraged to attempt the last point, and has triumphed where once he presumed not to make the most distant approach but with fear and trembling, and previous study how to come off in case of a high resentment.

To bring these illustrations home; this lady, I suppose, in her resentment intended only at first to vex and plague me; and finding she could do it to purpose, her desire of revenge became stronger in her than the desire of life; and now she is willing to die as an event which she supposes will cut my heart-strings asunder. And still the more to be revenged puts on the Christian, and forgives me.

But I'll have none of her forgiveness! My own heart tells me I do not deserve it; and I cannot bear it!—And what is it but a mere *verbal* forgiveness, as ostentatiously as cruelly given with a view to magnify herself, and wound me deeper? A little, dear, specious—but let me stop—lest I blaspheme!

READING over the above, I am ashamed of my ramblings: but what wouldst have me do?—Seest thou not that I am but seeking to run out of myself in hope to lose myself; yet, that I am unable to do either?

If *ever* thou lovedst but half so fervently as I love—but of that thy heavy soul is not capable.

Send me word by thy next, I conjure thee, in the names of all her kindred saints and angels, that she is living, and likely to live!—If thou sendest ill news; thou wilt be answerable for the consequence, whether it be fatal to the messenger or to

Thy LOVELACE

Letter 473: MR BELFORD TO ROBERT LOVELACE, ESQ.

Wednesday, 11 o'clock

DR H. has just been here. He tarried with me till the minister had done praying by the lady; and then we were both admitted. Mr Goddard (who came while the doctor and the clergyman were with her) went away with them when they went. They took a solemn and everlasting leave of her, as I have no scruple to say, blessing her, and being blessed by her; and wishing (when it came to be their lot) for an exit as happy as hers is likely to be.

She had again earnestly requested of the doctor his opinion how long it was *now* probable that she could continue: and he told her that he apprehended she would hardly see tomorrow night. She said she should number the hours with greater pleasure than ever she numbered any in her life on the most joyful occasion.

How unlike poor Belton's last hours, hers! See the infinite difference in the effects, on the same awful and affecting occasion, between a good and a bad conscience!

This moment a man is come from Miss Howe with a letter. Perhaps I shall be able to send you the contents.

SHE endeavoured several times with earnestness, but in vain, to read the letter of her dear friend—The writing, she said, was too fine for her grosser sight, and the lines staggered under her eye. And indeed she trembled so, she could not hold the paper: and at last desired Mrs Lovick to read it to her, the messenger waiting for an answer.

Thou wilt see in Miss Howe's letter, how different the expression of the same impatiency and passionate love is, when dictated by the gentler mind of a woman, from that which results from a mind so boisterous and knotty as thine. For Mrs Lovick will transcribe it; and I shall send it—to be read in this place, if thou wilt.

[*Letter 473.1: Miss Howe to Miss Clarissa Harlowe*]

Tuesday, Sept. 5

Oh my dearest friend!

WHAT will become of your poor Anna Howe! I see by your writing, as well as read by your own account (which, were you not very, *very* ill, you would have touched more tenderly), how it is with you!—Why have I thus long delayed to attend you!—Could I think that the comfortings of a faithful friend were as nothing to a gentle mind in distress, that I could be prevailed upon to forbear visiting you so much as *once* in all this time!—I, as well as everybody else, to desert and abandon my dear creature to strangers!—What will become of me if you be as bad as my apprehensions make you!

I will set out this moment, little as the encouragement is that you give me to do so!—My mother is willing I should!—Why, oh why, was she not *before* willing!

Yet she persuades me too (lest I should be fatally affected were I to find my fears too well justified) to wait the return of this messenger, who rides our swiftest horse—God speed him with good news to me—else—but, oh! my dearest, dearest friend, what else!—One line from your hand by him!—Send me but *one* line to bid me attend you!—I will set out the moment, the very moment, I receive it—I am now actually ready to do so!—And if you love me, as I love you, the sight of me will revive you to my hopes. But why, why, when I can think this, did I not go up sooner?

Blessed Heaven! deny not to my prayers, my friend, my monitress, my adviser, at a time so critical to myself!

But methinks your style and sentiments are too well connected, too full of life and vigour to give cause for so much despair as the staggering pen seems to threaten.

I am sorry I was not at home (I *must* add thus much though the servant is ready mounted at the door) when Mr Belford's servant came with your affecting letter. I was at Miss Lloyd's. My mamma sent it to me; and I came home that instant. But he was gone. He would not stay, it seems. Yet I wanted to ask him a hundred thousand questions. But why delay I thus my messenger? I have a multitude of things to say to you. To advise with you about! You shall direct me in everything. I will obey the holding up of your finger. But, if *you* leave me—what is the world, or anything in it, to

Your ANNA HOWE?

The effect this letter had on the lady, who is so near the end which the fair writer so much apprehends and deplores, obliged Mrs Lovick to make many breaks in reading it, and many changes of voice.

This *is* a friend, said the divine lady (taking the letter in her hand, and kissing it), worth wishing to live for—Oh my dear Anna Howe! How uninterruptedly sweet and noble has been our friendship!—But we shall one day, I hope (and that must comfort us both), meet, never to part again! Then, divested of the shades of body, shall we be all light and all mind—Then how unalloyed, how perfect, will be our friendship! Our love then will have one and the same adorable object, and we shall enjoy it and each other to all eternity!

She said her dear friend was so earnest for a line or two, that she would fain write if she could: and she tried; but to no purpose. She could dictate, however, she believed, and desired Mrs Lovick would take pen and paper. Which she did, and then she dictated to *her*. I would have withdrawn; but at her desire stayed.

She wandered a good deal at first—She took notice that she did—And when she got into a little train, not pleasing herself, she apologized to Mrs Lovick for making her begin again and again; and said that third time should go, let it be as it would.

She dictated the farewell part, without hesitation; and when she came to the blessing and subscription, she took the pen, and dropping on her knees, supported by Mrs Lovick, wrote the conclusion; but Mrs Lovick was forced to guide her hand.

You will find the sense surprisingly entire, her weakness considered.

I made the messenger wait while I transcribed it. I have endeavoured to imitate the subscriptive part.

[*Letter 473.2: Miss Clarissa Harlowe to Miss Howe*]

Wed. near 3 o'clock

My dearest Miss Howe,
You must not be surprised—nor grieved—that Mrs Lovick writes for me. Although I cannot obey you and write with my *pen*, yet my *heart* writes by hers—Accept it so—It is the nearest to obedience I can!

And now, what *ought* I to say? What *can* I say?—But why should you not know the truth? Since soon you must—very soon.

Know then, and let your tears be those, if of pity, of *joyful* pity! for I permit you to shed a few to embalm, as I may say, a fallen blossom—Know then that the good doctor, and the pious clergyman, and the worthy apothecary, have just now with joint benedictions taken their last leave of me: and the former bids me hope—do, my dearest, let me say *hope*—for my enlargement before tomorrow sunset.

Adieu, therefore, my dearest friend! Be this your consolation, as it is mine, that in God's good time we shall meet in a blessed eternity, never more to part!—Once more, then, adieu and be happy!—which a generous nature cannot be, unless to its power it makes others so too.

God for ever bless you! prays, dropt on my bended
Knees, altho' ſupported upon them,

Your Grateful, Obliged, Affectionate,
Clar. Harlowe.

When I had transcribed and sealed this letter, by her direction, I gave it to the messenger myself; who told me that Miss Howe waited for nothing but his return, to set out for London.

Thy servant is just come; so I will close here. Thou art a merciless master. The two fellows are *battered* to death by thee, to use a female word; and all female words, though we are not sure of their derivation, have very significant meanings. I believe, in their hearts, they wish the angel in the heaven that is ready to receive her, and thee at thy proper place, that there might be an end of their *flurries*; another word of the same gender.

What a letter hast thou sent me!—Poor Lovelace!—is all the answer I will return.

(*Five o'clock.*) Colonel Morden is this moment arrived.

Letter 474: MR BELFORD TO ROBERT LOVELACE, ESQ.

Eight in the evening

I HAD but just time in my former to tell you that Colonel Morden was arrived. He was on horseback, attended by two servants, and alit at the door just as the clock struck five. Mrs Smith was then below in her back shop, weeping, her husband with her, who was as much affected as she; Mrs Lovick having left them a little before, in tears likewise; for they had been bemoaning one another; joining in opinion that the admirable lady would not live the night over. She had told them it was *her* opinion too, from some numbnesses, which she called the forerunners of death, and from an increased inclination to doze.

The colonel, as Mrs Smith told me afterwards, asked with great impatience, the moment he alit, how Miss Harlowe was? She answered, Alive; but, she feared, drawing on apace. Good God! said he, with his hands and eyes lifted up. Can I see her? My name is Morden. I have the honour to be nearly related to her. Step up, pray; and let her know (She is sensible, I hope) that I am here. Who is with her?

Nobody but her nurse, and Mrs Lovick, a widow gentlewoman who is as careful of her as if she were her mother.

And *more* careful too, interrupted he, or she is not careful at all—

Except a gentleman be with her, one Mr Belford, continued Mrs Smith, who has been the best friend she has had.

If Mr Belford be with her, surely I may—But, pray, step up and let Mr Belford know that I shall take it for a favour to speak with him first.

Mrs Smith came up to me in my new apartment. I had but just dispatched your servant, and was asking her nurse if I might be again admitted; who answered that she was dozing in the elbow-chair, having refused to lie down, saying she should soon, she hoped, lie down for good.

The colonel, who is really a fine gentleman, received me with great politeness. After the first compliments, My kinswoman, sir, said he, is more obliged to you than to any of her own family. For my part, I have been endeavouring to move so many rocks in her favour; and, little thinking the dear creature so very bad, have neglected to attend her, as I ought to have done the moment I arrived; and *would*, had I known how ill she was, and what a task I should have had with the family. But, sir, your friend has been excessively to blame; and you being so *intimately* his friend has made her fare the worse for your civilities to her. But is there no hope of her recovery?

The doctors have left her with the melancholy declaration that there is none.

Has she had good attendance, sir? A skilful physician? I hear these good folks have been very civil and obliging to her—

Who could be otherwise, said Mrs Smith, weeping? She is the sweetest lady in the world!

The character, said the colonel, lifting up his eyes and one hand, that she has from every living creature!—Good God! How could your accursed friend—

And how could her cruel parents, interrupted I?—We may as easily account for *him*, as for *them*.

Too true! returned he, the vileness of the profligates of our sex considered, whenever they can get any of the other into their power.

I satisfied him about the care that had been taken of her; and told him of the friendly and even *paternal* attendance she had had from Dr H. and Mr Goddard.

He was impatient to attend her, having not seen her, as he said, since she was twelve years old; and that then she gave promises of being one of the finest women in England.

She *was* so, replied I, a very few months ago: and, though emaciated, she will appear to you to have confirmed those promises: for her features are so regular and exact, her proportion so fine, and her manner so inimitably graceful, that were she only skin and bone, she must be a beauty.

Mrs Smith, at his request, stepped up, and brought us down word that Mrs Lovick and her nurse were with her; and that she was in so sound a sleep, leaning upon the former in her elbow-chair, that she neither heard her enter the room, nor go out. The colonel begged, if not improper, that he might see her, though sleeping. He said that his impatience would not let him stay till she awaked. Yet he would not have her disturbed; and should be glad to contemplate her sweet features when she saw not him; and asked if she thought he could not go in and come out, without disturbing her?

She believed he might, she answered; for her chair's back was towards the door.

He said he would take care to withdraw if she awoke, that his sudden appearance might not surprise her.

Mrs Smith, stepping up before us, bid Mrs Lovick and the nurse not stir when we entered: and then we went up softly together.

We beheld the lady in a charming attitude. Dressed, as I told you before, in her virgin white, she was sitting in her elbow-chair, Mrs Lovick close by her in another chair, with her left arm round her neck, supporting it as it were; for it seems the lady had bid her do so, saying she had been a mother to her, and she would delight herself in thinking she was in her mamma's arms; for she found herself drowsy; perhaps, she said, for the last time she should ever be so.

One faded cheek rested upon the good woman's bosom, the kindly warmth of which had overspread it with a faint, but charming flush; the other paler, and hollow, as if already iced over by death. Her hands, white as the lily, with her meandering veins more transparently blue than ever I had seen even hers (veins so soon, alas! to be choked up by the congealment of that purple stream, which already so languidly creeps rather than flows through them!), her hands hanging lifelessly, one before her, the other grasped by the right hand of the kind widow, whose tears bedewed the sweet face which her motherly bosom supported, though unfelt by the fair sleeper; and either insensibly to the good woman, or what she would not disturb her to wipe off, or to change her posture. Her aspect was sweetly calm and serene: and though she started now and then, yet her sleep seemed easy; her breath indeed short and quick; but tolerably free, and not like that of a dying person.

In this heart-moving attitude she appeared to us when we approached her, and came to have her lovely face before us.

The colonel sighing often, gazed upon her with his arms folded, and with the most profound and affectionate attention; till at last, on her starting, and fetching her breath with greater difficulty than before, he retired to a screen that was drawn before her *house*, as she calls it, which as I have heretofore observed stands under one of the windows. This screen was placed there, at the time she found herself obliged to take to her chamber; and in the depth of our concern, and the fulness of other discourse at our first interview, I had forgotten to apprise the colonel of what he would probably see.

Retiring thither, he drew out his handkerchief, and drowned in grief seemed unable to speak: but, on casting his eye behind the screen, he soon broke silence; for, struck with the shape of the coffin, he lifted up a purplish coloured cloth that was spread over it, and, starting back, Good God! said he, what's here!

Mrs Smith standing next him: Why, said he, with great emotion, is my cousin suffered to indulge her sad reflections with such an object before her?—

Alas! sir, replied the good woman, who should control her? We are all strangers about her, in a manner: and yet we have expostulated with her upon this sad occasion.

I ought, said I (stepping softly up to him, the lady again falling into a doze), to have apprised you of this. I was here when it was brought in, and never was so shocked in my life. But she had none of her friends about her, and no reason to hope for any of them to come near her; and, assured she should not recover, she was resolved to leave as little as possible, especially as to what related to her person, to her executor. But it is not a shocking object to her, though it be to everybody else.

Curse upon the hard-heartedness of those, said he, who occasioned her to make so sad a provision for herself! What must her reflections have been all the time she was thinking of it, and giving orders about it? And what must they be every time she turns her head towards it? These uncommon geniuses—But indeed she *should* have been controlled in it, had I been here.

The lady fetched a profound sigh, and, starting, it broke off our talk; and the colonel then withdrew further behind the screen, that his sudden appearance might not surprise her.

Where am I! said she. How drowsy I am! How long have I dozed? Don't go, sir (for I was retiring). I am very stupid, and shall be more and more so, I suppose.

She then offered to raise herself; but, being ready to faint through weakness, was forced to sit down again, reclining her head on her chair-back; and, after a few moments, I believe now, my good friends, said she, all your kind trouble will soon be over. I have slept, but am not refreshed, and my fingers' ends seem numbed— have no feeling! (holding them up)—'Tis time to send the letter to my good Mrs Norton.

Shall I, madam, send my servant post with it?

Oh no, sir, I thank you. It will reach the dear woman too soon (as she will think) by the post.

I told her this was not post-day.[1]

Is it Wednesday still? said she. Bless me! I know not how the time goes: but very tediously, 'tis plain. And now I think I must soon take to my bed. All will be most conveniently and with least trouble over there—Will it not, Mrs Lovick?—I think, sir, turning to me, I have left nothing to these last incapacitating hours: nothing either to say, or to do: I bless God, I have not: if I *had*, how unhappy should I be? Can you, sir, remind me of anything necessary to be done or said to make your office easy?

If, madam, your cousin Morden should come, you would be glad to see him, I presume?

I am too weak to wish to see my cousin now. It would but discompose me, and him too. Yet if he come while I *can* see, I will see him, were it but to thank him for former favours, and for his present kind intentions to me. Has anybody been here from him?

He has called, and will be here, madam, in half an hour; but he feared to surprise you.

Nothing can surprise me now, except my mamma were to favour me with her last blessing in person. That would be a welcome surprise to me even yet. But did my cousin come purposely to town to see me?

Yes, madam. I took the liberty to let him know by a line last Monday, how ill you were.

You are very kind, sir. I am and have been greatly obliged to you. But I think I shall be pained to see him now, because he will be concerned to see me. And yet, as I am not so ill as I shall presently be—the sooner he comes the better. But if he come, what shall I do about the screen? He will chide me very probably; and I cannot bear chiding now. Perhaps (leaning upon Mrs Lovick and Mrs Smith) I can walk into the next apartment to receive him.

She motioned to rise; but was ready to faint again, and forced to sit still.

The colonel was in a perfect agitation behind the screen, to hear this discourse; and twice, unseen by his cousin, was coming from it towards her; but retreated for fear of surprising her too much.

I stepped to him, and favoured his retreat; she only saying: Are you going, Mr Belford? Are you sent for down? Is my cousin come? For she heard somebody step softly cross the room; and thought it [to be] me, her hearing being more perfect than her sight.

I told her, I believed he was; and she said: We must make the best of it, Mrs Lovick and Mrs Smith. I shall otherwise most grievously shock my poor cousin: for he loved me dearly once. Pray give me a few of the doctor's last drops in water, to keep up my spirits for this one interview; and that is all, I believe, that can concern me now.

The colonel (who heard all this) sent in his name; and I, pretending to go down to him, introduced the afflicted gentleman; she having first ordered the screen to be put as close to the window as possible, that he might not see what was behind it; while he, having heard what she had said about it, was determined to take no notice of it.

He folded the angel in his arms as she sat, dropping down on one knee; for, supporting herself upon the two elbows of the chair, she attempted to rise, but could not. Excuse, my dear cousin, said she, excuse me, that I cannot stand up— I did not expect this favour now. But I am glad of this opportunity to thank you for all your generous goodness to me.

I never, my best-beloved and dearest cousin, said he (with eyes running over), shall forgive myself that I did not attend you sooner. Little did I think you were so ill; nor do any of your friends believe it. If they did—

If they did, repeated she, interrupting him, I should have had more compassion from them. I am sure I should. But pray, sir, how did you leave them? Are *you* reconciled to them? If you are not, I beg, if you love your poor Clarissa, that you will: for every widened difference augments but my fault; since *that* is the foundation of all.

I had been expecting to hear from them in your favour, my dear cousin, said he, for some hours, when this gentleman's letter arrived, which hastened me up: but I have the account of your grandfather's estate to make up with you, and have bills and drafts upon their banker for the sums due to you; which they desire you may receive, lest you should have occasion for money. And this is such an earnest of an approaching reconciliation, that I dare to answer for all the rest being according to your wishes, if—

Ah! sir, interrupted she, with frequent breaks and pauses, I wish, I wish this does not rather show that were I to live, they would have nothing more to say to me. I never had any pride in being independent of them: all my actions, when I might have made myself *more* independent, show this—But what avail these reflections now?—I only beg, sir, that you, and *this* gentleman—to whom I am exceedingly obliged—will adjust those matters—according to the will I have written. Mr Belford will excuse me; but it was in truth more necessity than choice that made me think of giving him the trouble he so kindly accepts. Had I had the happiness to see you, my cousin, sooner—or to know that you still honoured me with your regard—I should not have had the assurance to ask this favour of *him*— But—though the friend of Mr Lovelace, he is a man of honour, and he will make peace rather than break it. And, my dear cousin, let me beg of you—to contribute your part to it—and remember that, while I have nearer relations than my cousin Morden, dear as you are and always were to me, you have no title to avenge my wrongs upon him who has been the occasion of them. But I wrote to you my mind on this subject; and my reasons; and hope I need not further urge them.

I must do Mr Lovelace so much justice, answered he, wiping his eyes, as to witness how sincerely he repents him of his ungrateful baseness to you, and how ready he is to make you all the amends in his power. He owns *his* wickedness, and *your* merit. If he did not, I could not pass it over, though you *have* nearer relations: for, my dear cousin, did not your grandfather leave me in trust for you? And should I think myself concerned for your fortune, and not for your honour?—But, since he is so desirous to do you justice, I have the less to say; and you may make yourself entirely easy on that account.

I thank you, thank you, sir, said she: all is now as I wished: but I am very faint, very low. I am sorry I cannot hold up; that I cannot better deserve the honour of this visit: but it will not be—And saying this, she sunk down in her chair, and was silent.

Hereupon we both withdrew, leaving word that we would be at the Bedford Head, if anything extraordinary happened.

We bespoke a little repast, having neither of us dined; and while it was getting ready, you may guess at the subject of our discourse. Both joined in lamentation for the lady's desperate state: admired her manifold excellencies: severely condemned you and her friends. Yet, to bring him into better opinion of you, I read to him some passages from your last letters, which showed your concern for the wrongs you had done her, and your deep remorse: and he said it was a dreadful thing to labour under the sense of a guilt so irremediable.

We procured Mr Goddard (Dr H. being not at home) once more to visit her, and to call upon us on his return. He was so good as to do so; but he tarried with her not five minutes; and told us that she was drawing on apace; that he feared she would not live till morning; and that she wished to see Colonel Morden directly.

The colonel made excuses where none were needed: and though our little refection was just brought in, he went away immediately.

I could not touch a morsel; and took pen and ink to amuse myself, and oblige you, knowing how impatient you would be for a few lines: for, from what I have recited, you will see it was impossible I could withdraw to write when your servant came at half an hour after five, or have an opportunity for it till now; and *this* is accidental: and yet your poor fellow was afraid to go away with the verbal message I sent, importing, as no doubt he told you, that the colonel was with us, the lady excessively ill, and that I could not stir to write a line.

Ten o'clock

THE colonel sent to me afterwards, that the lady having been in convulsions, he was so much disordered that he could not possibly attend me.

I have sent every half hour to know how she does: and just now I have the pleasure to hear that her convulsions have left her; and that she is gone to rest in a much quieter way than could be expected.

Her poor cousin is very much indisposed; yet will not stir out of the house while she is in such a way; but intends to lie down on a couch, having refused any other accommodation.

Letter 475: MR BELFORD [TO ROBERT LOVELACE, ESQ.]

(In continuation)

Soho, six o'clock, Sept. 7

THE lady is still alive. The colonel having just sent his servant to let me know that she inquired after me about an hour ago, I am dressing to attend her. Joel begs of me to dispatch him back, though but with one line to gratify your present impatience. He expects, he says, to find you at Knightsbridge, let him make what haste he can back; and if he has not a line or two to pacify you, he is afraid you will pistol him; for he apprehends that you are hardly yourself. I therefore dispatch this; and will have another ready as soon as I can, with particulars. But you must have a little patience; for how can I withdraw every half hour to write, if I am admitted to the lady's presence, or if I am with the colonel?

Smith's, 8 o'clock in the morning

THE lady is in a slumber. Mrs Lovick, who sat up with her, says she had a better night than was expected; for although she slept little, she seemed easy; and the easier for the pious frame she was in; all her waking moments being taken up in devotion, or in an ejaculatory silence; her hands and eyes often lifted up, and her lips moving with a fervour worthy of these her last hours.

Ten o'clock

THE colonel being earnest to see his cousin as soon as she awaked, we were both admitted. We observed in her, as soon as we entered, strong symptoms of her approaching dissolution, notwithstanding what the women had flattered us with from her last night's tranquillity. The colonel and I, each loath to say what we thought, looked upon one another with melancholy countenances.

The colonel told her he should send a servant to her uncle Antony's, for some papers he had left there; and asked if she had any commands that way?—She thought not, she said, speaking more inwardly than she did the day before. She had indeed a letter ready to be sent to her good Mrs Norton; and there was a request intimated in it. But it was time enough, if it were signified to those whom it concerned when all was over. However, it might be sent then by the servant who was going that way. And she caused it to be given to the colonel for that purpose.

Her breath being very short, she desired another pillow; and having two before, this made her in a manner sit up in her bed; and she spoke then with more distinctness; and seeing us greatly concerned, forgot her own sufferings to comfort us; and a charming lecture she gave us, though a brief one, upon the happiness of a timely preparation and upon the hazards of a late repentance, when the mind, as she observed, was so much weakened, as well as the body, as to render a poor soul unable to contend with its own infirmities.

I beseech ye, my good friends, proceeded she, mourn not for one who mourns not, nor has cause to mourn, for herself. On the contrary, rejoice with me that all my worldly troubles are so near their end. Believe me, sirs, that I would not, if I might, choose to live, although the pleasantest part of my life were to come over again: and yet eighteen years of it, out of nineteen, have been *very* pleasant. To be so much exposed to temptation, and to be so liable to fail in the trial, who would not rejoice that all her dangers are over!—All I wished was pardon and blessing from my dear parents. Easy as my departure seems to promise to be, it would have been still easier had I had that pleasure. BUT GOD ALMIGHTY WOULD NOT LET ME DEPEND FOR COMFORT UPON ANY BUT HIMSELF.

She then repeated her request, in the most earnest manner, to her *cousin*, that he would not *heighten* her fault by seeking to avenge her death; to *me*, that I would endeavour to make up all breaches, and use the power I had with my friend to prevent all future mischiefs *from* him, as well as that which this trust might give me to prevent any *to* him.

She made some excuses to her *cousin* for having not been able to alter her will to join him in the executorship with me; and to *me* for the trouble she had given and yet should give me.

She had fatigued herself so much (growing sensibly weaker) that she sunk her head upon her pillows, ready to faint; and we withdrew to the window, looking upon one another; but could not tell what to say; and yet both seemed inclinable to speak: but the motion passed over in silence. Our eyes only spoke; and that in a manner neither's were used to; mine, at least, not till I knew this admirable creature.

The colonel withdrew to dismiss his messenger, and send away the letter to Mrs Norton. I took the opportunity to retire likewise; and to write thus far. And Joel returning to take it; I now close here.

Eleven o'clock

Letter 476: MR BELFORD [TO ROBERT LOVELACE, ESQ.]

(In continuation)

THE colonel tells me that he has written to Mr John Harlowe by his servant, 'That they might spare themselves the trouble of debating about a reconciliation; for that his dear cousin would probably be no more, before they could resolve.'

He asked me after his cousin's means of subsisting; and whether she had accepted of any favour from *me*: he was sure, he said, she would not from *you*.

I acquainted him with the truth of her parting with some of her apparel. This wrung his heart; and bitterly did he exclaim as well against you, as against her implacable relations.

He wished he had not come to England at all, or had come time enough; and hoped I would apprise him of the whole mournful story, at a proper season. He added that he had thoughts when he came over of fixing here for the remainder of his days: but now, as it was impossible his cousin could recover, he would go abroad again, and resettle himself at Florence or Leghorn.

THE lady has been giving orders with great presence of mind about her body: directing her nurse and the maid of the house to put her into her coffin as soon as she was cold. Mr Belford, she said, would know the rest by her will.

SHE has just now given from her bosom, where she always wore it, a miniature picture set in gold of Miss Howe: she gave it to Mrs Lovick, desiring her to fold it up in white paper, and direct it *To Charles Hickman, Esq.*; and to give it to me, when she was departed, for that gentleman.

She looked upon the picture before she gave it her—*Sweet and ever-amiable friend—companion—sister—lover*! said she—and kissed it four several times, once at each tender appellation.

YOUR other servant is come—Well may you be impatient!—Well may you!—But do you think I can leave off in the middle of a conversation, to run and set down what offers, and send it away piecemeal as I write?—If I *could*, must I not lose one half, while I put down the other?

The event is nearly as interesting to *me* as it is to *you*. If you are more grieved than I, there can be but one reason for it; and that's at your heart! I had rather lose all the friends I have in the world (yourself included) than this divine lady; and shall be unhappy whenever I think of her sufferings, and her merit; though I have nothing to reproach myself upon the former.

I say not this, just now, so much to reflect upon you, as to express my own grief; though your conscience I suppose will make you think otherwise.

Your poor fellow, who says that he begs for *his life*, in desiring to be dispatched back with a letter, tears this from me. Else, perhaps (for I am just sent for down), a quarter of an hour would make you—not *easy* indeed—but *certain*—And that, in a *state* like yours to a *mind* like yours, is a relief.

Thursday afternoon, 4 o'clock

Letter 477: MR BELFORD TO RICHARD MOWBRAY, ESQ.

Thursday afternoon

Dear Mowbray,

I AM glad to hear you are in town. Throw yourself the moment this comes to your hand (if possible with Tourville) in the way of the man who least of all men deserves the love of the worthy heart; but most that of thine and his: else, the news I shall most probably send him within an hour or two, will make annihilation the greatest blessing he has to wish for.

You will find him between Piccadilly and Kensington, most probably on horseback, riding backwards and forwards in a crazy way; or put up, perhaps, at some inn or tavern in the way; a waiter possibly, if so, watching for his servant's return to him from me.

HIS man Will is just come to me. He will carry this to you in his way back, and be your director. Hie away, in a coach or any how. Your being with him may save either his or a servant's life. See the blessed effects of triumphant libertinism! Sooner or later it comes home to us, and all concludes in gall and bitterness! Adieu.

J. BELFORD

Letter 478: MR LOVELACE TO JOHN BELFORD, ESQ.

CURSE upon the colonel, and curse upon the writer of the last letter I received, and upon all the world! Thou to pretend to be as much interested in my Clarissa's fate as myself! 'Tis well for one of us that this was not said to me, instead of written—Living or dying, she is mine—and only mine. Have I not earned her dearly?—Is not damnation likely to be the purchase to me, though a happy eternity will be hers?

An eternal separation! Oh God! Oh God!—How can I bear that thought!—But yet there is life—Yet, therefore, hope—enlarge my hope, and thou shalt be my good genius, and I will forgive thee everything.

For this last time—but it must not, shall not, be the *last*—let me hear the moment thou receivest this—what I *am* to be—for at present I am

The most miserable of men

Rose, at Knightsbridge, 5 o'clock

My fellow tells me that thou art sending Mowbray and Tourville to me. I want them not. My soul's sick of them, and of all the world; but most of myself—Yet, as they send me word they will come to me immediately, I will wait for them, and for thy next. Oh Belford! let it not be—But hasten it, hasten it, be it what it may!

Letter 479: MR BELFORD TO ROBERT LOVELACE, ESQ.

Seven o'clock, Thursday even. Sept. 7

I HAVE only to say at present—Thou wilt do well to take a tour to Paris; or wherever else thy destiny shall lead thee!!!——

JOHN BELFORD

Letter 480: MR MOWBRAY TO JOHN BELFORD, ESQ.

Uxbridge, Sept. 7, between 11 and 12 at night

Dear Jack,

I SEND by poor Lovelace's desire, for *particulars* of the fatal breviate thou sentest him this night. He cannot bear to set pen to paper; yet wants to know every minute passage of Miss Harlowe's departure. Yet, why he should, I cannot see; for, if she is gone, she is gone; and who can help it?

I never heard of such a woman in my life. What great matters has she suffered, that grief should kill her thus?

I wish the poor fellow had never known her. From first to last, what trouble has she cost him! The charming fellow has been half lost to us, ever since he pursued her. And what is there in one woman more than another, for matter of that?

It was well we were with him when your note came. You showed your true friendship in your foresight. Why, Jack, the poor fellow was quite beside himself—mad as any man ever was in Bedlam.

Will brought him the letter, just after we had joined him at the Bohemia Head,[1] where he had left word at the Rose at Knightsbridge he should be; for he had been sauntering up and down, backwards and forwards, expecting us, and his fellow, Will, as soon as he delivered it, got out of his way; and when he opened it, never was such a piece of scenery. He trembled like a devil at receiving it: fumbled at the seal, his fingers in a palsy, like Tom Doleman's; his hand shake, shake, shake, that he tore the letter in two before he could come at the contents: and when he had read them, off went his hat to one corner of the room, his wig to the other— Damnation seize the world! and a whole volley of such-like *execratious* wishes; running up and down the room, and throwing up the sash, and pulling it down, and smiting his forehead with his double fist, with such force as would have felled an ox, and stamping and tearing, that the landlord ran in, and faster out again. And this was the distraction-scene for some time.

In vain was all Jemmy or I could say to him. I offered once to take hold of his hands, because he was going to do himself a mischief, as I believed, looking about for his pistols which he had laid upon the table, but which Will unseen had taken out with him (a faithful honest dog, that Will; I shall for ever love the fellow for it), and he hit me a damned dowse of the chops, as made my nose bleed. 'Twas well 'twas he; for I hardly knew how to take it.

Jemmy raved at him, and told him how wicked it was in him to be so brutish to abuse a friend, and run mad for a woman. And then he said he was sorry for it; and then Will ventured in with water and a towel; and the dog rejoiced, as I could see by his looks, that I *had it* rather than he.

And so, by degrees, we brought him a little to his reason, and he promised to behave more like a man. And so I forgave him: and we rode on in the dark to here at Doleman's. And we all tried to shame him out of his mad ungovernable foolishness: for we told him as how she was but a woman, and an obstinate, perverse woman too; and how could he help it?

And you know, Jack (as we told him, moreover), that it was a shame to manhood for a man who had served twenty and twenty women as bad or worse, let him have served Miss Harlowe never so bad, should give himself such *obstropulous* airs, because she would die: and we advised him never to attempt a woman proud of her character and *virtue*, as they call it, any more: for why? The conquest did not pay trouble; and what was there in one woman more than another? Hey, you know, Jack!—And thus we comforted him, and advised him.

But yet his damned addled pate runs upon this lady as much now she's dead as it did when she was living. For, I suppose, Jack, it is no joke. She is certainly and *bona fide* dead; i'n't she? If not, thou deservest to be doubly damned for thy fooling, I tell thee that. So he will have me write for particulars of her *departure*.

He won't bear the word *dead* on any account. A squeamish puppy! How love unmans, and softens, and enervates! And such a *noble* fellow as this too! Rot him for an idiot, and an oaf! I have no patience with the foolish *duncical* dog—upon my soul, I have not!

So send the account, and let him howl over it, as I suppose he will.

But he must and shall go abroad: and in a month or two, Jemmy, and you and I will join him, and he'll soon get the better of this chicken-hearted folly, never fear; and will then be ashamed of himself: and then we'll not spare him; though *now*, poor fellow, it were pity to lay him on so thick as he deserves. And do thou, till then, spare all reflections upon him; for, it seems, thou hast *worked* him unmercifully.

I was willing to give thee some account of the hand we have had with the tearing fellow, who had certainly been a lost man had we not been with him; or he would have killed somebody or other—I have no doubt of it. And *now* he is but very middling; sits grinning like a man in straw[2]; curses and swears, and is confounded gloomy; and creeps into holes and corners like an old hedgehog hunted for his grease. And so adieu, Jack. Tourville and all of us wish for thee; for no one has the influence upon him that thou hast.

R. MOWBRAY

As I promised him that I would write for the particulars abovesaid, I write this after all are gone to bed; and the fellow is to set out with it by daybreak.

Letter 481: MR BELFORD TO ROBERT LOVELACE, ESQ.

Thursday night

I MAY as well try to write; since, were I to go to bed, I shall not sleep. I never had such a weight of grief upon my mind in my life, as upon the demise of this admirable woman; whose soul is now rejoicing in the regions of light.

You may be glad to know the particulars of her happy exit. I will try to proceed;

for all is hush and still; the family retired; but not one of them, and least of all her poor cousin, I dare say, to rest.

At four o'clock, as I mentioned in my last, I was sent for down; and as thou usedst to like my descriptions, I will give thee the woeful scene that presented itself to me, as I approached the bed.

The colonel was the first that took my attention, kneeling on the side of the bed, the lady's right hand in both his, which his face covered, bathing it with his tears; although she had been comforting him, as the women since told him, in elevated strains but broken accents.

On the other side of the bed sat the good widow; her face overwhelmed with tears, leaning her head against the bed's head in a most disconsolate manner; and turning her face to me, as soon as she saw me: Oh Mr Belford, cried she, with folded hands—the dear lady—a heavy sob not permitting her to say more.

Mrs Smith, with clasped fingers and uplifted eyes, as if imploring help from the only Power which could give it, was kneeling down at the bed's feet, tears in large drops trickling down her cheeks.

Her nurse was kneeling between the widow and Mrs Smith, her arms extended. In one hand she held an ineffectual cordial, which she had just been offering to her dying mistress; her face was swollen with weeping (though used to such scenes as this) and she turned her eyes towards me, as if she called upon me by them to join in the helpless sorrow; a fresh stream bursting from them as I approached the bed.

The maid of the house, with her face upon her folded arms as she stood leaning against the wainscot, more audibly expressed her grief than any of the others.

The lady had been silent a few minutes, and speechless as they thought, moving her lips without uttering a word; one hand, as I said, in her cousin's. But when Mrs Lovick on my approach pronounced my name, Oh! Mr Belford, said she in broken periods; and with a faint inward voice, but very distinct nevertheless—Now!— Now!—(I bless God for His mercies to his poor creature) will all soon be over—A few—a very few moments—will end this strife—and I shall be happy!

Comfort here, sir—turning her head to the colonel—Comfort my cousin—see!— the blamable kindness—He would not wish me to be happy—so *soon*!

Here, she stopped, for two or three minutes, earnestly looking upon him: then resuming, My dearest cousin, said she, be comforted—What is dying but the common lot?—The mortal frame may *seem* to labour—but that is all!—It is not so hard to die, as I believed it to be!—The preparation is the difficulty—I bless God, I have had time for that—the rest is worse to beholders than to me!—I am all blessed hope—hope itself.

She *looked* what she said, a sweet smile beaming over her countenance.

After a short silence, Once more, my dear cousin, said she, but still in broken accents, commend me most dutifully to my father and mother—there she stopped. And then proceeding—to my sister, to my brother, to my uncles—and tell them I bless them with my parting breath—for all their goodness to me—even for their displeasure, I bless them—Most happy has been to me my punishment here!— happy indeed!

· She was silent for a few moments, lifting up her eyes and the hand her cousin held not between his. Then, *Oh death!* said she, *where is thy sting!*[1] (The words I remember to have heard in the Burial Service read over my uncle and poor

Belton.) And after a pause—*It is good for me that I was afflicted!*[2]—Words of Scripture, I suppose.

Then turning towards us who were lost in speechless sorrow—Oh dear, *dear* gentlemen, said she, you know not what *foretastes*—what *assurances*—And there she again stopped, and looked up, as if in a thankful rapture, sweetly smiling.

Then turning her head towards me—Do *you*, sir, tell your friend that I forgive him! And I pray to God to forgive him!—Again pausing, and lifting up her eyes as if praying that He would—Let him know how happily I die—And that such as my own, I wish to be his last hour.

She was again silent for a few moments: and then resuming—My sight fails me!—Your voices only—(for we both applauded her Christian, her divine frame, though in accents as broken as her own); and the voice of grief is alike in all. Is not this Mr Morden's hand? pressing one of his with that he had just let go. Which is Mr Belford's? holding out the other. I gave her mine. God Almighty bless you both, said she, and make you both—in your last hour—for you *must* come to this—happy as I am.

She paused again, her breath growing shorter; and, after a few minutes: And now, my dearest cousin, give me your hand—nearer—still nearer—drawing it towards her; and she pressed it with her dying lips—God protect you, dear, dear sir—and once more, receive my best and most grateful thanks—and tell my dear Miss Howe—and vouchsafe to see, and to tell my worthy Mrs Norton—she will be one day, I fear not, though now lowly in her fortunes, a saint in heaven—Tell them both, that I remember them with thankful blessings in my last moments!—And pray God to give them happiness here for many, many years, for the sake of their friends and lovers; and an heavenly crown hereafter; and such assurances of it as I have, through the all-satisfying merits of my blessed Redeemer.

Her sweet voice and broken periods methinks still fill my ears, and never will be out of my memory.

After a short silence, in a more broken and faint accent—And you, Mr Belford, pressing my hand, may God preserve you and make you sensible of all your errors—You see, in me, how all ends—may *you* be—And down sunk her head upon her pillow, she fainting away, and drawing from us her hands.

We thought she was then gone; and each gave way to a violent burst of grief.

But soon showing signs of returning life, our attention was again engaged; and I besought her, when a little recovered, to complete in my favour her half-pronounced blessing. She waved her hand to us both, and bowed her head six several times, as we have since recollected, as if distinguishing every person present; not forgetting the nurse and the maid-servant; the latter having approached the bed, weeping, as if crowding in for the divine lady's last blessing; and she spoke faltering and inwardly: Bless—bless—bless—you all—and now—and now (holding up her almost lifeless hands for the last time)—come—Oh come—blessed Lord—JESUS!

And with these words, the last but half-pronounced, expired: such a smile, such a charming serenity over-spreading her sweet face at the instant as seemed to manifest her eternal happiness already begun.

Oh Lovelace!—But I can write no more!

*

I RESUME my pen to add a few lines.

While warm, though pulseless, we pressed each her hand with our lips; and then retired into the next room.

We looked at each other with intent to speak: but, as if one motion governed as one cause affected both, we turned away silent.

The colonel sighed as if his heart would burst: at last, his face and hands uplifted, his back towards me, Good Heaven! said he to himself, support me!—And is it thus, Oh flower of nature!—then pausing—And must we no more—*never more!*—my blessed, blessed cousin! uttering some other words which his sighs made inarticulate—and then, as if recollecting himself—Forgive me, sir!—Excuse me, Mr Belford! and sliding by me: anon I hope to see you, sir—And downstairs he went, and out of the house, leaving me a statue.

When I recovered myself, it was almost to repine at what I *then* called an unequal dispensation; forgetting her happy preparation, and still happier departure; and that she had but drawn a common lot, triumphing in it; and leaving behind her every one less assured of happiness, though equally certain that it would one day be their own lot.

She departed exactly at 40 minutes after 6 o'clock, as by her watch on the table.

And thus died Miss CLARISSA HARLOWE, in the blossom of her youth and beauty: and who, her tender years considered, has not left behind her her superior in extensive knowledge, and watchful prudence; nor hardly her equal for unblemished virtue, exemplary piety, sweetness of manners, discreet generosity, and true Christian charity: and these all set off by the most graceful modesty and humility; yet on all proper occasions manifesting a noble presence of mind and true magnanimity: so that she may be said to have been not only an ornament to her sex, but to human nature.

A better pen than mine may do her fuller justice—Thine, I mean, oh Lovelace! For well dost thou know how much she excelled in the graces both of mind and person, natural and acquired, all that is woman. And thou also canst best account for the causes of her immature death, through those calamities which in so short a space of time from the highest pitch of felicity (every one in a manner adoring her) brought her to an exit so happy for herself, but that it was so *early*, so much to be deplored by all who had the honour of her acquaintance.

This task, then, I leave to thee: but now I can write no more, only that I am a sympathiser in every part of thy distress, except (and yet it is cruel to say it) in that which arises from thy guilt.

One o'clock, Friday morning

Letter 482: MR BELFORD TO ROBERT LOVELACE, ESQ.

Nine, Friday morn.

I HAVE no opportunity to write at length, having necessary orders to give on the melancholy occasion. Joel, who got to me by six in the morning, and whom I dispatched instantly back with the letter I had ready from last night, gives me but an indifferent account of the state of your mind. I wonder not at it; but time (and nothing else can) will make it easier to you: if (that is to say) you have compounded with your conscience; else it may be heavier every day than other.

TOURVILLE tells me what a way you are in. I hope you will not think of coming hither. The lady in her will desires you may not see her. Four copies are making of it. It is a long one; for she gives her reasons for all she wills. I will write to you more particularly as soon as possibly I can.

THREE letters are just brought by a servant in livery, directed *To Miss Clarissa Harlowe*. I will send copies of them to you. The contents are enough to make one mad. How would this poor lady have rejoiced to receive them—and yet, if she had, she would not have been enabled to say, as she nobly did,[a] *that God would not let her depend for comfort upon any but Himself*—And, indeed, for some days past, she had seemed to have got above all worldly considerations—Her *fervent love, even for her Miss Howe*, as she acknowledged, having given way to *supremer fervours*.[b]

Letter 483: MRS NORTON TO MISS CLARISSA HARLOWE

Wednesday, Sept. 6

AT length, my best beloved Miss Clary, everything is in the wished train—for all your relations are unanimous in your favour—Even your brother and sister are with the foremost to be reconciled to you.

I knew it must end thus!—By patience and persevering sweetness, what a triumph have you gained!

This happy change is owing to letters received from your physician, from your cousin Morden, and from Mr Brand.

Colonel Morden will be with you no doubt before this can reach you, with his pocket-book filled with money-bills, that nothing may be wanting to make you easy.

And *now*, all our hopes, all our prayers are that this good news may restore you to spirits and health; and that (so long withheld) it may not come too late.

I know how much your dutiful heart will be raised with the joyful tidings I write you, and still shall more particularly tell you of, when I have the happiness to see you: which will be by next Saturday at furthest; perhaps on Friday afternoon, by the time you can receive this.

For this day, by the general voice being sent for, I was received by everyone with great goodness and condescension, and *entreated* (for that was the word they were pleased to use, when I needed *no* entreaty I am sure) to hasten up to you, and to assure you of all their affectionate regards to you: and your father bid me say all the kind things that were in my *heart* to say, in order to comfort and raise you up; and they would hold themselves bound to make them good.

How agreeable is this commission to your Norton! My heart will overflow with kind speeches, never fear!—I am already meditating what I shall say to cheer and raise you up, in the names of everyone dear and near to you. And sorry I am that

a   See p. 1356.
b   See p. 1342.

I cannot this moment set out, as I might, instead of writing, would they favour my eager impatience with their chariot; but as it was not offered, it would be presumption to have asked for it: and tomorrow a hired chaise and pair will be ready; but at what hour I know not.

How I long once more to fold my dear precious young lady to my fond, my *more* than fond, my *maternal* bosom!

Your sister will write to you, and send her letter with this, by a particular hand. I must not let them see what I write, because of my wish about the chariot.

Your uncle Harlowe will also write, and (I doubt not) in the kindest terms: for they are all extremely alarmed and troubled at the dangerous way your doctor represents you to be in; as well as delighted with the character he gives you. Would to heaven the good gentleman had written *sooner*! And yet he writes that you know not he has *now* written. But it is all our confidence and our consolation, that he would not have written at all had he thought it too late.

They will prescribe no conditions to you, my dear young lady; but will leave all to your own duty and discretion. Only your brother and sister declare they will never yield to call Mr Lovelace brother: nor will your father, I believe, be easily brought to think of him for a son.

I am to bring you down with me as soon as your health and inclination will permit. You will be received with open arms. Everyone longs to see you. All the servants please themselves that they shall be permitted to kiss your hands. The pert Betty's note is already changed; and she now runs over in your just praises. What friends does prosperity make! What enemies adversity! It always was, and always will be so, in every state of life from the throne to the cottage—But let all be forgotten now on this jubilee change: and may you, my dearest miss, be capable of rejoicing in this good news; as I know you *will* rejoice if capable of anything.

God preserve you to our happy meeting! And I will, if I may say so, weary Heaven with my incessant prayers to preserve and restore you afterwards!

I need not say how much I am, my dear young lady,

> Your ever-affectionate and devoted
> JUDITH NORTON

An unhappy delay as to the chaise will make it Saturday morning before I can fold you to my fond heart.

Letter 484: MISS ARABELLA HARLOWE TO MISS CLARISSA HARLOWE

Wed. morning, Sept. 6

Dear sister,

WE have just heard that you are exceedingly ill. We all loved you as never young creature was loved: you are sensible of that, sister Clàry. And you have been very naughty—but we could not be angry always.

We are indeed more afflicted with the news of your being so very ill than I can express: for I see not but, after this separation (as we understand that your misfortune has been greater than your fault, and that, however unhappy, you have demeaned yourself like the good young creature you used to be) we shall love you better, if possible, than ever.

Take comfort therefore, sister Clary; and don't be too much cast down—
Whatever your mortifications may be from such noble prospects overclouded, and
from the reflections you will have from within on your faulty step, and from the
sullying of such a charming character by it, you will receive none from any of us:
and as an earnest of your papa's and mamma's favour and reconciliation, they
assure you by me of their blessing and hourly prayers.

If it will be any comfort to you, and my mother finds this letter is received as we
expect (which we shall know by the good effect it will have upon your health), she
will herself go to town to you. Meantime, the good woman you so dearly love will
be hastened up to you; and she writes by this opportunity to acquaint you of it,
and of all our returning love.

I hope you'll rejoice at this good news. Pray let us hear that you do. Your next
grateful letter on this occasion, especially if it gives us the pleasure of hearing you
are better upon this news, will be received with the same (if not greater) delight
that we *used* to have in all your prettily penned epistles. Adieu, my dear Clary! I
am

Your loving sister, and true friend,
ARABELLA HARLOWE

Letter 485: [JOHN HARLOWE] TO HIS DEAR NIECE MISS CLARISSA HARLOWE

Wed. Sept. 6

WE were greatly grieved, my beloved Miss Clary, at your fault; but we are still
more, if possible, to hear you are so very ill; and we are sorry things have been
carried so far.

We know your talents, my dear, and how movingly you could write, whenever
you pleased; so that nobody could ever deny you anything; and, believing you
depended on your pen, and little thinking you were so ill, and that you have lived
so regular a life, and were so truly penitent, are much troubled everyone of us,
your brother and all, for being so severe. Forgive my part in it, my dearest Clary.
I am your *second papa*, you know. And you *used* to love me.

I hope you'll soon be able to come down, and after a while when your indulgent
parents can spare you, that you will come to me for a whole month, and rejoice my
heart as you used to do. But if, through illness, you cannot so soon come down as
we wish, I will go up to you: for I long to see you. I never more longed to see you
in my life; and you was always the darling of my heart, you know.

My brother Antony desires his hearty commendations to you, and joins with me
in the tenderest assurance that all shall be well, and, if possible, better than ever;
for we now have been so long without you that we know the miss of you, and even
hunger and thirst, as I may say, to see you, and to take you once more to our
hearts: whence indeed you was never banished so far as our concern for the
unhappy step made *us* think and *you* believe you were. Your sister and brother
both talk of seeing you in town: so does my dear sister your indulgent mother.

God restore your health, if it be His will: else, I know not what will become of

Your truly loving uncle, and second papa,
JOHN HARLOWE

Letter 486: MR BELFORD TO ROBERT LOVELACE, ESQ.

Friday night, Sept. 8, past ten

I WILL now take up the account of our proceedings from my letter of last night, which contained the dying words of this incomparable lady.

As soon as we had seen the last scene closed (so blessedly for herself!), we left the body to the care of the good women, who according to the orders she had given them that very night removed her into that last house which she had displayed so much fortitude in providing.

In the morning, between 7 and 8 o'clock, according to appointment, the colonel came to me here. He was very much out of order. We went together, accompanied by Mrs Lovick and Mrs Smith, into the deceased's chamber. We could not help taking a view of the lovely corpse, and admiring the charming serenity of her noble aspect. The women declared they never saw death so lovely before; and that she looked as if in an easy slumber, the colour having not quite left her cheeks and lips.

I unlocked the drawer in which (as I mentioned in a former*a*) she had deposited her papers. I told you in mine of Monday last that she had the night before sealed up with three black seals a parcel inscribed. *As soon as I am certainly dead, this to be broken open by Mr Belford.* I accused myself for having not done it overnight. But really I was then incapable of anything.

I broke it open accordingly, and found in it no less than eleven letters, each sealed with her own seal and black wax, one of which was directed to me.

I will enclose a copy of it.

[*Letter 486.1: Clarissa Harlowe*] *to John Belford, Esq.*

Sunday evening, Sept. 3

Sir,

I TAKE this last and solemn occasion to repeat to you my thanks for all your kindness to me at a time when I most needed countenance and protection.

A few considerations I beg leave, as now, at your perusal of this, from the dead, to press upon you, with all the warmth of a sincere friendship.

By the time you will see this, you will have had an instance, I humbly trust, of the comfortable importance of a pacified conscience, in the last hours of one who, *to* the last hour, will wish your eternal welfare.

The great Duke of Luxemburgh,[1] as I have heard, on his death-bed declared that he would then much rather have had it to reflect upon that he had administered a cup of cold water to a worthy poor creature in distress, than that he had won so many battles as he had triumphed for—And, as one well observes, all the sentiments of worldly grandeur vanish at that unavoidable moment which decides the destiny of all men.

If then, sir, at the tremendous hour, it be thus with the conquerors of armies and the subduers of nations, let me in very few words (many are not needed) ask what, at that period, must be the reflections of those (if capable of reflection) who have lived a life of sense and offence; whose study and whose pride most ingloriously has been to seduce the innocent, and to ruin the weak, the unguarded, and the

a See p. 1329.

friendless; made still more friendless by *their* base seductions?—Oh! Mr Belford, weigh, ponder, and reflect upon it, now that in health and in vigour of mind and body, the reflections will most avail you—What an ungrateful, what an unmanly, what a meaner than reptile pride is this!

In the next place, sir, let me beg of you for *my sake* who AM or, as *now* you will best read it, *have been*, driven to the necessity of applying to you to be the executor of my will, that you will bear, according to that generosity which I think to be in you, with all my friends, and particularly with my brother (who is really a worthy young man, but perhaps a little too headstrong in his first resentments and conceptions of things), if anything by reason of this trust should fall out disagreeably; and that you will study to make peace, and to reconcile all parties; and more especially that you, who seem to have a great influence upon your *still more* headstrong friend, will interpose, if occasion be, to prevent *further* mischief— for surely, sir, that violent spirit may sit down satisfied with the evils he has already wrought; and particularly with the wrongs, the heinous and ignoble wrongs, he has in me done to my family, wounded in the tenderest part of its honour.

To this request I have already your repeated promise. I claim the observance of it, therefore, as a debt from you: and though I hope I need not doubt it, yet was I willing on this solemn, this *last* occasion, thus earnestly to reinforce it.

I have another request to make to you: it is only that you will be pleased, by a particular messenger, to forward the enclosed letters as directed.

And now, sir, having the presumption to think that an *useful* member is lost to society by means of the unhappy step which has brought my life so soon to its period, let me hope that I may be an humble instrument in the hands of Providence to reform a man of your parts and abilities; and then I shall think that loss will be more abundantly repaired to the world, while it will be, by God's goodness, my gain: and I shall have this further hope that once more I shall have an opportunity, in a blessed eternity, to thank you, as I now repeatedly do, for the good you have done to, and the trouble you will have taken for, sir,

> Your obliged servant,
> CLARISSA HARLOWE

The other letters are directed to her father, to her mother, one to her two uncles, to her brother, to her sister, to her Aunt Hervey, to her cousin Morden, to Miss Howe, to Mrs Norton, and lastly one to you, in performance of her promise *that a letter should be sent you when she arrived at her Father's house!*——I will withhold this last till I can be assured that you will be fitter to receive it than Tourville tells me you are at present.

Copies of all these are sealed up and entitled, *Copies of my ten posthumous letters, for* J. Belford, *Esq.*; and put in among the bundle of papers left to my direction, which I have not yet had leisure to open.

No wonder, while able, that she was always writing, since thus only of late could she employ that time which heretofore, from the long days she made, caused so many beautiful works to spring from her fingers. It is my opinion that there never was a lady so young, who wrote so much and with such celerity. Her thoughts keeping pace, as I have seen, with her pen, she hardly ever stopped or hesitated; and very seldom blotted out, or altered. It was a natural talent she was mistress of, among many other extraordinary ones.

I gave the colonel his letter, and ordered Harry instantly to get ready to carry the others.

Meantime (retiring into the next apartment) we opened the will. We were both so much affected in perusing it, that at one time the colonel, breaking off, gave it to me to read on; at another, I gave it back to him to proceed with; neither of us being able to read it through without such tokens of sensibility as affected the voices of each.

Mrs Lovick, Mrs Smith, and her nurse, were still more touched when we read those articles in which they are respectively remembered: but I will avoid mentioning the particulars (except in what relates to the thread of my narration) as I shall send you a copy of it in proper time.

The colonel told me he was ready to account with me for the moneys he had brought up from her friends; which would enable me, as he said, directly to execute the legacy parts of it; and he would needs at that instant force into my hands a paper relating to that subject. I put it in my pocket-book without looking into it; telling him that as I hoped he would do all in his power to promote a literal performance of the will, I must beg his advice and assistance in the execution of it.

Her request to be buried with her ancestors made a letter of the following import necessary, which I prevailed upon the colonel to write; being unwilling myself (so *early* at least) to appear officious in the eye of a family which probably wishes not any communication with me.

[*Letter 486.2: Colonel Morden*] *to James Harlowe, Jun., Esq.*]

Sir,

THE letter which the bearer of this brings with him, will, I presume, make it unnecessary to acquaint you and my cousins with the death of the most excellent of women. But I am requested by her executor, who will soon send you a copy of her last will, to acquaint her father (which I choose to do by your means) that in it she earnestly desires to be laid in the family vault, at the feet of her grandfather.

If her father will not admit of it, she has directed her body to be buried in the churchyard of the parish where she died.

I need not tell you that a speedy answer to this is necessary.

Her beatification commenced yesterday afternoon, exactly at 40 minutes after six.

I can write no more, than that I am

                                                          Yours, etc.
Friday morn. Sept. 8   WM. MORDEN

By the time this was written, and by the colonel's leave transcribed, Harry came booted and spurred, his horse at the door; and I delivered him the letters to the family, with those to Mrs Norton and Miss Howe (eight in all) together with the above of the colonel to Mr James Harlowe; and gave him orders to make the utmost dispatch with them.

The colonel and I have bespoke mourning for our selves and servants.

Letter 487: MR BELFORD TO ROBERT LOVELACE, ESQ.

Sat. ten o'clock

POOR Mrs Norton is come. She was set down at the door; and would have gone upstairs directly. But Mrs Smith and Mrs Lovick being together and in tears, and the former hinting too suddenly to the truly venerable woman the fatal news, she sunk down at her feet in fits; so that they were forced to breathe a vein to bring her to herself; and to a capacity of exclamation: and then she run on to Mrs Lovick and to me, who entered just as she recovered, in praise of the lady, in lamentations for her, and invectives against you: but yet so circumscribed were her invectives that I could observe in them the woman well-educated, and in her lamentations the passion christianized, as I may say.

She was impatient to see the corpse. The women went up with her. But they owned that they were too much affected themselves on this occasion to describe her extremely affecting behaviour.

With trembling impatience she pushed aside the coffin-lid. She bathed the face with her tears, and kissed her cheeks and forehead, as if she were living. It was *her* indeed, she said! Her sweet young lady! Her very self! Nor had death, which changed all things, a power to alter her lovely features! She admired the serenity of her aspect. She no doubt was happy, she said, as she had written to her she should be: but how many miserable creatures had she left behind her!—The good woman lamenting that she herself had lived to be one of them.

It was with difficulty they prevailed upon her to quit the corpse; and when they went into the next apartment, I joined them, and acquainted her with the kind legacy her beloved young lady had left her: but this rather augmented than diminished her concern. She ought, she said, to have attended her in person. What was the world to her, wringing her hands, now the child of her bosom and of her heart was no more? Her principal consolation, however, was that she should not long survive her. She hoped, she said, that she did not sin in wishing she might not.

It was easy to observe by the similitude of sentiments shown in this and other particulars, that the divine lady owed to this excellent woman many of her good notions.

I thought it would divert the poor gentlewoman, and not altogether unsuitably, if I were to put her upon furnishing mourning for herself; as it would rouse her by a seasonable and necessary employment from that dismal lethargy of grief which generally succeeds the too violent anguish with which a gentle nature is accustomed to be torn upon the first communication of the unexpected loss of a dear friend. I gave her therefore the thirty guineas bequeathed to her and to her son for mourning; the only mourning which the fair testatrix has mentioned: and desired her to lose no time in preparing her own, as I doubted not that she would accompany the corpse, if it were permitted to be carried down.

The colonel proposes to attend the hearse, if his kindred give him not fresh cause of displeasure; and will take with him a copy of the will. And being intent to give the family some favourable impressions of me, he will also, at his own desire, take with him the copy of the posthumous letter to me.

He is so kind as to promise me a minute account of all that shall pass on the melancholy occasion. And we have begun a friendship and settled a correspondence, which but one incident can possibly happen to interrupt to the end of our lives. And that I hope will not happen.

But what must be the grief, the remorse, that will seize upon the hearts of this hitherto inexorable family, on the receiving of the posthumous letters, and that of the colonel apprising them of what has happened!

I have given orders to an undertaker, on the supposition that the body will be permitted to be carried down; and the women intend to fill the coffin with aromatic herbs.

The colonel has obliged me to take the bills and drafts which he brought up with him, for the considerable sums accrued since the grandfather's death from the lady's estate.

I could have shown to Mrs Norton the copies of the two letters which she missed by coming up. But her grief wants not the heightenings which the reading of them would have given her.

I HAVE been dipping into the copies of the posthumous letters to the family which Harry has carried down. Well may I call this admirable lady divine. They are all calculated to give comfort rather than reproach, though their cruelty to her merited nothing but reproach. But were I in any of their places, how much rather had I that she had quitted scores with me by the most severe recriminations, than that she should thus nobly triumph over me by a generosity that has no example?

I will enclose some of them, which I desire you to return as soon as you can.

Letter 488: [MISS CLARISSA HARLOWE] TO THE EVER-HONOURED JAMES HARLOWE, SEN., ESQ.

Most dear sir!
WITH exulting confidence now does your emboldened daughter come into your awful presence by these lines, who dared not but upon this occasion to look up to you with hopes of favour and forgiveness; since when this comes to your hands it will be out of her power ever to offend you more.

And now let me bless you, my honoured papa, and bless you, as I write, upon my knees, for all the benefits I have received from your indulgence: for your fond love to me in the days of my prattling innocence: for the virtuous education you gave me: and for the crown of all, the happy end which, through Divine Grace, by means of that virtuous education, I hope by the time you will receive this I shall have made. And let me beg of you, dear venerable sir, to blot from your remembrance, if possible, the last unhappy eight months; and then I shall hope to be remembered with advantage for the pleasure you had the goodness to take in your Clarissa.

Still on her knees, let your poor penitent implore your forgiveness of all her faults and follies; more especially of that fatal error which threw her out of your protection.

When you know, sir, that I have never been faulty in my will: that ever since my calamity became irretrievable, I have been in a state of preparation: that I have the strongest assurances that the Almighty has accepted my unfeigned repentance; and that by this time you will (as I humbly presume to hope) have been the means of adding one to the number of the blessed; you will have reason for joy rather than sorrow. Since, had I escaped the snares by which I was entangled, I might have wanted those exercises which I look upon now as so many mercies dispensed to wean me betimes from a world that presented itself to me with prospects too alluring: and, in that case (too easily satisfied with *worldly* felicity) I might not have attained to that blessedness which now, on your reading of this, I humbly presume (through the Divine goodness) I am rejoicing in.

That the Almighty in His own good time will bring you, sir, and my ever-honoured mother, after a series of earthly felicities, of which may my unhappy fault be the only interruption (and very grievous I know that must have been), to rejoice in the same blessed state, is the repeated prayer of, sir,

Your now happy daughter,
CLARISSA HARLOWE

Letter 489: [MISS CLARISSA HARLOWE] TO THE EVER-HONOURED MRS HARLOWE

Honoured madam,
THE last time I had the boldness to write to you, it was with all the consciousness of a self-convicted criminal supplicating her offended judge for mercy and pardon. I now, by these lines, approach you with more assurance; but nevertheless with the highest degree of reverence, gratitude, and duty. The reason of my assurance, my letter to my papa will give: and as I humbly on my knees implored *his* pardon, so now, in the same dutiful manner, do I supplicate yours, for the grief and trouble I have given you.

Every vein of my heart has bled for an unhappy rashness; which (although involuntary as to the act) from the moment it was committed carried with it its own punishment; and was accompanied with a true and sincere penitence.

God, who has been a witness of my distresses, knows that great as they have been, the greatest of all was the distress that I knew I must have given to you, madam, and to my father, by a step that had so very ugly an appearance in your eyes and his; and indeed, in all my family's: a step so unworthy of *your* daughter and of the education you had given her!

But HE, I presume to hope, has forgiven me; and at the instant this will reach your hands, I humbly trust I shall be rejoicing in the blessed fruits of His forgiveness. And be this your comfort, my ever-honoured mamma, that the principal end of your pious care for me is attained, though not in the way so much hoped for.

May the grief which my fatal error has given to you both, be the only grief that shall ever annoy you in this world!—May you, madam, long live to sweeten the cares, and heighten the comforts of my papa!—May my sister's continued and if possible augmented duty happily make up to you the loss you have sustained in me! And whenever my brother and she change their single state, may it be with such satisfaction to you both as may make you forget my offence; and remember me only in those days in which you took pleasure in me: and, at last, may a happy meeting with your forgiven penitent in the eternal mansions augment the bliss of her who, purified by sufferings, already, when this salutes your hands, presumes she shall be

The forever happy
CLARISSA HARLOWE

Letter 490: [MISS CLARISSA HARLOWE] TO JAMES HARLOWE, JUN., ESQ.

Sir,

THERE was but one time, but one occasion, after the rash step I was precipitated upon, that I could hope to be excused looking up to you in the character of a brother and a friend. And NOW is that time, and THIS the occasion. Now, at reading this, will you pity your late unhappy sister! NOW will you forgive her faults, both supposed and real. And NOW will you afford to her *memory* that kind concern which you refused to her before!

I write, my brother, in the first place, to beg your pardon for the offence my unhappy step gave to you and to the rest of a family so dear to me.

Virgin purity should not so behave as to be suspected: yet, when you come to know all my story, you will find further room for pity, if not for *more* than pity, for your late unhappy sister!

Oh that passion had not been deaf! That misconception would have given way to inquiry! That your rigorous heart, if it could not itself be softened (moderating the power you had obtained over everyone) had permitted other hearts more indulgently to expand!

But I write not to give pain. I had rather you should think me faulty still, than take to yourself the consequence that will follow from acquitting me.

Abandoning therefore a subject which I had not intended to touch upon (for I hope, at the writing of this, I am above the spirit of recrimination) let me tell you, sir, that my next motive for writing to you in this last and most solemn manner is to beg of you to forego any active resentments (which may endanger a life so precious to all your friends) against the man to whose elaborate baseness I owe my worldly ruin.

For ought an innocent man to run an *equal* risk with a guilty one?—a *more* than equal risk, as the guilty one has been long inured to acts of violence and is skilled in the arts of offence?

You would not arrogate to yourself God's province, who has said, *Vengeance is mine, and I will repay it.*[1] If you would, I tremble for the consequence; for will it not be suitable to the Divine justice to punish the *presumptuous* innocent (as you would be in this case) in the *very* error, and that by the hand of the *self-defending* guilty—reserving *him* for a future day of vengeance for his accumulated crimes?

Leave then the poor wretch to the Divine justice. Let your sister's fault die with her. At least let it not be revived in blood. Life is a short stage where longest. A little time hence, the now green head will be gray, if it lives this little time: and if Heaven will afford him time for repentance, why should not *you?*

Then think, my brother, what will be the consequence to your dear parents if the guilty wretch who has occasioned to them the loss of a daughter should likewise deprive them of their best hope, an only son, more worth in the family account than several daughters?

Would you add, my brother, to those distresses which you hold your sister so inexcusable for having (although from involuntary and undesigned causes) given?

Seek not then, I beseech you, to extend the evil consequences of your sister's error. His conscience, when it shall please God to touch it, will be sharper than your sword.

I have still another motive for writing to you in this solemn manner: it is, to entreat you to watch over your passions. The principal fault I know you to be guilty of is the violence of your temper when you think yourself in the right: which you would oftener be but for that very violence.

You have several times brought your life into danger by it.

Is not the man guilty of a high degree of self-partiality, who is less able to *bear* contradiction than apt to *give* it?—How often with you has impetuosity brought on abasement?—a consequence too natural.

Let me then caution you, dear sir, against a warmth of temper, an impetuosity when moved, and you so *ready* to be moved, that may hurry you into unforeseen difficulties; and which it is in some measure a sin not to endeavour to restrain. God enable you to do it for the sake of your own peace and safety, as well present as future! And for the sake of your family and friends who all see your fault, but are tender of speaking to you of it!

As for me, my brother, my punishment has been seasonable. God gave me grace to make a right use of my sufferings. I early repented. I never loved the man half so much as I hated his actions, when I saw what he was capable of. I gave up my whole *heart* to a better hope. God blessed my penitence, and my reliance upon Him. And now I presume to say, I AM HAPPY.

May Heaven preserve you in safety, health, and honour, and long continue your life for a comfort and stay to your honoured parents: and may you in the change of your single state meet with a wife as agreeable to everyone else, as to yourself, and be happy in a hopeful race, and not have one Clarissa among them to embitter your comforts when she should give you *most* comfort. But may my example be of use to warn the dear creatures whom once I hoped to live to see and to cherish, of the evils with which this deceitful world abounds, are the prayers of

> Your affectionate sister,
> CLARISSA HARLOWE

Letter 491: [MISS CLARISSA HARLOWE] TO MISS HARLOWE

Now may you, my dear Arabella, unrestrained by the severity of your virtue, let fall a pitying tear on the past faults and sufferings of your late unhappy sister; since, now, she can never offend you more. The Divine mercy, which first inspired her with repentance (an *early* repentance it was; since it preceded her sufferings) for an error which she offers not to extenuate although perhaps it were capable of some extenuation, has *now*, at the instant that you are reading this, as I humbly hope, blessed her with the fruits of it.

Thus already, even while she writes, in imagination, purified and exalted, she the more fearlessly writes to her sister; and NOW is assured of pardon for all those little occasions of displeasure which her frowarder youth might give you; and for the disgrace which her fall has fixed upon you, and upon her family.

May you, my sister, continue to bless those dear and honoured relations, whose indulgence so well deserves your utmost gratitude, with those cheerful instances of duty and obedience which have hitherto been so acceptable to *them*, and praiseworthy in *you!* And may you when a suitable proposal shall offer, fill up more worthily that chasm which the loss they have sustained in me has made in their family!

Thus, my Arabella! my only sister! and for many happy years, my friend! most fervently prays that sister whose affection for you no acts of unkindness, no misconstruction of her conduct, could cancel! And who NOW, made perfect (as she hopes) through sufferings, styles herself,

The happy
CLARISSA HARLOWE

Letter 492: [MISS CLARISSA HARLOWE] TO JOHN AND ANTONY HARLOWE,
ESQRS.

Honoured sirs,

WHEN these lines reach your hands, your late unhappy niece will have known the end of all her troubles; and as she humbly hopes, will be rejoicing in the mercies of a gracious God who has declared that He will forgive the truly penitent of heart.

I write, therefore, my dear uncles, and to you both in one letter (since your fraternal love has made you both but as one person), to give you comfort, and not distress; for however sharp my afflictions have been, they have been but of short duration; and I am betimes (happily as I hope) arrived at the end of a painful journey.

At the same time, I write to thank you both for all your kind indulgence to me, and to beg your forgiveness of my last, my *only* great fault to you and to my family.

The ways of Providence are unsearchable. Various are the means made use of by it, to bring poor sinners to a sense of their duty. Some are drawn by love; others are driven by terrors, to their Divine refuge. I had for eighteen years out of nineteen rejoiced in the favour and affection of everyone. No trouble came near my heart. I seemed to be one of those designed to be drawn by the silken cords of love—But perhaps I was too apt to value myself upon the love and favour of everyone: the merit of the good I delighted to do, and of the inclinations which were given me, and which I could not help having, I was perhaps too ready to attribute to myself; and now, being led to account for the cause of my temporary calamities, find I had a secret pride to be punished for, which I had not fathomed: and it was necessary perhaps that some sore and terrible misfortunes should befall me in order to mortify my pride and my vanity.

Temptations were accordingly sent. I shrunk in the day of trial. My discretion, which had been so cried up, was found wanting when it came to be weighed in an equal balance. I was betrayed, fell, and became the byword of my companions, and a disgrace to my family, which had prided itself in me perhaps too much. But as my fault was not that of a culpable will, when my pride was sufficiently mortified (although I was surrounded by dangers, and entangled in snares) I was not suffered to be totally lost: but, purified by sufferings, I was fitted for the change I have NOW, at the time you will receive this, so newly and as I humbly hope so happily experienced.

Rejoice with me then, dear sirs, that I have weathered so great a storm. Nor let it be matter of concern that I am cut off in the bloom of youth. 'There is no inquisition in the grave, whether we lived ten or an hundred years; and the day of death is better than the day of our birth.'[1]

Once more, dear sirs, accept my grateful thanks for all your goodness to me, from my early childhood to the day, the unhappy day, of my error! Forgive that error!—And God give us a happy meeting in a blessed eternity, prays,

Your most dutiful and obliged kinswoman,
CLARISSA HARLOWE

Mr Belford gives the Lady's posthumous letters to Mrs Hervey, Miss Howe, and Mrs Norton, at length likewise: but although every letter varies in style as well as matter from the others; yet, as they are written on the same subject, and are pretty long, it is thought proper to abstract them.

[*Letter 492.1: Miss Clarissa Harlowe to Mrs Hervey*]

That to her Aunt Hervey is written in the same pious and generous strain with the others preceding, seeking to give comfort rather than distress. 'The Almighty, I hope, *says she*, has received and blessed my penitence, and I am happy. Could I have been more than so at the end of what is called a happy life of 20, or 30, or 40 years to come? And what are 20, or 30, or 40 years to look back upon, when passed?— In half of either of these periods, what friends might I not have mourned for? what temptations from worldly prosperity might I not have encountered with? And in such a case, immersed in earthly pleasures, how little likelihood that, in my last stage, I should have been blessed with such a preparation and resignation as I have now been blessed with?'

She proceeds as follows: 'Thus much, madam, of comfort to you and myself from this dispensation. As to my dear parents, I hope they will console themselves, that they have still many blessings left, which ought to balance the troubles my error has given them: that, unhappy as I have been to be the interrupter of their felicities, they never, till this my fault, knew any *heavy evil:* that afflictions patiently borne may be turned into blessings: that uninterrupted happiness is not to be expected in this life: that, after all, they have not, as I humbly presume to hope, the probability of the everlasting perdition of their child to deplore: and that, in short, when my story comes to be fully known, they will have the comfort to know that my sufferings will redound more to my honour than to my disgrace.

'These considerations will, I hope, make their temporary loss of but *one* child out of *three* (unhappily circumstanced too as she was) matter of greater consolation than affliction. And the rather, as we may hope for a happy meeting once more, never to be separated either by time or offences.'

She concludes this letter with an address to her cousin Dolly Hervey, whom she calls her amiable cousin; and thankfully remembers for the part she took in her afflictions: 'Oh my dear cousin, let your worthy heart be guarded against those delusions, which have been fatal to my worldly happiness!—That pity which you bestowed upon *me* demonstrates a gentleness of nature, which may possibly subject you to misfortunes, if your eye be permitted to mislead your judgement—But a strict observance of your filial duty, my dearest cousin, and the precepts of so prudent a mother as you have the happiness to have (enforced by so sad an example in your own family as I have set) will, I make no doubt, with the Divine assistance, be your guard and security.'

[Letter 492.2: Miss Clarissa Harlowe to Miss Howe]

The posthumous letter to Miss Howe is extremely tender and affectionate. She pathetically calls upon her 'to rejoice that all her Clarissa's troubles are now at an end. That the state of temptation and trial, of doubt and uncertainty, is now over with her, and that she has happily escaped the snares that were laid for her soul. The rather to rejoice, as that her misfortunes were of such a nature that it was impossible she could be tolerably happy in this life.'

She 'thankfully acknowledges the favours she had received from Mrs Howe and Mr Hickman; and expresses her concern for the trouble she has occasioned to the former, as well as to her; and prays that all the earthly blessings they used to wish to each other may singly devolve upon *her*.'

She beseeches her 'that she will not suspend the day which shall supply to herself the friend she will have lost in her, and give to herself a still nearer and dearer relation.'

She tells her 'that her choice (a choice made with the approbation of all her friends) has fallen upon a sincere, an honest, a virtuous, and what is more than all, a *pious* man; a man who although he admires her person, is still more in love with the graces of her mind. And as those graces are improvable with every added year of life, which will impair the transitory ones of person, what a firm basis, infers she, has Mr Hickman chosen to built his love upon!'

She prays 'that God will bless them together; and that the remembrance of her, and of what she has suffered, may not interrupt their mutual happiness; she desires them to think of nothing but what she now is; and that a time will come when they shall meet again, never to be divided.

'To the Divine protection meantime she commits her; and charges her, by the love that has always subsisted between them, that she will not mourn too heavily for her; and again calls upon her, after a gentle tear which she will allow her to let fall in memory of their uninterrupted friendship, to rejoice that she is so early released; and that she is purified by her sufferings, and is made as she assuredly trusts, by God's goodness, eternally happy.'

The posthumous letters to Mr LOVELACE *and Mr* MORDEN *will be occasionally inserted hereafter: as will also the substance of that written to Mrs* NORTON.

Letter 493: MR BELFORD TO ROBERT LOVELACE, ESQ.

Sat. afternoon, Sept. 9

I UNDERSTAND that thou breathest nothing but revenge against *me*, for treating thee with so much freedom; and against the accursed woman and her infernal crew. I am not at all concerned for thy menaces against myself. It is my design to make thee *feel*. It gives me pleasure to find my intention answered. And I congratulate thee that thou hast not lost that sense.

As to the cursed crew, well do they deserve the fire *here*, that thou threatenest them with, and the fire here*after* that seems to await them. But I have this moment received news which will, in all likelihood, save thee the guilt of punishing the old wretch for her share of wickedness as thy agent. But if that happens to her which is likely to happen, wilt thou not tremble for what may befall the principal?

Not to keep thee longer in suspense; last night, it seems, the infamous woman got so heartily intoxicated with her beloved liquor, arrack punch, at the expense of Colonel Salter, that, mistaking her way, she fell down a pair of stairs and broke her leg: and now, after a dreadful night, she lies foaming, raving, roaring, in a burning fever, that wants not any other fire to scorch her into a feeling more exquisite and durable than any thy vengeance could make her suffer.

The wretch has requested me to come to her: and lest I should refuse a common messenger, sent her vile associate Sally Martin; who not finding me at Soho, came hither; another part of her business being to procure the divine lady's pardon for the old creature's wickedness to her.

This devil incarnate Sally was never so shocked in her life, as when I told her the lady was dead.

She took out her salts to keep her from fainting; and when a little recovered, she accused herself for her part of the injuries the lady had sustained; as she said Polly Horton would do for hers; and shedding tears, declared that the world never produced such another woman. She called her the ornament and glory of her sex; acknowledged that her ruin was owing more to their instigations than even (savage as thou art) to thy own vileness: since thou wert inclined to have done her justice more than once, had they not kept up thy profligate spirit to its height.

This wretch would fain have been admitted to a sight of the corpse. But I refused her request with execrations.

She could forgive herself, she said, for everything but her insults upon the admirable lady at Rowland's: since all the rest was but in pursuit of a livelihood to which she had been reduced, as she boasted, from better expectations, and which hundreds follow as well as she. I did not ask her, *By whom reduced?*

At going away, she told me that the old monster's bruises are of more dangerous consequence than the fracture: that a mortification is apprehended: and that the vile wretch has so much compunction of heart on recollecting her treatment of Miss Harlowe, and is so much set upon procuring her forgiveness, that she is sure the news she has to carry her will hasten her end.

Sat. night

THY servant gives me a dreadful account of thy raving unmanageableness. I wonder not at it. But as nothing violent is lasting, I dare say that thy habitual gaiety of heart will quickly get the better of thy frenzy: and the rather do I judge so, as thy fits are of the raving kind (suitable to thy natural impetuosity) and not of that melancholy species which seizes slower souls.

For this reason I will proceed in writing to thee, that my narrative may not be broken by thy discomposure; and that the contents of it may find thee, and help thee to reflection, when thou shalt be restored.

Harry is returned from carrying the posthumous letters to the family and to Miss Howe; and that of the colonel which acquaints James Harlowe with his sister's death, and with her desire to be interred near her grandfather.

Harry was not admitted into the presence of any of the family. They were all assembled together, it seems, at Harlowe Place, on occasion of the colonel's letter which informed them of the lady's dangerous way[a]; and were comforting themselves, as Harry was told, with hopes that Mr Morden had made the worst of her state in order to quicken their resolutions.

It is easy then to judge what must be their grief and surprise on receiving the fatal news which the letters Harry sent in to them communicated.

He stayed there long enough to find the whole house in confusion; the servants running different ways; lamenting and wringing their hands as they run; the female servants particularly; as if somebody (poor Mrs Harlowe no doubt, and perhaps Mrs Hervey too) were in fits.

All were in such disorder that he could get no commands, nor obtain any notice of himself. The servants seemed more inclined to execrate than welcome him—Oh master! Oh young man! cried three or four together, what dismal tidings have you brought!—They helped him to his horse (which with great civility they had put up on his arrival) at the very first word: and he went to an inn; and pursued on foot his way to Mrs Norton's; and finding her come to town, left the letter he carried down for her with her son (a fine youth) who, when he heard the fatal news, burst out into a flood of tears—first lamenting the lady's death, and then crying out, What, what, would become of his poor mother?—How would she support herself, when she should find on her arrival in town that the dear lady who was so deservedly the darling of her heart was no more!

He proceeded to Miss Howe's, with the letter for her. That lady, he was told, had just given orders for a young man, a tenant's son, to post to London to bring her news of her dear friend's condition, and whether she should herself be encouraged by an account of her being still alive to make her a visit; everything being ordered to be in readiness for her going up, on his return with the news she wished and prayed for with the utmost impatience. And Harry was just in time to prevent the man's setting out.

He had the precaution to desire to speak with Miss Howe's woman or maid, and communicated to her the fatal tidings, that she might break them to her young lady. The maid was herself so affected that her old lady (who, Harry said, seemed

a See p. 1357.

to be everywhere at once) came to see what ailed her; and was herself so struck with the communication, that she was forced to sit down in a chair; Oh the sweet creature! said she—And is it come to this!—Oh my poor Nancy!—How shall I be able to break the matter to my Nancy!

Mr Hickman was in the house. He hastened in to comfort the old lady—but he could not restrain his own tears. He feared, he said, when he was last in town that this sad event would soon happen: but little thought it would be so very soon!— But she is happy, I am sure, said he!

Mrs Howe, when a little recovered, went up in order to break the news to her daughter. She took the letter, and her salts in her hand. And Harry could perceive that they had occasion for them. For the housekeeper soon came hurrying down into the kitchen, her face overspread with tears—Her young mistress had fainted away, she said—nor did she wonder at it—Never did there live a lady more deserving of general admiration and lamentation than Miss Clarissa Harlowe! And never was there a stronger friendship dissolved by death than between her young lady and her. She hurried with a lighted wax-candle, and with feathers to burn under the nose of her young mistress; which showed that she continued in fits.

Mr Hickman afterwards, with his usual humanity, directed that Harry should be taken care of all night; it being then the close of day. He asked him after my health. He expressed himself excessively afflicted, as well for the deprivation as for the just grief of the lady whom he so passionately loves. But he called the departed lady an angel of light. We dreaded, said he (tell your master) to read the letter sent—but we needed not—'Tis a blessed letter, written by a blessed hand!—But the consolation she aims to give will for the present heighten the sense we all shall have of the loss of so excellent a creature! Tell Mr Belford that I thank God I am not the man who had the unmerited honour to call himself her brother.

I know how terribly this *great* catastrophe (as I may call it, since so many persons are interested in it) affects *thee*. I should have been glad to have had particulars of the distress which the first communication of it must have given to the Harlowes. Yet who but must pity the unhappy mother?

The answer which James Harlowe returned to Colonel Morden's letter of notification of his sister's death, and to her request as to interment, will give a faint idea of what their concern must be. Here follows a copy of it.

[*Letter 494.1: James Harlowe, Jun.*] *to William Morden, Esq.*

Saturday, Sept. 9

Dear cousin,

I CANNOT find words to express what we all suffer on the mournfullest news that ever was communicated to us. My sister Arabella (but, alas! I have now no *other* sister) was preparing to follow Mrs Norton up; and I had resolved to escort her, and to have looked in upon the dear creature.

God be merciful to us all! To what purpose did the doctor write if she was so near her end!—Why, as everybody says, did he not send sooner?—or why at all?

The most admirable young creature that ever swerved!—not one friend to be with her!—Alas! sir, I fear my mother will never get over this shock—She has been in hourly fits ever since she received the fatal news. My poor father has the gout thrown into his stomach; and Heaven knows—Oh cousin, Oh sir!—I meant nothing but the honour of the family; yet have I all the weight thrown upon me—(Oh this cursed Lovelace! may I perish if he escape the deserved vengeance!*a*)

We had begun to please ourselves that we should soon see her here—Good Heaven! that her next entrance into this house, after she abandoned us so precipitately, should be in a coffin!

We can have nothing to do with her executor (another strange step of the dear creature's!). He cannot expect we will—nor, if he be a gentleman, will he think of acting. Do you therefore be pleased, sir, to order an undertaker to convey the body down to us.

My mother says she shall be for ever unhappy if she may not in death see the dear creature whom she could not see in life: be so kind therefore as to direct the lid to be only half screwed down—that (if my poor mother cannot be prevailed upon to dispense with so shocking a spectacle) she may be obliged—She was the darling of her heart!

If we know her will in relation to the funeral, it shall be punctually complied with: as shall everything in it that is fit or reasonable to be performed; and this without the intervention of strangers.

Will you not, dear sir, favour us with your presence at this melancholy time? Pray do—and pity and excuse what passed at our last meeting with that generosity which is natural to the brave and the wise. Everyone's respects attend you. And I am, sir,

> Your inexpressibly afflicted cousin and servant,
> JA. HARLOWE, Jun.

Everything that is fit or reasonable, to be performed! (repeated I to the colonel from the above letter on his reading it to me): that is everything which she has directed, that *can* be performed. I hope, colonel, that I shall have no contention with them. I wish no more for *their* acquaintance than they do for *mine*. But you, sir, must be the mediator between them and me; for I shall insist upon a literal performance in every article.

The colonel was so kind as to declare that he would join to support me in my resolution.

Letter 495: MR BELFORD TO ROBERT LOVELACE, ESQ.

Sunday morn. 8 o'clock, Sept. 10

I STAYED at Smith's till I saw the last of all that was mortal of the divine lady.

As she has directed rings by her will to several persons, with her hair to be set in crystal, the afflicted Mrs Norton cut off before the coffin was closed four charming ringlets; one of which the colonel took for a locket, which he says he will cause to be made, and wear next his heart in memory of his beloved cousin.

Between four and five in the morning, the corpse was put into the hearse; the coffin before being filled, as intended, with flowers and aromatic herbs, and proper care taken to prevent the corpse suffering (to the eye) from the jolting of the hearse.

Poor Mrs Norton is extremely ill. I gave particular directions to Mrs Smith's

a The words thus enclosed ( ) were omitted in the transcript to Mr Lovelace.

maid (whom I have ordered to attend the good woman in a mourning chariot) to take care of her. The colonel, who rides with his servants within view of the hearse, says that he will see my orders in relation to her enforced.

When the hearse moved off and was out of sight, I locked up the lady's chamber, into which all that had belonged to her was removed.

I expect to hear from the colonel as soon as he is got down, by a servant of his own.

Letter 496: MR MOWBRAY TO JOHN BELFORD, ESQ.

Uxbridge, Sunday morn. 9 o'clock

Dear Jack,

I SEND you enclosed a letter from Mr Lovelace; which, though written in the cursed algebra, I know to be such a one as will show what a *queer* way he is in; for he read it to us with the air of a tragedian. You will see by it what the mad fellow had intended to do, if we had not all of us interposed. He was actually setting out with a surgeon of this place, to have the lady opened and embalmed—Rot me if it be not my full persuasion that if he had, her heart would have been found to be either iron or marble.

We have got Lord M. to him. His lordship is also much afflicted at the lady's death. His sisters and nieces, he says, will be ready to break their hearts. What a rout's here about a woman? For after all she was no more.

We have taken a pailful of black bull's blood from him; and this has lowered him a little. But he threatens Colonel Morden, he threatens you for your cursed reflections (cursed reflections indeed, Jack!), and curses all the world and himself still.

Last night his mourning (which is full as deep as for a wife) was brought home, and his fellow's mourning too. And though 8 o'clock, he would put it on and make them attend him in theirs.

Everybody blames him on this lady's account. But I see not for why. She was a *vixen* in her virtue. And her relations are ten times more to blame than he. I will prove this to the teeth of them all. If *they* could use her ill, why should they expect *him* to use her well?—You or I, or Tourville, in his shoes would have done as he has done. Are not all the girls forewarned?—'Has he done by her as that caitiff *Miles* did to the farmer's daughter, whom he tricked up to town (a pretty girl also, just such another as Bob's Rosebud!) under a notion of waiting on a lady—*Drilled* her on, pretending the lady was abroad. Drank her light-hearted; then carried her to a play; then it was too late, you know, to see the pretended lady: then to a bagnio: ruined her, as they call it, and all the same day. Kept her on (an ugly dog too!) a fortnight or three weeks; then left her to the mercy of the people of the bagnio (never paying for anything), who stripped her of all her clothes, and because she would not take on, threw her into prison; where she died in want and in despair!'—A true story thou knowest, Jack—This fellow deserved to be damned. But has our Bob been such a villain as this?—and would he not have *married* this flinty-hearted lady?—*so he is justified very evidently*.

Why then should such cursed qualms take him?—Who would have thought he had been such *poor blood*? Now (rot the puppy!) to see him sit silent in a corner, when he has tired himself with his mock-majesty and with his argumentation (who so fond of *argufying* as he?) and teaching his shadow to make mouths against the wainscot—Lords-zounter, if I have patience with him!

But he has had no rest for these ten days: that's the thing!—You must write to him; and prithee coax him, Jack, and send him what he writes for, and give him all his way: there will be no bearing him else. And get the lady buried as fast as you can; and don't let him know where.

This letter should have gone yesterday. We told him it did. But were in hopes he would not have inquired after it again. But he raves as he has not any answer.

What he *vouchsafed* to read of other of your letters has given my lord such a curiosity as makes him desire you to continue your accounts. Pray do: but not in your hellish *Arabick*; and we will let the poor fellow only into what we think fitting for his present way.

I live a cursed dull poking life here. With what I so lately saw of poor Belton, and what I now see of this charming fellow, I shall be crazy as he soon, or as dull as thou, Jack; so must seek for better company in town than either of you. I have been forced to read sometimes to divert me; and you know I hate reading. It presently sets me into a fit of drowsiness, and then I yawn and stretch like a devil.

Yet in Dryden's *Palamon and Arcite* have I just now met with a passage that has in it much of our Bob's case. These are some of the lines.[1]

Mr Mowbray then recites some lines from that poem describing a distracted man, and runs the parallel; and then priding himself in his performance; says:

Let me tell you that had I begun to write as early as you and Lovelace, I might have cut as good a figure as either of you. Why not? But boy or man I ever hated a book. 'Tis a folly to lie. I loved action, my boy. I hated droning; and have led in former days more boys from their book than ever my master made to profit by it. Kicking and cuffing and orchard-robbing were my early glory.

But I am tired of writing. I never wrote such a long letter in my life. My wrists and my fingers and thumb ache damnably. The pen is an hundredweight at the least. And my eyes are ready to drop out of my head upon the paper—the cramp but this minute in my fingers. Rot the goose and the goose-quill! I will write no more long letters for a twelvemonth to come. Yet one word: We think the mad fellow coming to.   Adieu.

Letter 497: MR LOVELACE TO JOHN BELFORD, ESQ.

Uxbridge, Sat. Sept. 9

Jack,

I THINK it absolutely right that my ever-dear and beloved lady should be opened and embalmed. It must be done out of hand—this very afternoon. Your acquaintance Tomkins and old Anderson of this place, whom I will bring with me, shall be the surgeons. I have talked to the latter about it.

I will see everything done with that decorum which the case, and the sacred person of my beloved require.

Everything that can be done to preserve the charmer from decay shall also be done. And when she *will* descend to her original dust, or cannot be kept longer, I will then have her laid in my family vault between my own father and mother. Myself, as I am in my soul, so in person, chief mourner. But her heart, to which I have such unquestionable pretensions, in which once I had so large a share, and which I will prize above my own, I *will* have. I will keep it in spirits. It shall never be out of my sight. And all the charges of sepulture too shall be mine.

Surely nobody will dispute my right to her. Whose was she living? Whose is she dead, but mine?—Her cursed parents, whose barbarity to her no doubt was the *true* cause of her death, have long since renounced her. She left *them* for *me*. She chose *me* therefore: and I was her husband. What though I treated her like a villain? Do I not pay for it now? Would she not have been mine had I not? Nobody will dispute but she would. And has she not forgiven me?—I am then in *statu quo prius* with her—am I not?—as if I had never offended? Whose then can she be but mine?

I will free you from your executorship and all your cares.

Take notice, Belford, that I do hereby actually discharge you, and everybody, from all cares and troubles relating to her. And as to her last testament I will execute it myself.

There were no articles between us, no settlements; and she is mine, as you see I have proved to a demonstration: nor could she dispose of herself but as I pleased. D—nation seize me then if I make not good my right against all opposers!

Her bowels, if her friends are very solicitous about them, and very humble and sorrowful (and none have they of their own), shall be sent down to them—to be laid with *her* ancestors—unless she has ordered otherwise. For, except that she shall not be committed to the unworthy earth so long as she can be kept out of it, her will shall be performed in everything.

I send in the meantime for a lock of her hair.

I charge you stir not in any part of her will, but by my express direction. I will order everything myself. For am I not her husband? And being forgiven by her, am I not the chosen of her heart? What else signifies her forgiveness?

The two insufferable wretches you have sent me, plague me to death, and would treat me like a babe in strings. Damn the fellows, what can they mean by it?—Yet that crippled monkey Doleman joins with them. And, as I hear them whisper, they have sent for Lord M.—to control me, I suppose.

What can they mean by this usage of me? Sure all the world is run mad but myself. They treat me as they ought every one of themselves to be treated. The whole world is but one great Bedlam. G—d confound it, and everything in it, since now my beloved Clarissa Lovelace—no more Harlowe—Curse upon that name and everyone called by it.

What I write to you for is:

1. To forbid you intermeddling with anything relating to her. To forbid Morden intermeddling also. If I remember right, he has threatened me, and cursed me, and used me ill. And let him be gone from her if he would avoid my resentments.

2. To send me a lock of her hair instantly by the bearer.

3. To engage Tomkins to have everything ready for the opening and embalming. I shall bring Anderson with me.

4. To get her will and everything ready for my perusal and consideration.

I will have possession of her dear heart this very night; and let Tomkins provide a proper receptacle and spirits, till I can get a golden one made for it.

I will take her papers. And as no one can do her memory justice equal to myself, and I will not spare myself, who can better show the world what she was, and what a villain he that could use her ill? And the world shall also see, what implacable and unworthy parents she had.

All shall be set forth in words at length. No mincing of the matter. Names undisguised as well as facts. For as I shall make the worst figure in it myself, and have a right to treat myself as nobody else shall; who will control me? Who dare call me to account?

Let me know if the damned mother be yet the subject of the devil's own vengeance—if the old wretch be dead or alive? Some exemplary mischief I must yet do. My revenge shall sweep away that devil and all my opposers of the cruel Harlowe family, from the face of the earth. Whole hecatombs ought to be offered up to the *manes* of my Clarissa Lovelace.

Although her will may in some respects cross mine, yet I expect to be observed. I will be the interpreter of hers.

Next to mine, hers shall be observed, for she is my wife; and shall be to all eternity. I will never have another.

Adieu, Jack. I am preparing to be with you. I charge you, as you value my life or your own, do not oppose me in anything relating to my Clarissa Lovelace.

My temper is entirely altered. I know not what it is to laugh, or smile, or be pleasant. I am grown choleric and impatient, and will not be controlled.

I write this in characters, as I used to do, that nobody but you should know what I write. For never was any man plagued with impertinents, as I am.

R. LOVELACE

In a separate paper enclosed in the above

LET me tell thee, in characters still, that I am in a dreadful way just now. My brain is all boiling like a caldron over a fiery furnace. What a devil is the matter with me, I wonder! I never was so strange in my life.

In truth, Jack, I have been a most execrable villain. And when I consider all my actions by this angel of a woman, and in her the piety, the charity, the wit, the beauty I have *helped* to destroy, and the good to the world I have thereby been a means of frustrating, I can pronounce damnation upon myself. How then can I expect mercy anywhere else!

I believe I shall have no patience with you when I see you. Your damned stings and reflections have almost turned my brain.

But here Lord M. they tell me is come! D—n him, and those who sent for him!

I know not what I have written! But her dear heart and a lock of her hair I will have, let who will be the gainsayers! For is she not mine? Whose else can she be? She has no father nor mother, no sister, no brother; no relations but me. And my beloved is mine; and I am hers: and that's enough—But oh!

> She's out! The damp of death has quench'd her quite!
> Those spicy doors, her lips, are shut, close lock'd,
> Which never gale of life shall open more![1]

And is it so! Is it *indeed* so?—Good God! Good God!—But they will not let me write on. I must go down to this officious peer—who the devil sent for him?

Letter 498: MR BELFORD TO RICHARD MOWBRAY, ESQ.

Sunday, Sept. 10, 4 in the afternoon

I HAVE yours, with our unhappy friend's enclosed. I am glad my lord is with him. As I presume that his frenzy will be but of short continuance, I most earnestly wish that on his recovery he could be prevailed upon to go abroad. Mr Morden, who is inconsolable, has seen by the will, that the case was more than a common seduction; and had dropped hints already, that he looks upon himself on that account to be freed from his promises made to the dying lady, which were that he would not seek to avenge her death. You must make the recovery of his health the motive for urging him on this head; for, if you hint at his own safety, he will not stir, but rather seek the colonel.

As to the lock of hair, you may easily pacify him (as you once saw the angel) with hair near the colour, if he be intent upon it.

At my lord's desire I will write on, and in my common hand; that you may judge what is and what is not fit to read to Mr Lovelace at present. But as I shall not forbear reflections as I go along, in hopes to reach his heart on his recovery; I think it best to direct myself to him still; and that as if he were not disordered.

As I shall not have leisure to take copies, and yet am willing to have the whole subject before me, for my own future contemplation, I must insist upon a return of my letters some time hence. Mr Lovelace knows that this is one of my conditions; and has hitherto complied with it.

Thy letter, Mowbray, is an inimitable performance. Thou art a strange impenetrable creature. But let me most earnestly conjure thee, and the idle flutterer Tourville, from what ye have seen of poor Belton's exit; from our friend Lovelace's frenzy, and the occasion of it; and from the terrible condition in which the wretched Sinclair lies; to set about an immediate change of life and manners. For my own part, I am determined, be your resolutions what they may, to take the advice I give,

As witness
J. BELFORD

Letter 499: MR BELFORD TO ROBERT LOVELACE, ESQ.

OH Lovelace! I have a scene to paint in relation to the wretched Sinclair, that if I do it justice will make thee seriously ponder and reflect, or nothing can. I will lead to it in order; and that in my usual hand, that thy compeers may be able to read it as well as thyself.

When I had written the preceding letter; not knowing what to do with myself; recollecting and in vain wishing for that delightful and improving conversation, which I had now for ever lost; I thought I had as good begin the task which I had for some time past *resolved* to begin; that is to say, to go to church; and see if I could not reap some benefit from what I should hear there. Accordingly I determined to go to hear the celebrated preacher at St James's church. But as if the devil (for so I was then ready to conclude) thought himself concerned to prevent my intention, a visit was made me just as I was dressed, which took me off from my purpose.

Whom should this be from, but Sally Martin, accompanied by Mrs Carter, the sister of the infamous Sinclair; the same, I suppose I need not tell you, who keeps the bagnio near Bloomsbury.

These told me that the surgeon, apothecary, and physician, had all given the wretched woman over; but that she said she could not die nor be at rest till she saw me: and they besought me to accompany them in the coach they came in, if I had one spark of charity, of *Christian* charity as they called it, left.

I was very loath to be diverted from my purpose by a request so unwelcome, and from people so hated; but at last went, and we got thither by ten: where a scene so shocking presented itself to me, that the death of poor desponding Belton is not, I think, to be compared with it.

The old wretch had once put her leg out by her rage and violence, and had been crying, scolding, cursing, ever since the preceding evening, that the surgeon had told her it was impossible to save her; and that a mortification had begun to show itself; insomuch that purely in compassion to their own *ears*, they had been forced to send for another surgeon, purposely to tell her, though against his judgement, and (being a friend of the other) to seem to convince *him*, that he mistook her case; and that if she would be patient, she might recover. But nevertheless her apprehensions of death and her antipathy to the thoughts of dying were so strong, that their imposture had not the intended effect, and she was raving, crying, cursing, and even howling, more like a wolf than a human creature, when I came; so that as I went upstairs, I said surely this noise, this howling, cannot be from the unhappy woman! Sally said it was, and assured me that it was nothing to the noise she had made all night; and stepping into her room before me, Dear *Madam* Sinclair, said she, forbear this noise! It is more like that of a bull than a woman!— Here comes Mr Belford; and you'll fright him away if you bellow at this rate.

There were no less than eight of her cursed daughters surrounding her bed when I entered; one of her partners, Polly Horton, at their head; and now Sally, her other partner, and *Madam* Carter, as they called her (for they are all *madams* with one another) made the number ten: All in shocking dishabille and without stays, except Sally, Carter, and Polly; who, not daring to leave her, had not been in bed all night.

The other seven seemed to have been but just up, risen perhaps from their customers in the fore-house, and their nocturnal orgies, with faces, three or four of them, that had run, the paint lying in streaky seams not half blowzed off, discovering coarse wrinkled skins: the hair of some of them of divers colours; obliged to the blacklead comb where black was affected; the artificial jet, however, yielding apace to the natural brindle: that of others plaistered with oil and powder; the oil predominating: but every one's hanging about her ears and neck in broken curls, or ragged ends; and each at my entrance taken with one motion, stroking their matted locks with both hands under their coifs, mobs, or pinners, every one of which was awry. They were all slipshod; stockingless some; only under-petticoated all; their gowns, made to cover straddling hoops, hanging trollopy, and tangling about their heels; but hastily wrapped round them as soon as I came upstairs. And half of them (unpadded, shoulder-bent, pallid-lipped, feeble-jointed wretches) appearing from a blooming nineteen or twenty perhaps overnight, haggard well-worn strumpets of thirty-eight or forty.

I am the more particular in describing to thee the appearance these creatures made in my eyes when I came into the room, because I believe thou never sawest any of them, much less a group of them, thus unprepared for being seen.ª I, for my part, never did before; nor had I now but upon this occasion been thus *favoured*. If thou *hadst*, I believe thou wouldst hate a profligate woman as one of Swift's Yahoos, or Virgil's obscene Harpies' squirting their ordure upon the Trojan trenchers; since the persons of such in their retirements are as filthy as their minds—Hate them as much as I do; and as much as I admire and next to adore a truly virtuous and elegant woman: for to me it is evident that as a neat and clean woman must be an angel of a creature, so a sluttish one is the impurest animal in nature.

But these were the veterans, the chosen band; for now and then flitted in, to the number of half a dozen or more, by turns, subordinate sinners, undergraduates, younger than some of the chosen phalanx, but not less obscene in their appearance, though indeed not so much beholden to the plastering fucus; yet unpropped by stays, squalid, loose in attire, sluggish-haired, under-petticoated only as the former, eyes half opened, winking and pinking, mispatched, yawning, stretching, as if from the unworn-off effects of the midnight revel; all armed in succession with supplies of cordials, of which every one present was either taster or partaker under the direction of the Praetorian Dorcas, who now and then popped in to see her slops duly given and taken.

But when I approached the *old wretch*, what a spectacle presented itself to my eyes!

Her misfortune has not at all sunk but rather, as I thought, increased her flesh; rage and violence perhaps swelling her muscly features. Behold her then, spreading the whole tumbled bed with her huge quaggy carcase: her mill-post arms held up, her broad hands clenched with violence; her big eyes goggling and flaming-red as we may suppose those of a salamander; her matted grizzly hair made irreverend by her wickedness (her clouted head-dress being half off) spread about her fat ears and brawny neck; her livid lips parched, and working violently; her broad chin in convulsive motion; her wide mouth by reason of the contraction of her forehead (which seemed to be half-lost in its own frightful furrows) splitting her face, as it were, into two parts; and her huge tongue hideously rolling in it; heaving, puffing as if for breath, her bellows-shaped and various-coloured breasts ascending by turns to her chin and descending out of sight with the violence of her gaspings.

This was the spectacle, as recollection has enabled me to describe it, that this wretch made to my eye when I approached her bed-side, surrounded, as I said, by her suffragans and daughters, who surveyed her with scowling frighted attention, which one might easily see had more in it of horror and self-concern (and *self-condemnation* too) than of love or pity; as who should say, See! what we ourselves must one day be!

As soon as she saw me, her naturally big voice, more hoarsened by her ravings, broke upon me: Oh Mr Belford! Oh sir! see what I am come to!—See what I am

ª Whoever has seen Dean Swift's *Lady's Dressing Room* will think this description of Mr Belford not only more natural but more decent painting, as well as better justified by the design, and by the use that may be made of it.

brought to!—To have such a cursed crew about me, and not one of them to take care of me!—But to let me tumble down *stairs* so distant from the room I went from! so distant from the room I meant to go to! Oh cursed by every careless devil!—May this or worse be their fate, every one of them!

And then she cursed and swore more vehemently, and the more, as two or three of them were excusing themselves on the score of their being at that time as unable to help themselves as she.

As soon as she had cleared the passage of her throat by the oaths and curses which her wild impatience made her utter, she began in a more hollow and whining strain to bemoan herself. And here, said she—Heaven grant me patience! (clenching and unclenching her hands)—am I to die thus miserably!—of a broken leg in my old age!—snatched away by means of my own intemperance! Self-do! Self-undone!—No time for my affairs! No time to repent!—And in a few hours (Oh!—Oh!—with another long howling O—h!—U—gh—o! a kind of screaming key terminating it) who knows, who can tell *where* I shall be!—Oh! that indeed I never, never, had had a being!

What could one say to such a wretch as this! whose whole life has been spent in the most diffusive wickedness, and who has more souls to answer for, of both sexes, than the best divine in England ever saved?—Yet I told her she must be patient: that her violence made her worse: and that if she would compose herself, she might get into a frame more proper for her present circumstances.

Who, I? interrupted she: *I* get into a better frame! *I*, who can neither cry, nor pray! Yet already feel the torments of the damned! What mercy can I expect! What hope is left for me?——Then, that sweet creature! That incomparable Miss Harlowe!——She, it seems, is dead and gone!——Oh that cursed man! Had it not been for *him*! I had never had this, the most crying of all my sins, to answer for! And then she set up another howl.

And *is* she dead?—Indeed dead? proceeded she, when her howl was over—— Oh what an angel have I been the means of destroying!—For though it was that wicked man's fault that ever she was in my house, yet it was mine, and yours, and yours, and yours, devils as we all were (turning to Sally, to Polly, and to one or two more), that he did not do her justice! And that, *that* is my curse, and will one day be yours! And then again she howled.

I still advised patience. I said that if her time was so short as she apprehended it to be, the more ought she to endeavour to compose herself: and then she would at least die with more ease to herself—and satisfaction to her friends, I was *going* to say—but the word *die* put her into a violent raving, and thus she broke in upon me.

Die, did you say, sir?—*die!*—I *will not*, I *cannot* die!—I know not *how* to die!— *Die*, sir!—And *must* I then die!—leave this world!—I cannot bear it!—And who brought *you* hither, sir (her eyes striking fire at me), who brought you hither to tell me I must *die*, sir?—I cannot, I will not leave this world. Let others die who wish for another! who expect a better!—I have had my plagues in this; but would compound for all future hopes, so as I may be nothing after this! And then she howled and bellowed by turns.

By my faith, Lovelace, I trembled in every joint; and looking upon *her* who spoke this, and roared thus, and upon the *company* round me, I more than once thought myself to be in one of the infernal mansions!

Yet will I proceed and try for thy good, if I can shock thee but half as much with my descriptions as I was shocked by what I saw and heard.

Sally—Polly—Sister Carter! said she, did you not tell me I might *recover*? Did not the *surgeon* tell me I might?

And so you *may*, cried Sally; Mr Garon says you may if you'll be patient. But, as I have often told you this blessed morning, you are readier to take despair from your own fears than comfort from all the hope we can give you.

Yet, cried the wretch, interrupting, does not Mr Belford (and to *him* you have told the truth, though you won't to *me*; does not he) tell me I shall *die*?—I cannot bear it! I cannot bear the *thoughts* of dying!—

And then, but that half a dozen at once endeavoured to keep down her violent hands, would she have beaten herself; as it seems she had often attempted to do, from the time the surgeon popped out the word *mortification* to her.

Well, but to what purpose, said I (turning aside to her sister, and to Sally and Polly), are these hopes given her, if the gentlemen of the faculty give her over? You should let her know the worst, and then she *must* submit; for there is no running away from death. If she has any matters to settle, put her upon settling them; and do not, by telling her she will live when there is no room to expect it, take from her the opportunity of doing needful things. Do the surgeons actually give her over?

They do, whispered they. Her gross habit, they say, gives no hopes. We have sent for both surgeons, whom we expect every minute.

Both the surgeons (who are French, for Mrs Sinclair has heard Tourville launch out in the praise of French surgeons) came in while we were thus talking. I retired to the further end of the room, and threw up a window for a little air, being half poisoned by the effluvia arising from so many contaminated carcasses; which gave me no imperfect idea of the stench of gaols, which corrupting the ambient air give what is called the prison distemper.

I came back to the bedside, when the surgeons had inspected the fracture; and asked them if there were any expectation of her life?

One of them whispered me, there was none: that she had a strong fever upon her, which alone in such a habit would probably do the business; and that the mortification had visibly gained upon her since they were there six hours ago.

Will amputation save her? Her affairs and her mind want settling. A few days added to her life may be of service to her in both respects.

They told me the fracture was high in her leg; that the knee was greatly bruised; that the mortification in all probability had spread half-way of the *femur*: and then, getting me between them (three or four of the women joining us, and listening with their mouths open, and all the signs of ignorant wonder in their faces, as there appeared of self-sufficiency in those of the artists), did they by turns fill my ears with an anatomical description of the leg and thigh, running over with terms of art; of the *tarsus*, the *metatarsus*, the *tibia*, the *fibula*, the *patella*, the *os tali*, the *os tibiae*, the *tibialis posticus* and *tibialis anticus*, up to the *os femoris*, to the *acetabulum* of the *os ischion*, the *great trochanter*, [*glutaeus*], *triceps*, *levidus*, and *little rotators*; in short, of all the muscles, cartilages, and bones, that constitute the leg and thigh from the great toe to the hip; as if they would show me that all their science had penetrated their heads no farther than their mouths; while Sally lifted up her hands with a Laud bless me! Are all surgeons so learned!—But at last both the gentlemen declared, that if she and her friends would consent to amputation, they would whip off her leg in a moment.

Mrs Carter asked to what purpose, if the operation would not save her?

Very true, they said; but it might be a satisfaction to the patient's friends, that all was done that could be done.

And so the poor wretch was to be lanced and quartered, as I may say, for an experiment only! And, without any hope of benefit from the operation, was to pay the surgeons for tormenting her!

I cannot but say I have a mean opinion of both these gentlemen who, though they make a figure it seems in their way of living, and boast not only a French extraction but a Paris education, never will make any in their practice.

How unlike my honest English friend Tomkins, a plain, serious, intelligent man, whose art lies deeper than in words; who always avoids parade and jargon: and endeavours to make every one as much a judge of what he is about as himself.

All the time the surgeons run on with their anatomical process, the wretched woman most frightfully roared and bellowed; which the gentlemen (who showed themselves to be of the class of those who are not affected with the evils they do not *feel*) took no other notice of than by raising *their* voices to be *heard*, as she raised *hers*—being evidently more solicitous to increase their acquaintance, and to propagate the notion of their skill, than to attend to the clamours of the poor wretch whom they were called in to relieve; though by this very means, like the dog and the shadow in the fable, they lost both aims with me; for I never was deceived in one rule which I made early; to wit, *that the stillest water is the deepest*, while the bubbling stream only betrays shallowness; and that stones and pebbles lie there so near the surface to point out the best place to ford a river dry-shod.

As nobody cared to tell the unhappy wretch what everyone apprehended must follow, and what the surgeons convinced me soon would, I undertook to be the denouncer of her doom. Accordingly, the operators being withdrawn, I sat down by the bedside, and said, Come, Mrs Sinclair, let me advise you to forbear these ravings at the carelessness of those who I find at the time could take no care of themselves; and since the accident *has* happened, and cannot be remedied, to resolve to make the best of the matter: for all this violence but enrages the malady, and you will probably fall into a delirium if you give way to it, which will deprive you of that reason which you ought to make the best of, for the time it may be lent you.

She turned her head towards me, and hearing me speak with a determined *voice*, and seeing me assume as determined an *air*, became more calm and attentive.

I went on, telling her that I was glad from the hints she had given to find her concerned for her past misspent life, and particularly for the part she had had in the ruin of the most excellent woman on earth; that if she would compose herself, and patiently submit to the consequence of an evil she had brought upon herself, it might possibly be happy for her yet. Meantime, continued I, tell me, with temper and calmness, why you was so desirous to see me?

She seemed to be in great confusion of thought, and turned her head this way and that; and at last after much hesitation said, Alas for me! I hardly know *what* I wanted with you. When I awoke from my intemperate trance, and found what a cursed way I was in, my conscience smote me, and I was for catching like a drowning wretch at every straw. I wanted to see everybody and anybody but those I did see; everybody whom I thought could give me comfort. Yet could I expect none from you neither; for you had declared yourself my enemy, although I had never done you harm: for what, Jackey, in her old tone, whining through her nose, was Miss Harlowe to you?—But *she* is happy!—but oh! what will become of *me?*— Yet tell me (for the surgeons have told *you* the truth, no doubt) tell me, shall I do well again? May I recover? If I *may*, I will begin a new course of life: as I hope to be saved I will. I'll renounce you all—every one of you (looking round her) and scrape all I can together, and live a life of penitence; and when I die, leave it all to charitable uses—I will, by my soul—every doit of it to charity—But this once, lifting up her rolling eyes and folded hands (with a wry-mouthed earnestness, in which every muscle and feature of her face bore its part), this one time—good God of heaven and earth, but this once! this once! repeating those words five or six times, spare thy poor creature, and every hour of my life shall be penitence and atonement: upon my soul it shall!

Less vehement! a little less vehement! said I—It is not for me, who have led so free a life, as you but too well know, to talk to you in a reproaching strain, and to set before you the iniquity you have lived in, and the many souls you have helped to destroy. But as you are in so penitent a way, if I might advise, it should be to send for a good clergyman, the purity of whose life and manners may make all these things come from him with a better grace than they can from me.

How, sir! What, sir! interrupting me; send for a parson!—Then you indeed think I shall die! Then you think there is no room for hope!—A parson, sir!—Who sends for a parson while there is any hope left? The sight of a parson would be death immediate to me!—I cannot, cannot die!—Never tell me of it!—What! die!— What! cut off in the midst of my sins!

And then she began to rave again.

I cannot bear, said I, rising from my seat with a stern air, to see a reasonable creature behave so outrageously!—Will this vehemence, think you, mend the matter? Will it avail you anything? Will it not rather shorten the life you are so desirous to have lengthened, and deprive you of the only opportunity you can ever have to settle your affairs for both worlds?—This is but the common lot: and if it will be *yours* soon, looking at *her*, it will be also *yours*, and *yours*, and *yours*, speaking with a raised voice, and turning to every trembling devil round her (for they all shook at my forcible application); and *mine* also. And you have reason to be thankful that you did not perish in that act of intemperance which brought you to this: for it might have been your neck, as *well* as your leg; and then you had not had the opportunity you now have for repentance—And the Lord have mercy upon you! into what a state might you have awaked?

Then did the poor wretch set up an inarticulate frightful howl, such a one as I never before heard uttered, as if already pangs infernal had taken hold of her; and seeing everyone half-frighted, and me motioning to withdraw, Oh pity me, pity me, Mr Belford, cried she, her words interrupted by groans. I find you think I shall die! And *what* I may be, and *where*, in a very few hours—who can tell?

I told her it was in vain to flatter her: it was my opinion she would not recover.

I was going to re-advise her to calm her spirits, and endeavour to resign herself, and to make the best of the opportunity yet left her; but this declaration set her into a most outrageous raving. She would have torn her hair and beaten her breast, had not some of the wretches held her hands by force, while others kept her as steady as they could, lest she should again put out her new-set leg: so that, seeing her thus incapable of advice, and in a perfect frenzy, I told Sally Martin that there was no bearing the room; and that their best way was to send for a minister to pray by her and to reason with her, as soon as she should be capable of it.

And so I left them; and never was so sensible of the benefit of fresh air, as I was the moment I entered the street.

Nor is it to be wondered at, when it is considered that to the various ill smells that will be always found in a close sick-bed room (since generally when the physician comes, the air is shut out), *this* of Mrs Sinclair was the more particularly offensive as, to the scent of plaisters, embrocations, and ointments, were added the stenches of spirituous liquors, burnt and unburnt, of all denominations: for one or other of the creatures, under pretence of colics, gripes, qualms, or insurrections, were continually calling for supplies of these, all the time I was there. And yet this is thought to be a genteel house of the sort: and all the prostitutes in it are prostitutes of price, and their visitors people of note.

Oh Lovelace! what lives do most of us rakes and libertines lead! What company do we keep! And for *such* company, what society renounce or endeavour to make like these!

What woman, nice in her person and of purity in her mind and manners, did she know what miry wallowers the generality of men of our class are in themselves and constantly trough and sty with, but would detest the thoughts of associating with such filthy sensualists, whose favourite taste carries them to mingle with the dregs of stews, brothels, and common-sewers.

Yet, to such a choice are many worthy women betrayed by that false and inconsiderate notion, raised and propagated no doubt by the author of all delusion, *that a reformed rake makes the best husband.* We rakes, indeed, are bold enough to suppose that women in general are as much rakes in their *hearts*, as the libertines some of them suffer themselves to be taken with are in their *practice.* A supposition therefore which it behoves persons of true honour of that sex to discountenance, by rejecting the address of every man whose character will not stand the test of that virtue which is the glory of a woman: and indeed, I may say, of a man too. Why should it not?

How, indeed, can it be, if this point be duly weighed, that a man who thinks *alike of all the sex*, and knows it to be in the *power* of a wife to do him the greatest dishonour man can receive, and doubts not her *will* to do it if opportunity offer and importunity be not wanting: that *such* a one, from *principle*, should be a good husband to *any* woman? And, indeed, little do innocents think what a total revolution of manners, what a change of fixed habits, nay, what a conquest of a *bad nature*, is required to make a man a good husband, a worthy father, and true friend, from *principle*; especially when it is considered that it is not in a man's own power to reform when he will. *This* (to say nothing of my own experience) thou hast found in the progress of thy attempts upon the divine Miss Harlowe. For whose remorses could be either deeper or more frequent? and whose more transient?

Don't be disgusted that I mingle such grave reflections as these with my narratives. It becomes me in my present way of thinking to do so, when I see in Miss Harlowe how all human excellence, and in poor Belton how all inhuman libertinism, and am near seeing in this abandoned woman how all diabolical profligateness, end. And glad should I be, for your own sake, for your splendid family's sake, and for the sake of all your intimates and acquaintance, that you were labouring under the same impressions that so *we*, who have been companions in (and promoters of one another's) wickedness, might join in a general atonement to the utmost of our power.

I came home reflecting upon all these things, more edifying to me than any sermon I could have heard preached: and I shall conclude this long letter with observing that although I left the wretched howler in a high frenzy fit, which was excessively shocking to the bystanders; yet her frenzy is the happiest part of her dreadful condition: for when she is *herself*, as it is called, what must be her reflections upon her past profligate life, throughout which it has been her constant delight and business, devil-like, to make others as wicked as herself! What must her terrors be (a hell already begun in her mind!) on looking forward to the dreadful state she is now upon the verge of!—But I drop my trembling pen.

To have done with so shocking a subject at once, we shall take notice that Mr Belford, in a future letter, writes that the miserable woman to the surprise of the operators themselves (through hourly increasing tortures of body and mind) held out so long as till Thursday Sept. 21. And then died in such agonies as terrified into a transitory penitence all the wretches about her.

Letter 500: COLONEL MORDEN TO JOHN BELFORD, ESQ.

Sunday night, Sept. 10

Dear sir,

ACCORDING to my promise, I send you an account of matters here. Poor Mrs Norton was so very ill upon the road that, slowly as the hearse moved and the chariot followed, I was afraid we should not have got her to St Albans. We put up there as I had intended. I was in hopes that she would have been better for the stop: but I was forced to leave her behind me. I ordered the servant-maid you was so considerately kind as to send down with her to be very careful of her; and left the chariot to attend her. She deserves all the regard that can be paid her; not only upon my cousin's account, but on her own. She is an excellent woman.

When we were within five miles of Harlowe Place, I put on a hand-gallop. I ordered the hearse to proceed more slowly still, the cross-road we were in being rough, and having more time before us than I wanted; for I wished not the hearse to be in till near dusk.

I got to my cousin's about 4 o'clock. You may believe I found a mournful house. You desire me to be very minute.

At my entrance into the court, they were all in motion. Every servant whom I saw had swelled eyes, and looked with so much concern that at first I apprehended some new disaster had happened in the family.

Mr John and Mr Antony Harlowe and Mrs Hervey were there. They all helped on one another's grief, as they had before each other's hardness of heart.

My cousin James met me at the entrance of the hall. His countenance expressed a fixed concern; and he desired me to excuse his behaviour the last time I was there.

My cousin Arabella came to me full of tears and grief. Oh cousin! said she, hanging upon my arm, I dare not ask you any questions!—About the approach of the hearse, I suppose she meant.

I myself was full of grief; and without going farther or speaking, sat down in the hall, in the first chair.

The brother sat down on one hand of me, the sister on the other. Both were silent. The latter in tears.

Mr Antony Harlowe came to me soon after. His face was overspread with all the appearance of woe. He requested me to walk into the parlour; where, as he said, were all his fellow-mourners.

I attended him in. My cousins James and Arabella followed me.

A perfect concert of grief, as I may say, broke out the moment I entered the parlour.

My cousin Harlowe, the dear creature's father, as soon as he saw me said, Oh cousin, cousin, of all our family you are the only one who have nothing to reproach yourself with!—You are a happy man!

The poor mother bowing her head to me in speechless grief sat with her handkerchief held to her eyes with one hand. The other hand was held by her sister Hervey between both hers; Mrs Hervey weeping upon it.

Near the window sat Mr John Harlowe. His face and his body were turned from the sorrowing company. His eyes were red and swelled.

My cousin Antony, at his re-entering the parlour, went towards Mrs Harlowe— Don't—dear sister, said he!—Then towards my cousin Harlowe—Don't—dear brother!—Don't thus give way—And without being able to say another word went to a corner of the parlour and, wanting himself the comfort he would fain have given, sunk into a chair and audibly sobbed.

Miss Arabella followed her uncle Antony as he walked in before me; and seemed as if she would have spoken to the pierced mother some words of comfort. But she was unable to utter them, and got behind her mother's chair; and inclining her face over it on the unhappy lady's shoulder, seemed to claim the consolation that indulgent parent used, but then was unable to afford her.

Young Mr Harlowe with all his vehemence of spirit was now subdued. His self-reproaching conscience, no doubt, was the cause of it.

And what, sir, must their thoughts be which at that moment in a manner deprived them all of motion, and turned their speech into sighs and groans!—How to be pitied, how greatly to be pitied, all of them! But how much to be cursed that abhorred Lovelace, who as it seems by arts uncommon and a villainy without example has been the sole author of a woe so complicated and extensive!—God judge me, as—But I stop—The man is your friend!—He already suffers, you tell me, in his intellect—Restore him Heaven to that—If I find the matter come out, as I *apprehend* it will—Indeed her own hints of his usage of her, as in her will, and in her first letter to me, are enough!—Nor think, my beloved cousin, thou darling of my heart! that thy gentle spirit, breathing charity and forgiveness to the vilest of men, shall avail him!

But once more I stop—Forgive me, sir!—Who could behold such a scene, who could recollect it, in order to describe it (as minutely as you wished me to relate how this unhappy family were affected on this sad occasion), every one of the mourners nearly related to himself, and not be exasperated against the author of all?

As I was the only person (grieved as I was myself) from whom any of them at that instant could derive comfort: Let us not, said I, my dear cousin, approaching the inconsolable mother, give way to a grief which however just can now avail us nothing. We hurt ourselves, and cannot recall the dear creature for whom we mourn. Nor would you wish it, if you knew with what assurances of eternal happiness she left the world—She is happy, madam!—Depend upon it, she is happy! And comfort yourselves with that assurance.

Oh cousin, cousin! cried the unhappy mother, withdrawing her hand from her sister Hervey, and pressing mine with it, You know not what a child I have lost!— Then in a lower voice, And *how* lost!—That it is that makes the loss insupportable.

They all joined in a kind of melancholy chorus, and each accused him and herself, and some of them one another. But the eyes of all in turn were cast upon my cousin James as the person who had kept up the general resentment against so sweet a creature. While he was hardly able to bear his own remorse: nor Miss Harlowe hers; she breaking out into words, How tauntingly did I write to her! How barbarously did I insult her! Yet how patiently did she take it!—Who would have thought she had been so near her end!—Oh brother, brother!—but for *you!*— But for *you!*—

Double not upon me, said he, my own woes!—I have everything before me that has passed!—I thought only to reclaim a dear creature that had erred! I intended not to break her tender heart!—But it was the villainous Lovelace who did that— Not any of us!—Yet, cousin, did she not attribute all to *me?*—I fear she did!—Tell me only, did she name *me*, did she *speak* of me in her last hours? I hope she, who could forgive the greatest villain on earth, and plead that he may be safe from our vengeance; I *hope* she could forgive *me*.

She died blessing you all; and justified rather than condemned your severity to her.

Then they set up another general lamentation. We see, said her father; enough we see in her heart-piercing letters to us what a happy frame she was in a few days before her death: but did it hold to the last? Had she no repinings? Had the dear child no heart-burnings?

None at all!—I never saw, and never shall see, so blessed a *departure*: and no wonder, for I never heard of such a *preparation*. Every hour for weeks together was taken up in it. Let this be our comfort—We need only to wish for so happy an end for ourselves and for those who are nearest to our hearts. We may any of us be grieved for acts of unkindness to her: but had all happened that once she wished for, she could not have made a happier, perhaps not so happy, an end.

Dear soul! and dear sweet soul! the father, uncles, sister, my cousin Hervey, cried out all at once in accents of anguish inexpressibly affecting.

We must for ever be disturbed for those acts of unkindness to so sweet a child, cried the unhappy mother!—Indeed, indeed (softly to her sister Hervey) I have been too passive, much too passive in this case!—The temporary quiet I have been so studious all my life to preserve has cost me everlasting disquiet!—

There she stopped.

Dear sister! was all Mrs Hervey could say.

I have done but half my duty to the dearest and most meritorious of children, resumed the sorrowing mother!—Nay, *not* half!—How have we hardened our hearts against her!—

Again her tears choked up the passage of her words.

My *dearest, dearest sister!* again was all Mrs Hervey could say.

Would to Heaven, proceeded, exclaiming, the poor mother, I had but *once* seen her! Then turning to my cousin James and his sister—Oh my son! Oh my Arabella! if WE were to receive as little mercy—

And there again she stopped, her tears interrupting her further speech: everyone, all the time, remaining silent; their countenances showing a grief in their hearts too big for expression.

Now you see, Mr Belford, that my dearest cousin could be allowed all her merit!—What a dreadful thing is after-reflection upon a conduct so perverse and unnatural?

Oh this cursed friend of yours, Mr Belford! This detested Lovelace!—To him, to him is owing—

Pardon me, sir. I will lay down my pen till I have recovered my temper.

One in the morning

In vain, sir, have I endeavoured to compose myself to rest. You wished me to be very particular, and I cannot help it. This melancholy subject fills my whole mind. I will proceed, though it be midnight.

About six o'clock the hearse came to the outward gate. The parish church is at some distance; but the wind sitting fair, the afflicted family were struck, just before it came, into a fresh fit of grief on hearing the funeral bell tolled in a very solemn manner. A respect as it proved, and as they all guessed, paid to the memory of the dear deceased out of officious love, as the hearse passed near the church.

Judge, when their grief was so great in expectation of it, what it must be when it arrived.

A servant came in to acquaint us with what its lumbering heavy noise up the paved inner court-yard apprised us of before.

He spoke not. He could not speak. He looked, bowed, and withdrew.

I stepped out. No one else could then stir. Her brother, however, soon followed me.

When I came to the door, I beheld a sight very affecting.

You have heard, sir, how universally my dear cousin was beloved. By the poor and middling sort especially, no young lady was ever so much beloved. And with reason: she was the common patroness of all the honest poor in her neighbourhood.

It is natural for us in every deep and sincere grief to interest all we know in what is so concerning to ourselves. The servants of the family, it seems, had told *their* friends, and those *theirs*, that though living, their dear young lady could not be received nor looked upon, her body was permitted to be brought home. The space of time was so confined, that those who knew when she died must easily guess near the time the hearse was to come. A hearse, passing through country villages, and from London, however slenderly attended (for the chariot, as I have said, waited upon poor Mrs Norton) takes everyone's attention. Nor was it hard to guess whose *this* must be, though not adorned by escutcheons, when the cross-roads to Harlowe Place were taken, as soon as it came within six miles of it: so that the hearse and the solemn tolling of the bell had drawn together at least fifty of the neighbouring men, women, and children, and some of good appearance. Not a soul of them, it seems, with a dry eye; and each lamenting the death of this admired lady who, as I am told, never stirred out, but somebody was the better for her.

These, when the coffin was taken out of the hearse, crowding about it, hindered for a few moments its being carried in; the young people struggling who should bear it; and yet with respectful *whisperings* rather than clamorous *contention*. A mark of veneration I had never before seen paid, upon any occasion in all my travels, from the under-bred many, from whom noise is generally inseparable in all their emulations. At last six maidens were permitted to carry it in by the six handles.

The corpse was thus borne, with the most solemn respect, into the hall, and placed for the present upon two stools there. The plates, and emblems, and inscription, set every one gazing upon the lid, and admiring. The more, when they were told that all was of her own ordering. They wished to be permitted a sight of the corpse; but rather mentioned this as their wish than their hope. When they had all satisfied their curiosity, and remarked upon the emblems, they dispersed, with blessings upon her memory, and with tears and lamentations; pronouncing her to be happy; and inferring that were *she* not so, what would become of them? While others ran over with repetitions of the good she delighted to do. Nor were there wanting those among them who heaped curses upon the man who was the author of her fall.

The servants of the family then got about the coffin. They could not before. And that afforded a new scene of sorrow: but a silent one; for they spoke only by their eyes, and by sighs, looking upon the lid and upon one another, by turns, with hands lifted up. The presence of their young master possibly might awe them, and cause their grief to be expressed only in dumb show.

As for Mr James Harlowe (who had accompanied me, but withdrew when he saw the crowd), he stood looking upon the lid when the people had left it, with a fixed attention: yet I dare say knew not a symbol or letter upon it at that moment, had the question been asked him. In a profound reverie he stood, his arms folded, his head on one side, and marks of stupefaction imprinted upon every feature.

But when the corpse was carried into the lesser parlour adjoining to the hall, which she used to call *her* parlour, and put on a table in the middle of the room, and the father and mother, the two uncles, her Aunt Hervey, and her sister came in (joining her brother and me, with trembling feet, and eager woe), the scene was still more affecting. Their sorrow was heightened no doubt by the remembrance of their unforgiving severity: and now seeing before them the receptacle that contained the glory of their family, who so lately was driven thence by their indiscreet violence (never, never more to be restored to them!), no wonder that their grief was more than common grief.

They would have withheld the mother, it seems, from coming in: but when they could not, though undetermined before, they all bore her company, led on by an impulse they could not resist. The poor lady but just cast her eye upon the coffin, and then snatched it away, retiring with passionate grief towards the window; yet addressing herself, with clasped hands, as if to her beloved daughter; Oh my child! my child! cried she; thou pride of my hope! Why was I not permitted to speak pardon and peace to thee!—Oh forgive thy cruel mother!

Her son (his heart then softened, as his eyes showed) besought her to withdraw: and her woman looking in at that moment, he called her to assist him in conducting her lady into the middle parlour: and then returning, met his father going out at the door, who also had but just cast his eye on the coffin, and yielded to my entreaties to withdraw.

His grief was too deep for utterance, till he saw his son coming in; and then, fetching a heavy groan, Never, said he, was sorrow like my sorrow!—Oh son! son!—in a reproaching accent, his face turned from him.

I attended him through the middle parlour, endeavouring to console him. His lady was there in agonies. She took his eye. He made a motion towards her: Oh my dear, said he—but turning short, his eyes as full as his heart, he hastened through to the great parlour: and when there, he desired me to leave him to himself.

Her uncles and her sister looked and turned away, looked and turned away, very often upon the emblems, in silent sorrow. Mrs Hervey would have read to them the inscription—These words she did read, *Here the wicked cease from troubling:* but could read no further. Her tears fell in large drops upon the plate she was contemplating, and yet she was desirous of gratifying a curiosity that mingled impatience with her grief because she could *not* gratify it, although she often wiped her eyes as they flowed.

Judge you, Mr Belford (for you have great humanity), how *I* must be affected. Yet was I forced to try to comfort them all.

But here I will close this letter in order to send it to you in the morning early. Nevertheless, I will begin another upon supposition that my doleful prolixity will not be disagreeable to you. Indeed I am altogether indisposed for rest, as I mentioned before. So can do nothing but write. I have also more melancholy scenes to paint. My pen, if I may so say, is untired. These scenes are fresh in my memory: and I myself, perhaps, may owe to you the favour of a reviewal of them, with such other papers as you shall think proper to oblige me with, when heavy grief has given way to milder melancholy.

My servant, in his way to you with this letter, shall call at St Albans upon the good woman, that he may inform you how she does. Miss Arabella asked me after her, when I withdrew to my chamber; to which she complaisantly accompanied me. She was much concerned at the bad way we left her in; and said her mother would be more so.

No wonder that the dear departed, who foresaw the remorse that would fall to the lot of this unhappy family when they came to have the news of her death confirmed to them, was so grieved for their apprehended grief, and endeavoured to comfort them by her posthumous letters. But it was still a greater generosity in her to try to excuse them to me, as she did when we were alone together a few hours before she died; and to aggravate more than (as far as I can find) she ought to have done, the only error she was ever guilty of. The more freely however perhaps (exalted creature!) that I might think the better of her friends, although at her own expense. I am, dear sir,

Your faithful and obedient servant,
WM. MORDEN

Letter 501: COLONEL MORDEN [TO JOHN BELFORD, ESQ.]

(In continuation)

When the unhappy mourners were all retired, I directed the lid of the coffin to be unscrewed, and caused some fresh aromatics and flowers to be put into it.

The corpse was very little altered, notwithstanding the journey. The sweet smile remained.

The maids who brought the flowers were ambitious of strewing them about it: they poured forth fresh lamentations over her; each wishing she had been so happy as to have been allowed to attend her in London. One of them particularly, who is it seems my cousin Arabella's personal servant, was more clamorous in her grief than the rest; and the moment she turned her back, all the others allowed she had reason for it. I inquired afterwards about her, and found that this creature was set over my dear cousin when she was confined to her chamber by their indiscreet severity.

Good Heaven! that they should treat, and suffer thus to be treated, a young lady who was qualified to give laws to all her family!

When my cousins were told that the lid was unscrewed, they pressed in again, all but the mournful father and mother, as if by consent. Mrs Hervey kissed her pale lips. Flower of the world! was all she could say; and gave place to Miss Arabella; who kissing the forehead of *her* whom she had so cruelly treated could only say to my cousin James (looking upon the corpse, and upon him), Oh brother!—While he, taking the fair lifeless hand, kissed it, and retreated with precipitation.

Her two uncles were speechless. They seemed to wait each other's example whether to look upon the corpse or not. I ordered the lid to be replaced; and then they pressed forward, as the others again did, to take a last farewell of the casket which so lately contained so rich a jewel.

Then it was that the grief of each found fluenter expression; and the fair corpse was addressed to (with all the tenderness that the sincerest love and warmest admiration could inspire) by each, according to their different degrees of relationship, as if none of them had before looked upon her. She was their very niece, both uncles said; the injured saint, her uncle Harlowe; the same smiling sister, Arabella!—the dear creature! all of them—The same benignity of countenance! The same sweet composure! The same natural dignity—*She* was questionless happy! That sweet smile betokened *her* being so; *themselves* most unhappy!—And then, once more, the brother took the lifeless hand, and vowed revenge upon it on the cursed author of all this distress.

The unhappy parents proposed to take one last view and farewell of their once darling daughter. The father was got to the parlour door, after the inconsolable mother: but neither of them were able to enter it. The mother said, she must once more see the child of her heart, or she should never enjoy herself. But they both agreed to refer their melancholy curiosity till the next day; and hand in hand retired inconsolable and speechless both, their faces overspread with woe, and turned from each other as unable each to behold the distress of the other.

When all were withdrawn, I retired, and sent for my cousin James, and acquainted him with his sister's request in relation to the discourse to be pronounced at her interment; telling him how necessary it was that the minister, whoever he were to be, should have the earliest notice given him that the case would admit.

He lamented the death of the Reverend Dr Lewen who, as he said, was a great admirer of his sister, as she was of him, and would have been the fittest of all men for that office.

He spoke with great asperity of Mr Brand, upon whose light inquiry after his sister's character in town he was willing to lay some of the blame due to himself.

Mr Melvill, Dr Lewen's assistant, must he said be the man; and he praised him for his abilities, his elocution, and unexceptionable manners; and promised to engage him early in the morning.

He called out his sister, and she was of his opinion. So I left this upon them.

They both, with no little warmth, hinted their disapprobation of you, sir, for their sister's executor, on the score of your intimate friendship with the author of her ruin.

You must not resent anything I shall communicate to you of what they say on this occasion. Depending that you will not, I shall write with the greater freedom.

I told them how much my dear cousin was obliged to your friendship and humanity: the injunctions she had laid you under, and your own inclination to observe them. I said, that you were a man of honour: that you were desirous of consulting me because you would not willingly give offence to any of them; and that I was very fond of cultivating your favour and correspondence.

They said there was no need of an executor out of their family, and they hoped that you, sir, would relinquish so *unnecessary* a trust, as they called it. My cousin James declared that he would write to you as soon as the funeral was over, to desire that you would do so, upon proper assurances that all that the will prescribed should be performed.

I said you were a man of resolution: that I thought he would hardly succeed; for that you made a point of honour of it.

I then showed them their sister's posthumous letter to you; in which she confesses her obligations to you, and regard for you, and for your future welfare.[a] You may believe, sir, they were extremely affected with the perusal of it.

They were surprised that I had given up to you the proceed of her grandfather's estate since his death. I told them plainly that they must thank themselves if anything disagreeable to them occurred from their sister's devise; deserted and thrown into the hands of strangers as she had been.

They said they would report all I had said to their father and mother; adding that great as their trouble was, they found they had more still to come. But if Mr Belford *were to be* the executor of her will, contrary to their hopes, they besought me to take the trouble of transacting everything with you; that a friend of the man to whom they owed all their calamity might not appear to them.

They were extremely moved at the text their sister had chosen for the subject of the funeral discourse.[b] I had extracted from the will that article, supposing it probable that I might not so soon have an opportunity to show them the will itself, as would otherwise have been necessary, on account of the interment: which cannot be delayed.

a See p. 1367.
b See the will, p. 1419.

Monday morning between eight and nine

THE unhappy family are preparing for a mournful meeting at breakfast. Mr James Harlowe, who has had as little rest as I, has written to Mr Melvill, who has promised to draw up a brief eulogium on the deceased. Miss Howe is expected here by and by, to see for the last time her beloved friend.

Miss Howe, by her messenger, desires she may not be taken any notice of. She shall not tarry six minutes, was the word. Her desire will be easily granted her.

Her servant who brought the request, if it were denied was to return and meet her; for she was ready to set out in her chariot when he got on horseback.

If he met her not with the refusal, he was to stay here till she came. I am, sir,

Your faithful humble servant,
WILLIAM MORDEN

Letter 502: COLONEL MORDEN [TO JOHN BELFORD, ESQ.]

(In continuation)

Monday afternoon, Sept. 11
Sir,

WE are such bad company here to one another, that it is some relief to retire and write.

I was summoned to breakfast about half an hour after nine. Slowly did the mournful congress meet. Each, listless and spiritless, took our place with swollen eyes, inquiring, without expecting any tolerable account, how each had rested.

The sorrowing mother gave for answer that she should never more know what rest was.

By the time we were well seated, the bell ringing, the outward gate opening, a chariot rattling over the pavement of the courtyard, put them into emotion.

I left them; and was just time enough to give Miss Howe my hand as she alighted: her maid in tears remaining in the chariot.

I think you told me, sir, you never saw Miss Howe. She is a fine graceful young lady. A fixed melancholy on her whole aspect overclouded a vivacity and fire, which nevertheless darted now and then through the awful gloom. I shall ever respect her for her love to my dear cousin.

Never did I think, said she as she gave me her hand, to enter more these doors: but, living or dead, my *Clarissa* brings me after her anywhither!

She entered with me the little parlour. The moment she saw the coffin, she withdrew her hand from mine, and with impatience pushed aside the lid. As impatiently she removed the face-cloth. In a wild air, she clasped her uplifted hands together; and now looked upon the corpse, now up to Heaven as if appealing her woes to that? Her bosom heaved and fluttered discernible through her handkerchief, and at last she broke silence: Oh sir!—see you not here!—see you not here—the glory of her sex?—thus by the most villainous of yours—thus—laid low!

Oh my blessed friend, said she!—my sweet companion!—my lovely monitress!—kissing her lips at every tender invocation. And is this all!—is it all of my CLARISSA'S story!

Then, after a short pause and a profound sigh, she turned to me and then to her breathless friend—But *is* she, *can* she be really dead!—Oh no! no!—She only sleeps—Awake, my beloved friend! My sweet clay-cold friend, awake! Let thy Anna Howe revive thee, my dear creature!—by her warm breath revive thee! And, kissing her again, Let my warm lips animate thy cold ones!

Then, sighing again as from the bottom of her heart, and with an air as if disappointed that she answered not: And can such perfection end thus!—And art thou really and indeed flown from thy Anna Howe!—Oh my unkind CLARISSA!

She was silent a few moments, and then seeming to recover herself, she turned to me—Forgive, forgive, Mr Morden, this wild frenzy!—I am not myself!—I never shall be!—You know not the excellence, no, not *half* the excellence that is thus laid low!—Repeating, This cannot, surely, be all of my CLARISSA's story!

Again pausing, One tear, my beloved friend, didst thou allow me!—But this *dumb* sorrow!—Oh for a tear to ease my full-swollen heart that is just bursting!—

But why, sir, why, Mr Morden, was she sent *hither*? Why not to *me*?—She has no father, no mother, no relations; no, not *one!*—They had all renounced her. I was her sympathizing friend—And had not I the best right to my dear creature's remains?—And must names without nature be preferred to such a love as mine?

Again she kissed her lips, each cheek, her forehead—and sighed as if her heart would break—

But why, why, said she, was I withheld from seeing my dearest dear friend before she commenced angel?—Delaying still, and *too easily persuaded* to delay the friendly visit that my heart panted after; what pain will this reflection give me!—Oh my blessed friend! Who knows, who knows, had I come in time, what my cordial comfortings might have done for thee!

But—looking round her, as if she apprehended seeing some of the family—one more kiss, my angel, my friend, my ever-to-be-regretted lost companion! And let me fly this hated house, which I never loved but for thy sake!—Adieu, then, my dearest CLARISSA!—*Thou* art happy, I doubt not, as thou assuredst me in thy last letter!—Oh may we meet and rejoice together where no villainous *Lovelaces*, no hard-hearted *relations*, will ever shock our innocence, or ruffle our felicity!

Again she was silent, unable to go, though seeming to intend it; struggling as it were with her grief, and heaving with anguish: at last, happily, a flood of tears gushed from her eyes—Now!—now!—said she, shall I—shall I—be easier. But for this kindly relief my heart would have burst asunder—More, many more tears than these are due to my CLARISSA, whose counsel has done for me what mine could not do for her!—But why, looking earnestly upon her, her hands clasped and lifted up—but why do I thus lament the HAPPY? And that thou art so, is my comfort. It is, it is, my dear creature! kissing her again.

Excuse me, sir (turning to me, who was as much moved as herself); I loved the dear creature as never woman loved another. Excuse my frantic grief. How has the glory of her sex fallen a victim to villainy, and to hard-heartedness!

Madam, said I, they all have it!—Now indeed they have it.—

And let them have it!—I should belie my love for the friend of my heart were I to pity them!—But how unhappy am I (looking upon the corpse) that I saw her not before these eyes were shut, before these lips were for ever closed!—Oh! sir, you

know not the wisdom that continually flowed from these lips when she spoke!—
nor what a friend I have lost!

Then, surveying the lid, she seemed to take in at once the meaning of the
emblems: and this gave her so much fresh grief, that though she several times
wiped her eyes, she was unable to read the inscription and texts: turning therefore
to me: Favour me, sir, I pray you, by a line with the description of these emblems,
and with these texts: and if I might be allowed a lock of the dear creature's
hair—

I told her that her executor would order both; and would also send her a copy
of her will; in which she would find the most grateful remembrances of her love for
her whom she calls *the sister of her heart*.

Justly, said she, does she call me so; for we had but one heart, but one soul,
between us: and now my better half is torn from me—*what shall I do?*

But looking round her, on a servant's stepping by the door, as if again she had
apprehended it was some of the family: Once more, said she, a solemn, an
everlasting adieu!—Alas! for *me*, a solemn, an everlasting adieu!

Then again embracing her face with both her hands, and kissing it, and
afterwards the hands of the dear deceased, first one, then the other, she gave me
her hand; and quitting the room with precipitation, rushed into her chariot; and
when there, with profound sighs and a fresh burst of tears, unable to speak, she
bowed her head to me and was driven away.

The inconsolable company saw how much I had been moved, on my return to
them. Mr James Harlowe had been telling them what had passed between him and
me: and finding myself unfit for company, and observing that they broke off talk
at my coming in; I thought it proper to leave them to their consultations.

And here I will put an end to this letter; for indeed, sir, the very recollection of
this affecting scene has left me nearly as unable to proceed as I was, just after it,
to converse with my cousins. I am, sir, with great truth,

Your most obedient humble servant,
WILLIAM MORDEN

Letter 503: COLONEL MORDEN [TO JOHN BELFORD, ESQ.]

Tuesday morning, Sept. 12

THE good Mrs Norton is arrived, a little amended in her spirits: owing to the very
posthumous letters, as I may call them, which you, Mr Belford, as well as I,
apprehended would have had fatal effects upon her.

I cannot but attribute this to the right turn of her mind. It seems she has been
inured to afflictions; and has lived in a constant hope of a *better* life and, having no
acts of unkindness to the dear deceased to reproach herself with, is most
considerately resolved to exert her *utmost* fortitude in order to comfort the
sorrowing mother.

Oh Mr Belford, how does the character of my dear departed cousin rise upon
me from every mouth!—Had she been my own child, or my sister!—But do you
think that the man who occasioned this great, this extended ruin—But I forbear.

The will is not to be looked into till the funeral rites are performed. Preparations are making for the solemnity; and the servants, as well as principals of all the branches of the family are put into deep mourning.

I have seen Mr Melvill. He is a serious and sensible man. I have given him particulars to go upon in the discourse he is to pronounce at the funeral: but had the less need to do this as I find he is extremely well acquainted with the whole unhappy story; and was a personal admirer of my dear cousin, and a sincere lamenter of her misfortunes and death. The Reverend Dr Lewen, who is but very lately dead, was his particular friend, and had once intended to recommend him to her favour.

I AM just returned from attending the afflicted parents in an effort they made to see the corpse of their beloved child. They had requested my company and that of the good Mrs Norton. A last leave the mother said she *must* take.

An *effort* however it was, and no more. The moment they came in sight of the coffin, before the lid could be put aside, Oh my dear, said the father retreating, I cannot, I find I cannot, bear it!—Had I—had I—had I never been hard-hearted!—Then turning round to his lady, he had but just time to catch her in his arms, and prevent her sinking on the floor. Oh my dearest life! said he, This is too much!—too much indeed!—Let us, let us retire. Mrs Norton, who (attracted by the awful receptacle) had but just left the good lady, hastened to her—Dear, dear woman, cried the unhappy parent, flinging her arms about her neck, Bear me, bear me, hence!—Oh my child! my child! my own Clarissa Harlowe! Thou pride of my life so lately!—Never, never more must I behold thee!

I supported the unhappy father, Mrs Norton the sinking mother, into the next parlour. She threw herself on a settee there: he into an elbow-chair by her: the good woman at her feet, her arms clasped round her waist. The two mothers, as I may call them, of my beloved cousin, thus tenderly engaged!—What a variety of distress in these woeful scenes!

The unhappy father, in endeavouring to comfort his lady, loaded himself. Would to God, my dear, said he, would to God I had no more to charge myself with than you have!—*You* relented!—*You* would have prevailed upon *me* to relent!

The greater my fault, said she, when I knew that displeasure was carried too high, to acquiesce as I did! What a barbarous parent was I, to let two angry children make me forget that I was mother to a third—to *such* a third!—

Mrs Norton used arguments and prayers to comfort her—Oh my dear Norton, answered the unhappy lady, You was the dear creature's *more natural* mother!—Would to heaven I had no more to answer for than *you have!*

Thus the unhappy pair unavailingly recriminated, till my cousin Hervey entered and, with Mrs Norton, conducted up to her own chamber the inconsolable mother. The two uncles and Mr Hervey came in at the same time, and prevailed upon the afflicted father to retire with them to his—both giving up all thoughts of ever seeing more the child whose death was so deservedly regretted by them.

Time only, Mr Belford, can combat with advantage such a heavy deprivation as this. Advice will not do while the loss is recent. Nature will have way given to it (and so it ought) till sorrow has in a manner exhausted itself; and then reason and religion will come in seasonably with their powerful aids to raise the drooping heart.

I see here no face that is the same I saw at my first arrival. Proud and haughty every countenance then, unyielding to entreaty: now, how greatly are they humbled!—The utmost distress is apparent in every protracted feature, and in every bursting muscle of each disconsolate mourner. Their eyes, which so lately flashed anger and resentment, now are turned to everyone that approaches them, as if imploring pity!—*Could ever wilful hard-heartedness be more severely punished?*

The following lines of Juvenal are, upon the whole, applicable to this house and family. I have resolved them many times since Sunday evening:

> Humani generis mores tibi nosse volenti
> Sufficit una domus: paucos consume dies, et
> Dicere te miserum, postquam illinc veneris, aude.[1]

Let me add that Mrs Norton has communicated to the family the posthumous letter sent her. This letter affords a foundation for *future* consolation to them; but at *present* it has new-pointed their grief by making them reflect on their cruelty to so excellent a daughter, niece, and sister.[a] I am, dear sir,

Your faithful humble servant,
WM. MORDEN

This letter contains in substance: 'Her thanks to the good woman for her care of her in her infancy; for her good instructions and the excellent example she had set her: with self-accusations of a vanity and presumption which lay lurking in her heart unknown to herself till her calamities (obliging her to look into herself) brought them to light.

'She expatiates upon the benefit of afflictions to a mind modest, fearful, and diffident.

'She comforts her on her early death; having finished, as she says, her *probatory course*, at so early a time of life, when many are not ripened by the sunshine of Divine grace for a better till they are 50, 60, or 70 years of age.

'I hope, *says she*, that my father will grant the request I have made to him in my last will, to let you pass the remainder of your days at my *dairy-house*, as it used to be called, where once I promised myself to be happy in you. Your discretion, prudence, and economy, my dear good woman, will make your presiding over the concerns of that house, as beneficial to them, as it can be convenient to you. For *your* sake, my dear Mrs Norton, I hope they will make you this offer. And if they do, I hope you will accept of it, for *theirs*.'

She remembers herself to her foster-brother in a very kind manner: and charges her, for his sake, that she will not take too much to heart what has befallen her.

She concludes as follows: 'Remember me, in the last place, to all my kind well-wishers of your acquaintance; and to those whom I used to call MY POOR. They will be GOD's poor, if they trust in Him. I have taken such care that I hope they will not be losers by my death. Bid them therefore rejoice; and do you also, my reverend comforter and sustainer (as well in my darker, as in my fairer days), likewise rejoice that I am so soon delivered from the evils that were before me; and that I am NOW, when this comes to your hand, as I humbly trust, exulting in the mercies of a gracious God who has conducted me through the greatest trials in safety, and put so happy an end to all my temptations and distresses: and who, I most humbly trust, will in his own good time give us a joyful meeting in the regions of eternal blessedness.'

a [*Letter 503.1: Miss Clarissa Harlowe to Mrs Norton*]

Letter 504: COLONEL MORDEN TO JOHN BELFORD, ESQ.

(In continuation)

Thursday night, Sept. 14

WE are just returned from the solemnization of the last mournful rite. My cousin James and his sister, Mr and Mrs Hervey and *their* daughter, a young lady whose affection for my departed cousin shall ever bind me to her; my cousins John and Antony Harlowe, myself, and some other more distant relations of the names of Fuller and Allinson (who to testify their respect to the memory of the dear deceased had put themselves in mourning, self-invited) attended it.

The father and mother would have joined in these last honours had they been able: but they were both very much indisposed; and continue to be so.

The inconsolable mother told Mrs Norton that the two mothers of the sweetest child in the world ought not on this occasion to be separated. She therefore desired her to stay with her.

The whole solemnity was performed with great decency and order. The distance from Harlowe Place to the church is about half a mile. All the way the corpse was attended by great numbers of people of all conditions.

It was nine when it entered the church. Every corner of which was crowded. Such a profound, such a silent respect did I never see paid at the funeral of princes. An attentive sadness overspread the face of all.

The eulogy pronounced by Mr Melvill was a very pathetic one. He wiped his own eyes often; and made everybody present still oftener wipe theirs.

The auditors were most particularly affected when he told them that the solemn text was her own choice.

He enumerated her fine qualities, naming with honour their late worthy pastor for his authority.

Every enumerated excellence was witnessed to in different parts of the church in respectful whispers by different persons, as of their own knowledge, as I have been since informed.

When he pointed to the pew where (doing credit to religion by her example) she used to sit or kneel, the whole auditory, as one person, turned to the pew with the most respectful solemnity, as if she had been herself there.

When the gentleman attributed condescension and mingled dignity to her, a buzzing approbation was given to the attribute throughout the church; and a poor neat woman under my pew added, 'That she was indeed all graciousness and would speak to anybody.'

Many eyes ran over when he mentioned her charities, her well-judged charities. And her reward was decreed from every mouth, with interjections from some, and these words from others, 'The poor will dearly miss her.'

The *cheerful giver*, whom God is said *to love*,[1] was allowed to be *her*: and a young lady, I am told, said it was Miss Clarissa Harlowe's care to find out the unhappy, upon a sudden distress, before the sighing heart was overwhelmed by it.

She had a set of poor people, chosen for their remarkable honesty and ineffectual industry. These voluntarily paid their last attendance on their benefactress; and mingling in the church as they could crowd near the [aisle] where the corpse was on stands, it was the less wonder that her praises from the preacher met with such general and such grateful whispers of approbation.

Some it seems there were who knowing her unhappy story remarked upon the dejected looks of the brother, and the drowned eyes of the sister. 'Oh what would they now give, they'd warrant, had they not been so hard-hearted!'—Others pursued, as I may say, the severe father and unhappy mother into their chambers at home: 'They answered for their relenting now that it was too late!—What must be their grief?—No *wonder* they could not be present!'

Several expressed their astonishment, as people do every hour, 'that a man could live whom such perfections could not engage to be just to her,' to be *humane*, I may say—and who, her rank and fortune considered, could be so disregardful of his own *interest*, had he had no other motive to be just!—

The good divine, led by his text, just touched upon the unhappy step that was the cause of her untimely fate. He attributed it to the state of things below, in which there could not be absolute perfection. He very politely touched upon the noble disdain she showed (though earnestly solicited by a whole splendid family) to join interests with a man whom she found unworthy of her esteem and confidence; and who courted her with the utmost earnestness to accept of him.

What he most insisted upon was the happy end she made; and thence drew consolation to her relations, and instruction to the auditory.

In a word, his performance was such as heightened the reputation which he had before in a very eminent degree obtained.

When the corpse was to be carried down into the vault (a very spacious one within the church), there was great crowding to see the coffin-lid, and the devices upon it. Particularly two gentlemen, muffled up in cloaks, pressed forward. These it seems were Mr Mullins and Mr Wyerley: both of them professed admirers of my dear cousin.

When they came near the coffin, and cast their eyes upon the lid: 'In that little space, said Mr Mullins, is included all human excellence!'—And then Mr Wyerley, unable to contain himself, was forced to quit the church; and we hear is very ill.

It is said that Mr Solmes was in a remote part of the church, wrapped round in a horseman's coat: and that he shed tears several times. But I saw him not.

Another gentleman was there incognito, in a pew near the entrance of the vault, who had not been taken notice of but for his great emotion when he looked over his pew at the time the coffin was carried down to its last place. This was Miss Howe's worthy Mr Hickman.

My cousins John and Antony, and their nephew James, chose not to descend into the vault among their departed ancestors.

Miss Harlowe was extremely affected. Her *conscience*, as well as her love, was concerned on the occasion. She would go down with the corpse of her dear, her only sister, she said: but her brother would not permit it. And her overwhelmed eye pursued the coffin till she could see no more of it: and then she threw herself on the seat, and was near fainting away.

I accompanied it down, that I might not only satisfy myself, but you, sir, her executor, that it was deposited, as she had directed, at the feet of her grandfather.

Mr Melvill came down, contemplated the lid, and shed a few tears over it. I was so well satisfied with his discourse and behaviour, that I presented him on the solemn spot with a ring of some value; and thanked him for his performance.

And here I left the remains of my beloved cousin; having bespoken my own place by the side of her coffin.

On my return to Harlowe Place, I contented myself with sending my compliments to the sorrowing parents, and retired to my chamber. Nor am I ashamed to own, that I could not help giving way to a repeated fit of humanity as soon as I entered it.

I am, sir,
Your most faithful and obedient servant,
WM. MORDEN

P.S. You will have a letter from my cousin James, who hopes to prevail upon you to relinquish the executorship. It has not my encouragement.

Letter 505: MR BELFORD TO WILLIAM MORDEN, ESQ.

Saturday, Sept. 16

Dear sir,

I ONCE had thoughts to go down privately, in order, disguised, to see the last solemnity performed. But there was no need to give myself this melancholy trouble, since your last letter so naturally describes all that passed that I have every scene before my eyes.

You crowd me, sir, methinks, into the silent slow procession—now with the sacred bier do I enter the awful porch: now measure I with solemn paces the venerable [aisle]: now, emulative of a relationship to her, placed in a near pew to the eye-attracting coffin, do I listen to the moving eulogy: now, through the buzz of gaping, eye-swollen crowds, do I descend into the clammy vault, as a true executor, to see that part of her will performed with my own eyes. There, with a soul filled with musing, do I number the surrounding monuments of mortality, and contemplate the present stillness of so many once busy vanities crowded all into one poor vaulted nook, as if the living grudged room for the corps[es] of those, which when animated, the earth, the air, and the waters, could hardly find room for. Then seeing her placed at the feet of him whose earthly delight she was; and who, as I find, ascribes to the pleasure she gave him the prolongation of his own life[a]; sighing, and with averted face, I quit the solemn mansion, the symbolic coffin, and forever, the glory of her sex, and ascend with those who, in a few years, after a very short blaze of life, will fill up other spaces of the same vault, which now (while they mourn only for her whom they jointly persecuted) they press with their feet.

Nor do your affecting descriptions permit me *here* to stop: but, ascended, I mingle my tears and my praises with those of the numerous spectators. I accompany the afflicted mourners back to their uncomfortable mansion; and make one in the general concert of unavailing woe; till retiring, as I imagine as *they* retire, like them in reality, I give up to new scenes of solitary and sleepless grief; reflecting upon the perfections I have seen the end of; and having no relief but from an indignation which makes me approve of the resentments of others against the

a   See p. 53.

unhappy man, and those *equally unhappy relations of hers*, to whom the irreparable loss is owing.

Forgive me, sir, these reflections; and permit me with this to send you what you declined receiving till the Funeral was over—

He gives him then an account of the money and effects which he sends him down by this opportunity, for the legatees at Harlowe Place and in its neighbourhood; which he desires him to dispose of according to the will.

He also sends him an account of other steps he has taken in pursuance of the will; and desires to know if Mr Harlowe expects the discharge of the funeral expenses from the effects in his hands; and the reimbursement of the sums advanced to the testatrix since her grandfather's death.

These expeditious proceedings, says he, will convince Mr James Harlowe that I am resolved to see the will completely executed; and yet, by my manner of doing it, that I desire not to give unnecessary mortifications to the family, since everything that relates to them shall pass through your hands.

Letter 506: MR JAMES HARLOWE TO JOHN BELFORD, ESQ.

Harlowe Place, Friday night, Sept. 15

Sir,

I HOPE from the character my worthy cousin Morden gives you, that you will excuse the application I make to you, to oblige a whole family in an affair that much concerns their peace, and cannot equally concern anybody else. You will immediately judge, sir, that this is the executorship which my sister has given you the trouble of by her last will.

We shall all think ourselves extremely obliged to you, if you please to relinquish this trust to our own family; these reasons pleading for our expectation of this favour from you:

First, because she never would have had the thought of troubling you, sir, if she had believed any of her near relations would have taken it upon themselves.

Secondly, I understand that she recommends to you in the will to trust to the honour of any of our family for the performance of such of the articles as are of a domestic nature. We are *any* of us, and *all* of us, if you request it, willing to stake our honours upon this occasion: and all you can wish for, as a man of honour, is that the trust be executed.

We are the more concerned, sir, to wish you to decline this office, because of your short and accidental knowledge of the dear testatrix, and long and intimate acquaintance with the man to whom *she* owed her ruin, and *we* the greatest loss and disappointment (her manifold excellencies considered) that ever befell a family.

You will allow due weight, I dare say, to this plea, if you make our case your own: and so much the readier, when I assure you that your interfering in this matter so much against our inclinations (excuse, sir, my plain dealing) will very probably occasion an opposition in some points, where otherwise there might be none.

What therefore I propose is, not that my father should assume this trust: he is too much afflicted to undertake it—nor yet myself—I might be thought too much concerned in interest: but that it may be allowed to devolve upon my two uncles; whose known honour, and whose affection to the dear deceased, nobody ever doubted: and they will treat with you, sir, through my cousin Morden, as to the points they will undertake to perform.

The trouble you have already had will well entitle you to the legacy she bequeaths you, together with the reimbursement of all the charges you have been at and allowance of the legacies you have discharged, although you should not have qualified yourself to act as an executor; as I presume you have not *yet* done; nor will *now* do.

Your compliance, sir, will oblige a family who have already distress enough upon them, in the circumstance that occasions this application to you; and more particularly, sir,

Your most humble servant,
JAMES HARLOWE, Jun.

I send this by one of my servants, who will attend your dispatch.

Letter 507: MR BELFORD TO JAMES HARLOWE, JUN., ESQ.

Saturday, Sept. 16

Sir,

You will excuse *my* plain-dealing in turn: for I must observe that if I had not the just opinion I have of the sacred nature of the office I have undertaken, some passages in the letter you have favoured me with would convince me that I ought *not* to excuse myself from acting in it.

I need name only one of them. You are pleased to say that your uncles, if the trust be relinquished to them, will *treat with me*, through Colonel Morden, *as to the points they will undertake to perform.*

Permit me, sir, to say that it is the duty of an executor to see *every point* performed that *can* be performed. Nor will I leave the performance of mine to any other persons, especially where a qualifying is so directly intimated, and where all the branches of your family have shown themselves, with respect to the incomparable lady, to have but one mind.

You are pleased to urge that she recommends to me the leaving to the honour of any of your family such of the articles as are of a *domestic nature.* But admitting this to be so, does it not imply that the *other* articles are still to obtain my care?—but even these, you will find by the will, she gives not up; and to that I refer you.

I am sorry for the hints you give of an *opposition*, where, as you say, there might be none, if I did not interfere. I see not, sir, why your animosity against a man who cannot be defended should be carried to such a height against one who never gave you offence: and this only because he is acquainted with that man. I will not say all I might say on this occasion.

As to the legacy to myself, I assure you, sir, that neither my circumstances nor my temper will put me upon being a gainer by the executorship. I shall take pleasure to tread in the steps of the admirable testatrix in all I may; and rather will increase than diminish her Poor's Fund.

With regard to the trouble that may attend the execution of the trust, I shall not, in honour to her memory, value ten times more than this can give me. I have indeed two other executorships on my hands; but they sit light upon me. And survivors cannot better or more charitably bestow their time.

I conceive that every article, but that relating to the Poor's Fund, may be performed in two months' time at furthest.

Occasions of litigation or offence shall not proceed from me. You need only apply to Colonel Morden, who shall command me in everything that the will allows me to oblige your family in. I do assure you that I am as unwilling to obtrude myself upon it, as any of it can wish.

I own that I have not yet proved the will; nor shall I do it till next week at soonest, that you may have time for amicable objections if such you think fit to make through the colonel's mediation. But let me observe to you, sir, 'That an executor's power, in such instances as I have exercised it, is the same before the probate, as after it. He can even, without taking *that* out, *commence* an action, although he cannot *declare* upon it: and these acts of administration make him liable to actions himself.' I am therefore very *proper* in the steps I have taken in part of the execution of this sacred trust; and want not *allowance* on the occasion.

Permit me to add that when you have perused the will, and coolly considered everything, it is my hope that you will yourself be of opinion that there can be no room for dispute or opposition: and that if your family will join to expedite the execution, it will be the most natural and easy way of shutting up the whole affair, and to have done with a man, so causelessly as to his *own* particular the object of your dislike; as is, sir,

Your very humble servant (notwithstanding),
JOHN BELFORD

The WILL

To which the following Preamble, written on a separate paper, was stitched with black silk.

To my EXECUTOR

I HOPE I may be excused for expatiating, in diverse parts of this solemn last act, upon subjects of importance. For I have heard of so many instances of confusion and disagreement in families, and so much doubt and difficulty, for want of absolute clearness in the testaments of departed persons, that I have often concluded (were there to be no other reasons but those which respect the peace of surviving friends) that this last act, as to its designation and operation, ought not to be the last in its composition or making; but should be the result of cool deliberation; and (as is more *frequently* than *justly* said) of a *sound mind* and *memory*; which too seldom are to be met with but in *sound health*. All pretences of insanity of mind are likewise prevented when a testator gives reasons for what he wills: all cavils about words are obviated: the obliged are assured; and they enjoy the benefit for whom the benefit was intended. Hence have I for some time past employed myself in penning down heads of such a disposition; which, as reasons offered, I have altered and added to; so that I never was absolutely destitute of a *will*, had I been taken off ever so suddenly. These minutes and imperfect sketches enabled me, as God has graciously given me time and sedateness, to digest them into the form in which they appear.'

I CLARISSA HARLOWE, now, by strange melancholy accidents, lodging in the parish of St Paul, Covent Garden, being of sound and perfect mind and memory, as I hope these presents, drawn up by myself and written with my own hand, will testify; do (this second day of September[a]) in the year of our Lord ——[b] make and publish this my last will and testament, in manner and form following:

In the first place, I desire that my body may lie unburied three days after my decease, or till the pleasure of my father be known concerning it. But the occasion of my death not admitting of doubt, I will not on any account that it be opened; and it is my desire that it shall not be touched but by those of my own sex.

I have always earnestly requested that my body might be deposited in the family vault with those of my ancestors. If it might be granted, I could now wish that it may be placed at the feet of my dear and honoured grandfather. But as I have, by one very unhappy step been thought to disgrace my whole lineage, and therefore this last honour may be refused to my corpse; in this case, my desire is that it may be interred in the churchyard belonging to the parish in which I shall die; and that in the most private manner, between the hours of eleven and twelve at night; attended only by Mrs Lovick and Mr and Mrs Smith, and their maid-servant.

But it is my desire that the same fees and dues may be paid which are usually paid for those who are laid in the best ground, as it is called, or even in the Chancel. And I bequeath five pounds to be given at the direction of the churchwardens to twenty poor people the Sunday after my interment; and this whether I shall be buried here or elsewhere.

I have already given verbal directions that after I am dead (and laid out in the manner I have ordered) I may be put into my coffin as soon as possible: it is my desire that I may not be unnecessarily exposed to the view of anybody; except any of my relations should vouchsafe for the last time to look upon me.

And I could wish, if it might be avoided without making ill-will between Mr Lovelace and my executor, that the former might not be permitted to see my corpse. But if, as he is a man very uncontrollable, and as I am nobody's, he insist upon viewing *her dead* whom he ONCE before saw in a manner dead, let his gay curiosity be gratified. Let him behold and triumph over the wretched remains of one who has been made a victim to his barbarous perfidy: but let some good person, as by my desire, give him a paper whilst he is viewing the ghastly spectacle, containing those few words only: 'Gay, cruel heart! behold here the remains of the once ruined, yet now happy, Clarissa Harlowe!—See what thou thyself must quickly be—and REPENT!—'

Yet to show that I die in perfect charity with *all the world*, I do most sincerely forgive Mr Lovelace the wrongs he has done me.

If my father can pardon the error of his unworthy child so far as to suffer her corpse to be deposited at the feet of her grandfather, as above requested, I could wish (my misfortunes being so notorious) that a short discourse might be pronounced over my remains before they be interred. The subject of the discourse I shall determine before I conclude this writing.

So much written about what deserves not the least consideration and about what will be nothing when this writing comes to be opened and read will be excused when my present unhappy circumstances and absence from all my natural friends are considered.

And NOW with regard to the worldly matters which I shall die possessed of, as well as to those which of right appertain to me either by the will of my said grandfather or otherwise; thus do I dispose of them:

In the first place, I give and bequeath all the real estates in or to which I have any claim or title by the said will to my ever-honoured father James Harlowe, Esq., and that rather than to my brother and sister, to whom I had once thoughts of devising them, because if they survive my father, those estates will assuredly vest in them, or one of them, by virtue of his

a   A blank at the writing was left for this date; and filled up on this day. See p. 1311.
b   The date of the year is left blank for particular reasons.

favour and indulgence, as the circumstances of things with regard to marriage settlements or otherwise may require; or as they may respectively merit by the continuance of their duty.

The house late my grandfather's, called *The Grove*, and by him in honour of me and of some of my voluntary employments, *my dairy-house*, and the furniture thereof as it now stands (the pictures and large iron chest of old plate excepted), I also bequeath to my said father; only begging it as a favour that he will be pleased to permit my dear Mrs Norton to pass the remainder of her days in that house; and to have and enjoy the apartments in it known by the name of *the housekeeper's apartments*, with the furniture in them; and which (plain and neat) was bought for me by my grandfather, who delighted to call me his housekeeper; and which therefore in his lifetime I used as such: the office to go with the apartments. And I am the more earnest in this recommendation, as I had once thought to have been very happy there with the good woman; and because I think her prudent management will be as beneficial to my father as his favour can be convenient to her.

But with regard to what has accrued from that estate since my grandfather's death, and to the sum of nine hundred and seventy pounds which proved to be the moiety of the money that my said grandfather had by him at his death, and which moiety he bequeathed to me for my sole and separate use (as he did the other moiety, in like manner, to my sister[a]) and which sum (that I might convince my brother and sister that I wished not for an independence upon my father's pleasure) I gave into my father's hands, together with the management and produce of the whole estate devised to me—These sums, however considerable when put together, I hope I may be allowed to dispose of absolutely, as my love and my gratitude (not confined wholly to my own family, which is very wealthy in all its branches) may warrant: and which therefore I shall dispose of in the manner hereafter mentioned. But it is my will and express direction that my father's account of the above-mentioned produce may be taken and established absolutely (and without contravention or question) as he shall be pleased to give it to my cousin Morden, or to whom else he shall choose to give it; so as that the said account be not subject to litigation, or to the control of my executor or any other person.

My father of his love and bounty was pleased to allow me the same quarterly sums that he allowed my sister for apparel and other requisites; and (pleased with me then) used to say that those sums should not be deducted from the estate and effects bequeathed to me by my grandfather: but having *mortally* offended him (as I fear it may be said) by one unhappy step, it may be expected that he will reimburse himself those sums—It is therefore my will and direction that he shall be allowed to pay and satisfy himself for all such quarterly or other sums which he was so good as to advance me from the time of my grandfather's death; and that his account of such sums shall likewise be taken without questioning: the money, however, which I left behind me in my escritoire being to be taken in part of those disbursements.

My grandfather, who in his goodness and favour to me knew no bounds, was pleased to bequeath to me all the family pictures at his late house, some of which are very masterly performances; with command that if I died unmarried, or if married and had no descendants, they should then go to that son of his (if more than one should be then living) whom I should think would set most value by them. Now, as I know that my honoured uncle, John Harlowe, Esq., was pleased to express some concern that they were not left to him, as eldest son; and as he has a gallery where they may be placed to advantage: and as I have reason to believe that he will bequeath them to my father if he survive him; who, no doubt, will leave them to my brother; I therefore bequeath all the said family pictures to my said uncle John Harlowe. In these pictures, however, I include not one of my own, drawn when I was about fourteen years of age; which I shall hereafter in another article bequeath.

My said honoured grandfather having a great fondness for the old family plate, which he would never permit to be changed, having lived as he used to say to see a great deal of it come into request again in the revolution of fashions; and having left the same to me with a

a See p. 78.

command to keep it entire; and with power at my death to bequeath it to whomsoever I pleased that I thought would forward his desire; which was as he expresses it that it should be kept *to the end of time*: this family plate, which is deposited in a large iron chest in the strong room at his late dwelling-house, I bequeath entire to my honoured uncle Antony Harlowe, Esq., with the same injunctions which were laid on me; not doubting but he will confirm and strengthen them by his own last will.

I bequeath to my ever-valued friend Mrs Judith Norton, to whose piety and care, seconding the piety and care of my ever-honoured and excellent mother, I owe morally speaking the qualifications which for eighteen years of my life made me beloved and respected, the full sum of six hundred pounds to be paid her within three months after my death.

I bequeath also to the same good woman thirty guineas for mourning for her and for her son my foster-brother.

To Mrs Dorothy Hervey, the only sister of my honoured mother, I bequeath the sum of fifty guineas for a ring; and I beg of her to accept of my thankful acknowledgements for all her goodness to me from my infancy; and particularly for her patience with me in the several altercations that happened between my brother and sister, and me, before my unhappy departure from Harlowe Place.

To my kind and much-valued cousin Miss Dolly Hervey, daughter of my aunt Hervey, I bequeath my watch and equipage and my best Mechlin and Brussels head-dresses and ruffles; also my gown and petticoat of flowered silver of my own work; which having been made up but a few days before I was confined to my chamber, I never wore.

To the same young lady I bequeath likewise my harpsichord, my chamber-organ and all my music-books.

As my sister has a very pretty library; and as my beloved Miss Howe has also her late father's, as well as her own, I bequeath all my books in general, with the cases they are in, to my said cousin Dolly Hervey. As they are not ill-chosen for a woman's library, I know that she will take the greater pleasure in them (when her friendly grief is mellowed by time into a remembrance more sweet than painful) because they were mine; and because there are observations in many of them of my own writing; and some very judicious ones written by the truly reverend Dr Lewen.

I also bequeath to the same young lady twenty-five guineas for a ring to be worn in remembrance of her true friend.

If I live not to see my worthy cousin William Morden, Esq., I desire my humble and grateful thanks may be given to him for his favours and goodness to me; and particularly for his endeavours to reconcile my other friends to me, at a time when I was doubtful whether he would forgive me himself. As he is in great circumstances, I will only beg of him to accept of two or three trifles in remembrance of a kinswoman who always honoured *him* as much as he loved *her*. Particularly, of that piece of flowers which my uncle Robert, his father, was very earnest to obtain in order to carry it abroad with him.

I desire him likewise to accept of the little miniature picture set in gold, which his worthy father made me sit for to the famous Italian master whom he brought over with him; and which he presented to me that I might bestow it as he was pleased to say upon the man whom one day I should be most inclined to favour.

To the same gentleman I also bequeath my rose diamond ring, which was a present from his good father to me; and will be the more valuable to him on that account.

I humbly request Mrs Annabella Howe, the mother of my dear Miss Howe, to accept of my respectful thanks for all her favours and goodness to me when I was so frequently a visitor to her beloved daughter; and of a ring of twenty-five guineas price.

My picture at whole length, which is in my late grandfather's closet (excepted in an article above from the family pictures), drawn when I was near fourteen years of age; about which time my dear Miss Howe and I began to know, to distinguish and to love one another—so dearly—I cannot express how dearly—I bequeath to that sister of my heart: of whose friendship, as well in adversity as prosperity, when I was deprived of all other comfort and comforters, I have had such instances as that our love can only be exceeded in that state of perfection in which I hope to rejoice with her hereafter to all eternity.

I bequeath also to the same dear friend my best diamond ring, which is in the private drawer of my escritoire with other jewels. As also all my finished and framed pieces of needlework; the flower-piece excepted, which I have already bequeathed to my cousin Morden.

These pieces have all been taken down, as I have heard[a]; and my relations will have no heart to put them up again: but if my good mother chooses to keep back any one piece (the above capital piece, as it is called, excepted) not knowing but some time hence she may bear the sight of it; I except that also from this general bequest; and direct it to be presented to her.

My whole-length picture in the Vandyke taste,[b] that used to hang in my own parlour, as I was permitted to call it, I bequeath to my Aunt Hervey, except my mother shall think fit to keep it herself.

I bequeath to the worthy Charles Hickman, Esq., the locket with the miniature picture which I have constantly worn, and shall continue to wear near my heart till the approach of my last hour,[c] of the lady whom he best loves. It must be the most acceptable present that can be made him, next to the *hand* of the dear original. And oh my dear Miss Howe, let it not be long before you permit his claim to the *latter*—for indeed you know not the value of a virtuous mind in that sex; and how preferable such a mind is to one distinguished by the more dazzling flights of unruly wit; although the latter were to be joined by that specious outward appearance which is too, too often permitted to attract the hasty eye and susceptible heart.

I make it my earnest request to my dear Miss Howe that she will not put herself into mourning for me. But I desire her acceptance of a ring with my hair; and that Mr Hickman will also accept of the like; each of the value of fifteen guineas.

I bequeath to Lady Betty Lawrance, and to her sister Lady Sarah Sadleir, and to the right honourable Lord M. and to their worthy nieces Miss Charlotte and Miss Martha Montague, each an enamelled ring, with a cypher Cl. H. with my hair in crystal, and round the inside of each, the day, month, and year of my death: each ring, with brilliants, to cost twenty guineas. And this as a small token of the grateful sense I have of the honour of their good opinions and kind wishes in my favour; and of their truly noble offer to me of a very considerable annual provision, when they apprehended me to be entirely destitute of any.

To the reverend and learned Doctor Arthur Lewen, by whose instructions I have been equally delighted and benefited, I bequeath twenty guineas for a ring. If it should please God to call him to Himself before he can receive this small bequest, it is my will that his worthy daughter may have the benefit of it.

In token of the grateful sense I have of the civilities paid me by Mrs and Miss Howe's domestics, from time to time in my visits there, I bequeath thirty guineas to be divided among them, as their dear young mistress shall think proper.

To each of my worthy companions and friends Miss Biddy Lloyd, Miss Fanny Alston, Miss Rachel Biddulph, and Miss Cartwright Campbell, I bequeath five guineas for a ring.

To my late maidservant Hannah Burton, an honest, faithful creature, who loved *me*, reverenced my *mother*, and respected my *sister*, and never sought to do anything unbecoming of her character, I bequeath the sum of fifty pounds, to be paid within one month after my decease, she labouring under ill health: and if that ill health continue, I commend her for farther assistance to my good Mrs Norton, to be put upon my Poor's Fund, hereafter to be mentioned.

a   See p. 509.
b   See p. 509.
c   See p. 1357.

To the coachman, groom and two footmen, and five maids at Harlowe Place, I bequeath ten pounds each; to the helper five pounds.

To my sister's maid Betty Barnes, I bequeath ten pounds, to show that I resent not former disobligations; which I believe were owing more to the insolence of office, and to natural pertness, than to personal ill-will.

All my wearing apparel, of whatever sort, that I have not been obliged to part with, or which is not already bequeathed (my linen excepted), I desire Mrs Norton will accept of.

The trunks and boxes in which my clothes are sealed up, I desire may not be opened, but in presence of Mrs Norton (or of some one deputed by her) and of Mrs Lovick.

To the worthy Mrs Lovick abovementioned, from whom I have received great civilities, and even maternal kindnesses; and to Mrs Smith (with whom I lodge) from whom *also* I have received great kindnesses; I bequeath all my linen, and all my unsold laces; to be divided equally between them, as they shall agree; or, in case of disagreement, the same to be sold, and the money arising to be equally shared by them.

And I bequeath to the same two good women, as a further token of my thankful acknowledgements of their kind love and compassionate concern for me, the sum of twenty guineas each.

To Mr Smith, the husband of Mrs Smith above-named, I bequeath the sum of ten guineas, in acknowledgement of his civilities to me.

To Sarah, the honest maid-servant of Mrs Smith, to whom (having no servant of my own) I have been troublesome, I bequeath five guineas; and ten guineas more in lieu of a suit of my wearing-apparel, which once, with some linen, I thought of leaving to her. With this she may purchase what may be more suitable to her liking and degree.

To the honest and careful widow Ann Shelburne, my nurse, over and above her wages, and the little customary perquisites that may belong to her, I bequeath the sum of ten guineas. Hers is a careful and (to persons of such humanity and tenderness) a melancholy employment, attended in the latter part of life with great watching and fatigue, which is hardly ever enough considered.

The few books I have at my present lodgings, I desire Mrs Lovick to accept of; and that she be permitted, if she please, to take a copy of my book of *meditations*, as I used to call it; being extracts from the best of books; which she seemed to approve of, although suited particularly to my own case. As for the book itself, perhaps my good Mrs Norton will be glad to have it, as it is written all with my own hand.

In the middle drawer of my escritoire at Harlowe Place, are many letters and copies of letters, put up according to their dates, which I have written or received in a course of years (ever since I learned to write) from and to my grandfather, my father and mother, my uncles, my brother and sister, on occasional little absences; my late uncle Morden, my cousin Morden; Mrs Norton, and Miss Howe, and other of my companions and friends before my confinement at my father's: as also from the three reverend gentlemen, Dr Blome, Mr Arnold, and Mr Tompkins, now with God; and the very reverend Dr Lewen, on serious subjects. As these letters exhibit a correspondence that no young person of my sex need to be ashamed of, allowing for the time of life when mine were written; and as many excellent things are contained in those written to me; and as Miss Howe, to whom most of them have been communicated, wished formerly to have them, if she survived me: for these reasons I bequeath them to my said dear friend Miss Anna Howe; and the rather as she had for some years past a very considerable share in the correspondence.

I do hereby make, constitute and ordain, John Belford, of Edgworth in the county of Middlesex, Esq., the sole executor of this my last will and testament; having previously obtained his leave to do so. I have given the reasons which induced me to ask this gentleman to take upon him this trouble, to Miss Howe. I therefore refer to her on this subject.

But I do most earnestly beg of him, the said Mr Belford, that in the execution of this trust he will (as he has repeatedly promised) studiously endeavour to promote peace with, and suppress resentments in everyone; so as that all farther mischiefs may be prevented, as well *from* as *to* his friend. And in order to this, I beseech him to cultivate the friendship of my worthy cousin Morden; who, as I presume to hope (when he understands it to be my dying request), will give him his advice and assistance in every article where it may be necessary; and who will perhaps be so good as to interpose with my relations, if any difficulty should arise about carrying any of the articles of this my last will into execution, and to soften them into the wished-for condescension—for it is my earnest request to Mr Belford that he will not seek by law, or by any sort of violence, either by word or deed, to extort the performance from *them*. If there be any articles of a merely domestic nature that my relations shall think unfit to be carried into execution; such articles I leave entirely to my said cousin Morden and Mr Belford to vary, or totally dispense with, as they shall agree upon the matter; or, if they two differ in opinion, they will be pleased to be determined by a third person, to be chosen by them both.

Having been pressed by Miss Howe and her mother to collect the particulars of my sad story, and given expectation that I would, in order to do my character justice with all my friends and companions: but not having time before me for the painful task, it has been a pleasure to me to find, by extracts kindly communicated to me by my said executor, that I may safely trust my fame to the justice done me by Mr Lovelace in his letters to him my said executor. And as Mr Belford has engaged to contribute what is in his power towards a compilement to be made of all that relates to my story, and knows my whole mind in this respect; it is my desire that he will cause two copies to be made of this collection; one to remain with Miss Howe, the other with himself; and that he will show or lend his copy, if required, to my Aunt Hervey, for the satisfaction of any of my family; but under such restrictions as the said Mr Belford shall think fit to impose; that neither any other person's safety may be endangered, nor his own honour suffer, by the communication.

I bequeath to my said executor, the sum of one hundred guineas, as a grateful though insufficient acknowledgement of the trouble he will be at in the execution of the trust he has so kindly undertaken. I desire him likewise to accept of twenty guineas for a ring. And that he will reimburse himself for all the charges and expenses which he shall be at in the execution of this trust.

In the worthy Dr H. I have found a physician, a father and a friend. I beg of him, as a testimony of my gratitude, to accept of twenty guineas for a ring.

I have the same obligations to the kind and skilful Mr Goddard, who attended me as my apothecary. His very moderate bill I have discharged down to yesterday. I have always thought it incumbent upon testators to shorten all they can the trouble of their executors. I know I under-rate the value of Mr Goddard's attendances, when over and above what may accrue from yesterday, to the hour that will finish all, I desire fifteen guineas for a ring may be presented to him.

To the reverend Mr —— who frequently attended me and prayed by me in my last stages, I also bequeath fifteen guineas for a ring.

There are a set of honest indigent people whom I used to call *my poor*, and to whom Mrs Norton conveys relief each month or at shorter periods, in proportion to their necessities, from a sum I deposited in her hands and from time to time recruited as means accrued to me; but now nearly, if not wholly expended: NOW, that my fault may be as little aggravated as possible by the sufferings of the worthy people whom Heaven gave me a heart to relieve; and as the produce of my grandfather's estate (including the moiety of the sums he had by him and was pleased to give me at his death as above-mentioned) together with what I shall further appropriate to the same use in the subsequent articles, will, as I hope, more than answer all my legacies and bequests; it is my will and desire that the remainder, be it little or much, shall become a fund to be appropriated, and I hereby direct that it be appropriated, to the like purposes with the sums which I put into Mrs Norton's hands as aforesaid—And this under the direction and management of the said Mrs Norton, who knows my whole mind in this particular. And in case of her death, or of her desire to be acquitted of the management thereof; it is my earnest request to my dear Miss Howe that she will take it upon herself: and at her own death that she will transfer what shall remain undisposed of at the *time*, to such persons, and with such limitations, restrictions and provisos, as she shall think will best answer my intention. For, as to the management and distribution of all or any part of it while in Mrs Norton's hands or her own, I will that it be entirely discretional, and without account, either to my executor or any other person.

Although Mrs Norton, as I have hinted, knows my whole mind in this respect; yet it may be proper to mention in this last solemn act, that my intention is that this fund be entirely set apart and appropriated to relieve temporarily, from the interest thereof (as I dare say it will be put out to the best advantage) or even from the principal, if need be, the honest, industrious, labouring poor only; when sickness, lameness, unforeseen losses, or other accidents disable them from following their lawful callings; or to assist such honest people of large families as shall have a child of good inclinations to put out to service, trade or husbandry.

It has always been a rule with me in my little donations, to endeavour to aid and set forward the sober and industrious poor. Small helps, if seasonably afforded, will do for such; and so the fund may be of more extensive benefit: an ocean of wealth will not be sufficient for the idle and dissolute: whom, therefore, since they will be always in want, it will be no charity to relieve, if worthier creatures shall by that means be deprived of such assistance as may set the wheels of their industry going, and put them in a sphere of useful action.

But it is my express will and direction that let this fund come out to be ever so considerable, it shall be applied only in support of the *temporary exigencies* of the persons I have described; and that no one family or person receive from it, at one time, or in one year, more than the sum of twenty pounds.

It is my will and desire that the set of jewels which was my grandmother's, and presented to me soon after her death by my grandfather, be valued; and the worth of them paid to my executor, if any of my family choose to have them; or otherwise, that they be sold and go to the augmentation of my Poor's Fund—But if they may be deemed an equivalent for the sums my father was pleased to advance to me since the death of my grandfather, I desire that they may be given up to him.

I presume that the diamond necklace, solitaire and buckles, which were properly my own, presented by my mother's uncle Sir Josias Brookland, will not be purchased by anyone of my family, for a too obvious reason: in this case I desire that they may be sent to my executor; and that he will dispose of them to the best advantage; and apply the money to the uses of my will.

In the beginning of this tedious writing, I referred to the latter part of it, the naming of the subject of the discourse which I wished might be delivered at my funeral, if permitted to be interred with my ancestors: I think the following will be suitable to my case. I hope the alteration of the words *her* and *she*, for *him* and *her* may be allowable.

'Let not *her* that is deceived trust in vanity; for vanity shall be *her* recompense. *She* shall be accomplished before *her* time; and *her* branch shall not be green. *She* shall shake off *her* unripe grape as the vine and shall cast off *her* flower as the blighted olive.'[a]

But if I am to be interred in town, let only the usual Burial Service be read over my corpse.

If my body be permitted to be carried down, I bequeath ten pounds to be given to the poor of the parish, at the discretion of the churchwardens, within a fortnight after my interment.

If any necessary matter be omitted in this my will; or if anything appear doubtful or contradictory, as possibly may be the case; since, besides my inexperience in these matters, I am now at this time very weak and ill; having put off the finishing hand a little too long, in hopes of obtaining the last forgiveness of my honoured friends; in which case I should have

a   Job xv. 31, 32, 33.

acknowledged the favour with a suitable warmth of duty, and filled up some blanks which I left to the very last,[a] in a more agreeable manner to myself than now I have been enabled to do—In case of such omissions and imperfections, I desire that my cousin Morden will be so good as to join with Mr Belford in considering them, and in comparing them with what I have more explicitly written; and if, after *that*, any doubt remain, that they will be pleased to apply to Miss Howe, who knows my whole heart: and I desire that their construction may be established: and I hereby establish it, provided it be unanimous, and direct it to be put in force, as if I had so written and determined myself.

And now, oh my blessed REDEEMER, do I, with a lively faith, humbly lay hold of Thy meritorious death and sufferings; hoping to be washed clean in Thy precious blood from all my sins: in the bare hope of the happy consequences of which, how light do those sufferings seem (grievous as they were at the time) which I confidently trust will be a means, by Thy grace, to work out for me a more exceeding and eternal weight of glory!

Clari∫sa Harlowe.

Signed, sealed, published, and declared, the day and year above-written, by the said Clarissa Harlowe, as her last will and testament; contained in seven sheets of paper, all written with her own hand, and every sheet signed and sealed by herself, in the presence of us:

> John Williams
> Arthur Bedall
> Elizabeth Swanton

Letter 508: COLONEL MORDEN TO JOHN BELFORD, ESQ.

Sat. Sept. 16

I HAVE been employed in a most melancholy task. In reading the will of the dear deceased.

The unhappy mother and Mrs Norton chose to be absent on the affecting occasion. But Mrs Harlowe made it her earnest request that every article of it should be fulfilled.

They were all extremely touched with the preamble.

The first words of the will—'I Clarissa Harlowe, now by strange melancholy accidents, lodging' etc., drew tears from some, sighs from all.

The directions for her funeral, in case she were or were not permitted to be carried down; the mention of her orders having been given for the manner of her being laid out, and the presence of mind so visible throughout the whole, obtained their admiration, expressed by hands and eyes lifted up, and by falling tears.

When I read the direction, 'That her body was not to be viewed except any of her relations should vouchsafe for the last time to look upon her', they turned away, and turned to me, three or four times alternately. Mrs Hervey and Miss Arabella sobbed; the uncles wiped their eyes; the brother looked down; the father wrung his hands.

I was obliged to stop at the words, 'That she was *nobody's*.'

But when I came to the address to be made to the accursed man, 'if he were not to be diverted from seeing *her* dead whom once before he had seen in a manner dead'—execration, and either vows or wishes of revenge, filled every mouth.

a See p. 1311.

These were still more fervently renewed when they came to hear read her forgiveness of even this man.

You remember, sir, on our first reading of the will in town, the observations I made on the foul play which it is evident the excellent creature met with from this abandoned man, and what I said upon the occasion. I am not used to repeat things of that nature.

The dear creature's noble contempt of the *nothing*, as she as nobly calls it, about which she had been giving such particular directions, to wit, her body; and her apologizing for the particularity of those directions from the circumstances she was in—had the same, and as strong an effect upon me, as when I first read the animated paragraph; and, pointed by my eye (by turns cast upon them all), affected them all.

When the article was read which bequeathed to the father the grandfather's estate, and the reason assigned for it (so generous and so dutiful), the father could sit no longer, but withdrew, wiping his eyes and lifting up his hands at Mr James Harlowe; who arose to attend him to the door, as Arabella likewise did—all he could say—Oh son! son!—Oh girl! girl!—as if he reproached them for the parts they had acted and put him upon acting.

But yet on some occasions this brother and sister showed themselves to be true will-disputants.

Let tongue and eyes express what they will, Mr Belford, the reading of a will, where a person dies worth anything considerable, generally affords a true test of love to the deceased.

The clothes, the thirty guineas for mourning to Mrs Norton, with the recommendation of the good woman for housekeeper at *The Grove*, were thought sufficient, had the article of £600 which was called monstrous been omitted. Some other passages in the will were called *flights, and such whimsies as distinguish people of imagination from those of judgement.*

My cousin Dolly Hervey was grudged the library. Miss Harlowe said that as she and her sister never bought the same books, she would take that to herself, and would *make it up* to her cousin Dolly *one way or other.*

I intend, Mr Belford, to save you the trouble of interposing—the library shall be my cousin Dolly's.

Mrs Hervey could hardly keep her seat. On *this* occasion, however, she only said, that her late dear and *ever* dear niece, was *too good* to her and *hers.* But, *at another time,* she declared, with tears, that she could not forgive herself for a letter she wrote[a] (looking at Miss Arabella, whom, it seems, unknown to anybody, she had consulted before she wrote it) and which, she said, must have wounded a spirit that now, she saw, had been too deeply wounded before.

Oh my aunt, said Arabella, no more of that!—Who would have thought that the dear creature had been such a penitent?

Mr John and Mr Antony Harlowe were so much affected with the articles in their favour (bequeathed to them without a word or hint of reproach or recrimination) that they broke out into self accusations; and lamented that their sweet niece, as they called her, was now got above all grateful acknowledgement and returns.

a   See p. 503.

Indeed, the mutual upbraidings and grief of all present, upon those articles in which everyone was remembered for good, so often interrupted me, that the reading took up above six hours. But curses upon the accursed man were a refuge to which they often resorted, to exonerate themselves.

How wounding a thing, Mr Belford, is a generous and well-distinguished forgiveness! What revenge can be more effectual and more noble, were revenge intended, and were it wished to strike remorse into a guilty or ungrateful heart! But my dear cousin's motives were all duty and love. She seems indeed to have been, as much as mortal could be, LOVE itself. Love sublimed by a purity, by a true delicacy, that hardly any woman before her could boast of. Oh Mr Belford, what an example would she have given in every station of life (as wife, mother, mistress, friend), had her lot fallen upon a man blessed with a mind like her own!

The £600 bequeathed to Mrs Norton, the library to Miss Hervey, and the remembrances to Miss Howe, were not the only articles grudged. Yet to what purpose did they regret the pecuniary bequests, when the Poor's Fund, and not themselves, would have had the benefit had not those legacies been bequeathed?

But enough passed to convince me that my cousin was absolutely right in her choice of an executor out of the family. Had she chosen one in it, I dare say that her will would have been no more regarded than if it had been the will of a dead king; than that of Louis XIV in particular; so flagrantly broken through by his nephew the Duke of Orleans before he was cold. The only will of that monarch perhaps which was ever disputed.

But little does Mr James Harlowe think that while he is grasping at hundreds, he will most probably lose thousands, if he be my survivor. A man of a spirit so selfish and narrow shall not be my heir.

You will better conceive, Mr Belford, than I can express, how much they were touched at the hint that the dear creature had been obliged to part with some of her clothes.

Silent reproach seized every one of them when I came to the passage where she mentions that she deferred filling up some blanks, in hopes of receiving their last blessing and forgiveness.

I will only add that they could not bear to hear read the concluding part, so solemnly addressed to her Redeemer. They all arose from their seats, and crowded out of the apartment we were in. And then, as I afterwards found, separated in order to seek that consolation in solitary retirement, which, though they could not hope for from their own reflections, yet at the time they had less reason to expect in each other's company. I am, sir,

Your faithful and obedient servant,
WM. MORDEN

Letter 509: MR BELFORD TO THE RIGHT HONOURABLE LORD M.

London, Sept. 14

My lord,

I AM very apprehensive that the affair between Mr Lovelace and the late excellent Miss Clarissa Harlowe will be attended with further bad consequences, notwithstanding her dying injunctions to the contrary. I would therefore humbly propose that your lordship and his other relations will forward the purpose your kinsman lately had to go abroad; where I hope he will stay till all is blown over. But as he will not stir if he know the true motives of your wishes, the avowed inducement, as I hinted once to Mr Mowbray, may be such as respects his own health both of person and mind. To Mr Mowbray and Mr Tourville all countries are alike; and they perhaps will accompany him.

I am glad to hear that he is in a way of recovery: but this the rather induces me to press the matter. And I think no time should be lost.

Your lordship has heard that I have the honour to be the executor of this admirable lady's last will. I transcribe from it the following paragraph.

He then transcribes the article which so gratefully mentions this nobleman and the ladies of his family, in relation to the rings she bequeaths them, about which he desires their commands.

Letter 510: MISS MONTAGUE TO JOHN BELFORD, ESQ.

M. Hall, Friday, Sept. 15

Sir,

MY lord having the gout in his right hand, his lordship, and Lady Sarah, and Lady Betty, have commanded me to inform you that before your letter came Mr Lovelace was preparing for a foreign tour. We shall endeavour to hasten him away on the motives you suggest.

We are all extremely affected with the dear lady's death. Lady Betty and Lady Sarah have been indisposed ever since they heard of it. They had pleased themselves, as had my sister and self, with the hopes of cultivating her acquaintance and friendship after he was gone abroad, upon her own terms. Her kind remembrance of each of us has renewed, though it could not heighten, our regrets for so irreparable a loss. We shall order Mr Finch, our goldsmith, to wait on you. He has our directions about the rings. They will be long, long worn in memory of the dear testatrix.

Everybody is assured that you will do all in your power to prevent *farther* ill consequences from this melancholy affair. My lord desires his compliments to you. I am, sir,

Your humble servant,
CH. MONTAGUE

This collection having run into a much greater length than was wished, it is thought proper to omit several letters that passed between Colonel Morden, Miss Howe, Mr Belford, and Mr Hickman, in relation to the execution of the lady's will, etc.

It is however necessary to observe on this subject, that the unhappy mother, being supported by the two uncles, influenced the afflicted father to overrule all his son's objections, and to direct a literal observation of the will; and at the same time to give up all the sums which he was empowered by it to reimburse himself; as also to take upon himself to defray the funeral expenses.

Mr Belford so much obliged Miss Howe by his steadiness, equity, and dispatch,

*and by his readiness to contribute to the directed collection, that she voluntarily
entered into a correspondence with him, as the representative of her beloved friend.
In the course of which, he communicated to her (in confidence) the letters which
passed between him and Mr Lovelace and, by Colonel Morden's consent, those
which passed between that gentleman and himself.*

[*Letter 510.1: Mr Belford to Charles Hickman, Esq.*]

*He sent with the first parcel of letters which he had transcribed out of shorthand
for Miss Howe, a letter to Mr Hickman, dated the 16th of September; in which he
expresses himself as follows:*

'But I ought, sir, in this parcel to have kept out one letter. It is that which relates
to the interview between yourself and Mr Lovelace, at Mr Dormer's.ᵃ In which Mr
Lovelace treats you with an air of levity, which neither your person, your character,
nor your commission, deserved; but which was his usual way of treating everyone
whose business he was not pleased with. I hope, sir, you have too much greatness
of mind to be disturbed at this letter, should Miss Howe communicate it to you;
and the rather, as it is impossible that you should suffer with her on that account.'
*He then excuses Mr Lovelace as a good-natured man with all his faults; and gives
instances of his still greater freedoms with himself.*

[*Letter 510.2: Mr Hickman to John Belford, Esq.*]

To this Mr Hickman answers, in his letter of the 18th:
'As to Mr Lovelace's treatment of me in the letter you are pleased to mention,
I shall not be concerned at it, whatever it be. I went to him prepared to expect odd
behaviour from him; and was not disappointed. I argue to myself, in all such cases
as this, as Miss Howe from her ever-dear friend argues, *that if the reflections thrown
upon me are just, I ought not only to forgive them, but to endeavour to profit by
them*: if unjust, *that I ought to despise them, and the reflecter too; since it would be
inexcusable to strengthen by anger an enemy whose malice might be disarmed by
contempt.* And, moreover, I should be almost sorry to find myself spoken well of
by a man who could treat, as he treated, a lady who was an ornament to her sex
and to human nature.
'I thank you, however, sir, adds he, for your consideration for me in this
particular; and for your whole letter, which gives me so desirable an instance of
that friendship which you honoured me with the assurances of, when I was last in
town; and which I as cordially embrace, as wish to cultivate.'

[*Letter 510.3: Miss Howe to John Belford, Esq.*]

*Miss Howe, in hers of the 20th, acknowledging the receipt of the letters, and papers,
and legacies, sent with Mr Belford's letter to Mr Hickman, assures him* 'that no use
shall be made of his communications, but what he shall approve of.'
He had mentioned with compassion the distresses of the Harlowe family—'Persons
of a *pitiful nature*, says she, *may* pity them. I am not one of those. You, I think, pity
the infernal man likewise; while I from my heart grudge him his frenzy, because

a See p. 1091.

it deprives him of that remorse which, I hope, on his recovery will never leave him. At times, sir, let me tell you, that I hate your whole sex for his sake; even men of unblamable characters; whom at those times I cannot but look upon as persons I have not yet *found out*.

'If my dear creature's personal jewels, proceeds she, be sent up to you for sale, I desire that I may be the purchaser of them, at the *highest* price—of the necklace and solitaire particularly.

'Oh what tears did the perusal of my beloved's will cost me!—But I must not touch upon the heart-piercing subject. I can neither take it up, nor quit it, but with execration of the villain whom all the world must execrate.'

Mr Belford, in his answer, promises that she shall be the purchaser of the jewels if they come into his hands.

He acquaints her that the family had given Colonel Morden the keys of all that belonged to the dear departed: that the unhappy mother had (as the will allows) ordered a piece of needlework to be set aside for her, and had desired Mrs Norton to get the little book of Meditations *transcribed, and to let her have the original, as it was all of her dear daughter's hand-writing; and as it might, when she could bear to look into it, administer consolation to herself. And that she had likewise reserved for herself her picture in the Vandyke taste.*

Mr Belford sends with this letter to Miss Howe the lady's memorandum-book; and promises to send her copies of the several posthumous letters. He tells her that Mr Lovelace being upon the recovery, he had enclosed the posthumous letter directed for him to Lord M., that his lordship might give it to him, or not, as he should find he could bear it. The following is a copy of that letter.

[Letter 510.4: *Miss Clarissa Harlowe*] to *Mr Lovelace*

Thursday, Aug. 24

I TOLD you in the letter I wrote to you on *Tuesday* last,[a] that you should have another sent you when I had got to *my father's house*.

I presume to say that I am *now*, at your receiving of this, arrived there; and I invite you to follow me, as soon as you can be *prepared* for so great a journey.

Not to allegorize further—my fate is *now*, at your perusal of this, accomplished. My doom is unalterably fixed: and I am either a miserable, or a happy being to all eternity. If *happy*, I owe it solely to the Divine mercy: if *miserable*, to your undeserved cruelty—And consider now, for your own sake, gay, cruel, fluttering, unhappy man! consider whether the barbarous and perfidious treatment I have met with from you was worthy of the hazard of your immortal soul; since your wicked views were not to be effected but by the wilful breach of the most solemn

---

[a] See p. 1233. The reader may observe by the date of this letter, that it was written within two days of the allegorical one, to which it refers; and while the lady was labouring under the increased illness occasioned by the hurries and terrors which Mr Lovelace had put her into, to avoid the visit he was so earnest to make her at Smith's—so early written, perhaps, that she might not be surprised by death into a seeming breach of her word.

High as her Christian spirit soars in this letter, the reader has seen, in Letter 467 and in other places, that that exalted spirit carried her to still more divine elevations as she drew nearer to her end.

vows that ever were made by man; and those aided by a violence and baseness unworthy of a human creature.

In time then, once more, I wish you to consider your ways. Your golden dream cannot long last. Your present course can yield you pleasure no longer than you can keep off thought or reflection. A hardened insensibility is the only foundation on which your inward tranquillity is built. When once a dangerous sickness seizes you; when once effectual remorse breaks in upon you; how dreadful will be your condition! How poor a triumph will you then find it to have been able, by a series of black perjuries and studied baseness, under the name of gallantry or intrigue to betray poor inexperienced young creatures, who perhaps knew nothing but their duty till they knew you!—Not one good action in the hour of languishing to recollect, not one worthy intention to revolve, it will be all conscience and horror; and you will wish to have it in your power to compound for annihilation.

Reflect, sir, that I can have no other motive in what I write than your good, and the safety of other innocent creatures who may be drawn in by your wicked arts and perjuries. You have not, in my wishes for your future welfare, the wishes of a suppliant wife, endeavouring for her *own* sake as well as for *yours*, to induce you to reform those ways. They are wholly disinterested, as undeserved, but I should mistrust my own penitence were I capable of wishing to recompense evil for evil— if, black as your offences have been against me, I could not forgive as I wish to be forgiven.

I repeat, therefore, that I *do* forgive you. And may the Almighty forgive you too! Nor have I, at the writing of this, any other essential regrets than what are occasioned by the grief I have given to parents who till I knew you were the most indulgent of parents; by the scandal given to the other branches of my family; by the disreputation brought upon my sex; and by the offence given to virtue in my fall.

As to myself, you have only robbed me of what once were my favourite expectations in the transient life I shall have quitted when you receive this. You have only been the cause that I have been cut off in the bloom of youth, and of curtailing a life that might have been agreeable to myself, or otherwise, as had suited the designs and ends of Providence. I have reason to be thankful for being taken away from the evil of supporting my part of a yoke, with a man so *unhappy* I will only say that, in all probability, every hour I had lived with him might have brought with it some new trouble. And I am (indeed through sharp afflictions and distresses) indebted to you, *secondarily*, as I humbly presume to hope, for so many years of glory as might have proved years of danger, temptation, and anguish, had they been added to my mortal life.

So, sir, though no thanks to your *intention*, you have done me *real service*; and in return, I wish you happy. But such has been your life hitherto, that you can have no time to lose in setting about your repentance. Repentance to such as have lived only carelessly and in the omission of their regular duties, and who never aimed to draw any poor creatures into evil, is not so easy a task, nor so much in our own power as some imagine. How difficult a grace then to be obtained where the guilt is premeditated, wilful, and complicated!

To say I once respected you with a preference is what I ought to blush to own, since at the very time I was far from thinking you even a moral man; though I little thought that you, or indeed that any man breathing, could be what you have proved yourself to be. But, indeed, sir, I have long been greatly above you: for from my heart I have despised you, and all your ways, ever since I saw what manner of man you were.

Nor is it to be wondered that I should be able so to do, when that preference was not grounded on ignoble motives. For I was weak enough, and presumptuous enough, to hope to be a means in the hand of Providence to reclaim a man whom I thought worthy of the attempt.

Nor have I yet, as you will see by the pains I take on this solemn occasion to awaken you out of your sensual dream, given over all hopes of this nature.

Hear me therefore, oh Lovelace! as one speaking from the dead—Lose no time—Set about your repentance instantly—Be no longer the instrument of Satan to draw poor souls into those subtle snares which at last shall entangle your own feet. Seek not to multiply your offences till they become beyond the *power*, as I may say, of the Divine mercy to forgive; since *justice*, no less than *mercy*, is an attribute of the Almighty.

Tremble and reform, when you read what is *the portion of the wicked man from God*. Thus it is written:

'The triumphing of the wicked is short, and the joy of the hypocrite but for a moment. He is cast into a net by his own feet—he walketh upon a snare. Terrors shall make him afraid on every side, and shall drive him to his feet. His strength shall be hunger-bitten, and destruction shall be ready at his side. The first-born of death shall devour his strength. His remembrance shall perish from the earth; and he shall have no name in the streets. He shall be chased out of the world. He shall neither have son nor nephew among his people. They that have seen him, shall say, Where is he? He shall fly away as a dream: he shall be chased away as a vision of the night. His meat is the gall of asps within him. He shall flee from the iron weapon, and the bow of steel shall strike him through. A fire not blown shall consume him. The heaven shall reveal his iniquity, and the earth shall rise up against him. The worm shall feed sweetly on him. He shall be no more remembered—This is the fate of him that knoweth not God'—[1]

Whenever you shall be inclined to consult the sacred oracles, from whence the above threatenings are extracted, you will find doctrines and texts which a truly penitent and contrite heart may lay hold of for its consolation.

May yours, Mr Lovelace, become such! And may you be enabled to escape the fate denounced against the abandoned man, and be entitled to the mercies of a long-suffering and gracious God, is the sincere prayer of

CLARISSA HARLOWE

Letter 511: MR LOVELACE TO JOHN BELFORD, ESQ.

M. Hall, Thursday, Sept. 14

EVER since the fatal seventh of this month, I have been lost to myself, and to all the joys of life. I might have gone farther back than that fatal seventh; which, for the future, I will never see anniversarily revolve but in fables; only till that cursed day I had some gleams of hope now and then darting in upon me.

They tell me of an odd letter I wrote to you.[a] I remember I did write. But very little of the contents of what I wrote do I remember.

I have been in a cursed way. Methinks something has been working strangely retributive. I never was such a fool as to disbelieve a Providence: yet am I not for resolving into judgements everything that temporarily chances to wear an avenging face. Yet if we must be punished either here or hereafter for our misdeeds, better *here* say I, than *hereafter*. Have I not then an interest to think my punishment already not only begun, but completed; since what I have suffered, and do suffer, passes all description?

To give but one instance of the *retributive*—here I, who was the barbarous cause of the loss of senses for a week together to the most inimitable of women, have been punished with the loss of my own—preparative to—who knows what?— When, oh when, shall I know a joyful hour?

I am kept excessively low; and excessively low I *am*. This sweet creature's posthumous letter sticks close to me. All her excellencies rise up hourly to my remembrance.

Yet dare I not to indulge in these melancholy reflections. I find my head strangely working again?—Pen, begone!

Friday, Sept. 15

I RESUME, in a spritely vein, I hope—Mowbray and Tourville have just now—

But what of Mowbray and Tourville!—What's the world?—What's anybody in it?—

Yet are they highly exasperated against thee for the last letter thou wrotest to them[b]—such an unfriendly, such a merciless—

But it won't do!—I must again lay down my pen—Oh Belford, Belford! I am still, I am still, most miserably absent from myself! Shall never, never, more be what I was!

SATURDAY, Sunday, Nothing done. Incapable of anything—

Monday, Sept. 18

HEAVY, damnably heavy, and sick at soul, by Jupiter!—I must come into their expedient. I must see what change of climate will do.

You tell these fellows, and you tell me, of repenting and reforming—but I can do neither. He who *can*, must not have the *extinction* of a Clarissa Harlowe to answer for—Harlowe!—Curse upon the name!—And curse upon myself for not changing it, as I might have done!—Yet have I no need of urging a curse upon myself—I have it effectually.

'To say I once respected you with a preference'[c]—In what stiff language does maidenly modesty on these nice occasions express itself!—*To say I once loved you* is the English; and there is truth and ease in the expression—'To say I once loved you,' then let it be, 'is what I ought to blush to own.'

And dost thou own it?—Excellent creature! and dost thou then own it?—What music in these words from such an angel!—What would I give that she were in being, and *could* and *would* own that she loved me?

a   See his delirious letter, p. 1383, Letter 497.
b   This letter appears not.
c   See p. 1426.

'But indeed, sir, I have long been greatly above you.'

Long, my blessed charmer!—Long indeed—for you have been *ever* greatly above me, and above your sex, and above all the world.

'That preference was not grounded on ignoble motives.'

What a wretch was I to be so distinguished by her, and yet to be so unworthy of her hope to reclaim me!

Then, how generous her motives! Not for her *own* sake merely, not altogether for *mine*, did she hope to reclaim me; but equally for the sake of innocents who might otherwise be ruined by me.

And now, *why* did she write this letter, and *why* direct it to be given me when an event the most deplorable had taken place, but for my good, and with a view to the safety of innocents she knew not?—And *when* was this letter written? Was it not at the time, at the very time that I had been pursuing her, as I may say, from place to place; when her soul was bowed down by calamity and persecution; and herself was denied all forgiveness from relations the most implacable?

Exalted creature!—And couldst thou at *such a time*, and *so early*, and in *such circumstances*, have so far subdued thy own just resentments as to wish happiness to the principal author of all thy distresses? Wish happiness to him who had robbed thee 'of all thy favourite expectations in this life?' To him who had been the cause 'that thou were cut off in the bloom of youth?'

Heavenly aspirer!—What a frame must thou be in, to be able to use the word ONLY, in mentioning these important deprivations!—And as this was before thou puttedst off mortality, may I not presume that thou now,

> — with pitying eye,
> Not derogating from thy perfect bliss,
> Surveyst all heav'n around, and wishest for me?[1]

'Consider my ways'—Dear life of my life! Of what avail is consideration now, when I have lost the dear creature for whose sake alone it was worth while to *have* consideration?—Lost her beyond retrieve—swallowed up by the greedy grave—for *ever* lost her—that, *that's* the sting—

Matchless woman!—How does this reflection wound me!

'Your golden dream cannot long last,'—Divine prophetess! my golden dream is *already* over. 'Thought and reflection *are* no longer to be kept off'—No *longer continues* that 'hardened insensibility' thou chargest upon me—'Remorse *has* broken in upon me'—'Dreadful *is* my condition!'—'It *is* all conscience and horror with me!'—A thousand vultures in turn are preying upon my heart!

But no more of these fruitless reflections—since I am incapable of writing anything else; since my pen will slide into this gloomy subject, whether I will or not; I will once more quit it; nor will I again resume it till I can be more *its master*, and my own.

All I took pen to write for, is however unwritten. It was, in few words, to wish you to proceed with your communications as usual. And why should you not?—since in her ever-to-be-lamented death I know everything shocking and grievous—Acquaint me, then, with all thou knowest, which I do *not* know: how her relations, her cruel relations take it; and whether now the barbed dart of after-reflection sticks not in their hearts, as in mine, up to the very feathers.

I WILL soon quit this kingdom. For now my Clarissa is no more, what is there in it (in the world indeed) worth living for?—But should I not first, by some masterly mischief, avenge her and myself upon her cursed family?

The accused woman, they tell me, has broken her leg. Why was it not her neck?—All, all, but what is owing to her relations is the fault of that woman, and of her hellborn nymphs. *The greater the virtue, the nobler the triumph* was a sentence forever in their mouths—I have had it several times in my head to set fire to the execrable house; and to watch at the doors and windows, that not a devil in it escape the consuming flames. Had the house stood by itself, I had certainly done it.

But it seems the old wretch is in the way to be rewarded, without my help. A shocking letter is received of somebody's, in relation to her—yours I suppose—too shocking for me, they say, to see at present.[a]

They govern me as a child in strings: yet did I suffer so much in my fever that I am willing to bear with them, till I can get tolerably well.

At present I can neither eat, drink, nor sleep. Yet are my disorders nothing to what they were: for, Jack, my brain was on fire day and night: and had it not been of the *asbestos* kind, it had all been consumed.

I had no distinct ideas, but of dark and confused misery: *it was all conscience and horror* indeed! Thoughts of hanging, drowning, shooting; then rage, violence, mischief, and despair, took their turns with me. My lucid intervals still worse, giving me to reflect upon what I *was* the hour before, and what I was likely to be the next, and perhaps for life—The sport of enemies! the laughter of fools! and the hanging-sleeved, go-carted property of hired slaves; who were perhaps to find their account in manacling, and (abhorred thought!) in personally abusing me by blows and stripes!

Who can bear such reflections as these? To be made to *fear* only, to such a one as me, and to fear such wretches too!—What a thing was this but *remotely* to apprehend! And yet, for a man to be in such a state as to render it necessary for his dearest friends to suffer this to be done for his own sake, and in order to prevent further mischief!—There is no thinking of these things!

I will *not* think of them, therefore: but will either get a train of cheerful ideas, or hang myself by tomorrow morning.

> —To be a dog, and dead,
> Were paradise, to such a life as mine.[2]

Letter 512: MR LOVELACE TO JOHN BELFORD, ESQ.

Wed. Sept. 20

I WRITE to demand back again my last letter. I own it was my mind at the different times I wrote it; and, whatever ailed me, I could not *help* writing it. Such a gloomy impulse came upon me, and increased as I wrote, that for my soul I could not forbear running into the miserable.

'Tis strange, very strange, that a man's conscience should be able to force his

a See Letter 499.

fingers to write whether he will or not; and to run him into a subject he more than once, at the very time, resolved not to think of.

Nor is it less strange that (no new reason occurring) he should, in a day or two more, so totally change his mind; have his mind, I should rather say, so wholly illuminated by gay hopes, and rising prospects as to be ashamed of what he had written.

For, on reperusal of a copy of my letter, which fell into my hands by accident, in the handwriting of my cousin Charlotte, who unknown to me had transcribed it, I find it to be such a letter as an enemy would rejoice to see.

This I know, that were I to have continued but one week more in the way I was in when I wrote the latter part of it, I should have been confined, and in straw the next: for I now recollect that all my distemper was returning upon me with irresistible violence—and that in spite of water-gruel and soupe-maigre.

I own that I am still excessively grieved at the disappointment this admirable woman made it so much her whimsical choice to give me. But since it has thus fallen out; since she was determined to leave the world; and since she actually ceases *to be*; ought I, who have such a share of life and health in hand, to indulge gloomy reflections upon an event that is passed; and *being* passed, cannot be recalled?—Have I not had a specimen of what will be my case, if I do?

For, Belford ('tis a folly to deny it), I have been, to use an old word, quite *bestraught*.

Why, why, did my mother bring me up to bear no control? Why was I so educated as that to my very tutors it was a request that I should not know what contradiction or disappointment was?—Ought she not to have known what cruelty there was in her kindness?

What a punishment, to have my first very great disappointment touch my intellect!—And intellects once touched—but that I cannot bear to think of—only thus far; the very repentance and amendment wished me so heartily by my kind and cross dear have been invalidated and postponed, who knows for how long? the *amendment* at least—can a madman be capable of either?

Once touched, therefore, I must endeavour to banish those gloomy reflections, which might *otherwise* have brought on the right turn of mind; and this, to express myself in Lord M.'s style, that my wits may not be sent a *wool-gathering*.

For, let me moreover own to thee, that Dr Hale, who was my good *Astolfo* (you read Ariosto, Jack) and has brought me back my *wit-jar*,[1] had much ado by starving diet, by profuse phlebotomy, by flaying blisters, eyelet-hole-cupping, a dark room, a midnight solitude in a midday sun, to effect my recovery. And now, for my comfort, he tells me that I may still have returns upon full moons—horrible! most horrible!—and must be as careful of myself at both equinoctials as Caesar was warned to be of the Ides of March.

How my heart sickens at looking back upon what I was. Denied the sun, and all comfort: *all* my visitors, low-born, tiptoe attendants: even those tiptoe slaves never approaching me but periodically, armed with gallipots, boluses, and cephalic draughts; delivering their orders to me in hated whispers; and answering other curtain-holding impertinents, inquiring how I was, and how I took their execrable potions, whisperingly too! What a cursed still-life this!—Nothing active in me, or about me, but the worm that never dies.

Again I hasten from the recollection of scenes which *will*, at times, obtrude themselves upon me.

Adieu, Belford!

But return me my last letter—and build nothing upon its contents. I *must*, I *will*, I have *already*, overcome these fruitless gloominesses. Every hour my constitution rises stronger and stronger to befriend me; and, except a tributary sigh now and then to the memory of my heart's beloved, it gives me hope that I shall quickly be what I was—life, spirit, gaiety, and once more the plague of a sex that has been my plague, and will be every man's plague, at one time or other of his life.

I repeat my desire, however, that you will write to me as usual. I hope you have good store of particulars by you to communicate, when I can better bear to hear of the dispositions that were made for all that was mortal of my beloved Clarissa.

But it will be the joy of my heart to be told that her implacable friends are plagued with remorse. Such things as those you may *now* send me: for company in misery is some relief; especially when a man can think those he hates as miserable as himself.

Once more adieu, Jack!

Letter 513: MR LOVELACE TO JOHN BELFORD, ESQ.

I AM preparing to leave this kingdom. Mowbray and Tourville promise to give me their company in a month or two.

I'll give thee my route.

I shall first to Paris; and for amusement and diversion sake try to renew some of my old friendships: thence to some of the German courts: thence, perhaps to Vienna: thence descend through Bavaria and the Tyrol to Venice, where I shall keep the carnival: thence to Florence and Turin: thence again over mount Cenis to France: and, when I return again to Paris, shall expect to see my friend Belford, who by that time I doubt not will be all crusted and bearded over with penitence, self-denial and mortification; a very anchorite, only an itinerant one, journeying over in hope to cover a multitude of his own sins, by proselyting his old companion.

But let me tell thee, Jack, if stock rises on, as it has done since I wrote my last letter, I am afraid thou wilt find a difficult task in succeeding, should such be thy purpose.

Nor, I verily think, can thy own penitence and reformation hold. Strong habits are not so easily rooted out. Old Satan has had too much benefit from thy faithful services, for a series of years, to let thee so easily get out of his clutches. He knows what will do with thee. A fine strapping *bona roba*, in the Chartres taste,[1] but well-limbed, clear-complexioned, and Turkish-eyed; thou the first man with her, or made to believe so, which is the same thing; how will thy frosty face shine upon such an object! How will thy tristful visage be illumined by it! A composition will be made between thee and the grand tempter: thou wilt promise to do him suit and service till old age and inability come. And then will he, in all probability, be sure of thee for ever. For, wert thou to outlive thy present reigning appetites, he will trump up some other darling sin, or make a now secondary one darling, in order to keep thee firmly attached to his infernal interests. Thou wilt continue resolving to amend, but never amending, till grown old before thou art aware (*a dozen years after thou art old with everybody else*), thy för-time-built tenement having lasted its allotted period, he claps down upon thy grizzled head the universal trapdoor: and then all will be over with thee in his own way.

Thou wilt think these hints uncharacteristic from me. But yet I cannot help warning thee of the danger thou art actually in; which is the greater, as thou seemest not to know it. A few words more, therefore, on this subject.

Thou hast made good resolutions. If thou keepest them not, thou wilt never be able to keep any. But, nevertheless, the devil and thy time of life are against thee: and six to one thou failest. Were it only that thou hast *resolved*, six to one thou failest. And if thou dost, thou wilt become the scoff of men and the triumph of devils.—Then how will I laugh at thee! For this warning is not from principle. Perhaps I wish it were: but I never lied to man, and hardly ever said truth to woman. The first is what all free livers cannot say: the second, what every one can.

I am mad again, by Jupiter!—But, thank my stars, not gloomily so!—Farewell, farewell, farewell, for the third or fourth time, concludes

Thy LOVELACE

I believe Charlotte and you are in private league together. Letters, I find, have passed between her, and you, and Lord M. I have been kept strangely in the dark of late: But will soon break upon you all, as the sun upon a midnight thief. Remember that you never sent me the copy of my beloved's will.

Letter 514: MR BELFORD TO ROBERT LOVELACE, ESQ.

Friday, Sept. 22

JUST as I was sitting down to answer yours of the 14th to the 18th, in order to give you all the consolation in my power, came your revoking letter of Wednesday.

I am really concerned, and disappointed that your first was so soon followed by one so contrary to it.

The shocking letter you mention, which your friends withhold from you, is indeed from me. They may now, I see, show you anything. Ask them, then, for that letter, if you think it worth while to read aught about the true mother of your mind.

I WILL suppose that thou hast just read the letter thou callest shocking; and which I intended to be so. And let me ask what thou thinkest of it? Dost thou not tremble at the horrors the vilest of women labours with on the apprehensions of death and future judgement?—How fit the reflections that must have been raised by the perusal of this letter upon thy yet unclosed eyelet-holes? Will not some serious thoughts mingle with thy melilot, and tear off the callus of thy mind as that may flay the leather from thy back, and as thy epispastics may strip the parchment from thy plotting head? If not, then indeed is thy conscience seared, and no hopes will lie for thee.

Mr Belford then gives an account of the wretched Sinclair's terrible exit, which he had just then received.

If this move thee not, I have news to acquaint thee with, of another dismal catastrophe that is but within this hour come to my ear, of another of thy blessed agents. Thy TOMLINSON!—Dying, and, in all probability, before this can reach thee, dead, in Maidstone Gaol. As thou sayest in thy first letter, 'something strangely retributive seems to be working.'

This his case. He was at the head of a gang of smugglers, endeavouring to carry off run goods, landed last Tuesday, when a party of dragoons came up with them in the evening. Some of his comrades fled. M'Donald being surrounded, attempted to fight his way through, and wounded his man; but having received a shot in his neck, and being cut deeply in the head by a broadsword, he fell from his horse, was taken, and carried to Maidstone Gaol: and there my informant left him, just dying, and assured of hanging if he recover.

Absolutely destitute, he got a kinsman of his to apply to me, and, if in town, to the rest of the confraternity, for something, not to *support* him was the word (for he expected not to live till the fellow returned), but to bury him.

I never employed him but once; and then he ruined my project. I now thank Heaven that he did. But I sent him three guineas; and promised him more, as from you, and Mowbray and Tourville, if he live a few days, or to take his trial. And I put it upon you to make further inquiry of him, and to give him what you think fit.

His messenger tells me that he is very penitent: that he weeps continually. He cries out that he has been the vilest of men: yet palliates that his necessities made him worse than he should otherwise have been (an excuse which none of *us* can plead): but that what touched him most of all was a vile imposture he was put upon to serve a certain gentleman of fortune, to the ruin of the most excellent woman that ever lived; and who, he had heard, was dead of grief.

Let me consider, Lovelace—*Whose turn can be next?*—I wish it may not be thine. But since thou givest me one piece of advice (which I should indeed have thought out of character, hadst thou not taken pains to convince me that it proceeds not from *principle*) I will give thee another: and that is, prosecute, as fast as thou canst, thy intended tour. Change of scene and of climate may establish thy health: while this gross air and the approach of winter may thicken thy blood; and with the help of a conscience that is upon the struggle with thee, and like a cunning wrestler watches its opportunity to give thee another fall, may make thee miserable for thy life.

I return your revoked letter. Don't destroy it, however. The same dialect may one day come in fashion with you again.

As to the family at Harlowe Place, I have most affecting letters from Colonel Morden relating to their grief and distress. You, to whom the occasion is owing, do well to rejoice in their compunction: but, as one well observes, *averse as they were to you, they must and they would have been reconciled in time, had you done her justice.*

I should be sorry if I could not say that what you have warned me of in *sport* makes me tremble in *earnest*. I hope (for this is a serious subject with me, though nothing can be so with you) that I never shall deserve, by my apostasy, to be the scoff of men, and the triumph of devils.

All that you say of the difficulty of conquering rooted habits is but too true. Those, and time of life, are indeed too much against me: but, when I reflect upon the ends (some untimely) of those of our companions whom we have formerly lost; upon Belton's miserable exit; upon the howls and screams of Sinclair, which are still in my ears; and now upon your miserable Tomlinson; and compare their ends with the happy and desirable end of the inimitable Miss Harlowe: I hope I have reason to think my footing morally secure. Your caution nevertheless will be of use, however you might design it: and since I know my weak side, I will endeavour to fortify myself in that quarter by marriage, as soon as I can make myself worthy of the confidence and esteem of some virtuous woman; and by this means, become the subject of your envy, rather than of your scoffs.

I have already begun my retributory purposes, as I may call them. I have settled an annual sum for life upon poor John Loftus, whom I disabled while he was endeavouring to protect his young mistress from my lawless attempts. I rejoice that I succeeded not in that; as I do in recollecting many others of the like sort, in which I miscarried.

Poor Farley, who had become a bankrupt, I have set up again: but have declared that the annual allowance I make her shall cease if I hear she returns to her former courses: and I have made her accountable for her conduct to the good widow Lovick, whom I have taken, at a handsome salary, for my housekeeper at Edgware (for I have let the house at Watford); and she is to dispense the quarterly allotment to her, as she merits.

This good woman shall have other matters of the like nature under her care, as we grow better acquainted: and I make no doubt that she will answer my expectations, and that I shall be both confirmed and improved by her conversation: for she shall generally sit at my own table.

The undeserved sufferings of Miss Clarissa Harlowe, her exalted merit, her exemplary preparation, and her happy end, will be standing subjects with us.

She shall read *to* me, when I have no company; write *for* me, out of books, passages she shall recommend. Her years (turned of fifty) and her good character will secure me from scandal; and I have great pleasure in reflecting that I shall be better myself for making her happy.

Then, whenever I am in danger, I will read some of the admirable lady's papers: whenever I would abhor my former ways, I will read some of thine, and copies of my own.

The consequence of all this will be that I shall be the delight of my own relations of both sexes, who were wont to look upon me as a lost man. I shall have good order in my own family, because I shall give the example myself. I shall be visited and respected, not perhaps by Lovelace, by Mowbray, and by Tourville, because they cannot see me upon the *old* terms, and will not perhaps see me upon the *new*, but by the best and worthiest gentlemen, clergy as well as laity, all around me. I shall look upon my past follies with contempt; upon my old companions with pity. Oaths and curses shall be for ever banished from my mouth: in their place shall succeed conversation becoming a rational being and a gentleman. And instead of acts of *offence*, subjecting me perpetually to acts of *defence*, will I endeavour to atone for my past evils by doing all the good in my power, and by becoming an universal benefactor to the extent of that power.

Now, tell me, Lovelace, upon this faint sketch of what I hope to *do*, and to *be*, if this be not a scheme infinitely preferable to the wild, the pernicious, the dangerous ones, both to body and soul, which we have pursued?

I wish I could make my sketch as amiable to you as it appears to me. I wish it with all my soul: for I always loved you. It has been my misfortune that I did: for this led me into infinite riots and follies, which otherwise I verily think I should not have been guilty of.

You have a great deal more to answer for than I have, were it only in the temporal ruin of this admirable woman. Let me now, while yet you have youth, and health, and intellect, prevail upon you: for I am afraid, very much afraid, that such is the enormity of this single wickedness, in depriving the world of such a shining light, that if you do not quickly reform, it will be out of your power to reform at all; and that Providence, which has already given you the fates of your agents Sinclair and Tomlinson to take warning by, will not let the principal offender escape, if he slight the warning.

You will perhaps laugh at me for these serious reflections. Do, if you will. I had rather you should laugh at me for continuing in this way of thinking and acting, than triumph over me, as you threaten, on my swerving from purposes I have determined upon with such good reason, and from such good examples.

And so much for this subject at present.

I should be glad to know when you intend to set out. I have too much concern for your welfare not to wish you in a thinner air, and more certain climate.

What have Tourville and Mowbray to do, that they cannot set out with you? They will not covet my company, I dare say; and I shall not be able to endure theirs when you are gone: take them therefore with you.

I will not, however, forswear making you a visit at Paris, at your return from Germany and Italy: but hardly with the hope of reclaiming you, if due reflection upon what I have set before you and upon what you have written in your two last will not by that time have done it.

I suppose I shall see you before you go. Once more I wish you were gone. This heavy island air cannot do for you what that of the continent will.

I do not think I ought to communicate with you, as I used to do, on this side the Channel: let me then hear from you on the opposite shore, and you shall command the pen, as you please; and, honestly, the power, of

J. BELFORD

Letter 515: MR LOVELACE TO JOHN BELFORD, ESQ.

Tuesday, Sept. 26

FATE, I believe in my conscience, spins threads for tragedies, on purpose for thee to weave with—Thy Watford uncle, poor Belton, the fair inimitable (exalted creature! and is she to be found in such a list!), the accursed woman, and Tomlinson, seem to have been all doomed to give thee a theme for the dismal and the horrible!—And, by my soul, as Lord M. would phrase it, *thou dost work it going.*

That's the horrid thing: a man cannot begin to *think*, but *causes* for thought crowd in upon him: the gloomy takes place; and mirth and gaiety abandon his heart for ever!

Poor M'Donald!—I am really sorry for the fellow—He was an useful, faithful, solemn varlet, who could act incomparably any part given him, and knew not what a blush was—He really took honest pains for me in the last affair; which has cost him and me so dearly in reflection. Often gravelled, as we both were, yet was he never daunted—Poor M'Donald, I must once more say!—For carrying on a solemn piece of roguery, he had no equal.

I was so solicitous to know if he were really as bad as thou hast a knack of painting everybody whom thou singlest out to exercise thy murdering pen upon, that I dispatched a man and horse to Maidstone, as soon as I had thine; and had word brought me that he died in two hours after he had received thy three guineas. And all thou wrotest of his concern in relation to the ever-dear Miss Harlowe, it seems, was true.

I can't help it, Belford!—I have only to add that it is happy that the poor fellow lived not to be hanged; as it seems he would have been: for who knows, as he had got into such a penitential strain, what might have been in his dying speech?

When a man has not *great* good to comfort himself with, it is right to make the best of the *little* that may offer. There never was any discomfort happened to mortal man, but some little ray of consolation would dart in, if the wretch was not so much a wretch as to *draw*, instead of *undraw*, the curtain to keep it out.

And so much, at this time and for ever, for poor Captain Tomlinson, as I called him.

Your solicitude to get me out of this heavy changeable climate exactly tallies with everybody's here. They all believe that travelling will establish me. Yet I think I am quite well. Only these plaguy *news* and *fulls*, and the *equinoctials* fright me a little when I think of them; and that is always: for the whole family are continually ringing these changes in my ears, and are more sedulously intent than I can well account for, to get me out of the kingdom.

But wilt thou write often when I am gone? Wilt thou then piece the thread where thou brokest it off? Wilt thou give me the particulars of *their* distress, who were my *auxiliaries* in bringing on the event that affects me?—Nay, *principals* rather: since, say what thou wilt, what did I do worth a woman's breaking her heart for?

Faith and troth, Jack, I have had very hard usage, as I have often said—to have such a plaguy ill name given me, pointed at, screamed out upon, run away from, as a mad dog would be; all my own friends ready to renounce me!—

Yet I think I deserve it all: for have I not been as ready to give up myself, as others are to condemn me?

What madness, what folly, this!—Who will take the part of a man that condemns himself?—Who can? He that pleads guilty to an indictment, leaves no room for aught but the sentence. Out upon me for an impolitic wretch! I have not the art of the least artful of any of our Christian princes; who every day are guilty of ten times worse breaches of faith; and yet, issuing out a manifesto, they wipe their mouths, and go on from infraction to infraction, from robbery to robbery; commit devastation upon devastation; and destroy—for their *glory!* And are rewarded with the names of *conquerors*, and are dubbed *Le Grand*; praised, and even deified by orators and poets, for their butcheries and depredations.

While I, a poor, single, harmless prowler; at least *comparatively* harmless; in order to satisfy my hunger, steal but one poor lamb; and every mouth is opened, every hand is lifted up against me.

Nay, as I have just now heard, I am to be *manifestoed* against, though no prince: for Miss Howe threatens to have the case published to the whole world.

I have a good mind not to oppose it; and to write an answer to it as soon as it comes forth, and exculpate myself by throwing all the fault upon the old ones. And this I have to plead, supposing all that my worst enemies can allege against me were true—That I am not answerable for all the extravagant and unforeseen consequences that this affair has been attended with.

And this I will prove demonstrably by a case, which, but a few hours ago, I put to Lord M. and to the two Misses Montague. This it is:

Suppose *A*, a miser, had hid a parcel of gold in a *secret place*, in order to keep it there till he could lend it out at extravagant interest.

Suppose *B* in such great want of this treasure, as to be unable to *live without it.*

And suppose *A*, the *miser*, has such an opinion of *B*, the *wanter*, that he would rather lend it to him, than to any mortal living; but yet, though he has *no other* use in the world for it, insists upon very unconscionable terms.

B would gladly pay *common* interest for it; but would be undone (in *his own* opinion at least, and that is everything to him) if he complied with the miser's terms; since he would be sure to be soon thrown into *gaol* for the debt, and made a *prisoner for life.* Wherefore guessing (being an arch, penetrating fellow) where the *sweet hoard* lies, he *searches* for it when the miser is in a *profound sleep*, finds it, and runs away with it.

B, in this case, can be only a *thief*, that's plain, Jack.

Here Miss Montague put in very smartly. A thief, sir, said she, that steals what is and ought to be dearer to me than my life, deserves less to be forgiven, than he who murders me.

But what is this, cousin Charlotte, said I, that is dearer to you than your life? Your *honour*, you'll say—I will not talk to a lady (I never did) in a way she cannot answer me—But in the instance for which I put my case (allowing all you attribute to the phantom) what honour is lost, where the *will* is not violated, and the person cannot help it? But, with respect to the case put, how knew we, till the theft *was committed*, that the miser did actually set so romantic a value upon the treasure?

Both my cousins were silent; and my lord cursed me, because he could not answer me; and I proceeded.

Well then, the result is that *B* can only be a thief; that's plain—To pursue, therefore, my case—

Suppose this same miserly *A*, on awaking and searching for, and finding his treasure gone, takes it so much to heart, that he starves himself;

Who but himself is to blame for that?—Would either equity, law, or conscience, hang *B* for a murder?

And now to apply, said I—

None of your applications, cried my cousins, both in a breath.

None of your applications, and be d—ned to you, the passionate peer.

Well then, returned I, I am to conclude it to be a case so plain that it needs none; looking at the two girls, who tried for a blush apiece. And I hold myself, of consequence, acquitted of the *death*.

Not so, cried my lord (peers are judges, thou knowest, Jack, in the last resort): for if by committing an unlawful act, a capital crime is the consequence, you are answerable to both.

Say you so, my good lord?—But will you take upon you to say, supposing (as in the present case) a rape (saving your presence, cousin Charlotte, saving your presence, cousin Patty); is death the *natural* consequence of a rape?—Did you ever hear, my lord, or did you, ladies, that it was?—And if not the *natural* consequence, and a lady will destroy herself, whether by a lingering death as of grief; or by the dagger, as Lucretia did[1]; is there more than one fault the *man*'s?— Is not the other *hers*?—Were it not so, let me tell you, my dears, chucking each of my blushing cousins under the chin, we either have had no men so wicked as young Tarquin was, or no women so virtuous as Lucretia, in the space of—how many thousand years, my lord?—And so Lucretia is recorded as a single wonder!

You may believe I was cried out upon. People who cannot answer will rave: and this they all did. But I insisted upon it to them, and so I do to you, Jack, that I ought to be acquitted of everything but a common theft, a private larceny as the lawyers call it, in this point. And were my life to be a forfeit to the law, it would not be for murder.

Besides, as I told them, there was a circumstance strongly in my favour in this case: for I would have been glad, with all my soul, to have purchased my forgiveness by a compliance with the terms I first boggled at. And this I offered; and my lord, and Lady Betty, and Lady Sarah, and my two cousins, and all my cousins' cousins, to the fourteenth generation, would have been bound for me—But it would not do: the sweet miser would break her heart, and die; and how could I help it?

Upon the whole, Jack, had not the lady died, would there have been half so much said of it as there is? Was I the cause of her death? or could I help it? And have there not been, in a million of cases like this, nine hundred and ninety-nine thousand that have not ended as this has ended?—How hard, then, is my fate!— Upon my soul, I won't bear it as I have done; but, instead of taking guilt to myself, claim pity. And this (since yesterday cannot be recalled) is the only course I can pursue to make myself easy. Proceed anon.

Letter 516: MR LOVELACE TO JOHN BELFORD, ESQ.

BUT what a pretty scheme of life hast thou drawn out for thyself, and thy old widow! By my soul, Jack, I am mightily taken with it. There is but one thing wanting in it; and that will come of course: only to be in the commission and one of the quorum.[1] Thou art already provided with a clerk as good as thou'lt want; for thou understandest law, and she conscience: a good Lord Chancellor between ye!—I should take prodigious pleasure to hear thee decide in a bastard case, upon thy new notions and old remembrances.

But raillery apart (all gloom at heart, by Jupiter! although the pen and the countenance assume airs of levity!): if after all thou canst so easily repent and reform as thou thinkest thou canst: if thou canst thus shake off thy old sins and thy old habits: and if thy old master will so readily dismiss so tried and so faithful a servant, and permit thee thus calmly to enjoy thy new system; no room for scandal; all temptation ceasing: and if at last (thy reformation warranted and approved by time) thou marriest and livest honest—why, Belford, I cannot but say that if all these IF's come to pass, thou standest a good chance to be a happy man!

All I think, as I told thee in my last, is that the devil knows his own interest too well to let thee off so easily. Thou thyself tellest me that we cannot repent when we will. And indeed I found it so: for, in my lucid intervals, I made good resolutions: but, as health turned its blithe side to me, and opened my prospects of recovery, all my old inclinations and appetites returned; and this letter, perhaps, will be a thorough conviction to thee that I *am* as wild a fellow as ever, or in the way to be so.

Thou askest me very seriously if, upon the faint sketch thou hast drawn, thy new scheme be not infinitely preferable to any of those which we have so long pursued?—Why, Jack—let me reflect—Why, Belford—I can't say but it is. It is really, as Biddy[2] in the play says, a good comfortable scheme.

But when thou tellest me that it was thy misfortune to love me, because thy value for me made thee a wickeder man than otherwise thou wouldst have been; I desire thee to revolve this assertion: and I am persuaded that thou wilt not find thyself in so right a train as thou imaginest.

No false colourings, no glosses, does a true penitent aim at. Debasement, diffidence, mortification, contrition, are all near of kin, Jack, and inseparable from a repentant spirit—If thou knowest not this, thou art not got three steps (out of threescore) towards repentance and amendment. And let me remind thee, before the grand accuser comes to do it, that thou wert ever above being a passive follower in iniquity. Though thou hadst not so good an invention as he to whom thou writest, thou hadst as active an heart for mischief as ever I met with in man.

Then for improving an hint, thou wert always a true Englishman. I never started a roguery that did not come out of *thy* forge in a manner ready anvilled and hammered for execution, when I have sometimes been at a loss to make anything of it myself.

What indeed made me appear to be more wicked than thee was that I being a handsome fellow, and thou an ugly one, when we had started a game, and hunted it down, the poor frighted puss generally chose to throw herself into my paws, rather than into thine: and then, disappointed, hast thou wiped thy blubber-lips, and marched off to start a new game, calling me a wicked fellow all the while.

In short, Belford, thou wert an excellent *starter* and *setter*. The old women were not afraid for their daughters when they saw such a face as thine. But when *I* came, whip, was the key turned upon their girls. And yet all signified nothing; for love, upon occasion, will draw an elephant through a keyhole. But for thy HEART, Belford, who ever doubted *that?*

Nor even in this affair, that sticks most upon me, and which my conscience makes such a handle of against me, art thou so innocent as thou fanciest thyself. Thou wilt stare at this: but it is true; and I will convince thee of it in an instant.

Thou sayest thou wouldst have saved the lady from the ruin she met with. Thou art a pretty fellow for this: for *how* wouldst thou have saved her? What methods didst thou *take* to save her?

Thou knewest my designs all along. Hadst thou a mind to make thyself a good title to the merit to which thou now pretendest to lay claim, thou shouldest, like a true knight-errant, have sought to set the lady free from her enchanted castle. Thou shouldst have apprised her of her danger; have stolen in when the giant was out of the way; or hadst thou the true spirit of chivalry upon thee, and nothing else would have done, have killed the giant; and then something wouldst thou have had to brag of.

'Oh but the giant was my friend: he reposed a confidence in me: and I should have betrayed my friend, and his confidence!' This thou wouldst have pleaded, no doubt. But try this plea upon thy present principles, and thou wilt see what a caitiff thou wert to let it have weight with thee, upon an occasion where a breach of confidence is more excusable than to keep the secret.

Thou canst not pretend, and I know thou wilt not, that thou wert afraid of thy life by taking such a measure: for a braver fellow lives not, nor a more fearless, than Jack Belford. I remember several instances, and thou canst not forget them, where thou hast ventured thy bones, thy neck, thy life, against numbers, in a cause of roguery; and hadst thou had a spark of that virtue which now thou art willing to flatter thyself thou hast, thou wouldst surely have run a risk to save an innocence and a virtue, that it became every man to protect and espouse. This is the truth of the case, greatly as it makes against myself. But I hate an hypocrite from my soul.

I believe I should have killed thee at the *time*, if I could, hadst thou betrayed me thus. But I am sure *now*, that I would have thanked thee for it, with all my heart; and thought thee more a father, and a friend, than my real father, and my best friend—And it was natural for thee to think, with so exalted a merit as this lady had, that this would have been the case, when consideration took place of passion; or, rather, when that damned fondness for intrigue ceased, which never was my pride so much as it is now, upon reflection, my curse.

Set about defending thyself, and I will probe thee still deeper, and convict thee still more effectually, that thou hast more guilt than merit even in this affair. And as to all the others in which we have hunted in couples, thou wert always the forwardest whelp, and more ready by far to run away with me, than I with thee. Yet canst thou now compose thy horse-muscles, and cry out how much more hast thou, Lovelace, to answer for, than I have!—saying *nothing*, neither, when thou sayest this, were it *true*—for thou wilt not be tried, when the time comes, by *comparison*.

In short, thou mayest, at this rate, so miserably deceive thyself that, notwithstanding all thy self-denial and mortification, when thou closest thy eyes thou mayest perhaps open them in a place where thou thoughtest least to be.

However, consult thy old woman on this subject. I shall be thought to be out of character if I go on in this strain. But really, as to a title to merit in this affair, I do assure thee, Jack, that thou less deservest praise than an horse-pond: and I wish I had the sousing of thee.

I AM actually now employed in taking leave of my friends in the country. I had once thoughts of taking Tomlinson, as I called him, with me: but his destiny has frustrated that intention.

Next Monday I think to see you in town; and then you, and I, and Mowbray, and Tourville, will laugh off that evening together. They will both accompany me (as I expect *you* will) to Dover, if not cross the water. I must leave you and them good friends. They take extremely amiss the treatment you have given them in your last letters. They say you strike at their understandings. I laugh at them; and tell them that those people who have *least* are the most apt to be angry when it is called in question.

Make up all the papers and narratives you can spare me against the time. The will particularly I expect to take with me. Who knows but that those things which will help to secure *you* in the way you are got into may convert *me?*

Thou talkest of a wife, Jack: what thinkest thou of our Charlotte? Her family and fortune, I doubt, according to thy scheme, are a little too high. Will those be an objection? Charlotte is a smart girl. For piety (thy present turn) I cannot say much: yet she is as serious as most of her sex at her time of life—would flaunt it a little, I believe too, like the rest of them, were her reputation under covert.

But it won't do neither, now I think of it—Thou art so homely, and so awkward a creature! Hast such a boatswain-like air!—People would think she had picked thee up in Wapping, or Rotherhithe; or in going to see some new ship launched, or to view the docks at Chatham, or Portsmouth. So gaudy and so clumsy! Thy tawdriness won't do with Charlotte!—so sit thee down contented, Belford.

Yet would I fain secure thy morals too, if matrimony will do it.

Let me see!—now I have it.

Has not the widow Lovick a daughter, or a niece? It is not every girl of *fortune* and *family* that will go to prayers with thee *once or twice a day*. But since thou art for taking a wife to mortify with, what if thou marriest the widow herself?—She will then have a double concern in thy conversion. You and she may *tête à tête* pass many a comfortable winter's evening together, comparing *experiences*, as the good folks call them.

I am serious, Jack. Faith I am. And I would have thee take it into thy wise consideration.

Letter 517: MR BELFORD TO COLONEL MORDEN

Thursday, Sept. 21

GIVE me leave, dear sir, to address myself to you in a very serious and solemn manner on a subject that I must not, cannot dispense with; as I promised the divine lady that I would do everything in my power to prevent that further mischief which she was so very apprehensive of.

I will not content myself with distant hints. It is with very great concern that I have just now heard of a declaration which you are said to have made to your relations at Harlowe Place, that you will not rest till you have avenged your cousin's wrongs upon Mr Lovelace.

Far be it from me to offer to defend the unhappy man, or even *unduly* to extenuate his crime: but yet I must say, that the family, by their persecutions of the dear lady at first, and by their implacableness afterwards, ought *at least* to *share* the blame with him. There is even great reason to believe that a lady of such a religious turn, her virtue neither to be surprised nor corrupted, her will inviolate, would have got over a *mere personal* injury; especially as he would have done all that was in his power to repair it; and as, from the application of all his family in his favour, and other circumstances attending his sincere and voluntary offer, the lady might have condescended, with greater glory to herself than if he had never offended.

When I have the pleasure of seeing you next, I will acquaint you, sir, with all the circumstances of this melancholy story; from which you will see that Mr Lovelace was extremely ill-treated at first by the whole family, this admirable lady excepted. This exception, I know, heightens his crime: but as his principal intention was but to try her virtue; and that he became so earnest a suppliant to her for marriage; and as he has suffered so deplorably in the loss of his reason for not having it in his power to repair her wrongs; I presume to hope that much is to be pleaded against such a resolution as you are said to have made.

I will read to you at the same time some passages from letters of his; two of which (one but this moment received) will convince you that the unhappy man, who is but now recovering his intellects, needs no greater punishment than what he has from his own reflections.

I have just now read over the *copies* of the dear lady's posthumous letters. I send them all to you, except that directed for Mr Lovelace; which I reserve till I have the pleasure of seeing you. Let me entreat you to read once more *that* to yourself; and *that* to her brother[a]; which latter I now send you; as they are in point to the present subject.

I think, sir, they are unanswerable. Such, at least, is the effect they have upon me, that I hope I shall never be provoked to draw my sword again in a private quarrel.

To the weight these must needs have upon you, let me add that the unhappy man has given no *new* occasion of offence since your visit to him at Lord M.s, when you were so well satisfied of his intention to repair his crimes, that you yourself urged to your dear cousin *her* forgiveness of him.

Let me *also* (though I presume to hope there is no need, when you coolly consider everything) remind you of your own promise to your departing cousin; relying upon which, her last moments were the easier.

My dear Colonel Morden, the highest injury was to *her:* her family all have a share in the *cause*: *she* forgives it: why should we not endeavour to imitate what we admire?

You asked me, sir, when in town, if a brave man could be a premeditatedly base one? Generally speaking, I believe bravery and baseness are incompatible. But Mr Lovelace's character, in the instance before us, affords a proof of the truth of the common observation that there is no general rule but has its exceptions: for England, I believe, as gallant a nation as it is deemed to be, has not in it a braver spirit than his; nor a man who has greater skill at his weapons; nor more *calmness* with his skill.

I mention not this with a thought that it can affect Colonel Morden; who, if he be not withheld by SUPERIOR MOTIVES, as well as influenced by those I have reminded him of, will tell me that this skill and this bravery will make him the more worthy of being called upon by him.

To these SUPERIOR motives then I refer myself: and with the greater confidence; as a pursuit ending in blood would not, at *this time*, have the plea lie for it with *anybody*, which sudden passion might have with *some:* but would be construed by *all* to be a cool and deliberate act of revenge for an evil absolutely irretrievable: an act which a brave and noble spirit, such as the gentleman's to whom I now write, is not capable of.

a See p. 1373. Letter 490.

Excuse me, sir, for the sake of my executorial duty and promise, keeping in eye the dear lady's *personal injunctions* as well as *written will*, enforced by *letters posthumous*. Every article of which (solicitous as we *both* are to see it duly performed) she would have dispensed with, rather than farther mischief should happen on her account. I am,

Dear sir, Your affectionate and faithful servant,
JOHN BELFORD

The following is the posthumous letter to Colonel Morden referred to in the above.

Letter 518: [MISS CLARISSA HARLOWE] SUPERSCRIBED: TO MY BELOVED COUSIN, WILLIAM MORDEN, ESQ. TO BE DELIVERED AFTER MY DEATH

My dearest cousin,
As it is uncertain, from my present weak state, whether if living I may be in a condition to receive as I ought the favour you intend me of a visit, when you come to London, I take this opportunity to return you while able, the humble acknowledgements of a grateful heart for all your goodness to me from childhood till now: and more particularly for your present kind interposition in my favour— God Almighty for ever bless you, dear sir, for the kindness you endeavoured to procure for me.

One principal end of my writing to you in this solemn manner is to beg of you, which I do with the utmost earnestness, that when you come to hear the particulars of my story, you will not suffer *active* resentment to take place in your generous breast on my account.

Remember, my dear cousin, that vengeance is God's province; and he has undertaken to repay it; nor will you, I hope, invade that province—especially as there is no necessity for you to attempt to vindicate my fame; since the offender himself (before he is called upon) has stood forth and offered to do me all the justice that you could have extorted from him had I lived: and when your own person may be endangered by running an *equal* risk with a *guilty man*.

Duelling, sir, I need not tell *you* who have adorned a public character, is not only an usurpation of the Divine prerogative; but it is an insult upon magistracy and good government. 'Tis an impious act. 'Tis an attempt to take away a life that ought not to depend upon a private sword: an act, the consequence of which is to hurry a soul (all its sins upon its head) into perdition; endangering that of the poor triumpher—since neither intend to give to the other that *chance*, as I may call it, for the Divine mercy, in an opportunity for repentance, which each presumes to hope for himself.

Seek not then, I beseech you, sir, to aggravate my fault by a pursuit of blood, which must necessarily be deemed a consequence of it. Give not the unhappy man the merit (were you assuredly to be the victor) of falling by your hand. At present he is the perfidious, the ungrateful deceiver; but will not the forfeiture of his life, and the probable loss of his soul, be a dreadful expiation for having made me miserable for *a few months* only, and through that misery, by the Divine favour, happy to all eternity?

In such a case, my cousin, where shall the evil stop? And who shall avenge on you?—And who on your avenger?

Let the poor man's conscience then, dear sir, avenge me. He will one day find punishment more than enough from that. Leave him to the chance of repentance. If the Almighty will give him time for it, why should you deny it him?—Let him still be the guilty aggressor; and let no one say Clarissa Harlowe is now amply revenged in his fall; or, in the case of yours (which Heaven avert!), that her fault, instead of being buried in her grave, is perpetuated and aggravated by a loss far greater than that of herself.

Often, sir, has the *more* guilty been the vanquisher of the *less*. An Earl of Shrewsbury, in the reign of Charles II as I have read, endeavouring to revenge the greatest injury that man can do to man, met with his death at Barn Elms from the hand of the ignoble duke[1] who had vilely dishonoured him. Nor can it be thought an unequal dispensation, were it *generally* to happen that the usurper of the Divine prerogative should be punished for his presumption by the man whom he sought to destroy, and who, however *previously* criminal, is put in this case upon a necessary act of self-defence.

May Heaven protect you, sir, in all your ways; and, once more I pray, reward you for all your kindness to me: a kindness so worthy of *your* heart, and so exceedingly grateful to *mine:* that of seeking to make peace, and to reconcile parents to a once beloved child; uncles to a niece late their favourite; and a brother and sister to a sister whom once they thought not unworthy of that tender relation. A kindness so greatly preferable to the vengeance of the murdering sword.

Be a comforter, dear sir, to my honoured parents, as you have been to me: and may we, through the Divine goodness to us both, meet in that blessed eternity, into which as I humbly trust I shall have entered when you read this.

So prays, and to her latest hour will pray, my dear cousin Morden, my friend, my guardian, but not my avenger—(Dear sir! remember that!)——

> Your ever-affectionate and obliged
> CLARISSA HARLOWE

Letter 519: COLONEL MORDEN TO JOHN BELFORD, ESQ.

Sat. Sept. 23

Dear sir,

I AM very sorry that anything you have heard I have said should give you uneasiness.

I am obliged to you for the letters you have communicated to me; and still further for your promise to favour me with others occasionally.

All that relates to my dear cousin I shall be glad to see, be it from whom it will.

I leave to your own discretion what may or may not be proper for Miss Howe to see from so free a pen as mine.

I admire her spirit. Were she a *man*, do you think, sir, *she* would at *this time* have your advice to take upon such a subject as that you write upon?

Fear not, however, that your communications shall put me upon any measures that otherwise I should not have taken. The wickedness, sir, is of such a nature as admits not of aggravation.

Yet I do assure you that I have not made any resolutions that will be a tie upon me.

I have indeed expressed myself with vehemence upon the occasion. Who could forbear to do so? But it is not my way to resolve in matters of moment till opportunity brings the execution of my purposes within my reach. We shall see what manner of spirit this young man will be acted by, on his recovery. If he continue to brave and defy a family which he has so irreparably injured—if—But resolutions depending upon future contingencies are best left to future determination, as I just now hinted.

Meantime, I will own that I think my cousin's arguments unanswerable. No *good* man but must be concluded by them—But, alas! sir, who is *good*?

As to your arguments; I hope you will believe me when I assure you as I now do, that your opinion and your reasonings have, and will always have, great and deserved weight with me: and that I respect you still more than I did, if possible, for your expostulations in favour of the end of my cousin's pious injunctions to me. They come from *you*, sir, with the greatest propriety, as her executor and representative; and likewise as you are a man of humanity, and a well-wisher to both parties.

I am not exempt from violent passions, sir, any more than your friend; but then I hope they are only capable of being raised by other people's insolence, and not by my own arrogance. If ever I am stimulated by my imperfections and my resentments to act against my judgement and my cousin's injunctions; some such reflections as these that follow will run away with my reason. Indeed they are always present with me.

In the first place; my own disappointment: who came over with the hope of passing the remainder of my days in the conversation of a kinswoman so beloved; and to whom I had a double relation, as her cousin and trustee.

Then I reflect, too, too often perhaps for my engagements to her in her last hours, that the dear creature could only forgive for *herself*. She no doubt is happy: but who shall forgive for a *whole family* in all its branches made miserable for their lives?

That the more faulty her friends were as to *her*, the more enormous his ingratitude, and the more inexcusable—What! sir, was it not enough that she suffered what she did *for him*, but the barbarian must make her suffer for her sufferings for *his sake*?—Passion makes me express this weakly: passion refuses strength sometimes, where the propriety of a resentment *prima facie* declares expression to be needless. I leave it to *you*, sir, to give this reflection its due force.

That the author of this diffusive mischief perpetrated it premeditatedly, wantonly, in the gaiety of his heart. To *try* my cousin, say you, sir? To try the virtue of a Clarissa, sir!—Had she then given him any cause to doubt her virtue?—It could not be—If he avers that she did—I am indeed called upon—But I will have patience.

That he carried her, as now it appears, to a vile brothel, purposely to put her out of all human resource; himself out of the reach of all humane remorse: and that, finding her proof against all the common arts of delusion, base and unmanly arts were there used to effect his wicked purposes. *Once dead*, the injured saint in her will says, *he has seen her*.

That I could not know this when I saw him at M. Hall: that, the object of his attempts considered, I could not suppose there was such a monster breathing as he: that it was natural for me to impute her refusal of him rather to transitory resentment, to consciousness of human frailty and mingled doubts of the sincerity of his offers, than to villainies which had given the irreversible blow, and had at that instant brought her down to the gates of death, which in a very few days enclosed her.

That he is a man of defiance: a man who thinks to awe everyone by his insolent darings, and by his pretensions to superior courage and skill.

That, disgrace as he is to his name and to the character of a gentleman, the man would not want his merit who, in vindication of the *dishonoured* distinction, should expunge and blot him out of the worthy list.

That the injured family has a son who, however unworthy of such a sister, is of a temper vehement, unbridled, fierce, unequal therefore (as he has once indeed been found) to a contention with this man: the loss of which son by a violent death, on such an occasion, by a hand so justly hated, would complete the misery of the whole family: and who nevertheless resolves to call him to account, if I do not: his very *misbehaviour* perhaps to such a sister stimulating his perverse heart to do her memory the *more signal* justice; though the attempt might be fatal to him.

Then, sir, to be a witness, as I am every hour, to the calamity and distress of a family to which I am related; every one of whom, however averse to an alliance with him while it had *not* taken place, would no doubt have been soon reconciled to the admirable creature, had the man (to whom for his family and fortunes it was not a disgrace to be allied) done her but common justice!

To see them hang their pensive heads; mope about shunning one another; though formerly never used to meet but to rejoice in each other; afflicting themselves with reflections that the last time they respectively saw the dear creature it was here, or there, at such a place, in such an attitude; and could they have thought that it would have been the *last*?

Everyone of them reviving instances of her excellencies that will for a long time make their very blessings curse to them!

Her closet, her chamber, her cabinet, given up to me to disfurnish, in order to answer (now *too late* obliging!) the legacies bequeathed; unable themselves to enter them; and even making use of less convenient back-stairs, that they may avoid passing by the doors of her apartment!

Her parlour locked up; the walks, the retirements, the summer-house in which she delighted and used to pursue her charming works; *that*, in particular, from which she went to the fatal interview; shunned, or hurried by, or over!

Her perfections nevertheless called up to remembrance and enumerated: incidents and graces, unheeded before or passed over in the group of her numberless perfections, now brought into notice and dwelt upon!

The very servants allowed to expatiate upon these praiseful topics to their principals! Even eloquent in their praises—the distressed principals listening and weeping! Then to see them break in upon the zealous applauders, by their impatience and remorse, and throw abroad their helpless hands and exclaim; then again to see them listen to hear more of her praises and weep again—they even encouraging the servants to repeat how they used to be stopped by strangers to ask after her, and by those who knew her to be told of some new instances to her honour—how aggravating all this!

In *dreams* they see her, and *desire* to see her: always an angel, and accompanied by angels: always clad in robes of light: always endeavouring to comfort *them*, who declare that they shall never more know comfort!

What an example she set! How she indited! How she drew! How she wrought! How she talked! How she sung! How she prayed! Her voice, music! Her accent, harmony!

Her conversation how instructive! how sought after! The delight of persons of all ages, of both sexes, of all ranks! Yet how humble, how condescending! Never were dignity and humility so illustriously mingled!

At other times, how generous, how noble, how charitable, how judicious in her charities! In every action laudable! In every attitude attractive! In every appearance, whether full-dressed, or in the housewife's more humble garb, equally elegant and equally lovely! *Like* or *resembling* Miss Clarissa Harlowe they now remember to be a praise denoting the highest degree of approveable excellence, with everyone, whatever person, action, or rank, spoken of.

The desirable daughter; the obliging kinswoman; the affectionate sister (all envy now subsided!); the faithful, the warm friend; the affable, the kind, the benevolent mistress!—Not one fault remembered! All their severities called cruelties: mutually accusing each other; each him and herself; and all to raise *her* character, and torment themselves.

Such, sir, is the angel of whom the vilest of men has deprived the world! You, sir, who know more of the barbarous machinations and practices of this strange man can help me to still more inflaming reasons, were they needed, why a man *not perfect* may stand excused to the generality of the world, if he should pursue his vengeance.

But I will force myself from the subject, after I have repeated that I have not yet made any resolutions that can bind me. Whenever I do, I shall be glad they may be such as may merit the honour of your approbation.

I send you back the copies of the posthumous letters. I see the humanity of your purpose in the transmission of them to me; and I thank you most heartily for it. I presume that it is owing to the same laudable consideration, that you kept back the copy of that to the wicked man himself.

I intend to wait upon Miss Howe in person with the diamond ring, and such other of the effects bequeathed to her as are here. I am, sir,

Your most faithful and obliged servant,
WM. MORDEN

[Letter 519.1: Mr Belford to Colonel Morden]

Mr Belford, in his answer to this letter, farther enforces the lady's dying injunctions; and rejoices that the colonel has made no vindictive resolutions; and hopes everything from his prudence and consideration, and from his promise given to the dying lady.

He refers to the seeing him in town an account of the dreadful ends of two of the

greatest criminals in his cousin's affair. 'This, says he, together with Mr Lovelace's disorder of mind, looks as if Providence had already taken the punishment of these unhappy wretches into its own hands.'

He desires a day's notice of his coming to town, lest otherwise he may be absent at the time.

This he does, though he tells him not the reason, with a view to prevent a meeting between him and Mr Lovelace; who may be in town (as he apprehends) about the same time, in his way to go abroad.

Letter 520: COLONEL MORDEN TO JOHN BELFORD, ESQ.

Tuesday, Sept. 26

Dear sir,

I CANNOT help congratulating myself as well as you, that we have already got through with the family every article of the will where *they* have any concern.

You left me a discretional power, in many instances; and, in pursuance of it, I have had my dear cousin's personal jewels valued; and will account to you for them at the highest price, when I come to town, as well as for other matters that you were pleased to entrust to my management.

These jewels I have presented to my cousin Dolly Hervey, in acknowledgement of her love to the dear departed. I have told Miss Howe of this; and she is as well pleased with what I have done, as if she had been the purchaser of them herself. As that young lady has jewels of her own, she could only have wished to purchase these for her beloved friend's sake.

The grandmother's jewels are also valued; and the money will be paid me, for you, to be carried to the uses of the will.

Mrs Norton is preparing by general consent to enter upon her office as housekeeper at *The Grove*. But it is my opinion that she will not be long on this side Heaven.

I waited upon Miss Howe myself, as I told you I would, with what was bequeathed to her and her mother. If I make a few observations with regard to that young lady, so dear to my beloved cousin, you will not be displeased perhaps, as you have not a personal acquaintance with her.

There never was a firmer and nobler friendship in women than that which the wretched man has put an end to between my dear cousin and Miss Howe.

Friendship, generally speaking, Mr Belford, is too fervent a flame for female minds to manage: a light that but in few of their hands burns steady, and often hurries the sex into flight and absurdity. Like other extremes, it is hardly ever durable. Marriage, which is the highest state of friendship, generally absorbs the most vehement friendships of female to female; and that whether the wedlock be happy or not.

What female mind is capable of two fervent friendships at the same time?

This I mention as a *general observation*: but the friendship that subsisted between these two ladies affords a remarkable exception to it: which I account for from those qualities and attainments in *both*, which, were they more common, would furnish more exceptions still in favour of the sex. Both had an *enlarged*, and even a *liberal* education: both had minds thirsting after virtuous knowledge. Great readers both: great writers—(and *early familiar writing* I take to be one of the greatest openers and improvers of the mind that man or woman can be employed in). Both generous. High in fortune; therefore above that dependence each on the other that frequently destroys the familiarity which is the cement of friendship. Both excelling in *different ways*, in which neither sought to emulate the other. Both blessed with clear and distinguishing faculties; with solid sense; and from their first intimacy (I have many of my lights, sir, from Mrs Norton) each seeing something in the other to *fear*, as well as *love*; yet making it an indispensable condition of their friendship each to tell the other of her failings; and to be thankful for the freedom taken. One by nature *gentle*; the other *made so* by her *love* and *admiration* of her exalted friend—impossible that there could be a friendship better calculated for duration.

I must however take the liberty to blame Miss Howe for her behaviour to Mr Hickman. And I infer from it, that even women of sense are not to be trusted with power.

By the way, I am sure I need not desire you not to communicate to this fervent young lady the liberties I take with her character.

I dare say my cousin could not approve of Miss Howe's behaviour to this gentleman: a behaviour which is talked of by as many as know Mr Hickman and her. Can a *wise* young lady be easy under such censure?—She *must* know it.

Mr Hickman is really a very worthy man. Everybody speaks well of him. But he is gentle-dispositioned, and he adores Miss Howe; and love admits not of an air of even due dignity to the object of it. Yet will he hardly ever get back the reins he has yielded up; unless she, by carrying too far the power she seems at present too sensible of, should, when she has no favours to confer which he has not a right to demand, provoke him to throw off the too heavy yoke. And should he do so, and then treat her with negligence, Miss Howe of all the women I know will be the least able to support herself under it. She will then be *more* unhappy than she ever made him: for a man who is uneasy at home can divert himself abroad; which a woman cannot so easily do without scandal.

Permit me to take further notice as to Miss Howe, that it is very obvious to me that she has, by her haughty behaviour to this worthy man, involved herself in one difficulty from which she knows not how to extricate herself with that grace which accompanies all her actions. She intends to have Mr Hickman. I believe she does not dislike him. And it will cost her no small pains to descend from the elevation she has climbed to.

Another inconveniency, she will suffer from her having taught everybody (for she is above disguise) to think by her treatment of Mr Hickman much more meanly of him than he deserves to be thought of. And must *she* not suffer dishonour in *his* dishonour?

Mrs Howe is much disturbed at her daughter's behaviour to the gentleman. He is very deservedly a favourite of hers. But (*another* failing in Miss Howe!) her mother has not all the authority with her that her daughter's good sense ought to permit her to have. It is very difficult, Mr Belford, for people of *different* or *contrary* dispositions (though no bad people neither) to mingle REVERENCE with their *love* for each other; even where *nature* has called for *love* in the relationship.

Miss Howe is *open, generous, noble*. The mother has not any of these fine qualities. Parents, in order to preserve their children's veneration for them, should take great care not to let them see anything in their conduct or behaviour, or principles, which they themselves would not approve of in others.

But, after all, I see that there is something so charmingly brilliant and frank in Miss Howe's disposition, although at present visibly overclouded by grief, that it is impossible not to love her even for her failings. She *may*, and I hope she *will*, make Mr Hickman an obliging wife. And if she do, she will have an additional merit with me; since she cannot be apprehensive of check or control; and may therefore by her *generosity* and *prudence* lay an obligation upon her husband by the performance of what is no more than her *duty*.

Her mother both *loves* and *fears* her. Yet is Mrs Howe a woman of vivacity, and ready enough I dare say to cry out when she is pained. But, alas! she has, as I hinted above, *weakened her authority* by the *narrowness of her mind*.

Yet once she praised her daughter to me for the generosity of her spirit, with so much *warmth* that had I not known the old lady's character, I should have thought her generous *herself*. And yet I have always observed that people even of narrow tempers are ready to praise generous ones—and thus have I accounted for it, that such persons generally find it to their purpose, that all the world should be open-minded but themselves.

The old lady applied herself to me to urge to the young one the contents of the will, in order to hasten her to fix a day for her marriage: but desired that I would not let Miss Howe know that she did.

I took the liberty upon it to tell the young lady that I hoped that *her* part of a will, so soon and so punctually in almost all its other articles fulfilled, would not be the only one that would be slighted.

Her answer was she would consider of it: and made me a curtsy with such an air as showed me that she thought me more out of my sphere than I could allow her to think me had I been permitted to argue the point with her.

I found both Miss Howe and her own servant-maid in deep mourning. This, it seems, had occasioned a great debate at first between her mother and her. Her mother had the words of the will on her side; and Mr Hickman's interest in her view; as her daughter had said that she would wear it for six months at least. But the young lady carried her point—'Strange, said she, if I who shall mourn the heavy, the irreparable loss to the last hour of my life should not show my concern to the world for a few months.'

Mr Hickman for his part was so far from uttering an opposing word on this occasion, that on the very day that Miss Howe put on hers, he waited on her in a new suit of mourning as for a near relation. His servants and equipage made the same respectful appearance.

Whether the mother was consulted by him in it, I cannot say; but the daughter knew nothing of it till she saw him in it. She looked at him with surprise, and asked him for whom he mourned?

The dear, and ever-dear Miss Harlowe, he said.

She was at a loss, it seems—At last—All the world ought to mourn for my Clarissa, said she; but who, man (that was her address to him), thinkest thou to oblige by this appearance?

It is more than *appearance*, madam. I love not my own sister, worthy as she is, better than I loved Miss Clarissa Harlowe. I oblige *myself* by it. And if I disoblige not you, that is all I have to wish.

She surveyed him, I am told, from head to foot. She knew not, at first, whether to be angry or pleased—At length: I thought at first, said she, that you might have a bolder and freer motive—but (as my mamma says) you may be a well-meaning man, though generally a little wrong-headed—however, as the world is censorious, and may think us nearer of kin than I would have it supposed, I must take care, honest friend, that I am not seen abroad in your company.

But let me add, Mr Belford, that if this compliment of Mr Hickman (or this *more* than compliment as I may well call it, since the worthy man speaks not of my dear cousin without emotion) does not produce a short day, I shall think Miss Howe has less generosity in her temper than I am willing to allow her.

You will excuse me, Mr Belford, I dare say, for the particularities which you have invited and encouraged.

Having now seen everything that relates to the will of my dear cousin brought to a desirable issue, I will set about making my own. I shall follow the dear creature's example, and give my reasons for every article, that there may be no room for after-contention.

What but a fear of death, a fear unworthy of a creature who knows that he must one day as surely die as he was born, can hinder any one from making such a disposition?

I hope soon to pay my respects to you in town. Meantime, I am, with great respect, dear sir,

Your faithful and affectionate humble servant,

WM. MORDEN

Letter 521: MR BELFORD TO MISS HOWE

Thursday, Sept. 28

Madam,

I DO myself the honour to send you with this, according to my promise,[a] copies of the posthumous letters written by your exalted friend.

These will be accompanied with other letters, particularly a copy of one from Mr Lovelace, begun to be written on the 14th, and continued down to the 18th.[b] You will judge by it, madam, of the dreadful anguish that his spirits labour with, and of his deep remorse.

Mr Lovelace sent for this letter back. I complied; but I first took a copy of it. As I have not told him that I have done so, you will be pleased to forbear communicating of it to anybody but Mr Hickman. That gentleman's perusal of it will be the same as if nobody but yourself saw it.

One of the letters of Colonel Morden's which I enclose, you will observe, madam, is only a copy.[c] The true reason for which, as I will ingenuously acknowledge is some free but respectful observations which the colonel has made upon you, madam, for declining to carry into execution your part of your dear friend's last requests. I have therefore, in respect to that worthy gentleman (having a caution from him on that head) omitted those parts.

a See p. 1425.
b See p. 1427.
c See p. 1449.

Will you allow me, madam, however, to tell you that I myself could not have believed that my inimitable testatrix's own Miss Howe would have been the most backward in performing such a part of her dear friend's last will as is entirely in her own power to perform—especially when that performance would make one of the most deserving men in England happy; and whom, I presume, she proposes to honour with her hand?

Excuse me, madam. I have a most sincere veneration for you; and would not disoblige you for the world.

I will not presume to make remarks on the letters I send you: nor upon the informations I have to give you of the dreadful end of two unhappy wretches who were the greatest criminals in the affair of your adorable friend. These are the infamous *Sinclair*, and a person whom you have read of no doubt in the letters of the charming innocent by the name of Captain *Tomlinson*.

The wretched woman died in the extremest tortures and despondency: the man from wounds got in defending himself in carrying on a contraband trade: both accusing themselves in their last hours for the parts they had acted against the most excellent of women, as of the crime they had most remorse for.

Give me leave to say, madam, that if your compassion be not excited for the poor man who suffers from his own anguish of mind, as you will see by his letter; and for the unhappy family whose remorse, as you will see by Colonel Morden's, is so deep: your terror must. And yet I shall not wonder if the just sense of the irreparable loss you have sustained hardens a heart against pity which, on a less extraordinary occasion, would want its principal grace, if it were not compassionate.

I am, madam, with the greatest respect and gratitude,

Your most obliged and faithful humble servant,

J. BELFORD

Letter 522: MISS HOWE TO JOHN BELFORD, ESQ.

Sat. Sept. 30

Sir,

I LITTLE thought I ever could have owed so much obligation to any man, as you have laid me under. And yet what you have sent me has almost broken my heart, and ruined my eyes.

I am surprised, though agreeably, that you have so soon, and so well, got over that part of the trust you have engaged in which relates to the family.

It may be presumed, from the exits you mention of two of the infernal man's accomplices, that the thunderbolt will not stop short of the principal. Indeed I have some pleasure to think it seems rolling along towards the devoted head that has plotted all the mischief. But let me however say that, although I think Mr Morden not altogether in the wrong in his reasons for resenting, as he is the dear creature's kinsman and trustee; yet I think you very much in the right in endeavouring to dissuade him from it, as you are her executor, and act in pursuance of her earnest request.

But what a letter is that of the infernal man! I cannot observe upon it. Neither can I, for very different reasons, upon my dear creature's posthumous letters;

particularly on that to him. Oh! Mr Belford! what numberless perfections died when my Clarissa drew her last breath!

If decency be observed in his letters (for I have not yet had patience to read above two or three of them, besides this horrid one which I return you enclosed), I may some time hence be curious to look, by *their* means, into the hearts of wretches which, though they must be the abhorrence of virtuous minds, will when laid open (as I presume they are in them) afford a *proper warning* to those who read them, and teach them to *detest men of such profligate characters*.

If your reformation be sincere, you will not be offended that I except you not on this occasion—And thus have I helped you to a criterion to try yourself by.

By this letter of the wicked man it is apparent that there are still wickeder women. But see what a guilty commerce with the devils of your sex will bring those to, whose morals ye have ruined!—for these women were once innocent: it was *man* that made them otherwise. The first bad man, perhaps, threw them upon worse men: those upon still worse; till they commenced devils incarnate—The height of wickedness, or of shame, is not arrived at all at once, as I have somewhere heard observed.

But this man, this monster rather, for *him* to curse these women, and to curse the dear creature's family (implacable as the latter were) in order to lighten a burden he voluntarily took up and groans under is *meanness* added to *wickedness:* and in vain will he one day find his low plea of sharing with her friends, and with those common wretches, a guilt which will be adjudged him as all his own; though they too may meet with their punishment: as it is evidently begun; in the first, in their ineffectual reproaches of one another; in the second, as you have told me.

This letter of the abandoned wretch I have not shown to anybody; not even to Mr Hickman: for, sir, I must tell you I do not as *yet* think it the same thing as only seeing it myself.

Mr Hickman, like the rest of his sex, would grow upon indulgence. One distinction from me would make him pay two to himself. Insolent creepers, or encroachers, all of you! To show any of you a *favour* today, you would expect it as a *right* tomorrow.

I am, as you see, very open and sincere with you; and design in another letter to be still more so, in answer to your call, and Colonel Morden's call, upon me in a point that concerns me to explain myself upon to my beloved creature's executor, and to her *only tender* and *only worthy* relation.

I cannot but highly applaud Colonel Morden for his generosity to Miss Dolly Hervey.

Oh that he had arrived time enough to save my inimitable friend from the machinations of the vilest of men, and from the envy and malice of the most selfish and implacable of brothers and sisters!

ANNA HOWE

Monday, Oct. 2

WHEN you question me, sir, as you do and on a subject so affecting to me, in the character of the representative of my best-beloved friend, and have in every particular hitherto acted up to that character, you are entitled to my regard: especially as in your questioning of me you are joined by a gentleman whom I look upon as the dearest and nearest (because worthiest) relation of my dear friend: and who, it seems, has been so severe a censurer of my conduct, that your politeness will not permit you to send me his letter, with others of his; but a copy only, in which the passages reflecting upon me are omitted.

I presume, however, that what is meant by this alarming freedom of the colonel's is no more than what you both have already hinted to me; as if you thought I were not inclined to pay so much regard to my beloved creature's last will in my own case, as I would have others pay to it. A charge that I ought not to be quite silent under.

You have observed, no doubt, that I have seemed to value myself upon the freedom I take in declaring my sentiments without reserve upon every subject that I pretend to touch upon: and I can hardly question that I have, or shall, in your opinion, by my unceremonious treatment of you upon so short an acquaintance, run into the error of those who, wanting to be thought above hypocrisy and flattery, fall into rusticity, if not ill-manners; a common fault with such who, not caring to correct constitutional failings, seek to gloss them over by some *nominal* virtue; when all the time perhaps it is native arrogance; or at least a contracted rust, that they will not, because it would give them pain, submit to have filed off.

You see, sir, that I can, however, be as free with myself as with you: and, by what I am going to write, you will find me still more free: and yet I am aware that such of my sex as will not assume some little dignity, and exact respect from yours, will render themselves cheap; and perhaps, for their modesty and diffidence, be repaid with scorn and insult.

But the scorn I will endeavour not to deserve; and the insult I will not bear.

In some of the dear creature's papers, which you have had in your possession, and must again have for transcription, you will find several friendly but severe reprehensions of me, on account of a natural, or at least an *habitual*, warmth of temper which she was pleased to impute to me.

I was thinking to give you her charge against me in her own words, from one of her letters delivered to *me* with her own hands, on taking leave of me, on the last visit she honoured me with. But I will supply that charge by confession of more than it imports; to wit, 'That I am haughty, uncontrollable, and violent in my temper'; *this I say:* 'Impatient of contradiction,' *was my beloved's charge* (from anybody but her dear self, she should have said); 'and aim not at that affability, that gentleness next to meekness, which in the letter I was going to communicate she tells me are the peculiar and indispensable characteristics of a real fine lady; who, she is pleased to say, should appear to be gall-less as a dove; and never should know what warmth or high spirit is, but in the cause of religion or virtue; or in cases where her own honour, the honour of a friend, or that of an innocent person, is concerned.'

Now, sir, as I must needs plead guilty to this indictment, do you think I ought not to resolve upon a single life?—I, who have such an opinion of your sex, that I think there is not one man in an hundred whom a woman of sense and spirit can either *honour* or *obey*, though you make us promise *both*, in that solemn form of words which unites or rather *binds* us to you in marriage?

When I look round upon all the married people of my acquaintance, and see how *they* live, and what *they* bear, who live *best*, I am confirmed in my dislike to the state.

Well do your sex contrive to bring us up fools and idiots in order to make us bear the yoke you lay upon our shoulders; and that we may not despise you from our hearts (as we certainly should if we were brought up as you are) for your ignorance, as much as you often make us do (as it is) for your insolence.

These, sir, are some of my notions. And, with these notions, let me repeat my question, *Do you think I ought to marry at all?*

If I marry either a sordid or an imperious wretch, can I, do you think, live with him? And ought a man of a contrary character, for the sake of either of our reputations, to be plagued with me?

Long did I stand out against all the offers made me, and against all the persuasions of my mother; and, to tell you the truth, the *longer* and with the *more* obstinacy, as the person my choice would have at first fallen upon was neither approved by my mother, nor by my dear friend. This riveted me to my pride, and to my opposition: for although I was convinced after a while that my choice would neither have been prudent nor happy; and that the specious wretch was not what he had made me believe he was; yet could I not easily think of any other man: and indeed from the detection of him took a settled aversion to the whole sex.

At last Mr Hickman offered himself; a man worthy of a better choice. He had the good fortune (he thinks it so) to be agreeable (and to make his proposals agreeable) to my mother.

As to myself; I own that were I to have chosen a brother, Mr Hickman should have been the man; virtuous, sober, sincere, friendly, as he is. But I wished not to marry: nor knew I the man in the world whom I could think deserving of my beloved friend. But neither of our parents would let us live single.

The accursed Lovelace was proposed warmly to *her* at one time; and, while she was yet but indifferent to him, they by ungenerous usage of him (for then, sir, he was not known to be Beelzebub himself) and by endeavouring to force her inclinations in favour first of one worthless man, then of another, in antipathy to him, through her foolish brother's caprice, turned that indifference (from the natural generosity of her soul) into a regard which she never otherwise would have had for a man of his character.

Mr Hickman was proposed to me. I refused him again and again. He persisted: my mother his advocate. My mother made my beloved friend his advocate too. I told him my aversion to all men: to him: to matrimony—Still he persisted. I used him with tyranny: led indeed partly by my temper, partly by design; hoping thereby to get rid of him; till the poor man (his character unexceptionably uniform) still persisting, made himself a merit with me by his patience. This brought down my pride (I never, sir, was accounted very ungenerous, nor quite ungrateful) and gave me, at one time, an inferiority in my own opinion to him; which lasted just long enough for my friends to prevail upon me to promise him encouragement; and to receive his addresses.

Having so done, when the weather-glass of my pride got up again, I found I had gone too far to recede. My mother and my friend both held me to it. Yet I tried him; I vexed him an hundred ways; and not so much neither with design to vex him, as to make him hate me and decline his suit.

He bore this, however; and got nothing but my pity: yet still my mother and my friend, having obtained my promise (made, however, not to *him*, but to *them*) and being well assured that I valued no man *more* than Mr Hickman (who never once disobliged me in word or deed or look, except by his foolish perseverance) insisted upon the performance.

While my dear friend was in her unhappy uncertainty, I could not think of marriage: and now, what encouragement have I?—She, my monitress, my guide, my counsel, gone, for ever gone!—by whose advice and instructions I hoped to acquit myself tolerably in the state into which I could not avoid entering. For, sir, my mother is so partially Mr Hickman's friend, that I am sure, should any difference arise, she would always censure me, and acquit him; even were he ungenerous enough to remember me in his day.

This, sir, being my situation, consider how difficult it is for me to think of marriage. Whenever we approve, we can find an hundred good reasons to justify our approbation. Whenever we dislike, we can find a thousand to justify our dislike. Everything in the latter case is an impediment: every shadow a bugbear— Thus can I enumerate and swell perhaps only *imaginary* grievances: 'I must go whither he would have me to go: visit whom he would have me to visit: well as I love to write (though now, alas! my grand inducement to write is over), it must be to whom he pleases.' And Mrs Hickman (who as Miss Howe cannot do wrong) would hardly ever be able to do right. Thus, the tables turned upon me, I am reminded of my broken-vowed obedience; Madamed up perhaps to matrimonial perfection, and all the wedded warfare practised comfortably over between us (for I shall not be passive under insolent treatment) till we become curses to each other, a byword to our neighbours and the jest of our own servants.

But there must be *bear* and *forbear*, methinks some wise body will tell me: but why must I be teazed into a state where that *must* be necessarily the case; when now I can do as I please, and wish only to be let alone to do as best pleases me? And what, in effect, does my mother say? 'Anna Howe, you now do everything that pleases you: you now have nobody to control you: you go and you come; you dress and you undress; you rise and you go to rest; just as you think best: but you must be happier still, child!—'

As how, madam?

'Why, you must marry, my dear, and have none of these options; but in everything do as your husband commands you.'

This is very hard, you will own, sir, for such a one as me to think of. And yet, engaged to enter into that state as I am, how can I help myself? My mother presses me; my friend, my beloved friend, writing as from the dead, presses me; and you and Mr Morden, as executors of her will, remind me; the man is not afraid of me (I am sure were I *the* man, I should not have half his courage); and I think I ought to conclude to punish him (the only effectual way I have to do it) for his perverse adherence and persecution, as many other persons are punished, with the grant of his own wishes.

Let me then assure you, sir, that when I can find in the words of my charming friend in her will, writing of her cousin Hervey, that my grief for her is *mellowed by time into a remembrance more sweet than painful*, that I may not be utterly unworthy of the passion a man of some merit has for me, I will answer the request of my dear friend, so often repeated, and so earnestly pressed; and Mr Hickman shall find, if he continue to deserve my gratitude, that my endeavours shall not be wanting to make him amends for the patience he has had, and must still for a little while longer have, with me: and then will it be his own fault (I hope not mine) if our marriage answer not those happy *prognostics, which filled her* generous *presaging mind*, upon this view, as she once for *my* encouragement, and to induce me to encourage *him*, told me.

Thus, sir, have I, in a very free manner accounted to you, as to the executor of my beloved friend, for all that relates to you, as such, to know; and even for more than I needed to do, against myself: only that you will find as much against me in some of *her* letters; and so, *losing* nothing, I *gain* the character of *ingenuity* with you.

And thus much for the double reprimand on my delaying my part of the performance of my dear friend's will.

And now let me remind you of one great article relating to yourself, while you are admonishing me on this subject: it is furnished me by her posthumous letter to you—I hope you will not forget that the most benevolent of her sex expresses herself as earnestly concerned for your thorough reformation, as she does for my marrying. You'll see to it then that her wishes are as completely answered in that particular, as you are desirous they should be in all others.

I have, I own, disobeyed the dear creature in one article; and that is where she desires that I will not put myself into mourning. I could not help it.

I send this and mine of Saturday last together: and will not add another word, after I have told you that I think myself

Your obliged servant,
A. Howe

Letter 524: MR BELFORD TO MISS HOWE

Thursday night, Oct. 5

I RETURN you, madam, my most respectful thanks for your condescending hint in relation to the pious wishes of your exalted friend for my thorough reformation.

I will only say, that it shall be my earnest and unwearied endeavour to make those generous wishes effectual: and I hope for the Divine blessing upon such my endeavours, or else I know they will be in vain.

I cannot, madam, express how much I think myself obliged to you for your further condescension, in writing to me so frankly the state of your past and present mind in relation to the single and matrimonial life. If the lady by whom, as the executor of her inimitable friend, I am thus honoured, *has* failings, never were failings so lovely in woman!—How much more lovely, indeed, than the virtues of many of her sex!

I might have ventured into the hands of such a lady the colonel's letter without transcription or omission. That worthy gentleman exceedingly admires you; and his caution was the effect of his politeness only, and of his regard for you.

I send you, madam, a letter from Lord M. to myself; and the copies of three others written in consequence of that. These will acquaint you with Mr Lovelace's departure from England, and with other particulars which you will be curious to know.

Be pleased to keep to yourself such of the contents as your own prudence will suggest to you ought not to be seen by anybody else.

I am, madam, with the profoundest and most grateful respect,

> Your faithful and obliged humble servant,
> JOHN BELFORD

Letter 525: LORD M. TO JOHN BELFORD, ESQ.

> M. Hall, Friday, Sept. 29

Dear sir,

MY kinsman Lovelace is now setting out for London; proposing to see you, and then to go to Dover and so embark. God send him well out of the kingdom!

On Monday he will be with you, I believe. Pray let me be favoured with an account of all your conversations; for Mr Mowbray and Mr Tourville are to be there too; and whether you think he is grown quite his own man again. What I mostly write for, is to wish you to keep Colonel Morden and him asunder, and so to give you notice of his going to town. I should be very loath there should be any mischief between them, as you gave me notice that the colonel threatened my nephew. But my kinsman would not bear that; so nobody let him know that he did. But I hope there is no fear: for the colonel does not, as I hear, threaten now. For his own sake, I am glad of that; for there is not such a man in the world as my kinsman is said to be, at all the weapons—as well he was not; he would not be so daring.

We shall all here miss the wild fellow. To be sure there is no man better company when he pleases.

Pray, do you never travel thirty or forty mile? I should be glad to see you here at M. Hall. It will be charity, when my kinsman is gone; for we suppose you will be his chief correspondent: although he has promised to write to my nieces often. But he is very apt to forget his promises; to us his relations particularly. God preserve us all; Amen! prays

> Your very humble servant,
> M.

Letter 526: MR BELFORD TO LORD M.

London, Tuesday night, Oct. 3

My lord,

I OBEY your lordship's commands with great pleasure.

Yesterday in the afternoon Mr Lovelace made me a visit at my lodgings. As I was in expectation of one from Colonel Morden about the same time, I thought proper to carry him to a tavern which neither of us frequented (on pretence of an half-appointment); ordering notice to be sent me thither, if the colonel came: And Mr Lovelace sent to Mowbray, and Tourville, and Mr Doleman of Uxbridge (who came to town to take leave of him), to let them know where to find us.

Mr Lovelace is *too well* recovered, I was going to say. I never saw him more gay, lively, and handsome. We had a good deal of bluster about some parts of the trust I have engaged in; and upon freedoms I had treated him with; in which, he would have it, that I had exceeded our agreed-on limits: but on the arrival of our three old companions, and a nephew of Mr Doleman's (who had a good while been desirous to pass an hour with Mr Lovelace), it blew off for the present.

Mr Mowbray and Mr Tourville had also taken some exceptions at the freedoms of my pen; and Mr Lovelace, after his way, took upon him to reconcile us; and did it at the expense of all three; and with such an infinite run of humour and raillery, that we had nothing to do but laugh at what he said, and at one another. I can deal tolerably with him at my pen; but in conversation he has no equal. In short, it was his day. He was glad, he said, to find himself alive; and his two friends clapping and rubbing their hands twenty times in an hour, declared, that now once more he was all himself; the charmingest fellow in the world; and they would follow him to the furthest part of the globe.

I threw a bur upon his coat now and then; but none would stick.

Your lordship knows that there are many things which occasion a roar of applause in conversation, when the heart is *open* and men are *resolved* to be merry, which will neither bear repeating nor thinking of afterwards. Common things, in the mouth of a man we admire and whose wit has passed upon us for sterling, become in a gay hour *uncommon*. We watch every turn of such a one's countenance, and are resolved to laugh when he smiles, even before he utters what we are expecting to flow from his lips.

Mr Doleman and his nephew took leave of us by twelve. Mowbray and Tourville grew very noisy by one; and were carried off by two. Wine never moves Mr Lovelace, notwithstanding a vivacity which generally helps on over-gay spirits. As to myself, the little part I had taken in their gaiety kept me unconcerned.

The clock struck three before I could get him into any serious or attentive way—so natural to him is gaiety of heart; and such strong hold had the liveliness of the evening taken of him. His conversation you know, my lord, when his heart is free, runs off to the bottom without any dregs.

But after that hour, and when we thought of parting, he became a little more serious: and then he told me his designs, and gave me a plan of his intended tour; wishing heartily that I could have accompanied him.

We parted about four; he not a little dissatisfied with me; for we had some talk about subjects which, he said, he loved not to think of; to wit, Miss Harlowe's will;

my executorship; papers I had in confidence communicated to that admirable lady (with no unfriendly design, I assure your lordship); and he insisting upon, and I refusing, the return of the letters he had written to me from the time that he had made his first addresses to her.

He would see me once again, he said; and it would be upon very ill terms if I complied not with his request. Which I bid him not expect. But, that I might not deny him everything, I told him that I would give him a copy of the will; though I was sure, I said, when he read it, he would wish he had never seen it.

I had a message from him about eleven this morning, desiring me to name a place at which to dine with him, and Mowbray, and Tourville, for the last time: and soon after another from Colonel Morden, inviting me to pass the evening with him at the Bedford Head in Covent Garden. And, that I might keep them at distance from one another, I appointed Mr Lovelace at the Eagle in Suffolk Street.

There I met him, and the two others. We began where we left off at our last parting; and were very high with each other. But, at last, all was made up, and he offered to forget and forgive everything, on condition that I would correspond with him while abroad, and continue the series which had been broken through by his illness; and particularly give him, as I had offered, a copy of the lady's will.

I promised him: and he then fell to rallying me on my gravity, and on my reformation schemes, as he called them. As we walked about the room, expecting dinner to be brought in, he laid his hand upon my shoulder, then pushed me from him with a curse; walking round me, and surveying me from head to foot; then calling for the observation of the others, he turned round upon his heel, and, with one of his peculiar wild airs, 'Ha, ha, ha, ha, burst he out, that these sour-faced proselytes should take it into their heads that they cannot be pious, without forfeiting both their good-nature and good manners!—Why Jack, turning me about, prithee look up, man!—Dost thou not know that religion, if it has taken proper hold of the heart, is the most cheerful *countenance-maker* in the world?—I have heard my beloved Miss Harlowe say so: And she knew, or nobody did. And was not *her* aspect a benign proof of the observation? But by these wamblings in thy cursed gizzard, and thy awkward grimaces, I see thou'rt but a novice in it yet!—Ah, Belford, Belford, thou hast a confounded parcel of briars and thorns to trample over barefoot, before religion will illumine these gloomy features!'

I give your lordship this account, in answer to your desire to know if I think him the man he was?

In our conversation at dinner, he was balancing whether he should set out the next morning, or the morning after. But finding he had nothing to do, and Colonel Morden being in town (which, however, I told him not of), I turned the scale; and he agreed upon setting out tomorrow morning; they to see him embark; and I promised to accompany them for a morning's ride (as they proposed their horses); but said that I must return in the afternoon.

With much reluctance they let me go to my evening's appointment: they little thought with whom: for Mr Lovelace had put it as a case of honour to all of us, whether, as he had been told that Mr Morden and Mr James Harlowe had thrown out menaces against him, he ought to leave the kingdom till he had thrown himself in their way.

Mowbray gave his opinion that he ought to leave it like a man of honour, as he was; and if he did not take those gentlemen to task for their opprobrious speeches, that at least he should be seen by them in public before he went away; else they might give themselves airs, as if he had left the kingdom in fear of them.

To this he himself so much inclined, that it was with difficulty I persuaded him that, as they had neither of them proceeded to a direct and formal challenge; as they knew he had not made himself difficult of access; and as he had already done the family injury enough; and it was Miss Harlowe's earnest desire that he would be content with that; he had no reason, from any point of honour, to delay his journey; especially as he had so just a motive for his going as the establishing of his health; and as he might return the sooner, if he saw occasion for it.

I found the colonel in a very solemn way. We had a good deal of discourse upon the subject of letters which had passed between us in relation to Miss Harlowe's will, and to her family.

He has some accounts to settle with his banker; which, he says, will be adjusted tomorrow; and on Thursday he proposes to go down again to take leave of his friends; and then intends to set out directly for Italy.

I wish Mr Lovelace could have been prevailed upon to take any other tour than that of France and Italy. I did propose Madrid to him: but he laughed at me, and told me that the proposal was in character from a mule; and from one who was become as grave as a Spaniard of the old cut, at ninety.

I expressed to the colonel my apprehensions that his cousin's dying injunctions would not have the force upon him that were to be wished.

They have great force upon me, Mr Belford, said he; or one world would not have held Mr Lovelace and me thus long. But my intention is to go to Florence; not to lay my bones there, as upon my cousin's death I told you I thought to do; but to settle all my affairs in those parts, and then to come over and reside upon a little paternal estate in Kent, which is strangely gone to ruin in my absence. Indeed, were I to meet Mr Lovelace, either here or abroad, I might not be answerable for the consequence.

He would have engaged me for tomorrow. But having promised to attend Mr Lovelace on his journey, as I have mentioned, I said I was obliged to go out of town, and was uncertain as to the time of my return in the evening. And so I am to see him on Thursday morning at my own lodgings.

I will do myself the honour to write again to your lordship tomorrow night. Meantime, I am, my lord,

Your lordship's, etc.

Letter 527: MR BELFORD TO LORD M.

Wed. night, Oct. 4

My lord,

I AM just returned from attending Mr Lovelace as far as Gad's Hill near Rochester. He was exceeding gay all the way. Mowbray and Tourville are gone on with him. They will see him embark, and under sail; and promise to follow him in a month or two; for they say, there is no living without him, now he is once more himself.

He and I parted with great and even solemn tokens of affection; but yet not without gay intermixtures, as I will acquaint your lordship.

Taking me aside, and clasping his arms about me, 'Adieu, dear Belford! said he: may you proceed in the course you have entered upon!—Whatever airs I give myself, this charming creature has fast hold of me *here* (clapping his hand upon his heart); and I must either appear what you see me, or be what I so lately was—Oh the divine creature!' lifting up his eyes—

'But if I live to come to England, and you remain fixed in your present way and can give me encouragement, I hope rather to follow your example than to ridicule you for it. This will (for I had given him a copy of it) I will make the companion of my solitary hours. You have told me part of its melancholy contents; and that, and her posthumous letter, shall be my study; and they will prepare me for being your disciple, if you hold on.

'*You*, Jack, may marry, continued he; and I have a wife in my eye for you—Only thou'rt such an awkward mortal' (he saw me affected, and thought to make me smile): 'But we don't make ourselves, except it be worse, by our dress. Thou art in mourning now, as well as I: but if ever thy ridiculous turn lead thee again to be Beau-Brocade, I will *bedizen* thee, as the girls say, on my return, to my own fancy, and according to thy own natural appearance—Thou shalt doctor my soul, and I will doctor thy body: thou shalt see what a clever fellow I will make of thee.

'And for *me*, I never *will*, I never *can*, marry—That I will not take a few liberties, and that I will not try to start some of my former game, I won't promise—Habits are not easily shaken off—But they shall be by way of weaning. So *return* and *reform* shall go together.

'And now, thou sorrowful monkey, what aileth thee?' I do love him, my lord.

'Adieu!—And once more adieu!—embracing me—And when thou thinkest thou hast made thyself an interest *out yonder* (looking up) then put in a word for thy Lovelace.'

Joining company, he recommended to me to write often; and promised to let me quickly hear from him; and that he would write to your lordship, and to all his family round; for he said that you had all been more kind to him than he had deserved.

And so we parted.

I hope, my lord, for all your noble family's sake, that we shall see him soon return, and reform as he promises.

I return your lordship my humble thanks for the honour of your invitation to M. Hall. The first letter I receive from Mr Lovelace shall give me the opportunity of embracing it. I am, my lord,

> Your most faithful and obedient servant,
> J. BELFORD

Letter 528: MR BELFORD TO LORD M.

Thursday morning, Oct. 5

IT may be some satisfaction to your lordship, to have a brief account of what has just now passed between Colonel Morden and me.

We had a good deal of discourse about the Harlowe family, and those parts of the lady's will which still remain unexecuted; after which the colonel addressed himself to me in a manner which gave me some surprise.

He flattered himself, he said, from my present happy turn, and from my good constitution, that I should live a great many years. It was therefore his request, that I would consent to be *his* executor; since it was impossible for him to make a better choice, or pursue a better example than his cousin had set.

His heart, he said, was in it: there were some things in his cousin's will and *his* analogous; and he had named one person with me, with whom he was sure I would not refuse to be joined; and to whom he intended to apply for his consent when he had obtained mine.[a] (Intimating, as far as I could gather, that it was Mr Hickman, son of Sir Charles Hickman; to whom I know your lordship is not a stranger: for he said everyone who was dear to his beloved cousin must be so to him: and he knew that the gentleman whom he had thoughts of would have, besides my advice and assistance, the advice of one of the most sensible ladies in England.)

He took my hand, seeing me under some surprise: You must not hesitate, much less deny me, Mr Belford. Indeed you must not. Two things I will assure you of: that I have, as I hope, made everything so clear, that you cannot have any litigation: and that I have done so justly, and I hope it will be thought so generously, by all my relations, that a mind like yours will rather have pleasure than pain in the execution of this trust. And this is what I think every honest man, who hopes to find an honest man for his executor, should do.

I told him that I was greatly obliged to him for his good opinion of me: that it was so much every man's *duty* to be an honest man, that it could not be self-praise to say that I had no doubt to be found so. But if I accepted of this trust, it must be on condition—

I could name no condition, he said, interrupting me, which he would refuse to comply with.

This condition, I told him, was, that as there was as great a probability of his being *my* survivor as I *his*, he would permit me to name *him* for mine; and in that case a week should not pass before I made my will.

With all his heart, he said; and the readier, as he had no apprehensions of suddenly dying; for what he had done and requested was really the effect of the satisfaction he had taken in the part I had already acted as his cousin's executor; and in my ability, he was pleased to add: as well as in pursuance of his cousin's advice in the preamble to her will; to wit, 'That this was a work which should be set about in full health, both of body and mind.'

I told him that I was pleased to hear him say that he was not in any apprehension of suddenly dying; as this gave me assurance that he had laid aside all thoughts of acting contrary to his beloved cousin's dying request.

Does it argue, said he smiling, that if I were to pursue a vengeance so justifiable in my own opinion, I must be in apprehension of falling by Mr Lovelace's hand?— I will assure you that I have no fears of that sort—But I know this is an ungrateful subject to you. Mr Lovelace is your friend; and I will allow that a *good* man may have a friendship for a *bad one*, so far as to wish him well, without countenancing him in his evil.

I will assure you, added he, that I have not yet made any resolutions either way.

   a What is between crotchets thus (), Mr Belford omitted in the transcription of this Letter to Miss Howe.

I have told you what force my cousin's repeated requests have with me. Hitherto they have withheld me—but let us quit this subject.

This, sir (giving me a sealed-up parcel), is my will. It is witnessed. I made no doubt of prevailing upon you to do me the requested favour. I have a duplicate to leave with the other gentleman; and an attested copy which I shall deposit at my banker's. At my return, which will be in six or eight months at farthest, I will allow you to make an exchange of yours, if you will have it so. I have only now to take leave of my relations in the country. And so, God protect you, Mr Belford! You will soon hear of me again.

He then very solemnly embraced me, as I did him: and we parted.

I heartily congratulate with your lordship on the narrow escape each gentleman has had from the other: for I apprehend that they could not have met without fatal consequences.

Time, I hope, which subdues all things, will subdue their resentments. I am, my lord,

Your lordship's most faithful and obedient servant,
J. BELFORD

Several other letters passed between Miss Howe and Mr Belford, relating to the disposition of the papers and letters; to the Poor's Fund; and to other articles of the lady's will: wherein the method of proceeding in each case was adjusted. After which the papers were returned to Mr Belford, that he might order the two directed copies of them to be taken.

In one of these letters Mr Belford requests Miss Howe to give the character of the friend she so dearly loved: 'A task, he imagines, that will be as agreeable to herself, as worthy of her pen.

'I am more especially curious to know, *says he*, what was that particular disposition of her time, which I find mentioned in a letter which I have just dipped into, where her sister is enviously reproaching her on that score.[a] This information may perhaps enable me, *says he*, to account for what has often surprised me; how, at so tender an age, this admirable lady became mistress of such extraordinary and such various qualifications.'

This request produced the following letter.

Letter 529: MISS HOWE TO JOHN BELFORD, ESQ.

Thursday, October 12

Sir,

I AM incapable of doing justice to the character of my beloved friend; and that not only from want of talents, but from grief; which I think rather increases than diminishes by time; and which will not let me sit down to a task that requires so much thought, and a greater degree of accuracy than I ever believed myself mistress of.

And yet I so well approve of your motion, that I will throw into your hands a few materials that may serve by way of supplement, as I may say, to those you will be able to collect from the papers themselves, from Colonel Morden's letters to you,

a See p. 192.

particularly that of Sept. 23[a]; and from the letters of the detestable wretch himself who, I find, has done her justice, although to his own condemnation: all these together will enable *you*, who seem to be so great an admirer of her virtues, to perform the task; and I think better than any person I know. But I make it my request, that if you do anything in this way, you will let me see it—If I find it not to my mind, I will add or diminish, as justice shall require.

She was a wonderful creature from her *infancy:* but I suppose you intend to give a character of her at those years when she was qualified to be an example to other young ladies, rather than a history of her life.

Perhaps, nevertheless, you will choose to give a description of her person: and as you knew not the dear creature when her heart was easy, I will tell you what yet, in part, you can confirm;

That her shape was so fine, her proportion so exact, her features so regular, her complexion so lovely, and her whole person and manner was so distinguishedly charming, that she could not move without being admired and followed by the eyes of everyone, though strangers who never saw her before. Colonel Morden's letter, above referred to, will confirm this.

In her dress she was elegant beyond imitation.

Her stature rather tall than middling: in her whole aspect and air, a dignity that bespoke the mind that animated all.

This *native* dignity, as I may call it, induced some superficial persons who knew not how to account for the reverence which involuntarily filled their hearts on her appearance to impute pride to her. But she knew not what pride, in the bad sense of the word, was.

You may throw in these sentences of hers, if you touch upon this subject:

'Persons of accidental or shadowy merit may be proud: but inborn worth must be always as much above conceit as arrogance.'

'Who can be better or more worthy than they should be? And, who shall be proud of talents they give not to themselves?'

'The darkest and most contemptible ignorance is that of not knowing one's self; and that all we have, and all we excel in, is the gift of God.'

'All human excellence is but comparative—there are persons who excel us, as much as we fancy we excel the meanest.'

'In the general scale of beings, the lowest is as useful, and as much a link of the great chain, as the highest.'

'The excellence that makes every other excellence amiable is HUMILITY.'

'There is but one pride pardonable; that of being above doing a base or dishonourable action.'

Such were the sentiments by which this admirable young lady endeavoured to conduct herself, and to regulate her conduct to others.

And in truth, never were affability and complacency (graciousness, some have called it) more eminent in any person, man or woman, than in her, to those who put it in her power to oblige them: insomuch that the benefited has sometimes not known which to prefer; the grace bestowed, or the manner in which it was conferred.

It has been observed, that what was said of Henry IV of France might be said

---

a   See Letter 519.

of her manner of refusing a request; that she generally sent from her presence the person refused nearly as well satisfied as if she had granted it.

Then she was so nobly sincere!—You cannot, sir, expatiate too much upon her sincerity. I dare say that in all her letters, in all the wretch's letters, her sincerity will not be found to be once impeachable, although her calamities were so heavy, the horrid wretch's wiles so subtle, and her struggles to free herself from them so active.

Severe as she always was in her reprehensions of a wilful and studied vileness; yet no one accused her judgement, or thought her severe in a wrong place: for her charity was so great that she always chose to defend or acquit, where the fault was not so flagrant that it became a piece of justice to condemn it.

You must everywhere insist upon it, that had it not been for the stupid persecutions of her relations, she never would have been in the power of this horrid profligate: and yet she was frank enough to acknowledge that were *person*, and *address*, and *alliance*, to be allowably the *principal* attractives, it would not have been difficult for her eye to mislead her heart.

When she was last with me, three happy weeks together! in every visit he made her, he left her more dissatisfied with him than before.

In obedience to her friends' commands on her coming to me, she never would see him out of my company; and would often say, when he was gone,[a] Oh my Nancy, this is not THE man'—At other times, 'Gay, giddy creature! he has always something to be forgiven for.' At others, 'This man will much sooner excite one's fears, than attract one's love.' And then would she repeat, 'This is not THE man— All that the world says of him cannot be untrue—But what title have I to charge him, who intend not to have him?'—In short, had she been left to a judgement and discretion, which nobody ever questioned who had *either*, she would have discovered enough of him, to make her discard him for ever.

Her [ingenuousness] in acknowledging any error she was drawn into, you must also insist upon.

'Next to not erring, she used to say, was the owning of an error: and that the offering at an excuse in a blamable matter was the undoubted mark of a disingenuous or perverse mind.'

Yet one of her expressions upon a like subject deserves to be remembered: being upbraided by a severe censurer, upon a person's proving base, whom she had frequently defended; 'You had more penetration, madam, than such a young creature as I can pretend to have. But although human depravity may, I doubt, oftener justify the person who judges harshly, than them who judge favourably, yet will I not part with my charity; although, for the future, I will endeavour to make it consistent with caution and prudence.'

If you mention the beauties and graces of her pen, you may take notice that it was always matter of surprise to her, that the sex are generally so averse as they are to writing; since the pen, next to the needle, of all employments is the most proper and best adapted to their geniuses; and this as well for improvement as amusement: 'Who sees not, would she say, that those women who take delight in writing excel the men in all the graces of the familiar style? The gentleness of their minds, the delicacy of their sentiments (improved by the manner of their education)

---

a   See p. 72.

and the liveliness of their imaginations, qualify them to a high degree of preference for this employment: while men of learning, as they are called (of mere learning, however), aiming to get above that natural ease and freedom which distinguish this (and indeed every other kind of writing), when they think they have best succeeded are got above, or rather *beneath*, all natural beauty.'

And one hint you may give to the sex, if you please, who are generally too careless in their orthography (a consciousness of a defect in which generally keeps them from writing)—She used to say, 'It was a proof that a woman understood the derivation and sense of the words she used, and that she stopped not at *sound*, when she spelled accurately.'

You may take notice of the admirable facility she had in learning languages: that she read with great ease both Italian and French, and could hold a conversation in either, though she was not fond of doing so (and that she was *not*, be pleased to call it a fault): that she had begun to apply herself to Latin.

But that, notwithstanding all her acquirements, she was an excellent ECONOMIST and HOUSEWIFE. And these qualifications, you must take notice, she was particularly fond of inculcating upon all her reading and writing companions of the sex: for it was a maxim with her, 'That a woman who neglects the *useful* and the *elegant*, which distinguish *her own sex*, for the sake of obtaining the learning which is supposed more peculiar to the *other*, incurs more *contempt* by what she *foregoes* than she gains *credit* by what she *acquires*.

'Let our sex therefore (she used to say) seek to make themselves mistresses of all that is excellent and not incongruous to their sex in the *other*; but without losing anything commendable in *their own*.'

Perhaps you will not think it amiss further to observe on this head, as it will show that precept and example always went hand in hand with her, that her dairy at her grandfather's was the delight of everyone who saw it; and she, of all who saw her in it: for, in the same hour, whenever she pleased, she was the most elegant dairymaid that ever was seen, or the finest lady that ever graced a circle.

Yet was this admirable creature mistress of all these domestic qualifications, without the least intermixture of narrowness. She used to say, 'That, to define true generosity, it must be called the happy medium between parsimony and profusion.'

She was as much above reserve as disguise. So communicative, that no young lady could be in her company half an hour, and not carry away instruction with her, whatever was the topic. Yet all sweetly insinuated; nothing given with the air of prescription: so that while she seemed to ask a question for information-sake, she dropped in the needful instruction, and left the instructed unable to decide whether the thought (which being started, she, the instructed, could improve) came primarily from herself, or from the sweet instructress.

The Goths and Vandals in those branches of science which she aimed at acquiring, she knew how to detect and expose; and all from nature.

Propriety, another word for *nature*, was her law, as it is the foundation of all true judgement.

Her skill in needleworks you will find mentioned perhaps in some of the letters. That piece which she bequeaths to her cousin Morden is indeed a capital piece; a performance so admirable that that gentleman's father, who resided chiefly abroad, was (as is mentioned in her will) very desirous to obtain it, in order to carry it to Italy with him, to show the curious of *other* countries (as he used to say) for the honour of *his own*, that the cloistered confinement was not necessary to make English women excel in any of those fine arts, which nuns and recluses value themselves upon.

Her quickness at these sort of works was astonishing; and a great encouragement to herself to prosecute them.

Mr Morden's father would have been continually making her presents would she have permitted him: and he used to call them, and so did her grandfather, tributes due to a merit so sovereign, and not presents.

I say nothing of her skill in music, and of her charming voice when it accompanied her fingers, though very extraordinary, because she had her equals in both.

If she could not avoid cards without incurring the censure of particularity, she would play; but then she always declared against playing high. 'Except for trifles, she used to say, she would not submit to *chance* what she was already sure of.'

At other times, 'She should make her friends a very ill compliment, if she supposed they would wish to be possessed of what of right belonged to her; and she should be very unworthy, if she desired to make herself a title to what was theirs.

'High gaming, in short, she used to say, was a sordid vice; an immorality; the child of avarice; and a direct breach of that commandment which forbids us to covet what is our neighbour's.'

You will have occasion to mention her charities. Her will gives you hints of the peculiar nature of those: indeed, for the prudent distribution of them, she had neither example nor equal.

You may, if you desire to be particular in the account of them, consult Mrs Norton upon this subject; and when I see what she will furnish, I shall perhaps make an addition to it.

In all her readings, and in her conversations upon them, she was fonder of finding beauties than blemishes: yet she used to lament that certain writers of the first class, who were capable of exalting virtue and of putting vice out of countenance, too generally employed themselves in works of imagination only, upon subjects merely speculative, disinteresting, and unedifying; from which no good moral or example could be drawn.

All she said, and all she did, was accompanied with a natural ease and dignity which set her above affectation, or the suspicion of it. For, with all her excellencies, she was forwarder to *hear* than *speak*; and hence no doubt derived no small part of her improvement.

You are curious to know the particular distribution of her time; which you suppose will help you to account for what you own yourself surprised at, to wit, how so young a lady could make herself mistress of so many accomplishments.

I will premise that she was from infancy inured to rise early in a morning, by an excellent and, as I may say, a learned woman, Mrs Norton, to whose care, wisdom, and example, she was beholden for the groundwork of her taste and acquirements, which meeting with such a genius, made it the less wonder that she surpassed most of her age and sex.

She used to say, 'It was incredible to think what might be done by early rising, and by long days well filled up.'

It may be added, that had she calculated according to the practice of *too many*, she had actually lived more years at *sixteen*, than *they* had at *twenty-six*.

She used to say, 'That no one could spend their time properly, who did not live by some rule: who did not appropriate the hours, as near as might be, to particular purposes and employments.'

In conformity to this self-set lesson, the usual distribution of the twenty-four hours, when left to her own choice, was as follows:

For REST she allotted SIX hours only.

She thought herself not so well, and so clear in her intellects (so *much alive*, she used to say) if she exceeded this proportion. If she slept not, she chose to rise sooner. And in winter had her fire laid, and a taper ready burning to light it; not loving to give trouble to servants, 'whose harder work, and later hours of going to bed, she used to say, required consideration.'

I have blamed her for her greater regard to them than to herself: but this was her answer: 'I have my choice: who can wish for more? Why should I oppress others to gratify myself? You see what free-will enables one to do; while imposition would make a light burden heavy.'

Her first THREE morning hours

were generally passed in her study, and in her closet-duties: and were occasionally augmented by those she saved from rest: and in these passed her epistolary amusements.

TWO hours she generally allotted to domestic management

These at different times of the day, as occasions required; all the housekeeper's bills, in ease of her mother, passing through her hands. For she was a perfect mistress of the four principal rules of arithmetic.

FIVE hours to her needle, drawings, music, etc.

In these she included the assistance and inspection she gave to her own servants, and to her sister's servants, in the needleworks required for the family: for her sister is a MODERN. In these she also included Dr Lewen's conversation visits; with whom likewise she held a correspondence by letters. That reverend gentleman delighted himself and her, twice or thrice a week if his health permitted, with these visits: and she always preferred his company to any other engagement.

TWO hours she allotted to her two first meals.

But if conversation, or the desire of friends, or the falling in of company or guests, required it to be otherwise, she never scrupled to oblige; and would *borrow*, as she called it, from other distributions. And as she found it very hard not to exceed in this appropriation, she put down

ONE hour more to dinner-time conversation,

to be added or subtracted, as occasions offered, or the desire of her friends required: and yet found it difficult, as she often said, to keep this account even; especially if Dr Lewen obliged them with his company at their table: which however he seldom did; for, being a valetudinarian, and in a regimen, he generally made his visits in the afternoon.

ONE hour to visits to the neighbouring poor;

to a select number of whom, and to their children, she used to give brief instructions and good books: and as this happened not every day, and seldom above twice a week, she had two or three hours at a time to bestow in this benevolent employment.

The remaining FOUR hours

were occasionally allotted to supper, to conversation, or to reading after supper to the family. This allotment she called *her fund*, upon which she used to draw to satisfy her other debits: and in this she included visits received and returned, shows, spectacles, etc. which, in a country-life not occurring every day, she used to think a great allowance, no less than *two* artificial days in *six*, for amusements only: and she was wont to say that it was hard if she could not steal time out of such a fund as this for an excursion of even two or three days in a month.

If it be said that her relations or the young neighbouring ladies had but little of her time, it will be considered that besides those four hours in the twenty-four, great part of the time she was employed in her needleworks she used to converse as she worked: and it was a custom she had introduced among her acquaintance, that the young ladies in their visits used frequently in a neighbourly way (in the winter evenings especially) to bring their work with them; and one of half a dozen of her select acquaintance used by turns to read to the rest as they were at work.

This was her usual method, when at her own command, for *six* days in the week.

The SEVENTH DAY

she kept, as it ought to be kept: and as some part of it was frequently employed in works of mercy, the hour she allotted to visiting the neighbouring poor was occasionally supplied from this day, and added to her fund.

But I must observe that when in her grandfather's lifetime she was three or four weeks at a time his housekeeper and guest, as also at either of her uncles, her usual distribution of time was varied: but still she had an eye to it as nearly as circumstances would admit.

When I had the happiness of having her for my guest for a fortnight or so, she likewise dispensed with her rules. In her account book, since her ever-to-be-lamented death, I have found this memorandum: 'From *such a day*, to *such a day*, all holidays, at my dear Miss Howe's.' At her return: 'Account resumed *such a day*,' naming it; and then she proceeded regularly as before.

Once a week she used to reckon with herself; when, if within the 144 hours contained in the six days she had made her account even, she noted it accordingly: if otherwise, she carried the debit to the next week's account; as thus: *Debtor to the article of benevolent visits* so many hours. And so of the rest.

But it was always an especial part of her care that, whether visiting or visited, she showed in all companies an entire ease, satisfaction, and cheerfulness, as if she kept no such particular account, and as if she did not make herself answerable to herself for her occasional exceedings.

This method, which to others will appear perplexing and unnecessary, her early hours and custom had made easy and pleasant to her.

And indeed, as I used to tell her, greatly as I admired her in all her methods, I could not bring myself to this (though I *had* to early hours, and find the benefit of it) might I have had the world for my reward.

She used to answer: 'I do not think ALL I do necessary for another to do: nor even for myself: but when it is more pleasant to me to keep such an account than to let it alone; why may I not proceed in my supererogatories?—There can be no harm in it. It keeps up my attention to accounts; which one day may be of use to me in more material instances. Those who will not keep a *strict* account, seldom long keep *any*. I neglect not more useful employments for it. And it teaches me to be covetous of time; the only thing of which we can be *allowably* covetous; since we live but once in this world; and when gone, are gone from it for ever.'

Oh Mr Belford! I can write no further on this subject. For, looking into the account-book for other particulars, I met with a most affecting memorandum; which, being written on the extreme edge of the paper, with a fine pen, and in the dear creature's smallest hand, I saw not before—This it is; written, I suppose, at some calamitous period *after* the day named in it—Help me to a curse to blast the monster who gave occasion for it!—

'APRIL 10. The account concluded!—

And with it, all my worldly hopes and prospects!!!'

I TAKE up my pen; but not to apologize for my execration—Once more I pray to God to avenge me of him!—*Me* I say—for mine is the loss—Hers the gain.

Oh sir! you *did* not, you *could* not know her, as I knew her! Never was such an excellence!—So warm, yet so cool a friend!—So much what I wish to be, but never shall be!—for, alas, my stay, my adviser, my monitress, my directress, is gone! forever gone!

She honoured me with the title of *the sister of her heart*: but I was only so in the love I bore her (a love beyond a sister's—infinitely beyond *her* sister's!); in the hatred I have to every mean and sordid action; and in my love of virtue: for, otherwise, I am of a high and haughty temper, as I have acknowledged before, and very violent in my passions.

In short, she was the nearest perfection of any creature I ever knew. She never preached to me lessons she practised not. She lived the life she taught. All humility, meekness, self-accusing, others-acquitting, though the shadow of the fault hardly hers, the substance theirs whose only honour was their relation to her.

To lose such a friend, such a guide—if ever my violence was justifiable, it is upon this recollection!—for she only lived to make me sensible of my failings, but not long enough to enable me to conquer them; as I was resolved to endeavour to do.

Once more then let me execrate—But now violence and passion again predominate!—And how can it be otherwise?

But I force myself from the subject, having lost the purpose for which I resumed my pen.

A. HOWE

Letter 530: MR LOVELACE TO JOHN BELFORD, ESQ.

Paris, Octob. 14–25

> —Timor et minae
> Scandunt eodem quo dominus: neque
> Decedit aerata triremi, et
> Post equitem sedet atra cura.[1]

IN a language so expressive as the English, I hate the pedantry of tagging or prefacing what I write with Latin scraps; and ever was a censurer of the motto-mongers among our weekly and daily scribblers. But these verses of Horace are so applicable to my case that, whether on shipboard, whether in my post-chaise, or in my inn at night, I am not able to put them out of my head. Dryden once I thought said well in these bouncing lines:

> Man makes his Fate according to his mind.
> The weak, low spirit Fortune makes her slave:
> But she's a drudge, when hector'd by the brave.
> If Fate weave common thread, I'll change the doom,
> And with new purple weave a nobler loom.[2]

And in these:

> Let Fortune empty her whole quiver on me,
> I have a soul, that, like an ample shield,
> Can take in all, and verge enough for more.
> Fate was not mine: Nor am I Fate's—
> Souls know no conquerors—[3]

But in the first quoted lines, considering them closely, there is nothing but blustering absurdity: in the other, the poet says not truth; for CONSCIENCE is the conqueror of souls: at least it is the conqueror of mine: and who ever thought it a narrow one?

But this is occasioned partly by poring over the affecting will, and posthumous letter. What an army of texts has she drawn up in array against me in the latter!—But yet, Jack, do they not show me that, two or three thousand years ago, there were as wicked fellows as myself?—They do—and that's some consolation.

But the generosity of her mind displayed in both is what stings me most. And the more still, as it is now out of my power any way in the world to be even with her.

I ought to have written to you sooner. But I loitered two days at Calais for an answer to a letter I wrote to engage my former travelling valet, De la Tour; an ingenious, ready fellow, as you have heard me say. I *have* engaged him, and he is now with me.

I shall make no stay here; but intend for some of the Electoral courts.[4] That of Bavaria, I think, will engage me longest. Perhaps I may step out of my way (if I can be out of my way anywhere) to those of Dresden and Berlin: and it is not impossible that you may have one letter from me at Vienna. And then perhaps I may fall down into Italy by the Tyrol; and so, taking Turin in my way, return to Paris; where I hope to see Mowbray and Tourville: nor do I despair of you.

This a good deal differs from the plan I gave you. But you may expect to hear from me as I move; and whether I shall pursue this route, or the other.

I have my former lodgings in the Rue St Antoine: which I shall hold, notwithstanding my tour: so they will be ready to accommodate any two of you if you come hither before my return: and for this I have conditioned.

I write to Charlotte; and that is writing to all my relations at once.

Do thou, Jack, inform me duly of everything that passes: particularly, how thou proceedest in thy reformation scheme: how Mowbray and Tourville go on in my absence: whether thou hast any chance for a wife (I am the more solicitous on this head, because thou seemest to think that thy mortification will not be complete, nor thy reformation secure, till thou art shackled): how the Harlowes proceed in their penitentials: if Miss Howe be married, or near being so: how honest Doleman goes on with his empiric, now he has dismissed his regulars, or they him; and if any likelihood of his perfect recovery. Be sure be very minute: for every trifling occurrence relating to those we value becomes interesting when we are at a distance from them. Finally, prepare thou to piece thy broken thread, if thou wouldst oblige

Thy LOVELACE

Letter 531: MR BELFORD TO ROBERT LOVELACE, ESQ.

London, Oct. 25

I WRITE to show you that I am incapable of slighting even the minutest requests of an absent and distant friend. Yet you may believe that there cannot be any great alterations in the little time that you have been out of England, with respect to the subjects of your inquiry. Nevertheless I will answer to each for the reason above given; and for the reason you mention, that even trifles and chit-chat are agreeable from friend to friend, and of friends, and even of those to whom we give the importance of deeming them our *foes*.

First, then, as to my reformation scheme, as you call it, I hope I go on very well. I wish you had entered upon the like, and could say so too. You would then find infinitely more peace of mind than you are likely ever otherwise to be acquainted with. When I look back upon the sweep that has been made among us in the two or three past years, and forward upon what may still happen, I hardly think myself secure; though of late I have been guided by other lights than those of sense and appetite, which have hurried so many of our confraternity into worldly ruin, if not into eternal perdition.

I am very earnest in my wishes to be admitted into the nuptial state. But I think I ought to pass some time as a probationary, till by steadiness in my good resolutions, I can convince some woman whom I could love and honour, and whose worthy example might confirm my morals that there is *one* libertine who had the grace to reform before age or disease put it out of his power to sin on.

The Harlowes continue inconsolable; and I daresay will to the end of their lives.

Miss Howe is not yet married; but I have reason to think will soon. I have the honour of corresponding with her; and the more I know of her, the more I admire the nobleness of her mind. She must be conscious that she is superior to half *our* sex, and to most of *her own*; which may make her give way to a temper naturally hasty and impatient: but, if she meet with condescension in her man (and who would not veil to a superiority so visible, if it be not exacted with arrogance?), I dare say she will make an excellent wife.

As to Doleman, the poor man goes on trying and hoping with his empiric. I cannot but say that as the latter is a sensible and judicious man, and not rash, opinionative, or over-sanguine, I have great hopes (little as I think of quacks and nostrum-mongers in general) that he will do him good, if his case will admit of it. My reasons are, that the man pays a *regular* and *constant* attendance upon him: watches with his own eye every change and new symptom of his patient's malady: varies his applications as the indications vary: fetters not himself to rules laid down by the fathers of the art, who lived many hundred years ago; when diseases and the causes of them were different, as the modes of living were different from what they are now, as well as climates and accidents: that he is to have his reward, not in daily fees; but (after the first five guineas for medicines) in proportion as the patient himself shall find amendment.

As to Mowbray and Tourville; what novelties can be expected in so short a time, from men who have not sense enough to strike out or pursue new lights, either good or bad? Now, especially, that thou art gone, who wert the soul of all enterprise, and in particular *their* soul. Besides, I see them but seldom. I suppose they'll be at Paris before you can return from Germany; for they cannot live without you: and you gave them such a specimen of your recovered volatility, in the last evening's conversation, as equally delighted *them* and concerned *me*.

I wish, with all my heart, that thou wouldst bend thy course towards the Pyreneans. I should then (if thou writest to thy cousin Montague an account of what is most observable in thy tour) put in for a copy of thy letters. I wonder thou wilt not; since then thy subjects would be as new to thyself, as to

Thy BELFORD

Letter 532: MR LOVELACE TO JOHN BELFORD, ESQ.

Paris, Oct. 16–27

I FOLLOW my last of the 14/25th, on occasion of a letter just now come to hand from Joseph Leman. The fellow is conscience-ridden, Jack; and tells me, 'That he cannot rest either day or night for the mischiefs which he fears he has been, and may still further be, the means of doing.' He wishes, 'if it please God, and if it please *me*, that he had never seen my honour's face.'

And what is the cause of his present concern, as to his own peculiar; what, but 'the *slights* and *contempts* which he receives from every one of the Harlowes; from those particularly, he says, whom he has endeavoured to serve as faithfully as his engagements to *me* would let him serve them? And I always made him believe, he tells me (*poor weak soul as he was from his cradle!*), that serving me was serving both, *in the long run*. But this, and the death of his dear young lady, is a grief, he declares, that he shall never *claw off*, were he to live to the age of *Matthew-Salem*:

althoff, and *howsomever*, he is sure that he shall not live *a month to an end*, being strangely pined, and his stomach nothing like what it was: and Mrs Betty being also (now she *has got his love*) very *crass and slighting*: but, thank his God for punishing her! she is in a poor way *herself*.

'But the chief occasion of troubling my honour now is not his own griefs only, *althoff* they are very great; but to prevent future mischiefs to me: for he can assure me that Colonel Morden has set out from them all, with a full resolution to *have his will of me*: and he is well assured that he said, and swore to it, *as how* he was resolved that he would either have my honour's heart's blood, or I should have his; or *some such-like sad threatenings*: and that all the family rejoice in it, and hope I shall *come short home*.'

This is the substance of Joseph's letter; and I have one from Mowbray which has a hint to the same effect. And I recollect now, that thou wert very importunate with me to go to Madrid rather than to France and Italy, the last evening we passed together.

What I desire of thee is, by the first dispatch, to let me faithfully know all that thou knowest on this head.

I can't bear to be threatened, Jack. Nor shall any man, unquestioned, give himself airs in my absence, if I know it, that shall make me look mean in anybody's eyes: that shall give my friends pain for me: that shall put them upon wishing me to change my intentions, or my plan, to avoid him. Upon such despicable terms as these, thinkest thou that I could bear to live?

But why, if such were his purpose, did he not let me know it before I left England? Was he unable to work himself up to a resolution till he knew me to be out of the kingdom?

As soon as I can inform myself where to direct to him, I will write to know his purpose; for I cannot bear suspense, in such a case as this: that solemn act, were it even to be marriage or hanging, which must be done tomorrow, I had rather should be done today. My mind tires and sickens with impatience on ruminating upon scenes that can afford neither variety nor certainty. To dwell twenty days in expectation of an event that may be decided in a quarter of an hour, is grievous.

If he come to Paris, although I should be on my tour, he will very easily find out my *lodgings*: for I every day see some or other of my countrymen, and divers of them have I entertained *here*. I go frequently to the opera, and to the play, and appear at court, and at all public places. And, on my quitting this city, will leave a direction whither my letters from England, or elsewhere, shall from time to time be forwarded. Were I sure that his intention is what Joseph Leman tells me it is, I would stay here, or shorten his course to me, let him be where he would.

I cannot get off my regrets on account of this dear lady for the blood of me. If the colonel and I are to meet, as he has done me no injury and loves the memory of his cousin, we shall engage with the same sentiments as to the object of our dispute: and that, you know, is no very common case.

In short, I am as much convinced that I have done wrong as he can be; and regret it as much. But I will not bear to be threatened by any man in the world, however conscious of having deserved blame.

Adieu, Belford! Be sincere with me. No palliation, as thou valuest

Thy LOVELACE

Letter 533: MR BELFORD TO ROBERT LOVELACE, ESQ.

London, October 26

I CANNOT think, my dear Lovelace, that Colonel Morden has either threatened you in those gross terms mentioned by the vile, hypocritical, and ignorant Joseph Leman, or intends to follow you. They are the words of people of that fellow's class; and not of a gentleman: not of Colonel Morden, I am sure. You'll observe that Joseph pretends not to say that he heard him speak them.

I have been very solicitous to sound the colonel, for your sake and for his own, and for the sake of the injunctions of the excellent lady to me, as well as to him, on that subject. He is (and you will not wonder that he should be) extremely affected; and owns that he has expressed himself in terms of resentment on the occasion. Once he said to me that had his beloved cousin's case been that of a common seduction; and had she been drawn in by what Bishop Burnet calls the delicacy of intrigue¹ (her own infirmity or credulity contributing to her fall), he could have forgiven you. But, in so many words, he assured me that he had not taken any resolutions; nor had he declared himself to the family in such a way as should bind him to resent: on the contrary, he has owned that his cousin's injunctions have hitherto had the force upon him which I could wish they should have.

He went abroad in a week after you. When he took his leave of me, he told me that his design was to go to Florence; and that he would settle his affairs there; and then return to England, and here pass the remainder of his days.

I was indeed apprehensive that if you and he were to meet, something unhappy might fall out: and as I knew that you proposed to take Italy, and very likely Florence, in your return to France, I was very solicitous to prevail upon you to take the court of Spain into your plan. I am still so. And if you are not to be prevailed upon to do that, let me entreat you to avoid Florence or Leghorn in your return, as you have visited both heretofore. At least, let not the proposal of a meeting come from you.

It would be matter of serious reflection to me, if the *very fellow*, this *Joseph Leman*, who gave you such an opportunity to turn all the artillery of his masters against themselves, and to play them upon one another to favour your plotting purposes, should be the instrument in the devil's hand (unwittingly too) to avenge them all upon *you*: for should you even get the better of the colonel, would the mischief end there?—It would but add remorse to your present remorse; since the interview *must* end in death; for he would not, I am confident, take his life at your hand. The Harlowes would, moreover, prosecute you in a legal way. You hate *them*; and *they* would be gainers by *his* death: rejoicers in yours—and have you not done mischief enough already?

Let *me* therefore (and through me all your friends) have the satisfaction to hear that you are resolved to avoid this gentleman. Time will subdue all things. Nobody doubts your bravery. Nor will it be known that your plan is changed through persuasion.

Young Harlowe talks of calling you to account. This is a plain evidence that Mr Morden has not taken the quarrel upon himself for their family.

I am in no apprehension of anybody but Colonel Morden. I know it will not be

a means to prevail upon you to oblige me, to say that I am well assured that this
gentleman is a skilful swordsman; and that he is as cool and sedate as skilful. But
yet I will add, that if I had a value for my life he should be the last man, except
yourself, with whom I would choose to have a contention.

I have, as you required, been very candid and sincere with you. I have not aimed
at palliation. If you seek not Colonel Morden, it is my opinion he will not seek you:
for he is a man of principle. But if you seek him, I believe he will not shun you.

Let me re-urge (it is the effect of my love for you!) that you know your own guilt
in this affair, and should not be again an aggressor. It would be pity that so brave
a man as the colonel should drop, were you and he to meet: and on the other hand,
it would be dreadful, that you should be sent to your account unprepared for it;
and pursuing a fresh violence. Moreover, seest thou not in the deaths of two of thy
principal agents, the handwriting upon the wall against thee?

My zeal on this occasion may make me guilty of repetition. Indeed I know not
how to quit the subject. But if what I have written, added to your own remorse and
consciousness, cannot prevail, all that I might further urge will be ineffectual.

Adieu therefore! Mayest thou repent of the past: and may no new violences add
to thy heavy reflections, and overwhelm thy future hopes, is the wish of

Thy true friend,
JOHN BELFORD

Letter 534: MR LOVELACE TO JOHN BELFORD, ESQ.

Munich, Nov. 11–22

I RECEIVED yours this moment, just as I was setting out for Vienna.

As to going to Madrid or one single step out of the way, to avoid Colonel
Morden, let me perish, if I do!—You cannot think me so mean a wretch.

And so you own that he *has* threatened me; but not in gross and ungentlemanly
terms, you say. If he has threatened me like a gentleman, I will resent his threats
like a gentleman. But he has not done as a man of honour, if he has threatened me
at all behind my back. I would scorn to threaten any man to whom I *knew* how to
address myself either personally or by pen and ink.

As to what you mention of my guilt; of the handwriting on the wall; of a legal
prosecution if he meet his fate from my hand; of his skill, coolness, courage, and
such-like poltroon stuff; what can you mean by it? Surely you cannot believe that
such insinuations as those will weaken either my hands or my heart—No more of
this sort of nonsense, I beseech you, in any of your future letters.

He had not taken any resolutions, you say, when you saw him. He *must* and *will*
take resolutions, one way or other, very quickly; for I wrote to him yesterday,
without waiting for this your answer to my last. I could not avoid it. I could not
(as I told you in that) live in suspense. I have directed my letter to Florence. Nor
could I suffer my friends to live in suspense as to my safety or otherwise. But I
have couched it in such moderate terms, that he has fairly his option. He will be
the challenger, if he take it in the sense in which he may so handsomely avoid
taking it. And if he does, it will demonstrate that malice and revenge were the
predominant passions with him; and that he was determined but to settle his

affairs, and then *take his resolutions,* as you phrase it—Yet, if we are to meet (for I know what *my* option would be, in *his* case, on *such a letter,* complaisant as it is), I wish *he* had a worse, *I* a better cause. It would be sweet revenge to him, were I to fall by his hand. But what should I be the better for killing him?

I will enclose the copy of the letter I sent him.

ON reperusing yours in a cooler moment, I cannot but thank you for your friendly love and good intentions. My value for you, from the first hour of our acquaintance till now, I have never found misplaced; regarding at least your *intention:* thou must, however, own a good deal of blunder of the over-do and under-do kind, with respect to the part thou actedst between me and the beloved of my heart. But thou art really an honest fellow, and a sincere and warm friend. I could almost wish I had not written to Florence till I had received thy letter now before me. But it is gone. Let it go. If he wish peace, and to avoid violence, he will have a fair opportunity to embrace the one and shun the other—If not—he must take his fate.

But be this as it may, you may contrive to let young Harlowe know (he is a menacer too!) that I shall be in England in March next, at farthest.

This of Bavaria is a gallant and polite court. Nevertheless, being uncertain whether my letter may meet with the colonel at Florence, I shall quit it, and set out, as I intended, for Vienna; taking care to have any letter or message from him conveyed to me there: which will soon bring me back hither, or to any other place to which I shall be invited.

As I write to Charlotte, I have nothing more to add, after compliments to all friends, than that I am

Wholly yours.
LOVELACE

[Letter 534.1: Mr Lovelace] to William Morden, Esq.

(Enclosed in the above)

Munich, Nov. 10–21

Sir,

I HAVE heard, with a great deal of surprise, that you have thought fit to throw out some menacing expressions against me.

I should have been very glad that you had thought I had punishment enough in my own mind, for the wrongs I have done to the most excellent of women; and that it had been possible for two persons so ardently joining in one love (especially as I was desirous, to the utmost of my power, to repair those wrongs) to have lived, if not on amicable terms, in such a way as not to put either to the pain of hearing of threatenings thrown out in absence, which either ought to be despised for if he had not spirit to take notice of them.

Now, sir, if what I have heard be owing only to warmth of temper, or to sudden passion, while the loss of all other losses the most deplorable to me was recent, I not only excuse, but commend you for it. But if you are really *determined* to meet me on any other account (which, I own to you, is not however what I wish) it would be very blamable, and very unworthy of the character I desire to maintain as well with you as with every other gentleman, to give you a difficulty in doing it.

Being uncertain when this letter may meet you, I shall set out tomorrow for Vienna; where any letter directed to the post-house in that city, or to Baron Windisgratz's (at the Favorita) to whom I have commendations, will come to hand.

Meantime, believing you to be a man too generous to make a wrong construction of what I am going to declare, and knowing the value which the dearest of all creatures had for you, and your relationship to her; I will not scruple to assure you that the most acceptable return will be that Colonel Morden chooses to be upon an amicable, rather than upon any other footing, with

His sincere admirer, and humble servant,
R. LOVELACE

Letter 535: MR LOVELACE TO JOHN BELFORD, ESQ.

Linz, { Nov. 28
       { Dec. 9

I AM now on my way to Trent, in order to meet Colonel Morden, in pursuance of his answer to my letter enclosed in my last. I had been at Pressburg, and had intended to visit some other cities of Hungary: but having obliged myself to return first to Vienna, I there met with his letter: which follows.

[*Letter 535.1: Colonel Morden to Robert Lovelace, Esq.*]

Munich, { Nov. 21
        { Dec. 2

Sir,
YOUR letter was at Florence four days before I arrived there.

That I might not appear unworthy of your favour, I set out for this city the very next morning. I knew not but that the politeness of this court might have engaged, beyond his intention, a gentleman who has only his pleasures to pursue.

But being disappointed in my hope of finding you here, it becomes me to acquaint you that I have such a desire to stand well in the opinion of a man of your spirit, that I cannot hesitate a moment upon the option which I am sure Mr Lovelace in my situation (thus called upon) would make.

I own, sir, that I have on all occasions spoken of your treatment of my ever-dear cousin as it deserved. It would have been very surprising if I had not. And it behoves me (now you have given me so noble an opportunity of explaining myself) to convince you that no words fell from my lips, of you, merely because you were absent. I acquaint you therefore that I will attend your appointment; and would, were it to the farthest part of the globe.

I shall stay some days at this court; and if you please to direct for me at M. Klienfurt's in this city, whether I remain here or not your commands will come safely and speedily to the hands of, sir,

Your most humble servant,
WM. MORDEN

So you see, Belford, that the colonel, by his ready, his even eagerly expressed acceptance of the offered interview, *was determined*. And is it not much better to bring such a point as this to an issue, than to give pain to friends for my safety, or continue in a suspense myself; as I must do, if I imagined that another had aught against me?

This was my reply:

[*Letter 535.2: Mr Lovelace to Colonel Morden*]

Vienna, $\begin{cases} \text{Nov. 25} \\ \text{Dec. } 6 \end{cases}$

Sir,

I HAVE this moment the favour of yours. I will suspend a tour I was going to take into Hungary, and instantly set out for Munich: and, if I find you not there, will proceed to Trent. This city being on the confines of Italy, will be most convenient as I presume, to you in your return to Tuscany; and I shall hope to meet you in it on the 3/14 of December.

I shall bring with me only a French valet and an English footman. Other particulars may be adjusted when I have the honour to see you. Till when I am, sir,

Your most obedient servant,
R. LOVELACE

Now, Jack, I have no manner of apprehension of the event of this meeting. And I think I may say he seeks me; not I him. And so let him take the consequence.

What is infinitely nearer to my heart is my ingratitude to the most excellent of women—my *premeditated* ingratitude!—yet all the while enabled to distinguish and to adore her excellencies, in spite of the mean opinion of the sex which I had imbibed from early manhood.

But this lady has asserted the worthiness of her sex, and most gloriously has she exalted it with me now. Yet, surely, as I have said and written an hundred times, there cannot be such another woman.

But while my loss in her is the greatest of any man's, and while she was nearer to me than to any other person in the world, and once she herself wished to be so, what an insolence in any man breathing to pretend to avenge her on *me!*—Happy! happy! thrice happy! had I known how to value, as I ought to have valued, the glory of such a preference!

I will aggravate to myself this aggravation of the colonel's pretending to call me to account for my treatment of a lady so much *my own*, lest, in the approaching interview, my heart should relent for one so nearly related to her, and who means honour and justice to her memory; and I should thereby give him advantages which otherwise he cannot have. For I know that I shall be inclined to trust to my skill, to save a man who was so much and so justly valued by her; and shall be loath to give way to my resentment as a threatened man. And in this respect only am I sorry for his skill, and his courage, lest I should be obliged, in my own defence, to add a chalk to a score that is already too long.

INDEED, indeed, Belford, I am, and shall be to my latest hour, the most miserable of beings. Such exalted generosity!—Why didst thou put into my craving hands the copy of her will? Why sentest thou to me the posthumous letter?—What though I was earnest to see the will? Thou knewest what they *both* were (*I* did not); and that it would be cruel to oblige me.

The meeting of twenty Colonel Mordens, were there twenty to meet in turn, would be nothing to me; would not give me a moment's concern as to my own safety: But my reflections upon my vile ingratitude to so superior an excellence will ever be my curse.

Had she been a Miss Howe to me, and treated me as if I were a Hickman, I had had a call for revenge; and policy (when I had intended to be a husband) might have justified my attempts to humble her. But a meek and gentle temper was hers, though a true heroine, whenever honour or virtue called for an exertion of spirit.

Nothing but my cursed devices stood in the way of my happiness. Rememberest thou not how repeatedly, from the *first*, I poured cold water upon her rising flame, by meanly and ungratefully turning upon her the *injunctions*, which *virgin delicacy* and *filial duty* induced her to lay me under, before I got her into my power?[a]

Did she not tell me, and did I not know it if she had not told me, *that she could not be guilty of affectation or tyranny to the man whom she intended to marry?* [b] I knew, as she once upbraided me, that from the time I had got her from her father's house, *I had a plain path before me.* [c] True did she say, and I triumphed in the discovery, that from that time *I had held her soul in suspense an hundred times.*[d] My ipecacuanha trial alone was enough to convince an infidel that she had a mind in which love and tenderness would have presided, had I permitted the charming buds to put forth and blow.[e]

She *would have had no reserves*, as once she told me, *had I not given her cause of doubt.* [f] And did she not own to thee *that once she could have loved me; and, could she have made me good, would have made me happy?* [g] Oh Belford! here was love; a love of the noblest kind!—A love, as she hints in her posthumous letter, [h] that extended to the soul; and which she not only avowed in her dying hours, but contrived to let me know it after death in that letter filled with warnings and exhortations, which had for their sole end my eternal welfare!

The cursed women, indeed, endeavoured to excite my vengeance, and my pride, by preaching to me eternally her doubts, her want of love, and her contempt of me. And my pride was, at times, too much excited by their vile insinuations. But had it even been as they said; well might she, who had been used to be courted and admired by every desiring eye, and worshipped by every respectful heart—well might *such* a woman be allowed to draw back, when she found herself kept in

a   See p. 422. See also Letters 115, 142, 143 and many other places.

b   See p. 843. It may be observed further that all Clarissa's occasional lectures to Miss Howe on that young lady's treatment of Mr Hickman prove that she was herself above affectation and tyranny. See, more particularly, the advice she gives to that friend of her heart, Letter 435, p. 1263: 'Oh my dear,' says she in this letter, 'that it had been my lot (as I was not permitted to live single) to have met with a man by whom I could have acted generously and unreservedly!' etc. etc.

c   See pp. 798, 825.

d   See p. 829.

e   Letters 211, 212.

f   See p. 843.

g   See p. 1341.

h   See p. 1425.

suspense, *as to the great question of all*, by a designing and intriguing spirit; pretending awe and distance as reasons for reining in a fervour, which if real, cannot be reined-in—Divine creature! Her very doubts, her reserves (so justly doubting) would have been my assurance, and my glory!—And what other trial needed her virtue? What other needed a purity so angelic (blessed with such a command of her passions in the bloom of youth), had I not been a villain—and a wanton, a conceited, a proud fool, as well as a villain?

These reflections sharpened, rather than their edge by time rebated, accompany me in whatever I do, and wherever I go; and mingle with all my diversions and amusements. And yet I go into gay and splendid company. I have made new acquaintance in the different courts I have visited. I am both esteemed and sought after, by persons of rank and merit. I visit the colleges, the churches, the palaces. I frequent the theatre: am present at every public exhibition; and see all that is worth seeing, that I had not seen before, in the cabinets of the curious: am sometimes admitted to the toilette of an eminent toast, and make one with distinction at the assemblies of others—yet can think of nothing, nor of anybody with delight, but of my CLARISSA. Nor have I seen one woman with advantage to herself, but as she resembles in stature, air, complexion, voice, or in some feature, that charmer, that only charmer, of my soul.

What greater punishment, than to have these astonishing perfections, which she was mistress of, strike my remembrance with such force, when I have nothing left me but the remorse of having deprived myself and the world of such a blessing? Now and then, indeed, am I capable of a gleam of comfort, arising (not ungenerously) from the moral certainty which I have of her everlasting happiness, in spite of all the machinations and devices which I set on foot to ensnare her virtue, and to bring down so pure a mind to my own level.

> For can I be, at *worst* (Avert that worst,
> Oh Thou SUPREME, who only canst avert it!)
> So much a wretch, so very far abandon'd,
> But that I must, ev'n in the horrid'st gloom,
> Reap intervenient joy, at least some respite
> From pain and anguish, in *her* bliss—For why?
> This *very* soul must suffer—Not *another*.
> It *can't* be *mine*, if it could envy her,
> Or at her happiness repine—[1]

IF I find myself thus miserable abroad, I will soon return to England and follow your example, I think—turn hermit, or some plaguy thing or other, and see what a constant course of penitence and mortification will do for me. There is no living at this rate—d—n me if there be!

If any mishap should befall me, you'll have the particulars of it from De la Tour. He indeed knows not a word of English: but every modern tongue is yours. He is a trusty and ingenious fellow: and if anything happen, will have some other papers which I shall have ready sealed up, for you to transmit to Lord M. And since thou art so expert, and so ready at executorships, prithee, Belford, accept of the office for me, as well as for my Clarissa—CLARISSA LOVELACE let me call her.

By all that's good, I am bewitched to her memory. Her very name, with mine joined to it, ravishes my soul, and is more delightful to me than the sweetest music.

Had I carried her (I must still recriminate) to any other place, than to that accursed woman's—for the potion was her invention and mixture; and all the persisted-in violence was at her instigation, and at that of her wretched daughters, *who have now amply revenged upon me their own ruin, which they lay at my door.*

But this looks so like the confession of a thief at the gallows, that possibly thou wilt be apt to think I am intimidated in prospect of the approaching interview. But far otherwise. On the contrary, most cheerfully do I go to meet the colonel; and I would tear my heart out of my breast with my own hands, were it capable of fear or concern on that account.

Thus much only I know, that if I should kill him (which I will not do, if I can help it) I shall be far from being easy in my mind: *that* shall I never be more. But as the meeting is evidently of his own seeking, against an option fairly given to the contrary, and I cannot avoid it, I'll think of that hereafter. It is but repenting and mortifying for all at once: for I am as sure of victory as I am that I now live, let him be as skilful a swordsman as he will: since, besides that I am no unfleshed novice, this is a sport that, when provoked to it, I love as well as my food. And, moreover, I shall be as *calm and undisturbed* as the bishop at his prayers: while he, as is evident by his letter, must be actuated by revenge and passion.

Doubt not, therefore, Jack, that I shall give a good account of this affair. Meantime, I remain

Yours most affectionately, etc.
LOVELACE

Letter 536: MR LOVELACE TO JOHN BELFORD, ESQ.

Trent, Dec. 3–14

TOMORROW is to be the Day, that will in all probability send either one or two ghosts to attend the *manes* of my CLARISSA.

I arrived here yesterday; and inquiring for an English gentleman of the name of Morden, soon found out the colonel's lodgings. He had been in town two days; and left his name at every probable place.

He was gone to ride out; and I left *my* name, and where to be found: and in the evening he made me a visit.

He was plaguy gloomy. That was not I. But yet he told me that I had acted like a man of true spirit in my first letter; and with honour, in giving him so readily this meeting. He wished I had in other respects; and then we might have seen each other upon better terms than now we did.

I said there was no recalling what was passed; and that I wished some things had not been done, as well as he.

To recriminate now, he said, would be as exasperating as unavailable. And as I had so cheerfully given him this opportunity, words should give place to business—*Your* choice, Mr Lovelace, of time, of place, of weapon, shall be *my* choice.

The two latter be yours, Mr Morden. The time tomorrow, or next day, as you please.

Next day, then, Mr Lovelace; and we'll ride out tomorrow, to fix the place.

Agreed, sir.

Well; now, Mr Lovelace, do you choose the weapon.

I said, I believed we might be upon an equal foot with the single rapier; but, if he thought otherwise, I had no objection to a pistol.

I will only say, replied he, that the chances may be more equal by the sword, because we can neither of us be to seek in that: and you'd stand, says he, a worse chance, as I apprehend, with a pistol; and yet I have brought two; that you may take your choice of either: for, added he, I never missed a mark at pistol-distance, since I knew how to hold one.

I told him, that he spoke like himself: that I was expert enough that way, to embrace it, if he chose it; though not so sure of my mark as he pretended to be. Yet the devil's in't, colonel, if I, who have slit a bullet in two upon a knife's-edge, hit not my man. So I have no objection to a pistol, if it be *your* choice. No man, I'll venture to say, has a steadier hand or eye than I have.

They may both be of use to you, sir, at the sword, as well as at the pistol: the sword therefore be the thing, if you please.

With all my heart.

We parted with a solemn sort of ceremonious civility: and this day I called upon him; and we rode out together to fix upon the place: and both being of one mind, and hating to put off for the morrow what could be done today, would have decided it then: but De la Tour, and the colonel's valet, who attended us, being unavoidably let into the secret, joined to beg we would have with us a surgeon from Brixen, whom La Tour had fallen in with there, and who had told him he was to ride next morning to bleed a person in a fever, at a lone cottage which, by the surgeon's description, was not far from the place where we then were, if it were not that very cottage within sight of us.

They undertook so to manage it, that the surgeon should know nothing of the matter till his assistance was called in. And La Tour being, as I assured the colonel, a ready-contriving fellow (whom I ordered to obey him as myself were the chance to be in *his* favour), we both agreed to defer the decision till tomorrow, and to leave the whole about the surgeon to the management of our two valets; enjoining them absolute secrecy: and so rode back again by different ways.

We fixed upon a little lone valley for the spot—ten tomorrow morning the time——and single rapier the word. Yet I repeatedly told him that I value myself so much upon my skill in that weapon, that I would wish him to choose any other.

He said it was a gentleman's weapon; and he who understood it not, wanted a qualification that he ought to suffer for not having: but that, as to him, one weapon was as good as another throughout all the instruments of offence.

So, Jack, you see I take no advantage of him: but my devil must deceive me, if he take not his life, or his death, at my hands, before eleven tomorrow morning.

His valet and mine are to be present; but both strictly enjoined to be impartial and inactive: and, in return for my civility of the like nature, he commanded *his* to be assisting to me, if he fell.

We are to ride thither, and to dismount when at the place; and his footman and mine are to wait at an appointed distance, with a chaise to carry off to the borders of the Venetian territories the survivor, if one drop; or to assist either or both, as occasion may demand.

And thus, Belford, is the matter settled.

A shower of rain has left me nothing else to do: and therefore I write this letter; though I might as well have deferred it till tomorrow twelve o'clock, when I doubt not to be able to write again, to assure you how much I am

Yours, etc.
LOVELACE

Letter 537: F. J. DE LA TOUR TO JOHN BELFORD, ESQ., NEAR SOHO SQUARE, LONDON.

(Translation)

Trent, December 18. N. S.

Sir,

I HAVE melancholy news to inform you of, by order of the Chevalier Lovelace. He showed me his letter to you before he sealed it; signifying that he was to meet the Chevalier Morden on the 15th. Wherefore, as the occasion of the meeting is so well known to you, I shall say nothing of it here.

I had taken care to have ready, within a little distance, a surgeon and his assistant, to whom, under an oath of secrecy, I had revealed the matter (though I did not own it to the two gentlemen); so that they were prepared with bandages, and all things proper. For well was I acquainted with the bravery and skill of my Chevalier; and had heard the character of the other; and knew the animosity of both. A post-chaise was ready, with each of their footmen, at a little distance.

The two chevaliers came exactly at their time: they were attended by Monsieur Margate (the colonel's gentleman) and myself. They had given orders overnight, and now repeated them in each other's presence, that we should observe a strict impartiality between them: and that, if one fell, each of us should look upon himself, as to any needful help, or retreat, as the servant of the survivor, and take his commands accordingly.

After a few compliments, both the gentlemen, with the greatest presence of mind that I ever beheld in men, stripped to their shirts, and drew.

They parried with equal judgement several passes. My chevalier drew the first blood, making a desperate push, which by a sudden turn of his antagonist missed going clear through him, and wounded him on the fleshy part of the ribs of his right side; which part the sword tore out, being on the extremity of the body: but, before he could recover himself, his adversary, in return, pushed him into the inside of the left arm, near the shoulder: and the sword, by raking his breast as it passed, being followed by a great effusion of blood, the colonel said, sir, I believe you have enough.

My chevalier swore by G—d, he was not hurt: 'twas a pin's point: and so made another pass at his antagonist; which he, with a surprising dexterity, received under his arm, and run my dear chevalier into the body: who immediately fell; saying, The luck is yours, sir—Oh my beloved Clarissa!—Now art thou—Inwardly he spoke three or four words more. His sword dropped from his hand. Mr Morden threw his down, and ran to him, saying in French—Ah monsieur, you are a dead man!—Call to God for mercy!

We gave the signal agreed upon to the footmen; and they to the surgeons; who instantly came up.

Colonel Morden, I found, was too well used to the bloody work; for he was as cool as if nothing so extraordinary had happened, assisting the surgeons, though his own wound bled much. But my dear chevalier fainted away two or three times running, and vomited blood besides.

However, they stopped the bleeding for the present; and we helped him into the voiture; and then the colonel suffered his own wound to be dressed; and appeared concerned that my chevalier was between whiles (when he could speak, and struggle) extremely outrageous—Poor gentleman! He had made quite sure of victory!

The colonel, against the surgeons' advice, would mount on horseback to pass into the Venetian territories; and generously gave me a purse of gold to pay the surgeons; desiring me to make a present to the footman; and to accept of the remainder, as a mark of his satisfaction in my conduct; and in my care and tenderness of my master.

The surgeons told him, that my chevalier could not live over the day.

When the colonel took leave of him, Mr Lovelace said in French, You have well revenged the dear creature.

I have, sir, said Mr Morden, in the same language: and perhaps shall be sorry that you called upon me to this work, while I was balancing whether to obey, or disobey, the dear angel.

There is a fate in it! replied my chevalier—a cursed fate!—or this could not have been!—But be ye all witnesses, that I have provoked my destiny, and acknowledge, that I fall by a man of honour.

Sir, said the colonel, with the piety of a confessor (wringing Mr Lovelace's hand), snatch these few fleeting moments, and commend yourself to God.

And so he rode off.

The voiture proceeded slowly with my chevalier; yet the motion set both his wounds bleeding afresh; and it was with difficulty they again stopped the blood.

We brought him alive to the first cottage; and he gave orders to me to dispatch to you the packet I herewith send sealed up; and bid me write to you the particulars of this most unhappy affair, and to give you thanks, in his name, for all your favours and friendship to him.

Contrary to all expectation, he lived over the night: but suffered much, as well from his impatience and disappointment, as from his wounds; for he seemed very unwilling to die.

He was delirious, at times, in the two last hours; and then several times cried out, Take her away! Take her away! but named nobody. And sometimes praised some lady (that Clarissa, I suppose, whom he had called upon when he received his death's wound) calling her, Sweet Excellence! Divine Creature! Fair Sufferer!— And once he said, Look down, blessed Spirit, look down!—And there stopped— his lips however moving.

At nine in the morning, he was seized with convulsions, and fainted away; and it was a quarter of an hour before he came out of them.

His few last words I must not omit, as they show an ultimate composure; which may administer some consolation to his honourable friends.

Blessed—said he, addressing himself no doubt to Heaven; for his dying eyes were lifted up—a strong convulsion prevented him for a few moments saying more—But recovering, he again with great fervour (lifting up his eyes, and his spread hands) pronounced the word *Blessed*—Then, in a seeming ejaculation, he spoke inwardly so as not to be understood: at last, he distinctly pronounced these three words,

LET THIS EXPIATE!

And then, his head sinking on his pillow, he expired; at about half an hour after ten.

He little thought, poor gentleman! his end so near: so had given no direction about his body. I have caused it to be embowelled, and deposited in a vault, till I have orders from England.

This is a favour that was procured with difficulty; and would have been refused, had he not been an Englishman of rank: a nation with reason respected in every Austrian government—for he had refused ghostly attendance, and the Sacraments in the Catholic way. May his soul be happy, I pray God!

I have had some trouble also on account of the manner of his death, from the Magistracy here: who have taken the requisite informations in the affair. And it has cost me some money. Of which, and of my dear Chevalier's effects, I will give you a faithful account in my next. And so, waiting at this place your commands, I am, sir,

Your most faithful and obedient servant,
F. J. DE LA TOUR

CONCLUSION

Supposed to be written by Mr Belford

WHAT remains to be mentioned for the satisfaction of such of the readers as may be presumed to have interested themselves in the fortunes of those other principals in the story, who survived Mr Lovelace, will be found summarily related as follows:

The news of Mr LOVELACE'S unhappy end was received with as much grief by his own relations, as it was with exultation by the Harlowe family, and by Miss Howe. His own family were *most* to be pitied, because, being sincere admirers of the inimitable lady, they were greatly grieved for the injustice done her; and now had the *additional* mortification of losing the only male of it by a violent death.

That his fate was deserved was still a heightening of their calamity, as they had for that very reason, and his unpreparedness for it, but too much grounds for apprehension with regard to his future happiness. While the other family from their unforgiving spirit, and even the noble young lady above-mentioned from her lively resentments, found his death some little, some temporary, alleviation of the heavy loss they had sustained, principally through his means.

Temporary alleviation, we repeat, as to the Harlowe family; for THEY were far from being happy or easy in their reflections upon their own conduct.

Mrs HARLOWE lived about two years and an half after the much-lamented death of her excellent daughter.

Mr HARLOWE survived his lady about half a year.

BOTH, in their last hours, comforted themselves, that they should be restored to their BLESSED daughter, as they always (from the time that they were acquainted with her happy *exit*) called her.

They both lived, however, to see their son *James*, and their daughter *Arabella*, married: but not to take joy in either of their nuptials.

Mr JAMES HARLOWE married a woman of family, an orphan, and is obliged at a very great expense to support her claim to estates, which were his principal inducement to make his addresses to her; but which to this day he has not recovered; nor is likely to recover; having very powerful adversaries to contend with, and a title to assert which admits of litigation; and he not blessed with so much patience as is necessary to persons embarrassed in law.

What is further observable with regard to him is that the match was entirely of his own head, against the advice of his father, mother, and uncles, who warned him of marrying in this lady a lawsuit for life. His ungenerous behaviour to his wife, for what she cannot help, and for what is as much her misfortune as his, has occasioned such estrangements between them (she being a woman of spirit) as, were the lawsuits determined, and even more favourably than probably they will be, must make him unhappy to the end of his life. He attributes all his misfortunes, when he opens himself to the *few* friends he has, to his vile and cruel treatment of his angelic sister. He confesses these misfortunes to be just, without having temper to acquiesce in the acknowledged justice. One month in every year he puts on mourning, and that month commences with him on the 7th of September, during which he shuts himself up from all company. Finally, he is looked upon, and often calls himself, THE MOST MISERABLE OF BEINGS.

ARABELLA'S fortune became a temptation to a man of quality to make his addresses to her: his title an inducement with her to approve of him. Brothers and sisters, when they are not friends are generally the sharpest enemies to each other. He thought too much was done for her in the settlements. She thought not enough. And for some years past they have so heartily hated each other, that if either know a joy, it is in being told of some new misfortune or displeasure that happens to the other. Indeed, before they came to an open rupture, they were continually loading each other, by way of exonerating themselves (*to the additional disquiet of the whole family*), with the *principal* guilt of their implacable behaviour and sordid cruelty to their admirable sister. May the reports that are spread of this lady's further unhappiness from her lord's free life; a fault she *justly* thought so odious in Mr Lovelace (though that would not have been an insuperable objection with her to his addresses); and of his public slights and contempt of her, and even sometimes of his *personal abuses*, which are said to be owing to her impatient spirit and violent passions; be utterly groundless. For, what a heart must that be, which would wish she might be as great a torment to herself, as she had aimed to be to her sister? Especially as she regrets to this hour, and declares that she shall to the last of her life, her cruel treatment of that sister; and (as well as her brother) is but too ready to attribute to *that* her own unhappiness.

Mr ANTONY and Mr JOHN HARLOWE are still (at the writing of this) living: but often declare that, with their beloved niece, they lost all the joy of their lives: and lament without reserve, in all companies, the unnatural part they were induced to take against her.

Mr SOLMES is also still living, if a man of his cast may be said to live; for his general behaviour and sordid manners are such as justify the aversion the excellent lady had to him. He has moreover found his addresses rejected by several women of far inferior fortunes (great as his own are) to those of the lady to whom he was encouraged to aspire.

Mr MOWBRAY and Mr TOURVILLE having lost the man in whose conversation they so much delighted; shocked and awakened by the several unhappy catastrophes before their eyes; and having always rather *ductile* than *dictating* hearts; took their friend Belford's advice: converted the remainder of their fortunes into annuities for life; and retired, the one into Yorkshire, the other into Nottinghamshire, of which counties they are natives: their friend Belford managing their concerns for them, and corresponding with them, and having more and more hopes every time he sees them (which is once or twice a year, when they come to town) that they will become more and more worthy of their names and families.

It cannot be amiss to mention what became of the two sisters in iniquity, *Sally Martin*, and *Polly Horton*; names so frequently occurring in the foregoing collection.

After the death of the profligate Sinclair, they kept on the infamous trade with too much success; till an accident happened in the house—a gentleman of family killed in it in a fray, contending with another for a new-vamped face. Sally was accused of holding the gentleman's arm, while his more favoured adversary run him through the heart, and then made off. And she being tried for her life, narrowly escaped.

This accident obliged them to break up house-keeping, and not having been frugal enough of their ill-gotten gains (lavishing upon one, what they got by another), they were compelled for subsistence sake, to enter themselves as under-managers at such another house as their own had been. In which service, soon after, Sally died of a fever and surfeit got by a debauch: and the other, about a month after, by a violent cold, occasioned through carelessness in a salivation. Two creatures who wanted not sense, and had had (what is deemed to be) a good modern education; their parents having lived reputably; and once having much better hopes of them: but who were in a great measure answerable for their miscarriages, by indulging them in the fashionable follies and luxury of an age given up to those amusements and pleasures which are so apt to set people of but *middle fortunes* above all the useful employments of life; and to make young women an easy prey to rakes and libertines.

Happier scenes open for the remaining characters; for it might be descending too low to mention the untimely ends of *Dorcas*, and of *William*, Mr Lovelace's wicked servant; and the pining and consumptive ones of *Betty Barnes* and *Joseph Leman*, unmarried both, and in less than a year after the happy death of their excellent young lady.

The good Mrs NORTON passed the small remainder of her life as happily as she wished, in her beloved foster-daughter's dairy-house, as it used to be called: *as she wished*, we repeat; for she had too strong aspirations after another life to be greatly attached to this.

She laid out the greatest part of her time in doing good by her advice, and by the prudent management of the Fund committed to her direction. Having lived an exemplary life from her youth upwards; and seen her son happily settled in the world; she departed with ease and calmness, without pang or agony, like a tired traveller falling into a sweet slumber: her last words expressing her hope of being restored to the child of her bosom; and to her own excellent father and mother, to whose care and pains she owed that good education to which she was indebted for all her other blessings.

The Poor's Fund, which was committed to her care, she resigned a week before her death into the hands of Mrs Hickman, according to the direction of the will, and all the accounts and disbursements with it; which she had kept with such an exactness, that that lady declares that she will follow her method, and only wishes to do as well.

Miss HOWE was not to be persuaded to quit her mourning for her dear friend, until six months were fully expired: and then she made Mr HICKMAN one of the happiest men in the world. A woman of her fine sense and understanding, married to a man of virtue and good-nature (who had no past capital errors to reflect upon and to abate his joys, and whose behaviour to *Mrs Hickman* is as affectionate as it was respectful to *Miss Howe*), could not do otherwise. They are already blessed with two fine children; a daughter, to whom by joint consent they have given the name of her beloved friend; and a son, who bears that of his father.

She has allotted to Mr Hickman, who takes delight in doing good (and that as much for its own sake, as to oblige her), *his part* of the management of the Poor's Fund; to be accountable for it, as she pleasantly says, to *her*. She has appropriated every Thursday morning for *her part* of that management; and takes so much delight in the task, that she declares it is one of the most agreeable of her amusements. And the more agreeable, as she teaches everyone whom she benefits *to bless the memory of her departed friend*; to whom she attributes the merit of all *her own* charities, as well as that of those which she dispenses in pursuance of her will.

She has declared that this Fund shall never fail while she lives. She has even engaged her mother to contribute annually to it. And Mr Hickman has appropriated twenty pounds a year to the same. In consideration of which she allows him to recommend four objects yearly to partake of it. *Allows*, is her style; for she assumes the whole prerogative of dispensing this charity; the *only* prerogative she does or has occasion to assume. In every other case, there is but *one will* between them; and that is generally his or hers, as either speak first upon any subject, be it what it will. MRS HICKMAN, she sometimes as pleasantly as generously tells him, must not *quite* forget that she was once MISS HOWE, because if he had not loved her as such, and with all her foibles, she had never been Mrs *Hickman*. Nevertheless she seriously, on all occasions and that to others, as well as to himself, confesses, that she owes him *unreturnable* obligations for his patience *with* her in HER day, and for his generous behaviour *to* her in HIS.

And still the more highly does she esteem and love him, as she reflects upon his past kindness to her beloved friend; and on that dear friend's good opinion of him. Nor is it less grateful to her, that the worthy man joins most sincerely with her in all those respectful and affectionate recollections, which make the memory of the departed precious to survivors.

Mr BELFORD was not so destitute of humanity and affection as to be unconcerned at the unhappy fate of his most intimate friend. But when he reflects upon the untimely ends of several of his companions, but just mentioned in the preceding history[a]—on the shocking despondency and death of his poor friend *Belton*—on the signal justice which overtook the wicked *Tomlinson*—on the dreadful exit of the infamous *Sinclair*—on the deep remorses of his more valued friend—and on the other hand on the example, set him by the most excellent of her sex—and on her blessed preparation, and happy departure—and when he considers, as he often does with awe and terror, that his *wicked habits* were so *rooted* in his depraved heart, that all *these warnings*, and this *lovely example*, seemed to be *but necessary* to enable him to subdue them, and to reform; and that such awakening calls are hardly ever afforded to men of his cast, or (if they are) but seldom attended with such happy effects in the prime of youth, and in the full vigour of constitution—when he reflects upon all these things, he adores the mercy, which through these calls has snatched him as a *brand out of the fire*: and thinks himself obliged to make it his endeavour to find out and to reform any of those who may have been endangered by his means; as well as to repair, to the utmost of his power, any damage or mischiefs which he may have occasioned to others.

With regard to the trust with which he was honoured by the inimitable lady, he

---

a See pp. 1170, and 1453, 1474.

had the pleasure of acquitting himself of it in a very few months, to everybody's satisfaction; even to that of the unhappy family; who sent him their thanks on the occasion. Nor was he, at delivering up his accounts, contented with resigning the legacy bequeathed to him to the uses of the will. So that the Poor's Fund, as it is called, is become a very considerable sum; and will be a lasting bank for relief of objects who best deserve relief.

There was but one earthly blessing which remained for Mr Belford to wish for, in order, morally speaking, to secure to him all his other blessings; and that was the greatest of all worldly ones, a virtuous and prudent wife. So free a liver as he had been, he did not think that he could be worthy of such a one till upon an impartial examination of himself, he found the pleasure he had in his new resolutions so great, and his abhorrence of his former courses so sincere, that he was the less apprehensive of a deviation.

Upon this presumption, having also kept in his mind some encouraging hints from Mr Lovelace; and having been so happy as to have it in his power to oblige Lord M. and that whole noble family by some services grateful to them (the request for which from his unhappy friend was brought over, among other papers, with the dead body, by De la Tour) he besought that nobleman's leave to make his addresses to Miss CHARLOTTE MONTAGUE, the eldest of his lordship's two nieces: and making at the same time such proposals of settlements as were not objected to, his lordship was pleased to use his powerful interest in his favour. And his worthy niece having no engagement, she had the goodness to honour Mr Belford with her hand; and thereby made him as completely happy as a man *can be*, who has enormities to reflect upon which in a course of years, the deaths of some of the injured parties, and the irreclaimableness of others, have put it out of his power to atone for.

Happy is the man who in time of health and strength sees and reforms the errors of his ways!—But how much more happy he, who has no capital and wilful errors to repent of!—How unmixed and sincere must the joys of such a one come to him!

Lord M. added bountifully in his lifetime, as did also the two ladies his sisters, to the fortune of their worthy niece. And as Mr Belford has been blessed with a son by her, his lordship at his death (which happened just three years after the untimely one of his unhappy nephew) was pleased to devise to that son, and to his descendants for ever (and in case of his death unmarried, to any other children of his niece) his Hertfordshire estate (*designed for Mr Lovelace*) which he made up to the value of a moiety of his real estates; bequeathing also a moiety of his personal to the same lady.

Miss PATTY MONTAGUE, a fine young lady (to whom her noble uncle at his death devised the other moiety of his real and personal estates, including his seat in Berkshire) lives at present with her excellent sister Mrs Belford; to whom she removed upon Lord M.'s death: but, in all probability, will soon be the lady of a worthy baronet, of ancient family, fine qualities, and ample fortunes, just returned from his travels with a character superior to the *very* good one he set out with: a case that very seldom happens, although the *end of travel is improvement*.

Colonel MORDEN, who with so many virtues and accomplishments, cannot be unhappy, in several letters to the executor, with whom he corresponds from Florence (having, since his unhappy affair with Mr Lovelace, changed his purpose of coming so soon to reside in England as he had intended), declares that although he thought himself obliged either to accept of what he took to be a challenge, as such; or tamely to acknowledge that he gave up all resentment of his cousin's wrongs; and in a manner to beg pardon for having spoken freely of Mr Lovelace behind his back; and although at *the time* he owns he was not sorry to be called upon, as he was, to take either the one course or the other; yet now, coolly reflecting upon his beloved cousin's reasonings against duelling; and upon the price it had too probably cost the unhappy man; he wishes he had more fully considered those words in his cousin's posthumous letter: 'If God will allow him time for repentance, why should you deny it him?'

To conclude: the worthy Widow LOVICK continues to live with Mr Belford; and by her prudent behaviour, piety, and usefulness, has endeared herself to her lady, and to the whole family.

POSTSCRIPT

THE author of the foregoing work has been favoured, in the course of its publication, with many anonymous letters, in which the writers have *differently* expressed their wishes as to what they apprehended of the catastrophe.

Most of those directed to him by the gentler sex turn in favour of what they call a *fortunate ending*; and some of them, enamoured as they declare with the principal character, are warmly solicitous to have her *happy*.

These letters having been written on the perusal of the first four volumes only, before the complicated adjustment of the several parts to one another could be seen, or fully known, it may be thought superfluous, now the whole work is before the public, to enter upon this argument, because it is presumed that the catastrophe necessarily follows the natural progress of the story: but as the notion of *poetical justice* seems to have generally obtained among the fair sex, and must be confessed to have the appearance of good nature and humanity, it may not be amiss to give it a brief consideration.

Nor can it be deemed impertinent to touch upon this subject at the conclusion of a work which is designed to inculcate upon the human mind, under the guise of an amusement, the great lessons of Christianity, in an age *like the present*; which seems to expect from the poets and dramatic writers (that is to say, from the authors of works of invention) that they should make it one of their principal rules, to propagate another sort of dispensation, under the name of *poetical justice*, than that with which God by Revelation teaches us he has thought fit to exercise mankind; whom, placing here only in a state of *probation*, he hath so intermingled good and evil as to necessitate them to look forward for a more equal distribution of both.

The history, or rather the dramatic narrative of CLARISSA, is formed on this religious plan; and is therefore well justified in deferring to extricate suffering virtue till it meets with the completion of its reward.

But we have no need to shelter our conduct under the sanction of religion (an authority perhaps not of the greatest weight with modern critics) since we are justified in it by the greatest master of reason, and the best judge of composition that ever was. The learned reader knows we must mean ARISTOTLE; whose sentiments in this matter we shall beg leave to deliver in the words of a very amiable writer of our own country.

'The English writers of tragedy, *says Mr Addison*,[a] are possessed with a notion that when they represent a virtuous or innocent person in distress, they ought not to leave him till they have delivered him out of his troubles, or made him triumph over his enemies.

'This *error* they have been led into by a *ridiculous* doctrine in *modern criticism*, that they are obliged to an *equal distribution* of *rewards* and *punishments* and an impartial execution of *poetical justice*.

a   *Spectator*, No. 40.

'Who were the first that established this rule, I know not; but I am sure it has no foundation in NATURE, in REASON, or in the PRACTICE OF THE ANCIENTS.

'We find, that (*in the dispensations of* PROVIDENCE) good and evil happen alike to ALL MEN on this side the grave: and as the principal design of tragedy is to raise commiseration and terror in the minds of the audience, we shall defeat this great end if we always make virtue and innocence happy and successful.

'Whatever crosses and disappointments a good man suffers in the *body* of the tragedy, they will make but small impression on our minds, when we know that in the *last act*, he is to arrive at the end of his wishes and desires.

'When we see him engaged in the depth of his afflictions, we are apt to comfort ourselves because we are sure he will find his way out of them, and that his grief, how great soever it may be at present, will soon terminate in gladness.

'For this reason, the ancient writers of tragedy treated men in their *plays* as they are dealt with in the *world*, by making virtue sometimes happy and sometimes miserable, as they found it in the fable which they made choice of, or as it might affect their audience in the most agreeable manner.

'Aristotle considers the tragedies that were written in either of those kinds; and observes that those which ended unhappily had always pleased the people, and carried away the prize in the public disputes of the stage from those that ended happily.[a]

a   This was at a time when the entertainments of the stage were committed to the care of the magistrates; when the prizes contended for were given by the state; when of consequence the emulation among writers was ardent; and when learning was at the highest pitch of glory in that renowned commonwealth.

It cannot be supposed that the Athenians, in this their highest age of taste and politeness, were less humane, less tender-hearted, than we of the present. But they were not afraid of being moved, nor ashamed of showing themselves to be so, at the distresses they saw well painted and represented. In short, they were of the opinion, with the wisest of men, *that it was better to go to the house of mourning than to the house of mirth*; and had fortitude enough to trust themselves with their own generous grief, because they found their hearts mended by it.

Thus also Horace, and the politest Romans in the Augustan age, wished to be affected:

Ac ne forte putes me, quae facere ipse recusem,
Cum recte tract[e]nt alii, laudare maligne;
Ille per extentum funem mihi posse videtur
Ire poeta, meum qui pectus inaniter angit,
Irritat, mulcet; falsis terroribus implet,
Ut magus; et modo me Thebis, modo ponit Athenis.

Thus Englished by Mr Pope:

Yet lest you think I railly more than teach,
Or praise malignly *Arts* I cannot reach,
Let me, for once, presume t'instruct the times
To know the *Poet* from the *Man of Rhymes*.
'Tis He who gives my breast a thousand pains,
Can make me *feel* each passion that he feigns;
Enrage—compose—with more than magic Art,
With *Pity* and with *Terror* tear my heart;
And snatch me o'er the earth, or thro' the air,
To Thebes, to Athens, when he will, and where.[1]

'Terror and commiseration leave a *pleasing anguish* in the mind, and fix the audience in such a serious composure of thought as is much more lasting and delightful, than any little transient starts of joy and satisfaction.

'Accordingly we find that more of our English tragedies have succeeded, in which the favourites of the audience sink under their calamities, than those in which they recover themselves out of them.

'The best plays of this kind are *The Orphan, Venice Preserved, Alexander the Great, Theodosius, All for Love, Oedipus, Oroonoko, Othello*, etc.

'*King Lear* is an admirable tragedy of the same kind, as Shakespeare wrote it: but as it is reformed according to the *chimerical notion* of poetical (*or, as we may say, anti-providential*) justice, in my humble opinion it has lost half its beauty.[a]

'At the same time I must allow that there are very noble tragedies which have been framed upon the other plan, and have ended happily; as indeed most of the good tragedies which have been written since the starting of the above-mentioned criticism have taken this turn: as *The Mourning Bride, Tamerlane,*[b] *Ulysses, Phaedra and Hippolytus,*[3] with most of Mr Dryden's. I must also allow that many of Shakespeare's, and several of the celebrated tragedies of antiquity are cast in the same form. I do not therefore dispute against this way of writing tragedies; but against the criticism that would establish this as the *only* method; and by that means would very much cramp the English tragedy, and perhaps give a wrong bent to the genius of our writers.'

Thus far Mr Addison.

Our fair readers are also desired to attend to what a celebrated critic[c] of a neighbouring nation says on the nature and design of tragedy, from the rules laid down by the same great ancient.

'Tragedy, says he, makes man *modest*, by representing the great masters of the earth humbled; and it makes him *tender* and *merciful*, by showing him the *strange accidents of life*, and the *unforeseen disgraces* to which the most important persons are subject.

'But because man is naturally timorous and compassionate, he may fall into other extremes. Too much fear may shake his constancy of mind, and too much compassion may enfeeble his equity.' 'Tis the business of tragedy to regulate these two weaknesses. It prepares and arms him against *disgraces*, by showing them so frequent in the most considerable persons; and he will cease to fear extraordinary accidents, when he sees them happen to the *highest* (and still more efficacious, we may add, the example will be, when he sees them happen to the *best*) part of mankind.

---

a Yet so different seems to be the modern taste from that of the ancients, that the altered *King Lear* of Mr Tate is constantly acted on the English stage, in preference to the original, though written by Shakespeare himself! Whether this *strange* preference be owing to the false delicacy or affected tenderness of the players, or to that of the audience, has not for many years been tried. And perhaps the former have not the courage to try the public taste upon it. And yet if it were *ever* to be tried, *now* seems to be the time, when an *actor* and a *manager* [Garrick],[2] in the *same person*, is in being, who deservedly engages the public favour in all he undertakes, and who owes so much, and is gratefully sensible that he does, to that great master of the human passions.

b Yet in *Tamerlane* two of the most amiable characters, Moneses and Aspasia, suffer death.

c Rapin, on Aristotle's *Poetics*.[4]

'But as the end of tragedy is to teach men not to fear too weakly *common misfortunes*, it proposes also to teach them to spare their compassion for objects that *deserve it*. For there is an *injustice* in being moved at the afflictions of those who *deserve to be miserable*. We may see, without pity, Clytemnestra slain by her son Orestes in *Aeschylus*, because she had murdered Agamemnon her husband; and we cannot see Hippolytus die by the plot of his stepmother Phaedra, in *Euripides*, without compassion, because he died not but for being chaste and virtuous.'

These are the great authorities so favourable to the stories that end unhappily: yet the writer of the *History of Clarissa* is humbly of opinion that he might have been excused referring to them for the vindication of *his* catastrophe, even by those who are advocates for the contrary opinion; since the notion of *poetical justice*, founded on the *modern rules*, has hardly ever been more strictly observed in works of this nature, than in the present performance, if any regard at all be to be paid to the *Christian system* on which it is formed.

For, is not Mr *Lovelace*, who could persevere in his villainous views, against the strongest and most frequent convictions and remorses that ever were sent to awaken and reclaim a wicked man—is not this great, this wilful transgressor, condignly *punished*; and his punishment brought on through the intelligence of the very Joseph Leman whom he had corrupted[a]; and by means of the very women whom he had debauched[b]—is not Mr *Belton*, who has an uncle's *hastened* death to answer for[c]—are not the *whole Harlowe family*—is not the vile *Tomlinson*—are not the infamous *Sinclair*, and her *wretched partners*—and even the wicked *servants* who with their eyes open contributed their parts to the carrying on of the vile schemes of their respective principals—*are they not all likewise exemplarily punished*?

On the other hand, is not Miss Howe, for her noble friendship to the exalted lady in her calamities—is not Mr Hickman, for his unexceptionable morals and integrity of life—is not the repentant and not ungenerous Belford—is not the worthy Norton—*made signally happy*?

And who that are in earnest in their profession of Christianity but will rather envy than regret the triumphant death of Clarissa, whose piety from her early childhood; whose diffusive charity; whose steady virtue; whose Christian humility; whose forgiving spirit; whose meekness, whose resignation, HEAVEN *only* could reward?[d]

The length of the piece has been objected to by some, who had seen only the first four volumes, and who perhaps looked upon it as a mere *novel* or *romance*; and yet of *these* there are not wanting works of equal length.

They were of opinion that the story moved too slowly, particularly in the first and second volumes, which are chiefly taken up with the altercations between Clarissa and the several persons of her family.

a See pp. 1475–7.
b See p. 1484.
c See p. 1242.
d It may not be amiss to remind the reader, that so early in the work as pp. 332–3 the dispensations of Providence in her distresses are justified by herself. And thus she ends her reflections: 'I shall not live always—May my closing scene be happy!'
  She had her wish. It was happy.

But is it not true that those altercations are the foundation of the whole, and therefore a necessary part of the work? The letters and conversations, where the story makes the slowest progress, are presumed to be *characteristic*. They give occasion likewise to suggest many interesting *personalities*, in which a good deal of the instruction essential to a work of this nature is conveyed. And it will, moreover, be remembered that the author at his first setting out, apprised the reader, that the story was to be looked upon as the vehicle only to the instruction.

To all which we may add, that there was frequently a necessity to be very circumstantial and minute, in order to preserve and maintain that air of probability, which is necessary to be maintained in a story designed to represent real life; and which is rendered extremely busy and active by the plots and contrivances formed and carried on by one of the principal characters.

In a word, *if* in the *History* before us it shall be found that the spirit is duly diffused throughout; that the characters are various and natural; well distinguished, and uniformly supported and maintained: *if* there be a variety of incidents sufficient to excite attention, and those so conducted as to keep the reader always awake; the length then must add proportionably to the pleasure that every person of taste receives from a well-drawn picture of nature. But where the contrary of all these qualities shock the understanding, the extravagant performance will be judged tedious though no longer than a fairy tale.

TABLE OF LETTERS

TABLE OF LETTER NUMBERS IN OTHER EDITIONS

1st ed., 7 vols. [C1] (see pp. 15–16)	3rd ed., 8 vols. [C3], and the Shakespeare Head edition*	Everyman Library ed., 4 vols. (1932 etc.)	This edition (following 1st ed.; see p.31)
i I – XLV [L1] [L45]	i I – XLV [L1] [L45]	i I – XCIX [L1] [L99]	L1 omits L43
ii I – XLVI [L46] [L93]	ii I – LI [L46] [L96]		omits L66, 67
iii I – LXXVIII [L94] [L173]	iii I – LXX [L97] [L166]	ii I – CXXXIII [L100] [L228]	omits L122
iv I – LVI [L174] [L231]	iv I – LIX [L167] [L225]		omits L208
v I – LXII [L232] [L293]	v I – XLIII [L226] [L268]	iii I – CLXXV [L229] [L361]	omits L249
vi I – CXX [L294] [L418]	vi I – CI [L269] [L369]		
vii I – CXIII [L419] [L537]	vii I – CXI [L370] [L480]	iv I – CLXXV [L362] [L537]	omits L468, L469
	viii I – LVII [L481] [L537]		L537

* The Shakespeare Head *Clarissa* occupies vols. v–xii of the edition of Richardson's *Novels* by W. King and A. Bott (Oxford, 1925–34). The numbering follows the third edition [C3].

NOTES

For abbreviations and signs, see p. 11.

L7   1. *wooing as the English did . . . Edward the Sixth*. Henry VIII invaded Scotland (the 'Rough Wooing') in 1544 and 1545, attempting to force a marriage between his seven-year-old son (not Edward VI until 1547) and the four-year-old Mary Queen of Scots, sent to France in 1548.

L10   1. *Hannibal . . . attack the Romans upon their own territories*. His advice to Antiochus when in defeat he fled from Carthage to Ephesus in 195 B.C. (Livy, xxxiv, 60:2, 3).

L20   1. *the old Roman and his lentils*. Some moral story contrasting traditional self-sufficient Roman frugality with corrupt, ensnaring luxury: cf. the story referred to by Plutarch in his life of Cato the Censor, in which Manius Curius Dentatus, the plebeian hero (consul in 290, 284, 275, 274 B.C.), was cooking his rustic supper of turnips when visited by the ambassadors of the Samnites, whom he had conquered; they unsuccessfully offered him a large present of gold, for his favour.

L21   1. *same vacuity of thought . . . Dryden's clown whistle*. 'He trudg'd along unknowing what he sought, / And whistled as he went for want of thought'. *Fables Ancient and Modern* (1700), 'Cymon and Iphigenia, from Boccaccio', 85.

L31   1. *He who seems virtuous . . . but his art*. Sir Robert Howard, *The Vestal Virgin, or, The Roman Ladies. A Tragedy* (1664), I.
2. *Clarissa! . . . first leaps of life*. Thomas Otway (1652–85), *The History and Fall of Caius Marius. A Tragedy* (1680), I, i, 305–7 ('Lavinia' in the original).
3. *Love various minds . . . with revenge it glows*. Dryden, *Tyrannic Love, or, The Royal Martyr. A Tragedy* (1669), II, i, 292–7.
4. *Perdition catch my soul, but I do love her*. Shakespeare, *Othello*, II, iii, 339.
5. *The cause of love . . . the lover's mind*. *Tyrannic Love*, III, i, 122–3.
6. *Beauty! . . . no certain what, nor where*. Abraham Cowley (1618–67), *The Mistress* (1668), 'Beauty'.
7. *Full many a lady . . . ev'ry creature's best*. Shakespeare, *The Tempest*, III, i, 40–48.

L32.4   1. *He that is first in his own cause . . . and searcheth him*. Proverbs 18:17.
2. *the plain Dunstable of the matter*. Plain speaking: '[as] plain [as the road to] Dunstable', proverbial from 1546 (*ODEP³*, 209), joking on 'dunce'.
3. *gnat-strainers and camel swallowers*. 'Ye blind guides which strain at a gnat and swallow a camel'. Matthew 23:24.
4. *Dunmow flitch . . . was never claimed*. The flitch of bacon is awarded in Dunmow, Essex, to the couple who can swear at the church door that they have never quarrelled during the previous year, or wished themselves unmarried.

L35   1. *Dryden's lion . . . What though this mighty soul . . . his hunters tears*. *Absalom and Achitophel. Part I* (1681), 445–54.

L44   1. *wild oats . . . black oxen*. '[To sow one's] wild oats', proverbial from 1542 (*ODEP³*, 889); 'the black ox has trod on his foot' (i.e. he has met adversity), proverbial from 1525 (*ODEP³*, 64).

L46   1. *King William cravat*. A long wide neck-cloth fashionable at the end of the seventeenth century in the reign of William III.

L47   1. *the case of a celebrated bard . . . refused the honours that they may justly claim*. Perhaps Pope, of whom SR often made unfavourable remarks in his letters (EK, 574–8).

L48   1. *the Cocoa Tree in Pall Mall*. A chocolate house (more raffish than a coffee house), frequented by Tories; it stood on the south side of Pall Mall from 1698 to 1757, when it moved across the road.

2. *resolution . . . of old Tom Wharton*. Thomas Wharton (1648–1715), 2nd Baron; created Earl (1706) and Lord Lieutenant of Ireland (1708–10); a notorious rake, but an able politician. He was the father of the flighty Duke of Wharton, with whom SR had some political connections (EK, 20–24).

L54   1. *Ode to Wisdom*. Written by the learned Elizabeth Carter (1717–1806) of Deal, a friend of Dr Johnson (but only later of SR). The latter printed the *Ode* here without the author's permission, from a MS. copy that was circulating. SR commissioned the music and had it engraved at considerable cost, as he says in an exculpatory letter to Miss Carter, as an embellishment to his novel, 'which is perhaps too solemn' (EK, 214–16). In [C1], [C2] and [C3] the music was printed on a fold-out sheet, next to the verses, and in the fourth edition it was re-engraved to fit a single page. It is printed below on p. 1534.

L68   1. *Coventry Act*. 1670: declared nose-slitting and mutilation such as that inflicted by Charles II's cronies on Sir John Coventry, a Tory MP, to be a capital offence.

2. *the three estates . . . our political union*. The crown (executive), the lords and commons (the legislature).

L75   1. *a Thomas à Kempis*. Some volume containing the *De Imitatione Christi* (*On the Following* [or *Imitation*] *of Christ*), a work of ascetic piety by one Thomas, born at Kempen (c. 1379–1471), printed, translated, retranslated, scores of times. There were several English translations; that by George Stanhope (see Glossary: *Stanhope's Gospels*), with meditations, and prayers for sick persons, first published in 1698, was popular at this time. The eleventh edition of it was published in 1726.

L81   1. *What old Greek was it that said . . . and his son, her*. An apophthegm of Themistocles (c. 528–462 B.C.), the Athenian statesman, quoted by Plutarch in his life of Cato the Censor.

L90   1. *There will be joy in Heaven . . .* 'over one sinner that repenteth, more than over ninety and nine just persons, that need no repentance'. Luke 15:7.

L91   1. *close borderers . . . as the poet tells us Wit and Madness are*. 'Great Wits are sure to Madness near ally'd' Dryden, *Absalom and Achitophel. Part I* (1681), 163; a version of Seneca, *De Tranq. Animi*, xvii, 10: 'there was never any great genius without a mixture of madness'; in turn resting on Aristotle, *Problemata*, xxx, i.

L96   1. *plases are no inherittanses nowadays*. 'Service is no inheritance', proverbial from the fifteenth century (*ODEP³*, 716).

2. *to throe my hat at her, or so*. To defy her; 'To throw one's cap at . . .', proverbial from the sixteenth century (*ODEP³*, 101).

L97   1. *Oh ecstasy! . . . into her bosom*. Nathaniel Lee (?1649–1692), *The Rival Queens, or, The Death of Alexander the Great. A Tragedy* (1667), III, i.

L98   1. *[swear] like a trooper*. An earlier use in print than recorded by *ODEP³* or *OED*.

2. *As Shakespeare says . . . audacious eloquence*. *A Midsummer Night's Dream*, V, i, 102.

L103   1. *throw out a tub to the whale*. The mariners' ancient defence against a pursuing sea monster (see Swift, *A Tale of a Tub*, ed. Guthkelch and Nichol Smith, 1920 etc., pp. xviii–xxx).

L106   1. *Clodius . . . Calpurnia*. Publius Clodius Pulcher (born c. 92, murdered 52 B.C.), patrician demagogue, enemy of Cicero, and gangster, was tried in 61 B.C. for masquerading as a woman at the festival of the Bona Dea (see Glossary: dea bona). Portia was the wife of Brutus, Calpurnia of Julius Caesar.

L110 1. *I have read ... not the man for the woman.* 1 Corinthians 11:9; and Samuel Butler (1612–80), *Hudibras: Epistle to his Lady*, 273: 'For Women first were made for Men, / Not Men for them ...'

2. *good men of old.* Job.

3. *she'll be more than woman ... if I succeed not.* Untraced.

L115 1. *like Tiresias, can tell what they think.* The legendary seer of Thebes was briefly turned into a woman when he struck two coupling snakes; he was blinded, either because he saw Athena bathing, or because when asked whether man or woman had more pleasure in love, he answered that woman did.

2. *every woman is a rake in her heart.* 'But every woman is at heart a Rake'; Pope, *Of the Characters of Women: An Epistle to a Lady* (1735), 216.

L116 1. *nothing new under the sun.* Ecclesiastes 1:9.

2. *Lord Shaftesbury's test.* The 3rd Earl of Shaftesbury (1671–1731), in 'Sensus Communis: An Essay on the Freedom of Wit and Humour' (1709), reprinted in *Characteristics* (1711), vol. i, suggested ridicule as a test of truth.

3. *Habitual evils ... Dissimulation.* Nicholas Rowe (1674–1718), *Ulysses. A Tragedy* (1705; revised 1714), I, i.

L118 1. *eat the calf in the cow's belly.* i.e. spend rents before they fall due; proverbial in the eighteenth century (*ODEP³*, 216).

L123 1. *the jay in the fable* (sometimes a jackdaw) was to become king and decked himself in the bright, moulted feathers of the other birds: cf. *Fables of Aesop*, trans. S. A. Handford (Penguin, 1964 etc.), 76.

L128 1. *his brother Orson.* Fr. *oursin*, little bear; in the romance, *Valentine and Orson* were the twin sons of Belisant, sister of King Pepin and wife of Alexander, Emperor of Constantinople. Orson was carried off and suckled by a she-bear, becoming the terror of France.

L130 1. *Hanover Square ... the new streets about Grosvenor Square.* The Grosvenor estate began building development of the latter square and surrounding streets from 1725. Hanover Square had been laid out in 1717.

L131 1 *like a farcical dean and chapter, choose ...* In the Church of England, the dean and chapter of a cathedral 'elect' their bishop in accordance with the royal *congé d'élire*, which nominates one candidate.

L132 1. *a dove ... go tame about house and breed.* Perhaps an unspecific reference to Steele's comedy *The Tender Husband, or, The Accomplish'd Fools* (1705), II, ii (*Sir Charles Grandison*, ed. J. Harris, i, 251: note on the same phrase, which does not, however, occur in so many words in any available text of the play).

L139 1. *listens ... as if she was among beans.* A country belief held that the scent of flowering beans made a person light-headed.

2. *yet what shall a man get to lose his soul.* 'For what is a man profited, if he shall gain the whole world, and lose his own soul'. Matthew 16:26.

L142 1. *Your Israelitish hankerings after the Egyptian onions.* 'And the children of Israel said unto [Moses and Aaron], Would to God we had died by the hand of the Lord in the land of Egypt, when we sat by the flesh-pots ...'. Exodus 16:3.

L147 1. *Mr Highmore.* Joseph Highmore (1692–1780), portrait painter (two of SR in the National Portrait Gallery, one in the Stationers' Company's Hall), also painted twelve pictures to illustrate *Pamela*, from which a set of prints was made. The portrait of Clarissa 'in the Vandyke taste' is not now known, but Highmore's picture of 'the assembled Harlowes, the *accusing* brother, and the *accused* sister on her return from Miss Howe's as represented at the beginning' (EK, 189, quoting SR to Lady Bradshaigh, mid-January 1749) is in the Paul Mellon Collection, Yale Center for British Art, New Haven, Conn., and is reproduced on the cover of this volume.

L149   1. *the wise man's observation . . . the medicine of life.* Ecclesiasticus 6:16.

L154   1. *The wise and active . . . impossibility they fear.* Nicholas Rowe, *The Ambitious Stepmother. A Tragedy* (1700), I, i.

       2. *Fairer to be seen . . . in blossoms new.* Dryden, 'Palamon and Arcite, or, The Knight's Tale, from Chaucer, Book I', *Fables Ancient and Modern* (1700), 170–72.

L155   1. Apart from specific titles (e.g. Stanhope's *Gospels*), for which see the Glossary, the items in this list are:

       A sacramental piece of the Bishop of Man. Thomas Wilson (1663–1755), whose son, also the Rev. Thomas Wilson, was a correspondent of S R's. He wrote several works of piety, including *The Principles and Duties of Christianity* (1707) and *A Short and Plain Instruction for the better Understanding of the Lord's Supper* (1733); his most famous and widely-read volume, *The Sacra Privata, or, Private Meditations and Prayers*, does not seem to have been printed until 1781.

       another of Dr Gauden, Bishop of Exeter. John Gauden (1605–62), Bishop of Exeter (later of Worcester), to whom was attributed *Eikon Basilike* (1649; very often reprinted), purporting to set out Charles I's religious meditations during his imprisonment.

       a Telemachus in French, another in English. François de Salignac de la Mothe Fénelon (1651–1715), Archbishop of Cambrai, wrote a prose epic about the son of. Ulysses which was first published in 1699; an English translation was printed by S R's press in 1728.

       that genteel comedy of Mr Cibber, The Careless Husband. First acted 1704; printed 1705 etc. Cibber was a friend of S R, and took a close interest in *Clarissa*.

L157   1. *Scipio.* Publius Cornelius Scipio Africanus (236–183 B.C.).

       2. *Shakespeare says well . . . The bloom of gaudy years.* Bysshe, *Art of English Poetry* (1710), and similar anthologies, all s.v. 'Youth', assign this line (or near it) and two others to Shakespeare, *Troilus and Cressida*. The two lines not quoted here are perhaps related to V, iii, 33, but the passage is not in Shakespeare's play as now printed, nor in Dryden's reworking of it, *Troilus and Cressida, or, Truth Found too Late* (1679).

       3. *the following lines, from Congreve . . . In winter's cold embraces die. Imitations of Horace*; *Odes*, Book I, ix (iii, 12–15).

L157.1   1. *what the learned bishop . . . the delicacy of intrigue.* Gilbert Burnet (1643–1715), later Bishop of Salisbury, *Some letters containing an Account of what seem'd most remarkable in . . . Italy . . . &c., in the Years 1685 and 1686 . . . to the Rt. Hon. R. B[oyle[. . .* (Antwerp, 1686; Amsterdam, 1686), and in collections: [C3] nominates this as Lovelace's phrase for Burnet's 'Intanglements of Amour'.

L159   1. *the text.* 2 Samuel 12:7.

       2. *my Gloriana.* The beautiful victim of Augustus in *Gloriana, or, The Court of Augustus Caesar. A Tragedy* (1676) by Nathaniel Lee.

       3. *Mark her majestic fabric . . . unworthy of the god.* The emperor's description of Almeyda in Dryden, *Don Sebastian, King of Portugal. A Tragedy* (1690), II, i.

       4. *The bloom of op'ning flow'rs . . . the world's first spring.* Rowe, *Tamerlane. A Tragedy* (first acted 1701; printed 1702), I, i, 139–41.

L161   1. *His tongue . . . he pleas'd the ear.* Satan in *Paradise Lost*, II, 113.

L167   1. *Mercury, as the fabulist tells us . . .* Cf. *Fables of Aesop*, trans. S. A. Handford (Penguin, 1964 etc.), p. 155.

L169   1. *Sweet are the joys that come with willingness.* 'Sweet is the love that comes with willingness': Indamora's reproach in Dryden, *Aureng-Zebe* (1676), II, i.

L171   1. *How like Boileau's parson . . . my double chin.* In *Le Lutrin* (1674), a mock heroic poem on 'The Reading Desk' by Nicholas Boileau-Despréaux (1636–1711), Chant I, 66, the sybaritic bishop is discovered waiting for his dinner, 'Son menton sur son sein descend à double étage . . .'.

L174 1. *To you, great gods!... but my heart is free.* Altered from Dryden and Lee, *Oedipus. A Tragedy* (acted 1678, printed 1679), III, i.

L174.3 1. *On what slight strings . . . men build their glory!* Untraced.

L175 1. *Old Terence has taken notice . . . lovers falling in.* Publius Terentius Afer (*c.* 190–*c.* 159 B.C.), *Andria*, 555.
2. *Shakespeare says . . . the roughest day.* Altered from *Macbeth*, I, iii, 147–8: '. . . Time and the hour run . . .'.

L183 1. *The stake he has in his country, and his reversions.* The local political influence he has, and the property he expects to inherit on the deaths of relatives.

L190 1. *to return evil for good.* '. . . render . . .': 1 Samuel 25:21.
2. *my old friend Wycherl[e]y.* William Wycherley (?1640–1716), Restoration comedy writer, wit and poet.

L191 1. *It is resistance that inflames desire . . . to make possession hard.* The Emperor's reply to Indamora (see L169 *n* 1) in Dryden's *Aureng-Zebe*, II, i.
2. *it is in Josephus . . . he reigned in his place.* Hazael 'spread a wet cloth in the nature of a net over [Benhadad], and strangled him; and took his dominion.' Josephus (see Glossary), *Antiquities of the Jews*, IX. iv. 92; trans. W. Whiston (1737); also trans. Sir Roger L'Estrange (1706; reprinted 1725).

L192 1. *the royal cully of France . . . was Maintenoned into it . . .* In *c.* 1683 Louis XIV secretly married, as his second wife, Françoise d'Aubigné (1635–1719), who had been his mistress and whom he had made Marquise de Maintenon (1675).

L193 1. *of Montaigne's taste . . . a glory to subdue a girl of family.* 'I have not much been given to mercenary and common acquaintances. I have coveted to set an edge on that sensual pleasure by difficulty, by desire, and for some glory. And liked Tiberius his fashions, who in his amours was swayed as much by modesty and nobleness as by any other quality . . .' Montaigne (1533–92), *Essays*, trans. John Florio (1603 etc.), III, iii, 'Of Three Commerces or Societies' (Everyman (1910), ii, 47): suggested by John Carroll.

L194 1. *Venice Preserved . . . as a benefit play.* Thomas Otway, *Venice Preserved, or, A Plot Discovered. A Tragedy* (1682), advertised as a performance for the benefit of one or more of the players or someone connected with the theatre.

L195 1. *[whatever it be].* Alteration from [C3], which also adds a reference back to p. 608; [C1] reads 'with Mrs Townsend', who is not named by Anna Howe until L196.

L197 1. *far fetched and dear-bought . . . is a proverb.* 'Dear bought and far fetched are dainties for ladies'; proverbial since *c.* 1350 (*ODEP³*, 173).

L198 1. *come in for her snack.* Get her share.
2. *St James's Church.* A fashionable church on the south side of Piccadilly, built in 1684 by Wren; Samuel Clarke (1675–1729), the philosopher and controversialist, was the rector.
3. *throw out my handkerchief.* The Grand Signior (Sultan of Turkey) chose his sleeping partner from the ladies of the harem by throwing a handkerchief to the 'lucky woman'.

L202 1. *An unseen hand . . . For destiny plays us all.* Slightly altered ('our' for 'their') from Abraham Cowley's pindaric ode on 'Destiny', ii, 11–15.

L203 1. *Malmsey . . . Cyprus . . . the generous products of the Cape.* Strong sweet wines.

L206 1. *St Stephen's Chapel.* In the ancient royal palace of Westminster, the chamber where the House of Commons met, which gave the system of two facing blocks of benches.
2. *two or three boroughs . . . I had rather you were for the shire.* Lovelace's family's political influence allows them to nominate borough Members of Parliament, and even (more prestigiously) one of the two county M.P.s, though that would be more problematical.
3. *a courtier . . . a malcontent.* i.e. neither a supporter of the government in

expectation of office, nor an extreme member of the opposition despising all perquisites.

4. *Archibald Hutcheson . . . Mr Secretary Craggs.* Hutcheson, London barrister and amateur economist, two of whose anti-Walpole pamphlets were printed by SR, was an independent Tory M.P. for the government borough of Hastings (1713–22), and a harrier of the ruined South Sea Company. James Craggs (1686–1721) was Secretary for State for the Southern Department from 1719 until he died of smallpox at the height of the South Sea crisis.

L207   1. *Waller says, Women are born to be controlled.* Edmund Waller (1606–87): 'For women (born to be controlled) / Stoop to the forward and the bold', *Of Love*, 13–14.

L209   1. *Henceforth, oh watchful fair one . . . bring thee to it.* Shakespeare, *Troilus and Cressida*, IV, v, 233–40 and 260–62 (adapted).

L210   1. *the Upper Flask.* A tavern near the top of Hampstead Hill; the Flask was an inn near the bottom.

L211   1. *Cocoa Tree.* See L48 n 1.

L214   1. *The falling out of lovers . . .* 'is the beginning of love': Terence, *Andria* (see L175 n 1), 555; proverbial in English since c. 1530 (*ODEP³*, 242).

L217.3 1. *lines translated from Juvenal . . . celestial sense.* Juvenal, *Satire XV*, 131–47: Nahum Tate (1652–1715) contributed the translation of XV to *The Satires of . . . Juvenalis by Mr Dryden and several other eminent Hands* (1693).

L218   1. *are we not told that in being well deceived consists the whole of human happiness.* 'For, if we take an examination of what is generally understood by *happiness*, as it has respect either to the understanding or the senses, we shall find all its properties and adjuncts will herd under this short definition: that it is a perpetual possession of being well deceived.' Swift, *A Tale of a Tub* (1704), Section IX, 'A Digression concerning . . . Madness . . .'.

L219   1. *Doctors' Commons . . . a licence.* The College of Doctors of Civil Law in St Paul's Churchyard, who practised in the ecclesiastical courts, dealing with marriage, divorce etc.; abolished in 1857.
2. *women have no souls . . .* Lovelace's remark is a misinterpretation of Talmudic law (see e.g. A. Steinsaltz, *The Essential Talmud*, trans. C. Galai (N.Y., 1976), pp. 137 ff.). The notion is old; cf. Lewis Wager, *The Repentance of Mary Magdalen* (1566). 'Jew' was altered to 'Turk' in [C3].
3. *there is no sex in ethereals.* Jesus said that angels do not marry (e.g. Matthew 22:30).

L220   1. *the pious task continued for one month, and no more.* The propriety of mothers suckling their own children was a question that exercised SR. He added a footnote to this passage referring the reader to *Pamela, Part the Second* (1741), Letter xlv, where this matter, disputed by Mr B. (against) and Pamela (for), is discussed; as it is further in Letters xlvi and xlvii.

L221   1. *these lines of Shakespeare . . . Begin to water. Julius Caesar*, III, i, 282.
2. *a white sheet.* The garb of a public penitent, especially a fornicator.

L222   1. *Cowley . . . had defined it . . . where the reader must.* Abraham Cowley, 'Ode of Wit', *Miscellanies* (1656).
2. *Wit, like a luxuriant vine . . . on the ground.* Cowley, 'On the Death of Mrs Philips', *Occasional Verses* (1668).
    3. *Devils believe and tremble.* 'Thou believest that there is one God; thou doest well: the devils also believe and tremble'. James 2:19.

L225   1. *the simple history of Dorastus and Faunia.* Robert Greene's prose romance *Pandosto: the Triumph of Time* (1588), one of the sources of Shakespeare's *Winter's Tale*, was thereafter frequently reprinted under its running title *The History of*

Dorastus and Faunia, or, The Royal Shepherdess, and in broadside versions.
2. *Bowing, I kneel'd ... ev'ry burning sinew ach'd with bliss.* Untraced.

L228 1. *substantial food ... other angels. '... manna ... the corn of heaven ... angel's food ...'.* Psalms 78:24, 25.
2. *'Tis nobler like a lion ... throws out the scraps of love.* From *Valentinian. A Tragedy* as *'tis altered by the late Earl of Rochester* (1685), IV, ii.
3. *She reigns more fully ... new-discover'd beauties.* Nathaniel Lee, *Caesar Borgia, Son of Pope Alexander the Sixth. A Tragedy* (1679), II, i.

L229 1. *with such a love as Herod loved his Mariamne.* Herod the Great (73 B.C.–4 B.C.), King of Judea, had killed Mariamne's father and brother to marry her, one of the most beautiful and accomplished of women. He had her, and his two sons by her, killed also, because he suspected her as descended from the former royal house; but after her death he used to rave for his Mariamne (Josephus, *Antiquities of the Jews*, XV. iv and x; Addison, *Spectator* (1711), No. 171). Elijah Fenton (1683–1730) wrote *Mariamne. A Tragedy* (1723).
2. *Nor was Nick Rowe ever half so diligent to learn Spanish.* '[Rowe] afterwards applied to the Earl of Oxford for some public employment. Oxford enjoined him to study Spanish, and when, some time afterwards, he came again, and said he had mastered it, dismissed him with this congratulation, "Then, Sir, I envy you the pleasure of reading *Don Quixote* in the original" ' (Johnson, *Lives of the Poets*, 1779–81).

L231 1. *I have sent for a Blunt's chariot.* Thomas Blount (or Blunt), FRS (*fl.* 1668), invented a carriage with improved suspension and action, 'for the ease of both man and horse'. Pepys went to see it.
2. *Hudibras ... admire the sleight of hand.* Butler, *Hudibras, Part First*, III, 1–6.
3. *The rosy-finger'd morn ... a glorious day.* Dryden, *Albion and Albianus. An Opera* (1685), II.

L232 1. *the great Macedonian.* Alexander the Great.

L233 1. *I started up ... Ithuriel's spear.* Milton, *Paradise Lost*, IV, 812.

L235 1. *Shakespeare advises well: Oppose not ... the naked ford.* Not from Shakespeare as in Bysshe, *Art of English Poetry* (1710), s.v. 'Rage', but from the rearrangement of Shakespeare's play by Dryden, *Troilus and Cressida, or, Truth Found too Late* (1679), V, ii.

L237 1. *Hudibras's metaphysicians ... metaphysic wit can fly.* Butler, *Hudibras, Part First*, I. 149–50.

L238 1. *the condition of David's sow.* 'As drunk as David's sow': proverbial since 1652 (*ODEP*³, 206).

L241 1. *The post, general and penny.* The private penny post service operated in and near London.

L243 1. *Hercules-like ... I could tear in pieces.* The vengeful Nessus gave Deianira, Hercules' wife, a shirt which unknown to her was poisoned. She gave it to Hercules as she thought to regain his love. In agony, he threw himself on a funeral pyre.

L246 1. *Mandeville's rule, That private vices are public benefits.* Bernard Mandeville (1670–1733), a cynical Dutch physician resident in London, wrote a complex, stylishly paradoxical work (a poem with added prose essays), *The Fable of the Bees, or, Private Vices Public Benefits* (1714; enlarged 1723); *Part II*, (1729). Mandeville's paradox was often (wilfully) misread. He was universally attacked by contemporary churchmen, but was not (or said he was not) advocating a vicious life.

L251 1. *at the sign of the Castle.* The Castle Inn on Hampstead Heath.
2. *the Tombs.* In Westminster Abbey; part of the London tourist attractions.

L252.1   1. *did not discover his foot before.* 'The Devil is known by his (cloven) foot';
proverbial from *c.* 1600 (*ODEP*³, 182).
2. *Phalaris . . . artist.* Perillus invented the brazen bull for Phalaris, tyrant of Acragas
in Sicily (6th century B.C.), to roast his victims, and was himself the test victim.

L254   1. *Lycurgus's institutions.* By tradition, the ancient constitution of Sparta (8th or 9th
century B.C.).
2. *annual Parliaments.* Parliaments elected each year, a long-standing demand of
opponents of royal and (especially) ministerial power.

L259   1. *the skull of king Philip and that of another man.* Untraced.
2. *Matt Prior's two lines . . . but not today.* 'Dear Robert quoth the Saint [St John,
Lord Bolingbroke] . . . / Let this be wrought, which Mat. doth say: / Yea, quoth the
Erle [of Oxford]; but not today.' Matthew Prior (1664–1721), *Erle Robert's Mice*
(1712; and in collections of his poems). He is asking for the sinecure post of Teller
of the Exchequer as a hedge against political misfortune; in 1699, the Auditorship
had been taken in this way by Charles, Lord Halifax.

L260   1. *their English treaty.* The English government used the Catalans to fight their
battles in Spain, during the War of the Spanish Succession, in return guaranteeing
separatist constitutional rights; but by the Peace of Utrecht in 1713, they abandoned
them to the oppression of France and Spain.

L261   1. *Paper X.* The following scraps of verse that Clarissa's delirium has assembled
from her recollection have been identified:
Lead me, where my own thoughts . . . appease thee. Otway, *Venice Preserved*, IV,
213–16.
Death only can be dreadful . . . a friend. Dryden and Lee, *Oedipus*, III, i, 74–7.
Oh! you have done an act . . . a blister there. *Hamlet*, III, iv, 40–44.
Then down I laid my head . . . destin'd is to mourn [burn]. Abraham Cowley, *The
Mistress*, 'The Despair', 25–33.
Oh my Miss Howe! . . . the pangs of my affliction. Otway, *Venice Preserved*, IV,
406–10.
When honour's lost . . . from infamy. Samuel Garth, *The Dispensary* (1699 . . . 1706
etc.), *ad fin.*
I could a tale . . . thy soul. *Hamlet*, I, v, 15.
For life can never be sincerely . . . the Best. Dryden, *Absalom and Achitophel. Part
I*, 43–4.
2. *A less complicated villainy cost a Tarquin.* According to Roman legend, Sextus,
son of King Tarquinius Superbus (*c.* 500 B.C.), violated Lucretia, wife of Tarquinius
Collatinus, as she slept. She committed suicide and the Tarquins were expelled from
Rome, which became a republic.

L263   1. *Lucretia-like vengeance.* See L261 *n* 2.

L264   1. *Horace, as translated by Cowley . . . He must find Quiet too.* 'Odi profanum
vulgus', *Odes*, Book II, i; in Abraham Cowley's *Several Discourses by way of Essays
in Verse and Prose*, 'Of Greatness'.

L266   1. *the old dismal thirtieth of January strain.* The anniversary of the execution of
Charles I in 1649, in the Anglican church a day of fasting, humiliation and
commemorative sermons.
2. *a dead psalm melody.* The customary psalm sung at the gallows before a hanging.

L267   1. *the host's tale in Ariosto . . . the sex. Orlando Furioso*, Canto XXVIII, Stanzas
1–64: Jocundo and King Astolfo share Fiametta in an anti-female *fabliau* that shows
all women to be complaisant.

L272   1. *Glanville . . . Baxter . . . The Royal Insignificant.* Joseph Glanvill, FRS (1636–80),
Saducismus Triumphatus (1681), attempting a 'scientific' proof of witchcraft; Richard
Baxter (1615–91), theologian and controversialist, *The Certainty of the Worlds of
Spirits* (1691); James VI of Scotland and I of England (1566–1625), *Daemonologie*
(1597).

L277 1. *an Heraclitus to the family . . . a Democritus among my private friends.* Heraclitus of Ephesus (*c.* 500 B.C.), the 'weeping philospher'; Democritus of Abdera (*c.* 400 B.C.), the 'laughing philosopher'.

L287 1. *the canonical hour at church.* The prescribed hours, usually 8 a.m. to 3 p.m., within which marriages may legally be performed.

L289 1. *Monmouth Street.* A street west of Covent Garden, near Seven Dials, where new and second-hand clothes shops were located; cf. 'And cut out clothes for all the Town; / And sent them out to Monmouth Street' (Matthew Prior, *Alma*, or, *The Progress of the Mind*, in *Poems on Several Occasions* (1718), Canto I, para. 17).

L294 1. *laudanum and wet cloth.* See L191 *n* 2.
2. *honest White Kennet.* The Rev. White Kennett (1660–1728), Bishop of Peterborough, *The History of England from the Commencement of the Reign of Charles I to the end of the Reign of William II*, in a booksellers' collaborative *Complete History of England . . .*, iii (1706; reprinted 1719), p. 417.

L296 1. *Evil communication*[*s*] . . . 'corrupt good manners'. 1 Corinthians 15:33.

L309 1. *faithful are the wounds of a friend* . . . 'but the kisses of an enemy deceitful'. Proverbs 27:5.

L313 1. *Taylor's Holy Living and Dying.* Jeremy Taylor (1613–67), Bishop of Down and Connor, *The Rule and Exercises of Holy Living* (1650), . . . *of Holy Dying* (1651); usually bound together after 1658; became one of the standard works of religious meditation in English.

L321 1. *the Italian eunuchs.* Male falsettists, used in the fashionable Italian opera of the seventeenth and eighteenth centuries. The voice could be produced by castration.

L322 1. *narrate . . . the Scottish phrase.* A Scottish law term, to set out the facts in a legal document, the *narration*.

L323 1. *Laudanum and wet cloth . . . long ago.* See L191 *n* 2.

L325 1. *Philomela . . . her barbarous Tereus.* Pandion, King of Athens, had two daughters, Procne and Philomela. The former was married to his ally, Tereus, King of Thrace. Tereus pretended that Procne had died; he asked for Philomela, and when she arrived, seduced or raped her, then cut out her tongue. She wove her story in an embroidery and sent it to her sister, who paid Tereus back by serving him the flesh of their child, Itys. When he realized this, he chased the sister with an axe, but at that moment the gods turned him into a hoopoe, Procne into a swallow, and Philomela into a nightingale (Ovid, *Metamorphoses*, vi, 424 ff. '. . . Lean'd her breast up-till a thorn . . . / *Fie, fie, fie!* now would she cry; / Tereu, tereu! by and by.' Richard Bamfield (1574–1627), 'Philomel'.

L326 1. *the true father of a certain monarque.* Said to be a chamberlain to Anne of Austria, wife of Louis XIII and mother of Louis XIV; he is also one of the candidates for 'the man in the Iron Mask'.

L333 1. *tongue was ready to cleave . . . her mouth.* Psalms 137:6.
2. *doubled down the useful places, as honest Matt Prior says.* 'He bought her Sermons, Psalms, and Graces; / And doubled down the useful places.' Matthew Prior, 'Hans Carvel', 51–2, in *Poems on Several Occasions* (1718).
3. *an Old Bailey forecast.* A threat of prosecution for murder at the Old Bailey if Clarissa died.

L336 1. *Otway's apothecary . . . nor the world's law.* Adapted from Thomas Otway, *The History and Fall of Caius Marius. A Tragedy* (1680), V, 277 . . . 302; cf. Shakespeare, *Romeo and Juliet*, IV, i, 40 . . . 73.

L341 1. *the help of the post-office bullet.* Letters were opened as a matter of course in the Post Office by government order.

L344 1. *the noble Sarmatians . . . Novogrod . . . whip in his hand.* Cf. Herodotus IV, 1–4, on the Scythians.

L346 1. *Swift's Digressions in Praise of Digressions.* Specifically, Section VII of *A Tale of a Tub* (1704).

2. *Prior's Alma . . . the English custom.* Matthew Prior, *Alma, or, The Progress of the Mind*, Canto II, para. 29: 'Turn we this globe and let us see, / How diff'rent nations disagree, / In what we wear, or eat and drink . . .'.

3. *a descendant of old Chancellor More, I believe.* Sir Thomas More (1478–1535), Lord Chancellor, executed by Henry VIII (and now canonized): 'See me safe up [on to the scaffold]; for my coming down I can shift for myself.'

L350 1. *what Mr Addison says of liberty . . . pleasure to the day.* 'A Letter from Italy to the Rt. Hon. Charles, Lord Halifax. In the year 1701', para. 13, in *Remarks on Several Parts of Italy* (1715; 1718).

L359 1. *sweet singer of Israel . . . rivers of oil.* 2. Samuel 1:26: David says 'thy [Jonathan's] love to me was wonderful, passing the love of women' . . . Job 29:2–6. Italicizations in the text mark changes.

2. *the words of Job . . . house appointed for all living.* Job 30:23.

L364 1. *the poet says of unfeigned affection . . . speaks most plain.* Dryden, *Troilus and Cressida, or, Truth Found too Late* (1679), III, ii.

2. *meditation . . . extracted by the lady from the Scriptures.* The meditation following is made up of Job 6:2–4; 7:4–7; 3:20, 21, 23, 25, 26; 19:23, 24.

3. *the two sages of antiquity, to laugh and to weep.* Democritus and Heraclitus (see L299 *n* 1).

4. *The Sacred Classics, written by one Blackwall.* Anthony Blackwall (1674–1730), *The Sacred Classics defended and illustrated*, in two parts (1725–31).

L365 1. *time . . . give increase to hers.* William Congreve, *The Mourning Bride* (1697), I, i: '*Leonora*: . . . grant that time may bring her some relief. *Almeiria*: O no, time gives increase to my afflictions . . .'.

L366 1. *the Lebeck's Head in Chandos Street.* Le Beck was a celebrated cook who had a picture of himself as a sign to his house. The sign continued as an inn.

L367 1. *the generality of ladies were rakes in their hearts.* See L115 *n* 2.

L370 1. *trusty Trojan.* The Trojans were (in Homer and Virgil) truthful, brave, loyal; cf. 'he worked like a Trojan'.

2. *Anchises . . . the Ilion bonfire . . . Creüsa.* Aeneas bore his aged father, Anchises, from Troy (Ilium) as it was burned by the Greeks, leaving his wife behind.

3. *maiden queen . . . sister-queen . . . a succession four deep.* Queen Elizabeth of England . . . Mary Queen of Scots . . . James VI and I, Charles I, Charles II and James VII and II.

4. *Time . . . afflictions.* See L365 *n* 1.

5. *one of the former . . . a dead dog.* George Whitefield (1714–70): E K, 553, quoting an anachronistic note by SR: either 1 Samuel 24:14 (David) or 2 Samuel 9:8 (Mephibosheth).

6. *rose-bound beaver.* The ecclesiastical shovel-hat, in which the broad brim was pulled up at each side by a string attached to the crown by a rosette.

7. *Dryden's Alexander's Feast.* Published 1697.

8. *Sir Richard . . . Addison's Cato . . . laws to my little senate.* Sir Richard Steele (1672–1729) . . . Pope, Prologue to Addison's *Cato. A Tragedy* (1713), 23: 'while Cato gives his little senate laws'.

L371 1. *The poet says well . . . and stand aghast.* Rowe, *The Fair Penitent. A Tragedy* (1703), V.

2. *the old man in the fable with his bundle of sticks.* 'Divided, men are vulnerable; it is union that makes them strong.' *Fables of Aesop*, trans. S. A. Handford (Penguin, 1964 etc.), 177

3. *Shakespeare . . . we fear of death. Measure for Measure*, III, i, 118 ff.

L379 1. *If I justify myself . . . perverse.* Job 9:20 ('heart' for 'mouth').

2. *as he did, who says . . . iniquity in my bosom.* Adapted from Job 31:35, 36, 34.

L389 1. *he hath overwhelmed . . . his friend.* Job 6:27.

L396 1. *the relish of salvation in it, as Shakespeare says.* *Hamlet*, III, iii, 92.

L413 1. *Monimia . . . Theodosius.* SR lists several of the Restoration tragedies, staples of
the eighteenth-century stage, which he has frequently made Lovelace quote: e.g.
Thomas Otway, *The Orphan, or, The Unhappy Marriage* (1680) and *Venice
Preserved, or, A Plot Discovered* (1682); Nathaniel Lee, *Theodosius, or, The Force
of Love* (1680).
2. *Nick Rowe . . . a fitter title.* Nicholas Rowe (1674–1718), *The Fair Penitent* (1703).
3. *a whining Tom Essence. Tom Essence. A Comedy* was printed in 1677; on the
evidence of Walpole's *Anecdotes*, it is assigned to Thomas Rawlins (d. 1670).
4. *Meditation.* Another collection of texts from the Book of Job, 19:2, 4; 6:14 etc.

L416 1. *Tenderly kneeling . . . her soft'ning eyes.* Untraced.
2. *White's.* A fashionable chocolate house in St James's Street.
3. *Pultowa.* The battle at which, in 1709, Charles XII of Sweden was routed by the
army of Peter the Great.

L417 1. *a hole . . . of Elden.* A deep pot-hole in the limestone Peak District of Derbyshire.
2. *That I do love her . . . fears to die.* Nathaniel Lee, *Mithridates, King of Pontus. A
Tragedy* (1678), I, ii.

L418 1. *On being hunted after . . .* This meditation is almost completely made up of verses
from the Book of Psalms (some adapted).

L419 1. *Give sorrow words . . . bids it break. Macbeth,* IV, iii, 209.
2. *as Juvenal says, Tears . . . manhood.* See L217.3 *n* 1.
3. *many a man . . . going up Holborn Hill.* Cf. 'He will ride (backward) up Holborn
Hill'; proverbial from 1592 (*ODEP³*, 672); i.e. he will ride in a cart in the ritual
procession from Newgate to be hanged on Tyburn Tree, near the present Marble
Arch.
4. *Oh that I less could fear . . . faster melts away.* Dryden, *All for Love, or, The World
well Lost* (1678), V, 131–4.
5. *When the sun sets . . . our imagination's weight.* Dryden and Lee, *Oedipus* (1679),
VI, i, 80–90.
6. *a poetical divine . . . darkness all behind.* John Norris (1657–1711), *A Collection
of Miscellanies: consisting of Poems, Essays, Discourses and Letters* (1687; 1692;
1730, 9th ed.), 'The Meditation'.
7. *[Mr Pomfret] in his Prospect of Death . . .* John Pomfret (1667–1702), *A Prospect
of Death* (1700; and *Poems*, often reprinted); erroneously attributed by SR in [CI]
to Lord Roscommon, hence 'the noble poet' below, never corrected.

L422 1. *Madam Maintenon . . . losses.* See L192 *n* 1.

L424 1. *as Ratcliffe said.* Dr John Radcliffe (the usual spelling; 1650–1714), a leading
physician to whose name were attracted many medical stories.
2. *Alas! he's gone . . . Ah! whither fled?* Untraced.

L442 1. *Chamont . . .* In Otway's tragedy *The Orphan, or, The Unhappy Marriage* (1680),
a 'soldier of fortune', brother of the tragic heroine, Monimia. His impetuosity
precipitates the death of his sister and the suicide of her lover, Castalio, who is
guiltless of harming her.

L444 1. *the poor limed soul . . . divine Quarles's.* Cf. 'Oh, limed soul, that struggling to be
free, / Art more ingaged.' Shakespeare, *Hamlet*, III, iii, 68); quoted Bysshe *sub*
'Repentance'. Francis Quarles (1592–1644) in his *Emblems* (1635) several times
represents the soul as an ensnared or caged bird, just as Lovelace represents (L170)
Clarissa at Mrs Sinclair's as 'the ensnared volatile', but I have not found 'limed' in
Quarles's verses, i.e. caught by fowlers' bird-lime.
2. *Mr Daniel de Foe . . . a chapel there.* 'Whenever God erects a House of Prayer, /

The Devil always builds a Chapel there: / And 'twill be found upon Examination, / The latter has the largest Congregation'. Defoe, *The True-Born Englishman, a Satire* (1701), 56–9; *ODEP*, 309.

3. *Juvenal . . . Nobilitas sola est . . . virtus.* Juvenal, *Satire VIII*, 20: 'Virtue remains the true and only nobility'.

4. *Uvaque conspecta livorem ducit ab uva.* Juvenal, *Satire II*, 81: 'One tainted grape blights another'.

5. *by the poet . . . forma petita ruit.* Untraced: 'You will keep the beautiful girl with difficulty. Her sought-for figure flees, pursued now by entreaties, now by gold.'

6. *that of Horace . . . vetitum nefas.* Horace, *Odes I*, iii, 25–6: 'Bold to endure everything, mankind rushes through forbidden wrong.'

7. *Ovid . . . Adulator nullus amicus erit.* 'A sycophant will never be a friend.' Does not seem to be Ovid.

L449   1. *Dame Elizabeth Carteret on her monument in Westminster Abbey.* The engaging late baroque, high-relief carving of Lady Elizabeth Carteret (1659–1717), widow of Sir Philip Carteret, is no longer to be seen in the Abbey. A drawing of it by G. Shepherd, engraved by T. Sutherland, is reproduced in William Combe, *The History of the Abbey Church of St Peter's, Westminster, its Antiquities and Monuments* published by Rudolph Ackerman (1812), ii; and is one of the interesting illustrations in M. A. Doody, *A Natural Passion: A Study of the Novels of Samuel Richardson*, (OUP, 1974), plate 3 (a), discussed on pp. 129–31.

L453   1. *as Prior says, What serious is, thou turn'st to farce.* 'What should be great you turn to farce:/I wish the Ladle in your A——'. *The Ladle* (1703), 139–40.

L458   1. *Howard . . . From death we rose . . . dying only pray.* Untraced.
        2. *in the earth.* Genesis 4:14.

L459   1. *the good King Hezekiah, you may have them prolonged.* 'Thus saith the Lord . . . I have heard thy [Hezekiah's] prayer . . . I will heal thee . . . And I will add unto thy days fifteen years'. 2 Kings 20:5, 6.

L463   1. *like Addison's Angel, direct, and even enjoy, the storm.* 'So when an angel by divine command / With rising tempests shakes a guilty land, / Such as of late o'er pale Britannia past, / Calm and serene he drives the furious blast; / And pleas'd th' Almighty's orders to perform, / Rides in the whirlwind, and directs the storm.' Joseph Addison, *The Campaign: A Poem to His Grace, the Duke of Marlborough* (1705).
        2. *whose mind . . . for all things fram'd.* Untraced.

L466   1. *bring the dog by his ears, like another Habakkuk.* 'Then the angel of the Lord took [Habbacuc] by the crown, and bare him by the hair of his head, and through the vehemency of his spirit set him in Babylon over the lions' den.' The History of the Destruction of Bel and the Dragon (Apocrypha), 36.

L474   1. *this was not post-day.* Tuesday, Thursday and Saturday were the days the postal services left London.

L480   1. *the Bohemia Head.* Probably the King of Bohemia's Head at Turnham Green.
        2. *like a man in straw.* Like one of the inmates of Bedlam, who slept in straw.

L481   1. *Oh death . . . where is thy sting!* 1 Corinthians 15:55.
        2. *It is good for me that I was afflicted.* Psalms 119:71.

L486   1. *The great Duke of Luxemburgh.* François Henri de Montmorency-Bouteville (1628–95), Duc de Luxembourg (1661), made Marshal of France by Louis XIV (1675); he several times defeated William III.

L490   1. *Vengeance is mine, and I will repay it.* Romans 12:19; Deuteronomy 32:35 etc.

L492   1. *There is no inquisition in the grave . . . the day of our birth.* Ecclesiasticus 41:4 and Ecclesiastes 7:1.

L496   1. *in Dryden's Palamon and Arcite*. 'Palamon and Arcite, or, The Knight's Tale', *Fables Ancient and Modern* (1700), i, 522–42.

L497   1. *She's out! The damp of death . . . shall open more.* Ziphanes in Nathaniel Lee, *Mithridates, King of Pontus* (1678), v, ii.

L499   1. *Virgil's obscene Harpies. Aeneid*, iii, 209 ff.: 'With virgin-faces, but with wombs obscene, / Foul paunches and with ordure still unclean: / With claws for hands and looks for ever lean' (Dryden's translation).

L503   1. *The following lines of Juvenal . . . veneris, aude.* 'If you wish to know about human behaviour a single [private] house has it all; spend a few days there, and on your return, complain of your own misery if you dare.' Juvenal, *Satire XIII*, 159–61. (This is a mis-reading of the text, however; *domus* refers to the police court of Rutulius Gallicus, the urban prefect.)

L504   1. *The cheerful giver, whom God is said to love . . .* 2 Corinthians 9:7.

L510.4   1. *The triumphing of the wicked is short . . . knoweth not God.* Job 20:5, 18:11, 12 etc.

L511   1. *with pitying eye . . . and wishest for me?* Untraced.
       2. *To be a dog . . . life as mine.* Rowe, *Tamerlane. A Tragedy* I, i, 294–5.

L512   1. *my good Astolfo . . . my wit-jar.* Ariosto, *Orlando Furioso*, Canto XXXIX, Stanza 7.

L513   1. *A fine strapping bona roba, in the Chartres taste.* A young whore to suit 'Colonel' Francis Chartres (or Charteris, 1675–1732), a rich debauchee whose conviction for the rape of a teenager and subsequent pardon, notoriously at the behest of Walpole, became a political issue in 1730.

L515   1. *by the dagger, as Lucretia did.* See L261 n 2.

L516   1. *to be in the commission* [of the peace] *and one of the quorum.* One of the senior members of the bench of Justices of the Peace for a county, some of whom (quorum) had to be present to constitute a legal sitting.
       2. *Biddy.* The niece in Steele's comedy *The Tender Husband* (1705), II, ii.

L518   1. *An Earl of Shrewsbury . . . the hand of the ignoble duke.* 'The Duke of Buckingham and [Anna Marie Brudenel, Countess of Shrewsbury] remained for a long period both happy and perfectly contented . . . until Lord Shrewsbury, who never before had shown the least uneasiness at his lady's misconduct, thought proper to resent it' (Count Antony Hamilton, *Memoirs of the Count de Gramont*, trans. etc. by Horace Walpole . . . with additional notes by Sir Walter Scott and Mrs Jameson, n.d., p. 338). Shrewsbury was killed in a duel by George, second Duke of Buckingham, on 16 March 1667.

L530   1. [*sed*] *Timor et minae . . . sedet atra cura.* '[But] Fear and Threats mount to the same place as the owner does, nor does black Care leave the brass-bound galley and even sits behind the horseman.' Horace, *Odes*, Book III, i, 37–40.
       2. *Man makes his Fate . . . a nobler loom.* Dryden, *The Conquest of Granada by the Spaniards. A Tragedy, in two parts* (1670; 1671), *Part I*, II, i.
       3. *Let Fortune empty . . . know no conquerors.* Dryden, *Don Sebastian, King of Portugal. A Tragedy* (1689), I, i.
       4. *Electoral courts.* The courts of the German 'electors', princes and prince-bishops who nominally elected the Holy Roman Emperor: e.g. the Electors of Cologne and Mainz, and of course George II, who was also Elector of Hanover.

L533   1. *Bishop Burnet calls the delicacy of intrigue.* See L157.1 n 1.

L535   1. *For can . . . repine.* Untraced. Perhaps S R's own verses; they were docked after 'bliss—' in later editions.

·POSTSCRIPT 1. *Ac ne forte . . . when he will, and where.* Pope, *The First Epistle of the Second Book of Horace, Imitated* (1737), sub-titled 'To Augustus', 338–47; the passage from Horace forms lines 208–13 of the Roman poet's own *Epistle to Augustus*, which was printed on the facing pages of Pope's text.

2. *the altered King Lear of Mr Tate . . . and a manager*. Nahum Tate in *The History of King Lear* (acted 1680, printed 1681) adapted Shakespeare's play to the requirements of the Restoration tragic stage, with a much enlarged star part for Cordelia, and satisfied convention with the introduction of an attempted rape of her. His piece is attacked by Richardson for its 'happy ending'. Dr Johnson, however, asserted that 'the general suffrage' preferred Cordelia to retire 'with victory and felicity', and the adaptation held the stage for a century and a half . . . David Garrick (1717–79) took over the management of Drury Lane in 1747; he appeared fifty-nine times as Lear in Tate's version; in 1756 he launched his own adaptation which restored much of Shakespeare's writing, especially in Acts I–III, but kept Tate's rearranged plot.

3. *The Mourning Bride, Tamerlane, Ulysses, Phaedra and Hippolytus*. By, respectively, Congreve (first acted 1697); the next two by Nicholas Rowe (first acted 1701 and 1705); the last by Addison's friend Edmund Smith (first acted 1707).

4. *Rapin, on Aristotle's Poetics*. René Rapin (1621–87), S.J., *Réflexions sur la Poétique* (1673), translated by Thomas Rymer as *Reflections on Aristotle's Treatise of Poesie* (1674; and in *The Whole Critical Works of M. Rapin*, 1706, vol. 2; 3rd edition 1731).

GLOSSARY OF WORDS
AND PHRASES

Aaron's rod '. . . Aaron cast down his rod before Pharaoh, and before his servants and it
became a serpent . . . For [the magicians of Egypt] cast down every man his rod, and they
became serpents: but Aaron's rod swallowed their rods.' Exodus 7:10–12.

achievement-motto Heraldic motto.

alt (*in*) Excited, 'keyed up' (from music).

amuse Divert attention, cheat, deceive.

anchoret Original form of 'anchorite': a hermit.

animal organs Bodily parts (as distinct from mental faculties).

arrack An Eastern distilled spirit (from dates, rice, coconuts etc.).

awfully Causing dread.

bagnio (*lit.* a bath, bathhouse) A brothel.

bait (*n*. and *vb*) Rest for refreshment.

Barbados Cordial flavoured with orange and/or lemon peel.

battalia Battle array.

beaver Hat made from the fur of the beaver; worn by both sexes.

bestraught Distracted (distraught), frenzied.

biscake A kind of bread, as ship's biscuit.

Blackwell Hall In the City to the south of Guildhall; it housed a weekly market of the
closely controlled wholesale trade in woollen cloth.

blowzed off Dishevelled, frowzy.

brays Pounds, crushes to powder.

break squares Break order, cause mischief.

breathe a vein Open a vein for bleeding.

breviate Summary, brief statement, lawyer's brief.

bull's feather A horn, mark of cuckoldry.

buskin-airs In the tragic style; high-flown: from 'buskins', the characteristic footwear of
ancient tragic actors.

callus A thickened and toughened piece of skin.

camlet Light fabric woven of a mixture of fibres such as silk and wool (or goat's hair).

caput mortuum Death's head or skull; in alchemy the sign for what remains after distillation.

carry the county Win a (parliamentary) election; be popular.

cellula adiposa Fatty tissue.

cephalic draughts Medicines to relieve headaches or disorders of the head.

chair A sedan chair; a closed vehicle for one person, placed between two poles and carried
by two men, one before and one behind.

chairman One who carries a *chair* (*q.v.*).

chaise A light pleasure or travelling four-wheeled carriage for two or three passengers.

character(*s*) Writing in shorthand or cipher.

chariot Light four-wheeled carriage with a single back seat for two.

cheapens Bargains for, haggles.

class (*it*) (*vb*) Take position or rank with.

clouterly Clumsy, clownish; cf. Spenser's rustic, Colin Clout (rag, tatter).

coifs Close-fitting caps, covering the ears and back of the head, tying under the chin.

common (*on the*) Prostitution.

compassionate (*vb*) Sympathize with, feel pity for.

compulsory Coercive, enforcing.

conceit (*vb*) Imagine, fancy.

condition (*vb*) Bargain with.

confessionaire One who has made confession (to a priest).

conscious Well aware, inwardly sensible.

control, controlled Check(ed), contradict(ed).

corking-pins The largest size of pins.

counterscarp (in fortification) The outer slope or wall of the ditch.

country Native district; also the people living there.

cousin(s) Any collateral relative(s) more distant than a brother or sister; a kinsman or kinswoman (e.g. nephew or niece).

couteau Knife.

cropsick Disordered in the stomach (from poultry-keeping).

crow's-foot The wrinkle at the outer corner of the eye.

cully Dupe, gull

cunning woman 'Wise woman', witch, fortune-teller.

cupping (in medicine) Drawing blood by scarifying the skin and applying a heated 'cupping glass' above the wound, which forms a vacuum as it cools.

dark closet A walk-in cupboard without a window.

dea bona Bona Dea, a Roman (good) goddess, worshipped exclusively by women.

debellare superbos To vanquish the proud (Virgil, *Aeneid*, vi, 853).

debonair (*adj.*) Courteous, affable. (*n.*) Graciousness and courtesy of manner.

devoted Doomed.

Dii majores The six male and six female Roman deities who were called the *dii maiorum gentium* (gods of the greater peoples): Juno, Vesta, Minerva, Ceres, Diana, Venus, Mars, Mercurius, Jovi, Neptunus, Vulcanus, Apollo.

dishabille Undress, lounging or leisure garb.

disreputable Bringing into disrepute.

dressed Arrayed in full or formal dress.

Drexelius on Eternity Jeremiah Drexel (1581–1638), S.J., wrote many volumes of piety for
• the use of young people, embellished by emblematic engravings: his *De Considerationes Aeternitatis* (1620) was translated as *Considerations on Eternity* (1710) and reprinted several times during the eighteenth century.

drilled her on Enticed her, drew her on.

Eaton's Styptic Dr Eaton's 'balsamic styptic' was advertised as a remedy for vomiting, as well as for bleeding and haemorrhoids (e.g. *Daily Journal*, 1 September 1731).

economist One who runs a family, a steward.

economy Household (accounts).

elf A malignant being, a demon.

elogy Characterization, biographical summary (usually commendatory, therefore the word has been displaced by 'eulogy').

enthusiasts People who consider themselves inspired, visionaries.

epispastics (in medicine) Substances used to produce blisters.

equipage Everything necessary for a journey, or for setting up house; especially coach, horses and servants.

estray (in law) A tame beast found, having no known owner, which if not claimed within a year and a day falls to the lord of the manor.

evidenceship One who gives evidence; an evidence, i.e. a professional or dishonest witness.

ex mero motu By one's own free will; (in law) 'of [his] mere motion' indicates the royal will.

fact Action, deed.

femme sole (in law; as opposed to *femme couvert*) A woman who does not have the protection of a husband, i.e. a spinster, a widow, a single woman, who as to her property is independent.

figaries Corrupt form of 'vagaries': whims, eccentricities.

flapped one side of it (of a hat) To bring down part of the brim or edge to shade the face.

flowered lawn Fine linen resembling cambric, embellished with embroidered flowers or a flower-like pattern.

fluster Make tipsy.

forestall Intercept or buy up goods before they reach the public market so as to raise the price.

formed his party Organized his side.

Francis Spira *A relation of the fearful Estate of Francis Spira in the Year 1548* (1638; many later editions up to the nineteenth century), a polemical work attributed to Nathaniel Bacon, based on a narrative by 'Matthew Girbaldus [Mofa], a lawyer of Padua', detailing the miserable death of an apostate from Protestantism who repented too late.

French prophets Group of French refugees from Louis XIV's persecution of the Calvinist Camisards in the Cévennes, who brought to London visionary beliefs, including prophesying. The name was also applied to English adherents of the sect.

frost-piece A person of frigid disposition.

fucus Paint or cosmetic.

gallery green-box (in the theatre) Box above one of the proscenium doors, at the stage end of the middle gallery and with (private) access to the green-room.

gantlope A form of gauntlet; *to run the gauntlet*: a military punishment in which the culprit was stripped and made to pass between two lines of soldiers who struck him with cudgels.

Geddes's Tracts The Rev. Michael Geddes (?1650–1713), Anglican priest, published *Miscellaneous Tracts* (1702, 1705, 1706; 3rd edition 1730) and *Several Tracts against Popery* . . . (1715).

gin (from 'engine') A snare, net or trap to catch small birds or animals.

gives Mis-gives, alarms.

glout (*vb*) Scowl, frown, look sullen.

Gothamite Inhabitant of Gotham, a mythical village proverbial for its fools.

gradatim Step by step, gradually.

grand climacteric The most critical stage in human life, usually the sixty-third year.

gummed taffaty Taffeta (a fabric woven of some proportion of silk) stiffened with gum.

habit A lady's travelling or riding dress.

hanging-sleeve coat A child's garment with loose sleeves.

higgler, higgling Huckster; one who sells (particularly country produce) round the doors in town; this kind of dealing.

home put A home thrust, a blow that goes directly to the heart.

honoured in a cover Distinguished by having his name used in the direction (address) of a sealed letter.

hostler Ostler; a stableman, especially at an inn; one who looks after horses.

Houses of Convocation Each province of the Church of England (Canterbury and York) had a synod consisting of an Upper House (of bishops) and a Lower House (of representatives of the non-episcopal clergy). The meetings of these bodies had fallen into abeyance in 1717.

humanity Both the study of Latin (literature) and the cultivation of civilized behaviour.

humour Inclination, disposition.

hypped Affected with hypochondria, morbidly depressed.

ignis fatuus A phosphorescent light flitting over a marsh (will o' the wisp); figuratively, a delusive light.

In Coelo Salus or Quies In Heaven, Safety (or Repose).

in petto (Italian, from Latin *in pectore*, in the bosom) Something reserved, kept back, not made public.

Inett's Devotions Probably *A Guide to the Devout Christian* (1688; 14th edition, 1741; later reprintings) by Dr John Inett (1647–1718). This popular devotional handbook is in three parts, of which Part I is 'Devotional Calendars'.

ingenuity Ingenuousness.

jet (*of the business*) The heart (or gist) of the matter.

joint-stool A stool made by parts jointed together, i.e. by a joiner; not a crude construction.

jointure Property held jointly by husband and wife, hence property reserved on the death of the husband for the wife's support.

jolter-headed Clumsy or heavy-headed.

Josephus Flavius Josephus (37–*c.* 100 A.D.), Jewish priest and Pharisee, author (in Greek) of a pro-Roman *History of the Jewish Wars* (from 170 B.C. to A.D. 80) and *Antiquities of the Jews* (from the Creation to A.D. 66).

julap Julep: a pleasant-tasting liquid medicine.

kemboed Akimbo: each hand on each hip.

kerb-bridle Curb-bridle: a strap or chain running under the lower jaw, linking the two upper branches of the bit, to restrain an unruly horse.

Lady Easy In Colley Cibber's comedy, *The Careless Husband*: see L155 n 1.

leading-strings 'Reins' used to restrain and support children learning to walk.

Lords-zounter ? Lord's wounds; cf. *zounds*.

lozenge (in heraldry) A diamond-shaped frame in which the arms of a spinster or a widow are emblazoned.

lustring A glossy silk fabric.

make a stoop (of a hawk on the wing) Drop violently to make a kill.

manes The spirit or shade of a departed person, to be revered.

medium Compromise, middle course.

megrims Vapours (*q.v.*), low spirits; cf. 'migraines'.

melilot The dried flowers of the *Yellow Melilot*, used in medicine to make plasters and poultices.

men in straw. Madmen (from the furnishing of Bedlam).

mended her markets Improved her bargaining position.

mercer A dealer in (usually costly) fabrics, silks etc., but sometimes a more general dealer.

meum and tuum Mine and thine (i.e. property rights).

minores Lesser.

miserum est aliena vivere quadra It is wretched to live at another's table (as a dependant).

mob(s) Close-fitting cap(s) worn by ladies at night, or in dishabille (*q.v.*)

modus Means, expedient, course of action.

Monument The fluted Roman Doric column, 202 ft high, erected 1671–7 in Fish Street Hill from a design by Sir Christopher Wren, to commemorate the Great Fire of London which broke out nearby.

Mulciber The 'softener', i.e. smelter; epithet applied to Vulcan, god of fire and smiths.

mundified Cleansed, purified.

Neapolitan saint St Januarius (d. *c.* 305), whose blood is carried in a glass phial in a cathedral procession on certain occasions and liquefies on the high altar.

Nelson's Feasts and Fasts Robert Nelson (1656–1715), *A Companion to Festivals and Fasts of the Church of England: with Collects and Prayers for each Solemnity* (1704; 16th edition by 1736), a popular manual of Anglican piety.

Niobe Wife of Amphion, king of Thebes. Apollo and Diana slew her beautiful children, of whom she was inordinately fond. She was changed to stone through grief, and continued to weep.

noless soless Nolens volens; willing or unwilling; willy-nilly.

Norris's Miscellanies The Rev. John Norris (1657–1711), a prolific writer, mystic and neoplatonist, *A Collection of Miscellanies, consisting of Poems, Essays, Discourses and Letters* (1687; 5th edition, revised, 1710; several times reprinted in the eighteenth century).

noverint universi Let all men know (the opening formula of some legal writs).

occasionally For some particular occasions.

Oons Wounds, i.e. God's wounds; cf. *Zounds*.

pad-nag (*it*) (*no*) An easy-going horse; (*vb*) amble, pussy-foot.

padusoy A strong, corded, grosgrain silk, used by both men and women for coats etc.

painful Painstaking, assiduous, diligent.

peculiars The group of (Clarissa's) intimates; perhaps from 'God's peculiar people', i.e. the Jews.

peery Fond of peering, inquisitive.

penny-rents Rents paid (or received) in money; hence, cash income.

pervicacious Obstinate, headstrong, wilful.

pervicacy Obstinacy, stubbornness.

petit-maîtres Effeminate men; fops, coxcombs.

phaeton A light, four-wheeled, open carriage with a back seat for one (or two), usually drawn by a pair of horses.

philosophy of temper Settled conduct of resignation; calmness.

phyllirea hedge (i.e. *phillyrea*) Mock-privet or jasmine-box; an evergreen hedging and wall plant with small greenish-white flowers.

pickeroon (i.e. picaroon) A thief, rogue, brigand.

piddle Toy with (food).

pieball (i.e. 'piebald') Of two different colours.

pinners Long flaps pinned to the sides of ladies' caps; see *mobs* and *coifs*.

pip A disease of poultry.

pius (Latin; SR incorrectly takes it to mean 'pious') One who acts according to duty, especially performing what the gods or parents require.

play (me) booty To act falsely (against me) for gain.

plumb man One who has £100,000 (a *plumb* or *plum*).

pockets Ladies wore two pockets, separate from and under their skirts, fixed to a tape tied round the waist.

pock-fretten The skin pitted with pock-marks.

podagra-man One who has gout in the foot.

Portugal six-and-thirty A coin worth thirty-six shillings, a double gold *escudo*, half the standard gold *dobra*.

posse (i.e. *posse comitatus*) The force which the sheriff of the county has the right to raise in pursuit of a malefactor.

post (vb) Ride or travel as fast as possible by changing horses at the 'post-houses', every twenty miles or so.

postponed Subordinated, relegated.

postulata Requirements, stipulations.

powdered beef Salted or cured (corned) beef.

Practice of Piety Lewis Bayly (1565–1613), Bishop of Bangor, *The Practice of Piety* (1613; 59th edition 1735), which rivalled *The Whole Duty of Man* as a religious handbook stressing the danger of damnation, the joys of salvation and the near approach of death.

pragmatical motives Conceited, self-important motives.

presently Immediately.

press-bed A bed set into an alcove, sometimes shut off by doors.

pretence(s) Claim(s).

pretend Claim.

pretender Claimant.

prevent Forestall.

proctor Legal agent, esp. in ecclesiastical courts.

puisne Lesser, insignificant; cf. 'puny'.

puss A hare; also applied to a girl or woman, denoting slyness.

put Push, shove; or perhaps throw (in a game).

rappee (i.e. rasped) A coarse dark snuff.

re infecta Without accomplishing the matter.

reach Try to vomit; retch.

receipt Recipe.

regimen A diet.

reins The seat of the feelings, emotions.

resentment(s) Feelings in general, as well as the modern sense of injury.

robings Trimmings on a lady's dress.

rock-water Clear, cold, spring water.

roup-cloaking chicken A complaining chicken suffering from a contagious disease known as roup.

rumpled my gorget Disarranged my neck-dress; i.e. upset.

sacque A loose gown worn by ladies.

saddling Putting on (equipment, e.g. spectacles).

salivation The treatment of veneral disease by compounds of mercury, which stimulated the flow of saliva.

salvo A bad excuse, an evasion, a quibble.

sap (by the) In besieging, by tunnelling or constructing a covered trench; i.e. slow, sure, secret.

sash-door A door with a sash-window in the upper half.

scandalum magnatum 'Scandal of magnates'; libel of, or attack on, those in authority, e.g. peers, grandees.

scarificators (in medicine) Agents for scarifying, i.e. lacerating the skin by making multiple incisions.

score (n. and vb) Record, account (of debt).

Scots snuff A 'dry snuff'; i.e. ground after fermentation of the stalks.

seelie Foolish, simple (silly).

se'nnight Seven-night, a week; cf. fortnight (fourteen-night), two weeks.

sensible Sensitive, having delicate feelings.

sentences Sententious remarks.

set (n.) A team of (normally six) matched horses to draw a carriage (an important status symbol).

set (vb) Indicate (point) game in hunting, e.g. by dogs (setters or pointers).

shreeve Sheriff.

sikeing Sighing or sobbing.

snack Share, portion.

sole See *femme sole*.

somnivolences Intended soporifics. The *OED* gives this (in common with several of Lovelace's words) as the earliest printed use.

souse upon Swindle, impose upon; or swoop on, pounce on.

sprindges (old form of 'springes') Snares for catching small birds.

stagger Wander, be in doubt.

Stanhope's Gospels George Stanhope (1660–1728), D.D., Dean of Canterbury, *A Paraphrase and Comment upon the Epistles and Gospels appointed to be used by the Church of England on all Sundays and Holy-Days throughout the Year*, 4 vols. (1705–8; often reprinted during the eighteenth century).

statu quo prius In the former situation.

stews Brothels.

stived Stifled, shut up in a closed place.

stomach (is down) Pride or obstinacy (is reduced).

story History.

stuff-damask A woollen cloth, figured or embroidered as if a more expensive material.

stylum veterum Old-fashioned expression.

tabret A small tabor or tambourine.

T'Antony, Tantony. Shortened version of St Antony.

telling Counting.

temper Temperament.

Temple Stairs At the river end of Middle Temple Lane, which ran south from Fleet Street at Temple Bar to the Thames, for the convenience of boat users.

tenant-courtesy Agreement not to exercise the power of taking over the land which the tenant may have when the landowner borrows from him against future rent payment.

tiddle Potter, fuss over.

toilette The articles for a lady's dressing; the table on which they stood; the process of dressing; the dress ensemble itself.

tostications (originally 'intoxication') Perplexities, distractions.

trusses (of a bird of prey) Seizes its quarry in its talons and carries it off.

trusty Trojan A boon companion, merry fellow.

turkey-worked Turkish (or Turkish-style) tapestry work.

umbrage Shade.

unmortified Not spiritually subdued (i.e. in the consciousness of approaching death).

unmortised Coming apart at the joints.

vapours A morbid state supposed to be produced by internal exhalations (usually of the stomach); depression, hysteria; also hypochondria.

veil (*your bonnets*) (*vb*) Show respect by doffing a cap or bonnet.

vend Sell.

viaticum The Eucharist administered to one who is dying.

vicinage Neighbourhood.

wafer A small disk of flour and gum which, when moistened, sealed a letter.

wafered on Attached by a wafer (*q.v.*).

Waltham disguises Disguises (black faces, women's clothes etc.) employed by the 'Waltham blacks', poachers and other protesters against the restrictions on the use of Waltham Chase in Hampshire.

wash-balls Balls of toilet or shaving soap.

Westminster Hall Within which at this time the law courts sat.

wet finger (*with a*) Effortlessly, easily.

wet wafer See *wafer*.

whale-ribbed canvas The stiffening of ladies' wide, hooped skirts: canvas with ribs or strips of whale-bone.

work it going Work twice as hard; cf. 'work double tides'.

woundily corned (of beef) Heavily cured or seasoned with salt.

yesterday was se'nnight A week ago yesterday.

yonker Youngster.

Zounds (*pron.* zoonds) God's wounds.

APPENDIX

The Music for the 'Ode to Wisdom' in Letter 54
See L54 n 1.

XIV